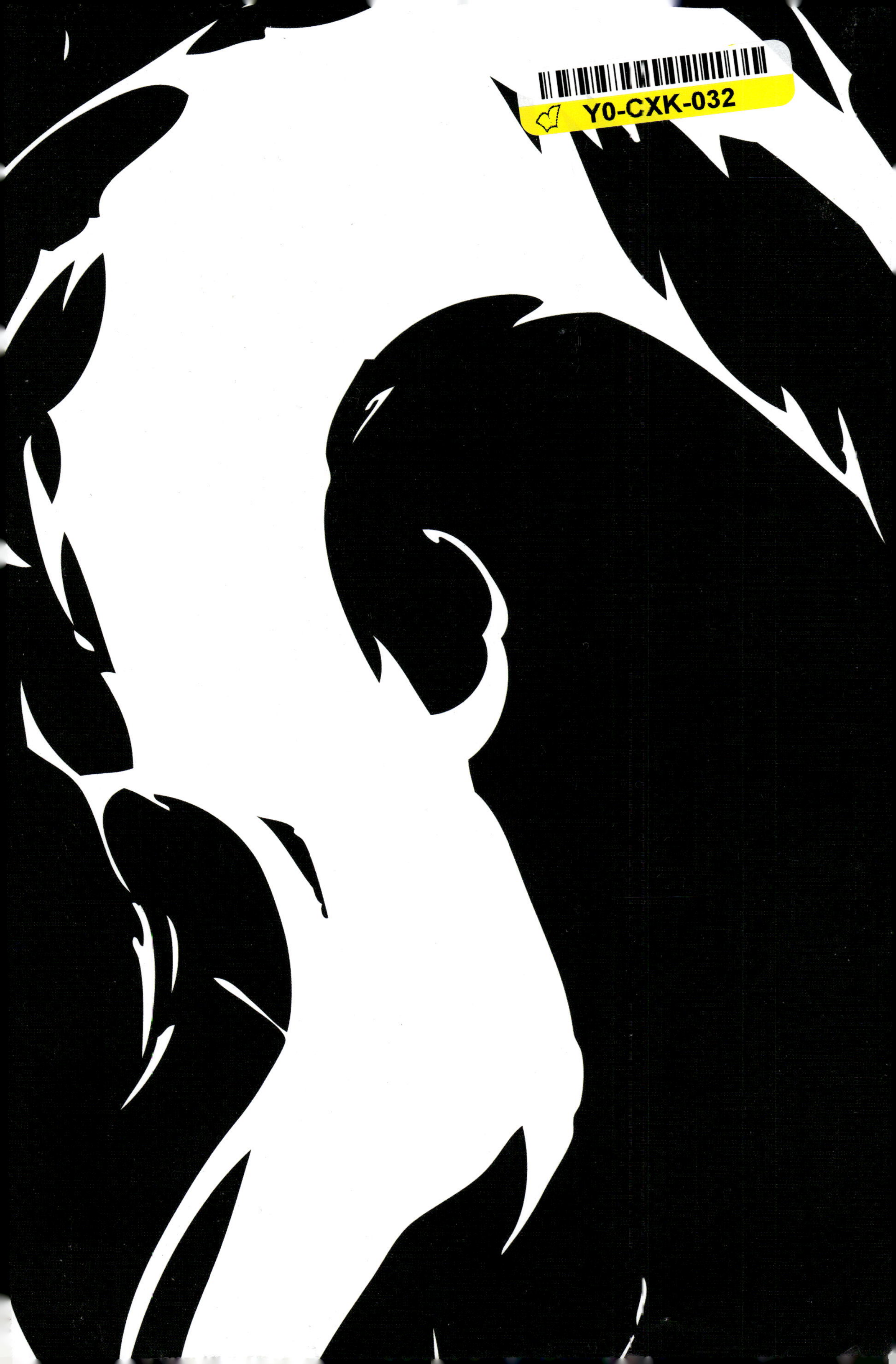

THE DARKNESS
COMPENDIUM
— VOLUME 2 —

FOR TOP COW PRODUCTIONS, INC.:
MARC SILVESTRI - CEO
MATT HAWKINS - PRESIDENT & COO
FILIP SABLIK - PUBLISHER
BRYAN ROUNTREE - EDITOR
ELENA SALCEDO - EVENT & LOGISTICS COORDINATOR
JESSI REID - SOCIAL MARKETING COORDINATOR

IMAGE COMICS, INC.

Robert Kirkman - chief operating officer
Erik Larsen - chief financial officer
Todd McFarlane - president
Marc Silvestri - chief executive officer
Jim Valentino - vice president

Eric Stephenson - publisher
Todd Martinez - sales & licensing coordinator
Jennifer de Guzman - pr & marketing director
Branwyn Bigglestone - accounts manager
Emily Miller - administrative assistant
Jamie Parreno - marketing assistant
Sarah deLaine - events coordinator
Kevin Yuen - digital rights coordinator
Tyler Shainline - production manager
Drew Gill - art director
Jonathan Chan - senior production artist
Monica Garcia - production artist
Vincent Kukua - production artist
Jana Cook - production artist
www.imagecomics.com

to find the comic shop
nearest you call:
1-888-COMICBOOK

Want more info? check out:
www.topcow.com and **www.thetopcowstore.com**
for news and exclusive Top Cow merchandise!

For this edition
Book Design and Layout by:
Phil Smith, Vincent Kukua & Jana Cook

The Darkness Compendium Volume 2
Softcover
April 2012. FIRST PRINTING. ISBN: 978-1-60706-403-9
Published by Image Comics Inc. Office of Publication: 2134 Allston Way, Second Floor, Berkeley, CA 94704. $69.99 U.S.D. Originally published in single magazine form as THE DARKNESS #41 - #89, THE DARKNESS: LODBROK'S HAND #1, THE DARKNESS: SHADOWS AND FLAME #1, THE DARKNESS: BUTCHER #1. The Darkness © 2012 Top Cow Productions, Inc. All rights reserved. The Darkness logos, and the likeness of all characters (human or otherwise) featured herein are registered trademarks of Top Cow Productions, Inc. Image Comics and the Image Comics logo are trademarks of Image Comics, Inc. The characters, events, and stories in this publication are entirely fictional. Any resemblance to actual persons (living or dead), events, institutions, or locales, without satiric intent, is coincidental. No portion of this publication may be reproduced or transmitted, in any form or by any means, without the express written permission of Top Cow Productions, Inc. **PRINTED IN SOUTH KOREA.**

TABLE OF CONTENTS

The Darkness Issue #41
cover art by: Dale Keown & Matt Milla

THE DARKNESS #41

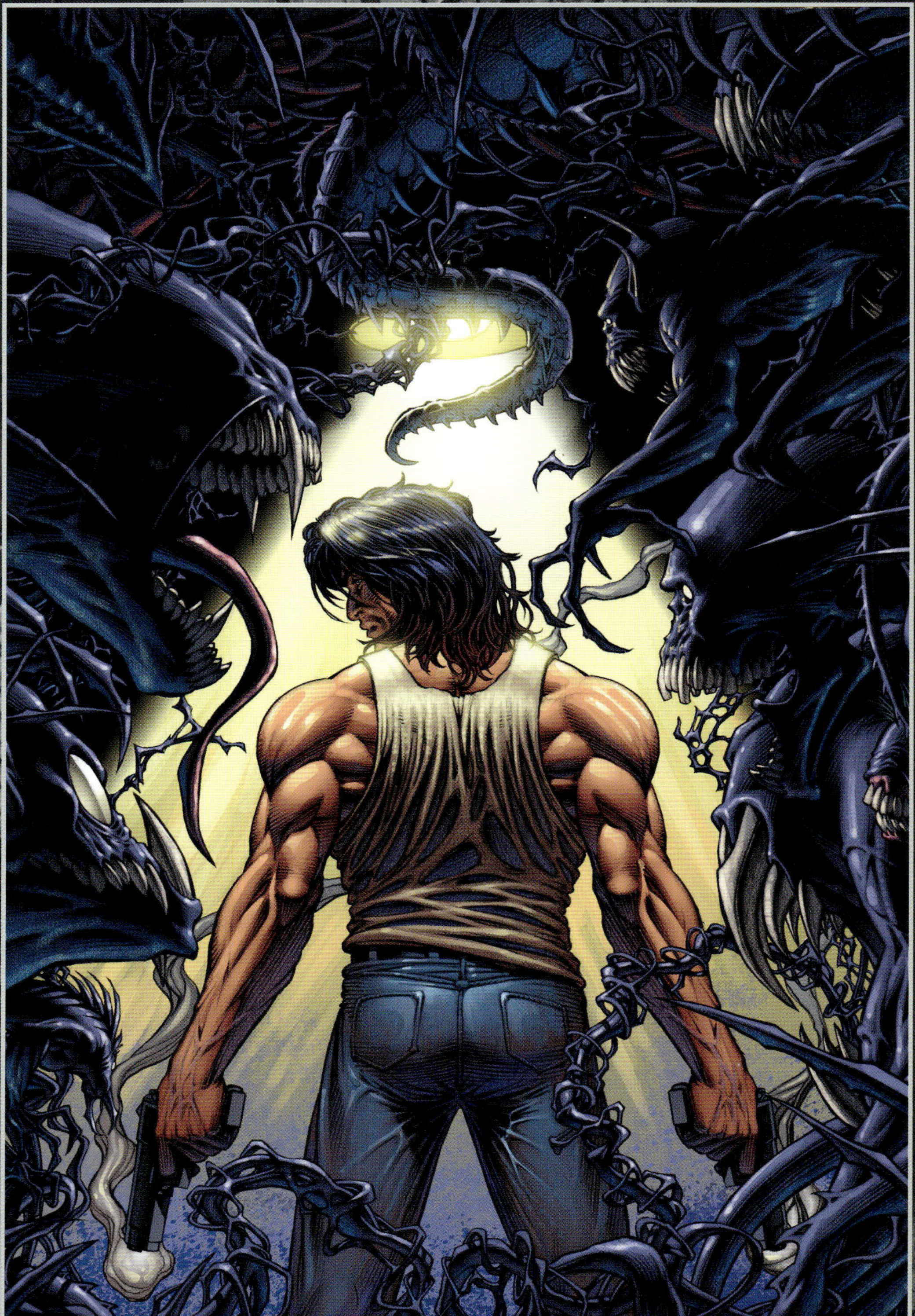

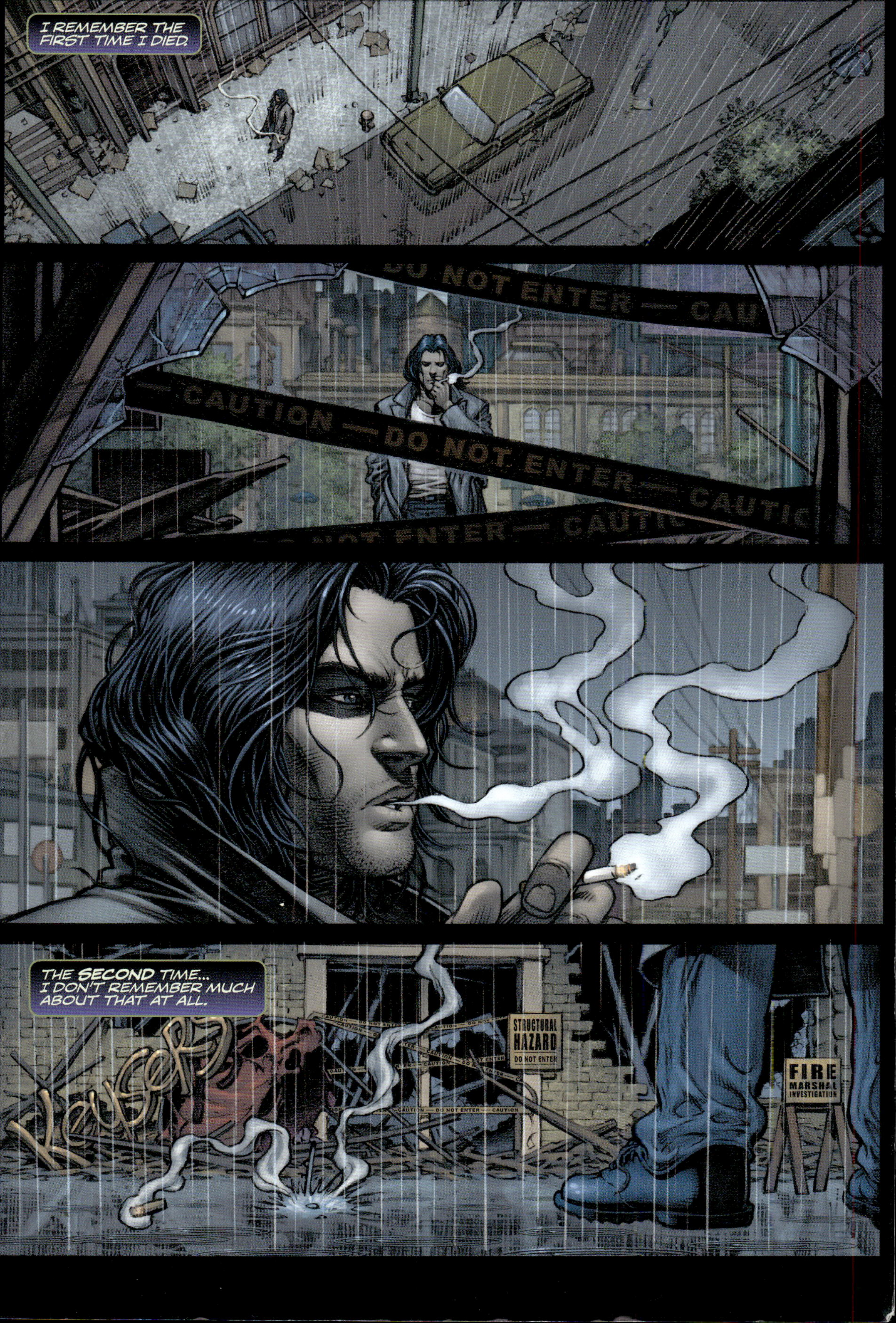
I REMEMBER THE FIRST TIME I DIED.
DO NOT ENTER — CAU
— CAUTION — DO NOT ENTER — CAUTI
THE SECOND TIME... I DON'T REMEMBER MUCH ABOUT THAT AT ALL.
STRUCTURAL HAZARD DO NOT ENTER
FIRE MARSHAL INVESTIGATION

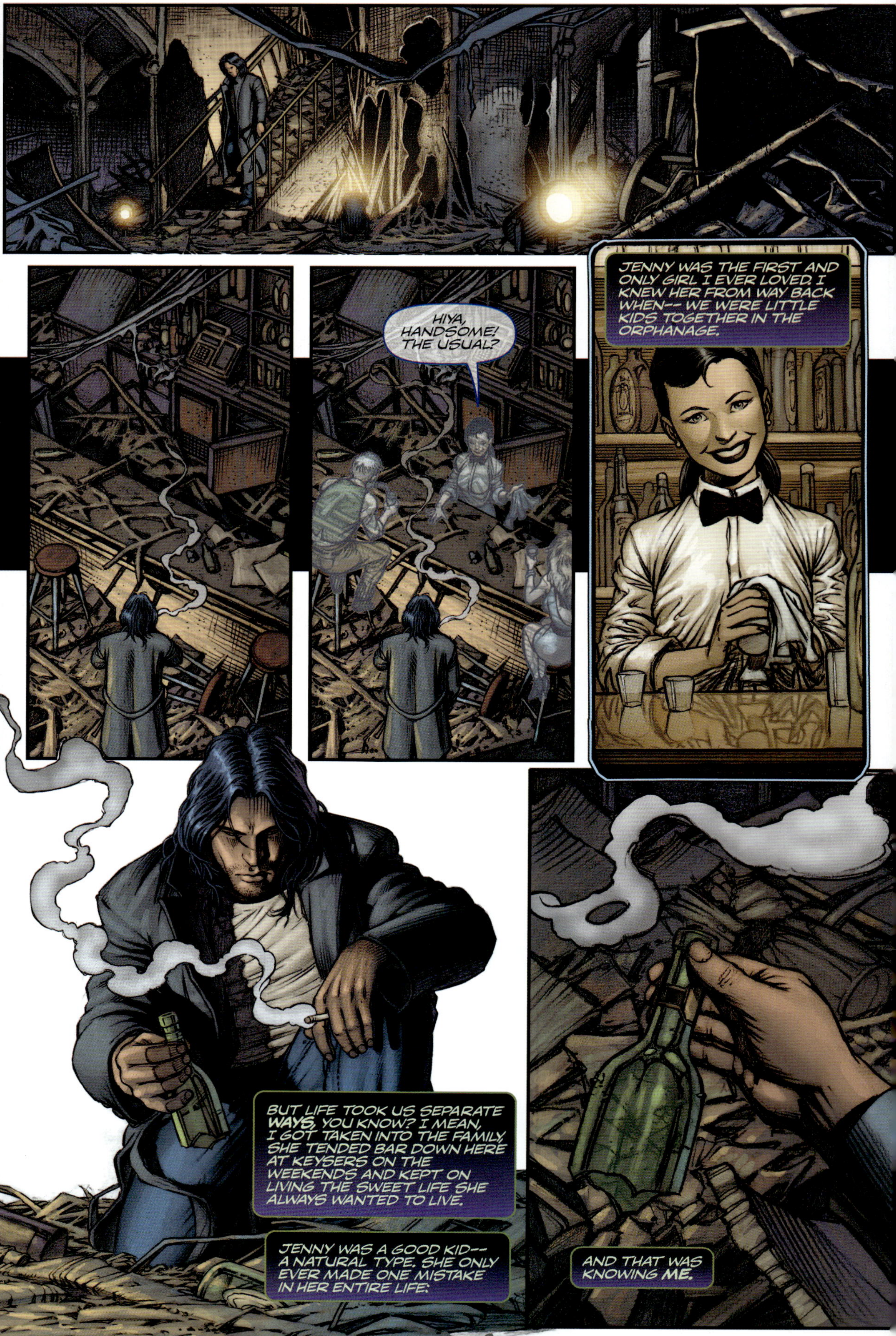

HIYA, HANDSOME! THE USUAL?
JENNY WAS THE FIRST AND ONLY GIRL I EVER LOVED. I KNEW HER FROM WAY BACK WHEN-- WE WERE LITTLE KIDS TOGETHER IN THE ORPHANAGE.
BUT LIFE TOOK US SEPARATE WAYS, YOU KNOW? I MEAN, I GOT TAKEN INTO THE FAMILY. SHE TENDED BAR DOWN HERE AT KEYSERS ON THE WEEKENDS AND KEPT ON LIVING THE SWEET LIFE SHE ALWAYS WANTED TO LIVE.
JENNY WAS A GOOD KID-- A NATURAL TYPE. SHE ONLY EVER MADE ONE MISTAKE IN HER ENTIRE LIFE:
AND THAT WAS KNOWING ME.

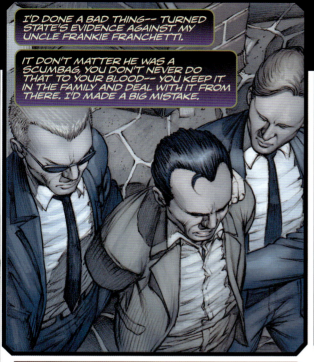

I'D DONE A BAD THING-- TURNED STATE'S EVIDENCE AGAINST MY UNCLE FRANKIE FRANCHETTI.

IT DON'T MATTER HE WAS A SCUMBAG, YOU DON'T NEVER DO THAT TO YOUR BLOOD-- YOU KEEP IT IN THE FAMILY AND DEAL WITH IT FROM THERE. I'D MADE A BIG MISTAKE.

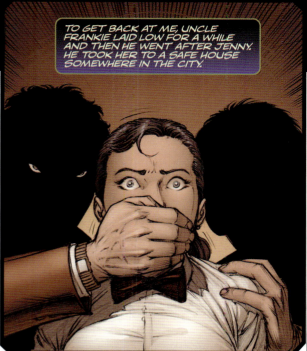

TO GET BACK AT ME, UNCLE FRANKIE LAID LOW FOR A WHILE AND THEN HE WENT AFTER JENNY. HE TOOK HER TO A SAFE HOUSE SOMEWHERE IN THE CITY.

THEN HE SENT ME A VIDEOTAPE OF HIS DEMANDS. WHAT HE WANTED WAS PRETTY SIMPLE: I'D HURT HIM, HE WANTED TO HURT ME BACK.

AND SO HE TOOK A GUN TO HER TEMPLE AND HE BLEW HER BRAINS OUT OF HER EAR BEFORE I EVER HAD A CHANCE TO SAVE HER.

I WATCHED THE WHOLE THING.

AND THAT WAS THE *FIRST* TIME I DIED.

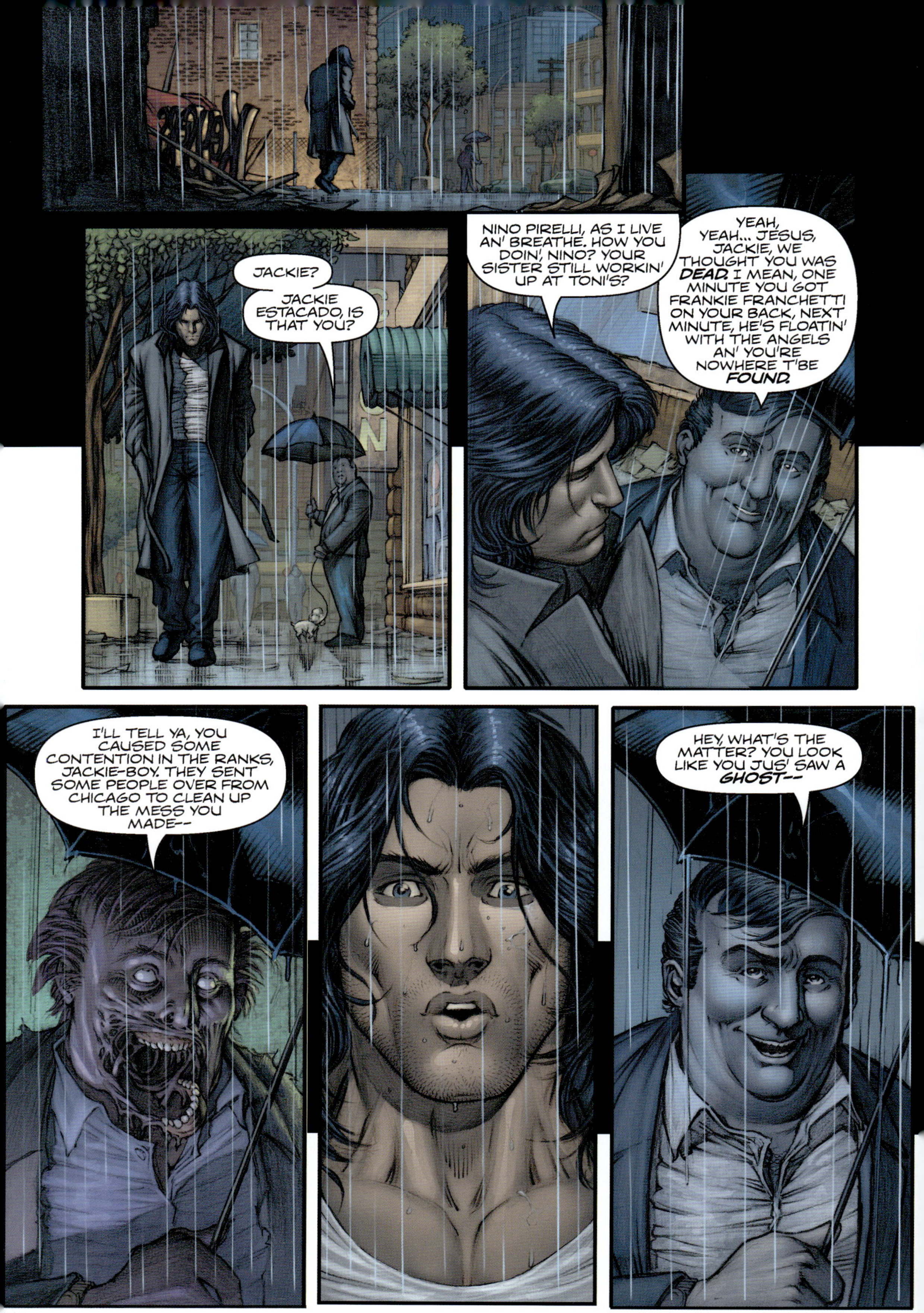
JACKIE?
JACKIE ESTACADO, IS THAT YOU?
NINO PIRELLI, AS I LIVE AN' BREATHE. HOW YOU DOIN', NINO? YOUR SISTER STILL WORKIN' UP AT TONI'S?
YEAH, YEAH... JESUS, JACKIE, WE THOUGHT YOU WAS DEAD. I MEAN, ONE MINUTE YOU GOT FRANKIE FRANCHETTI ON YOUR BACK, NEXT MINUTE, HE'S FLOATIN' WITH THE ANGELS AN' YOU'RE NOWHERE T'BE FOUND.
I'LL TELL YA, YOU CAUSED SOME CONTENTION IN THE RANKS, JACKIE-BOY. THEY SENT SOME PEOPLE OVER FROM CHICAGO TO CLEAN UP THE MESS YOU MADE--
HEY, WHAT'S THE MATTER? YOU LOOK LIKE YOU JUS' SAW A GHOST--

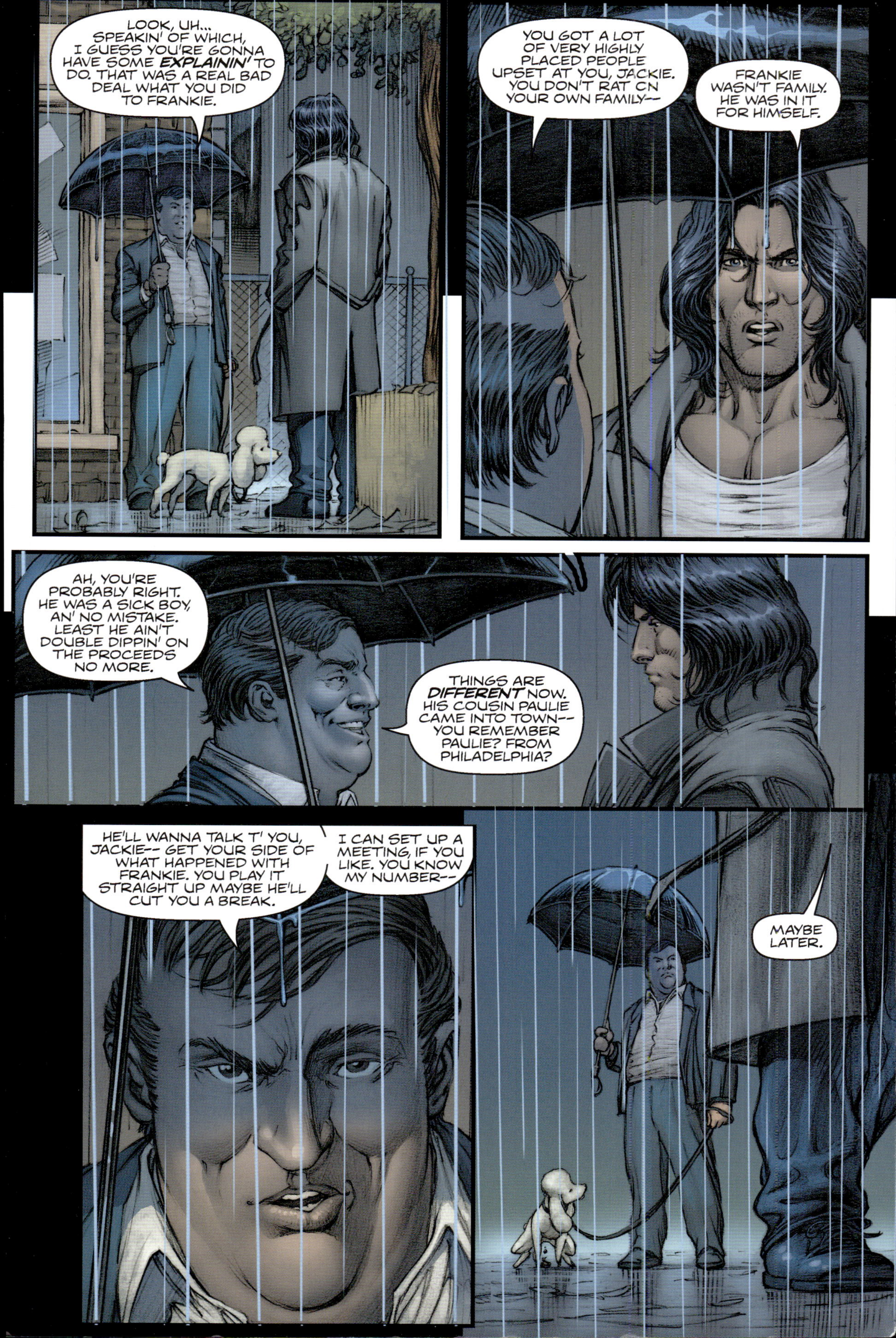
LOOK, UH... SPEAKIN' OF WHICH, I GUESS YOU'RE GONNA HAVE SOME EXPLAININ' TO DO. THAT WAS A REAL BAD DEAL WHAT YOU DID TO FRANKIE.
YOU GOT A LOT OF VERY HIGHLY PLACED PEOPLE UPSET AT YOU, JACKIE. YOU DON'T RAT ON YOUR OWN FAMILY--
FRANKIE WASN'T FAMILY. HE WAS IN IT FOR HIMSELF.
AH, YOU'RE PROBABLY RIGHT. HE WAS A SICK BOY, AN' NO MISTAKE. LEAST HE AIN'T DOUBLE DIPPIN' ON THE PROCEEDS NO MORE.
THINGS ARE DIFFERENT NOW. HIS COUSIN PAULIE CAME INTO TOWN-- YOU REMEMBER PAULIE? FROM PHILADELPHIA?
HE'LL WANNA TALK T' YOU, JACKIE-- GET YOUR SIDE OF WHAT HAPPENED WITH FRANKIE. YOU PLAY IT STRAIGHT UP MAYBE HE'LL CUT YOU A BREAK.
I CAN SET UP A MEETING, IF YOU LIKE. YOU KNOW MY NUMBER--
MAYBE LATER.

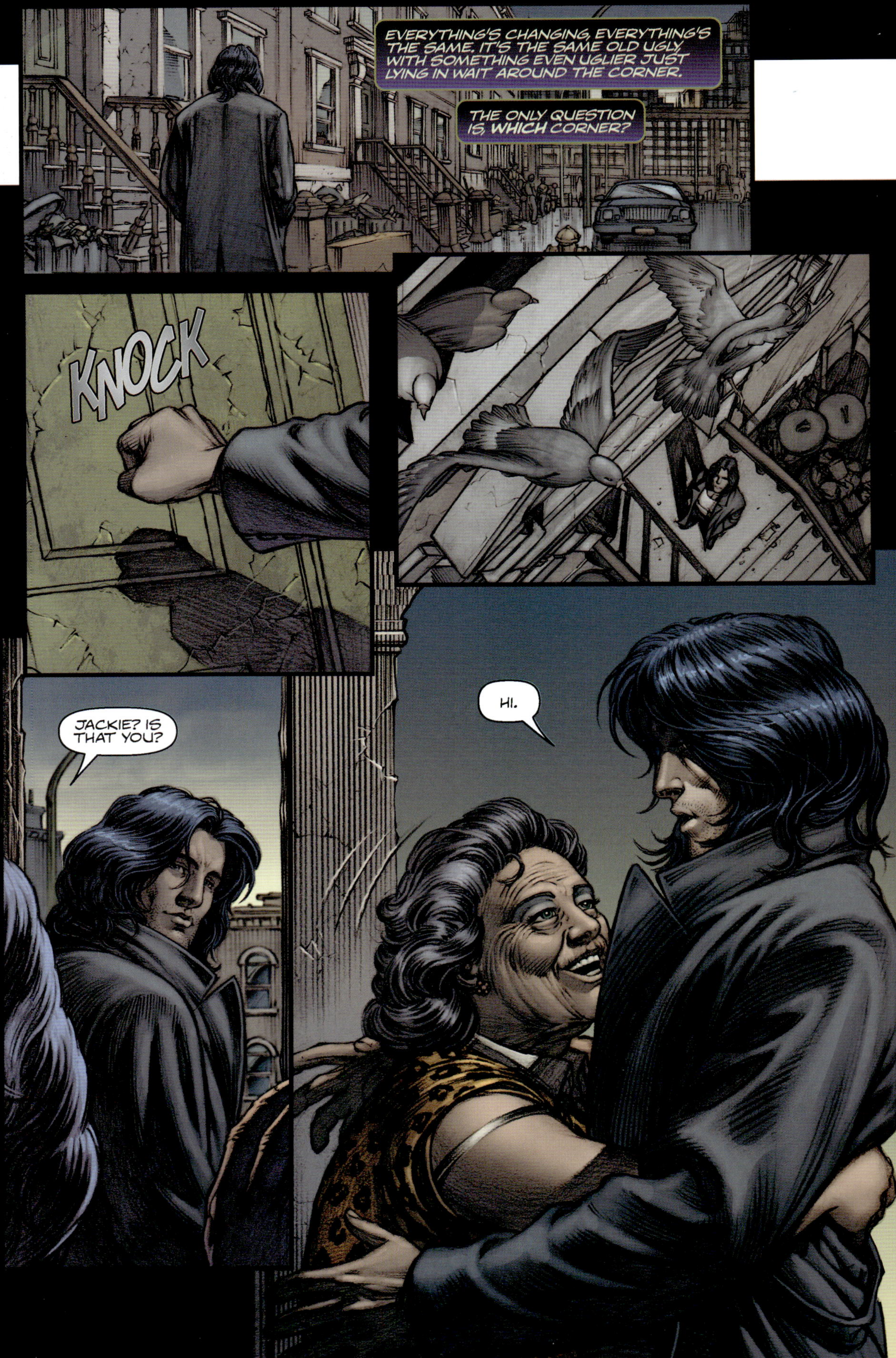
EVERYTHING'S CHANGING, EVERYTHING'S THE SAME. IT'S THE SAME OLD UGLY, WITH SOMETHING EVEN UGLIER JUST LYING IN WAIT AROUND THE CORNER.
THE ONLY QUESTION IS, WHICH CORNER?
KNOCK
JACKIE? IS THAT YOU?
HI.

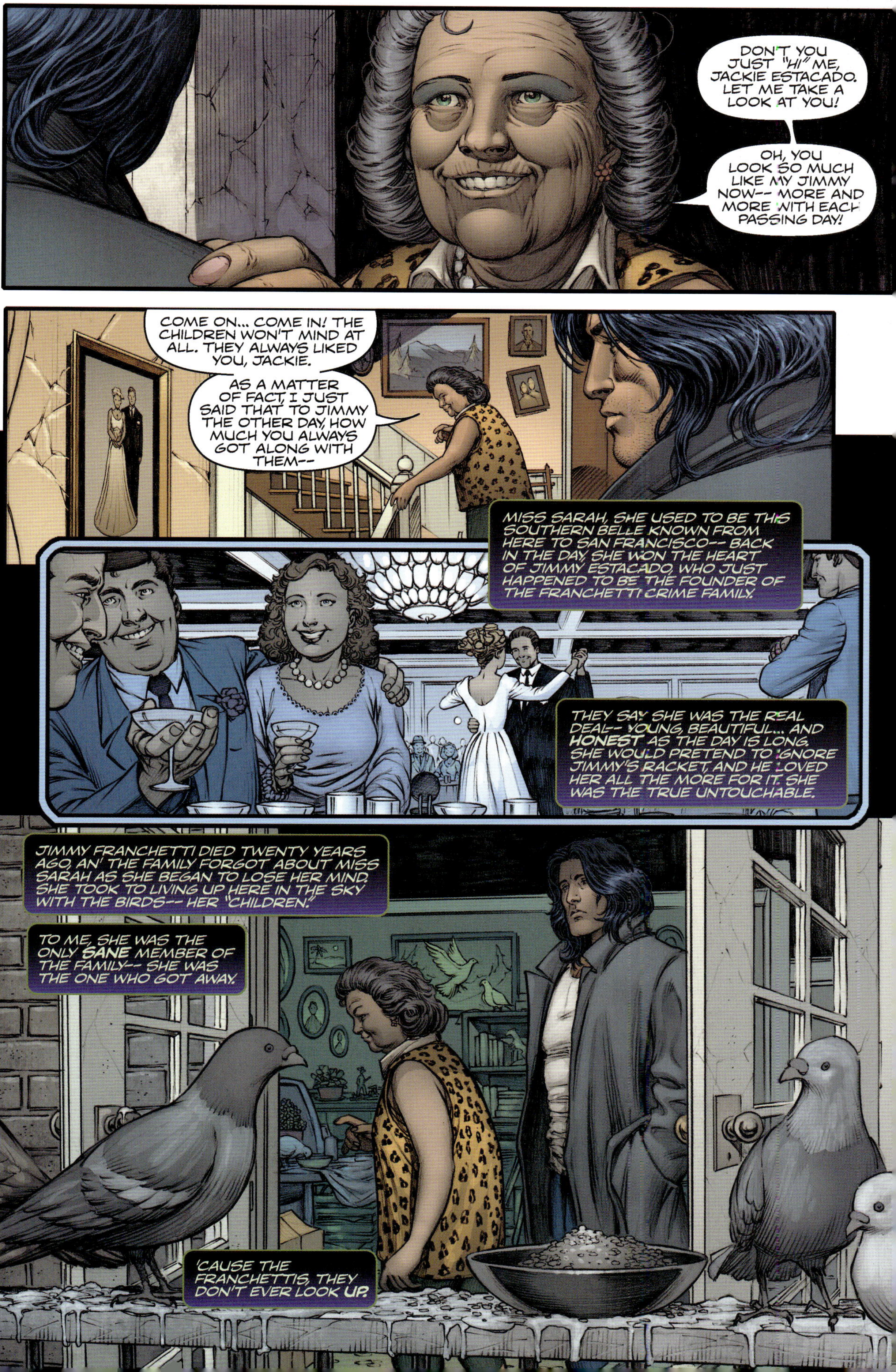
DON'T YOU JUST "HI" ME, JACKIE ESTACADO. LET ME TAKE A LOOK AT YOU!
OH, YOU LOOK SO MUCH LIKE MY JIMMY NOW-- MORE AND MORE WITH EACH PASSING DAY!
COME ON... COME IN! THE CHILDREN WON'T MIND AT ALL. THEY ALWAYS LIKED YOU, JACKIE.
AS A MATTER OF FACT, I JUST SAID THAT TO JIMMY THE OTHER DAY, HOW MUCH YOU ALWAYS GOT ALONG WITH THEM--
MISS SARAH, SHE USED TO BE THIS SOUTHERN BELLE KNOWN FROM HERE TO SAN FRANCISCO-- BACK IN THE DAY, SHE WON THE HEART OF JIMMY ESTACADO, WHO JUST HAPPENED TO BE THE FOUNDER OF THE FRANCHETTI CRIME FAMILY.
THEY SAY SHE WAS THE REAL DEAL-- YOUNG, BEAUTIFUL... AND HONEST AS THE DAY IS LONG. SHE WOULD PRETEND TO IGNORE JIMMY'S RACKET, AND HE LOVED HER ALL THE MORE FOR IT. SHE WAS THE TRUE UNTOUCHABLE.
JIMMY FRANCHETTI DIED TWENTY YEARS AGO, AN' THE FAMILY FORGOT ABOUT MISS SARAH AS SHE BEGAN TO LOSE HER MIND. SHE TOOK TO LIVING UP HERE IN THE SKY WITH THE BIRDS-- HER "CHILDREN."
TO ME, SHE WAS THE ONLY SANE MEMBER OF THE FAMILY-- SHE WAS THE ONE WHO GOT AWAY.
'CAUSE THE FRANCHETTIS, THEY DON'T EVER LOOK UP.

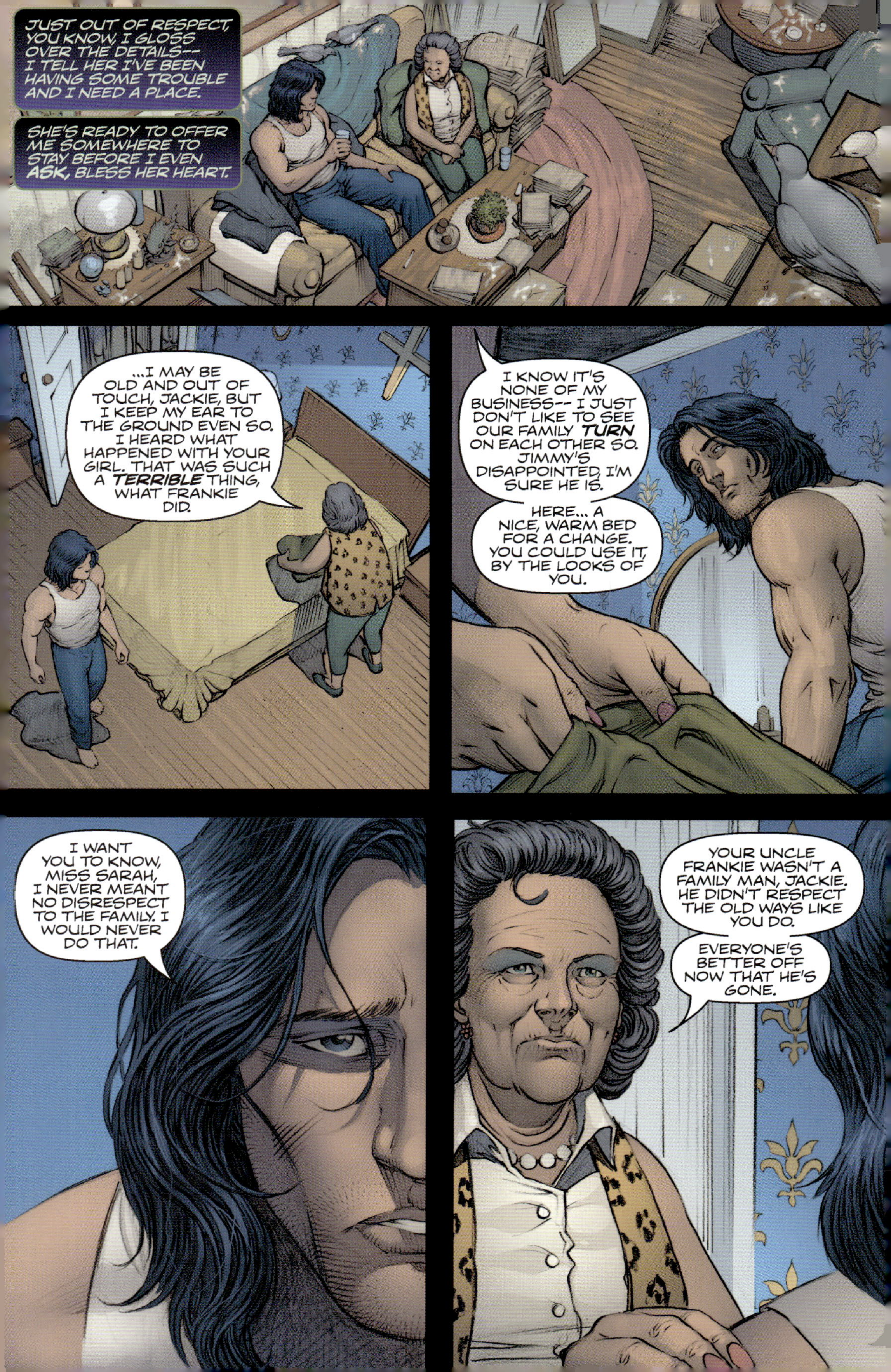
JUST OUT OF RESPECT, YOU KNOW, I GLOSS OVER THE DETAILS-- I TELL HER I'VE BEEN HAVING SOME TROUBLE AND I NEED A PLACE.
SHE'S READY TO OFFER ME SOMEWHERE TO STAY BEFORE I EVEN ASK, BLESS HER HEART.
...I MAY BE OLD AND OUT OF TOUCH, JACKIE, BUT I KEEP MY EAR TO THE GROUND EVEN SO. I HEARD WHAT HAPPENED WITH YOUR GIRL. THAT WAS SUCH A TERRIBLE THING, WHAT FRANKIE DID.
I KNOW IT'S NONE OF MY BUSINESS-- I JUST DON'T LIKE TO SEE OUR FAMILY TURN ON EACH OTHER SO. JIMMY'S DISAPPOINTED, I'M SURE HE IS.
HERE... A NICE, WARM BED FOR A CHANGE. YOU COULD USE IT, BY THE LOOKS OF YOU.
I WANT YOU TO KNOW, MISS SARAH, I NEVER MEANT NO DISRESPECT TO THE FAMILY. I WOULD NEVER DO THAT.
YOUR UNCLE FRANKIE WASN'T A FAMILY MAN, JACKIE. HE DIDN'T RESPECT THE OLD WAYS LIKE YOU DO.
EVERYONE'S BETTER OFF NOW THAT HE'S GONE.

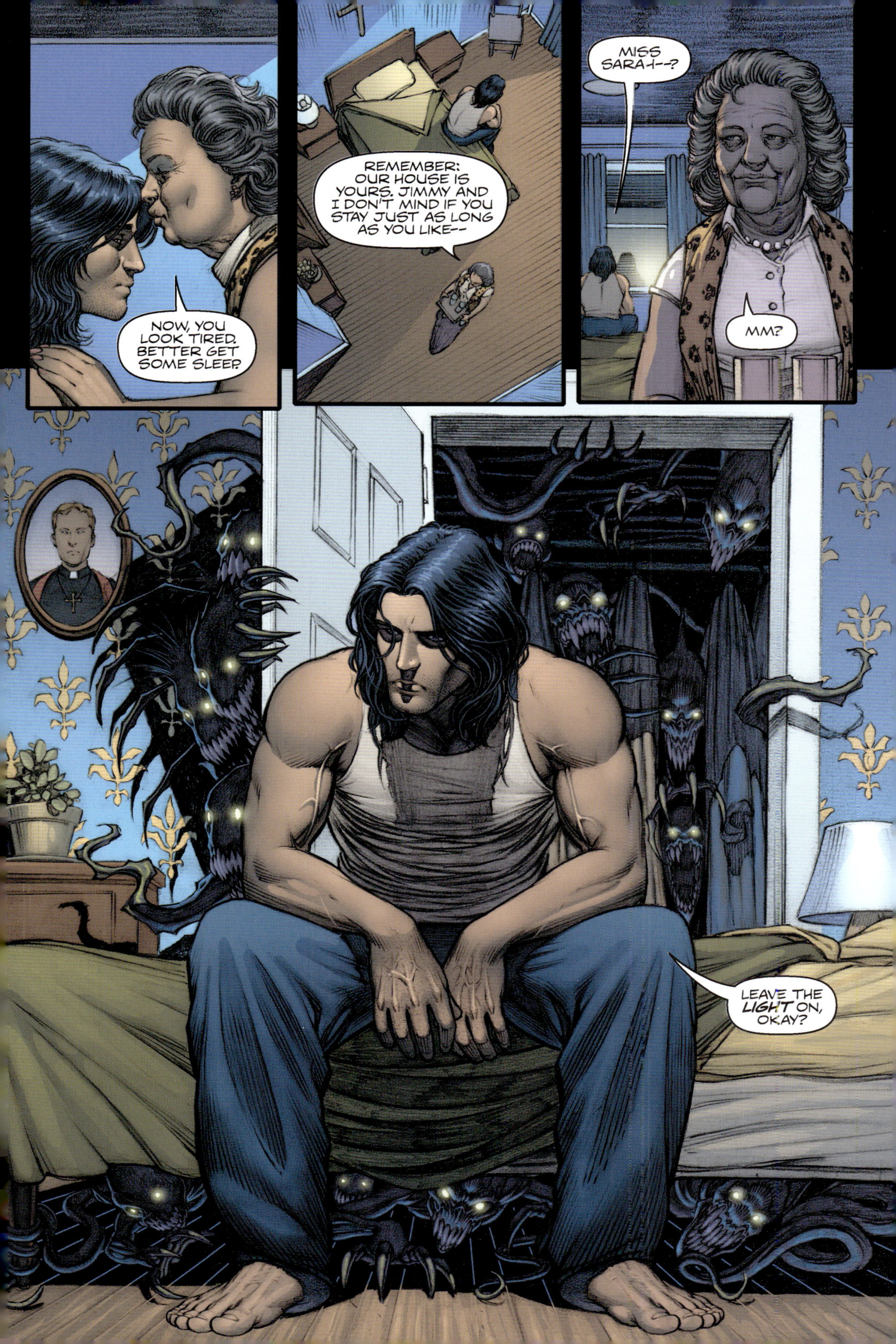
NOW, YOU LOOK TIRED. BETTER GET SOME SLEEP.
REMEMBER: OUR HOUSE IS YOURS. JIMMY AND I DON'T MIND IF YOU STAY JUST AS LONG AS YOU LIKE--
MISS SARA-I--?
MM?
LEAVE THE LIGHT ON, OKAY?

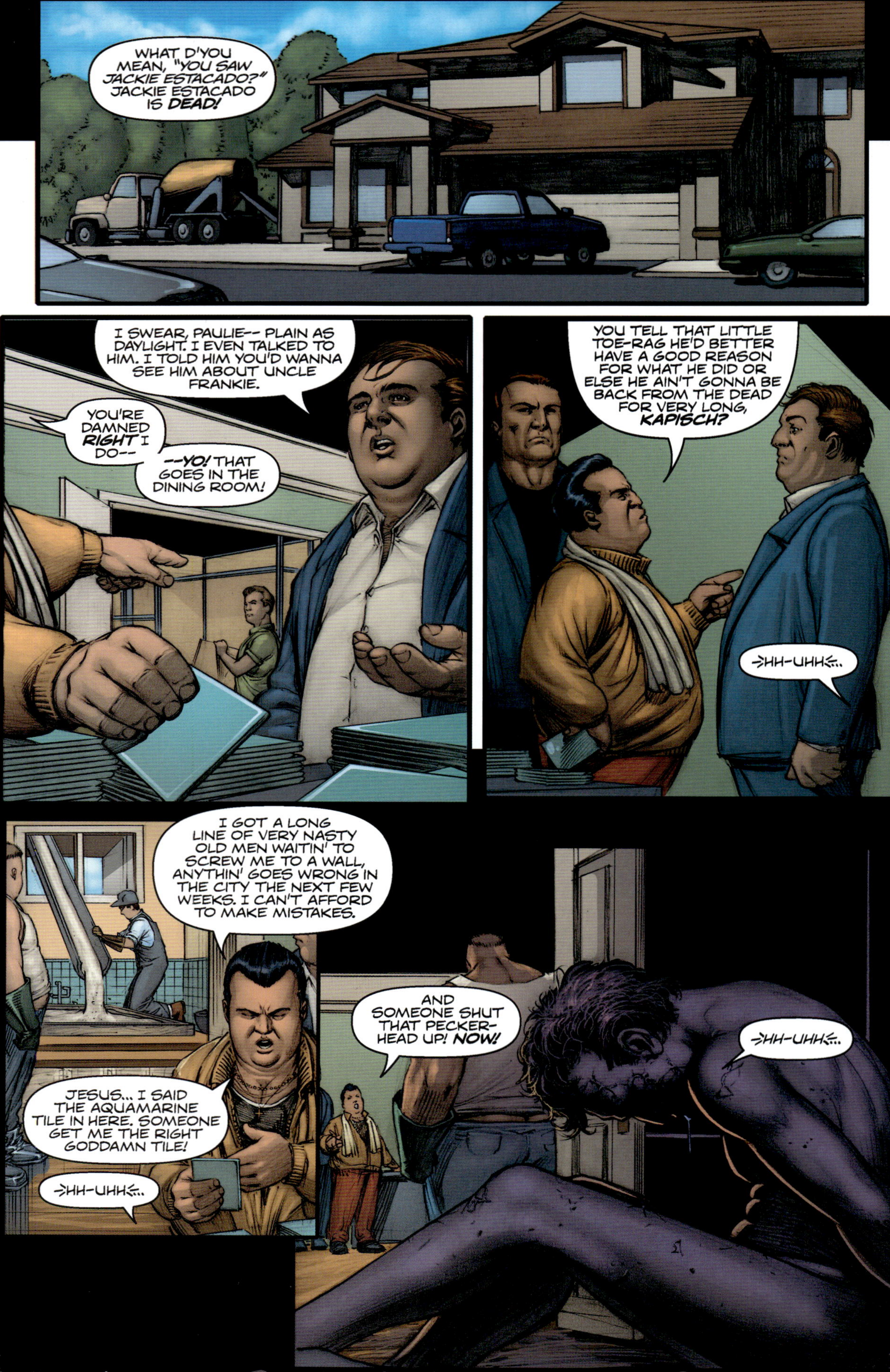

WHAT D'YOU MEAN, "YOU SAW JACKIE ESTACADO?" JACKIE ESTACADO IS *DEAD!*
I SWEAR, PAULIE-- PLAIN AS DAYLIGHT. I EVEN TALKED TO HIM. I TOLD HIM YOU'D WANNA SEE HIM ABOUT UNCLE FRANKIE.
YOU'RE DAMNED *RIGHT* I DO--
--YO! THAT GOES IN THE DINING ROOM!
YOU TELL THAT LITTLE TOE-RAG HE'D BETTER HAVE A GOOD REASON FOR WHAT HE DID OR ELSE HE AIN'T GONNA BE BACK FROM THE DEAD FOR VERY LONG, *KAPISCH?*
HH-UHH...
I GOT A LONG LINE OF VERY NASTY OLD MEN WAITIN' TO SCREW ME TO A WALL, ANYTHIN' GOES WRONG IN THE CITY THE NEXT FEW WEEKS. I CAN'T AFFORD TO MAKE MISTAKES.
JESUS... I SAID THE AQUAMARINE TILE IN HERE. SOMEONE GET ME THE RIGHT GODDAMN TILE!
HH-UHH...
AND SOMEONE SHUT THAT PECKER-HEAD UP! *NOW!*
HH-UHH...

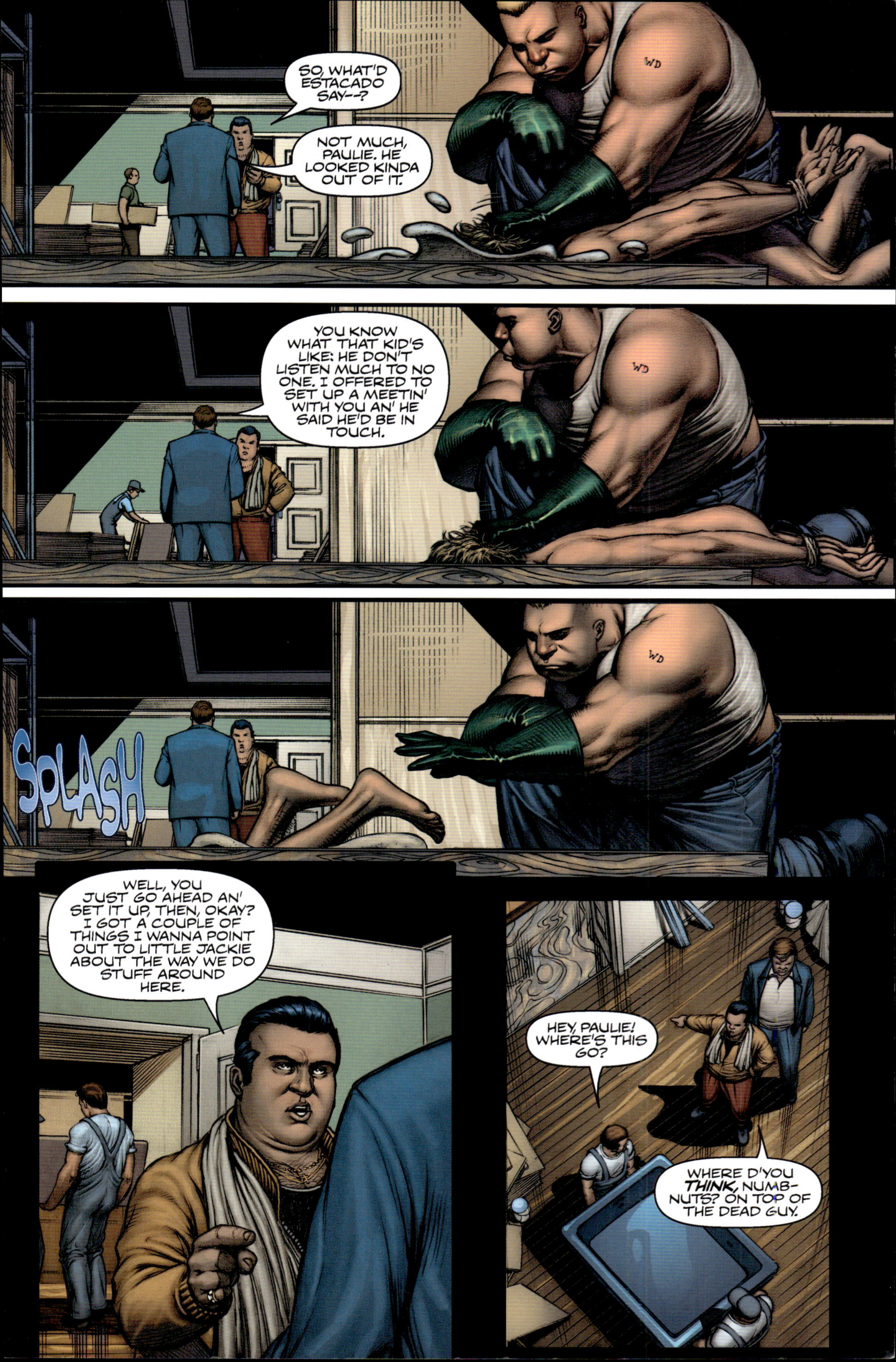

SO, WHAT'D ESTACADO SAY--?
NOT MUCH, PAULIE. HE LOOKED KINDA OUT OF IT.
WD
YOU KNOW WHAT THAT KID'S LIKE: HE DON'T LISTEN MUCH TO NO ONE. I OFFERED TO SET UP A MEETIN' WITH YOU AN' HE SAID HE'D BE IN TOUCH.
WD
SPLASH
WD
WELL, YOU JUST GO AHEAD AN' SET IT UP, THEN, OKAY? I GOT A COUPLE OF THINGS I WANNA POINT OUT TO LITTLE JACKIE ABOUT THE WAY WE DO STUFF AROUND HERE.
HEY, PAULIE! WHERE'S THIS GO?
WHERE D'YOU *THINK*, NUMB-NUTS? ON TOP OF THE DEAD GUY.

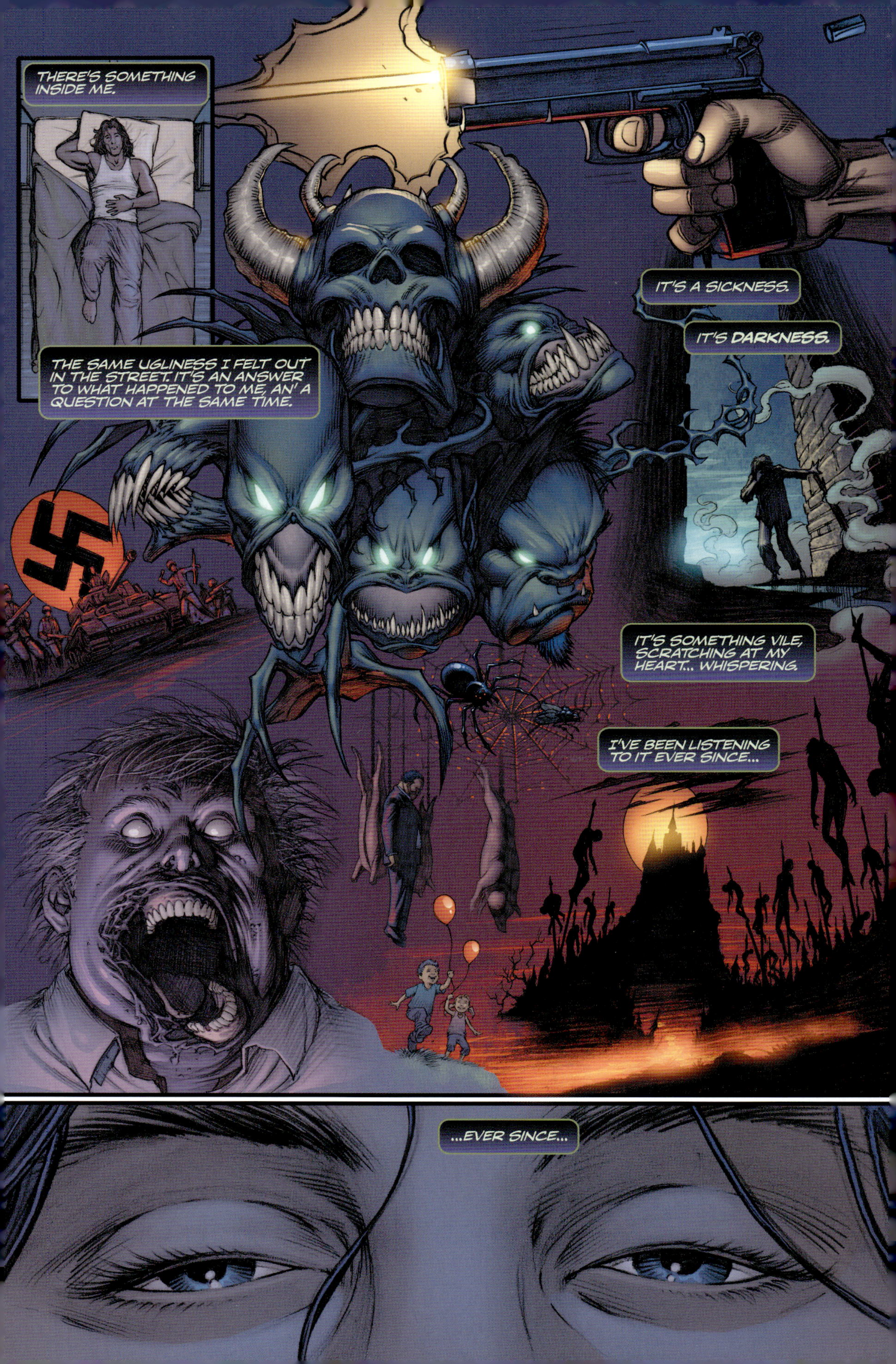
THERE'S SOMETHING INSIDE ME.
THE SAME UGLINESS I FELT OUT IN THE STREET. IT'S AN ANSWER TO WHAT HAPPENED TO ME, AN' A QUESTION AT THE SAME TIME.
IT'S A SICKNESS.
IT'S DARKNESS.
IT'S SOMETHING VILE, SCRATCHING AT MY HEART... WHISPERING.
I'VE BEEN LISTENING TO IT EVER SINCE...
...EVER SINCE...

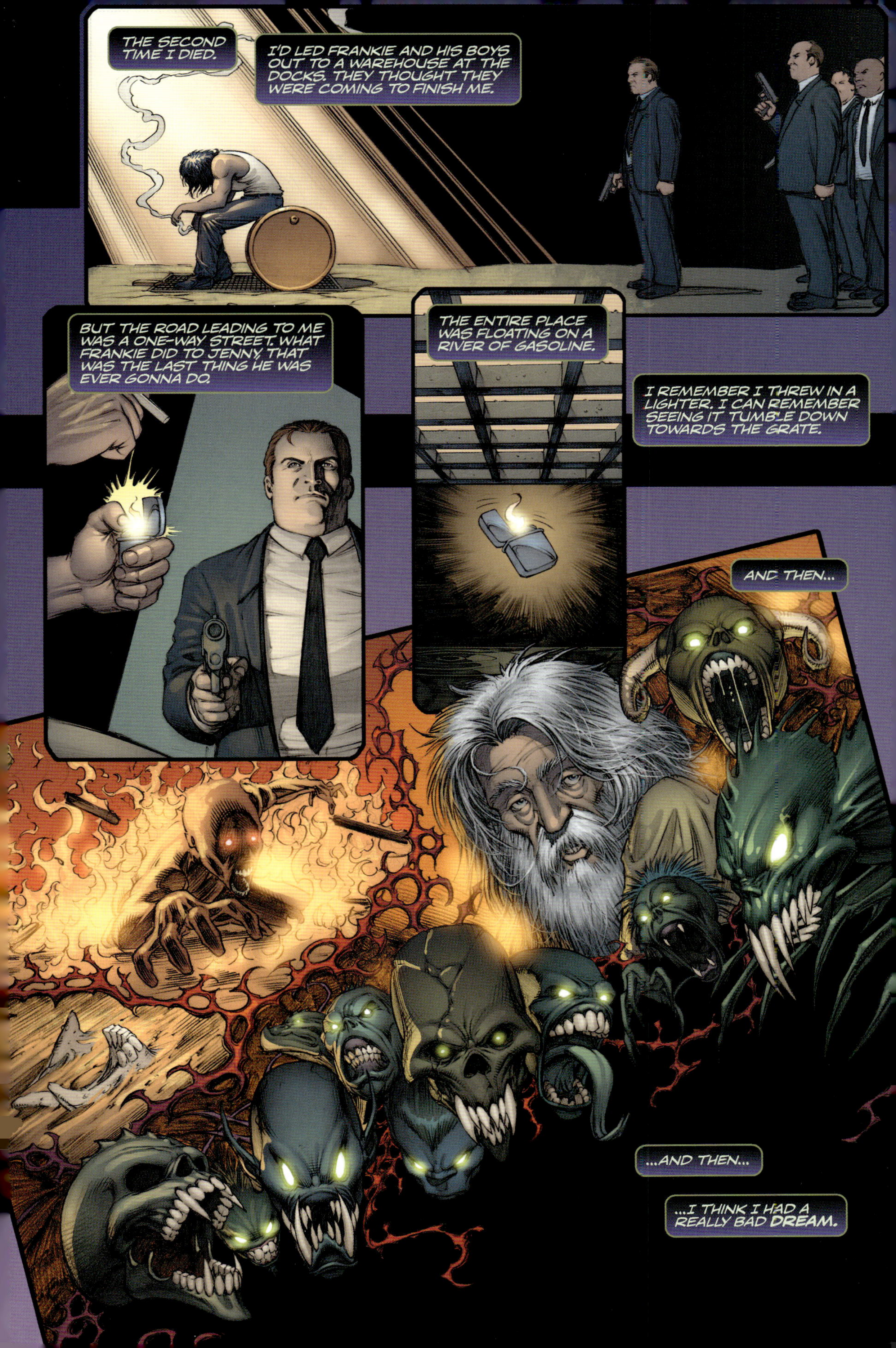
THE SECOND TIME I DIED.
I'D LED FRANKIE AND HIS BOYS OUT TO A WAREHOUSE AT THE DOCKS. THEY THOUGHT THEY WERE COMING TO FINISH ME.
BUT THE ROAD LEADING TO ME WAS A ONE-WAY STREET. WHAT FRANKIE DID TO JENNY, THAT WAS THE LAST THING HE WAS EVER GONNA DO.
THE ENTIRE PLACE WAS FLOATING ON A RIVER OF GASOLINE.
I REMEMBER I THREW IN A LIGHTER. I CAN REMEMBER SEEING IT TUMBLE DOWN TOWARDS THE GRATE.
AND THEN...
...AND THEN...
...I THINK I HAD A REALLY BAD DREAM.

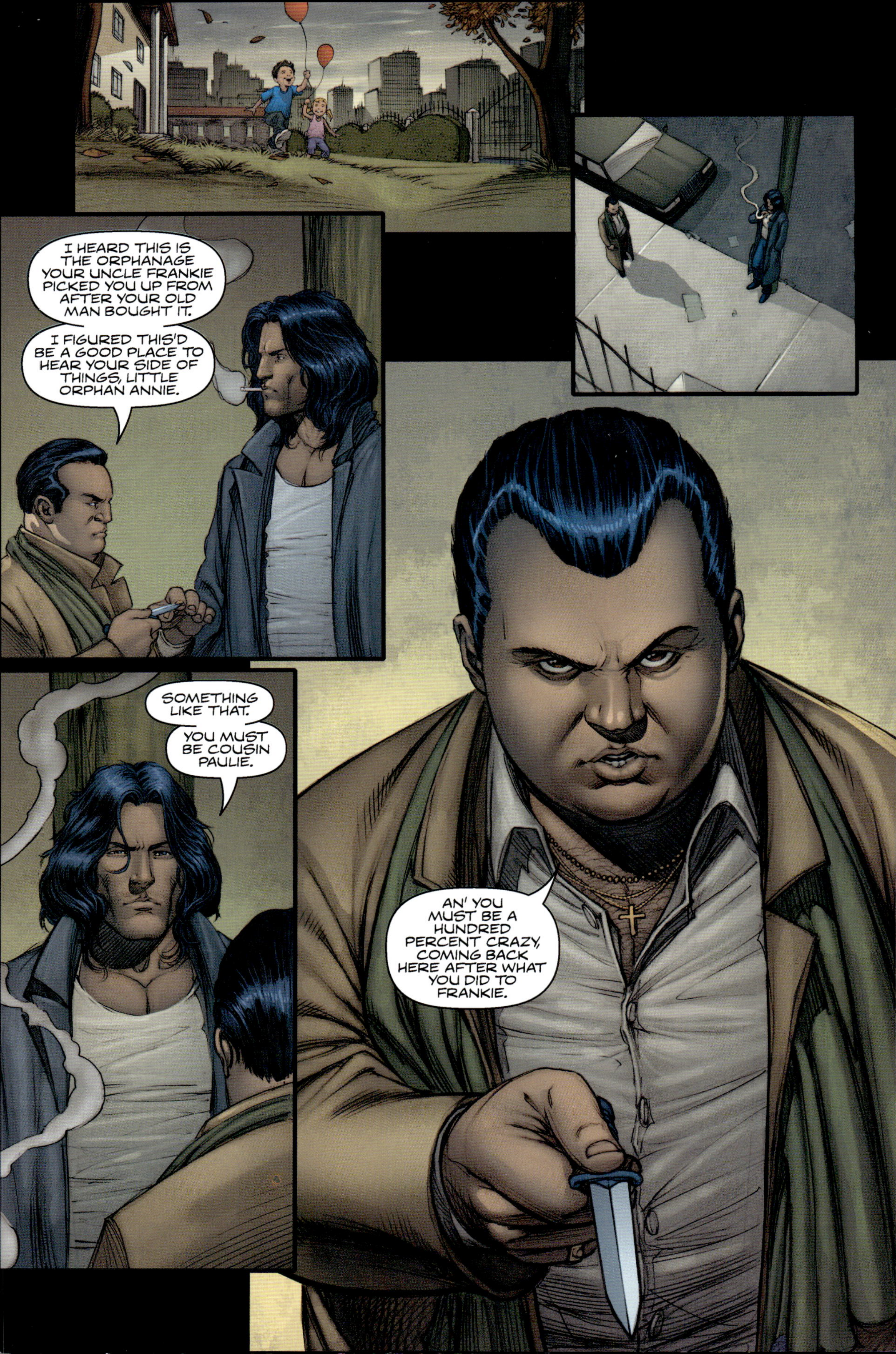
I HEARD THIS IS THE ORPHANAGE YOUR UNCLE FRANKIE PICKED YOU UP FROM AFTER YOUR OLD MAN BOUGHT IT.
I FIGURED THIS'D BE A GOOD PLACE TO HEAR YOUR SIDE OF THINGS, LITTLE ORPHAN ANNIE.
SOMETHING LIKE THAT.
YOU MUST BE COUSIN PAULIE.
AN' YOU MUST BE A HUNDRED PERCENT CRAZY, COMING BACK HERE AFTER WHAT YOU DID TO FRANKIE.

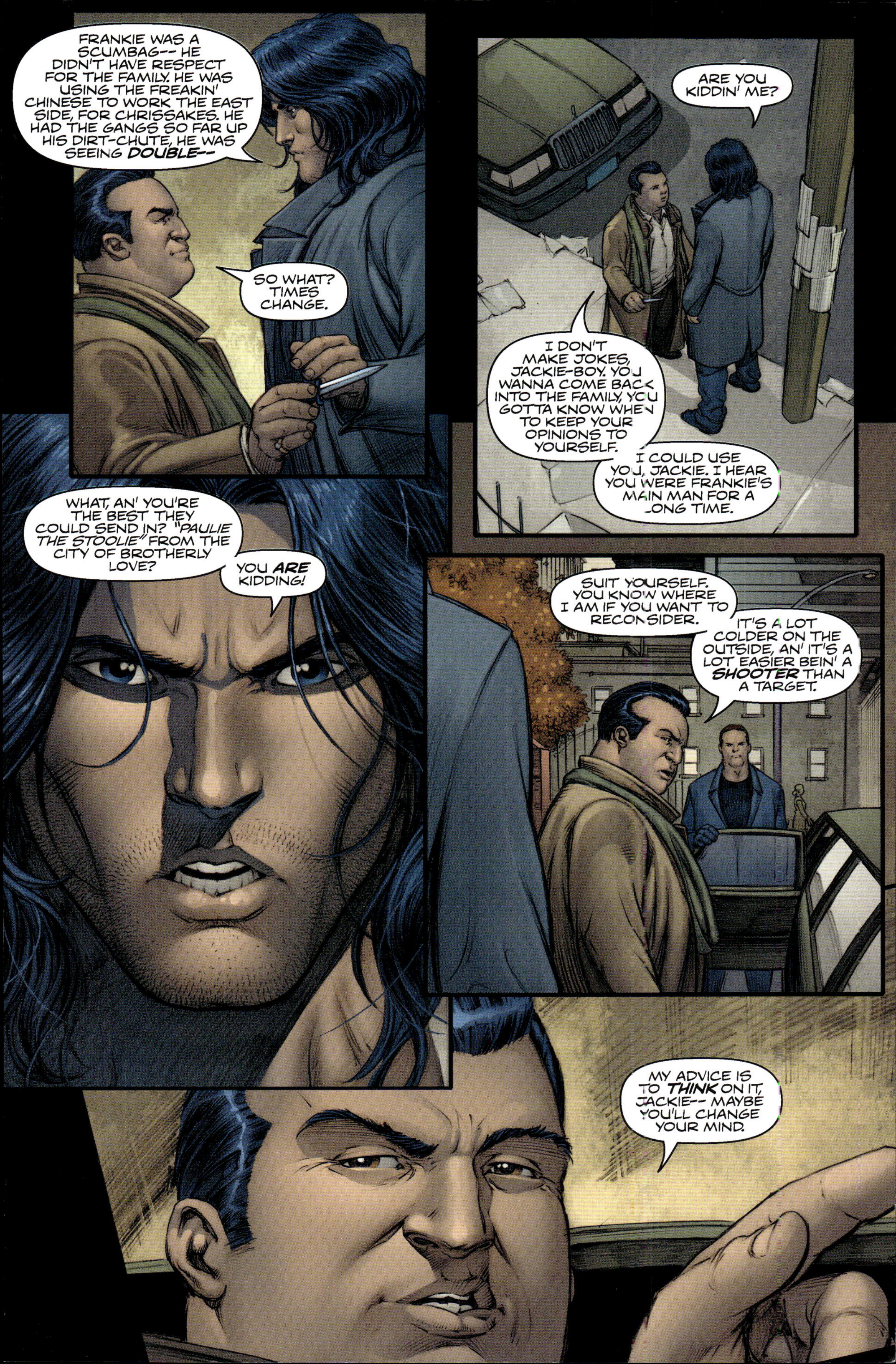
FRANKIE WAS A SCUMBAG-- HE DIDN'T HAVE RESPECT FOR THE FAMILY. HE WAS USING THE FREAKIN' CHINESE TO WORK THE EAST SIDE, FOR CHRISSAKES. HE HAD THE GANGS SO FAR UP HIS DIRT-CHUTE, HE WAS SEEING DOUBLE--
SO WHAT? TIMES CHANGE.
ARE YOU KIDDIN' ME?
I DON'T MAKE JOKES, JACKIE-BOY. YOU WANNA COME BACK INTO THE FAMILY, YOU GOTTA KNOW WHEN TO KEEP YOUR OPINIONS TO YOURSELF.
I COULD USE YOU, JACKIE. I HEAR YOU WERE FRANKIE'S MAIN MAN FOR A LONG TIME.
WHAT, AN' YOU'RE THE BEST THEY COULD SEND IN? "PAULIE THE STOOLIE" FROM THE CITY OF BROTHERLY LOVE?
YOU ARE KIDDING!
SUIT YOURSELF. YOU KNOW WHERE I AM IF YOU WANT TO RECONSIDER.
IT'S A LOT COLDER ON THE OUTSIDE, AN' IT'S A LOT EASIER BEIN' A SHOOTER THAN A TARGET.
MY ADVICE IS TO THINK ON IT, JACKIE-- MAYBE YOU'LL CHANGE YOUR MIND.

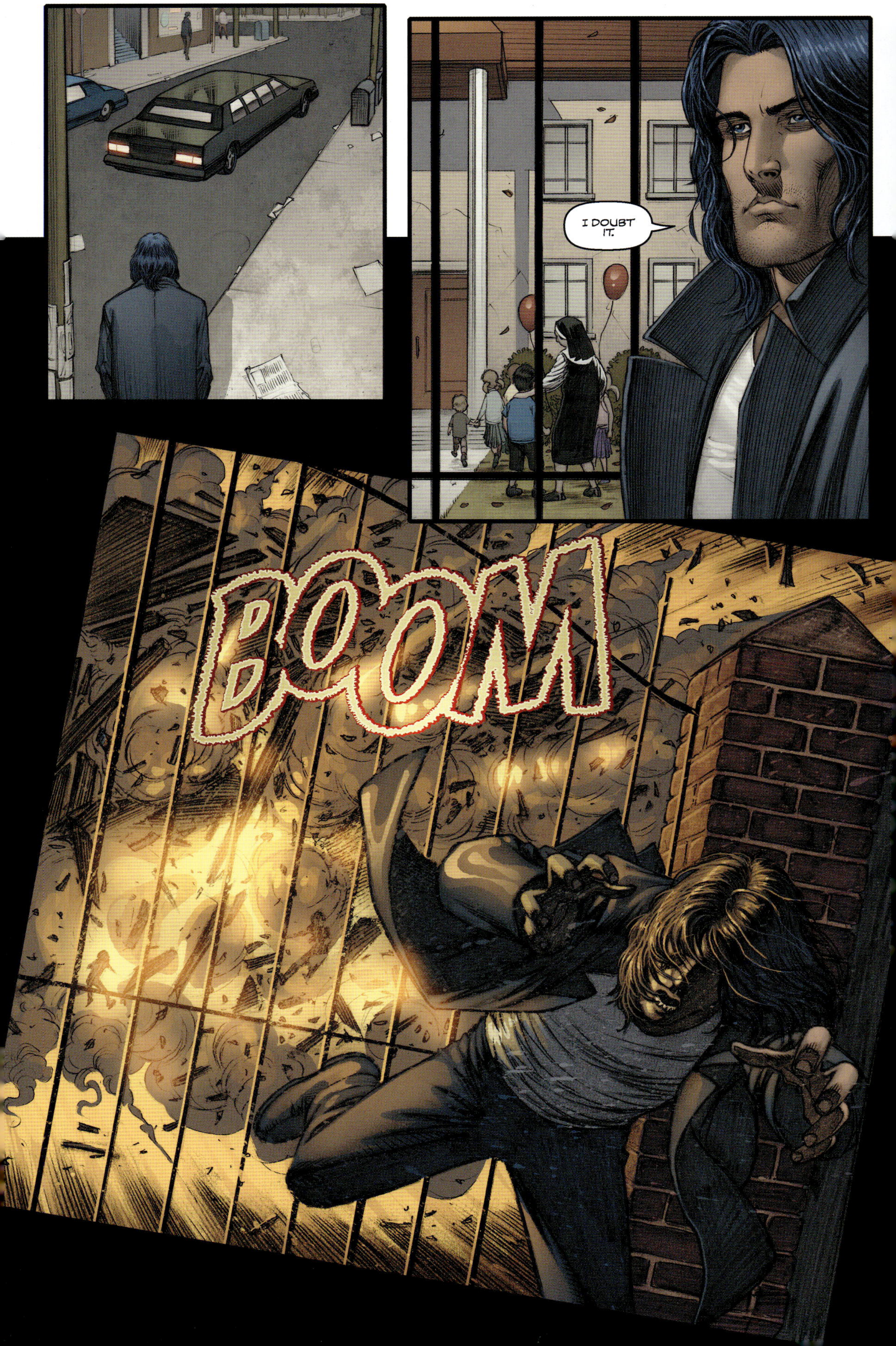
I DOUBT IT.
BOOM

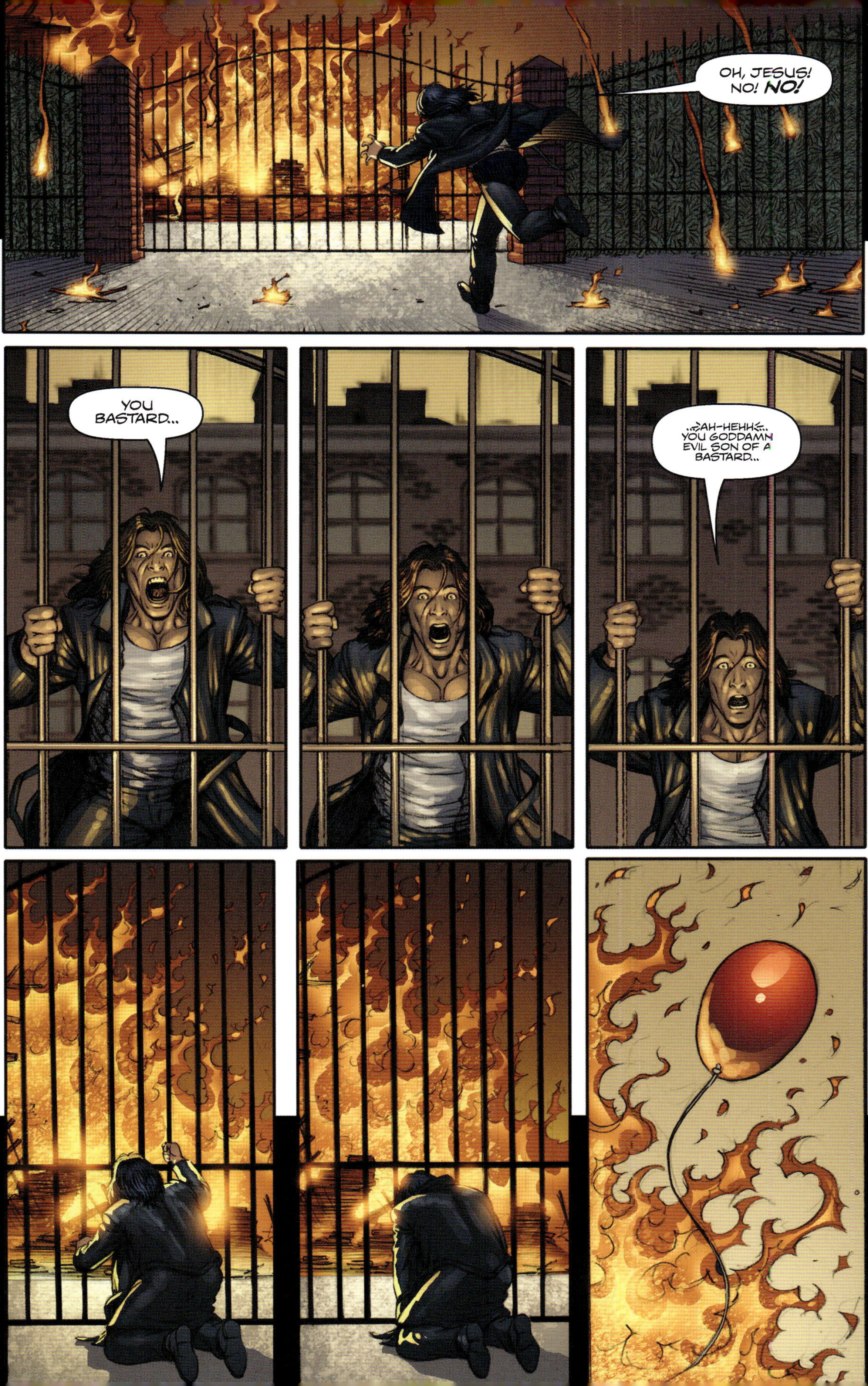

OH, JESUS! NO! **NO!**
YOU BASTARD...
..AH-HEHH.. YOU GODDAMN EVIL SON OF A BASTARD...

SO, WHAT HAPPENED, NINO? WAY I HEARD IT, YOU SOLD ESTACADO DOWN THE RIVER TO PAULIE, HUH?

HEY, THAT LITTLE PUNK WAS THE FIRST IN THE WATER WITH A PADDLE. YOU F#%@ WITH THE FAMILY, THIS IS WHAT HAPPENS.

YEAH, WELL GET THIS: THAT WAS THE SAME ORPHANAGE WHERE FRANKIE FRANCHETTI PICKED UP ESTACADO FROM WHEN HE WAS A LITTLE KID.

IS THAT RIGHT? IT'S A SMALL WORLD.

HAW! HEHH... PAULIE HAD HIM WATCH THE WHOLE THING! CAN YOU IMAGINE THE LOOK ON HIS FACE--?

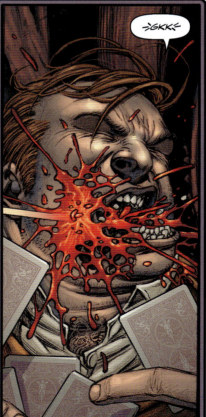

-»GKK«-

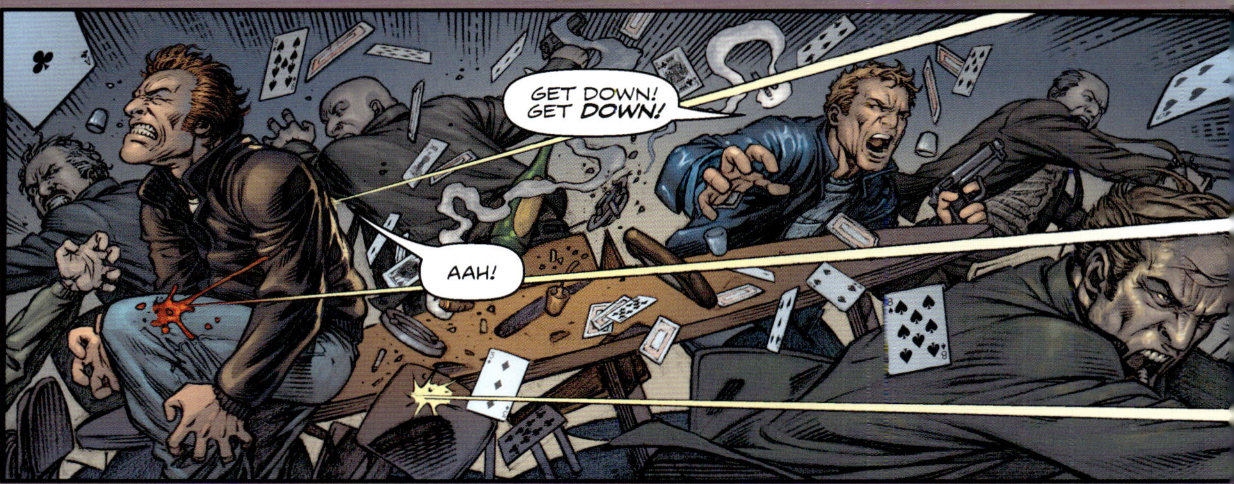
GET DOWN! GET DOWN!
AAH!

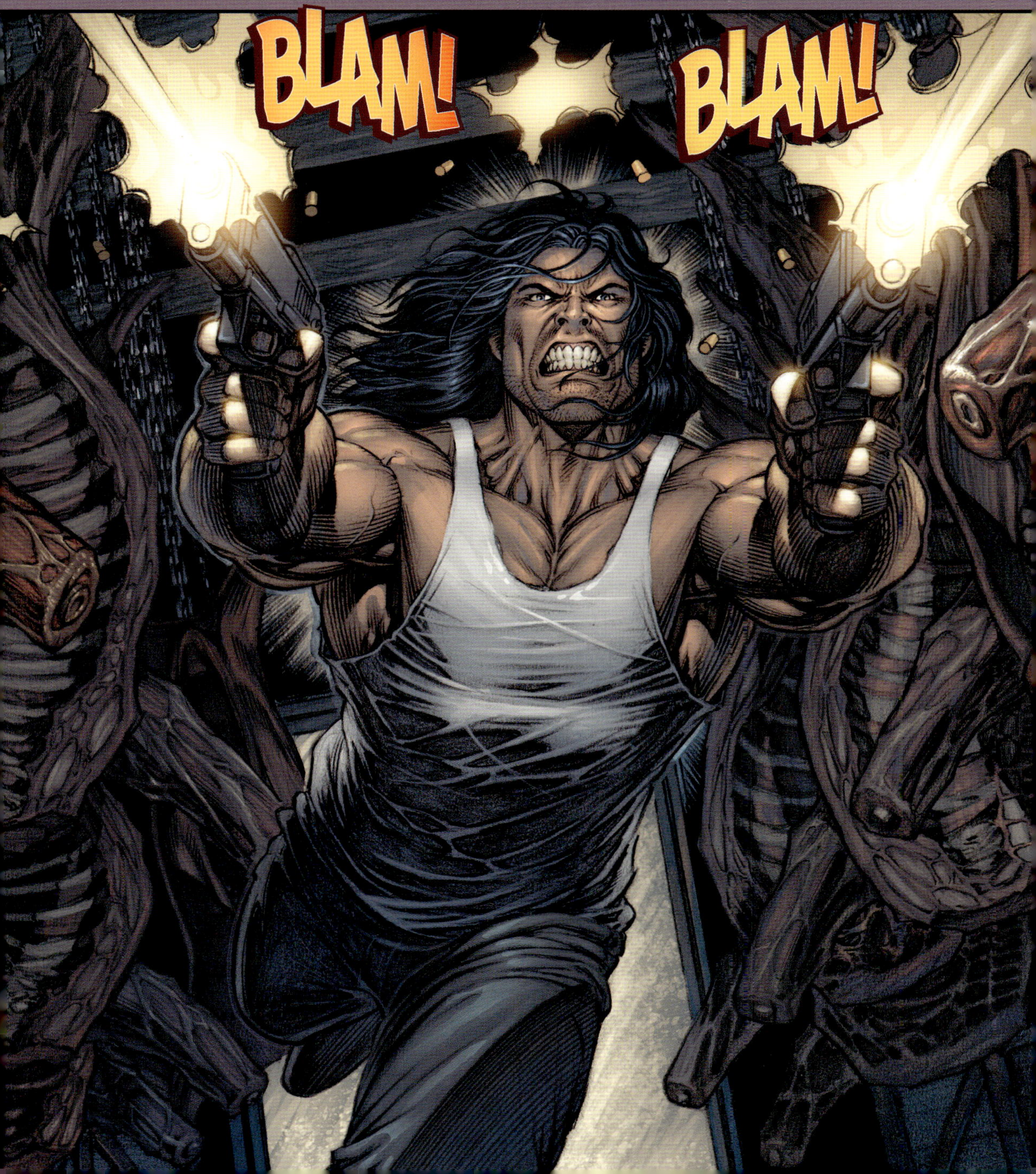
BLAM!
BLAM!

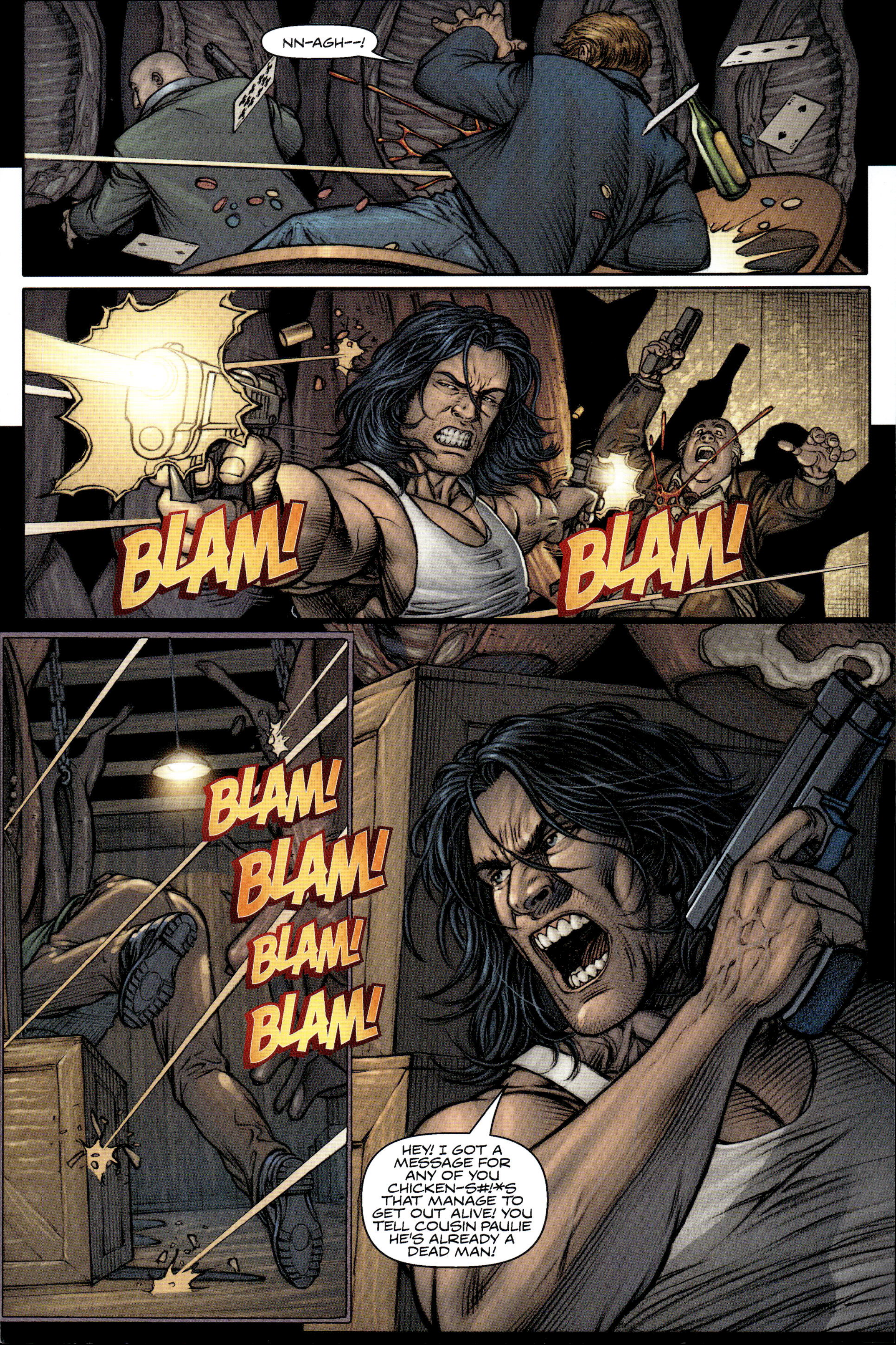
NN-AGH--!
BLAM!
BLAM!
BLAM!
BLAM!
BLAM!
BLAM!
HEY! I GOT A MESSAGE FOR ANY OF YOU CHICKEN-S#!*S THAT MANAGE TO GET OUT ALIVE! YOU TELL COUSIN PAULIE HE'S ALREADY A DEAD MAN!

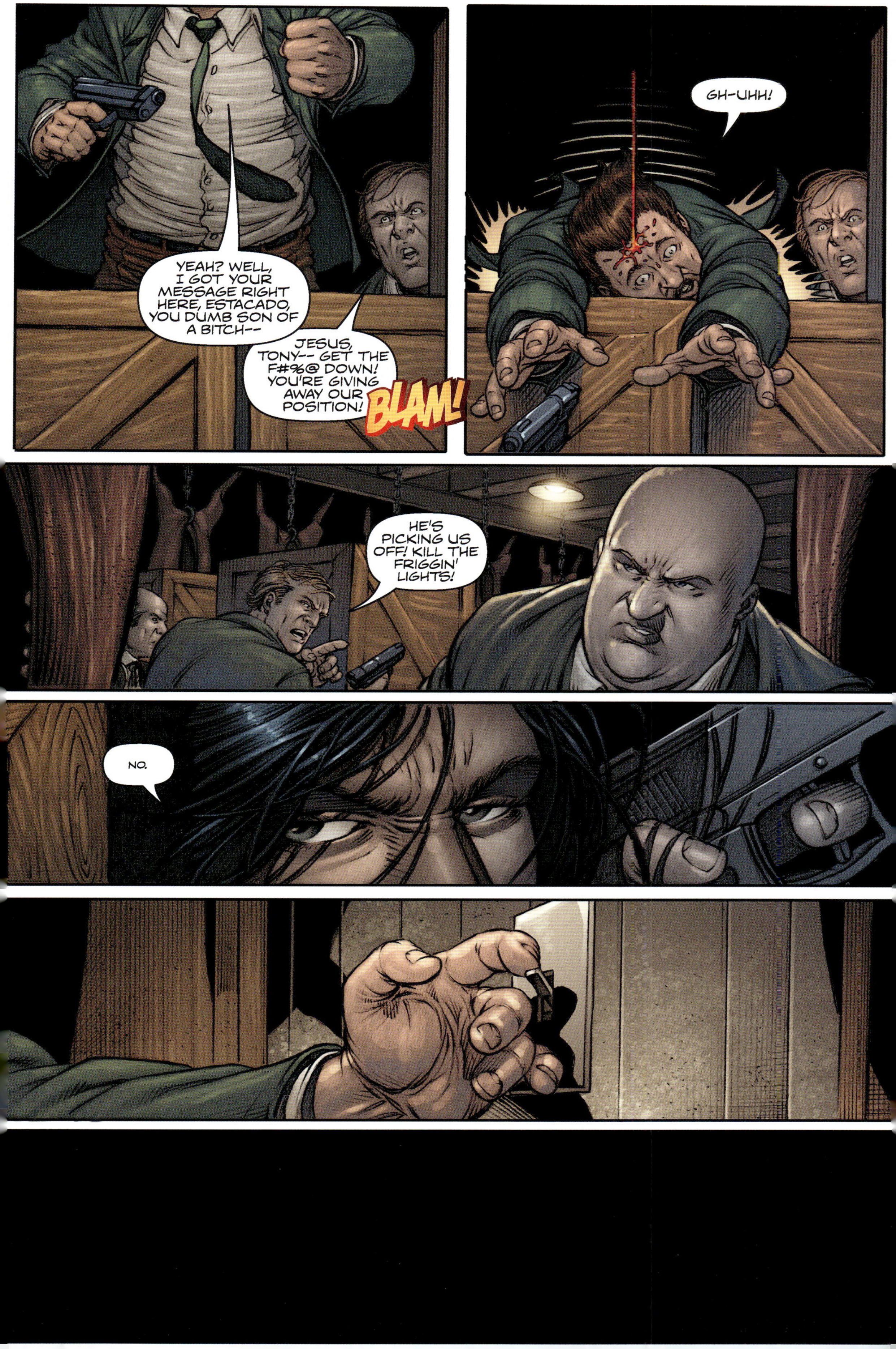
YEAH? WELL, I GOT YOUR MESSAGE RIGHT HERE, ESTACADO, YOU DUMB SON OF A BITCH--
JESUS, TONY-- GET THE F#%@ DOWN! YOU'RE GIVING AWAY OUR POSITION!
BLAM!
GH-UHH!
HE'S PICKING US OFF! KILL THE FRIGGIN' LIGHTS!
NO.

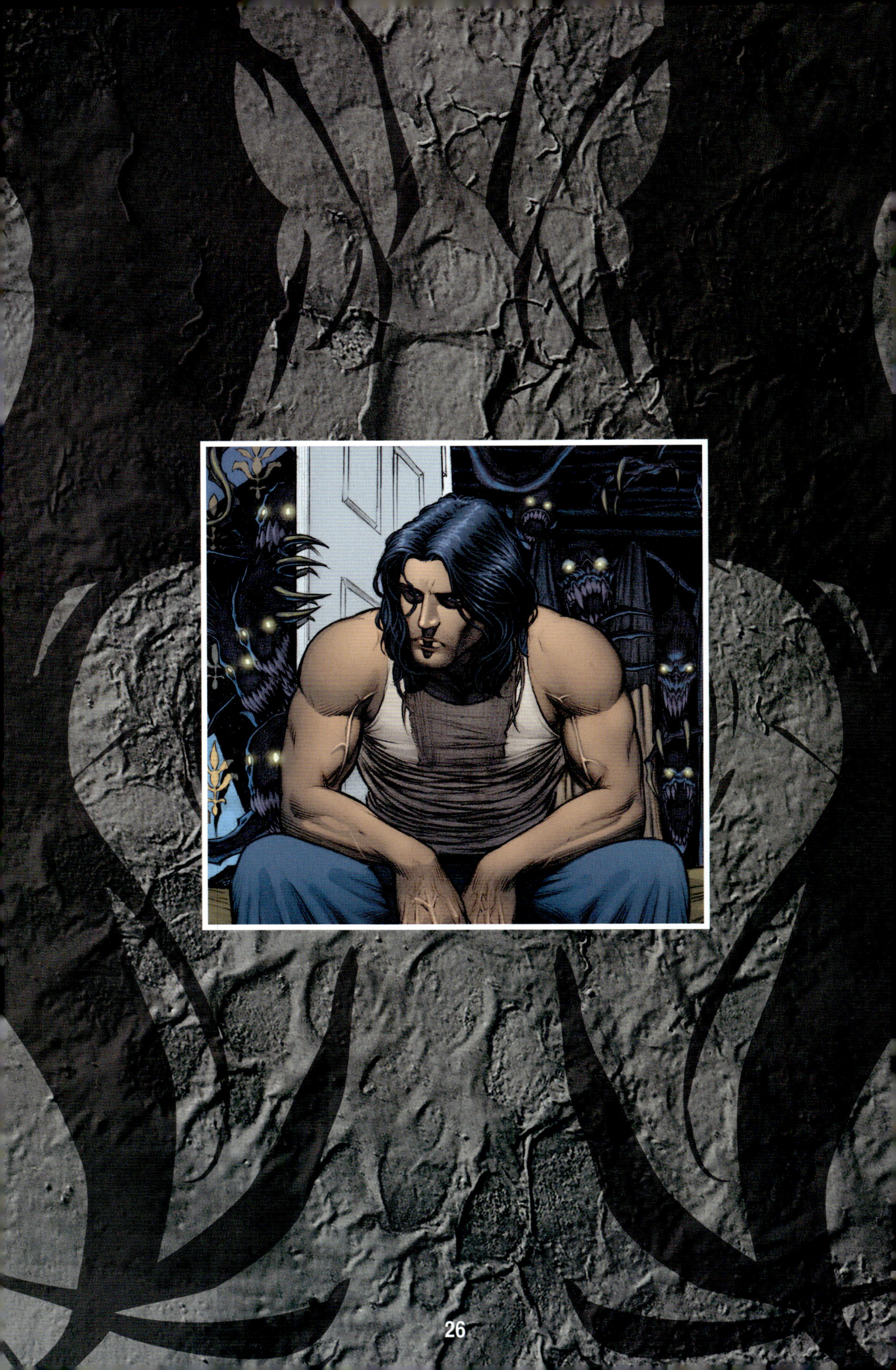

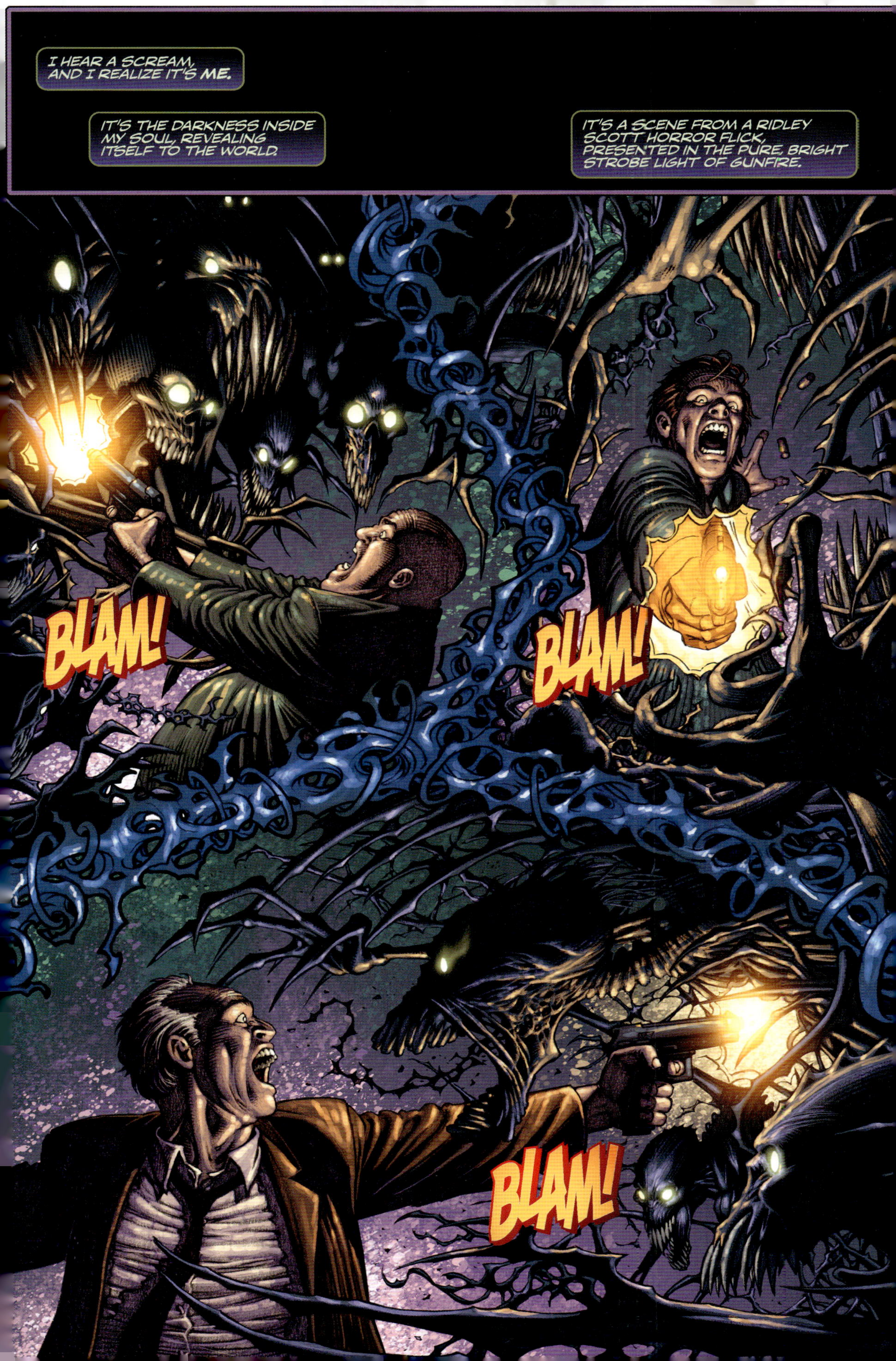
I HEAR A SCREAM, AND I REALIZE IT'S ME.
IT'S THE DARKNESS INSIDE MY SOUL, REVEALING ITSELF TO THE WORLD.
IT'S A SCENE FROM A RIDLEY SCOTT HORROR FLICK, PRESENTED IN THE PURE, BRIGHT STROBE LIGHT OF GUNFIRE.
BLAM!
BLAM!
BLAM!

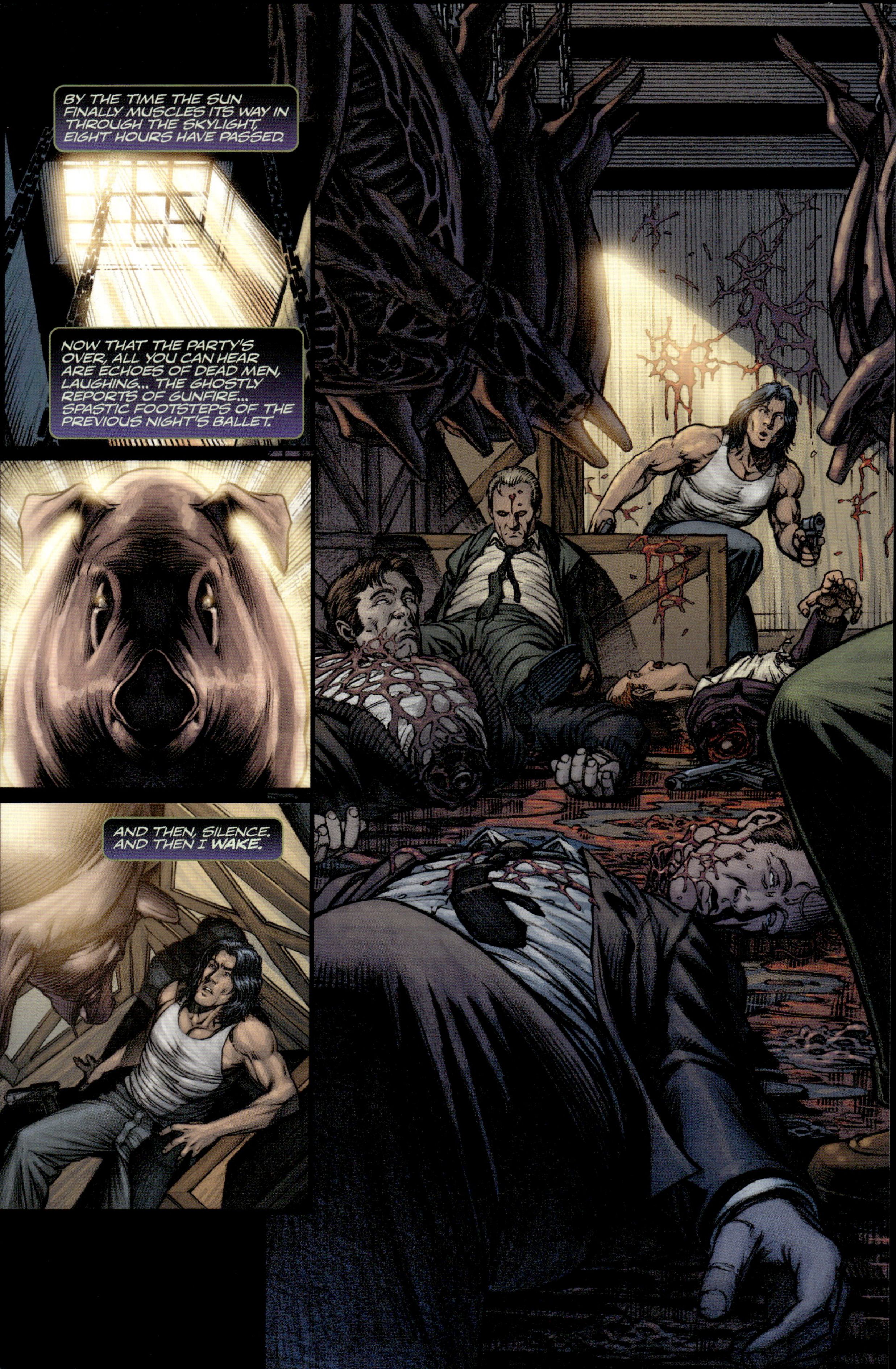

BY THE TIME THE SUN FINALLY MUSCLES ITS WAY IN THROUGH THE SKYLIGHT, EIGHT HOURS HAVE PASSED.
NOW THAT THE PARTY'S OVER, ALL YOU CAN HEAR ARE ECHOES OF DEAD MEN, LAUGHING... THE GHOSTLY REPORTS OF GUNFIRE... SPASTIC FOOTSTEPS OF THE PREVIOUS NIGHT'S BALLET.
AND THEN, SILENCE. AND THEN I **WAKE.**

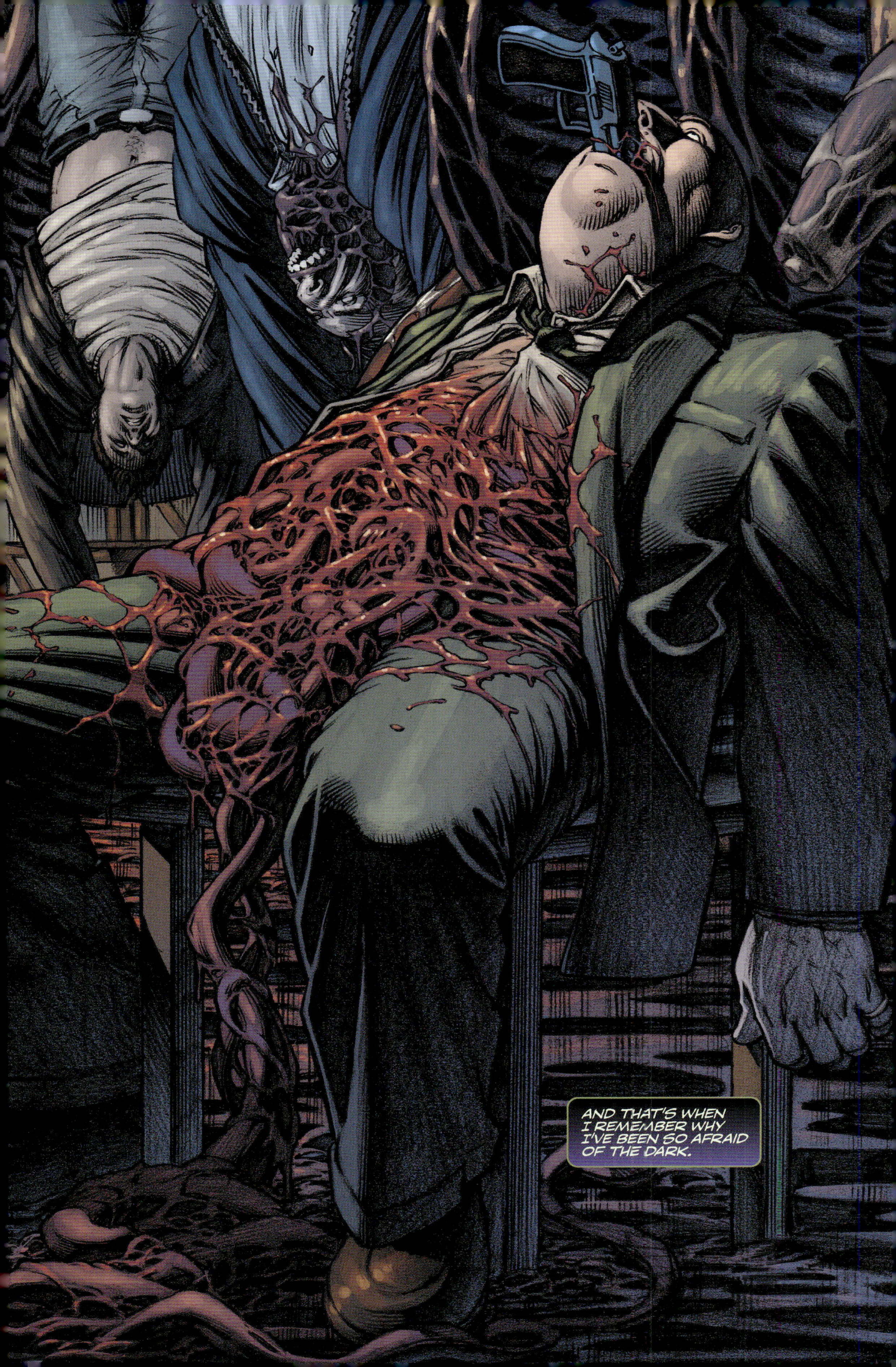
AND THAT'S WHEN I REMEMBER WHY I'VE BEEN SO AFRAID OF THE DARK.

The Darkness Issue #42
cover art by: Dale Keown & Matt Milla

THE DARKNESS #42

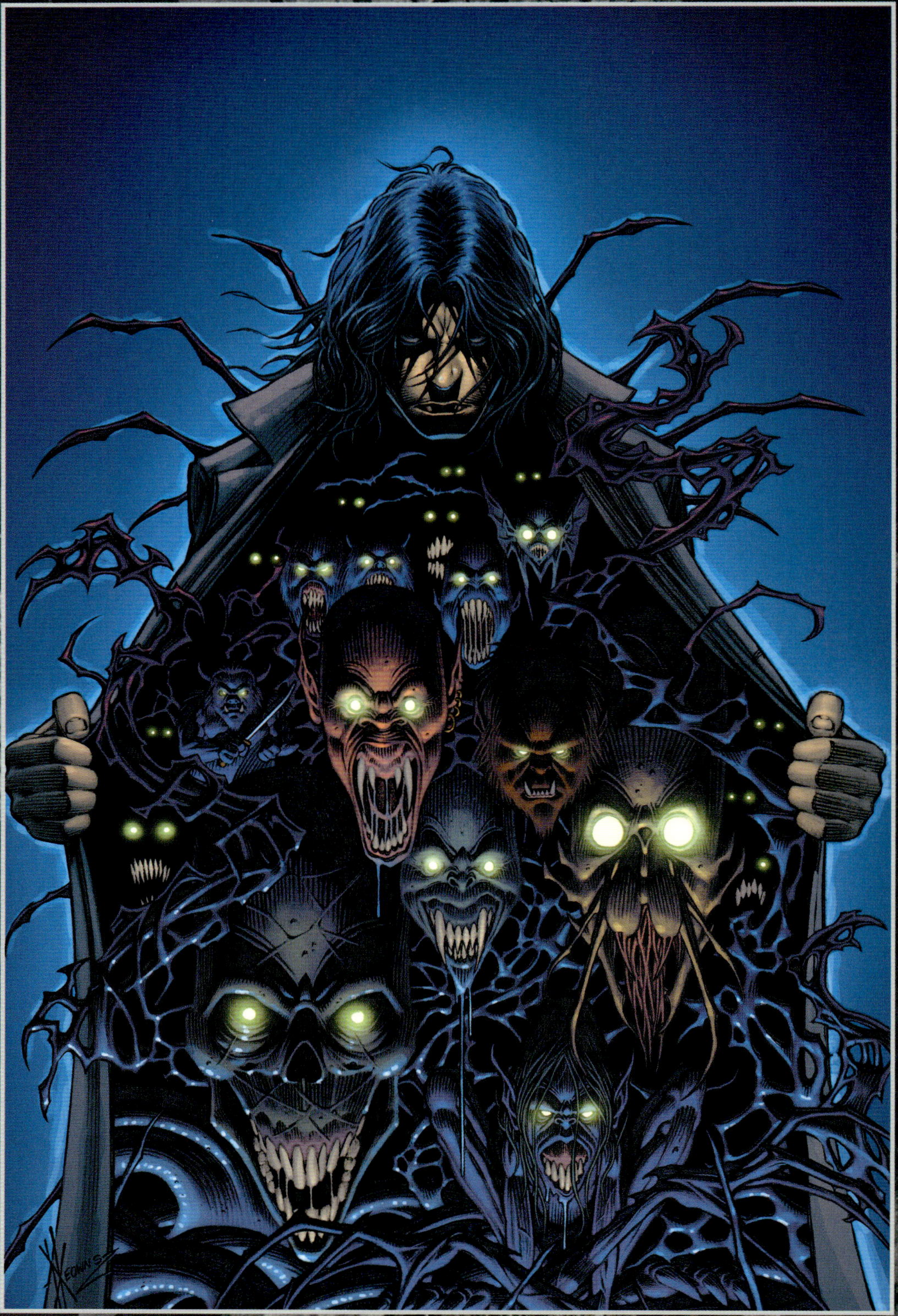

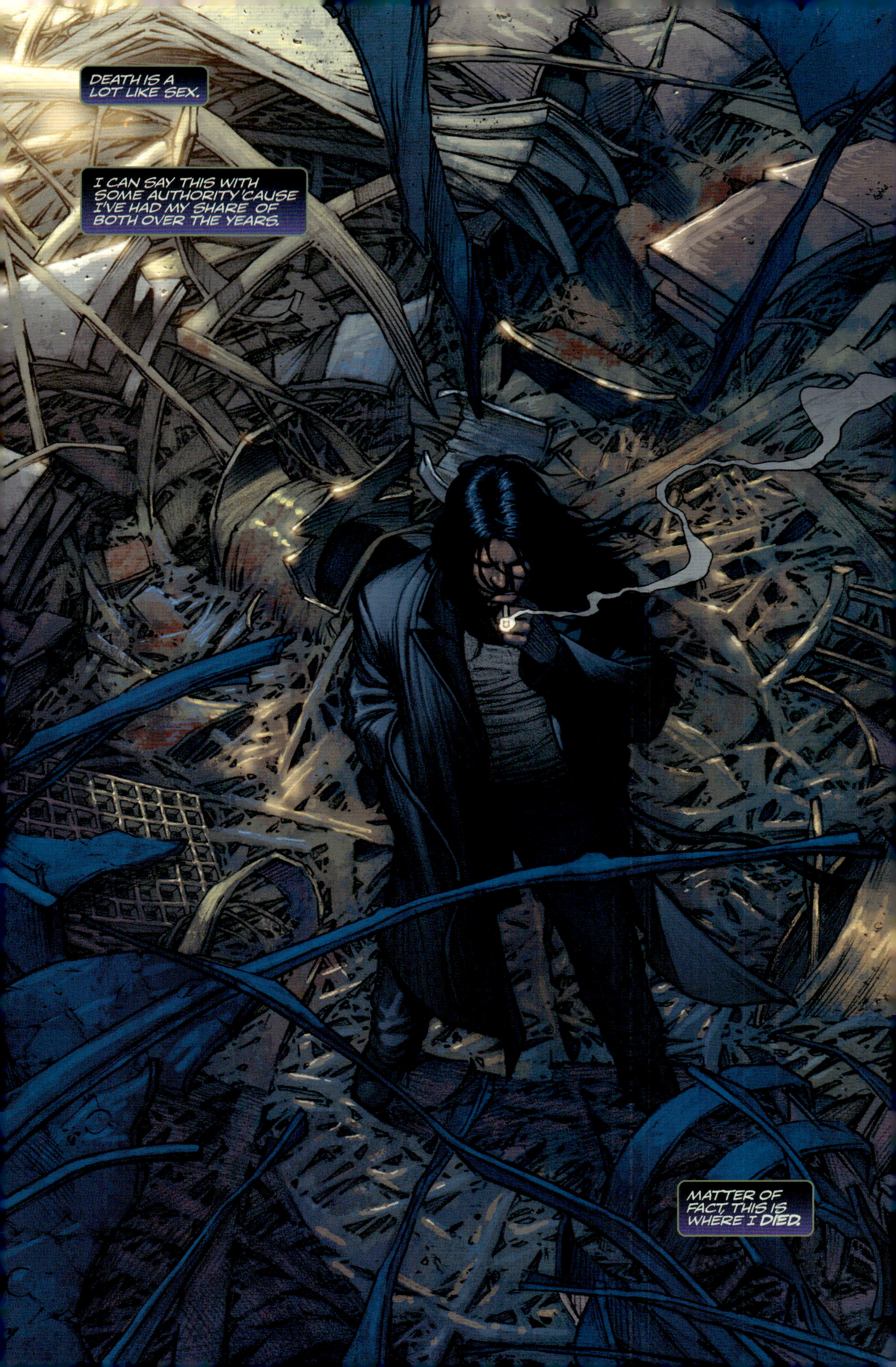
DEATH IS A LOT LIKE SEX.
I CAN SAY THIS WITH SOME AUTHORITY 'CAUSE I'VE HAD MY SHARE OF BOTH OVER THE YEARS.
MATTER OF FACT, THIS IS WHERE I DIED.

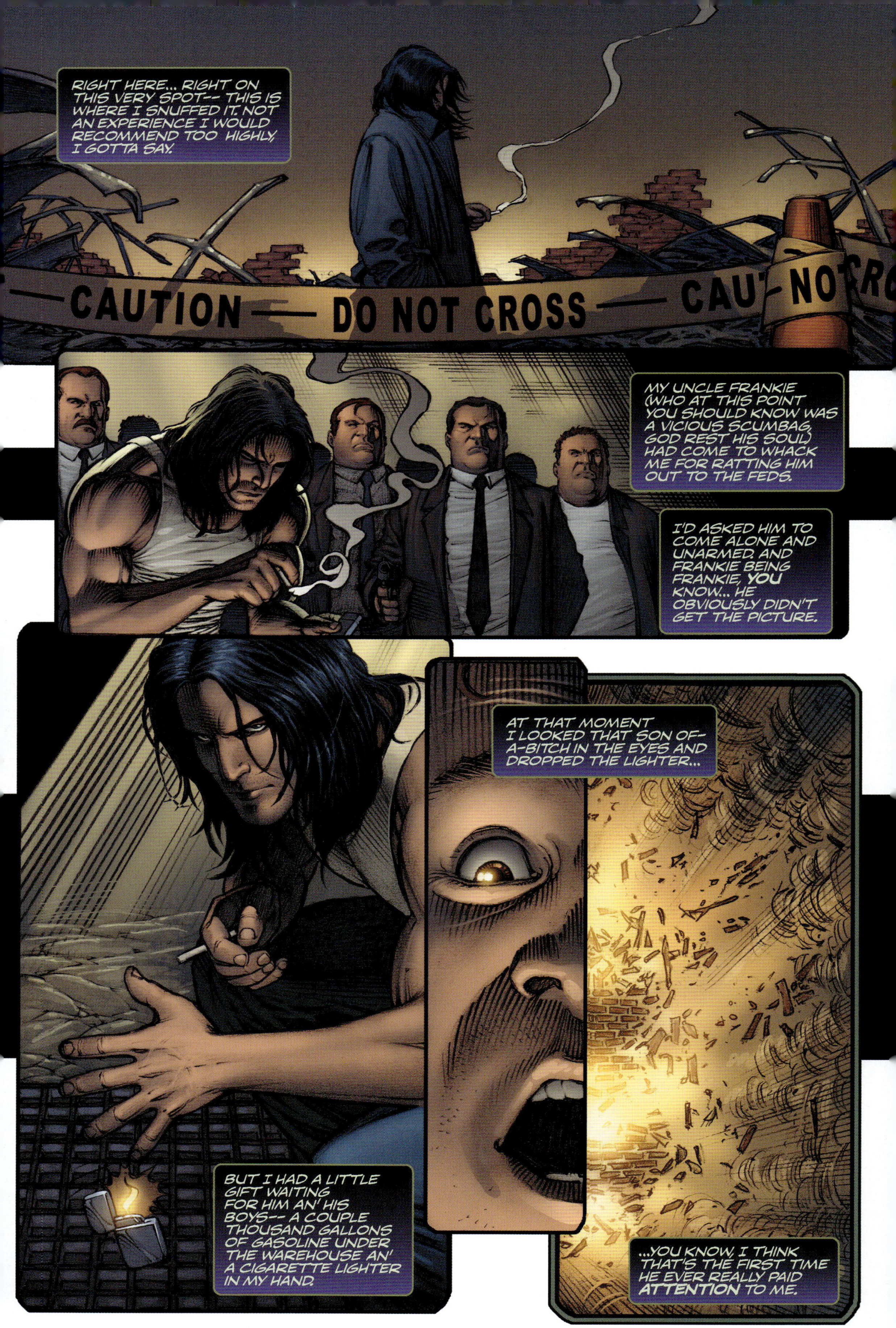
RIGHT HERE... RIGHT ON THIS VERY SPOT-- THIS IS WHERE I SNUFFED IT. NOT AN EXPERIENCE I WOULD RECOMMEND TOO HIGHLY, I GOTTA SAY.
CAUTION — DO NOT CROSS — CAUT
MY UNCLE FRANKIE (WHO AT THIS POINT YOU SHOULD KNOW WAS A VICIOUS SCUMBAG, GOD REST HIS SOUL) HAD COME TO WHACK ME FOR RATTING HIM OUT TO THE FEDS.
I'D ASKED HIM TO COME ALONE AND UNARMED. AND FRANKIE BEING FRANKIE, YOU KNOW... HE OBVIOUSLY DIDN'T GET THE PICTURE.
BUT I HAD A LITTLE GIFT WAITING FOR HIM AN' HIS BOYS-- A COUPLE THOUSAND GALLONS OF GASOLINE UNDER THE WAREHOUSE AN' A CIGARETTE LIGHTER IN MY HAND.
AT THAT MOMENT I LOOKED THAT SON OF-A-BITCH IN THE EYES AND DROPPED THE LIGHTER...
...YOU KNOW, I THINK THAT'S THE FIRST TIME HE EVER REALLY PAID ATTENTION TO ME.

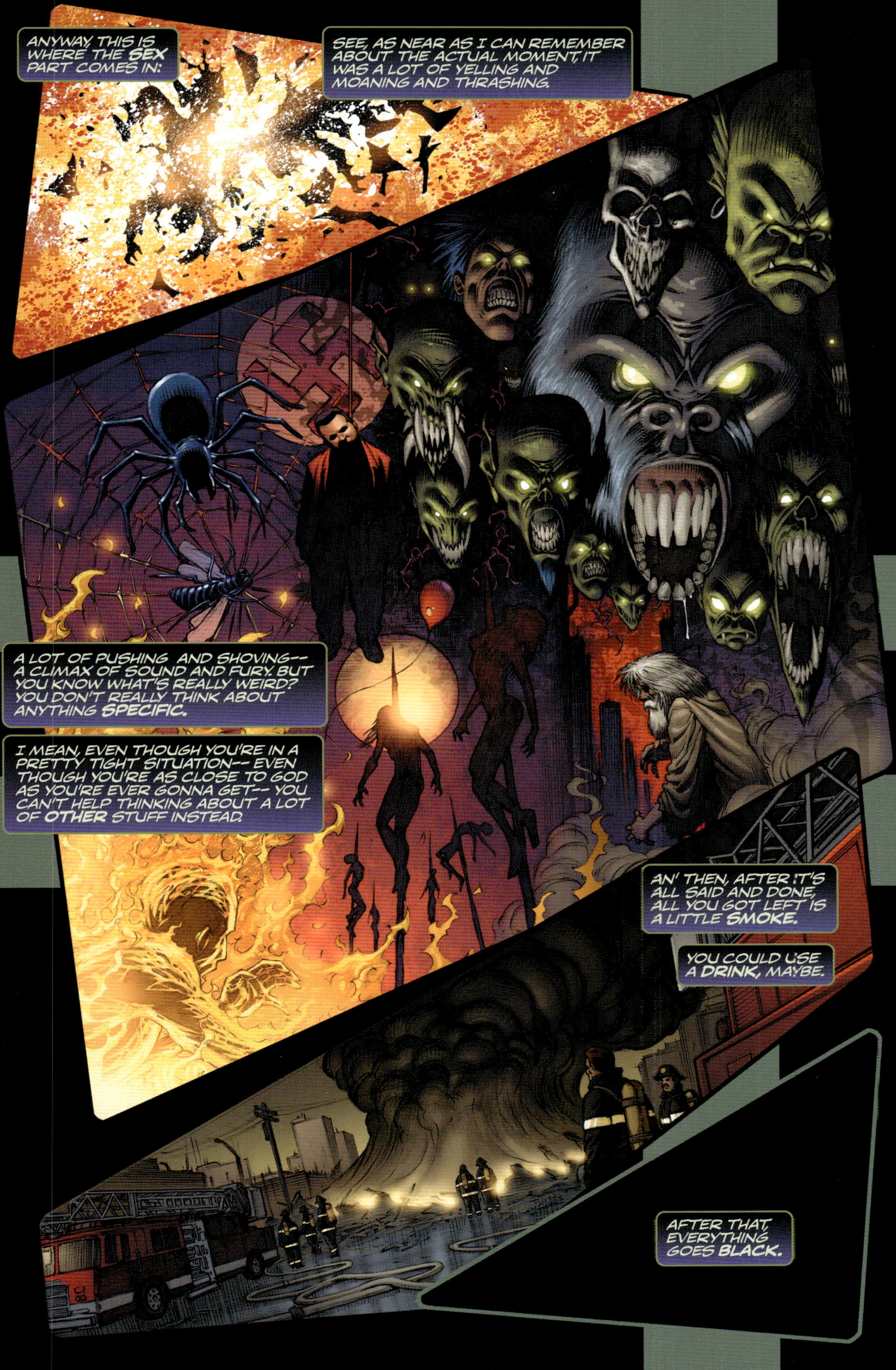
ANYWAY, THIS IS WHERE THE SEX PART COMES IN:
SEE, AS NEAR AS I CAN REMEMBER ABOUT THE ACTUAL MOMENT, IT WAS A LOT OF YELLING AND MOANING AND THRASHING.
A LOT OF PUSHING AND SHOVING-- A CLIMAX OF SOUND AND FURY. BUT YOU KNOW WHAT'S REALLY WEIRD? YOU DON'T REALLY THINK ABOUT ANYTHING SPECIFIC.
I MEAN, EVEN THOUGH YOU'RE IN A PRETTY TIGHT SITUATION-- EVEN THOUGH YOU'RE AS CLOSE TO GOD AS YOU'RE EVER GONNA GET-- YOU CAN'T HELP THINKING ABOUT A LOT OF OTHER STUFF INSTEAD.
AN' THEN, AFTER IT'S ALL SAID AND DONE, ALL YOU GOT LEFT IS A LITTLE SMOKE.
YOU COULD USE A DRINK, MAYBE.
AFTER THAT, EVERYTHING GOES BLACK.

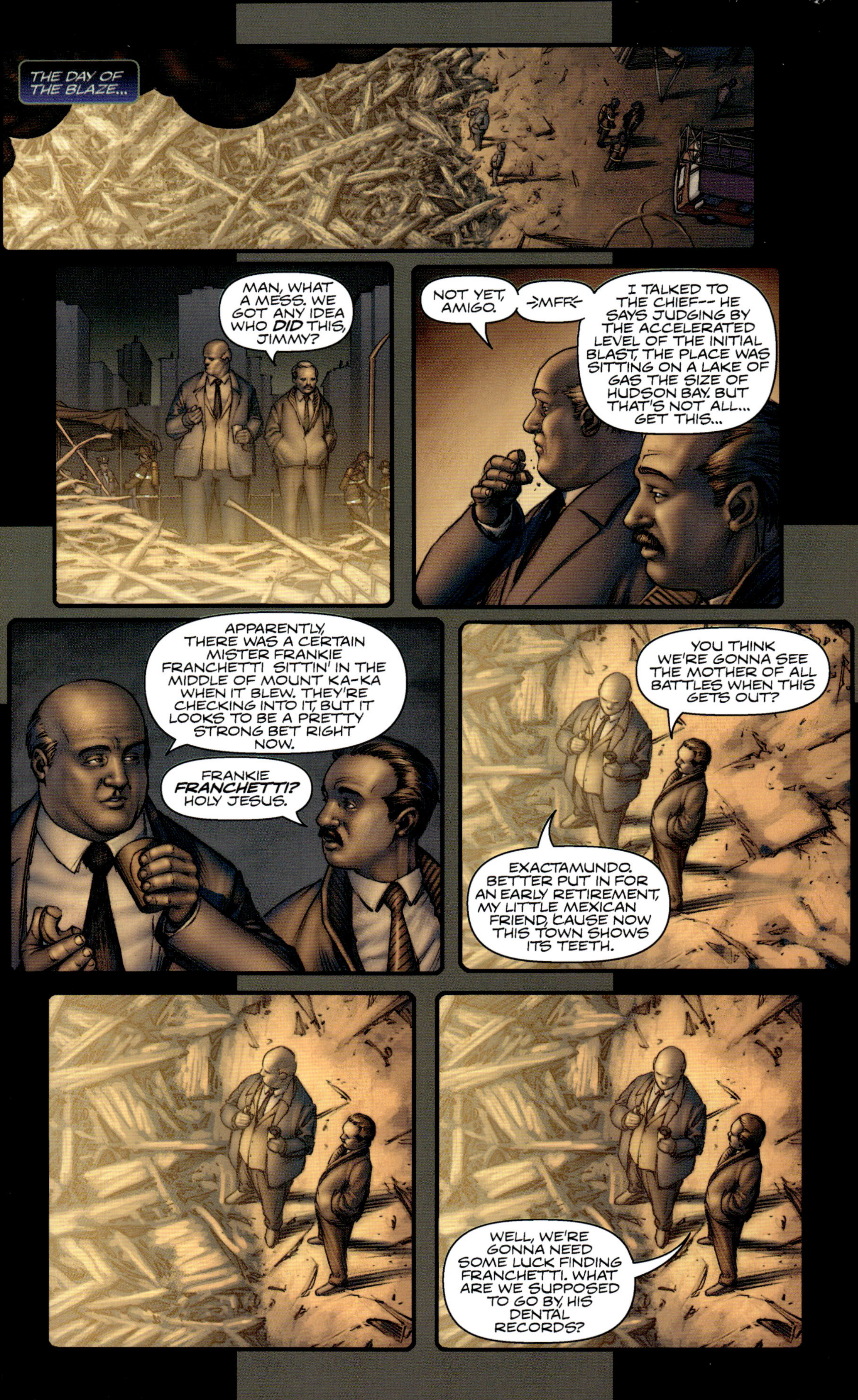
THE DAY OF THE BLAZE...
MAN, WHAT A MESS. WE GOT ANY IDEA WHO DID THIS, JIMMY?
NOT YET, AMIGO.
MFF
I TALKED TO THE CHIEF-- HE SAYS JUDGING BY THE ACCELERATED LEVEL OF THE INITIAL BLAST, THE PLACE WAS SITTING ON A LAKE OF GAS THE SIZE OF HUDSON BAY. BUT THAT'S NOT ALL... GET THIS...
APPARENTLY, THERE WAS A CERTAIN MISTER FRANKIE FRANCHETTI SITTIN' IN THE MIDDLE OF MOUNT KA-KA WHEN IT BLEW. THEY'RE CHECKING INTO IT, BUT IT LOOKS TO BE A PRETTY STRONG BET RIGHT NOW.
FRANKIE FRANCHETTI? HOLY JESUS.
YOU THINK WE'RE GONNA SEE THE MOTHER OF ALL BATTLES WHEN THIS GETS OUT?
EXACTAMUNDO. BETTER PUT IN FOR AN EARLY RETIREMENT, MY LITTLE MEXICAN FRIEND, CAUSE NOW THIS TOWN SHOWS ITS TEETH.
WELL, WE'RE GONNA NEED SOME LUCK FINDING FRANCHETTI. WHAT ARE WE SUPPOSED TO GO BY, HIS DENTAL RECORDS?

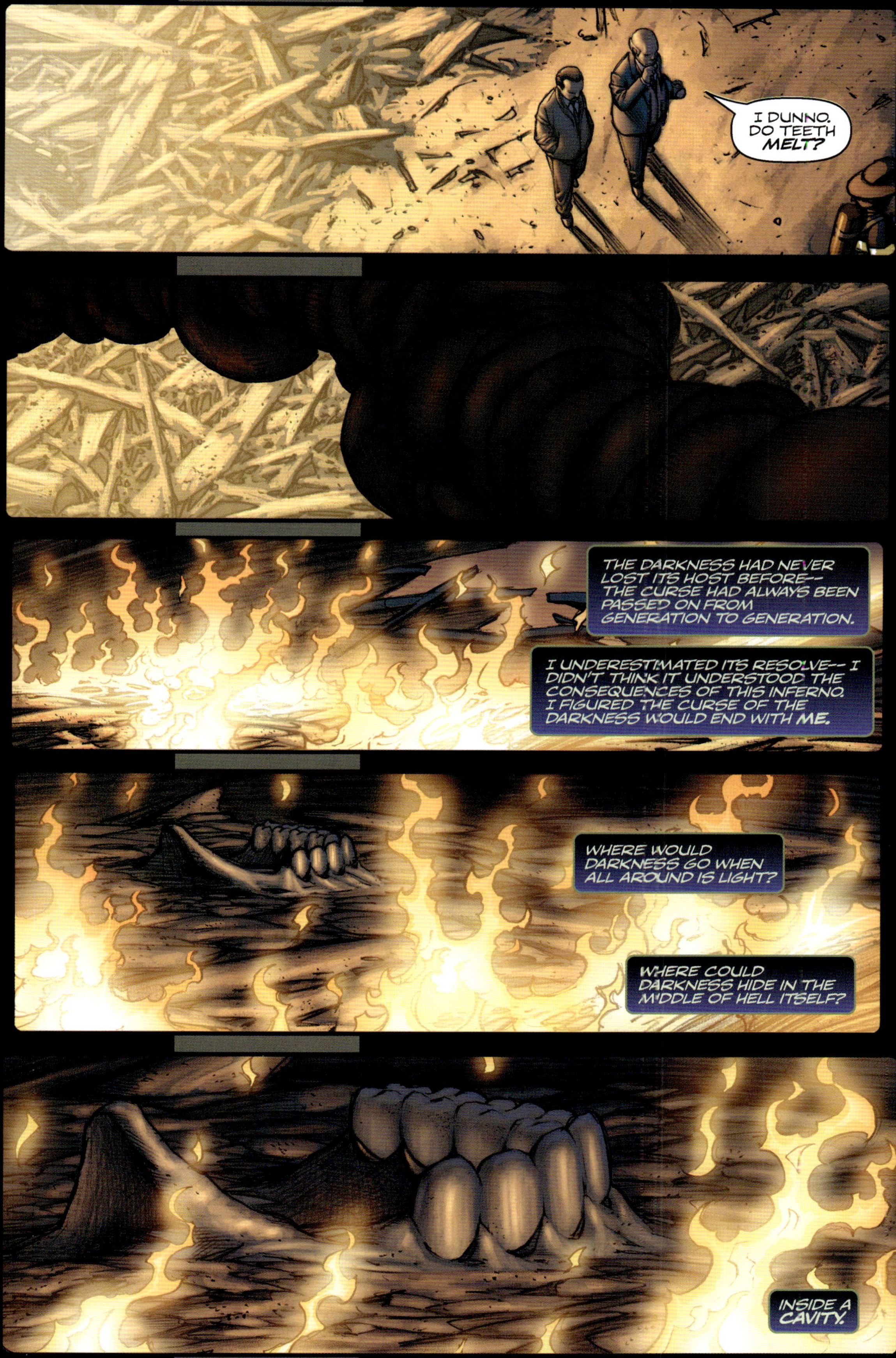
I DUNNO. DO TEETH MELT?
THE DARKNESS HAD NEVER LOST ITS HOST BEFORE-- THE CURSE HAD ALWAYS BEEN PASSED ON FROM GENERATION TO GENERATION.
I UNDERESTIMATED ITS RESOLVE-- I DIDN'T THINK IT UNDERSTOOD THE CONSEQUENCES OF THIS INFERNO. I FIGURED THE CURSE OF THE DARKNESS WOULD END WITH ME.
WHERE WOULD DARKNESS GO WHEN ALL AROUND IS LIGHT?
WHERE COULD DARKNESS HIDE IN THE MIDDLE OF HELL ITSELF?
INSIDE A CAVITY.

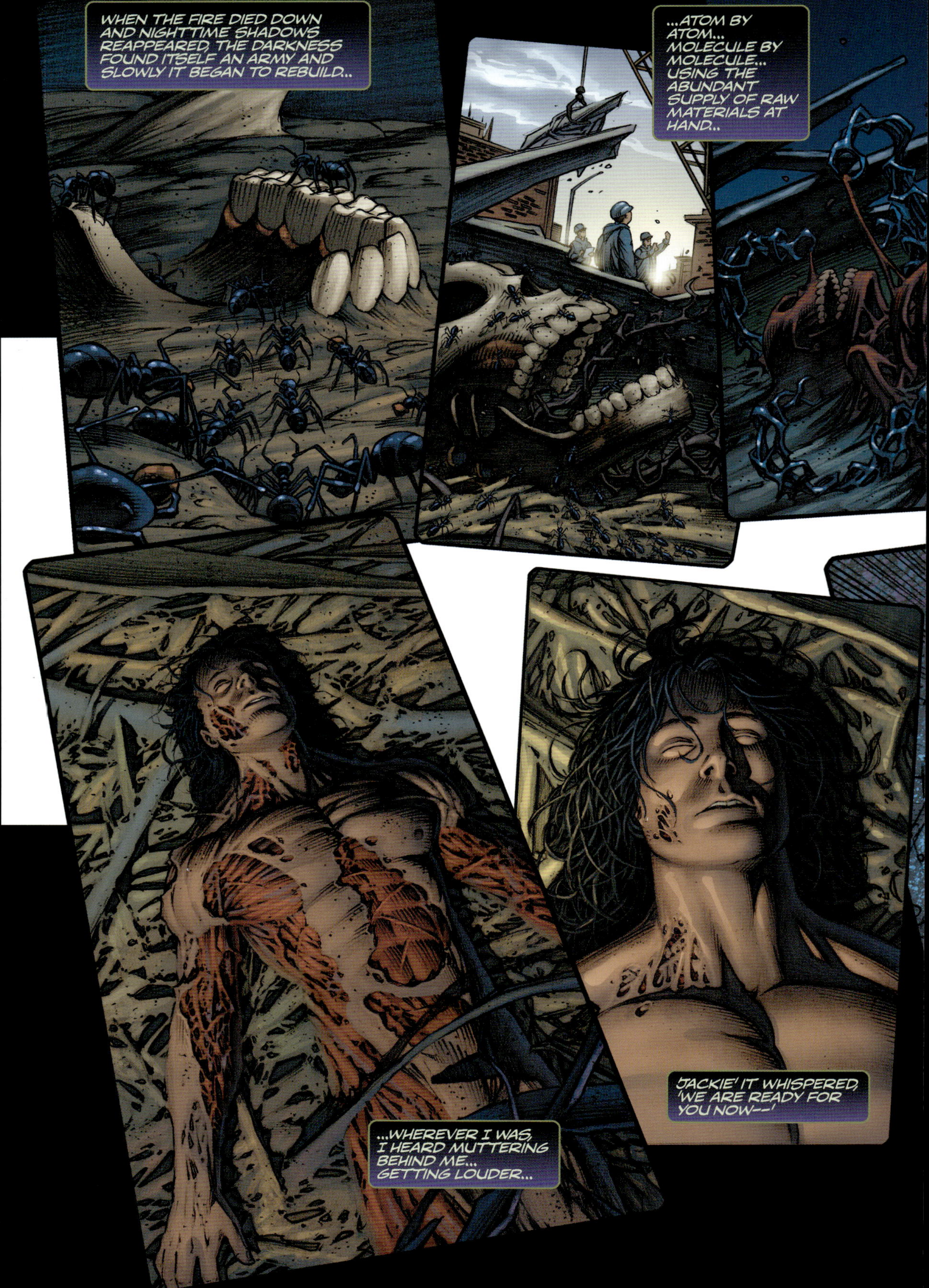
WHEN THE FIRE DIED DOWN AND NIGHTTIME SHADOWS REAPPEARED, THE DARKNESS FOUND ITSELF AN ARMY AND SLOWLY IT BEGAN TO REBUILD..
...ATOM BY ATOM... MOLECULE BY MOLECULE... USING THE ABUNDANT SUPPLY OF RAW MATERIALS AT HAND..
...WHEREVER I WAS, I HEARD MUTTERING BEHIND ME... GETTING LOUDER...
'JACKIE' IT WHISPERED, 'WE ARE READY FOR YOU NOW--'

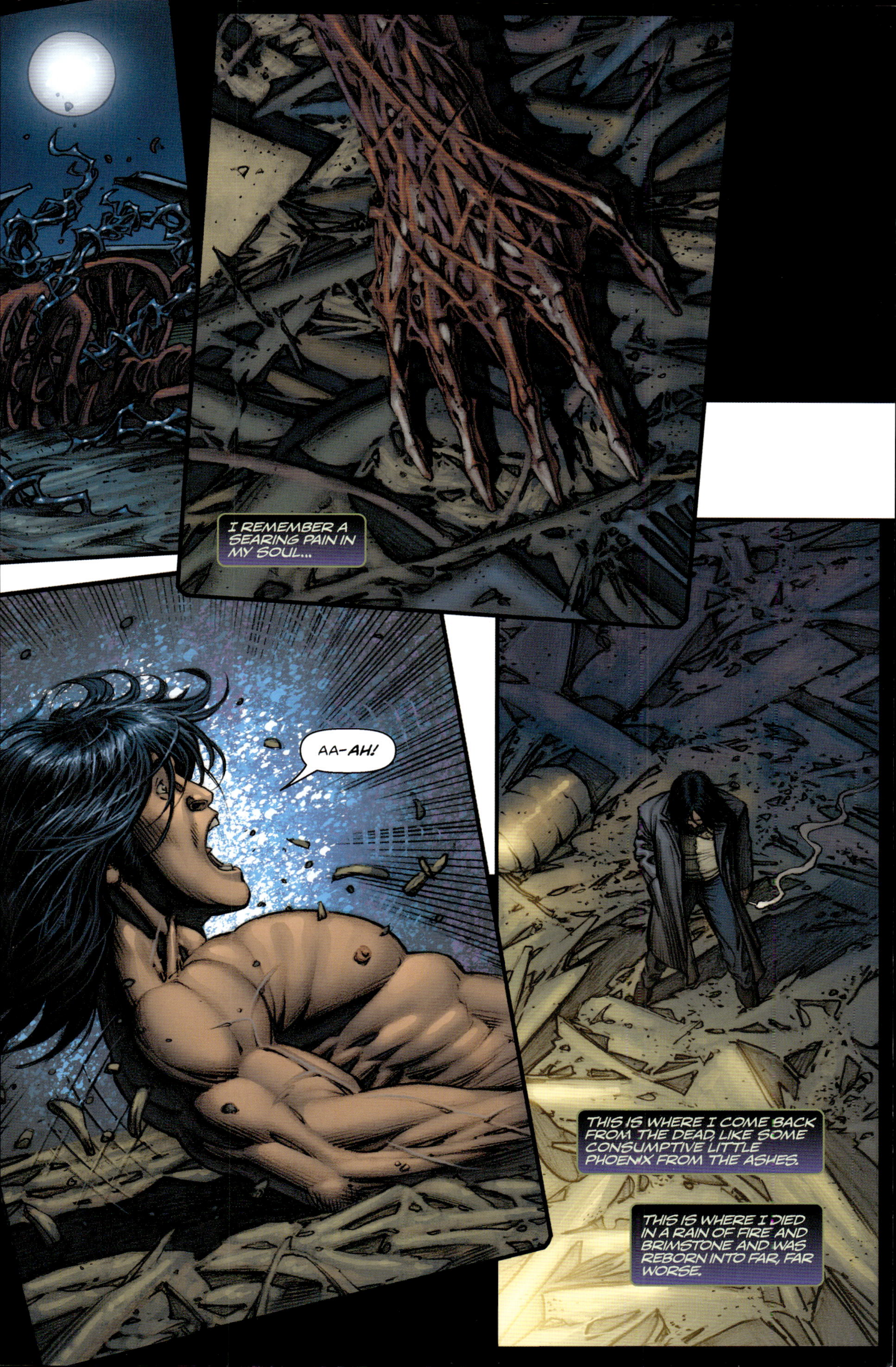
I REMEMBER A SEARING PAIN IN MY SOUL...
AA-AH!
THIS IS WHERE I COME BACK FROM THE DEAD, LIKE SOME CONSUMPTIVE LITTLE PHOENIX FROM THE ASHES.
THIS IS WHERE I DIED IN A RAIN OF FIRE AND BRIMSTONE AND WAS REBORN INTO FAR, FAR WORSE.

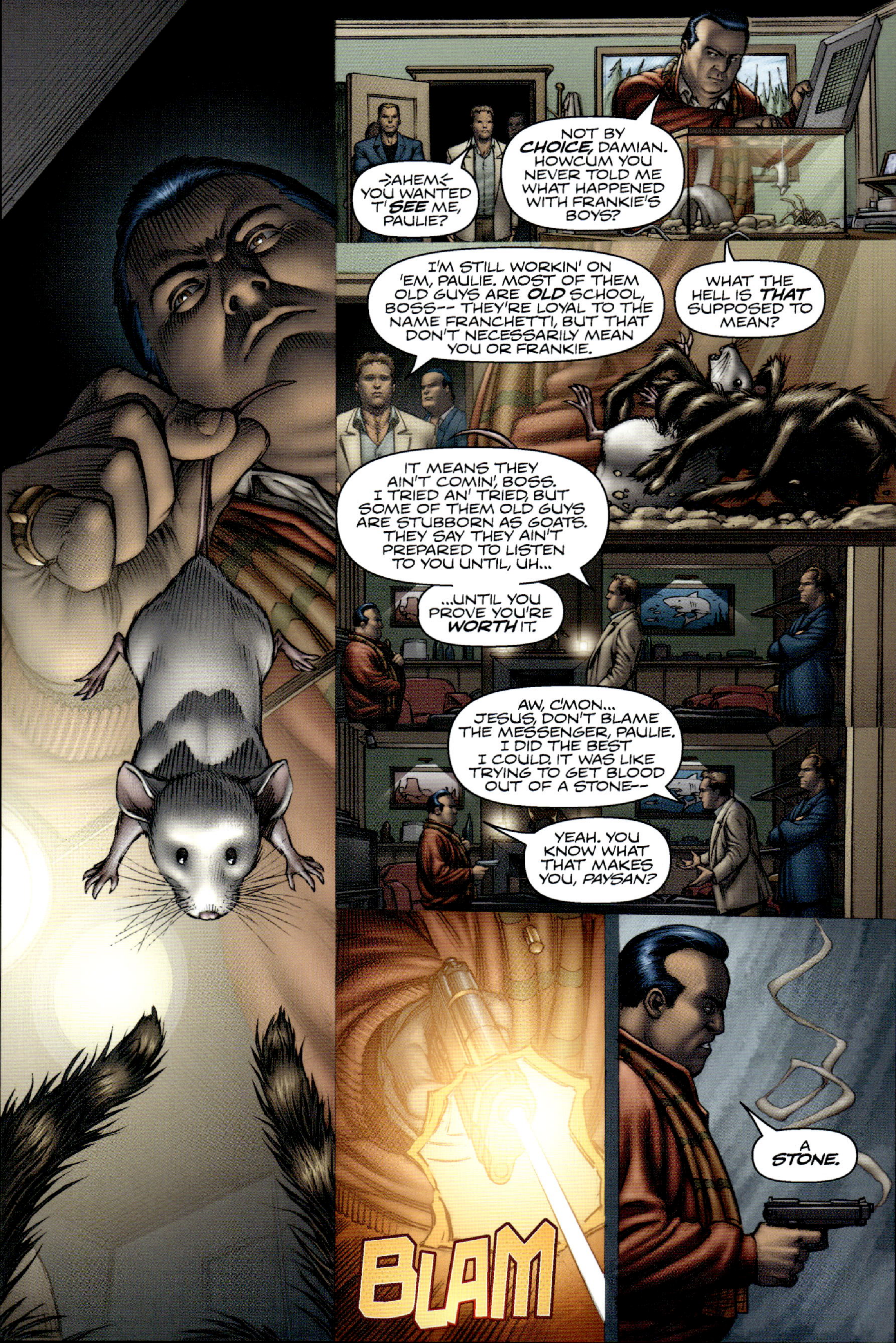

-AHEM- YOU WANTED T' SEE ME, PAULIE?
NOT BY CHOICE, DAMIAN. HOWCUM YOU NEVER TOLD ME WHAT HAPPENED WITH FRANKIE'S BOYS?
I'M STILL WORKIN' ON 'EM, PAULIE. MOST OF THEM OLD GUYS ARE OLD SCHOOL, BOSS-- THEY'RE LOYAL TO THE NAME FRANCHETTI, BUT THAT DON'T NECESSARILY MEAN YOU OR FRANKIE.
WHAT THE HELL IS THAT SUPPOSED TO MEAN?
IT MEANS THEY AIN'T COMIN', BOSS. I TRIED AN' TRIED, BUT SOME OF THEM OLD GUYS ARE STUBBORN AS GOATS. THEY SAY THEY AIN'T PREPARED TO LISTEN TO YOU UNTIL, UH...
...UNTIL YOU PROVE YOU'RE WORTH IT.
AW, C'MON... JESUS, DON'T BLAME THE MESSENGER, PAULIE. I DID THE BEST I COULD. IT WAS LIKE TRYING TO GET BLOOD OUT OF A STONE--
YEAH. YOU KNOW WHAT THAT MAKES YOU, PAYSAN?
BLAM
A STONE.

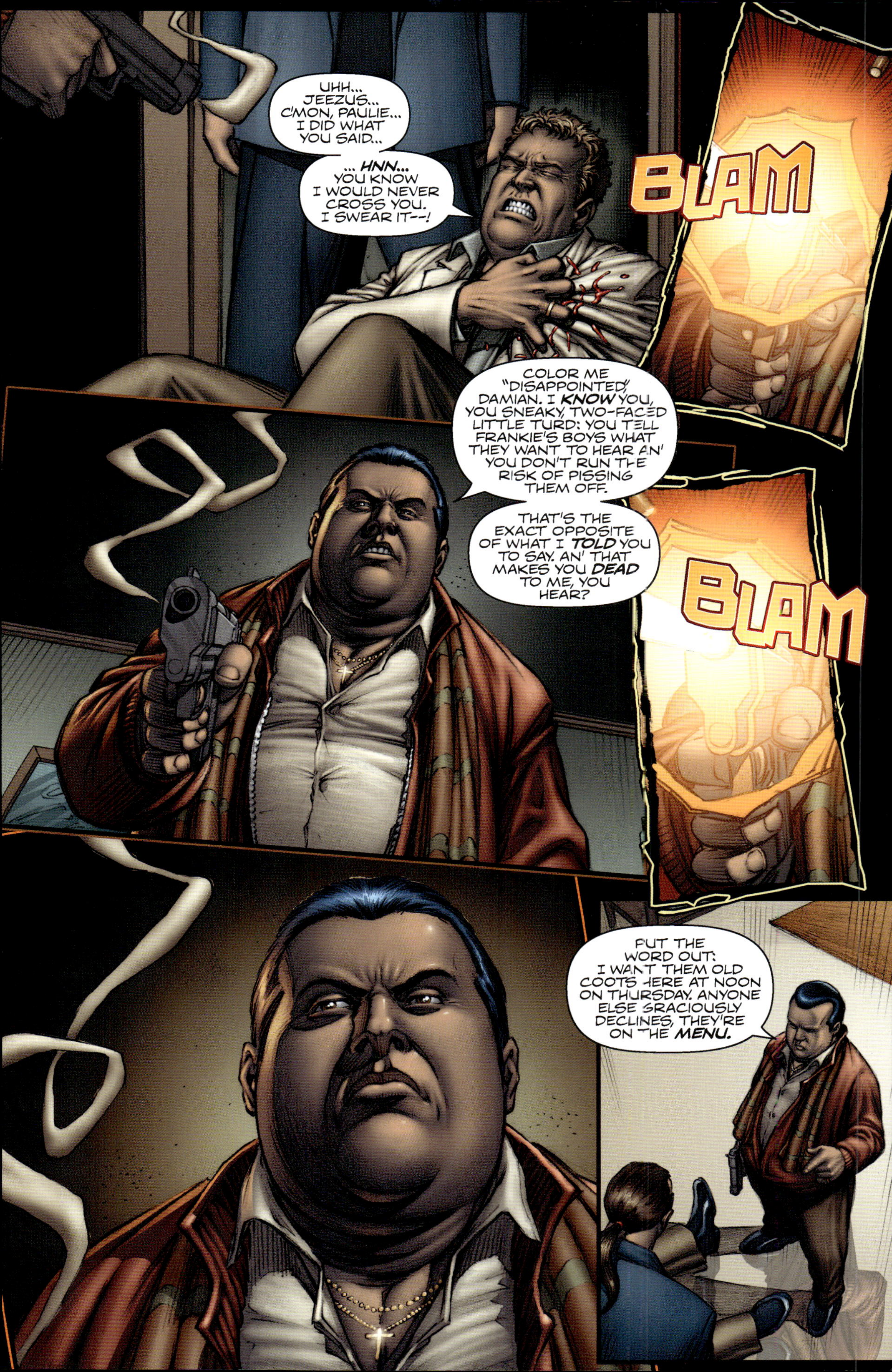
UHH... JEEZUS... C'MON, PAULIE... I DID WHAT YOU SAID...
... HNN... YOU KNOW I WOULD NEVER CROSS YOU. I SWEAR IT--!
BLAM
COLOR ME "DISAPPOINTED," DAMIAN. I KNOW YOU, YOU SNEAKY, TWO-FACED LITTLE TURD: YOU TELL FRANKIE'S BOYS WHAT THEY WANT TO HEAR AN' YOU DON'T RUN THE RISK OF PISSING THEM OFF.
THAT'S THE EXACT OPPOSITE OF WHAT I TOLD YOU TO SAY. AN' THAT MAKES YOU DEAD TO ME, YOU HEAR?
BLAM
PUT THE WORD OUT: I WANT THEM OLD COOTS HERE AT NOON ON THURSDAY. ANYONE ELSE GRACIOUSLY DECLINES, THEY'RE ON THE MENU.

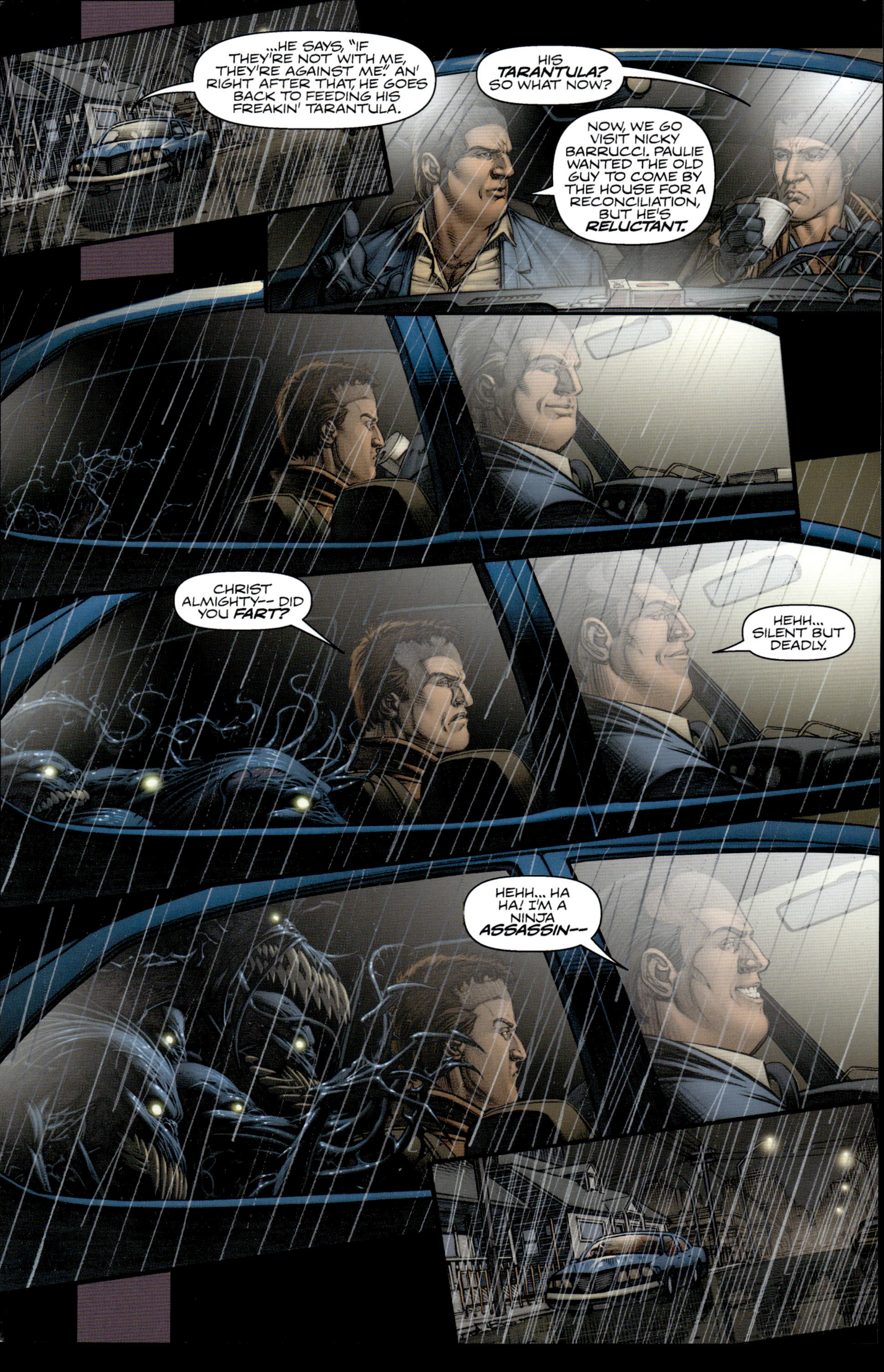
...HE SAYS, "IF THEY'RE NOT WITH ME, THEY'RE AGAINST ME." AN' RIGHT AFTER THAT, HE GOES BACK TO FEEDING HIS FREAKIN' TARANTULA.
HIS TARANTULA? SO WHAT NOW?
NOW, WE GO VISIT NICKY BARRUCCI. PAULIE WANTED THE OLD GUY TO COME BY THE HOUSE FOR A RECONCILIATION, BUT HE'S RELUCTANT.
CHRIST ALMIGHTY-- DID YOU FART?
HEHH... SILENT BUT DEADLY.
HEHH... HA HA! I'M A NINJA ASSASSIN--

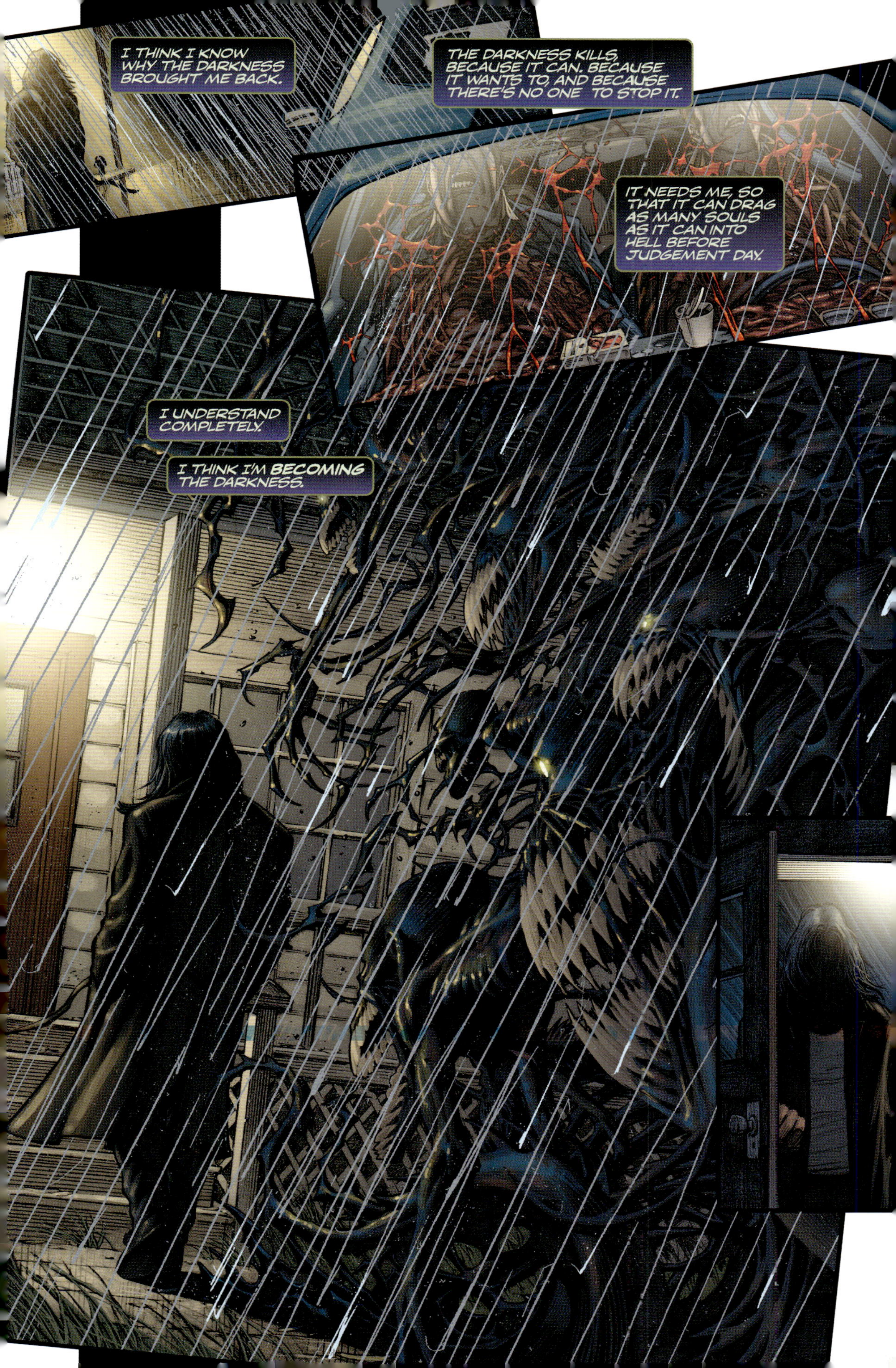

I THINK I KNOW WHY THE DARKNESS BROUGHT ME BACK.
THE DARKNESS KILLS, BECAUSE IT CAN, BECAUSE IT WANTS TO, AND BECAUSE THERE'S NO ONE TO STOP IT.
IT NEEDS ME, SO THAT IT CAN DRAG AS MANY SOULS AS IT CAN INTO HELL BEFORE JUDGEMENT DAY.
I UNDERSTAND COMPLETELY.
I THINK I'M **BECOMING** THE DARKNESS.

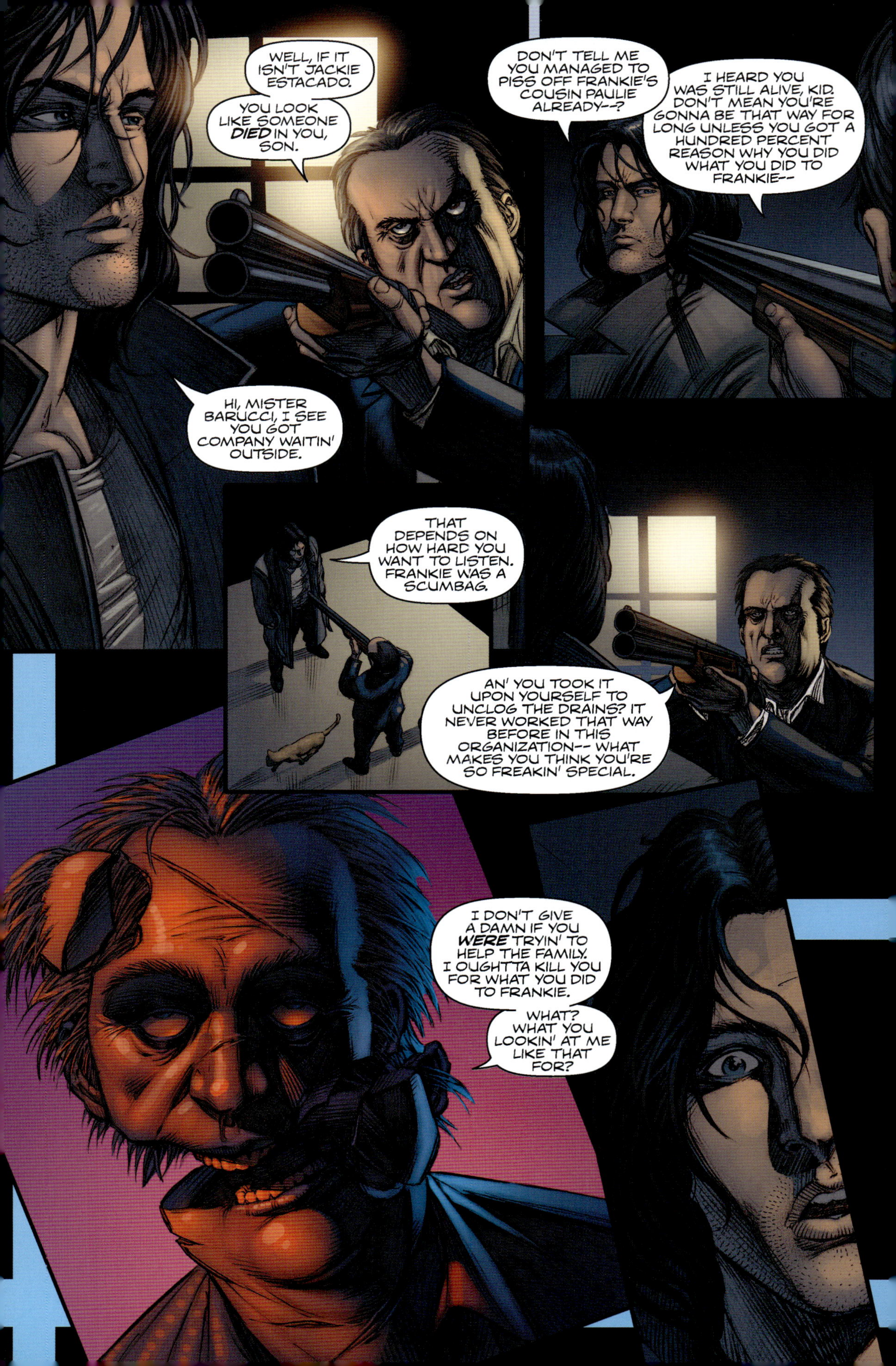
WELL, IF IT ISN'T JACKIE ESTACADO.
YOU LOOK LIKE SOMEONE *DIED* IN YOU, SON.
HI, MISTER BARUCCI, I SEE YOU GOT COMPANY WAITIN' OUTSIDE.
DON'T TELL ME YOU MANAGED TO PISS OFF FRANKIE'S COUSIN PAULIE ALREADY--?
I HEARD YOU WAS STILL ALIVE, KID. DON'T MEAN YOU'RE GONNA BE THAT WAY FOR LONG UNLESS YOU GOT A HUNDRED PERCENT REASON WHY YOU DID WHAT YOU DID TO FRANKIE--
THAT DEPENDS ON HOW HARD YOU WANT TO LISTEN. FRANKIE WAS A SCUMBAG.
AN' YOU TOOK IT UPON YOURSELF TO UNCLOG THE DRAINS? IT NEVER WORKED THAT WAY BEFORE IN THIS ORGANIZATION-- WHAT MAKES YOU THINK YOU'RE SO FREAKIN' SPECIAL.
I DON'T GIVE A DAMN IF YOU *WERE* TRYIN' TO HELP THE FAMILY. I OUGHT'TA KILL YOU FOR WHAT YOU DID TO FRANKIE.
WHAT? WHAT YOU LOOKIN' AT ME LIKE THAT FOR?

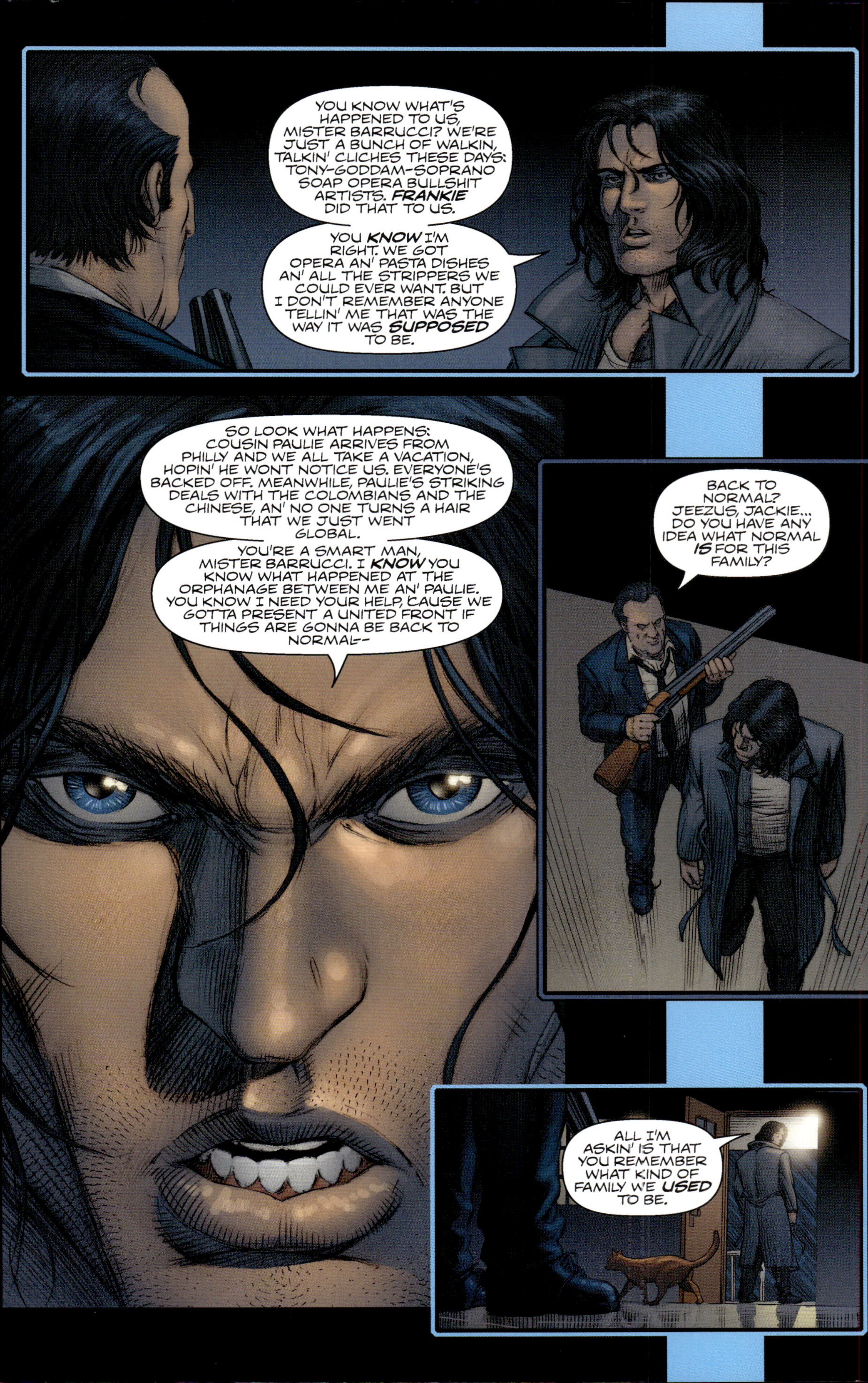

YOU KNOW WHAT'S HAPPENED TO US, MISTER BARRUCCI? WE'RE JUST A BUNCH OF WALKIN, TALKIN' CLICHES THESE DAYS: TONY-GODDAM-SOPRANO SOAP OPERA BULLSHIT ARTISTS. FRANKIE DID THAT TO US.
YOU KNOW I'M RIGHT. WE GOT OPERA AN' PASTA DISHES AN' ALL THE STRIPPERS WE COULD EVER WANT. BUT I DON'T REMEMBER ANYONE TELLIN' ME THAT WAS THE WAY IT WAS SUPPOSED TO BE.
SO LOOK WHAT HAPPENS: COUSIN PAULIE ARRIVES FROM PHILLY AND WE ALL TAKE A VACATION, HOPIN' HE WONT NOTICE US. EVERYONE'S BACKED OFF. MEANWHILE, PAULIE'S STRIKING DEALS WITH THE COLOMBIANS AND THE CHINESE, AN' NO ONE TURNS A HAIR THAT WE JUST WENT GLOBAL.
YOU'RE A SMART MAN, MISTER BARRUCCI. I KNOW YOU KNOW WHAT HAPPENED AT THE ORPHANAGE BETWEEN ME AN' PAULIE. YOU KNOW I NEED YOUR HELP, 'CAUSE WE GOTTA PRESENT A UNITED FRONT IF THINGS ARE GONNA BE BACK TO NORMAL--
BACK TO NORMAL? JEEZUS, JACKIE... DO YOU HAVE ANY IDEA WHAT NORMAL IS FOR THIS FAMILY?
ALL I'M ASKIN' IS THAT YOU REMEMBER WHAT KIND OF FAMILY WE USED TO BE.

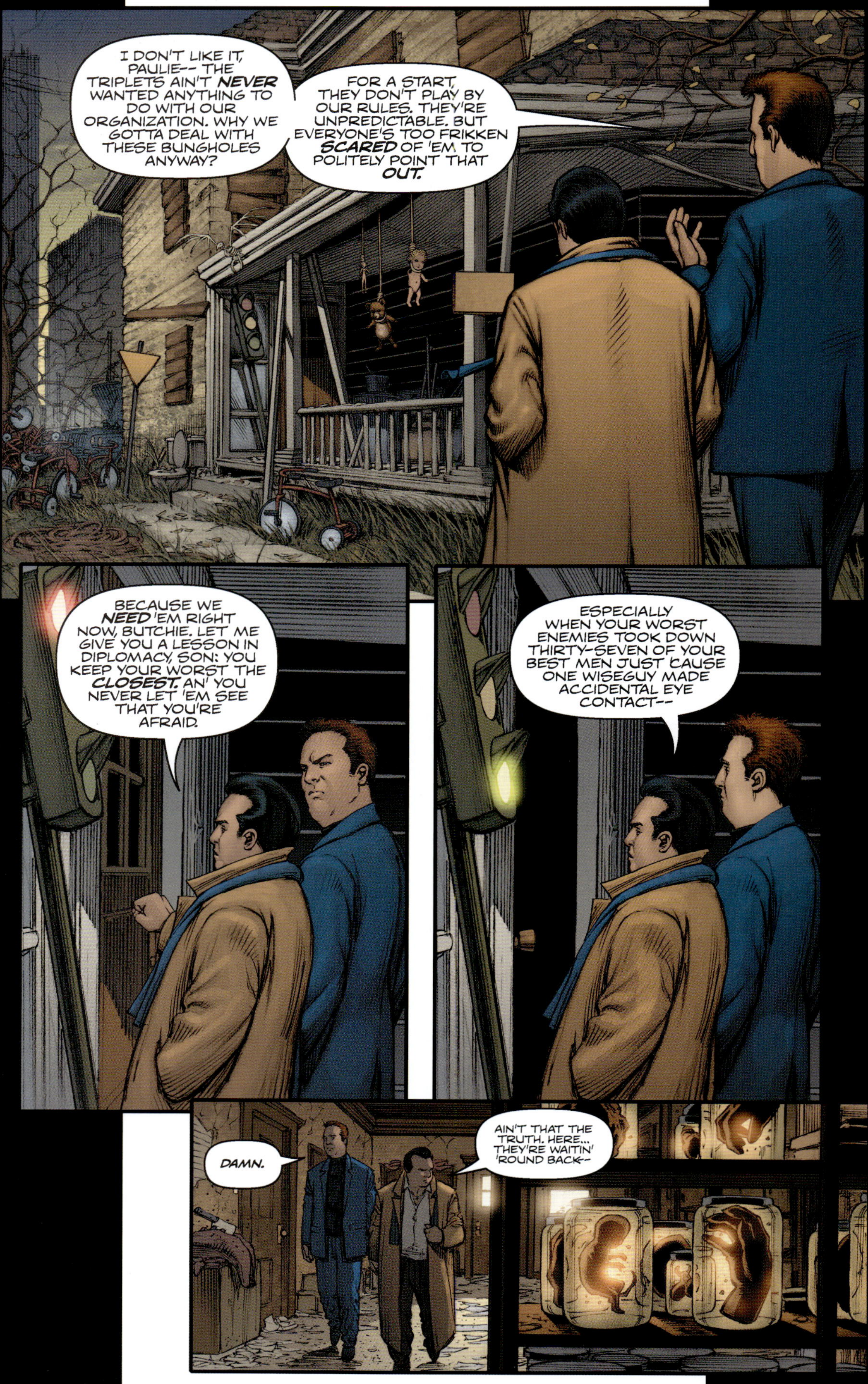
I DON'T LIKE IT, PAULIE-- THE TRIPLETS AIN'T NEVER WANTED ANYTHING TO DO WITH OUR ORGANIZATION. WHY WE GOTTA DEAL WITH THESE BUNGHOLES ANYWAY?
FOR A START, THEY DON'T PLAY BY OUR RULES. THEY'RE UNPREDICTABLE. BUT EVERYONE'S TOO FRIKKEN SCARED OF 'EM TO POLITELY POINT THAT OUT.
BECAUSE WE NEED 'EM RIGHT NOW, BUTCHIE. LET ME GIVE YOU A LESSON IN DIPLOMACY, SON: YOU KEEP YOUR WORST THE CLOSEST. AN' YOU NEVER LET 'EM SEE THAT YOU'RE AFRAID.
ESPECIALLY WHEN YOUR WORST ENEMIES TOOK DOWN THIRTY-SEVEN OF YOUR BEST MEN JUST 'CAUSE ONE WISEGUY MADE ACCIDENTAL EYE CONTACT--
DAMN.
AIN'T THAT THE TRUTH. HERE... THEY'RE WAITIN' 'ROUND BACK--

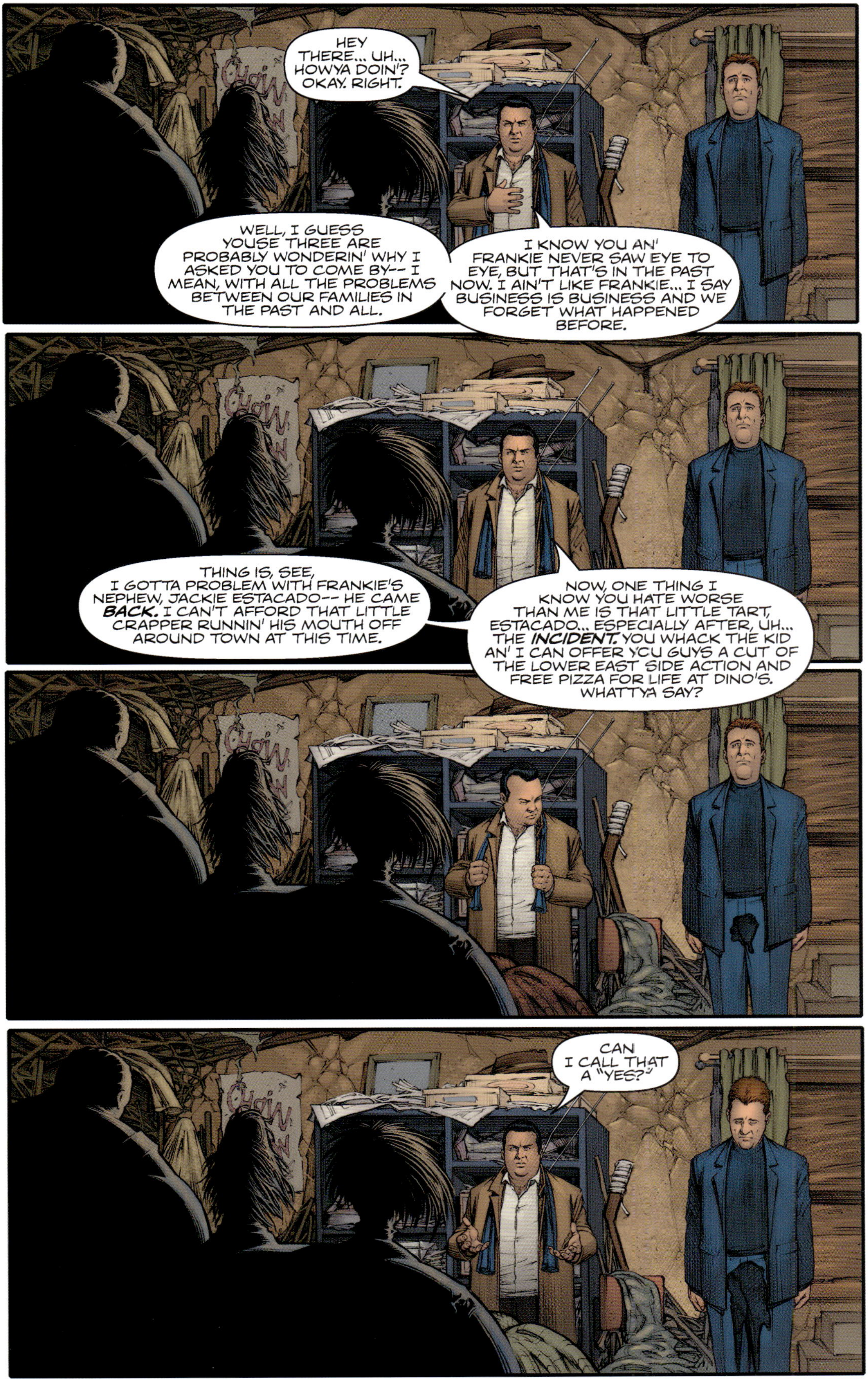
HEY THERE... UH... HOWYA DOIN'? OKAY. RIGHT.
WELL, I GUESS YOUSE THREE ARE PROBABLY WONDERIN' WHY I ASKED YOU TO COME BY-- I MEAN, WITH ALL THE PROBLEMS BETWEEN OUR FAMILIES IN THE PAST AND ALL.
I KNOW YOU AN' FRANKIE NEVER SAW EYE TO EYE, BUT THAT'S IN THE PAST NOW. I AIN'T LIKE FRANKIE... I SAY BUSINESS IS BUSINESS AND WE FORGET WHAT HAPPENED BEFORE.
THING IS, SEE, I GOTTA PROBLEM WITH FRANKIE'S NEPHEW, JACKIE ESTACADO-- HE CAME BACK. I CAN'T AFFORD THAT LITTLE CRAPPER RUNNIN' HIS MOUTH OFF AROUND TOWN AT THIS TIME.
NOW, ONE THING I KNOW YOU HATE WORSE THAN ME IS THAT LITTLE TART, ESTACADO... ESPECIALLY AFTER, UH... THE INCIDENT. YOU WHACK THE KID AN' I CAN OFFER YOU GUYS A CUT OF THE LOWER EAST SIDE ACTION AND FREE PIZZA FOR LIFE AT DINO'S. WHATTYA SAY?
CAN I CALL THAT A "YES?"

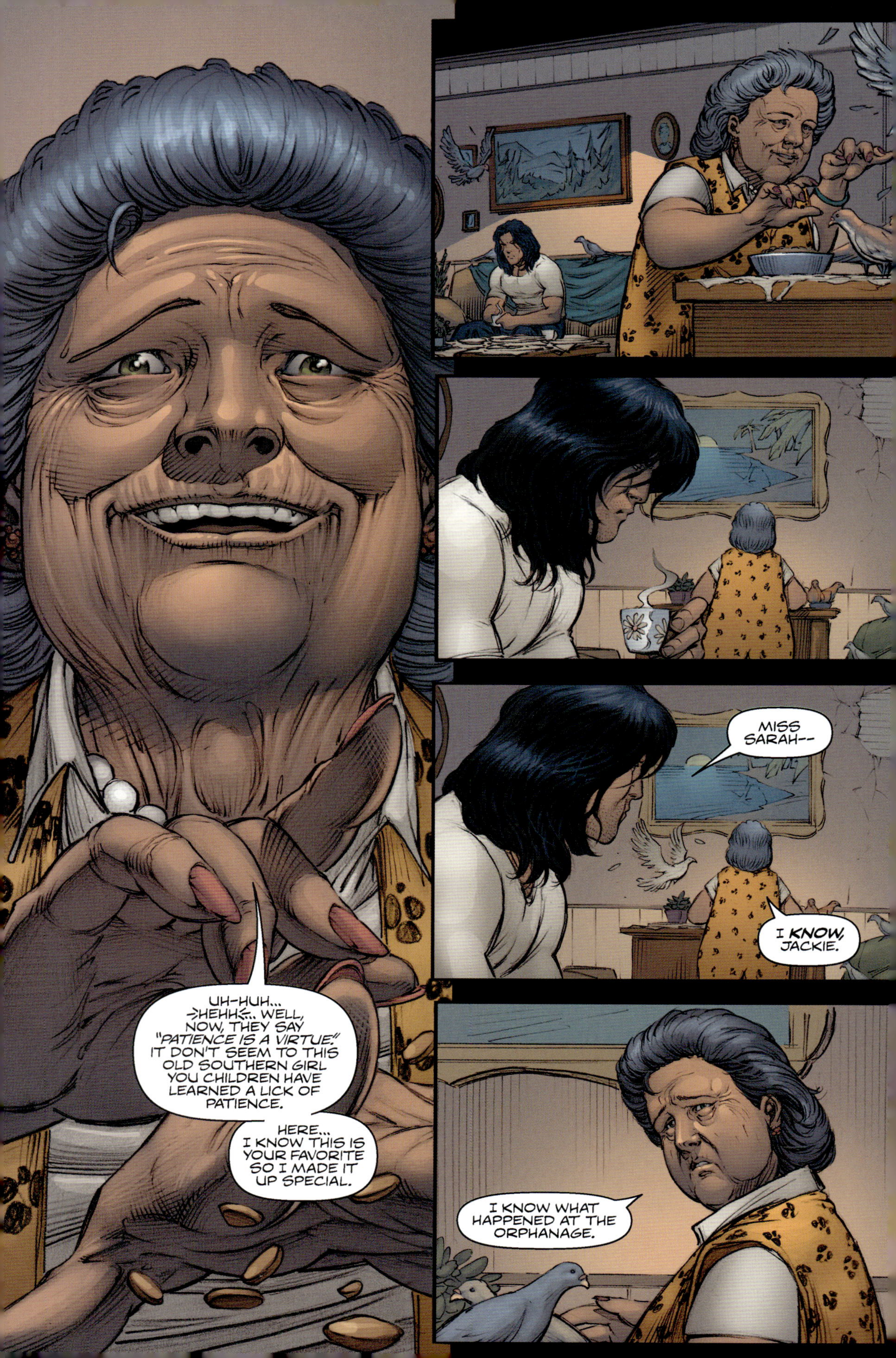
UH-HUH... ⪢HEHH⪡... WELL, NOW, THEY SAY "PATIENCE IS A VIRTUE." IT DON'T SEEM TO THIS OLD SOUTHERN GIRL YOU CHILDREN HAVE LEARNED A LICK OF PATIENCE.
HERE... I KNOW THIS IS YOUR FAVORITE SO I MADE IT UP SPECIAL.
MISS SARAH--
I KNOW, JACKIE.
I KNOW WHAT HAPPENED AT THE ORPHANAGE.

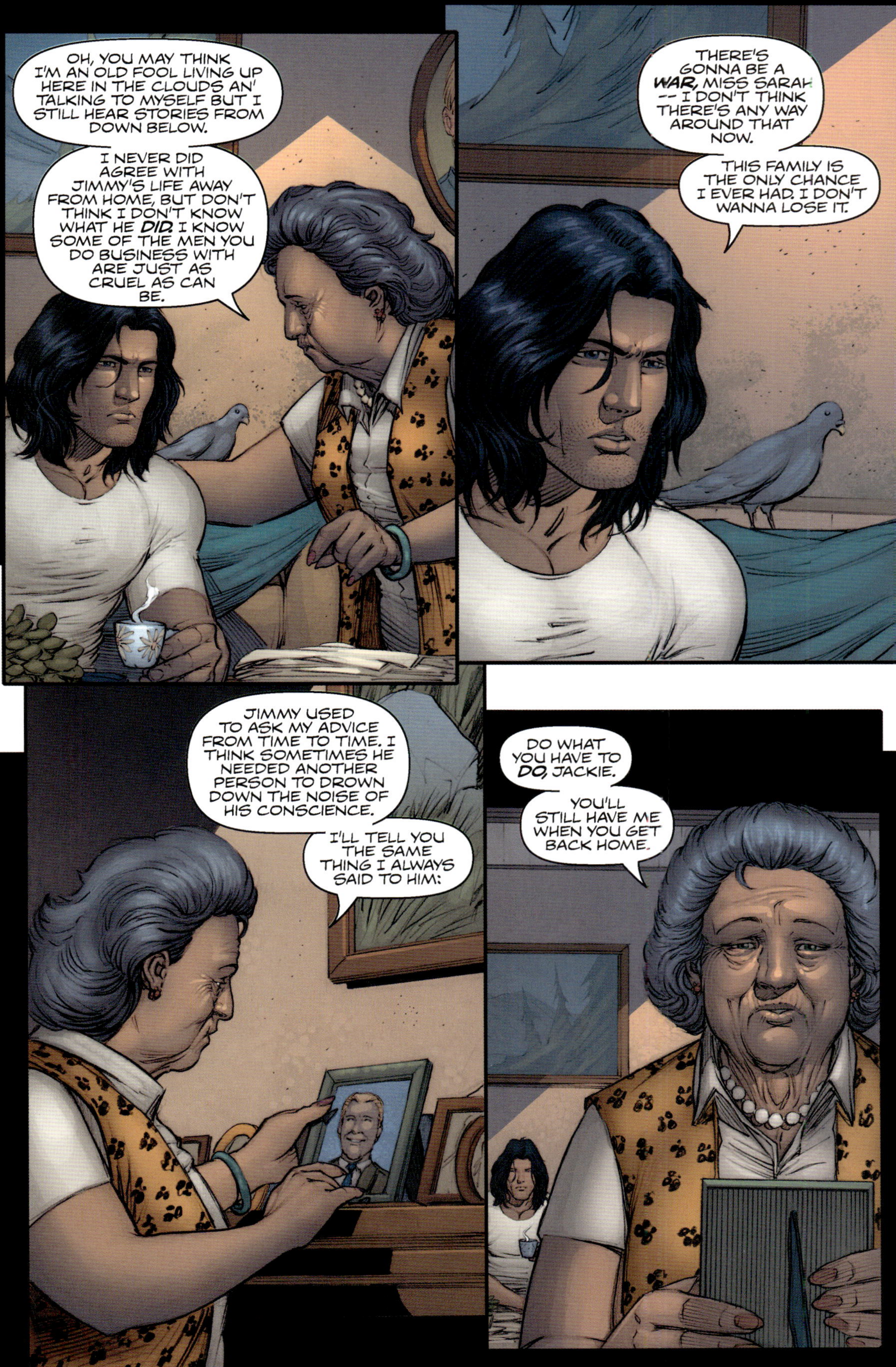
OH, YOU MAY THINK I'M AN OLD FOOL LIVING UP HERE IN THE CLOUDS AN' TALKING TO MYSELF BUT I STILL HEAR STORIES FROM DOWN BELOW.
I NEVER DID AGREE WITH JIMMY'S LIFE AWAY FROM HOME, BUT DON'T THINK I DON'T KNOW WHAT HE DID. I KNOW SOME OF THE MEN YOU DO BUSINESS WITH ARE JUST AS CRUEL AS CAN BE.
THERE'S GONNA BE A WAR, MISS SARAH -- I DON'T THINK THERE'S ANY WAY AROUND THAT NOW.
THIS FAMILY IS THE ONLY CHANCE I EVER HAD. I DON'T WANNA LOSE IT.
JIMMY USED TO ASK MY ADVICE FROM TIME TO TIME. I THINK SOMETIMES HE NEEDED ANOTHER PERSON TO DROWN DOWN THE NOISE OF HIS CONSCIENCE.
I'LL TELL YOU THE SAME THING I ALWAYS SAID TO HIM:
DO WHAT YOU HAVE TO DO, JACKIE.
YOU'LL STILL HAVE ME WHEN YOU GET BACK HOME.

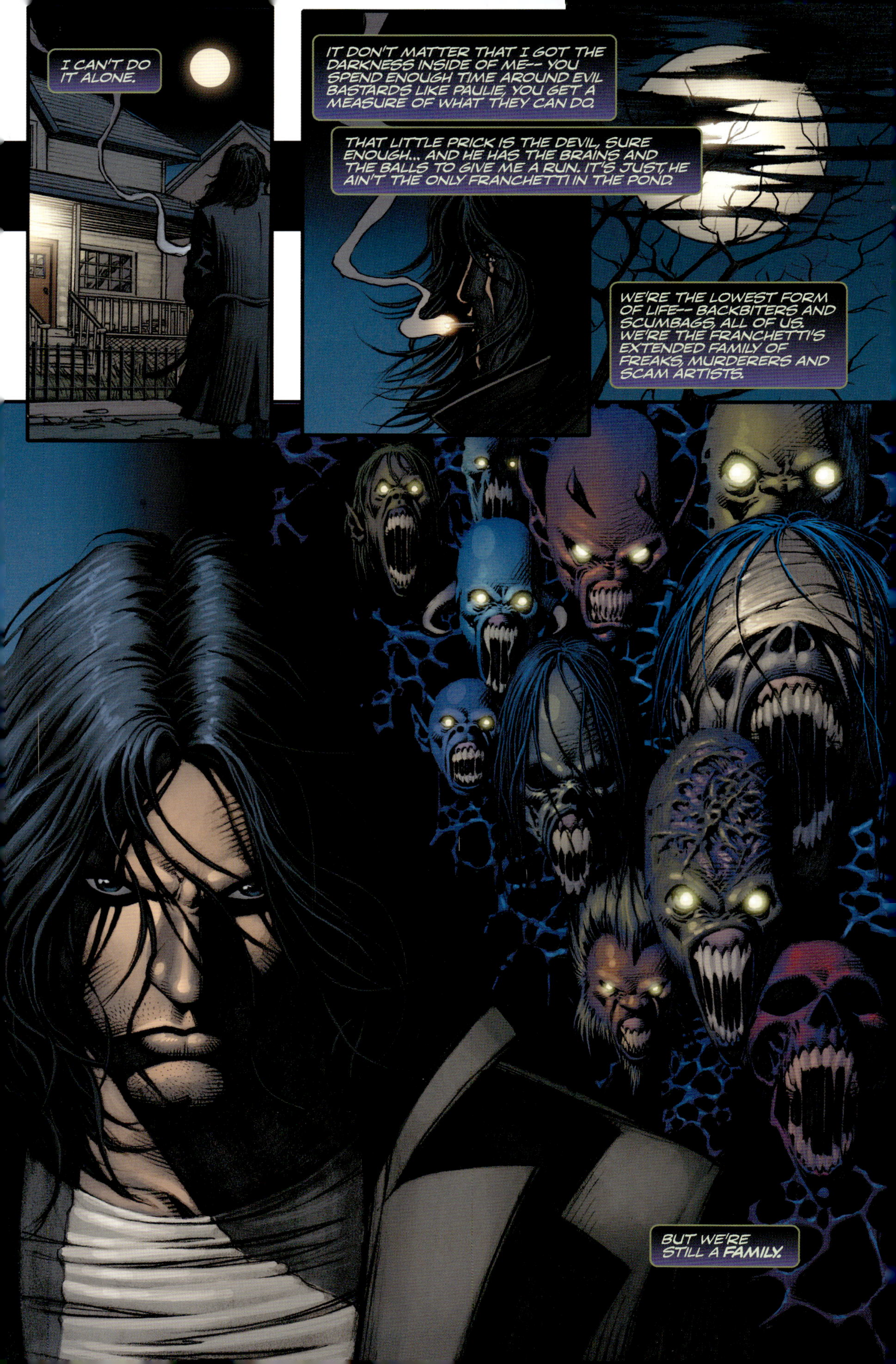
I CAN'T DO IT ALONE.
IT DON'T MATTER THAT I GOT THE DARKNESS INSIDE OF ME-- YOU SPEND ENOUGH TIME AROUND EVIL BASTARDS LIKE PAULIE, YOU GET A MEASURE OF WHAT THEY CAN DO.
THAT LITTLE PRICK IS THE DEVIL, SURE ENOUGH... AND HE HAS THE BRAINS AND THE BALLS TO GIVE ME A RUN. IT'S JUST, HE AIN'T THE ONLY FRANCHETTI IN THE POND.
WE'RE THE LOWEST FORM OF LIFE-- BACKBITERS AND SCUMBAGS, ALL OF US. WE'RE THE FRANCHETTI'S EXTENDED FAMILY OF FREAKS, MURDERERS AND SCAM ARTISTS.
BUT WE'RE STILL A **FAMILY.**

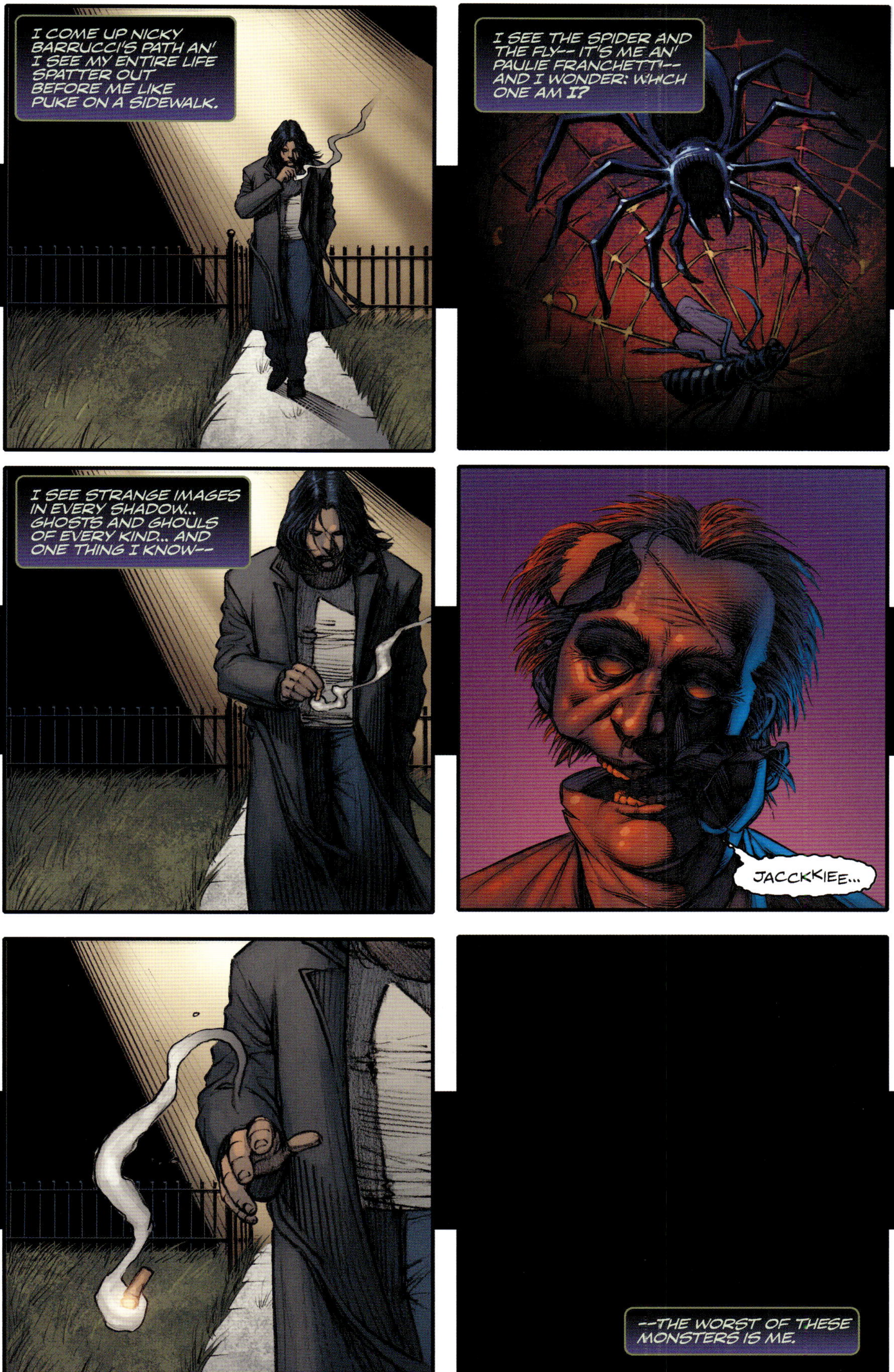
I COME UP NICKY BARRUCCI'S PATH AN' I SEE MY ENTIRE LIFE SPATTER OUT BEFORE ME LIKE PUKE ON A SIDEWALK.
I SEE THE SPIDER AND THE FLY-- IT'S ME AN' PAULIE FRANCHETTI-- AND I WONDER: WHICH ONE AM I?
I SEE STRANGE IMAGES IN EVERY SHADOW... GHOSTS AND GHOULS OF EVERY KIND... AND ONE THING I KNOW--
JACCKKIEE...
--THE WORST OF THESE MONSTERS IS ME.

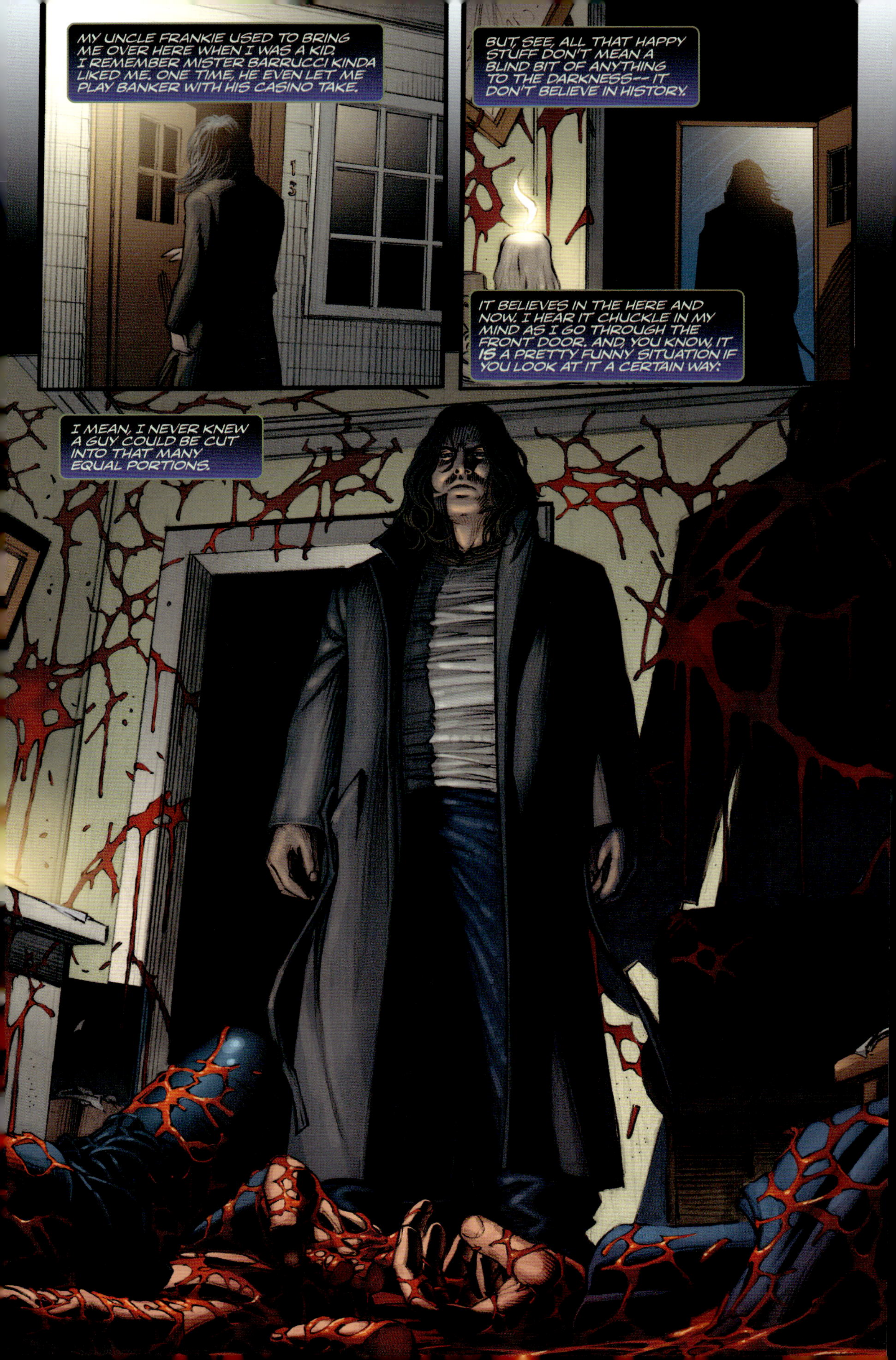
MY UNCLE FRANKIE USED TO BRING ME OVER HERE WHEN I WAS A KID. I REMEMBER MISTER BARRUCCI KINDA LIKED ME. ONE TIME, HE EVEN LET ME PLAY BANKER WITH HIS CASINO TAKE.
BUT, SEE, ALL THAT HAPPY STUFF DON'T MEAN A BLIND BIT OF ANYTHING TO THE DARKNESS-- IT DON'T BELIEVE IN HISTORY.
IT BELIEVES IN THE HERE AND NOW. I HEAR IT CHUCKLE IN MY MIND AS I GO THROUGH THE FRONT DOOR. AND, YOU KNOW, IT IS A PRETTY FUNNY SITUATION IF YOU LOOK AT IT A CERTAIN WAY:
I MEAN, I NEVER KNEW A GUY COULD BE CUT INTO THAT MANY EQUAL PORTIONS.

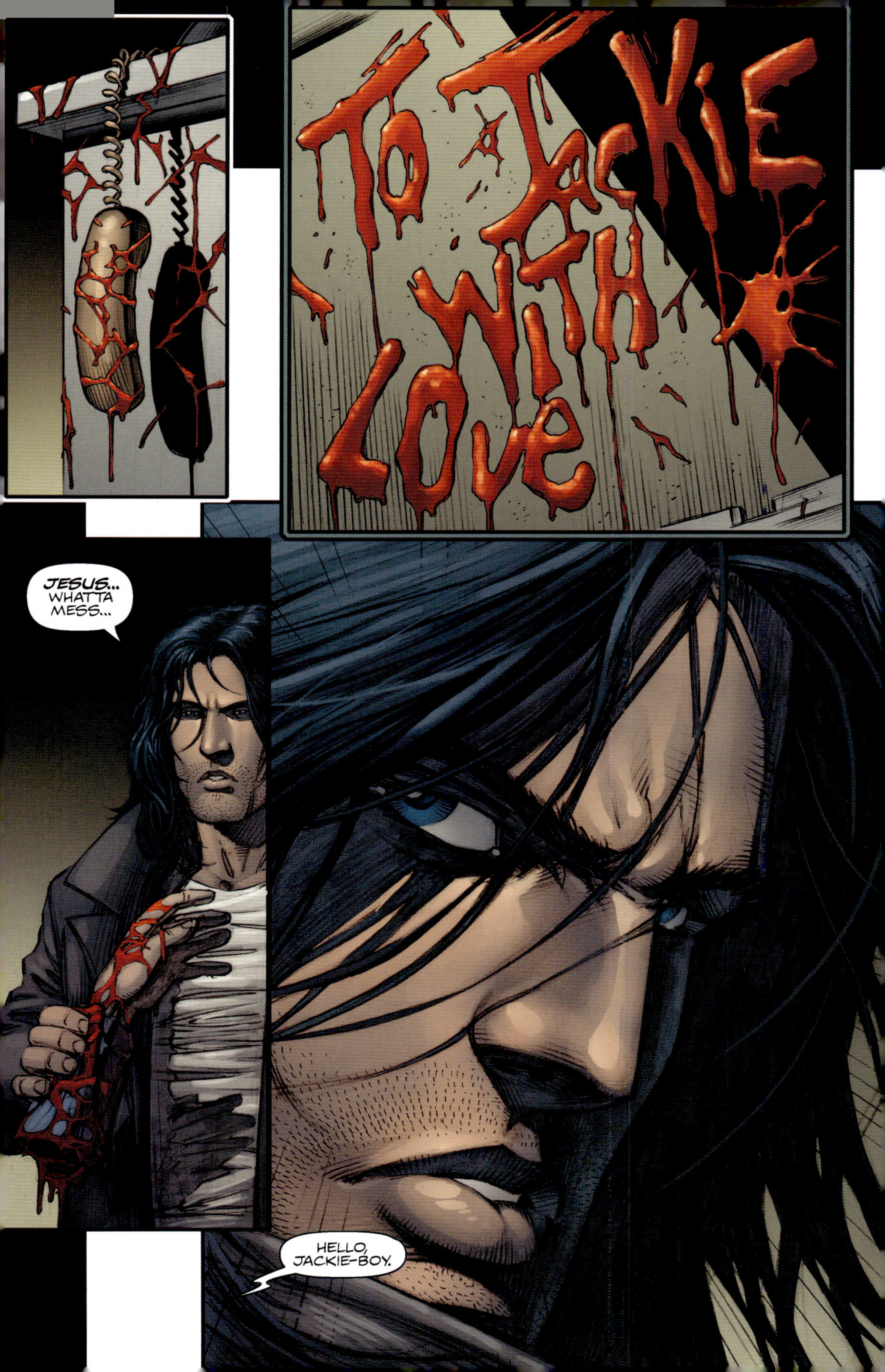
TO JACKIE WITH LOVE
JESUS... WHATTA MESS...
HELLO, JACKIE-BOY.

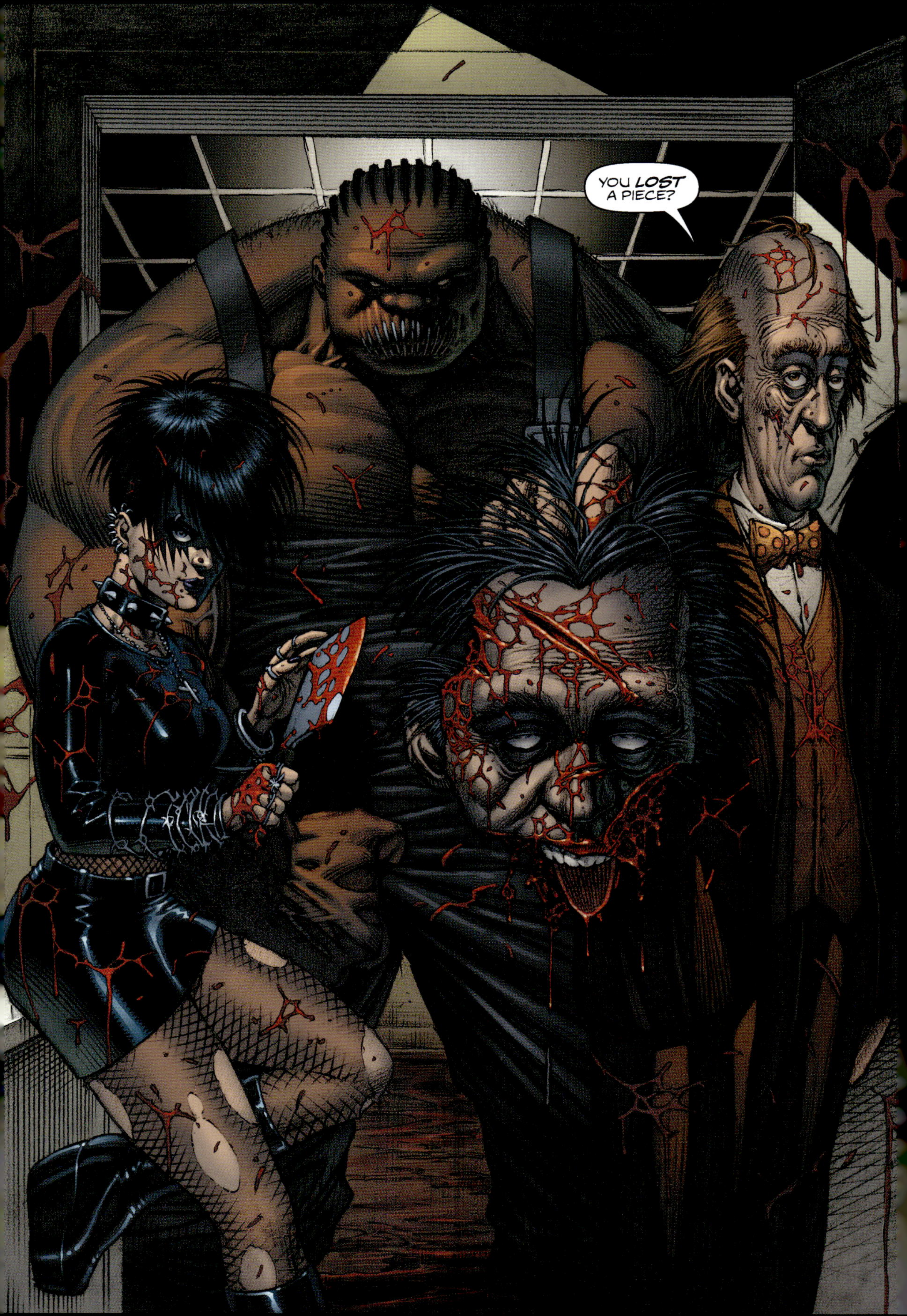
YOU LOST A PIECE?

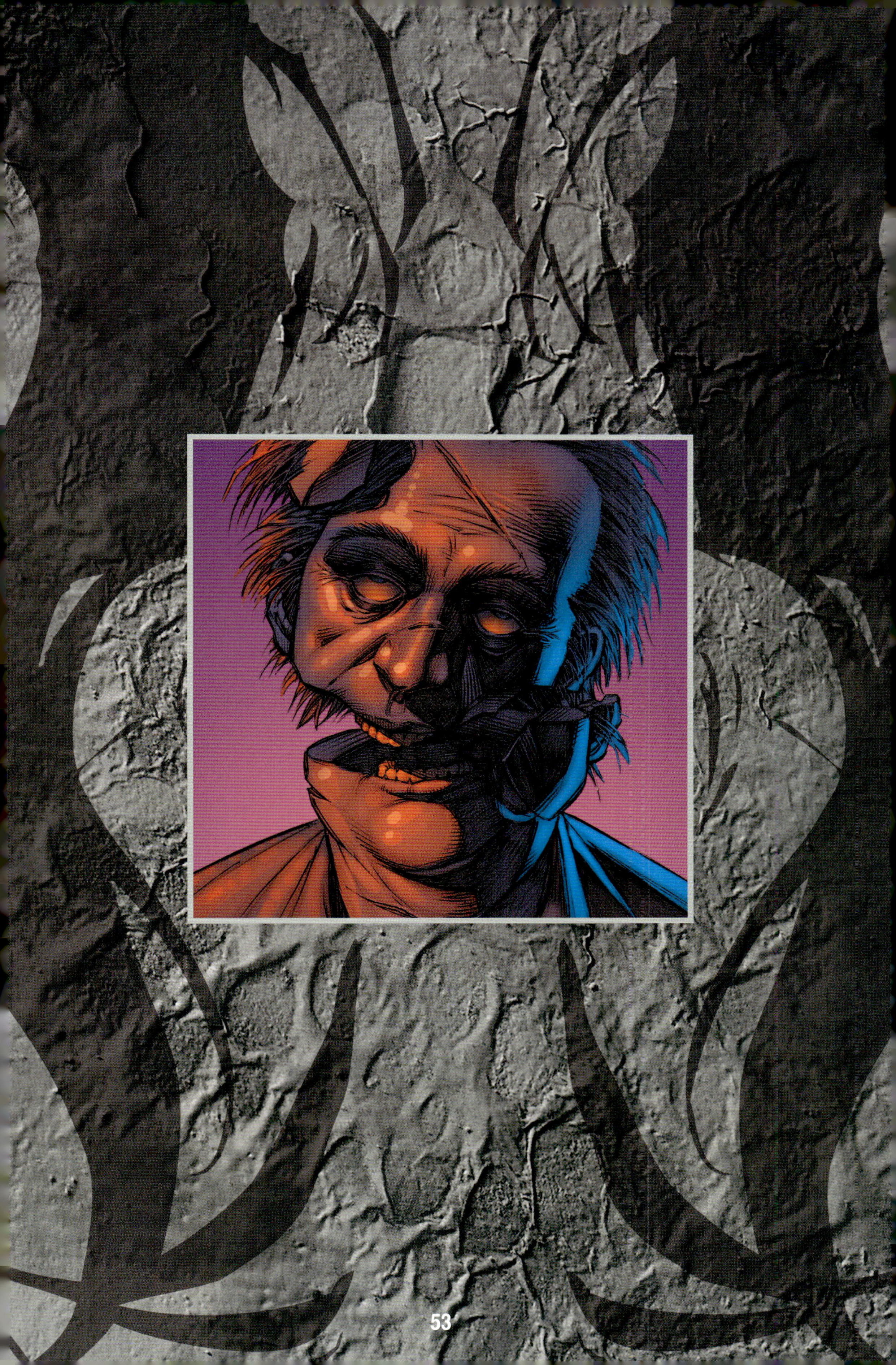

The Darkness Issue #43
cover art by: Dale Keown & Matt Milla

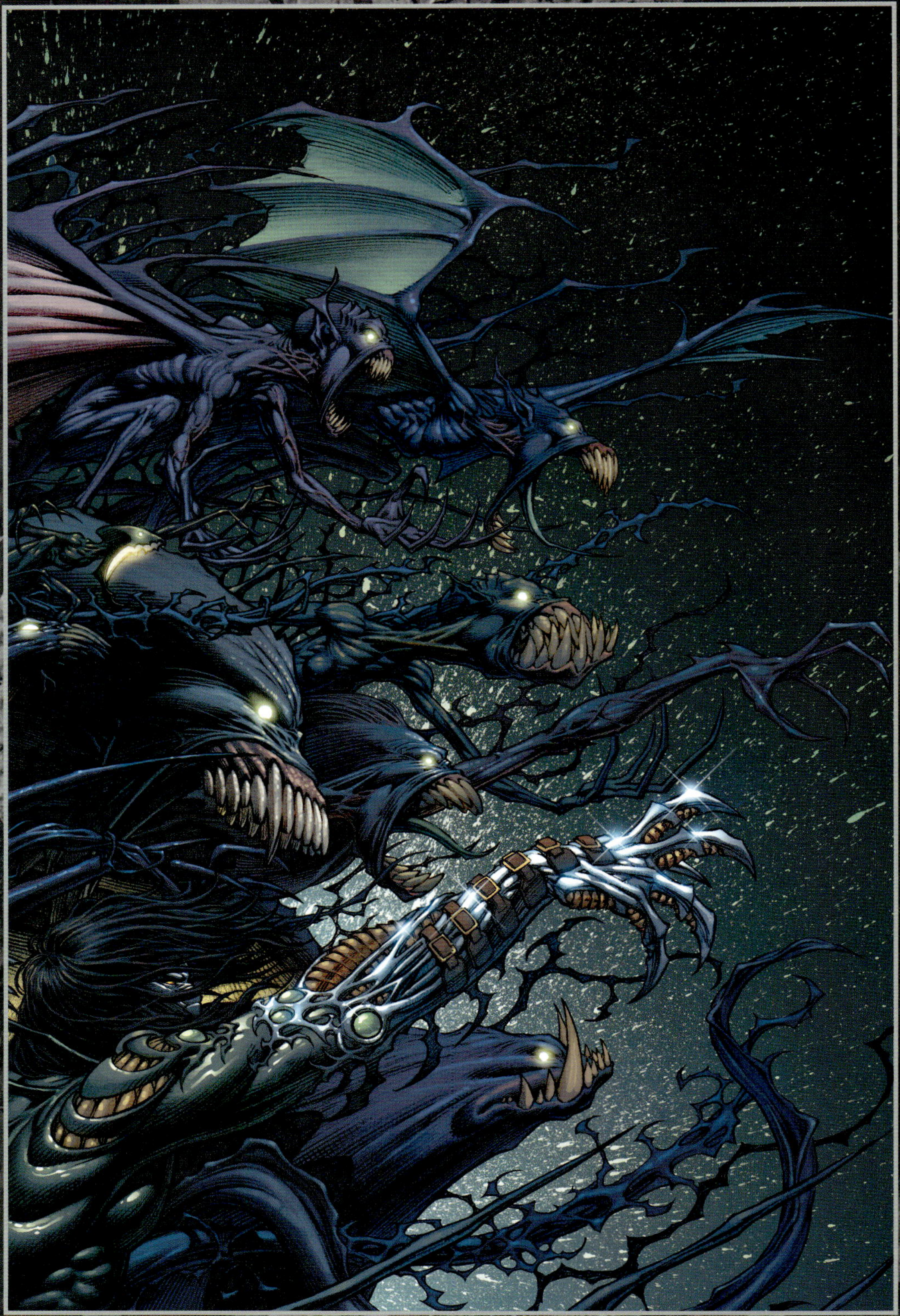

THE DARKNESS #43

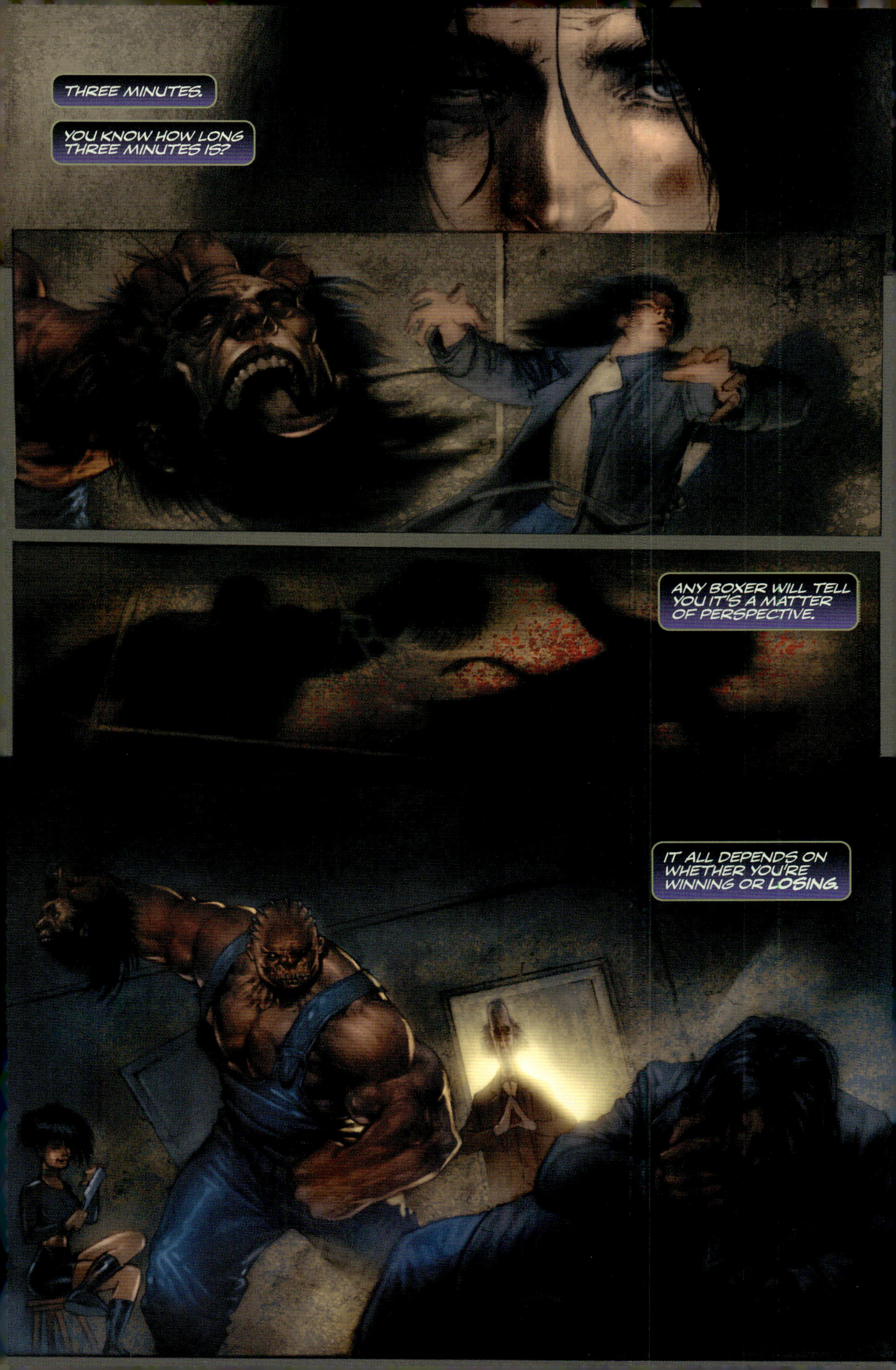
THREE MINUTES.
YOU KNOW HOW LONG THREE MINUTES IS?
ANY BOXER WILL TELL YOU IT'S A MATTER OF PERSPECTIVE.
IT ALL DEPENDS ON WHETHER YOU'RE WINNING OR **LOSING.**

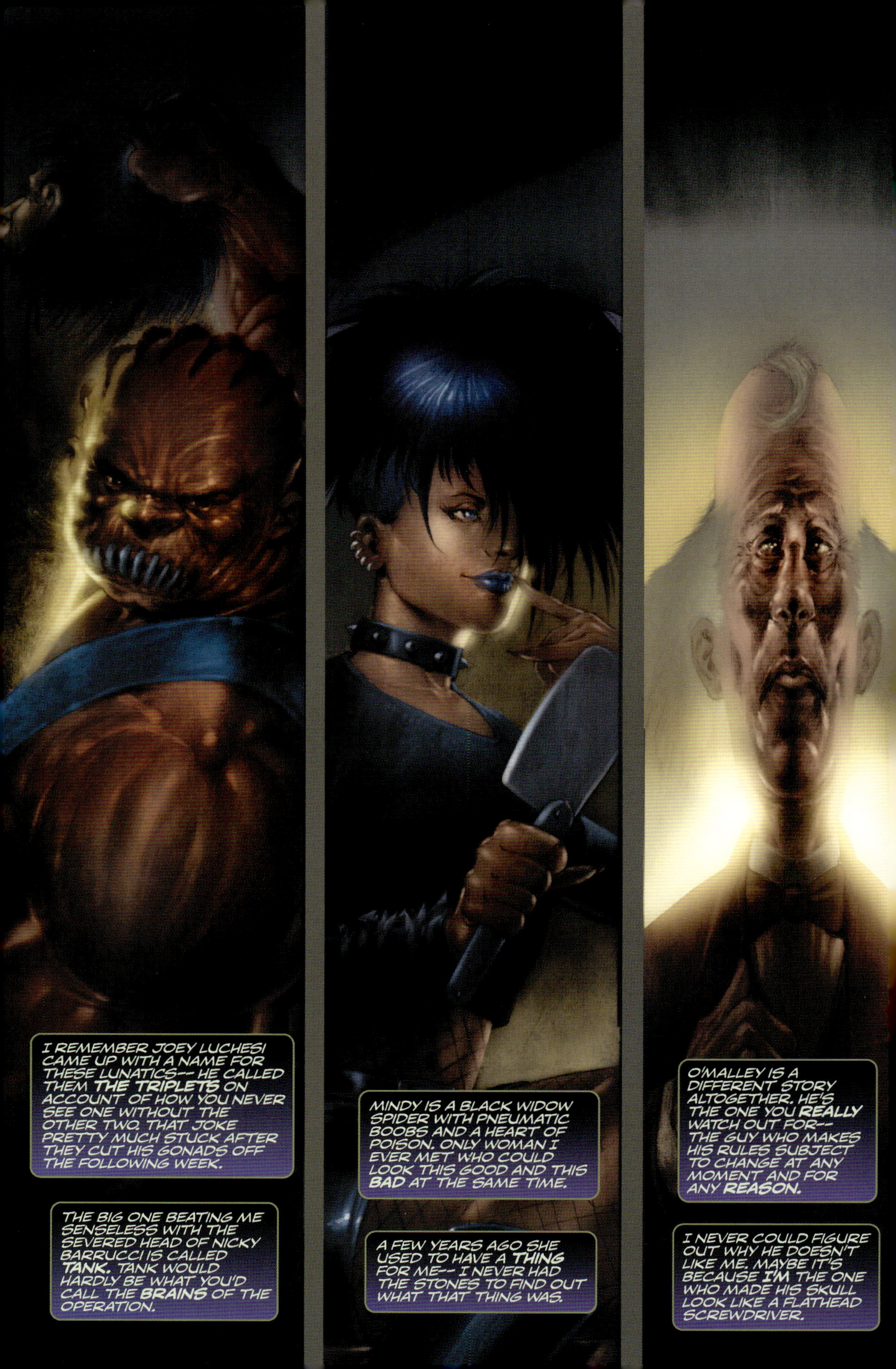
I REMEMBER JOEY LUCHESI CAME UP WITH A NAME FOR THESE LUNATICS-- HE CALLED THEM THE TRIPLETS ON ACCOUNT OF HOW YOU NEVER SEE ONE WITHOUT THE OTHER TWO. THAT JOKE PRETTY MUCH STUCK AFTER THEY CUT HIS GONADS OFF THE FOLLOWING WEEK.
THE BIG ONE BEATING ME SENSELESS WITH THE SEVERED HEAD OF NICKY BARRUCCI IS CALLED TANK. TANK WOULD HARDLY BE WHAT YOU'D CALL THE BRAINS OF THE OPERATION.
MINDY IS A BLACK WIDOW SPIDER WITH PNEUMATIC BOOBS AND A HEART OF POISON. ONLY WOMAN I EVER MET WHO COULD LOOK THIS GOOD AND THIS BAD AT THE SAME TIME.
A FEW YEARS AGO SHE USED TO HAVE A THING FOR ME-- I NEVER HAD THE STONES TO FIND OUT WHAT THAT THING WAS.
O'MALLEY IS A DIFFERENT STORY ALTOGETHER. HE'S THE ONE YOU REALLY WATCH OUT FOR-- THE GUY WHO MAKES HIS RULES SUBJECT TO CHANGE AT ANY MOMENT AND FOR ANY REASON.
I NEVER COULD FIGURE OUT WHY HE DOESN'T LIKE ME. MAYBE IT'S BECAUSE I'M THE ONE WHO MADE HIS SKULL LOOK LIKE A FLATHEAD SCREWDRIVER.

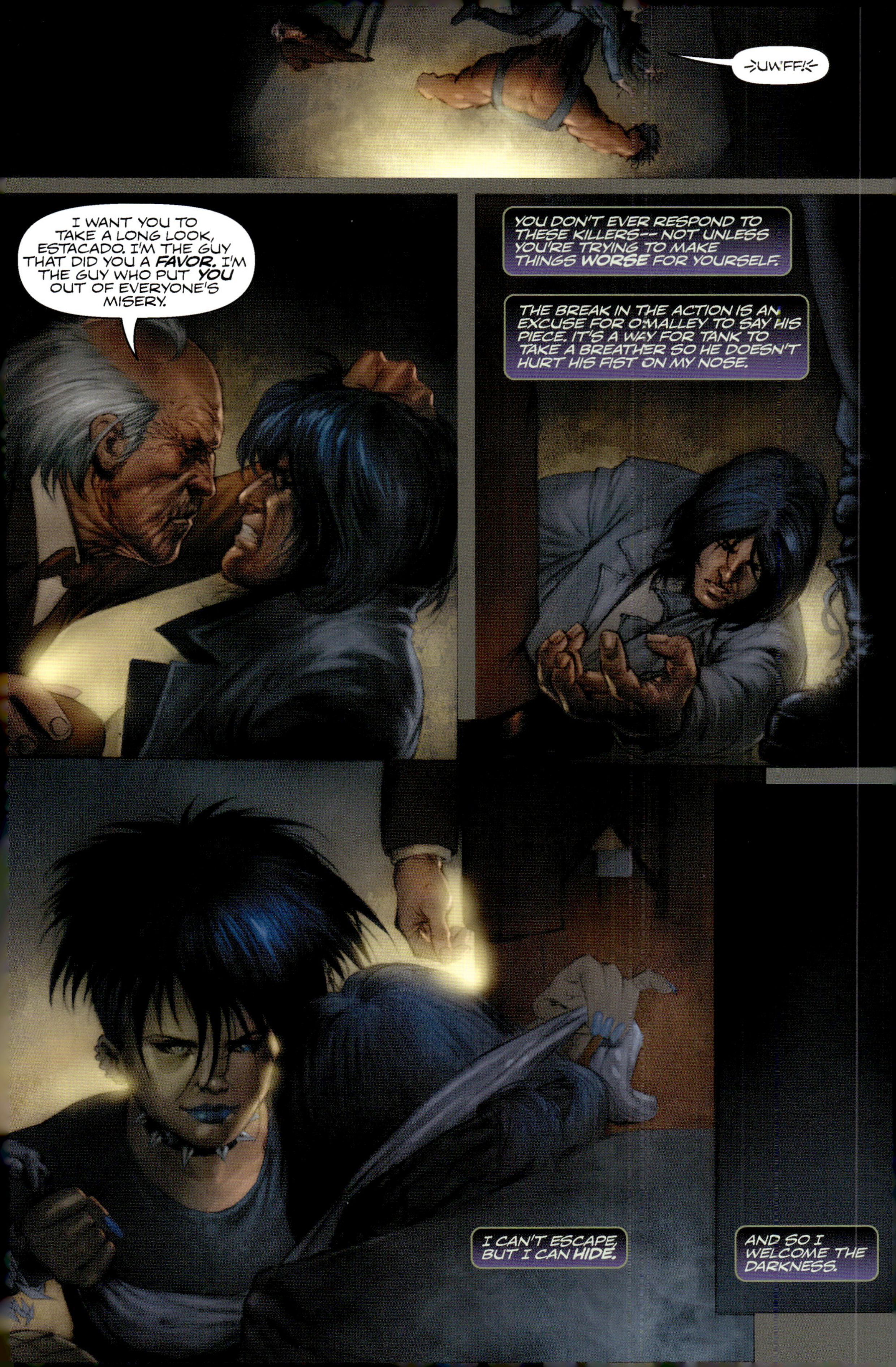

UWFF!
I WANT YOU TO TAKE A LONG LOOK, ESTACADO. I'M THE GUY THAT DID YOU A FAVOR. I'M THE GUY WHO PUT YOU OUT OF EVERYONE'S MISERY.
YOU DON'T EVER RESPOND TO THESE KILLERS-- NOT UNLESS YOU'RE TRYING TO MAKE THINGS WORSE FOR YOURSELF.
THE BREAK IN THE ACTION IS AN EXCUSE FOR O'MALLEY TO SAY HIS PIECE. IT'S A WAY FOR TANK TO TAKE A BREATHER SO HE DOESN'T HURT HIS FIST ON MY NOSE.
I CAN'T ESCAPE, BUT I CAN HIDE.
AND SO I WELCOME THE DARKNESS.

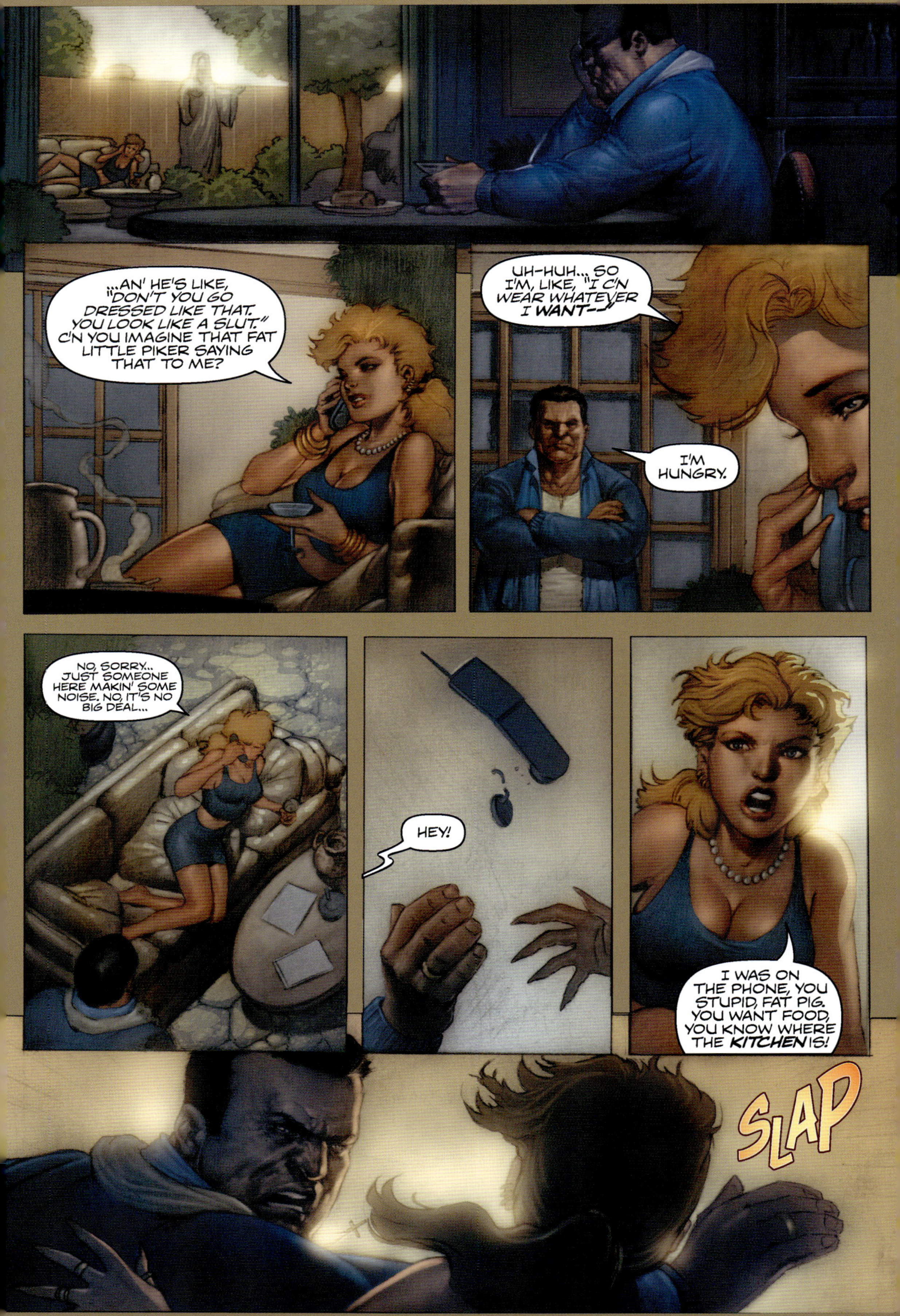
...AN' HE'S LIKE, "DON'T YOU GO DRESSED LIKE THAT. YOU LOOK LIKE A SLUT." C'N YOU IMAGINE THAT FAT LITTLE PIKER SAYING THAT TO ME?
UH-HUH... SO I'M, LIKE, "I C'N WEAR WHATEVER I WANT--"
I'M HUNGRY.
NO, SORRY... JUST SOMEONE HERE MAKIN' SOME NOISE. NO, IT'S NO BIG DEAL...
HEY!
I WAS ON THE PHONE, YOU STUPID, FAT PIG. YOU WANT FOOD, YOU KNOW WHERE THE KITCHEN IS!
SLAP

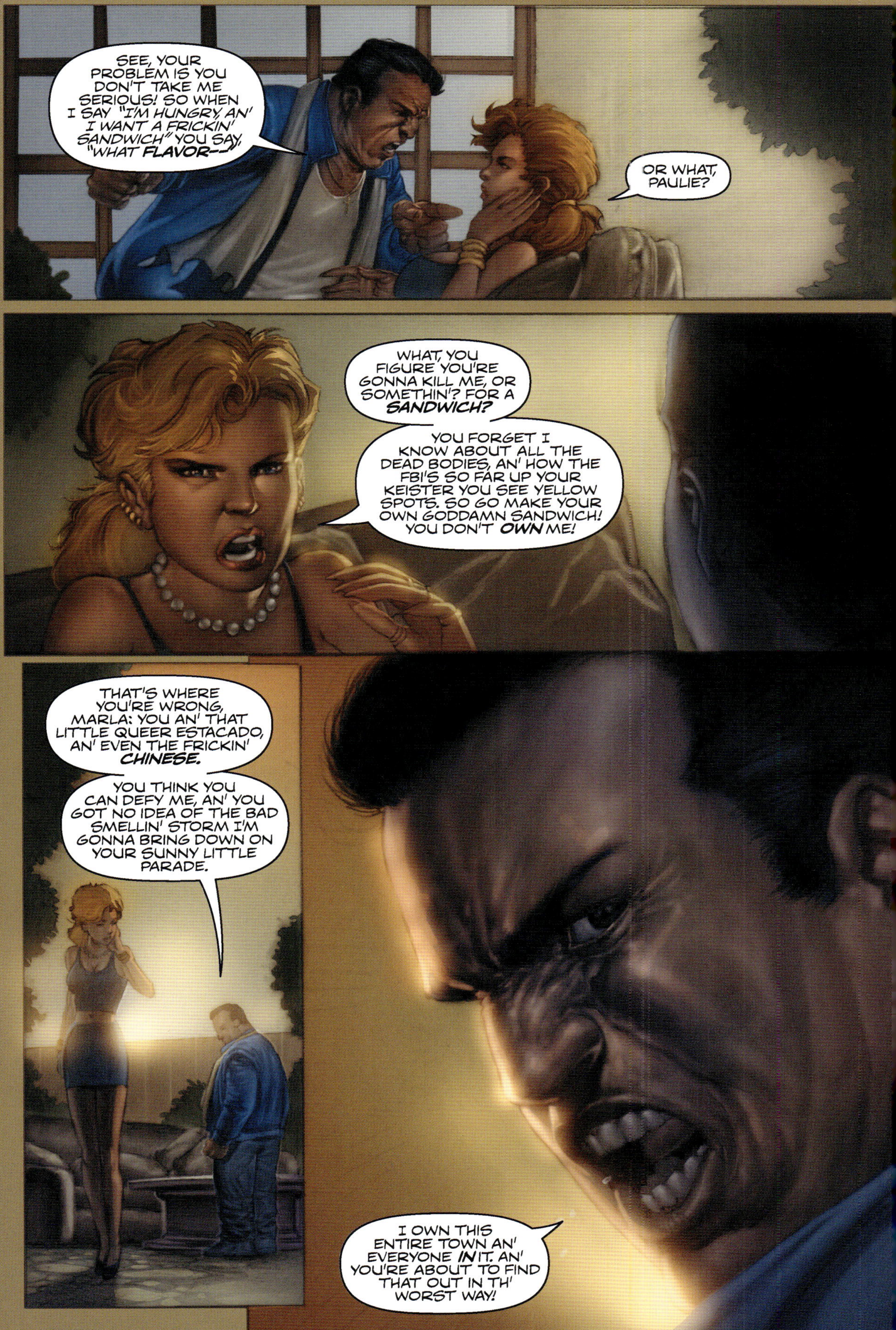
SEE, YOUR PROBLEM IS YOU DON'T TAKE ME SERIOUS! SO WHEN I SAY "I'M HUNGRY, AN' I WANT A FRICKIN' SANDWICH" YOU SAY, "WHAT FLAVOR--"
OR WHAT, PAULIE?
WHAT, YOU FIGURE YOU'RE GONNA KILL ME, OR SOMETHIN'? FOR A SANDWICH?
YOU FORGET I KNOW ABOUT ALL THE DEAD BODIES, AN' HOW THE FBI'S SO FAR UP YOUR KEISTER YOU SEE YELLOW SPOTS. SO GO MAKE YOUR OWN GODDAMN SANDWICH! YOU DON'T OWN ME!
THAT'S WHERE YOU'RE WRONG, MARLA: YOU AN' THAT LITTLE QUEER ESTACADO, AN' EVEN THE FRICKIN' CHINESE.
YOU THINK YOU CAN DEFY ME, AN' YOU GOT NO IDEA OF THE BAD SMELLIN' STORM I'M GONNA BRING DOWN ON YOUR SUNNY LITTLE PARADE.
I OWN THIS ENTIRE TOWN AN' EVERYONE IN IT. AN' YOU'RE ABOUT TO FIND THAT OUT IN TH' WORST WAY!

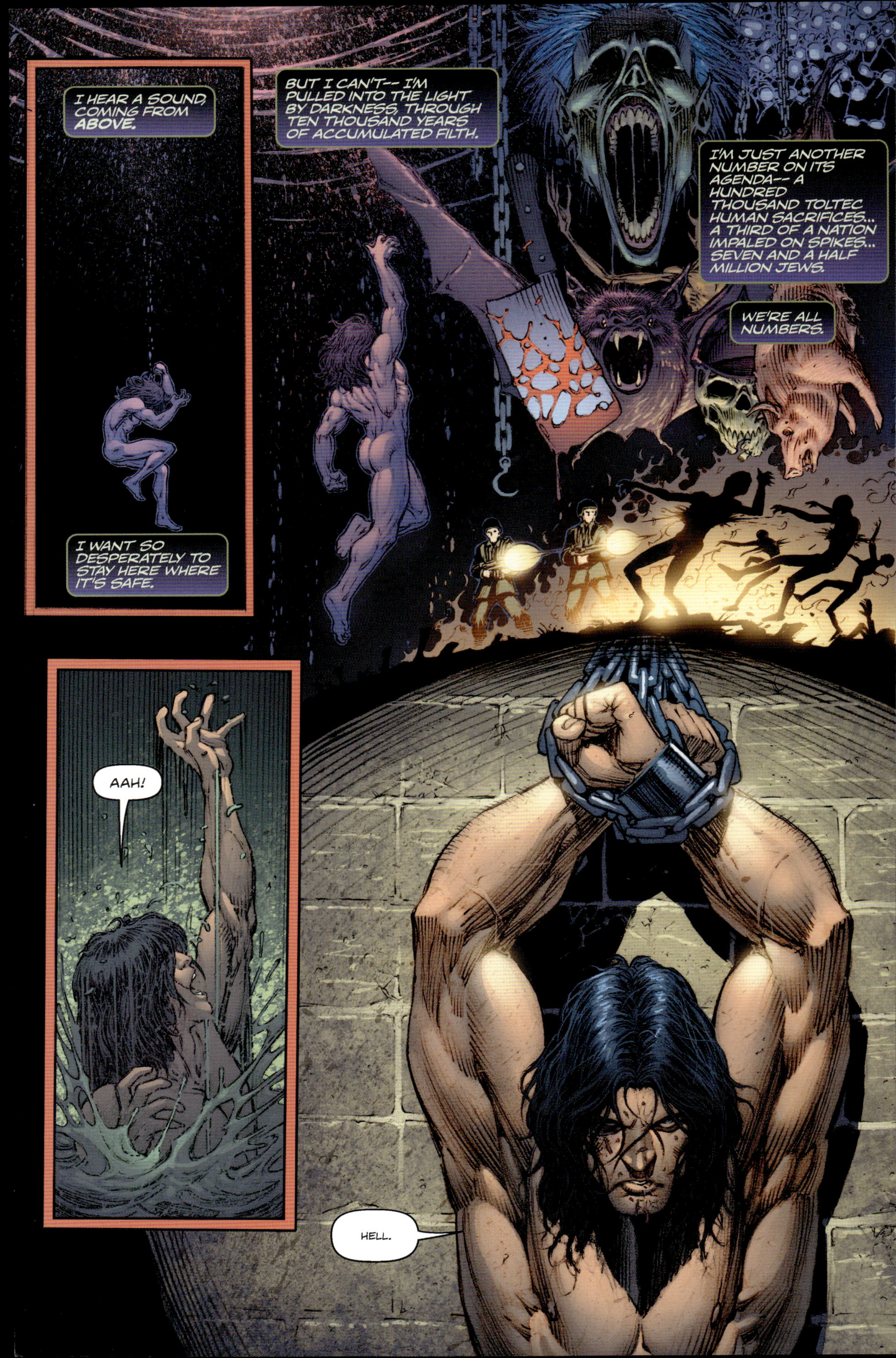
I HEAR A SOUND, COMING FROM **ABOVE.**
I WANT SO DESPERATELY TO STAY HERE WHERE IT'S SAFE.
BUT I CAN'T-- I'M PULLED INTO THE LIGHT BY DARKNESS, THROUGH TEN THOUSAND YEARS OF ACCUMULATED FILTH.
I'M JUST ANOTHER NUMBER ON ITS AGENDA-- A HUNDRED THOUSAND TOLTEC HUMAN SACRIFICES... A THIRD OF A NATION IMPALED ON SPIKES... SEVEN AND A HALF MILLION JEWS.
WE'RE ALL NUMBERS.
AAH!
HELL.

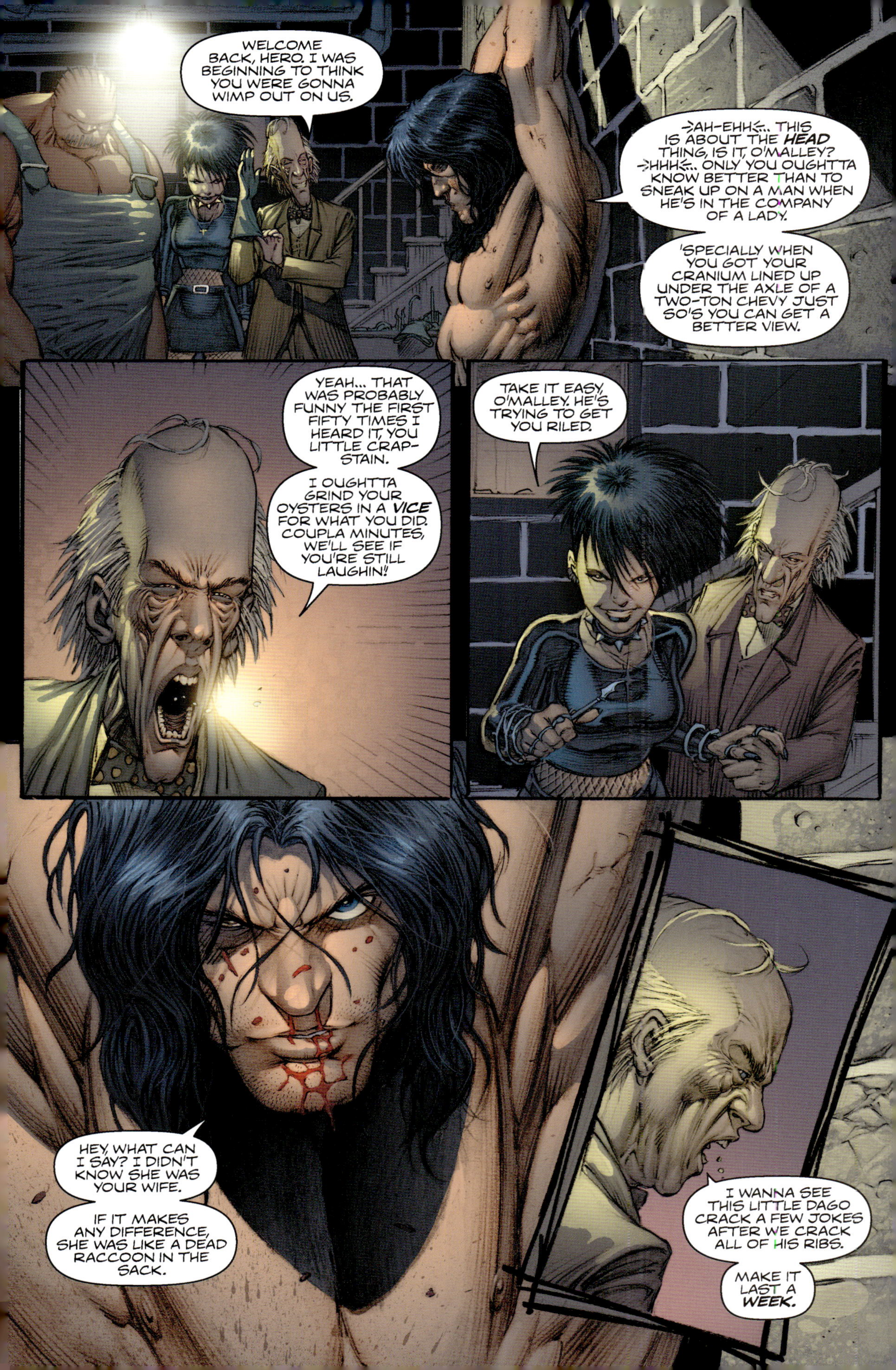
WELCOME BACK, HERO. I WAS BEGINNING TO THINK YOU WERE GONNA WIMP OUT ON US.
AH-EHH... THIS IS ABOUT THE *HEAD* THING, IS IT, O'MALLEY? HHH... ONLY YOU OUGHTTA KNOW BETTER THAN TO SNEAK UP ON A MAN WHEN HE'S IN THE COMPANY OF A LADY.
'SPECIALLY WHEN YOU GOT YOUR CRANIUM LINED UP UNDER THE AXLE OF A TWO-TON CHEVY JUST SO'S YOU CAN GET A BETTER VIEW.
YEAH... THAT WAS PROBABLY FUNNY THE FIRST FIFTY TIMES I HEARD IT, YOU LITTLE CRAP-STAIN.
I OUGHTTA GRIND YOUR OYSTERS IN A *VICE* FOR WHAT YOU DID. COUPLA MINUTES, WE'LL SEE IF YOU'RE STILL LAUGHIN'!
TAKE IT EASY, O'MALLEY. HE'S TRYING TO GET YOU RILED.
HEY, WHAT CAN I SAY? I DIDN'T KNOW SHE WAS YOUR WIFE.
IF IT MAKES ANY DIFFERENCE, SHE WAS LIKE A DEAD RACCOON IN THE SACK.
I WANNA SEE THIS LITTLE DAGO CRACK A FEW JOKES AFTER WE CRACK ALL OF HIS RIBS.
MAKE IT LAST A *WEEK.*

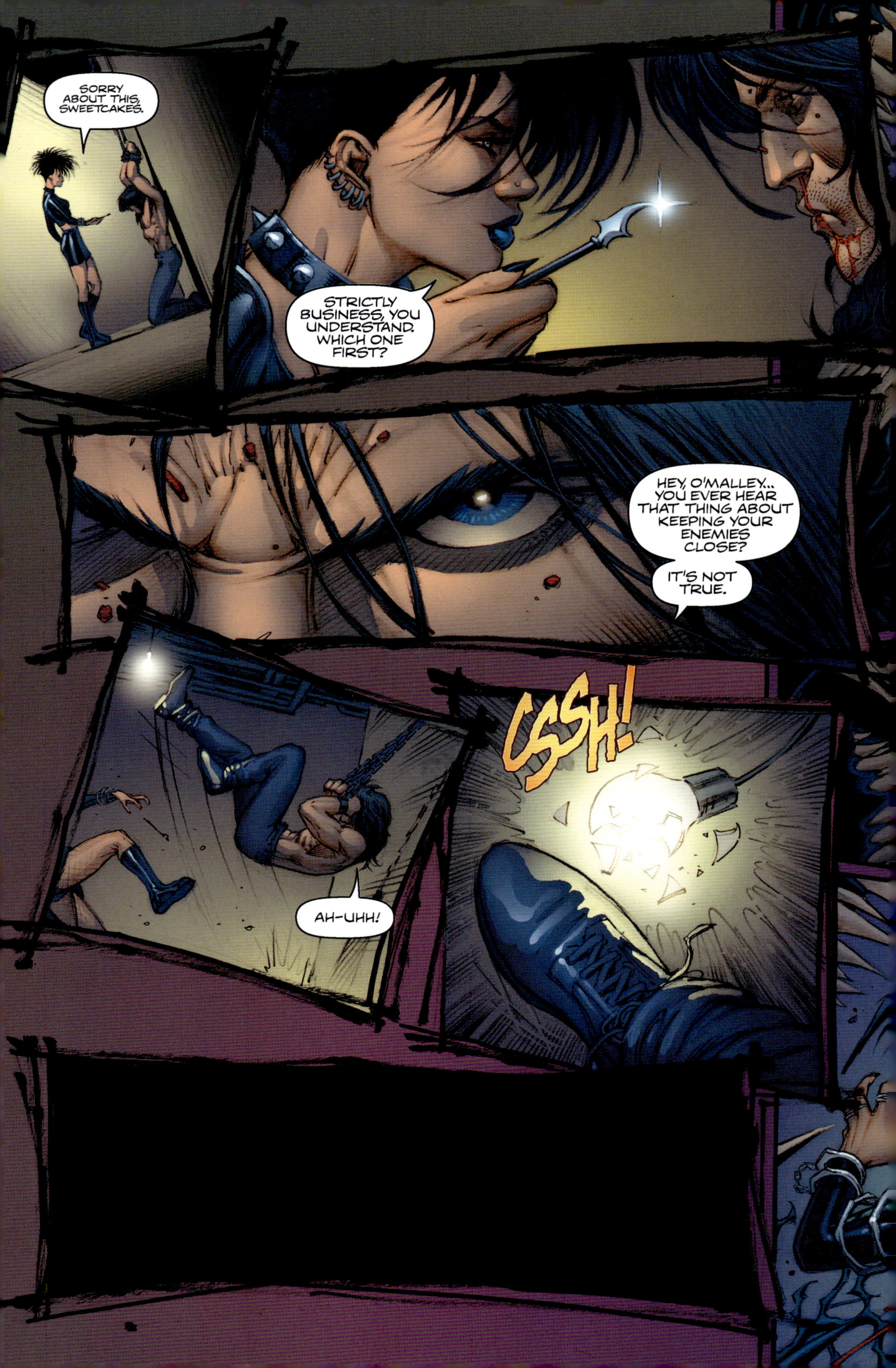
SORRY ABOUT THIS, SWEETCAKES.
STRICTLY BUSINESS, YOU UNDERSTAND. WHICH ONE FIRST?
HEY, O'MALLEY... YOU EVER HEAR THAT THING ABOUT KEEPING YOUR ENEMIES CLOSE?
IT'S NOT TRUE.
AH-UHH!
CSSH!

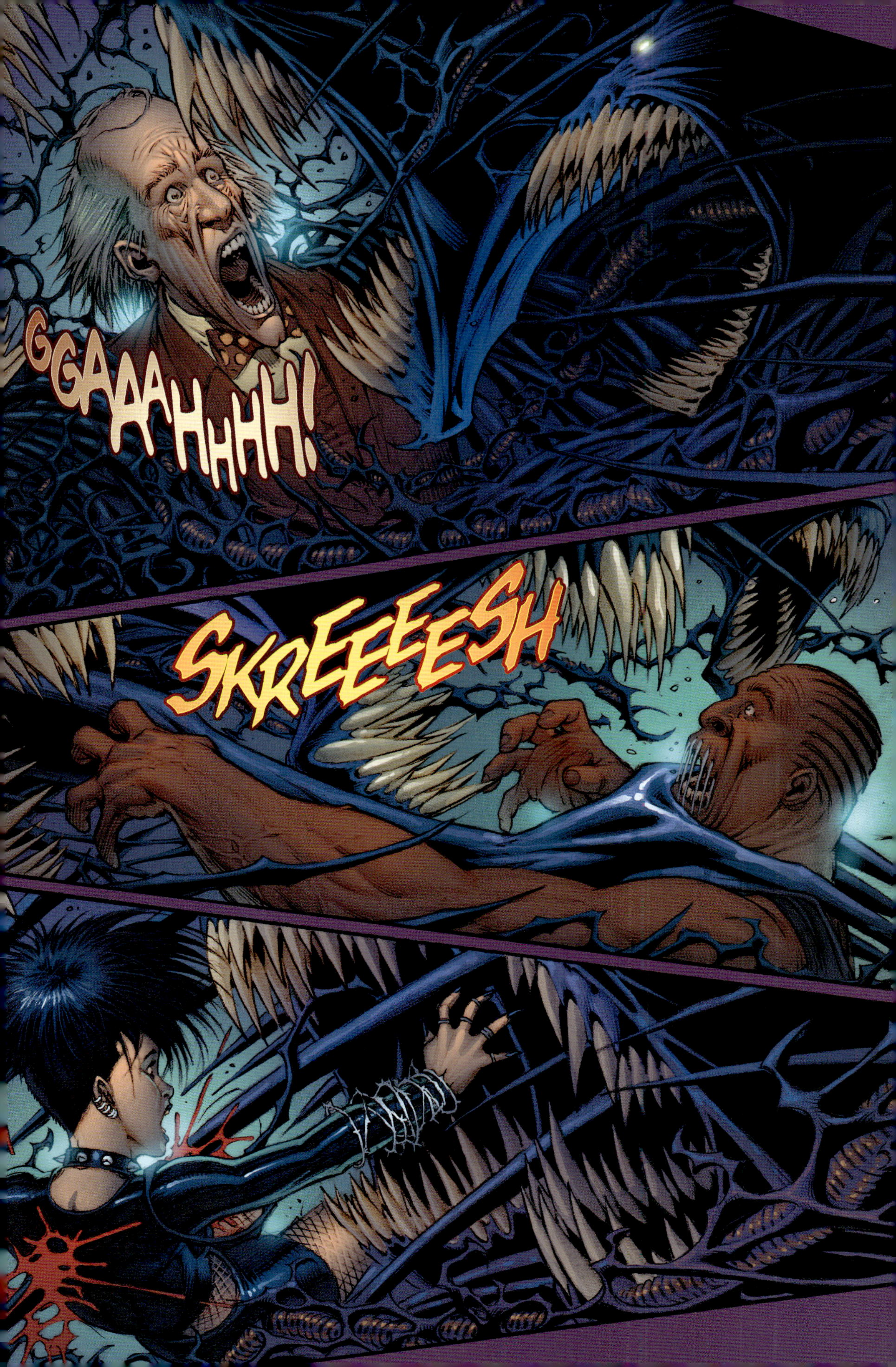
GGAAAHHHH!
SKREEEEESH

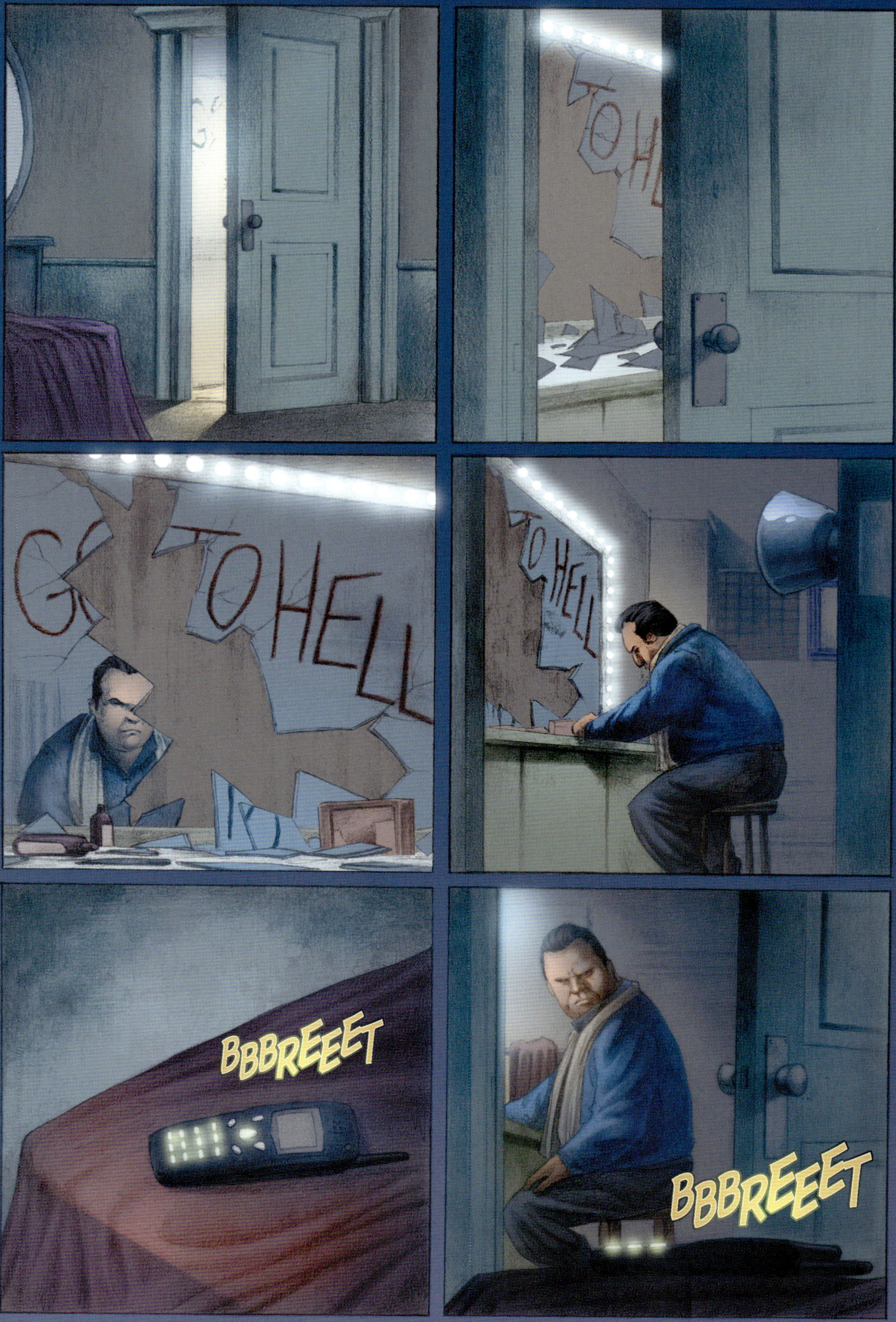
TO HELL
TO HELL
BBBREEET
BBBREEET

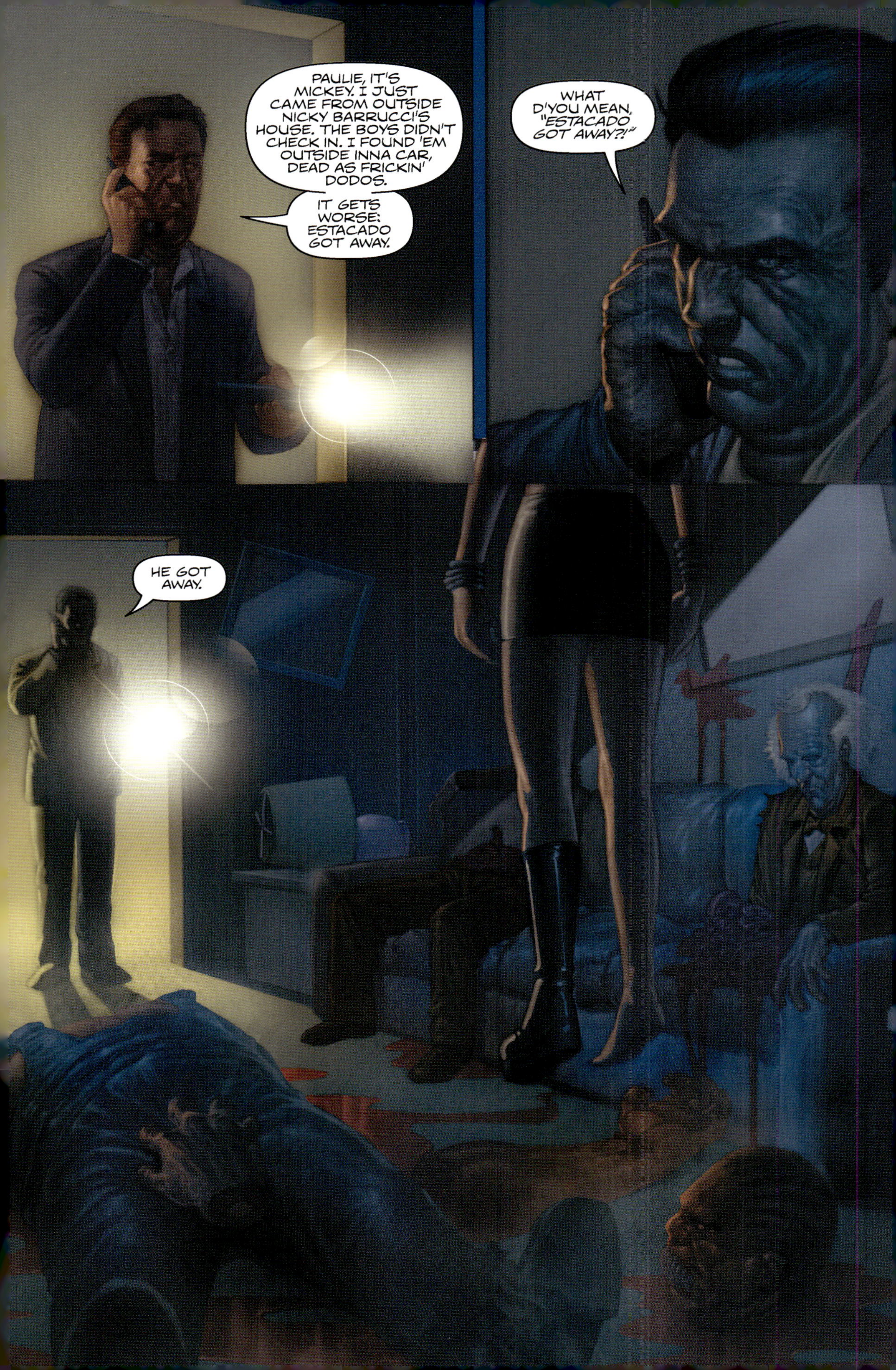
PAULIE, IT'S MICKEY. I JUST CAME FROM OUTSIDE NICKY BARRUCCI'S HOUSE. THE BOYS DIDN'T CHECK IN. I FOUND 'EM OUTSIDE INNA CAR, DEAD AS FRICKIN' DODOS.
IT GETS WORSE: ESTACADO GOT AWAY.
WHAT D'YOU MEAN, "ESTACADO GOT AWAY?!"
HE GOT AWAY.

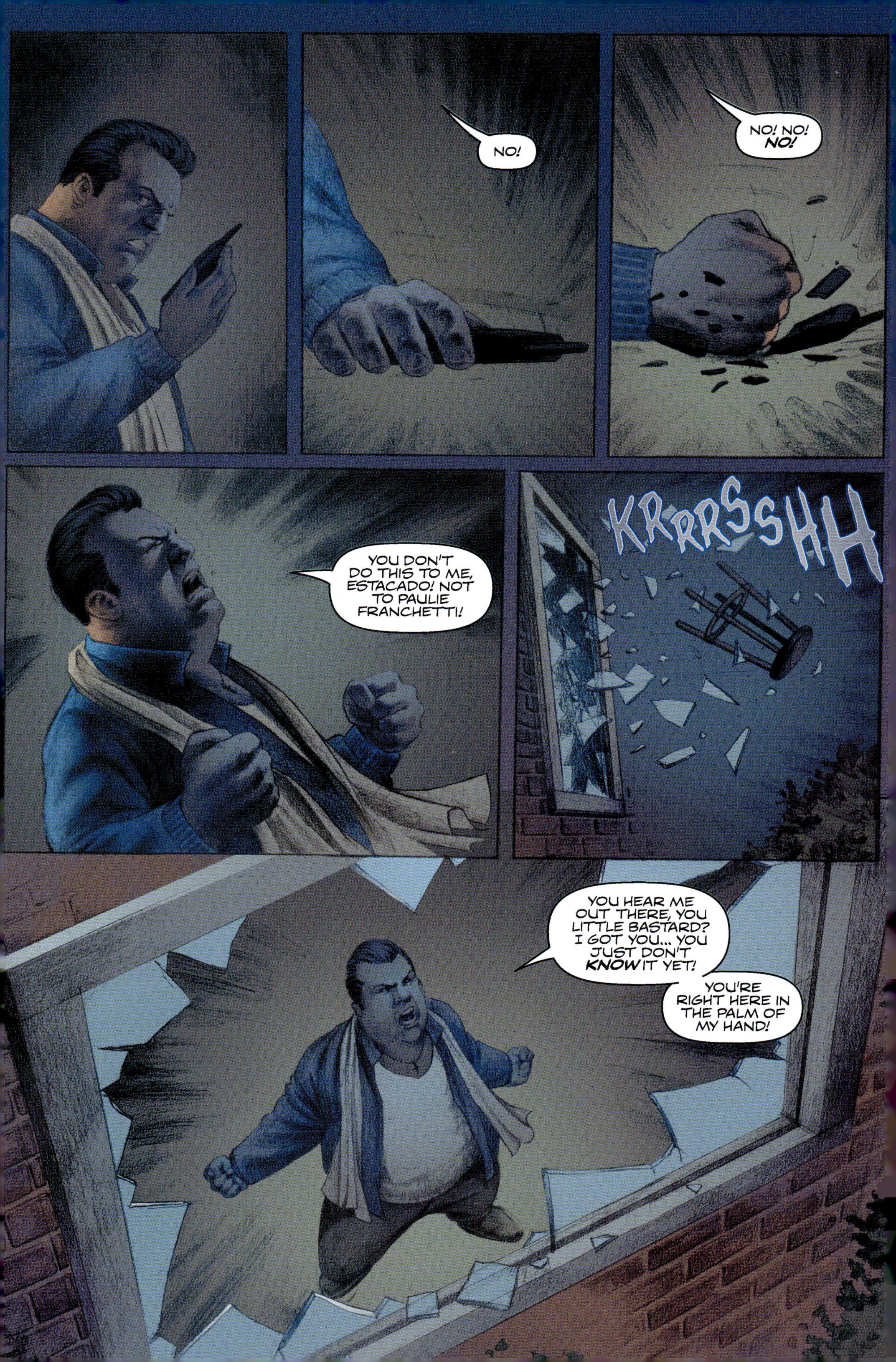
NO!
NO! NO! NO!
YOU DON'T DO THIS TO ME, ESTACADO! NOT TO PAULIE FRANCHETTI!
KRRRSSHH
YOU HEAR ME OUT THERE, YOU LITTLE BASTARD? I GOT YOU... YOU JUST DON'T KNOW IT YET!
YOU'RE RIGHT HERE IN THE PALM OF MY HAND!

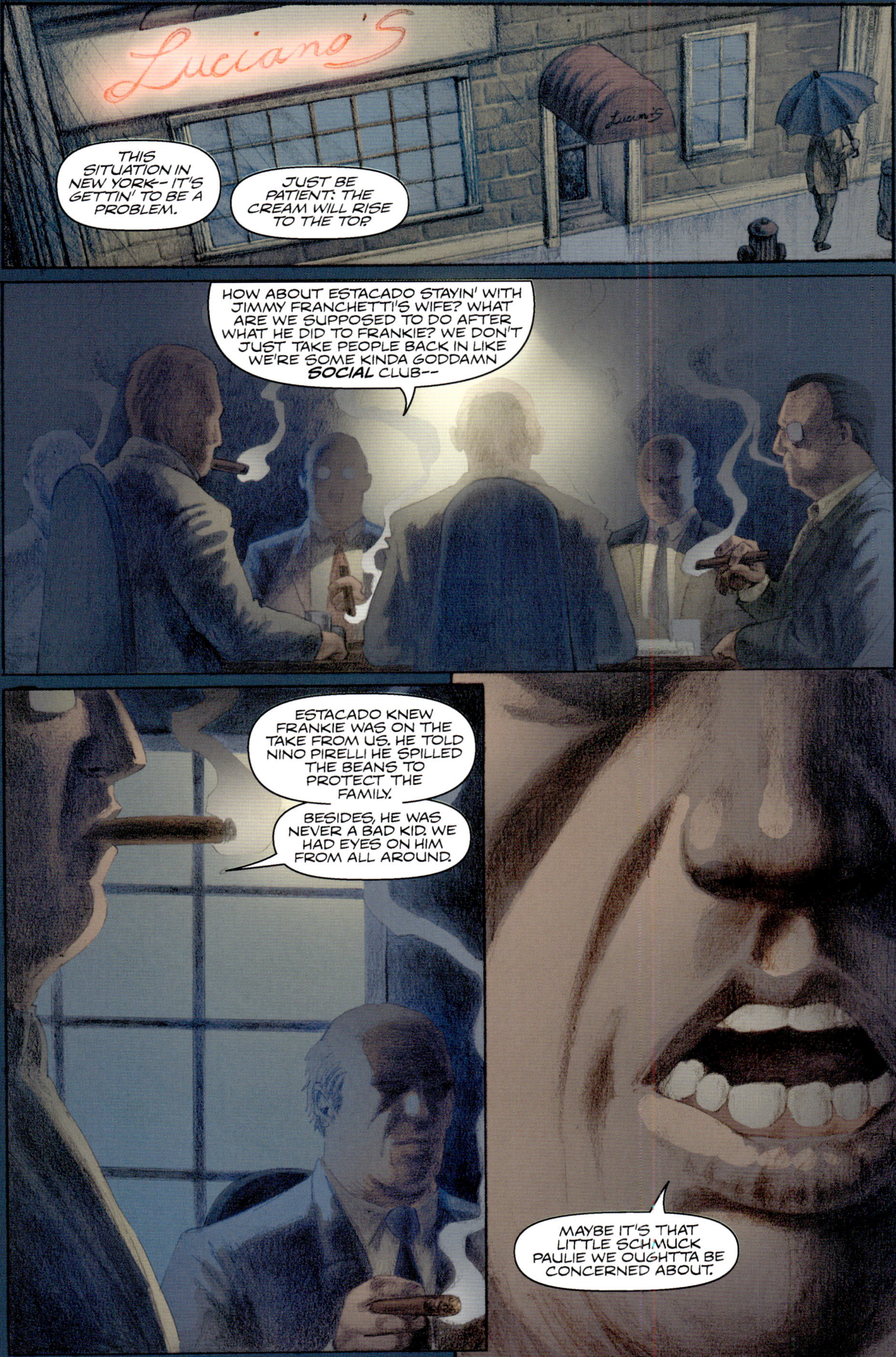
Luciano's
Luciano's
THIS SITUATION IN NEW YORK-- IT'S GETTIN' TO BE A PROBLEM.
JUST BE PATIENT: THE CREAM WILL RISE TO THE TOP.
HOW ABOUT ESTACADO STAYIN' WITH JIMMY FRANCHETTI'S WIFE? WHAT ARE WE SUPPOSED TO DO AFTER WHAT HE DID TO FRANKIE? WE DON'T JUST TAKE PEOPLE BACK IN LIKE WE'RE SOME KINDA GODDAMN SOCIAL CLUB--
ESTACADO KNEW FRANKIE WAS ON THE TAKE FROM US. HE TOLD NINO PIRELLI HE SPILLED THE BEANS TO PROTECT THE FAMILY.
BESIDES, HE WAS NEVER A BAD KID. WE HAD EYES ON HIM FROM ALL AROUND.
MAYBE IT'S THAT LITTLE SCHMUCK PAULIE WE OUGHTTA BE CONCERNED ABOUT.

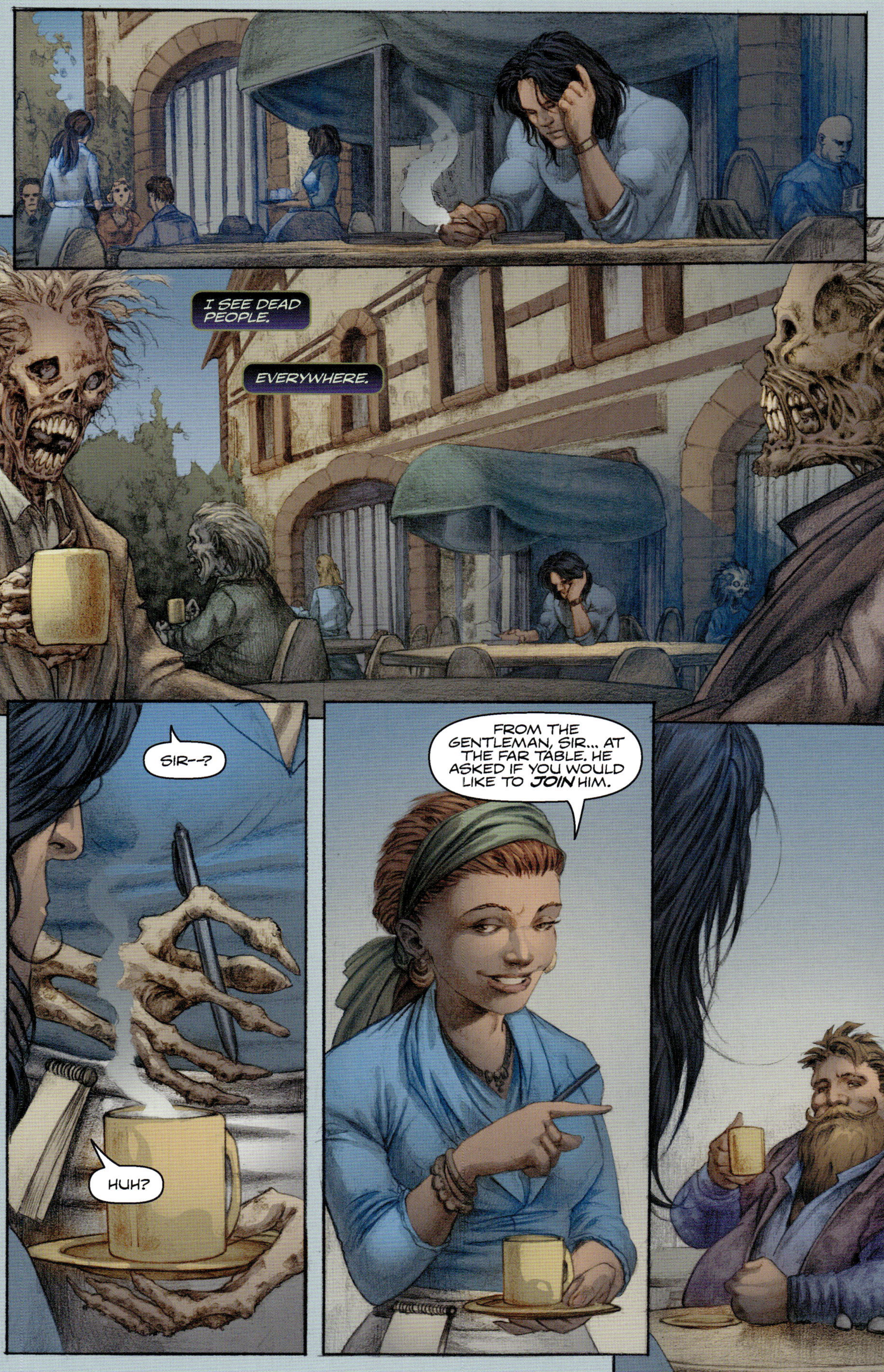
I SEE DEAD PEOPLE.
EVERYWHERE.
SIR--?
HUH?
FROM THE GENTLEMAN, SIR... AT THE FAR TABLE. HE ASKED IF YOU WOULD LIKE TO JOIN HIM.

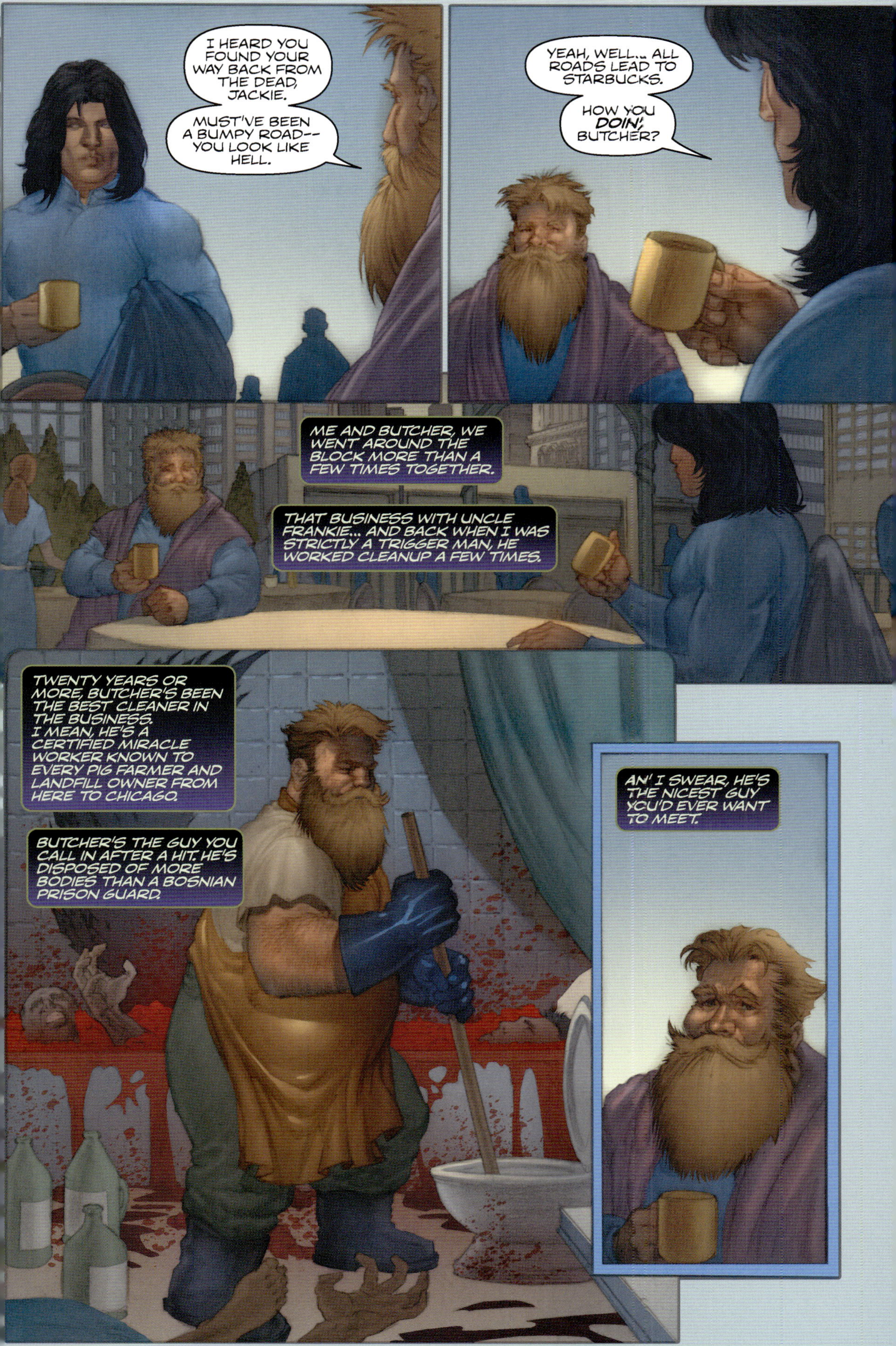
I HEARD YOU FOUND YOUR WAY BACK FROM THE DEAD, JACKIE.
MUST'VE BEEN A BUMPY ROAD-- YOU LOOK LIKE HELL.
YEAH, WELL... ALL ROADS LEAD TO STARBUCKS.
HOW YOU DOIN', BUTCHER?
ME AND BUTCHER, WE WENT AROUND THE BLOCK MORE THAN A FEW TIMES TOGETHER.
THAT BUSINESS WITH UNCLE FRANKIE... AND BACK WHEN I WAS STRICTLY A TRIGGER MAN, HE WORKED CLEANUP A FEW TIMES.
TWENTY YEARS OR MORE, BUTCHER'S BEEN THE BEST CLEANER IN THE BUSINESS. I MEAN, HE'S A CERTIFIED MIRACLE WORKER KNOWN TO EVERY PIG FARMER AND LANDFILL OWNER FROM HERE TO CHICAGO.
BUTCHER'S THE GUY YOU CALL IN AFTER A HIT. HE'S DISPOSED OF MORE BODIES THAN A BOSNIAN PRISON GUARD.
AN' I SWEAR, HE'S THE NICEST GUY YOU'D EVER WANT TO MEET.

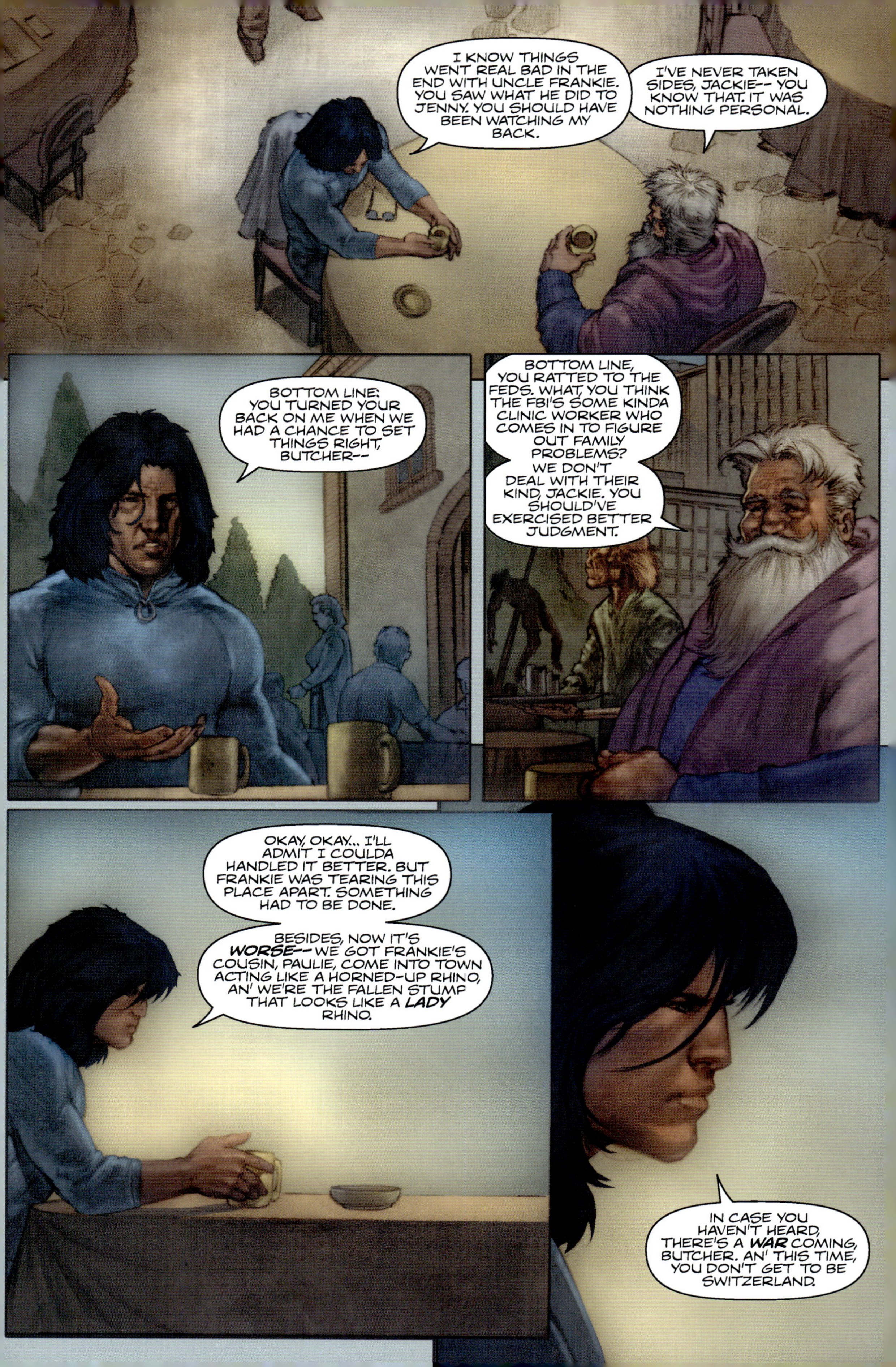
I KNOW THINGS WENT REAL BAD IN THE END WITH UNCLE FRANKIE. YOU SAW WHAT HE DID TO JENNY. YOU SHOULD HAVE BEEN WATCHING MY BACK.
I'VE NEVER TAKEN SIDES, JACKIE-- YOU KNOW THAT. IT WAS NOTHING PERSONAL.
BOTTOM LINE: YOU TURNED YOUR BACK ON ME WHEN WE HAD A CHANCE TO SET THINGS RIGHT, BUTCHER--
BOTTOM LINE, YOU RATTED TO THE FEDS. WHAT, YOU THINK THE FBI'S SOME KINDA CLINIC WORKER WHO COMES IN TO FIGURE OUT FAMILY PROBLEMS?
WE DON'T DEAL WITH THEIR KIND, JACKIE. YOU SHOULD'VE EXERCISED BETTER JUDGMENT.
OKAY, OKAY... I'LL ADMIT I COULDA HANDLED IT BETTER. BUT FRANKIE WAS TEARING THIS PLACE APART. SOMETHING HAD TO BE DONE.
BESIDES, NOW IT'S WORSE-- WE GOT FRANKIE'S COUSIN, PAULIE, COME INTO TOWN ACTING LIKE A HORNED-UP RHINO, AN' WE'RE THE FALLEN STUMP THAT LOOKS LIKE A LADY RHINO.
IN CASE YOU HAVEN'T HEARD, THERE'S A WAR COMING, BUTCHER. AN' THIS TIME, YOU DON'T GET TO BE SWITZERLAND.

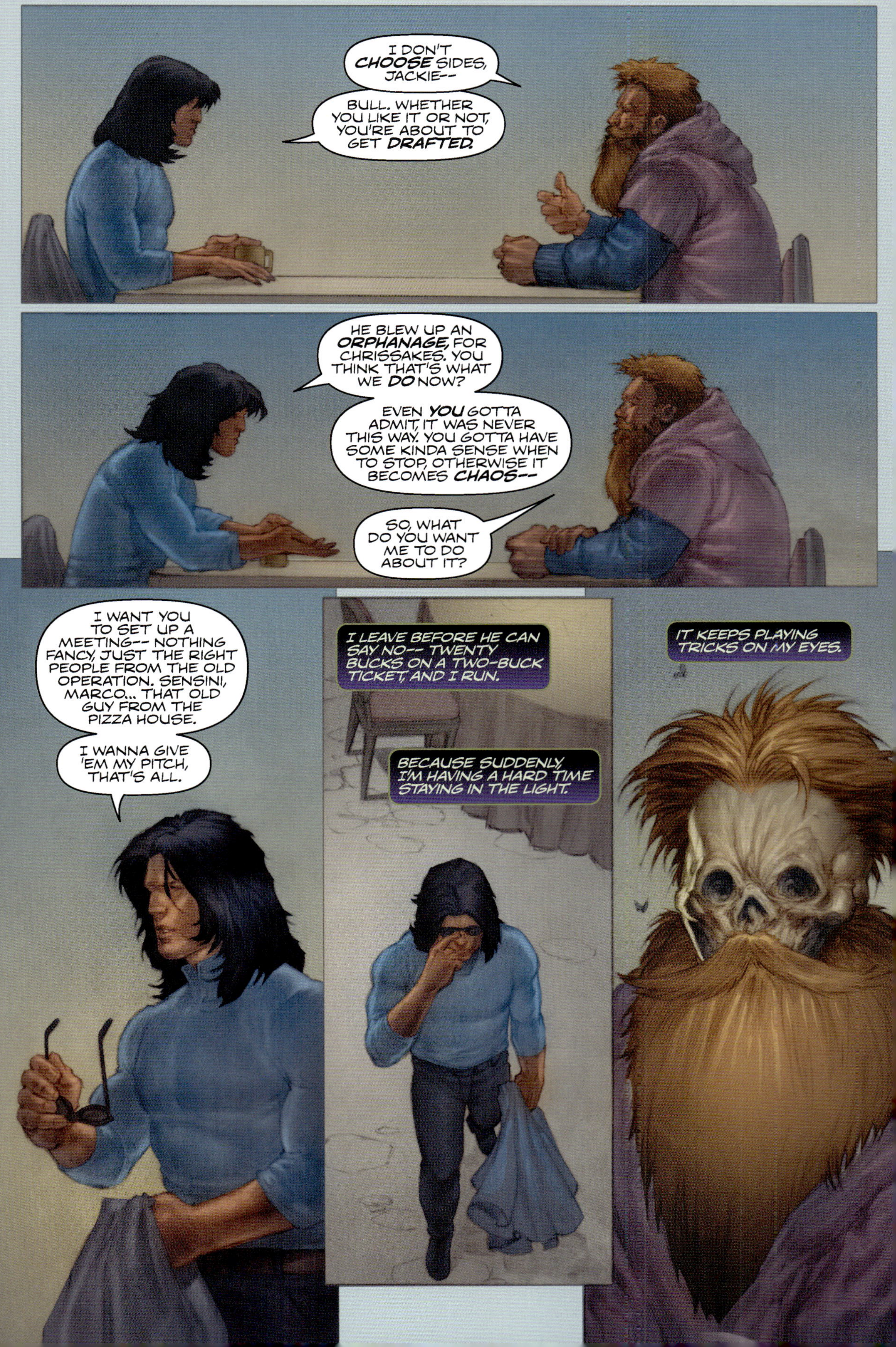
I DON'T CHOOSE SIDES, JACKIE--
BULL. WHETHER YOU LIKE IT OR NOT, YOU'RE ABOUT TO GET DRAFTED.
HE BLEW UP AN ORPHANAGE, FOR CHRISSAKES. YOU THINK THAT'S WHAT WE DO NOW?
EVEN YOU GOTTA ADMIT, IT WAS NEVER THIS WAY. YOU GOTTA HAVE SOME KINDA SENSE WHEN TO STOP, OTHERWISE IT BECOMES CHAOS--
SO, WHAT DO YOU WANT ME TO DO ABOUT IT?
I WANT YOU TO SET UP A MEETING-- NOTHING FANCY, JUST THE RIGHT PEOPLE FROM THE OLD OPERATION. SENSINI, MARCO... THAT OLD GUY FROM THE PIZZA HOUSE.
I WANNA GIVE 'EM MY PITCH, THAT'S ALL.
I LEAVE BEFORE HE CAN SAY NO-- TWENTY BUCKS ON A TWO-BUCK TICKET, AND I RUN.
BECAUSE SUDDENLY, I'M HAVING A HARD TIME STAYING IN THE LIGHT.
IT KEEPS PLAYING TRICKS ON MY EYES.

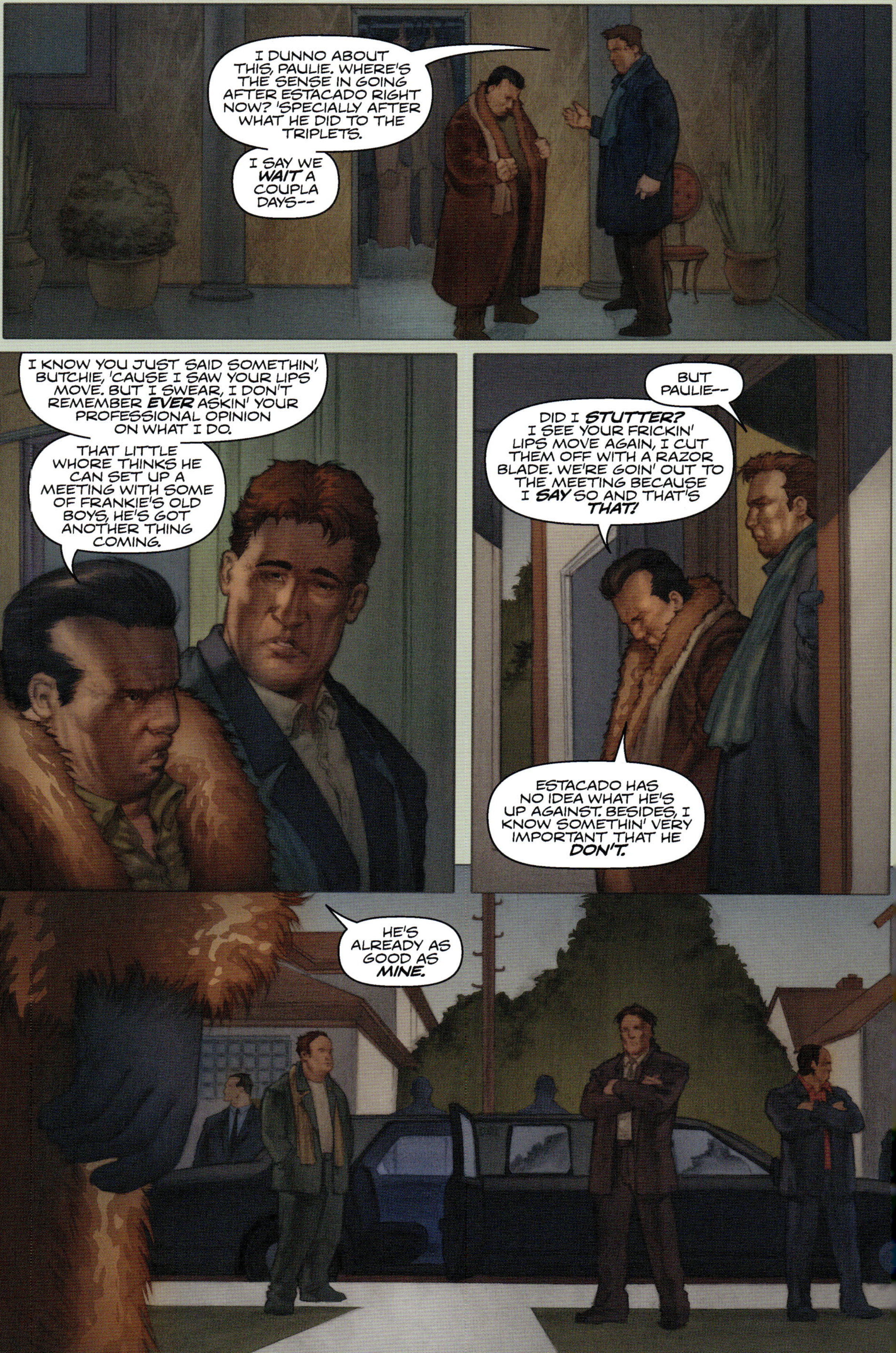
I DUNNO ABOUT THIS, PAULIE. WHERE'S THE SENSE IN GOING AFTER ESTACADO RIGHT NOW? 'SPECIALLY AFTER WHAT HE DID TO THE TRIPLETS.
I SAY WE WAIT A COUPLA DAYS--
I KNOW YOU JUST SAID SOMETHIN', BUTCHIE, 'CAUSE I SAW YOUR LIPS MOVE. BUT I SWEAR, I DON'T REMEMBER EVER ASKIN' YOUR PROFESSIONAL OPINION ON WHAT I DO.
THAT LITTLE WHORE THINKS HE CAN SET UP A MEETING WITH SOME OF FRANKIE'S OLD BOYS, HE'S GOT ANOTHER THING COMING.
BUT PAULIE--
DID I STUTTER? I SEE YOUR FRICKIN' LIPS MOVE AGAIN, I CUT THEM OFF WITH A RAZOR BLADE. WE'RE GOIN' OUT TO THE MEETING BECAUSE I SAY SO AND THAT'S THAT!
ESTACADO HAS NO IDEA WHAT HE'S UP AGAINST. BESIDES, I KNOW SOMETHIN' VERY IMPORTANT THAT HE DON'T.
HE'S ALREADY AS GOOD AS MINE.

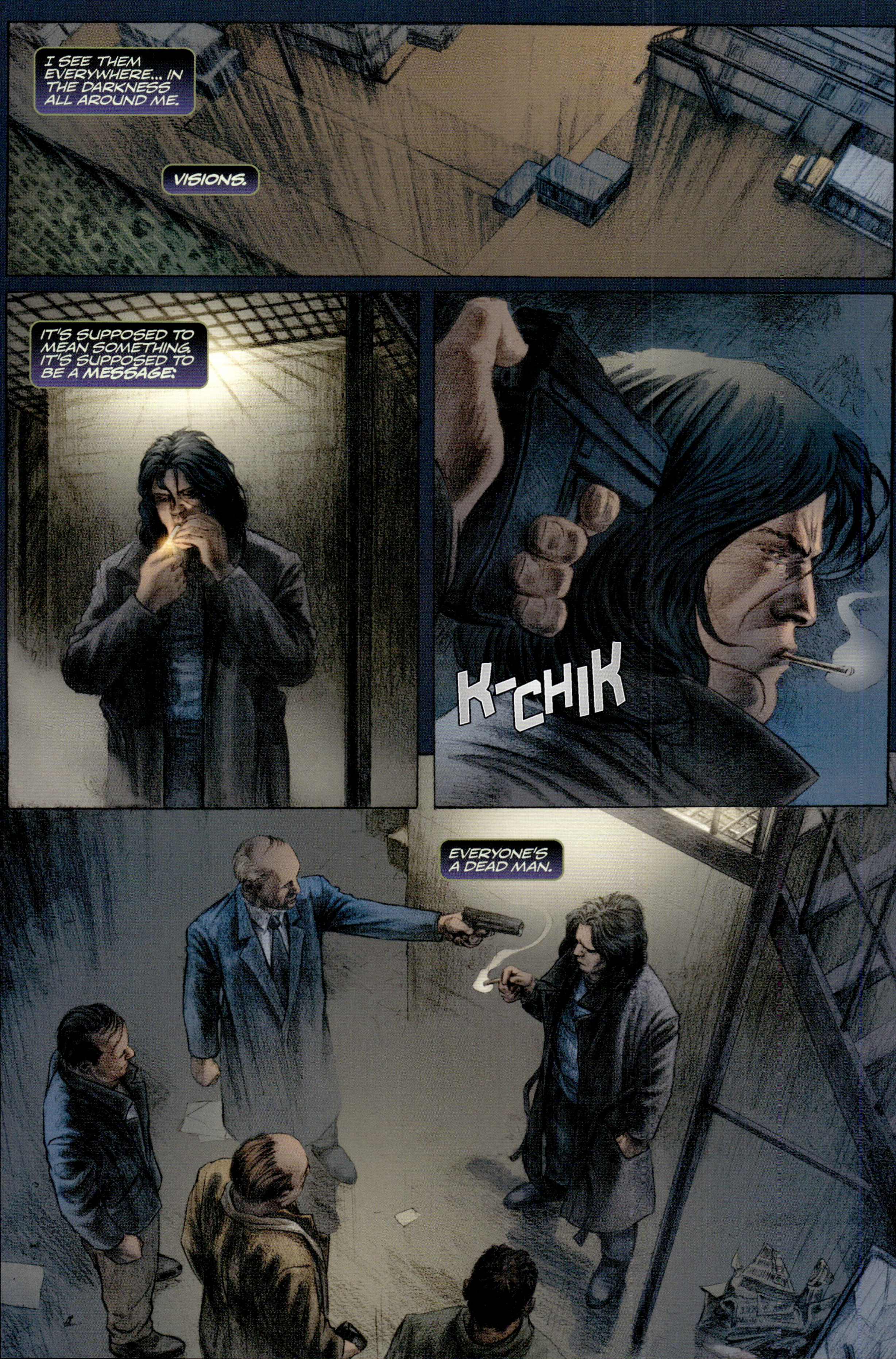
I SEE THEM EVERYWHERE... IN THE DARKNESS ALL AROUND ME.
VISIONS.
IT'S SUPPOSED TO MEAN SOMETHING. IT'S SUPPOSED TO BE A MESSAGE:
K-CHIK
EVERYONE'S A DEAD MAN.

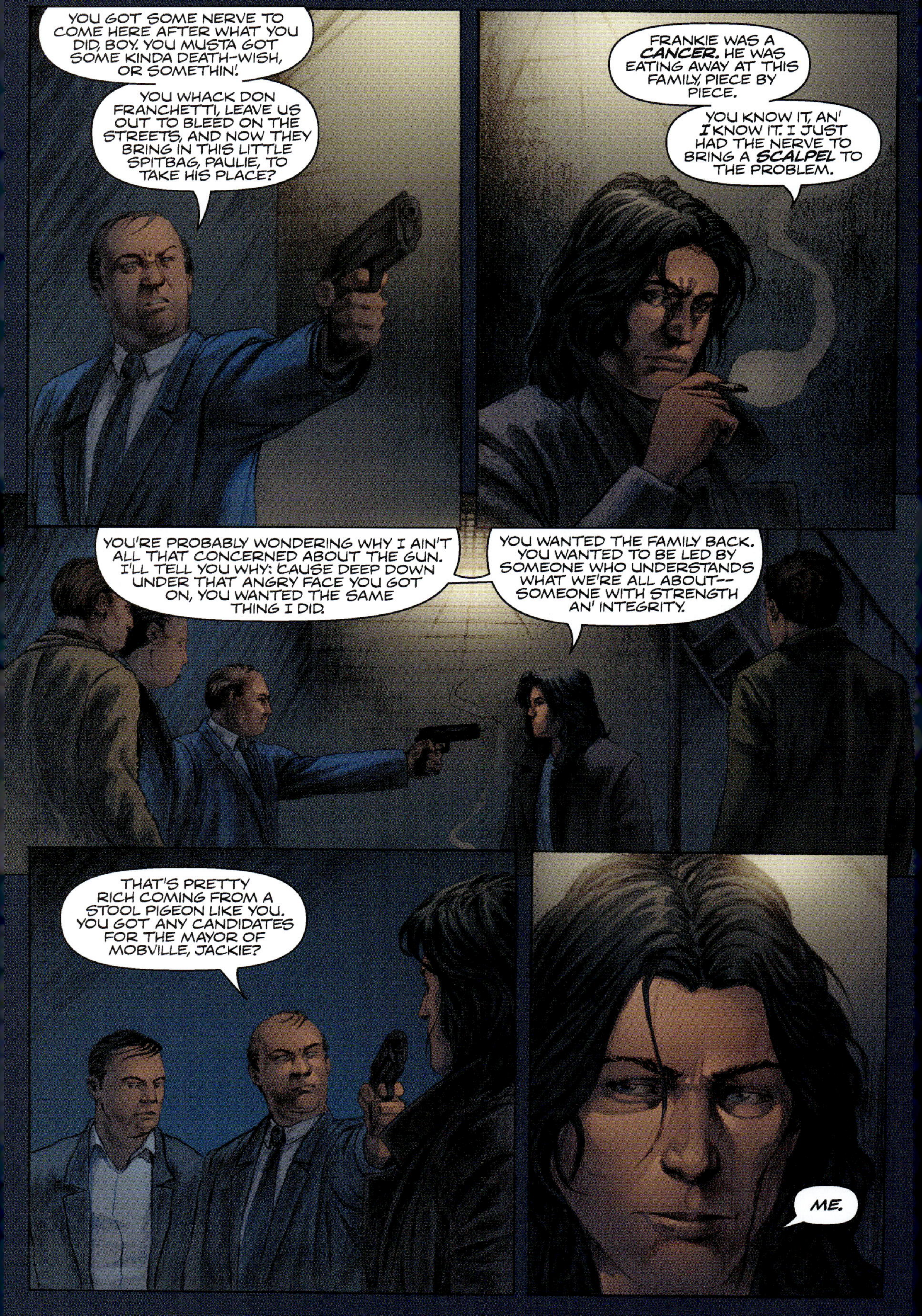
YOU GOT SOME NERVE TO COME HERE AFTER WHAT YOU DID, BOY. YOU MUSTA GOT SOME KINDA DEATH-WISH, OR SOMETHIN'.
YOU WHACK DON FRANCHETTI, LEAVE US OUT TO BLEED ON THE STREETS, AND NOW THEY BRING IN THIS LITTLE SPITBAG, PAULIE, TO TAKE HIS PLACE?
FRANKIE WAS A CANCER. HE WAS EATING AWAY AT THIS FAMILY, PIECE BY PIECE.
YOU KNOW IT, AN' I KNOW IT. I JUST HAD THE NERVE TO BRING A SCALPEL TO THE PROBLEM.
YOU'RE PROBABLY WONDERING WHY I AIN'T ALL THAT CONCERNED ABOUT THE GUN. I'LL TELL YOU WHY: CAUSE DEEP DOWN UNDER THAT ANGRY FACE YOU GOT ON, YOU WANTED THE SAME THING I DID.
YOU WANTED THE FAMILY BACK. YOU WANTED TO BE LED BY SOMEONE WHO UNDERSTANDS WHAT WE'RE ALL ABOUT-- SOMEONE WITH STRENGTH AN' INTEGRITY.
THAT'S PRETTY RICH COMING FROM A STOOL PIGEON LIKE YOU. YOU GOT ANY CANDIDATES FOR THE MAYOR OF MOBVILLE, JACKIE?
ME.

YOU? NOW I KNOW YOU'RE PULLIN' MY LEG--

I'M DEADLY SERIOUS. I ALWAYS STOOD IN THE BACK, DID WHAT MY UNCLE FRANKIE SAID I NEVER HAD THE AMBITION FOR IT BEFORE NOW.

SO WHY NOW, JACKIE? YOU WERE ALWAYS JUST ANOTHER PUNK WITH A GUN. YOU CAN KILL, BUT WHAT ELSE CAN YOU DO?

YOU SEE THAT WAREHOUSE OVER THERE?

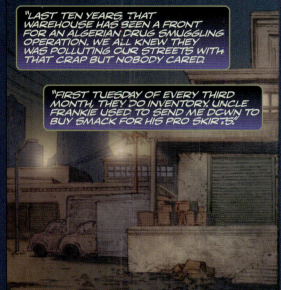

"LAST TEN YEARS, THAT WAREHOUSE HAS BEEN A FRONT FOR AN ALGERIAN DRUG SMUGGLING OPERATION. WE ALL KNEW THEY WAS POLLUTING OUR STREETS WITH THAT CRAP BUT NOBODY CARED.

"FIRST TUESDAY OF EVERY THIRD MONTH, THEY DO INVENTORY. UNCLE FRANKIE USED TO SEND ME DOWN TO BUY SMACK FOR HIS PRO SKIRTS."

LET'S SAY I SHUT THEM DOWN TONIGHT FOR GOOD-- END OF PROBLEM, ALL BY MYSELF.

THINK YOU'D TAKE ME SERIOUSLY AFTER THAT?

FINE. KNOCK YOURSELF OUT.

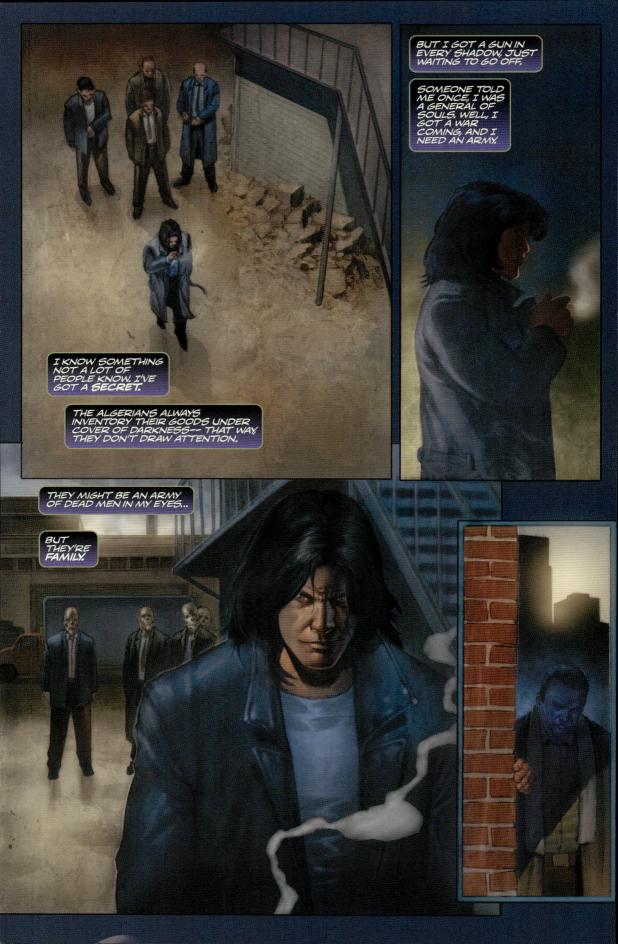

BUT I GOT A GUN IN EVERY SHADOW, JUST WAITING TO GO OFF.

SOMEONE TOLD ME ONCE, I WAS A GENERAL OF SOULS. WELL, I GOT A WAR COMING, AND I NEED AN ARMY.

I KNOW SOMETHING NOT A LOT OF PEOPLE KNOW. I'VE GOT A SECRET.

THE ALGERIANS ALWAYS INVENTORY THEIR GOODS UNDER COVER OF DARKNESS-- THAT WAY, THEY DON'T DRAW ATTENTION.

THEY MIGHT BE AN ARMY OF DEAD MEN IN MY EYES...

BUT THEY'RE FAMILY.

The Darkness Issue #44
cover art by: Dale Keown & Matt Milla

THE DARKNESS #44

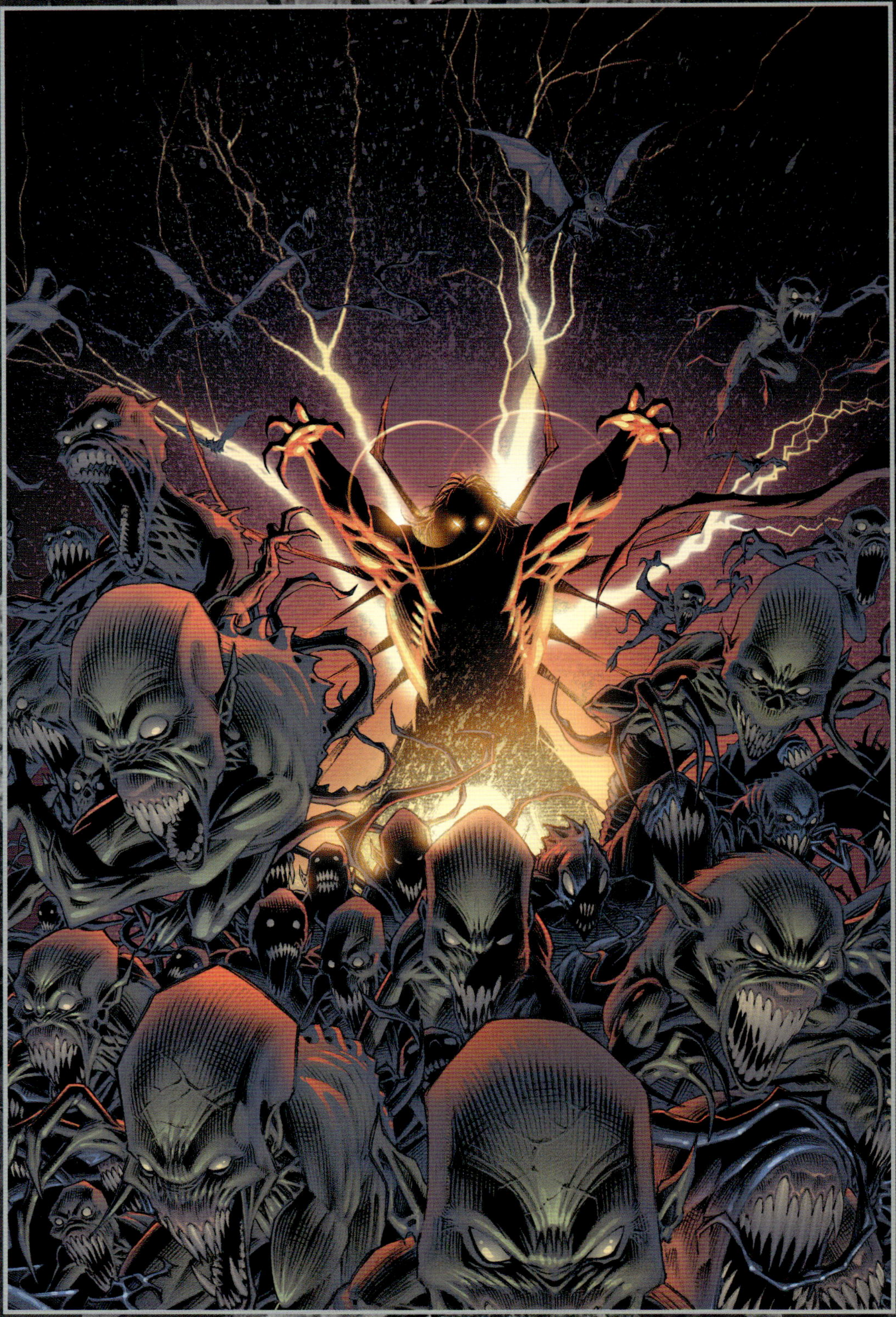

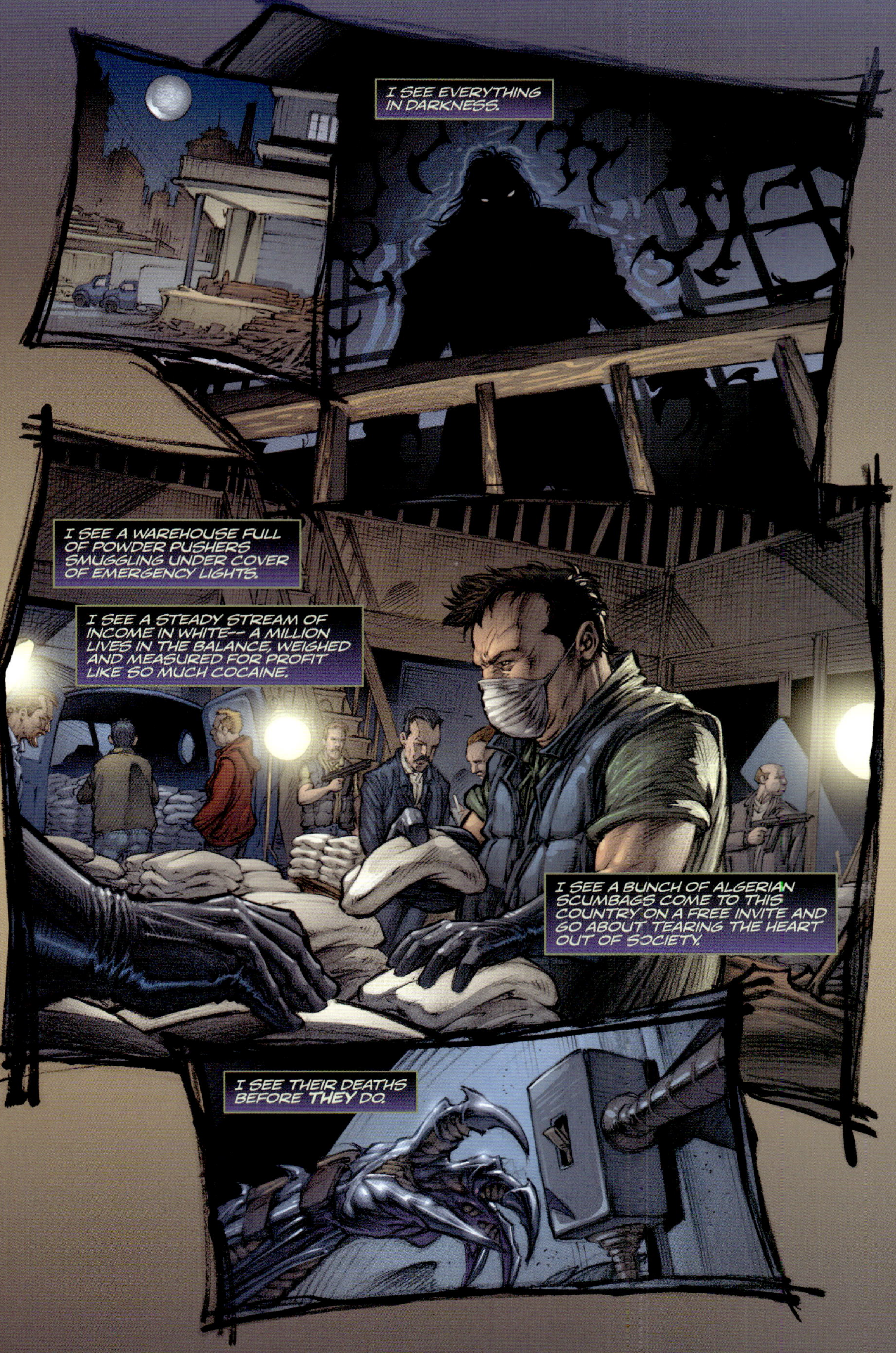
I SEE EVERYTHING IN DARKNESS.
I SEE A WAREHOUSE FULL OF POWDER PUSHERS SMUGGLING UNDER COVER OF EMERGENCY LIGHTS.
I SEE A STEADY STREAM OF INCOME IN WHITE-- A MILLION LIVES IN THE BALANCE, WEIGHED AND MEASURED FOR PROFIT LIKE SO MUCH COCAINE.
I SEE A BUNCH OF ALGERIAN SCUMBAGS COME TO THIS COUNTRY ON A FREE INVITE AND GO ABOUT TEARING THE HEART OUT OF SOCIETY.
I SEE THEIR DEATHS BEFORE THEY DO.

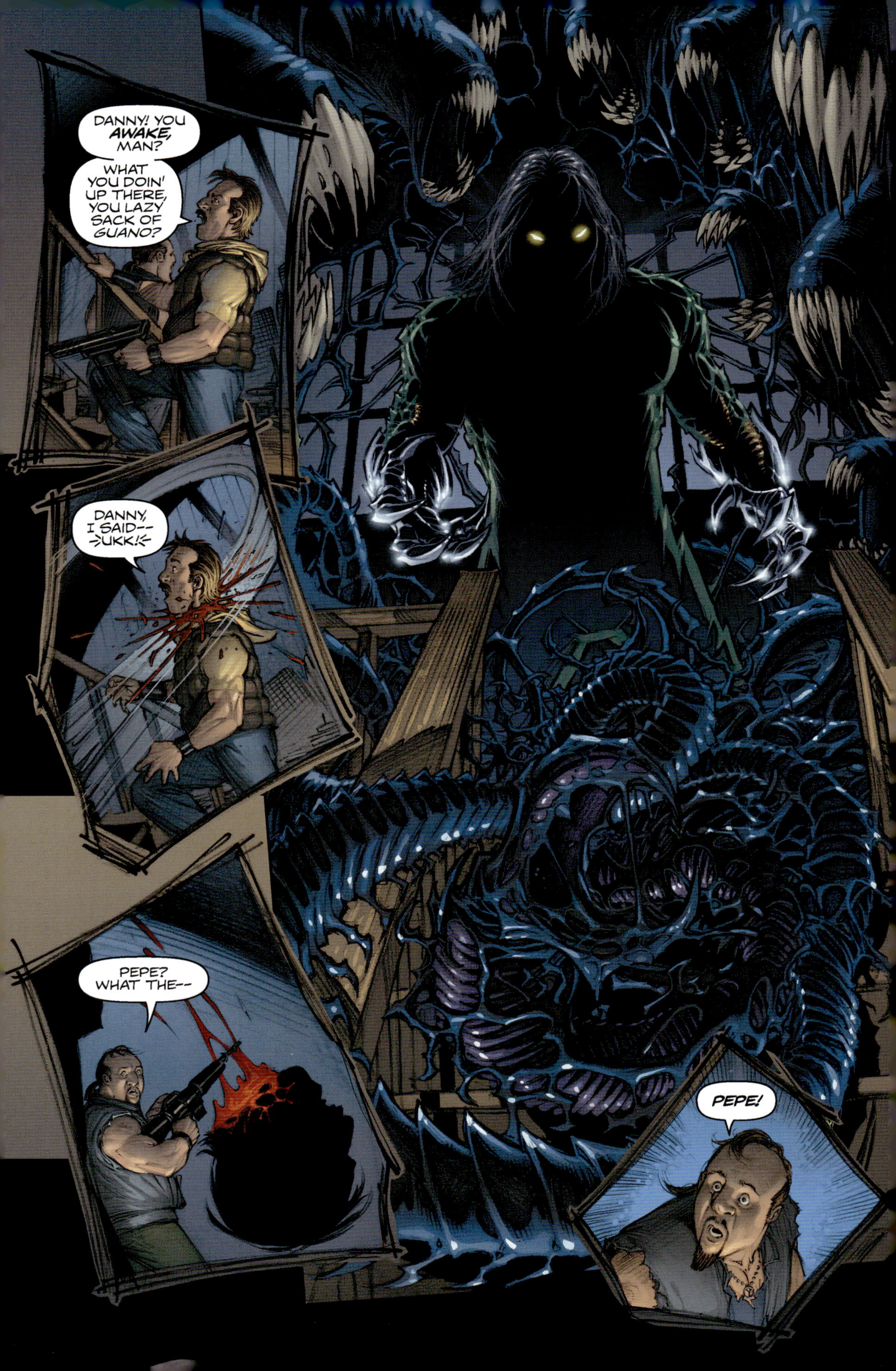
DANNY! YOU *AWAKE,* MAN?
WHAT YOU DOIN' UP THERE, YOU LAZY SACK OF GUANO?
DANNY, I SAID-- >UKK!<
PEPE? WHAT THE--
PEPE!

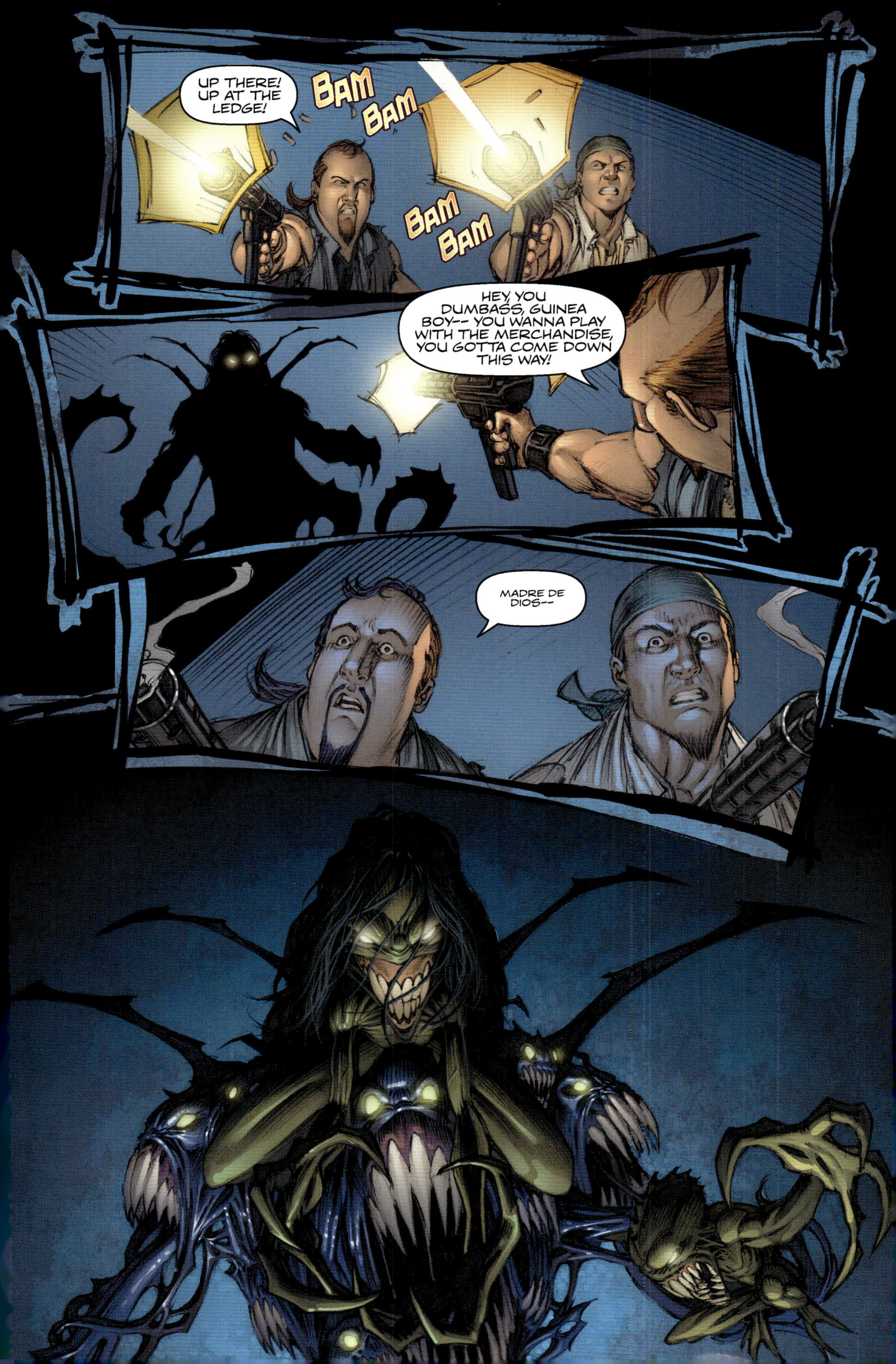
UP THERE! UP AT THE LEDGE!
BAM BAM
BAM BAM
HEY, YOU DUMBASS, GUINEA BOY-- YOU WANNA PLAY WITH THE MERCHANDISE, YOU GOTTA COME DOWN THIS WAY!
MADRE DE DIOS--

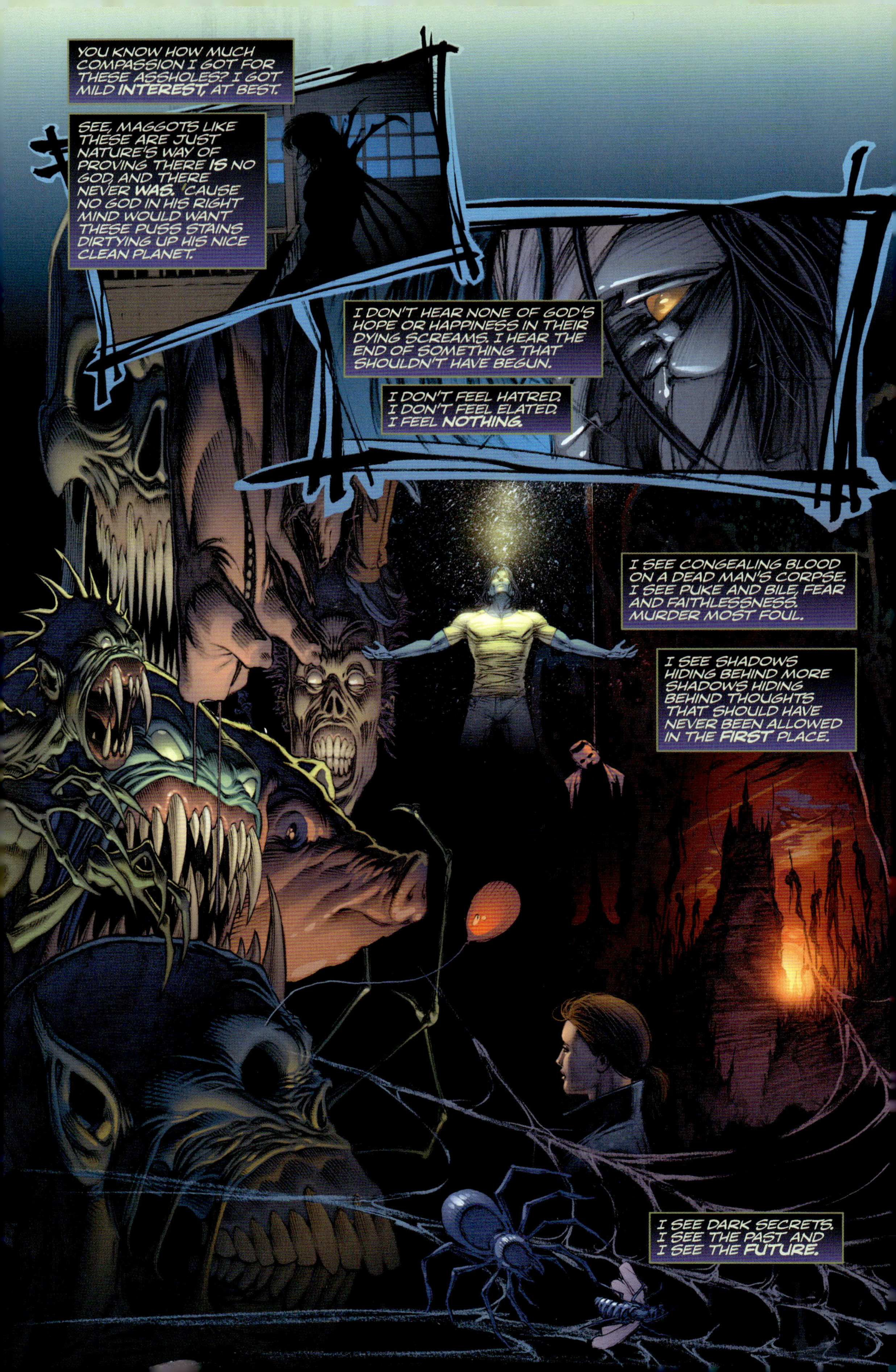
YOU KNOW HOW MUCH COMPASSION I GOT FOR THESE ASSHOLES? I GOT MILD INTEREST, AT BEST.
SEE, MAGGOTS LIKE THESE ARE JUST NATURE'S WAY OF PROVING THERE IS NO GOD, AND THERE NEVER WAS. 'CAUSE NO GOD IN HIS RIGHT MIND WOULD WANT THESE PUSS STAINS DIRTYING UP HIS NICE CLEAN PLANET.
I DON'T HEAR NONE OF GOD'S HOPE OR HAPPINESS IN THEIR DYING SCREAMS. I HEAR THE END OF SOMETHING THAT SHOULDN'T HAVE BEGUN.
I DON'T FEEL HATRED. I DON'T FEEL ELATED. I FEEL NOTHING.
I SEE CONGEALING BLOOD ON A DEAD MAN'S CORPSE. I SEE PUKE AND BILE, FEAR AND FAITHLESSNESS. MURDER MOST FOUL.
I SEE SHADOWS HIDING BEHIND MORE SHADOWS HIDING BEHIND THOUGHTS THAT SHOULD HAVE NEVER BEEN ALLOWED IN THE FIRST PLACE.
I SEE DARK SECRETS. I SEE THE PAST AND I SEE THE FUTURE.

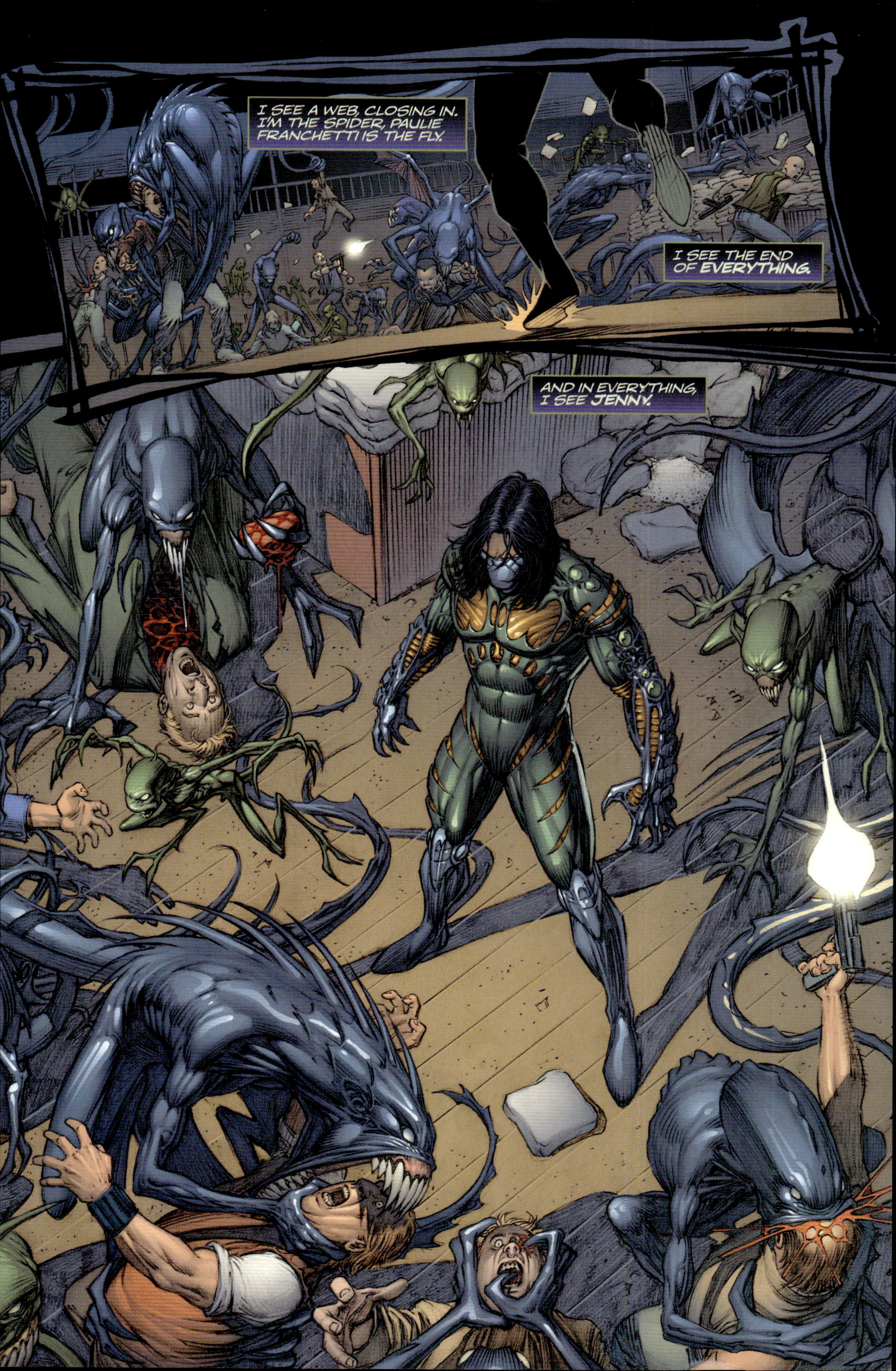
I SEE A WEB, CLOSING IN. I'M THE SPIDER, PAULIE FRANCHETTI IS THE FLY.
I SEE THE END OF EVERYTHING.
AND IN EVERYTHING, I SEE JENNY.

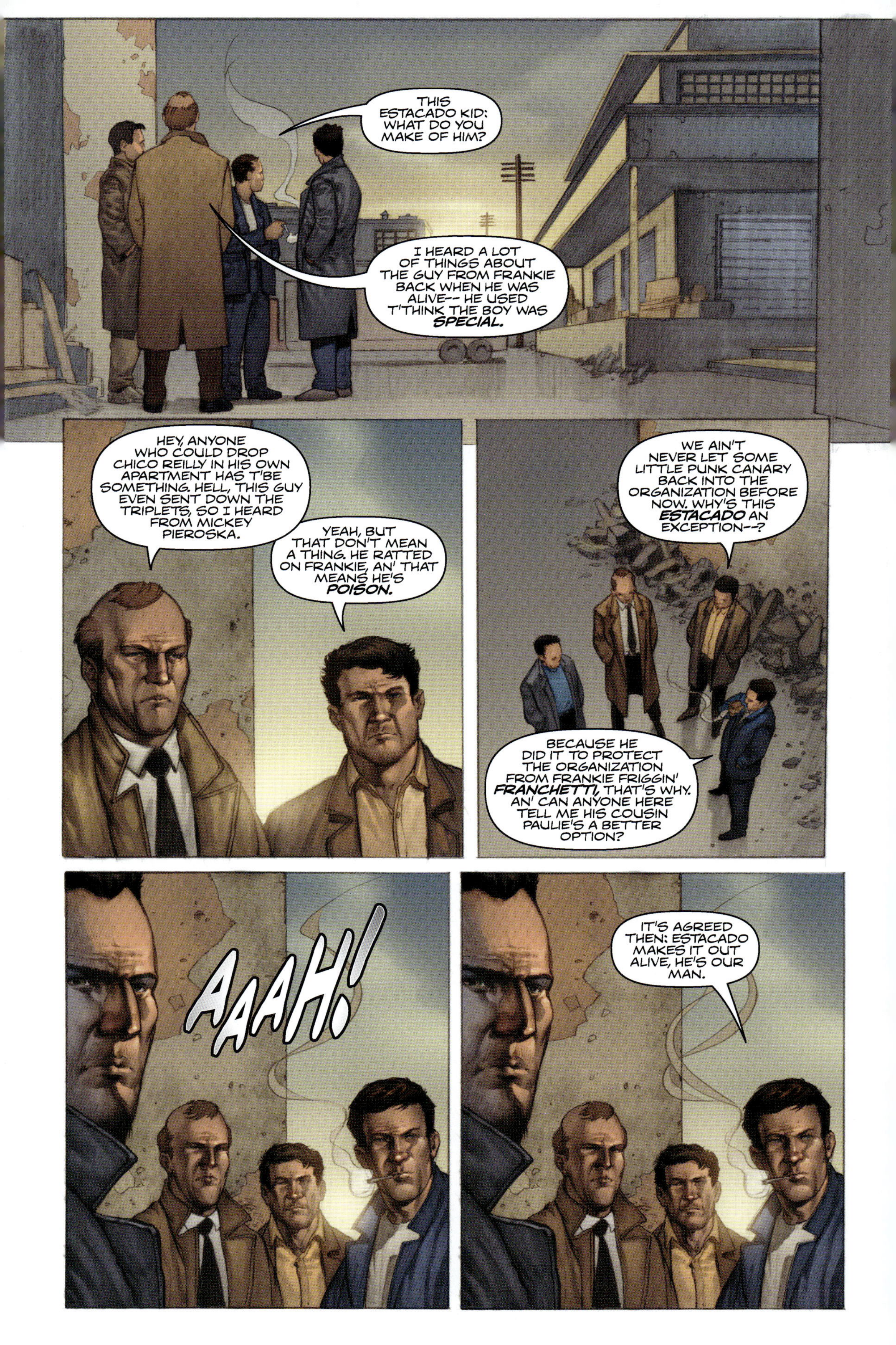
THIS ESTACADO KID: WHAT DO YOU MAKE OF HIM?
I HEARD A LOT OF THINGS ABOUT THE GUY FROM FRANKIE BACK WHEN HE WAS ALIVE-- HE USED T'THINK THE BOY WAS SPECIAL.
HEY, ANYONE WHO COULD DROP CHICO REILLY IN HIS OWN APARTMENT HAS T'BE SOMETHING. HELL, THIS GUY EVEN SENT DOWN THE TRIPLETS, SO I HEARD FROM MICKEY PIEROSKA.
YEAH, BUT THAT DON'T MEAN A THING. HE RATTED ON FRANKIE, AN' THAT MEANS HE'S POISON.
WE AIN'T NEVER LET SOME LITTLE PUNK CANARY BACK INTO THE ORGANIZATION BEFORE NOW. WHY'S THIS ESTACADO AN EXCEPTION--?
BECAUSE HE DID IT TO PROTECT THE ORGANIZATION FROM FRANKIE FRIGGIN' FRANCHETTI, THAT'S WHY. AN' CAN ANYONE HERE TELL ME HIS COUSIN PAULIE'S A BETTER OPTION?
AAAH!
IT'S AGREED THEN: ESTACADO MAKES IT OUT ALIVE, HE'S OUR MAN.

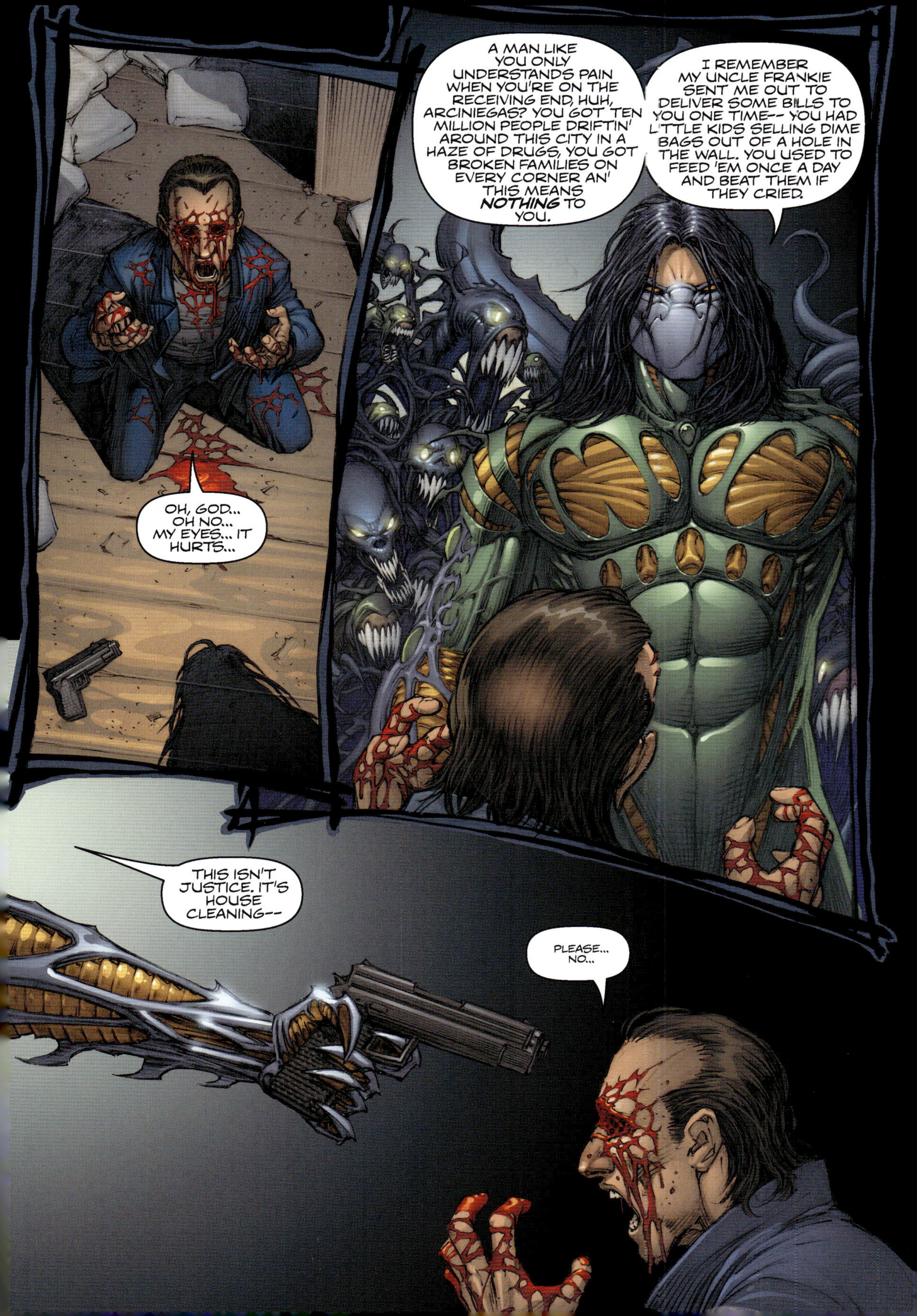
A MAN LIKE YOU ONLY UNDERSTANDS PAIN WHEN YOU'RE ON THE RECEIVING END, HUH, ARCINIEGAS? YOU GOT TEN MILLION PEOPLE DRIFTIN' AROUND THIS CITY IN A HAZE OF DRUGS, YOU GOT BROKEN FAMILIES ON EVERY CORNER AN' THIS MEANS **NOTHING** TO YOU.
I REMEMBER MY UNCLE FRANKIE SENT ME OUT TO DELIVER SOME BILLS TO YOU ONE TIME-- YOU HAD LITTLE KIDS SELLING DIME BAGS OUT OF A HOLE IN THE WALL. YOU USED TO FEED 'EM ONCE A DAY AND BEAT THEM IF THEY CRIED.
OH, GOD... OH NO... MY EYES... IT HURTS...
THIS ISN'T JUSTICE. IT'S HOUSE CLEANING--
PLEASE... NO...

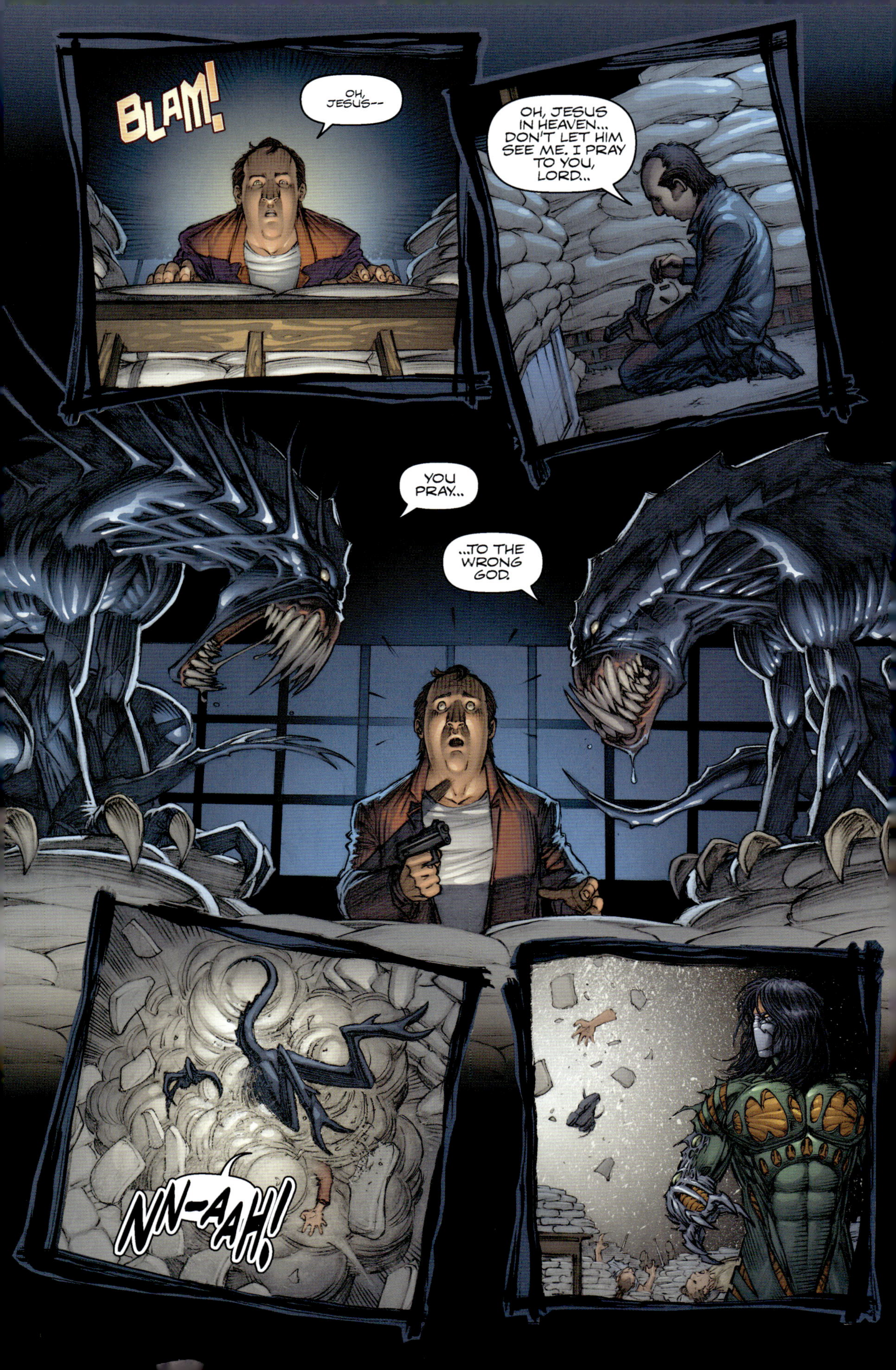
BLAM!
OH, JESUS--
OH, JESUS IN HEAVEN... DON'T LET HIM SEE ME. I PRAY TO YOU, LORD...
YOU PRAY...
...TO THE WRONG GOD.
NN-AAH!

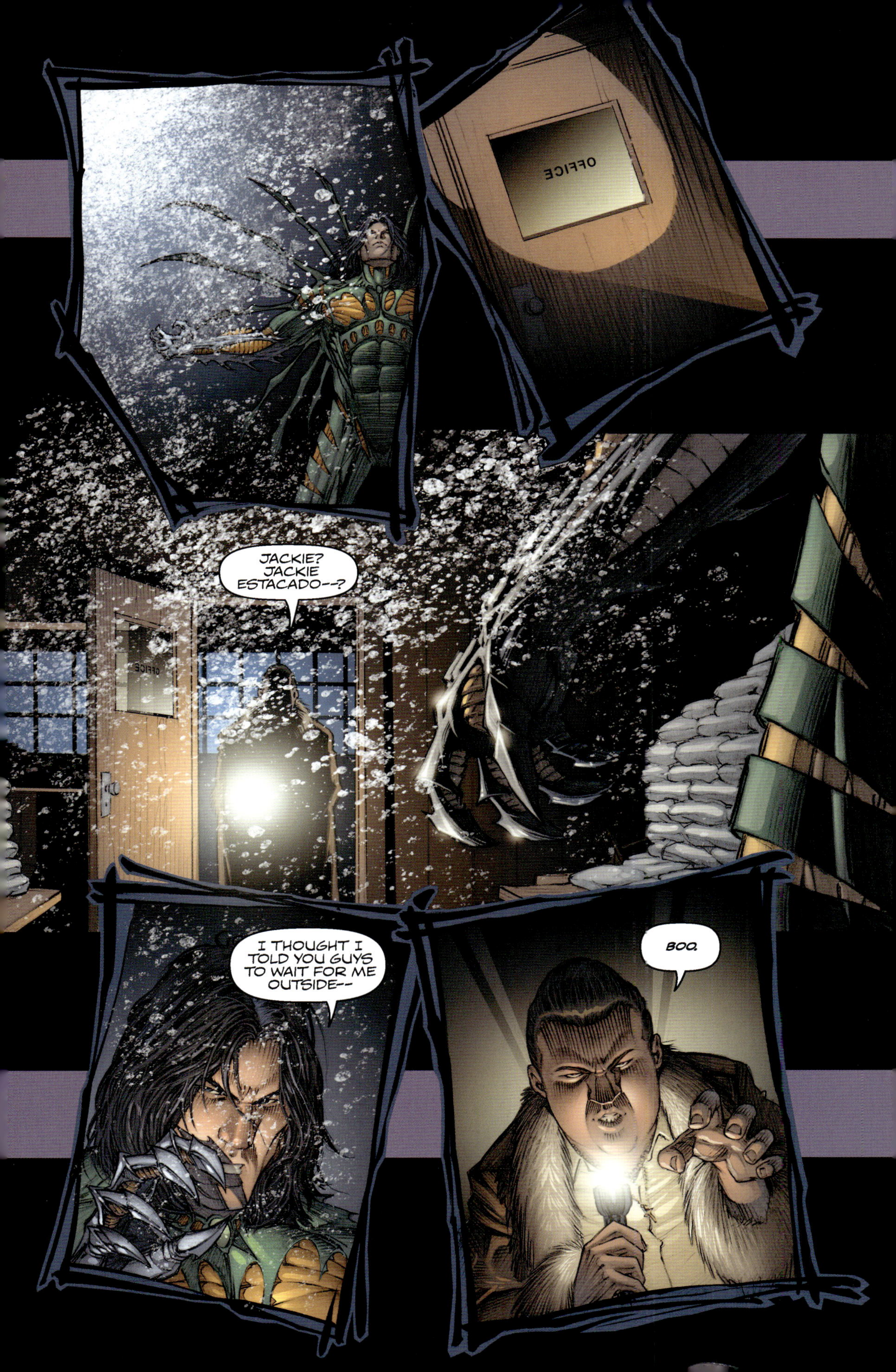
OFFICE
OFFICE
JACKIE? JACKIE ESTACADO--?
I THOUGHT I TOLD YOU GUYS TO WAIT FOR ME OUTSIDE--
BOO.

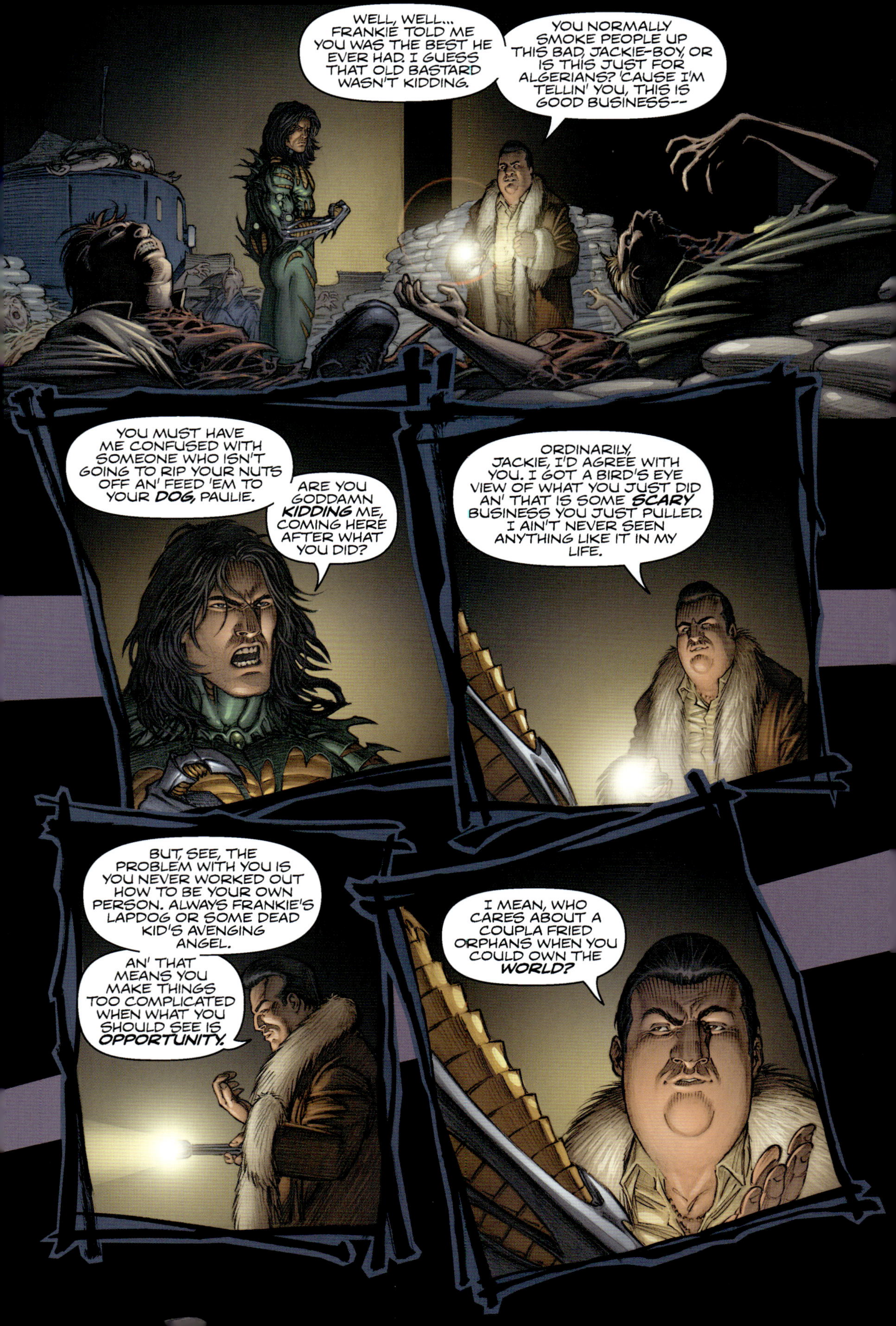
WELL, WELL... FRANKIE TOLD ME YOU WAS THE BEST HE EVER HAD. I GUESS THAT OLD BASTARD WASN'T KIDDING.
YOU NORMALLY SMOKE PEOPLE UP THIS BAD, JACKIE-BOY, OR IS THIS JUST FOR ALGERIANS? 'CAUSE I'M TELLIN' YOU, THIS IS GOOD BUSINESS--
YOU MUST HAVE ME CONFUSED WITH SOMEONE WHO ISN'T GOING TO RIP YOUR NUTS OFF AN' FEED 'EM TO YOUR DOG, PAULIE.
ARE YOU GODDAMN KIDDING ME, COMING HERE AFTER WHAT YOU DID?
ORDINARILY, JACKIE, I'D AGREE WITH YOU. I GOT A BIRD'S EYE VIEW OF WHAT YOU JUST DID AN' THAT IS SOME SCARY BUSINESS YOU JUST PULLED. I AIN'T NEVER SEEN ANYTHING LIKE IT IN MY LIFE.
BUT, SEE, THE PROBLEM WITH YOU IS YOU NEVER WORKED OUT HOW TO BE YOUR OWN PERSON. ALWAYS FRANKIE'S LAPDOG OR SOME DEAD KID'S AVENGING ANGEL.
AN' THAT MEANS YOU MAKE THINGS TOO COMPLICATED WHEN WHAT YOU SHOULD SEE IS OPPORTUNITY.
I MEAN, WHO CARES ABOUT A COUPLA FRIED ORPHANS WHEN YOU COULD OWN THE WORLD?

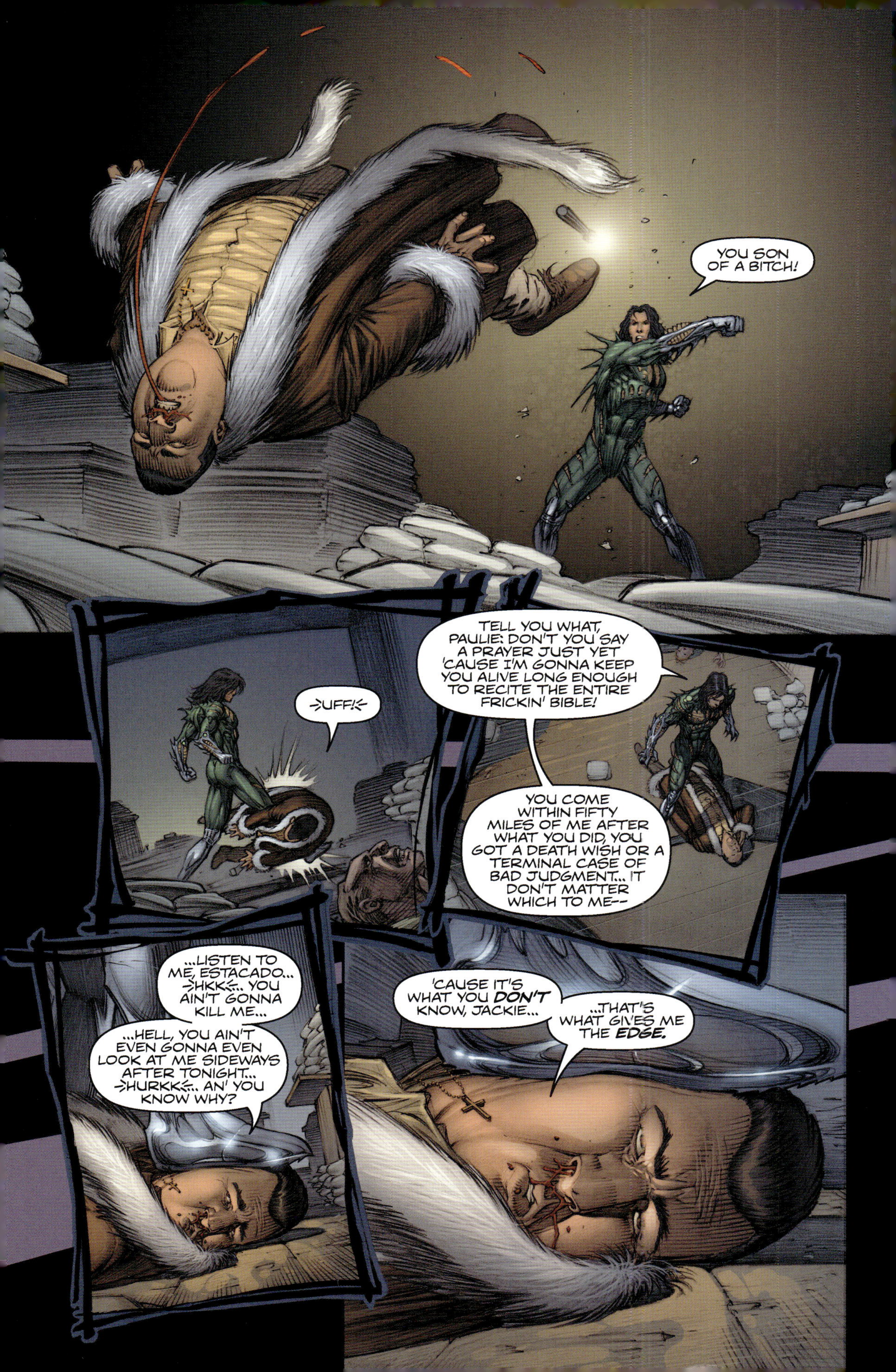

YOU SON OF A BITCH!
>UFF!<
TELL YOU WHAT, PAULIE: DON'T YOU SAY A PRAYER JUST YET 'CAUSE I'M GONNA KEEP YOU ALIVE LONG ENOUGH TO RECITE THE ENTIRE FRICKIN' BIBLE!
YOU COME WITHIN FIFTY MILES OF ME AFTER WHAT YOU DID, YOU GOT A DEATH WISH OR A TERMINAL CASE OF BAD JUDGMENT... IT DON'T MATTER WHICH TO ME--
...LISTEN TO ME, ESTACADO... >HKK<... YOU AIN'T GONNA KILL ME...
...HELL, YOU AIN'T EVEN GONNA EVEN LOOK AT ME SIDEWAYS AFTER TONIGHT... >HURKK<... AN' YOU KNOW WHY?
'CAUSE IT'S WHAT YOU **DON'T** KNOW, JACKIE...
...THAT'S WHAT GIVES ME THE **EDGE.**

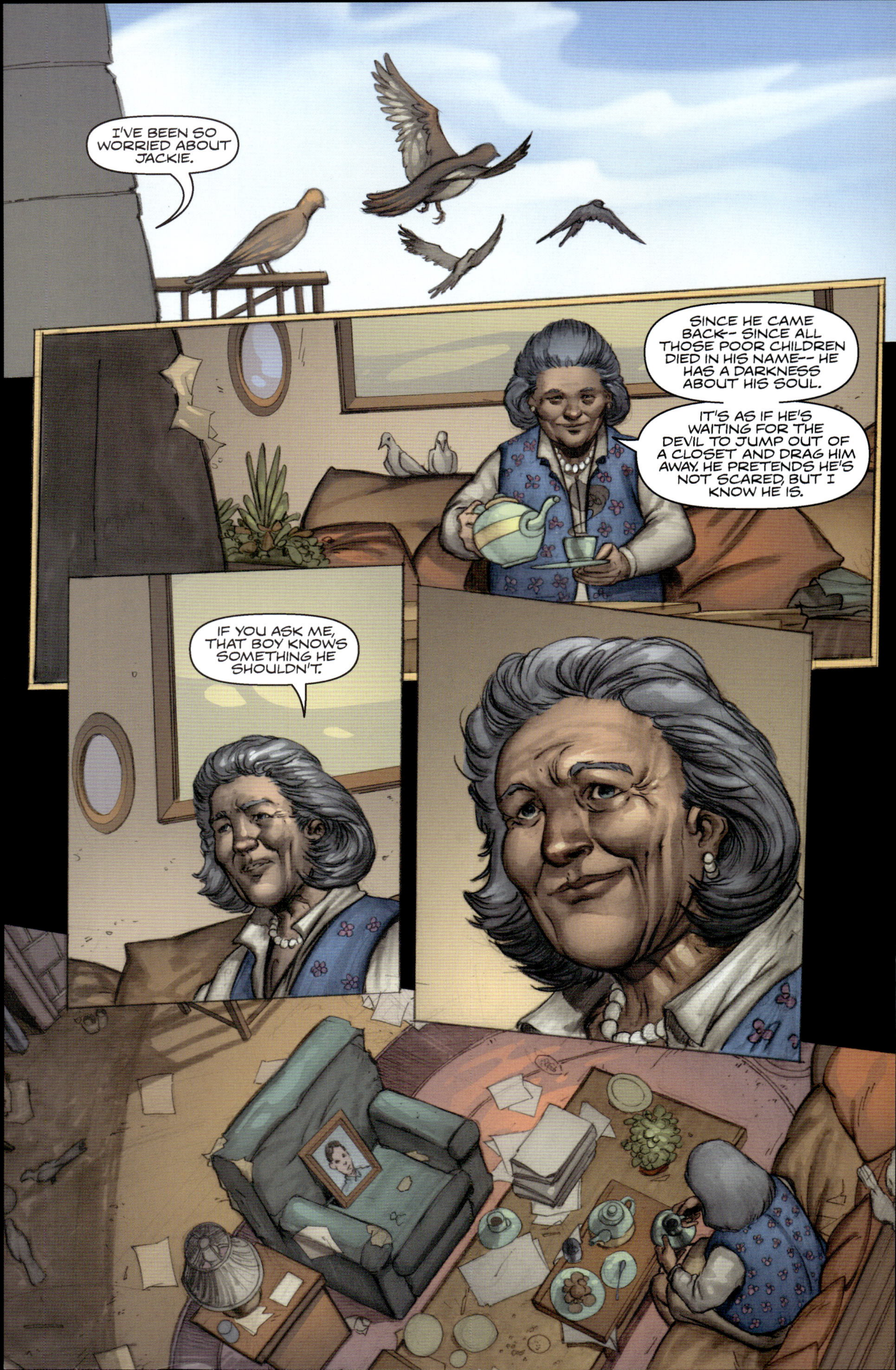
I'VE BEEN SO WORRIED ABOUT JACKIE.
SINCE HE CAME BACK-- SINCE ALL THOSE POOR CHILDREN DIED IN HIS NAME-- HE HAS A DARKNESS ABOUT HIS SOUL.
IT'S AS IF HE'S WAITING FOR THE DEVIL TO JUMP OUT OF A CLOSET AND DRAG HIM AWAY. HE PRETENDS HE'S NOT SCARED, BUT I KNOW HE IS.
IF YOU ASK ME, THAT BOY KNOWS SOMETHING HE SHOULDN'T.

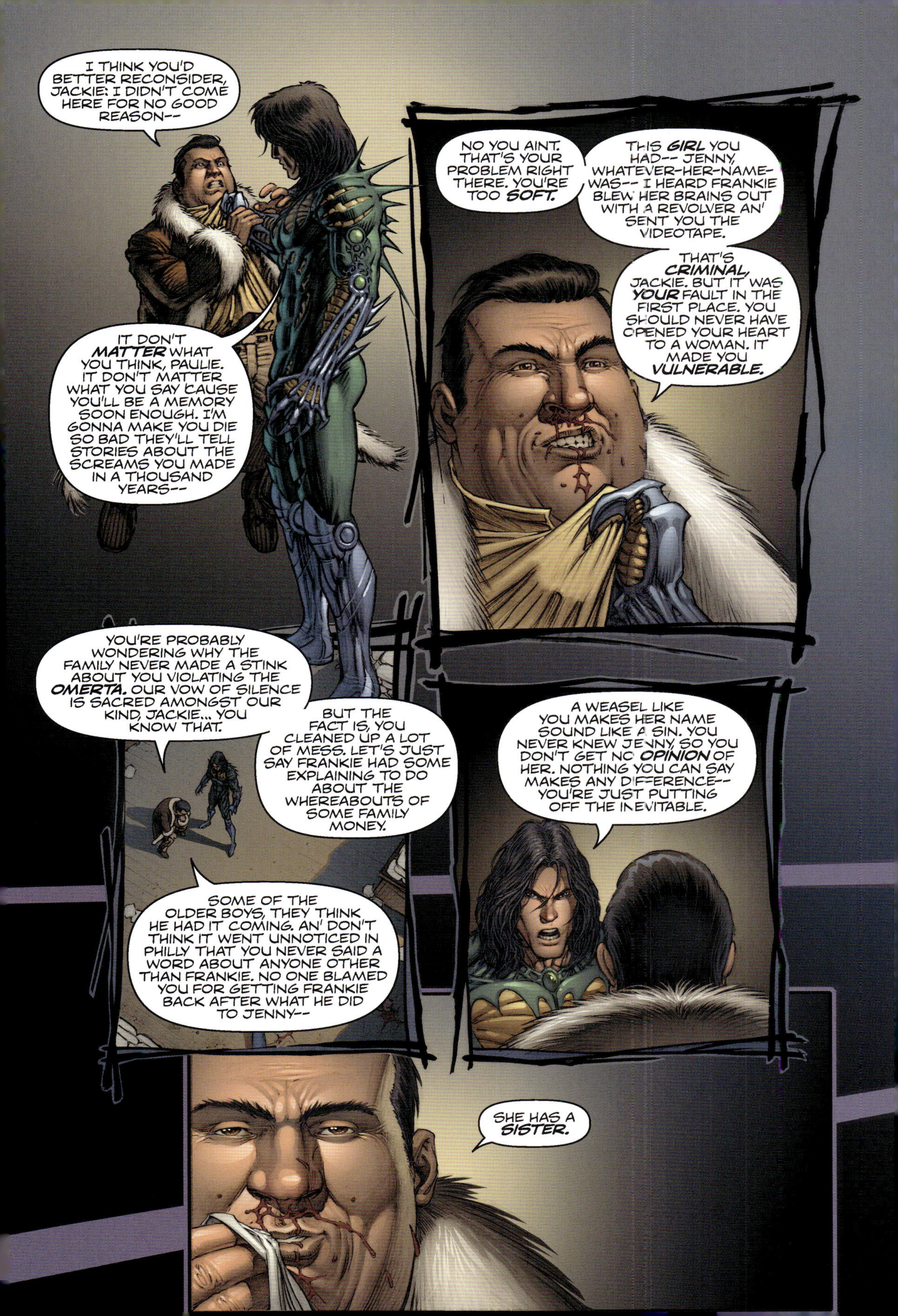
I THINK YOU'D BETTER RECONSIDER, JACKIE. I DIDN'T COME HERE FOR NO GOOD REASON--
IT DON'T MATTER WHAT YOU THINK, PAULIE. IT DON'T MATTER WHAT YOU SAY 'CAUSE YOU'LL BE A MEMORY SOON ENOUGH. I'M GONNA MAKE YOU DIE SO BAD THEY'LL TELL STORIES ABOUT THE SCREAMS YOU MADE IN A THOUSAND YEARS--
NO YOU AINT. THAT'S YOUR PROBLEM RIGHT THERE. YOU'RE TOO SOFT.
THIS GIRL YOU HAD-- JENNY, WHATEVER-HER-NAME-WAS-- I HEARD FRANKIE BLEW HER BRAINS OUT WITH A REVOLVER AN' SENT YOU THE VIDEOTAPE.
THAT'S CRIMINAL, JACKIE. BUT IT WAS YOUR FAULT IN THE FIRST PLACE. YOU SHOULD NEVER HAVE OPENED YOUR HEART TO A WOMAN. IT MADE YOU VULNERABLE.
YOU'RE PROBABLY WONDERING WHY THE FAMILY NEVER MADE A STINK ABOUT YOU VIOLATING THE OMERTA. OUR VOW OF SILENCE IS SACRED AMONGST OUR KIND, JACKIE... YOU KNOW THAT.
BUT THE FACT IS, YOU CLEANED UP A LOT OF MESS. LET'S JUST SAY FRANKIE HAD SOME EXPLAINING TO DO ABOUT THE WHEREABOUTS OF SOME FAMILY MONEY.
SOME OF THE OLDER BOYS, THEY THINK HE HAD IT COMING. AN' DON'T THINK IT WENT UNNOTICED IN PHILLY THAT YOU NEVER SAID A WORD ABOUT ANYONE OTHER THAN FRANKIE. NO ONE BLAMED YOU FOR GETTING FRANKIE BACK AFTER WHAT HE DID TO JENNY--
A WEASEL LIKE YOU MAKES HER NAME SOUND LIKE A SIN. YOU NEVER KNEW JENNY, SO YOU DON'T GET NO OPINION OF HER. NOTHING YOU CAN SAY MAKES ANY DIFFERENCE-- YOU'RE JUST PUTTING OFF THE INEVITABLE.
SHE HAS A SISTER.

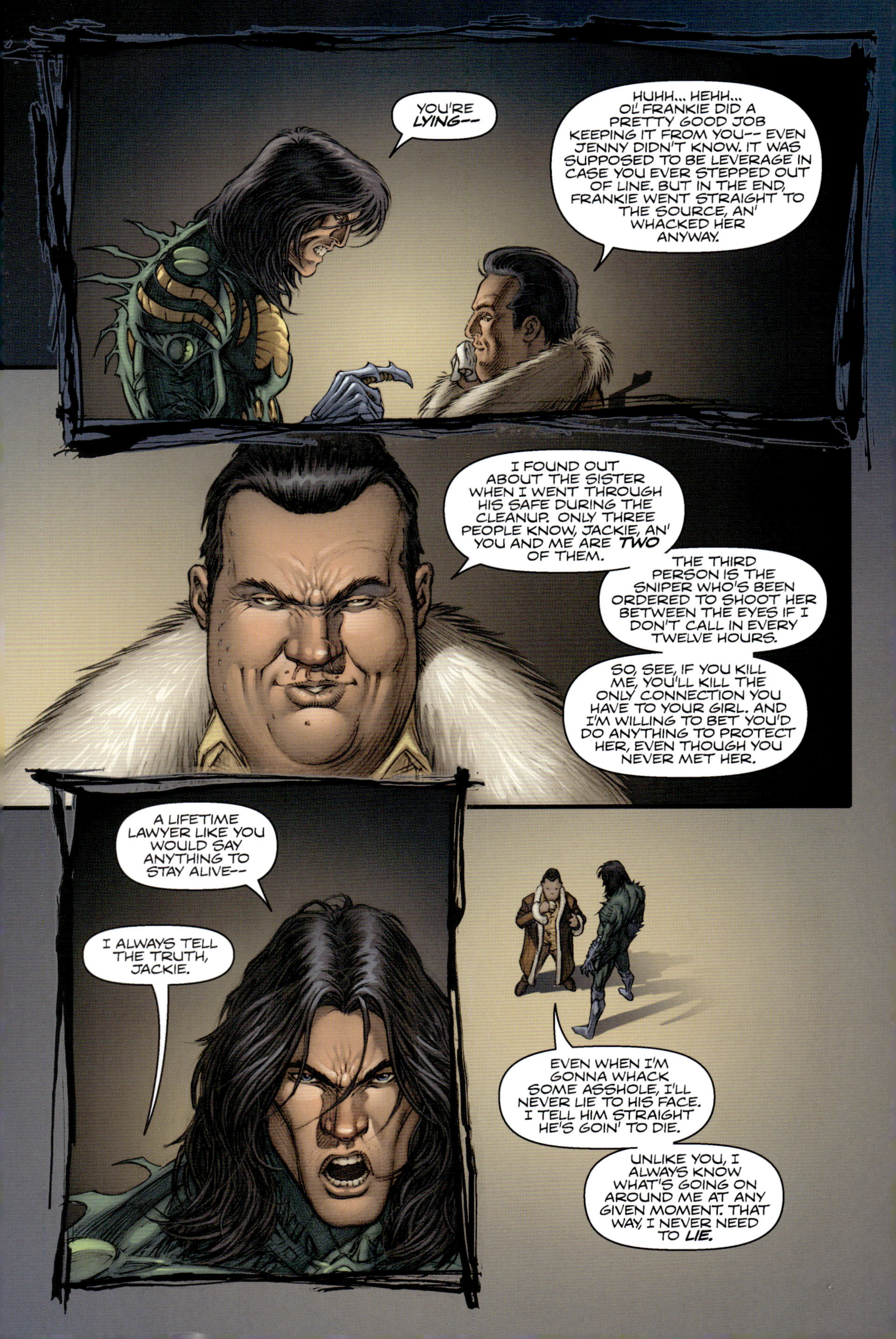

HUHH... HEHH... OL' FRANKIE DID A PRETTY GOOD JOB KEEPING IT FROM YOU-- EVEN JENNY DIDN'T KNOW. IT WAS SUPPOSED TO BE LEVERAGE IN CASE YOU EVER STEPPED OUT OF LINE. BUT IN THE END, FRANKIE WENT STRAIGHT TO THE SOURCE, AN' WHACKED HER ANYWAY.
YOU'RE LYING--
I FOUND OUT ABOUT THE SISTER WHEN I WENT THROUGH HIS SAFE DURING THE CLEANUP. ONLY THREE PEOPLE KNOW, JACKIE, AN' YOU AND ME ARE TWO OF THEM.
THE THIRD PERSON IS THE SNIPER WHO'S BEEN ORDERED TO SHOOT HER BETWEEN THE EYES IF I DON'T CALL IN EVERY TWELVE HOURS.
SO, SEE, IF YOU KILL ME, YOU'LL KILL THE ONLY CONNECTION YOU HAVE TO YOUR GIRL. AND I'M WILLING TO BET YOU'D DO ANYTHING TO PROTECT HER, EVEN THOUGH YOU NEVER MET HER.
A LIFETIME LAWYER LIKE YOU WOULD SAY ANYTHING TO STAY ALIVE--
I ALWAYS TELL THE TRUTH, JACKIE.
EVEN WHEN I'M GONNA WHACK SOME ASSHOLE, I'LL NEVER LIE TO HIS FACE. I TELL HIM STRAIGHT HE'S GOIN' TO DIE.
UNLIKE YOU, I ALWAYS KNOW WHAT'S GOING ON AROUND ME AT ANY GIVEN MOMENT. THAT WAY, I NEVER NEED TO LIE.

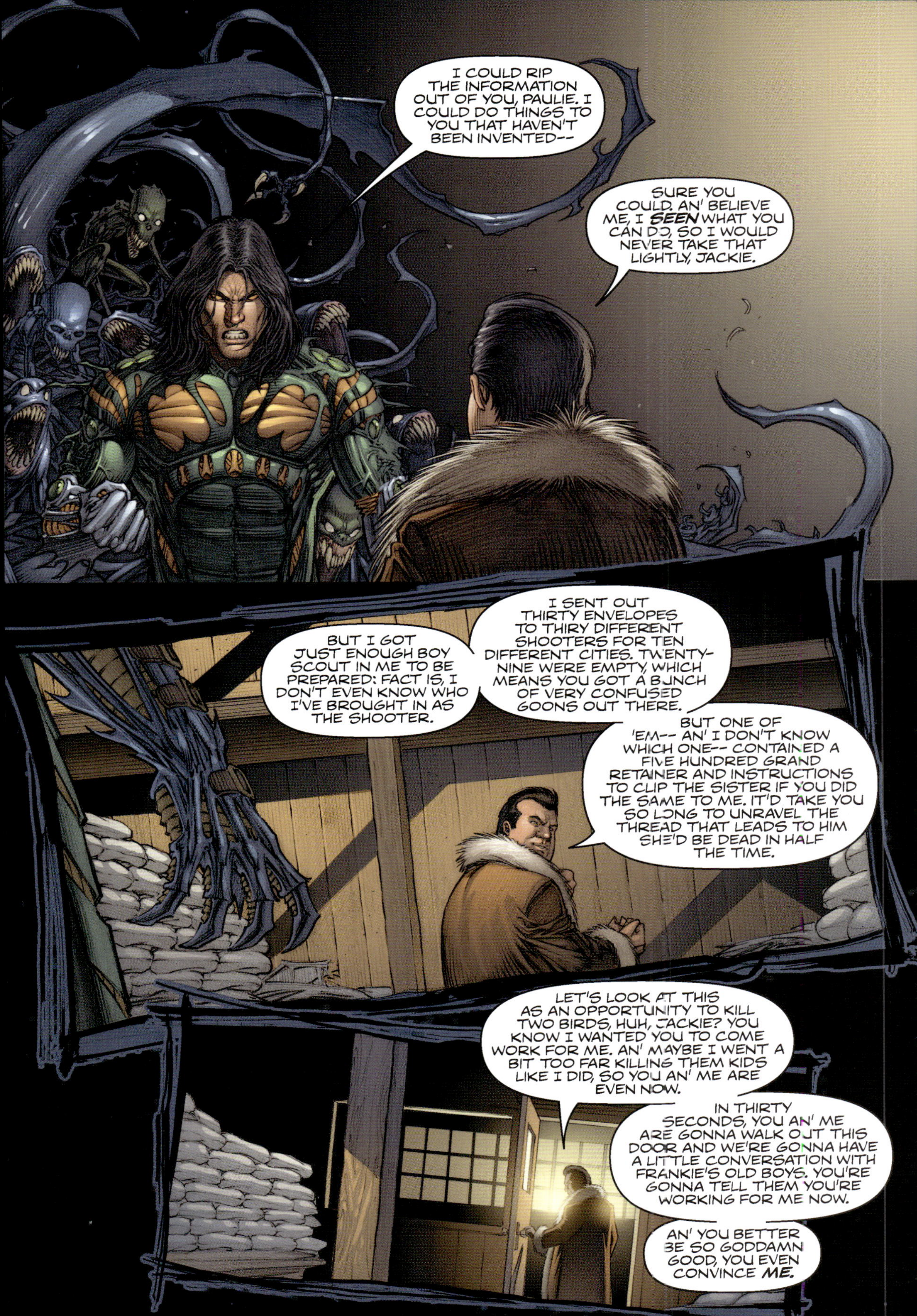
I COULD RIP THE INFORMATION OUT OF YOU, PAULIE. I COULD DO THINGS TO YOU THAT HAVEN'T BEEN INVENTED--
SURE YOU COULD. AN' BELIEVE ME, I SEEN WHAT YOU CAN DO, SO I WOULD NEVER TAKE THAT LIGHTLY, JACKIE.
BUT I GOT JUST ENOUGH BOY SCOUT IN ME TO BE PREPARED: FACT IS, I DON'T EVEN KNOW WHO I'VE BROUGHT IN AS THE SHOOTER.
I SENT OUT THIRTY ENVELOPES TO THIRY DIFFERENT SHOOTERS FOR TEN DIFFERENT CITIES. TWENTY-NINE WERE EMPTY, WHICH MEANS YOU GOT A BUNCH OF VERY CONFUSED GOONS OUT THERE.
BUT ONE OF 'EM-- AN' I DON'T KNOW WHICH ONE-- CONTAINED A FIVE HUNDRED GRAND RETAINER AND INSTRUCTIONS TO CLIP THE SISTER IF YOU DID THE SAME TO ME. IT'D TAKE YOU SO LONG TO UNRAVEL THE THREAD THAT LEADS TO HIM SHE'D BE DEAD IN HALF THE TIME.
LET'S LOOK AT THIS AS AN OPPORTUNITY TO KILL TWO BIRDS, HUH, JACKIE? YOU KNOW I WANTED YOU TO COME WORK FOR ME. AN' MAYBE I WENT A BIT TOO FAR KILLING THEM KIDS LIKE I DID, SO YOU AN' ME ARE EVEN NOW.
IN THIRTY SECONDS, YOU AN' ME ARE GONNA WALK OUT THIS DOOR AND WE'RE GONNA HAVE A LITTLE CONVERSATION WITH FRANKIE'S OLD BOYS. YOU'RE GONNA TELL THEM YOU'RE WORKING FOR ME NOW.
AN' YOU BETTER BE SO GODDAMN GOOD, YOU EVEN CONVINCE ME.

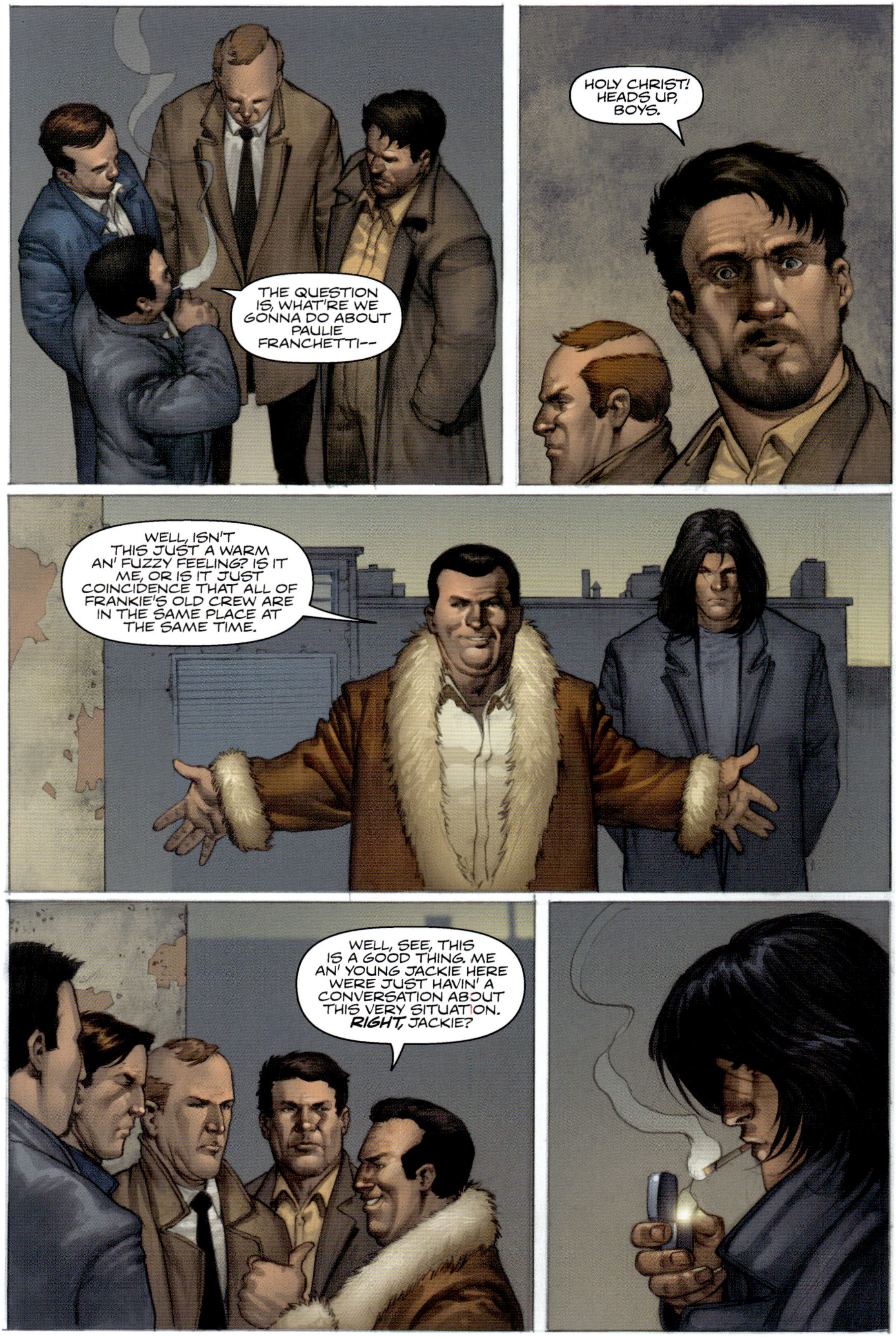
THE QUESTION IS, WHAT'RE WE GONNA DO ABOUT PAULIE FRANCHETTI--
HOLY CHRIST! HEADS UP, BOYS.
WELL, ISN'T THIS JUST A WARM AN' FUZZY FEELING? IS IT ME, OR IS IT JUST COINCIDENCE THAT ALL OF FRANKIE'S OLD CREW ARE IN THE SAME PLACE AT THE SAME TIME.
WELL, SEE, THIS IS A GOOD THING. ME AN' YOUNG JACKIE HERE WERE JUST HAVIN' A CONVERSATION ABOUT THIS VERY SITUATION. RIGHT, JACKIE?

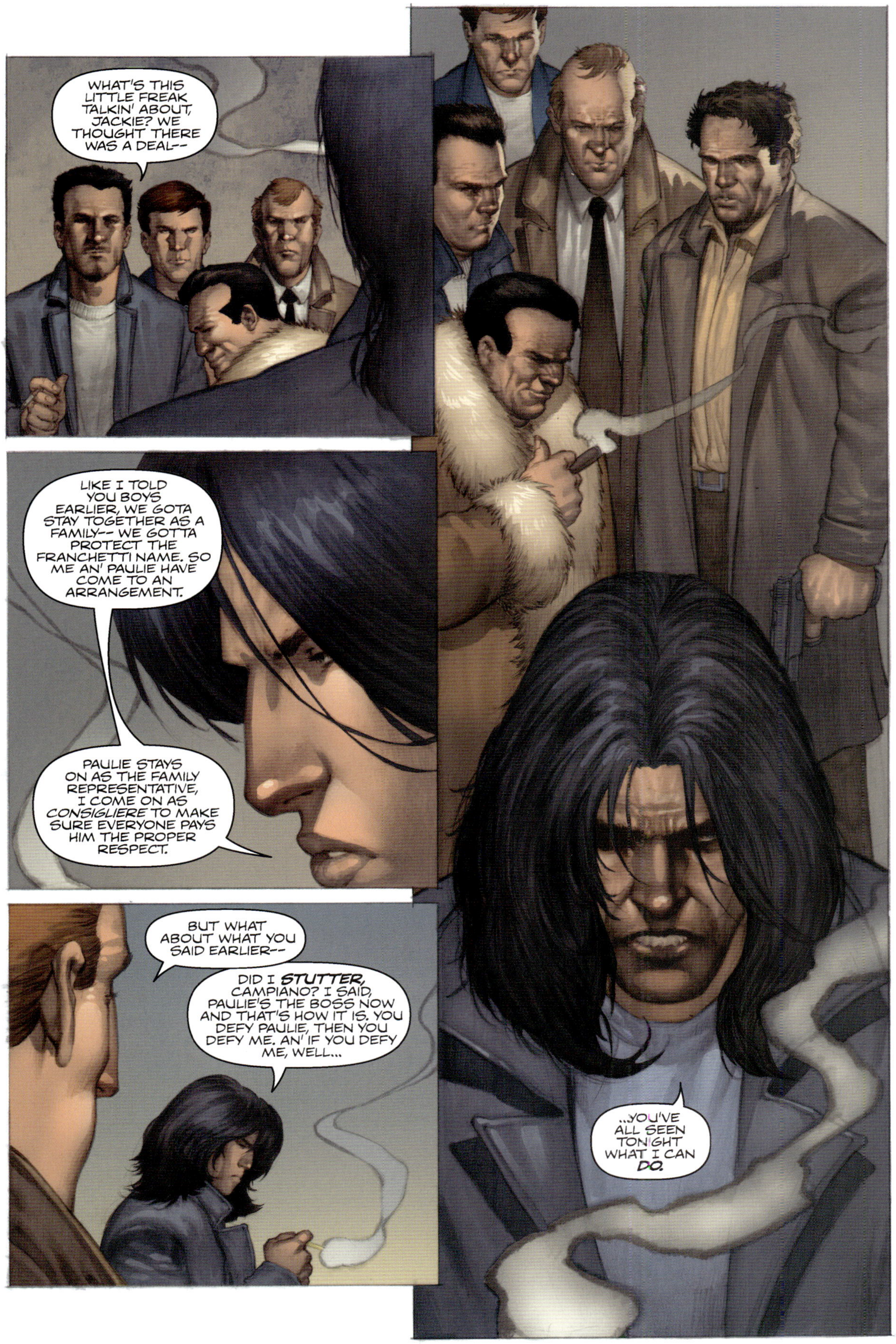
WHAT'S THIS LITTLE FREAK TALKIN' ABOUT, JACKIE? WE THOUGHT THERE WAS A DEAL--
LIKE I TOLD YOU BOYS EARLIER, WE GOTA STAY TOGETHER AS A FAMILY-- WE GOTTA PROTECT THE FRANCHETTI NAME. SO ME AN' PAULIE HAVE COME TO AN ARRANGEMENT.
PAULIE STAYS ON AS THE FAMILY REPRESENTATIVE, I COME ON AS CONSIGLIERE TO MAKE SURE EVERYONE PAYS HIM THE PROPER RESPECT.
BUT WHAT ABOUT WHAT YOU SAID EARLIER--
DID I STUTTER, CAMPIANO? I SAID, PAULIE'S THE BOSS NOW AND THAT'S HOW IT IS. YOU DEFY PAULIE, THEN YOU DEFY ME. AN' IF YOU DEFY ME, WELL...
...YOU'VE ALL SEEN TONIGHT WHAT I CAN DO.

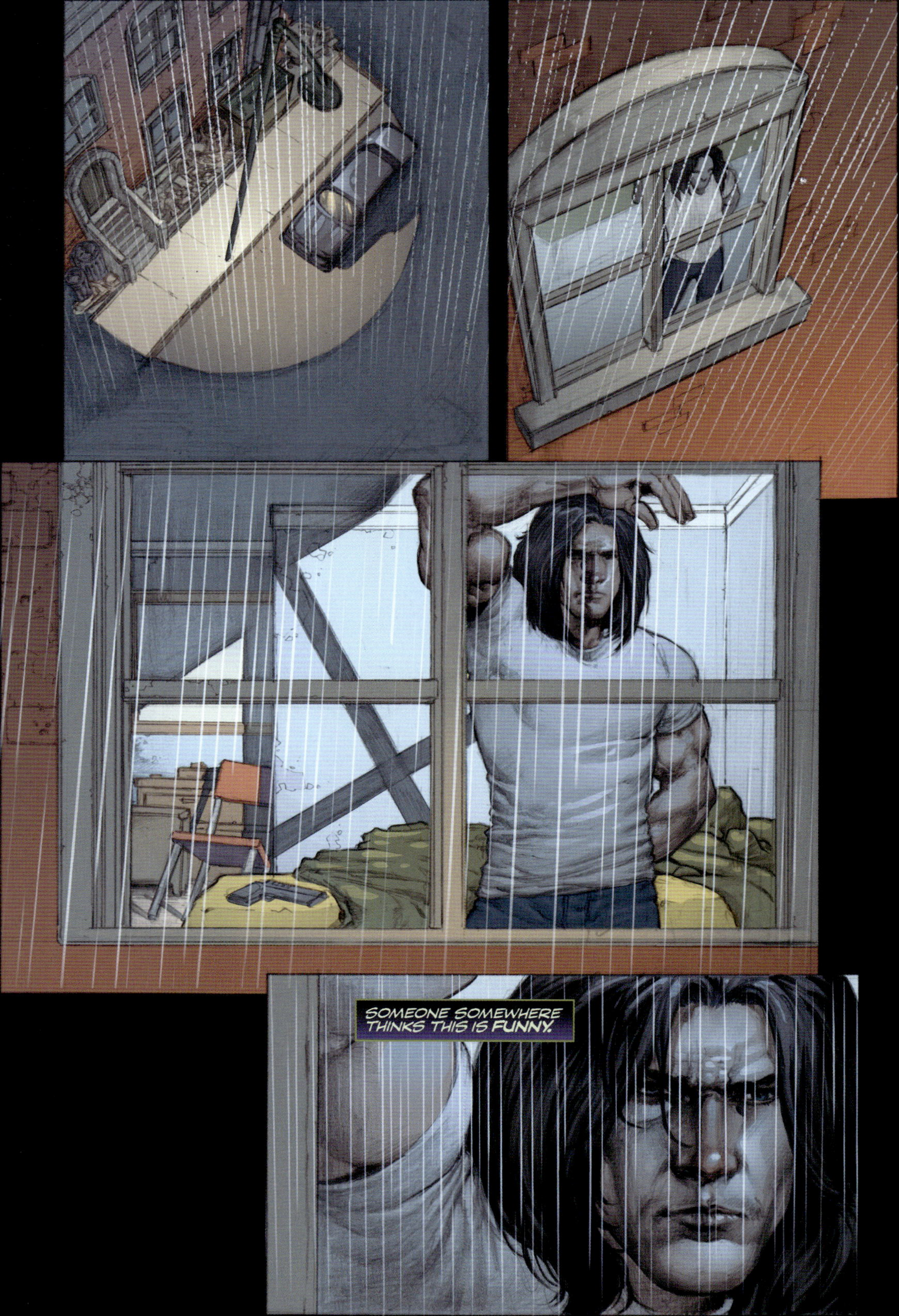
SOMEONE SOMEWHERE THINKS THIS IS FUNNY.

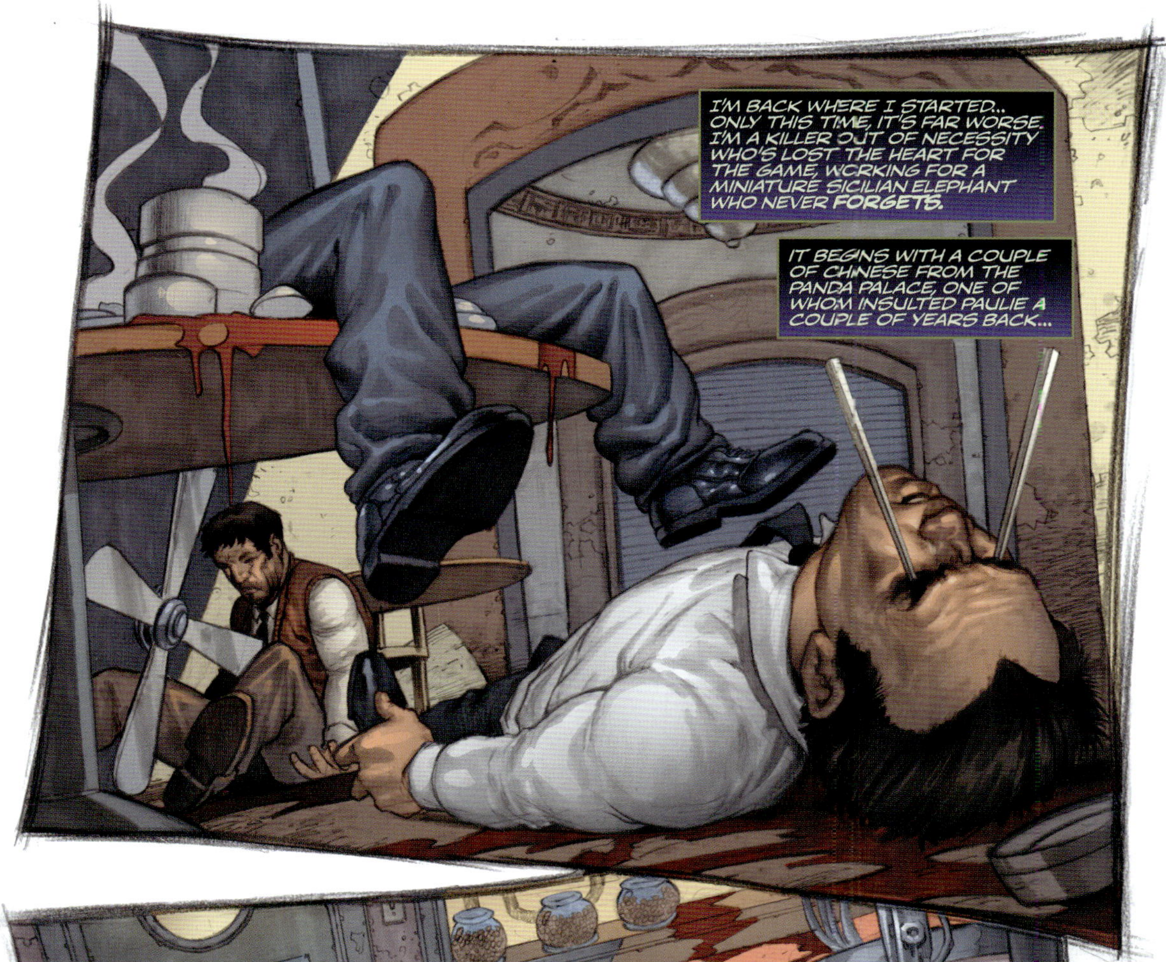
I'M BACK WHERE I STARTED... ONLY THIS TIME, IT'S FAR WORSE. I'M A KILLER OUT OF NECESSITY WHO'S LOST THE HEART FOR THE GAME, WORKING FOR A MINIATURE SICILIAN ELEPHANT WHO NEVER **FORGETS.**
IT BEGINS WITH A COUPLE OF CHINESE FROM THE PANDA PALACE, ONE OF WHOM INSULTED PAULIE A COUPLE OF YEARS BACK...

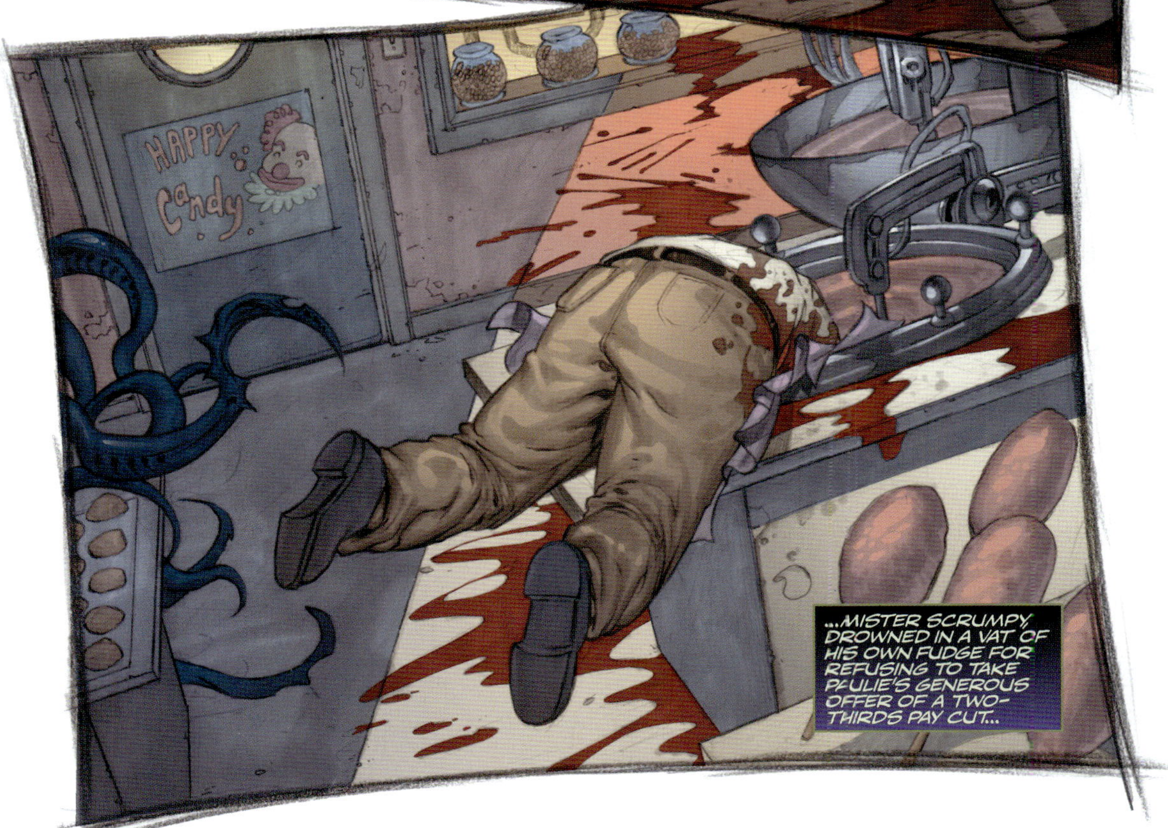
HAPPY Candy
...MISTER SCRUMPY DROWNED IN A VAT OF HIS OWN FUDGE FOR REFUSING TO TAKE PAULIE'S GENEROUS OFFER OF A TWO-THIRDS PAY CUT...

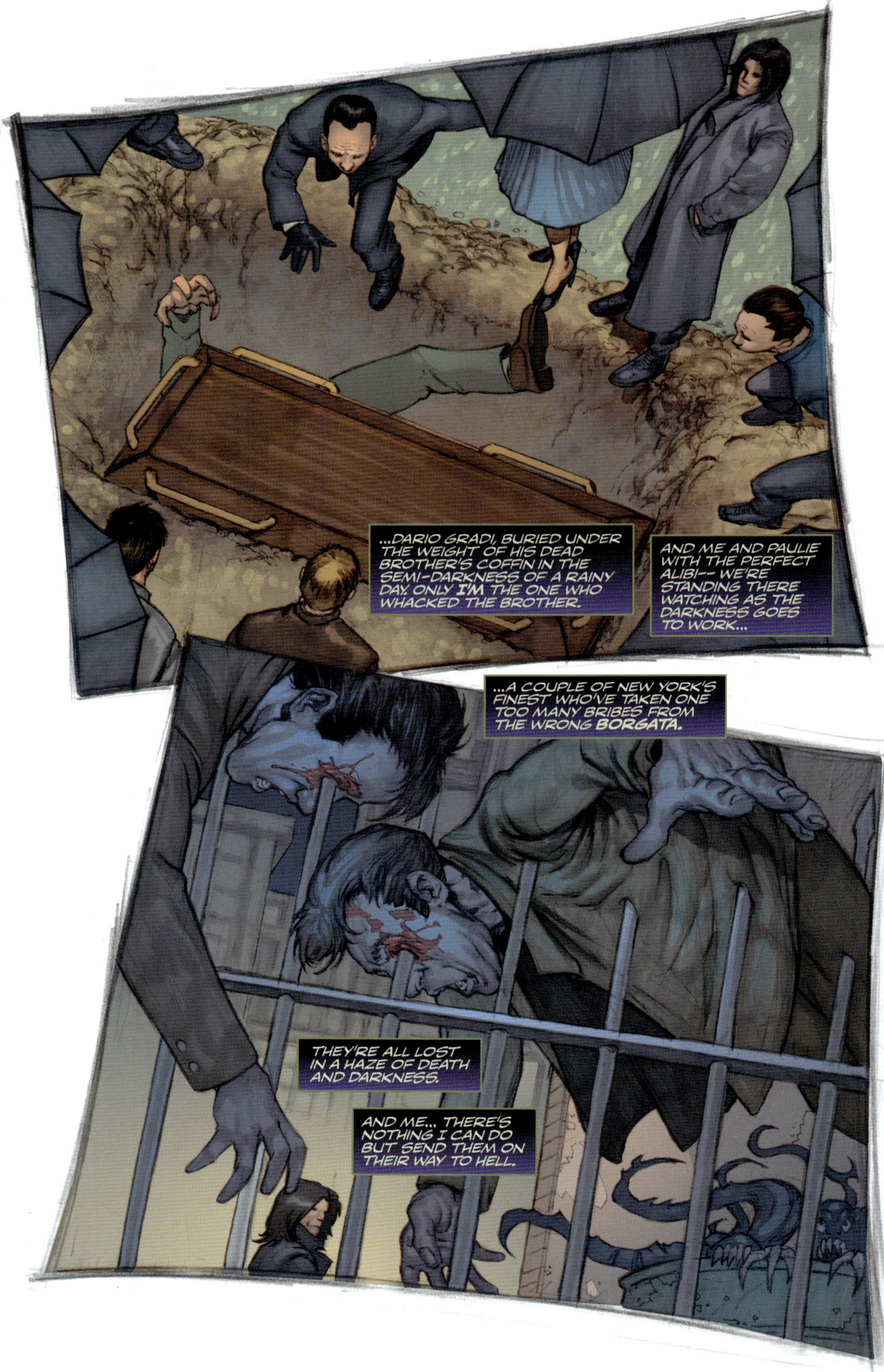
...DARIO GRADI, BURIED UNDER THE WEIGHT OF HIS DEAD BROTHER'S COFFIN IN THE SEMI-DARKNESS OF A RAINY DAY. ONLY I'M THE ONE WHO WHACKED THE BROTHER.
AND ME AND PAULIE WITH THE PERFECT ALIBI-- WE'RE STANDING THERE WATCHING AS THE DARKNESS GOES TO WORK...
...A COUPLE OF NEW YORK'S FINEST WHO'VE TAKEN ONE TOO MANY BRIBES FROM THE WRONG BORGATA.
THEY'RE ALL LOST IN A HAZE OF DEATH AND DARKNESS.
AND ME... THERE'S NOTHING I CAN DO BUT SEND THEM ON THEIR WAY TO HELL.

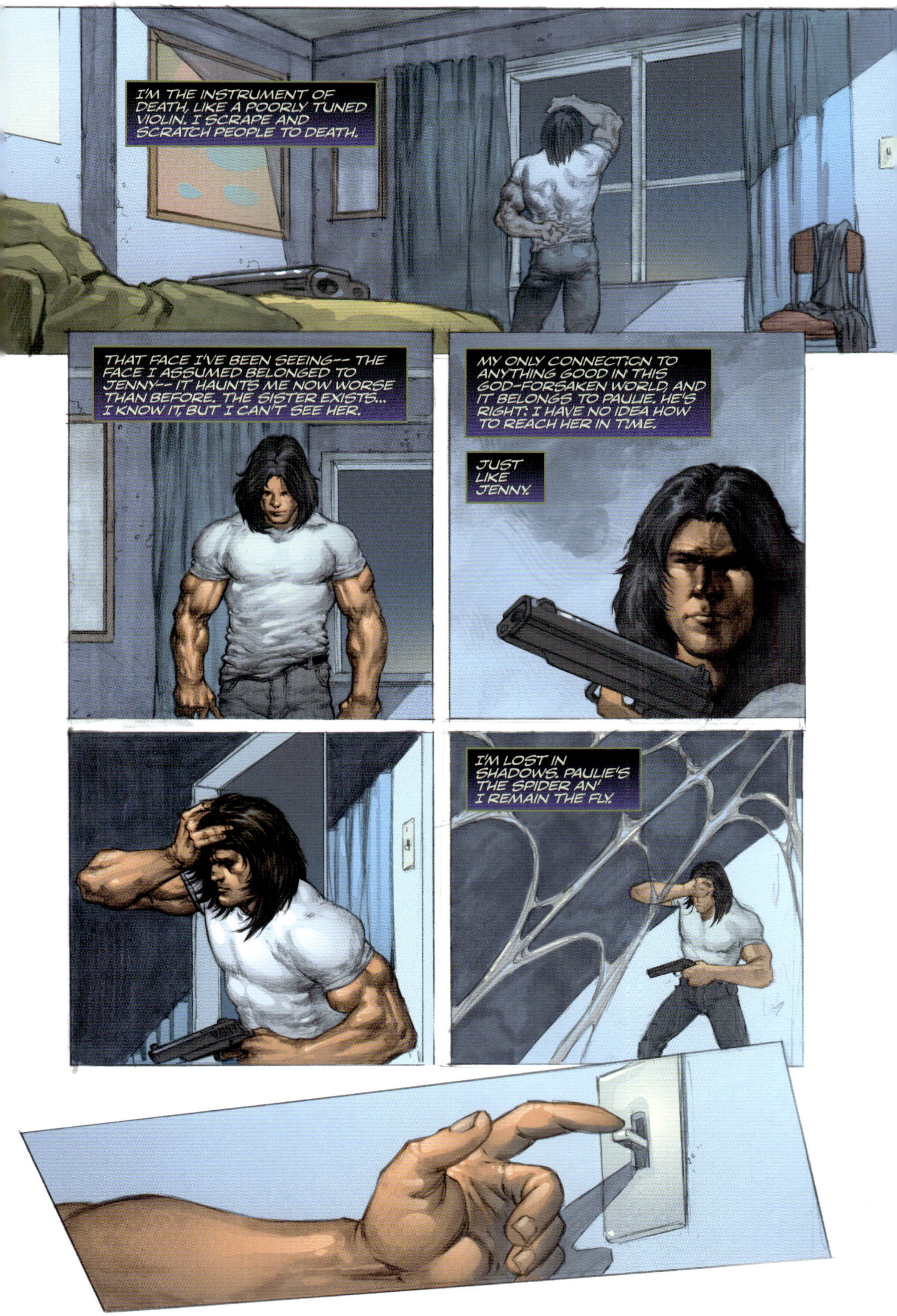
I'M THE INSTRUMENT OF DEATH, LIKE A POORLY TUNED VIOLIN. I SCRAPE AND SCRATCH PEOPLE TO DEATH.
THAT FACE I'VE BEEN SEEING-- THE FACE I ASSUMED BELONGED TO JENNY-- IT HAUNTS ME NOW WORSE THAN BEFORE. THE SISTER EXISTS... I KNOW IT, BUT I CAN'T SEE HER.
MY ONLY CONNECTION TO ANYTHING GOOD IN THIS GOD-FORSAKEN WORLD, AND IT BELONGS TO PAULIE. HE'S RIGHT: I HAVE NO IDEA HOW TO REACH HER IN TIME.
JUST LIKE JENNY.
I'M LOST IN SHADOWS. PAULIE'S THE SPIDER AN' I REMAIN THE FLY.

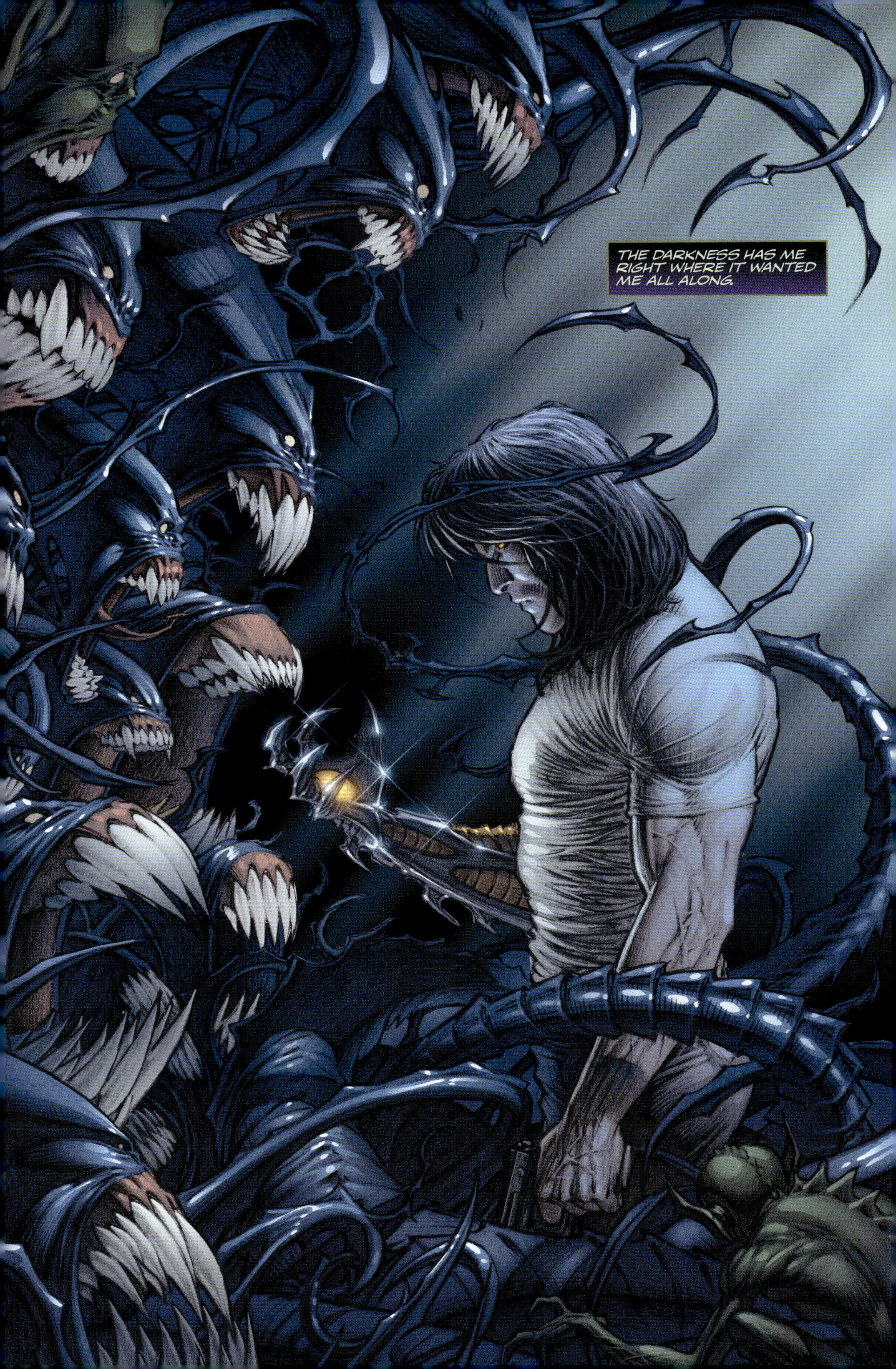
THE DARKNESS HAS ME RIGHT WHERE IT WANTED ME ALL ALONG.

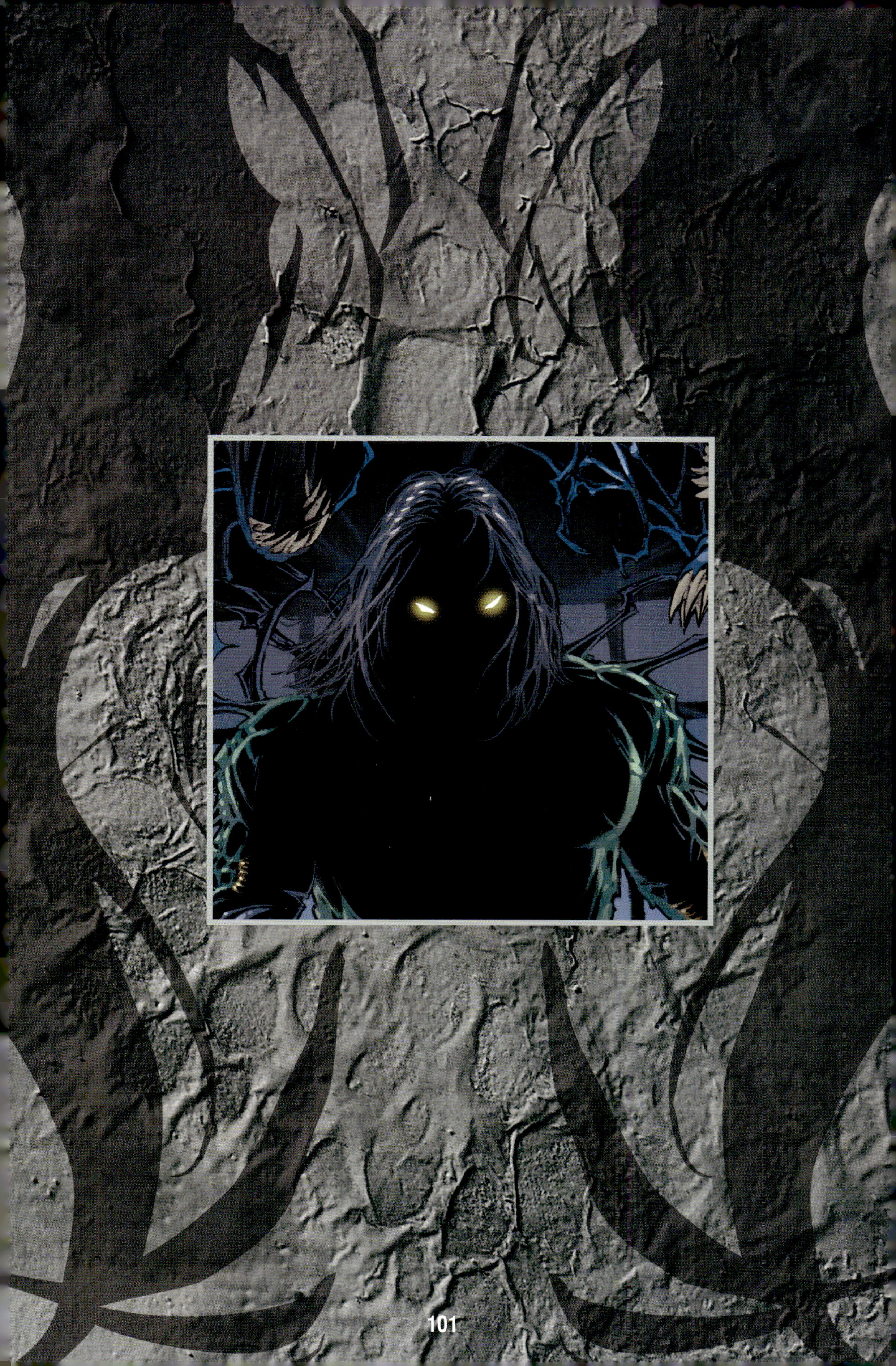

The Darkness Issue #45
cover art by: Dale Keown & Matt Milla

THE DARKNESS #45

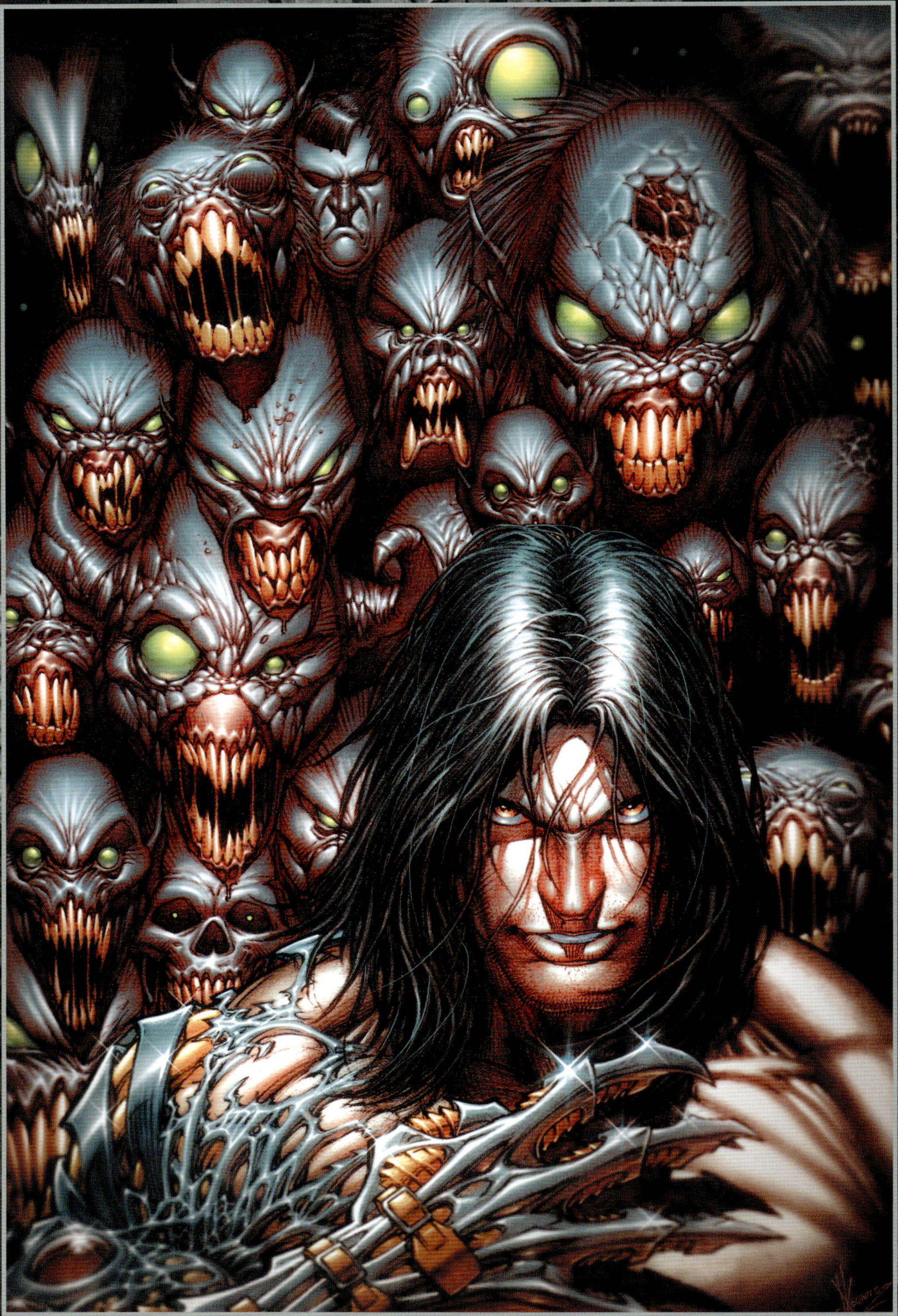

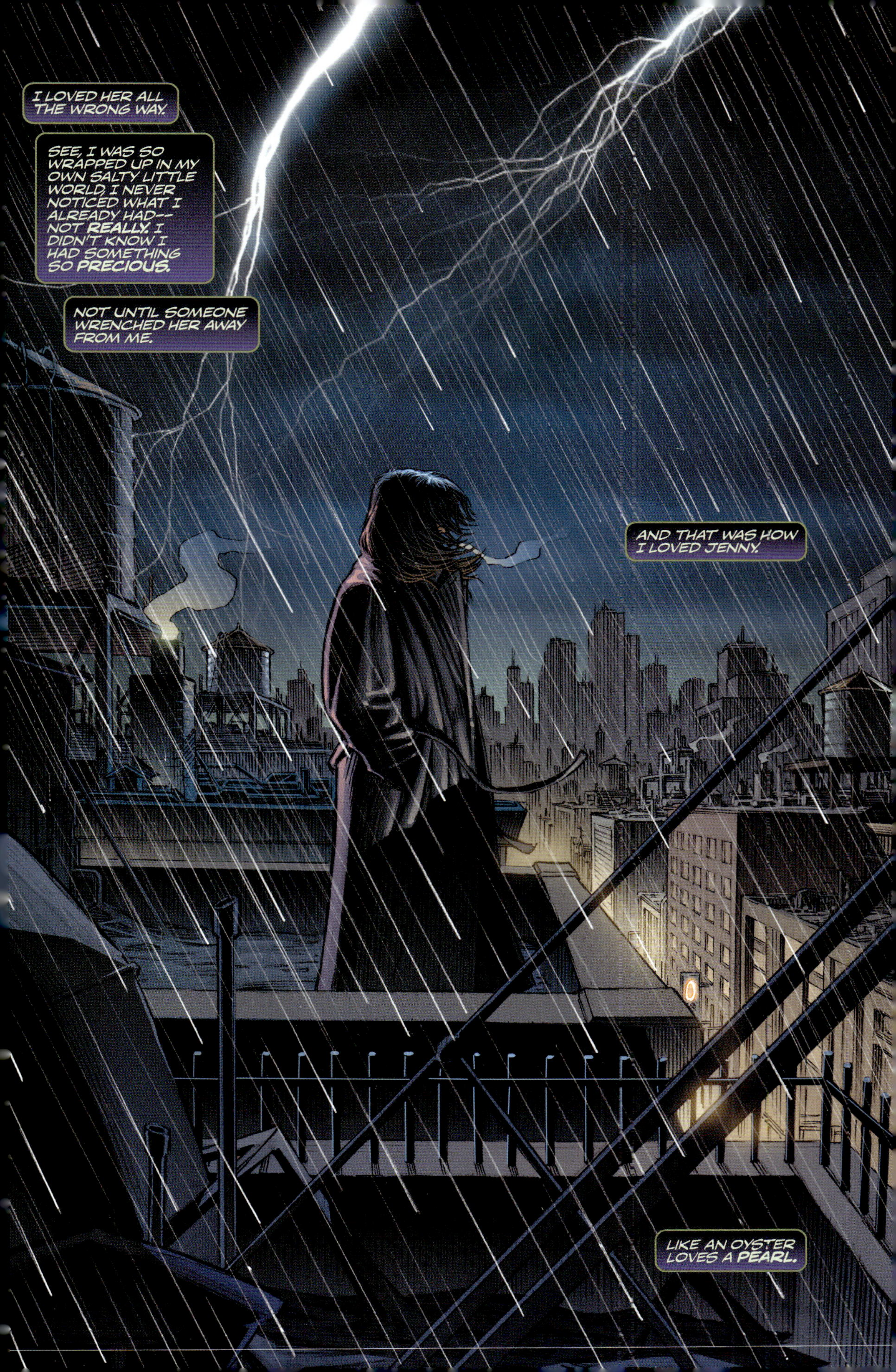
I LOVED HER ALL THE WRONG WAY.
SEE, I WAS SO WRAPPED UP IN MY OWN SALTY LITTLE WORLD, I NEVER NOTICED WHAT I ALREADY HAD-- NOT **REALLY.** I DIDN'T KNOW I HAD SOMETHING SO **PRECIOUS.**
NOT UNTIL SOMEONE WRENCHED HER AWAY FROM ME.
AND THAT WAS HOW I LOVED JENNY.
LIKE AN OYSTER LOVES A **PEARL.**

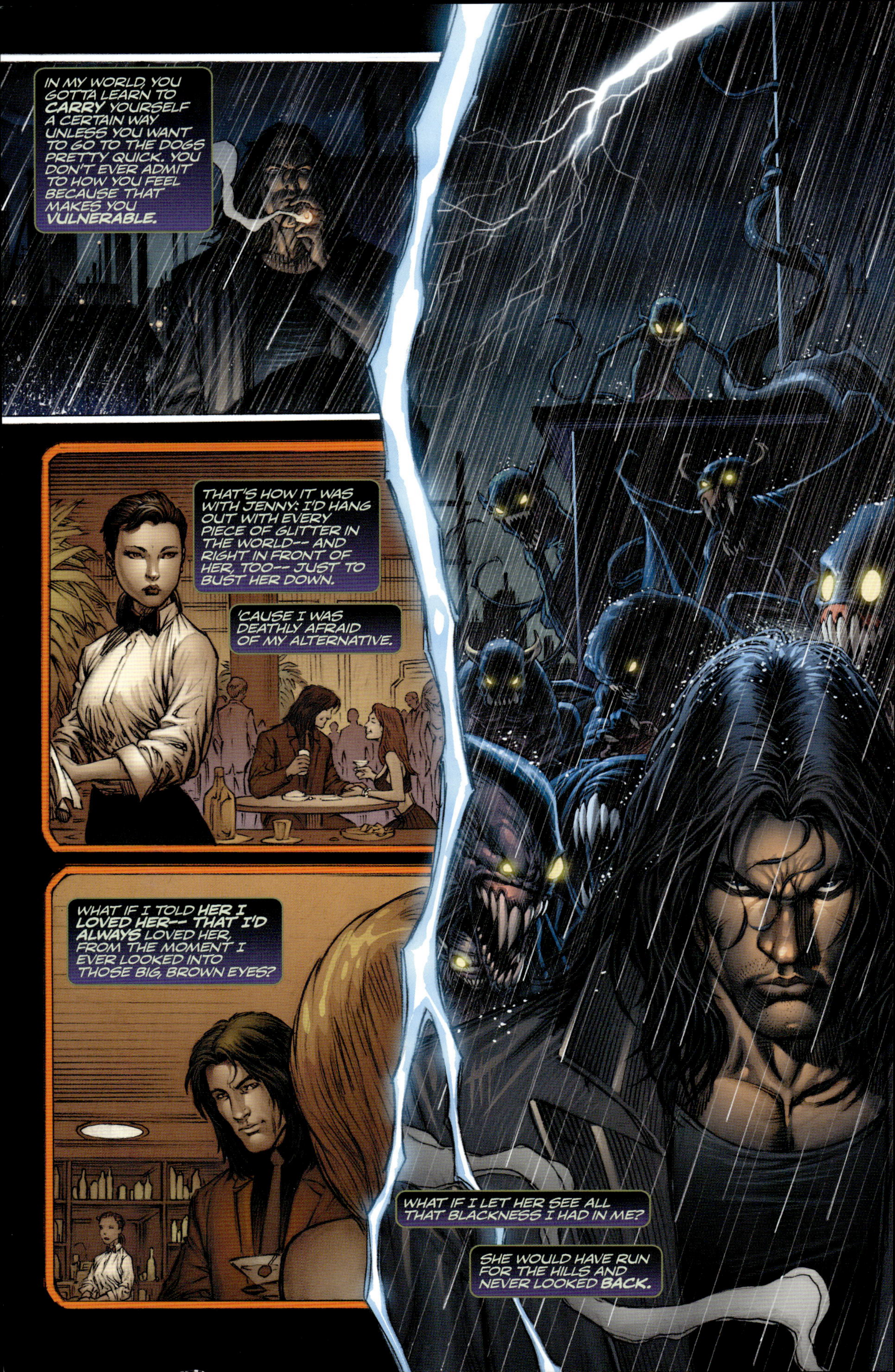

IN MY WORLD, YOU GOTTA LEARN TO CARRY YOURSELF A CERTAIN WAY UNLESS YOU WANT TO GO TO THE DOGS PRETTY QUICK. YOU DON'T EVER ADMIT TO HOW YOU FEEL BECAUSE THAT MAKES YOU VULNERABLE.
THAT'S HOW IT WAS WITH JENNY: I'D HANG OUT WITH EVERY PIECE OF GLITTER IN THE WORLD-- AND RIGHT IN FRONT OF HER, TOO-- JUST TO BUST HER DOWN.
'CAUSE I WAS DEATHLY AFRAID OF MY ALTERNATIVE.
WHAT IF I TOLD HER I LOVED HER-- THAT I'D ALWAYS LOVED HER, FROM THE MOMENT I EVER LOOKED INTO THOSE BIG, BROWN EYES?
WHAT IF I LET HER SEE ALL THAT BLACKNESS I HAD IN ME?
SHE WOULD HAVE RUN FOR THE HILLS AND NEVER LOOKED BACK.

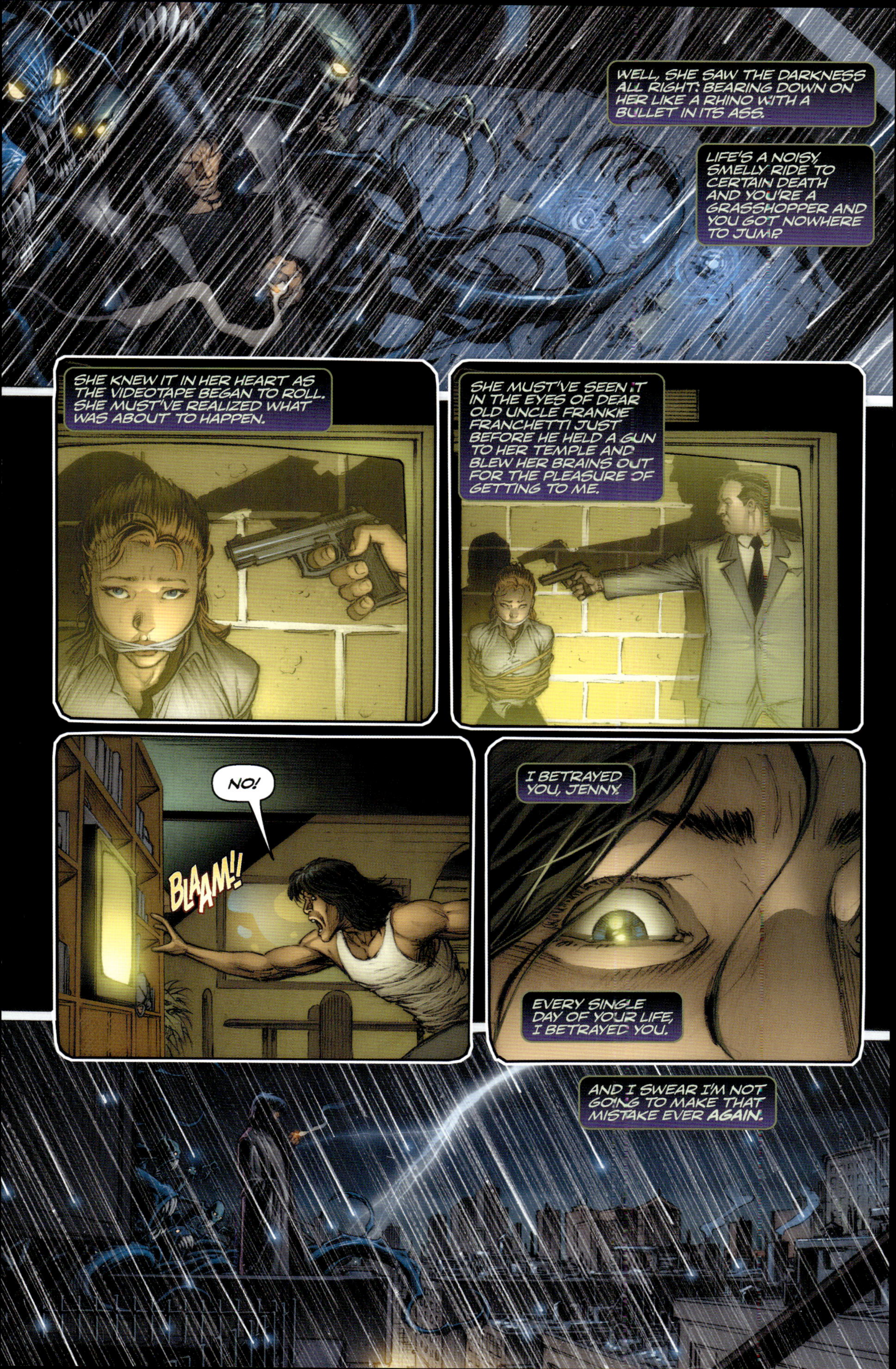
WELL, SHE SAW THE DARKNESS ALL RIGHT: BEARING DOWN ON HER LIKE A RHINO WITH A BULLET IN ITS ASS.
LIFE'S A NOISY, SMELLY RIDE TO CERTAIN DEATH AND YOU'RE A GRASSHOPPER AND YOU GOT NOWHERE TO JUMP.
SHE KNEW IT IN HER HEART AS THE VIDEOTAPE BEGAN TO ROLL. SHE MUST'VE REALIZED WHAT WAS ABOUT TO HAPPEN.
SHE MUST'VE SEEN IT IN THE EYES OF DEAR OLD UNCLE FRANKIE FRANCHETTI JUST BEFORE HE HELD A GUN TO HER TEMPLE AND BLEW HER BRAINS OUT FOR THE PLEASURE OF GETTING TO ME.
NO!
BLAAM!!
I BETRAYED YOU, JENNY.
EVERY SINGLE DAY OF YOUR LIFE, I BETRAYED YOU.
AND I SWEAR I'M NOT GOING TO MAKE THAT MISTAKE EVER AGAIN.

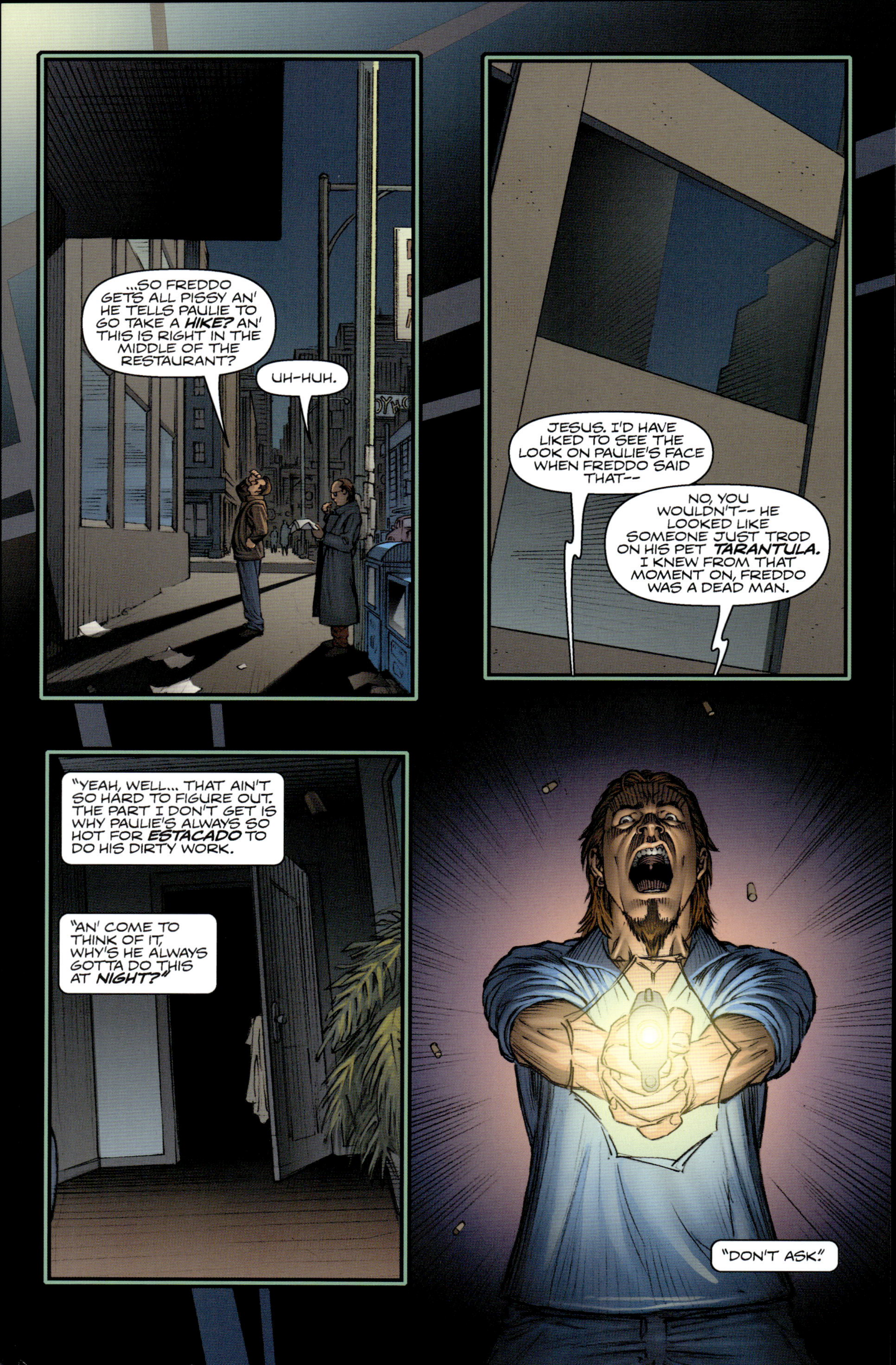
...SO FREDDO GETS ALL PISSY AN' HE TELLS PAULIE TO GO TAKE A HIKE? AN' THIS IS RIGHT IN THE MIDDLE OF THE RESTAURANT?
UH-HUH.
JESUS. I'D HAVE LIKED TO SEE THE LOOK ON PAULIE'S FACE WHEN FREDDO SAID THAT--
NO, YOU WOULDN'T-- HE LOOKED LIKE SOMEONE JUST TROD ON HIS PET TARANTULA. I KNEW FROM THAT MOMENT ON, FREDDO WAS A DEAD MAN.
"YEAH, WELL... THAT AIN'T SO HARD TO FIGURE OUT. THE PART I DON'T GET IS WHY PAULIE'S ALWAYS SO HOT FOR ESTACADO TO DO HIS DIRTY WORK.
"AN' COME TO THINK OF IT, WHY'S HE ALWAYS GOTTA DO THIS AT NIGHT?"
"DON'T ASK."

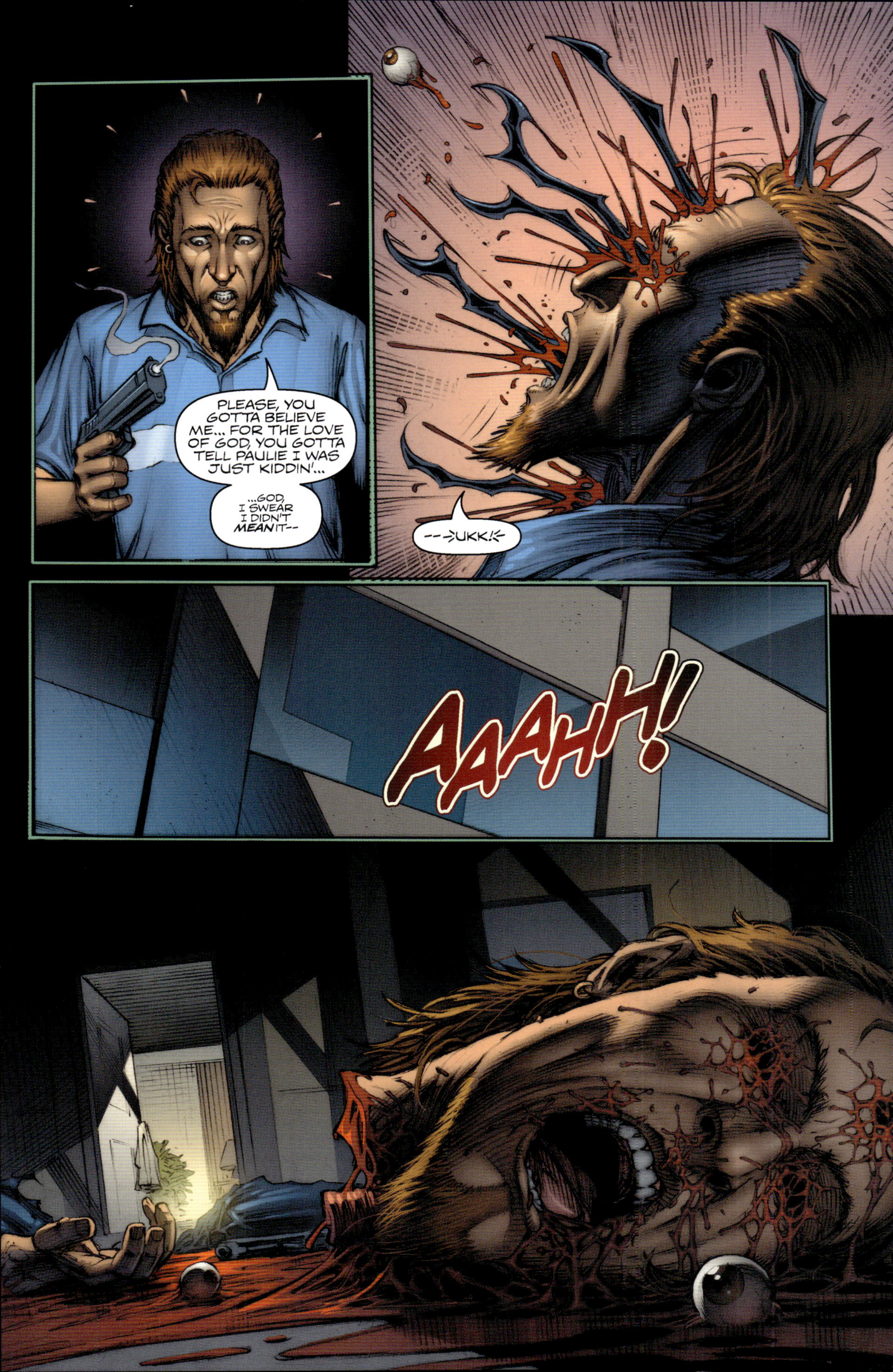

PLEASE, YOU GOTTA BELIEVE ME... FOR THE LOVE OF GOD, YOU GOTTA TELL PAULIE I WAS JUST KIDDIN'...
...GOD, I SWEAR I DIDN'T MEAN IT--
--UKK!
AAAHH!

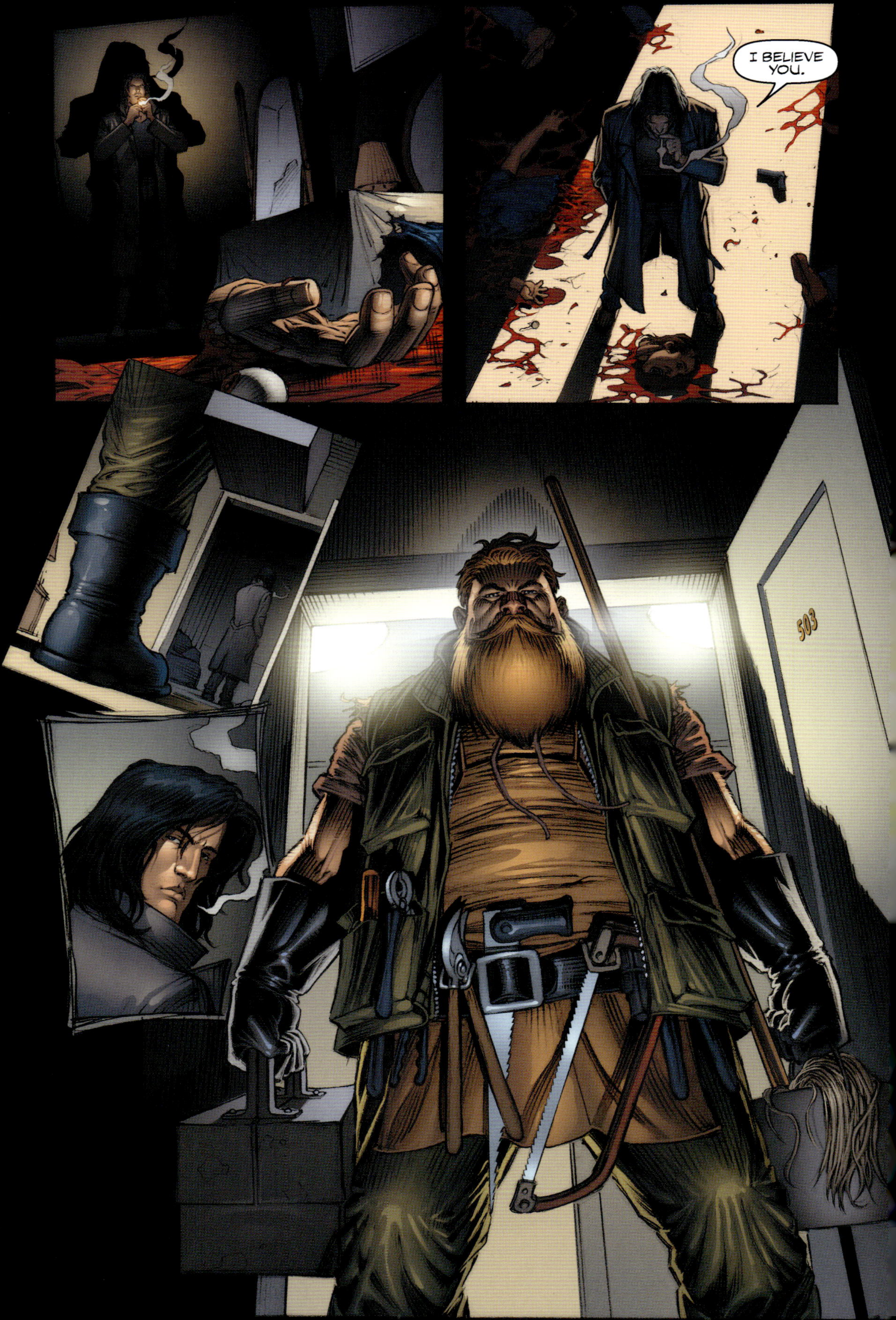
I BELIEVE YOU.
503

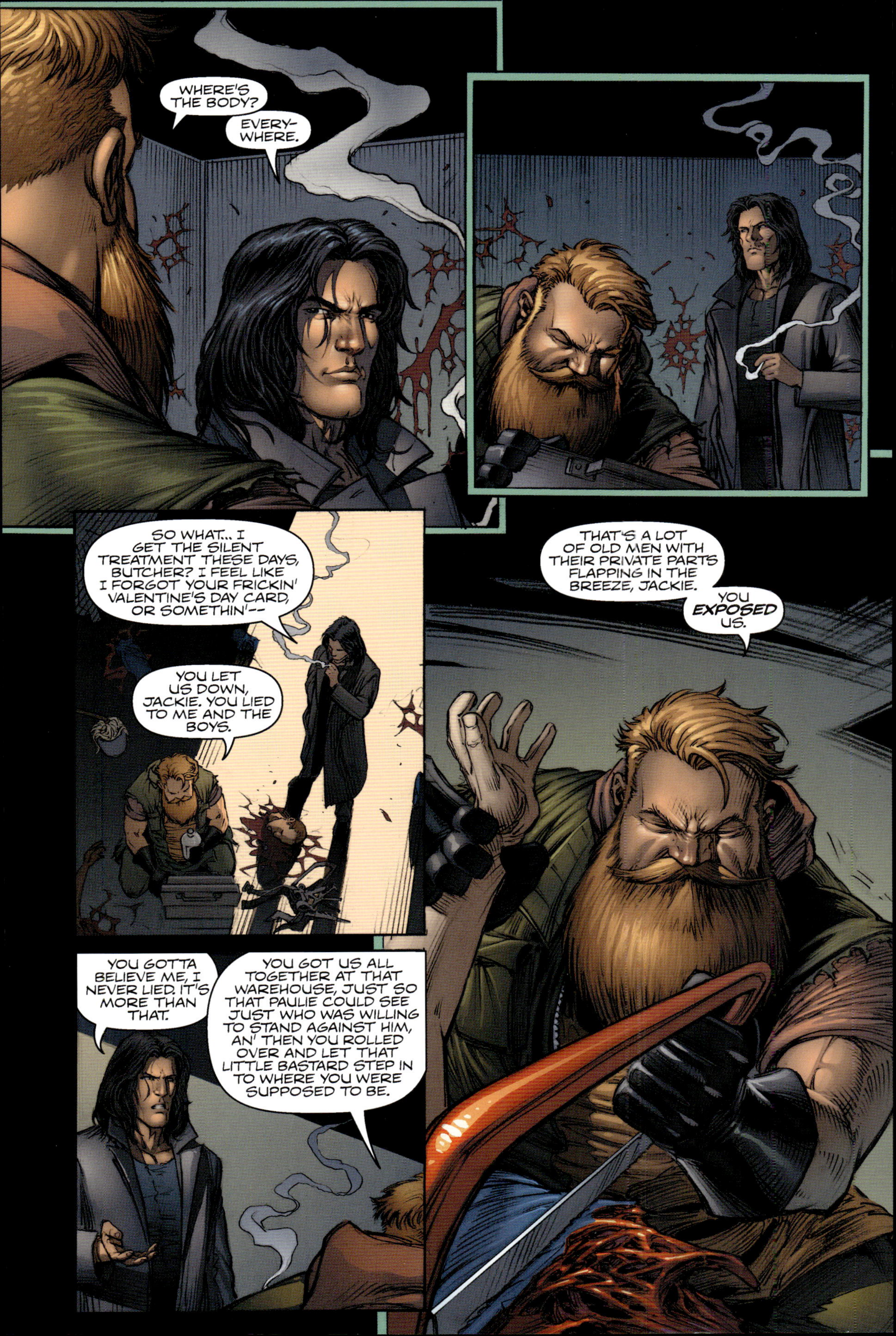
WHERE'S THE BODY?
EVERY-WHERE.
SO WHAT... I GET THE SILENT TREATMENT THESE DAYS, BUTCHER? I FEEL LIKE I FORGOT YOUR FRICKIN' VALENTINE'S DAY CARD, OR SOMETHIN'--
YOU LET US DOWN, JACKIE. YOU LIED TO ME AND THE BOYS.
THAT'S A LOT OF OLD MEN WITH THEIR PRIVATE PARTS FLAPPING IN THE BREEZE, JACKIE.
YOU **EXPOSED** US.
YOU GOTTA BELIEVE ME, I NEVER LIED. IT'S MORE THAN THAT.
YOU GOT US ALL TOGETHER AT THAT WAREHOUSE, JUST SO THAT PAULIE COULD SEE JUST WHO WAS WILLING TO STAND AGAINST HIM, AN' THEN YOU ROLLED OVER AND LET THAT LITTLE BASTARD STEP IN TO WHERE YOU WERE SUPPOSED TO BE.

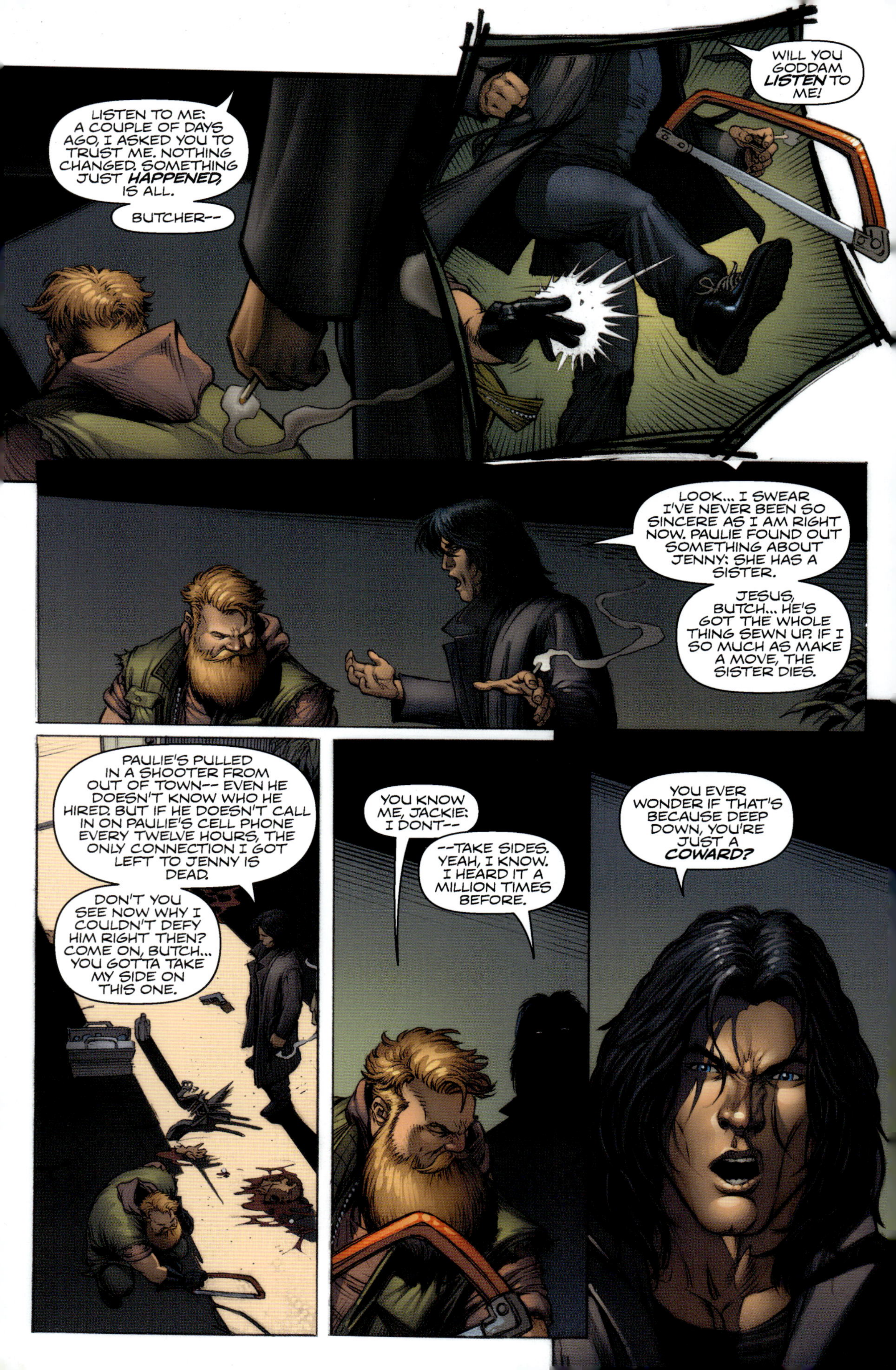
LISTEN TO ME: A COUPLE OF DAYS AGO, I ASKED YOU TO TRUST ME. NOTHING CHANGED. SOMETHING JUST HAPPENED, IS ALL.
BUTCHER--
WILL YOU GODDAM LISTEN TO ME!
LOOK... I SWEAR I'VE NEVER BEEN SO SINCERE AS I AM RIGHT NOW. PAULIE FOUND OUT SOMETHING ABOUT JENNY: SHE HAS A SISTER.
JESUS, BUTCH... HE'S GOT THE WHOLE THING SEWN UP. IF I SO MUCH AS MAKE A MOVE, THE SISTER DIES.
PAULIE'S PULLED IN A SHOOTER FROM OUT OF TOWN-- EVEN HE DOESN'T KNOW WHO HE HIRED. BUT IF HE DOESN'T CALL IN ON PAULIE'S CELL PHONE EVERY TWELVE HOURS, THE ONLY CONNECTION I GOT LEFT TO JENNY IS DEAD.
DON'T YOU SEE NOW WHY I COULDN'T DEFY HIM RIGHT THEN? COME ON, BUTCH... YOU GOTTA TAKE MY SIDE ON THIS ONE.
YOU KNOW ME, JACKIE: I DONT--
--TAKE SIDES. YEAH, I KNOW. I HEARD IT A MILLION TIMES BEFORE.
YOU EVER WONDER IF THAT'S BECAUSE DEEP DOWN, YOU'RE JUST A COWARD?

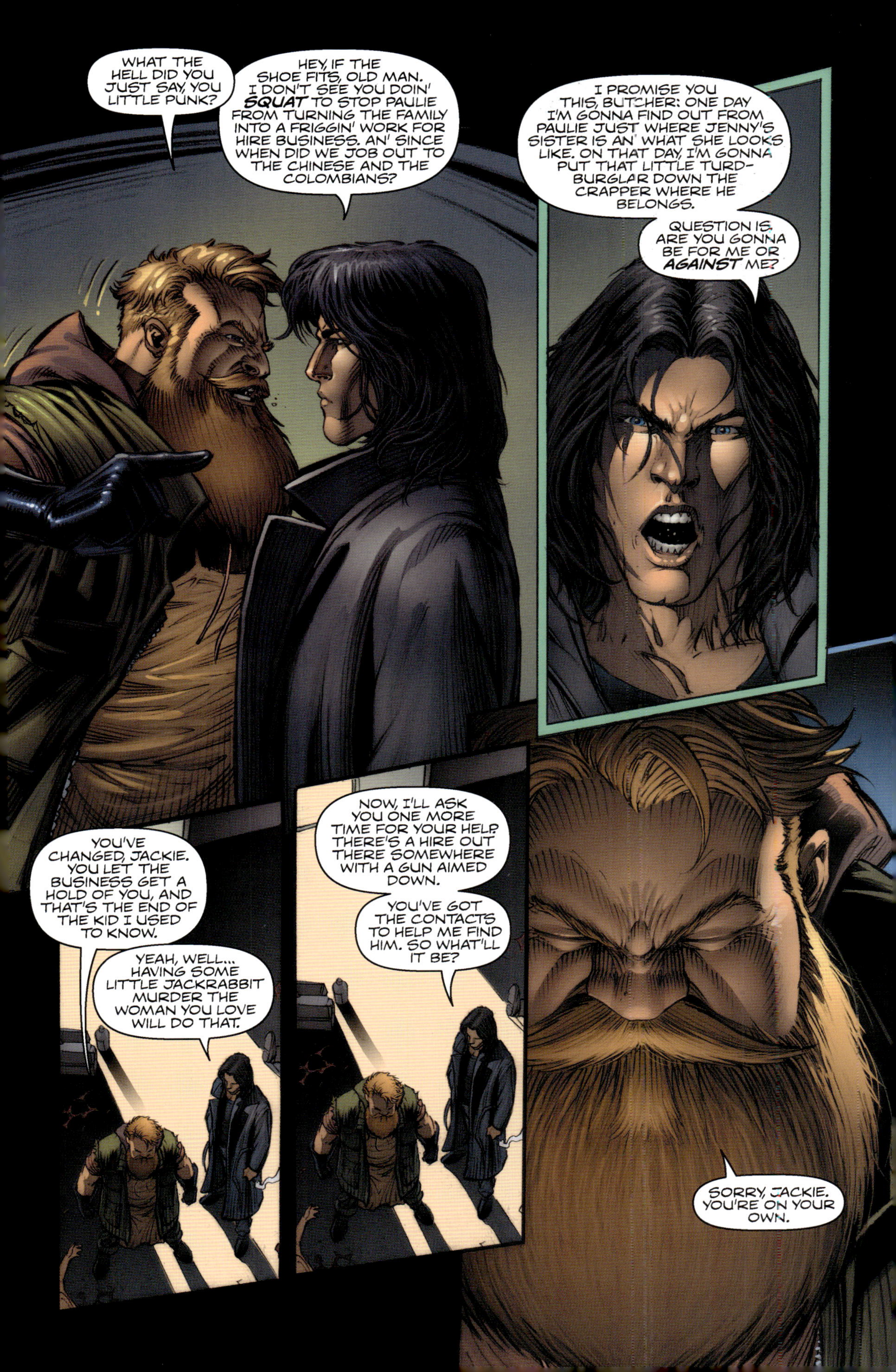
WHAT THE HELL DID YOU JUST SAY, YOU LITTLE PUNK?
HEY, IF THE SHOE FITS, OLD MAN. I DON'T SEE YOU DOIN' SQUAT TO STOP PAULIE FROM TURNING THE FAMILY INTO A FRIGGIN' WORK FOR HIRE BUSINESS. AN' SINCE WHEN DID WE JOB OUT TO THE CHINESE AND THE COLOMBIANS?
I PROMISE YOU THIS, BUTCHER: ONE DAY I'M GONNA FIND OUT FROM PAULIE JUST WHERE JENNY'S SISTER IS AN' WHAT SHE LOOKS LIKE. ON THAT DAY, I'M GONNA PUT THAT LITTLE TURD-BURGLAR DOWN THE CRAPPER WHERE HE BELONGS.
QUESTION IS. ARE YOU GONNA BE FOR ME OR AGAINST ME?
YOU'VE CHANGED, JACKIE. YOU LET THE BUSINESS GET A HOLD OF YOU, AND THAT'S THE END OF THE KID I USED TO KNOW.
YEAH, WELL... HAVING SOME LITTLE JACKRABBIT MURDER THE WOMAN YOU LOVE WILL DO THAT.
NOW, I'LL ASK YOU ONE MORE TIME FOR YOUR HELP. THERE'S A HIRE OUT THERE SOMEWHERE WITH A GUN AIMED DOWN.
YOU'VE GOT THE CONTACTS TO HELP ME FIND HIM. SO WHAT'LL IT BE?
SORRY, JACKIE. YOU'RE ON YOUR OWN.

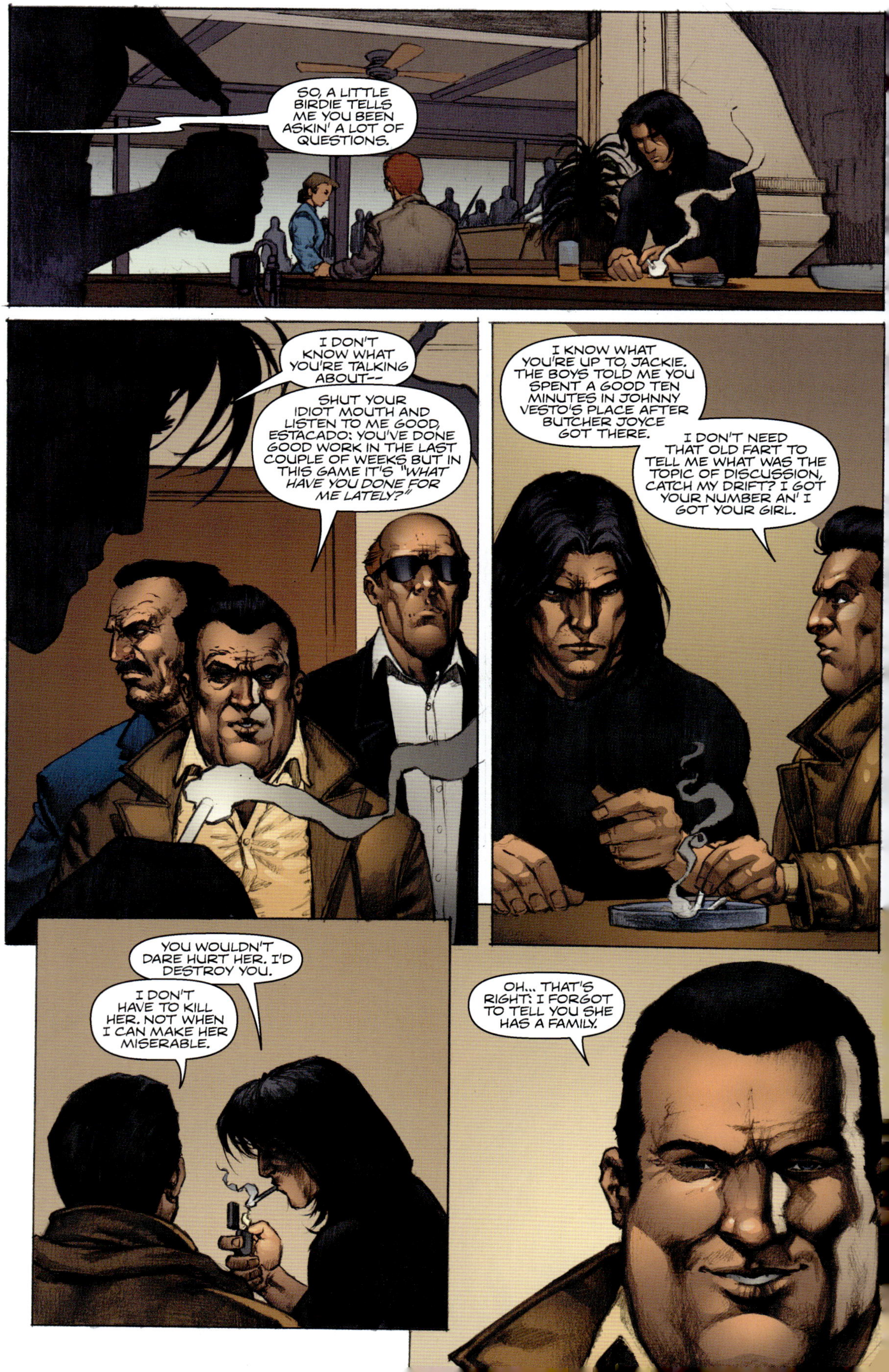
SO, A LITTLE BIRDIE TELLS ME YOU BEEN ASKIN' A LOT OF QUESTIONS.
I DON'T KNOW WHAT YOU'RE TALKING ABOUT--
SHUT YOUR IDIOT MOUTH AND LISTEN TO ME GOOD, ESTACADO: YOU'VE DONE GOOD WORK IN THE LAST COUPLE OF WEEKS BUT IN THIS GAME IT'S "WHAT HAVE YOU DONE FOR ME LATELY?"
I KNOW WHAT YOU'RE UP TO, JACKIE. THE BOYS TOLD ME YOU SPENT A GOOD TEN MINUTES IN JOHNNY VESTO'S PLACE AFTER BUTCHER JOYCE GOT THERE.
I DON'T NEED THAT OLD FART TO TELL ME WHAT WAS THE TOPIC OF DISCUSSION, CATCH MY DRIFT? I GOT YOUR NUMBER AN' I GOT YOUR GIRL.
YOU WOULDN'T DARE HURT HER. I'D DESTROY YOU.
I DON'T HAVE TO KILL HER. NOT WHEN I CAN MAKE HER MISERABLE.
OH... THAT'S RIGHT: I FORGOT TO TELL YOU SHE HAS A FAMILY.

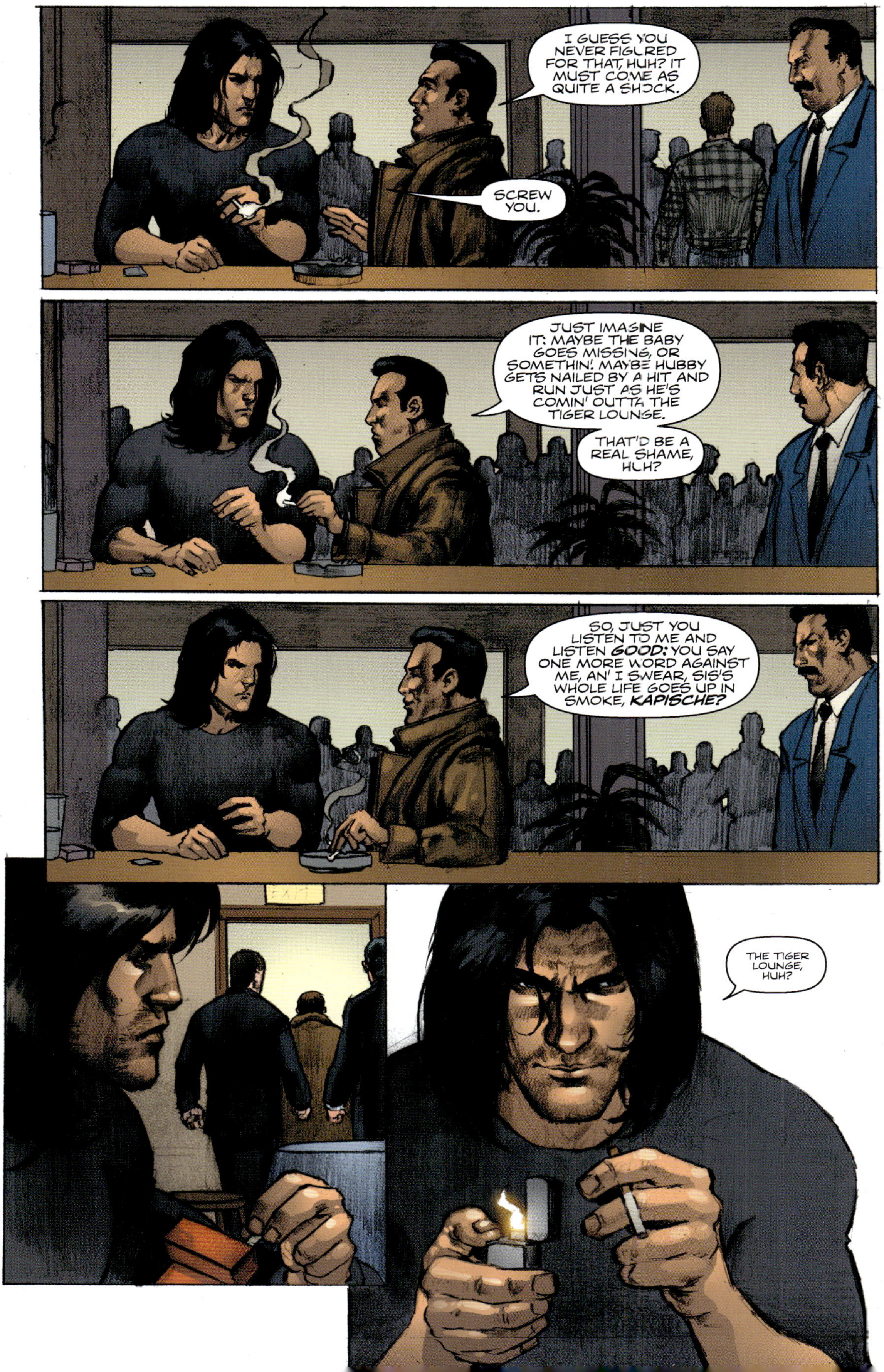
I GUESS YOU NEVER FIGURED FOR THAT, HUH? IT MUST COME AS QUITE A SHOCK.
SCREW YOU.
JUST IMAGINE IT: MAYBE THE BABY GOES MISSING, OR SOMETHIN'. MAYBE HUBBY GETS NAILED BY A HIT AND RUN JUST AS HE'S COMIN' OUTTA THE TIGER LOUNGE.
THAT'D BE A REAL SHAME, HUH?
SO, JUST YOU LISTEN TO ME AND LISTEN GOOD: YOU SAY ONE MORE WORD AGAINST ME, AN' I SWEAR, SIS'S WHOLE LIFE GOES UP IN SMOKE, KAPISCHE?
EXIT
THE TIGER LOUNGE, HUH?

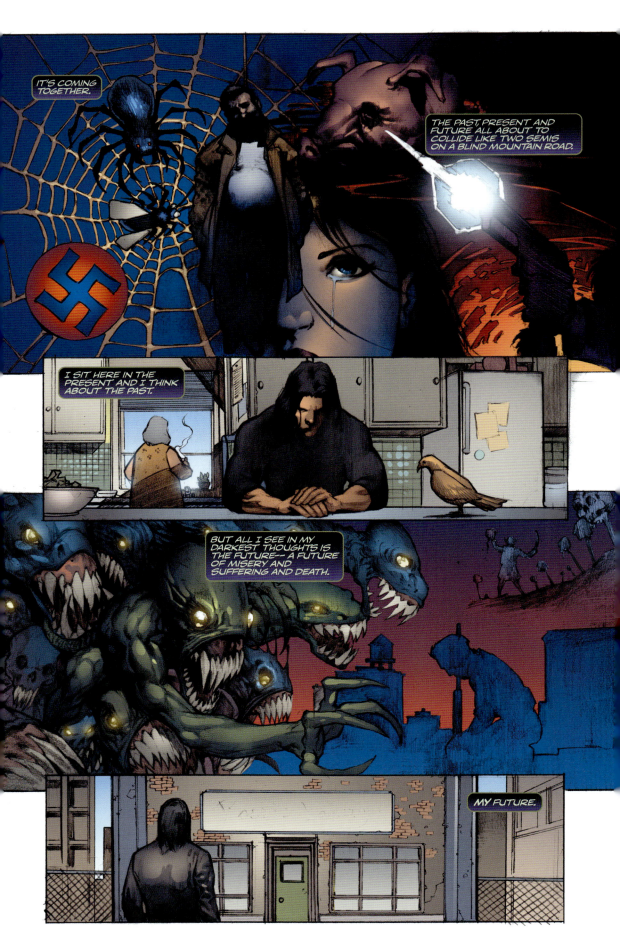

IT'S COMING TOGETHER.

THE PAST, PRESENT AND FUTURE ALL ABOUT TO COLLIDE LIKE TWO SEMIS ON A BLIND MOUNTAIN ROAD.

I SIT HERE IN THE PRESENT AND I THINK ABOUT THE PAST.

BUT ALL I SEE IN MY DARKEST THOUGHTS IS THE FUTURE-- A FUTURE OF MISERY AND SUFFERING AND DEATH.

MY FUTURE.

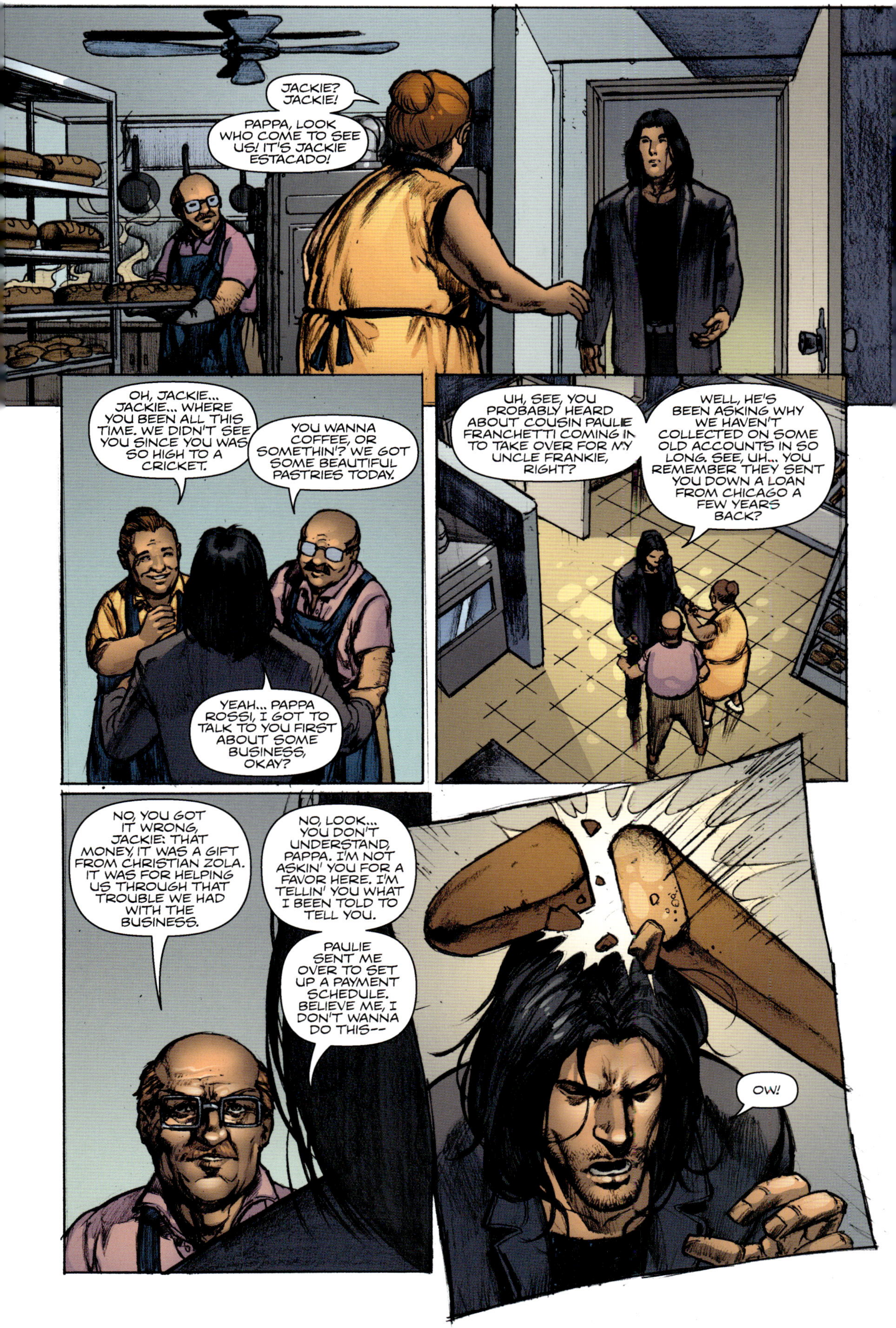
JACKIE? JACKIE!
PAPPA, LOOK WHO COME TO SEE US! IT'S JACKIE ESTACADO!
OH, JACKIE... JACKIE... WHERE YOU BEEN ALL THIS TIME. WE DIDN'T SEE YOU SINCE YOU WAS SO HIGH TO A CRICKET.
YOU WANNA COFFEE, OR SOMETHIN'? WE GOT SOME BEAUTIFUL PASTRIES TODAY.
YEAH... PAPPA ROSSI, I GOT TO TALK TO YOU FIRST ABOUT SOME BUSINESS, OKAY?
UH, SEE, YOU PROBABLY HEARD ABOUT COUSIN PAULIE FRANCHETTI COMING IN TO TAKE OVER FOR MY UNCLE FRANKIE, RIGHT?
WELL, HE'S BEEN ASKING WHY WE HAVEN'T COLLECTED ON SOME OLD ACCOUNTS IN SO LONG. SEE, UH... YOU REMEMBER THEY SENT YOU DOWN A LOAN FROM CHICAGO A FEW YEARS BACK?
NO, YOU GOT IT WRONG, JACKIE: THAT MONEY, IT WAS A GIFT FROM CHRISTIAN ZOLA. IT WAS FOR HELPING US THROUGH THAT TROUBLE WE HAD WITH THE BUSINESS.
NO, LOOK... YOU DON'T UNDERSTAND, PAPPA. I'M NOT ASKIN' YOU FOR A FAVOR HERE. I'M TELLIN' YOU WHAT I BEEN TOLD TO TELL YOU.
PAULIE SENT ME OVER TO SET UP A PAYMENT SCHEDULE. BELIEVE ME, I DON'T WANNA DO THIS--
OW!

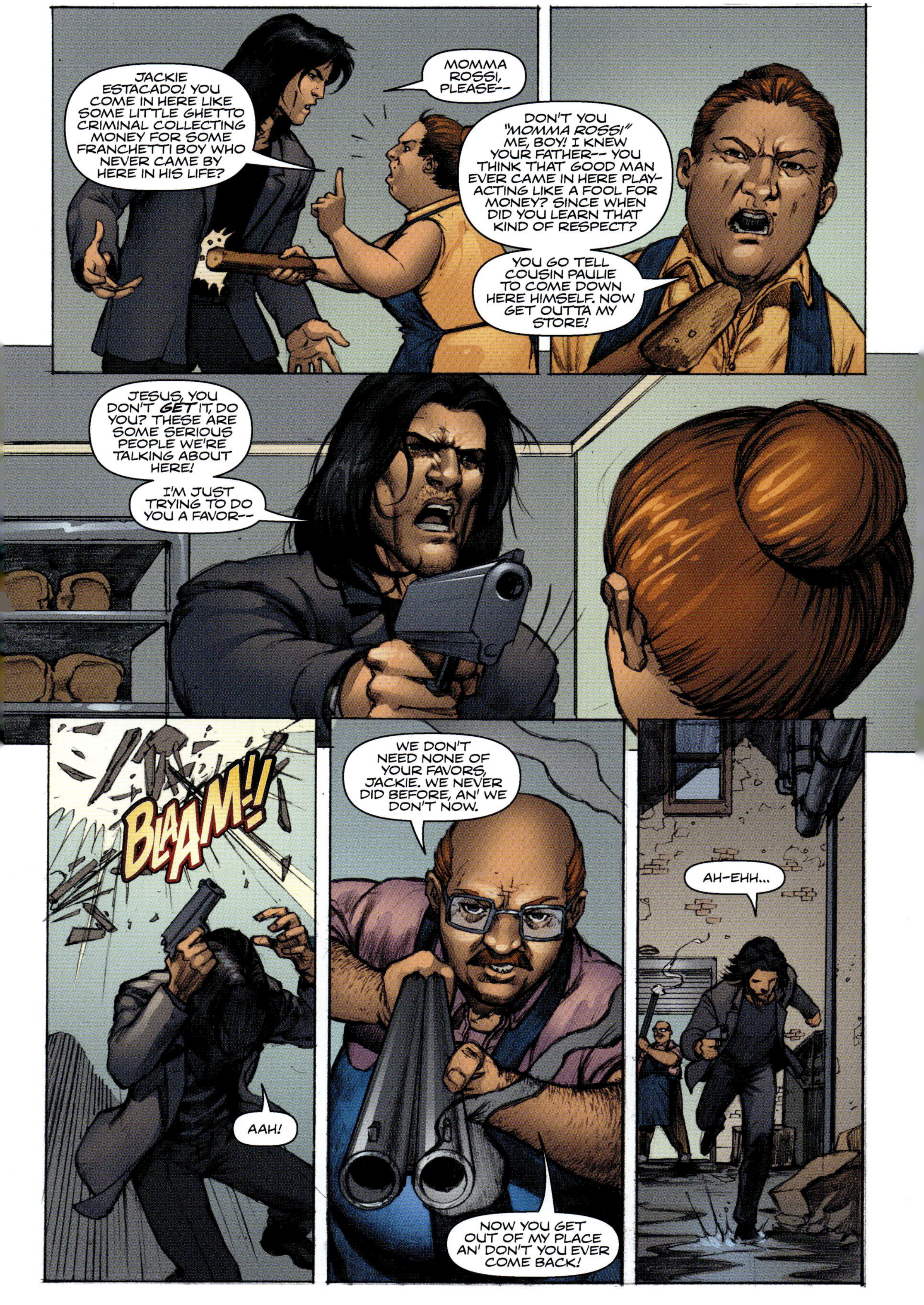
JACKIE ESTACADO! YOU COME IN HERE LIKE SOME LITTLE GHETTO CRIMINAL COLLECTING MONEY FOR SOME FRANCHETTI BOY WHO NEVER CAME BY HERE IN HIS LIFE?
MOMMA ROSSI, PLEASE--
DON'T YOU "MOMMA ROSSI" ME, BOY! I KNEW YOUR FATHER-- YOU THINK THAT GOOD MAN EVER CAME IN HERE PLAY-ACTING LIKE A FOOL FOR MONEY? SINCE WHEN DID YOU LEARN THAT KIND OF RESPECT?
YOU GO TELL COUSIN PAULIE TO COME DOWN HERE HIMSELF. NOW GET OUTTA MY STORE!
JESUS, YOU DON'T GET IT, DO YOU? THESE ARE SOME SERIOUS PEOPLE WE'RE TALKING ABOUT HERE!
I'M JUST TRYING TO DO YOU A FAVOR--
BLAAM!!
AAH!
WE DON'T NEED NONE OF YOUR FAVORS, JACKIE. WE NEVER DID BEFORE, AN' WE DON'T NOW.
NOW YOU GET OUT OF MY PLACE AN' DON'T YOU EVER COME BACK!
AH-EHH...

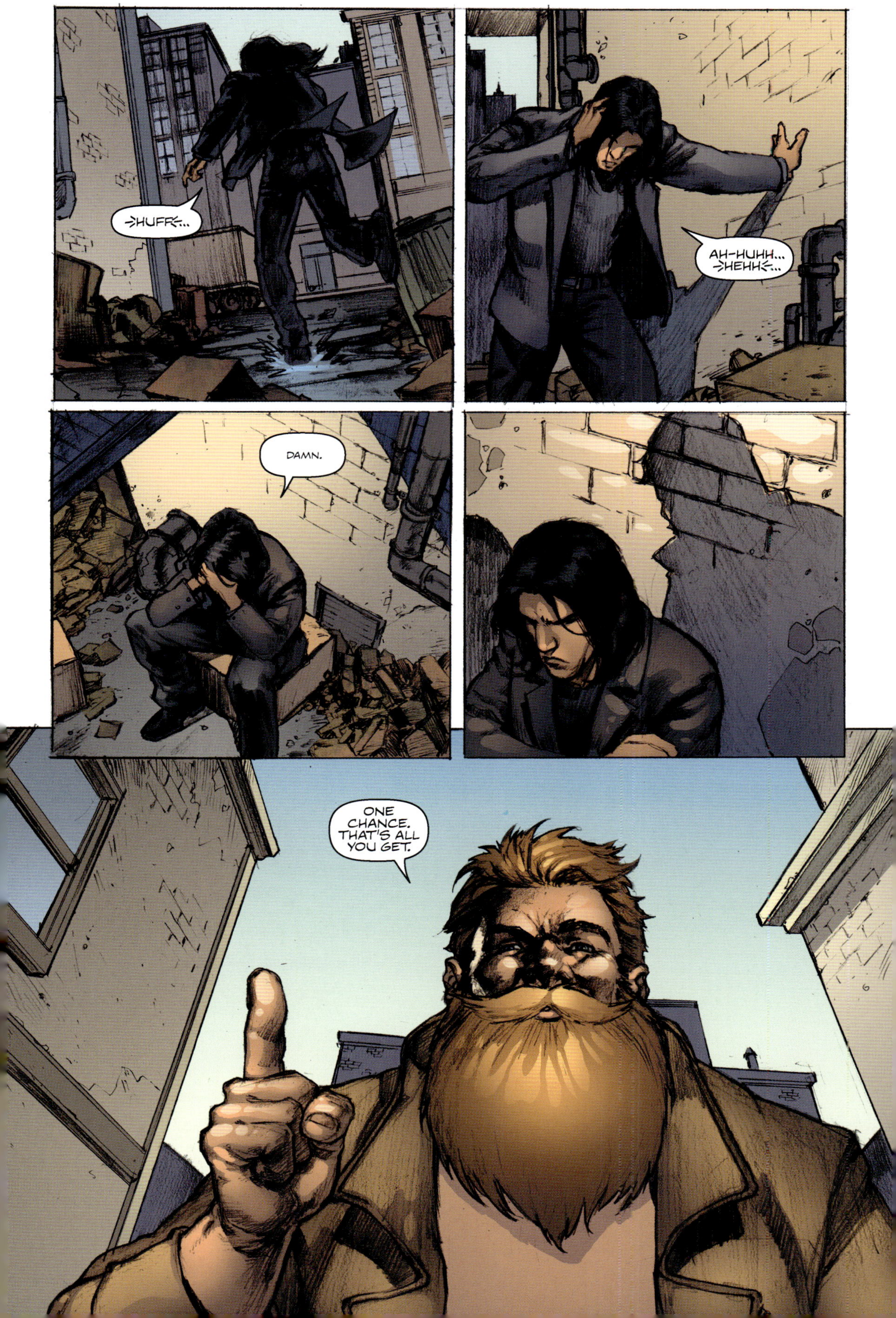
HUFF...
AH-HUHH... HEHH...
DAMN.
ONE CHANCE. THAT'S ALL YOU GET.

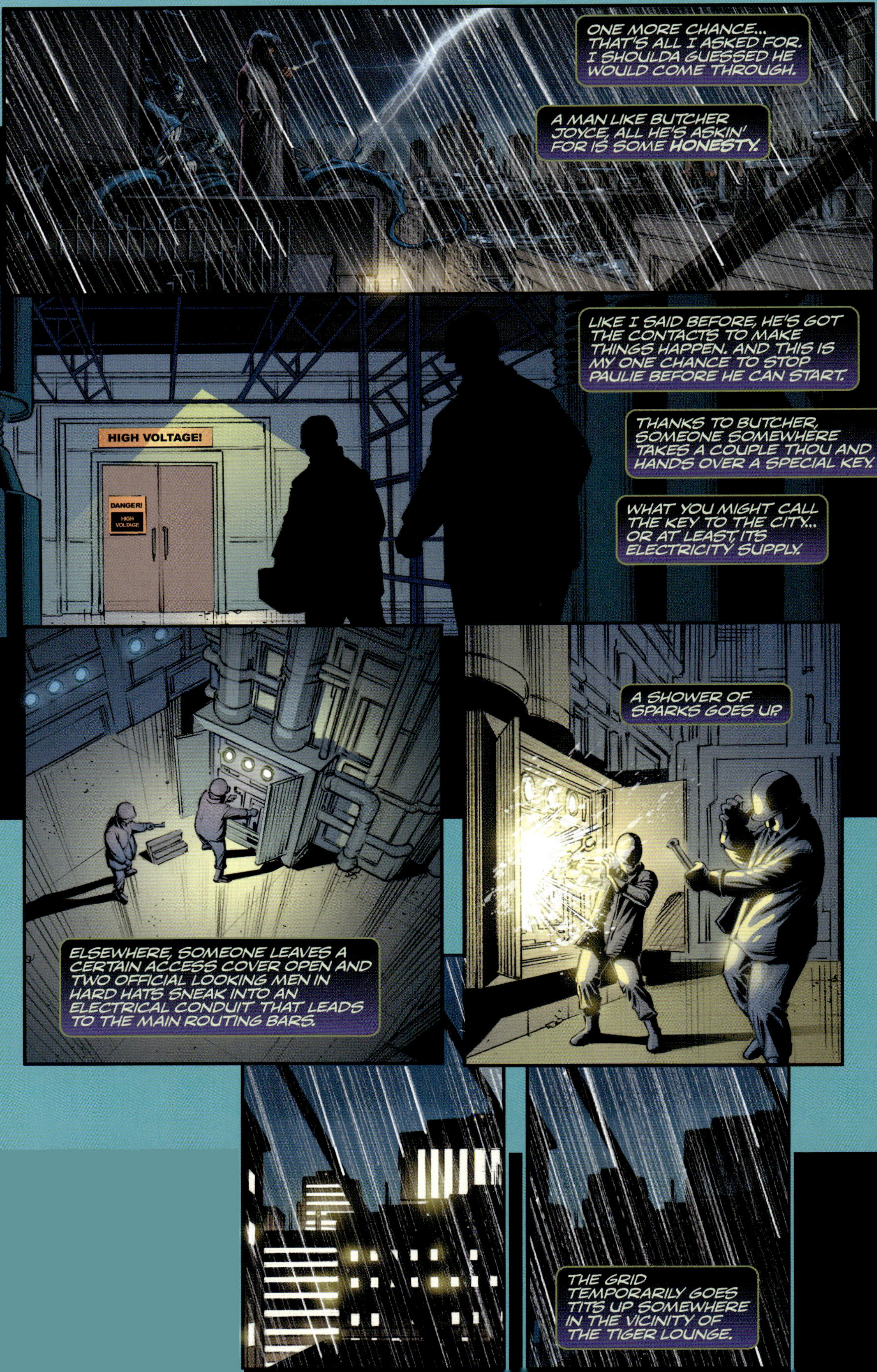
ONE MORE CHANCE... THAT'S ALL I ASKED FOR. I SHOULDA GUESSED HE WOULD COME THROUGH.
A MAN LIKE BUTCHER JOYCE, ALL HE'S ASKIN' FOR IS SOME HONESTY.
LIKE I SAID BEFORE, HE'S GOT THE CONTACTS TO MAKE THINGS HAPPEN. AND THIS IS MY ONE CHANCE TO STOP PAULIE BEFORE HE CAN START.
THANKS TO BUTCHER, SOMEONE SOMEWHERE TAKES A COUPLE THOU AND HANDS OVER A SPECIAL KEY.
WHAT YOU MIGHT CALL THE KEY TO THE CITY... OR AT LEAST, ITS ELECTRICITY SUPPLY.
HIGH VOLTAGE!
DANGER!
HIGH VOLTAGE
ELSEWHERE, SOMEONE LEAVES A CERTAIN ACCESS COVER OPEN AND TWO OFFICIAL LOOKING MEN IN HARD HATS SNEAK INTO AN ELECTRICAL CONDUIT THAT LEADS TO THE MAIN ROUTING BARS.
A SHOWER OF SPARKS GOES UP.
THE GRID TEMPORARILY GOES TITS UP SOMEWHERE IN THE VICINITY OF THE TIGER LOUNGE.

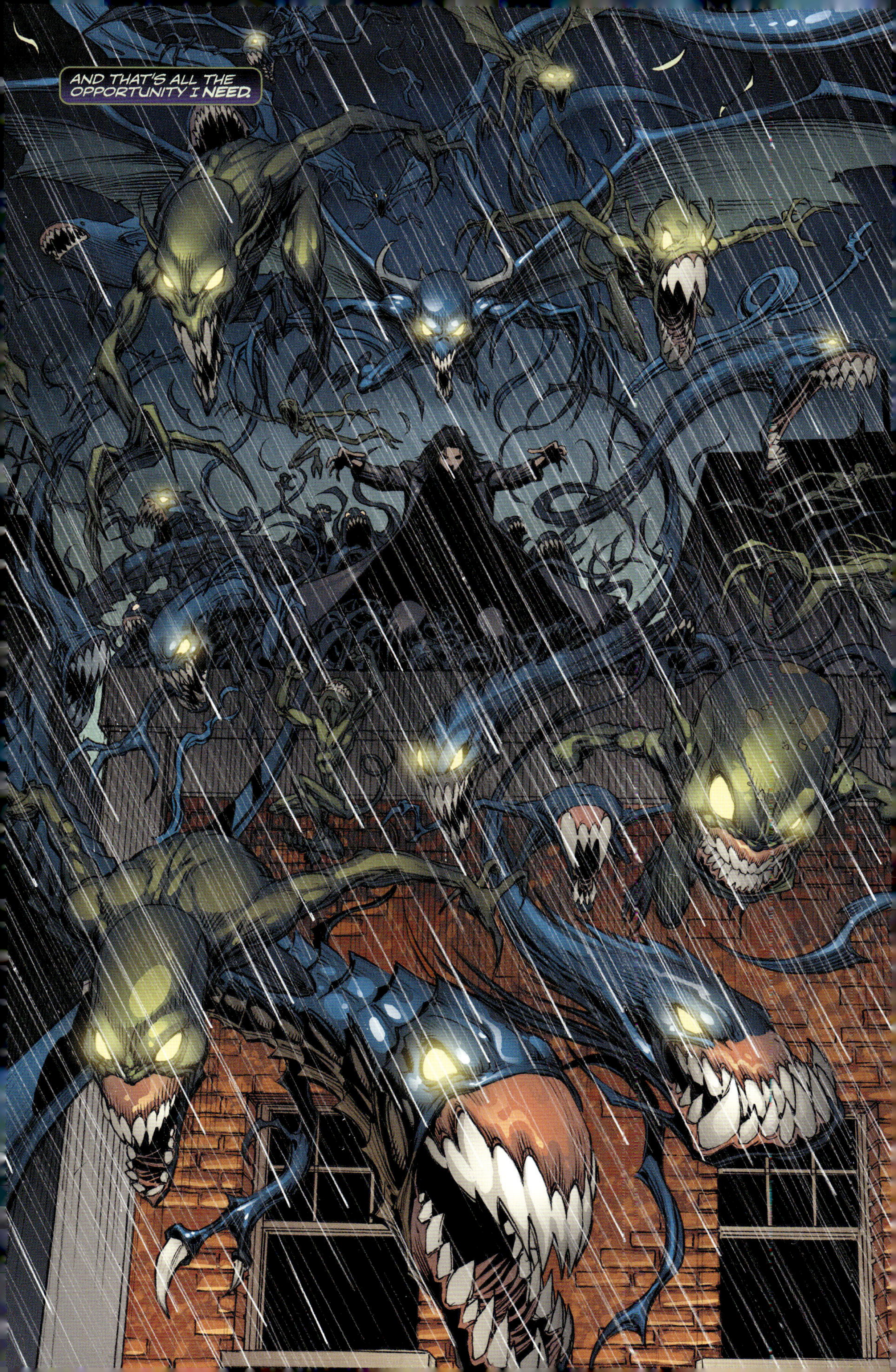
AND THAT'S ALL THE OPPORTUNITY I **NEED**.

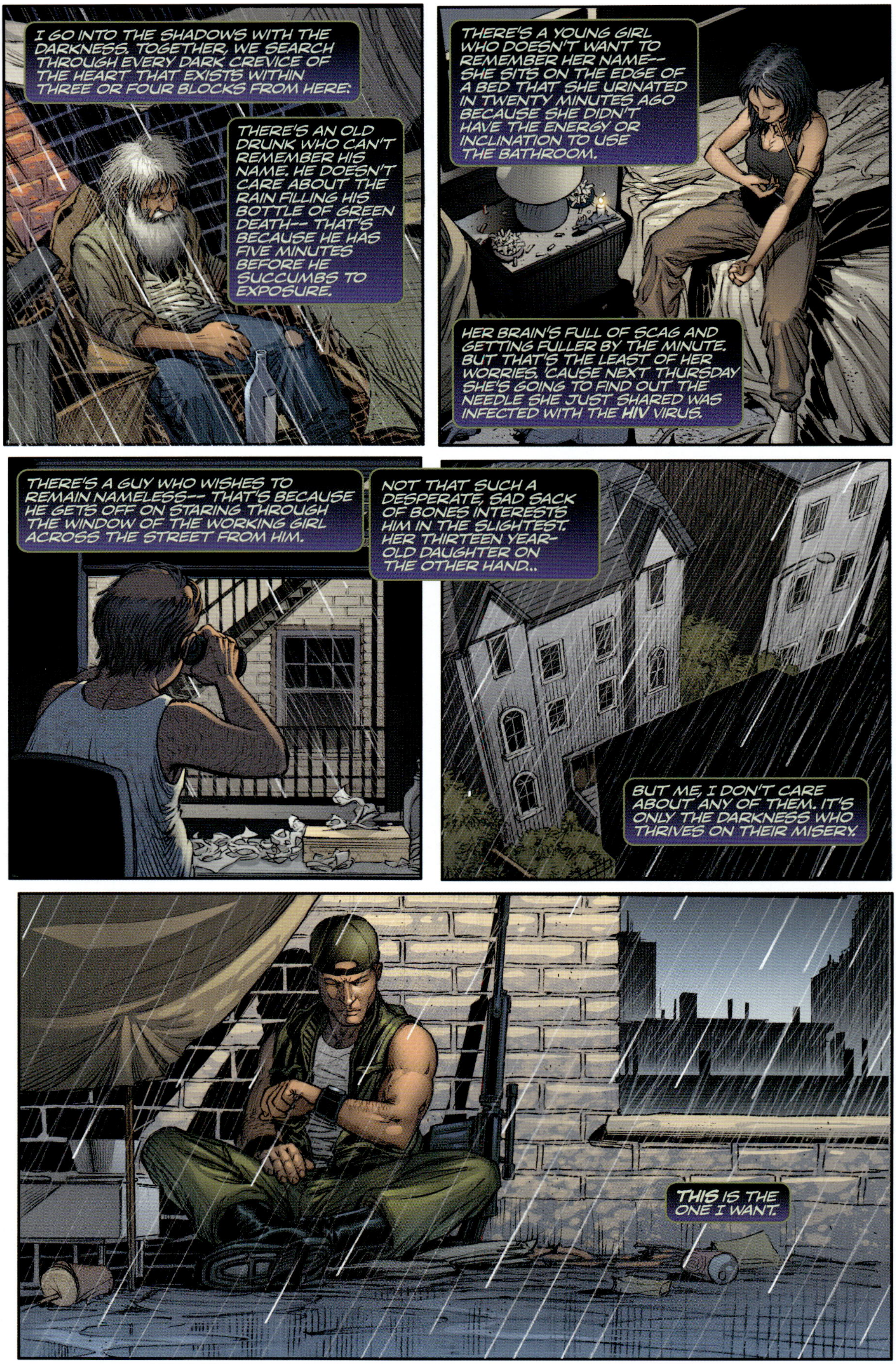
I GO INTO THE SHADOWS WITH THE DARKNESS. TOGETHER, WE SEARCH THROUGH EVERY DARK CREVICE OF THE HEART THAT EXISTS WITHIN THREE OR FOUR BLOCKS FROM HERE:
THERE'S AN OLD DRUNK WHO CAN'T REMEMBER HIS NAME. HE DOESN'T CARE ABOUT THE RAIN FILLING HIS BOTTLE OF GREEN DEATH-- THAT'S BECAUSE HE HAS FIVE MINUTES BEFORE HE SUCCUMBS TO EXPOSURE.
THERE'S A YOUNG GIRL WHO DOESN'T WANT TO REMEMBER HER NAME-- SHE SITS ON THE EDGE OF A BED THAT SHE URINATED IN TWENTY MINUTES AGO BECAUSE SHE DIDN'T HAVE THE ENERGY OR INCLINATION TO USE THE BATHROOM.
HER BRAIN'S FULL OF SCAG AND GETTING FULLER BY THE MINUTE. BUT THAT'S THE LEAST OF HER WORRIES. 'CAUSE NEXT THURSDAY SHE'S GOING TO FIND OUT THE NEEDLE SHE JUST SHARED WAS INFECTED WITH THE HIV VIRUS.
THERE'S A GUY WHO WISHES TO REMAIN NAMELESS-- THAT'S BECAUSE HE GETS OFF ON STARING THROUGH THE WINDOW OF THE WORKING GIRL ACROSS THE STREET FROM HIM.
NOT THAT SUCH A DESPERATE, SAD SACK OF BONES INTERESTS HIM IN THE SLIGHTEST. HER THIRTEEN YEAR-OLD DAUGHTER ON THE OTHER HAND...
BUT ME, I DON'T CARE ABOUT ANY OF THEM. IT'S ONLY THE DARKNESS WHO THRIVES ON THEIR MISERY.
THIS IS THE ONE I WANT.

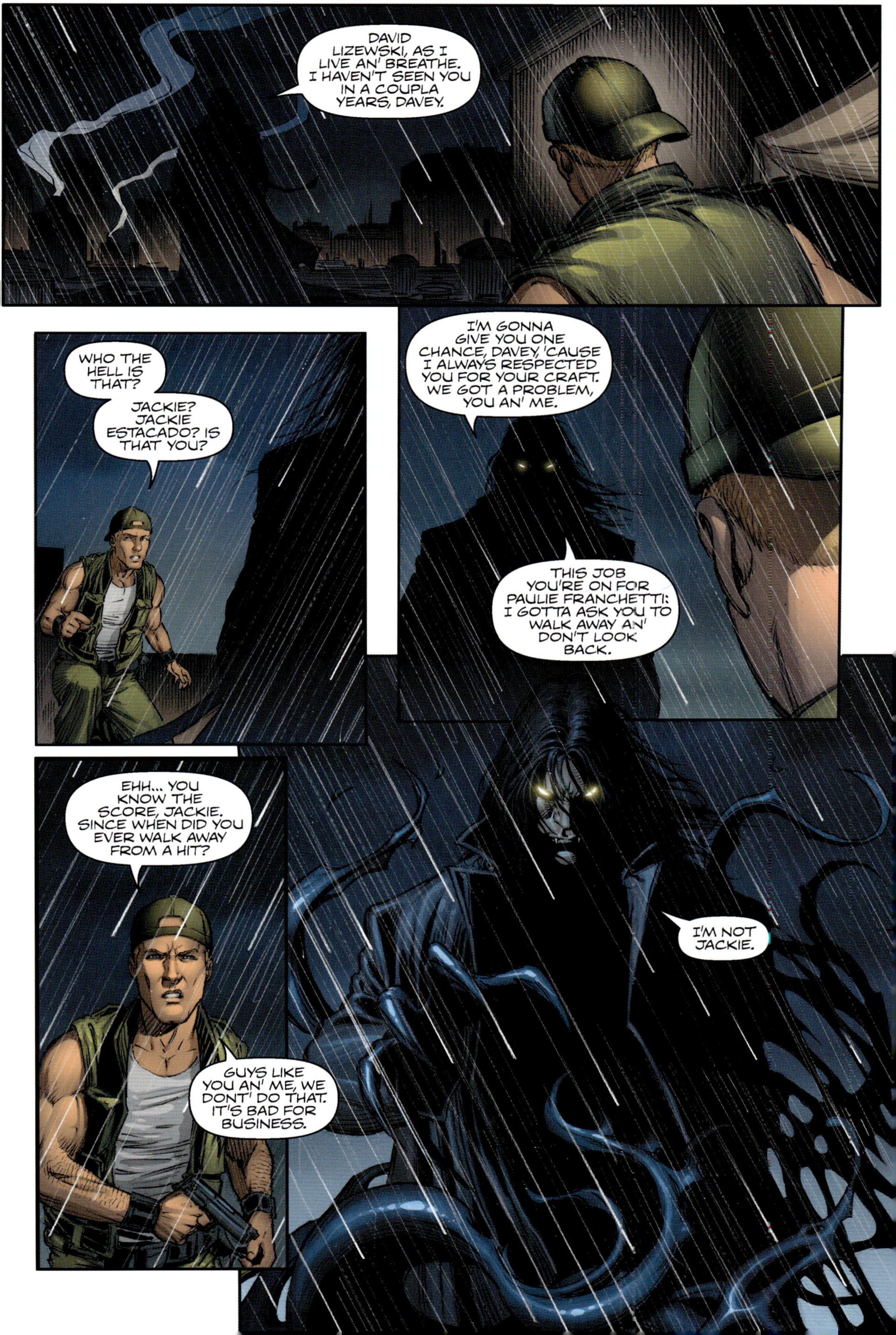
DAVID LIZEWSKI, AS I LIVE AN' BREATHE. I HAVEN'T SEEN YOU IN A COUPLA YEARS, DAVEY.
WHO THE HELL IS THAT?
JACKIE? JACKIE ESTACADO? IS THAT YOU?
I'M GONNA GIVE YOU ONE CHANCE, DAVEY, 'CAUSE I ALWAYS RESPECTED YOU FOR YOUR CRAFT. WE GOT A PROBLEM, YOU AN' ME.
THIS JOB YOU'RE ON FOR PAULIE FRANCHETTI: I GOTTA ASK YOU TO WALK AWAY AN' DON'T LOOK BACK.
EHH... YOU KNOW THE SCORE, JACKIE. SINCE WHEN DID YOU EVER WALK AWAY FROM A HIT?
GUYS LIKE YOU AN' ME, WE DONT' DO THAT. IT'S BAD FOR BUSINESS.
I'M NOT JACKIE.

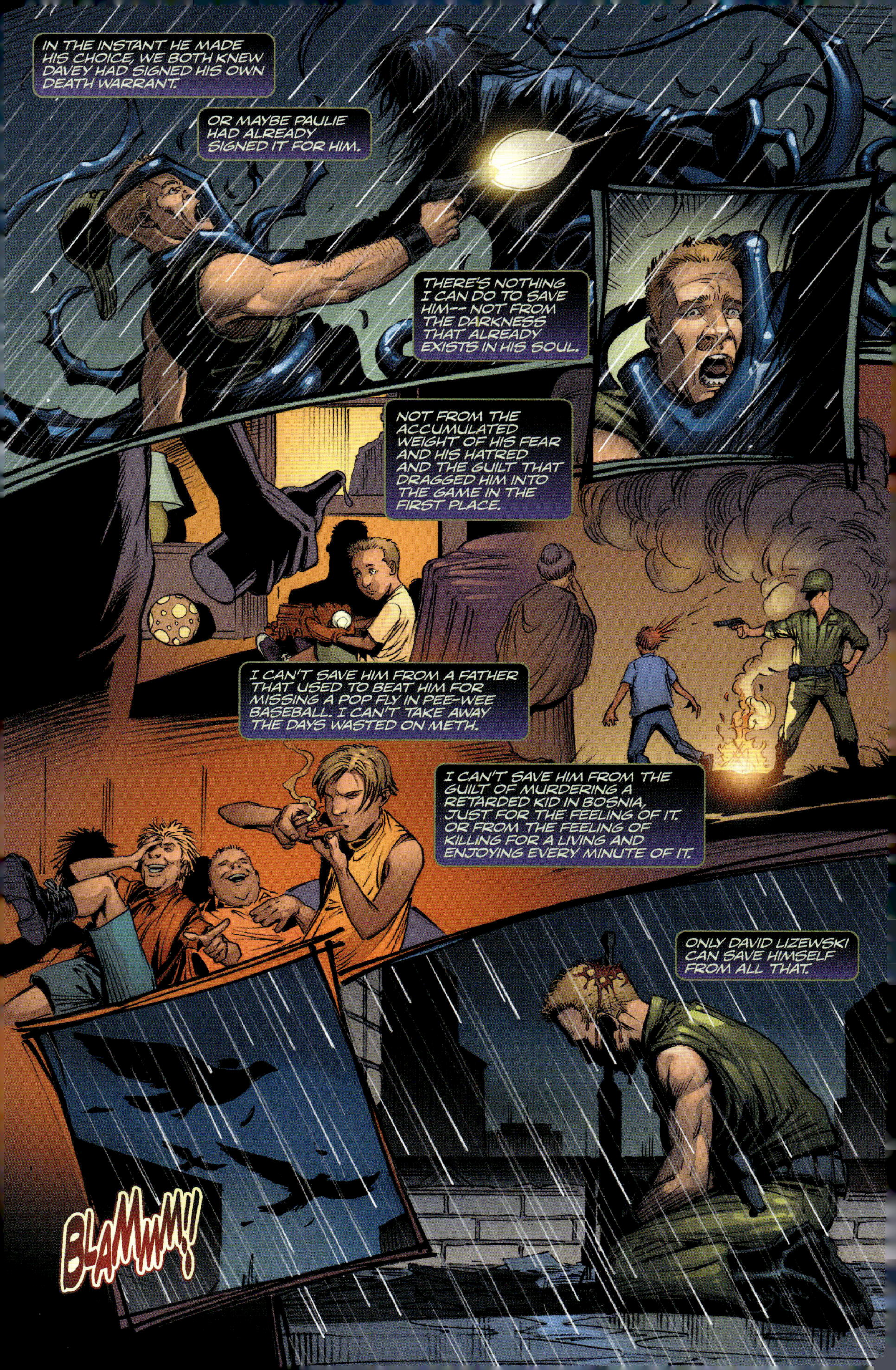
IN THE INSTANT HE MADE HIS CHOICE, WE BOTH KNEW DAVEY HAD SIGNED HIS OWN DEATH WARRANT.
OR MAYBE PAULIE HAD ALREADY SIGNED IT FOR HIM.
THERE'S NOTHING I CAN DO TO SAVE HIM-- NOT FROM THE DARKNESS THAT ALREADY EXISTS IN HIS SOUL.
NOT FROM THE ACCUMULATED WEIGHT OF HIS FEAR AND HIS HATRED AND THE GUILT THAT DRAGGED HIM INTO THE GAME IN THE FIRST PLACE.
I CAN'T SAVE HIM FROM A FATHER THAT USED TO BEAT HIM FOR MISSING A POP FLY IN PEE-WEE BASEBALL. I CAN'T TAKE AWAY THE DAYS WASTED ON METH.
I CAN'T SAVE HIM FROM THE GUILT OF MURDERING A RETARDED KID IN BOSNIA, JUST FOR THE FEELING OF IT. OR FROM THE FEELING OF KILLING FOR A LIVING AND ENJOYING EVERY MINUTE OF IT.
ONLY DAVID LIZEWSKI CAN SAVE HIMSELF FROM ALL THAT.
BLAMMM!

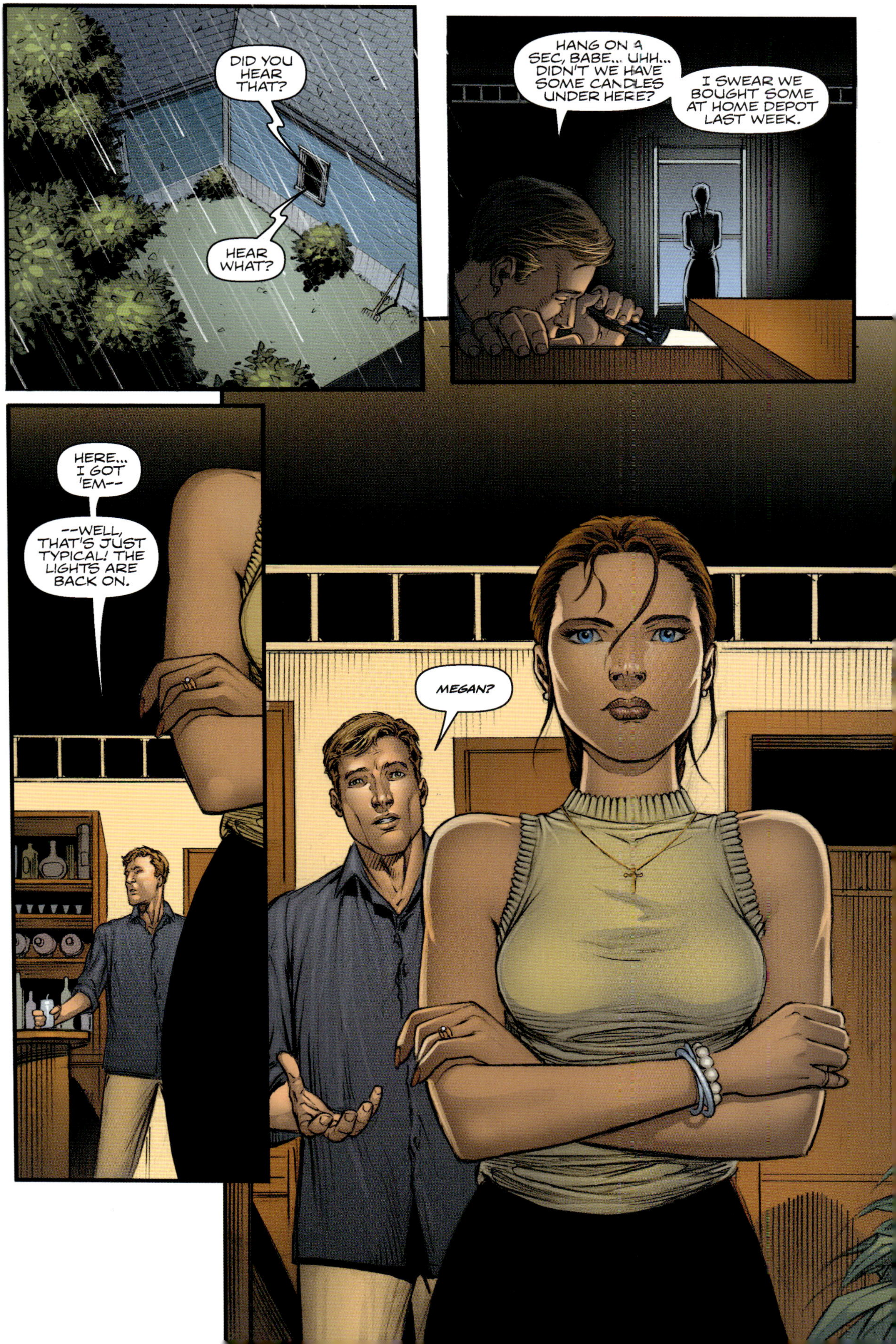
DID YOU HEAR THAT?
HEAR WHAT?
HANG ON A SEC, BABE... UHH... DIDN'T WE HAVE SOME CANDLES UNDER HERE?
I SWEAR WE BOUGHT SOME AT HOME DEPOT LAST WEEK.
HERE... I GOT 'EM--
--WELL, THAT'S JUST TYPICAL! THE LIGHTS ARE BACK ON.
MEGAN?

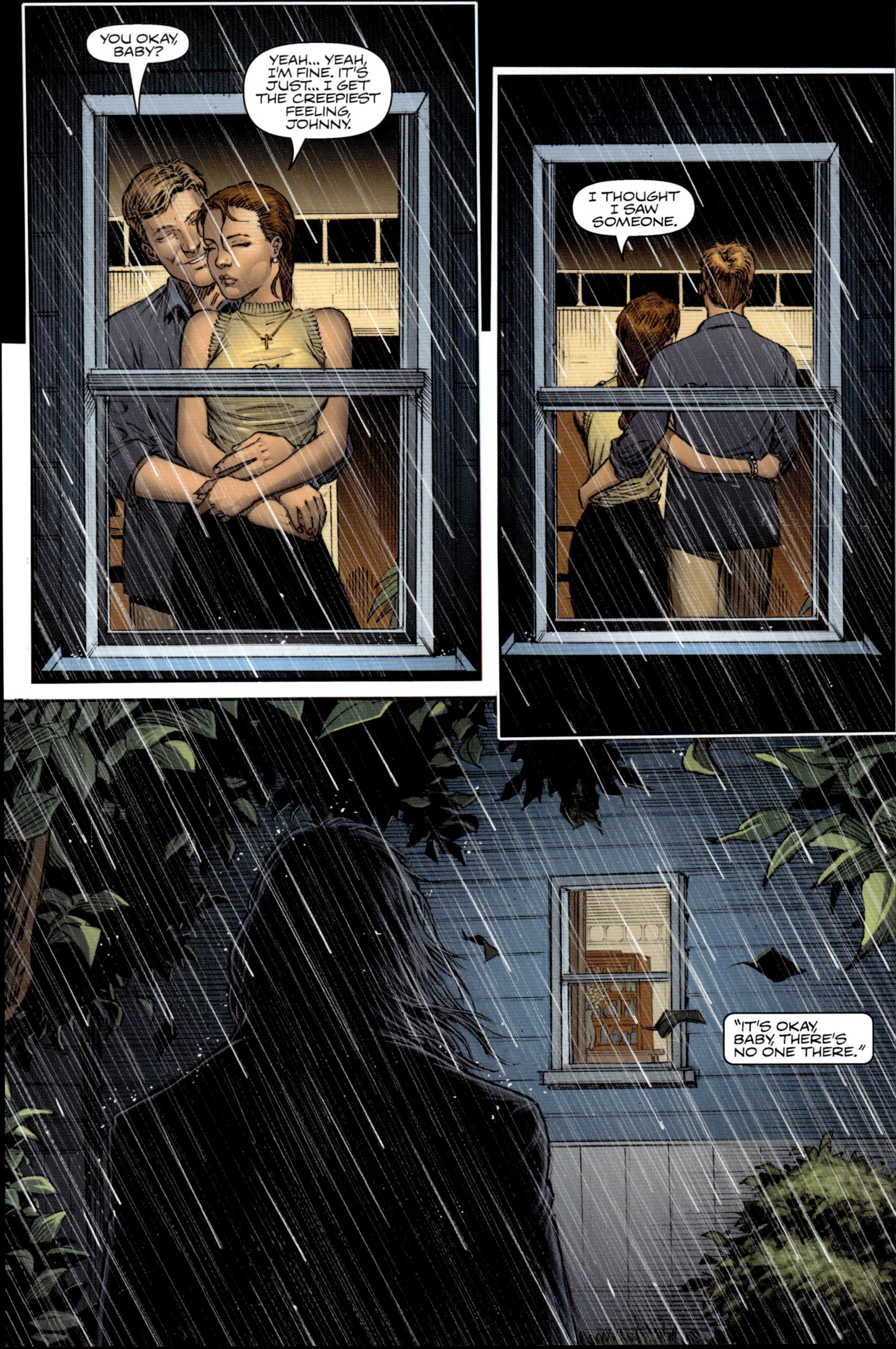
YOU OKAY, BABY?
YEAH... YEAH, I'M FINE. IT'S JUST... I GET THE CREEPIEST FEELING, JOHNNY.
I THOUGHT I SAW SOMEONE.
"IT'S OKAY, BABY, THERE'S NO ONE THERE."

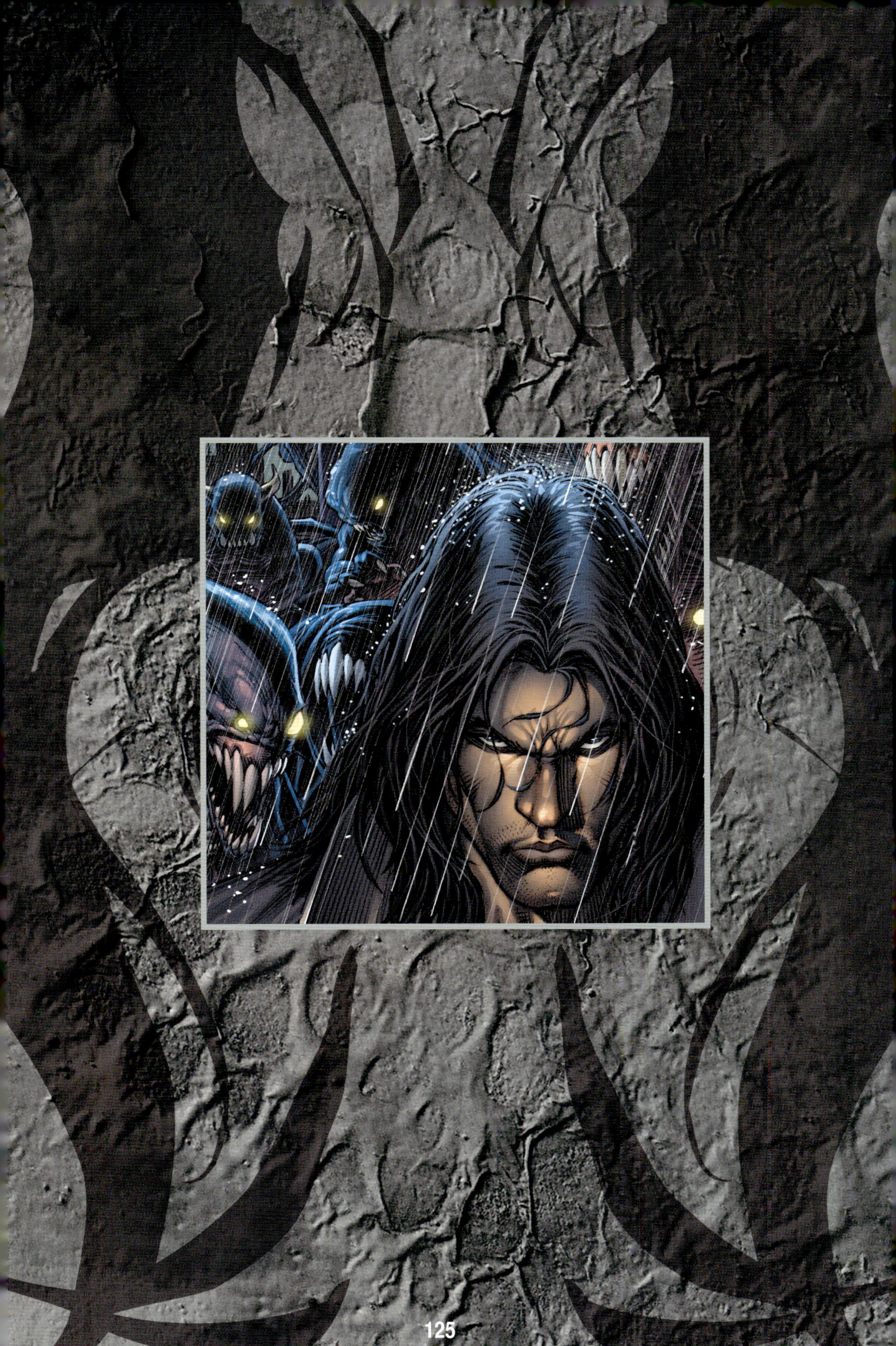

cover art by: Dale Keown & Matt Milla

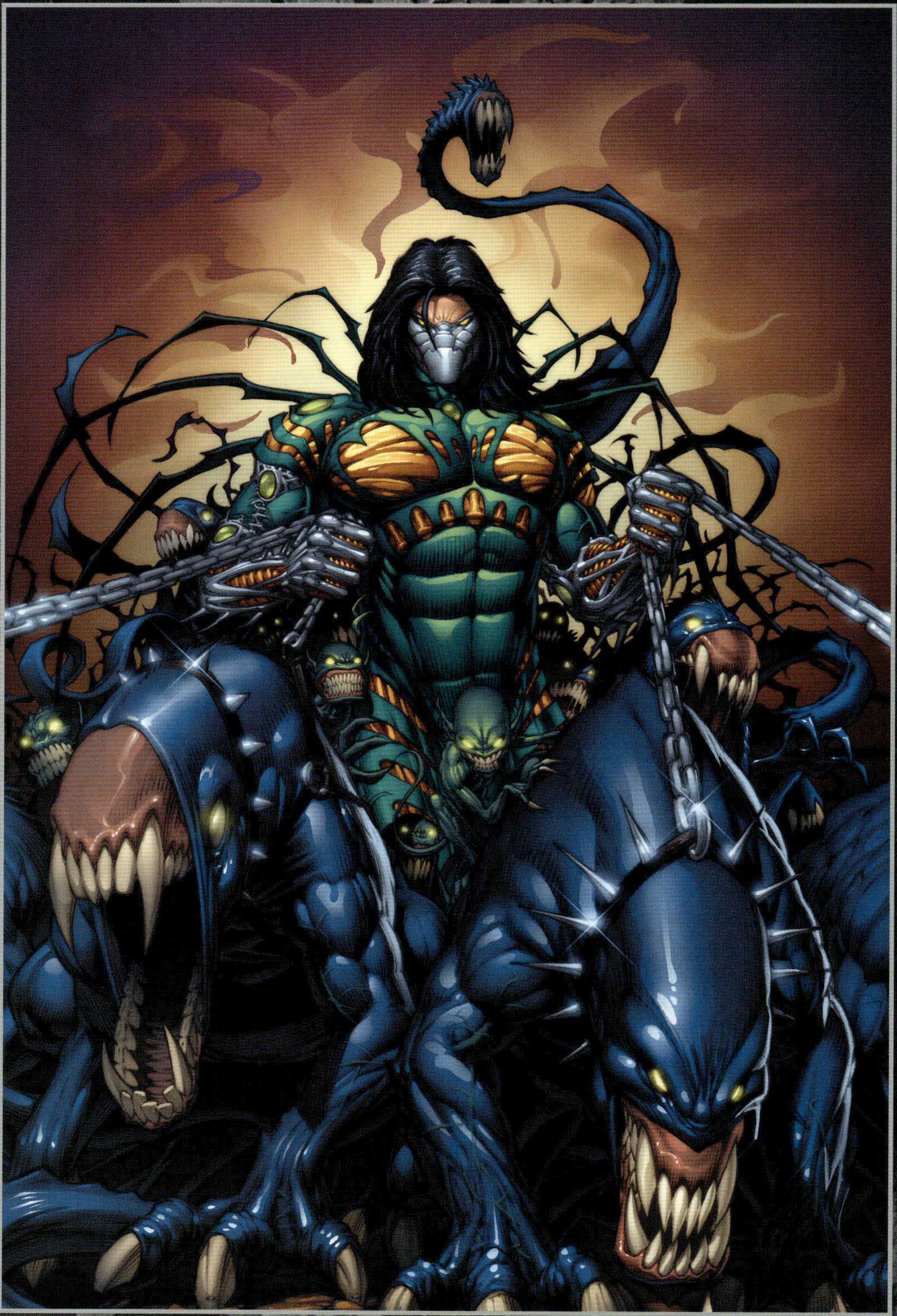

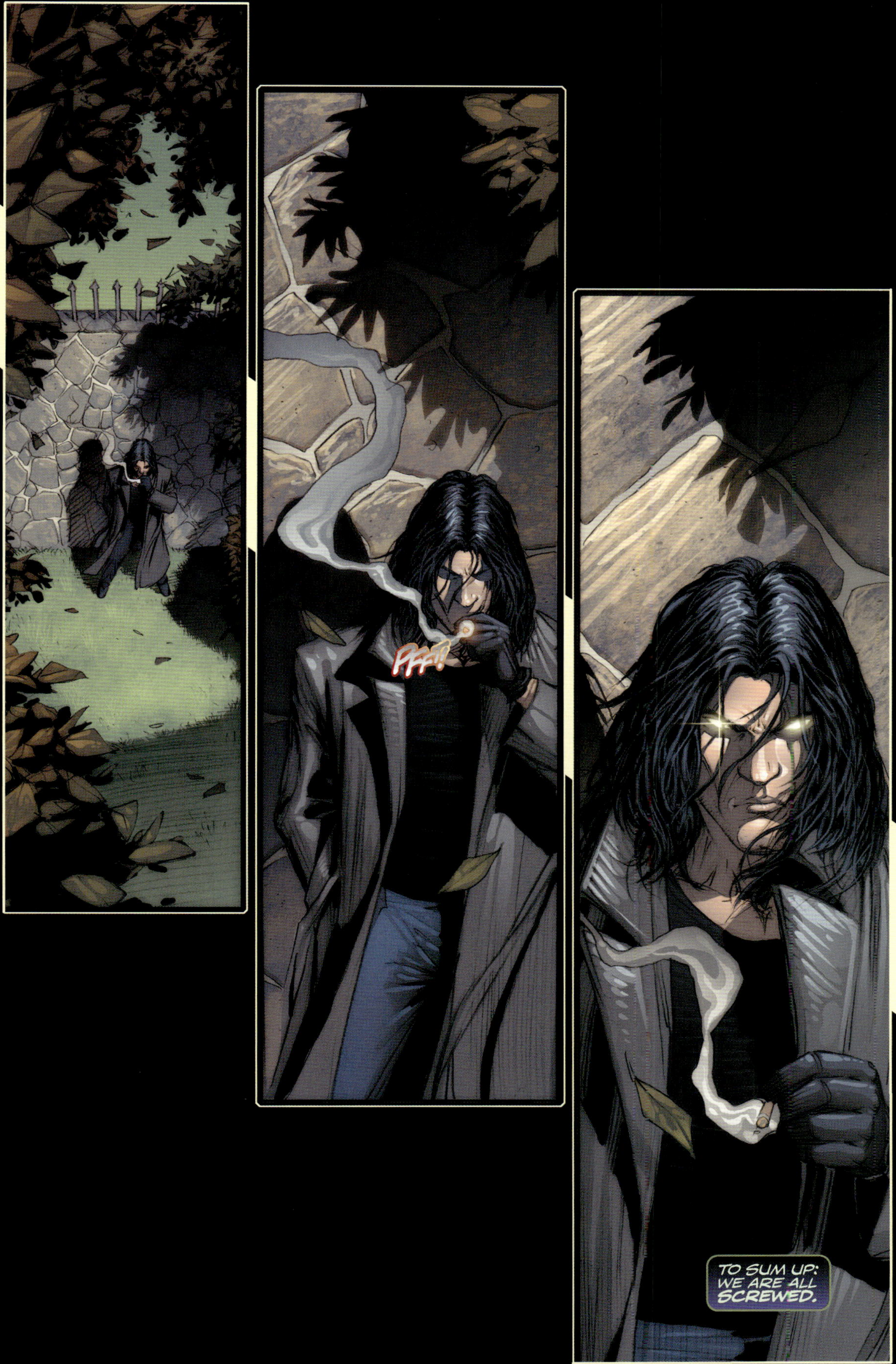
PFFT!
TO SUM UP: WE ARE ALL SCREWED.

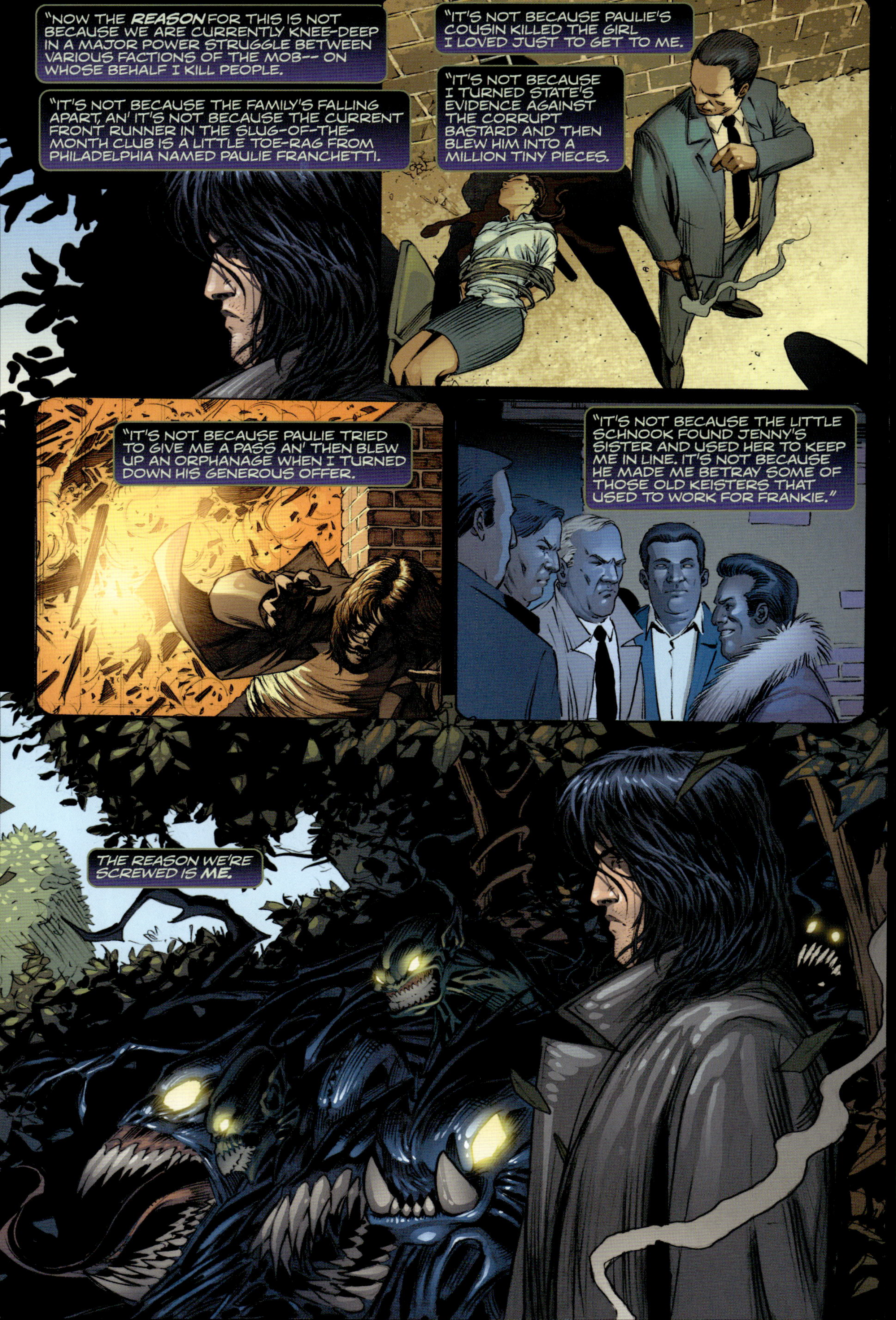
"NOW THE *REASON* FOR THIS IS NOT BECAUSE WE ARE CURRENTLY KNEE-DEEP IN A MAJOR POWER STRUGGLE BETWEEN VARIOUS FACTIONS OF THE MOB-- ON WHOSE BEHALF I KILL PEOPLE.
"IT'S NOT BECAUSE THE FAMILY'S FALLING APART, AN' IT'S NOT BECAUSE THE CURRENT FRONT RUNNER IN THE SLUG-OF-THE-MONTH CLUB IS A LITTLE TOE-RAG FROM PHILADELPHIA NAMED PAULIE FRANCHETTI.
"IT'S NOT BECAUSE PAULIE'S COUSIN KILLED THE GIRL I LOVED JUST TO GET TO ME.
"IT'S NOT BECAUSE I TURNED STATE'S EVIDENCE AGAINST THE CORRUPT BASTARD AND THEN BLEW HIM INTO A MILLION TINY PIECES.
"IT'S NOT BECAUSE PAULIE TRIED TO GIVE ME A PASS AN' THEN BLEW UP AN ORPHANAGE WHEN I TURNED DOWN HIS GENEROUS OFFER.
"IT'S NOT BECAUSE THE LITTLE SCHNOOK FOUND JENNY'S SISTER AND USED HER TO KEEP ME IN LINE. IT'S NOT BECAUSE HE MADE ME BETRAY SOME OF THOSE OLD KEISTERS THAT USED TO WORK FOR FRANKIE."
*THE REASON WE'RE SCREWED IS **ME**.*

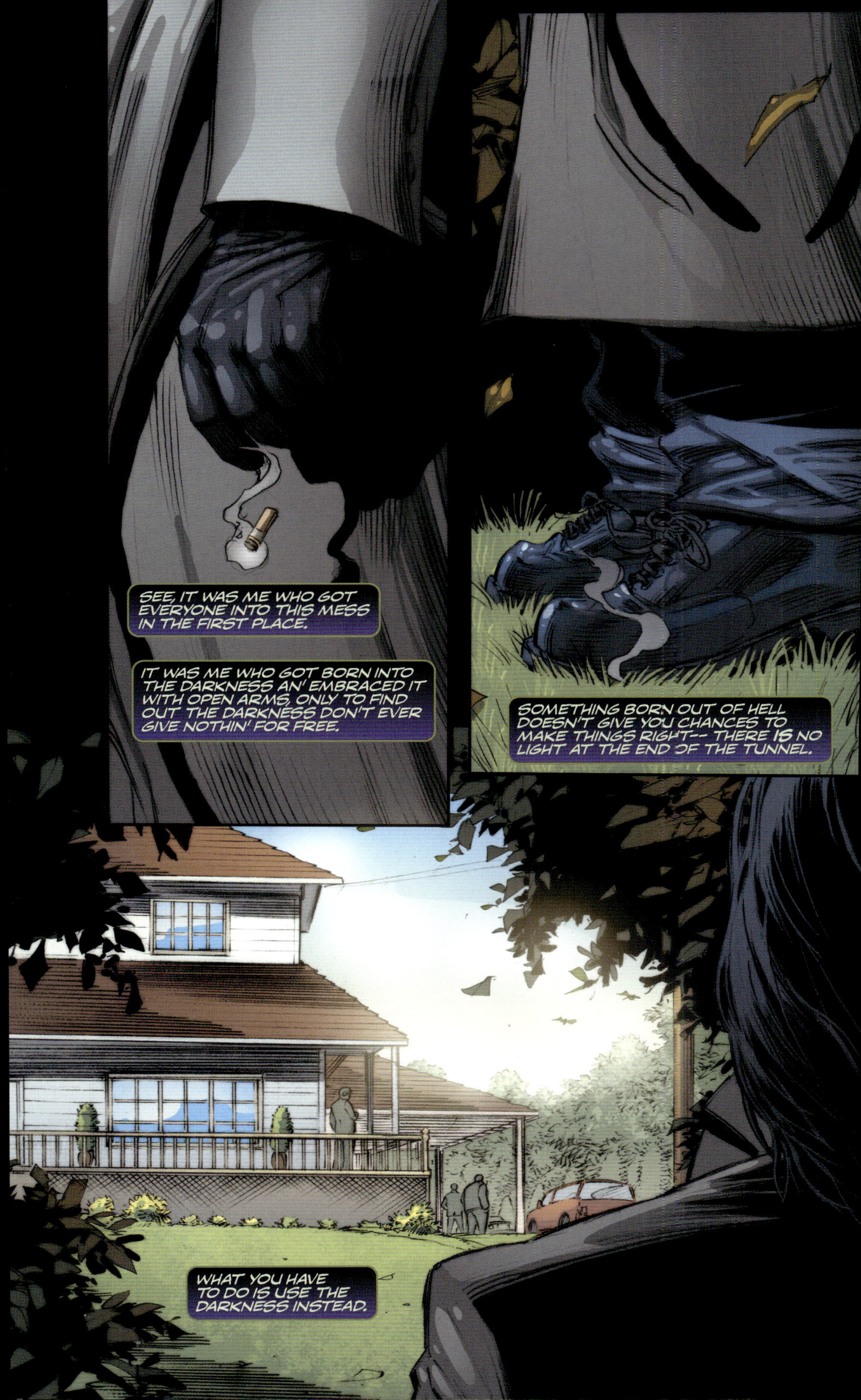
SEE, IT WAS ME WHO GOT EVERYONE INTO THIS MESS IN THE FIRST PLACE.
IT WAS ME WHO GOT BORN INTO THE DARKNESS AN' EMBRACED IT WITH OPEN ARMS, ONLY TO FIND OUT THE DARKNESS DON'T EVER GIVE NOTHIN' FOR FREE.
SOMETHING BORN OUT OF HELL DOESN'T GIVE YOU CHANCES TO MAKE THINGS RIGHT-- THERE IS NO LIGHT AT THE END OF THE TUNNEL.
WHAT YOU HAVE TO DO IS USE THE DARKNESS INSTEAD.

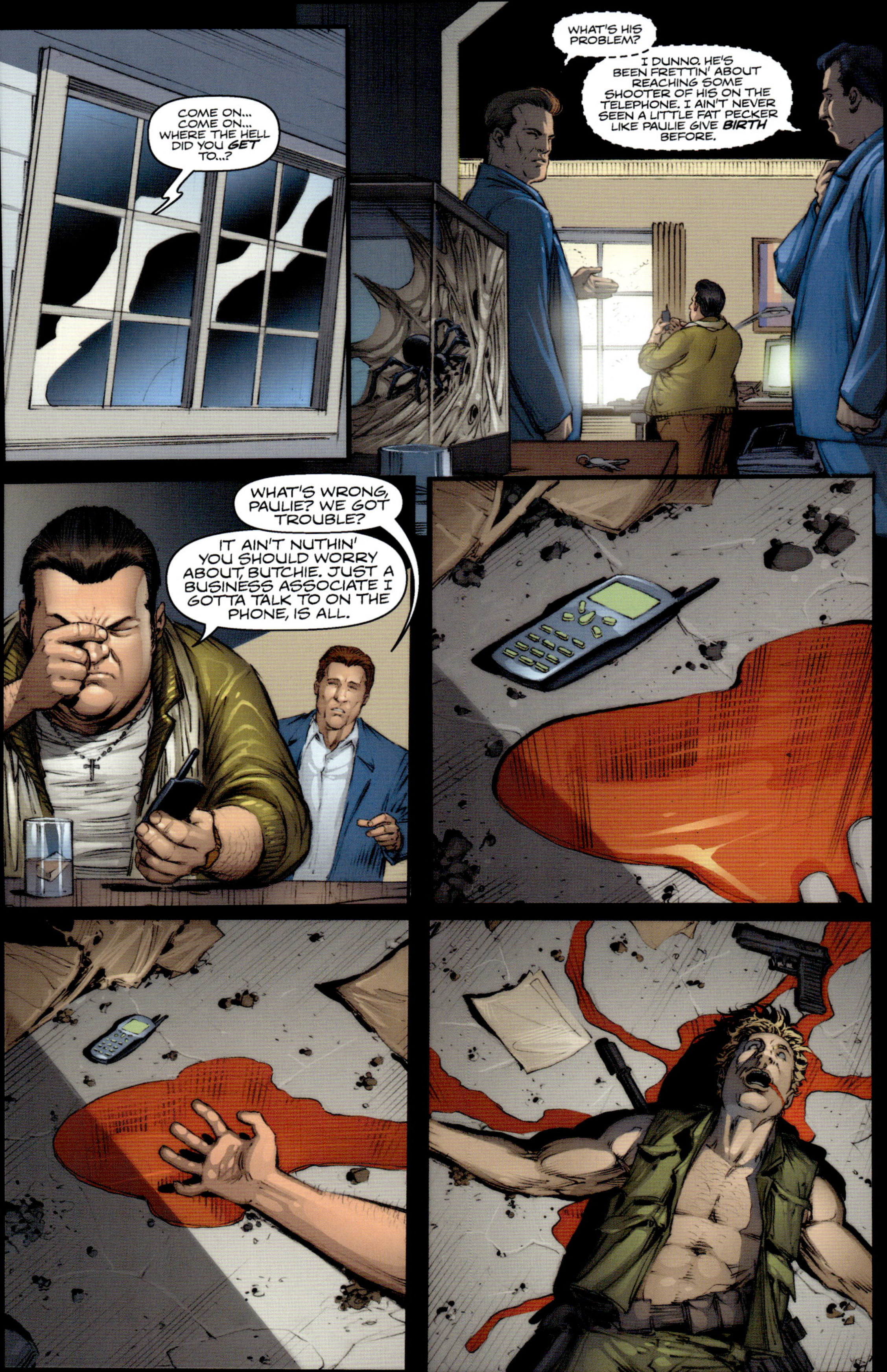
COME ON... COME ON... WHERE THE HELL DID YOU *GET* TO...?
WHAT'S HIS PROBLEM?
I DUNNO. HE'S BEEN FRETTIN' ABOUT REACHING SOME SHOOTER OF HIS ON THE TELEPHONE. I AIN'T NEVER SEEN A LITTLE FAT PECKER LIKE PAULIE GIVE *BIRTH* BEFORE.
WHAT'S WRONG, PAULIE? WE GOT TROUBLE?
IT AIN'T NUTHIN' YOU SHOULD WORRY ABOUT, BUTCHIE. JUST A BUSINESS ASSOCIATE I GOTTA TALK TO ON THE PHONE, IS ALL.

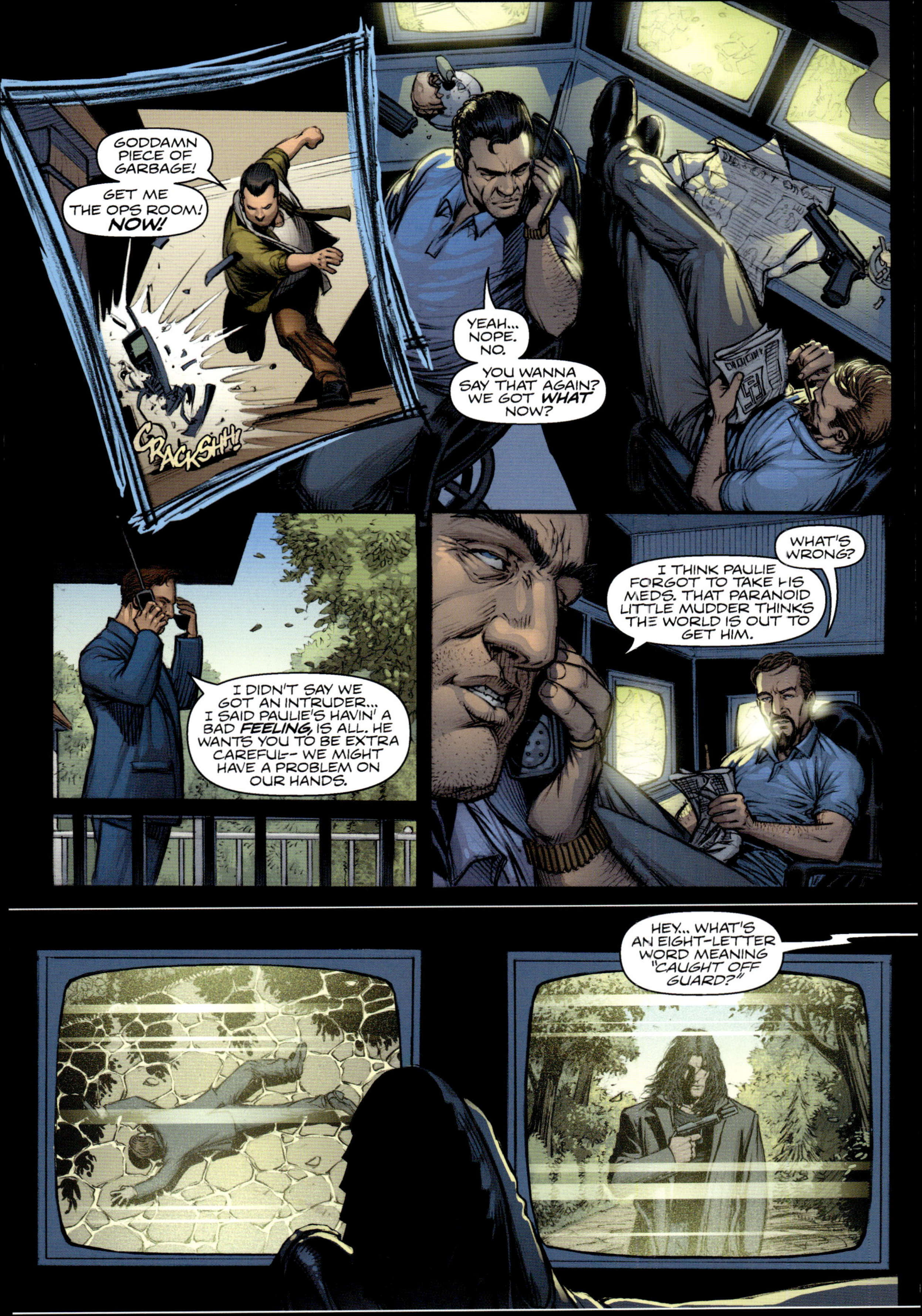
GODDAMN PIECE OF GARBAGE!
GET ME THE OPS ROOM! NOW!
CRACKSHH!
YEAH... NOPE. NO.
YOU WANNA SAY THAT AGAIN? WE GOT WHAT NOW?
I DIDN'T SAY WE GOT AN INTRUDER... I SAID PAULIE'S HAVIN' A BAD FEELING, IS ALL. HE WANTS YOU TO BE EXTRA CAREFUL-- WE MIGHT HAVE A PROBLEM ON OUR HANDS.
WHAT'S WRONG?
I THINK PAULIE FORGOT TO TAKE HIS MEDS. THAT PARANOID LITTLE MUDDER THINKS THE WORLD IS OUT TO GET HIM.
HEY... WHAT'S AN EIGHT-LETTER WORD MEANING "CAUGHT OFF GUARD?"

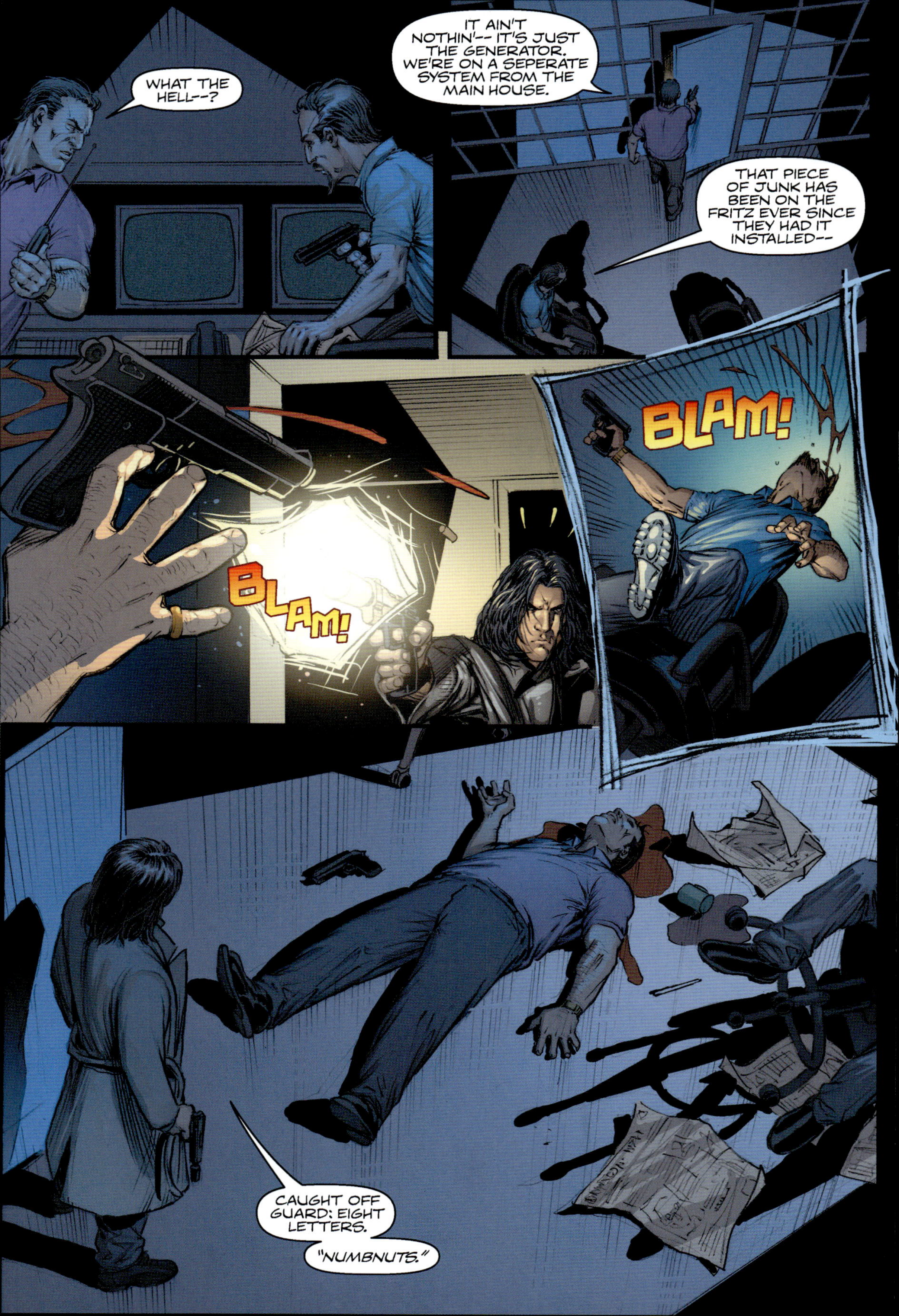
WHAT THE HELL--?
IT AIN'T NOTHIN'-- IT'S JUST THE GENERATOR. WE'RE ON A SEPERATE SYSTEM FROM THE MAIN HOUSE.
THAT PIECE OF JUNK HAS BEEN ON THE FRITZ EVER SINCE THEY HAD IT INSTALLED--
BLAM!
BLAM!
CAUGHT OFF GUARD: EIGHT LETTERS.
"NUMBNUTS."

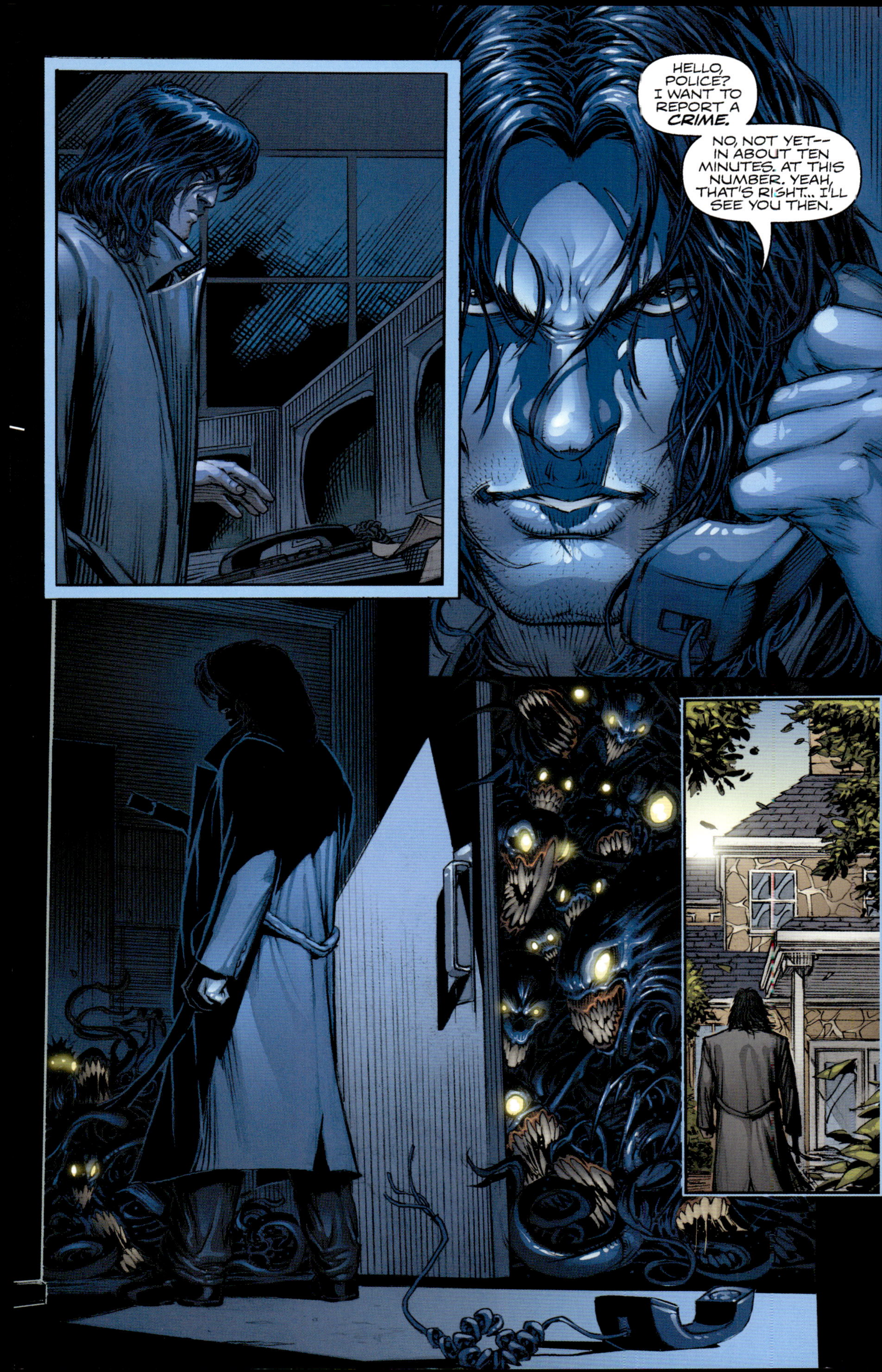
HELLO, POLICE? I WANT TO REPORT A CRIME.
NO, NOT YET-- IN ABOUT TEN MINUTES. AT THIS NUMBER. YEAH, THAT'S RIGHT... I'LL SEE YOU THEN.

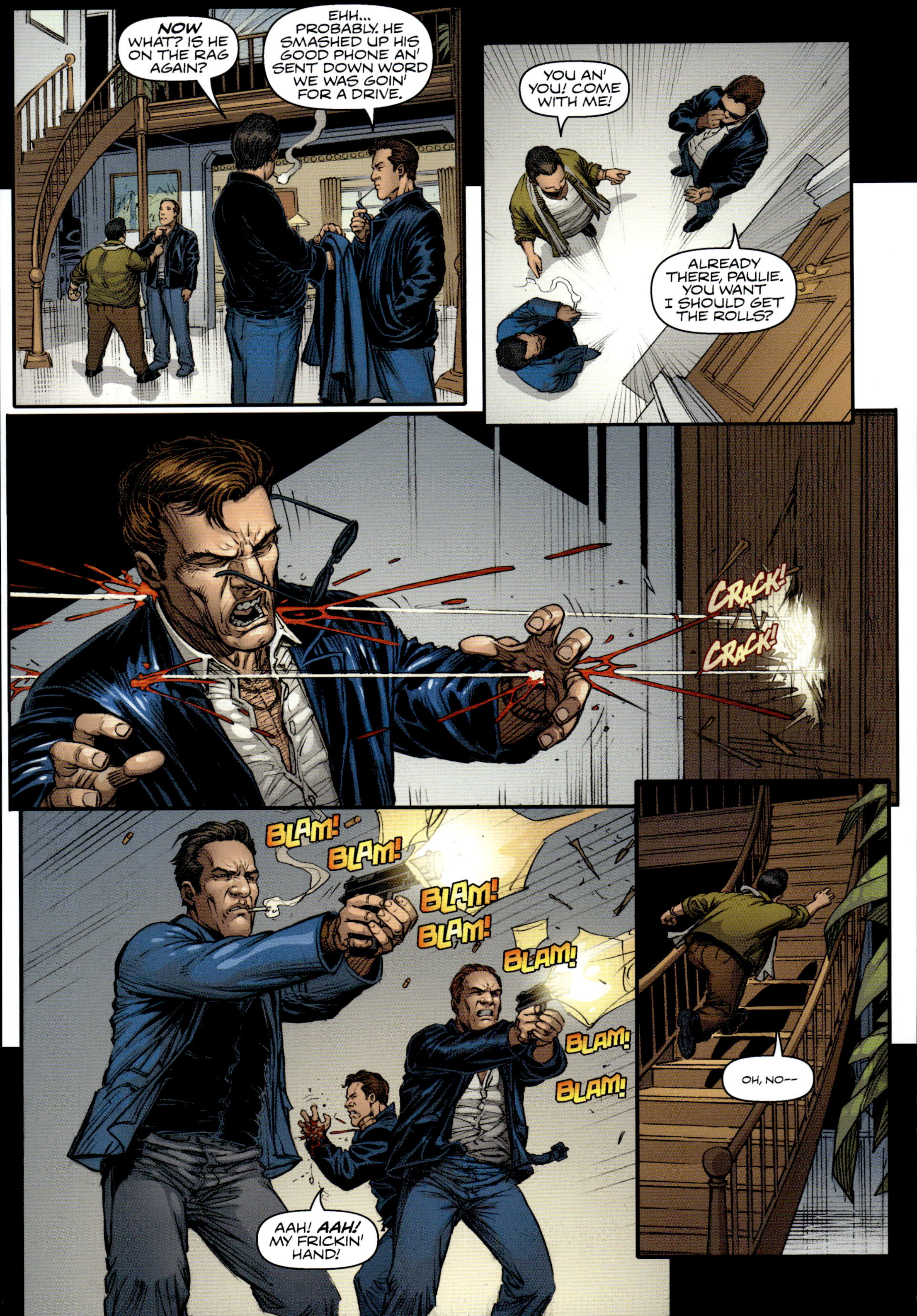
NOW WHAT? IS HE ON THE RAG AGAIN?
EHH... PROBABLY. HE SMASHED UP HIS GOOD PHONE AN' SENT DOWN WORD WE WAS GOIN' FOR A DRIVE.
YOU AN' YOU! COME WITH ME!
ALREADY THERE, PAULIE. YOU WANT I SHOULD GET THE ROLLS?
CRACK!
CRACK!
BLAM!
BLAM!
BLAM!
BLAM!
BLAM!
BLAM!
BLAM!
AAH! AAH! MY FRICKIN' HAND!
OH, NO--

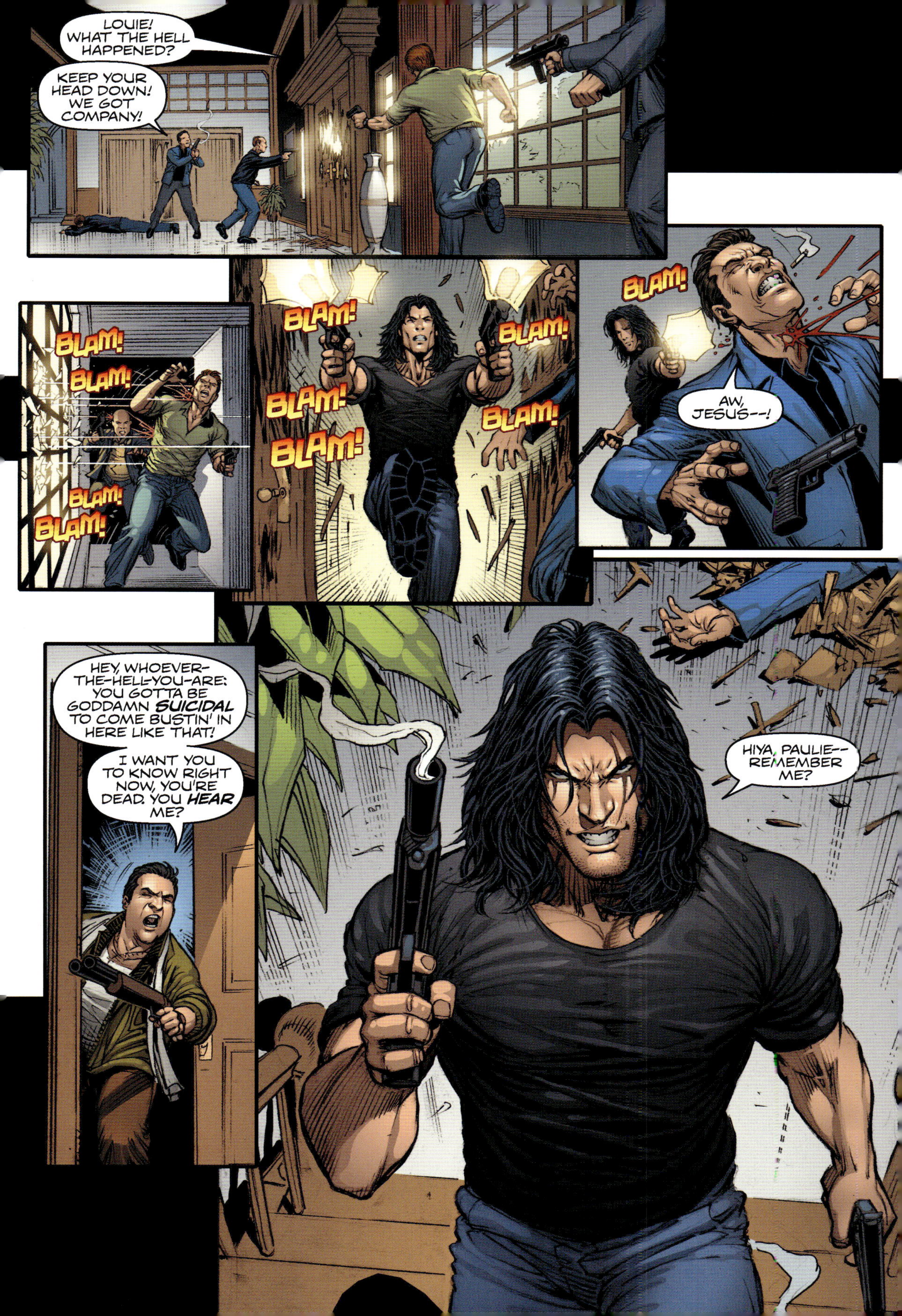
LOUIE! WHAT THE HELL HAPPENED?
KEEP YOUR HEAD DOWN! WE GOT COMPANY!
BLAM!
BLAM!
BLAM! BLAM!
BLAM!
BLAM!
BLAM!
BLAM!
BLAM!
BLAM!
BLAM!
AW, JESUS--!
HEY, WHOEVER-THE-HELL-YOU-ARE: YOU GOTTA BE GODDAMN SUICIDAL TO COME BUSTIN' IN HERE LIKE THAT!
I WANT YOU TO KNOW RIGHT NOW, YOU'RE DEAD. YOU HEAR ME?
HIYA, PAULIE-- REMEMBER ME?

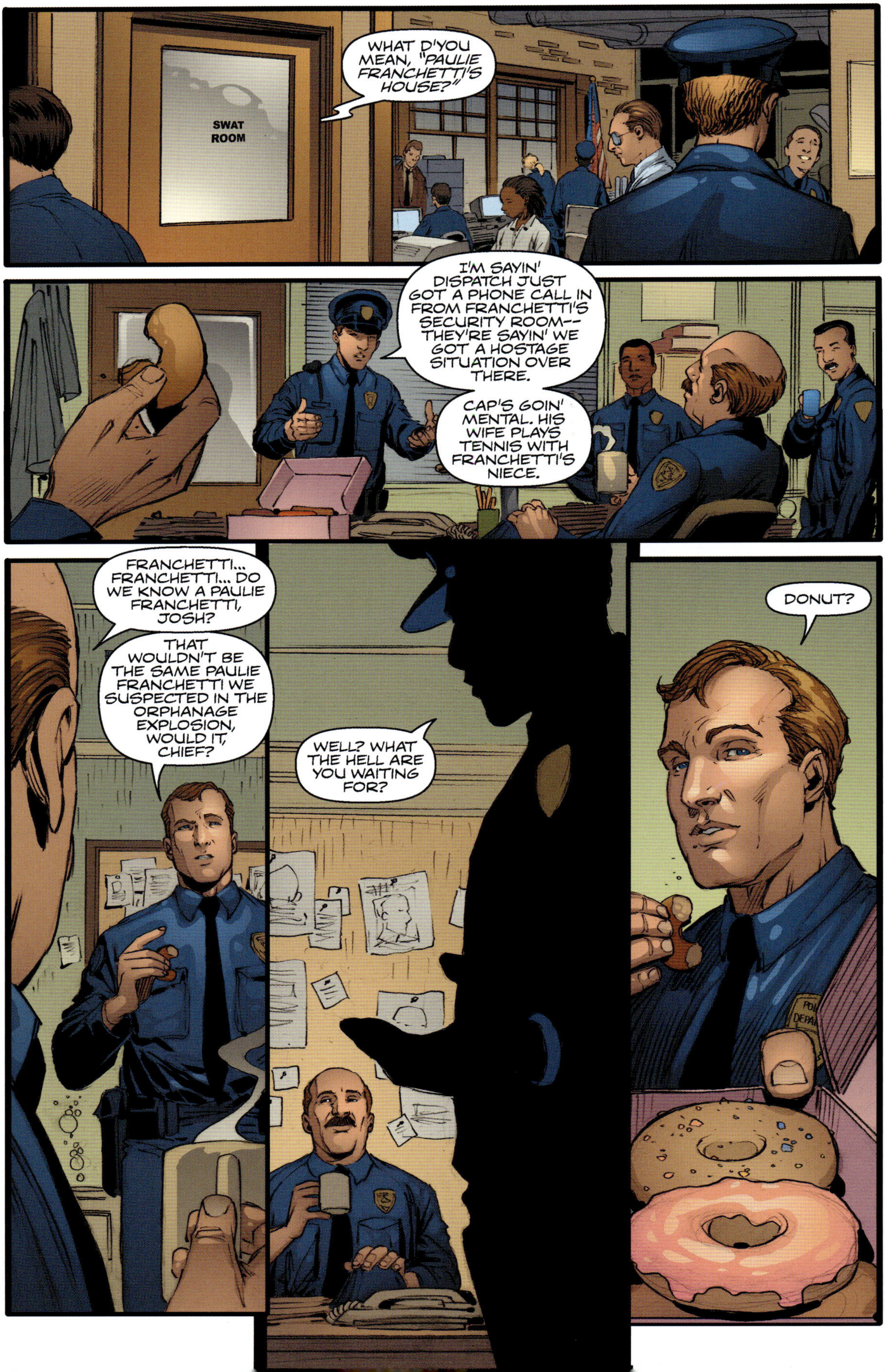
SWAT ROOM
WHAT D'YOU MEAN, "PAULIE FRANCHETTI'S HOUSE?"
I'M SAYIN' DISPATCH JUST GOT A PHONE CALL IN FROM FRANCHETTI'S SECURITY ROOM-- THEY'RE SAYIN' WE GOT A HOSTAGE SITUATION OVER THERE.
CAP'S GOIN' MENTAL. HIS WIFE PLAYS TENNIS WITH FRANCHETTI'S NIECE.
FRANCHETTI... FRANCHETTI... DO WE KNOW A PAULIE FRANCHETTI, JOSH?
THAT WOULDN'T BE THE SAME PAULIE FRANCHETTI WE SUSPECTED IN THE ORPHANAGE EXPLOSION, WOULD IT, CHIEF?
WELL? WHAT THE HELL ARE YOU WAITING FOR?
DONUT?

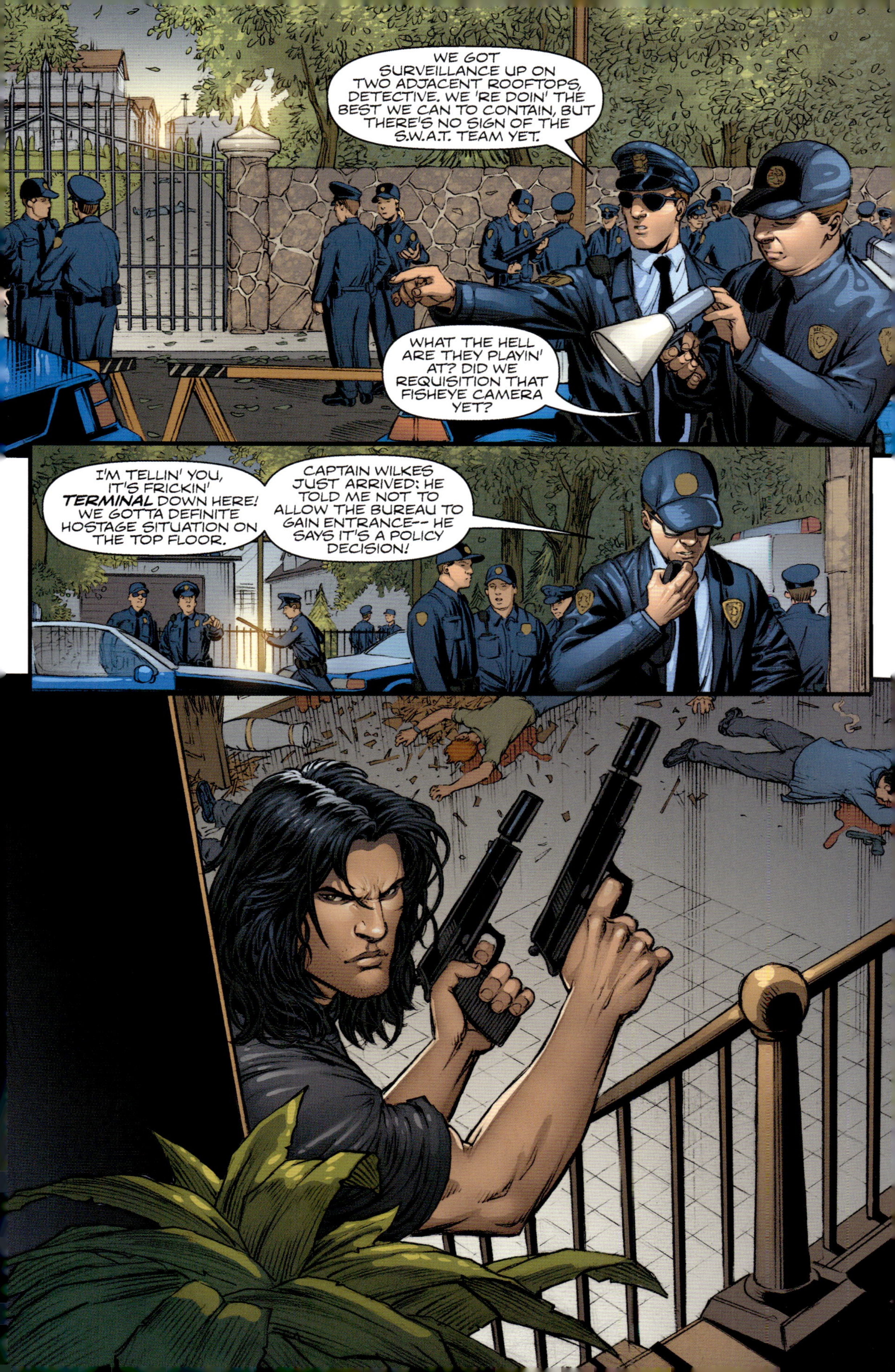
WE GOT SURVEILLANCE UP ON TWO ADJACENT ROOFTOPS, DETECTIVE. WE 'RE DOIN' THE BEST WE CAN TO CONTAIN, BUT THERE'S NO SIGN OF THE S.W.A.T. TEAM YET.
WHAT THE HELL ARE THEY PLAYIN' AT? DID WE REQUISITION THAT FISHEYE CAMERA YET?
I'M TELLIN' YOU, IT'S FRICKIN' **TERMINAL** DOWN HERE! WE GOTTA DEFINITE HOSTAGE SITUATION ON THE TOP FLOOR.
CAPTAIN WILKES JUST ARRIVED: HE TOLD ME NOT TO ALLOW THE BUREAU TO GAIN ENTRANCE-- HE SAYS IT'S A POLICY DECISION!

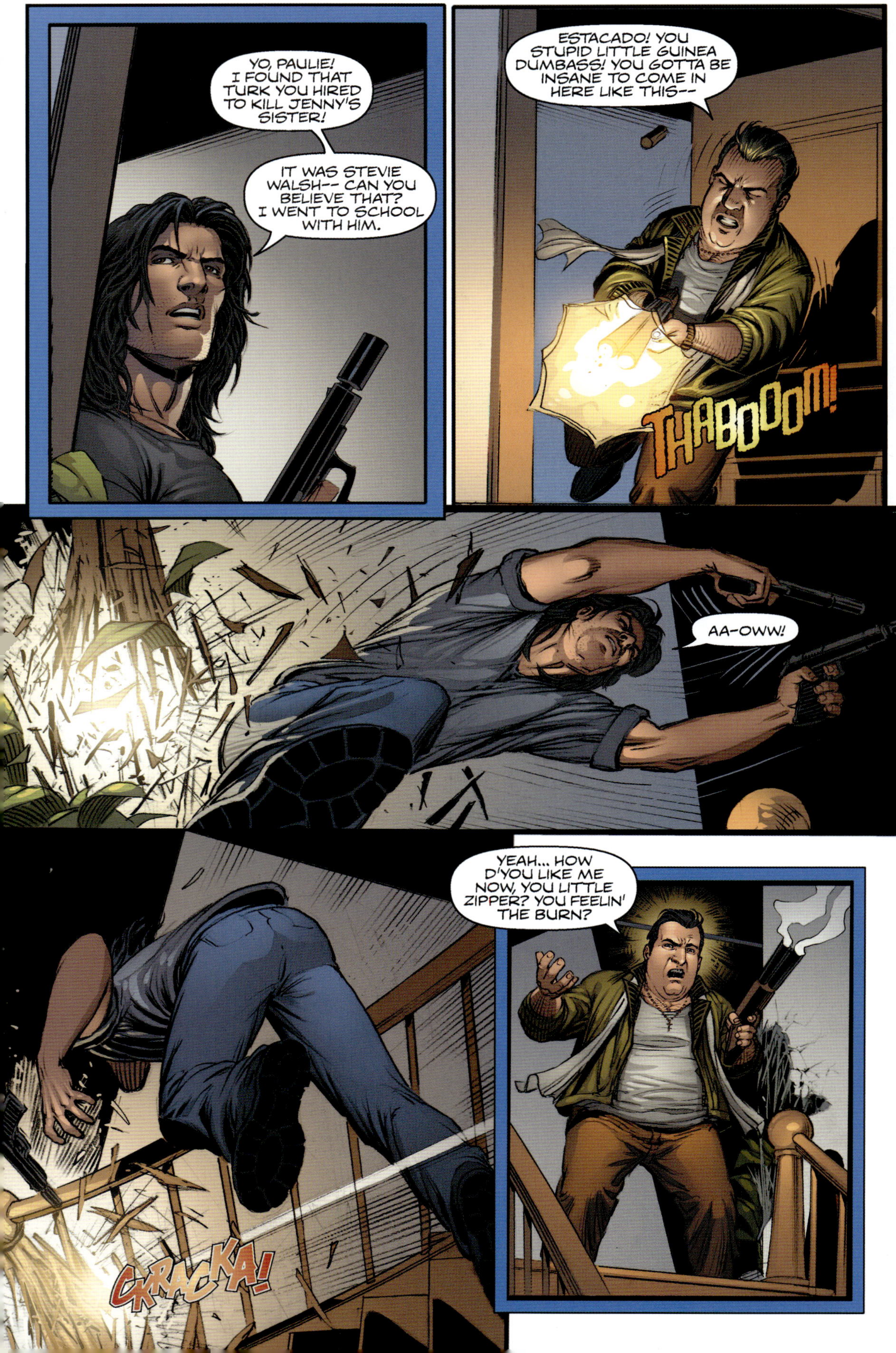
YO, PAULIE! I FOUND THAT TURK YOU HIRED TO KILL JENNY'S SISTER!
IT WAS STEVIE WALSH-- CAN YOU BELIEVE THAT? I WENT TO SCHOOL WITH HIM.
ESTACADO! YOU STUPID LITTLE GUINEA DUMBASS! YOU GOTTA BE INSANE TO COME IN HERE LIKE THIS--
THABOOOM!
AA-OWW!
CKRACKA!
YEAH... HOW D'YOU LIKE ME NOW, YOU LITTLE ZIPPER? YOU FEELIN' THE BURN?

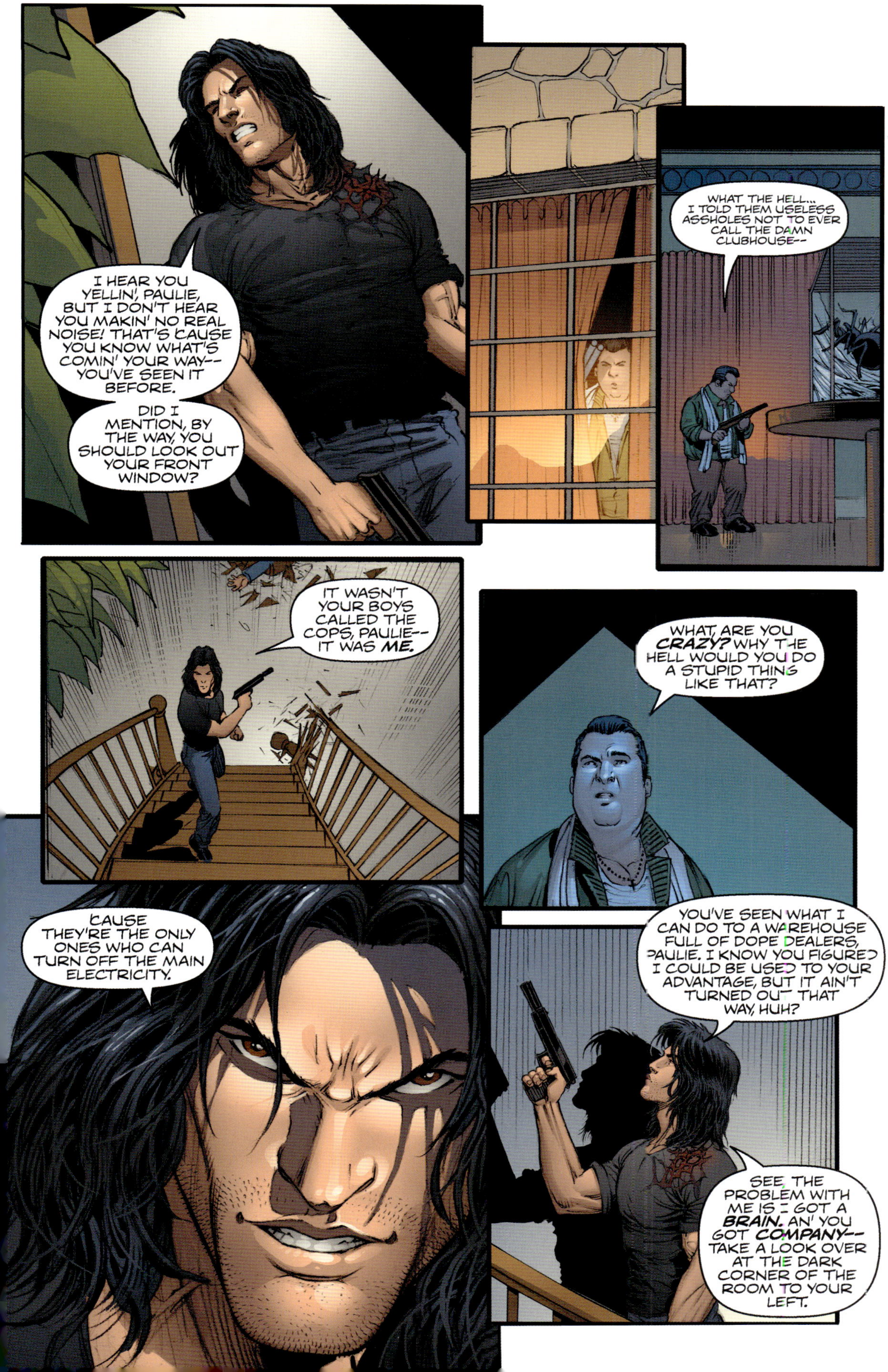

I HEAR YOU YELLIN', PAULIE, BUT I DON'T HEAR YOU MAKIN' NO REAL NOISE! THAT'S CAUSE YOU KNOW WHAT'S COMIN' YOUR WAY-- YOU'VE SEEN IT BEFORE.
DID I MENTION, BY THE WAY, YOU SHOULD LOOK OUT YOUR FRONT WINDOW?
WHAT THE HELL... I TOLD THEM USELESS ASSHOLES NOT TO EVER CALL THE DAMN CLUBHOUSE--
IT WASN'T YOUR BOYS CALLED THE COPS, PAULIE-- IT WAS ME.
WHAT, ARE YOU CRAZY? WHY THE HELL WOULD YOU DO A STUPID THING LIKE THAT?
CAUSE THEY'RE THE ONLY ONES WHO CAN TURN OFF THE MAIN ELECTRICITY.
YOU'VE SEEN WHAT I CAN DO TO A WAREHOUSE FULL OF DOPE DEALERS, PAULIE. I KNOW YOU FIGURED I COULD BE USED TO YOUR ADVANTAGE, BUT IT AIN'T TURNED OUT THAT WAY, HUH?
SEE, THE PROBLEM WITH ME IS I GOT A BRAIN. AN' YOU GOT COMPANY-- TAKE A LOOK OVER AT THE DARK CORNER OF THE ROOM TO YOUR LEFT.

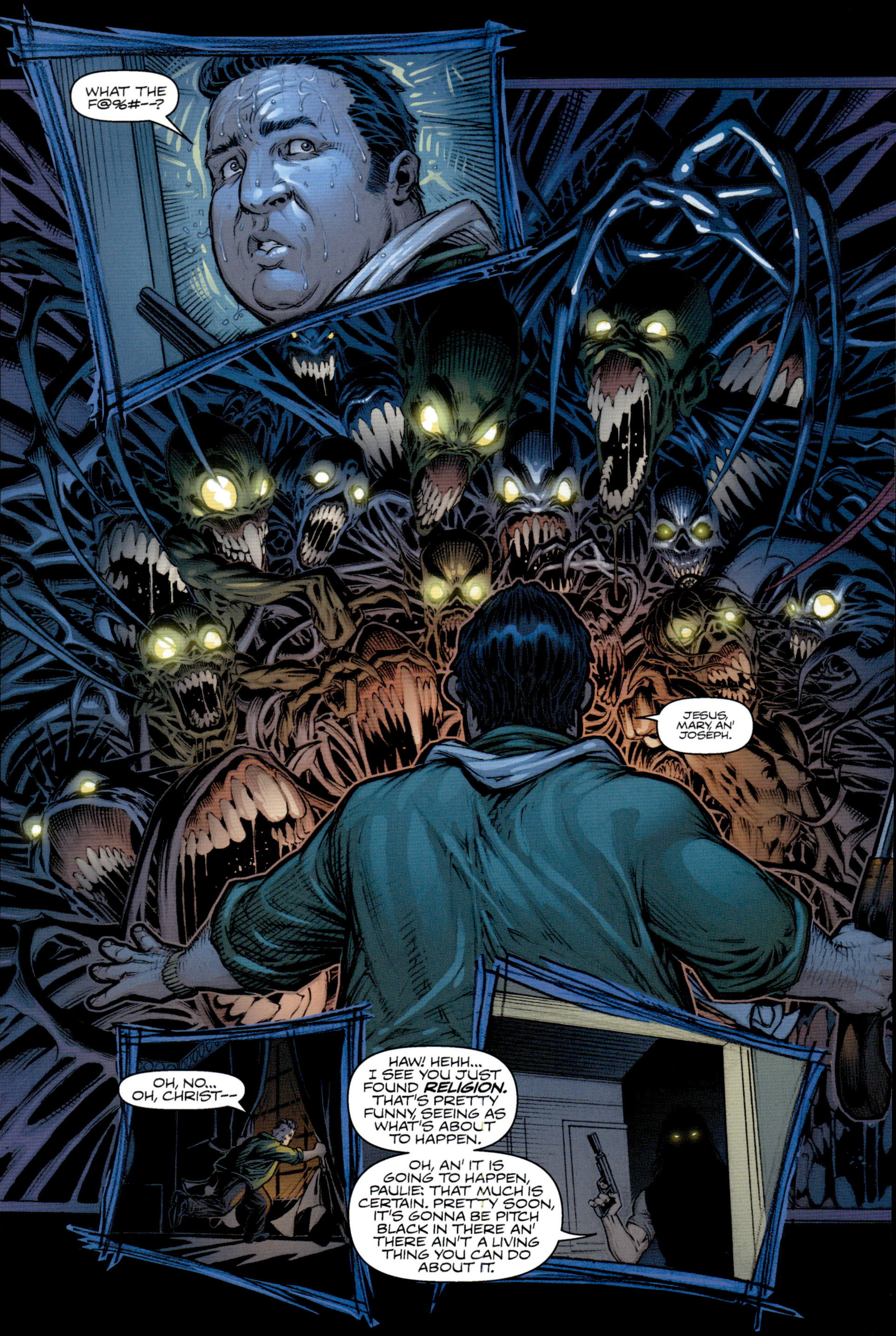
WHAT THE F@%#--?
JESUS, MARY, AN' JOSEPH.
OH, NO... OH, CHRIST--
HAW! HEHH... I SEE YOU JUST FOUND RELIGION. THAT'S PRETTY FUNNY, SEEING AS WHAT'S ABOUT TO HAPPEN.
OH, AN' IT IS GOING TO HAPPEN, PAULIE: THAT MUCH IS CERTAIN. PRETTY SOON, IT'S GONNA BE PITCH BLACK IN THERE AN' THERE AIN'T A LIVING THING YOU CAN DO ABOUT IT.

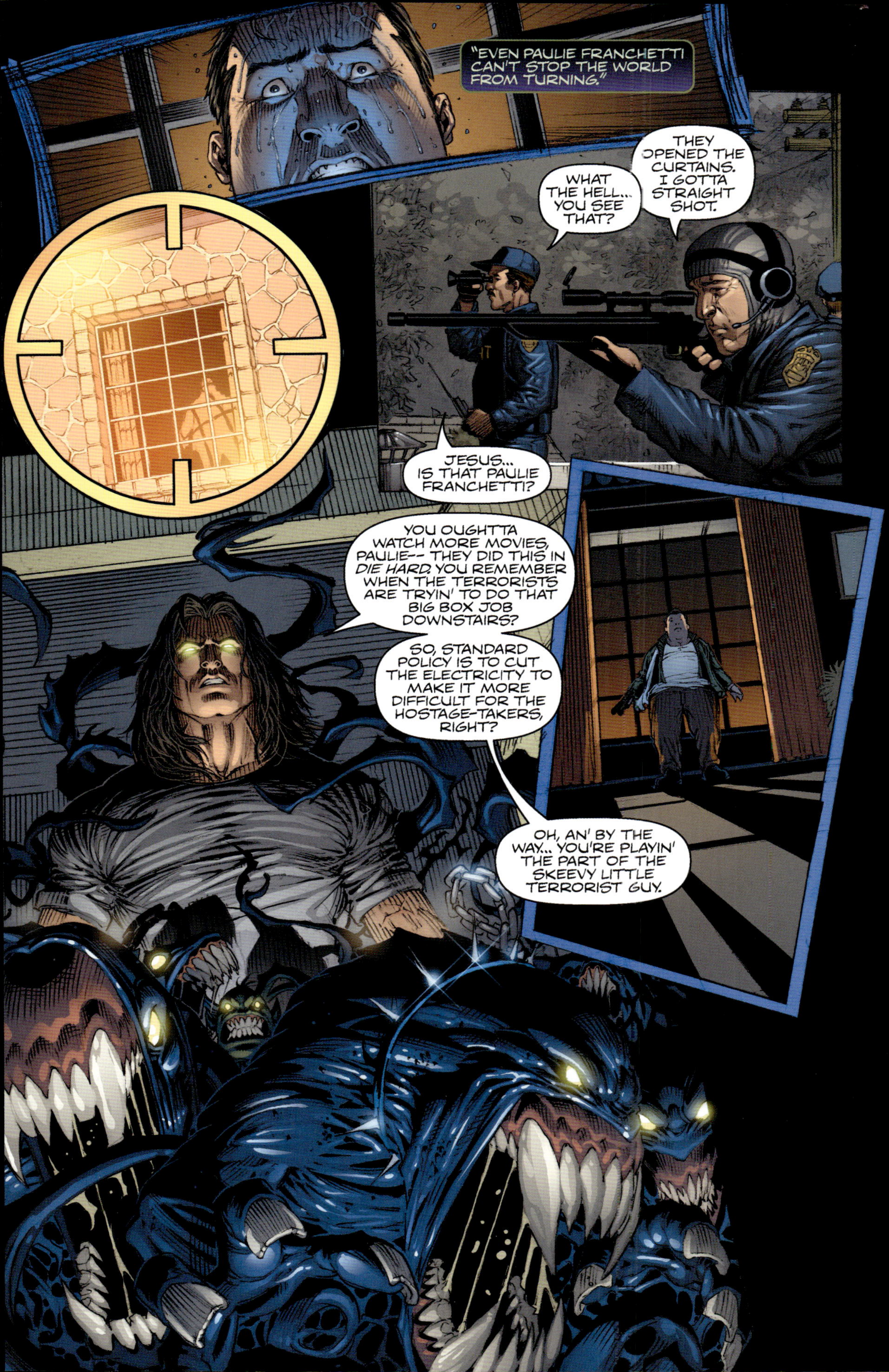
"EVEN PAULIE FRANCHETTI CAN'T STOP THE WORLD FROM TURNING."
WHAT THE HELL... YOU SEE THAT?
THEY OPENED THE CURTAINS. I GOTTA STRAIGHT SHOT.
JESUS... IS THAT PAULIE FRANCHETTI?
YOU OUGHTTA WATCH MORE MOVIES, PAULIE-- THEY DID THIS IN DIE HARD. YOU REMEMBER WHEN THE TERRORISTS ARE TRYIN' TO DO THAT BIG BOX JOB DOWNSTAIRS?
SO, STANDARD POLICY IS TO CUT THE ELECTRICITY TO MAKE IT MORE DIFFICULT FOR THE HOSTAGE-TAKERS, RIGHT?
OH, AN' BY THE WAY... YOU'RE PLAYIN' THE PART OF THE SKEEVY LITTLE TERRORIST GUY.

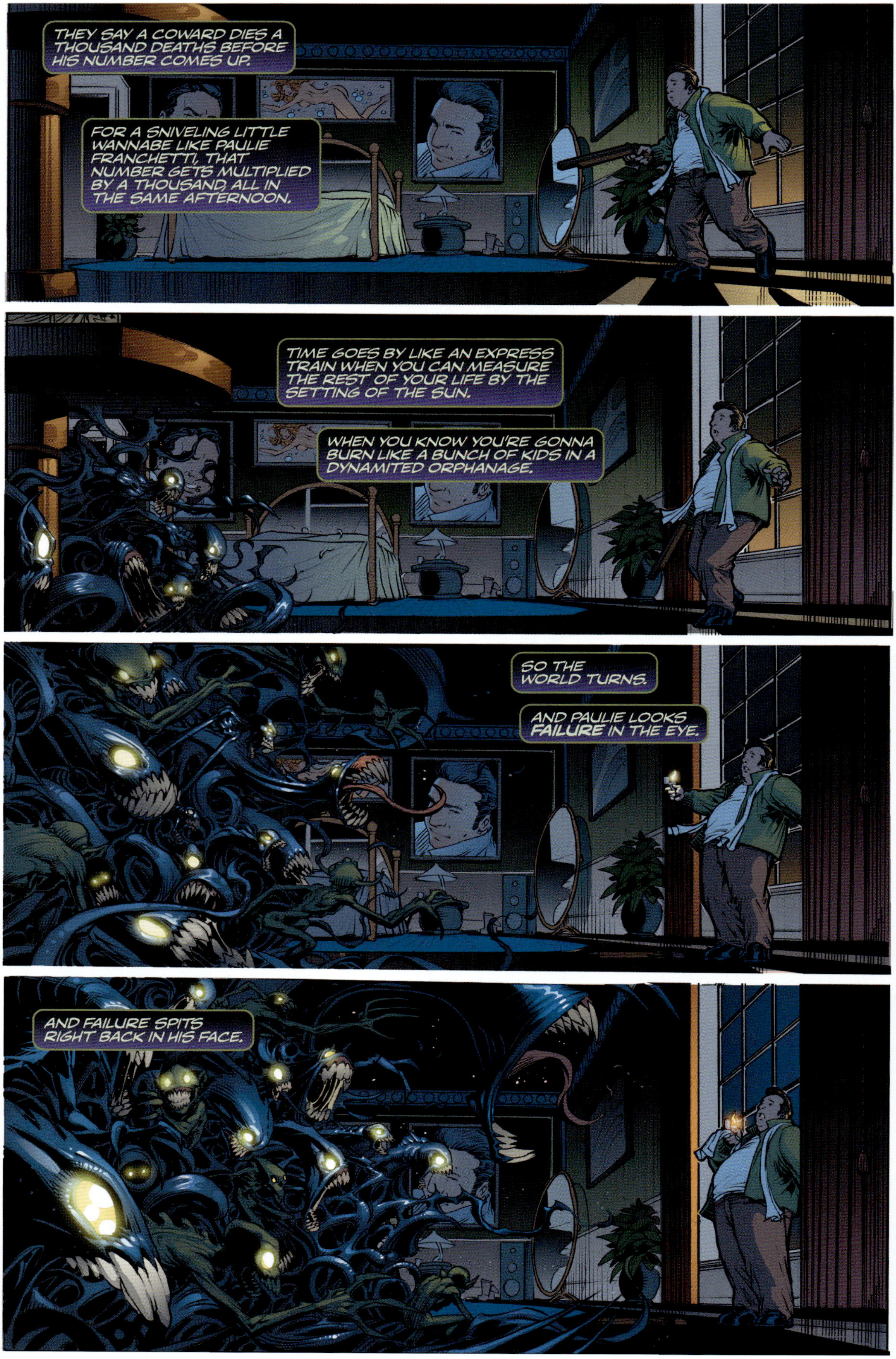
THEY SAY A COWARD DIES A THOUSAND DEATHS BEFORE HIS NUMBER COMES UP.
FOR A SNIVELING LITTLE WANNABE LIKE PAULIE FRANCHETTI, THAT NUMBER GETS MULTIPLIED BY A THOUSAND, ALL IN THE SAME AFTERNOON.
TIME GOES BY LIKE AN EXPRESS TRAIN WHEN YOU CAN MEASURE THE REST OF YOUR LIFE BY THE SETTING OF THE SUN.
WHEN YOU KNOW YOU'RE GONNA BURN LIKE A BUNCH OF KIDS IN A DYNAMITED ORPHANAGE.
SO THE WORLD TURNS.
AND PAULIE LOOKS FAILURE IN THE EYE.
AND FAILURE SPITS RIGHT BACK IN HIS FACE.

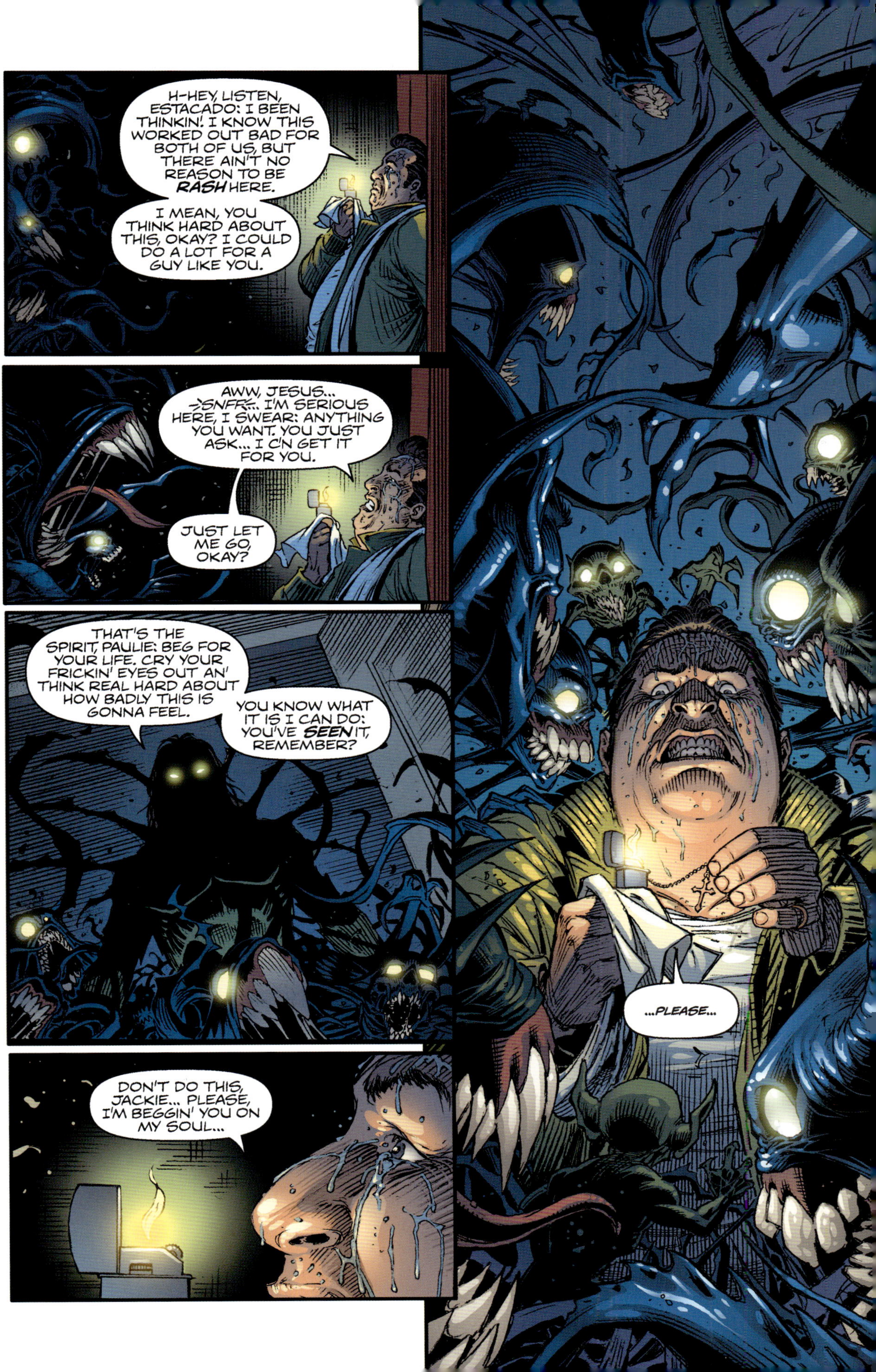
H-HEY, LISTEN, ESTACADO: I BEEN THINKIN'. I KNOW THIS WORKED OUT BAD FOR BOTH OF US, BUT THERE AIN'T NO REASON TO BE RASH HERE.
I MEAN, YOU THINK HARD ABOUT THIS, OKAY? I COULD DO A LOT FOR A GUY LIKE YOU.
AWW, JESUS... >SNFF<... I'M SERIOUS HERE, I SWEAR: ANYTHING YOU WANT. YOU JUST ASK... I C'N GET IT FOR YOU.
JUST LET ME GO, OKAY?
THAT'S THE SPIRIT, PAULIE: BEG FOR YOUR LIFE. CRY YOUR FRICKIN' EYES OUT AN' THINK REAL HARD ABOUT HOW BADLY THIS IS GONNA FEEL.
YOU KNOW WHAT IT IS I CAN DO: YOU'VE SEEN IT, REMEMBER?
DON'T DO THIS, JACKIE... PLEASE, I'M BEGGIN' YOU ON MY SOUL...
...PLEASE...

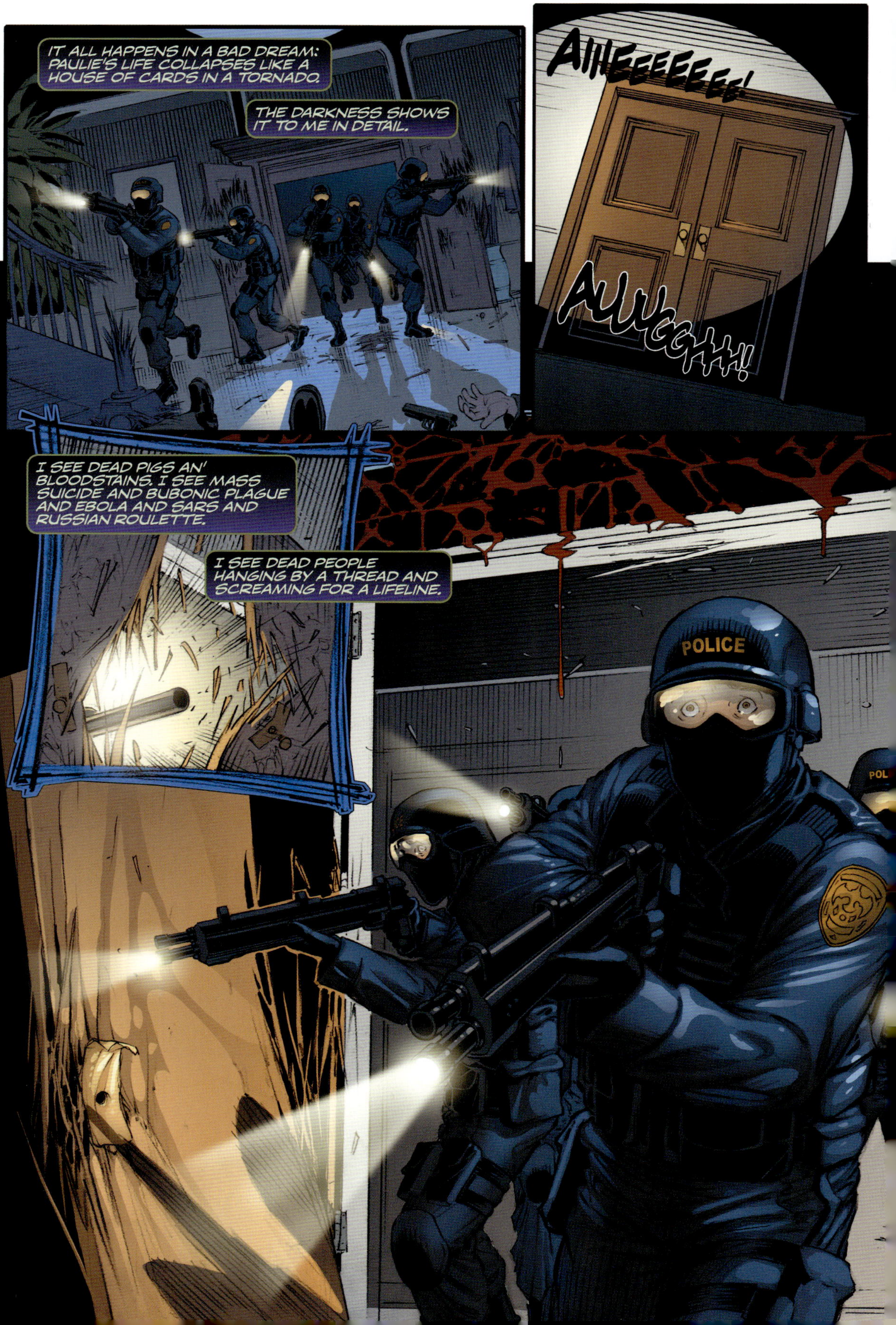
IT ALL HAPPENS IN A BAD DREAM: PAULIE'S LIFE COLLAPSES LIKE A HOUSE OF CARDS IN A TORNADO.
THE DARKNESS SHOWS IT TO ME IN DETAIL.
AIIEEEEEEEE!
AUUGGHHH!
I SEE DEAD PIGS AN' BLOODSTAINS. I SEE MASS SUICIDE AND BUBONIC PLAGUE AND EBOLA AND SARS AND RUSSIAN ROULETTE.
I SEE DEAD PEOPLE HANGING BY A THREAD AND SCREAMING FOR A LIFELINE.
POLICE

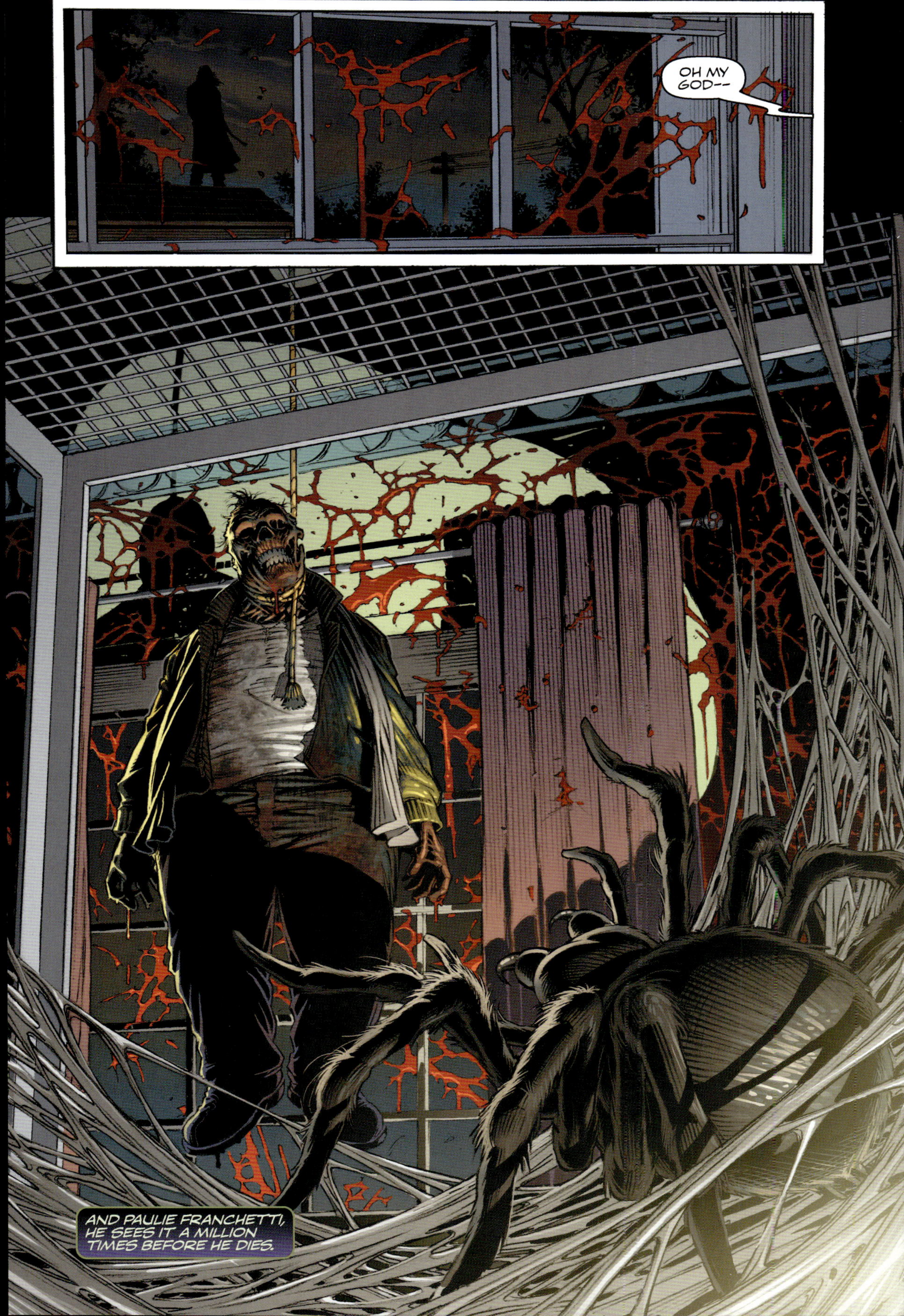
OH MY GOD--
AND PAULIE FRANCHETTI, HE SEES IT A MILLION TIMES BEFORE HE DIES.

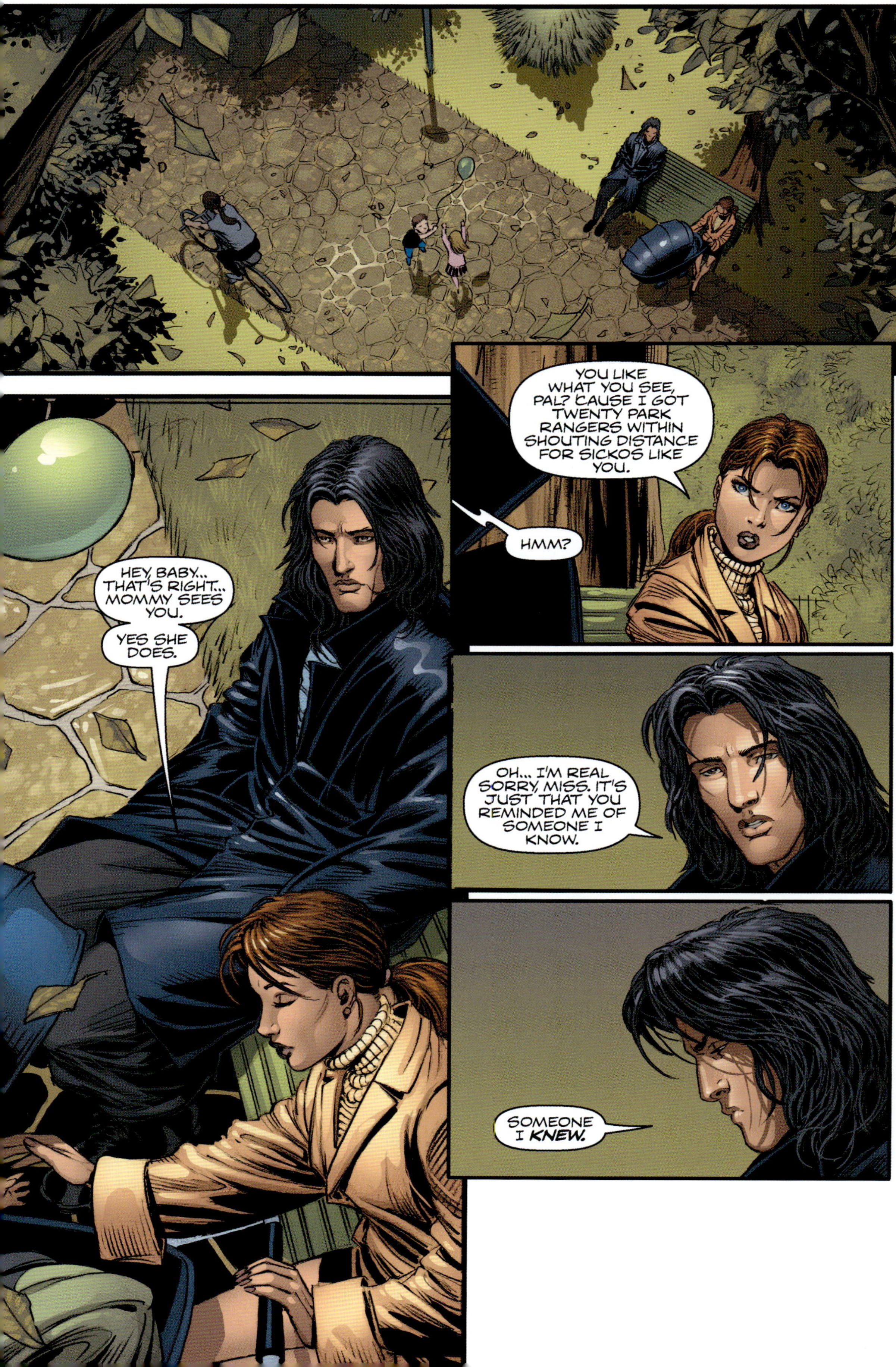
HEY, BABY... THAT'S RIGHT... MOMMY SEES YOU.
YES SHE DOES.
YOU LIKE WHAT YOU SEE, PAL? CAUSE I GOT TWENTY PARK RANGERS WITHIN SHOUTING DISTANCE FOR SICKOS LIKE YOU.
HMM?
OH... I'M REAL SORRY, MISS. IT'S JUST THAT YOU REMINDED ME OF SOMEONE I KNOW.
SOMEONE I *KNEW.*

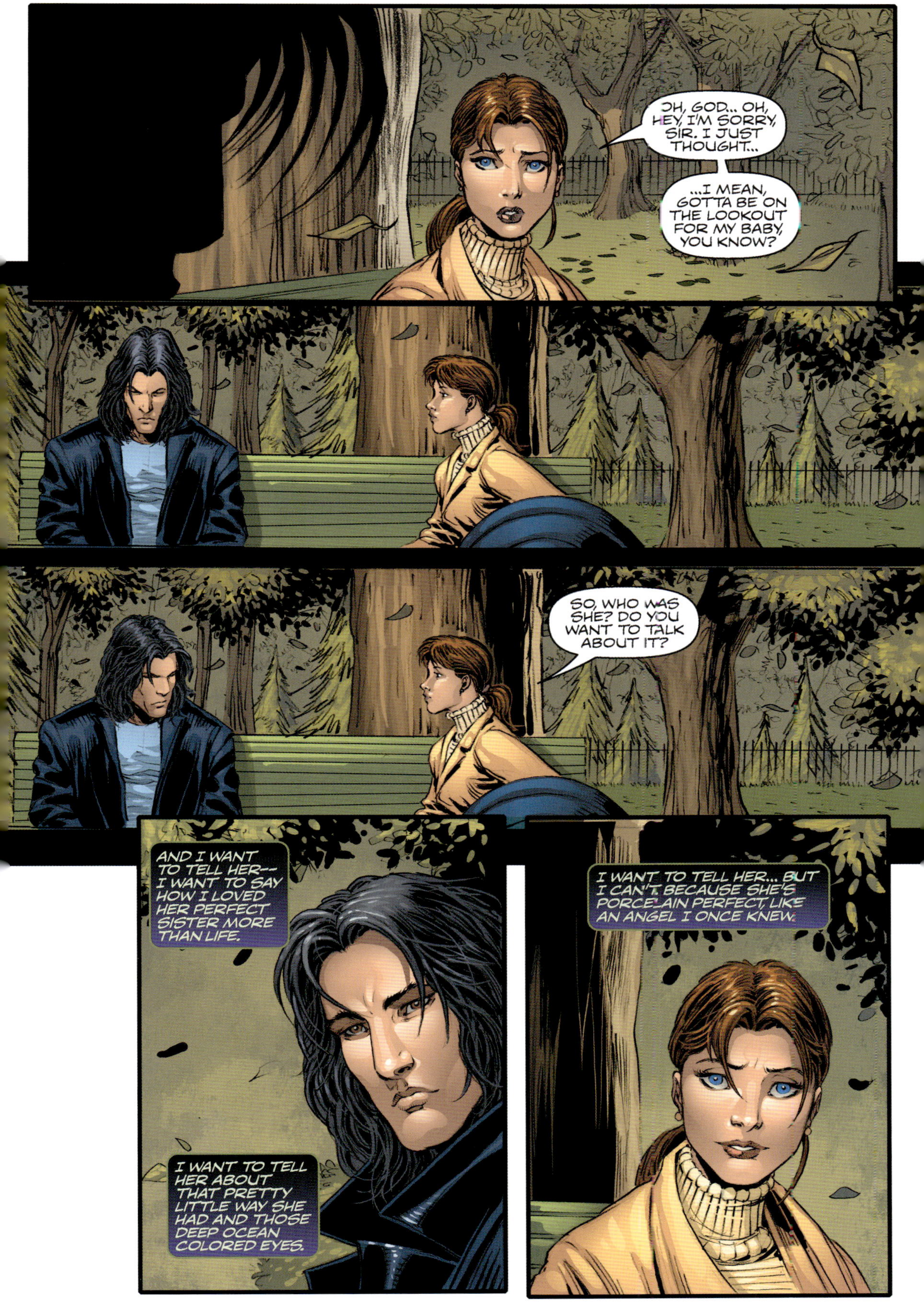
OH, GOD... OH, HEY, I'M SORRY, SIR. I JUST THOUGHT...
...I MEAN, GOTTA BE ON THE LOOKOUT FOR MY BABY, YOU KNOW?
SO, WHO WAS SHE? DO YOU WANT TO TALK ABOUT IT?
AND I WANT TO TELL HER-- I WANT TO SAY HOW I LOVED HER PERFECT SISTER MORE THAN LIFE.
I WANT TO TELL HER ABOUT THAT PRETTY LITTLE WAY SHE HAD AND THOSE DEEP OCEAN COLORED EYES.
I WANT TO TELL HER... BUT I CAN'T, BECAUSE SHE'S PORCELAIN PERFECT, LIKE AN ANGEL I ONCE KNEW.

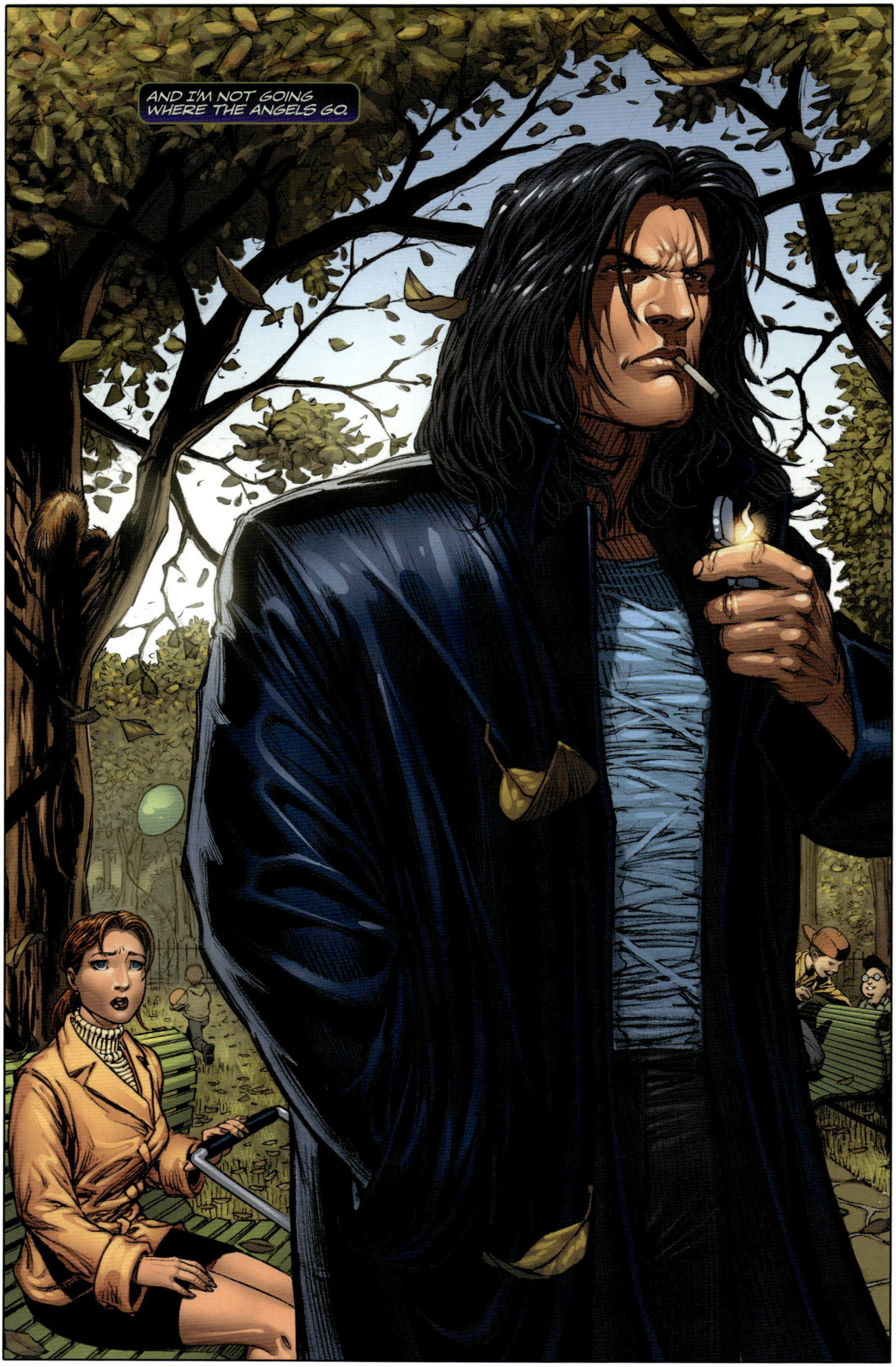
AND I'M NOT GOING WHERE THE ANGELS GO.

The Darkness Issue #47
cover art by: Dale Keown

THE DARKNESS #47

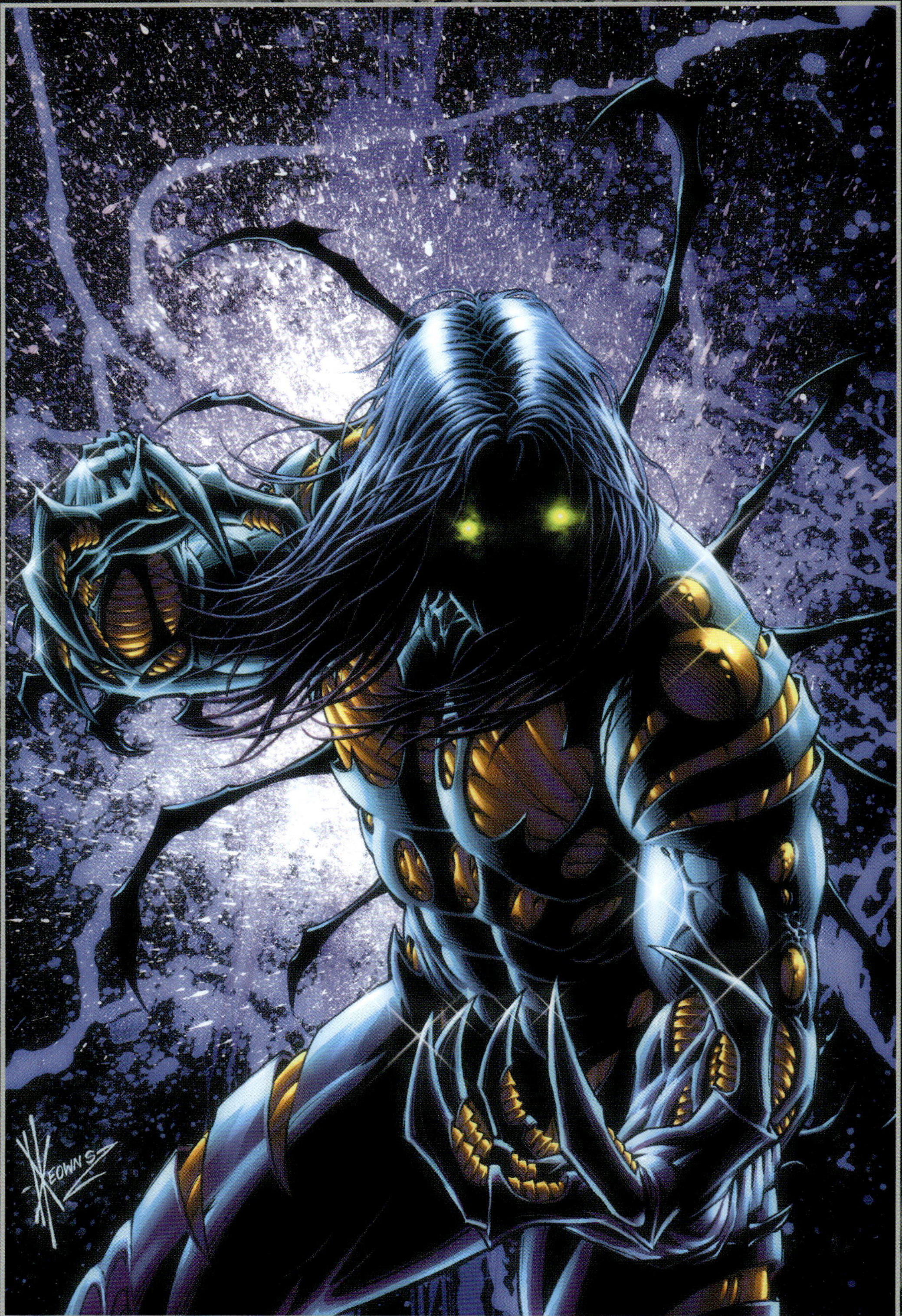
KEOWN

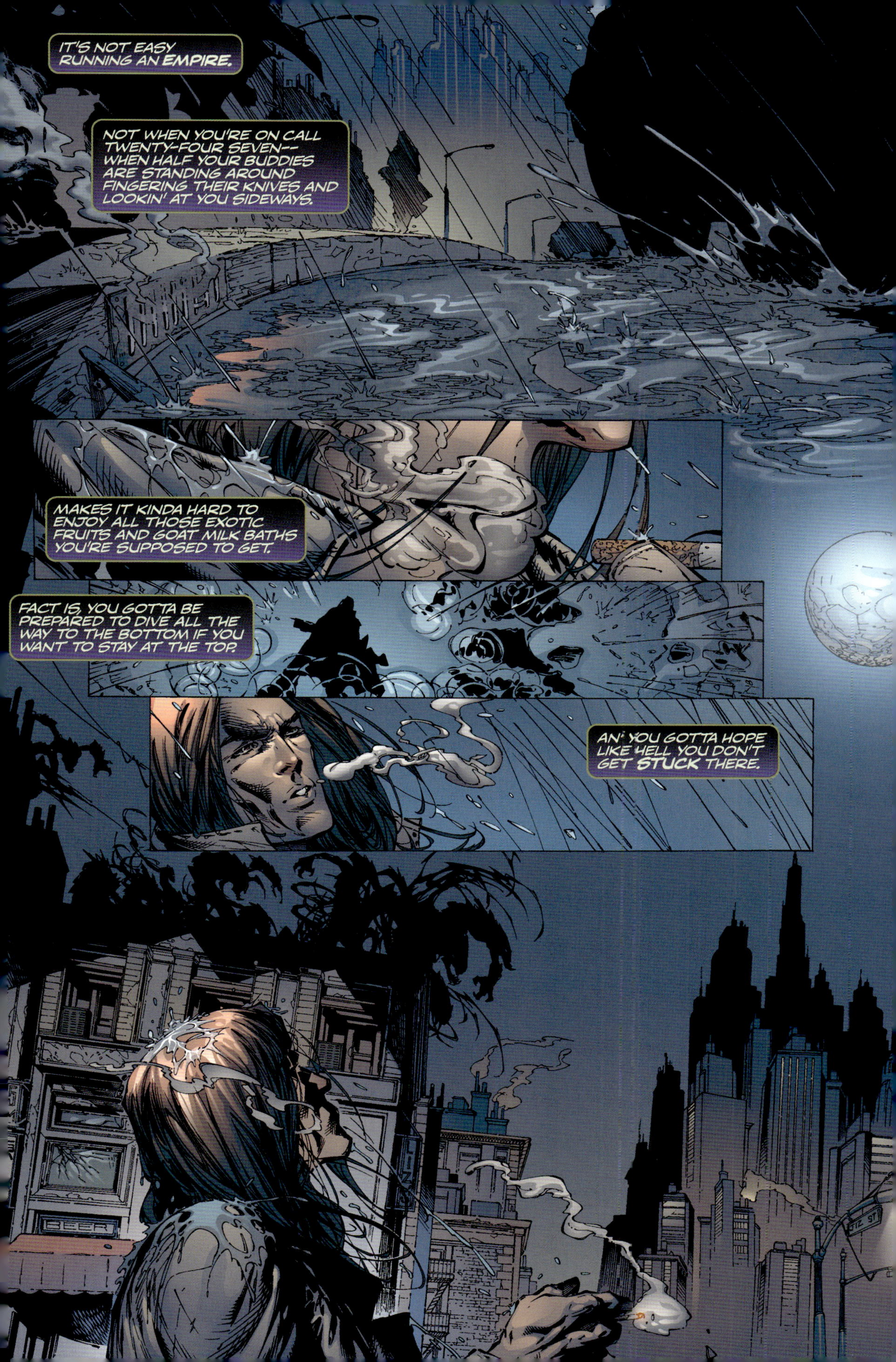
IT'S NOT EASY RUNNING AN EMPIRE.
NOT WHEN YOU'RE ON CALL TWENTY-FOUR SEVEN-- WHEN HALF YOUR BUDDIES ARE STANDING AROUND FINGERING THEIR KNIVES AND LOOKIN' AT YOU SIDEWAYS.
MAKES IT KINDA HARD TO ENJOY ALL THOSE EXOTIC FRUITS AND GOAT MILK BATHS YOU'RE SUPPOSED TO GET.
FACT IS, YOU GOTTA BE PREPARED TO DIVE ALL THE WAY TO THE BOTTOM IF YOU WANT TO STAY AT THE TOP.
AN' YOU GOTTA HOPE LIKE HELL YOU DON'T GET STUCK THERE.
BEER

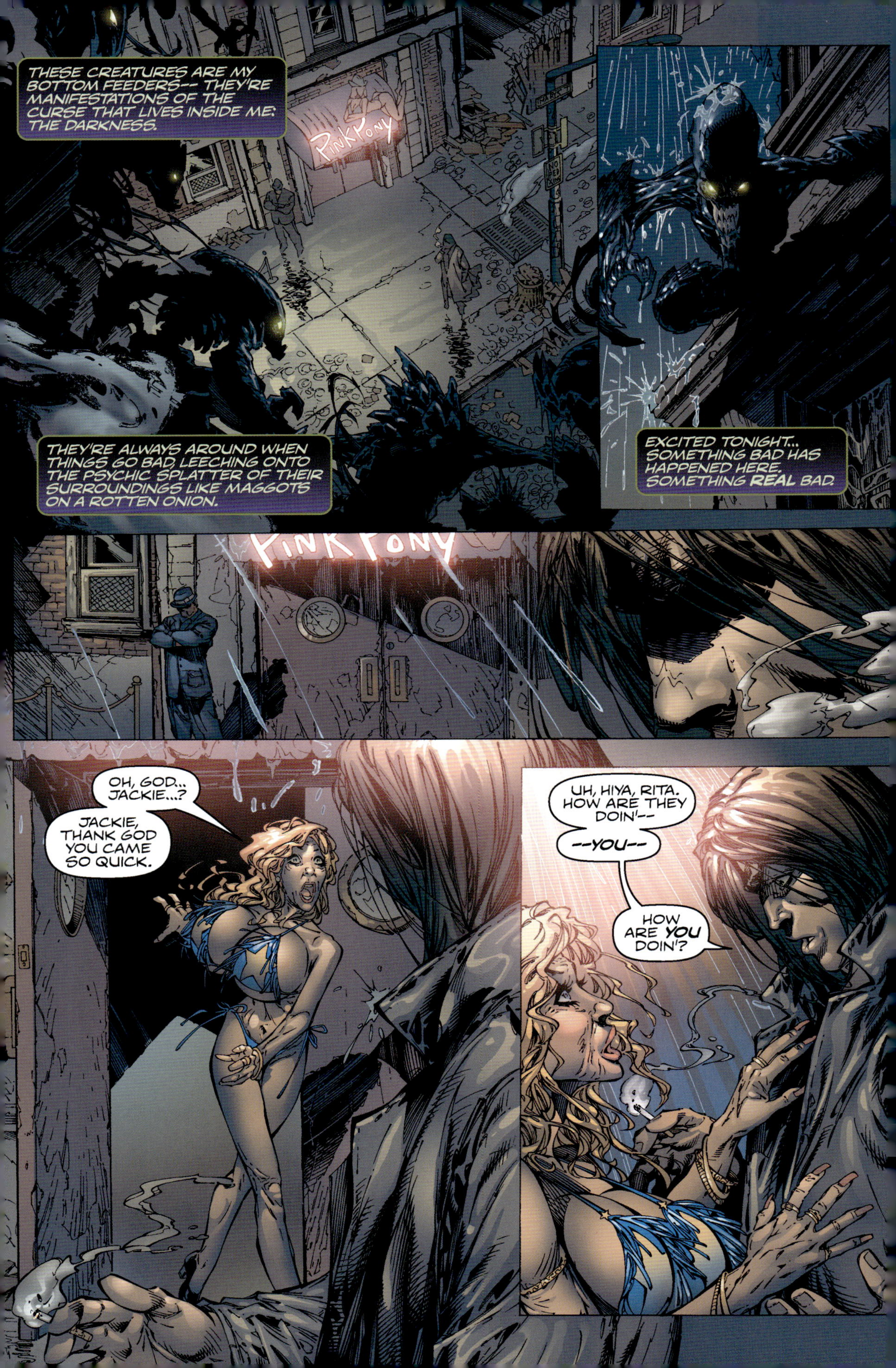
THESE CREATURES ARE MY BOTTOM FEEDERS-- THEY'RE MANIFESTATIONS OF THE CURSE THAT LIVES INSIDE ME: THE DARKNESS.
PINK PONY
THEY'RE ALWAYS AROUND WHEN THINGS GO BAD, LEECHING ONTO THE PSYCHIC SPLATTER OF THEIR SURROUNDINGS LIKE MAGGOTS ON A ROTTEN ONION.
EXCITED TONIGHT... SOMETHING BAD HAS HAPPENED HERE. SOMETHING **REAL** BAD.
PINK PONY
OH, GOD... JACKIE...?
JACKIE, THANK GOD YOU CAME SO QUICK.
UH, HIYA, RITA. HOW ARE THEY DOIN'--
--YOU--
HOW ARE **YOU** DOIN'?

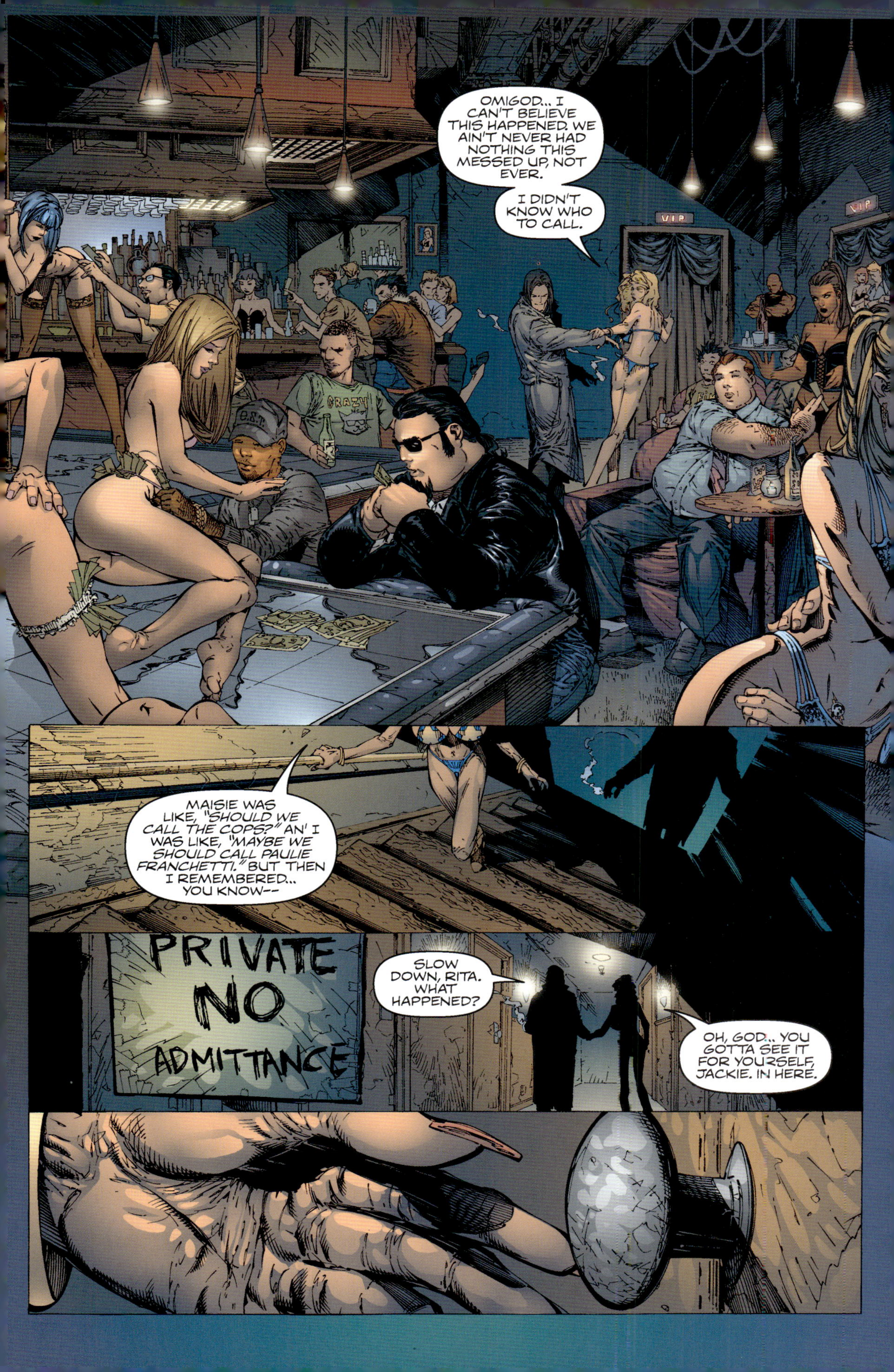
OMIGOD... I CAN'T BELIEVE THIS HAPPENED. WE AIN'T NEVER HAD NOTHING THIS MESSED UP, NOT EVER.
I DIDN'T KNOW WHO TO CALL.
VIP
VIP
CRAZY
MAISIE WAS LIKE, "SHOULD WE CALL THE COPS?" AN' I WAS LIKE, "MAYBE WE SHOULD CALL PAULIE FRANCHETTI." BUT THEN I REMEMBERED... YOU KNOW--
PRIVATE NO ADMITTANCE
SLOW DOWN, RITA. WHAT HAPPENED?
OH, GOD... YOU GOTTA SEE IT FOR YOURSELF, JACKIE. IN HERE.

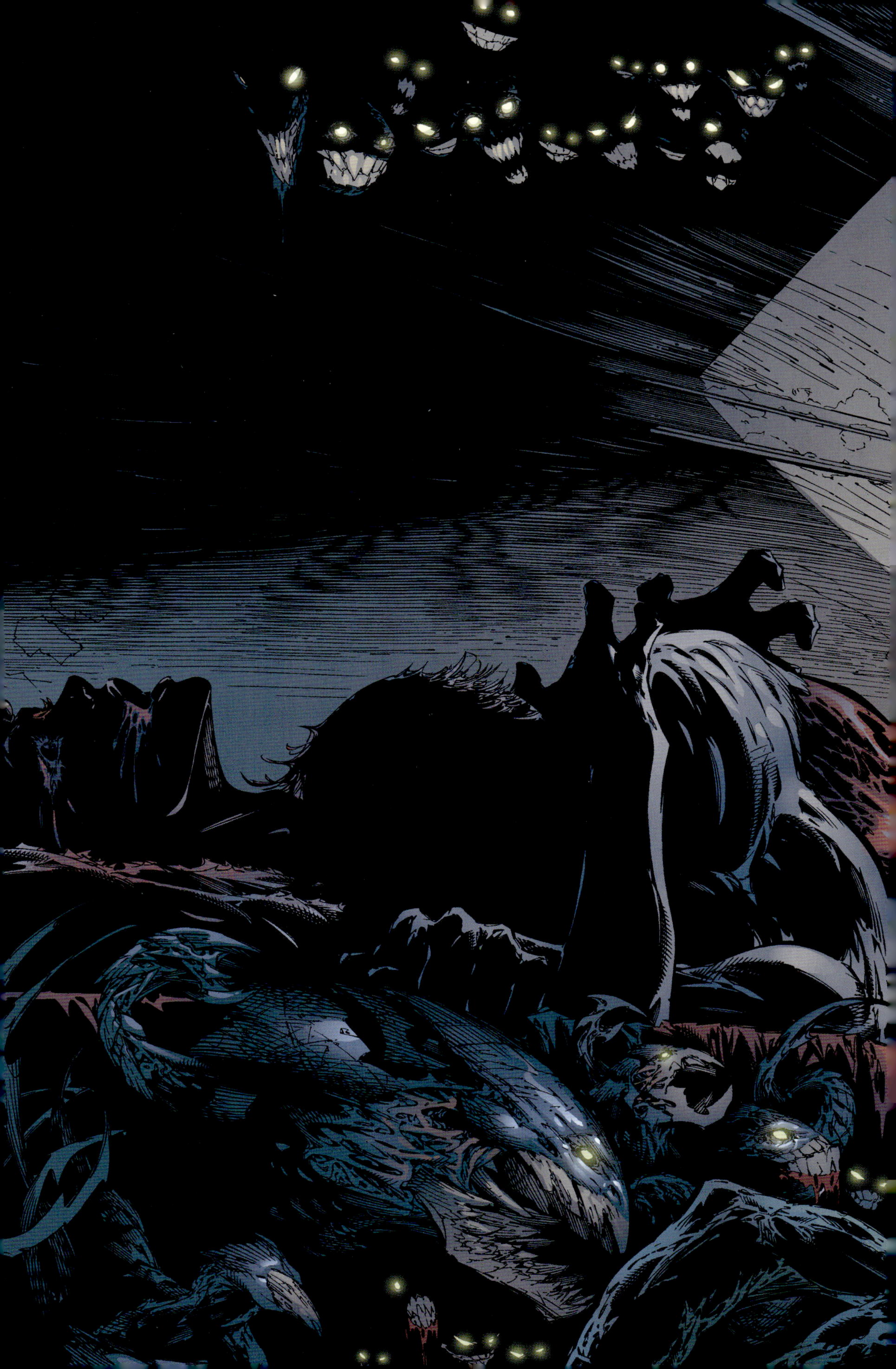

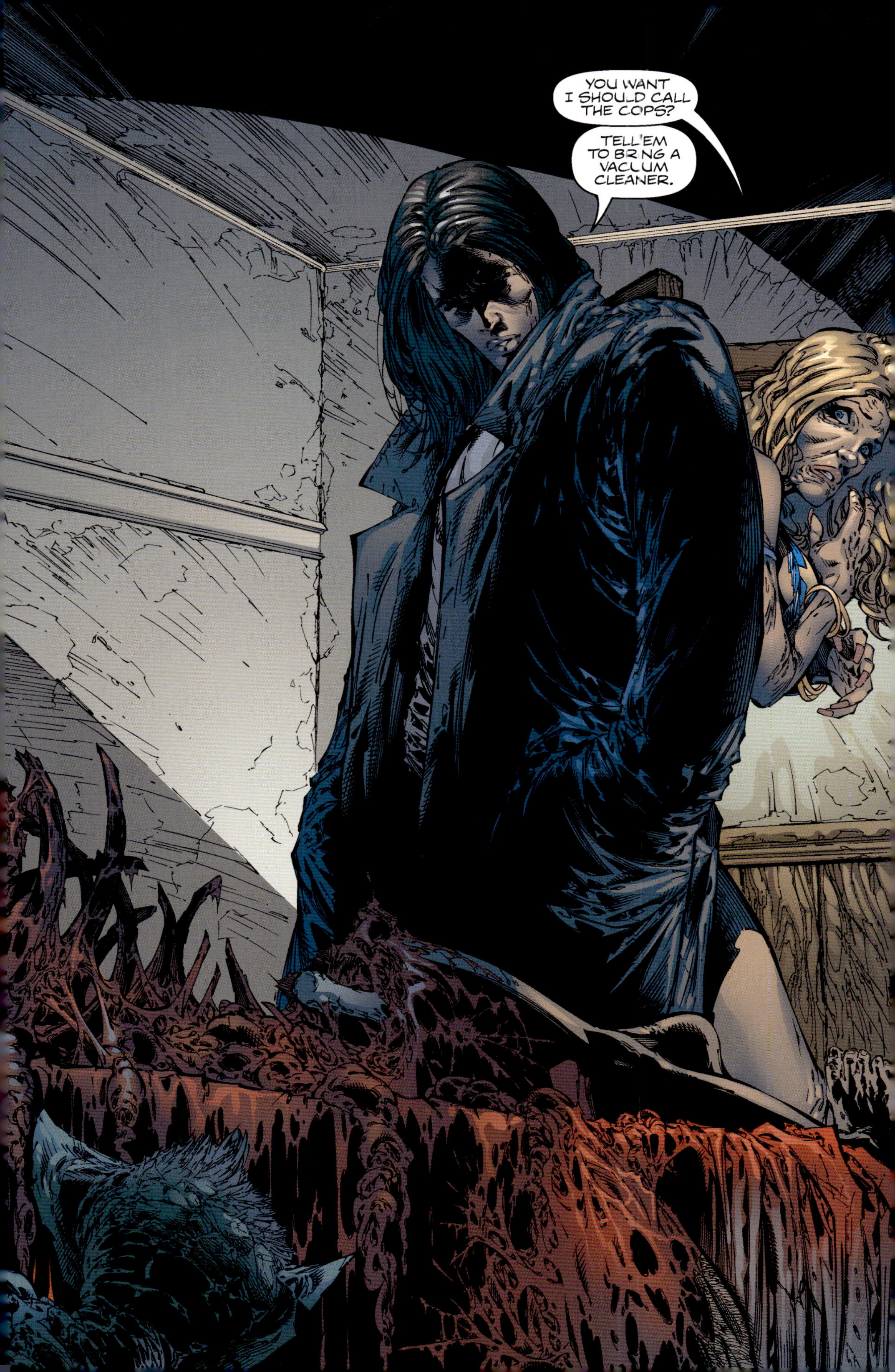
YOU WANT I SHOULD CALL THE COPS?
TELL'EM TO BRING A VACUUM CLEANER.

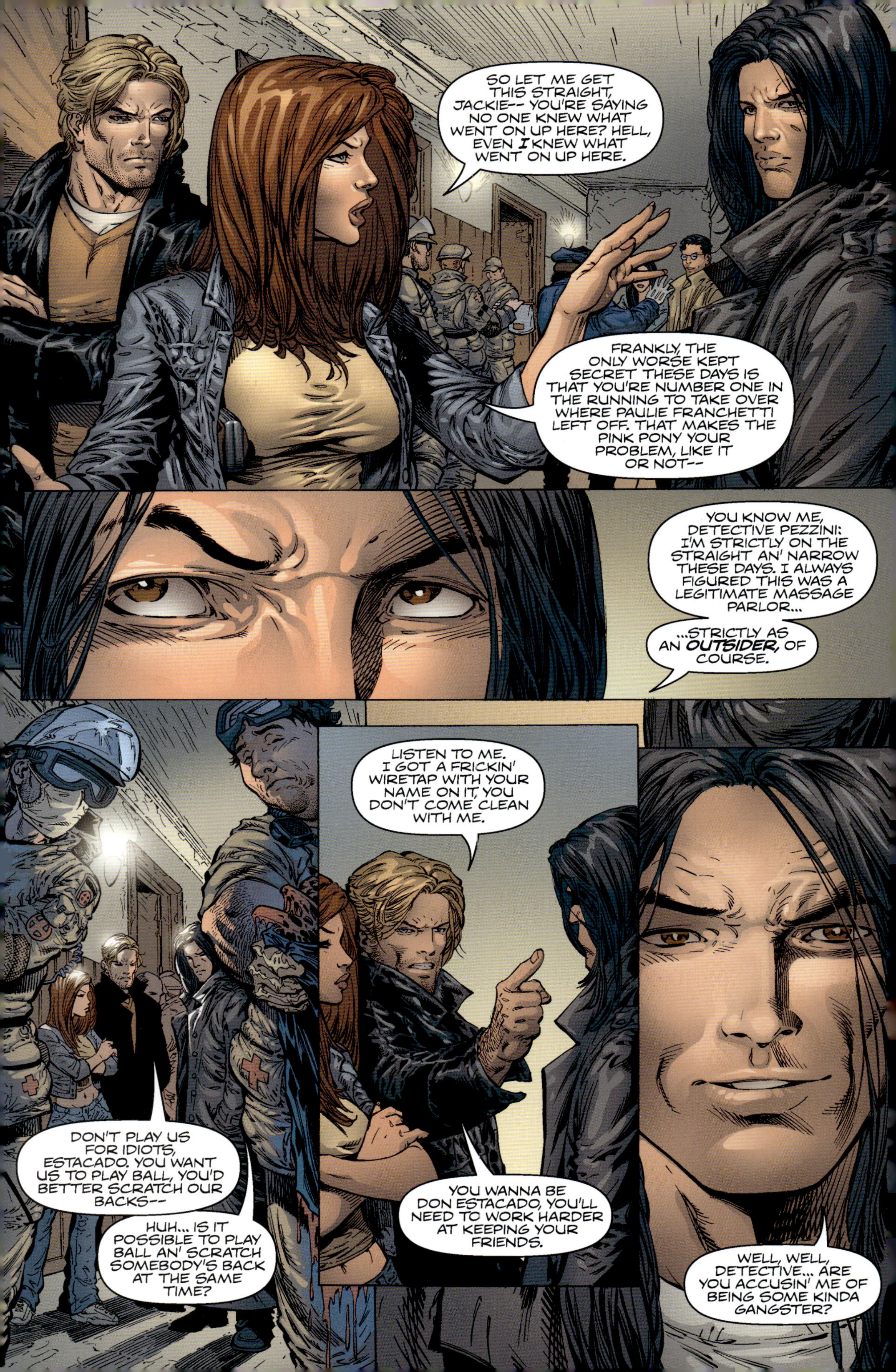
SO LET ME GET THIS STRAIGHT, JACKIE-- YOU'RE SAYING NO ONE KNEW WHAT WENT ON UP HERE? HELL, EVEN I KNEW WHAT WENT ON UP HERE.
FRANKLY, THE ONLY WORSE KEPT SECRET THESE DAYS IS THAT YOU'RE NUMBER ONE IN THE RUNNING TO TAKE OVER WHERE PAULIE FRANCHETTI LEFT OFF. THAT MAKES THE PINK PONY YOUR PROBLEM, LIKE IT OR NOT--
YOU KNOW ME, DETECTIVE PEZZINI: I'M STRICTLY ON THE STRAIGHT AN' NARROW THESE DAYS. I ALWAYS FIGURED THIS WAS A LEGITIMATE MASSAGE PARLOR...
...STRICTLY AS AN OUTSIDER, OF COURSE.
DON'T PLAY US FOR IDIOTS, ESTACADO. YOU WANT US TO PLAY BALL, YOU'D BETTER SCRATCH OUR BACKS--
HUH... IS IT POSSIBLE TO PLAY BALL AN' SCRATCH SOMEBODY'S BACK AT THE SAME TIME?
LISTEN TO ME. I GOT A FRICKIN' WIRETAP WITH YOUR NAME ON IT, YOU DON'T COME CLEAN WITH ME.
YOU WANNA BE DON ESTACADO, YOU'LL NEED TO WORK HARDER AT KEEPING YOUR FRIENDS.
WELL, WELL, DETECTIVE... ARE YOU ACCUSIN' ME OF BEING SOME KINDA GANGSTER?

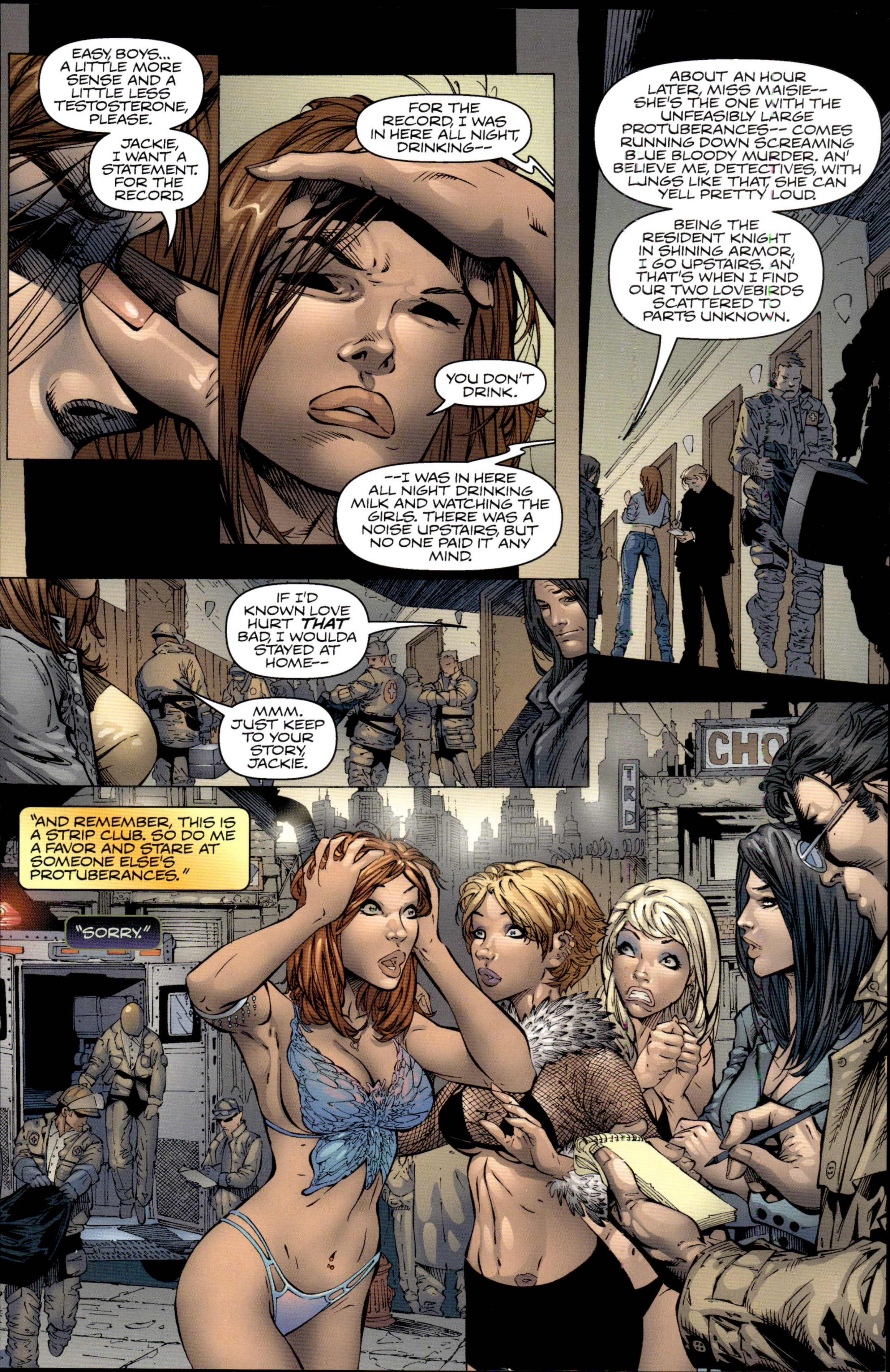
EASY, BOYS... A LITTLE MORE SENSE AND A LITTLE LESS TESTOSTERONE, PLEASE.
JACKIE, I WANT A STATEMENT. FOR THE RECORD.
FOR THE RECORD, I WAS IN HERE ALL NIGHT, DRINKING--
YOU DON'T DRINK.
--I WAS IN HERE ALL NIGHT DRINKING MILK AND WATCHING THE GIRLS. THERE WAS A NOISE UPSTAIRS, BUT NO ONE PAID IT ANY MIND.
ABOUT AN HOUR LATER, MISS MAISIE-- SHE'S THE ONE WITH THE UNFEASIBLY LARGE PROTUBERANCES-- COMES RUNNING DOWN SCREAMING BLUE BLOODY MURDER. AN' BELIEVE ME, DETECTIVES, WITH LUNGS LIKE THAT, SHE CAN YELL PRETTY LOUD.
BEING THE RESIDENT KNIGHT IN SHINING ARMOR, I GO UPSTAIRS. AN' THAT'S WHEN I FIND OUR TWO LOVEBIRDS SCATTERED TO PARTS UNKNOWN.
IF I'D KNOWN LOVE HURT THAT BAD, I WOULDA STAYED AT HOME--
MMM. JUST KEEP TO YOUR STORY, JACKIE.
"AND REMEMBER, THIS IS A STRIP CLUB. SO DO ME A FAVOR AND STARE AT SOMEONE ELSE'S PROTUBERANCES."
"SORRY."
CHO

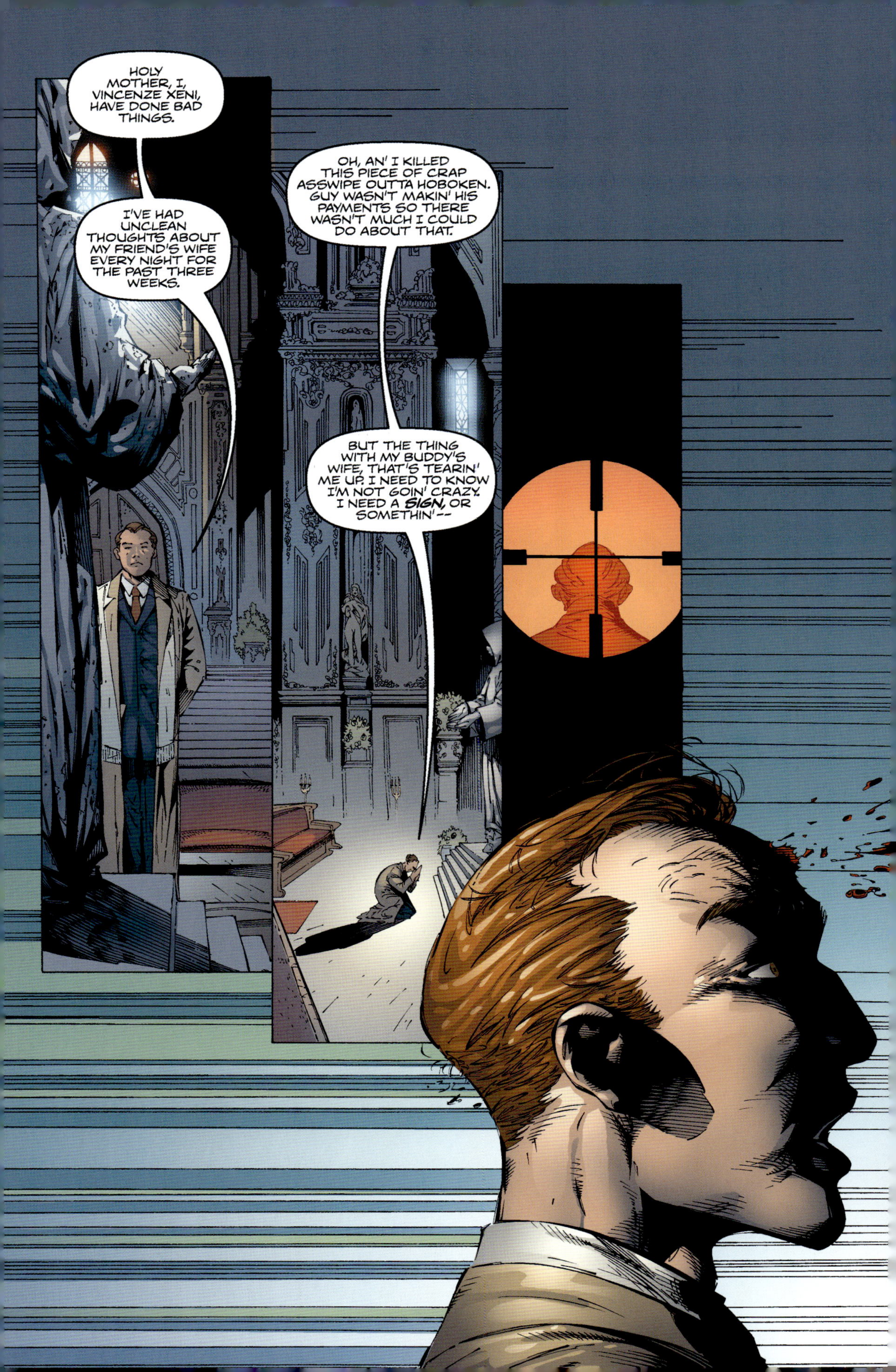
HOLY MOTHER, I, VINCENZE XENI, HAVE DONE BAD THINGS.
I'VE HAD UNCLEAN THOUGHTS ABOUT MY FRIEND'S WIFE EVERY NIGHT FOR THE PAST THREE WEEKS.
OH, AN' I KILLED THIS PIECE OF CRAP ASSWIPE OUTTA HOBOKEN. GUY WASN'T MAKIN' HIS PAYMENTS SO THERE WASN'T MUCH I COULD DO ABOUT THAT.
BUT THE THING WITH MY BUDDY'S WIFE, THAT'S TEARIN' ME UP. I NEED TO KNOW I'M NOT GOIN' CRAZY. I NEED A SIGN, OR SOMETHIN'--

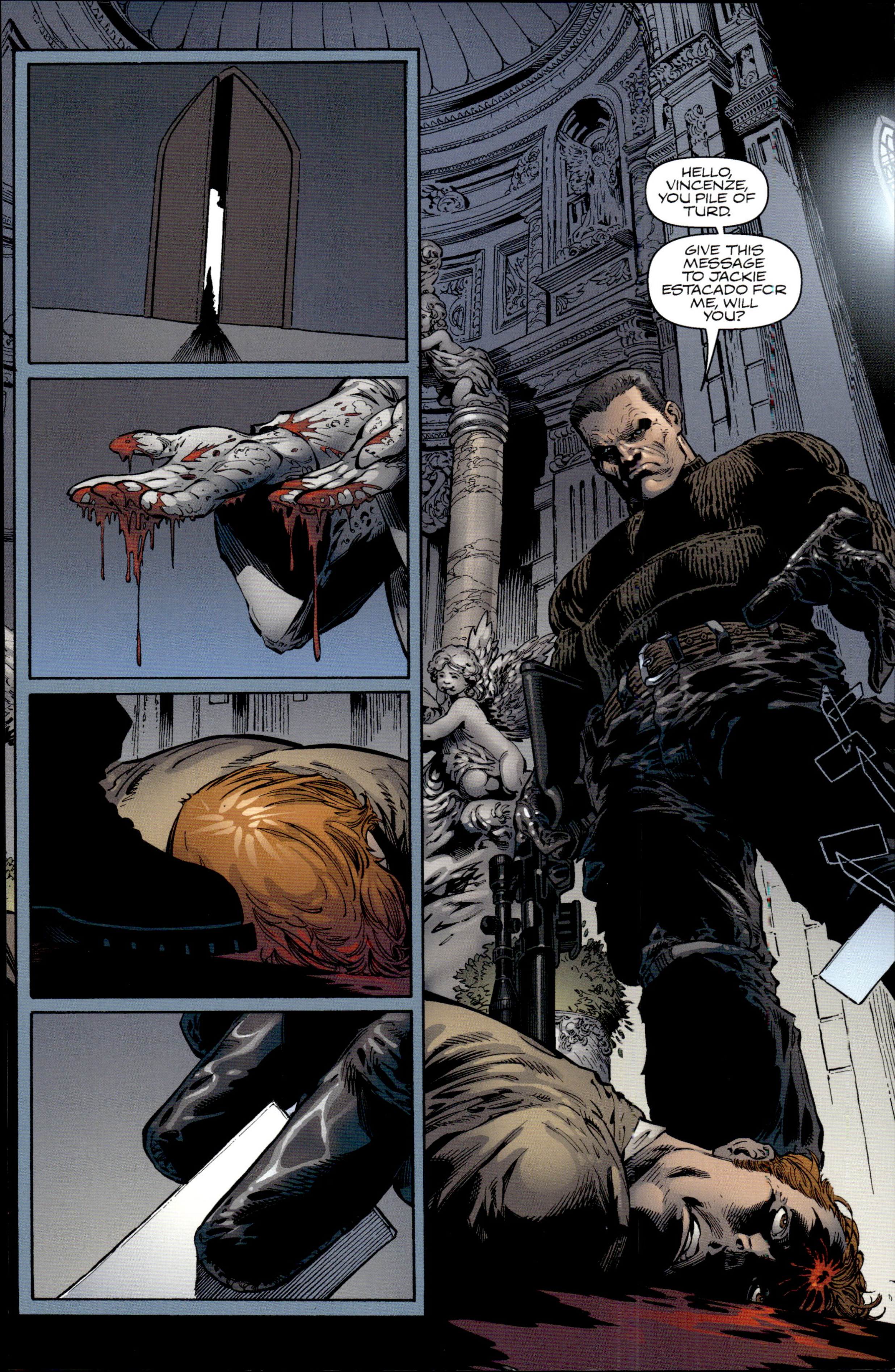
HELLO, VINCENZE, YOU PILE OF TURD.
GIVE THIS MESSAGE TO JACKIE ESTACADO FOR ME, WILL YOU?

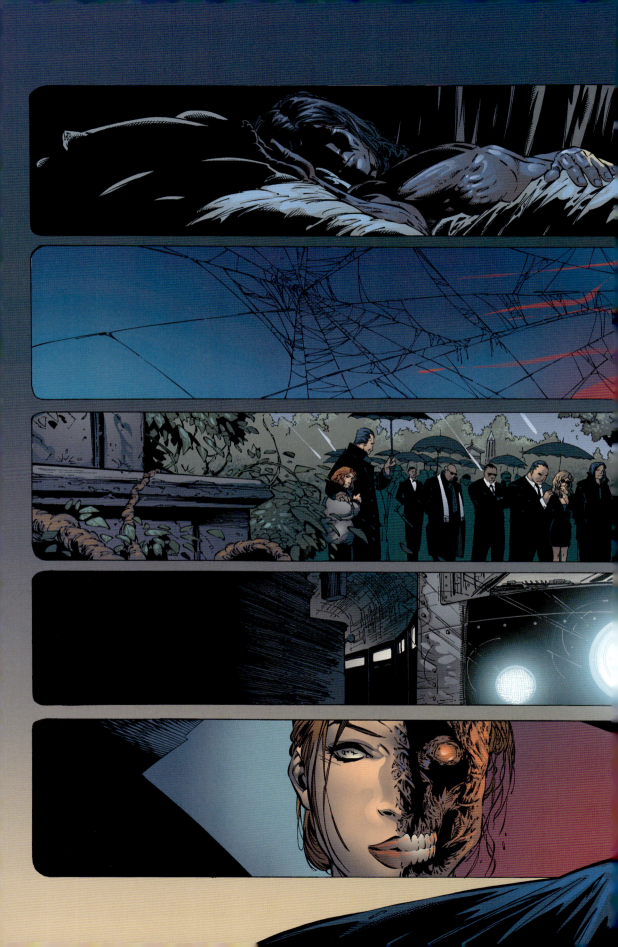

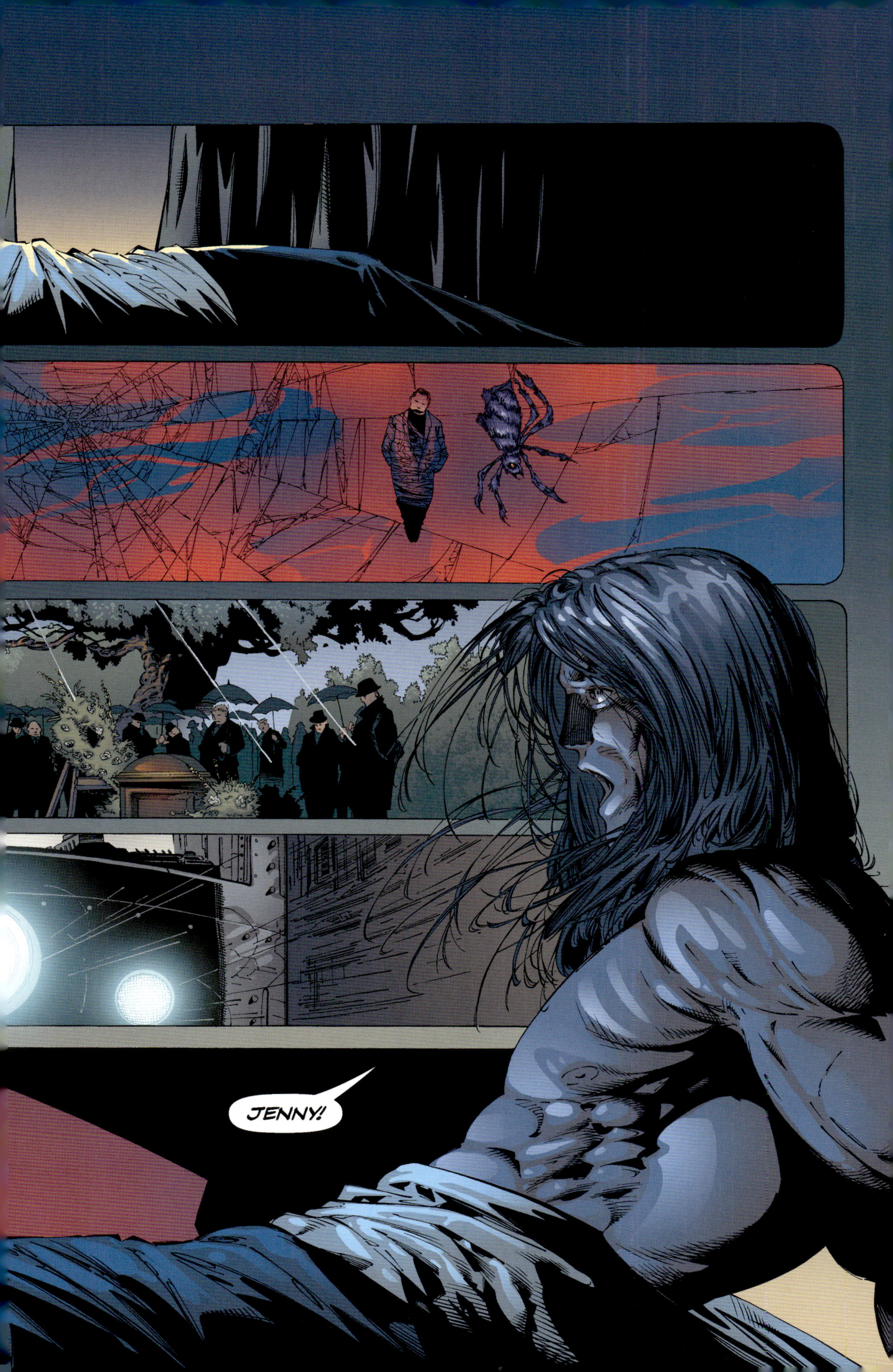
JENNY!

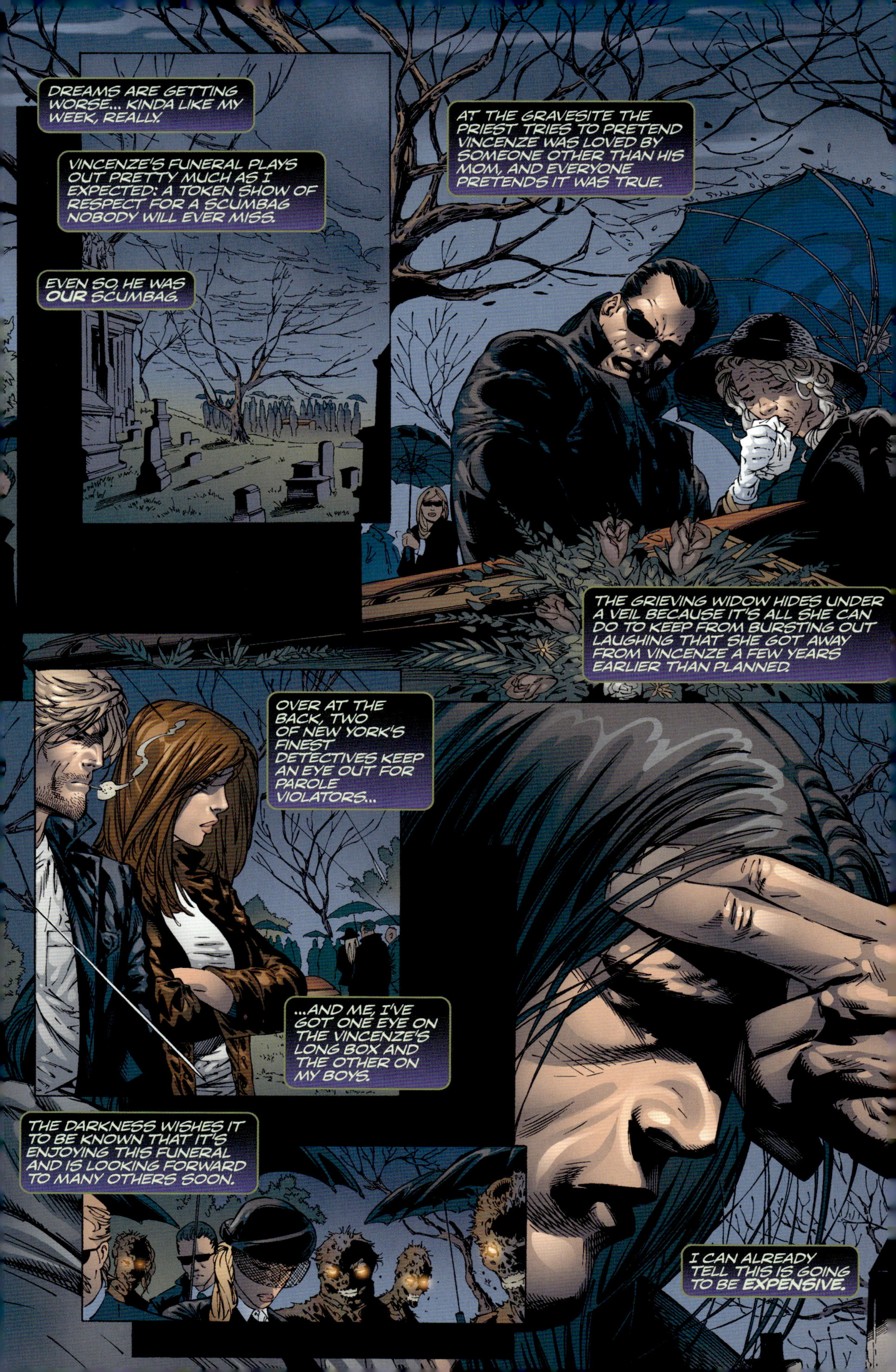
DREAMS ARE GETTING WORSE... KINDA LIKE MY WEEK, REALLY.
VINCENZE'S FUNERAL PLAYS OUT PRETTY MUCH AS I EXPECTED: A TOKEN SHOW OF RESPECT FOR A SCUMBAG NOBODY WILL EVER MISS.
EVEN SO, HE WAS OUR SCUMBAG.
AT THE GRAVESITE THE PRIEST TRIES TO PRETEND VINCENZE WAS LOVED BY SOMEONE OTHER THAN HIS MOM, AND EVERYONE PRETENDS IT WAS TRUE.
THE GRIEVING WIDOW HIDES UNDER A VEIL BECAUSE IT'S ALL SHE CAN DO TO KEEP FROM BURSTING OUT LAUGHING THAT SHE GOT AWAY FROM VINCENZE A FEW YEARS EARLIER THAN PLANNED.
OVER AT THE BACK, TWO OF NEW YORK'S FINEST DETECTIVES KEEP AN EYE OUT FOR PAROLE VIOLATORS...
...AND ME, I'VE GOT ONE EYE ON THE VINCENZE'S LONG BOX AND THE OTHER ON MY BOYS.
THE DARKNESS WISHES IT TO BE KNOWN THAT IT'S ENJOYING THIS FUNERAL AND IS LOOKING FORWARD TO MANY OTHERS SOON.
I CAN ALREADY TELL THIS IS GOING TO BE EXPENSIVE.

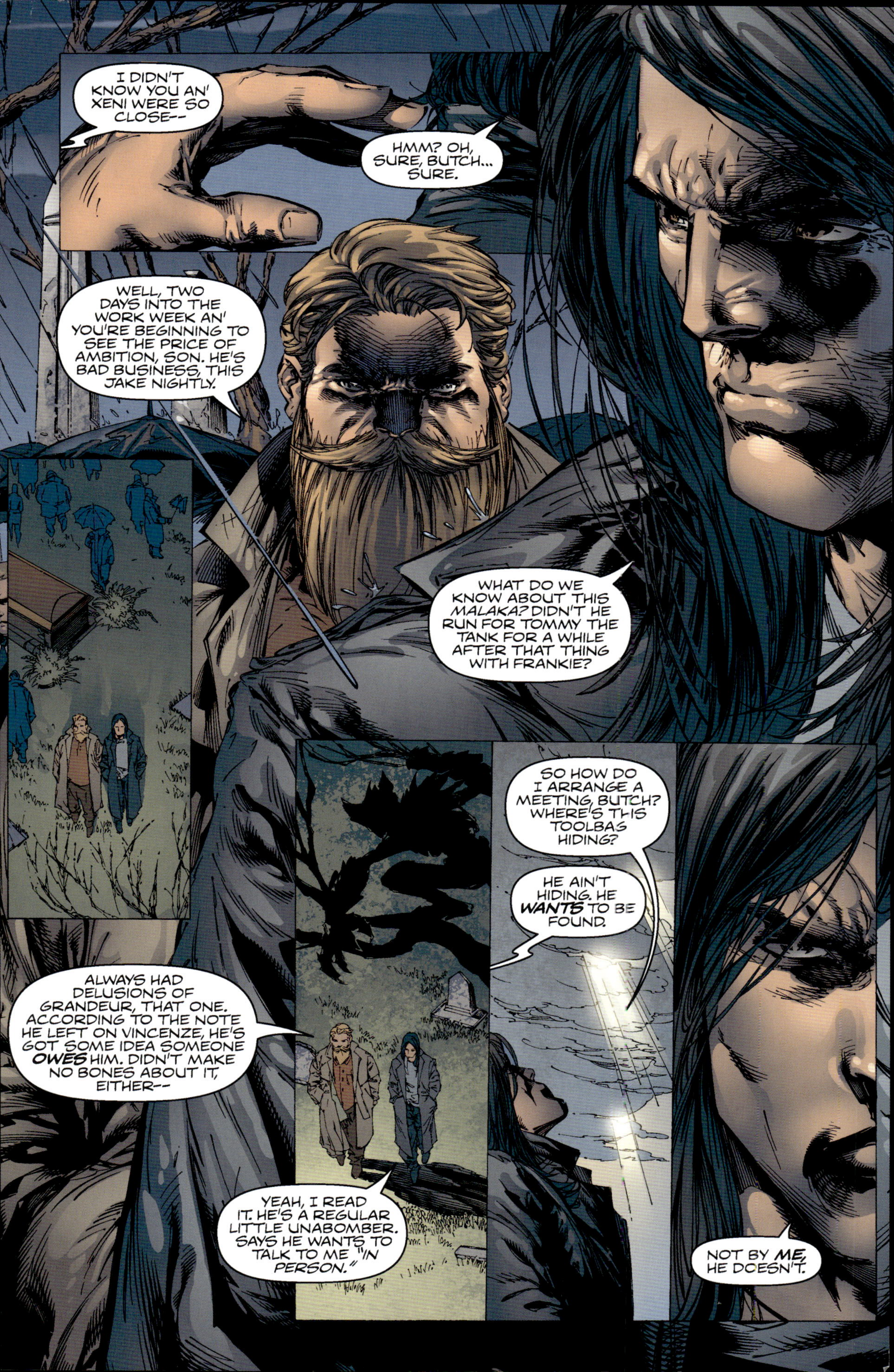
I DIDN'T KNOW YOU AN' XENI WERE SO CLOSE--
HMM? OH, SURE, BUTCH... SURE.
WELL, TWO DAYS INTO THE WORK WEEK AN' YOU'RE BEGINNING TO SEE THE PRICE OF AMBITION, SON. HE'S BAD BUSINESS, THIS JAKE NIGHTLY.
WHAT DO WE KNOW ABOUT THIS *MALAKA*? DIDN'T HE RUN FOR TOMMY THE TANK FOR A WHILE AFTER THAT THING WITH FRANKIE?
ALWAYS HAD DELUSIONS OF GRANDEUR, THAT ONE. ACCORDING TO THE NOTE HE LEFT ON VINCENZE, HE'S GOT SOME IDEA SOMEONE ***OWES*** HIM. DIDN'T MAKE NO BONES ABOUT IT, EITHER--
YEAH, I READ IT. HE'S A REGULAR LITTLE UNABOMBER. SAYS HE WANTS TO TALK TO ME *"IN PERSON."*
SO HOW DO I ARRANGE A MEETING, BUTCH? WHERE'S THIS TOOLBAG HIDING?
HE AIN'T HIDING. HE ***WANTS*** TO BE FOUND.
NOT BY ***ME***, HE DOESN'T.

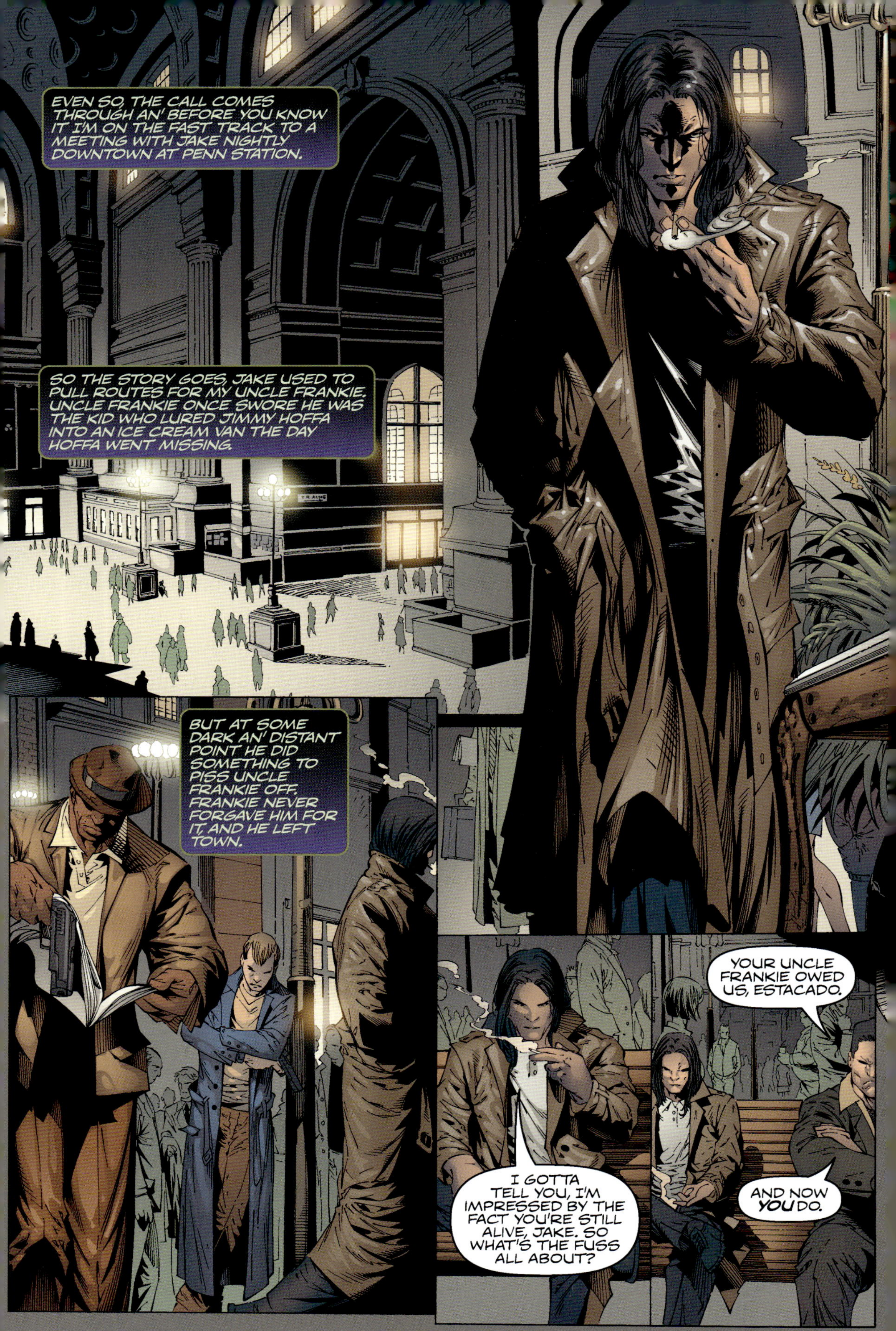
EVEN SO, THE CALL COMES THROUGH AN' BEFORE YOU KNOW IT I'M ON THE FAST TRACK TO A MEETING WITH JAKE NIGHTLY DOWNTOWN AT PENN STATION.
SO THE STORY GOES, JAKE USED TO PULL ROUTES FOR MY UNCLE FRANKIE. UNCLE FRANKIE ONCE SWORE HE WAS THE KID WHO LURED JIMMY HOFFA INTO AN ICE CREAM VAN THE DAY HOFFA WENT MISSING.
BUT AT SOME DARK AN' DISTANT POINT HE DID SOMETHING TO PISS UNCLE FRANKIE OFF. FRANKIE NEVER FORGAVE HIM FOR IT, AND HE LEFT TOWN.
I GOTTA TELL YOU, I'M IMPRESSED BY THE FACT YOU'RE STILL ALIVE, JAKE. SO WHAT'S THE FUSS ALL ABOUT?
YOUR UNCLE FRANKIE OWED US, ESTACADO.
AND NOW YOU DO.

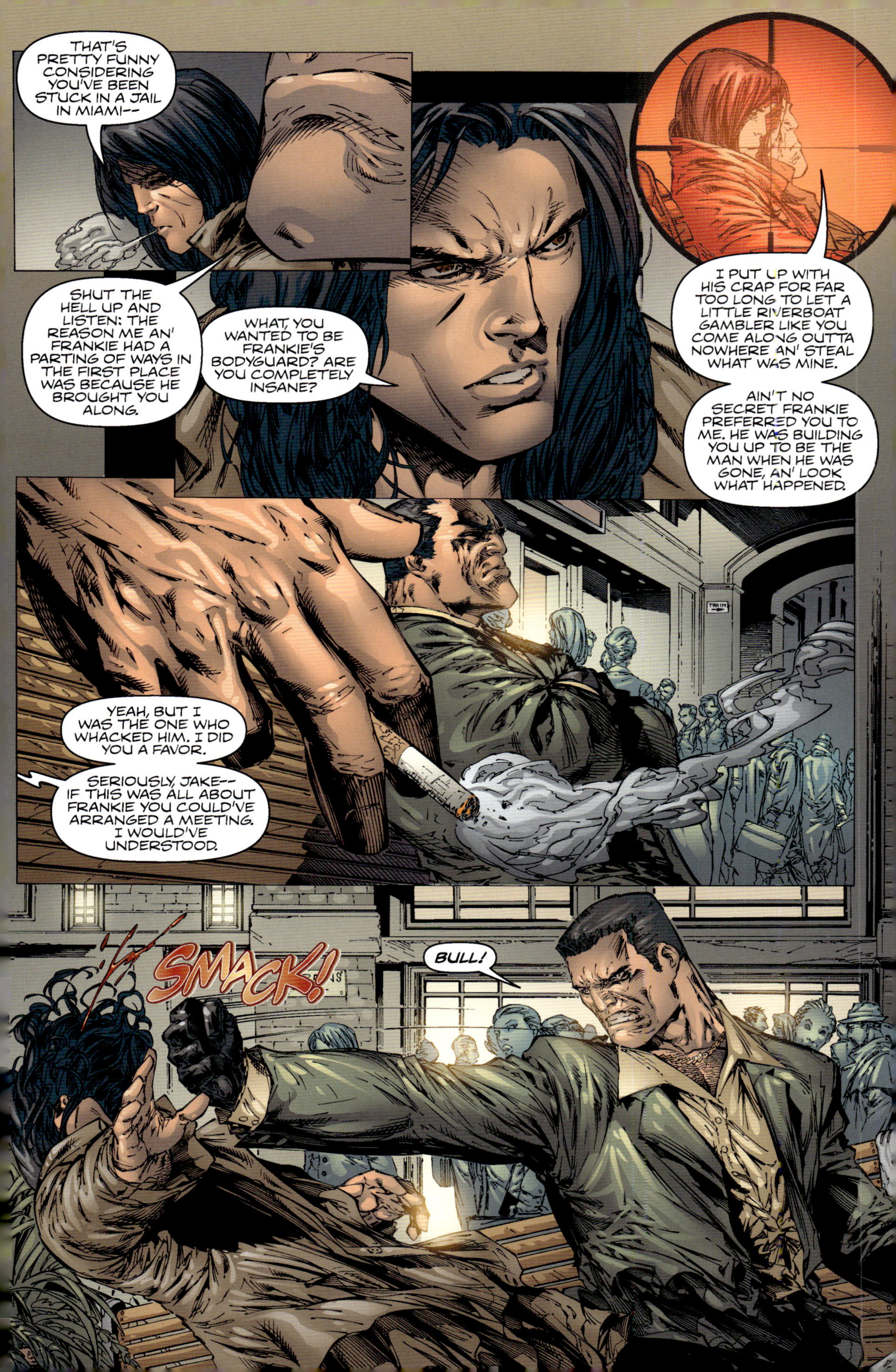

THAT'S PRETTY FUNNY CONSIDERING YOU'VE BEEN STUCK IN A JAIL IN MIAMI--
SHUT THE HELL UP AND LISTEN: THE REASON ME AN' FRANKIE HAD A PARTING OF WAYS IN THE FIRST PLACE WAS BECAUSE HE BROUGHT YOU ALONG.
WHAT, YOU WANTED TO BE FRANKIE'S BODYGUARD? ARE YOU COMPLETELY INSANE?
I PUT UP WITH HIS CRAP FOR FAR TOO LONG TO LET A LITTLE RIVERBOAT GAMBLER LIKE YOU COME ALONG OUTTA NOWHERE AN' STEAL WHAT WAS MINE.
AIN'T NO SECRET FRANKIE PREFERRED YOU TO ME. HE WAS BUILDING YOU UP TO BE THE MAN WHEN HE WAS GONE, AN' LOOK WHAT HAPPENED.
YEAH, BUT I WAS THE ONE WHO WHACKED HIM. I DID YOU A FAVOR.
SERIOUSLY, JAKE-- IF THIS WAS ALL ABOUT FRANKIE YOU COULD'VE ARRANGED A MEETING. I WOULD'VE UNDERSTOOD.
TRAIN
SMACK!
BULL!

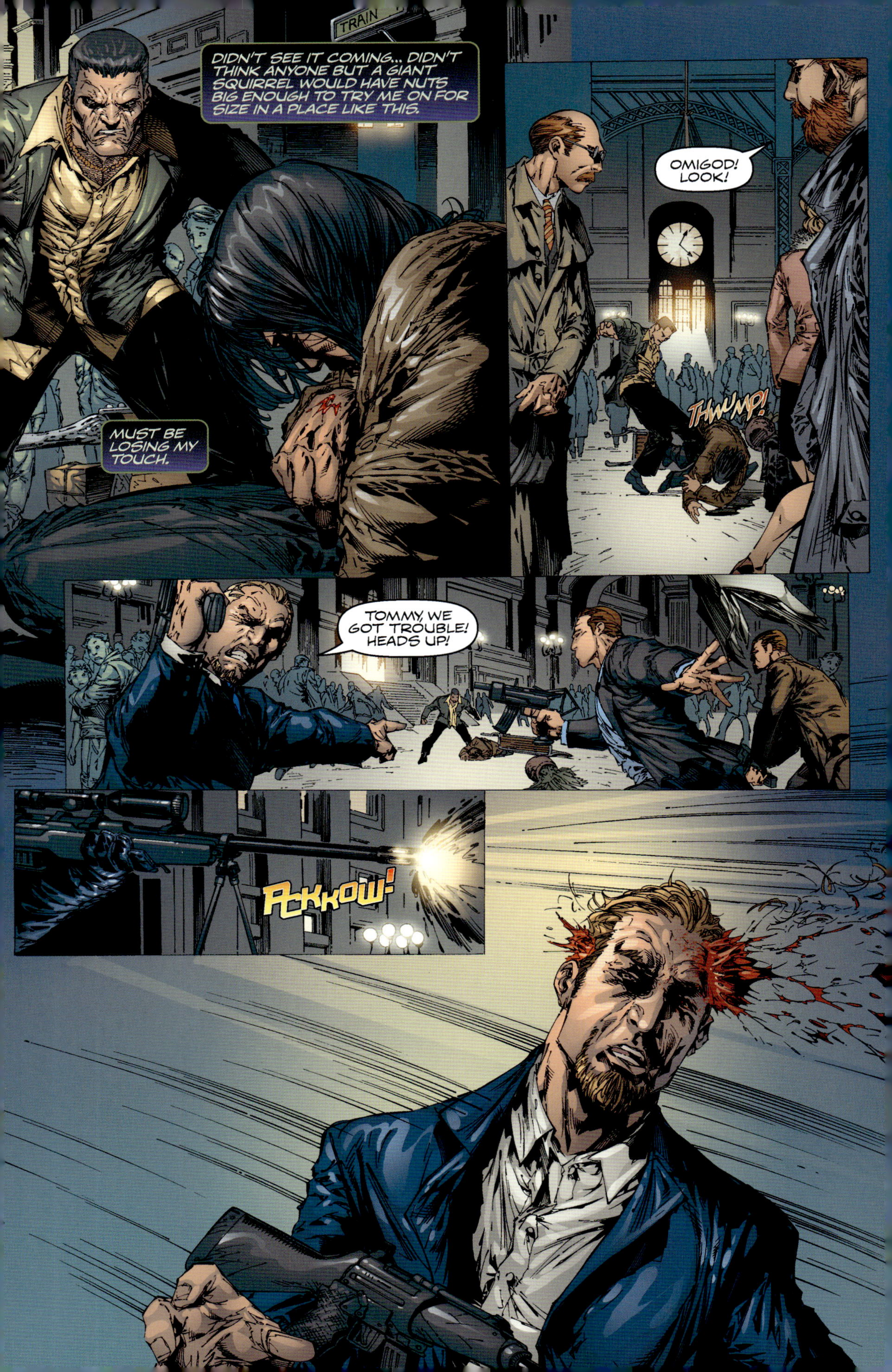
TRAIN
DIDN'T SEE IT COMING... DIDN'T THINK ANYONE BUT A GIANT SQUIRREL WOULD HAVE NUTS BIG ENOUGH TO TRY ME ON FOR SIZE IN A PLACE LIKE THIS.
MUST BE LOSING MY TOUCH.
OMIGOD! LOOK!
THWUMP!
TOMMY, WE GOT TROUBLE! HEADS UP!
ACKKOW!

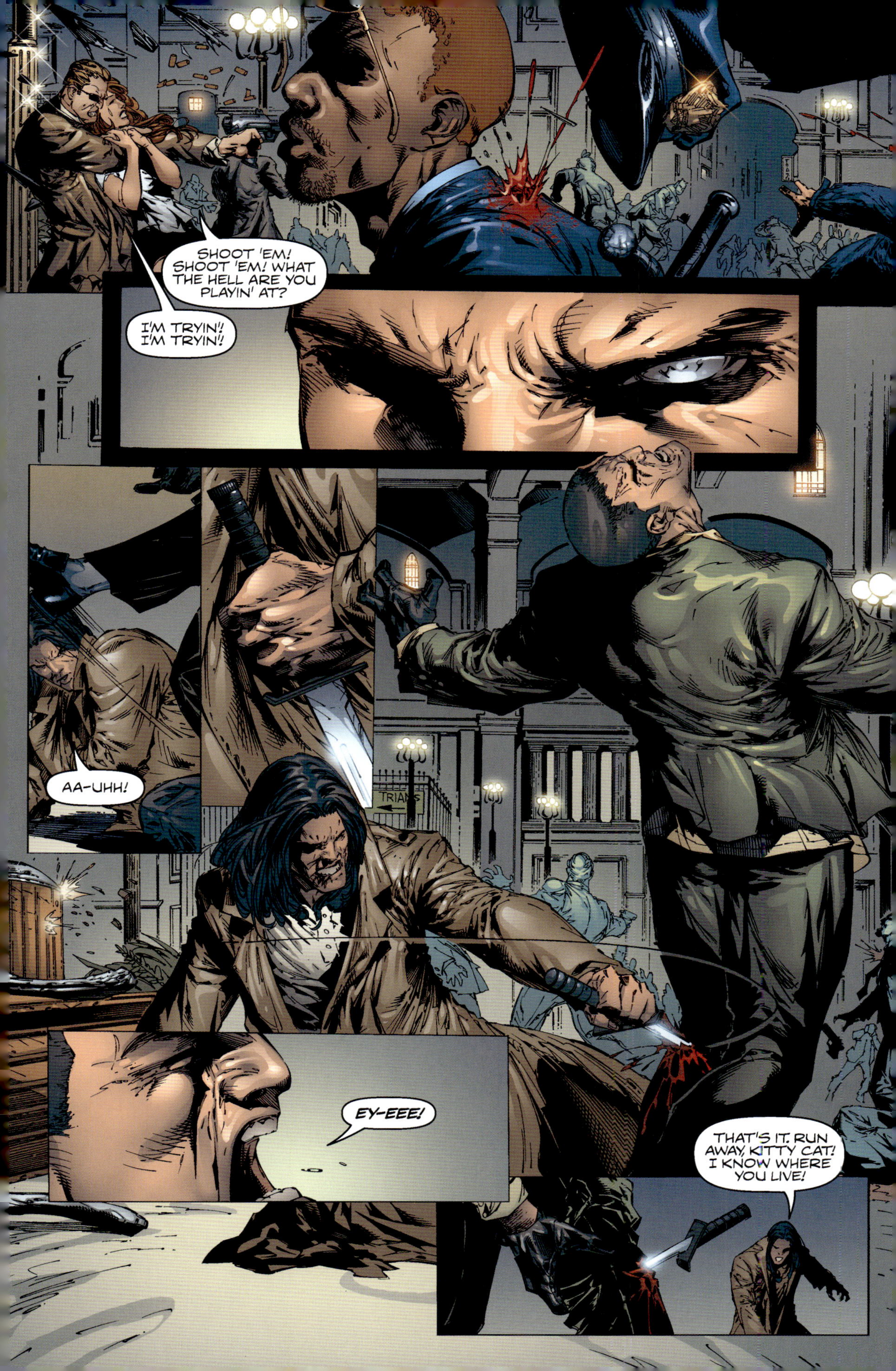
SHOOT 'EM! SHOOT 'EM! WHAT THE HELL ARE YOU PLAYIN' AT?
I'M TRYIN'! I'M TRYIN'!
AA-UHH!
EY-EEE!
THAT'S IT. RUN AWAY, KITTY CAT! I KNOW WHERE YOU LIVE!

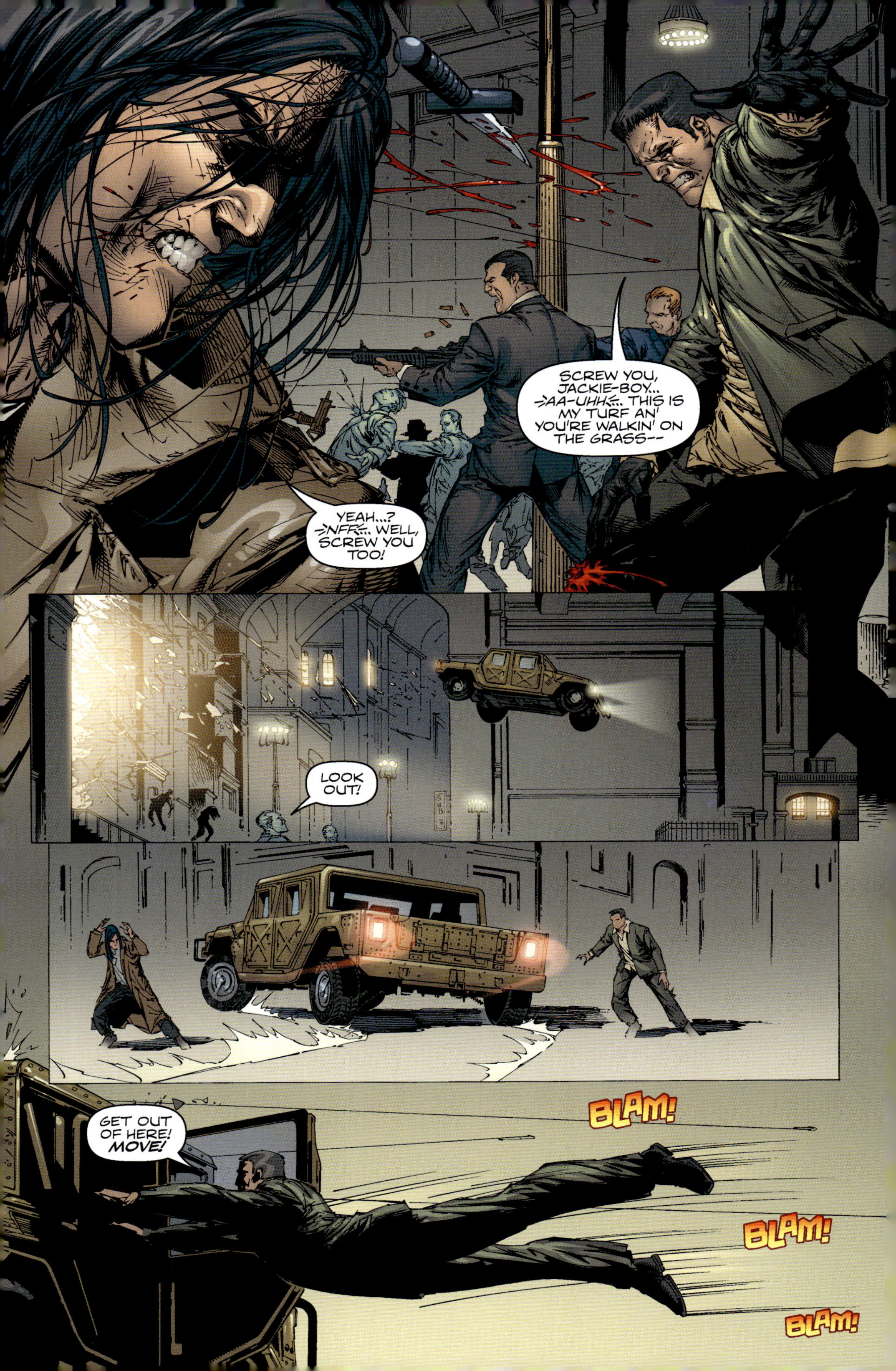
SCREW YOU, JACKIE-BOY.. -AA-UHH-.. THIS IS MY TURF AN' YOU'RE WALKIN' ON THE GRASS--
YEAH...? -NFF-.. WELL, SCREW YOU TOO!
LOOK OUT!
GET OUT OF HERE! MOVE!
BLAM!
BLAM!
BLAM!

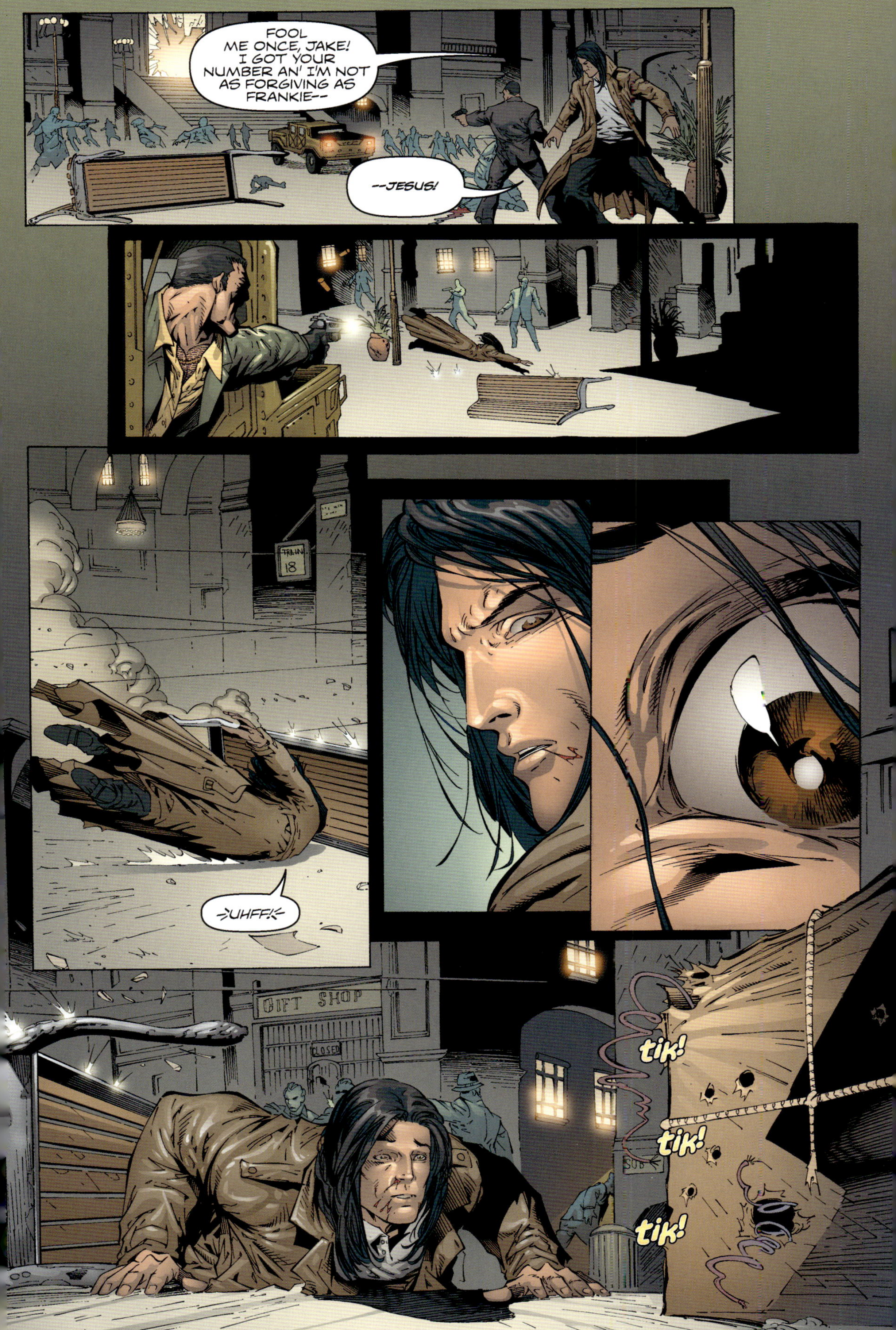
FOOL ME ONCE, JAKE! I GOT YOUR NUMBER AN' I'M NOT AS FORGIVING AS FRANKIE--
--JESUS!
TRAIN 18
UHFF!
GIFT SHOP
CLOSED
tik!
tik!
tik!

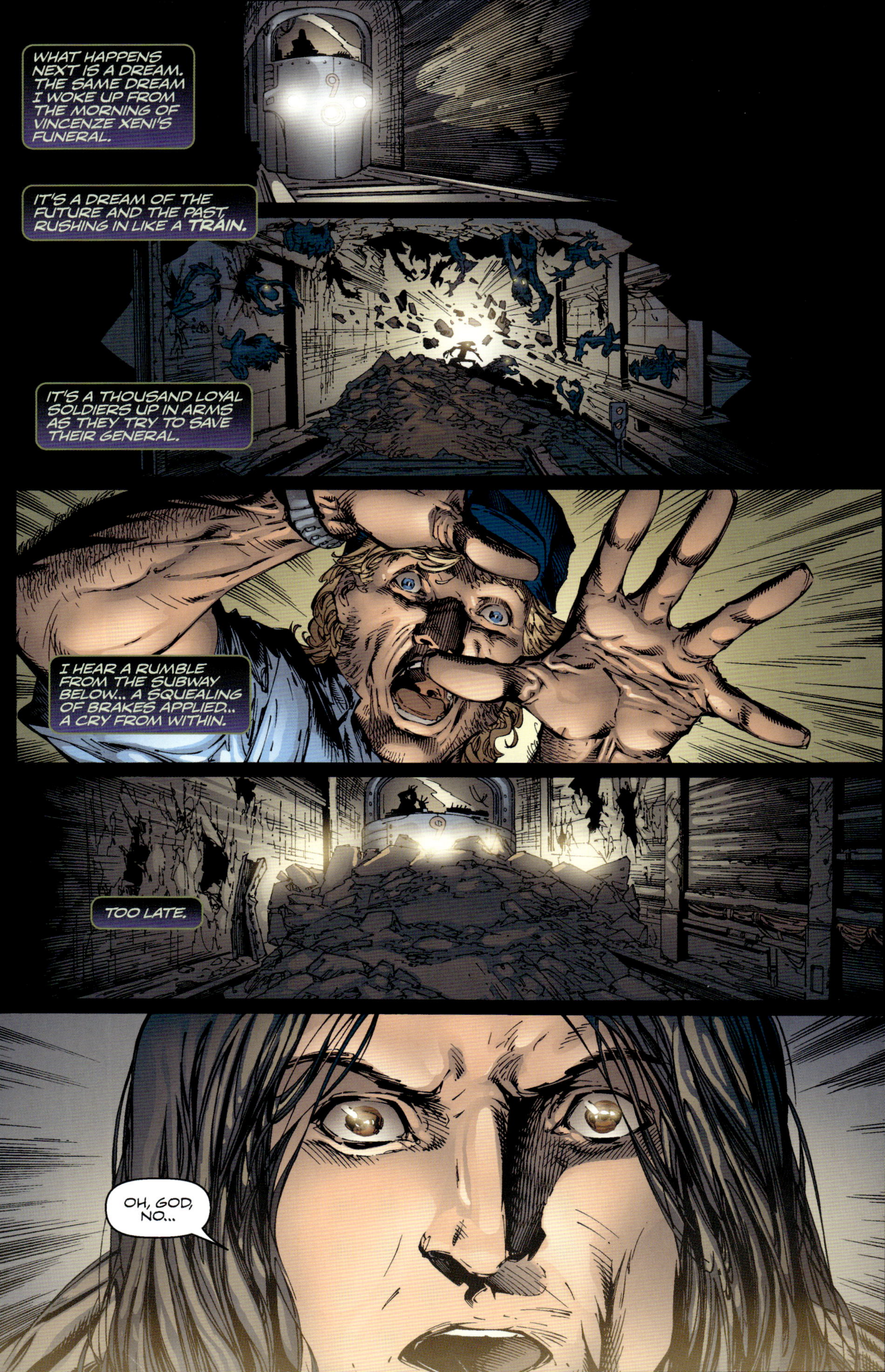
WHAT HAPPENS NEXT IS A DREAM. THE SAME DREAM I WOKE UP FROM THE MORNING OF VINCENZE XENI'S FUNERAL.
IT'S A DREAM OF THE FUTURE AND THE PAST, RUSHING IN LIKE A TRAIN.
IT'S A THOUSAND LOYAL SOLDIERS UP IN ARMS AS THEY TRY TO SAVE THEIR GENERAL.
I HEAR A RUMBLE FROM THE SUBWAY BELOW... A SQUEALING OF BRAKES APPLIED.. A CRY FROM WITHIN.
TOO LATE.
OH, GOD, NO...

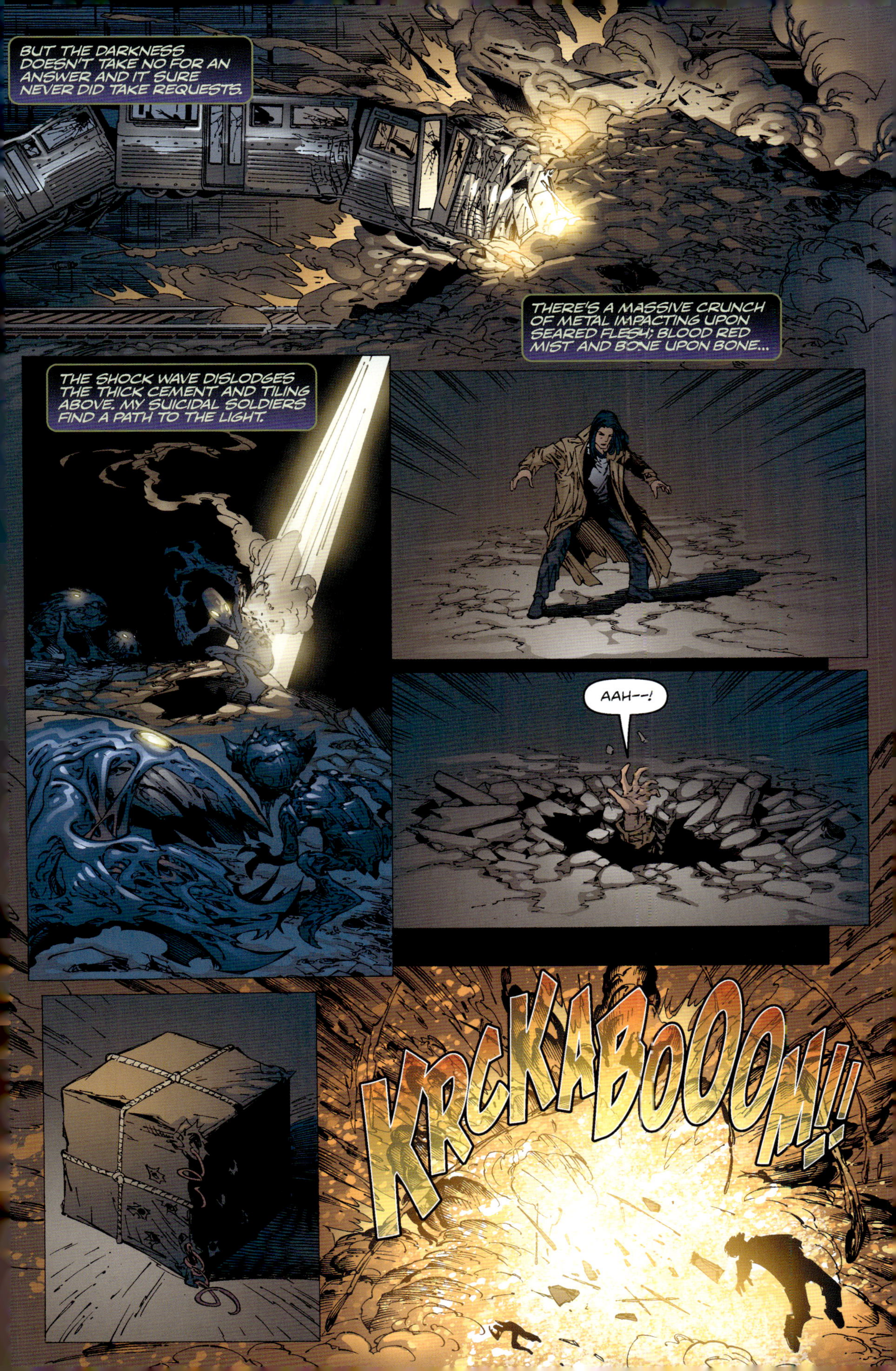

BUT THE DARKNESS DOESN'T TAKE NO FOR AN ANSWER AND IT SURE NEVER DID TAKE REQUESTS.
THERE'S A MASSIVE CRUNCH OF METAL IMPACTING UPON SEARED FLESH; BLOOD RED MIST AND BONE UPON BONE...
THE SHOCK WAVE DISLODGES THE THICK CEMENT AND TILING ABOVE. MY SUICIDAL SOLDIERS FIND A PATH TO THE LIGHT.
AAH--!
KRCKABOOOM!!

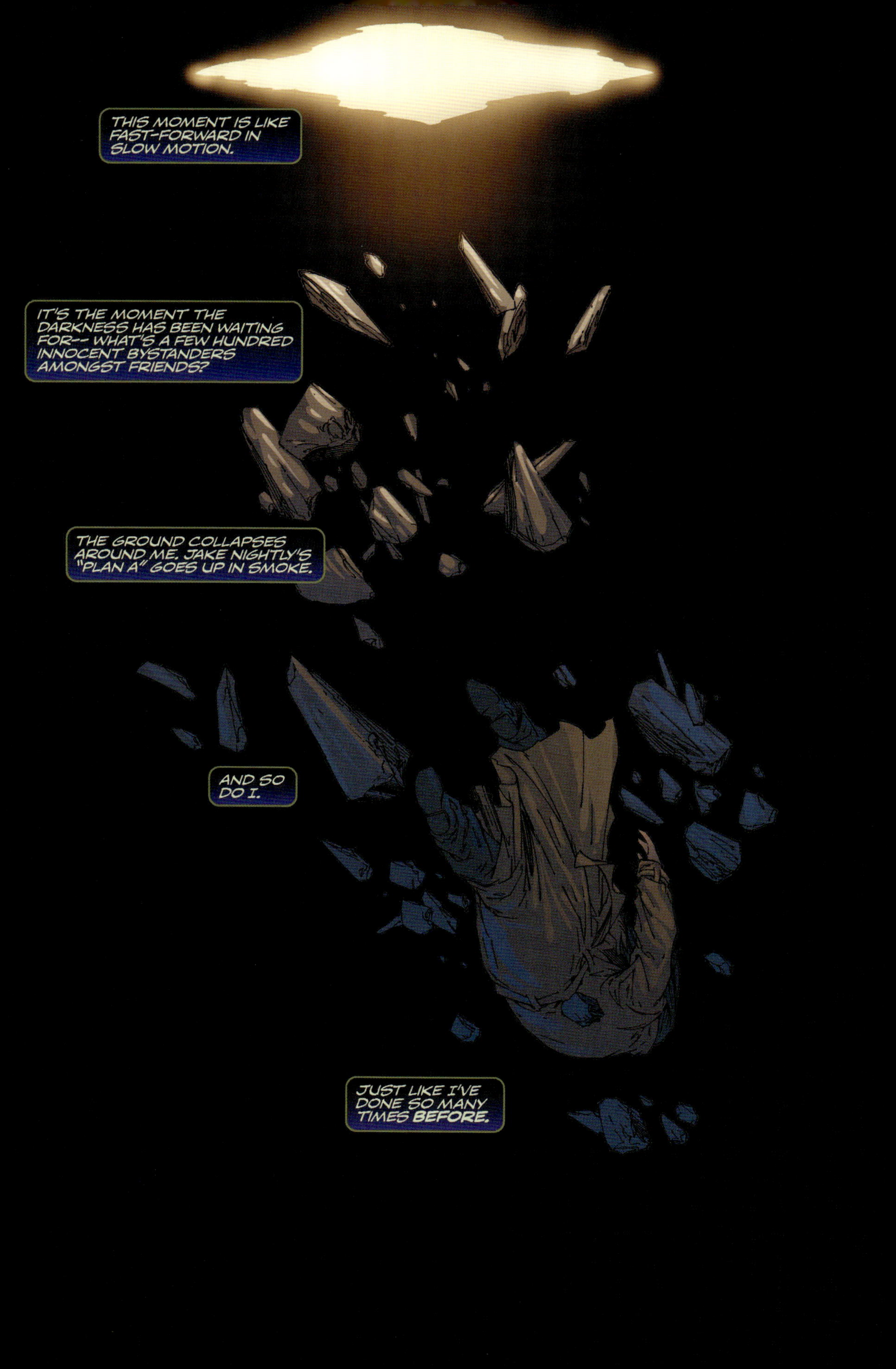
THIS MOMENT IS LIKE FAST-FORWARD IN SLOW MOTION.
IT'S THE MOMENT THE DARKNESS HAS BEEN WAITING FOR-- WHAT'S A FEW HUNDRED INNOCENT BYSTANDERS AMONGST FRIENDS?
THE GROUND COLLAPSES AROUND ME. JAKE NIGHTLY'S "PLAN A" GOES UP IN SMOKE.
AND SO DO I.
JUST LIKE I'VE DONE SO MANY TIMES BEFORE.

The Darkness Issue #48

cover art by: Chris Gossett, Paul Schrier, & Matt Milla

THE DARKNESS #48

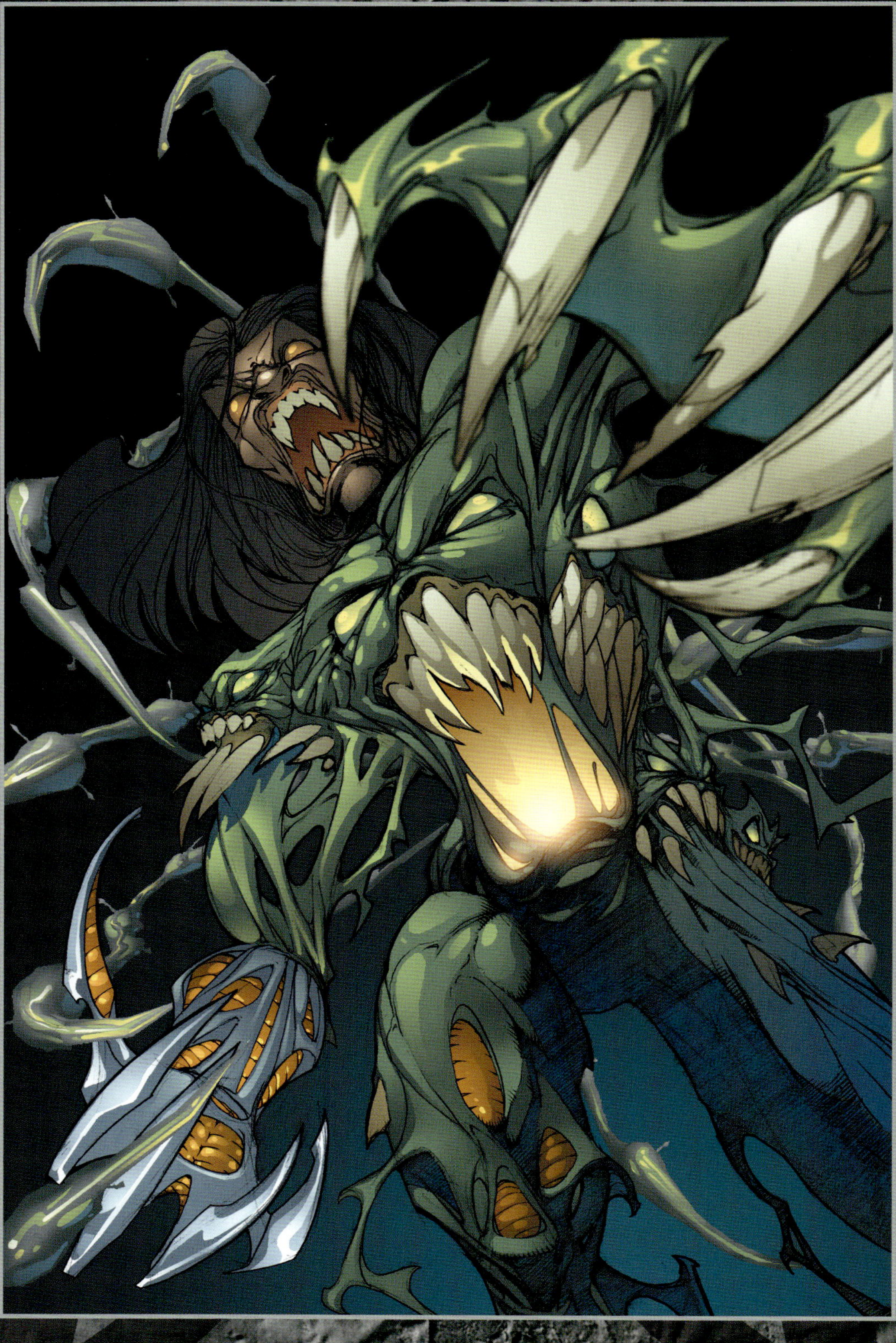

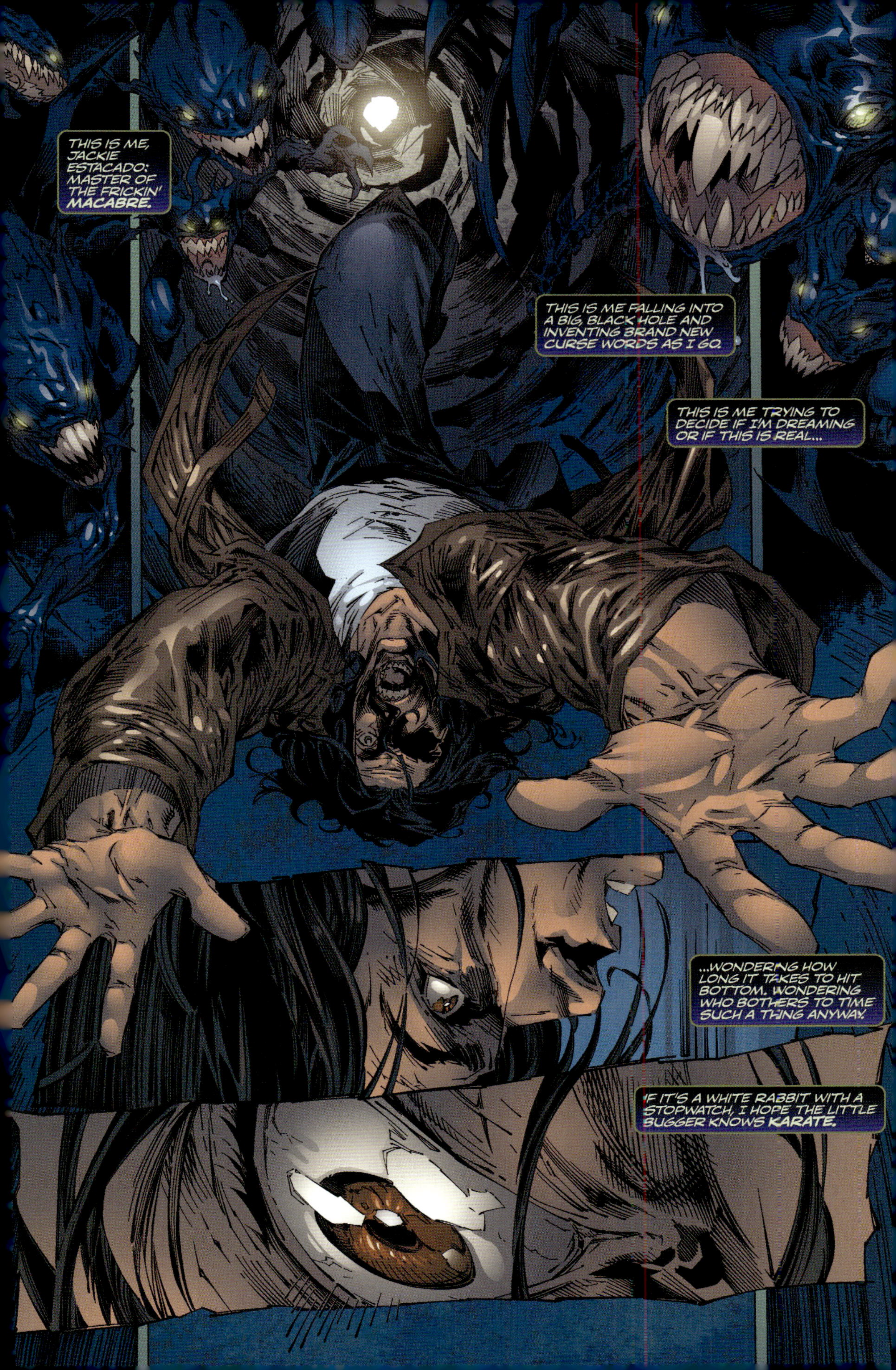

THIS IS ME, JACKIE ESTACADO: MASTER OF THE FRICKIN' MACABRE.
THIS IS ME FALLING INTO A BIG, BLACK HOLE AND INVENTING BRAND NEW CURSE WORDS AS I GO.
THIS IS ME TRYING TO DECIDE IF I'M DREAMING OR IF THIS IS REAL...
...WONDERING HOW LONG IT TAKES TO HIT BOTTOM. WONDERING WHO BOTHERS TO TIME SUCH A THING ANYWAY.
IF IT'S A WHITE RABBIT WITH A STOPWATCH, I HOPE THE LITTLE BUGGER KNOWS KARATE.

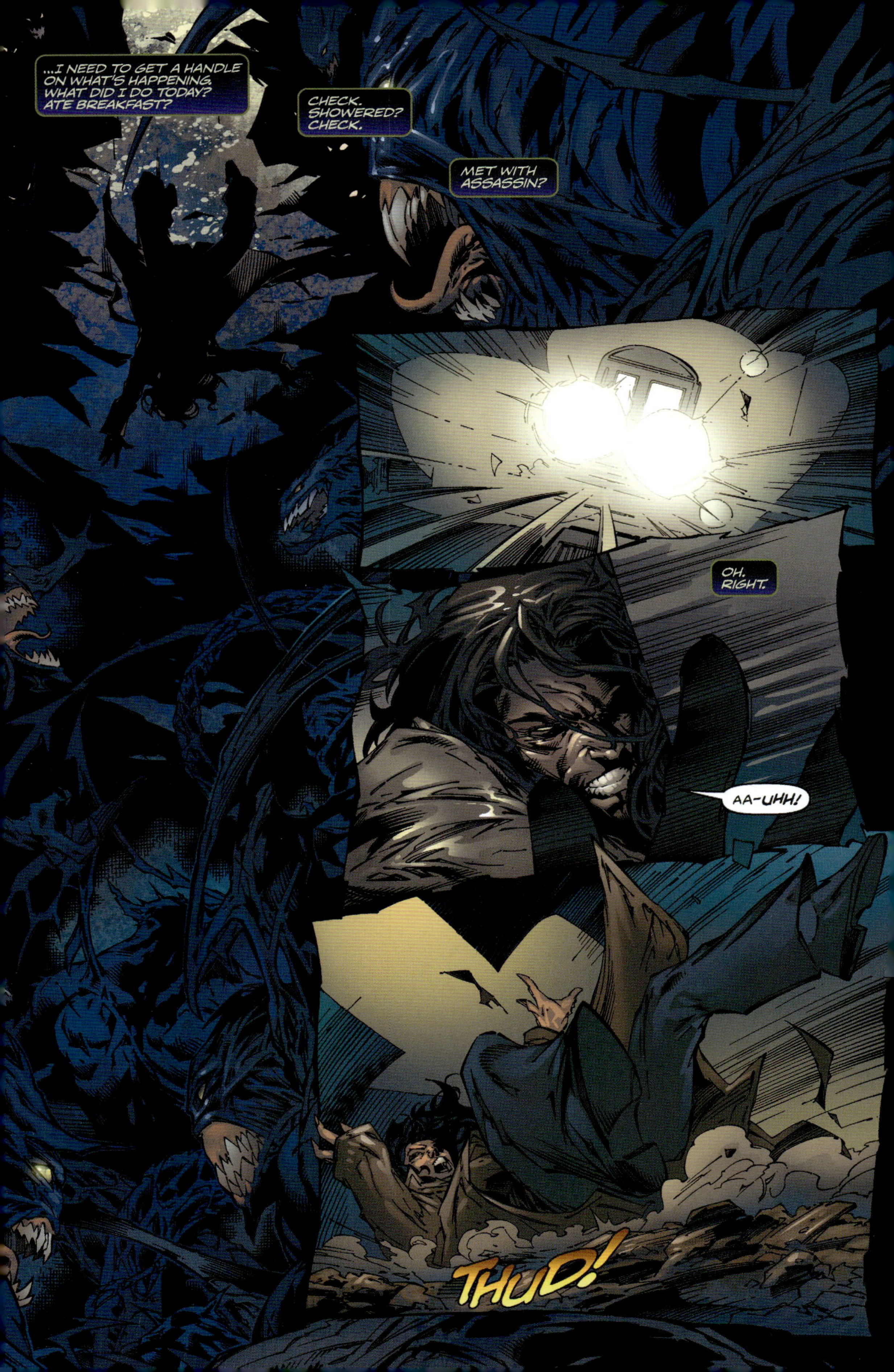
...I NEED TO GET A HANDLE ON WHAT'S HAPPENING. WHAT DID I DO TODAY? ATE BREAKFAST?
CHECK. SHOWERED? CHECK.
MET WITH ASSASSIN?
OH. RIGHT.
AA-UHH!
THUD!

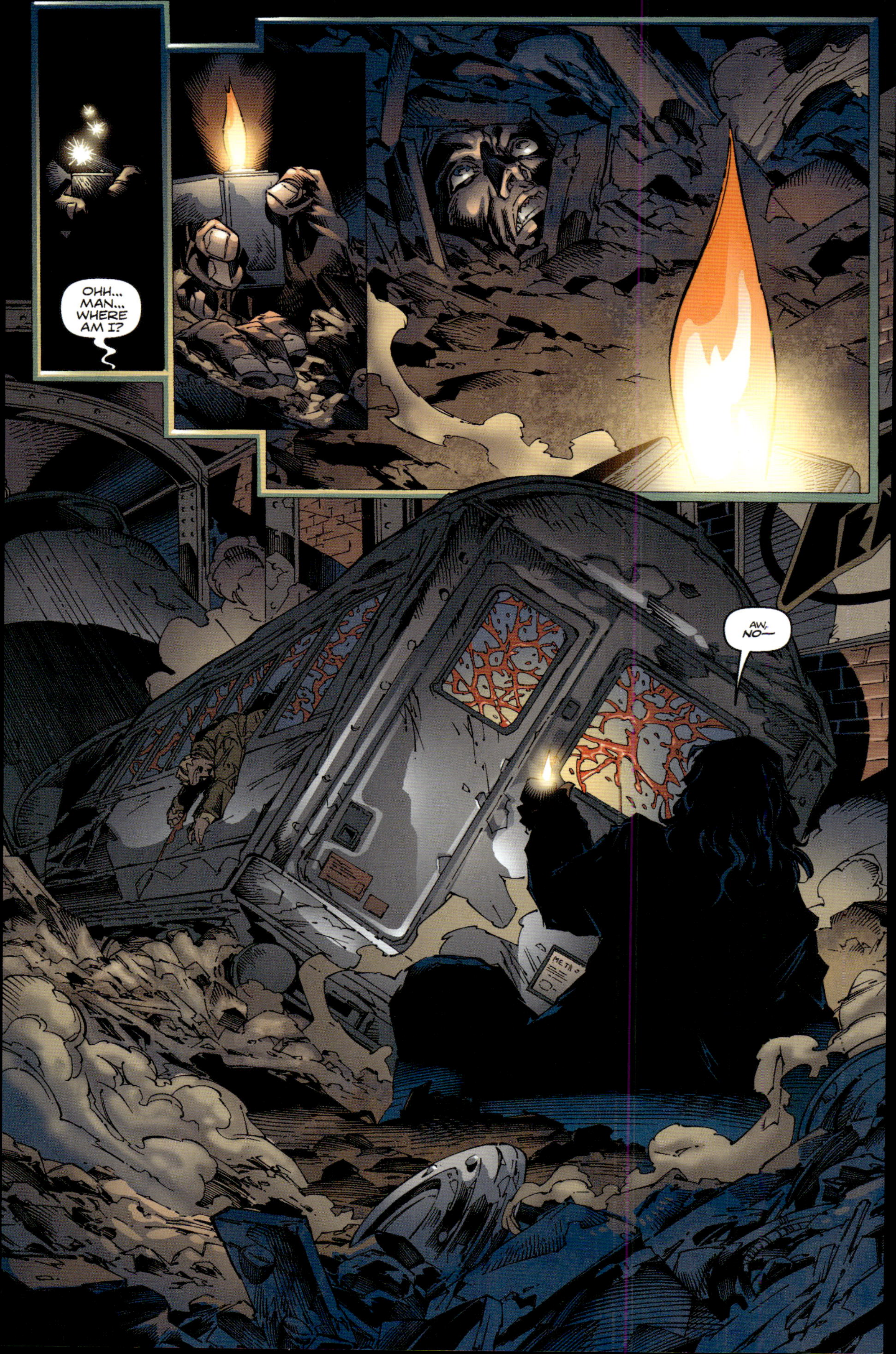
OHH... MAN... WHERE AM I?
AW, NO—

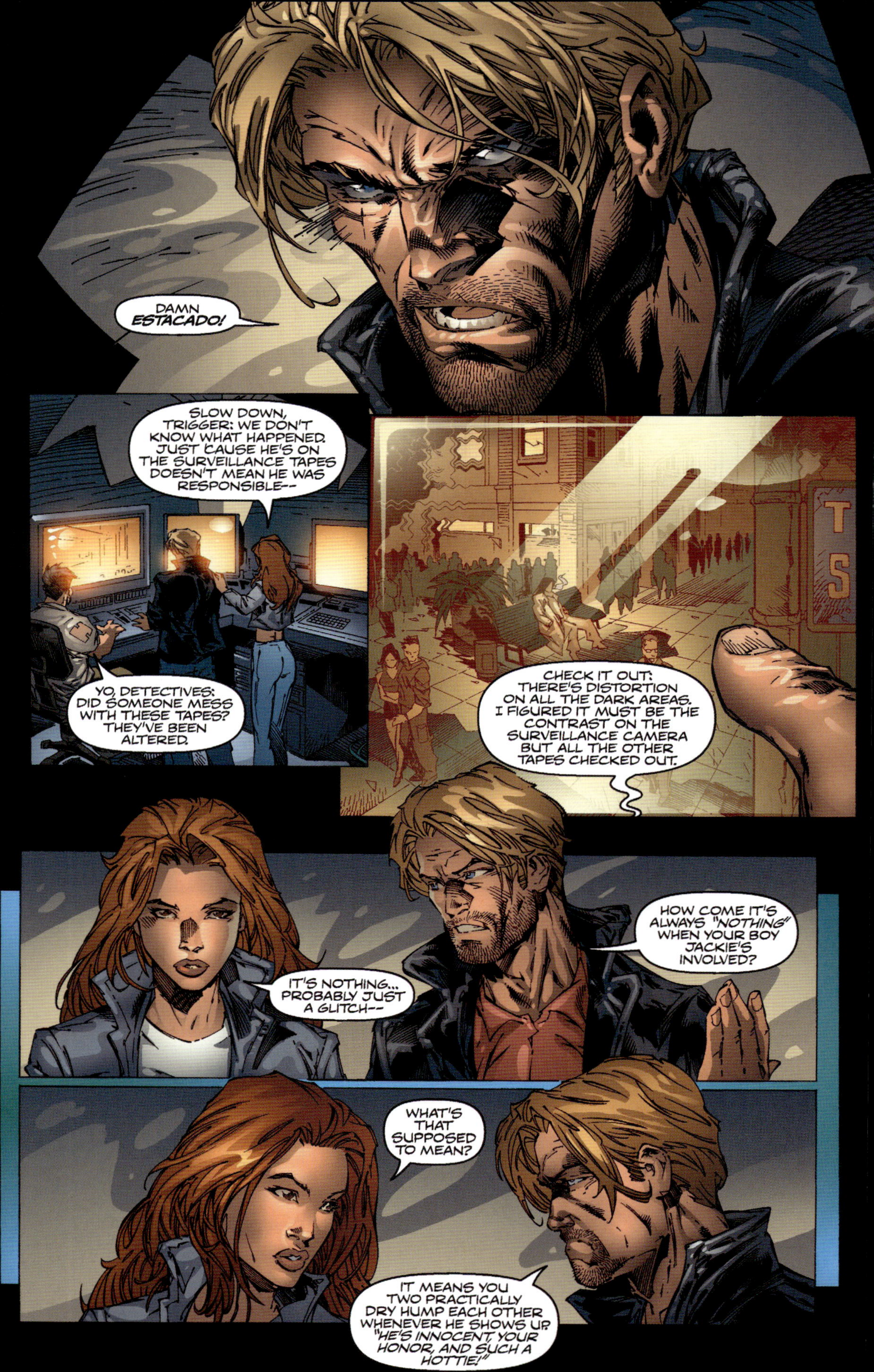
DAMN ESTACADO!
SLOW DOWN, TRIGGER: WE DON'T KNOW WHAT HAPPENED. JUST 'CAUSE HE'S ON THE SURVEILLANCE TAPES DOESN'T MEAN HE WAS RESPONSIBLE--
YO, DETECTIVES: DID SOMEONE MESS WITH THESE TAPES? THEY'VE BEEN ALTERED.
CHECK IT OUT: THERE'S DISTORTION ON ALL THE DARK AREAS. I FIGURED IT MUST BE THE CONTRAST ON THE SURVEILLANCE CAMERA BUT ALL THE OTHER TAPES CHECKED OUT.
IT'S NOTHING... PROBABLY JUST A GLITCH--
HOW COME IT'S ALWAYS "NOTHING" WHEN YOUR BOY JACKIE'S INVOLVED?
WHAT'S THAT SUPPOSED TO MEAN?
IT MEANS YOU TWO PRACTICALLY DRY HUMP EACH OTHER WHENEVER HE SHOWS UP. "HE'S INNOCENT, YOUR HONOR, AND SUCH A HOTTIE!"

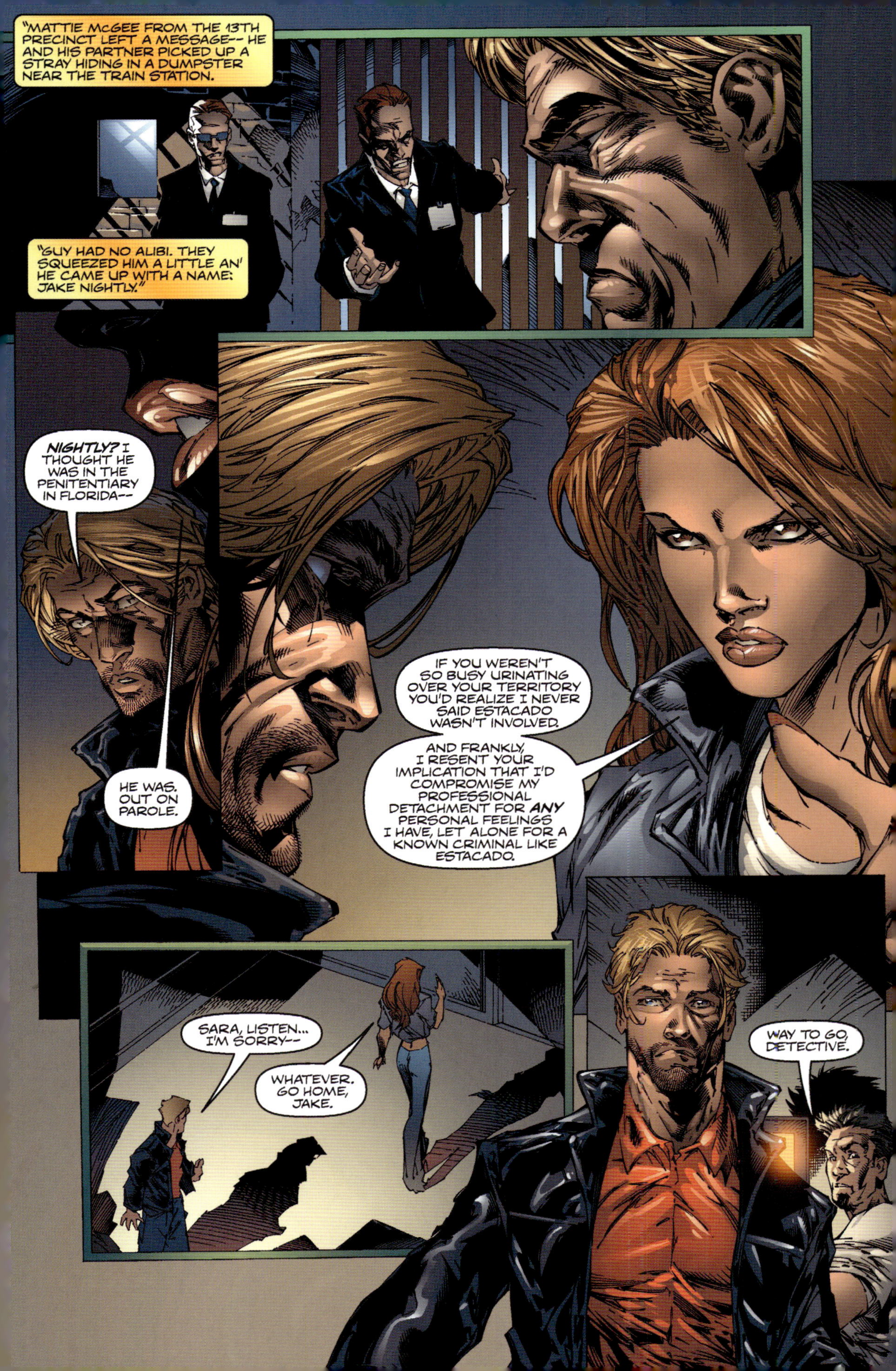
"MATTIE McGEE FROM THE 13TH PRECINCT LEFT A MESSAGE-- HE AND HIS PARTNER PICKED UP A STRAY HIDING IN A DUMPSTER NEAR THE TRAIN STATION.
"GUY HAD NO ALIBI. THEY SQUEEZED HIM A LITTLE AN' HE CAME UP WITH A NAME: JAKE NIGHTLY."
NIGHTLY? I THOUGHT HE WAS IN THE PENITENTIARY IN FLORIDA--
HE WAS. OUT ON PAROLE.
IF YOU WEREN'T SO BUSY URINATING OVER YOUR TERRITORY YOU'D REALIZE I NEVER SAID ESTACADO WASN'T INVOLVED.
AND FRANKLY, I RESENT YOUR IMPLICATION THAT I'D COMPROMISE MY PROFESSIONAL DETACHMENT FOR ANY PERSONAL FEELINGS I HAVE, LET ALONE FOR A KNOWN CRIMINAL LIKE ESTACADO.
SARA, LISTEN... I'M SORRY--
WHATEVER. GO HOME, JAKE.
WAY TO GO, DETECTIVE.

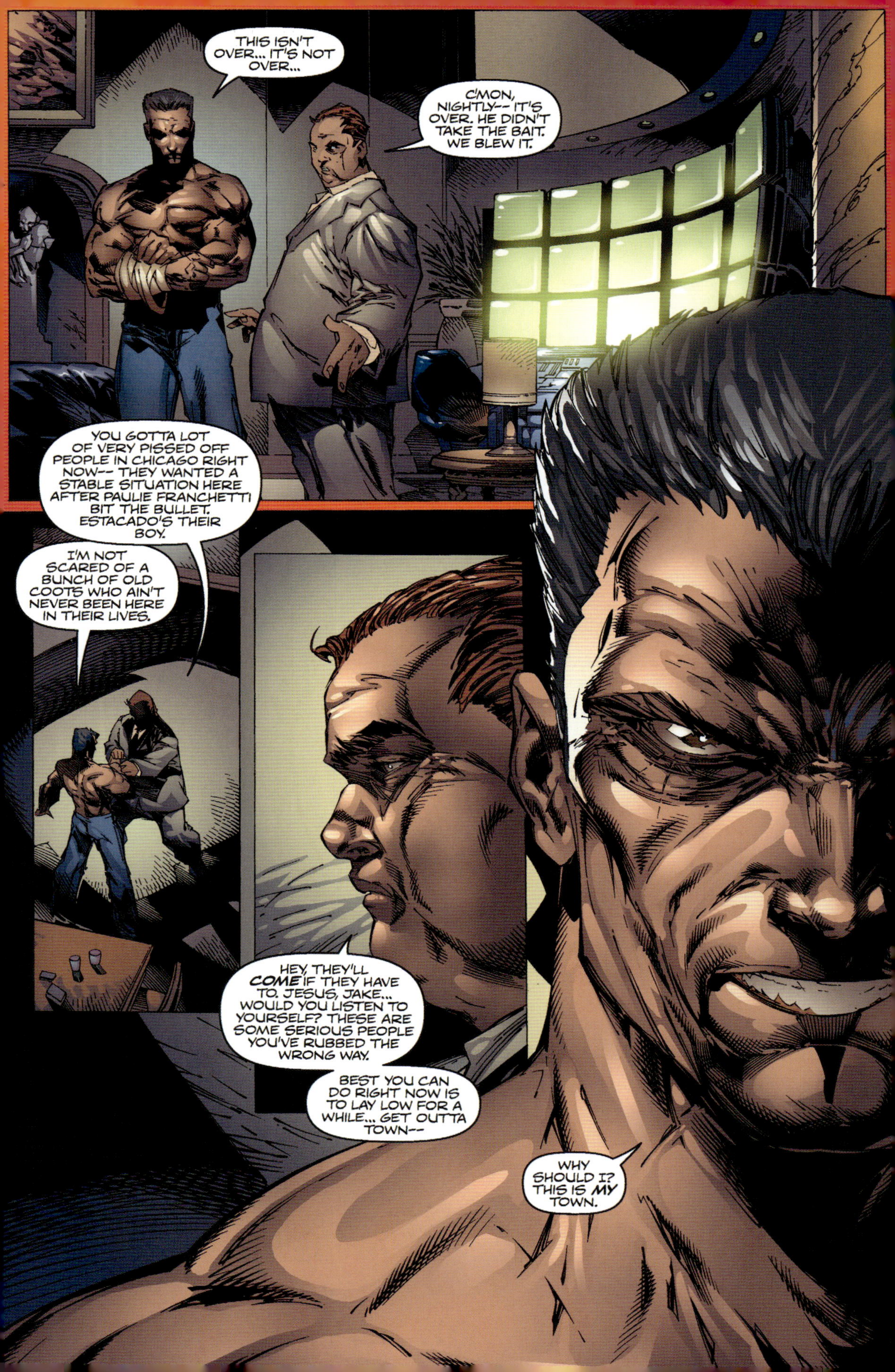
THIS ISN'T OVER... IT'S NOT OVER...
C'MON, NIGHTLY-- IT'S OVER. HE DIDN'T TAKE THE BAIT. WE BLEW IT.
YOU GOTTA LOT OF VERY PISSED OFF PEOPLE IN CHICAGO RIGHT NOW-- THEY WANTED A STABLE SITUATION HERE AFTER PAULIE FRANCHETTI BIT THE BULLET. ESTACADO'S THEIR BOY.
I'M NOT SCARED OF A BUNCH OF OLD COOTS WHO AIN'T NEVER BEEN HERE IN THEIR LIVES.
HEY, THEY'LL **COME** IF THEY HAVE TO. JESUS, JAKE... WOULD YOU LISTEN TO YOURSELF? THESE ARE SOME SERIOUS PEOPLE YOU'VE RUBBED THE WRONG WAY.
BEST YOU CAN DO RIGHT NOW IS TO LAY LOW FOR A WHILE... GET OUTTA TOWN--
WHY SHOULD I? THIS IS **MY** TOWN.

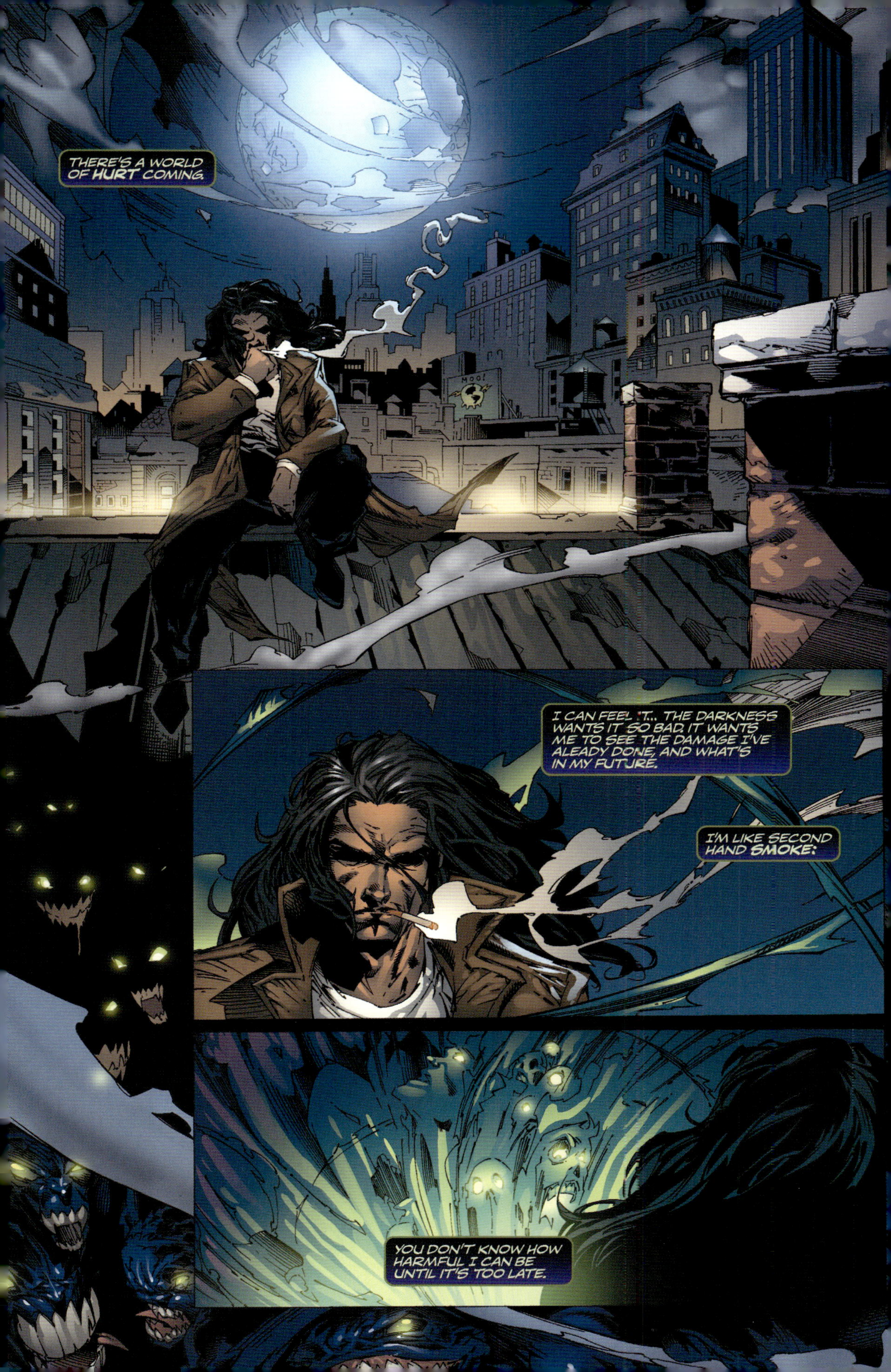
THERE'S A WORLD OF HURT COMING.
I CAN FEEL IT... THE DARKNESS WANTS IT SO BAD, IT WANTS ME TO SEE THE DAMAGE I'VE ALEADY DONE, AND WHAT'S IN MY FUTURE.
I'M LIKE SECOND HAND SMOKE:
YOU DON'T KNOW HOW HARMFUL I CAN BE UNTIL IT'S TOO LATE.

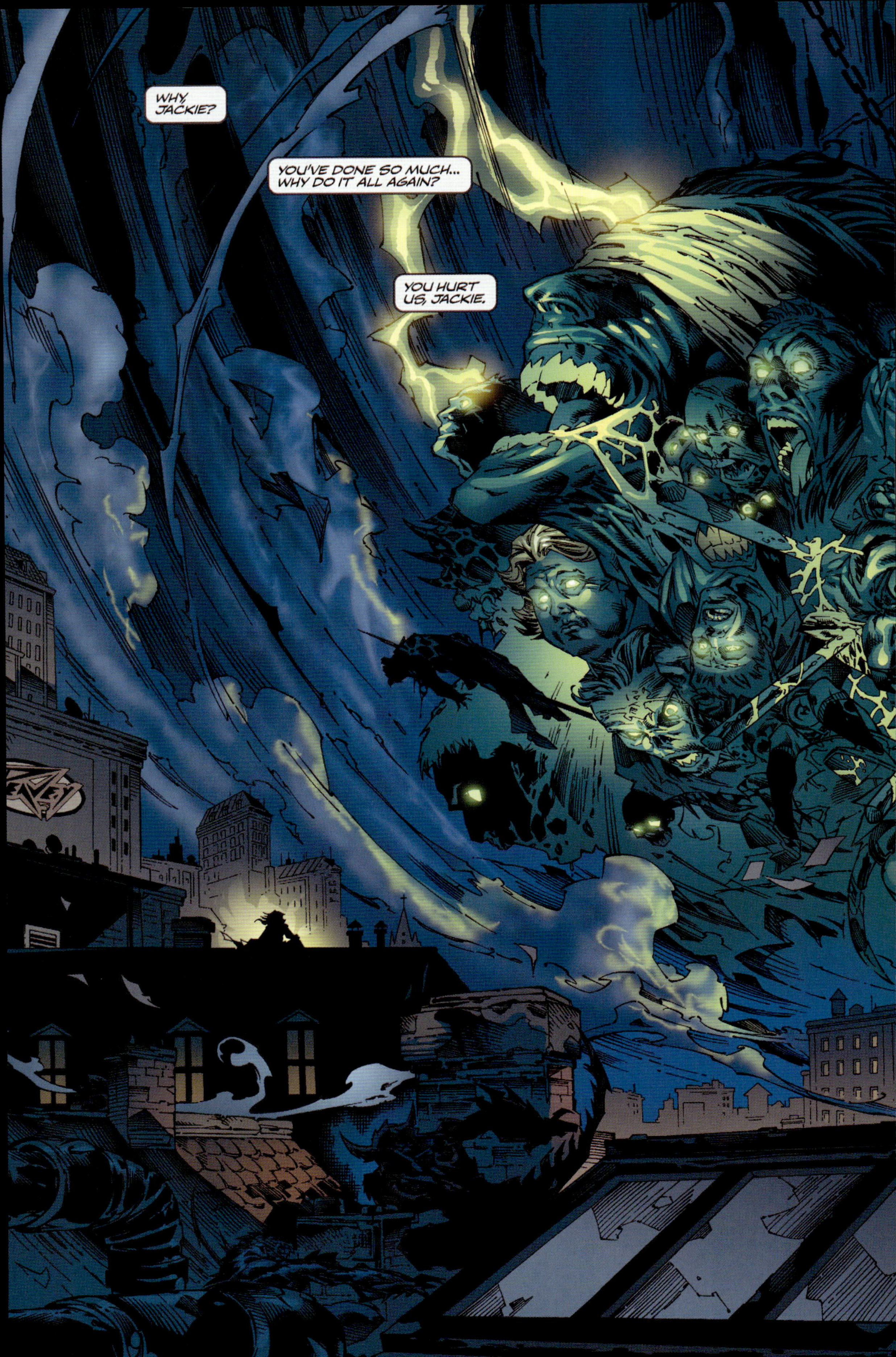
WHY, JACKIE?
YOU'VE DONE SO MUCH... WHY DO IT ALL AGAIN?
YOU HURT US, JACKIE.

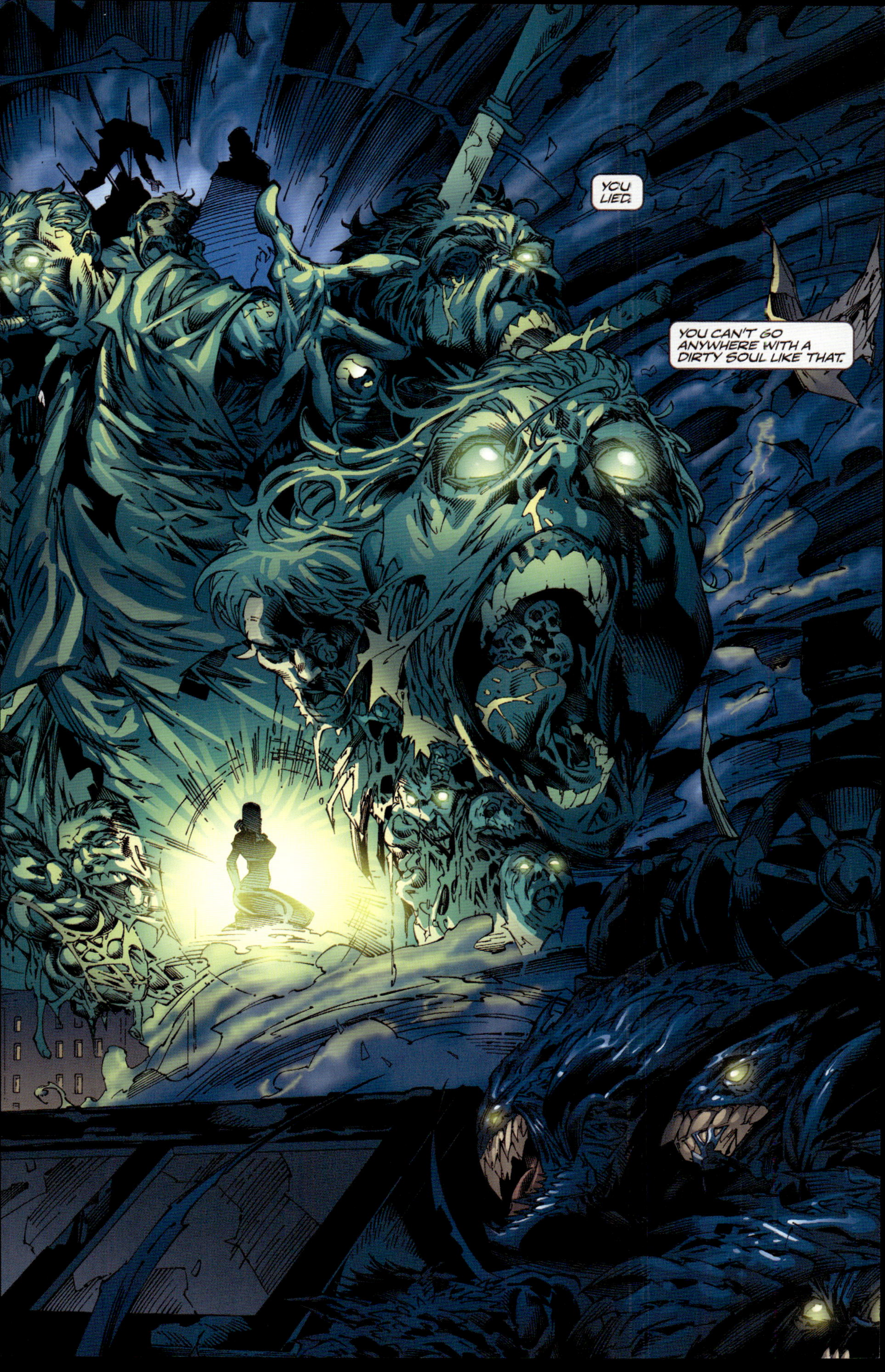
YOU LIED.
YOU CAN'T GO ANYWHERE WITH A DIRTY SOUL LIKE THAT.

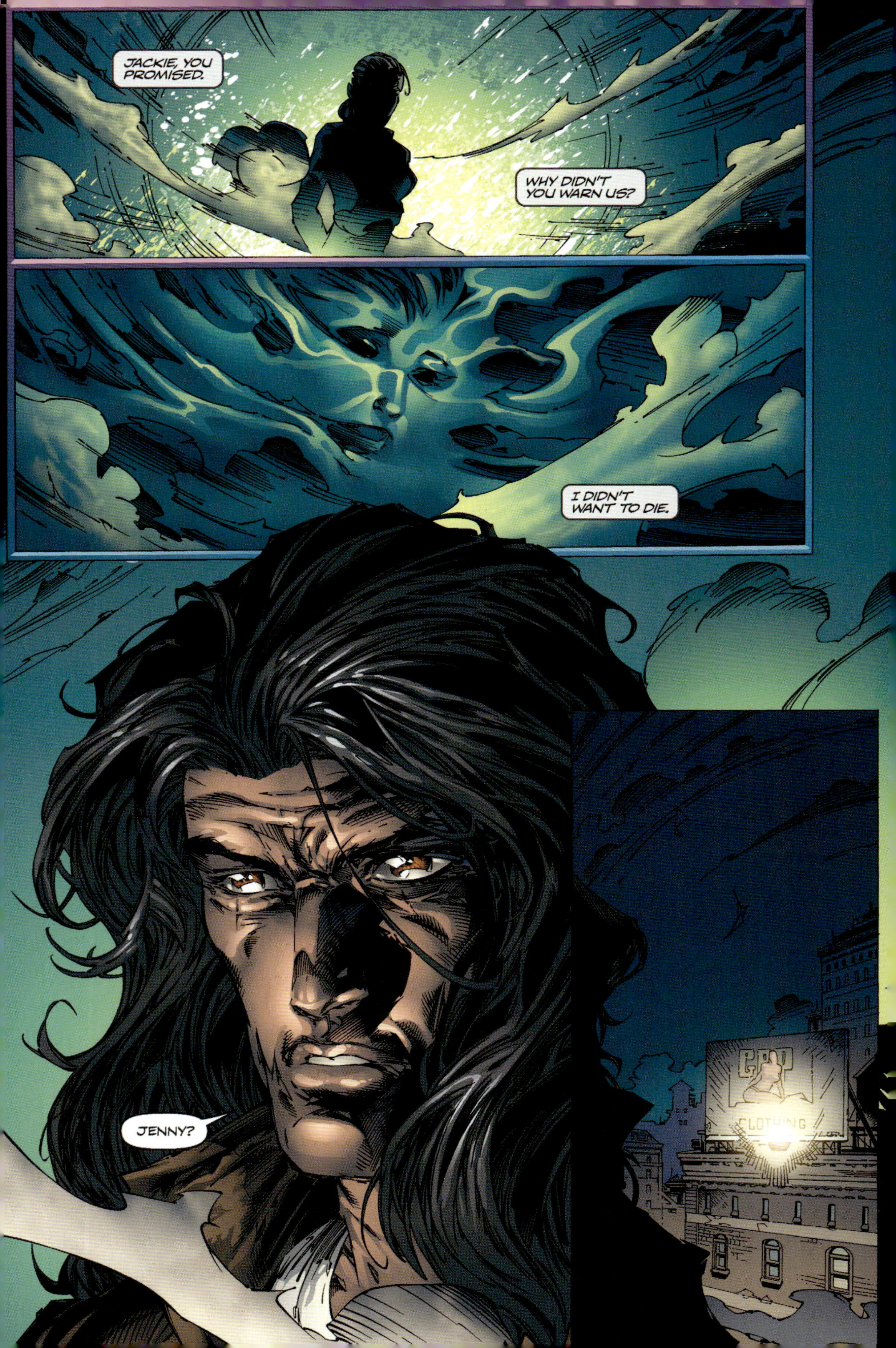
JACKIE, YOU PROMISED.
WHY DIDN'T YOU WARN US?
I DIDN'T WANT TO DIE.
JENNY?
CLOTHING

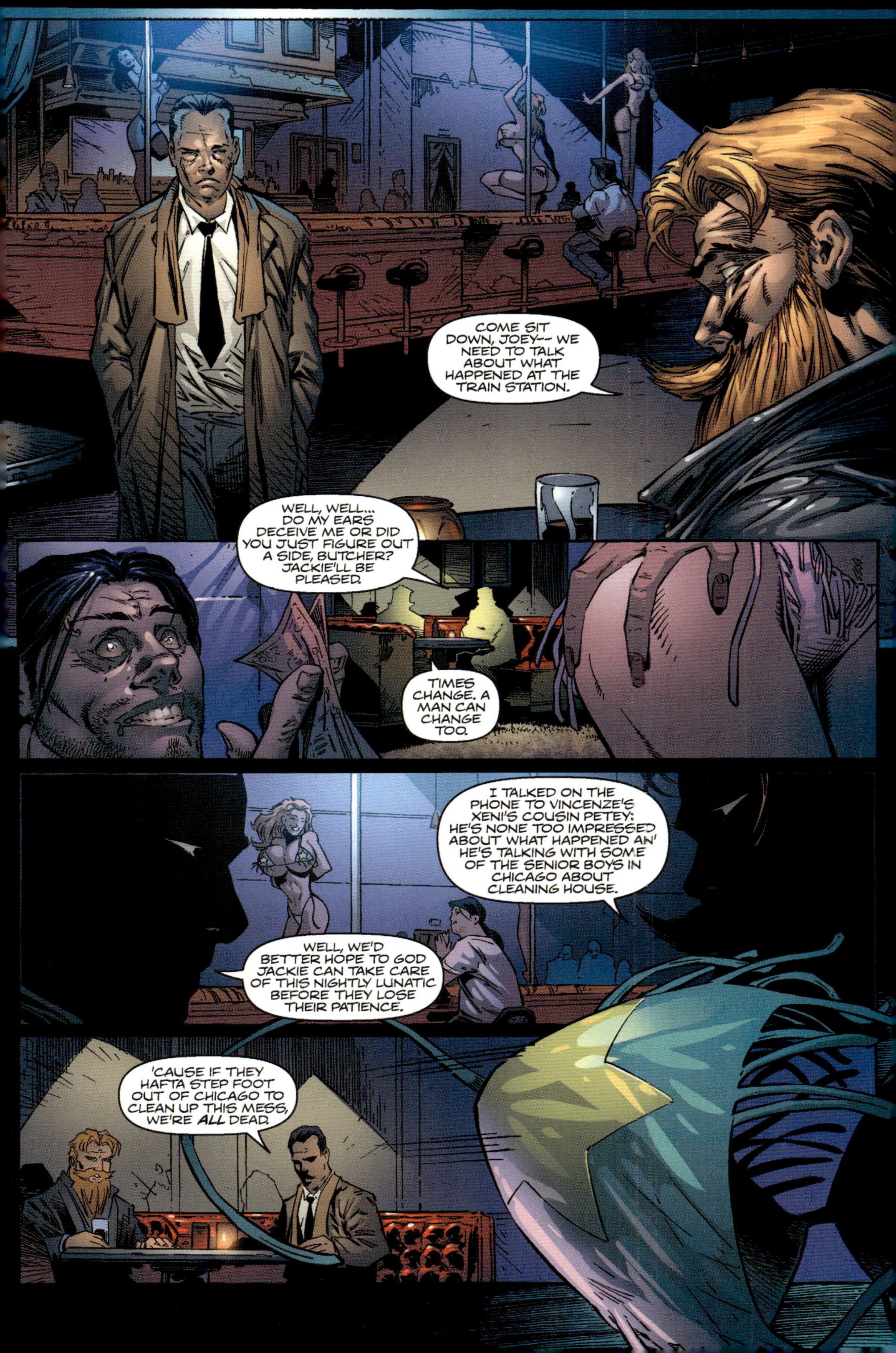
COME SIT DOWN, JOEY-- WE NEED TO TALK ABOUT WHAT HAPPENED AT THE TRAIN STATION.
WELL, WELL... DO MY EARS DECEIVE ME OR DID YOU JUST FIGURE OUT A SIDE, BUTCHER? JACKIE'LL BE PLEASED.
TIMES CHANGE. A MAN CAN CHANGE TOO.
I TALKED ON THE PHONE TO VINCENZE'S XENI'S COUSIN PETEY: HE'S NONE TOO IMPRESSED ABOUT WHAT HAPPENED AN' HE'S TALKING WITH SOME OF THE SENIOR BOYS IN CHICAGO ABOUT CLEANING HOUSE.
WELL, WE'D BETTER HOPE TO GOD JACKIE CAN TAKE CARE OF THIS NIGHTLY LUNATIC BEFORE THEY LOSE THEIR PATIENCE.
'CAUSE IF THEY HAFTA STEP FOOT OUT OF CHICAGO TO CLEAN UP THIS MESS, WE'RE ALL DEAD.

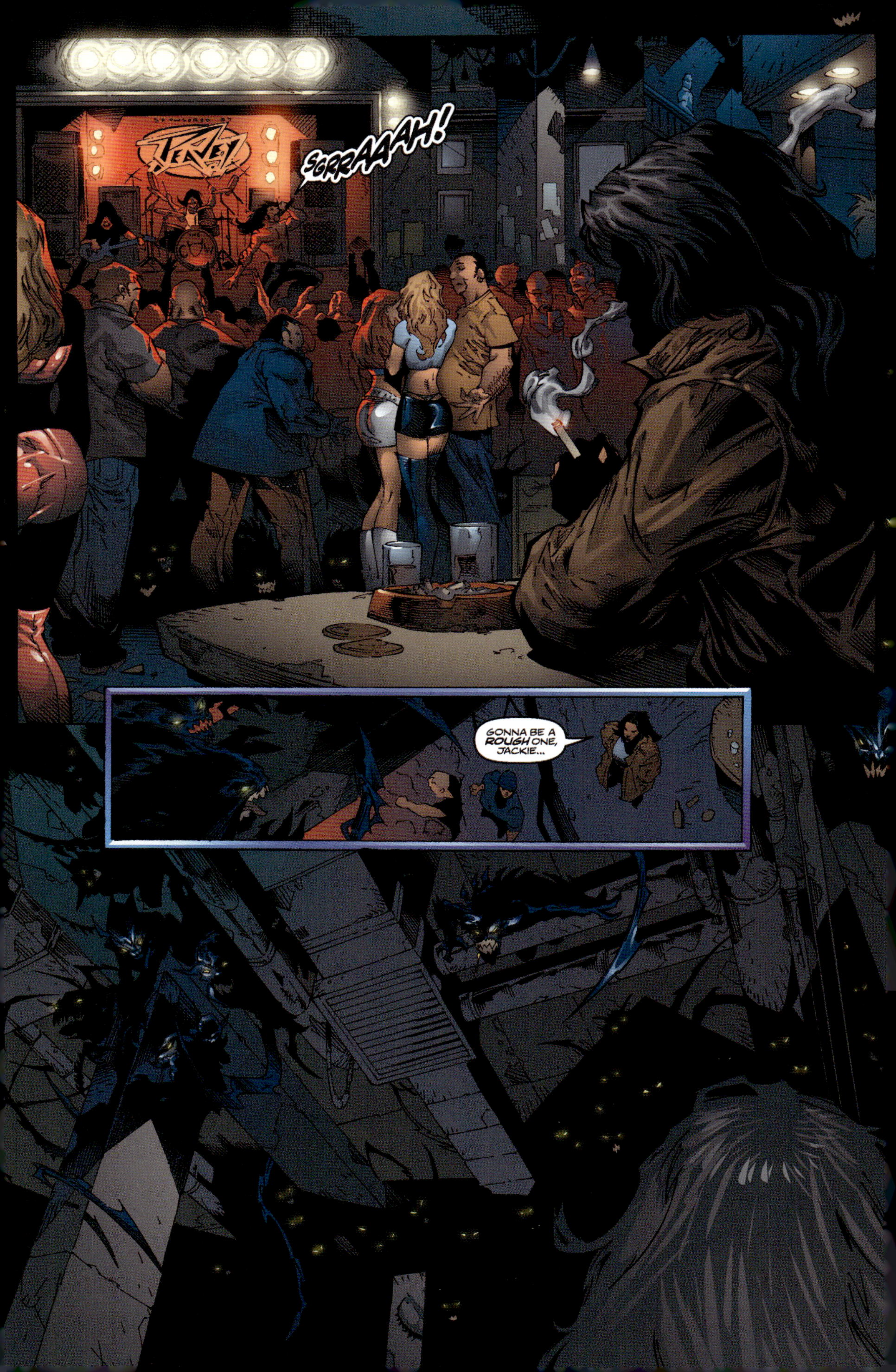
SCRRAAAH!
GONNA BE A ROUGH ONE, JACKIE...

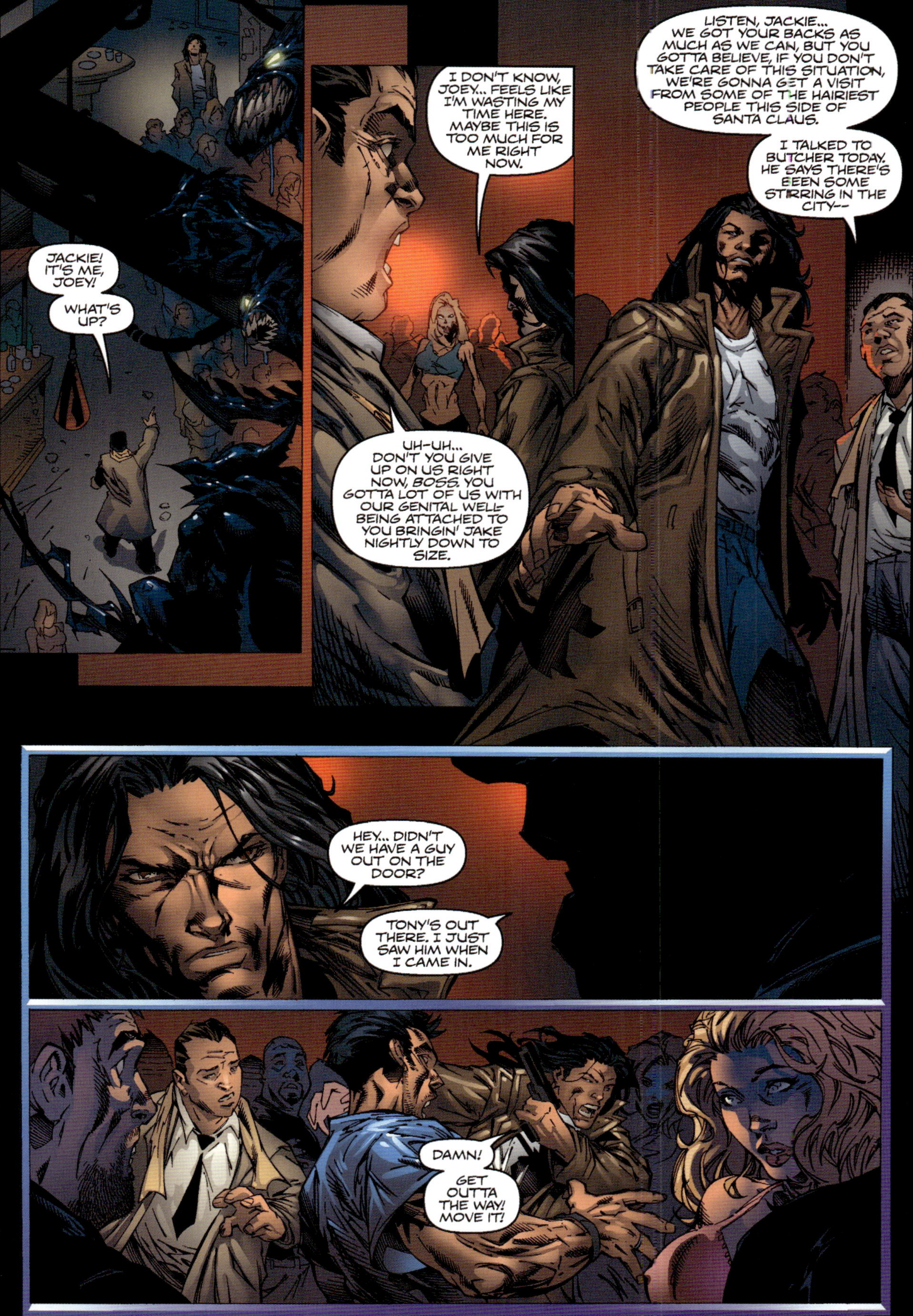
JACKIE! IT'S ME, JOEY!
WHAT'S UP?
I DON'T KNOW, JOEY... FEELS LIKE I'M WASTING MY TIME HERE. MAYBE THIS IS TOO MUCH FOR ME RIGHT NOW.
UH-UH... DON'T YOU GIVE UP ON US RIGHT NOW, BOSS. YOU GOTTA LOT OF US WITH OUR GENITAL WELL-BEING ATTACHED TO YOU BRINGIN' JAKE NIGHTLY DOWN TO SIZE.
LISTEN, JACKIE... WE GOT YOUR BACKS AS MUCH AS WE CAN, BUT YOU GOTTA BELIEVE, IF YOU DON'T TAKE CARE OF THIS SITUATION, WE'RE GONNA GET A VISIT FROM SOME OF THE HAIRIEST PEOPLE THIS SIDE OF SANTA CLAUS.
I TALKED TO BUTCHER TODAY. HE SAYS THERE'S BEEN SOME STIRRING IN THE CITY--
HEY... DIDN'T WE HAVE A GUY OUT ON THE DOOR?
TONY'S OUT THERE. I JUST SAW HIM WHEN I CAME IN.
DAMN!
GET OUTTA THE WAY! MOVE IT!

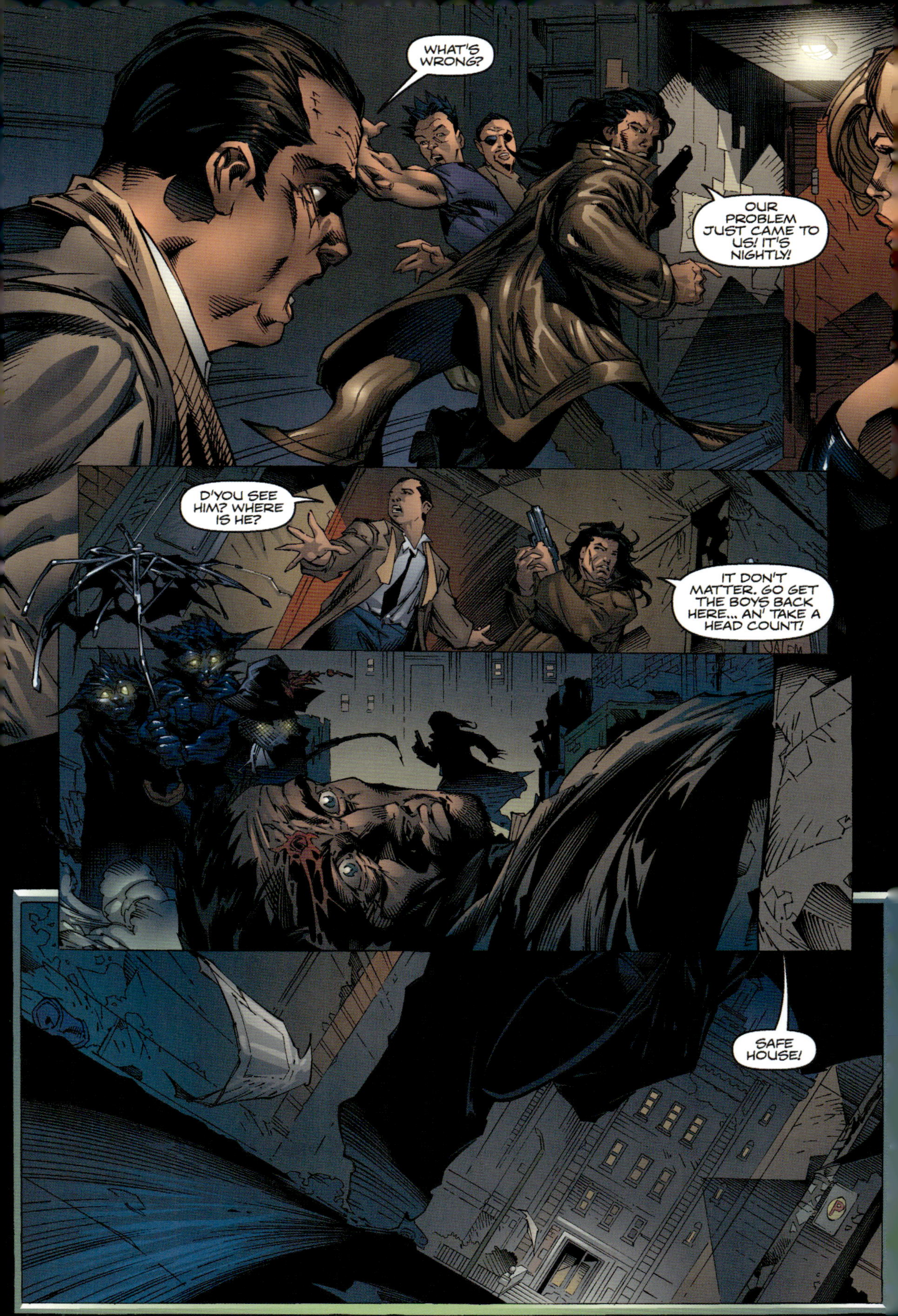
WHAT'S WRONG?
OUR PROBLEM JUST CAME TO US! IT'S NIGHTLY!
D'YOU SEE HIM? WHERE IS HE?
IT DON'T MATTER. GO GET THE BOYS BACK HERE... AN' TAKE A HEAD COUNT!
SAFE HOUSE!

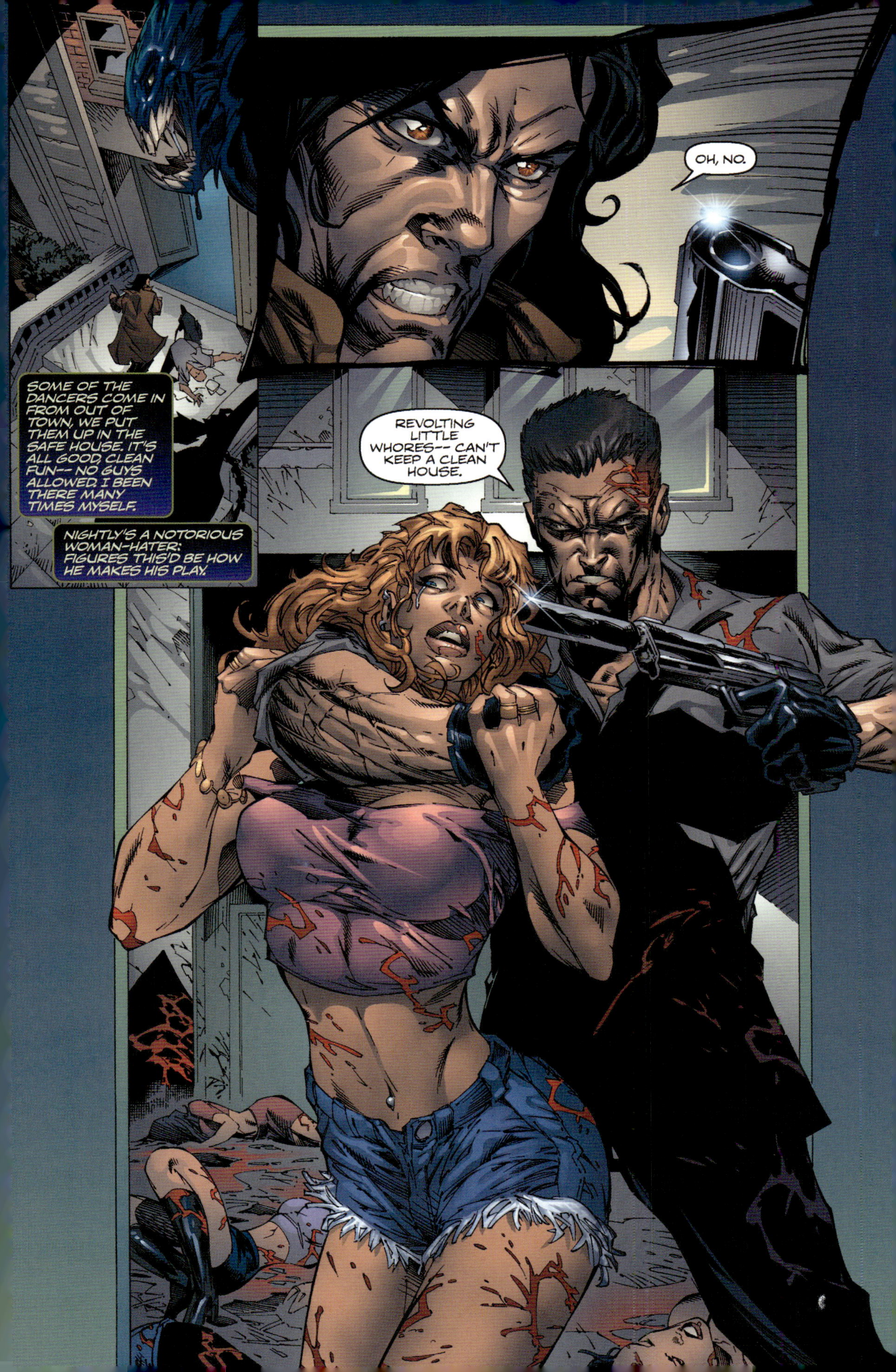
OH, NO.
SOME OF THE DANCERS COME IN FROM OUT OF TOWN, WE PUT THEM UP IN THE SAFE HOUSE. IT'S ALL GOOD CLEAN FUN-- NO GUYS ALLOWED. I BEEN THERE MANY TIMES MYSELF.
NIGHTLY'S A NOTORIOUS WOMAN-HATER: FIGURES THIS'D BE HOW HE MAKES HIS PLAY.
REVOLTING LITTLE WHORES-- CAN'T KEEP A CLEAN HOUSE.

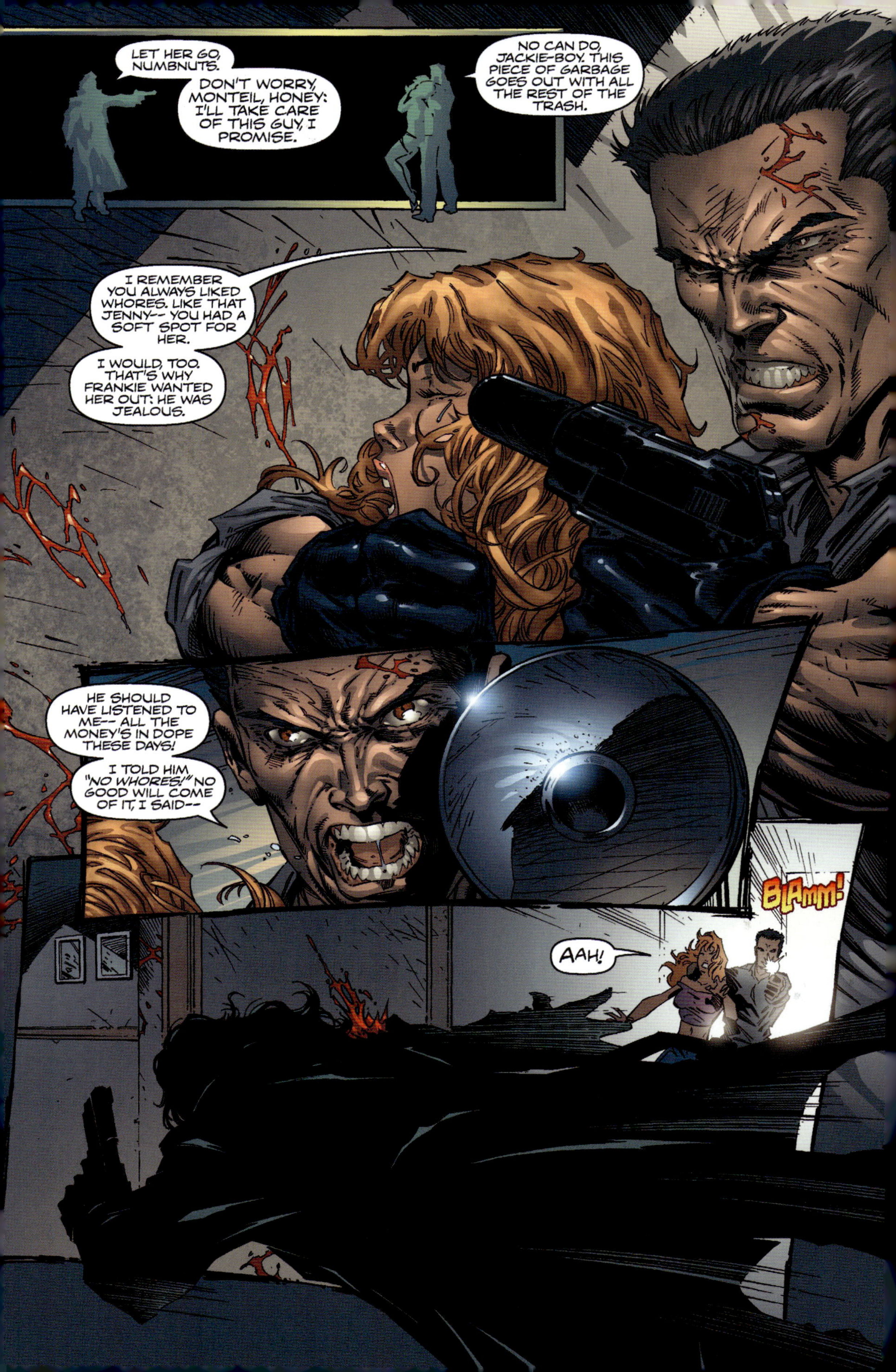
LET HER GO, NUMBNUTS.
DON'T WORRY, MONTEIL, HONEY: I'LL TAKE CARE OF THIS GUY, I PROMISE.
NO CAN DO, JACKIE-BOY. THIS PIECE OF GARBAGE GOES OUT WITH ALL THE REST OF THE TRASH.
I REMEMBER YOU ALWAYS LIKED WHORES. LIKE THAT JENNY-- YOU HAD A SOFT SPOT FOR HER.
I WOULD, TOO. THAT'S WHY FRANKIE WANTED HER OUT: HE WAS JEALOUS.
HE SHOULD HAVE LISTENED TO ME-- ALL THE MONEY'S IN DOPE THESE DAYS!
I TOLD HIM "NO WHORES!" NO GOOD WILL COME OF IT, I SAID--
BLAMM!
AAH!

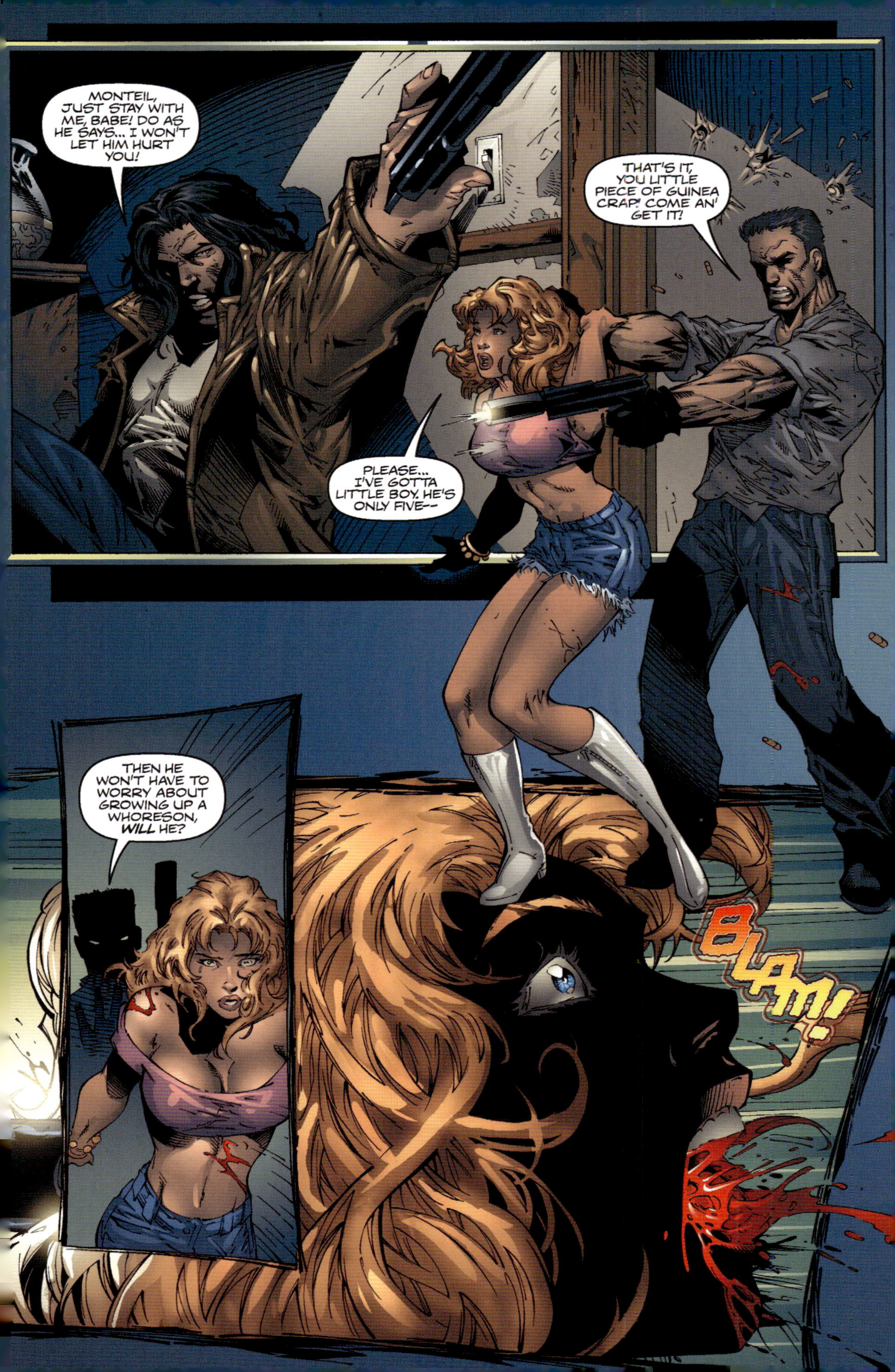
MONTEIL, JUST STAY WITH ME, BABE! DO AS HE SAYS... I WON'T LET HIM HURT YOU!
THAT'S IT, YOU LITTLE PIECE OF GUINEA CRAP! COME AN' GET IT!
PLEASE... I'VE GOTTA LITTLE BOY. HE'S ONLY FIVE--
THEN HE WON'T HAVE TO WORRY ABOUT GROWING UP A WHORESON, WILL HE?
BLAM!

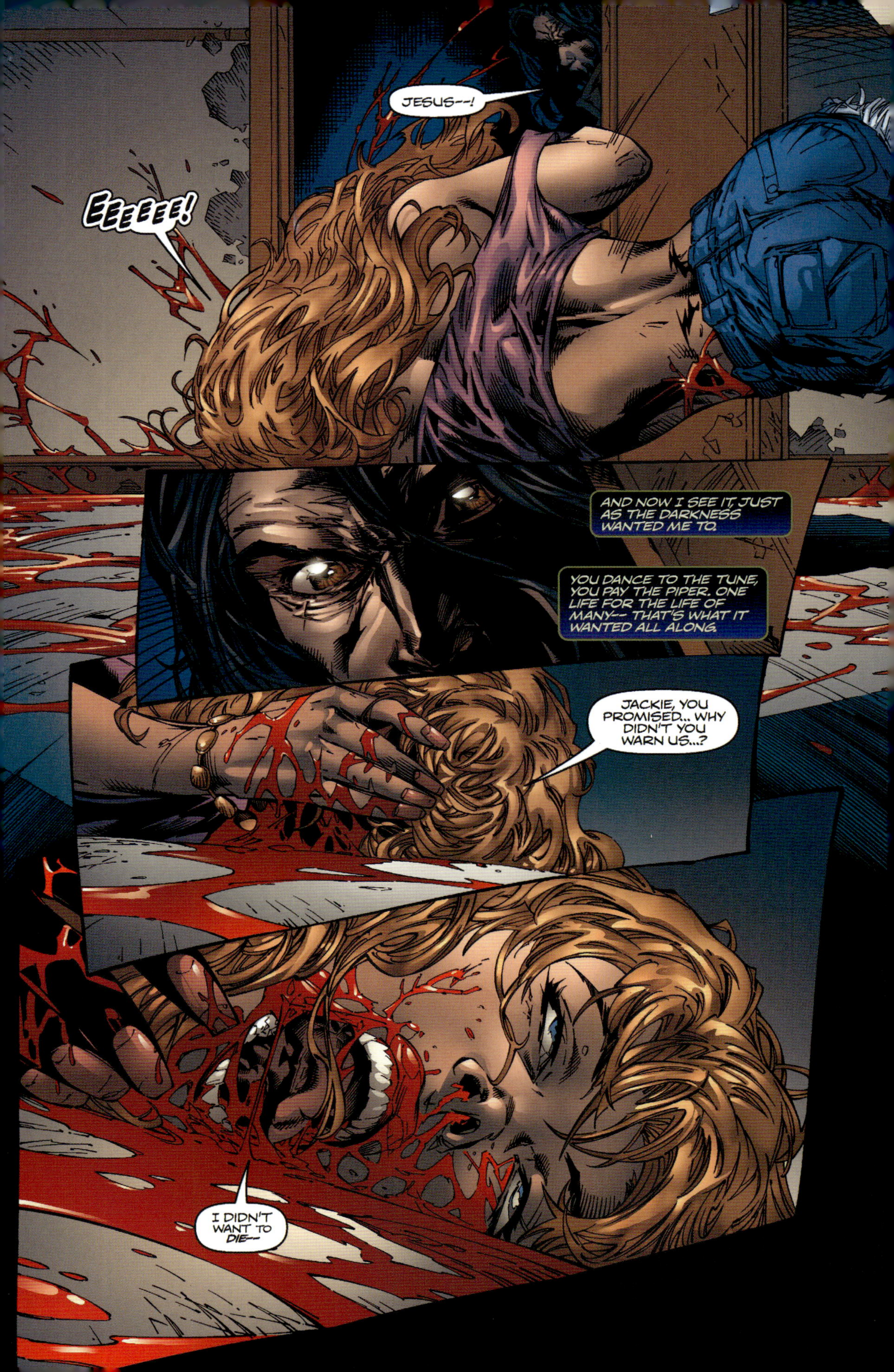
JESUS--!
EEEEEE!
AND NOW I SEE IT, JUST AS THE DARKNESS WANTED ME TO.
YOU DANCE TO THE TUNE, YOU PAY THE PIPER. ONE LIFE FOR THE LIFE OF MANY-- THAT'S WHAT IT WANTED ALL ALONG.
JACKIE, YOU PROMISED... WHY DIDN'T YOU WARN US...?
I DIDN'T WANT TO DIE--

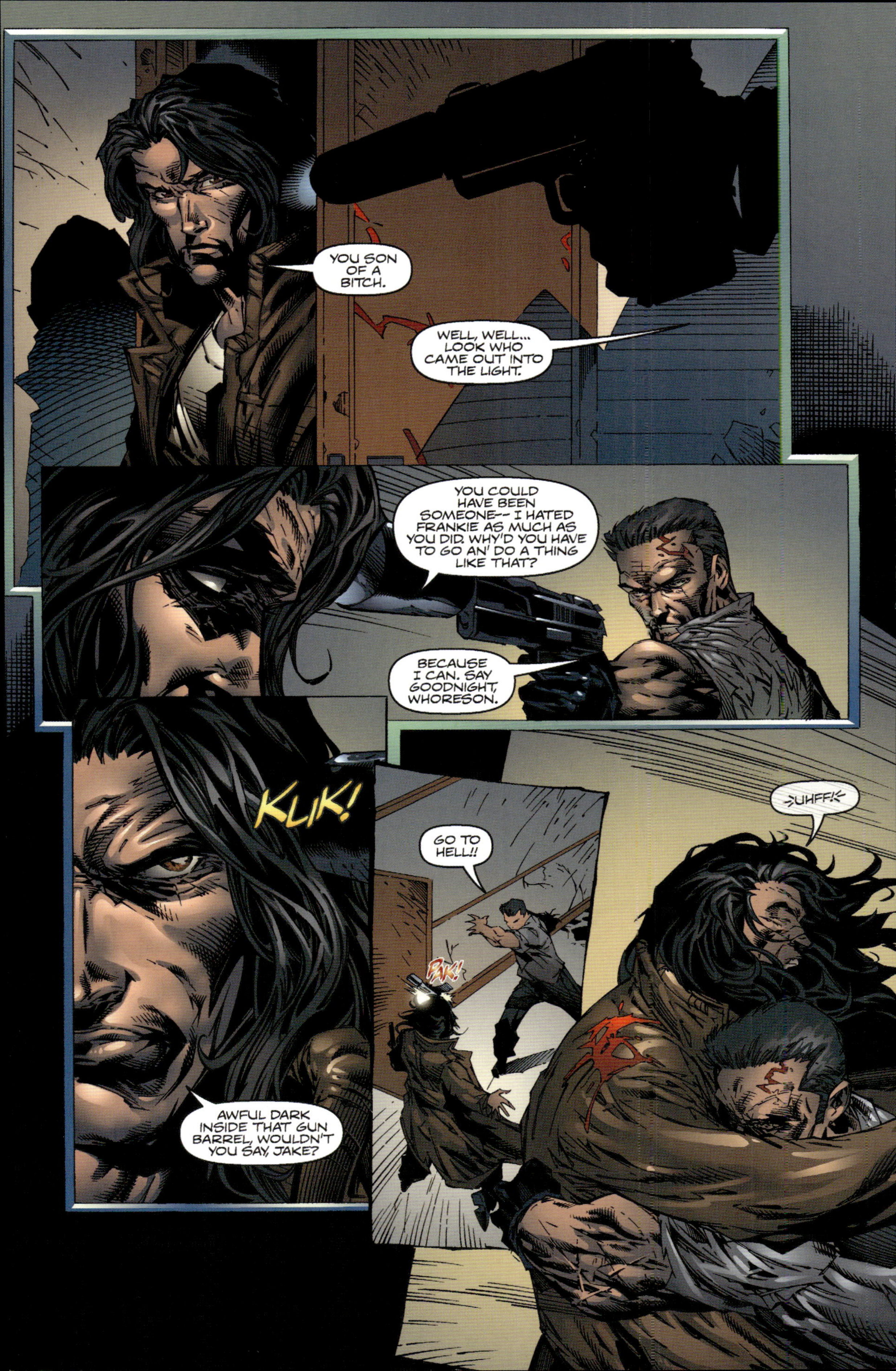
YOU SON OF A BITCH.
WELL, WELL... LOOK WHO CAME OUT INTO THE LIGHT.
YOU COULD HAVE BEEN SOMEONE-- I HATED FRANKIE AS MUCH AS YOU DID. WHY'D YOU HAVE TO GO AN' DO A THING LIKE THAT?
BECAUSE I CAN. SAY GOODNIGHT, WHORESON.
KLIK!
AWFUL DARK INSIDE THAT GUN BARREL, WOULDN'T YOU SAY, JAKE?
GO TO HELL!!
PAK!
UHFF!

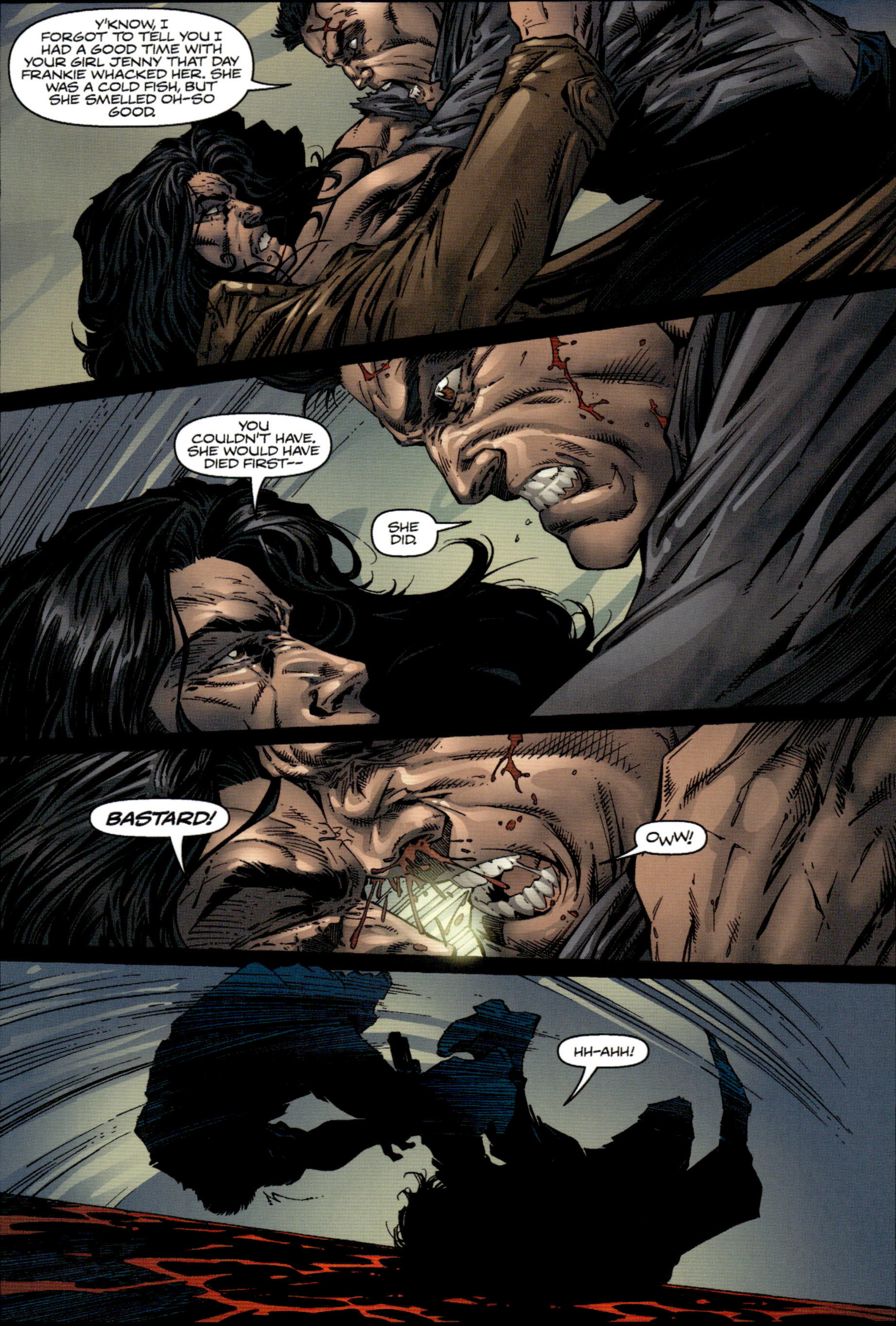
Y'KNOW, I FORGOT TO TELL YOU I HAD A GOOD TIME WITH YOUR GIRL JENNY THAT DAY FRANKIE WHACKED HER. SHE WAS A COLD FISH, BUT SHE SMELLED OH-SO GOOD.
YOU COULDN'T HAVE. SHE WOULD HAVE DIED FIRST--
SHE DID.
BASTARD!
OWW!
HH-AHH!

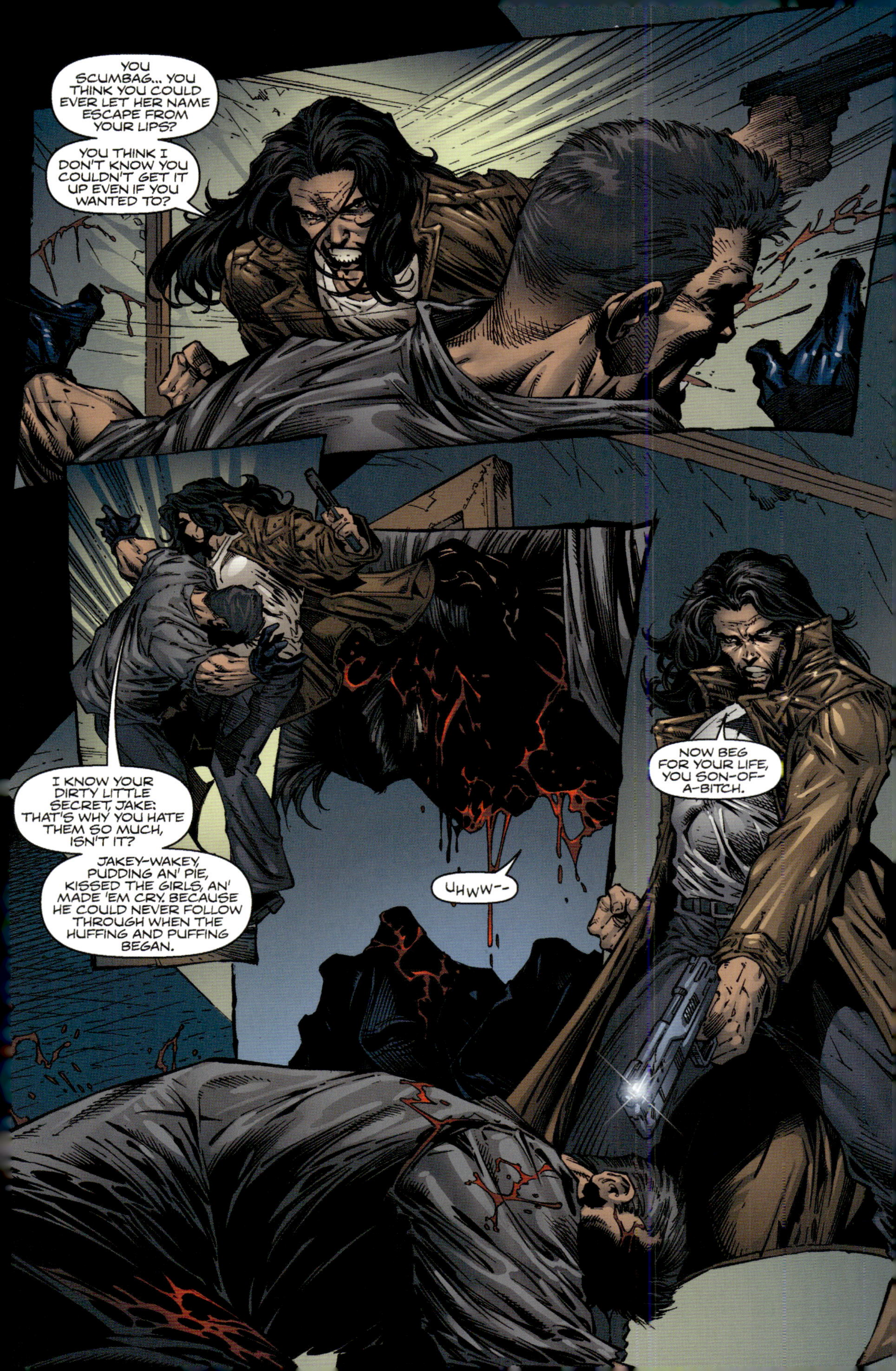
YOU SCUMBAG... YOU THINK YOU COULD EVER LET HER NAME ESCAPE FROM YOUR LIPS?
YOU THINK I DON'T KNOW YOU COULDN'T GET IT UP EVEN IF YOU WANTED TO?
I KNOW YOUR DIRTY LITTLE SECRET, JAKE: THAT'S WHY YOU HATE THEM SO MUCH, ISN'T IT?
JAKEY-WAKEY, PUDDING AN' PIE, KISSED THE GIRLS, AN' MADE 'EM CRY. BECAUSE HE COULD NEVER FOLLOW THROUGH WHEN THE HUFFING AND PUFFING BEGAN.
UHWW--
NOW BEG FOR YOUR LIFE, YOU SON-OF-A-BITCH.

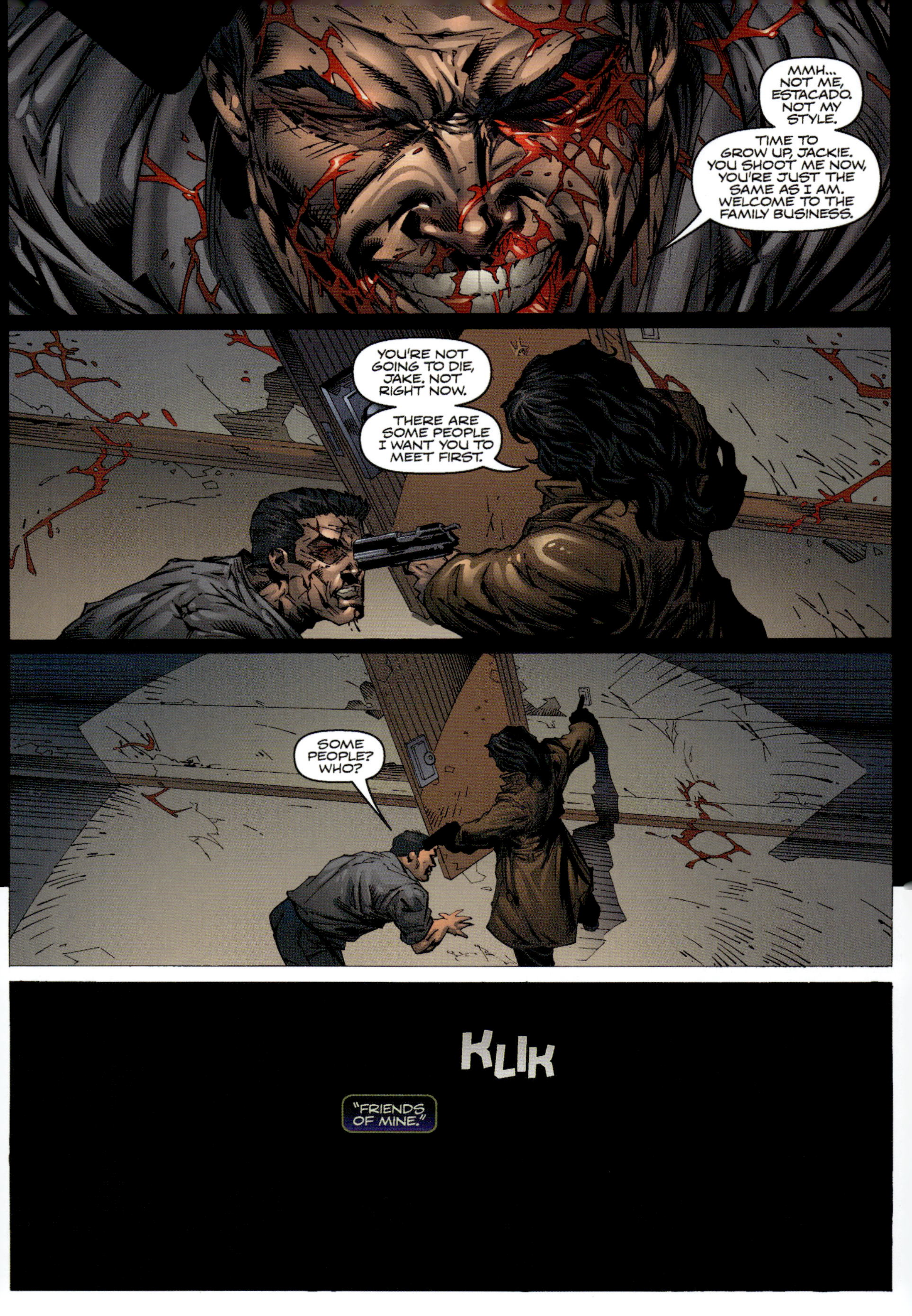
MMH... NOT ME, ESTACADO. NOT MY STYLE.
TIME TO GROW UP, JACKIE. YOU SHOOT ME NOW, YOU'RE JUST THE SAME AS I AM. WELCOME TO THE FAMILY BUSINESS.
YOU'RE NOT GOING TO DIE, JAKE. NOT RIGHT NOW.
THERE ARE SOME PEOPLE I WANT YOU TO MEET FIRST.
SOME PEOPLE? WHO?
KLIK
"FRIENDS OF MINE."

The Darkness Issue #49
cover art by: Vatche Mavlian & Brian Buccellato

THE DARKNESS #49

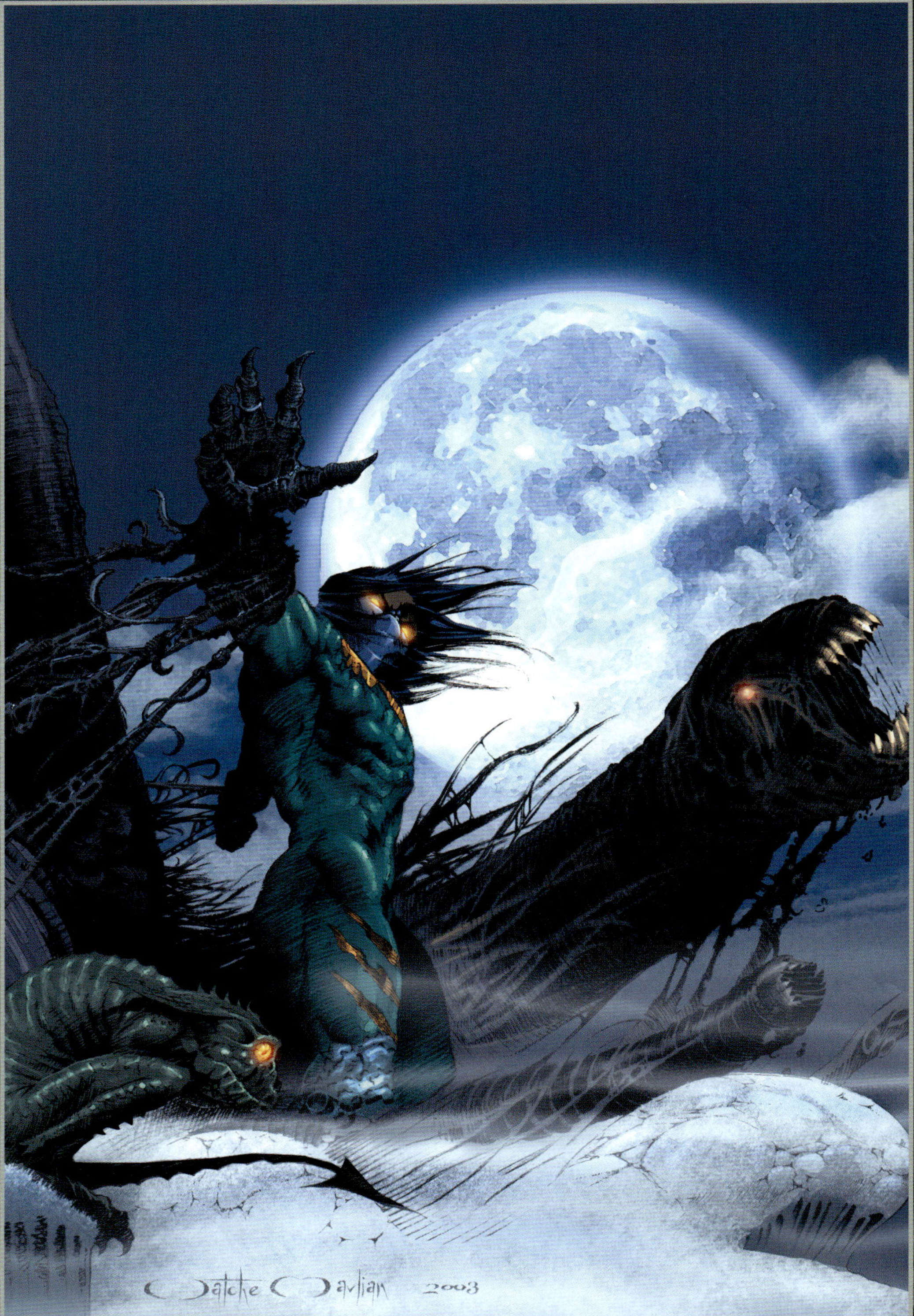
Vatche Mavlian 2003

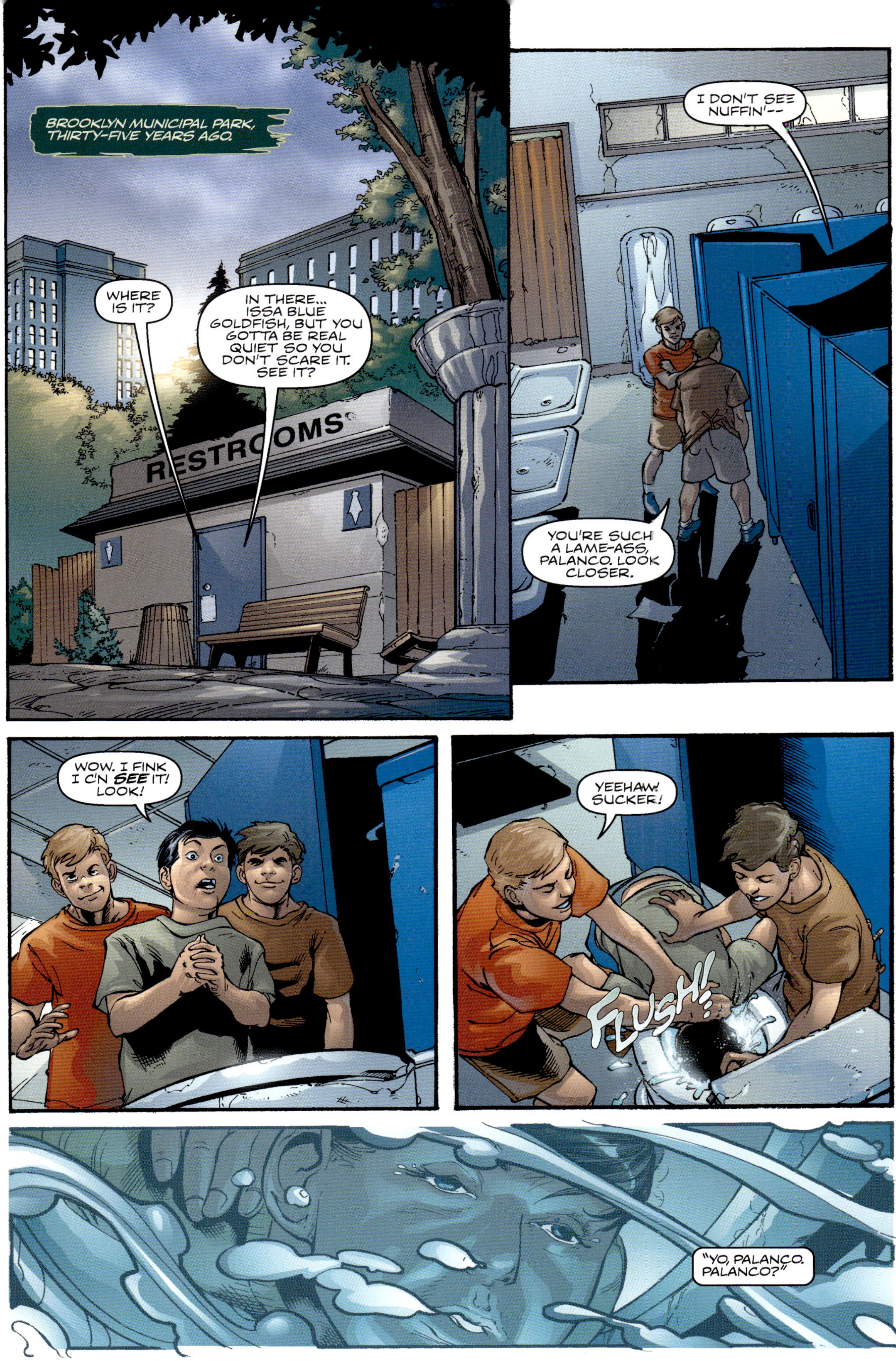
BROOKLYN MUNICIPAL PARK, THIRTY-FIVE YEARS AGO.
WHERE IS IT?
IN THERE... ISSA BLUE GOLDFISH, BUT YOU GOTTA BE REAL QUIET SO YOU DON'T SCARE IT. SEE IT?
RESTROOMS
I DON'T SEE NUFFIN'--
YOU'RE SUCH A LAME-ASS, PALANCO. LOOK CLOSER.
WOW. I FINK I C'N *SEE* IT! LOOK!
YEEHAW! SUCKER!
FLUSH!
"YO, PALANCO. PALANCO?"

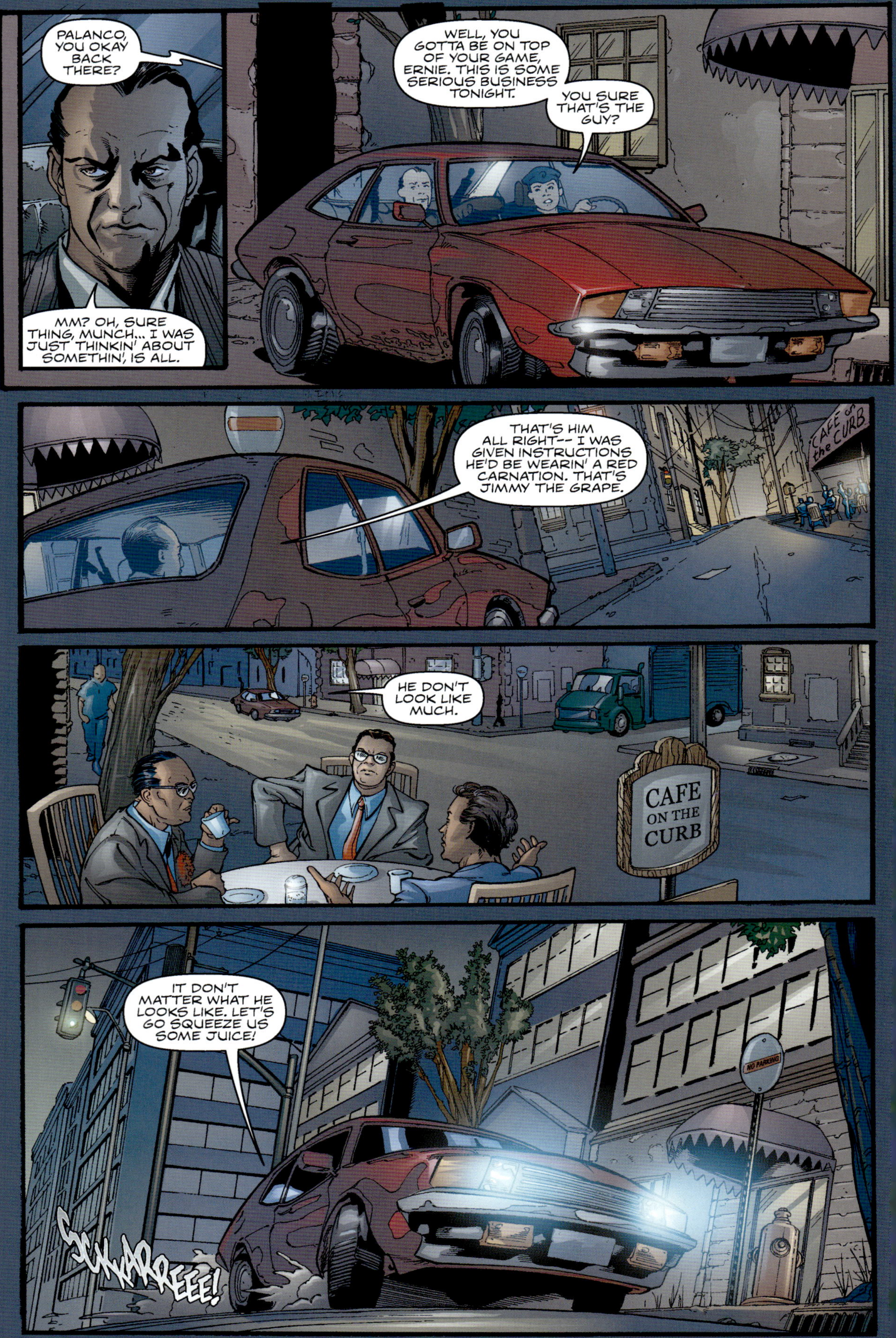

PALANCO, YOU OKAY BACK THERE?
MM? OH, SURE THING, MUNCH... I WAS JUST THINKIN' ABOUT SOMETHIN', IS ALL.
WELL, YOU GOTTA BE ON TOP OF YOUR GAME, ERNIE. THIS IS SOME SERIOUS BUSINESS TONIGHT.
YOU SURE THAT'S THE GUY?
THAT'S HIM ALL RIGHT-- I WAS GIVEN INSTRUCTIONS HE'D BE WEARIN' A RED CARNATION. THAT'S JIMMY THE GRAPE.
CAFE on the CURB
HE DON'T LOOK LIKE MUCH.
CAFE ON THE CURB
IT DON'T MATTER WHAT HE LOOKS LIKE. LET'S GO SQUEEZE US SOME JUICE!
NO PARKING
SCKKARRREEE!

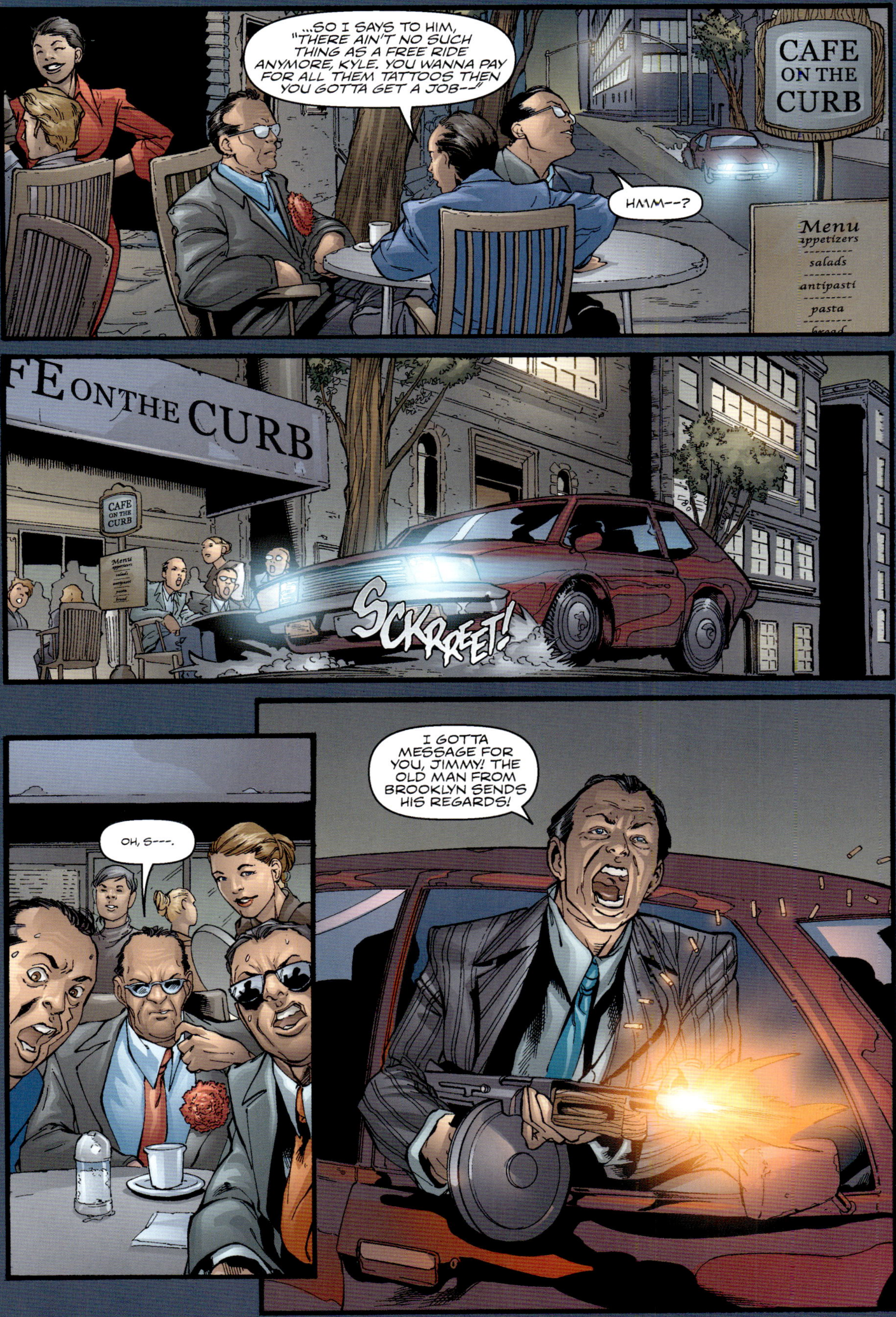
...SO I SAYS TO HIM, "THERE AIN'T NO SUCH THING AS A FREE RIDE ANYMORE, KYLE. YOU WANNA PAY FOR ALL THEM TATTOOS THEN YOU GOTTA GET A JOB--"
CAFE ON THE CURB
HMM--?
Menu appetizers salads antipasti pasta
FE ON THE CURB
SCKRREET!
I GOTTA MESSAGE FOR YOU, JIMMY! THE OLD MAN FROM BROOKLYN SENDS HIS REGARDS!
OH, S---.

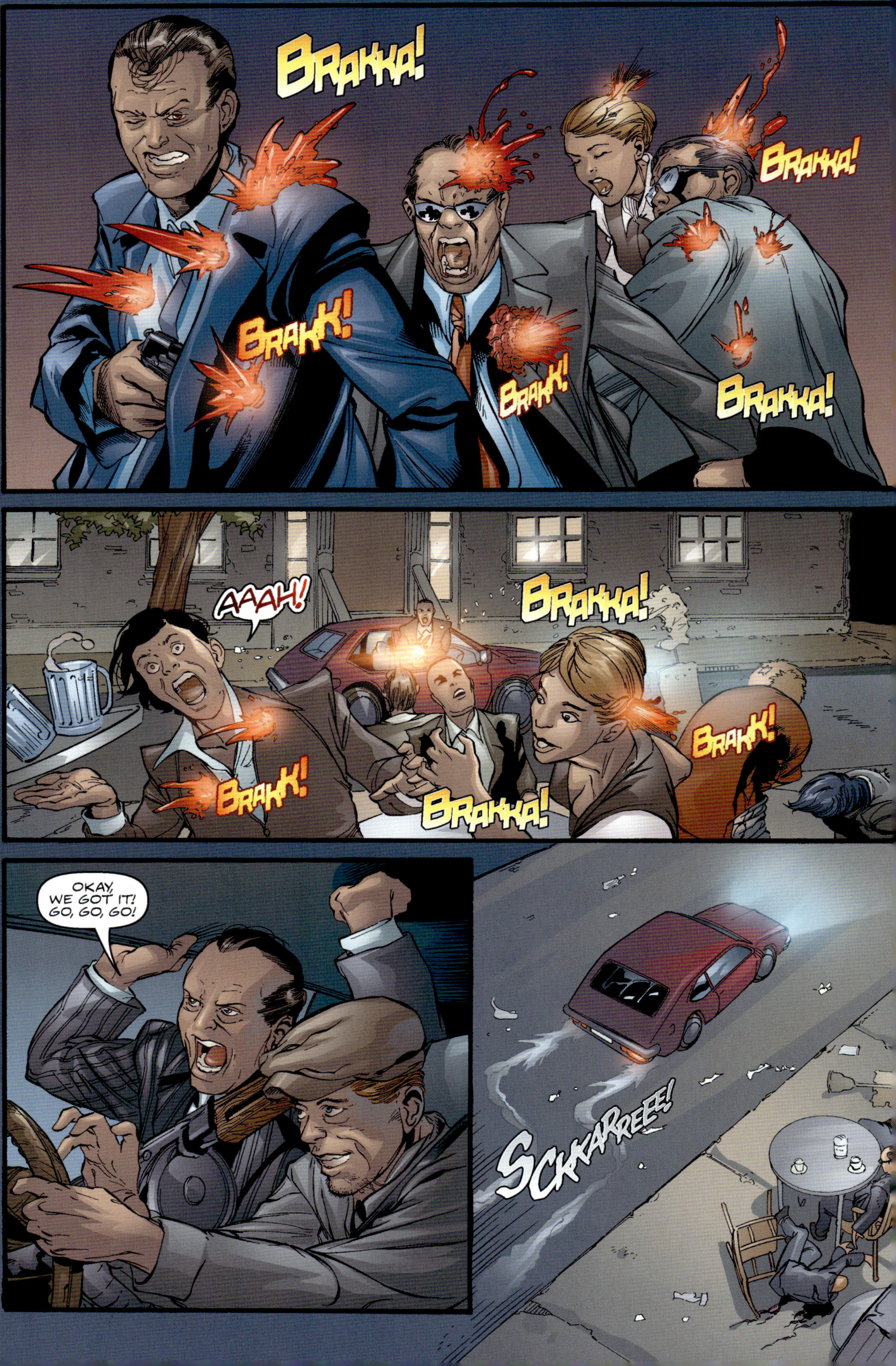
BRAKKA!
BRAKK!
BRAKK!
BRAKKA!
BRAKKA!
AAAH!
BRAKKA!
BRAKK!
BRAKK!
BRAKKA!
OKAY, WE GOT IT! GO, GO, GO!
SCKKARREEE!

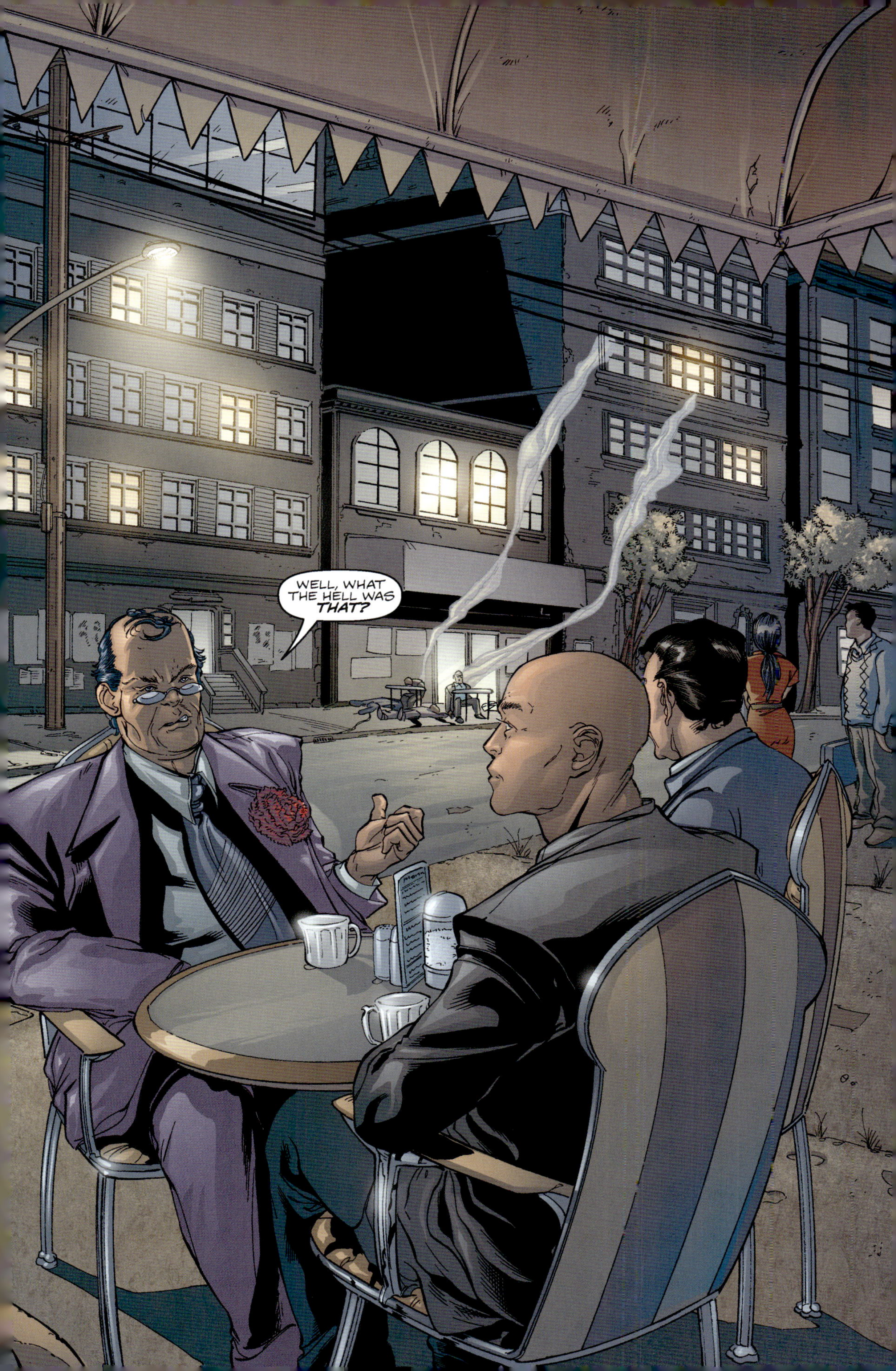
WELL, WHAT THE HELL WAS *THAT?*

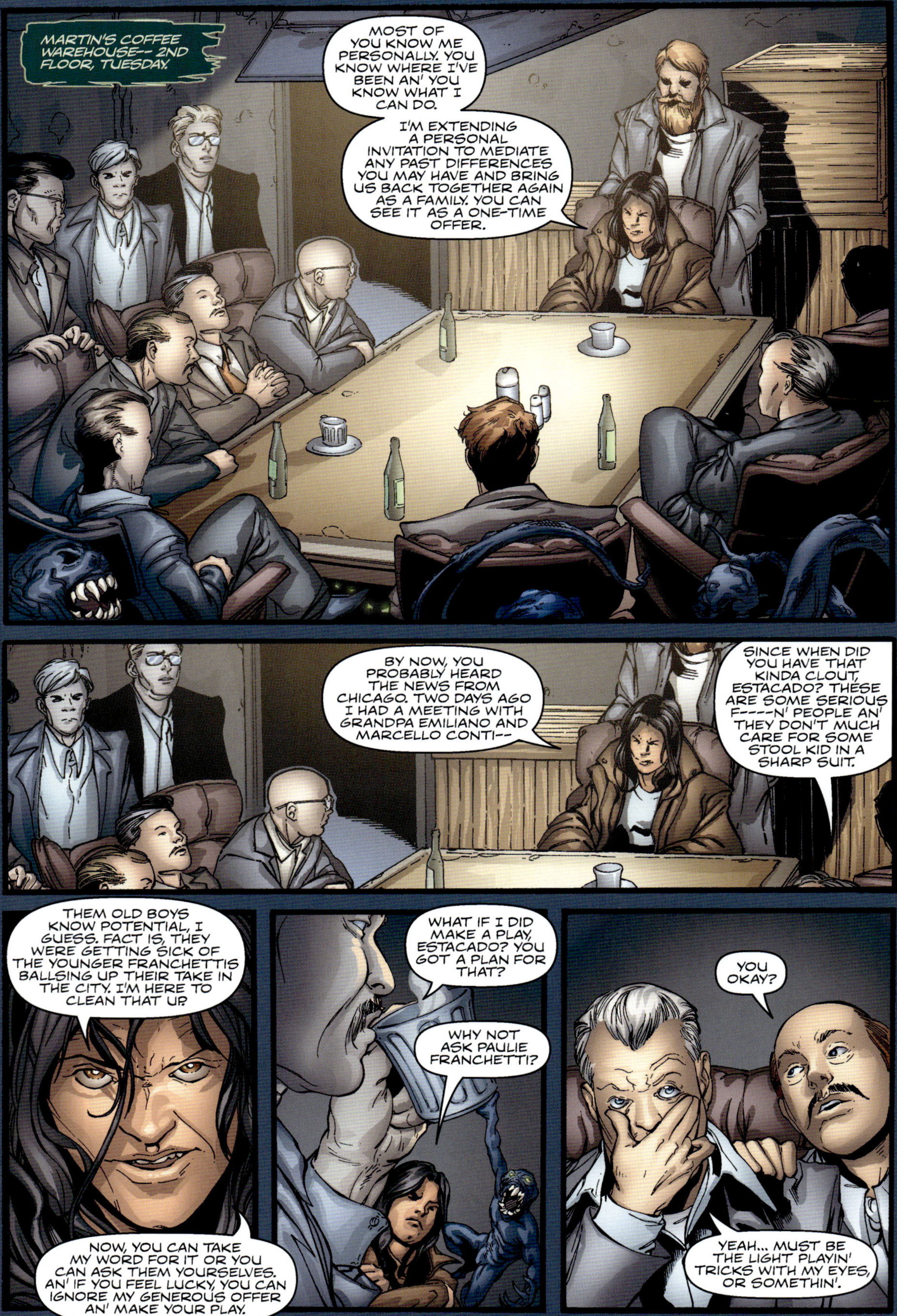
MARTIN'S COFFEE WAREHOUSE-- 2ND FLOOR, TUESDAY.
MOST OF YOU KNOW ME PERSONALLY. YOU KNOW WHERE I'VE BEEN AN' YOU KNOW WHAT I CAN DO.
I'M EXTENDING A PERSONAL INVITATION TO MEDIATE ANY PAST DIFFERENCES YOU MAY HAVE AND BRING US BACK TOGETHER AGAIN AS A FAMILY. YOU CAN SEE IT AS A ONE-TIME OFFER.
BY NOW, YOU PROBABLY HEARD THE NEWS FROM CHICAGO. TWO DAYS AGO I HAD A MEETING WITH GRANDPA EMILIANO AND MARCELLO CONTI--
SINCE WHEN DID YOU HAVE THAT KINDA CLOUT, ESTACADO? THESE ARE SOME SERIOUS F----N' PEOPLE AN' THEY DON'T MUCH CARE FOR SOME STOOL KID IN A SHARP SUIT.
THEM OLD BOYS KNOW POTENTIAL, I GUESS. FACT IS, THEY WERE GETTING SICK OF THE YOUNGER FRANCHETTIS BALLSING UP THEIR TAKE IN THE CITY. I'M HERE TO CLEAN THAT UP.
NOW, YOU CAN TAKE MY WORD FOR IT OR YOU CAN ASK THEM YOURSELVES. AN' IF YOU FEEL LUCKY, YOU CAN IGNORE MY GENEROUS OFFER AN' MAKE YOUR PLAY.
WHAT IF I DID MAKE A PLAY, ESTACADO? YOU GOT A PLAN FOR THAT?
WHY NOT ASK PAULIE FRANCHETTI?
YOU OKAY?
YEAH... MUST BE THE LIGHT PLAYIN' TRICKS WITH MY EYES, OR SOMETHIN'.

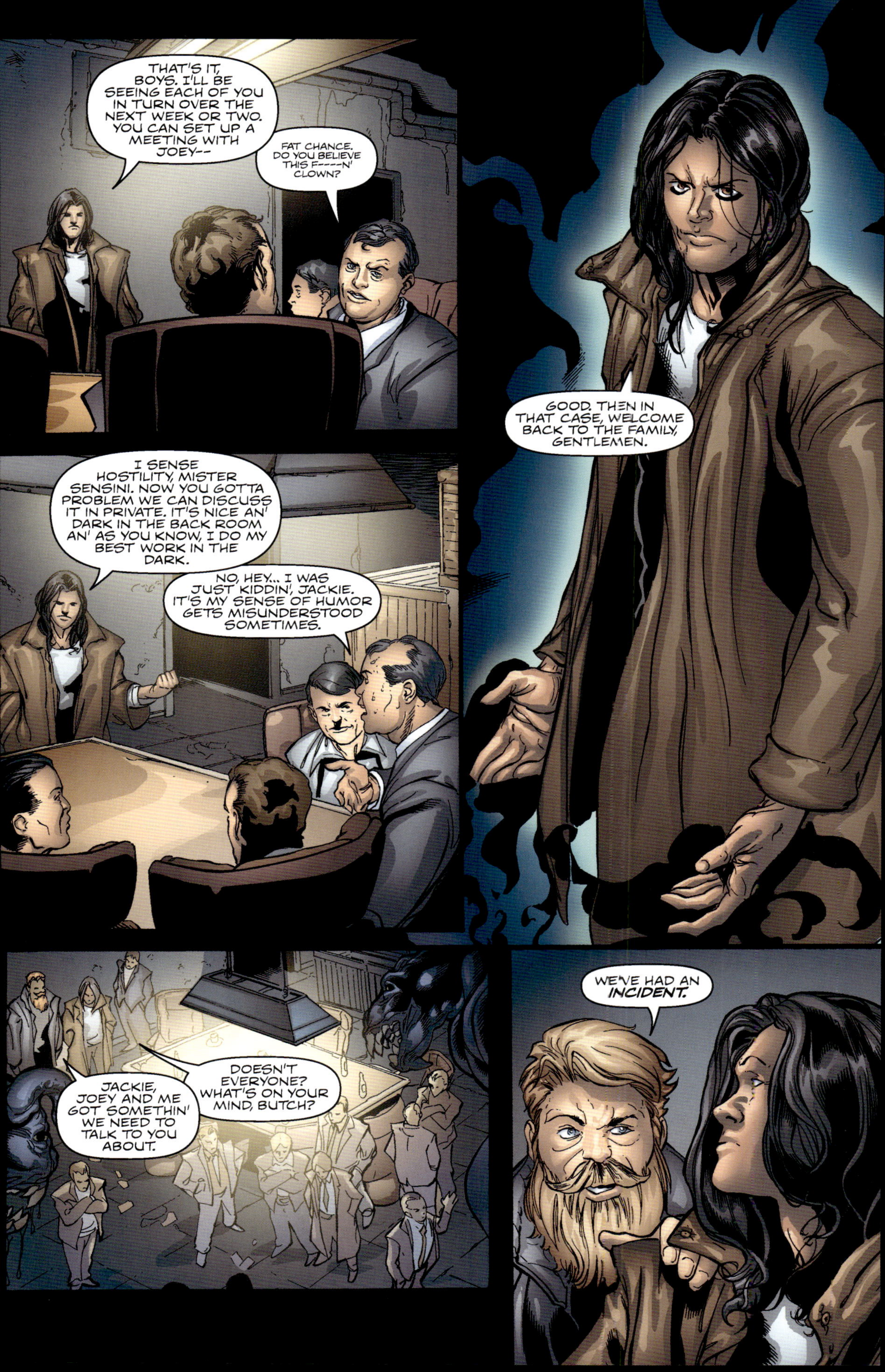
THAT'S IT, BOYS. I'LL BE SEEING EACH OF YOU IN TURN OVER THE NEXT WEEK OR TWO. YOU CAN SET UP A MEETING WITH JOEY--
FAT CHANCE. DO YOU BELIEVE THIS F----N' CLOWN?
I SENSE HOSTILITY, MISTER SENSINI. NOW YOU GOTTA PROBLEM WE CAN DISCUSS IT IN PRIVATE. IT'S NICE AN' DARK IN THE BACK ROOM AN' AS YOU KNOW, I DO MY BEST WORK IN THE DARK.
NO, HEY... I WAS JUST KIDDIN', JACKIE. IT'S MY SENSE OF HUMOR GETS MISUNDERSTOOD SOMETIMES.
GOOD. THEN IN THAT CASE, WELCOME BACK TO THE FAMILY, GENTLEMEN.
JACKIE, JOEY AND ME GOT SOMETHIN' WE NEED TO TALK TO YOU ABOUT.
DOESN'T EVERYONE? WHAT'S ON YOUR MIND, BUTCH?
WE'VE HAD AN *INCIDENT.*

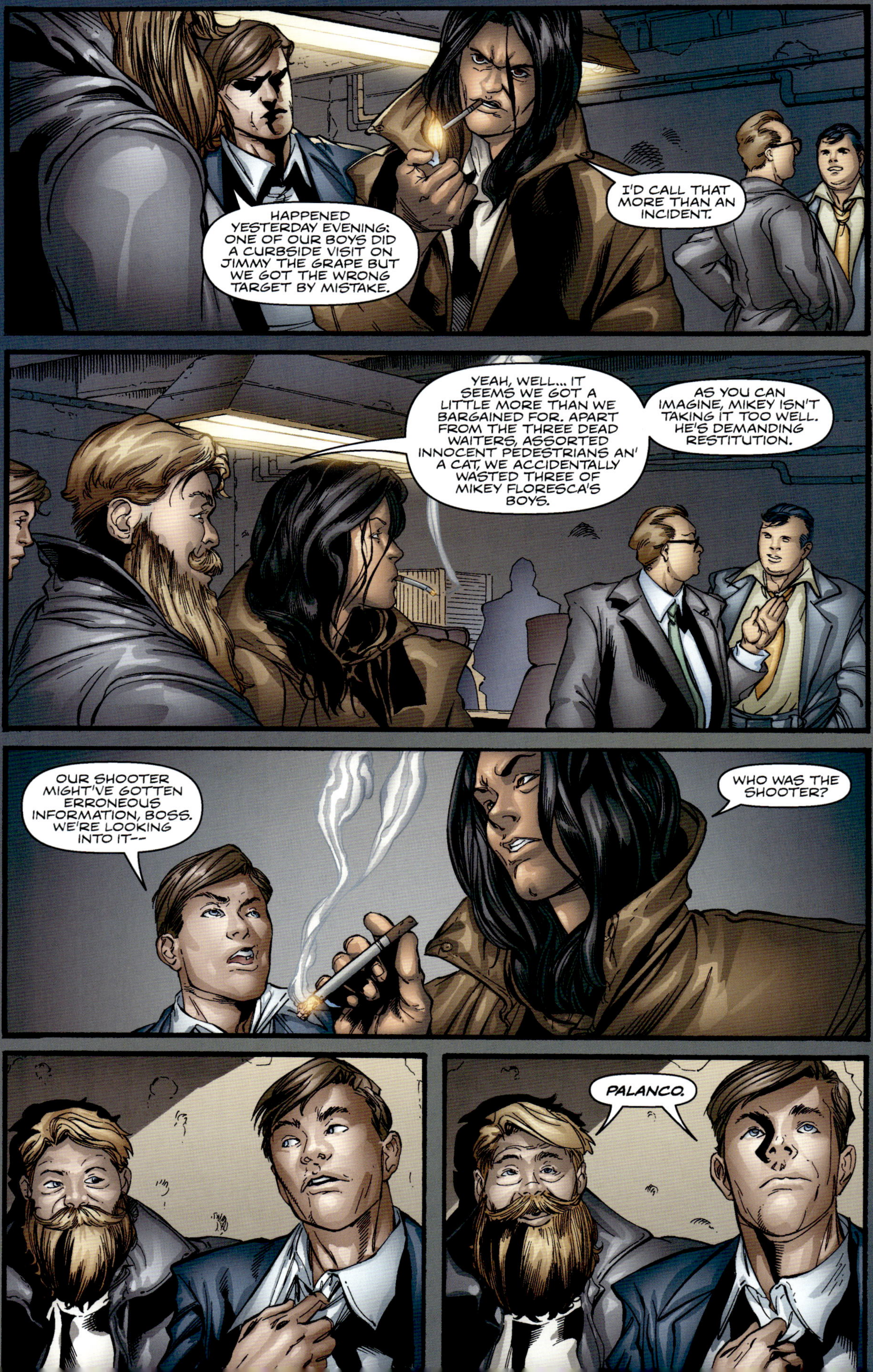
HAPPENED YESTERDAY EVENING: ONE OF OUR BOYS DID A CURBSIDE VISIT ON JIMMY THE GRAPE BUT WE GOT THE WRONG TARGET BY MISTAKE.
I'D CALL THAT MORE THAN AN INCIDENT.
YEAH, WELL... IT SEEMS WE GOT A LITTLE MORE THAN WE BARGAINED FOR. APART FROM THE THREE DEAD WAITERS, ASSORTED INNOCENT PEDESTRIANS AN' A CAT, WE ACCIDENTALLY WASTED THREE OF MIKEY FLORESCA'S BOYS.
AS YOU CAN IMAGINE, MIKEY ISN'T TAKING IT TOO WELL. HE'S DEMANDING RESTITUTION.
OUR SHOOTER MIGHT'VE GOTTEN ERRONEOUS INFORMATION, BOSS. WE'RE LOOKING INTO IT--
WHO WAS THE SHOOTER?
PALANCO.

BELCHER STREET, MANHATTAN-- TUESDAY EVENING.

THERE ARE MANY THINGS IN THIS UNIVERSE THAT DEFY DESCRIPTION, BUT THE NAME ERNIE PALANCO EXPLAINS MOST OF THEM.

IN THIS CITY, PALANCO IS A LEGEND FOR ALL THE WRONG REASONS.

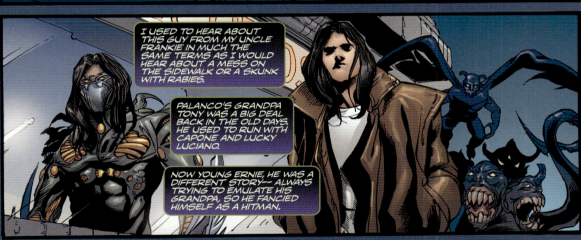

I USED TO HEAR ABOUT THIS GUY FROM MY UNCLE FRANKIE IN MUCH THE SAME TERMS AS I WOULD HEAR ABOUT A MESS ON THE SIDEWALK OR A SKUNK WITH RABIES.

PALANCO'S GRANDPA TONY WAS A BIG DEAL BACK IN THE OLD DAYS. HE USED TO RUN WITH CAPONE AND LUCKY LUCIANO.

NOW YOUNG ERNIE, HE WAS A DIFFERENT STORY-- ALWAYS TRYING TO EMULATE HIS GRANDPA, SO HE FANCIED HIMSELF AS A HITMAN.

ERNIE'S GOT IT ALL DOWN PAT: THE GUNS AND THE DUDS... HE EVEN GETS A FEW SMALL JOBS COURTESY OF THE BOYS BACK HOME. IN SHORT, HE'S PRETTY MUCH A CARBON COPY OF THE OLD MAN.

EXCEPT THAT HE'S A F-----G IDIOT.

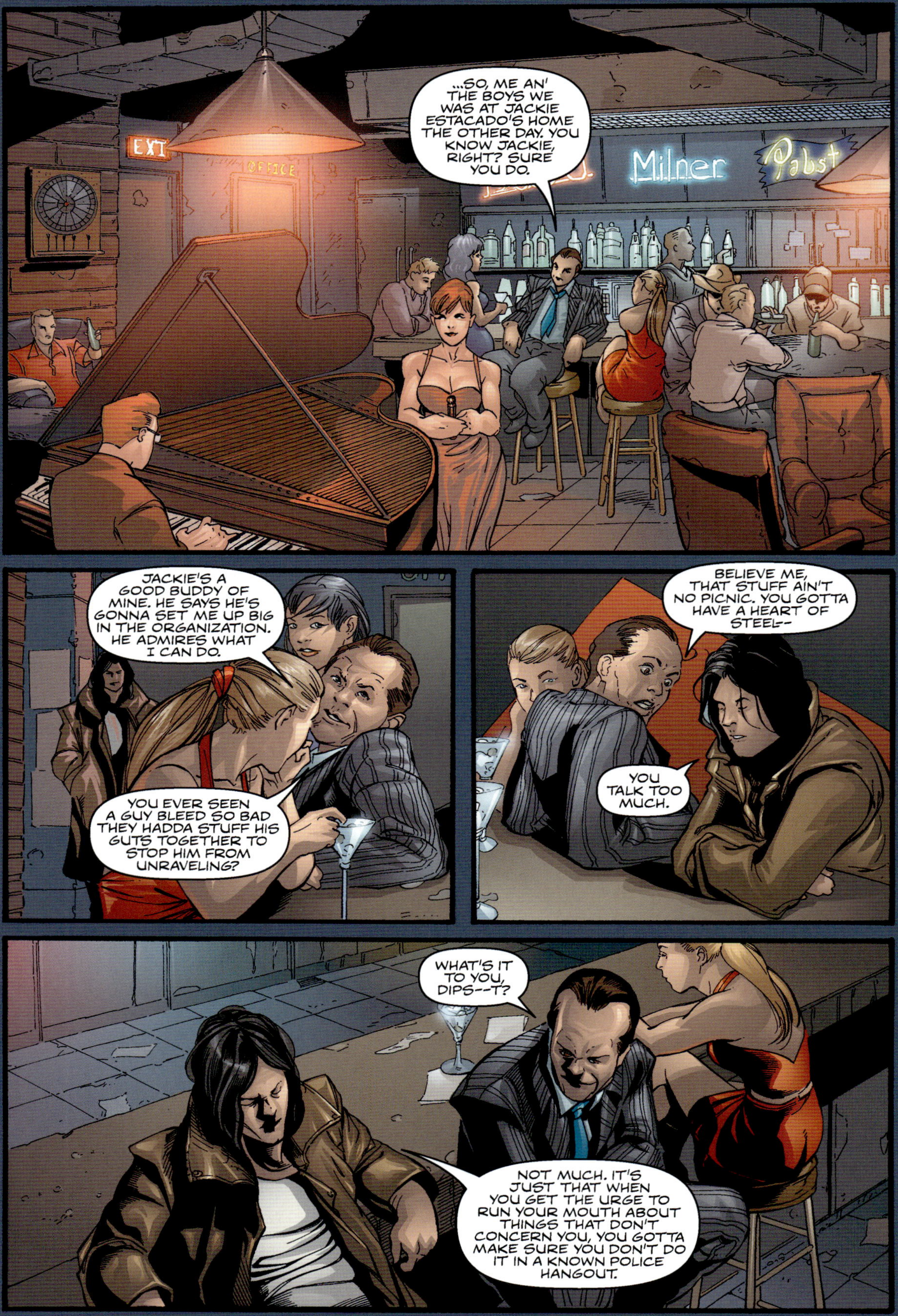
...SO, ME AN' THE BOYS WE WAS AT JACKIE ESTACADO'S HOME THE OTHER DAY. YOU KNOW JACKIE, RIGHT? SURE YOU DO.
EXIT
OFFICE
Milner
Pabst
JACKIE'S A GOOD BUDDY OF MINE. HE SAYS HE'S GONNA SET ME UP BIG IN THE ORGANIZATION. HE ADMIRES WHAT I CAN DO.
YOU EVER SEEN A GUY BLEED SO BAD THEY HADDA STUFF HIS GUTS TOGETHER TO STOP HIM FROM UNRAVELING?
BELIEVE ME, THAT STUFF AIN'T NO PICNIC. YOU GOTTA HAVE A HEART OF STEEL--
YOU TALK TOO MUCH.
WHAT'S IT TO YOU, DIPS--T?
NOT MUCH. IT'S JUST THAT WHEN YOU GET THE URGE TO RUN YOUR MOUTH ABOUT THINGS THAT DON'T CONCERN YOU, YOU GOTTA MAKE SURE YOU DON'T DO IT IN A KNOWN POLICE HANGOUT.

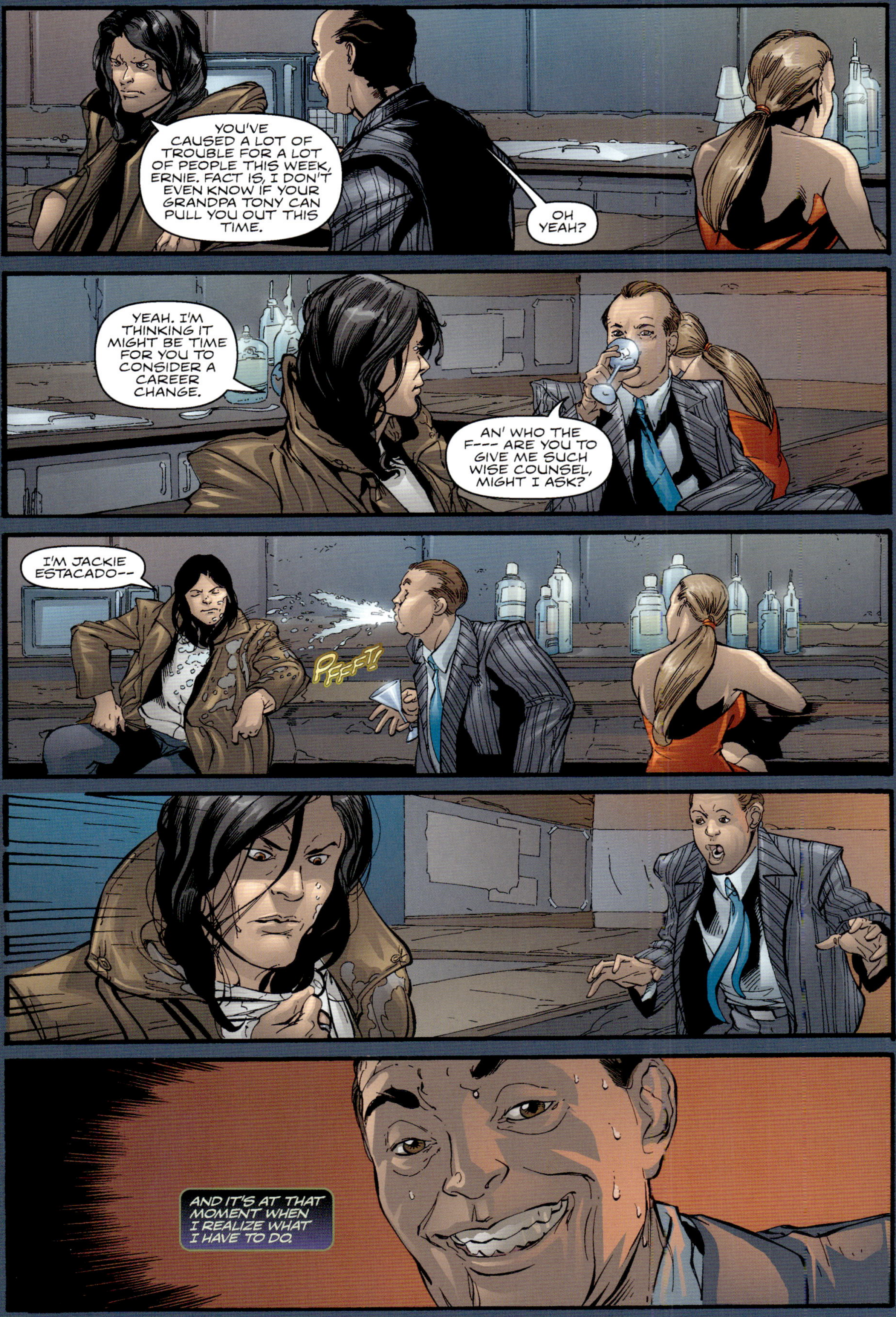
YOU'VE CAUSED A LOT OF TROUBLE FOR A LOT OF PEOPLE THIS WEEK, ERNIE. FACT IS, I DON'T EVEN KNOW IF YOUR GRANDPA TONY CAN PULL YOU OUT THIS TIME.
OH YEAH?
YEAH. I'M THINKING IT MIGHT BE TIME FOR YOU TO CONSIDER A CAREER CHANGE.
AN' WHO THE F--- ARE YOU TO GIVE ME SUCH WISE COUNSEL, MIGHT I ASK?
I'M JACKIE ESTACADO--
PFFFT!
AND IT'S AT THAT MOMENT WHEN I REALIZE WHAT I HAVE TO DO.

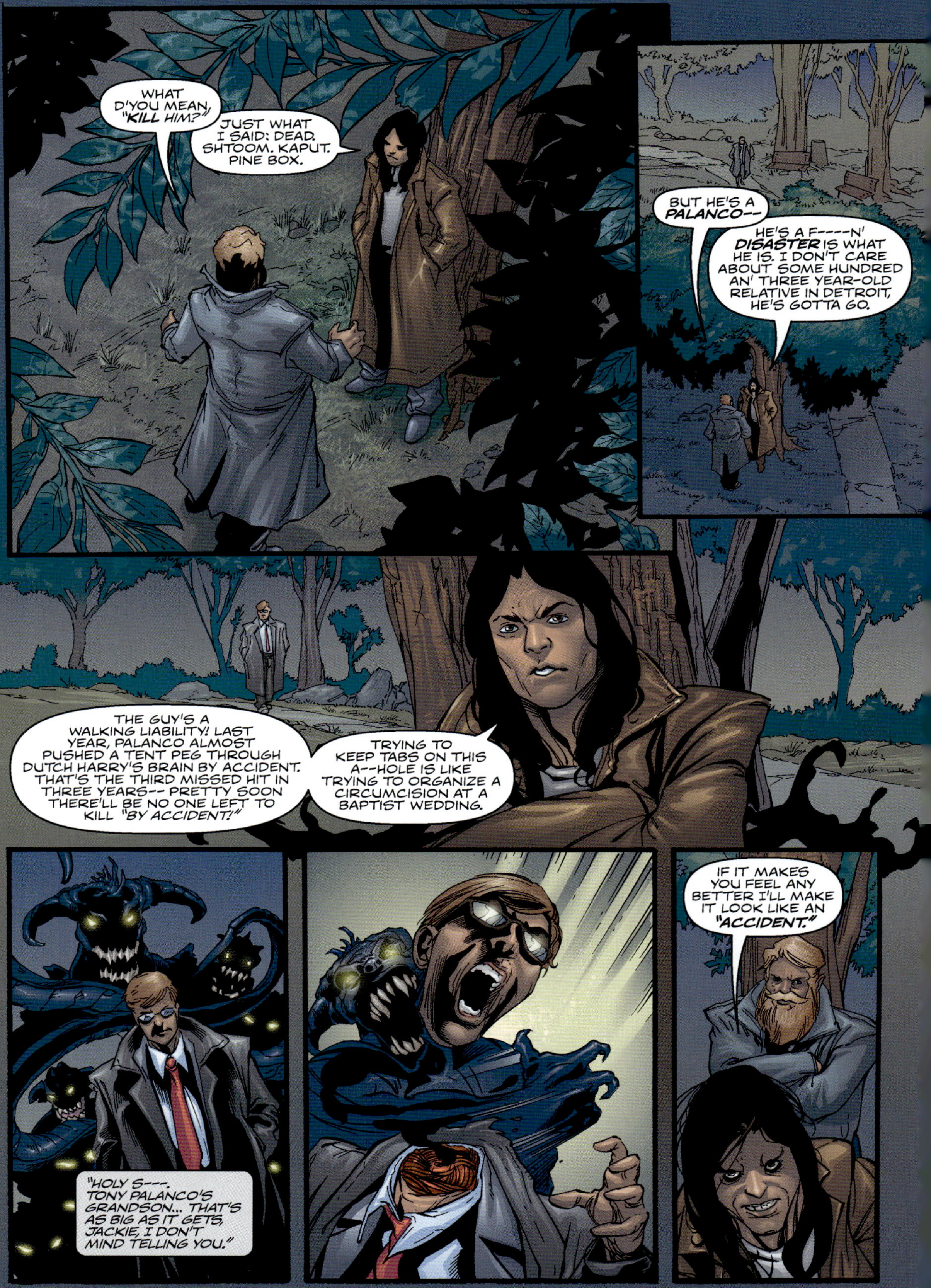
WHAT D'YOU MEAN, "KILL HIM?"
JUST WHAT I SAID: DEAD. SHTOOM. KAPUT. PINE BOX.
BUT HE'S A PALANCO--
HE'S A F----N' DISASTER IS WHAT HE IS. I DON'T CARE ABOUT SOME HUNDRED AN' THREE YEAR-OLD RELATIVE IN DETROIT, HE'S GOTTA GO.
THE GUY'S A WALKING LIABILITY! LAST YEAR, PALANCO ALMOST PUSHED A TENT PEG THROUGH DUTCH HARRY'S BRAIN BY ACCIDENT. THAT'S THE THIRD MISSED HIT IN THREE YEARS-- PRETTY SOON THERE'LL BE NO ONE LEFT TO KILL "BY ACCIDENT!"
TRYING TO KEEP TABS ON THIS A--HOLE IS LIKE TRYING TO ORGANIZE A CIRCUMCISION AT A BAPTIST WEDDING.
"HOLY S---. TONY PALANCO'S GRANDSON... THAT'S AS BIG AS IT GETS, JACKIE, I DON'T MIND TELLING YOU."
IF IT MAKES YOU FEEL ANY BETTER I'LL MAKE IT LOOK LIKE AN "ACCIDENT."

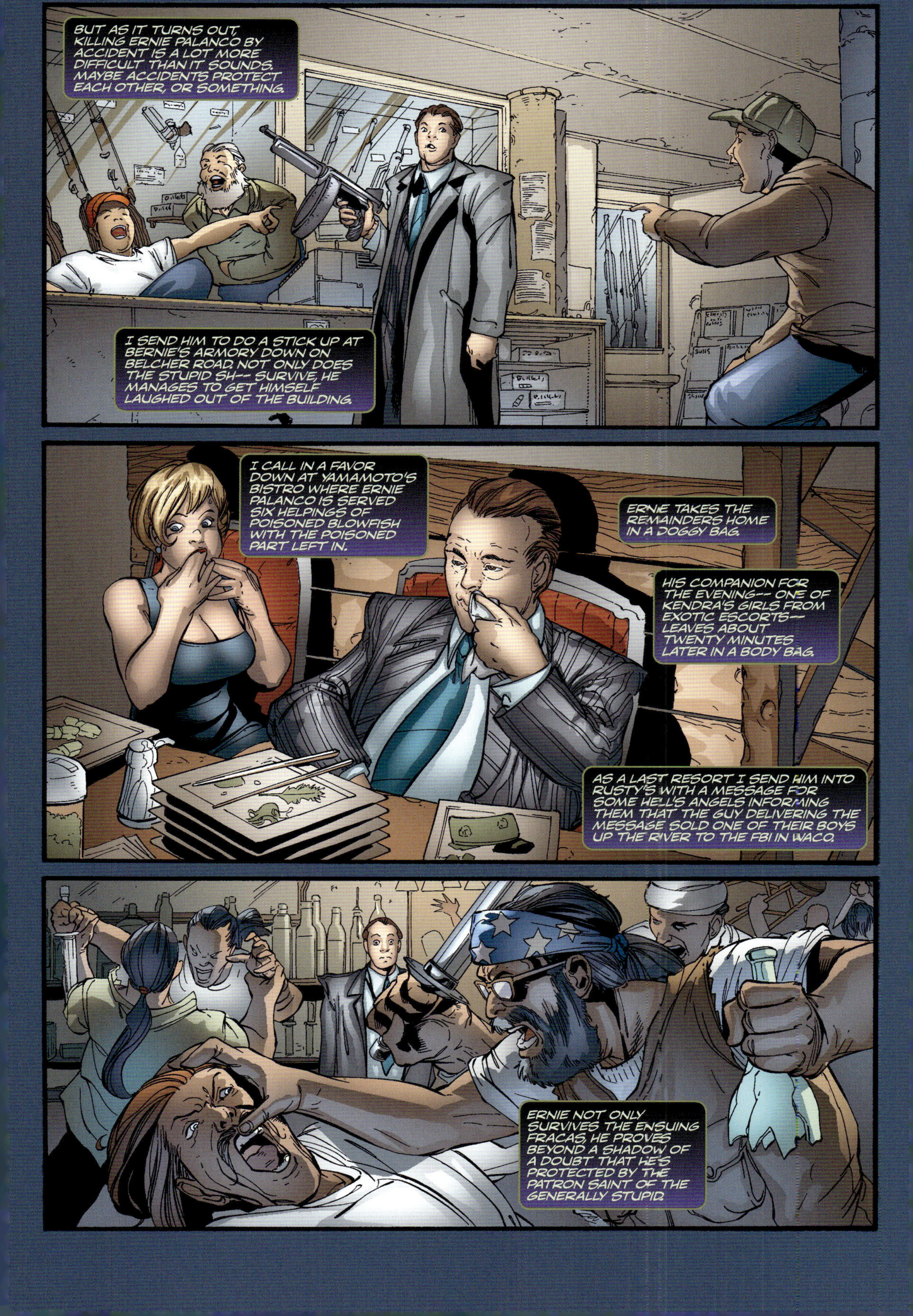
BUT AS IT TURNS OUT, KILLING ERNIE PALANCO BY ACCIDENT IS A LOT MORE DIFFICULT THAN IT SOUNDS. MAYBE ACCIDENTS PROTECT EACH OTHER, OR SOMETHING.
I SEND HIM TO DO A STICK UP AT BERNIE'S ARMORY DOWN ON BELCHER ROAD. NOT ONLY DOES THE STUPID SH-- SURVIVE, HE MANAGES TO GET HIMSELF LAUGHED OUT OF THE BUILDING.
I CALL IN A FAVOR DOWN AT YAMAMOTO'S BISTRO WHERE ERNIE PALANCO IS SERVED SIX HELPINGS OF POISONED BLOWFISH WITH THE POISONED PART LEFT IN.
ERNIE TAKES THE REMAINDERS HOME IN A DOGGY BAG.
HIS COMPANION FOR THE EVENING-- ONE OF KENDRA'S GIRLS FROM EXOTIC ESCORTS-- LEAVES ABOUT TWENTY MINUTES LATER IN A BODY BAG.
AS A LAST RESORT I SEND HIM INTO RUSTY'S WITH A MESSAGE FOR SOME HELL'S ANGELS INFORMING THEM THAT THE GUY DELIVERING THE MESSAGE SOLD ONE OF THEIR BOYS UP THE RIVER TO THE FBI IN WACO.
ERNIE NOT ONLY SURVIVES THE ENSUING FRACAS, HE PROVES BEYOND A SHADOW OF A DOUBT THAT HE'S PROTECTED BY THE PATRON SAINT OF THE GENERALLY STUPID.

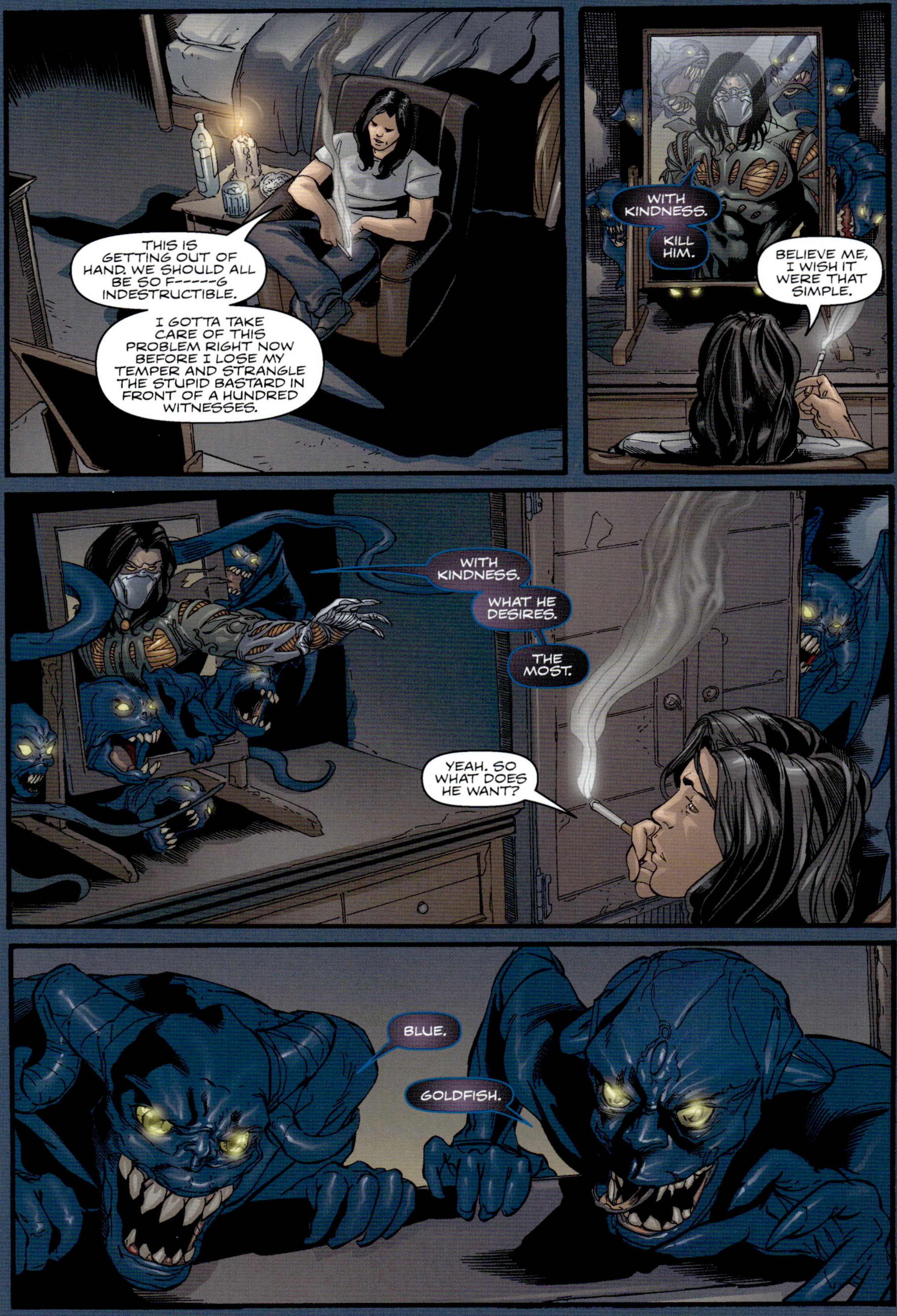
THIS IS GETTING OUT OF HAND. WE SHOULD ALL BE SO F-----G INDESTRUCTIBLE.
I GOTTA TAKE CARE OF THIS PROBLEM RIGHT NOW BEFORE I LOSE MY TEMPER AND STRANGLE THE STUPID BASTARD IN FRONT OF A HUNDRED WITNESSES.
WITH KINDNESS.
KILL HIM.
BELIEVE ME, I WISH IT WERE THAT SIMPLE.
WITH KINDNESS.
WHAT HE DESIRES.
THE MOST.
YEAH. SO WHAT DOES HE WANT?
BLUE.
GOLDFISH.

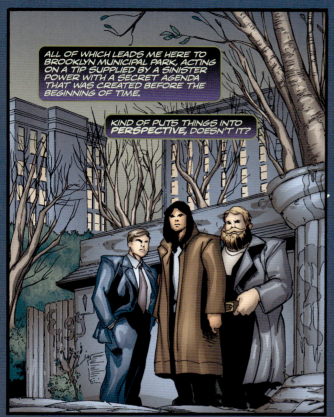

ALL OF WHICH LEADS ME HERE TO BROOKLYN MUNICIPAL PARK, ACTING ON A TIP SUPPLIED BY A SINISTER POWER WITH A SECRET AGENDA THAT WAS CREATED BEFORE THE BEGINNING OF TIME.

KIND OF PUTS THINGS INTO *PERSPECTIVE*, DOESN'T IT?

YO, JACKIE. WORD UP?

IT'S *"WHAT'S UP?"* AN' WHAT'S UP IS THAT WE GOTTA PROBLEM OUT HERE IN THE PARK, ERNIE. I FIGURED YOU WAS THE GUY TO HELP US TAKE CARE OF IT.

WE GOT WORD SOME FREAKIN' CHILD MOLESTERS HAVE BEEN USING THE TOILETS AS A PLACE TO TAKE KIDS. I DON'T WANNA EVEN SOIL MY LIPS TO TELL YOU WHAT THEY BEEN DOING IN THERE.

MISTER ESTACADO WANTS YOU TO TAKE CARE OF THE PROBLEM, KAPISCHE?

WHERE DO I SIGN UP?

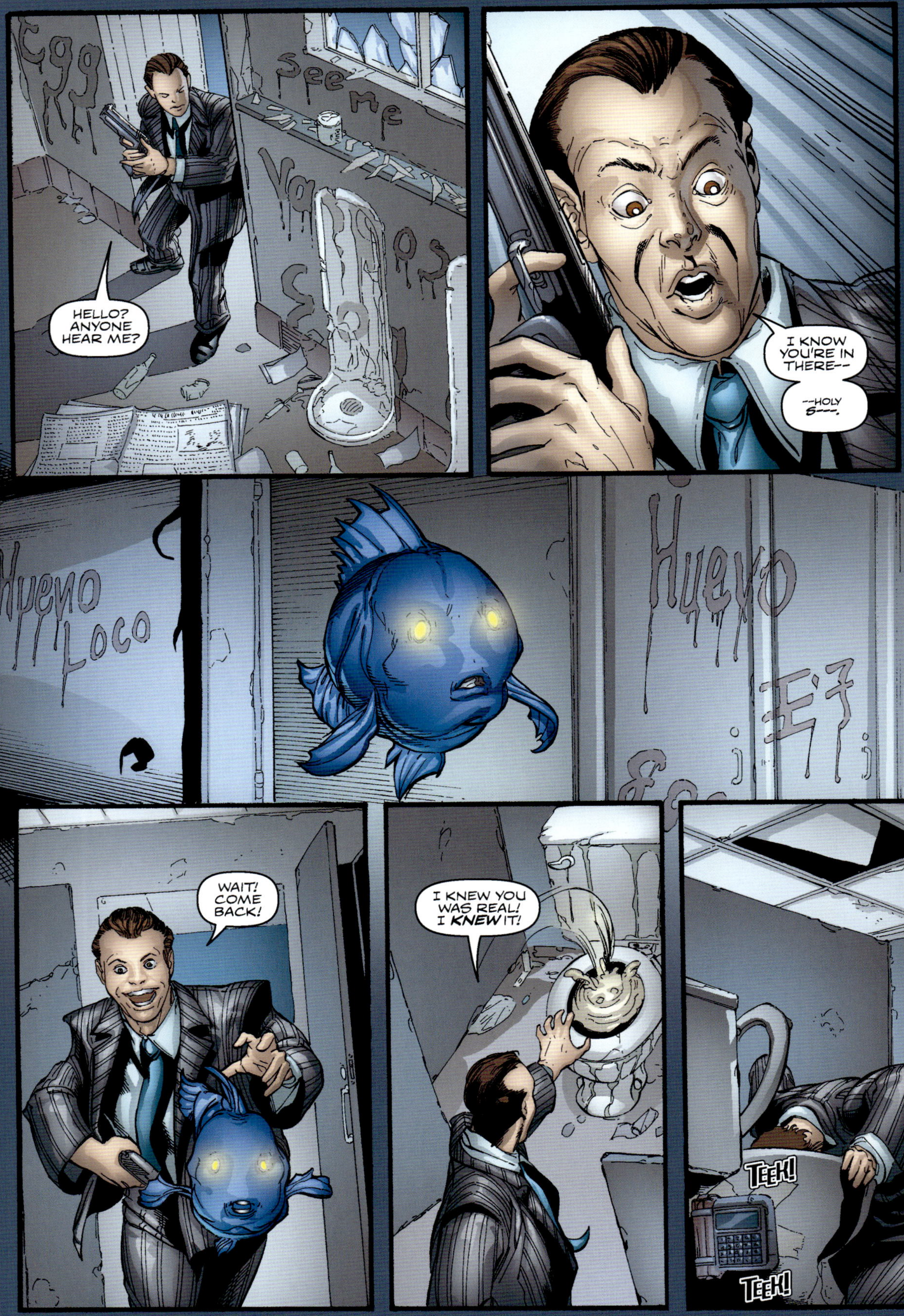
HELLO? ANYONE HEAR ME?
I KNOW YOU'RE IN THERE--
--HOLY S---.
WAIT! COME BACK!
I KNEW YOU WAS REAL! I KNEW IT!
TEEK!
TEEK!

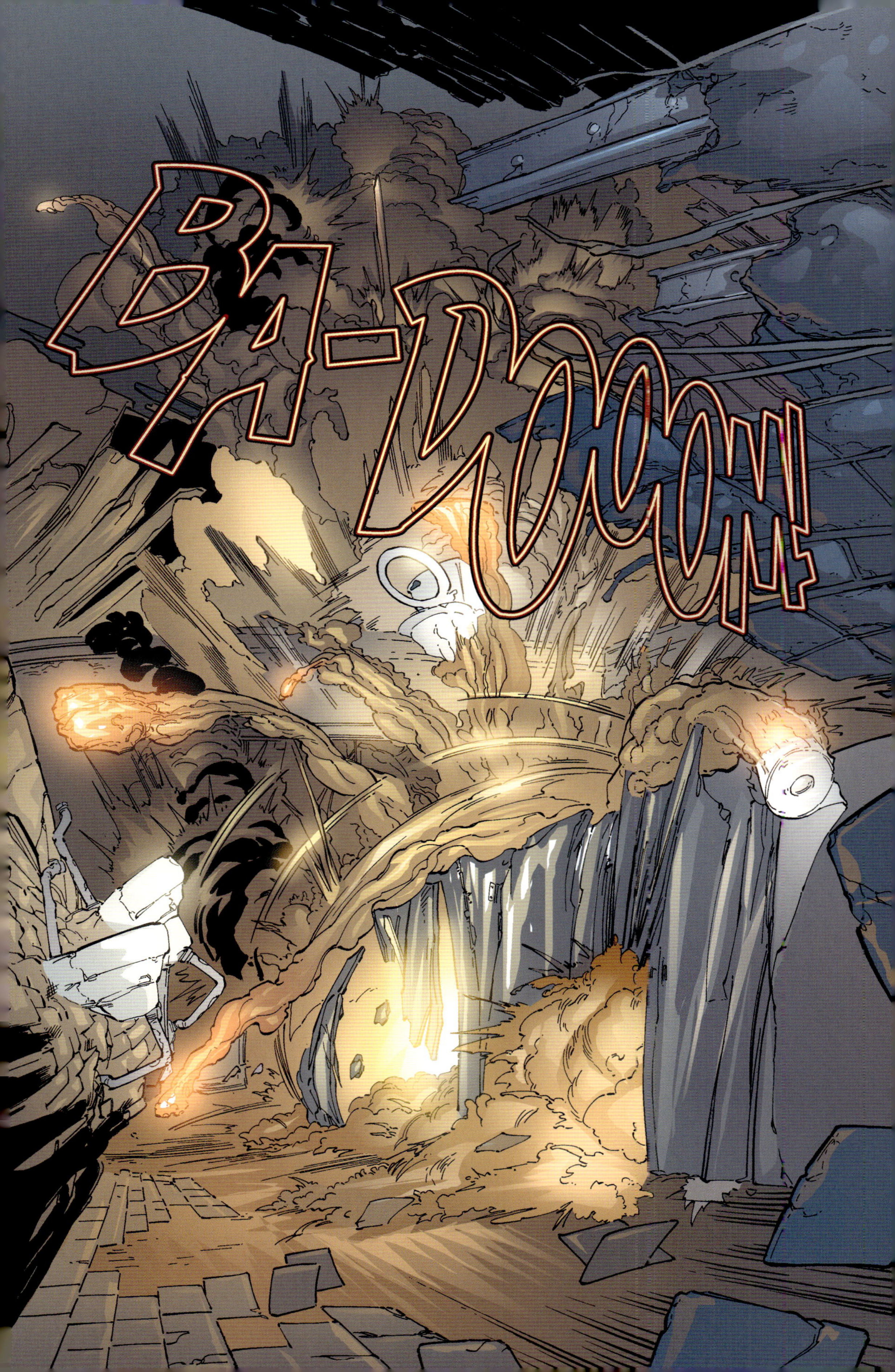
BA-DOOOOM!

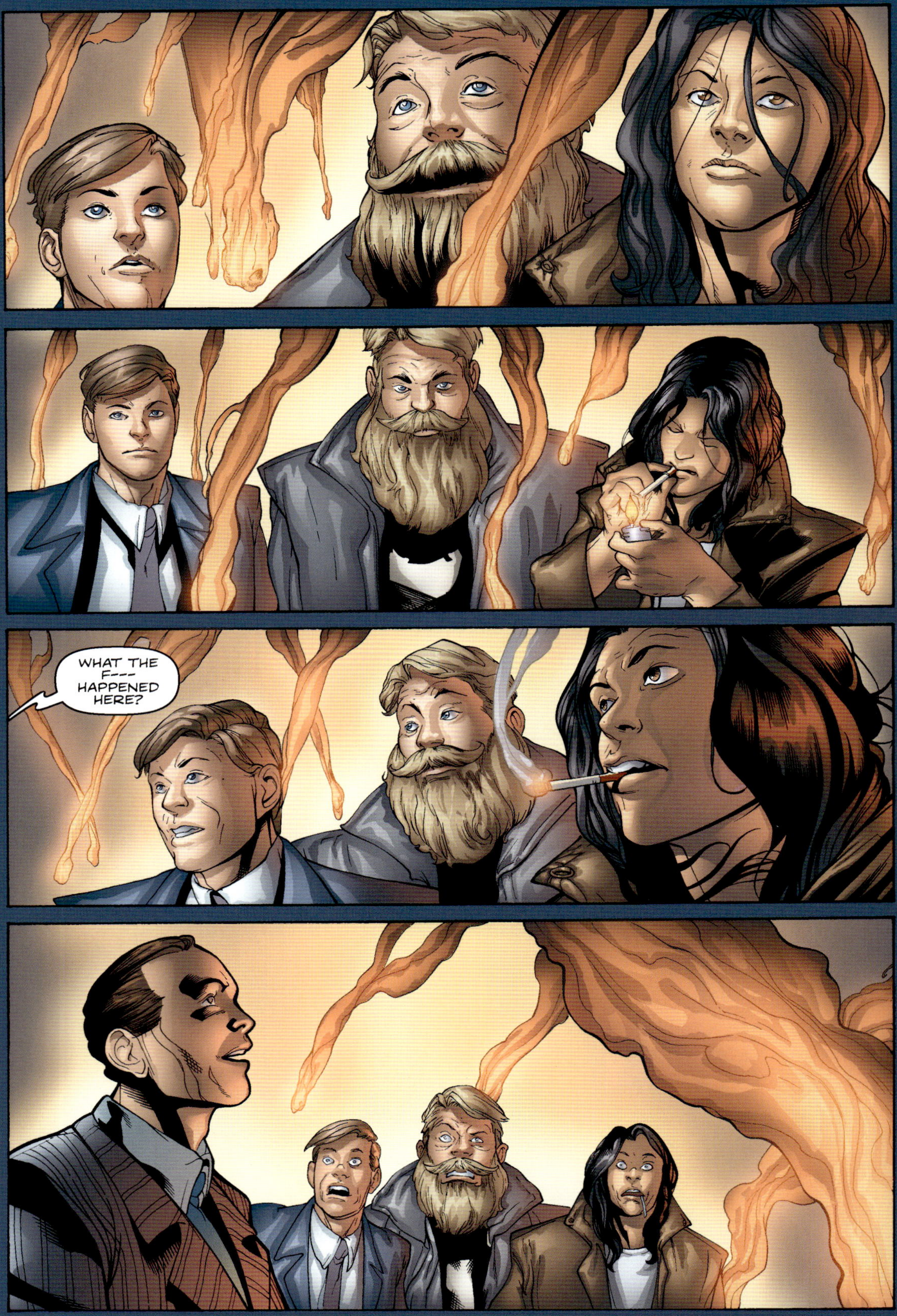
WHAT THE F--- HAPPENED HERE?

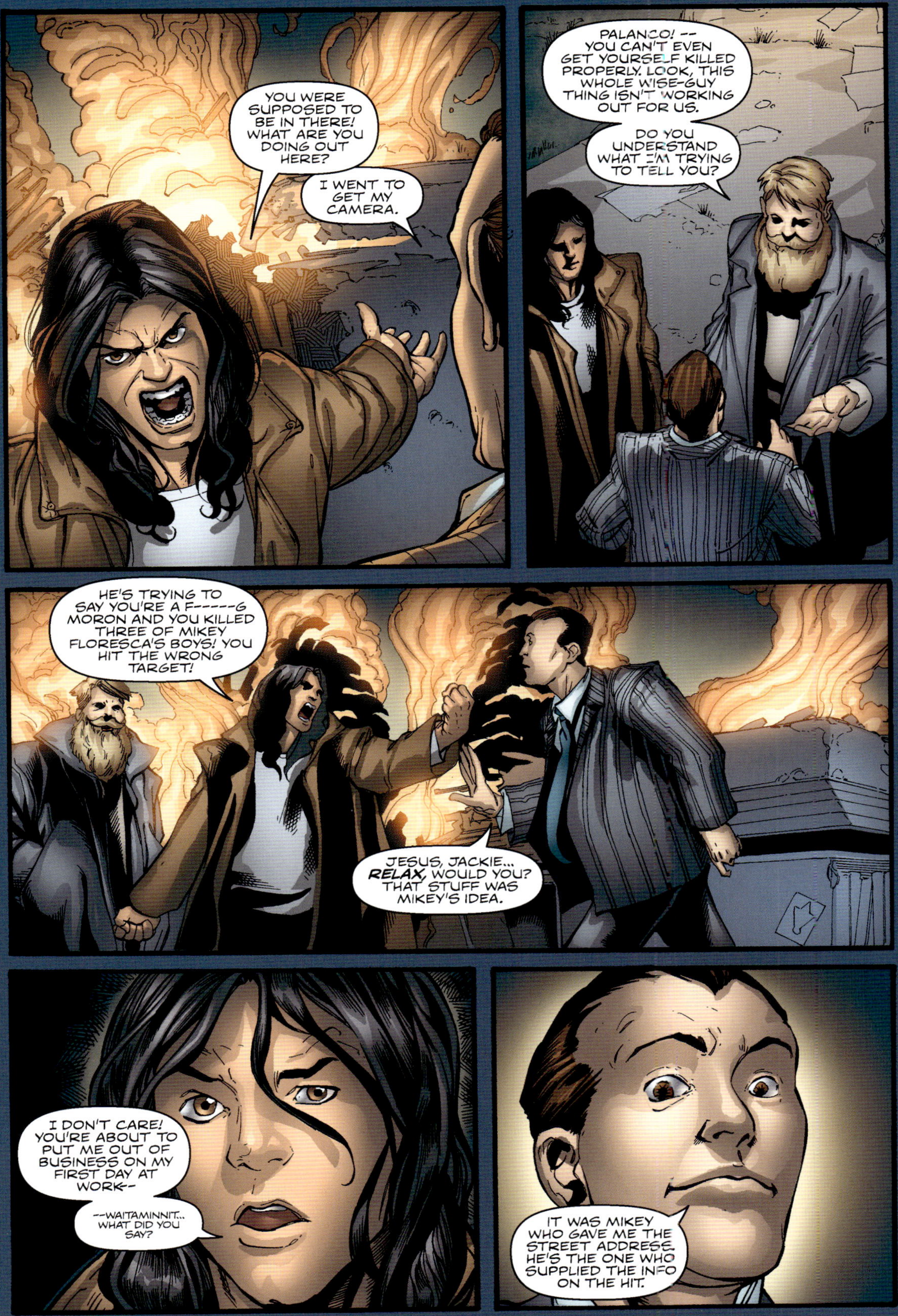
YOU WERE SUPPOSED TO BE IN THERE! WHAT ARE YOU DOING OUT HERE?
I WENT TO GET MY CAMERA.
PALANCO! -- YOU CAN'T EVEN GET YOURSELF KILLED PROPERLY. LOOK, THIS WHOLE WISE-GUY THING ISN'T WORKING OUT FOR US.
DO YOU UNDERSTAND WHAT I'M TRYING TO TELL YOU?
HE'S TRYING TO SAY YOU'RE A F-----G MORON AND YOU KILLED THREE OF MIKEY FLORESCA'S BOYS! YOU HIT THE WRONG TARGET!
JESUS, JACKIE... RELAX, WOULD YOU? THAT STUFF WAS MIKEY'S IDEA.
I DON'T CARE! YOU'RE ABOUT TO PUT ME OUT OF BUSINESS ON MY FIRST DAY AT WORK--
--WAITAMINNIT... WHAT DID YOU SAY?
IT WAS MIKEY WHO GAVE ME THE STREET ADDRESS. HE'S THE ONE WHO SUPPLIED THE INFO ON THE HIT.

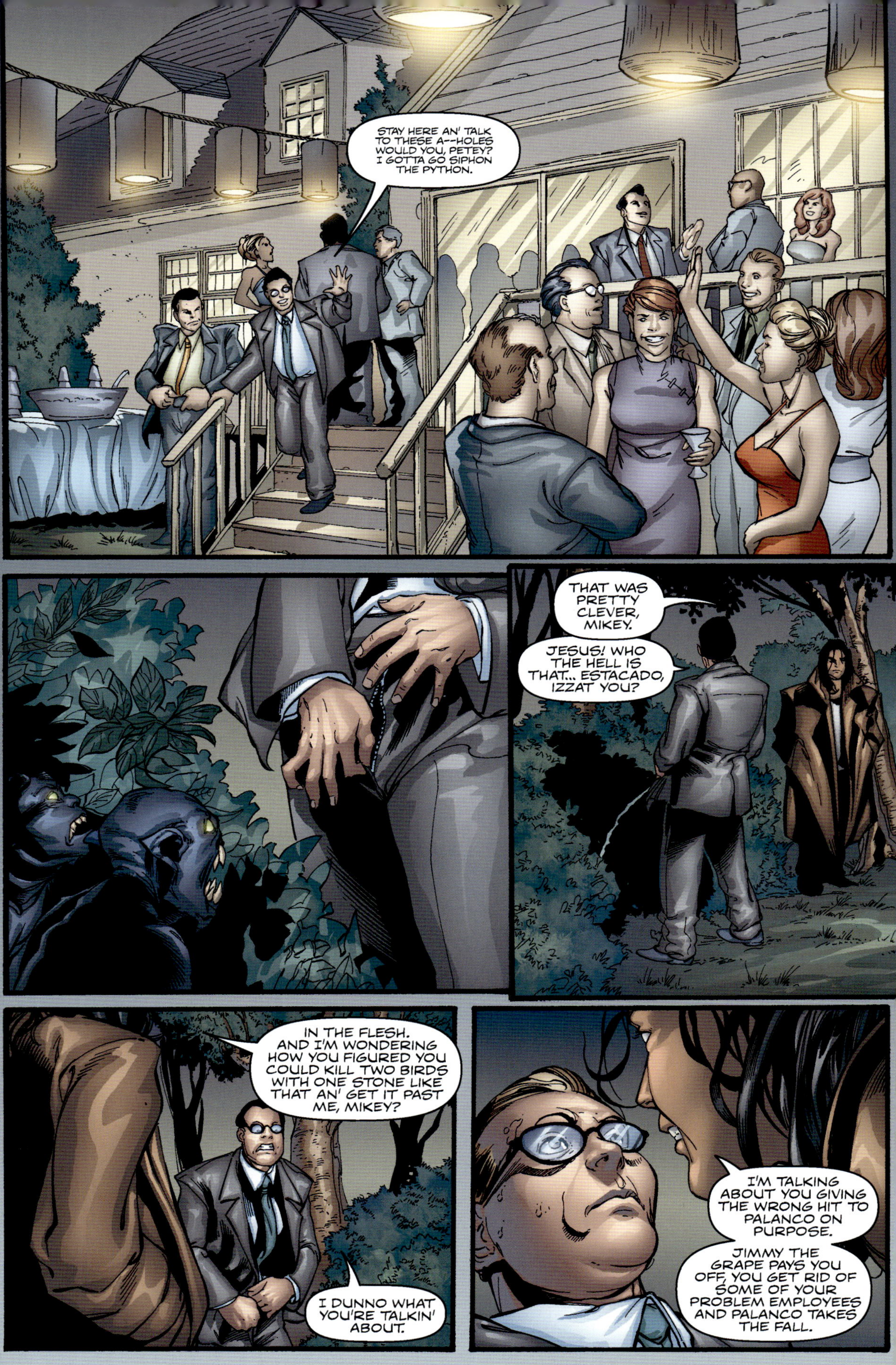
STAY HERE AN' TALK TO THESE A--HOLES WOULD YOU, PETEY? I GOTTA GO SIPHON THE PYTHON.
THAT WAS PRETTY CLEVER, MIKEY.
JESUS! WHO THE HELL IS THAT... ESTACADO, IZZAT YOU?
IN THE FLESH. AND I'M WONDERING HOW YOU FIGURED YOU COULD KILL TWO BIRDS WITH ONE STONE LIKE THAT AN' GET IT PAST ME, MIKEY?
I DUNNO WHAT YOU'RE TALKIN' ABOUT.
I'M TALKING ABOUT YOU GIVING THE WRONG HIT TO PALANCO ON PURPOSE.
JIMMY THE GRAPE PAYS YOU OFF, YOU GET RID OF SOME OF YOUR PROBLEM EMPLOYEES AND PALANCO TAKES THE FALL.

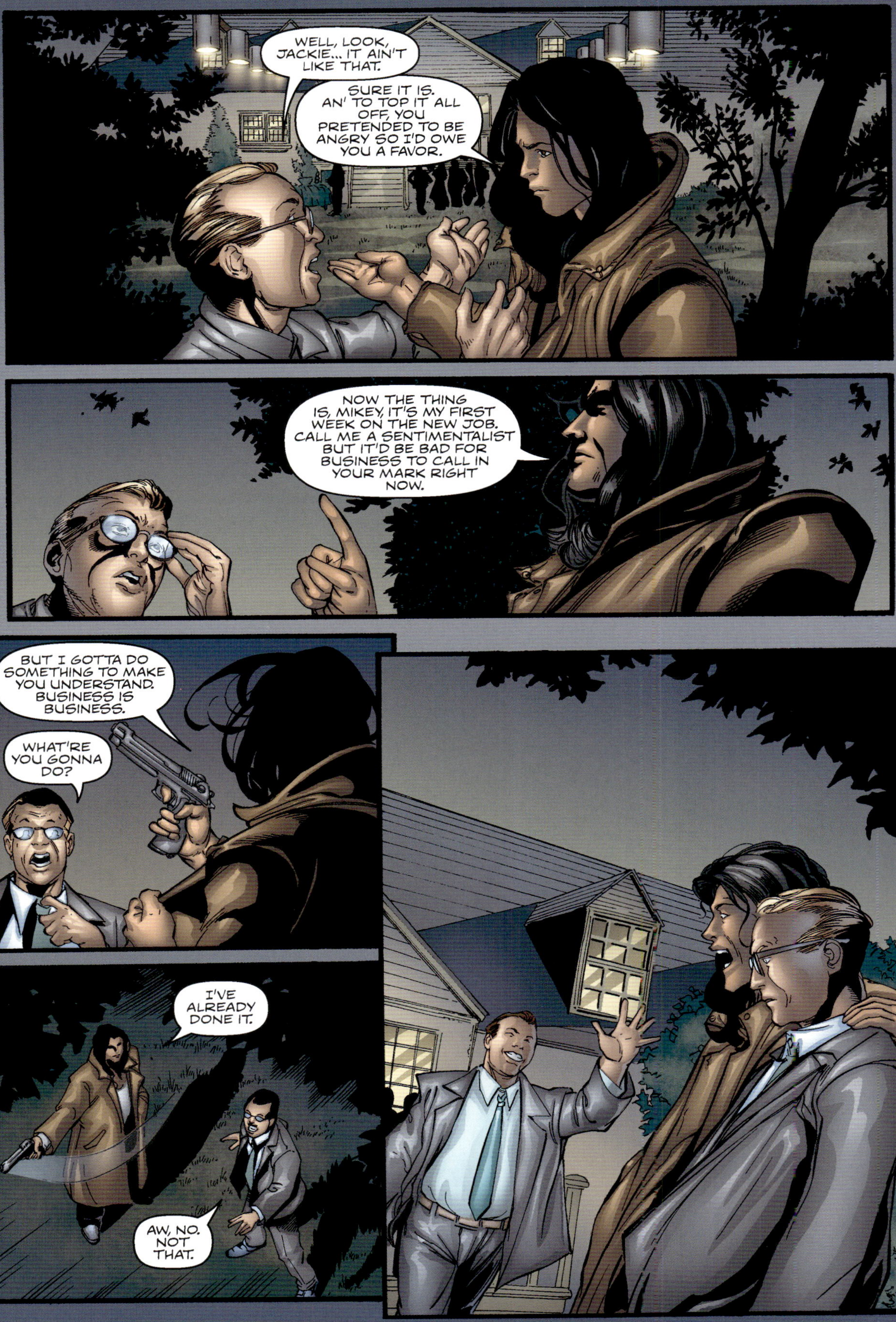
WELL, LOOK, JACKIE... IT AIN'T LIKE THAT.
SURE IT IS. AN' TO TOP IT ALL OFF, YOU PRETENDED TO BE ANGRY SO I'D OWE YOU A FAVOR.
NOW THE THING IS, MIKEY, IT'S MY FIRST WEEK ON THE NEW JOB. CALL ME A SENTIMENTALIST BUT IT'D BE BAD FOR BUSINESS TO CALL IN YOUR MARK RIGHT NOW.
BUT I GOTTA DO SOMETHING TO MAKE YOU UNDERSTAND. BUSINESS IS BUSINESS.
WHAT'RE YOU GONNA DO?
I'VE ALREADY DONE IT.
AW, NO. NOT THAT.

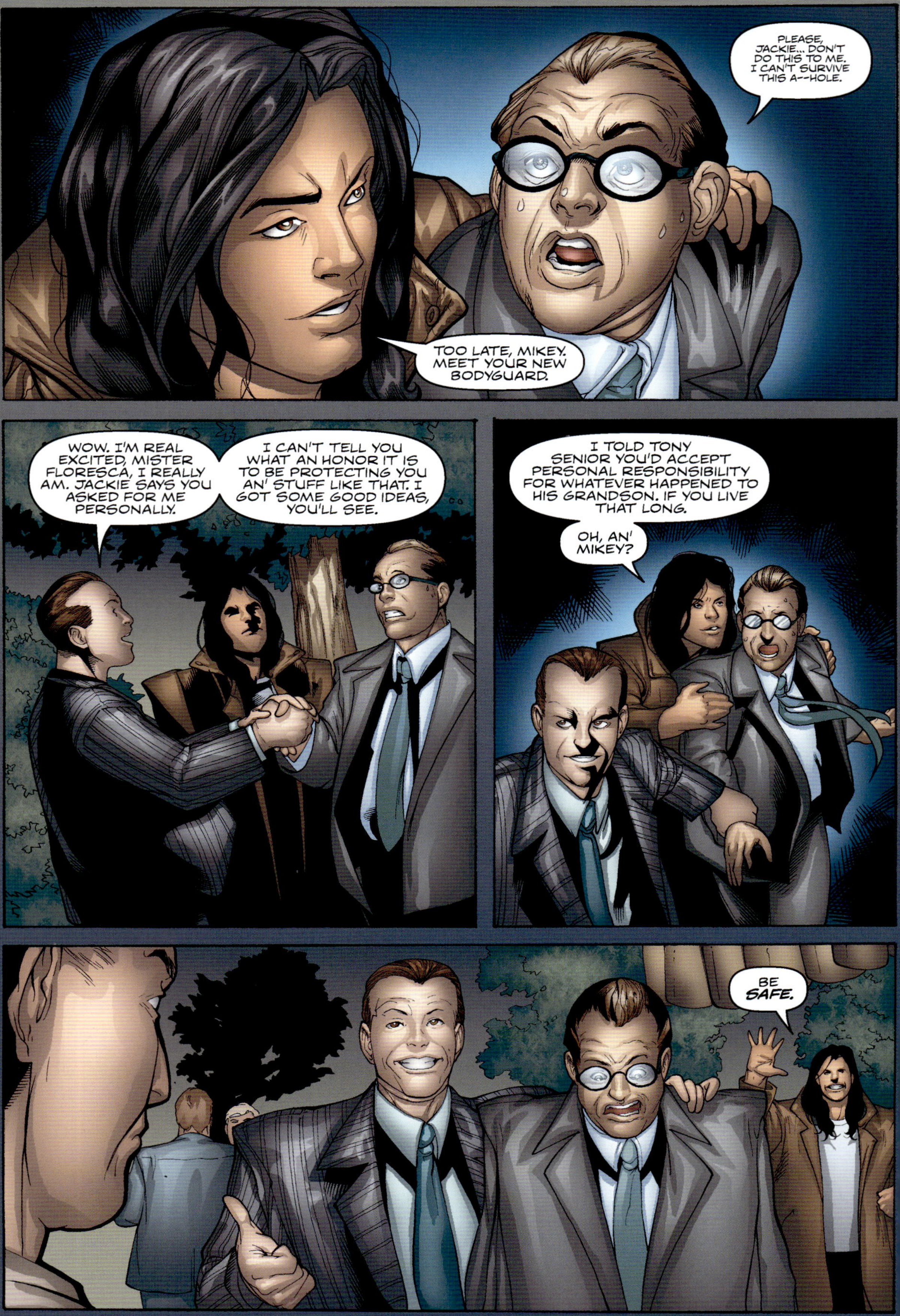
PLEASE, JACKIE... DON'T DO THIS TO ME. I CAN'T SURVIVE THIS A--HOLE.
TOO LATE, MIKEY. MEET YOUR NEW BODYGUARD.
WOW. I'M REAL EXCITED, MISTER FLORESCA, I REALLY AM. JACKIE SAYS YOU ASKED FOR ME PERSONALLY.
I CAN'T TELL YOU WHAT AN HONOR IT IS TO BE PROTECTING YOU AN' STUFF LIKE THAT. I GOT SOME GOOD IDEAS, YOU'LL SEE.
I TOLD TONY SENIOR YOU'D ACCEPT PERSONAL RESPONSIBILITY FOR WHATEVER HAPPENED TO HIS GRANDSON. IF YOU LIVE THAT LONG.
OH, AN' MIKEY?
BE SAFE.

The Darkness Issue #50

cover art by: Dale Keown and Matt Milla

THE DARKNESS #50

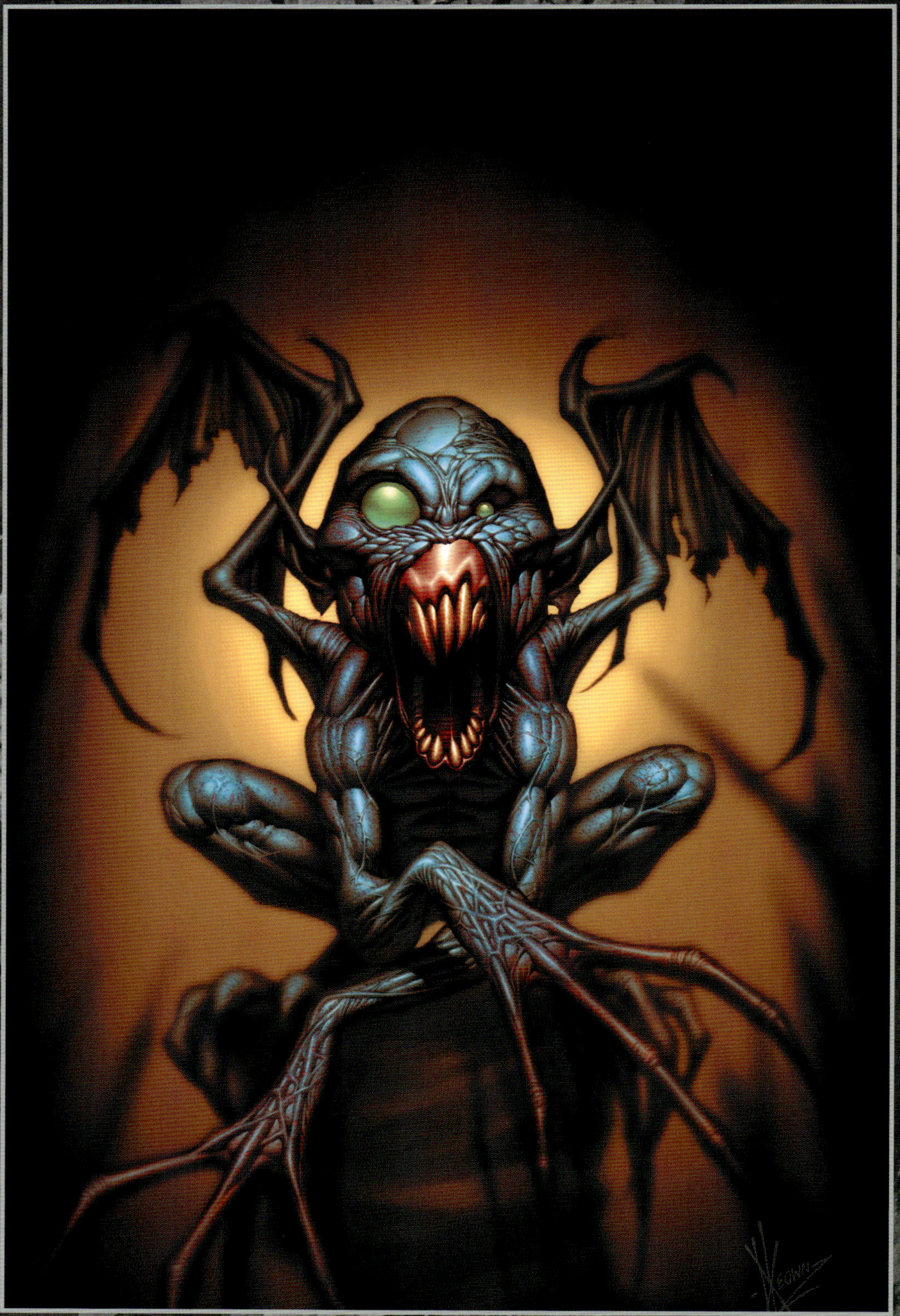

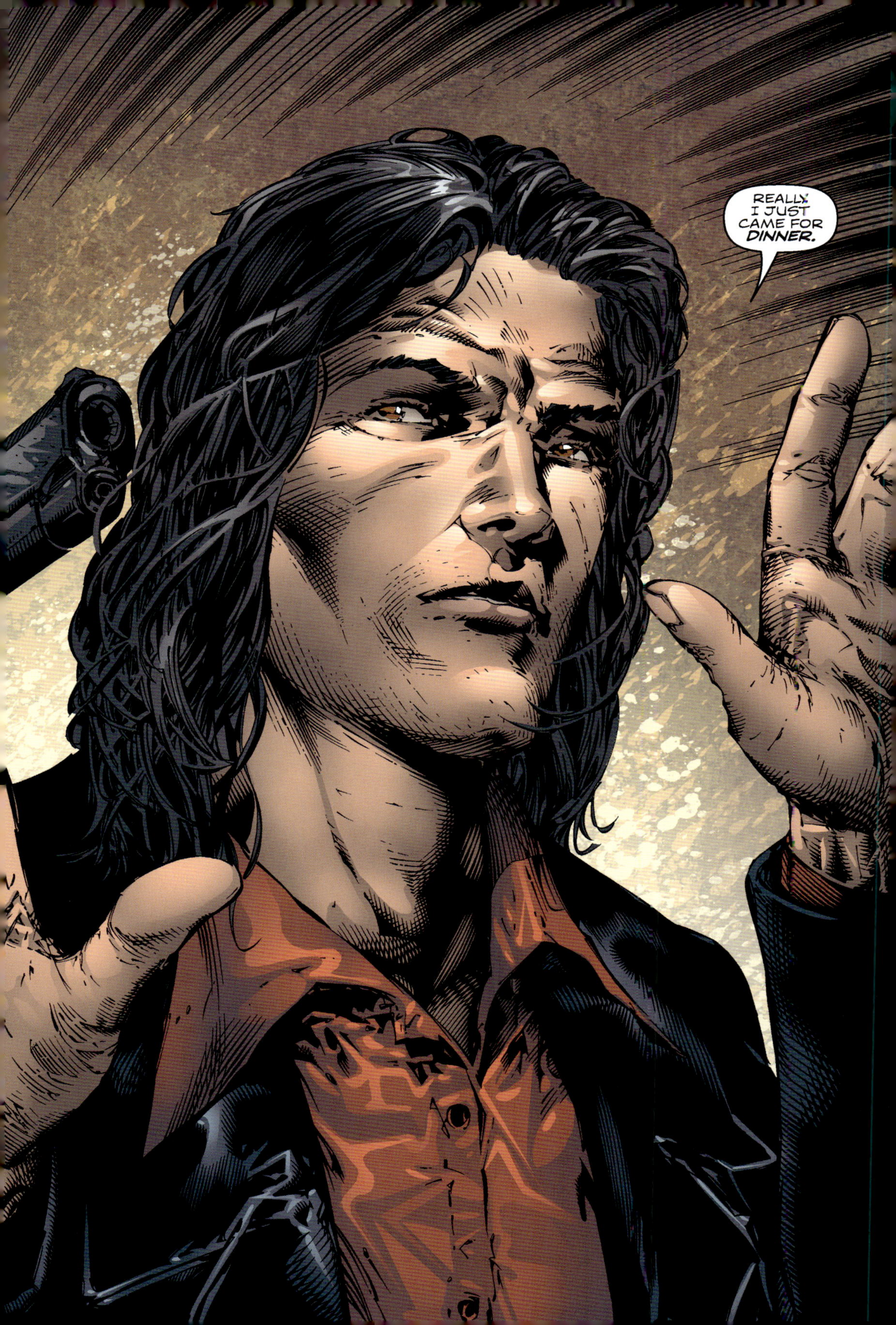
REALLY, I JUST CAME FOR DINNER.

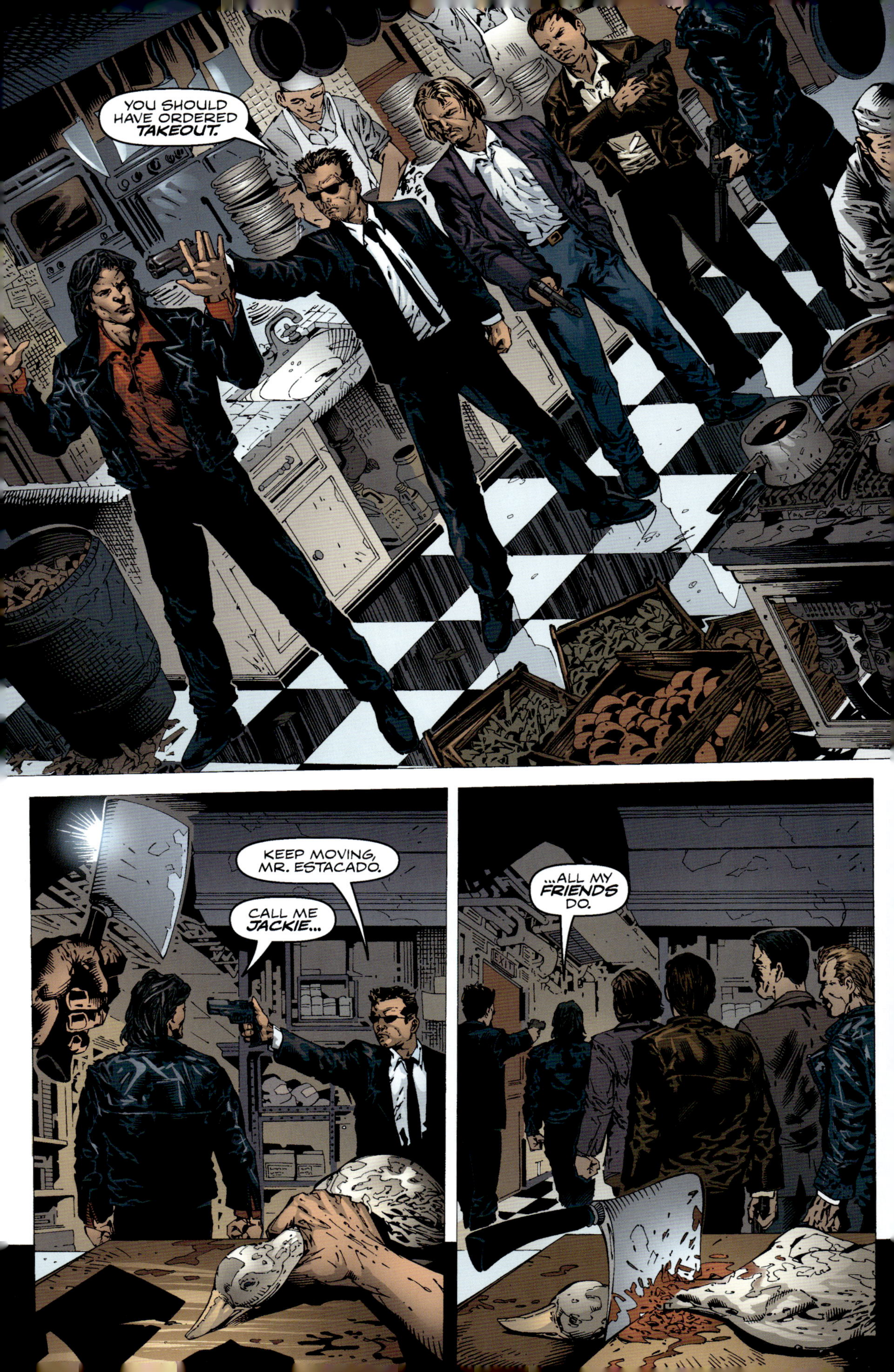

YOU SHOULD HAVE ORDERED TAKEOUT.
KEEP MOVING, MR. ESTACADO.
CALL ME JACKIE...
...ALL MY FRIENDS DO.
EXIT

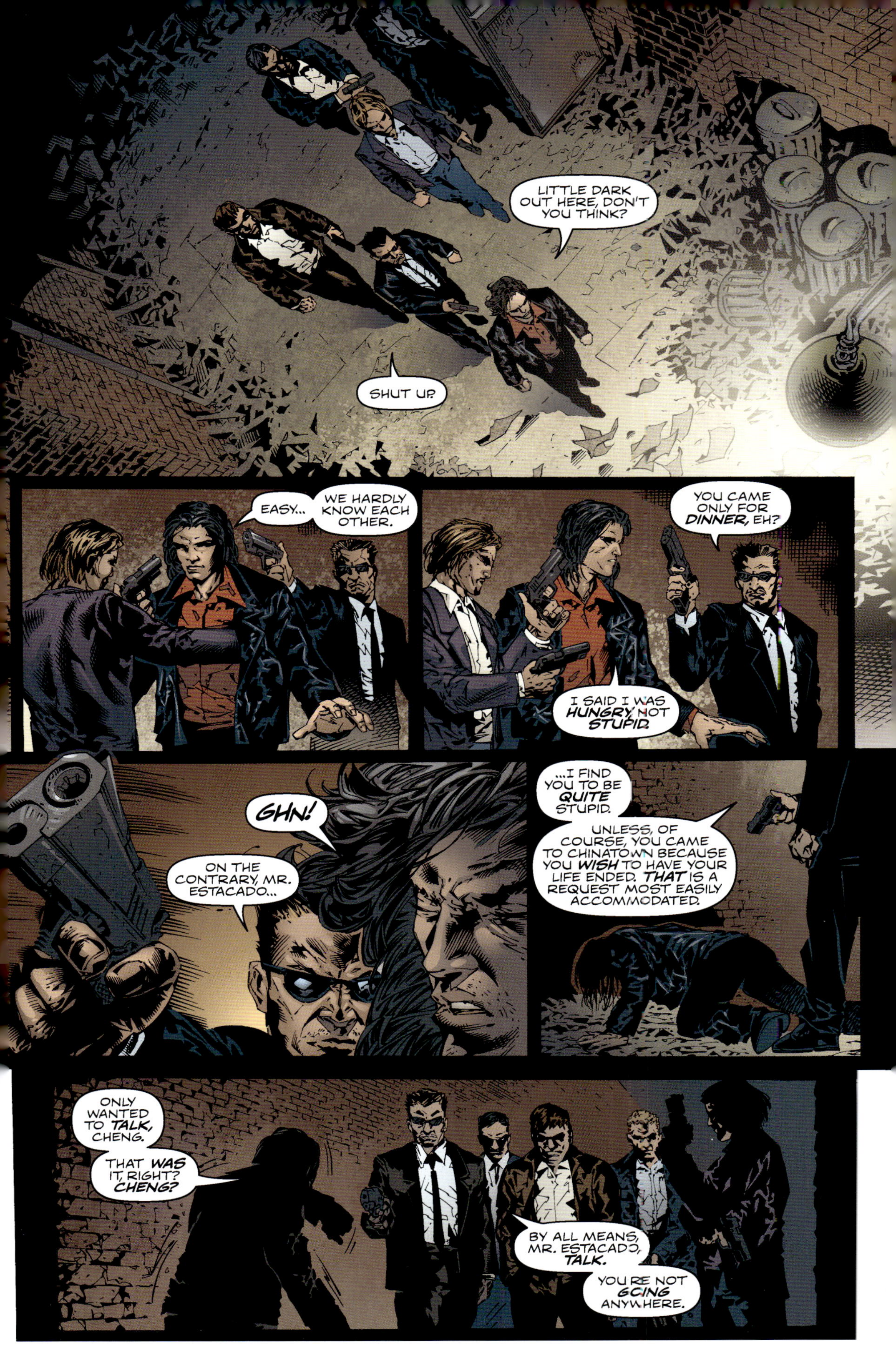
LITTLE DARK OUT HERE, DON'T YOU THINK?
SHUT UP.
EASY...
WE HARDLY KNOW EACH OTHER.
YOU CAME ONLY FOR DINNER, EH?
I SAID I WAS HUNGRY, NOT STUPID.
GHN!
ON THE CONTRARY, MR. ESTACADO...
...I FIND YOU TO BE QUITE STUPID.
UNLESS, OF COURSE, YOU CAME TO CHINATOWN BECAUSE YOU WISH TO HAVE YOUR LIFE ENDED. THAT IS A REQUEST MOST EASILY ACCOMMODATED.
ONLY WANTED TO TALK, CHENG.
THAT WAS IT, RIGHT? CHENG?
BY ALL MEANS, MR. ESTACADO, TALK.
YOU'RE NOT GOING ANYWHERE.

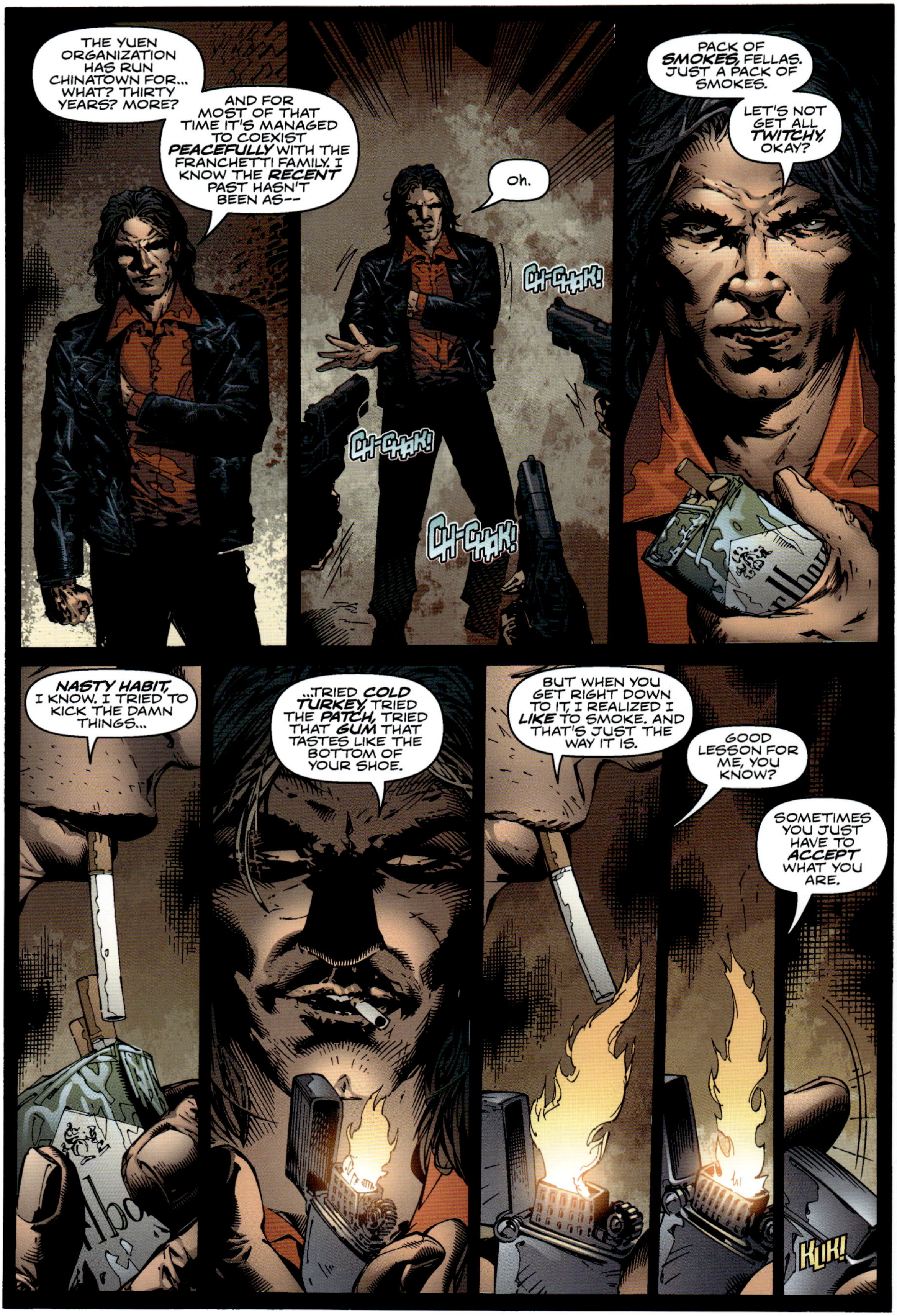

THE YUEN ORGANIZATION HAS RUN CHINATOWN FOR... WHAT? THIRTY YEARS? MORE?
AND FOR MOST OF THAT TIME IT'S MANAGED TO COEXIST PEACEFULLY WITH THE FRANCHETTI FAMILY. I KNOW THE RECENT PAST HASN'T BEEN AS--
Oh.
CH-CHAK!
CH-CHAK!
CH-CHAK!
PACK OF SMOKES, FELLAS. JUST A PACK OF SMOKES.
LET'S NOT GET ALL TWITCHY, OKAY?
NASTY HABIT, I KNOW. I TRIED TO KICK THE DAMN THINGS...
...TRIED COLD TURKEY, TRIED THE PATCH, TRIED THAT GUM THAT TASTES LIKE THE BOTTOM OF YOUR SHOE.
BUT WHEN YOU GET RIGHT DOWN TO IT, I REALIZED I LIKE TO SMOKE. AND THAT'S JUST THE WAY IT IS.
GOOD LESSON FOR ME, YOU KNOW?
SOMETIMES YOU JUST HAVE TO ACCEPT WHAT YOU ARE.
KLIK!

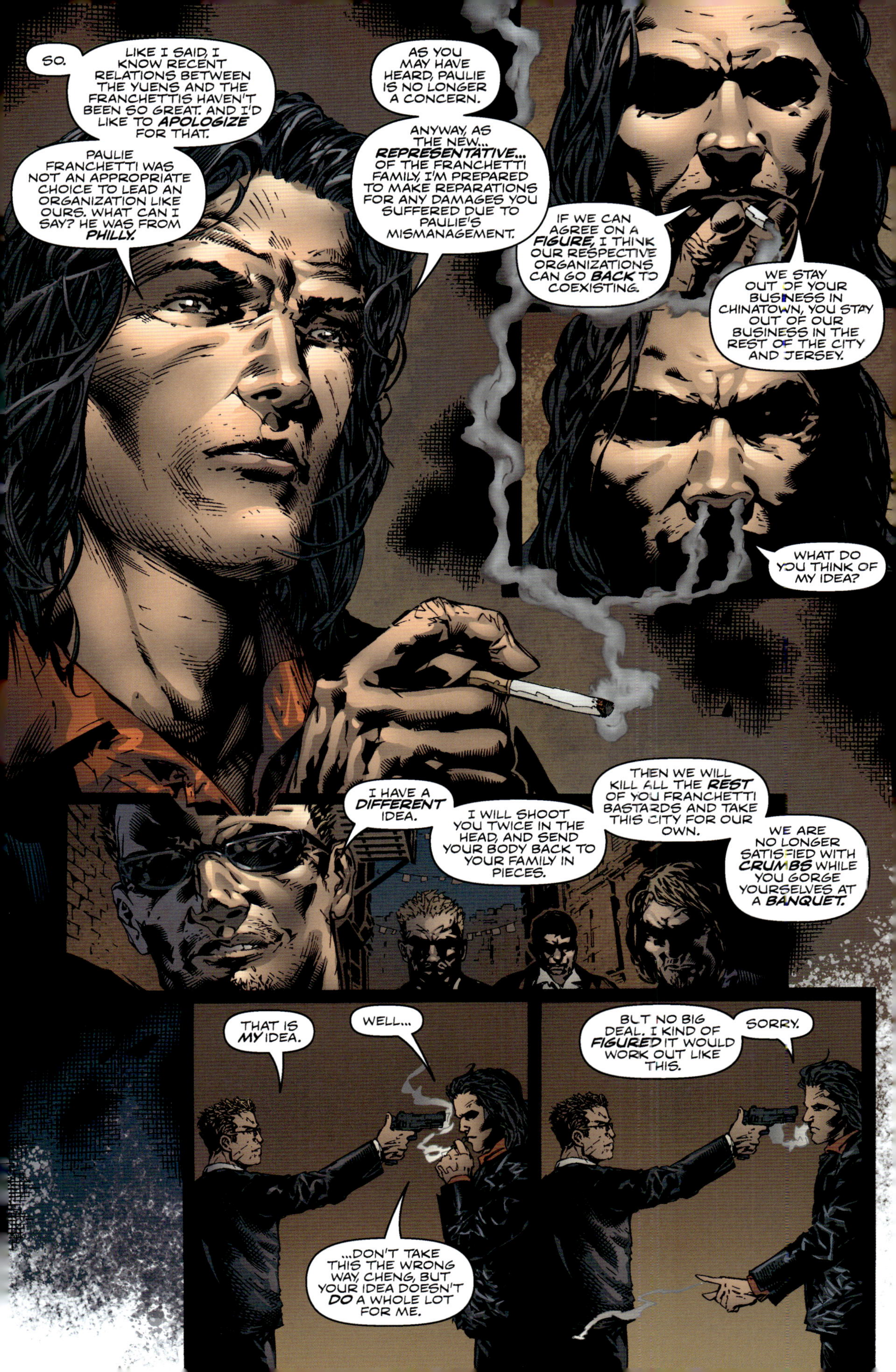
SO.
LIKE I SAID, I KNOW RECENT RELATIONS BETWEEN THE YUENS AND THE FRANCHETTIS HAVEN'T BEEN SO GREAT. AND I'D LIKE TO APOLOGIZE FOR THAT.
PAULIE FRANCHETTI WAS NOT AN APPROPRIATE CHOICE TO LEAD AN ORGANIZATION LIKE OURS. WHAT CAN I SAY? HE WAS FROM PHILLY.
AS YOU MAY HAVE HEARD, PAULIE IS NO LONGER A CONCERN.
ANYWAY, AS THE NEW... REPRESENTATIVE... OF THE FRANCHETTI FAMILY, I'M PREPARED TO MAKE REPARATIONS FOR ANY DAMAGES YOU SUFFERED DUE TO PAULIE'S MISMANAGEMENT.
IF WE CAN AGREE ON A FIGURE, I THINK OUR RESPECTIVE ORGANIZATIONS CAN GO BACK TO COEXISTING.
WE STAY OUT OF YOUR BUSINESS IN CHINATOWN, YOU STAY OUT OF OUR BUSINESS IN THE REST OF THE CITY AND JERSEY.
WHAT DO YOU THINK OF MY IDEA?
I HAVE A DIFFERENT IDEA.
I WILL SHOOT YOU TWICE IN THE HEAD, AND SEND YOUR BODY BACK TO YOUR FAMILY IN PIECES.
THEN WE WILL KILL ALL THE REST OF YOU FRANCHETTI BASTARDS AND TAKE THIS CITY FOR OUR OWN.
WE ARE NO LONGER SATISFIED WITH CRUMBS WHILE YOU GORGE YOURSELVES AT A BANQUET.
THAT IS MY IDEA.
WELL...
...DON'T TAKE THIS THE WRONG WAY, CHENG, BUT YOUR IDEA DOESN'T DO A WHOLE LOT FOR ME.
BUT NO BIG DEAL. I KIND OF FIGURED IT WOULD WORK OUT LIKE THIS.
SORRY.

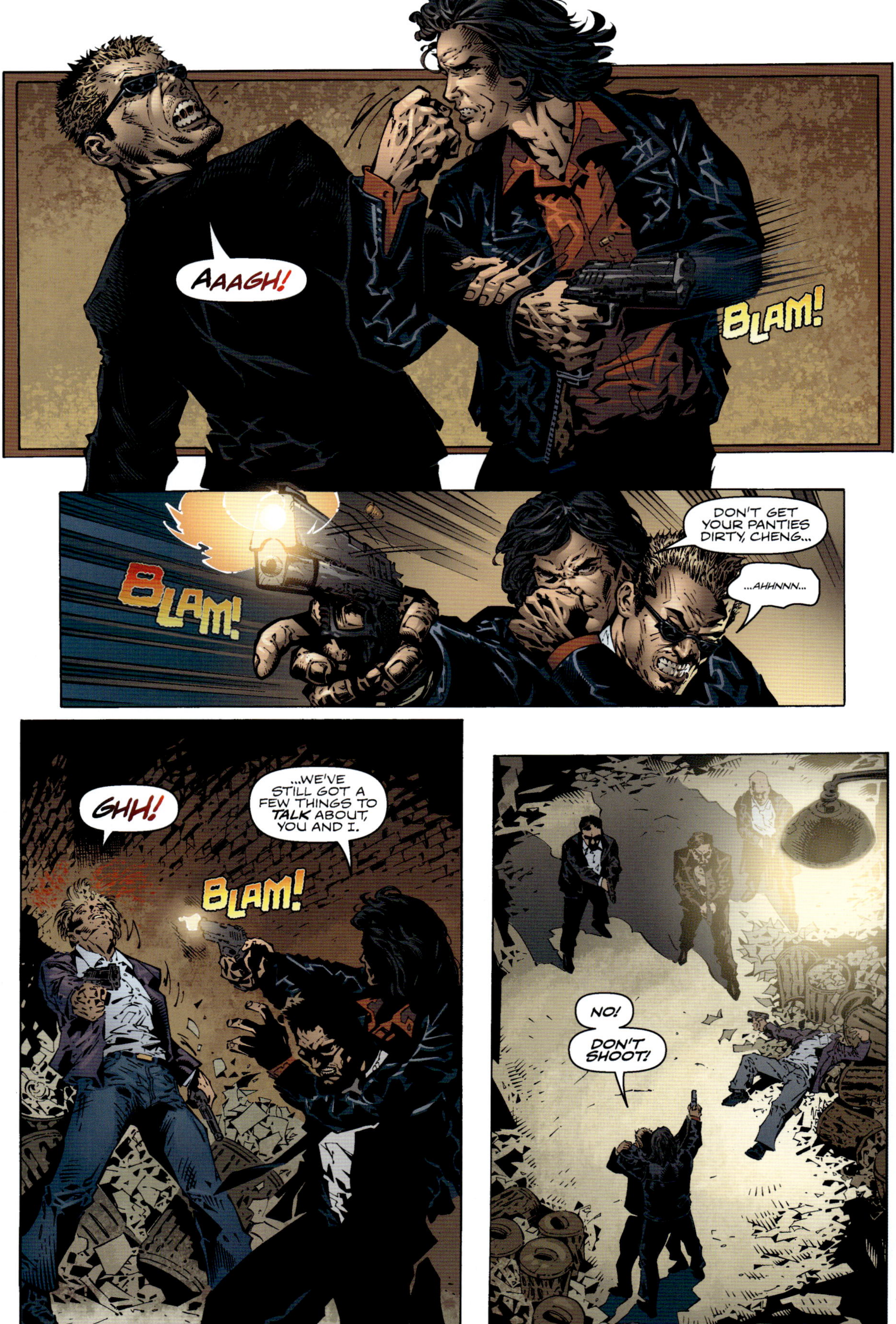
AAAGH!
BLAM!
BLAM!
DON'T GET YOUR PANTIES DIRTY, CHENG...
...AHHNNN...
GHH!
...WE'VE STILL GOT A FEW THINGS TO TALK ABOUT, YOU AND I.
BLAM!
NO! DON'T SHOOT!

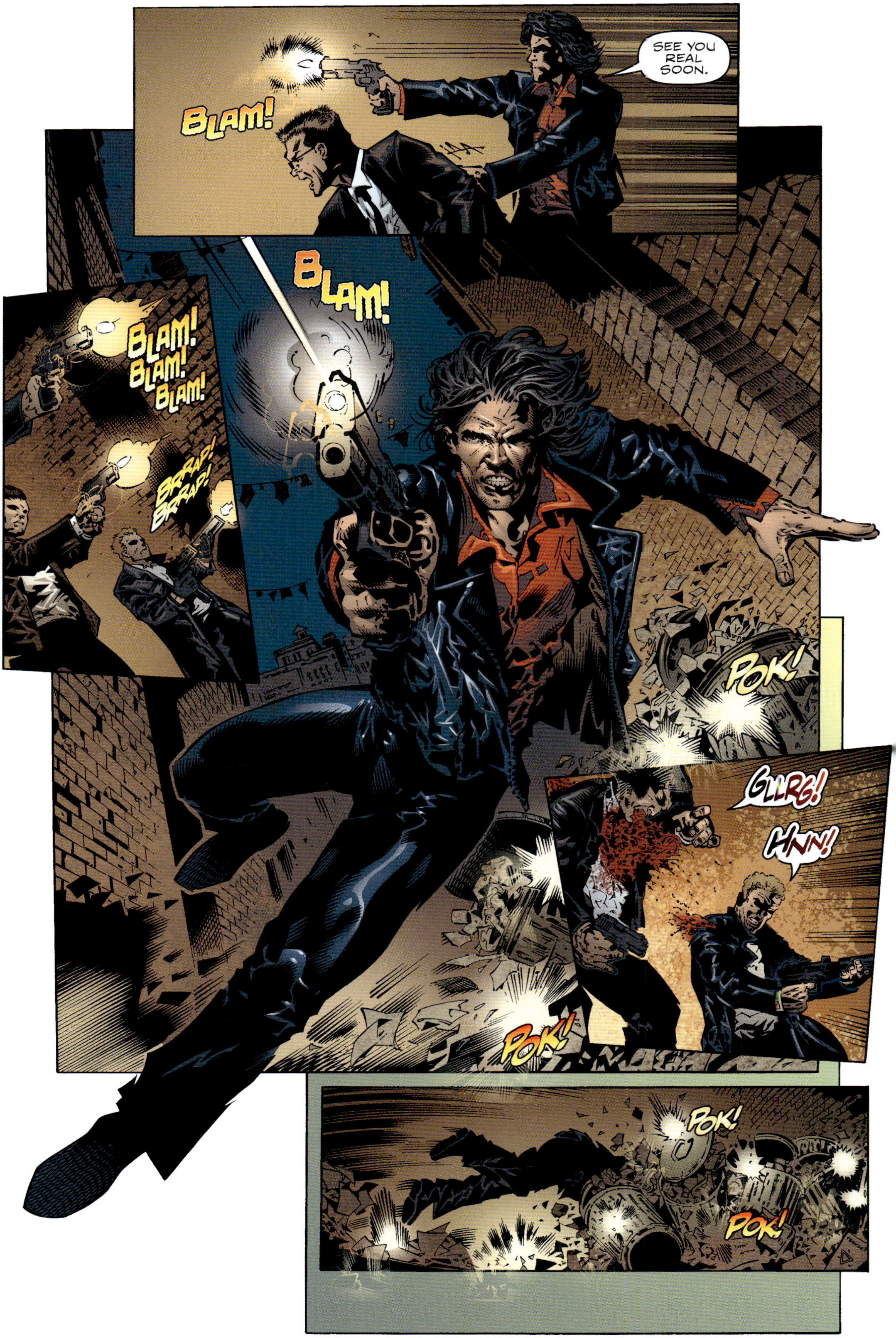
SEE YOU REAL SOON.
BLAM!
BLAM!
BLAM! BLAM! BLAM!
BRRAP! BRRAP!
POK!
GLLRG!
HNN!
POK!
POK!
POK!

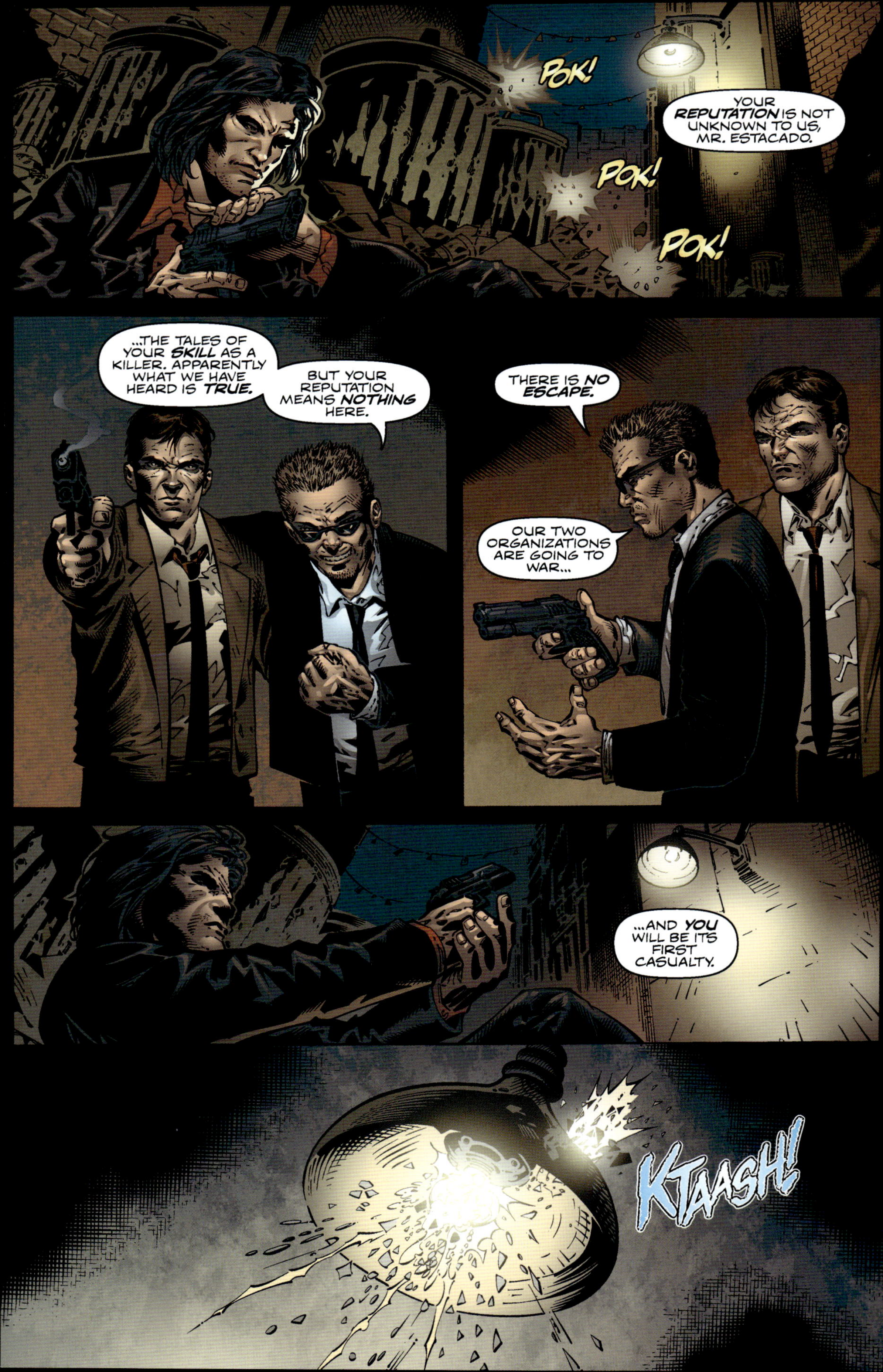
POK!
YOUR REPUTATION IS NOT UNKNOWN TO US, MR. ESTACADO.
POK!
POK!
...THE TALES OF YOUR SKILL AS A KILLER. APPARENTLY WHAT WE HAVE HEARD IS TRUE.
BUT YOUR REPUTATION MEANS NOTHING HERE.
THERE IS NO ESCAPE.
OUR TWO ORGANIZATIONS ARE GOING TO WAR...
...AND YOU WILL BE ITS FIRST CASUALTY.
KTAASH!

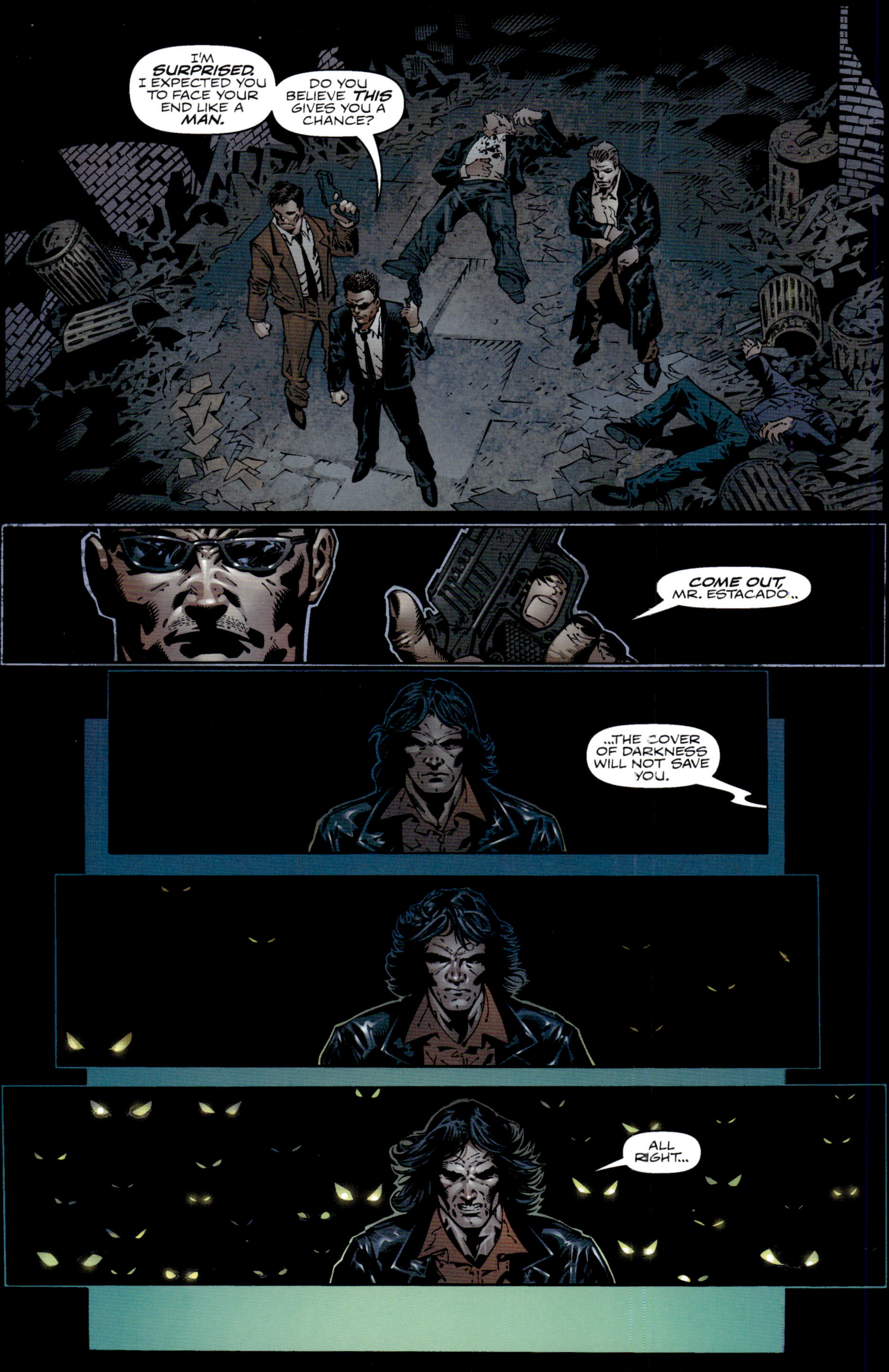

I'M SURPRISED. I EXPECTED YOU TO FACE YOUR END LIKE A MAN.
DO YOU BELIEVE THIS GIVES YOU A CHANCE?
COME OUT, MR. ESTACADO...
...THE COVER OF DARKNESS WILL NOT SAVE YOU.
ALL RIGHT...

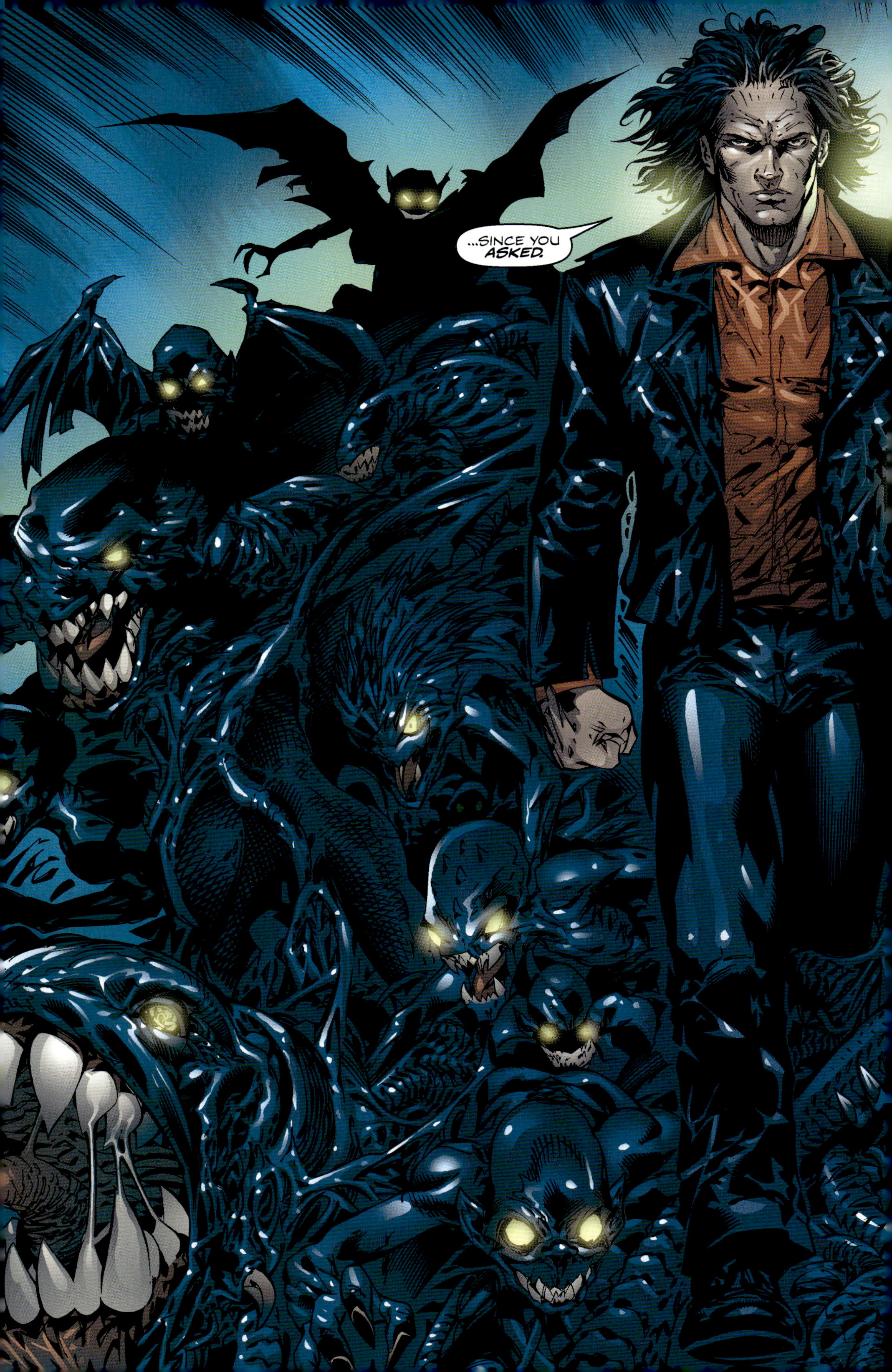
...SINCE YOU ASKED.

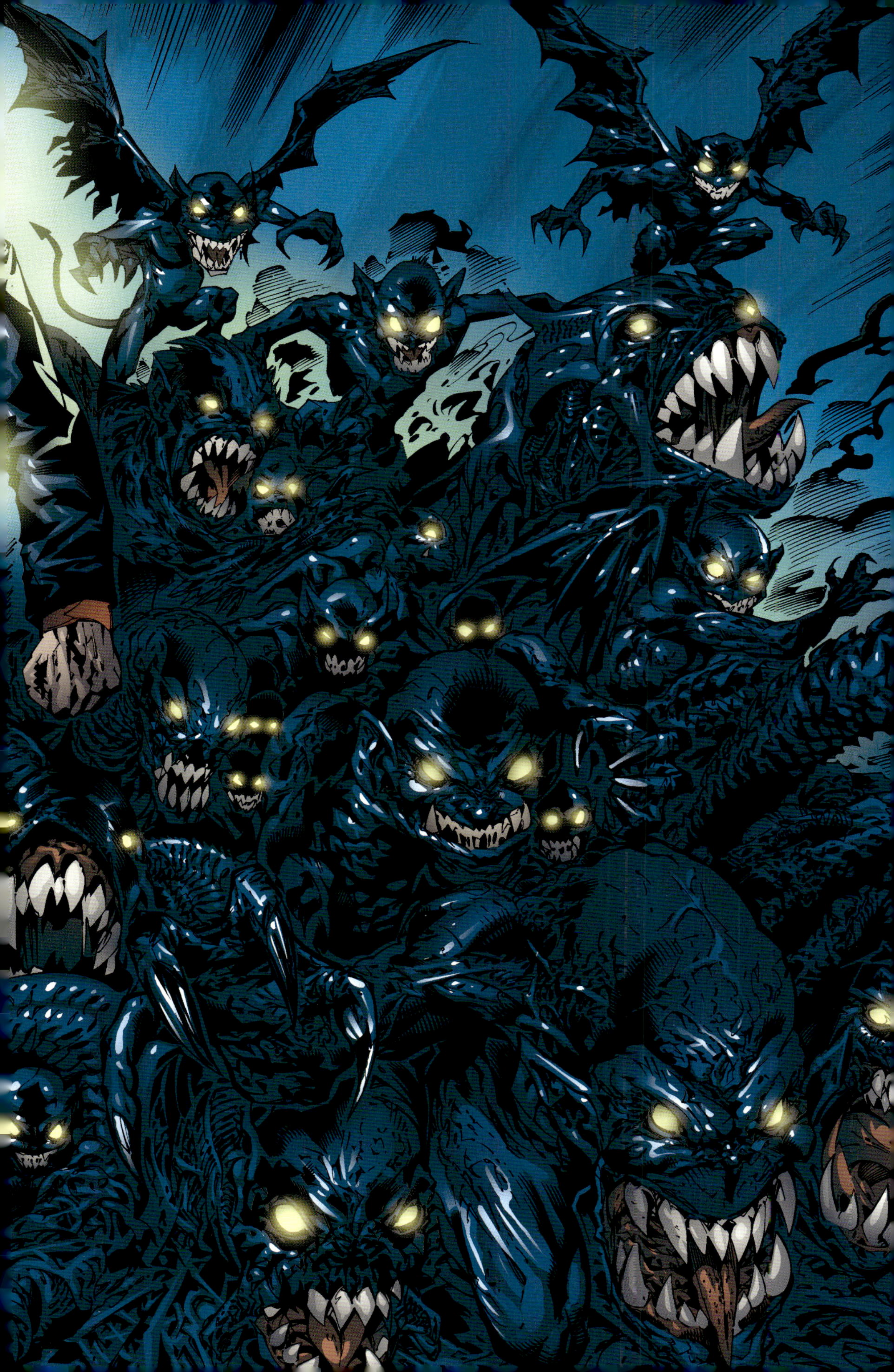

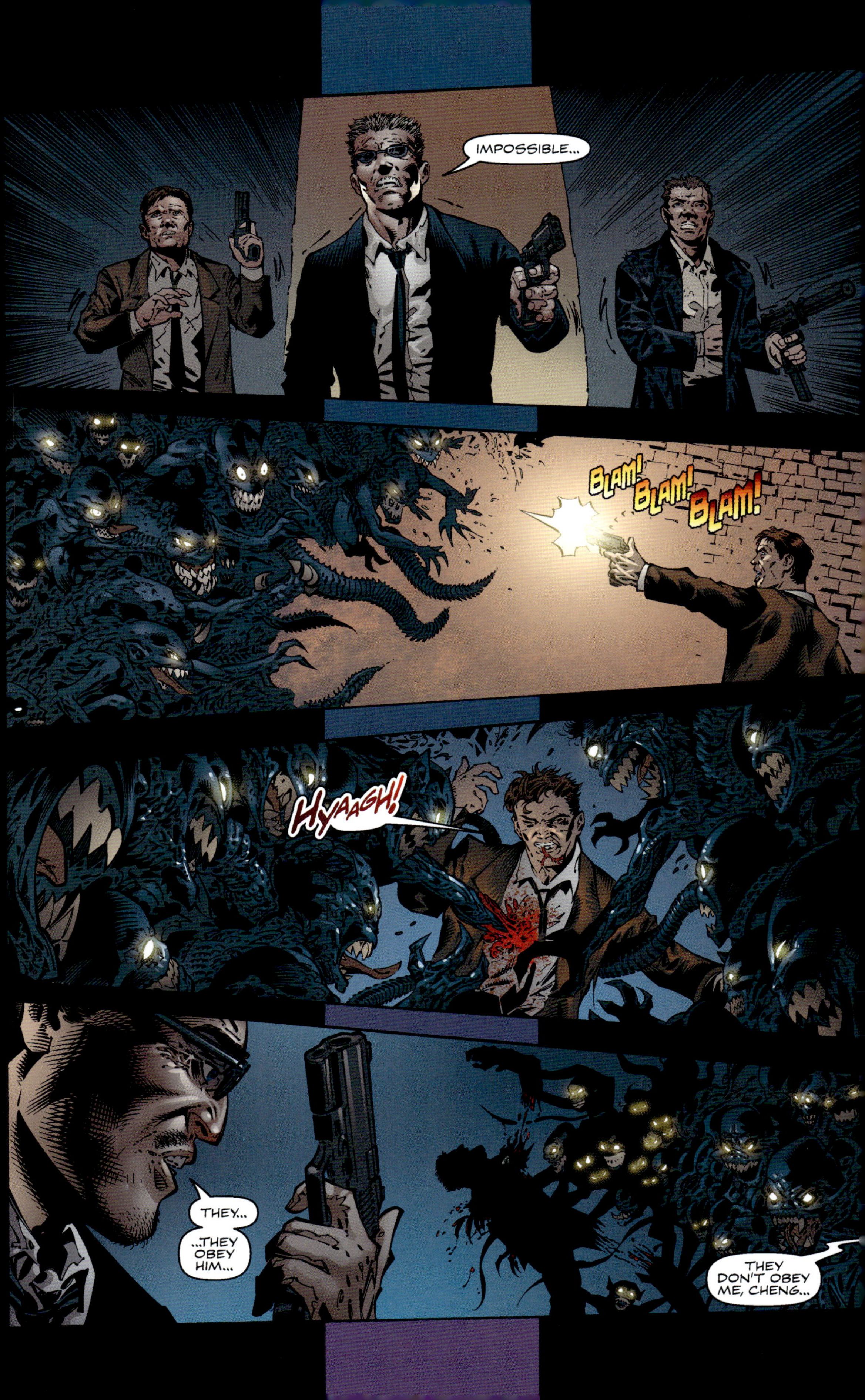
IMPOSSIBLE...
BLAM! BLAM! BLAM!
HYAAGH!
THEY...
...THEY OBEY HIM...
THEY DON'T OBEY ME, CHENG...

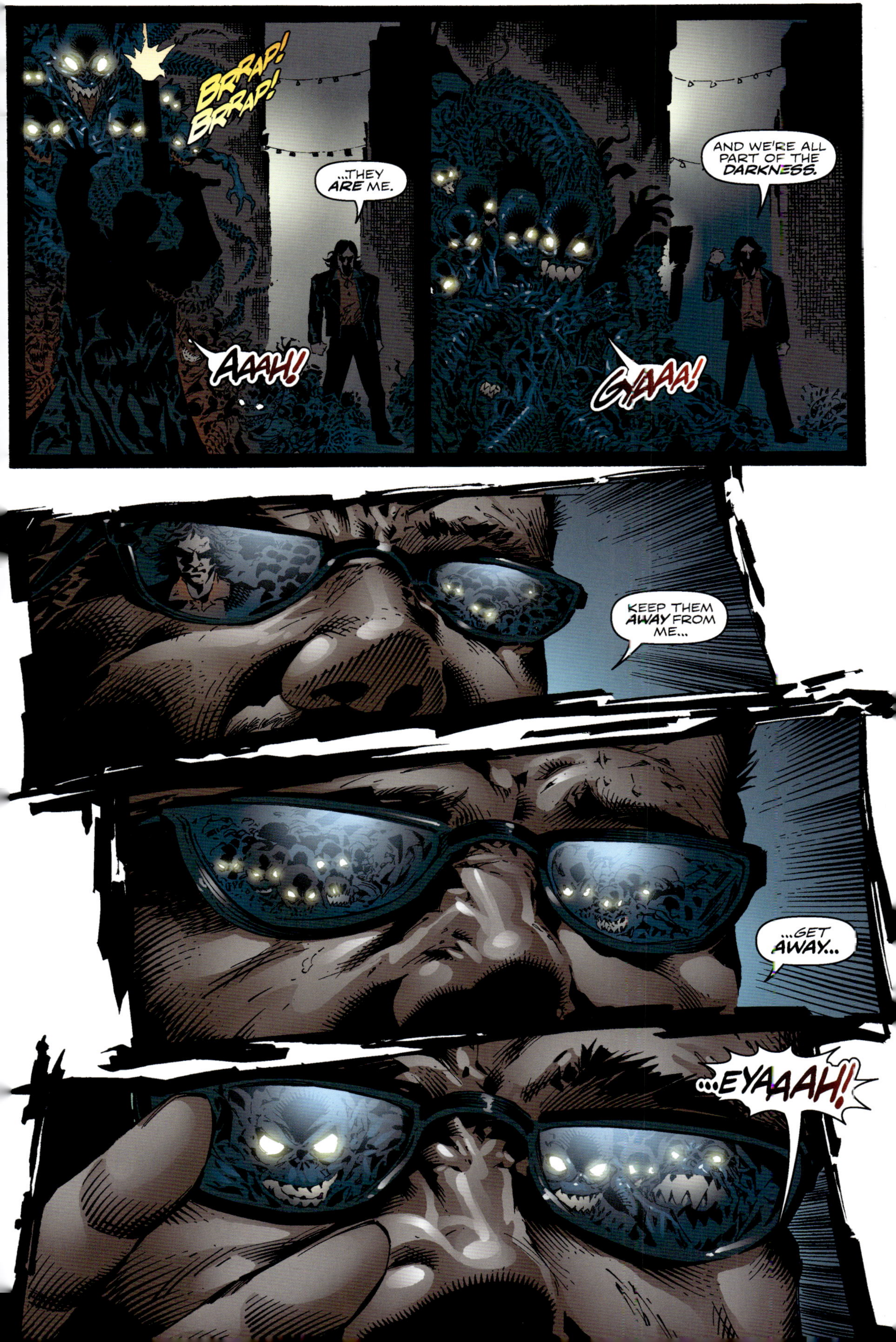
BRRAP! BRRAP!
...THEY ARE ME.
AAAH!
AND WE'RE ALL PART OF THE DARKNESS.
GYAAA!
KEEP THEM AWAY FROM ME...
...GET AWAY...
...EYAAAH!

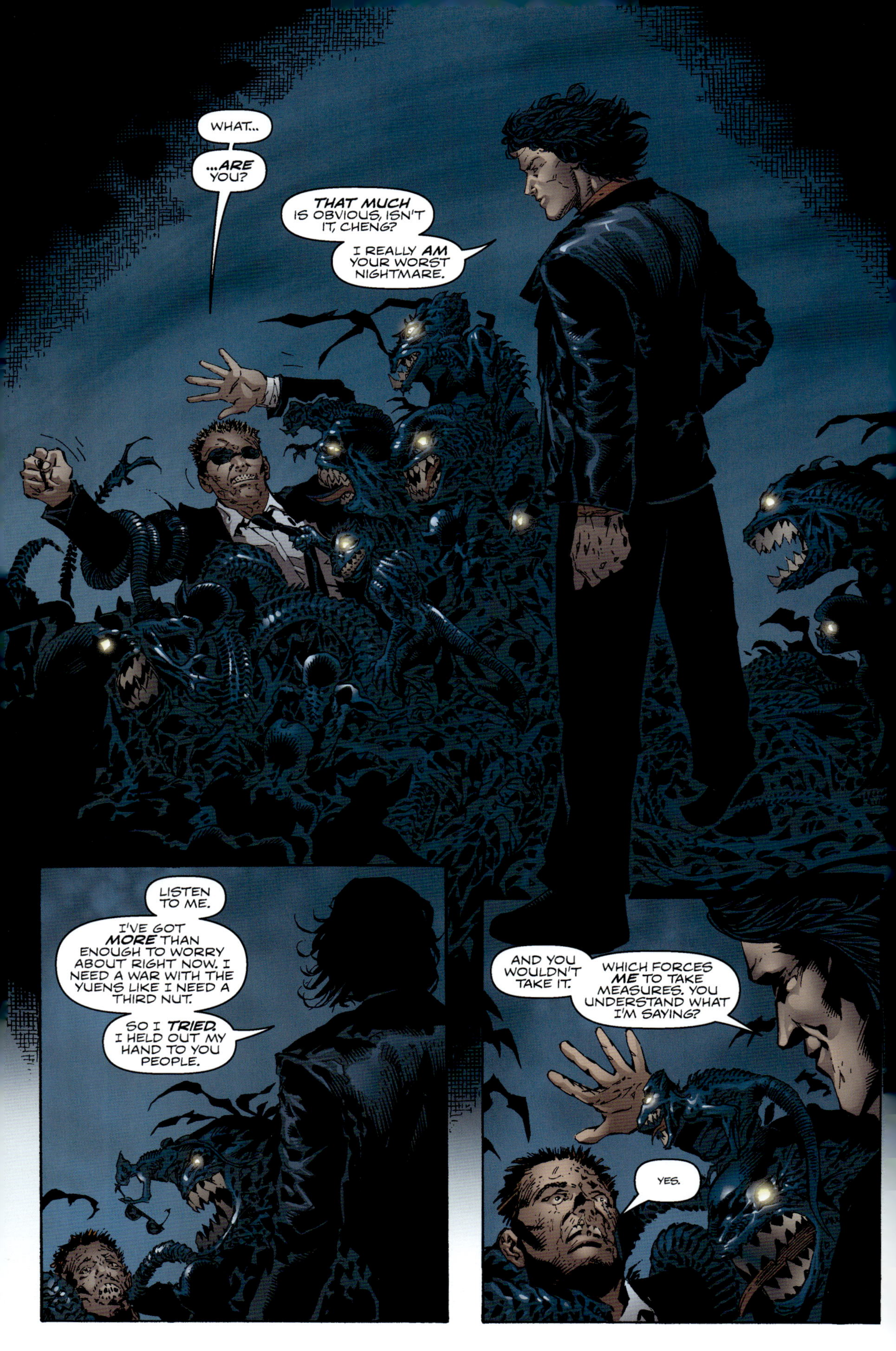
WHAT...
...ARE YOU?
THAT MUCH IS OBVIOUS, ISN'T IT, CHENG?
I REALLY AM YOUR WORST NIGHTMARE.
LISTEN TO ME.
I'VE GOT MORE THAN ENOUGH TO WORRY ABOUT RIGHT NOW. I NEED A WAR WITH THE YUENS LIKE I NEED A THIRD NUT.
SO I TRIED. I HELD OUT MY HAND TO YOU PEOPLE.
AND YOU WOULDN'T TAKE IT.
WHICH FORCES ME TO TAKE MEASURES. YOU UNDERSTAND WHAT I'M SAYING?
YES.

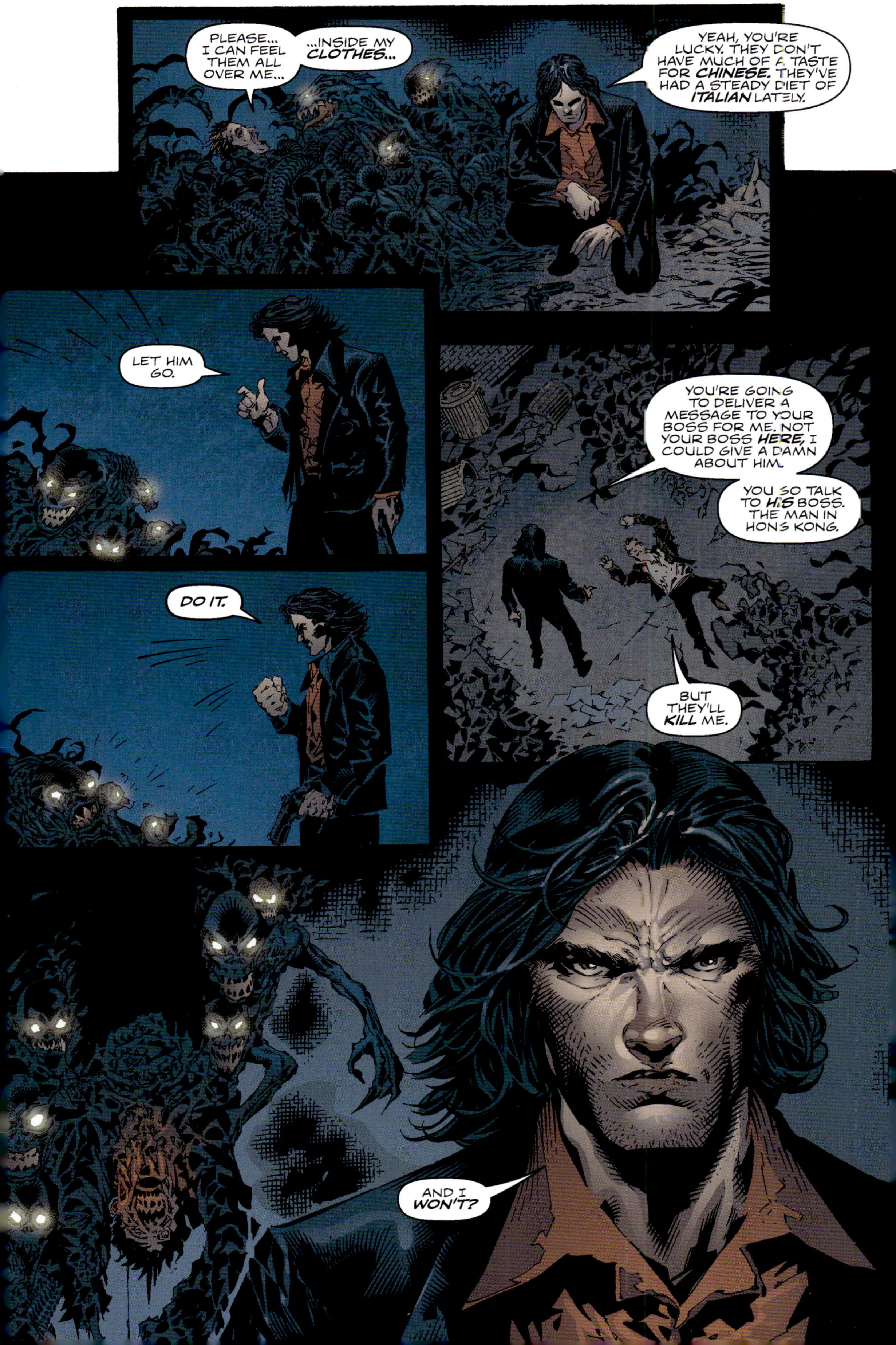
PLEASE... I CAN FEEL THEM ALL OVER ME...
...INSIDE MY CLOTHES...
YEAH, YOU'RE LUCKY. THEY DON'T HAVE MUCH OF A TASTE FOR CHINESE. THEY'VE HAD A STEADY DIET OF ITALIAN LATELY.
LET HIM GO.
DO IT.
YOU'RE GOING TO DELIVER A MESSAGE TO YOUR BOSS FOR ME. NOT YOUR BOSS HERE, I COULD GIVE A DAMN ABOUT HIM.
YOU GO TALK TO HIS BOSS. THE MAN IN HONG KONG.
BUT THEY'LL KILL ME.
AND I WON'T?

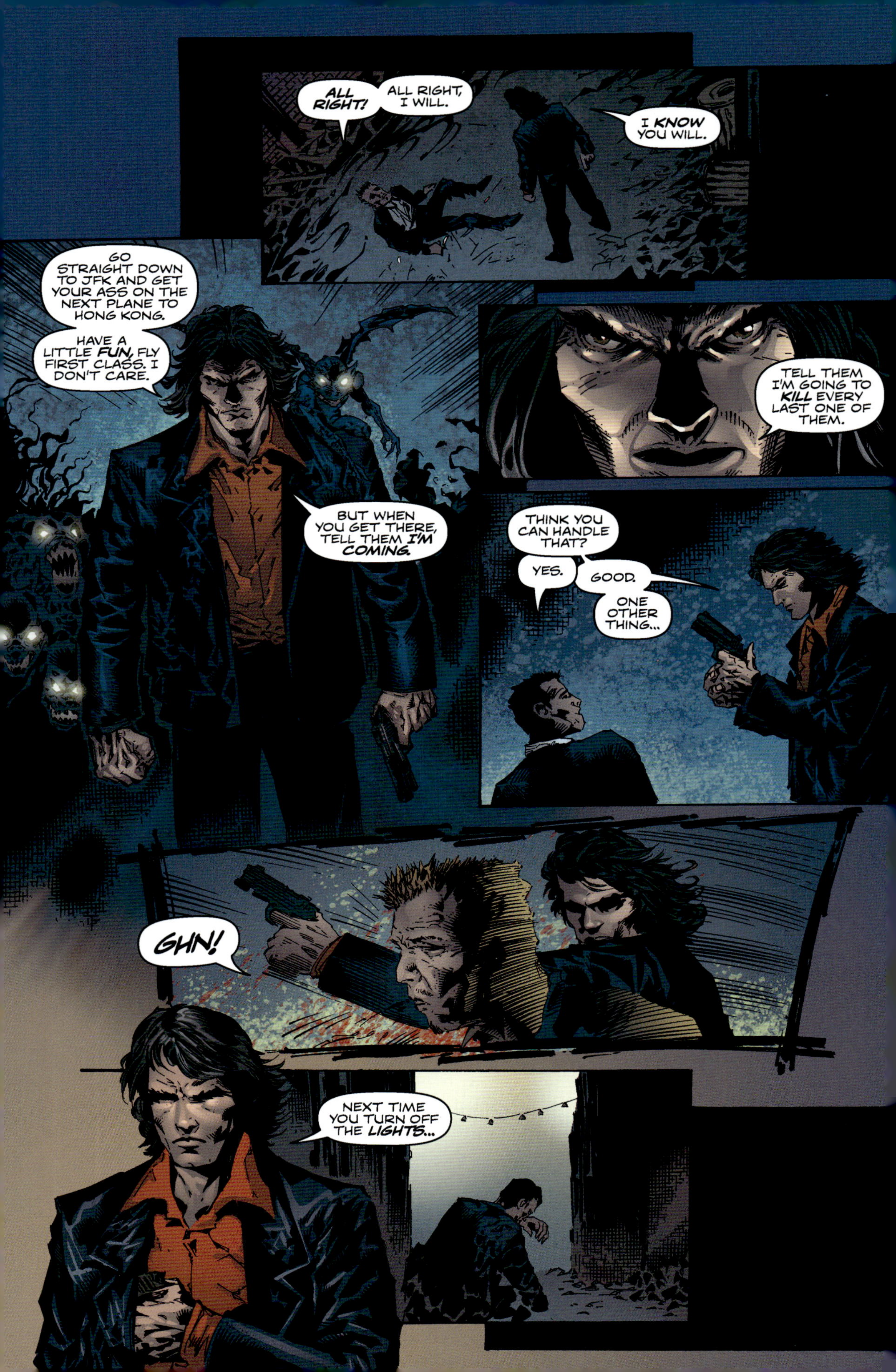
ALL RIGHT!
ALL RIGHT, I WILL.
I KNOW YOU WILL.
GO STRAIGHT DOWN TO JFK AND GET YOUR ASS ON THE NEXT PLANE TO HONG KONG.
HAVE A LITTLE FUN, FLY FIRST CLASS. I DON'T CARE.
BUT WHEN YOU GET THERE, TELL THEM I'M COMING.
TELL THEM I'M GOING TO KILL EVERY LAST ONE OF THEM.
THINK YOU CAN HANDLE THAT?
YES.
GOOD.
ONE OTHER THING...
GHN!
NEXT TIME YOU TURN OFF THE LIGHTS...

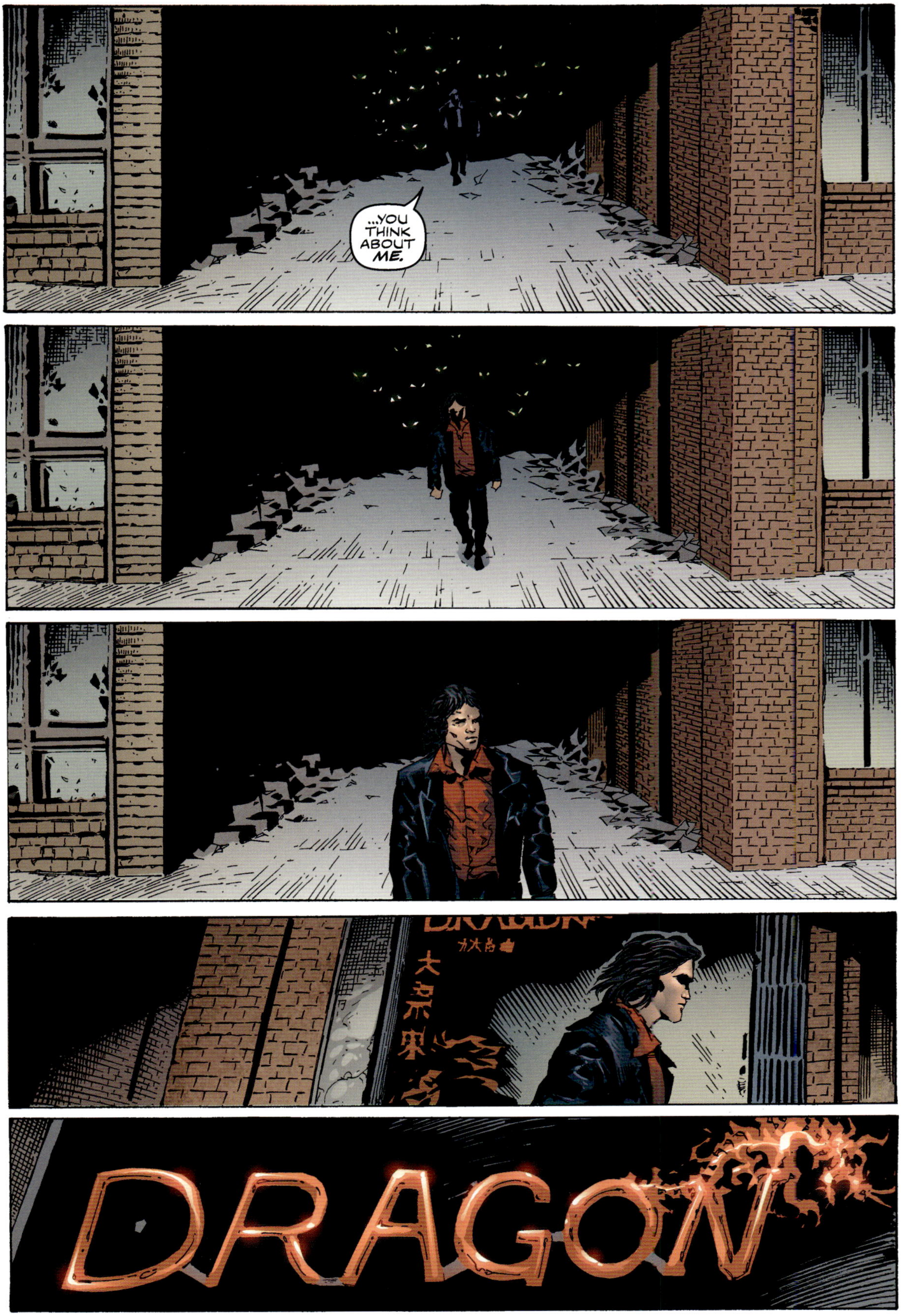
...YOU THINK ABOUT ME.
DRAGON

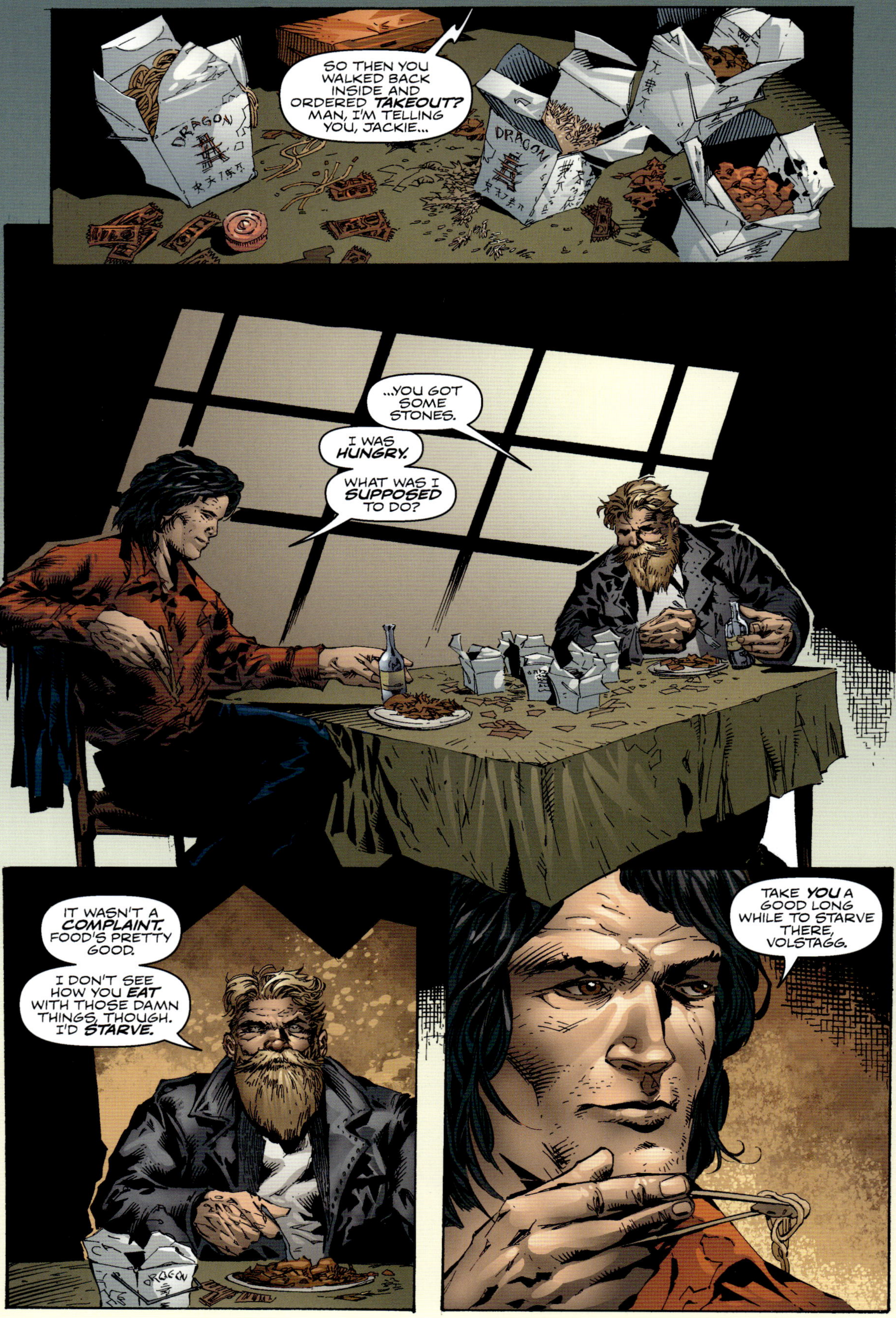
SO THEN YOU WALKED BACK INSIDE AND ORDERED TAKEOUT? MAN, I'M TELLING YOU, JACKIE...
...YOU GOT SOME STONES.
I WAS HUNGRY.
WHAT WAS I SUPPOSED TO DO?
IT WASN'T A COMPLAINT. FOOD'S PRETTY GOOD.
I DON'T SEE HOW YOU EAT WITH THOSE DAMN THINGS, THOUGH. I'D STARVE.
TAKE YOU A GOOD LONG WHILE TO STARVE THERE, VOLSTAGG.

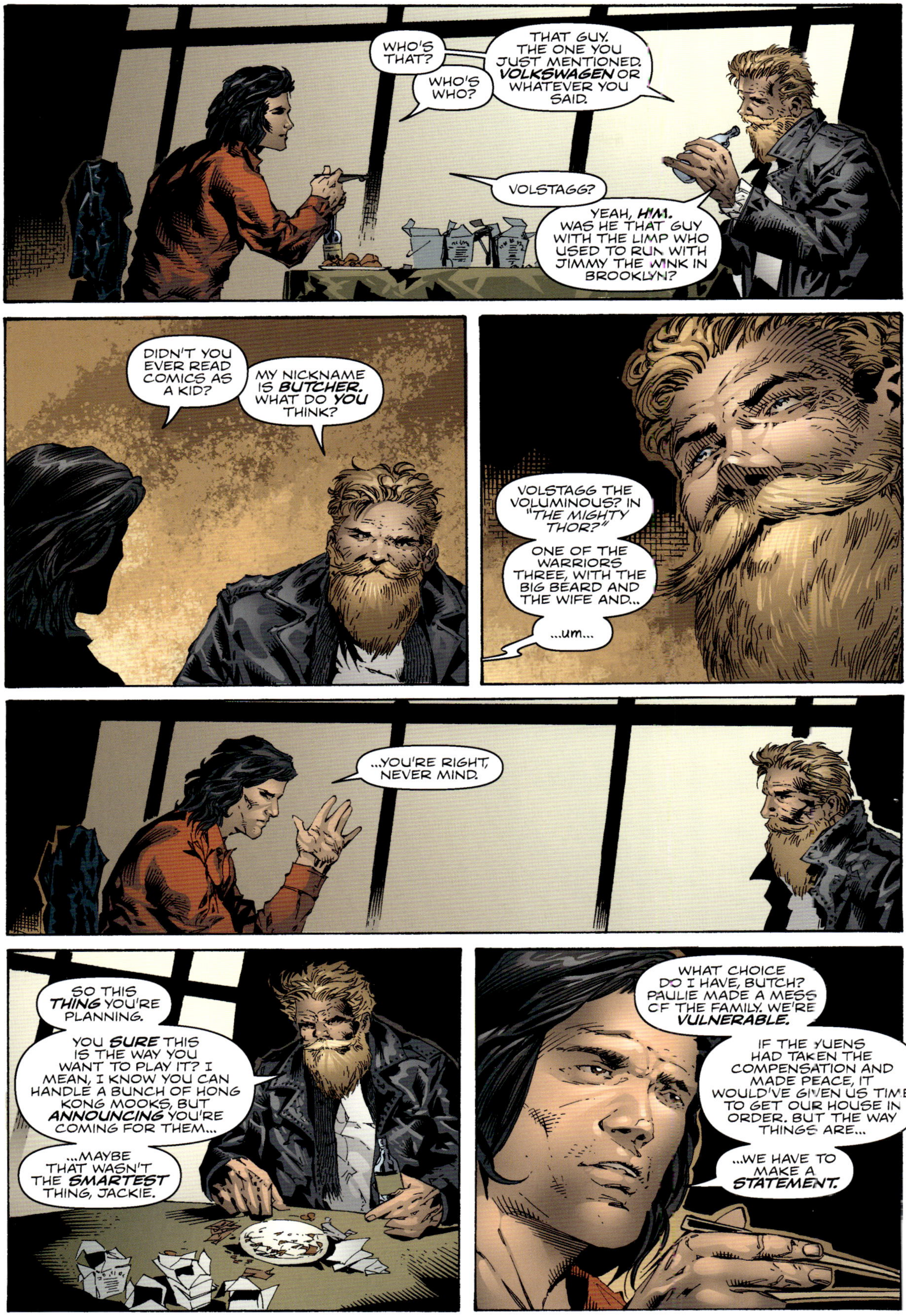
WHO'S THAT?
THAT GUY. THE ONE YOU JUST MENTIONED. VOLKSWAGEN OR WHATEVER YOU SAID.
WHO'S WHO?
VOLSTAGG?
YEAH, HIM. WAS HE THAT GUY WITH THE LIMP WHO USED TO RUN WITH JIMMY THE WINK IN BROOKLYN?
DIDN'T YOU EVER READ COMICS AS A KID?
MY NICKNAME IS BUTCHER. WHAT DO YOU THINK?
VOLSTAGG THE VOLUMINOUS? IN "THE MIGHTY THOR?"
ONE OF THE WARRIORS THREE, WITH THE BIG BEARD AND THE WIFE AND...
...um...
...YOU'RE RIGHT, NEVER MIND.
SO THIS THING YOU'RE PLANNING.
YOU SURE THIS IS THE WAY YOU WANT TO PLAY IT? I MEAN, I KNOW YOU CAN HANDLE A BUNCH OF HONG KONG MOOKS, BUT ANNOUNCING YOU'RE COMING FOR THEM...
...MAYBE THAT WASN'T THE SMARTEST THING, JACKIE.
WHAT CHOICE DO I HAVE, BUTCH? PAULIE MADE A MESS OF THE FAMILY. WE'RE VULNERABLE.
IF THE YUENS HAD TAKEN THE COMPENSATION AND MADE PEACE, IT WOULD'VE GIVEN US TIME TO GET OUR HOUSE IN ORDER. BUT THE WAY THINGS ARE...
...WE HAVE TO MAKE A STATEMENT.

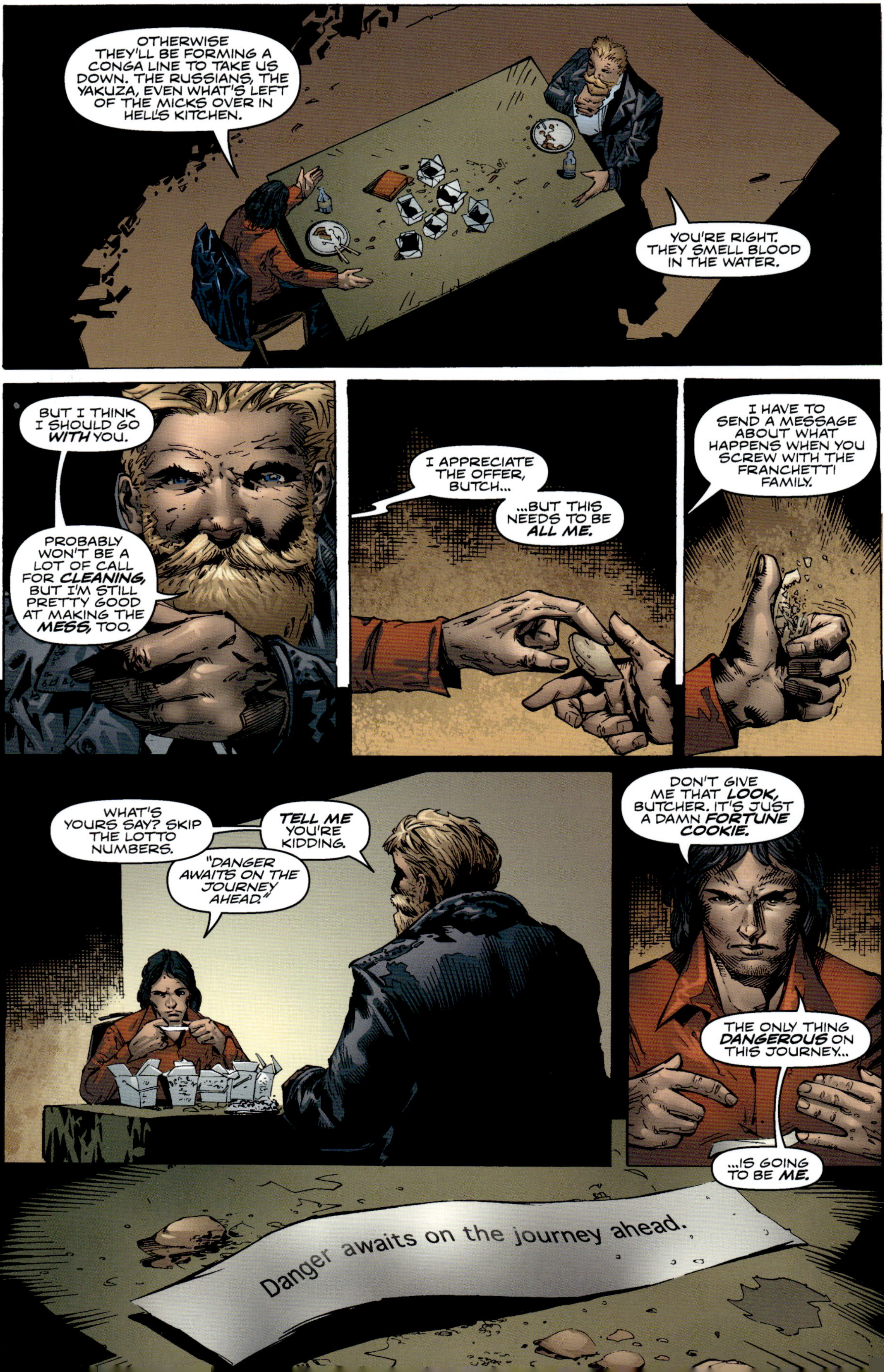
OTHERWISE THEY'LL BE FORMING A CONGA LINE TO TAKE US DOWN. THE RUSSIANS, THE YAKUZA, EVEN WHAT'S LEFT OF THE MICKS OVER IN HELL'S KITCHEN.
YOU'RE RIGHT. THEY SMELL BLOOD IN THE WATER.
BUT I THINK I SHOULD GO *WITH* YOU.
PROBABLY WON'T BE A LOT OF CALL FOR *CLEANING*, BUT I'M STILL PRETTY GOOD AT MAKING THE *MESS*, TOO.
I APPRECIATE THE OFFER, BUTCH...
...BUT THIS NEEDS TO BE *ALL ME.*
I HAVE TO SEND A MESSAGE ABOUT WHAT HAPPENS WHEN YOU SCREW WITH THE FRANCHETTI FAMILY.
WHAT'S YOURS SAY? SKIP THE LOTTO NUMBERS.
"DANGER AWAITS ON THE JOURNEY AHEAD."
TELL ME YOU'RE KIDDING.
DON'T GIVE ME THAT *LOOK*, BUTCHER. IT'S JUST A DAMN *FORTUNE COOKIE.*
THE ONLY THING *DANGEROUS* ON THIS JOURNEY...
...IS GOING TO BE *ME.*
Danger awaits on the journey ahead.

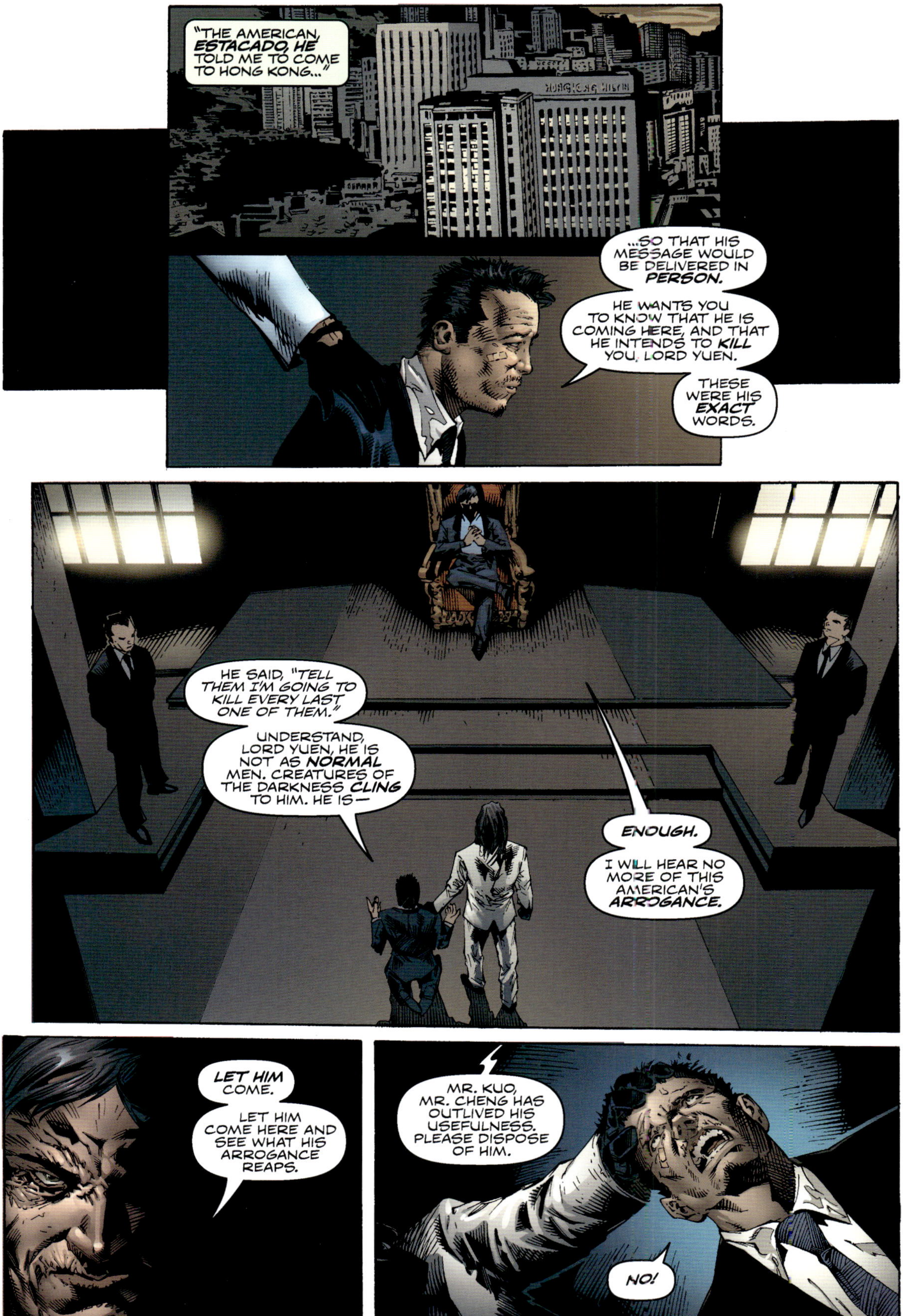
"THE AMERICAN, ESTACADO, HE TOLD ME TO COME TO HONG KONG..."
...SO THAT HIS MESSAGE WOULD BE DELIVERED IN PERSON.
HE WANTS YOU TO KNOW THAT HE IS COMING HERE, AND THAT HE INTENDS TO KILL YOU, LORD YUEN.
THESE WERE HIS EXACT WORDS.
HE SAID, "TELL THEM I'M GOING TO KILL EVERY LAST ONE OF THEM."
UNDERSTAND, LORD YUEN, HE IS NOT AS NORMAL MEN. CREATURES OF THE DARKNESS CLING TO HIM. HE IS—
ENOUGH.
I WILL HEAR NO MORE OF THIS AMERICAN'S ARROGANCE.
LET HIM COME.
LET HIM COME HERE AND SEE WHAT HIS ARROGANCE REAPS.
MR. KUO, MR. CHENG HAS OUTLIVED HIS USEFULNESS. PLEASE DISPOSE OF HIM.
NO!

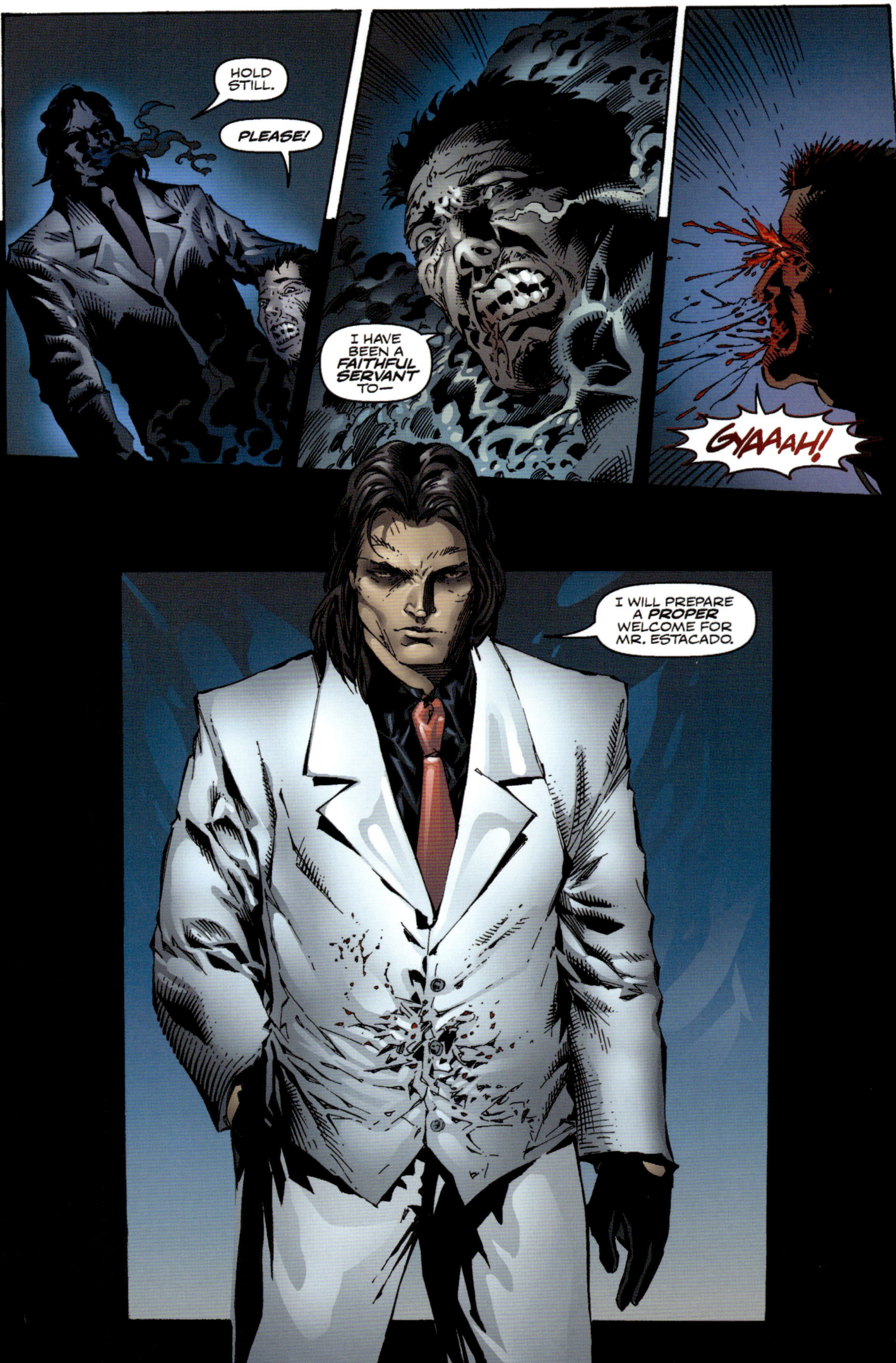

HOLD STILL.
PLEASE!
I HAVE BEEN A FAITHFUL SERVANT TO—
GYAAAH!
I WILL PREPARE A PROPER WELCOME FOR MR. ESTACADO.

The Darkness Issue #51

cover art by: Dale Keown and Matt Milla

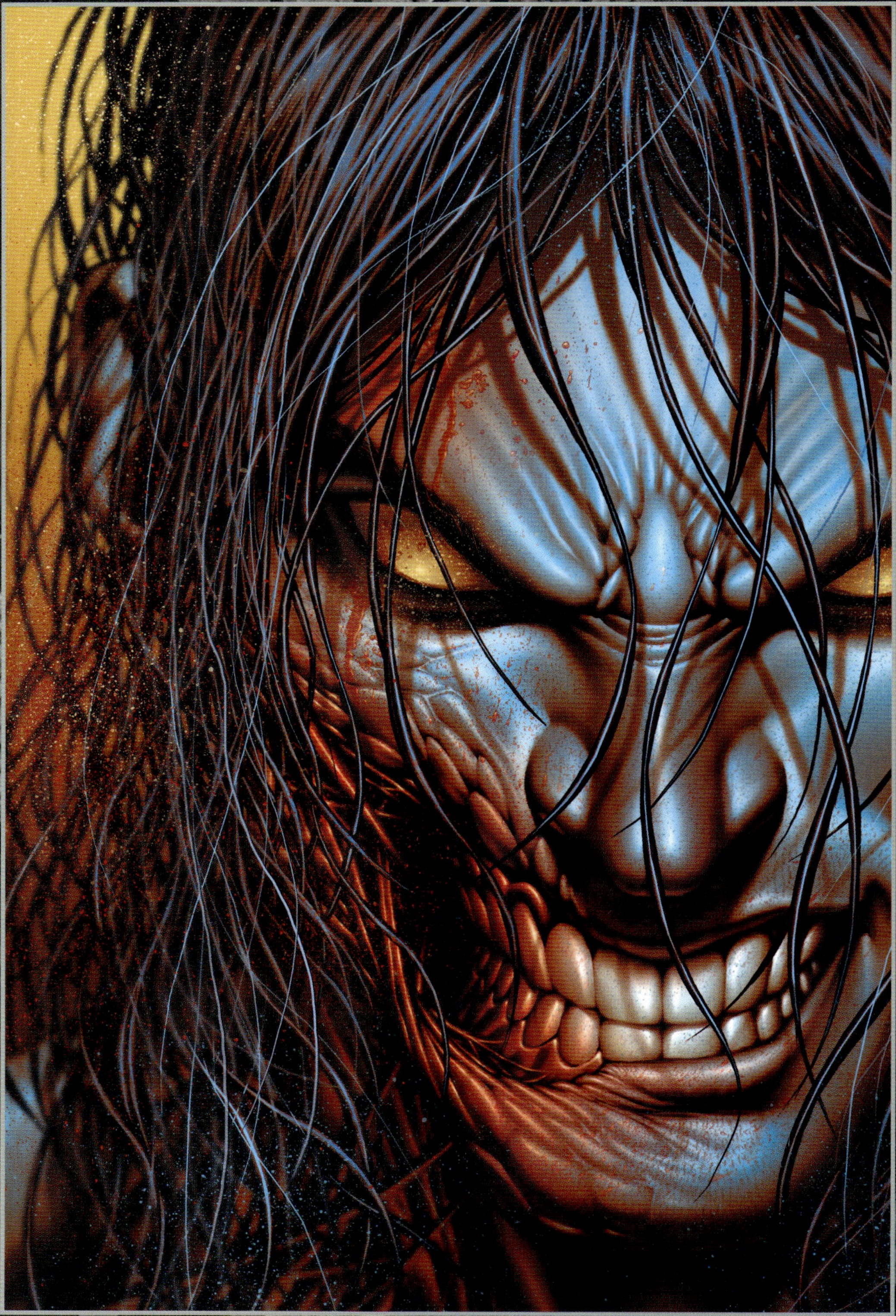

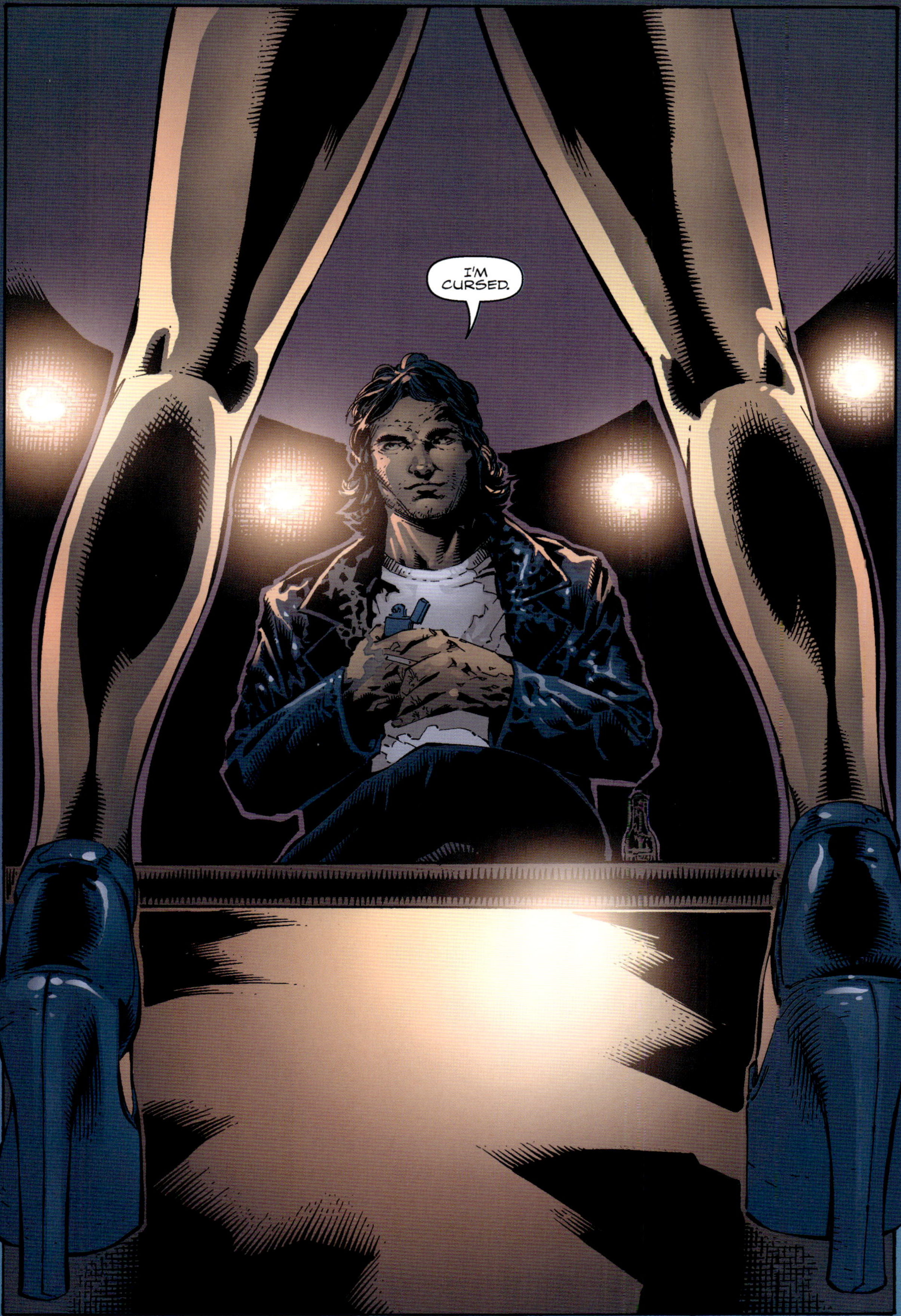
I'M CURSED.

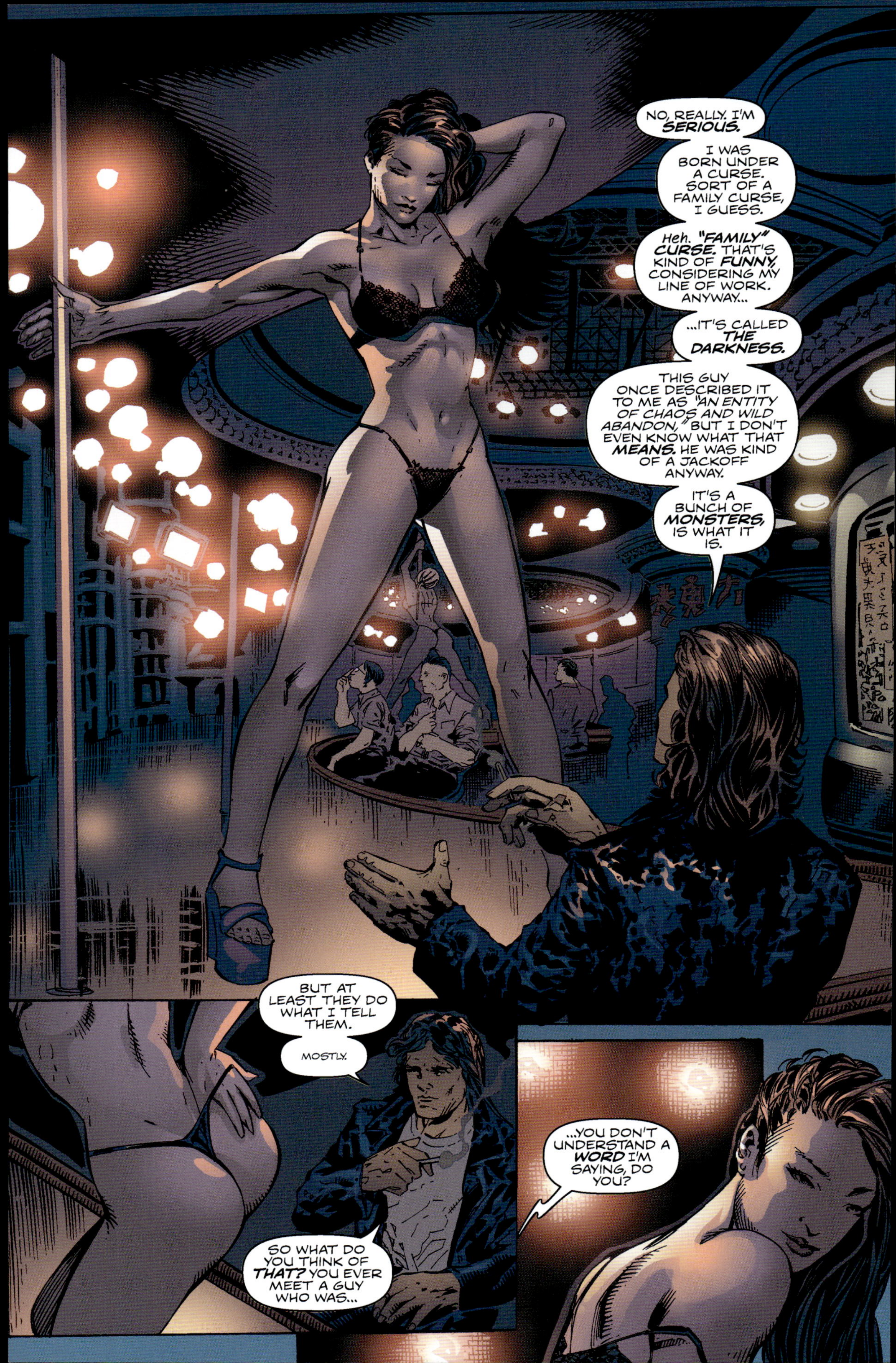

NO, REALLY. I'M SERIOUS.
I WAS BORN UNDER A CURSE. SORT OF A FAMILY CURSE, I GUESS.
Heh. "FAMILY" CURSE. THAT'S KIND OF FUNNY, CONSIDERING MY LINE OF WORK. ANYWAY...
...IT'S CALLED THE DARKNESS.
THIS GUY ONCE DESCRIBED IT TO ME AS "AN ENTITY OF CHAOS AND WILD ABANDON," BUT I DON'T EVEN KNOW WHAT THAT MEANS. HE WAS KIND OF A JACKOFF ANYWAY.
IT'S A BUNCH OF MONSTERS, IS WHAT IT IS.
BUT AT LEAST THEY DO WHAT I TELL THEM.
MOSTLY.
SO WHAT DO YOU THINK OF THAT? YOU EVER MEET A GUY WHO WAS...
...YOU DON'T UNDERSTAND A WORD I'M SAYING, DO YOU?

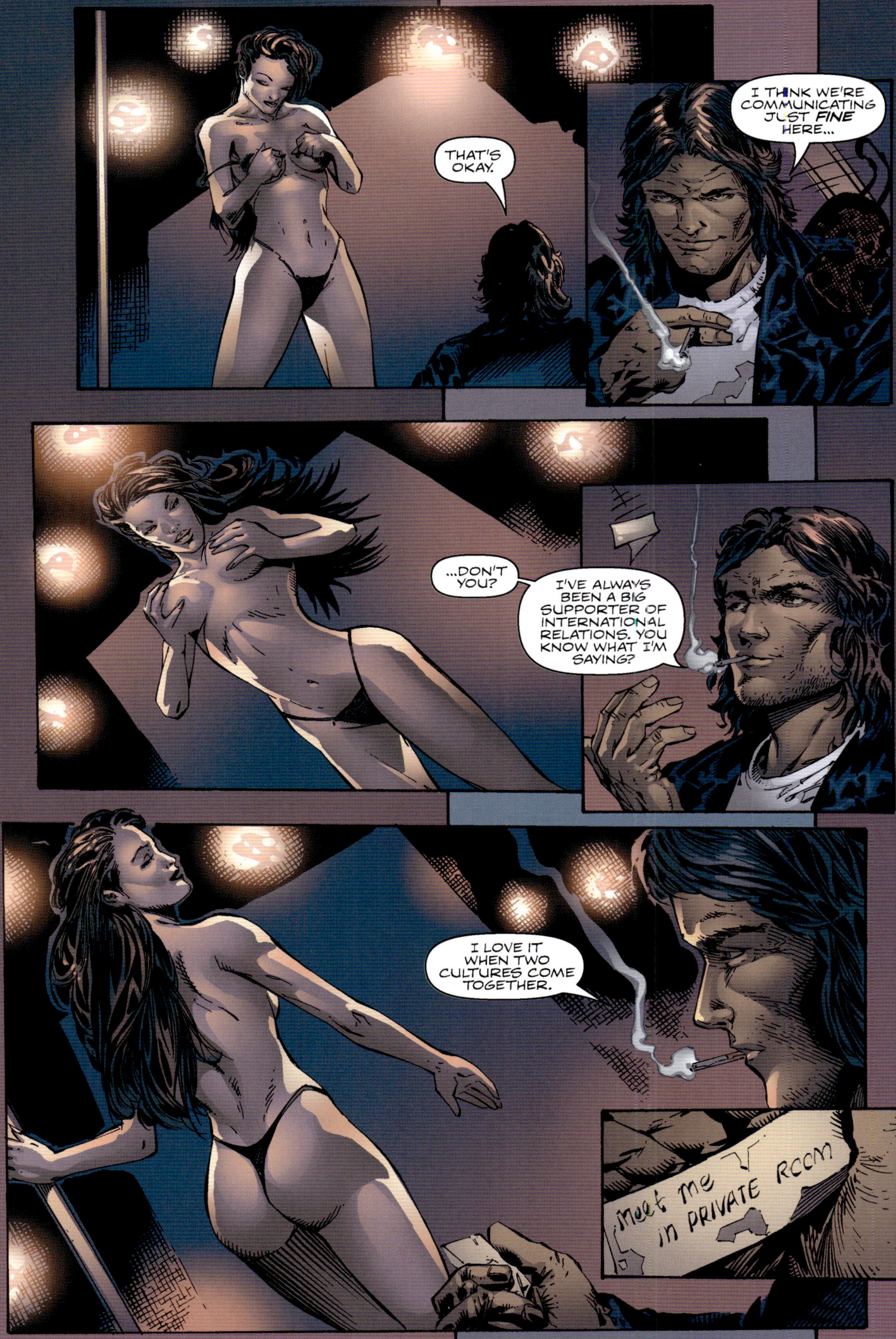
THAT'S OKAY.
I THINK WE'RE COMMUNICATING JUST FINE HERE...
...DON'T YOU?
I'VE ALWAYS BEEN A BIG SUPPORTER OF INTERNATIONAL RELATIONS. YOU KNOW WHAT I'M SAYING?
I LOVE IT WHEN TWO CULTURES COME TOGETHER.
Meet me in PRIVATE ROOM

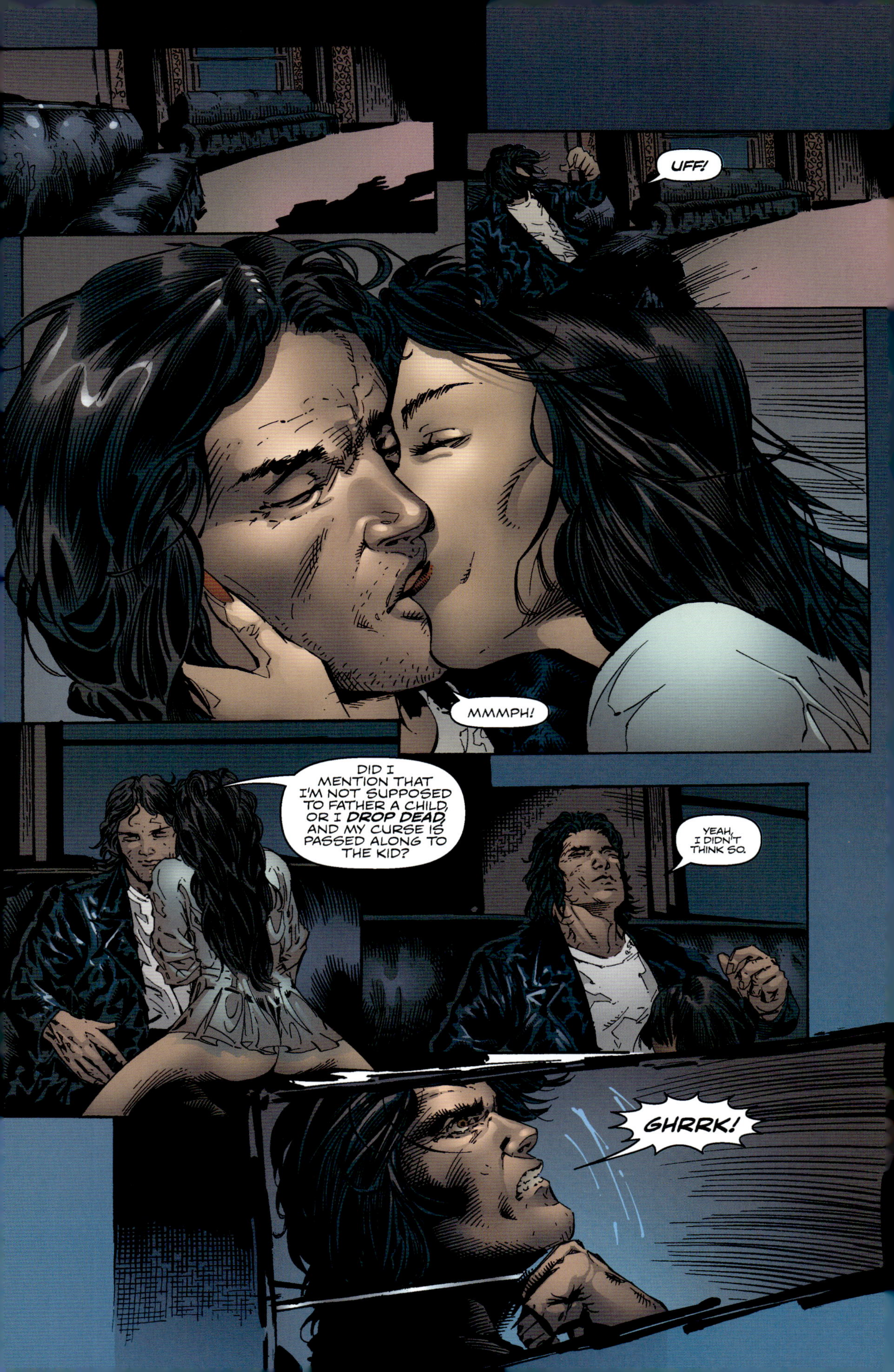
UFF!
MMMPH!
DID I MENTION THAT I'M NOT SUPPOSED TO FATHER A CHILD, OR I DROP DEAD, AND MY CURSE IS PASSED ALONG TO THE KID?
YEAH, I DIDN'T THINK SO.
GHRRK!

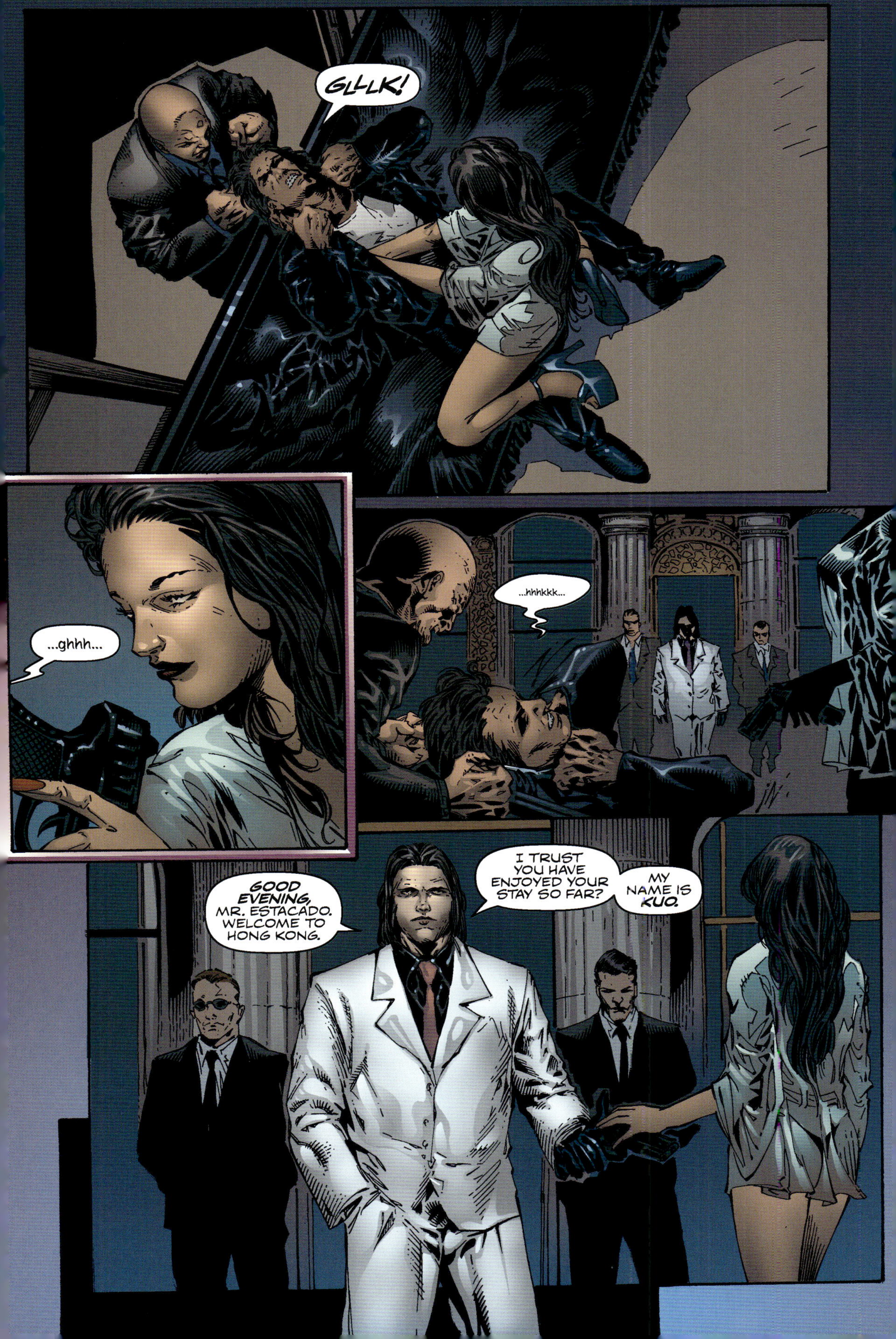
GLLLK!
...ghhh...
...hhhkkk...
GOOD EVENING, MR. ESTACADO. WELCOME TO HONG KONG.
I TRUST YOU HAVE ENJOYED YOUR STAY SO FAR?
MY NAME IS KUO.

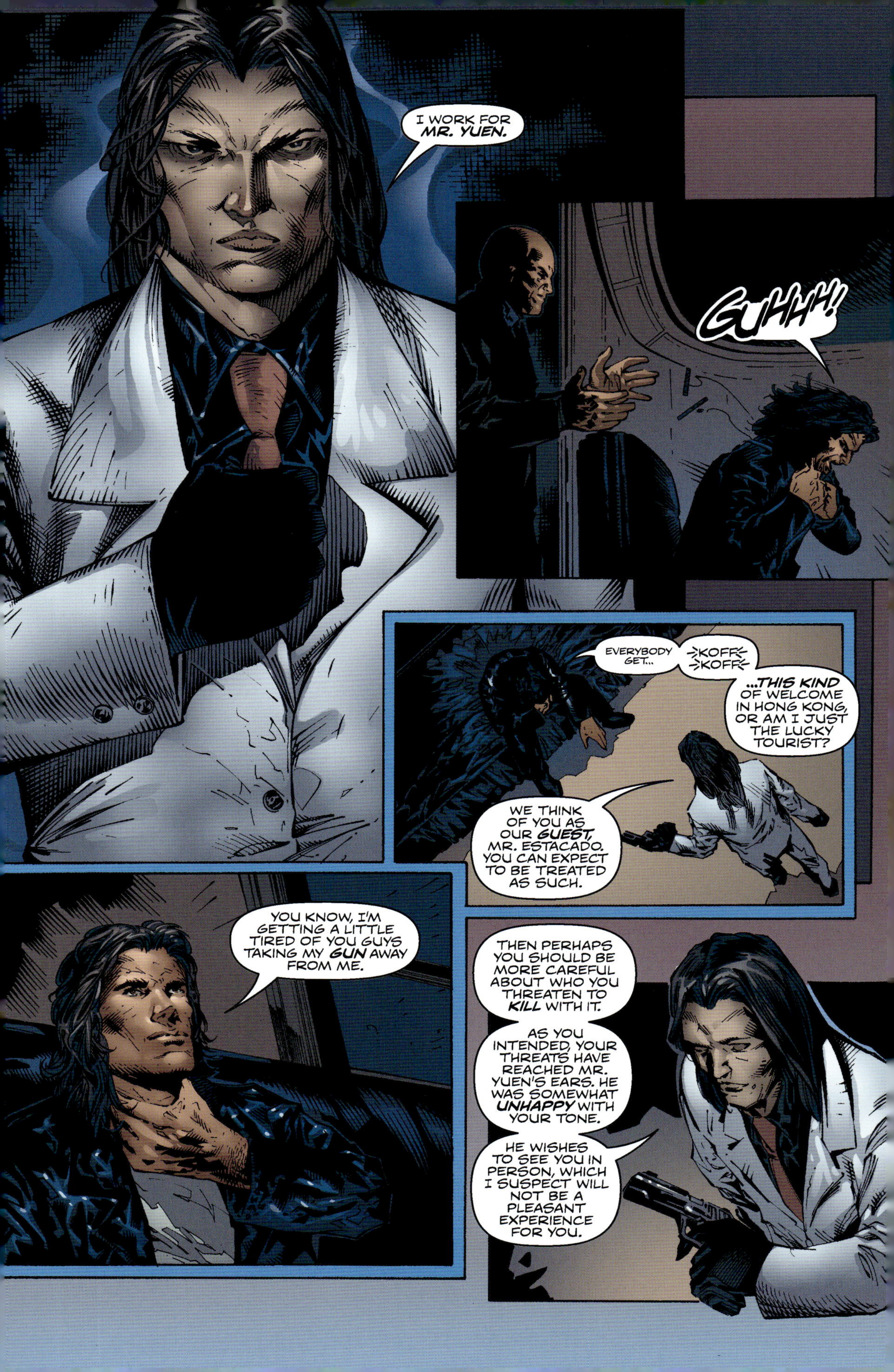
I WORK FOR MR. YUEN.
GUHHH!
EVERYBODY GET...
KOFF KOFF
...THIS KIND OF WELCOME IN HONG KONG, OR AM I JUST THE LUCKY TOURIST?
WE THINK OF YOU AS OUR GUEST, MR. ESTACADO. YOU CAN EXPECT TO BE TREATED AS SUCH.
YOU KNOW, I'M GETTING A LITTLE TIRED OF YOU GUYS TAKING MY GUN AWAY FROM ME.
THEN PERHAPS YOU SHOULD BE MORE CAREFUL ABOUT WHO YOU THREATEN TO KILL WITH IT.
AS YOU INTENDED, YOUR THREATS HAVE REACHED MR. YUEN'S EARS. HE WAS SOMEWHAT UNHAPPY WITH YOUR TONE.
HE WISHES TO SEE YOU IN PERSON, WHICH I SUSPECT WILL NOT BE A PLEASANT EXPERIENCE FOR YOU.

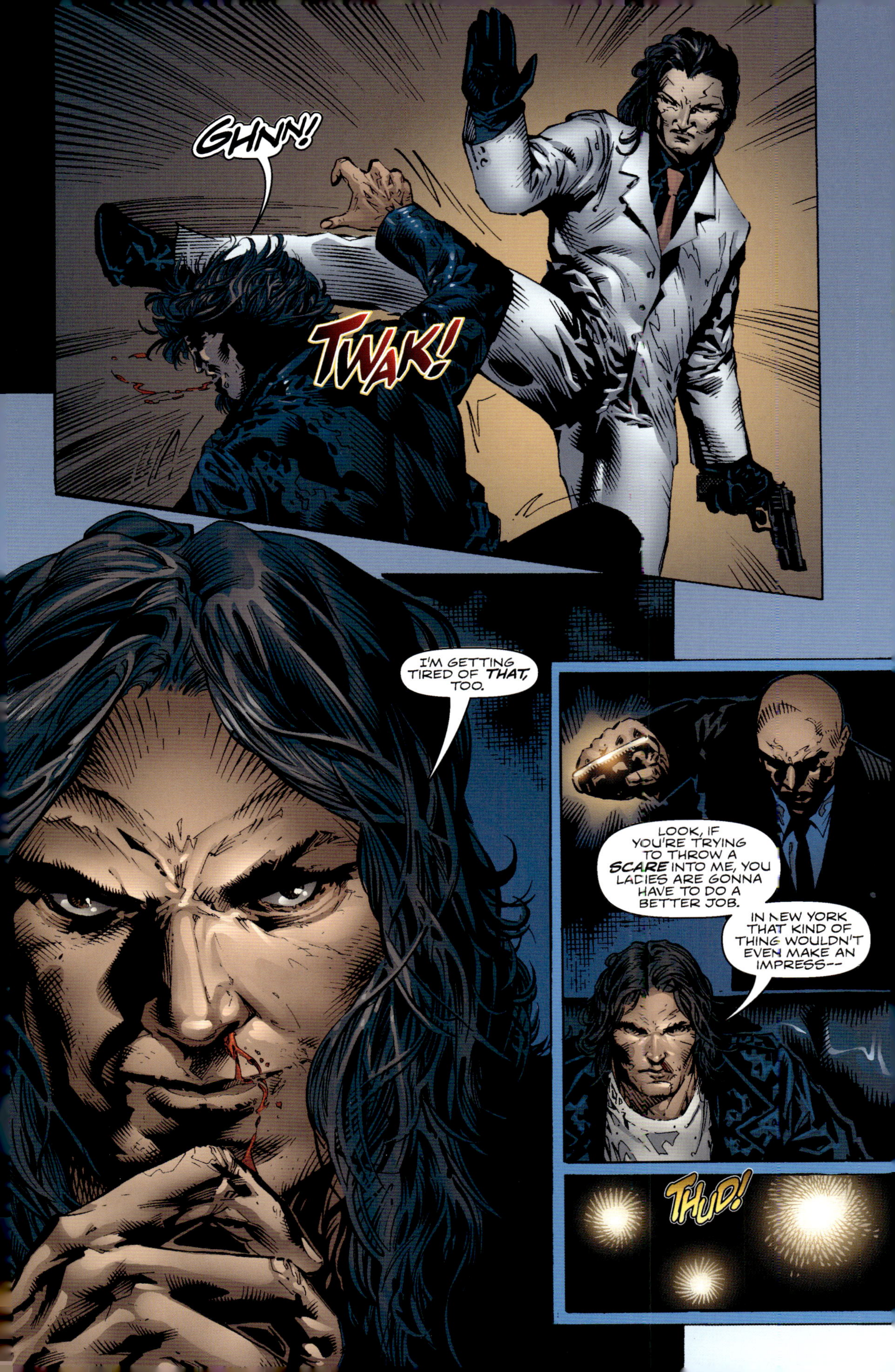
GHNN!
TWAK!
I'M GETTING TIRED OF THAT, TOO.
LOOK, IF YOU'RE TRYING TO THROW A SCARE INTO ME, YOU LADIES ARE GONNA HAVE TO DO A BETTER JOB.
IN NEW YORK THAT KIND OF THING WOULDN'T EVEN MAKE AN IMPRESS--
THUD!

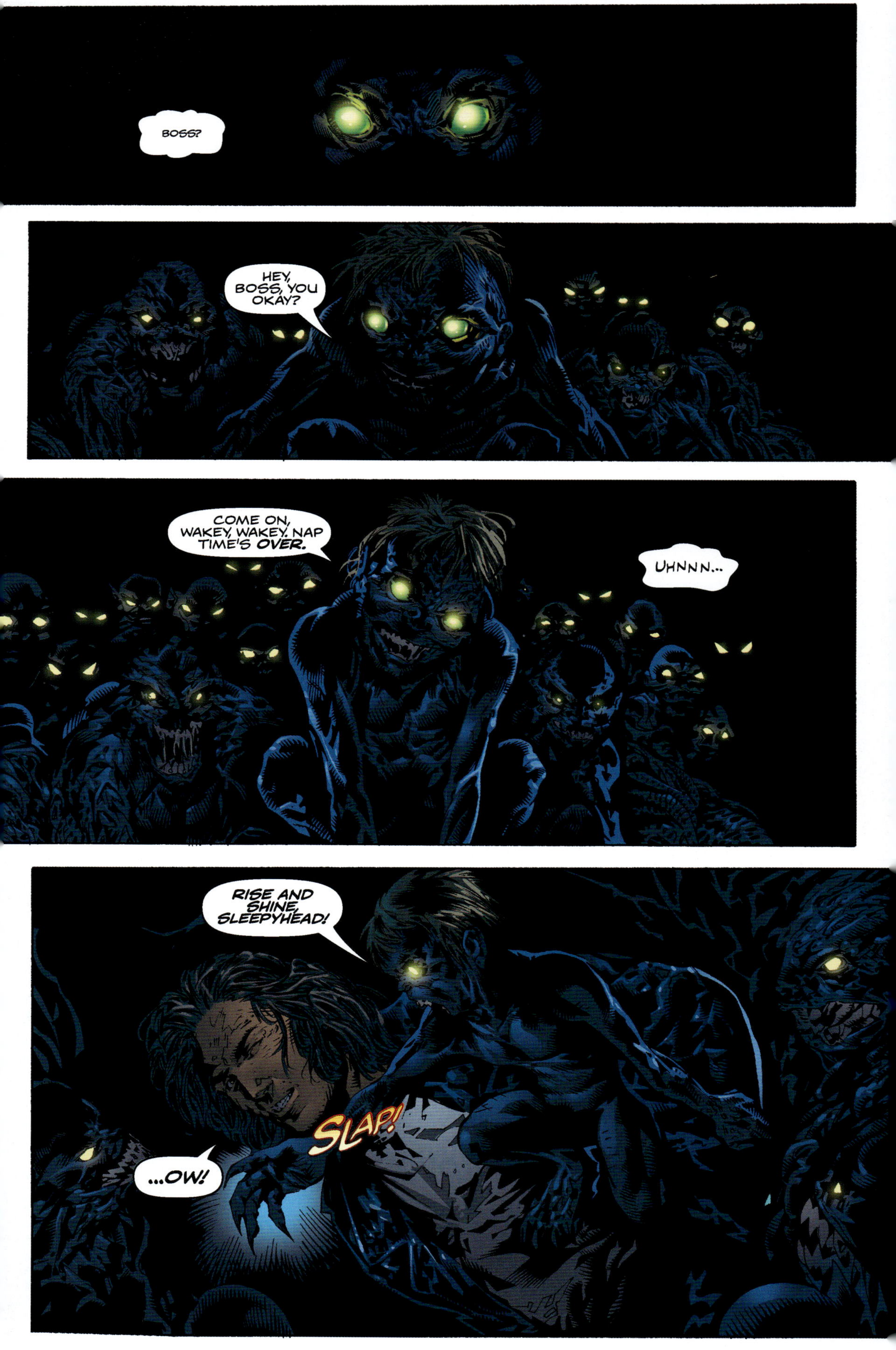
BOSS?
HEY, BOSS, YOU OKAY?
COME ON, WAKEY, WAKEY. NAP TIME'S *OVER.*
UHNNN...
RISE AND SHINE, SLEEPYHEAD!
SLAP!
...OW!

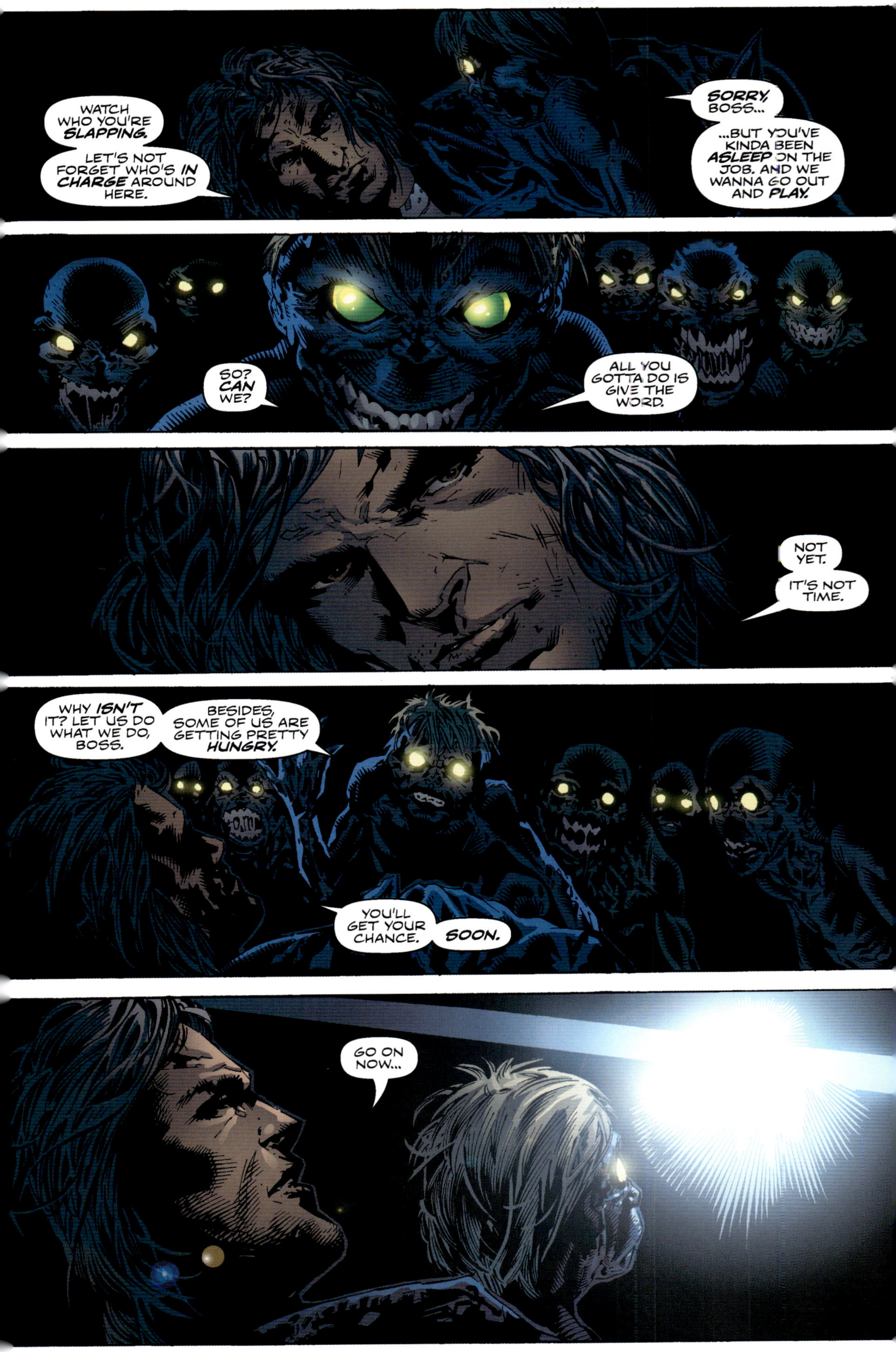

WATCH WHO YOU'RE SLAPPING.
LET'S NOT FORGET WHO'S IN CHARGE AROUND HERE.
SORRY, BOSS...
...BUT YOU'VE KINDA BEEN ASLEEP ON THE JOB. AND WE WANNA GO OUT AND PLAY.
SO? CAN WE?
ALL YOU GOTTA DO IS GIVE THE WORD.
NOT YET.
IT'S NOT TIME.
WHY ISN'T IT? LET US DO WHAT WE DO, BOSS.
BESIDES, SOME OF US ARE GETTING PRETTY HUNGRY.
YOU'LL GET YOUR CHANCE.
SOON.
GO ON NOW...

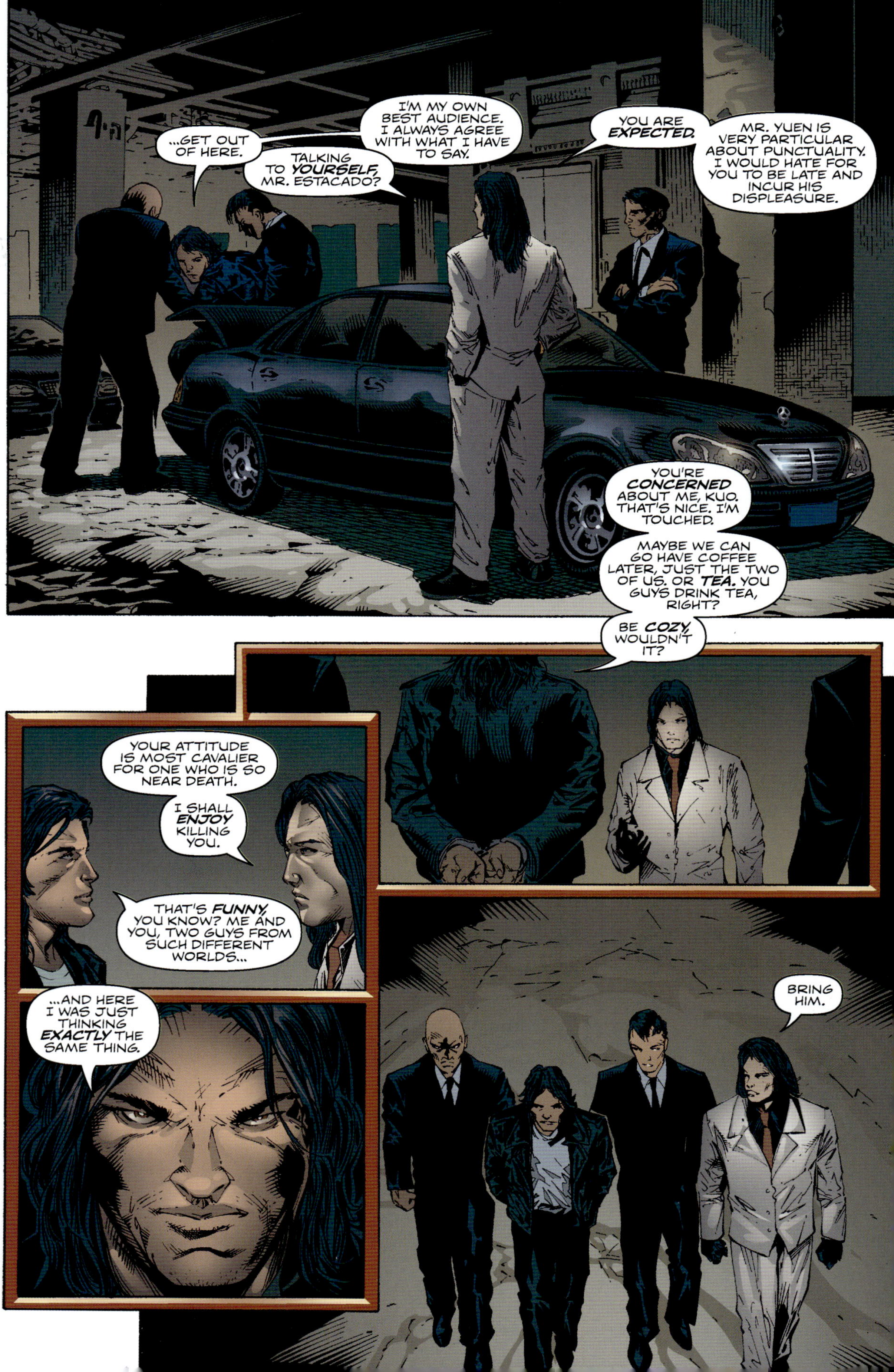
...GET OUT OF HERE.
TALKING TO YOURSELF, MR. ESTACADO?
I'M MY OWN BEST AUDIENCE. I ALWAYS AGREE WITH WHAT I HAVE TO SAY.
YOU ARE EXPECTED.
MR. YUEN IS VERY PARTICULAR ABOUT PUNCTUALITY. I WOULD HATE FOR YOU TO BE LATE AND INCUR HIS DISPLEASURE.
YOU'RE CONCERNED ABOUT ME, KUO. THAT'S NICE. I'M TOUCHED.
MAYBE WE CAN GO HAVE COFFEE LATER, JUST THE TWO OF US. OR TEA. YOU GUYS DRINK TEA, RIGHT?
BE COZY, WOULDN'T IT?
YOUR ATTITUDE IS MOST CAVALIER FOR ONE WHO IS SO NEAR DEATH.
I SHALL ENJOY KILLING YOU.
THAT'S FUNNY, YOU KNOW? ME AND YOU, TWO GUYS FROM SUCH DIFFERENT WORLDS...
...AND HERE I WAS JUST THINKING EXACTLY THE SAME THING.
BRING HIM.

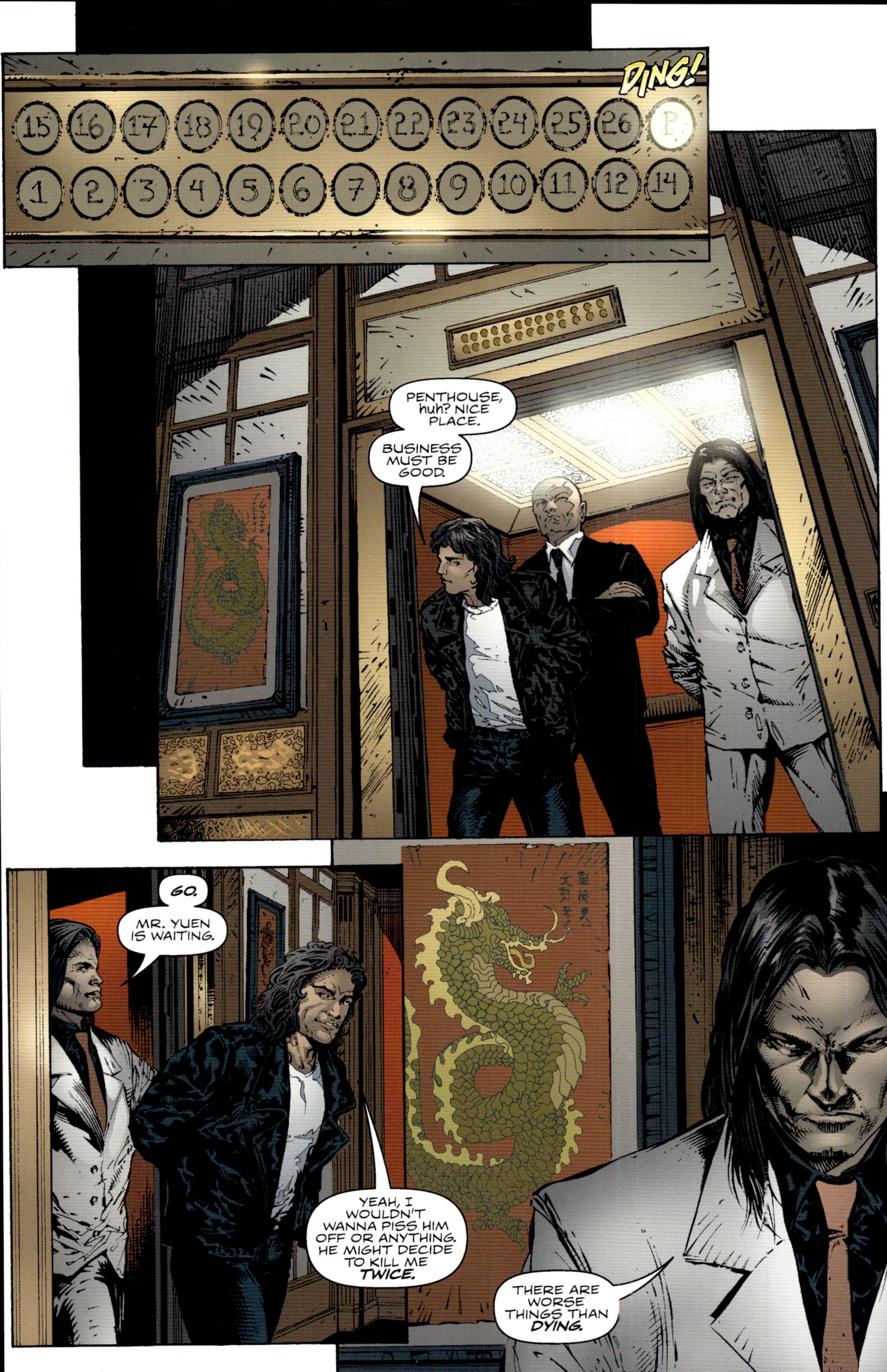
DING!
15 16 17 18 19 20 21 22 23 24 25 26 P
1 2 3 4 5 6 7 8 9 10 11 12 14
PENTHOUSE, huh? NICE PLACE.
BUSINESS MUST BE GOOD.
GO.
MR. YUEN IS WAITING.
YEAH, I WOULDN'T WANNA PISS HIM OFF OR ANYTHING. HE MIGHT DECIDE TO KILL ME *TWICE.*
THERE ARE WORSE THINGS THAN *DYING.*

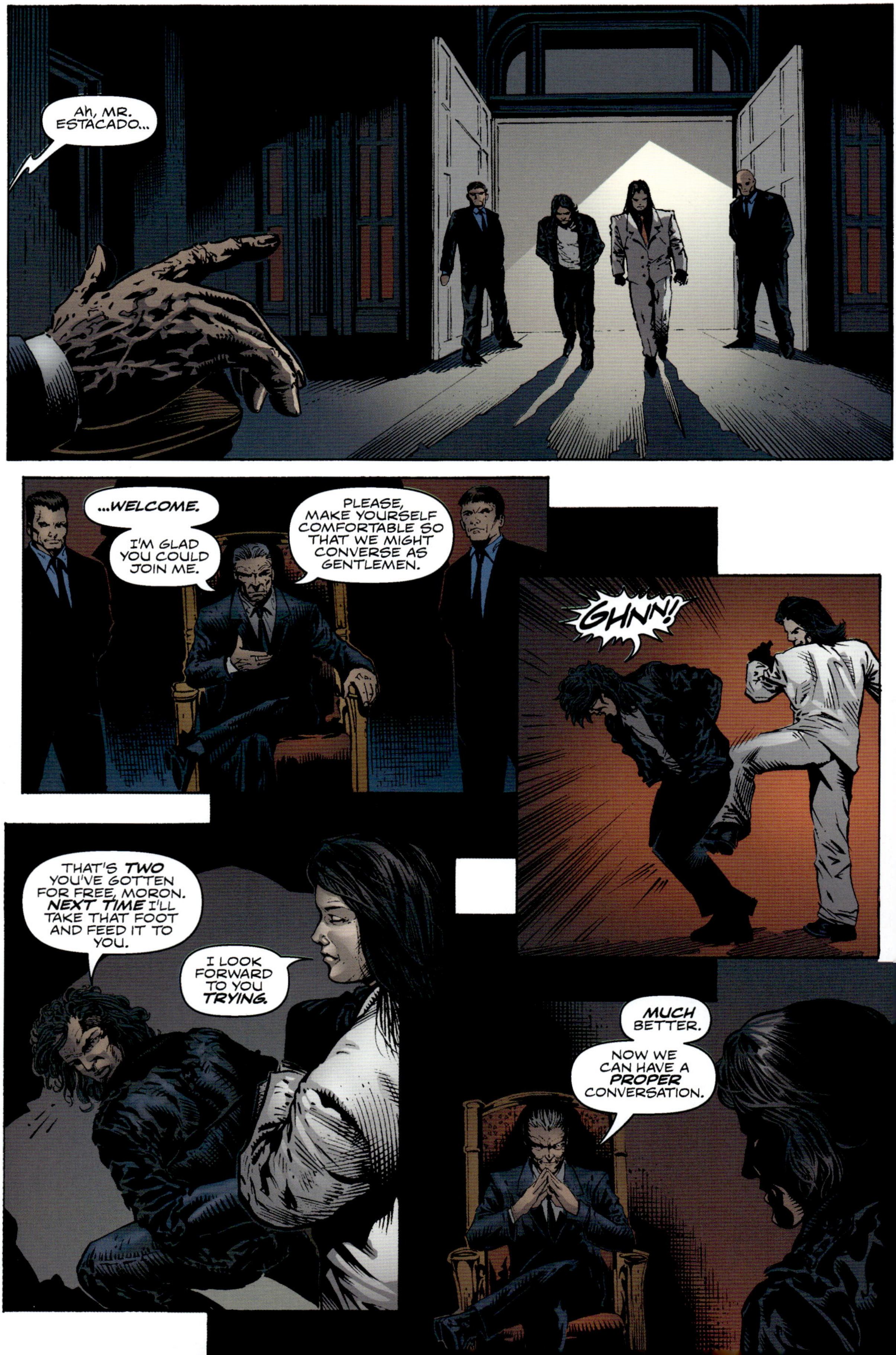
Ah, MR. ESTACADO...
...WELCOME.
I'M GLAD YOU COULD JOIN ME.
PLEASE, MAKE YOURSELF COMFORTABLE SO THAT WE MIGHT CONVERSE AS GENTLEMEN.
GHNN!
THAT'S TWO YOU'VE GOTTEN FOR FREE, MORON. NEXT TIME I'LL TAKE THAT FOOT AND FEED IT TO YOU.
I LOOK FORWARD TO YOU TRYING.
MUCH BETTER.
NOW WE CAN HAVE A PROPER CONVERSATION.

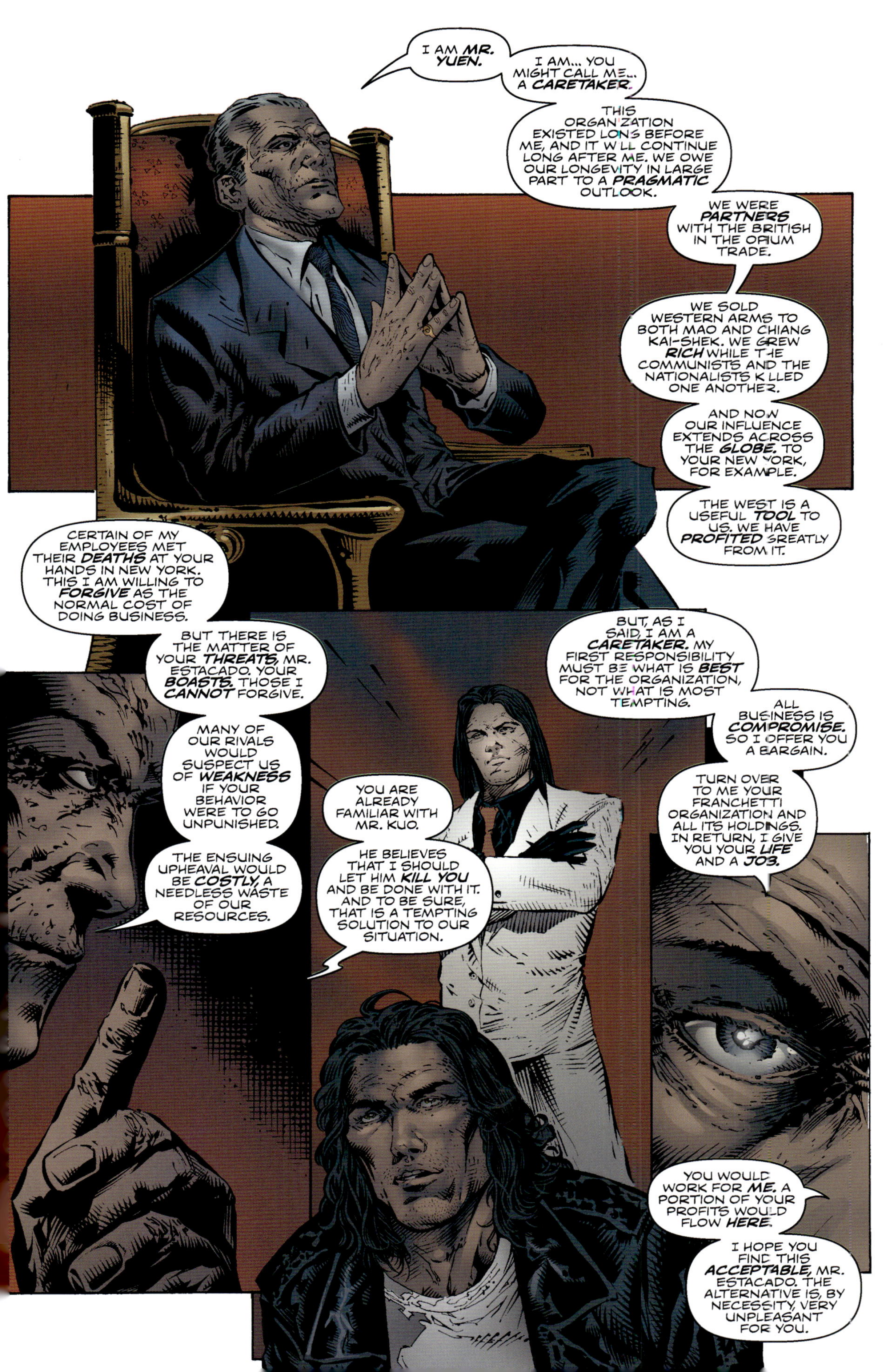
I AM MR. YUEN.
I AM... YOU MIGHT CALL ME... A CARETAKER.
THIS ORGANIZATION EXISTED LONG BEFORE ME, AND IT WILL CONTINUE LONG AFTER ME. WE OWE OUR LONGEVITY IN LARGE PART TO A PRAGMATIC OUTLOOK.
WE WERE PARTNERS WITH THE BRITISH IN THE OPIUM TRADE.
WE SOLD WESTERN ARMS TO BOTH MAO AND CHIANG KAI-SHEK. WE GREW RICH WHILE THE COMMUNISTS AND THE NATIONALISTS KILLED ONE ANOTHER.
AND NOW OUR INFLUENCE EXTENDS ACROSS THE GLOBE. TO YOUR NEW YORK, FOR EXAMPLE.
THE WEST IS A USEFUL TOOL TO US. WE HAVE PROFITED GREATLY FROM IT.
CERTAIN OF MY EMPLOYEES MET THEIR DEATHS AT YOUR HANDS IN NEW YORK. THIS I AM WILLING TO FORGIVE AS THE NORMAL COST OF DOING BUSINESS.
BUT THERE IS THE MATTER OF YOUR THREATS, MR. ESTACADO. YOUR BOASTS. THOSE I CANNOT FORGIVE.
MANY OF OUR RIVALS WOULD SUSPECT US OF WEAKNESS IF YOUR BEHAVIOR WERE TO GO UNPUNISHED.
THE ENSUING UPHEAVAL WOULD BE COSTLY, A NEEDLESS WASTE OF OUR RESOURCES.
YOU ARE ALREADY FAMILIAR WITH MR. KUO.
HE BELIEVES THAT I SHOULD LET HIM KILL YOU AND BE DONE WITH IT. AND TO BE SURE, THAT IS A TEMPTING SOLUTION TO OUR SITUATION.
BUT, AS I SAID, I AM A CARETAKER. MY FIRST RESPONSIBILITY MUST BE WHAT IS BEST FOR THE ORGANIZATION, NOT WHAT IS MOST TEMPTING.
ALL BUSINESS IS COMPROMISE. SO I OFFER YOU A BARGAIN.
TURN OVER TO ME YOUR FRANCHETTI ORGANIZATION AND ALL ITS HOLDINGS. IN RETURN, I GIVE YOU YOUR LIFE AND A JOB.
YOU WOULD WORK FOR ME. A PORTION OF YOUR PROFITS WOULD FLOW HERE.
I HOPE YOU FIND THIS ACCEPTABLE, MR. ESTACADO. THE ALTERNATIVE IS, BY NECESSITY, VERY UNPLEASANT FOR YOU.

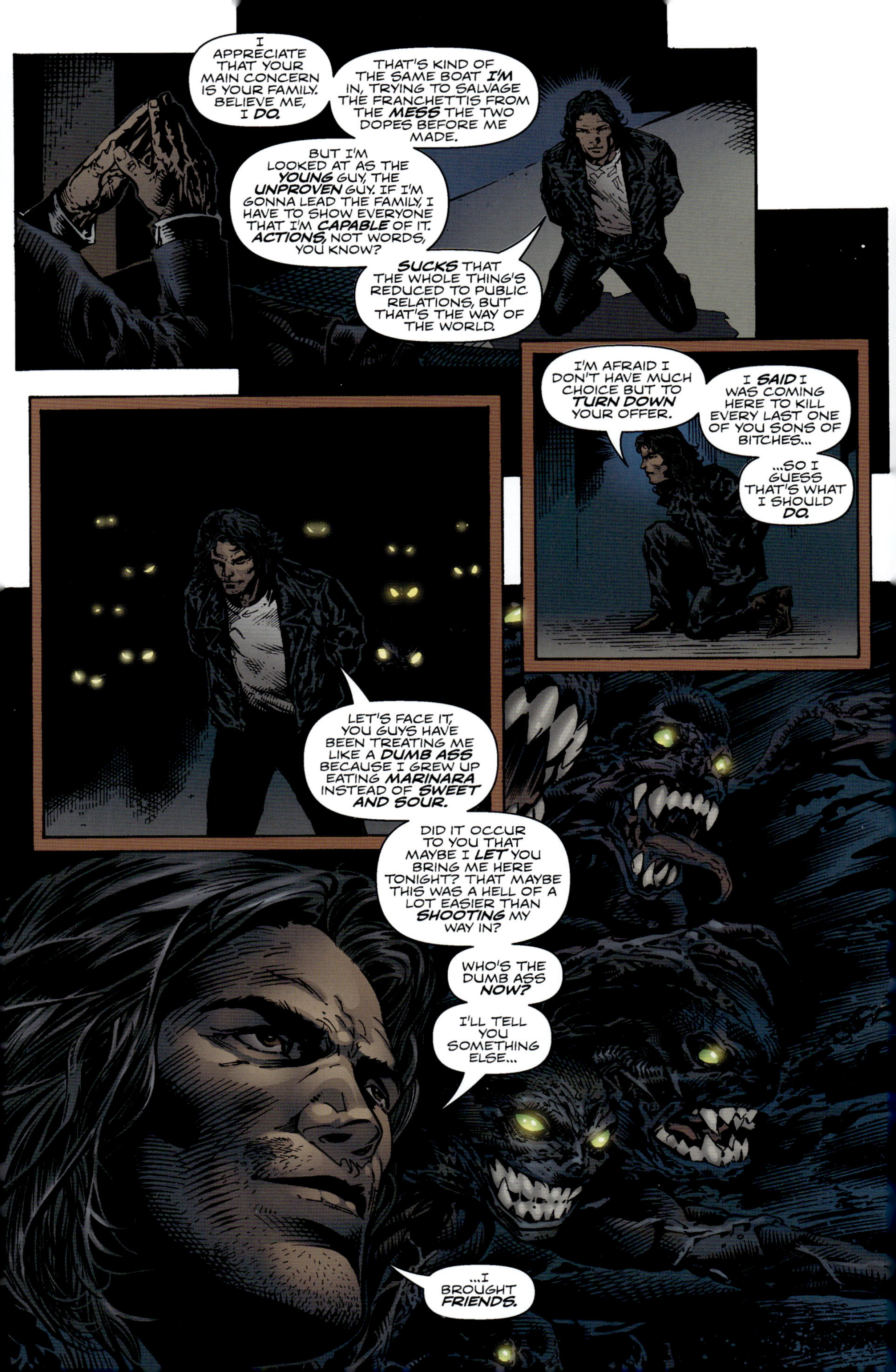
I APPRECIATE THAT YOUR MAIN CONCERN IS YOUR FAMILY. BELIEVE ME, I DO.
THAT'S KIND OF THE SAME BOAT I'M IN, TRYING TO SALVAGE THE FRANCHETTIS FROM THE MESS THE TWO DOPES BEFORE ME MADE.
BUT I'M LOOKED AT AS THE YOUNG GUY, THE UNPROVEN GUY. IF I'M GONNA LEAD THE FAMILY, I HAVE TO SHOW EVERYONE THAT I'M CAPABLE OF IT. ACTIONS, NOT WORDS, YOU KNOW?
SUCKS THAT THE WHOLE THING'S REDUCED TO PUBLIC RELATIONS, BUT THAT'S THE WAY OF THE WORLD.
I'M AFRAID I DON'T HAVE MUCH CHOICE BUT TO TURN DOWN YOUR OFFER.
I SAID I WAS COMING HERE TO KILL EVERY LAST ONE OF YOU SONS OF BITCHES...
...SO I GUESS THAT'S WHAT I SHOULD DO.
LET'S FACE IT, YOU GUYS HAVE BEEN TREATING ME LIKE A DUMB ASS BECAUSE I GREW UP EATING MARINARA INSTEAD OF SWEET AND SOUR.
DID IT OCCUR TO YOU THAT MAYBE I LET YOU BRING ME HERE TONIGHT? THAT MAYBE THIS WAS A HELL OF A LOT EASIER THAN SHOOTING MY WAY IN?
WHO'S THE DUMB ASS NOW?
I'LL TELL YOU SOMETHING ELSE...
...I BROUGHT FRIENDS.

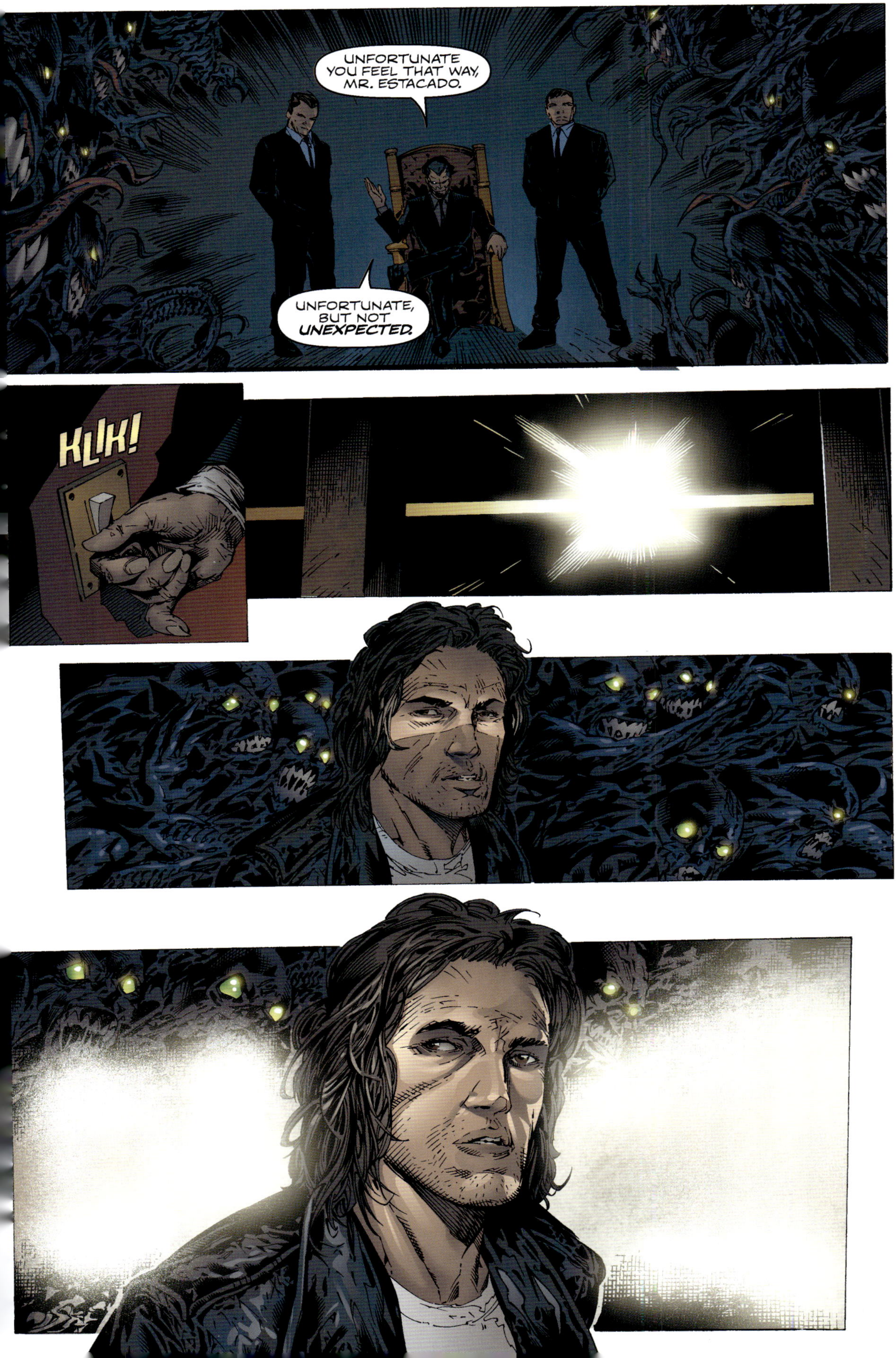
UNFORTUNATE YOU FEEL THAT WAY, MR. ESTACADO.
UNFORTUNATE, BUT NOT UNEXPECTED.
KLIK!

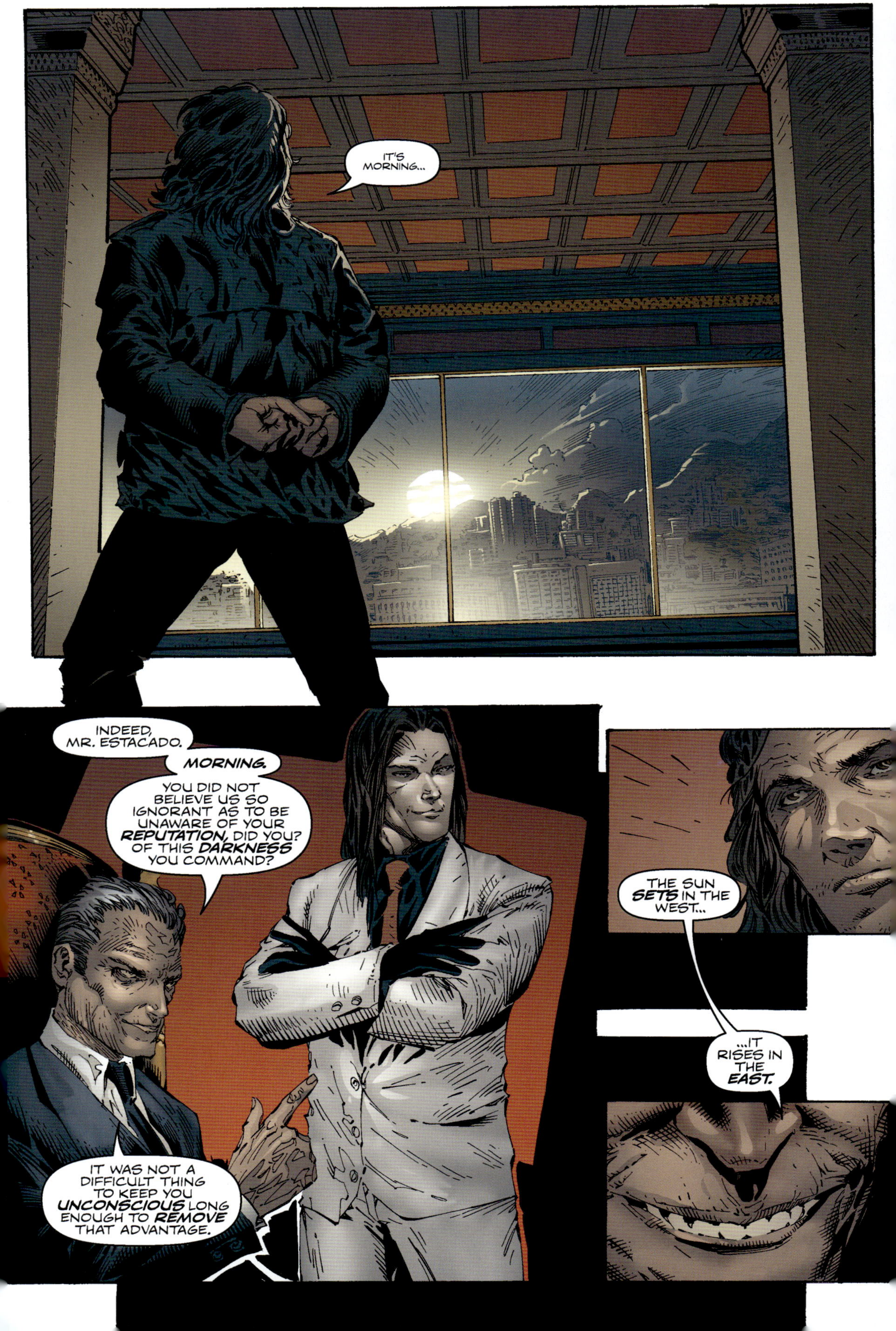
IT'S MORNING...
INDEED, MR. ESTACADO.
MORNING.
YOU DID NOT BELIEVE US SO IGNORANT AS TO BE UNAWARE OF YOUR REPUTATION, DID YOU? OF THIS DARKNESS YOU COMMAND?
IT WAS NOT A DIFFICULT THING TO KEEP YOU UNCONSCIOUS LONG ENOUGH TO REMOVE THAT ADVANTAGE.
THE SUN SETS IN THE WEST...
...IT RISES IN THE EAST.

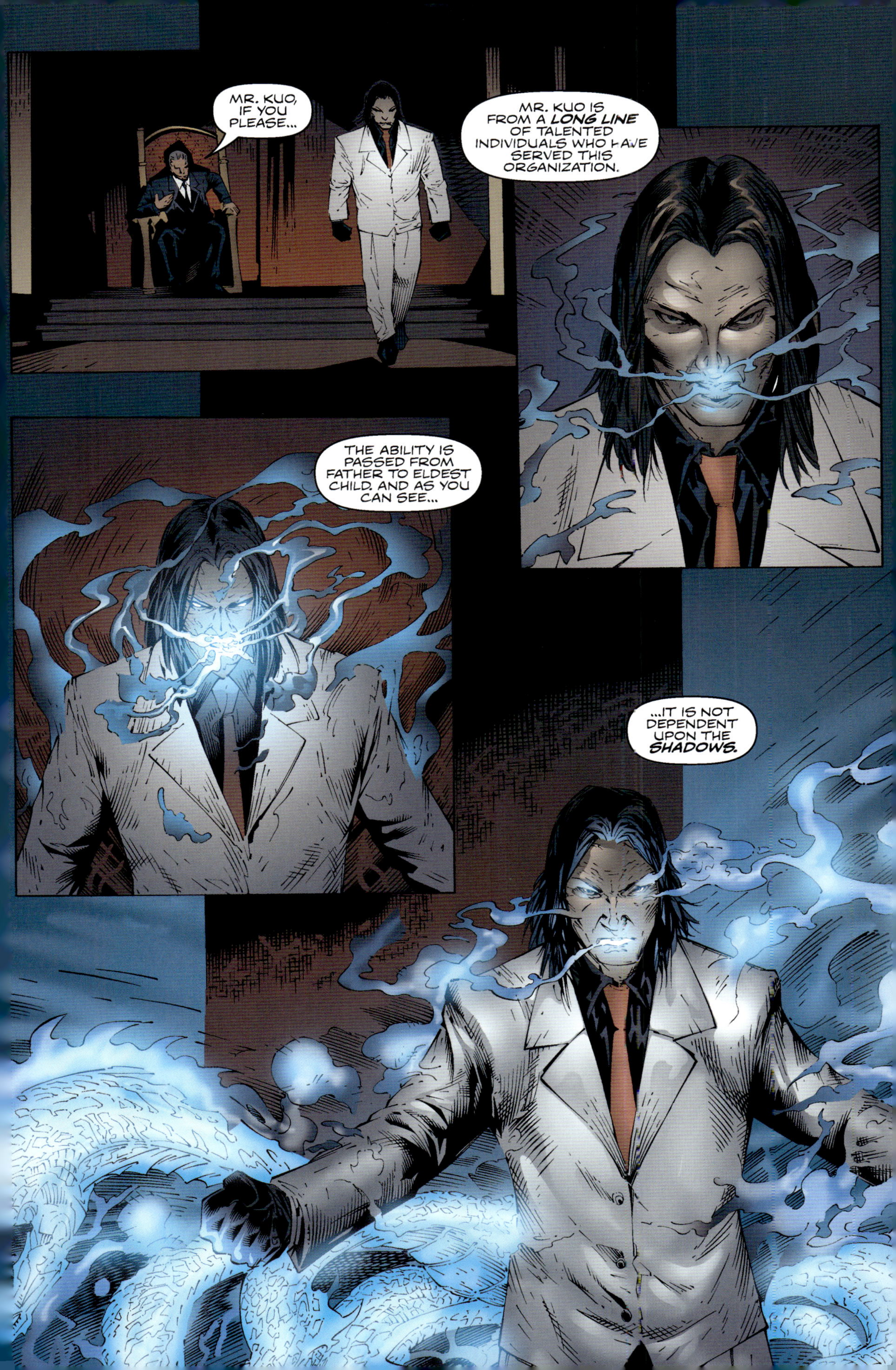
MR. KUO, IF YOU PLEASE...
MR. KUO IS FROM A LONG LINE OF TALENTED INDIVIDUALS WHO HAVE SERVED THIS ORGANIZATION.
THE ABILITY IS PASSED FROM FATHER TO ELDEST CHILD. AND AS YOU CAN SEE...
...IT IS NOT DEPENDENT UPON THE SHADOWS.

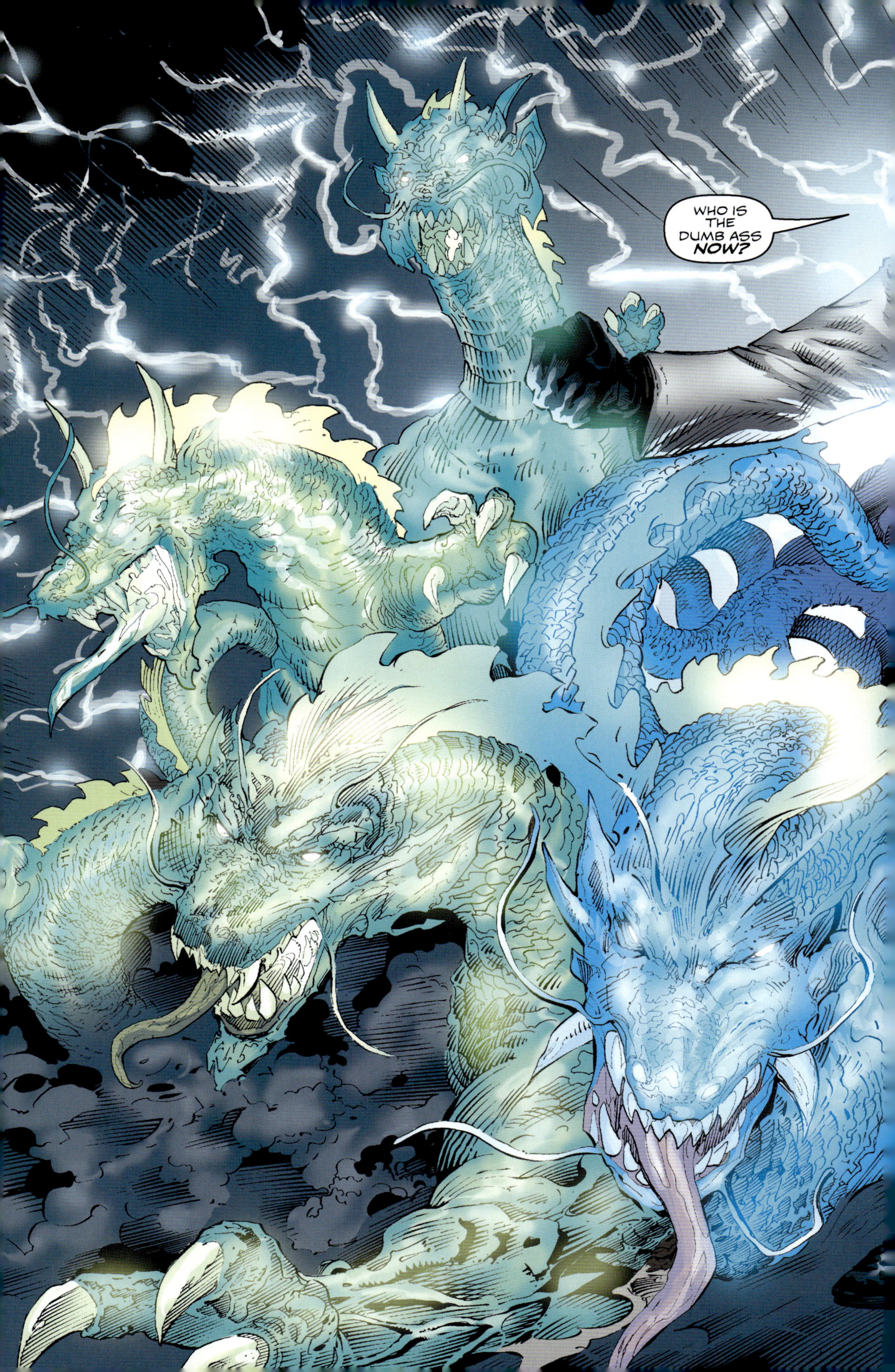
WHO IS THE DUMB ASS NOW?

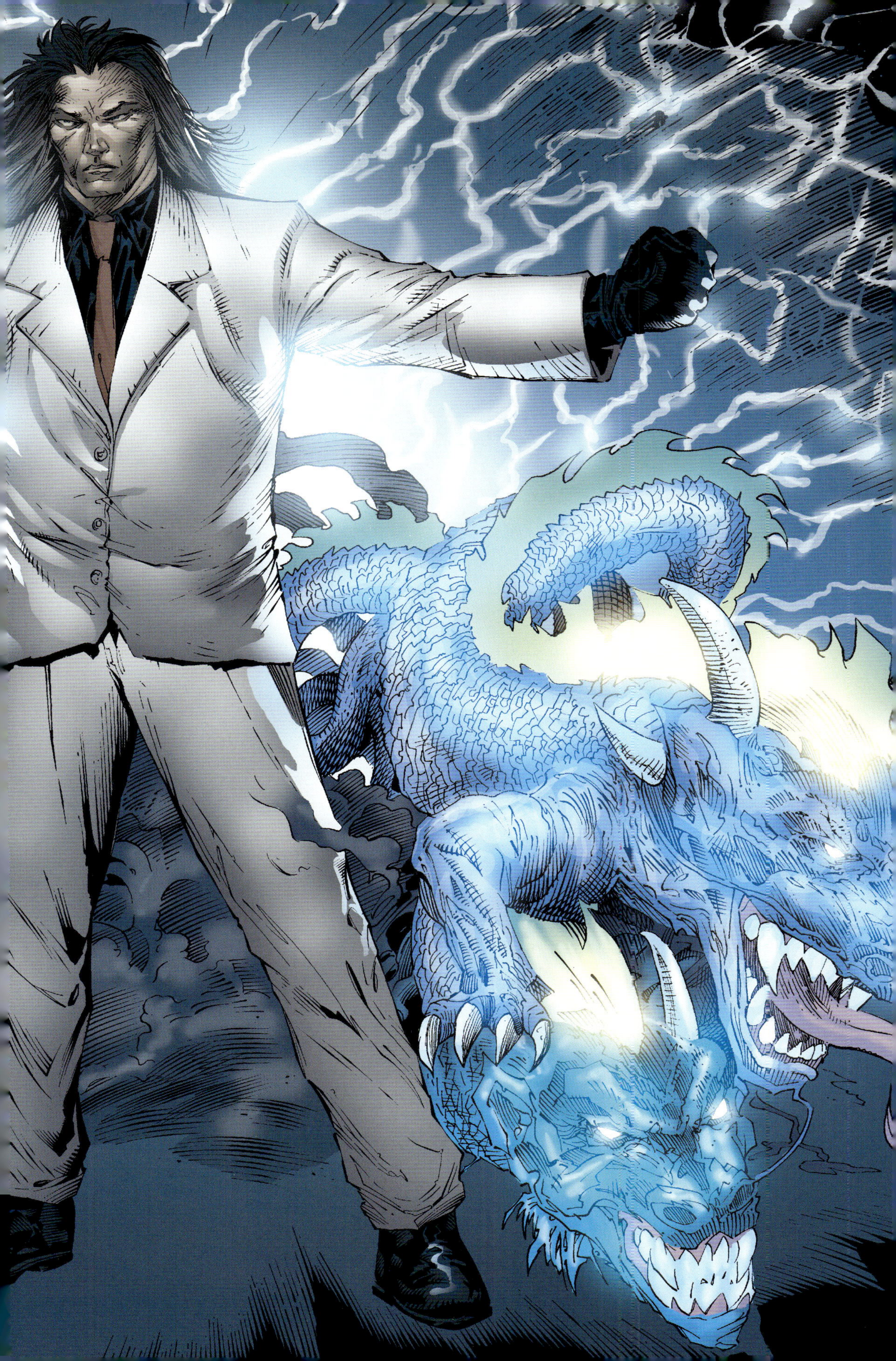

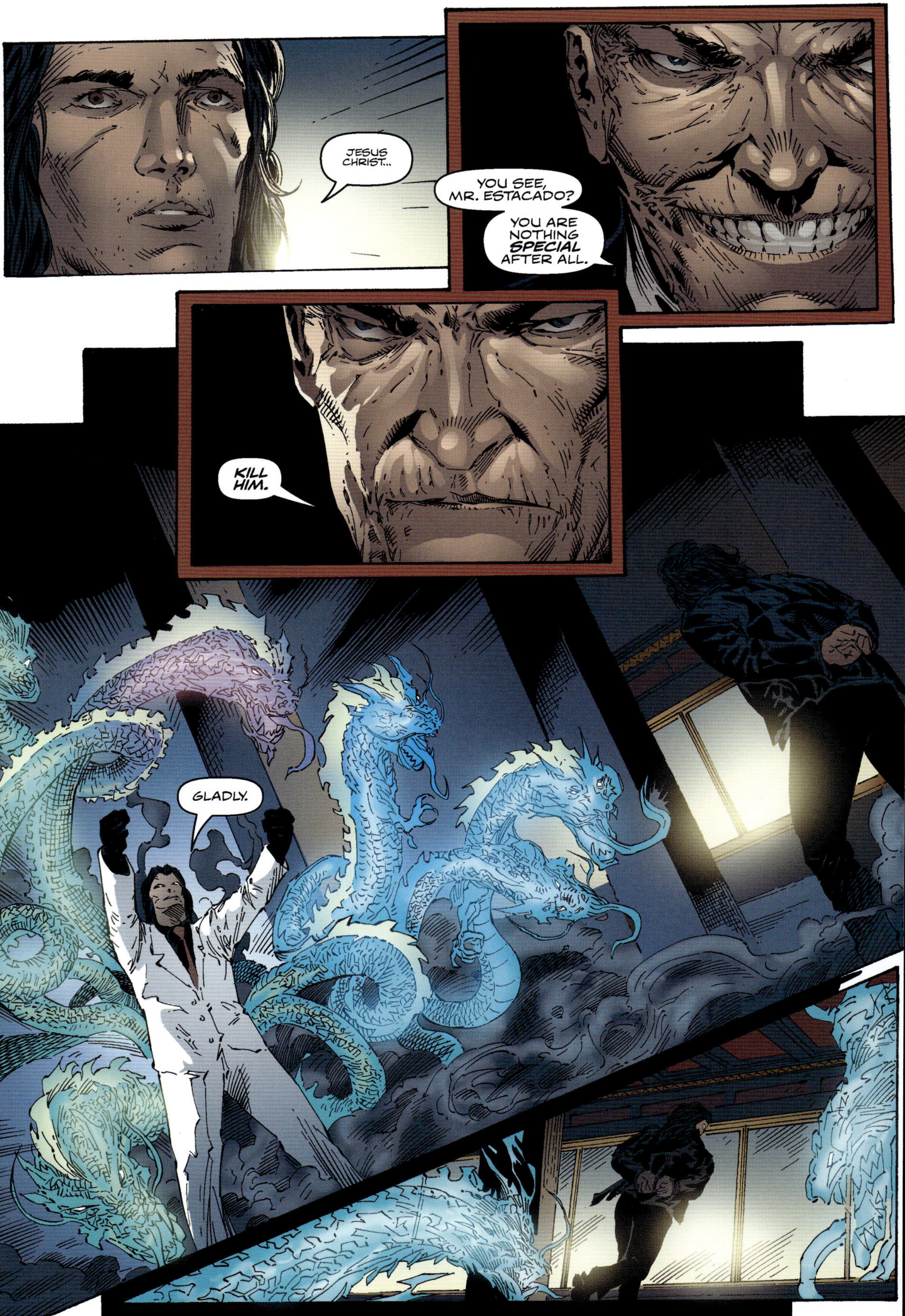
JESUS CHRIST...
YOU SEE, MR. ESTACADO?
YOU ARE NOTHING SPECIAL AFTER ALL.
KILL HIM.
GLADLY.

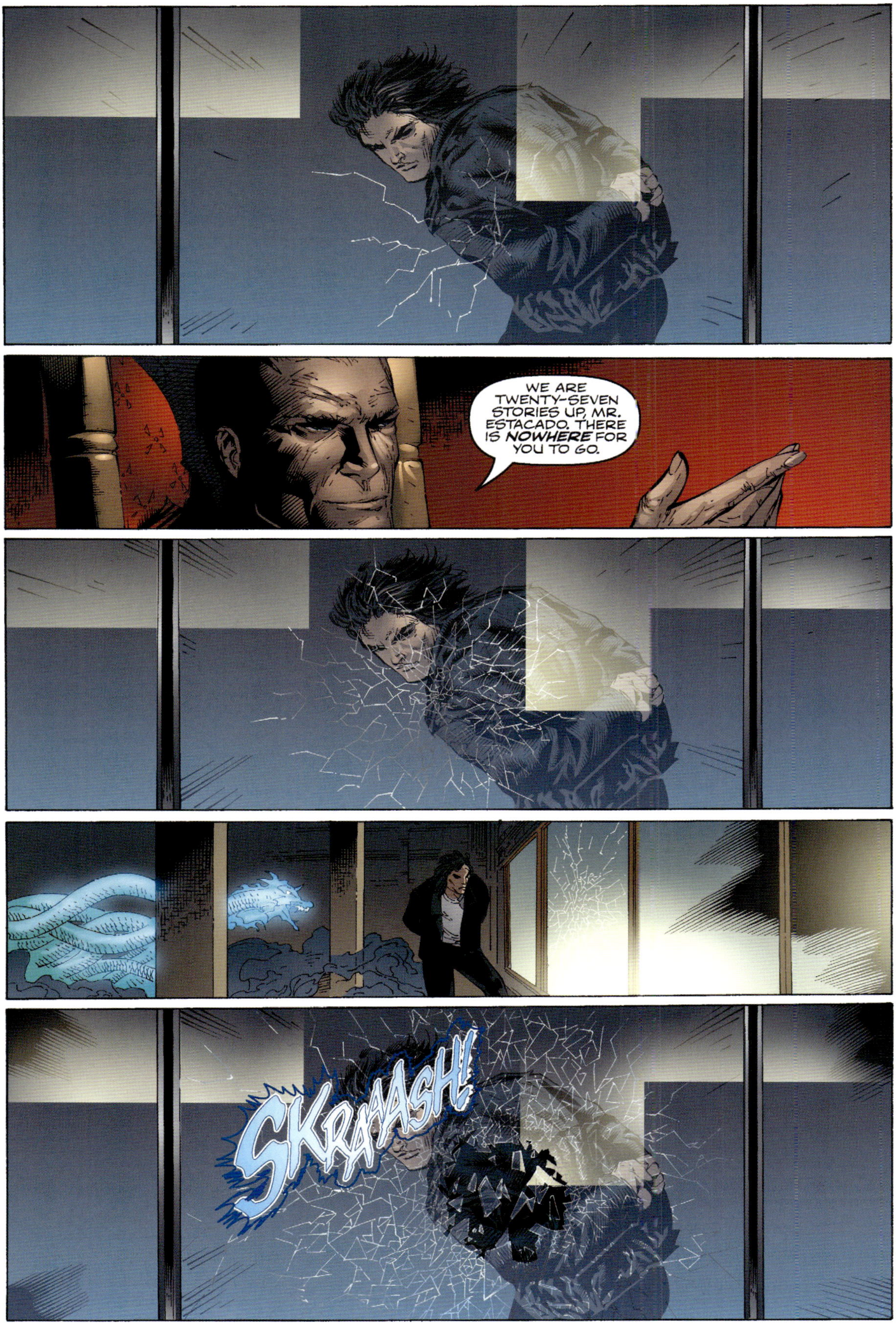
WE ARE TWENTY-SEVEN STORIES UP, MR. ESTACADO. THERE IS **NOWHERE** FOR YOU TO GO.
SKRAAASH!

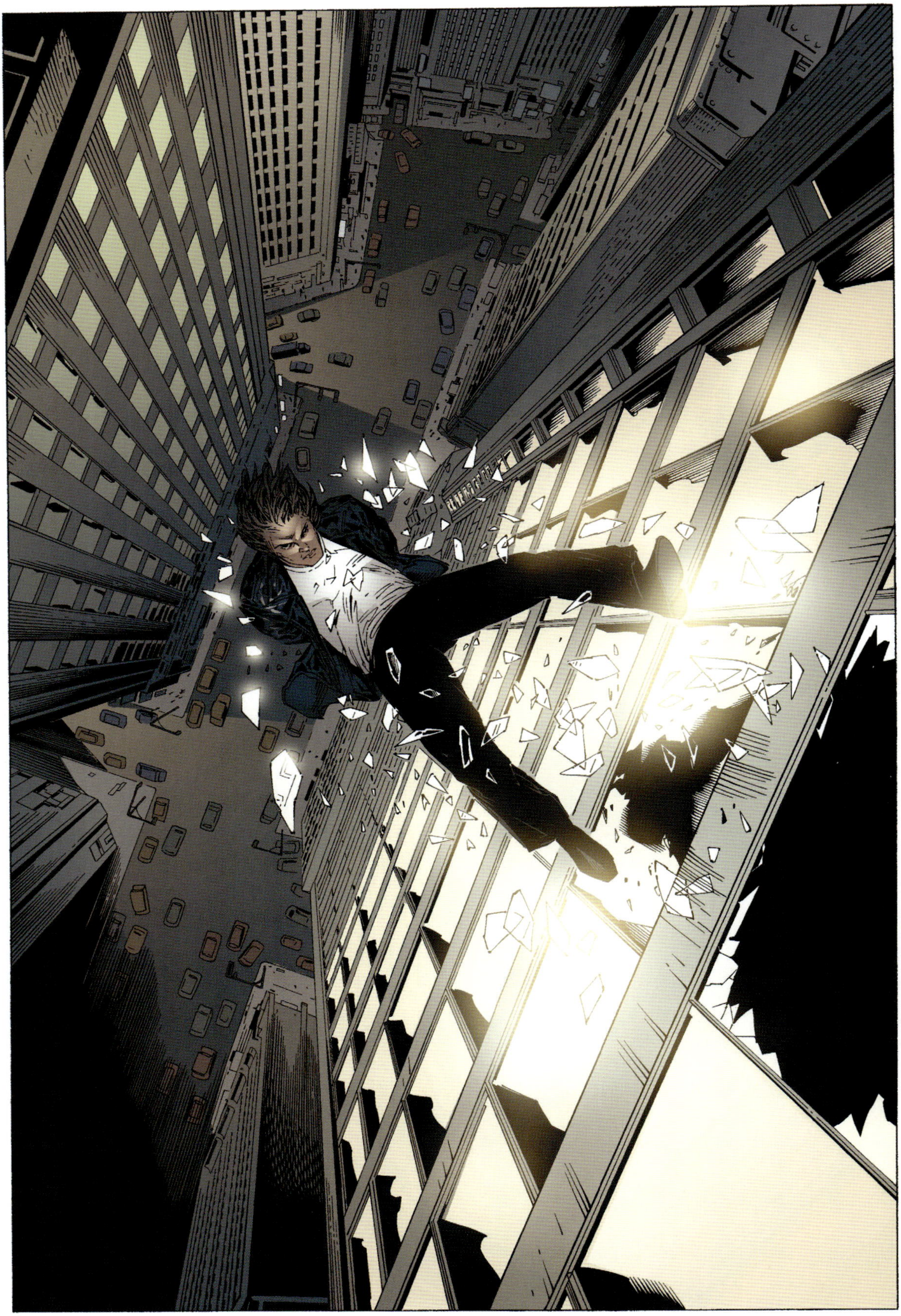

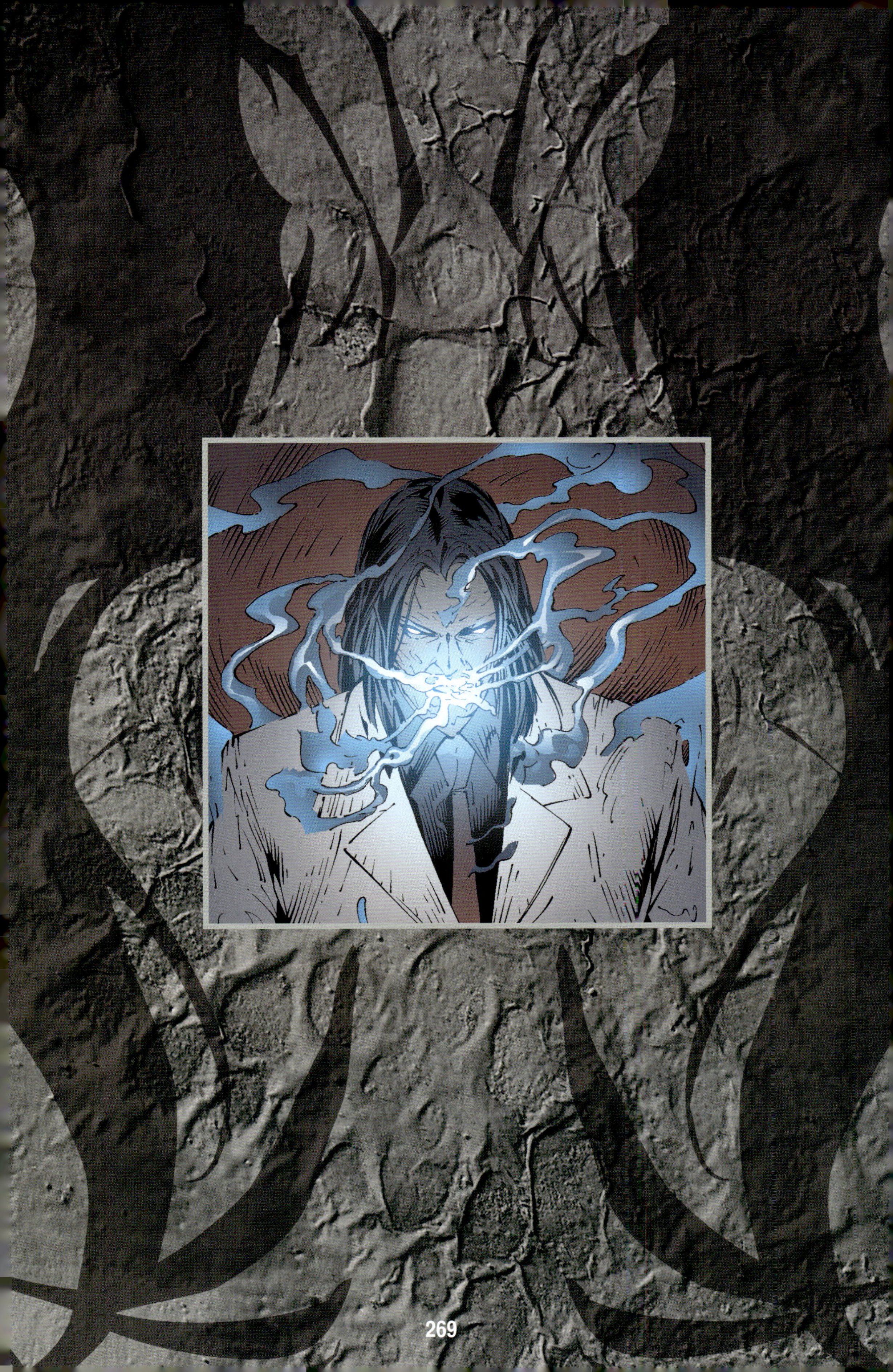

The Darkness Issue #52
cover art by: Dale Keown and Matt Milla

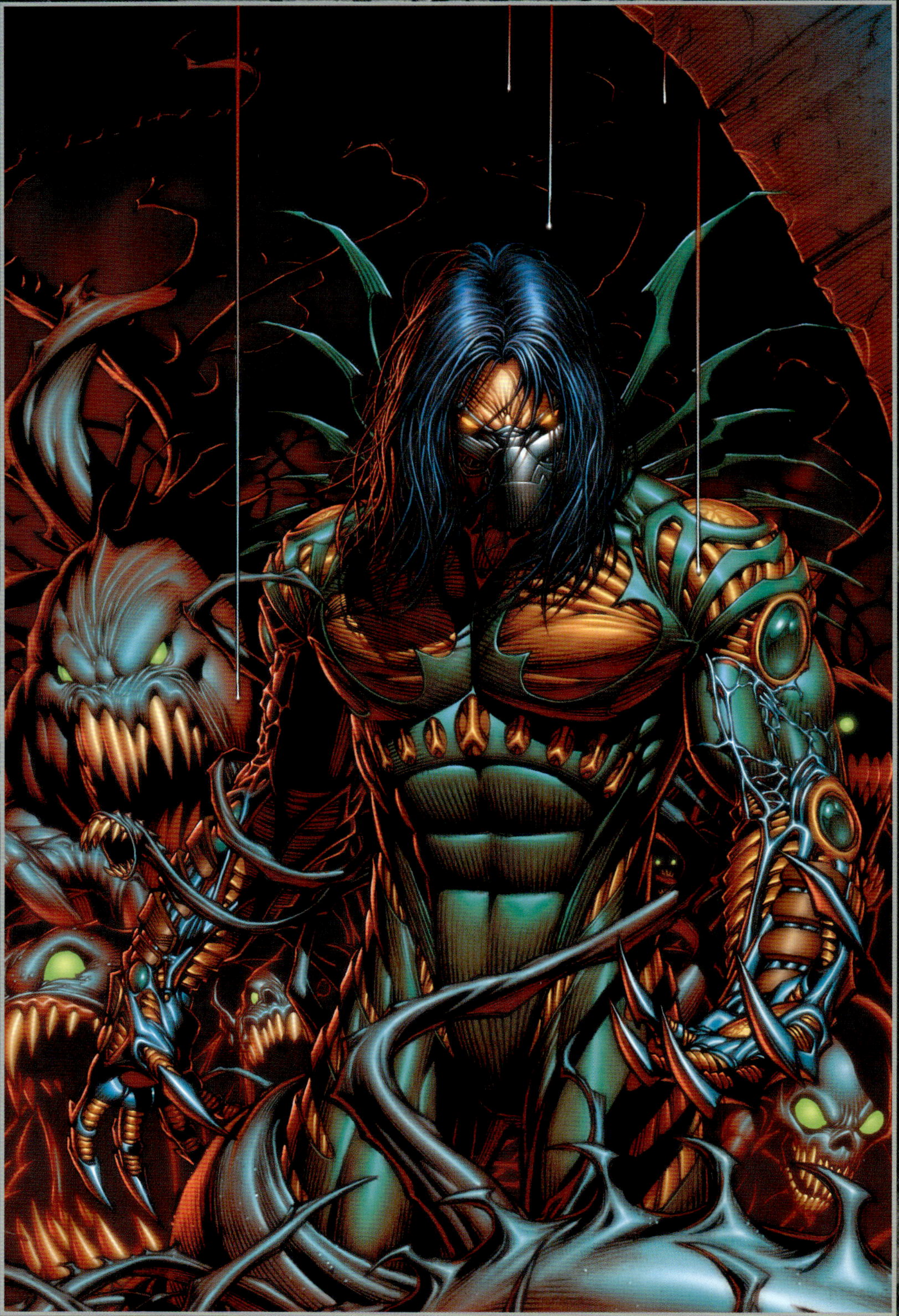

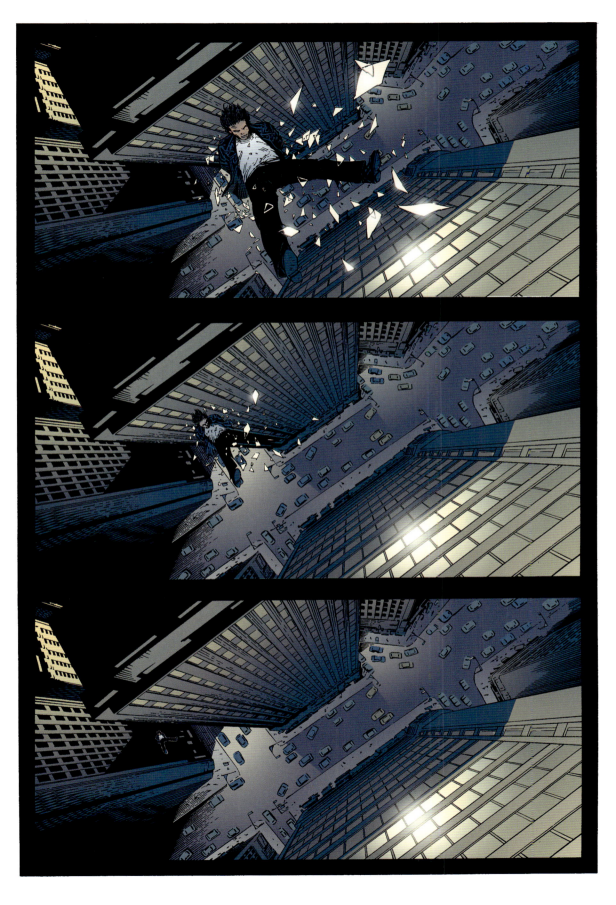

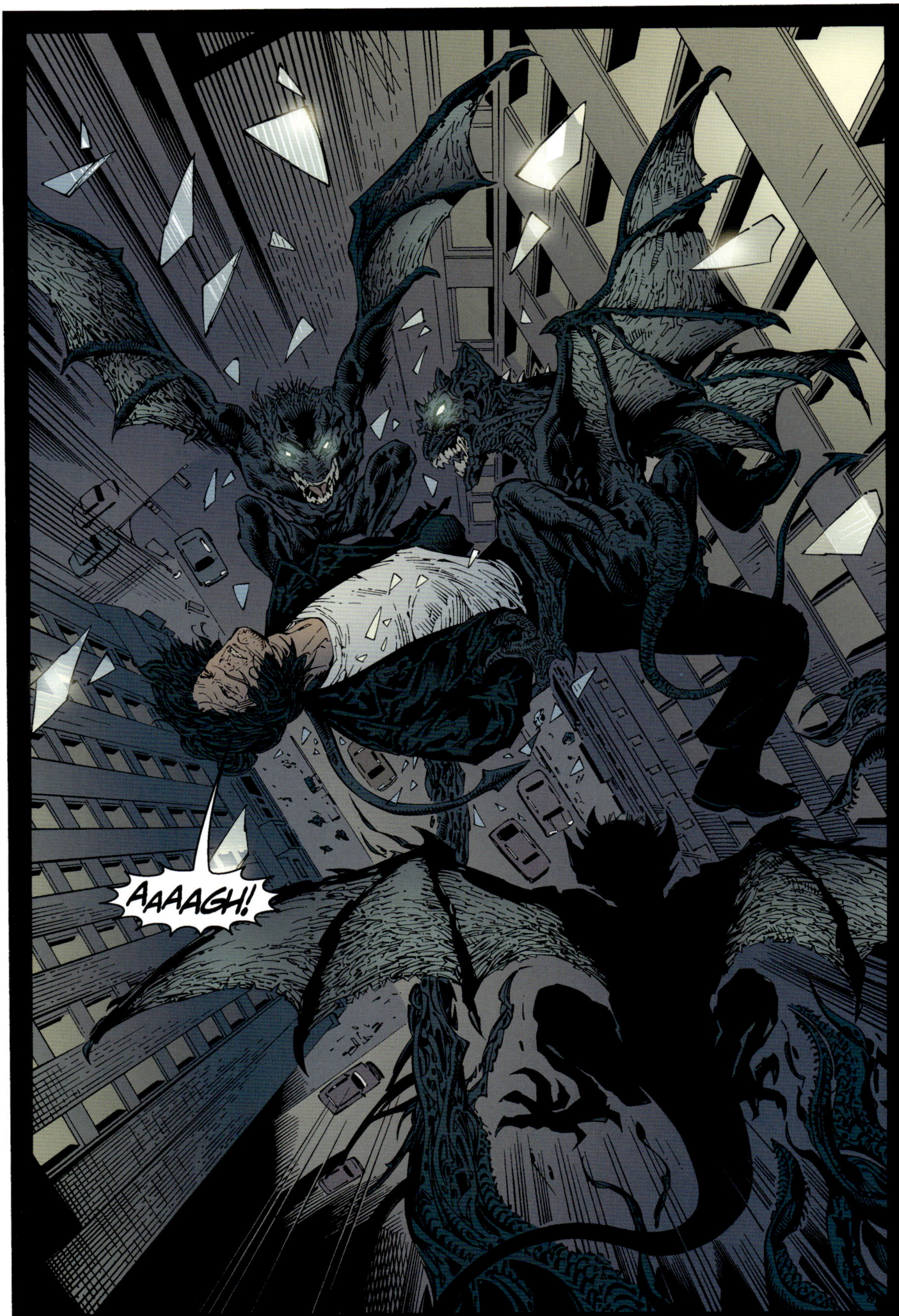
AAAAGH!

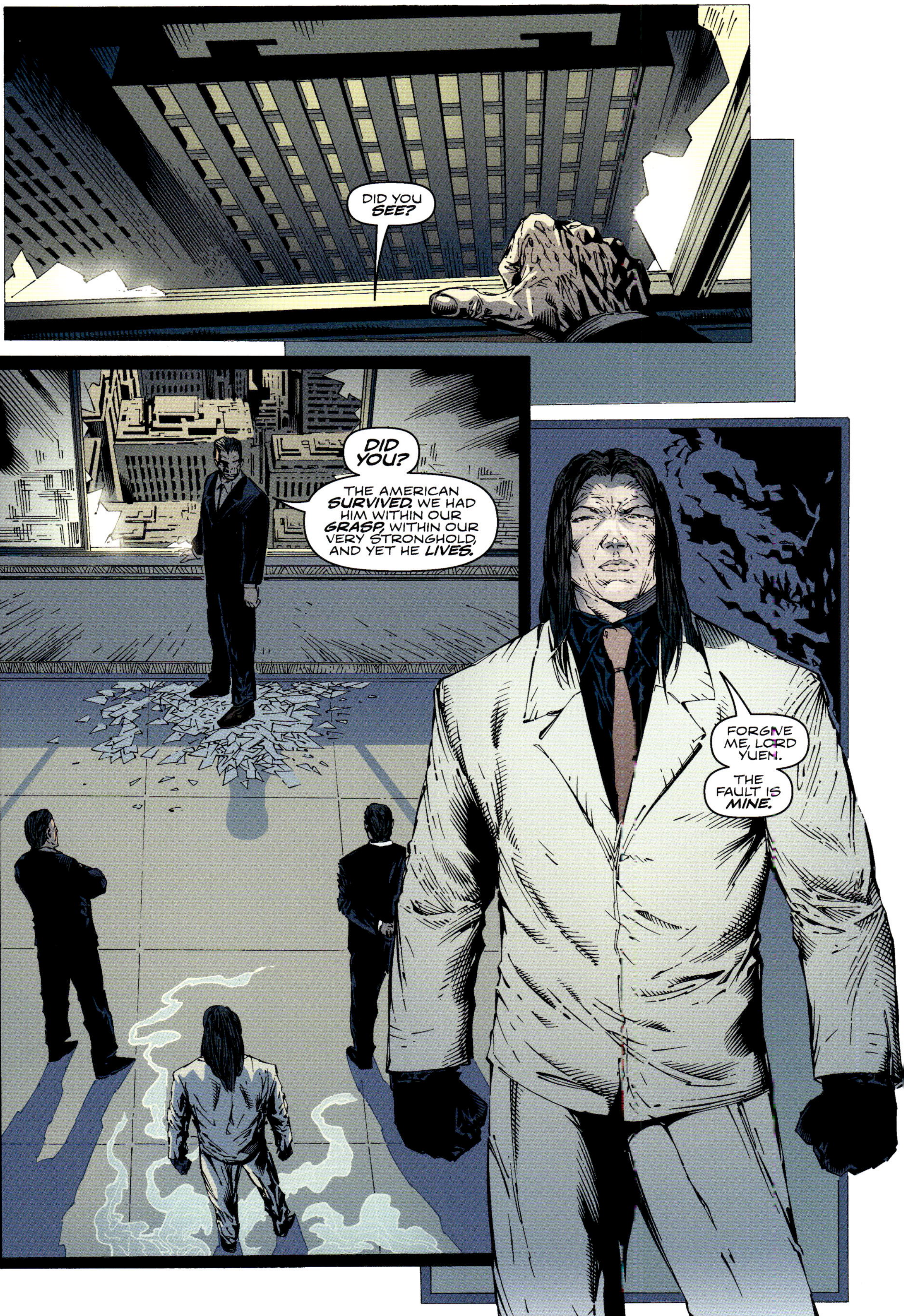
DID YOU *SEE?*
DID YOU?
THE AMERICAN *SURVIVED.* WE HAD HIM WITHIN OUR *GRASP,* WITHIN OUR VERY STRONGHOLD, AND YET HE *LIVES.*
FORGIVE ME, LORD YUEN.
THE FAULT IS *MINE.*

YOUR **APOLOGIES** ARE OF NO USE TO ME, KUO.

GATHER THE MEN...

...**ALL** OF THEM...

...AND GO INTO THE STREETS.

I WANT ESTACADO **FOUND** AND I WANT HIM **EXECUTED.**

DO THIS THING **BEFORE** NIGHTFALL.

YES, LORD YUEN. THE AMERICAN WILL NOT SEE ANOTHER SUNSET.

KUO...

...DO NOT SQUANDER THE **GIFT** YOU HAVE INHERITED.

I WILL AWAIT NEWS OF YOUR SUCCESS AT THE **ESTATE.**

I WILL NOT ACCEPT **FAILURE** IN THIS.

NO, LORD...

...IT WILL BE AS YOU SAY.

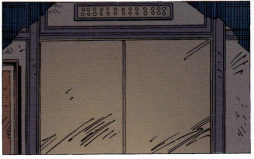

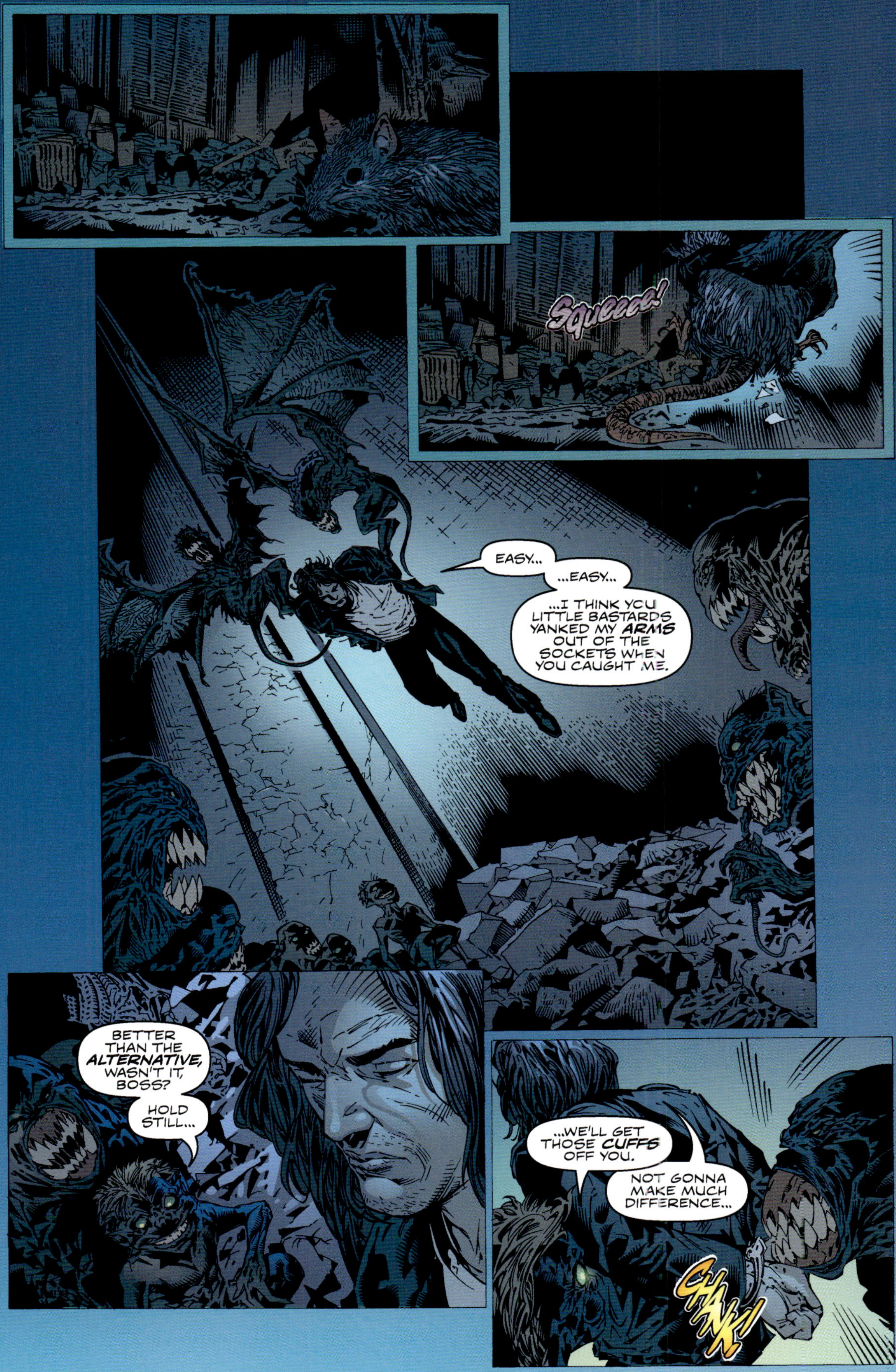
Squeeee!
EASY...
...EASY...
...I THINK YOU LITTLE BASTARDS YANKED MY ARMS OUT OF THE SOCKETS WHEN YOU CAUGHT ME.
BETTER THAN THE ALTERNATIVE, WASN'T IT, BOSS?
HOLD STILL...
...WE'LL GET THOSE CUFFS OFF YOU.
NOT GONNA MAKE MUCH DIFFERENCE...
CHANK!

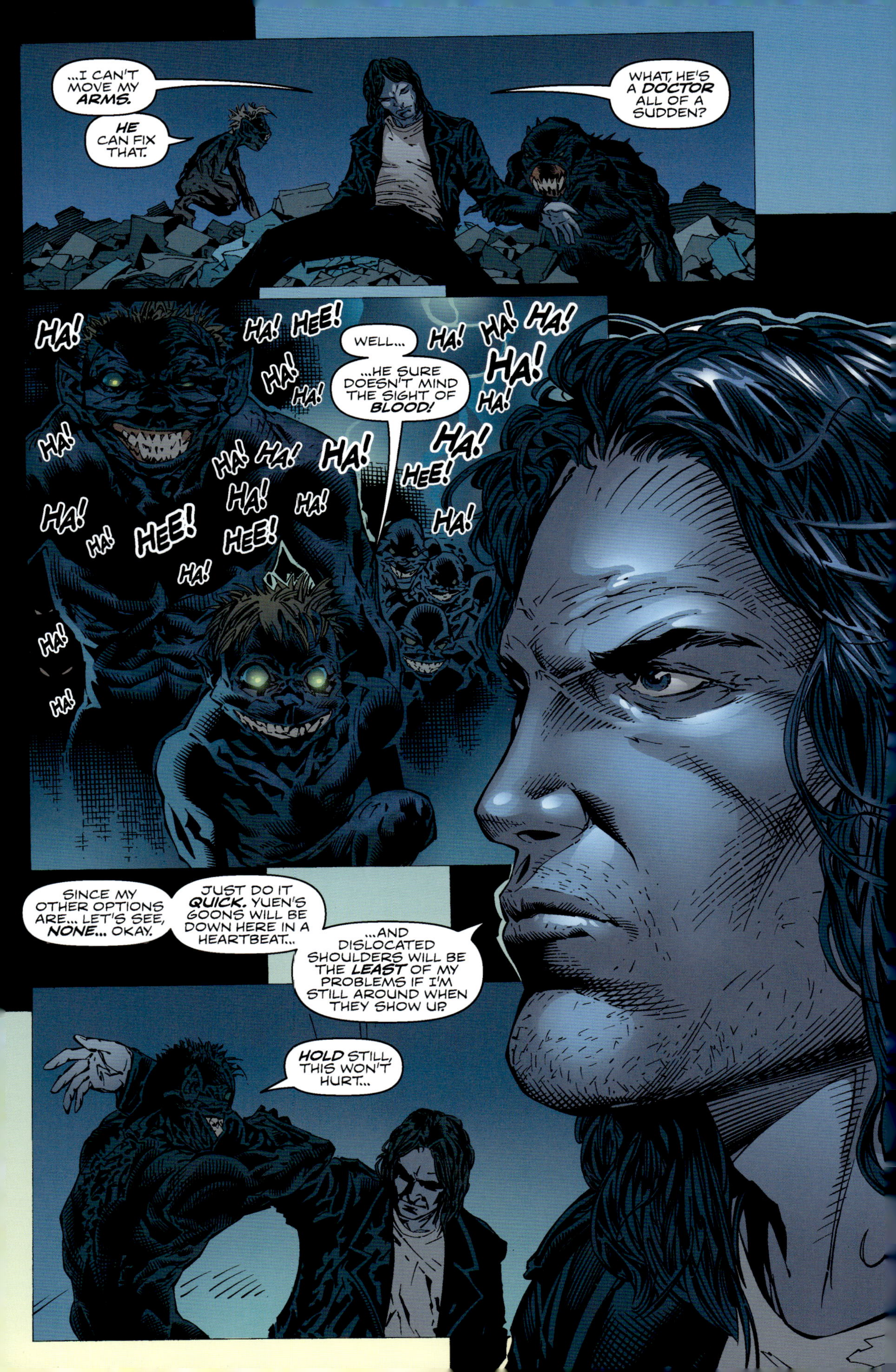
...I CAN'T MOVE MY ARMS.
HE CAN FIX THAT.
WHAT, HE'S A DOCTOR ALL OF A SUDDEN?
HA! HA! HEE! HA! HA!
WELL...
...HE SURE DOESN'T MIND THE SIGHT OF BLOOD!
HA! HA! HA! HA! HA!
HA! HA! HA! HA! HA! HEE! HA! HA! HA! HEE! HEE! HA! HA! HA!
SINCE MY OTHER OPTIONS ARE... LET'S SEE, NONE... OKAY.
JUST DO IT QUICK. YUEN'S GOONS WILL BE DOWN HERE IN A HEARTBEAT...
...AND DISLOCATED SHOULDERS WILL BE THE LEAST OF MY PROBLEMS IF I'M STILL AROUND WHEN THEY SHOW UP.
HOLD STILL, THIS WON'T HURT...

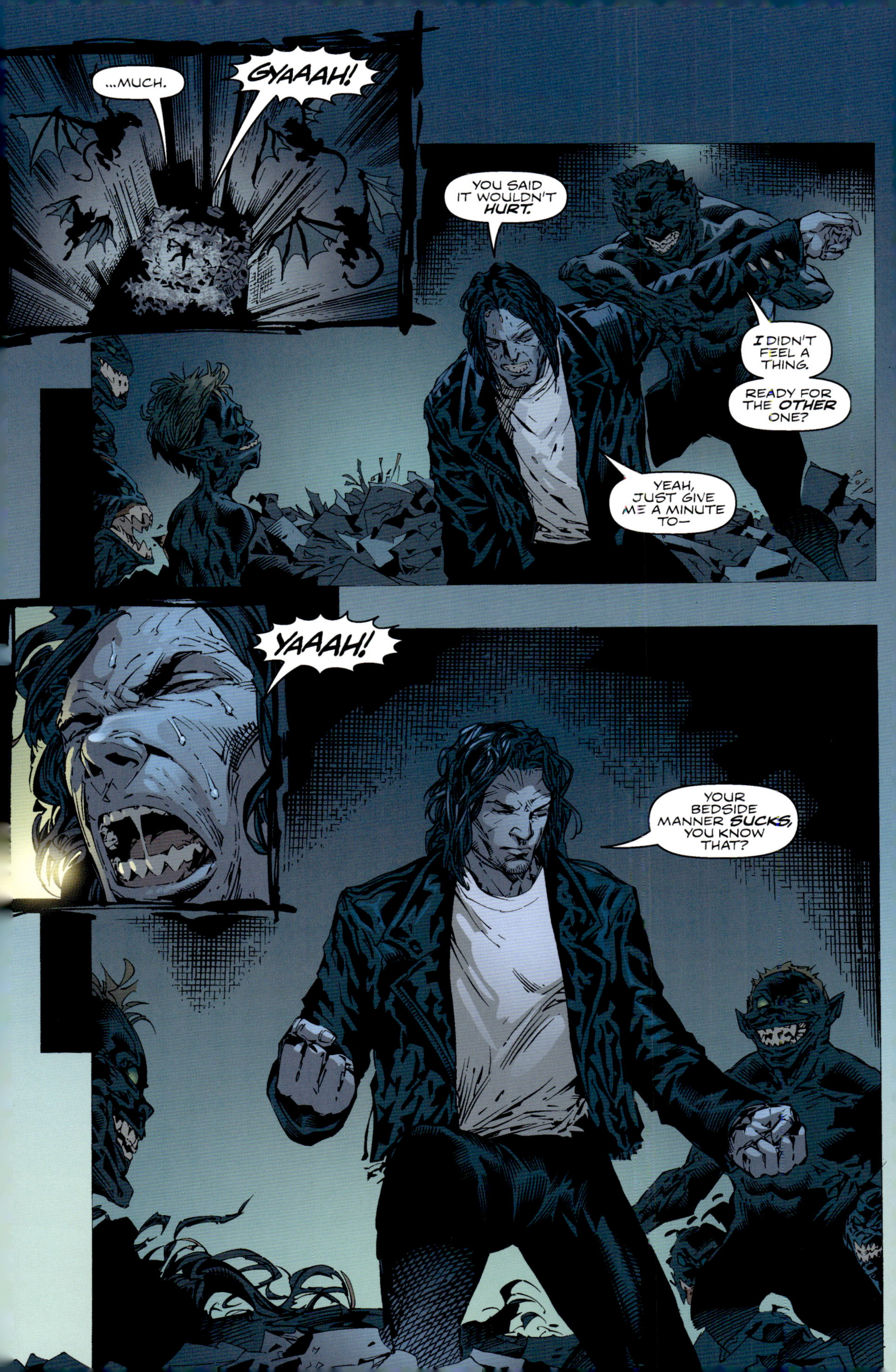
...MUCH.
GYAAAH!
YOU SAID IT WOULDN'T HURT.
I DIDN'T FEEL A THING.
READY FOR THE OTHER ONE?
YEAH, JUST GIVE ME A MINUTE TO—
YAAAH!
YOUR BEDSIDE MANNER SUCKS, YOU KNOW THAT?

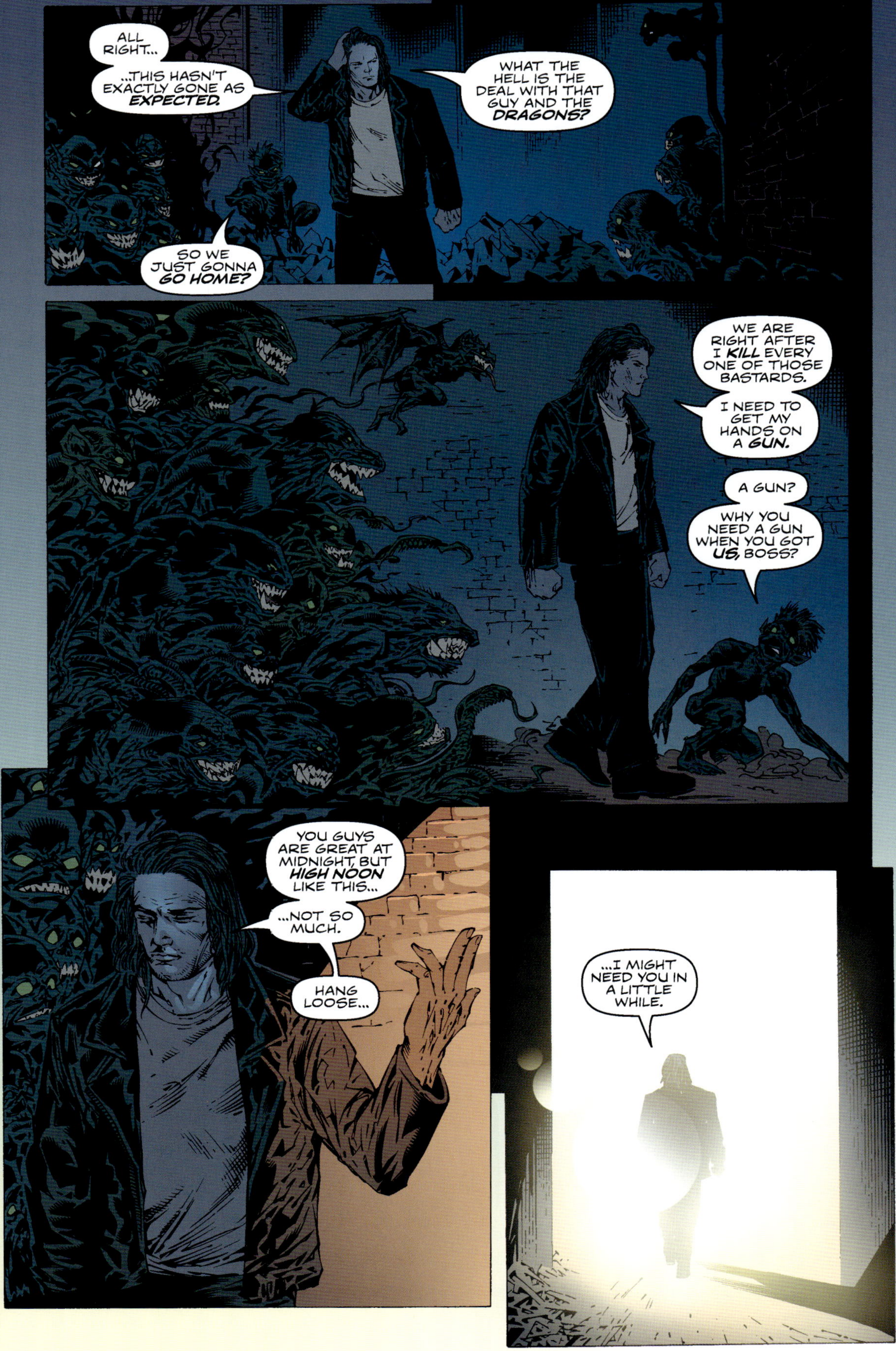

ALL RIGHT...
...THIS HASN'T EXACTLY GONE AS EXPECTED.
WHAT THE HELL IS THE DEAL WITH THAT GUY AND THE DRAGONS?
SO WE JUST GONNA GO HOME?
WE ARE RIGHT AFTER I KILL EVERY ONE OF THOSE BASTARDS.
I NEED TO GET MY HANDS ON A GUN.
A GUN?
WHY YOU NEED A GUN WHEN YOU GOT US, BOSS?
YOU GUYS ARE GREAT AT MIDNIGHT, BUT HIGH NOON LIKE THIS...
...NOT SO MUCH.
HANG LOOSE...
...I MIGHT NEED YOU IN A LITTLE WHILE.

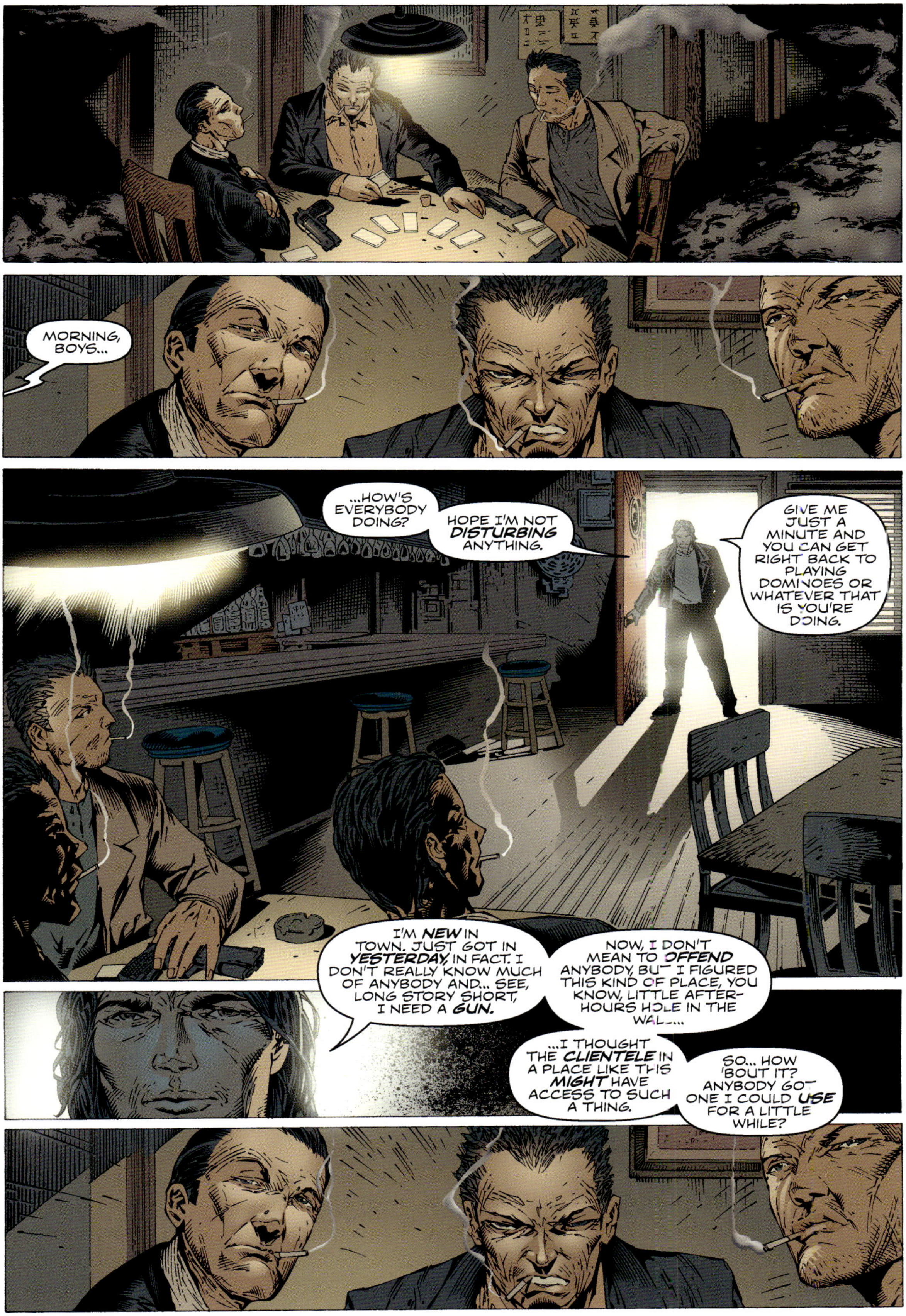
MORNING, BOYS...
...HOW'S EVERYBODY DOING?
HOPE I'M NOT DISTURBING ANYTHING.
GIVE ME JUST A MINUTE AND YOU CAN GET RIGHT BACK TO PLAYING DOMINOES OR WHATEVER THAT IS YOU'RE DOING.
I'M NEW IN TOWN. JUST GOT IN YESTERDAY, IN FACT. I DON'T REALLY KNOW MUCH OF ANYBODY AND... SEE, LONG STORY SHORT, I NEED A GUN.
NOW, I DON'T MEAN TO OFFEND ANYBODY, BUT I FIGURED THIS KIND OF PLACE, YOU KNOW, LITTLE AFTER-HOURS HOLE IN THE WALL...
...I THOUGHT THE CLIENTELE IN A PLACE LIKE THIS MIGHT HAVE ACCESS TO SUCH A THING.
SO... HOW 'BOUT IT? ANYBODY GOT ONE I COULD USE FOR A LITTLE WHILE?

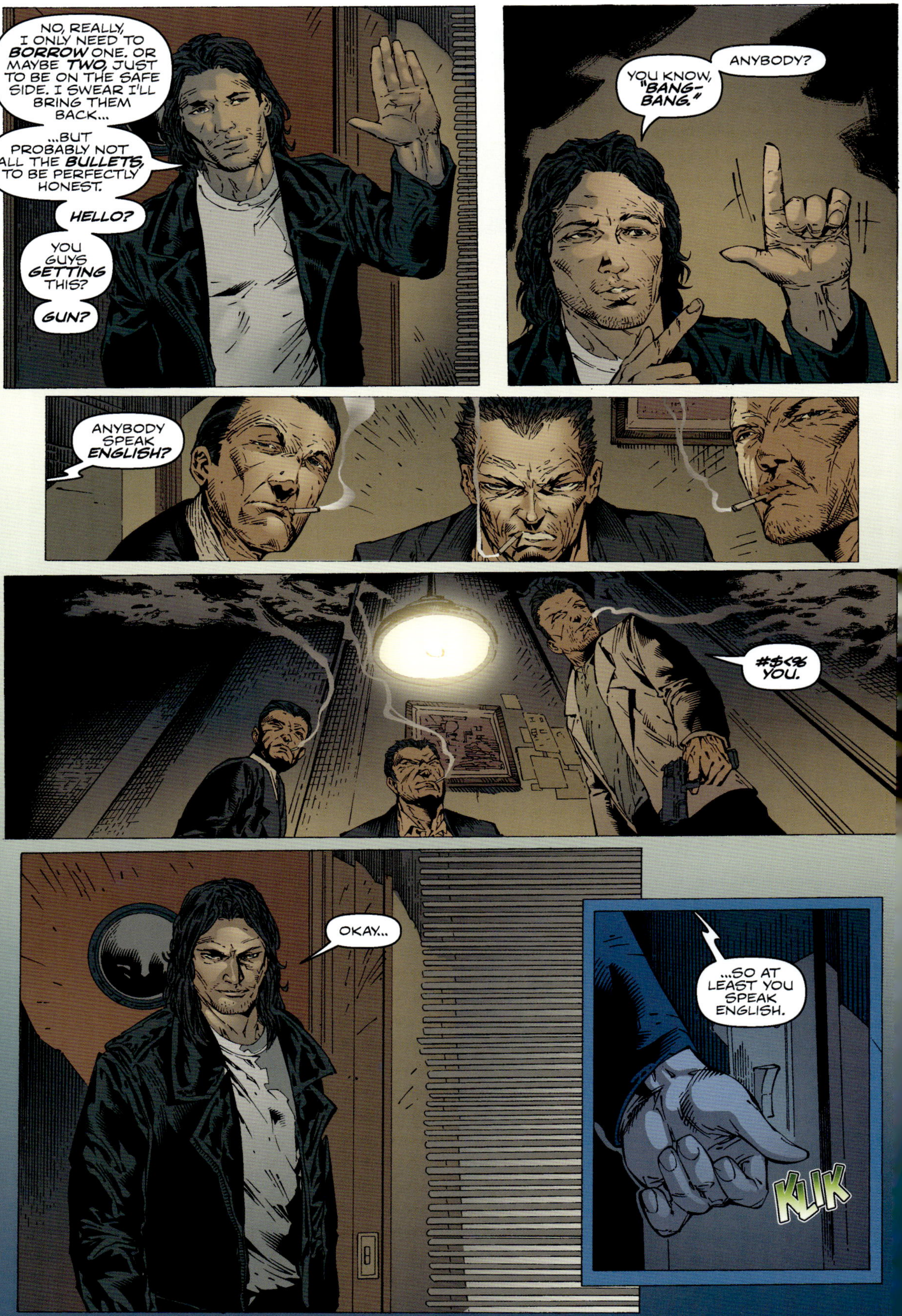

NO, REALLY, I ONLY NEED TO BORROW ONE. OR MAYBE TWO, JUST TO BE ON THE SAFE SIDE. I SWEAR I'LL BRING THEM BACK...
...BUT PROBABLY NOT ALL THE BULLETS, TO BE PERFECTLY HONEST.
HELLO?
YOU GUYS GETTING THIS?
GUN?
YOU KNOW, "BANG-BANG."
ANYBODY?
ANYBODY SPEAK ENGLISH?
#$<%6 YOU.
OKAY...
...SO AT LEAST YOU SPEAK ENGLISH.
KLIK

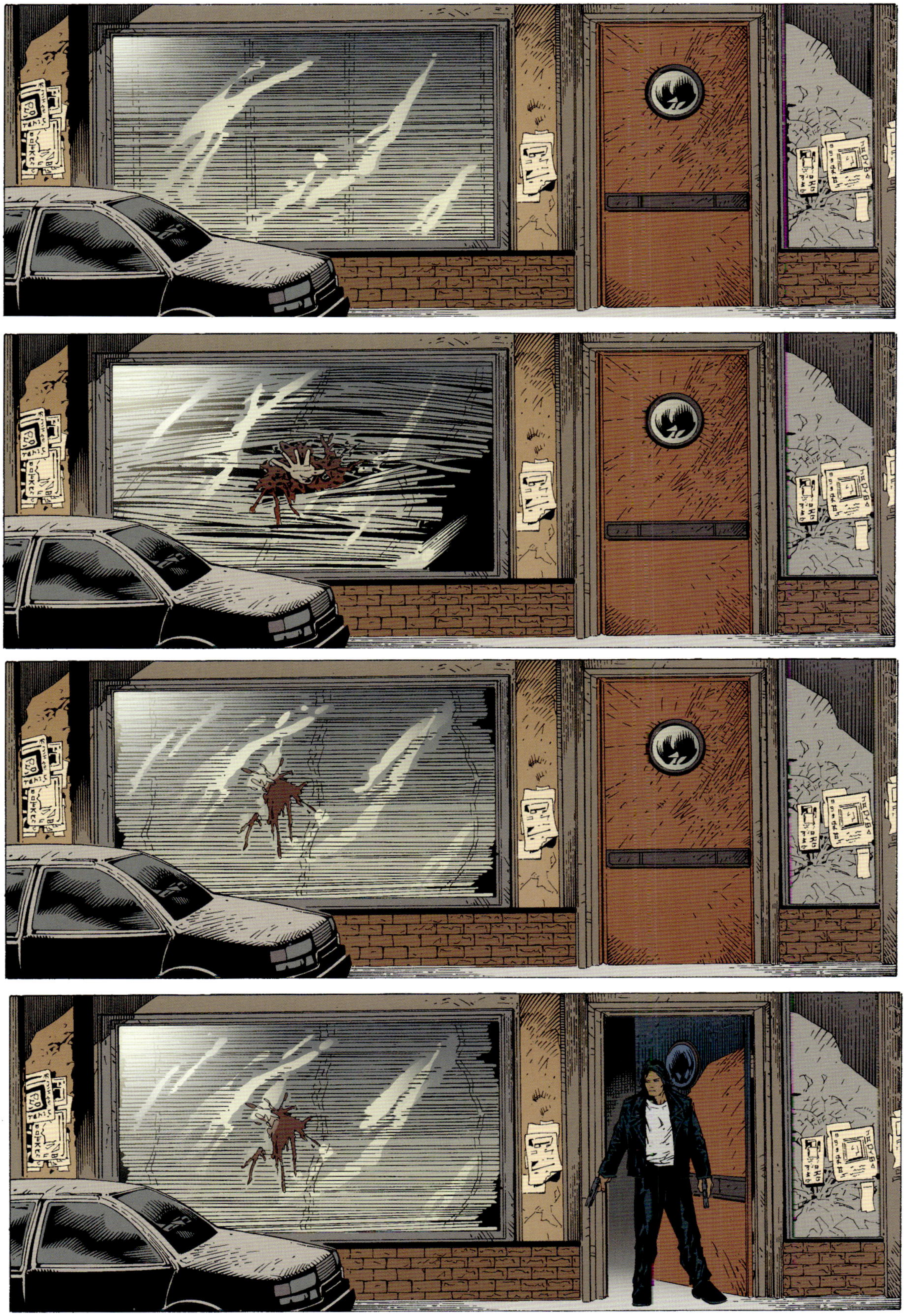

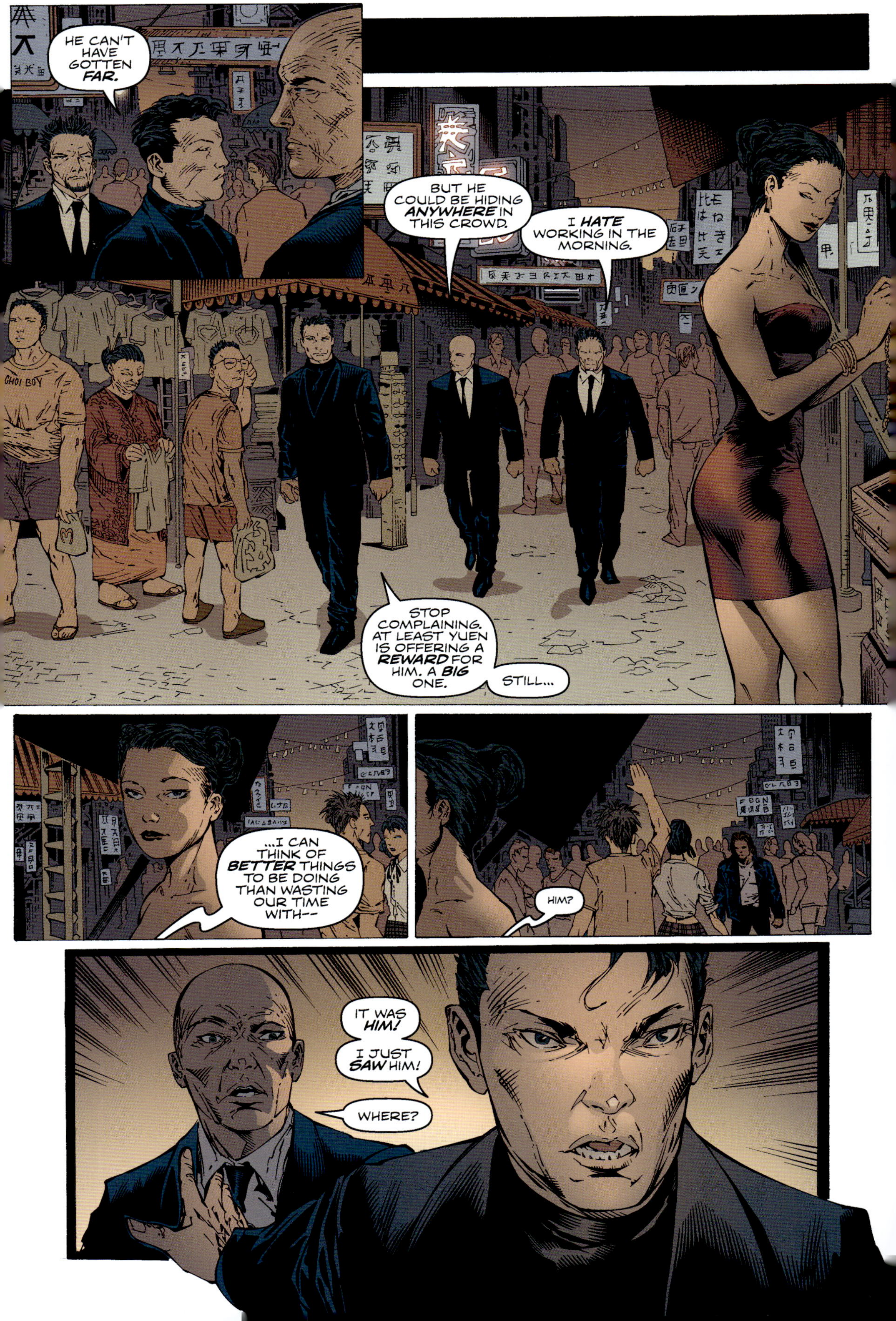
HE CAN'T HAVE GOTTEN FAR.
BUT HE COULD BE HIDING ANYWHERE IN THIS CROWD.
I HATE WORKING IN THE MORNING.
CHOI BOY
STOP COMPLAINING. AT LEAST YUEN IS OFFERING A REWARD FOR HIM. A BIG ONE.
STILL...
...I CAN THINK OF BETTER THINGS TO BE DOING THAN WASTING OUR TIME WITH--
HIM?
IT WAS HIM!
I JUST SAW HIM!
WHERE?

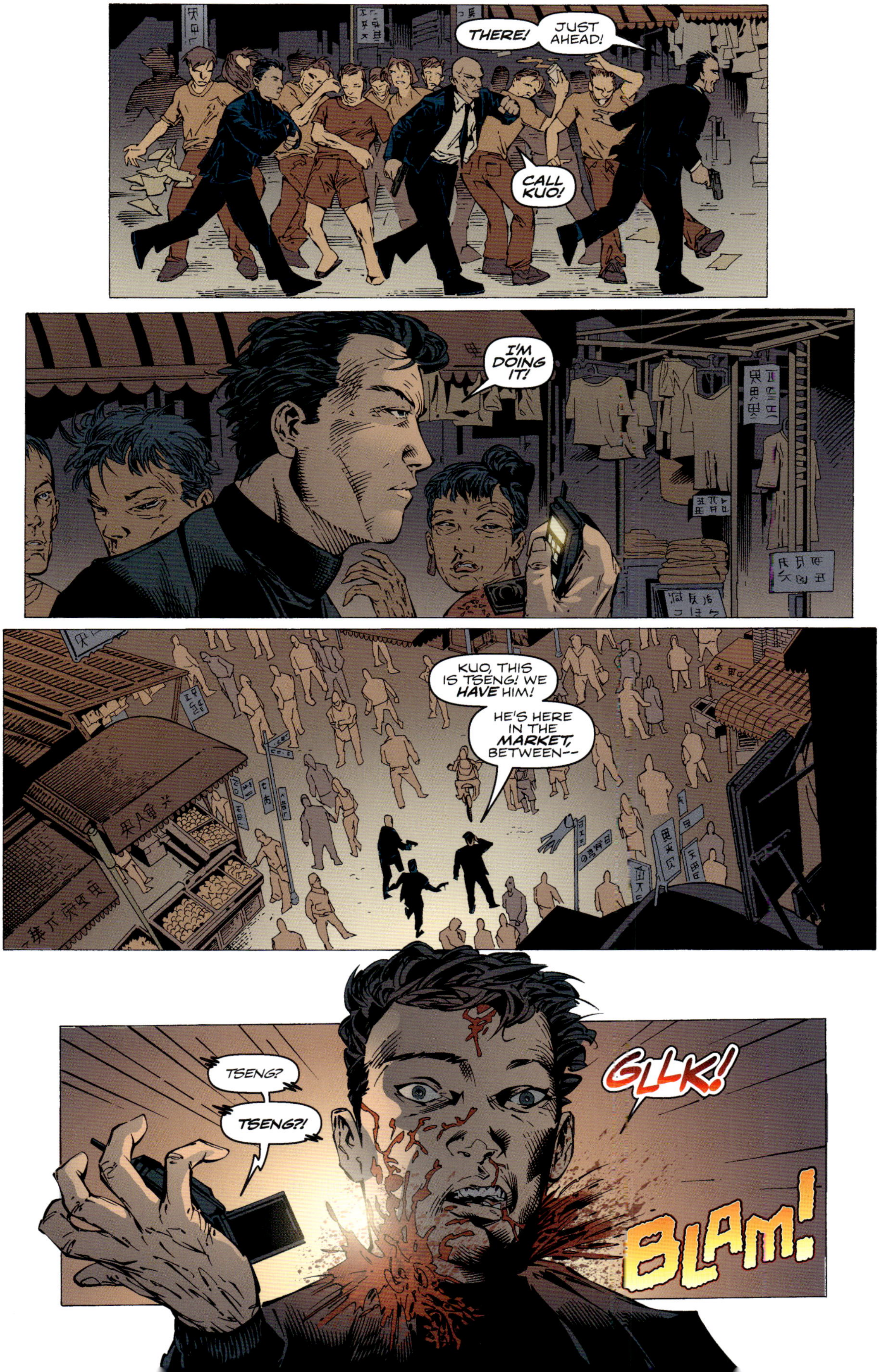
THERE!
JUST AHEAD!
CALL KUO!
I'M DOING IT!
KUO, THIS IS TSENG! WE HAVE HIM!
HE'S HERE IN THE MARKET, BETWEEN--
TSENG?
TSENG?!
GLLK!
BLAM!

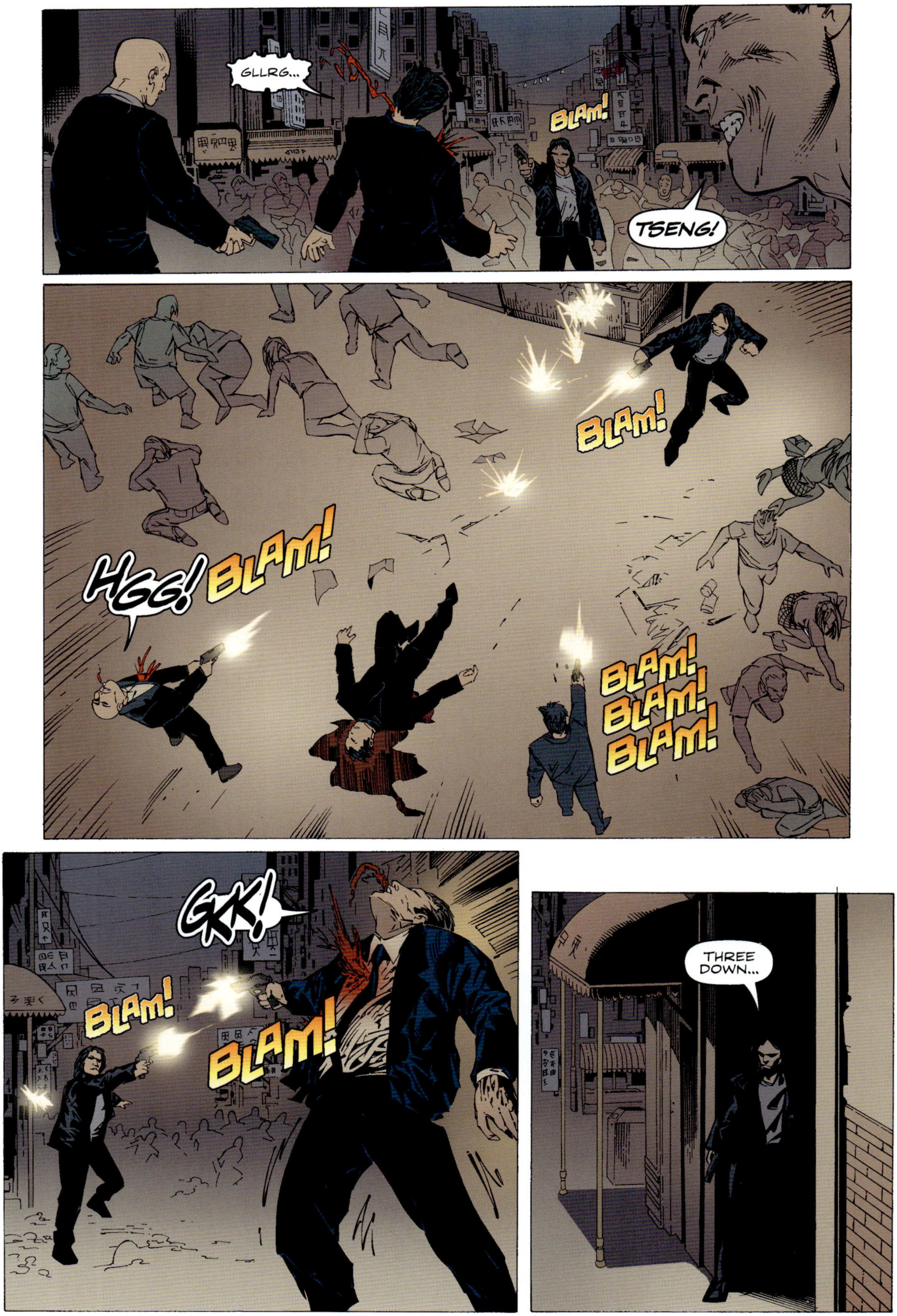
GLLRG...
BLAM!
TSENG!
BLAM!
HGG!
BLAM!
BLAM!
BLAM!
BLAM!
GKK!
BLAM!
BLAM!
THREE DOWN...

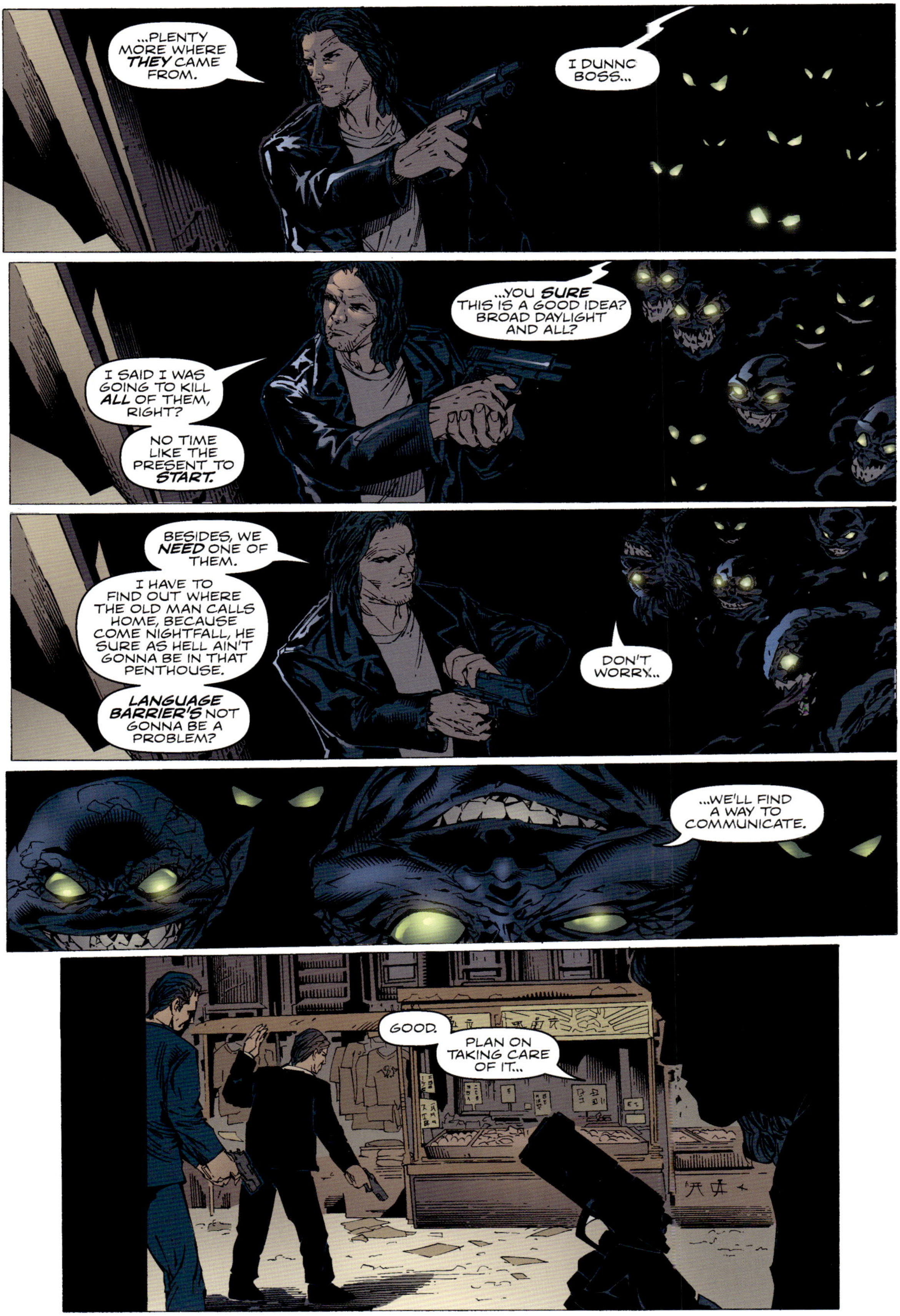

...PLENTY MORE WHERE THEY CAME FROM.
I DUNNO BOSS...
...YOU SURE THIS IS A GOOD IDEA? BROAD DAYLIGHT AND ALL?
I SAID I WAS GOING TO KILL ALL OF THEM, RIGHT?
NO TIME LIKE THE PRESENT TO START.
BESIDES, WE NEED ONE OF THEM.
I HAVE TO FIND OUT WHERE THE OLD MAN CALLS HOME, BECAUSE COME NIGHTFALL, HE SURE AS HELL AIN'T GONNA BE IN THAT PENTHOUSE.
LANGUAGE BARRIER'S NOT GONNA BE A PROBLEM?
DON'T WORRY...
...WE'LL FIND A WAY TO COMMUNICATE.
GOOD.
PLAN ON TAKING CARE OF IT...

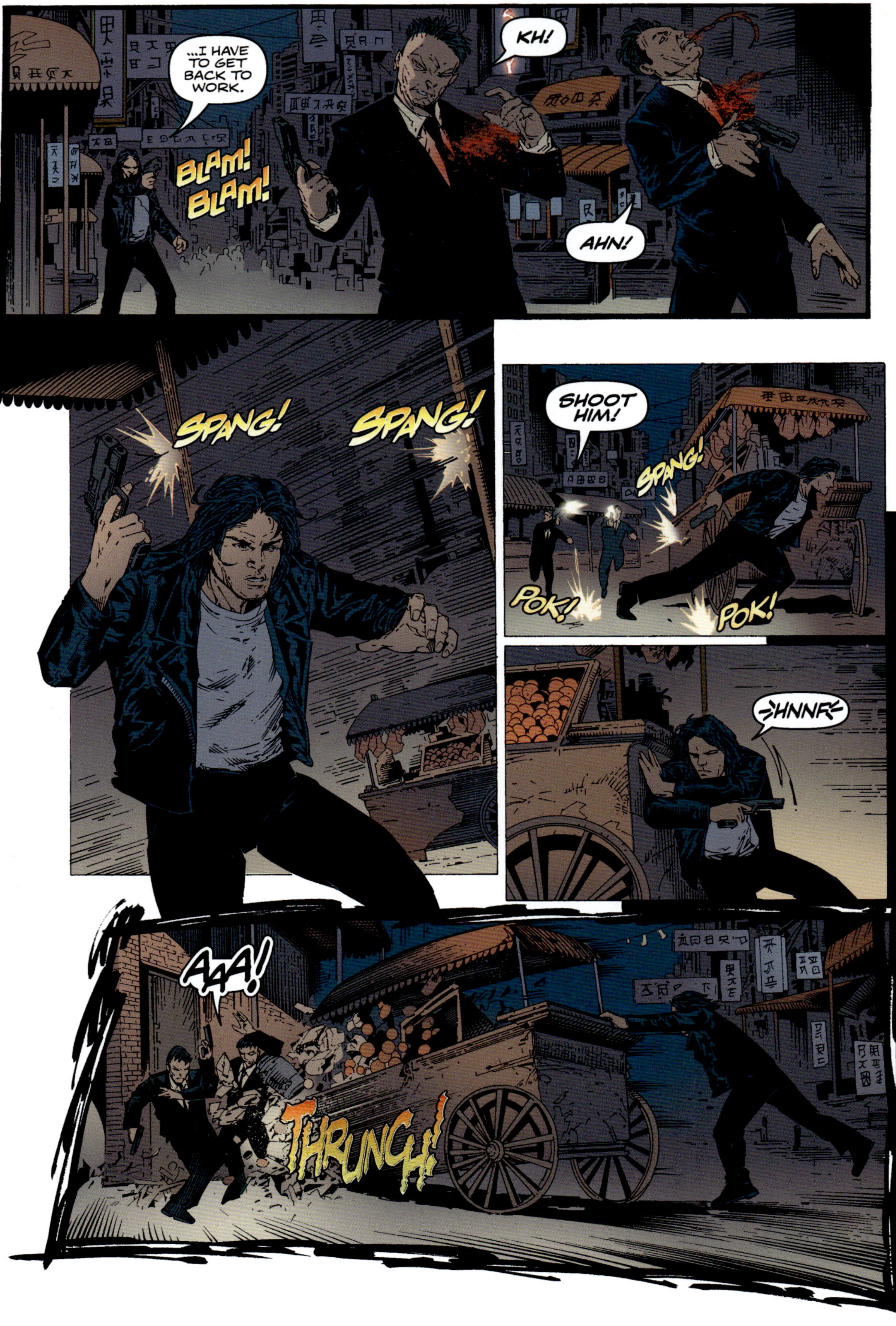
...I HAVE TO GET BACK TO WORK.
BLAM! BLAM!
KH!
AHN!
SPANG!
SPANG!
SHOOT HIM!
SPANG!
POK!
POK!
HNNF
AAA!
THRUNCH!

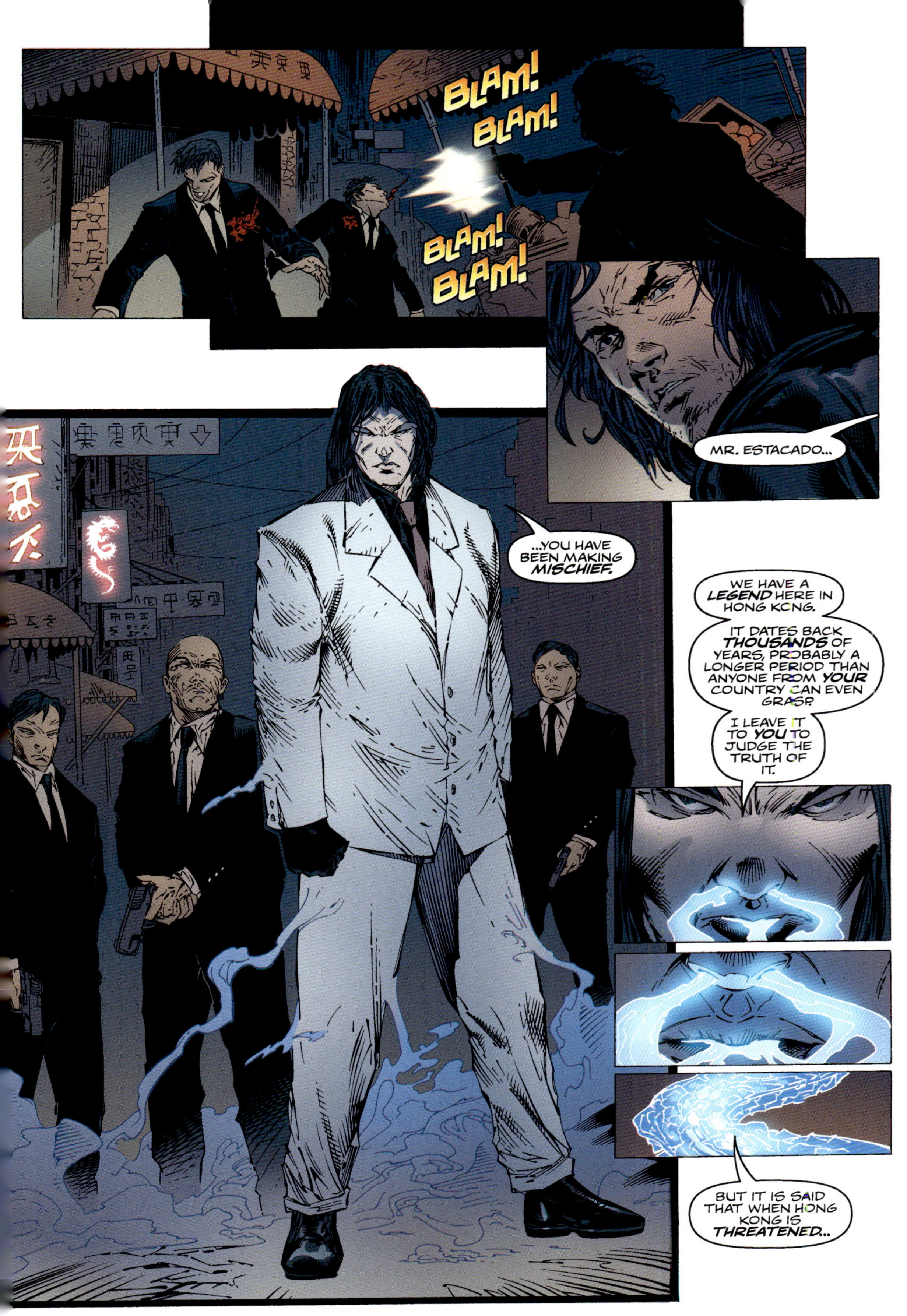

BLAM! BLAM!
BLAM! BLAM!
MR. ESTACADO...
...YOU HAVE BEEN MAKING MISCHIEF.
WE HAVE A LEGEND HERE IN HONG KONG.
IT DATES BACK THOUSANDS OF YEARS, PROBABLY A LONGER PERIOD THAN ANYONE FROM YOUR COUNTRY CAN EVEN GRASP.
I LEAVE IT TO YOU TO JUDGE THE TRUTH OF IT.
BUT IT IS SAID THAT WHEN HONG KONG IS THREATENED...

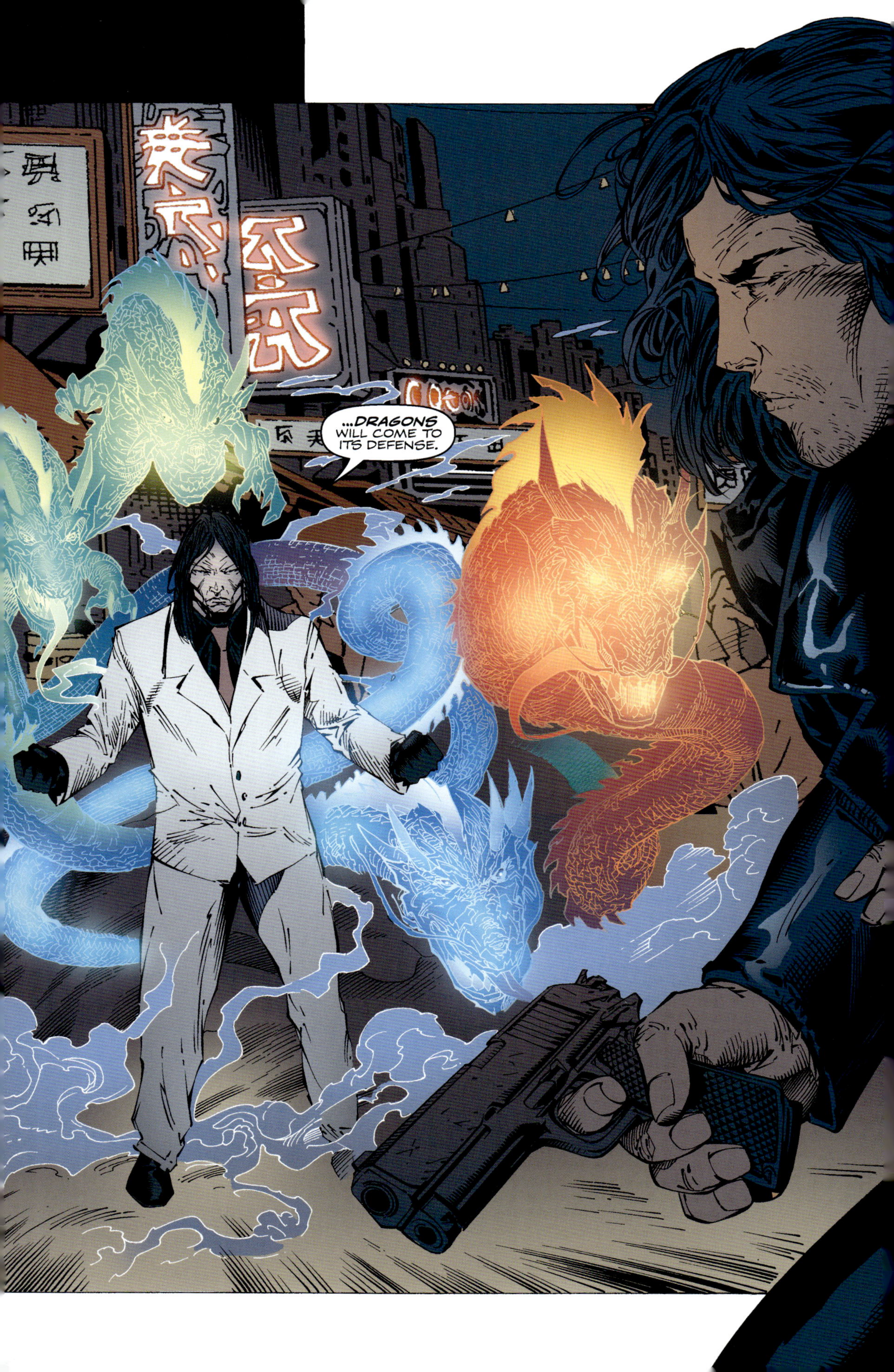
...DRAGONS WILL COME TO ITS DEFENSE.

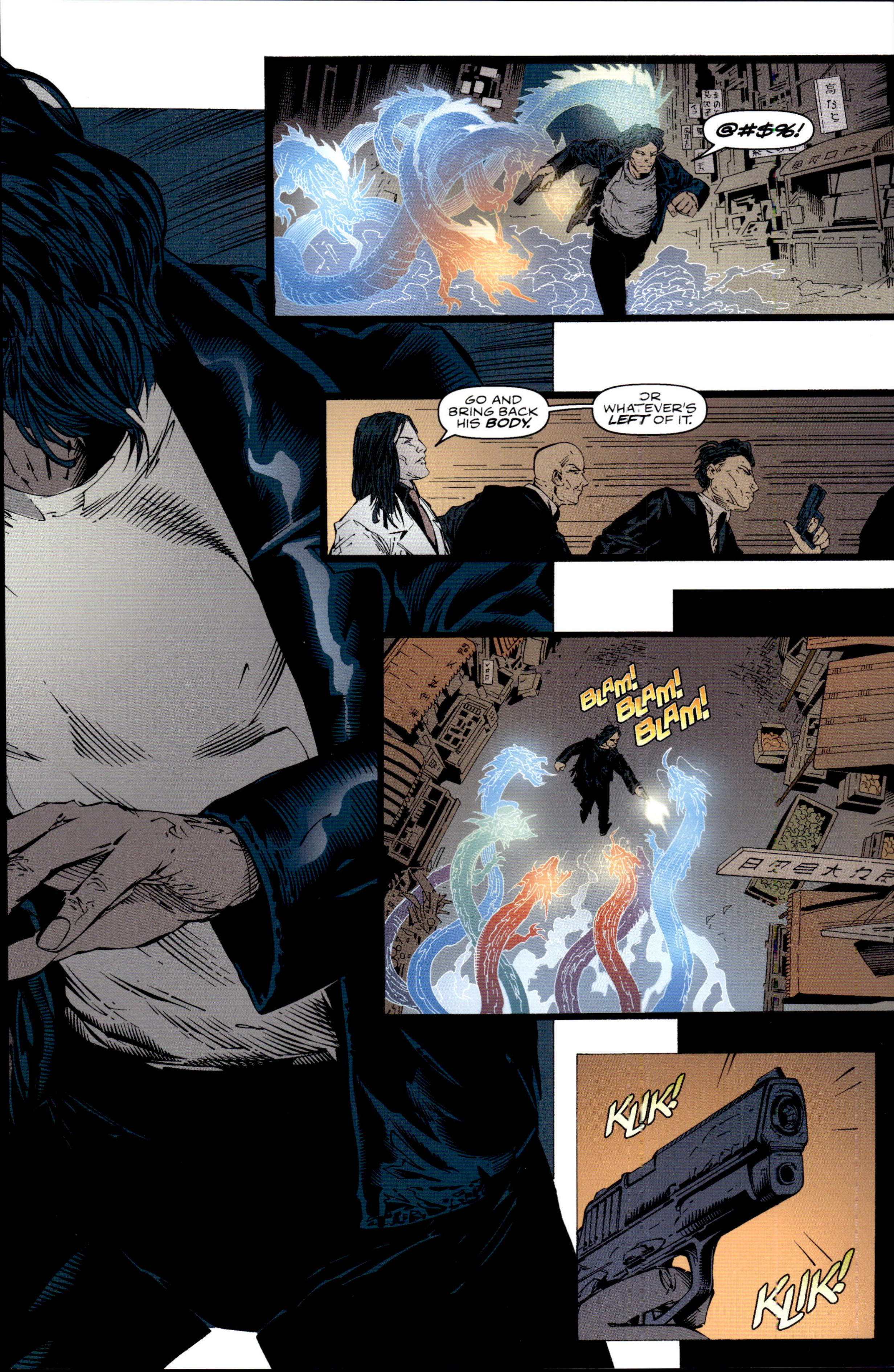
@#$%!
GO AND BRING BACK HIS BODY.
OR WHATEVER'S LEFT OF IT.
BLAM! BLAM! BLAM!
KLIK!
KLIK!

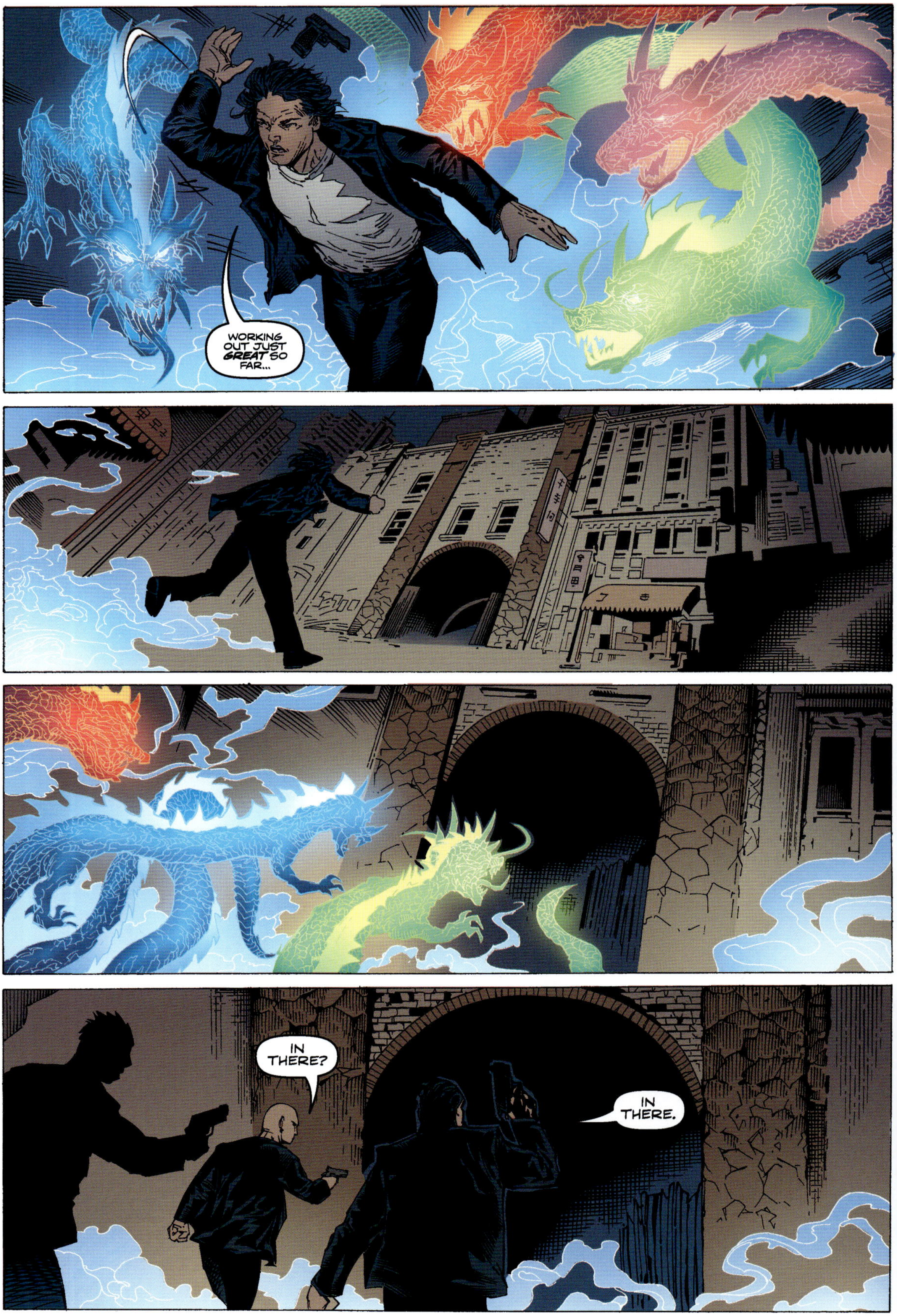
WORKING OUT JUST GREAT SO FAR...
IN THERE?
IN THERE.

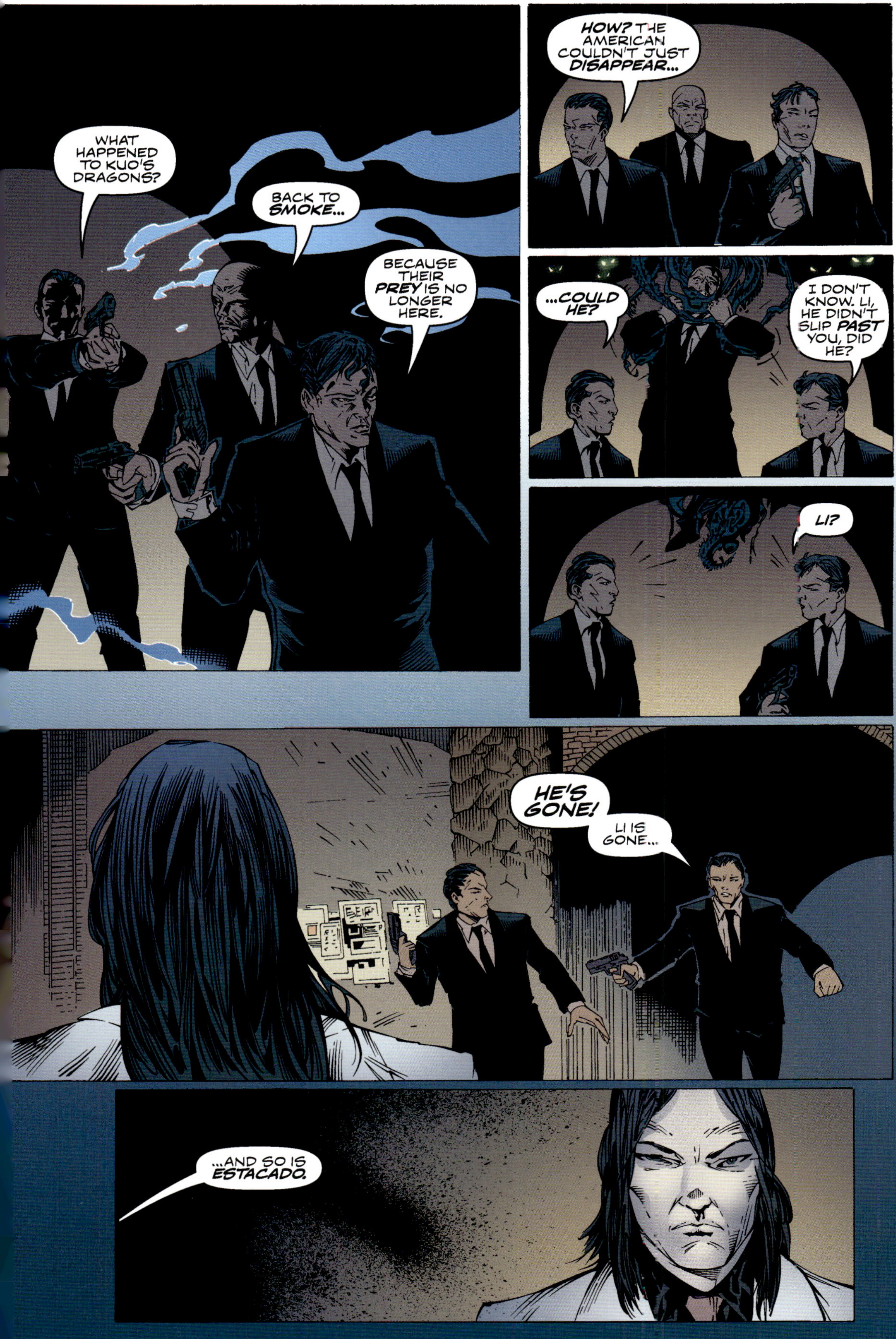

WHAT HAPPENED TO KUO'S DRAGONS?
BACK TO SMOKE...
BECAUSE THEIR PREY IS NO LONGER HERE.
HOW? THE AMERICAN COULDN'T JUST DISAPPEAR...
...COULD HE?
I DON'T KNOW. LI, HE DIDN'T SLIP PAST YOU, DID HE?
LI?
HE'S GONE!
LI IS GONE...
...AND SO IS ESTACADO.

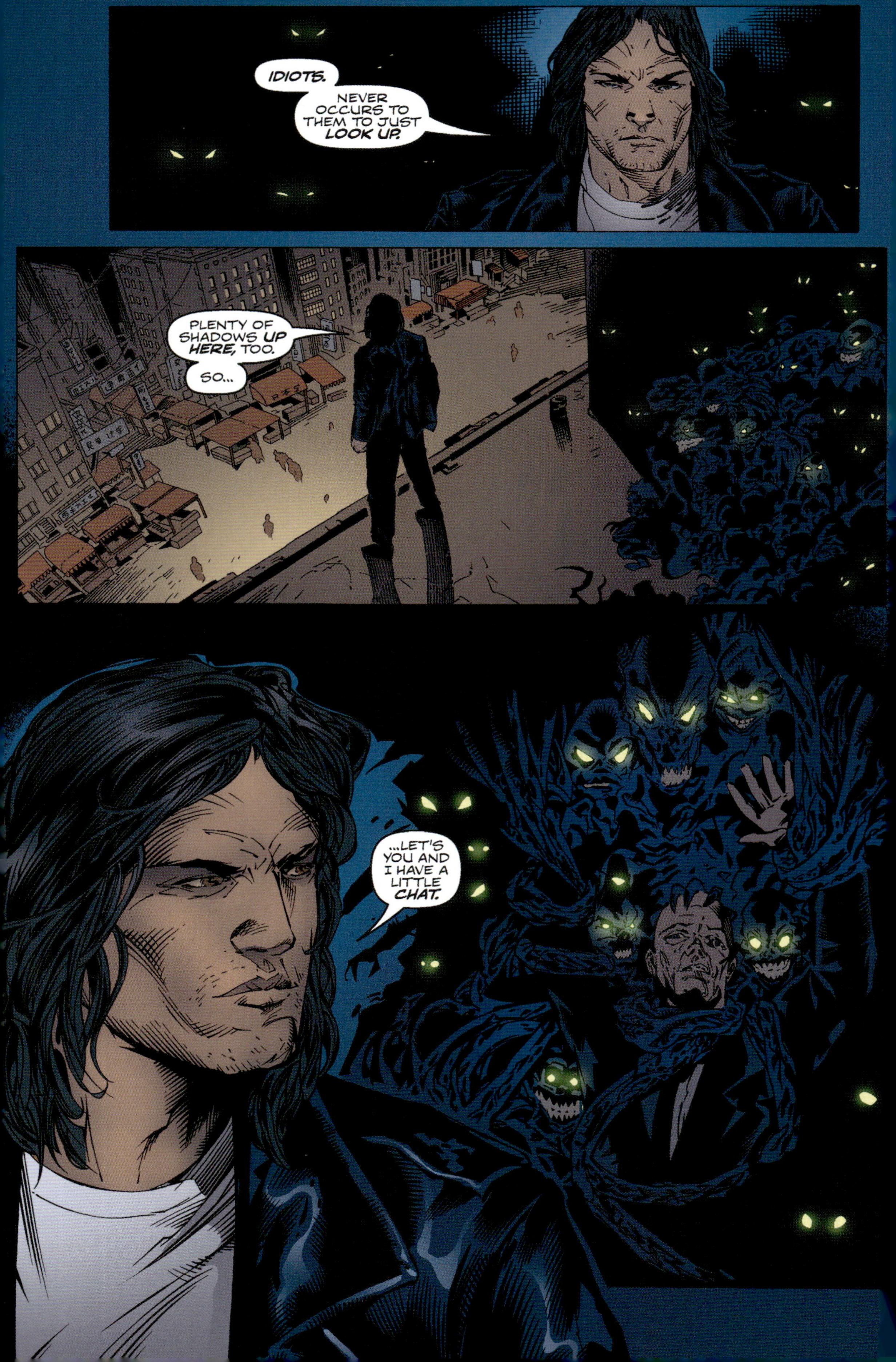
IDIOTS.
NEVER OCCURS TO THEM TO JUST LOOK UP.
PLENTY OF SHADOWS UP HERE, TOO.
SO...
...LET'S YOU AND I HAVE A LITTLE CHAT.

The Darkness Issue #53
cover art by: Dale Keown and Matt Milla

THE DARKNESS #53

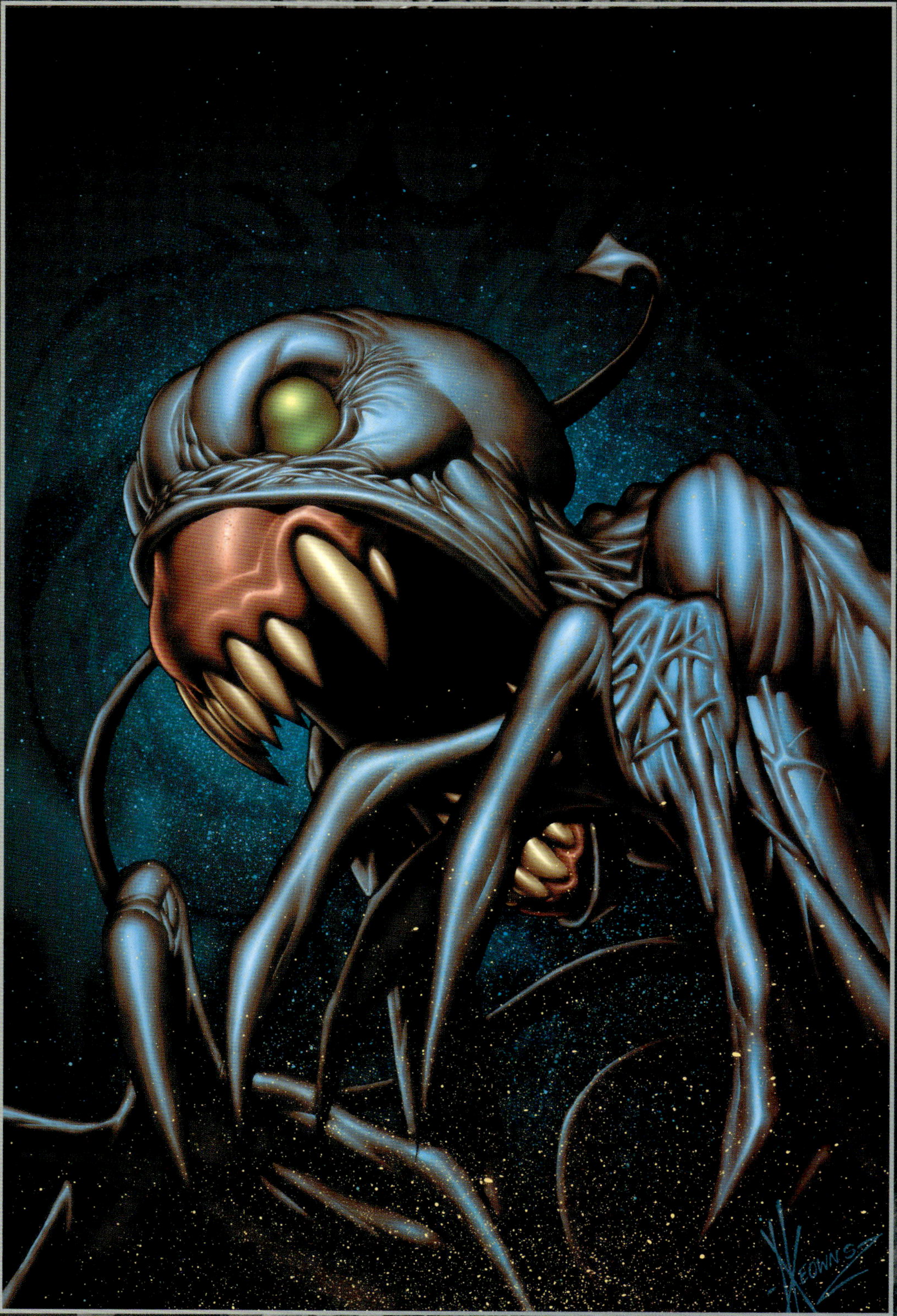
KEOWN

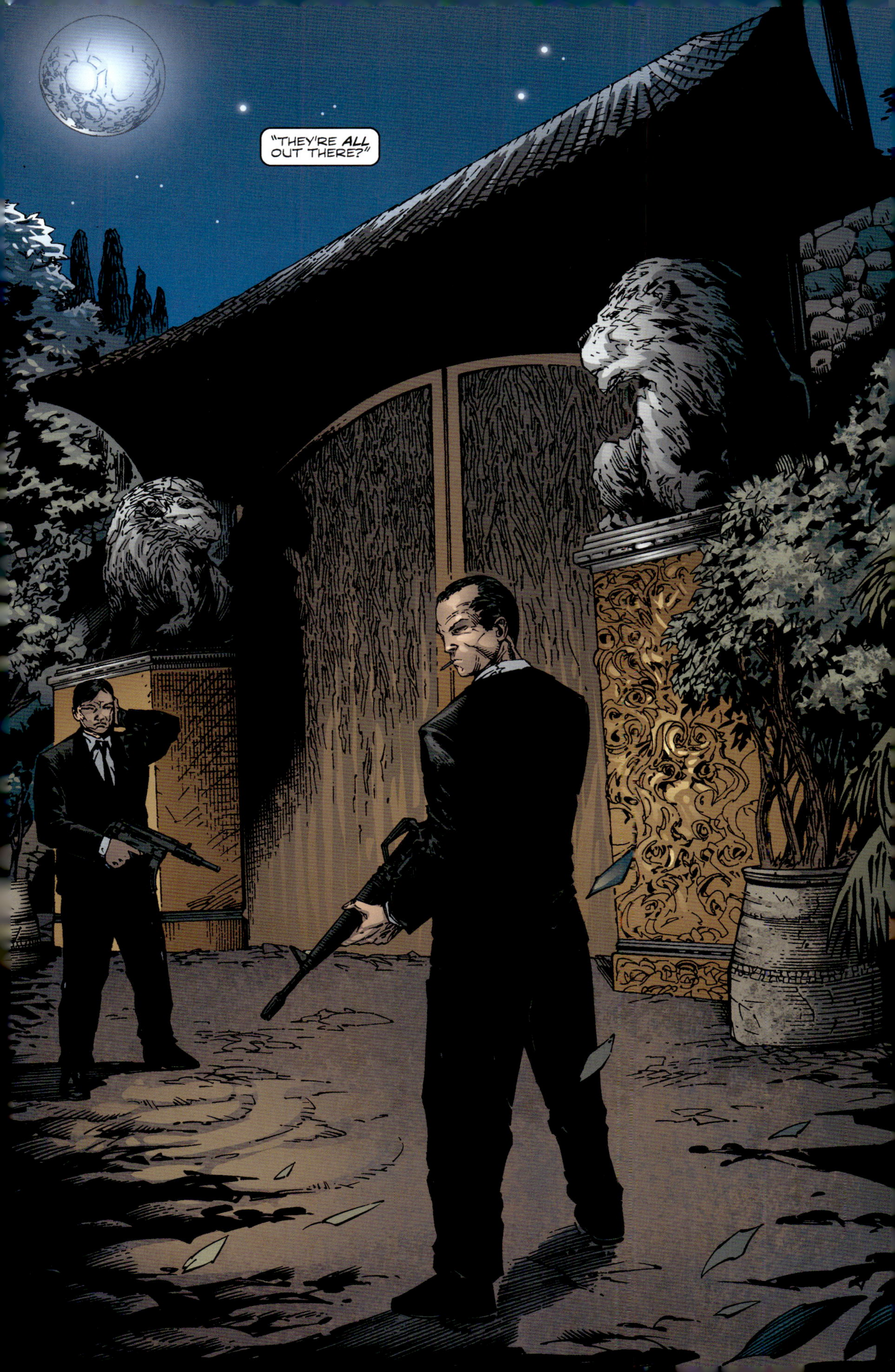
"THEY'RE ALL OUT THERE?"

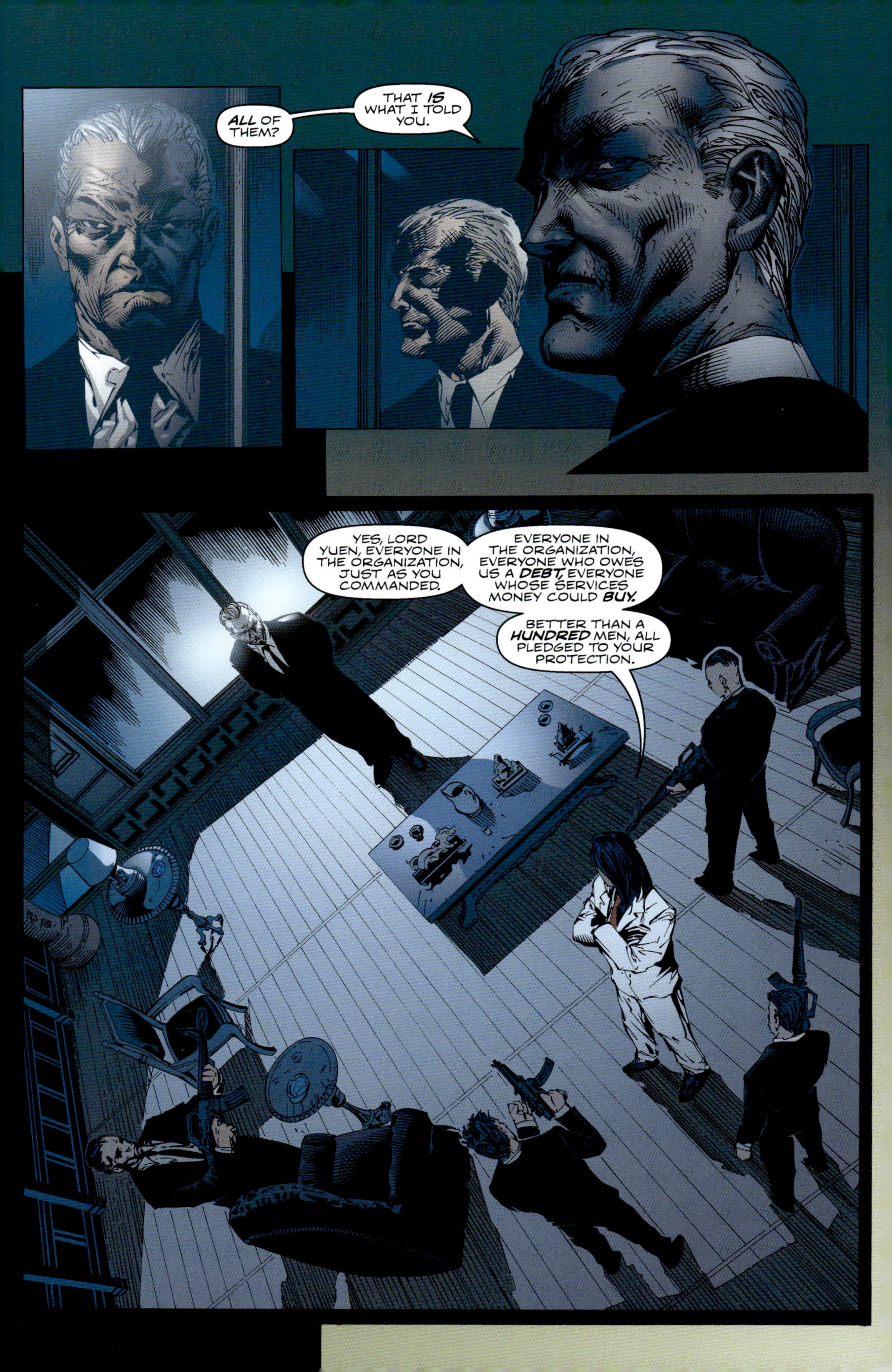
ALL OF THEM?
THAT IS WHAT I TOLD YOU.
YES, LORD YUEN, EVERYONE IN THE ORGANIZATION, JUST AS YOU COMMANDED.
EVERYONE IN THE ORGANIZATION, EVERYONE WHO OWES US A DEBT, EVERYONE WHOSE SERVICES MONEY COULD BUY.
BETTER THAN A HUNDRED MEN, ALL PLEDGED TO YOUR PROTECTION.

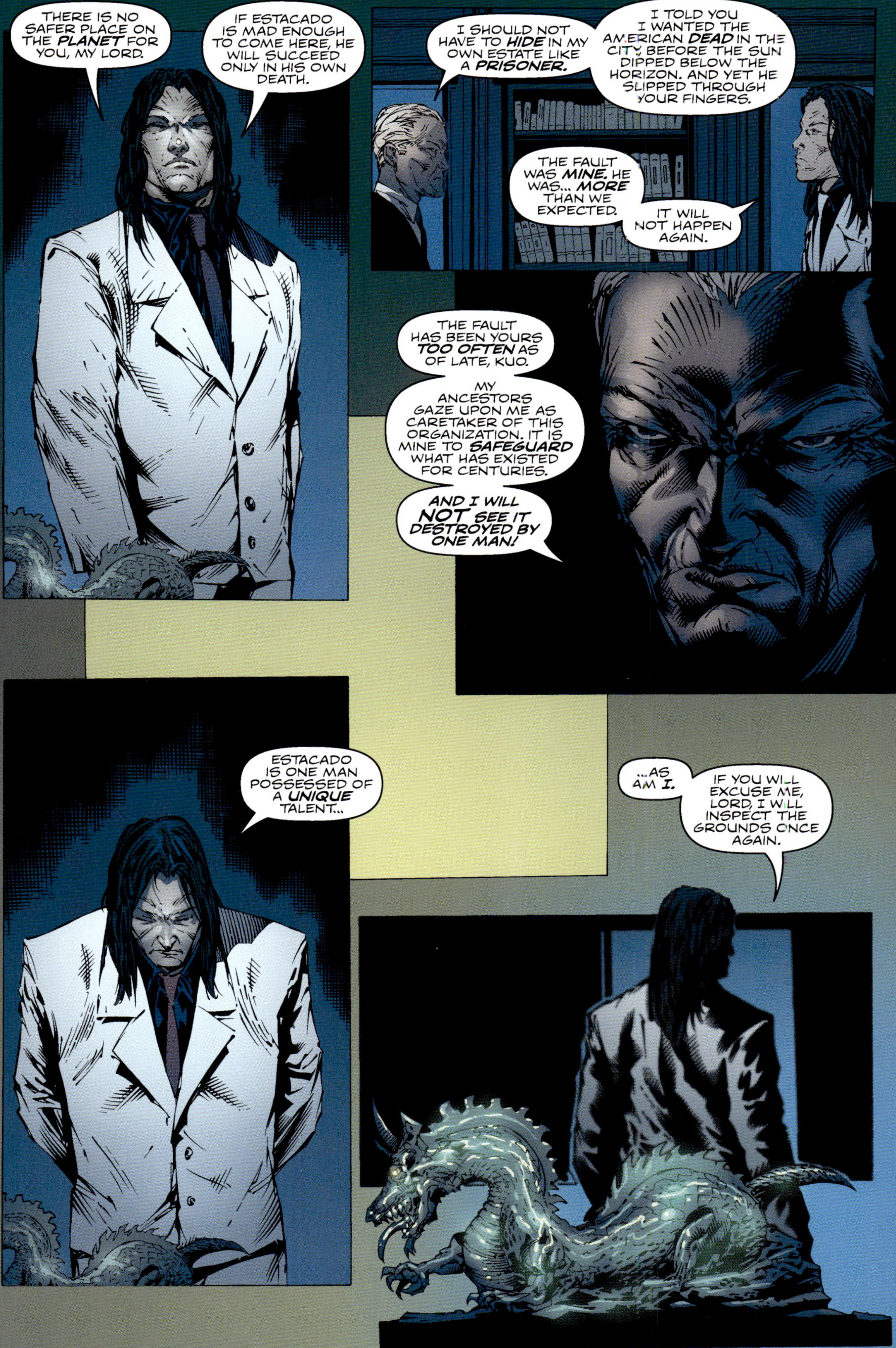
THERE IS NO SAFER PLACE ON THE PLANET FOR YOU, MY LORD.
IF ESTACADO IS MAD ENOUGH TO COME HERE, HE WILL SUCCEED ONLY IN HIS OWN DEATH.
I SHOULD NOT HAVE TO HIDE IN MY OWN ESTATE LIKE A PRISONER.
I TOLD YOU I WANTED THE AMERICAN DEAD IN THE CITY BEFORE THE SUN DIPPED BELOW THE HORIZON. AND YET HE SLIPPED THROUGH YOUR FINGERS.
THE FAULT WAS MINE. HE WAS... MORE THAN WE EXPECTED.
IT WILL NOT HAPPEN AGAIN.
THE FAULT HAS BEEN YOURS TOO OFTEN AS OF LATE, KUO.
MY ANCESTORS GAZE UPON ME AS CARETAKER OF THIS ORGANIZATION. IT IS MINE TO SAFEGUARD WHAT HAS EXISTED FOR CENTURIES.
AND I WILL NOT SEE IT DESTROYED BY ONE MAN!
ESTACADO IS ONE MAN POSSESSED OF A UNIQUE TALENT...
...AS AM I.
IF YOU WILL EXCUSE ME, LORD, I WILL INSPECT THE GROUNDS ONCE AGAIN.

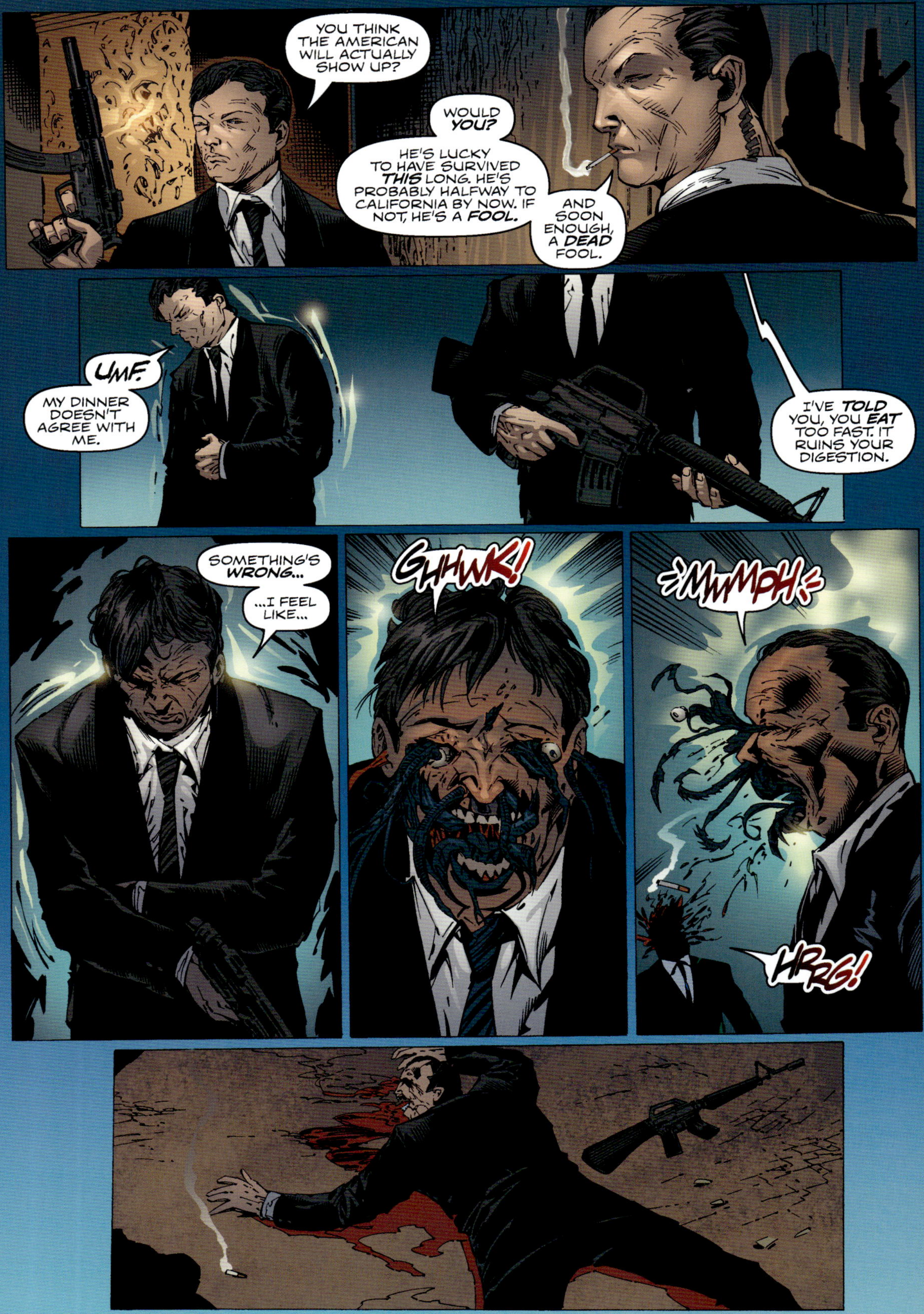
YOU THINK THE AMERICAN WILL ACTUALLY SHOW UP?
WOULD YOU?
HE'S LUCKY TO HAVE SURVIVED THIS LONG. HE'S PROBABLY HALFWAY TO CALIFORNIA BY NOW. IF NOT, HE'S A FOOL.
AND SOON ENOUGH, A DEAD FOOL.
UMF.
MY DINNER DOESN'T AGREE WITH ME.
I'VE TOLD YOU, YOU EAT TOO FAST. IT RUINS YOUR DIGESTION.
SOMETHING'S WRONG...
...I FEEL LIKE...
GHHWK!
MMMPH
HRRG!

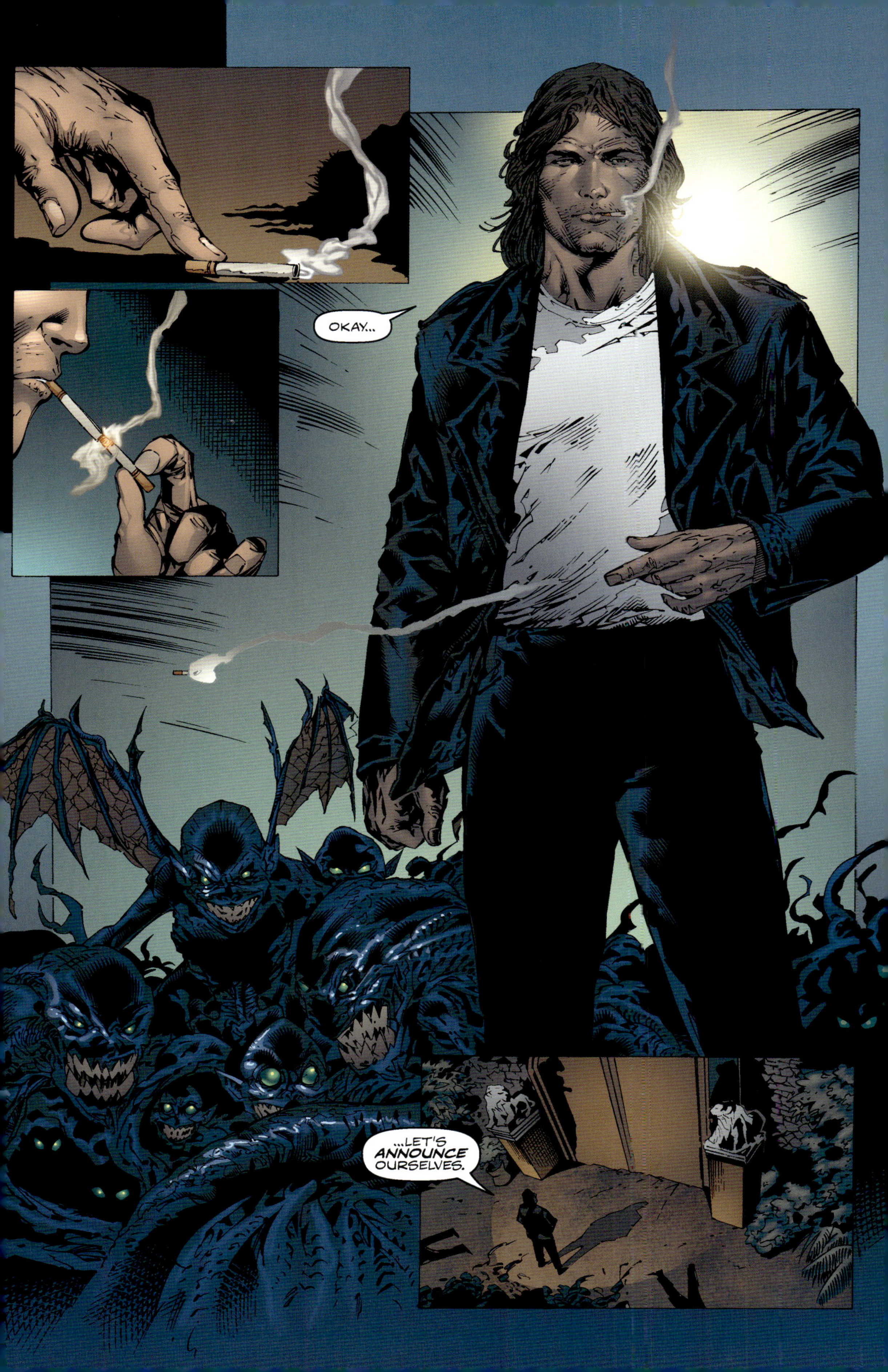
OKAY...
...LET'S ANNOUNCE OURSELVES.

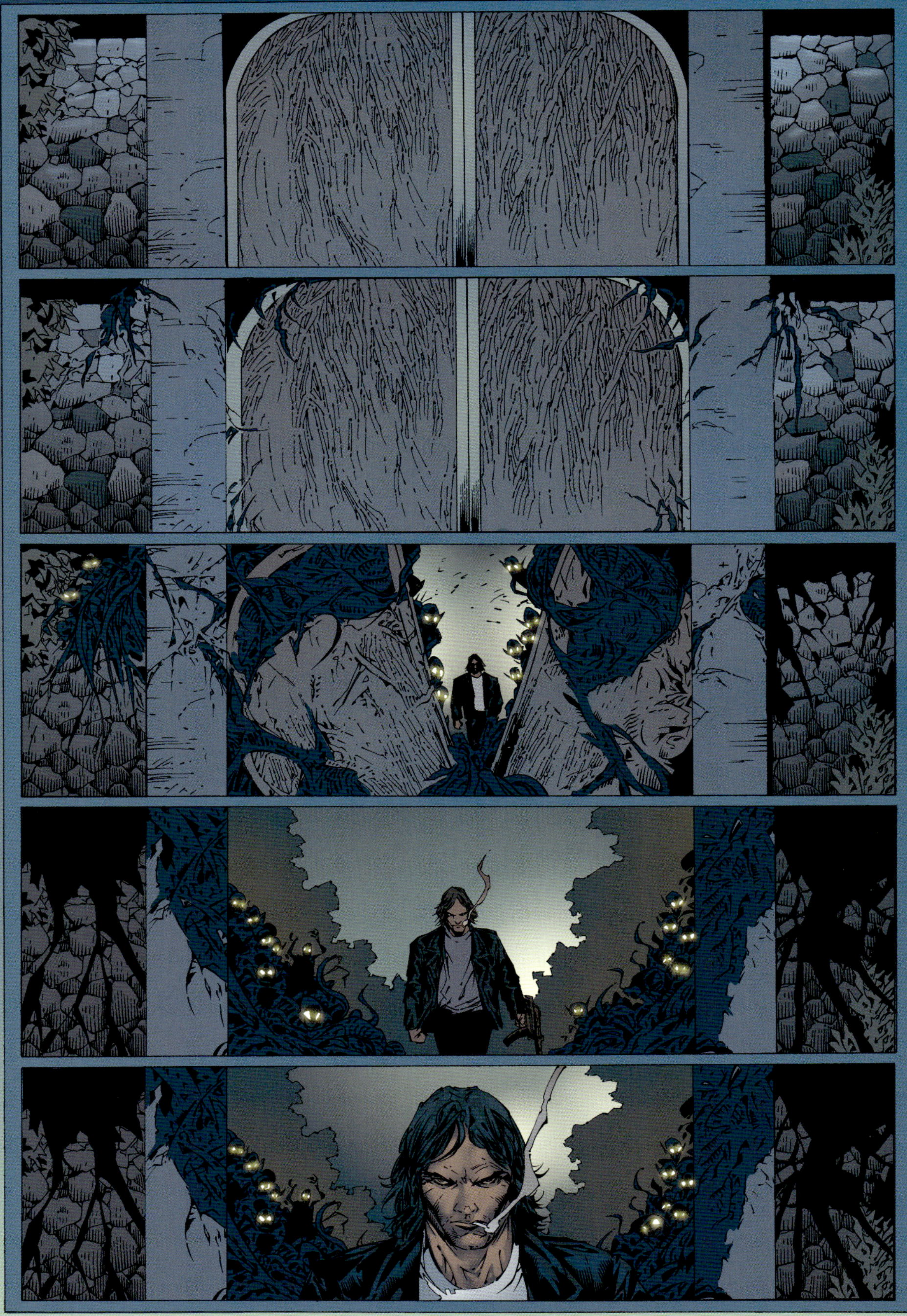

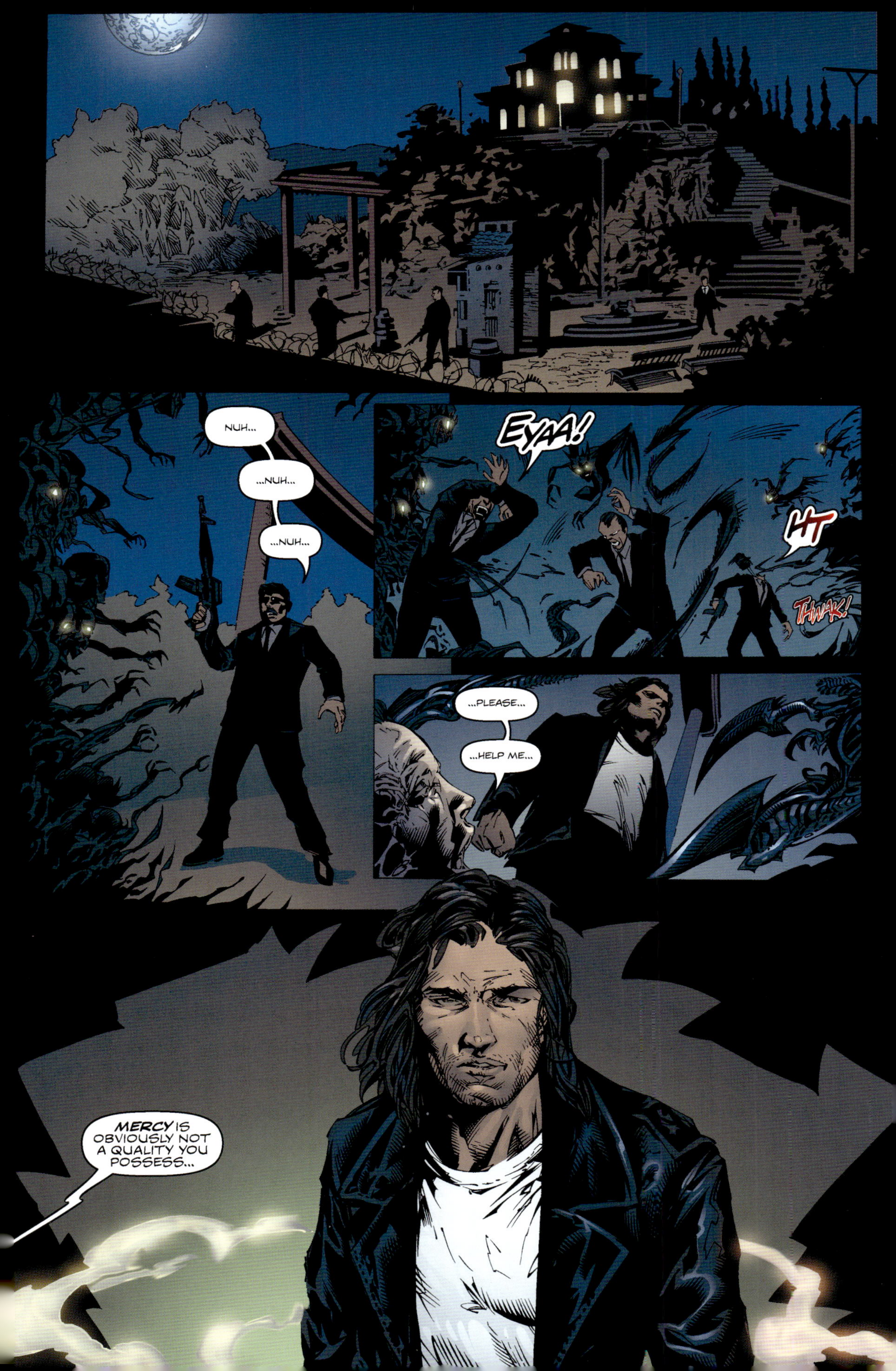
NUH...
...NUH...
...NUH...
EYAA!
HT
THWAK!
...PLEASE...
...HELP ME...
MERCY IS OBVIOUSLY NOT A QUALITY YOU POSSESS...

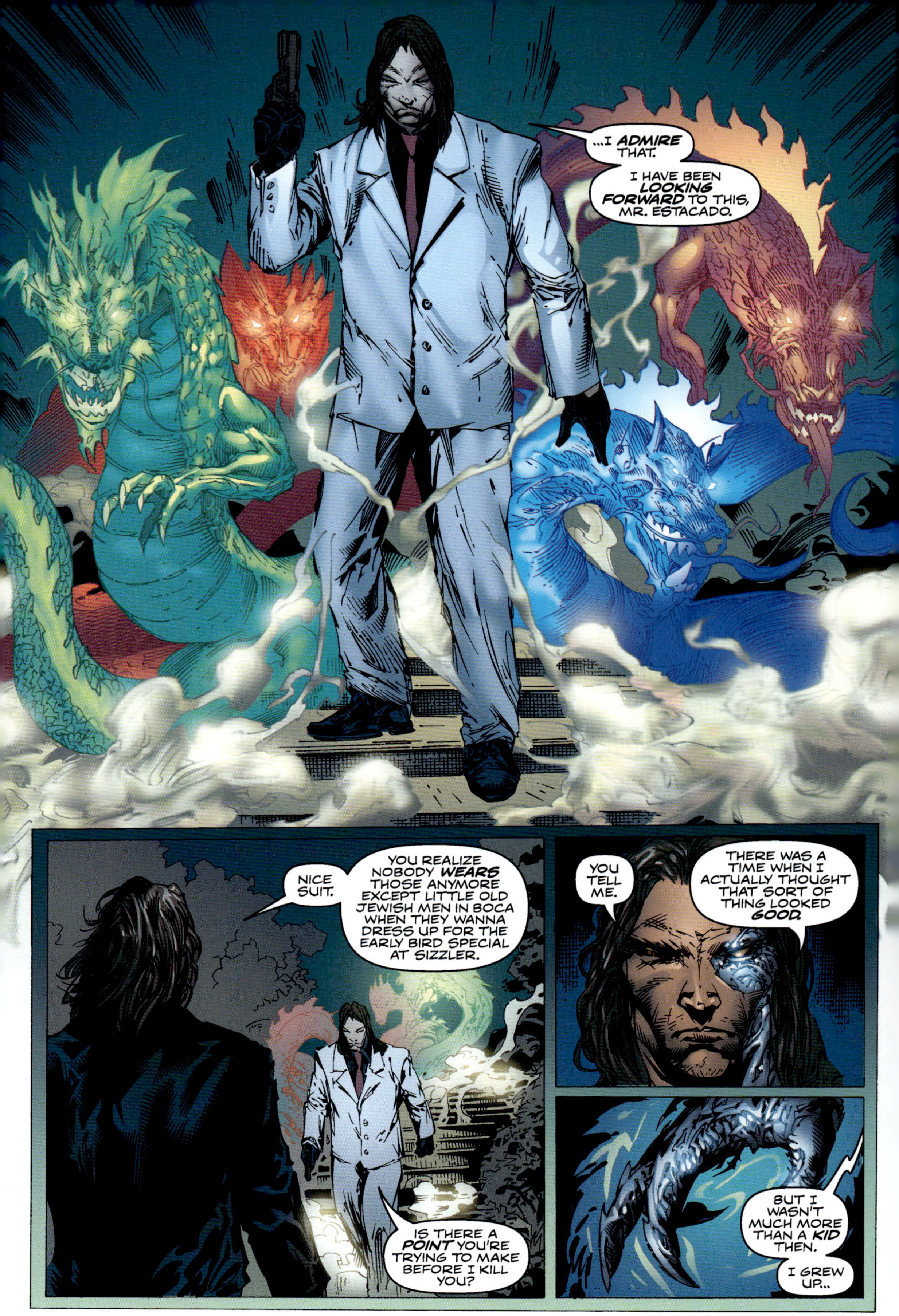
...I ADMIRE THAT.
I HAVE BEEN LOOKING FORWARD TO THIS, MR. ESTACADO.
NICE SUIT.
YOU REALIZE NOBODY WEARS THOSE ANYMORE EXCEPT LITTLE OLD JEWISH MEN IN BOCA WHEN THEY WANNA DRESS UP FOR THE EARLY BIRD SPECIAL AT SIZZLER.
IS THERE A POINT YOU'RE TRYING TO MAKE BEFORE I KILL YOU?
YOU TELL ME.
THERE WAS A TIME WHEN I ACTUALLY THOUGHT THAT SORT OF THING LOOKED GOOD.
BUT I WASN'T MUCH MORE THAN A KID THEN.
I GREW UP...

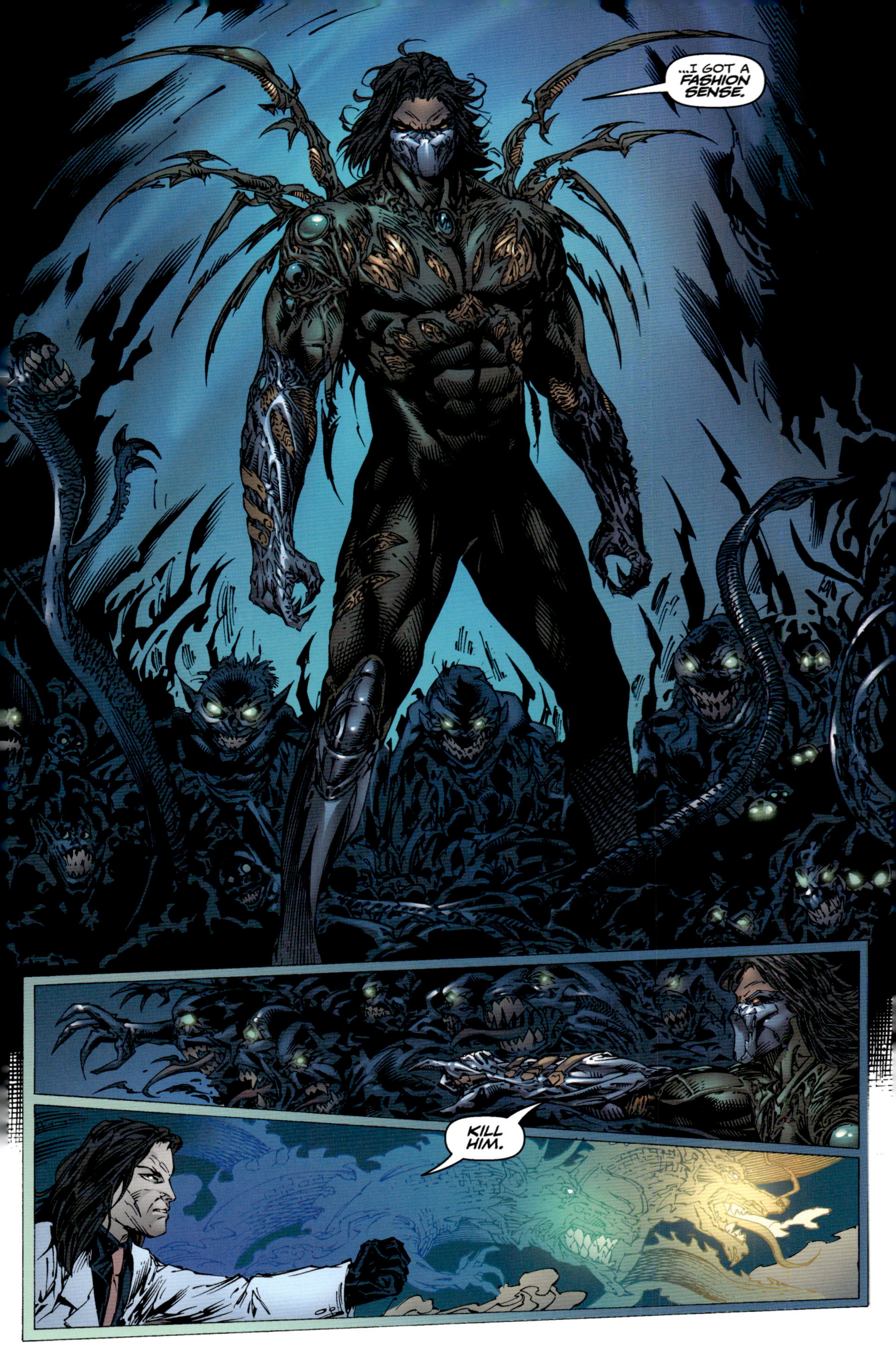
...I GOT A FASHION SENSE.
KILL HIM.

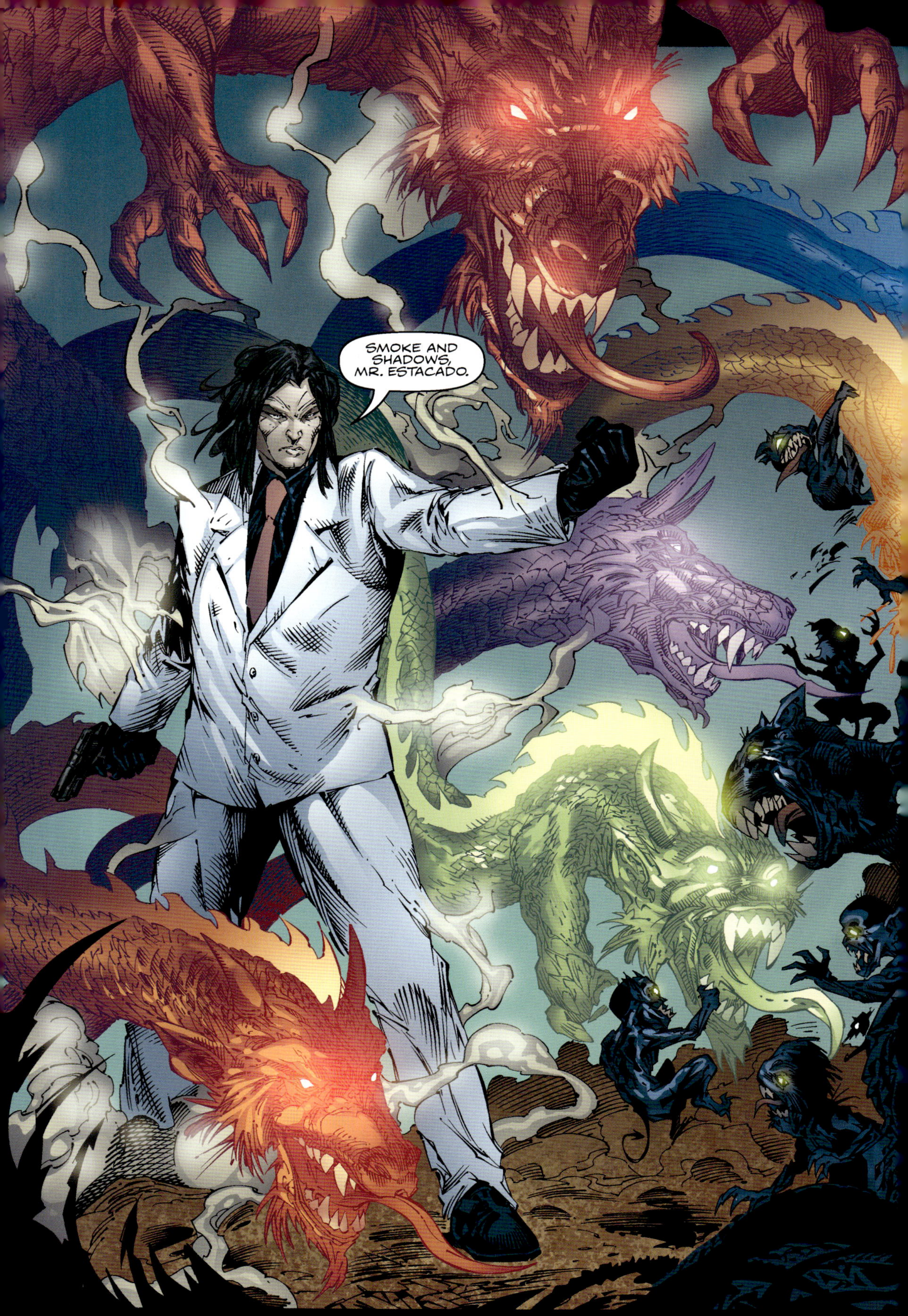
SMOKE AND SHADOWS, MR. ESTACADO.

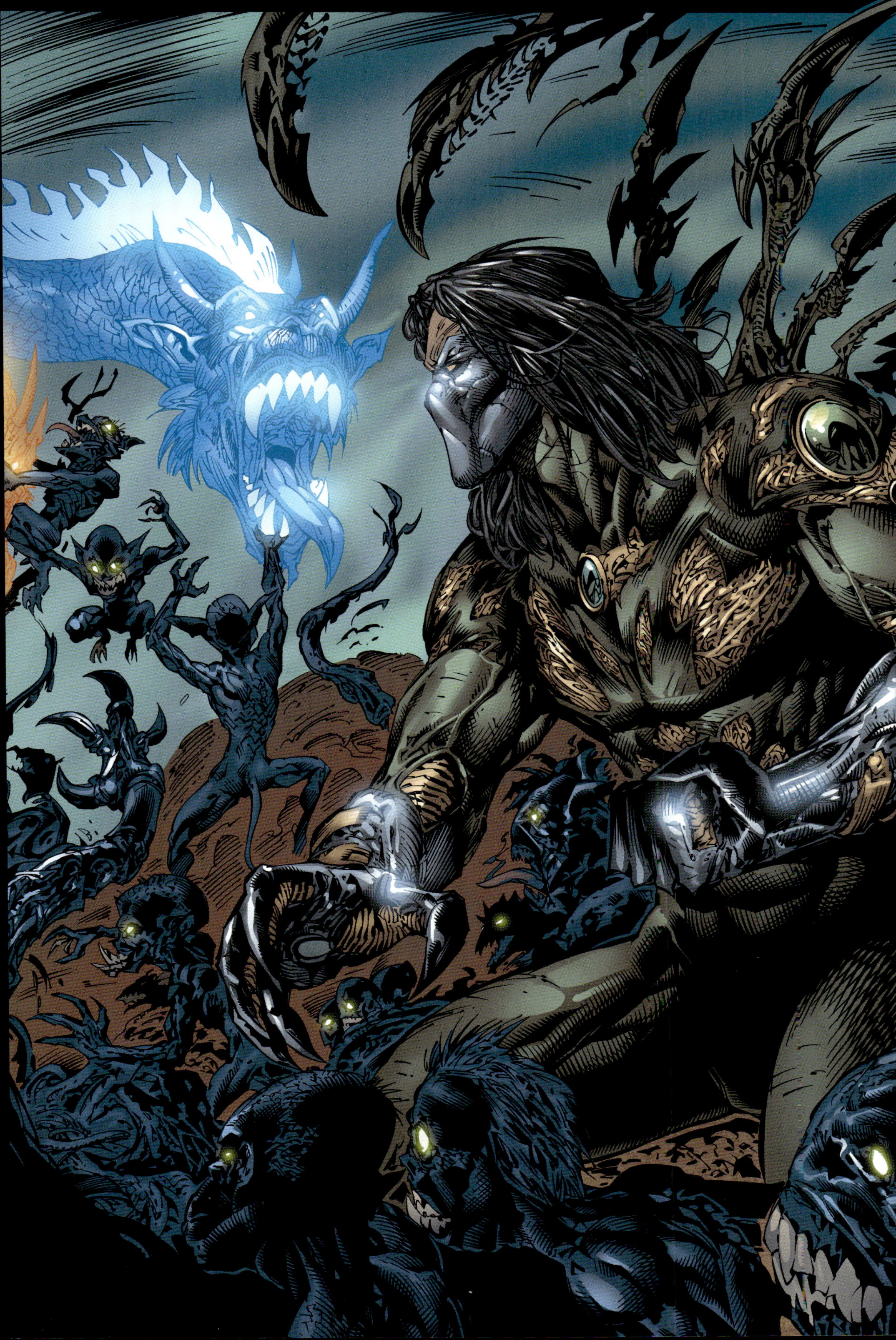

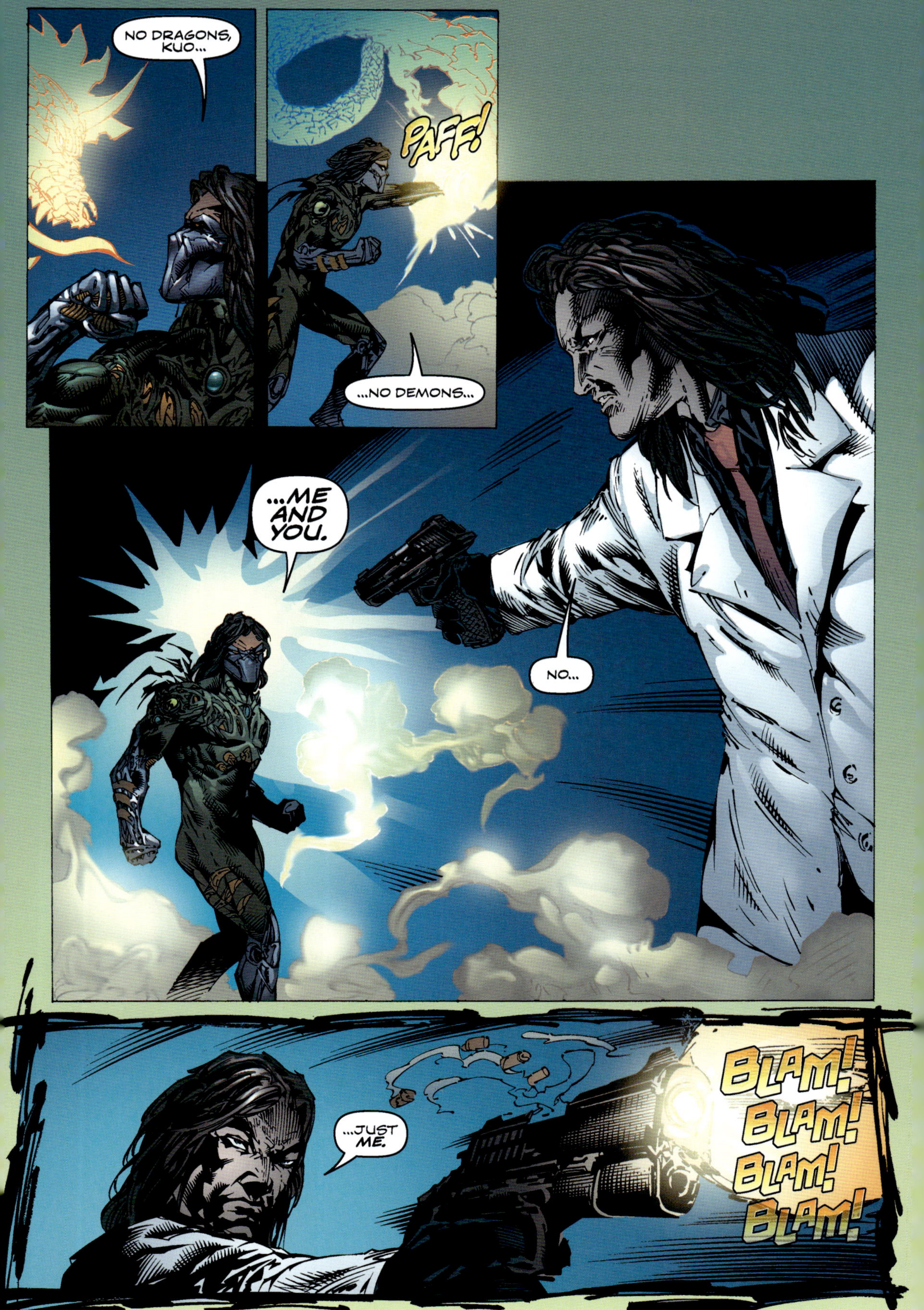
NO DRAGONS, KUO...
PAFF!
...NO DEMONS...
...ME AND YOU.
NO...
...JUST ME.
BLAM!
BLAM!
BLAM!
BLAM!

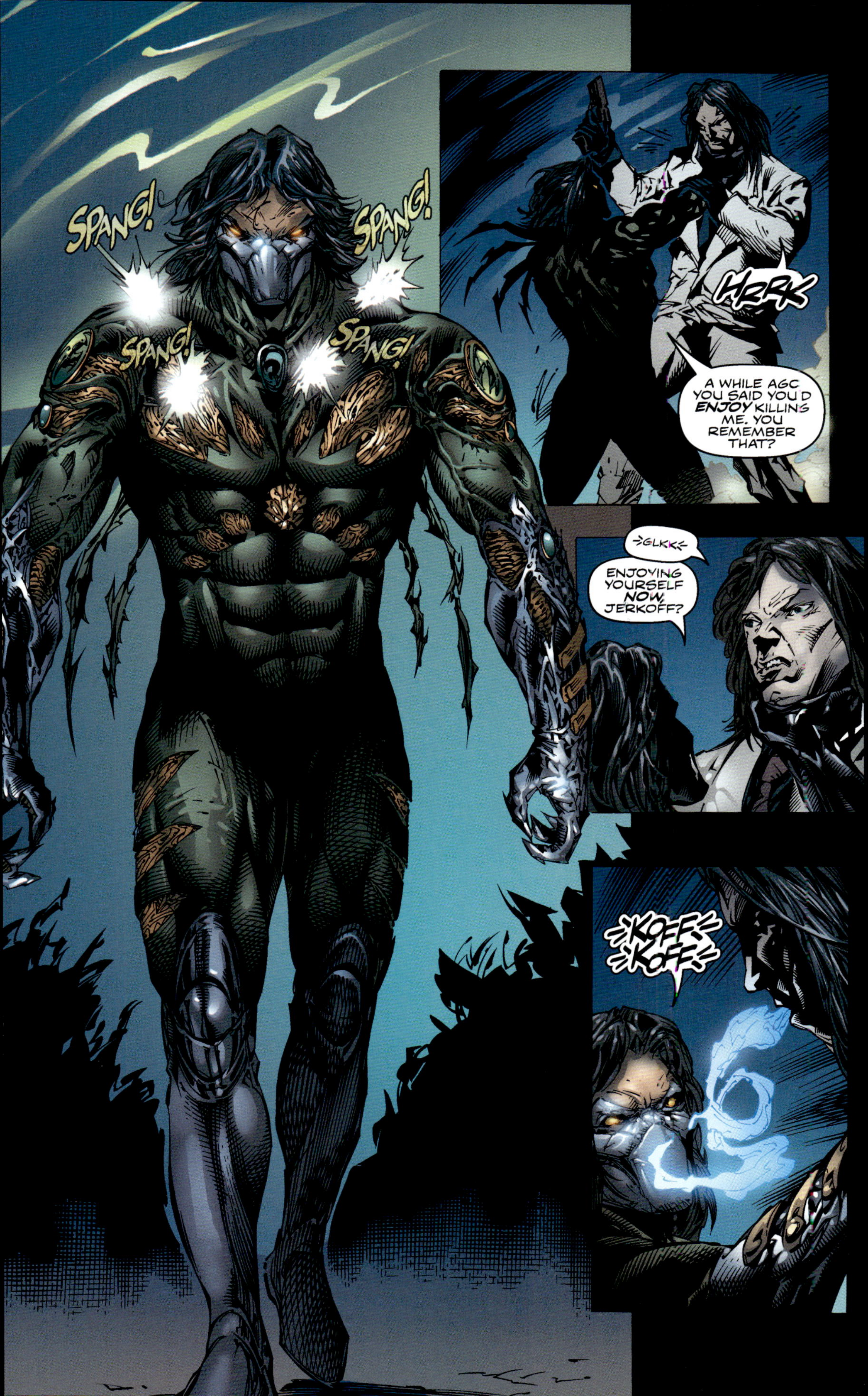
SPANG!
SPANG!
SPANG!
SPANG!
HERK
A WHILE AGO YOU SAID YOU'D ENJOY KILLING ME. YOU REMEMBER THAT?
>GLK<
ENJOYING YOURSELF NOW, JERKOFF?
KOFF KOFF

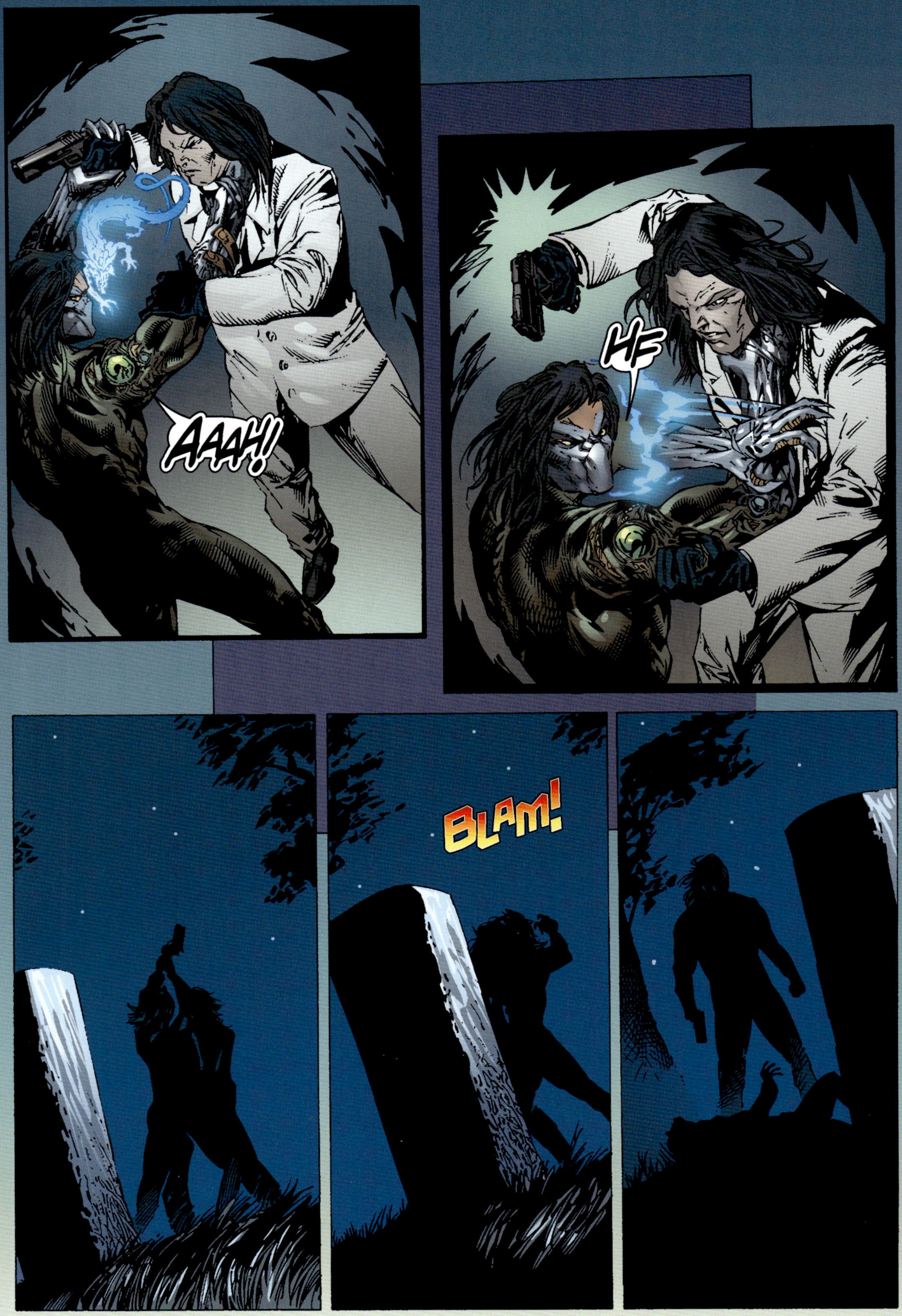
AAAH!
HF
BLAM!

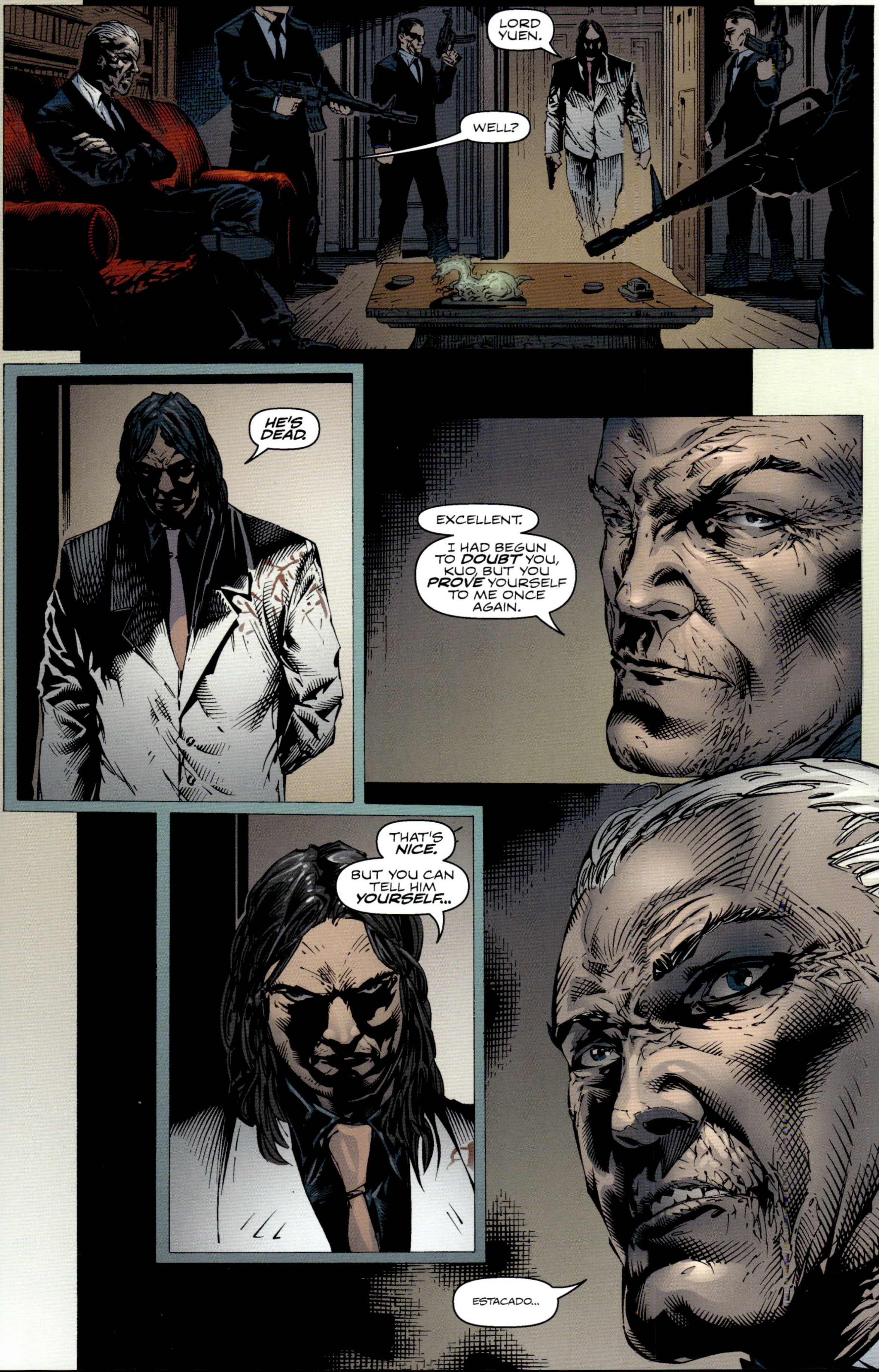
LORD YUEN.
WELL?
HE'S DEAD.
EXCELLENT.
I HAD BEGUN TO DOUBT YOU, KUO, BUT YOU PROVE YOURSELF TO ME ONCE AGAIN.
THAT'S NICE.
BUT YOU CAN TELL HIM YOURSELF...
ESTACADO...

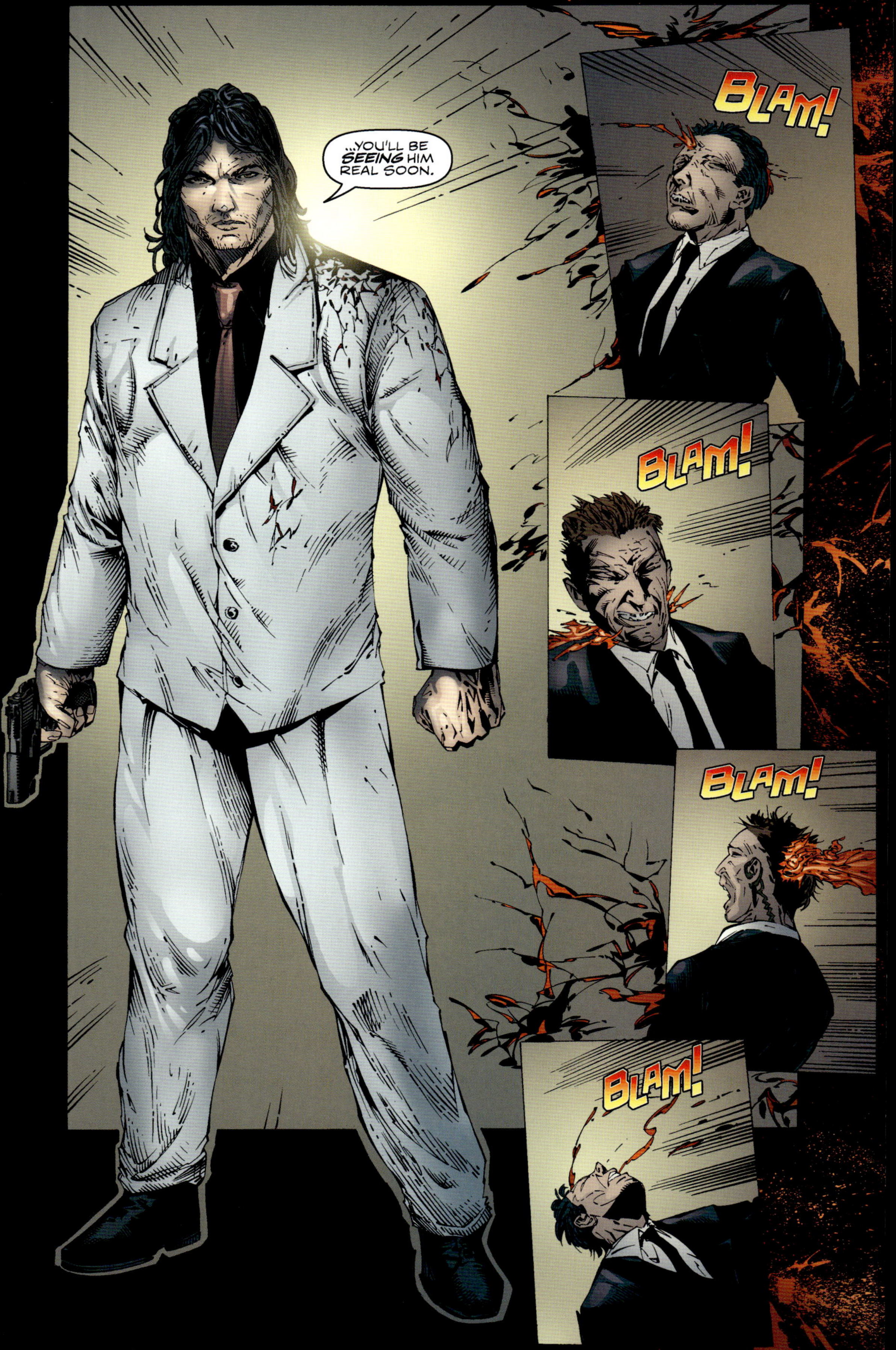
...YOU'LL BE SEEING HIM REAL SOON.
BLAM!
BLAM!
BLAM!
BLAM!

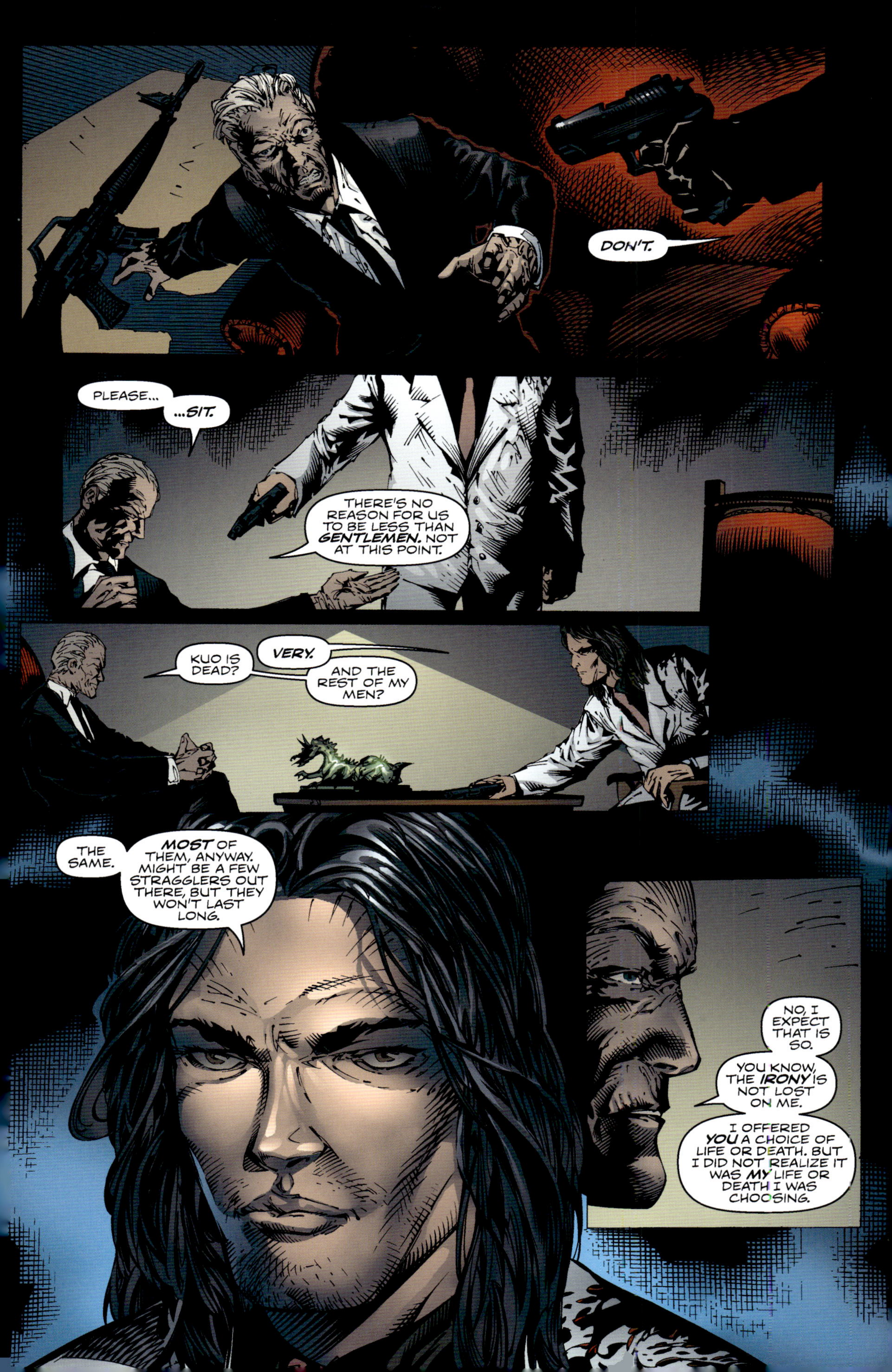
DON'T.
PLEASE...
...SIT.
THERE'S NO REASON FOR US TO BE LESS THAN GENTLEMEN. NOT AT THIS POINT.
KUO IS DEAD?
VERY.
AND THE REST OF MY MEN?
THE SAME.
MOST OF THEM, ANYWAY. MIGHT BE A FEW STRAGGLERS OUT THERE, BUT THEY WON'T LAST LONG.
NO, I EXPECT THAT IS SO.
YOU KNOW, THE IRONY IS NOT LOST ON ME.
I OFFERED YOU A CHOICE OF LIFE OR DEATH. BUT I DID NOT REALIZE IT WAS MY LIFE OR DEATH I WAS CHOOSING.

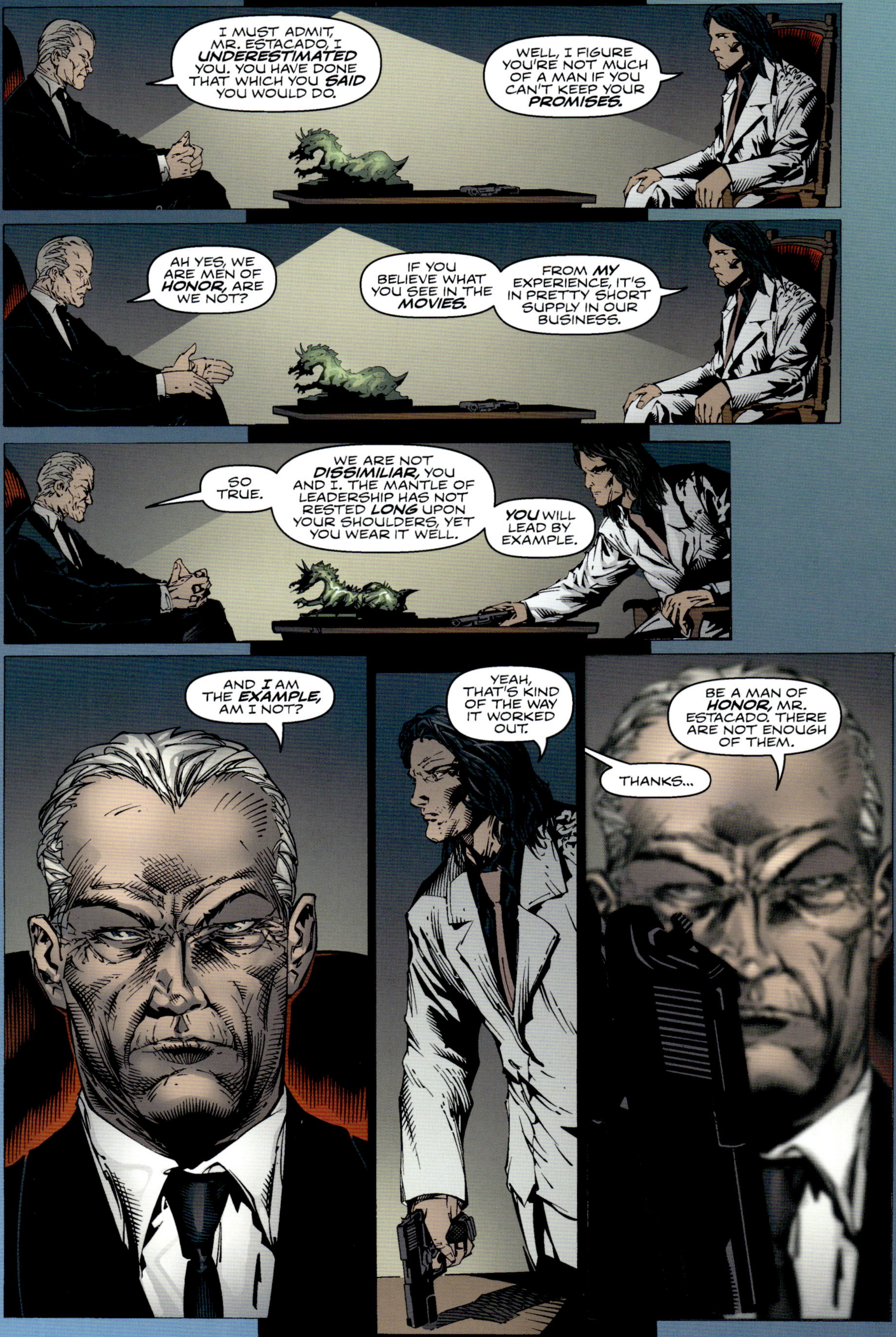
I MUST ADMIT, MR. ESTACADO, I UNDERESTIMATED YOU. YOU HAVE DONE THAT WHICH YOU SAID YOU WOULD DO.
WELL, I FIGURE YOU'RE NOT MUCH OF A MAN IF YOU CAN'T KEEP YOUR PROMISES.
AH YES, WE ARE MEN OF HONOR, ARE WE NOT?
IF YOU BELIEVE WHAT YOU SEE IN THE MOVIES.
FROM MY EXPERIENCE, IT'S IN PRETTY SHORT SUPPLY IN OUR BUSINESS.
SO TRUE.
WE ARE NOT DISSIMILIAR, YOU AND I. THE MANTLE OF LEADERSHIP HAS NOT RESTED LONG UPON YOUR SHOULDERS, YET YOU WEAR IT WELL.
YOU WILL LEAD BY EXAMPLE.
AND I AM THE EXAMPLE, AM I NOT?
YEAH, THAT'S KIND OF THE WAY IT WORKED OUT.
BE A MAN OF HONOR, MR. ESTACADO. THERE ARE NOT ENOUGH OF THEM.
THANKS...

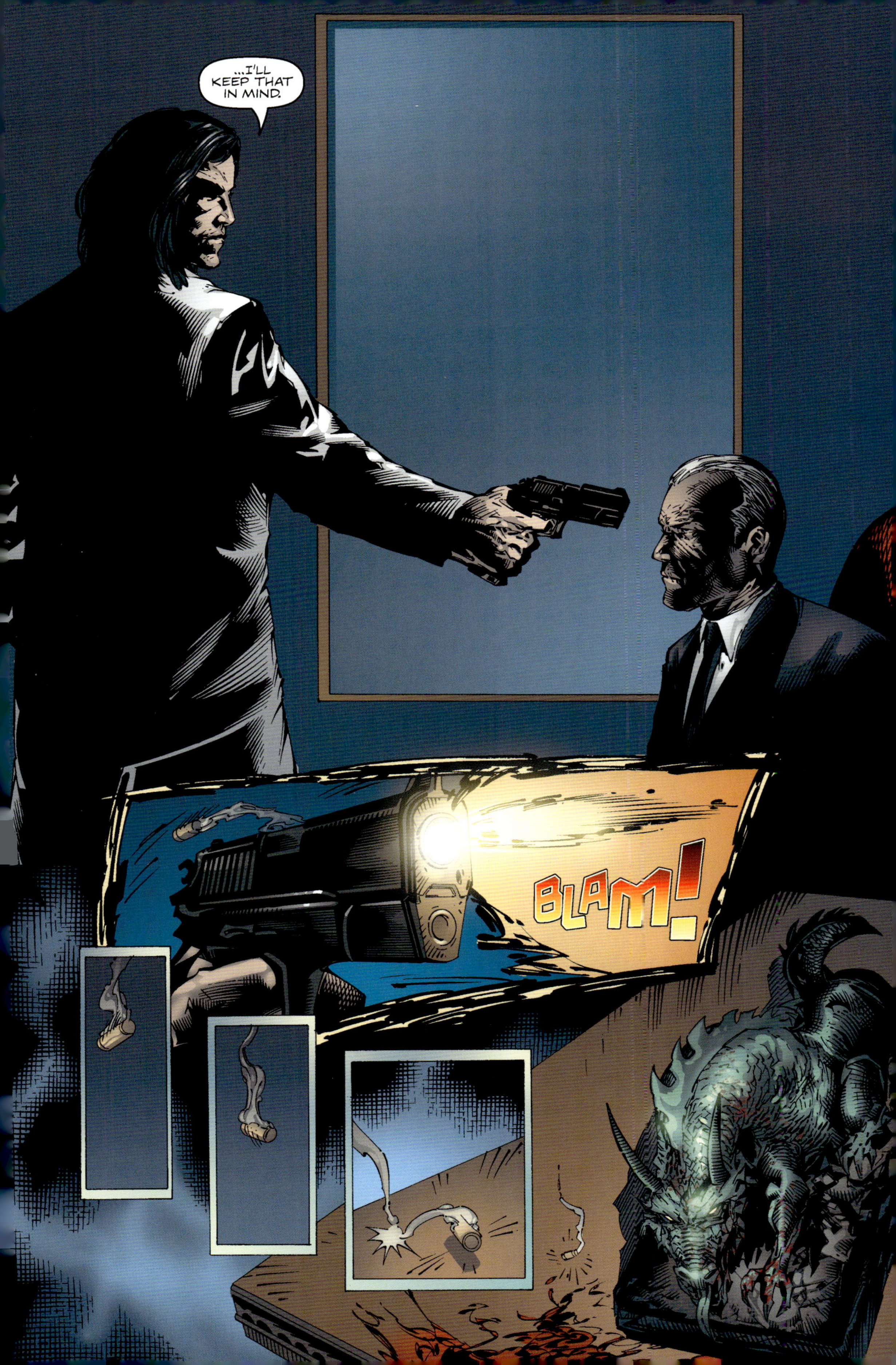
...I'LL KEEP THAT IN MIND.
BLAM!

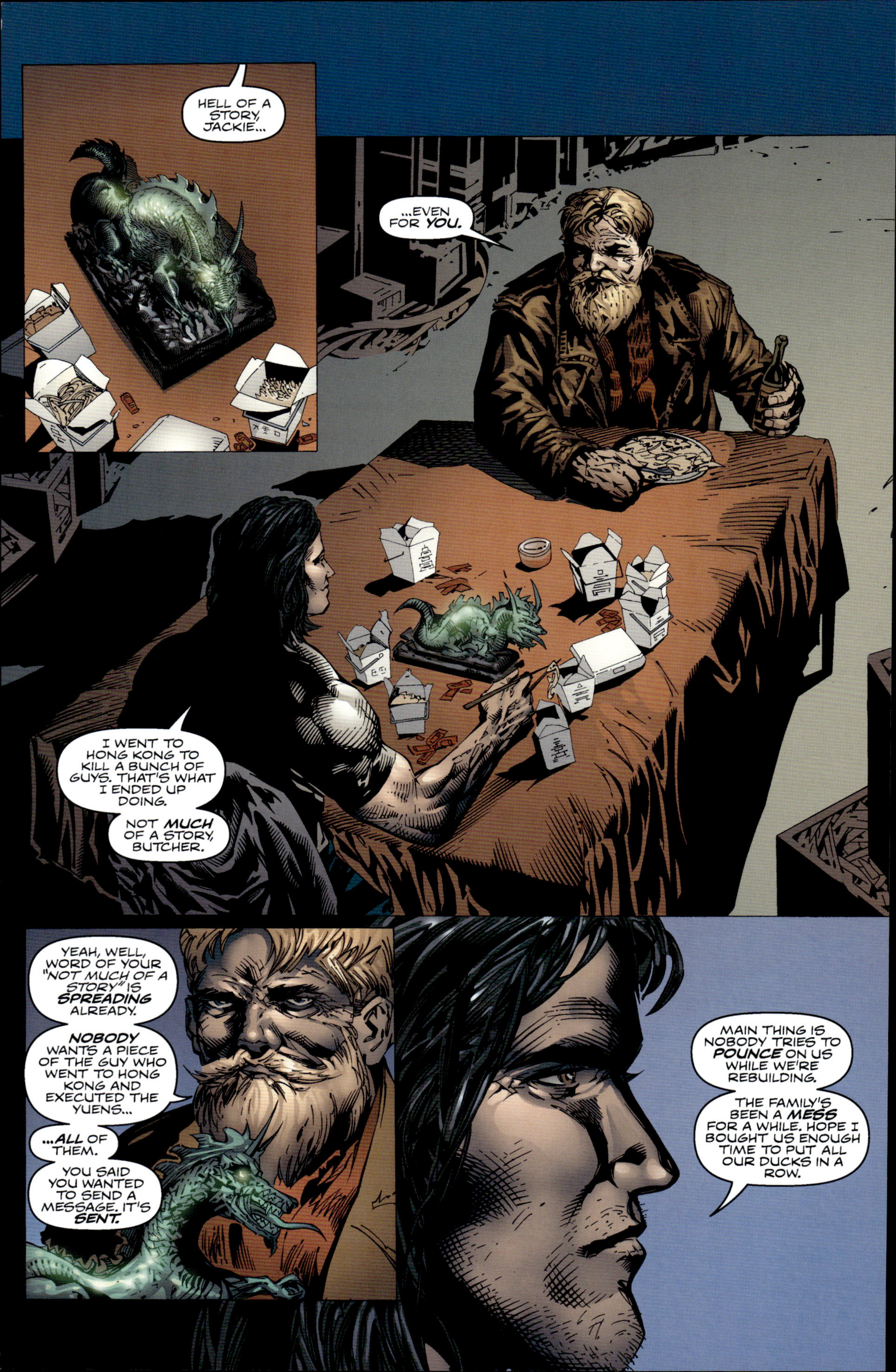
HELL OF A STORY, JACKIE...
...EVEN FOR YOU.
I WENT TO HONG KONG TO KILL A BUNCH OF GUYS. THAT'S WHAT I ENDED UP DOING.
NOT MUCH OF A STORY, BUTCHER.
YEAH, WELL, WORD OF YOUR "NOT MUCH OF A STORY" IS SPREADING ALREADY.
NOBODY WANTS A PIECE OF THE GUY WHO WENT TO HONG KONG AND EXECUTED THE YUENS...
...ALL OF THEM.
YOU SAID YOU WANTED TO SEND A MESSAGE. IT'S SENT.
MAIN THING IS NOBODY TRIES TO POUNCE ON US WHILE WE'RE REBUILDING.
THE FAMILY'S BEEN A MESS FOR A WHILE. HOPE I BOUGHT US ENOUGH TIME TO PUT ALL OUR DUCKS IN A ROW.

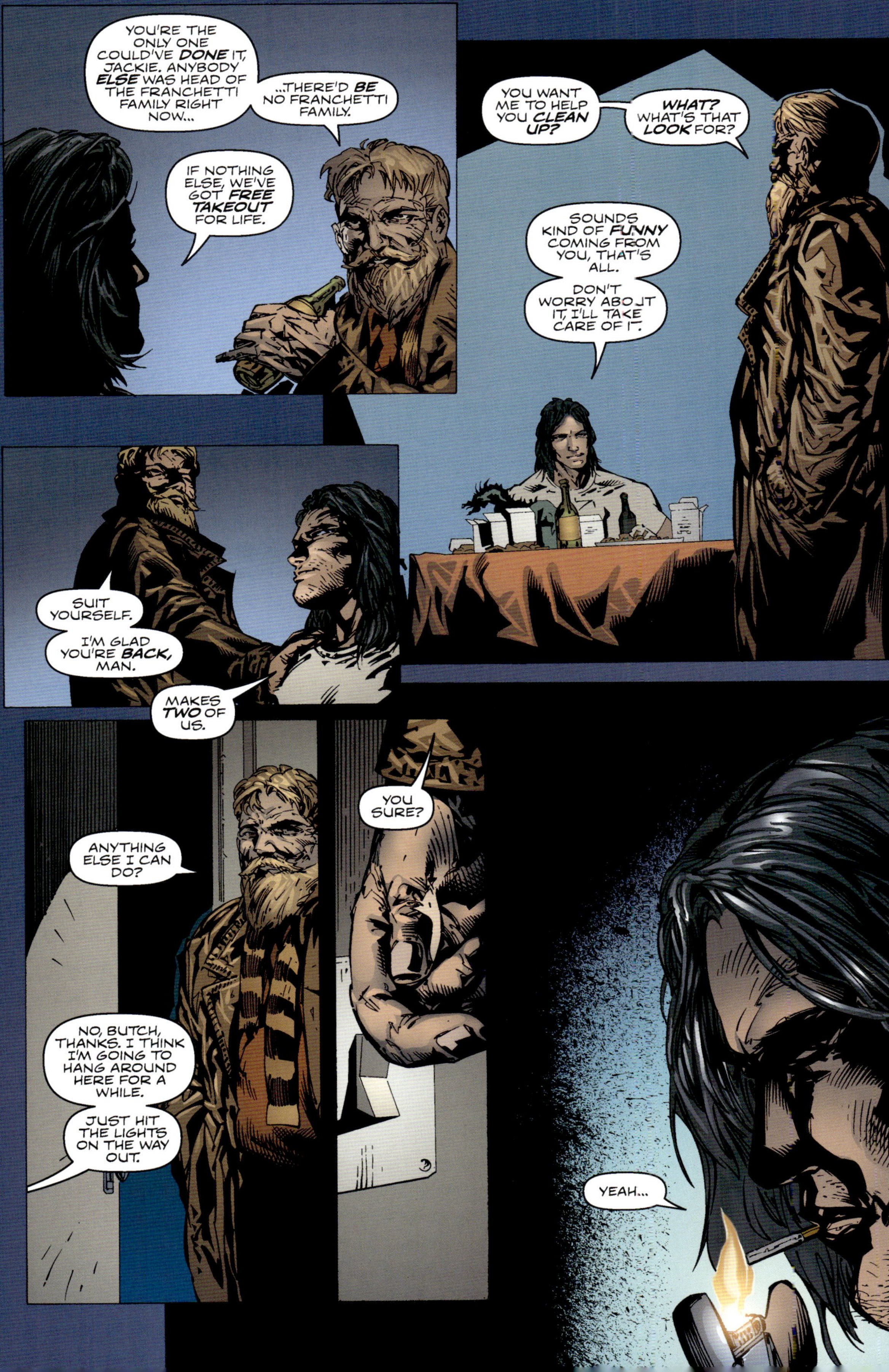

YOU'RE THE ONLY ONE COULD'VE DONE IT, JACKIE. ANYBODY ELSE WAS HEAD OF THE FRANCHETTI FAMILY RIGHT NOW...
...THERE'D BE NO FRANCHETTI FAMILY.
IF NOTHING ELSE, WE'VE GOT FREE TAKEOUT FOR LIFE.
YOU WANT ME TO HELP YOU CLEAN UP?
WHAT? WHAT'S THAT LOOK FOR?
SOUNDS KIND OF FUNNY COMING FROM YOU, THAT'S ALL.
DON'T WORRY ABOUT IT, I'LL TAKE CARE OF IT.
SUIT YOURSELF.
I'M GLAD YOU'RE BACK, MAN.
MAKES TWO OF US.
ANYTHING ELSE I CAN DO?
NO, BUTCH, THANKS. I THINK I'M GOING TO HANG AROUND HERE FOR A WHILE.
JUST HIT THE LIGHTS ON THE WAY OUT.
YOU SURE?
YEAH...

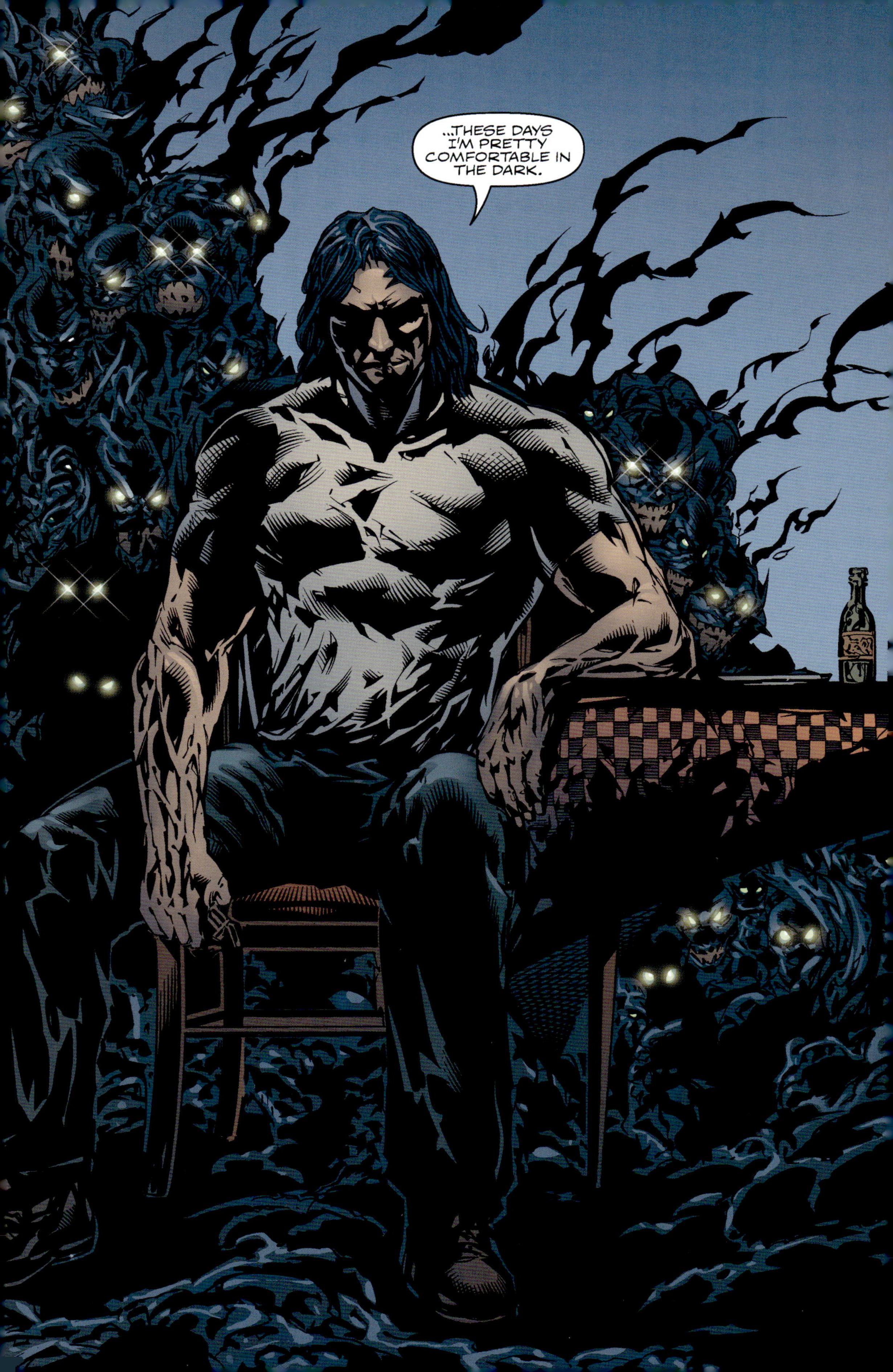
...THESE DAYS I'M PRETTY COMFORTABLE IN THE DARK.

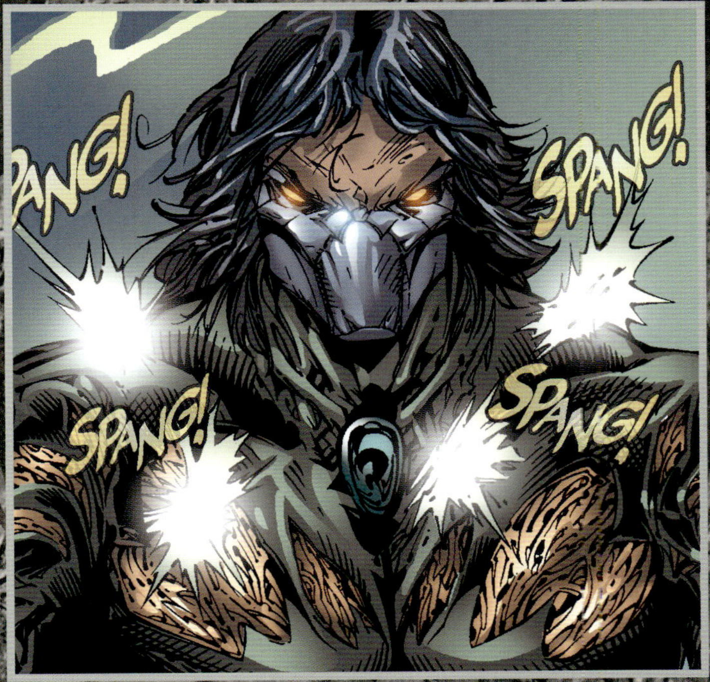
PANG!
SPANG!
SPANG!
SPANG!

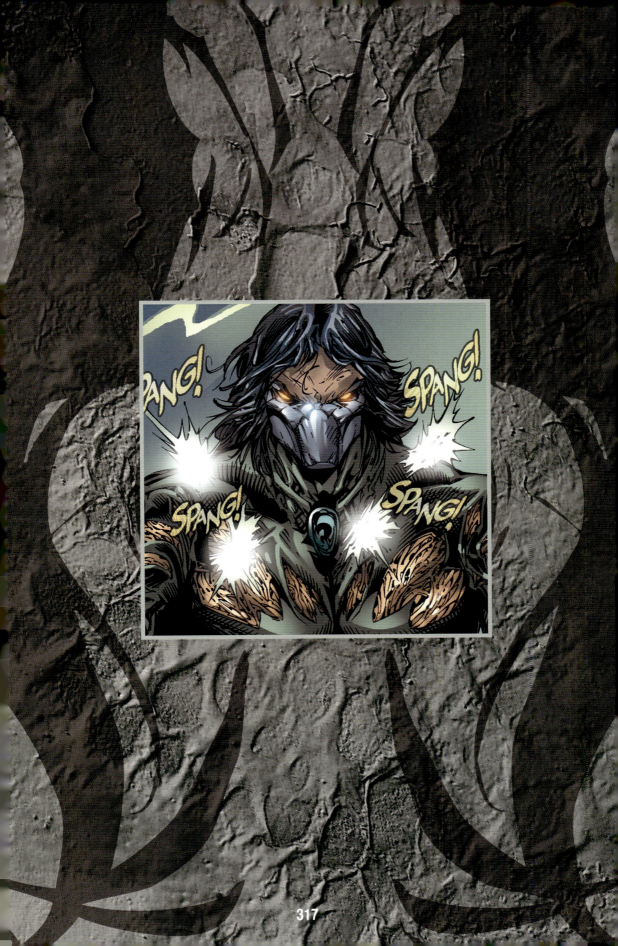

The Darkness Issue #54
cover art by: Dale Keown and Matt Milla

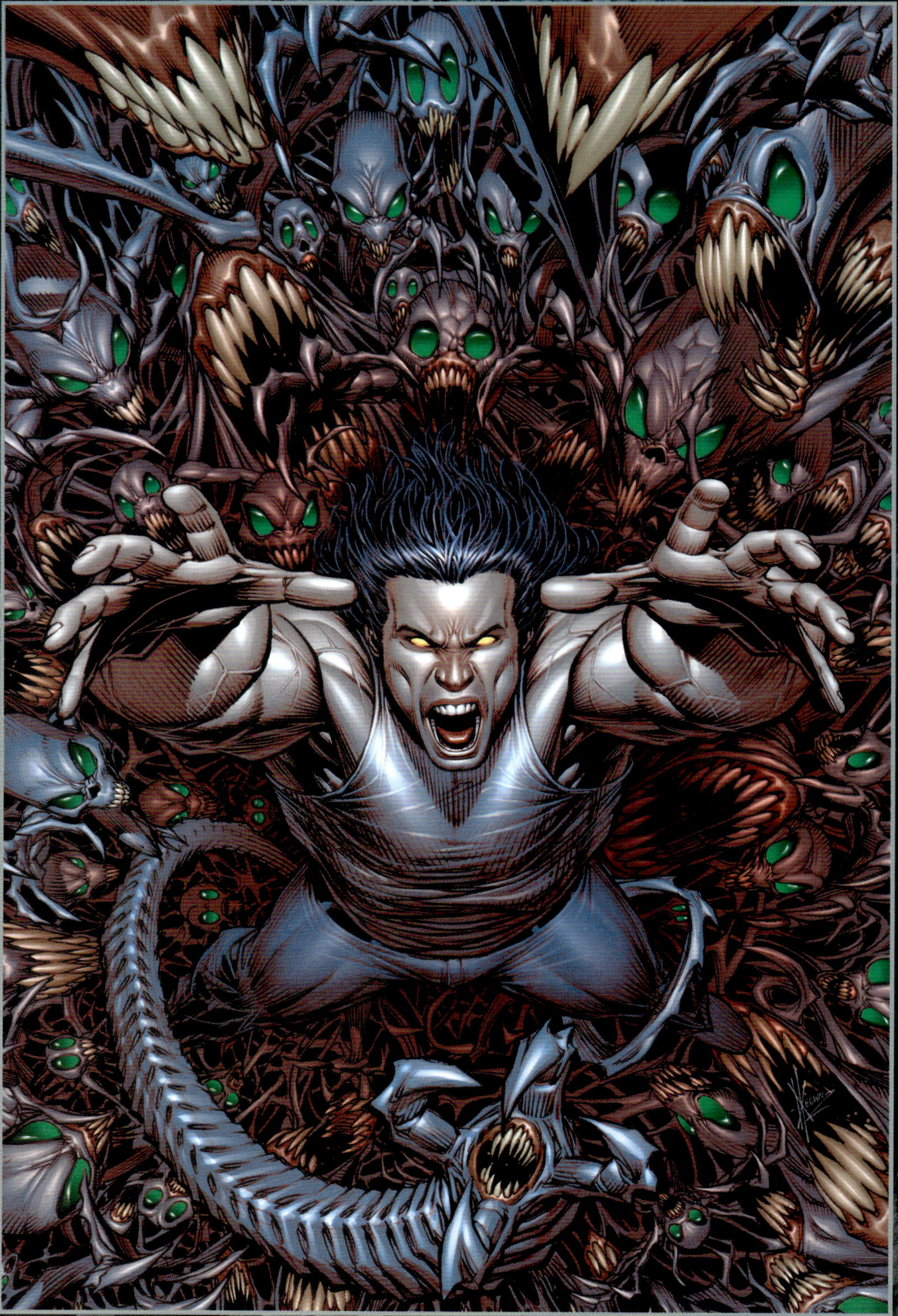

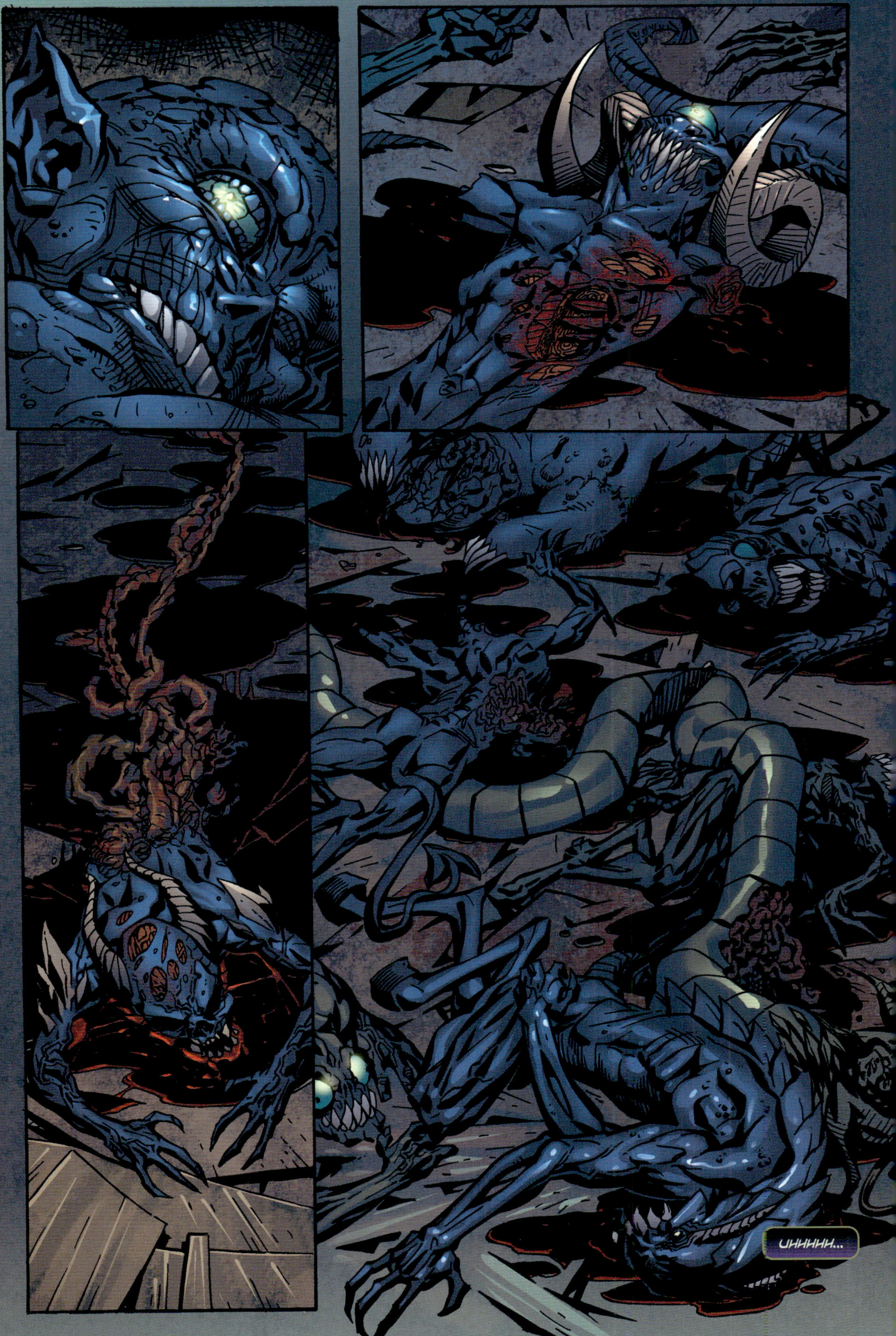
UHHHHH...

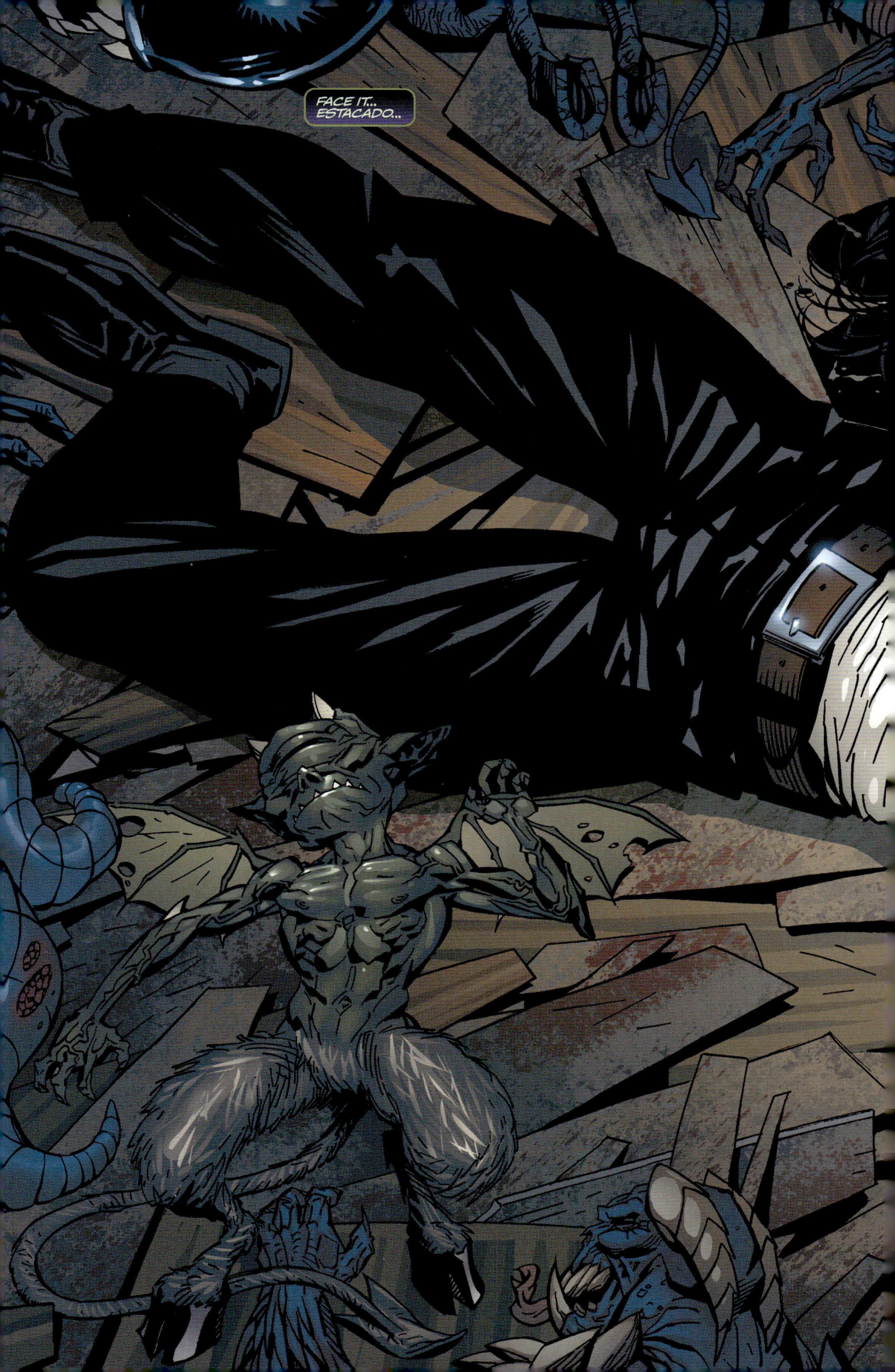
FACE IT...
ESTACADO...

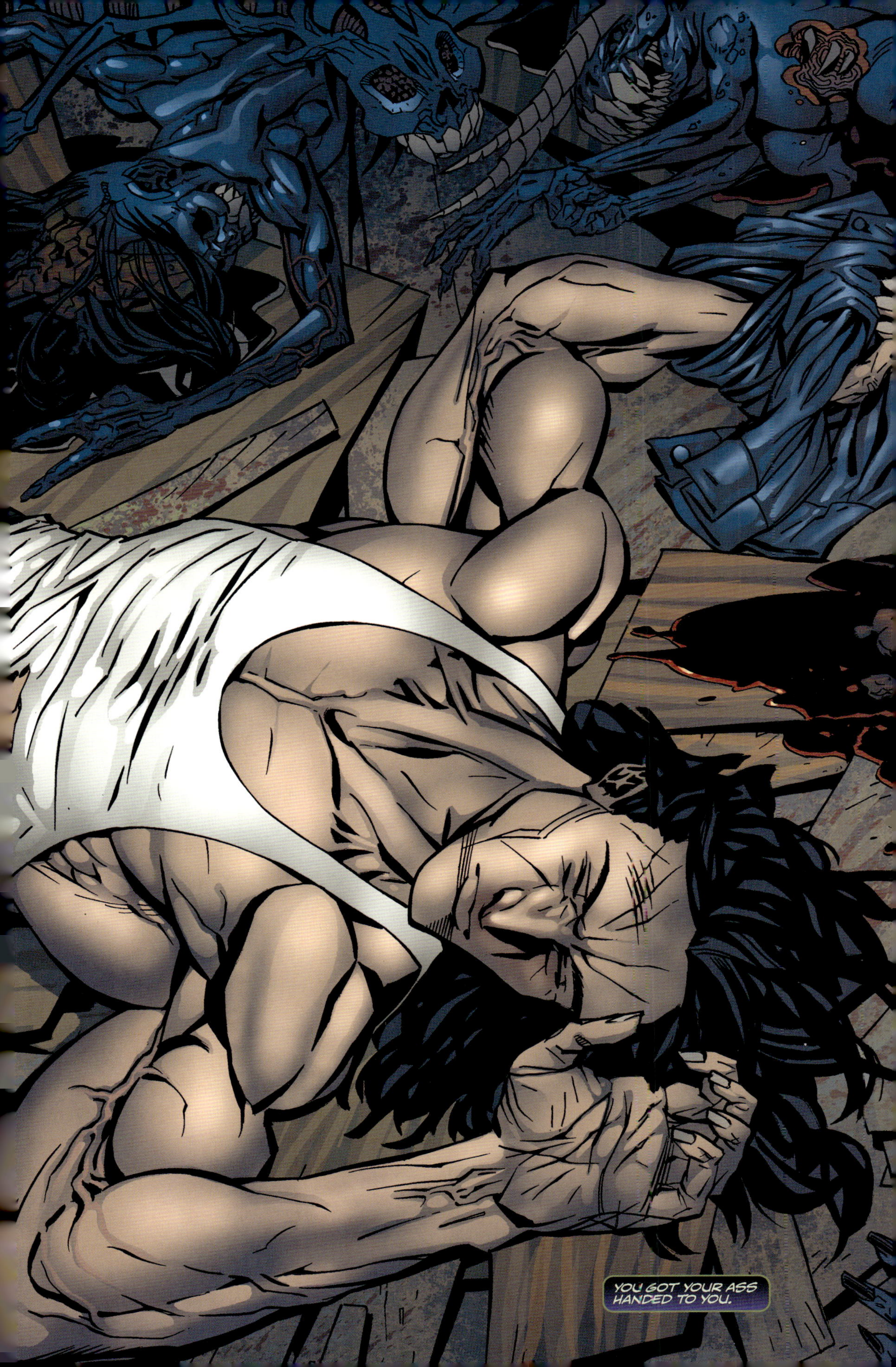
YOU GOT YOUR ASS HANDED TO YOU.

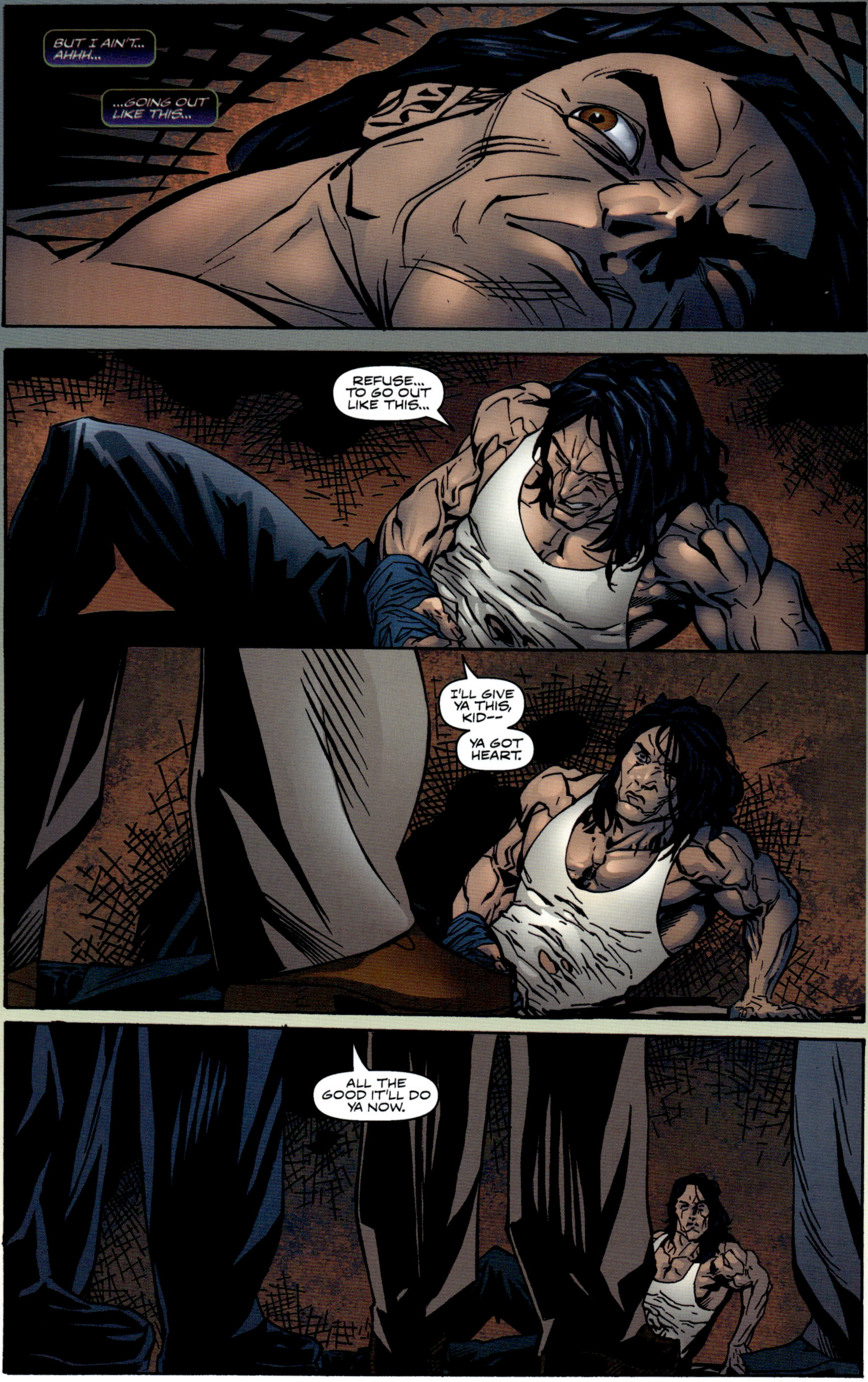
BUT I AIN'T... AHHH...
...GOING OUT LIKE THIS...
REFUSE... TO GO OUT LIKE THIS...
I'LL GIVE YA THIS, KID--
YA GOT HEART.
ALL THE GOOD IT'LL DO YA NOW.

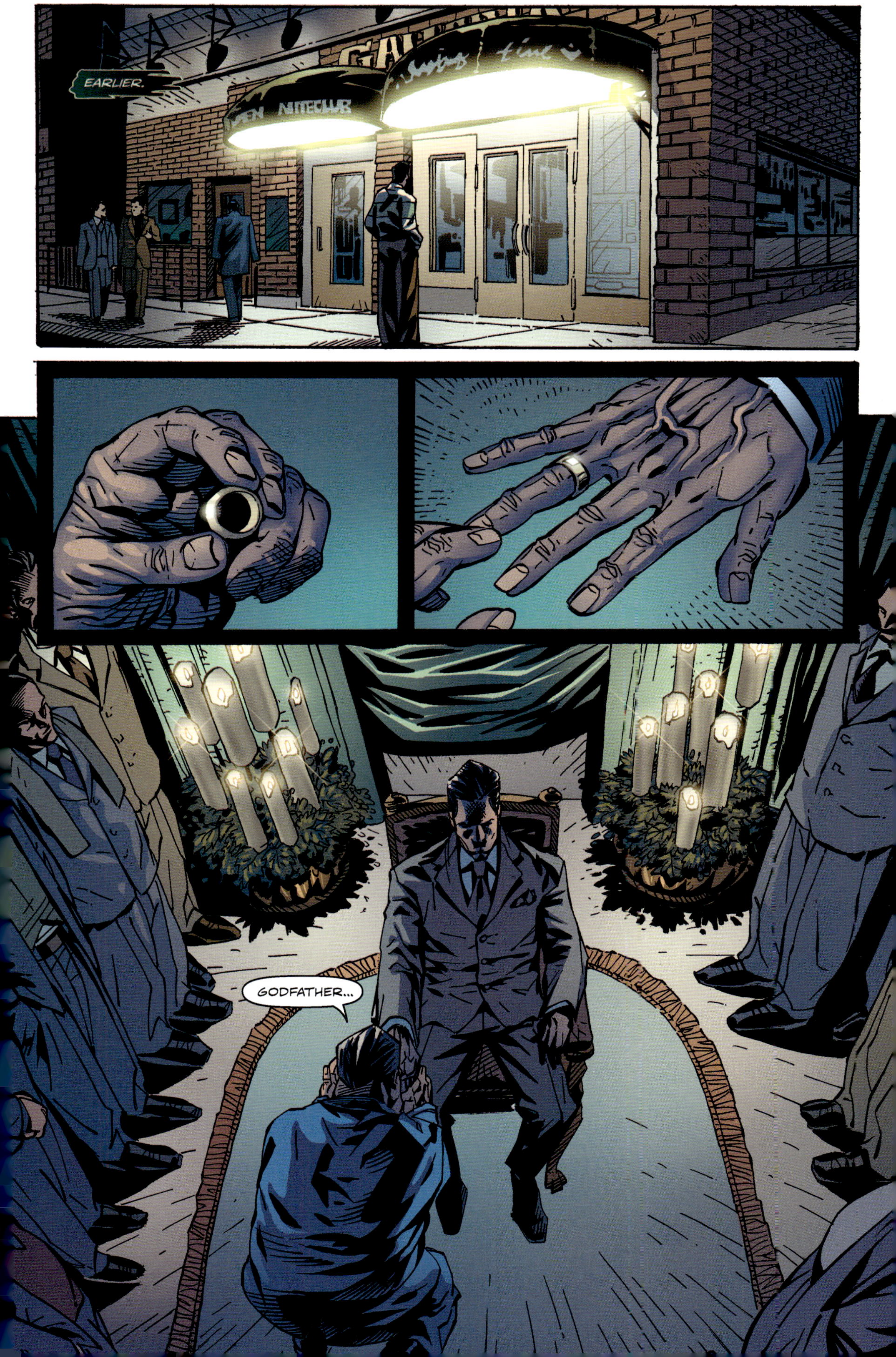
EARLIER.
GODFATHER...

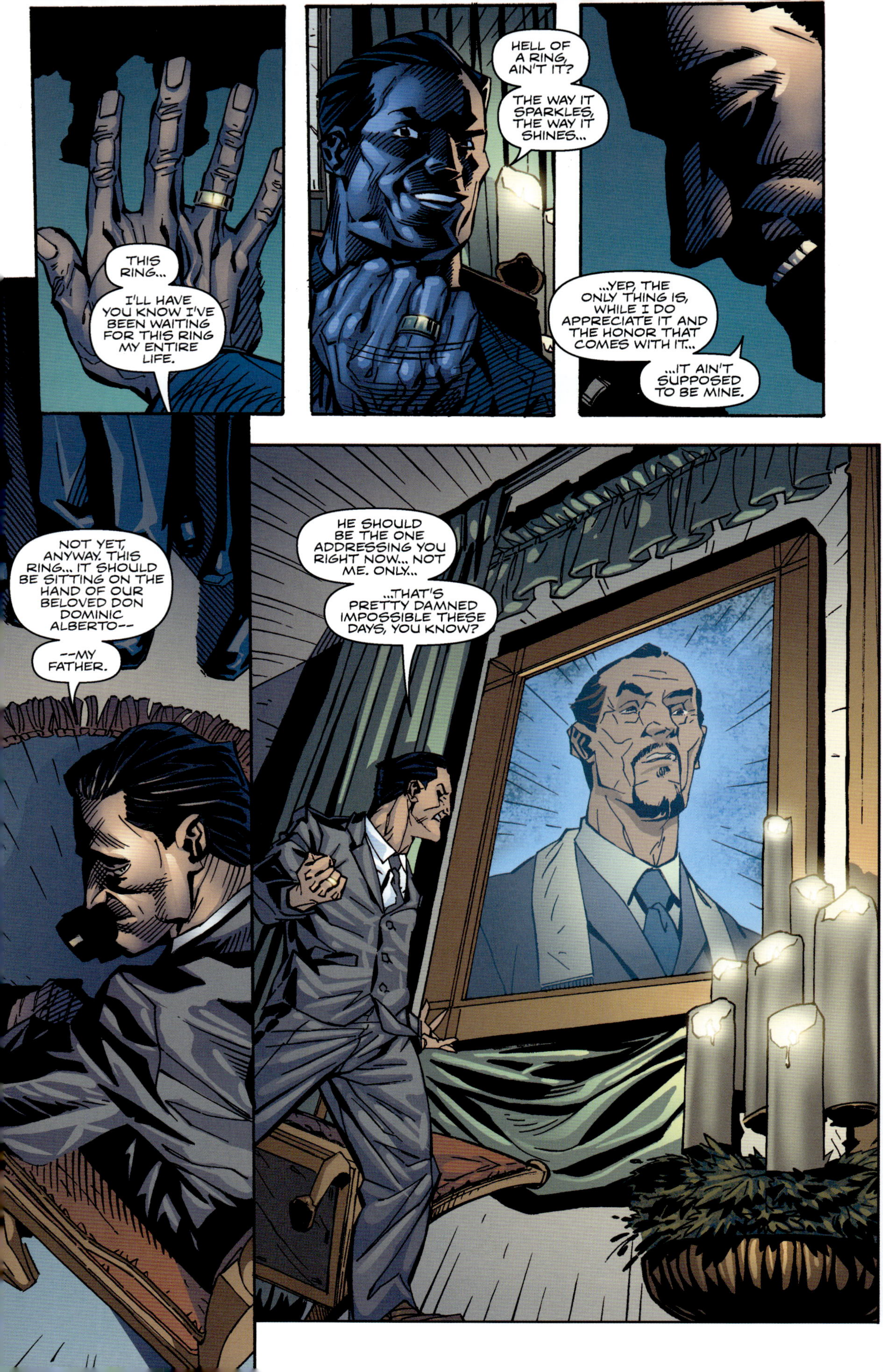
THIS RING...
I'LL HAVE YOU KNOW I'VE BEEN WAITING FOR THIS RING MY ENTIRE LIFE.
HELL OF A RING, AIN'T IT?
THE WAY IT SPARKLES, THE WAY IT SHINES...
...YEP, THE ONLY THING IS, WHILE I DO APPRECIATE IT AND THE HONOR THAT COMES WITH IT...
...IT AIN'T SUPPOSED TO BE MINE.
NOT YET, ANYWAY. THIS RING... IT SHOULD BE SITTING ON THE HAND OF OUR BELOVED DON DOMINIC ALBERTO--
--MY FATHER.
HE SHOULD BE THE ONE ADDRESSING YOU RIGHT NOW... NOT ME. ONLY...
...THAT'S PRETTY DAMNED IMPOSSIBLE THESE DAYS, YOU KNOW?

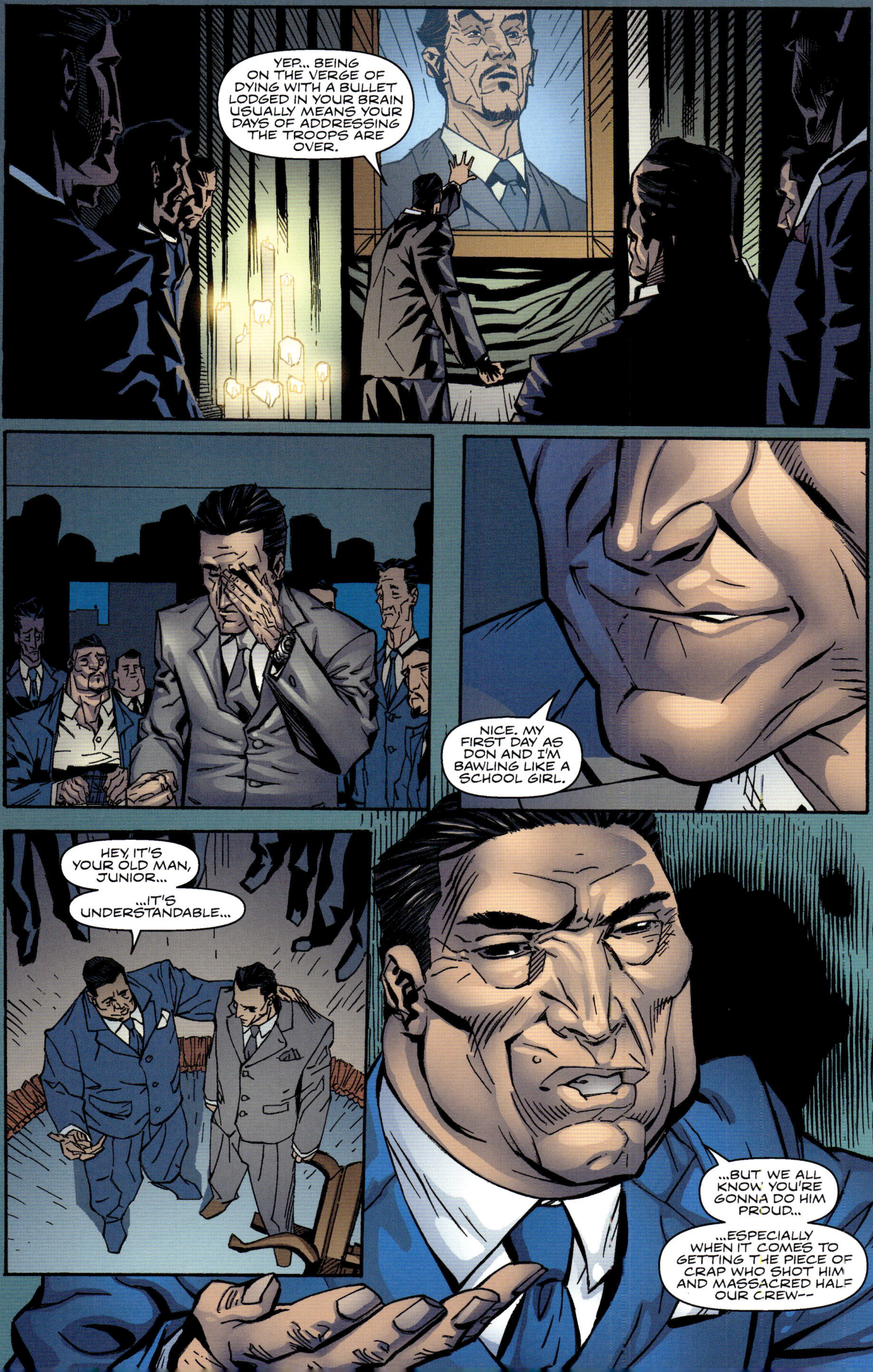
YEP... BEING ON THE VERGE OF DYING WITH A BULLET LODGED IN YOUR BRAIN USUALLY MEANS YOUR DAYS OF ADDRESSING THE TROOPS ARE OVER.
NICE. MY FIRST DAY AS DON AND I'M BAWLING LIKE A SCHOOL GIRL.
HEY, IT'S YOUR OLD MAN, JUNIOR...
...IT'S UNDERSTANDABLE...
...BUT WE ALL KNOW YOU'RE GONNA DO HIM PROUD...
...ESPECIALLY WHEN IT COMES TO GETTING THE PIECE OF CRAP WHO SHOT HIM AND MASSACRED HALF OUR CREW--

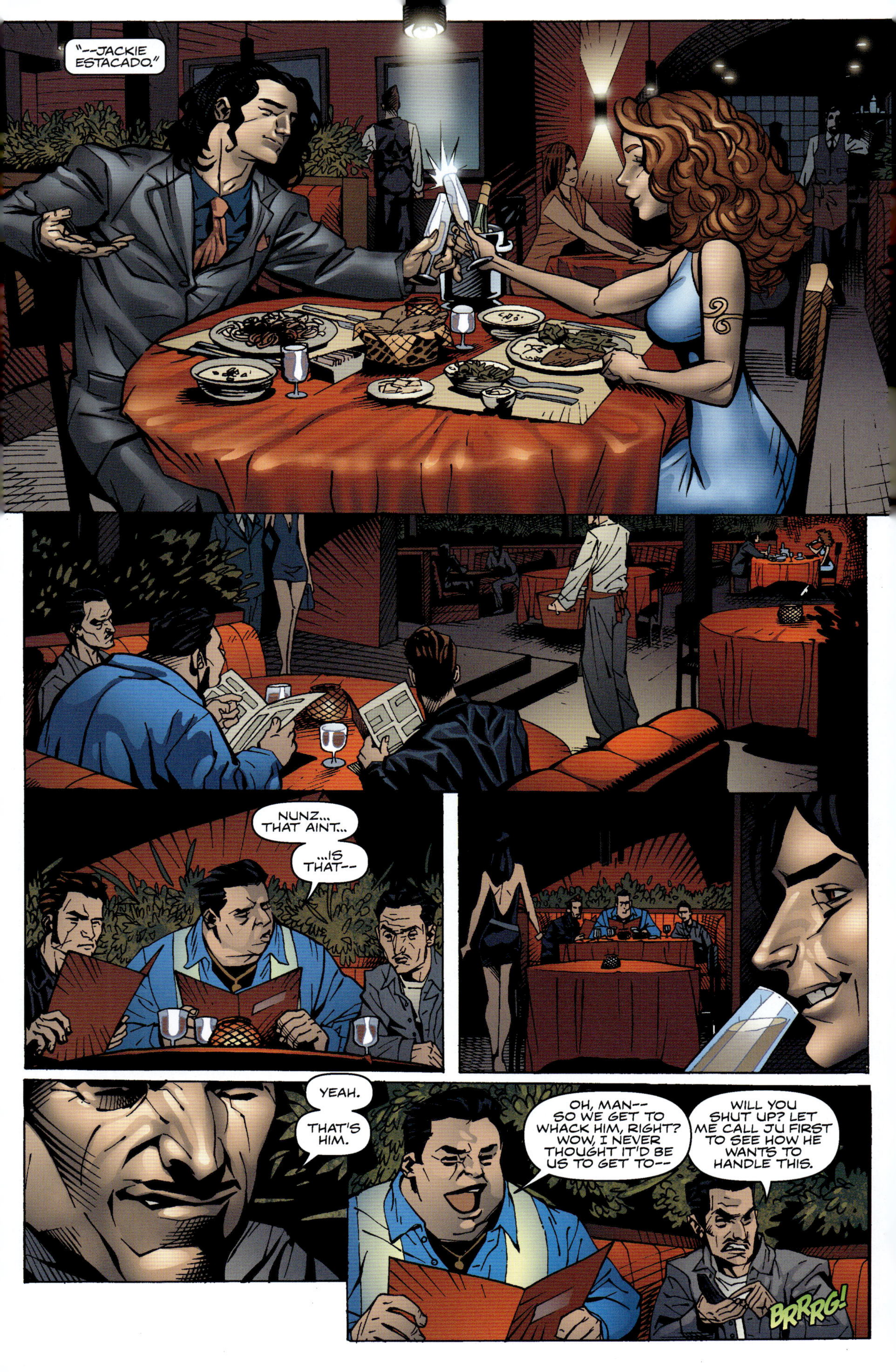
"--JACKIE ESTACADO."
NUNZ... THAT AINT...
...IS THAT--
YEAH.
THAT'S HIM.
OH, MAN-- SO WE GET TO WHACK HIM, RIGHT? WOW, I NEVER THOUGHT IT'D BE US TO GET TO--
WILL YOU SHUT UP? LET ME CALL JU FIRST TO SEE HOW HE WANTS TO HANDLE THIS.
BRRRG!

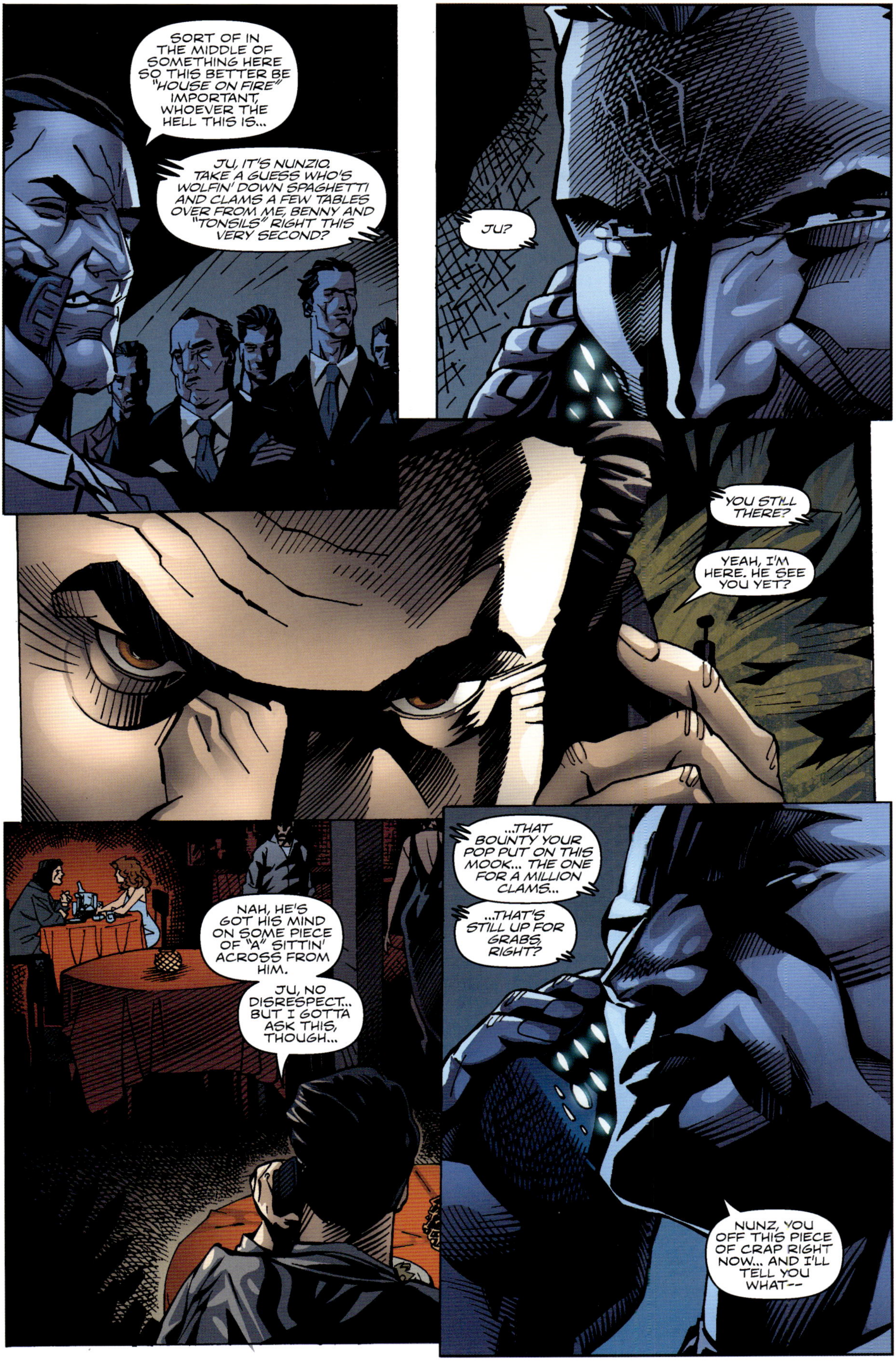
SORT OF IN THE MIDDLE OF SOMETHING HERE SO THIS BETTER BE "HOUSE ON FIRE" IMPORTANT, WHOEVER THE HELL THIS IS...
JU, IT'S NUNZIO. TAKE A GUESS WHO'S WOLFIN' DOWN SPAGHETTI AND CLAMS A FEW TABLES OVER FROM ME, BENNY AND "TONSILS" RIGHT THIS VERY SECOND?
JU?
YOU STILL THERE?
YEAH, I'M HERE. HE SEE YOU YET?
NAH, HE'S GOT HIS MIND ON SOME PIECE OF "A" SITTIN' ACROSS FROM HIM.
JU, NO DISRESPECT... BUT I GOTTA ASK THIS, THOUGH...
...THAT BOUNTY YOUR POP PUT ON THIS MOOK... THE ONE FOR A MILLION CLAMS...
...THAT'S STILL UP FOR GRABS, RIGHT?
NUNZ, YOU OFF THIS PIECE OF CRAP RIGHT NOW... AND I'LL TELL YOU WHAT--

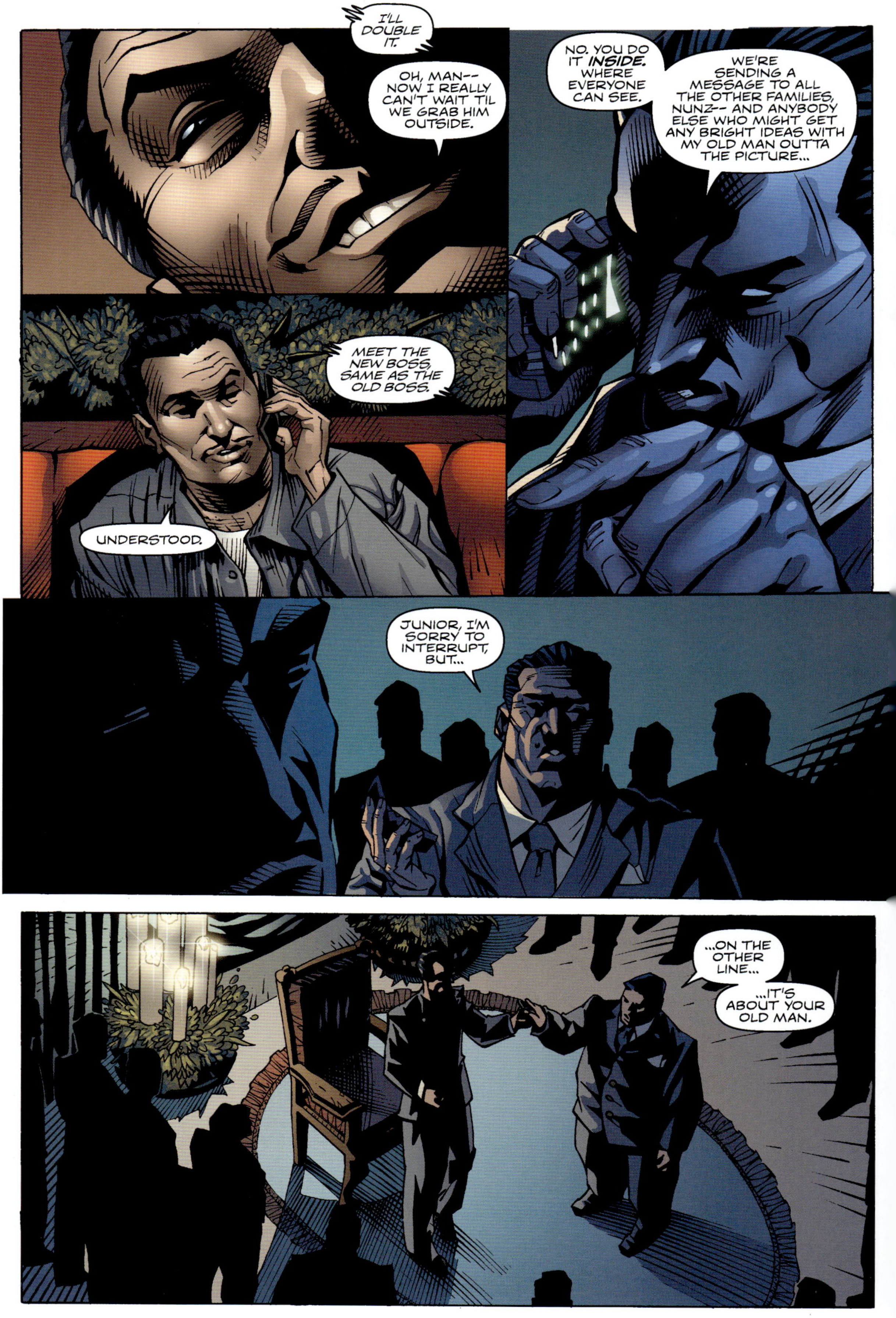

I'LL DOUBLE IT.
OH, MAN-- NOW I REALLY CAN'T WAIT TIL WE GRAB HIM OUTSIDE.
NO. YOU DO IT *INSIDE.* WHERE EVERYONE CAN SEE.
WE'RE SENDING A MESSAGE TO ALL THE OTHER FAMILIES, NUNZ-- AND ANYBODY ELSE WHO MIGHT GET ANY BRIGHT IDEAS WITH MY OLD MAN OUTTA THE PICTURE...
MEET THE NEW BOSS, SAME AS THE OLD BOSS.
UNDERSTOOD.
JUNIOR, I'M SORRY TO INTERRUPT, BUT...
...ON THE OTHER LINE...
...IT'S ABOUT YOUR OLD MAN.

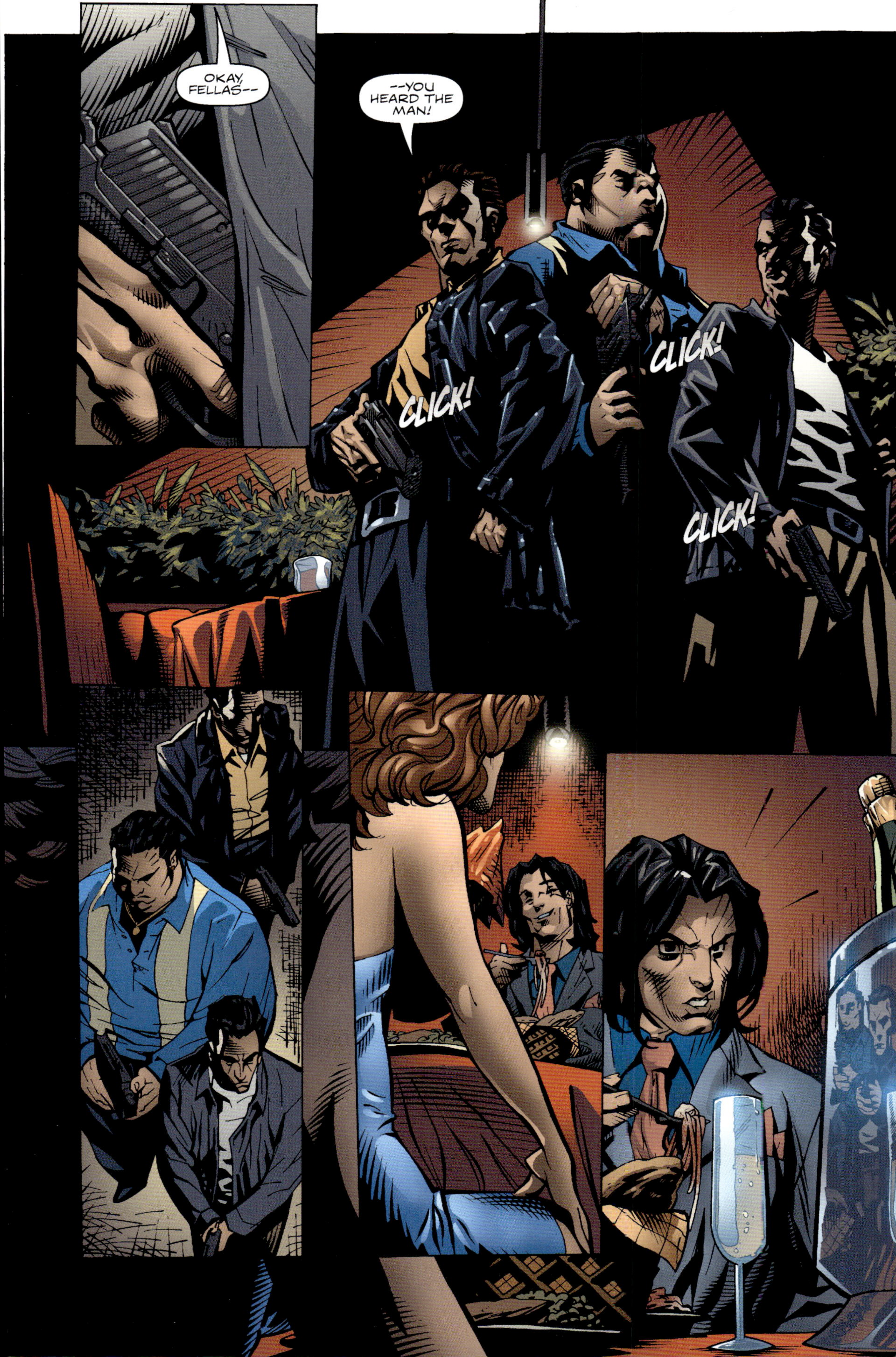
OKAY, FELLAS--
--YOU HEARD THE MAN!
CLICK!
CLICK!
CLICK!

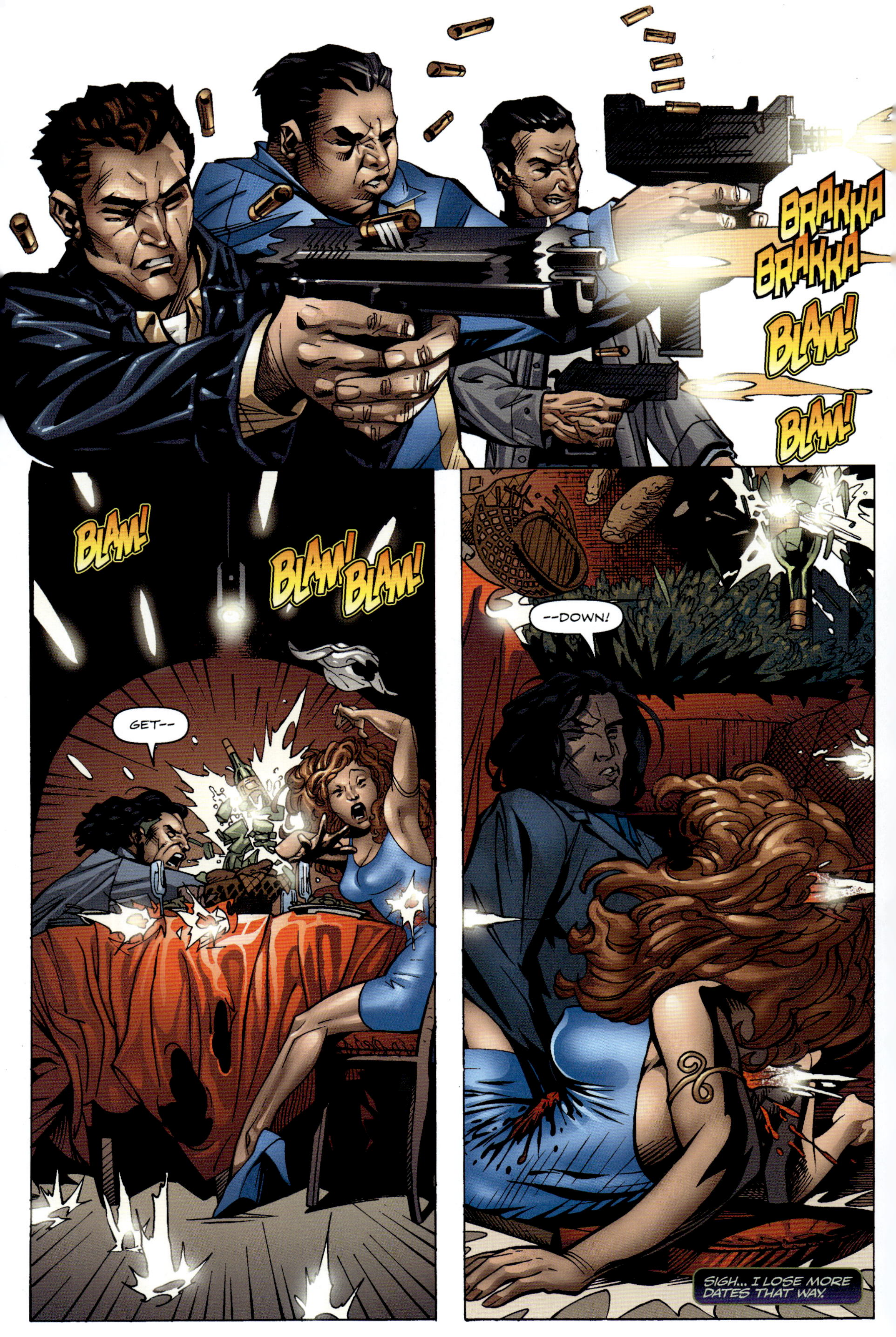
BRAKKA
BRAKKA
BLAM!
BLAM!
BLAM!
BLAM! BLAM!
GET--
--DOWN!
SIGH... I LOSE MORE DATES THAT WAY.

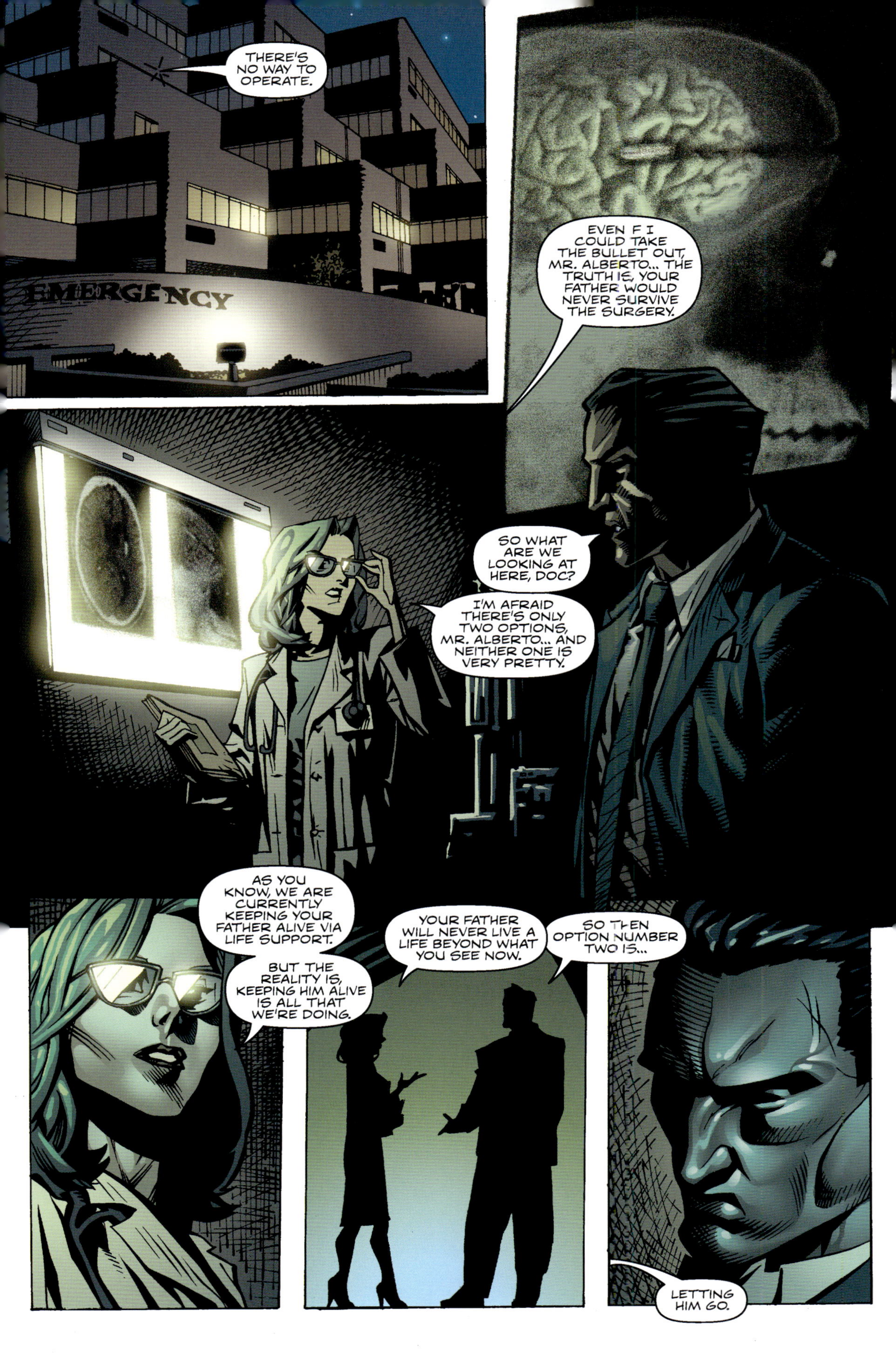
THERE'S NO WAY TO OPERATE.
EVEN F I COULD TAKE THE BULLET OUT, MR. ALBERTO... THE TRUTH IS, YOUR FATHER WOULD NEVER SURVIVE THE SURGERY.
EMERGENCY
SO WHAT ARE WE LOOKING AT HERE, DOC?
I'M AFRAID THERE'S ONLY TWO OPTIONS, MR. ALBERTO... AND NEITHER ONE IS VERY PRETTY.
AS YOU KNOW, WE ARE CURRENTLY KEEPING YOUR FATHER ALIVE VIA LIFE SUPPORT.
BUT THE REALITY IS, KEEPING HIM ALIVE IS ALL THAT WE'RE DOING.
YOUR FATHER WILL NEVER LIVE A LIFE BEYOND WHAT YOU SEE NOW.
SO THEN OPTION NUMBER TWO IS...
LETTING HIM GO.

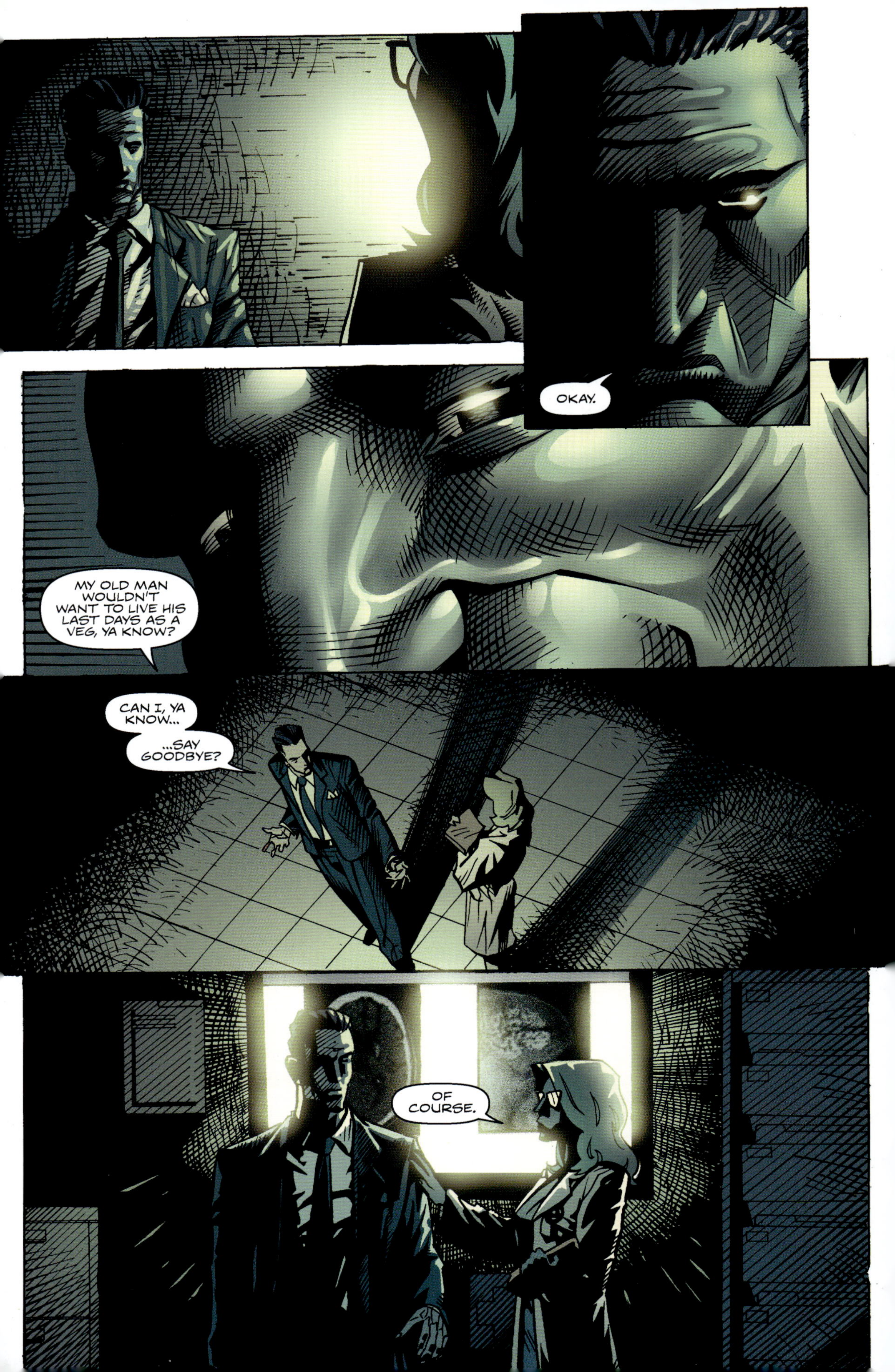
OKAY.
MY OLD MAN WOULDN'T WANT TO LIVE HIS LAST DAYS AS A VEG, YA KNOW?
CAN I, YA KNOW...
...SAY GOODBYE?
OF COURSE.

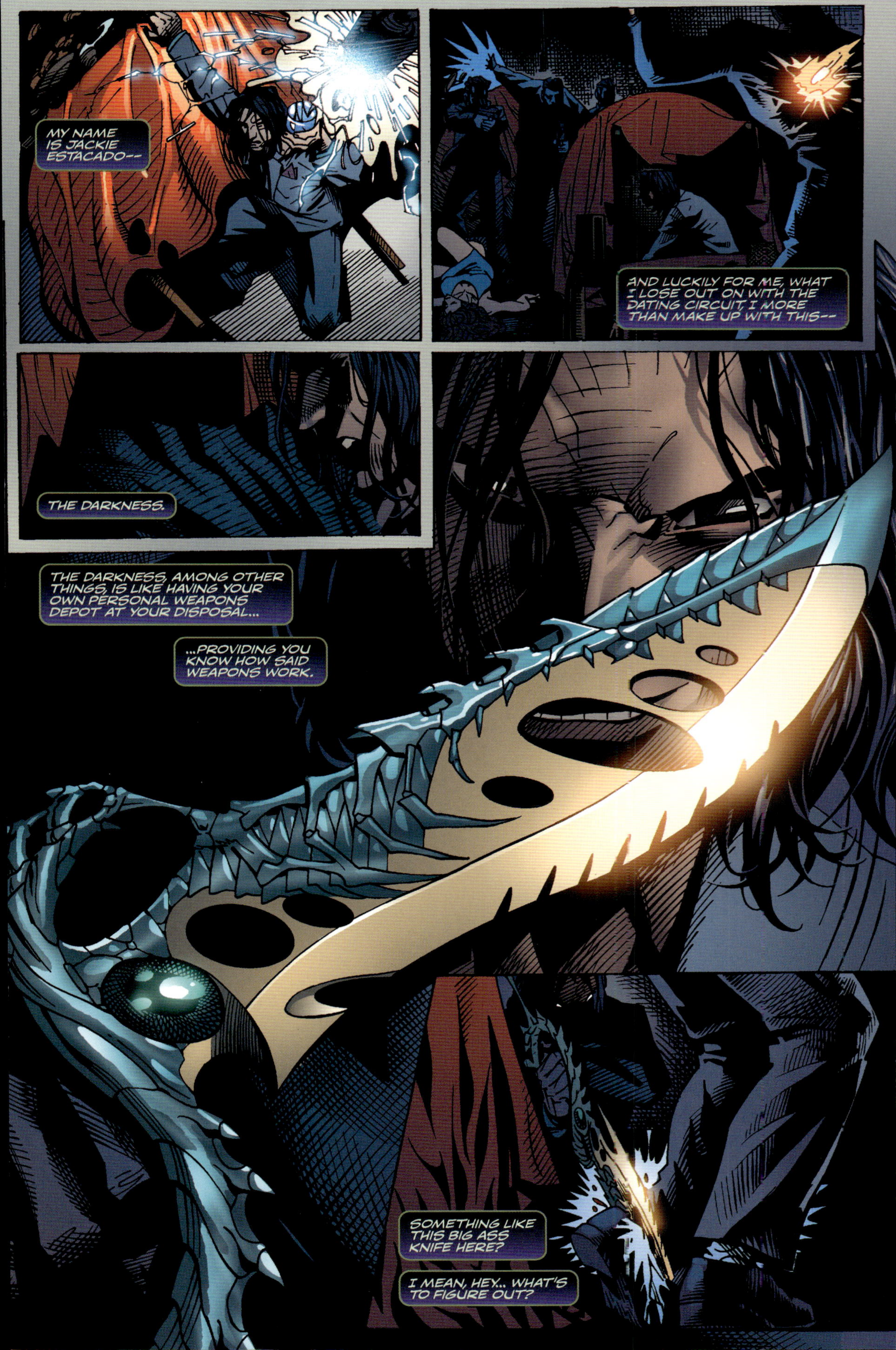
MY NAME IS JACKIE ESTACADO--
AND LUCKILY FOR ME, WHAT I LOSE OUT ON WITH THE DATING CIRCUIT, I MORE THAN MAKE UP WITH THIS--
THE DARKNESS.
THE DARKNESS, AMONG OTHER THINGS, IS LIKE HAVING YOUR OWN PERSONAL WEAPONS DEPOT AT YOUR DISPOSAL...
...PROVIDING YOU KNOW HOW SAID WEAPONS WORK.
SOMETHING LIKE THIS BIG ASS KNIFE HERE?
I MEAN, HEY... WHAT'S TO FIGURE OUT?

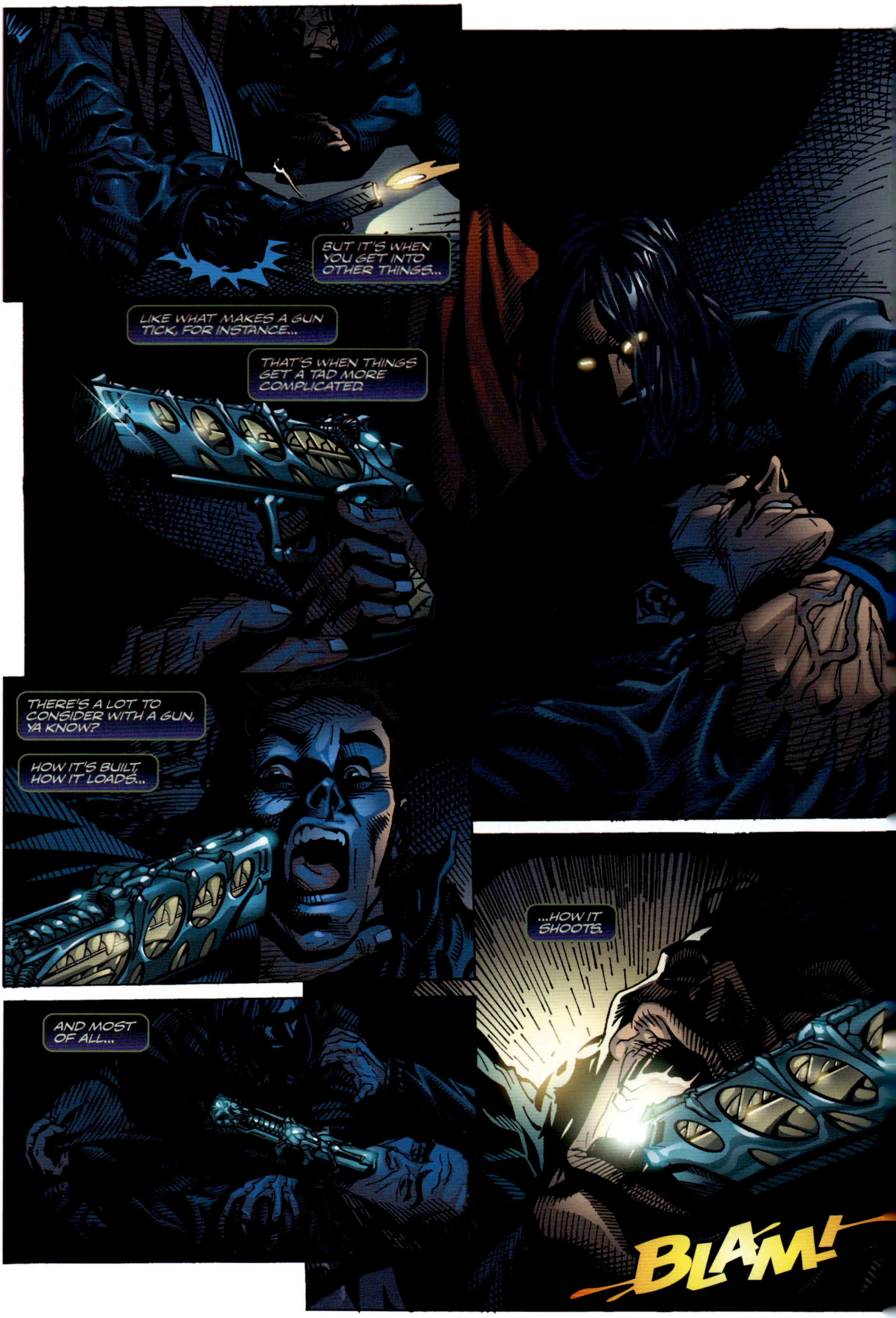
BUT IT'S WHEN YOU GET INTO OTHER THINGS...
LIKE WHAT MAKES A GUN TICK, FOR INSTANCE...
THAT'S WHEN THINGS GET A TAD MORE COMPLICATED.
THERE'S A LOT TO CONSIDER WITH A GUN, YA KNOW?
HOW IT'S BUILT, HOW IT LOADS...
...HOW IT SHOOTS.
AND MOST OF ALL...
BLAM!

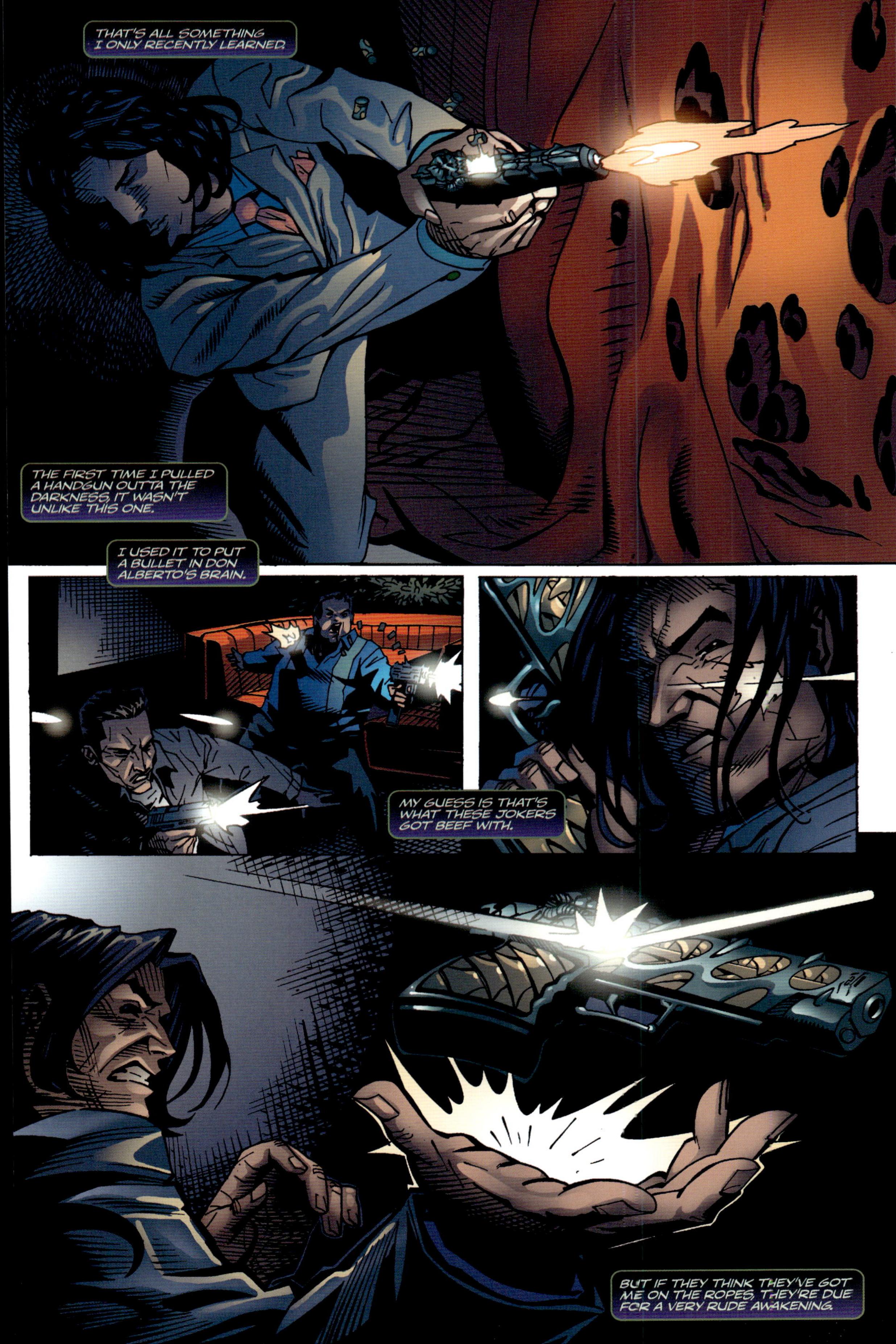
THAT'S ALL SOMETHING I ONLY RECENTLY LEARNED.
THE FIRST TIME I PULLED A HANDGUN OUTTA THE DARKNESS, IT WASN'T UNLIKE THIS ONE.
I USED IT TO PUT A BULLET IN DON ALBERTO'S BRAIN.
MY GUESS IS THAT'S WHAT THESE JOKERS GOT BEEF WITH.
BUT IF THEY THINK THEY'VE GOT ME ON THE ROPES, THEY'RE DUE FOR A VERY RUDE AWAKENING.

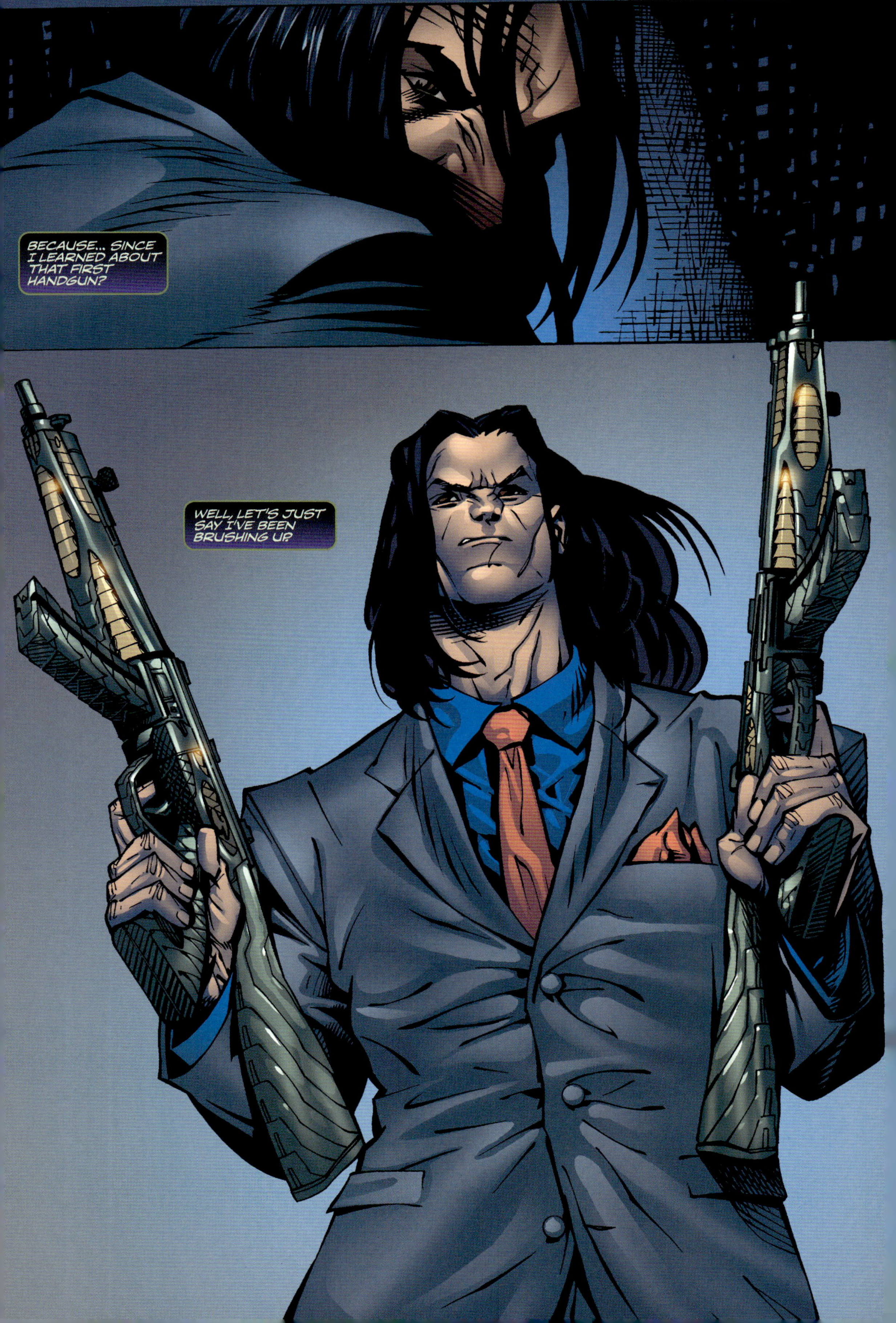
BECAUSE... SINCE I LEARNED ABOUT THAT FIRST HANDGUN?
WELL, LET'S JUST SAY I'VE BEEN BRUSHING UP.

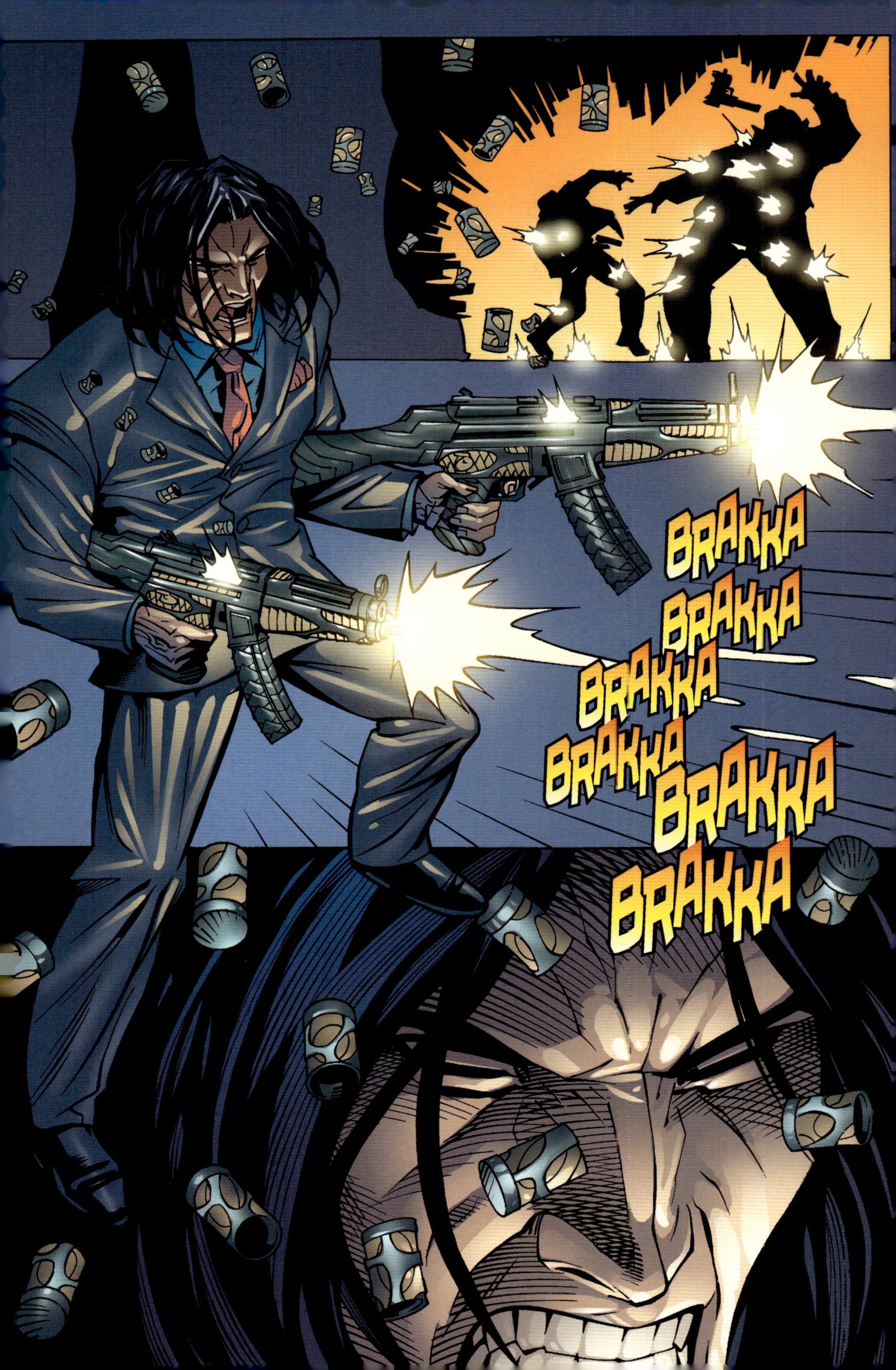
BRAKKA
BRAKKA
BRAKKA
BRAKKA
BRAKKA
BRAKKA

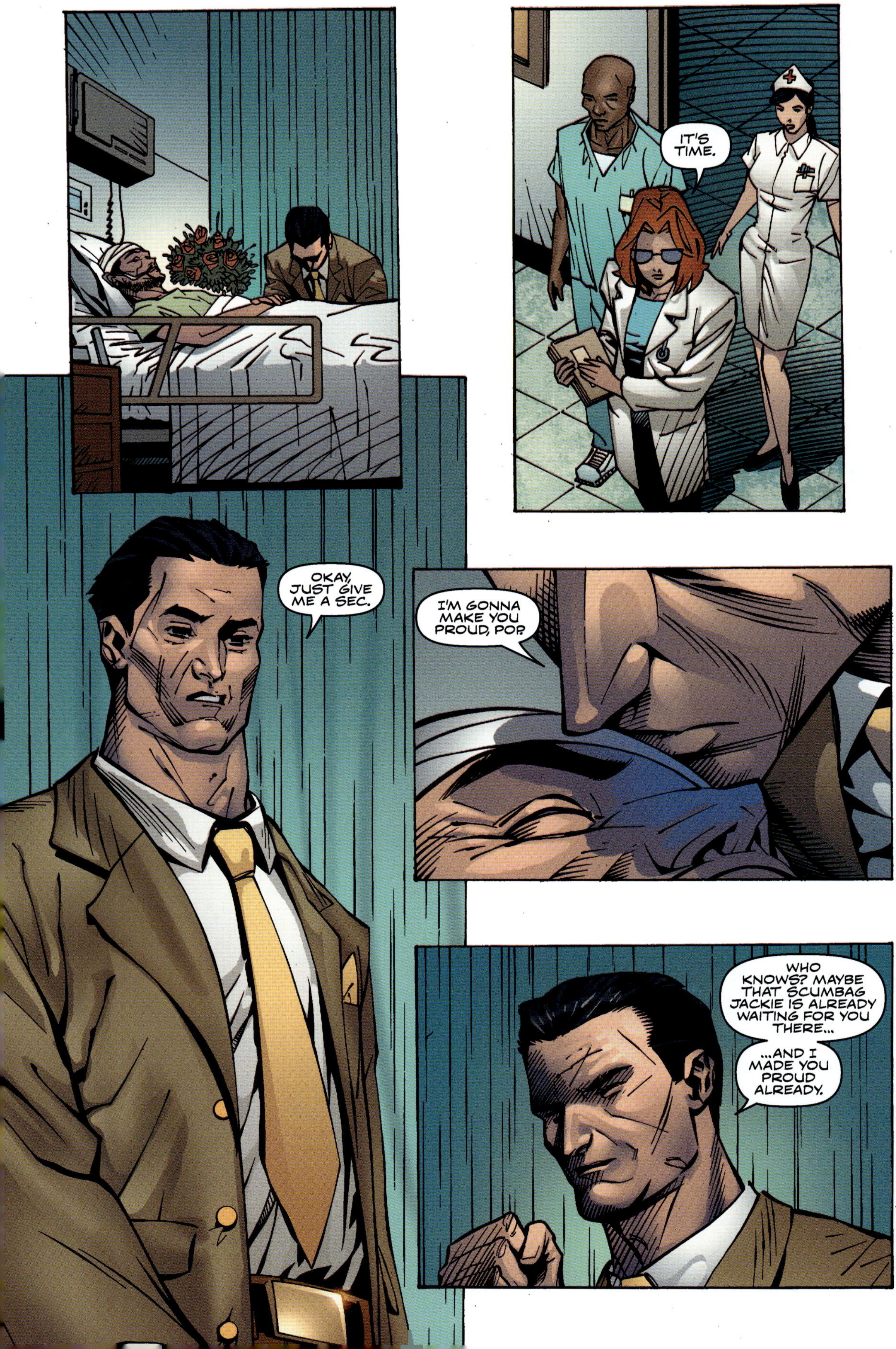
IT'S TIME.
OKAY, JUST GIVE ME A SEC.
I'M GONNA MAKE YOU PROUD, POP.
WHO KNOWS? MAYBE THAT SCUMBAG JACKIE IS ALREADY WAITING FOR YOU THERE...
...AND I MADE YOU PROUD ALREADY.

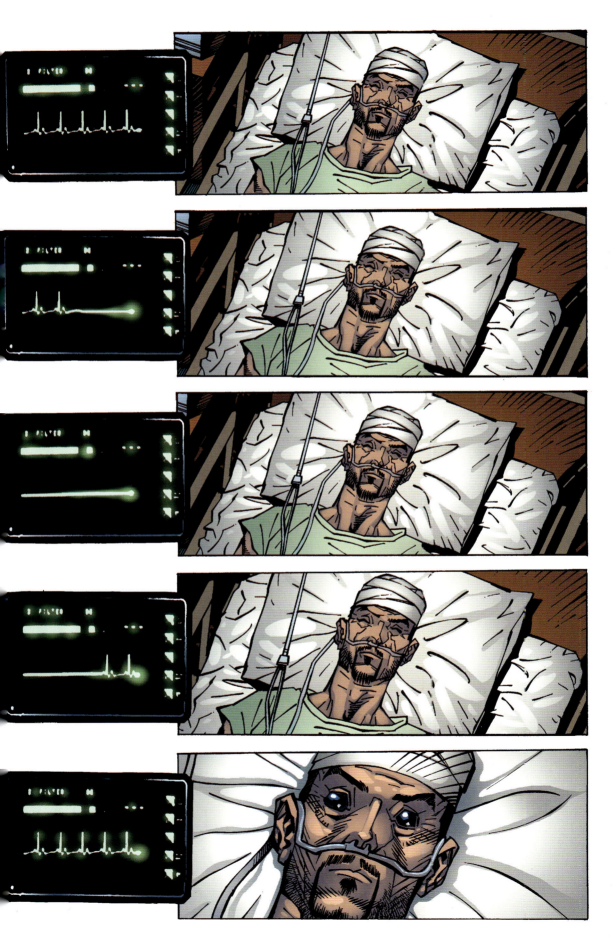

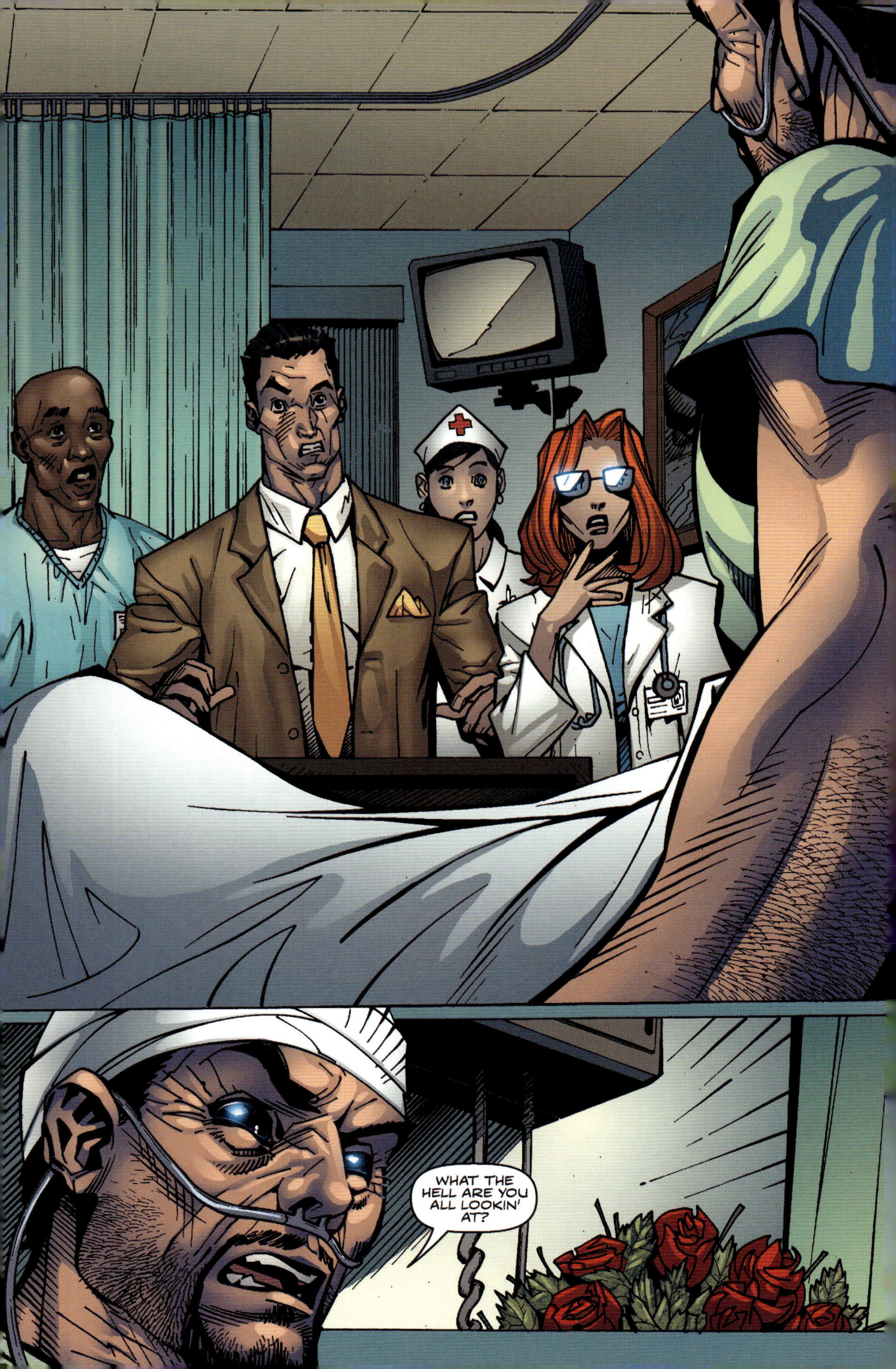
WHAT THE HELL ARE YOU ALL LOOKIN' AT?

The Darkness Issue #55

cover art by: Dale Keown and Matt Milla

THE DARKNESS #55

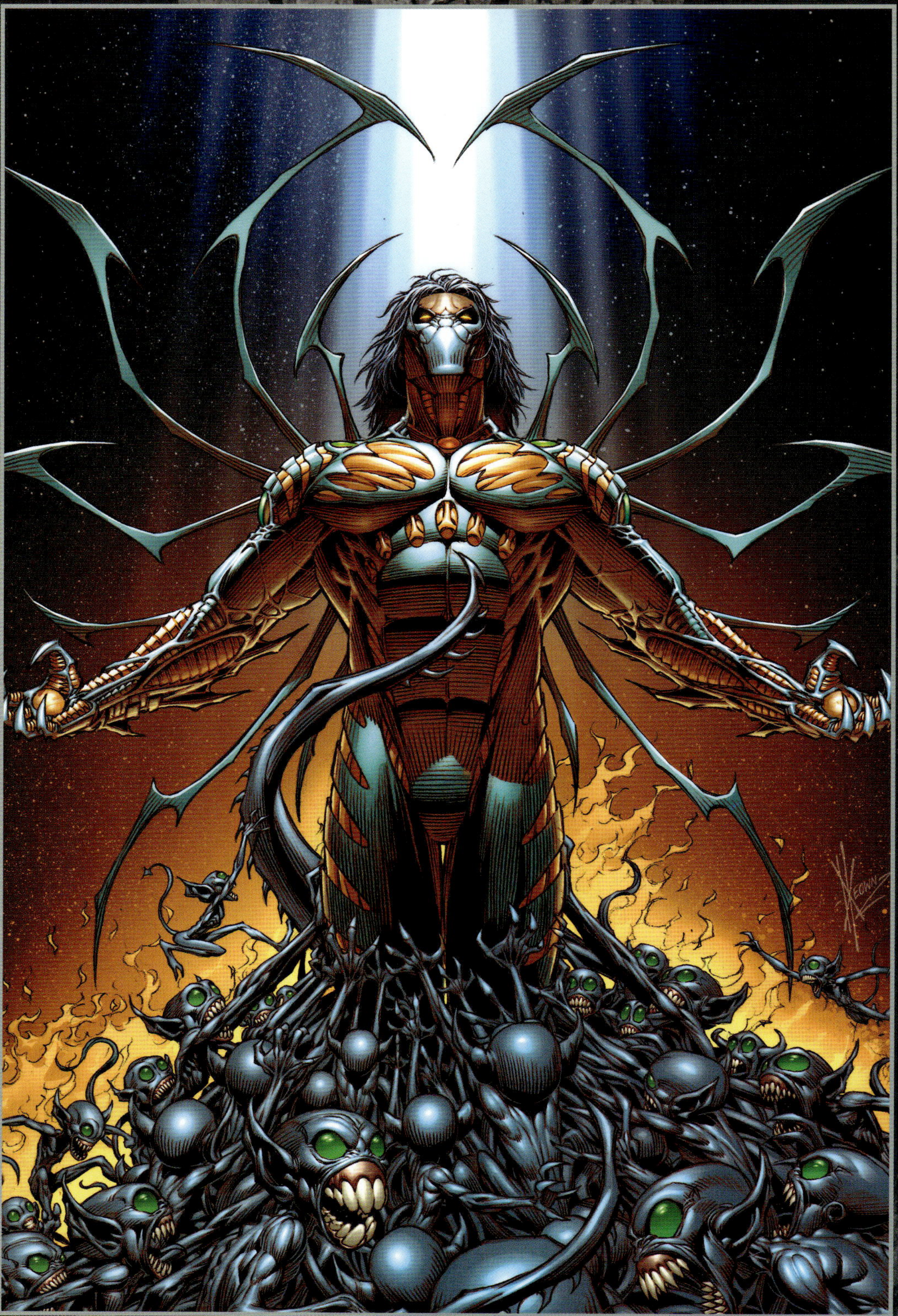

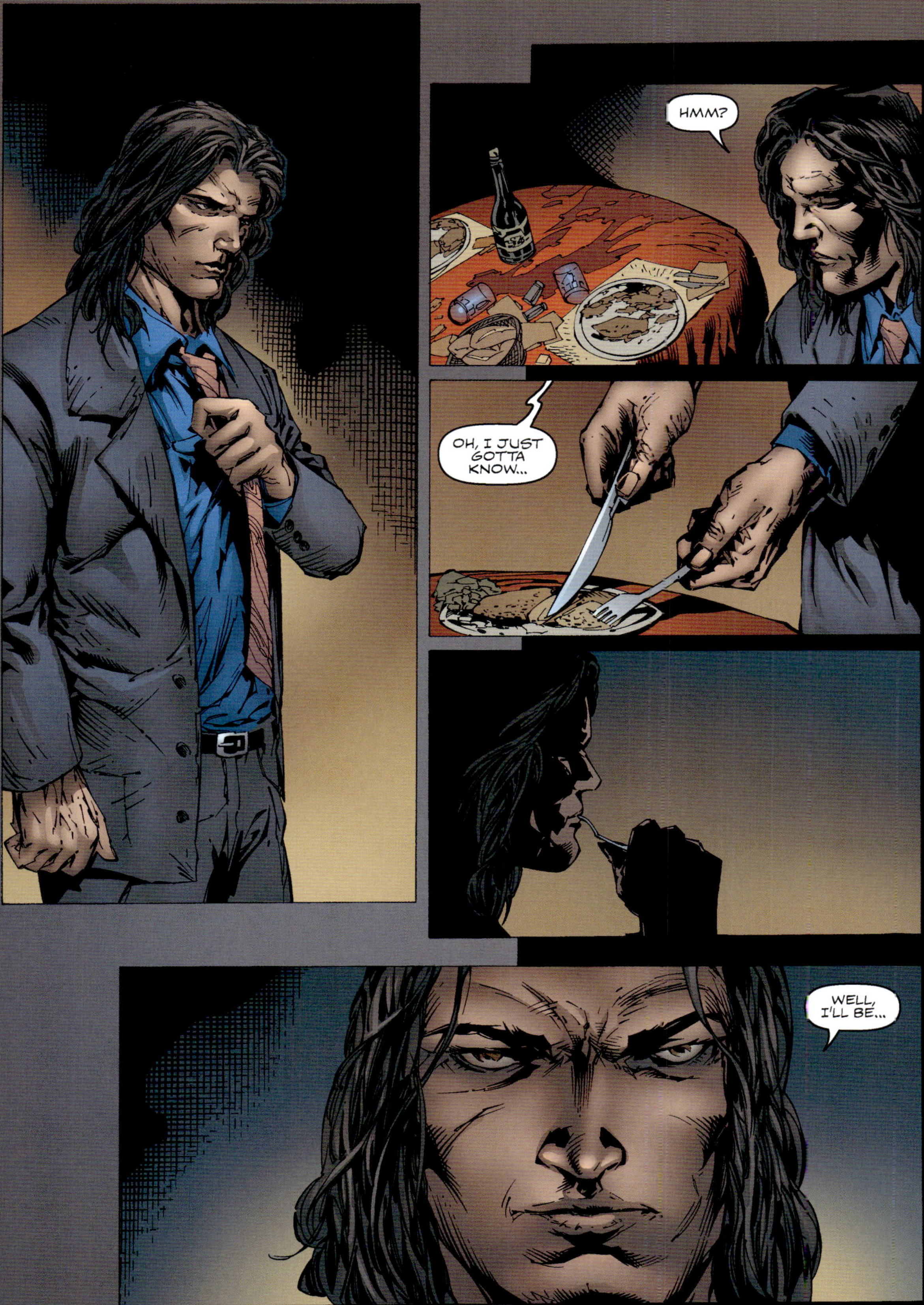
HMM?
OH, I JUST GOTTA KNOW...
WELL, I'LL BE...

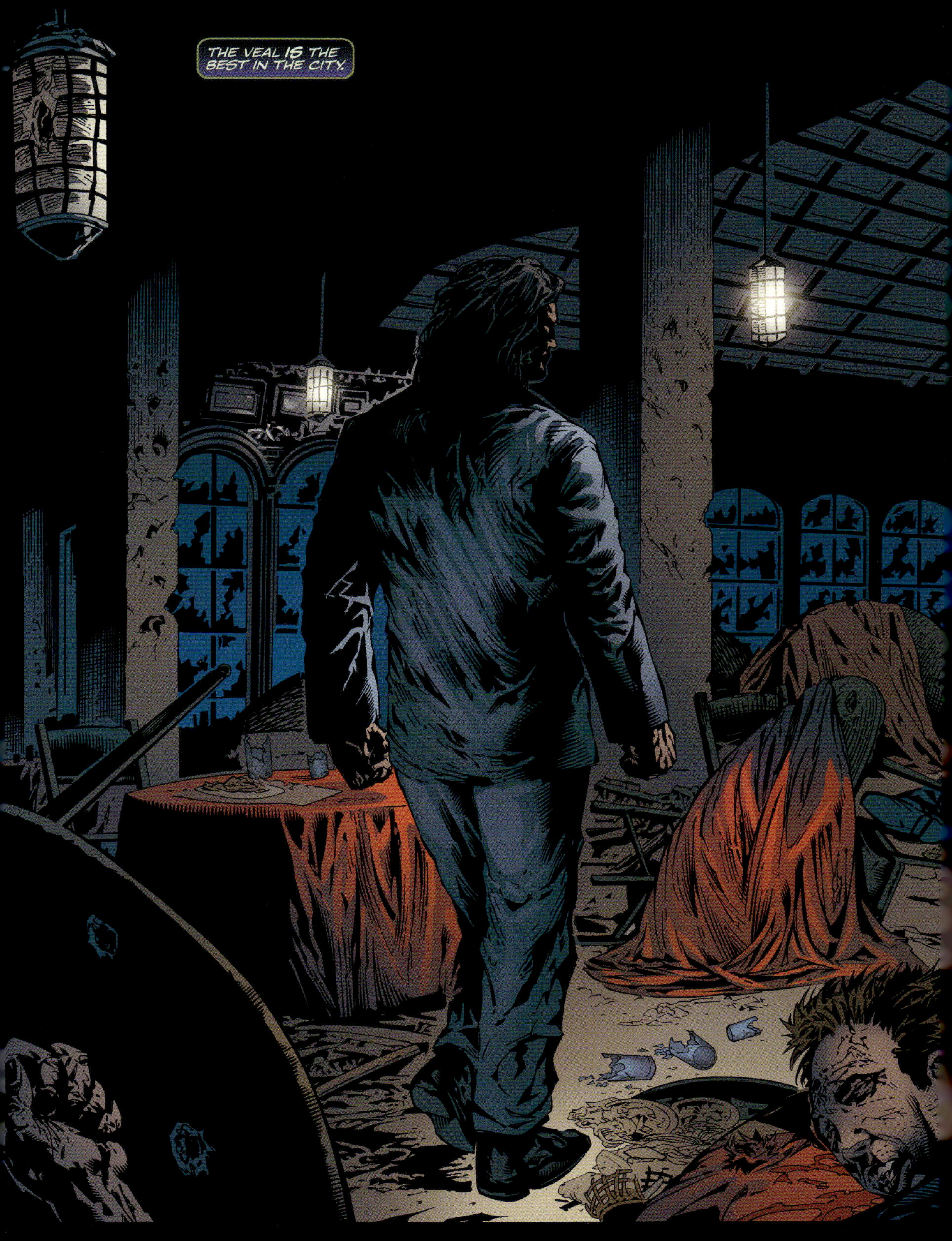
THE VEAL IS THE BEST IN THE CITY.

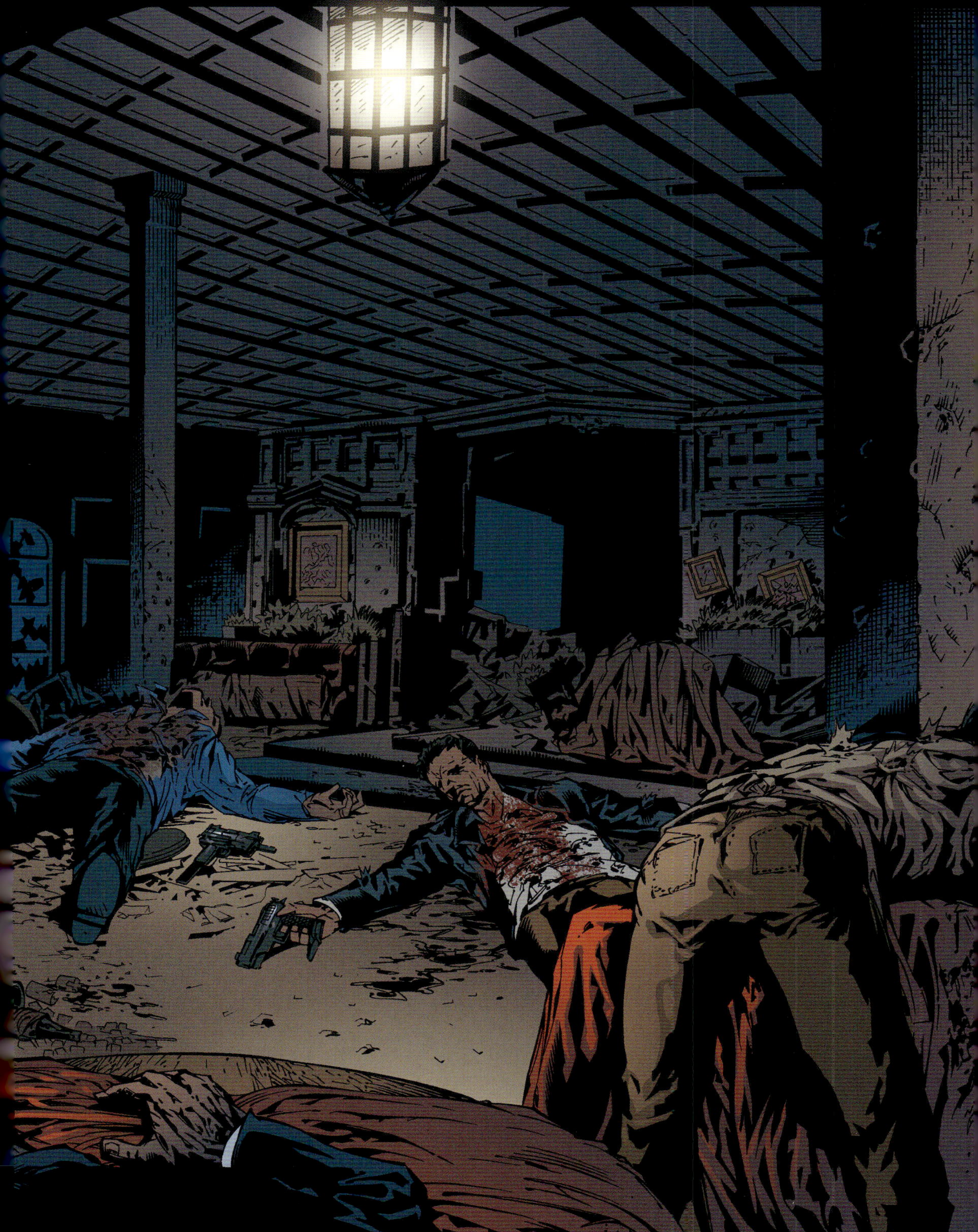

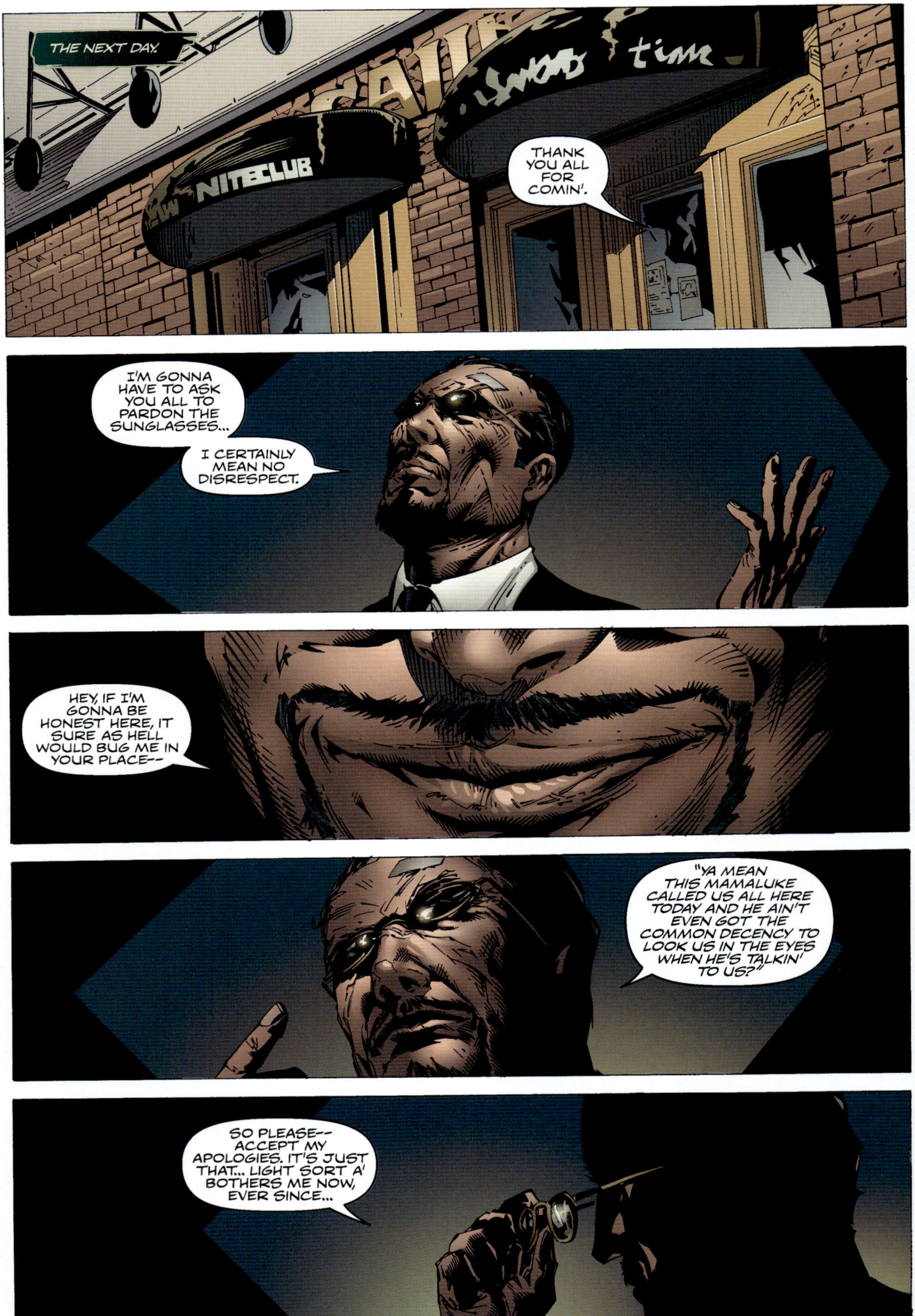
THE NEXT DAY.
NITECLUB
THANK YOU ALL FOR COMIN'.
I'M GONNA HAVE TO ASK YOU ALL TO PARDON THE SUNGLASSES...
I CERTAINLY MEAN NO DISRESPECT.
HEY, IF I'M GONNA BE HONEST HERE, IT SURE AS HELL WOULD BUG ME IN YOUR PLACE--
"YA MEAN THIS MAMALUKE CALLED US ALL HERE TODAY AND HE AIN'T EVEN GOT THE COMMON DECENCY TO LOOK US IN THE EYES WHEN HE'S TALKIN' TO US?"
SO PLEASE-- ACCEPT MY APOLOGIES. IT'S JUST THAT... LIGHT SORT A' BOTHERS ME NOW, EVER SINCE...

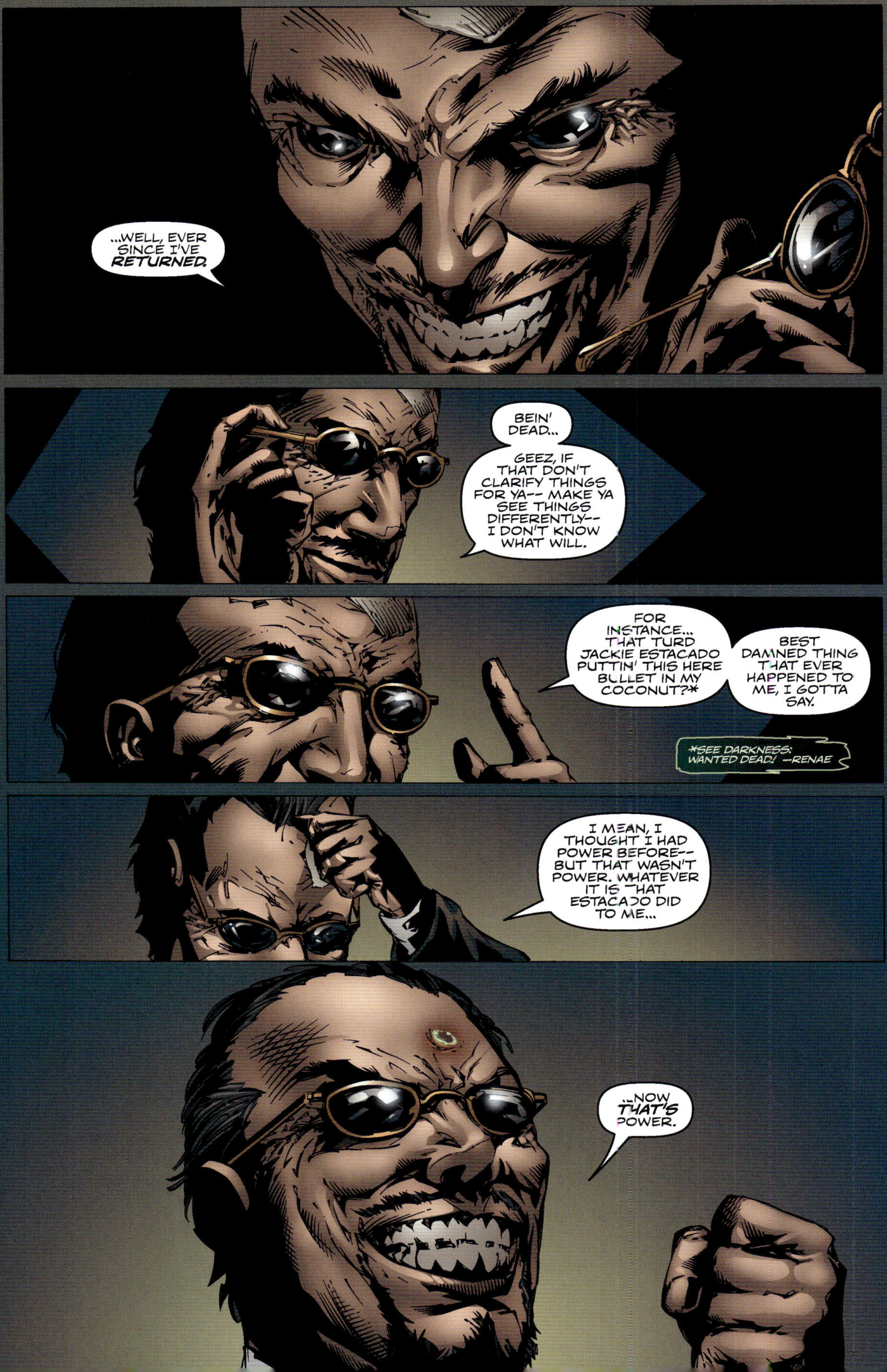
...WELL, EVER SINCE I'VE RETURNED.
BEIN' DEAD...
GEEZ, IF THAT DON'T CLARIFY THINGS FOR YA-- MAKE YA SEE THINGS DIFFERENTLY-- I DON'T KNOW WHAT WILL.
FOR INSTANCE... THAT TURD JACKIE ESTACADO PUTTIN' THIS HERE BULLET IN MY COCONUT?*
BEST DAMNED THING THAT EVER HAPPENED TO ME, I GOTTA SAY.
*SEE DARKNESS: WANTED DEAD! —RENAE
I MEAN, I THOUGHT I HAD POWER BEFORE-- BUT THAT WASN'T POWER. WHATEVER IT IS THAT ESTACADO DID TO ME...
...NOW THAT'S POWER.

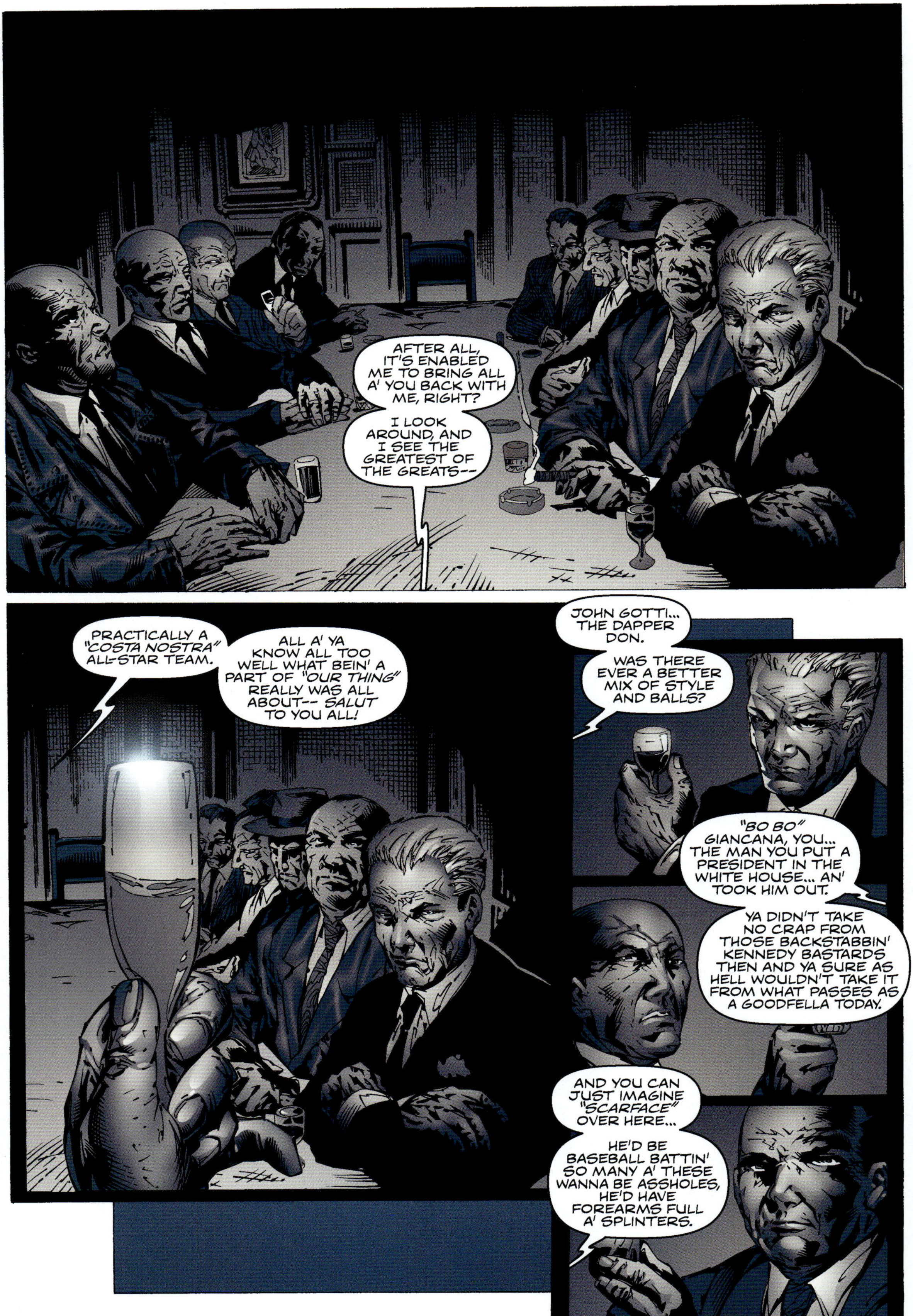

AFTER ALL, IT'S ENABLED ME TO BRING ALL A' YOU BACK WITH ME, RIGHT?
I LOOK AROUND, AND I SEE THE GREATEST OF THE GREATS--
PRACTICALLY A "COSTA NOSTRA" ALL-STAR TEAM.
ALL A' YA KNOW ALL TOO WELL WHAT BEIN' A PART OF "OUR THING" REALLY WAS ALL ABOUT-- SALUT TO YOU ALL!
JOHN GOTTI... THE DAPPER DON.
WAS THERE EVER A BETTER MIX OF STYLE AND BALLS?
"BO BO" GIANCANA, YOU... THE MAN YOU PUT A PRESIDENT IN THE WHITE HOUSE... AN' TOOK HIM OUT.
YA DIDN'T TAKE NO CRAP FROM THOSE BACKSTABBIN' KENNEDY BASTARDS THEN AND YA SURE AS HELL WOULDN'T TAKE IT FROM WHAT PASSES AS A GOODFELLA TODAY.
AND YOU CAN JUST IMAGINE "SCARFACE" OVER HERE...
HE'D BE BASEBALL BATTIN' SO MANY A' THESE WANNA BE ASSHOLES, HE'D HAVE FOREARMS FULL A' SPLINTERS.

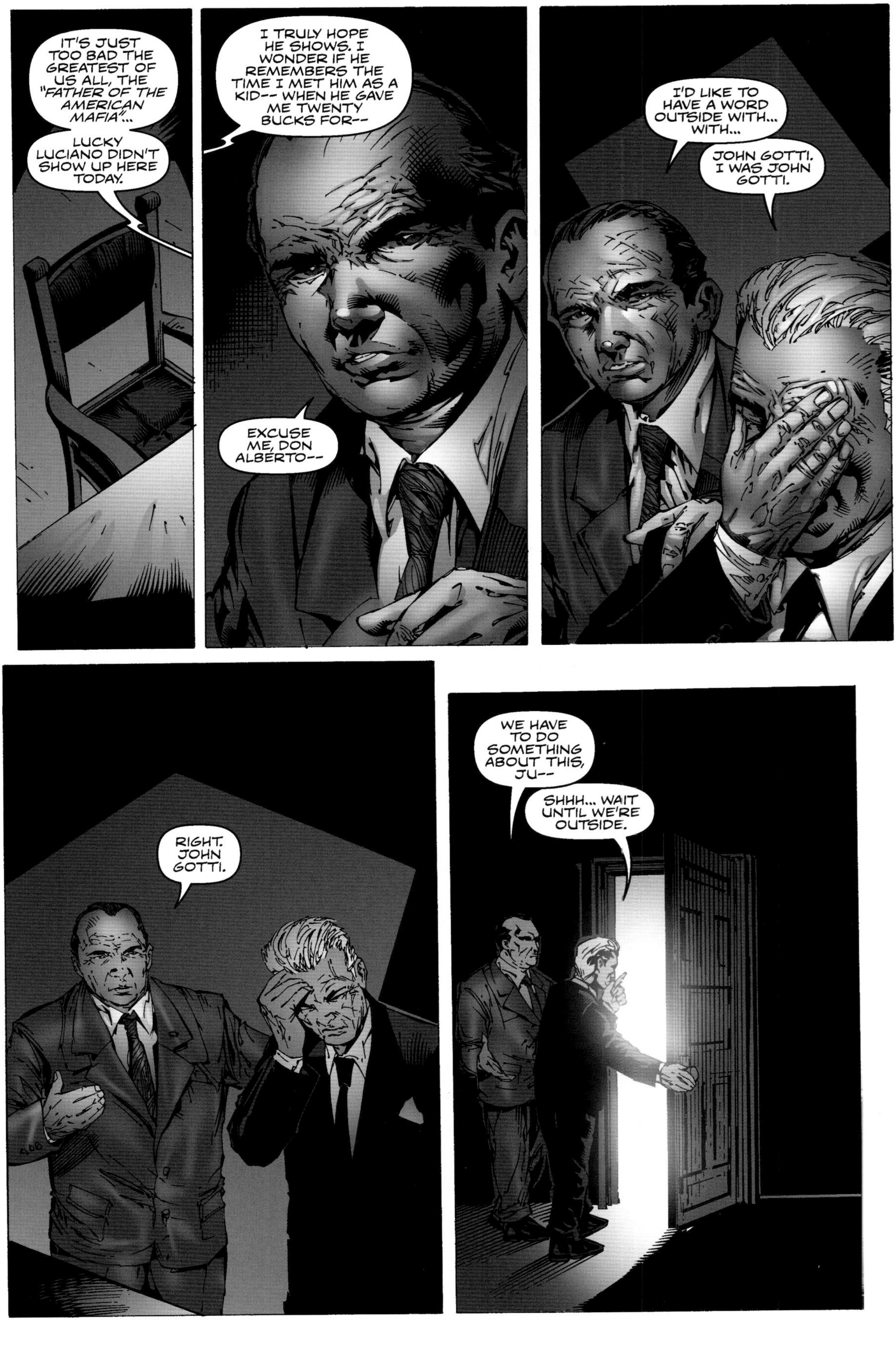
IT'S JUST TOO BAD THE GREATEST OF US ALL, THE "FATHER OF THE AMERICAN MAFIA"...
LUCKY LUCIANO DIDN'T SHOW UP HERE TODAY.
I TRULY HOPE HE SHOWS. I WONDER IF HE REMEMBERS THE TIME I MET HIM AS A KID-- WHEN HE GAVE ME TWENTY BUCKS FOR--
EXCUSE ME, DON ALBERTO--
I'D LIKE TO HAVE A WORD OUTSIDE WITH... WITH...
JOHN GOTTI. I WAS JOHN GOTTI.
RIGHT. JOHN GOTTI.
WE HAVE TO DO SOMETHING ABOUT THIS, JU--
SHHH... WAIT UNTIL WE'RE OUTSIDE.

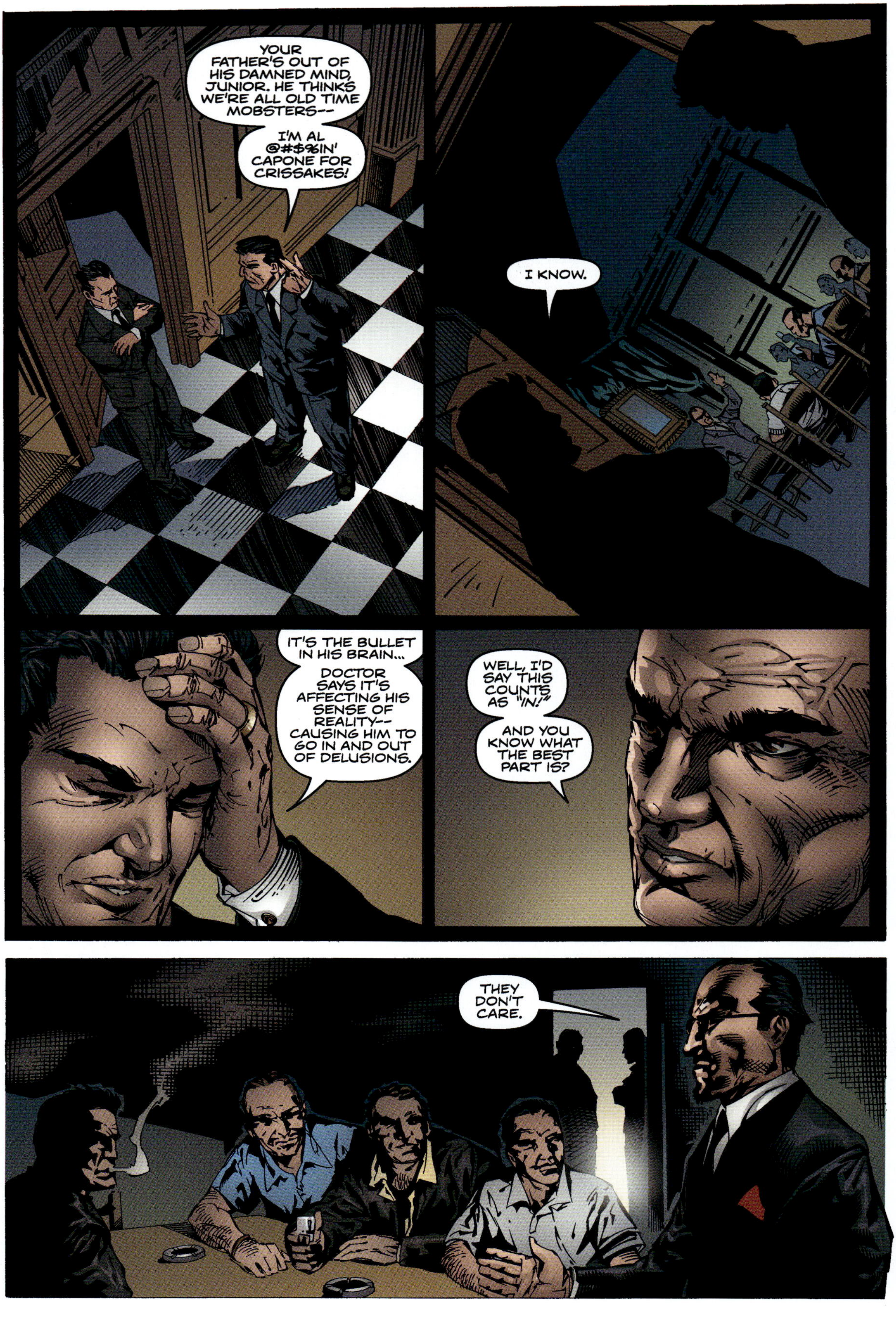
YOUR FATHER'S OUT OF HIS DAMNED MIND, JUNIOR. HE THINKS WE'RE ALL OLD TIME MOBSTERS--
I'M AL @#$%IN' CAPONE FOR CRISSAKES!
I KNOW.
IT'S THE BULLET IN HIS BRAIN...
DOCTOR SAYS IT'S AFFECTING HIS SENSE OF REALITY-- CAUSING HIM TO GO IN AND OUT OF DELUSIONS.
WELL, I'D SAY THIS COUNTS AS "IN!"
AND YOU KNOW WHAT THE BEST PART IS?
THEY DON'T CARE.

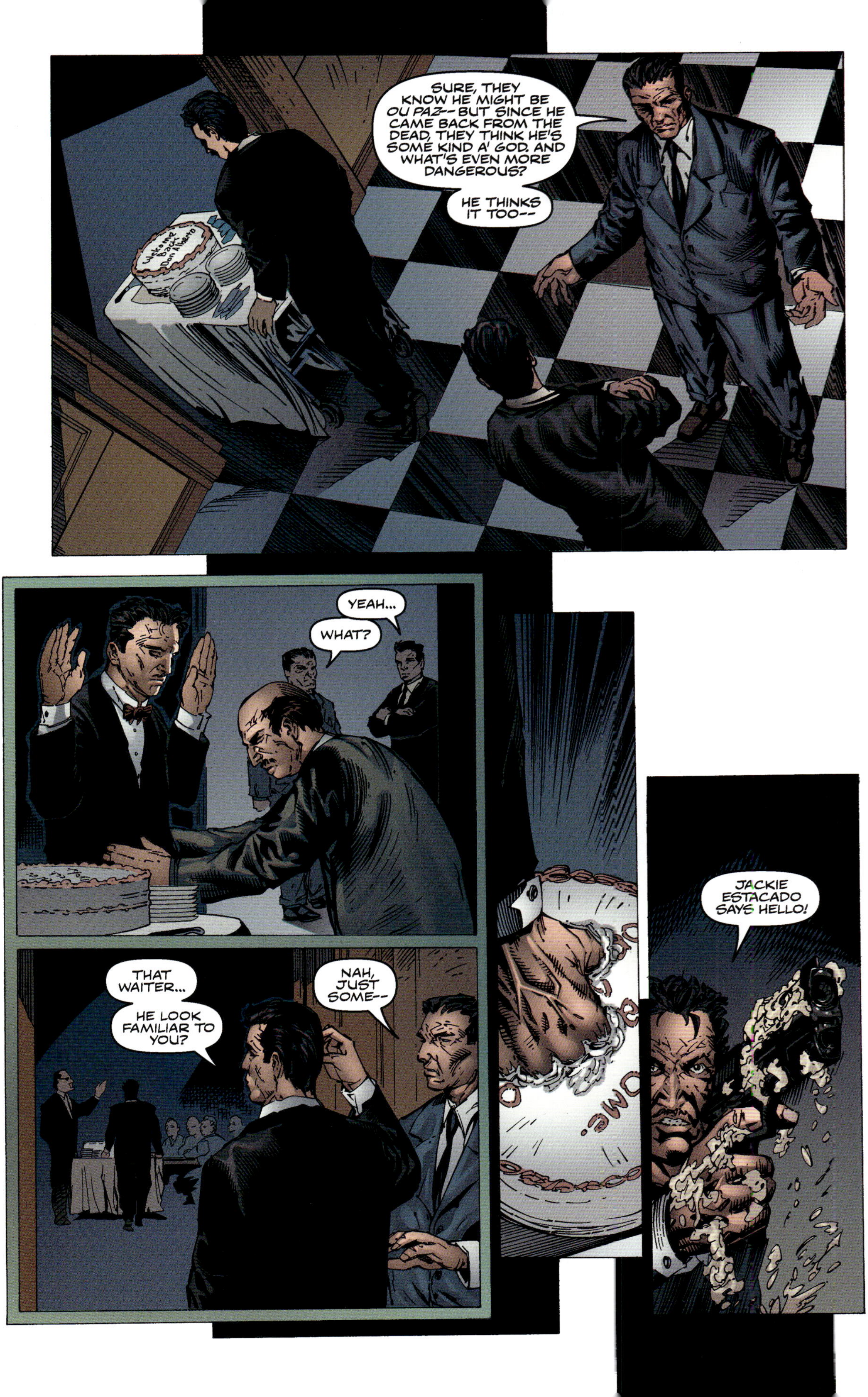
SURE, THEY KNOW HE MIGHT BE OU PAZ-- BUT SINCE HE CAME BACK FROM THE DEAD, THEY THINK HE'S SOME KIND A' GOD. AND WHAT'S EVEN MORE DANGEROUS?
HE THINKS IT TOO--
YEAH...
WHAT?
THAT WAITER...
HE LOOK FAMILIAR TO YOU?
NAH, JUST SOME--
JACKIE ESTACADO SAYS HELLO!

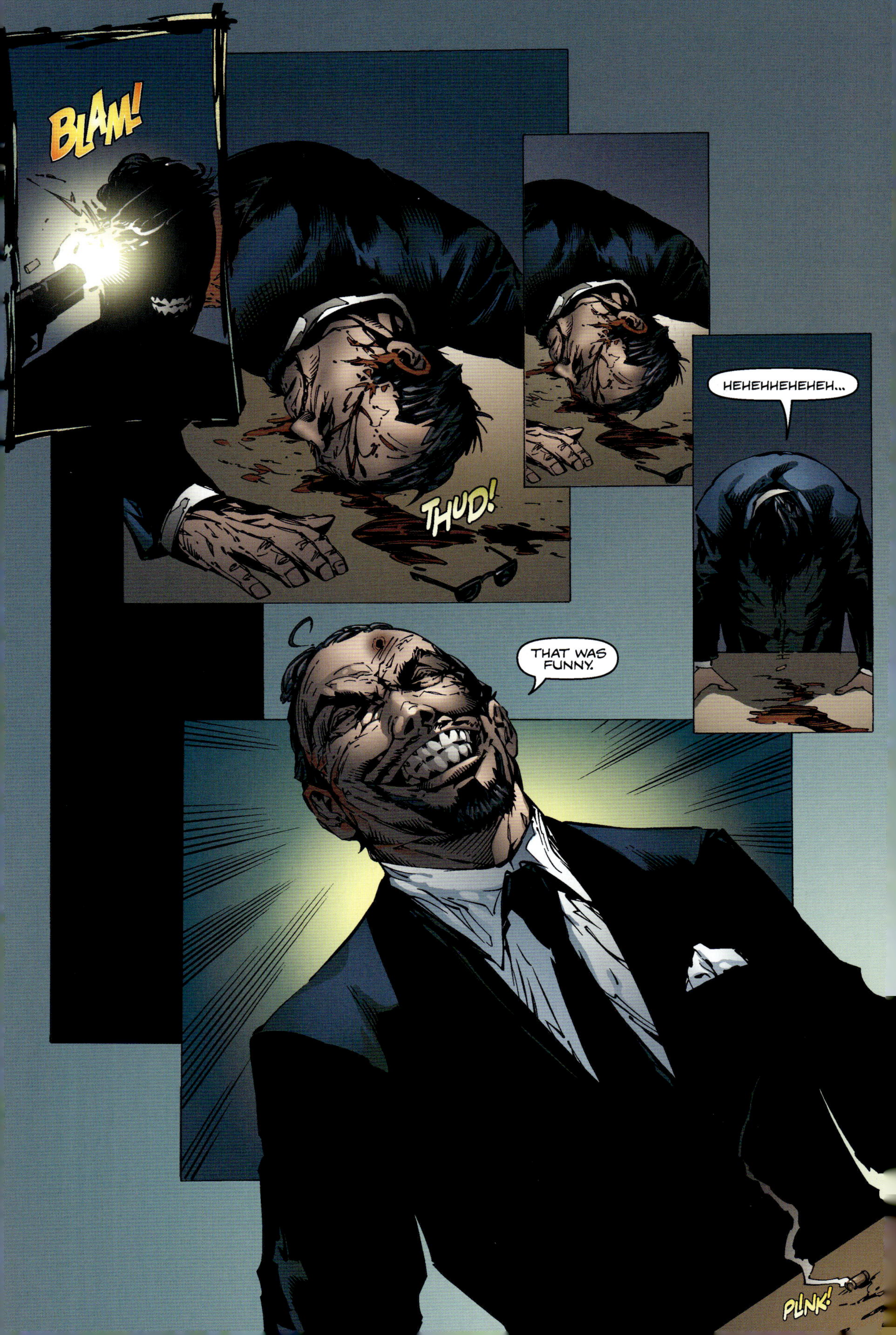
BLAM!
THUD!
HEHEHHEHEHEH...
THAT WAS FUNNY.
PLINK!

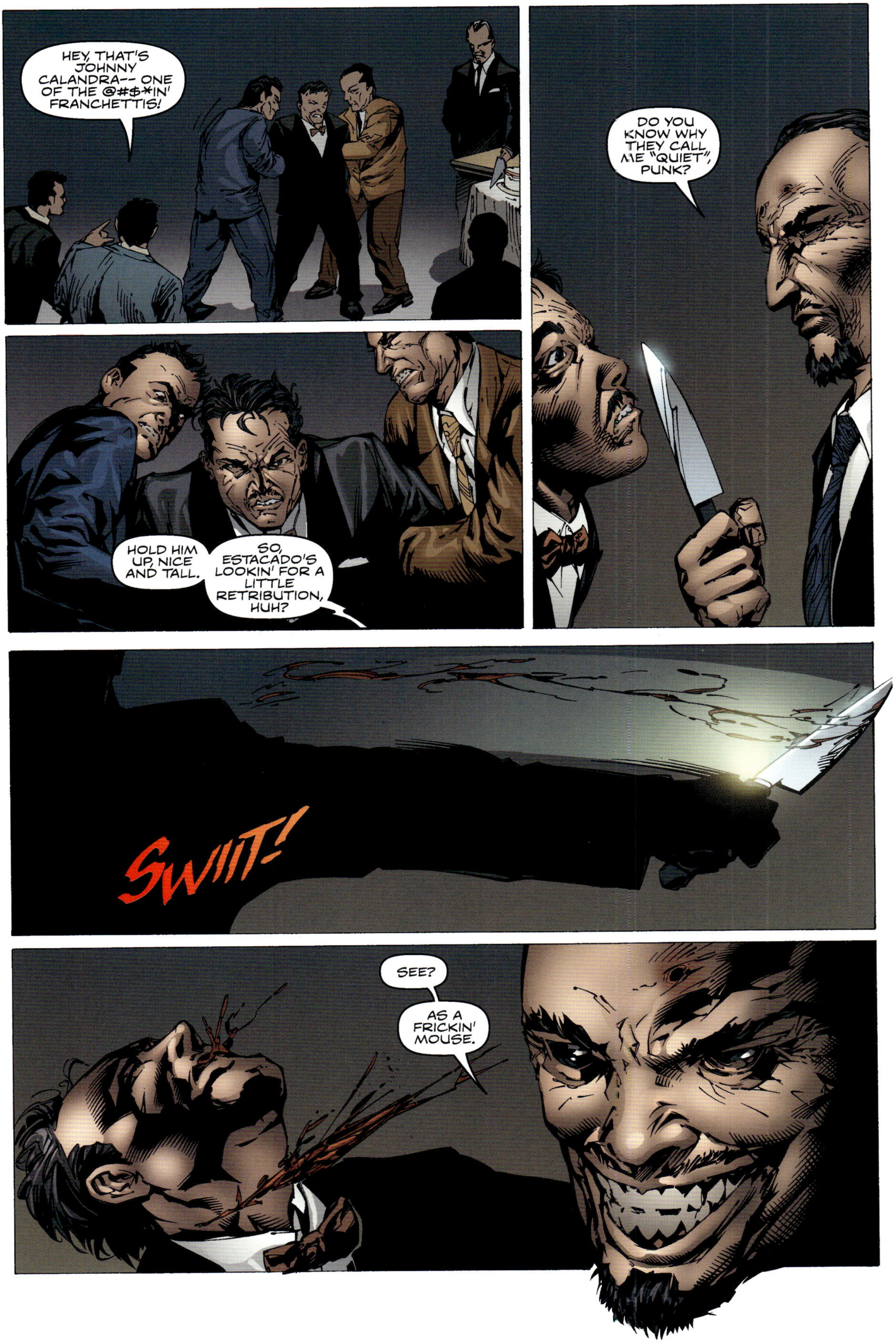
HEY, THAT'S JOHNNY CALANDRA-- ONE OF THE @#$*IN' FRANCHETTIS!
HOLD HIM UP, NICE AND TALL.
SO, ESTACADO'S LOOKIN' FOR A LITTLE RETRIBUTION, HUH?
DO YOU KNOW WHY THEY CALL ME "QUIET", PUNK?
SWIIT!
SEE?
AS A FRICKIN' MOUSE.

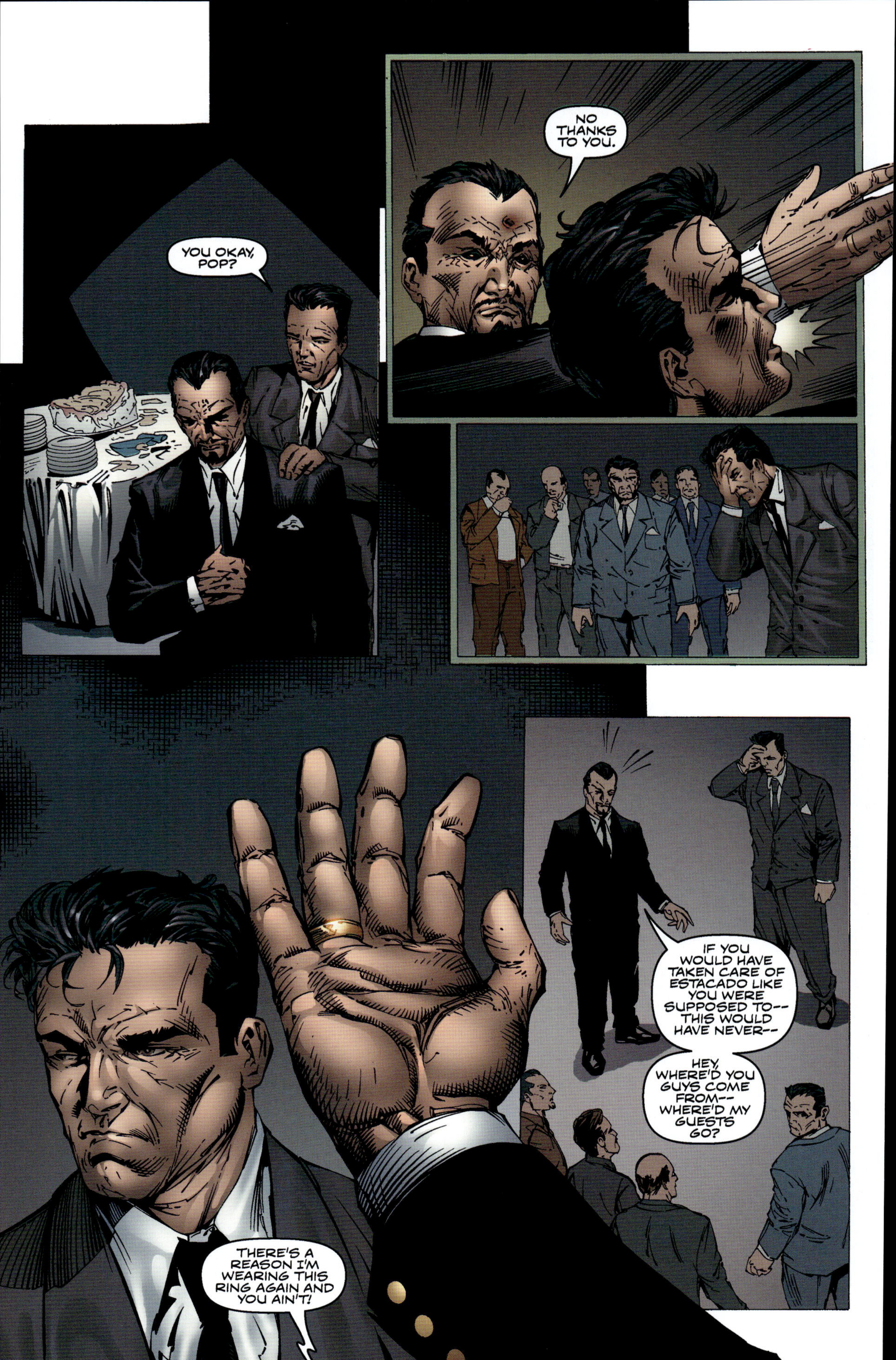

YOU OKAY, POP?
NO THANKS TO YOU.
IF YOU WOULD HAVE TAKEN CARE OF ESTACADO LIKE YOU WERE SUPPOSED TO-- THIS WOULD HAVE NEVER--
HEY, WHERE'D YOU GUYS COME FROM-- WHERE'D MY GUESTS GO?
THERE'S A REASON I'M WEARING THIS RING AGAIN AND YOU AIN'T!

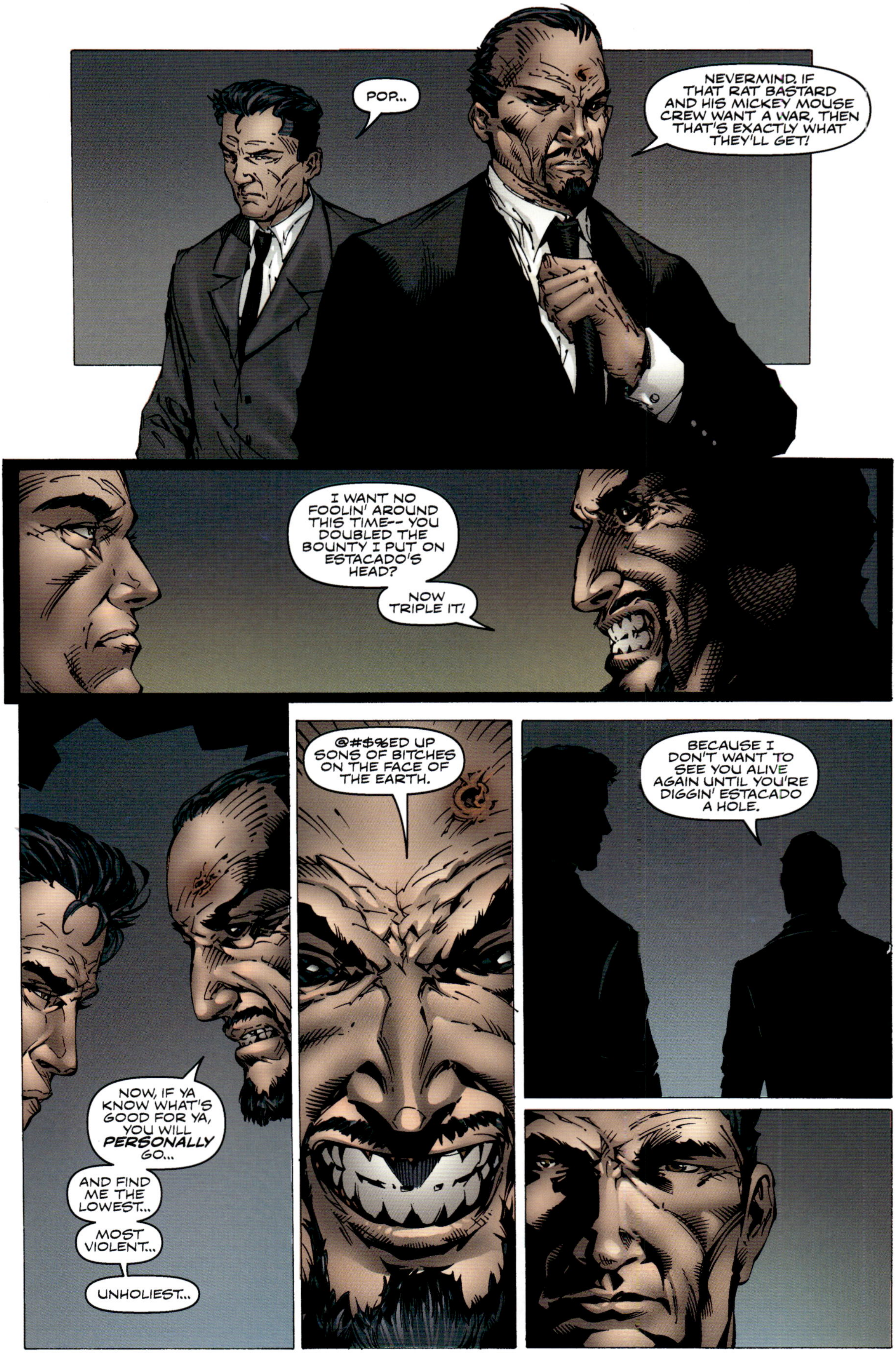

POP...
NEVERMIND. IF THAT RAT BASTARD AND HIS MICKEY MOUSE CREW WANT A WAR, THEN THAT'S EXACTLY WHAT THEY'LL GET!
I WANT NO FOOLIN' AROUND THIS TIME-- YOU DOUBLED THE BOUNTY I PUT ON ESTACADO'S HEAD?
NOW TRIPLE IT!
NOW, IF YA KNOW WHAT'S GOOD FOR YA, YOU WILL **PERSONALLY** GO...
AND FIND ME THE LOWEST...
MOST VIOLENT...
UNHOLIEST...
@#$%ED UP SONS OF BITCHES ON THE FACE OF THE EARTH.
BECAUSE I DON'T WANT TO SEE YOU ALIVE AGAIN UNTIL YOU'RE DIGGIN' ESTACADO A HOLE.

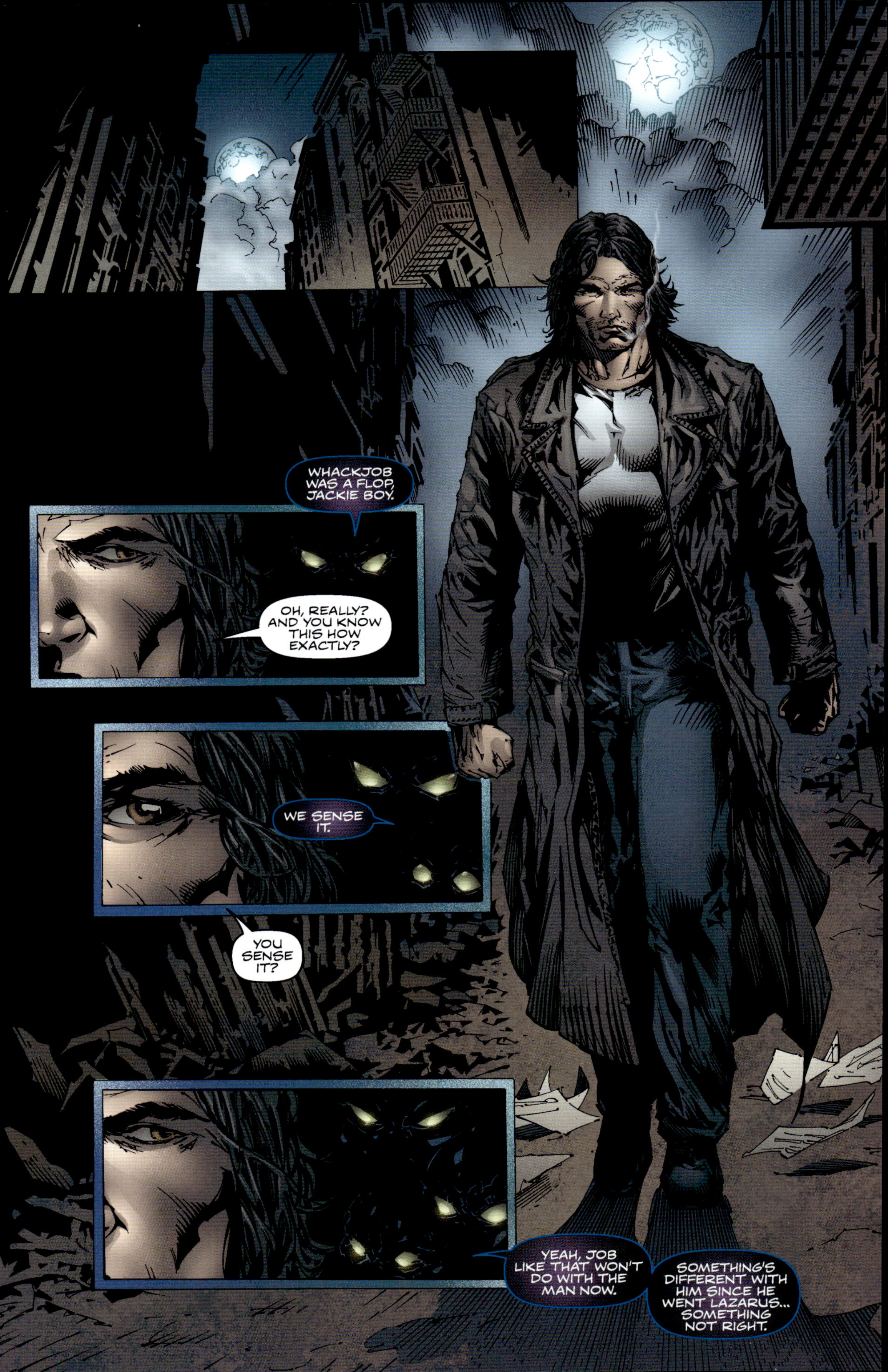
WHACKJOB WAS A FLOP, JACKIE BOY.
OH, REALLY? AND YOU KNOW THIS HOW EXACTLY?
WE SENSE IT.
YOU SENSE IT?
YEAH, JOB LIKE THAT WON'T DO WITH THE MAN NOW.
SOMETHING'S DIFFERENT WITH HIM SINCE HE WENT LAZARUS... SOMETHING NOT RIGHT.

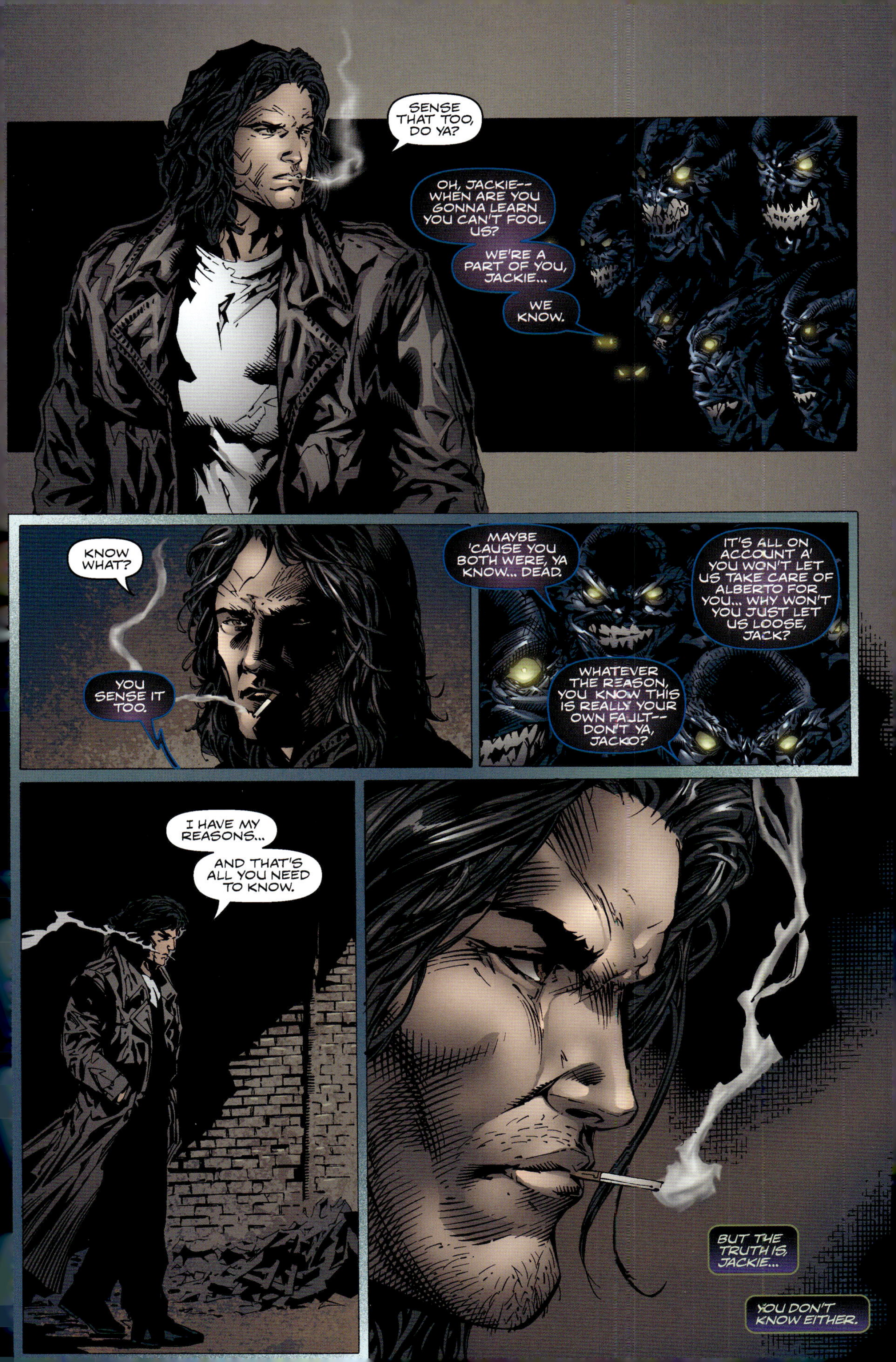
SENSE THAT TOO, DO YA?
OH, JACKIE-- WHEN ARE YOU GONNA LEARN YOU CAN'T FOOL US?
WE'RE A PART OF YOU, JACKIE...
WE KNOW.
KNOW WHAT?
YOU SENSE IT TOO.
MAYBE 'CAUSE YOU BOTH WERE, YA KNOW... DEAD.
IT'S ALL ON ACCOUNT A' YOU WON'T LET US TAKE CARE OF ALBERTO FOR YOU... WHY WON'T YOU JUST LET US LOOSE, JACK?
WHATEVER THE REASON, YOU KNOW THIS IS REALLY YOUR OWN FAULT-- DON'T YA, JACKO?
I HAVE MY REASONS...
AND THAT'S ALL YOU NEED TO KNOW.
BUT THE TRUTH IS, JACKIE...
YOU DON'T KNOW EITHER.

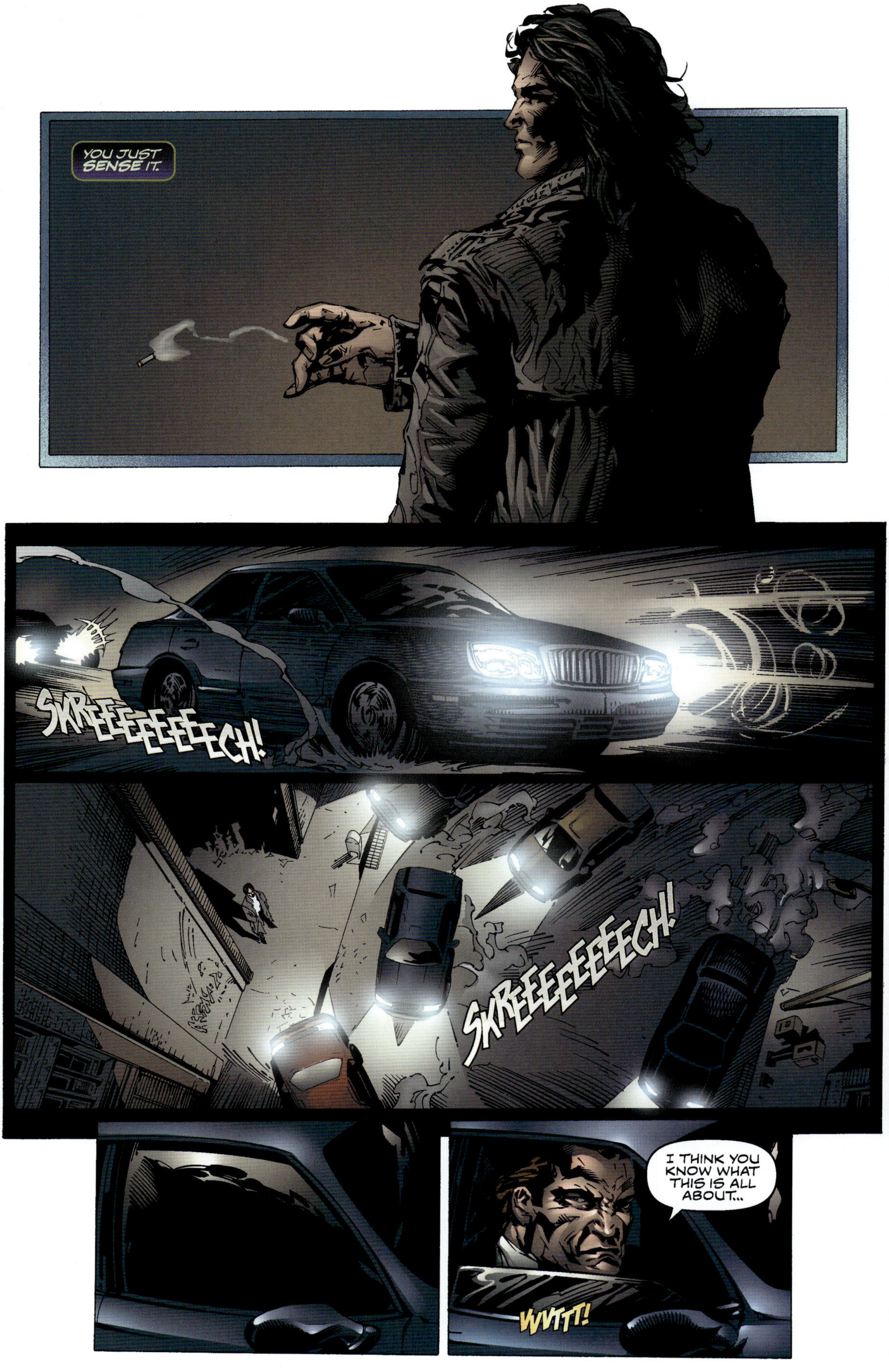
YOU JUST SENSE IT.
SKREEEEEEEEECH!
SKREEEEEEEEECH!
I THINK YOU KNOW WHAT THIS IS ALL ABOUT...
VVVTTT!

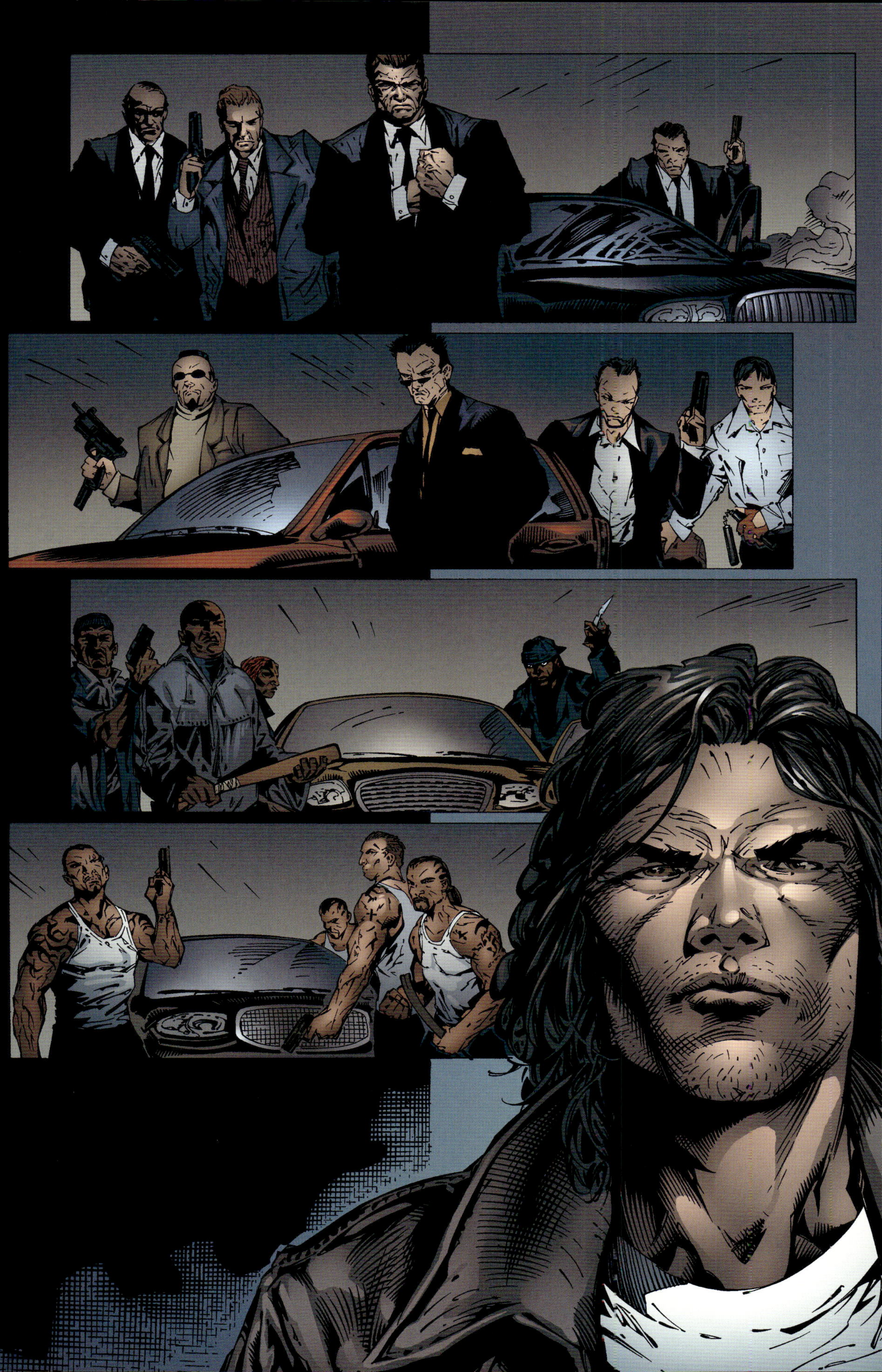

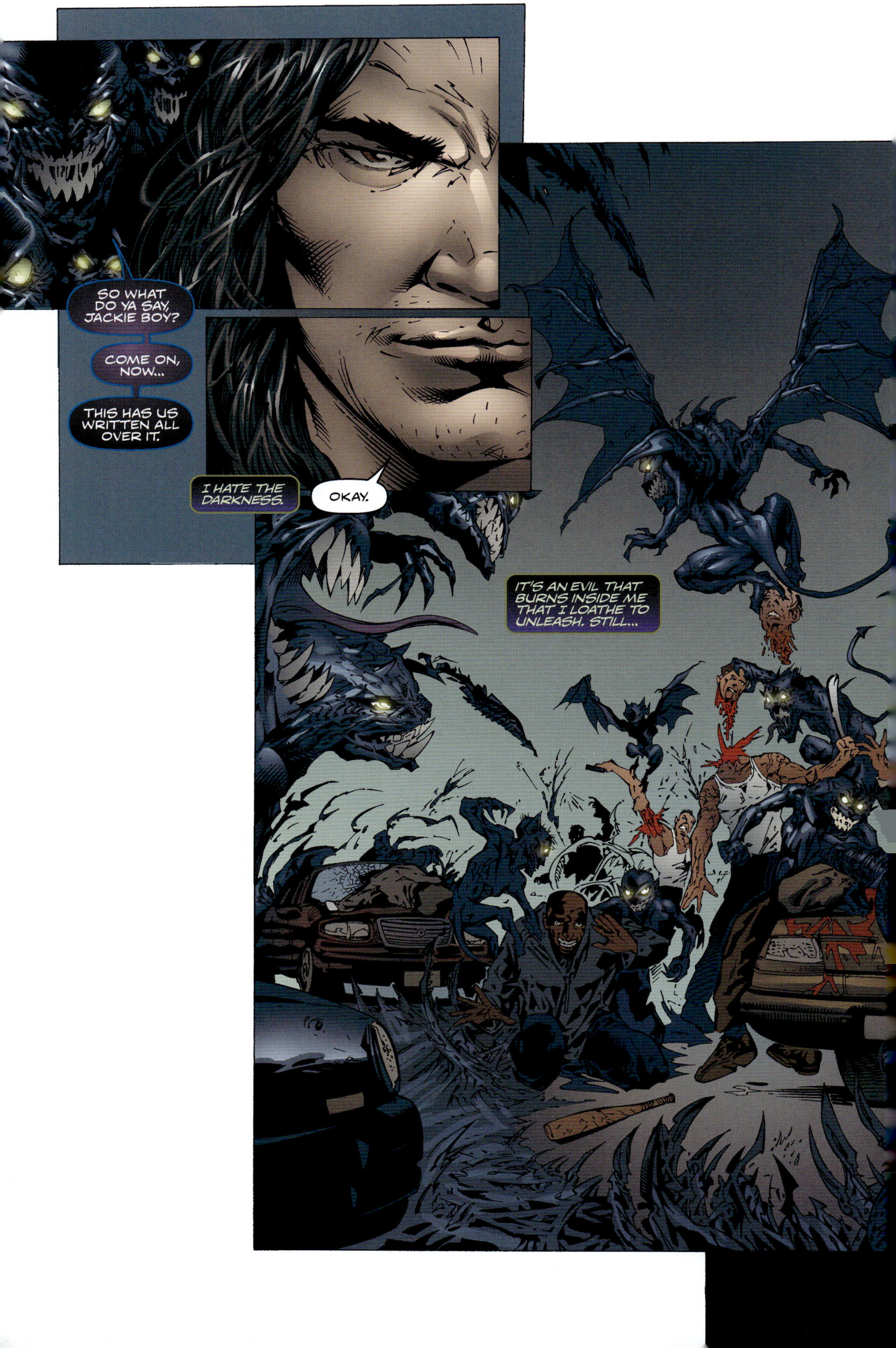
SO WHAT DO YA SAY, JACKIE BOY?
COME ON, NOW...
THIS HAS US WRITTEN ALL OVER IT.
I HATE THE DARKNESS.
OKAY.
IT'S AN EVIL THAT BURNS INSIDE ME THAT I LOATHE TO UNLEASH. STILL...

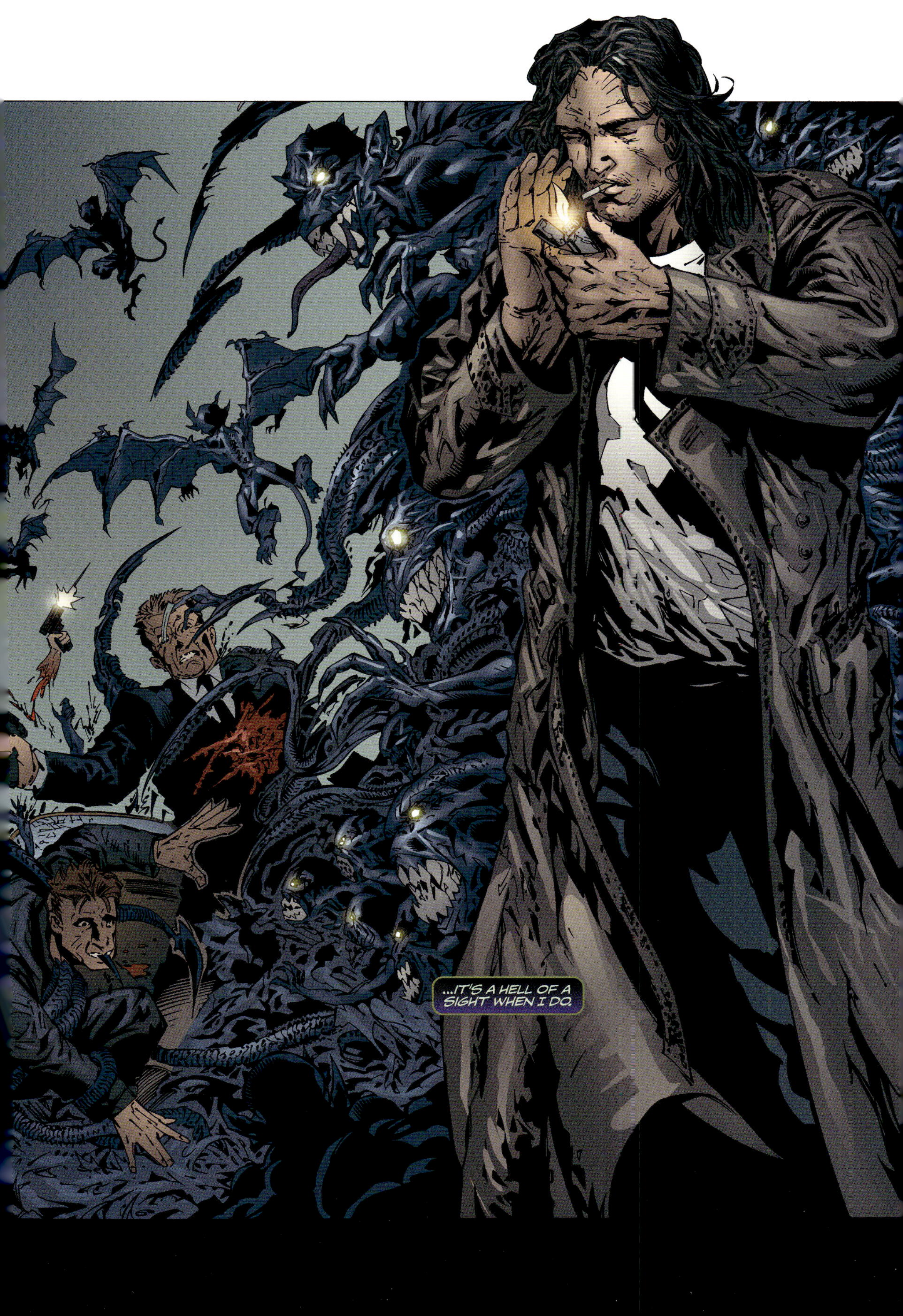
...IT'S A HELL OF A SIGHT WHEN I DO.

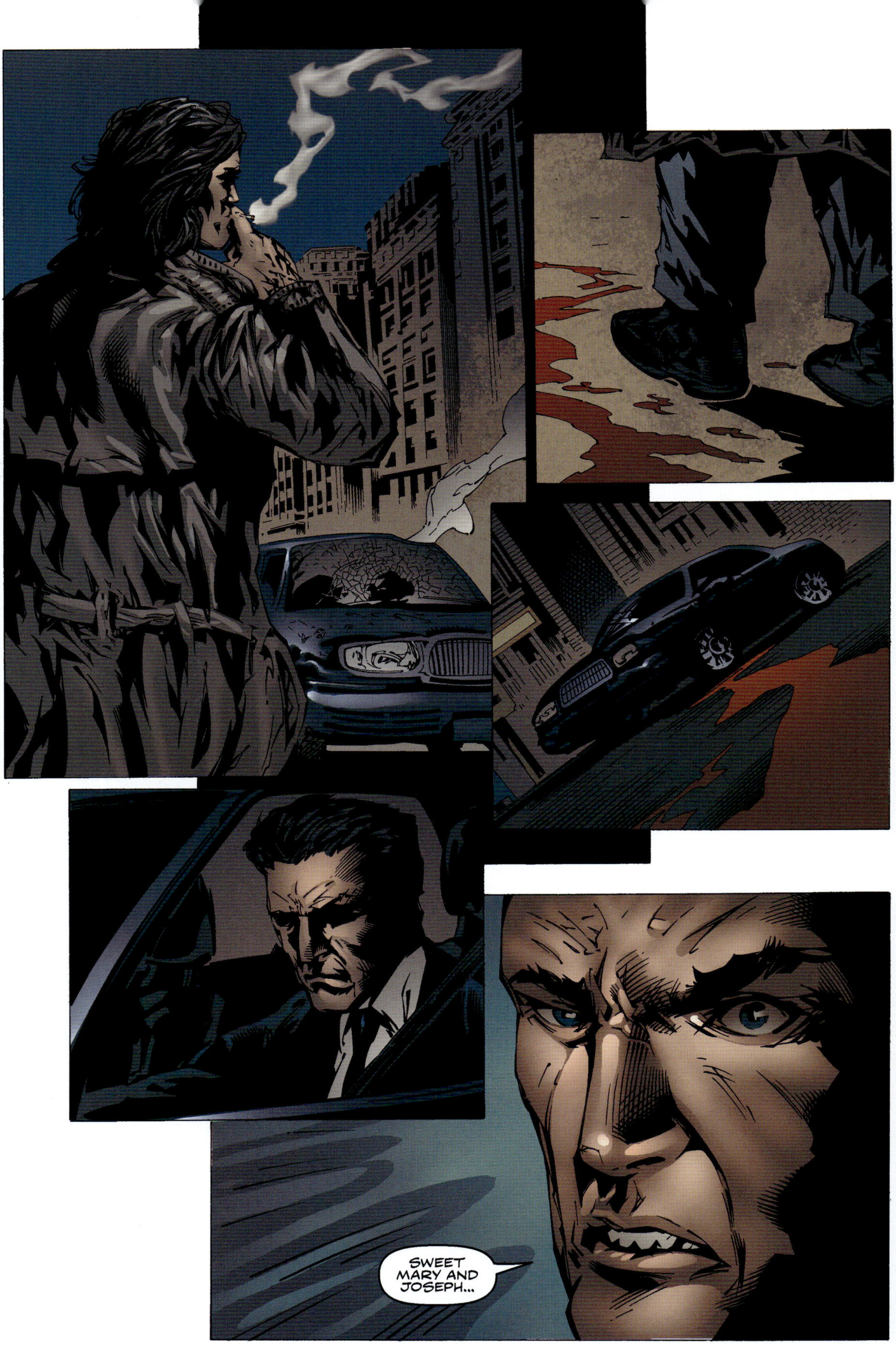
SWEET MARY AND JOSEPH...

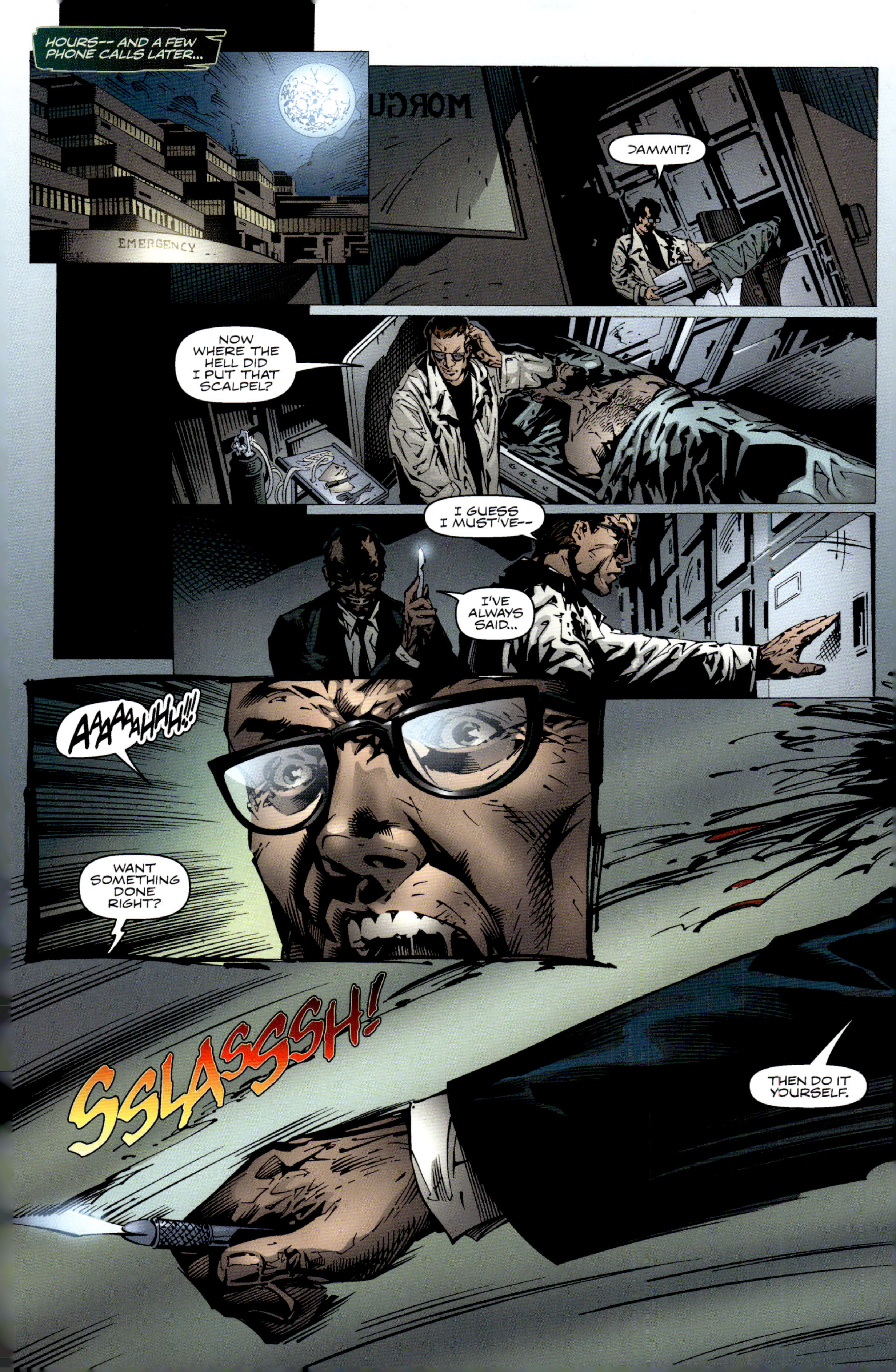
HOURS-- AND A FEW PHONE CALLS LATER...
EMERGENCY
MORGU
DAMMIT!
NOW WHERE THE HELL DID I PUT THAT SCALPEL?
I GUESS I MUST'VE--
I'VE ALWAYS SAID...
AAAAAHHH!!!
WANT SOMETHING DONE RIGHT?
SSLASSSH!
THEN DO IT YOURSELF.

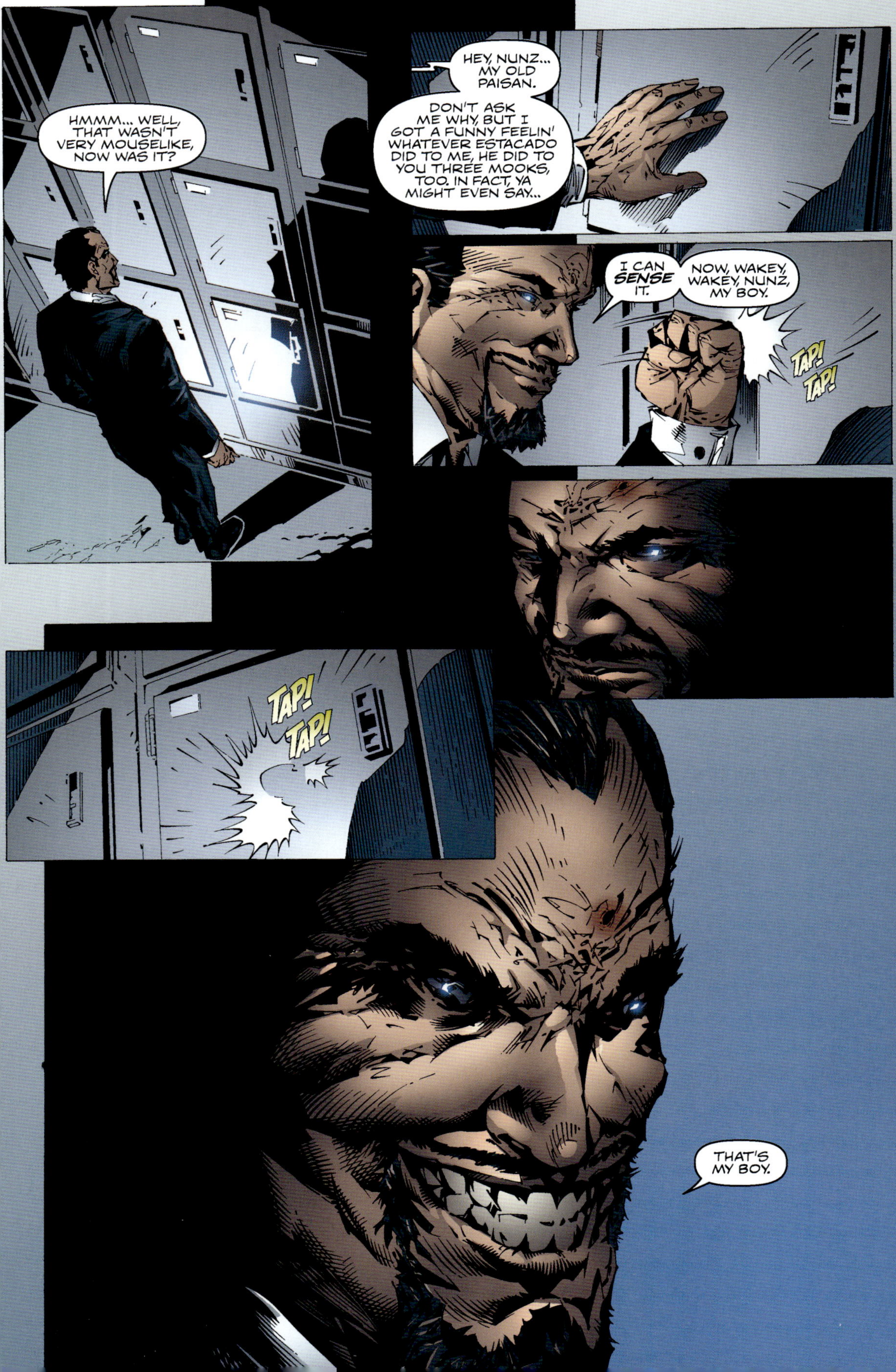
HMMM... WELL, THAT WASN'T VERY MOUSELIKE, NOW WAS IT?
HEY, NUNZ... MY OLD PAISAN.
DON'T ASK ME WHY, BUT I GOT A FUNNY FEELIN' WHATEVER ESTACADO DID TO ME, HE DID TO YOU THREE MOOKS, TOO. IN FACT, YA MIGHT EVEN SAY...
I CAN SENSE IT.
NOW, WAKEY, WAKEY, NUNZ, MY BOY.
TAP! TAP!
TAP! TAP!
THAT'S MY BOY.

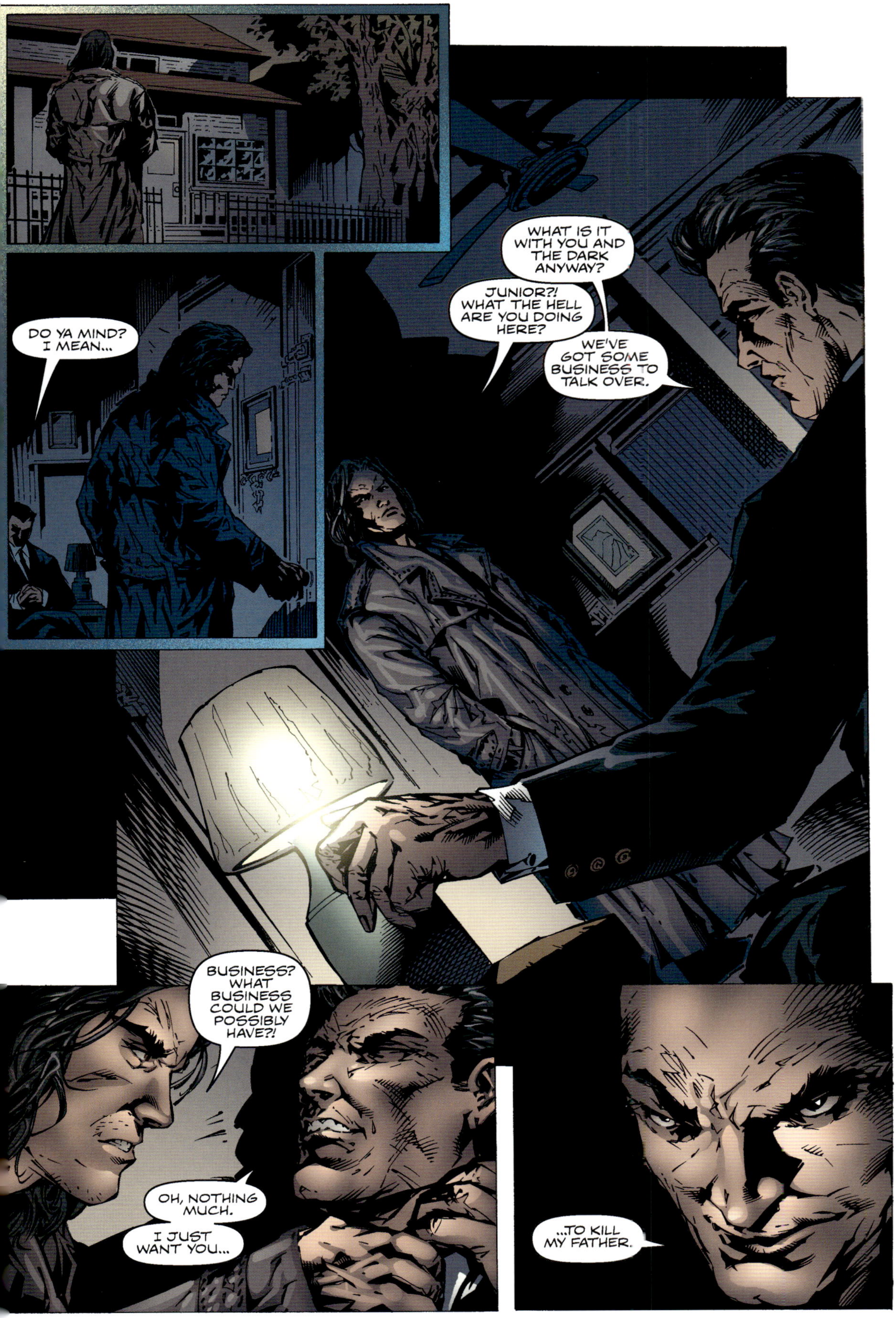
DO YA MIND? I MEAN...
WHAT IS IT WITH YOU AND THE DARK ANYWAY?
JUNIOR?! WHAT THE HELL ARE YOU DOING HERE?
WE'VE GOT SOME BUSINESS TO TALK OVER.
BUSINESS? WHAT BUSINESS COULD WE POSSIBLY HAVE?!
OH, NOTHING MUCH.
I JUST WANT YOU...
...TO KILL MY FATHER.

The Darkness Issue #56
cover art by: Dale Keown

THE DARKNESS #56

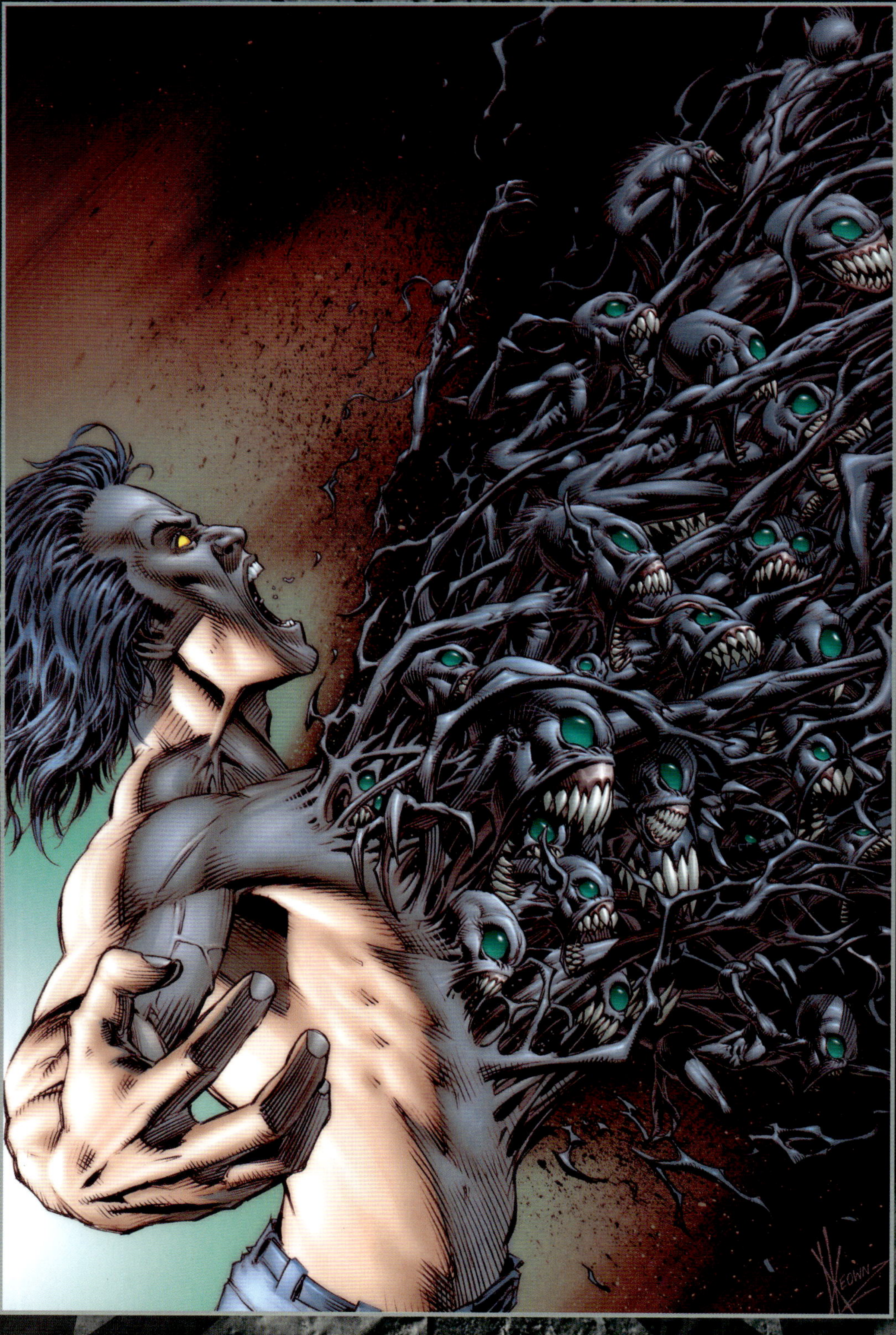
KEOWN

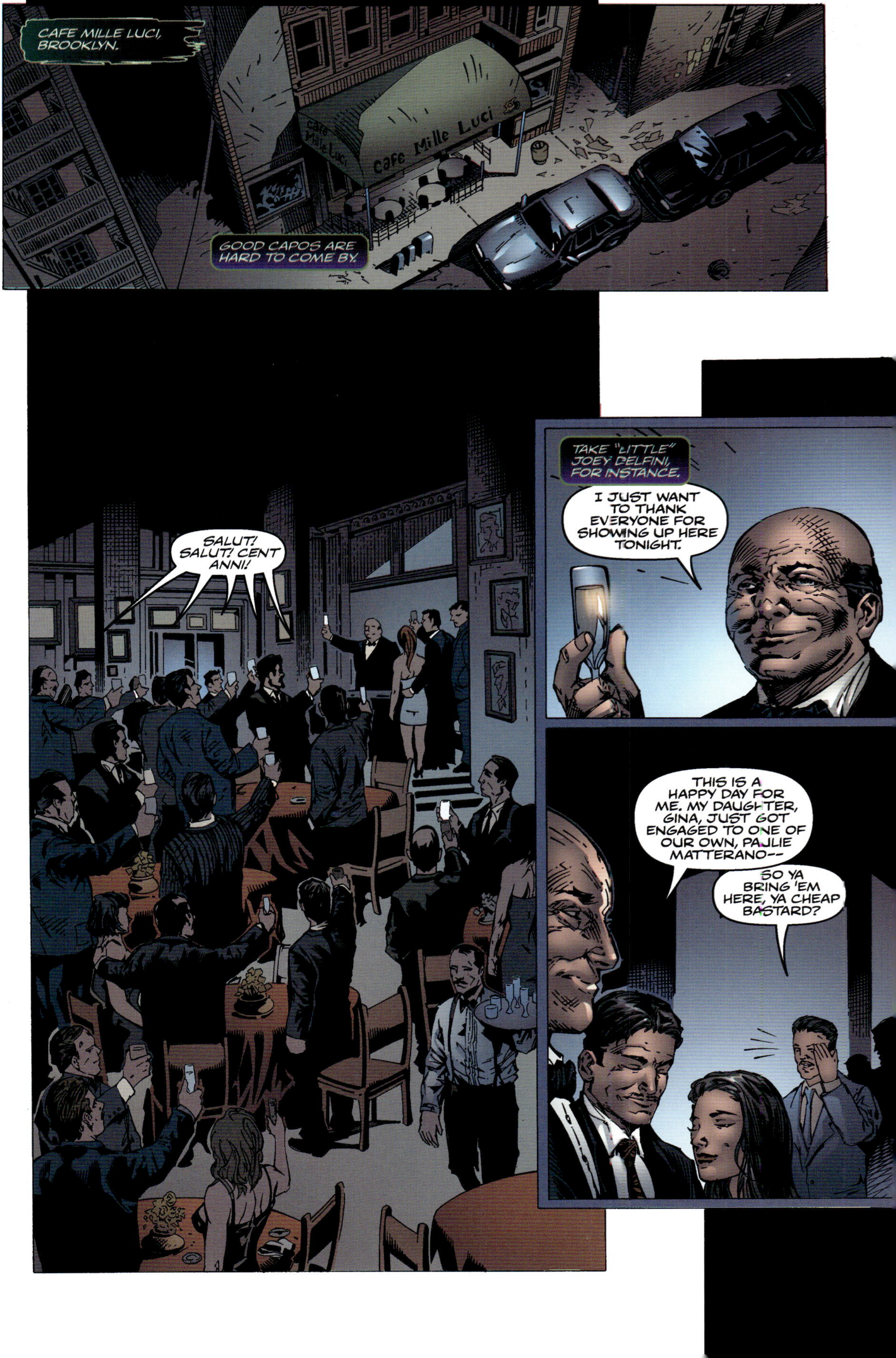
CAFE MILLE LUCI, BROOKLYN.
Cafe Mille Luci
GOOD CAPOS ARE HARD TO COME BY.
SALUT! SALUT! CENT ANNI!
TAKE "LITTLE" JOEY DELFINI, FOR INSTANCE.
I JUST WANT TO THANK EVERYONE FOR SHOWING UP HERE TONIGHT.
THIS IS A HAPPY DAY FOR ME. MY DAUGHTER, GINA, JUST GOT ENGAGED TO ONE OF OUR OWN, PAULIE MATTERANO--
SO YA BRING 'EM HERE, YA CHEAP BASTARD?

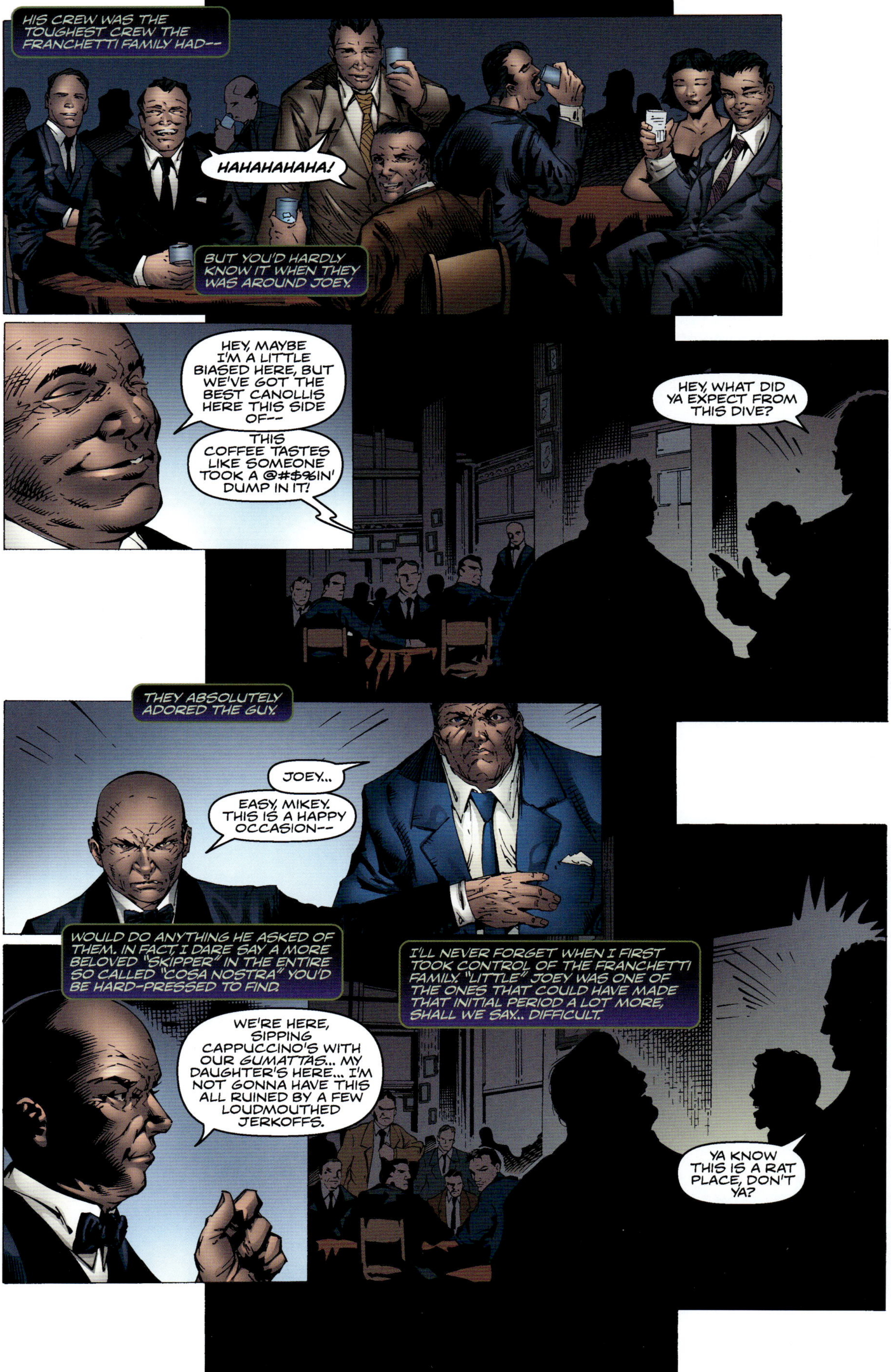
HIS CREW WAS THE TOUGHEST CREW THE FRANCHETTI FAMILY HAD--
HAHAHAHAHA!
BUT YOU'D HARDLY KNOW IT WHEN THEY WAS AROUND JOEY.
HEY, MAYBE I'M A LITTLE BIASED HERE, BUT WE'VE GOT THE BEST CANOLLIS HERE THIS SIDE OF--
THIS COFFEE TASTES LIKE SOMEONE TOOK A @#$%IN' DUMP IN IT!
HEY, WHAT DID YA EXPECT FROM THIS DIVE?
THEY ABSOLUTELY ADORED THE GUY.
JOEY...
EASY, MIKEY. THIS IS A HAPPY OCCASION--
WOULD DO ANYTHING HE ASKED OF THEM. IN FACT, I DARE SAY A MORE BELOVED "SKIPPER" IN THE ENTIRE SO CALLED "COSA NOSTRA" YOU'D BE HARD-PRESSED TO FIND.
WE'RE HERE, SIPPING CAPPUCCINO'S WITH OUR GUMATTAS... MY DAUGHTER'S HERE... I'M NOT GONNA HAVE THIS ALL RUINED BY A FEW LOUDMOUTHED JERKOFFS.
I'LL NEVER FORGET WHEN I FIRST TOOK CONTROL OF THE FRANCHETTI FAMILY. "LITTLE" JOEY WAS ONE OF THE ONES THAT COULD HAVE MADE THAT INITIAL PERIOD A LOT MORE, SHALL WE SAY.. DIFFICULT.
YA KNOW THIS IS A RAT PLACE, DON'T YA?

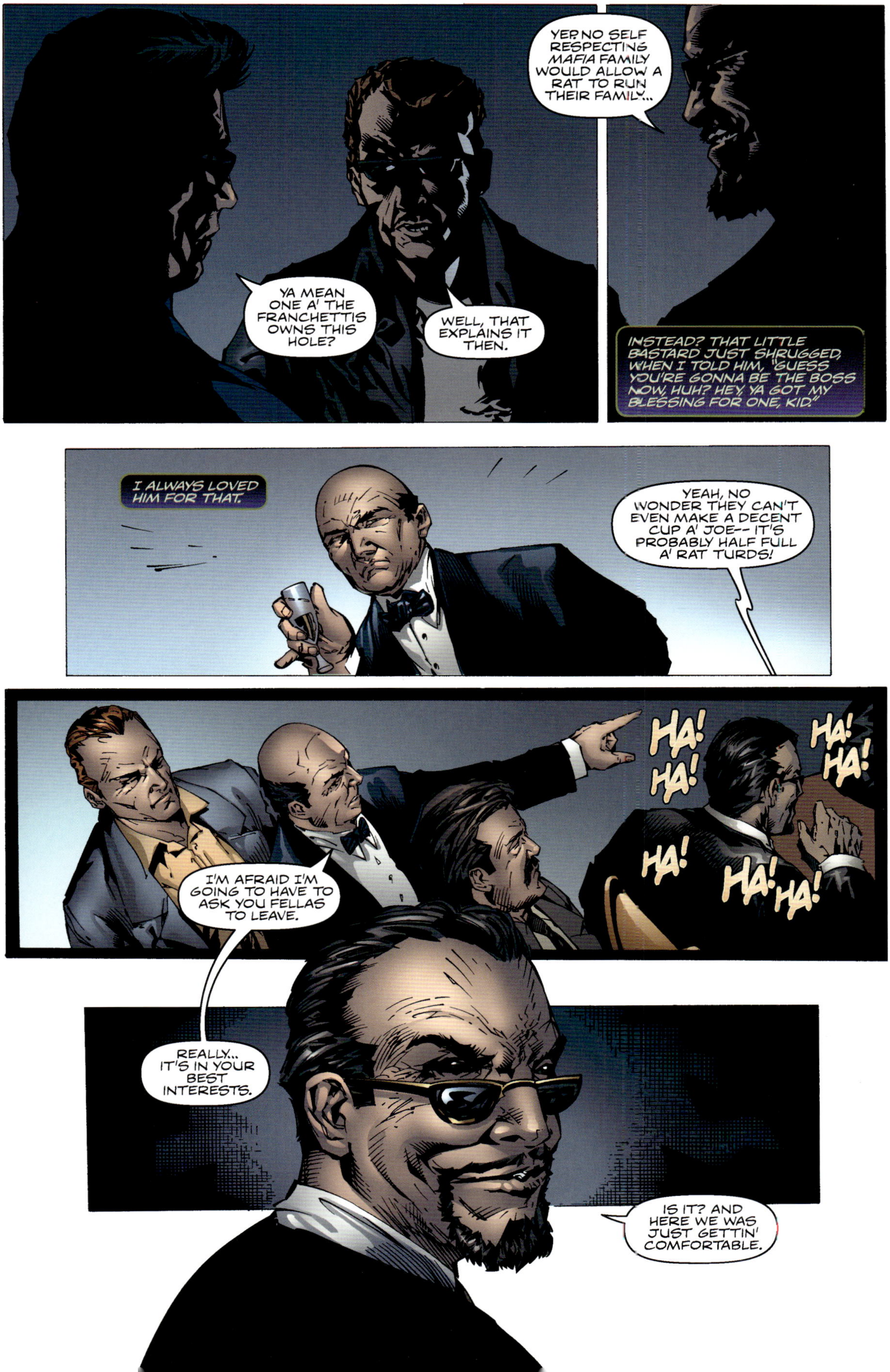
YEP. NO SELF RESPECTING MAFIA FAMILY WOULD ALLOW A RAT TO RUN THEIR FAMILY...
YA MEAN ONE A' THE FRANCHETTIS OWNS THIS HOLE?
WELL, THAT EXPLAINS IT THEN.
INSTEAD? THAT LITTLE BASTARD JUST SHRUGGED, WHEN I TOLD HIM, "GUESS YOU'RE GONNA BE THE BOSS NOW, HUH? HEY, YA GOT MY BLESSING FOR ONE, KID."
I ALWAYS LOVED HIM FOR THAT.
YEAH, NO WONDER THEY CAN'T EVEN MAKE A DECENT CUP A' JOE-- IT'S PROBABLY HALF FULL A' RAT TURDS!
HA! HA!
HA! HA!
HA!
HA! HA!
I'M AFRAID I'M GOING TO HAVE TO ASK YOU FELLAS TO LEAVE.
REALLY... IT'S IN YOUR BEST INTERESTS.
IS IT? AND HERE WE WAS JUST GETTIN' COMFORTABLE.

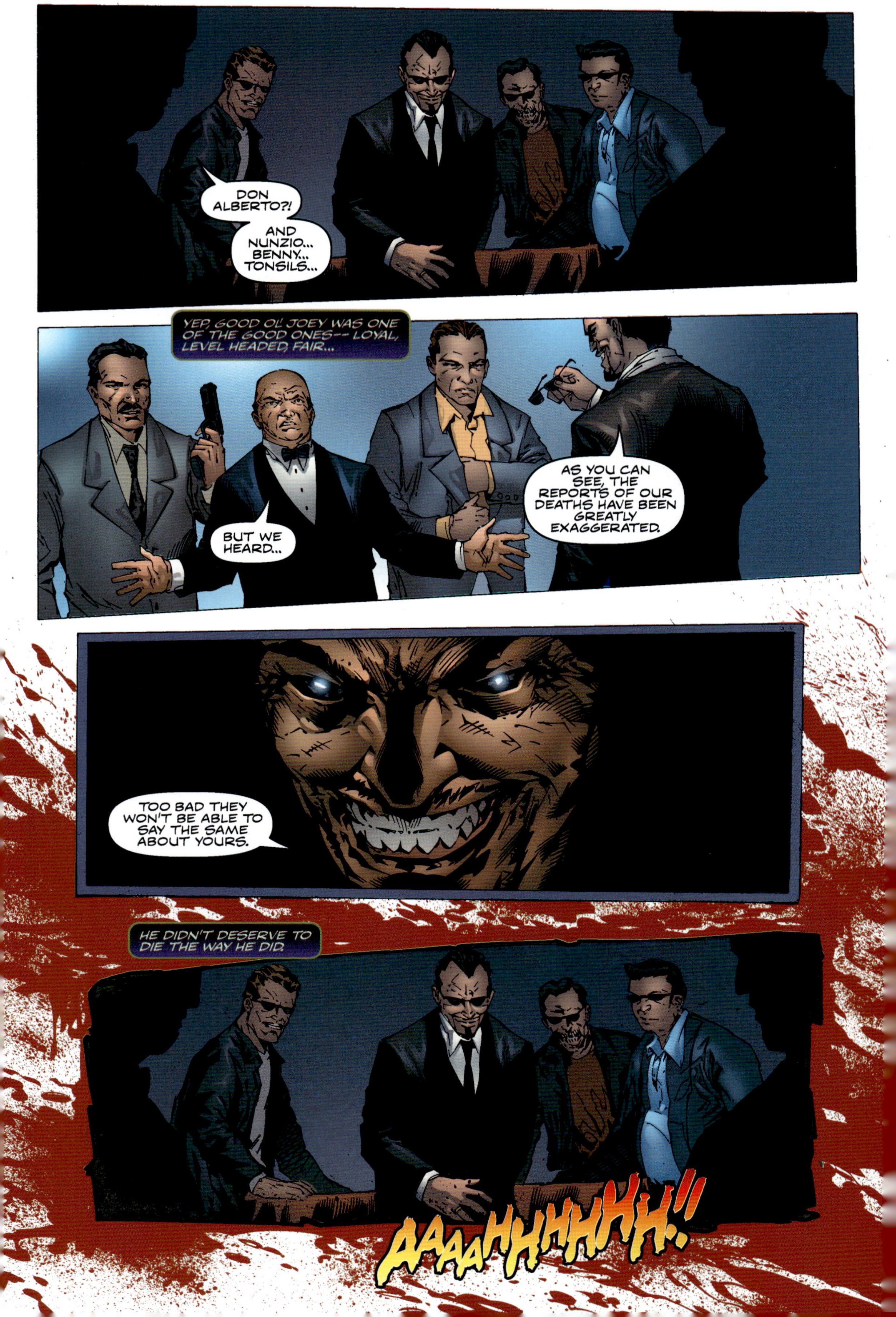
DON ALBERTO?!
AND NUNZIO... BENNY... TONSILS...
YEP, GOOD OL' JOEY WAS ONE OF THE GOOD ONES-- LOYAL, LEVEL HEADED, FAIR...
BUT WE HEARD...
AS YOU CAN SEE, THE REPORTS OF OUR DEATHS HAVE BEEN GREATLY EXAGGERATED.
TOO BAD THEY WON'T BE ABLE TO SAY THE SAME ABOUT YOURS.
HE DIDN'T DESERVE TO DIE THE WAY HE DID.
AAAAHHHHHH!!

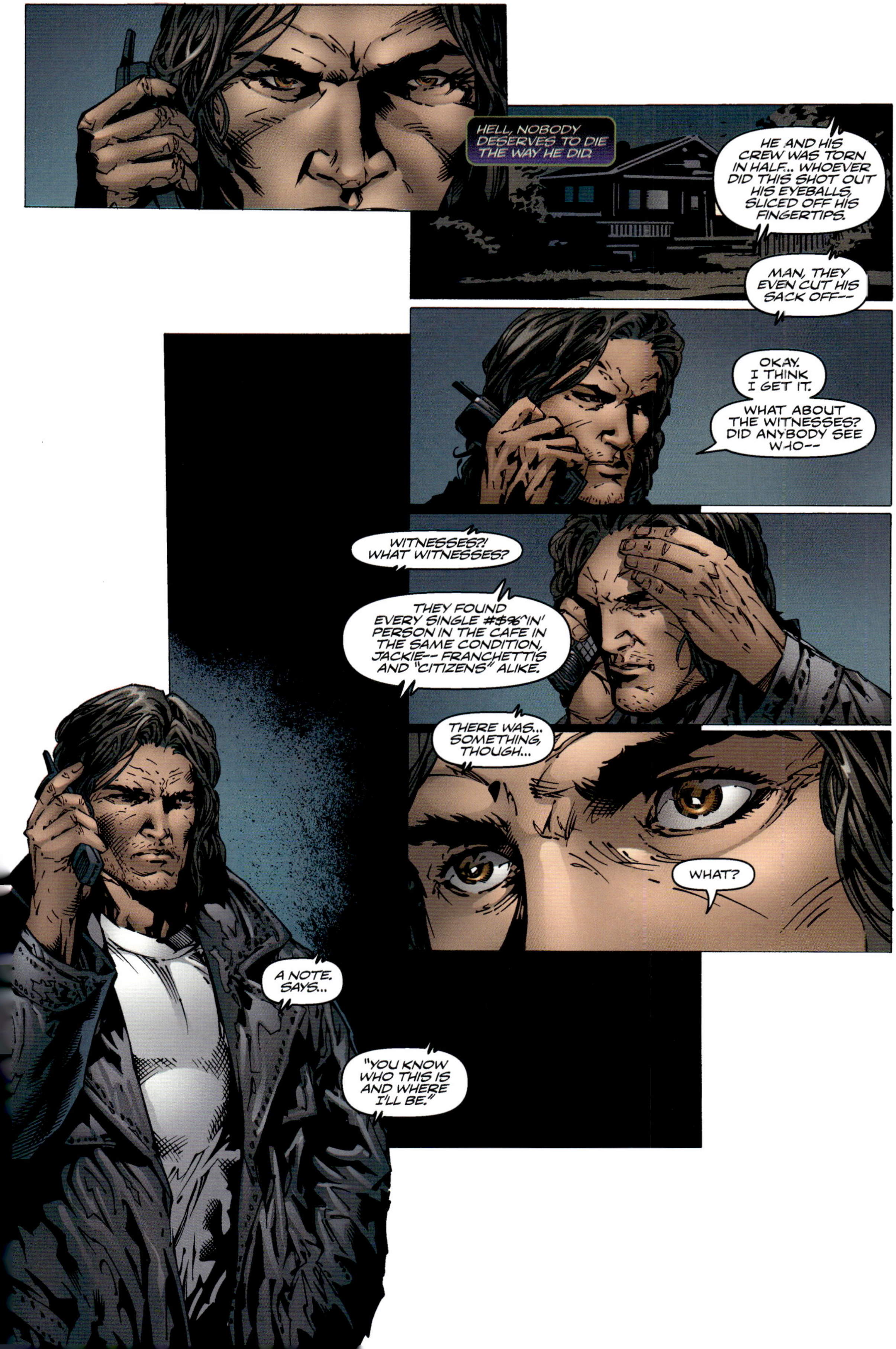
HELL, NOBODY DESERVES TO DIE THE WAY HE DID.
HE AND HIS CREW WAS TORN IN HALF... WHOEVER DID THIS SHOT OUT HIS EYEBALLS, SLICED OFF HIS FINGERTIPS.
MAN, THEY EVEN CUT HIS SACK OFF--
OKAY. I THINK I GET IT.
WHAT ABOUT THE WITNESSES? DID ANYBODY SEE WHO--
WITNESSES?! WHAT WITNESSES?
THEY FOUND EVERY SINGLE #$%^IN' PERSON IN THE CAFE IN THE SAME CONDITION, JACKIE-- FRANCHETTIS AND "CITIZENS" ALIKE.
THERE WAS... SOMETHING, THOUGH...
WHAT?
A NOTE. SAYS...
"YOU KNOW WHO THIS IS AND WHERE I'LL BE."

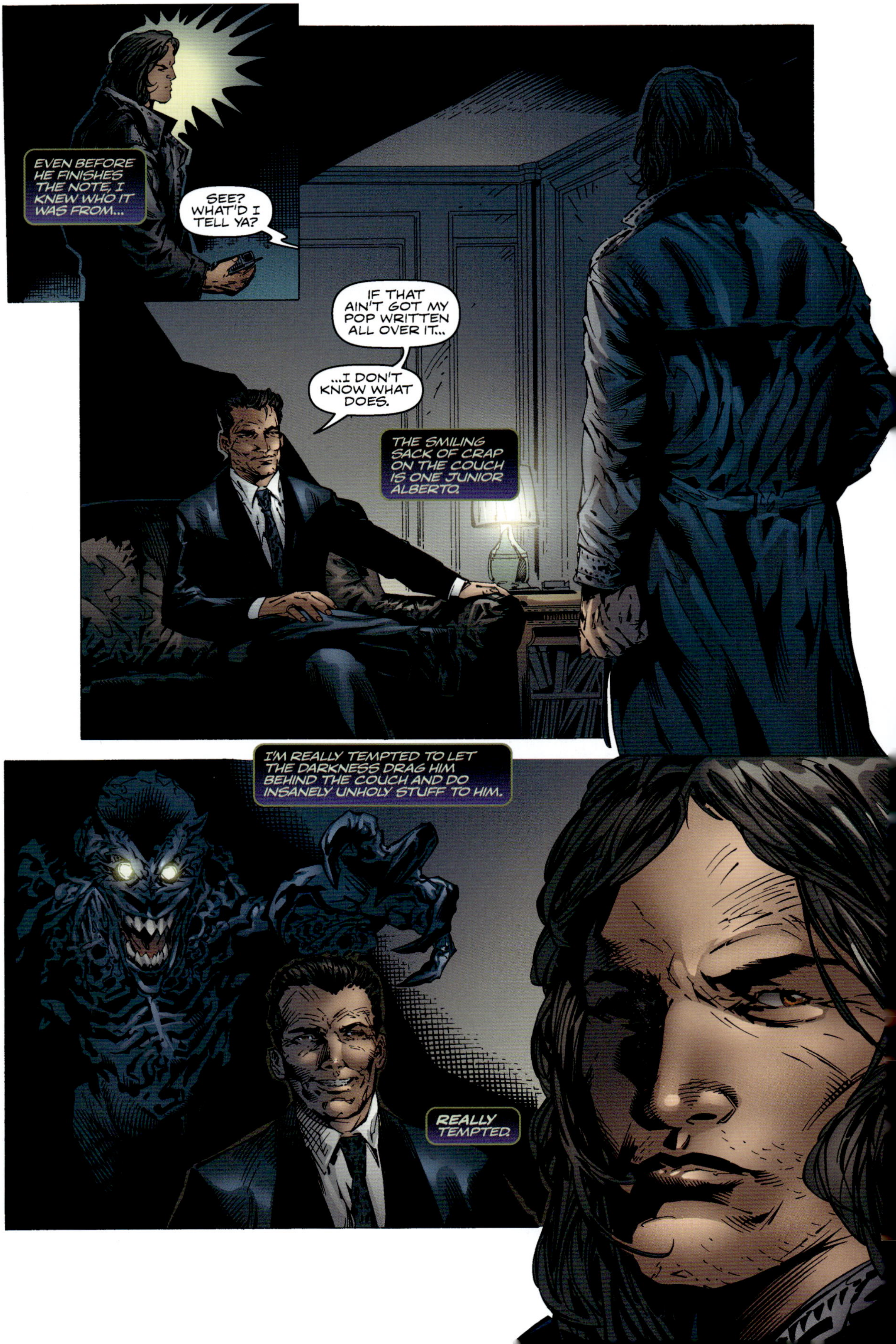

EVEN BEFORE HE FINISHES THE NOTE, I KNEW WHO IT WAS FROM...
SEE? WHAT'D I TELL YA?
IF THAT AIN'T GOT MY POP WRITTEN ALL OVER IT...
...I DON'T KNOW WHAT DOES.
THE SMILING SACK OF CRAP ON THE COUCH IS ONE JUNIOR ALBERTO.
I'M REALLY TEMPTED TO LET THE DARKNESS DRAG HIM BEHIND THE COUCH AND DO INSANELY UNHOLY STUFF TO HIM.
REALLY TEMPTED.

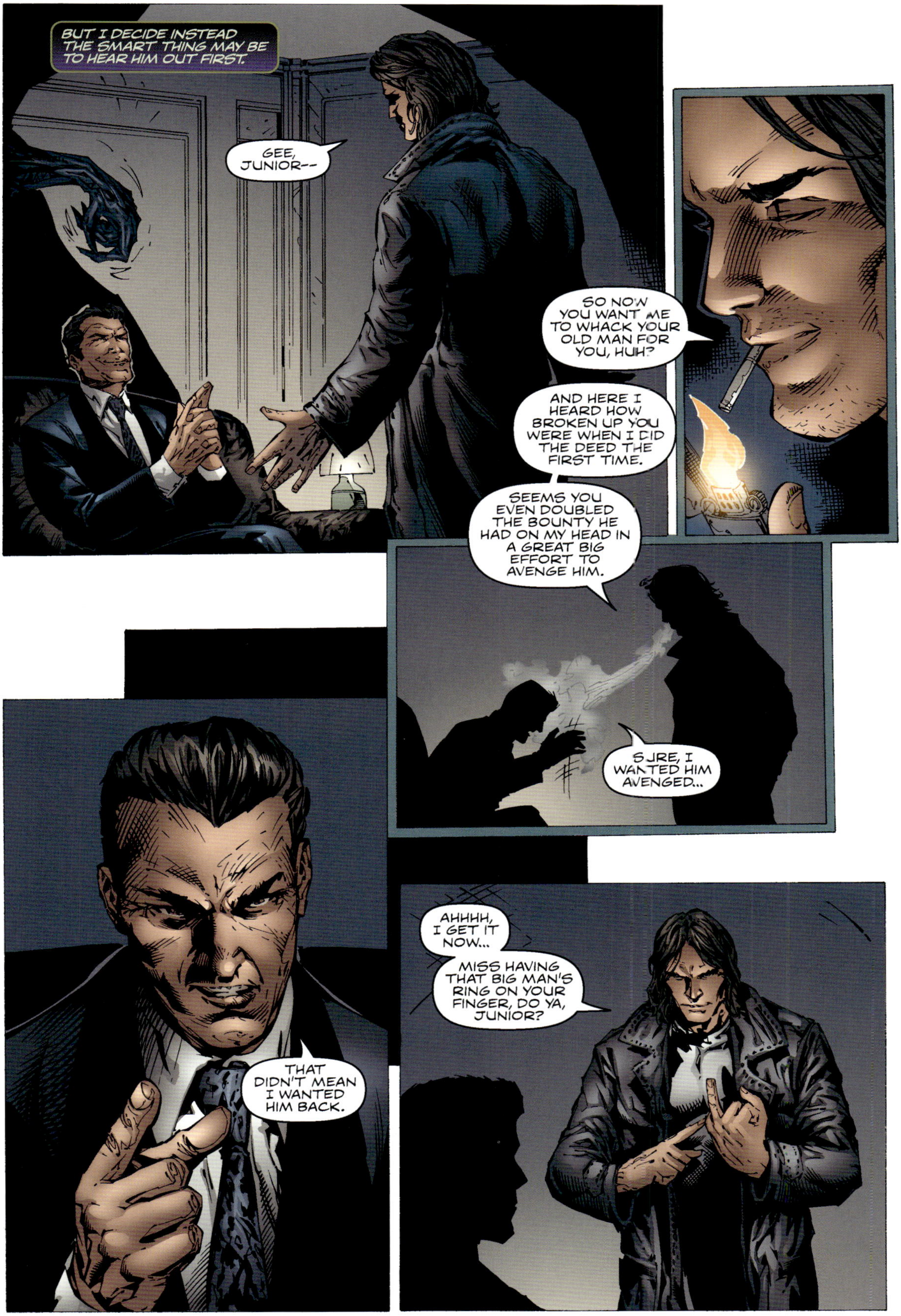
BUT I DECIDE INSTEAD THE SMART THING MAY BE TO HEAR HIM OUT FIRST.
GEE, JUNIOR--
SO NOW YOU WANT ME TO WHACK YOUR OLD MAN FOR YOU, HUH?
AND HERE I HEARD HOW BROKEN UP YOU WERE WHEN I DID THE DEED THE FIRST TIME.
SEEMS YOU EVEN DOUBLED THE BOUNTY HE HAD ON MY HEAD IN A GREAT BIG EFFORT TO AVENGE HIM.
SURE, I WANTED HIM AVENGED...
THAT DIDN'T MEAN I WANTED HIM BACK.
AHHHH, I GET IT NOW...
MISS HAVING THAT BIG MAN'S RING ON YOUR FINGER, DO YA, JUNIOR?

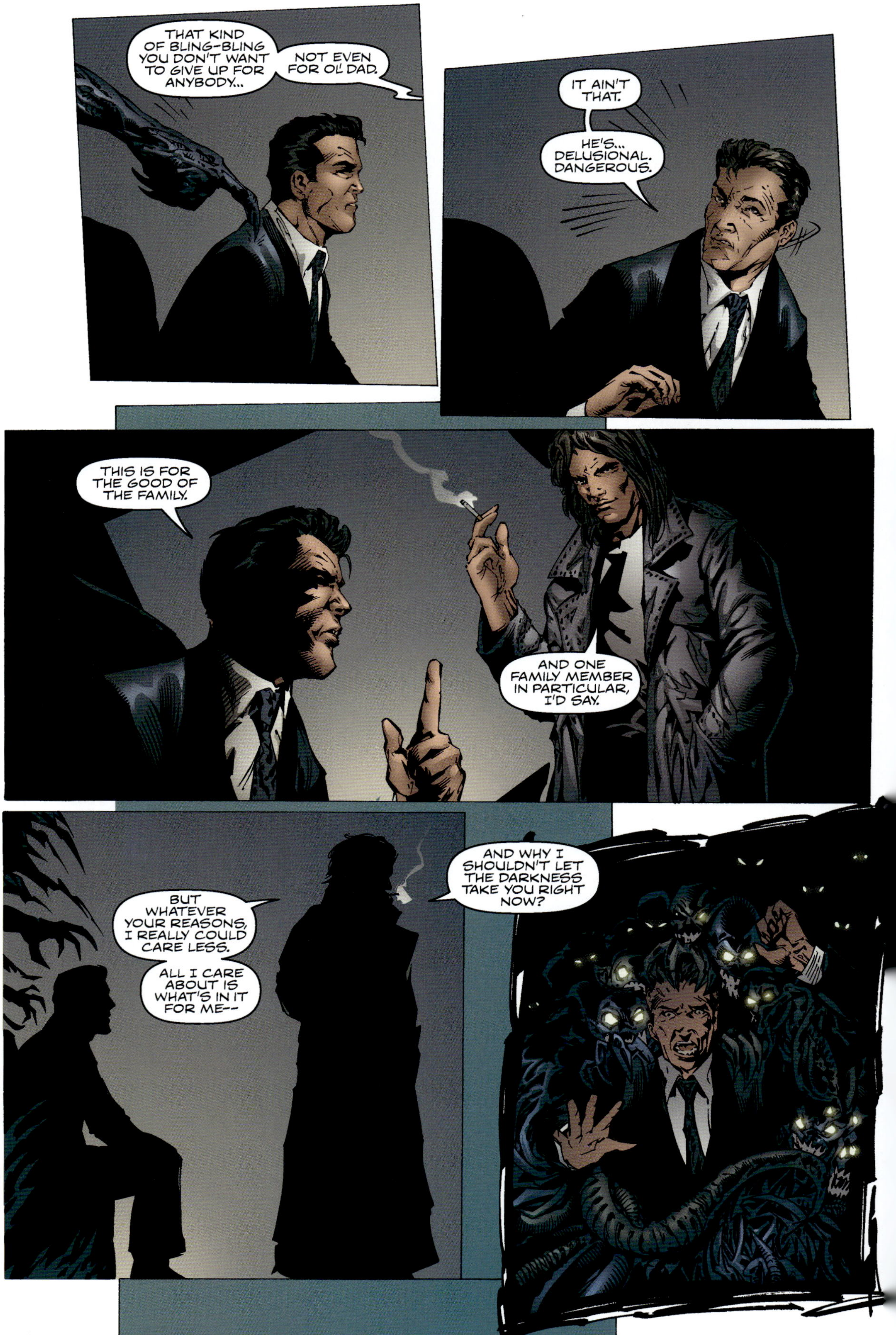
THAT KIND OF BLING-BLING YOU DON'T WANT TO GIVE UP FOR ANYBODY...
NOT EVEN FOR OL' DAD.
IT AIN'T THAT.
HE'S... DELUSIONAL. DANGEROUS.
THIS IS FOR THE GOOD OF THE FAMILY.
AND ONE FAMILY MEMBER IN PARTICULAR, I'D SAY.
BUT WHATEVER YOUR REASONS, I REALLY COULD CARE LESS.
ALL I CARE ABOUT IS WHAT'S IN IT FOR ME--
AND WHY I SHOULDN'T LET THE DARKNESS TAKE YOU RIGHT NOW?

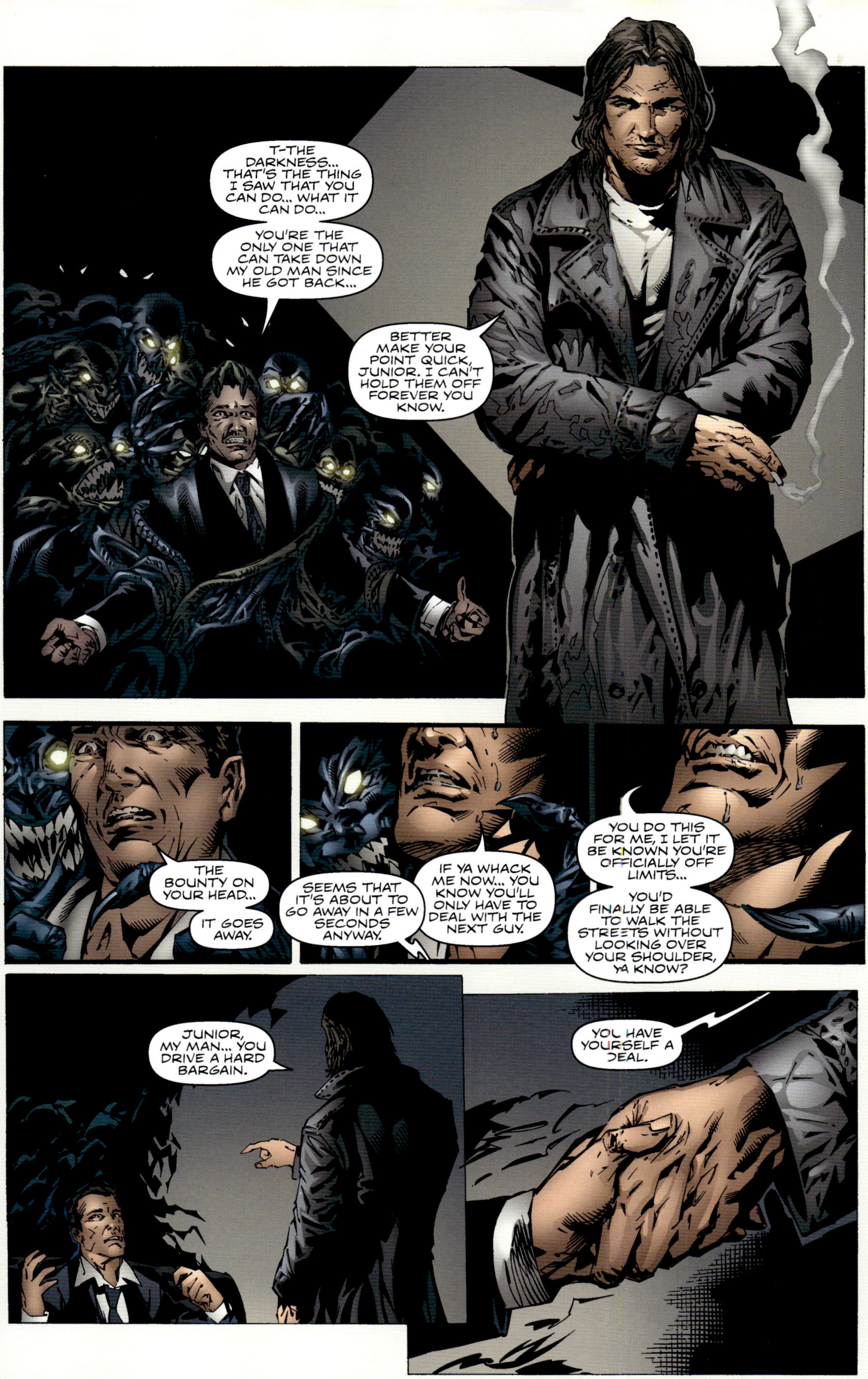
T-THE DARKNESS... THAT'S THE THING I SAW THAT YOU CAN DO... WHAT IT CAN DO...
YOU'RE THE ONLY ONE THAT CAN TAKE DOWN MY OLD MAN SINCE HE GOT BACK...
BETTER MAKE YOUR POINT QUICK, JUNIOR. I CAN'T HOLD THEM OFF FOREVER YOU KNOW.
THE BOUNTY ON YOUR HEAD...
IT GOES AWAY.
SEEMS THAT IT'S ABOUT TO GO AWAY IN A FEW SECONDS ANYWAY.
IF YA WHACK ME NOW... YOU KNOW YOU'LL ONLY HAVE TO DEAL WITH THE NEXT GUY.
YOU DO THIS FOR ME, I LET IT BE KNOWN YOU'RE OFFICIALLY OFF LIMITS...
YOU'D FINALLY BE ABLE TO WALK THE STREETS WITHOUT LOOKING OVER YOUR SHOULDER, YA KNOW?
JUNIOR, MY MAN... YOU DRIVE A HARD BARGAIN.
YOU HAVE YOURSELF A DEAL.

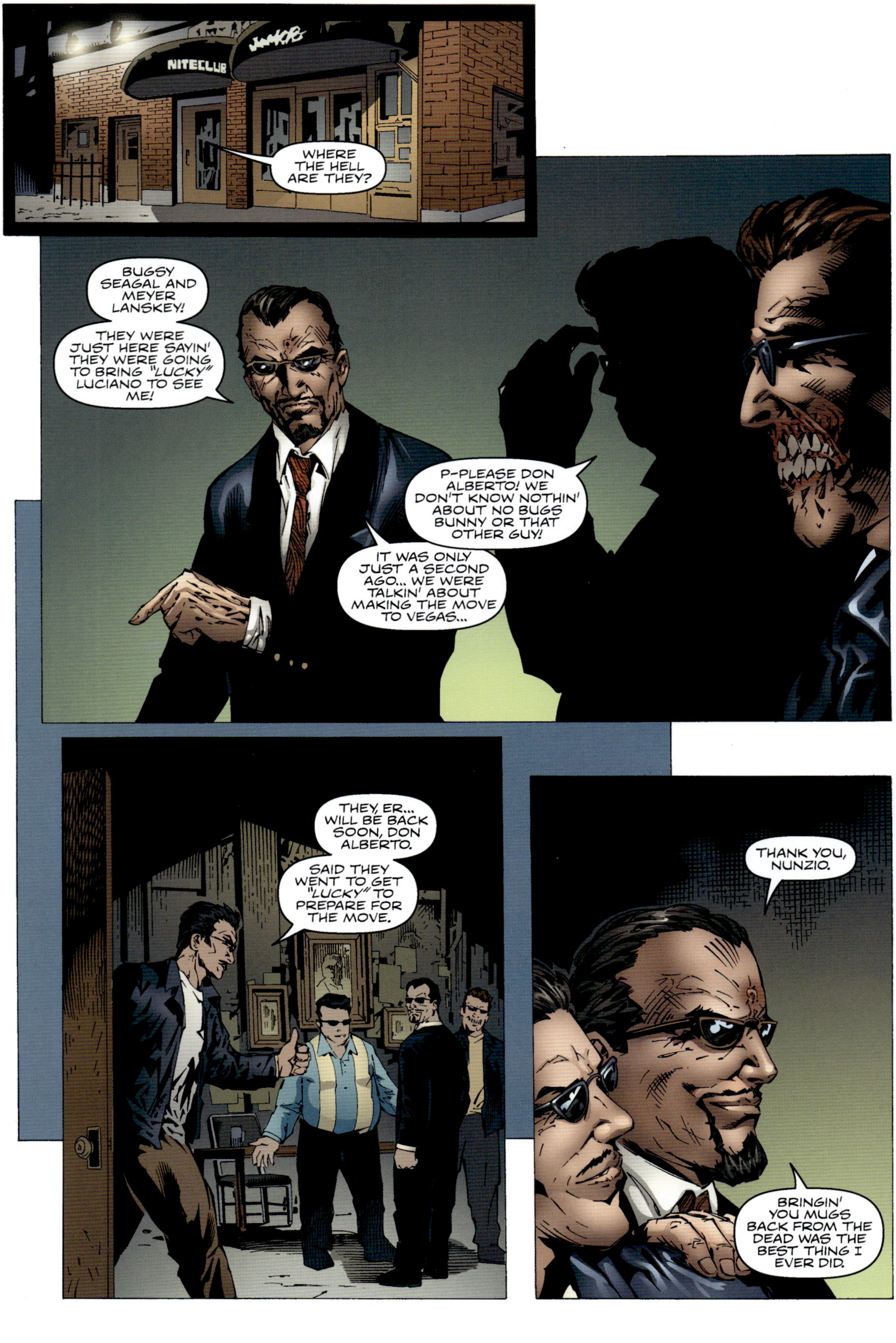
NITECLUB
WHERE THE HELL ARE THEY?
BUGSY SEAGAL AND MEYER LANSKEY!
THEY WERE JUST HERE SAYIN' THEY WERE GOING TO BRING "LUCKY" LUCIANO TO SEE ME!
P-PLEASE DON ALBERTO! WE DON'T KNOW NOTHIN' ABOUT NO BUGS BUNNY OR THAT OTHER GUY!
IT WAS ONLY JUST A SECOND AGO... WE WERE TALKIN' ABOUT MAKING THE MOVE TO VEGAS...
THEY, ER... WILL BE BACK SOON, DON ALBERTO.
SAID THEY WENT TO GET "LUCKY" TO PREPARE FOR THE MOVE.
THANK YOU, NUNZIO.
BRINGIN' YOU MUGS BACK FROM THE DEAD WAS THE BEST THING I EVER DID.

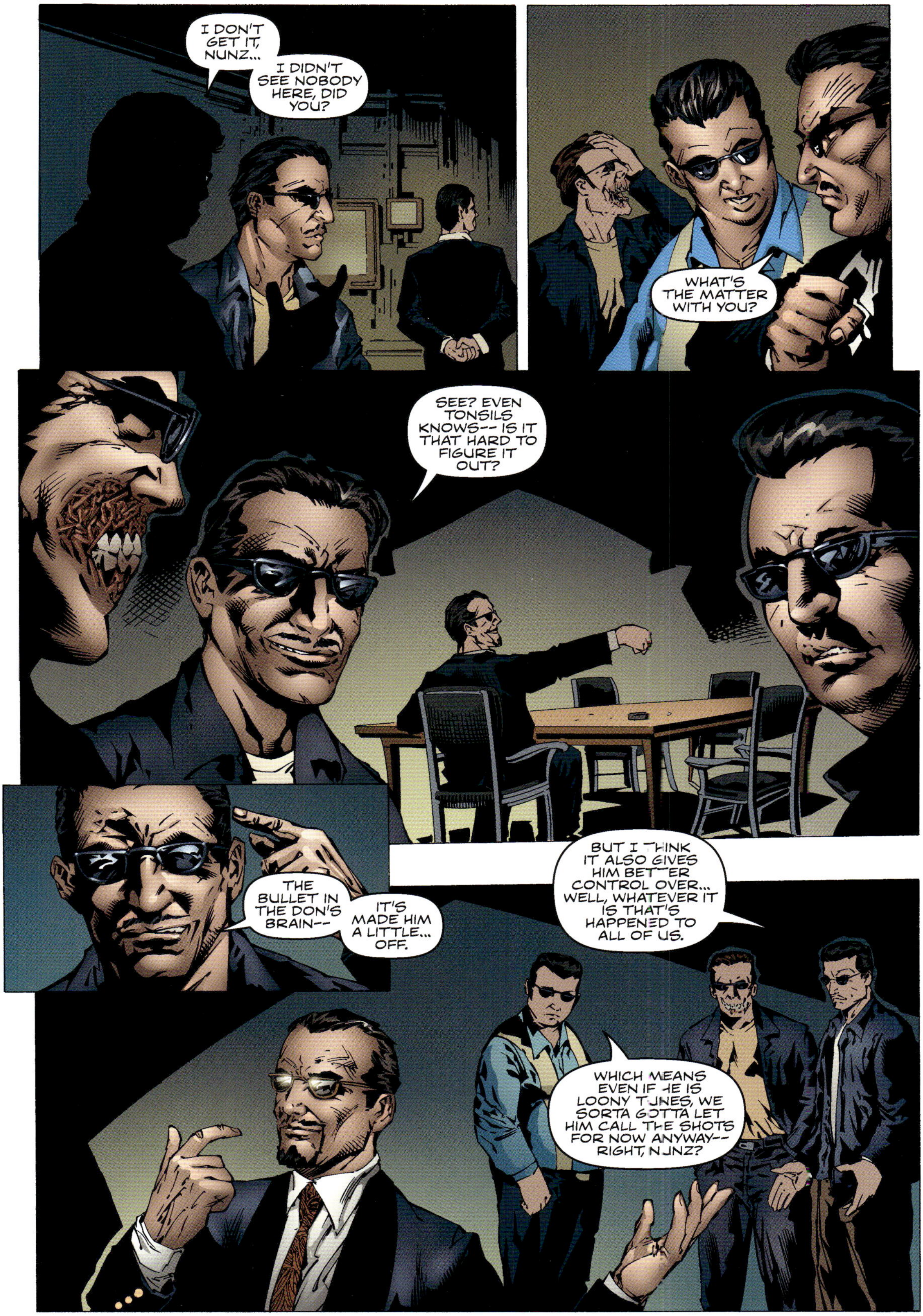
I DON'T GET IT, NUNZ...
I DIDN'T SEE NOBODY HERE, DID YOU?
WHAT'S THE MATTER WITH YOU?
SEE? EVEN TONSILS KNOWS-- IS IT THAT HARD TO FIGURE IT OUT?
THE BULLET IN THE DON'S BRAIN--
IT'S MADE HIM A LITTLE... OFF.
BUT I THINK IT ALSO GIVES HIM BETTER CONTROL OVER... WELL, WHATEVER IT IS THAT'S HAPPENED TO ALL OF US.
WHICH MEANS EVEN IF HE IS LOONY TUNES, WE SORTA GOTTA LET HIM CALL THE SHOTS FOR NOW ANYWAY-- RIGHT, NUNZ?

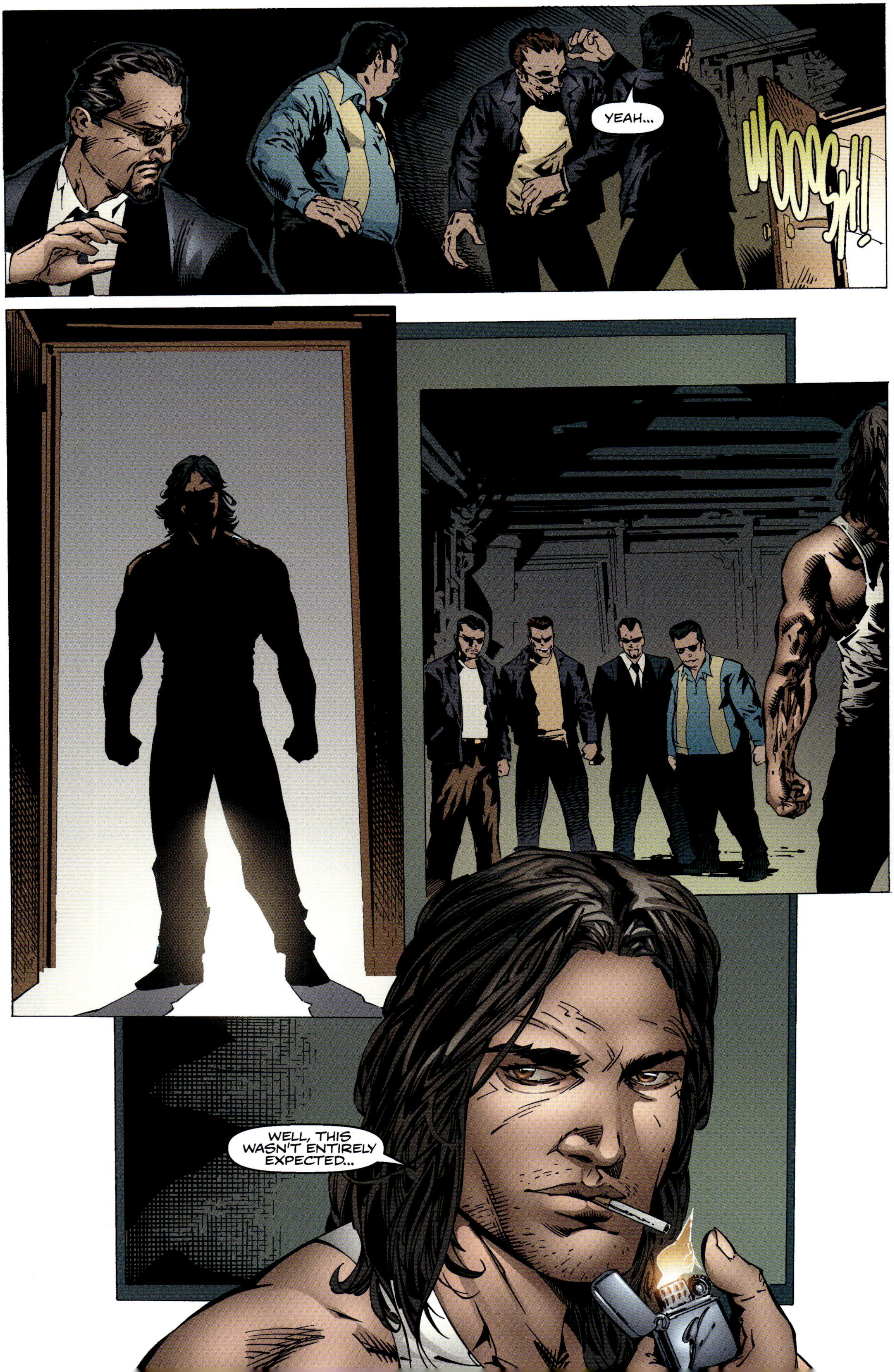
YEAH...
WOOOSH!!
WELL, THIS WASN'T ENTIRELY EXPECTED...

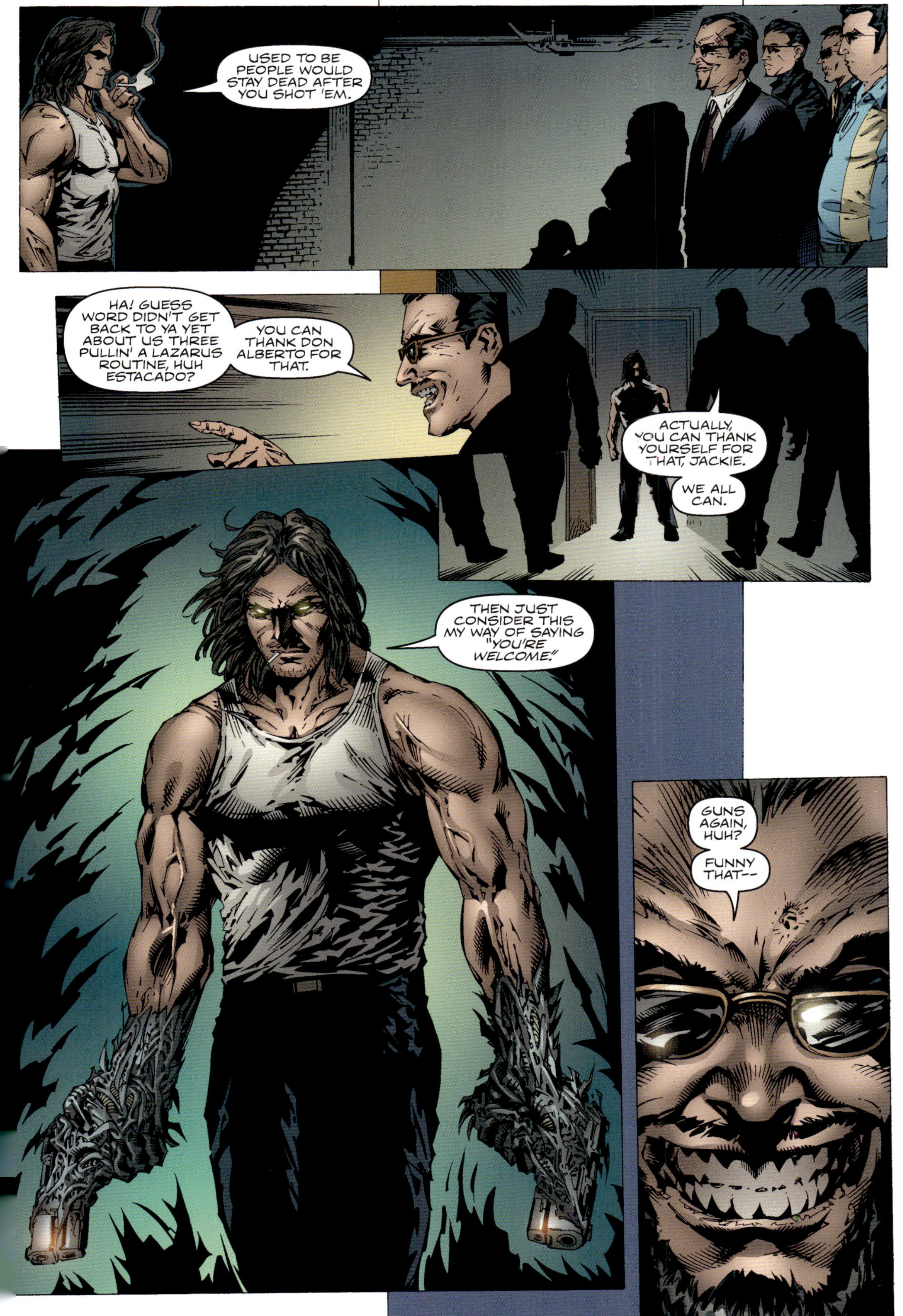
USED TO BE PEOPLE WOULD STAY DEAD AFTER YOU SHOT 'EM.
HA! GUESS WORD DIDN'T GET BACK TO YA YET ABOUT US THREE PULLIN' A LAZARUS ROUTINE, HUH ESTACADO?
YOU CAN THANK DON ALBERTO FOR THAT.
ACTUALLY, YOU CAN THANK YOURSELF FOR THAT, JACKIE.
WE ALL CAN.
THEN JUST CONSIDER THIS MY WAY OF SAYING "YOU'RE WELCOME."
GUNS AGAIN, HUH?
FUNNY THAT--

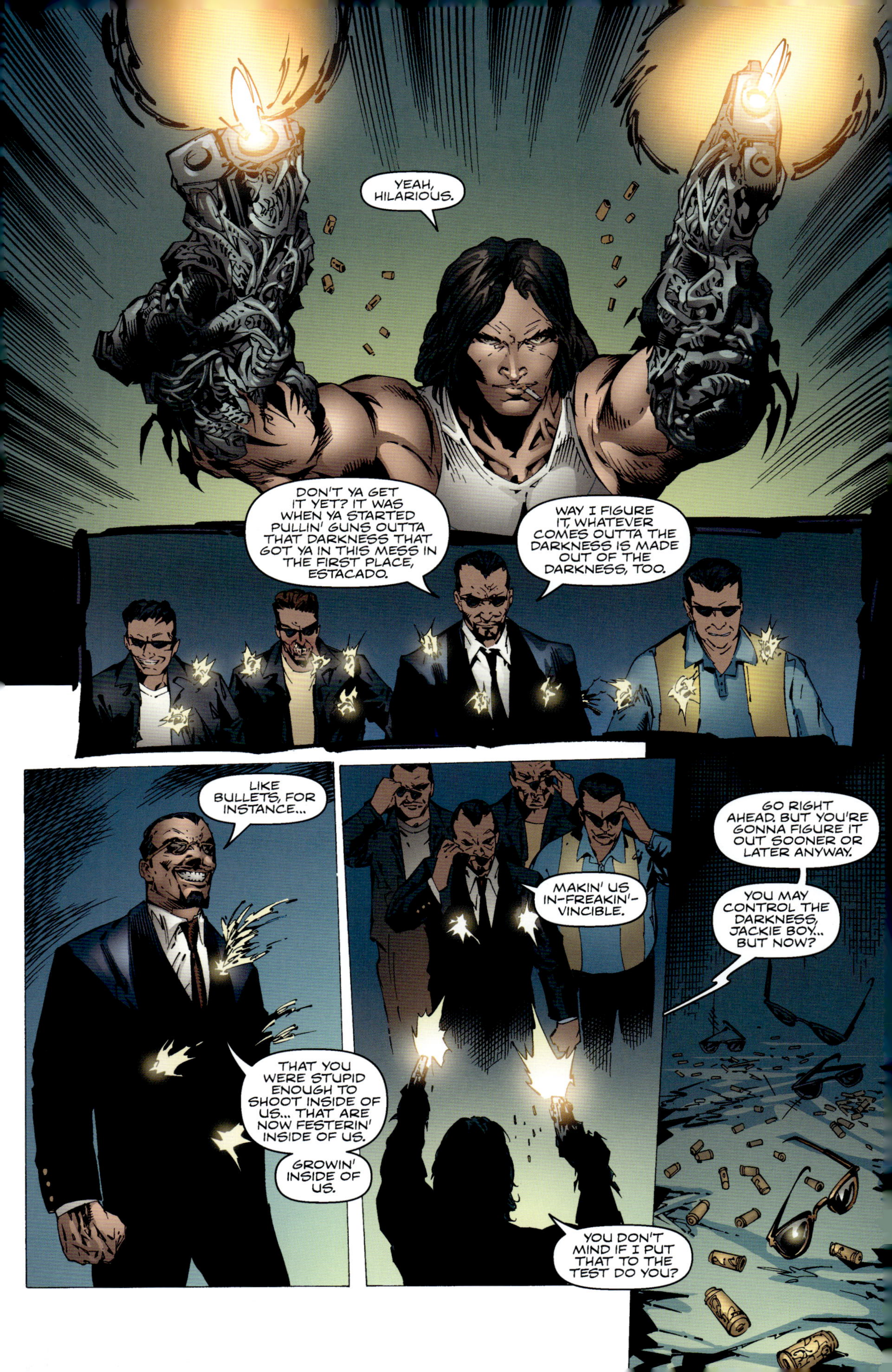

YEAH, HILARIOUS.
DON'T YA GET IT YET? IT WAS WHEN YA STARTED PULLIN' GUNS OUTTA THAT DARKNESS THAT GOT YA IN THIS MESS IN THE FIRST PLACE, ESTACADO.
WAY I FIGURE IT, WHATEVER COMES OUTTA THE DARKNESS IS MADE OUT OF THE DARKNESS, TOO.
LIKE BULLETS, FOR INSTANCE...
THAT YOU WERE STUPID ENOUGH TO SHOOT INSIDE OF US... THAT ARE NOW FESTERIN' INSIDE OF US.
GROWIN' INSIDE OF US.
MAKIN' US IN-FREAKIN'-VINCIBLE.
YOU DON'T MIND IF I PUT THAT TO THE TEST DO YOU?
GO RIGHT AHEAD, BUT YOU'RE GONNA FIGURE IT OUT SOONER OR LATER ANYWAY.
YOU MAY CONTROL THE DARKNESS, JACKIE BOY... BUT NOW?

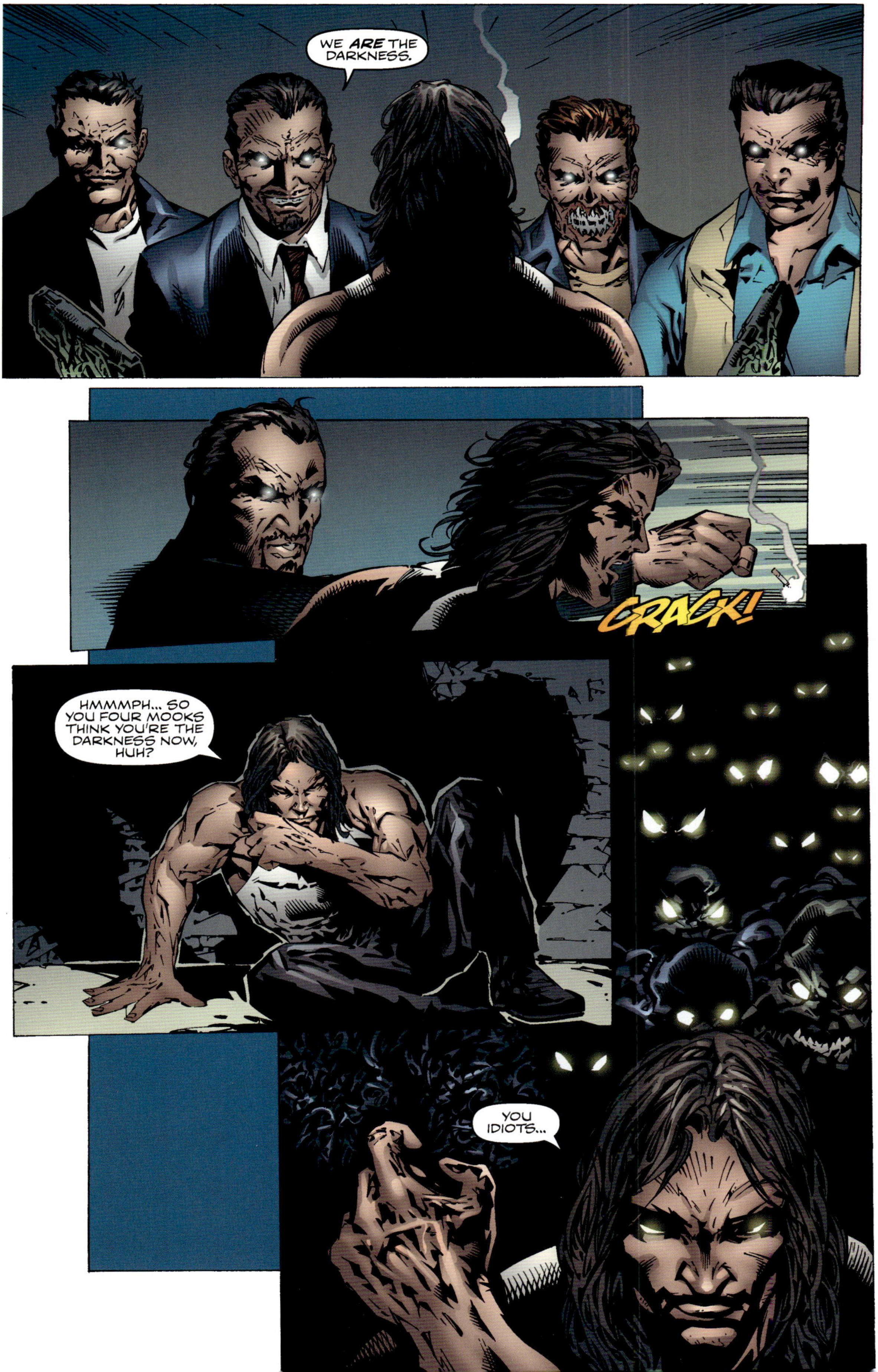
WE ARE THE DARKNESS.
CRACK!
HMMMPH... SO YOU FOUR MOOKS THINK YOU'RE THE DARKNESS NOW, HUH?
YOU IDIOTS...

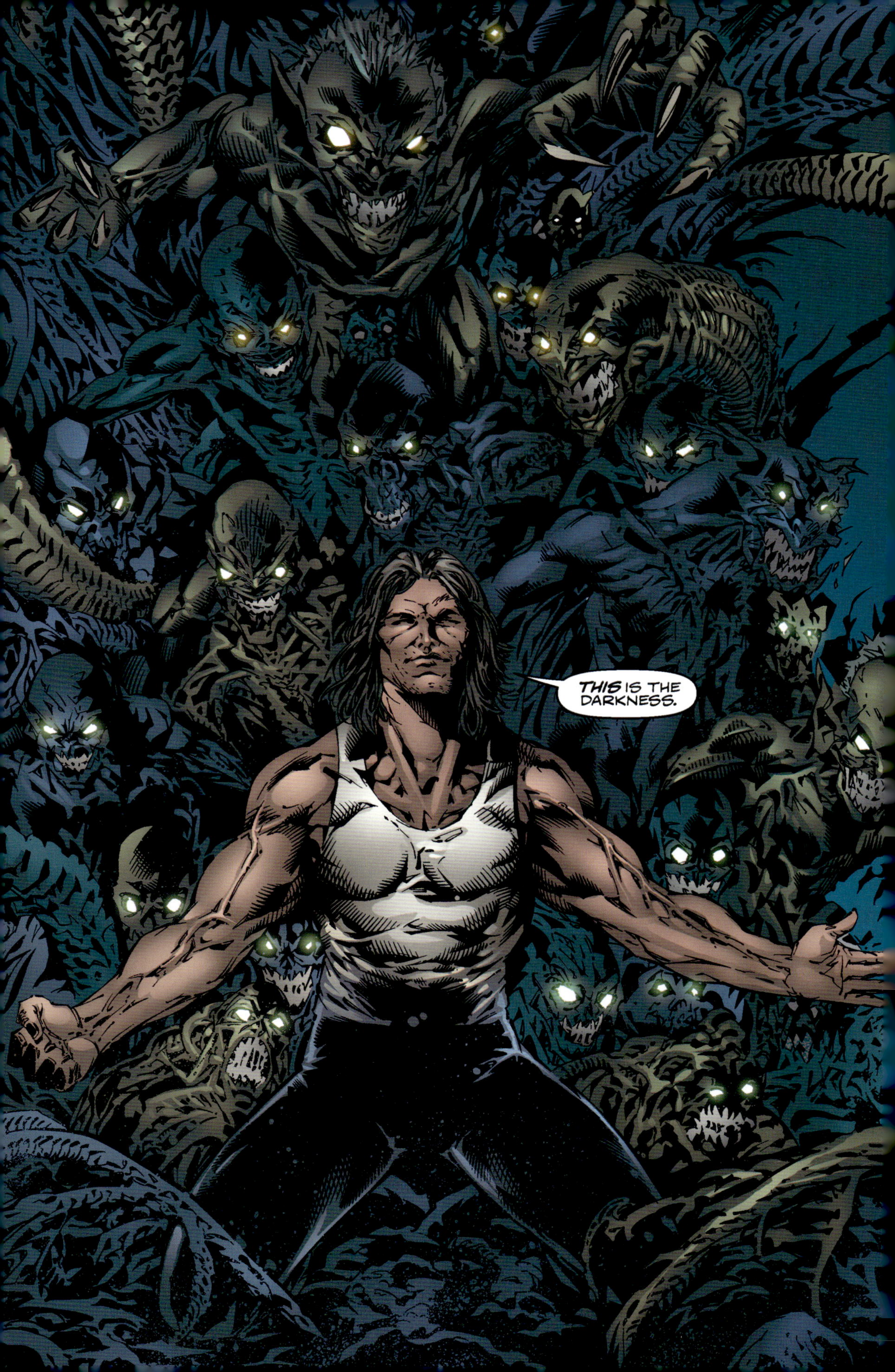
THIS IS THE DARKNESS.

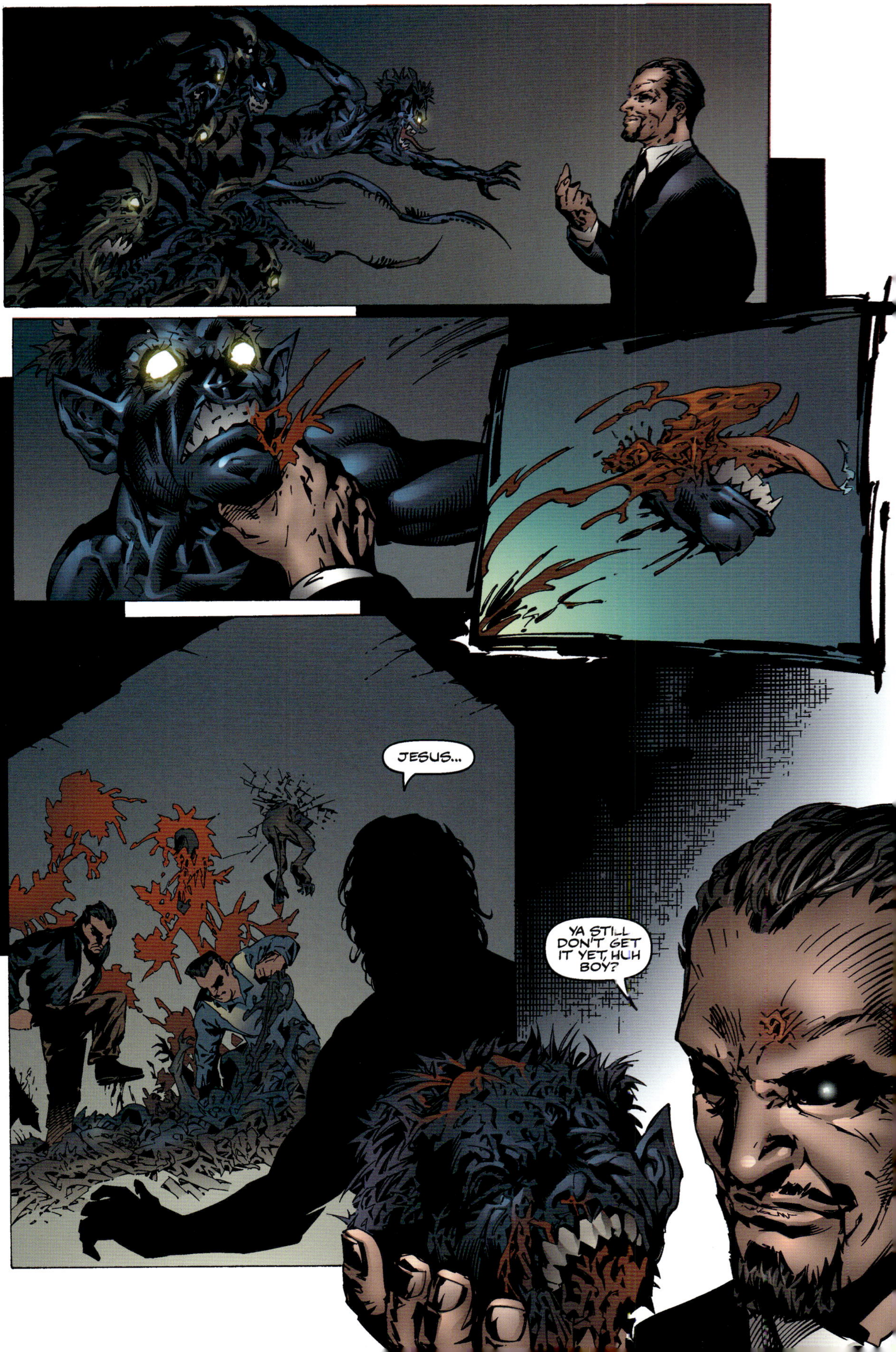
JESUS...
YA STILL DON'T GET IT YET, HUH BOY?

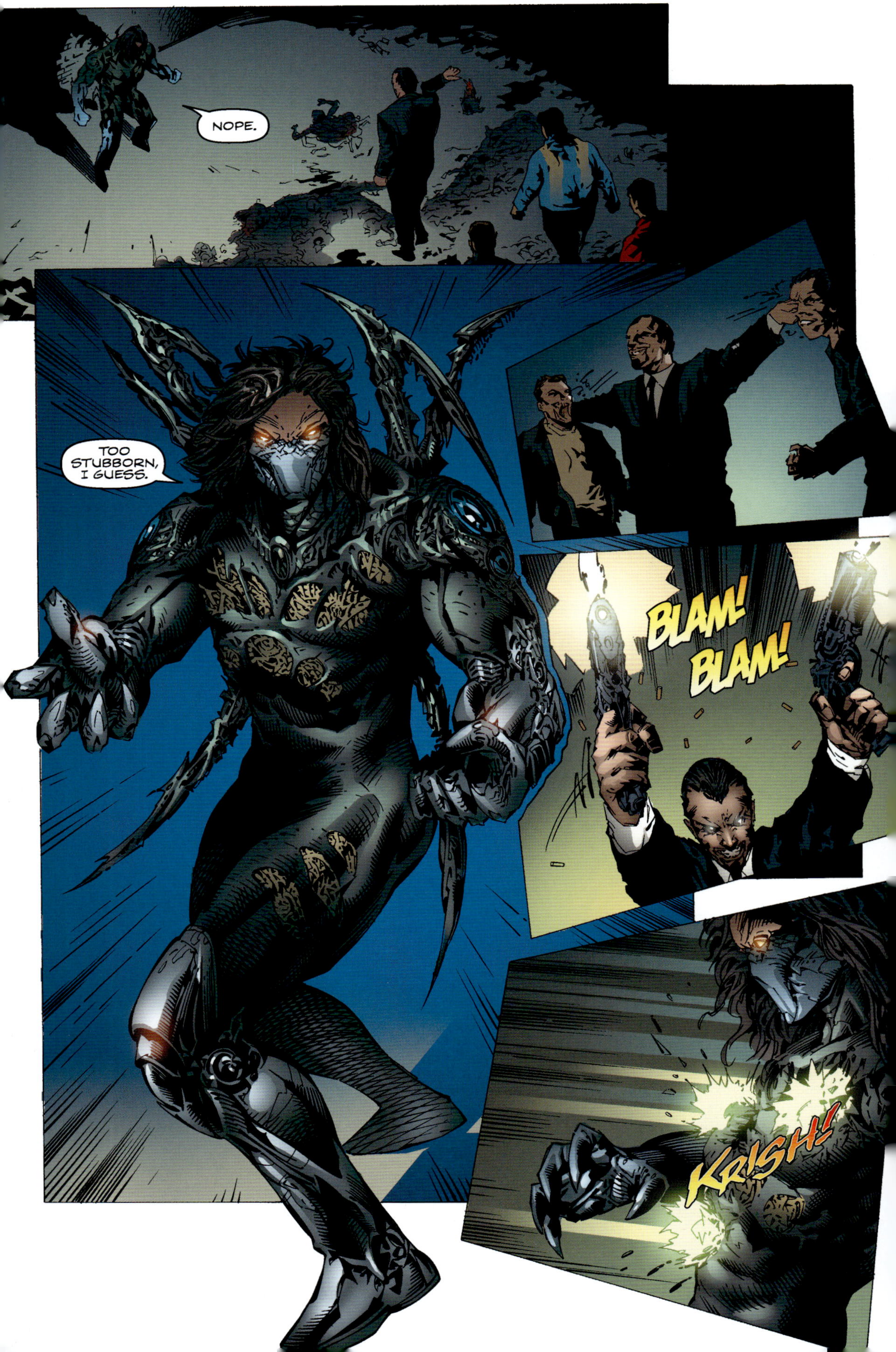
NOPE.
TOO STUBBORN, I GUESS.
BLAM! BLAM!
KRISH!

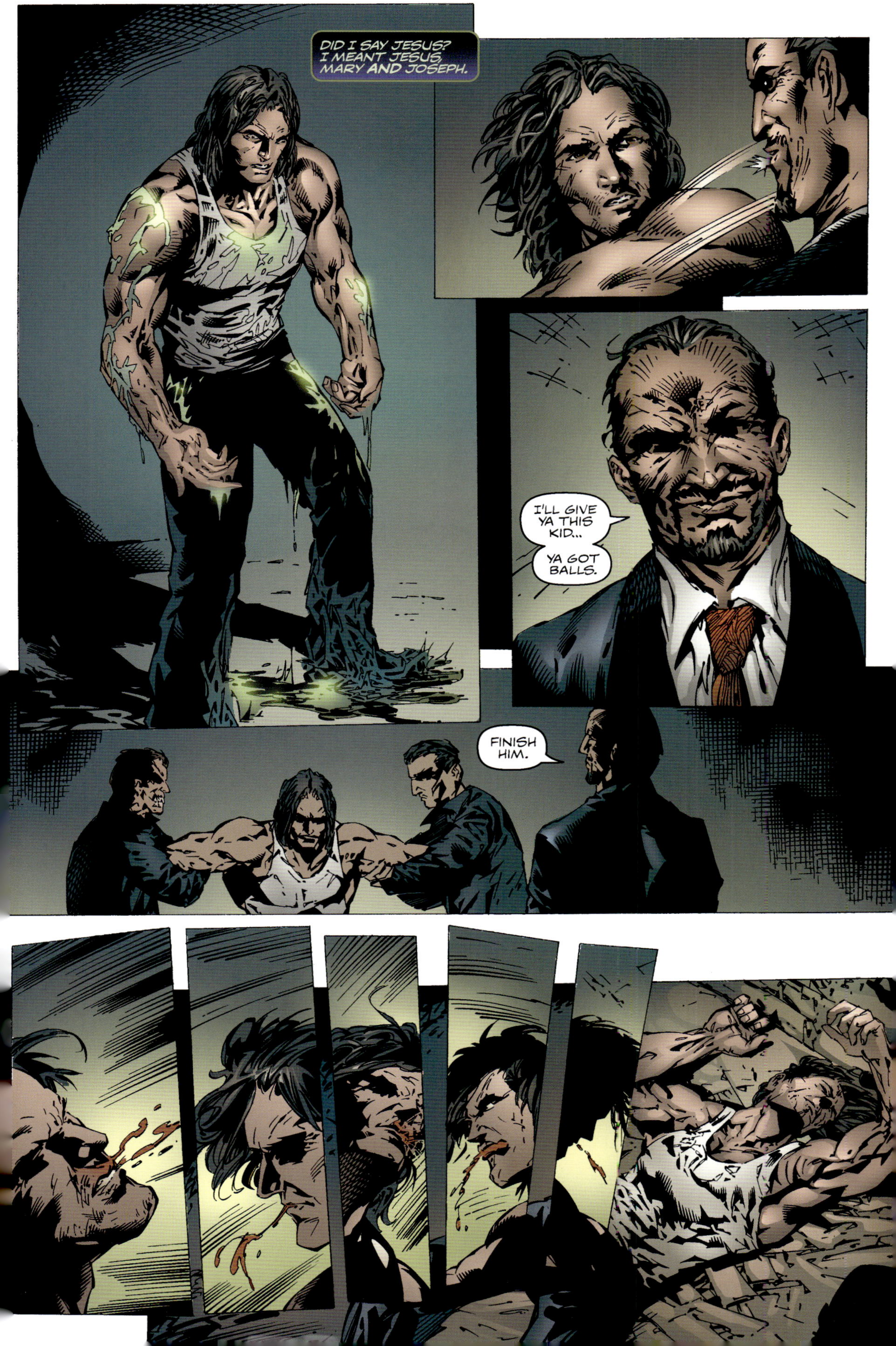
DID I SAY JESUS? I MEANT JESUS, MARY AND JOSEPH.
I'LL GIVE YA THIS KID...
YA GOT BALLS.
FINISH HIM.

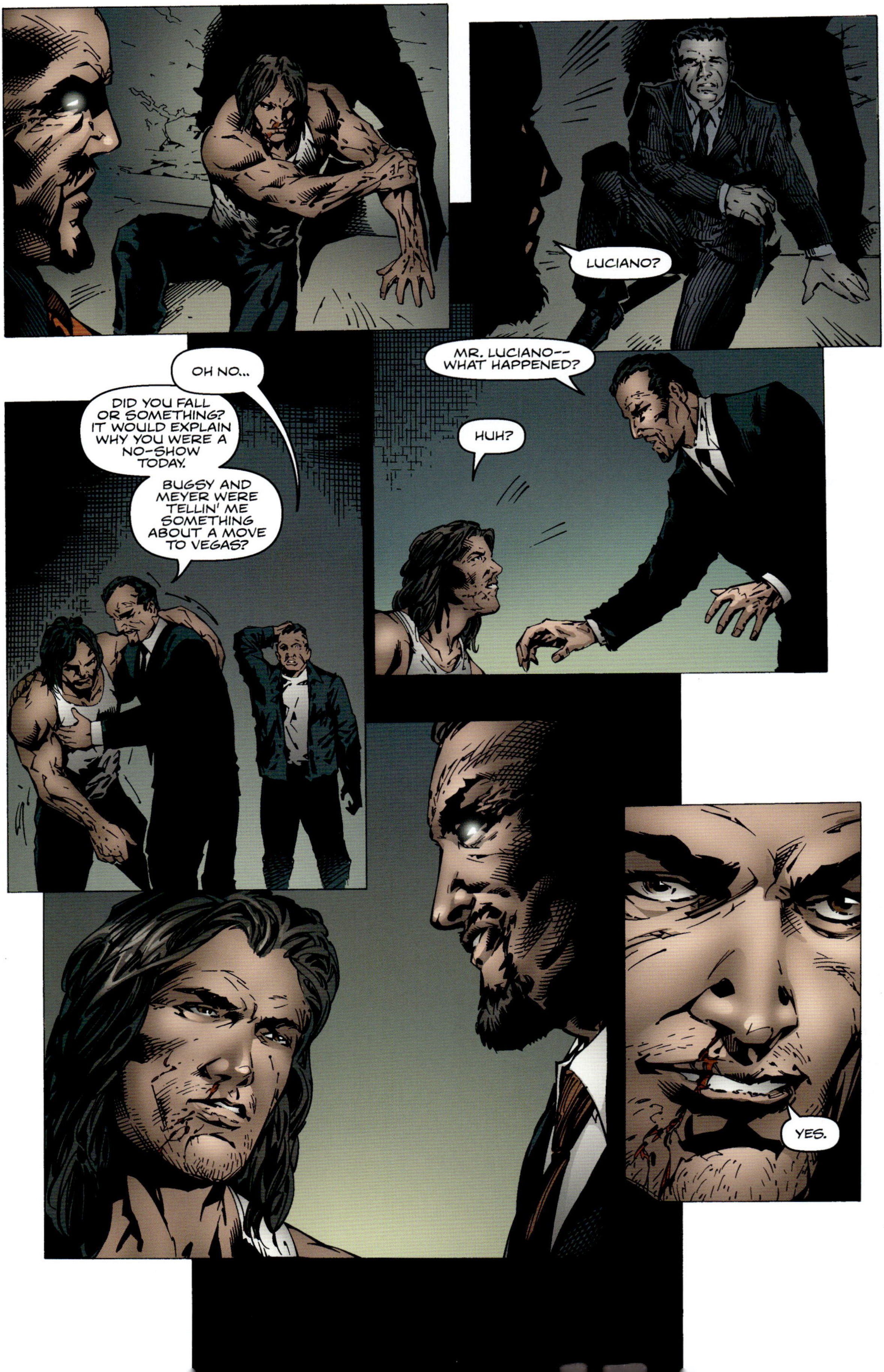
LUCIANO?
OH NO...
DID YOU FALL OR SOMETHING? IT WOULD EXPLAIN WHY YOU WERE A NO-SHOW TODAY.
BUGSY AND MEYER WERE TELLIN' ME SOMETHING ABOUT A MOVE TO VEGAS?
MR. LUCIANO-- WHAT HAPPENED?
HUH?
YES.

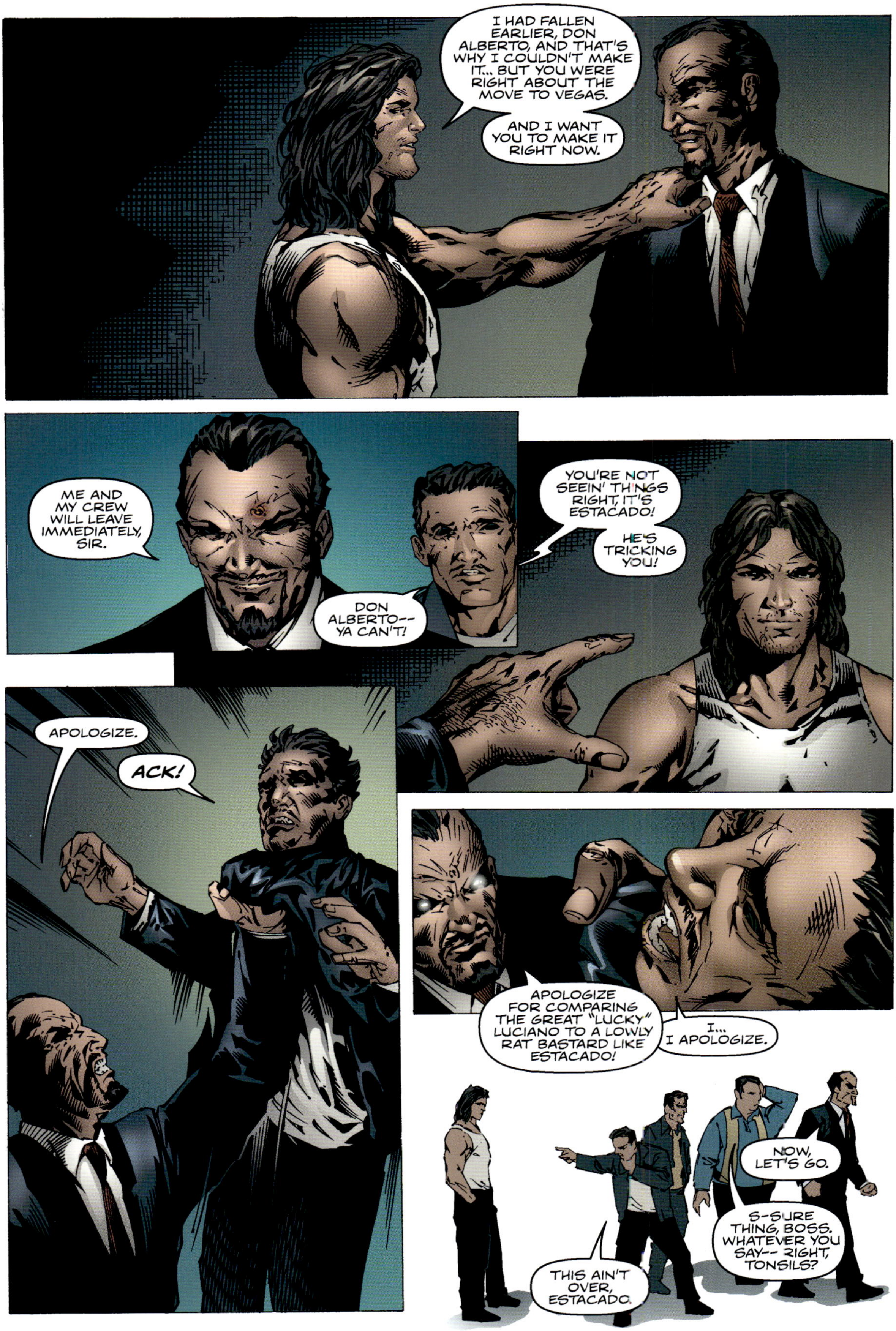
I HAD FALLEN EARLIER, DON ALBERTO, AND THAT'S WHY I COULDN'T MAKE IT... BUT YOU WERE RIGHT ABOUT THE MOVE TO VEGAS.
AND I WANT YOU TO MAKE IT RIGHT NOW.
ME AND MY CREW WILL LEAVE IMMEDIATELY, SIR.
DON ALBERTO-- YA CAN'T!
YOU'RE NOT SEEIN' THINGS RIGHT, IT'S ESTACADO!
HE'S TRICKING YOU!
APOLOGIZE.
ACK!
APOLOGIZE FOR COMPARING THE GREAT "LUCKY" LUCIANO TO A LOWLY RAT BASTARD LIKE ESTACADO!
I... I APOLOGIZE.
NOW, LET'S GO.
S-SURE THING, BOSS. WHATEVER YOU SAY-- RIGHT, TONSILS?
THIS AIN'T OVER, ESTACADO.

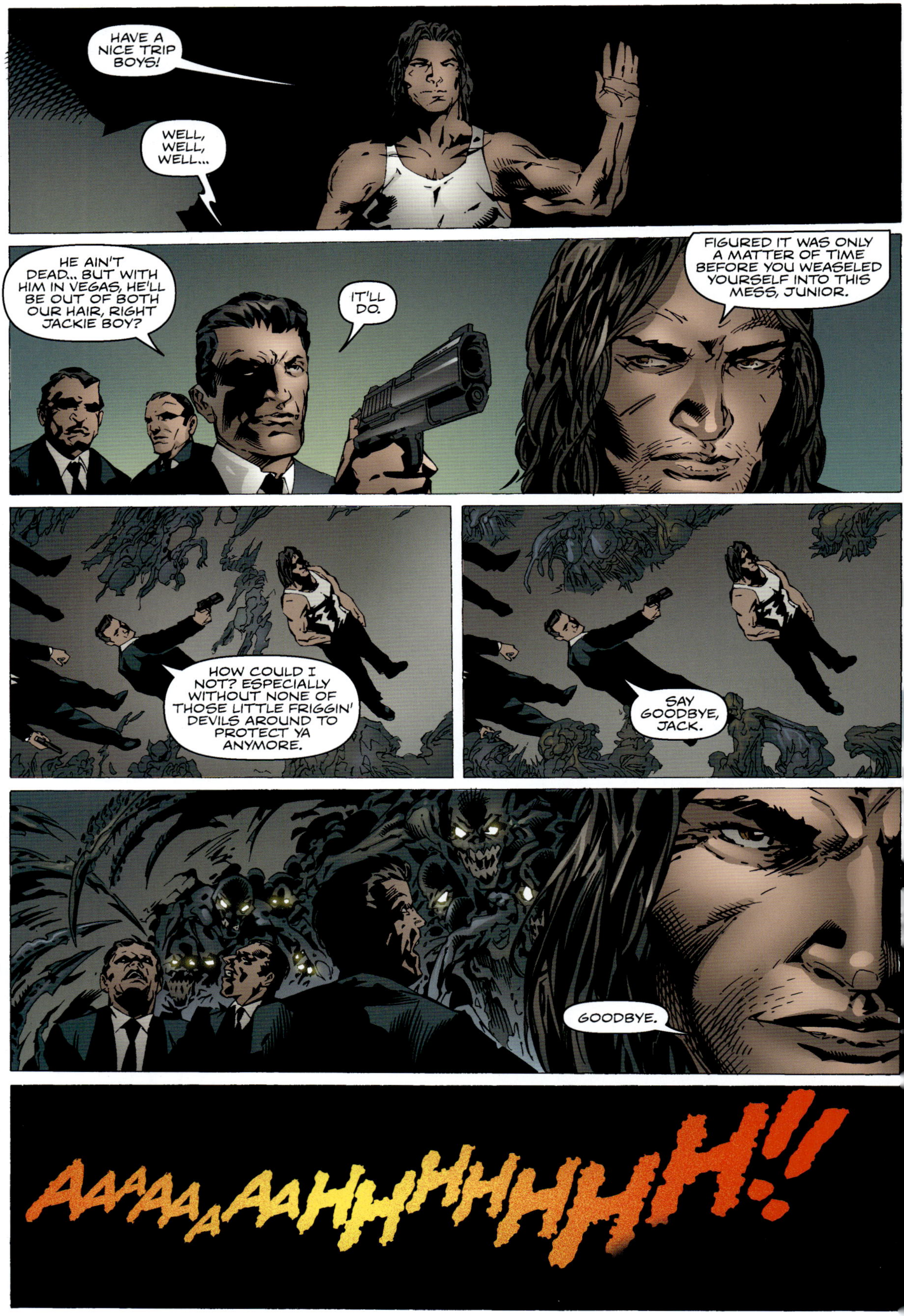
HAVE A NICE TRIP BOYS!
WELL, WELL, WELL...
HE AIN'T DEAD... BUT WITH HIM IN VEGAS, HE'LL BE OUT OF BOTH OUR HAIR, RIGHT JACKIE BOY?
IT'LL DO.
FIGURED IT WAS ONLY A MATTER OF TIME BEFORE YOU WEASELED YOURSELF INTO THIS MESS, JUNIOR.
HOW COULD I NOT? ESPECIALLY WITHOUT NONE OF THOSE LITTLE FRIGGIN' DEVILS AROUND TO PROTECT YA ANYMORE.
SAY GOODBYE, JACK.
GOODBYE.
AAAAAAAHHHHHHHH!!

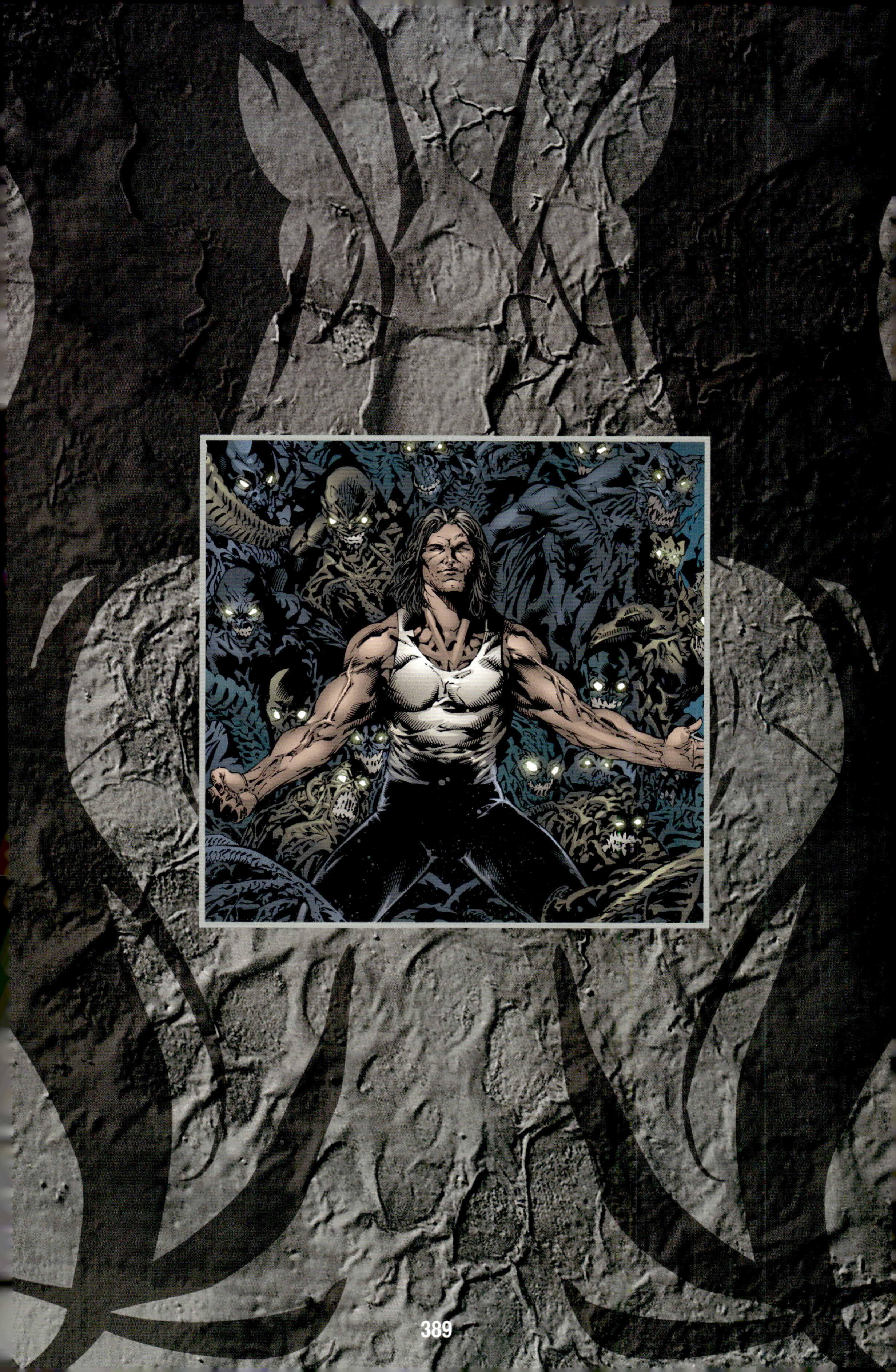

The Darkness Issue #57
cover art by: Dale Keown

THE DARKNESS #57

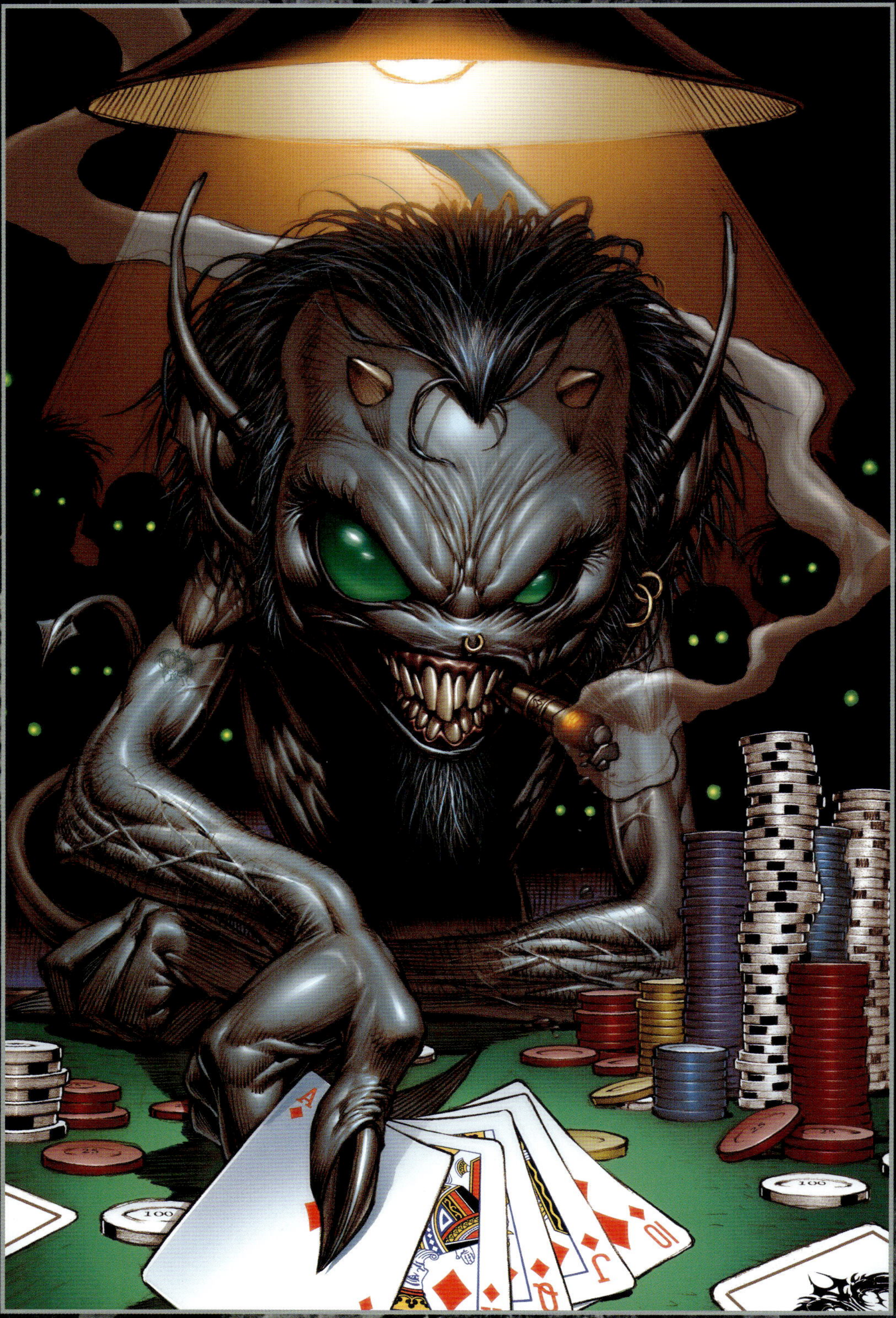

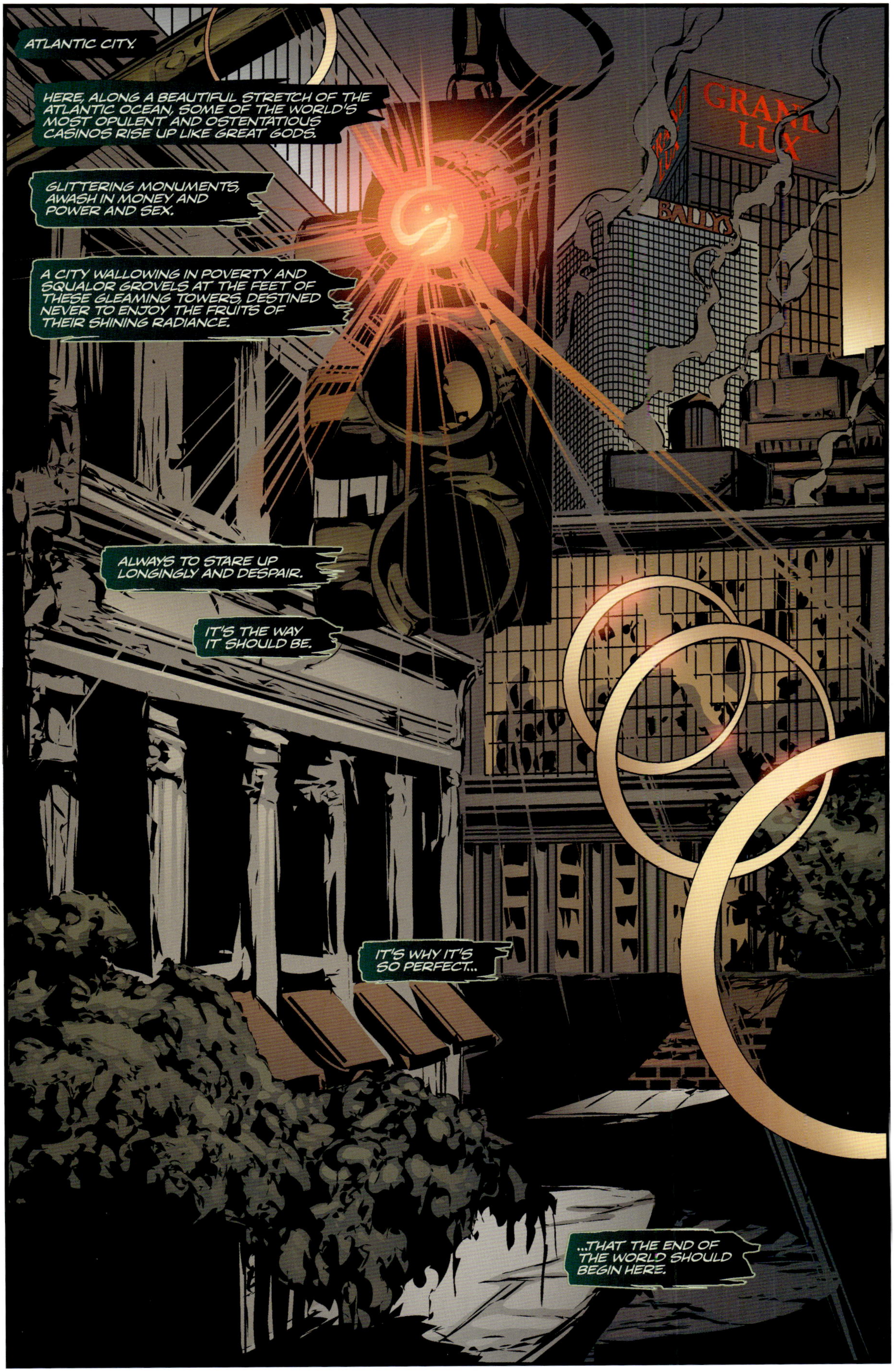
ATLANTIC CITY.
HERE, ALONG A BEAUTIFUL STRETCH OF THE ATLANTIC OCEAN, SOME OF THE WORLD'S MOST OPULENT AND OSTENTATIOUS CASINOS RISE UP LIKE GREAT GODS.
GLITTERING MONUMENTS, AWASH IN MONEY AND POWER AND SEX.
A CITY WALLOWING IN POVERTY AND SQUALOR GROVELS AT THE FEET OF THESE GLEAMING TOWERS, DESTINED NEVER TO ENJOY THE FRUITS OF THEIR SHINING RADIANCE.
ALWAYS TO STARE UP LONGINGLY AND DESPAIR.
IT'S THE WAY IT SHOULD BE.
IT'S WHY IT'S SO PERFECT...
...THAT THE END OF THE WORLD SHOULD BEGIN HERE.
GRAND LUX
BALLY'S

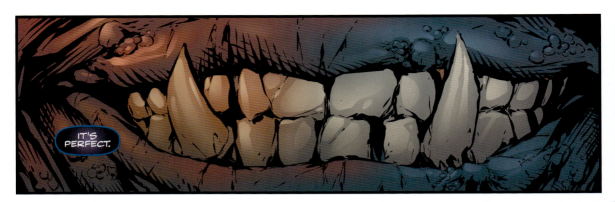

IT'S PERFECT.

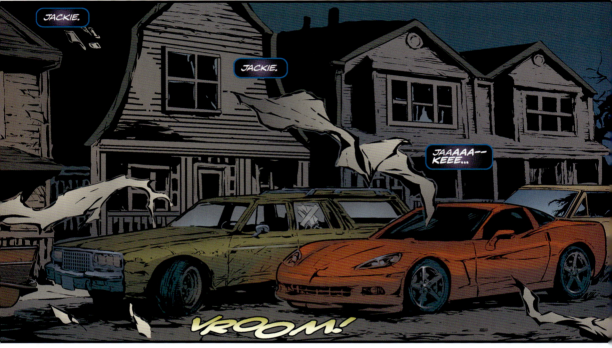

JACKIE.

JACKIE.

JAAAAAA-- KEEE...

VROOM!

JACKIE. JACKIE. JACKIE. JACKIE. JACKIE. JACKIE. JACKIE. JACKIE. JACKIE. JACKIE. JACKIE. JACKIE.

SHUT UP.

ARE YOU TIRED, JACKIE?

YOU'RE A BIG MAN NOW, JACKIE.

IT'S TOUGH TO BE THE BOSS.

EVERYONE WANTS A PIECE OF THE BOSS.

MAYBE YOU NEED A REST, JACKIE.

HE LOOKS SLEEPY.

HA. HA.

KNOCK! KNOCK! KNOCK!

LET US HANDLE THIS ONE.

NOBODY'S HOME...

NO KILLING TODAY.

LET'S TRY NEXT DOOR.

DELEGATE. DELEGATE, JACKIE.

JACKIE?...

YOU'RE A BAD KING, JACKIE.

YOU'RE SO MEAN TO USSSSS...

YES.

YES. MEAN.

YES.

YES.

TEASES US.

TUNK!

PUNISHES US.

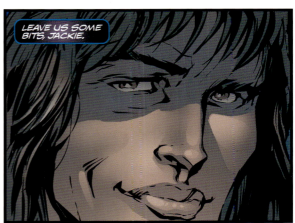

LEAVE US SOME BITS, JACKIE.

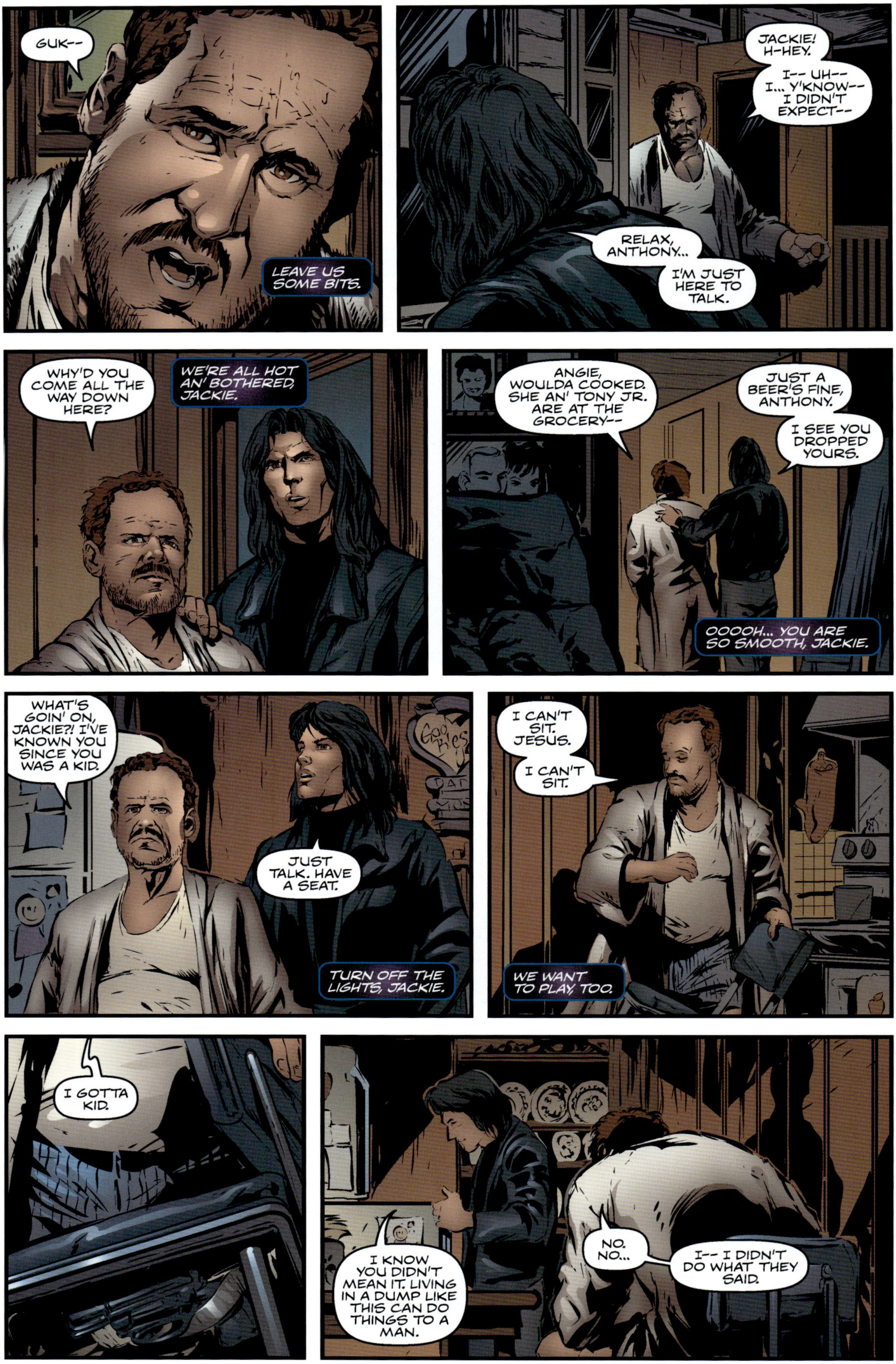
GUK--
LEAVE US SOME BITS.
JACKIE! H-HEY.
I-- UH-- I... Y'KNOW-- I DIDN'T EXPECT--
RELAX, ANTHONY...
I'M JUST HERE TO TALK.
WHY'D YOU COME ALL THE WAY DOWN HERE?
WE'RE ALL HOT AN' BOTHERED, JACKIE.
ANGIE, WOULDA COOKED. SHE AN' TONY JR. ARE AT THE GROCERY--
JUST A BEER'S FINE, ANTHONY.
I SEE YOU DROPPED YOURS.
OOOOH... YOU ARE SO SMOOTH, JACKIE.
WHAT'S GOIN' ON, JACKIE?! I'VE KNOWN YOU SINCE YOU WAS A KID.
JUST TALK. HAVE A SEAT.
TURN OFF THE LIGHTS, JACKIE.
I CAN'T SIT. JESUS.
I CAN'T SIT.
WE WANT TO PLAY, TOO.
I GOTTA KID.
I KNOW YOU DIDN'T MEAN IT. LIVING IN A DUMP LIKE THIS CAN DO THINGS TO A MAN.
NO. NO...
I-- I DIDN'T DO WHAT THEY SAID.

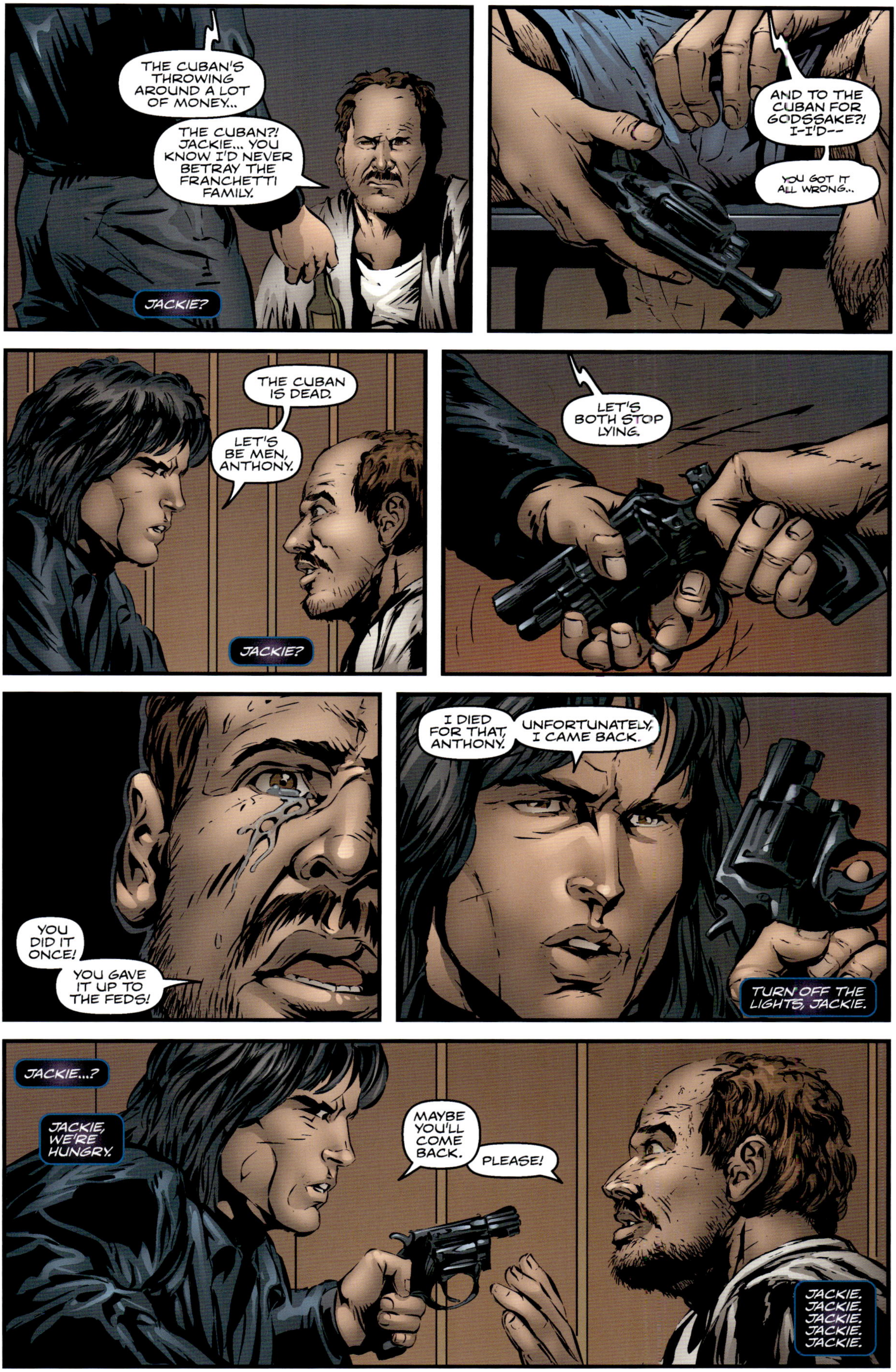
THE CUBAN'S THROWING AROUND A LOT OF MONEY...
THE CUBAN?! JACKIE... YOU KNOW I'D NEVER BETRAY THE FRANCHETTI FAMILY.
JACKIE?
AND TO THE CUBAN FOR GODSSAKE?! I-I'D--
YOU GOT IT ALL WRONG...
THE CUBAN IS DEAD.
LET'S BE MEN, ANTHONY.
JACKIE?
LET'S BOTH STOP LYING.
YOU DID IT ONCE!
YOU GAVE IT UP TO THE FEDS!
I DIED FOR THAT, ANTHONY.
UNFORTUNATELY, I CAME BACK.
TURN OFF THE LIGHTS, JACKIE.
JACKIE...?
JACKIE, WE'RE HUNGRY.
MAYBE YOU'LL COME BACK.
PLEASE!
JACKIE. JACKIE. JACKIE. JACKIE. JACKIE.

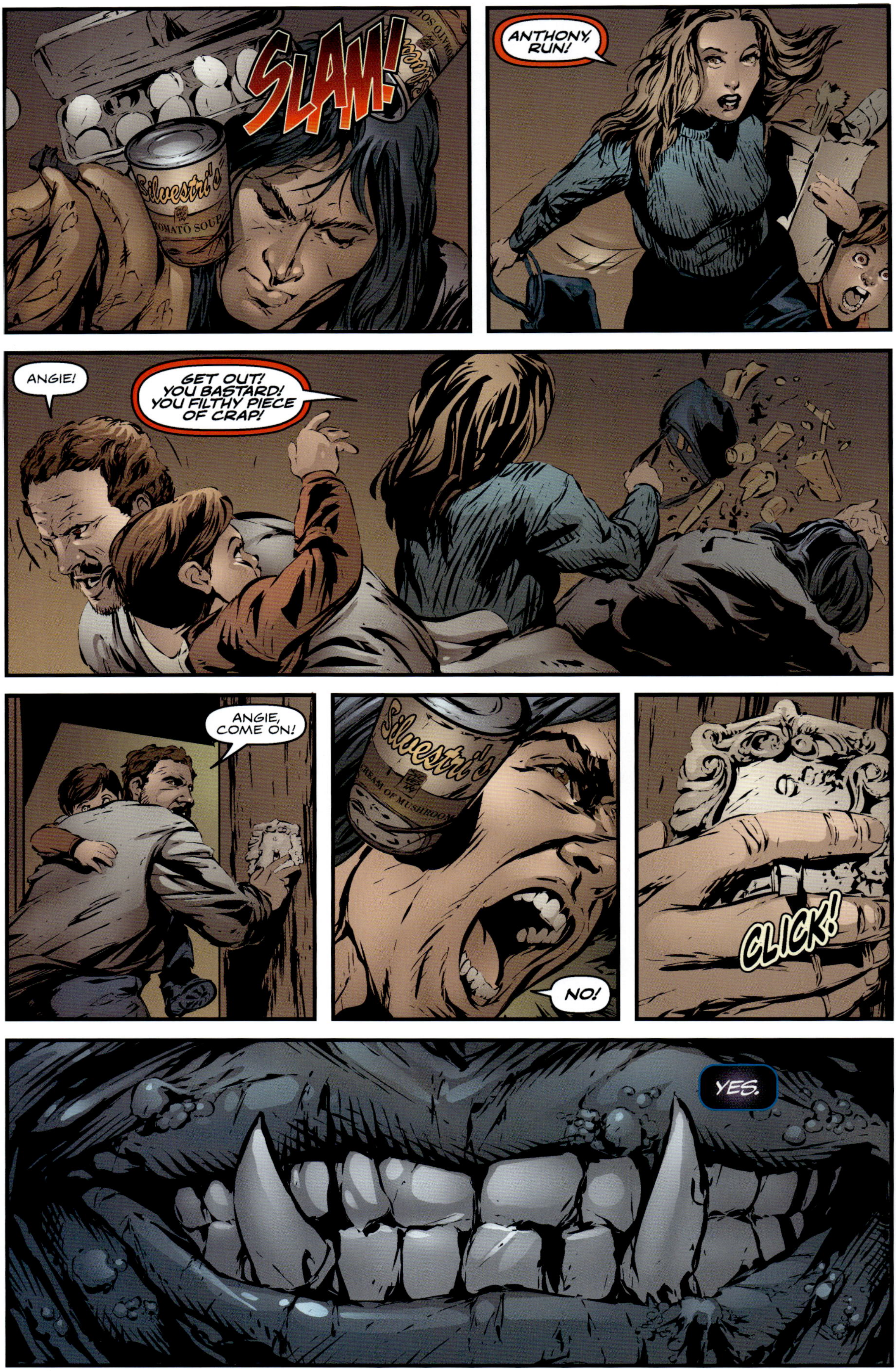
SLAM!
Silvestri's
TOMATO SOUP
ANTHONY, RUN!
ANGIE!
GET OUT! YOU BASTARD! YOU FILTHY PIECE OF CRAP!
ANGIE, COME ON!
Silvestri's
CREAM OF MUSHROOM
NO!
CLICK!
YES.

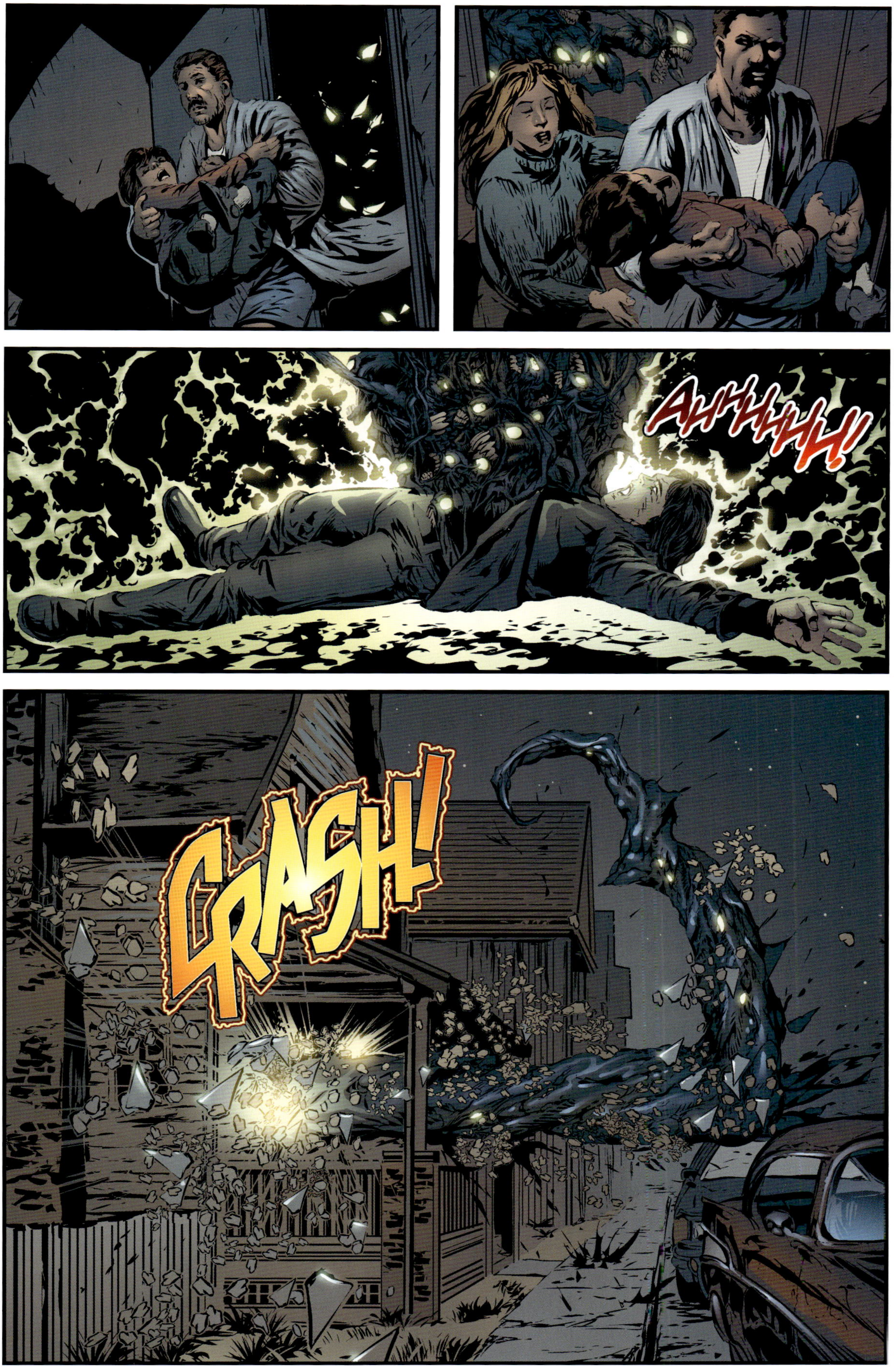
AHHHHH!
CRASH!

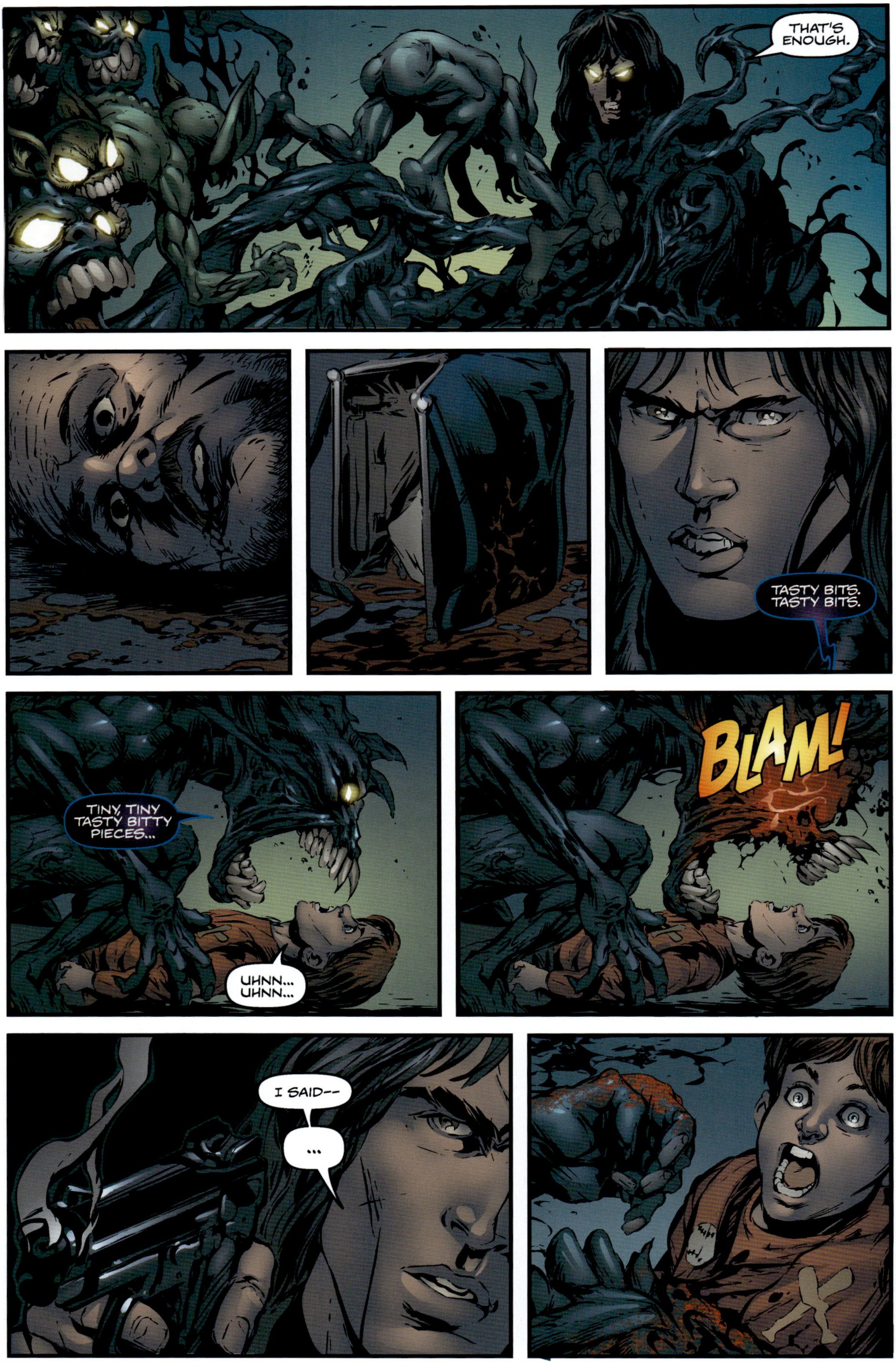
THAT'S ENOUGH.
TASTY BITS. TASTY BITS.
TINY, TINY TASTY BITTY PIECES...
UHNN... UHNN...
BLAM!
I SAID--
...

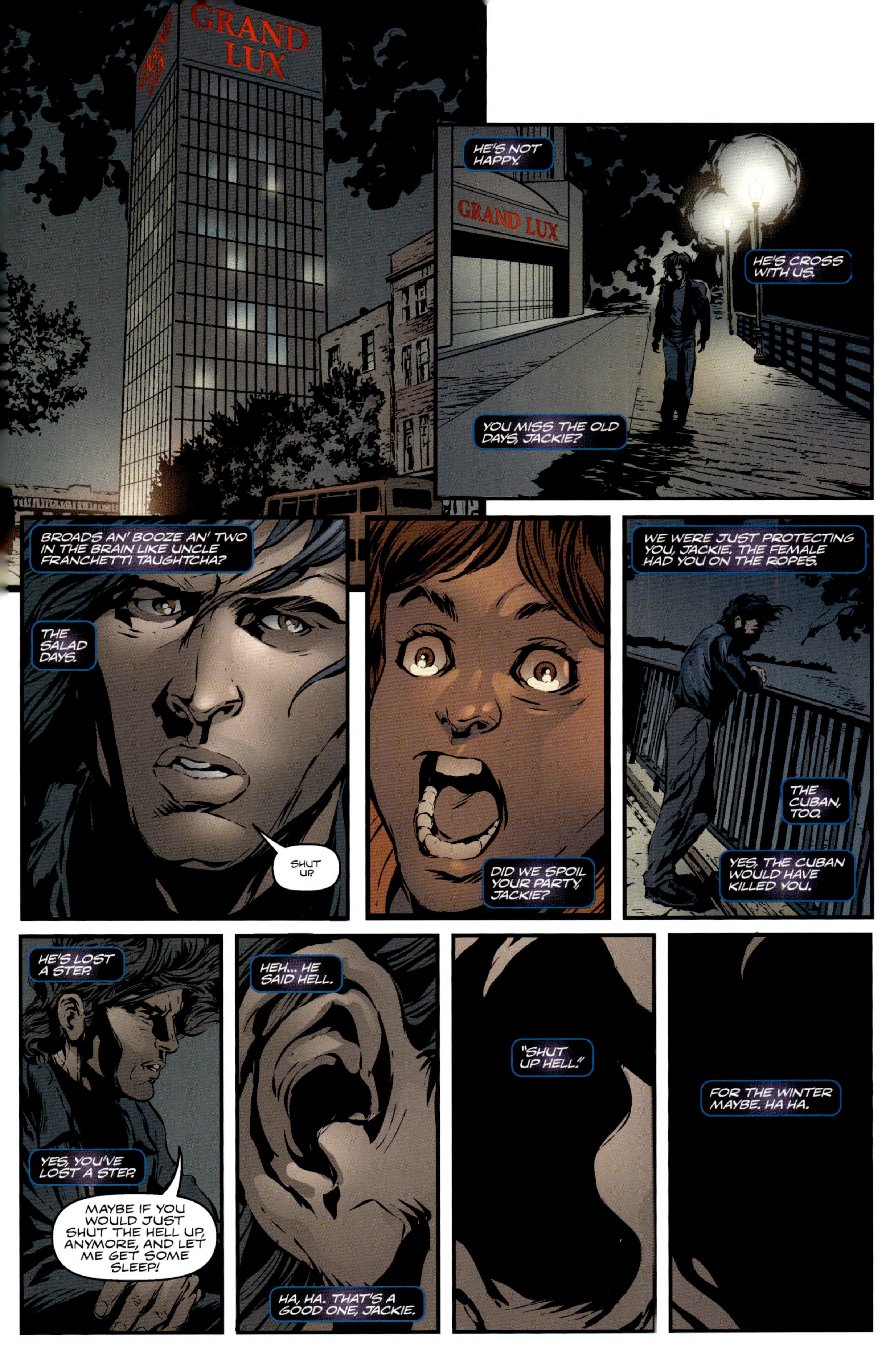
GRAND LUX
HE'S NOT HAPPY.
GRAND LUX
HE'S CROSS WITH US.
YOU MISS THE OLD DAYS, JACKIE?
BROADS AN' BOOZE AN' TWO IN THE BRAIN LIKE UNCLE FRANCHETTI TAUGHTCHA?
THE SALAD DAYS.
SHUT UP.
DID WE SPOIL YOUR PARTY, JACKIE?
WE WERE JUST PROTECTING YOU, JACKIE. THE FEMALE HAD YOU ON THE ROPES.
THE CUBAN, TOO.
YES, THE CUBAN WOULD HAVE KILLED YOU.
HE'S LOST A STEP.
YES, YOU'VE LOST A STEP.
MAYBE IF YOU WOULD JUST SHUT THE HELL UP, ANYMORE, AND LET ME GET SOME SLEEP!
HEH... HE SAID HELL.
HA, HA. THAT'S A GOOD ONE, JACKIE.
"SHUT UP HELL."
FOR THE WINTER MAYBE. HA HA.

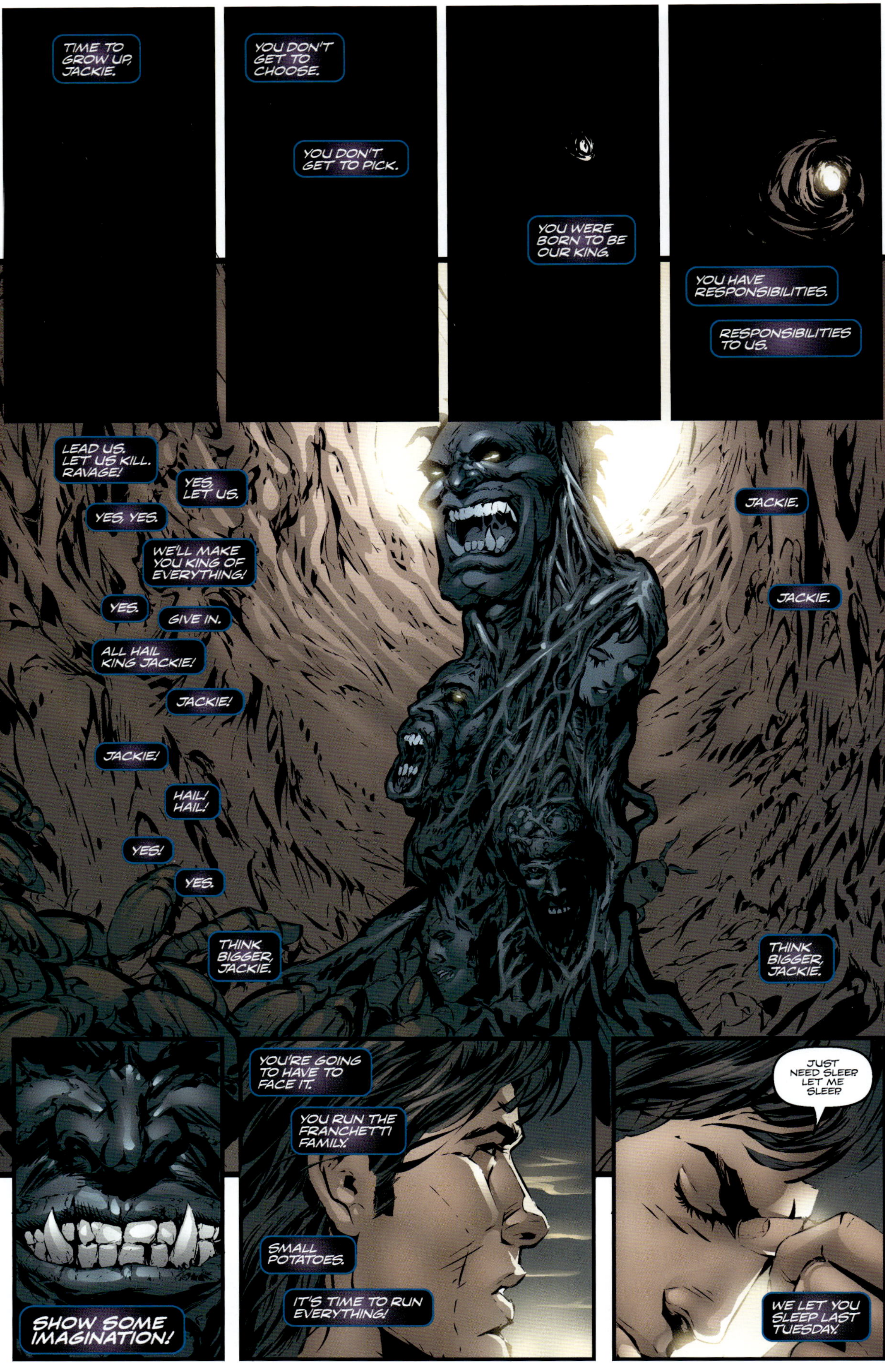
TIME TO GROW UP, JACKIE.
YOU DON'T GET TO CHOOSE.
YOU DON'T GET TO PICK.
YOU WERE BORN TO BE OUR KING.
YOU HAVE RESPONSIBILITIES.
RESPONSIBILITIES TO US.
LEAD US. LET US KILL. RAVAGE!
YES, LET US.
YES, YES.
WE'LL MAKE YOU KING OF EVERYTHING!
YES.
GIVE IN.
ALL HAIL KING JACKIE!
JACKIE!
JACKIE!
HAIL! HAIL!
YES!
YES.
JACKIE.
JACKIE.
THINK BIGGER, JACKIE.
THINK BIGGER, JACKIE.
SHOW SOME IMAGINATION!
YOU'RE GOING TO HAVE TO FACE IT.
YOU RUN THE FRANCHETTI FAMILY.
SMALL POTATOES.
IT'S TIME TO RUN EVERYTHING!
JUST NEED SLEEP. LET ME SLEEP.
WE LET YOU SLEEP LAST TUESDAY.

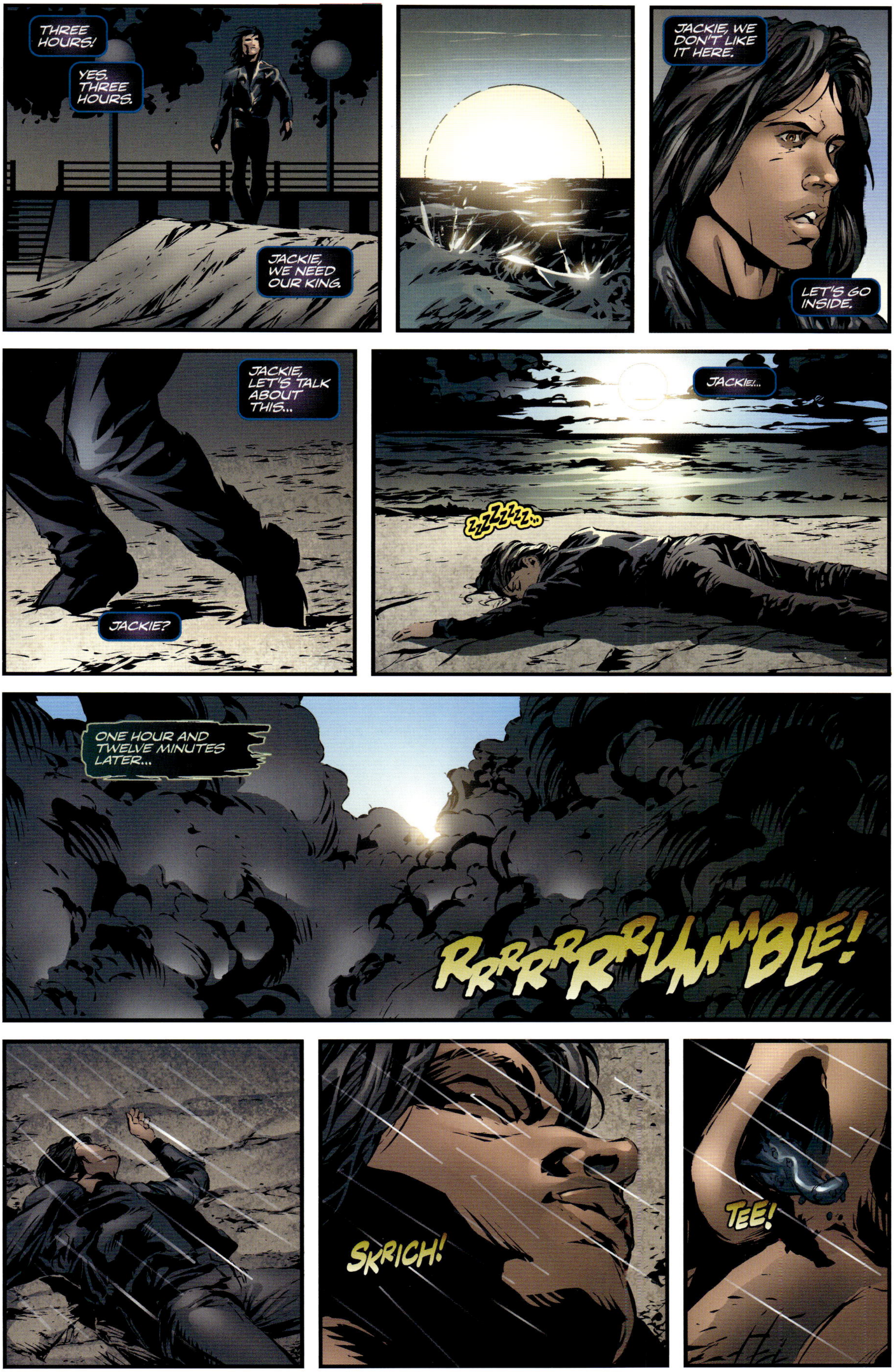
THREE HOURS!
YES. THREE HOURS.
JACKIE, WE NEED OUR KING.
JACKIE, WE DON'T LIKE IT HERE.
LET'S GO INSIDE.
JACKIE, LET'S TALK ABOUT THIS...
JACKIE?
JACKIE!...
ZZZZZZ...
ONE HOUR AND TWELVE MINUTES LATER...
RRRRRRRUMMBLE!
SKRICH!
TEE!

SHLORP!

TEE!

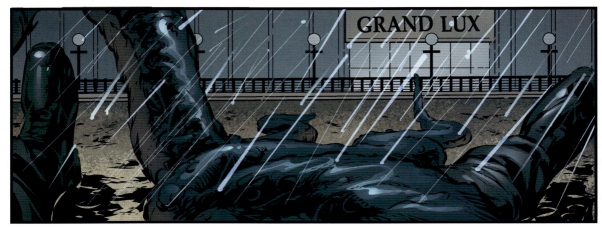

GRAND LUX

KRRRAK!

NNNUH...

I DON'T EVEN CARE... CHATTER AWAY GUYS...

I'M SO TIRED I COULD SLEEP THROUGH--

HELLO...?

GRAND LUX

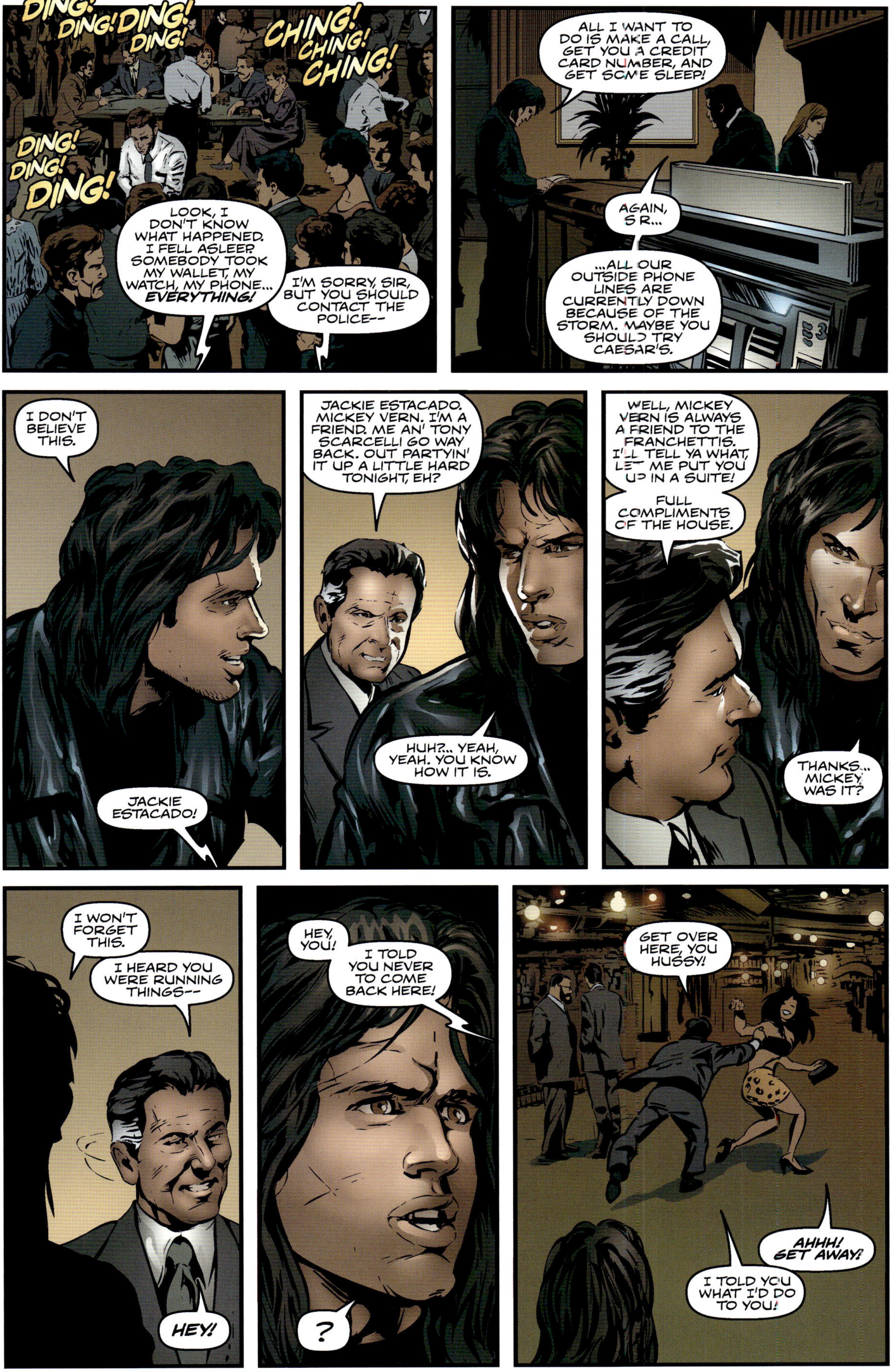
DING! DING! DING! DING!
CHING! CHING! CHING!
DING! DING! DING!
LOOK, I DON'T KNOW WHAT HAPPENED. I FELL ASLEEP. SOMEBODY TOOK MY WALLET, MY WATCH, MY PHONE... EVERYTHING!
I'M SORRY, SIR, BUT YOU SHOULD CONTACT THE POLICE--
ALL I WANT TO DO IS MAKE A CALL, GET YOU A CREDIT CARD NUMBER, AND GET SOME SLEEP!
AGAIN, SIR...
...ALL OUR OUTSIDE PHONE LINES ARE CURRENTLY DOWN BECAUSE OF THE STORM. MAYBE YOU SHOULD TRY CAESAR'S.
I DON'T BELIEVE THIS.
JACKIE ESTACADO!
JACKIE ESTACADO. MICKEY VERN. I'M A FRIEND. ME AN' TONY SCARCELLI GO WAY BACK. OUT PARTYIN' IT UP A LITTLE HARD TONIGHT, EH?
HUH?.. YEAH, YEAH. YOU KNOW HOW IT IS.
WELL, MICKEY VERN IS ALWAYS A FRIEND TO THE FRANCHETTIS. I'LL TELL YA WHAT, LET ME PUT YOU UP IN A SUITE!
FULL COMPLIMENTS OF THE HOUSE.
THANKS... MICKEY, WAS IT?
I WON'T FORGET THIS.
I HEARD YOU WERE RUNNING THINGS--
HEY!
HEY, YOU!
I TOLD YOU NEVER TO COME BACK HERE!
?
GET OVER HERE, YOU HUSSY!
AHHH! GET AWAY!
I TOLD YOU WHAT I'D DO TO YOU!

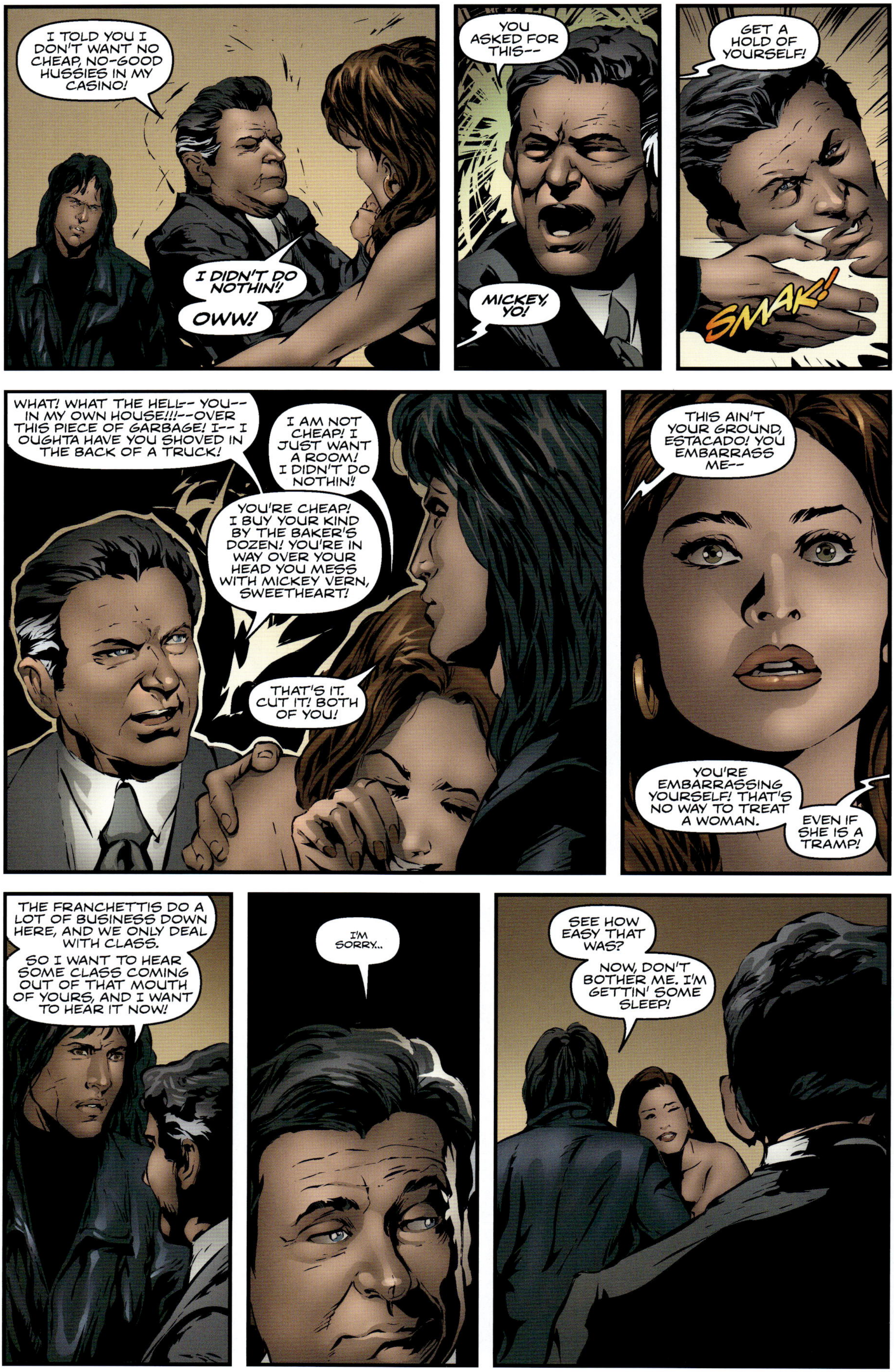

I TOLD YOU I DON'T WANT NO CHEAP, NO-GOOD HUSSIES IN MY CASINO!
I DIDN'T DO NOTHIN'!
OWW!
YOU ASKED FOR THIS--
MICKEY, YO!
GET A HOLD OF YOURSELF!
SMAK!
WHAT! WHAT THE HELL-- YOU-- IN MY OWN HOUSE!!!--OVER THIS PIECE OF GARBAGE! I-- I OUGHTA HAVE YOU SHOVED IN THE BACK OF A TRUCK!
I AM NOT CHEAP! I JUST WANT A ROOM! I DIDN'T DO NOTHIN'!
YOU'RE CHEAP! I BUY YOUR KIND BY THE BAKER'S DOZEN! YOU'RE IN WAY OVER YOUR HEAD YOU MESS WITH MICKEY VERN, SWEETHEART!
THAT'S IT. CUT IT! BOTH OF YOU!
THIS AIN'T YOUR GROUND, ESTACADO! YOU EMBARRASS ME--
YOU'RE EMBARRASSING YOURSELF! THAT'S NO WAY TO TREAT A WOMAN.
EVEN IF SHE IS A TRAMP!
THE FRANCHETTIS DO A LOT OF BUSINESS DOWN HERE, AND WE ONLY DEAL WITH CLASS.
SO I WANT TO HEAR SOME CLASS COMING OUT OF THAT MOUTH OF YOURS, AND I WANT TO HEAR IT NOW!
I'M SORRY...
SEE HOW EASY THAT WAS?
NOW, DON'T BOTHER ME. I'M GETTIN' SOME SLEEP!

THAT WAS-- I MEAN-- I THOUGHT HE WAS GOING TO EXPLODE. DID YOU SEE HOW RED HE GOT? YOU MUST BE ONE VERY IMPORTANT FELLA, MISTER. NOBODY BOSSES MICKEY VERN AROUND LIKE THAT.

NNN... YEAH... SURE... COULD YOU JUST PRESS FOURTEEN.

Y'KNOW, YOU HAVE ONE VERY GRATEFUL GIRL IN THIS TINY ELEVATOR. I CAN SHOW YOU HOW GRATEFUL, IF YOU GIVE ME A CHANCE.

MY NAME IS LORI, BY THE WAY. LORI PAPPALARDO.

MISS PAPPALARDO, NO OFFENSE, BUT RIGHT NOW, JENNIFER LOPEZ AND HER GIRL ARMY COULDN'T KEEP ME FROM A SHOWER AND EIGHT HOURS OF GOOD SHUT EYE.

DING!

YOU TAKE CARE OF YOURSELF.

JACKIE...

JACKIE...

YOU DIDN'T THINK WE'D LEAVE YOU ALL ALONE DID YOU, JACKIE?

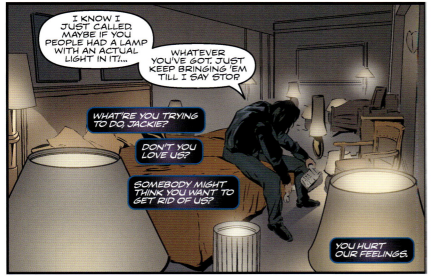

I KNOW I JUST CALLED. MAYBE IF YOU PEOPLE HAD A LAMP WITH AN ACTUAL LIGHT IN IT!...

WHATEVER YOU'VE GOT. JUST KEEP BRINGING 'EM TILL I SAY STOP.

WHAT'RE YOU TRYING TO DO, JACKIE?

DON'T YOU LOVE US?

SOMEBODY MIGHT THINK YOU WANT TO GET RID OF US?

YOU HURT OUR FEELINGS.

SOMEDAY YOU'LL BE SORRY.

YES, SOMEDAY YOU'LL NEED US.

GIVE US SOME BITS.

A NICE YOUNG ONE.

NNNN... GOD...

LEAVE HIM OUT OF THIS.

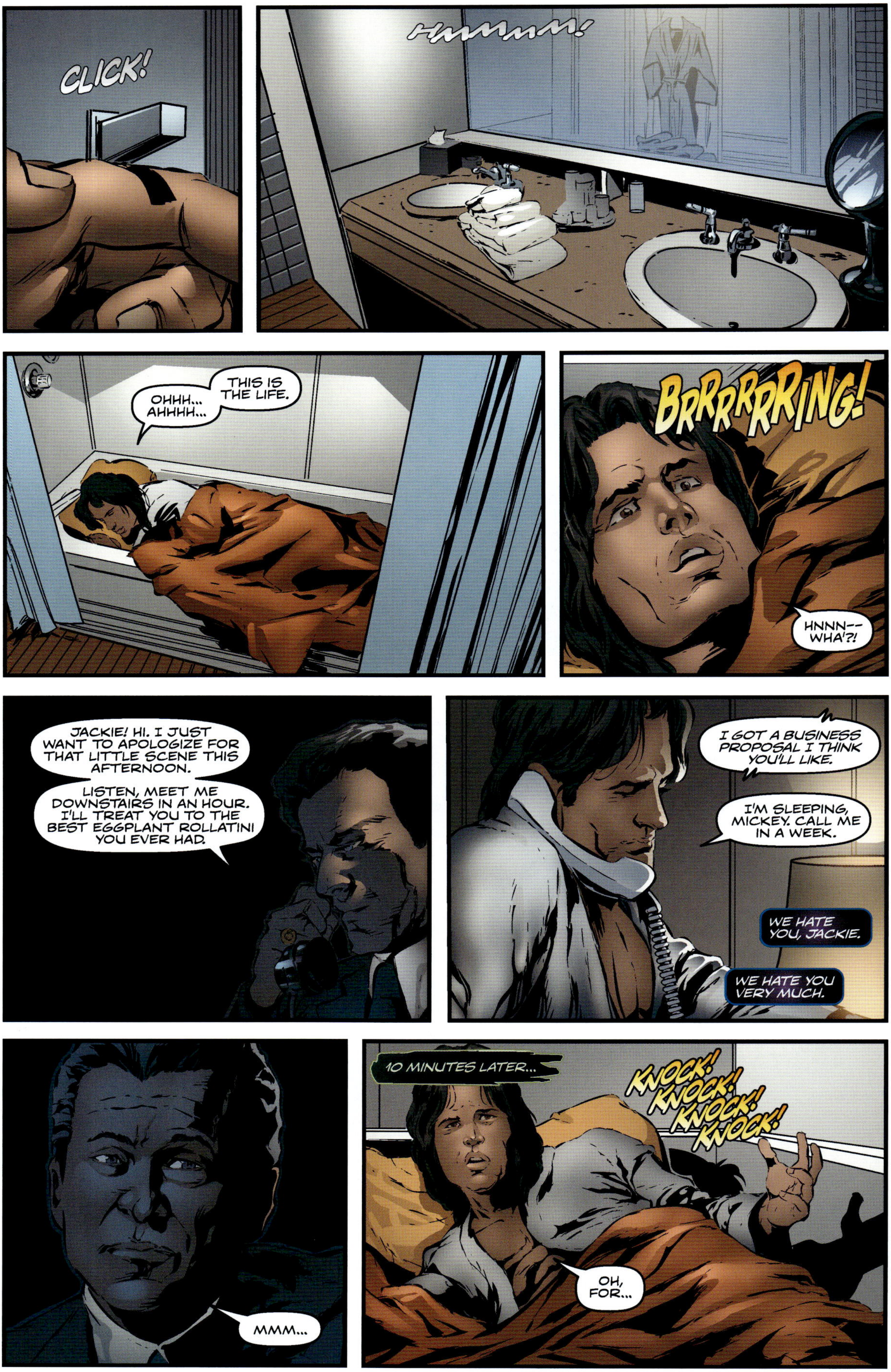
CLICK!
OHHH... AHHHH...
THIS IS THE LIFE.
BRRRRRRING!
HNNN-- WHA'?!
JACKIE! HI. I JUST WANT TO APOLOGIZE FOR THAT LITTLE SCENE THIS AFTERNOON.
LISTEN, MEET ME DOWNSTAIRS IN AN HOUR. I'LL TREAT YOU TO THE BEST EGGPLANT ROLLATINI YOU EVER HAD.
I GOT A BUSINESS PROPOSAL I THINK YOU'LL LIKE.
I'M SLEEPING, MICKEY. CALL ME IN A WEEK.
WE HATE YOU, JACKIE.
WE HATE YOU VERY MUCH.
MMM...
10 MINUTES LATER...
KNOCK! KNOCK! KNOCK! KNOCK!
OH, FOR...

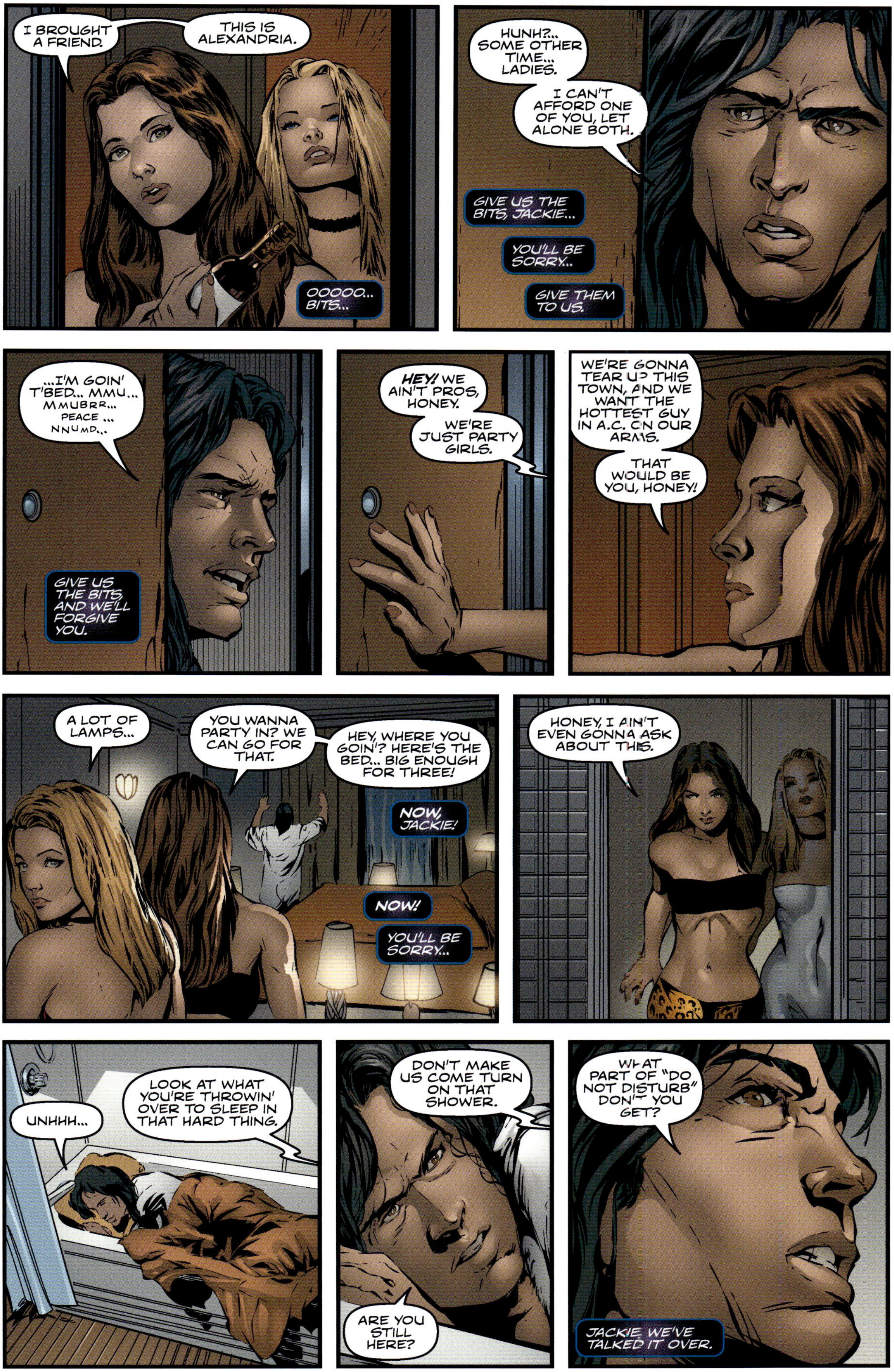
I BROUGHT A FRIEND.
THIS IS ALEXANDRIA.
OOOOO... BITS...
HUNH?.. SOME OTHER TIME... LADIES.
I CAN'T AFFORD ONE OF YOU, LET ALONE BOTH.
GIVE US THE BITS, JACKIE...
YOU'LL BE SORRY...
GIVE THEM TO US.
...I'M GOIN' T'BED... MMU... MMUBRR... PEACE ... NNUMD...
GIVE US THE BITS, AND WE'LL FORGIVE YOU.
HEY! WE AIN'T PROS, HONEY.
WE'RE JUST PARTY GIRLS.
WE'RE GONNA TEAR UP THIS TOWN, AND WE WANT THE HOTTEST GUY IN A.C. ON OUR ARMS.
THAT WOULD BE YOU, HONEY!
A LOT OF LAMPS...
YOU WANNA PARTY IN? WE CAN GO FOR THAT.
HEY, WHERE YOU GOIN'? HERE'S THE BED... BIG ENOUGH FOR THREE!
NOW, JACKIE!
NOW!
YOU'LL BE SORRY...
HONEY, I AIN'T EVEN GONNA ASK ABOUT THIS.
UNHHH...
LOOK AT WHAT YOU'RE THROWIN' OVER TO SLEEP IN THAT HARD THING.
DON'T MAKE US COME TURN ON THAT SHOWER.
ARE YOU STILL HERE?
WHAT PART OF "DO NOT DISTURB" DON'T YOU GET?
JACKIE, WE'VE TALKED IT OVER.

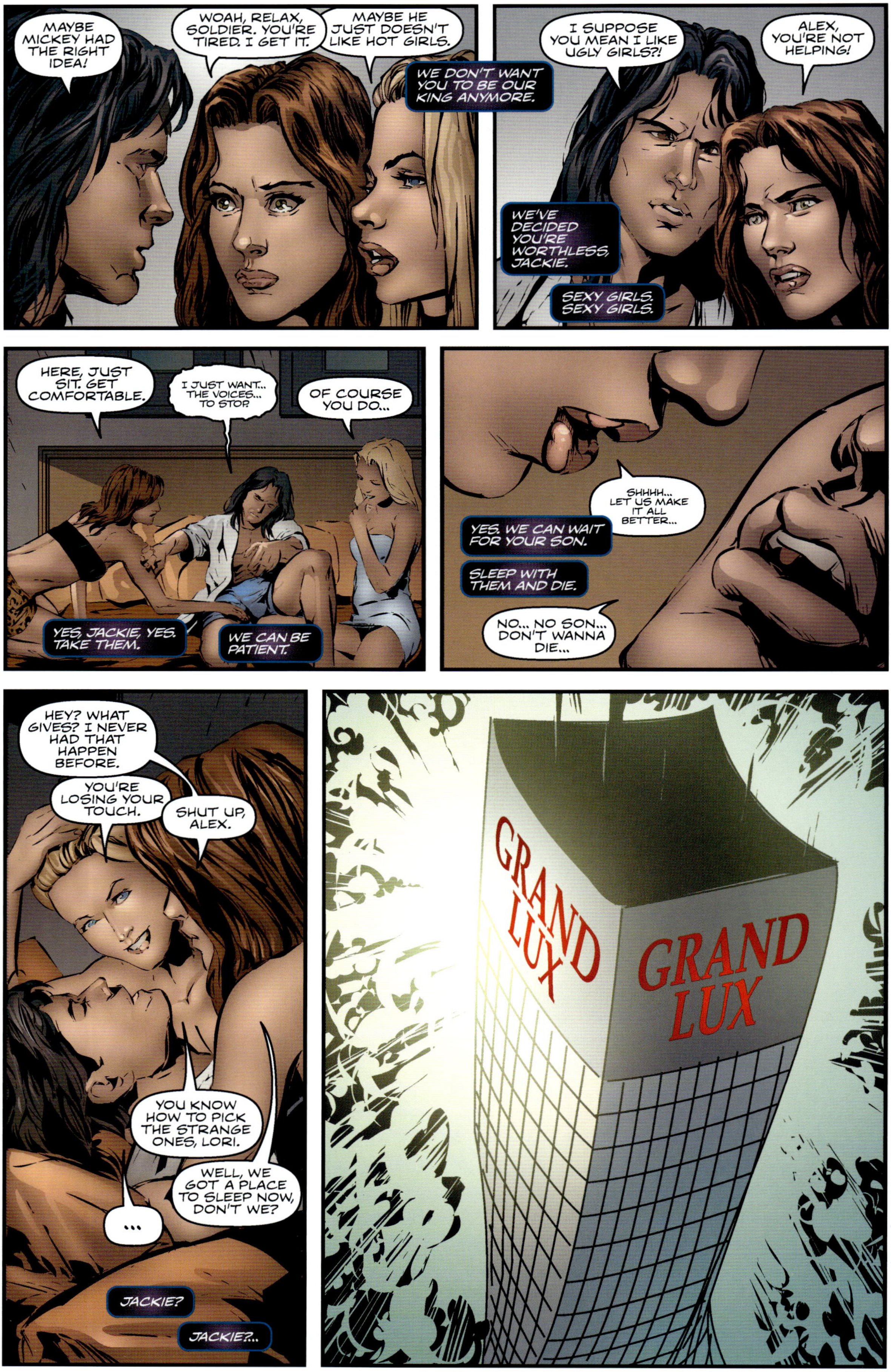
MAYBE MICKEY HAD THE RIGHT IDEA!
WOAH, RELAX, SOLDIER. YOU'RE TIRED. I GET IT.
MAYBE HE JUST DOESN'T LIKE HOT GIRLS.
WE DON'T WANT YOU TO BE OUR KING ANYMORE.
I SUPPOSE YOU MEAN I LIKE UGLY GIRLS?!
ALEX, YOU'RE NOT HELPING!
WE'VE DECIDED YOU'RE WORTHLESS, JACKIE.
SEXY GIRLS. SEXY GIRLS.
HERE, JUST SIT. GET COMFORTABLE.
I JUST WANT... THE VOICES... TO STOP.
OF COURSE YOU DO...
YES, JACKIE, YES. TAKE THEM.
WE CAN BE PATIENT.
SHHHH... LET US MAKE IT ALL BETTER...
YES. WE CAN WAIT FOR YOUR SON.
SLEEP WITH THEM AND DIE.
NO... NO SON... DON'T WANNA DIE...
HEY? WHAT GIVES? I NEVER HAD THAT HAPPEN BEFORE.
YOU'RE LOSING YOUR TOUCH.
SHUT UP, ALEX.
YOU KNOW HOW TO PICK THE STRANGE ONES, LORI.
WELL, WE GOT A PLACE TO SLEEP NOW, DON'T WE?
...
JACKIE?
JACKIE?...
GRAND LUX
GRAND LUX

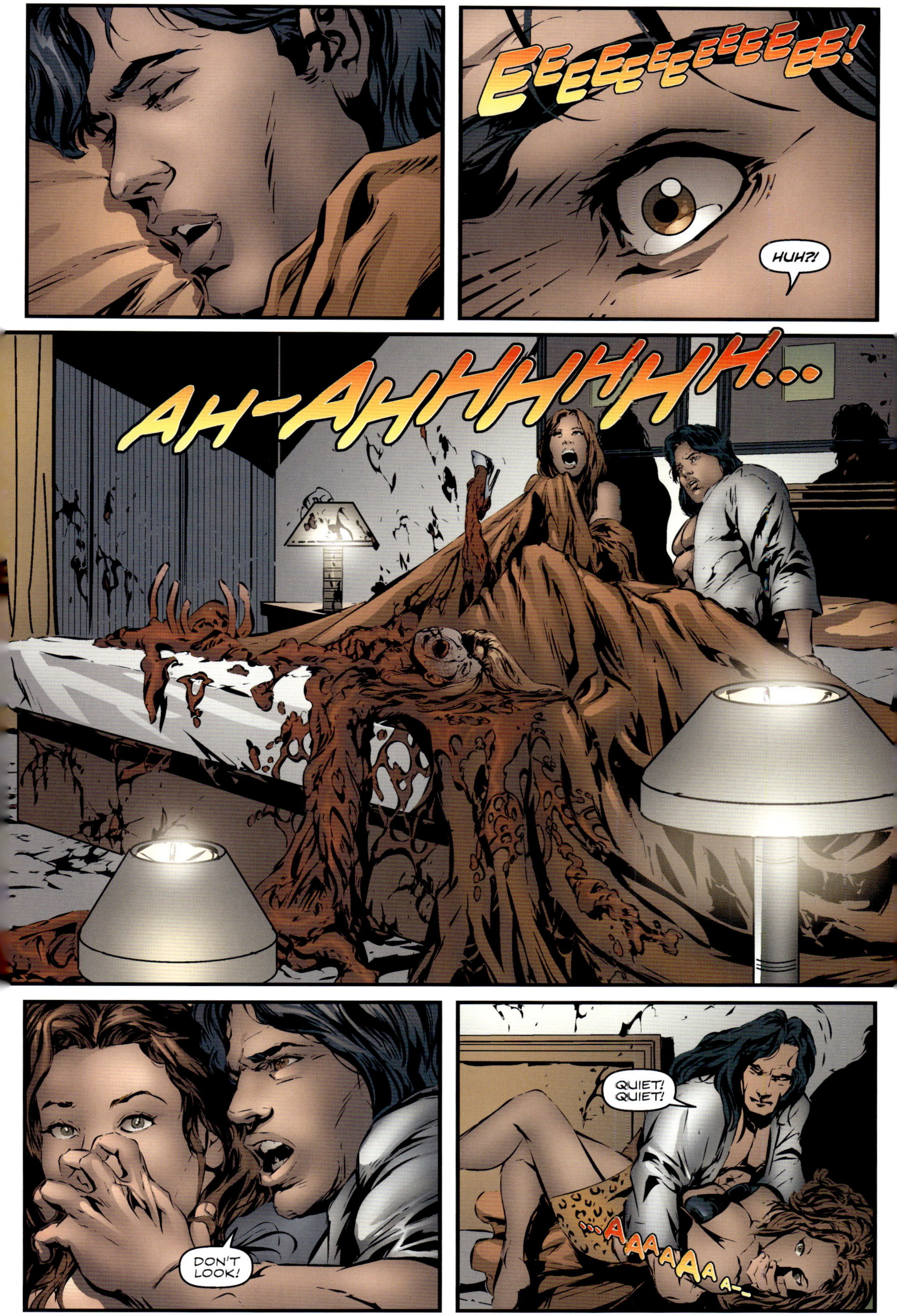
EEEEEEEEEEEE!
HUH?!
AH-AHHHHHH...
DON'T LOOK!
QUIET! QUIET!
...AAAAAA A--

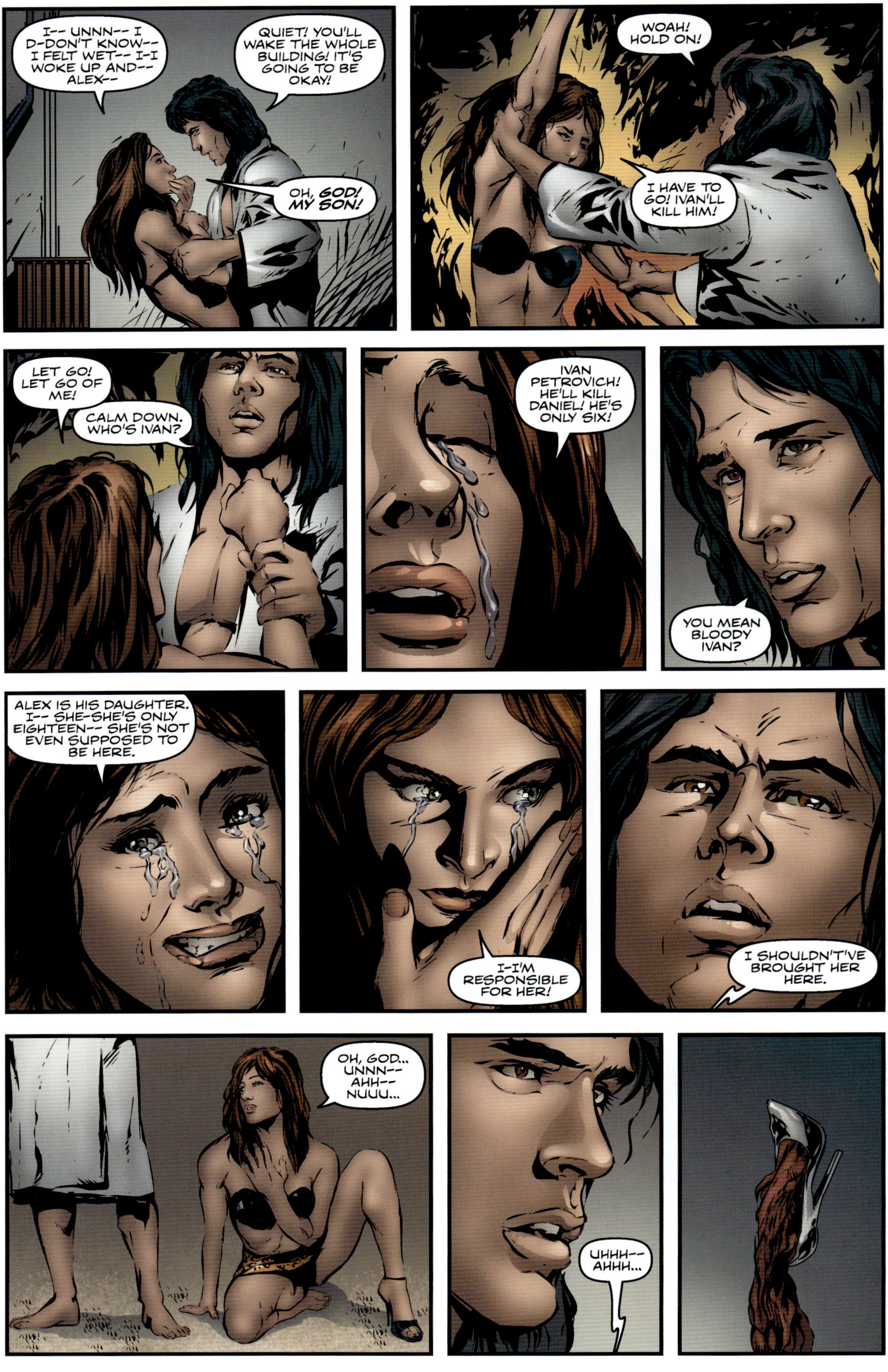
I-- UNNN-- I D-DON'T KNOW-- I FELT WET-- I-I WOKE UP AND-- ALEX--
QUIET! YOU'LL WAKE THE WHOLE BUILDING! IT'S GOING TO BE OKAY!
OH, GOD! MY SON!
WOAH! HOLD ON!
I HAVE TO GO! IVAN'LL KILL HIM!
LET GO! LET GO OF ME!
CALM DOWN. WHO'S IVAN?
IVAN PETROVICH! HE'LL KILL DANIEL! HE'S ONLY SIX!
YOU MEAN BLOODY IVAN?
ALEX IS HIS DAUGHTER. I-- SHE-SHE'S ONLY EIGHTEEN-- SHE'S NOT EVEN SUPPOSED TO BE HERE.
I-I'M RESPONSIBLE FOR HER!
I SHOULDN'T'VE BROUGHT HER HERE.
OH, GOD... UNNN-- AHH-- NUUU...
UHHH-- AHHH...

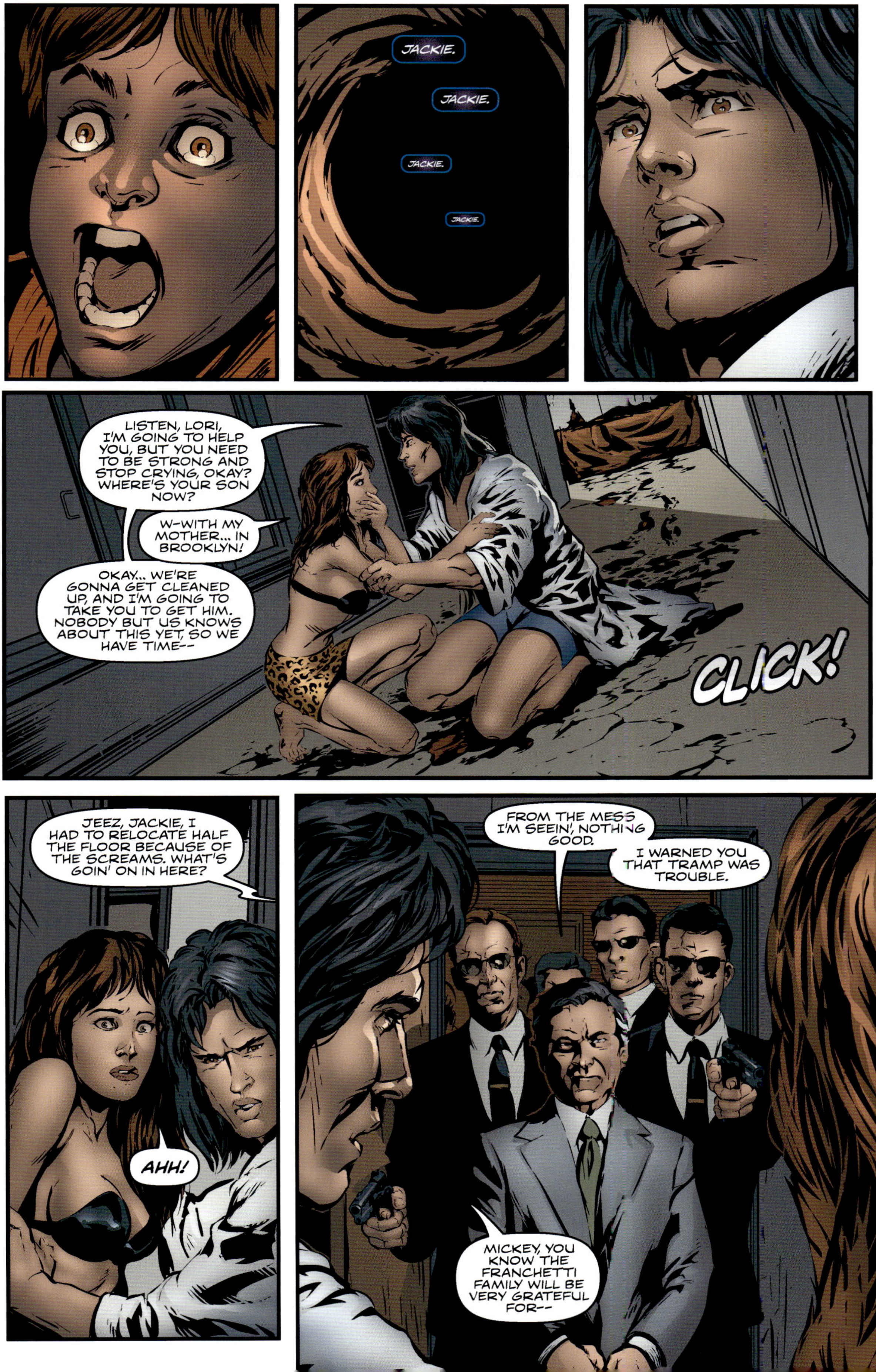
JACKIE.
JACKIE.
JACKIE.
JACKIE.
LISTEN, LORI, I'M GOING TO HELP YOU, BUT YOU NEED TO BE STRONG AND STOP CRYING, OKAY? WHERE'S YOUR SON NOW?
W-WITH MY MOTHER... IN BROOKLYN!
OKAY... WE'RE GONNA GET CLEANED UP, AND I'M GOING TO TAKE YOU TO GET HIM. NOBODY BUT US KNOWS ABOUT THIS YET, SO WE HAVE TIME--
CLICK!
JEEZ, JACKIE, I HAD TO RELOCATE HALF THE FLOOR BECAUSE OF THE SCREAMS. WHAT'S GOIN' ON IN HERE?
AHH!
FROM THE MESS I'M SEEIN', NOTHING GOOD.
I WARNED YOU THAT TRAMP WAS TROUBLE.
MICKEY, YOU KNOW THE FRANCHETTI FAMILY WILL BE VERY GRATEFUL FOR--

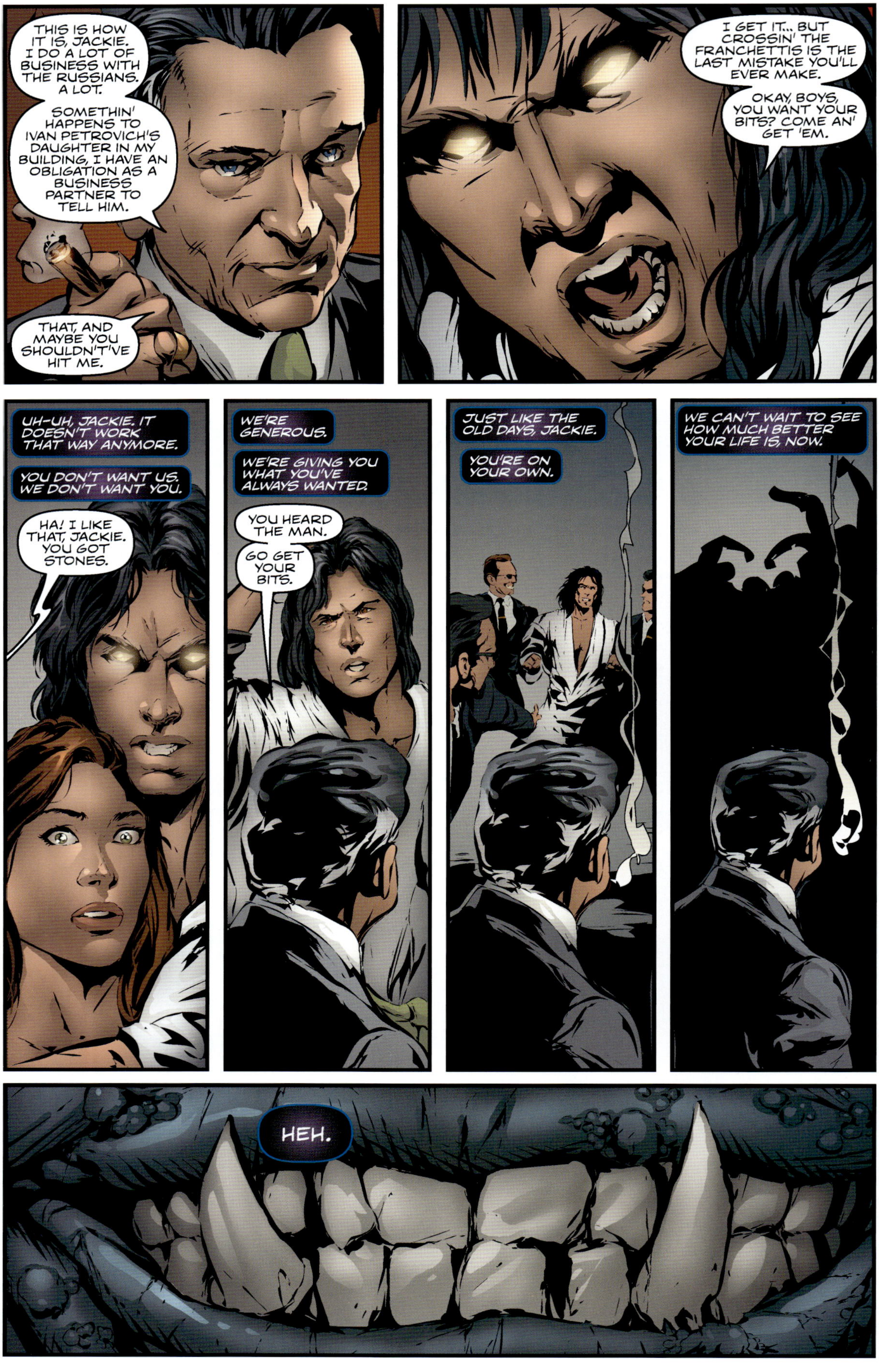
THIS IS HOW IT IS, JACKIE. I DO A LOT OF BUSINESS WITH THE RUSSIANS. A LOT.
SOMETHIN' HAPPENS TO IVAN PETROVICH'S DAUGHTER IN MY BUILDING, I HAVE AN OBLIGATION AS A BUSINESS PARTNER TO TELL HIM.
THAT, AND MAYBE YOU SHOULDN'T'VE HIT ME.
I GET IT... BUT CROSSIN' THE FRANCHETTIS IS THE LAST MISTAKE YOU'LL EVER MAKE.
OKAY, BOYS, YOU WANT YOUR BITS? COME AN' GET 'EM.
UH-UH, JACKIE. IT DOESN'T WORK THAT WAY ANYMORE.
YOU DON'T WANT US. WE DON'T WANT YOU.
HA! I LIKE THAT, JACKIE. YOU GOT STONES.
WE'RE GENEROUS.
WE'RE GIVING YOU WHAT YOU'VE ALWAYS WANTED.
YOU HEARD THE MAN.
GO GET YOUR BITS.
JUST LIKE THE OLD DAYS, JACKIE.
YOU'RE ON YOUR OWN.
WE CAN'T WAIT TO SEE HOW MUCH BETTER YOUR LIFE IS, NOW.
HEH.

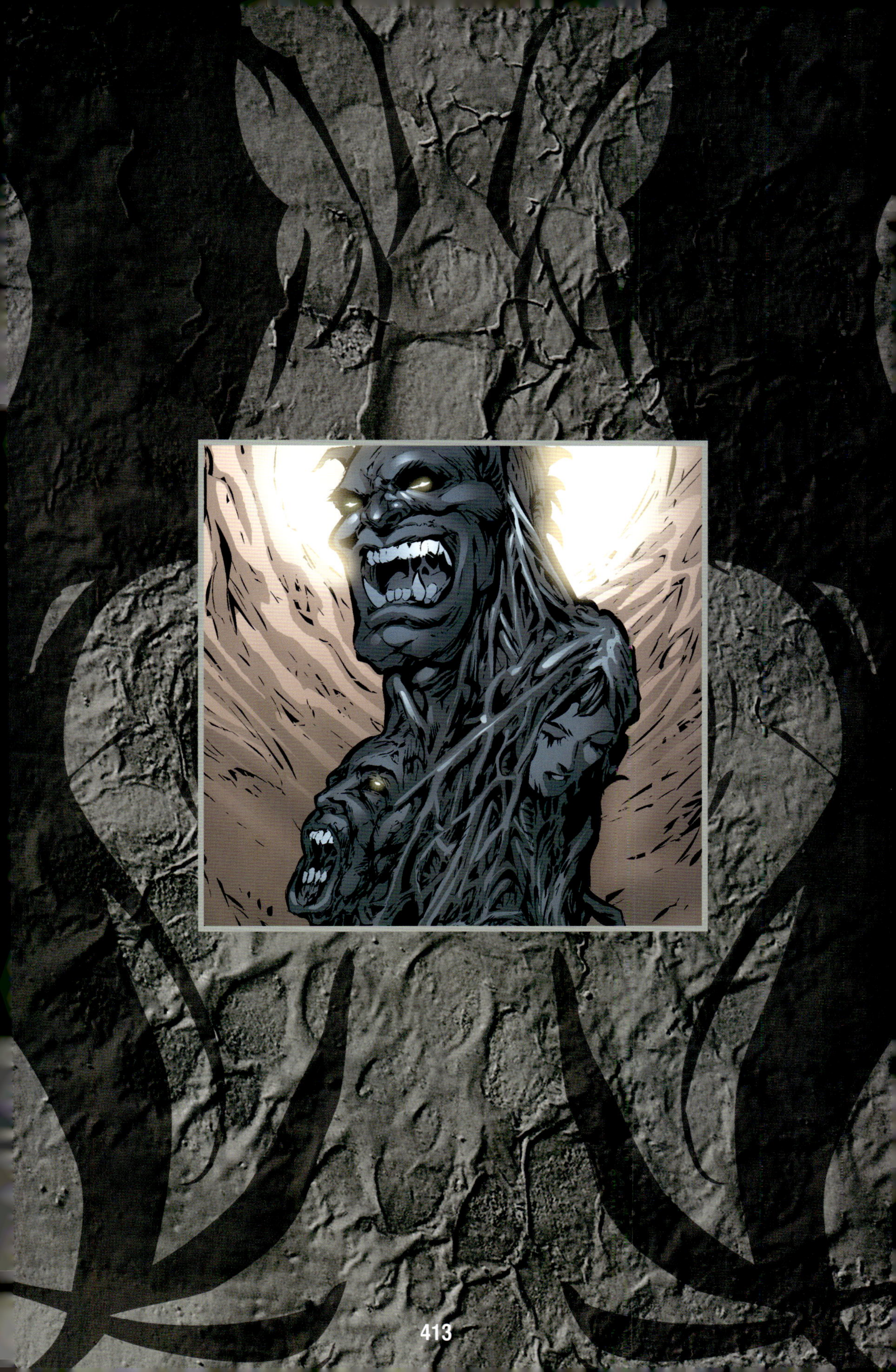

The Darkness Issue #58
cover art by: Dale Keown

THE DARKNESS #58

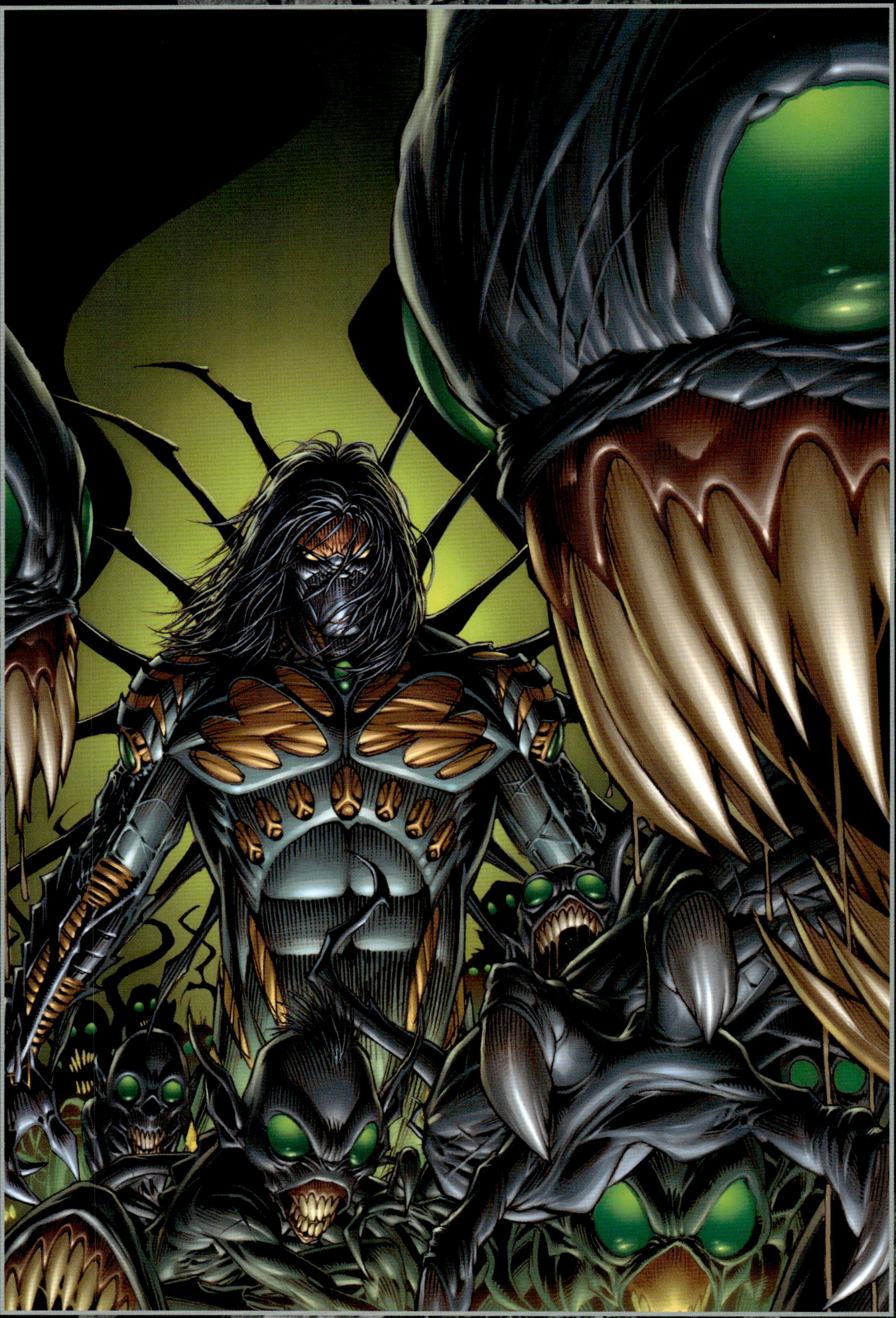

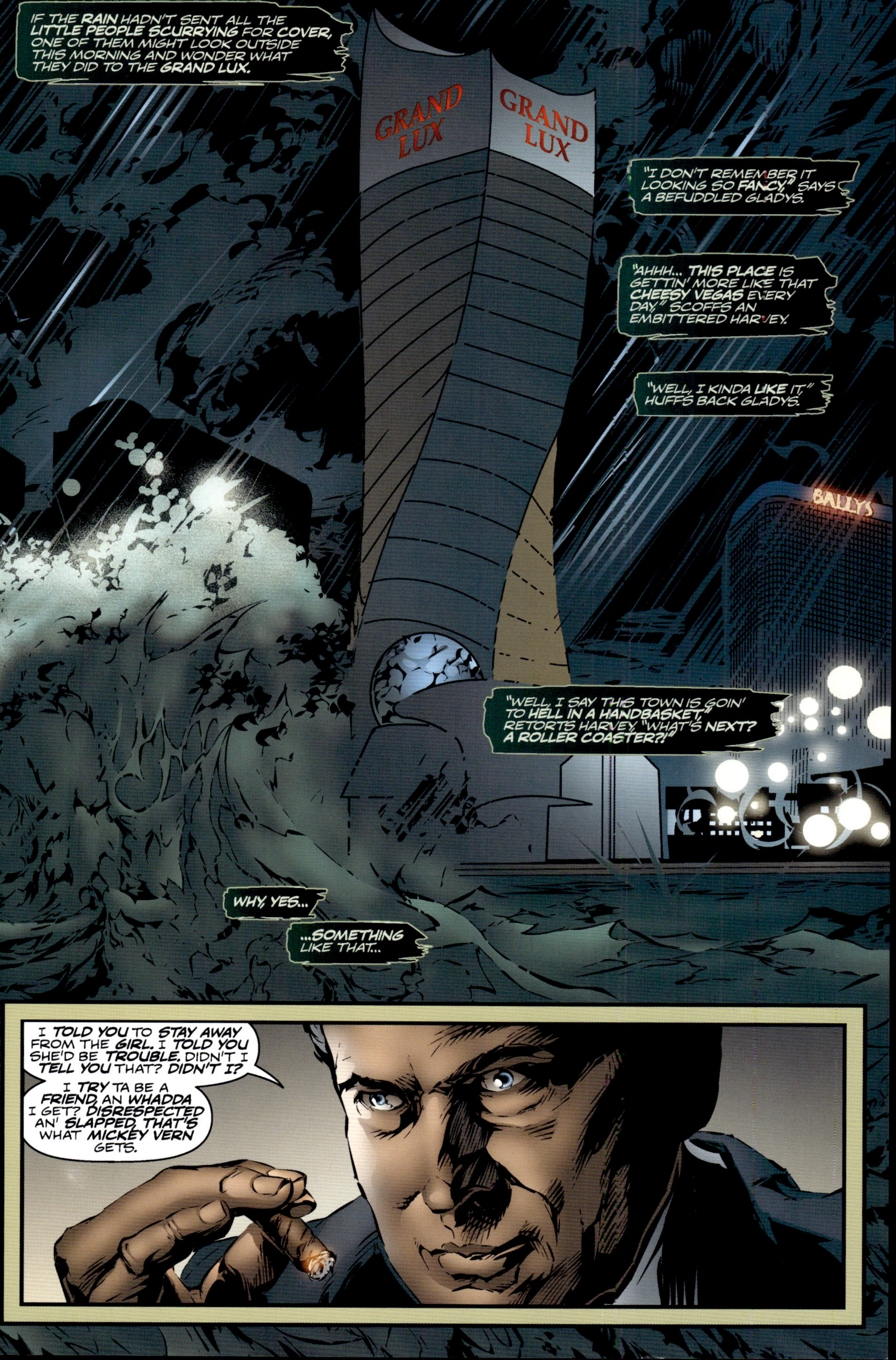
IF THE RAIN HADN'T SENT ALL THE LITTLE PEOPLE SCURRYING FOR COVER, ONE OF THEM MIGHT LOOK OUTSIDE THIS MORNING AND WONDER WHAT THEY DID TO THE GRAND LUX.
GRAND LUX
GRAND LUX
"I DON'T REMEMBER IT LOOKING SO FANCY," SAYS A BEFUDDLED GLADYS.
"AHHH... THIS PLACE IS GETTIN' MORE LIKE THAT CHEESY VEGAS EVERY DAY," SCOFFS AN EMBITTERED HARVEY.
"WELL, I KINDA LIKE IT," HUFFS BACK GLADYS.
BALLYS
"WELL, I SAY THIS TOWN IS GOIN' TO HELL IN A HANDBASKET," RETORTS HARVEY. "WHAT'S NEXT? A ROLLER COASTER?!"
WHY, YES...
...SOMETHING LIKE THAT...
I TOLD YOU TO STAY AWAY FROM THE GIRL. I TOLD YOU SHE'D BE TROUBLE. DIDN'T I TELL YOU THAT? DIDN'T I?
I TRY TA BE A FRIEND, AN WHADDA I GET? DISRESPECTED AN' SLAPPED. THAT'S WHAT MICKEY VERN GETS.

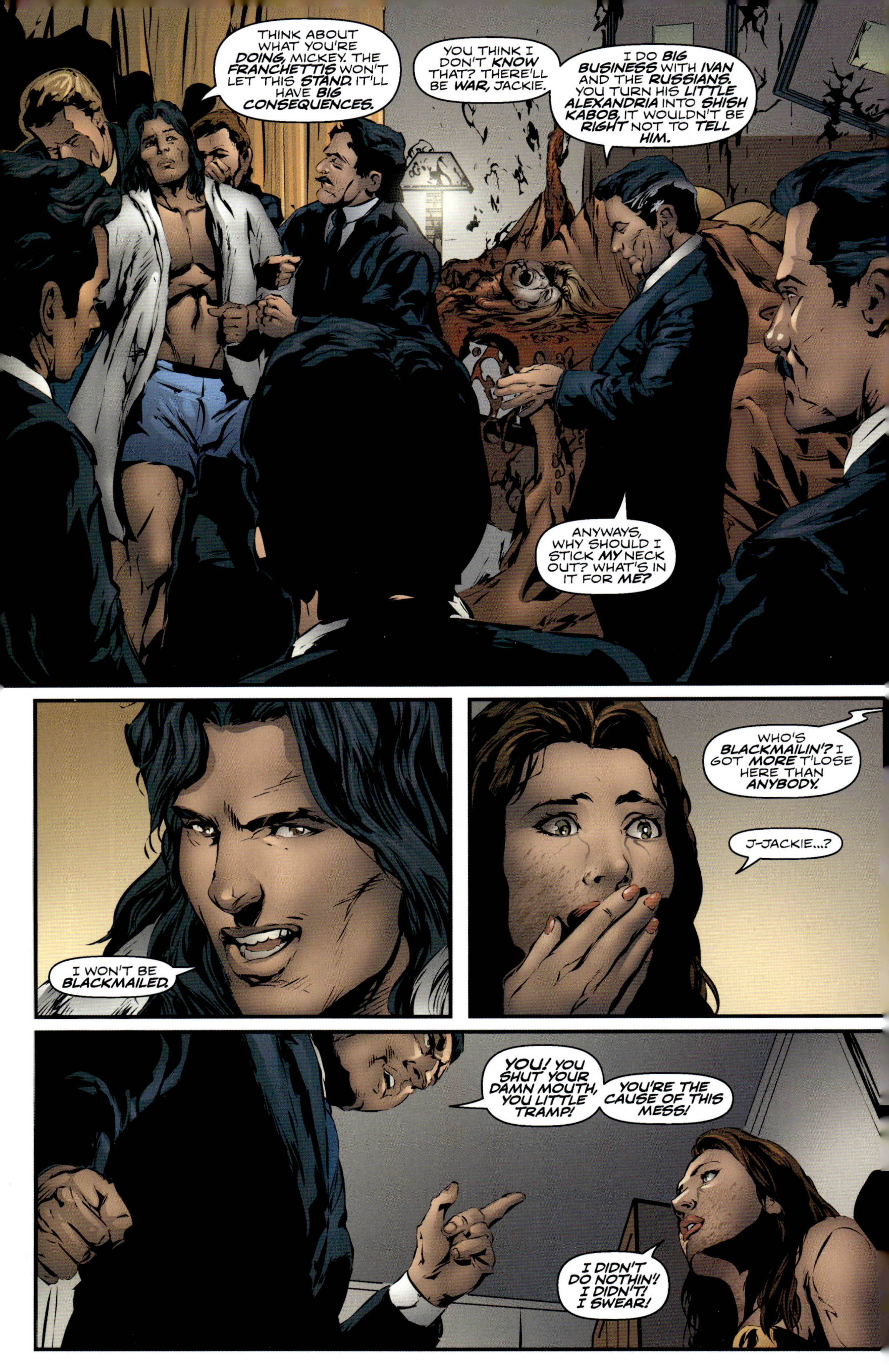
THINK ABOUT WHAT YOU'RE DOING, MICKEY. THE FRANCHETTIS WON'T LET THIS STAND. IT'LL HAVE BIG CONSEQUENCES.
YOU THINK I DON'T KNOW THAT? THERE'LL BE WAR, JACKIE.
I DO BIG BUSINESS WITH IVAN AND THE RUSSIANS. YOU TURN HIS LITTLE ALEXANDRIA INTO SHISH KABOB, IT WOULDN'T BE RIGHT NOT TO TELL HIM.
ANYWAYS, WHY SHOULD I STICK MY NECK OUT? WHAT'S IN IT FOR ME?
I WON'T BE BLACKMAILED.
WHO'S BLACKMAILIN'? I GOT MORE T'LOSE HERE THAN ANYBODY.
J-JACKIE...?
YOU! YOU SHUT YOUR DAMN MOUTH, YOU LITTLE TRAMP!
YOU'RE THE CAUSE OF THIS MESS!
I DIDN'T DO NOTHIN'! I DIDN'T! I SWEAR!

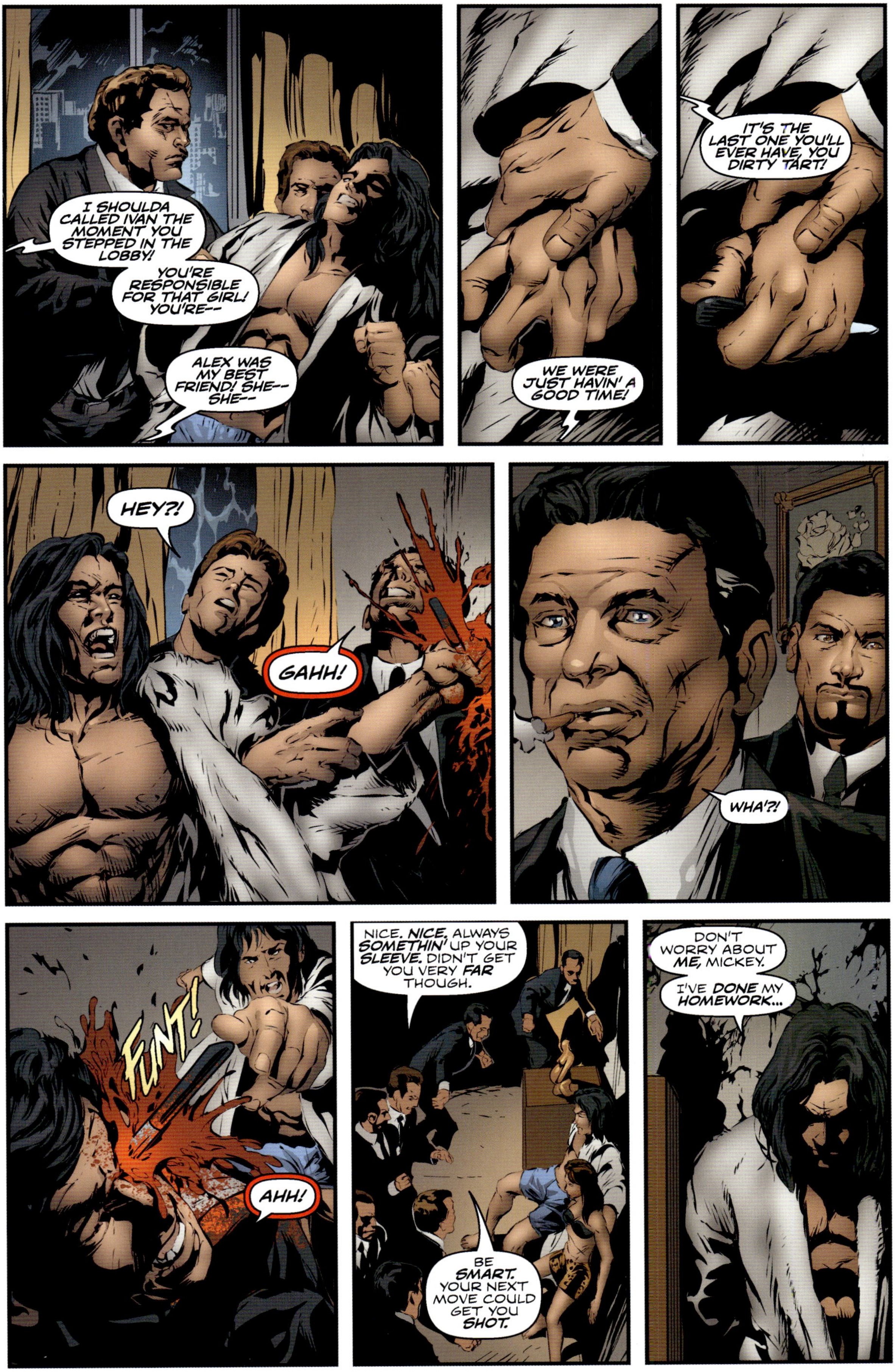
I SHOULDA CALLED IVAN THE MOMENT YOU STEPPED IN THE LOBBY!
YOU'RE RESPONSIBLE FOR THAT GIRL! YOU'RE--
ALEX WAS MY BEST FRIEND! SHE-- SHE--
WE WERE JUST HAVIN' A GOOD TIME!
IT'S THE LAST ONE YOU'LL EVER HAVE, YOU DIRTY TART!
HEY?!
GAHH!
WHA'?!
FUNT!
AHH!
NICE. NICE. ALWAYS SOMETHIN' UP YOUR SLEEVE. DIDN'T GET YOU VERY FAR THOUGH.
BE SMART. YOUR NEXT MOVE COULD GET YOU SHOT.
DON'T WORRY ABOUT ME, MICKEY.
I'VE DONE MY HOMEWORK...

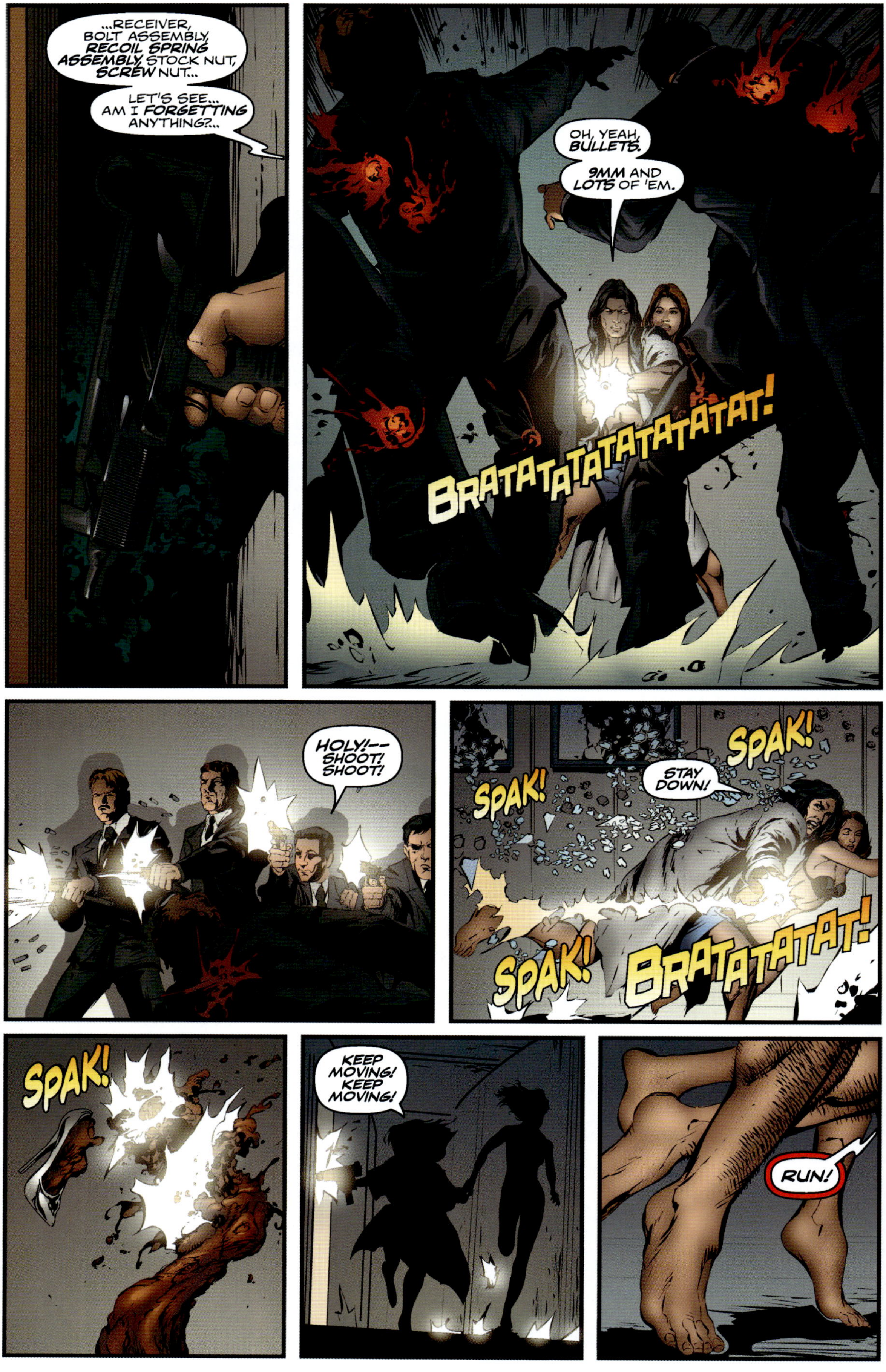
...RECEIVER, BOLT ASSEMBLY, RECOIL SPRING ASSEMBLY, STOCK NUT, SCREW NUT...
LET'S SEE... AM I FORGETTING ANYTHING?...
OH, YEAH, BULLETS.
9MM AND LOTS OF 'EM.
BRATATATATATATATAT!
HOLY!-- SHOOT! SHOOT!
SPAK!
SPAK!
STAY DOWN!
SPAK!
BRATATATAT!
SPAK!
KEEP MOVING! KEEP MOVING!
RUN!

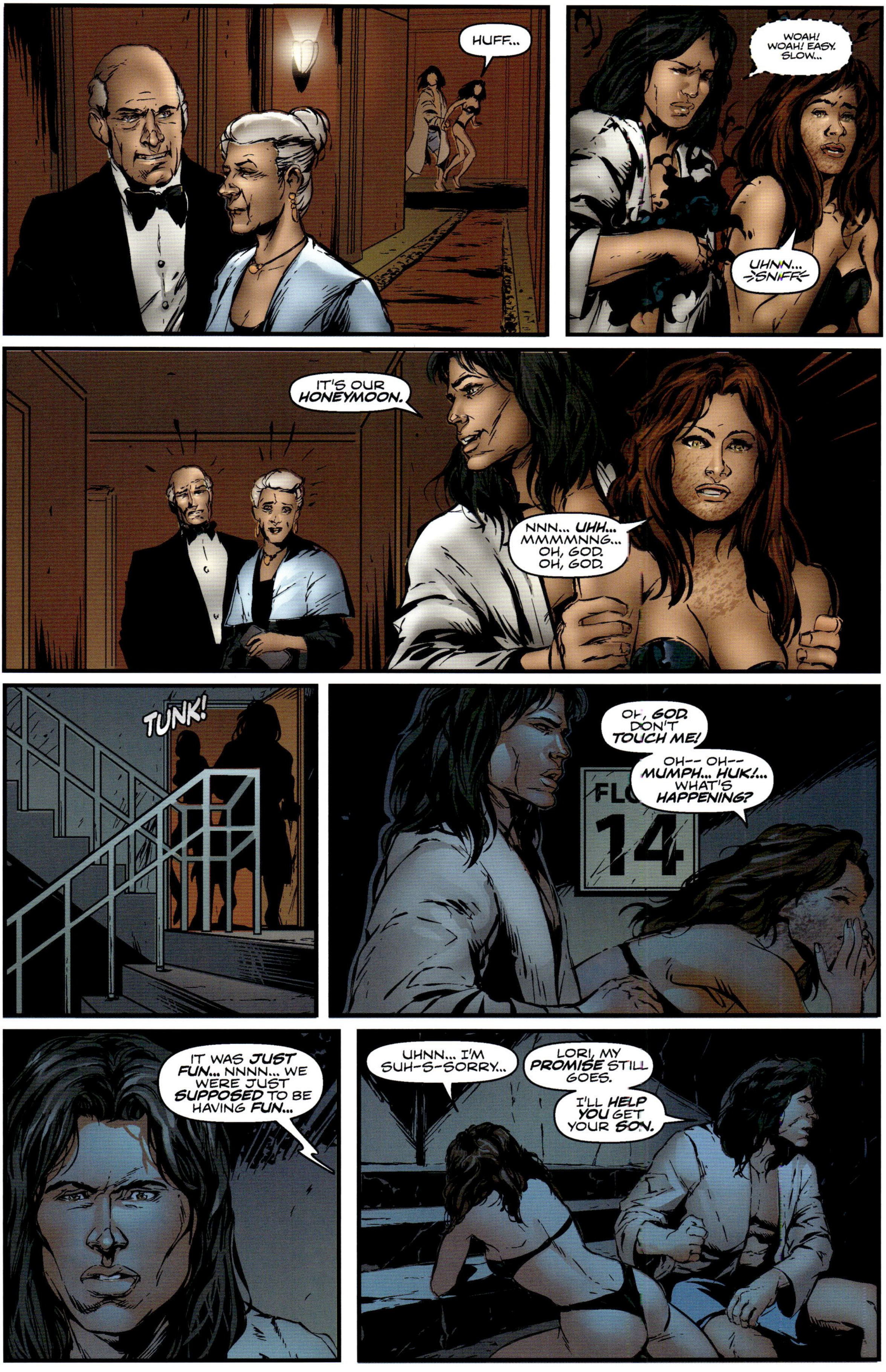
HUFF...
WOAH! WOAH! EASY. SLOW...
UHNN... SNIFF
IT'S OUR HONEYMOON.
NNN... UHH... MMMMNNG... OH, GOD. OH, GOD.
TUNK!
OH, GOD. DON'T TOUCH ME!
OH-- OH-- MUMPH... HUK!... WHAT'S HAPPENING?
FLO
14
IT WAS JUST FUN... NNNN... WE WERE JUST SUPPOSED TO BE HAVING FUN...
UHNN... I'M SUH-S-SORRY...
LORI, MY PROMISE STILL GOES.
I'LL HELP YOU GET YOUR SON.

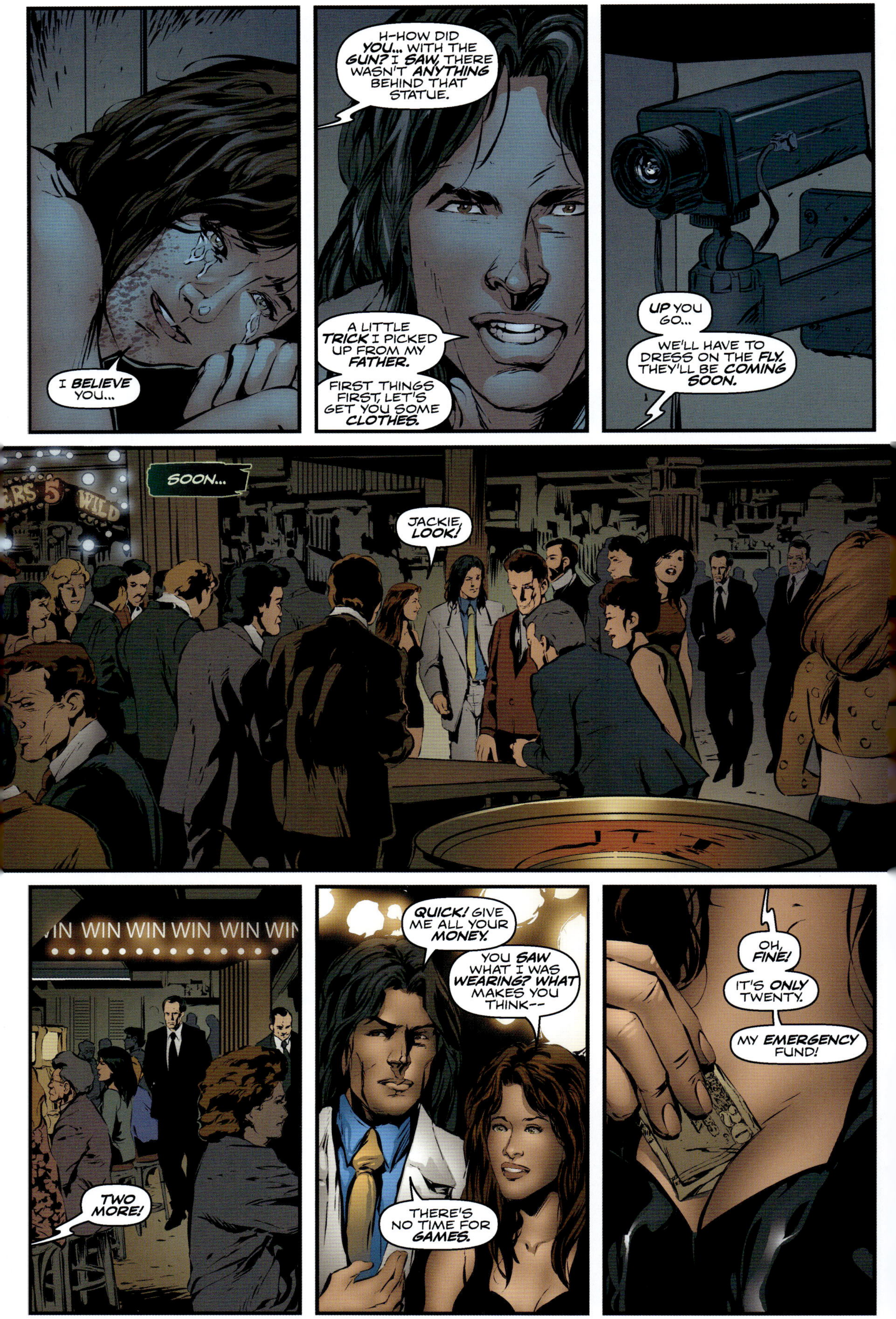
I BELIEVE YOU...
H-HOW DID YOU... WITH THE GUN? I SAW, THERE WASN'T ANYTHING BEHIND THAT STATUE.
A LITTLE TRICK I PICKED UP FROM MY FATHER.
FIRST THINGS FIRST, LET'S GET YOU SOME CLOTHES.
UP YOU GO...
WE'LL HAVE TO DRESS ON THE FLY. THEY'LL BE COMING SOON.
SOON...
JACKIE, LOOK!
WIN WIN WIN WIN WIN WIN
TWO MORE!
QUICK! GIVE ME ALL YOUR MONEY.
YOU SAW WHAT I WAS WEARING? WHAT MAKES YOU THINK--
THERE'S NO TIME FOR GAMES.
OH, FINE!
IT'S ONLY TWENTY.
MY EMERGENCY FUND!

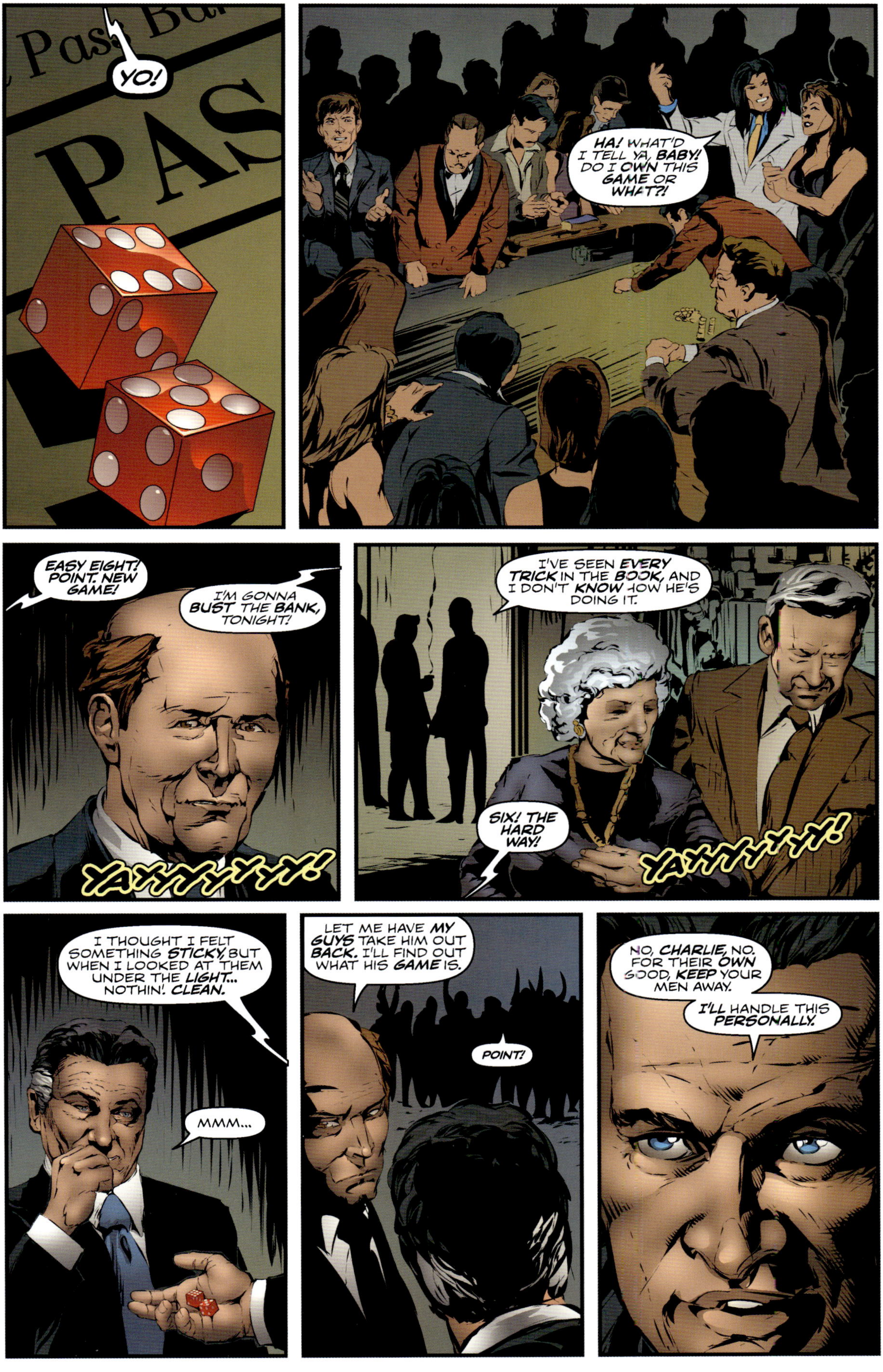

YO!
HA! WHAT'D I TELL YA, BABY! DO I OWN THIS GAME OR WHAT?!
EASY EIGHT! POINT. NEW GAME!
I'M GONNA BUST THE BANK, TONIGHT!
YAYYYYYYY!
I'VE SEEN EVERY TRICK IN THE BOOK, AND I DON'T KNOW HOW HE'S DOING IT.
SIX! THE HARD WAY!
YAYYYYYYY!
I THOUGHT I FELT SOMETHING STICKY, BUT WHEN I LOOKED AT THEM UNDER THE LIGHT... NOTHIN'. CLEAN.
MMM...
LET ME HAVE MY GUYS TAKE HIM OUT BACK. I'LL FIND OUT WHAT HIS GAME IS.
POINT!
NO, CHARLIE, NO. FOR THEIR OWN GOOD, KEEP YOUR MEN AWAY.
I'LL HANDLE THIS PERSONALLY.

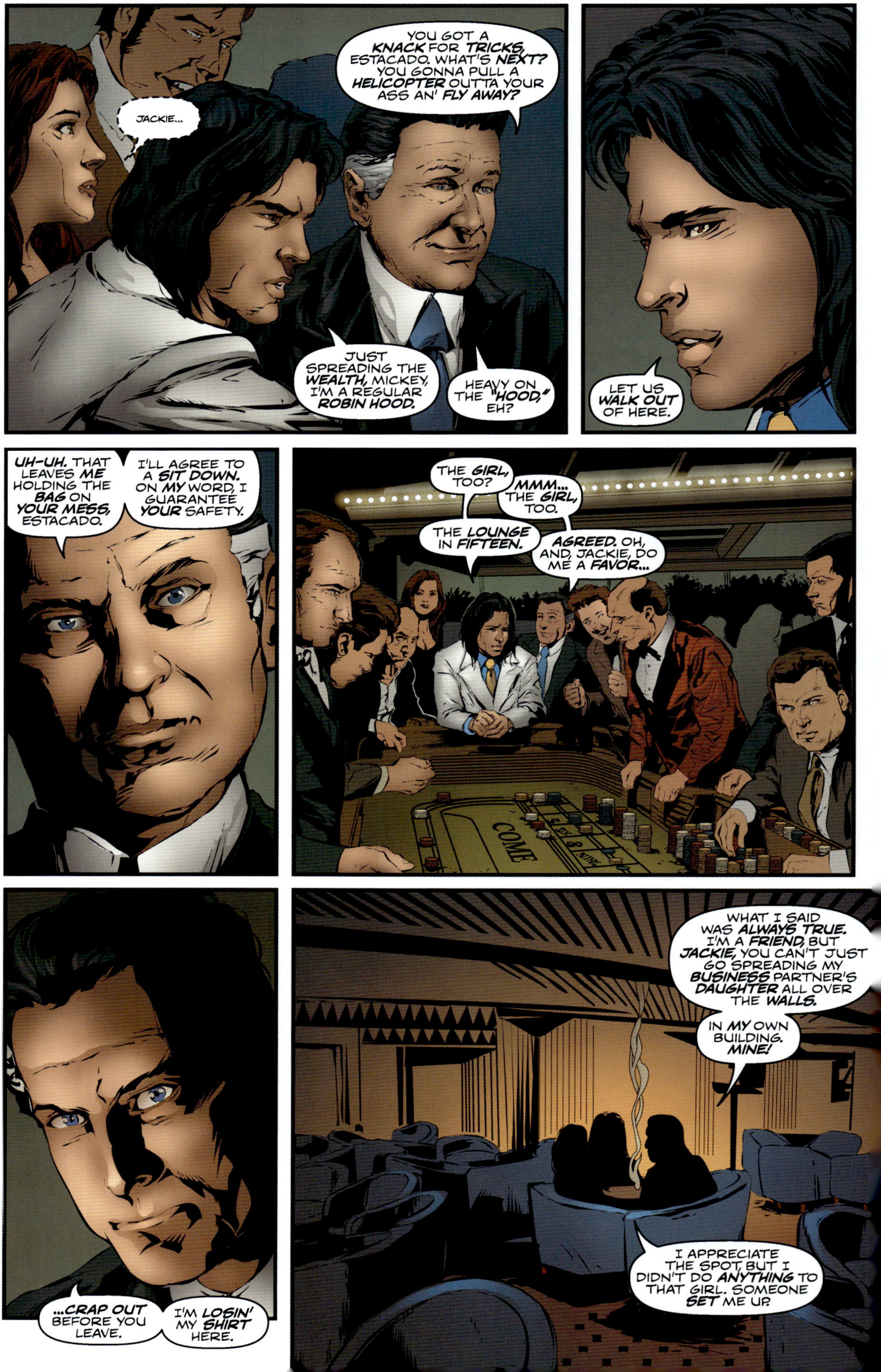

YOU GOT A KNACK FOR TRICKS, ESTACADO. WHAT'S NEXT? YOU GONNA PULL A HELICOPTER OUTTA YOUR ASS AN' FLY AWAY?
JACKIE...
JUST SPREADING THE WEALTH, MICKEY, I'M A REGULAR ROBIN HOOD.
HEAVY ON THE "HOOD," EH?
LET US WALK OUT OF HERE.
UH-UH. THAT LEAVES ME HOLDING THE BAG ON YOUR MESS, ESTACADO.
I'LL AGREE TO A SIT DOWN. ON MY WORD, I GUARANTEE YOUR SAFETY.
THE GIRL, TOO?
MMM... THE GIRL, TOO.
THE LOUNGE IN FIFTEEN.
AGREED. OH, AND, JACKIE, DO ME A FAVOR...
COME
...CRAP OUT BEFORE YOU LEAVE.
I'M LOSIN' MY SHIRT HERE.
WHAT I SAID WAS ALWAYS TRUE. I'M A FRIEND, BUT JACKIE, YOU CAN'T JUST GO SPREADING MY BUSINESS PARTNER'S DAUGHTER ALL OVER THE WALLS.
IN MY OWN BUILDING. MINE!
I APPRECIATE THE SPOT, BUT I DIDN'T DO ANYTHING TO THAT GIRL. SOMEONE SET ME UP.

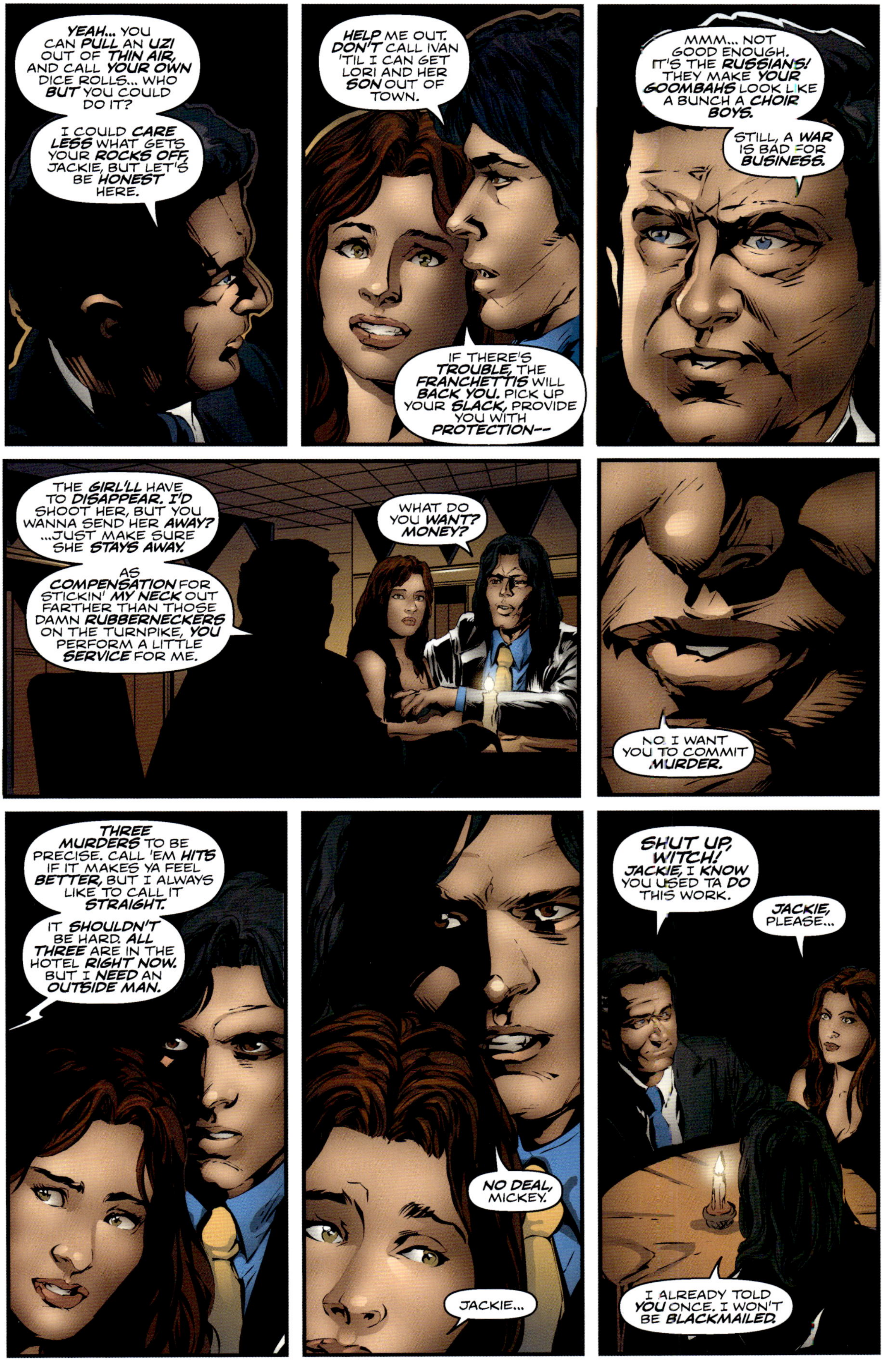
YEAH... YOU CAN PULL AN UZI OUT OF THIN AIR, AND CALL YOUR OWN DICE ROLLS... WHO BUT YOU COULD DO IT?
I COULD CARE LESS WHAT GETS YOUR ROCKS OFF, JACKIE, BUT LET'S BE HONEST HERE.
HELP ME OUT. DON'T CALL IVAN 'TIL I CAN GET LORI AND HER SON OUT OF TOWN.
IF THERE'S TROUBLE, THE FRANCHETTIS WILL BACK YOU. PICK UP YOUR SLACK, PROVIDE YOU WITH PROTECTION--
MMM... NOT GOOD ENOUGH. IT'S THE RUSSIANS! THEY MAKE YOUR GOOMBAHS LOOK LIKE A BUNCH A CHOIR BOYS.
STILL, A WAR IS BAD FOR BUSINESS.
THE GIRL'LL HAVE TO DISAPPEAR. I'D SHOOT HER, BUT YOU WANNA SEND HER AWAY? ...JUST MAKE SURE SHE STAYS AWAY.
AS COMPENSATION FOR STICKIN' MY NECK OUT FARTHER THAN THOSE DAMN RUBBERNECKERS ON THE TURNPIKE, YOU PERFORM A LITTLE SERVICE FOR ME.
WHAT DO YOU WANT? MONEY?
NO. I WANT YOU TO COMMIT MURDER.
THREE MURDERS TO BE PRECISE. CALL 'EM HITS IF IT MAKES YA FEEL BETTER, BUT I ALWAYS LIKE TO CALL IT STRAIGHT.
IT SHOULDN'T BE HARD. ALL THREE ARE IN THE HOTEL RIGHT NOW. BUT I NEED AN OUTSIDE MAN.
NO DEAL, MICKEY.
JACKIE...
SHUT UP, WITCH! JACKIE, I KNOW YOU USED TA DO THIS WORK.
JACKIE, PLEASE...
I ALREADY TOLD YOU ONCE. I WON'T BE BLACKMAILED.

I SAID... MEN ARE TALKING!

NO! THIS IS MY LIFE WE'RE TALKING ABOUT!

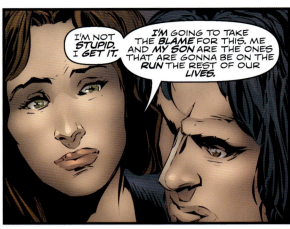

I'M NOT STUPID. I GET IT.

I'M GOING TO TAKE THE BLAME FOR THIS. ME AND MY SON ARE THE ONES THAT ARE GONNA BE ON THE RUN THE REST OF OUR LIVES.

JACKIE, PLEASE... I-I KNOW I DON'T HAVE THE RIGHT TO ASK YOU THIS...

BUT, JACKIE, WE HAVE A WAY OUT.

ALL RIGHT, MICKEY...

BUT I WANT A FEE.

SIXTY GRAND. LEGIT DOLLARS TO GO TO LORI AND HER SON.

I'M DOIN' YOU A FAVOR, YOU STUBBORN SON OF A--

JACKIE, NO...

TAKE IT OR LEAVE IT, MICKEY.

TAKE IT.

YOU'RE SO TENSE.

YOU THINK MICKEY'LL CROSS US?

I FEEL LIKE I JUST MADE A DEAL WITH THE DEVIL.

IT'S NOT HIM. I LIKE HIM. I THINK HE'S A GOOD MAN.

SOMETHING ELSE... I DON'T KNOW...

JAAACKIEEE...

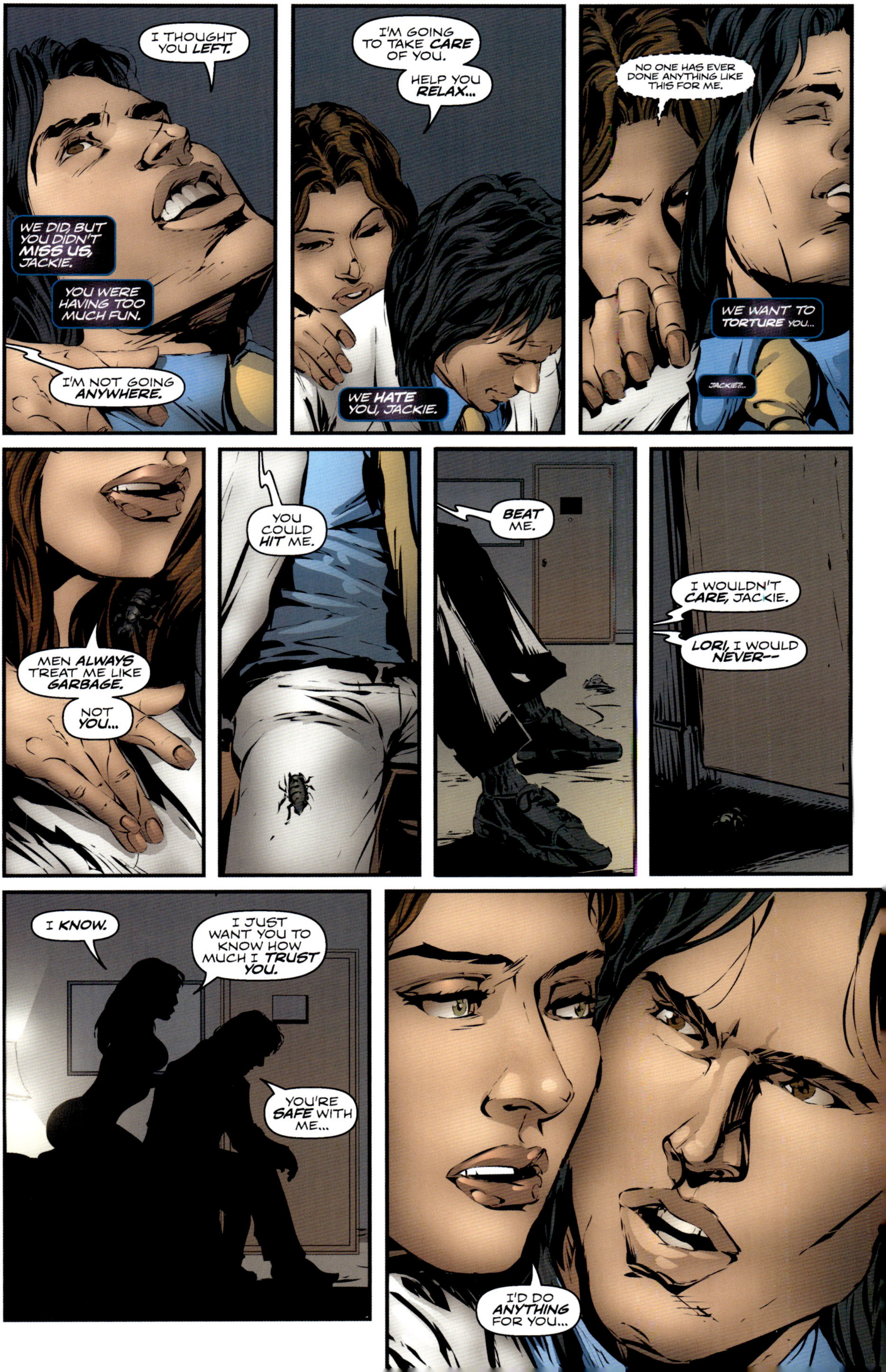
I THOUGHT YOU LEFT.
WE DID, BUT YOU DIDN'T MISS US, JACKIE.
YOU WERE HAVING TOO MUCH FUN.
I'M NOT GOING ANYWHERE.
I'M GOING TO TAKE CARE OF YOU.
HELP YOU RELAX...
WE HATE YOU, JACKIE.
NO ONE HAS EVER DONE ANYTHING LIKE THIS FOR ME.
WE WANT TO TORTURE YOU...
JACKIE?..
MEN ALWAYS TREAT ME LIKE GARBAGE.
NOT YOU...
YOU COULD HIT ME.
BEAT ME.
I WOULDN'T CARE, JACKIE.
LORI, I WOULD NEVER--
I KNOW.
I JUST WANT YOU TO KNOW HOW MUCH I TRUST YOU.
YOU'RE SAFE WITH ME...
I'D DO ANYTHING FOR YOU...

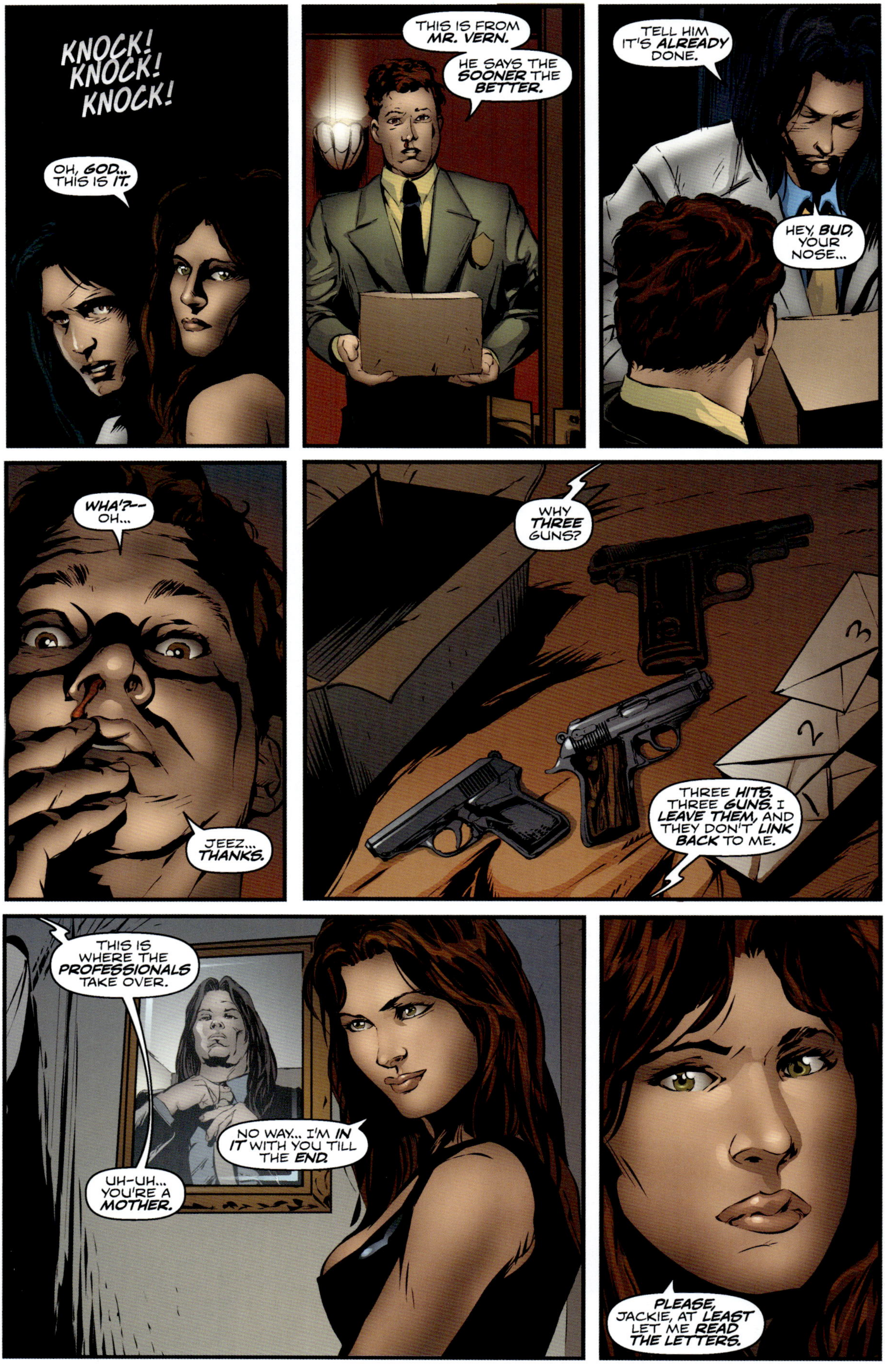
KNOCK! KNOCK! KNOCK!
OH, GOD... THIS IS IT.
THIS IS FROM MR. VERN.
HE SAYS THE SOONER THE BETTER.
TELL HIM IT'S ALREADY DONE.
HEY, BUD, YOUR NOSE...
WHA'?-- OH...
JEEZ... THANKS.
WHY THREE GUNS?
THREE HITS. THREE GUNS. I LEAVE THEM, AND THEY DON'T LINK BACK TO ME.
THIS IS WHERE THE PROFESSIONALS TAKE OVER.
NO WAY... I'M IN IT WITH YOU TILL THE END.
UH-UH... YOU'RE A MOTHER.
PLEASE, JACKIE, AT LEAST LET ME READ THE LETTERS.

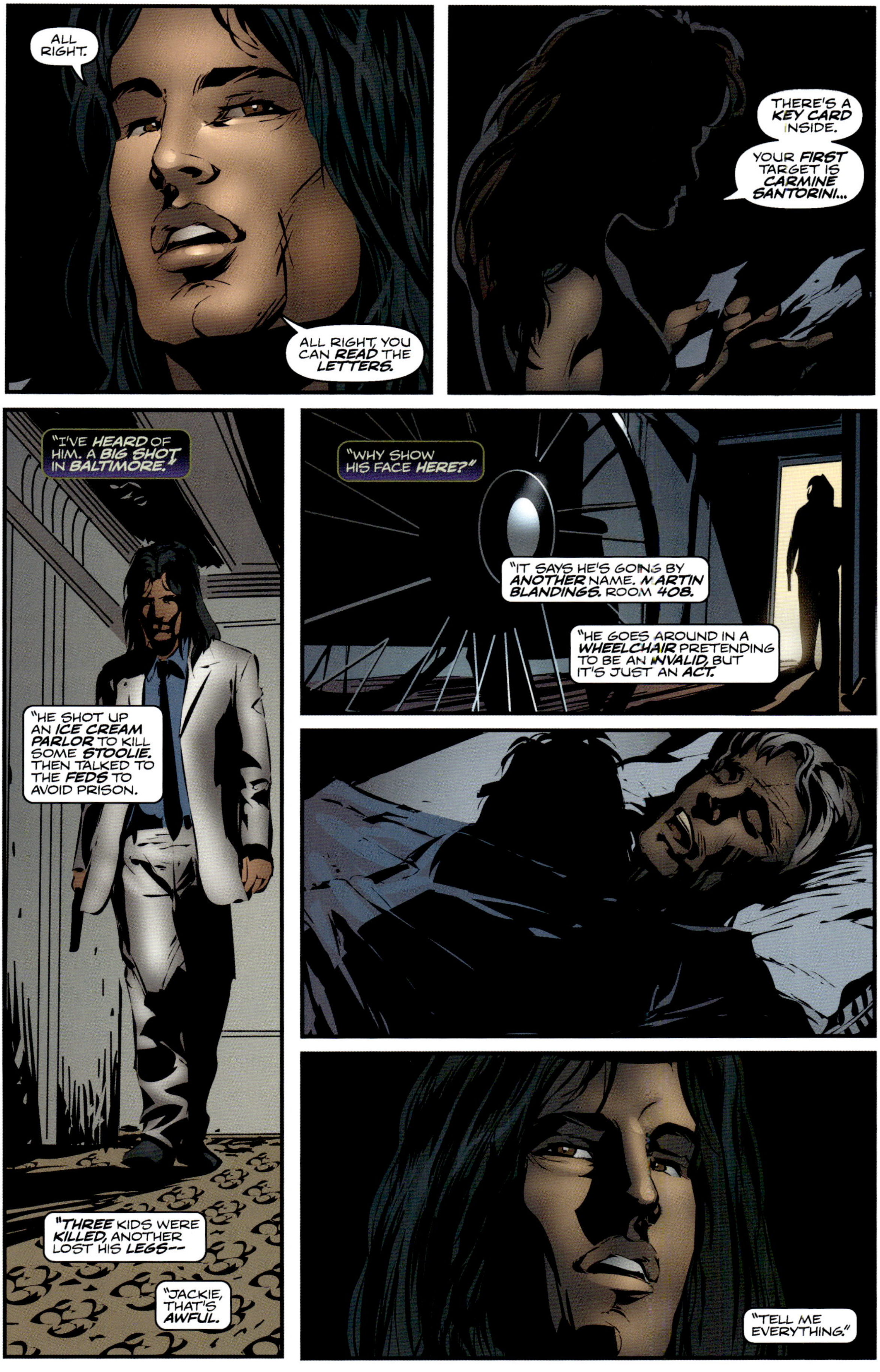
ALL RIGHT.
ALL RIGHT, YOU CAN READ THE LETTERS.
THERE'S A KEY CARD INSIDE.
YOUR FIRST TARGET IS CARMINE SANTORINI...
"I'VE HEARD OF HIM. A BIG SHOT IN BALTIMORE."
"HE SHOT UP AN ICE CREAM PARLOR TO KILL SOME STOOLIE. THEN TALKED TO THE FEDS TO AVOID PRISON.
"THREE KIDS WERE KILLED, ANOTHER LOST HIS LEGS--
"JACKIE, THAT'S AWFUL.
"WHY SHOW HIS FACE HERE?"
"IT SAYS HE'S GOING BY ANOTHER NAME. MARTIN BLANDINGS. ROOM 408.
"HE GOES AROUND IN A WHEELCHAIR PRETENDING TO BE AN INVALID, BUT IT'S JUST AN ACT.
"TELL ME EVERYTHING."

I *SHOT* HIM. THAT'S *IT*.

YOU'RE DOING THIS FOR *ME* AND MY *SON*. I CAN *HANDLE IT*. TELL ME WHAT *HAPPENED*.

JUST *READ* THE *SECOND* LETTER.

JACKIE, JUST TELL ME *THIS*... HE *DESERVED* IT, RIGHT?

HE WAS A *BAD MAN*?

YEAH.

THE *SECOND* ONE'S NAME IS *SANTIAGO FERRER*. HE CONSPIRED IN A PLOT TO KILL MICKEY. HE WANTS YOU TO *SEND A MESSAGE*...

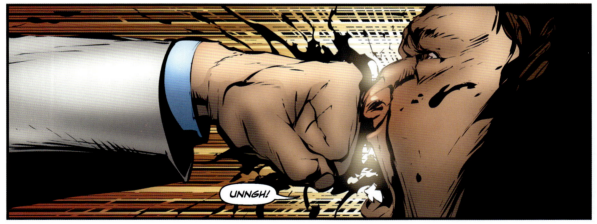

UNNGH!

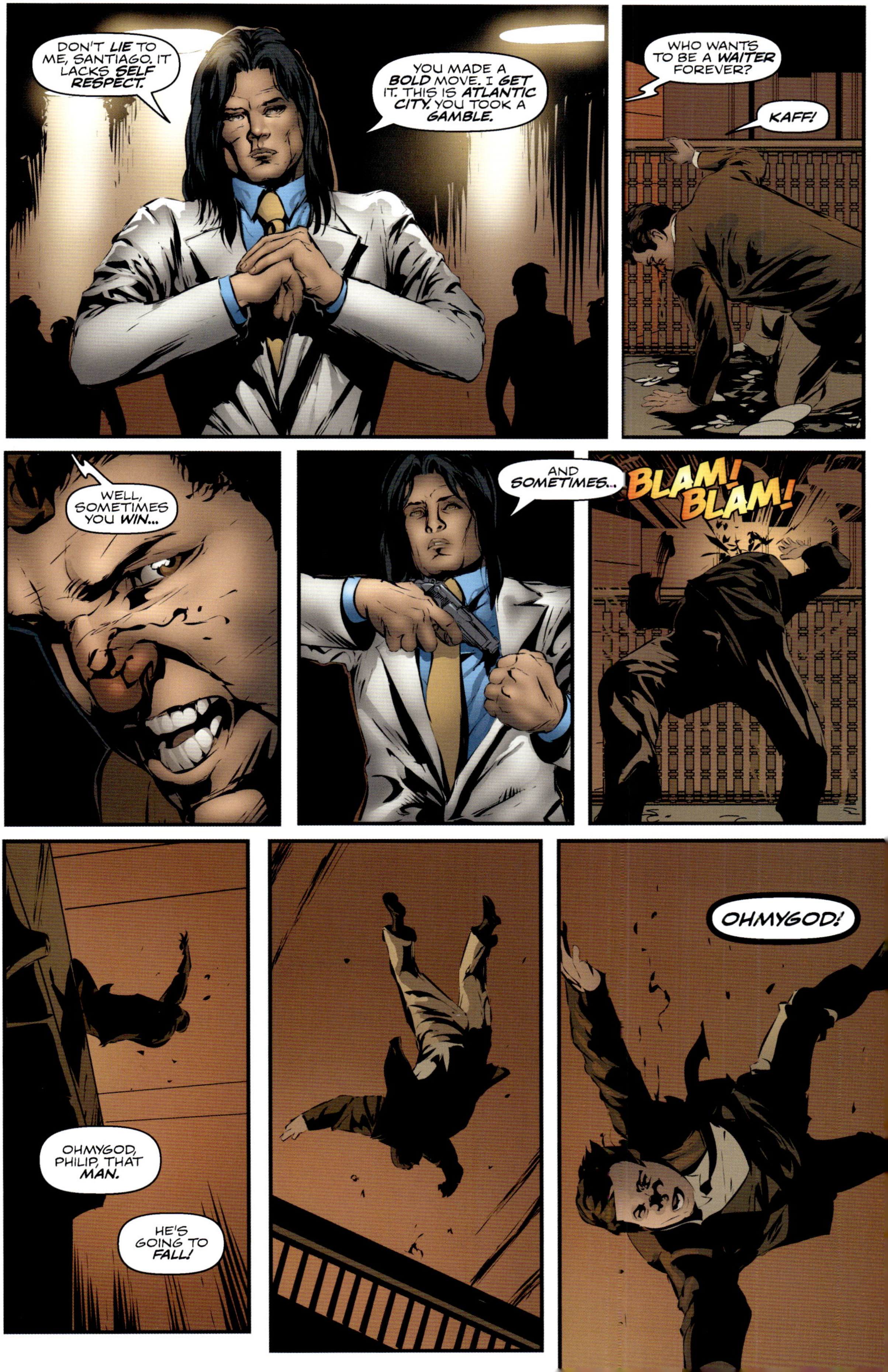
DON'T LIE TO ME, SANTIAGO. IT LACKS SELF RESPECT.
YOU MADE A BOLD MOVE. I GET IT. THIS IS ATLANTIC CITY. YOU TOOK A GAMBLE.
WHO WANTS TO BE A WAITER FOREVER?
KAFF!
WELL, SOMETIMES YOU WIN...
AND SOMETIMES...
BLAM! BLAM!
OHMYGOD, PHILIP, THAT MAN.
HE'S GOING TO FALL!
OHMYGOD!

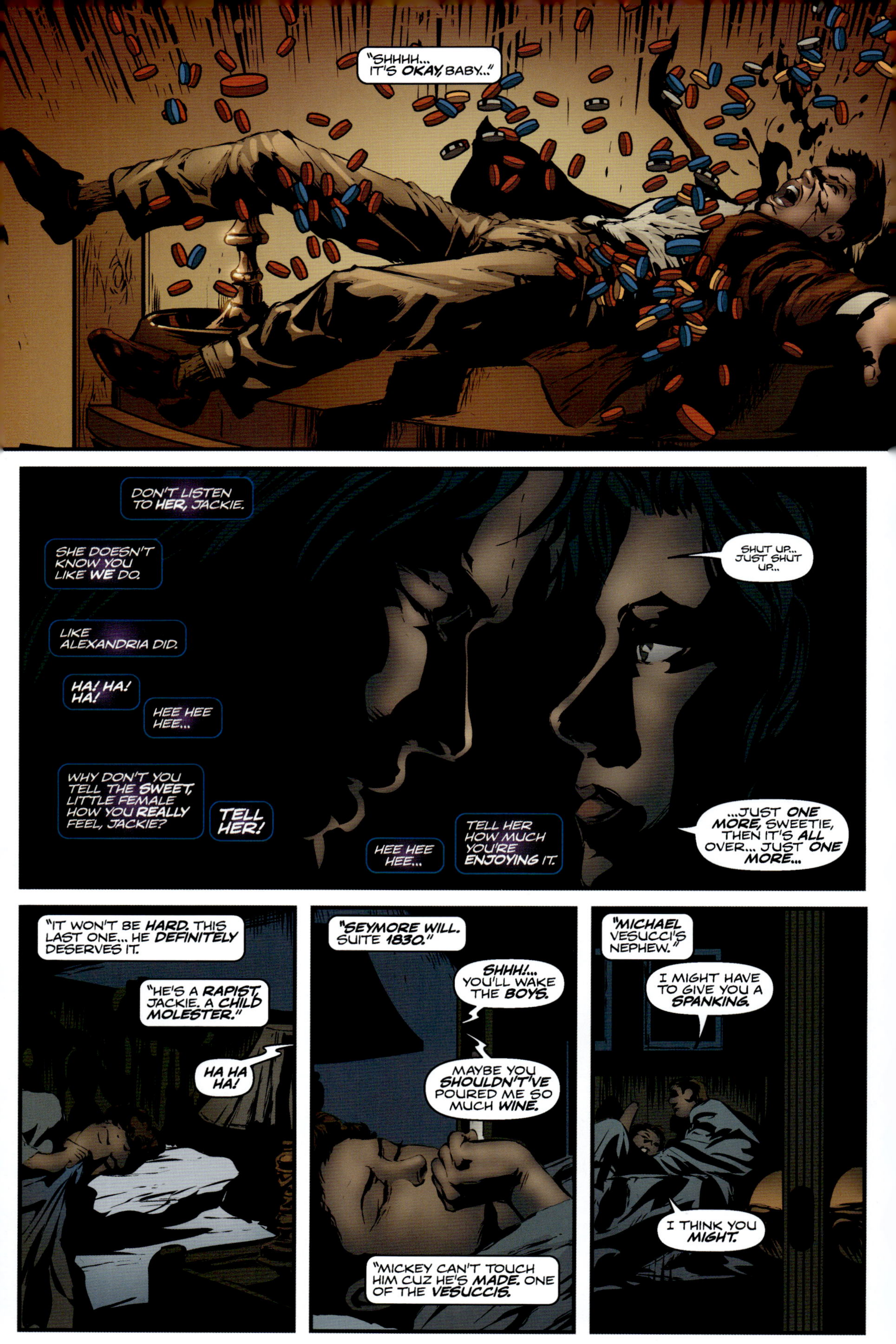
"SHHHH... IT'S OKAY, BABY..."
DON'T LISTEN TO HER, JACKIE.
SHE DOESN'T KNOW YOU LIKE WE DO.
LIKE ALEXANDRIA DID.
HA! HA! HA!
HEE HEE HEE...
WHY DON'T YOU TELL THE SWEET, LITTLE FEMALE HOW YOU REALLY FEEL, JACKIE?
TELL HER!
HEE HEE HEE...
TELL HER HOW MUCH YOU'RE ENJOYING IT.
SHUT UP... JUST SHUT UP...
...JUST ONE MORE, SWEETIE, THEN IT'S ALL OVER... JUST ONE MORE...
"IT WON'T BE HARD, THIS LAST ONE... HE DEFINITELY DESERVES IT.
"HE'S A RAPIST, JACKIE. A CHILD MOLESTER."
HA HA HA!
"SEYMORE WILL. SUITE 1830."
SHHH!... YOU'LL WAKE THE BOYS.
MAYBE YOU SHOULDN'T'VE POURED ME SO MUCH WINE.
"MICKEY CAN'T TOUCH HIM CUZ HE'S MADE. ONE OF THE VESUCCIS.
"MICHAEL VESUCCI'S NEPHEW."
I MIGHT HAVE TO GIVE YOU A SPANKING.
I THINK YOU MIGHT.

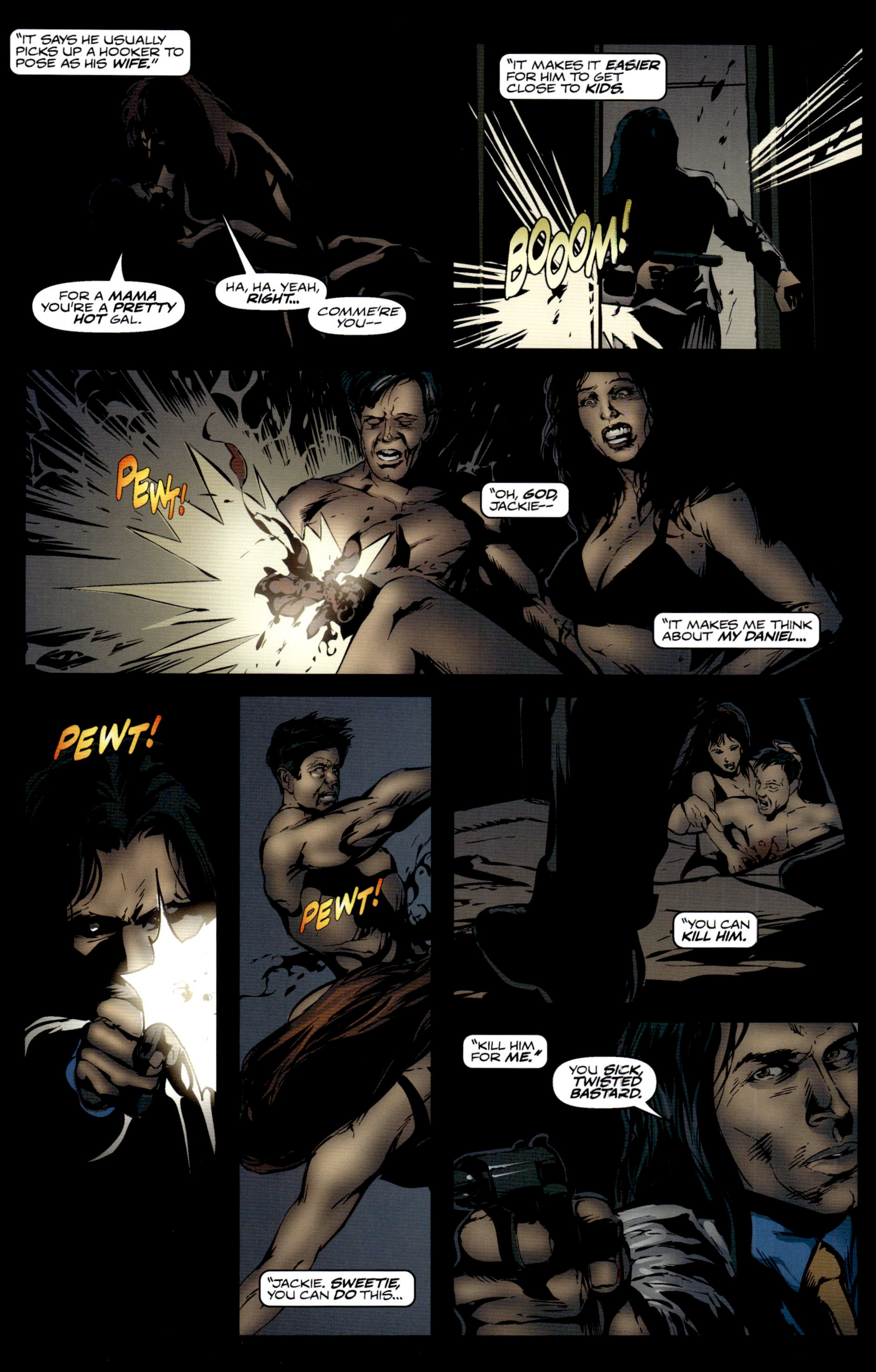
"IT SAYS HE USUALLY PICKS UP A HOOKER TO POSE AS HIS WIFE."
FOR A MAMA YOU'RE A PRETTY HOT GAL.
HA, HA. YEAH, RIGHT...
COMME'RE YOU--
"IT MAKES IT EASIER FOR HIM TO GET CLOSE TO KIDS.
BOOOM!
PEWT!
"OH, GOD, JACKIE--
"IT MAKES ME THINK ABOUT MY DANIEL...
PEWT!
PEWT!
"JACKIE. SWEETIE, YOU CAN DO THIS...
"YOU CAN KILL HIM.
"KILL HIM FOR ME."
YOU SICK, TWISTED BASTARD.

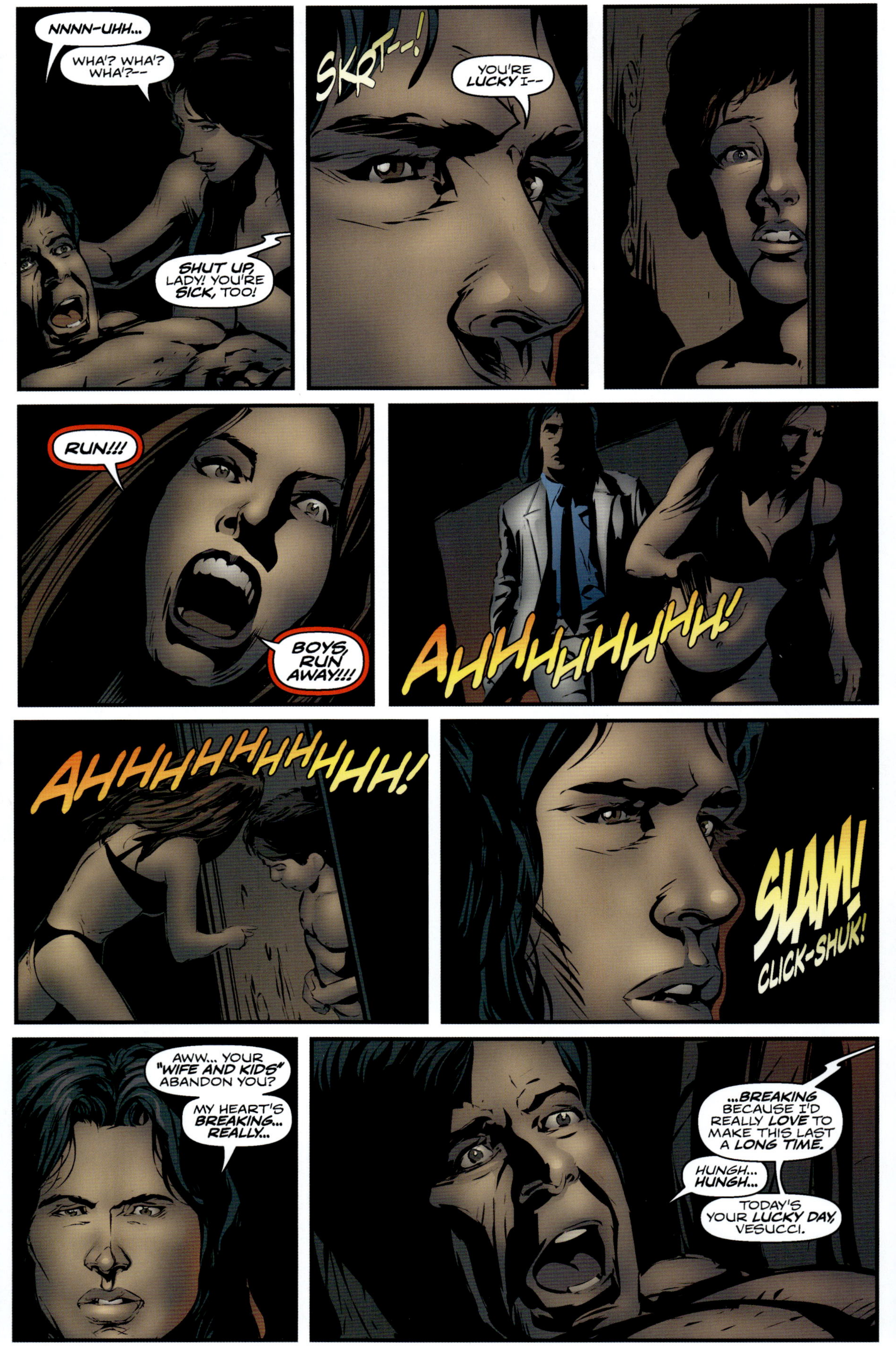

NNNN-UHH...
WHA'? WHA'? WHA'?--
SHUT UP, LADY! YOU'RE SICK, TOO!
SKRT--!
YOU'RE LUCKY I--
RUN!!!
BOYS, RUN AWAY!!!
AHHHHHHHH!
AHHHHHHHHHHH!
SLAM!
CLICK-SHUK!
AWW... YOUR "WIFE AND KIDS" ABANDON YOU?
MY HEART'S BREAKING... REALLY...
...BREAKING BECAUSE I'D REALLY LOVE TO MAKE THIS LAST A LONG TIME.
HUNGH... HUNGH...
TODAY'S YOUR LUCKY DAY, VESUCCI.

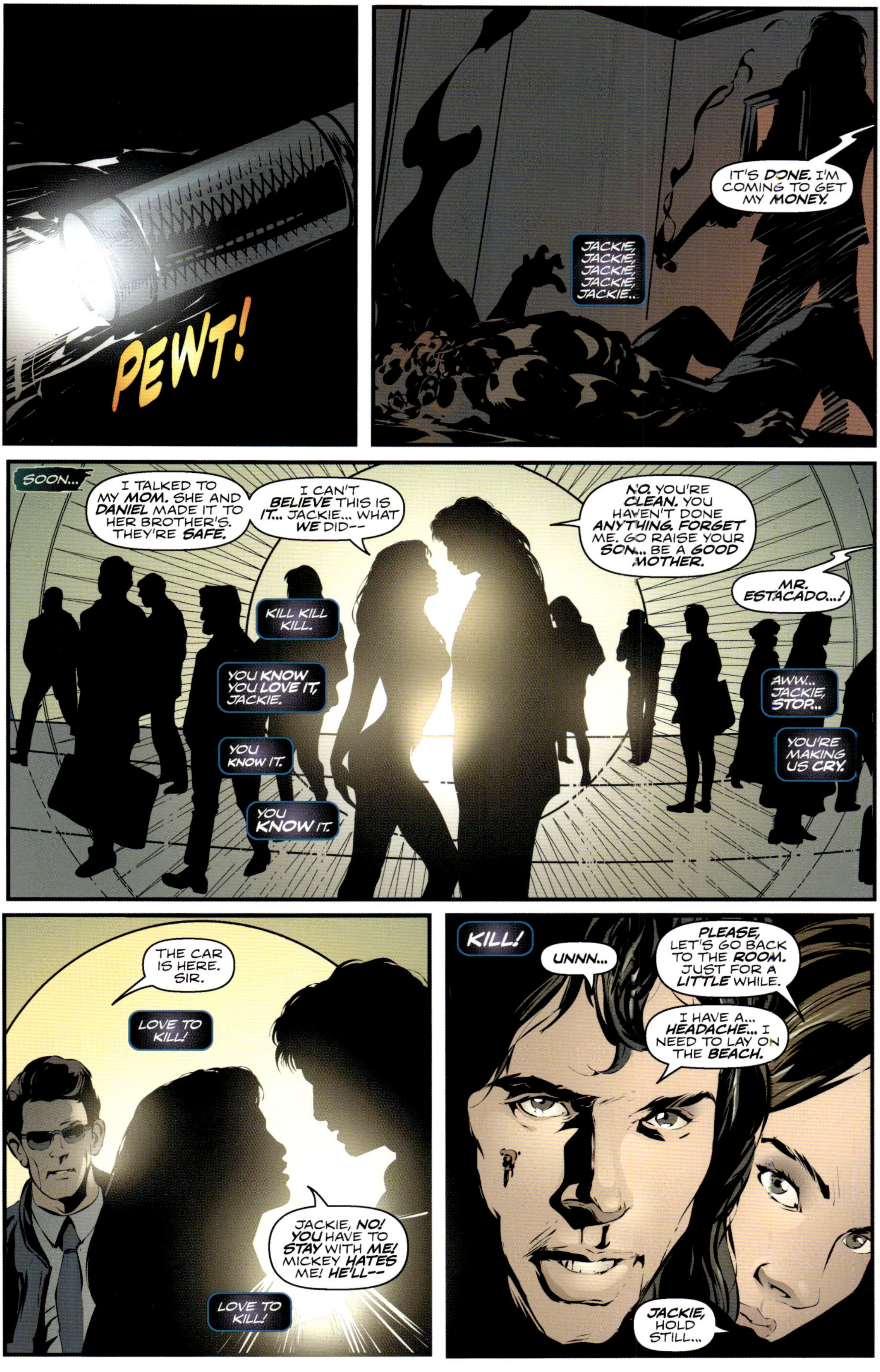
PEWT!
IT'S DONE. I'M COMING TO GET MY MONEY.
JACKIE, JACKIE, JACKIE, JACKIE, JACKIE...
SOON...
I TALKED TO MY MOM. SHE AND DANIEL MADE IT TO HER BROTHER'S. THEY'RE SAFE.
I CAN'T BELIEVE THIS IS IT... JACKIE... WHAT WE DID--
NO. YOU'RE CLEAN. YOU HAVEN'T DONE ANYTHING. FORGET ME. GO RAISE YOUR SON... BE A GOOD MOTHER.
MR. ESTACADO...!
KILL KILL KILL.
YOU KNOW YOU LOVE IT, JACKIE.
YOU KNOW IT.
YOU KNOW IT.
AWW... JACKIE, STOP...
YOU'RE MAKING US CRY.
THE CAR IS HERE. SIR.
LOVE TO KILL!
JACKIE, NO! YOU HAVE TO STAY WITH ME! MICKEY HATES ME! HE'LL--
LOVE TO KILL!
KILL!
UNNN...
PLEASE, LET'S GO BACK TO THE ROOM. JUST FOR A LITTLE WHILE.
I HAVE A... HEADACHE... I NEED TO LAY ON THE BEACH.
JACKIE, HOLD STILL...

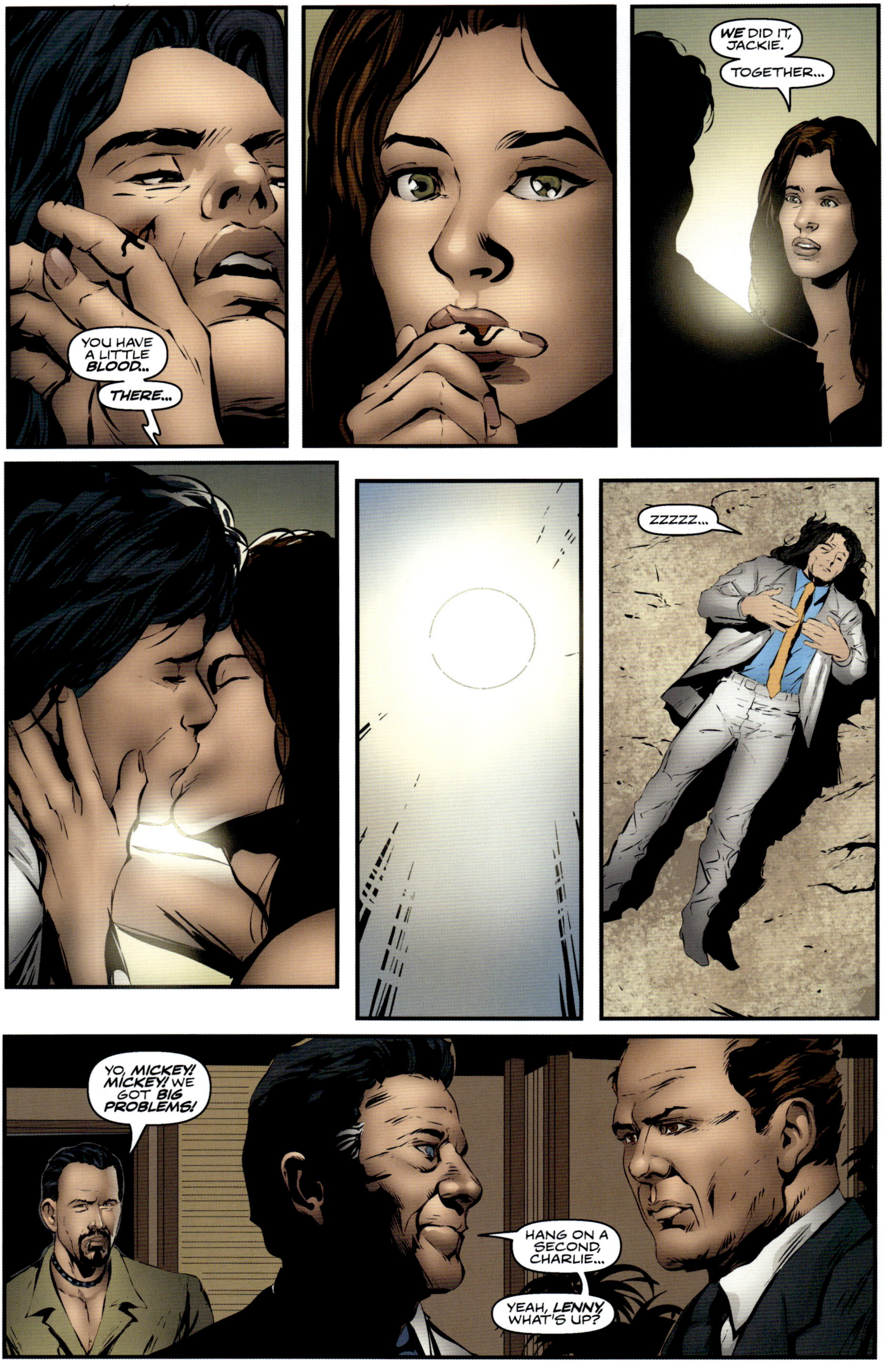
YOU HAVE A LITTLE BLOOD...
THERE...
WE DID IT, JACKIE.
TOGETHER...
ZZZZZ...
YO, MICKEY! MICKEY! WE GOT BIG PROBLEMS!
HANG ON A SECOND, CHARLIE...
YEAH, LENNY, WHAT'S UP?

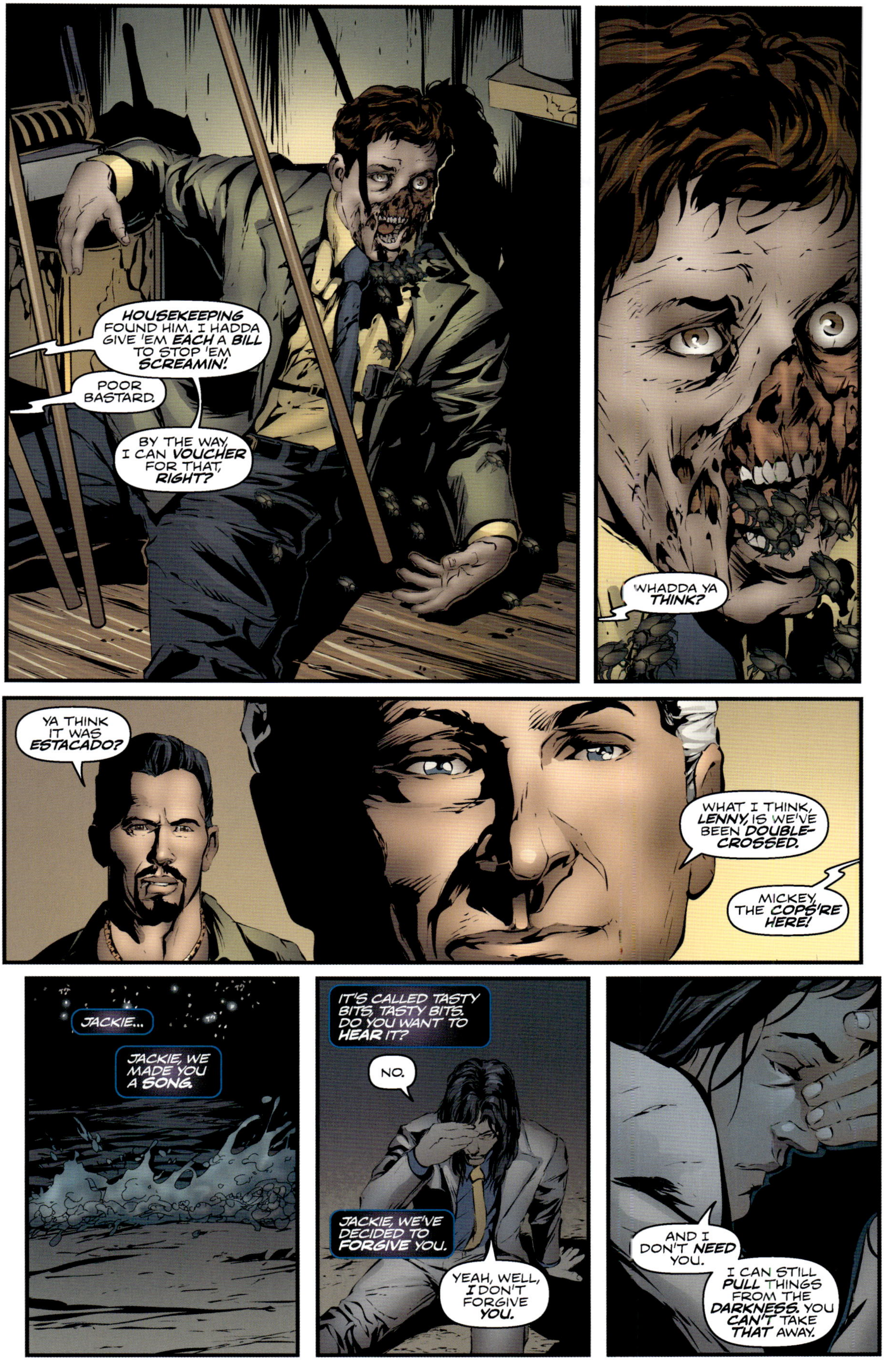

HOUSEKEEPING FOUND HIM. I HADDA GIVE 'EM EACH A BILL TO STOP 'EM SCREAMIN!
POOR BASTARD.
BY THE WAY, I CAN VOUCHER FOR THAT, RIGHT?
WHADDA YA THINK?
YA THINK IT WAS ESTACADO?
WHAT I THINK, LENNY, IS WE'VE BEEN DOUBLE-CROSSED.
MICKEY, THE COPS'RE HERE!
JACKIE...
JACKIE, WE MADE YOU A SONG.
IT'S CALLED TASTY BITS, TASTY BITS. DO YOU WANT TO HEAR IT?
NO.
JACKIE, WE'VE DECIDED TO FORGIVE YOU.
YEAH, WELL, I DON'T FORGIVE YOU.
AND I DON'T NEED YOU.
I CAN STILL PULL THINGS FROM THE DARKNESS. YOU CAN'T TAKE THAT AWAY.

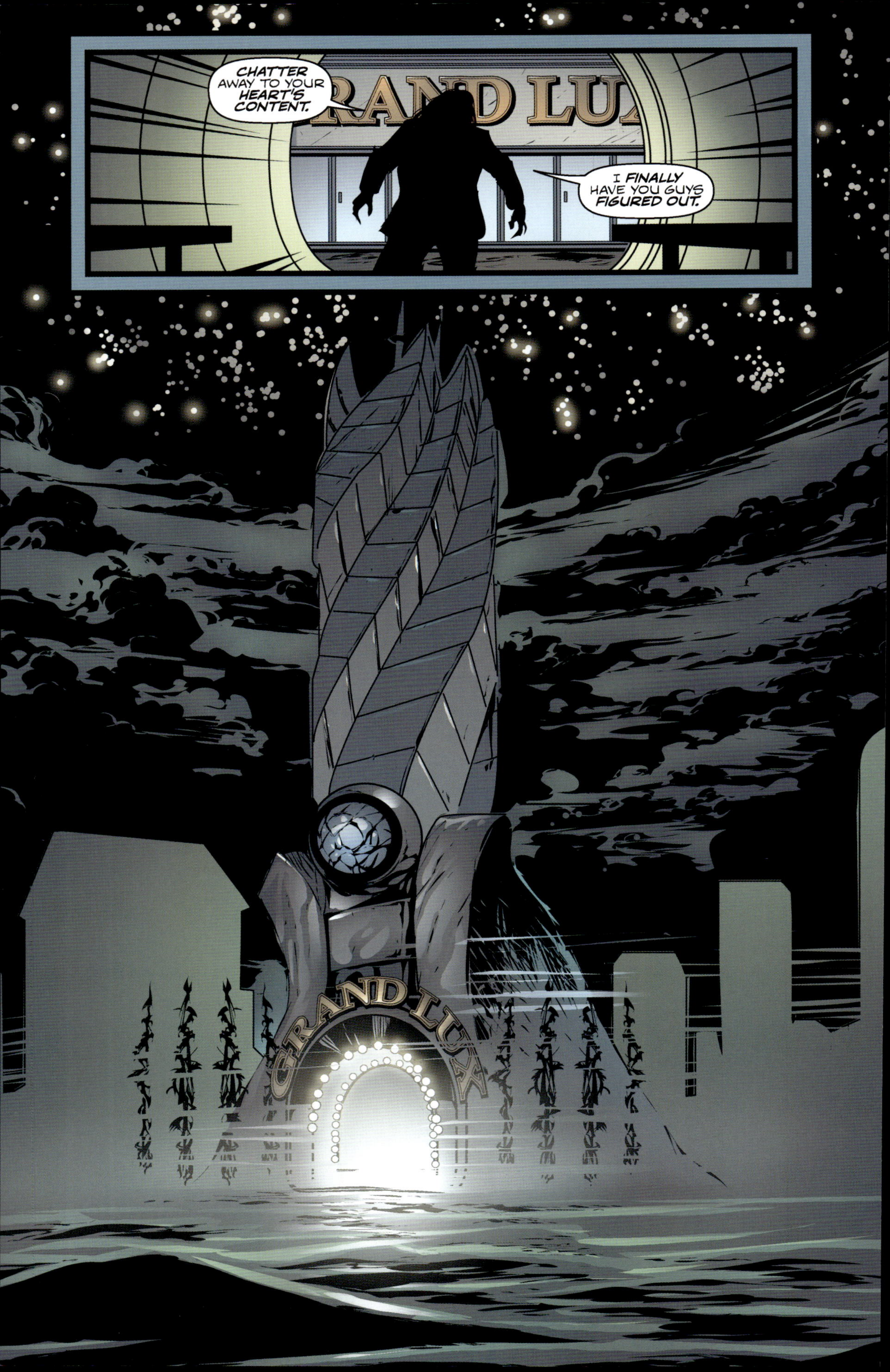

CHATTER AWAY TO YOUR HEART'S CONTENT.
I FINALLY HAVE YOU GUYS FIGURED OUT.
GRAND LUX
GRAND LUX

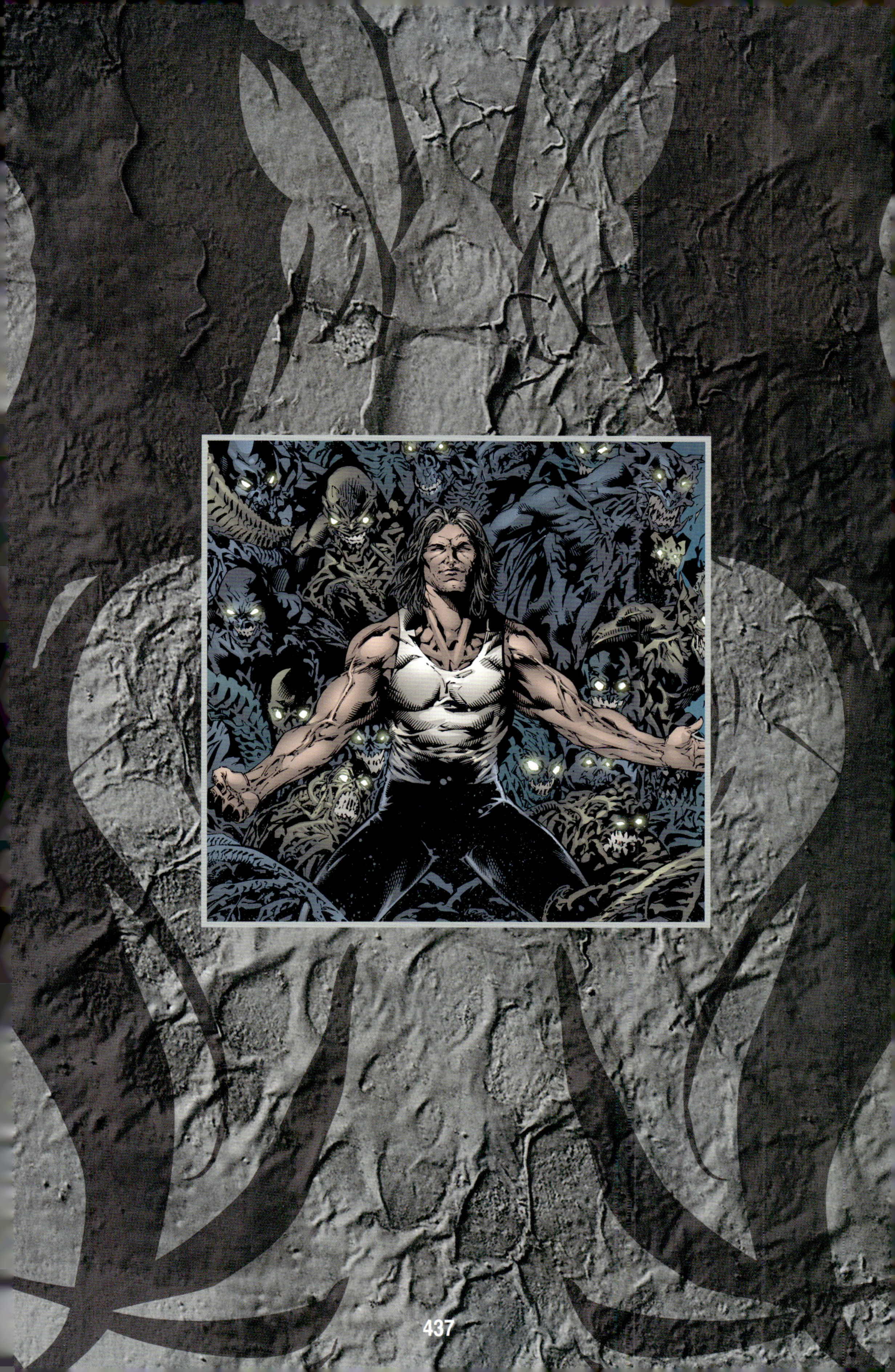

The Darkness Issue #59
cover art by: Dale Keown

THE DARKNESS #59

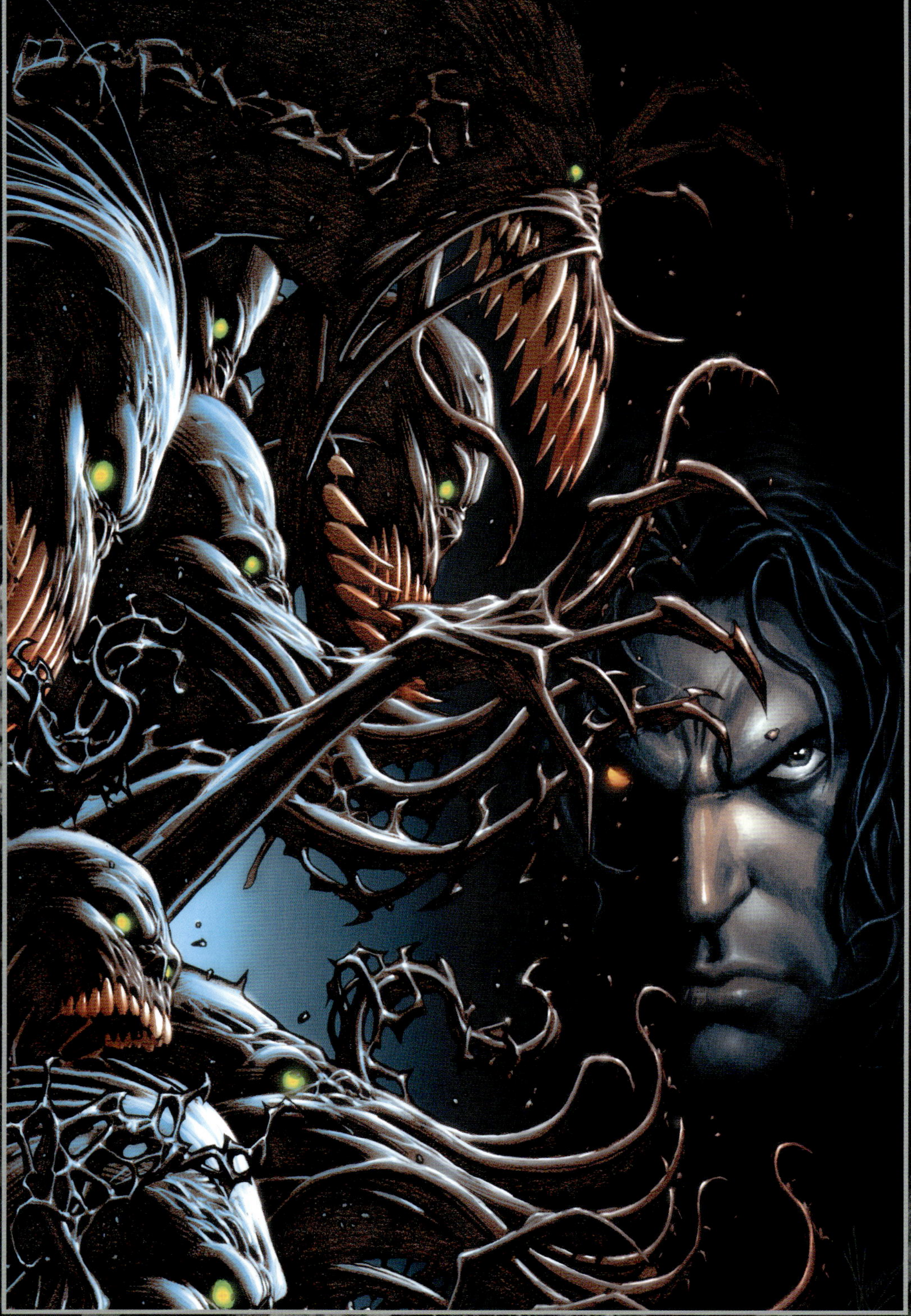

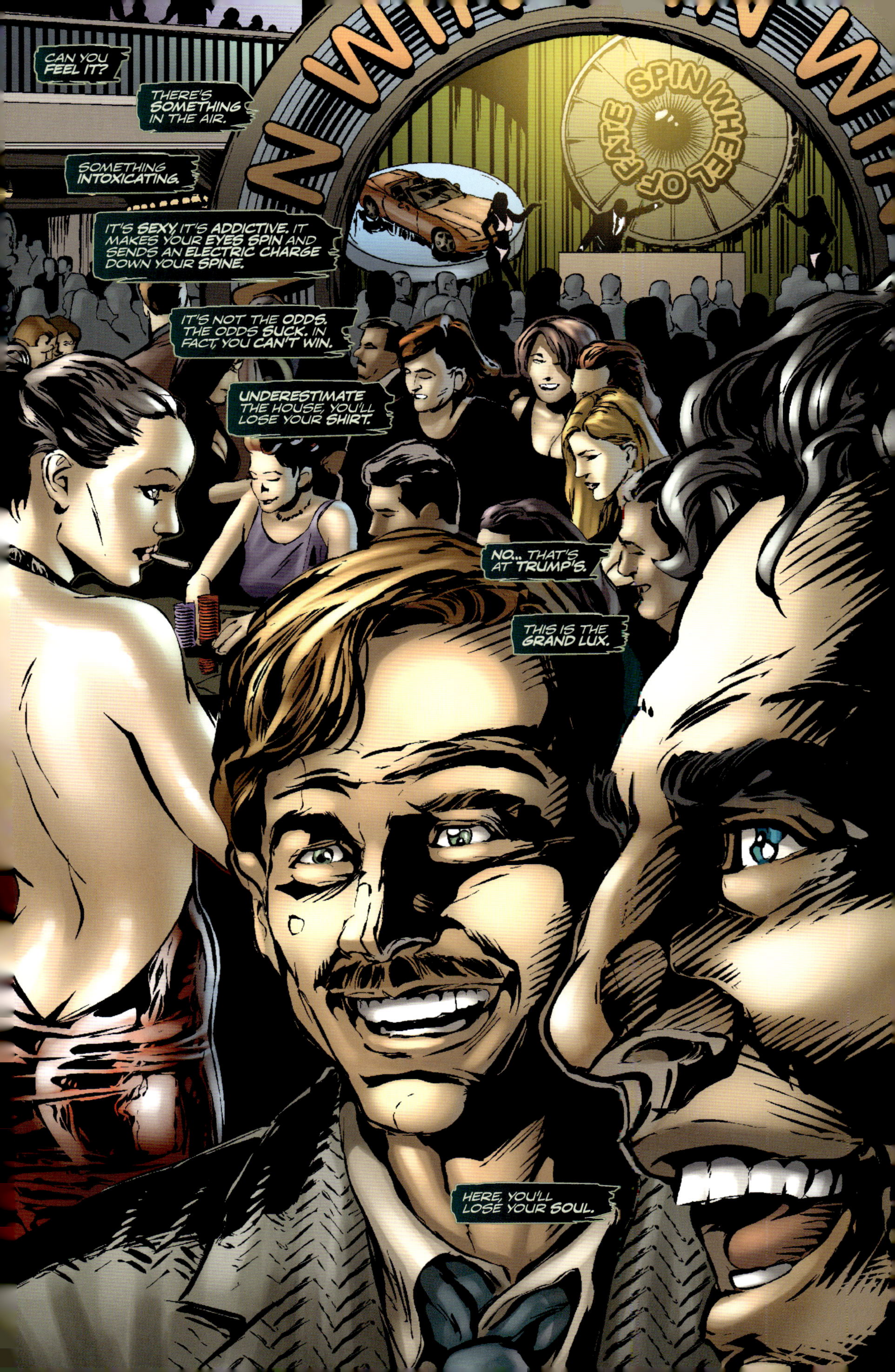

CAN YOU FEEL IT?
THERE'S SOMETHING IN THE AIR.
SOMETHING INTOXICATING.
IT'S SEXY, IT'S ADDICTIVE. IT MAKES YOUR EYES SPIN AND SENDS AN ELECTRIC CHARGE DOWN YOUR SPINE.
IT'S NOT THE ODDS. THE ODDS SUCK. IN FACT, YOU CAN'T WIN.
UNDERESTIMATE THE HOUSE, YOU'LL LOSE YOUR SHIRT.
NO... THAT'S AT TRUMP'S.
THIS IS THE GRAND LUX.
HERE, YOU'LL LOSE YOUR SOUL.
SPIN WHEEL OF FATE

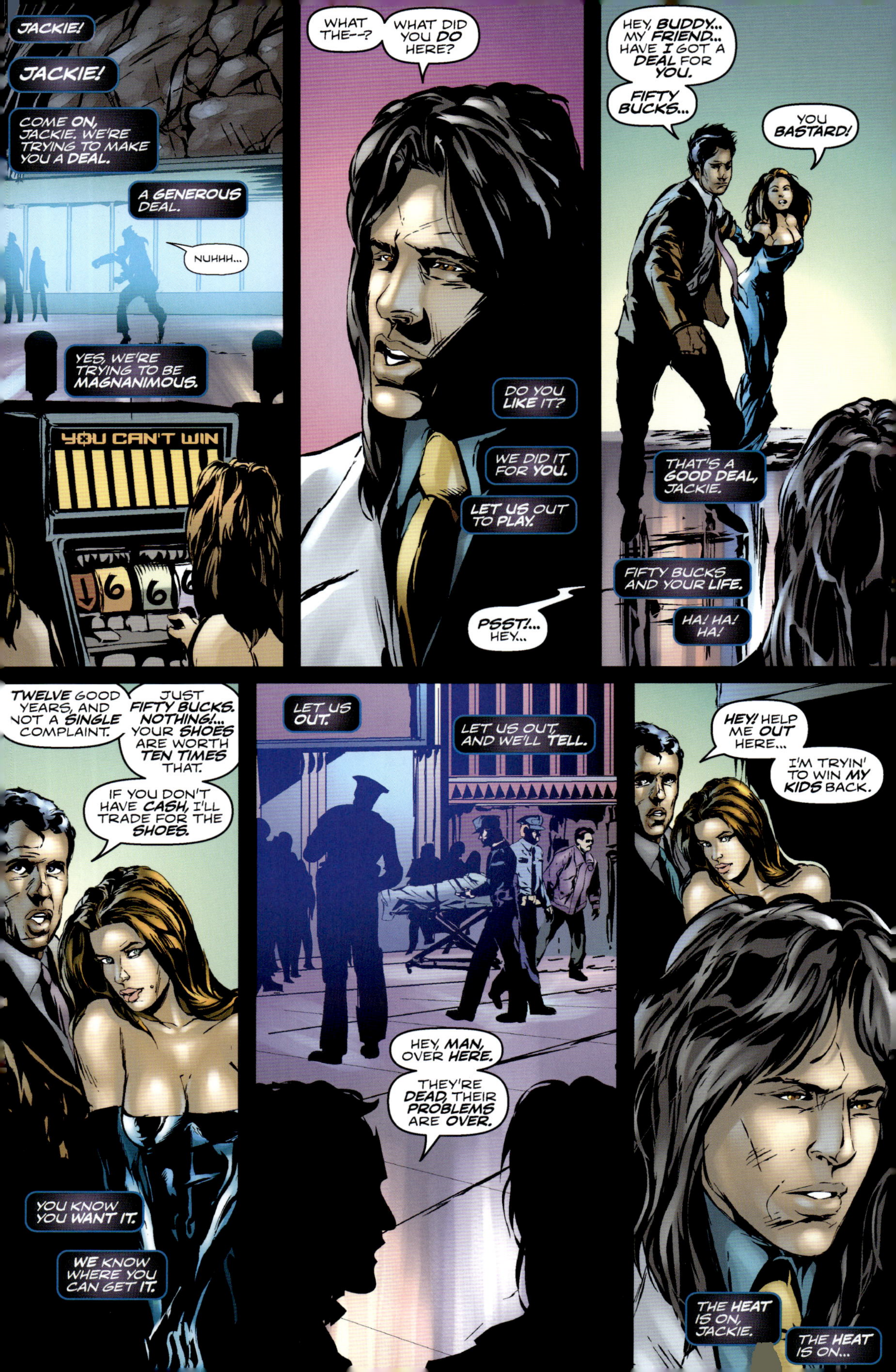
JACKIE!
JACKIE!
COME ON, JACKIE. WE'RE TRYING TO MAKE YOU A DEAL.
A GENEROUS DEAL.
NUHHH...
YES, WE'RE TRYING TO BE MAGNANIMOUS.
YOU CAN'T WIN
WHAT THE--?
WHAT DID YOU DO HERE?
DO YOU LIKE IT?
WE DID IT FOR YOU.
LET US OUT TO PLAY.
PSST!... HEY...
HEY, BUDDY... MY FRIEND... HAVE I GOT A DEAL FOR YOU.
FIFTY BUCKS...
YOU BASTARD!
THAT'S A GOOD DEAL, JACKIE.
FIFTY BUCKS AND YOUR LIFE.
HA! HA! HA!
TWELVE GOOD YEARS, AND NOT A SINGLE COMPLAINT.
JUST FIFTY BUCKS. NOTHING!... YOUR SHOES ARE WORTH TEN TIMES THAT.
IF YOU DON'T HAVE CASH, I'LL TRADE FOR THE SHOES.
YOU KNOW YOU WANT IT.
WE KNOW WHERE YOU CAN GET IT.
LET US OUT.
LET US OUT, AND WE'LL TELL.
HEY, MAN, OVER HERE.
THEY'RE DEAD. THEIR PROBLEMS ARE OVER.
HEY! HELP ME OUT HERE...
I'M TRYIN' TO WIN MY KIDS BACK.
THE HEAT IS ON, JACKIE.
THE HEAT IS ON...

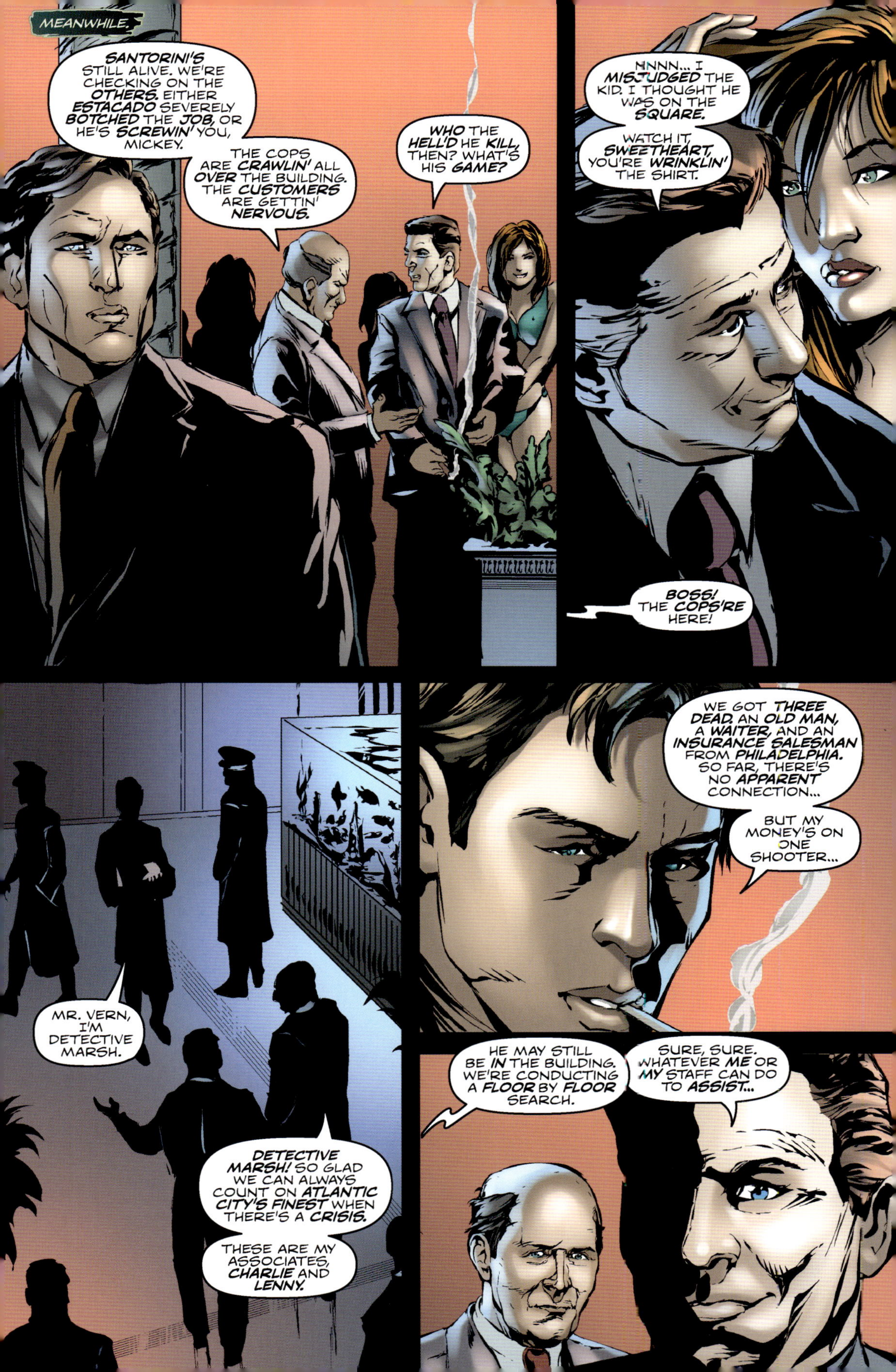
MEANWHILE.
SANTORINI'S STILL ALIVE. WE'RE CHECKING ON THE OTHERS. EITHER ESTACADO SEVERELY BOTCHED THE JOB, OR HE'S SCREWIN' YOU, MICKEY.
THE COPS ARE CRAWLIN' ALL OVER THE BUILDING. THE CUSTOMERS ARE GETTIN' NERVOUS.
WHO THE HELL'D HE KILL, THEN? WHAT'S HIS GAME?
HNNN... I MISJUDGED THE KID. I THOUGHT HE WAS ON THE SQUARE.
WATCH IT, SWEETHEART, YOU'RE WRINKLIN' THE SHIRT.
BOSS! THE COPS'RE HERE!
MR. VERN, I'M DETECTIVE MARSH.
DETECTIVE MARSH! SO GLAD WE CAN ALWAYS COUNT ON ATLANTIC CITY'S FINEST WHEN THERE'S A CRISIS.
THESE ARE MY ASSOCIATES, CHARLIE AND LENNY.
WE GOT THREE DEAD, AN OLD MAN, A WAITER, AND AN INSURANCE SALESMAN FROM PHILADELPHIA. SO FAR, THERE'S NO APPARENT CONNECTION...
BUT MY MONEY'S ON ONE SHOOTER...
HE MAY STILL BE IN THE BUILDING. WE'RE CONDUCTING A FLOOR BY FLOOR SEARCH.
SURE, SURE. WHATEVER ME OR MY STAFF CAN DO TO ASSIST...

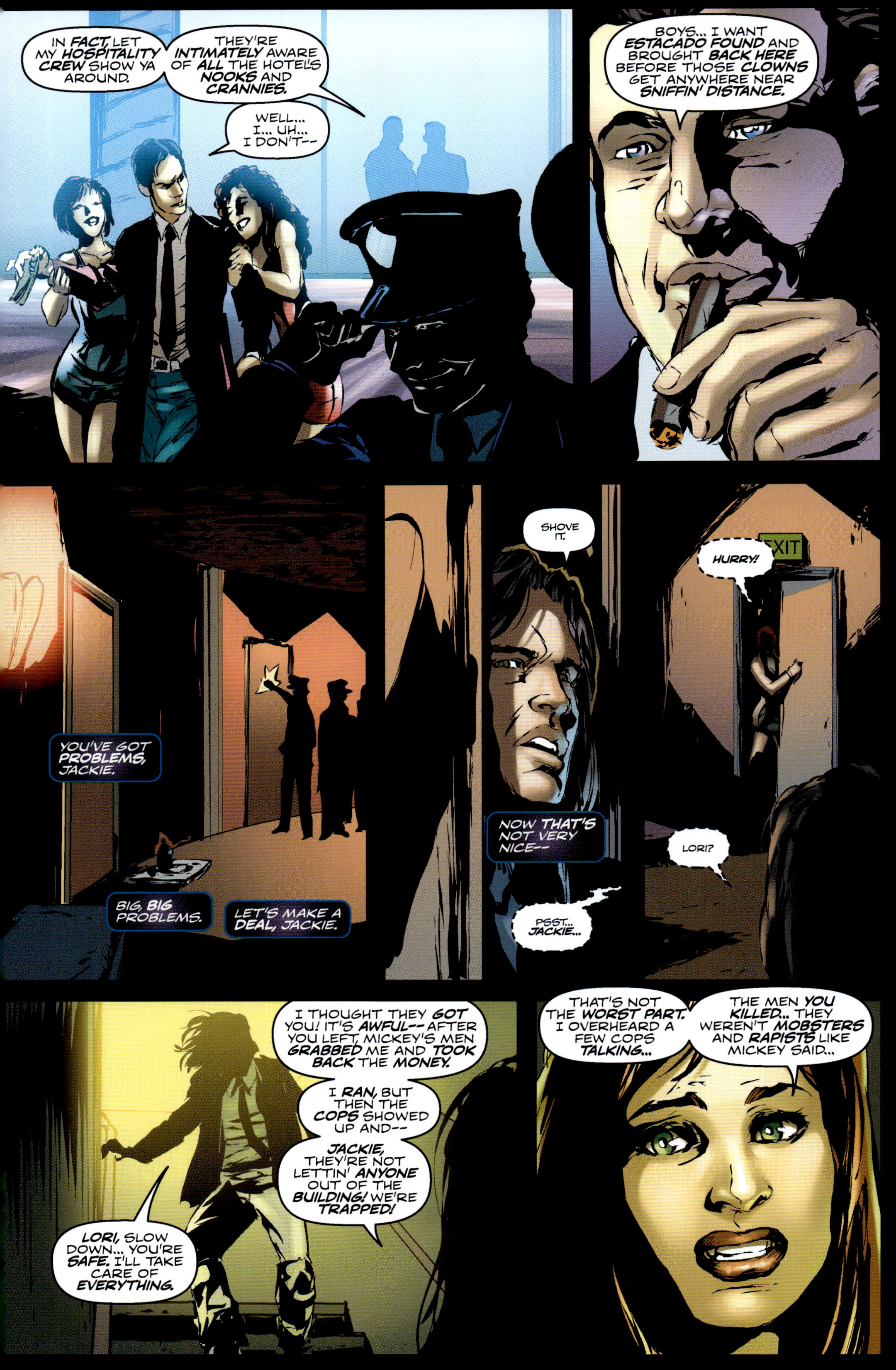
IN FACT, LET MY HOSPITALITY CREW SHOW YA AROUND.
THEY'RE INTIMATELY AWARE OF ALL THE HOTEL'S NOOKS AND CRANNIES.
WELL... I... UH... I DON'T--
BOYS... I WANT ESTACADO FOUND AND BROUGHT BACK HERE BEFORE THOSE CLOWNS GET ANYWHERE NEAR SNIFFIN' DISTANCE.
YOU'VE GOT PROBLEMS, JACKIE.
BIG, BIG PROBLEMS.
LET'S MAKE A DEAL, JACKIE.
SHOVE IT.
NOW THAT'S NOT VERY NICE--
PSST... JACKIE...
HURRY!
EXIT
LORI?
I THOUGHT THEY GOT YOU! IT'S AWFUL-- AFTER YOU LEFT, MICKEY'S MEN GRABBED ME AND TOOK BACK THE MONEY.
I RAN, BUT THEN THE COPS SHOWED UP AND--
JACKIE, THEY'RE NOT LETTIN' ANYONE OUT OF THE BUILDING! WE'RE TRAPPED!
LORI, SLOW DOWN... YOU'RE SAFE. I'LL TAKE CARE OF EVERYTHING.
THAT'S NOT THE WORST PART. I OVERHEARD A FEW COPS TALKING...
THE MEN YOU KILLED... THEY WEREN'T MOBSTERS AND RAPISTS LIKE MICKEY SAID...

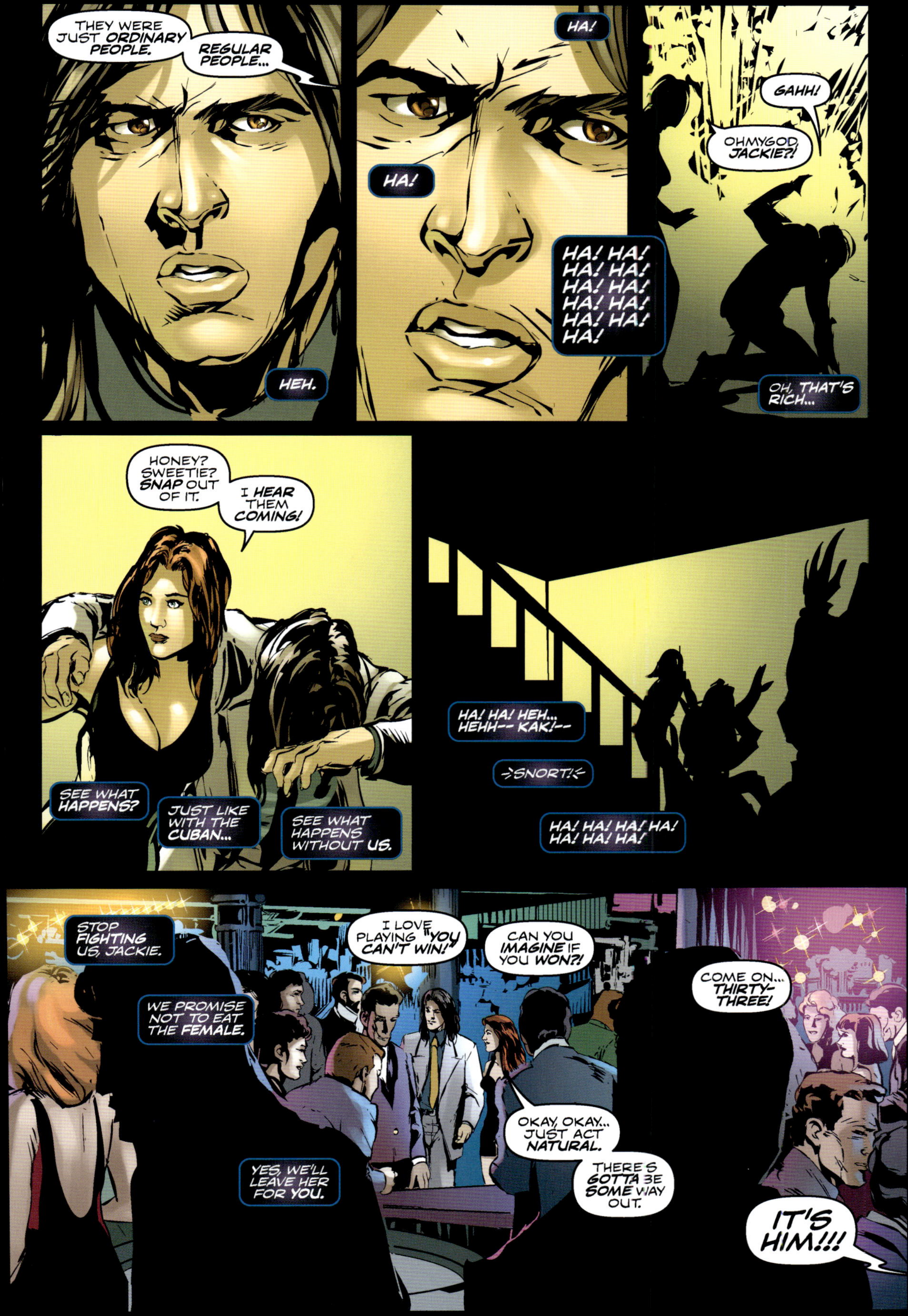
THEY WERE JUST ORDINARY PEOPLE.
REGULAR PEOPLE...
HEH.
HA!
HA!
HA! HA! HA! HA! HA! HA! HA! HA! HA! HA! HA!
GAHH!
OHMYGOD, JACKIE?!
OH, THAT'S RICH...
HONEY? SWEETIE? SNAP OUT OF IT.
I HEAR THEM COMING!
SEE WHAT HAPPENS?
JUST LIKE WITH THE CUBAN...
SEE WHAT HAPPENS WITHOUT US.
HA! HA! HEH... HEHH-- KAK!--
SNORT!
HA! HA! HA! HA! HA! HA! HA!
STOP FIGHTING US, JACKIE.
WE PROMISE NOT TO EAT THE FEMALE.
YES, WE'LL LEAVE HER FOR YOU.
I LOVE PLAYING "YOU CAN'T WIN!"
CAN YOU IMAGINE IF YOU WON?!
OKAY, OKAY... JUST ACT NATURAL.
THERE'S GOTTA BE SOME WAY OUT.
COME ON... THIRTY-THREE!
IT'S HIM!!!

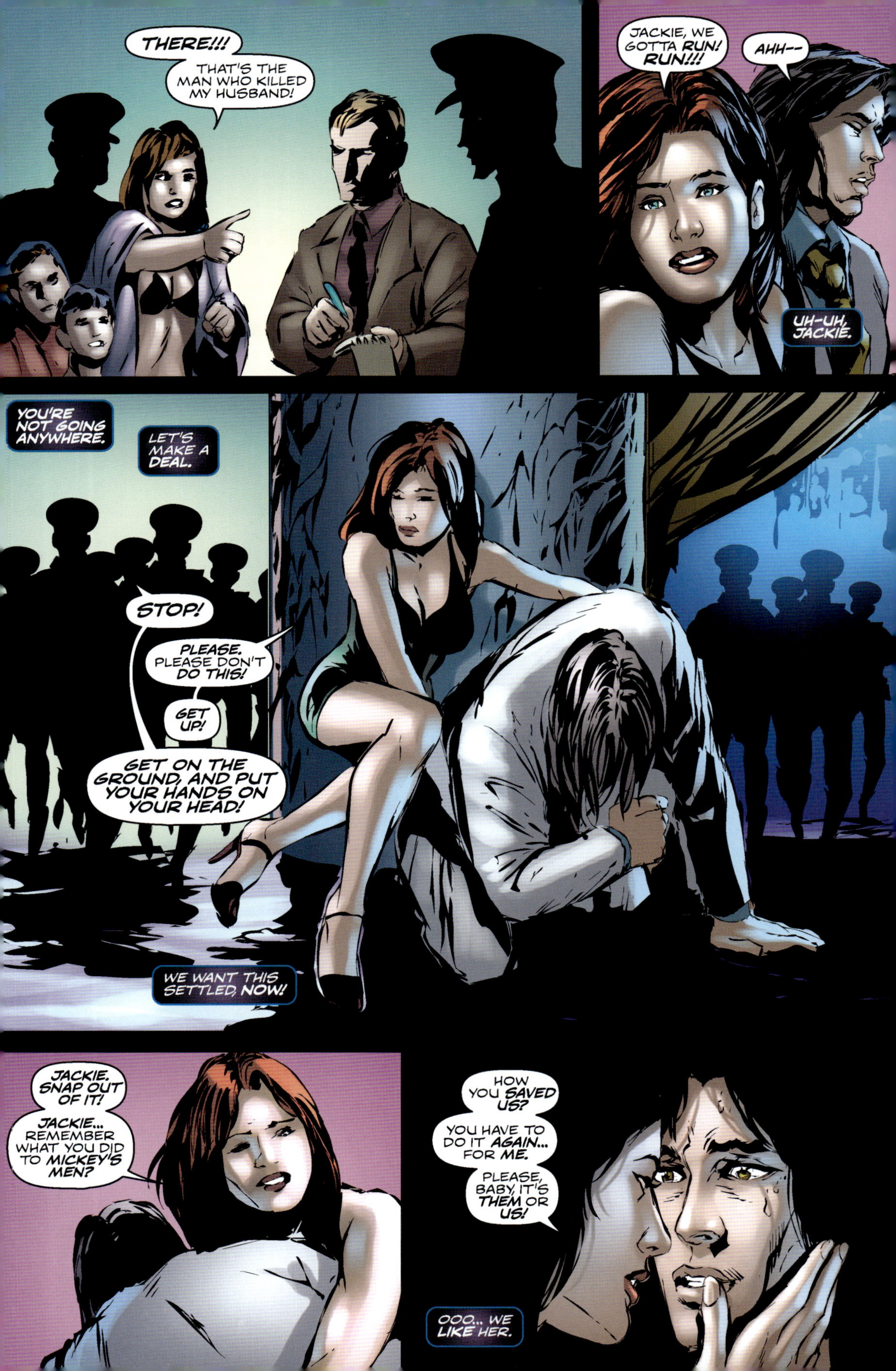
THERE!!! THAT'S THE MAN WHO KILLED MY HUSBAND!
JACKIE, WE GOTTA RUN! RUN!!!
AHH--
UH-UH, JACKIE.
YOU'RE NOT GOING ANYWHERE.
LET'S MAKE A DEAL.
STOP!
PLEASE. PLEASE DON'T DO THIS!
GET UP!
GET ON THE GROUND, AND PUT YOUR HANDS ON YOUR HEAD!
WE WANT THIS SETTLED, NOW!
JACKIE. SNAP OUT OF IT!
JACKIE... REMEMBER WHAT YOU DID TO MICKEY'S MEN?
HOW YOU SAVED US?
YOU HAVE TO DO IT AGAIN... FOR ME.
PLEASE, BABY, IT'S THEM OR US!
OOO... WE LIKE HER.

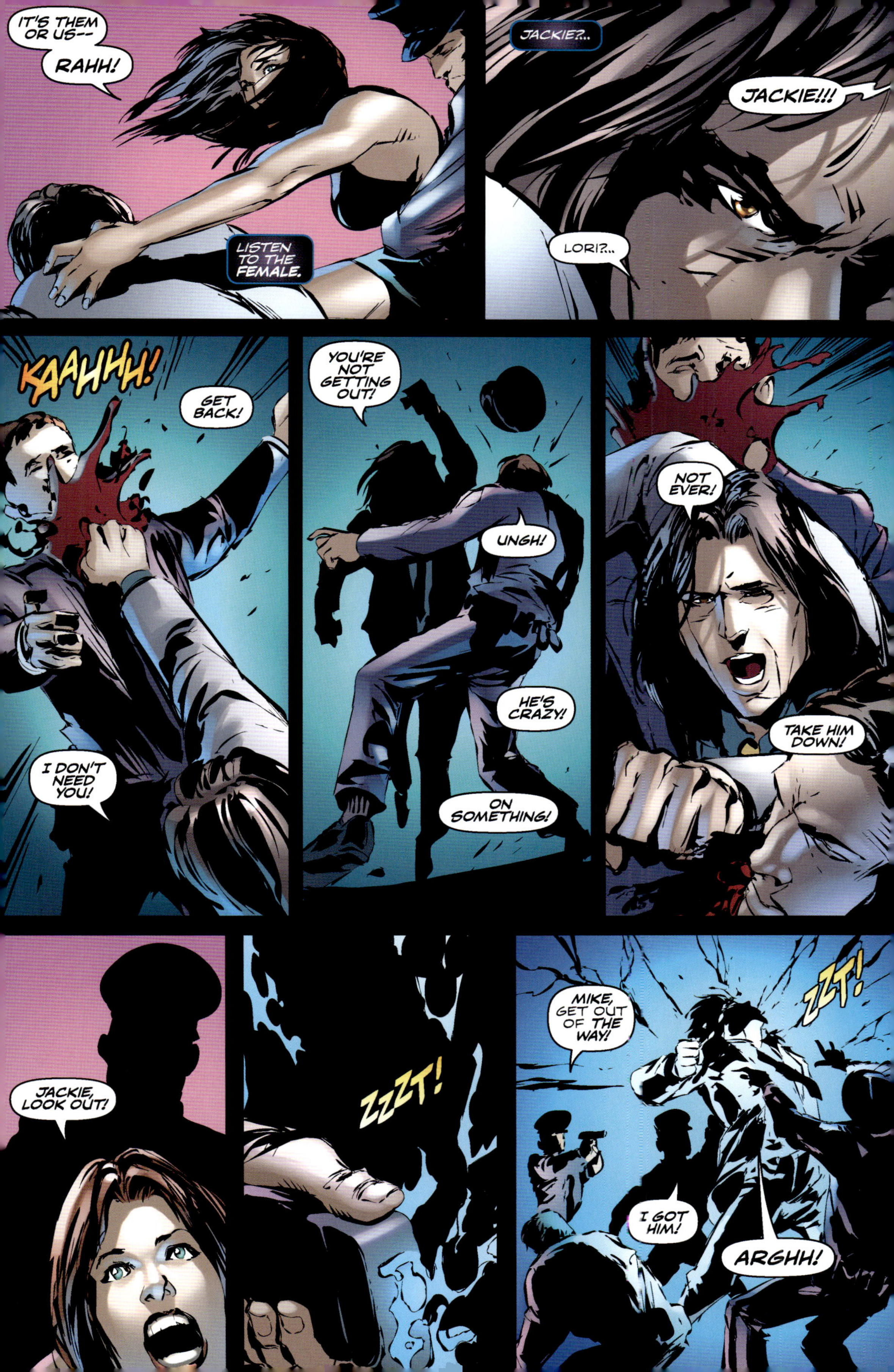

IT'S THEM OR US--
RAHH!
LISTEN TO THE FEMALE.
JACKIE?..
JACKIE!!!
LORI?..
KAAHHH!
GET BACK!
I DON'T NEED YOU!
YOU'RE NOT GETTING OUT!
UNGH!
HE'S CRAZY!
ON SOMETHING!
NOT EVER!
TAKE HIM DOWN!
JACKIE, LOOK OUT!
ZZZT!
MIKE, GET OUT OF THE WAY!
ZZT!
I GOT HIM!
ARGHH!

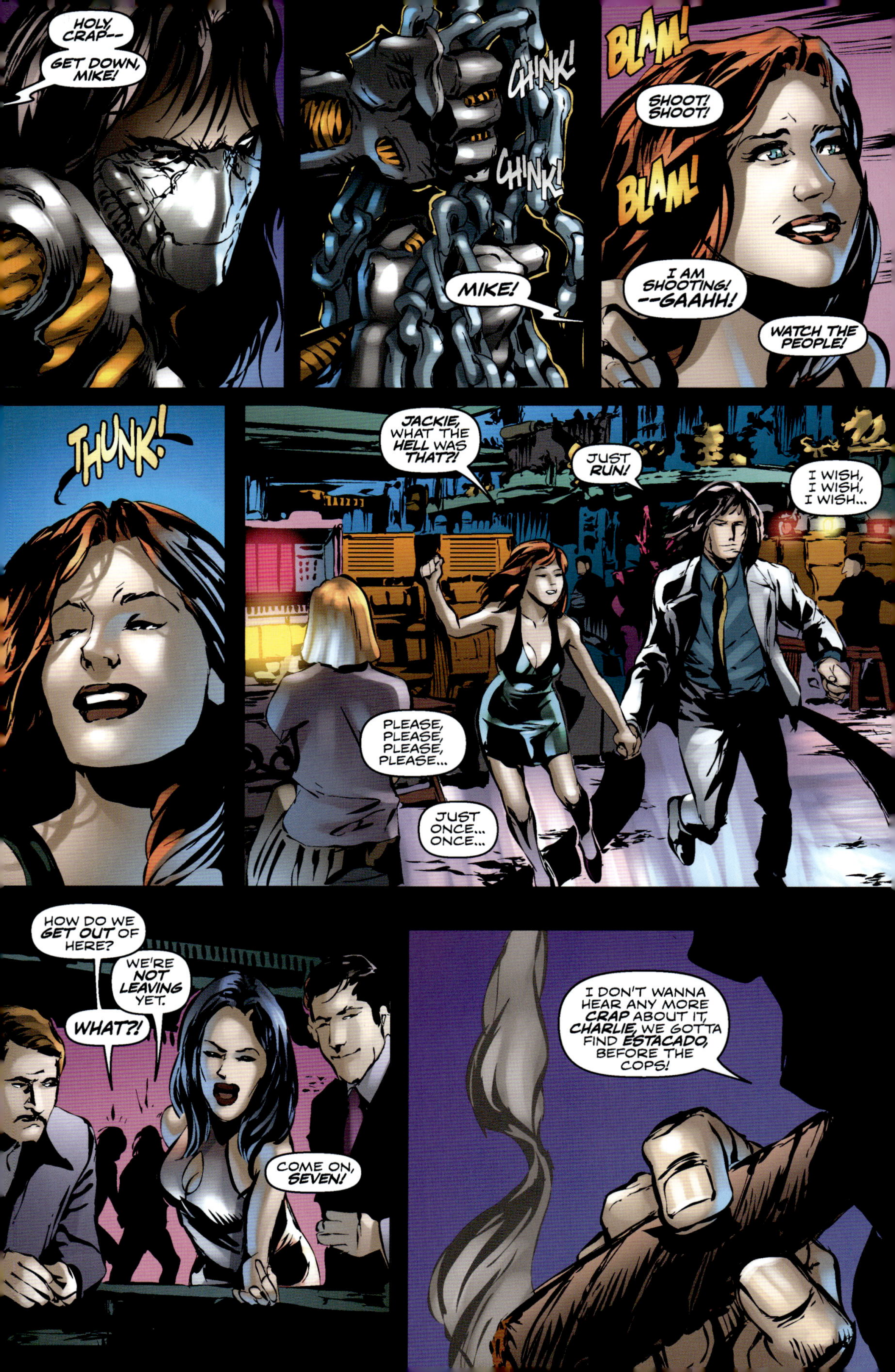
HOLY CRAP--
GET DOWN, MIKE!
CHINK!
CHINK!
MIKE!
BLAM!
SHOOT! SHOOT!
BLAM!
I AM SHOOTING! --GAAHH!
WATCH THE PEOPLE!
THUNK!
JACKIE, WHAT THE HELL WAS THAT?!
JUST RUN!
I WISH, I WISH, I WISH...
PLEASE, PLEASE, PLEASE, PLEASE...
JUST ONCE... ONCE...
HOW DO WE GET OUT OF HERE?
WE'RE NOT LEAVING YET.
WHAT?!
COME ON, SEVEN!
I DON'T WANNA HEAR ANY MORE CRAP ABOUT IT, CHARLIE, WE GOTTA FIND ESTACADO, BEFORE THE COPS!

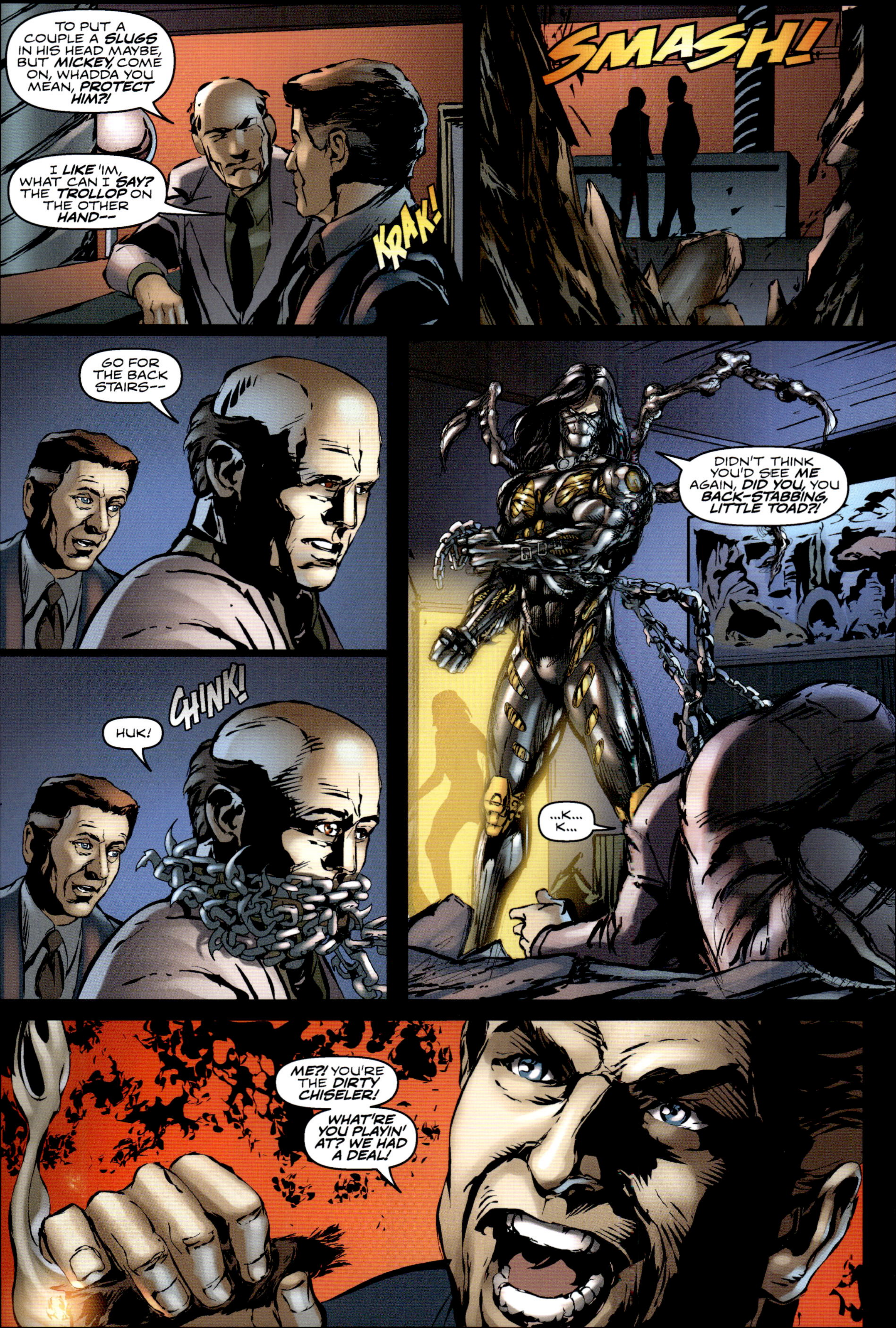
TO PUT A COUPLE A SLUGS IN HIS HEAD MAYBE, BUT MICKEY, COME ON, WHADDA YOU MEAN, PROTECT HIM?!
I LIKE 'IM, WHAT CAN I SAY? THE TROLLOP ON THE OTHER HAND--
KRAK!
SMASH!
GO FOR THE BACK STAIRS--
CHINK!
HUK!
DIDN'T THINK YOU'D SEE ME AGAIN, DID YOU, YOU BACK-STABBING, LITTLE TOAD?!
...K... K...
ME?! YOU'RE THE DIRTY CHISELER!
WHAT'RE YOU PLAYIN' AT? WE HAD A DEAL!

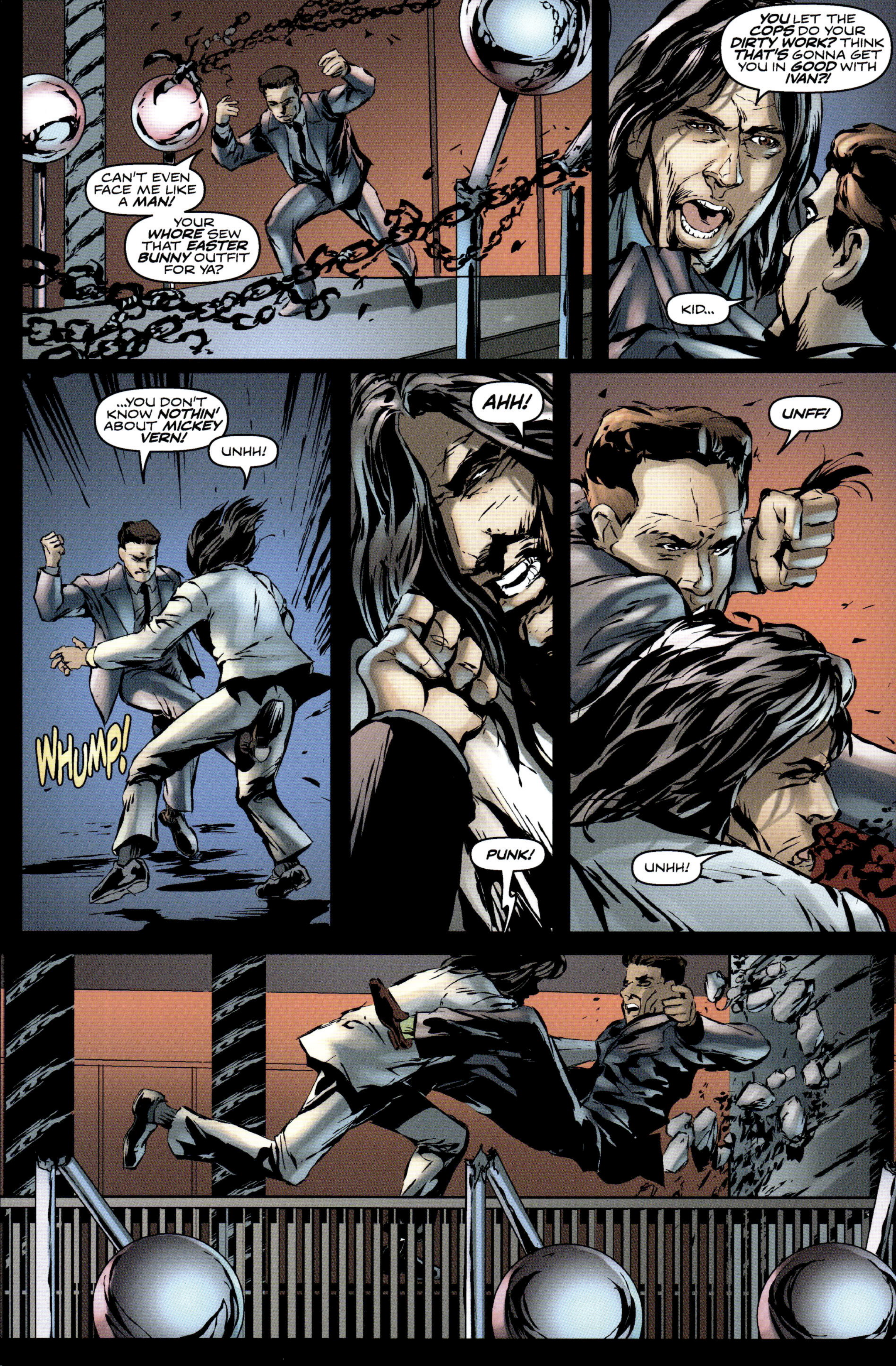
CAN'T EVEN FACE ME LIKE A MAN!
YOUR WHORE SEW THAT EASTER BUNNY OUTFIT FOR YA?
YOU LET THE COPS DO YOUR DIRTY WORK? THINK THAT'S GONNA GET YOU IN GOOD WITH IVAN?!
KID...
...YOU DON'T KNOW NOTHIN' ABOUT MICKEY VERN!
UNHH!
WHUMP!
AHH!
PUNK!
UNFF!
UNHH!

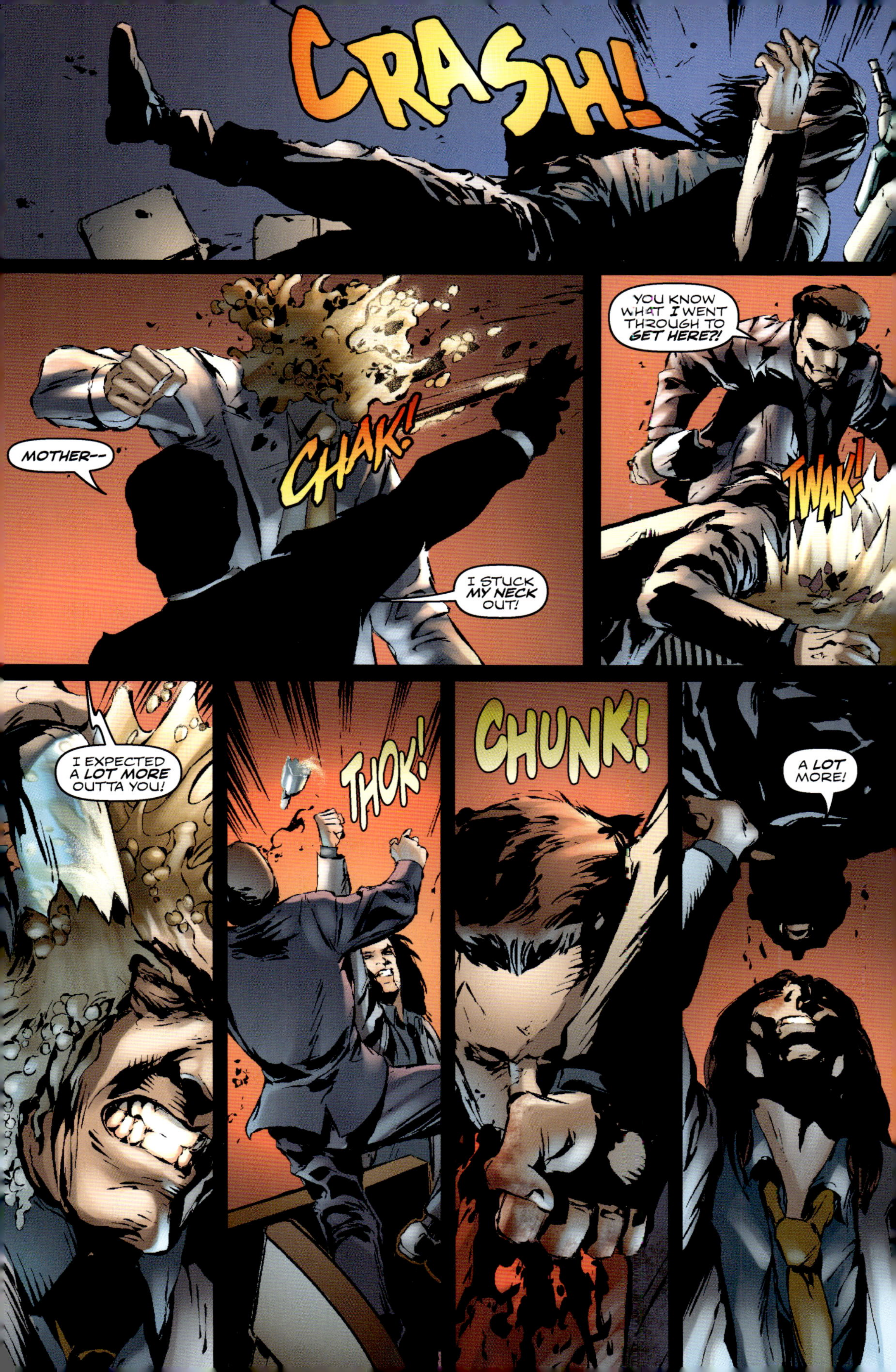
CRASH!
MOTHER--
CHAK!
I STUCK MY NECK OUT!
YOU KNOW WHAT I WENT THROUGH TO GET HERE?!
TWAK!
I EXPECTED A LOT MORE OUTTA YOU!
THOK!
CHUNK!
A LOT MORE!

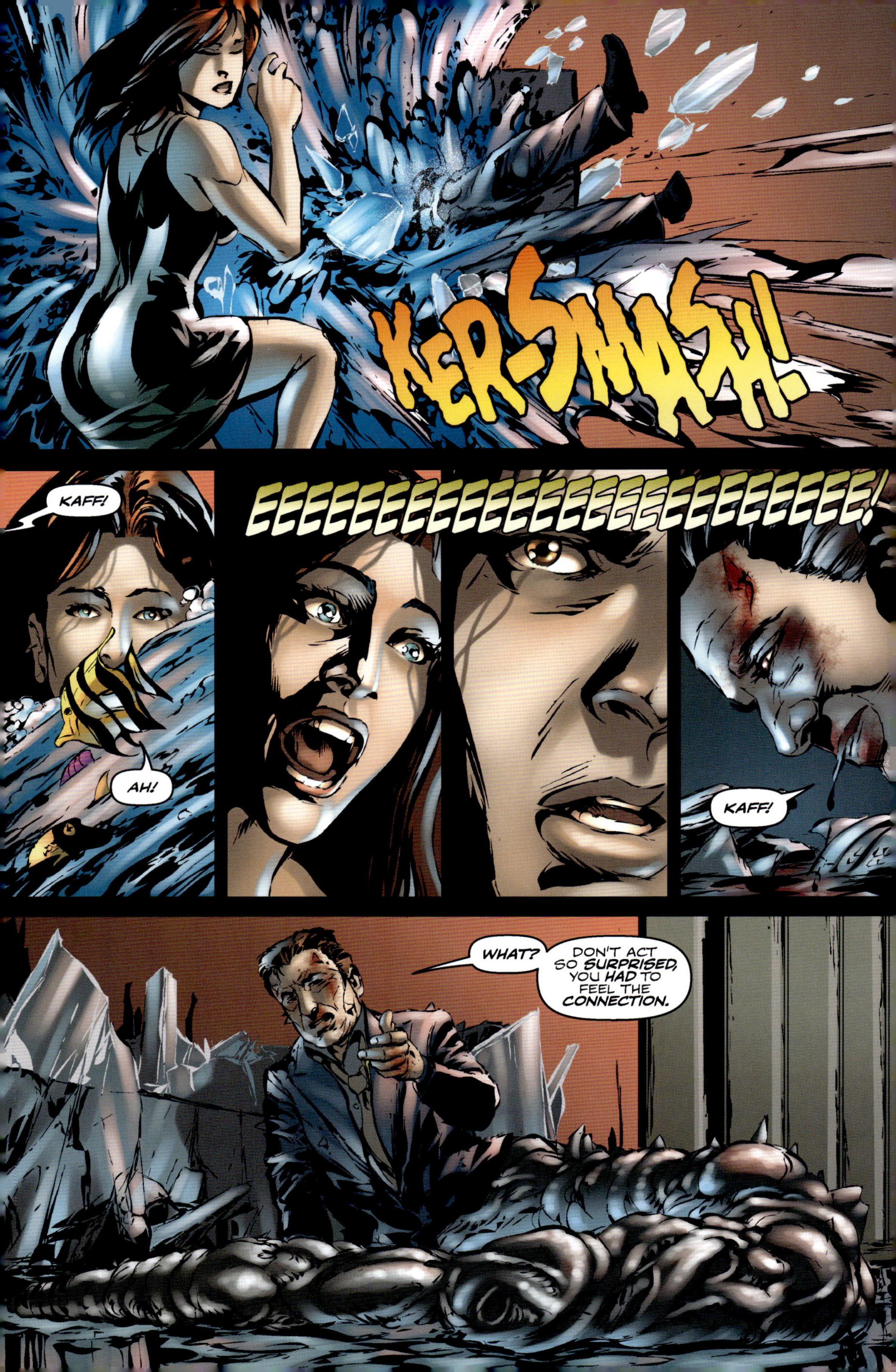
KER-SMASH!
KAFF!
AH!
EEEEEEEEEEEEEEEEEEEEEEEEEEE!
KAFF!
WHAT?
DON'T ACT SO SURPRISED, YOU HAD TO FEEL THE CONNECTION.

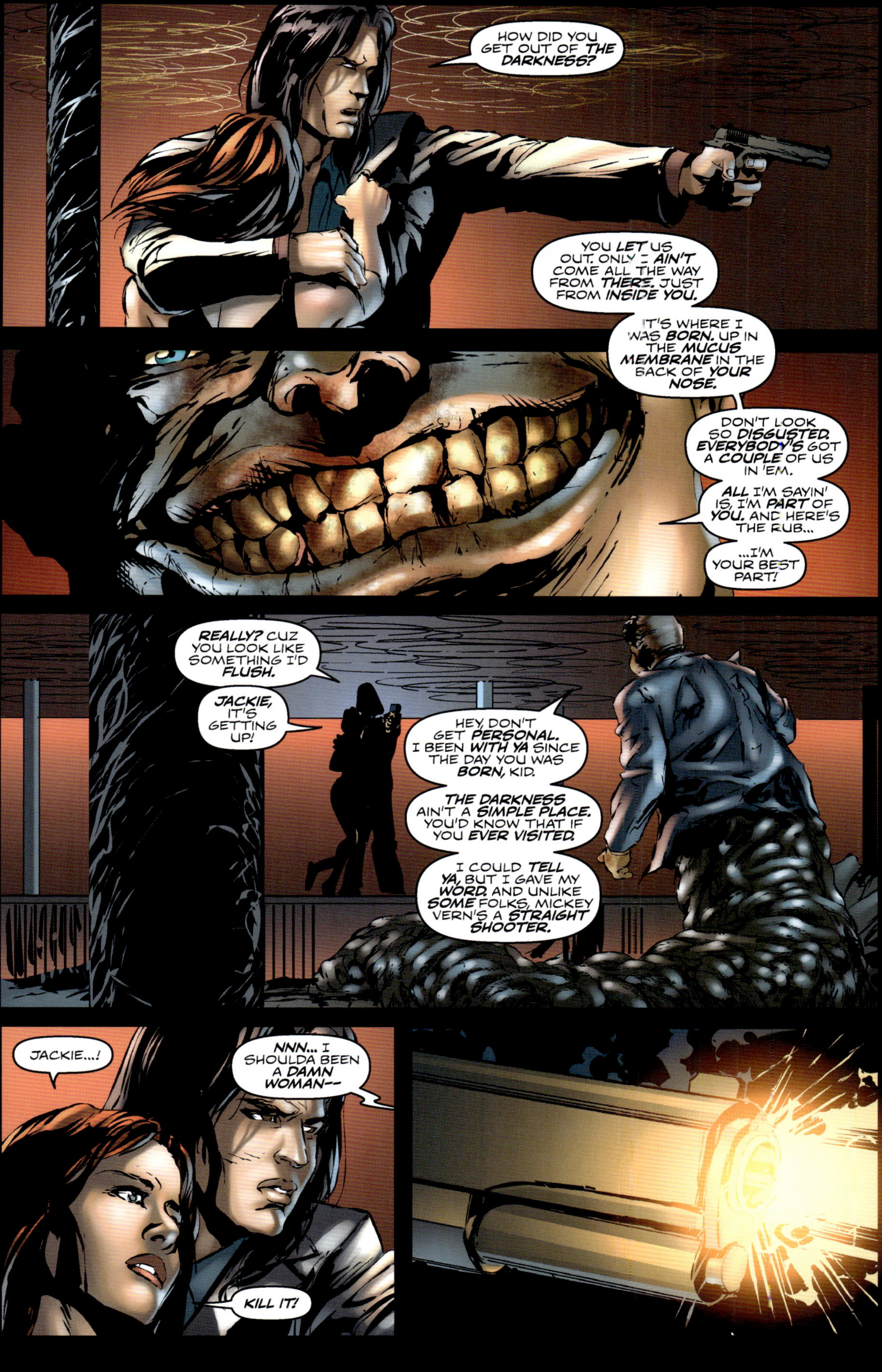
HOW DID YOU GET OUT OF THE DARKNESS?
YOU LET US OUT. ONLY I AIN'T COME ALL THE WAY FROM THERE. JUST FROM INSIDE YOU.
IT'S WHERE I WAS BORN. UP IN THE MUCUS MEMBRANE IN THE BACK OF YOUR NOSE.
DON'T LOOK SO DISGUSTED. EVERYBODY'S GOT A COUPLE OF US IN 'EM.
ALL I'M SAYIN' IS, I'M PART OF YOU. AND HERE'S THE RUB...
...I'M YOUR BEST PART!
REALLY? CUZ YOU LOOK LIKE SOMETHING I'D FLUSH.
JACKIE, IT'S GETTING UP!
HEY, DON'T GET PERSONAL. I BEEN WITH YA SINCE THE DAY YOU WAS BORN, KID.
THE DARKNESS AIN'T A SIMPLE PLACE. YOU'D KNOW THAT IF YOU EVER VISITED.
I COULD TELL YA, BUT I GAVE MY WORD. AND UNLIKE SOME FOLKS, MICKEY VERN'S A STRAIGHT SHOOTER.
JACKIE...!
NNN... I SHOULDA BEEN A DAMN WOMAN--
KILL IT!

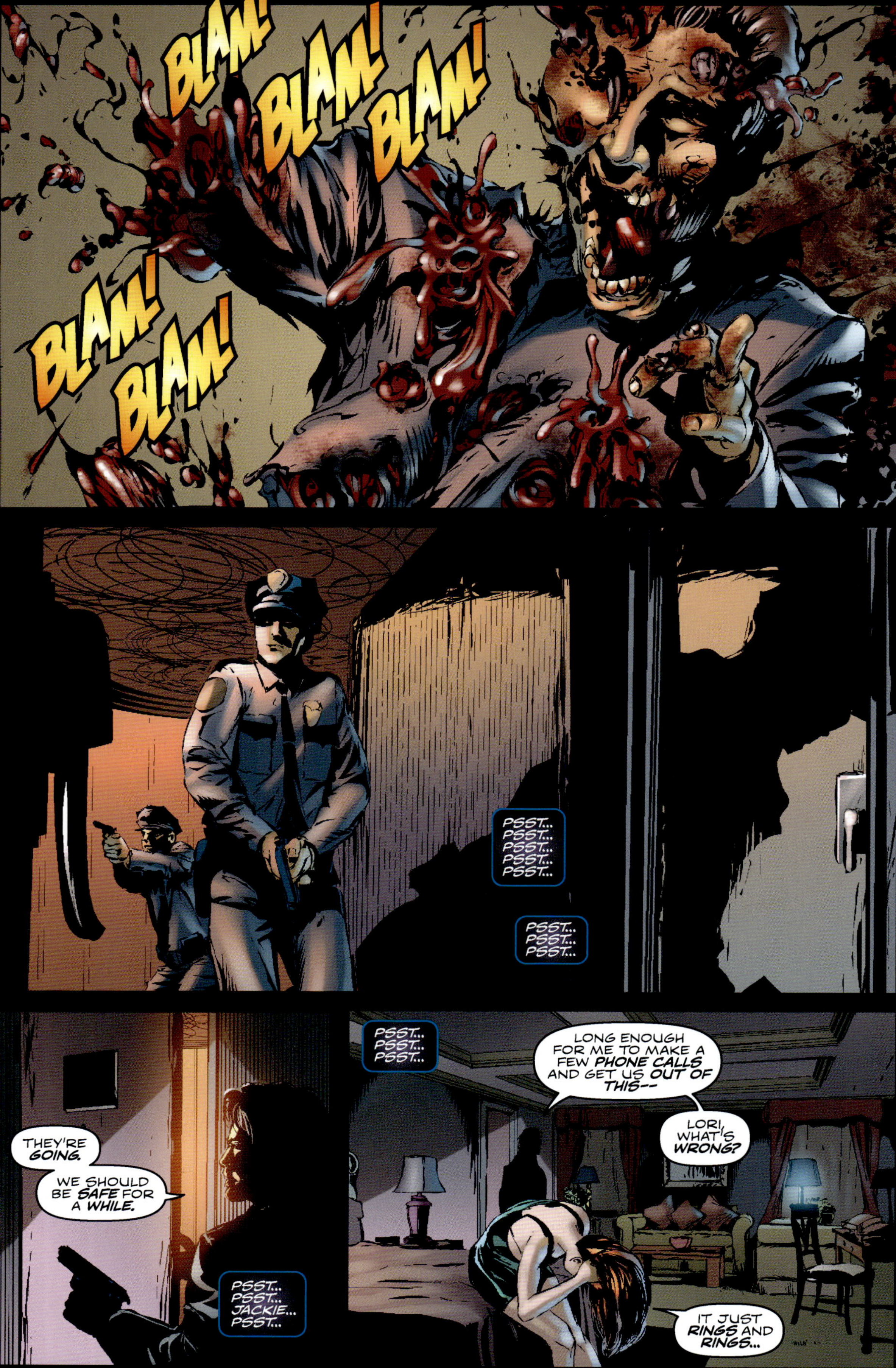
BLAM!
BLAM!
BLAM!
BLAM!
BLAM!
PSST... PSST... PSST... PSST... PSST...
PSST... PSST... PSST...
THEY'RE GOING.
WE SHOULD BE SAFE FOR A WHILE.
PSST... PSST... JACKIE... PSST...
PSST... PSST... PSST...
LONG ENOUGH FOR ME TO MAKE A FEW PHONE CALLS AND GET US OUT OF THIS--
LORI, WHAT'S WRONG?
IT JUST RINGS AND RINGS...

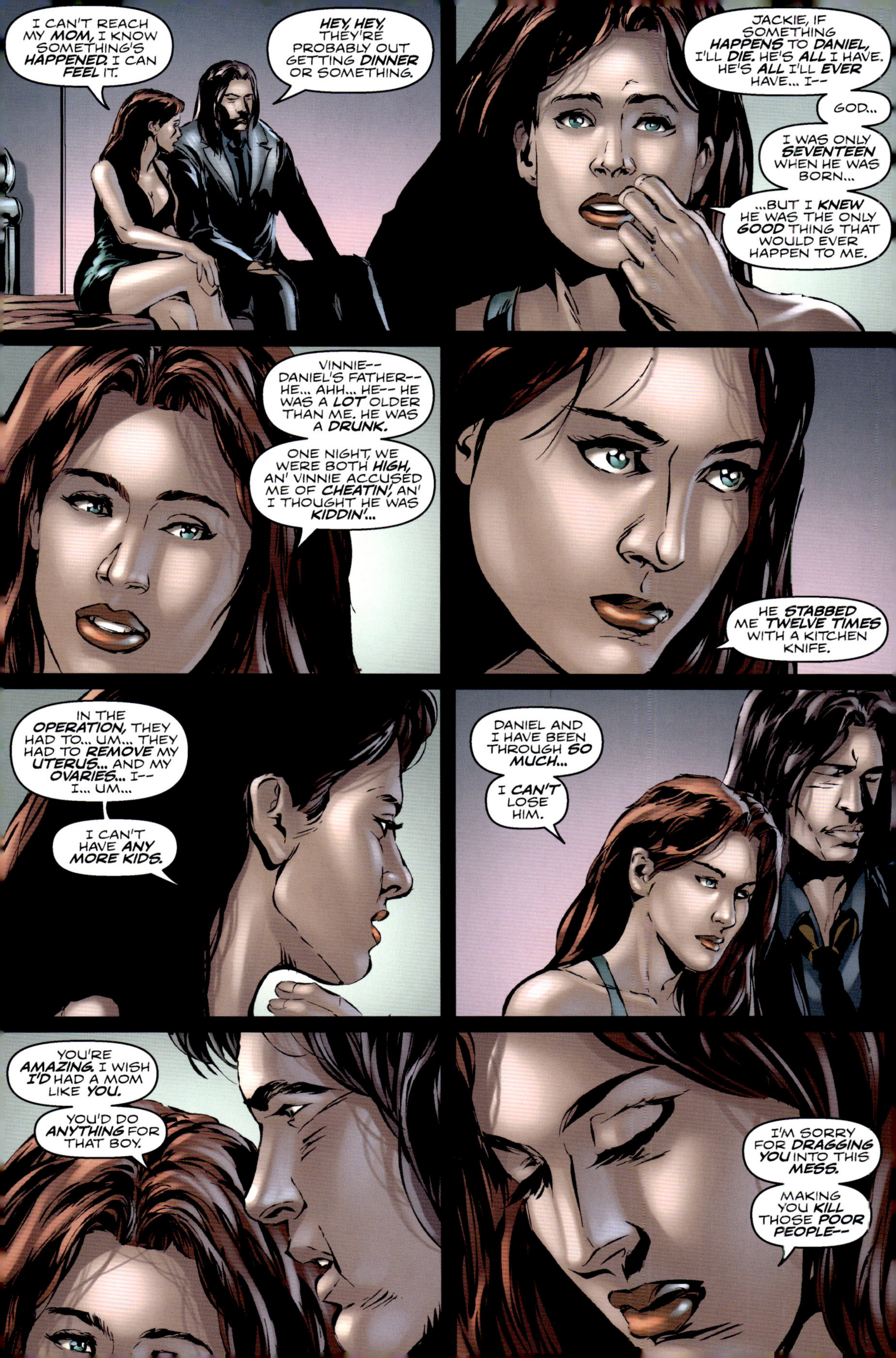

I CAN'T REACH MY MOM, I KNOW SOMETHING'S HAPPENED. I CAN FEEL IT.
HEY, HEY, THEY'RE PROBABLY OUT GETTING DINNER OR SOMETHING.
JACKIE, IF SOMETHING HAPPENS TO DANIEL, I'LL DIE. HE'S ALL I HAVE. HE'S ALL I'LL EVER HAVE... I--
GOD...
I WAS ONLY SEVENTEEN WHEN HE WAS BORN...
...BUT I KNEW HE WAS THE ONLY GOOD THING THAT WOULD EVER HAPPEN TO ME.
VINNIE-- DANIEL'S FATHER-- HE... AHH... HE-- HE WAS A LOT OLDER THAN ME. HE WAS A DRUNK.
ONE NIGHT, WE WERE BOTH HIGH, AN' VINNIE ACCUSED ME OF CHEATIN', AN' I THOUGHT HE WAS KIDDIN'...
HE STABBED ME TWELVE TIMES WITH A KITCHEN KNIFE.
IN THE OPERATION, THEY HAD TO... UM... THEY HAD TO REMOVE MY UTERUS... AND MY OVARIES... I-- I... UM...
I CAN'T HAVE ANY MORE KIDS.
DANIEL AND I HAVE BEEN THROUGH SO MUCH...
I CAN'T LOSE HIM.
YOU'RE AMAZING. I WISH I'D HAD A MOM LIKE YOU.
YOU'D DO ANYTHING FOR THAT BOY.
I'M SORRY FOR DRAGGING YOU INTO THIS MESS.
MAKING YOU KILL THOSE POOR PEOPLE--

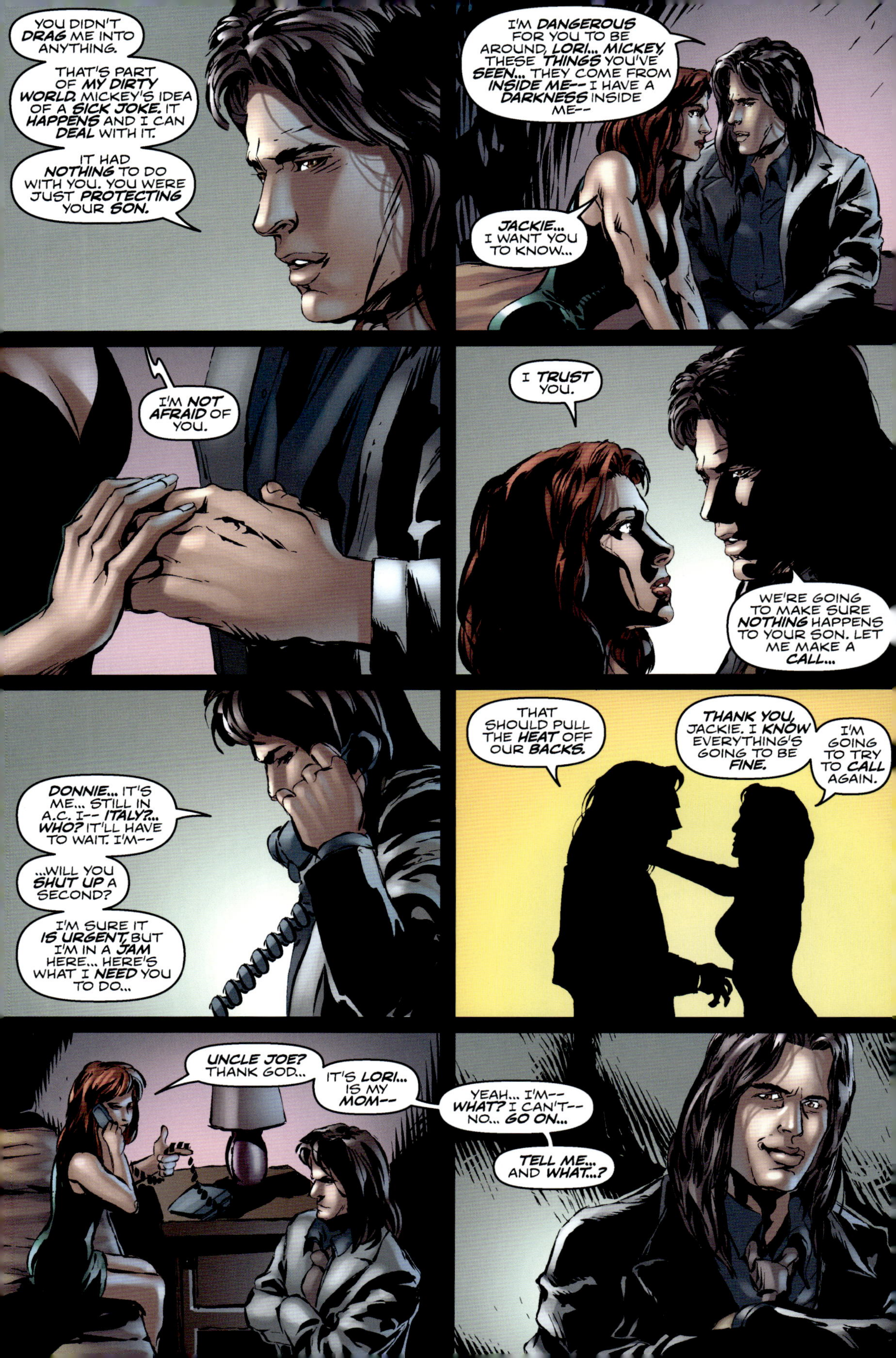
YOU DIDN'T DRAG ME INTO ANYTHING.
THAT'S PART OF MY DIRTY WORLD. MICKEY'S IDEA OF A SICK JOKE. IT HAPPENS AND I CAN DEAL WITH IT.
IT HAD NOTHING TO DO WITH YOU. YOU WERE JUST PROTECTING YOUR SON.
I'M DANGEROUS FOR YOU TO BE AROUND, LORI... MICKEY, THESE THINGS YOU'VE SEEN... THEY COME FROM INSIDE ME-- I HAVE A DARKNESS INSIDE ME--
JACKIE... I WANT YOU TO KNOW...
I'M NOT AFRAID OF YOU.
I TRUST YOU.
WE'RE GOING TO MAKE SURE NOTHING HAPPENS TO YOUR SON. LET ME MAKE A CALL...
DONNIE... IT'S ME... STILL IN A.C. I-- ITALY?.. WHO? IT'LL HAVE TO WAIT. I'M--
...WILL YOU SHUT UP A SECOND?
I'M SURE IT IS URGENT, BUT I'M IN A JAM HERE... HERE'S WHAT I NEED YOU TO DO...
THAT SHOULD PULL THE HEAT OFF OUR BACKS.
THANK YOU, JACKIE. I KNOW EVERYTHING'S GOING TO BE FINE.
I'M GOING TO TRY TO CALL AGAIN.
UNCLE JOE? THANK GOD...
IT'S LORI... IS MY MOM--
YEAH... I'M-- WHAT? I CAN'T-- NO... GO ON...
TELL ME... AND WHAT...?

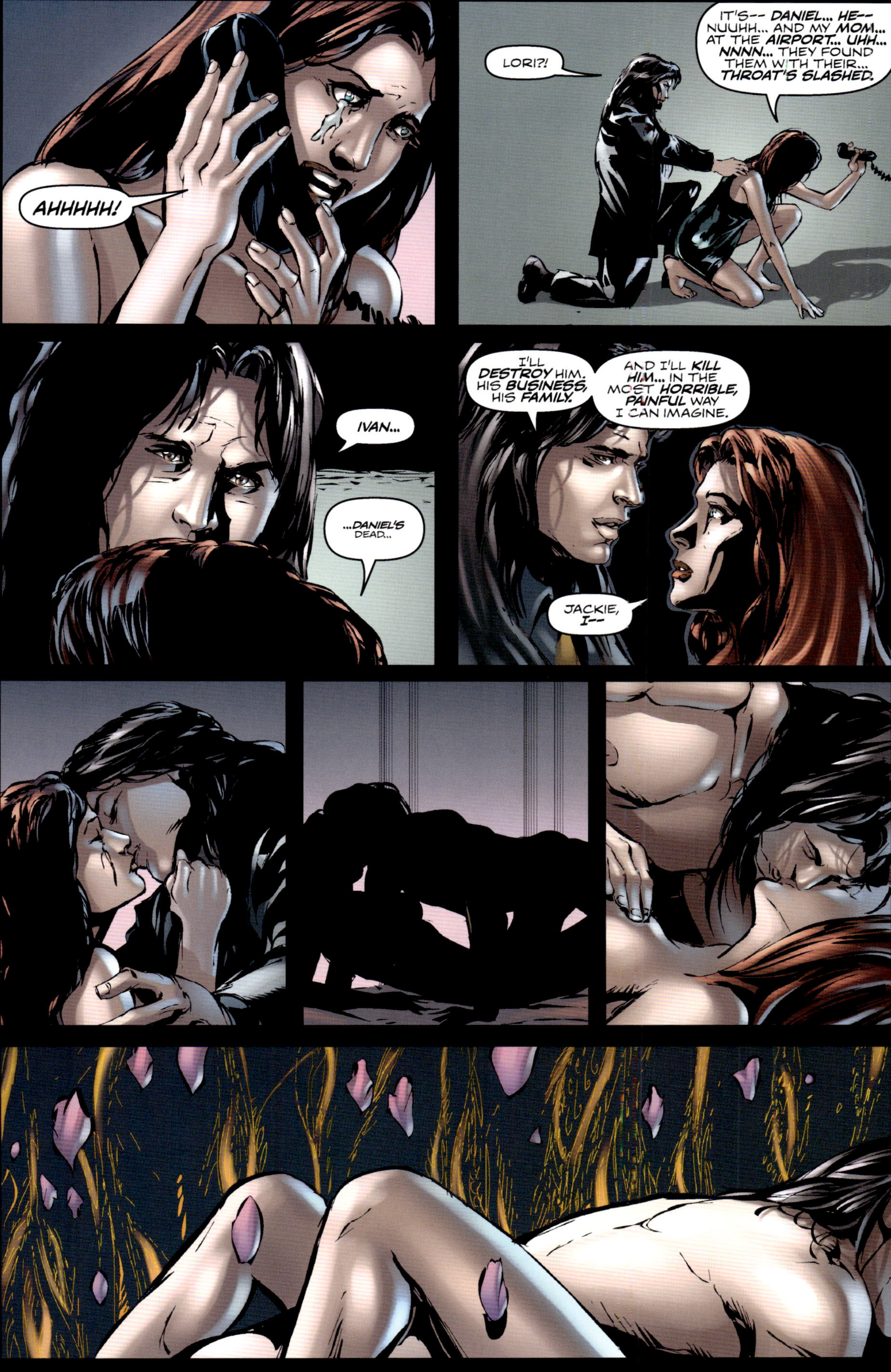
AHHHHH!
LORI?!
IT'S-- DANIEL... HE-- NUUHH... AND MY MOM... AT THE AIRPORT... UHH... NNNN... THEY FOUND THEM WITH THEIR... THROAT'S SLASHED.
IVAN...
...DANIEL'S DEAD...
I'LL DESTROY HIM. HIS BUSINESS, HIS FAMILY.
AND I'LL KILL HIM... IN THE MOST HORRIBLE, PAINFUL WAY I CAN IMAGINE.
JACKIE, I--

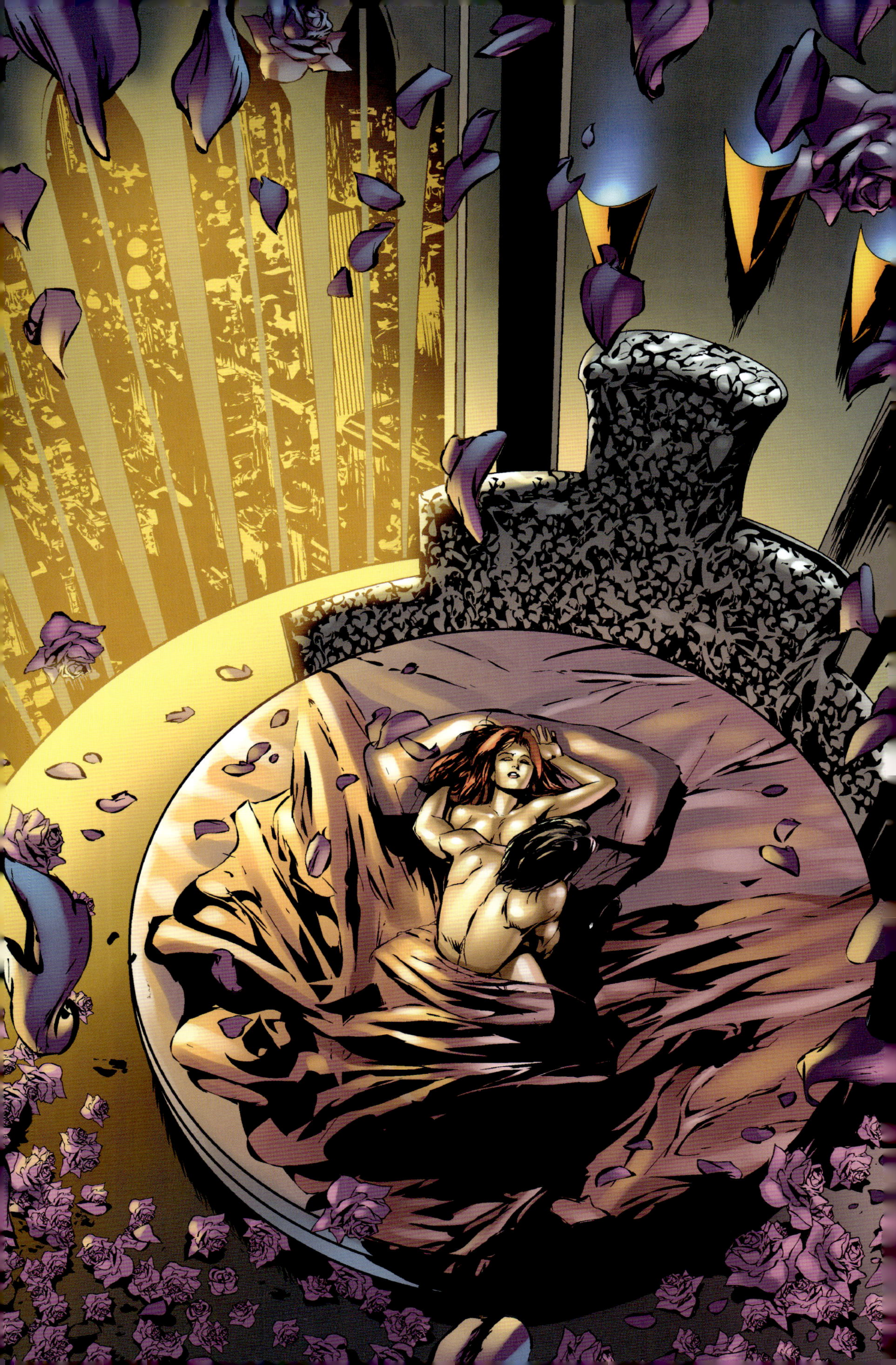

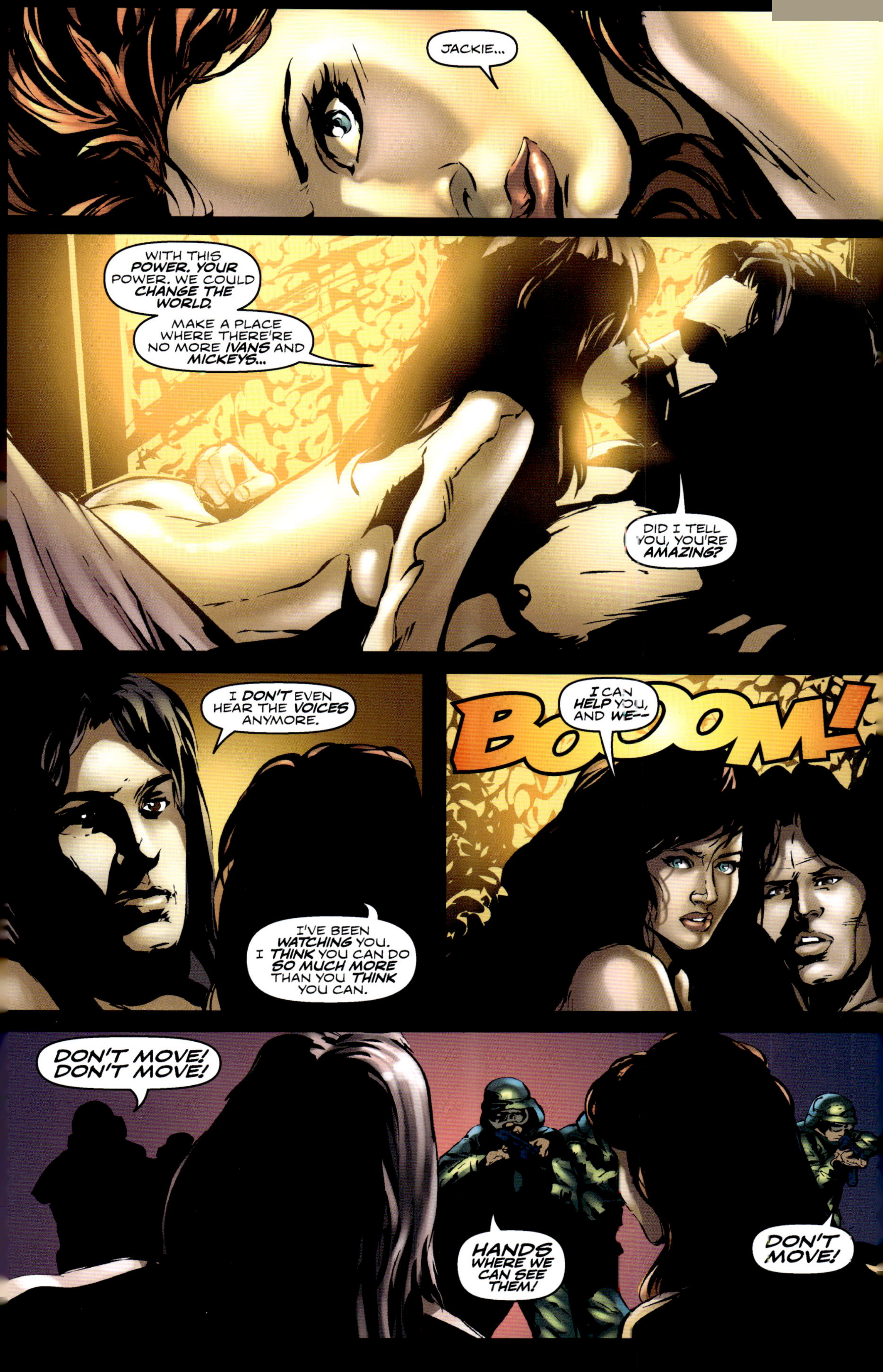
JACKIE...
WITH THIS POWER. YOUR POWER. WE COULD CHANGE THE WORLD.
MAKE A PLACE WHERE THERE'RE NO MORE IVANS AND MICKEYS...
DID I TELL YOU, YOU'RE AMAZING?
I DON'T EVEN HEAR THE VOICES ANYMORE.
I'VE BEEN WATCHING YOU. I THINK YOU CAN DO SO MUCH MORE THAN YOU THINK YOU CAN.
I CAN HELP YOU, AND WE--
BOOOM!
DON'T MOVE! DON'T MOVE!
HANDS WHERE WE CAN SEE THEM!
DON'T MOVE!

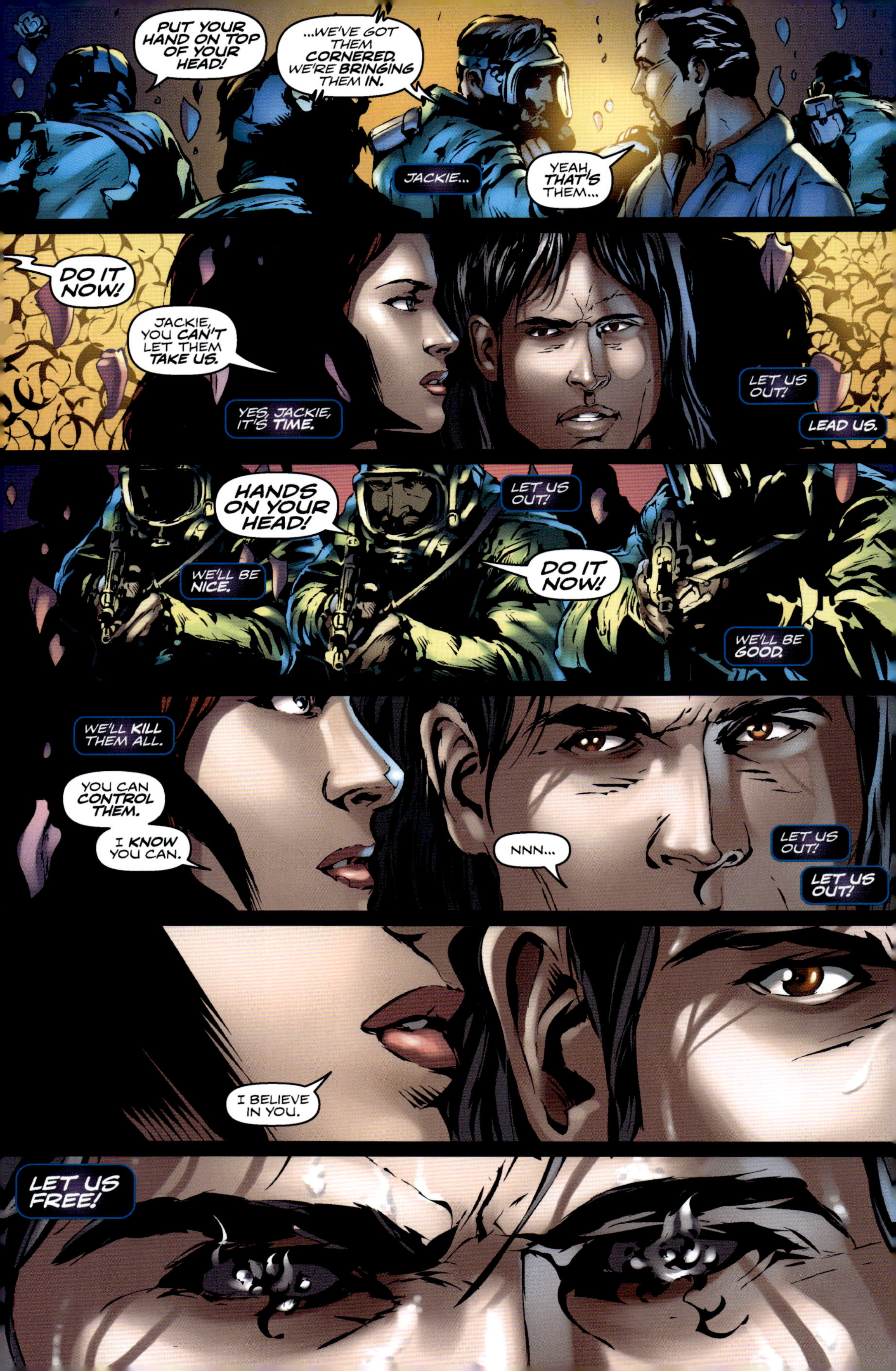
PUT YOUR HAND ON TOP OF YOUR HEAD!
...WE'VE GOT THEM CORNERED. WE'RE BRINGING THEM IN.
JACKIE...
YEAH, THAT'S THEM...
DO IT NOW!
JACKIE, YOU CAN'T LET THEM TAKE US.
YES, JACKIE, IT'S TIME.
LET US OUT!
LEAD US.
HANDS ON YOUR HEAD!
LET US OUT!
WE'LL BE NICE.
DO IT NOW!
WE'LL BE GOOD.
WE'LL KILL THEM ALL.
YOU CAN CONTROL THEM.
I KNOW YOU CAN.
NNN...
LET US OUT!
LET US OUT!
I BELIEVE IN YOU.
LET US FREE!

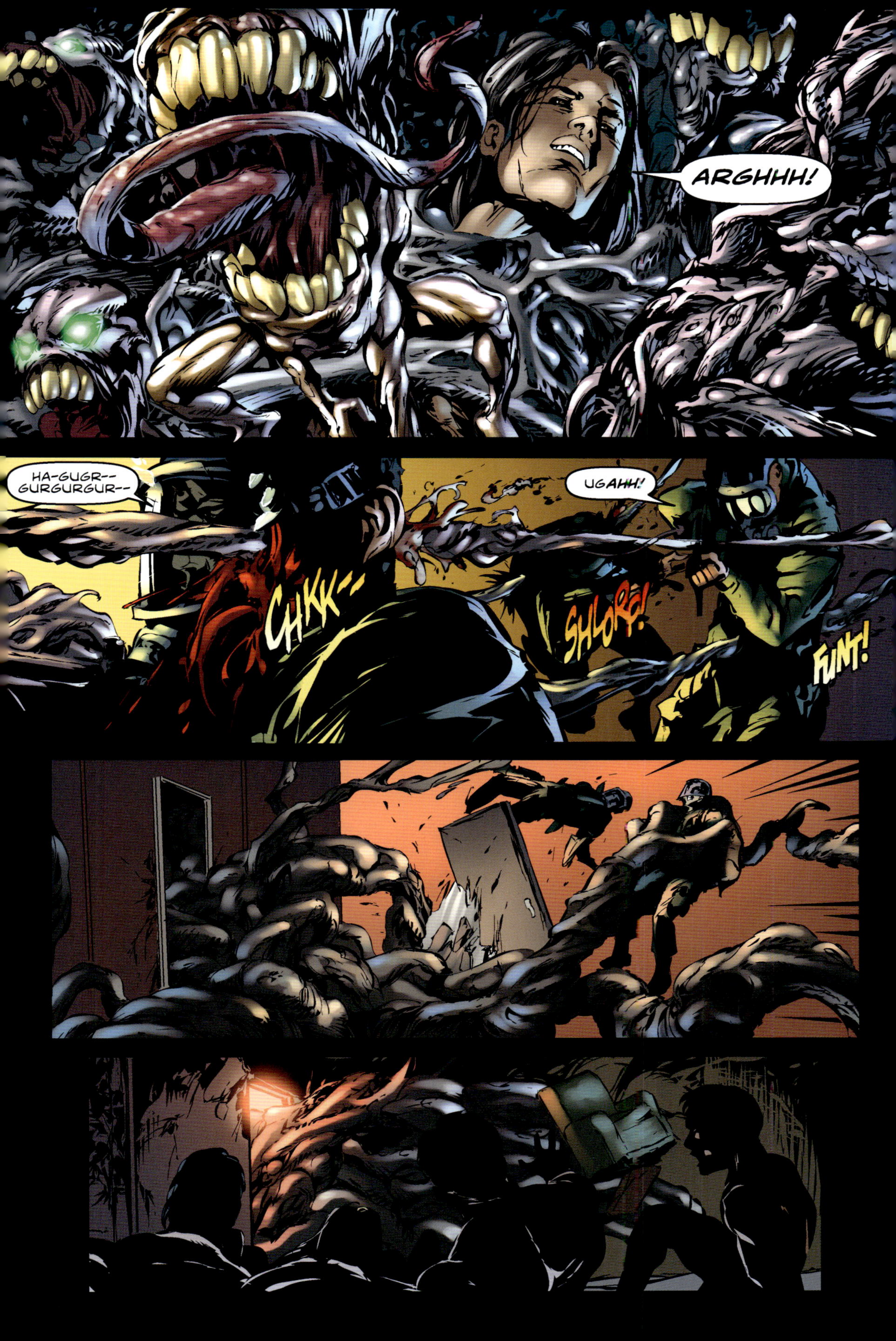
ARGHHH!
HA-GUGR--
GURGURGUR--
UGAHH!
CHKK--
SHLORG!
FUNT!

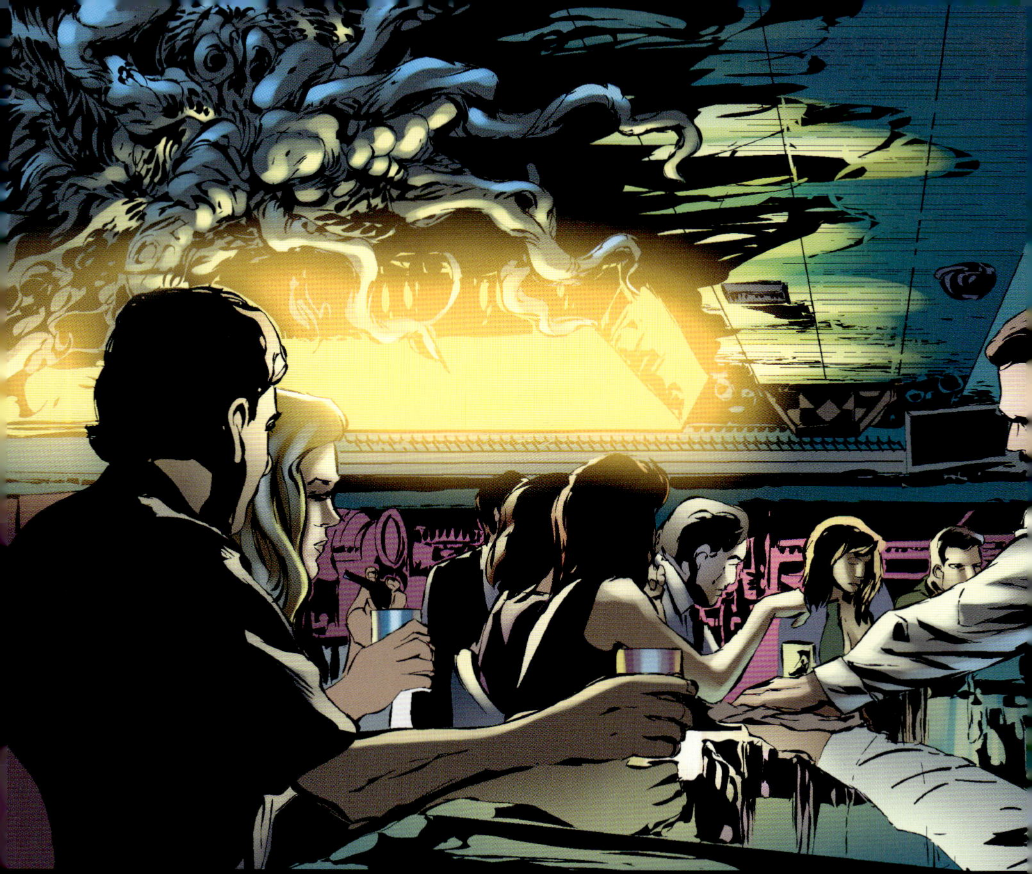

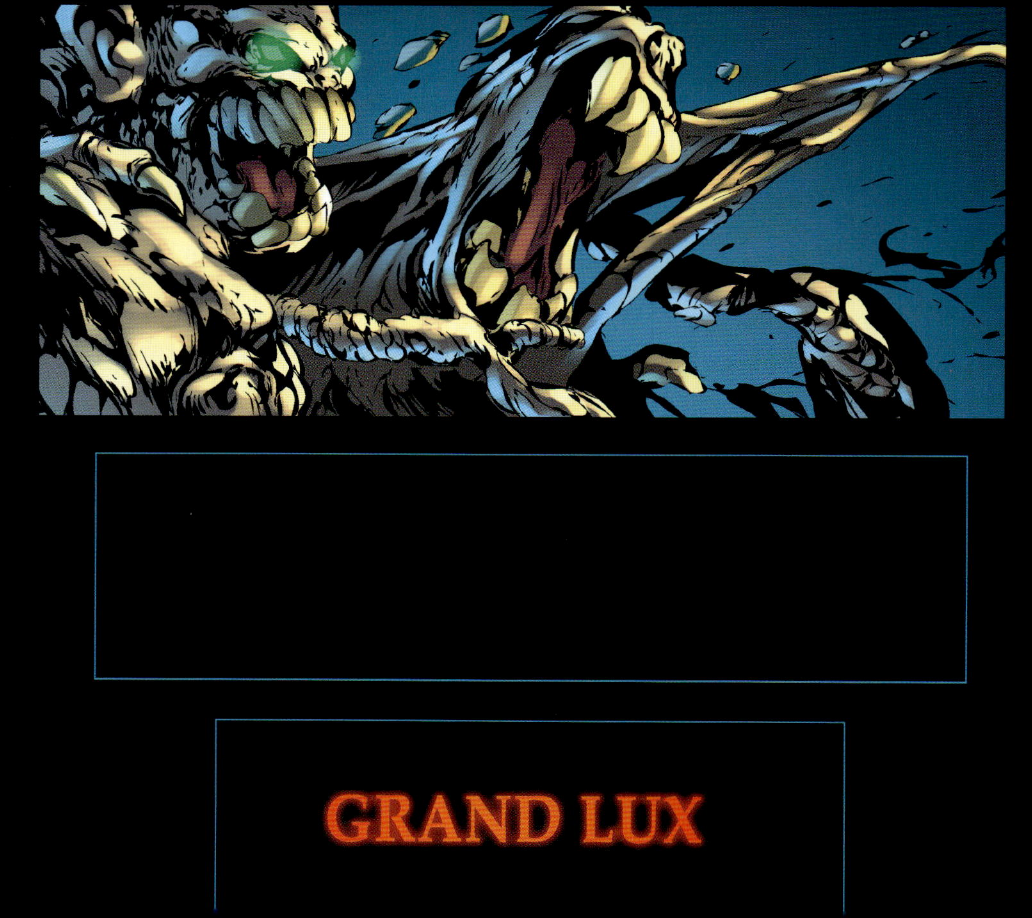

GRAND LUX

The Darkness Issue #60
cover art by: Dale Keown

THE DARKNESS #60

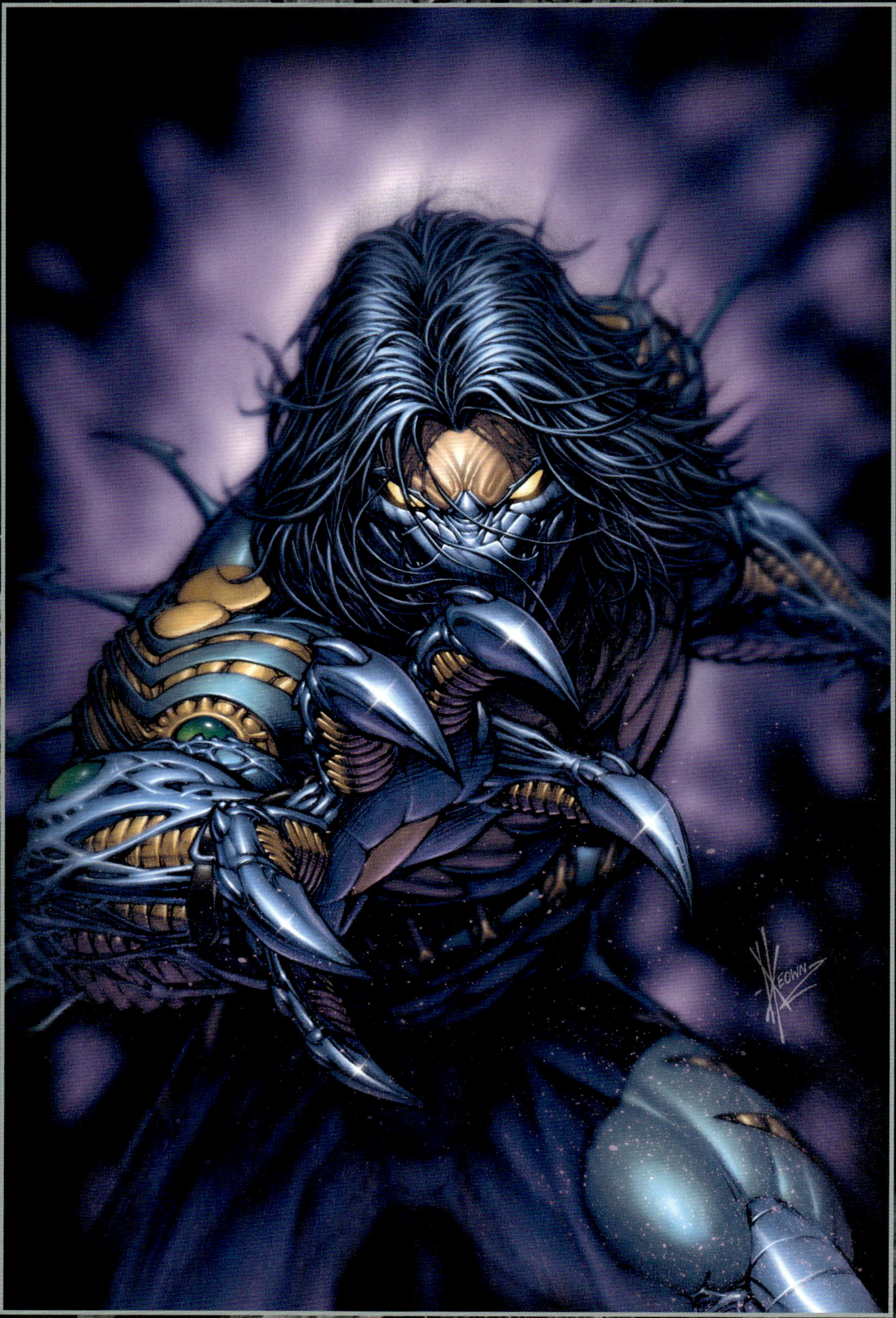
KEOWN

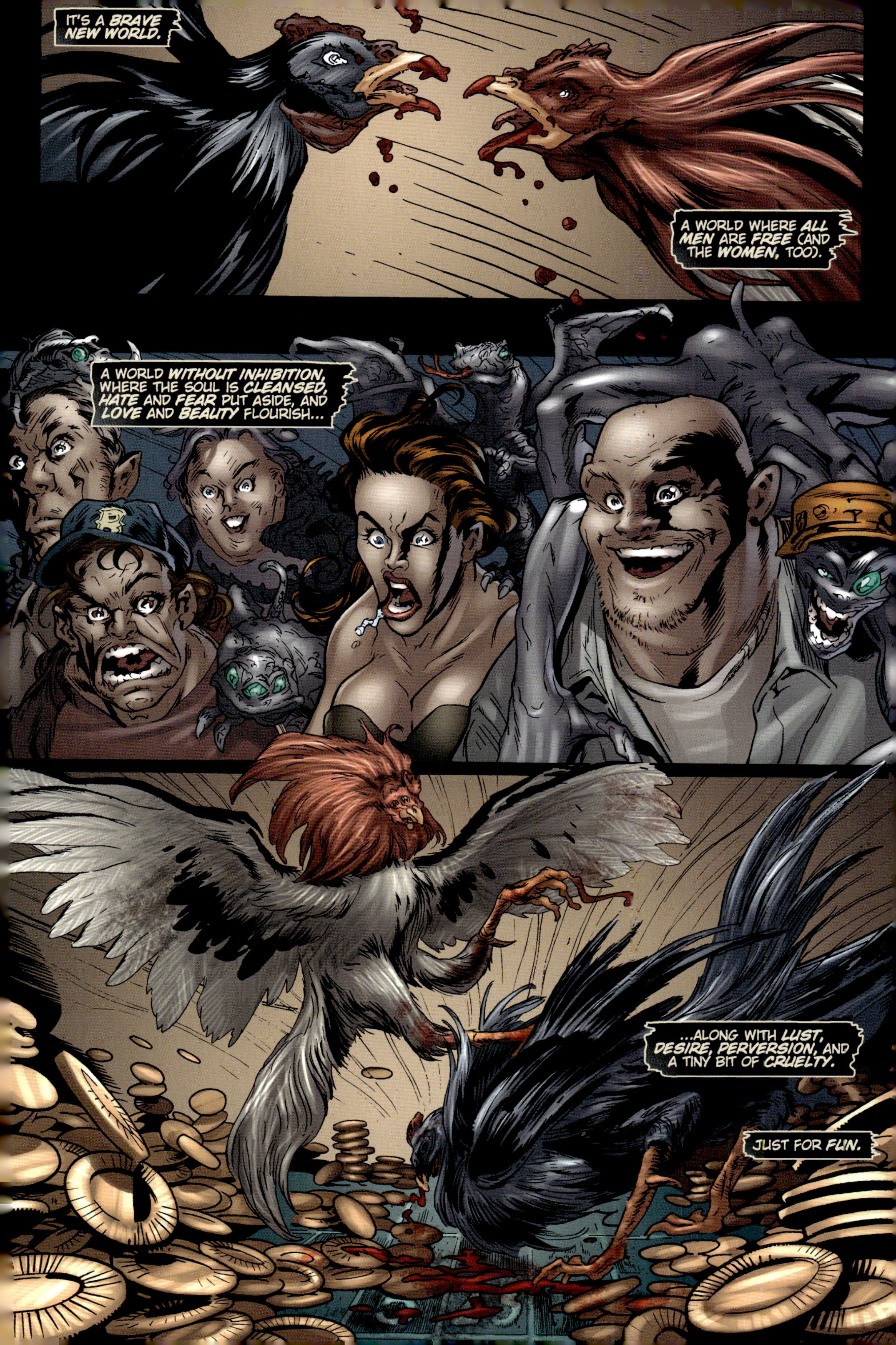
IT'S A BRAVE NEW WORLD.
A WORLD WHERE ALL MEN ARE FREE (AND THE WOMEN, TOO).
A WORLD WITHOUT INHIBITION, WHERE THE SOUL IS CLEANSED, HATE AND FEAR PUT ASIDE, AND LOVE AND BEAUTY FLOURISH...
...ALONG WITH LUST, DESIRE, PERVERSION, AND A TINY BIT OF CRUELTY.
JUST FOR FUN.

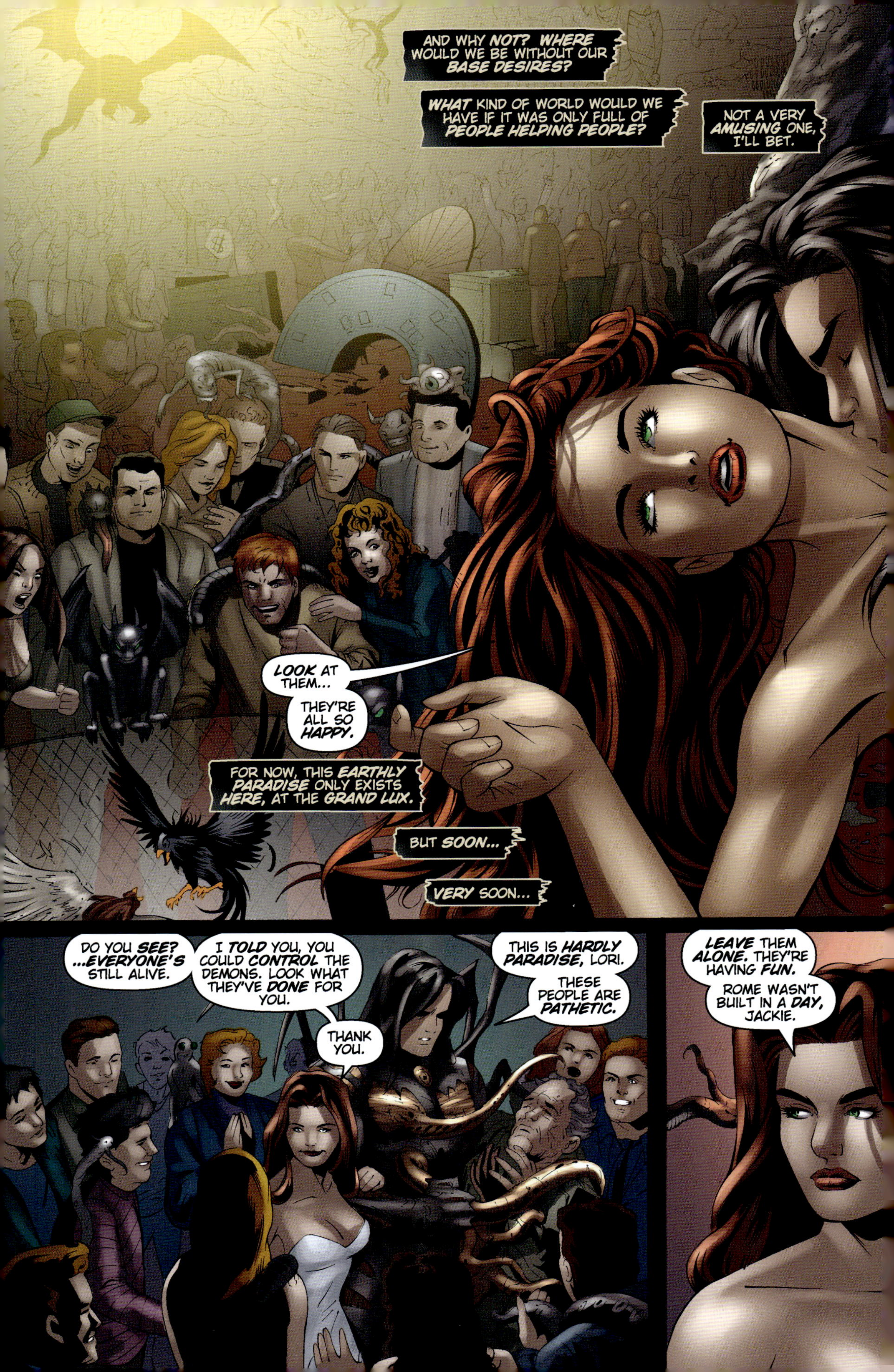
AND WHY NOT? WHERE WOULD WE BE WITHOUT OUR BASE DESIRES?
WHAT KIND OF WORLD WOULD WE HAVE IF IT WAS ONLY FULL OF PEOPLE HELPING PEOPLE?
NOT A VERY AMUSING ONE, I'LL BET.
LOOK AT THEM...
THEY'RE ALL SO HAPPY.
FOR NOW, THIS EARTHLY PARADISE ONLY EXISTS HERE, AT THE GRAND LUX.
BUT SOON...
VERY SOON...
DO YOU SEE? ...EVERYONE'S STILL ALIVE.
I TOLD YOU, YOU COULD CONTROL THE DEMONS. LOOK WHAT THEY'VE DONE FOR YOU.
THANK YOU.
THIS IS HARDLY PARADISE, LORI.
THESE PEOPLE ARE PATHETIC.
LEAVE THEM ALONE. THEY'RE HAVING FUN.
ROME WASN'T BUILT IN A DAY, JACKIE.

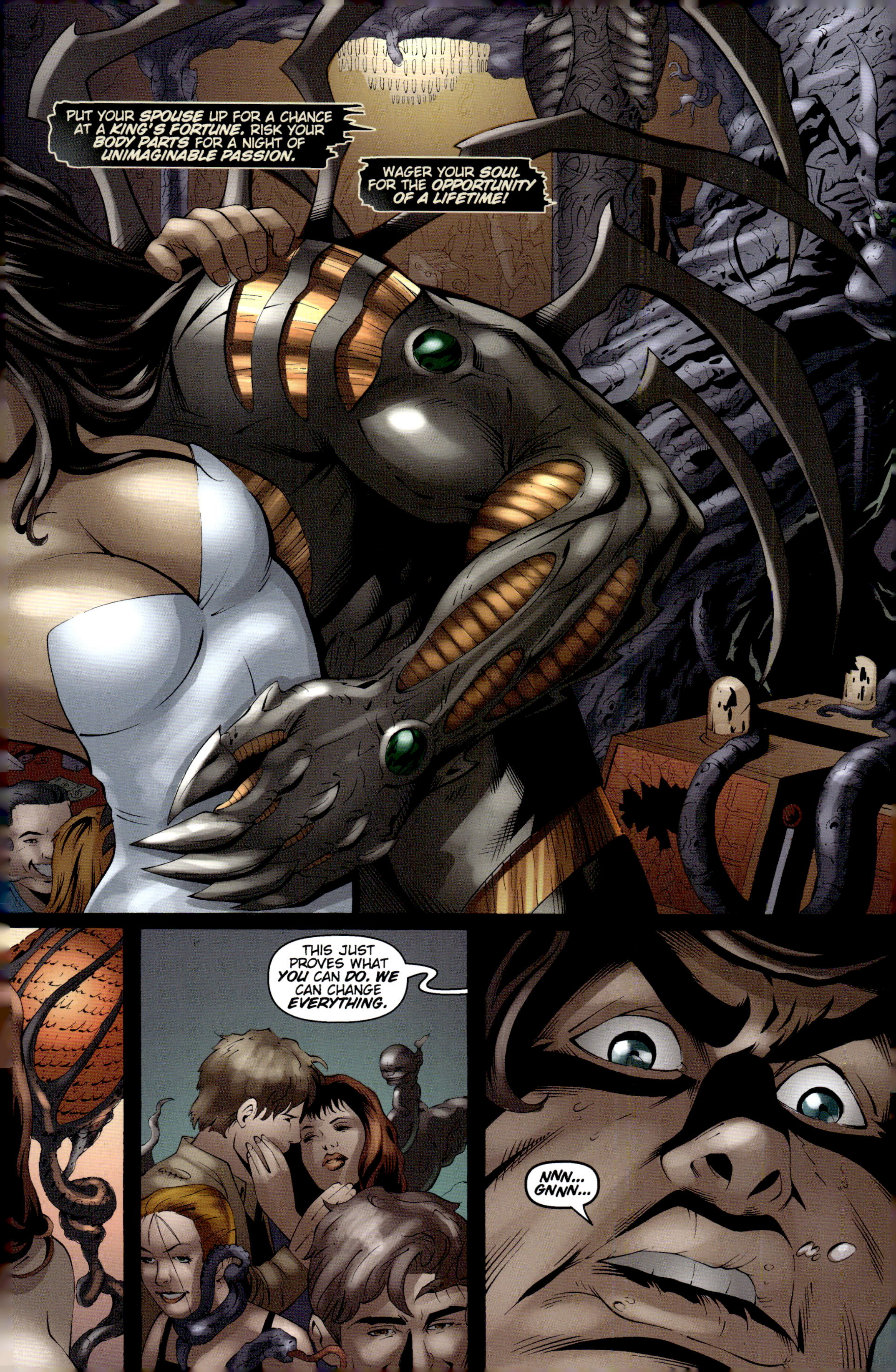
PUT YOUR SPOUSE UP FOR A CHANCE AT A KING'S FORTUNE. RISK YOUR BODY PARTS FOR A NIGHT OF UNIMAGINABLE PASSION.
WAGER YOUR SOUL FOR THE OPPORTUNITY OF A LIFETIME!
THIS JUST PROVES WHAT YOU CAN DO. WE CAN CHANGE EVERYTHING.
NNN... GNNN...

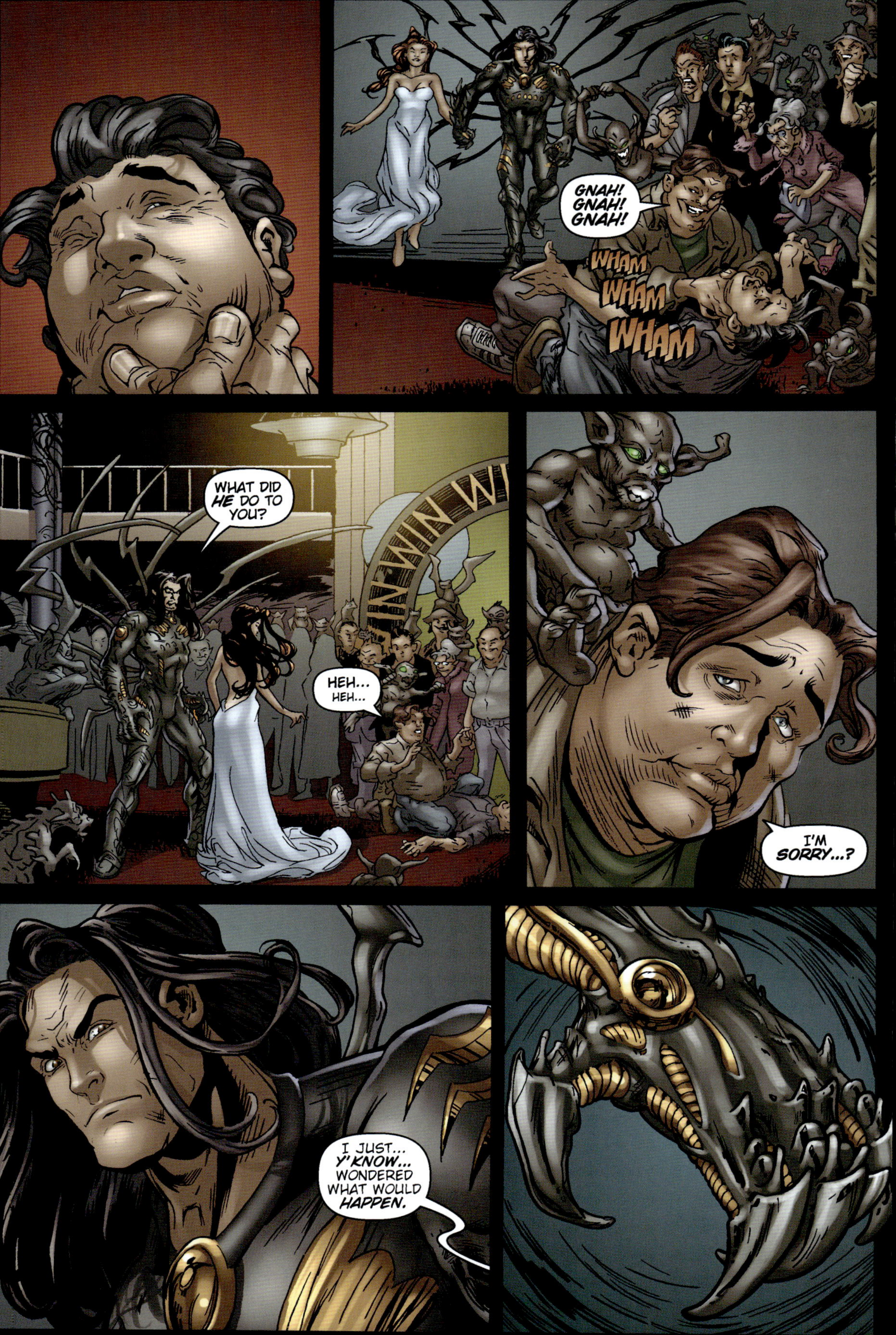
GNAH! GNAH! GNAH!
WHAM WHAM WHAM
WHAT DID HE DO TO YOU?
HEH... HEH...
I'M SORRY...?
I JUST... Y'KNOW... WONDERED WHAT WOULD HAPPEN.

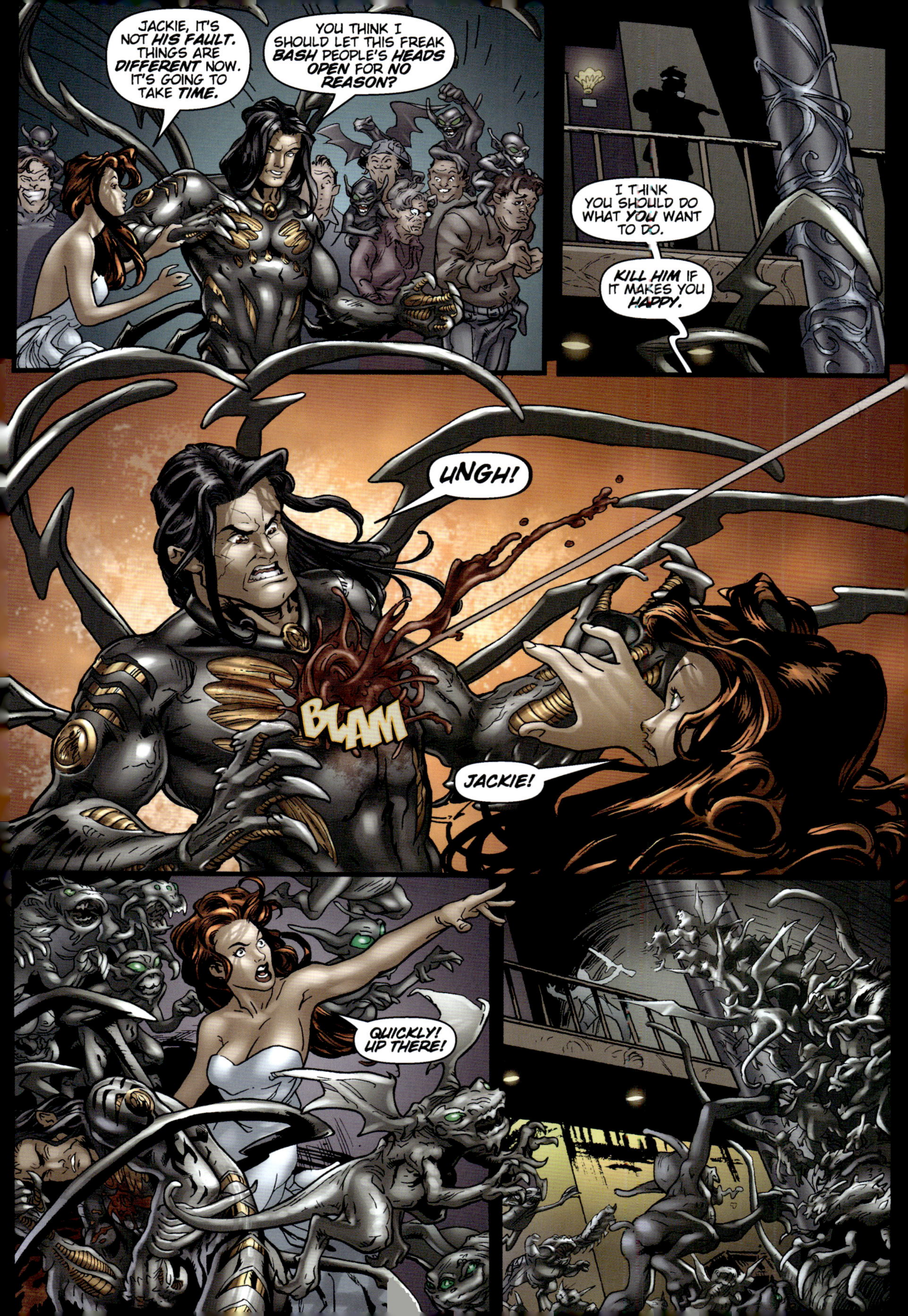
JACKIE, IT'S NOT HIS FAULT. THINGS ARE DIFFERENT NOW. IT'S GOING TO TAKE TIME.
YOU THINK I SHOULD LET THIS FREAK BASH PEOPLE'S HEADS OPEN FOR NO REASON?
I THINK YOU SHOULD DO WHAT YOU WANT TO DO.
KILL HIM IF IT MAKES YOU HAPPY.
UNGH!
BLAM
JACKIE!
QUICKLY! UP THERE!

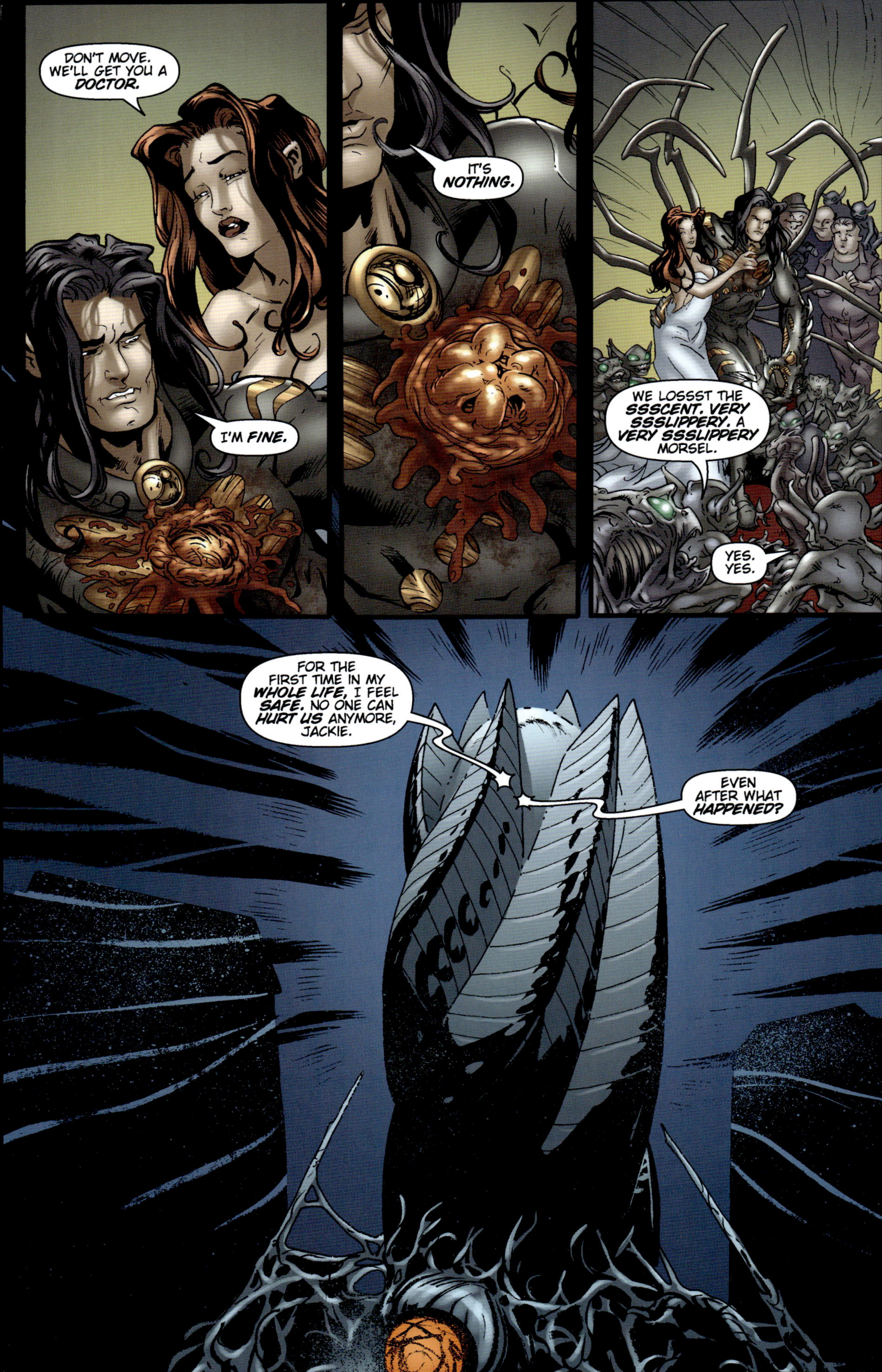
DON'T MOVE. WE'LL GET YOU A DOCTOR.
I'M FINE.
IT'S NOTHING.
WE LOSSST THE SSSCENT. VERY SSSLIPPERY. A VERY SSSLIPPERY MORSEL.
YES. YES.
FOR THE FIRST TIME IN MY WHOLE LIFE, I FEEL SAFE. NO ONE CAN HURT US ANYMORE, JACKIE.
EVEN AFTER WHAT HAPPENED?

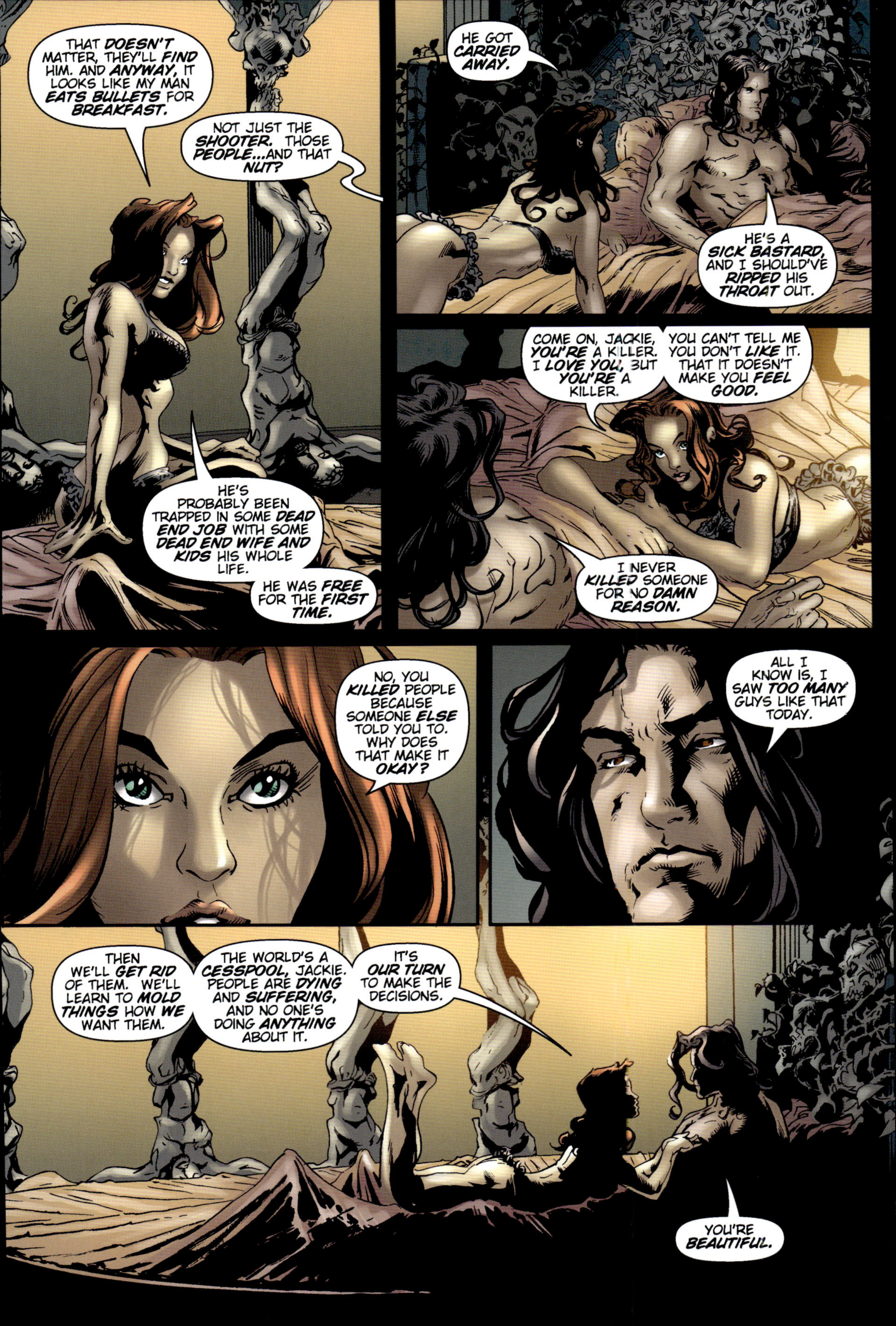
THAT DOESN'T MATTER, THEY'LL FIND HIM. AND ANYWAY, IT LOOKS LIKE MY MAN EATS BULLETS FOR BREAKFAST.
NOT JUST THE SHOOTER. THOSE PEOPLE...AND THAT NUT?
HE GOT CARRIED AWAY.
HE'S A SICK BASTARD, AND I SHOULD'VE RIPPED HIS THROAT OUT.
HE'S PROBABLY BEEN TRAPPED IN SOME DEAD END JOB WITH SOME DEAD END WIFE AND KIDS HIS WHOLE LIFE.
HE WAS FREE FOR THE FIRST TIME.
COME ON, JACKIE, YOU'RE A KILLER. I LOVE YOU, BUT YOU'RE A KILLER.
YOU CAN'T TELL ME YOU DON'T LIKE IT. THAT IT DOESN'T MAKE YOU FEEL GOOD.
I NEVER KILLED SOMEONE FOR NO DAMN REASON.
NO, YOU KILLED PEOPLE BECAUSE SOMEONE ELSE TOLD YOU TO. WHY DOES THAT MAKE IT OKAY?
ALL I KNOW IS, I SAW TOO MANY GUYS LIKE THAT TODAY.
THEN WE'LL GET RID OF THEM. WE'LL LEARN TO MOLD THINGS HOW WE WANT THEM.
THE WORLD'S A CESSPOOL, JACKIE. PEOPLE ARE DYING AND SUFFERING, AND NO ONE'S DOING ANYTHING ABOUT IT.
IT'S OUR TURN TO MAKE THE DECISIONS.
YOU'RE BEAUTIFUL.

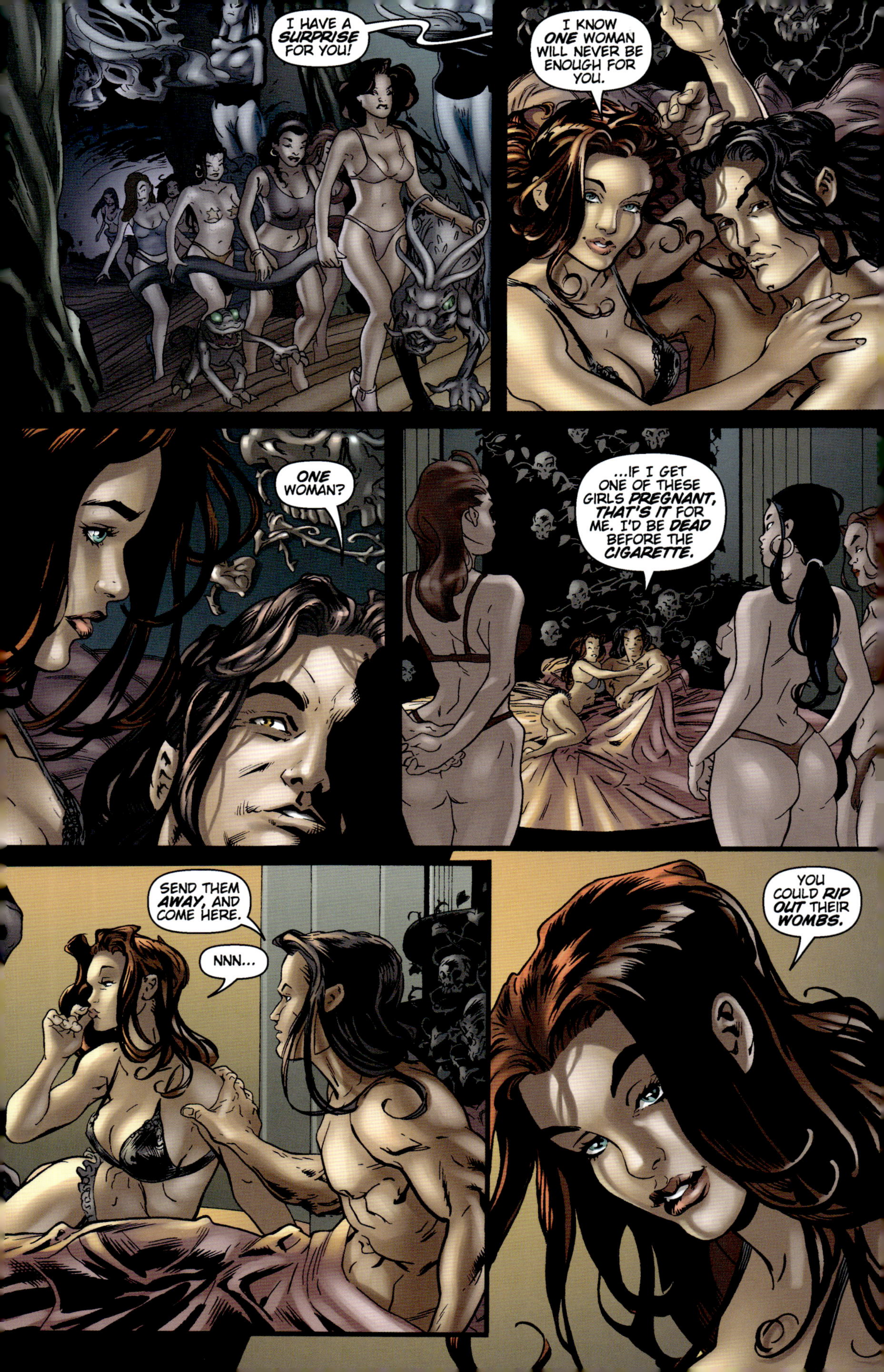
I HAVE A SURPRISE FOR YOU!
I KNOW ONE WOMAN WILL NEVER BE ENOUGH FOR YOU.
ONE WOMAN?
...IF I GET ONE OF THESE GIRLS PREGNANT, THAT'S IT FOR ME. I'D BE DEAD BEFORE THE CIGARETTE.
SEND THEM AWAY, AND COME HERE.
NNN...
YOU COULD RIP OUT THEIR WOMBS.

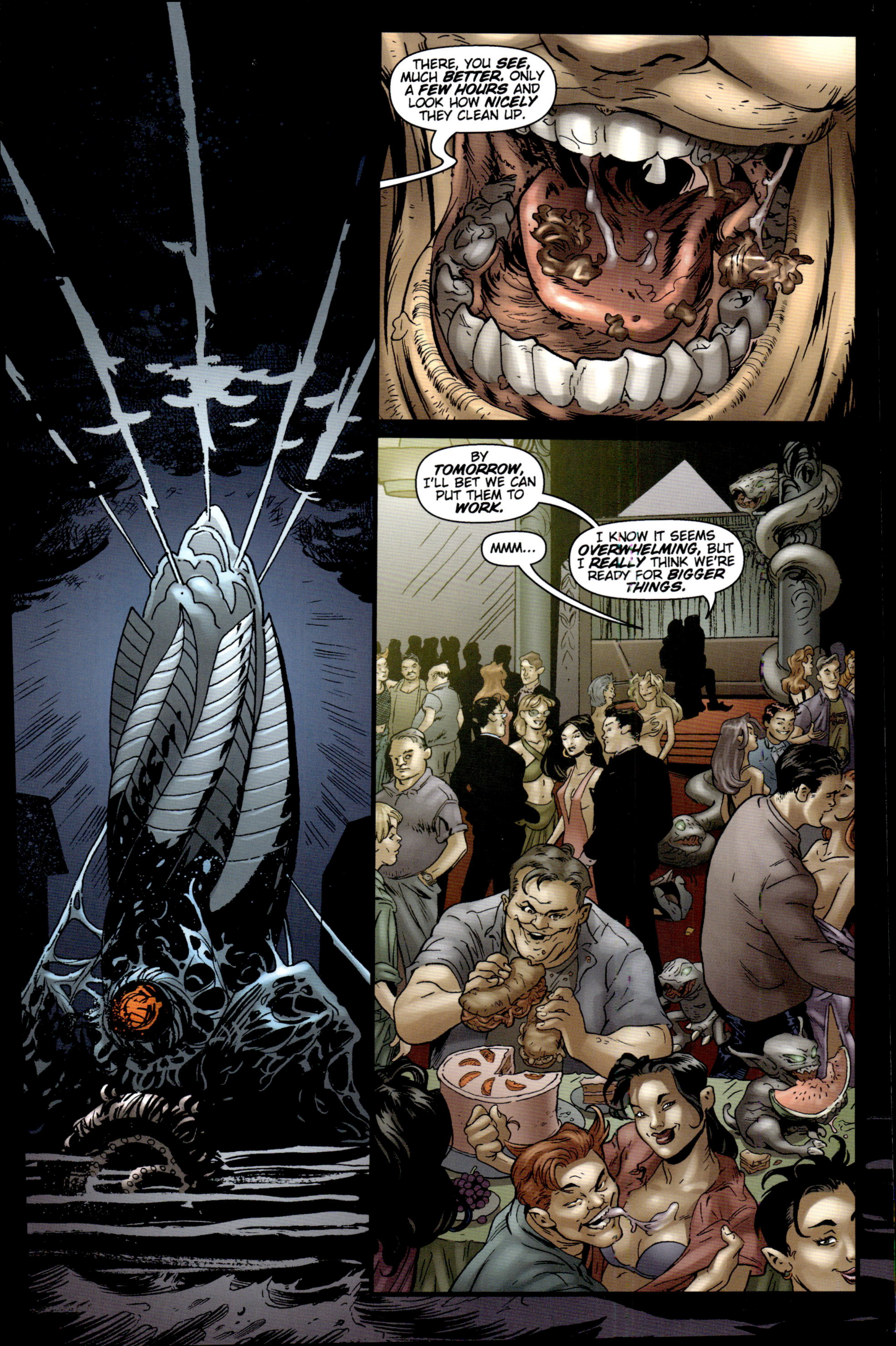
THERE, YOU SEE, MUCH BETTER. ONLY A FEW HOURS AND LOOK HOW NICELY THEY CLEAN UP.
BY TOMORROW, I'LL BET WE CAN PUT THEM TO WORK.
MMM...
I KNOW IT SEEMS OVERWHELMING, BUT I REALLY THINK WE'RE READY FOR BIGGER THINGS.

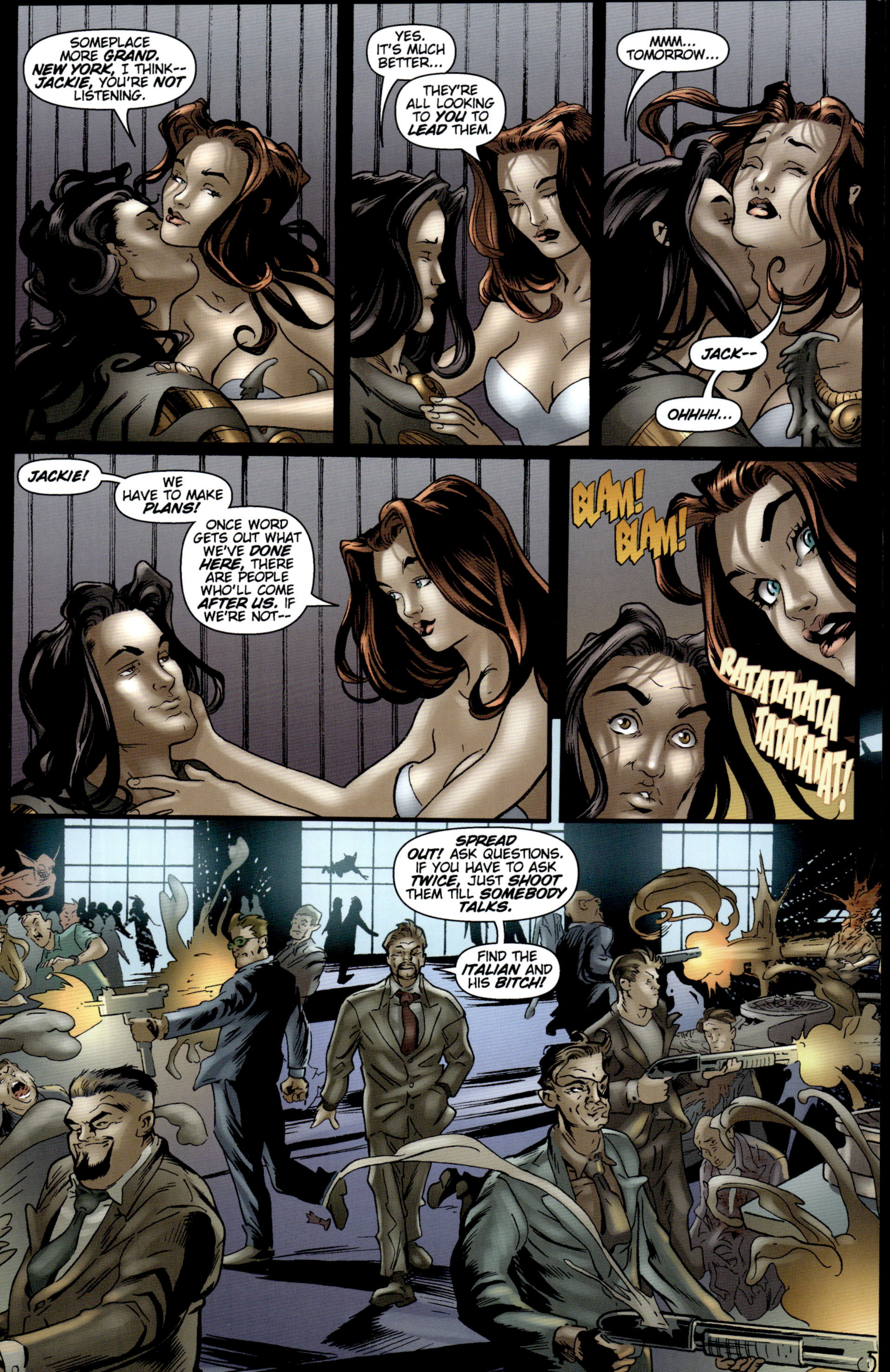
SOMEPLACE MORE GRAND. NEW YORK, I THINK-- JACKIE, YOU'RE NOT LISTENING.
YES. IT'S MUCH BETTER...
THEY'RE ALL LOOKING TO YOU TO LEAD THEM.
MMM... TOMORROW...
JACK--
OHHHH...
JACKIE!
WE HAVE TO MAKE PLANS!
ONCE WORD GETS OUT WHAT WE'VE DONE HERE, THERE ARE PEOPLE WHO'LL COME AFTER US. IF WE'RE NOT--
BLAM! BLAM!
BATATATATA TATATATAT!
SPREAD OUT! ASK QUESTIONS. IF YOU HAVE TO ASK TWICE, JUST SHOOT THEM TILL SOMEBODY TALKS.
FIND THE ITALIAN AND HIS BITCH!

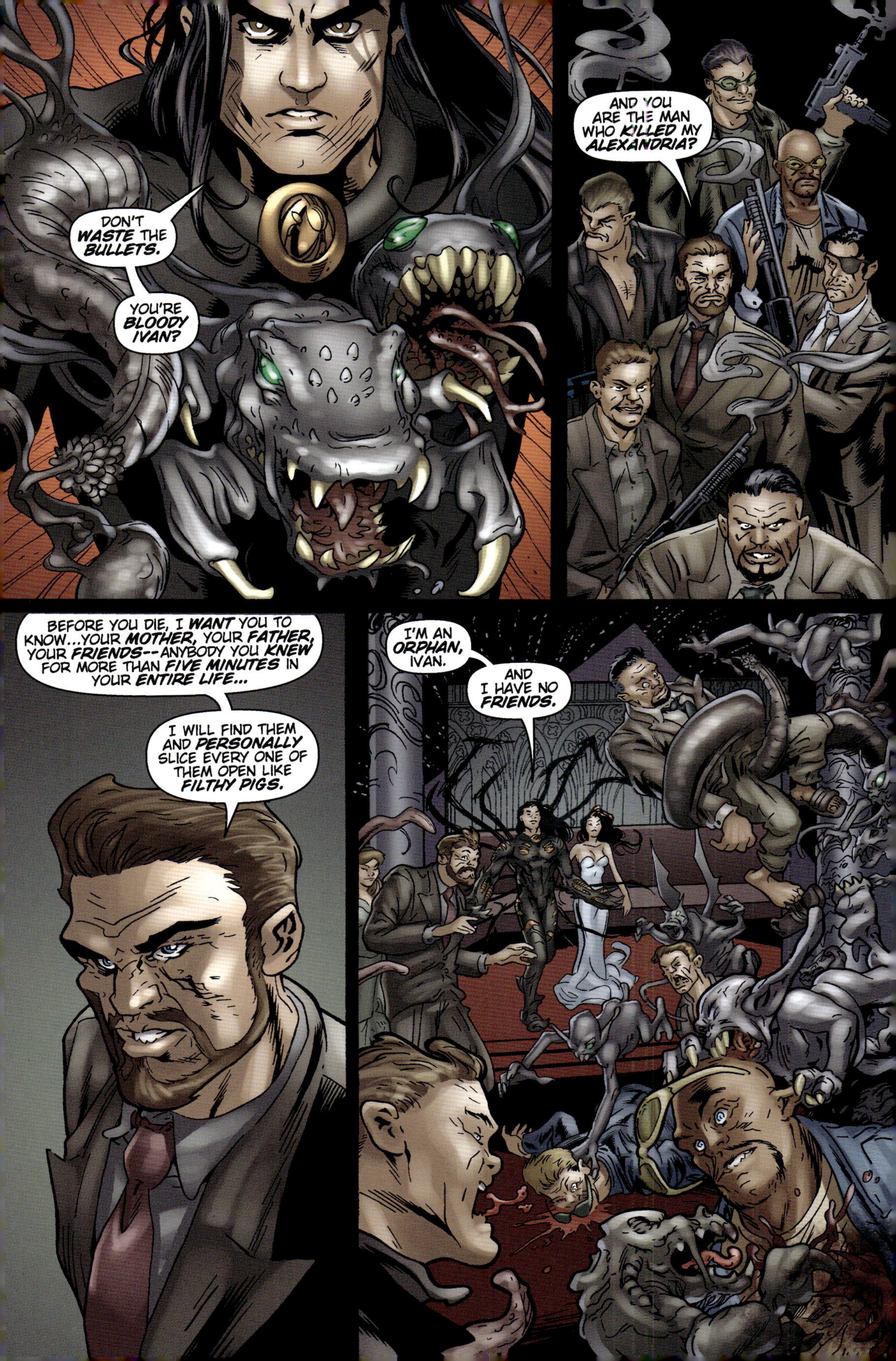
DON'T WASTE THE BULLETS.
YOU'RE BLOODY IVAN?
AND YOU ARE THE MAN WHO KILLED MY ALEXANDRIA?
BEFORE YOU DIE, I WANT YOU TO KNOW...YOUR MOTHER, YOUR FATHER, YOUR FRIENDS--ANYBODY YOU KNEW FOR MORE THAN FIVE MINUTES IN YOUR ENTIRE LIFE...
I WILL FIND THEM AND PERSONALLY SLICE EVERY ONE OF THEM OPEN LIKE FILTHY PIGS.
I'M AN ORPHAN, IVAN.
AND I HAVE NO FRIENDS.

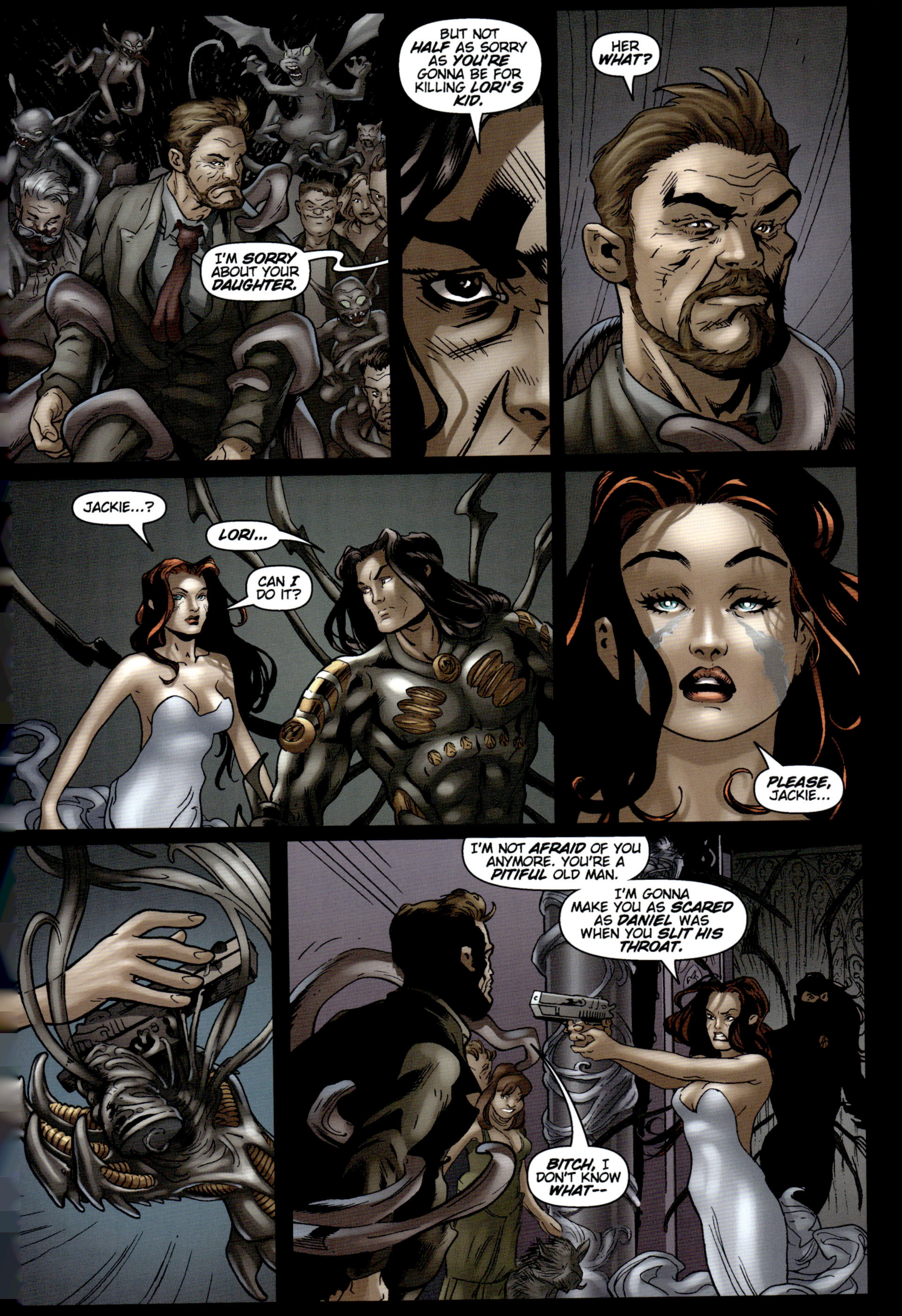
I'M SORRY ABOUT YOUR DAUGHTER.
BUT NOT HALF AS SORRY AS YOU'RE GONNA BE FOR KILLING LORI'S KID.
HER WHAT?
JACKIE...?
LORI...
CAN I DO IT?
PLEASE, JACKIE...
I'M NOT AFRAID OF YOU ANYMORE. YOU'RE A PITIFUL OLD MAN.
I'M GONNA MAKE YOU AS SCARED AS DANIEL WAS WHEN YOU SLIT HIS THROAT.
BITCH, I DON'T KNOW WHAT--

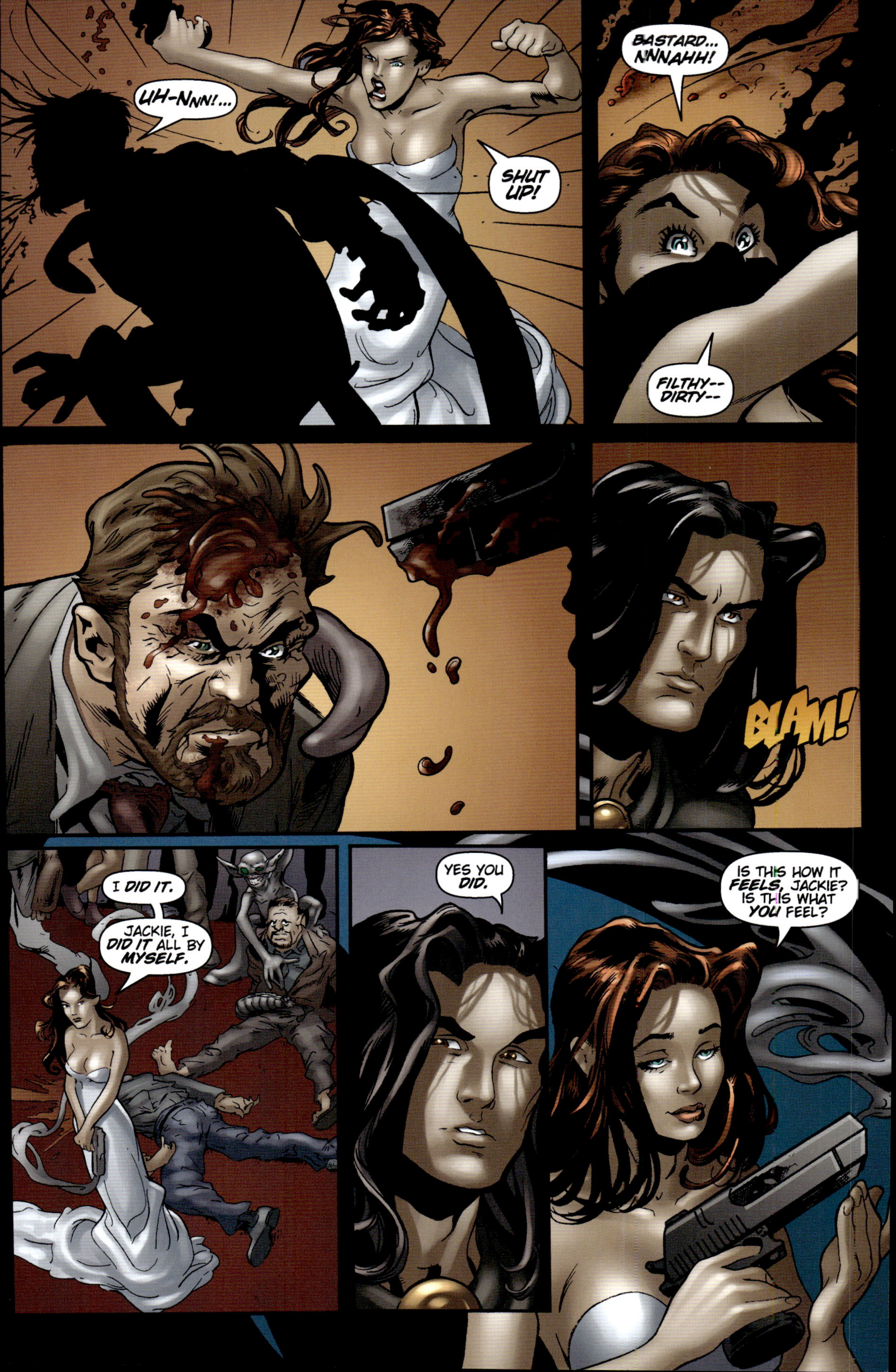
UH-NNN!...
SHUT UP!
BASTARD... NNNAHH!
FILTHY-- DIRTY--
BLAM!
I DID IT.
JACKIE, I DID IT ALL BY MYSELF.
YES YOU DID.
IS THIS HOW IT FEELS, JACKIE? IS THIS WHAT YOU FEEL?

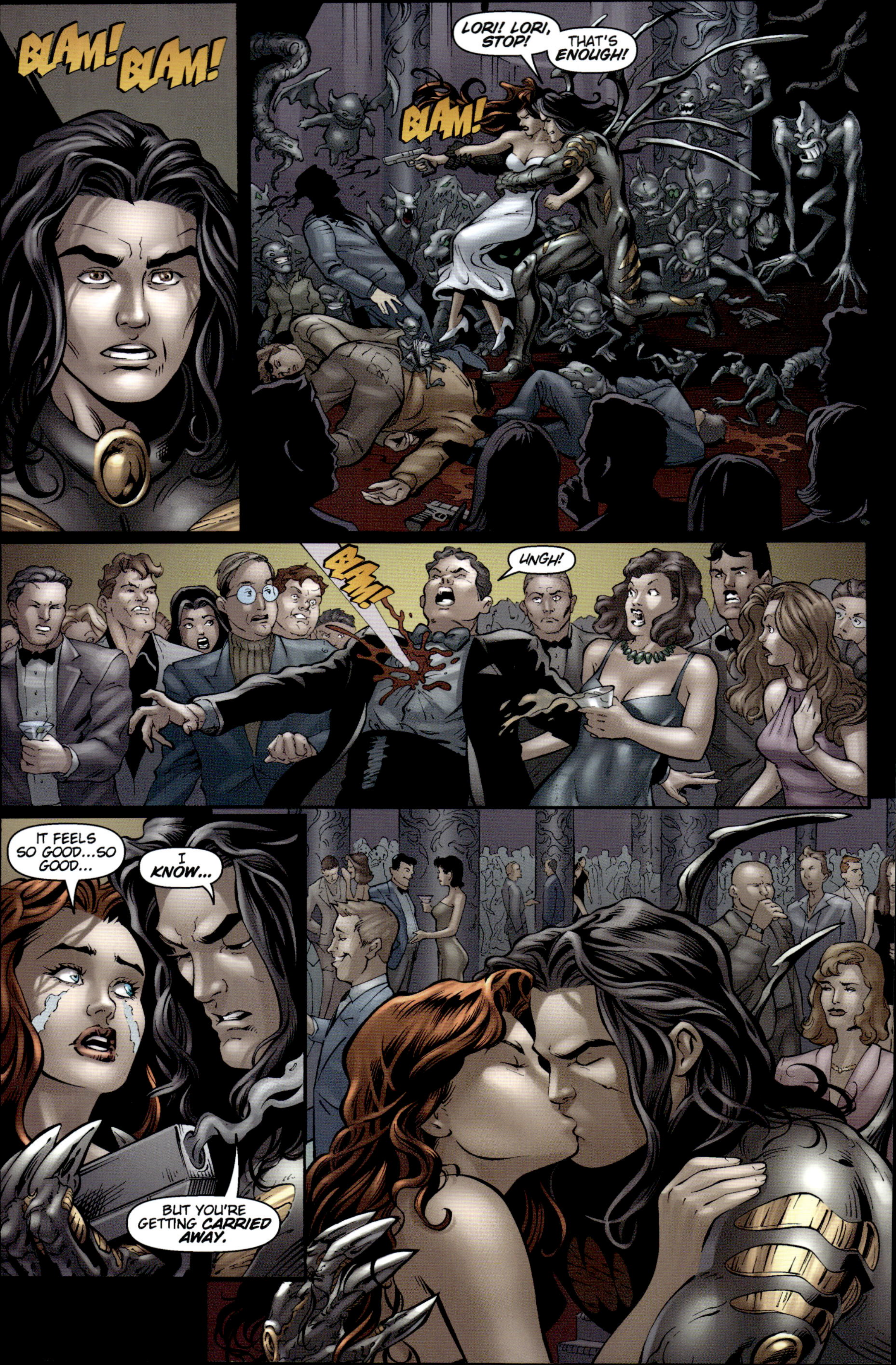
BLAM! BLAM!
LORI! LORI, STOP!
THAT'S ENOUGH!
BLAM!
BLAM!
UNGH!
IT FEELS SO GOOD...SO GOOD...
I KNOW...
BUT YOU'RE GETTING CARRIED AWAY.

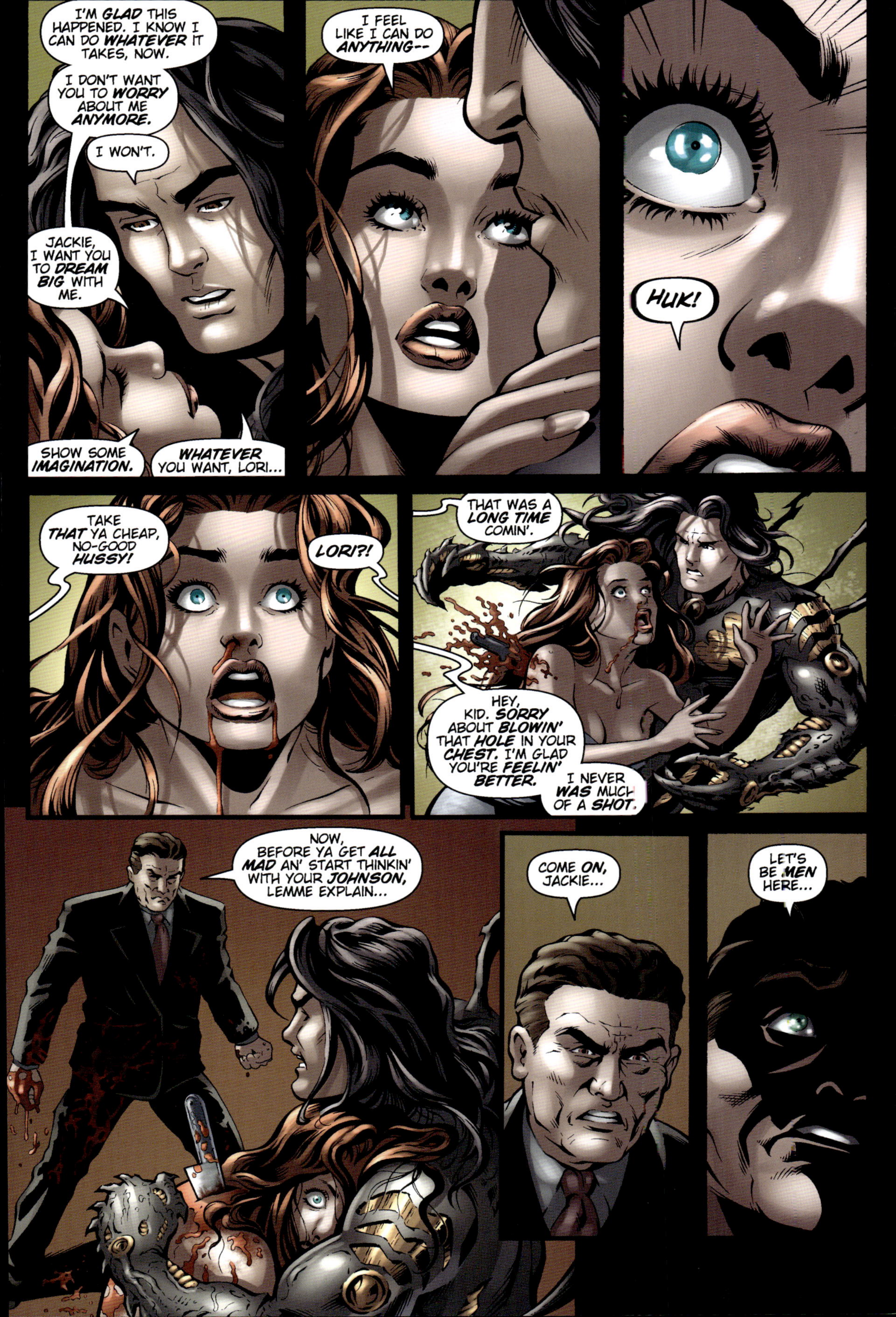
I'M GLAD THIS HAPPENED. I KNOW I CAN DO WHATEVER IT TAKES, NOW.
I DON'T WANT YOU TO WORRY ABOUT ME ANYMORE.
I WON'T.
JACKIE, I WANT YOU TO DREAM BIG WITH ME.
SHOW SOME IMAGINATION.
WHATEVER YOU WANT, LORI...
I FEEL LIKE I CAN DO ANYTHING--
HUK!
TAKE THAT YA CHEAP, NO-GOOD HUSSY!
LORI?!
THAT WAS A LONG TIME COMIN'.
HEY, KID. SORRY ABOUT BLOWIN' THAT HOLE IN YOUR CHEST. I'M GLAD YOU'RE FEELIN' BETTER.
I NEVER WAS MUCH OF A SHOT.
NOW, BEFORE YA GET ALL MAD AN' START THINKIN' WITH YOUR JOHNSON, LEMME EXPLAIN...
COME ON, JACKIE...
LET'S BE MEN HERE...

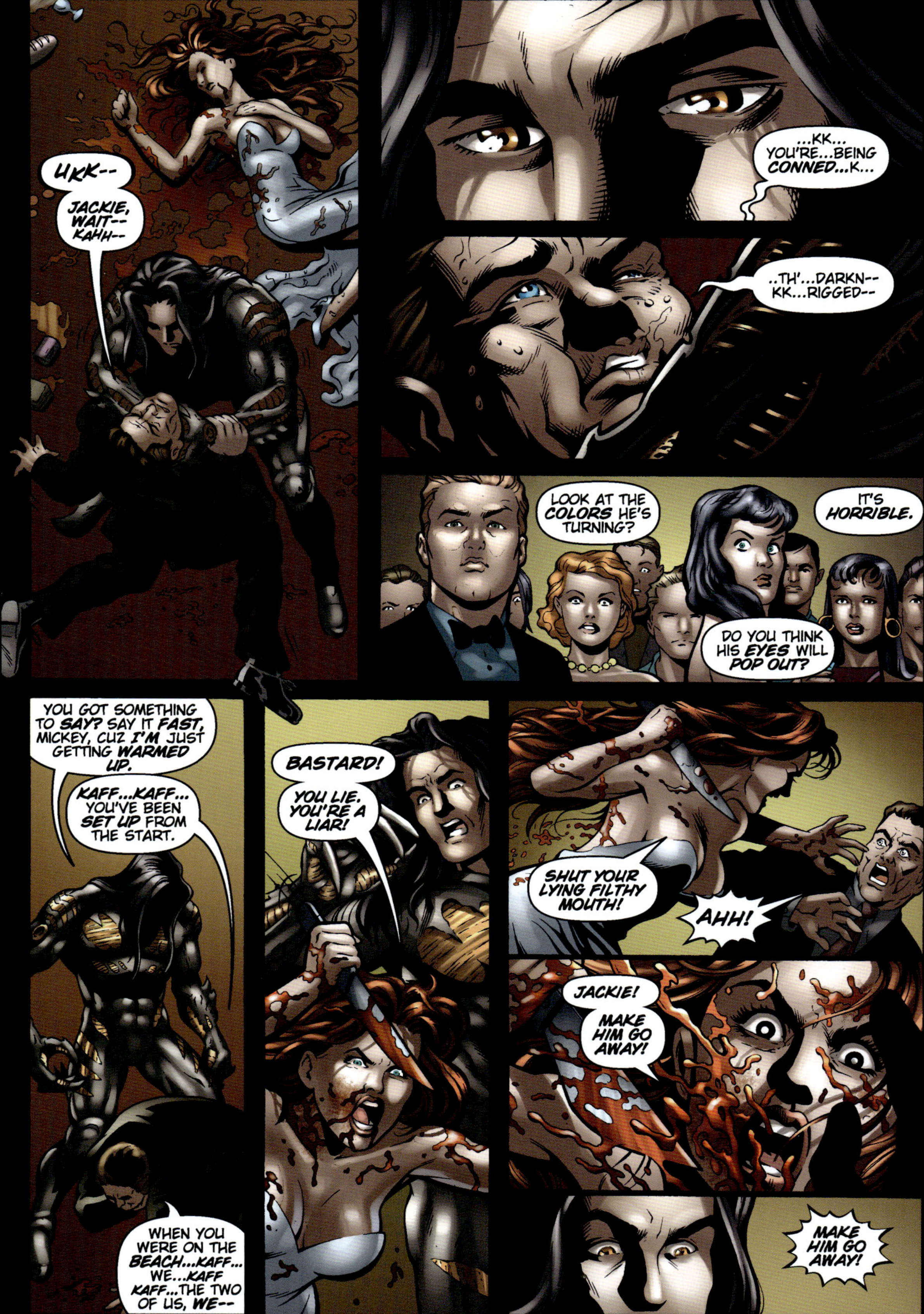
UKK--
JACKIE, WAIT-- KAHH--
...KK... YOU'RE...BEING CONNED...K...
..TH'...DARKN-- KK...RIGGED--
LOOK AT THE COLORS HE'S TURNING?
IT'S HORRIBLE.
DO YOU THINK HIS EYES WILL POP OUT?
YOU GOT SOMETHING TO SAY? SAY IT FAST, MICKEY, CUZ I'M JUST GETTING WARMED UP.
KAFF...KAFF... YOU'VE BEEN SET UP FROM THE START.
WHEN YOU WERE ON THE BEACH...KAFF... WE...KAFF KAFF...THE TWO OF US, WE--
BASTARD!
YOU LIE. YOU'RE A LIAR!
SHUT YOUR LYING FILTHY MOUTH!
AHH!
JACKIE!
MAKE HIM GO AWAY!
MAKE HIM GO AWAY!

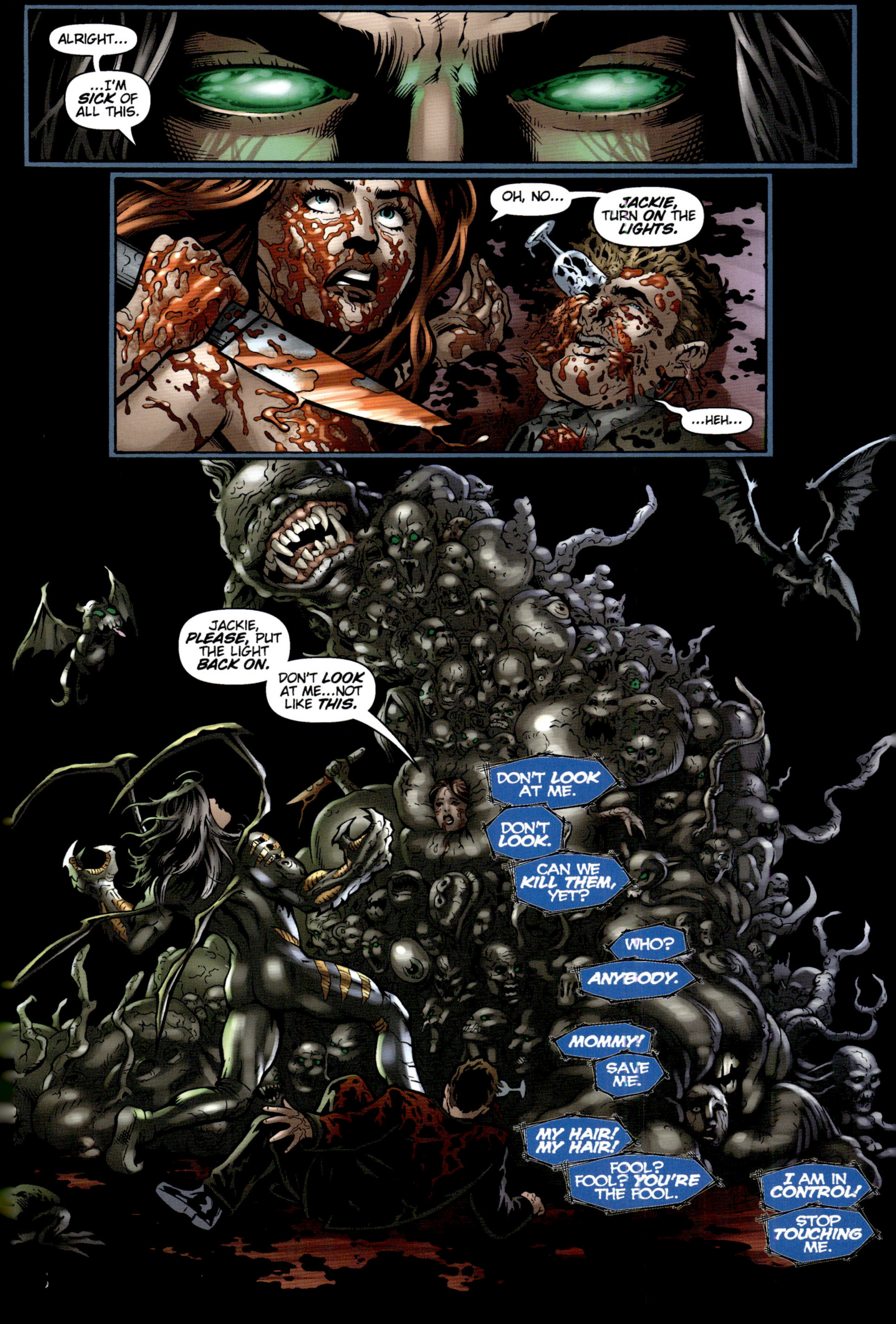
ALRIGHT...
...I'M SICK OF ALL THIS.
OH, NO...
JACKIE, TURN ON THE LIGHTS.
...HEH...
JACKIE, PLEASE, PUT THE LIGHT BACK ON.
DON'T LOOK AT ME...NOT LIKE THIS.
DON'T LOOK AT ME.
DON'T LOOK.
CAN WE KILL THEM, YET?
WHO?
ANYBODY.
MOMMY!
SAVE ME.
MY HAIR! MY HAIR!
FOOL? FOOL? YOU'RE THE FOOL.
I AM IN CONTROL!
STOP TOUCHING ME.

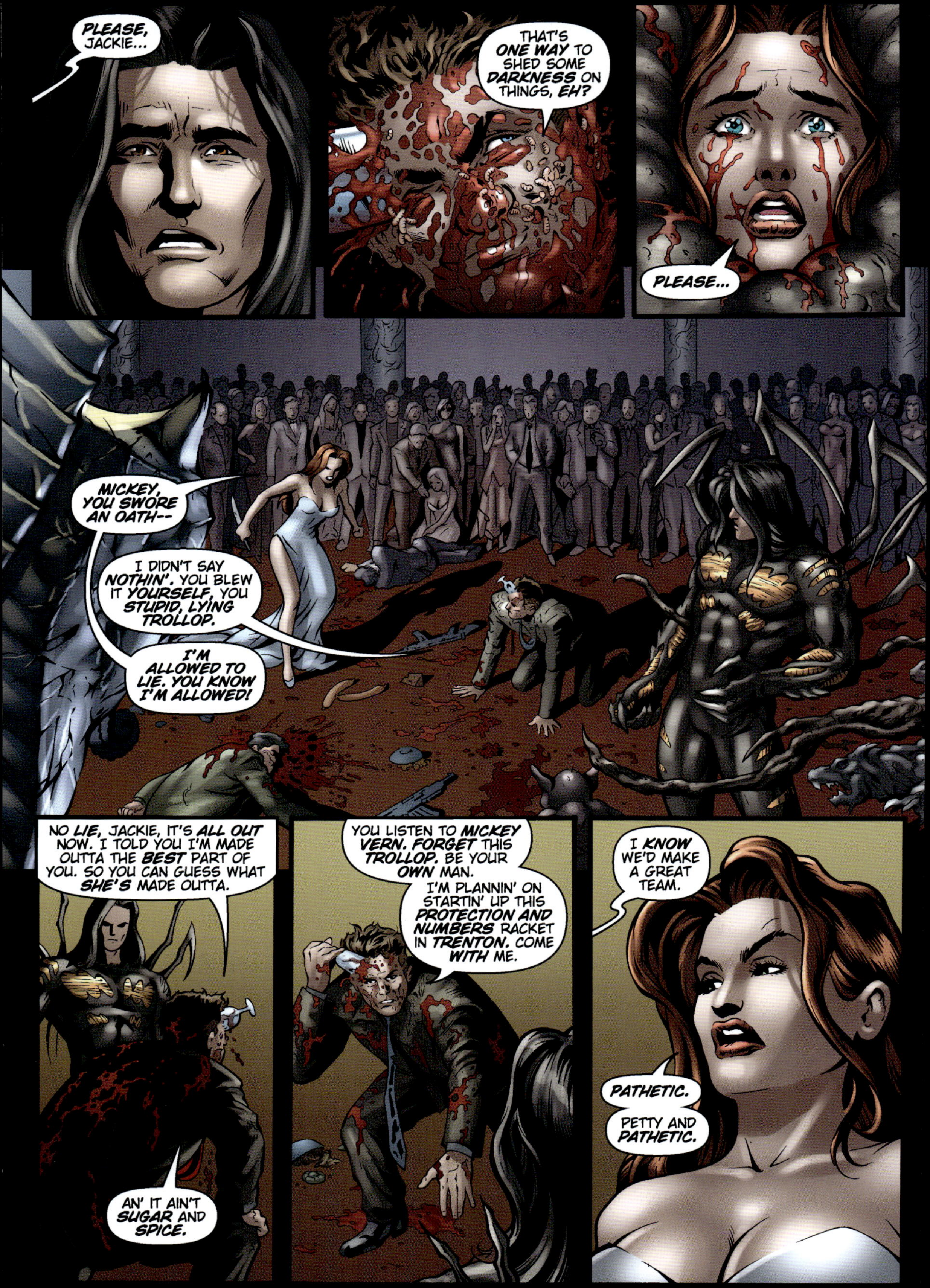
PLEASE, JACKIE...
THAT'S ONE WAY TO SHED SOME DARKNESS ON THINGS, EH?
PLEASE...
MICKEY, YOU SWORE AN OATH--
I DIDN'T SAY NOTHIN'. YOU BLEW IT YOURSELF, YOU STUPID, LYING TROLLOP.
I'M ALLOWED TO LIE. YOU KNOW I'M ALLOWED!
NO LIE, JACKIE, IT'S ALL OUT NOW. I TOLD YOU I'M MADE OUTTA THE BEST PART OF YOU. SO YOU CAN GUESS WHAT SHE'S MADE OUTTA.
AN' IT AIN'T SUGAR AND SPICE.
YOU LISTEN TO MICKEY VERN. FORGET THIS TROLLOP. BE YOUR OWN MAN.
I'M PLANNIN' ON STARTIN' UP THIS PROTECTION AND NUMBERS RACKET IN TRENTON. COME WITH ME.
I KNOW WE'D MAKE A GREAT TEAM.
PATHETIC.
PETTY AND PATHETIC.

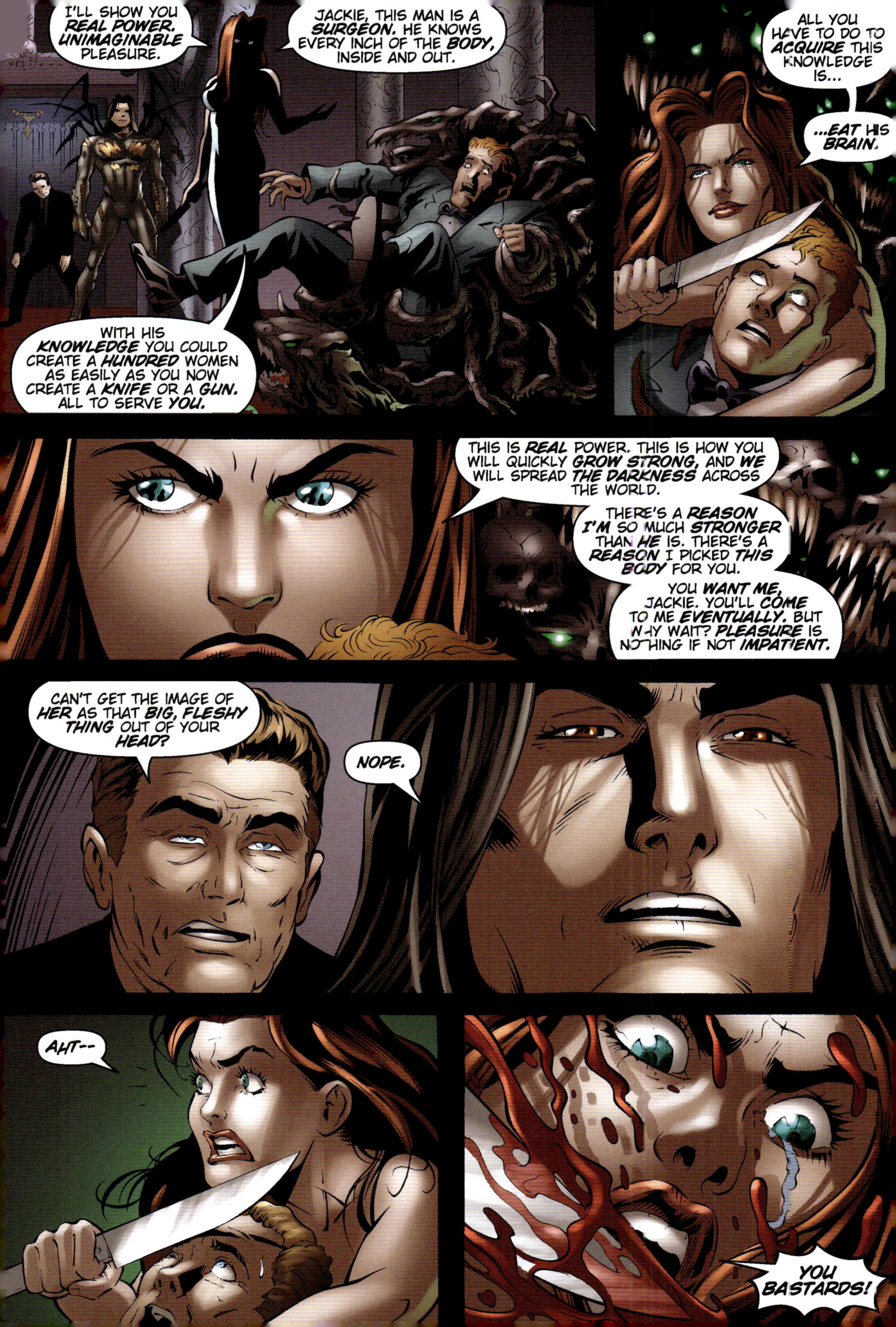

I'LL SHOW YOU REAL POWER. UNIMAGINABLE PLEASURE.
JACKIE, THIS MAN IS A SURGEON. HE KNOWS EVERY INCH OF THE BODY, INSIDE AND OUT.
WITH HIS KNOWLEDGE YOU COULD CREATE A HUNDRED WOMEN AS EASILY AS YOU NOW CREATE A KNIFE OR A GUN. ALL TO SERVE YOU.
ALL YOU HAVE TO DO TO ACQUIRE THIS KNOWLEDGE IS...
...EAT HIS BRAIN.
THIS IS REAL POWER. THIS IS HOW YOU WILL QUICKLY GROW STRONG, AND WE WILL SPREAD THE DARKNESS ACROSS THE WORLD.
THERE'S A REASON I'M SO MUCH STRONGER THAN HE IS. THERE'S A REASON I PICKED THIS BODY FOR YOU.
YOU WANT ME, JACKIE. YOU'LL COME TO ME EVENTUALLY. BUT WHY WAIT? PLEASURE IS NOTHING IF NOT IMPATIENT.
CAN'T GET THE IMAGE OF HER AS THAT BIG, FLESHY THING OUT OF YOUR HEAD?
NOPE.
AHT--
YOU BASTARDS!

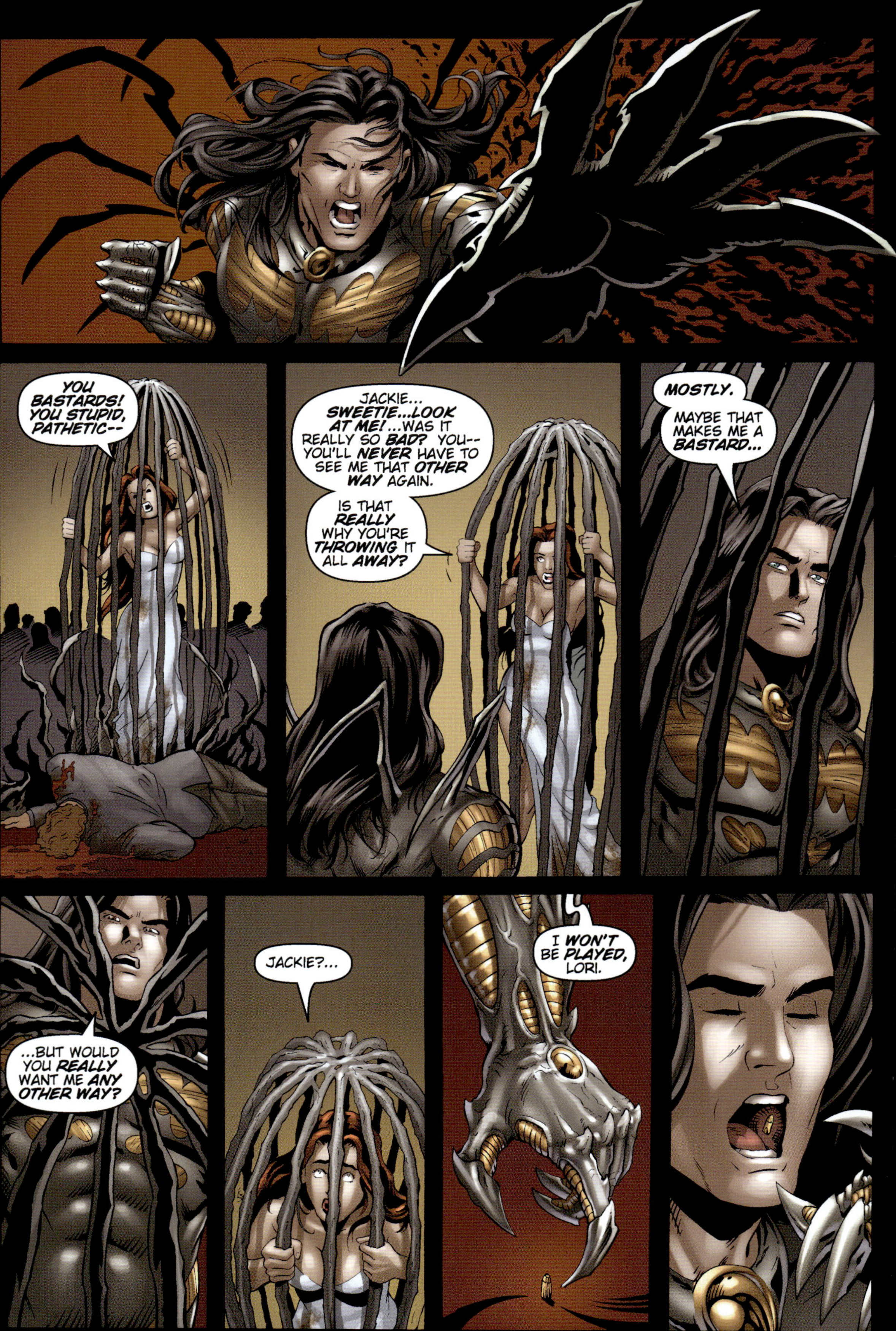
YOU BASTARDS! YOU STUPID, PATHETIC--
JACKIE... SWEETIE...LOOK AT ME! ...WAS IT REALLY SO BAD? YOU-- YOU'LL NEVER HAVE TO SEE ME THAT OTHER WAY AGAIN.
IS THAT REALLY WHY YOU'RE THROWING IT ALL AWAY?
MOSTLY.
MAYBE THAT MAKES ME A BASTARD...
...BUT WOULD YOU REALLY WANT ME ANY OTHER WAY?
JACKIE?...
I WON'T BE PLAYED, LORI.

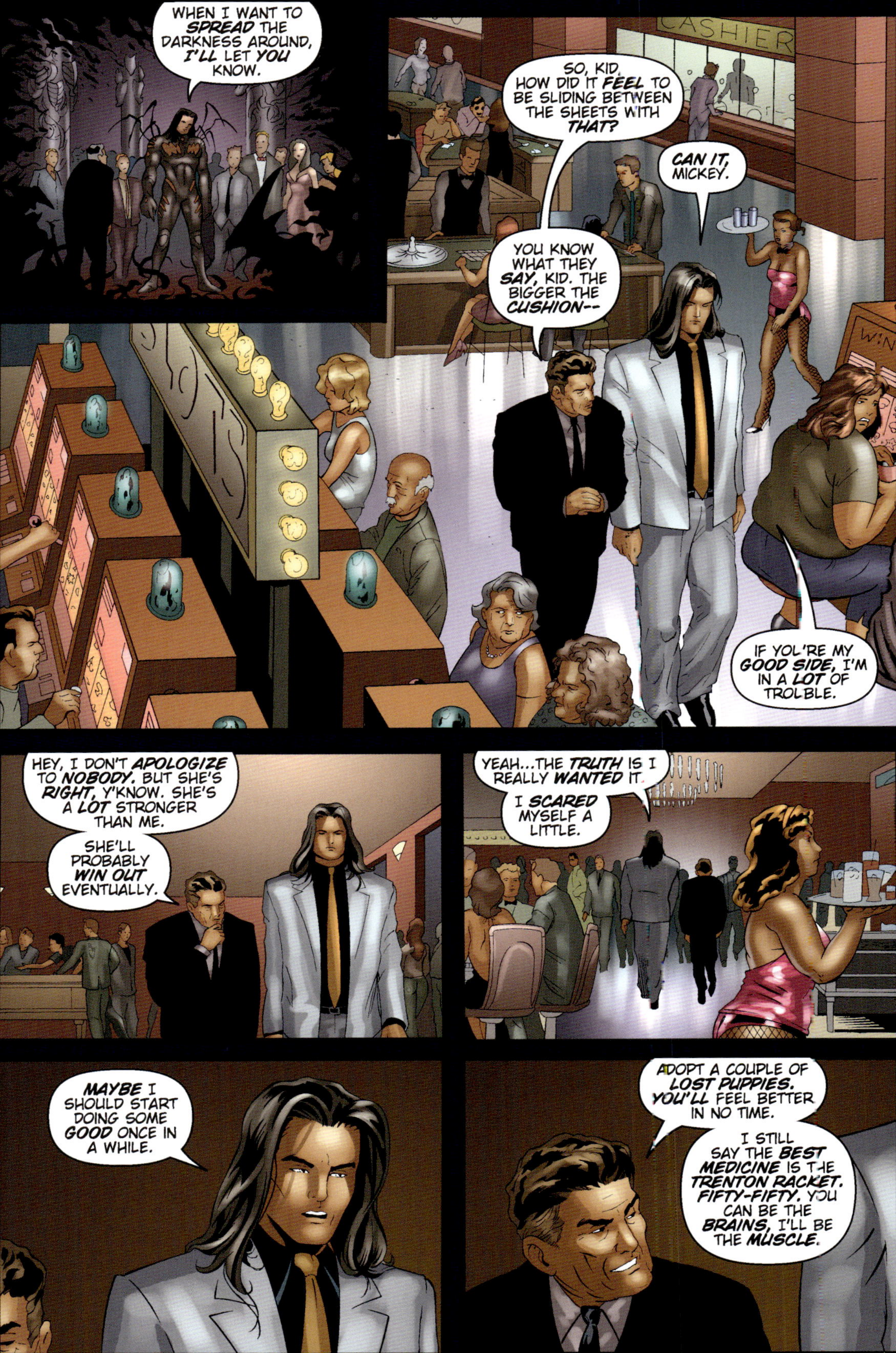

WHEN I WANT TO SPREAD THE DARKNESS AROUND, I'LL LET YOU KNOW.
SO, KID, HOW DID IT FEEL TO BE SLIDING BETWEEN THE SHEETS WITH THAT?
CAN IT, MICKEY.
YOU KNOW WHAT THEY SAY, KID. THE BIGGER THE CUSHION--
IF YOL'RE MY GOOD SIDE, I'M IN A LOT OF TROLBLE.
HEY, I DON'T APOLOGIZE TO NOBODY. BUT SHE'S RIGHT, Y'KNOW. SHE'S A LOT STRONGER THAN ME.
SHE'LL PROBABLY WIN OUT EVENTUALLY.
YEAH...THE TRUTH IS I REALLY WANTED IT.
I SCARED MYSELF A LITTLE.
MAYBE I SHOULD START DOING SOME GOOD ONCE IN A WHILE.
ADOPT A COUPLE OF LOST PUPPIES. YOU'LL FEEL BETTER IN NO TIME.
I STILL SAY THE BEST MEDICINE IS THE TRENTON RACKET. FIFTY-FIFTY. YOU CAN BE THE BRAINS, I'LL BE THE MUSCLE.

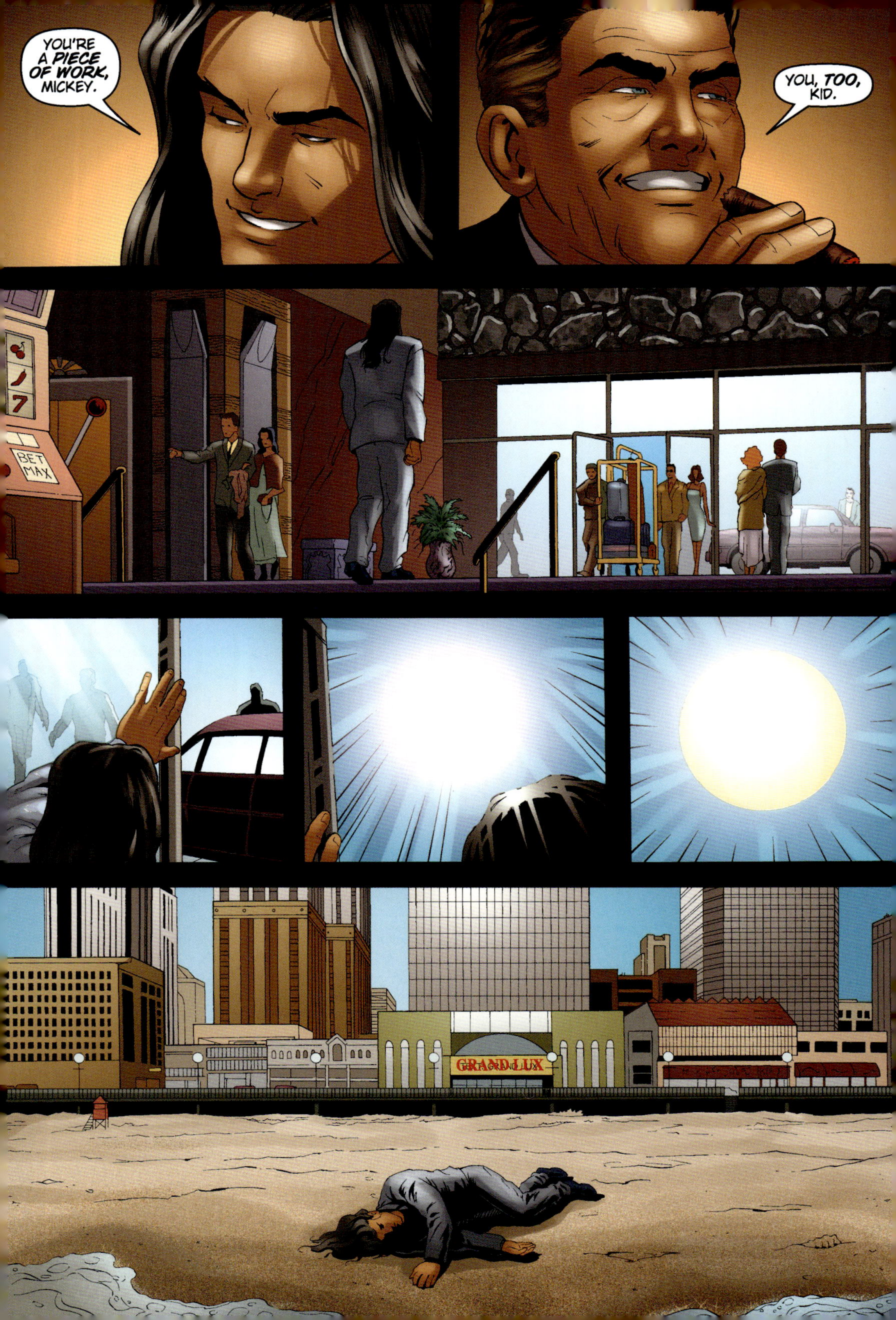
YOU'RE A PIECE OF WORK, MICKEY.
YOU, TOO, KID.
BET MAX
GRAND LUX

The Darkness Issue #61

cover art by: Dale Keown & Matt Milla

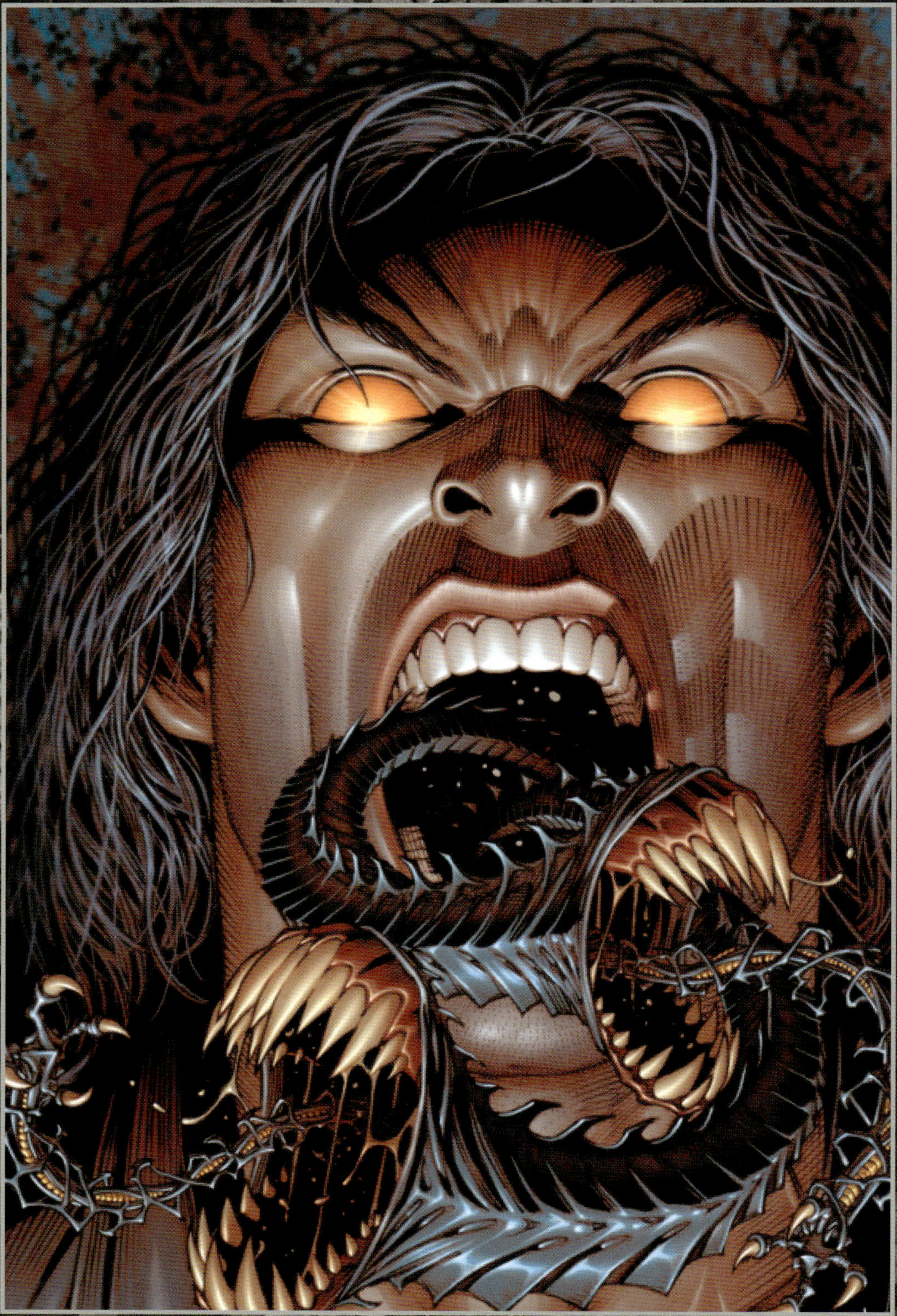

THE DARKNESS #61

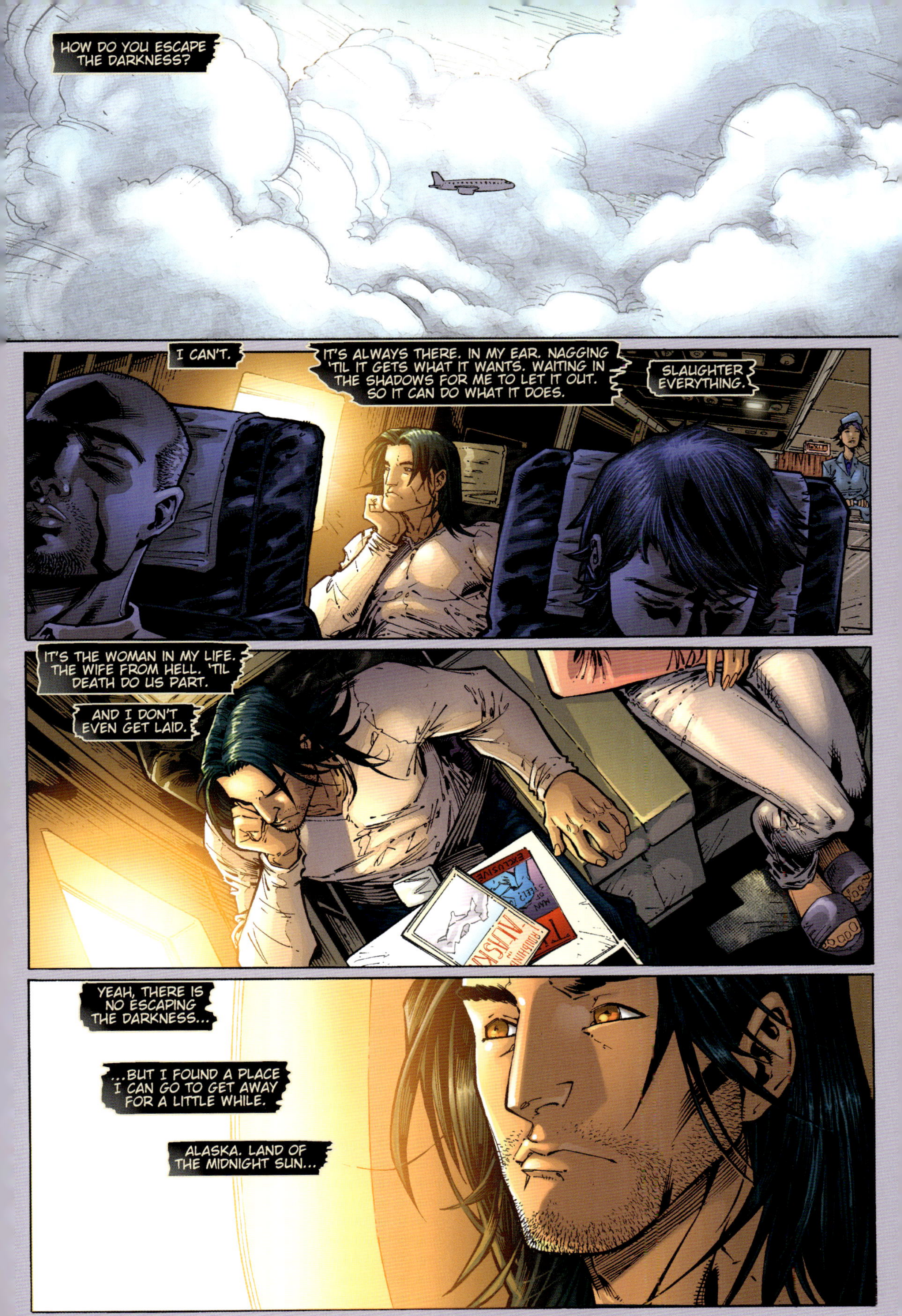
HOW DO YOU ESCAPE THE DARKNESS?
I CAN'T.
IT'S ALWAYS THERE. IN MY EAR. NAGGING 'TIL IT GETS WHAT IT WANTS. WAITING IN THE SHADOWS FOR ME TO LET IT OUT. SO IT CAN DO WHAT IT DOES.
SLAUGHTER EVERYTHING.
IT'S THE WOMAN IN MY LIFE. THE WIFE FROM HELL. 'TIL DEATH DO US PART.
AND I DON'T EVEN GET LAID.
EXCLUSIVE
ALASKA
YEAH, THERE IS NO ESCAPING THE DARKNESS...
...BUT I FOUND A PLACE I CAN GO TO GET AWAY FOR A LITTLE WHILE.
ALASKA. LAND OF THE MIDNIGHT SUN...

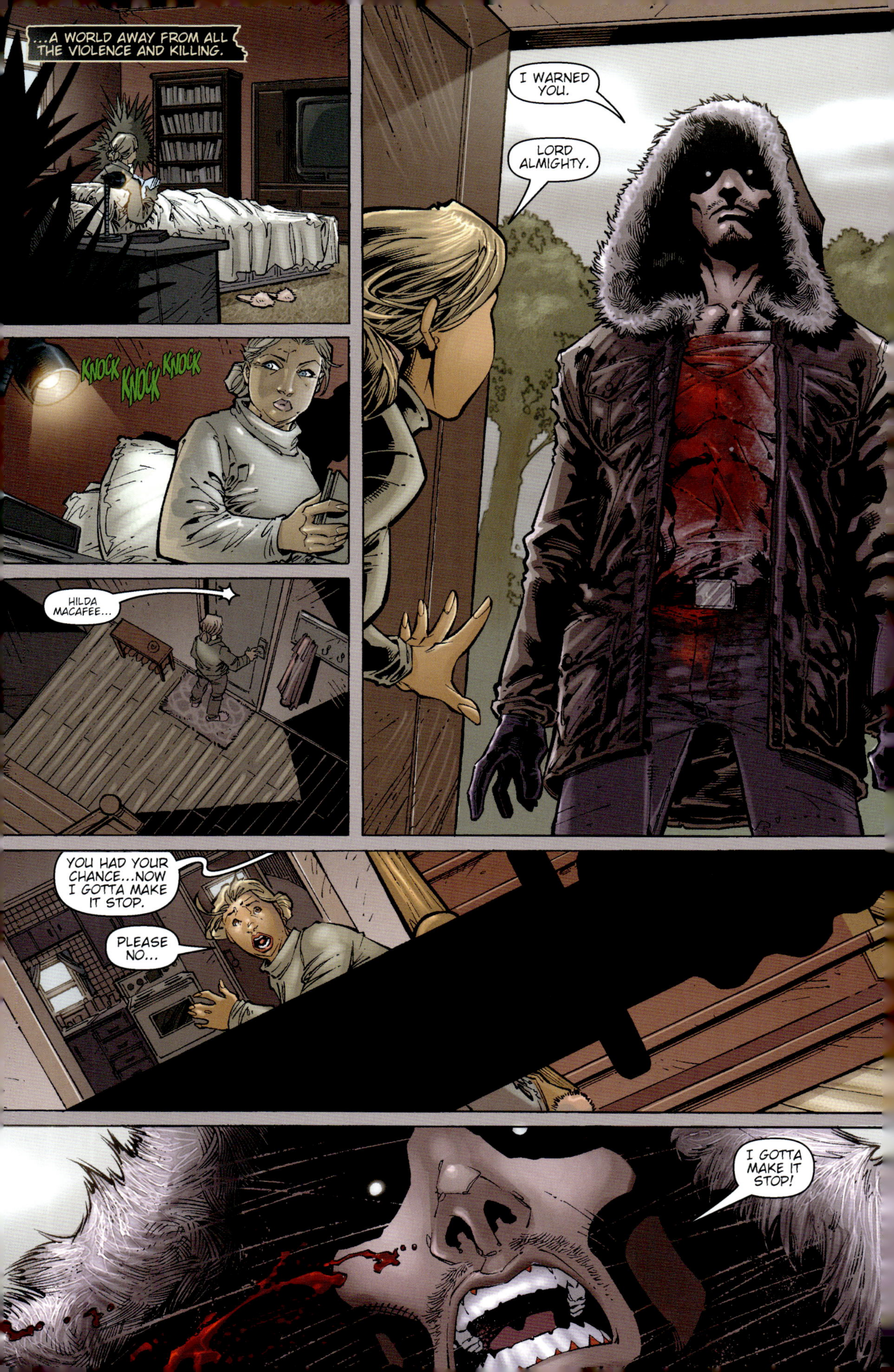
...A WORLD AWAY FROM ALL THE VIOLENCE AND KILLING.
KNOCK KNOCK KNOCK
HILDA MACAFEE...
I WARNED YOU.
LORD ALMIGHTY.
YOU HAD YOUR CHANCE...NOW I GOTTA MAKE IT STOP.
PLEASE NO...
I GOTTA MAKE IT STOP!

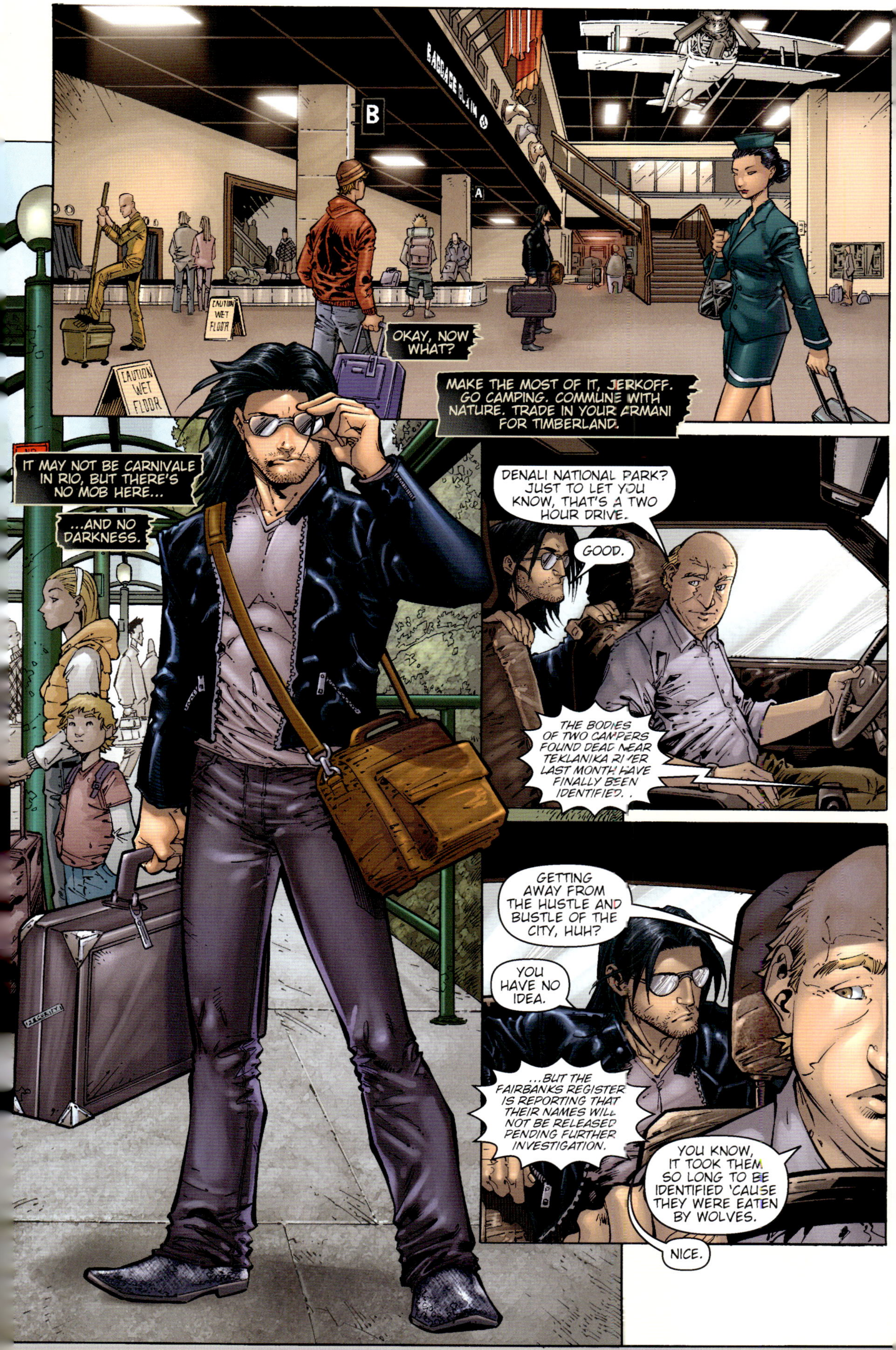
BAGGAGE CLAIM
B
A
CAUTION WET FLOOR
CAUTION WET FLOOR
OKAY, NOW WHAT?
MAKE THE MOST OF IT, JERKOFF. GO CAMPING. COMMUNE WITH NATURE. TRADE IN YOUR ARMANI FOR TIMBERLAND.
IT MAY NOT BE CARNIVALE IN RIO, BUT THERE'S NO MOB HERE...
...AND NO DARKNESS.
DENALI NATIONAL PARK? JUST TO LET YOU KNOW, THAT'S A TWO HOUR DRIVE.
GOOD.
THE BODIES OF TWO CAMPERS FOUND DEAD NEAR TEKLANIKA RIVER LAST MONTH HAVE FINALLY BEEN IDENTIFIED. .
GETTING AWAY FROM THE HUSTLE AND BUSTLE OF THE CITY, HUH?
YOU HAVE NO IDEA.
...BUT THE FAIRBANKS REGISTER IS REPORTING THAT THEIR NAMES WILL NOT BE RELEASED PENDING FURTHER INVESTIGATION.
YOU KNOW, IT TOOK THEM SO LONG TO BE IDENTIFIED 'CAUSE THEY WERE EATEN BY WOLVES.
NICE.

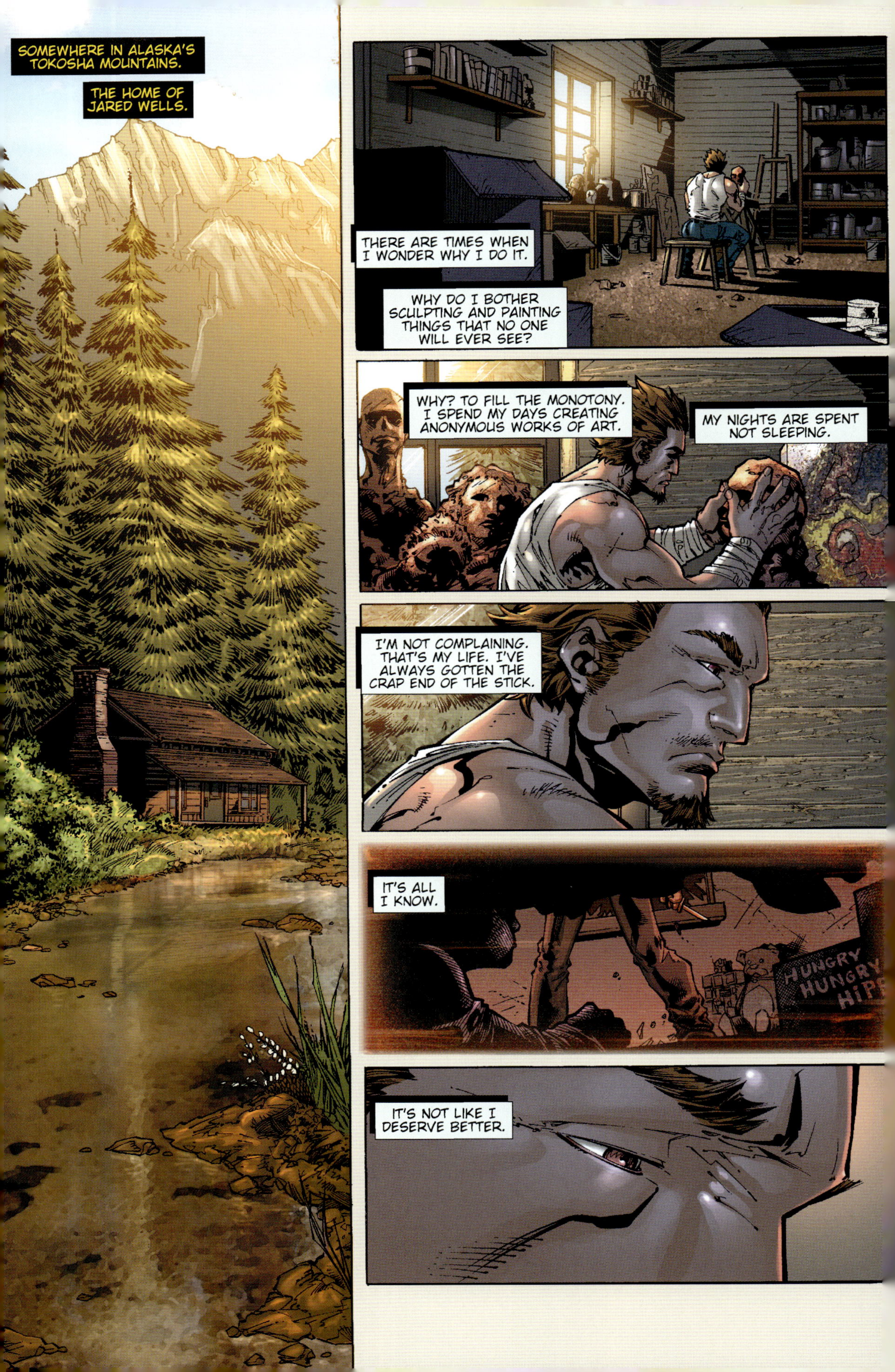
SOMEWHERE IN ALASKA'S TOKOSHA MOUNTAINS.
THE HOME OF JARED WELLS.
THERE ARE TIMES WHEN I WONDER WHY I DO IT.
WHY DO I BOTHER SCULPTING AND PAINTING THINGS THAT NO ONE WILL EVER SEE?
WHY? TO FILL THE MONOTONY. I SPEND MY DAYS CREATING ANONYMOUS WORKS OF ART.
MY NIGHTS ARE SPENT NOT SLEEPING.
I'M NOT COMPLAINING. THAT'S MY LIFE. I'VE ALWAYS GOTTEN THE CRAP END OF THE STICK.
IT'S ALL I KNOW.
HUNGRY HUNGRY HIPP
IT'S NOT LIKE I DESERVE BETTER.

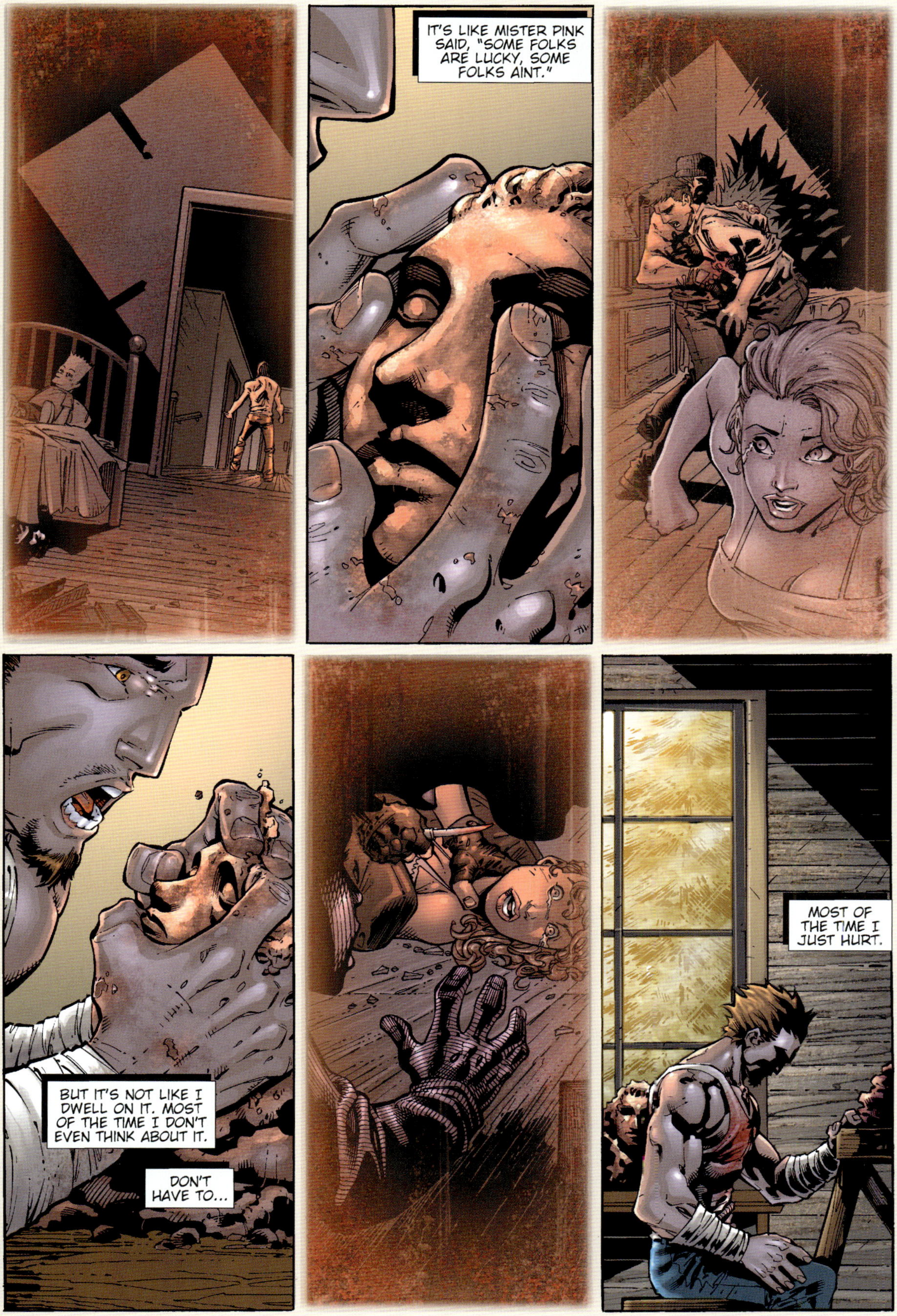
IT'S LIKE MISTER PINK SAID, "SOME FOLKS ARE LUCKY, SOME FOLKS AINT."
BUT IT'S NOT LIKE I DWELL ON IT. MOST OF THE TIME I DON'T EVEN THINK ABOUT IT.
DON'T HAVE TO...
MOST OF THE TIME I JUST HURT.

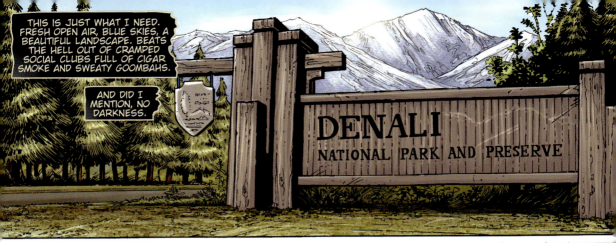

THIS IS JUST WHAT I NEED. FRESH OPEN AIR, BLUE SKIES, A BEAUTIFUL LANDSCAPE. BEATS THE HELL OUT OF CRAMPED SOCIAL CLUBS FULL OF CIGAR SMOKE AND SWEATY GOOMBAHS.

AND DID I MENTION, NO DARKNESS.

DENALI
NATIONAL PARK AND PRESERVE

ALL I GOTTA DO IS SET UP CAMP. GIMME TEN MINUTES TO PITCH MY TENT, AND WE'RE IN BUSINESS.

58 MINUTES LATER...

IT CAN'T BE THIS HARD. IT JUST CAN'T. I CAN BUILD AN M16 FROM NOTHING, BUT I CAN'T PITCH A FRIGGIN' TENT?!

THAT'S IT, TENT, YOU'RE DEAD!

I WOULDN'T DO THAT IF I WERE

YOU NEED A PERMIT TO HUNT TENTS AROUND HERE.

HA HA. VERY FUNNY.

YOU'VE GOT TO PUT TOGETHER THE FRAME FIRST.

RIGHT. CAN YOU POINT ME TO THE CLOSEST FOUR STAR HOTEL?

DON'T GIVE UP SO EASILY. WE CAN HELP YOU WITH THAT.

SOMEHOW I DOUBT IT. BUT KNOCK YOURSELVES OUT.

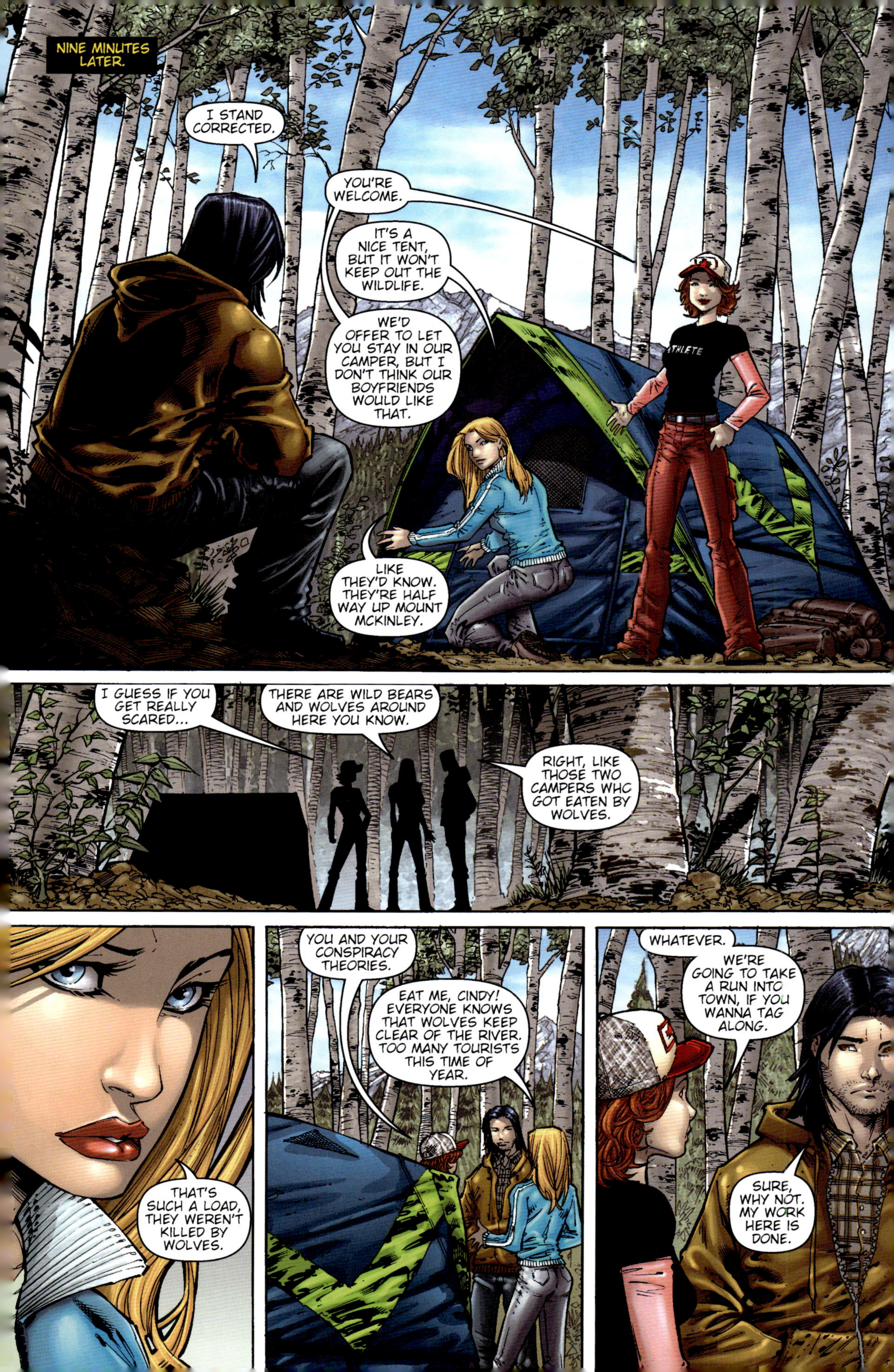
NINE MINUTES LATER.
I STAND CORRECTED.
YOU'RE WELCOME.
IT'S A NICE TENT, BUT IT WON'T KEEP OUT THE WILDLIFE.
WE'D OFFER TO LET YOU STAY IN OUR CAMPER, BUT I DON'T THINK OUR BOYFRIENDS WOULD LIKE THAT.
LIKE THEY'D KNOW. THEY'RE HALF WAY UP MOUNT MCKINLEY.
I GUESS IF YOU GET REALLY SCARED...
THERE ARE WILD BEARS AND WOLVES AROUND HERE YOU KNOW.
RIGHT, LIKE THOSE TWO CAMPERS WHC GOT EATEN BY WOLVES.
THAT'S SUCH A LOAD, THEY WEREN'T KILLED BY WOLVES.
YOU AND YOUR CONSPIRACY THEORIES.
EAT ME, CINDY! EVERYONE KNOWS THAT WOLVES KEEP CLEAR OF THE RIVER. TOO MANY TOURISTS THIS TIME OF YEAR.
WHATEVER.
WE'RE GOING TO TAKE A RUN INTO TOWN, IF YOU WANNA TAG ALONG.
SURE, WHY NOT. MY WORK HERE IS DONE.

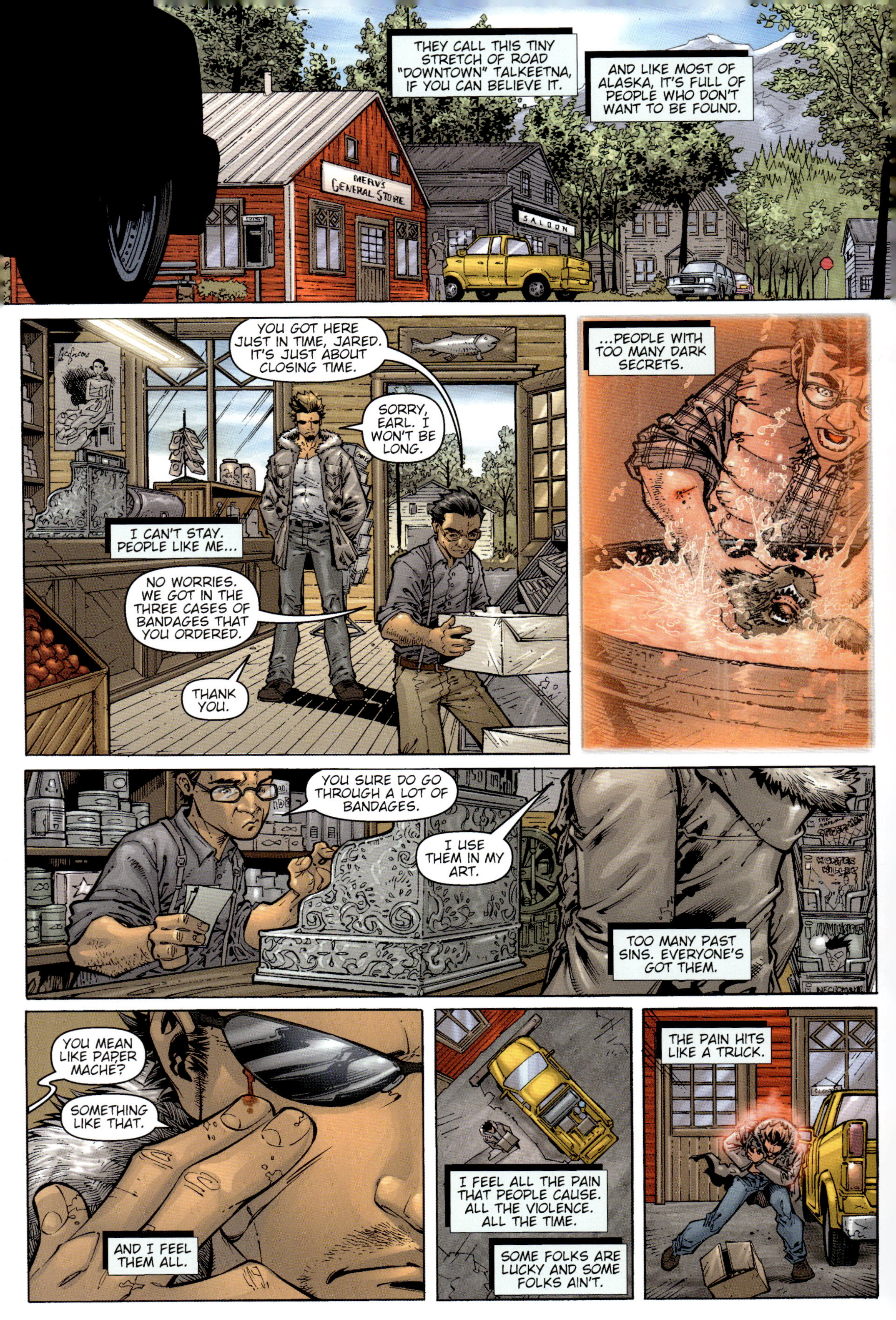
THEY CALL THIS TINY STRETCH OF ROAD "DOWNTOWN" TALKEETNA, IF YOU CAN BELIEVE IT.
AND LIKE MOST OF ALASKA, IT'S FULL OF PEOPLE WHO DON'T WANT TO BE FOUND.
MERV'S GENERAL STORE
SALOON
YOU GOT HERE JUST IN TIME, JARED. IT'S JUST ABOUT CLOSING TIME.
SORRY, EARL. I WON'T BE LONG.
I CAN'T STAY. PEOPLE LIKE ME...
NO WORRIES. WE GOT IN THE THREE CASES OF BANDAGES THAT YOU ORDERED.
THANK YOU.
...PEOPLE WITH TOO MANY DARK SECRETS.
YOU SURE DO GO THROUGH A LOT OF BANDAGES.
I USE THEM IN MY ART.
TOO MANY PAST SINS. EVERYONE'S GOT THEM.
YOU MEAN LIKE PAPER MACHE?
SOMETHING LIKE THAT.
AND I FEEL THEM ALL.
I FEEL ALL THE PAIN THAT PEOPLE CAUSE. ALL THE VIOLENCE. ALL THE TIME.
SOME FOLKS ARE LUCKY AND SOME FOLKS AIN'T.
THE PAIN HITS LIKE A TRUCK.

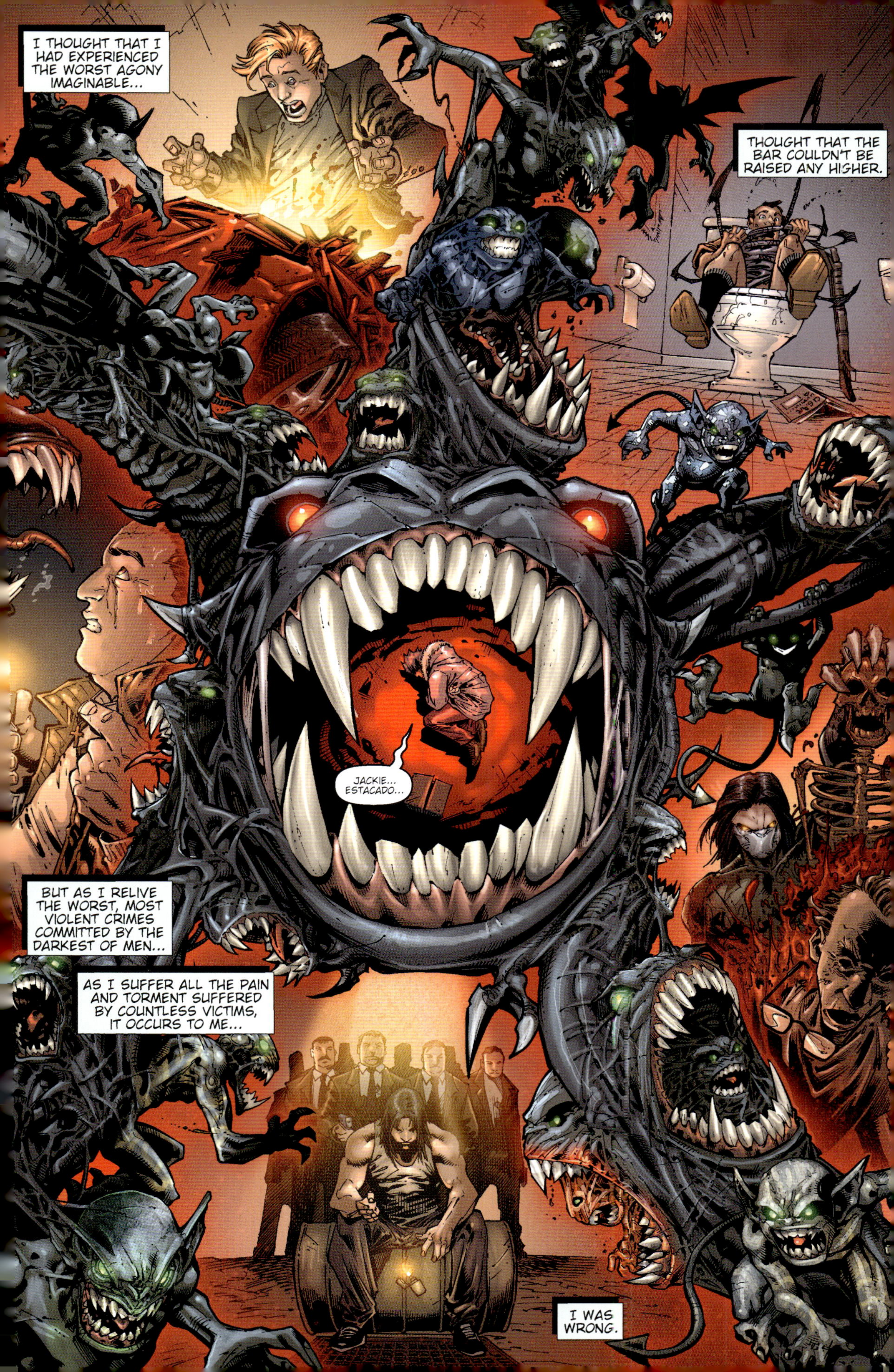

I THOUGHT THAT I HAD EXPERIENCED THE WORST AGONY IMAGINABLE...
THOUGHT THAT THE BAR COULDN'T BE RAISED ANY HIGHER.
JACKIE... ESTACADO...
BUT AS I RELIVE THE WORST, MOST VIOLENT CRIMES COMMITTED BY THE DARKEST OF MEN...
AS I SUFFER ALL THE PAIN AND TORMENT SUFFERED BY COUNTLESS VICTIMS, IT OCCURS TO ME...
I WAS WRONG.

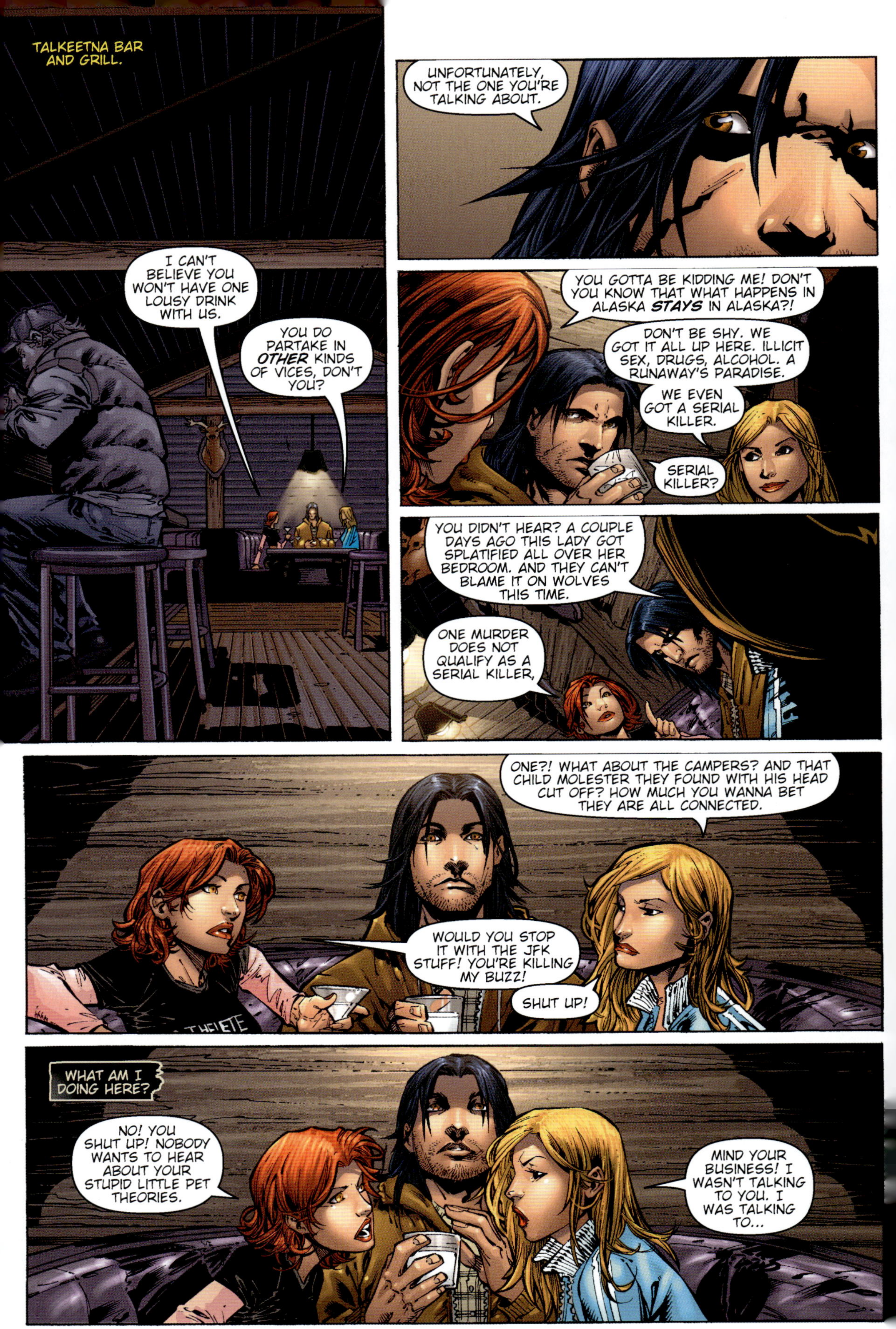
TALKEETNA BAR AND GRILL.
UNFORTUNATELY, NOT THE ONE YOU'RE TALKING ABOUT.
I CAN'T BELIEVE YOU WON'T HAVE ONE LOUSY DRINK WITH US.
YOU DO PARTAKE IN OTHER KINDS OF VICES, DON'T YOU?
YOU GOTTA BE KIDDING ME! DON'T YOU KNOW THAT WHAT HAPPENS IN ALASKA STAYS IN ALASKA?!
DON'T BE SHY. WE GOT IT ALL UP HERE. ILLICIT SEX, DRUGS, ALCOHOL. A RUNAWAY'S PARADISE.
WE EVEN GOT A SERIAL KILLER.
SERIAL KILLER?
YOU DIDN'T HEAR? A COUPLE DAYS AGO THIS LADY GOT SPLATIFIED ALL OVER HER BEDROOM. AND THEY CAN'T BLAME IT ON WOLVES THIS TIME.
ONE MURDER DOES NOT QUALIFY AS A SERIAL KILLER,
ONE?! WHAT ABOUT THE CAMPERS? AND THAT CHILD MOLESTER THEY FOUND WITH HIS HEAD CUT OFF? HOW MUCH YOU WANNA BET THEY ARE ALL CONNECTED.
WOULD YOU STOP IT WITH THE JFK STUFF! YOU'RE KILLING MY BUZZ!
SHUT UP!
WHAT AM I DOING HERE?
NO! YOU SHUT UP! NOBODY WANTS TO HEAR ABOUT YOUR STUPID LITTLE PET THEORIES.
MIND YOUR BUSINESS! I WASN'T TALKING TO YOU. I WAS TALKING TO...

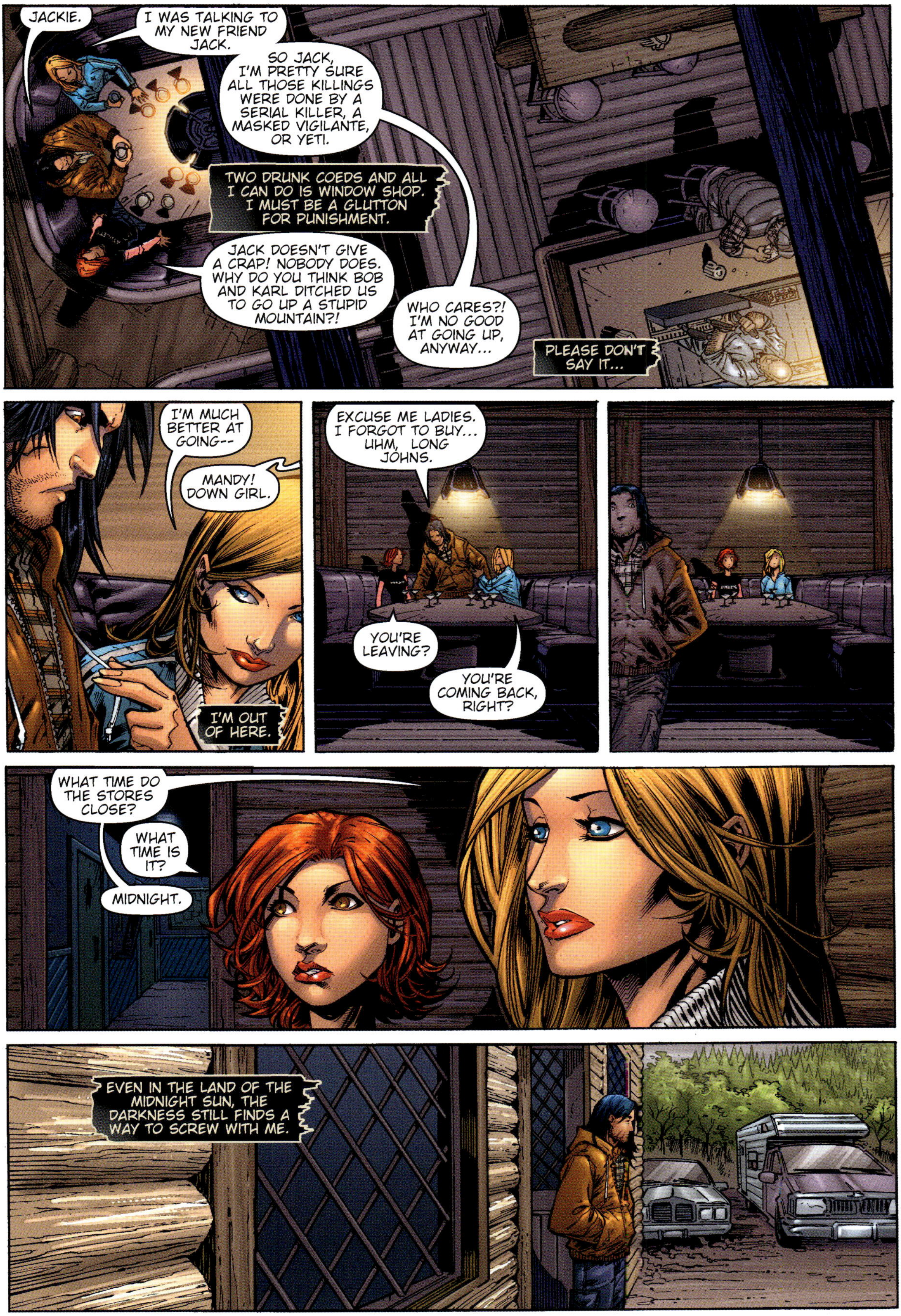
JACKIE.
I WAS TALKING TO MY NEW FRIEND JACK.
SO JACK, I'M PRETTY SURE ALL THOSE KILLINGS WERE DONE BY A SERIAL KILLER, A MASKED VIGILANTE, OR YETI.
TWO DRUNK COEDS AND ALL I CAN DO IS WINDOW SHOP. I MUST BE A GLUTTON FOR PUNISHMENT.
JACK DOESN'T GIVE A CRAP! NOBODY DOES. WHY DO YOU THINK BOB AND KARL DITCHED US TO GO UP A STUPID MOUNTAIN?!
WHO CARES?! I'M NO GOOD AT GOING UP, ANYWAY...
PLEASE DON'T SAY IT...
I'M MUCH BETTER AT GOING--
MANDY! DOWN GIRL.
I'M OUT OF HERE.
EXCUSE ME LADIES. I FORGOT TO BUY... UHM, LONG JOHNS.
YOU'RE LEAVING?
YOU'RE COMING BACK, RIGHT?
WHAT TIME DO THE STORES CLOSE?
WHAT TIME IS IT?
MIDNIGHT.
EVEN IN THE LAND OF THE MIDNIGHT SUN, THE DARKNESS STILL FINDS A WAY TO SCREW WITH ME.

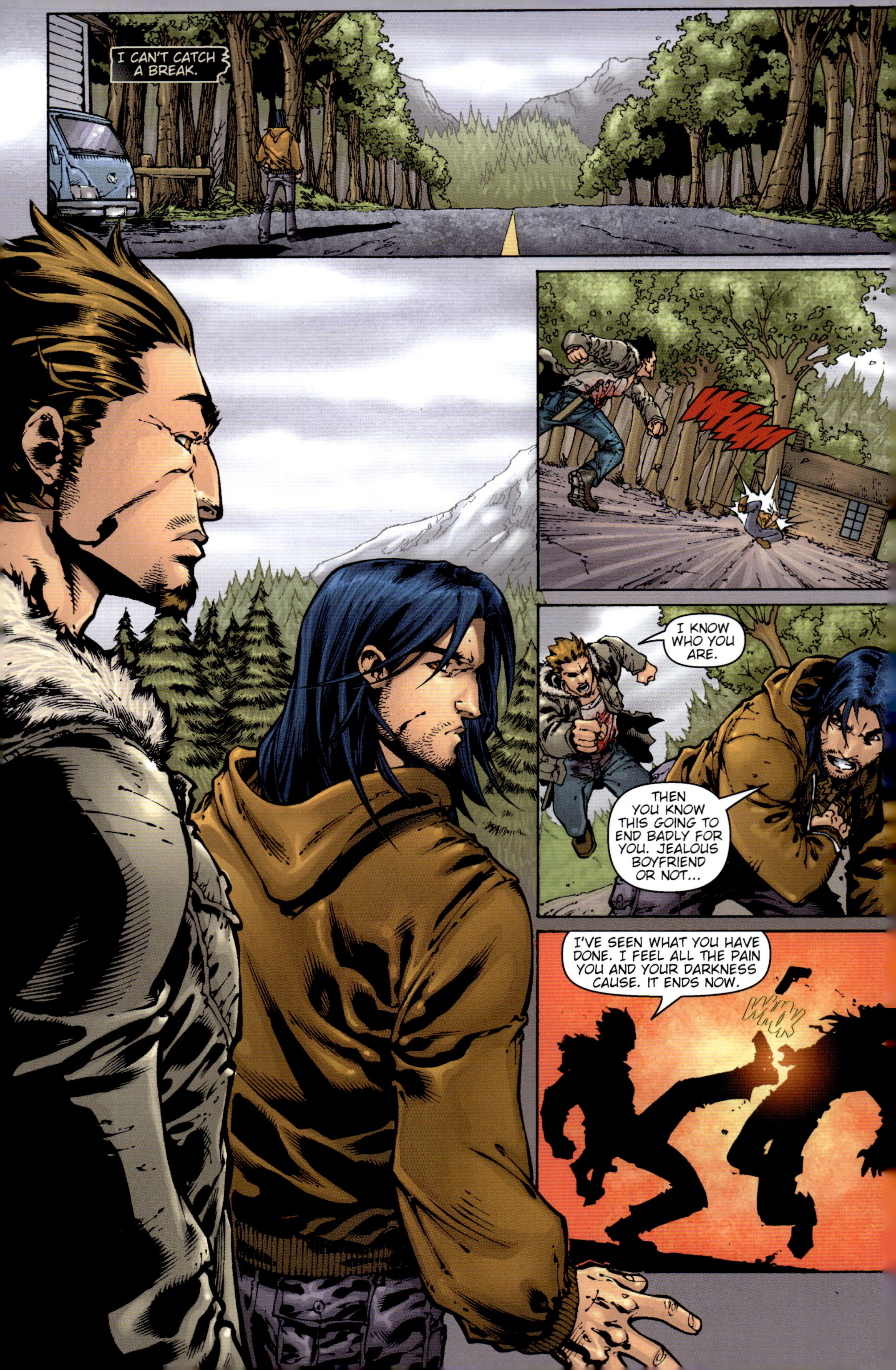

I CAN'T CATCH A BREAK.
WHAM
I KNOW WHO YOU ARE.
THEN YOU KNOW THIS GOING TO END BADLY FOR YOU. JEALOUS BOYFRIEND OR NOT...
I'VE SEEN WHAT YOU HAVE DONE. I FEEL ALL THE PAIN YOU AND YOUR DARKNESS CAUSE. IT ENDS NOW.
WHAK

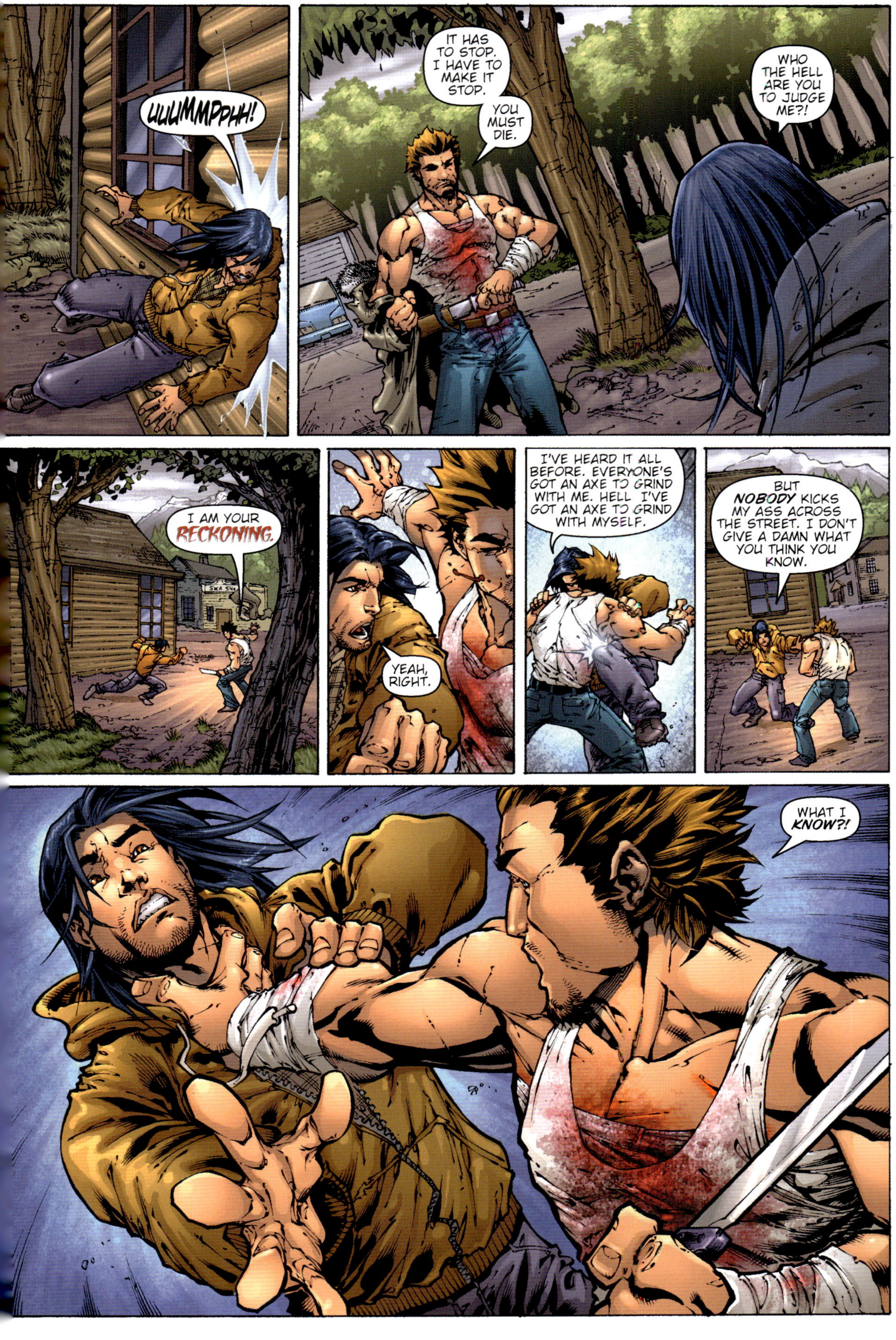
UUUMMPPHH!
IT HAS TO STOP. I HAVE TO MAKE IT STOP.
YOU MUST DIE.
WHO THE HELL ARE YOU TO JUDGE ME?!
I AM YOUR RECKONING.
YEAH, RIGHT.
I'VE HEARD IT ALL BEFORE. EVERYONE'S GOT AN AXE TO GRIND WITH ME. HELL I'VE GOT AN AXE TO GRIND WITH MYSELF.
BUT NOBODY KICKS MY ASS ACROSS THE STREET. I DON'T GIVE A DAMN WHAT YOU THINK YOU KNOW.
WHAT I KNOW?!

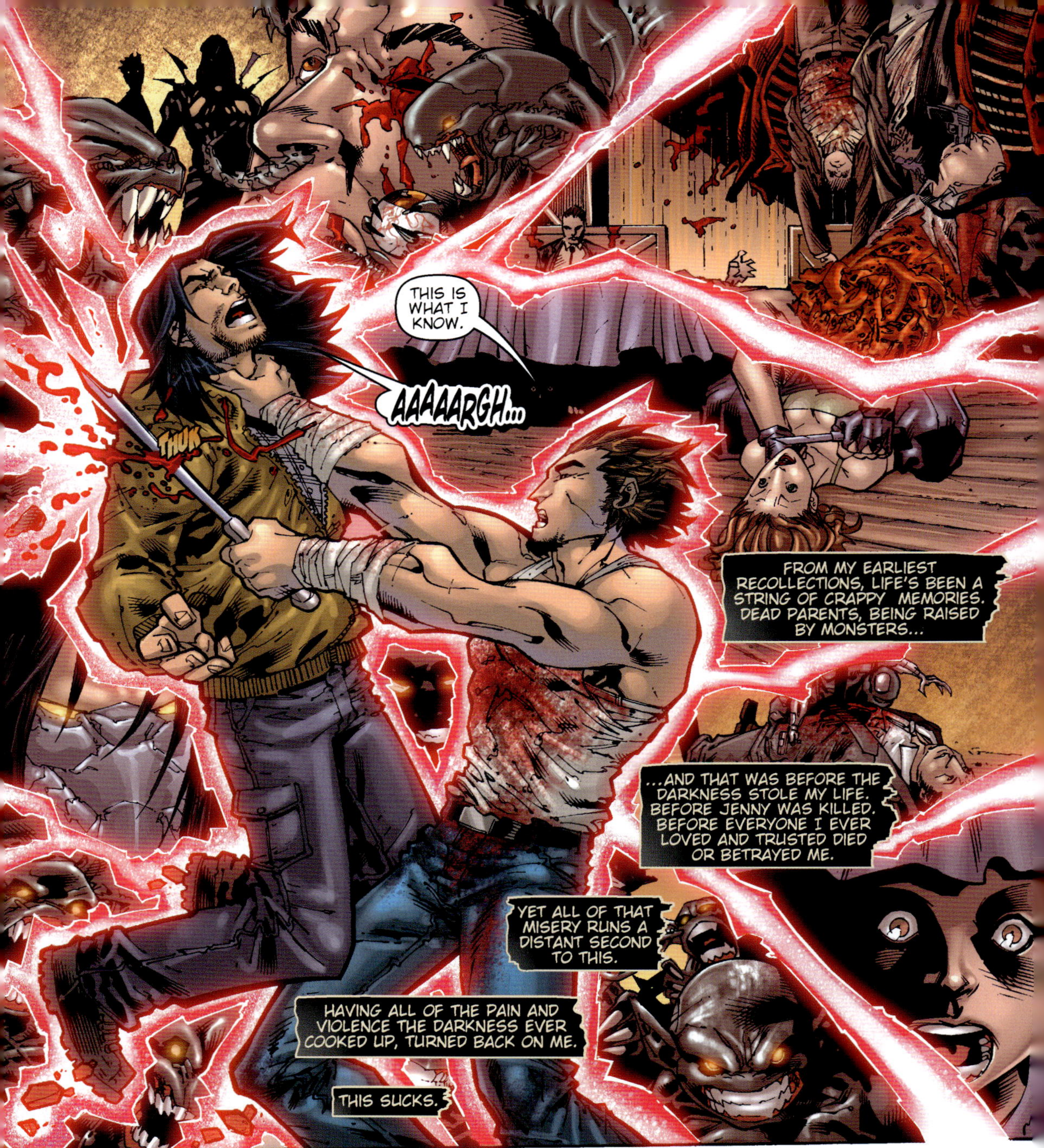
THIS IS WHAT I KNOW.
AAAAARGH...
THUK
FROM MY EARLIEST RECOLLECTIONS, LIFE'S BEEN A STRING OF CRAPPY MEMORIES. DEAD PARENTS, BEING RAISED BY MONSTERS...
...AND THAT WAS BEFORE THE DARKNESS STOLE MY LIFE. BEFORE JENNY WAS KILLED. BEFORE EVERYONE I EVER LOVED AND TRUSTED DIED OR BETRAYED ME.
YET ALL OF THAT MISERY RUNS A DISTANT SECOND TO THIS.
HAVING ALL OF THE PAIN AND VIOLENCE THE DARKNESS EVER COOKED UP, TURNED BACK ON ME.
THIS SUCKS.

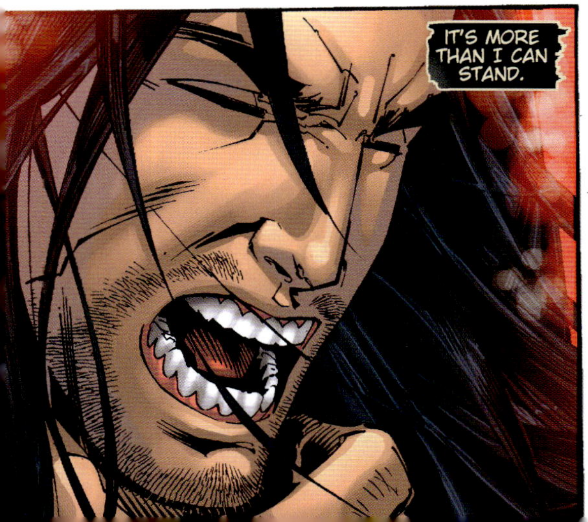
IT'S MORE THAN I CAN STAND.

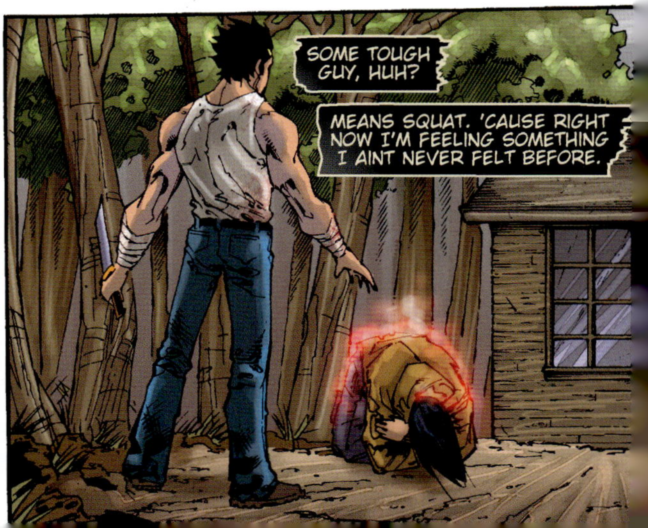
SOME TOUGH GUY, HUH?
MEANS SQUAT. 'CAUSE RIGHT NOW I'M FEELING SOMETHING I AINT NEVER FELT BEFORE.

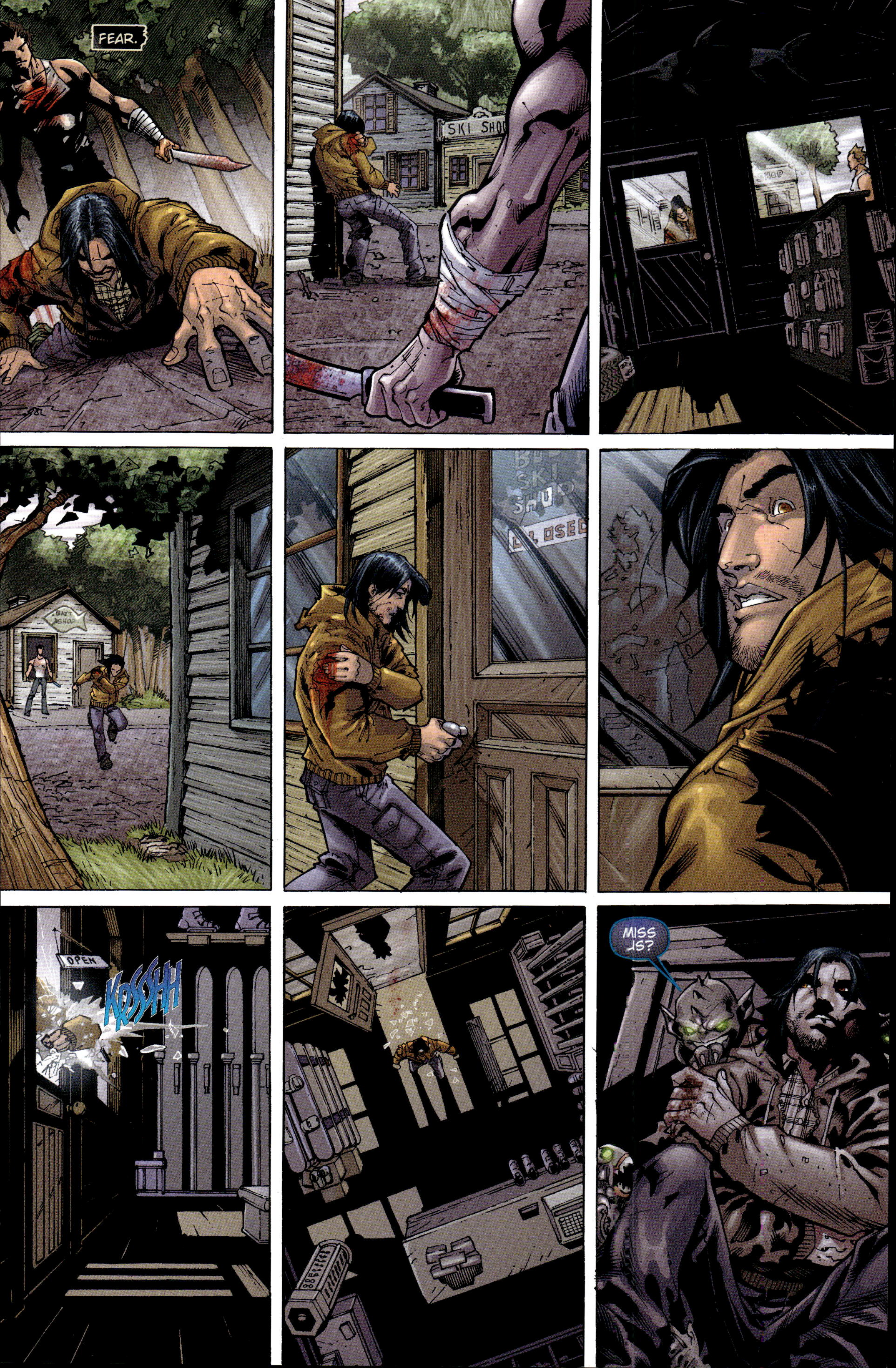
FEAR.
SKI SHO
BAIT SHOP
OPEN
KRSSHH
MISS JS?

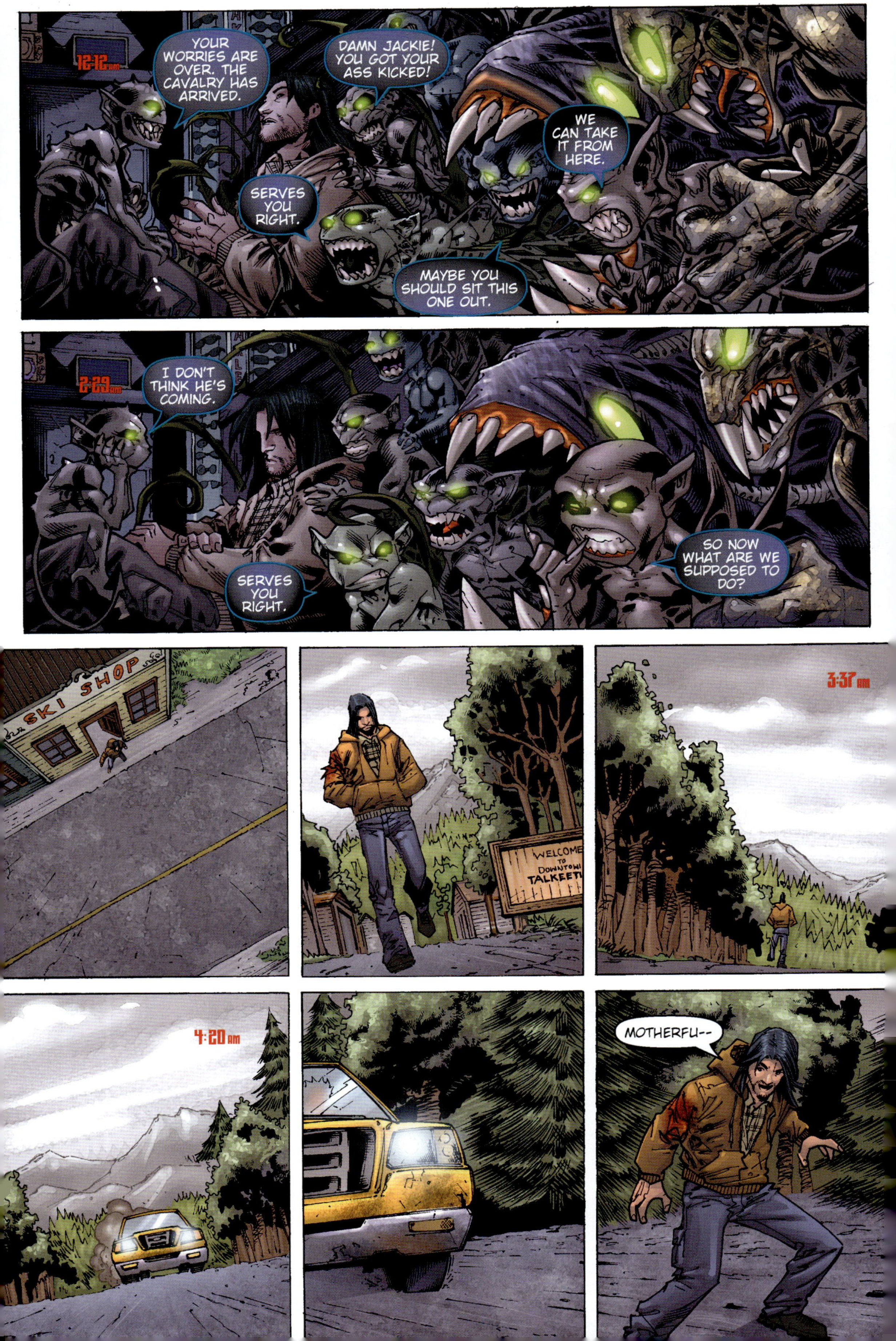
12:12 AM
YOUR WORRIES ARE OVER. THE CAVALRY HAS ARRIVED.
DAMN JACKIE! YOU GOT YOUR ASS KICKED!
WE CAN TAKE IT FROM HERE.
SERVES YOU RIGHT.
MAYBE YOU SHOULD SIT THIS ONE OUT.
2:29 AM
I DON'T THINK HE'S COMING.
SERVES YOU RIGHT.
SO NOW WHAT ARE WE SUPPOSED TO DO?
SKI SHOP
WELCOME TO DOWNTOWN TALKEET
3:37 AM
4:20 AM
MOTHERFU--

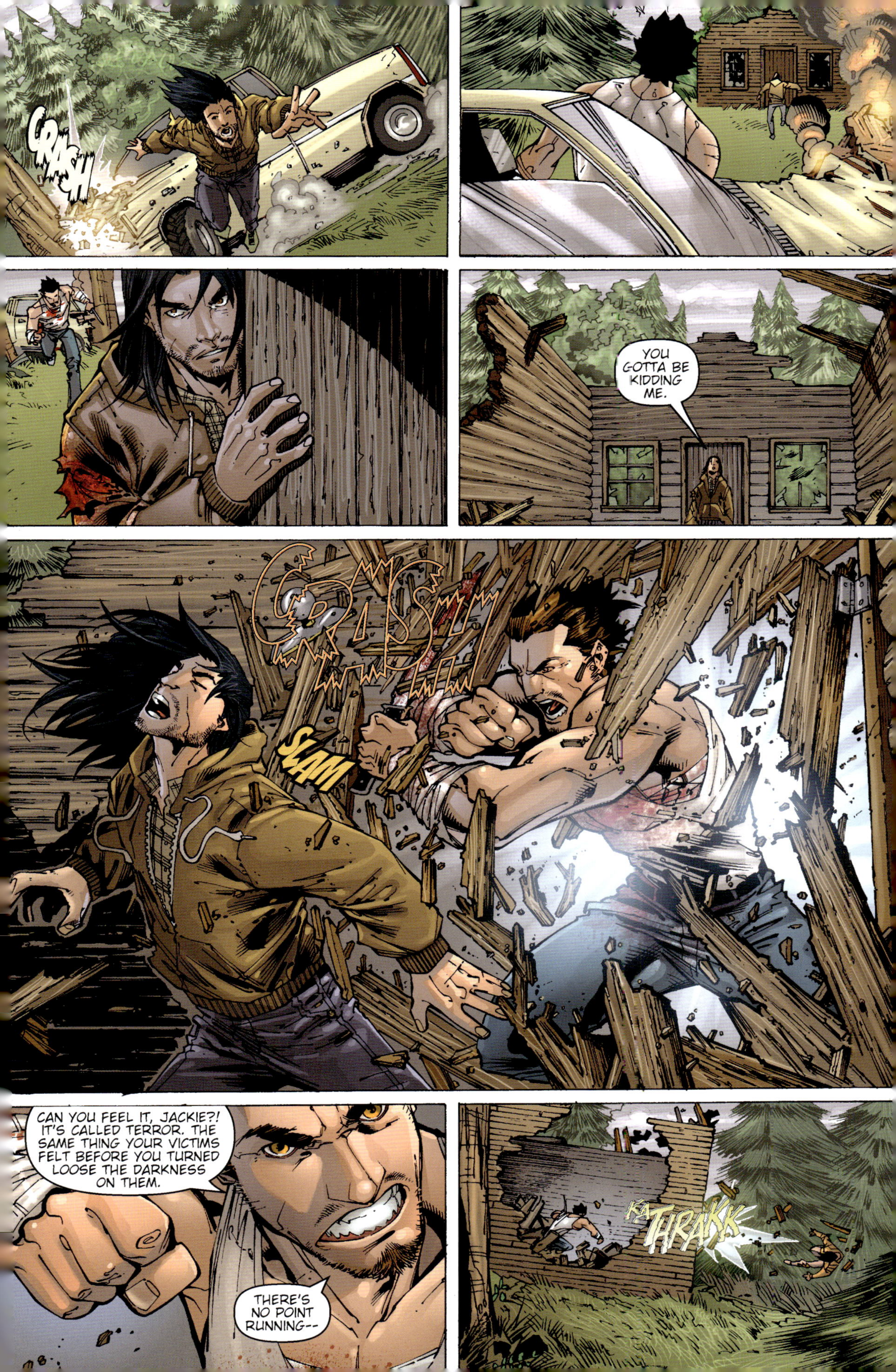
CRASH
YOU GOTTA BE KIDDING ME.
SLAM
CAN YOU FEEL IT, JACKIE?! IT'S CALLED TERROR. THE SAME THING YOUR VICTIMS FELT BEFORE YOU TURNED LOOSE THE DARKNESS ON THEM.
THERE'S NO POINT RUNNING--
KA THRAKK

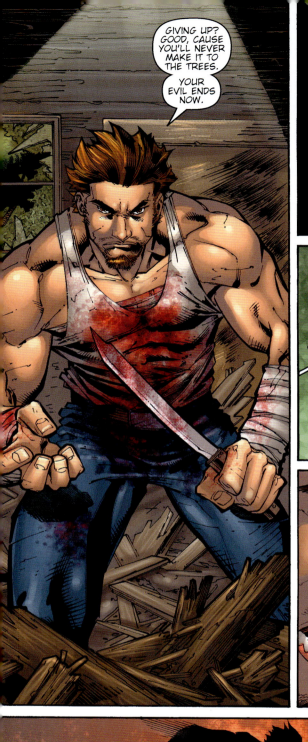

GIVING UP? GOOD, CAUSE YOU'LL NEVER MAKE IT TO THE TREES.

YOUR EVIL ENDS NOW.

MY EVIL?! WHAT ABOUT YOUR EVIL?

WHAT MAKES YOU ANY BETTER?! I KNOW WHAT YOU'VE DONE. WHEN YOU TURNED MY PAST ON ME, I GOT A LOOK INTO YOUR LIFE.

HOW IS THAT POSSIBLE? YOUR POWERS?

WHO CARES. YOU'RE A HYPOCRITE. I'VE SEEN THE PEOPLE *YOU* BUTCHERED.

THAT WOMAN WAS A BLACK WIDOW! SHE POISONED TWO HUSBANDS. SHE SUFFOCATED *THREE* OF HER OWN BABIES!

AND THOSE CAMPERS?! FUGITIVE TERRORISTS RESPONSIBLE FOR OVER A DOZEN BOMBINGS ACROSS AFRICA. I HAD TO KILL THEM, TO MAKE IT STOP!

THEY GOT WHAT THEY DESERVED!

I WASN'T TALKING ABOUT THAT. WHAT ABOUT EMILY?

DID SHE GET WHAT SHE DESERVED?

SHUT UP!

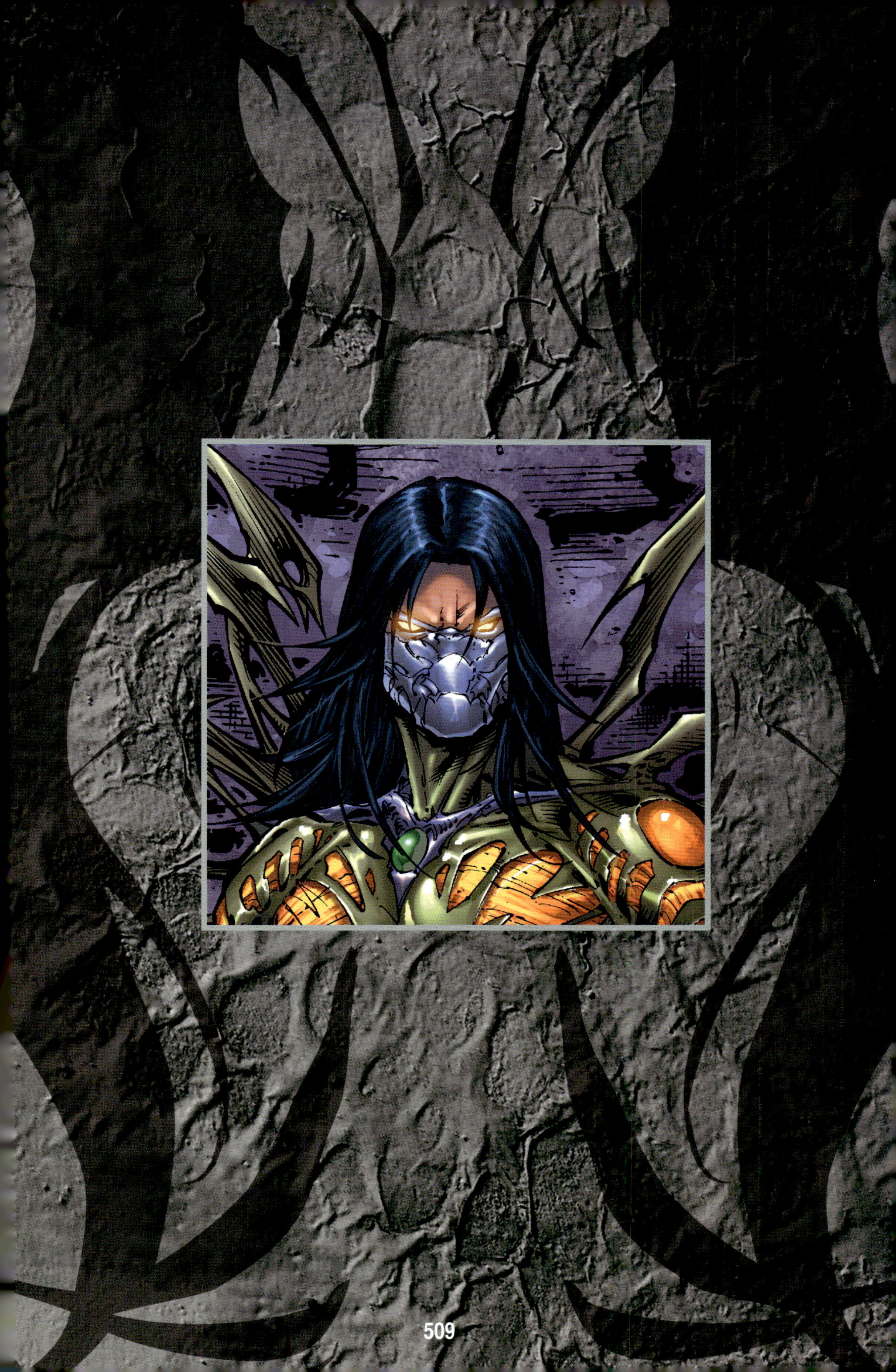

The Darkness Issue #62
cover art by: Dale Keown & Matt Milla

THE DARKNESS #62

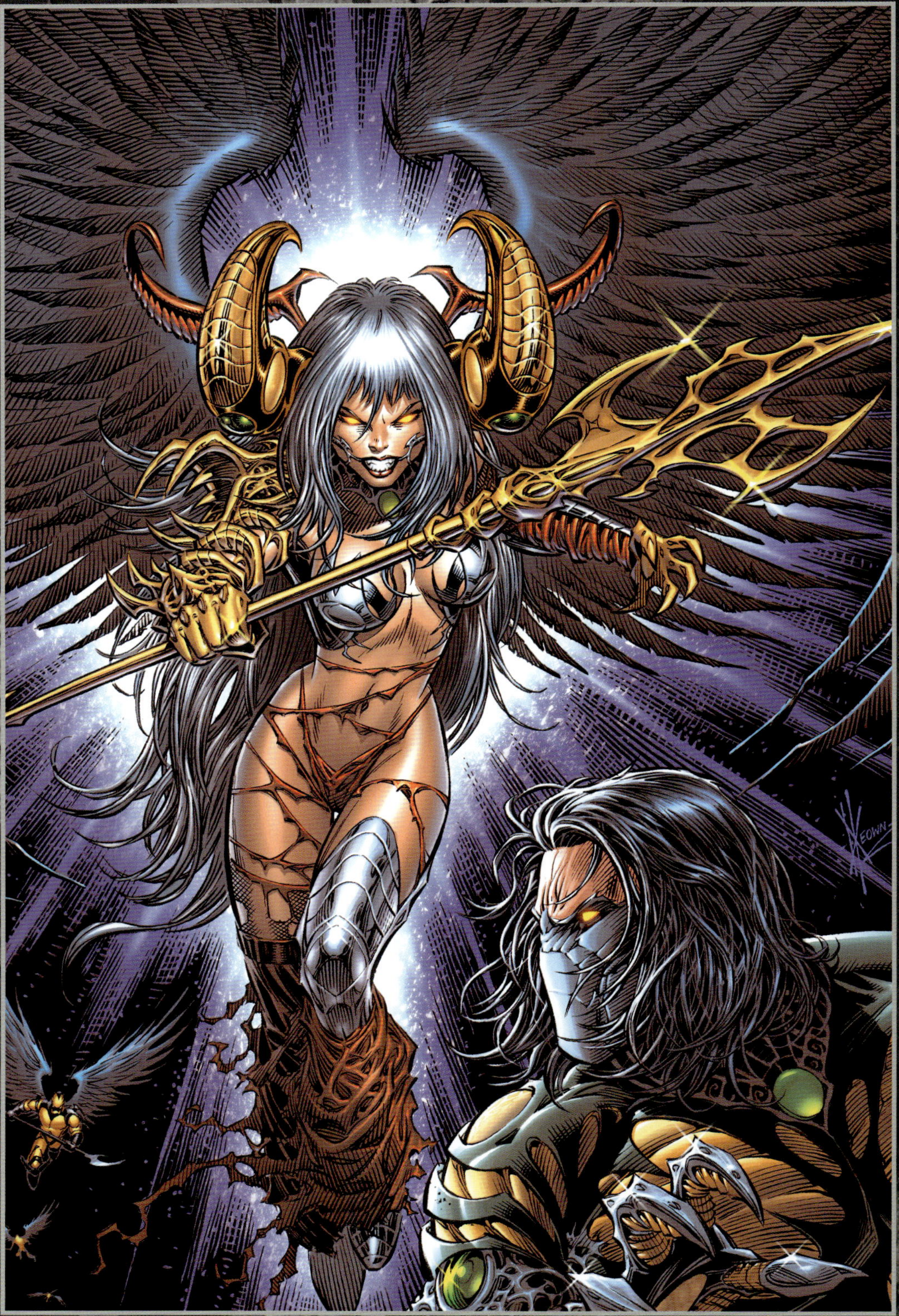

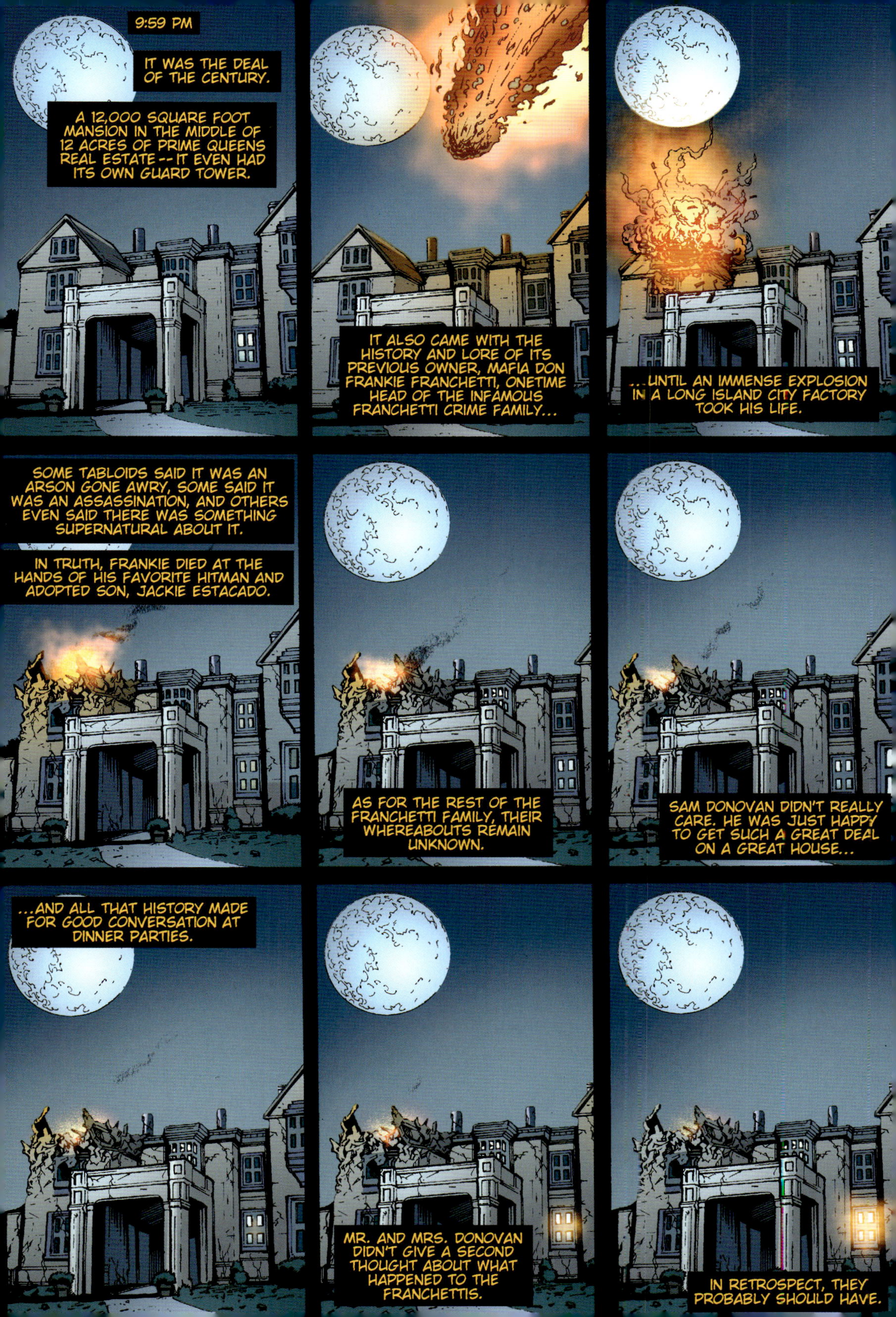
9:59 PM
IT WAS THE DEAL OF THE CENTURY.
A 12,000 SQUARE FOOT MANSION IN THE MIDDLE OF 12 ACRES OF PRIME QUEENS REAL ESTATE -- IT EVEN HAD ITS OWN GUARD TOWER.
IT ALSO CAME WITH THE HISTORY AND LORE OF ITS PREVIOUS OWNER, MAFIA DON FRANKIE FRANCHETTI, ONETIME HEAD OF THE INFAMOUS FRANCHETTI CRIME FAMILY...
...UNTIL AN IMMENSE EXPLOSION IN A LONG ISLAND CITY FACTORY TOOK HIS LIFE.
SOME TABLOIDS SAID IT WAS AN ARSON GONE AWRY, SOME SAID IT WAS AN ASSASSINATION, AND OTHERS EVEN SAID THERE WAS SOMETHING SUPERNATURAL ABOUT IT.
IN TRUTH, FRANKIE DIED AT THE HANDS OF HIS FAVORITE HITMAN AND ADOPTED SON, JACKIE ESTACADO.
AS FOR THE REST OF THE FRANCHETTI FAMILY, THEIR WHEREABOUTS REMAIN UNKNOWN.
SAM DONOVAN DIDN'T REALLY CARE. HE WAS JUST HAPPY TO GET SUCH A GREAT DEAL ON A GREAT HOUSE...
...AND ALL THAT HISTORY MADE FOR GOOD CONVERSATION AT DINNER PARTIES.
MR. AND MRS. DONOVAN DIDN'T GIVE A SECOND THOUGHT ABOUT WHAT HAPPENED TO THE FRANCHETTIS.
IN RETROSPECT, THEY PROBABLY SHOULD HAVE.

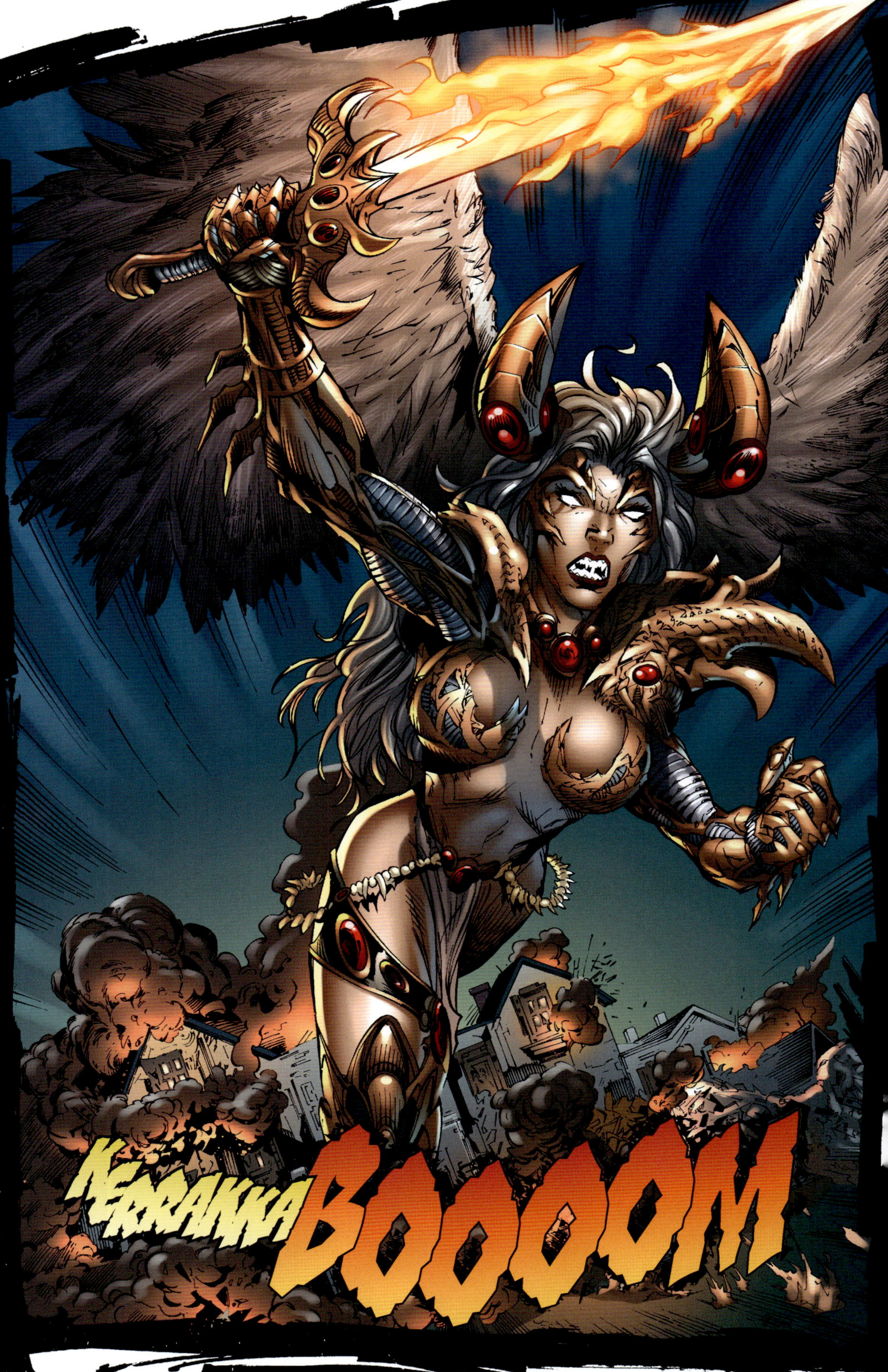
KERRAKKA
BOOOOM

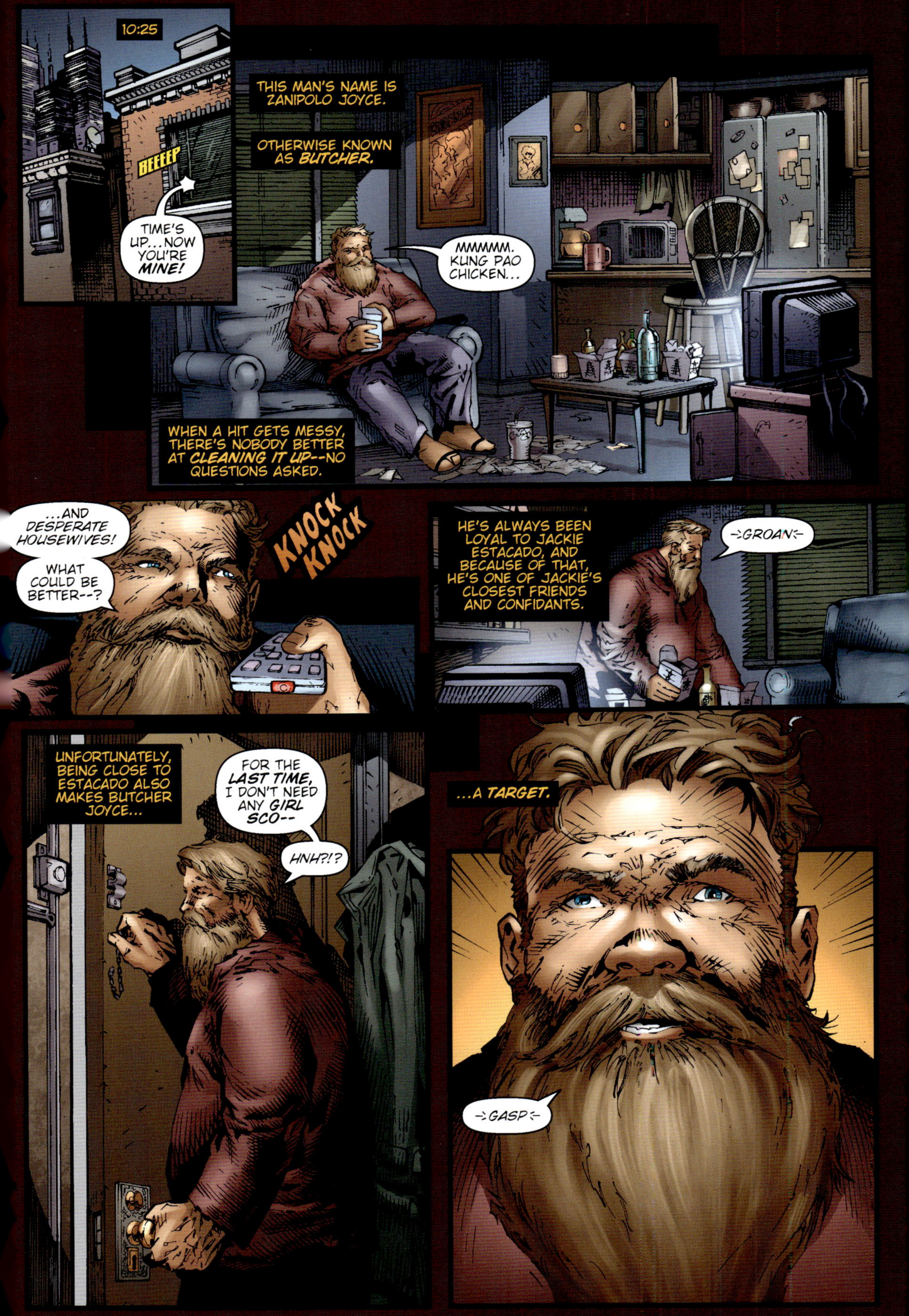
10:25
BEEEEP
TIME'S UP...NOW YOU'RE MINE!
THIS MAN'S NAME IS ZANIPOLO JOYCE.
OTHERWISE KNOWN AS BUTCHER.
MMMMM. KUNG PAO CHICKEN...
WHEN A HIT GETS MESSY, THERE'S NOBODY BETTER AT CLEANING IT UP--NO QUESTIONS ASKED.
...AND DESPERATE HOUSEWIVES!
WHAT COULD BE BETTER--?
KNOCK KNOCK
HE'S ALWAYS BEEN LOYAL TO JACKIE ESTACADO, AND BECAUSE OF THAT, HE'S ONE OF JACKIE'S CLOSEST FRIENDS AND CONFIDANTS.
GROAN
UNFORTUNATELY, BEING CLOSE TO ESTACADO ALSO MAKES BUTCHER JOYCE...
FOR THE LAST TIME, I DON'T NEED ANY GIRL SCO--
HNH?!?
...A TARGET.
GASP

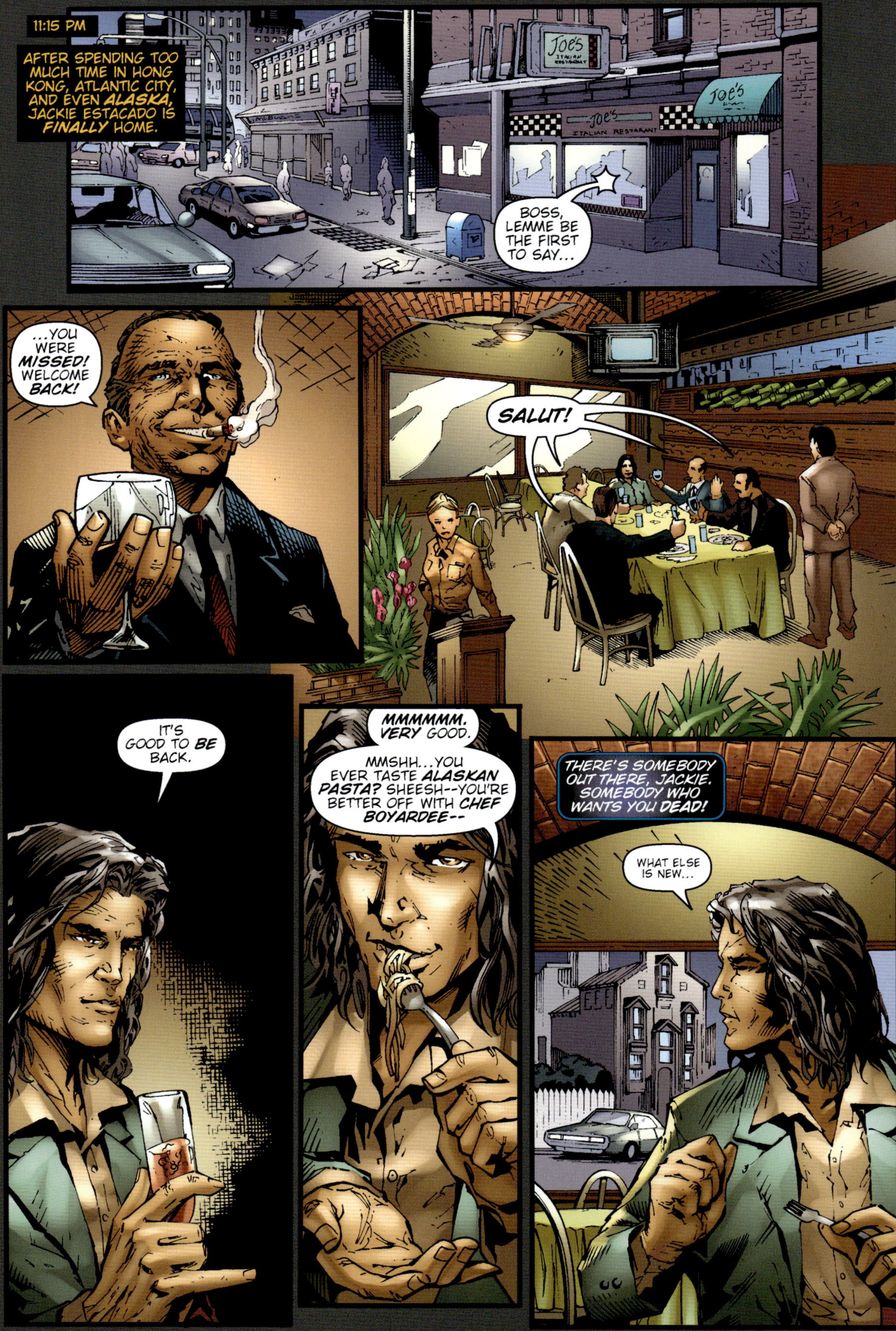

11:15 PM
AFTER SPENDING TOO MUCH TIME IN HONG KONG, ATLANTIC CITY, AND EVEN ALASKA, JACKIE ESTACADO IS FINALLY HOME.
JOE'S ITALIAN RESTAURANT
BOSS, LEMME BE THE FIRST TO SAY...
...YOU WERE MISSED! WELCOME BACK!
SALUT!
IT'S GOOD TO BE BACK.
MMMMMM. VERY GOOD.
MMSHH...YOU EVER TASTE ALASKAN PASTA? SHEESH--YOU'RE BETTER OFF WITH CHEF BOYARDEE--
THERE'S SOMEBODY OUT THERE, JACKIE. SOMEBODY WHO WANTS YOU DEAD!
WHAT ELSE IS NEW...

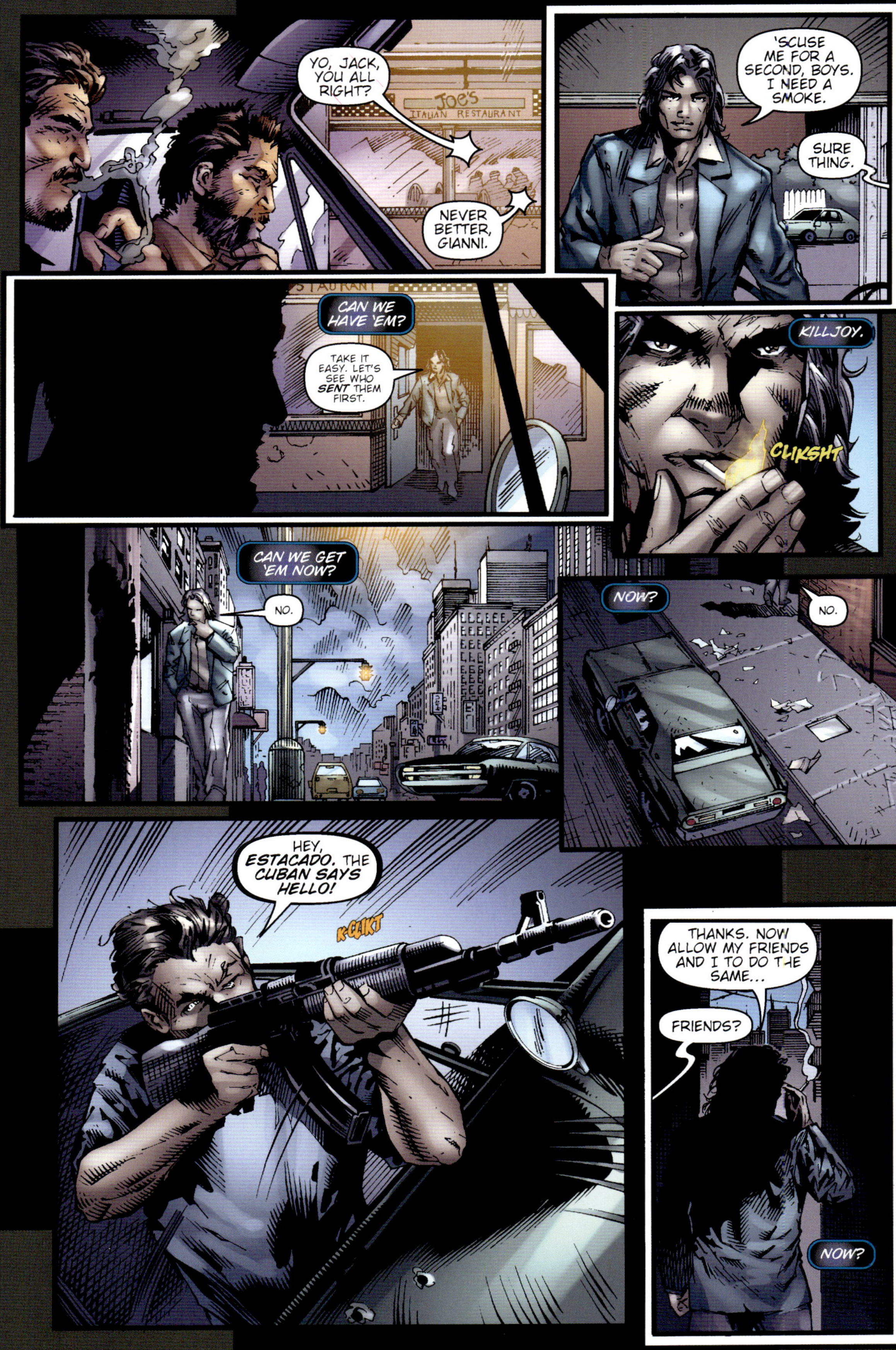
YO, JACK, YOU ALL RIGHT?
JOE'S ITALIAN RESTAURANT
NEVER BETTER, GIANNI.
'SCUSE ME FOR A SECOND, BOYS. I NEED A SMOKE.
SURE THING.
CAN WE HAVE 'EM?
TAKE IT EASY. LET'S SEE WHO SENT THEM FIRST.
KILLJOY.
CLIKSHT
CAN WE GET 'EM NOW?
NO.
NOW?
NO.
HEY, ESTACADO. THE CUBAN SAYS HELLO!
K-CLIKT
THANKS. NOW ALLOW MY FRIENDS AND I TO DO THE SAME...
FRIENDS?
NOW?

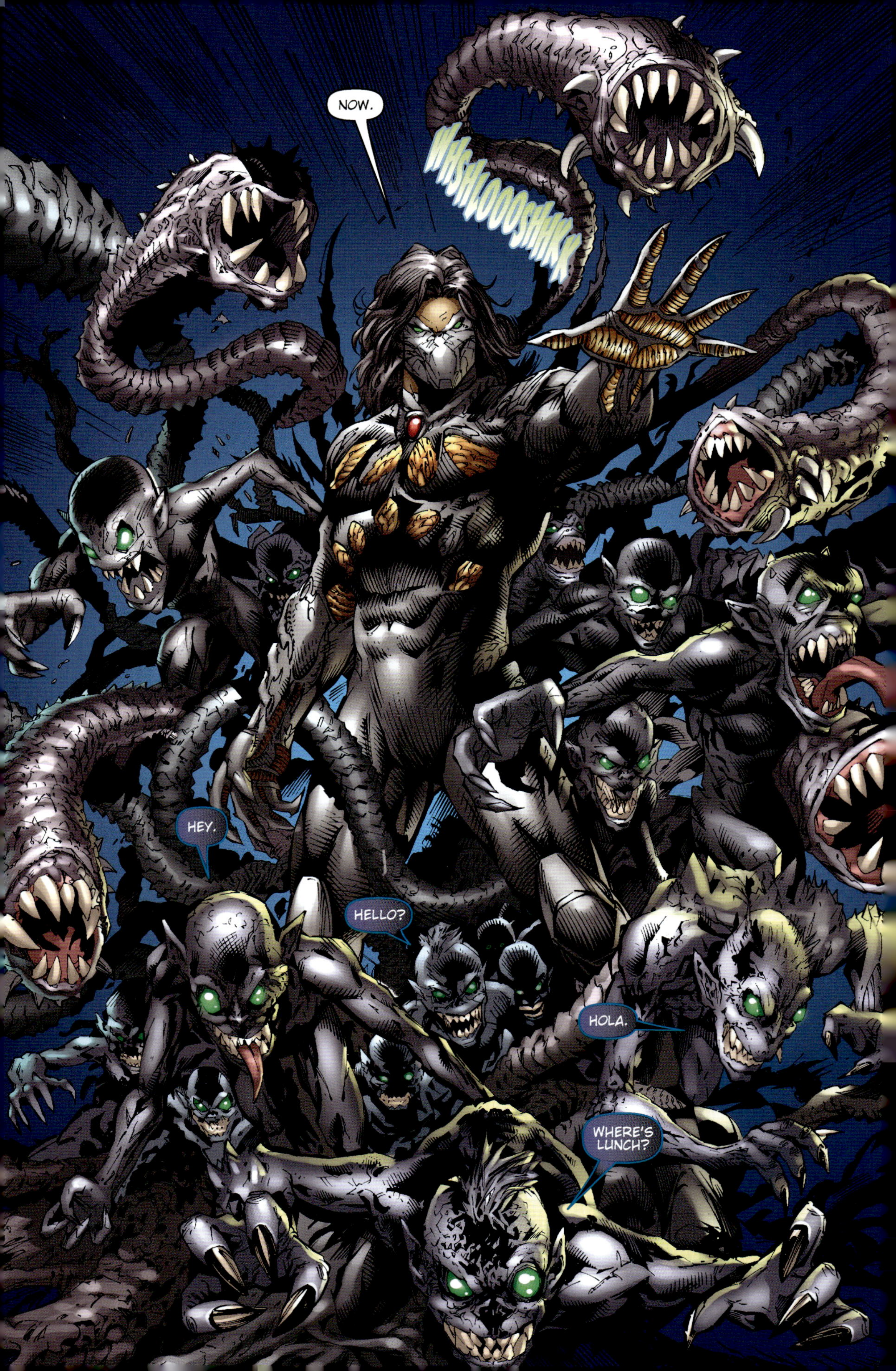
NOW.
WHSHLOOOSHHKK
HEY.
HELLO?
HOLA.
WHERE'S LUNCH?

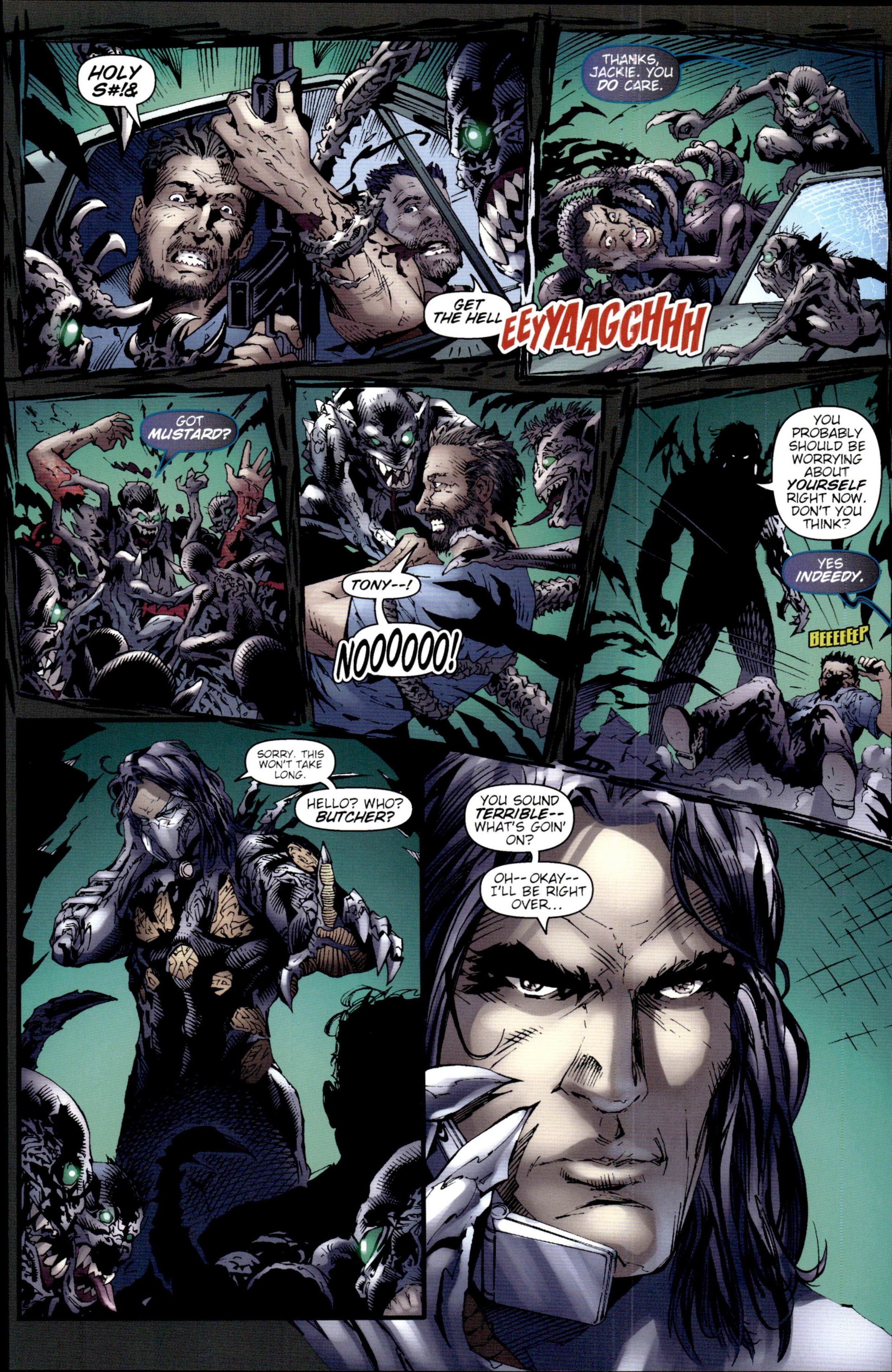

HOLY S#!&
GET THE HELL
EEYYAAGGHHH
THANKS, JACKIE. YOU DO CARE.
GOT MUSTARD?
TONY--!
NOOOOOO!
YOU PROBABLY SHOULD BE WORRYING ABOUT YOURSELF RIGHT NOW. DON'T YOU THINK?
YES INDEEDY.
BEEEEEP
SORRY. THIS WON'T TAKE LONG.
HELLO? WHO? BUTCHER?
YOU SOUND TERRIBLE-- WHAT'S GOIN' ON?
OH--OKAY-- I'LL BE RIGHT OVER...

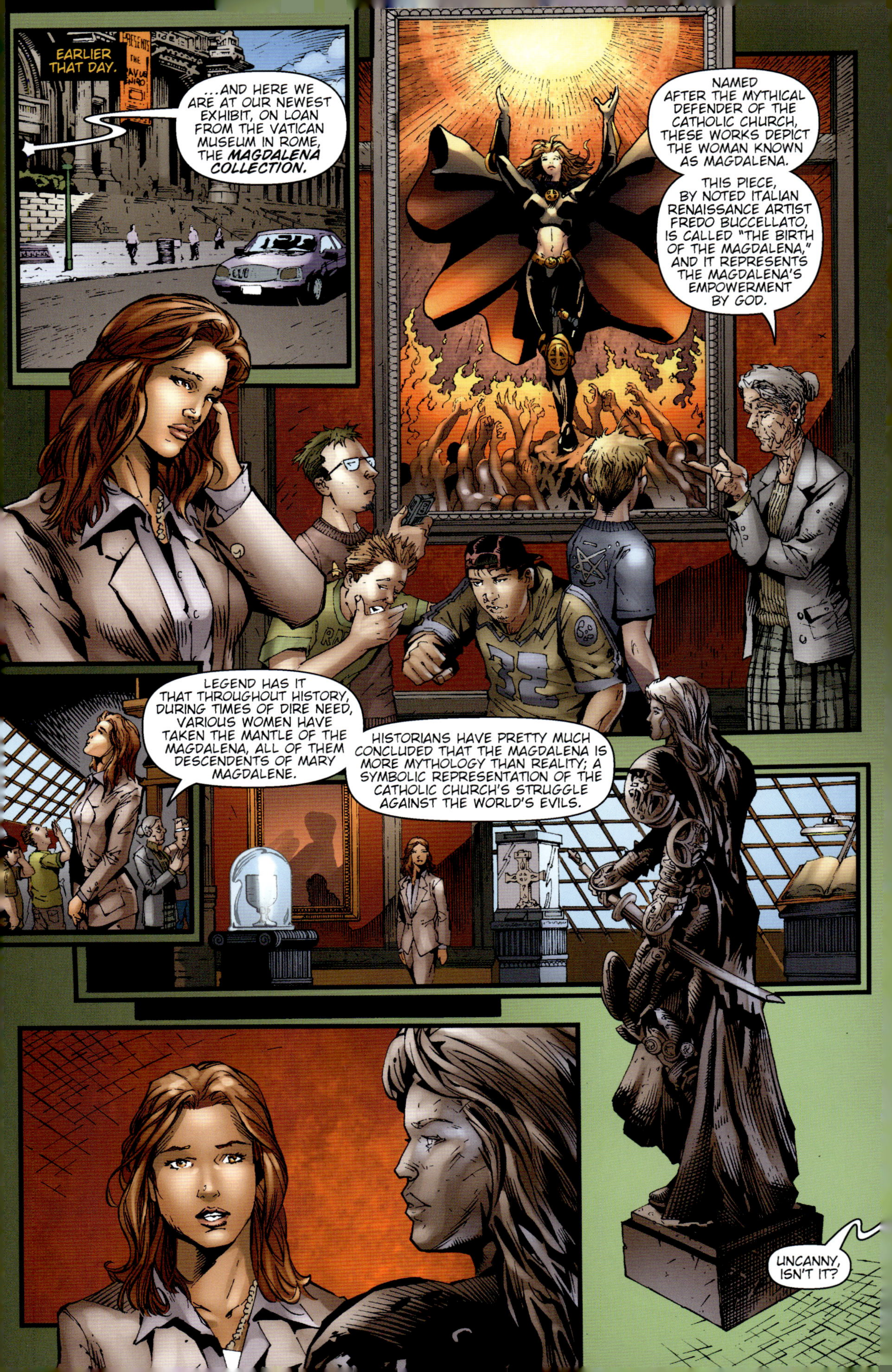
EARLIER THAT DAY.
...AND HERE WE ARE AT OUR NEWEST EXHIBIT, ON LOAN FROM THE VATICAN MUSEUM IN ROME, THE *MAGDALENA COLLECTION.*
NAMED AFTER THE MYTHICAL DEFENDER OF THE CATHOLIC CHURCH, THESE WORKS DEPICT THE WOMAN KNOWN AS MAGDALENA.
THIS PIECE, BY NOTED ITALIAN RENAISSANCE ARTIST FREDO BUCCELLATO, IS CALLED "THE BIRTH OF THE MAGDALENA," AND IT REPRESENTS THE MAGDALENA'S EMPOWERMENT BY GOD.
LEGEND HAS IT THAT THROUGHOUT HISTORY, DURING TIMES OF DIRE NEED, VARIOUS WOMEN HAVE TAKEN THE MANTLE OF THE MAGDALENA, ALL OF THEM DESCENDENTS OF MARY MAGDALENE.
HISTORIANS HAVE PRETTY MUCH CONCLUDED THAT THE MAGDALENA IS MORE MYTHOLOGY THAN REALITY; A SYMBOLIC REPRESENTATION OF THE CATHOLIC CHURCH'S STRUGGLE AGAINST THE WORLD'S EVILS.
UNCANNY, ISN'T IT?

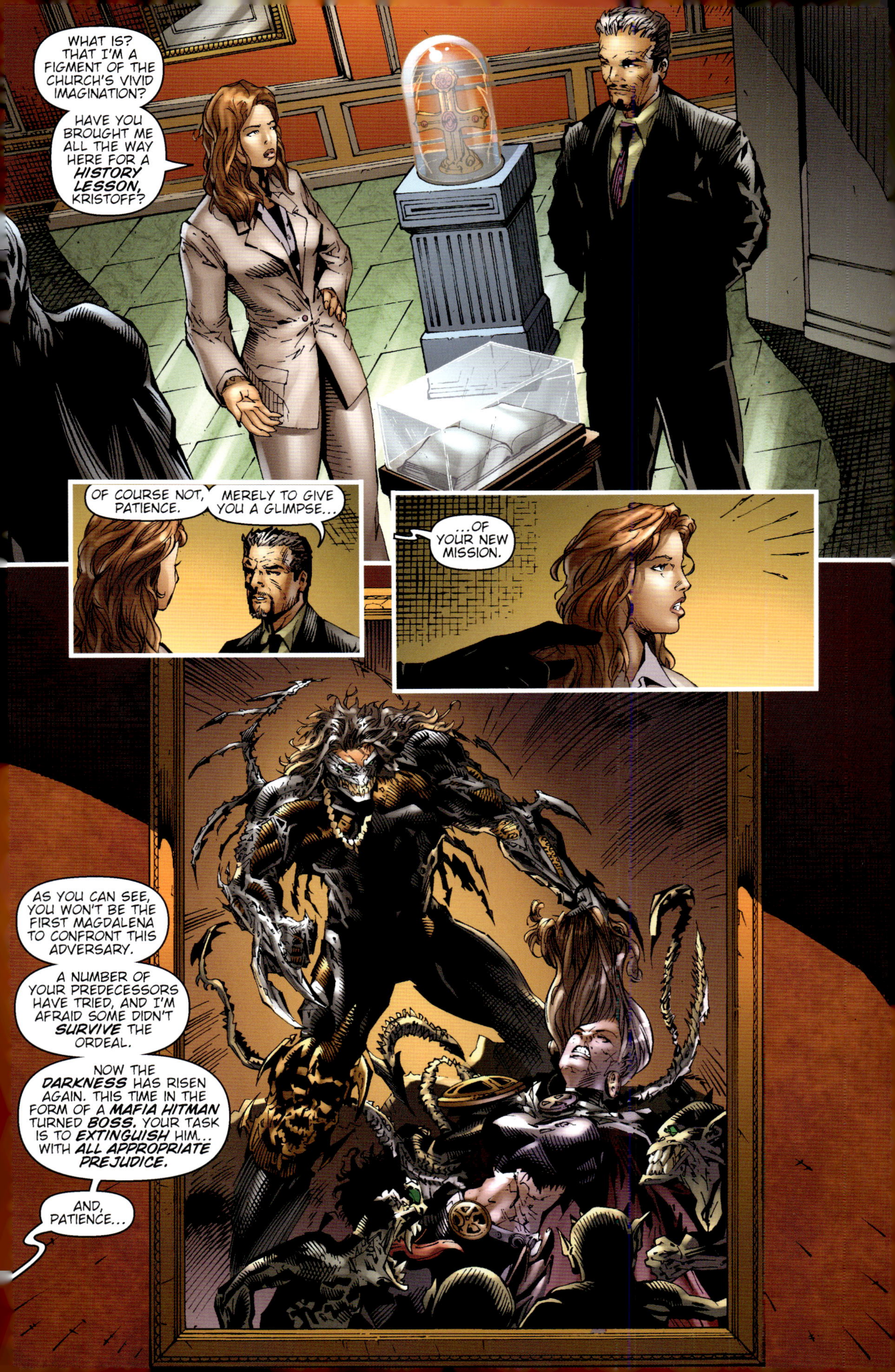
WHAT IS? THAT I'M A FIGMENT OF THE CHURCH'S VIVID IMAGINATION?
HAVE YOU BROUGHT ME ALL THE WAY HERE FOR A ***HISTORY LESSON,*** KRISTOFF?
OF COURSE NOT, PATIENCE.
MERELY TO GIVE YOU A GLIMPSE...
...OF YOUR NEW MISSION.
AS YOU CAN SEE, YOU WON'T BE THE FIRST MAGDALENA TO CONFRONT THIS ADVERSARY.
A NUMBER OF YOUR PREDECESSORS HAVE TRIED, AND I'M AFRAID SOME DIDN'T ***SURVIVE*** THE ORDEAL.
NOW THE ***DARKNESS*** HAS RISEN AGAIN. THIS TIME IN THE FORM OF A ***MAFIA HITMAN*** TURNED ***BOSS.*** YOUR TASK IS TO ***EXTINGUISH*** HIM... WITH ***ALL APPROPRIATE PREJUDICE.***
AND, PATIENCE...

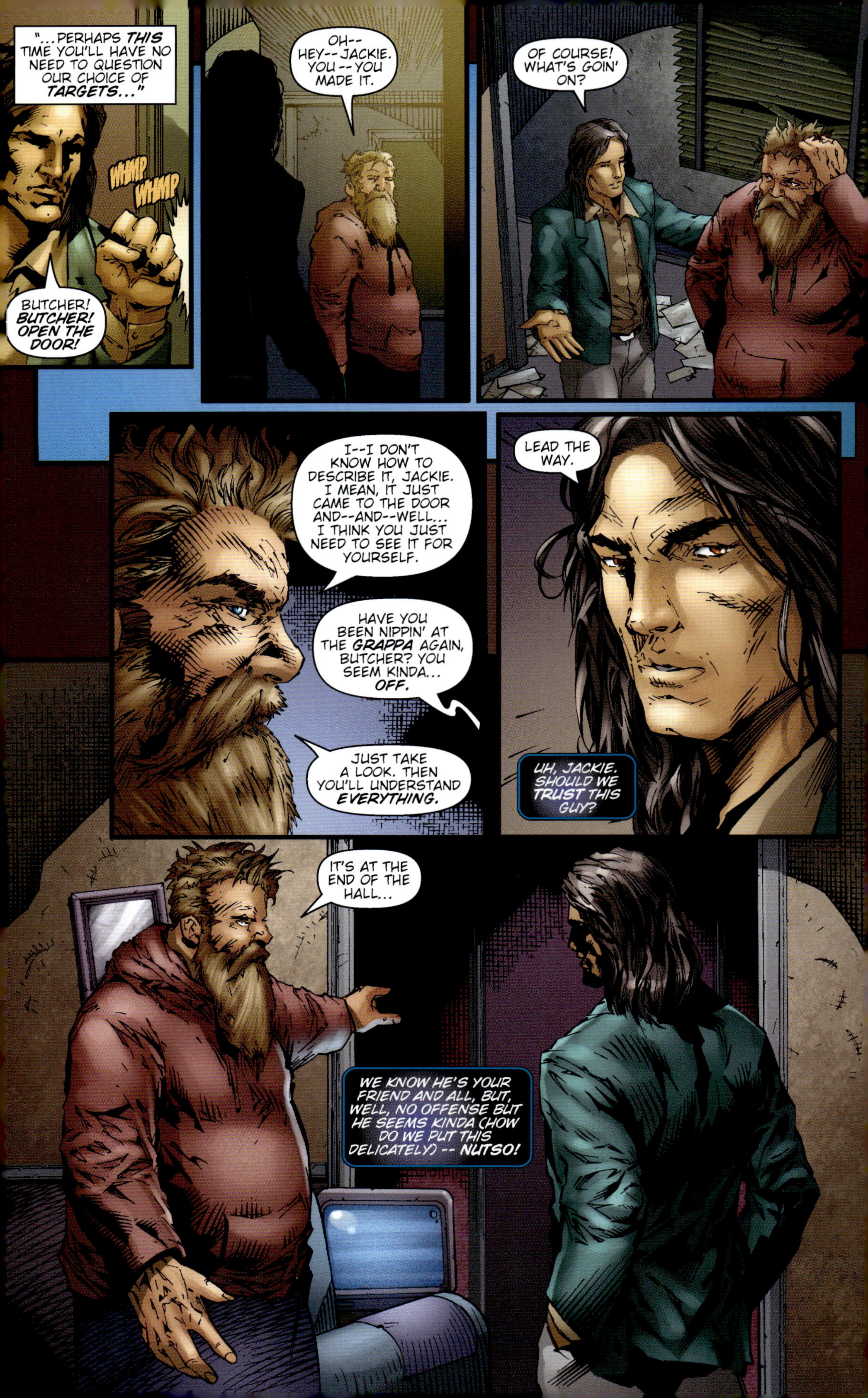

"...PERHAPS THIS TIME YOU'LL HAVE NO NEED TO QUESTION OUR CHOICE OF TARGETS..."
WHMP WHMP
BUTCHER! BUTCHER! OPEN THE DOOR!
OH-- HEY-- JACKIE. YOU --YOU MADE IT.
OF COURSE! WHAT'S GOIN' ON?
I--I DON'T KNOW HOW TO DESCRIBE IT, JACKIE. I MEAN, IT JUST CAME TO THE DOOR AND--AND--WELL... I THINK YOU JUST NEED TO SEE IT FOR YOURSELF.
HAVE YOU BEEN NIPPIN' AT THE GRAPPA AGAIN, BUTCHER? YOU SEEM KINDA... OFF.
JUST TAKE A LOOK. THEN YOU'LL UNDERSTAND EVERYTHING.
LEAD THE WAY.
UH, JACKIE. SHOULD WE TRUST THIS GUY?
IT'S AT THE END OF THE HALL...
WE KNOW HE'S YOUR FRIEND AND ALL, BUT, WELL, NO OFFENSE BUT HE SEEMS KINDA (HOW DO WE PUT THIS DELICATELY) -- NUTSO!

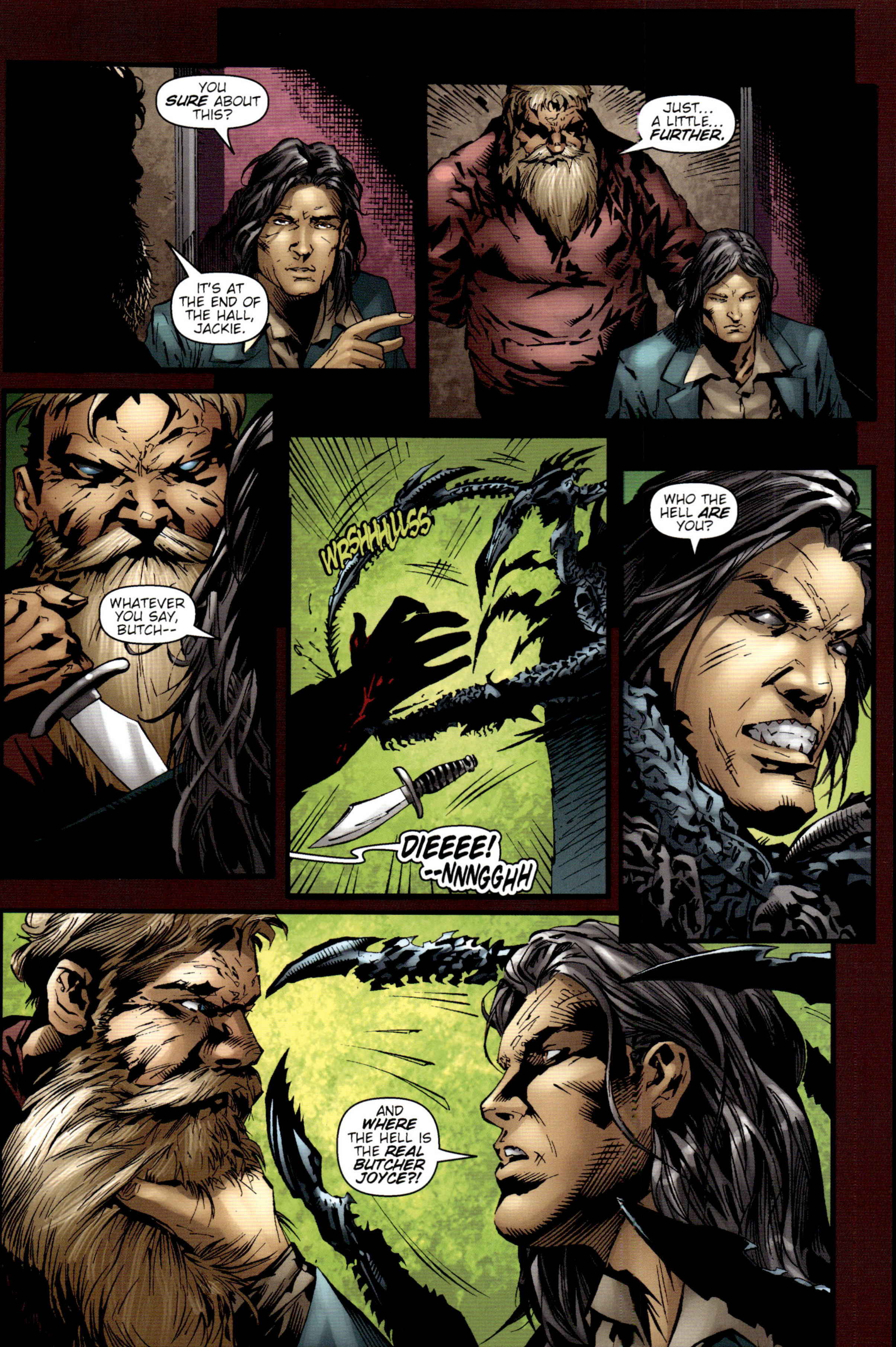

YOU SURE ABOUT THIS?
IT'S AT THE END OF THE HALL, JACKIE.
JUST... A LITTLE... FURTHER.
WHATEVER YOU SAY, BUTCH--
WRSHHHLLSS
DIEEEE! --NNNGGHH
WHO THE HELL ARE YOU?
AND WHERE THE HELL IS THE REAL BUTCHER JOYCE?!

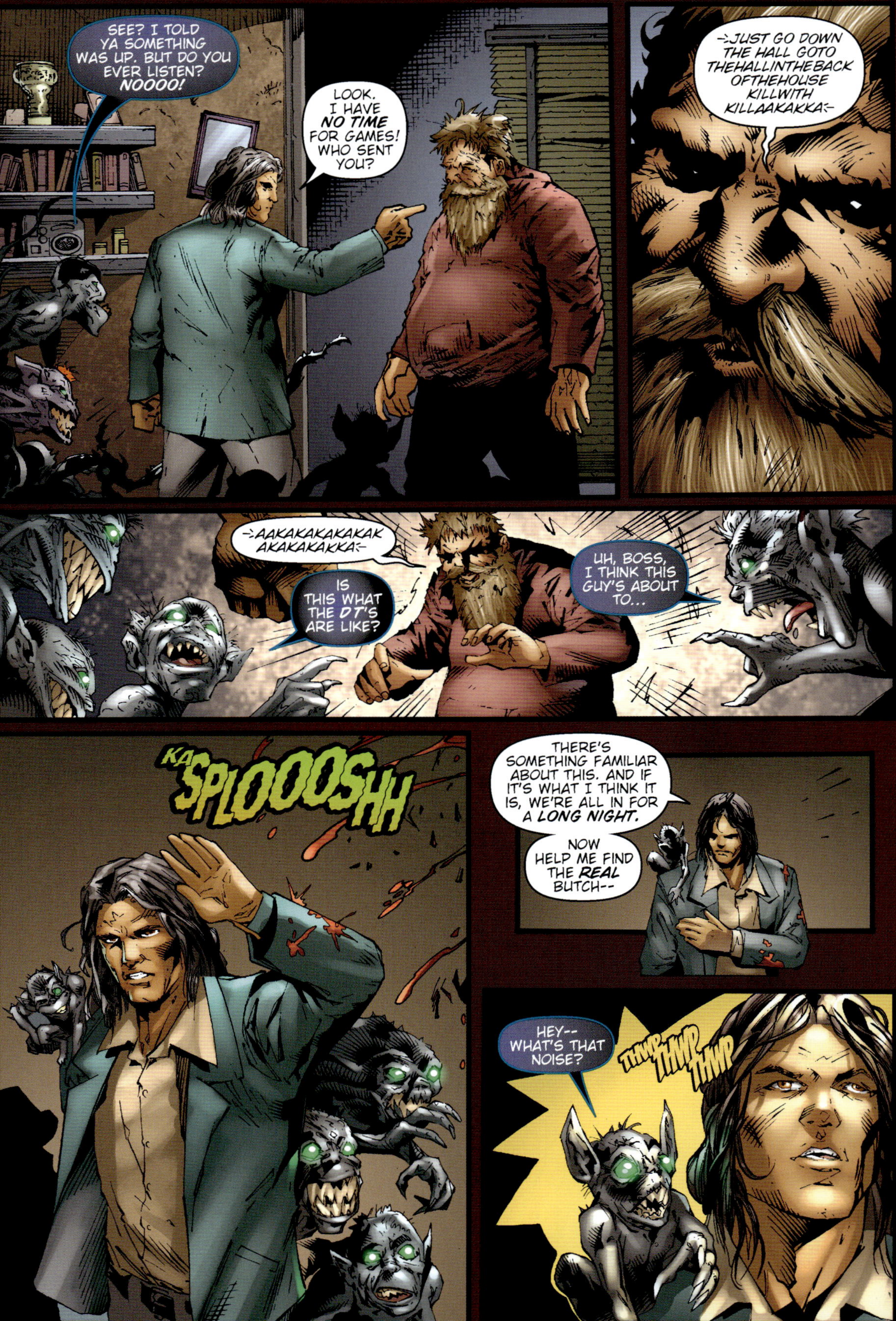

SEE? I TOLD YA SOMETHING WAS UP. BUT DO YOU EVER LISTEN? NOOOO!
LOOK. I HAVE NO TIME FOR GAMES! WHO SENT YOU?
-JUST GO DOWN THE HALL GOTO THEHALLINTHEBACK OFTHEHOUSE KILLWITH KILLAAKAKKA-
-AAKAKAKAKAKAK AKAKAKAKKA-
IS THIS WHAT THE DT'S ARE LIKE?
UH, BOSS, I THINK THIS GUY'S ABOUT TO...
KA SPLOOOSHH
THERE'S SOMETHING FAMILIAR ABOUT THIS. AND IF IT'S WHAT I THINK IT IS, WE'RE ALL IN FOR A LONG NIGHT.
NOW HELP ME FIND THE REAL BUTCH--
HEY-- WHAT'S THAT NOISE?
THWP THWP THWP

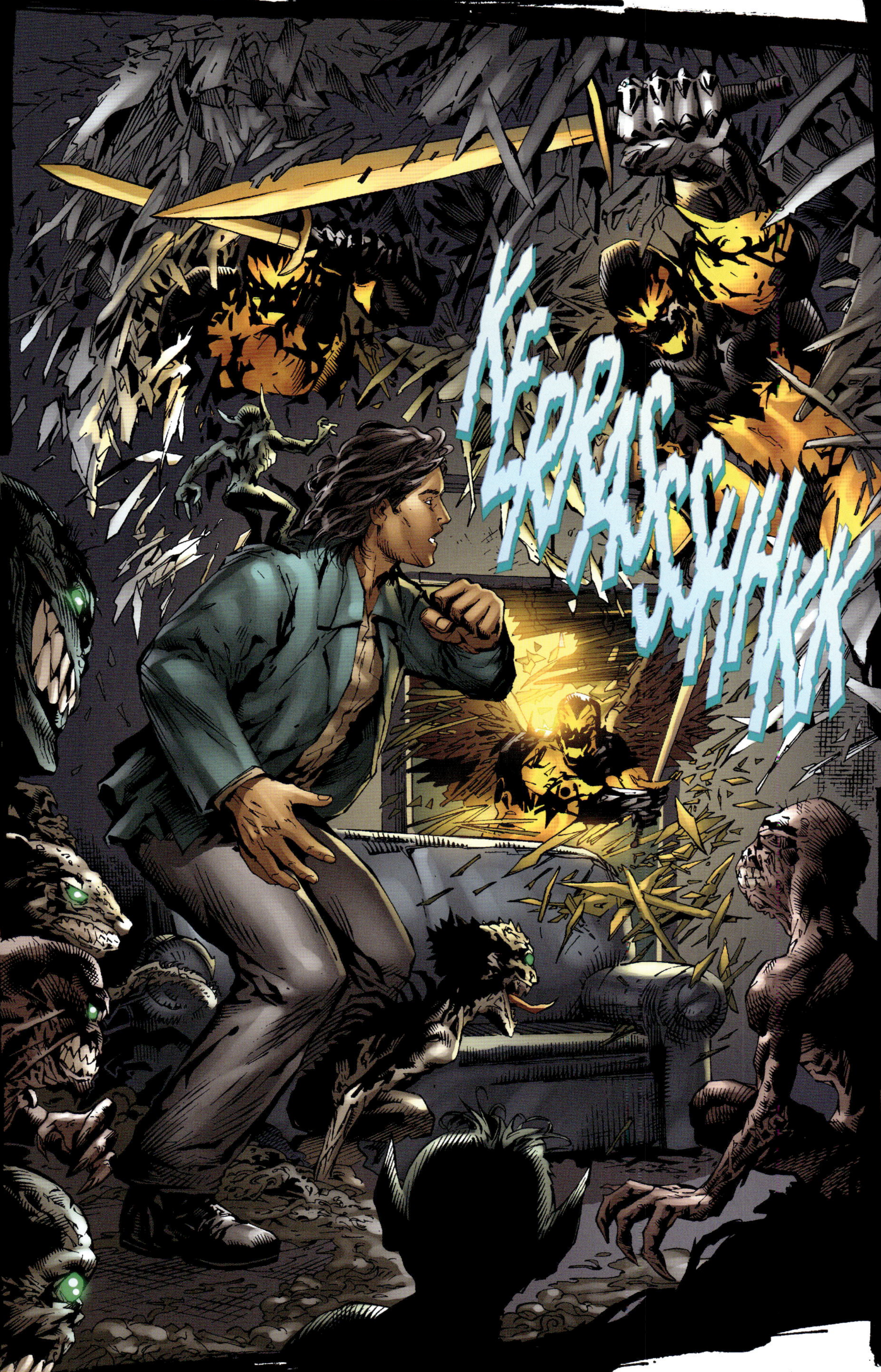

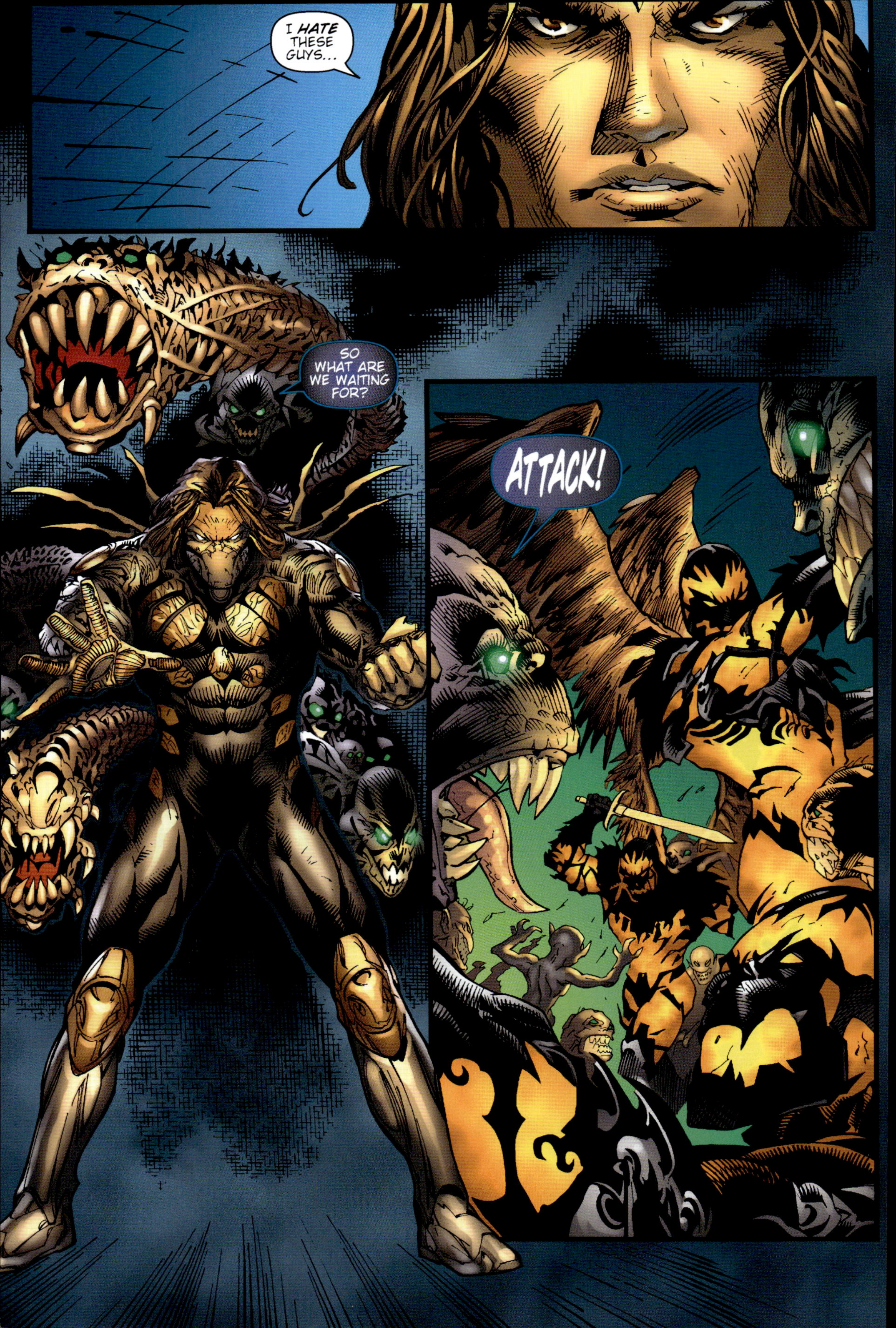
I HATE THESE GUYS...
SO WHAT ARE WE WAITING FOR?
ATTACK!

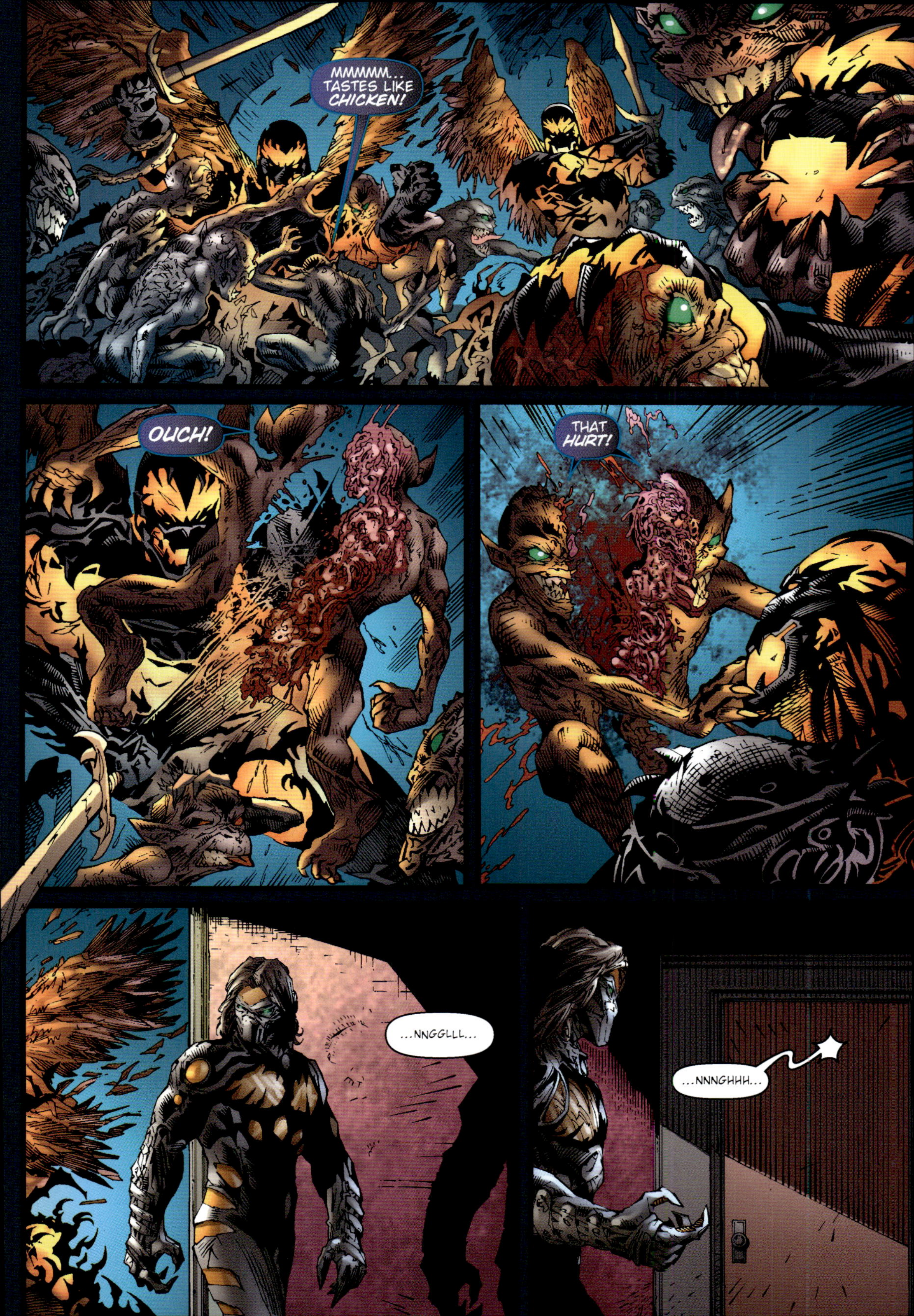
MMMMM... TASTES LIKE CHICKEN!
OUCH!
THAT HURT!
...NNGGLLL...
...NNNGHHH...

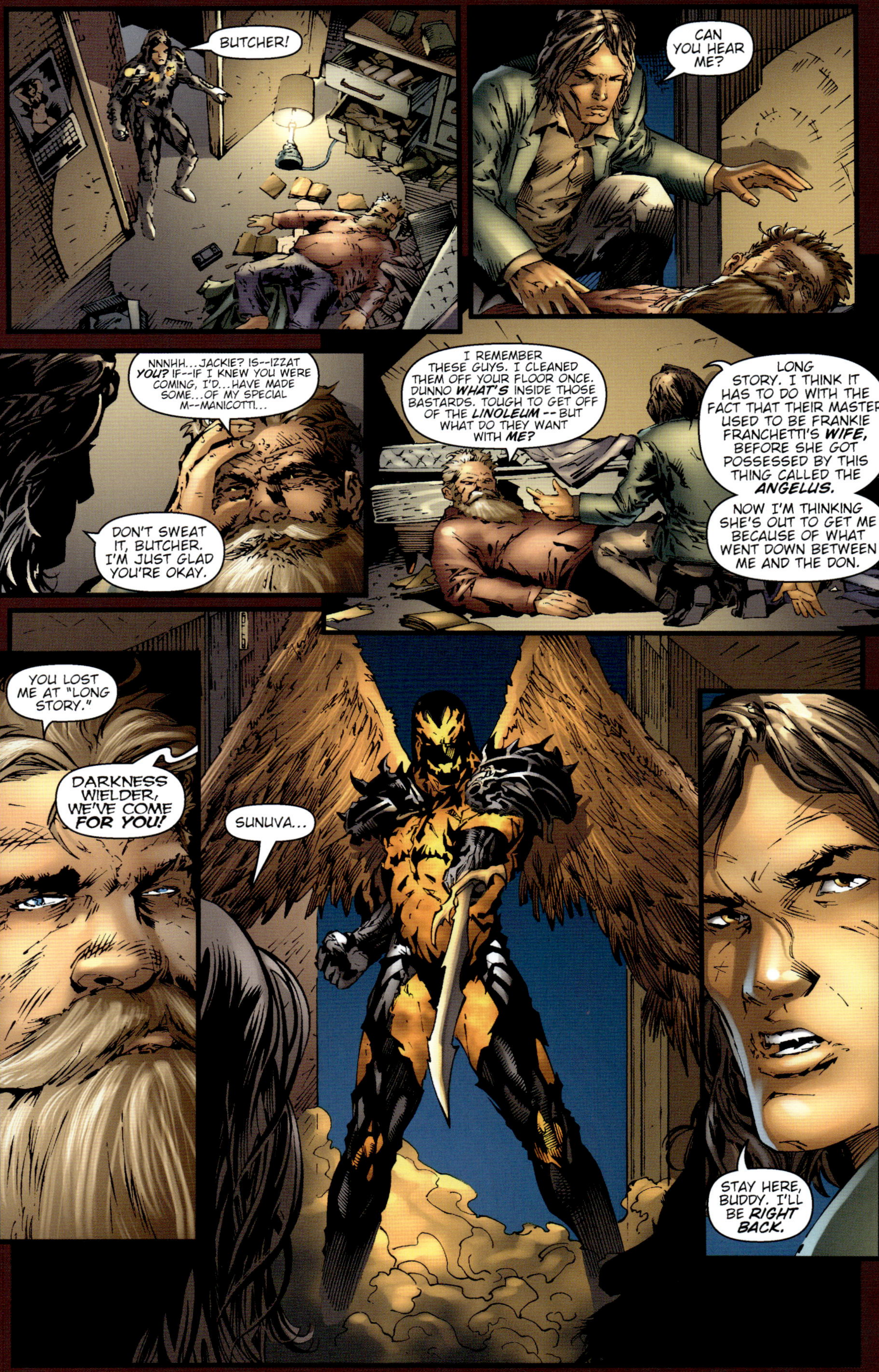
BUTCHER!
CAN YOU HEAR ME?
NNNHH...JACKIE? IS--IZZAT *YOU?* IF--IF I KNEW YOU WERE COMING, I'D...HAVE MADE SOME...OF MY SPECIAL M--MANICOTTI...
DON'T SWEAT IT, BUTCHER. I'M JUST GLAD YOU'RE OKAY.
I REMEMBER THESE GUYS. I CLEANED THEM OFF YOUR FLOOR ONCE. DUNNO ***WHAT'S*** INSIDE THOSE BASTARDS. TOUGH TO GET OFF OF THE ***LINOLEUM*** -- BUT WHAT DO THEY WANT WITH ***ME?***
LONG STORY. I THINK IT HAS TO DO WITH THE FACT THAT THEIR MASTER USED TO BE FRANKIE FRANCHETTI'S ***WIFE,*** BEFORE SHE GOT POSSESSED BY THIS THING CALLED THE ***ANGELUS.***
NOW I'M THINKING SHE'S OUT TO GET ME BECAUSE OF WHAT WENT DOWN BETWEEN ME AND THE DON.
YOU LOST ME AT "LONG STORY."
DARKNESS WIELDER, WE'VE COME ***FOR YOU!***
SUNUVA...
STAY HERE, BUDDY. I'LL BE ***RIGHT BACK.***

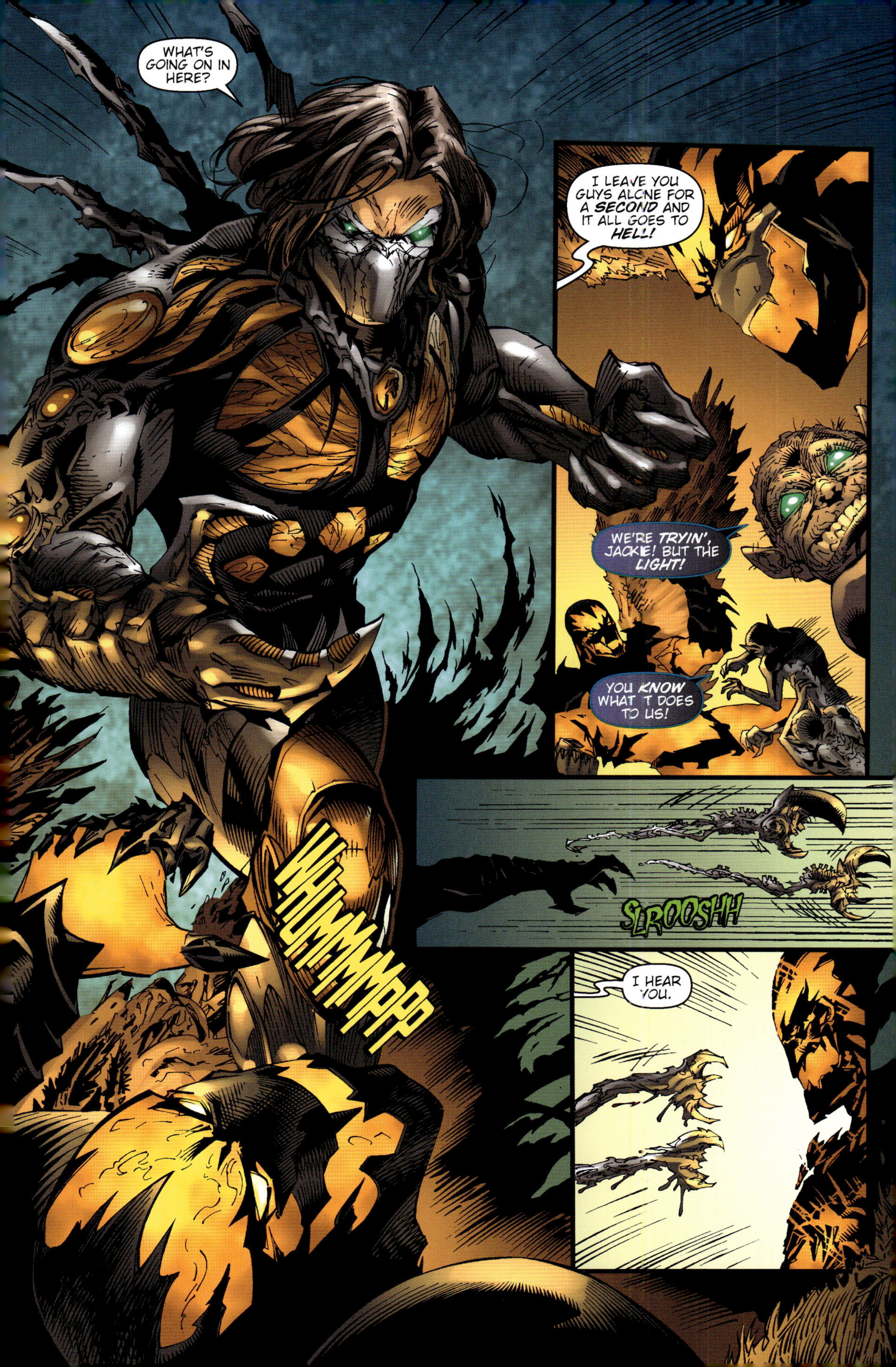
WHAT'S GOING ON IN HERE?
I LEAVE YOU GUYS ALONE FOR A SECOND AND IT ALL GOES TO HELL!
WE'RE TRYIN', JACKIE! BUT THE LIGHT!
YOU KNOW WHAT IT DOES TO US!
WHUMMMPP
SLROOSHH
I HEAR YOU.

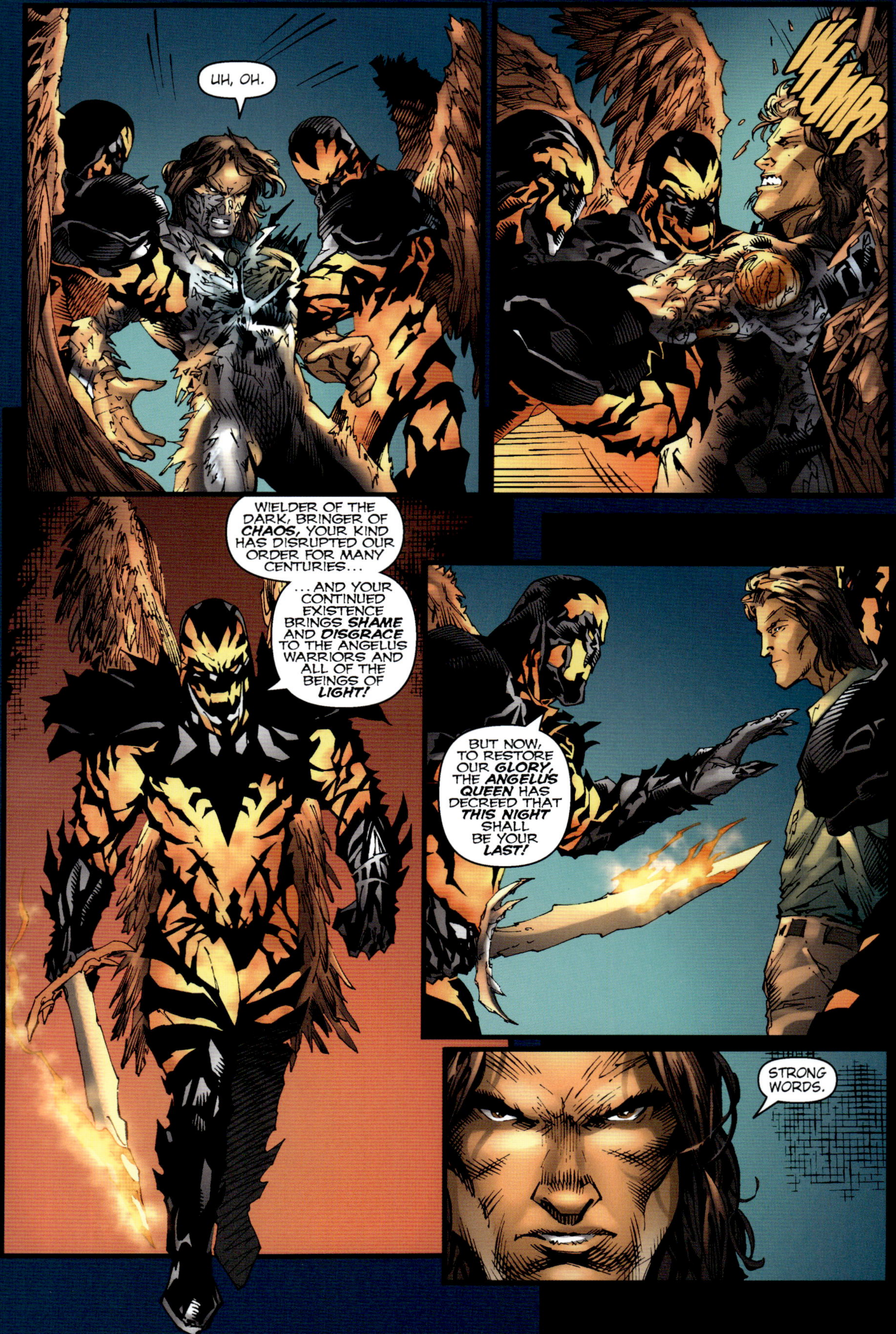

UH, OH.
WHMP
WIELDER OF THE DARK, BRINGER OF CHAOS, YOUR KIND HAS DISRUPTED OUR ORDER FOR MANY CENTURIES...
...AND YOUR CONTINUED EXISTENCE BRINGS SHAME AND DISGRACE TO THE ANGELUS WARRIORS AND ALL OF THE BEINGS OF LIGHT!
BUT NOW, TO RESTORE OUR GLORY, THE ANGELUS QUEEN HAS DECREED THAT THIS NIGHT SHALL BE YOUR LAST!
STRONG WORDS.

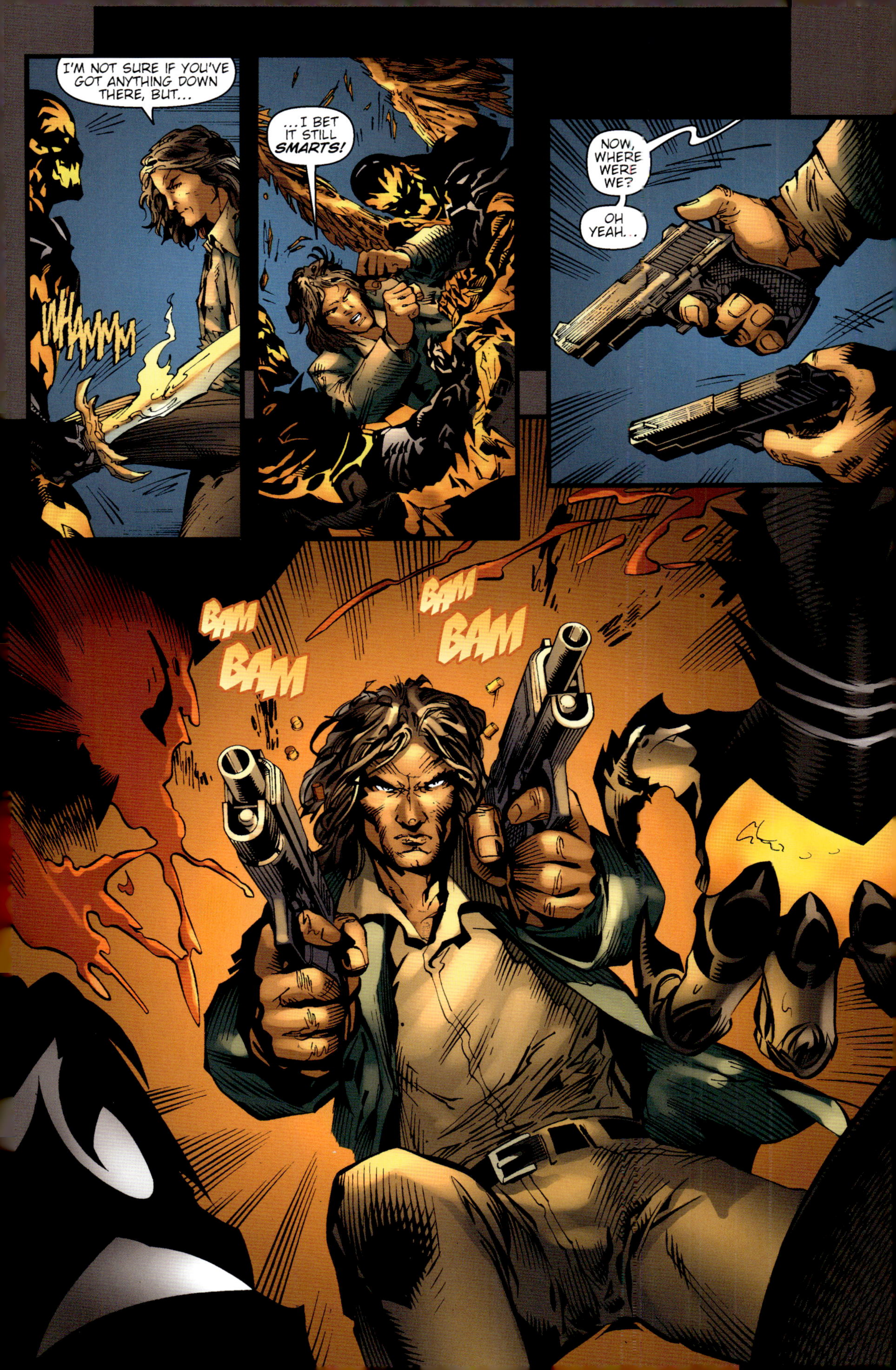
I'M NOT SURE IF YOU'VE GOT ANYTHING DOWN THERE, BUT...
WHAMMM
...I BET IT STILL SMARTS!
NOW, WHERE WERE WE?
OH YEAH...
BAM
BAM
BAM
BAM

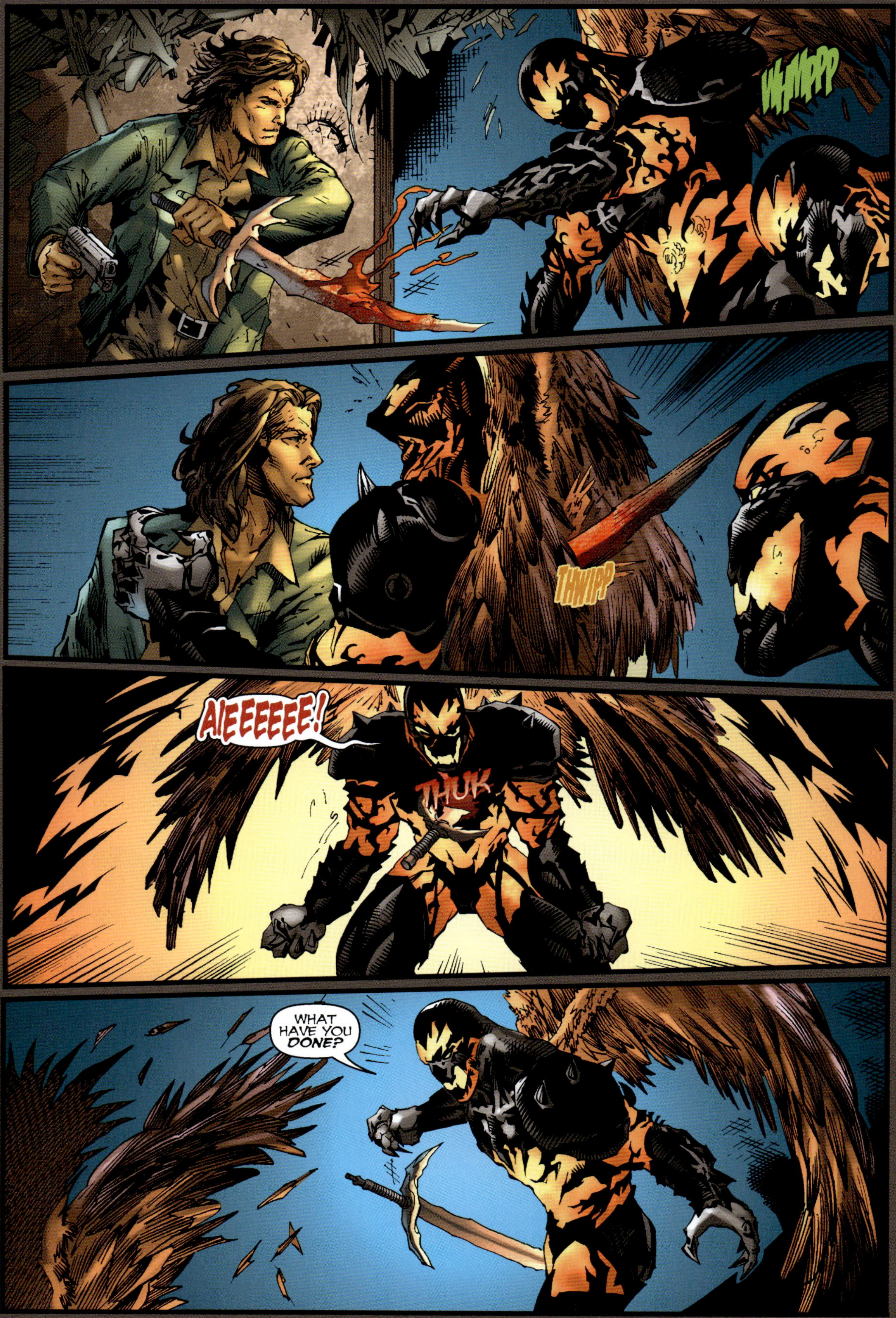
WHMPP
THWIPP
AIEEEEEE!
THUK
WHAT HAVE YOU DONE?

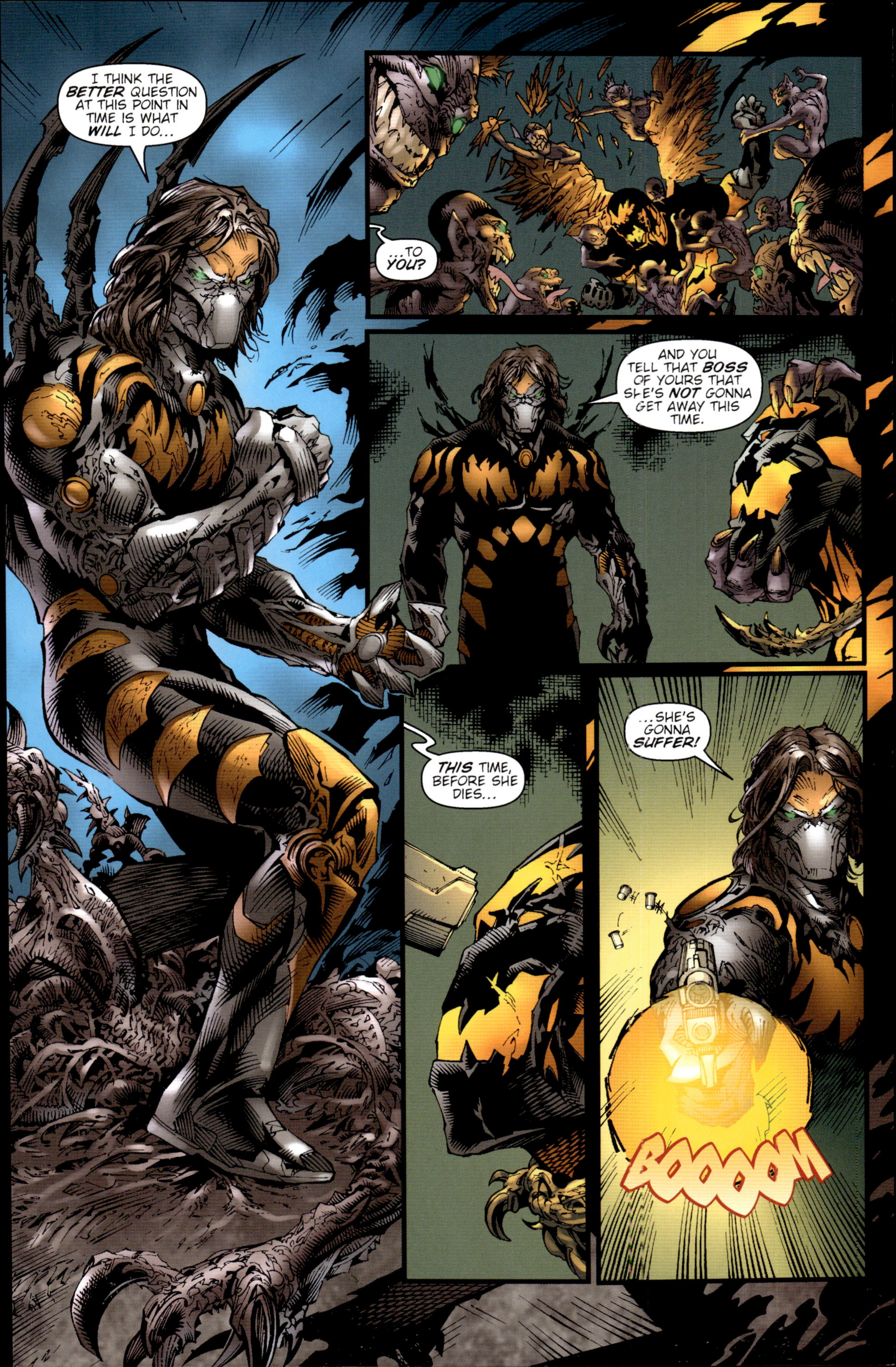
I THINK THE BETTER QUESTION AT THIS POINT IN TIME IS WHAT WILL I DO...
...TO YOU?
AND YOU TELL THAT BOSS OF YOURS THAT SHE'S NOT GONNA GET AWAY THIS TIME.
THIS TIME, BEFORE SHE DIES...
...SHE'S GONNA SUFFER!
BOOOOM

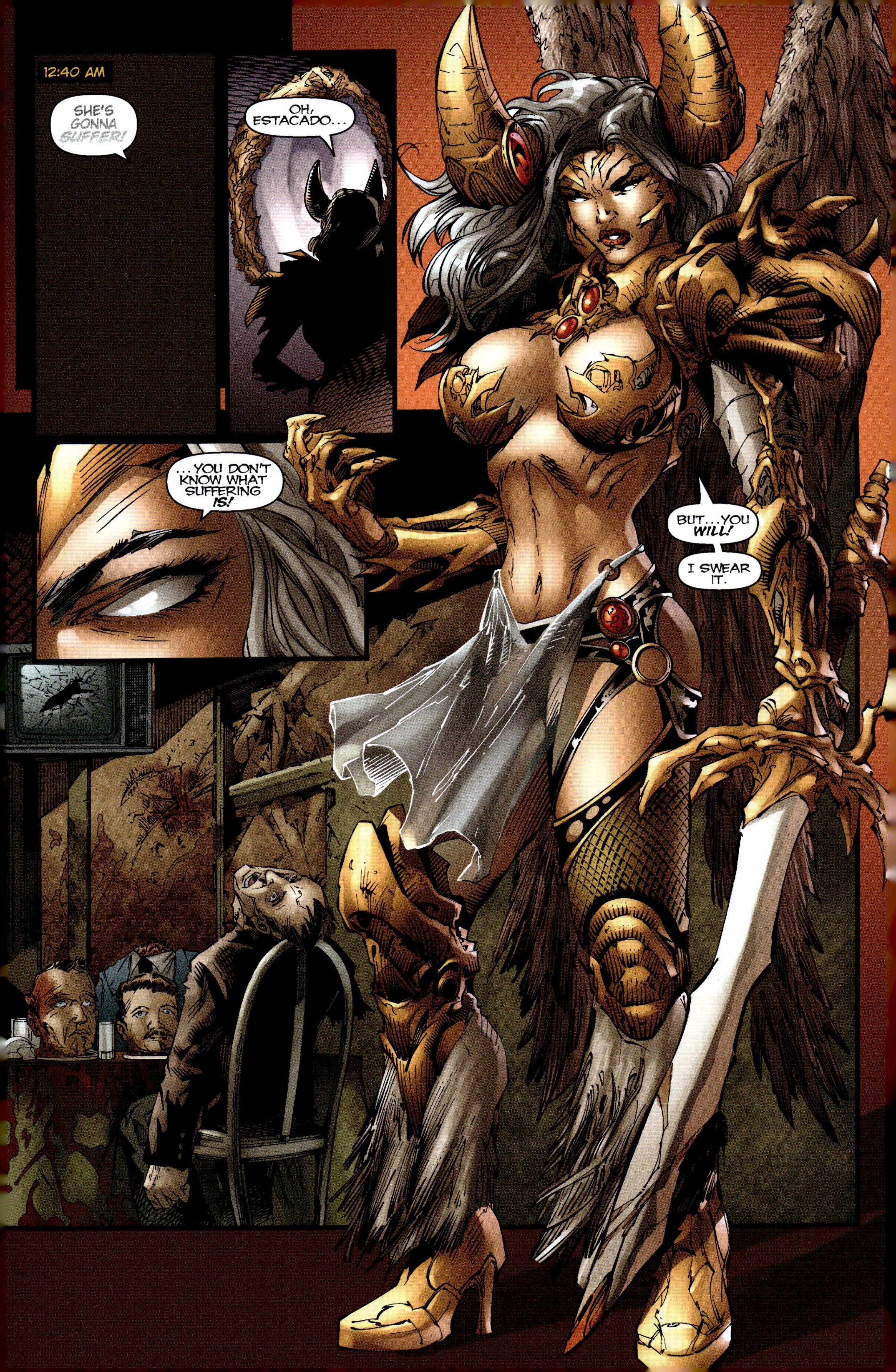
12:40 AM
SHE'S GONNA SUFFER!
OH, ESTACADO...
...YOU DON'T KNOW WHAT SUFFERING IS!
BUT...YOU WILL!
I SWEAR IT.

The Darkness Issue #63

cover art by: Dale Keown & Matt Milla

THE DARKNESS #63

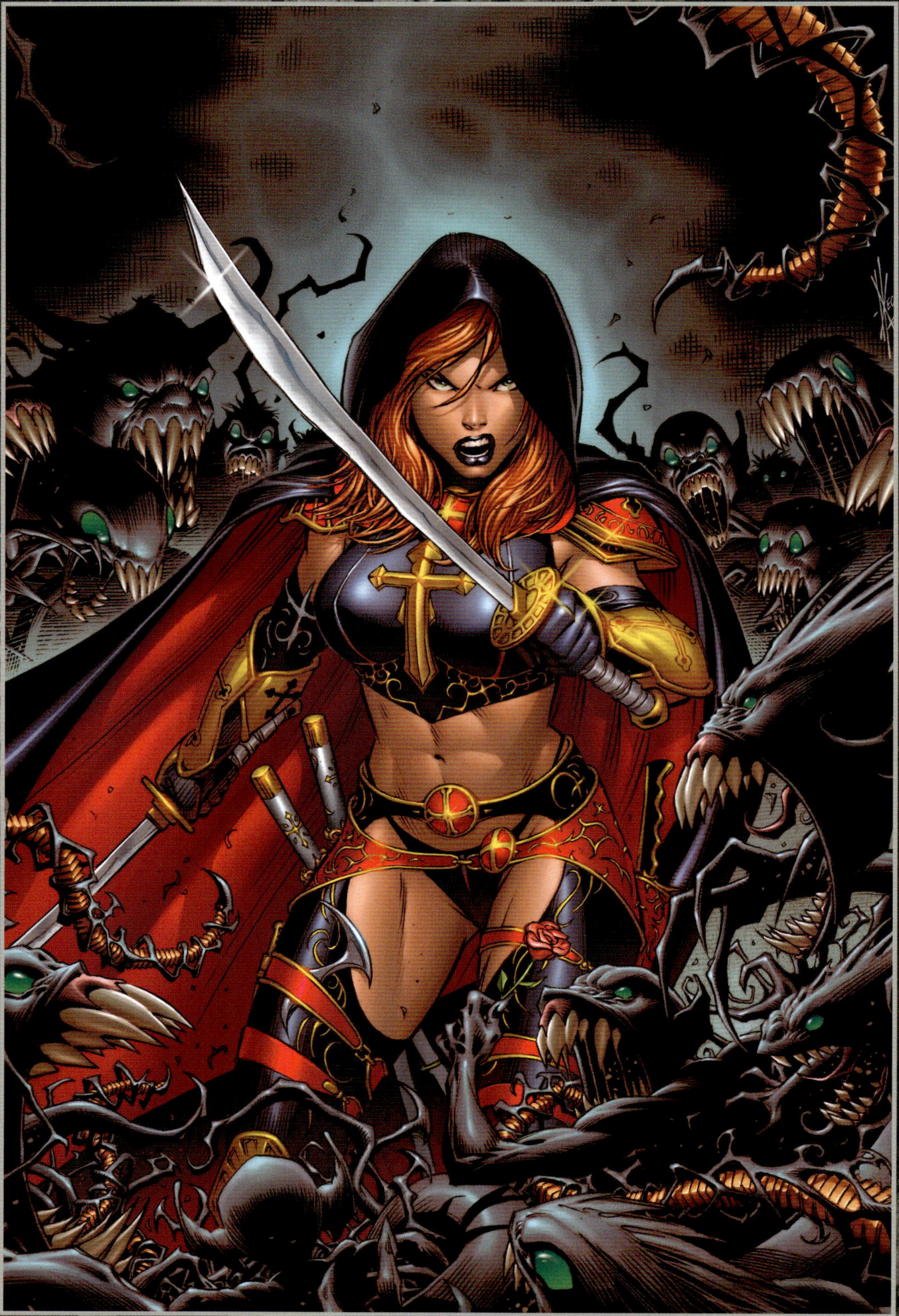

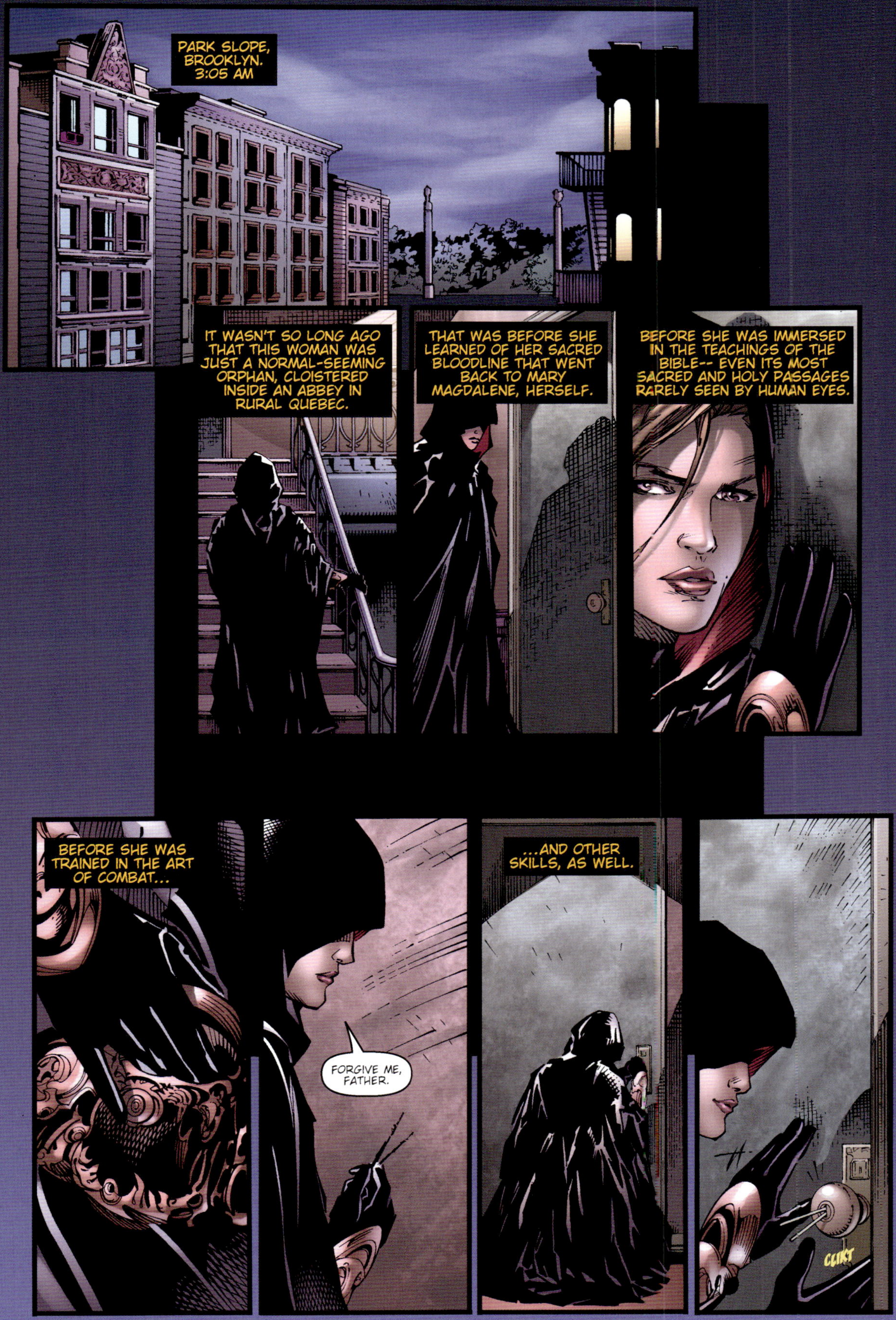
PARK SLOPE, BROOKLYN. 3:05 AM
IT WASN'T SO LONG AGO THAT THIS WOMAN WAS JUST A NORMAL-SEEMING ORPHAN, CLOISTERED INSIDE AN ABBEY IN RURAL QUEBEC.
THAT WAS BEFORE SHE LEARNED OF HER SACRED BLOODLINE THAT WENT BACK TO MARY MAGDALENE, HERSELF.
BEFORE SHE WAS IMMERSED IN THE TEACHINGS OF THE BIBLE-- EVEN ITS MOST SACRED AND HOLY PASSAGES RARELY SEEN BY HUMAN EYES.
BEFORE SHE WAS TRAINED IN THE ART OF COMBAT...
FORGIVE ME, FATHER.
...AND OTHER SKILLS, AS WELL.
CLIKT

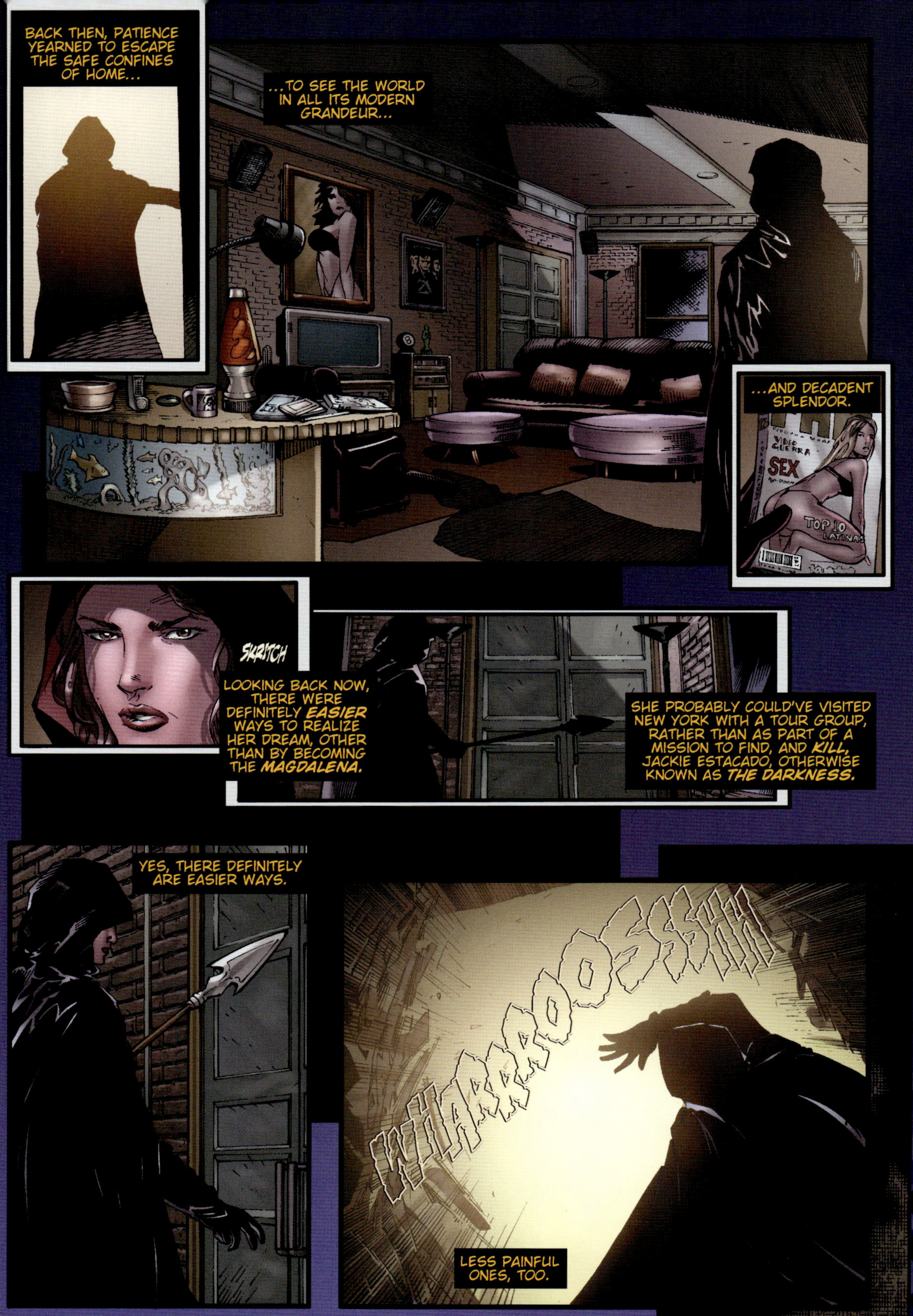
BACK THEN, PATIENCE YEARNED TO ESCAPE THE SAFE CONFINES OF HOME...
...TO SEE THE WORLD IN ALL ITS MODERN GRANDEUR...
...AND DECADENT SPLENDOR.
VIDEO GUERRA
SEX
TOP 10 LATINAS
SKRITCH
LOOKING BACK NOW, THERE WERE DEFINITELY EASIER WAYS TO REALIZE HER DREAM, OTHER THAN BY BECOMING THE MAGDALENA.
SHE PROBABLY COULD'VE VISITED NEW YORK WITH A TOUR GROUP, RATHER THAN AS PART OF A MISSION TO FIND, AND KILL, JACKIE ESTACADO, OTHERWISE KNOWN AS THE DARKNESS.
YES, THERE DEFINITELY ARE EASIER WAYS.
WHARROOSSHH
LESS PAINFUL ONES, TOO.

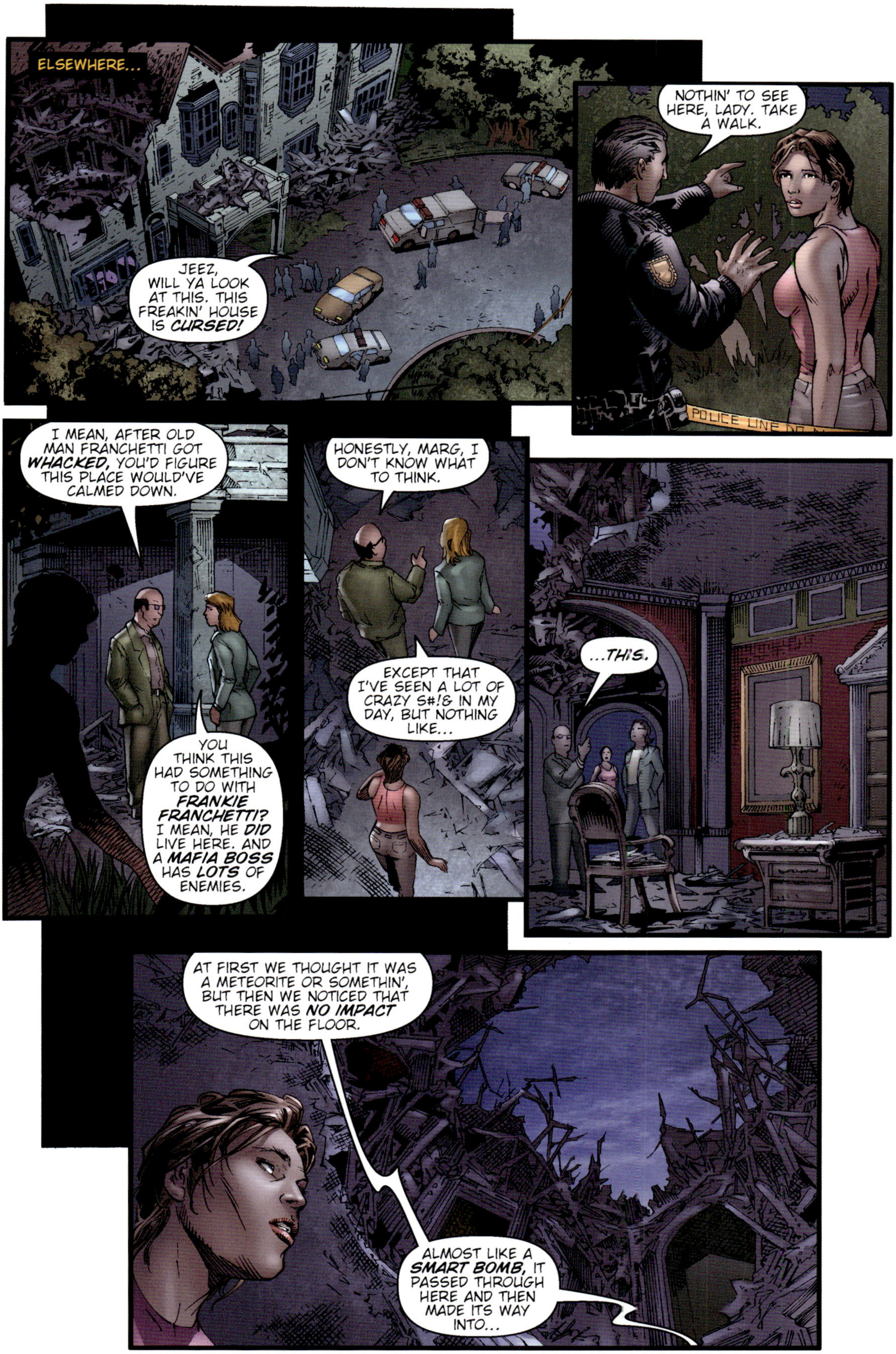
ELSEWHERE...
JEEZ, WILL YA LOOK AT THIS. THIS FREAKIN' HOUSE IS CURSED!
NOTHIN' TO SEE HERE, LADY. TAKE A WALK.
POLICE LINE
I MEAN, AFTER OLD MAN FRANCHETTI GOT WHACKED, YOU'D FIGURE THIS PLACE WOULD'VE CALMED DOWN.
YOU THINK THIS HAD SOMETHING TO DO WITH FRANKIE FRANCHETTI? I MEAN, HE DID LIVE HERE. AND A MAFIA BOSS HAS LOTS OF ENEMIES.
HONESTLY, MARG, I DON'T KNOW WHAT TO THINK.
EXCEPT THAT I'VE SEEN A LOT OF CRAZY S#!& IN MY DAY, BUT NOTHING LIKE...
...THIS.
AT FIRST WE THOUGHT IT WAS A METEORITE OR SOMETHIN', BUT THEN WE NOTICED THAT THERE WAS NO IMPACT ON THE FLOOR.
ALMOST LIKE A SMART BOMB, IT PASSED THROUGH HERE AND THEN MADE ITS WAY INTO...

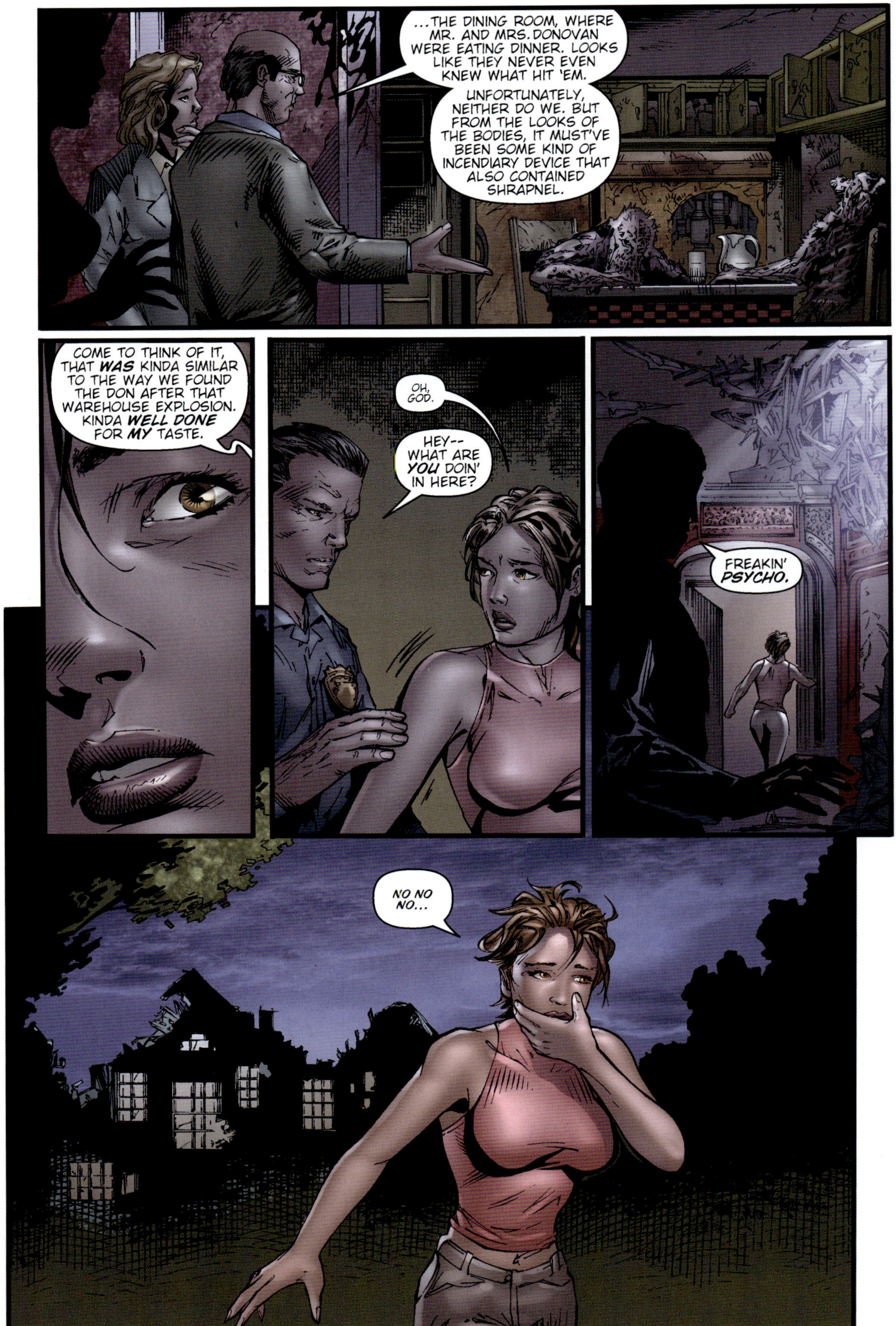
...THE DINING ROOM, WHERE MR. AND MRS. DONOVAN WERE EATING DINNER. LOOKS LIKE THEY NEVER EVEN KNEW WHAT HIT 'EM.
UNFORTUNATELY, NEITHER DO WE. BUT FROM THE LOOKS OF THE BODIES, IT MUST'VE BEEN SOME KIND OF INCENDIARY DEVICE THAT ALSO CONTAINED SHRAPNEL.
COME TO THINK OF IT, THAT **WAS** KINDA SIMILAR TO THE WAY WE FOUND THE DON AFTER THAT WAREHOUSE EXPLOSION. KINDA **WELL DONE** FOR **MY** TASTE.
OH, GOD.
HEY-- WHAT ARE **YOU** DOIN' IN HERE?
FREAKIN' **PSYCHO.**
NO NO NO...

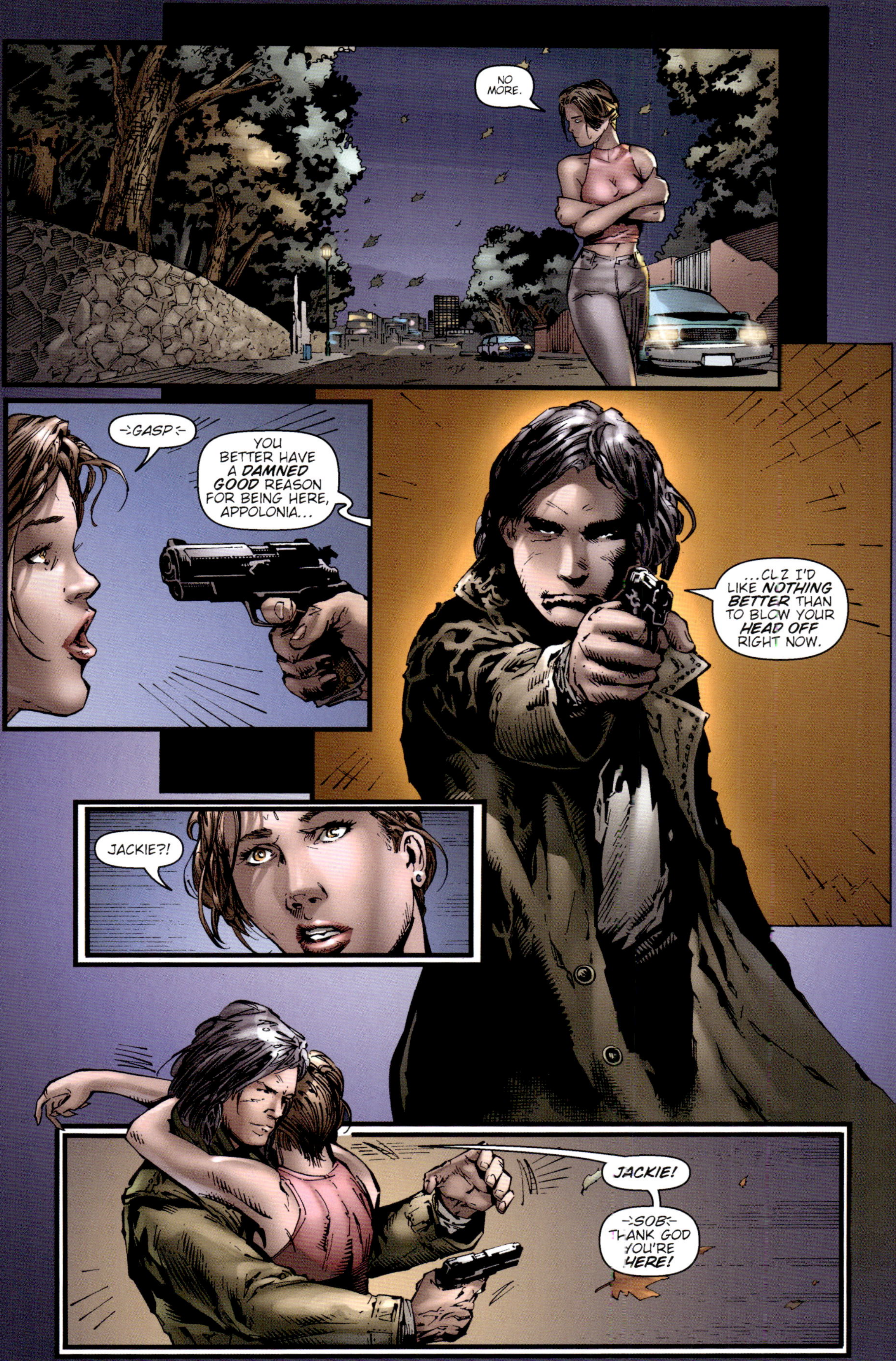
NO MORE.
-GASP-
YOU BETTER HAVE A DAMNED GOOD REASON FOR BEING HERE, APPOLONIA...
...CUZ I'D LIKE NOTHING BETTER THAN TO BLOW YOUR HEAD OFF RIGHT NOW.
JACKIE?!
JACKIE!
-SOB- THANK GOD YOU'RE HERE!

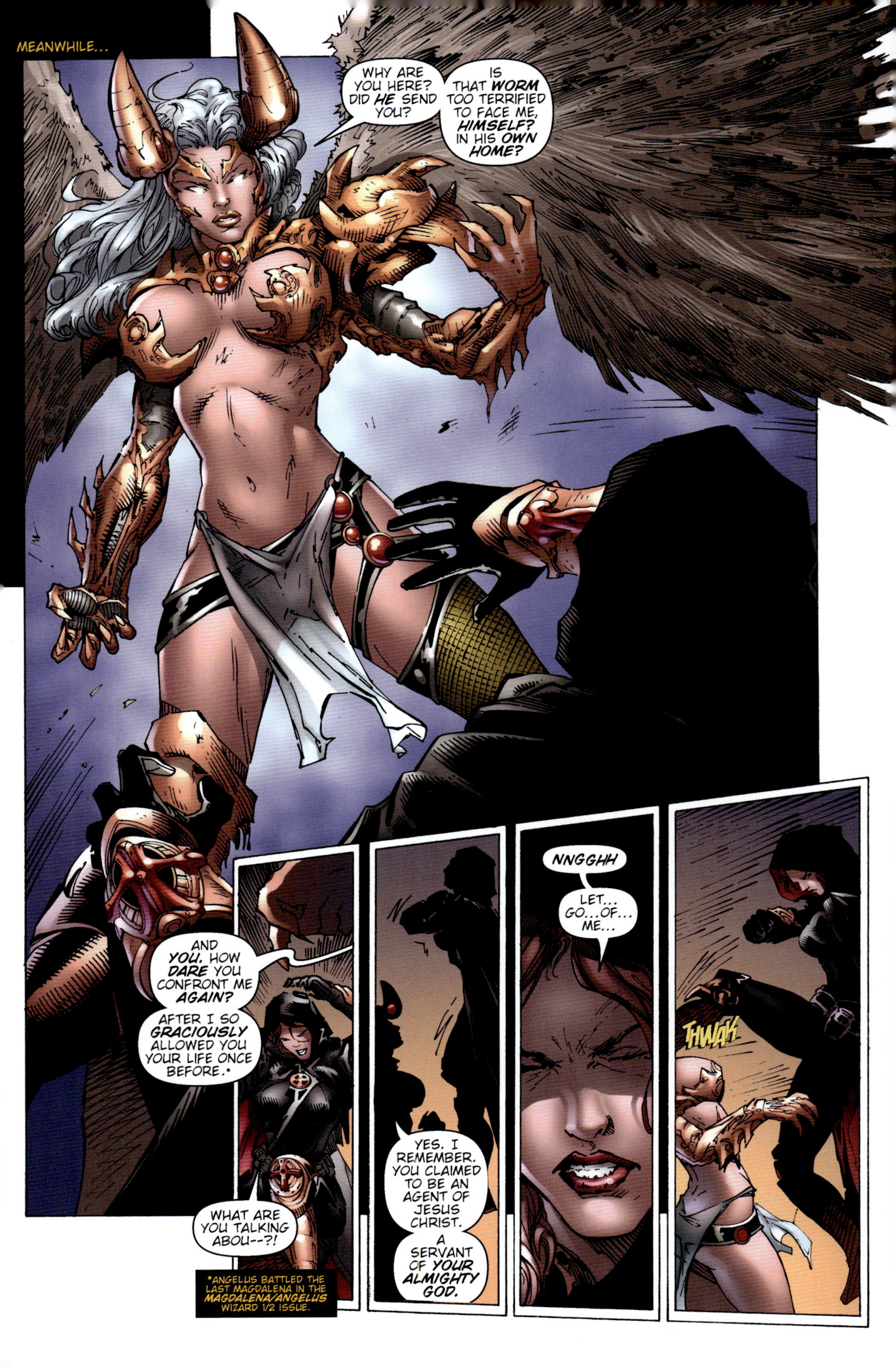
MEANWHILE...
WHY ARE YOU HERE? DID HE SEND YOU?
IS THAT WORM TOO TERRIFIED TO FACE ME, HIMSELF? IN HIS OWN HOME?
AND YOU. HOW DARE YOU CONFRONT ME AGAIN?
AFTER I SO GRACIOUSLY ALLOWED YOU YOUR LIFE ONCE BEFORE.*
WHAT ARE YOU TALKING ABOU--?!
*ANGELUS BATTLED THE LAST MAGDALENA IN THE MAGDALENA/ANGELUS WIZARD 1/2 ISSUE.
YES. I REMEMBER. YOU CLAIMED TO BE AN AGENT OF JESUS CHRIST.
A SERVANT OF YOUR ALMIGHTY GOD.
NNGGHH
LET... GO...OF... ME...
THWAK

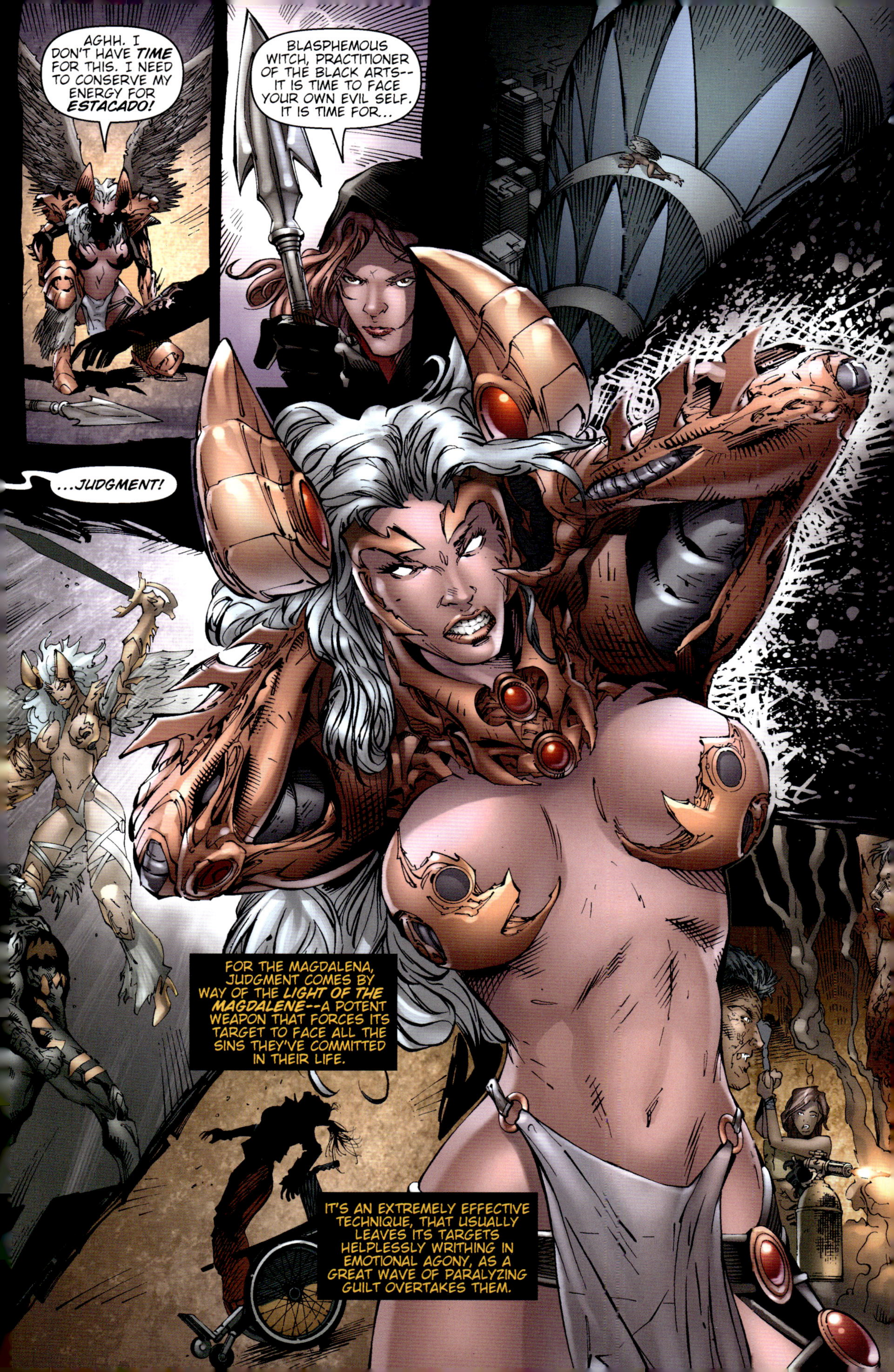
AGHH. I DON'T HAVE TIME FOR THIS. I NEED TO CONSERVE MY ENERGY FOR ESTACADO!
BLASPHEMOUS WITCH, PRACTITIONER OF THE BLACK ARTS-- IT IS TIME TO FACE YOUR OWN EVIL SELF. IT IS TIME FOR...
...JUDGMENT!
FOR THE MAGDALENA, JUDGMENT COMES BY WAY OF THE LIGHT OF THE MAGDALENE--A POTENT WEAPON THAT FORCES ITS TARGET TO FACE ALL THE SINS THEY'VE COMMITTED IN THEIR LIFE.
IT'S AN EXTREMELY EFFECTIVE TECHNIQUE, THAT USUALLY LEAVES ITS TARGETS HELPLESSLY WRITHING IN EMOTIONAL AGONY, AS A GREAT WAVE OF PARALYZING GUILT OVERTAKES THEM.

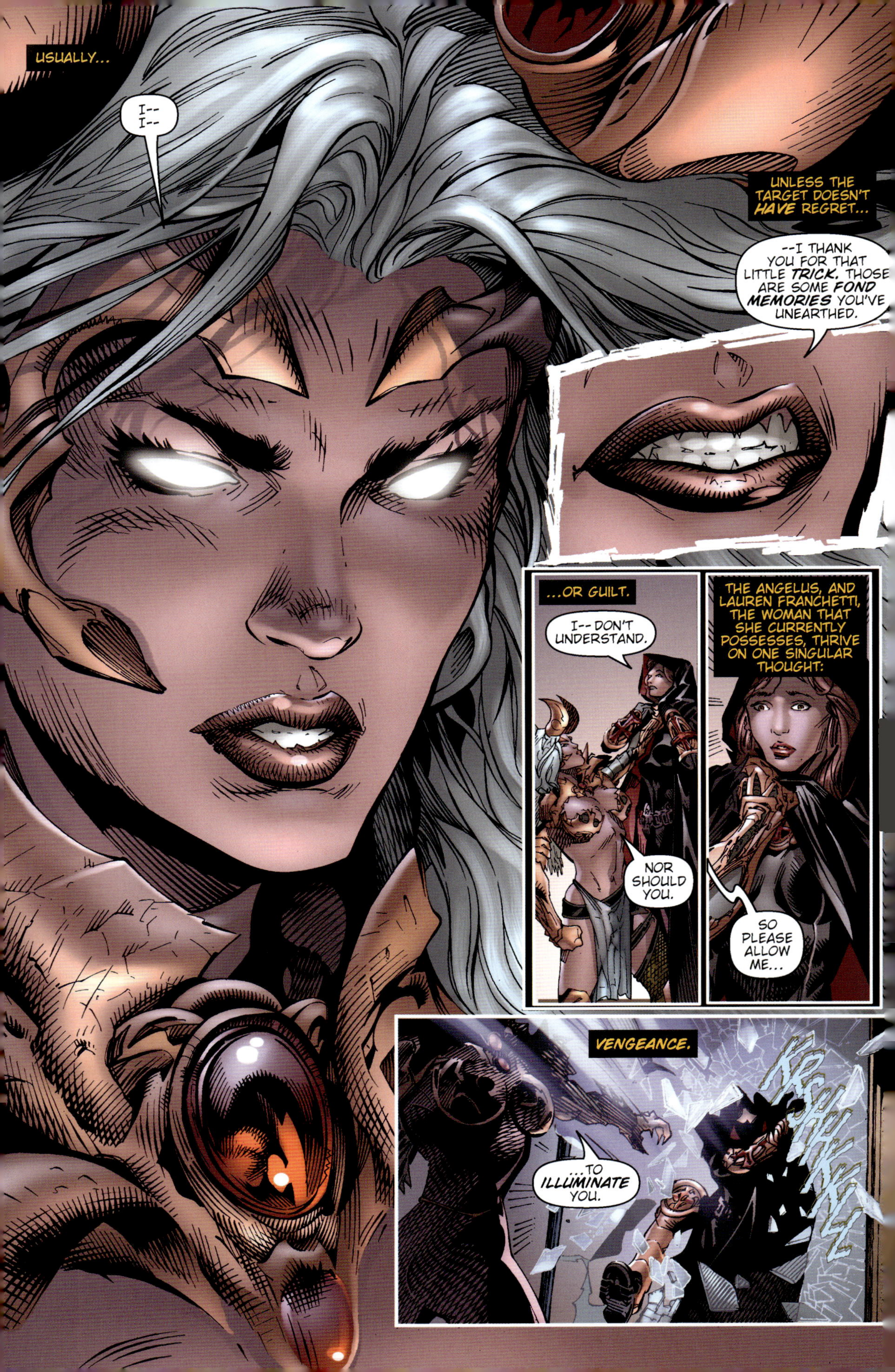
USUALLY...
I--
I--
UNLESS THE TARGET DOESN'T HAVE REGRET...
--I THANK YOU FOR THAT LITTLE TRICK. THOSE ARE SOME FOND MEMORIES YOU'VE UNEARTHED.
...OR GUILT.
I--DON'T UNDERSTAND.
NOR SHOULD YOU.
THE ANGELUS, AND LAUREN FRANCHETTI, THE WOMAN THAT SHE CURRENTLY POSSESSES, THRIVE ON ONE SINGULAR THOUGHT:
SO PLEASE ALLOW ME...
VENGEANCE.
...TO ILLUMINATE YOU.
KRSHKKL

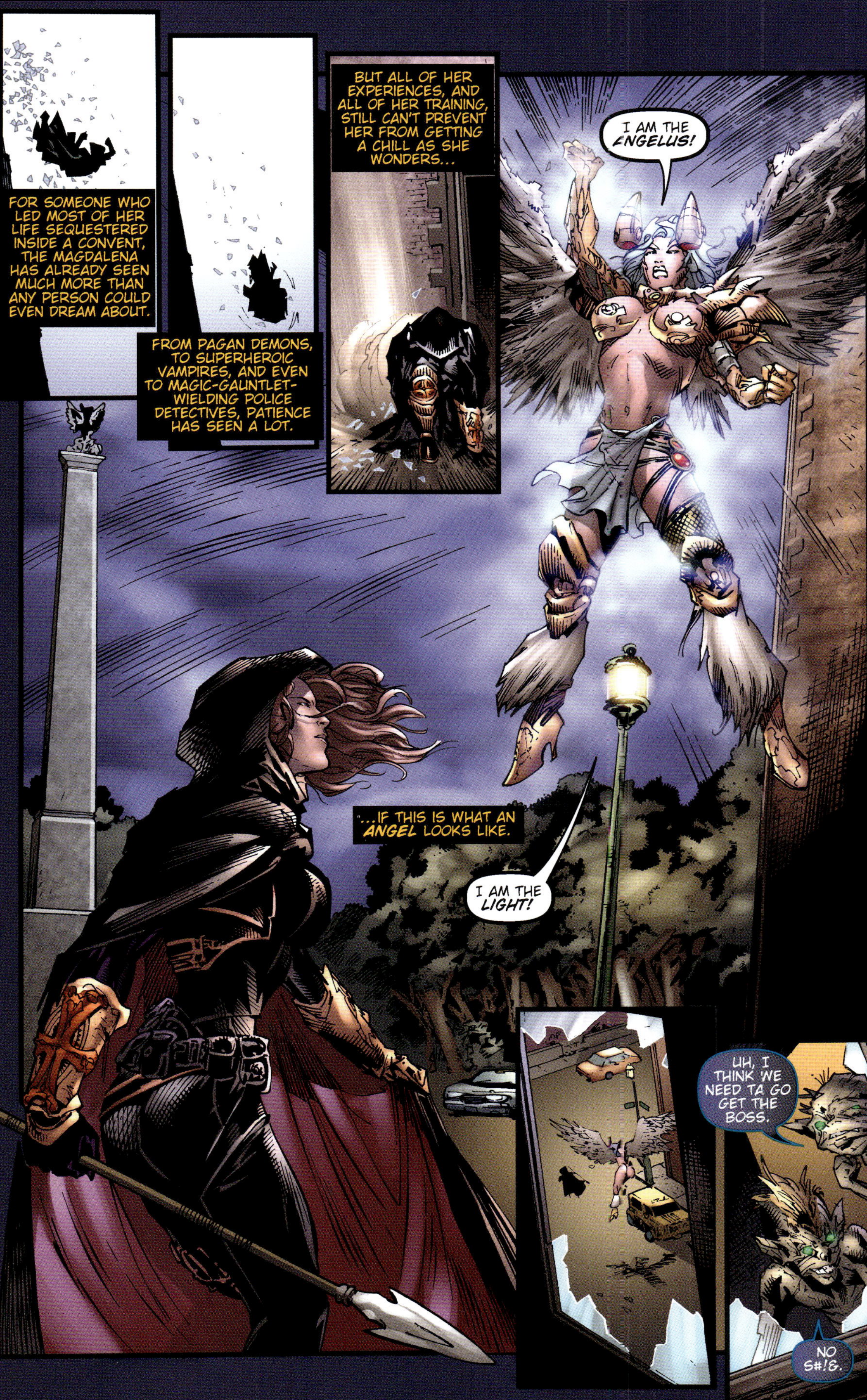
FOR SOMEONE WHO LED MOST OF HER LIFE SEQUESTERED INSIDE A CONVENT, THE MAGDALENA HAS ALREADY SEEN MUCH MORE THAN ANY PERSON COULD EVEN DREAM ABOUT.
FROM PAGAN DEMONS, TO SUPERHEROIC VAMPIRES, AND EVEN TO MAGIC-GAUNTLET-WIELDING POLICE DETECTIVES, PATIENCE HAS SEEN A LOT.
BUT ALL OF HER EXPERIENCES, AND ALL OF HER TRAINING, STILL CAN'T PREVENT HER FROM GETTING A CHILL AS SHE WONDERS...
I AM THE *ANGELUS!*
"...IF THIS IS WHAT AN *ANGEL* LOOKS LIKE.
I AM THE *LIGHT!*
UH, I THINK WE NEED TA GO GET THE BOSS.
NO S#!&.

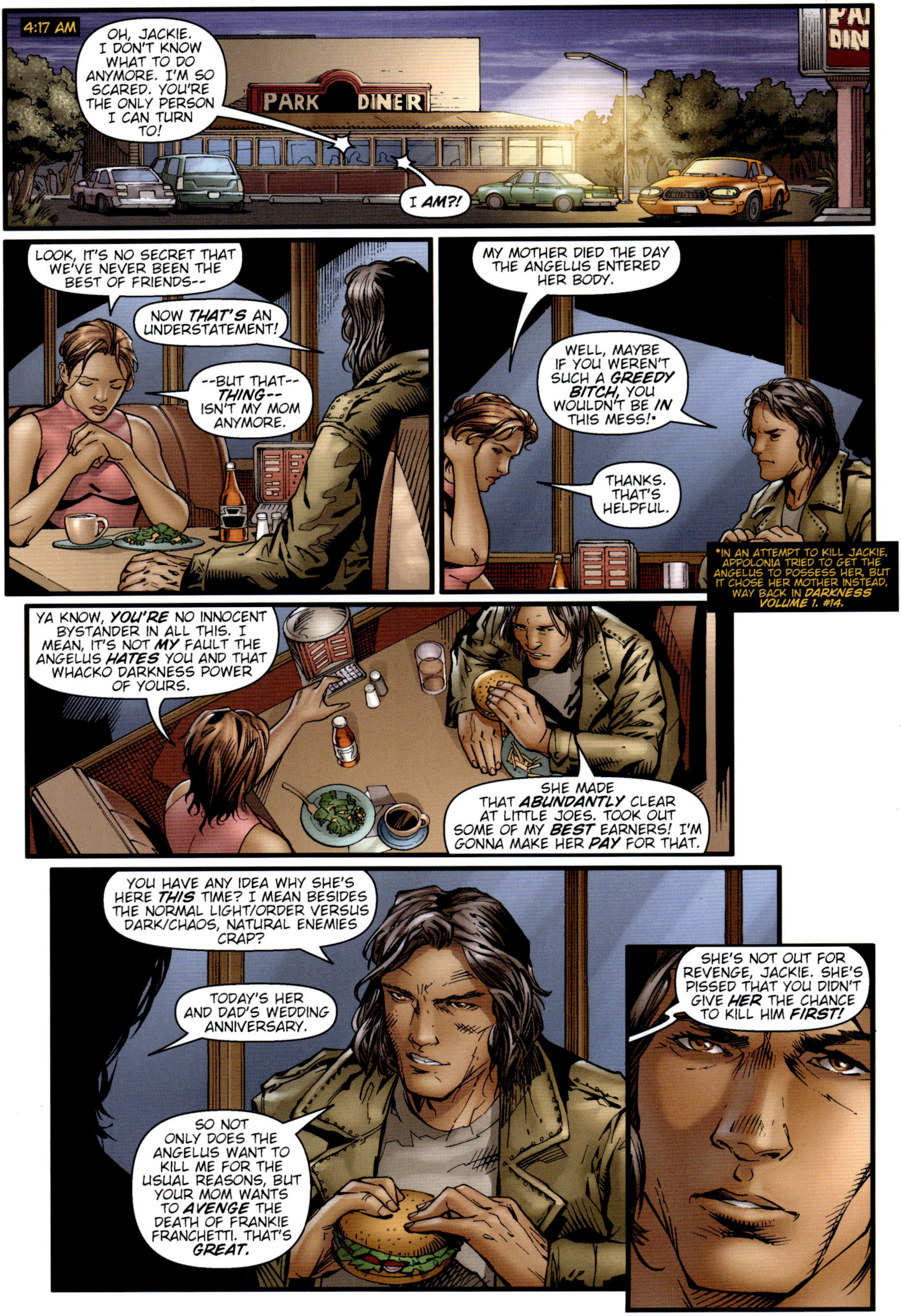
4:17 AM
PARK DINER
OH, JACKIE. I DON'T KNOW WHAT TO DO ANYMORE. I'M SO SCARED. YOU'RE THE ONLY PERSON I CAN TURN TO!
I AM?!
LOOK, IT'S NO SECRET THAT WE'VE NEVER BEEN THE BEST OF FRIENDS--
NOW THAT'S AN UNDERSTATEMENT!
--BUT THAT--THING--ISN'T MY MOM ANYMORE.
MY MOTHER DIED THE DAY THE ANGELUS ENTERED HER BODY.
WELL, MAYBE IF YOU WEREN'T SUCH A GREEDY BITCH, YOU WOULDN'T BE IN THIS MESS!*
THANKS. THAT'S HELPFUL.
*IN AN ATTEMPT TO KILL JACKIE, APPOLONIA TRIED TO GET THE ANGELUS TO POSSESS HER, BUT IT CHOSE HER MOTHER INSTEAD, WAY BACK IN DARKNESS VOLUME 1, #14.
YA KNOW, YOU'RE NO INNOCENT BYSTANDER IN ALL THIS. I MEAN, IT'S NOT MY FAULT THE ANGELUS HATES YOU AND THAT WHACKO DARKNESS POWER OF YOURS.
SHE MADE THAT ABUNDANTLY CLEAR AT LITTLE JOES. TOOK OUT SOME OF MY BEST EARNERS! I'M GONNA MAKE HER PAY FOR THAT.
YOU HAVE ANY IDEA WHY SHE'S HERE THIS TIME? I MEAN BESIDES THE NORMAL LIGHT/ORDER VERSUS DARK/CHAOS, NATURAL ENEMIES CRAP?
TODAY'S HER AND DAD'S WEDDING ANNIVERSARY.
SO NOT ONLY DOES THE ANGELUS WANT TO KILL ME FOR THE USUAL REASONS, BUT YOUR MOM WANTS TO AVENGE THE DEATH OF FRANKIE FRANCHETTI. THAT'S GREAT.
SHE'S NOT OUT FOR REVENGE, JACKIE. SHE'S PISSED THAT YOU DIDN'T GIVE HER THE CHANCE TO KILL HIM FIRST!

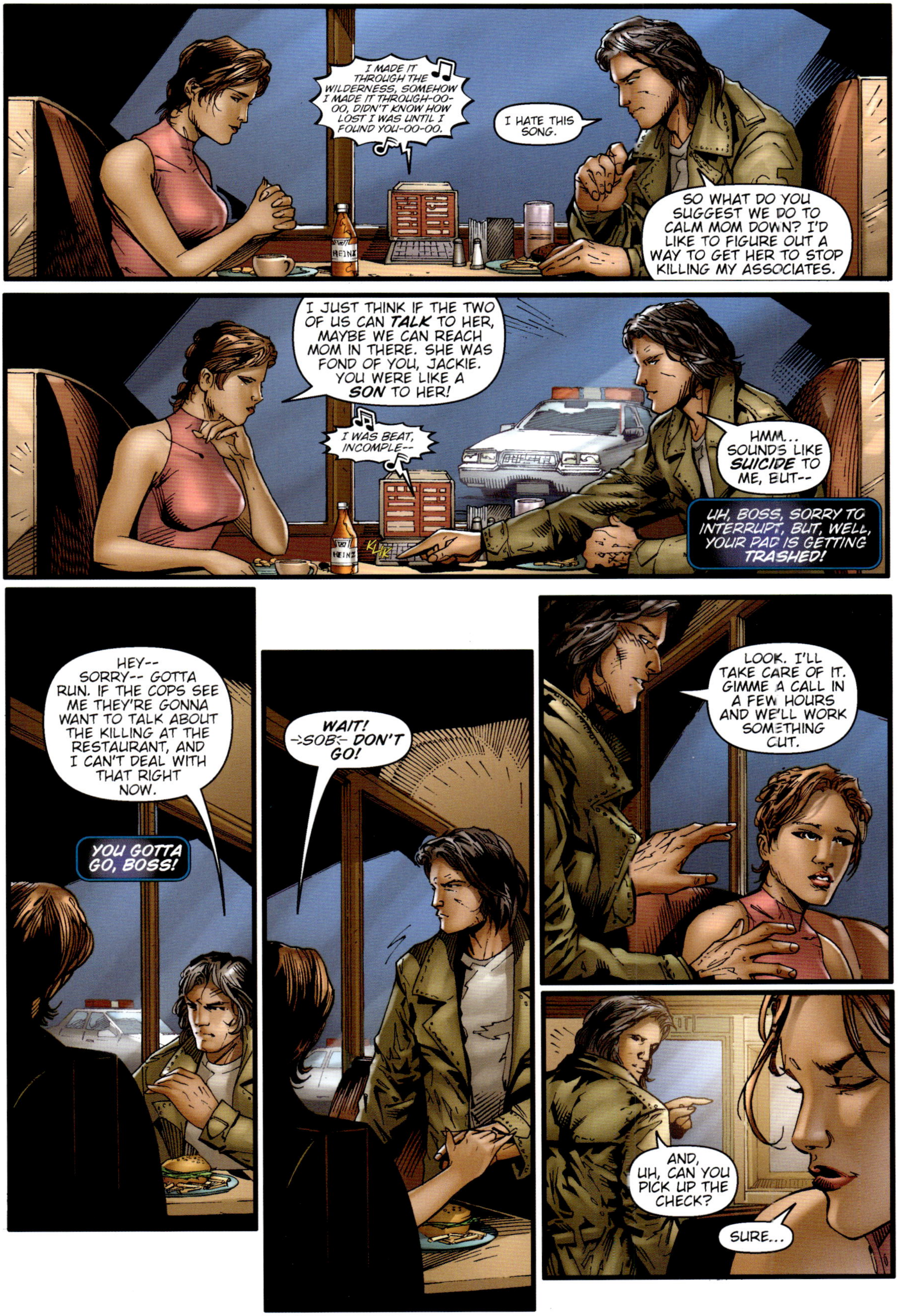
I MADE IT THROUGH THE WILDERNESS. SOMEHOW I MADE IT THROUGH-OO-OO, DIDN'T KNOW HOW LOST I WAS UNTIL I FOUND YOU-OO-OO.
I HATE THIS SONG.
SO WHAT DO YOU SUGGEST WE DO TO CALM MOM DOWN? I'D LIKE TO FIGURE OUT A WAY TO GET HER TO STOP KILLING MY ASSOCIATES.
I JUST THINK IF THE TWO OF US CAN TALK TO HER, MAYBE WE CAN REACH MOM IN THERE. SHE WAS FOND OF YOU, JACKIE. YOU WERE LIKE A SON TO HER!
I WAS BEAT, INCOMPLE--
HMM... SOUNDS LIKE SUICIDE TO ME, BUT--
KLIK
UH, BOSS, SORRY TO INTERRUPT, BUT, WELL, YOUR PAD IS GETTING TRASHED!
HEY-- SORRY-- GOTTA RUN. IF THE COPS SEE ME THEY'RE GONNA WANT TO TALK ABOUT THE KILLING AT THE RESTAURANT, AND I CAN'T DEAL WITH THAT RIGHT NOW.
YOU GOTTA GO, BOSS!
WAIT! -SOB- DON'T GO!
LOOK. I'LL TAKE CARE OF IT. GIMME A CALL IN A FEW HOURS AND WE'LL WORK SOMETHING OUT.
AND, UH, CAN YOU PICK UP THE CHECK?
SURE...

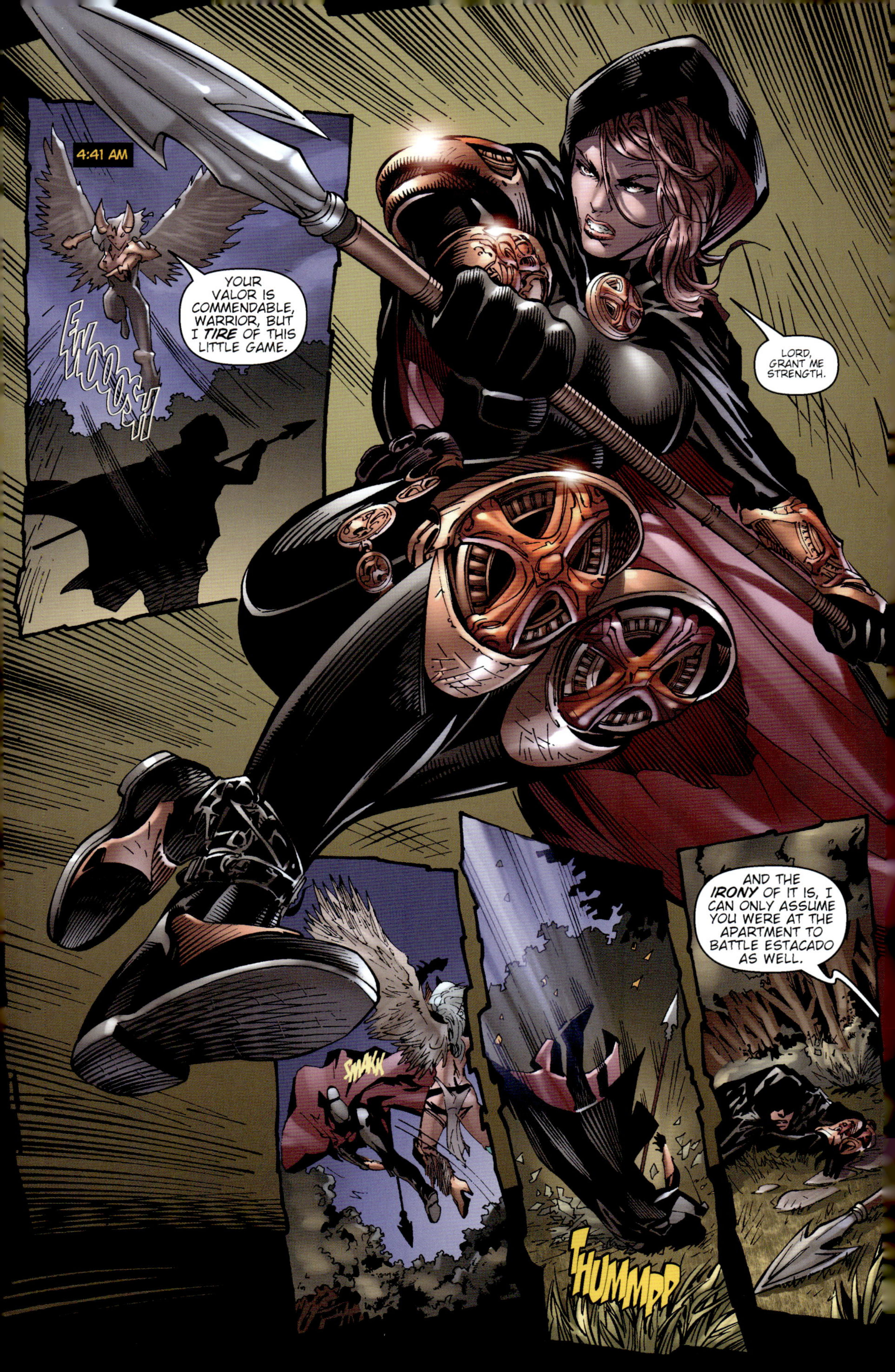
4:41 AM
YOUR VALOR IS COMMENDABLE, WARRIOR, BUT I TIRE OF THIS LITTLE GAME.
EVOOOSH
LORD, GRANT ME STRENGTH.
SWAKK
THUMMPP
AND THE IRONY OF IT IS, I CAN ONLY ASSUME YOU WERE AT THE APARTMENT TO BATTLE ESTACADO AS WELL.

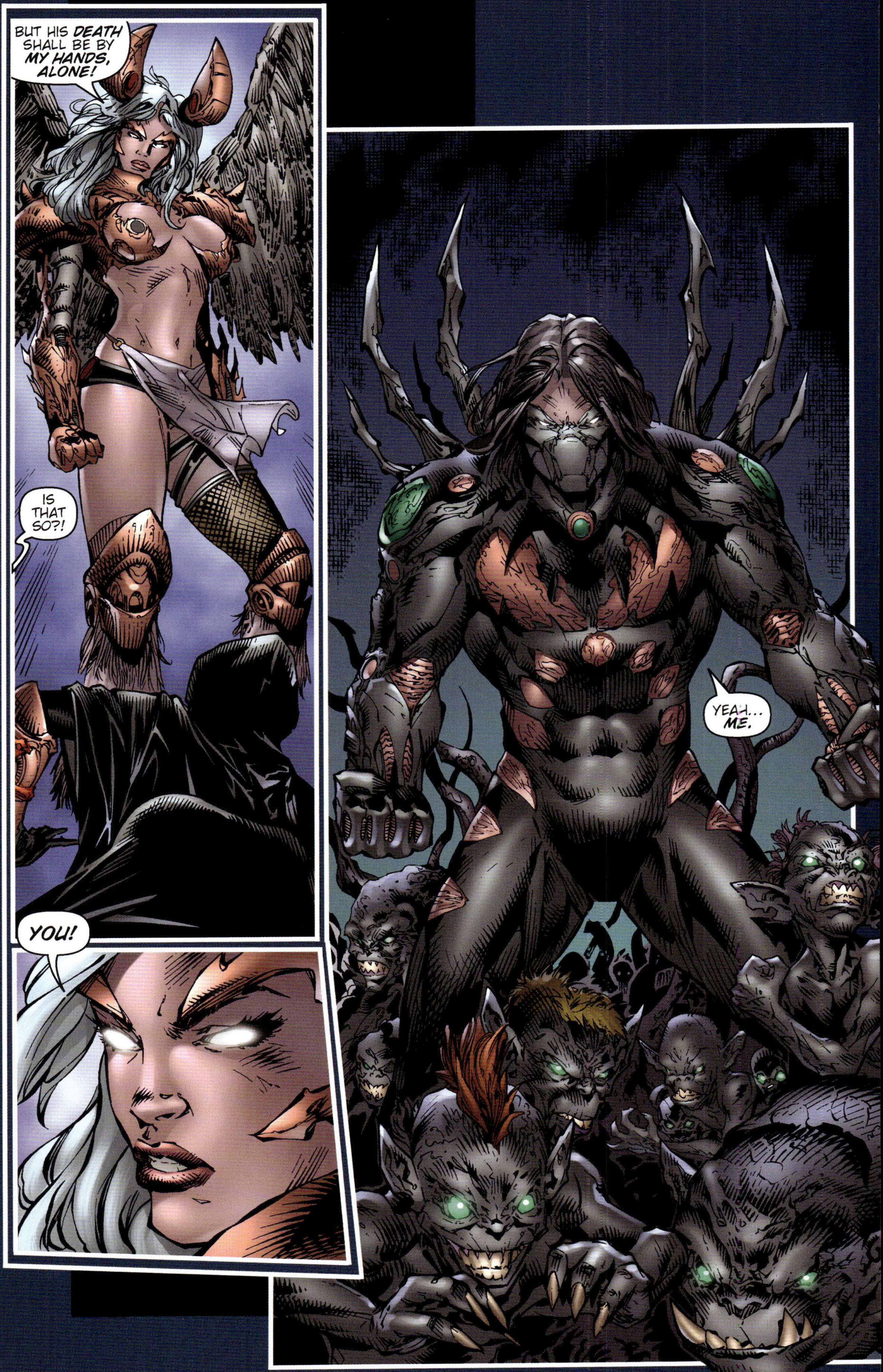

BUT HIS DEATH SHALL BE BY MY HANDS, ALONE!
IS THAT SO?!
YOU!
YEAH... ME.

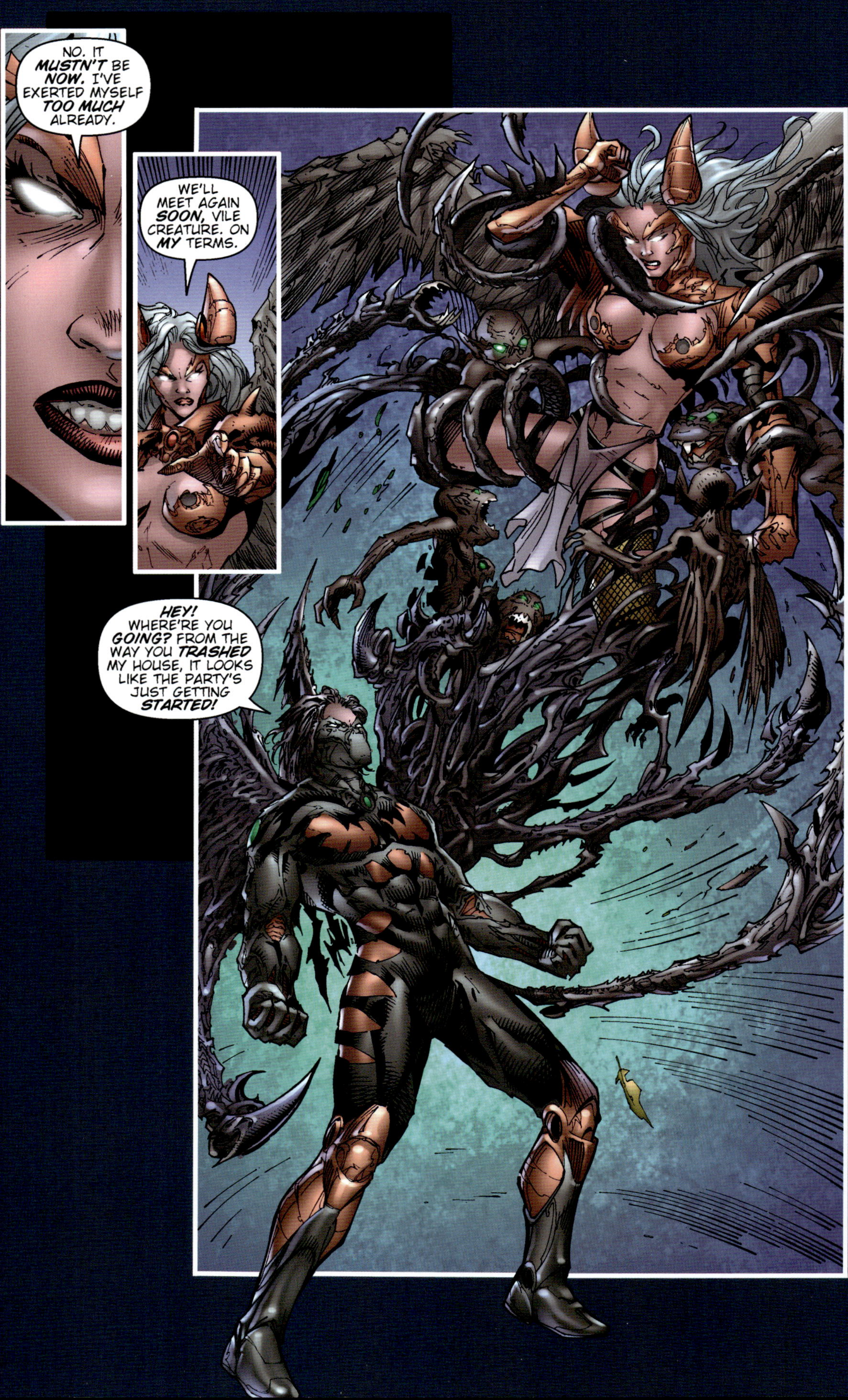
NO. IT MUSTN'T BE NOW. I'VE EXERTED MYSELF TOO MUCH ALREADY.
WE'LL MEET AGAIN SOON, VILE CREATURE. ON MY TERMS.
HEY! WHERE'RE YOU GOING? FROM THE WAY YOU TRASHED MY HOUSE, IT LOOKS LIKE THE PARTY'S JUST GETTING STARTED!

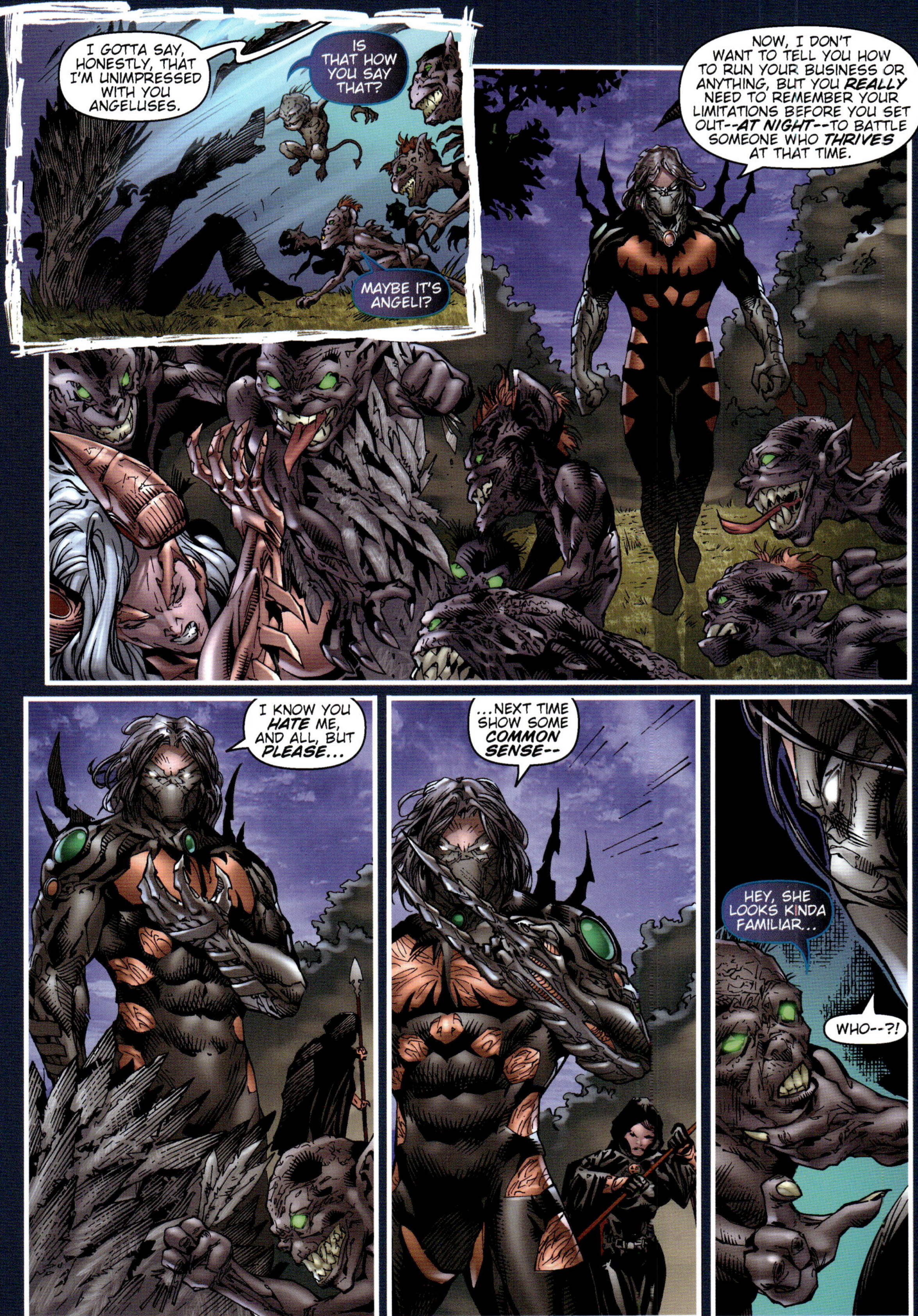
I GOTTA SAY, HONESTLY, THAT I'M UNIMPRESSED WITH YOU ANGELUSES.
IS THAT HOW YOU SAY THAT?
MAYBE IT'S ANGELI?
NOW, I DON'T WANT TO TELL YOU HOW TO RUN YOUR BUSINESS OR ANYTHING, BUT YOU REALLY NEED TO REMEMBER YOUR LIMITATIONS BEFORE YOU SET OUT--AT NIGHT--TO BATTLE SOMEONE WHO THRIVES AT THAT TIME.
I KNOW YOU HATE ME, AND ALL, BUT PLEASE...
...NEXT TIME SHOW SOME COMMON SENSE--
HEY, SHE LOOKS KINDA FAMILIAR...
WHO--?!

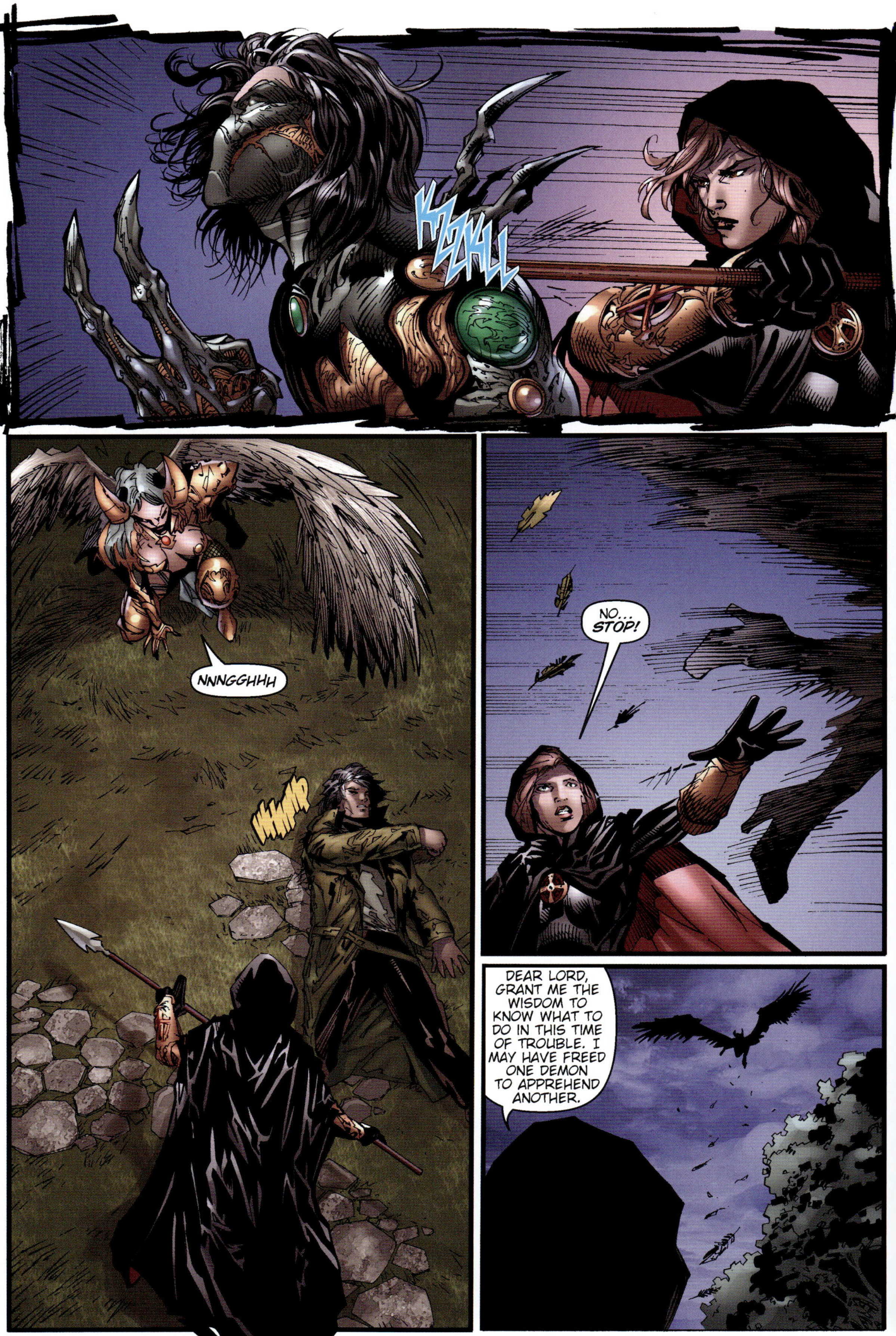
KZZKLL
NNNGGHHH
NO... STOP!
DEAR LORD, GRANT ME THE WISDOM TO KNOW WHAT TO DO IN THIS TIME OF TROUBLE. I MAY HAVE FREED ONE DEMON TO APPREHEND ANOTHER.

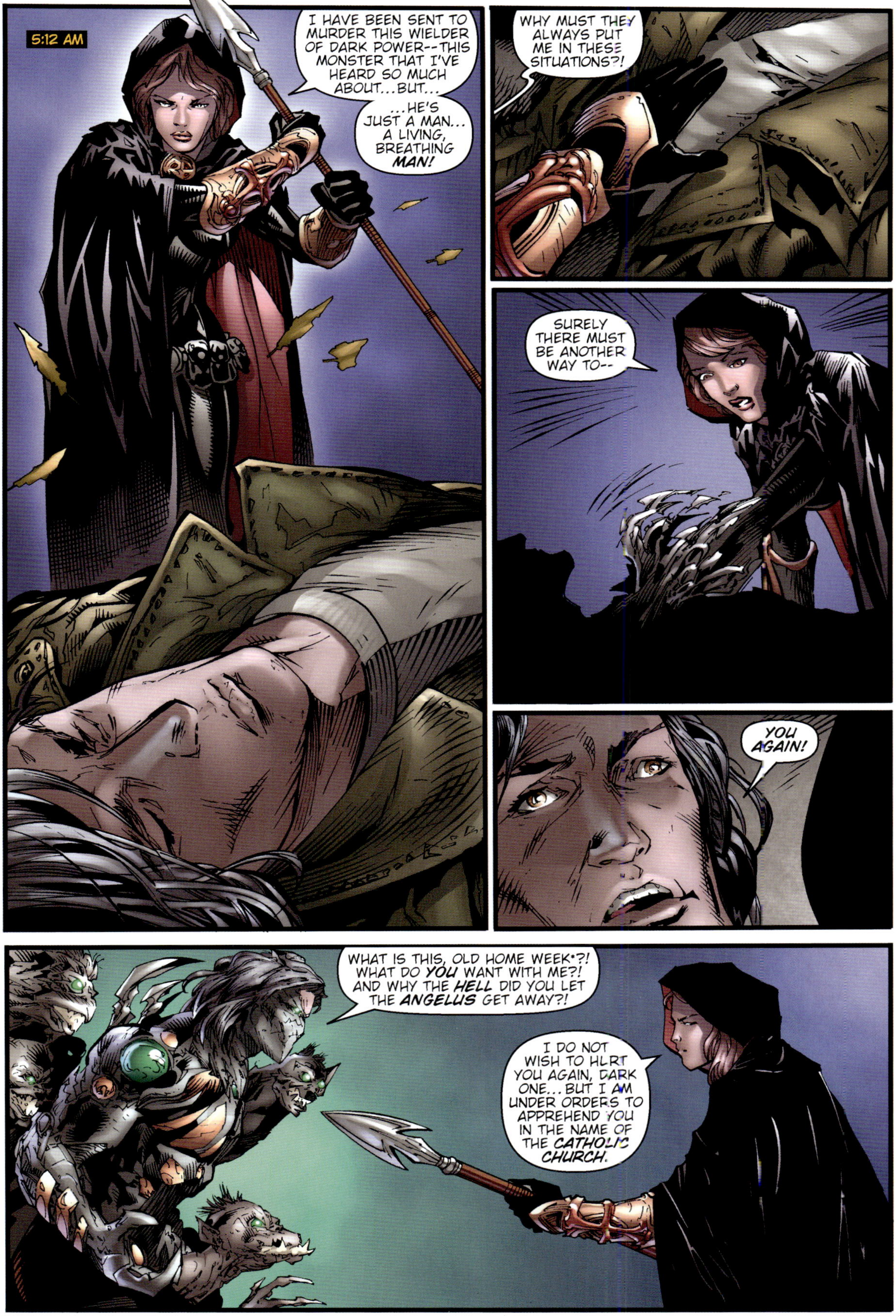
5:12 AM
I HAVE BEEN SENT TO MURDER THIS WIELDER OF DARK POWER--THIS MONSTER THAT I'VE HEARD SO MUCH ABOUT... BUT...
...HE'S JUST A MAN... A LIVING, BREATHING MAN!
WHY MUST THEY ALWAYS PUT ME IN THESE SITUATIONS?!
SURELY THERE MUST BE ANOTHER WAY TO--
YOU AGAIN!
WHAT IS THIS, OLD HOME WEEK*?! WHAT DO YOU WANT WITH ME?! AND WHY THE HELL DID YOU LET THE ANGELUS GET AWAY?!
I DO NOT WISH TO HURT YOU AGAIN, DARK ONE... BUT I AM UNDER ORDERS TO APPREHEND YOU IN THE NAME OF THE CATHOLIC CHURCH.

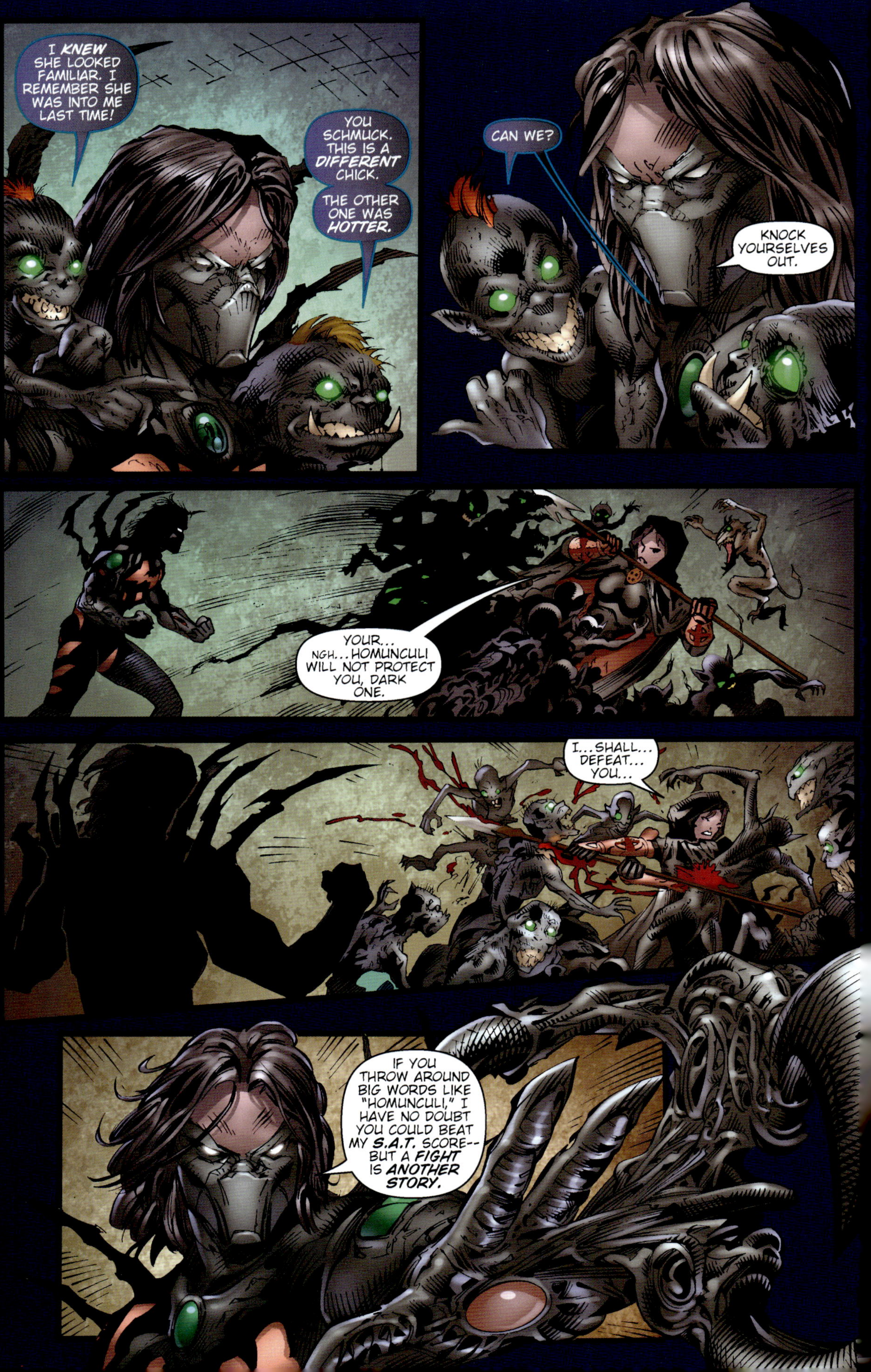
I KNEW SHE LOOKED FAMILIAR. I REMEMBER SHE WAS INTO ME LAST TIME!
YOU SCHMUCK. THIS IS A DIFFERENT CHICK.
THE OTHER ONE WAS HOTTER.
CAN WE?
KNOCK YOURSELVES OUT.
YOUR... NGH... HOMUNCULI WILL NOT PROTECT YOU, DARK ONE.
I...SHALL... DEFEAT... YOU...
IF YOU THROW AROUND BIG WORDS LIKE "HOMUNCULI," I HAVE NO DOUBT YOU COULD BEAT MY S.A.T. SCORE-- BUT A FIGHT IS ANOTHER STORY.

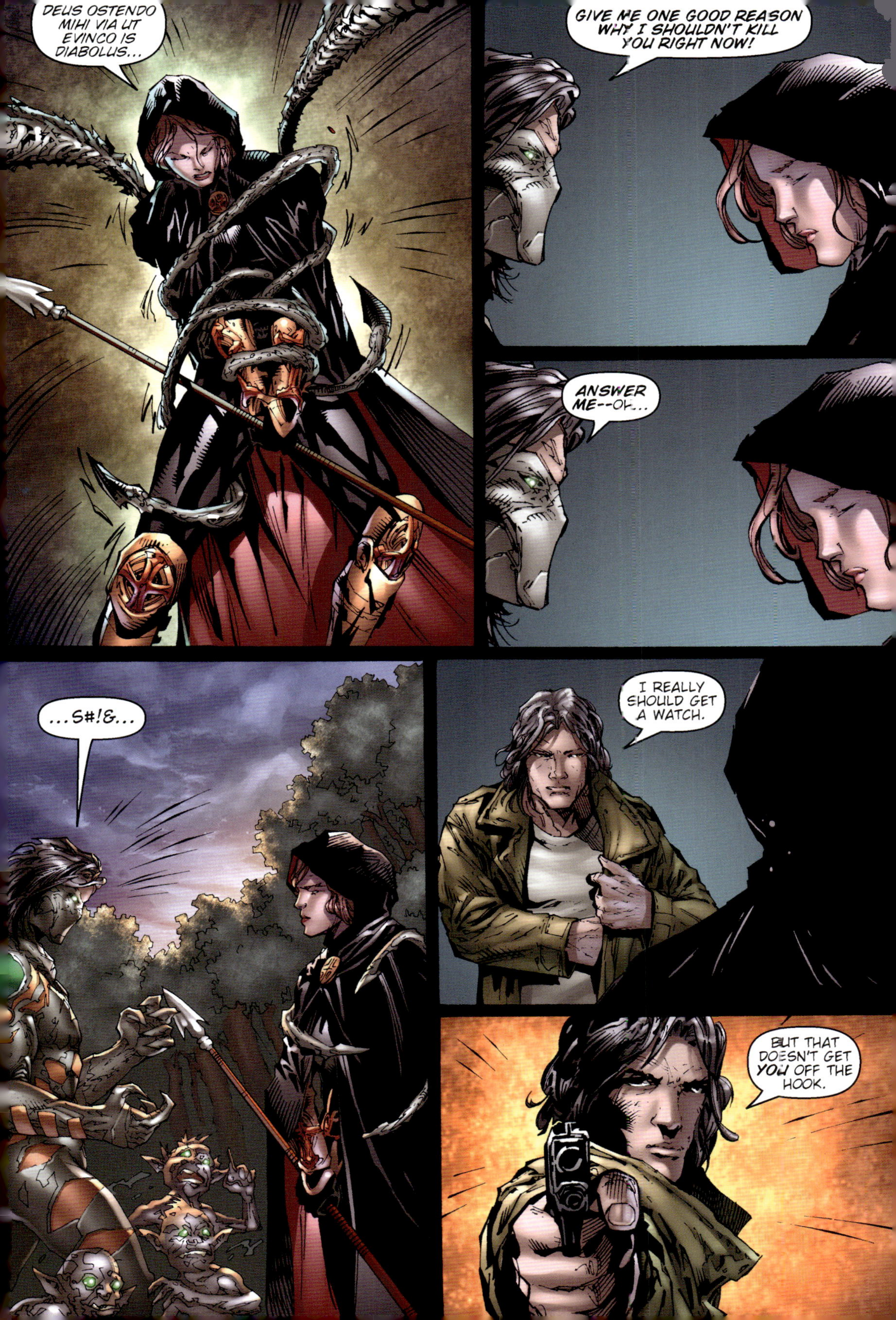
DEUS OSTENDO MIHI VIA UT EVINCO IS DIABOLUS...
GIVE ME ONE GOOD REASON WHY I SHOULDN'T KILL YOU RIGHT NOW!
ANSWER ME--OH...
...S#!&...
I REALLY SHOULD GET A WATCH.
BUT THAT DOESN'T GET YOU OFF THE HOOK.

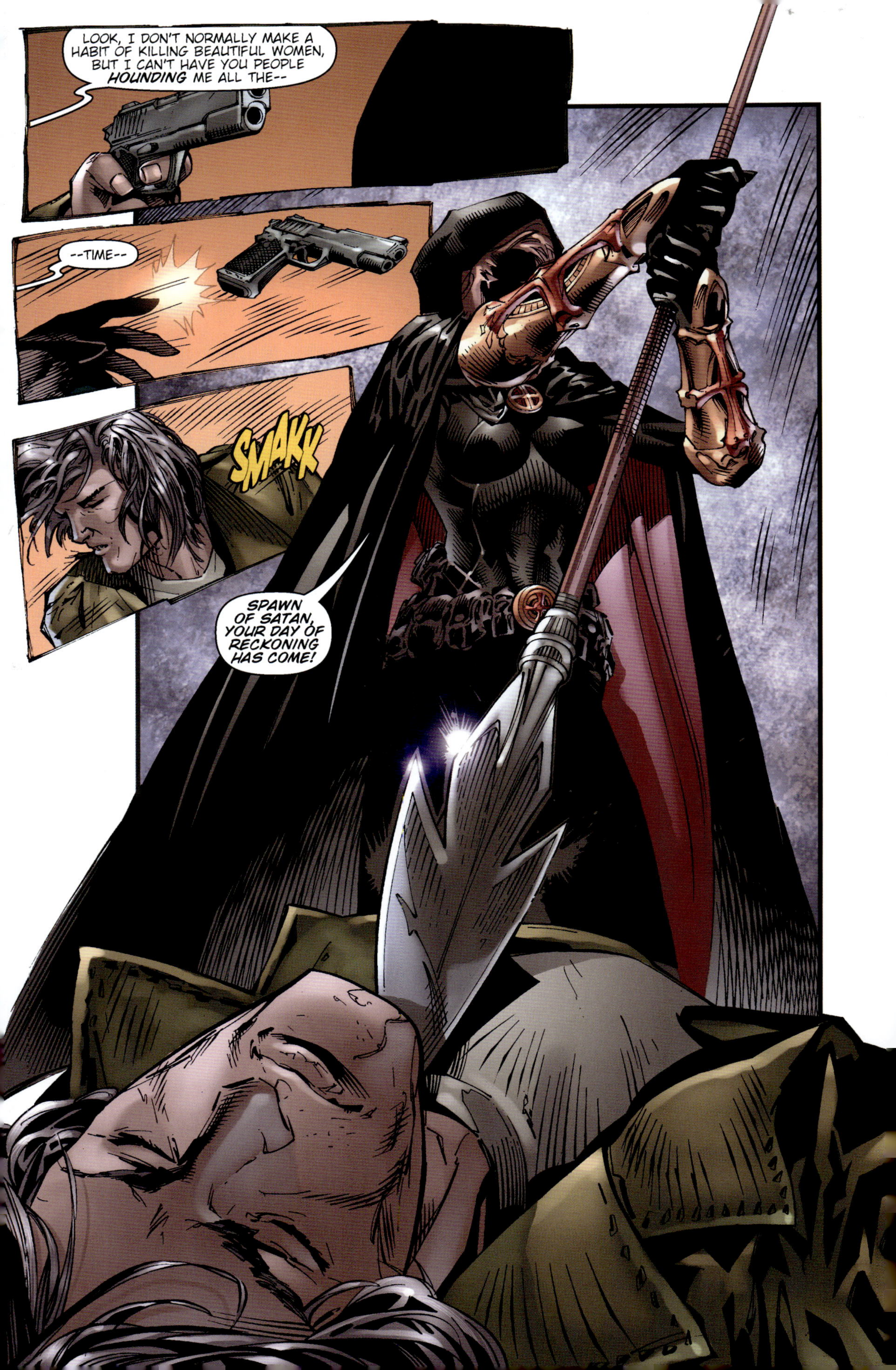
LOOK, I DON'T NORMALLY MAKE A HABIT OF KILLING BEAUTIFUL WOMEN, BUT I CAN'T HAVE YOU PEOPLE HOUNDING ME ALL THE--
--TIME--
SMAKK
SPAWN OF SATAN, YOUR DAY OF RECKONING HAS COME!

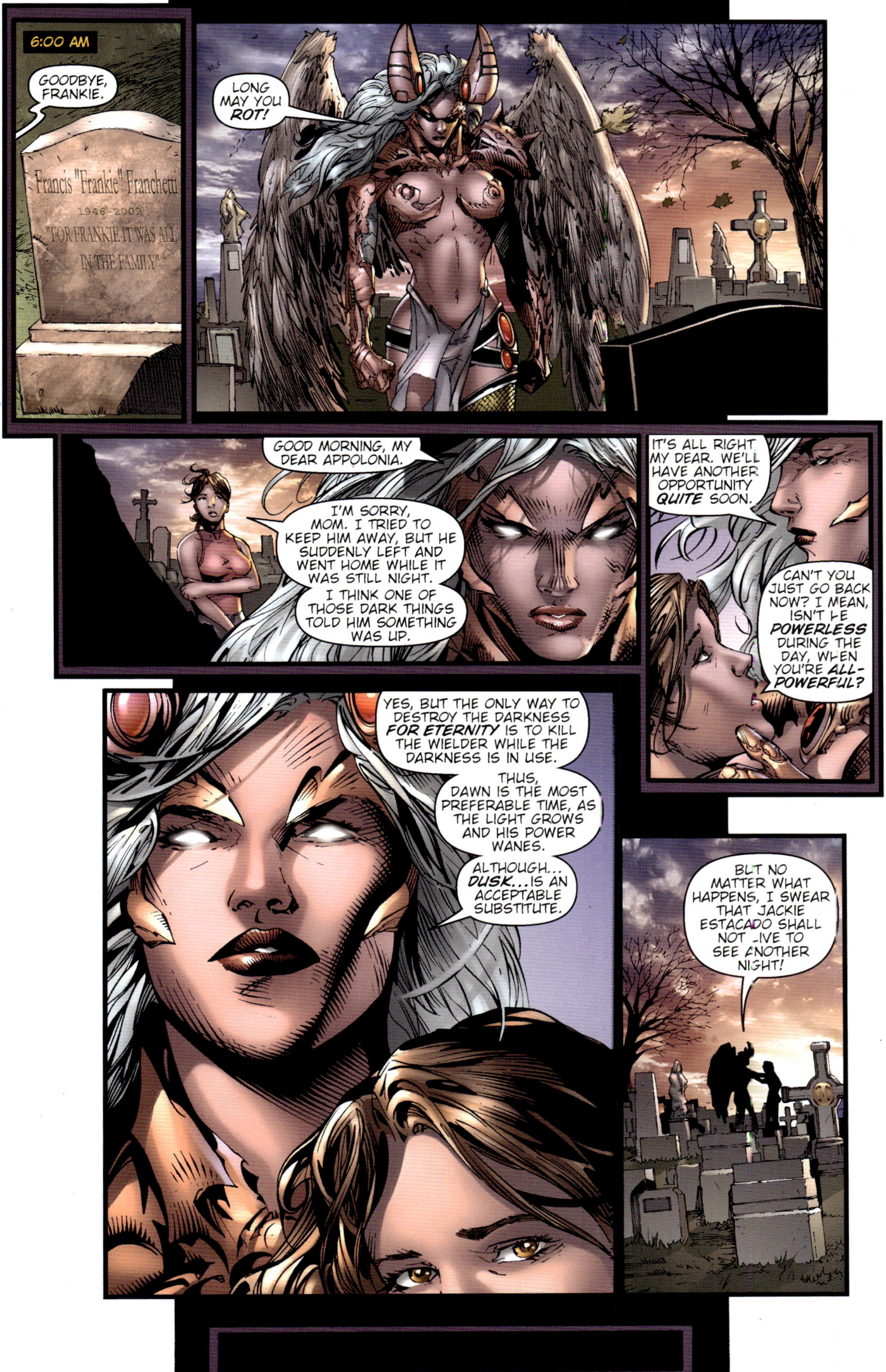
6:00 AM
GOODBYE, FRANKIE.
Francis "Frankie" Franchetti
1946-2002
"FOR FRANKIE IT WAS ALL IN THE FAMILY"
LONG MAY YOU ROT!
GOOD MORNING, MY DEAR APPOLONIA.
I'M SORRY, MOM. I TRIED TO KEEP HIM AWAY, BUT HE SUDDENLY LEFT AND WENT HOME WHILE IT WAS STILL NIGHT.
I THINK ONE OF THOSE DARK THINGS TOLD HIM SOMETHING WAS UP.
IT'S ALL RIGHT, MY DEAR. WE'LL HAVE ANOTHER OPPORTUNITY QUITE SOON.
CAN'T YOU JUST GO BACK NOW? I MEAN, ISN'T HE POWERLESS DURING THE DAY, WHEN YOU'RE ALL-POWERFUL?
YES, BUT THE ONLY WAY TO DESTROY THE DARKNESS FOR ETERNITY IS TO KILL THE WIELDER WHILE THE DARKNESS IS IN USE.
THUS, DAWN IS THE MOST PREFERABLE TIME, AS THE LIGHT GROWS AND HIS POWER WANES.
ALTHOUGH... DUSK... IS AN ACCEPTABLE SUBSTITUTE.
BUT NO MATTER WHAT HAPPENS, I SWEAR THAT JACKIE ESTACADO SHALL NOT LIVE TO SEE ANOTHER NIGHT!

The Darkness Issue #64

cover art by: Dale Keown & Matt Milla

THE DARKNESS #64

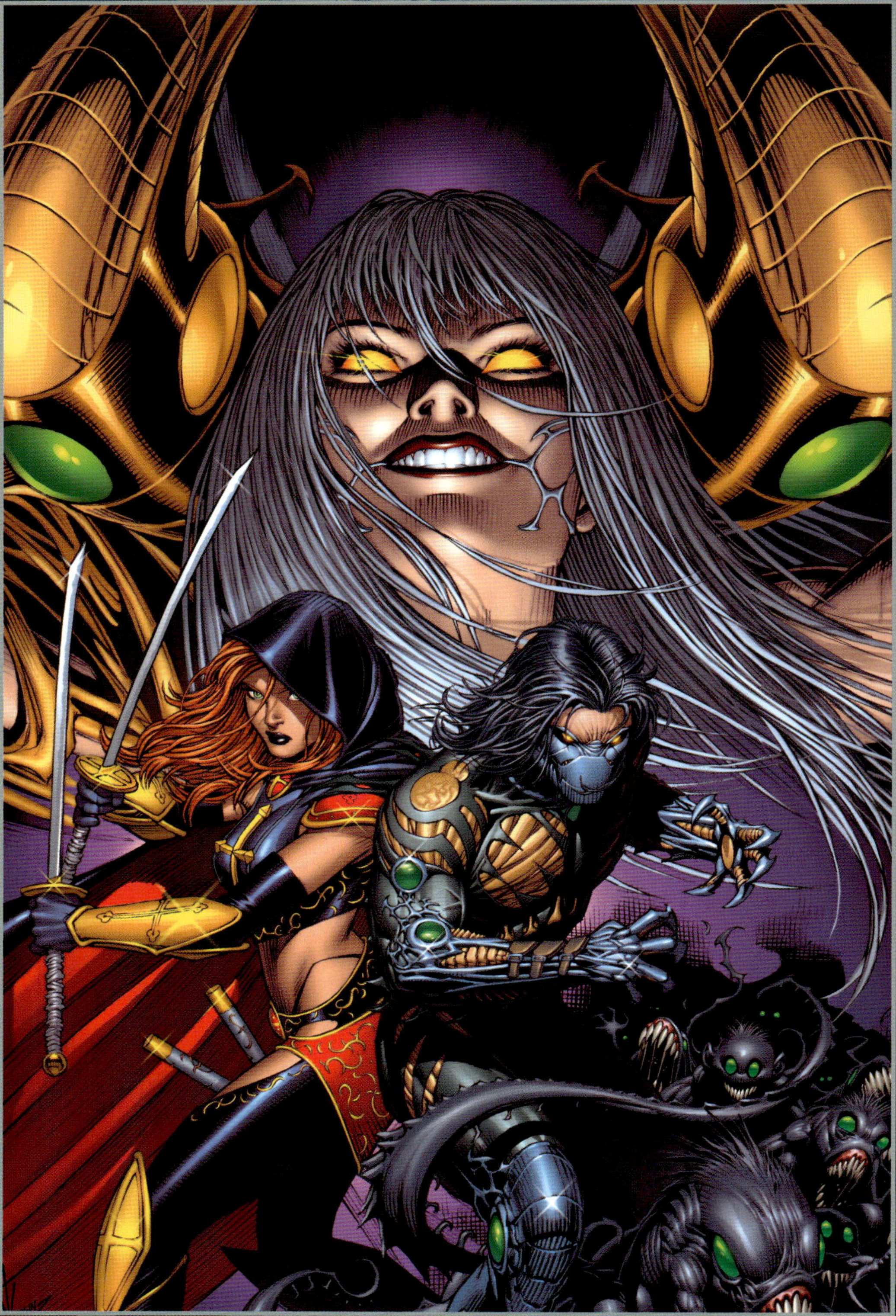

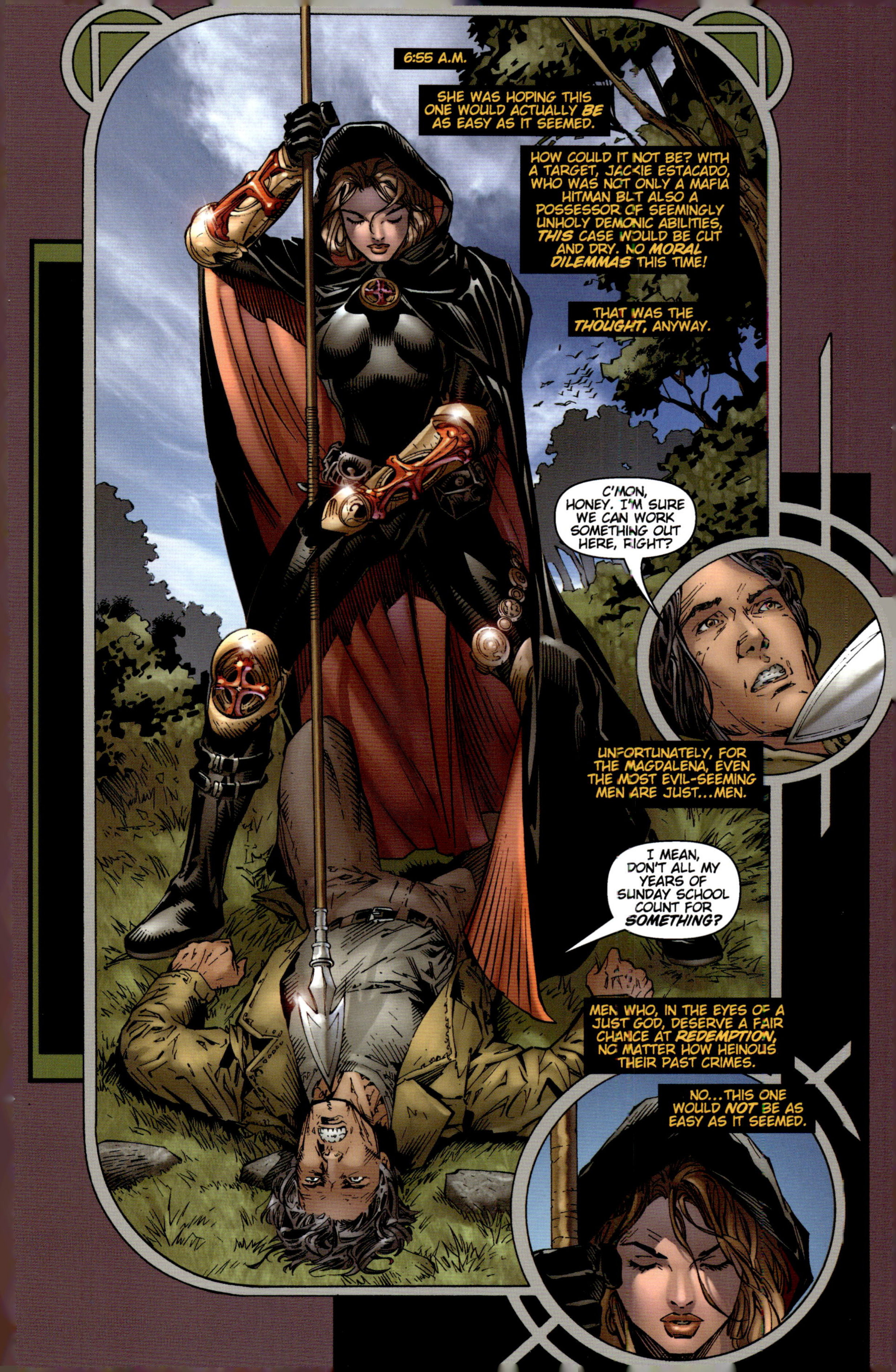

6:55 A.M.
SHE WAS HOPING THIS ONE WOULD ACTUALLY BE AS EASY AS IT SEEMED.
HOW COULD IT NOT BE? WITH A TARGET, JACKIE ESTACADO, WHO WAS NOT ONLY A MAFIA HITMAN BUT ALSO A POSSESSOR OF SEEMINGLY UNHOLY DEMONIC ABILITIES, THIS CASE WOULD BE CUT AND DRY. NO MORAL DILEMMAS THIS TIME!
THAT WAS THE THOUGHT, ANYWAY.
C'MON, HONEY. I'M SURE WE CAN WORK SOMETHING OUT HERE, RIGHT?
UNFORTUNATELY, FOR THE MAGDALENA, EVEN THE MOST EVIL-SEEMING MEN ARE JUST...MEN.
I MEAN, DON'T ALL MY YEARS OF SUNDAY SCHOOL COUNT FOR SOMETHING?
MEN WHO, IN THE EYES OF A JUST GOD, DESERVE A FAIR CHANCE AT REDEMPTION, NO MATTER HOW HEINOUS THEIR PAST CRIMES.
NO...THIS ONE WOULD NOT BE AS EASY AS IT SEEMED.

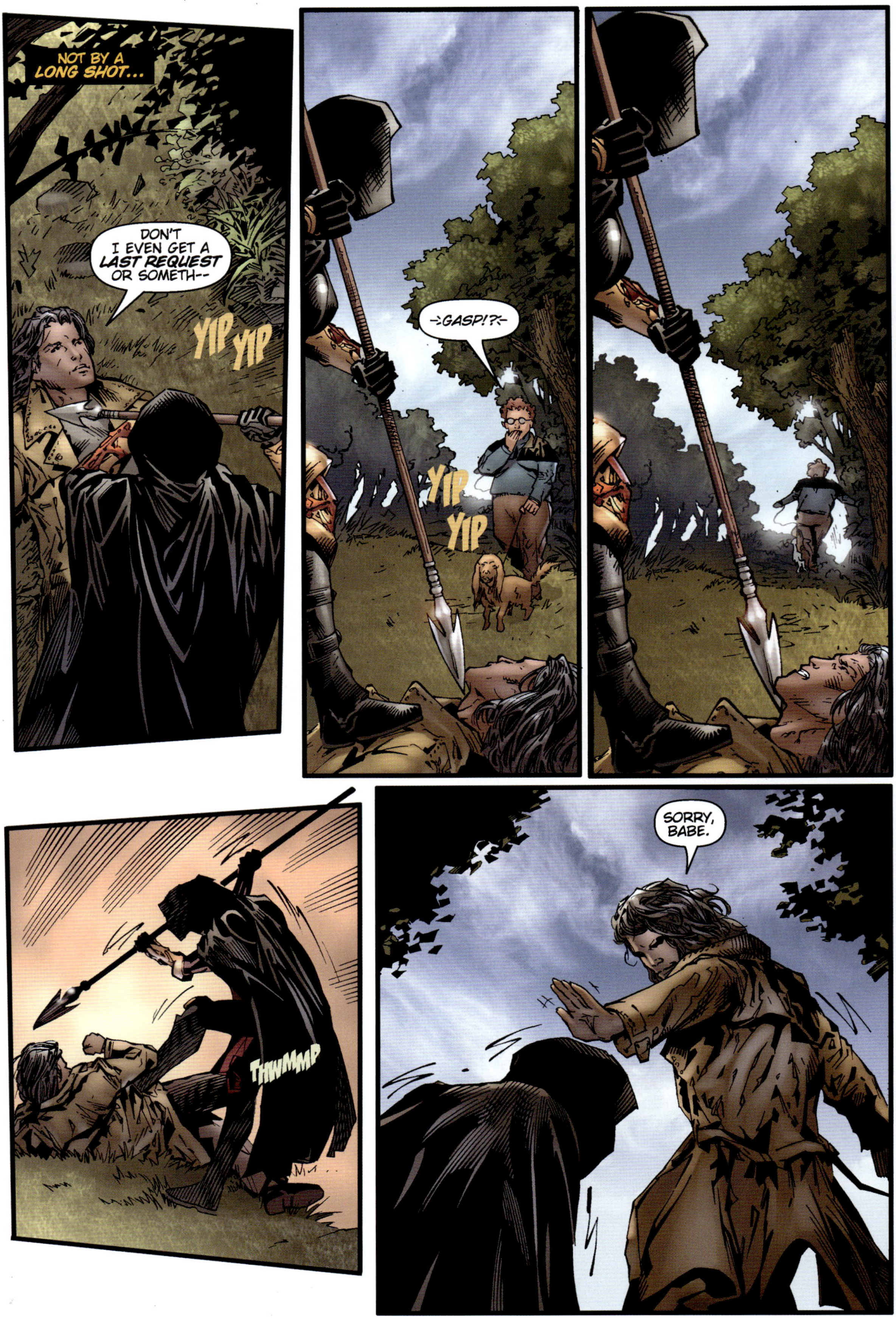
NOT BY A LONG SHOT...
DON'T I EVEN GET A LAST REQUEST OR SOMETH--
YIP YIP
-?GASP!?-
YIP YIP
THWMMP
SORRY, BABE.

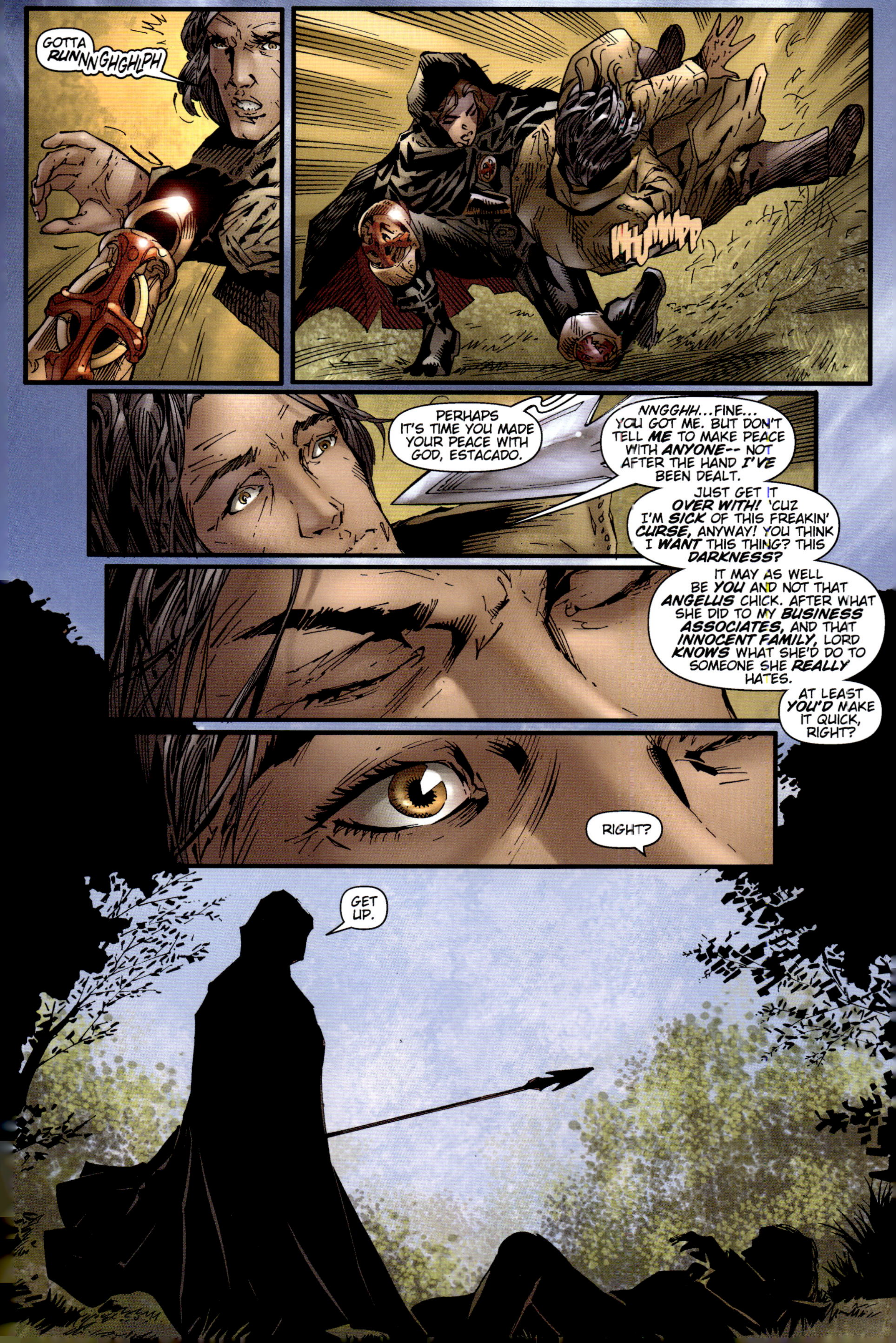
GOTTA RUNNNGHGHLPH
WHUMPF
PERHAPS IT'S TIME YOU MADE YOUR PEACE WITH GOD, ESTACADO.
NNGGHH...FINE... YOU GOT ME. BUT DON'T TELL ME TO MAKE PEACE WITH ANYONE-- NOT AFTER THE HAND I'VE BEEN DEALT.
JUST GET IT OVER WITH! 'CUZ I'M SICK OF THIS FREAKIN' CURSE, ANYWAY! YOU THINK I WANT THIS THING? THIS DARKNESS?
IT MAY AS WELL BE YOU AND NOT THAT ANGELUS CHICK. AFTER WHAT SHE DID TO MY BUSINESS ASSOCIATES, AND THAT INNOCENT FAMILY, LORD KNOWS WHAT SHE'D DO TO SOMEONE SHE REALLY HATES.
AT LEAST YOU'D MAKE IT QUICK, RIGHT?
RIGHT?
GET UP.

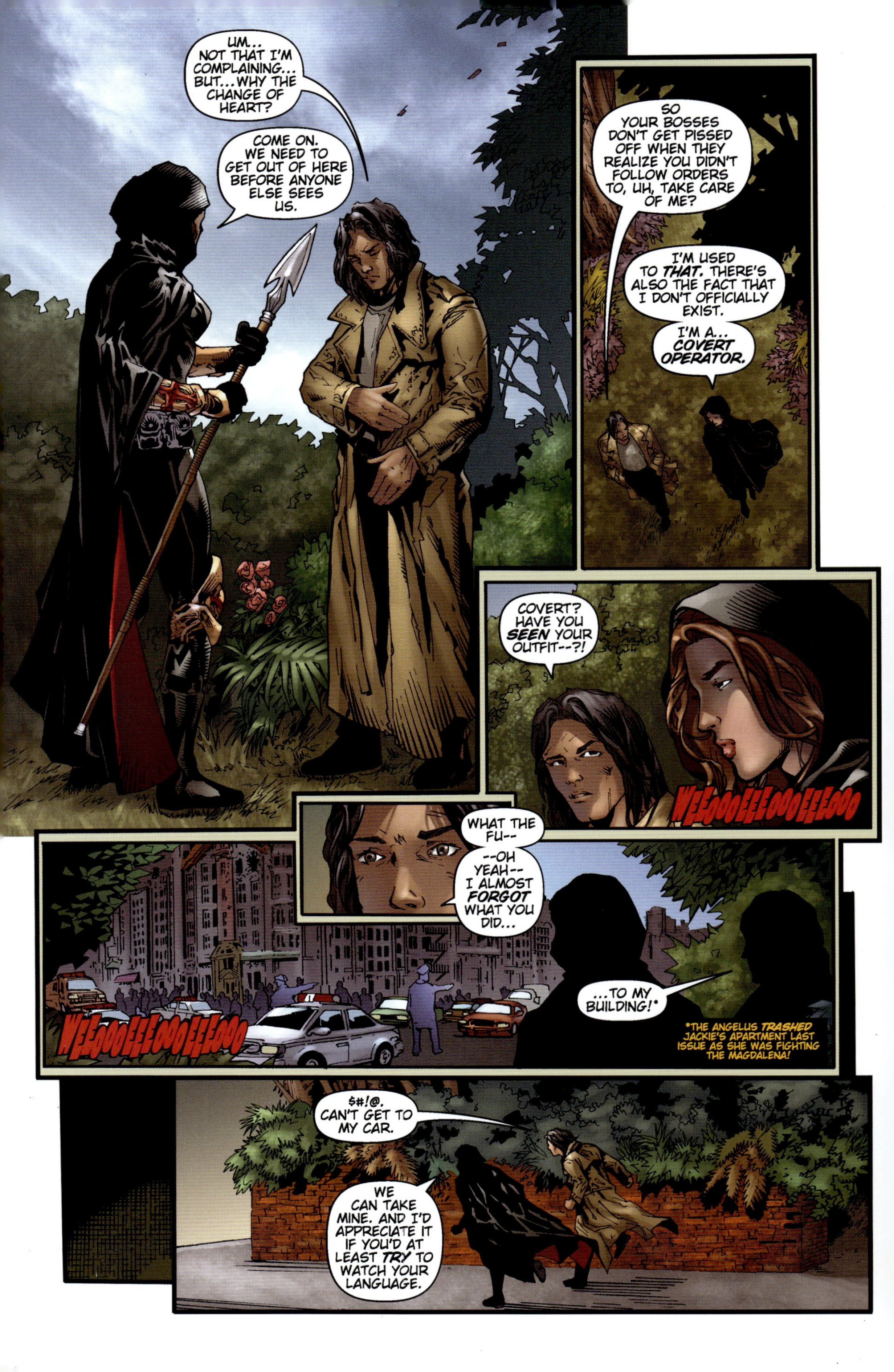
UM... NOT THAT I'M COMPLAINING... BUT...WHY THE CHANGE OF HEART?
COME ON. WE NEED TO GET OUT OF HERE BEFORE ANYONE ELSE SEES US.
SO YOUR BOSSES DON'T GET PISSED OFF WHEN THEY REALIZE YOU DIDN'T FOLLOW ORDERS TO, UH, TAKE CARE OF ME?
I'M USED TO THAT. THERE'S ALSO THE FACT THAT I DON'T OFFICIALLY EXIST.
I'M A... COVERT OPERATOR.
COVERT? HAVE YOU SEEN YOUR OUTFIT--?!
WEEOOOEEEOOOEEEOOO
WHAT THE FU--
--OH YEAH-- I ALMOST FORGOT WHAT YOU DID...
...TO MY BUILDING!*
WEEOOOEEEOOOEEEOOO
*THE ANGELUS TRASHED JACKIE'S APARTMENT LAST ISSUE AS SHE WAS FIGHTING THE MAGDALENA!
$#!@. CAN'T GET TO MY CAR.
WE CAN TAKE MINE. AND I'D APPRECIATE IT IF YOU'D AT LEAST TRY TO WATCH YOUR LANGUAGE.

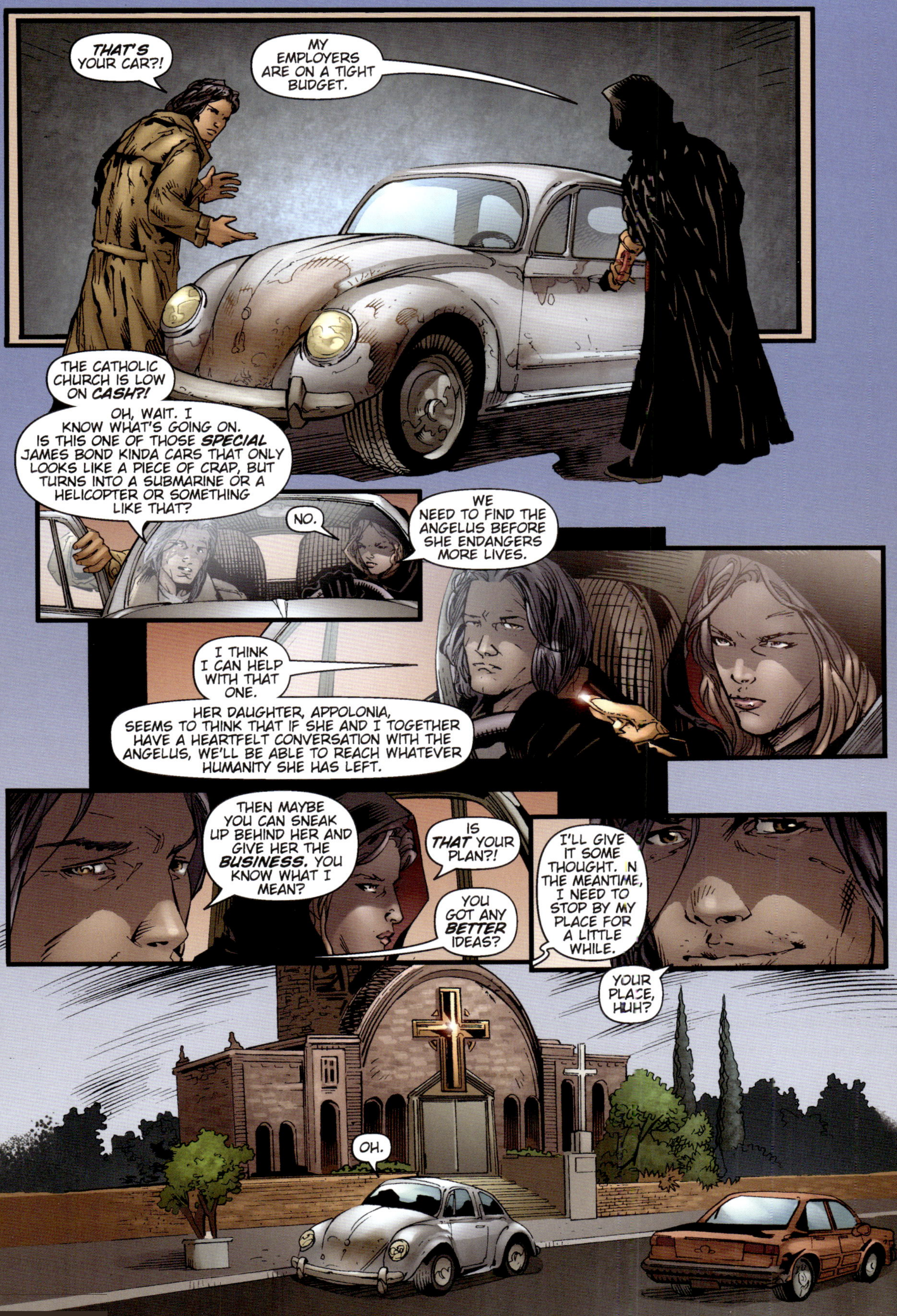
THAT'S YOUR CAR?!
MY EMPLOYERS ARE ON A TIGHT BUDGET.
THE CATHOLIC CHURCH IS LOW ON CASH?!
OH, WAIT. I KNOW WHAT'S GOING ON. IS THIS ONE OF THOSE SPECIAL JAMES BOND KINDA CARS THAT ONLY LOOKS LIKE A PIECE OF CRAP, BUT TURNS INTO A SUBMARINE OR A HELICOPTER OR SOMETHING LIKE THAT?
NO.
WE NEED TO FIND THE ANGELUS BEFORE SHE ENDANGERS MORE LIVES.
I THINK I CAN HELP WITH THAT ONE.
HER DAUGHTER, APPOLONIA, SEEMS TO THINK THAT IF SHE AND I TOGETHER HAVE A HEARTFELT CONVERSATION WITH THE ANGELUS, WE'LL BE ABLE TO REACH WHATEVER HUMANITY SHE HAS LEFT.
THEN MAYBE YOU CAN SNEAK UP BEHIND HER AND GIVE HER THE BUSINESS. YOU KNOW WHAT I MEAN?
IS THAT YOUR PLAN?!
YOU GOT ANY BETTER IDEAS?
I'LL GIVE IT SOME THOUGHT. IN THE MEANTIME, I NEED TO STOP BY MY PLACE FOR A LITTLE WHILE.
YOUR PLACE, HUH?
OH.

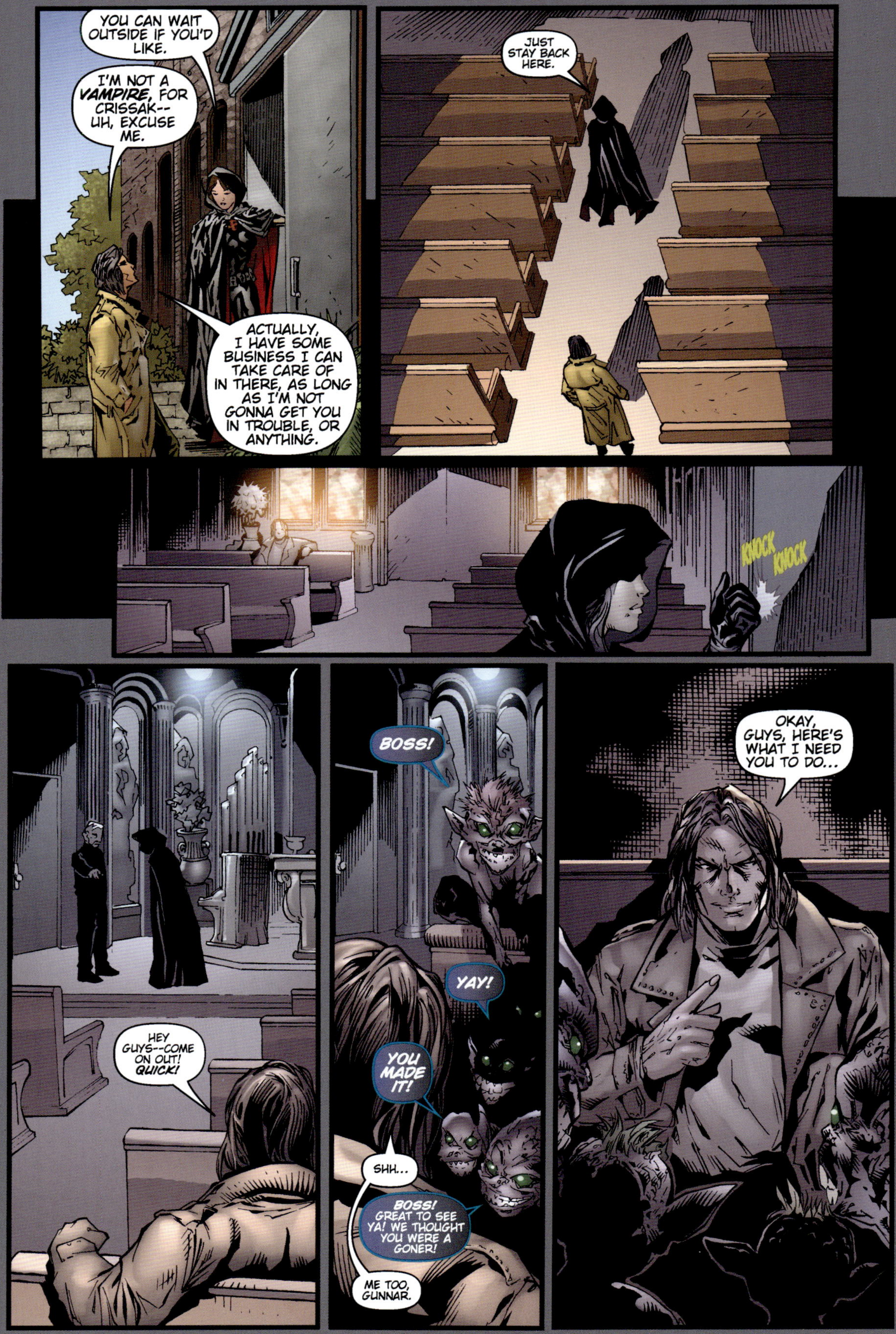
YOU CAN WAIT OUTSIDE IF YOU'D LIKE.
I'M NOT A VAMPIRE, FOR CRISSAK--UH, EXCUSE ME.
ACTUALLY, I HAVE SOME BUSINESS I CAN TAKE CARE OF IN THERE, AS LONG AS I'M NOT GONNA GET YOU IN TROUBLE, OR ANYTHING.
JUST STAY BACK HERE.
KNOCK KNOCK
HEY GUYS--COME ON OUT! QUICK!
BOSS!
YAY!
YOU MADE IT!
SHH...
BOSS! GREAT TO SEE YA! WE THOUGHT YOU WERE A GONER!
ME TOO, GUNNAR.
OKAY, GUYS, HERE'S WHAT I NEED YOU TO DO...

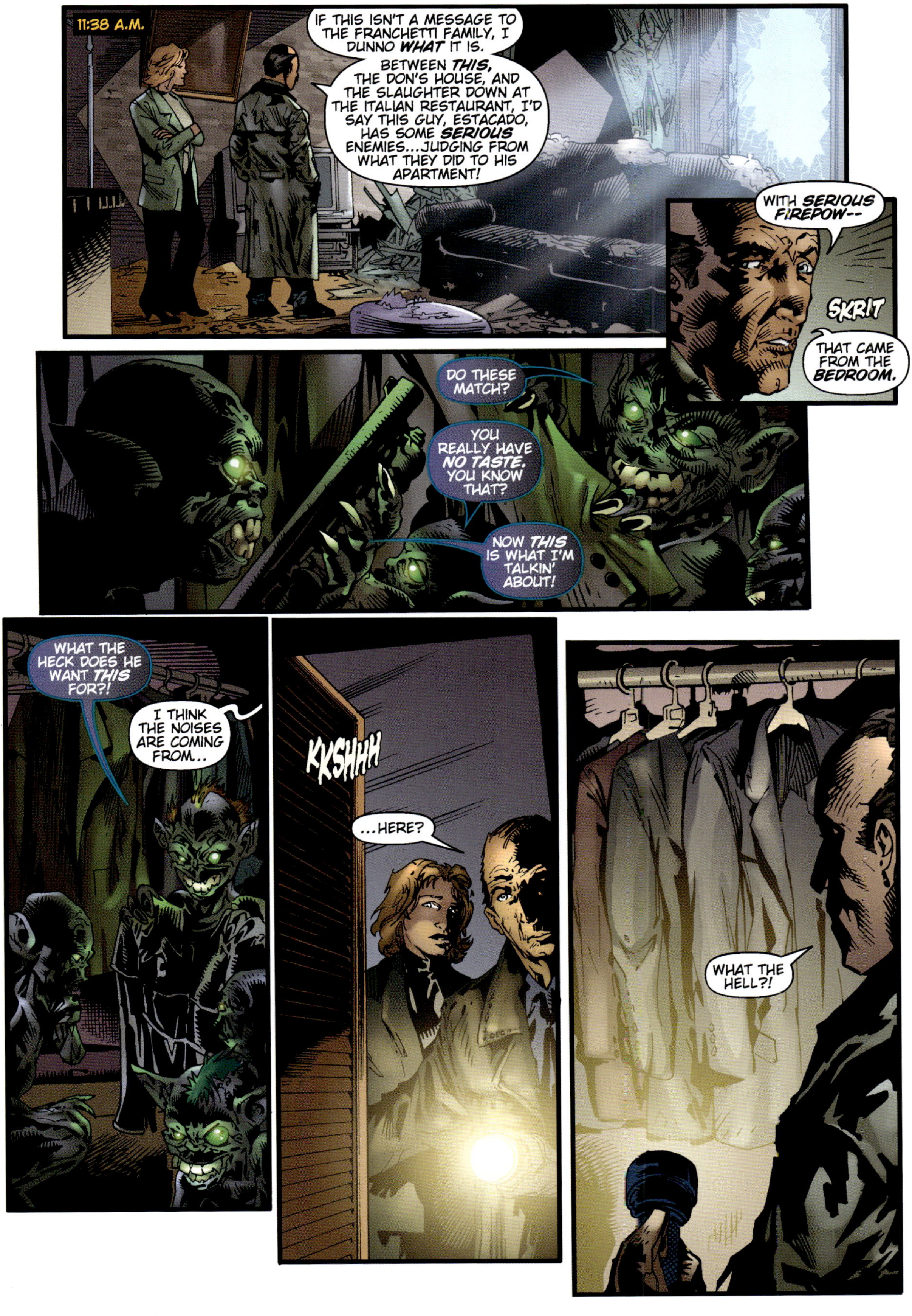
11:38 A.M.
IF THIS ISN'T A MESSAGE TO THE FRANCHETTI FAMILY, I DUNNO WHAT IT IS.
BETWEEN THIS, THE DON'S HOUSE, AND THE SLAUGHTER DOWN AT THE ITALIAN RESTAURANT, I'D SAY THIS GUY, ESTACADO, HAS SOME SERIOUS ENEMIES...JUDGING FROM WHAT THEY DID TO HIS APARTMENT!
WITH SERIOUS FIREPOW--
SKRIT
THAT CAME FROM THE BEDROOM.
DO THESE MATCH?
YOU REALLY HAVE NO TASTE. YOU KNOW THAT?
NOW THIS IS WHAT I'M TALKIN' ABOUT!
WHAT THE HECK DOES HE WANT THIS FOR?!
I THINK THE NOISES ARE COMING FROM..
KKSHHH
...HERE?
WHAT THE HELL?!

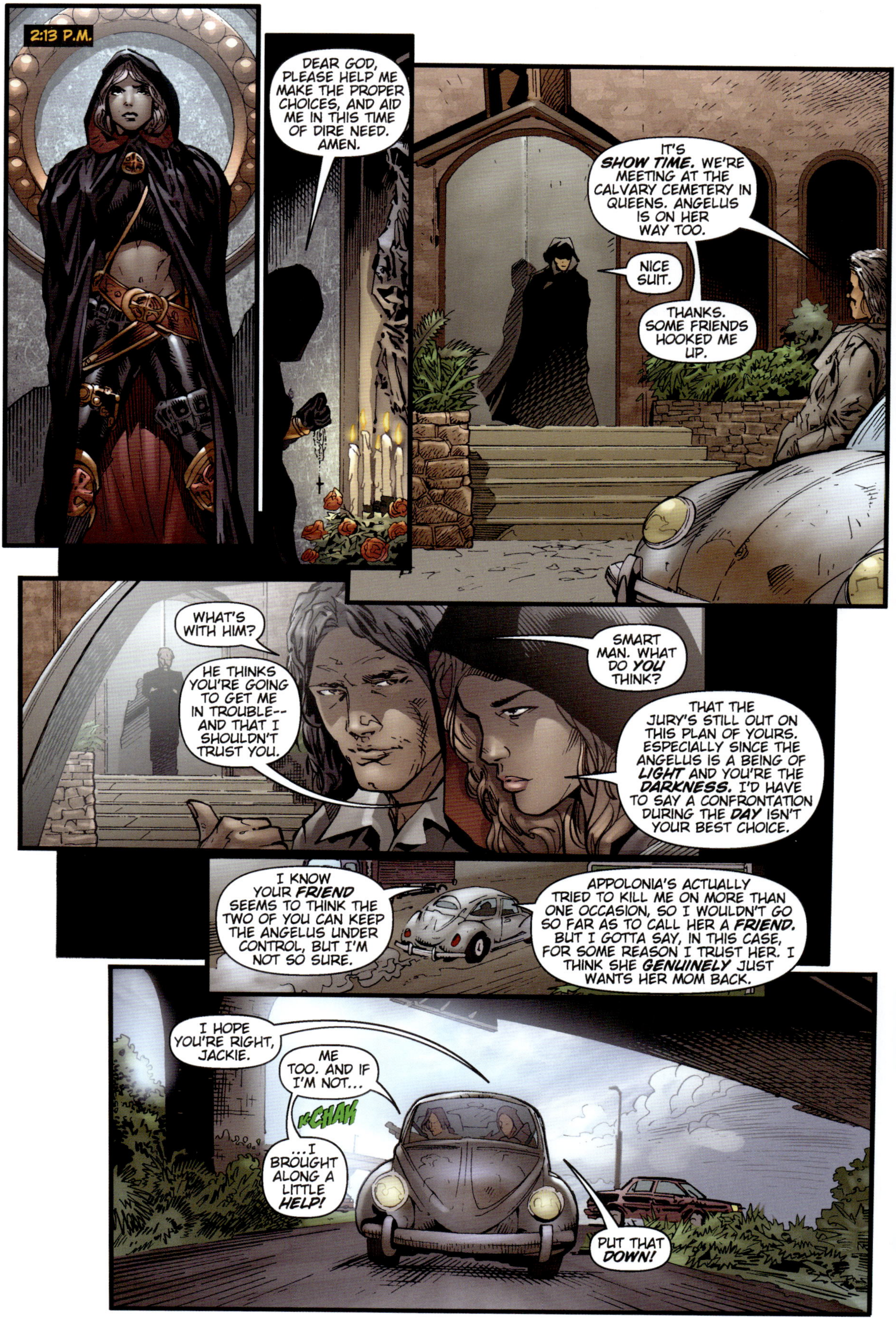

2:13 P.M.
DEAR GOD, PLEASE HELP ME MAKE THE PROPER CHOICES, AND AID ME IN THIS TIME OF DIRE NEED. AMEN.
IT'S SHOW TIME. WE'RE MEETING AT THE CALVARY CEMETERY IN QUEENS. ANGELUS IS ON HER WAY TOO.
NICE SUIT.
THANKS. SOME FRIENDS HOOKED ME UP.
WHAT'S WITH HIM?
HE THINKS YOU'RE GOING TO GET ME IN TROUBLE-- AND THAT I SHOULDN'T TRUST YOU.
SMART MAN. WHAT DO YOU THINK?
THAT THE JURY'S STILL OUT ON THIS PLAN OF YOURS. ESPECIALLY SINCE THE ANGELUS IS A BEING OF LIGHT AND YOU'RE THE DARKNESS. I'D HAVE TO SAY A CONFRONTATION DURING THE DAY ISN'T YOUR BEST CHOICE.
I KNOW YOUR FRIEND SEEMS TO THINK THE TWO OF YOU CAN KEEP THE ANGELUS UNDER CONTROL, BUT I'M NOT SO SURE.
APPOLONIA'S ACTUALLY TRIED TO KILL ME ON MORE THAN ONE OCCASION, SO I WOULDN'T GO SO FAR AS TO CALL HER A FRIEND. BUT I GOTTA SAY, IN THIS CASE, FOR SOME REASON I TRUST HER. I THINK SHE GENUINELY JUST WANTS HER MOM BACK.
I HOPE YOU'RE RIGHT, JACKIE.
ME TOO. AND IF I'M NOT...
K-CHAK
...I BROUGHT ALONG A LITTLE HELP!
PUT THAT DOWN!

4:11 P.M.

PAPA... ...I DON'T THINK I'VE EVER SAID THIS BEFORE, BUT I'M *SORRY*.

I KNOW IT WASN'T *YOUR* FAULT THAT YOU WERE AN INSENSITIVE, SADISTIC PRICK. IT'S THE WAY YOU WERE RAISED.

YOU DIDN'T TREAT MOM ANY WORSE THAN GRANDPA TREATED GRANDMA. IT'S THE WAY "THINGS WERE *DONE*..."

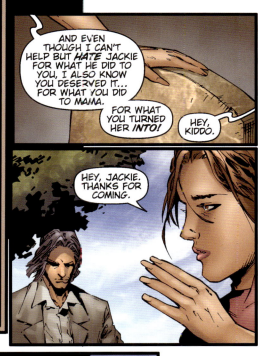

AND EVEN THOUGH I CAN'T HELP BUT *HATE* JACKIE FOR WHAT HE DID TO YOU, I ALSO KNOW YOU DESERVED IT... FOR WHAT YOU DID TO MAMA.

FOR WHAT YOU TURNED HER *INTO*!

HEY, KIDDO.

HEY, JACKIE. THANKS FOR COMING.

I'M SORRY IT HAD TO TURN OUT THIS WAY. I REALLY WAS HOPING WE COULD TALK SENSE INTO HER. BUT YOU KNOW MOM WHEN SHE SETS HER MIND TO SOMETHING...

WHAT THE HELL ARE YOU TALKING ABOU--

--OH--

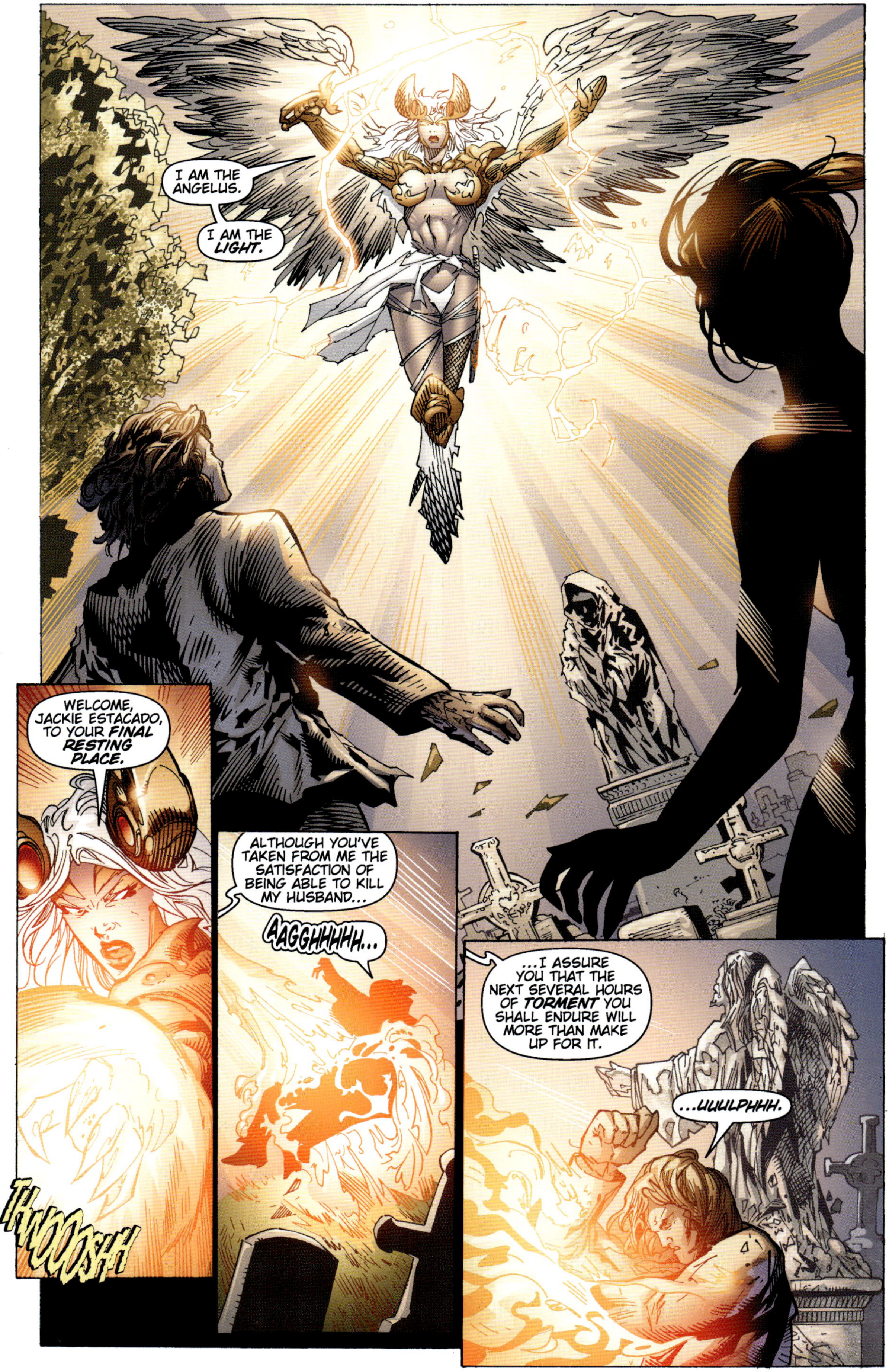
I AM THE ANGELUS.
I AM THE LIGHT.
WELCOME, JACKIE ESTACADO, TO YOUR FINAL RESTING PLACE.
THWOOOSHH
ALTHOUGH YOU'VE TAKEN FROM ME THE SATISFACTION OF BEING ABLE TO KILL MY HUSBAND...
AAGGHHHHH...
...I ASSURE YOU THAT THE NEXT SEVERAL HOURS OF TORMENT YOU SHALL ENDURE WILL MORE THAN MAKE UP FOR IT.
...UUULPHHH.

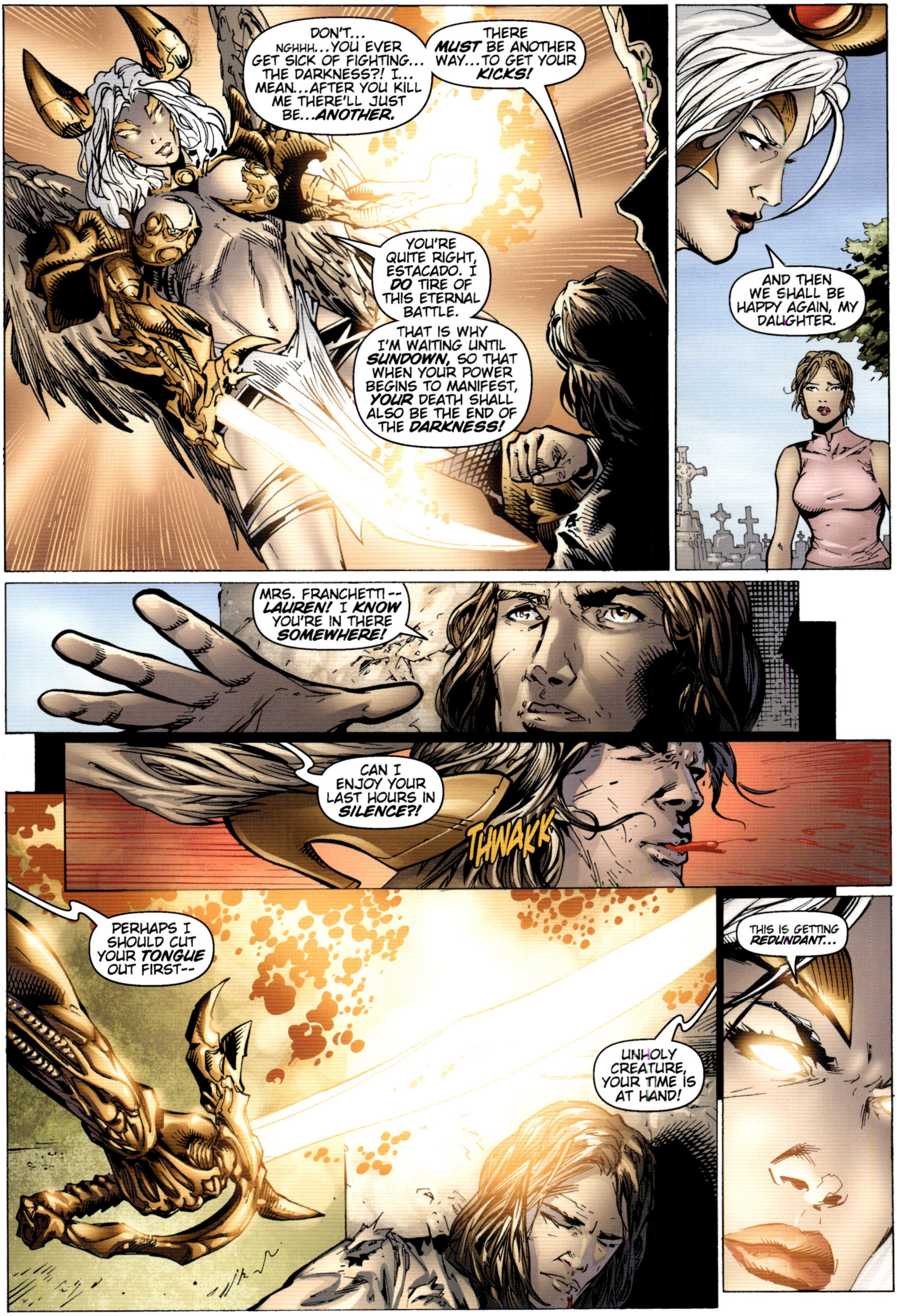
DON'T... NGHHH...YOU EVER GET SICK OF FIGHTING... THE DARKNESS?! I... MEAN...AFTER YOU KILL ME THERE'LL JUST BE...ANOTHER.
THERE MUST BE ANOTHER WAY...TO GET YOUR KICKS!
YOU'RE QUITE RIGHT, ESTACADO. I DO TIRE OF THIS ETERNAL BATTLE.
THAT IS WHY I'M WAITING UNTIL SUNDOWN, SO THAT WHEN YOUR POWER BEGINS TO MANIFEST, YOUR DEATH SHALL ALSO BE THE END OF THE DARKNESS!
AND THEN WE SHALL BE HAPPY AGAIN, MY DAUGHTER.
MRS. FRANCHETTI -- LAUREN! I KNOW YOU'RE IN THERE SOMEWHERE!
CAN I ENJOY YOUR LAST HOURS IN SILENCE?!
THWAKK
PERHAPS I SHOULD CUT YOUR TONGUE OUT FIRST--
THIS IS GETTING REDUNDANT...
UNHOLY CREATURE, YOUR TIME IS AT HAND!

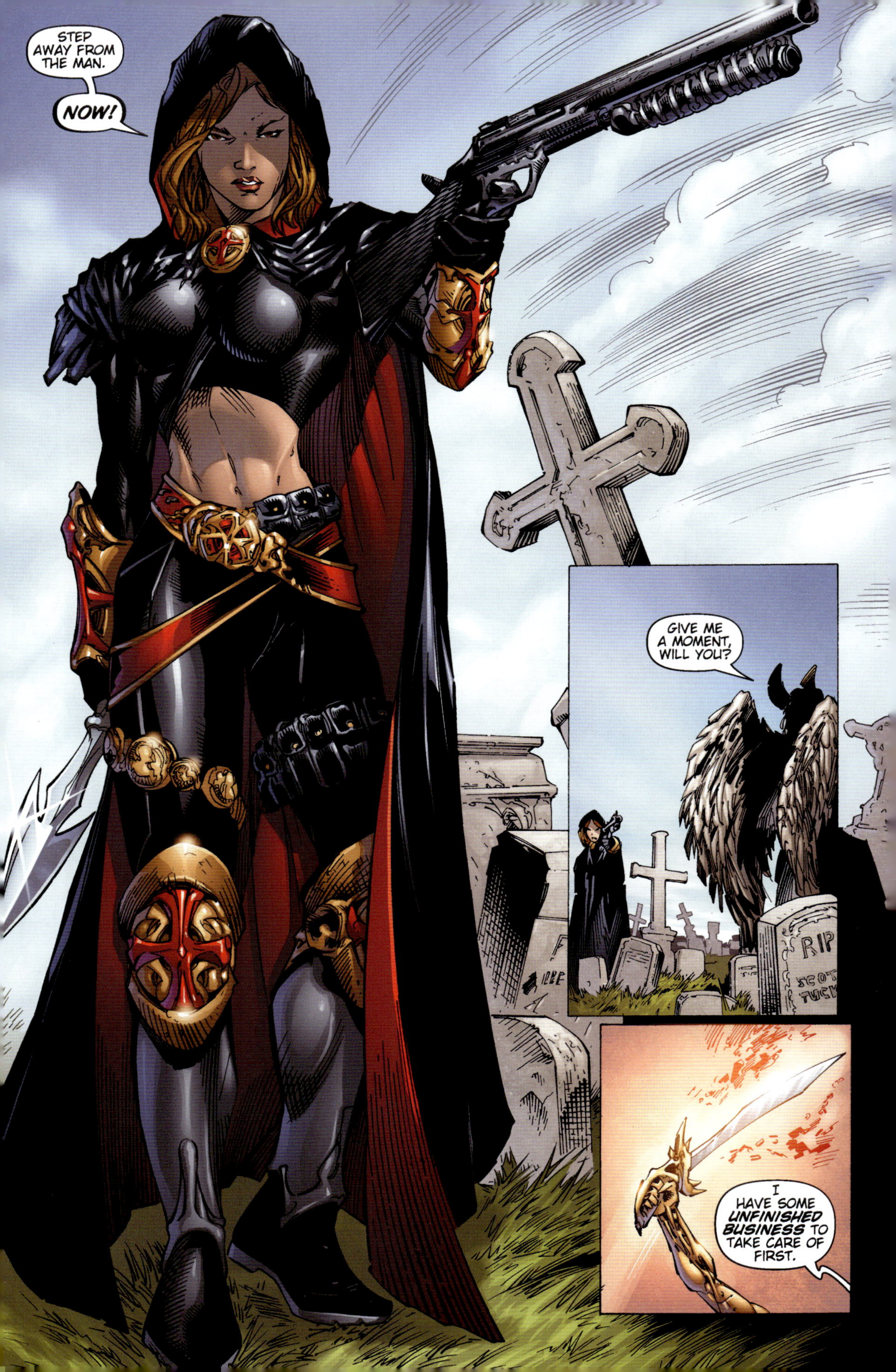
STEP AWAY FROM THE MAN.
NOW!
GIVE ME A MOMENT, WILL YOU?
I HAVE SOME UNFINISHED BUSINESS TO TAKE CARE OF FIRST.
RIP SCOT TUCK

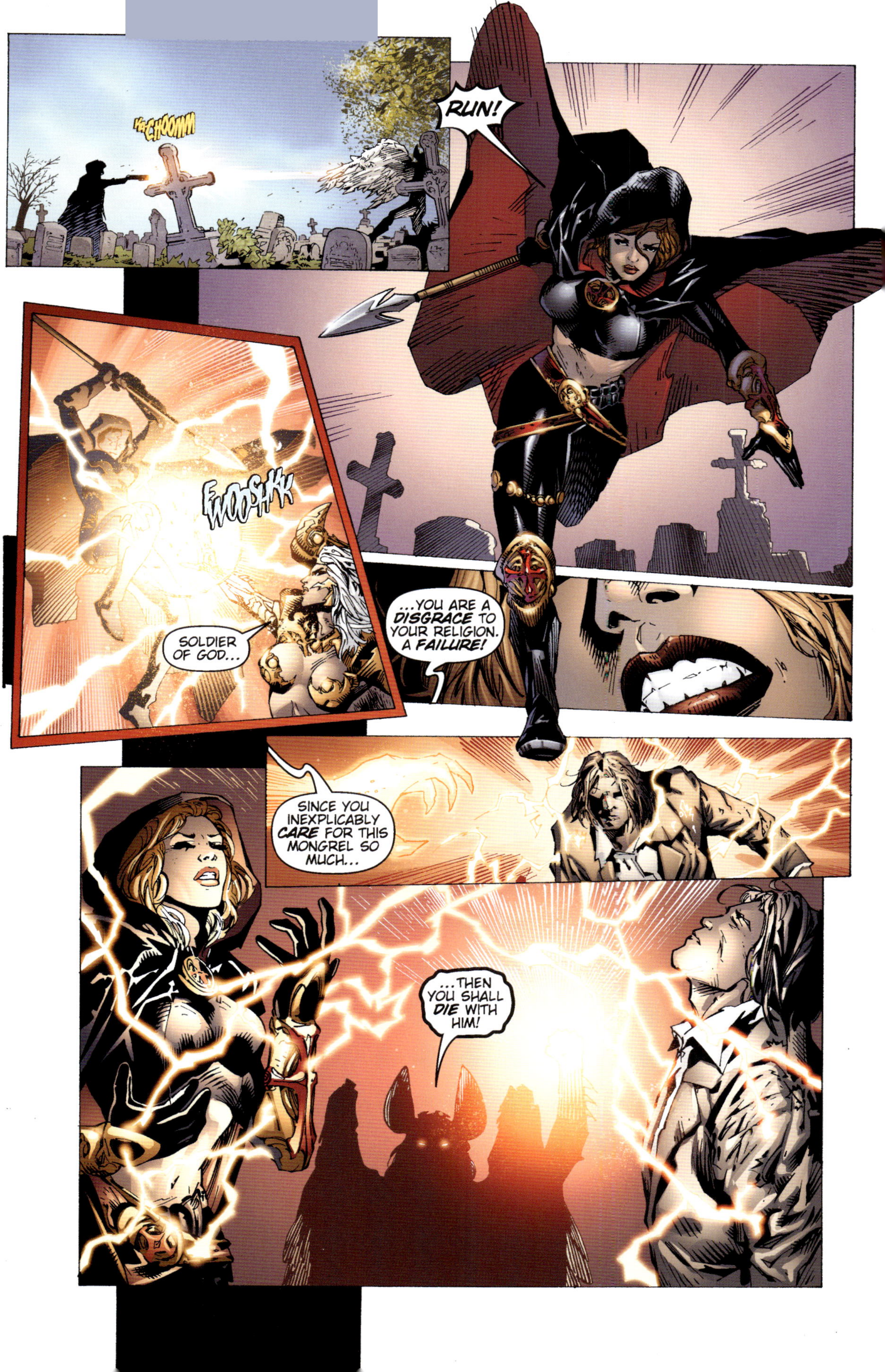

KA-CHOOMM
RUN!
FWOOSHKK
SOLDIER OF GOD...
...YOU ARE A DISGRACE TO YOUR RELIGION. A FAILURE!
SINCE YOU INEXPLICABLY CARE FOR THIS MONGREL SO MUCH...
...THEN YOU SHALL DIE WITH HIM!

I HAVE BEEN WAITING MILLENNIA FOR THIS OPPORTUNITY -- TO RESTORE GLORIOUS ORDER TO THIS EARTH.
I THOUGHT THAT YOU, A MEMBER OF THE CHURCH, WOULD SEE THE GOOD I'M DOING FOR EVERYONE.
NO MATTER. NOBODY SHALL STAND IN MY WAY.
NOBODY!
NNNGHHHLLL
WHMMP

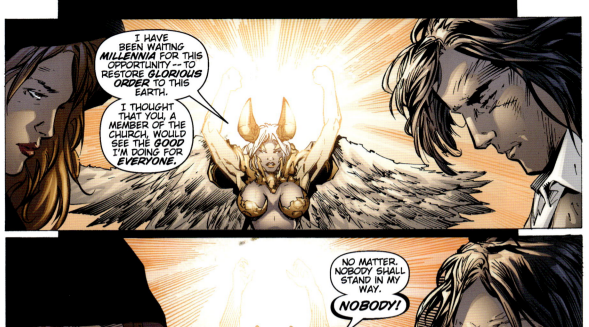

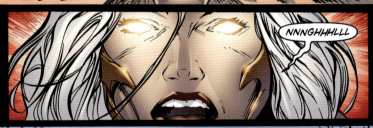

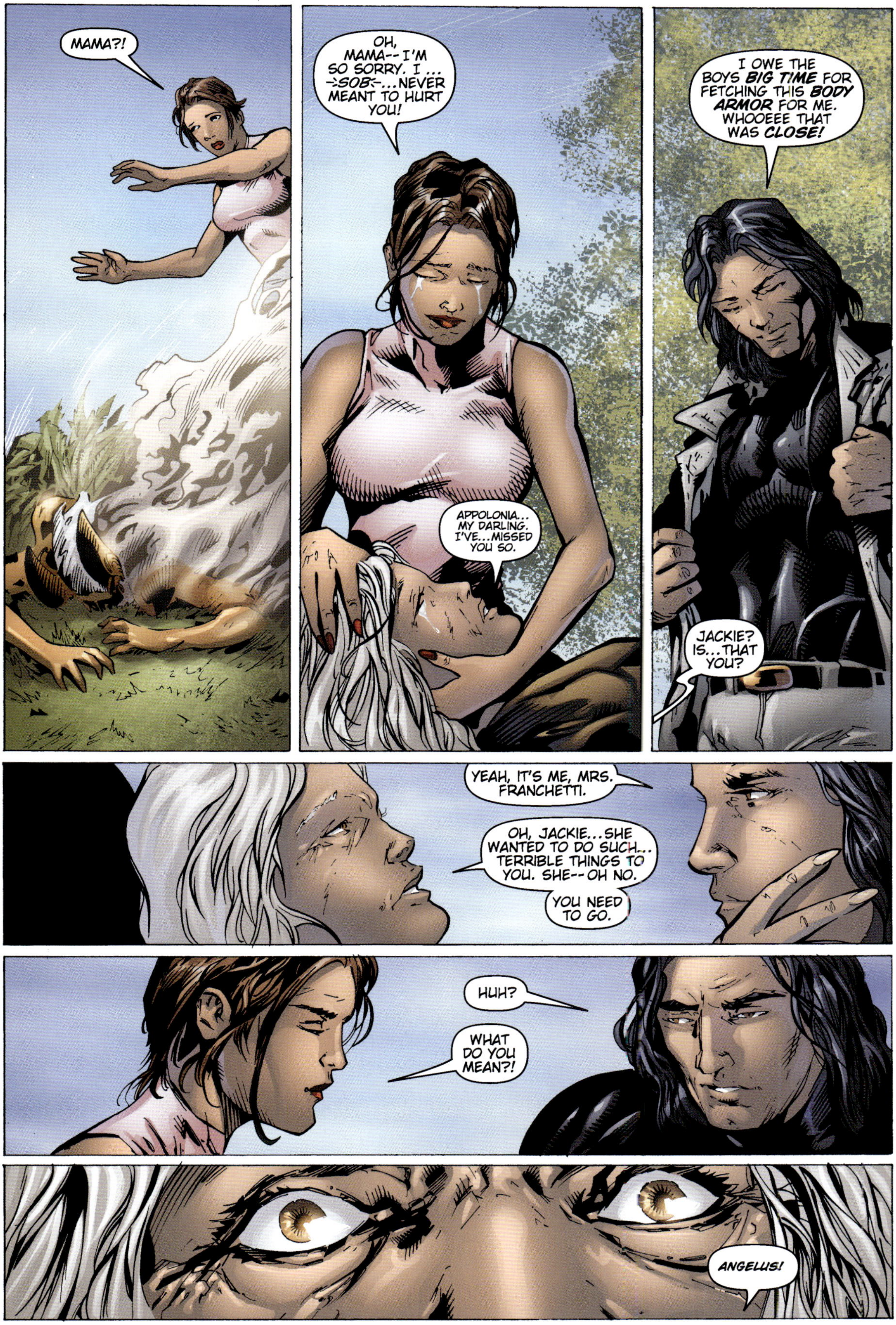
MAMA?!
OH, MAMA-- I'M SO SORRY. I ... -SOB-... NEVER MEANT TO HURT YOU!
APPOLONIA... MY DARLING. I'VE...MISSED YOU SO.
I OWE THE BOYS BIG TIME FOR FETCHING THIS BODY ARMOR FOR ME. WHOOEEE THAT WAS CLOSE!
JACKIE? IS...THAT YOU?
YEAH, IT'S ME, MRS. FRANCHETTI.
OH, JACKIE...SHE WANTED TO DO SUCH... TERRIBLE THINGS TO YOU. SHE--OH NO.
YOU NEED TO GO.
HUH?
WHAT DO YOU MEAN?!
ANGELUS!

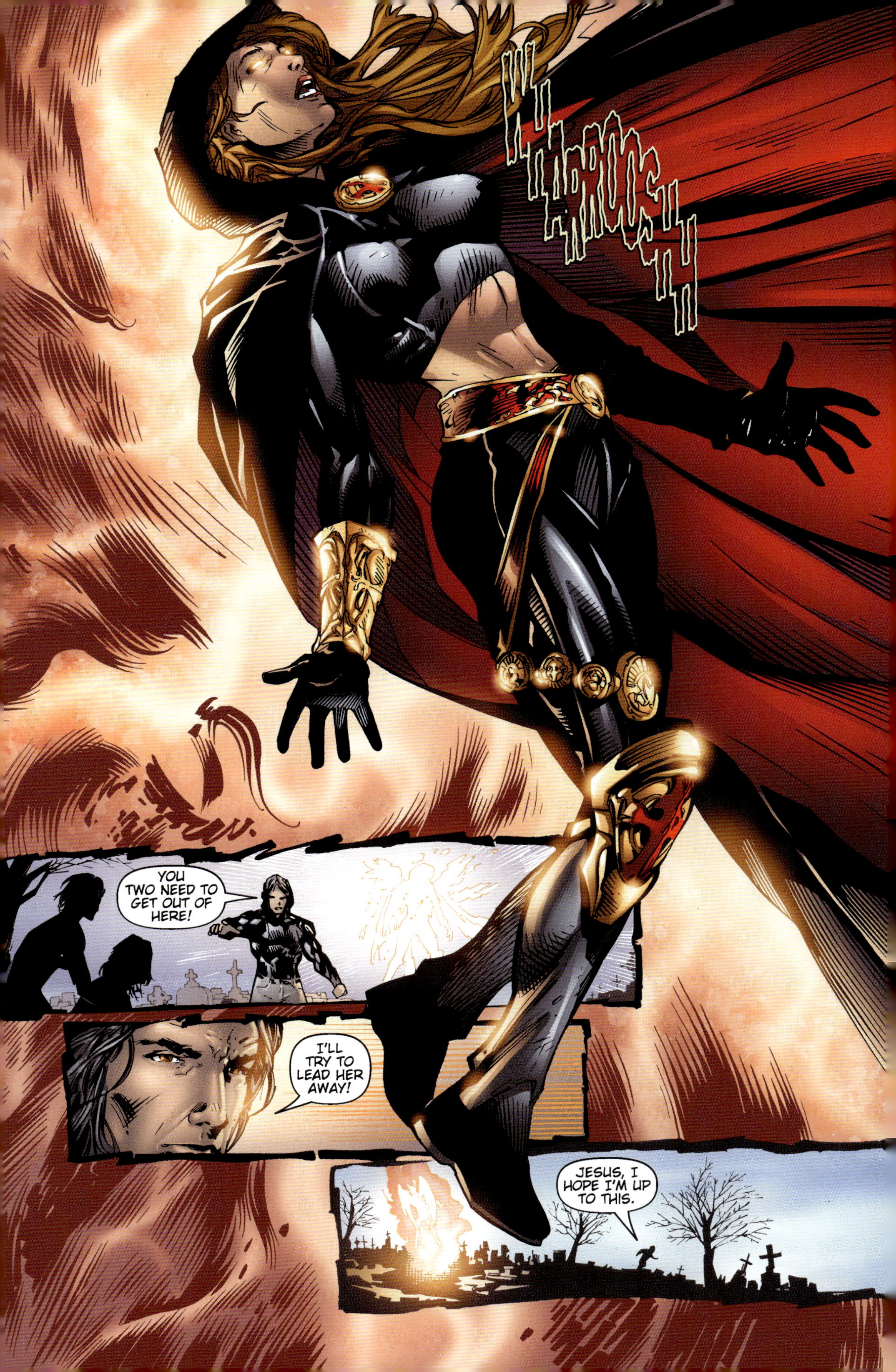
WHARROOSHH
YOU TWO NEED TO GET OUT OF HERE!
I'LL TRY TO LEAD HER AWAY!
JESUS, I HOPE I'M UP TO THIS.

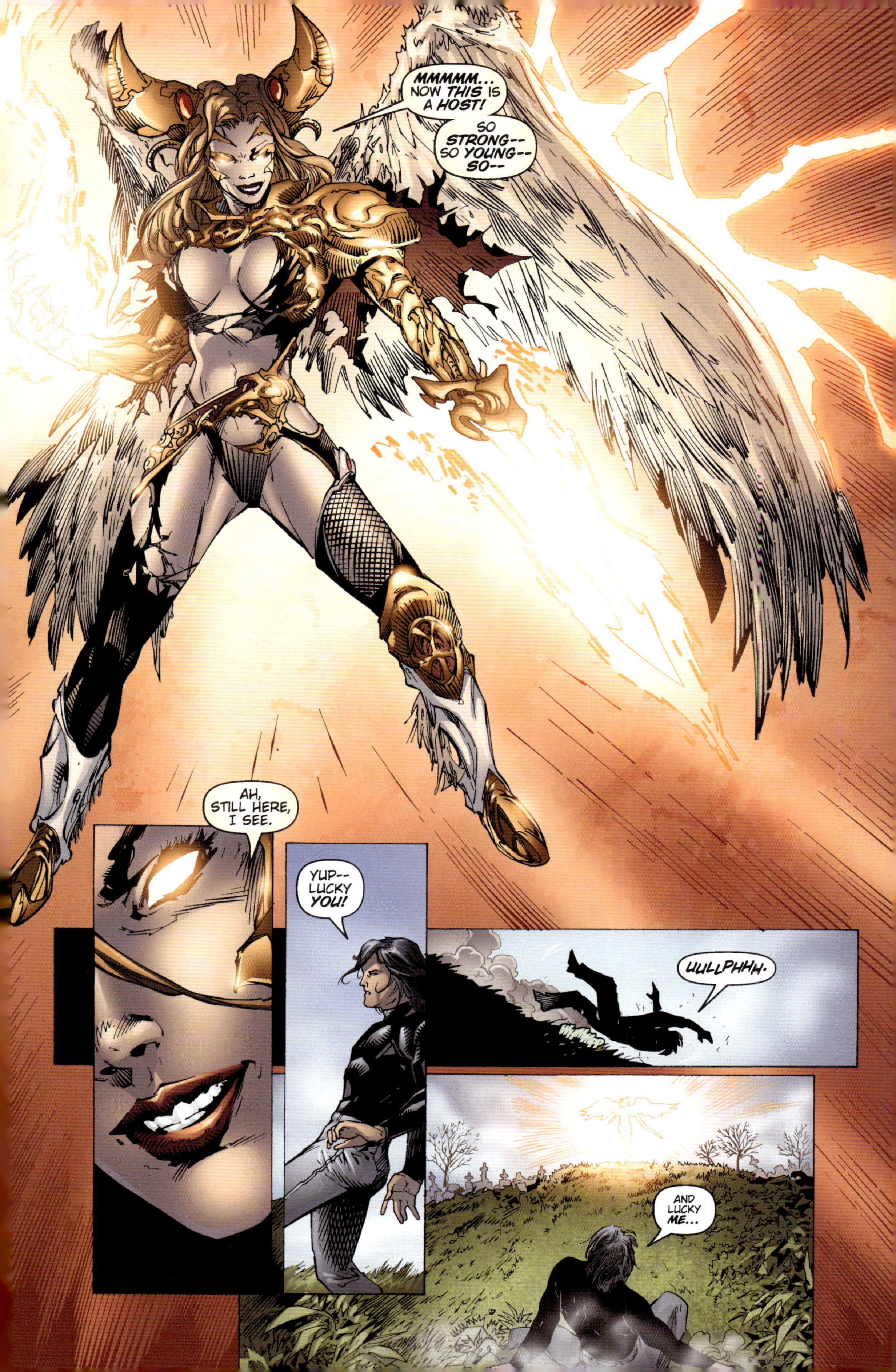
MMMMM... NOW THIS IS A HOST!
SO STRONG-- SO YOUNG-- SO--
AH, STILL HERE, I SEE.
YUP-- LUCKY YOU!
UULLPHHH.
AND LUCKY ME...

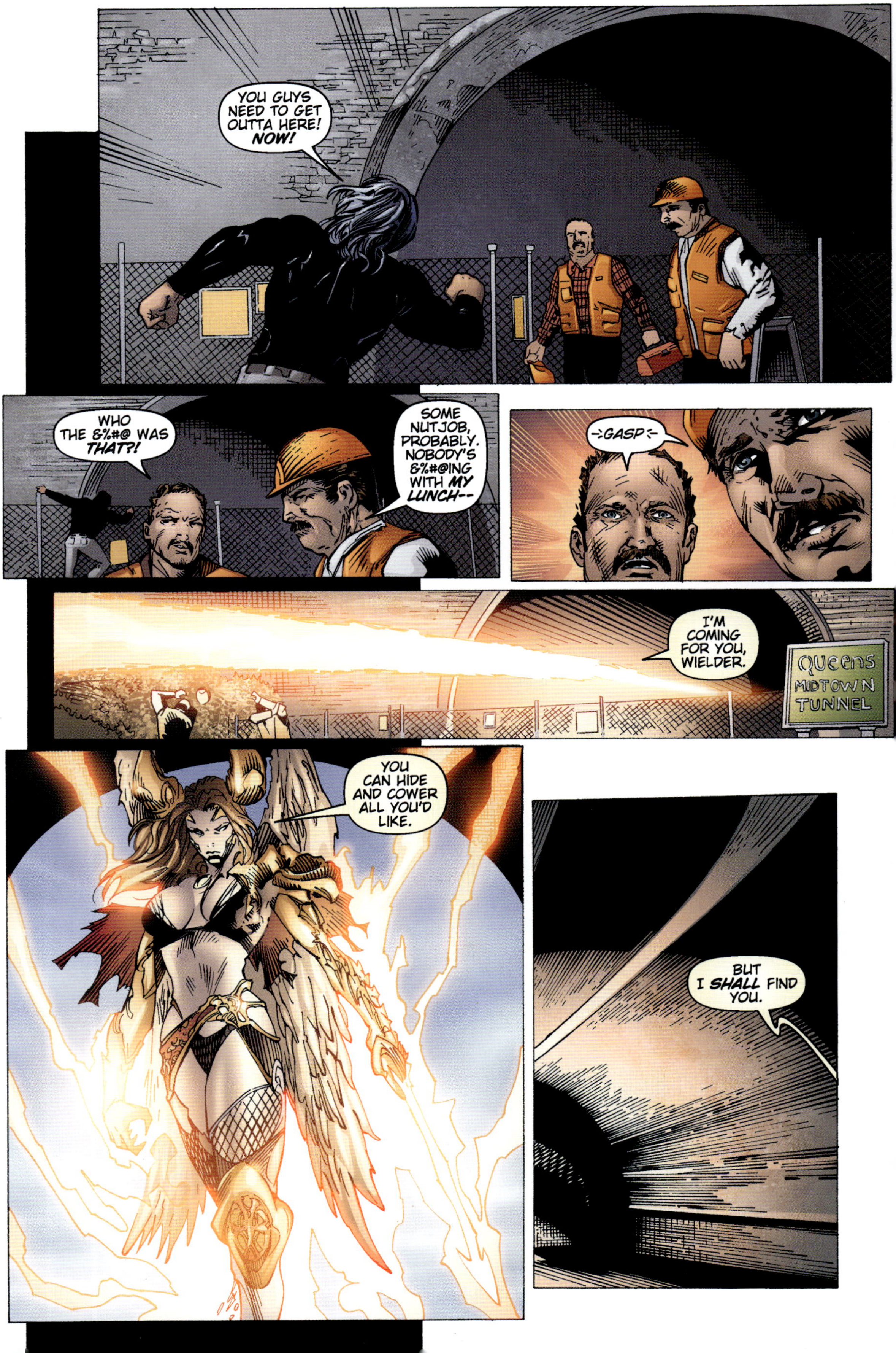
YOU GUYS NEED TO GET OUTTA HERE! NOW!
WHO THE &%#@ WAS THAT?!
SOME NUTJOB, PROBABLY. NOBODY'S &%#@ING WITH MY LUNCH--
-GASP-
I'M COMING FOR YOU, WIELDER.
QUEENS MIDTOWN TUNNEL
YOU CAN HIDE AND COWER ALL YOU'D LIKE.
BUT I SHALL FIND YOU.

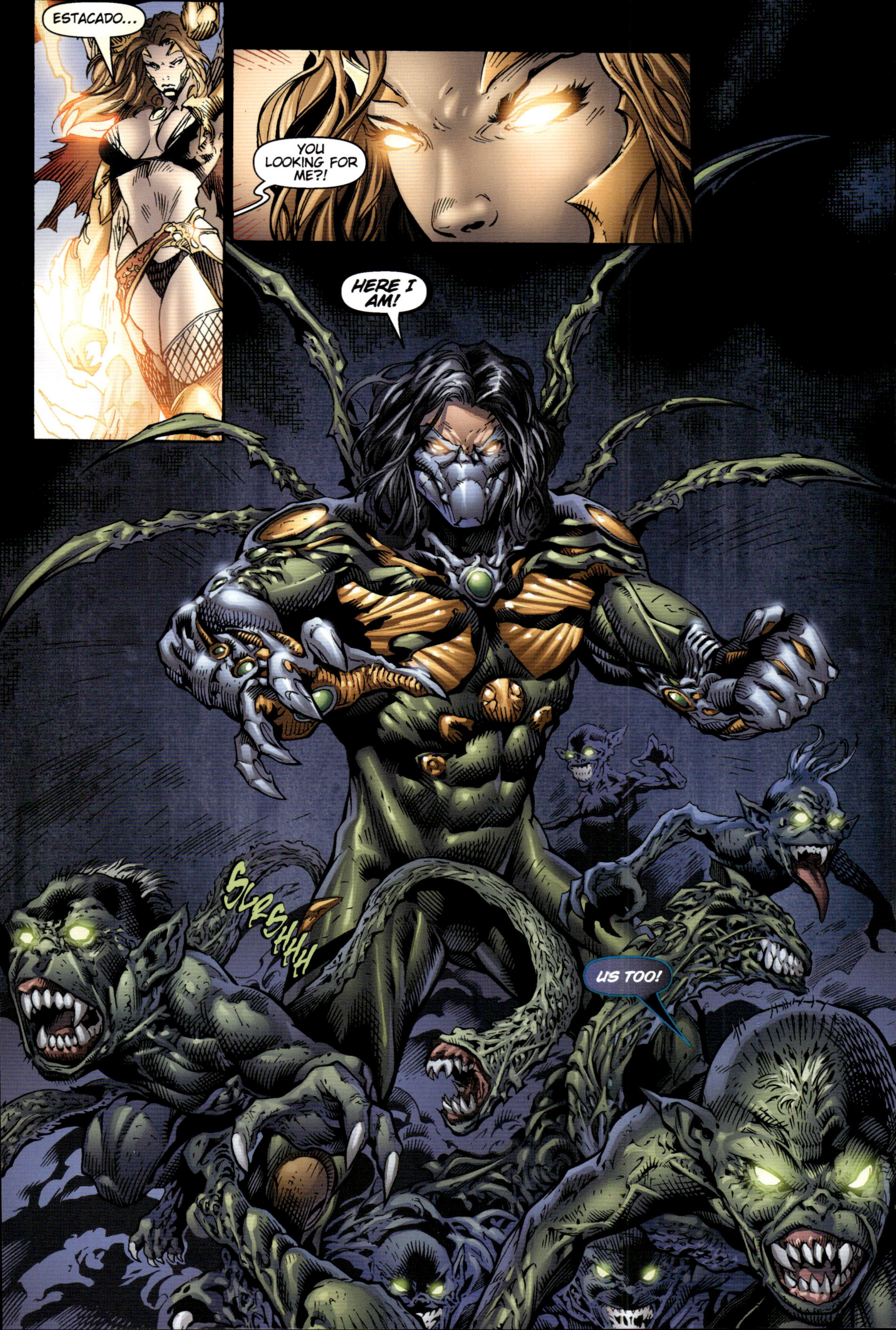
ESTACADO...
YOU LOOKING FOR ME?!
HERE I AM!
SURSHHH
US TOO!

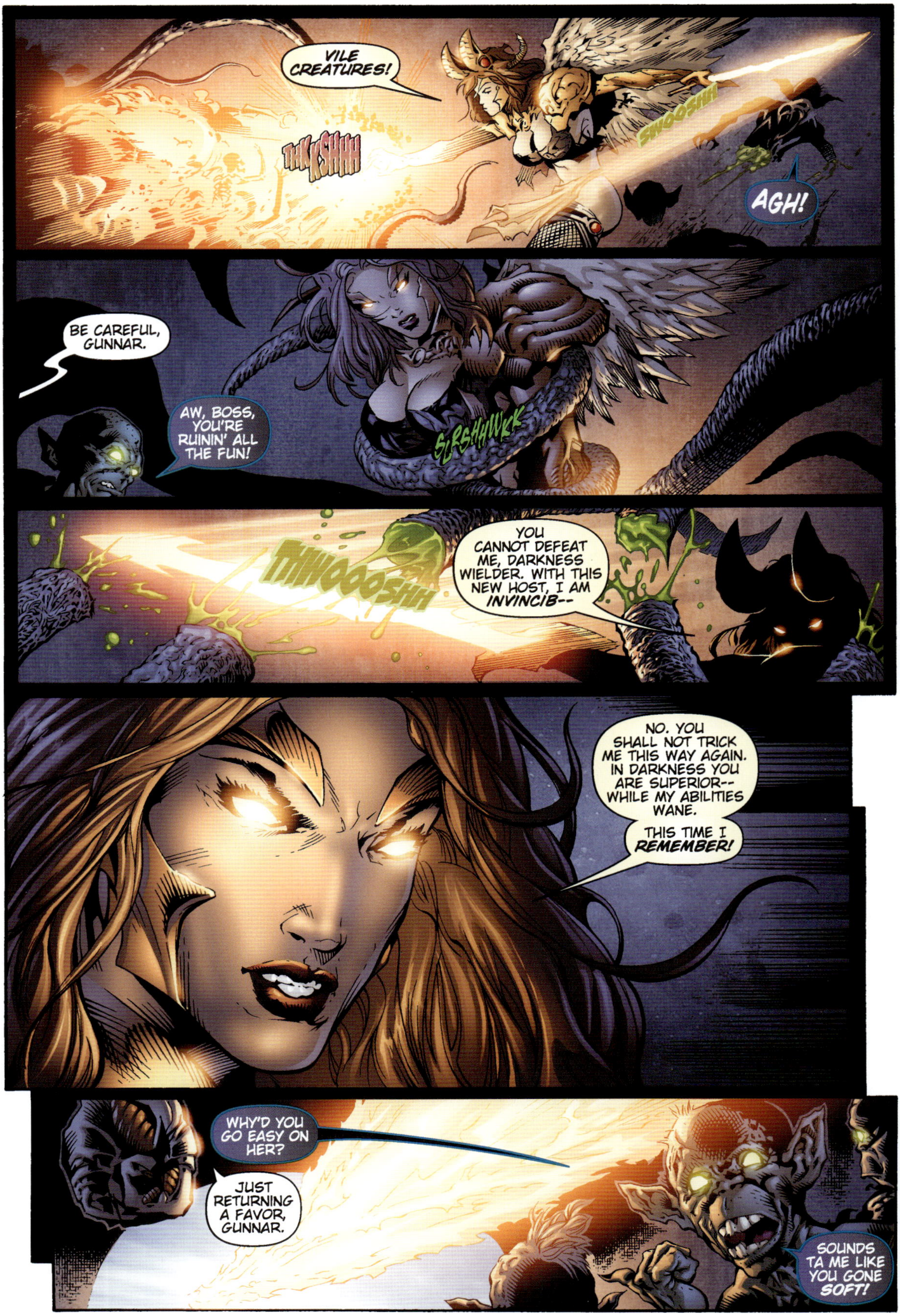
VILE CREATURES!
THKKSHHH
SWOOSHH
AGH!
BE CAREFUL, GUNNAR.
AW, BOSS, YOU'RE RUININ' ALL THE FUN!
SLRSHHWKK
THWOOOSHH
YOU CANNOT DEFEAT ME, DARKNESS WIELDER. WITH THIS NEW HOST, I AM *INVINCIB--*
NO. YOU SHALL NOT TRICK ME THIS WAY AGAIN. IN DARKNESS YOU ARE SUPERIOR-- WHILE MY ABILITIES WANE.
THIS TIME I *REMEMBER!*
WHY'D YOU GO EASY ON HER?
JUST RETURNING A FAVOR, GUNNAR.
SOUNDS TA ME LIKE YOU GONE *SOFT!*

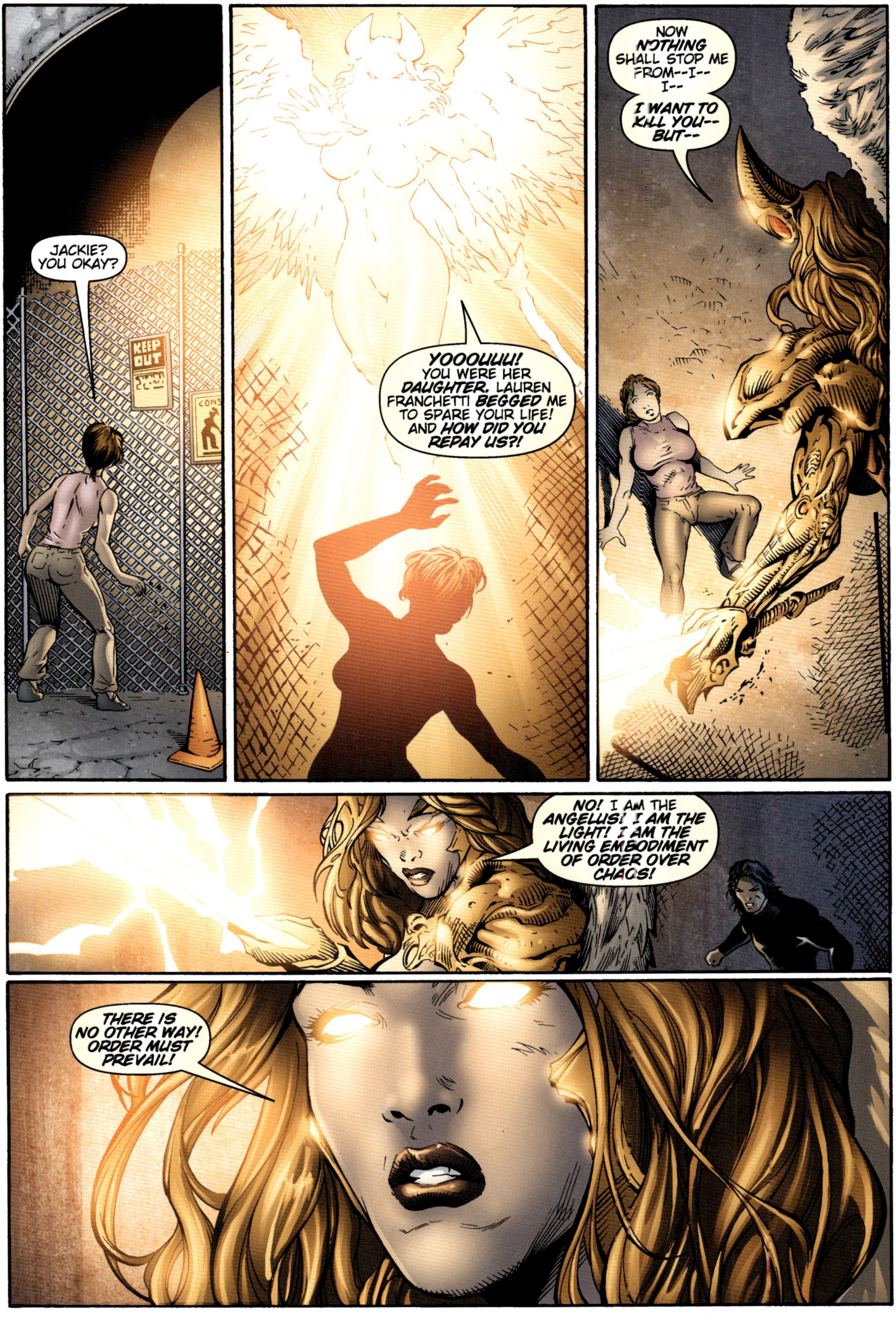
JACKIE? YOU OKAY?
KEEP OUT
YOOOUUU! YOU WERE HER DAUGHTER. LAUREN FRANCHETTI BEGGED ME TO SPARE YOUR LIFE! AND HOW DID YOU REPAY US?!
NOW NOTHING SHALL STOP ME FROM--I-- I--
I WANT TO KILL YOU-- BUT--
NO! I AM THE ANGELUS! I AM THE LIGHT! I AM THE LIVING EMBODIMENT OF ORDER OVER CHAOS!
THERE IS NO OTHER WAY! ORDER MUST PREVAIL!

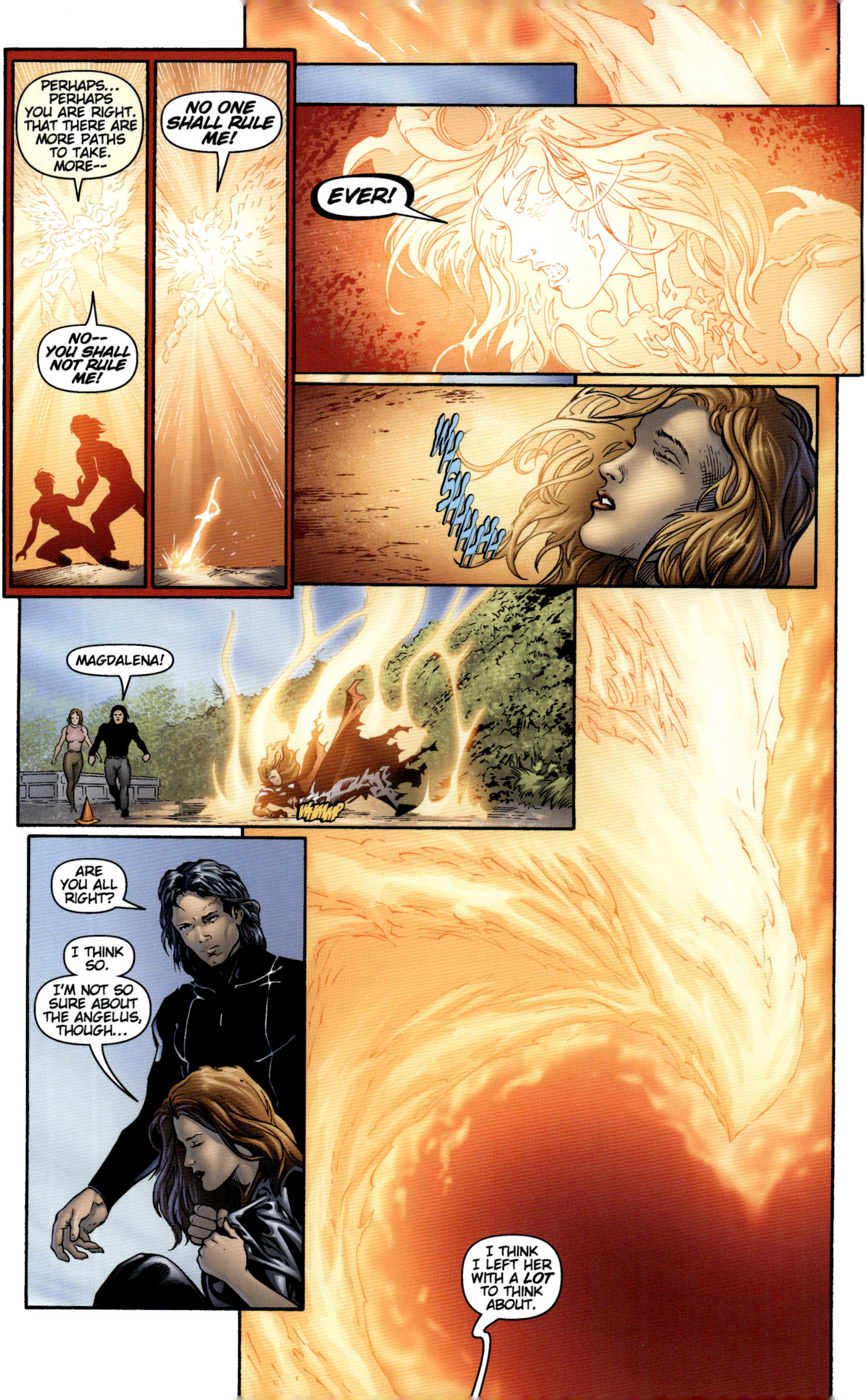
PERHAPS... PERHAPS YOU ARE RIGHT. THAT THERE ARE MORE PATHS TO TAKE. MORE--
NO-- YOU SHALL NOT RULE ME!
NO ONE SHALL RULE ME!
EVER!
WHSHHH
MAGDALENA!
WHUMP
ARE YOU ALL RIGHT?
I THINK SO.
I'M NOT SO SURE ABOUT THE ANGELUS, THOUGH...
I THINK I LEFT HER WITH A LOT TO THINK ABOUT.

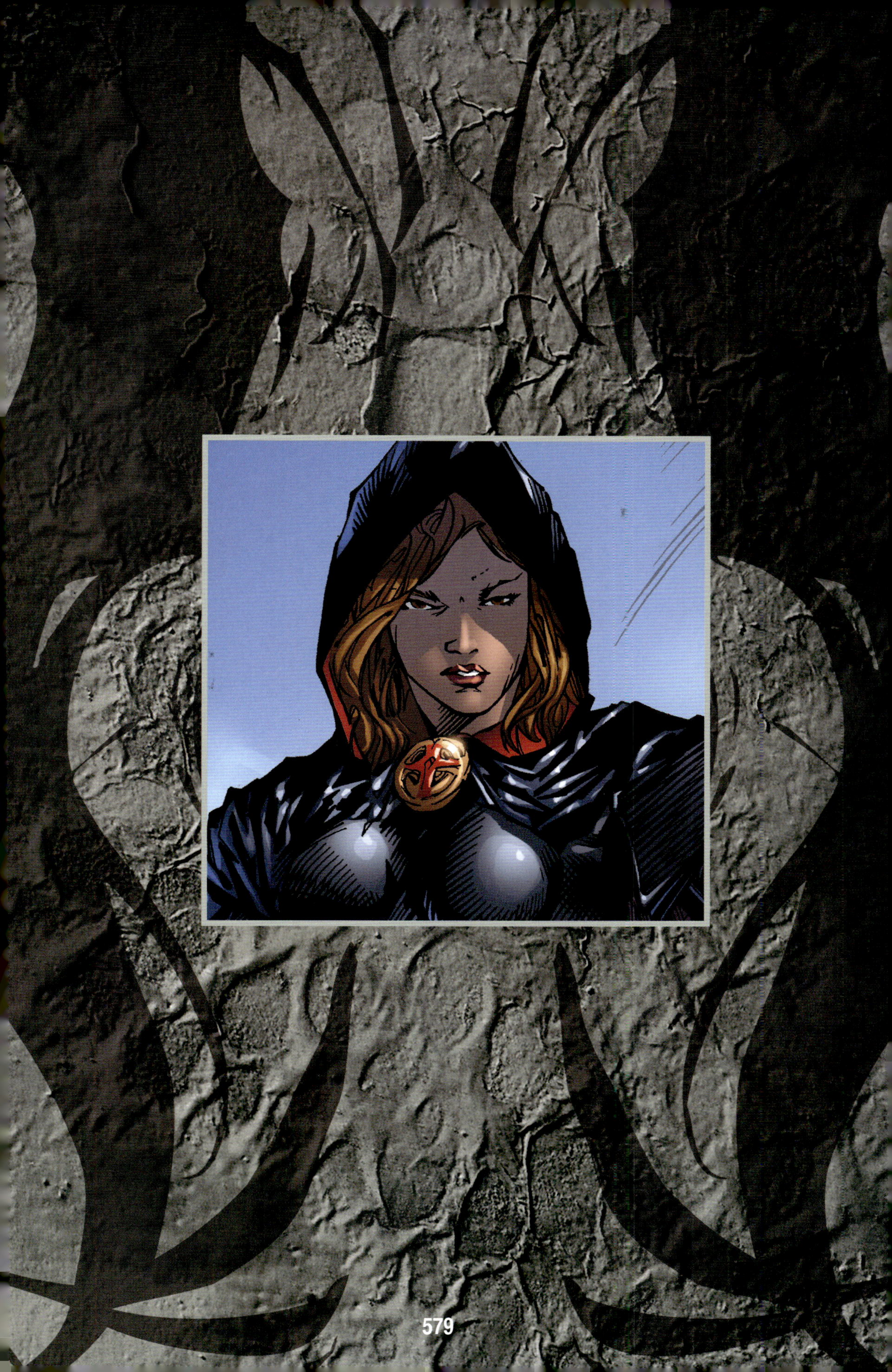

THE DARKNESS #65

The Darkness Issue #65
cover art by: Marc Silvestri, Joe Weems,
& Frank D'Armata

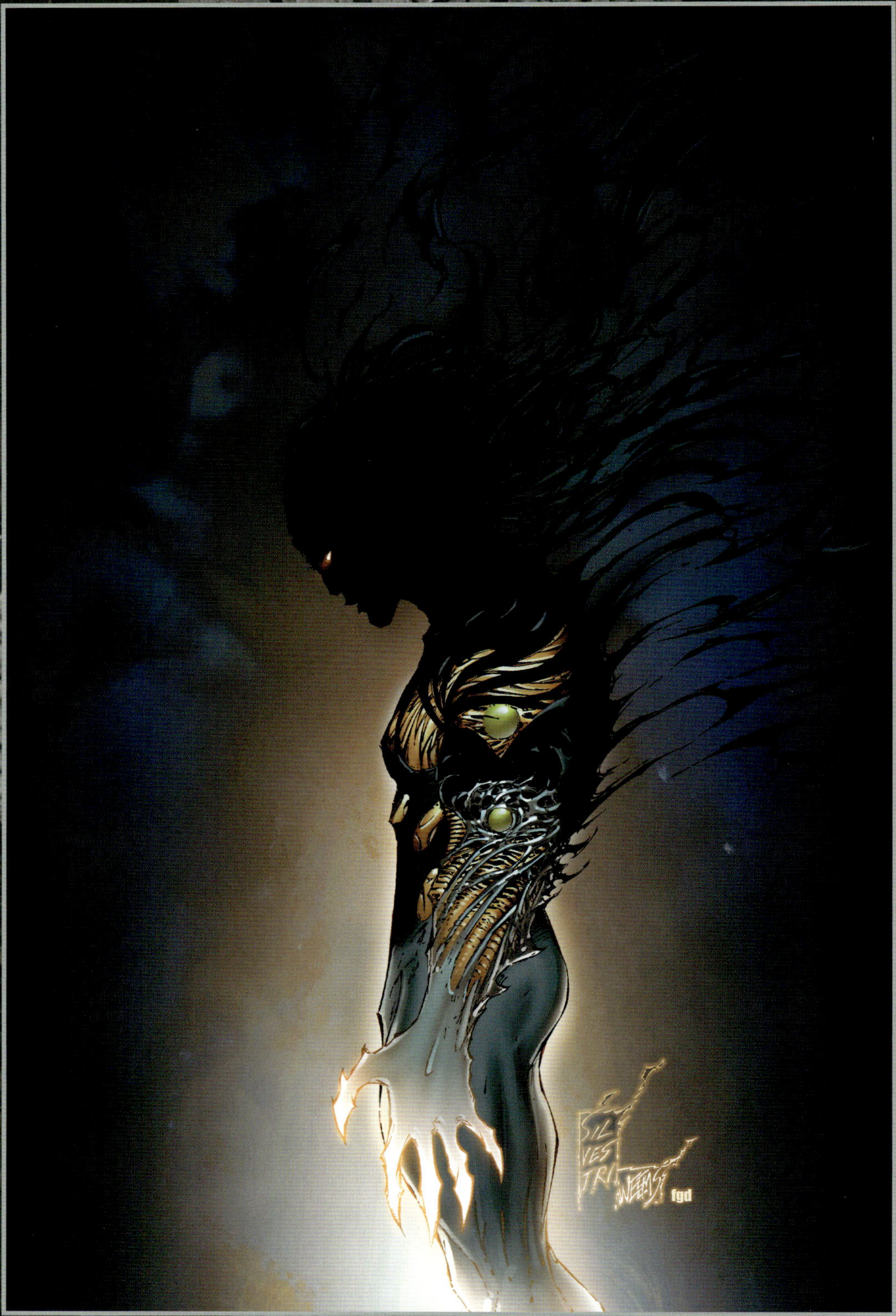

EDITORS NOTE: THIS ISSUE TAKES PLACE AFTER THE EVENTS OF FIRST BORN

THE EARTH WAS FORMLESS AND VOID AND DARKNESS WAS OVER THE SURFACE OF THE DEEP.

THEN GOD SAID, "LET THERE BE LIGHT."

AND THERE WAS LIGHT. AND GOD SAW THAT THE LIGHT WAS GOOD; AND GOD SEPARATED THE LIGHT FROM THE DARKNESS.

AND THE DARKNESS?

THE DARKNESS RESENTED IT.

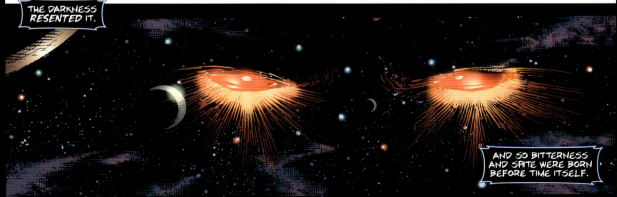

AND SO BITTERNESS AND SPITE WERE BORN BEFORE TIME ITSELF.

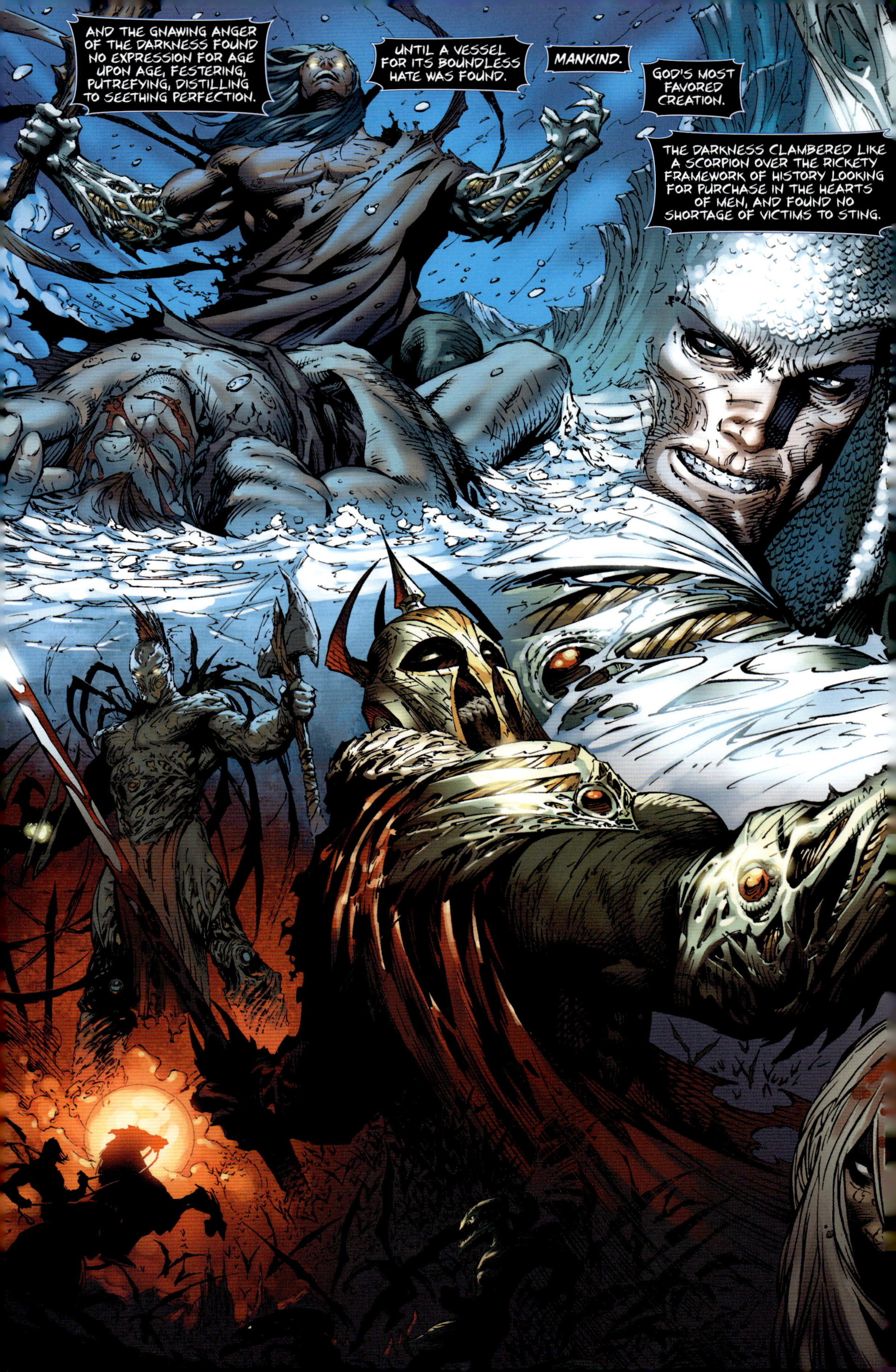
AND THE GNAWING ANGER OF THE DARKNESS FOUND NO EXPRESSION FOR AGE UPON AGE, FESTERING, PUTREFYING, DISTILLING TO SEETHING PERFECTION.
UNTIL A VESSEL FOR ITS BOUNDLESS HATE WAS FOUND.
MANKIND.
GOD'S MOST FAVORED CREATION.
THE DARKNESS CLAMBERED LIKE A SCORPION OVER THE RICKETY FRAMEWORK OF HISTORY LOOKING FOR PURCHASE IN THE HEARTS OF MEN, AND FOUND NO SHORTAGE OF VICTIMS TO STING.

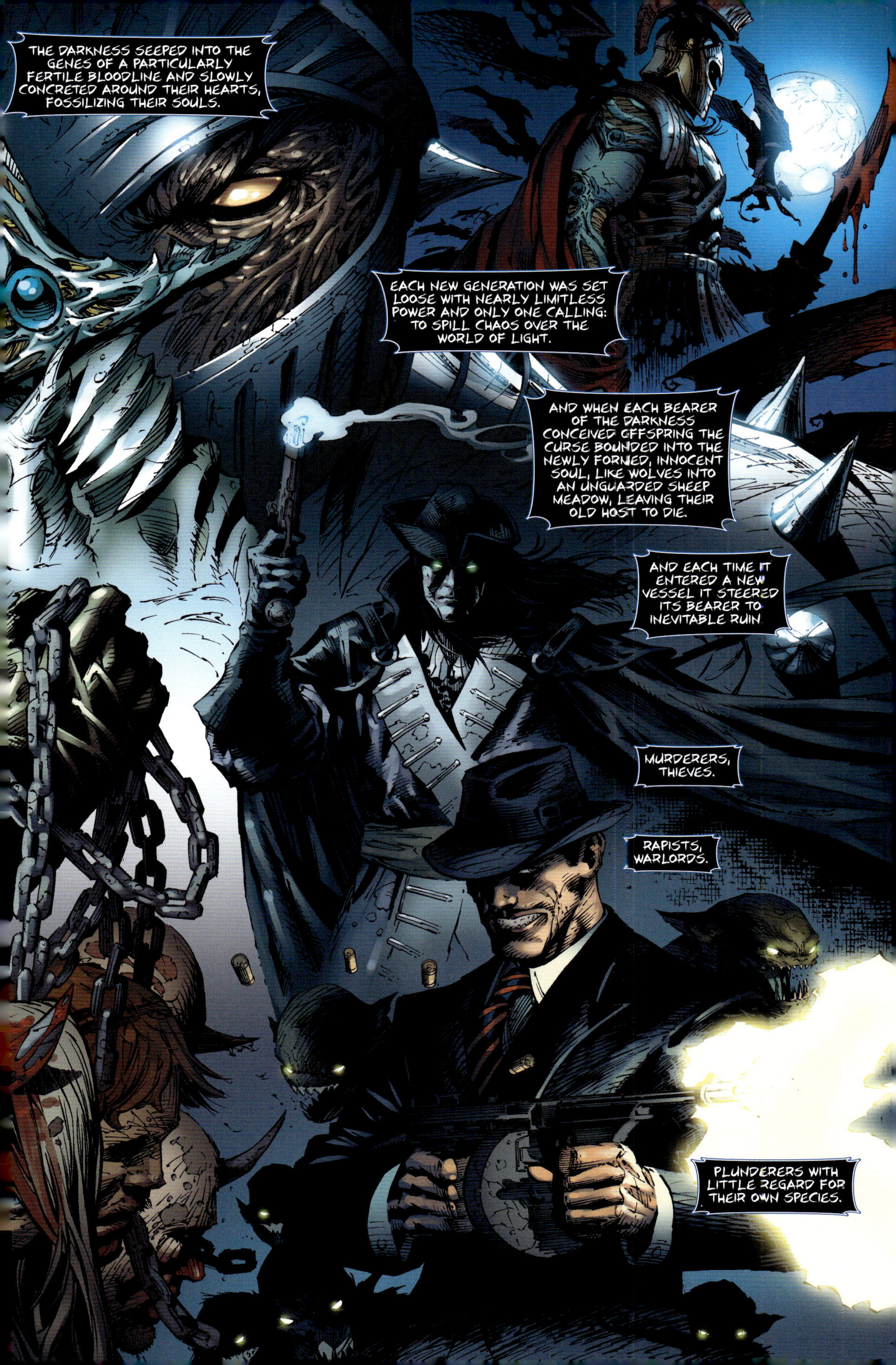
THE DARKNESS SEEPED INTO THE GENES OF A PARTICULARLY FERTILE BLOODLINE AND SLOWLY CONCRETED AROUND THEIR HEARTS, FOSSILIZING THEIR SOULS.
EACH NEW GENERATION WAS SET LOOSE WITH NEARLY LIMITLESS POWER AND ONLY ONE CALLING: TO SPILL CHAOS OVER THE WORLD OF LIGHT.
AND WHEN EACH BEARER OF THE DARKNESS CONCEIVED OFFSPRING THE CURSE BOUNDED INTO THE NEWLY FORMED, INNOCENT SOUL, LIKE WOLVES INTO AN UNGUARDED SHEEP MEADOW, LEAVING THEIR OLD HOST TO DIE.
AND EACH TIME IT ENTERED A NEW VESSEL IT STEERED ITS BEARER TO INEVITABLE RUIN.
MURDERERS, THIEVES.
RAPISTS, WARLORDS.
PLUNDERERS WITH LITTLE REGARD FOR THEIR OWN SPECIES.

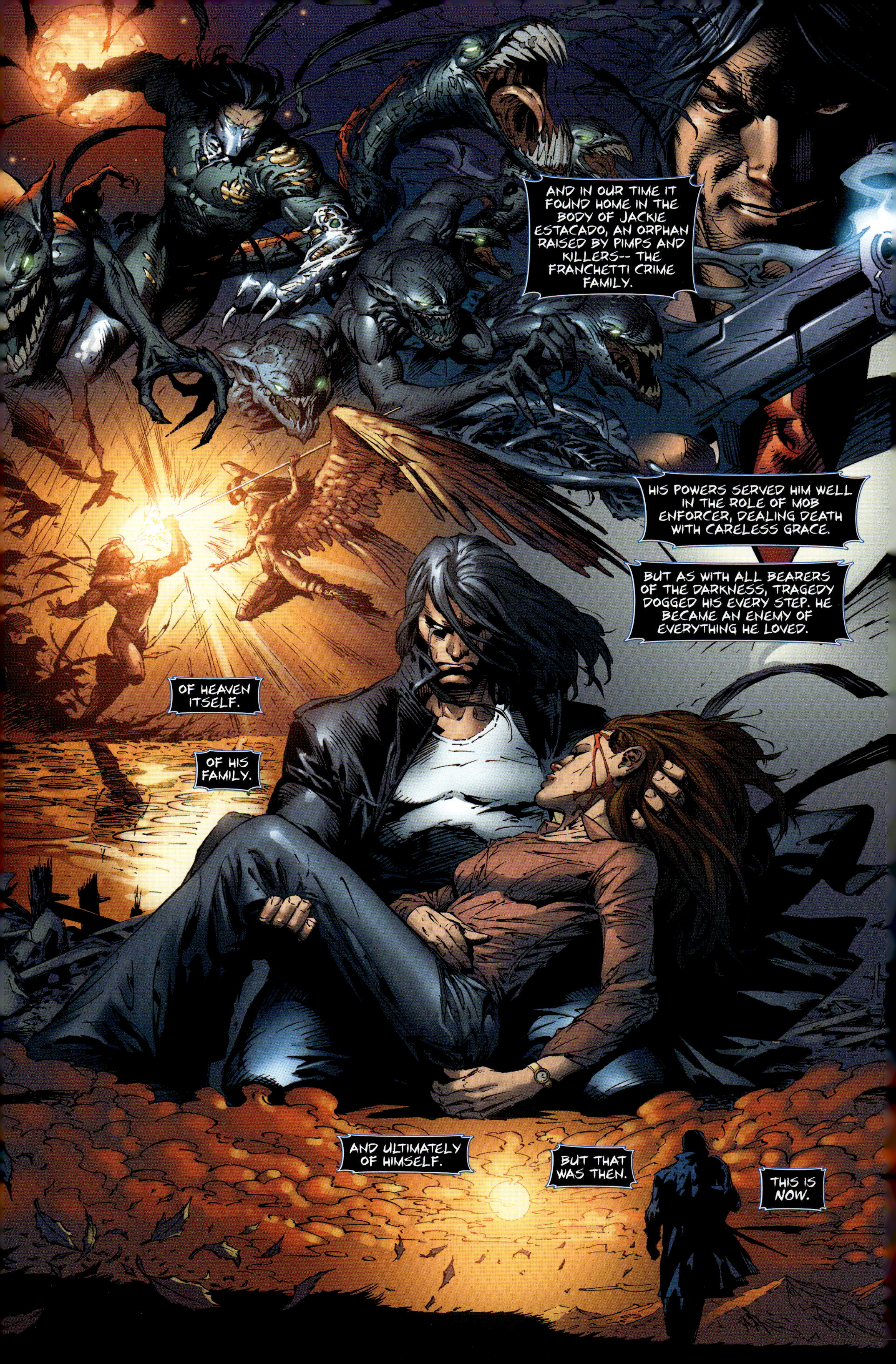
AND IN OUR TIME IT FOUND HOME IN THE BODY OF JACKIE ESTACADO, AN ORPHAN RAISED BY PIMPS AND KILLERS-- THE FRANCHETTI CRIME FAMILY.
HIS POWERS SERVED HIM WELL IN THE ROLE OF MOB ENFORCER, DEALING DEATH WITH CARELESS GRACE.
BUT AS WITH ALL BEARERS OF THE DARKNESS, TRAGEDY DOGGED HIS EVERY STEP. HE BECAME AN ENEMY OF EVERYTHING HE LOVED.
OF HEAVEN ITSELF.
OF HIS FAMILY.
AND ULTIMATELY OF HIMSELF.
BUT THAT WAS THEN.
THIS IS NOW.

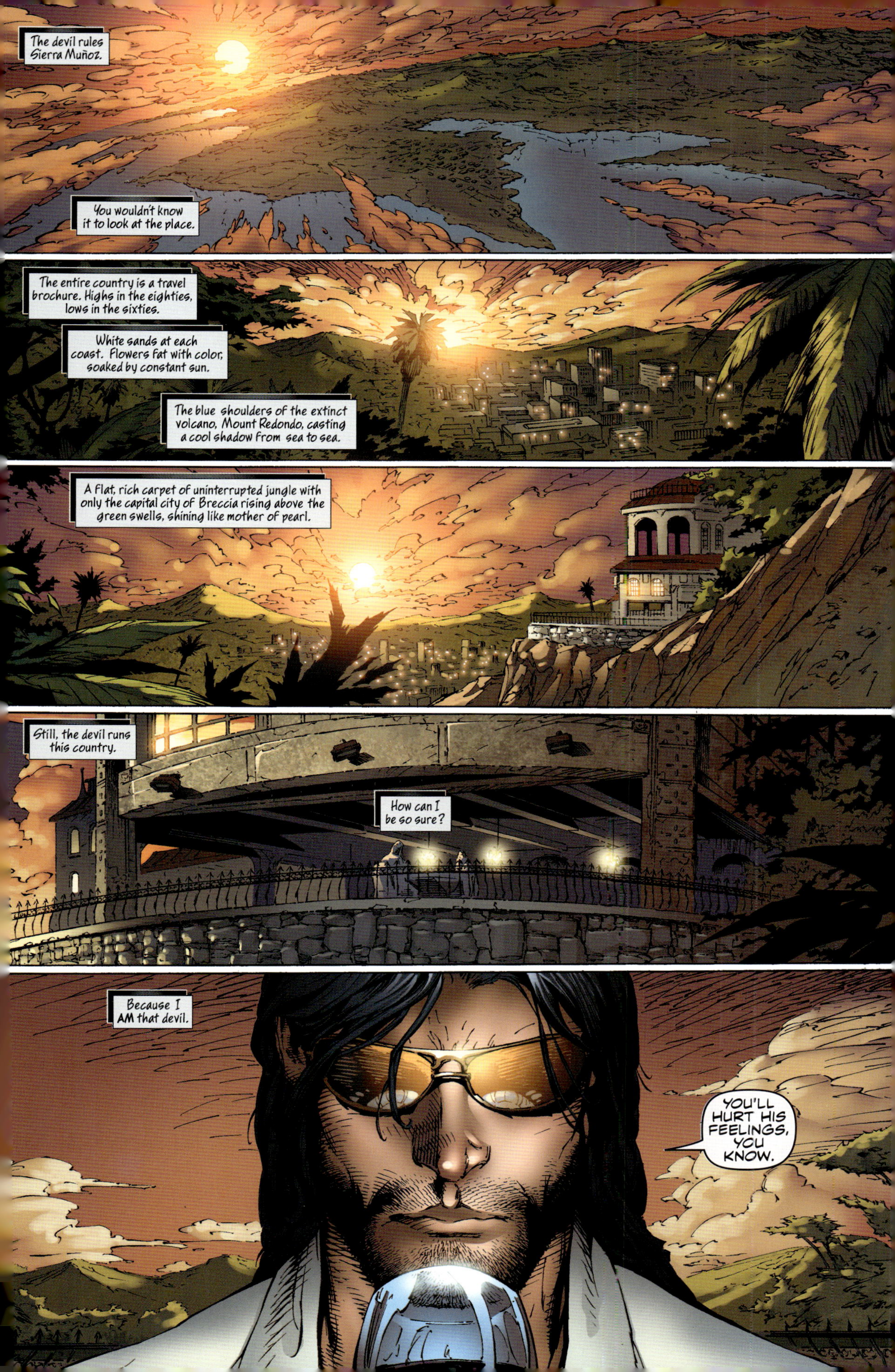
The devil rules Sierra Muñoz.
You wouldn't know it to look at the place.
The entire country is a travel brochure. Highs in the eighties, lows in the sixties.
White sands at each coast. Flowers fat with color, soaked by constant sun.
The blue shoulders of the extinct volcano, Mount Redondo, casting a cool shadow from sea to sea.
A flat, rich carpet of uninterrupted jungle with only the capital city of Breccia rising above the green swells, shining like mother of pearl.
Still, the devil runs this country.
How can I be so sure?
Because I AM that devil.
YOU'LL HURT HIS FEELINGS, YOU KNOW.

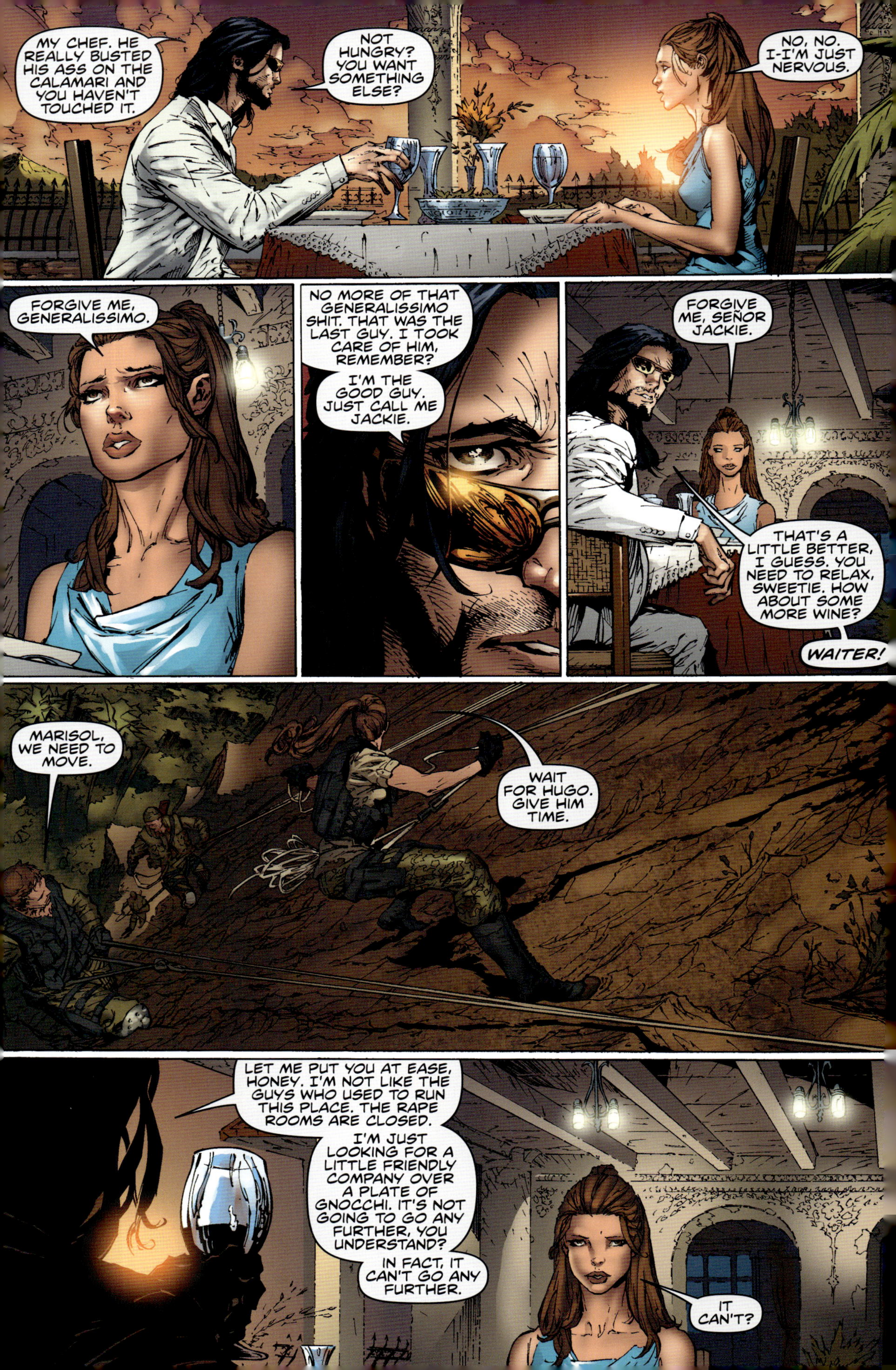
MY CHEF. HE REALLY BUSTED HIS ASS ON THE CALAMARI AND YOU HAVEN'T TOUCHED IT.
NOT HUNGRY? YOU WANT SOMETHING ELSE?
NO, NO. I-I'M JUST NERVOUS.
FORGIVE ME, GENERALISSIMO.
NO MORE OF THAT GENERALISSIMO SHIT. THAT WAS THE LAST GUY. I TOOK CARE OF HIM, REMEMBER?
I'M THE GOOD GUY. JUST CALL ME JACKIE.
FORGIVE ME, SEÑOR JACKIE.
THAT'S A LITTLE BETTER, I GUESS. YOU NEED TO RELAX, SWEETIE. HOW ABOUT SOME MORE WINE?
WAITER!
MARISOL, WE NEED TO MOVE.
WAIT FOR HUGO. GIVE HIM TIME.
LET ME PUT YOU AT EASE, HONEY. I'M NOT LIKE THE GUYS WHO USED TO RUN THIS PLACE. THE RAPE ROOMS ARE CLOSED.
I'M JUST LOOKING FOR A LITTLE FRIENDLY COMPANY OVER A PLATE OF GNOCCHI. IT'S NOT GOING TO GO ANY FURTHER, YOU UNDERSTAND?
IN FACT, IT CAN'T GO ANY FURTHER.
IT CAN'T?

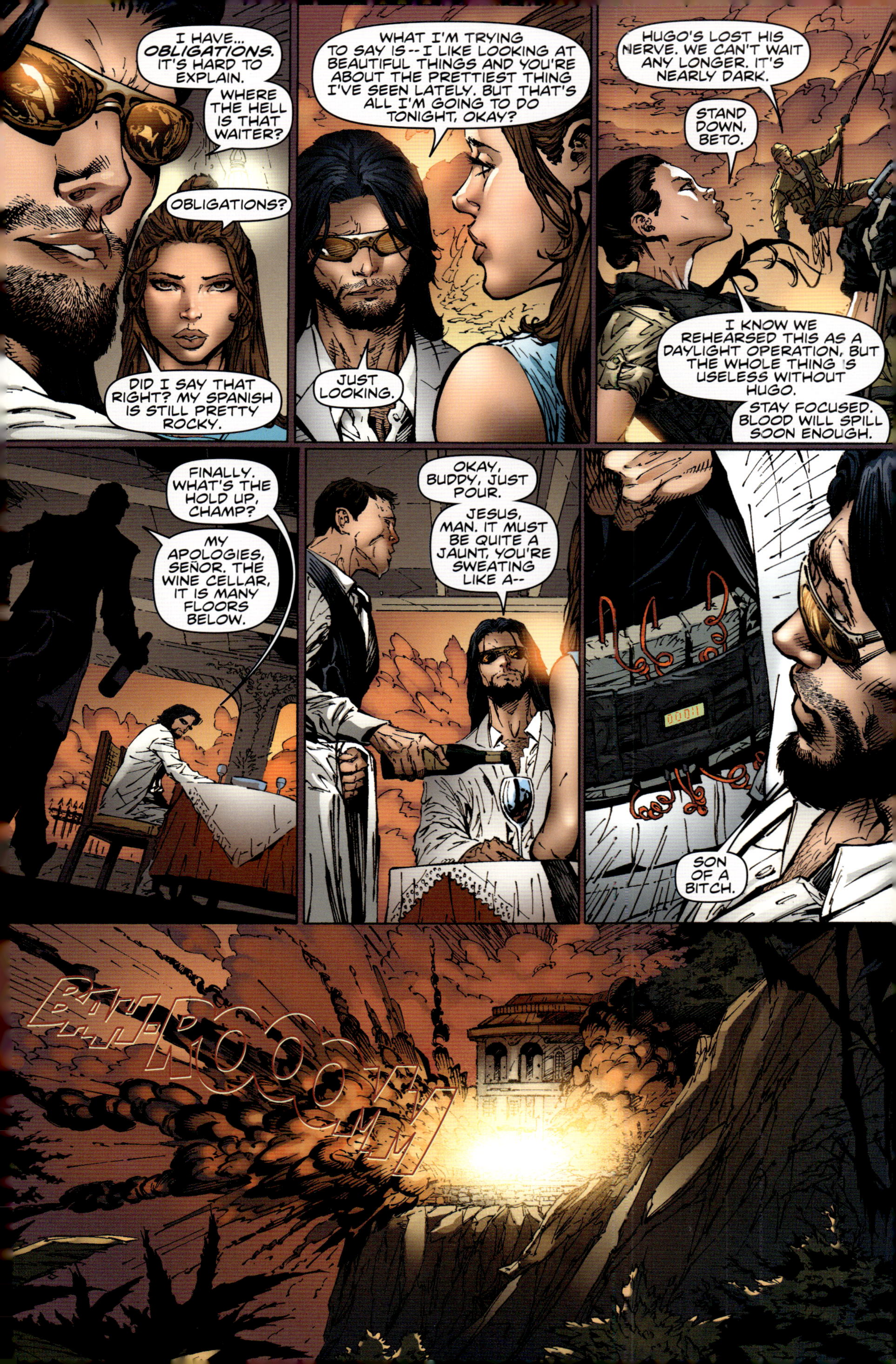
I HAVE... *OBLIGATIONS*. IT'S HARD TO EXPLAIN.
WHERE THE HELL IS THAT WAITER?
OBLIGATIONS?
DID I SAY THAT RIGHT? MY SPANISH IS STILL PRETTY ROCKY.
WHAT I'M TRYING TO SAY IS-- I LIKE LOOKING AT BEAUTIFUL THINGS AND YOU'RE ABOUT THE PRETTIEST THING I'VE SEEN LATELY. BUT THAT'S ALL I'M GOING TO DO TONIGHT, OKAY?
JUST LOOKING.
HUGO'S LOST HIS NERVE. WE CAN'T WAIT ANY LONGER. IT'S NEARLY DARK.
STAND DOWN, BETO.
I KNOW WE REHEARSED THIS AS A DAYLIGHT OPERATION, BUT THE WHOLE THING IS USELESS WITHOUT HUGO.
STAY FOCUSED. BLOOD WILL SPILL SOON ENOUGH.
FINALLY. WHAT'S THE HOLD UP, CHAMP?
MY APOLOGIES, SEÑOR. THE WINE CELLAR, IT IS MANY FLOORS BELOW.
OKAY, BUDDY, JUST POUR.
JESUS, MAN. IT MUST BE QUITE A JAUNT, YOU'RE SWEATING LIKE A--
SON OF A BITCH.
BHHROOOOM

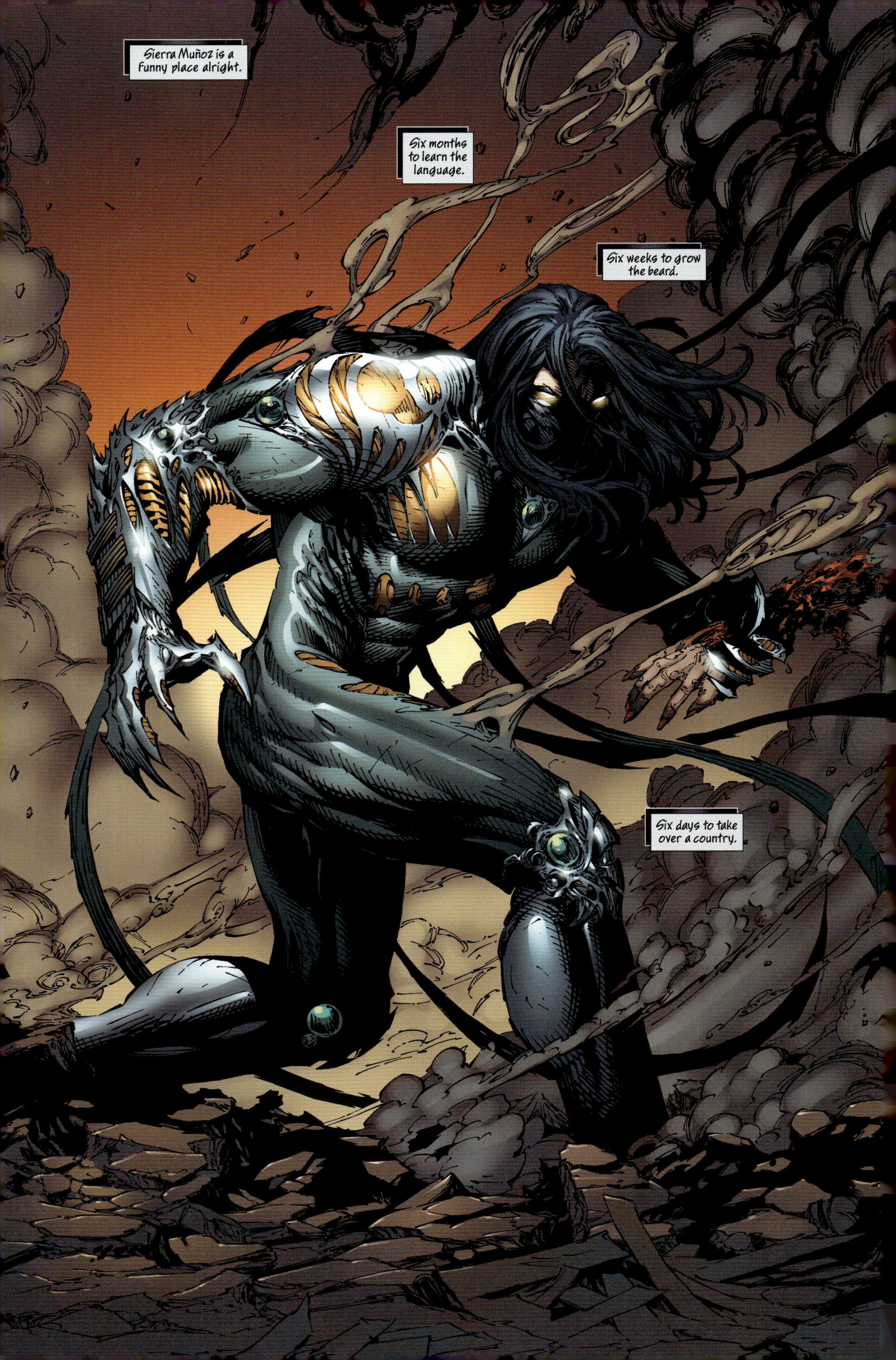
Sierra Muñoz is a funny place alright.
Six months to learn the language.
Six weeks to grow the beard.
Six days to take over a country.

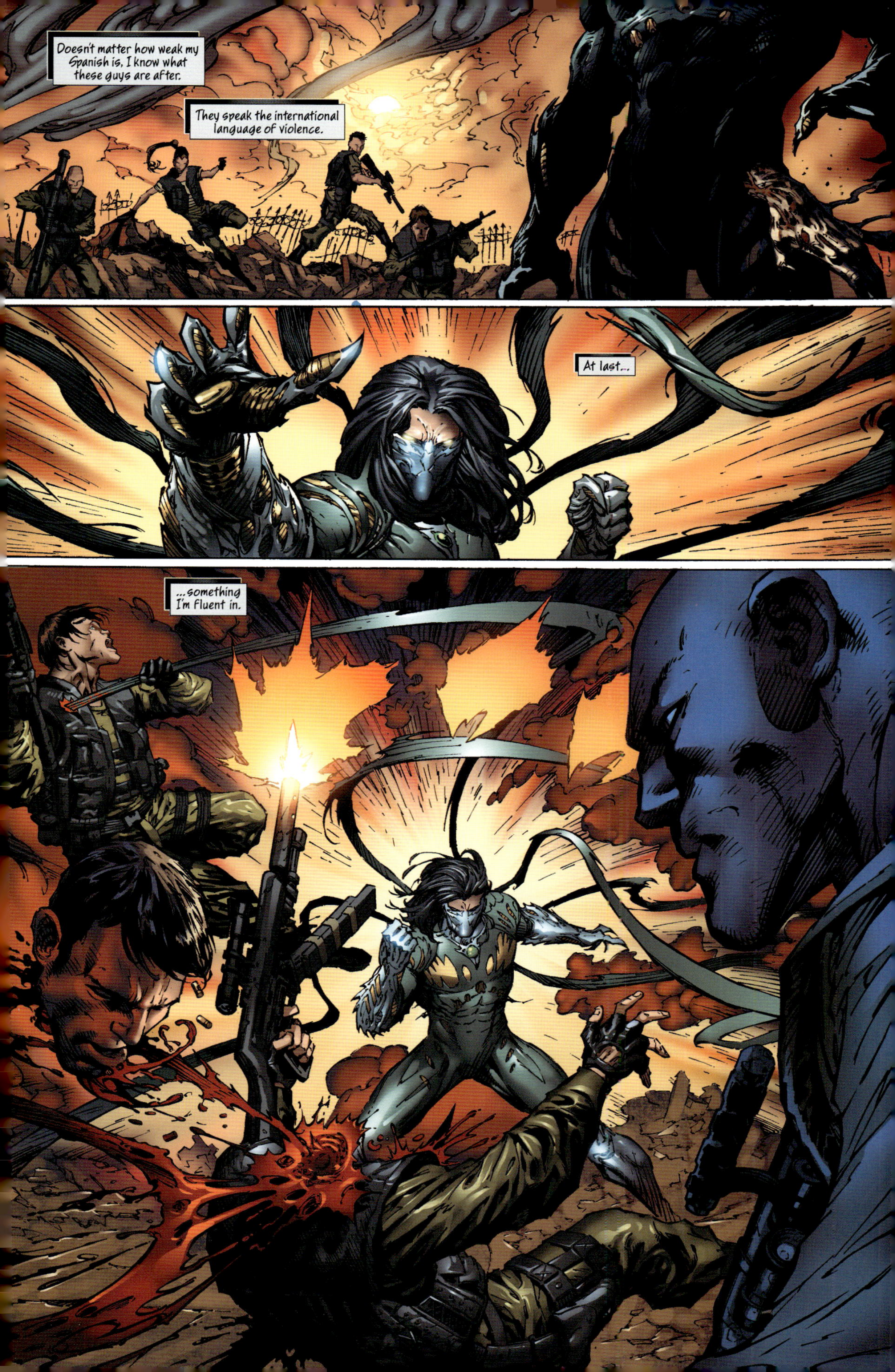
Doesn't matter how weak my Spanish is, I know what these guys are after.
They speak the international language of violence.
At last...
...something I'm fluent in.

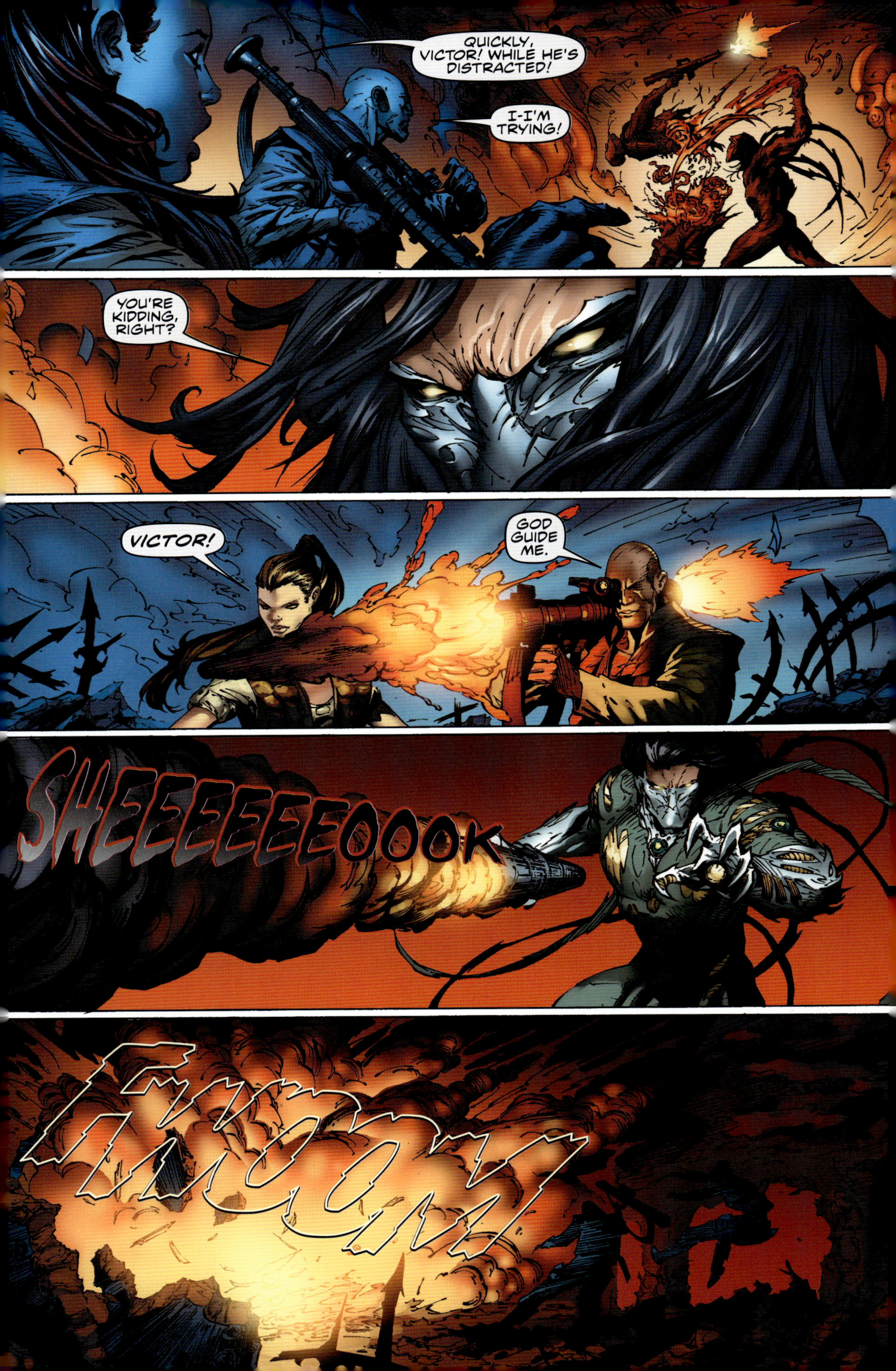
QUICKLY, VICTOR! WHILE HE'S DISTRACTED!
I-I'M TRYING!
YOU'RE KIDDING, RIGHT?
VICTOR!
GOD GUIDE ME.
SHEEEEEEOOOK

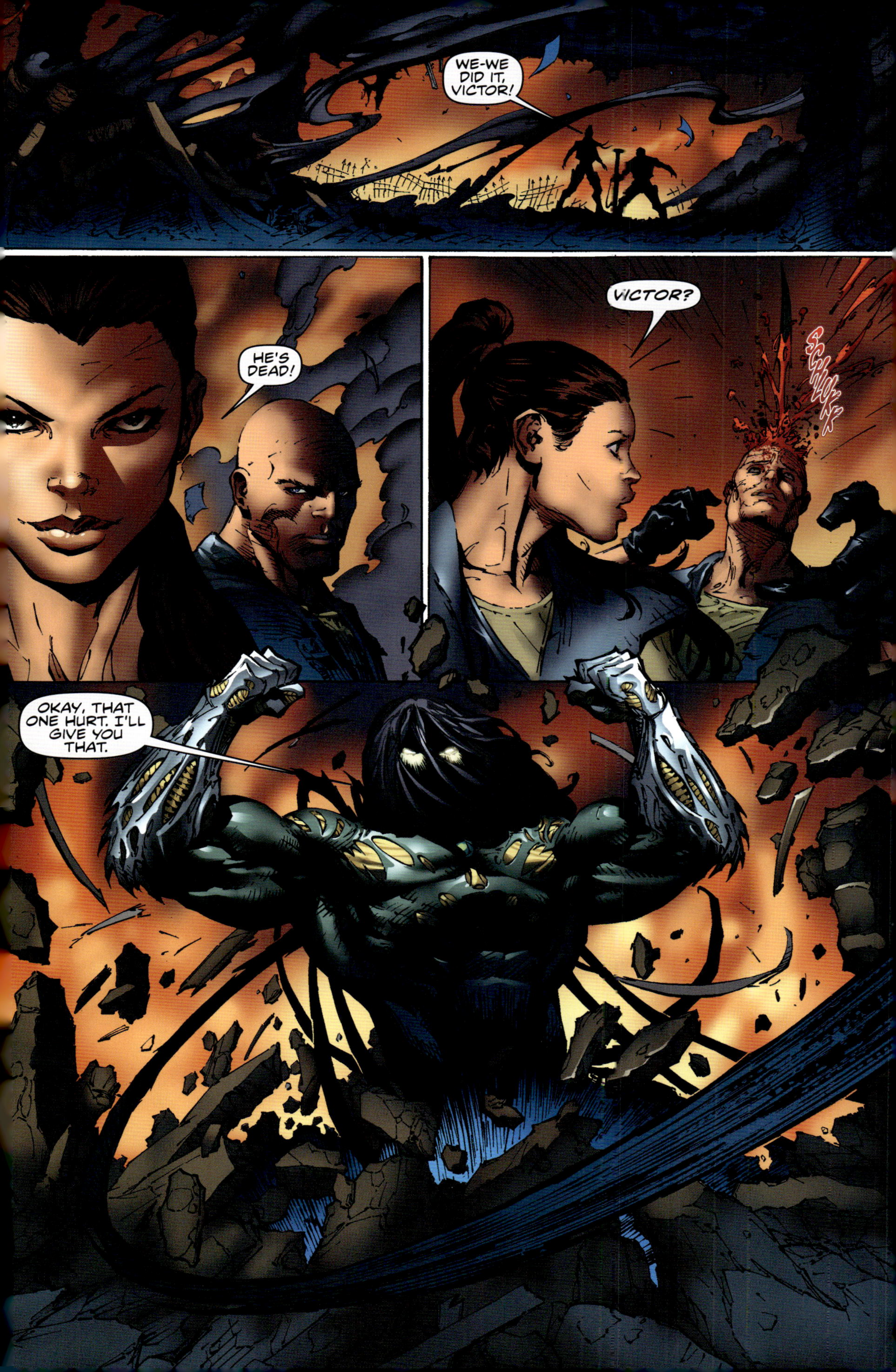
WE-WE DID IT, VICTOR!
HE'S DEAD!
VICTOR?
SCHLUKK
OKAY, THAT ONE HURT. I'LL GIVE YOU THAT.

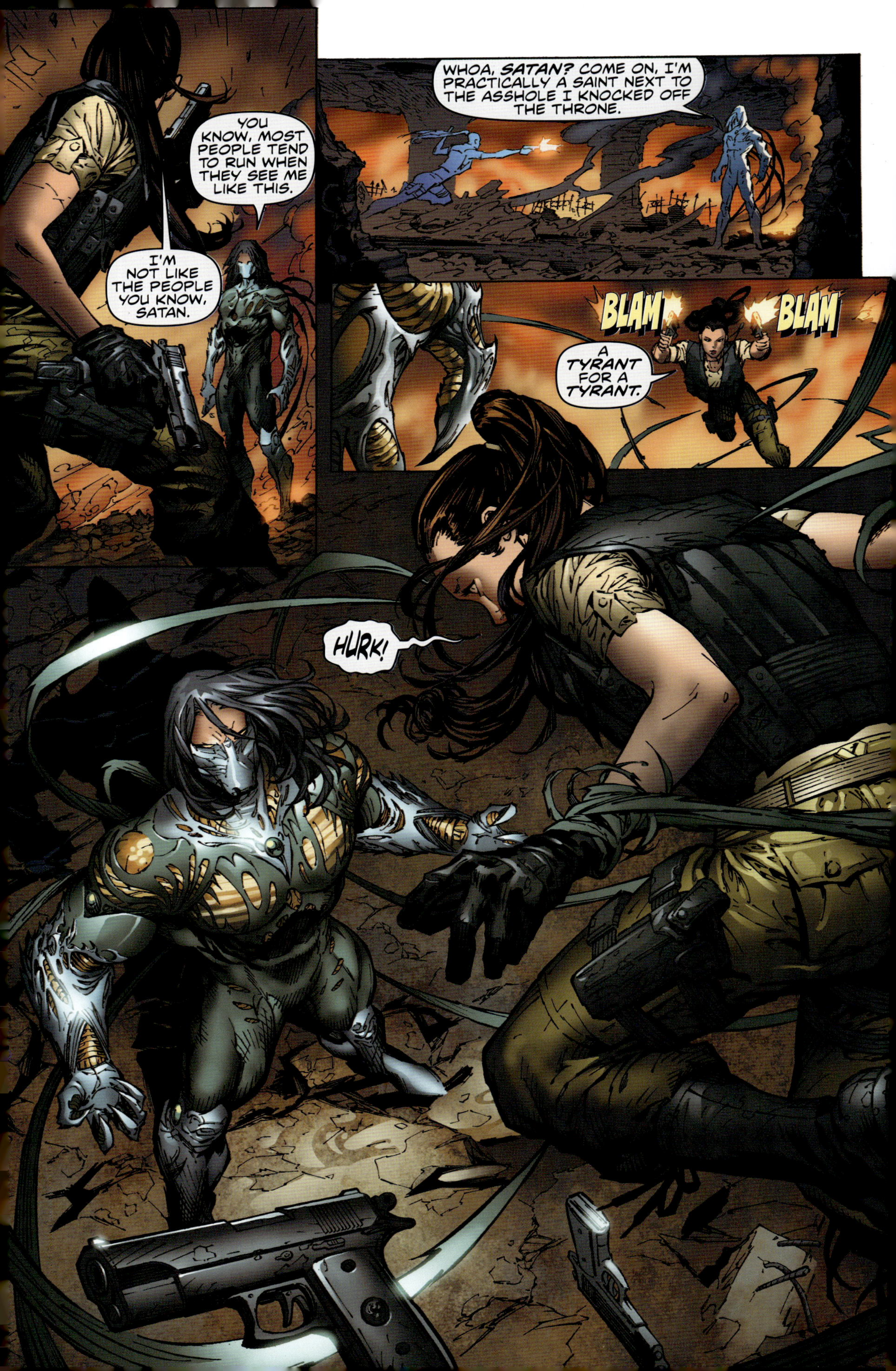
YOU KNOW, MOST PEOPLE TEND TO RUN WHEN THEY SEE ME LIKE THIS.
I'M NOT LIKE THE PEOPLE YOU KNOW, SATAN.
WHOA, SATAN? COME ON, I'M PRACTICALLY A SAINT NEXT TO THE ASSHOLE I KNOCKED OFF THE THRONE.
BLAM
BLAM
A TYRANT FOR A TYRANT.
HURK!

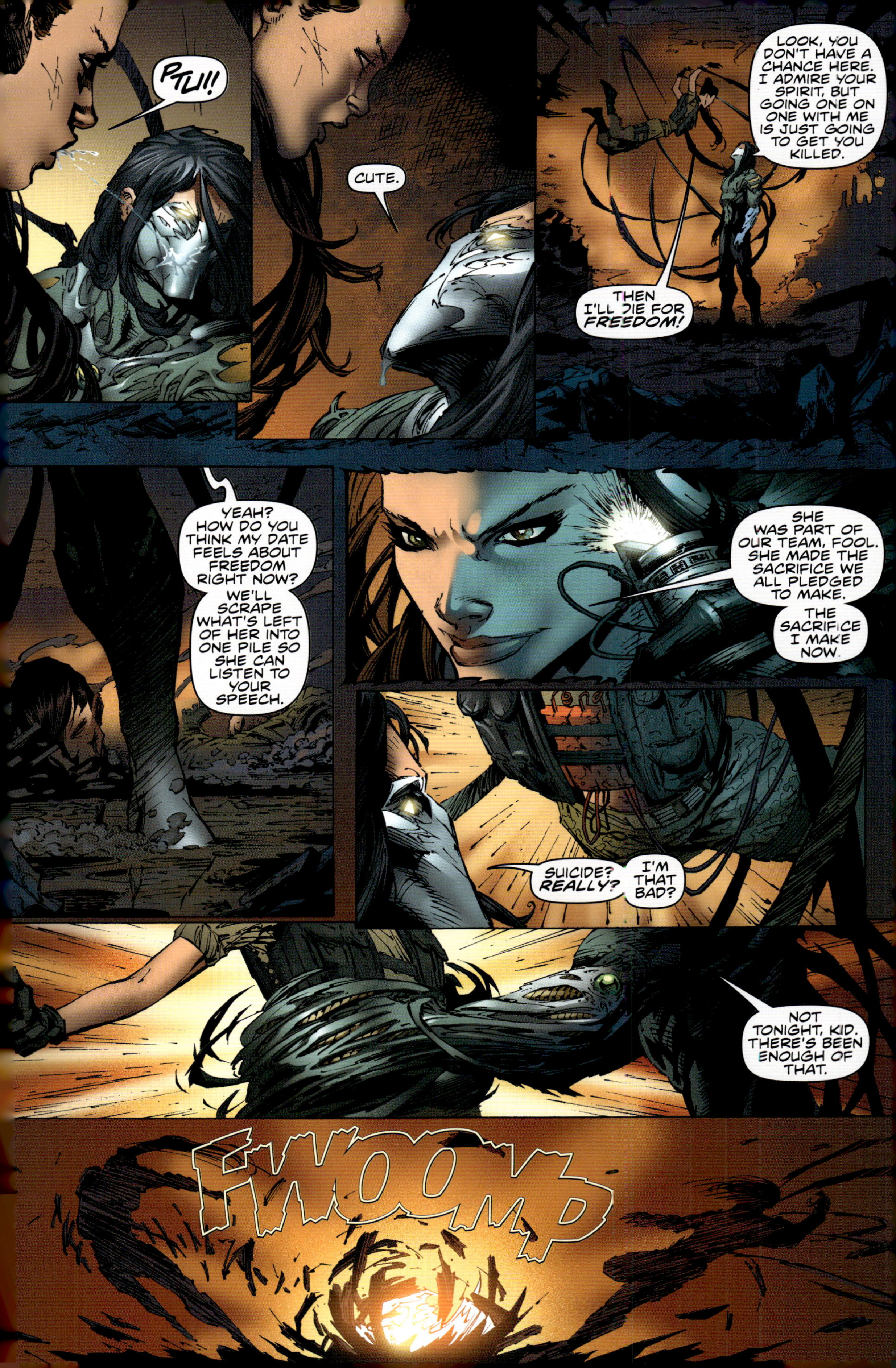
PTUI!!
CUTE.
LOOK, YOU DON'T HAVE A CHANCE HERE. I ADMIRE YOUR SPIRIT, BUT GOING ONE ON ONE WITH ME IS JUST GOING TO GET YOU KILLED.
THEN I'LL DIE FOR FREEDOM!
YEAH? HOW DO YOU THINK MY DATE FEELS ABOUT FREEDOM RIGHT NOW?
WE'LL SCRAPE WHAT'S LEFT OF HER INTO ONE PILE SO SHE CAN LISTEN TO YOUR SPEECH.
SHE WAS PART OF OUR TEAM, FOOL. SHE MADE THE SACRIFICE WE ALL PLEDGED TO MAKE.
THE SACRIFICE I MAKE NOW.
SUICIDE? REALLY?
I'M THAT BAD?
NOT TONIGHT, KID. THERE'S BEEN ENOUGH OF THAT.
FWOOMP

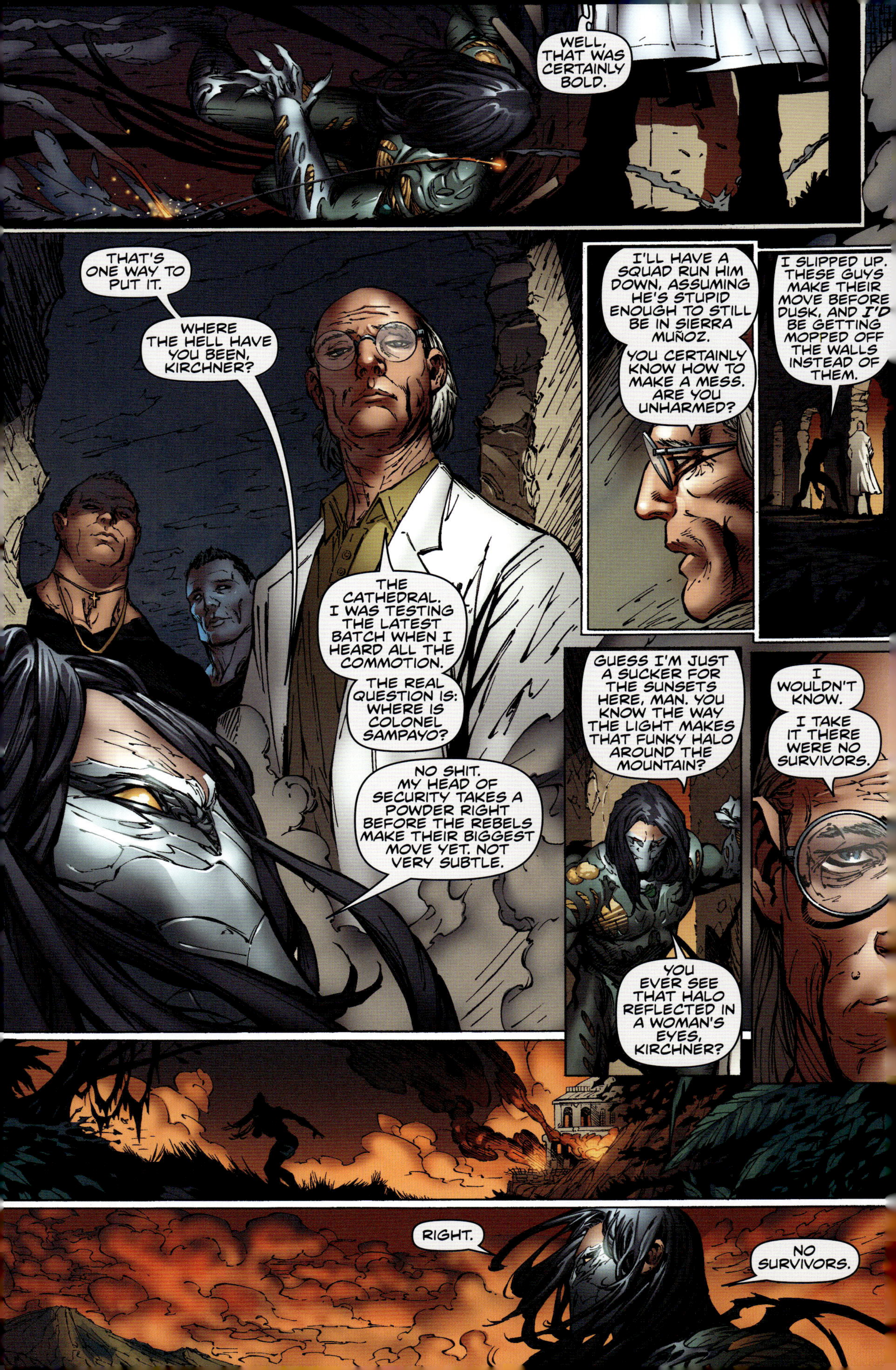
WELL, THAT WAS CERTAINLY BOLD.
THAT'S ONE WAY TO PUT IT.
WHERE THE HELL HAVE YOU BEEN, KIRCHNER?
THE CATHEDRAL. I WAS TESTING THE LATEST BATCH WHEN I HEARD ALL THE COMMOTION.
THE REAL QUESTION IS: WHERE IS COLONEL SAMPAYO?
NO SHIT. MY HEAD OF SECURITY TAKES A POWDER RIGHT BEFORE THE REBELS MAKE THEIR BIGGEST MOVE YET. NOT VERY SUBTLE.
I'LL HAVE A SQUAD RUN HIM DOWN, ASSUMING HE'S STUPID ENOUGH TO STILL BE IN SIERRA MUÑOZ.
YOU CERTAINLY KNOW HOW TO MAKE A MESS. ARE YOU UNHARMED?
I SLIPPED UP. THESE GUYS MAKE THEIR MOVE BEFORE DUSK, AND *I'D* BE GETTING MOPPED OFF THE WALLS INSTEAD OF THEM.
GUESS I'M JUST A SUCKER FOR THE SUNSETS HERE, MAN. YOU KNOW THE WAY THE LIGHT MAKES THAT FUNKY HALO AROUND THE MOUNTAIN?
YOU EVER SEE THAT HALO REFLECTED IN A WOMAN'S EYES, KIRCHNER?
I WOULDN'T KNOW.
I TAKE IT THERE WERE NO SURVIVORS.
RIGHT.
NO SURVIVORS.

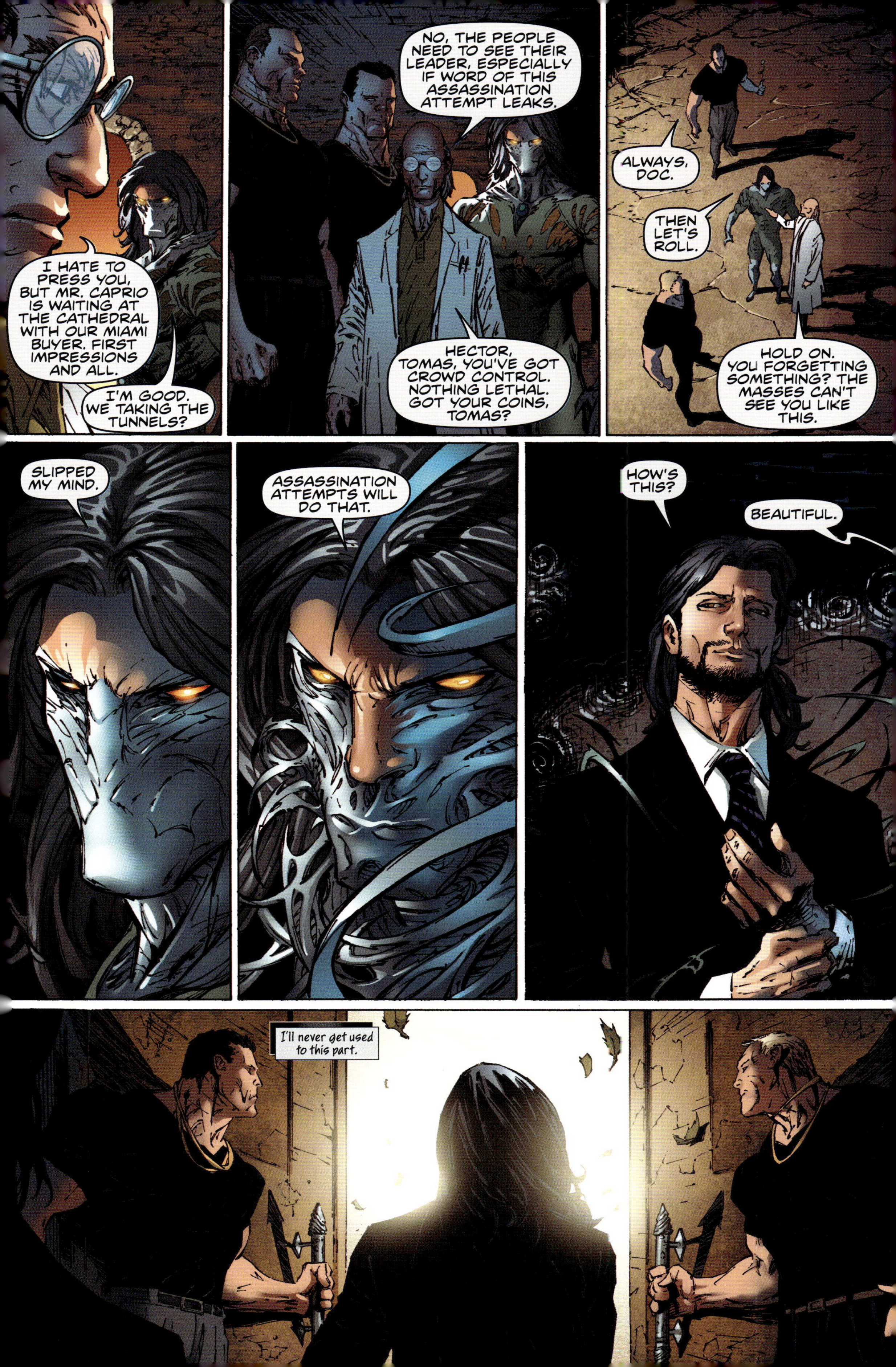
I HATE TO PRESS YOU, BUT MR. CAPRIO IS WAITING AT THE CATHEDRAL WITH OUR MIAMI BUYER. FIRST IMPRESSIONS AND ALL.
I'M GOOD. WE TAKING THE TUNNELS?
NO, THE PEOPLE NEED TO SEE THEIR LEADER, ESPECIALLY IF WORD OF THIS ASSASSINATION ATTEMPT LEAKS.
HECTOR, TOMAS, YOU'VE GOT CROWD CONTROL. NOTHING LETHAL. GOT YOUR COINS, TOMAS?
ALWAYS, DOC.
THEN LET'S ROLL.
HOLD ON. YOU FORGETTING SOMETHING? THE MASSES CAN'T SEE YOU LIKE THIS.
SLIPPED MY MIND.
ASSASSINATION ATTEMPTS WILL DO THAT.
HOW'S THIS?
BEAUTIFUL.
I'll never get used to this part.

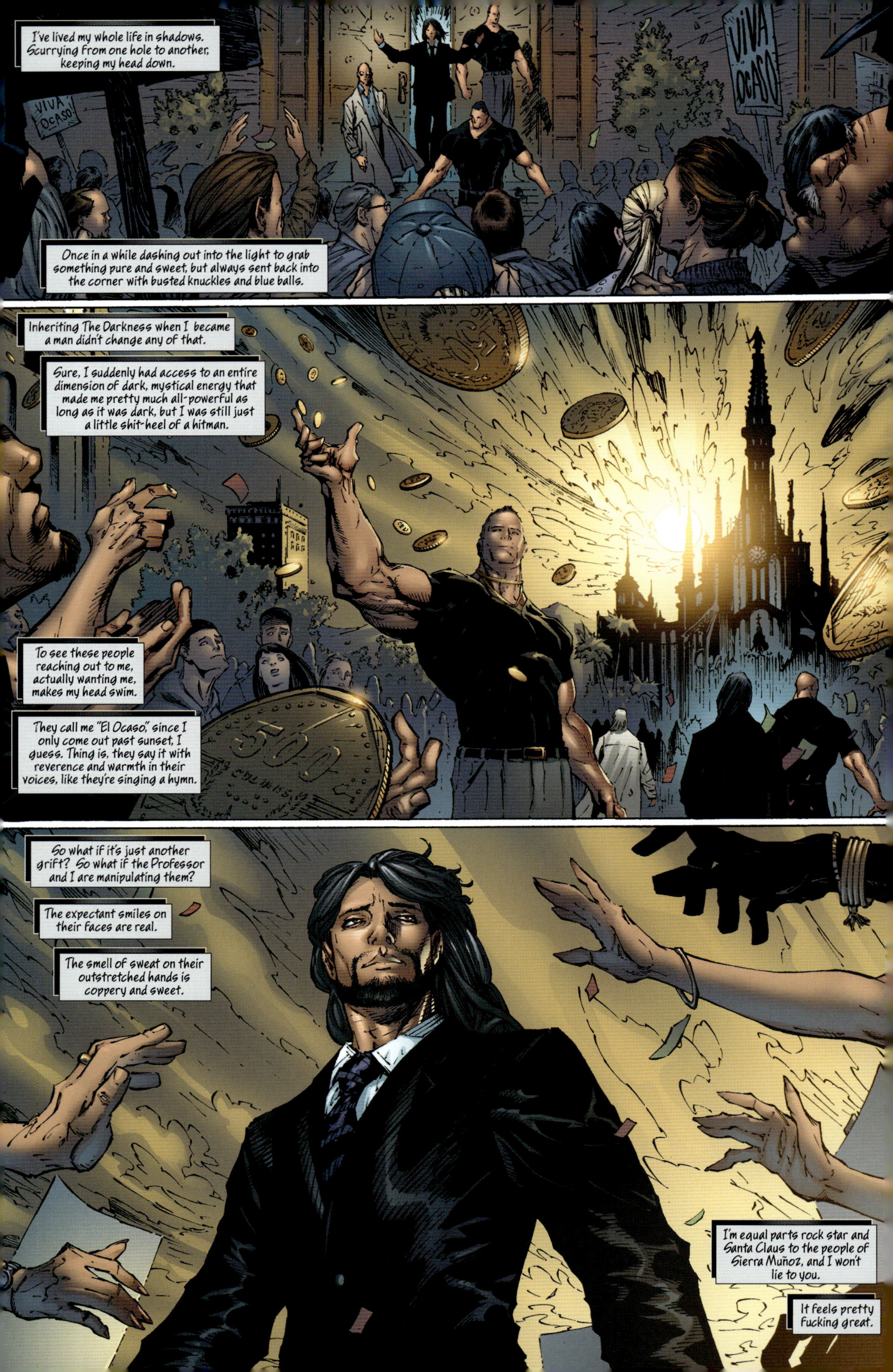
I've lived my whole life in shadows. Scurrying from one hole to another, keeping my head down.
VIVA OCASO
VIVA OCASO!
Once in a while dashing out into the light to grab something pure and sweet, but always sent back into the corner with busted knuckles and blue balls.
Inheriting The Darkness when I became a man didn't change any of that.
Sure, I suddenly had access to an entire dimension of dark, mystical energy that made me pretty much all-powerful as long as it was dark, but I was still just a little shit-heel of a hitman.
To see these people reaching out to me, actually wanting me, makes my head swim.
They call me "El Ocaso," since I only come out past sunset, I guess. Thing is, they say it with reverence and warmth in their voices, like they're singing a hymn.
So what if it's just another grift? So what if the Professor and I are manipulating them?
The expectant smiles on their faces are real.
The smell of sweat on their outstretched hands is coppery and sweet.
I'm equal parts rock star and Santa Claus to the people of Sierra Muñoz, and I won't lie to you.
It feels pretty fucking great.

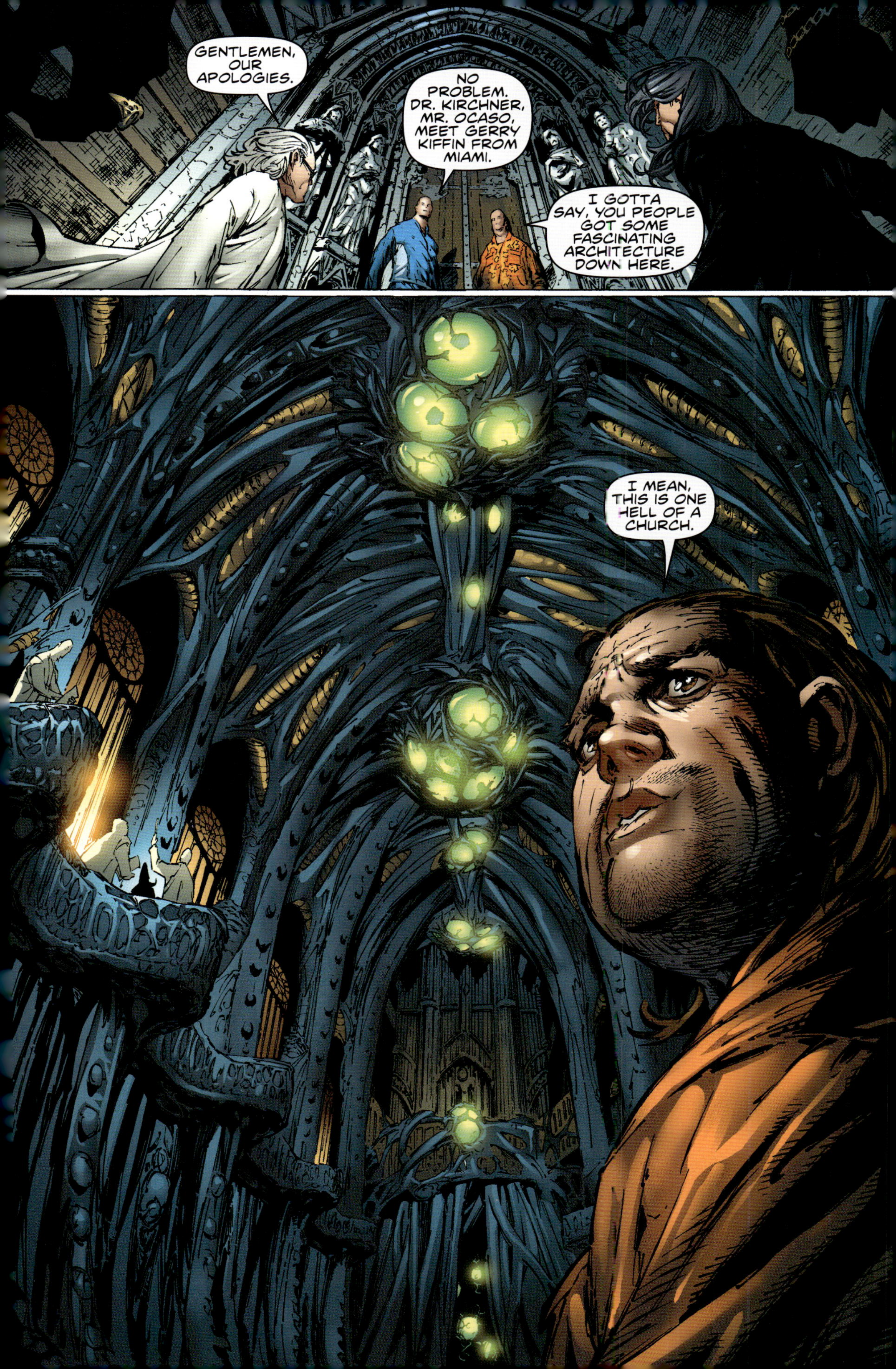
GENTLEMEN, OUR APOLOGIES.
NO PROBLEM. DR. KIRCHNER, MR. OCASO, MEET GERRY KIFFIN FROM MIAMI.
I GOTTA SAY, YOU PEOPLE GOT SOME FASCINATING ARCHITECTURE DOWN HERE.
I MEAN, THIS IS ONE HELL OF A CHURCH.

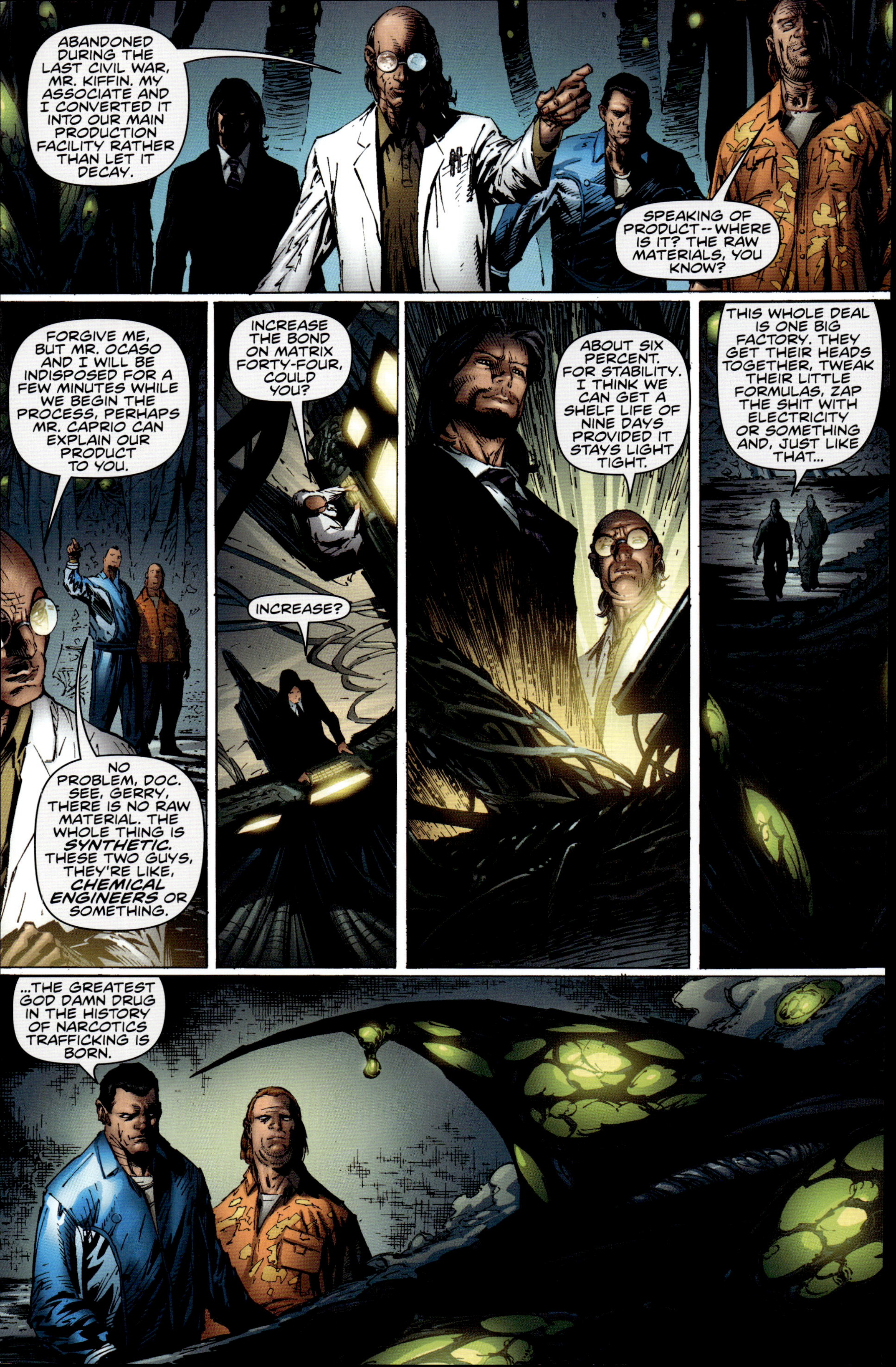
ABANDONED DURING THE LAST CIVIL WAR, MR. KIFFIN. MY ASSOCIATE AND I CONVERTED IT INTO OUR MAIN PRODUCTION FACILITY RATHER THAN LET IT DECAY.
SPEAKING OF PRODUCT--WHERE IS IT? THE RAW MATERIALS, YOU KNOW?
FORGIVE ME, BUT MR. OCASO AND I WILL BE INDISPOSED FOR A FEW MINUTES WHILE WE BEGIN THE PROCESS. PERHAPS MR. CAPRIO CAN EXPLAIN OUR PRODUCT TO YOU.
NO PROBLEM, DOC. SEE, GERRY, THERE IS NO RAW MATERIAL. THE WHOLE THING IS SYNTHETIC. THESE TWO GUYS, THEY'RE LIKE, CHEMICAL ENGINEERS OR SOMETHING.
INCREASE THE BOND ON MATRIX FORTY-FOUR, COULD YOU?
INCREASE?
ABOUT SIX PERCENT. FOR STABILITY. I THINK WE CAN GET A SHELF LIFE OF NINE DAYS PROVIDED IT STAYS LIGHT TIGHT.
THIS WHOLE DEAL IS ONE BIG FACTORY. THEY GET THEIR HEADS TOGETHER, TWEAK THEIR LITTLE FORMULAS, ZAP THE SHIT WITH ELECTRICITY OR SOMETHING AND, JUST LIKE THAT...
...THE GREATEST GOD DAMN DRUG IN THE HISTORY OF NARCOTICS TRAFFICKING IS BORN.

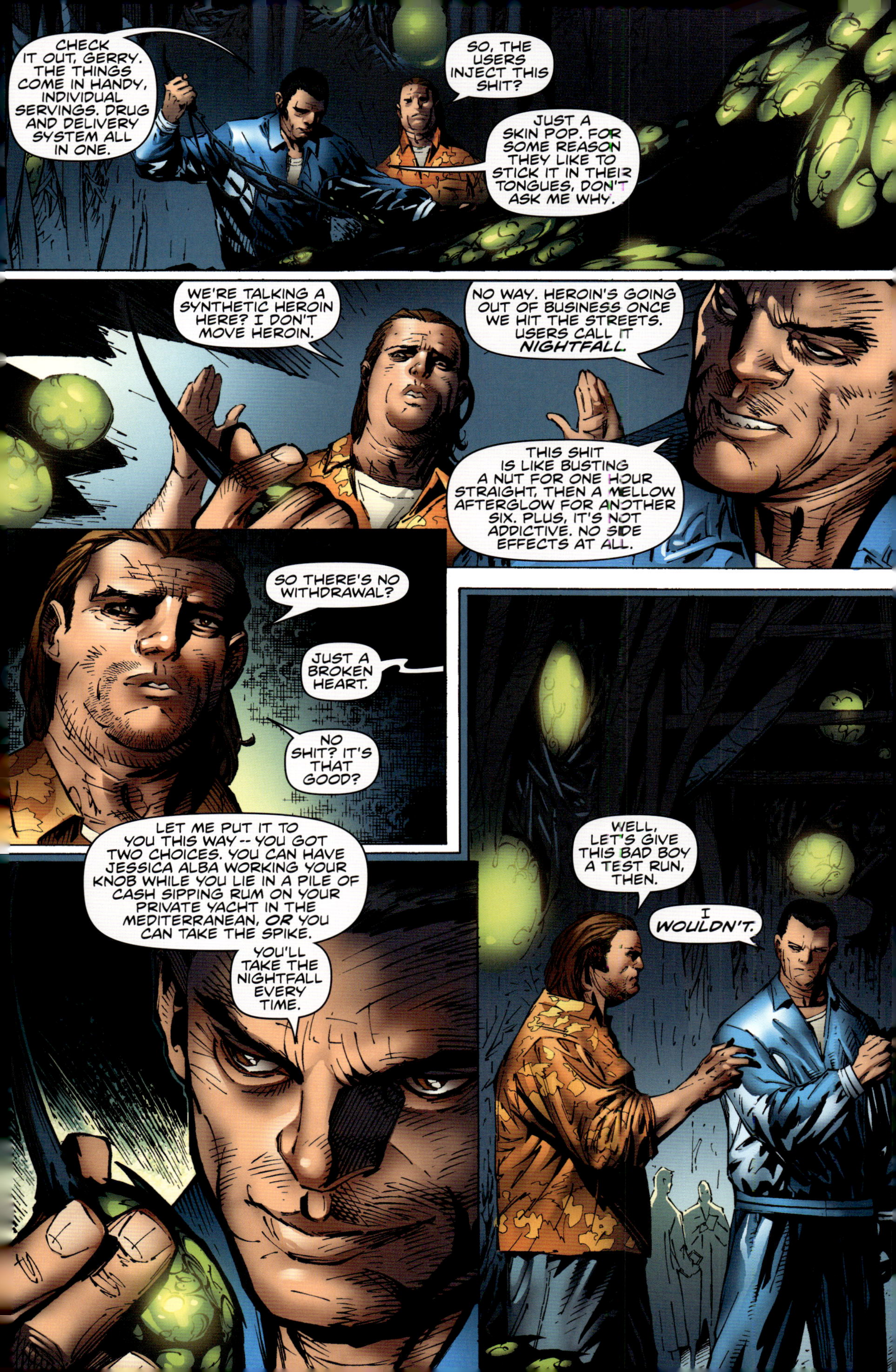
CHECK IT OUT, GERRY. THE THINGS COME IN HANDY, INDIVIDUAL SERVINGS. DRUG AND DELIVERY SYSTEM ALL IN ONE.
SO, THE USERS INJECT THIS SHIT?
JUST A SKIN POP. FOR SOME REASON THEY LIKE TO STICK IT IN THEIR TONGUES, DON'T ASK ME WHY.
WE'RE TALKING A SYNTHETIC HEROIN HERE? I DON'T MOVE HEROIN.
NO WAY. HEROIN'S GOING OUT OF BUSINESS ONCE WE HIT THE STREETS. USERS CALL IT NIGHTFALL.
THIS SHIT IS LIKE BUSTING A NUT FOR ONE HOUR STRAIGHT, THEN A MELLOW AFTERGLOW FOR ANOTHER SIX. PLUS, IT'S NOT ADDICTIVE. NO SIDE EFFECTS AT ALL.
SO THERE'S NO WITHDRAWAL?
JUST A BROKEN HEART.
NO SHIT? IT'S THAT GOOD?
LET ME PUT IT TO YOU THIS WAY -- YOU GOT TWO CHOICES. YOU CAN HAVE JESSICA ALBA WORKING YOUR KNOB WHILE YOU LIE IN A PILE OF CASH SIPPING RUM ON YOUR PRIVATE YACHT IN THE MEDITERRANEAN, OR YOU CAN TAKE THE SPIKE.
YOU'LL TAKE THE NIGHTFALL EVERY TIME.
WELL, LET'S GIVE THIS BAD BOY A TEST RUN, THEN.
I WOULDN'T.

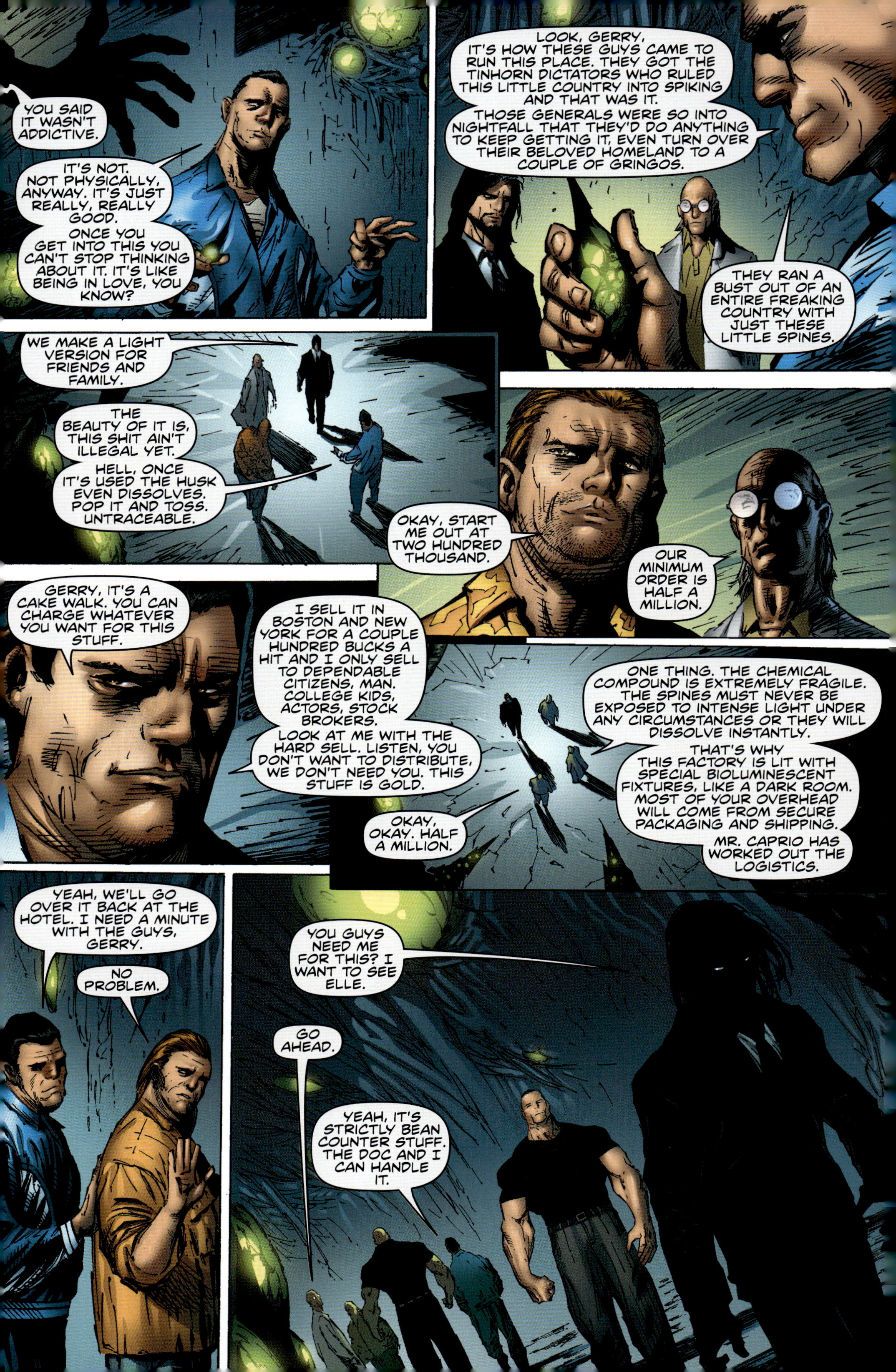
YOU SAID IT WASN'T ADDICTIVE.
IT'S NOT. NOT PHYSICALLY, ANYWAY. IT'S JUST REALLY, REALLY GOOD.
ONCE YOU GET INTO THIS YOU CAN'T STOP THINKING ABOUT IT. IT'S LIKE BEING IN LOVE, YOU KNOW?
LOOK, GERRY, IT'S HOW THESE GUYS CAME TO RUN THIS PLACE. THEY GOT THE TINHORN DICTATORS WHO RULED THIS LITTLE COUNTRY INTO SPIKING AND THAT WAS IT.
THOSE GENERALS WERE SO INTO NIGHTFALL THAT THEY'D DO ANYTHING TO KEEP GETTING IT, EVEN TURN OVER THEIR BELOVED HOMELAND TO A COUPLE OF GRINGOS.
THEY RAN A BUST OUT OF AN ENTIRE FREAKING COUNTRY WITH JUST THESE LITTLE SPINES.
WE MAKE A LIGHT VERSION FOR FRIENDS AND FAMILY.
THE BEAUTY OF IT IS, THIS SHIT AIN'T ILLEGAL YET.
HELL, ONCE IT'S USED THE HUSK EVEN DISSOLVES. POP IT AND TOSS. UNTRACEABLE.
OKAY, START ME OUT AT TWO HUNDRED THOUSAND.
OUR MINIMUM ORDER IS HALF A MILLION.
GERRY, IT'S A CAKE WALK. YOU CAN CHARGE WHATEVER YOU WANT FOR THIS STUFF.
I SELL IT IN BOSTON AND NEW YORK FOR A COUPLE HUNDRED BUCKS A HIT AND I ONLY SELL TO DEPENDABLE CITIZENS, MAN. COLLEGE KIDS, ACTORS, STOCK BROKERS.
LOOK AT ME WITH THE HARD SELL. LISTEN, YOU DON'T WANT TO DISTRIBUTE, WE DON'T NEED YOU. THIS STUFF IS GOLD.
OKAY, OKAY. HALF A MILLION.
ONE THING. THE CHEMICAL COMPOUND IS EXTREMELY FRAGILE. THE SPINES MUST NEVER BE EXPOSED TO INTENSE LIGHT UNDER ANY CIRCUMSTANCES OR THEY WILL DISSOLVE INSTANTLY.
THAT'S WHY THIS FACTORY IS LIT WITH SPECIAL BIOLUMINESCENT FIXTURES, LIKE A DARK ROOM. MOST OF YOUR OVERHEAD WILL COME FROM SECURE PACKAGING AND SHIPPING.
MR. CAPRIO HAS WORKED OUT THE LOGISTICS.
YEAH, WE'LL GO OVER IT BACK AT THE HOTEL. I NEED A MINUTE WITH THE GUYS, GERRY.
NO PROBLEM.
YOU GUYS NEED ME FOR THIS? I WANT TO SEE ELLE.
GO AHEAD.
YEAH, IT'S STRICTLY BEAN COUNTER STUFF. THE DOC AND I CAN HANDLE IT.

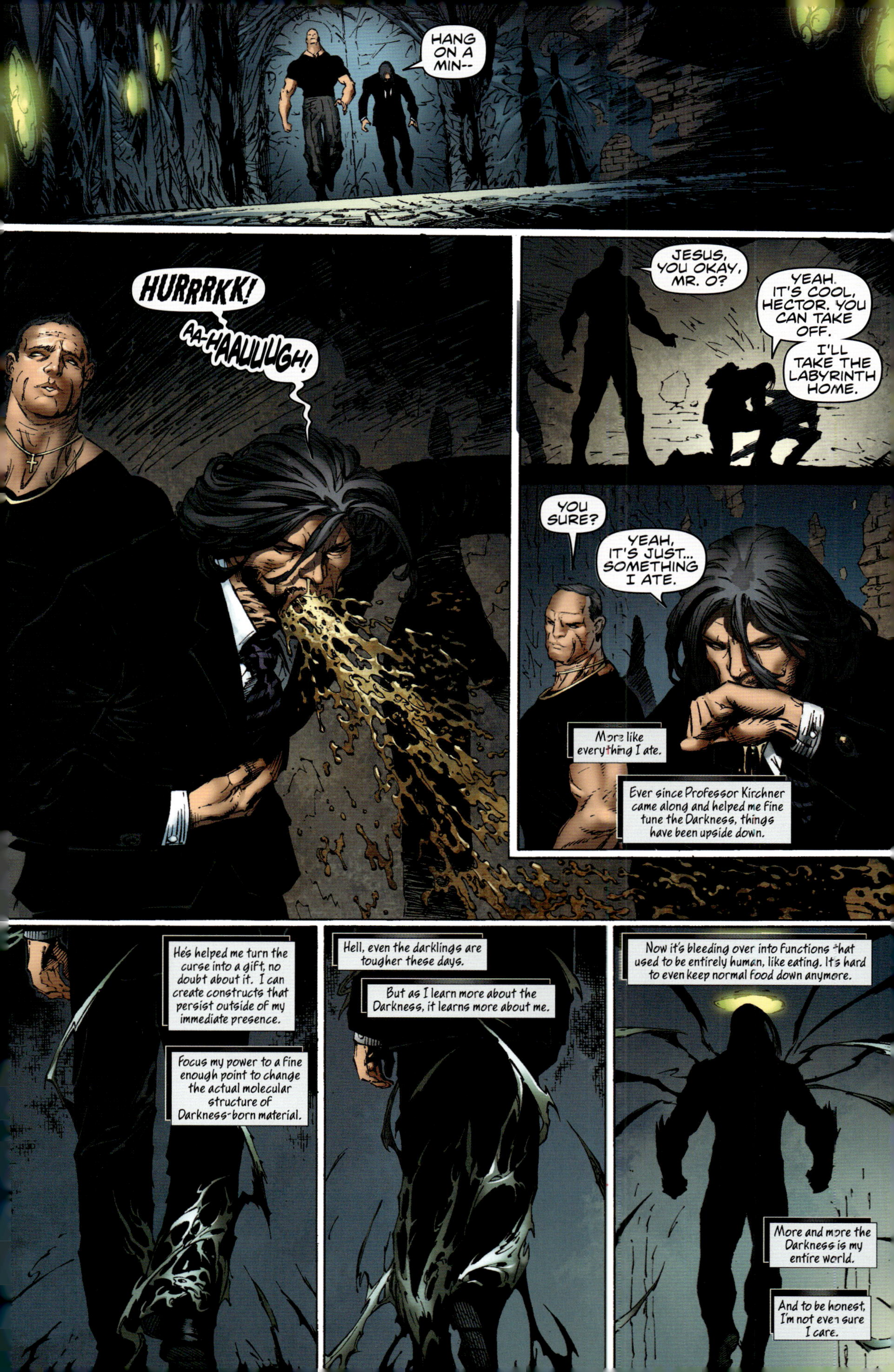
HANG ON A MIN--
HURRRKK!
AA-HAAUUUGH!
JESUS, YOU OKAY, MR. O?
YEAH. IT'S COOL, HECTOR. YOU CAN TAKE OFF.
I'LL TAKE THE LABYRINTH HOME.
YOU SURE?
YEAH, IT'S JUST... SOMETHING I ATE.
More like everything I ate.
Ever since Professor Kirchner came along and helped me fine tune the Darkness, things have been upside down.
He's helped me turn the curse into a gift, no doubt about it. I can create constructs that persist outside of my immediate presence.
Focus my power to a fine enough point to change the actual molecular structure of Darkness-born material.
Hell, even the darklings are tougher these days.
But as I learn more about the Darkness, it learns more about me.
Now it's bleeding over into functions that used to be entirely human, like eating. It's hard to even keep normal food down anymore.
More and more the Darkness is my entire world.
And to be honest, I'm not even sure I care.

CAN I OFFER YOU SOMETHING TO DRINK?

NAH. LET'S GET RIGHT DOWN TO BUSINESS.

I SUPPOSE YOU WANT A DEEPER DISCOUNT FOR OPENING MIAMI UP TO US. IS THAT IT?

NOT ENTIRELY. I'M LOOKING FOR SOMETHING MORE LIKE A BONUS.

A BONUS?

YEAH. FOR STARTERS, I GET ALL THE PRODUCT I CAN MOVE FOR FREE, AND ON TOP OF THAT A ONE TIME FEE OF FIVE MILLION.

WHAT THE HELL ARE YOU TALKING ABOUT?

I'M TALKING ABOUT YOUR PARTNER.

MR. OCASO?

COME ON, DOC.

JACKIE ESTACADO.

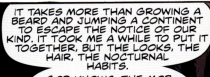

IT TAKES MORE THAN GROWING A BEARD AND JUMPING A CONTINENT TO ESCAPE THE NOTICE OF OUR KIND. IT TOOK ME A WHILE TO PUT IT TOGETHER, BUT THE LOOKS, THE HAIR, THE NOCTURNAL HABITS.

GOD KNOWS, THE MOB ISN'T WHAT IT USED TO BE, BUT THE FRANCHETTI FAMILY STILL HAS FRIENDS THAT WOULD PAY DEARLY TO SEE THAT KID WITH A CHALK OUTLINE AROUND HIM.

NOT TO MENTION MY FRIENDS IN THE DEA. MY HELP COULD PUT A STOP TO A NEWBORN DRUG SCOURGE BEFORE IT SWEEPS THE STATES.

HELL, THIS IS THE KIND OF SHIT PRESIDENTS LOVE TO START WARS OVER, YOU KNOW?

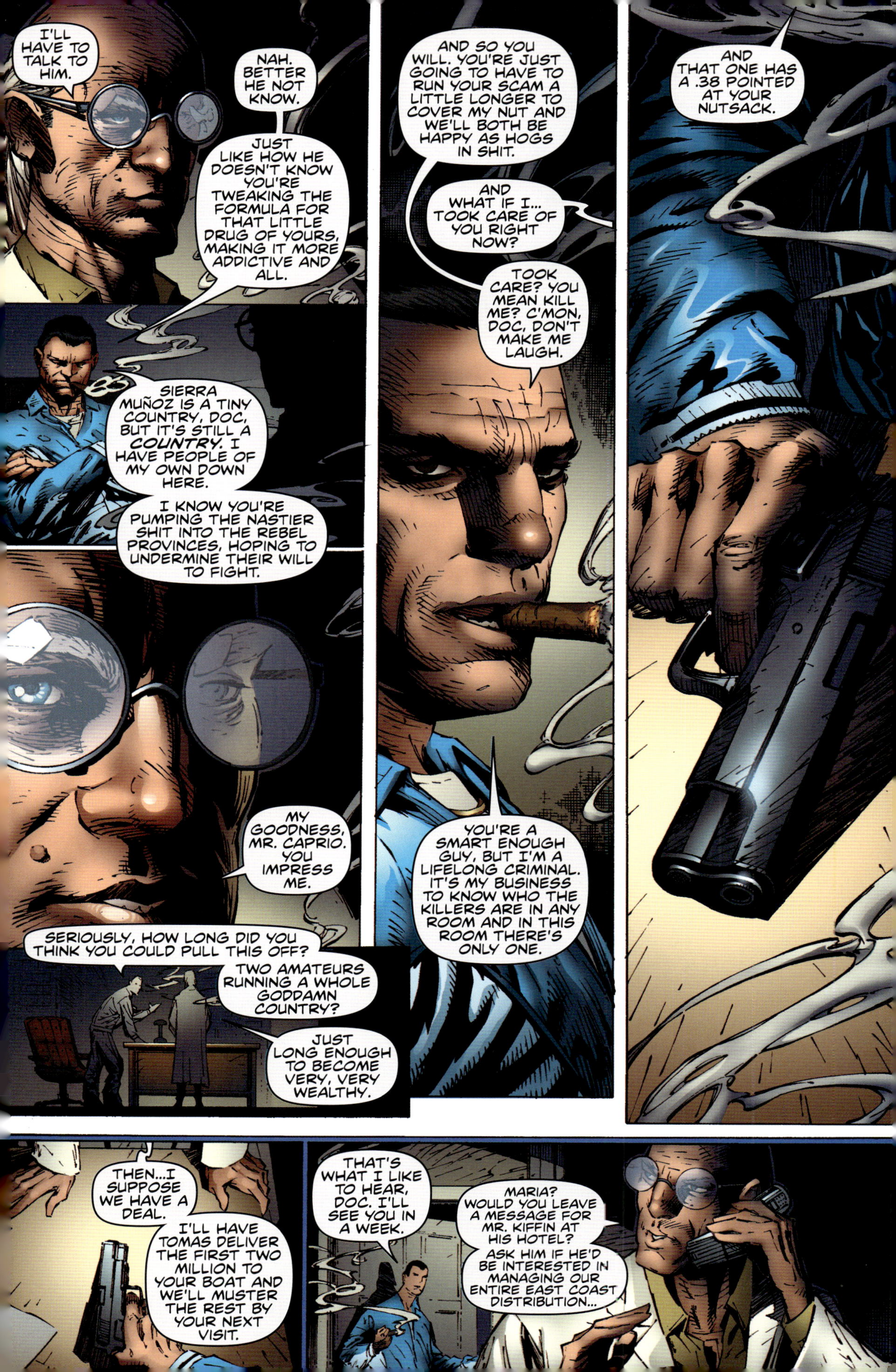
I'LL HAVE TO TALK TO HIM.
NAH. BETTER HE NOT KNOW.
JUST LIKE HOW HE DOESN'T KNOW YOU'RE TWEAKING THE FORMULA FOR THAT LITTLE DRUG OF YOURS, MAKING IT MORE ADDICTIVE AND ALL.
SIERRA MUÑOZ IS A TINY COUNTRY, DOC, BUT IT'S STILL A *COUNTRY*. I HAVE PEOPLE OF MY OWN DOWN HERE.
I KNOW YOU'RE PUMPING THE NASTIER SHIT INTO THE REBEL PROVINCES, HOPING TO UNDERMINE THEIR WILL TO FIGHT.
MY GOODNESS, MR. CAPRIO. YOU IMPRESS ME.
SERIOUSLY, HOW LONG DID YOU THINK YOU COULD PULL THIS OFF?
TWO AMATEURS RUNNING A WHOLE GODDAMN COUNTRY?
JUST LONG ENOUGH TO BECOME VERY, VERY WEALTHY.
AND SO YOU WILL. YOU'RE JUST GOING TO HAVE TO RUN YOUR SCAM A LITTLE LONGER TO COVER MY NUT AND WE'LL BOTH BE HAPPY AS HOGS IN SHIT.
AND WHAT IF I... TOOK CARE OF YOU RIGHT NOW?
TOOK CARE? YOU MEAN KILL ME? C'MON, DOC, DON'T MAKE ME LAUGH.
YOU'RE A SMART ENOUGH GUY, BUT I'M A LIFELONG CRIMINAL. IT'S MY BUSINESS TO KNOW WHO THE KILLERS ARE IN ANY ROOM AND IN THIS ROOM THERE'S ONLY ONE.
AND THAT ONE HAS A .38 POINTED AT YOUR NUTSACK.
THEN...I SUPPOSE WE HAVE A DEAL.
I'LL HAVE TOMAS DELIVER THE FIRST TWO MILLION TO YOUR BOAT AND WE'LL MUSTER THE REST BY YOUR NEXT VISIT.
THAT'S WHAT I LIKE TO HEAR, DOC. I'LL SEE YOU IN A WEEK.
MARIA? WOULD YOU LEAVE A MESSAGE FOR MR. KIFFIN AT HIS HOTEL?
ASK HIM IF HE'D BE INTERESTED IN MANAGING OUR ENTIRE EAST COAST DISTRIBUTION...

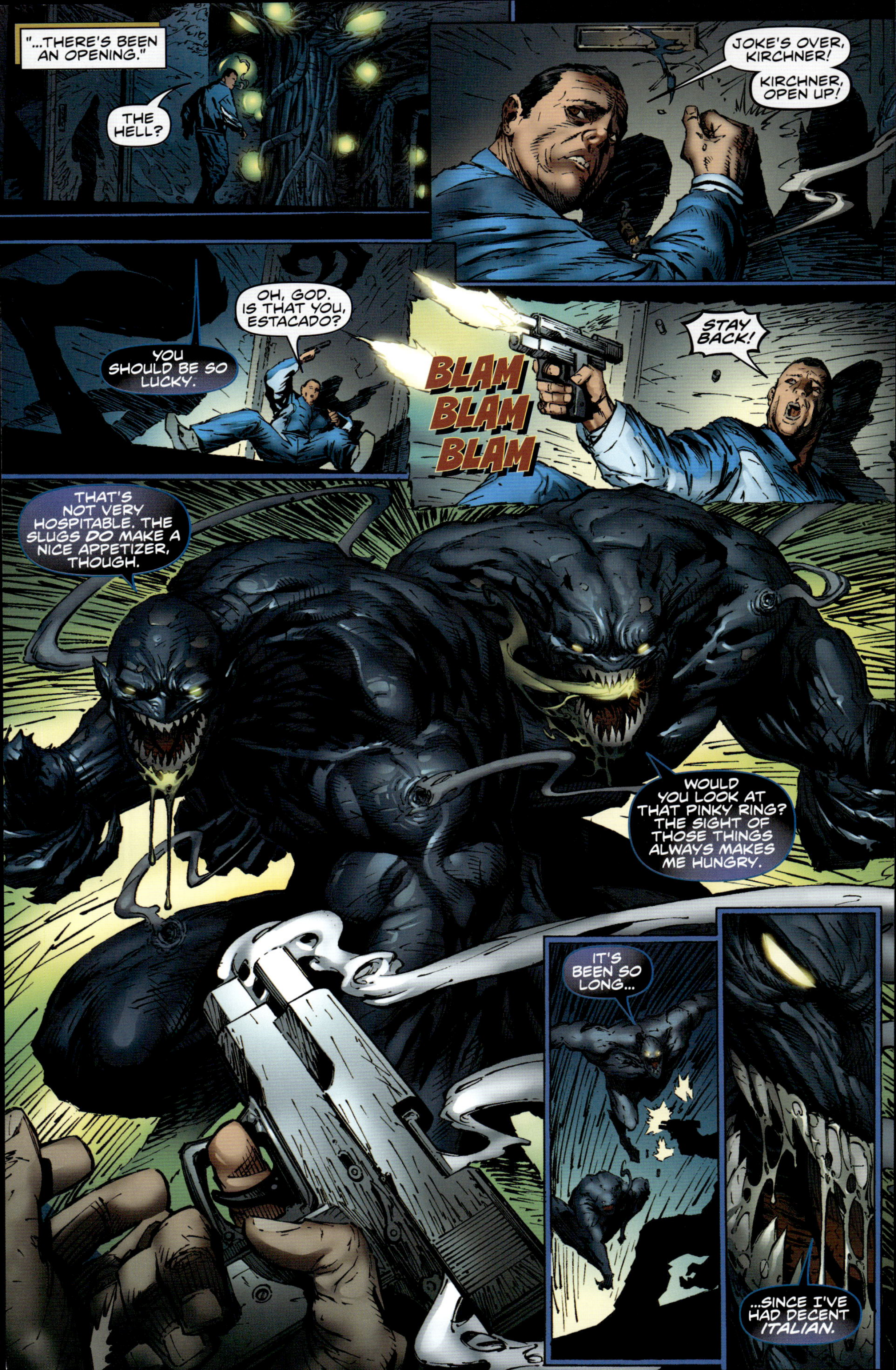

"...THERE'S BEEN AN OPENING."
THE HELL?
JOKE'S OVER, KIRCHNER!
KIRCHNER, OPEN UP!
YOU SHOULD BE SO LUCKY.
OH, GOD. IS THAT YOU, ESTACADO?
BLAM BLAM BLAM
STAY BACK!
THAT'S NOT VERY HOSPITABLE. THE SLUGS DO MAKE A NICE APPETIZER, THOUGH.
WOULD YOU LOOK AT THAT PINKY RING? THE SIGHT OF THOSE THINGS ALWAYS MAKES ME HUNGRY.
IT'S BEEN SO LONG...
...SINCE I'VE HAD DECENT ITALIAN.

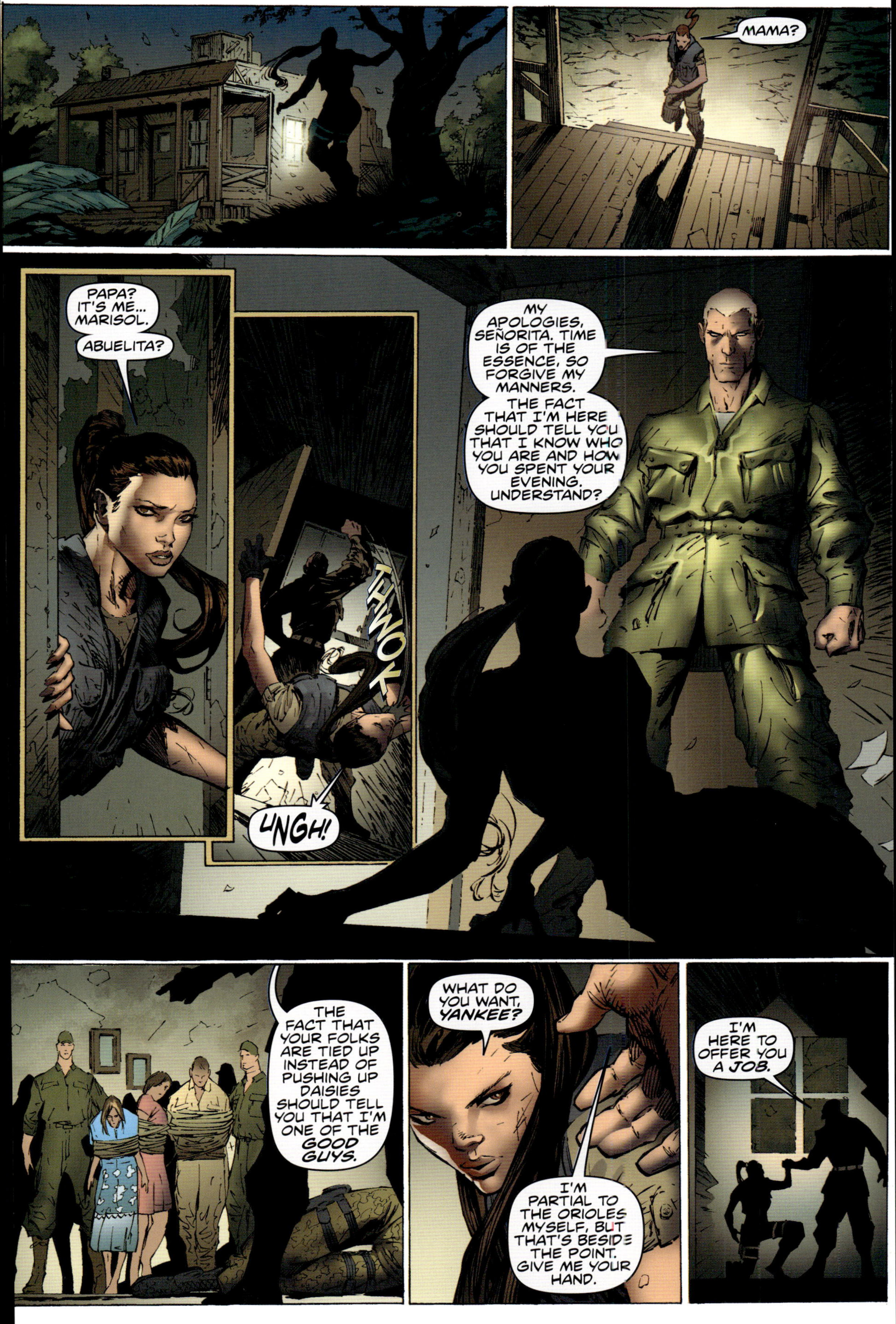
MAMA?
PAPA? IT'S ME... MARISOL.
ABUELITA?
THWOK
UNGH!
MY APOLOGIES, SEÑORITA. TIME IS OF THE ESSENCE, SO FORGIVE MY MANNERS.
THE FACT THAT I'M HERE SHOULD TELL YOU THAT I KNOW WHO YOU ARE AND HOW YOU SPENT YOUR EVENING. UNDERSTAND?
THE FACT THAT YOUR FOLKS ARE TIED UP INSTEAD OF PUSHING UP DAISIES SHOULD TELL YOU THAT I'M ONE OF THE GOOD GUYS.
WHAT DO YOU WANT, YANKEE?
I'M PARTIAL TO THE ORIOLES MYSELF, BUT THAT'S BESIDE THE POINT. GIVE ME YOUR HAND.
I'M HERE TO OFFER YOU A JOB.

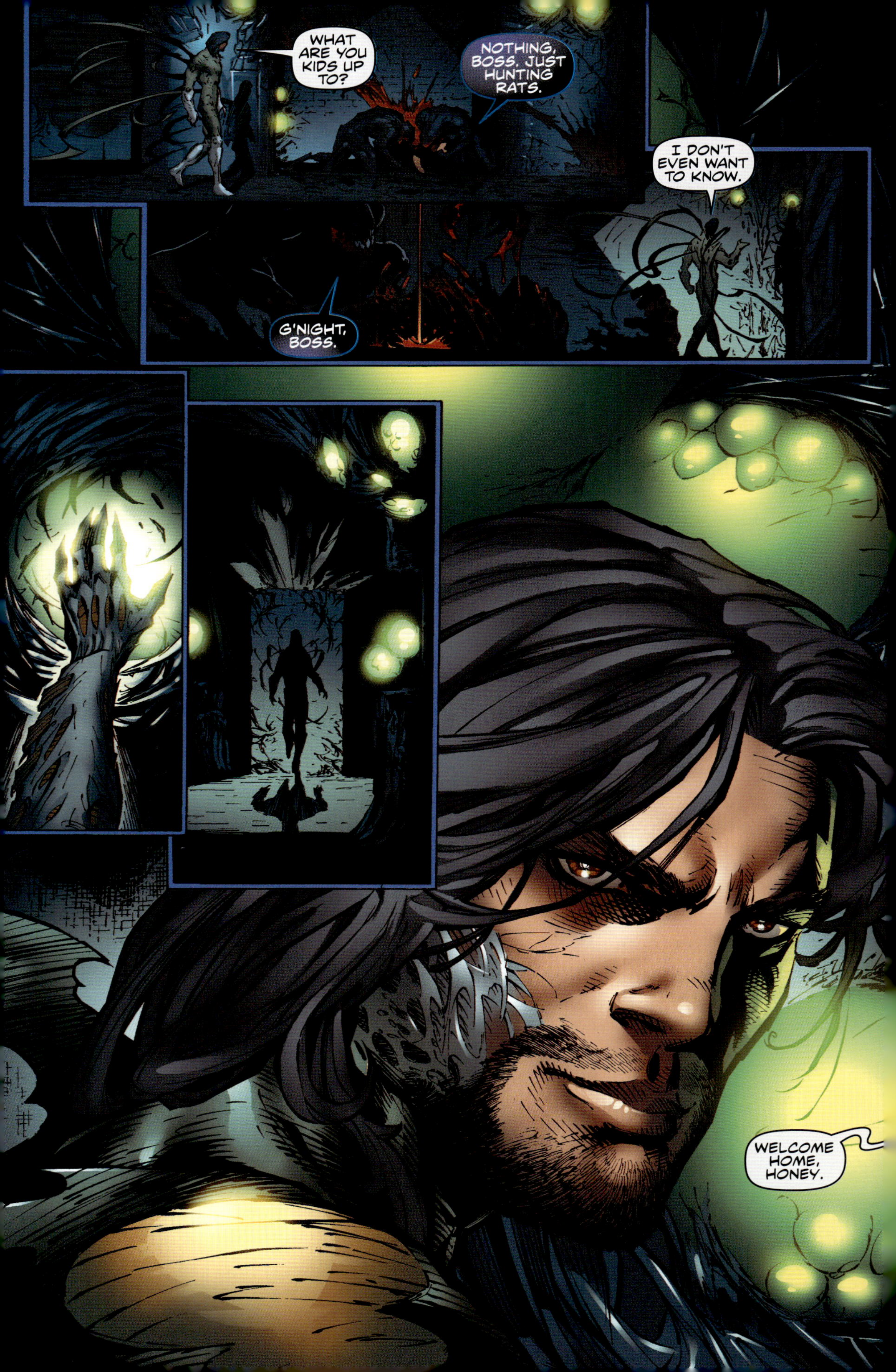
WHAT ARE YOU KIDS UP TO?
NOTHING, BOSS. JUST HUNTING RATS.
I DON'T EVEN WANT TO KNOW.
G'NIGHT, BOSS.
WELCOME HOME, HONEY.

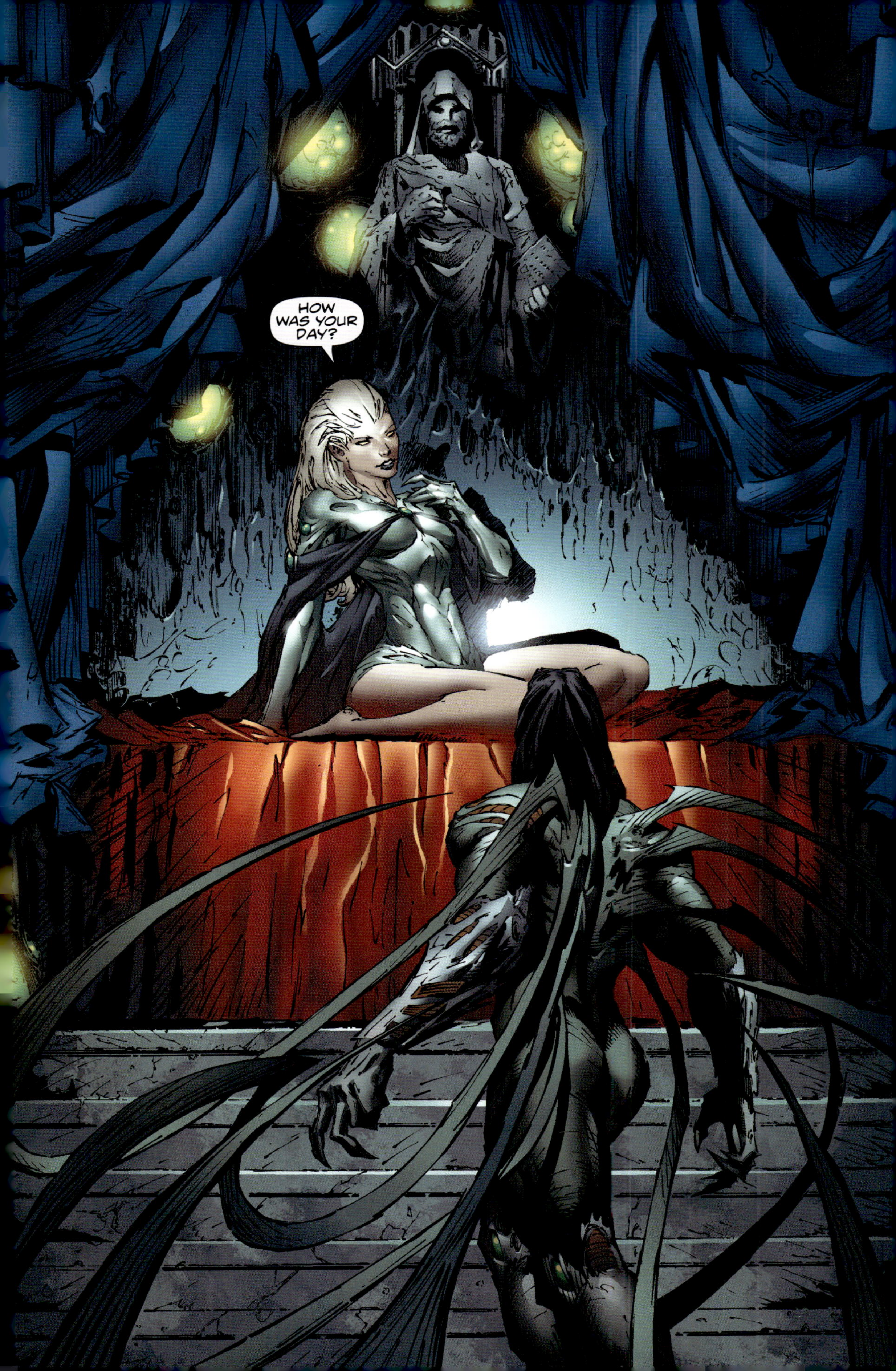
HOW WAS YOUR DAY?

The Darkness Issue #66
cover art by: Dale Keown

THE DARKNESS #66

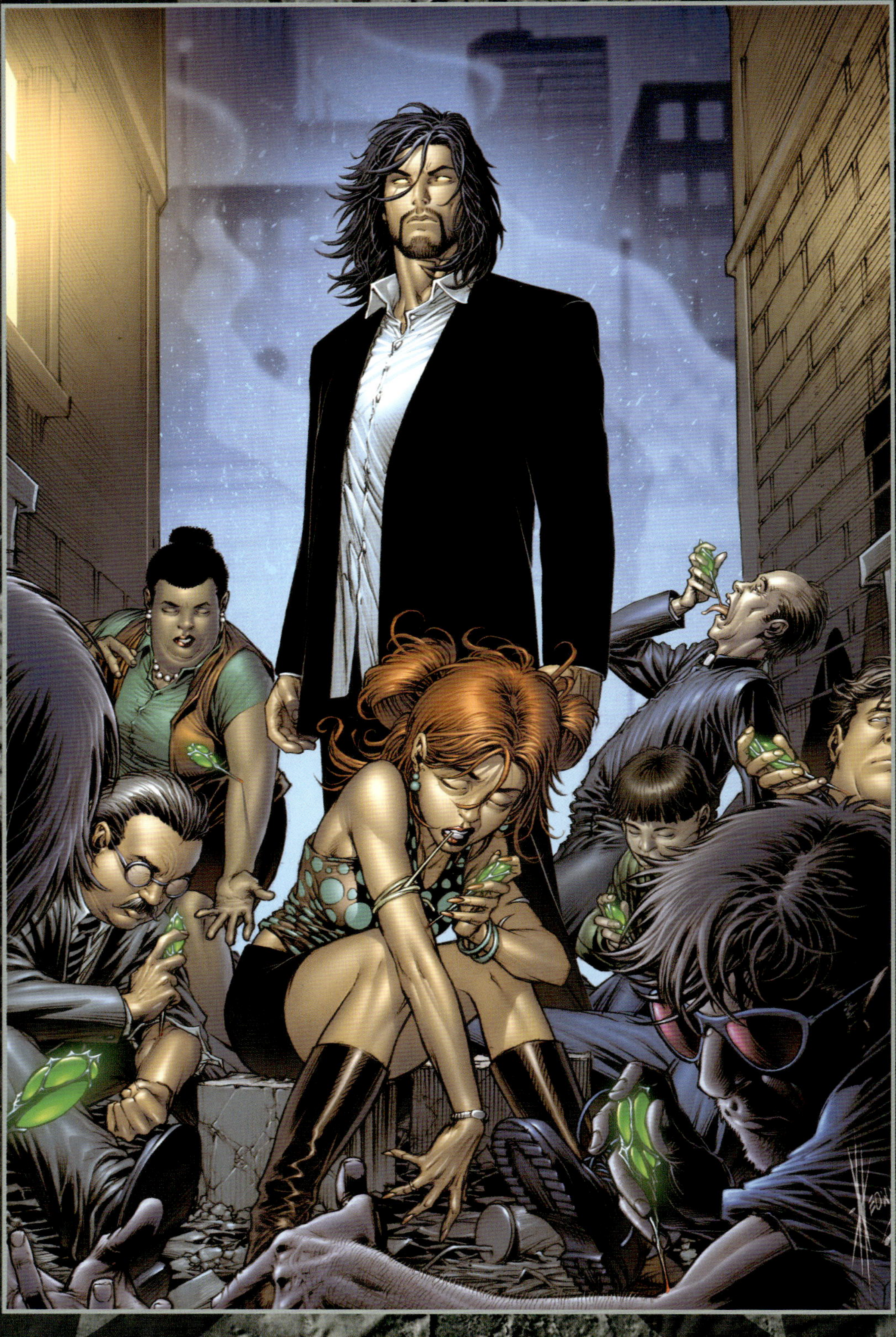

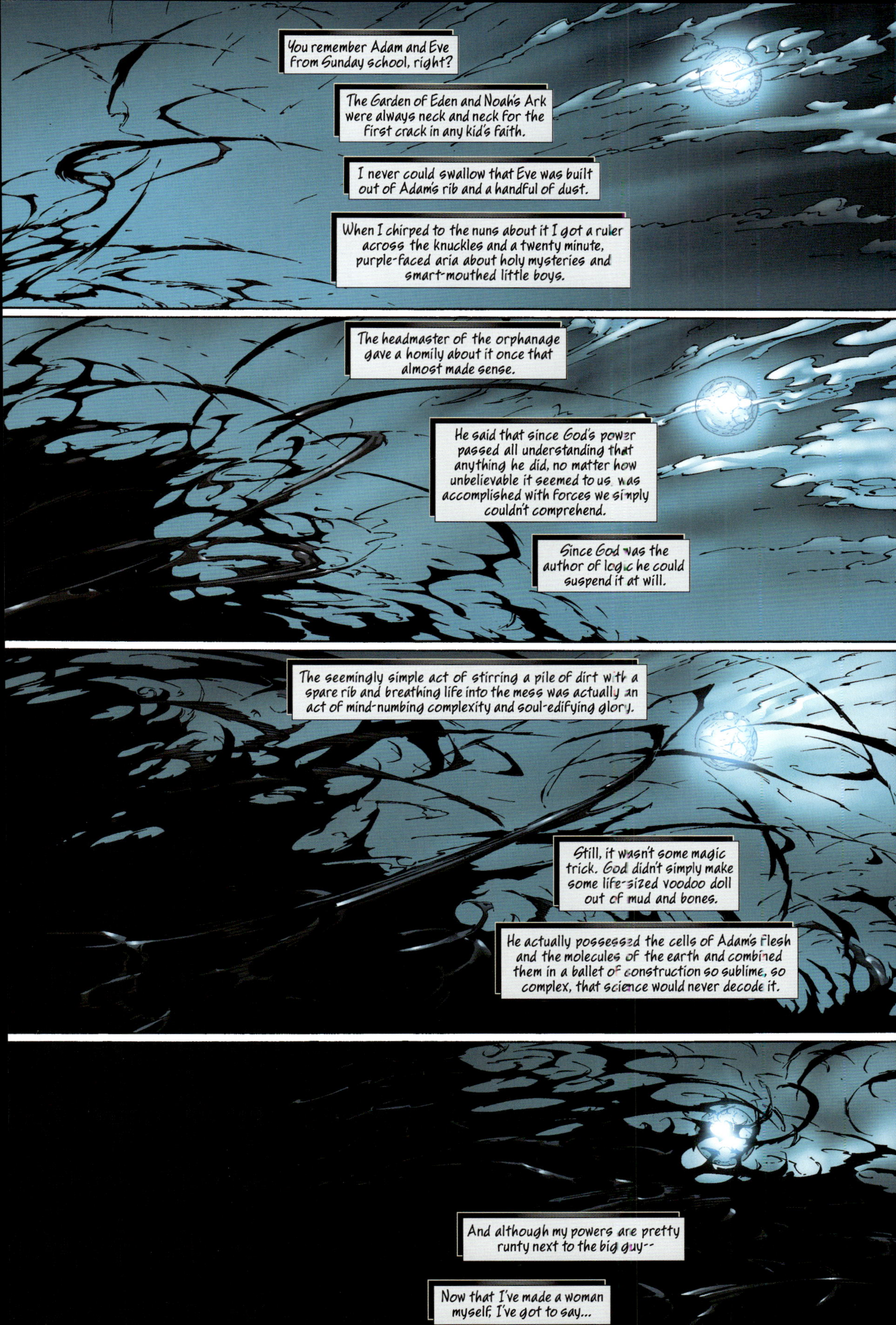
You remember Adam and Eve from Sunday school, right?
The Garden of Eden and Noah's Ark were always neck and neck for the first crack in any kid's faith.
I never could swallow that Eve was built out of Adam's rib and a handful of dust.
When I chirped to the nuns about it I got a ruler across the knuckles and a twenty minute, purple-faced aria about holy mysteries and smart-mouthed little boys.
The headmaster of the orphanage gave a homily about it once that almost made sense.
He said that since God's power passed all understanding that anything he did, no matter how unbelievable it seemed to us, was accomplished with forces we simply couldn't comprehend.
Since God was the author of logic he could suspend it at will.
The seemingly simple act of stirring a pile of dirt with a spare rib and breathing life into the mess was actually an act of mind-numbing complexity and soul-edifying glory.
Still, it wasn't some magic trick. God didn't simply make some life-sized voodoo doll out of mud and bones.
He actually possessed the cells of Adam's flesh and the molecules of the earth and combined them in a ballet of construction so sublime, so complex, that science would never decode it.
And although my powers are pretty runty next to the big guy--
Now that I've made a woman myself, I've got to say...

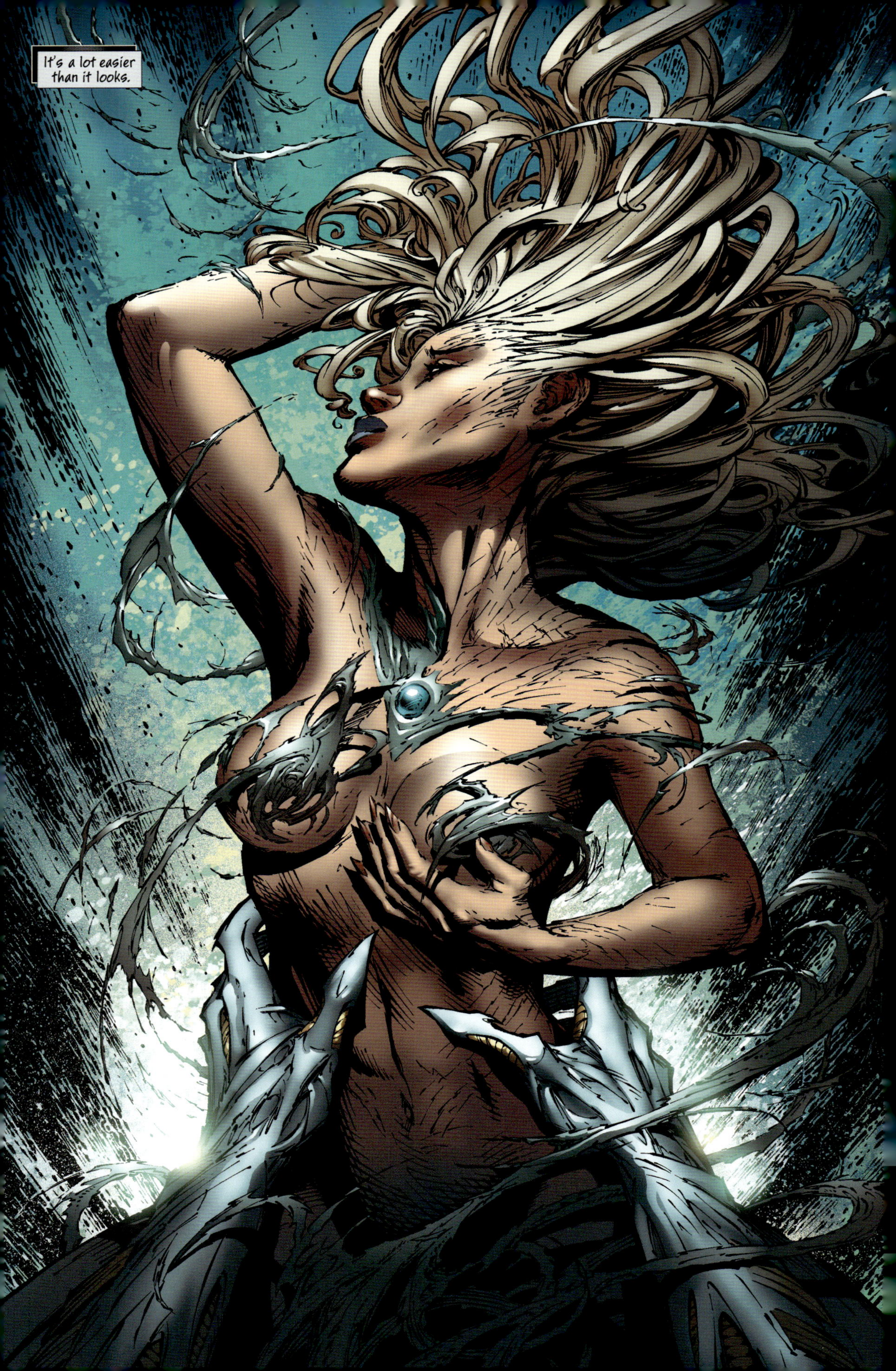
It's a lot easier than it looks.

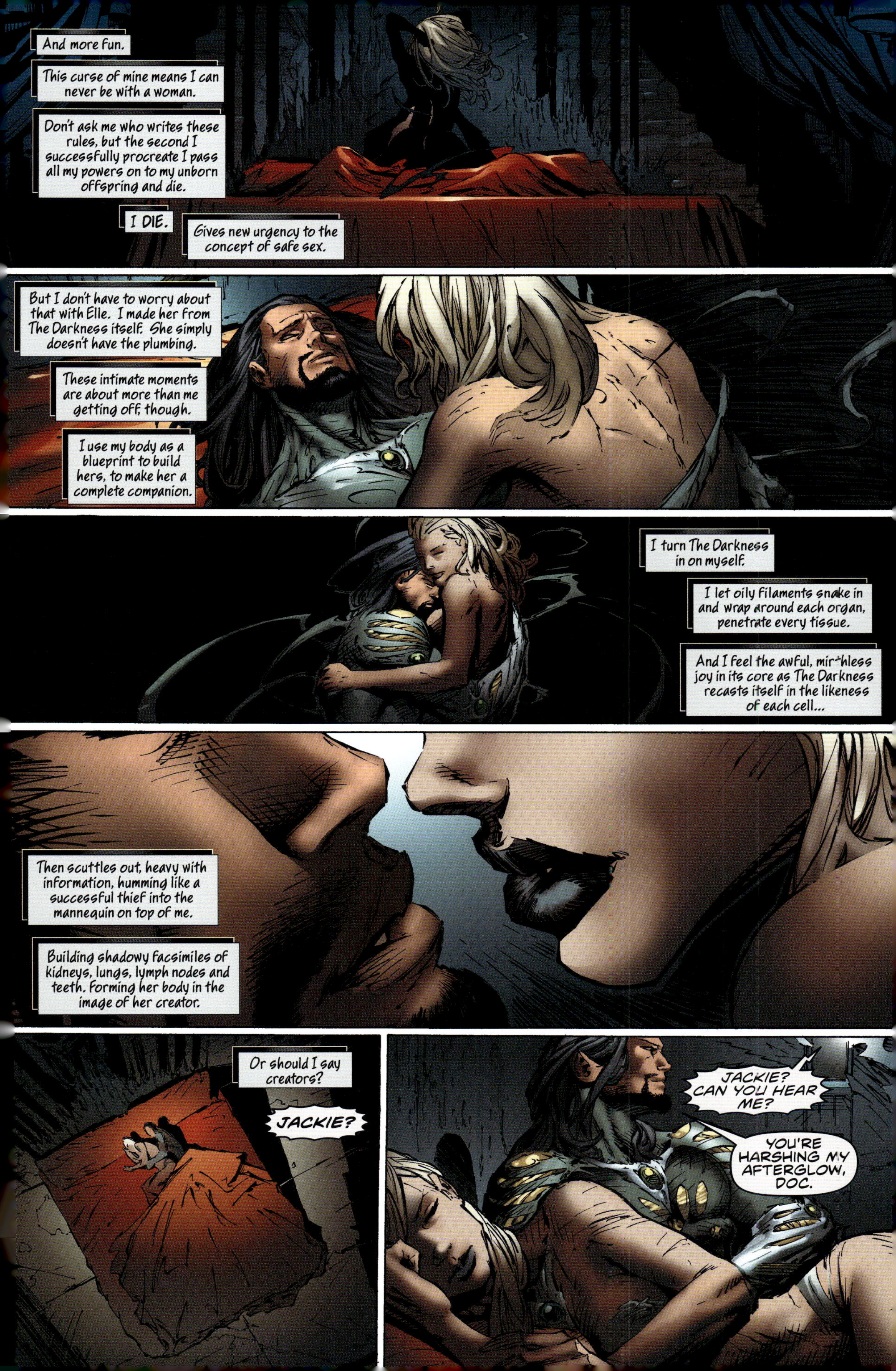

And more fun.
This curse of mine means I can never be with a woman.
Don't ask me who writes these rules, but the second I successfully procreate I pass all my powers on to my unborn offspring and die.
I DIE.
Gives new urgency to the concept of safe sex.
But I don't have to worry about that with Elle. I made her from The Darkness itself. She simply doesn't have the plumbing.
These intimate moments are about more than me getting off, though.
I use my body as a blueprint to build hers, to make her a complete companion.
I turn The Darkness in on myself.
I let oily filaments snake in and wrap around each organ, penetrate every tissue.
And I feel the awful, mirthless joy in its core as The Darkness recasts itself in the likeness of each cell...
Then scuttles out, heavy with information, humming like a successful thief into the mannequin on top of me.
Building shadowy facsimiles of kidneys, lungs, lymph nodes and teeth. Forming her body in the image of her creator.
Or should I say creators?
JACKIE?
JACKIE? CAN YOU HEAR ME?
YOU'RE HARSHING MY AFTERGLOW, DOC.

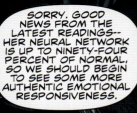

SORRY. GOOD NEWS FROM THE LATEST READINGS-- HER NEURAL NETWORK IS UP TO NINETY-FOUR PERCENT OF NORMAL, SO WE SHOULD BEGIN TO SEE SOME MORE AUTHENTIC EMOTIONAL RESPONSIVENESS.

GIVE ME SOME TIME TO WORK OUT HOW TO TRANSLATE HORMONAL INFORMATION AND WE'LL GIVE THAT A GO TOMORROW.

OKAY.

I HATE THE SOUND OF THAT MAN'S VOICE.

THAT'S NO WAY TO TALK. YOU WOULDN'T EXIST WITHOUT PROFESSOR KIRCHNER'S HELP.

BUT *YOU* MADE ME.

WITH THE DOC'S HELP, ELLE. WE'VE GONE OVER IT BEFORE.

I'VE TRIED TO USE THE DARKNESS TO MAKE COMPANIONS IN THE PAST, BUT THERE WAS ALWAYS SOMETHING HOLLOW ABOUT THEM.

KIRCHNER IS HELPING ME MAKE YOU MORE REAL, LIKE AN ACTUAL PERSON, YOU KNOW? SOMEONE I CAN SHARE MY LIFE WITH.

HE STILL CREEPS ME OUT.

SEE, WE'RE MAKING PROGRESS. YOU WEREN'T EVEN CAPABLE OF BEING CREEPED OUT YESTERDAY. DO YOU FEEL ANY DIFFERENT?

NO. I NEVER DO.

WHAT DID YOU DO TODAY?

I SAT AROUND AND WAITED FOR YOU TO COME HOME. I DID SOME TESTS DR. KIRCHNER DESIGNED FOR ME.

OH, AND I DRANK WATER FOR THE FIRST TIME.

REALLY? HOW'D YOU LIKE IT?

I LIKE YOU BETTER.

I LOVE YOU.

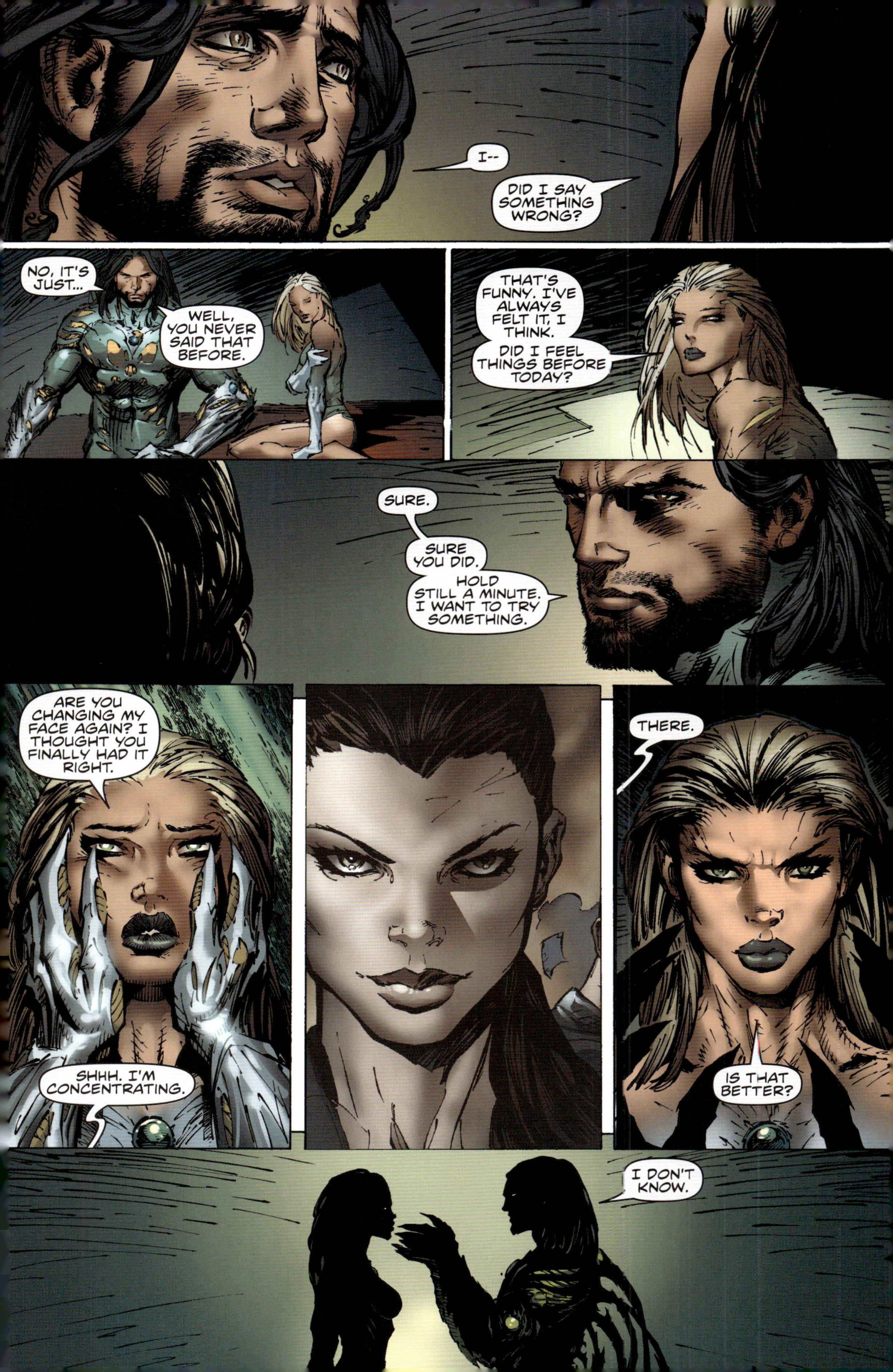
I--
DID I SAY SOMETHING WRONG?
NO, IT'S JUST...
WELL, YOU NEVER SAID THAT BEFORE.
THAT'S FUNNY. I'VE ALWAYS FELT IT, I THINK.
DID I FEEL THINGS BEFORE TODAY?
SURE.
SURE YOU DID.
HOLD STILL A MINUTE. I WANT TO TRY SOMETHING.
ARE YOU CHANGING MY FACE AGAIN? I THOUGHT YOU FINALLY HAD IT RIGHT.
SHHH. I'M CONCENTRATING.
THERE.
IS THAT BETTER?
I DON'T KNOW.

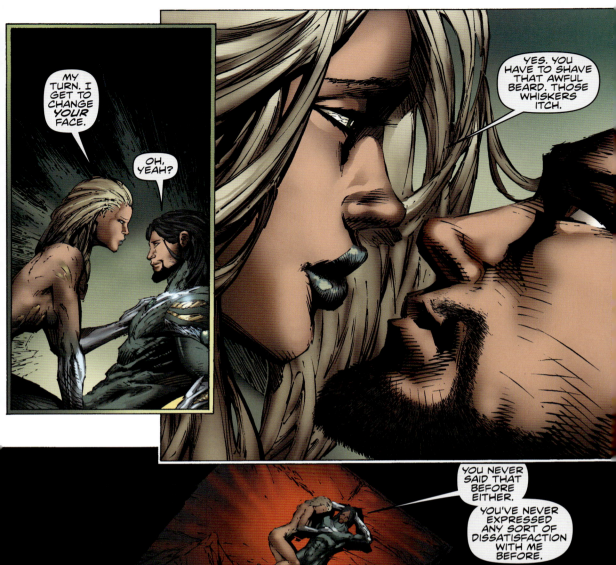

MY TURN. I GET TO CHANGE YOUR FACE.

OH, YEAH?

YES. YOU HAVE TO SHAVE THAT AWFUL BEARD. THOSE WHISKERS ITCH.

YOU NEVER SAID THAT BEFORE EITHER.

YOU'VE NEVER EXPRESSED ANY SORT OF DISSATISFACTION WITH ME BEFORE.

WELL, IT'S TRUE. THAT THING IS GROSS.

OKAY, I GET THE MESSAGE.

LISTEN, I'VE GOT TO RUN. WE'VE HAD SOME TROUBLE WITH THE LOCALS LATELY.

I'LL BE RIGHT HERE, BABY.

JUST LIKE ALWAYS.

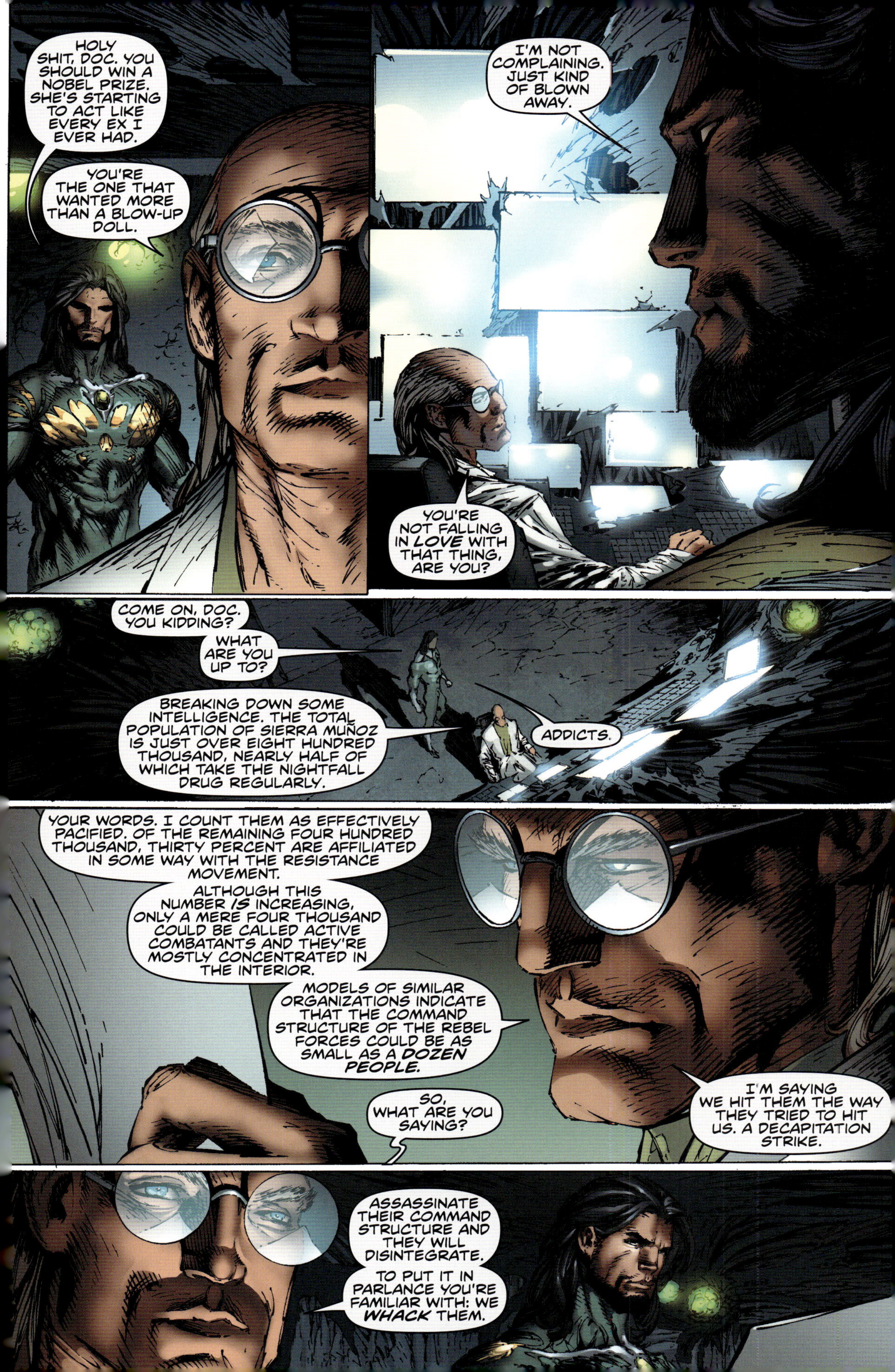

HOLY SHIT, DOC. YOU SHOULD WIN A NOBEL PRIZE. SHE'S STARTING TO ACT LIKE EVERY EX I EVER HAD.
YOU'RE THE ONE THAT WANTED MORE THAN A BLOW-UP DOLL.
I'M NOT COMPLAINING. JUST KIND OF BLOWN AWAY.
YOU'RE NOT FALLING IN LOVE WITH THAT THING, ARE YOU?
COME ON, DOC. YOU KIDDING?
WHAT ARE YOU UP TO?
BREAKING DOWN SOME INTELLIGENCE. THE TOTAL POPULATION OF SIERRA MUÑOZ IS JUST OVER EIGHT HUNDRED THOUSAND, NEARLY HALF OF WHICH TAKE THE NIGHTFALL DRUG REGULARLY.
ADDICTS.
YOUR WORDS. I COUNT THEM AS EFFECTIVELY PACIFIED. OF THE REMAINING FOUR HUNDRED THOUSAND, THIRTY PERCENT ARE AFFILIATED IN SOME WAY WITH THE RESISTANCE MOVEMENT.
ALTHOUGH THIS NUMBER IS INCREASING, ONLY A MERE FOUR THOUSAND COULD BE CALLED ACTIVE COMBATANTS AND THEY'RE MOSTLY CONCENTRATED IN THE INTERIOR.
MODELS OF SIMILAR ORGANIZATIONS INDICATE THAT THE COMMAND STRUCTURE OF THE REBEL FORCES COULD BE AS SMALL AS A DOZEN PEOPLE.
SO, WHAT ARE YOU SAYING?
I'M SAYING WE HIT THEM THE WAY THEY TRIED TO HIT US. A DECAPITATION STRIKE.
ASSASSINATE THEIR COMMAND STRUCTURE AND THEY WILL DISINTEGRATE.
TO PUT IT IN PARLANCE YOU'RE FAMILIAR WITH: WE WHACK THEM.

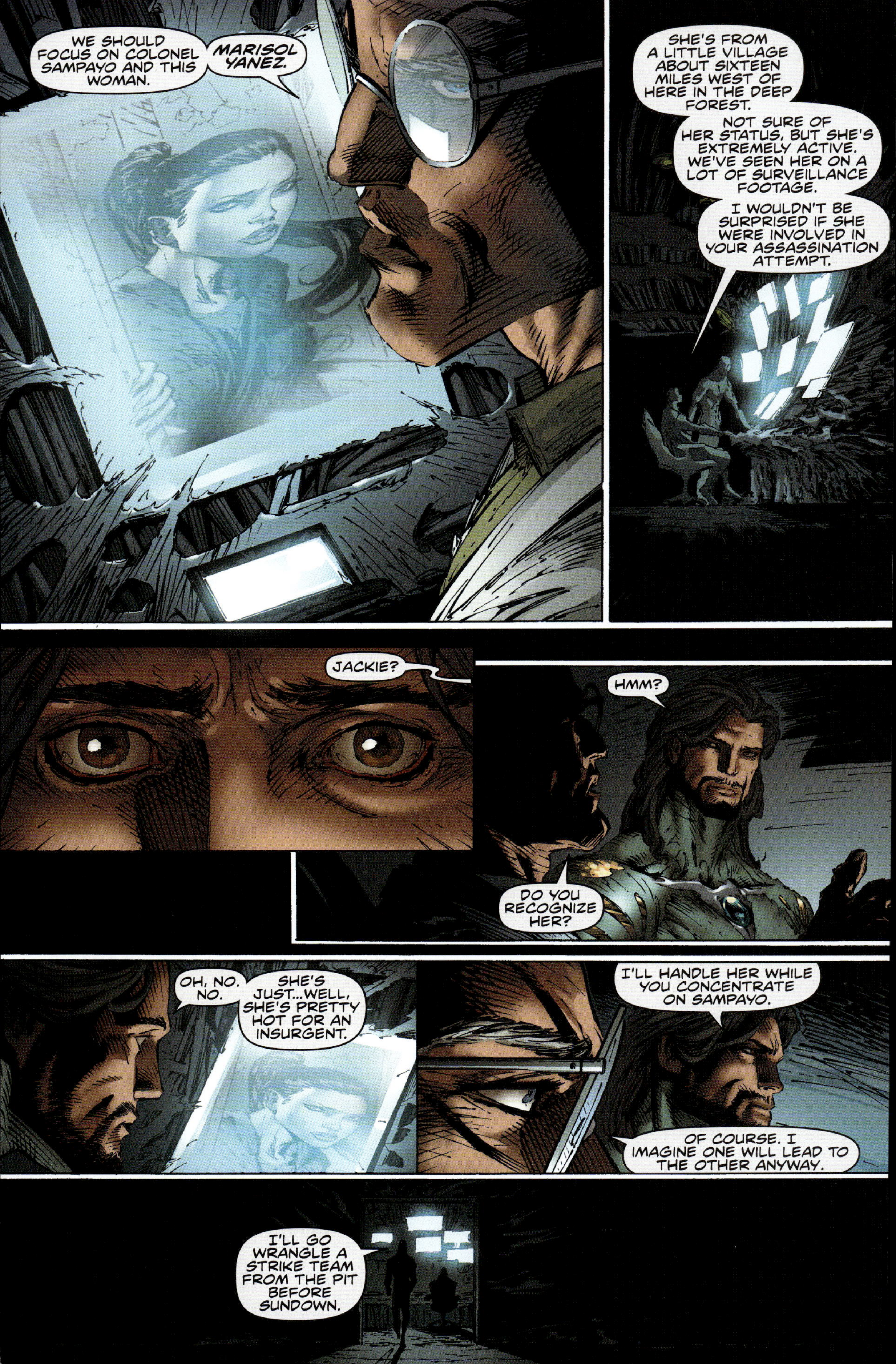
WE SHOULD FOCUS ON COLONEL SAMPAYO AND THIS WOMAN.
MARISOL YANEZ.
SHE'S FROM A LITTLE VILLAGE ABOUT SIXTEEN MILES WEST OF HERE IN THE DEEP FOREST.
NOT SURE OF HER STATUS, BUT SHE'S EXTREMELY ACTIVE. WE'VE SEEN HER ON A LOT OF SURVEILLANCE FOOTAGE.
I WOULDN'T BE SURPRISED IF SHE WERE INVOLVED IN YOUR ASSASSINATION ATTEMPT.
JACKIE?
HMM?
DO YOU RECOGNIZE HER?
OH, NO. NO.
SHE'S JUST...WELL, SHE'S PRETTY HOT FOR AN INSURGENT.
I'LL HANDLE HER WHILE YOU CONCENTRATE ON SAMPAYO.
OF COURSE. I IMAGINE ONE WILL LEAD TO THE OTHER ANYWAY.
I'LL GO WRANGLE A STRIKE TEAM FROM THE PIT BEFORE SUNDOWN.

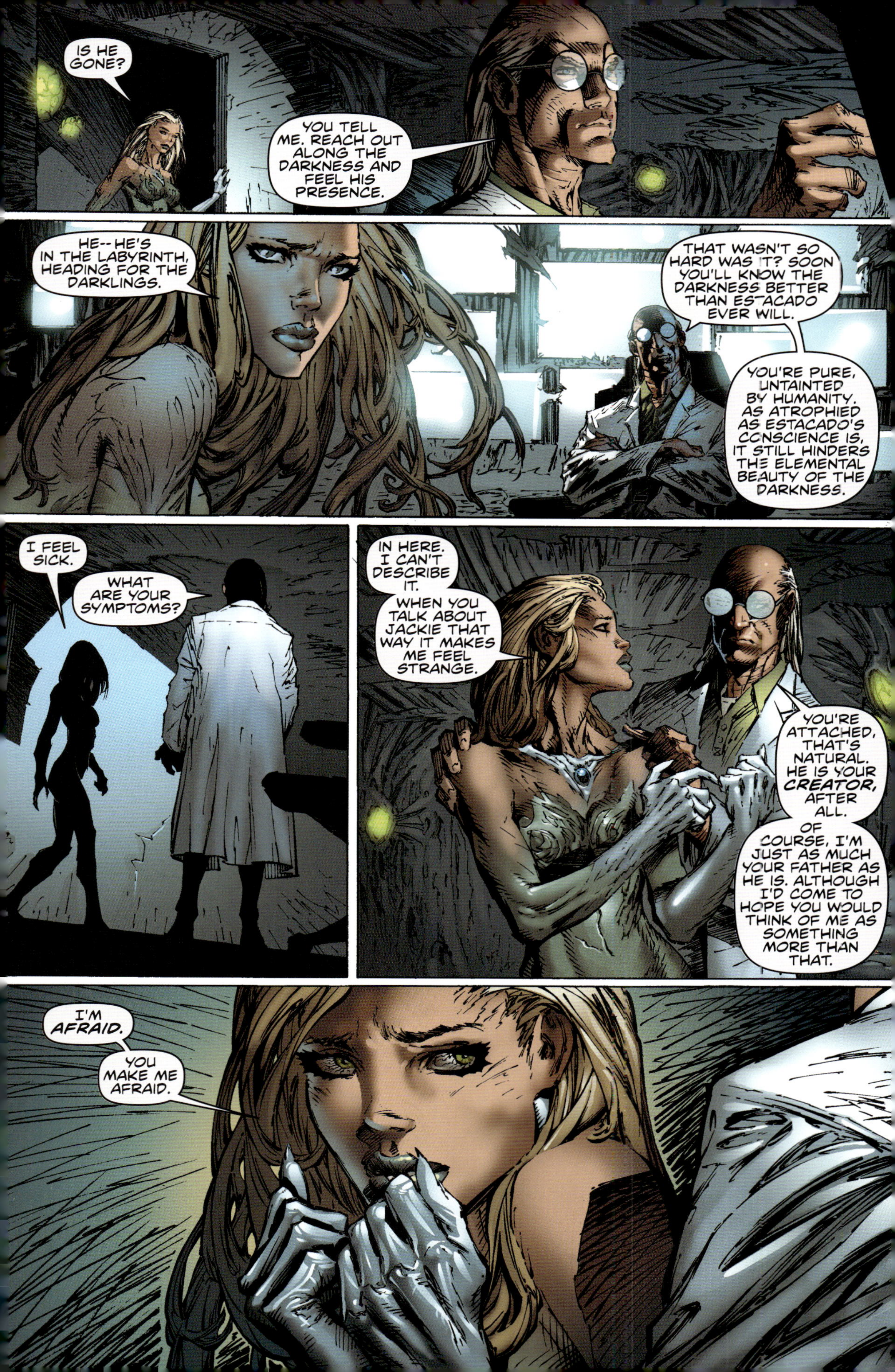
IS HE GONE?
YOU TELL ME. REACH OUT ALONG THE DARKNESS AND FEEL HIS PRESENCE.
HE--HE'S IN THE LABYRINTH, HEADING FOR THE DARKLINGS.
THAT WASN'T SO HARD WAS IT? SOON YOU'LL KNOW THE DARKNESS BETTER THAN ESTACADO EVER WILL.
YOU'RE PURE, UNTAINTED BY HUMANITY. AS ATROPHIED AS ESTACADO'S CONSCIENCE IS, IT STILL HINDERS THE ELEMENTAL BEAUTY OF THE DARKNESS.
I FEEL SICK.
WHAT ARE YOUR SYMPTOMS?
IN HERE. I CAN'T DESCRIBE IT.
WHEN YOU TALK ABOUT JACKIE THAT WAY IT MAKES ME FEEL STRANGE.
YOU'RE ATTACHED, THAT'S NATURAL. HE IS YOUR CREATOR, AFTER ALL.
OF COURSE, I'M JUST AS MUCH YOUR FATHER AS HE IS. ALTHOUGH I'D COME TO HOPE YOU WOULD THINK OF ME AS SOMETHING MORE THAN THAT.
I'M AFRAID.
YOU MAKE ME AFRAID.

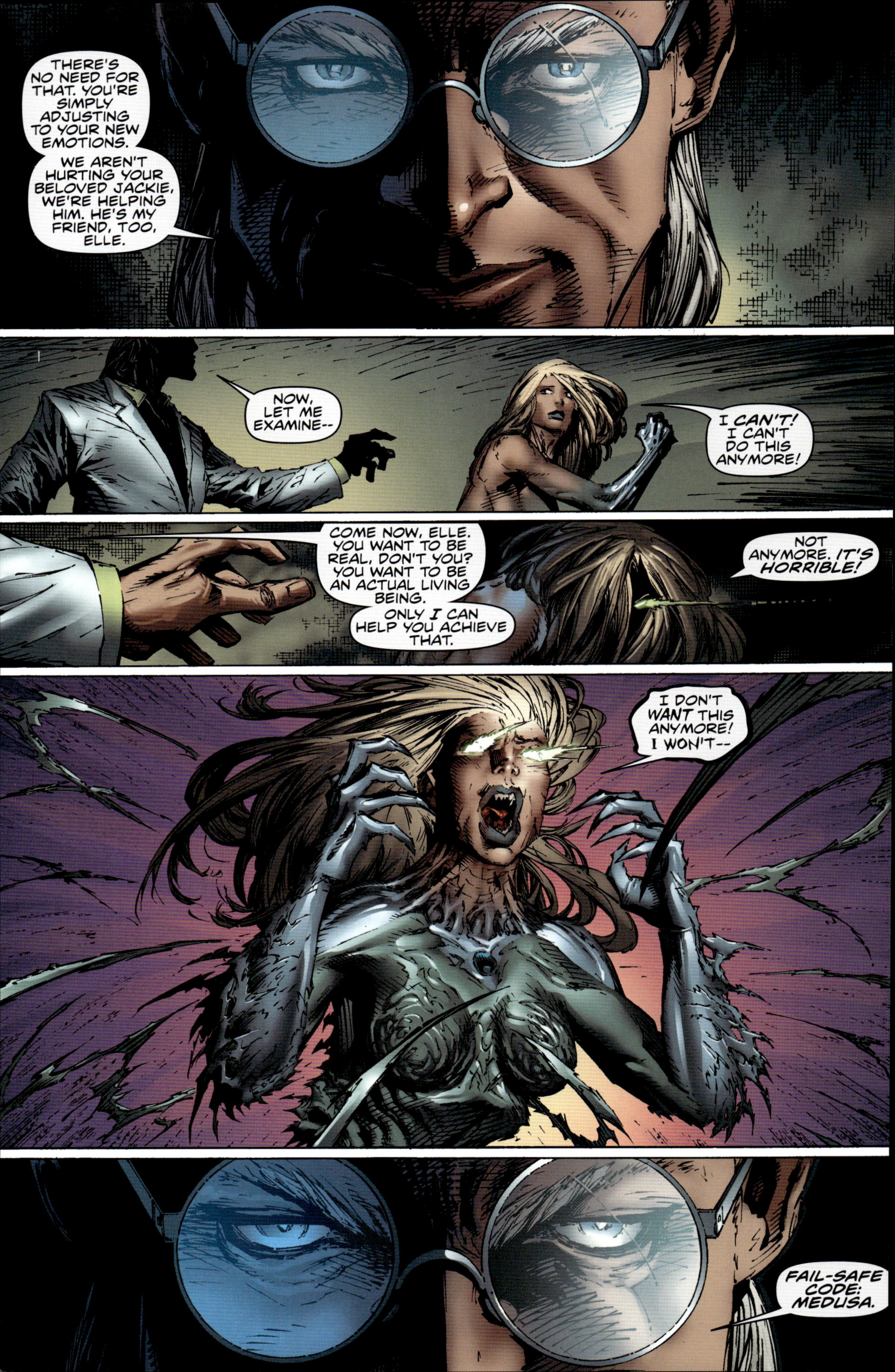
THERE'S NO NEED FOR THAT. YOU'RE SIMPLY ADJUSTING TO YOUR NEW EMOTIONS.
WE AREN'T HURTING YOUR BELOVED JACKIE, WE'RE HELPING HIM. HE'S MY FRIEND, TOO, ELLE.
NOW, LET ME EXAMINE--
I CAN'T! I CAN'T DO THIS ANYMORE!
COME NOW, ELLE. YOU WANT TO BE REAL, DON'T YOU? YOU WANT TO BE AN ACTUAL LIVING BEING.
ONLY I CAN HELP YOU ACHIEVE THAT.
NOT ANYMORE. IT'S HORRIBLE!
I DON'T WANT THIS ANYMORE! I WON'T--
FAIL-SAFE CODE: MEDUSA.

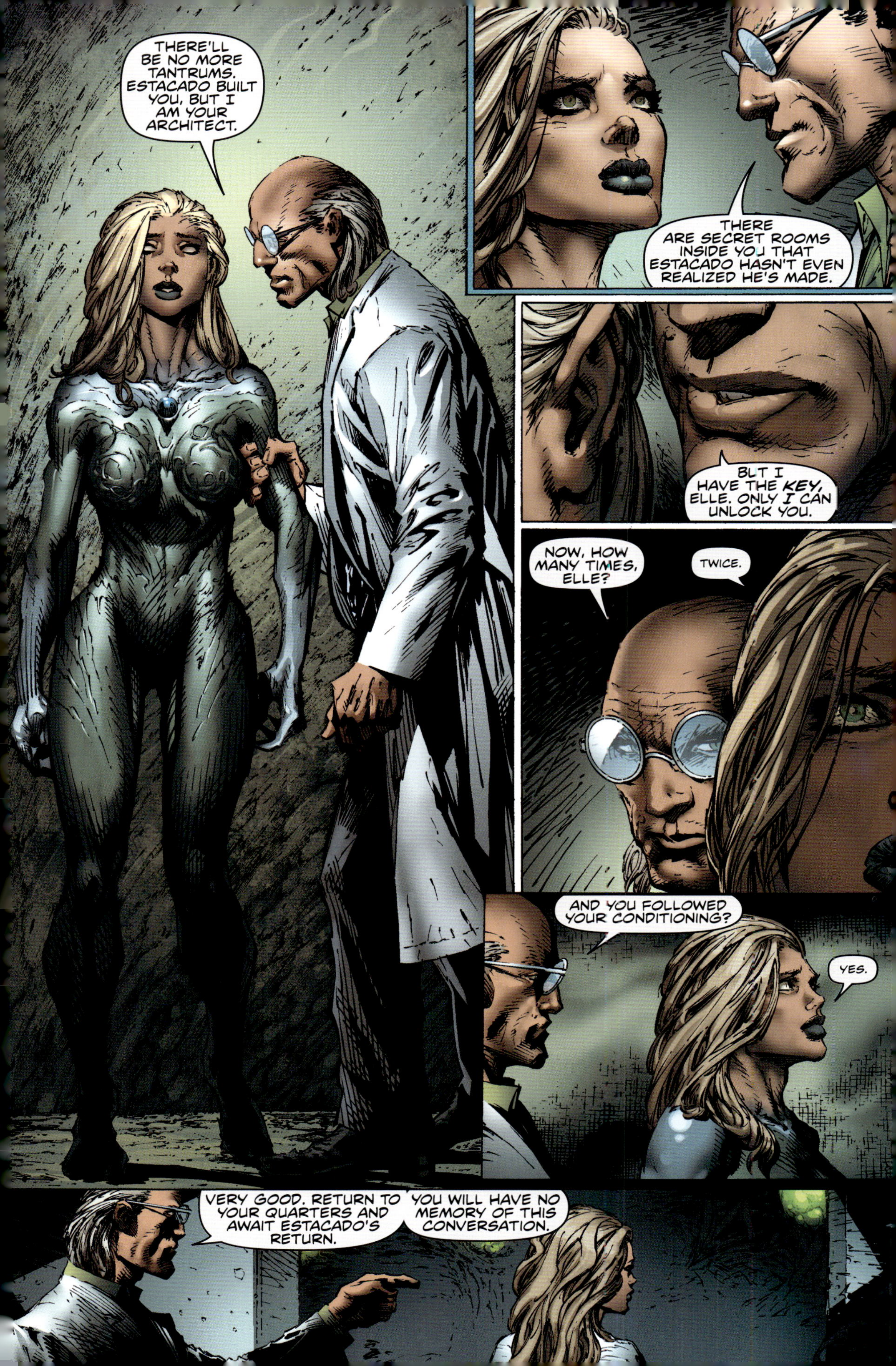
THERE'LL BE NO MORE TANTRUMS. ESTACADO BUILT YOU, BUT I AM YOUR ARCHITECT.
THERE ARE SECRET ROOMS INSIDE YOU THAT ESTACADO HASN'T EVEN REALIZED HE'S MADE.
BUT I HAVE THE KEY, ELLE. ONLY I CAN UNLOCK YOU.
NOW, HOW MANY TIMES, ELLE?
TWICE.
AND YOU FOLLOWED YOUR CONDITIONING?
YES.
VERY GOOD. RETURN TO YOUR QUARTERS AND AWAIT ESTACADO'S RETURN.
YOU WILL HAVE NO MEMORY OF THIS CONVERSATION.

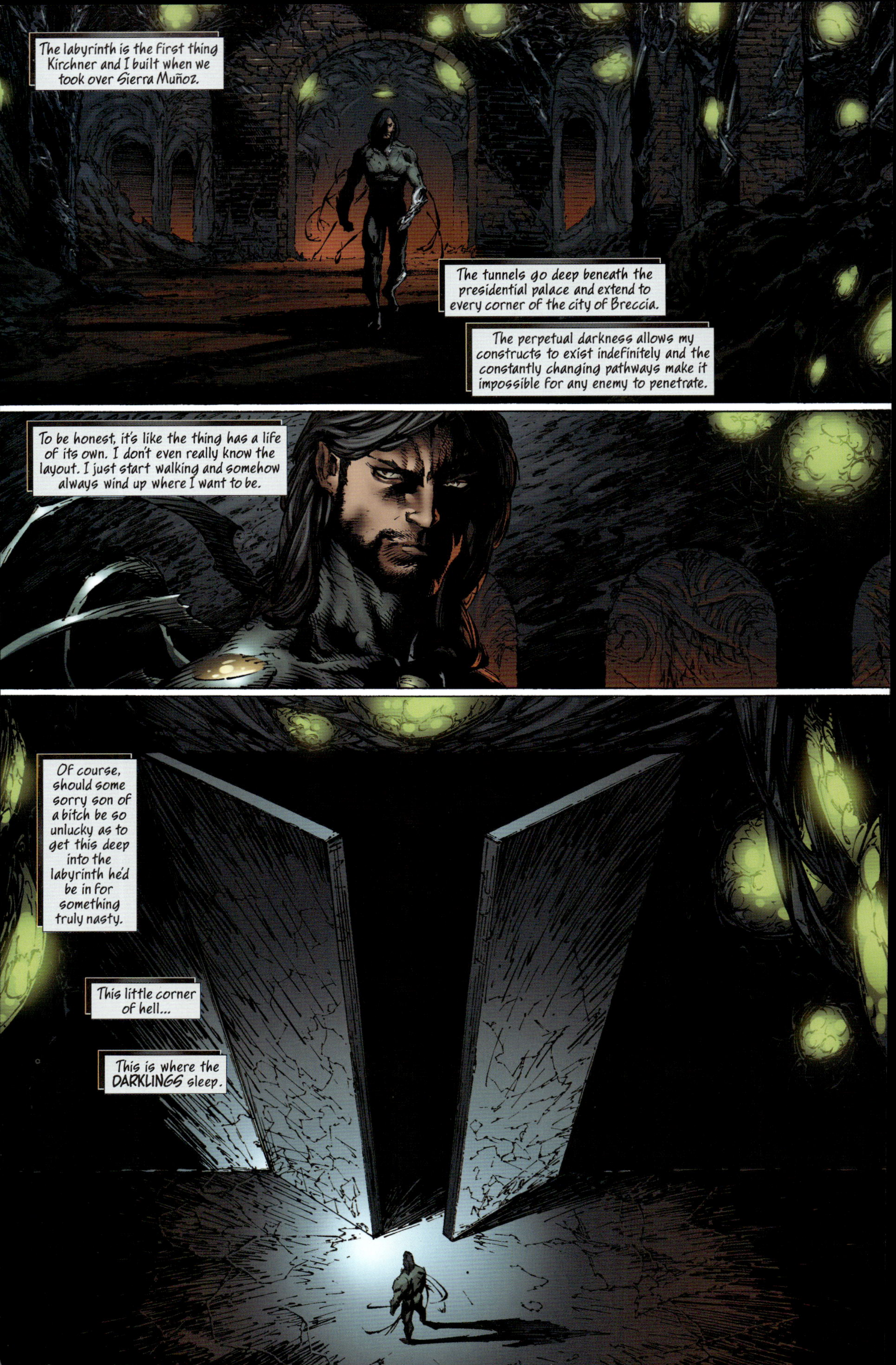
The labyrinth is the first thing Kirchner and I built when we took over Sierra Muñoz.
The tunnels go deep beneath the presidential palace and extend to every corner of the city of Breccia.
The perpetual darkness allows my constructs to exist indefinitely and the constantly changing pathways make it impossible for any enemy to penetrate.
To be honest, it's like the thing has a life of its own. I don't even really know the layout. I just start walking and somehow always wind up where I want to be.
Of course, should some sorry son of a bitch be so unlucky as to get this deep into the labyrinth he'd be in for something truly nasty.
This little corner of hell...
This is where the DARKLINGS sleep.

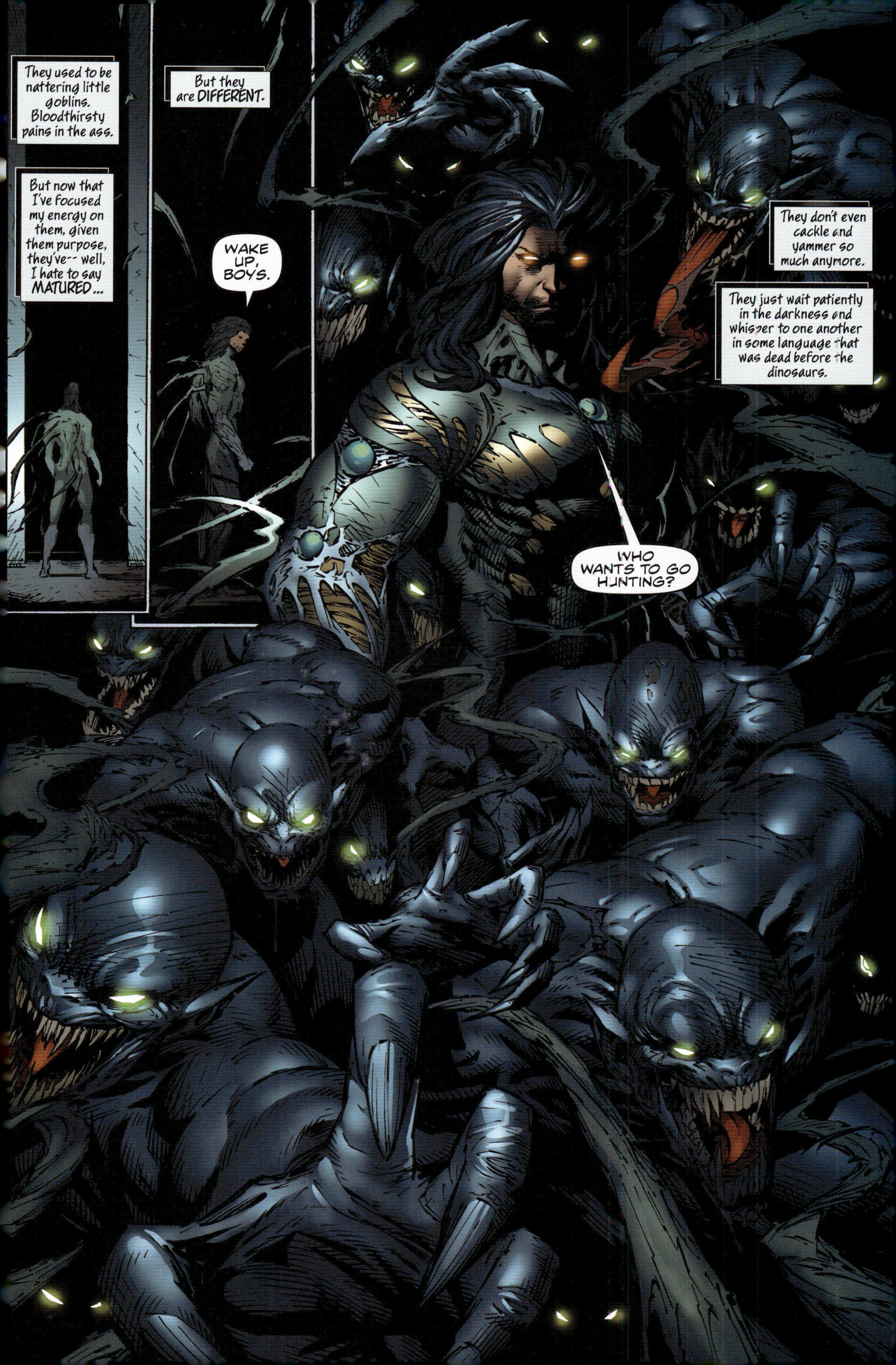
They used to be nattering little goblins. Bloodthirsty pains in the ass.
But now that I've focused my energy on them, given them purpose, they've-- well, I hate to say MATURED...
But they are DIFFERENT.
WAKE UP, BOYS.
They don't even cackle and yammer so much anymore.
They just wait patiently in the darkness and whisper to one another in some language that was dead before the dinosaurs.
WHO WANTS TO GO HUNTING?

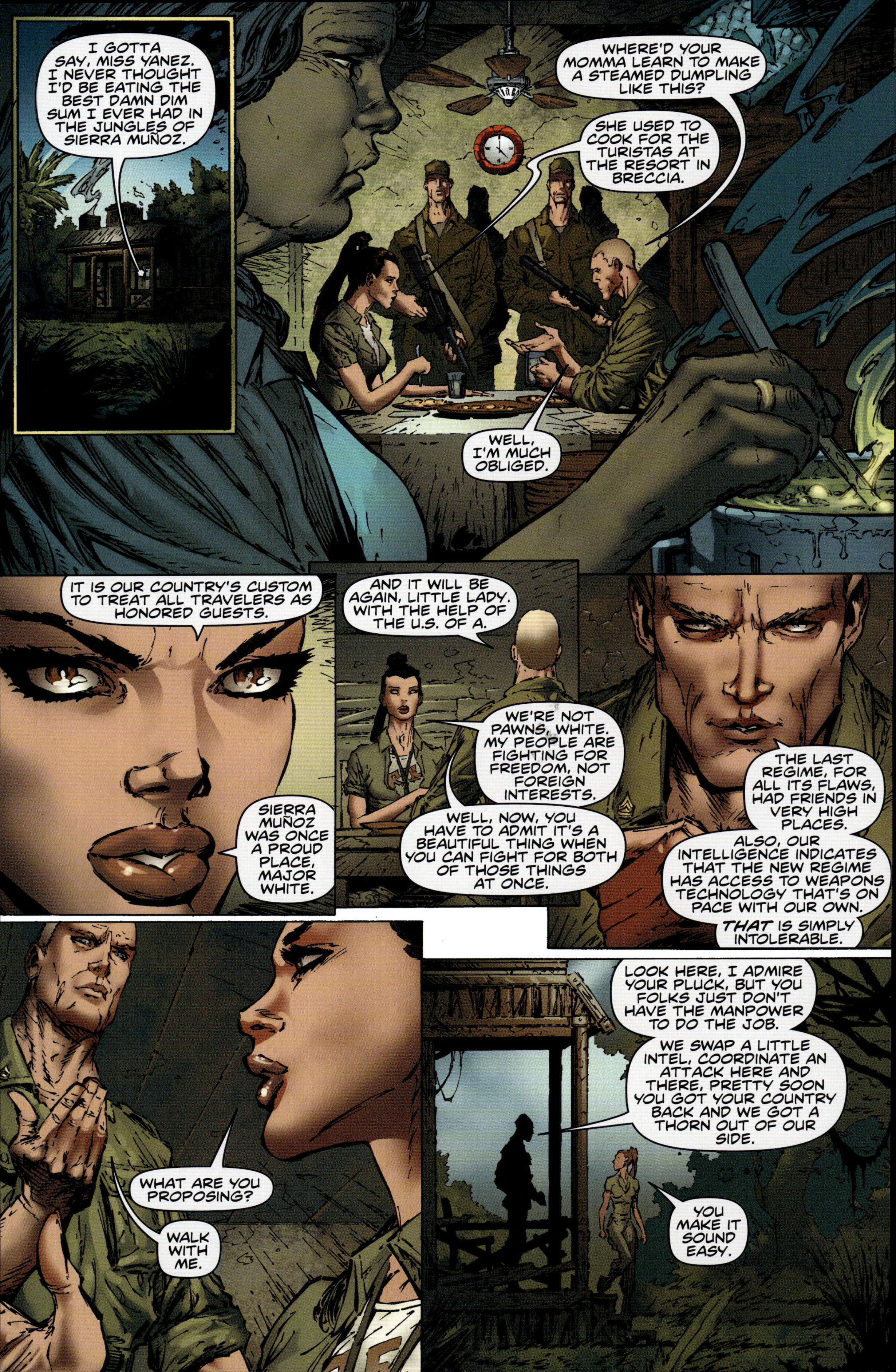

I GOTTA SAY, MISS YANEZ. I NEVER THOUGHT I'D BE EATING THE BEST DAMN DIM SUM I EVER HAD IN THE JUNGLES OF SIERRA MUÑOZ.
WHERE'D YOUR MOMMA LEARN TO MAKE A STEAMED DUMPLING LIKE THIS?
SHE USED TO COOK FOR THE TURISTAS AT THE RESORT IN BRECCIA.
WELL, I'M MUCH OBLIGED.
IT IS OUR COUNTRY'S CUSTOM TO TREAT ALL TRAVELERS AS HONORED GUESTS.
SIERRA MUÑOZ WAS ONCE A PROUD PLACE, MAJOR WHITE.
AND IT WILL BE AGAIN, LITTLE LADY. WITH THE HELP OF THE U.S. OF A.
WE'RE NOT PAWNS, WHITE. MY PEOPLE ARE FIGHTING FOR FREEDOM, NOT FOREIGN INTERESTS.
WELL, NOW, YOU HAVE TO ADMIT IT'S A BEAUTIFUL THING WHEN YOU CAN FIGHT FOR BOTH OF THOSE THINGS AT ONCE.
THE LAST REGIME, FOR ALL ITS FLAWS, HAD FRIENDS IN VERY HIGH PLACES.
ALSO, OUR INTELLIGENCE INDICATES THAT THE NEW REGIME HAS ACCESS TO WEAPONS TECHNOLOGY THAT'S ON PACE WITH OUR OWN. *THAT* IS SIMPLY INTOLERABLE.
WHAT ARE YOU PROPOSING?
WALK WITH ME.
LOOK HERE, I ADMIRE YOUR PLUCK, BUT YOU FOLKS JUST DON'T HAVE THE MANPOWER TO DO THE JOB.
WE SWAP A LITTLE INTEL, COORDINATE AN ATTACK HERE AND THERE, PRETTY SOON YOU GOT YOUR COUNTRY BACK AND WE GOT A THORN OUT OF OUR SIDE.
YOU MAKE IT SOUND EASY.

SINCE THAT NIGHTFALL DRUG SWEPT YOUR LITTLE HOMELAND HALF THE STANDING ARMY IS SO HIGH THEY COULDN'T BENCH PRESS A BROOMSTICK. IT WON'T BE HARD TO KNOCK THE FIGHT OUT OF THEM.

THAT'S NOT WHO YOU SHOULD BE WORRIED ABOUT. IT'S OCASO HIMSELF AND HIS PERSONAL GUARD.

THEY OPERATE OUT OF A SUBTERRANEAN FORTRESS UNDER THE PRESIDENTIAL PALACE THAT'S NEVER BEEN PENETRATED.

THEY STRIKE AT NIGHT AND CAN'T BE SEEN, SOME SAY CAN'T BE KILLED.

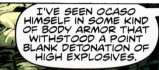

I'VE SEEN OCASO HIMSELF IN SOME KIND OF BODY ARMOR THAT WITHSTOOD A POINT BLANK DETONATION OF HIGH EXPLOSIVES.

AND THAT BODY ARMOR IS EXACTLY WHY WE WANT HIM.

WE COMBINE OUR FORCES IN A DIRECT ASSAULT ON THAT FORTRESS. OUR CREW HELPS YOU KNOCK DOWN THAT ELITE GUARD, TAKE OUT SOME INFRASTRUCTURE.

WE SNATCH OCASO AND WE'RE OFF IN A CLOUD OF DUST WITH A HEARTY "HI-YO, SILVER."

YOU FOLKS SETTLE EVERYTHING ELSE ON YOUR OWN TIME. A FEW MONTHS LATER OUR RICH AND POWERFUL FRIENDS, WELL, THEY COME DOWN AND MAKE FRIENDS WITH WHOEVER IS IN CHARGE.

MYSELF, I'D LIKE THAT TO BE YOU. NOT ENOUGH PRETTY FACES ON CNN THESE DAYS.

ENOUGH. LET'S SAY WE AGREE TO WORK WITH YOU. HOW SOON COULD YOU DEPLOY RESOURCES TO SIERRA MUÑOZ?

MA'AM, WITH ALL DUE RESPECT...

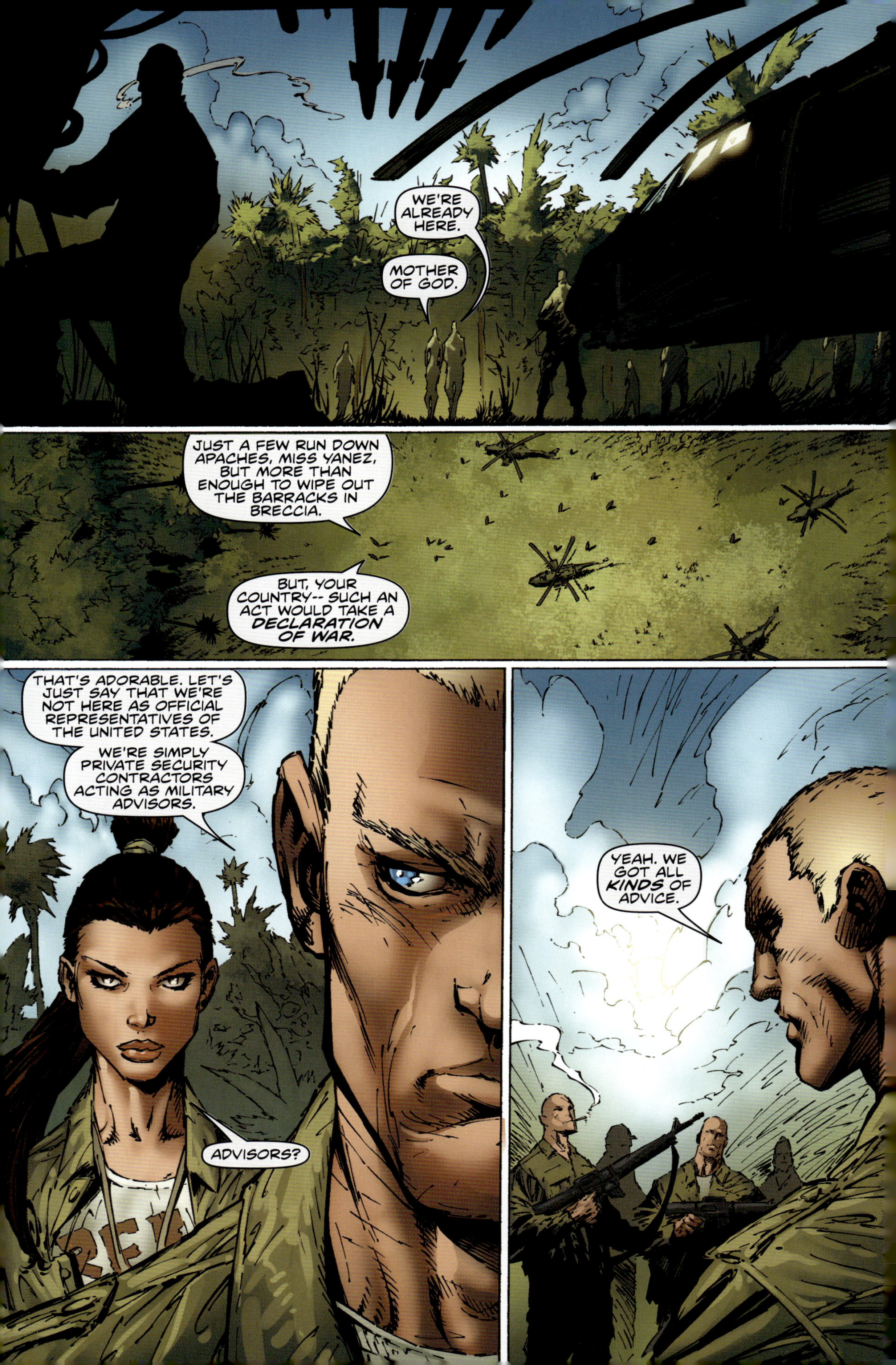
WE'RE ALREADY HERE.
MOTHER OF GOD.
JUST A FEW RUN DOWN APACHES, MISS YANEZ, BUT MORE THAN ENOUGH TO WIPE OUT THE BARRACKS IN BRECCIA.
BUT, YOUR COUNTRY-- SUCH AN ACT WOULD TAKE A *DECLARATION OF WAR.*
THAT'S ADORABLE. LET'S JUST SAY THAT WE'RE NOT HERE AS OFFICIAL REPRESENTATIVES OF THE UNITED STATES.
WE'RE SIMPLY PRIVATE SECURITY CONTRACTORS ACTING AS MILITARY ADVISORS.
ADVISORS?
YEAH. WE GOT ALL *KINDS* OF ADVICE.

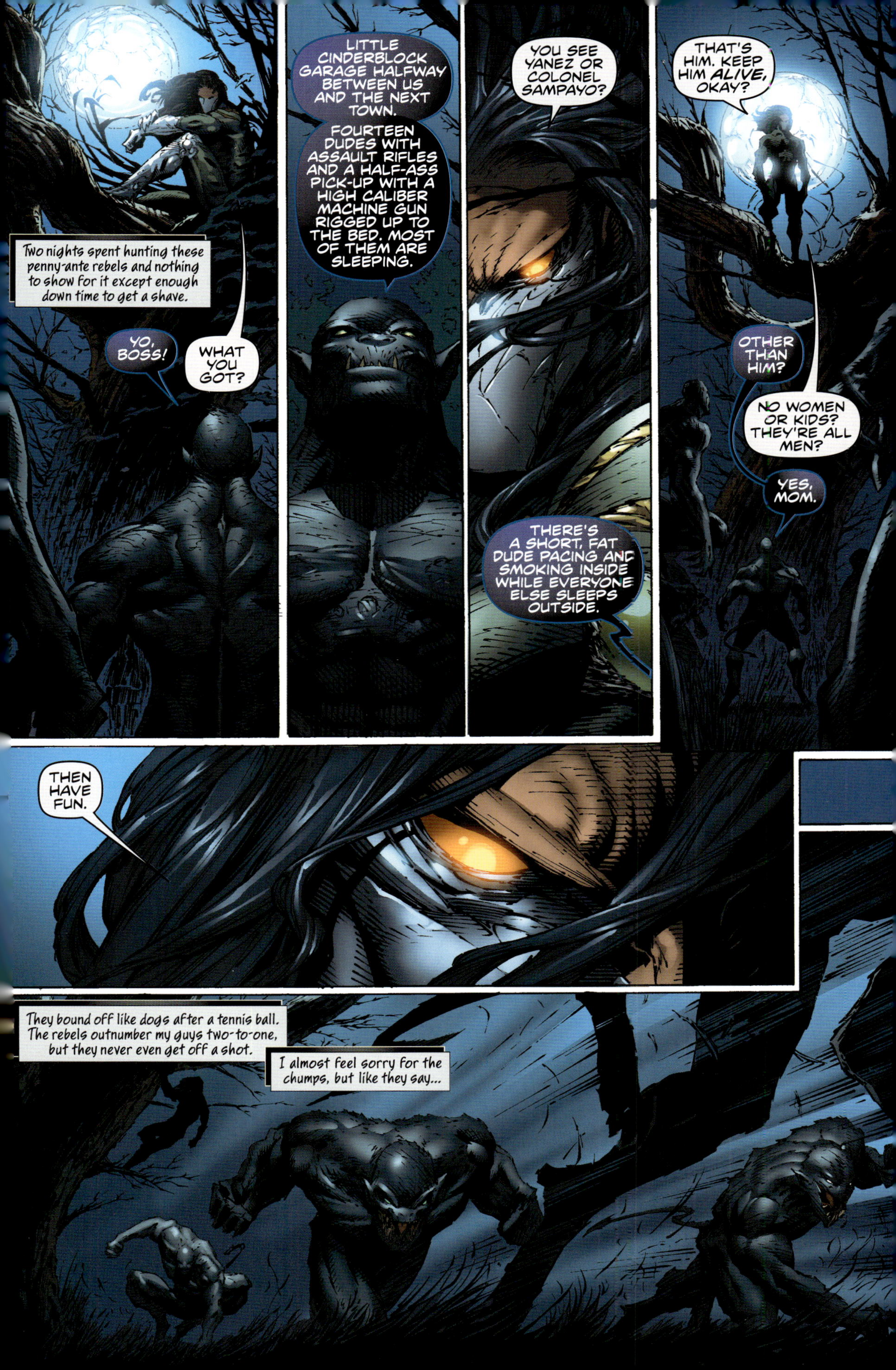
Two nights spent hunting these penny-ante rebels and nothing to show for it except enough down time to get a shave.
YO, BOSS!
WHAT YOU GOT?
LITTLE CINDERBLOCK GARAGE HALFWAY BETWEEN US AND THE NEXT TOWN.
FOURTEEN DUDES WITH ASSAULT RIFLES AND A HALF-ASS PICK-UP WITH A HIGH CALIBER MACHINE GUN RIGGED UP TO THE BED. MOST OF THEM ARE SLEEPING.
YOU SEE YANEZ OR COLONEL SAMPAYO?
THERE'S A SHORT, FAT DUDE PACING AND SMOKING INSIDE WHILE EVERYONE ELSE SLEEPS OUTSIDE.
THAT'S HIM. KEEP HIM ALIVE, OKAY?
OTHER THAN HIM?
NO WOMEN OR KIDS? THEY'RE ALL MEN?
YES, MOM.
THEN HAVE FUN.
They bound off like dogs after a tennis ball. The rebels outnumber my guys two-to-one, but they never even get off a shot.
I almost feel sorry for the chumps, but like they say...

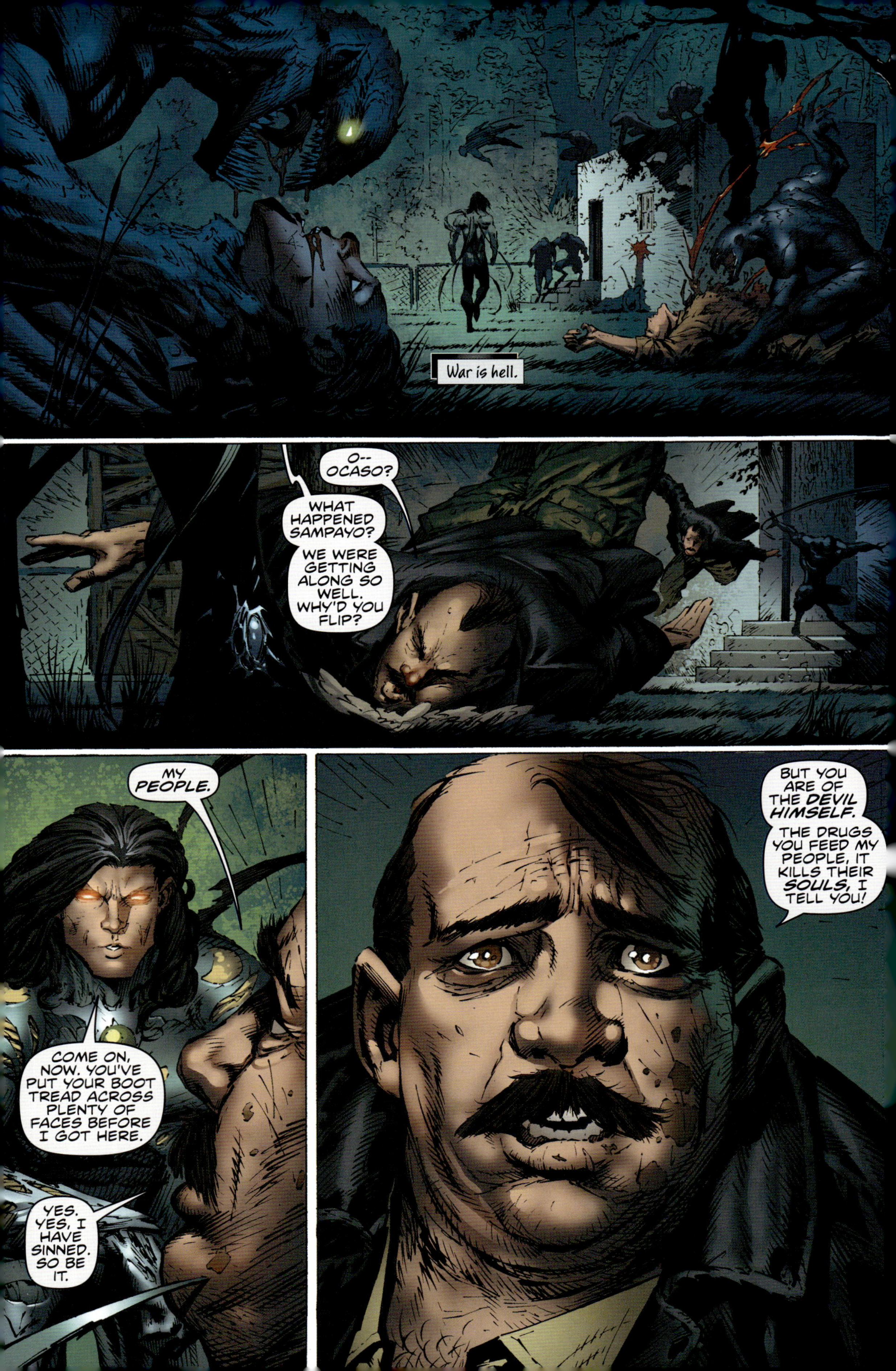
War is hell.
O-- OCASO?
WHAT HAPPENED SAMPAYO?
WE WERE GETTING ALONG SO WELL. WHY'D YOU FLIP?
MY PEOPLE.
COME ON, NOW. YOU'VE PUT YOUR BOOT TREAD ACROSS PLENTY OF FACES BEFORE I GOT HERE.
YES. YES, I HAVE SINNED. SO BE IT.
BUT YOU ARE OF THE DEVIL HIMSELF.
THE DRUGS YOU FEED MY PEOPLE, IT KILLS THEIR SOULS, I TELL YOU!

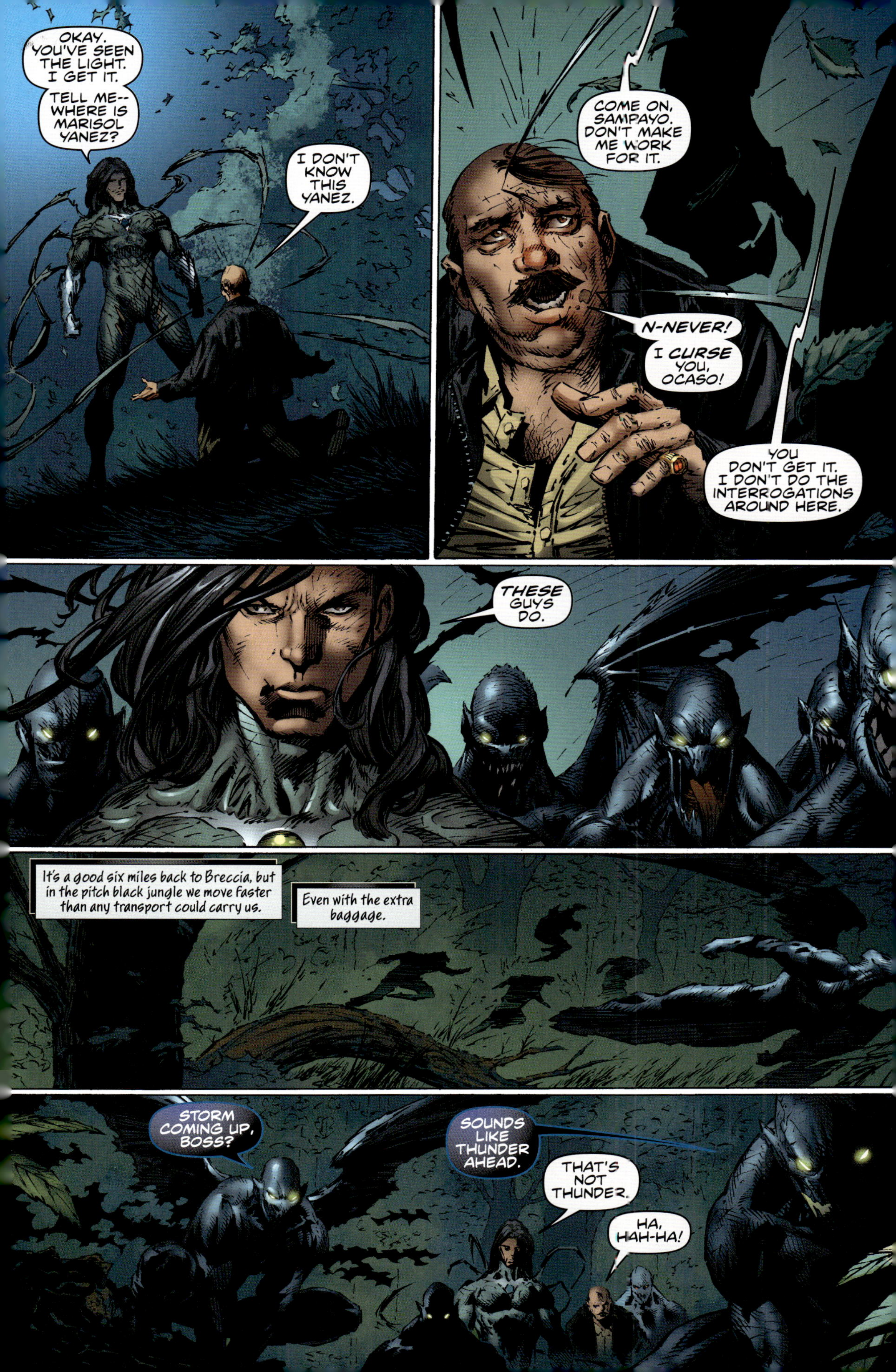

OKAY. YOU'VE SEEN THE LIGHT. I GET IT.
TELL ME-- WHERE IS MARISOL YANEZ?
I DON'T KNOW THIS YANEZ.
COME ON, SAMPAYO. DON'T MAKE ME WORK FOR IT.
N-NEVER!
I CURSE YOU, OCASO!
YOU DON'T GET IT. I DON'T DO THE INTERROGATIONS AROUND HERE.
THESE GUYS DO.
It's a good six miles back to Breccia, but in the pitch black jungle we move faster than any transport could carry us.
Even with the extra baggage.
STORM COMING UP, BOSS?
SOUNDS LIKE THUNDER AHEAD.
THAT'S NOT THUNDER.
HA, HAH-HA!

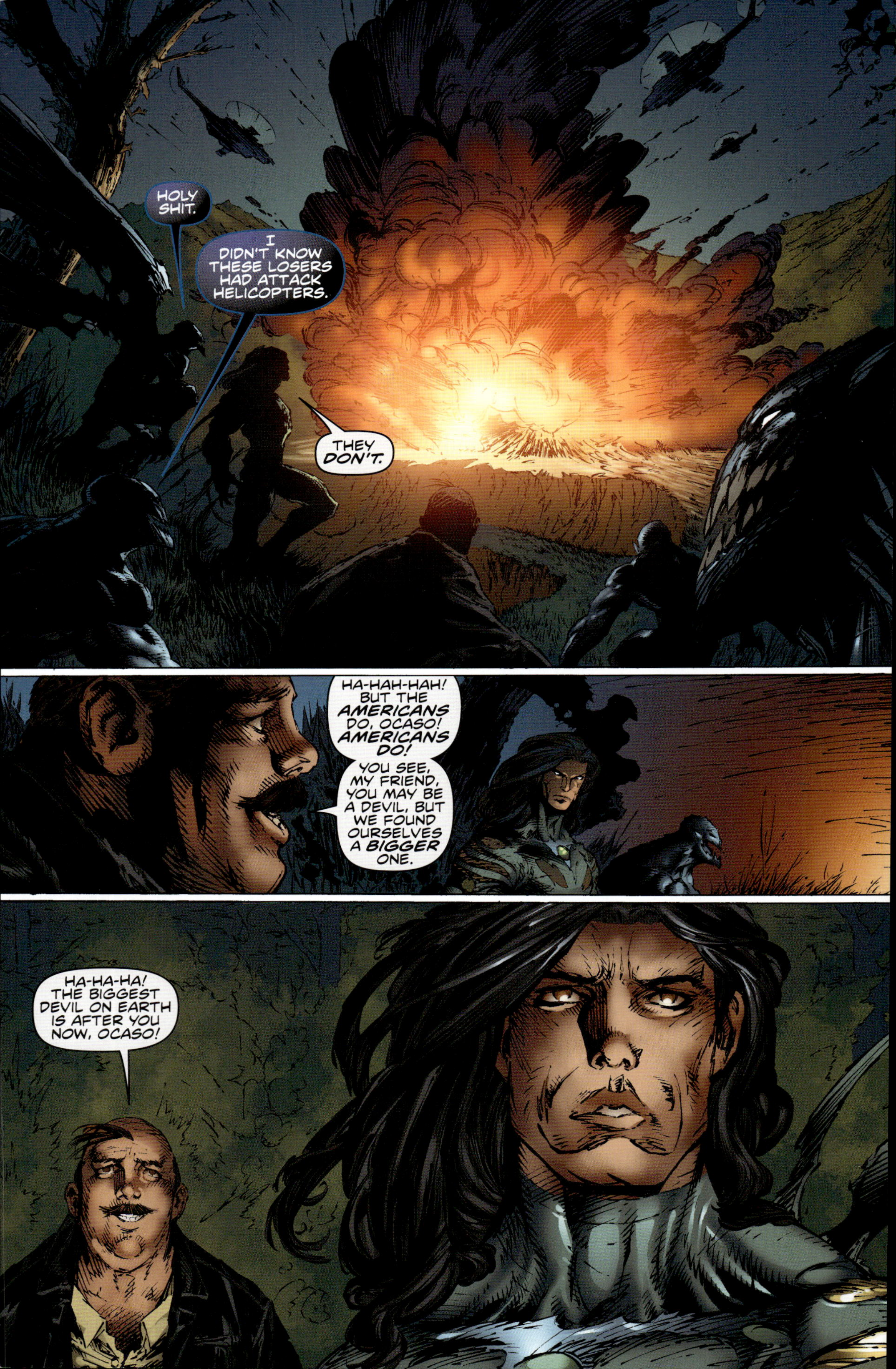
HOLY SHIT.
I DIDN'T KNOW THESE LOSERS HAD ATTACK HELICOPTERS.
THEY DON'T.
HA-HAH-HAH! BUT THE AMERICANS DO, OCASO! AMERICANS DO!
YOU SEE, MY FRIEND, YOU MAY BE A DEVIL, BUT WE FOUND OURSELVES A BIGGER ONE.
HA-HA-HA! THE BIGGEST DEVIL ON EARTH IS AFTER YOU NOW, OCASO!

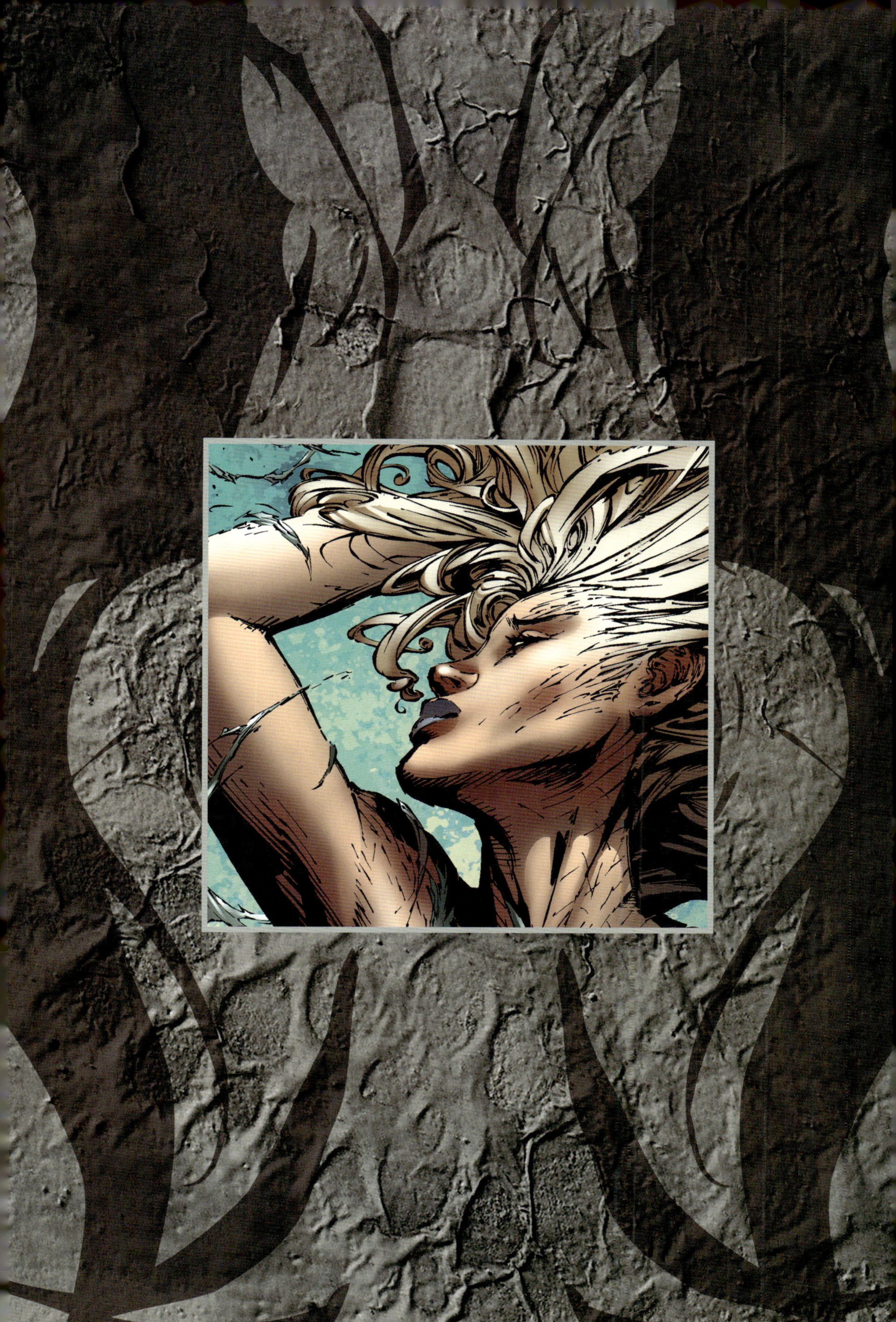

The Darkness Issue #67
cover art by: Dale Keown

THE DARKNESS #67

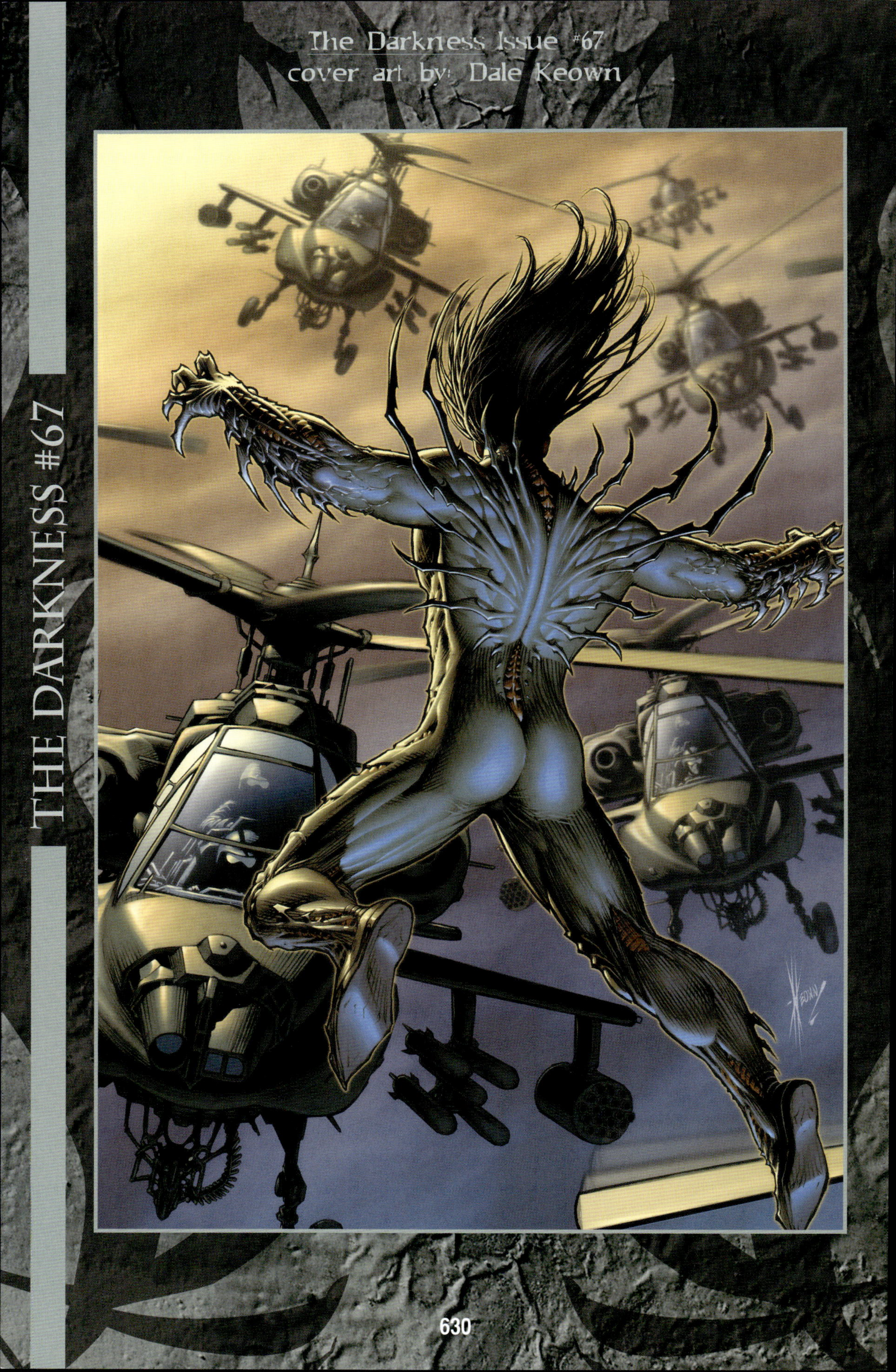

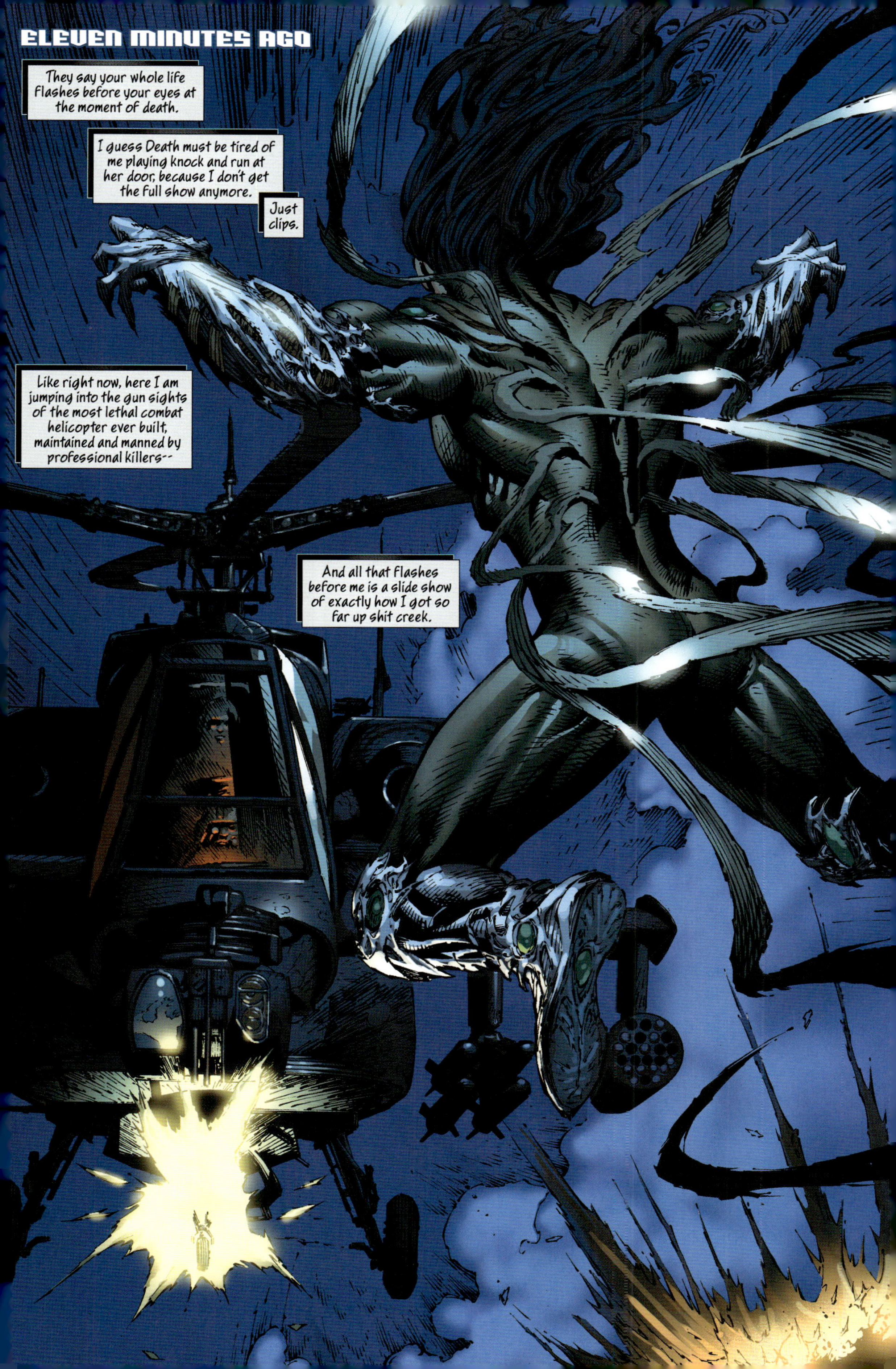
ELEVEN MINUTES AGO
They say your whole life flashes before your eyes at the moment of death.
I guess Death must be tired of me playing knock and run at her door, because I don't get the full show anymore.
Just clips.
Like right now, here I am jumping into the gun sights of the most lethal combat helicopter ever built, maintained and manned by professional killers--
And all that flashes before me is a slide show of exactly how I got so far up shit creek.

HELP ME OUT HERE.

EXACTLY WHY AM I KILLING YOU AGAIN?

BLUE JAYS.

AH, RIGHT, THE TORONTO BLUE JAYS.

SORRY, DOC. NO ONE'S SMART ENOUGH TO BET BASEBALL, NOT EVEN ROCKET SCIENTISTS.

CHEMICAL ENGINEER. I'M A CHEMICAL ENGINEER, NOT A ROCKET SCIENTIST. NOT THAT IT MATTERS.

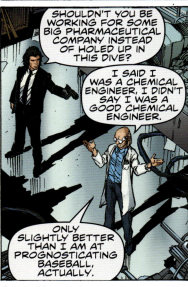

SHOULDN'T YOU BE WORKING FOR SOME BIG PHARMACEUTICAL COMPANY INSTEAD OF HOLED UP IN THIS DIVE?

I SAID I WAS A CHEMICAL ENGINEER, I DIDN'T SAY I WAS A GOOD CHEMICAL ENGINEER.

ONLY SLIGHTLY BETTER THAN I AM AT PROGNOSTICATING BASEBALL, ACTUALLY.

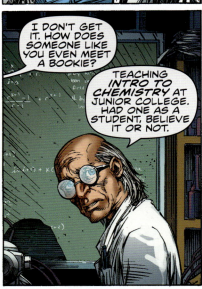

I DON'T GET IT. HOW DOES SOMEONE LIKE YOU EVEN MEET A BOOKIE?

TEACHING INTRO TO CHEMISTRY AT JUNIOR COLLEGE. HAD ONE AS A STUDENT, BELIEVE IT OR NOT.

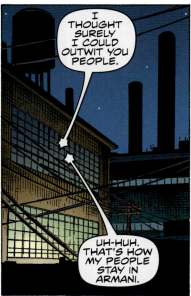

I THOUGHT SURELY I COULD OUTWIT YOU PEOPLE.

UH-HUH. THAT'S HOW MY PEOPLE STAY IN ARMANI.

TRUE. I ACTUALLY HAD SUCCESS IN MY FIRST SEASON BETTING FOOTBALL, BUT BASEBALL WAS MY UNDOING. I ACCRUED MASSIVE, UNRECOVERABLE DEBT WITH YOUR EMPLOYERS.
AND HERE YOU ARE.

THAT'S THE PART THAT DOESN'T ADD UP. I'M NOT EXACTLY CHEAP.
THE FAMILY DOESN'T SEND ME OUT FOR RUN-OF-THE-MILL DEADBEATS. IT'S LIKE TAKING A LAMBORGHINI TO WAL-MART FOR RAMEN NOODLES.

NO OFFENSE, BUT THERE'S GOTTA BE MORE TO THIS.

YOU'RE IN CHARGE HERE. CAN I TELL YOU WHILE I GET MY THINGS IN ORDER?

I'D LIKE MY DAUGHTER TO FIND THE PLACE IN A REASONABLE STATE ONCE I'M, WELL... YOU KNOW.

NOT LIKE YOU'RE GOING ANYWHERE.

ONCE MY DEBT BECAME UNMANAGEABLE I TRIED TO BARTER MY WAY OUT OF TROUBLE.

BARTER? WITH WHAT?

MY SKILLS AS A SCIENTIST. I PROMISED YOUR EMPLOYERS UNTRACEABLE EXPLOSIVES, CHEAP METHODS OF CONVERTING STANDARD COMMERCIAL AMMUNITION INTO ARMOR PIERCING ROUNDS, THAT SORT OF THING.

I PARLAYED THIS TASK INTO MONTHS OF GRACE, AND I DID WORK HARD TO LIVE UP TO MY PROMISES, BUT MY CREDITORS SOON WANTED TANGIBLE RESULTS.

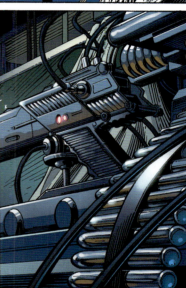

LET ME GUESS, YOU DIDN'T HAVE ANY.

NO. NO, I DIDN'T.

THAT IS, NOT UNTIL JUST RECENTLY.

BLANG

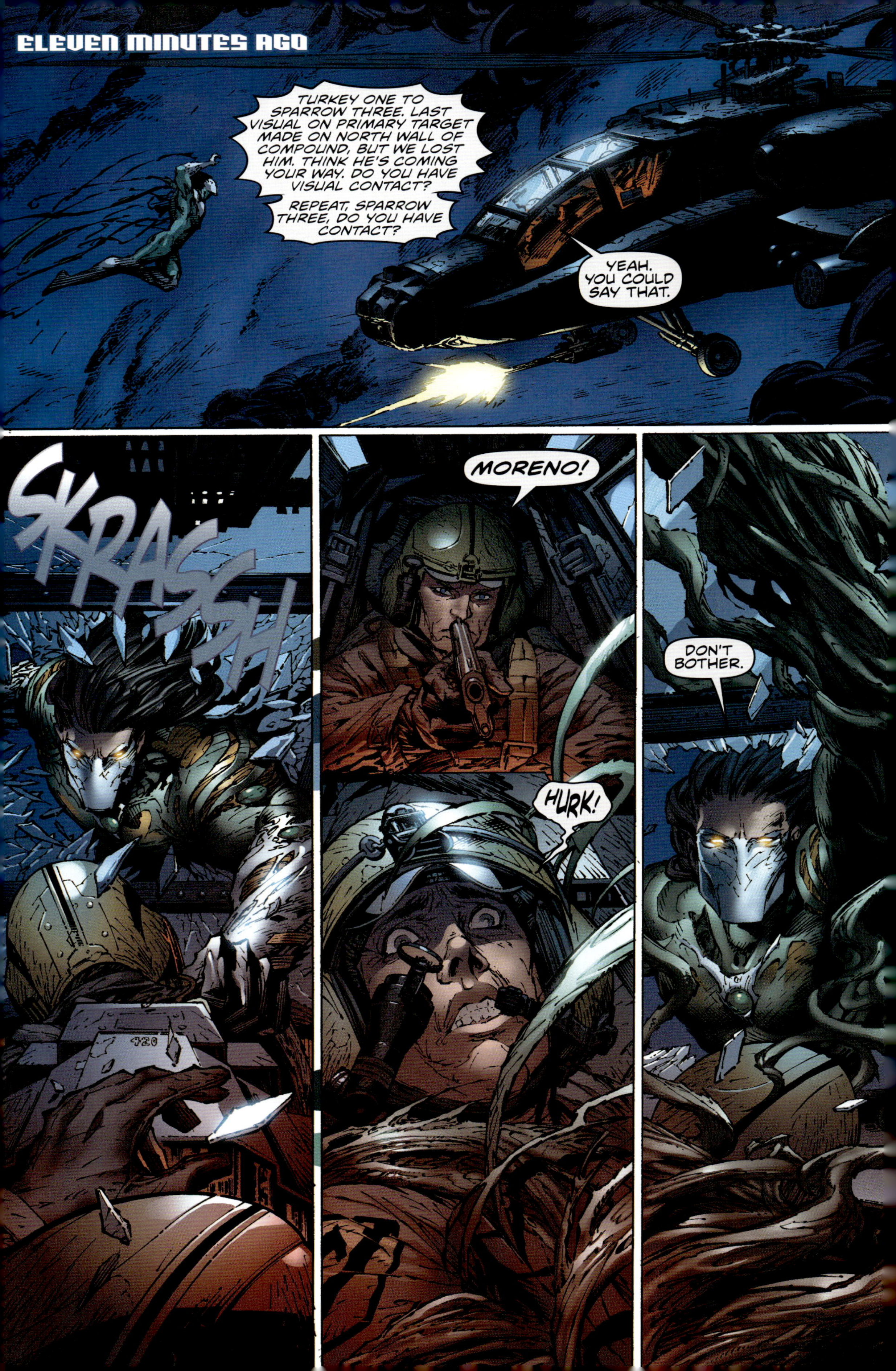
ELEVEN MINUTES AGO
TURKEY ONE TO SPARROW THREE. LAST VISUAL ON PRIMARY TARGET MADE ON NORTH WALL OF COMPOUND, BUT WE LOST HIM. THINK HE'S COMING YOUR WAY. DO YOU HAVE VISUAL CONTACT?
REPEAT, SPARROW THREE, DO YOU HAVE CONTACT?
YEAH. YOU COULD SAY THAT.
SKRASSH
420
MORENO!
HURK!
DON'T BOTHER.

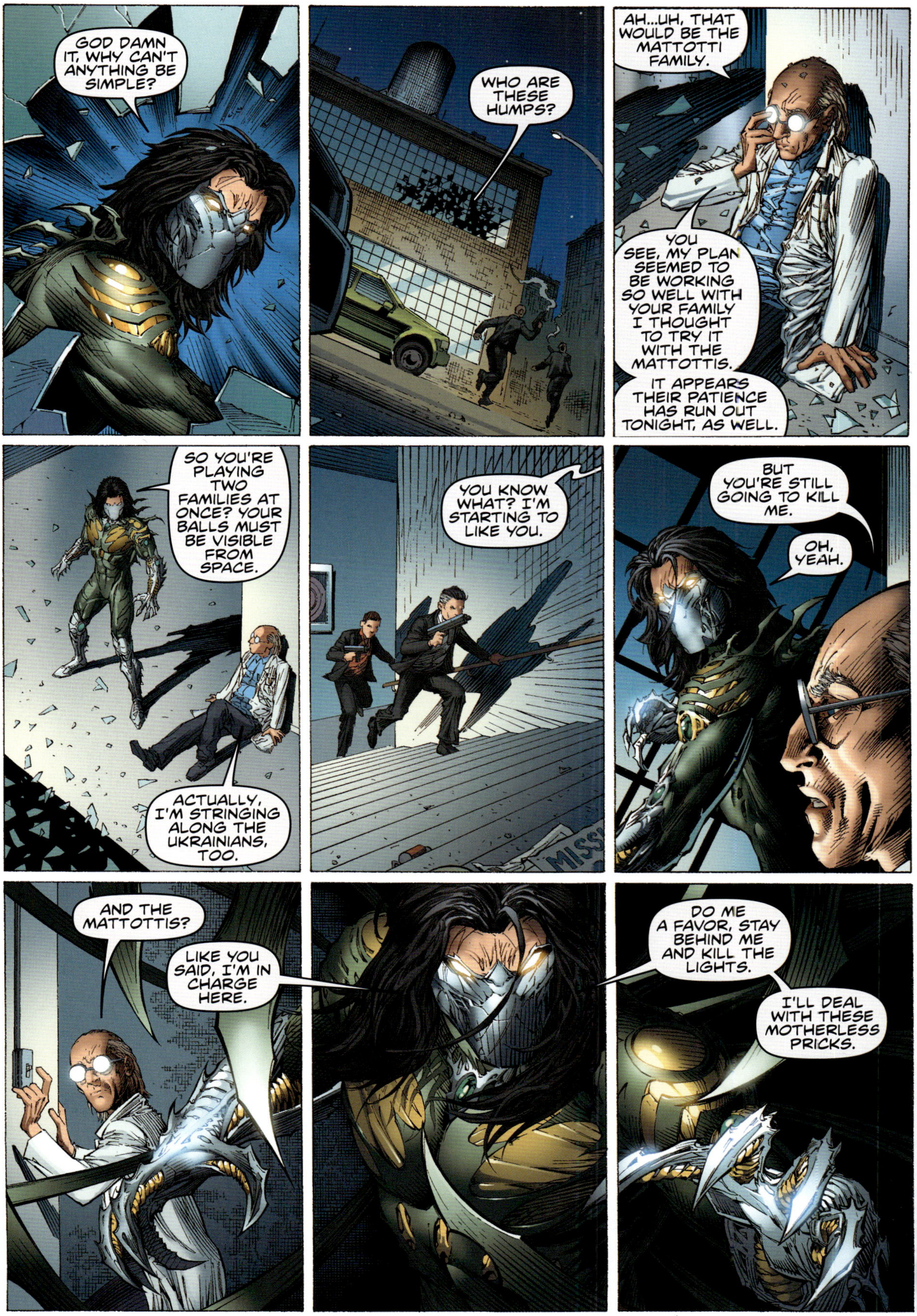
GOD DAMN IT, WHY CAN'T ANYTHING BE SIMPLE?
WHO ARE THESE HUMPS?
AH...UH, THAT WOULD BE THE MATTOTTI FAMILY.
YOU SEE, MY PLAN SEEMED TO BE WORKING SO WELL WITH YOUR FAMILY I THOUGHT TO TRY IT WITH THE MATTOTTIS.
IT APPEARS THEIR PATIENCE HAS RUN OUT TONIGHT, AS WELL.
SO YOU'RE PLAYING TWO FAMILIES AT ONCE? YOUR BALLS MUST BE VISIBLE FROM SPACE.
ACTUALLY, I'M STRINGING ALONG THE UKRAINIANS, TOO.
YOU KNOW WHAT? I'M STARTING TO LIKE YOU.
BUT YOU'RE STILL GOING TO KILL ME.
OH, YEAH.
AND THE MATTOTTIS?
LIKE YOU SAID, I'M IN CHARGE HERE.
DO ME A FAVOR, STAY BEHIND ME AND KILL THE LIGHTS.
I'LL DEAL WITH THESE MOTHERLESS PRICKS.

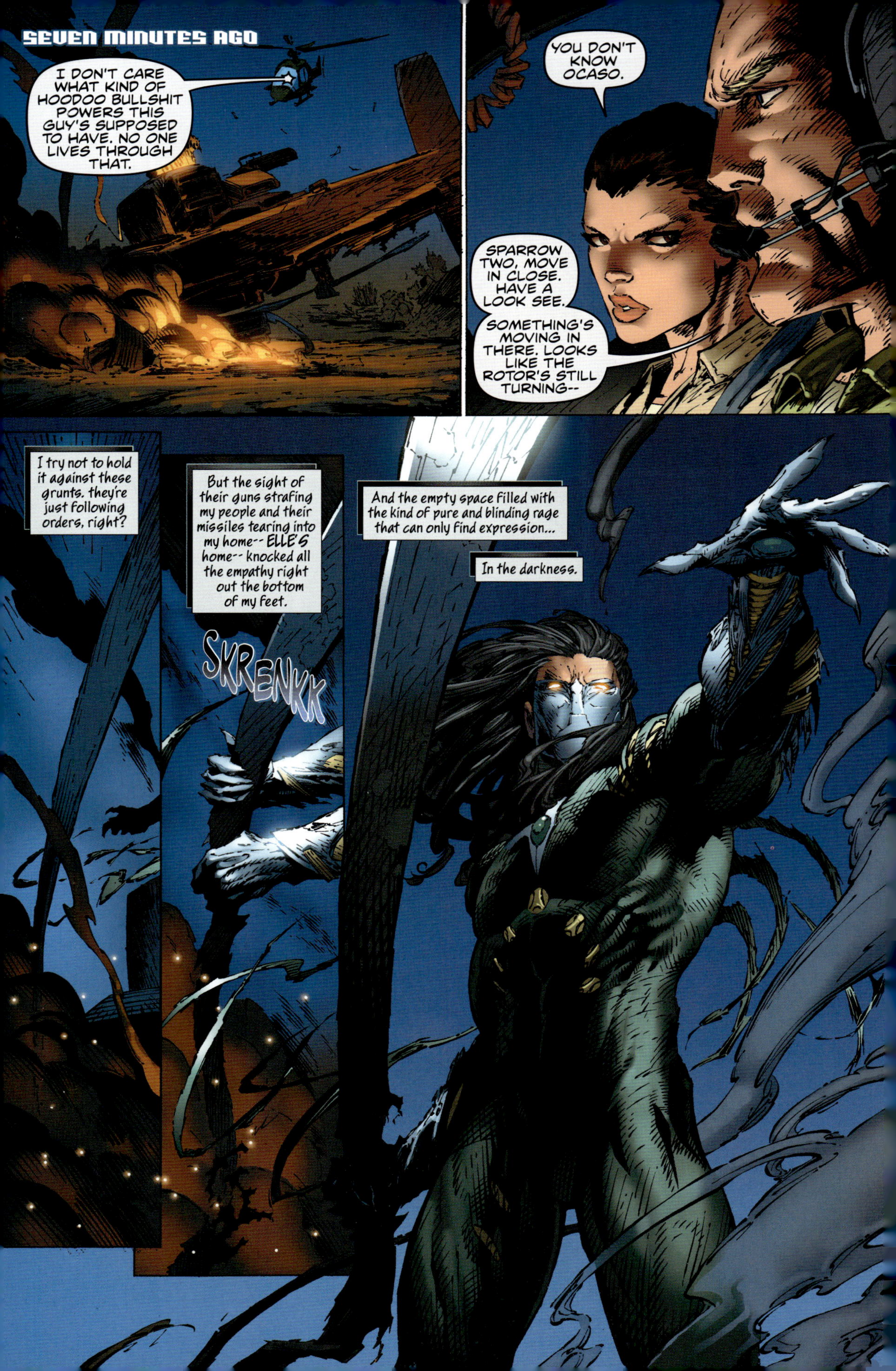
SEVEN MINUTES AGO
I DON'T CARE WHAT KIND OF HOODOO BULLSHIT POWERS THIS GUY'S SUPPOSED TO HAVE. NO ONE LIVES THROUGH THAT.
YOU DON'T KNOW OCASO.
SPARROW TWO, MOVE IN CLOSE. HAVE A LOOK SEE.
SOMETHING'S MOVING IN THERE. LOOKS LIKE THE ROTOR'S STILL TURNING--
I try not to hold it against these grunts. they're just following orders, right?
But the sight of their guns strafing my people and their missiles tearing into my home-- ELLE'S home-- knocked all the empathy right out the bottom of my feet.
SKRENKK
And the empty space filled with the kind of pure and blinding rage that can only find expression...
In the darkness.

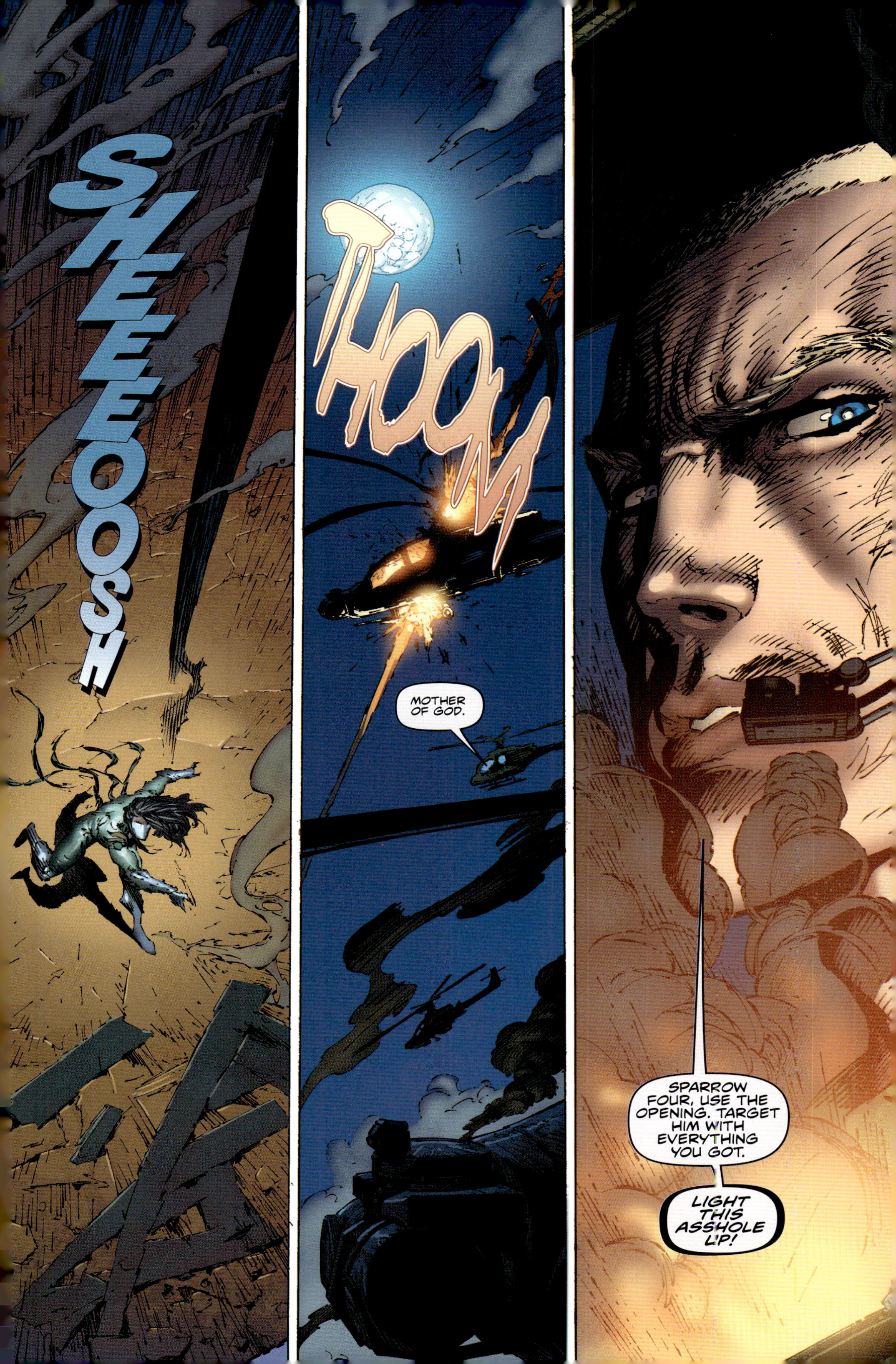
SHEEEOOSH
THOOM
MOTHER OF GOD.
SPARROW FOUR, USE THE OPENING. TARGET HIM WITH EVERYTHING YOU GOT.
LIGHT THIS ASSHOLE UP!

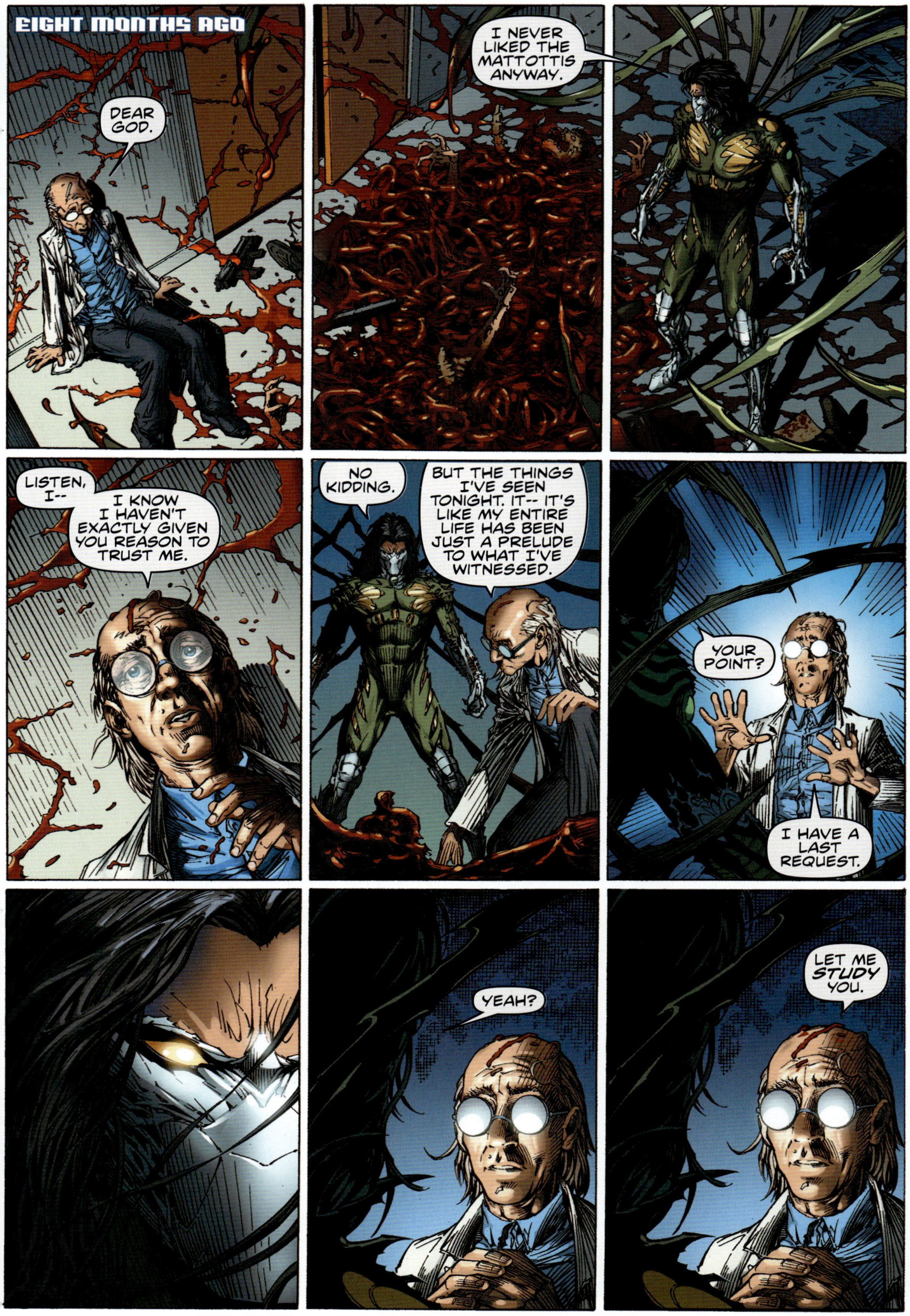
EIGHT MONTHS AGO
DEAR GOD.
I NEVER LIKED THE MATTOTTIS ANYWAY.
LISTEN, I--
I KNOW I HAVEN'T EXACTLY GIVEN YOU REASON TO TRUST ME.
NO KIDDING.
BUT THE THINGS I'VE SEEN TONIGHT. IT-- IT'S LIKE MY ENTIRE LIFE HAS BEEN JUST A PRELUDE TO WHAT I'VE WITNESSED.
YOUR POINT?
I HAVE A LAST REQUEST.
YEAH?
LET ME STUDY YOU.

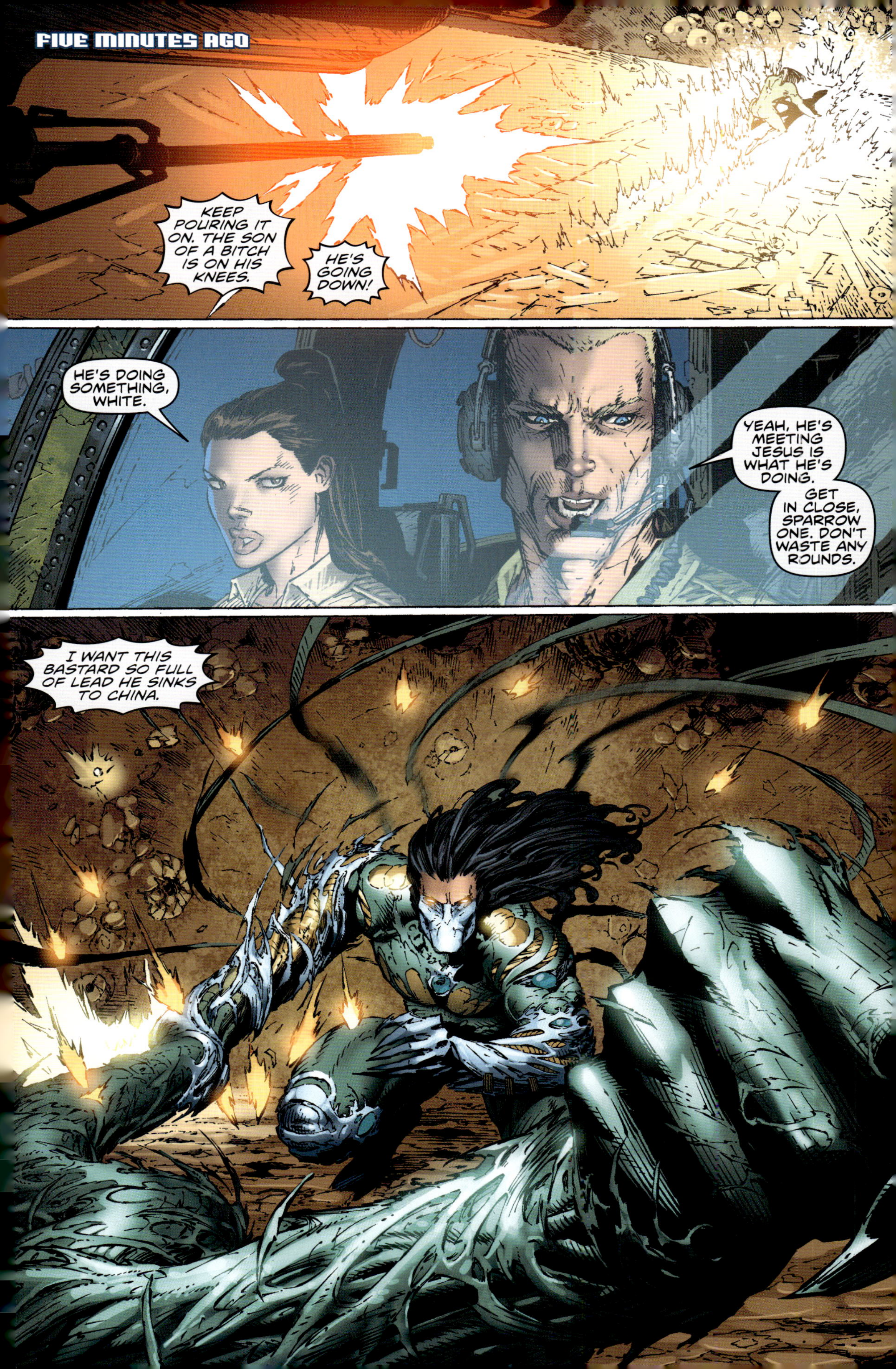
FIVE MINUTES AGO
KEEP POURING IT ON. THE SON OF A BITCH IS ON HIS KNEES.
HE'S GOING DOWN!
HE'S DOING SOMETHING, WHITE.
YEAH, HE'S MEETING JESUS IS WHAT HE'S DOING.
GET IN CLOSE, SPARROW ONE. DON'T WASTE ANY ROUNDS.
I WANT THIS BASTARD SO FULL OF LEAD HE SINKS TO CHINA.

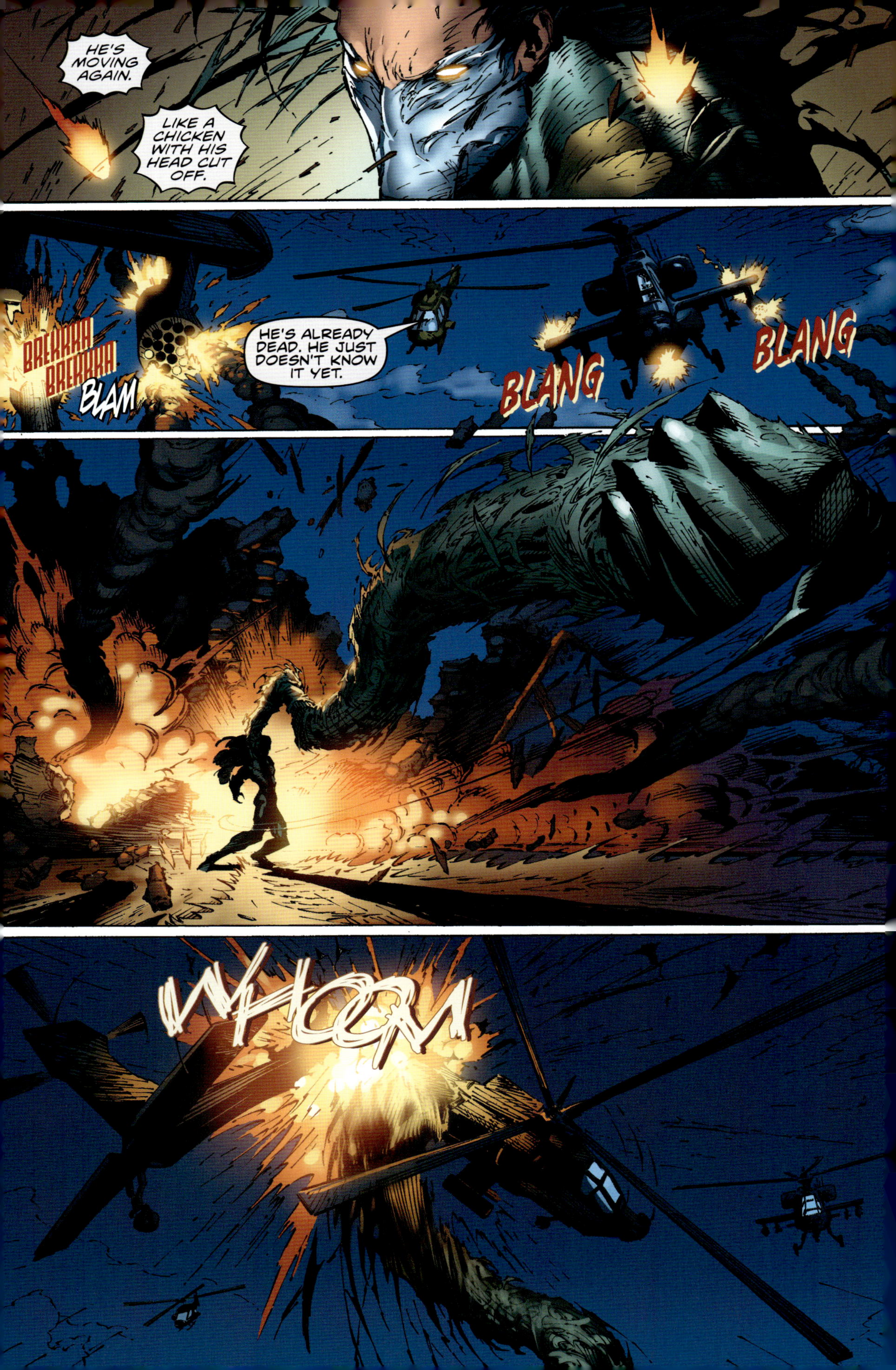
HE'S MOVING AGAIN.
LIKE A CHICKEN WITH HIS HEAD CUT OFF.
BREKKKA BREKKKA
BLAM
HE'S ALREADY DEAD. HE JUST DOESN'T KNOW IT YET.
BLANG
BLANG
WHOOM

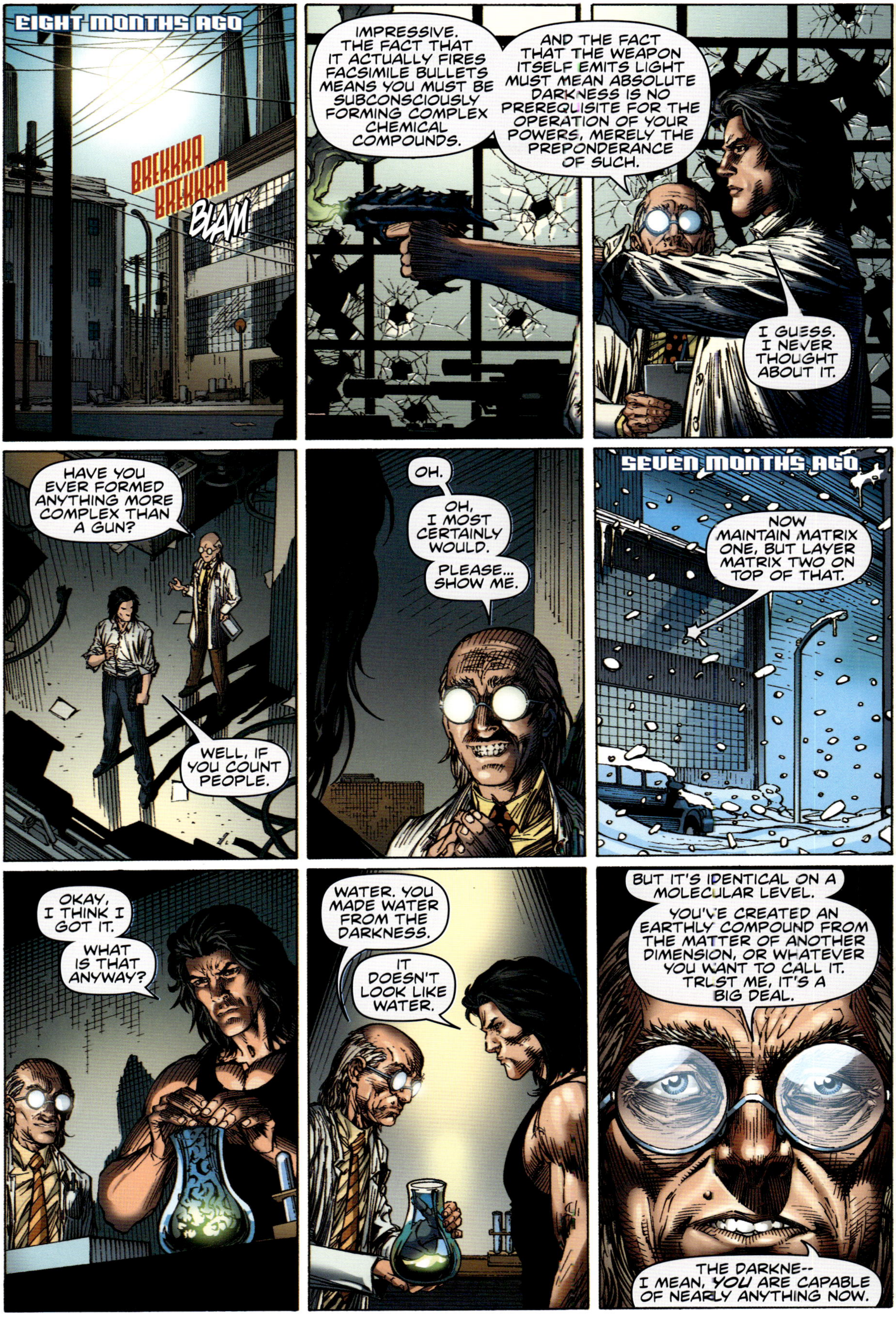
EIGHT MONTHS AGO
BREKKKA BREKKKA
BLAM
IMPRESSIVE. THE FACT THAT IT ACTUALLY FIRES FACSIMILE BULLETS MEANS YOU MUST BE SUBCONSCIOUSLY FORMING COMPLEX CHEMICAL COMPOUNDS.
AND THE FACT THAT THE WEAPON ITSELF EMITS LIGHT MUST MEAN ABSOLUTE DARKNESS IS NO PREREQUISITE FOR THE OPERATION OF YOUR POWERS, MERELY THE PREPONDERANCE OF SUCH.
I GUESS. I NEVER THOUGHT ABOUT IT.
HAVE YOU EVER FORMED ANYTHING MORE COMPLEX THAN A GUN?
WELL, IF YOU COUNT PEOPLE.
OH.
OH, I MOST CERTAINLY WOULD.
PLEASE... SHOW ME.
SEVEN MONTHS AGO
NOW MAINTAIN MATRIX ONE, BUT LAYER MATRIX TWO ON TOP OF THAT.
OKAY, I THINK I GOT IT.
WHAT IS THAT ANYWAY?
WATER. YOU MADE WATER FROM THE DARKNESS.
IT DOESN'T LOOK LIKE WATER.
BUT IT'S IDENTICAL ON A MOLECULAR LEVEL.
YOU'VE CREATED AN EARTHLY COMPOUND FROM THE MATTER OF ANOTHER DIMENSION, OR WHATEVER YOU WANT TO CALL IT. TRUST ME, IT'S A BIG DEAL.
THE DARKNE-- I MEAN, YOU ARE CAPABLE OF NEARLY ANYTHING NOW.

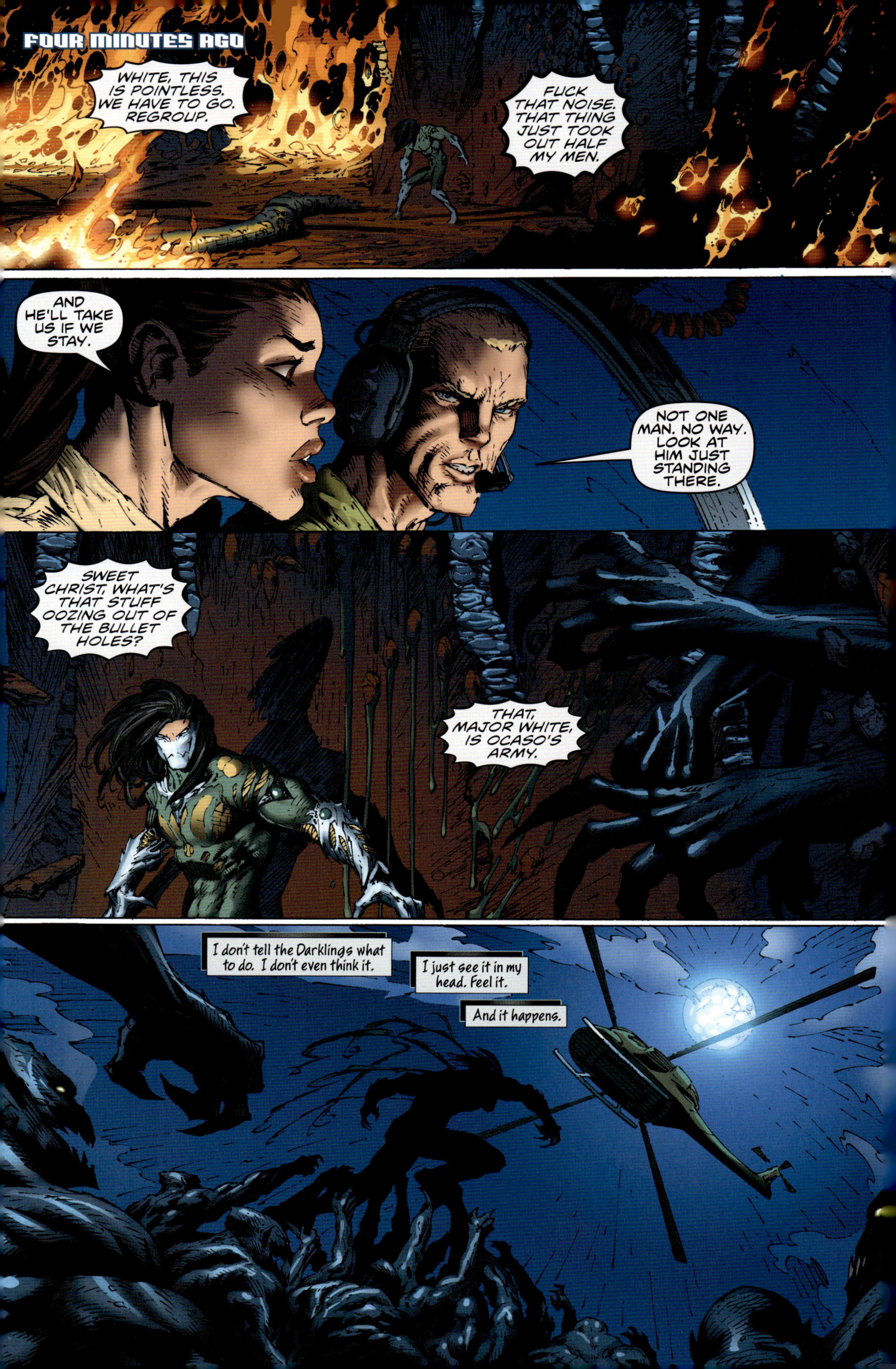
FOUR MINUTES AGO
WHITE, THIS IS POINTLESS. WE HAVE TO GO. REGROUP.
FUCK THAT NOISE. THAT THING JUST TOOK OUT HALF MY MEN.
AND HE'LL TAKE US IF WE STAY.
NOT ONE MAN. NO WAY. LOOK AT HIM JUST STANDING THERE.
SWEET CHRIST, WHAT'S THAT STUFF OOZING OUT OF THE BULLET HOLES?
THAT, MAJOR WHITE, IS OCASO'S ARMY.
I don't tell the Darklings what to do. I don't even think it.
I just see it in my head. Feel it.
And it happens.

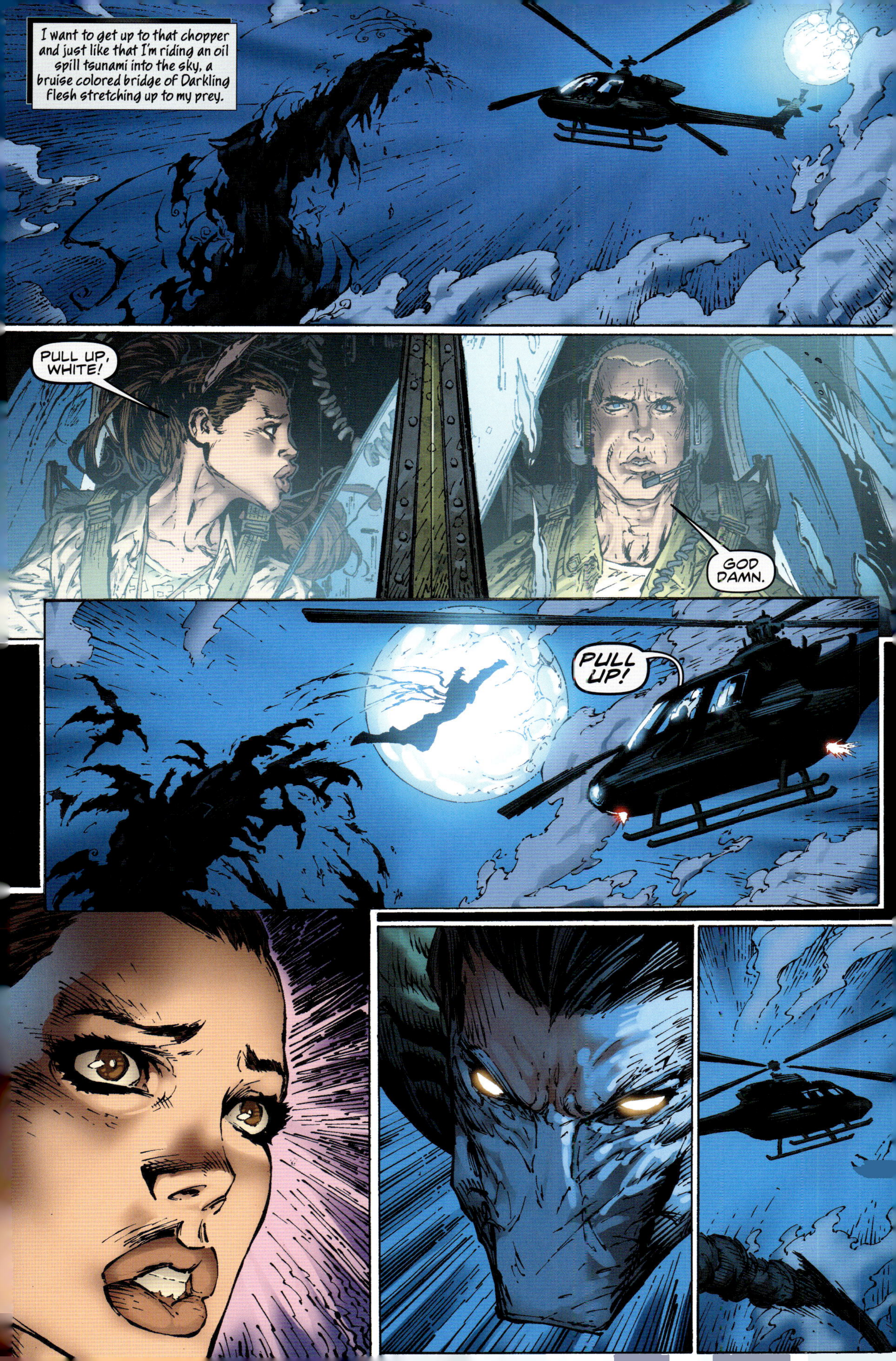
I want to get up to that chopper and just like that I'm riding an oil spill tsunami into the sky, a bruise colored bridge of Darkling flesh stretching up to my prey.
PULL UP, WHITE!
GOD DAMN.
PULL UP!

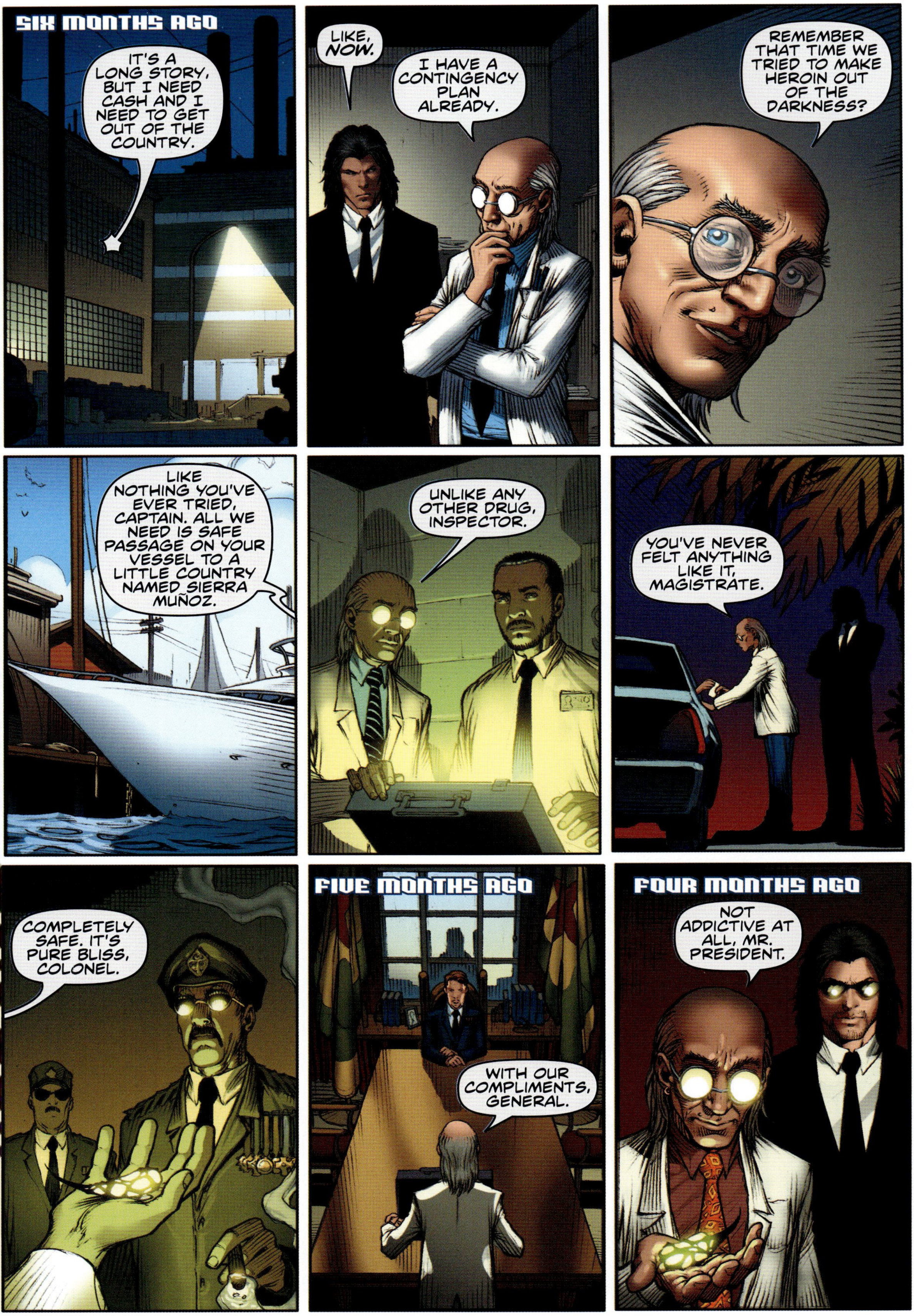
SIX MONTHS AGO
IT'S A LONG STORY, BUT I NEED CASH AND I NEED TO GET OUT OF THE COUNTRY.
LIKE, NOW.
I HAVE A CONTINGENCY PLAN ALREADY.
REMEMBER THAT TIME WE TRIED TO MAKE HEROIN OUT OF THE DARKNESS?
LIKE NOTHING YOU'VE EVER TRIED, CAPTAIN. ALL WE NEED IS SAFE PASSAGE ON YOUR VESSEL TO A LITTLE COUNTRY NAMED SIERRA MUÑOZ.
UNLIKE ANY OTHER DRUG, INSPECTOR.
YOU'VE NEVER FELT ANYTHING LIKE IT, MAGISTRATE.
COMPLETELY SAFE. IT'S PURE BLISS, COLONEL.
FIVE MONTHS AGO
WITH OUR COMPLIMENTS, GENERAL.
FOUR MONTHS AGO
NOT ADDICTIVE AT ALL, MR. PRESIDENT.

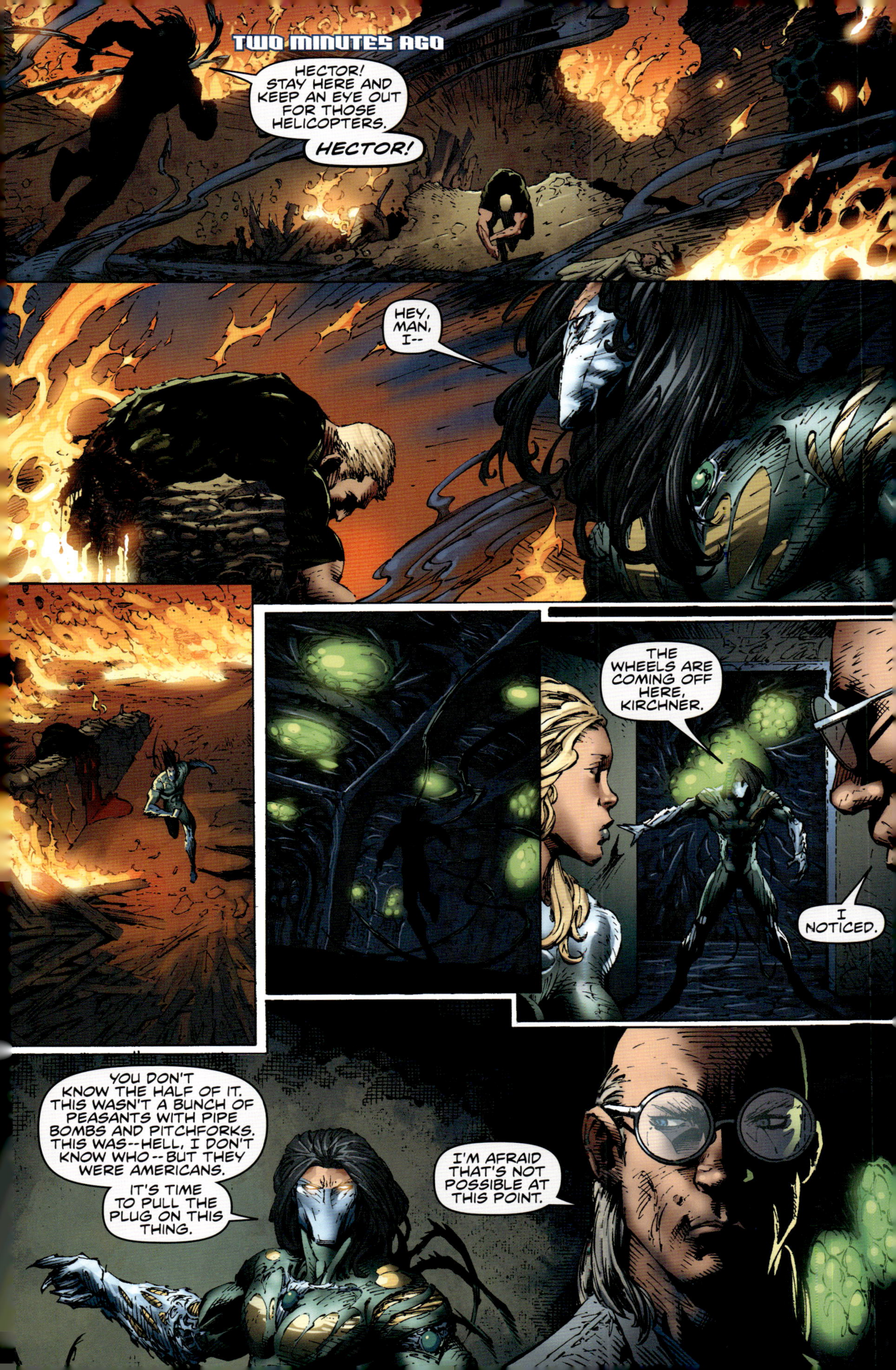
TWO MINUTES AGO
HECTOR! STAY HERE AND KEEP AN EYE OUT FOR THOSE HELICOPTERS.
HECTOR!
HEY, MAN, I--
THE WHEELS ARE COMING OFF HERE, KIRCHNER.
I NOTICED.
YOU DON'T KNOW THE HALF OF IT. THIS WASN'T A BUNCH OF PEASANTS WITH PIPE BOMBS AND PITCHFORKS. THIS WAS--HELL, I DON'T KNOW WHO--BUT THEY WERE AMERICANS.
IT'S TIME TO PULL THE PLUG ON THIS THING.
I'M AFRAID THAT'S NOT POSSIBLE AT THIS POINT.

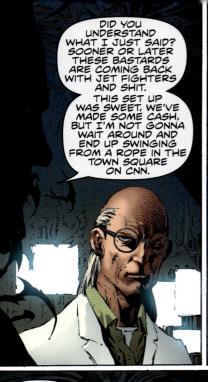

DID YOU UNDERSTAND WHAT I JUST SAID? SOONER OR LATER THESE BASTARDS ARE COMING BACK WITH JET FIGHTERS AND SHIT.

THIS SET UP WAS SWEET, WE'VE MADE SOME CASH, BUT I'M NOT GONNA WAIT AROUND AND END UP SWINGING FROM A ROPE IN THE TOWN SQUARE ON CNN.

WE CAN'T MOVE ELLE RIGHT NOW.

WE'LL WORK SOMETHING OUT, DOC. PUT HER IN ONE OF THE NIGHTFALL CONTAINERS OR SOMETHING.

YOU DON'T UNDERSTAND. ELLE AND I ARE WORKING ON A SPECIAL PROJECT AND WE'RE AT A CRITICAL JUNCTURE--

WHOA, WHOA. I DON'T CARE ABOUT YOUR EXPERIMENT. THIS IS OVER.

LET'S. GO.

NO.

ENOUGH.

COME ON, ELLE. KIRCHNER CAN HANDLE HIMSELF.

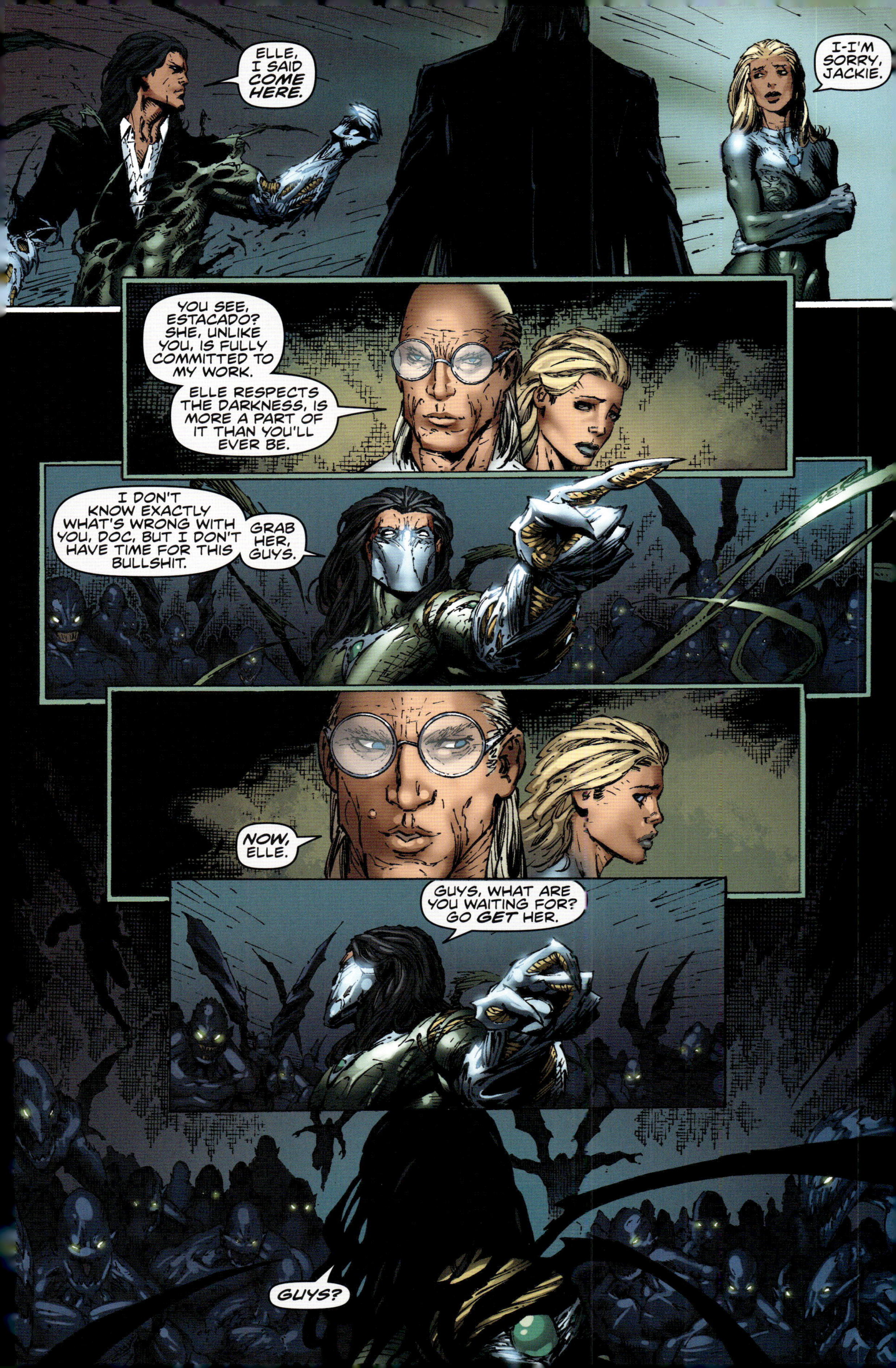
ELLE, I SAID COME HERE.
I-I'M SORRY, JACKIE.
YOU SEE, ESTACADO? SHE, UNLIKE YOU, IS FULLY COMMITTED TO MY WORK.
ELLE RESPECTS THE DARKNESS, IS MORE A PART OF IT THAN YOU'LL EVER BE.
I DON'T KNOW EXACTLY WHAT'S WRONG WITH YOU, DOC, BUT I DON'T HAVE TIME FOR THIS BULLSHIT.
GRAB HER, GUYS.
NOW, ELLE.
GUYS, WHAT ARE YOU WAITING FOR? GO GET HER.
GUYS?

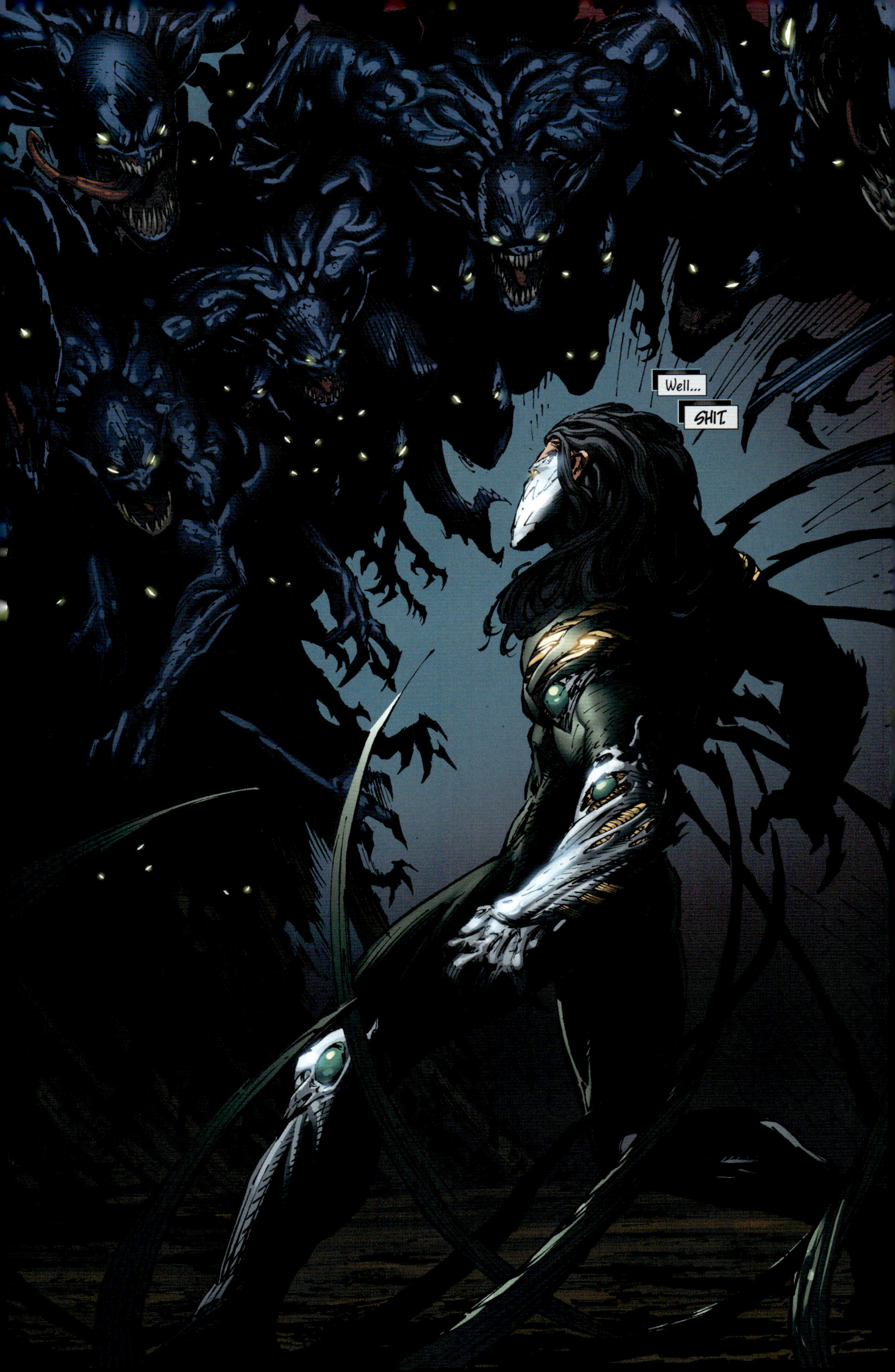
Well...
SHIT.

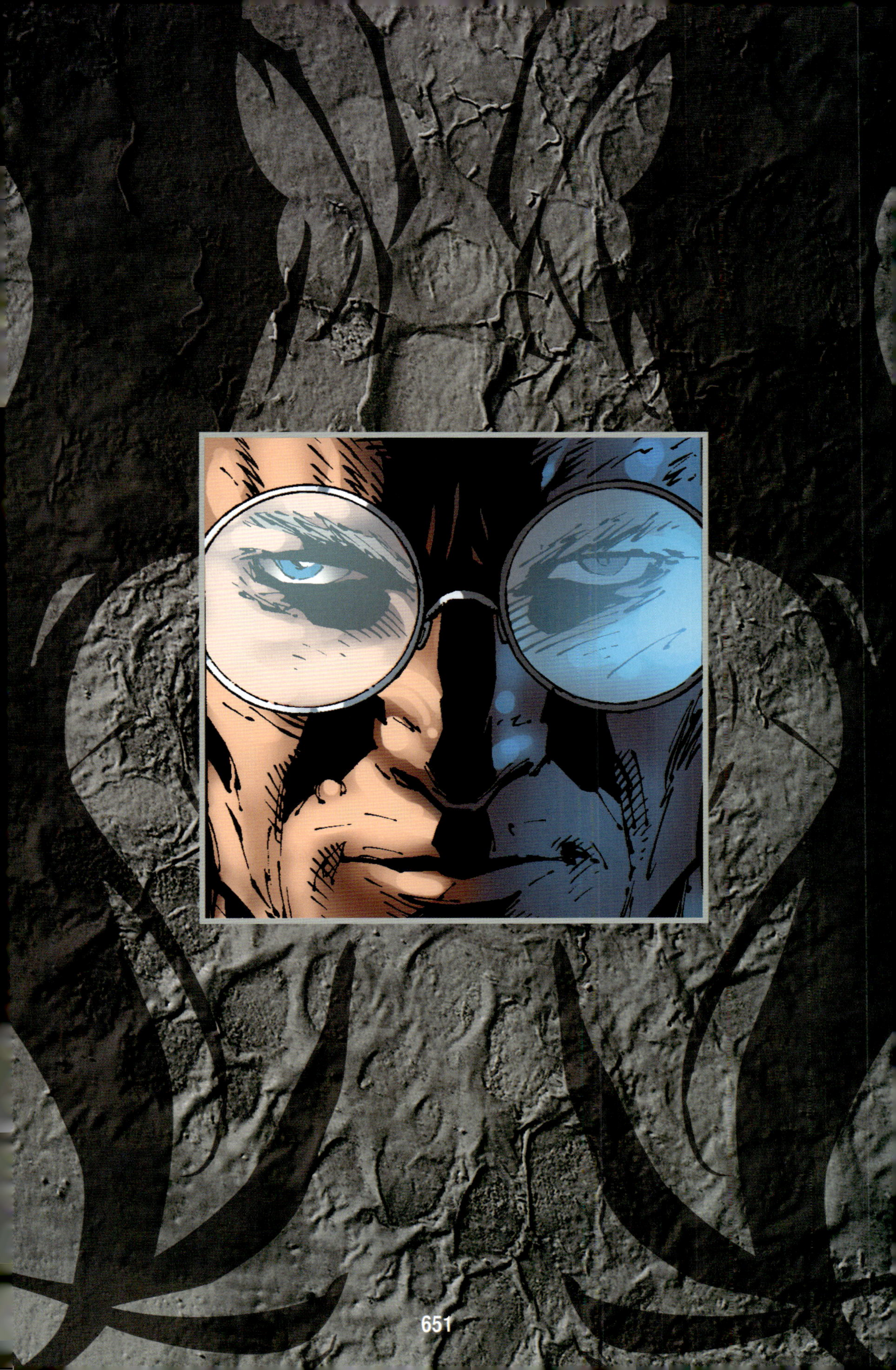

The Darkness Issue #68
cover art by: Dale Keown

THE DARKNESS #68

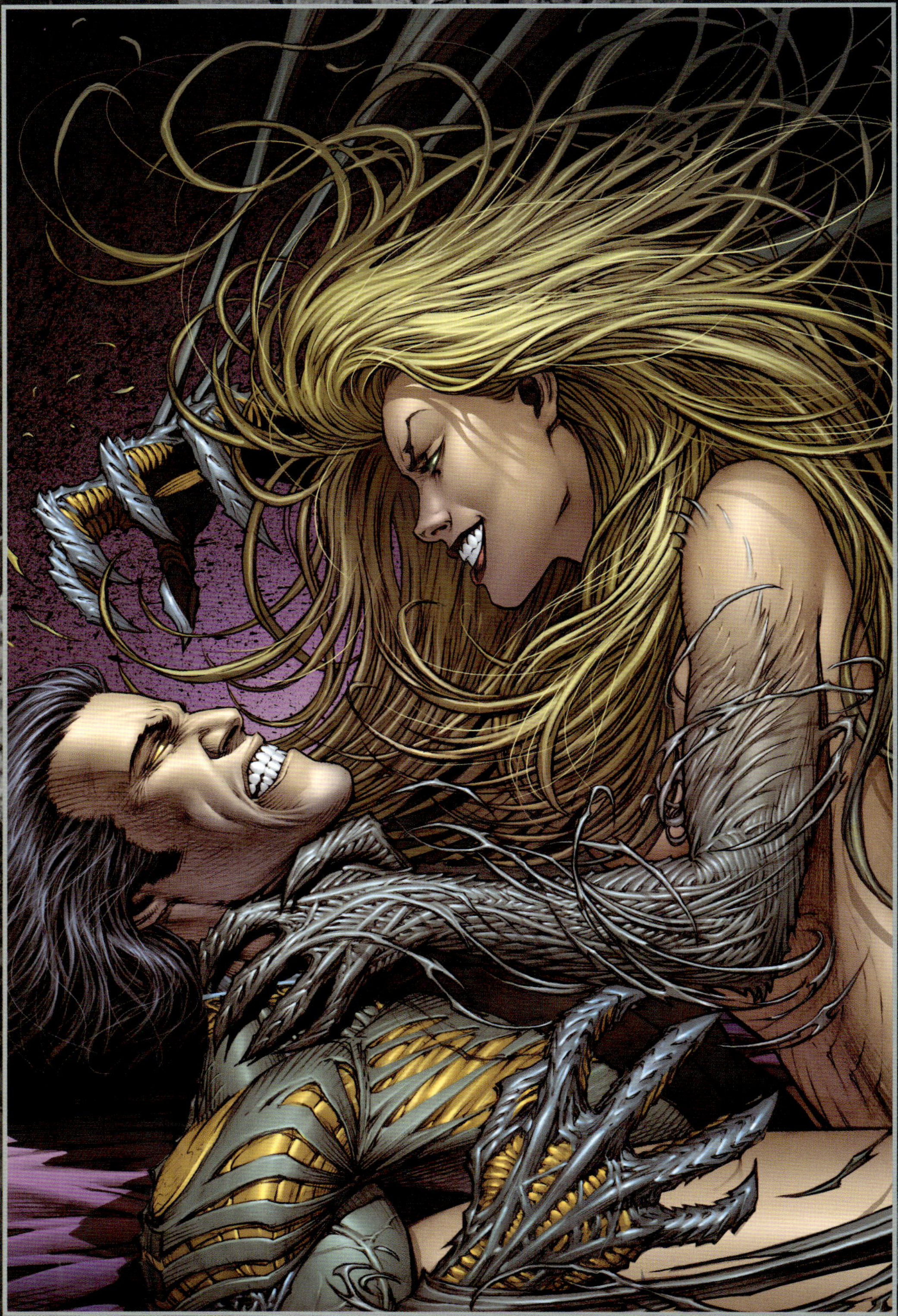

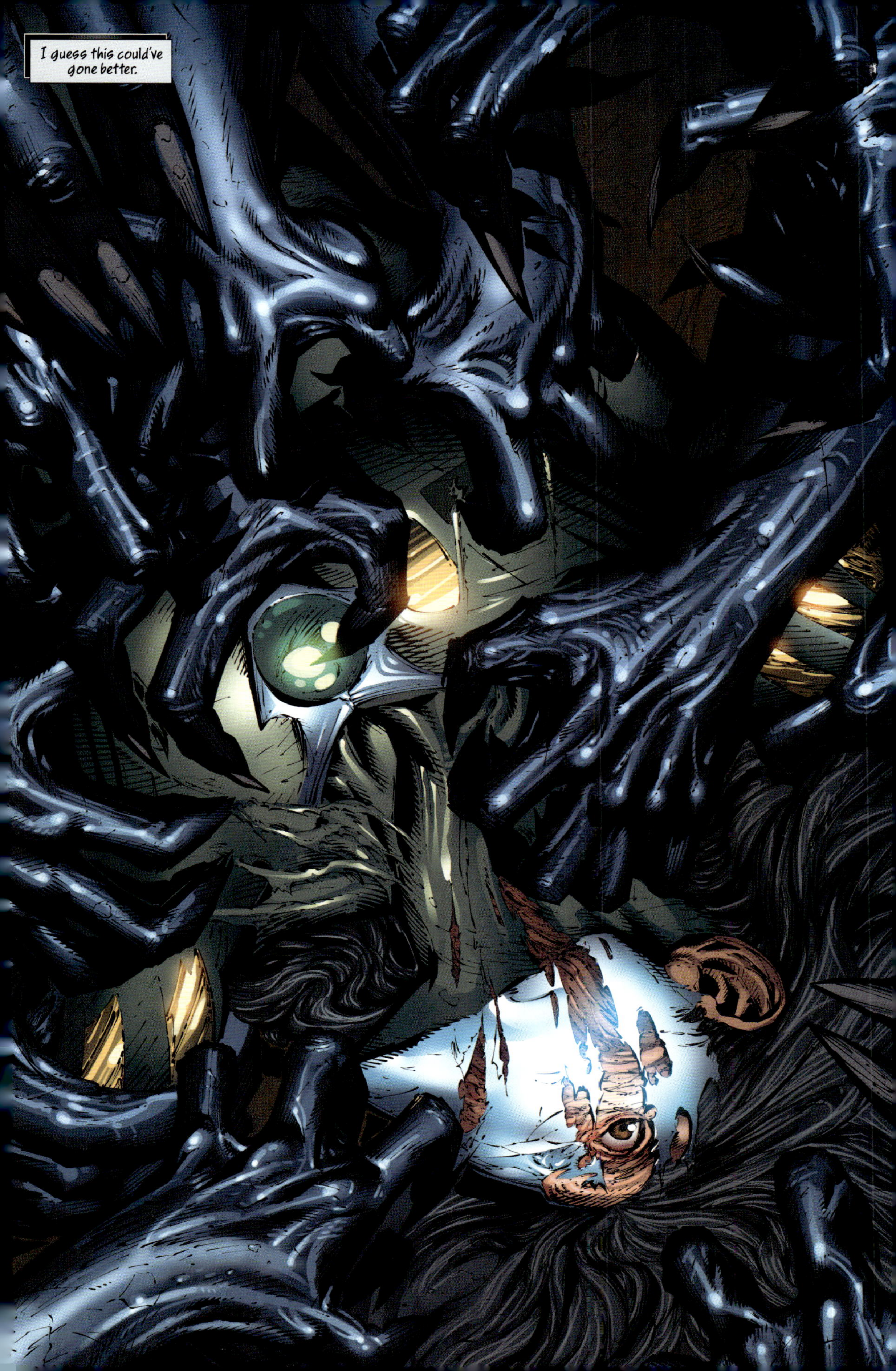
I guess this could've gone better.

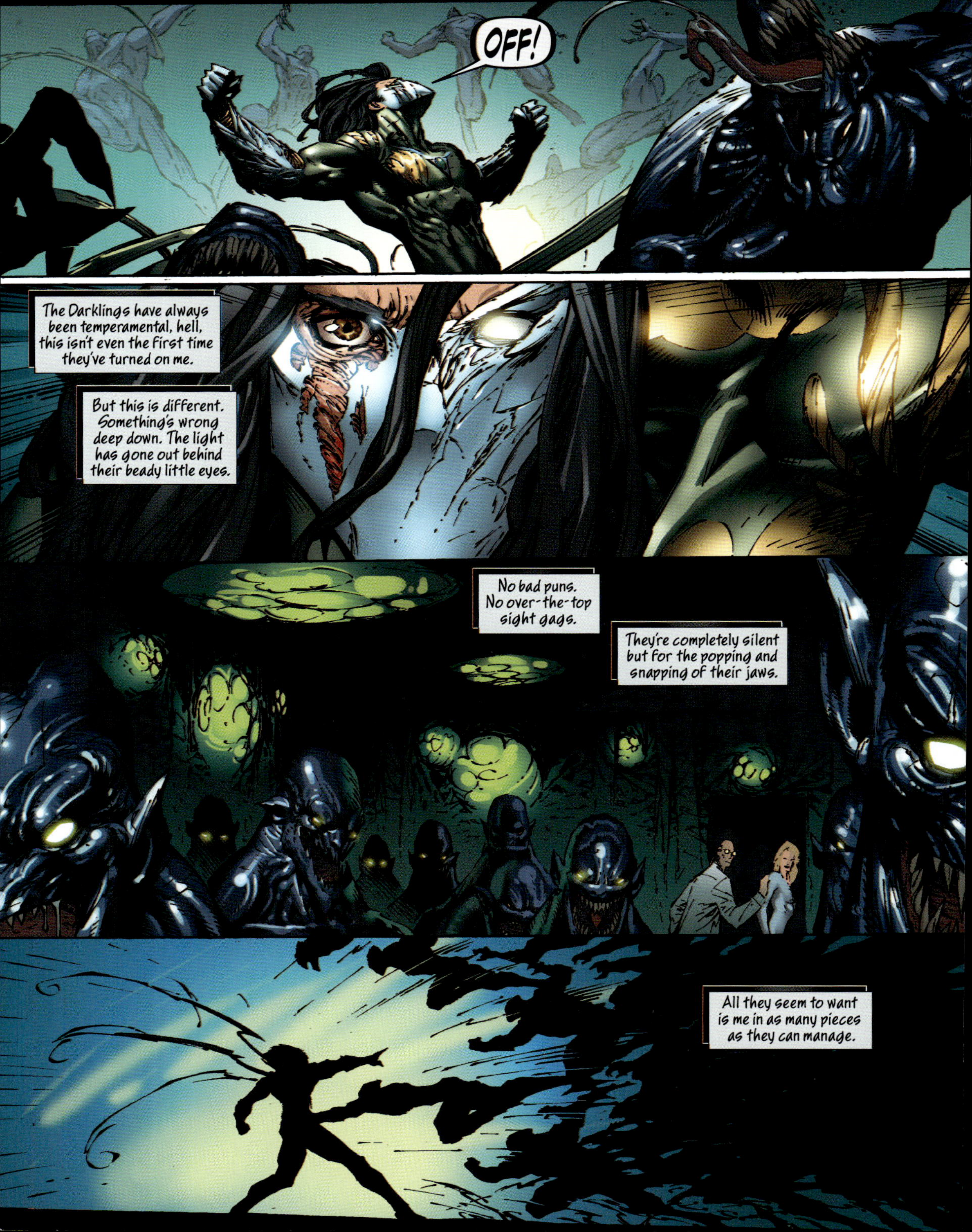
OFF!
The Darklings have always been temperamental, hell, this isn't even the first time they've turned on me.
But this is different. Something's wrong deep down. The light has gone out behind their beady little eyes.
No bad puns. No over-the-top sight gags.
They're completely silent but for the popping and snapping of their jaws.
All they seem to want is me in as many pieces as they can manage.

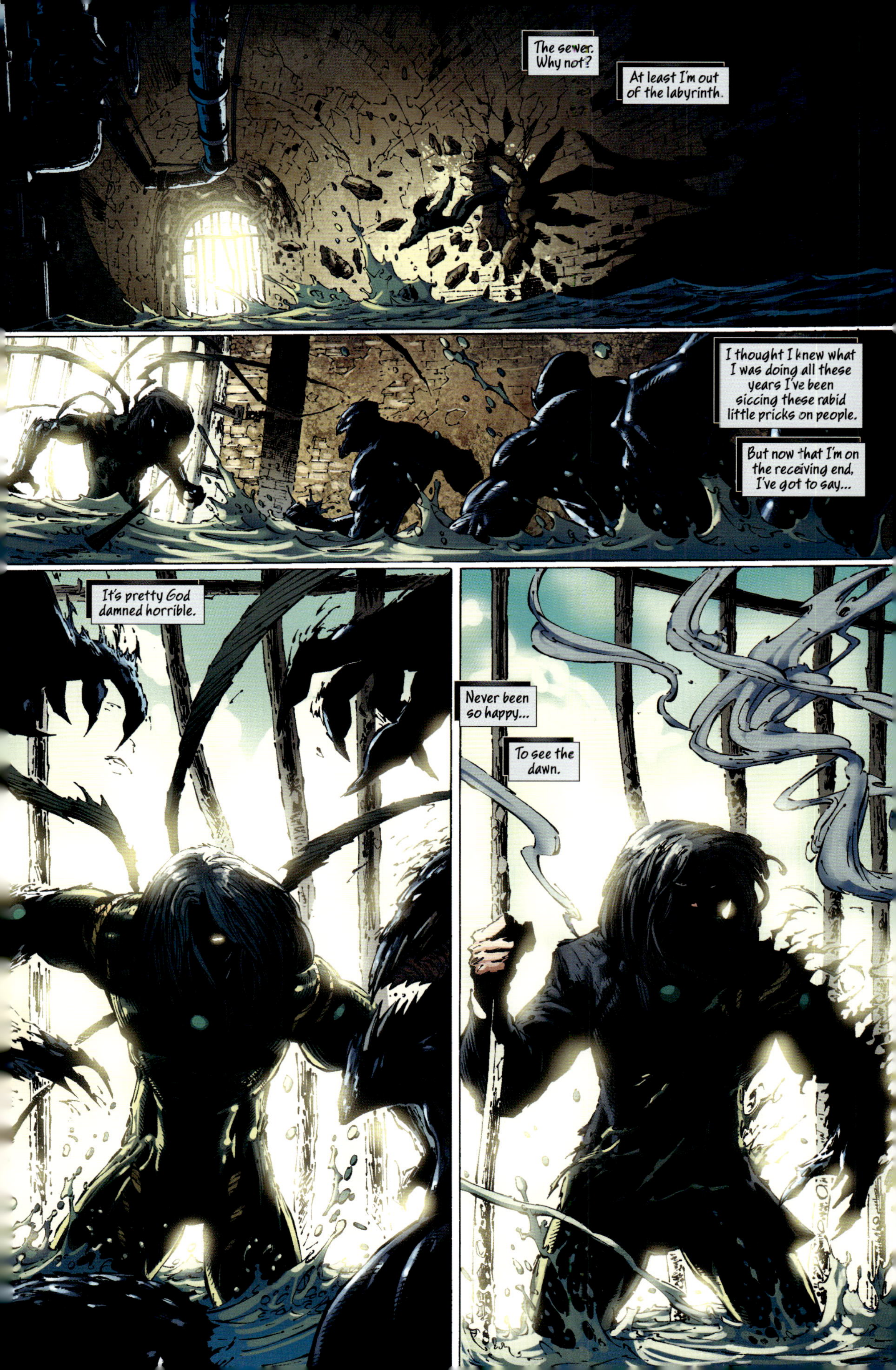
The sewer. Why not?
At least I'm out of the labyrinth.
I thought I knew what I was doing all these years I've been siccing these rabid little pricks on people.
But now that I'm on the receiving end, I've got to say...
It's pretty God damned horrible.
Never been so happy...
To see the dawn.

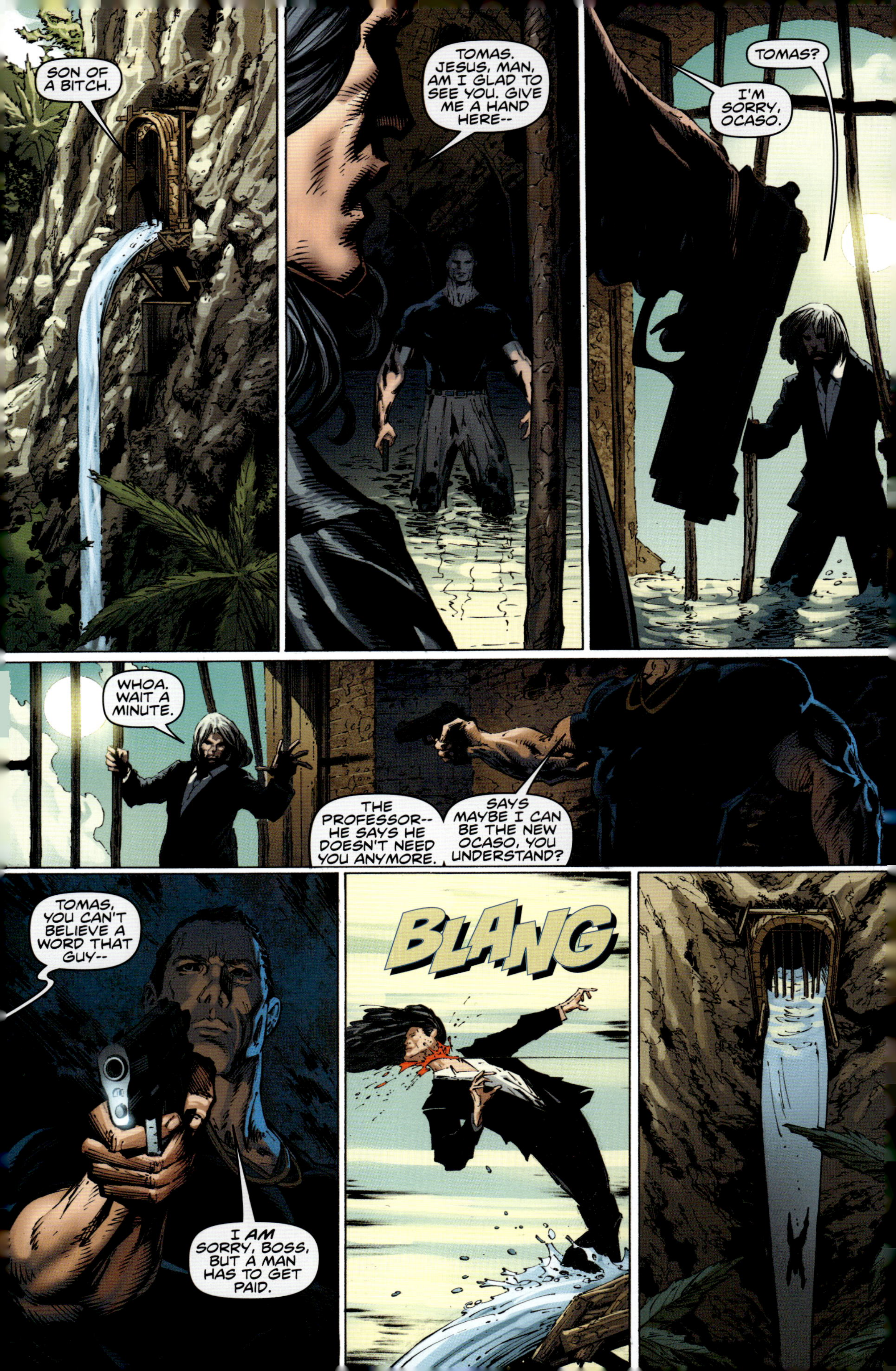
SON OF A BITCH.
TOMAS. JESUS, MAN, AM I GLAD TO SEE YOU. GIVE ME A HAND HERE--
TOMAS?
I'M SORRY, OCASO.
WHOA. WAIT A MINUTE.
THE PROFESSOR-- HE SAYS HE DOESN'T NEED YOU ANYMORE.
SAYS MAYBE I CAN BE THE NEW OCASO, YOU UNDERSTAND?
TOMAS, YOU CAN'T BELIEVE A WORD THAT GUY--
I *AM* SORRY, BOSS, BUT A MAN HAS TO GET PAID.
BLANG

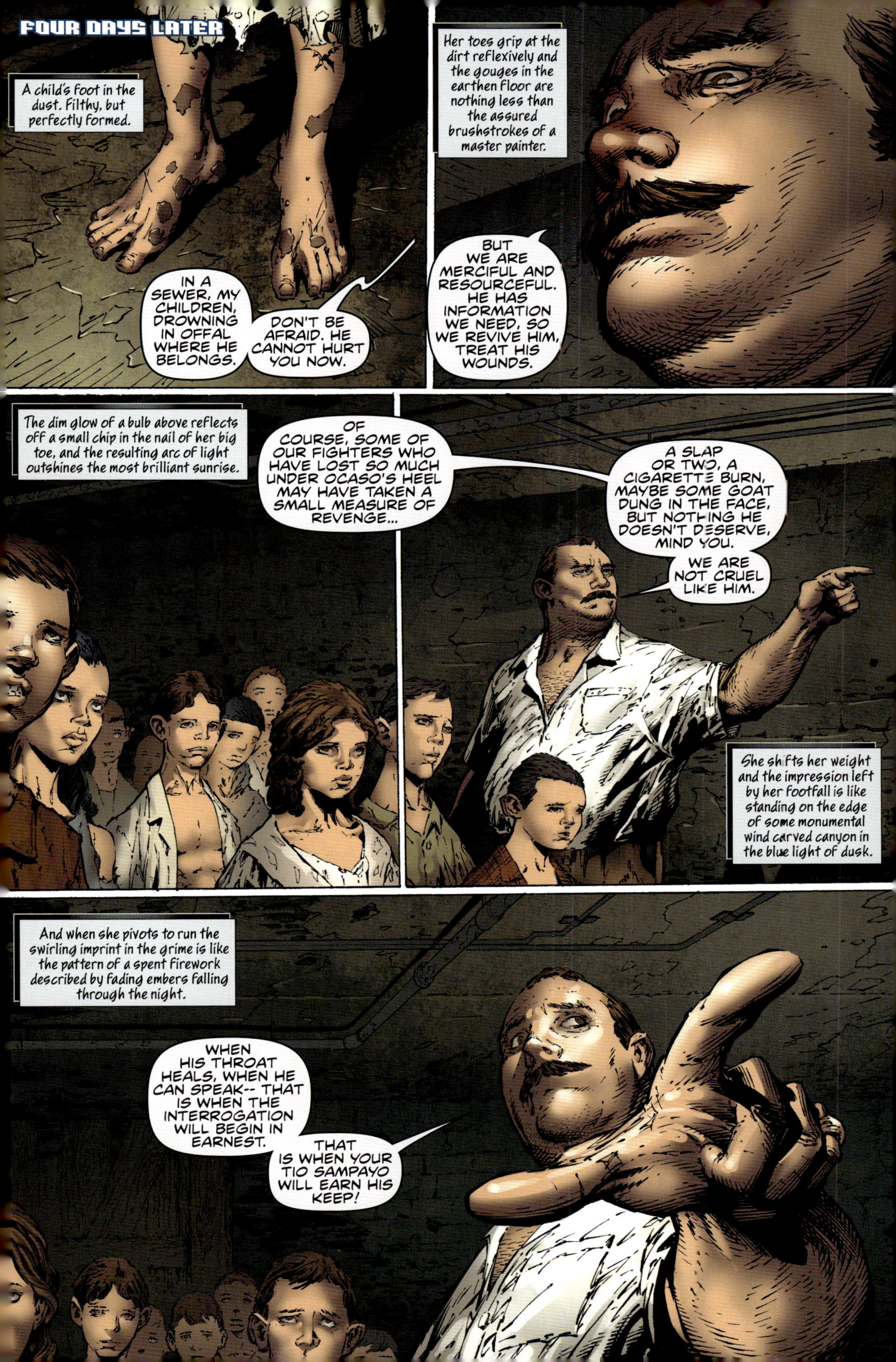
FOUR DAYS LATER
A child's foot in the dust. Filthy, but perfectly formed.
IN A SEWER, MY CHILDREN, DROWNING IN OFFAL WHERE HE BELONGS.
DON'T BE AFRAID. HE CANNOT HURT YOU NOW.
Her toes grip at the dirt reflexively and the gouges in the earthen floor are nothing less than the assured brushstrokes of a master painter.
BUT WE ARE MERCIFUL AND RESOURCEFUL. HE HAS INFORMATION WE NEED, SO WE REVIVE HIM, TREAT HIS WOUNDS.
The dim glow of a bulb above reflects off a small chip in the nail of her big toe, and the resulting arc of light outshines the most brilliant sunrise.
OF COURSE, SOME OF OUR FIGHTERS WHO HAVE LOST SO MUCH UNDER OCASO'S HEEL MAY HAVE TAKEN A SMALL MEASURE OF REVENGE...
A SLAP OR TWO, A CIGARETTE BURN, MAYBE SOME GOAT DUNG IN THE FACE, BUT NOTHING HE DOESN'T DESERVE, MIND YOU.
WE ARE NOT CRUEL LIKE HIM.
She shifts her weight and the impression left by her footfall is like standing on the edge of some monumental wind carved canyon in the blue light of dusk.
And when she pivots to run the swirling imprint in the grime is like the pattern of a spent firework described by fading embers falling through the night.
WHEN HIS THROAT HEALS, WHEN HE CAN SPEAK-- THAT IS WHEN THE INTERROGATION WILL BEGIN IN EARNEST.
THAT IS WHEN YOUR TIO SAMPAYO WILL EARN HIS KEEP!

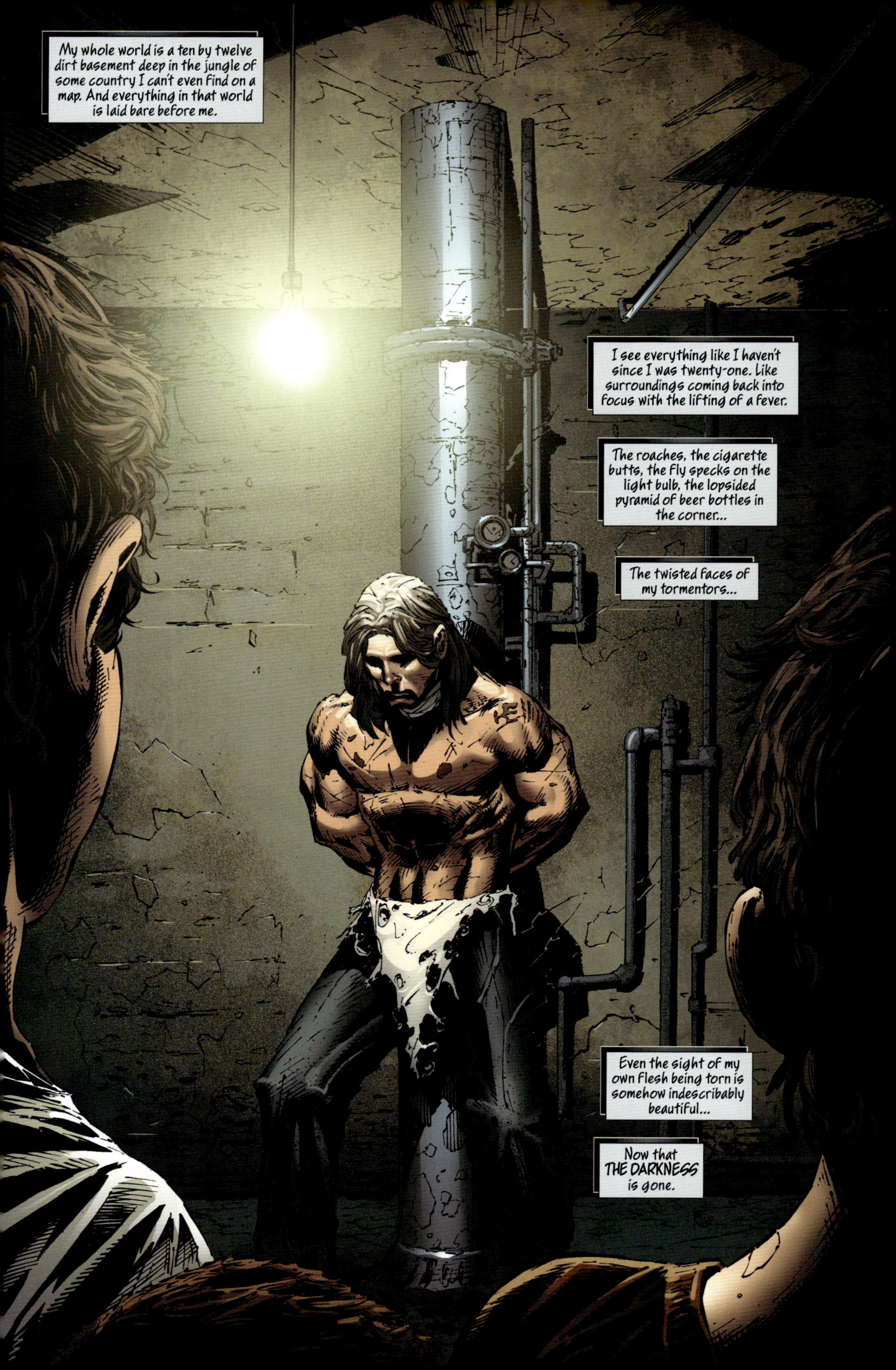
My whole world is a ten by twelve dirt basement deep in the jungle of some country I can't even find on a map. And everything in that world is laid bare before me.
I see everything like I haven't since I was twenty-one. Like surroundings coming back into focus with the lifting of a fever.
The roaches, the cigarette butts, the fly specks on the light bulb, the lopsided pyramid of beer bottles in the corner...
The twisted faces of my tormentors...
Even the sight of my own flesh being torn is somehow indescribably beautiful...
Now that THE DARKNESS is gone.

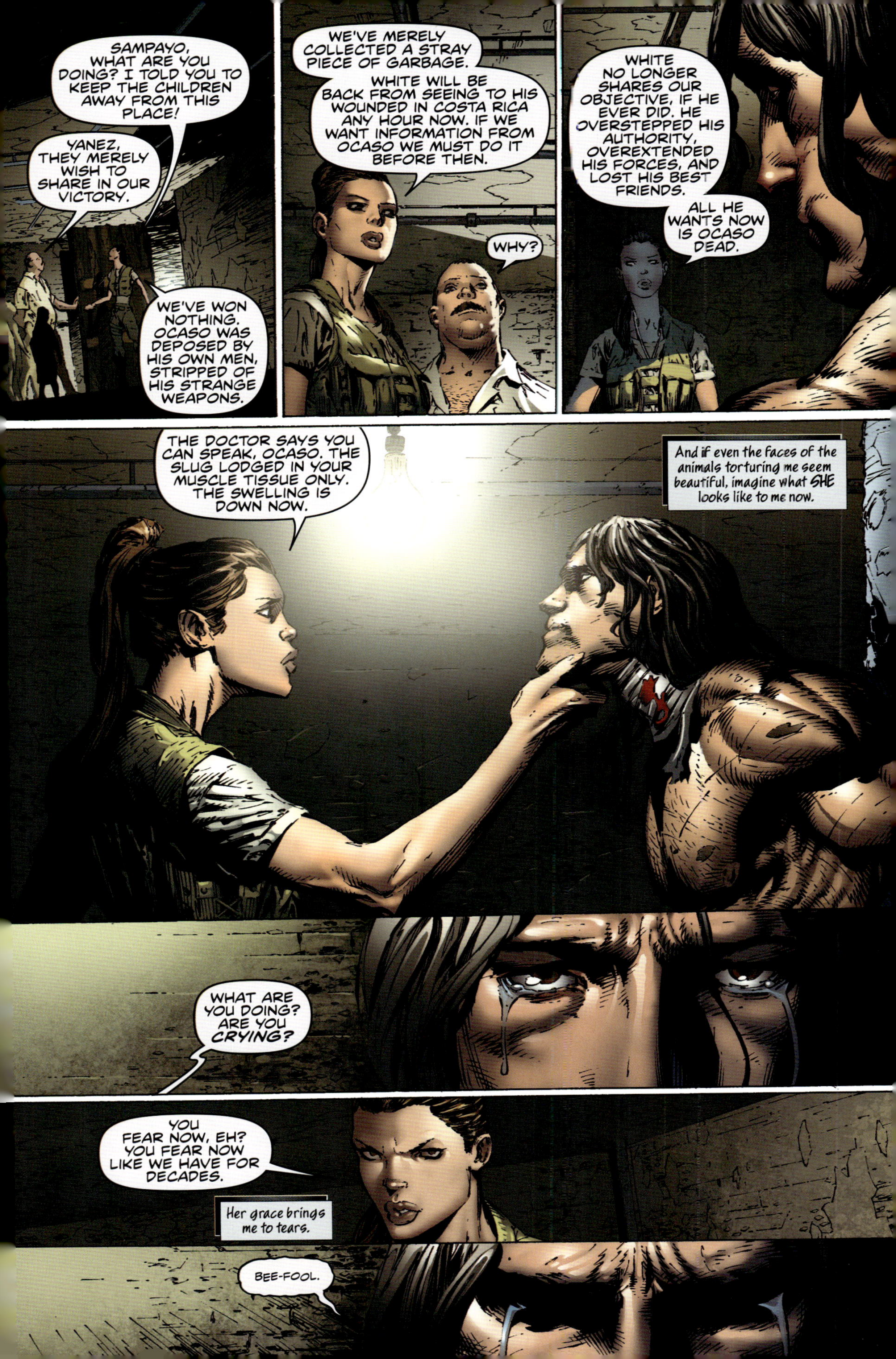

SAMPAYO, WHAT ARE YOU DOING? I TOLD YOU TO KEEP THE CHILDREN AWAY FROM THIS PLACE!
YANEZ, THEY MERELY WISH TO SHARE IN OUR VICTORY.
WE'VE WON NOTHING. OCASO WAS DEPOSED BY HIS OWN MEN, STRIPPED OF HIS STRANGE WEAPONS.
WE'VE MERELY COLLECTED A STRAY PIECE OF GARBAGE.
WHITE WILL BE BACK FROM SEEING TO HIS WOUNDED IN COSTA RICA ANY HOUR NOW. IF WE WANT INFORMATION FROM OCASO WE MUST DO IT BEFORE THEN.
WHY?
WHITE NO LONGER SHARES OUR OBJECTIVE, IF HE EVER DID. HE OVERSTEPPED HIS AUTHORITY, OVEREXTENDED HIS FORCES, AND LOST HIS BEST FRIENDS.
ALL HE WANTS NOW IS OCASO DEAD.
THE DOCTOR SAYS YOU CAN SPEAK, OCASO. THE SLUG LODGED IN YOUR MUSCLE TISSUE ONLY. THE SWELLING IS DOWN NOW.
And if even the faces of the animals torturing me seem beautiful, imagine what SHE looks like to me now.
WHAT ARE YOU DOING? ARE YOU CRYING?
YOU FEAR NOW, EH? YOU FEAR NOW LIKE WE HAVE FOR DECADES.
Her grace brings me to tears.
BEE-FOOL.

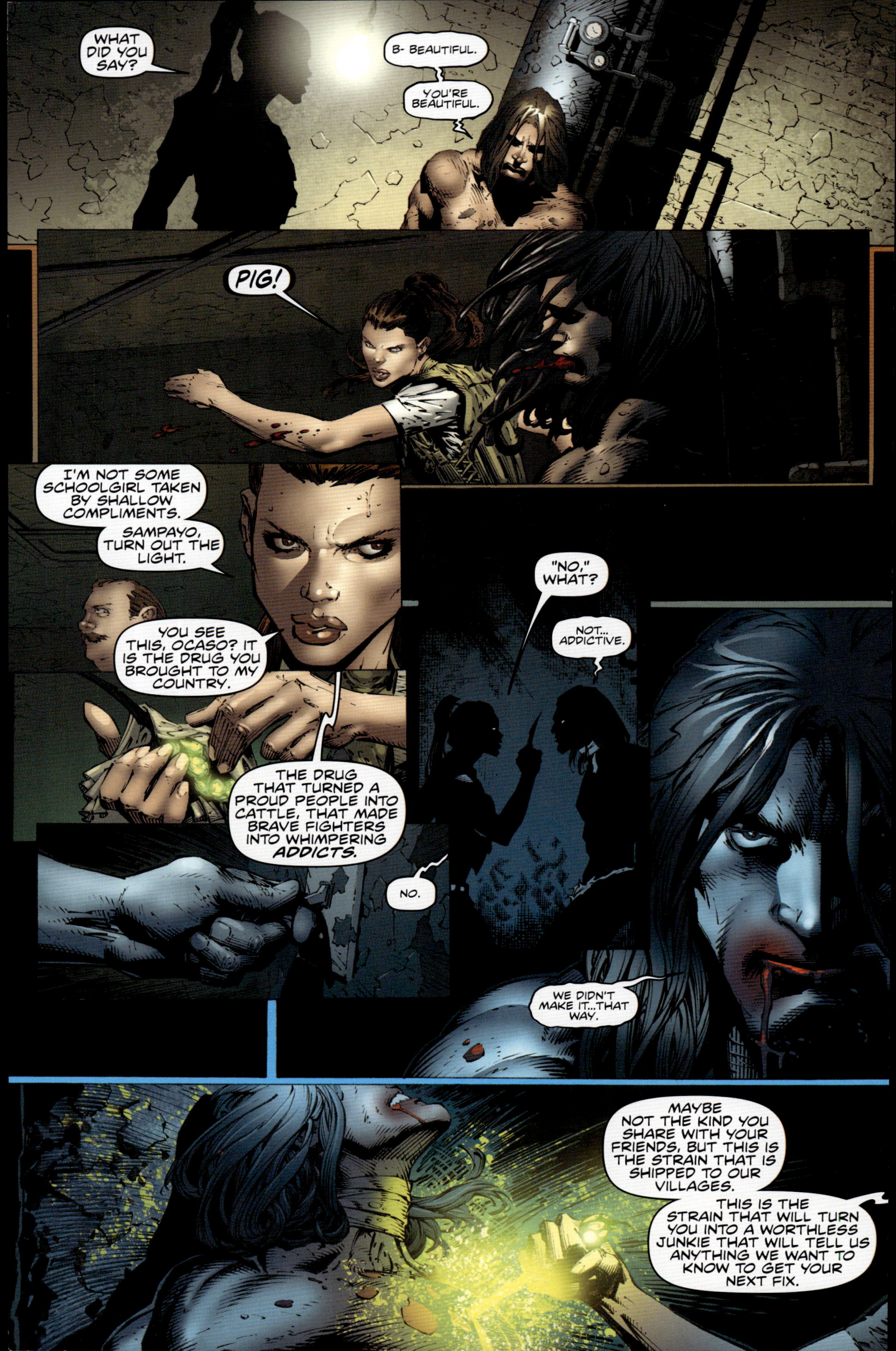
WHAT DID YOU SAY?
B- BEAUTIFUL.
YOU'RE BEAUTIFUL.
PIG!
I'M NOT SOME SCHOOLGIRL TAKEN BY SHALLOW COMPLIMENTS.
SAMPAYO, TURN OUT THE LIGHT.
YOU SEE THIS, OCASO? IT IS THE DRUG YOU BROUGHT TO MY COUNTRY.
THE DRUG THAT TURNED A PROUD PEOPLE INTO CATTLE, THAT MADE BRAVE FIGHTERS INTO WHIMPERING ADDICTS.
NO.
"NO," WHAT?
NOT... ADDICTIVE.
WE DIDN'T MAKE IT...THAT WAY.
MAYBE NOT THE KIND YOU SHARE WITH YOUR FRIENDS, BUT THIS IS THE STRAIN THAT IS SHIPPED TO OUR VILLAGES.
THIS IS THE STRAIN THAT WILL TURN YOU INTO A WORTHLESS JUNKIE THAT WILL TELL US ANYTHING WE WANT TO KNOW TO GET YOUR NEXT FIX.

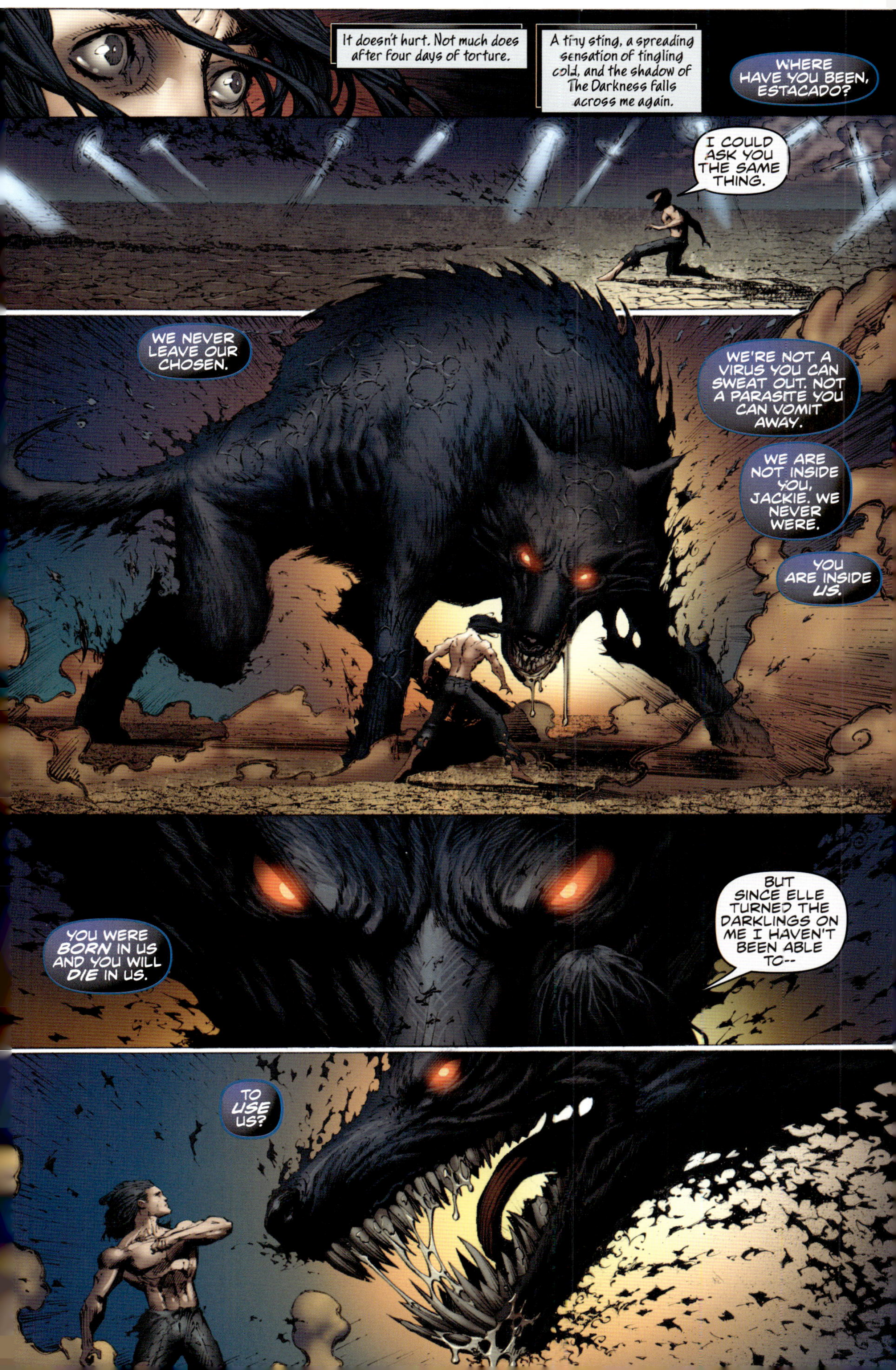
It doesn't hurt. Not much does after four days of torture.
A tiny sting, a spreading sensation of tingling cold, and the shadow of The Darkness falls across me again.
WHERE HAVE YOU BEEN, ESTACADO?
I COULD ASK YOU THE SAME THING.
WE NEVER LEAVE OUR CHOSEN.
WE'RE NOT A VIRUS YOU CAN SWEAT OUT. NOT A PARASITE YOU CAN VOMIT AWAY.
WE ARE NOT INSIDE YOU, JACKIE. WE NEVER WERE.
YOU ARE INSIDE US.
YOU WERE BORN IN US AND YOU WILL DIE IN US.
BUT SINCE ELLE TURNED THE DARKLINGS ON ME I HAVEN'T BEEN ABLE TO--
TO USE US?

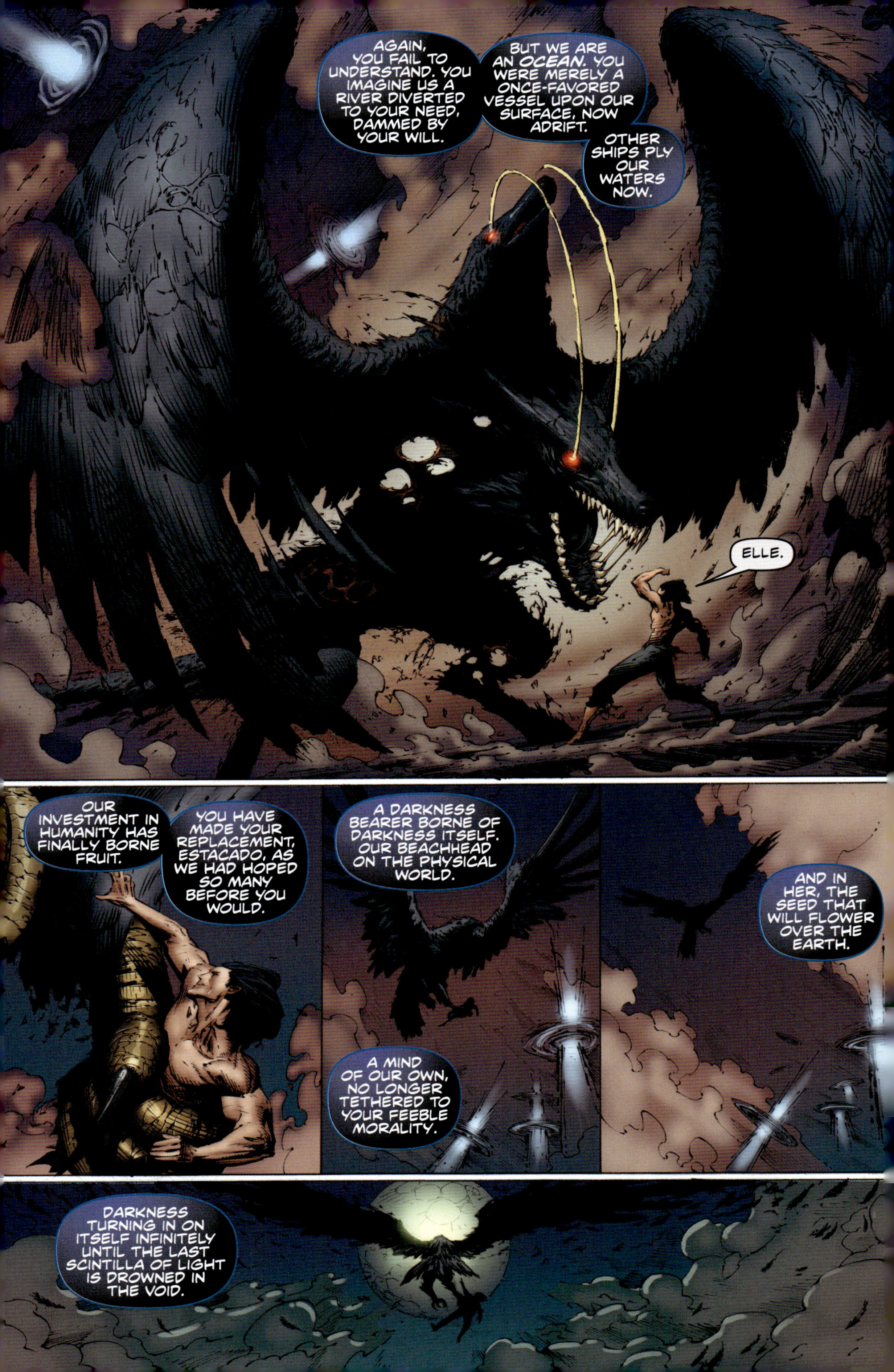
AGAIN, YOU FAIL TO UNDERSTAND. YOU IMAGINE US A RIVER DIVERTED TO YOUR NEED, DAMMED BY YOUR WILL.
BUT WE ARE AN OCEAN. YOU WERE MERELY A ONCE-FAVORED VESSEL UPON OUR SURFACE, NOW ADRIFT.
OTHER SHIPS PLY OUR WATERS NOW.
ELLE.
OUR INVESTMENT IN HUMANITY HAS FINALLY BORNE FRUIT.
YOU HAVE MADE YOUR REPLACEMENT, ESTACADO, AS WE HAD HOPED SO MANY BEFORE YOU WOULD.
A DARKNESS BEARER BORNE OF DARKNESS ITSELF. OUR BEACHHEAD ON THE PHYSICAL WORLD.
A MIND OF OUR OWN, NO LONGER TETHERED TO YOUR FEEBLE MORALITY.
AND IN HER, THE SEED THAT WILL FLOWER OVER THE EARTH.
DARKNESS TURNING IN ON ITSELF INFINITELY UNTIL THE LAST SCINTILLA OF LIGHT IS DROWNED IN THE VOID.

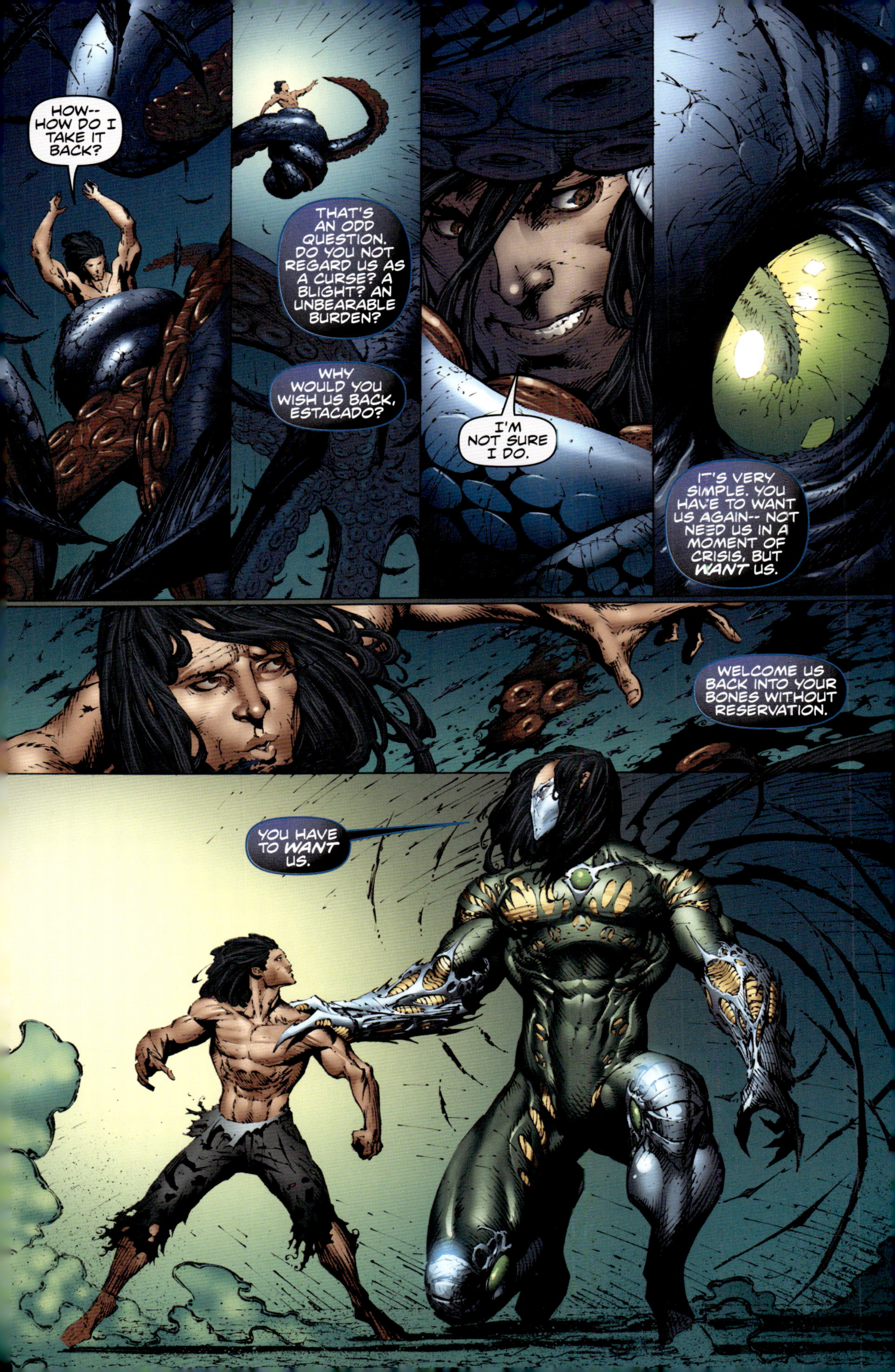
HOW-- HOW DO I TAKE IT BACK?
THAT'S AN ODD QUESTION. DO YOU NOT REGARD US AS A CURSE? A BLIGHT? AN UNBEARABLE BURDEN?
WHY WOULD YOU WISH US BACK, ESTACADO?
I'M NOT SURE I DO.
IT'S VERY SIMPLE. YOU HAVE TO WANT US AGAIN-- NOT NEED US IN A MOMENT OF CRISIS, BUT WANT US.
WELCOME US BACK INTO YOUR BONES WITHOUT RESERVATION.
YOU HAVE TO WANT US.

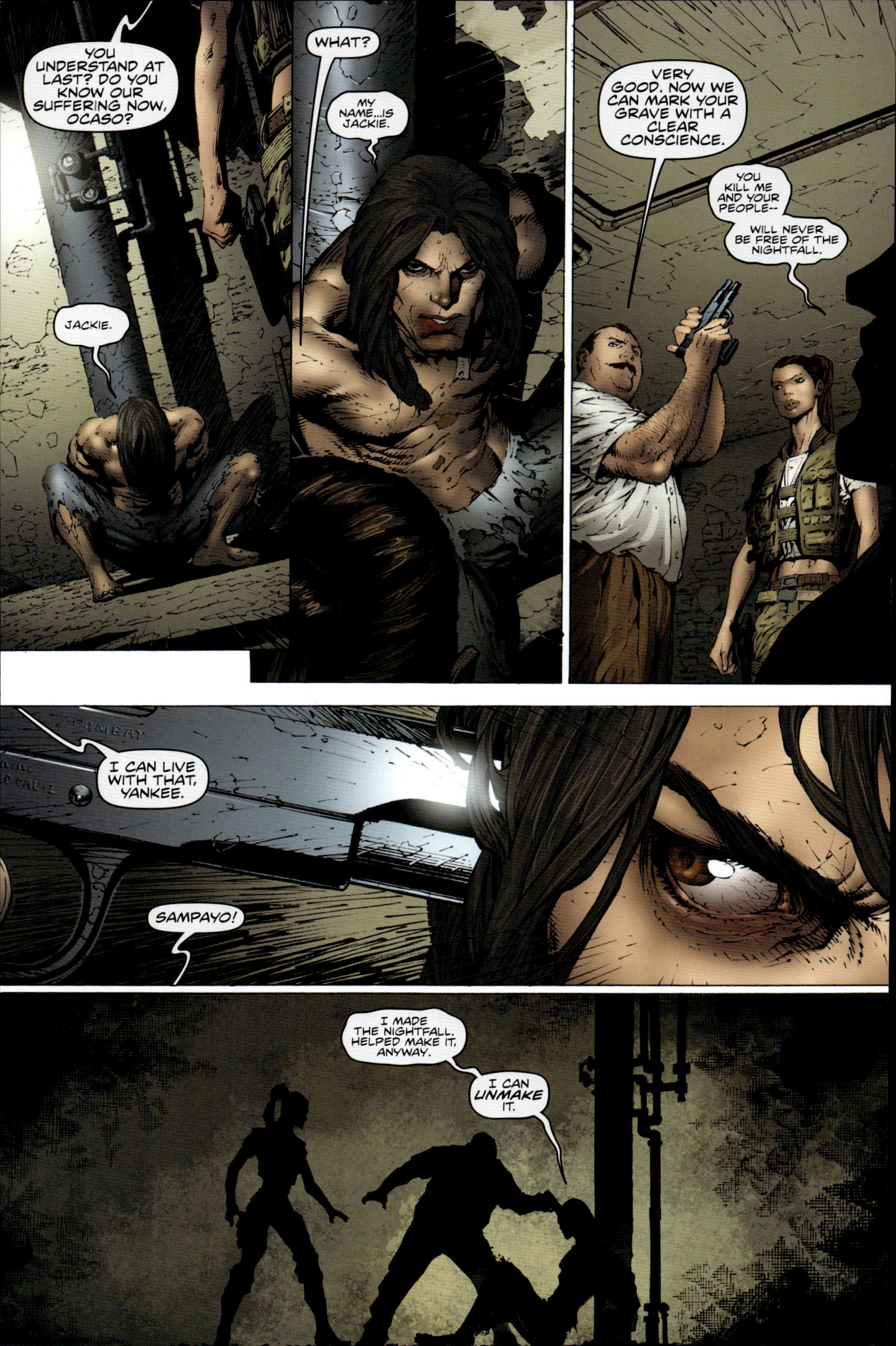

YOU UNDERSTAND AT LAST? DO YOU KNOW OUR SUFFERING NOW, OCASO?
JACKIE.
WHAT?
MY NAME...IS JACKIE.
VERY GOOD. NOW WE CAN MARK YOUR GRAVE WITH A CLEAR CONSCIENCE.
YOU KILL ME AND YOUR PEOPLE--
WILL NEVER BE FREE OF THE NIGHTFALL.
I CAN LIVE WITH THAT, YANKEE.
SAMPAYO!
I MADE THE NIGHTFALL. HELPED MAKE IT, ANYWAY.
I CAN UNMAKE IT.

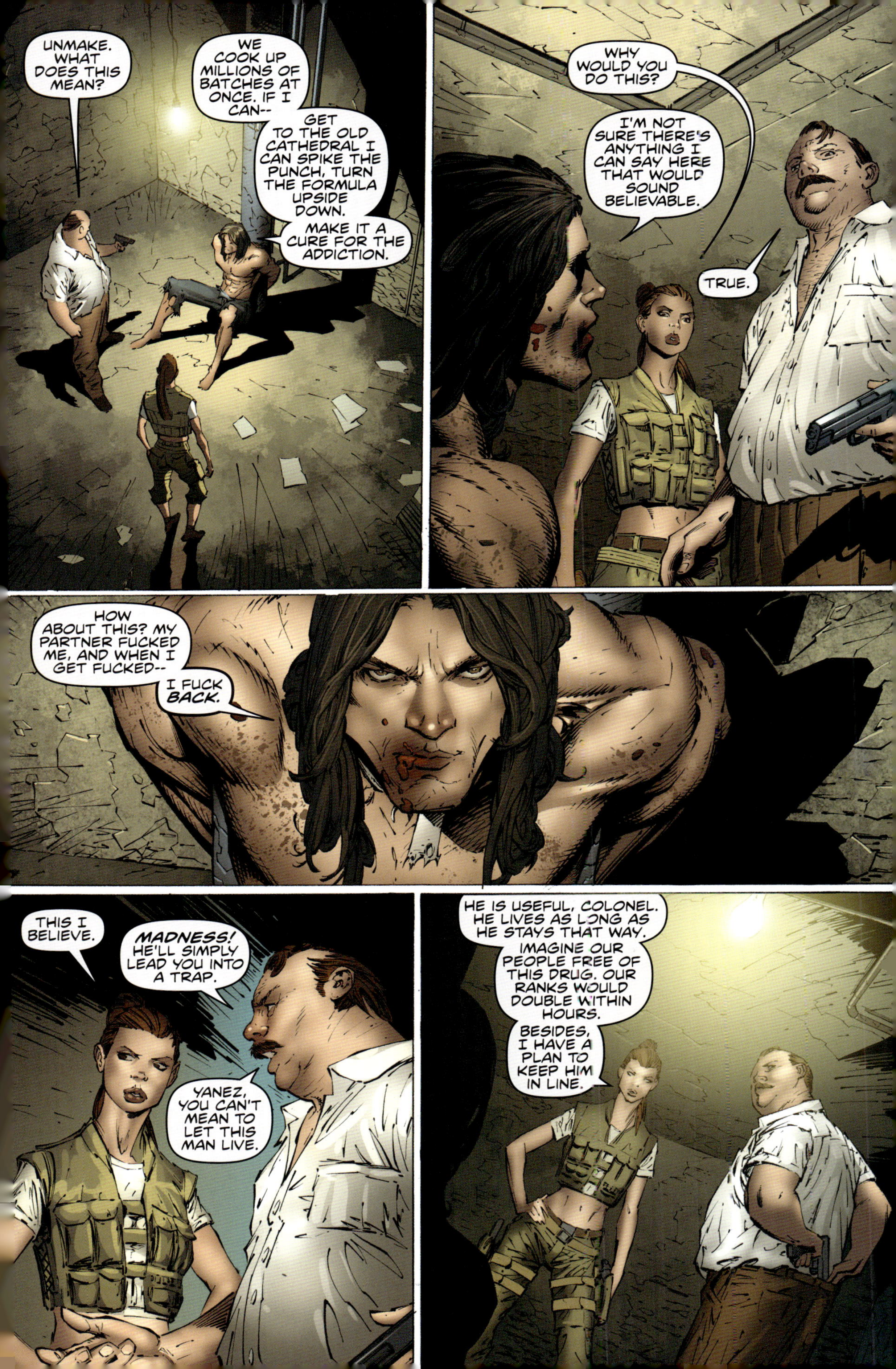
UNMAKE. WHAT DOES THIS MEAN?
WE COOK UP MILLIONS OF BATCHES AT ONCE. IF I CAN--
GET TO THE OLD CATHEDRAL I CAN SPIKE THE PUNCH, TURN THE FORMULA UPSIDE DOWN.
MAKE IT A CURE FOR THE ADDICTION.
WHY WOULD YOU DO THIS?
I'M NOT SURE THERE'S ANYTHING I CAN SAY HERE THAT WOULD SOUND BELIEVABLE.
TRUE.
HOW ABOUT THIS? MY PARTNER FUCKED ME, AND WHEN I GET FUCKED--
I FUCK *BACK.*
THIS I BELIEVE.
MADNESS! HE'LL SIMPLY LEAD YOU INTO A TRAP.
YANEZ, YOU CAN'T MEAN TO LET THIS MAN LIVE.
HE IS USEFUL, COLONEL. HE LIVES AS LONG AS HE STAYS THAT WAY.
IMAGINE OUR PEOPLE FREE OF THIS DRUG. OUR RANKS WOULD DOUBLE WITHIN HOURS.
BESIDES, I HAVE A PLAN TO KEEP HIM IN LINE.

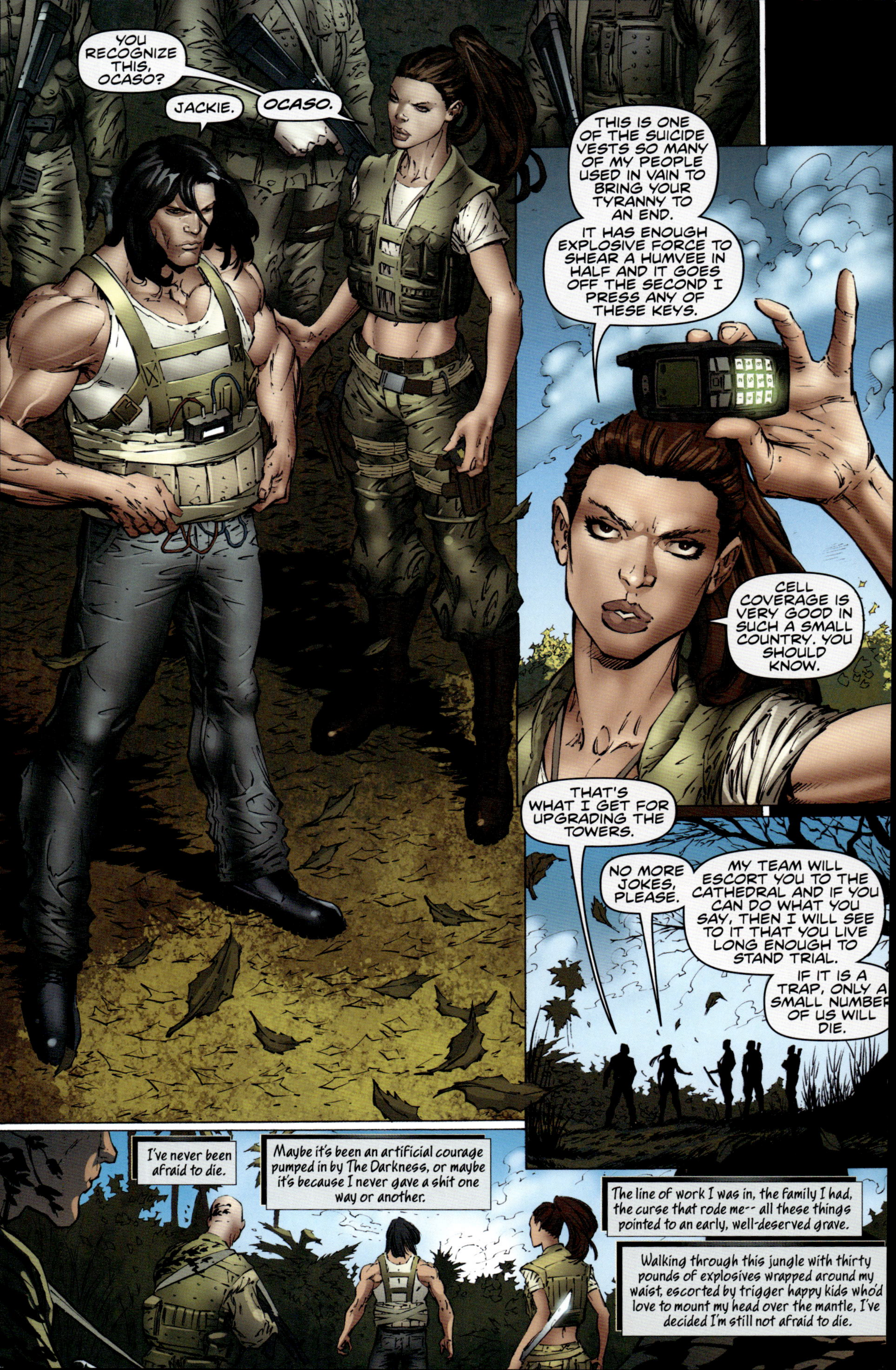
YOU RECOGNIZE THIS, OCASO?
JACKIE.
OCASO.
THIS IS ONE OF THE SUICIDE VESTS SO MANY OF MY PEOPLE USED IN VAIN TO BRING YOUR TYRANNY TO AN END.
IT HAS ENOUGH EXPLOSIVE FORCE TO SHEAR A HUMVEE IN HALF AND IT GOES OFF THE SECOND I PRESS ANY OF THESE KEYS.
CELL COVERAGE IS VERY GOOD IN SUCH A SMALL COUNTRY. YOU SHOULD KNOW.
THAT'S WHAT I GET FOR UPGRADING THE TOWERS.
NO MORE JOKES, PLEASE.
MY TEAM WILL ESCORT YOU TO THE CATHEDRAL AND IF YOU CAN DO WHAT YOU SAY, THEN I WILL SEE TO IT THAT YOU LIVE LONG ENOUGH TO STAND TRIAL.
IF IT IS A TRAP, ONLY A SMALL NUMBER OF US WILL DIE.
I've never been afraid to die.
Maybe it's been an artificial courage pumped in by The Darkness, or maybe it's because I never gave a shit one way or another.
The line of work I was in, the family I had, the curse that rode me-- all these things pointed to an early, well-deserved grave.
Walking through this jungle with thirty pounds of explosives wrapped around my waist, escorted by trigger happy kids who'd love to mount my head over the mantle, I've decided I'm still not afraid to die.

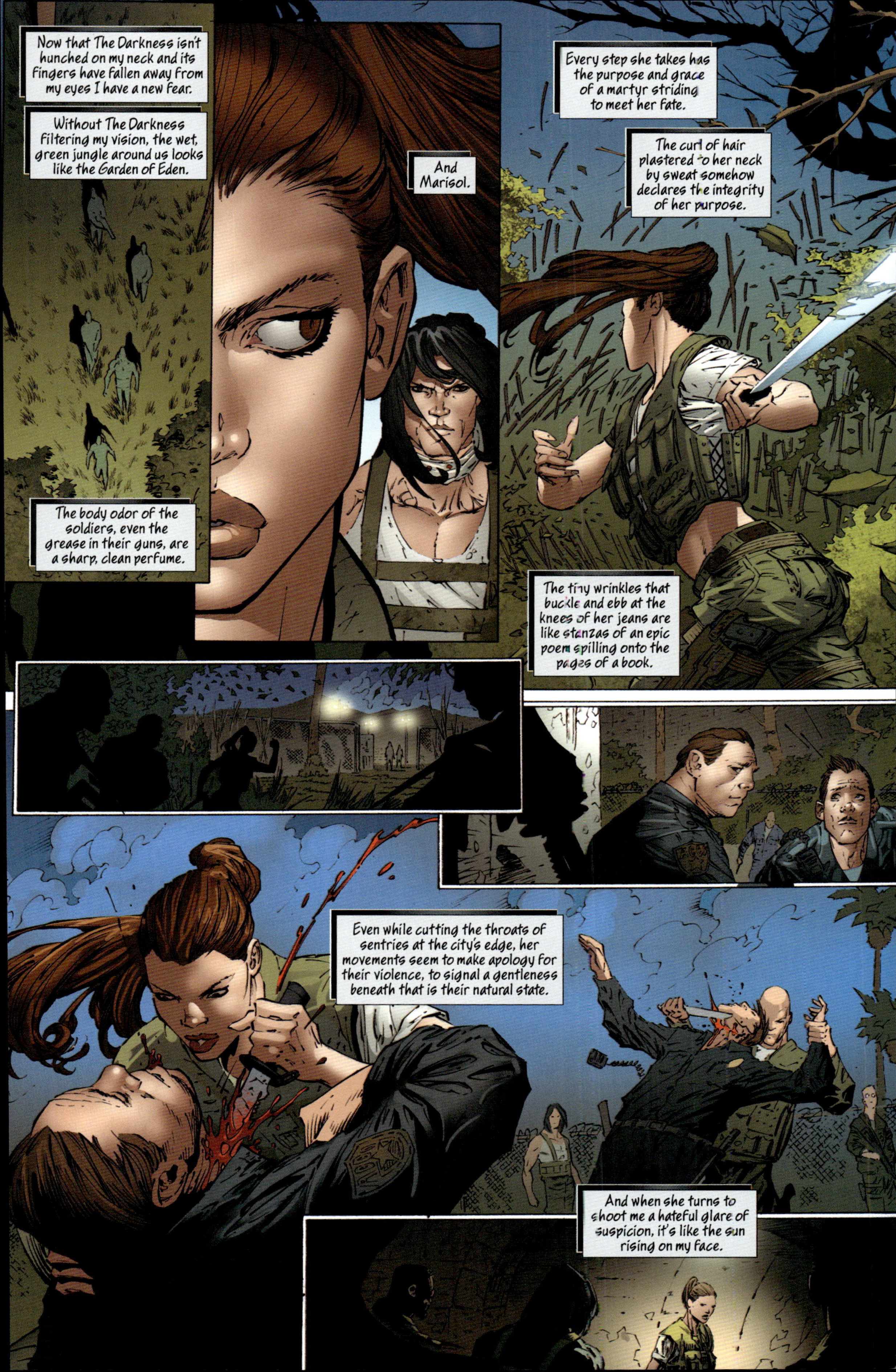
Now that The Darkness isn't hunched on my neck and its fingers have fallen away from my eyes I have a new fear.
Without The Darkness filtering my vision, the wet, green jungle around us looks like the Garden of Eden.
The body odor of the soldiers, even the grease in their guns, are a sharp, clean perfume.
And Marisol.
Every step she takes has the purpose and grace of a martyr striding to meet her fate.
The curl of hair plastered to her neck by sweat somehow declares the integrity of her purpose.
The tiny wrinkles that buckle and ebb at the knees of her jeans are like stanzas of an epic poem spilling onto the pages of a book.
Even while cutting the throats of sentries at the city's edge, her movements seem to make apology for their violence, to signal a gentleness beneath that is their natural state.
And when she turns to shoot me a hateful glare of suspicion, it's like the sun rising on my face.

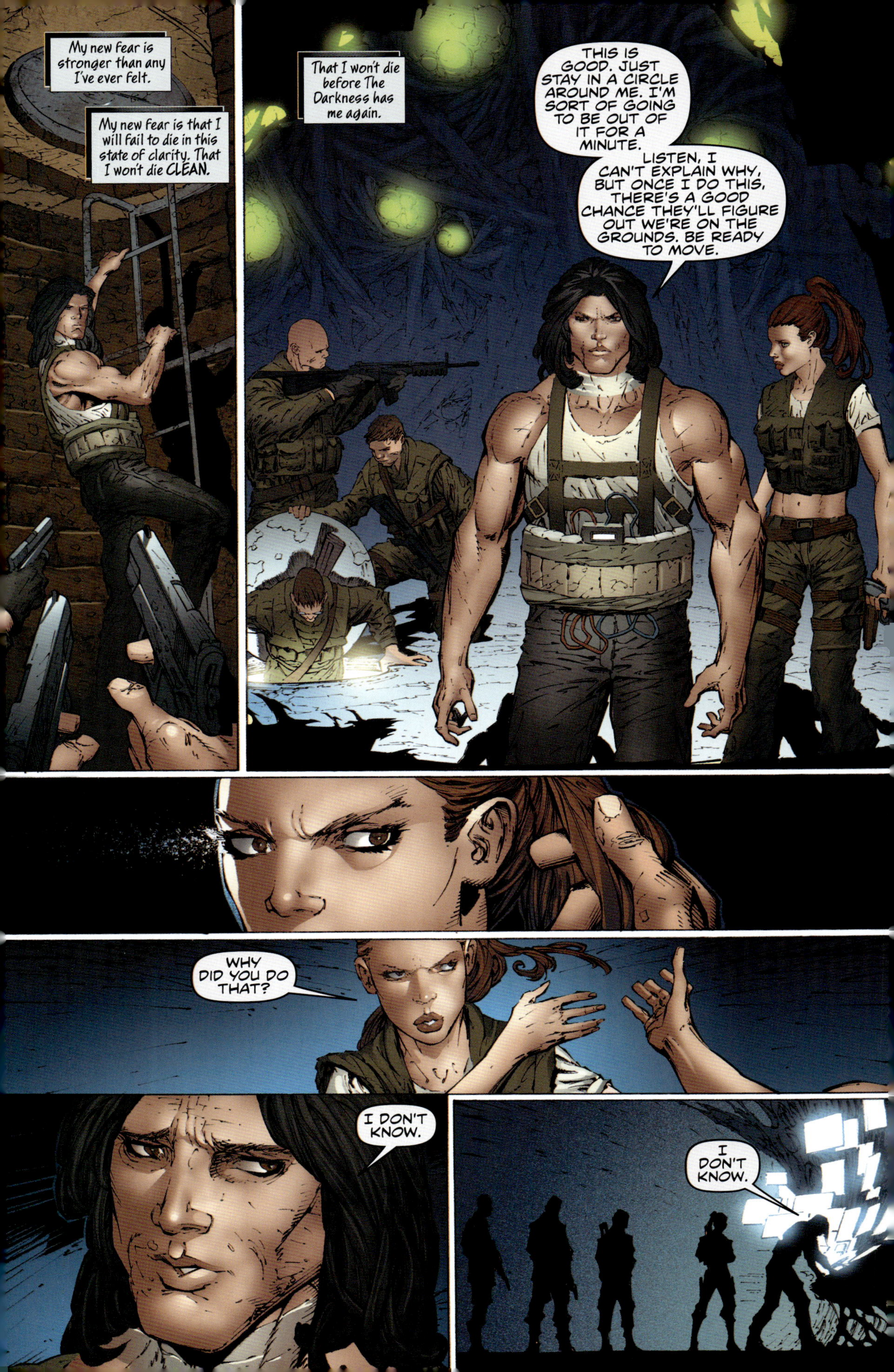
My new fear is stronger than any I've ever felt.
My new fear is that I will fail to die in this state of clarity. That I won't die CLEAN.
That I won't die before The Darkness has me again.
THIS IS GOOD. JUST STAY IN A CIRCLE AROUND ME. I'M SORT OF GOING TO BE OUT OF IT FOR A MINUTE.
LISTEN, I CAN'T EXPLAIN WHY, BUT ONCE I DO THIS, THERE'S A GOOD CHANCE THEY'LL FIGURE OUT WE'RE ON THE GROUNDS. BE READY TO MOVE.
WHY DID YOU DO THAT?
I DON'T KNOW.
I DON'T KNOW.

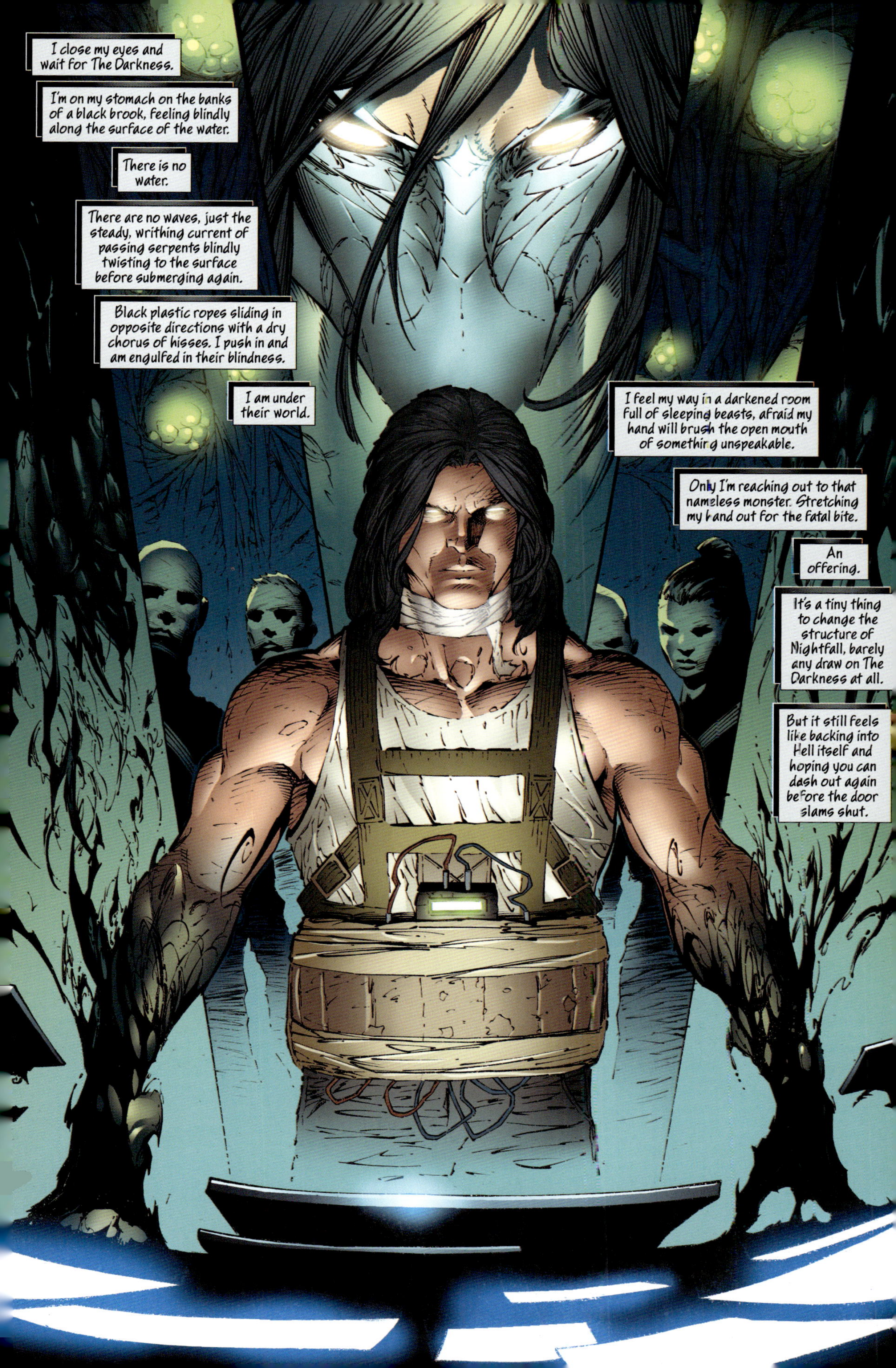
I close my eyes and wait for The Darkness.
I'm on my stomach on the banks of a black brook, feeling blindly along the surface of the water.
There is no water.
There are no waves, just the steady, writhing current of passing serpents blindly twisting to the surface before submerging again.
Black plastic ropes sliding in opposite directions with a dry chorus of hisses. I push in and am engulfed in their blindness.
I am under their world.
I feel my way in a darkened room full of sleeping beasts, afraid my hand will brush the open mouth of something unspeakable.
Only I'm reaching out to that nameless monster. Stretching my hand out for the fatal bite.
An offering.
It's a tiny thing to change the structure of Nightfall, barely any draw on The Darkness at all.
But it still feels like backing into Hell itself and hoping you can dash out again before the door slams shut.

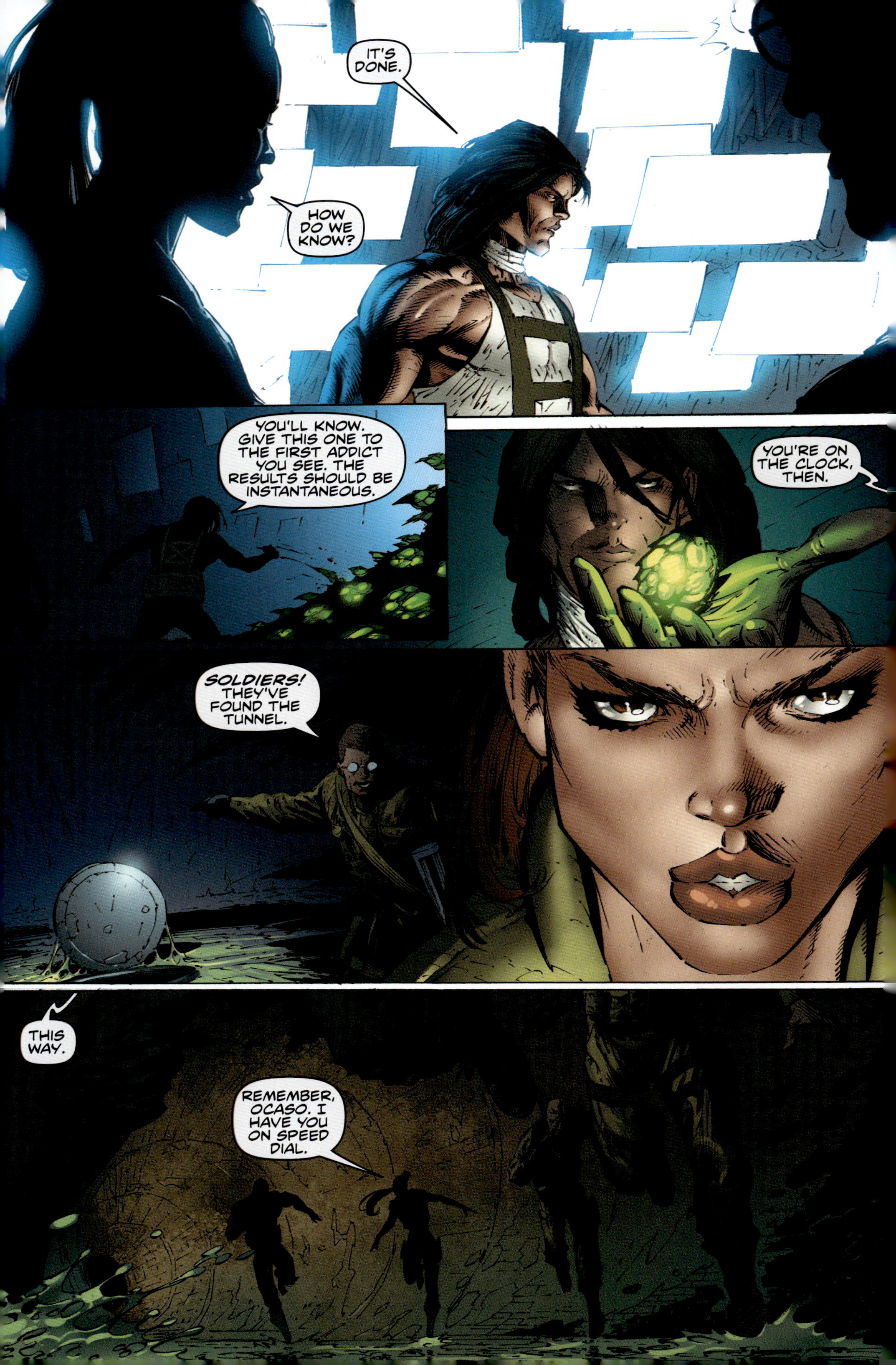
IT'S DONE.
HOW DO WE KNOW?
YOU'LL KNOW. GIVE THIS ONE TO THE FIRST ADDICT YOU SEE. THE RESULTS SHOULD BE INSTANTANEOUS.
YOU'RE ON THE CLOCK, THEN.
SOLDIERS! THEY'VE FOUND THE TUNNEL.
THIS WAY.
REMEMBER, OCASO. I HAVE YOU ON SPEED DIAL.

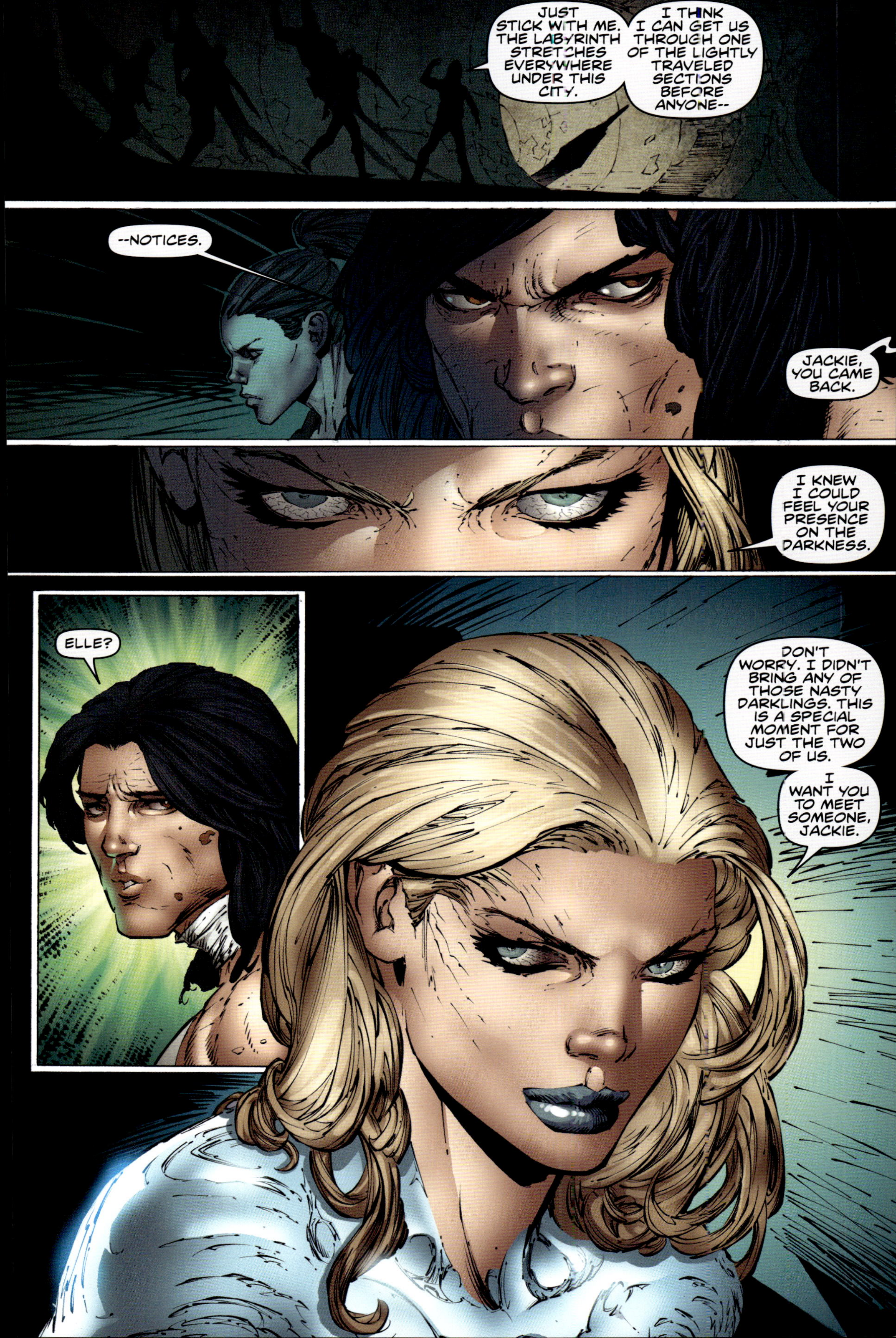
JUST STICK WITH ME. THE LABYRINTH STRETCHES EVERYWHERE UNDER THIS CITY.
I THINK I CAN GET US THROUGH ONE OF THE LIGHTLY TRAVELED SECTIONS BEFORE ANYONE--
--NOTICES.
JACKIE, YOU CAME BACK.
I KNEW I COULD FEEL YOUR PRESENCE ON THE DARKNESS.
ELLE?
DON'T WORRY. I DIDN'T BRING ANY OF THOSE NASTY DARKLINGS. THIS IS A SPECIAL MOMENT FOR JUST THE TWO OF US.
I WANT YOU TO MEET SOMEONE, JACKIE.

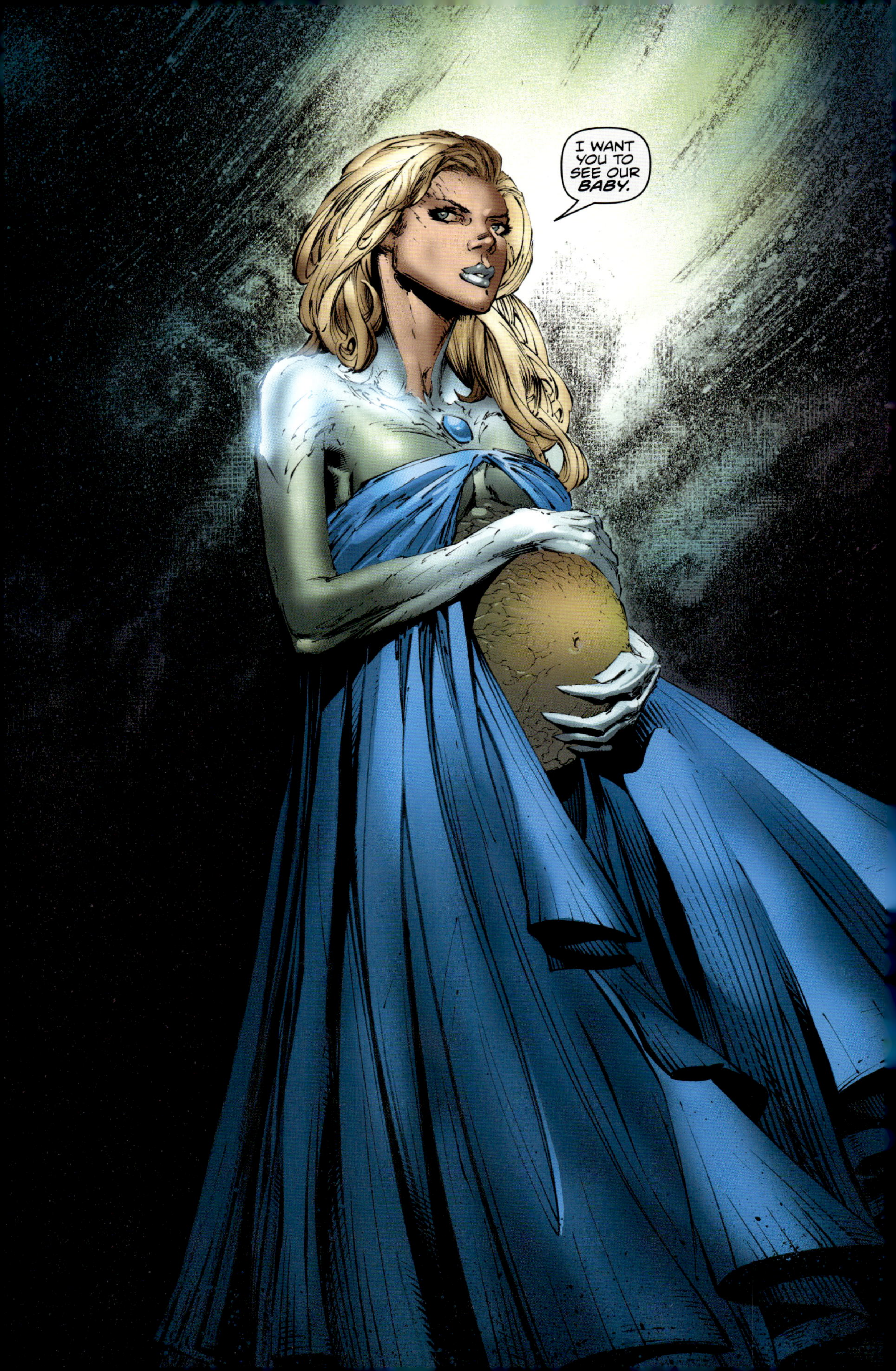
I WANT YOU TO SEE OUR BABY.

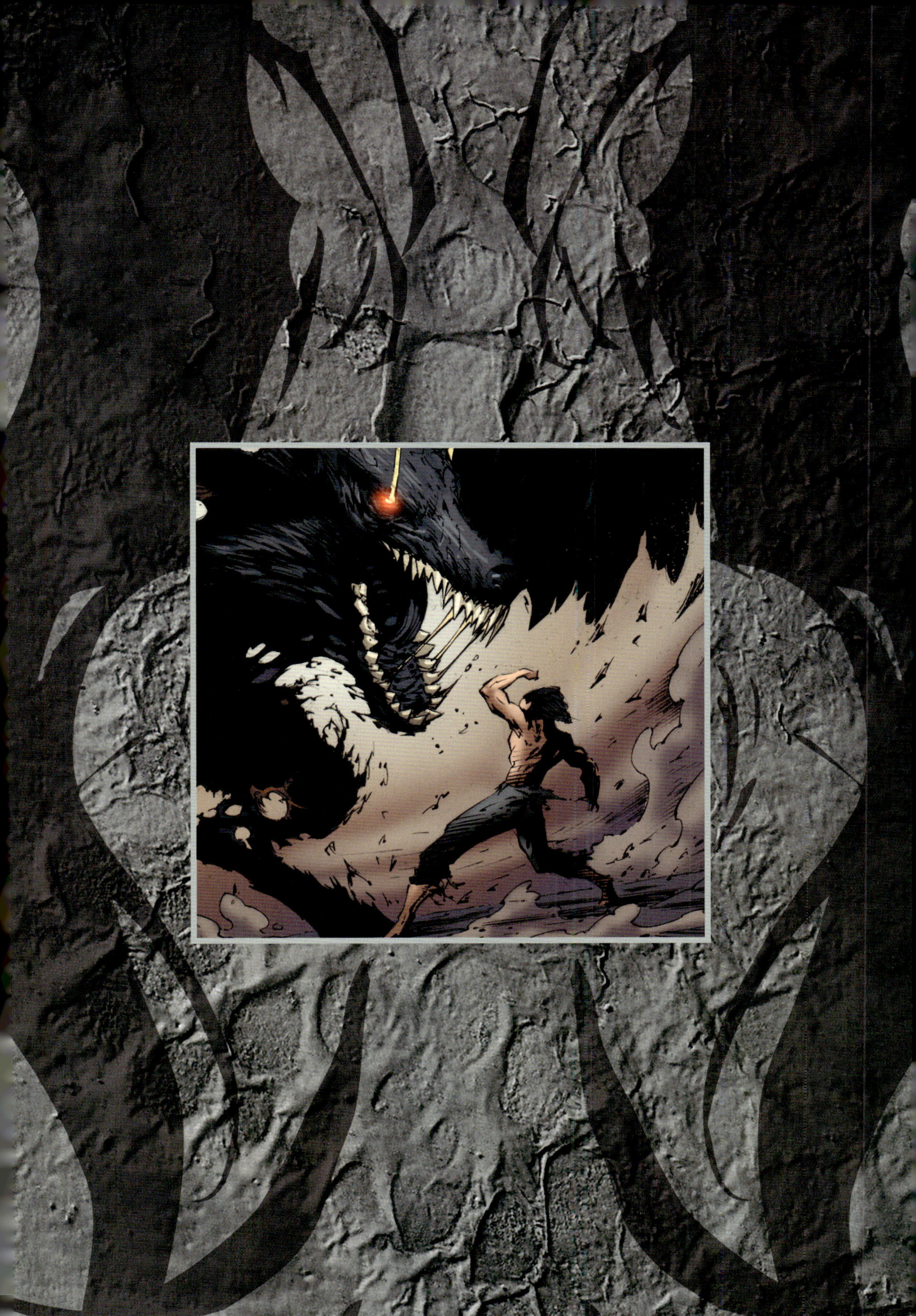

The Darkness Issue #69
cover art by: Dale Keown

THE DARKNESS #69

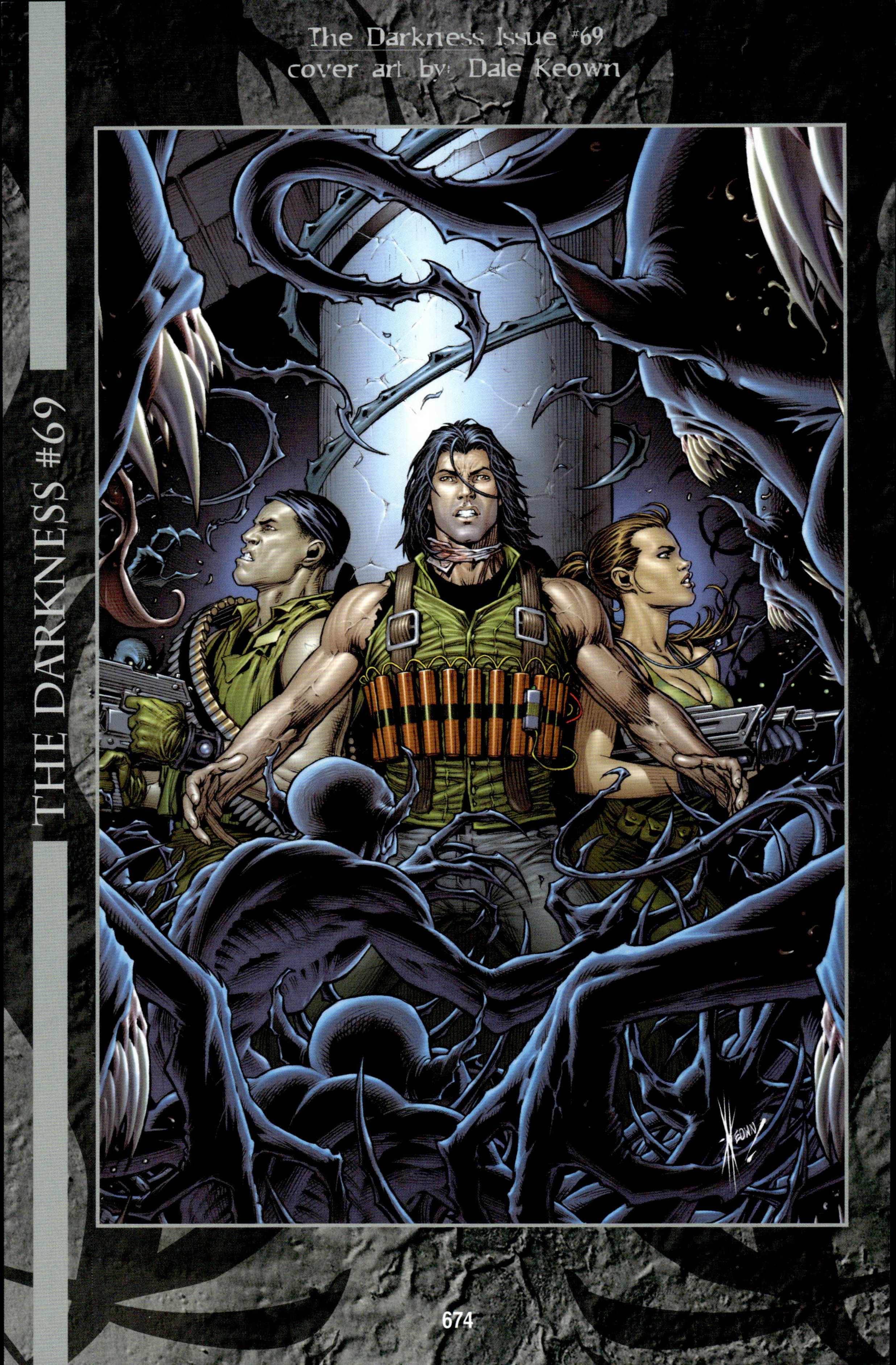

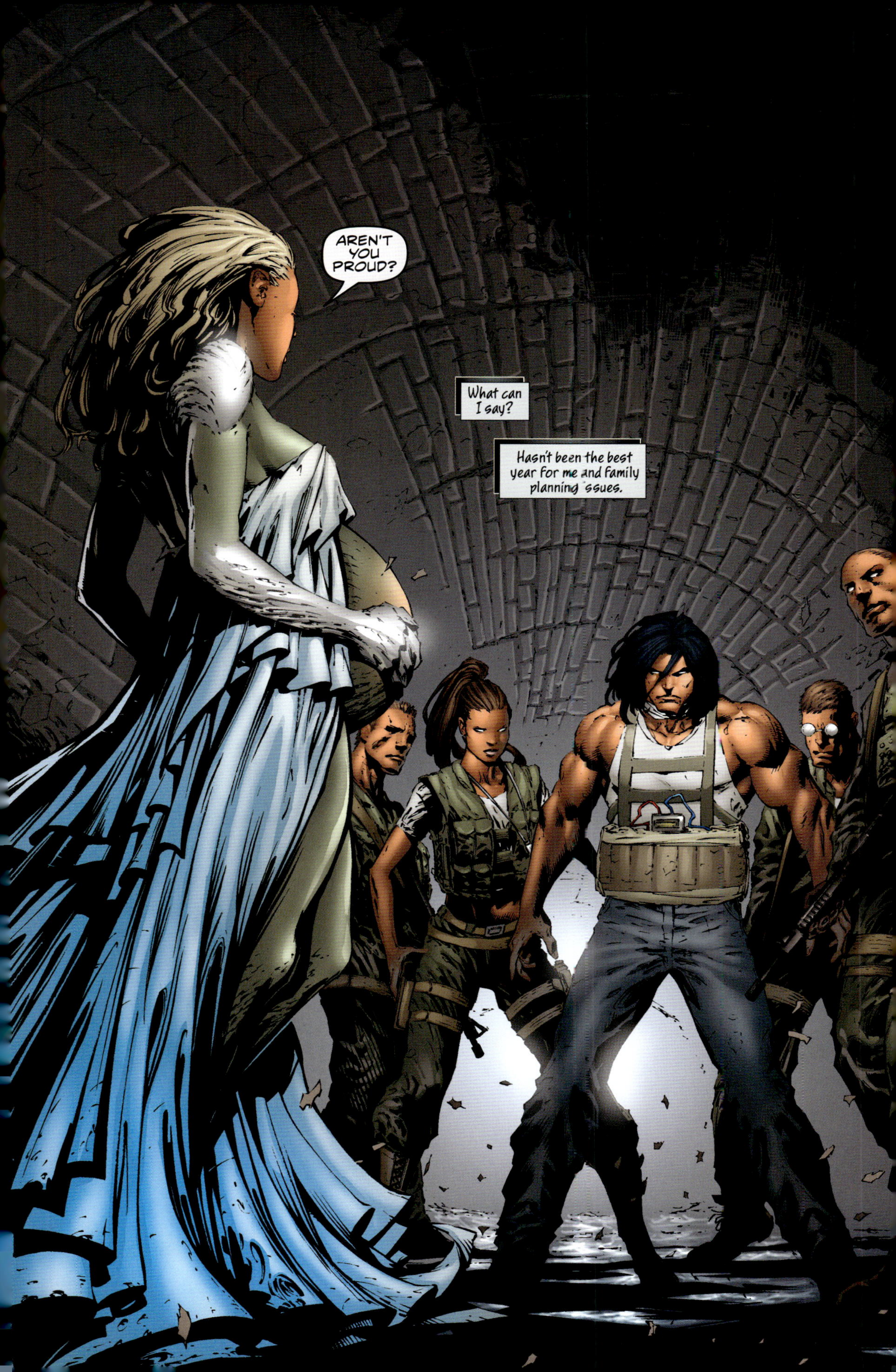
AREN'T YOU PROUD?
What can I say?
Hasn't been the best year for me and family planning issues.

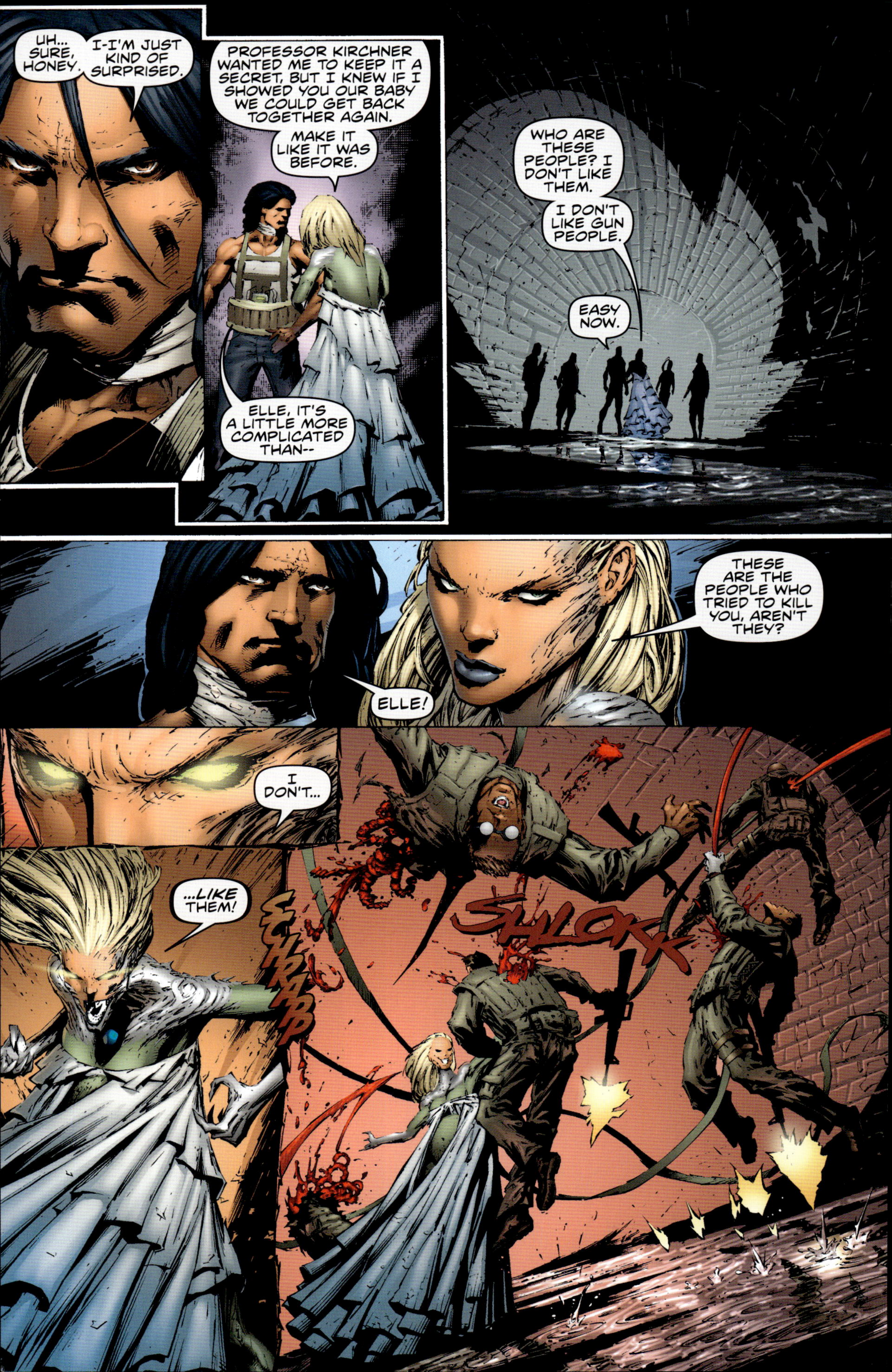
UH... SURE, HONEY.
I-I'M JUST KIND OF SURPRISED.
PROFESSOR KIRCHNER WANTED ME TO KEEP IT A SECRET, BUT I KNEW IF I SHOWED YOU OUR BABY WE COULD GET BACK TOGETHER AGAIN.
MAKE IT LIKE IT WAS BEFORE.
ELLE, IT'S A LITTLE MORE COMPLICATED THAN--
WHO ARE THESE PEOPLE? I DON'T LIKE THEM.
I DON'T LIKE GUN PEOPLE.
EASY NOW.
THESE ARE THE PEOPLE WHO TRIED TO KILL YOU, AREN'T THEY?
ELLE!
I DON'T...
...LIKE THEM!
SHLOKK

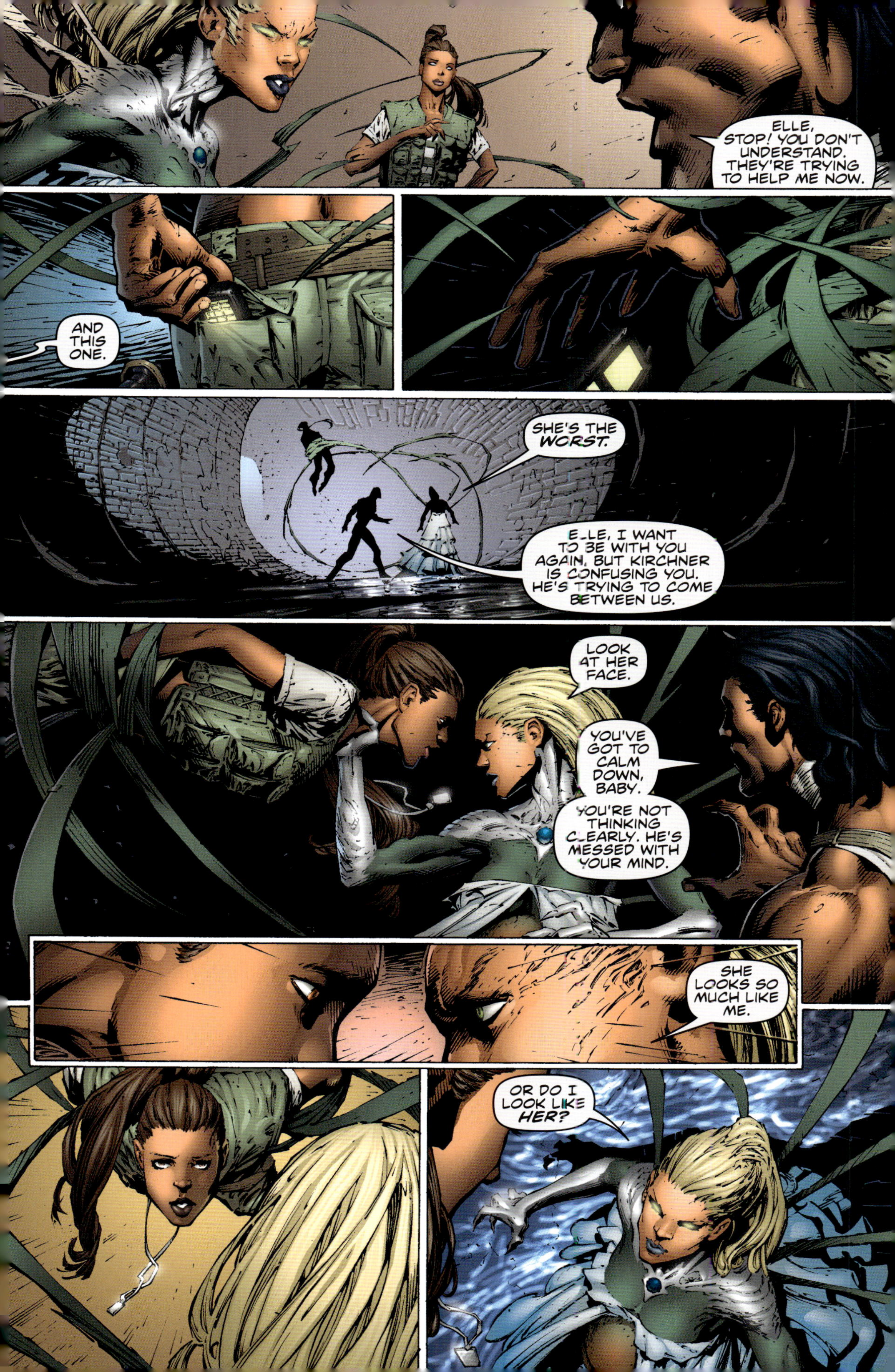
ELLE, STOP! YOU DON'T UNDERSTAND. THEY'RE TRYING TO HELP ME NOW.
AND THIS ONE.
SHE'S THE *WORST.*
ELLE, I WANT TO BE WITH YOU AGAIN, BUT KIRCHNER IS CONFUSING YOU. HE'S TRYING TO COME BETWEEN US.
LOOK AT HER FACE.
YOU'VE GOT TO CALM DOWN, BABY.
YOU'RE NOT THINKING CLEARLY. HE'S MESSED WITH YOUR MIND.
SHE LOOKS SO MUCH LIKE ME.
OR DO I LOOK LIKE *HER?*

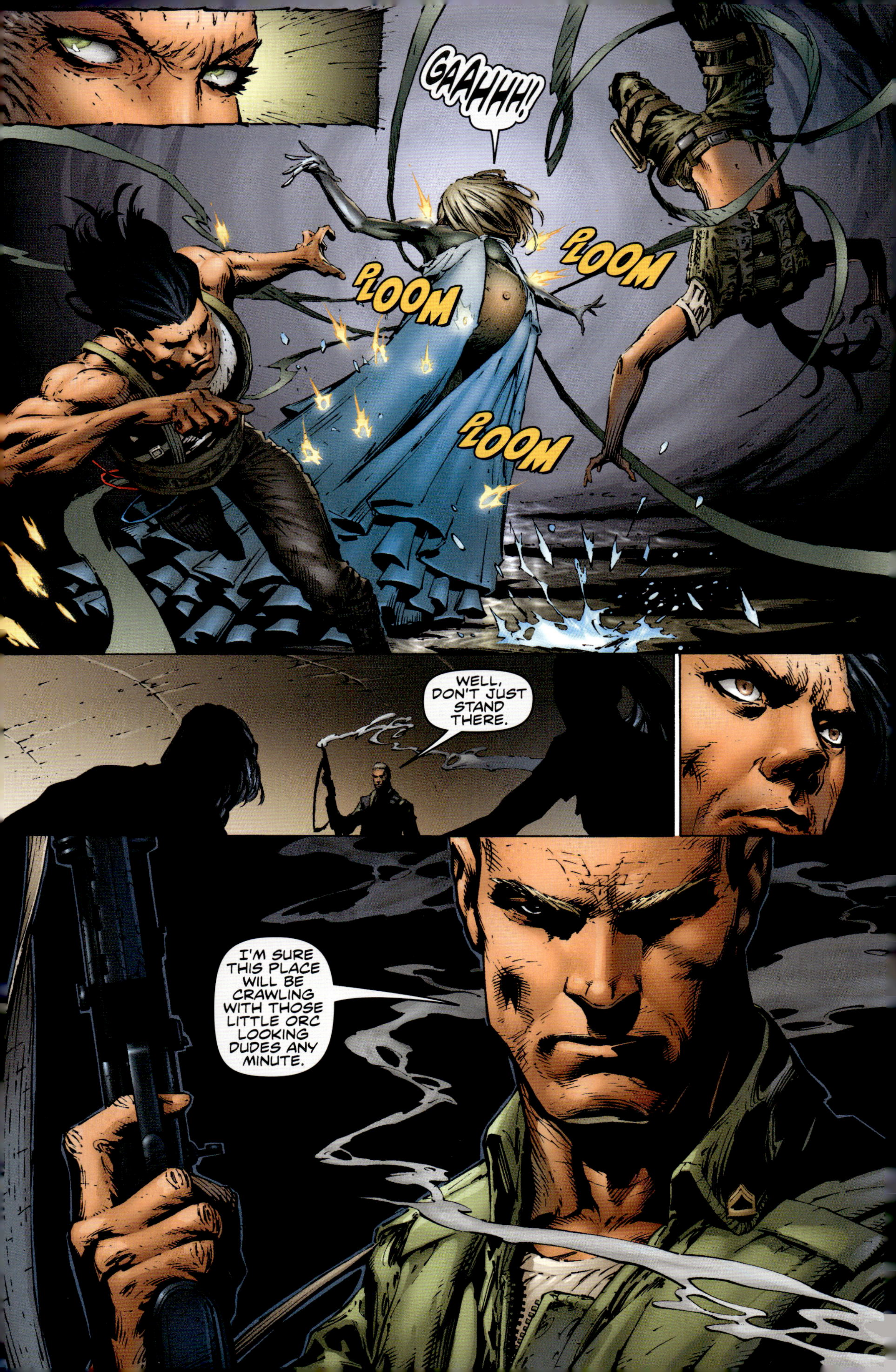
GAAHHH!
PLOOM
PLOOM
PLOOM
WELL, DON'T JUST STAND THERE.
I'M SURE THIS PLACE WILL BE CRAWLING WITH THOSE LITTLE ORC LOOKING DUDES ANY MINUTE.

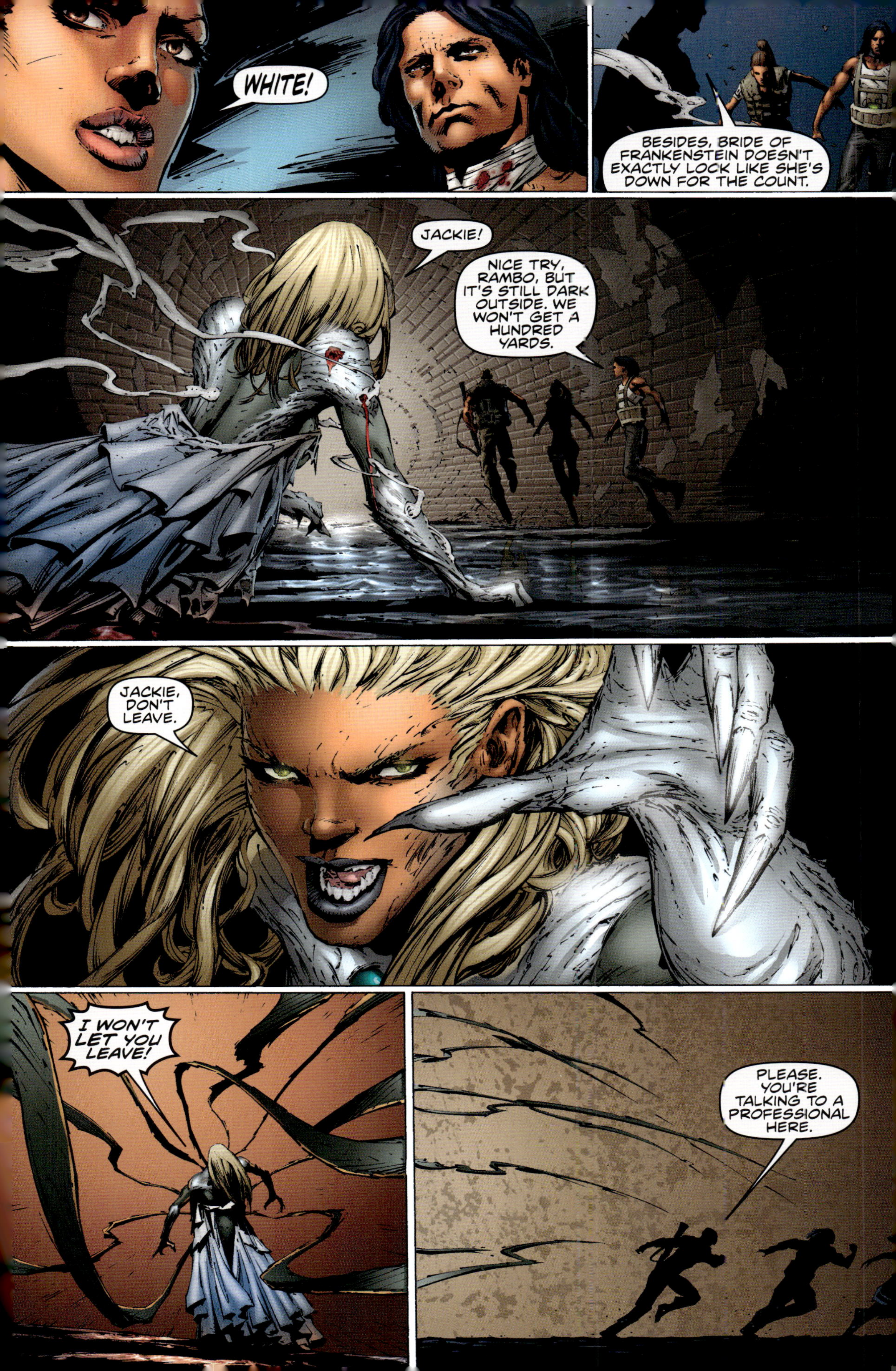
WHITE!
BESIDES, BRIDE OF FRANKENSTEIN DOESN'T EXACTLY LOOK LIKE SHE'S DOWN FOR THE COUNT.
JACKIE!
NICE TRY, RAMBO, BUT IT'S STILL DARK OUTSIDE. WE WON'T GET A HUNDRED YARDS.
JACKIE, DON'T LEAVE.
I WON'T LET YOU LEAVE!
PLEASE. YOU'RE TALKING TO A PROFESSIONAL HERE.

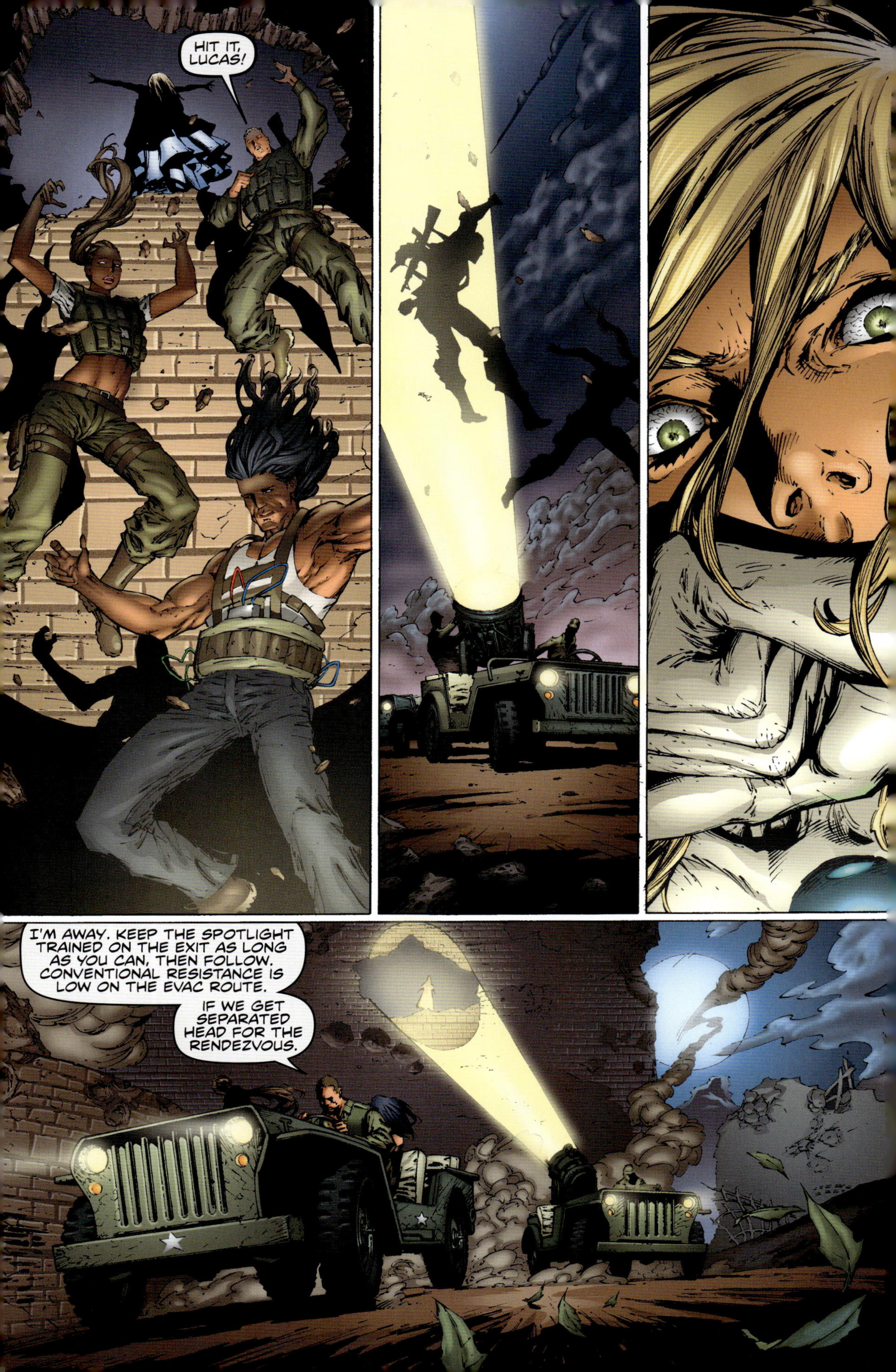
HIT IT, LUCAS!
I'M AWAY. KEEP THE SPOTLIGHT TRAINED ON THE EXIT AS LONG AS YOU CAN, THEN FOLLOW. CONVENTIONAL RESISTANCE IS LOW ON THE EVAC ROUTE.
IF WE GET SEPARATED HEAD FOR THE RENDEZVOUS.

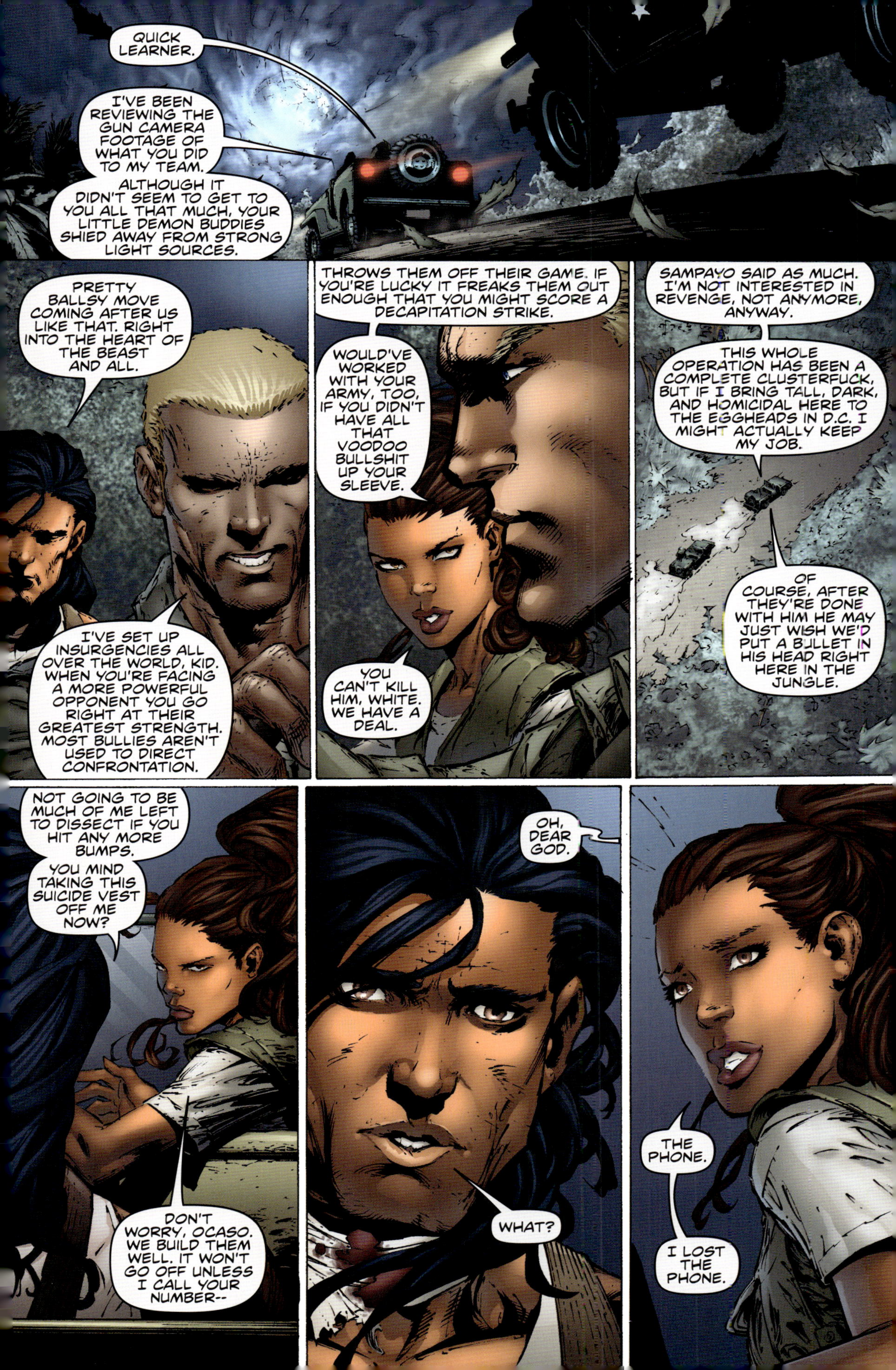
QUICK LEARNER.
I'VE BEEN REVIEWING THE GUN CAMERA FOOTAGE OF WHAT YOU DID TO MY TEAM.
ALTHOUGH IT DIDN'T SEEM TO GET TO YOU ALL THAT MUCH, YOUR LITTLE DEMON BUDDIES SHIED AWAY FROM STRONG LIGHT SOURCES.
PRETTY BALLSY MOVE COMING AFTER US LIKE THAT. RIGHT INTO THE HEART OF THE BEAST AND ALL.
I'VE SET UP INSURGENCIES ALL OVER THE WORLD, KID. WHEN YOU'RE FACING A MORE POWERFUL OPPONENT YOU GO RIGHT AT THEIR GREATEST STRENGTH. MOST BULLIES AREN'T USED TO DIRECT CONFRONTATION.
THROWS THEM OFF THEIR GAME. IF YOU'RE LUCKY IT FREAKS THEM OUT ENOUGH THAT YOU MIGHT SCORE A DECAPITATION STRIKE.
WOULD'VE WORKED WITH YOUR ARMY, TOO, IF YOU DIDN'T HAVE ALL THAT VOODOO BULLSHIT UP YOUR SLEEVE.
YOU CAN'T KILL HIM, WHITE. WE HAVE A DEAL.
SAMPAYO SAID AS MUCH. I'M NOT INTERESTED IN REVENGE, NOT ANYMORE, ANYWAY.
THIS WHOLE OPERATION HAS BEEN A COMPLETE CLUSTERFUCK, BUT IF I BRING TALL, DARK, AND HOMICIDAL HERE TO THE EGGHEADS IN D.C. I MIGHT ACTUALLY KEEP MY JOB.
OF COURSE, AFTER THEY'RE DONE WITH HIM HE MAY JUST WISH WE'D PUT A BULLET IN HIS HEAD RIGHT HERE IN THE JUNGLE.
NOT GOING TO BE MUCH OF ME LEFT TO DISSECT IF YOU HIT ANY MORE BUMPS.
YOU MIND TAKING THIS SUICIDE VEST OFF ME NOW?
DON'T WORRY, OCASO. WE BUILD THEM WELL. IT WON'T GO OFF UNLESS I CALL YOUR NUMBER--
OH, DEAR GOD.
WHAT?
THE PHONE.
I LOST THE PHONE.

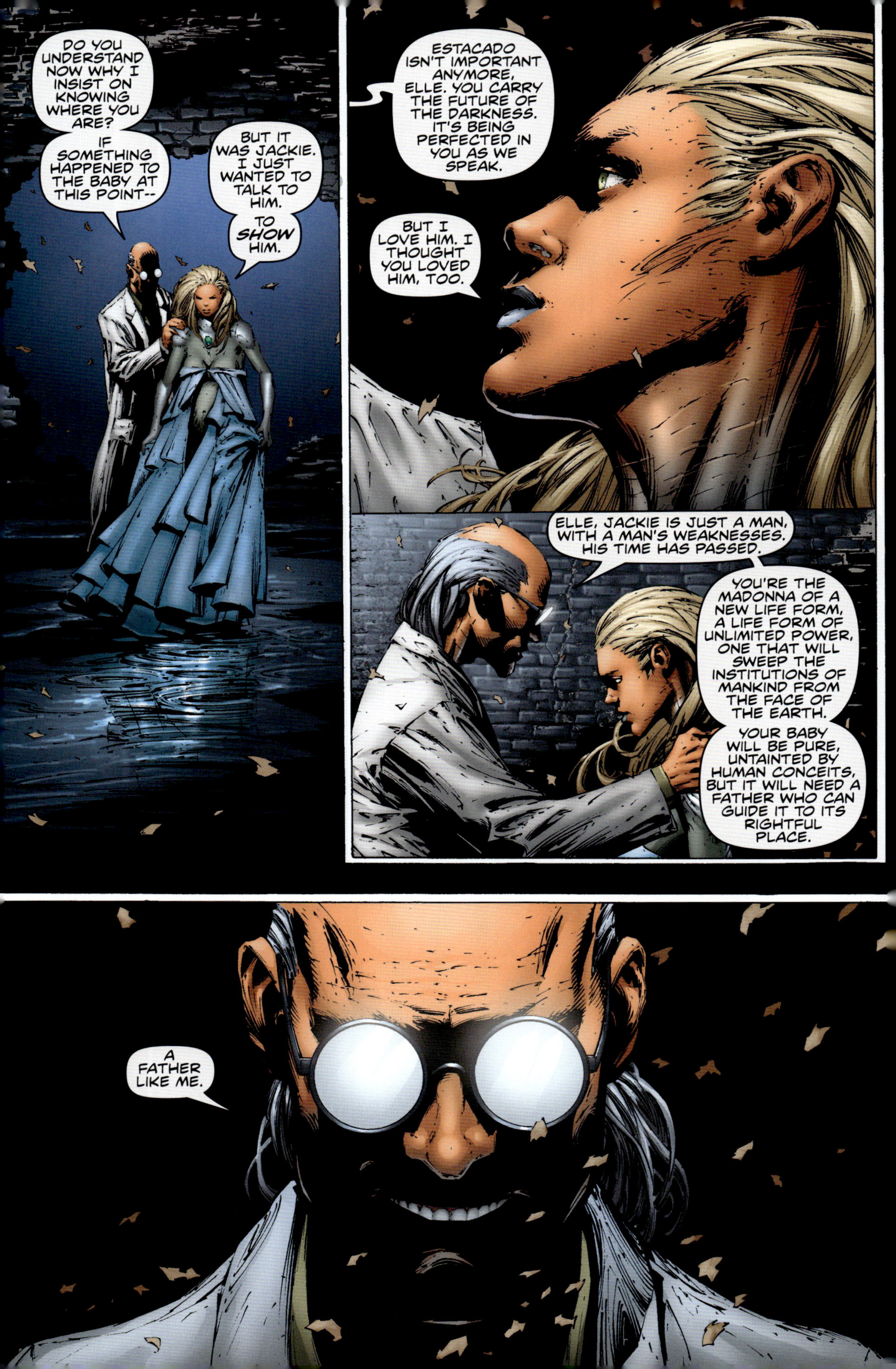
DO YOU UNDERSTAND NOW WHY I INSIST ON KNOWING WHERE YOU ARE?
IF SOMETHING HAPPENED TO THE BABY AT THIS POINT--
BUT IT WAS JACKIE. I JUST WANTED TO TALK TO HIM.
TO *SHOW* HIM.
ESTACADO ISN'T IMPORTANT ANYMORE, ELLE. YOU CARRY THE FUTURE OF THE DARKNESS. IT'S BEING PERFECTED IN YOU AS WE SPEAK.
BUT I LOVE HIM. I THOUGHT YOU LOVED HIM, TOO.
ELLE, JACKIE IS JUST A MAN, WITH A MAN'S WEAKNESSES. HIS TIME HAS PASSED.
YOU'RE THE MADONNA OF A NEW LIFE FORM, A LIFE FORM OF UNLIMITED POWER, ONE THAT WILL SWEEP THE INSTITUTIONS OF MANKIND FROM THE FACE OF THE EARTH.
YOUR BABY WILL BE PURE, UNTAINTED BY HUMAN CONCEITS, BUT IT WILL NEED A FATHER WHO CAN GUIDE IT TO ITS RIGHTFUL PLACE.
A FATHER LIKE ME.

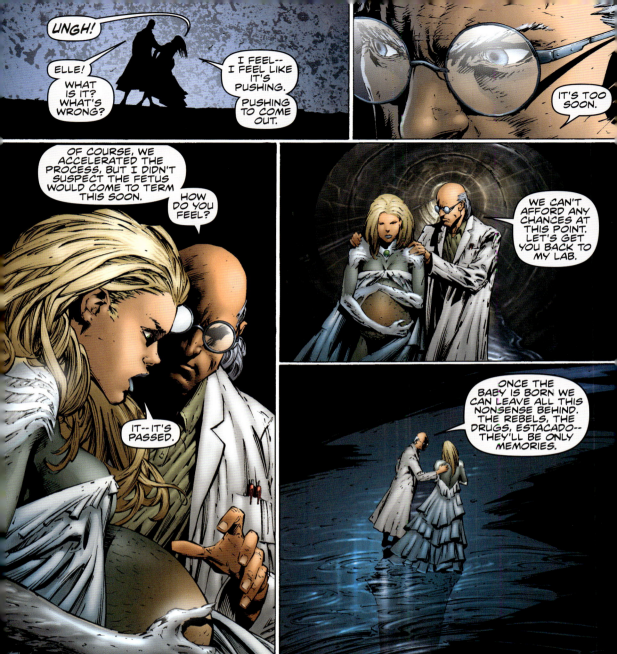

UNGH!

ELLE! WHAT IS IT? WHAT'S WRONG?

I FEEL-- I FEEL LIKE IT'S PUSHING. PUSHING TO COME OUT.

IT'S TOO SOON.

OF COURSE, WE ACCELERATED THE PROCESS, BUT I DIDN'T SUSPECT THE FETUS WOULD COME TO TERM THIS SOON. HOW DO YOU FEEL?

WE CAN'T AFFORD ANY CHANCES AT THIS POINT. LET'S GET YOU BACK TO MY LAB.

IT-- IT'S PASSED.

ONCE THE BABY IS BORN WE CAN LEAVE ALL THIS NONSENSE BEHIND. THE REBELS, THE DRUGS, ESTACADO-- THEY'LL BE ONLY MEMORIES.

WHAT'S THIS?

THE GIRL DROPPED IT, I THINK.

GIRL?

YOU KNOW, THE ONE WHO LOOKS LIKE ME.

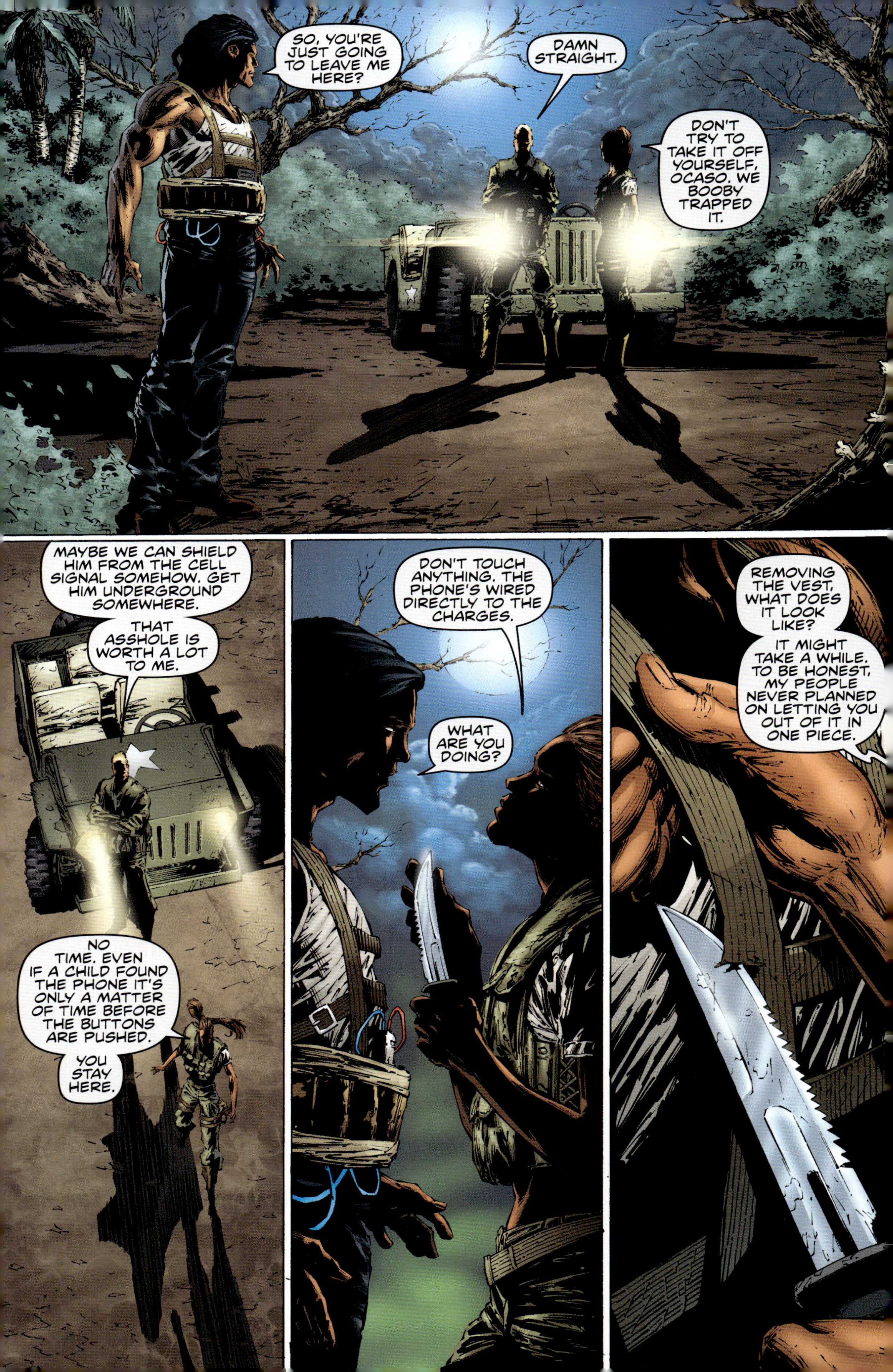
SO, YOU'RE JUST GOING TO LEAVE ME HERE?
DAMN STRAIGHT.
DON'T TRY TO TAKE IT OFF YOURSELF, OCASO. WE BOOBY TRAPPED IT.
MAYBE WE CAN SHIELD HIM FROM THE CELL SIGNAL SOMEHOW. GET HIM UNDERGROUND SOMEWHERE.
THAT ASSHOLE IS WORTH A LOT TO ME.
NO TIME. EVEN IF A CHILD FOUND THE PHONE IT'S ONLY A MATTER OF TIME BEFORE THE BUTTONS ARE PUSHED.
YOU STAY HERE.
DON'T TOUCH ANYTHING. THE PHONE'S WIRED DIRECTLY TO THE CHARGES.
WHAT ARE YOU DOING?
REMOVING THE VEST, WHAT DOES IT LOOK LIKE?
IT MIGHT TAKE A WHILE. TO BE HONEST, MY PEOPLE NEVER PLANNED ON LETTING YOU OUT OF IT IN ONE PIECE.

HOLD STILL.

MARISOL.

DON'T CALL ME THAT.

MARISOL. I DON'T KNOW HOW ELSE TO SAY THIS-- I'M NOT WORTH IT.

LOOK AT ME. I'M NOT KIDDING.

I DON'T DESERVE YOU RISKING YOUR LIFE TO SAVE ME.

QUIET, PLEASE. I'M TRYING TO CONCENTRATE.

ALL THE THINGS I DID TO YOUR COUNTRY-- FOR MONEY, I GUESS.

I WAS REALLY JUST RUNNING AWAY FROM ANOTHER MESS I'D MADE IN THE STATES.

LET GO, I'M WORKING HERE.

IT'S JUST-- MY WHOLE LIFE I'VE BEEN KICKED AROUND, YOU KNOW? I DON'T KNOW HOW TO DO ANYTHING BUT KICK BACK.

THERE'S NOTHING IN ME BUT SOME FUCKED UP LITTLE KID WHO WANTS TO HIT BACK UNTIL THERE'S NOTHING LEFT TO HIT.

I'VE PROBABLY KILLED HUNDREDS OF PEOPLE, AND UNTIL JUST A FEW DAYS AGO IT DIDN'T BOTHER ME ONE BIT. IT WAS JUST ANOTHER NATURAL FUNCTION TO ME, LIKE BREATHING.

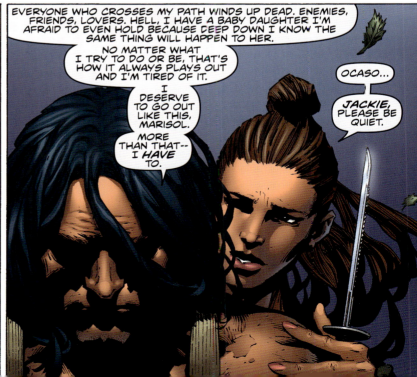

EVERYONE WHO CROSSES MY PATH WINDS UP DEAD. ENEMIES, FRIENDS, LOVERS. HELL, I HAVE A BABY DAUGHTER I'M AFRAID TO EVEN HOLD BECAUSE DEEP DOWN I KNOW THE SAME THING WILL HAPPEN TO HER.

NO MATTER WHAT I TRY TO DO OR BE, THAT'S HOW IT ALWAYS PLAYS OUT AND I'M TIRED OF IT.

I DESERVE TO GO OUT LIKE THIS, MARISOL.

MORE THAN THAT-- I HAVE TO.

OCASO...

JACKIE, PLEASE BE QUIET.

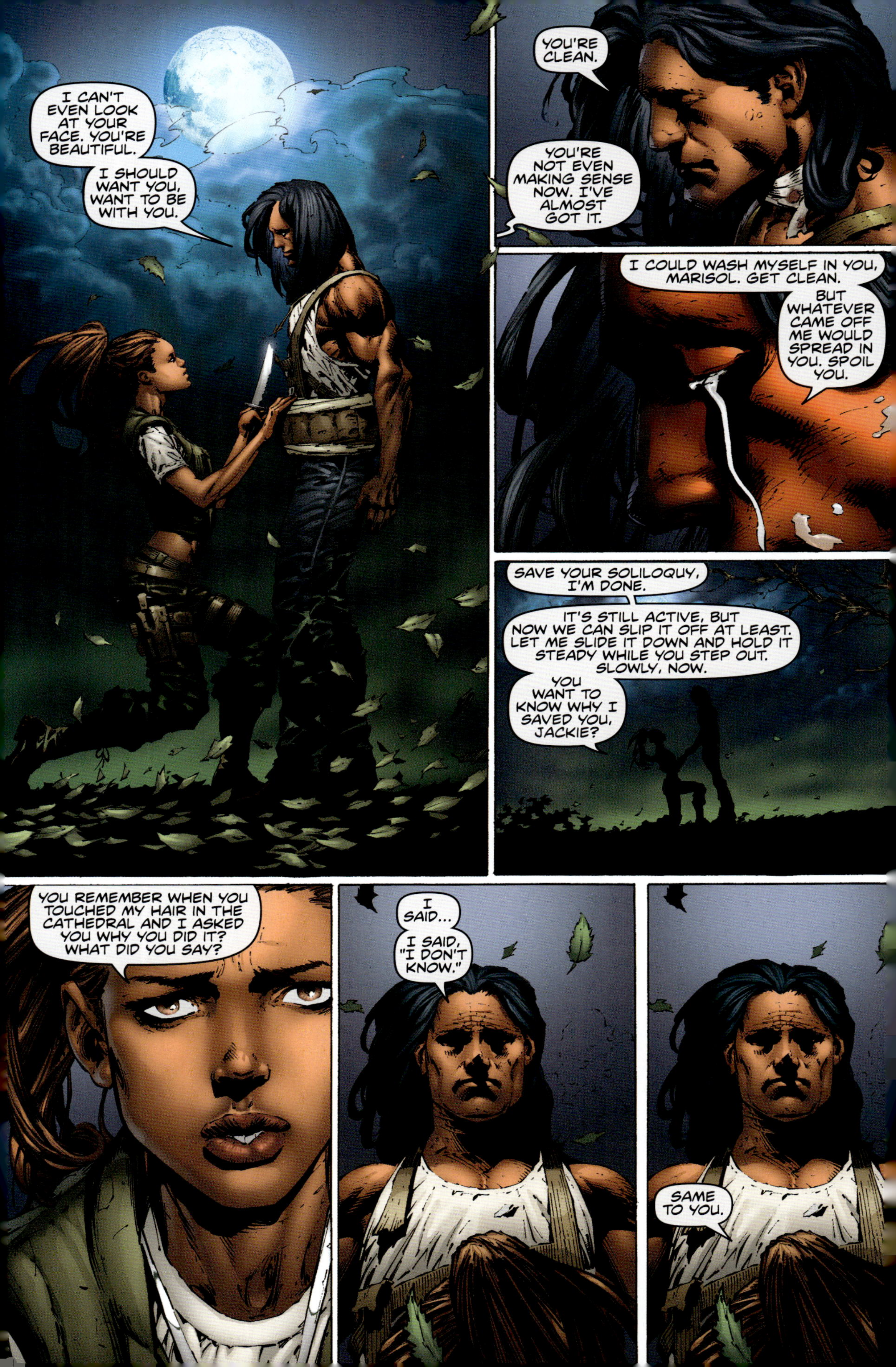
I CAN'T EVEN LOOK AT YOUR FACE. YOU'RE BEAUTIFUL.
I SHOULD WANT YOU, WANT TO BE WITH YOU.
YOU'RE CLEAN.
YOU'RE NOT EVEN MAKING SENSE NOW. I'VE ALMOST GOT IT.
I COULD WASH MYSELF IN YOU, MARISOL. GET CLEAN.
BUT WHATEVER CAME OFF ME WOULD SPREAD IN YOU. SPOIL YOU.
SAVE YOUR SOLILOQUY, I'M DONE.
IT'S STILL ACTIVE, BUT NOW WE CAN SLIP IT OFF AT LEAST. LET ME SLIDE IT DOWN AND HOLD IT STEADY WHILE YOU STEP OUT. SLOWLY, NOW.
YOU WANT TO KNOW WHY I SAVED YOU, JACKIE?
YOU REMEMBER WHEN YOU TOUCHED MY HAIR IN THE CATHEDRAL AND I ASKED YOU WHY YOU DID IT? WHAT DID YOU SAY?
I SAID...
I SAID, "I DON'T KNOW."
SAME TO YOU.

ESCORT HER DIRECTLY TO THE LAB. NO GAMES.

WATCH FOR ANY STRAY REBELS LOST IN THE LABYRINTH.

COMPUTER, GIVE ME A PLAYBACK SCREEN FOR THIS CORRIDOR.

REPLAY THIRTEEN MINUTES AGO.

TWELVE.

STOP.

ZOOM IN.

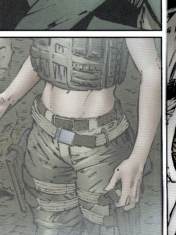

OH, JACKIE, YOU STUPID, STUPID LITTLE MAN.

WHY THE DARKNESS CHOSE YOU I'LL NEVER KNOW.

MEEP

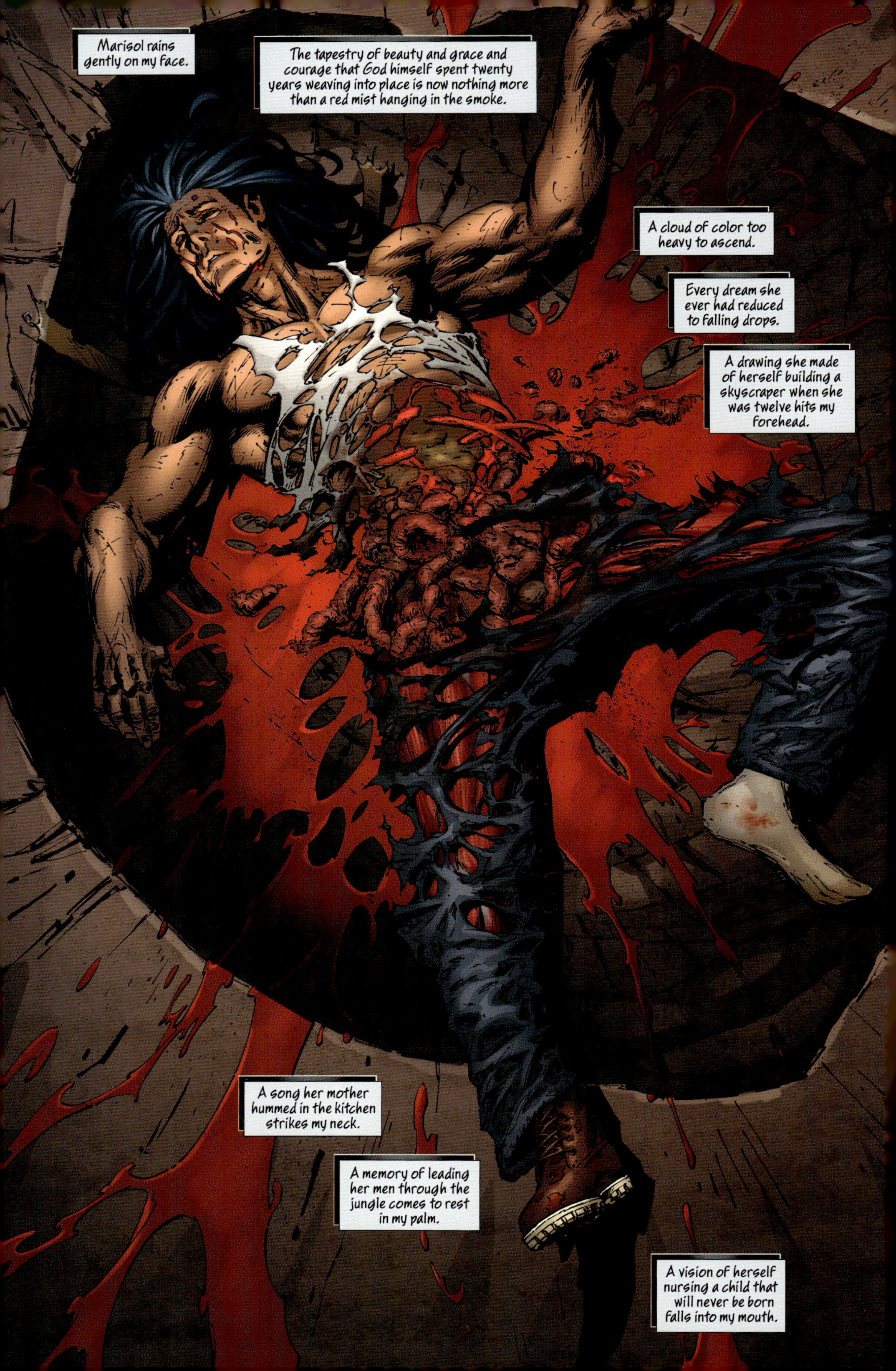
Marisol rains gently on my face.
The tapestry of beauty and grace and courage that God himself spent twenty years weaving into place is now nothing more than a red mist hanging in the smoke.
A cloud of color too heavy to ascend.
Every dream she ever had reduced to falling drops.
A drawing she made of herself building a skyscraper when she was twelve hits my forehead.
A song her mother hummed in the kitchen strikes my neck.
A memory of leading her men through the jungle comes to rest in my palm.
A vision of herself nursing a child that will never be born falls into my mouth.

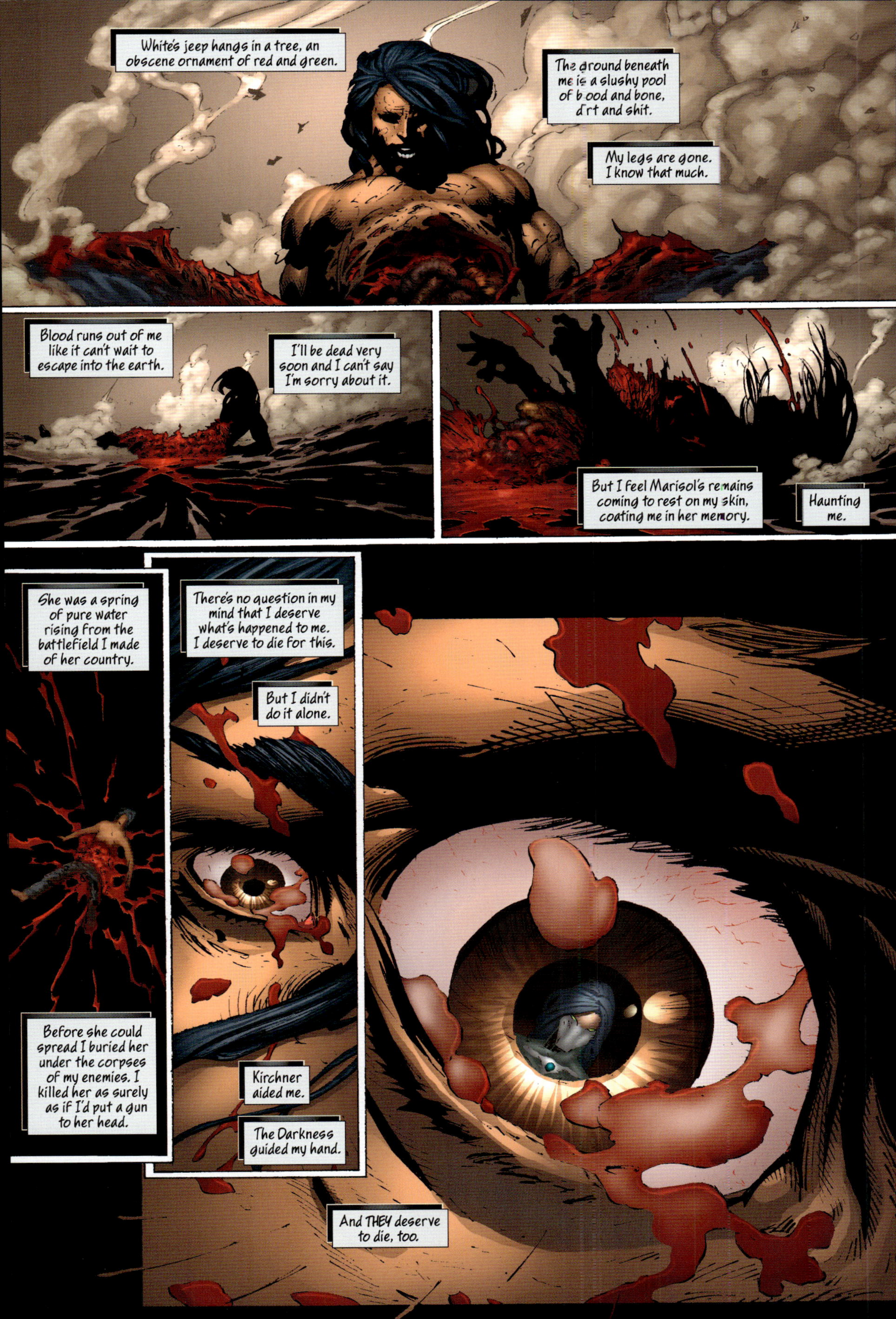
White's jeep hangs in a tree, an obscene ornament of red and green.
The ground beneath me is a slushy pool of blood and bone, dirt and shit.
My legs are gone. I know that much.
Blood runs out of me like it can't wait to escape into the earth.
I'll be dead very soon and I can't say I'm sorry about it.
But I feel Marisol's remains coming to rest on my skin, coating me in her memory.
Haunting me.
She was a spring of pure water rising from the battlefield I made of her country.
Before she could spread I buried her under the corpses of my enemies. I killed her as surely as if I'd put a gun to her head.
There's no question in my mind that I deserve what's happened to me. I deserve to die for this.
But I didn't do it alone.
Kirchner aided me.
The Darkness guided my hand.
And THEY deserve to die, too.

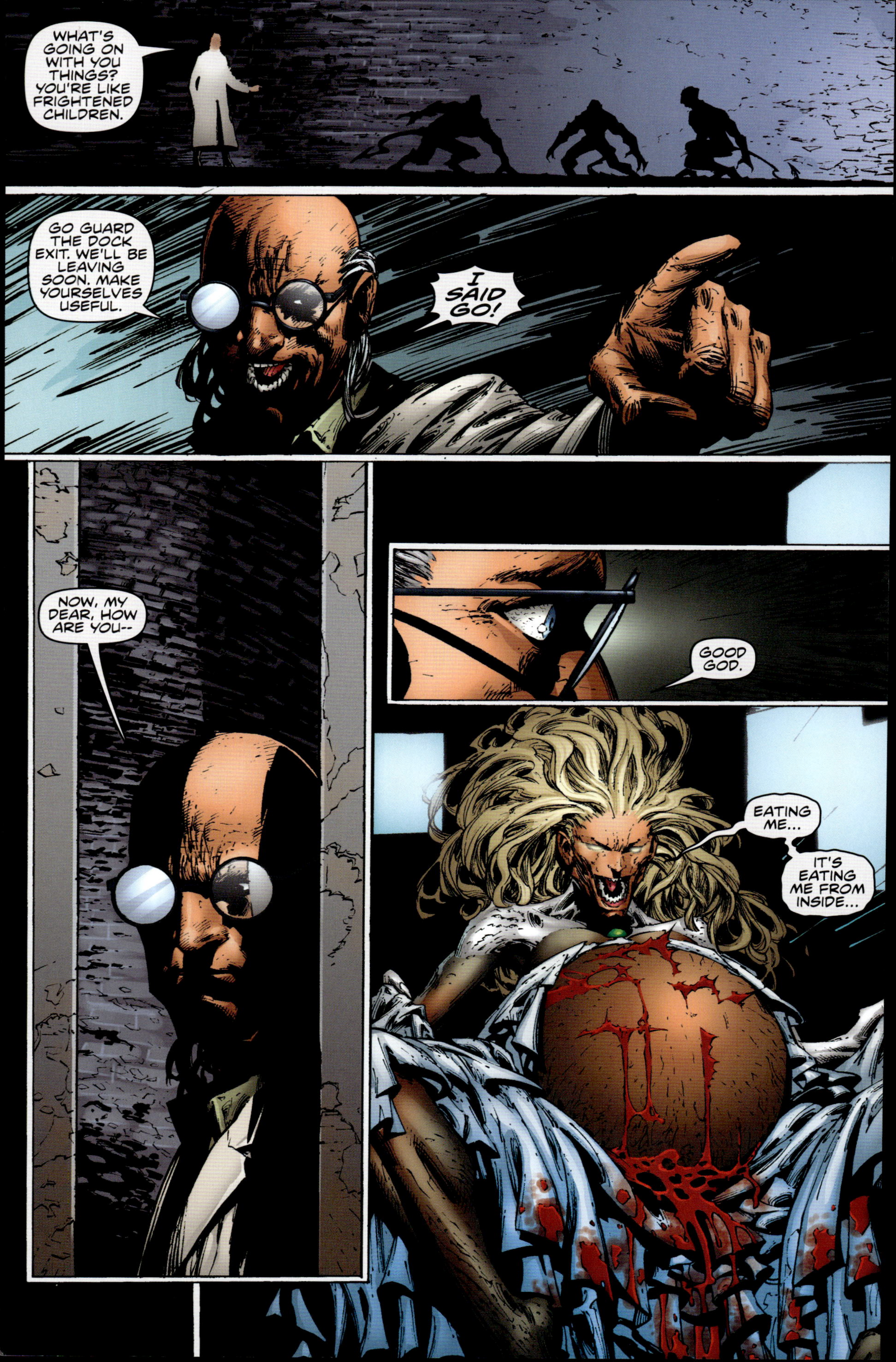
WHAT'S GOING ON WITH YOU THINGS? YOU'RE LIKE FRIGHTENED CHILDREN.
GO GUARD THE DOCK EXIT. WE'LL BE LEAVING SOON. MAKE YOURSELVES USEFUL.
I SAID GO!
NOW, MY DEAR, HOW ARE YOU--
GOOD GOD.
EATING ME...
IT'S EATING ME FROM INSIDE...

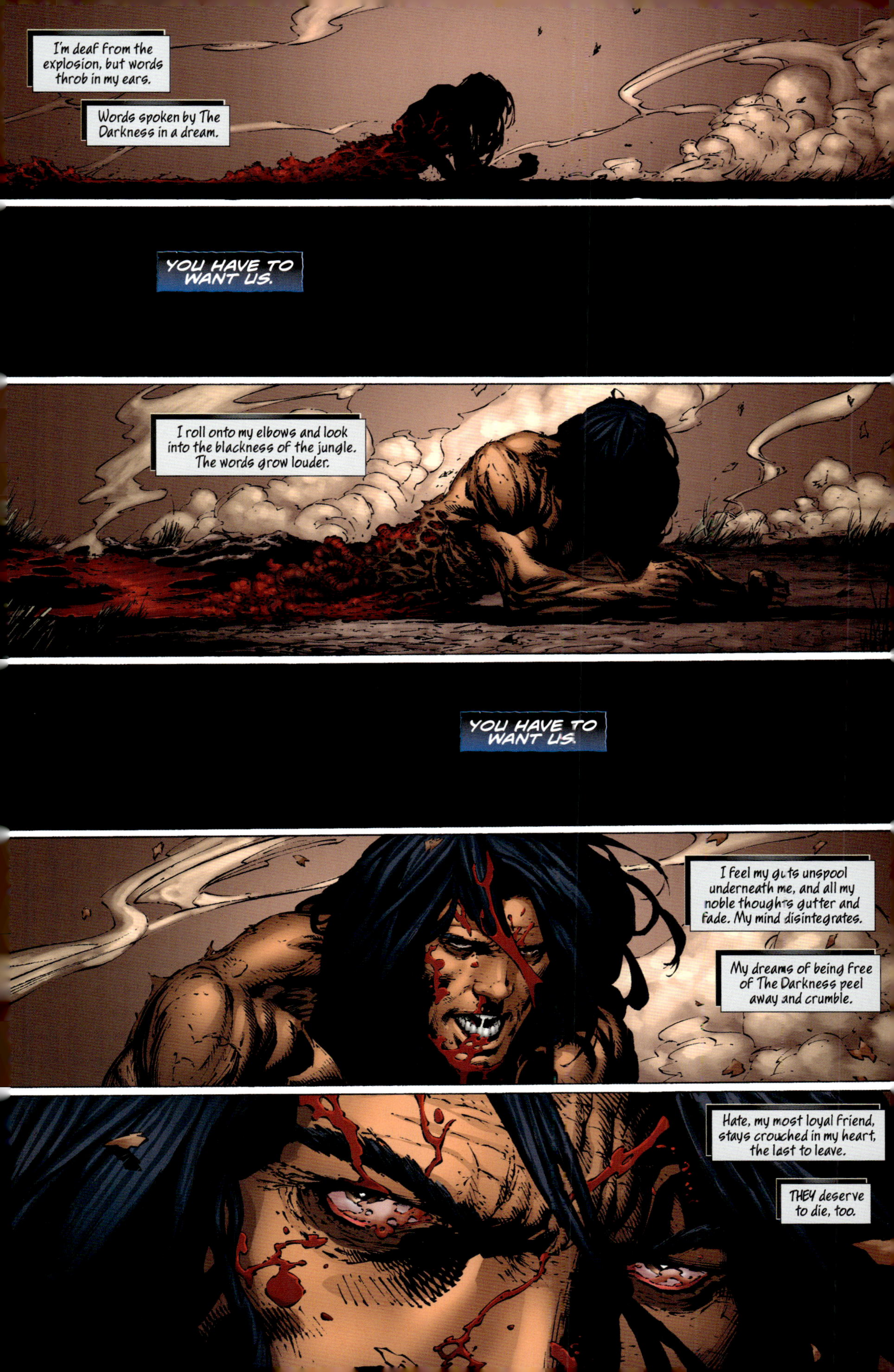
I'm deaf from the explosion, but words throb in my ears.
Words spoken by The Darkness in a dream.
YOU HAVE TO WANT US.
I roll onto my elbows and look into the blackness of the jungle. The words grow louder.
YOU HAVE TO WANT US.
I feel my guts unspool underneath me, and all my noble thoughts gutter and fade. My mind disintegrates.
My dreams of being free of The Darkness peel away and crumble.
Hate, my most loyal friend, stays crouched in my heart, the last to leave.
THEY deserve to die, too.

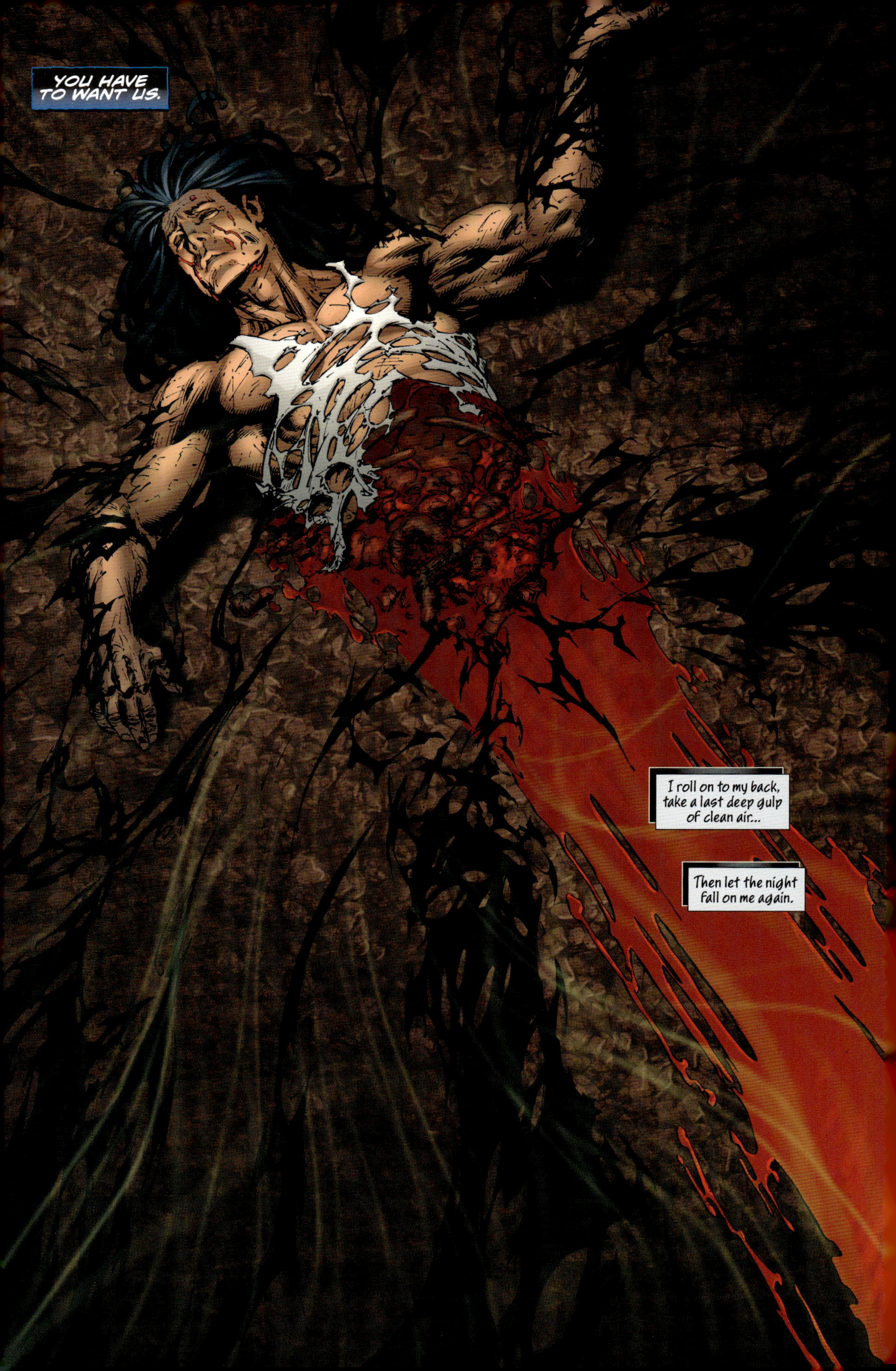
YOU HAVE TO WANT US.
I roll on to my back, take a last deep gulp of clean air...
Then let the night fall on me again.

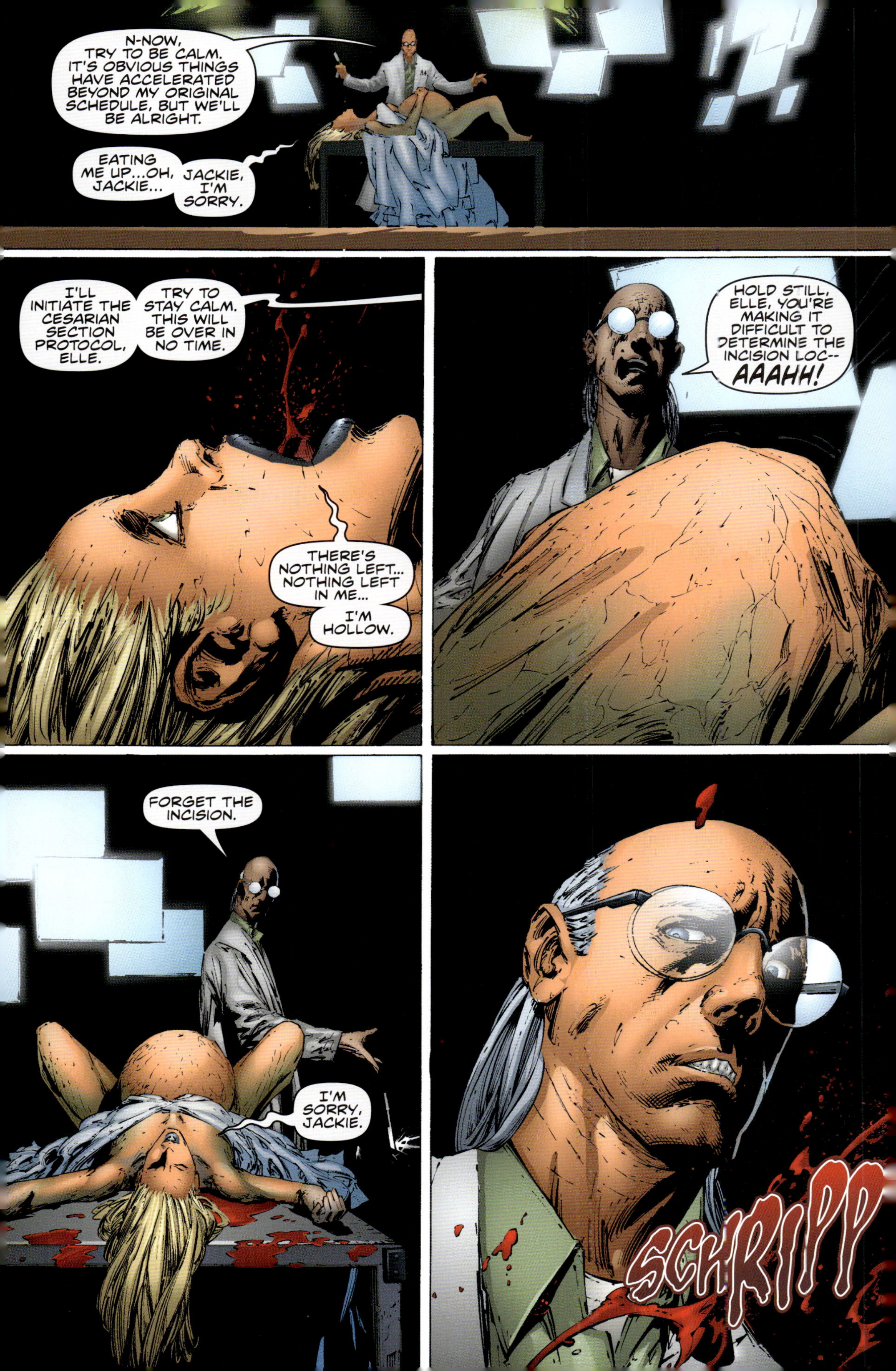
N-NOW, TRY TO BE CALM. IT'S OBVIOUS THINGS HAVE ACCELERATED BEYOND MY ORIGINAL SCHEDULE, BUT WE'LL BE ALRIGHT.
EATING ME UP...OH, JACKIE...
JACKIE, I'M SORRY.
I'LL INITIATE THE CESARIAN SECTION PROTOCOL, ELLE.
TRY TO STAY CALM. THIS WILL BE OVER IN NO TIME.
THERE'S NOTHING LEFT... NOTHING LEFT IN ME...
I'M HOLLOW.
HOLD STILL, ELLE, YOU'RE MAKING IT DIFFICULT TO DETERMINE THE INCISION LOC-- AAAHH!
FORGET THE INCISION.
I'M SORRY, JACKIE.
SCHRIPP

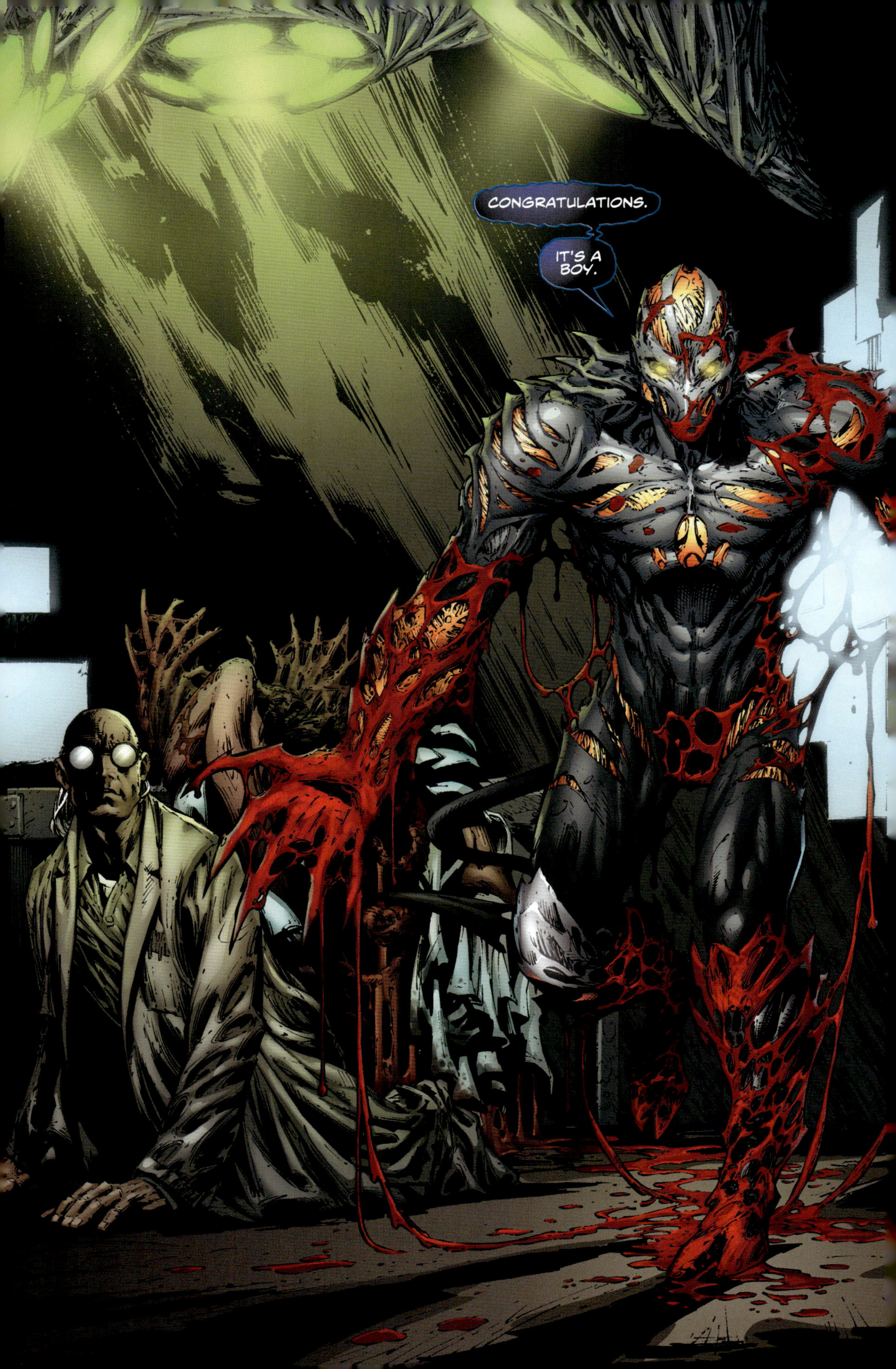
CONGRATULATIONS.
IT'S A BOY.

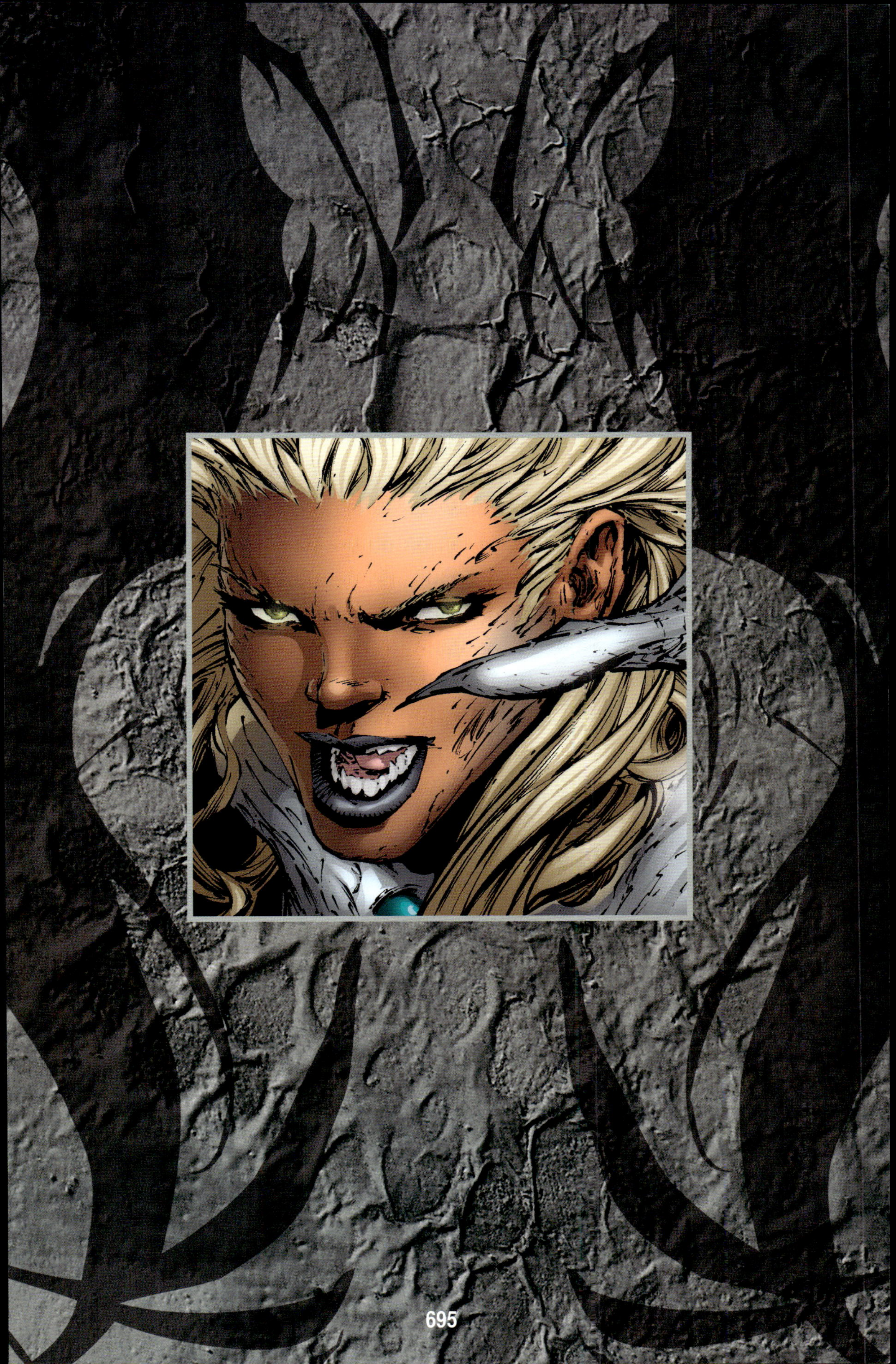

The Darkness Issue #70
cover art by: Dale Keown

THE DARKNESS #70

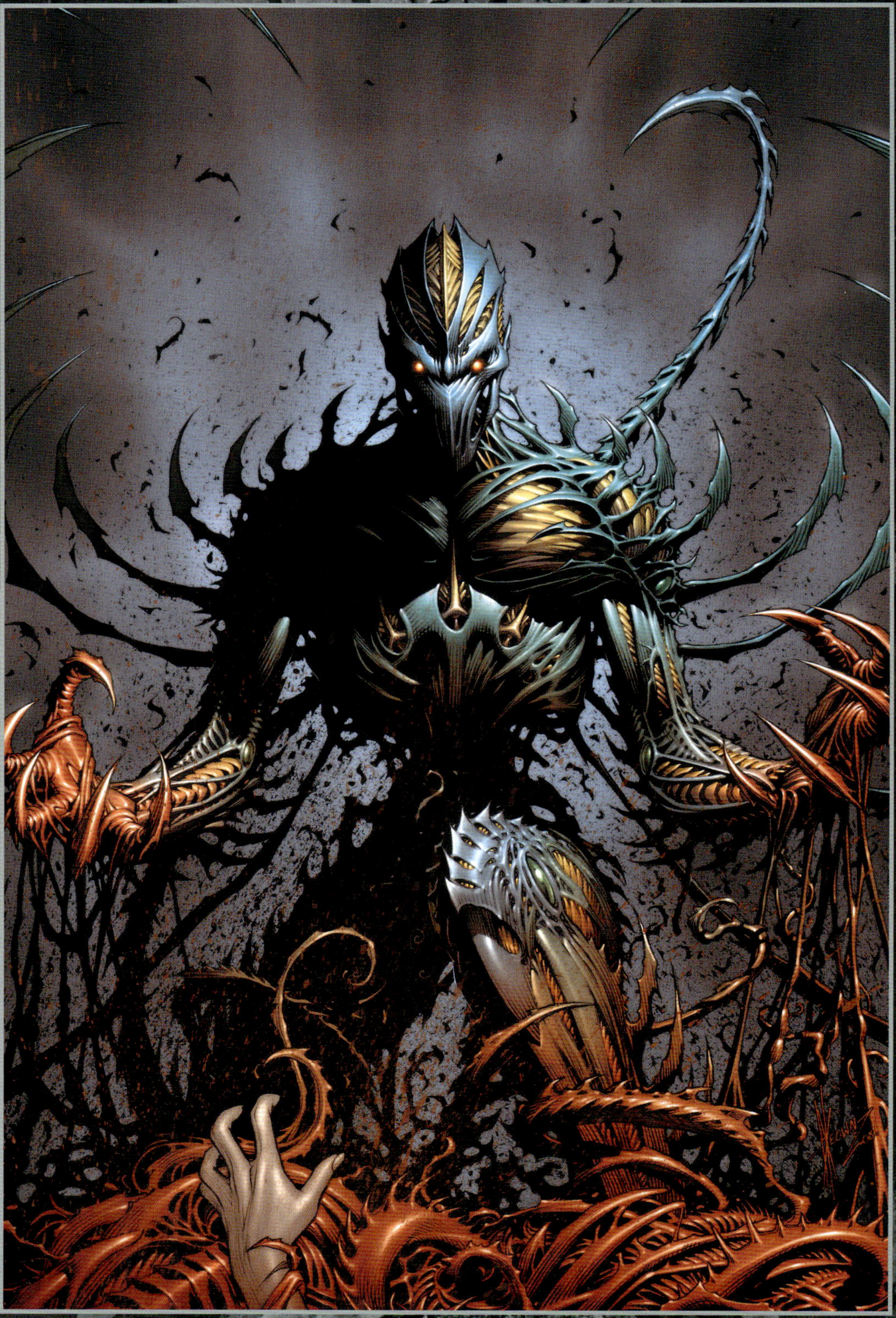

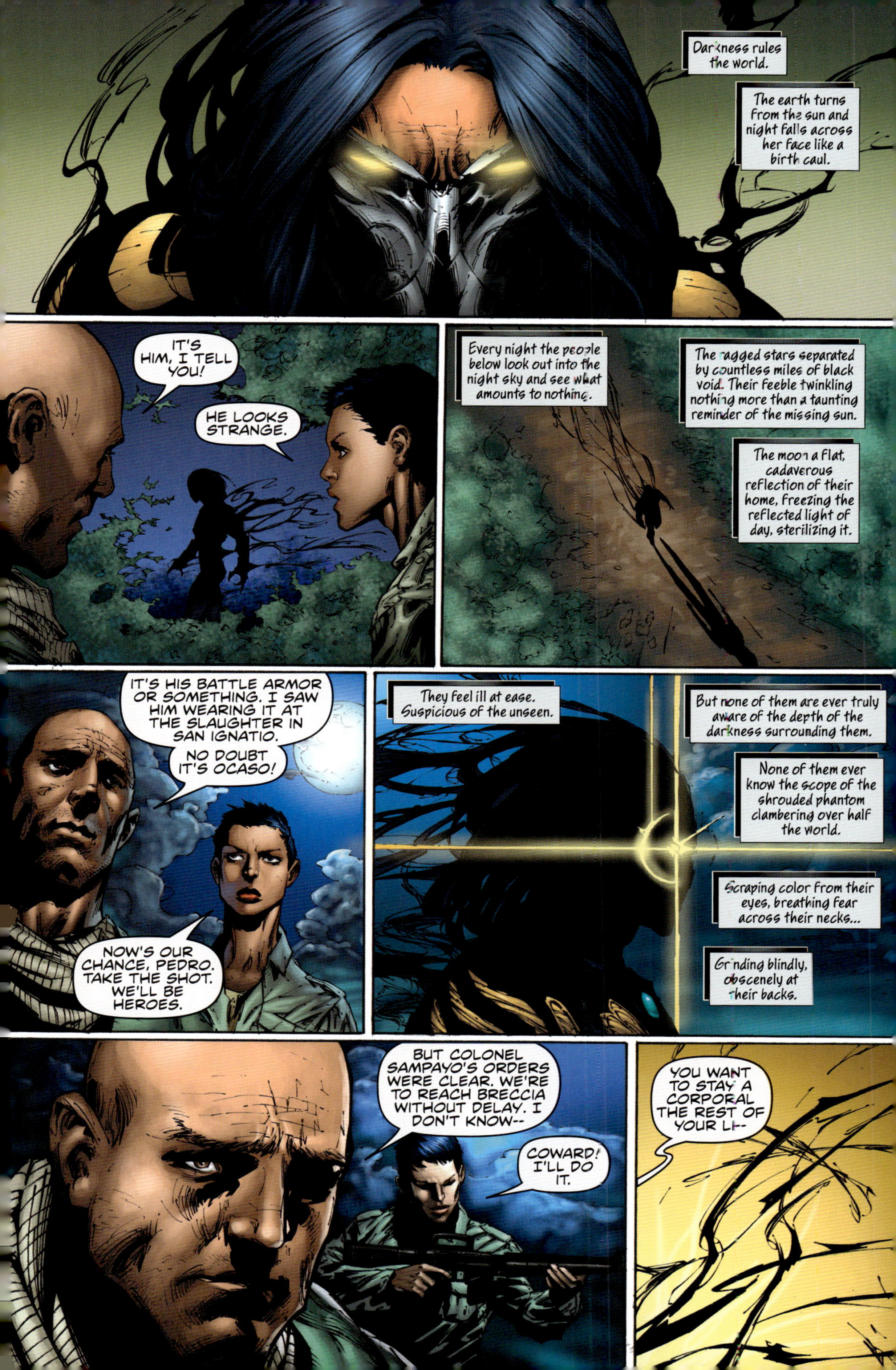

Darkness rules the world.
The earth turns from the sun and night falls across her face like a birth caul.
IT'S HIM, I TELL YOU!
HE LOOKS STRANGE.
Every night the people below look out into the night sky and see what amounts to nothing.
The ragged stars separated by countless miles of black void. Their feeble twinkling nothing more than a taunting reminder of the missing sun.
The moon a flat, cadaverous reflection of their home, freezing the reflected light of day, sterilizing it.
IT'S HIS BATTLE ARMOR OR SOMETHING. I SAW HIM WEARING IT AT THE SLAUGHTER IN SAN IGNATIO.
NO DOUBT IT'S OCASO!
NOW'S OUR CHANCE, PEDRO. TAKE THE SHOT. WE'LL BE HEROES.
They feel ill at ease. Suspicious of the unseen.
But none of them are ever truly aware of the depth of the darkness surrounding them.
None of them ever know the scope of the shrouded phantom clambering over half the world.
Scraping color from their eyes, breathing fear across their necks...
Grinding blindly, obscenely at their backs.
BUT COLONEL SAMPAYO'S ORDERS WERE CLEAR. WE'RE TO REACH BRECCIA WITHOUT DELAY. I DON'T KNOW--
COWARD! I'LL DO IT.
YOU WANT TO STAY A CORPORAL THE REST OF YOUR LI--

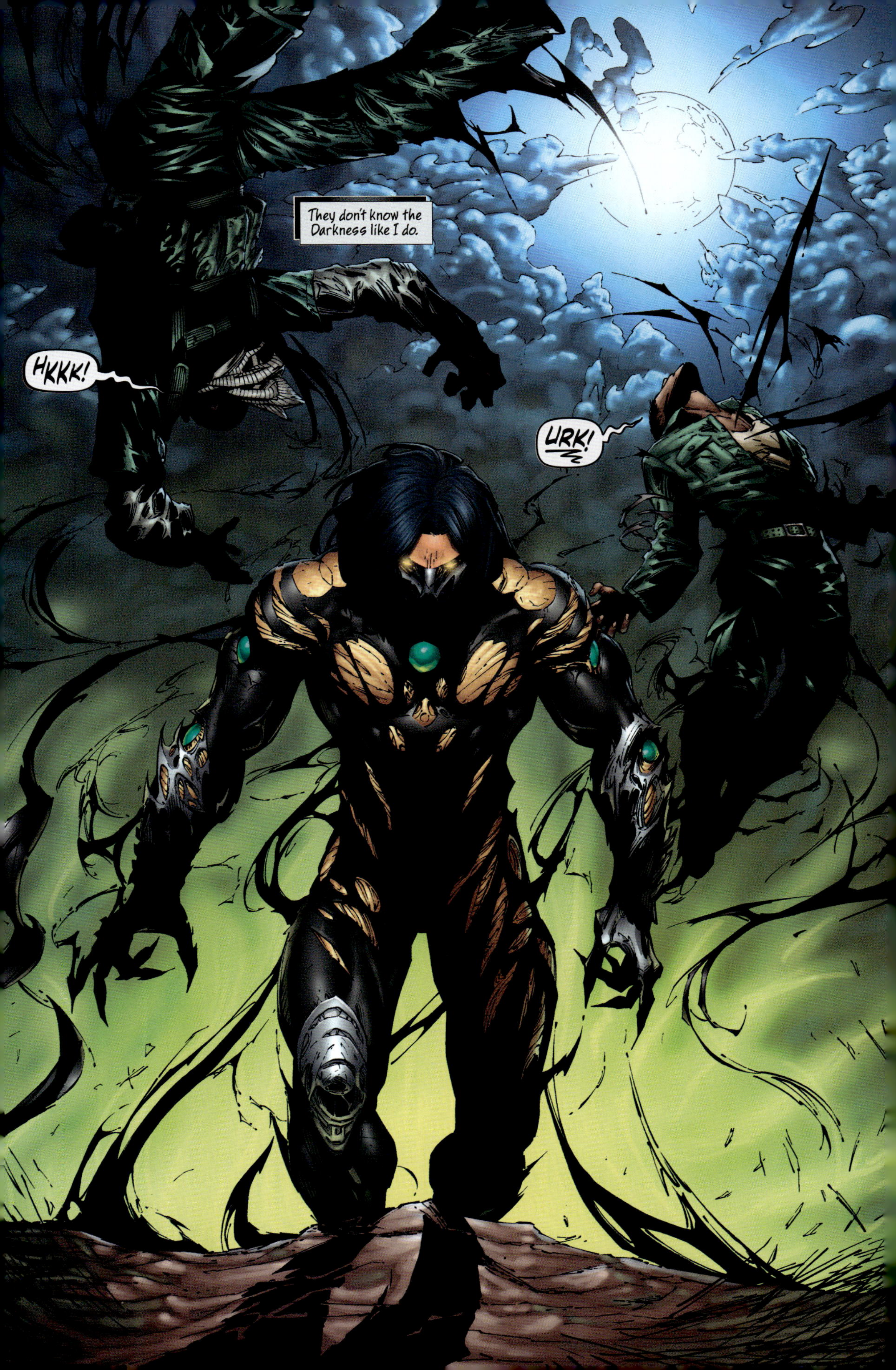
They don't know the Darkness like I do.
HKKK!
URK!

They were not born into its body, like I was.

I thought I could run away from it, but I'm in its blood. And like blood being pushed out of the heart, my escape is only temporary.

With its very next beat, the heart of the Darkness pulls me back along its veins.

So be it. No more running. No more questions.

Am I a good man polluted by a bad world, or am I a bad man poisoning a good world?

That question meant so much to me not very long ago.

Now it seems like the pathetic dream of some lost kid I barely remember.

LOOK WHO'S BACK!

THE PRODIGAL PUSSY.

WE'RE UNDER NEW MANAGEMENT NOW, ESTACADO.

YEAH, NO MORE OF YOUR PATHETIC HUMAN BULLSH--

SNAP

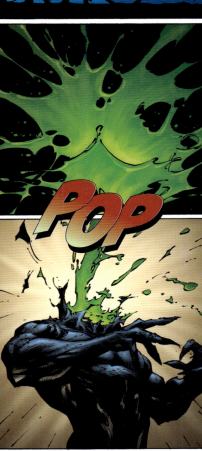

POP

SNAPP

POP POP POP

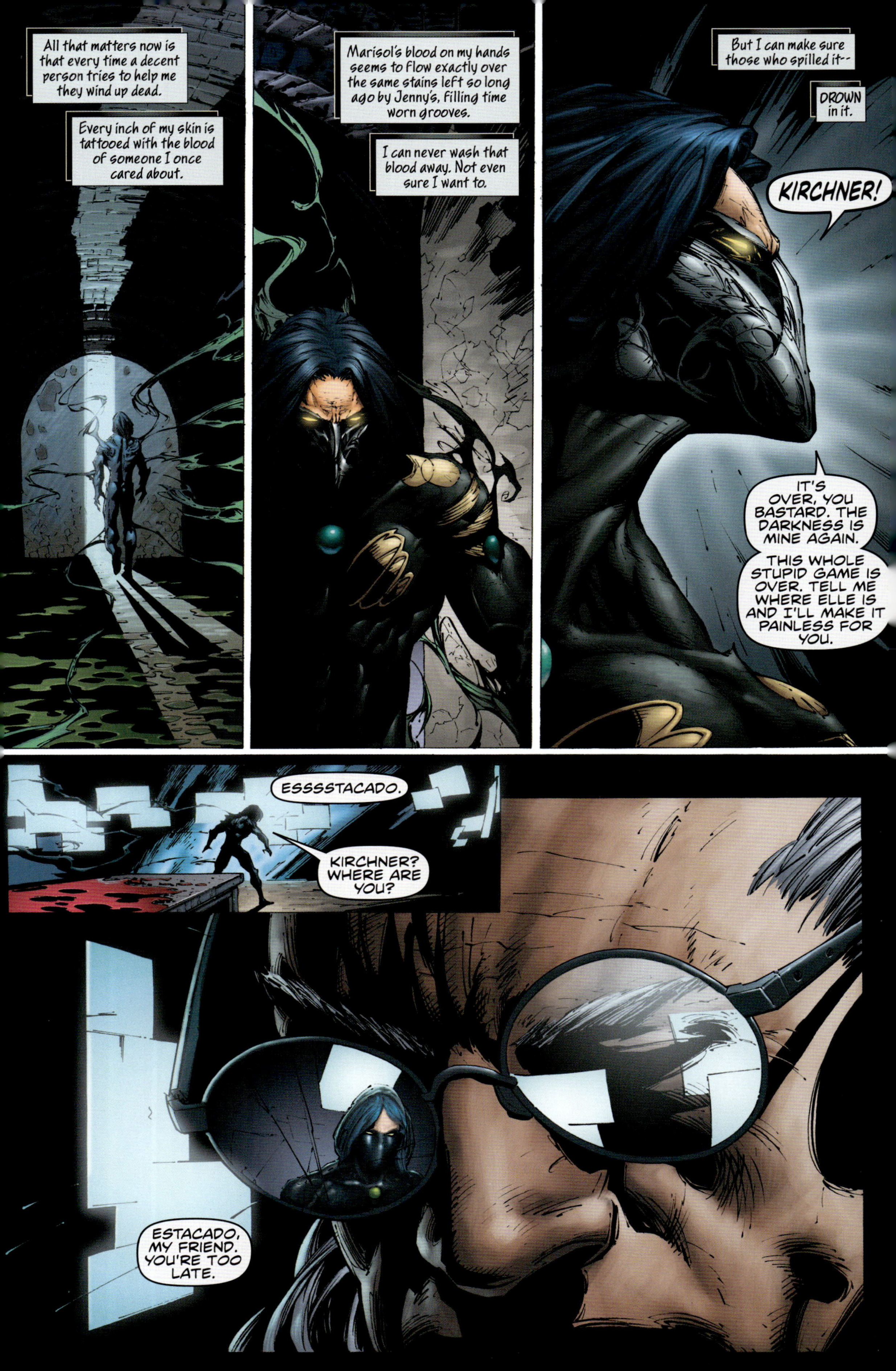
All that matters now is that every time a decent person tries to help me they wind up dead.
Every inch of my skin is tattooed with the blood of someone I once cared about.
Marisol's blood on my hands seems to flow exactly over the same stains left so long ago by Jenny's, filling time worn grooves.
I can never wash that blood away. Not even sure I want to.
But I can make sure those who spilled it-
DROWN in it.
KIRCHNER!
IT'S OVER, YOU BASTARD. THE DARKNESS IS MINE AGAIN.
THIS WHOLE STUPID GAME IS OVER. TELL ME WHERE ELLE IS AND I'LL MAKE IT PAINLESS FOR YOU.
ESSSSTACADO.
KIRCHNER? WHERE ARE YOU?
ESTACADO, MY FRIEND. YOU'RE TOO LATE.

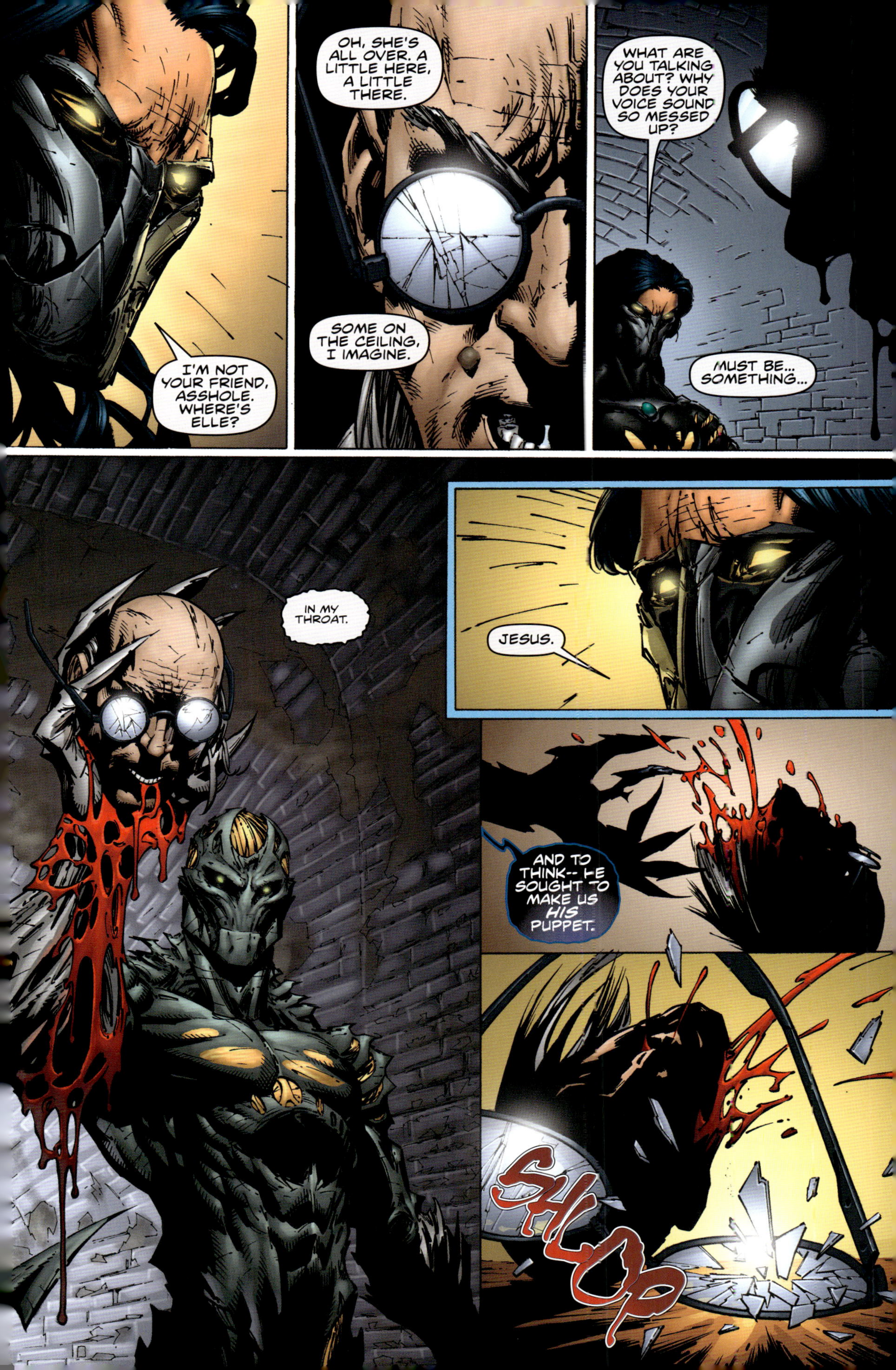
I'M NOT YOUR FRIEND, ASSHOLE. WHERE'S ELLE?
OH, SHE'S ALL OVER. A LITTLE HERE, A LITTLE THERE.
SOME ON THE CEILING, I IMAGINE.
WHAT ARE YOU TALKING ABOUT? WHY DOES YOUR VOICE SOUND SO MESSED UP?
MUST BE... SOMETHING...
IN MY THROAT.
JESUS.
AND TO THINK-- HE SOUGHT TO MAKE US HIS PUPPET.
SHLOP

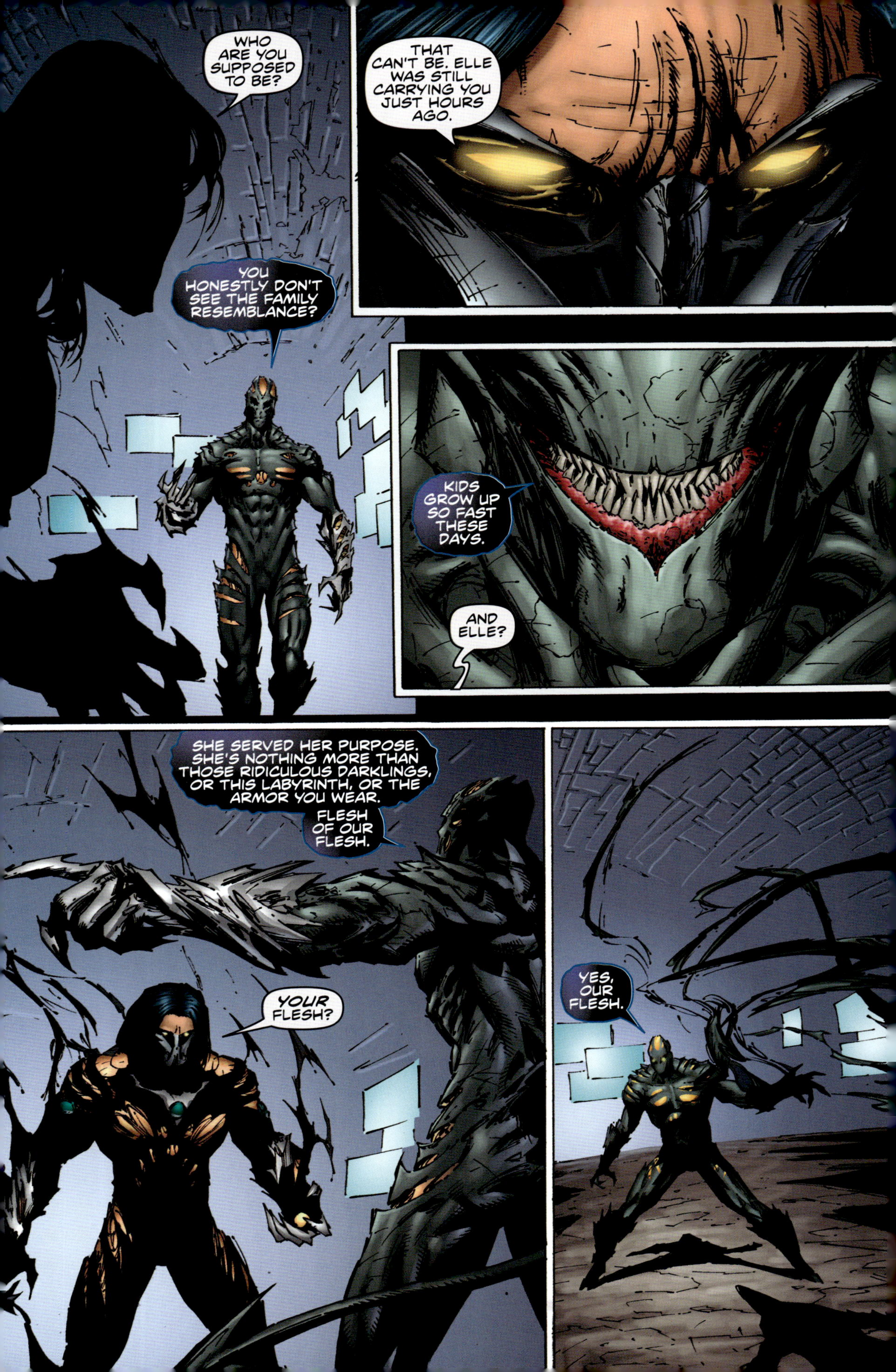
WHO ARE YOU SUPPOSED TO BE?
THAT CAN'T BE. ELLE WAS STILL CARRYING YOU JUST HOURS AGO.
YOU HONESTLY DON'T SEE THE FAMILY RESEMBLANCE?
KIDS GROW UP SO FAST THESE DAYS.
AND ELLE?
SHE SERVED HER PURPOSE. SHE'S NOTHING MORE THAN THOSE RIDICULOUS DARKLINGS, OR THIS LABYRINTH, OR THE ARMOR YOU WEAR.
FLESH OF OUR FLESH.
YOUR FLESH?
YES, OUR FLESH.

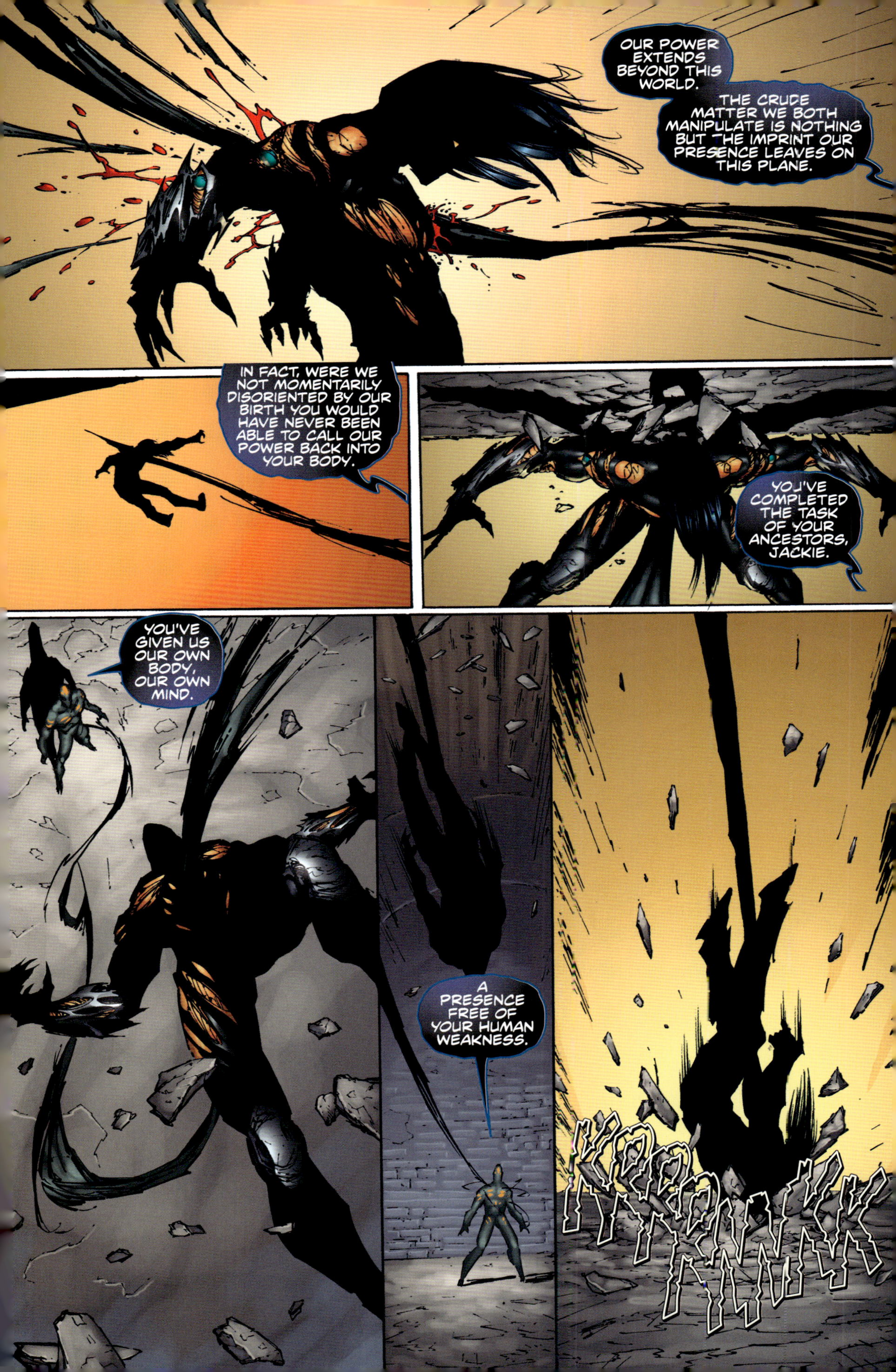
OUR POWER EXTENDS BEYOND THIS WORLD.
THE CRUDE MATTER WE BOTH MANIPULATE IS NOTHING BUT THE IMPRINT OUR PRESENCE LEAVES ON THIS PLANE.
IN FACT, WERE WE NOT MOMENTARILY DISORIENTED BY OUR BIRTH YOU WOULD HAVE NEVER BEEN ABLE TO CALL OUR POWER BACK INTO YOUR BODY.
YOU'VE COMPLETED THE TASK OF YOUR ANCESTORS, JACKIE.
YOU'VE GIVEN US OUR OWN BODY, OUR OWN MIND.
A PRESENCE FREE OF YOUR HUMAN WEAKNESS.

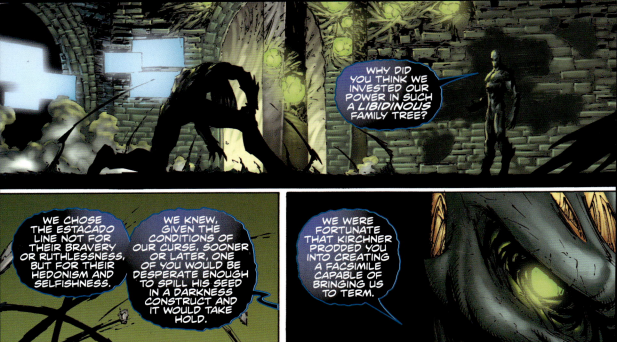

WHY DID YOU THINK WE INVESTED OUR POWER IN SUCH A *LIBIDINOUS* FAMILY TREE?

WE CHOSE THE ESTACADO LINE NOT FOR THEIR BRAVERY OR RUTHLESSNESS, BUT FOR THEIR HEDONISM AND SELFISHNESS.

WE KNEW, GIVEN THE CONDITIONS OF OUR CURSE, SOONER OR LATER, ONE OF YOU WOULD BE DESPERATE ENOUGH TO SPILL HIS SEED IN A DARKNESS CONSTRUCT AND IT WOULD TAKE HOLD.

WE WERE FORTUNATE THAT KIRCHNER PRODDED YOU INTO CREATING A FACSIMILE CAPABLE OF BRINGING US TO TERM.

AND NOW THE ONLY THING KEEPING US TETHERED TO HUMANITY AT ALL...

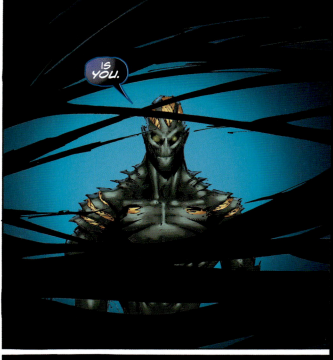

IS YOU.

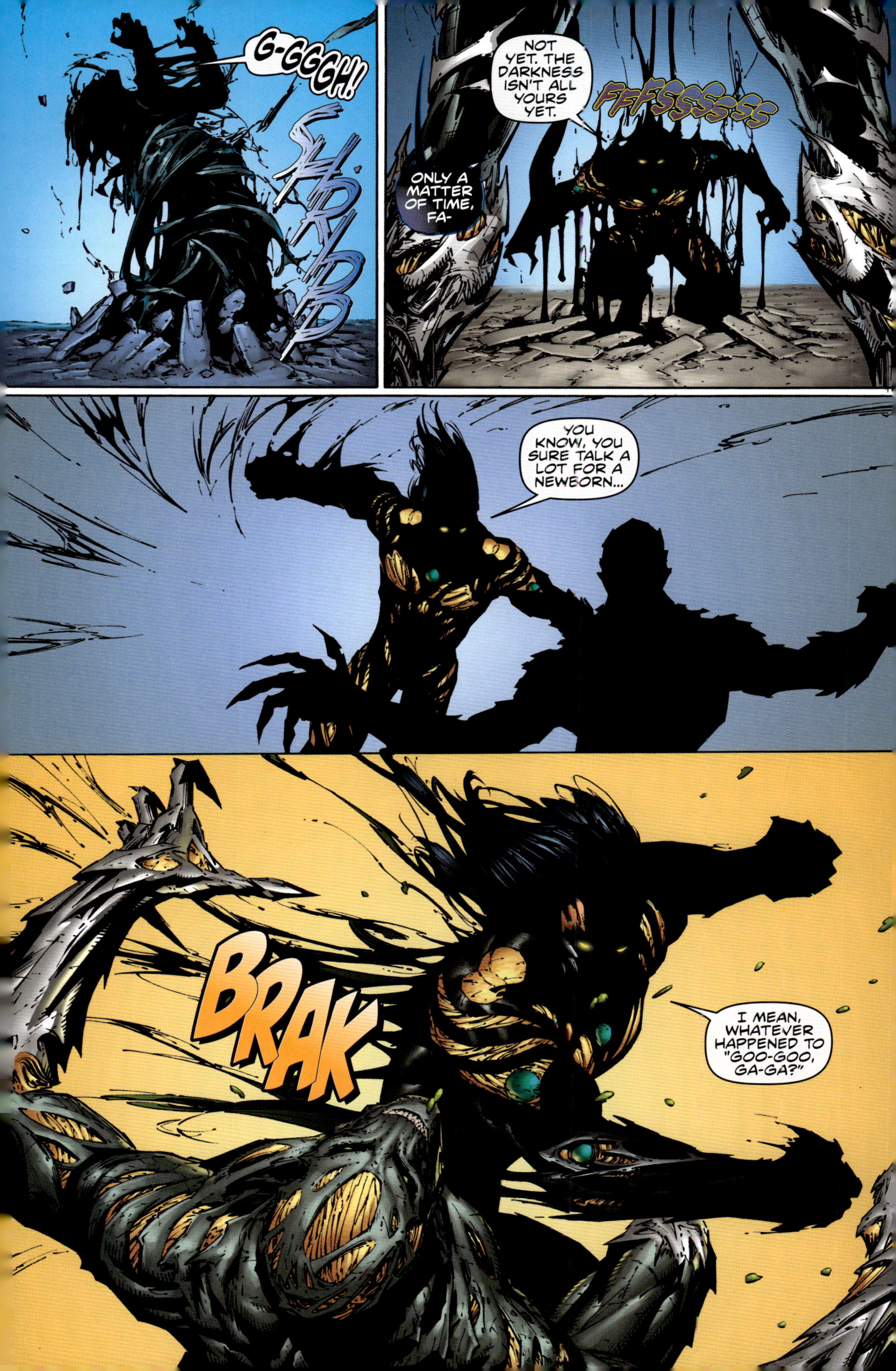
G-GGGH!
SHRDDD
NOT YET. THE DARKNESS ISN'T ALL YOURS YET.
FFFSSSSSSS
ONLY A MATTER OF TIME, FA-
YOU KNOW, YOU SURE TALK A LOT FOR A NEWBORN...
BRAK
I MEAN, WHATEVER HAPPENED TO "GOO-GOO, GA-GA?"

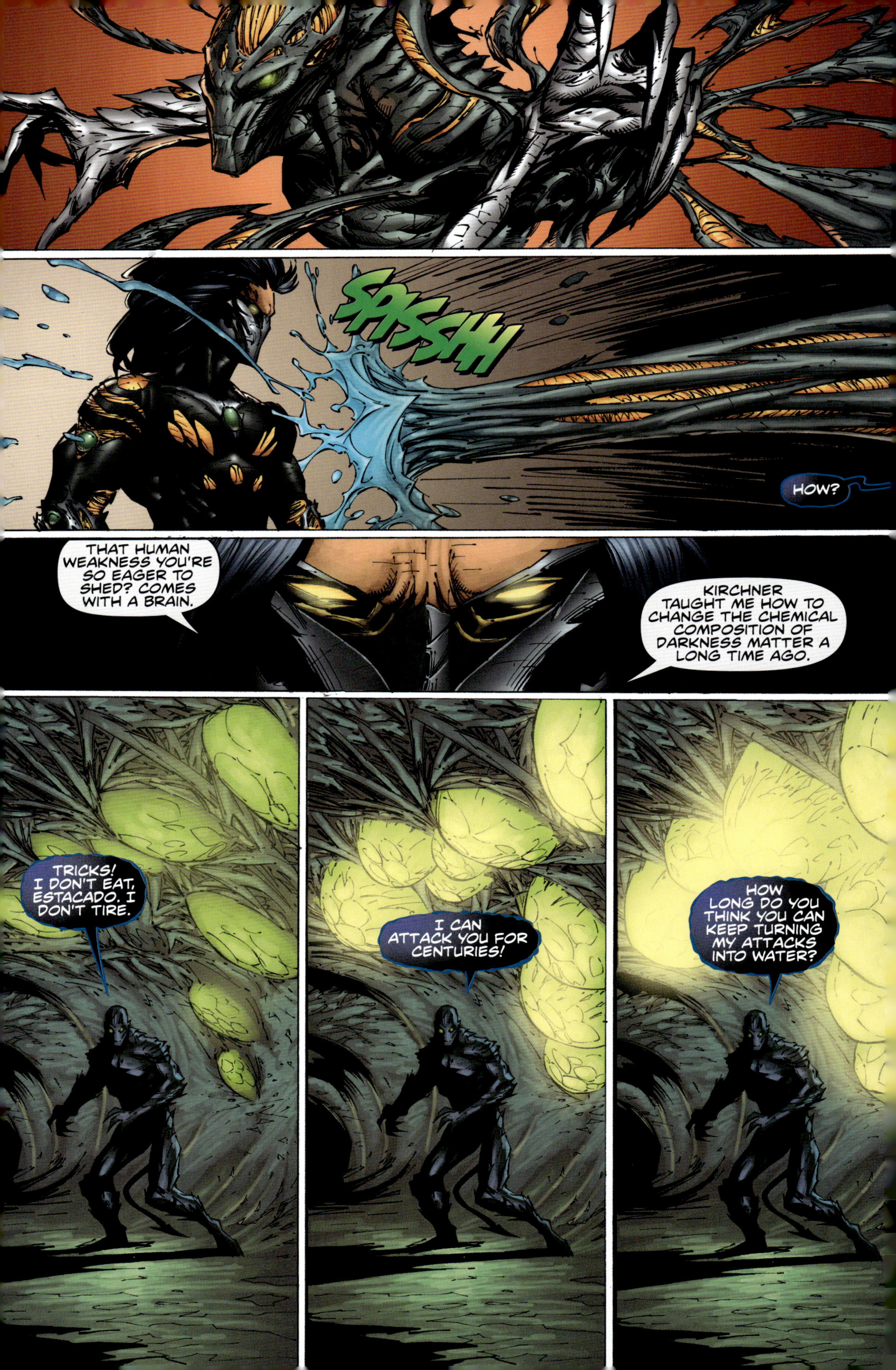
SPISSHH
HOW?
THAT HUMAN WEAKNESS YOU'RE SO EAGER TO SHED? COMES WITH A BRAIN.
KIRCHNER TAUGHT ME HOW TO CHANGE THE CHEMICAL COMPOSITION OF DARKNESS MATTER A LONG TIME AGO.
TRICKS! I DON'T EAT, ESTACADO. I DON'T TIRE.
I CAN ATTACK YOU FOR CENTURIES!
HOW LONG DO YOU THINK YOU CAN KEEP TURNING MY ATTACKS INTO WATER?

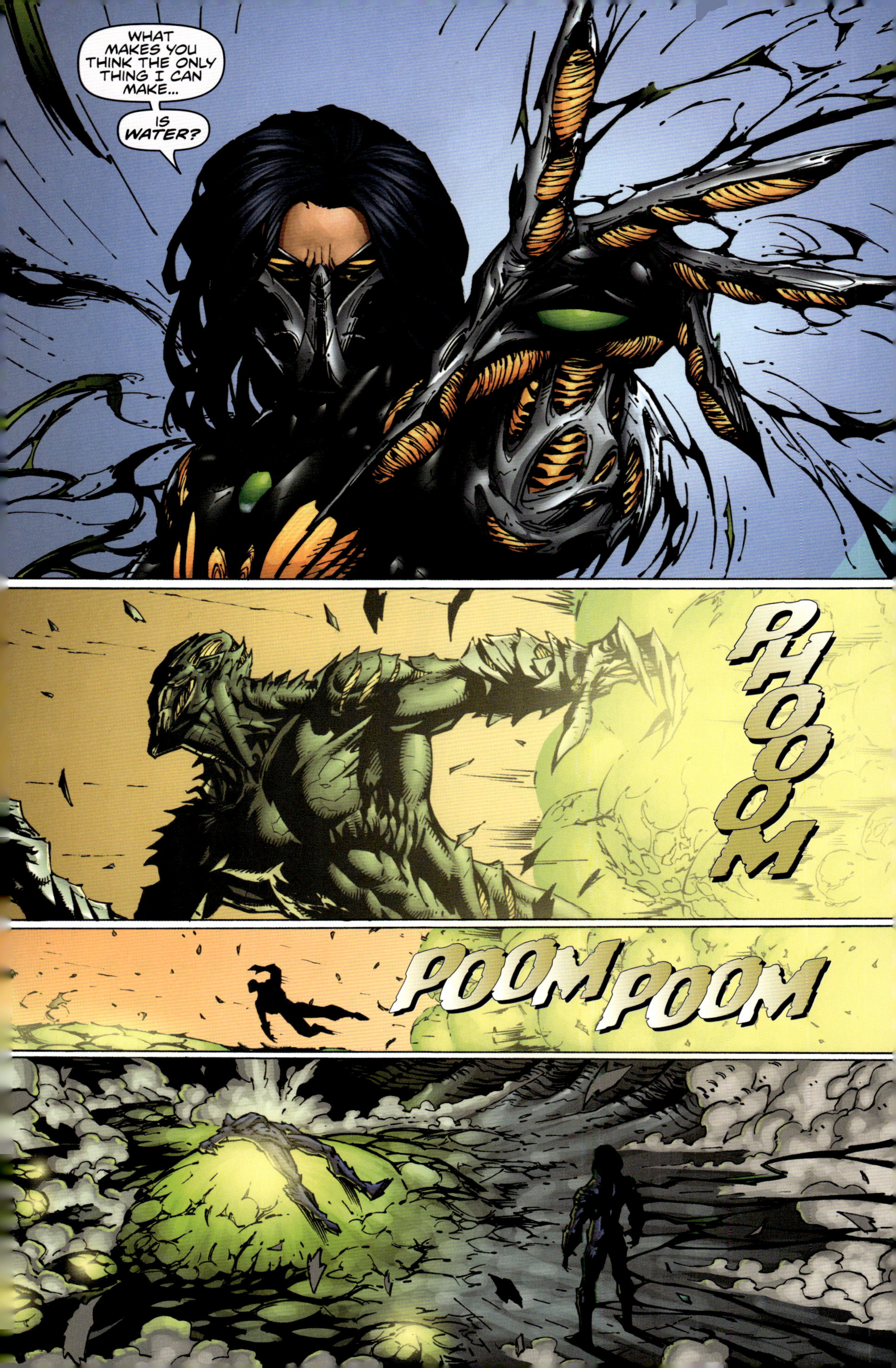
WHAT MAKES YOU THINK THE ONLY THING I CAN MAKE...
IS *WATER?*
PHOOOM
POOM POOM

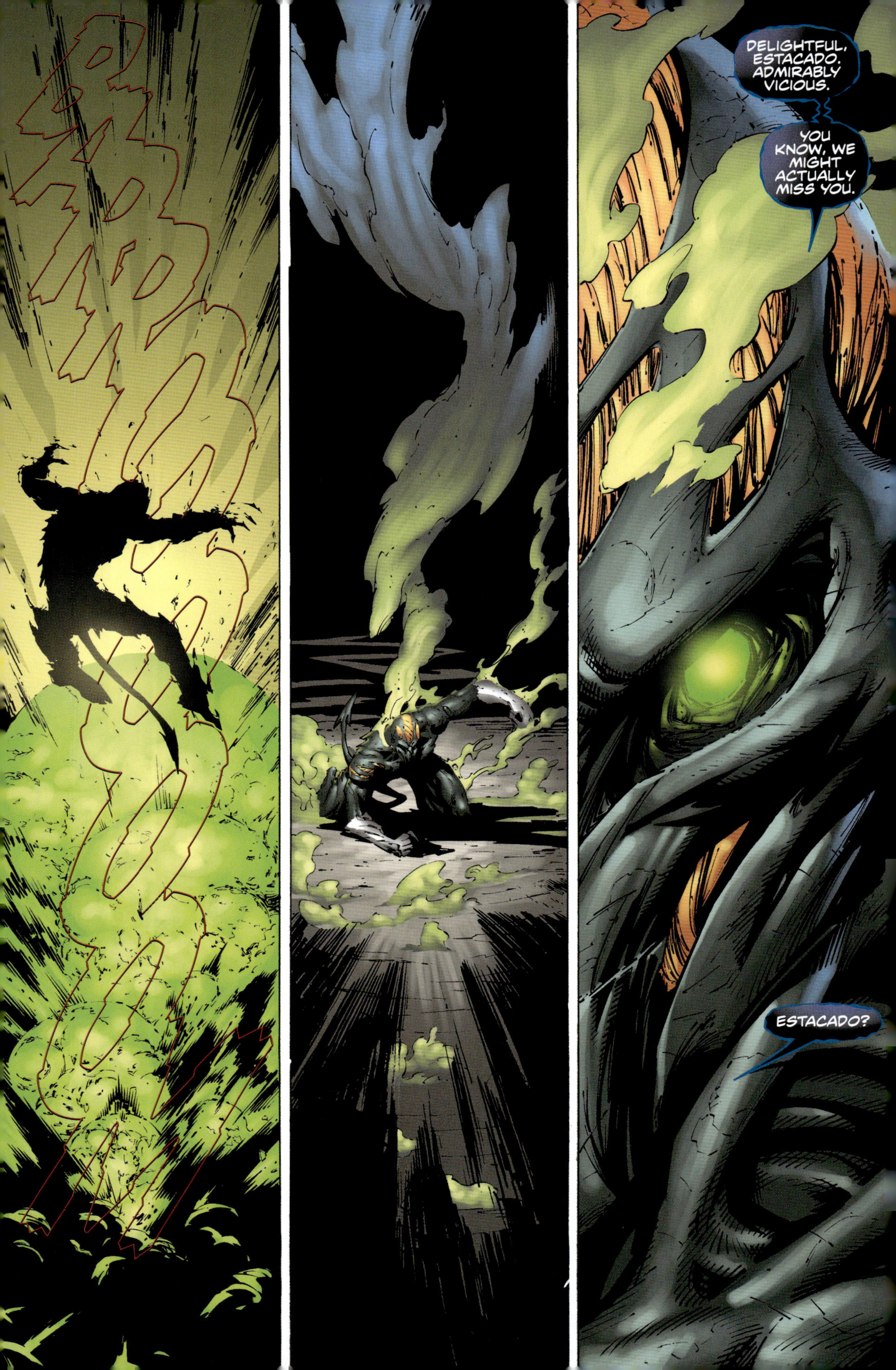
DELIGHTFUL, ESTACADO. ADMIRABLY VICIOUS.
YOU KNOW, WE MIGHT ACTUALLY MISS YOU.
ESTACADO?

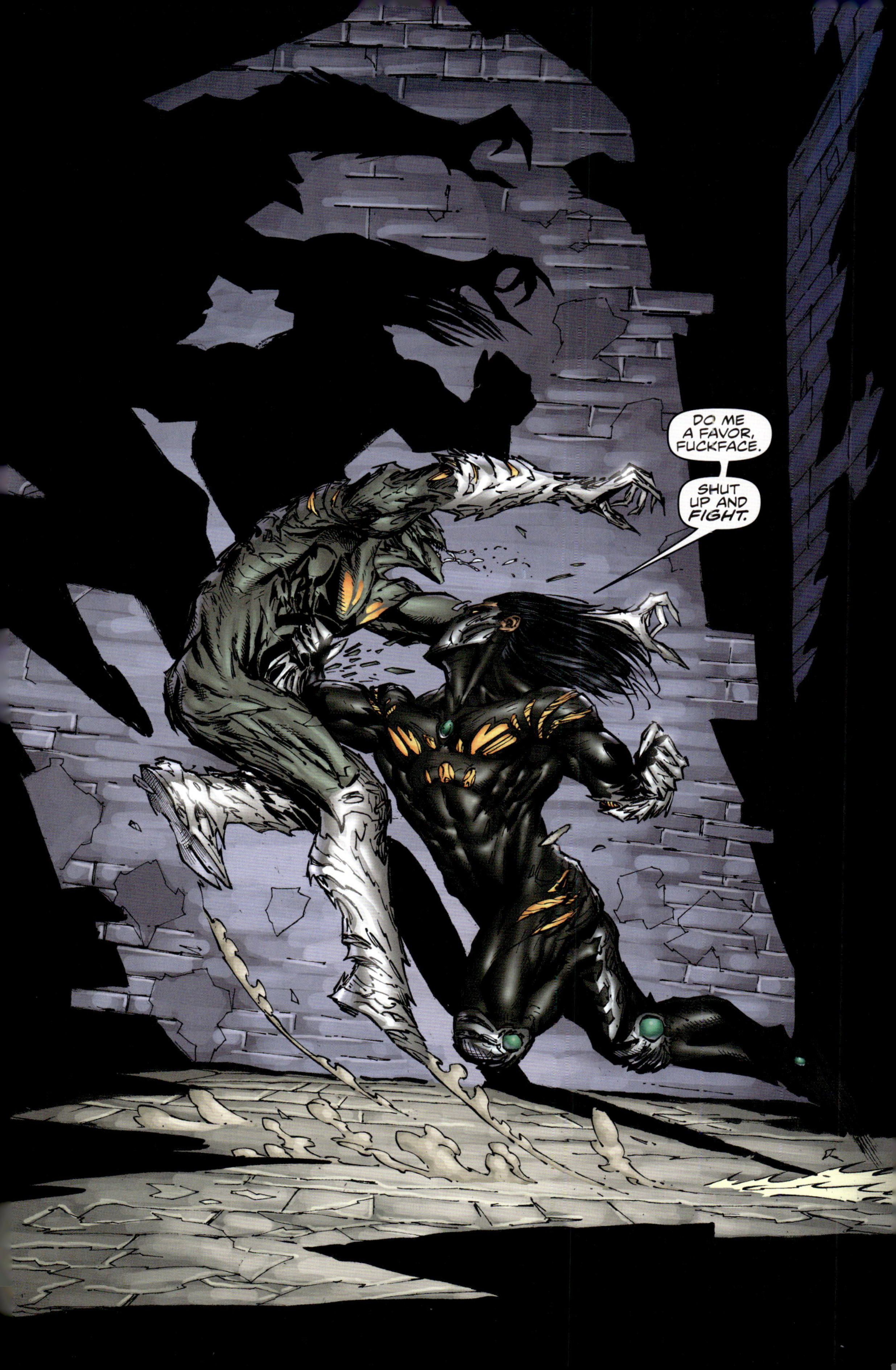
DO ME A FAVOR, FUCKFACE.
SHUT UP AND FIGHT.

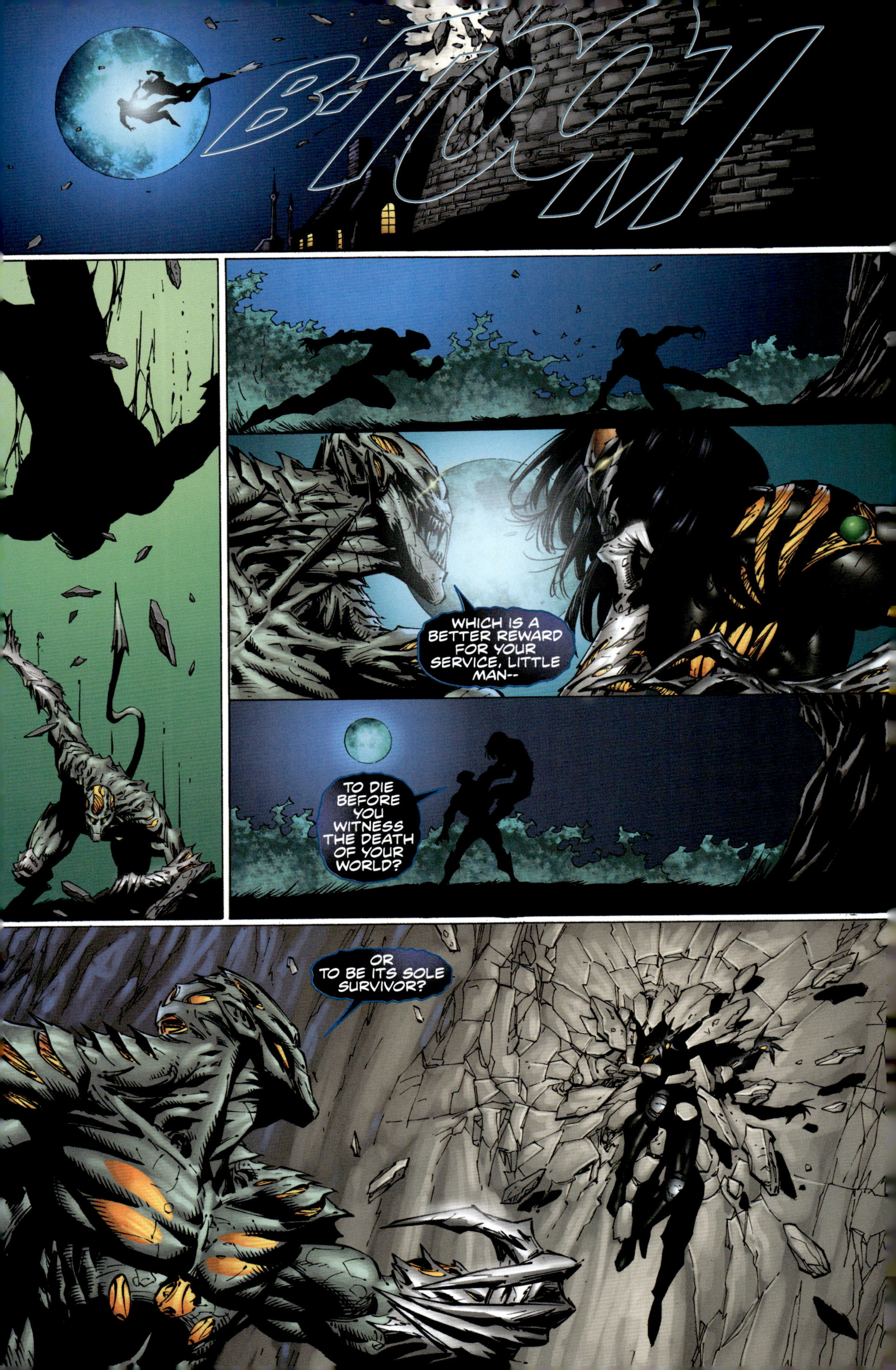
BTOOM
WHICH IS A BETTER REWARD FOR YOUR SERVICE, LITTLE MAN--
TO DIE BEFORE YOU WITNESS THE DEATH OF YOUR WORLD?
OR TO BE ITS SOLE SURVIVOR?

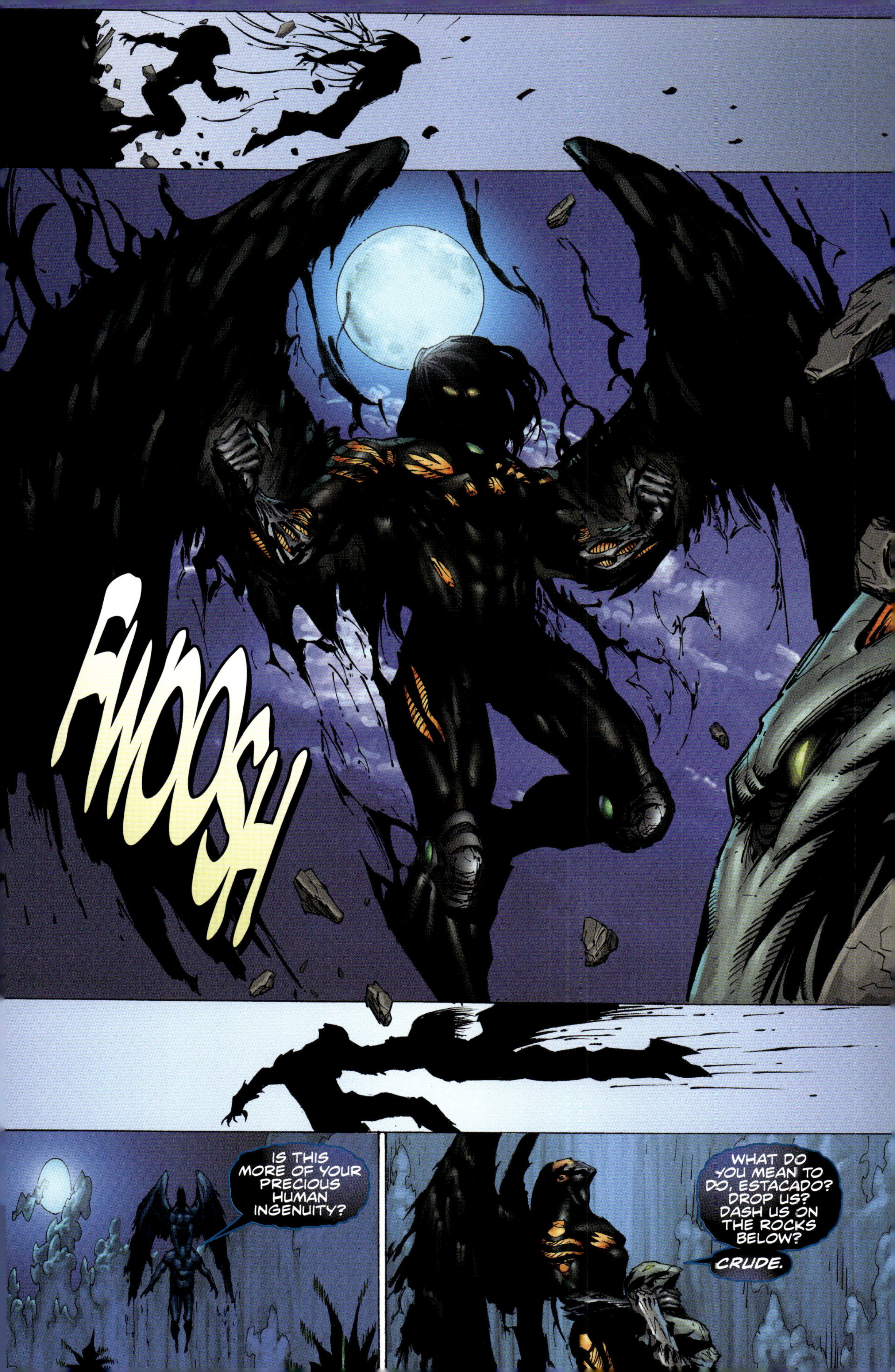
FWOOSH
IS THIS MORE OF YOUR PRECIOUS HUMAN INGENUITY?
WHAT DO YOU MEAN TO DO, ESTACADO? DROP US? DASH US ON THE ROCKS BELOW?
CRUDE.

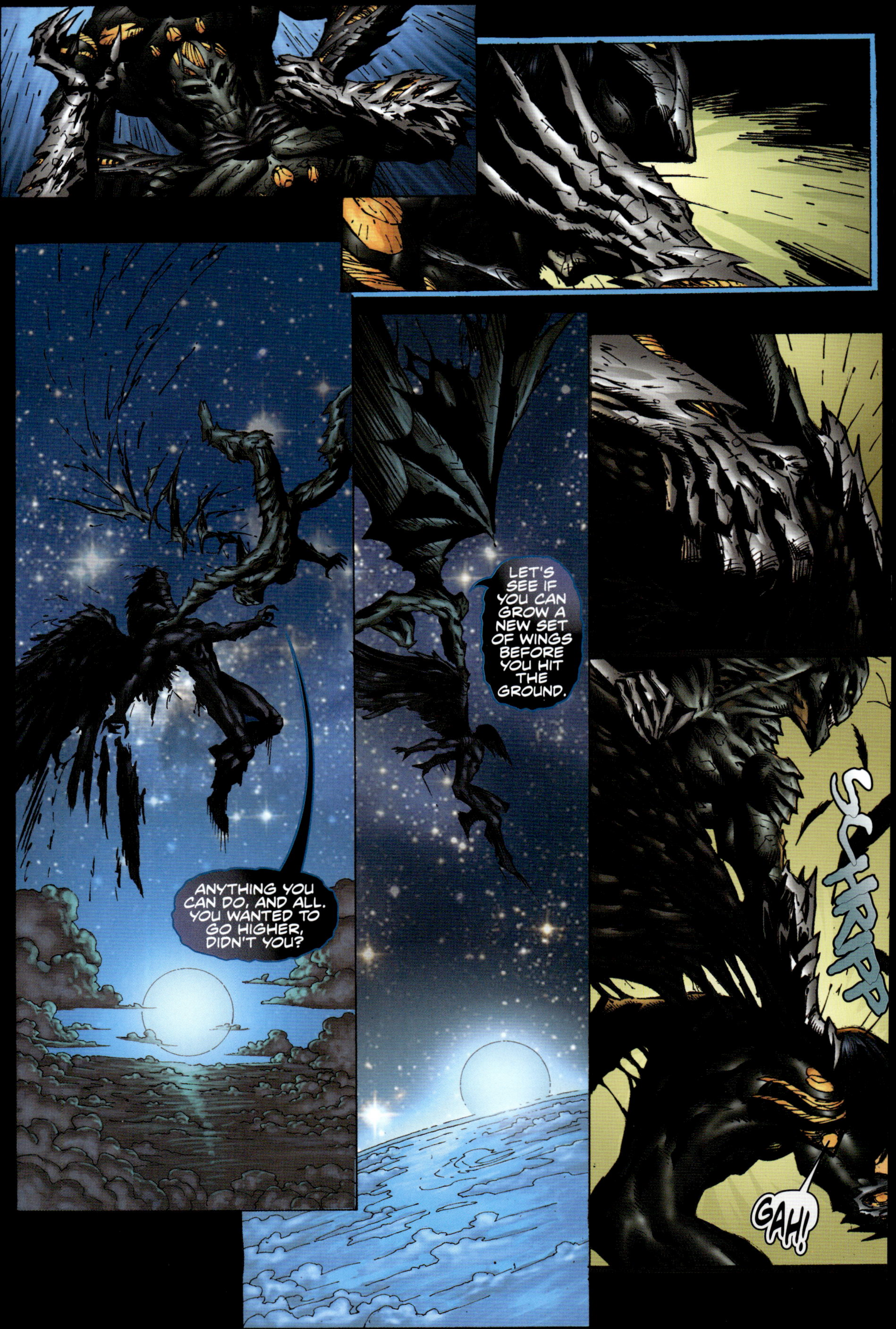
ANYTHING YOU CAN DO, AND ALL. YOU WANTED TO GO HIGHER, DIDN'T YOU?
LET'S SEE IF YOU CAN GROW A NEW SET OF WINGS BEFORE YOU HIT THE GROUND.
SCHRIPP
GAH!

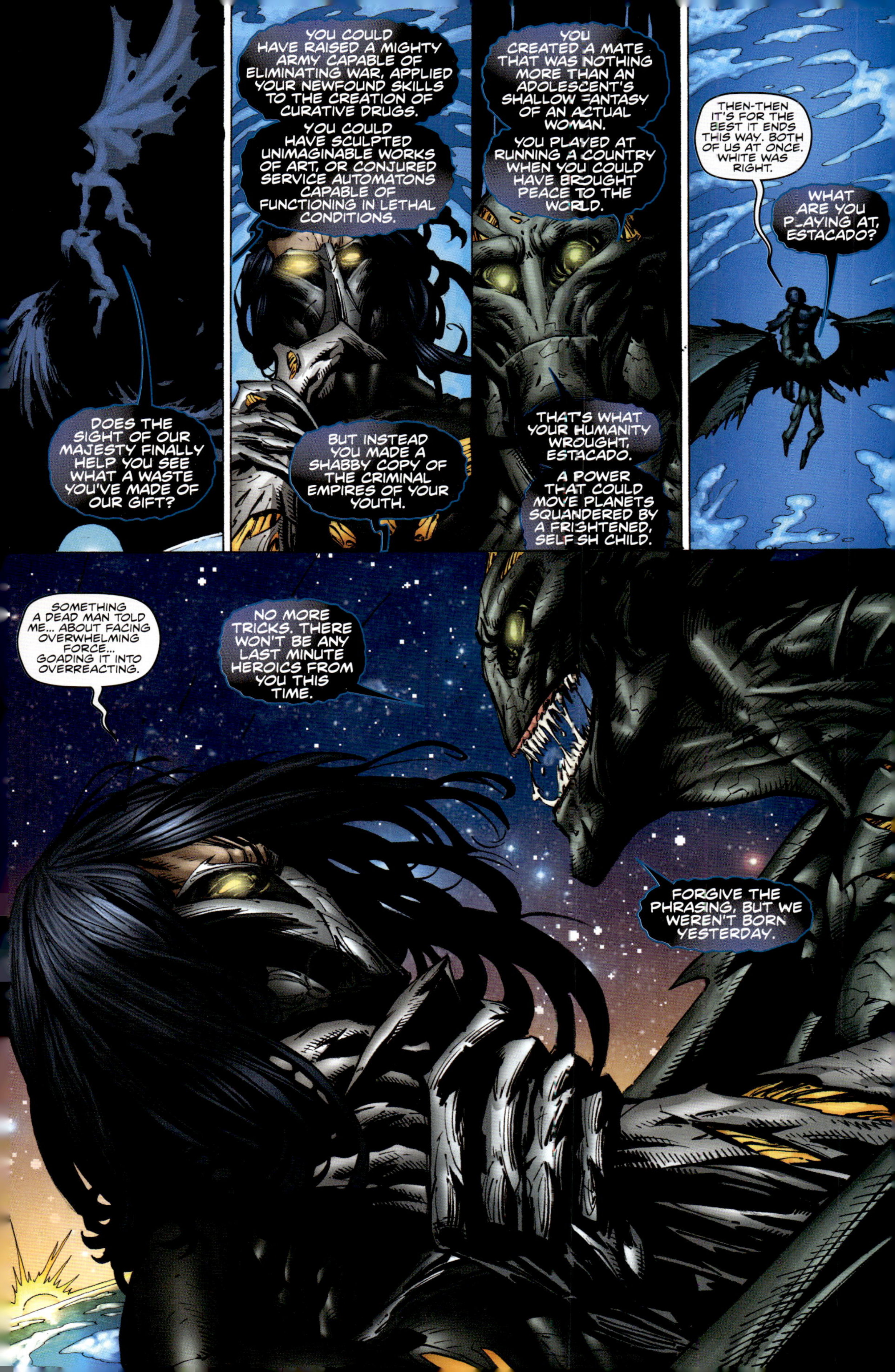
DOES THE SIGHT OF OUR MAJESTY FINALLY HELP YOU SEE WHAT A WASTE YOU'VE MADE OF OUR GIFT?
YOU COULD HAVE RAISED A MIGHTY ARMY CAPABLE OF ELIMINATING WAR, APPLIED YOUR NEWFOUND SKILLS TO THE CREATION OF CURATIVE DRUGS.
YOU COULD HAVE SCULPTED UNIMAGINABLE WORKS OF ART, OR CONJURED SERVICE AUTOMATONS CAPABLE OF FUNCTIONING IN LETHAL CONDITIONS.
BUT INSTEAD YOU MADE A SHABBY COPY OF THE CRIMINAL EMPIRES OF YOUR YOUTH.
YOU CREATED A MATE THAT WAS NOTHING MORE THAN AN ADOLESCENT'S SHALLOW FANTASY OF AN ACTUAL WOMAN.
YOU PLAYED AT RUNNING A COUNTRY WHEN YOU COULD HAVE BROUGHT PEACE TO THE WORLD.
THAT'S WHAT YOUR HUMANITY WROUGHT, ESTACADO.
A POWER THAT COULD MOVE PLANETS SQUANDERED BY A FRIGHTENED, SELFISH CHILD.
THEN-THEN IT'S FOR THE BEST IT ENDS THIS WAY. BOTH OF US AT ONCE. WHITE WAS RIGHT.
WHAT ARE YOU PLAYING AT, ESTACADO?
SOMETHING A DEAD MAN TOLD ME... ABOUT FACING OVERWHELMING FORCE... GOADING IT INTO OVERREACTING.
NO MORE TRICKS. THERE WON'T BE ANY LAST MINUTE HEROICS FROM YOU THIS TIME.
FORGIVE THE PHRASING, BUT WE WEREN'T BORN YESTERDAY.

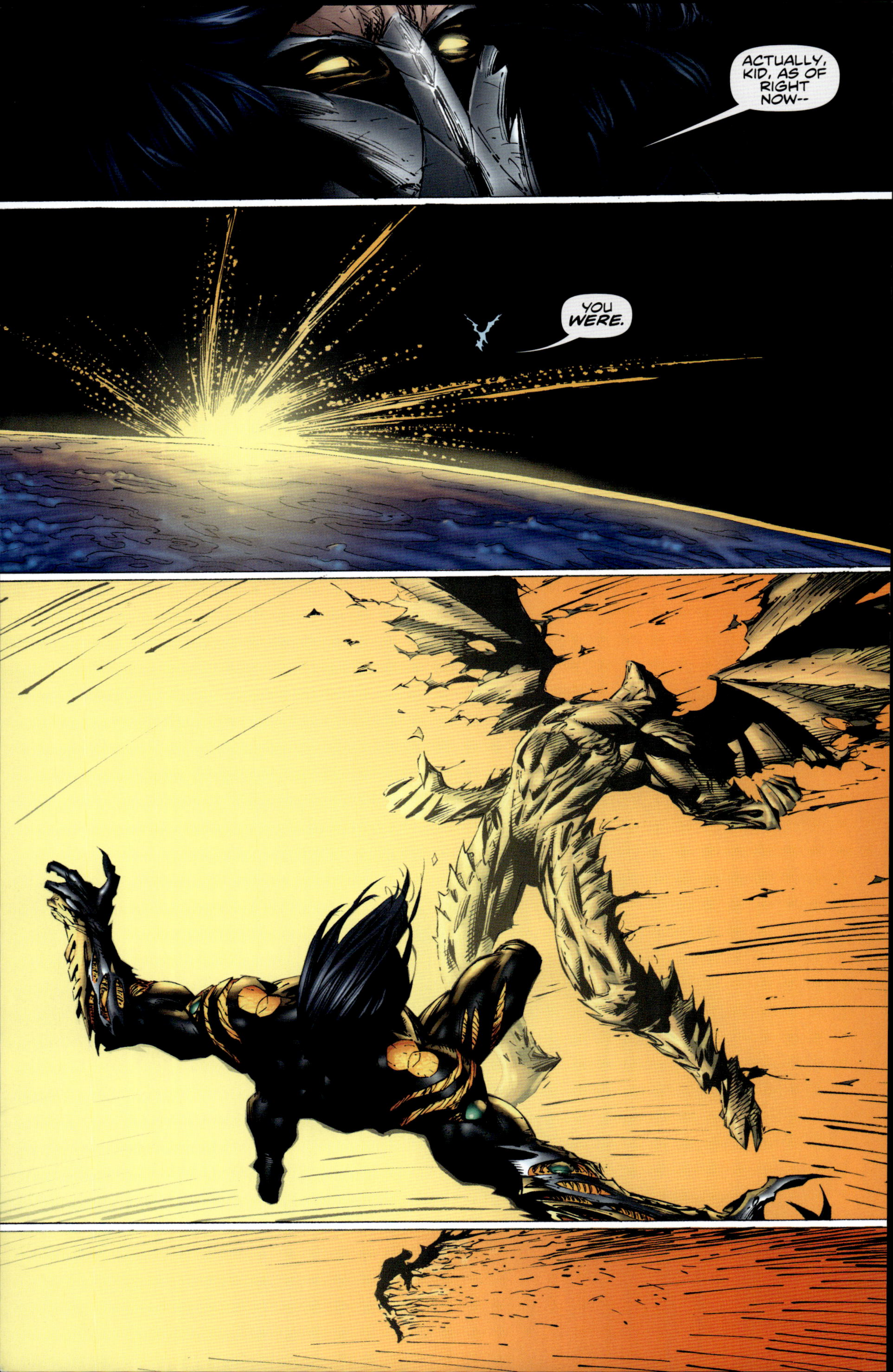
ACTUALLY, KID, AS OF RIGHT NOW--
YOU WERE.

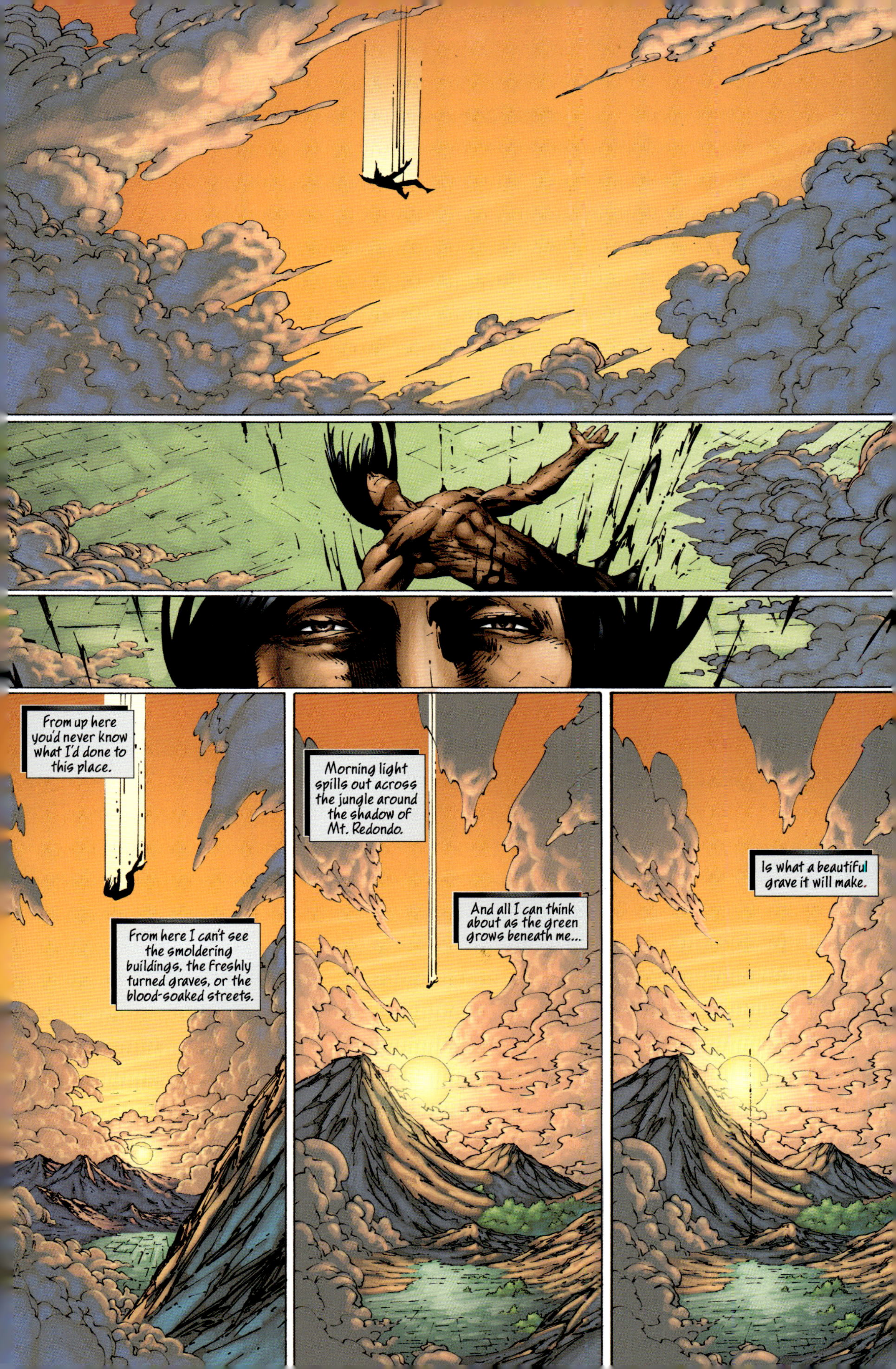
From up here you'd never know what I'd done to this place.
From here I can't see the smoldering buildings, the freshly turned graves, or the blood-soaked streets.
Morning light spills out across the jungle around the shadow of Mt. Redondo.
And all I can think about as the green grows beneath me...
Is what a beautiful grave it will make.

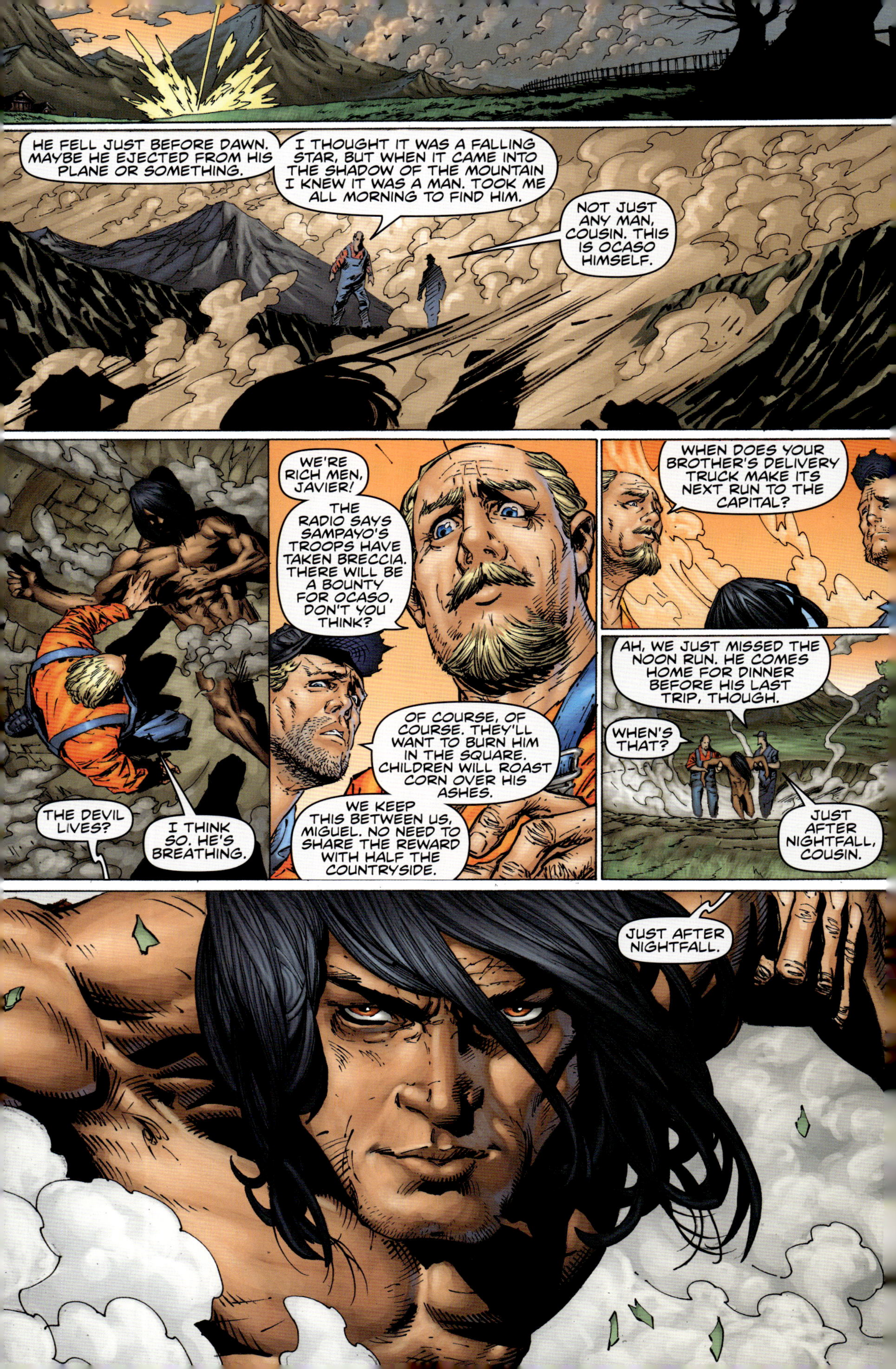

HE FELL JUST BEFORE DAWN. MAYBE HE EJECTED FROM HIS PLANE OR SOMETHING.
I THOUGHT IT WAS A FALLING STAR, BUT WHEN IT CAME INTO THE SHADOW OF THE MOUNTAIN I KNEW IT WAS A MAN. TOOK ME ALL MORNING TO FIND HIM.
NOT JUST ANY MAN, COUSIN. THIS IS OCASO HIMSELF.
THE DEVIL LIVES?
I THINK SO. HE'S BREATHING.
WE'RE RICH MEN, JAVIER!
THE RADIO SAYS SAMPAYO'S TROOPS HAVE TAKEN BRECCIA. THERE WILL BE A BOUNTY FOR OCASO, DON'T YOU THINK?
OF COURSE, OF COURSE. THEY'LL WANT TO BURN HIM IN THE SQUARE. CHILDREN WILL ROAST CORN OVER HIS ASHES.
WE KEEP THIS BETWEEN US, MIGUEL. NO NEED TO SHARE THE REWARD WITH HALF THE COUNTRYSIDE.
WHEN DOES YOUR BROTHER'S DELIVERY TRUCK MAKE ITS NEXT RUN TO THE CAPITAL?
AH, WE JUST MISSED THE NOON RUN. HE COMES HOME FOR DINNER BEFORE HIS LAST TRIP, THOUGH.
WHEN'S THAT?
JUST AFTER NIGHTFALL, COUSIN.
JUST AFTER NIGHTFALL.

The Darkness Issue #71

cover art by: Jorge Lucas and Lee Loughridge

THE DARKNESS #71

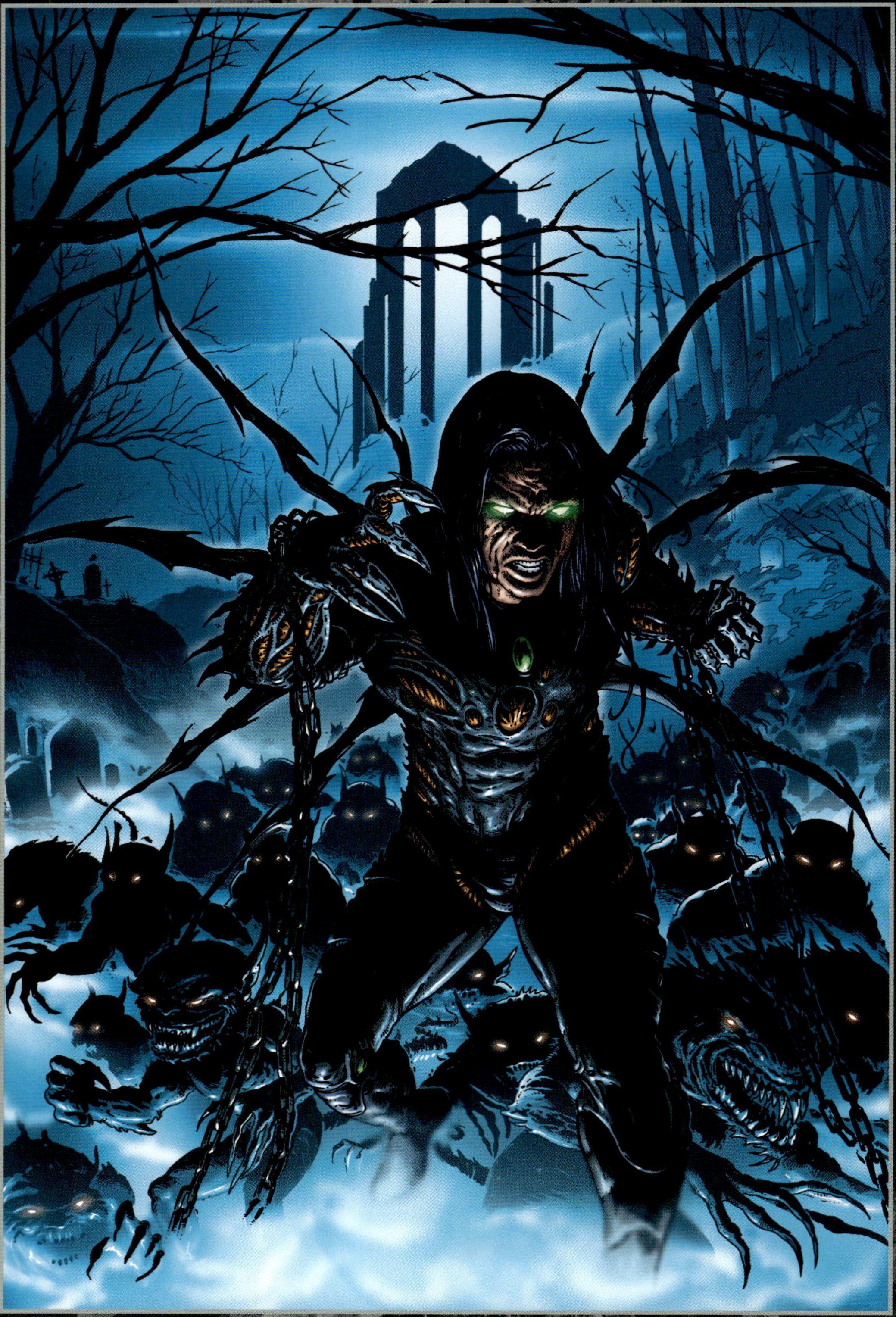

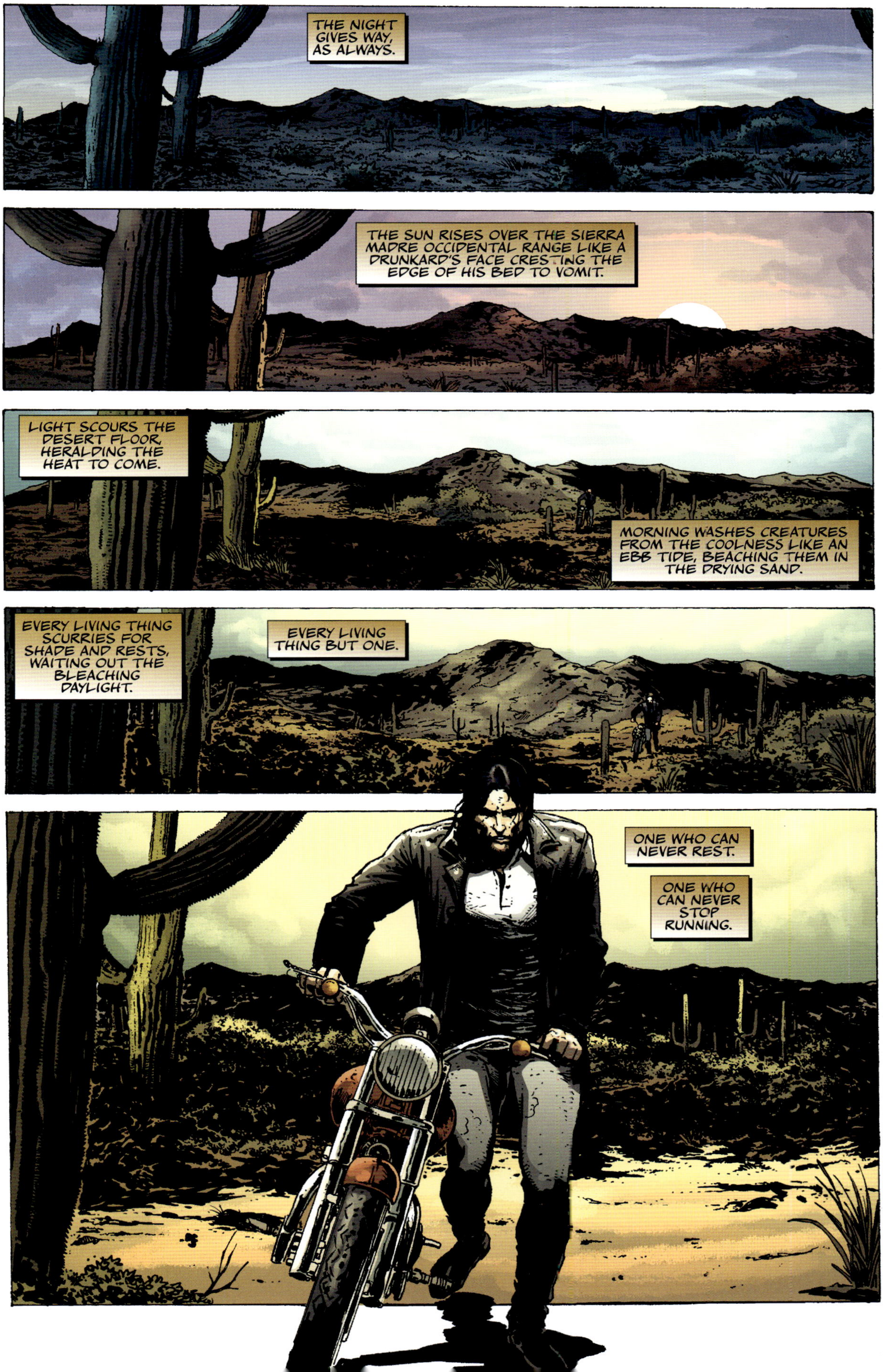
THE NIGHT GIVES WAY, AS ALWAYS.
THE SUN RISES OVER THE SIERRA MADRE OCCIDENTAL RANGE LIKE A DRUNKARD'S FACE CRESTING THE EDGE OF HIS BED TO VOMIT.
LIGHT SCOURS THE DESERT FLOOR, HERALDING THE HEAT TO COME.
MORNING WASHES CREATURES FROM THE COOLNESS LIKE AN EBB TIDE, BEACHING THEM IN THE DRYING SAND.
EVERY LIVING THING SCURRIES FOR SHADE AND RESTS, WAITING OUT THE BLEACHING DAYLIGHT.
EVERY LIVING THING BUT ONE.
ONE WHO CAN NEVER REST.
ONE WHO CAN NEVER STOP RUNNING.

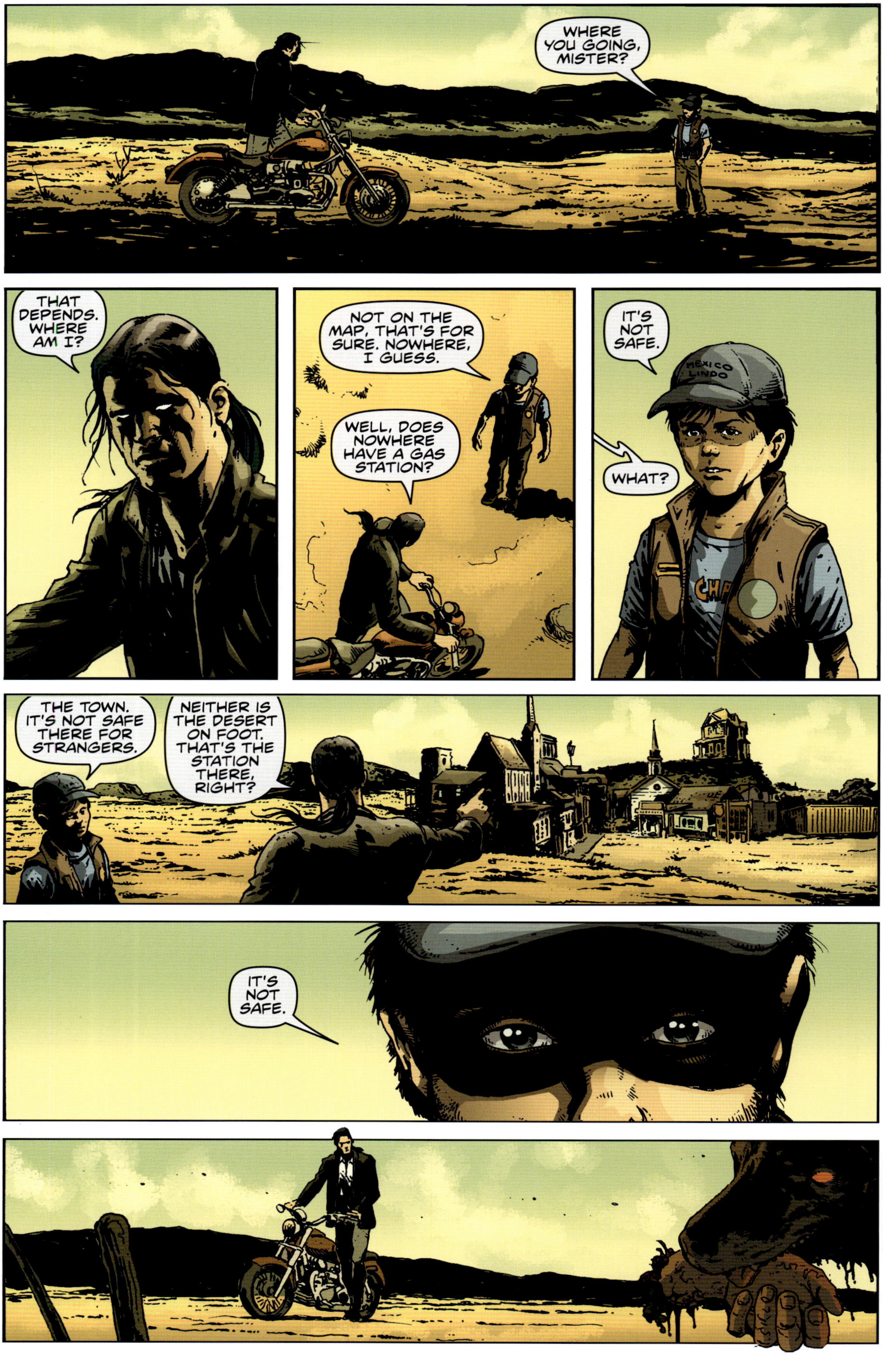
WHERE YOU GOING, MISTER?
THAT DEPENDS. WHERE AM I?
NOT ON THE MAP, THAT'S FOR SURE. NOWHERE, I GUESS.
WELL, DOES NOWHERE HAVE A GAS STATION?
IT'S NOT SAFE.
MEXICO LINDO
WHAT?
THE TOWN. IT'S NOT SAFE THERE FOR STRANGERS.
NEITHER IS THE DESERT ON FOOT. THAT'S THE STATION THERE, RIGHT?
IT'S NOT SAFE.

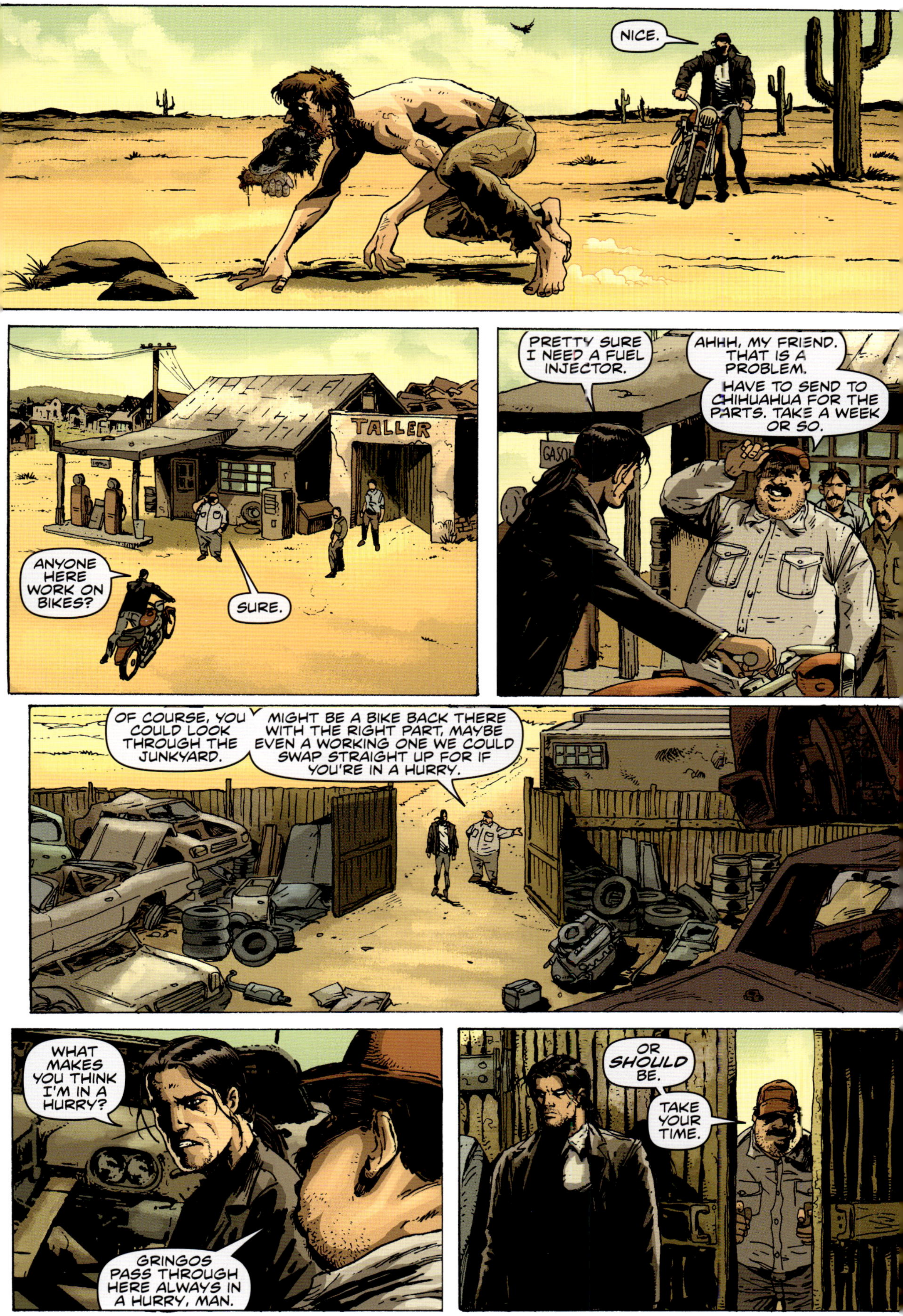
NICE.
TALLER
ANYONE HERE WORK ON BIKES?
SURE.
PRETTY SURE I NEED A FUEL INJECTOR.
AHHH, MY FRIEND. THAT IS A PROBLEM.
HAVE TO SEND TO CHIHUAHUA FOR THE PARTS. TAKE A WEEK OR SO.
OF COURSE, YOU COULD LOOK THROUGH THE JUNKYARD.
MIGHT BE A BIKE BACK THERE WITH THE RIGHT PART, MAYBE EVEN A WORKING ONE WE COULD SWAP STRAIGHT UP FOR IF YOU'RE IN A HURRY.
WHAT MAKES YOU THINK I'M IN A HURRY?
GRINGOS PASS THROUGH HERE ALWAYS IN A HURRY, MAN.
OR SHOULD BE.
TAKE YOUR TIME.

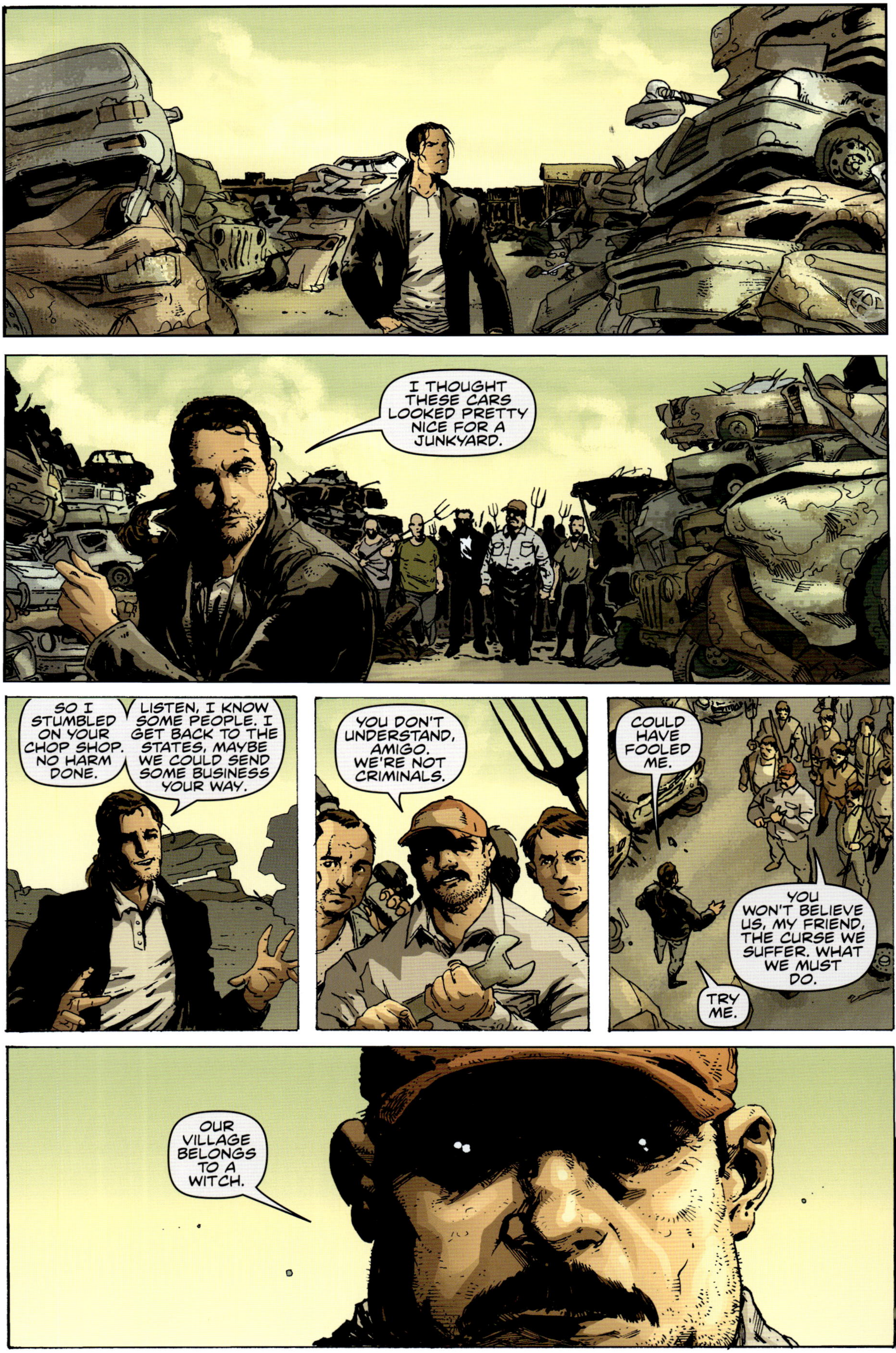
I THOUGHT THESE CARS LOOKED PRETTY NICE FOR A JUNKYARD.
SO I STUMBLED ON YOUR CHOP SHOP. NO HARM DONE.
LISTEN, I KNOW SOME PEOPLE. I GET BACK TO THE STATES, MAYBE WE COULD SEND SOME BUSINESS YOUR WAY.
YOU DON'T UNDERSTAND, AMIGO. WE'RE NOT CRIMINALS.
COULD HAVE FOOLED ME.
YOU WON'T BELIEVE US, MY FRIEND, THE CURSE WE SUFFER. WHAT WE MUST DO.
TRY ME.
OUR VILLAGE BELONGS TO A WITCH.

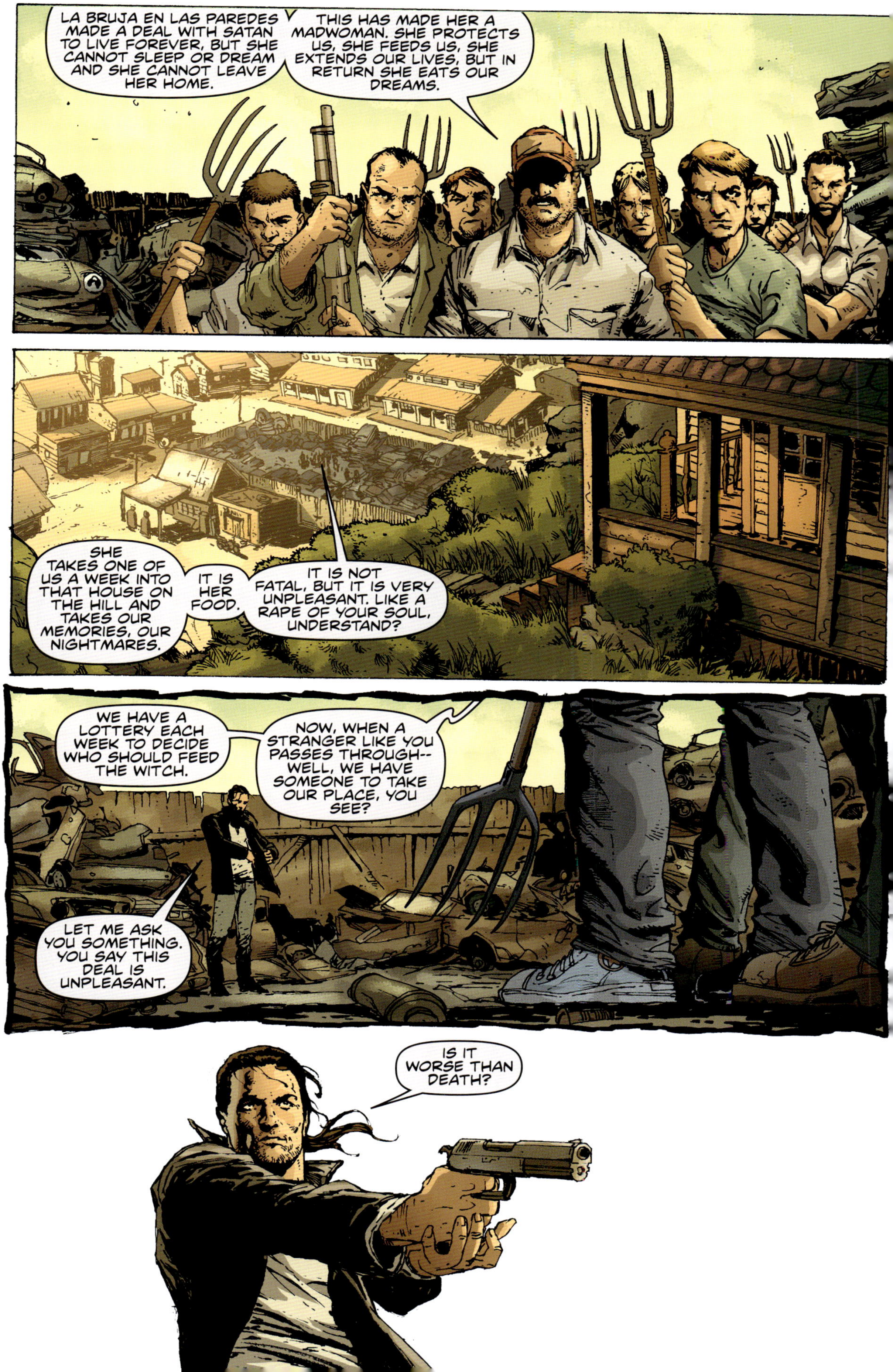
LA BRUJA EN LAS PAREDES MADE A DEAL WITH SATAN TO LIVE FOREVER, BUT SHE CANNOT SLEEP OR DREAM AND SHE CANNOT LEAVE HER HOME.
THIS HAS MADE HER A MADWOMAN. SHE PROTECTS US, SHE FEEDS US, SHE EXTENDS OUR LIVES, BUT IN RETURN SHE EATS OUR DREAMS.
SHE TAKES ONE OF US A WEEK INTO THAT HOUSE ON THE HILL AND TAKES OUR MEMORIES, OUR NIGHTMARES.
IT IS HER FOOD.
IT IS NOT FATAL, BUT IT IS VERY UNPLEASANT. LIKE A RAPE OF YOUR SOUL, UNDERSTAND?
WE HAVE A LOTTERY EACH WEEK TO DECIDE WHO SHOULD FEED THE WITCH.
NOW, WHEN A STRANGER LIKE YOU PASSES THROUGH-- WELL, WE HAVE SOMEONE TO TAKE OUR PLACE, YOU SEE?
LET ME ASK YOU SOMETHING. YOU SAY THIS DEAL IS UNPLEASANT.
IS IT WORSE THAN DEATH?

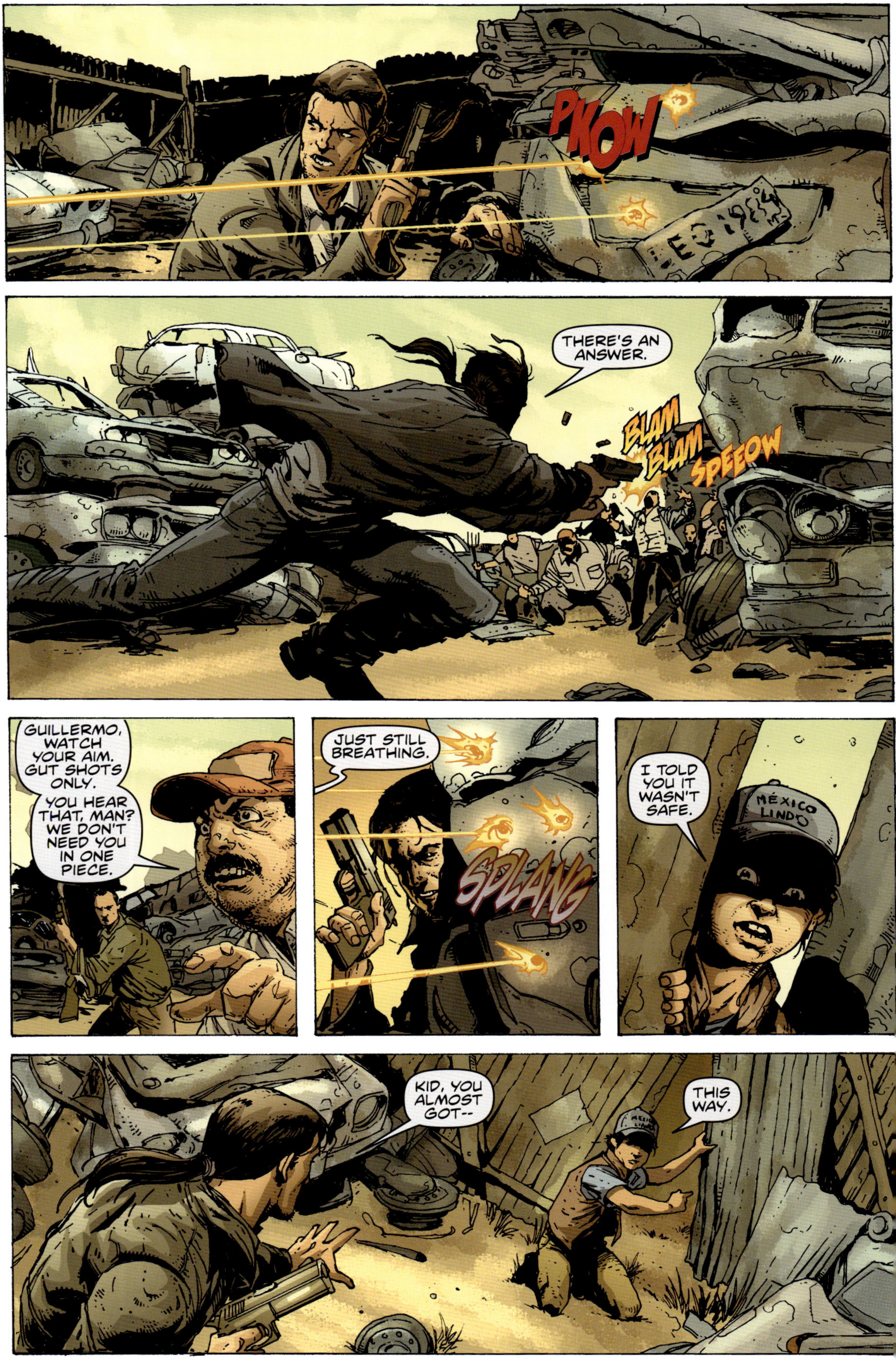
PKOW
THERE'S AN ANSWER.
BLAM
BLAM
SPEEOW
GUILLERMO, WATCH YOUR AIM. GUT SHOTS ONLY.
YOU HEAR THAT, MAN? WE DON'T NEED YOU IN ONE PIECE.
JUST STILL BREATHING.
SPLANG
I TOLD YOU IT WASN'T SAFE.
MÉXICO LINDO
KID, YOU ALMOST GOT--
THIS WAY.

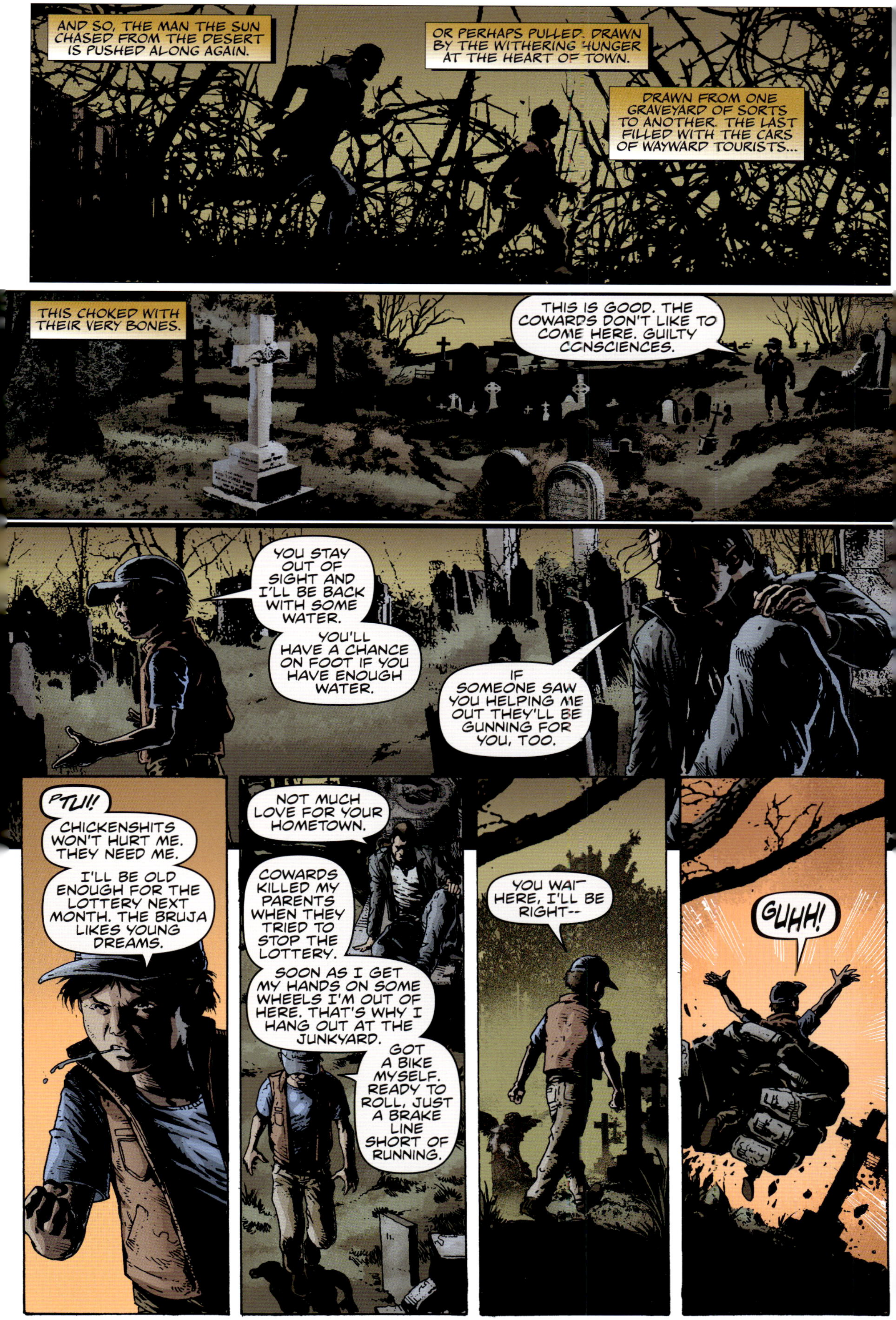
AND SO, THE MAN THE SUN CHASED FROM THE DESERT IS PUSHED ALONG AGAIN.
OR PERHAPS PULLED. DRAWN BY THE WITHERING HUNGER AT THE HEART OF TOWN.
DRAWN FROM ONE GRAVEYARD OF SORTS TO ANOTHER. THE LAST FILLED WITH THE CARS OF WAYWARD TOURISTS...
THIS CHOKED WITH THEIR VERY BONES.
THIS IS GOOD. THE COWARDS DON'T LIKE TO COME HERE. GUILTY CONSCIENCES.
YOU STAY OUT OF SIGHT AND I'LL BE BACK WITH SOME WATER.
YOU'LL HAVE A CHANCE ON FOOT IF YOU HAVE ENOUGH WATER.
IF SOMEONE SAW YOU HELPING ME OUT THEY'LL BE GUNNING FOR YOU, TOO.
PTU!!
CHICKENSHITS WON'T HURT ME. THEY NEED ME.
I'LL BE OLD ENOUGH FOR THE LOTTERY NEXT MONTH. THE BRUJA LIKES YOUNG DREAMS.
NOT MUCH LOVE FOR YOUR HOMETOWN.
COWARDS KILLED MY PARENTS WHEN THEY TRIED TO STOP THE LOTTERY.
SOON AS I GET MY HANDS ON SOME WHEELS I'M OUT OF HERE. THAT'S WHY I HANG OUT AT THE JUNKYARD.
GOT A BIKE MYSELF. READY TO ROLL, JUST A BRAKE LINE SHORT OF RUNNING.
YOU WAIT HERE, I'LL BE RIGHT--
GUHH!

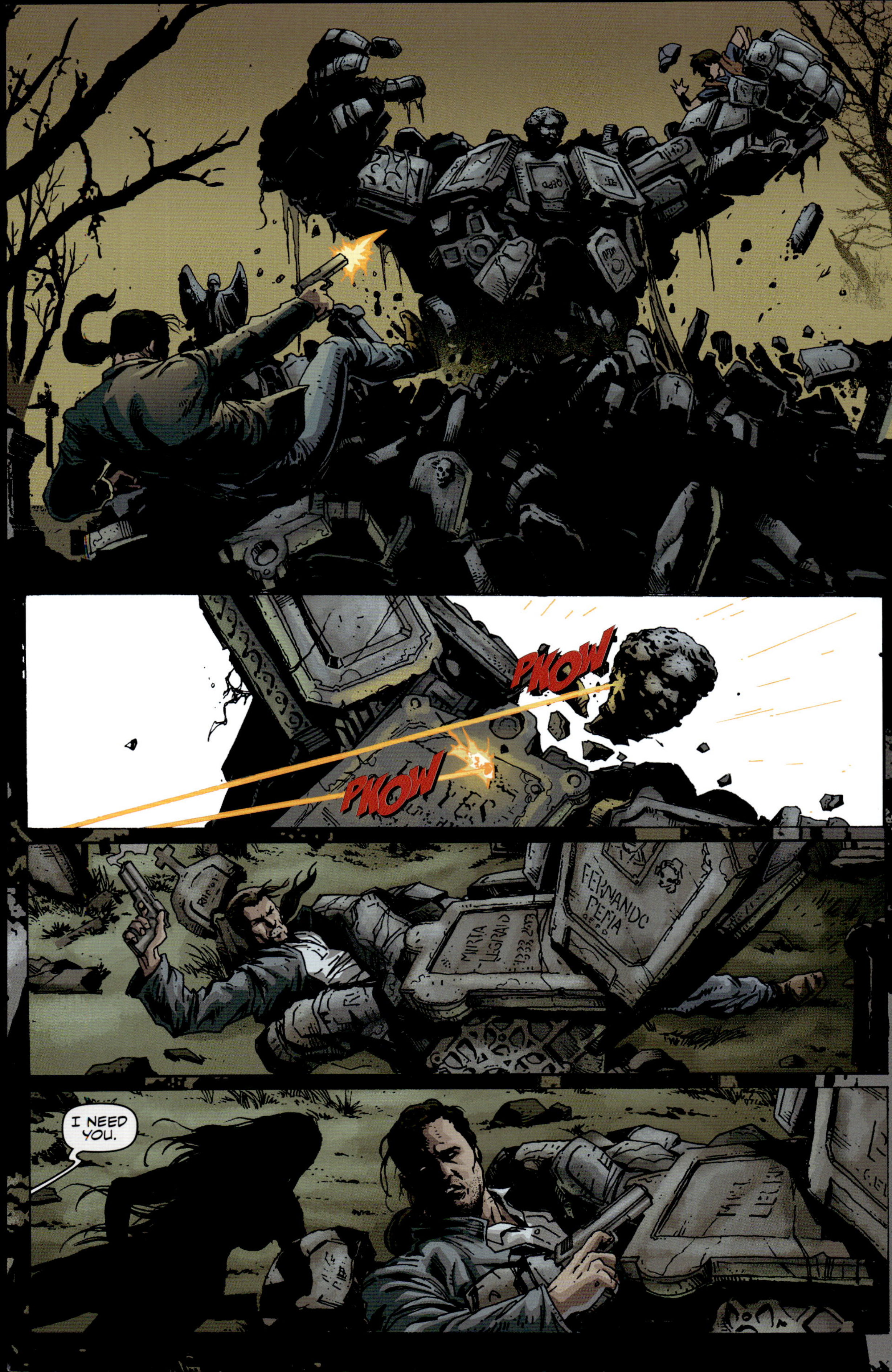
PKOW
PKOW
I NEED YOU.

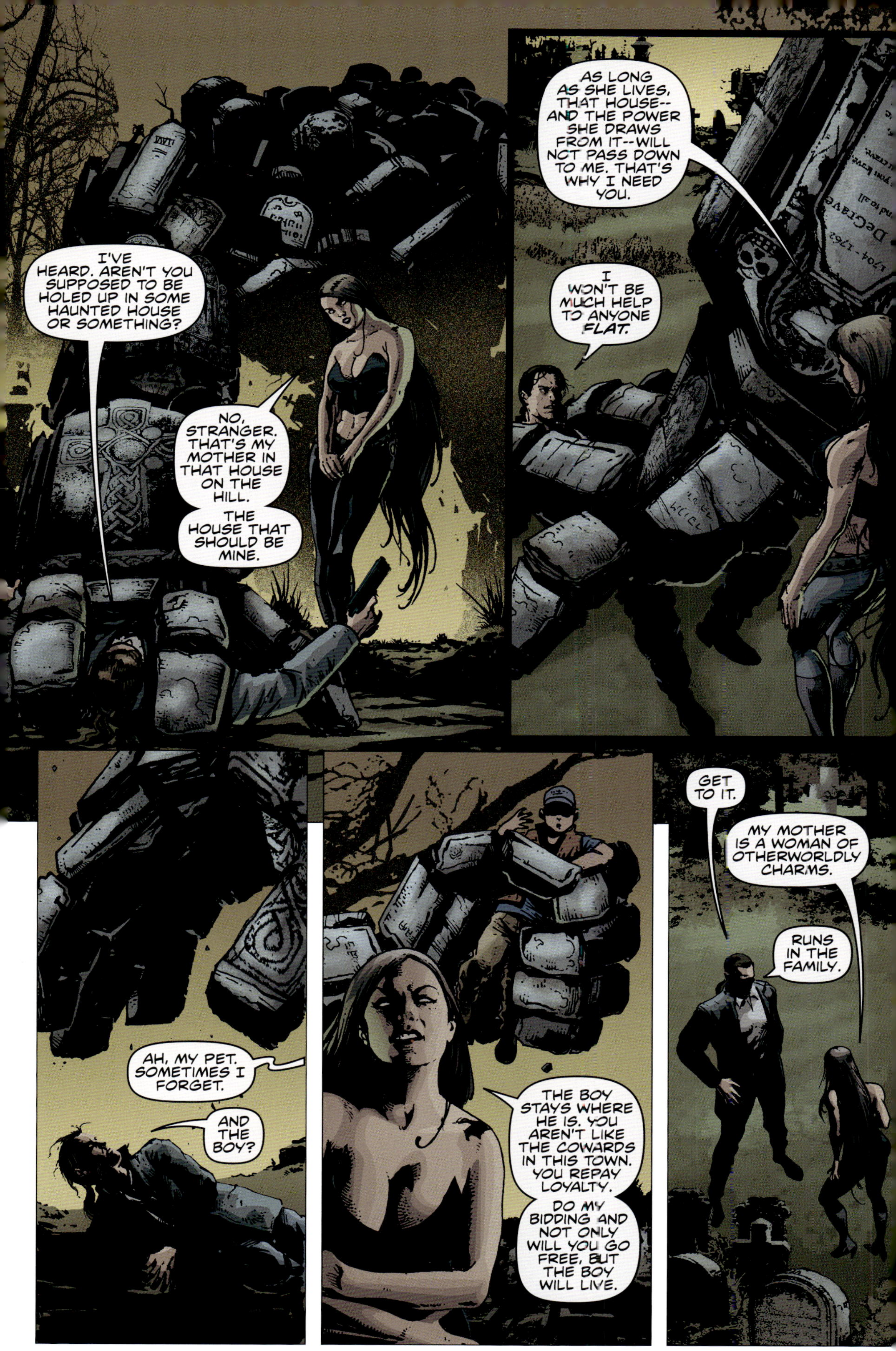
I'VE HEARD. AREN'T YOU SUPPOSED TO BE HOLED UP IN SOME HAUNTED HOUSE OR SOMETHING?
NO, STRANGER. THAT'S MY MOTHER IN THAT HOUSE ON THE HILL.
THE HOUSE THAT SHOULD BE MINE.
AS LONG AS SHE LIVES, THAT HOUSE--AND THE POWER SHE DRAWS FROM IT--WILL NOT PASS DOWN TO ME. THAT'S WHY I NEED YOU.
I WON'T BE MUCH HELP TO ANYONE FLAT.
AH, MY PET. SOMETIMES I FORGET.
AND THE BOY?
THE BOY STAYS WHERE HE IS. YOU AREN'T LIKE THE COWARDS IN THIS TOWN. YOU REPAY LOYALTY.
DO MY BIDDING AND NOT ONLY WILL YOU GO FREE, BUT THE BOY WILL LIVE.
GET TO IT.
MY MOTHER IS A WOMAN OF OTHERWORLDLY CHARMS.
RUNS IN THE FAMILY.

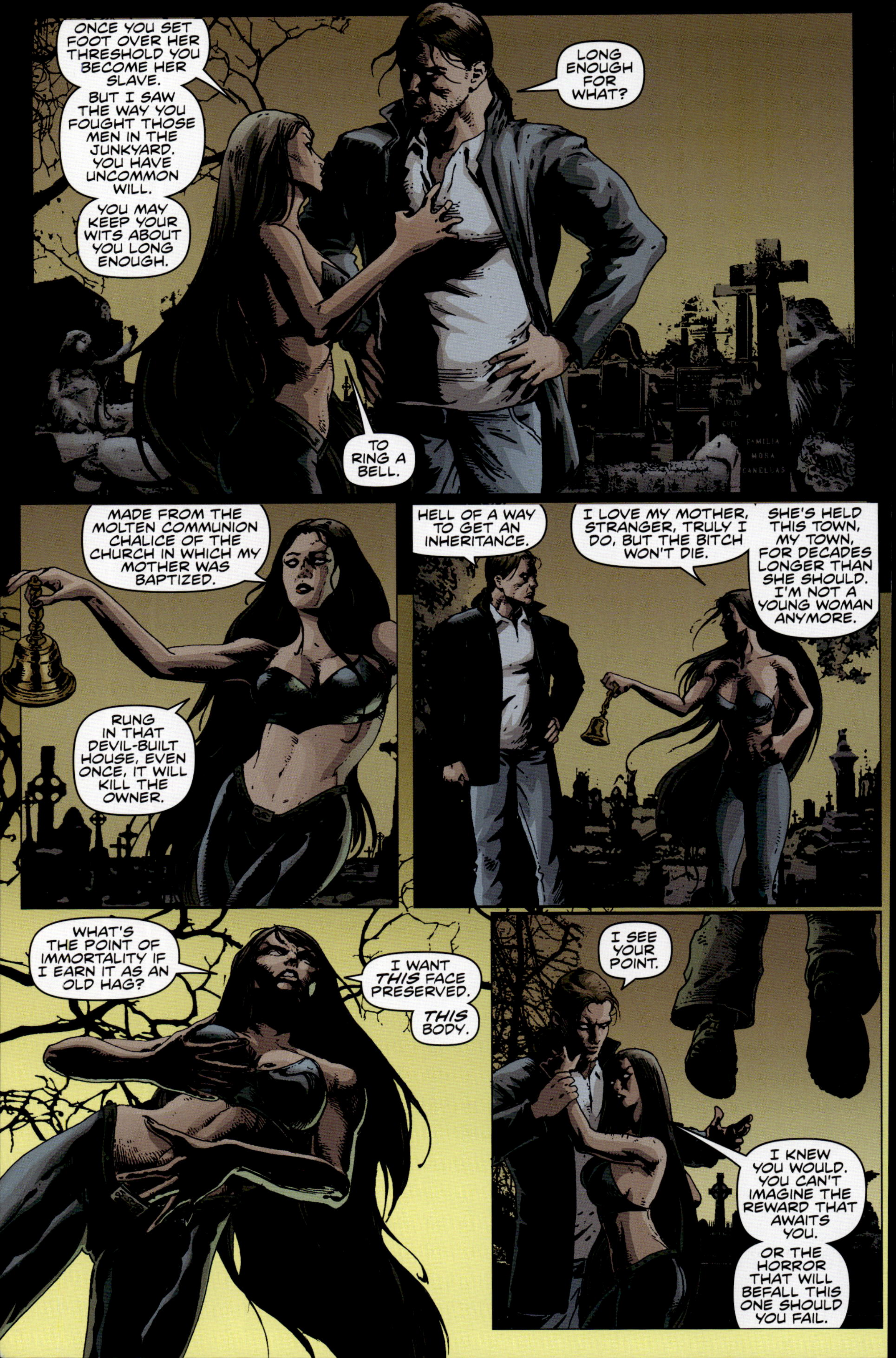
ONCE YOU SET FOOT OVER HER THRESHOLD YOU BECOME HER SLAVE.
BUT I SAW THE WAY YOU FOUGHT THOSE MEN IN THE JUNKYARD. YOU HAVE UNCOMMON WILL.
YOU MAY KEEP YOUR WITS ABOUT YOU LONG ENOUGH.
LONG ENOUGH FOR WHAT?
TO RING A BELL.
MADE FROM THE MOLTEN COMMUNION CHALICE OF THE CHURCH IN WHICH MY MOTHER WAS BAPTIZED.
RUNG IN THAT DEVIL-BUILT HOUSE, EVEN ONCE, IT WILL KILL THE OWNER.
HELL OF A WAY TO GET AN INHERITANCE.
I LOVE MY MOTHER, STRANGER, TRULY I DO, BUT THE BITCH WON'T DIE.
SHE'S HELD THIS TOWN, MY TOWN, FOR DECADES LONGER THAN SHE SHOULD. I'M NOT A YOUNG WOMAN ANYMORE.
WHAT'S THE POINT OF IMMORTALITY IF I EARN IT AS AN OLD HAG?
I WANT *THIS* FACE PRESERVED.
THIS BODY.
I SEE YOUR POINT.
I KNEW YOU WOULD. YOU CAN'T IMAGINE THE REWARD THAT AWAITS YOU.
OR THE HORROR THAT WILL BEFALL THIS ONE SHOULD YOU FAIL.

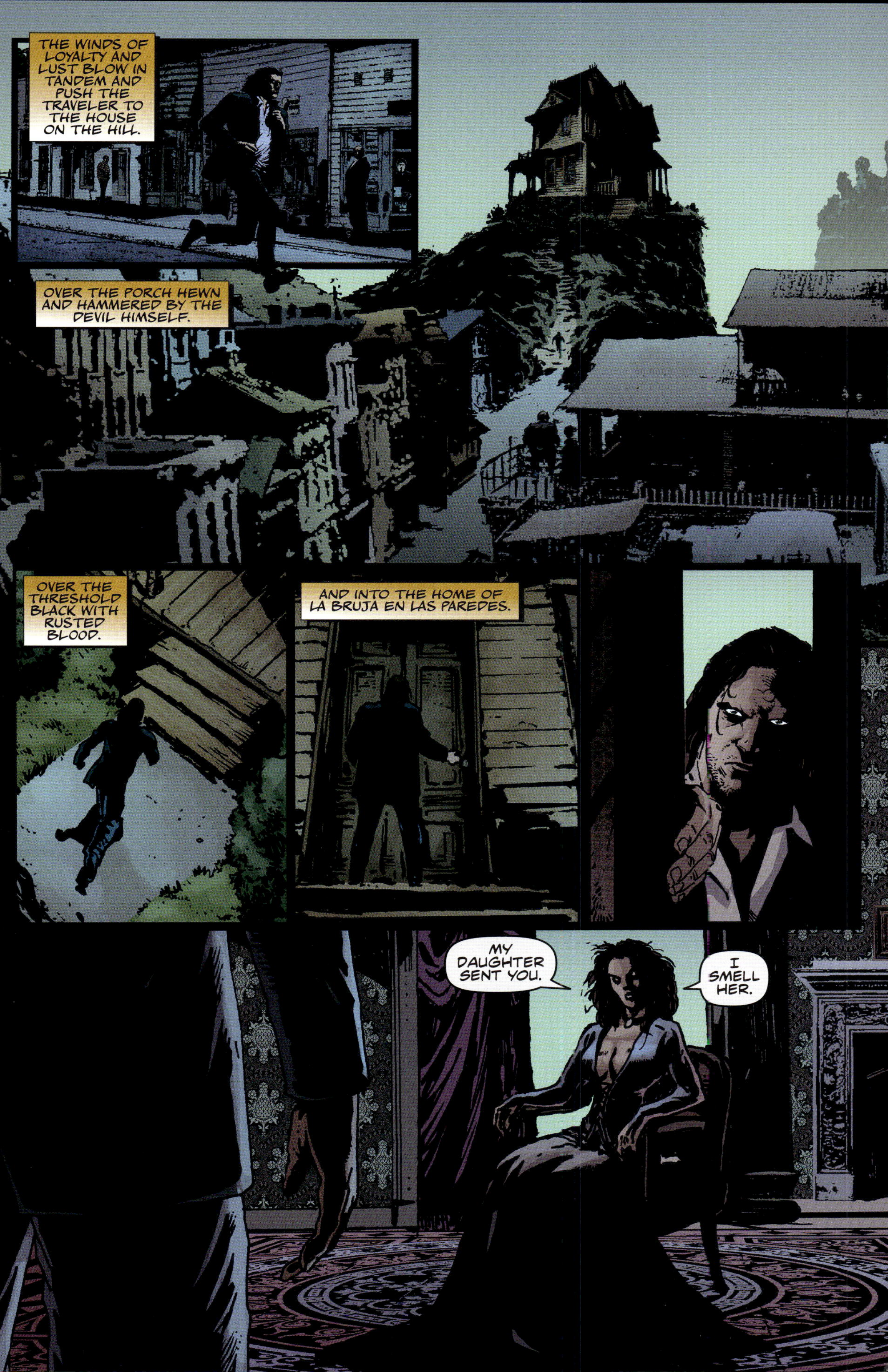
THE WINDS OF LOYALTY AND LUST BLOW IN TANDEM AND PUSH THE TRAVELER TO THE HOUSE ON THE HILL.
OVER THE PORCH HEWN AND HAMMERED BY THE DEVIL HIMSELF.
OVER THE THRESHOLD BLACK WITH RUSTED BLOOD.
AND INTO THE HOME OF LA BRUJA EN LAS PAREDES.
MY DAUGHTER SENT YOU.
I SMELL HER.

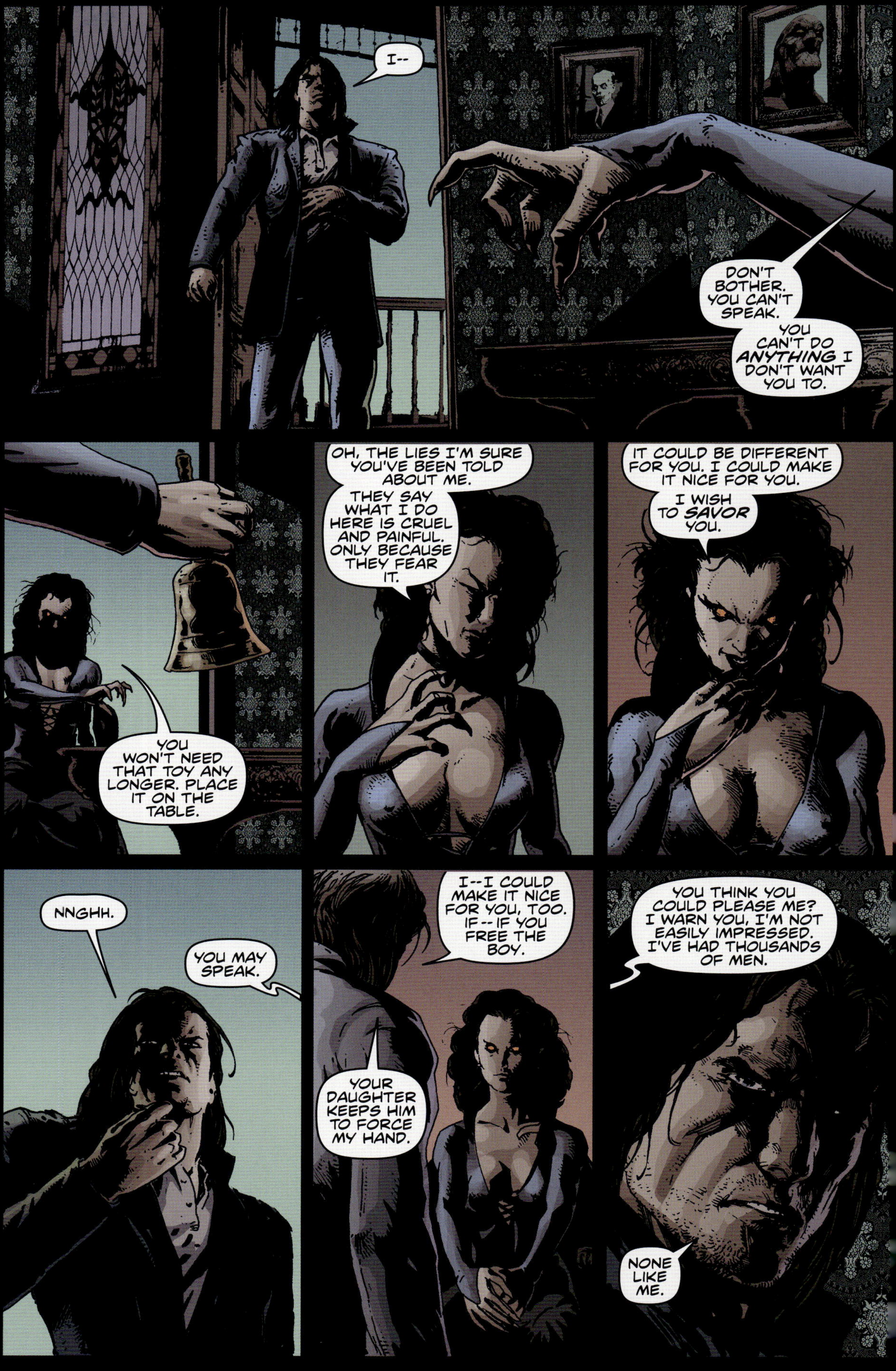
I--
DON'T BOTHER. YOU CAN'T SPEAK.
YOU CAN'T DO ANYTHING I DON'T WANT YOU TO.
YOU WON'T NEED THAT TOY ANY LONGER. PLACE IT ON THE TABLE.
OH, THE LIES I'M SURE YOU'VE BEEN TOLD ABOUT ME.
THEY SAY WHAT I DO HERE IS CRUEL AND PAINFUL. ONLY BECAUSE THEY FEAR IT.
IT COULD BE DIFFERENT FOR YOU. I COULD MAKE IT NICE FOR YOU.
I WISH TO SAVOR YOU.
NNGHH.
YOU MAY SPEAK.
I--I COULD MAKE IT NICE FOR YOU, TOO. IF--IF YOU FREE THE BOY.
YOUR DAUGHTER KEEPS HIM TO FORCE MY HAND.
YOU THINK YOU COULD PLEASE ME? I WARN YOU, I'M NOT EASILY IMPRESSED. I'VE HAD THOUSANDS OF MEN.
NONE LIKE ME.

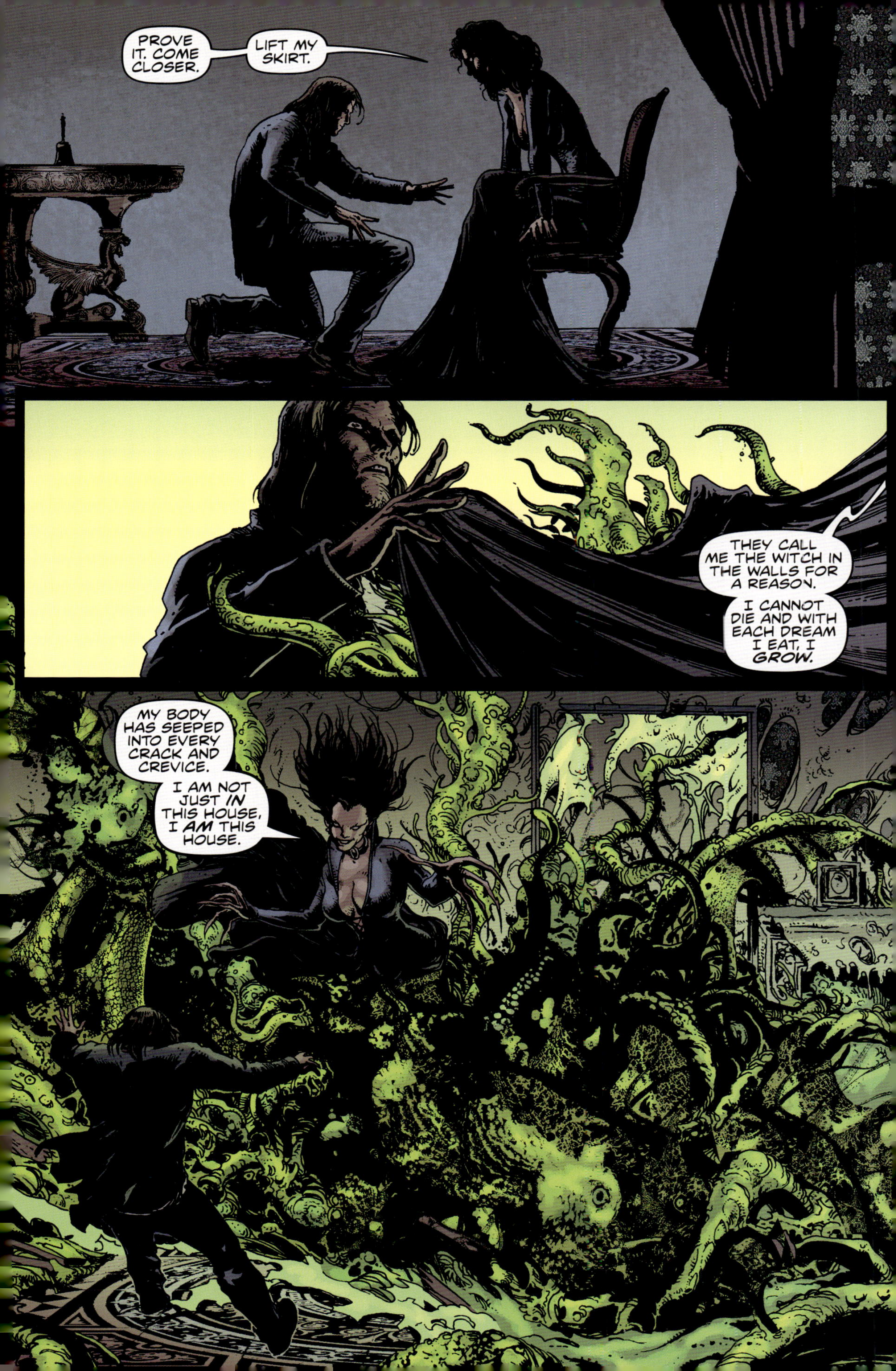
PROVE IT. COME CLOSER.
LIFT MY SKIRT.
THEY CALL ME THE WITCH IN THE WALLS FOR A REASON.
I CANNOT DIE AND WITH EACH DREAM I EAT, I *GROW.*
MY BODY HAS SEEPED INTO EVERY CRACK AND CREVICE.
I AM NOT JUST *IN* THIS HOUSE, I *AM* THIS HOUSE.

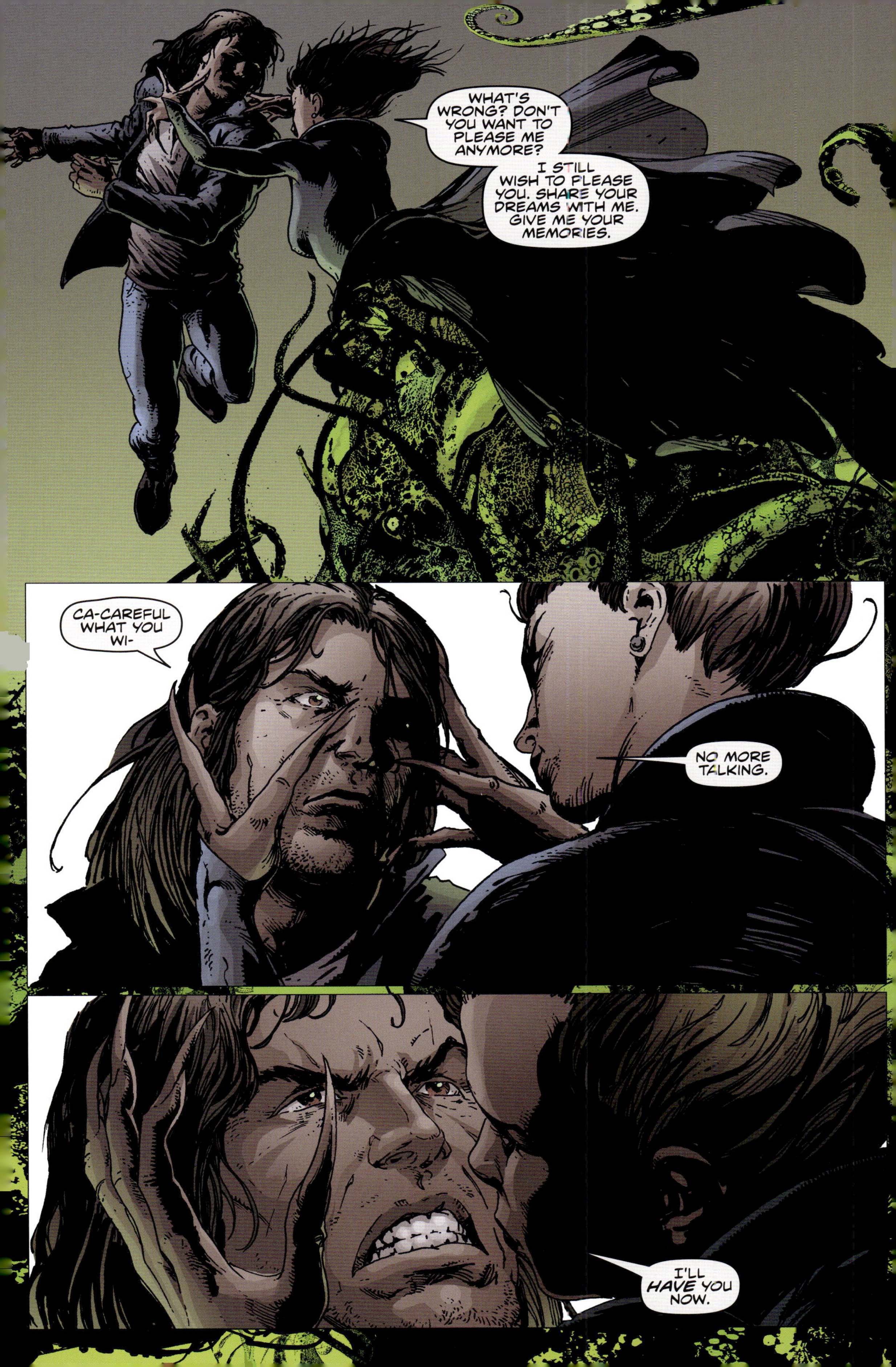
WHAT'S WRONG? DON'T YOU WANT TO PLEASE ME ANYMORE?
I STILL WISH TO PLEASE YOU. SHARE YOUR DREAMS WITH ME. GIVE ME YOUR MEMORIES.
CA-CAREFUL WHAT YOU WI-
NO MORE TALKING.
I'LL *HAVE* YOU NOW.

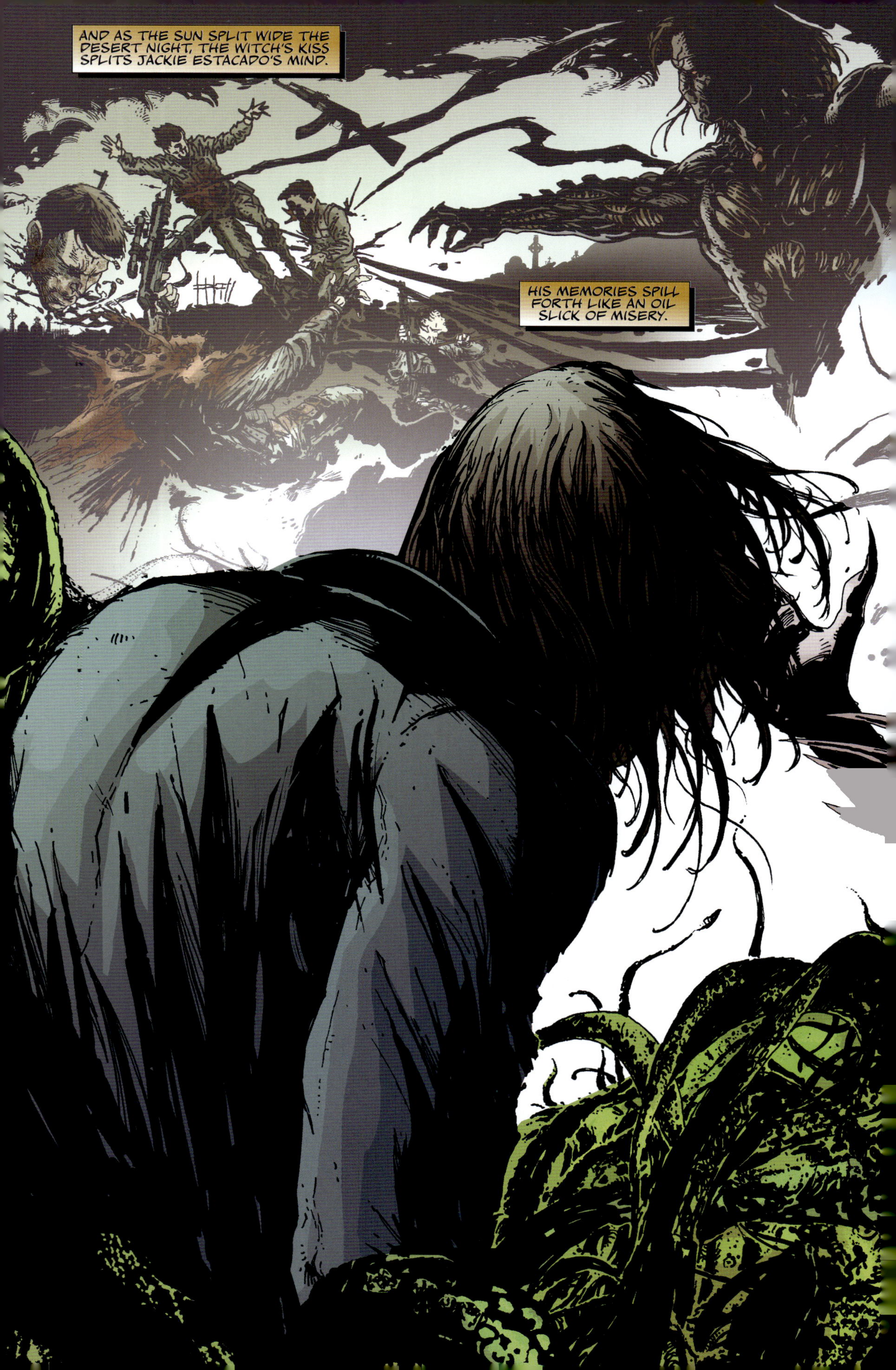
AND AS THE SUN SPLIT WIDE THE DESERT NIGHT, THE WITCH'S KISS SPLITS JACKIE ESTACADO'S MIND.
HIS MEMORIES SPILL FORTH LIKE AN OIL SLICK OF MISERY.

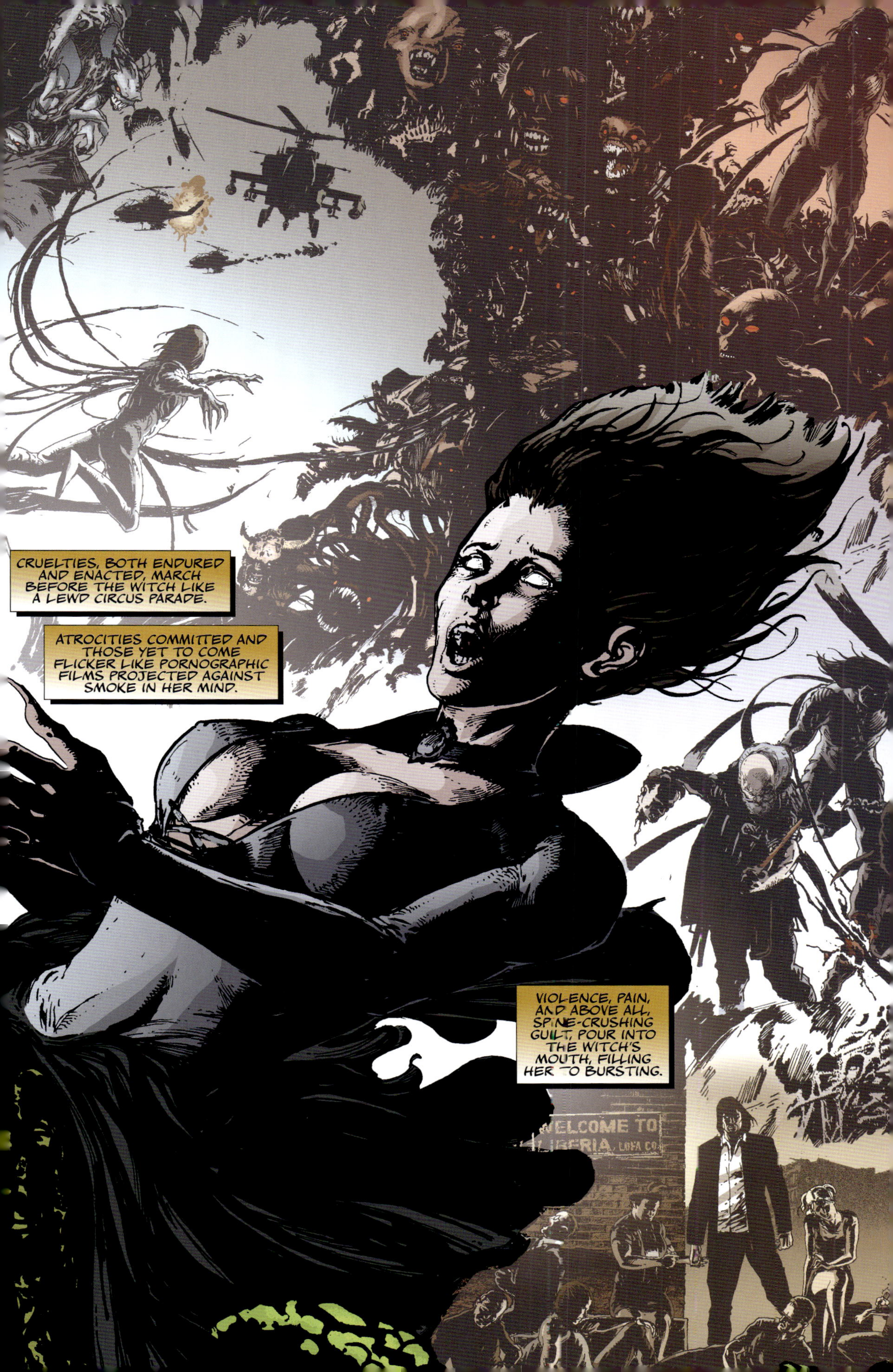
CRUELTIES, BOTH ENDURED AND ENACTED, MARCH BEFORE THE WITCH LIKE A LEWD CIRCUS PARADE.
ATROCITIES COMMITTED AND THOSE YET TO COME FLICKER LIKE PORNOGRAPHIC FILMS PROJECTED AGAINST SMOKE IN HER MIND.
VIOLENCE, PAIN, AND ABOVE ALL, SPINE-CRUSHING GUILT, POUR INTO THE WITCH'S MOUTH, FILLING HER TO BURSTING.
WELCOME TO LIBERIA. LOFA CO.

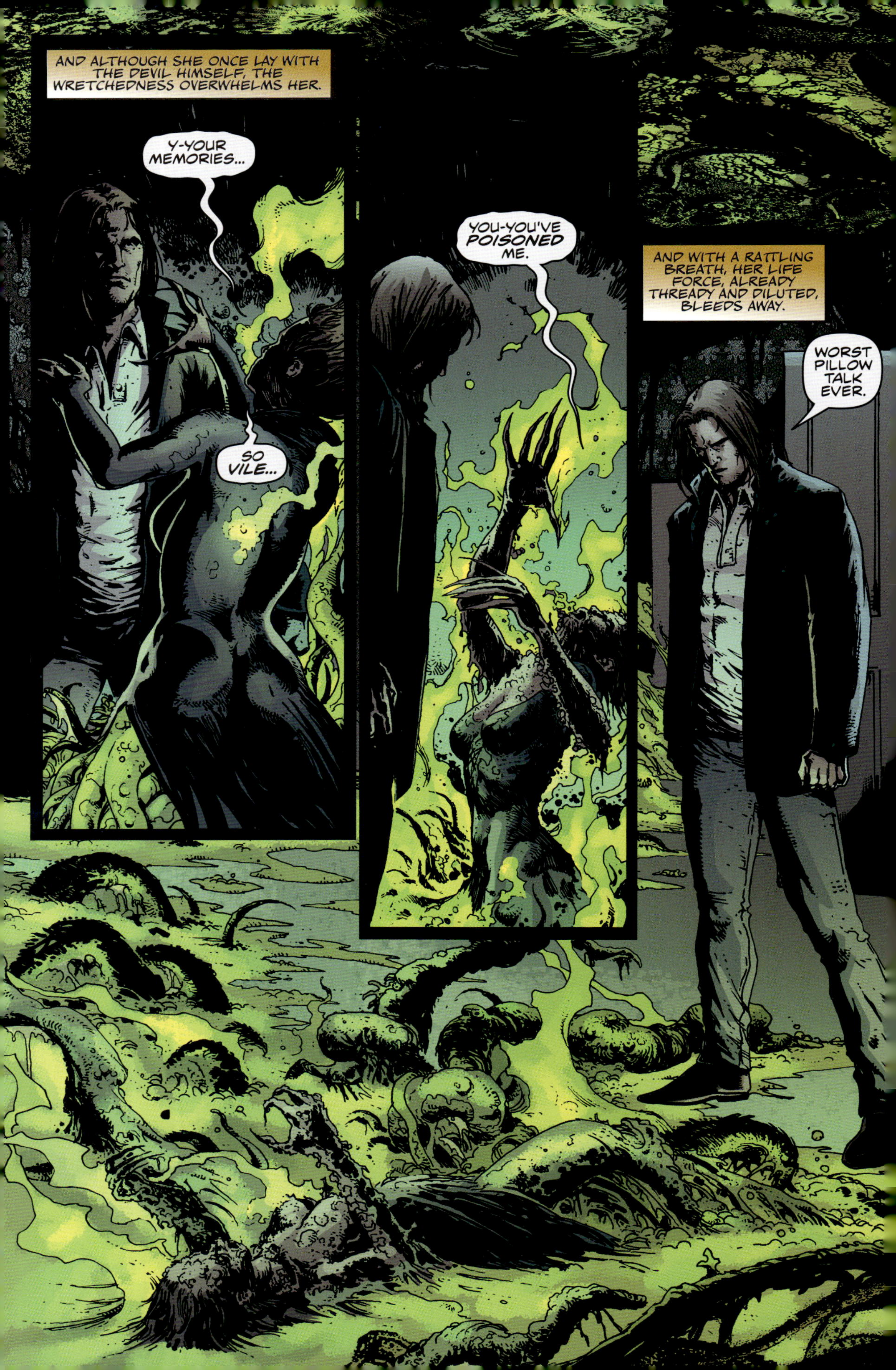
AND ALTHOUGH SHE ONCE LAY WITH THE DEVIL HIMSELF, THE WRETCHEDNESS OVERWHELMS HER.
Y-YOUR MEMORIES...
SO VILE...
YOU-YOU'VE POISONED ME.
AND WITH A RATTLING BREATH, HER LIFE FORCE, ALREADY THREADY AND DILUTED, BLEEDS AWAY.
WORST PILLOW TALK EVER.

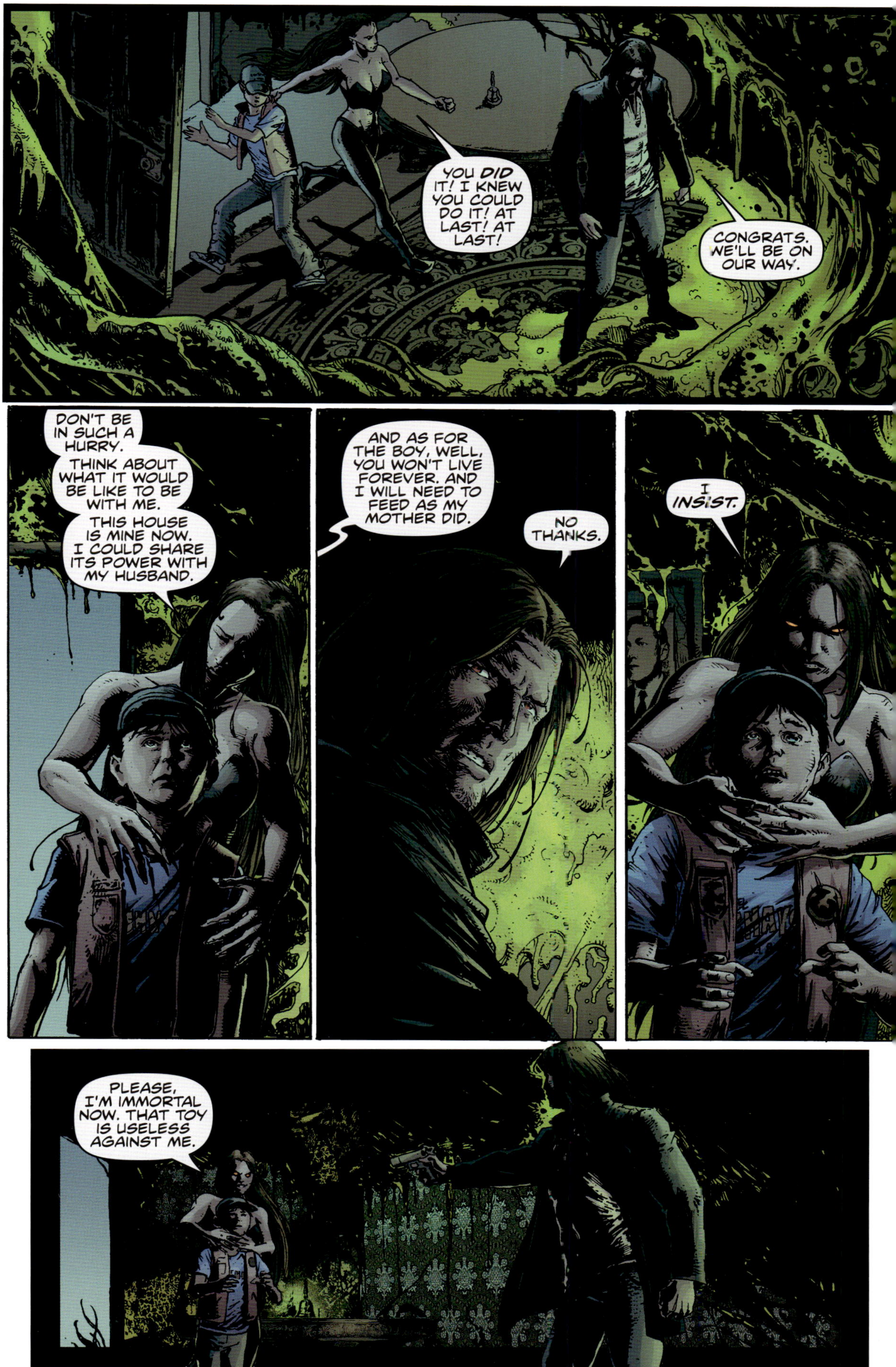
YOU DID IT! I KNEW YOU COULD DO IT! AT LAST! AT LAST!
CONGRATS. WE'LL BE ON OUR WAY.
DON'T BE IN SUCH A HURRY.
THINK ABOUT WHAT IT WOULD BE LIKE TO BE WITH ME.
THIS HOUSE IS MINE NOW. I COULD SHARE ITS POWER WITH MY HUSBAND.
AND AS FOR THE BOY, WELL, YOU WON'T LIVE FOREVER. AND I WILL NEED TO FEED AS MY MOTHER DID.
NO THANKS.
I INSIST.
PLEASE, I'M IMMORTAL NOW. THAT TOY IS USELESS AGAINST ME.

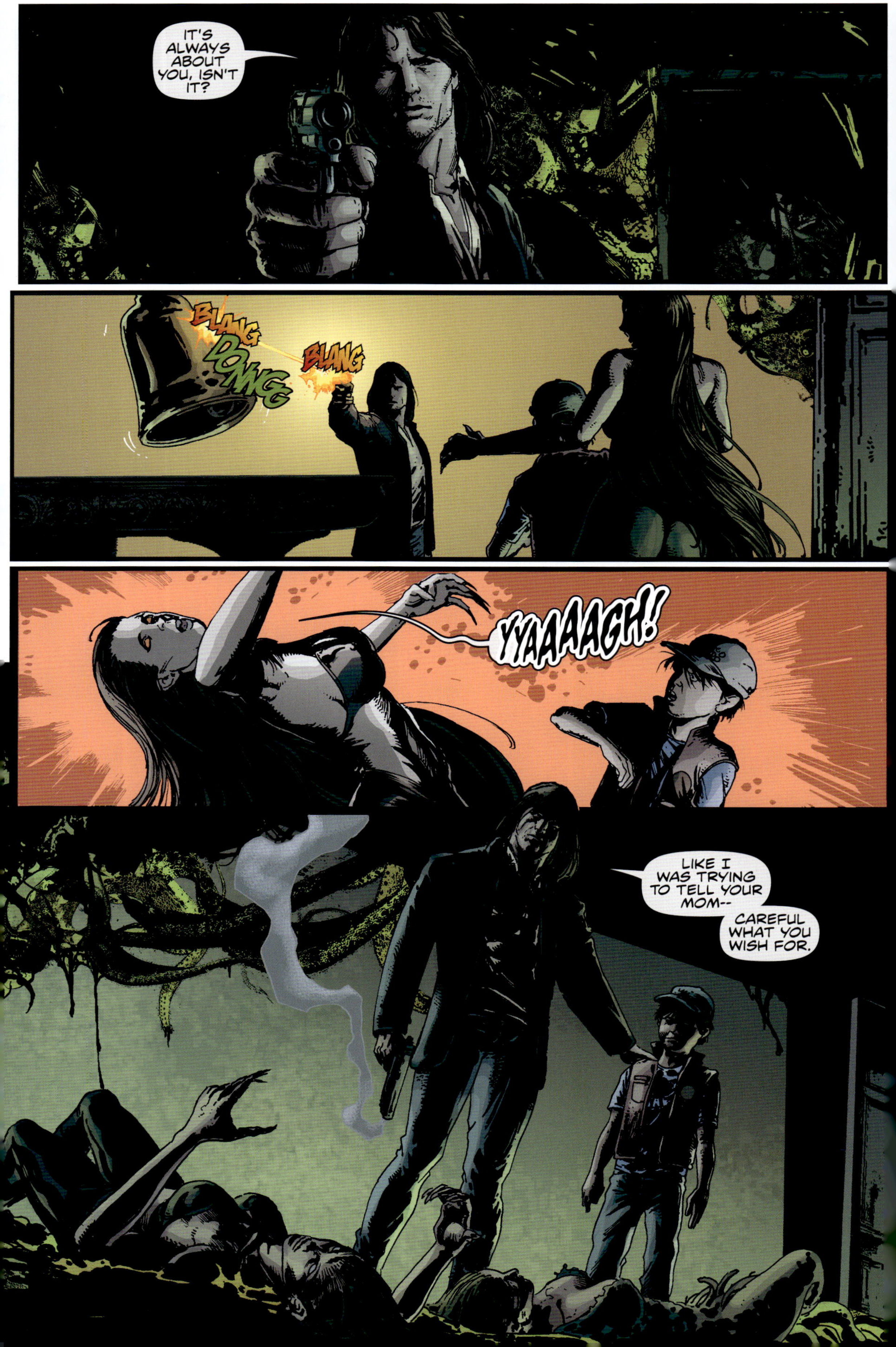
IT'S ALWAYS ABOUT YOU, ISN'T IT?
BLANG
DONNGG
BLANG
YYAAAAGH!
LIKE I WAS TRYING TO TELL YOUR MOM--
CAREFUL WHAT YOU WISH FOR.

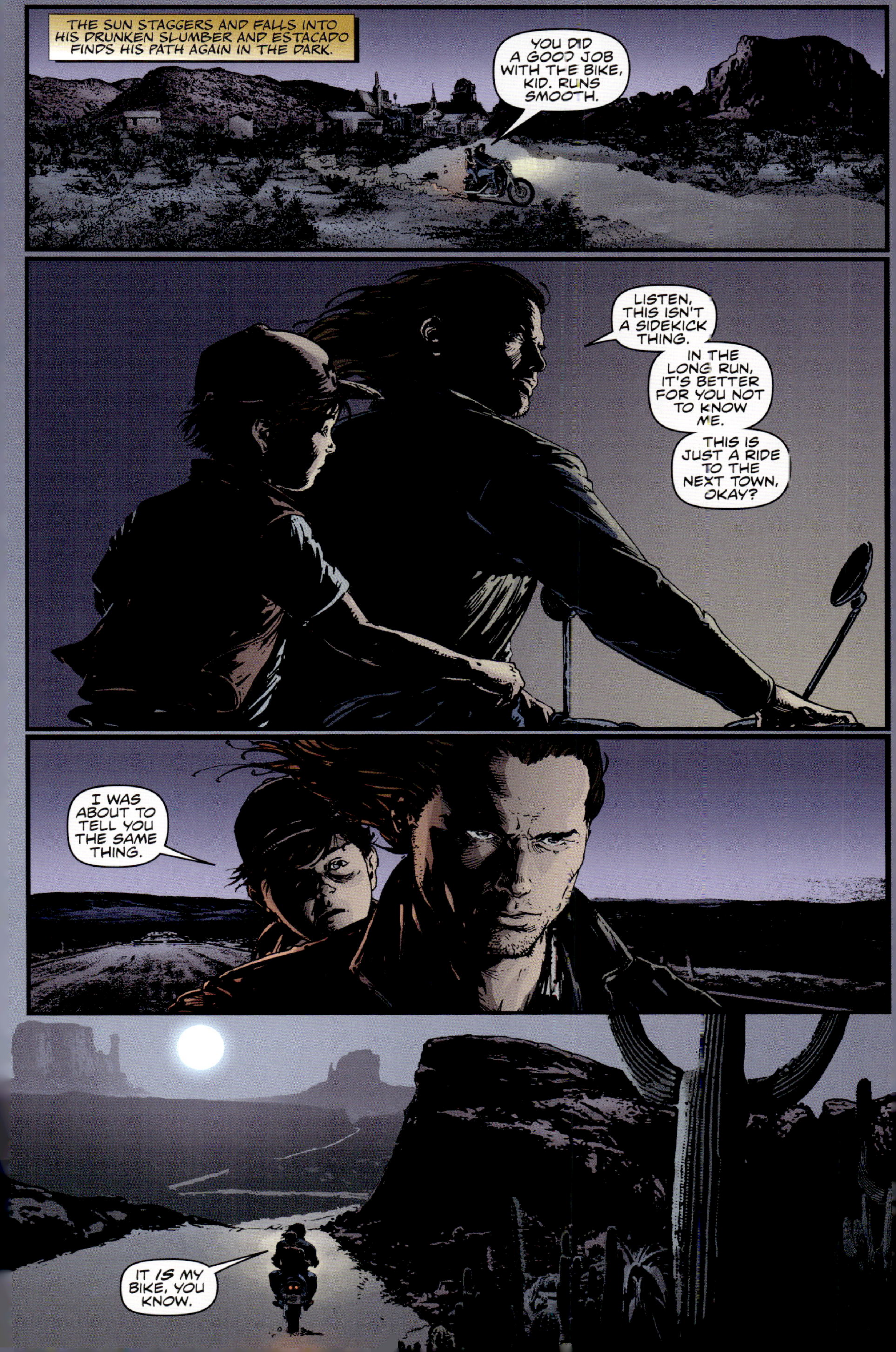
THE SUN STAGGERS AND FALLS INTO HIS DRUNKEN SLUMBER AND ESTACADO FINDS HIS PATH AGAIN IN THE DARK.
YOU DID A GOOD JOB WITH THE BIKE, KID. RUNS SMOOTH.
LISTEN, THIS ISN'T A SIDEKICK THING.
IN THE LONG RUN, IT'S BETTER FOR YOU NOT TO KNOW ME.
THIS IS JUST A RIDE TO THE NEXT TOWN, OKAY?
I WAS ABOUT TO TELL YOU THE SAME THING.
IT *IS* MY BIKE, YOU KNOW.

The Darkness Issue #72

cover art by: Jorge Lucas and Lee Loughridge

THE DARKNESS #72

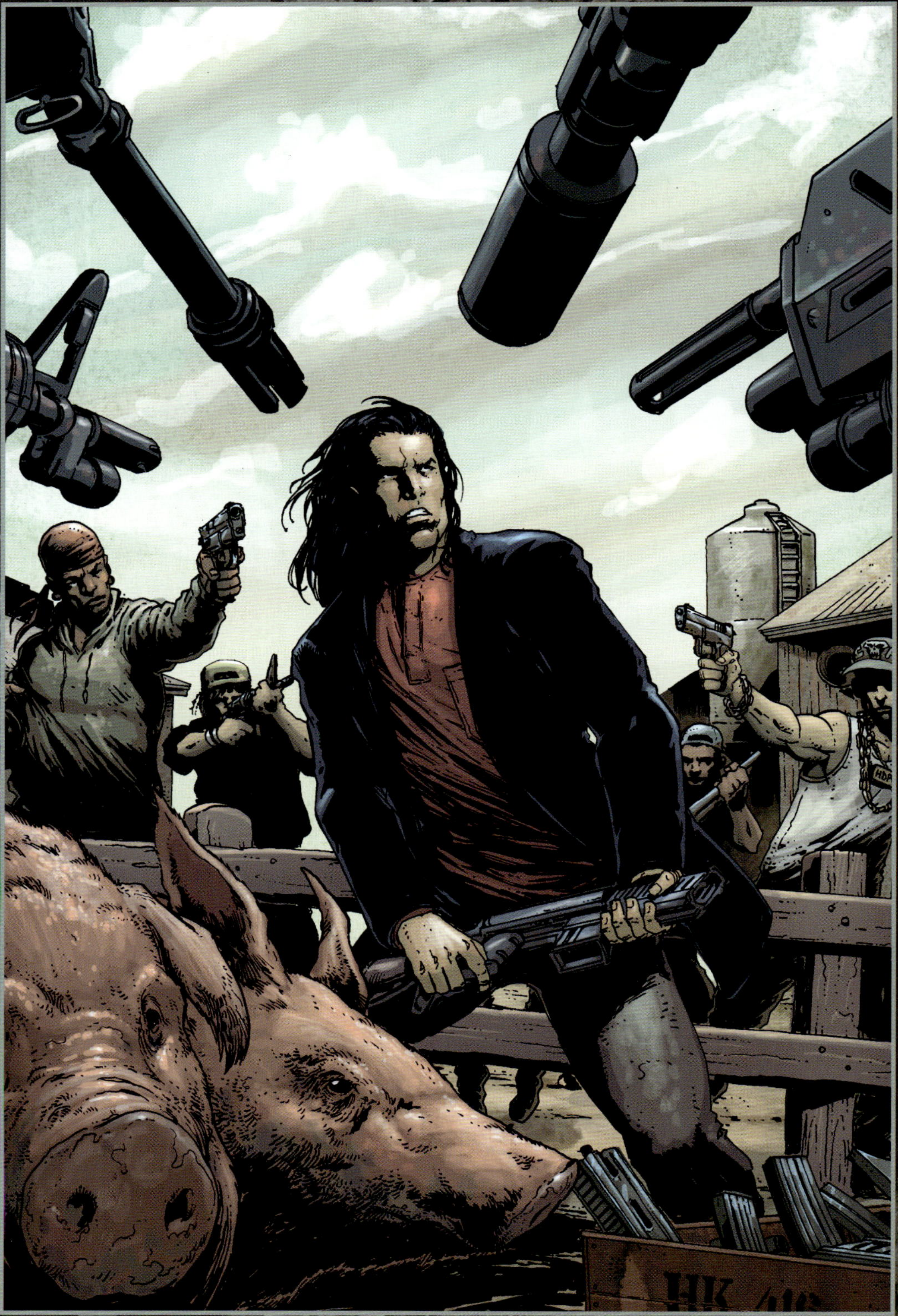
HK 416

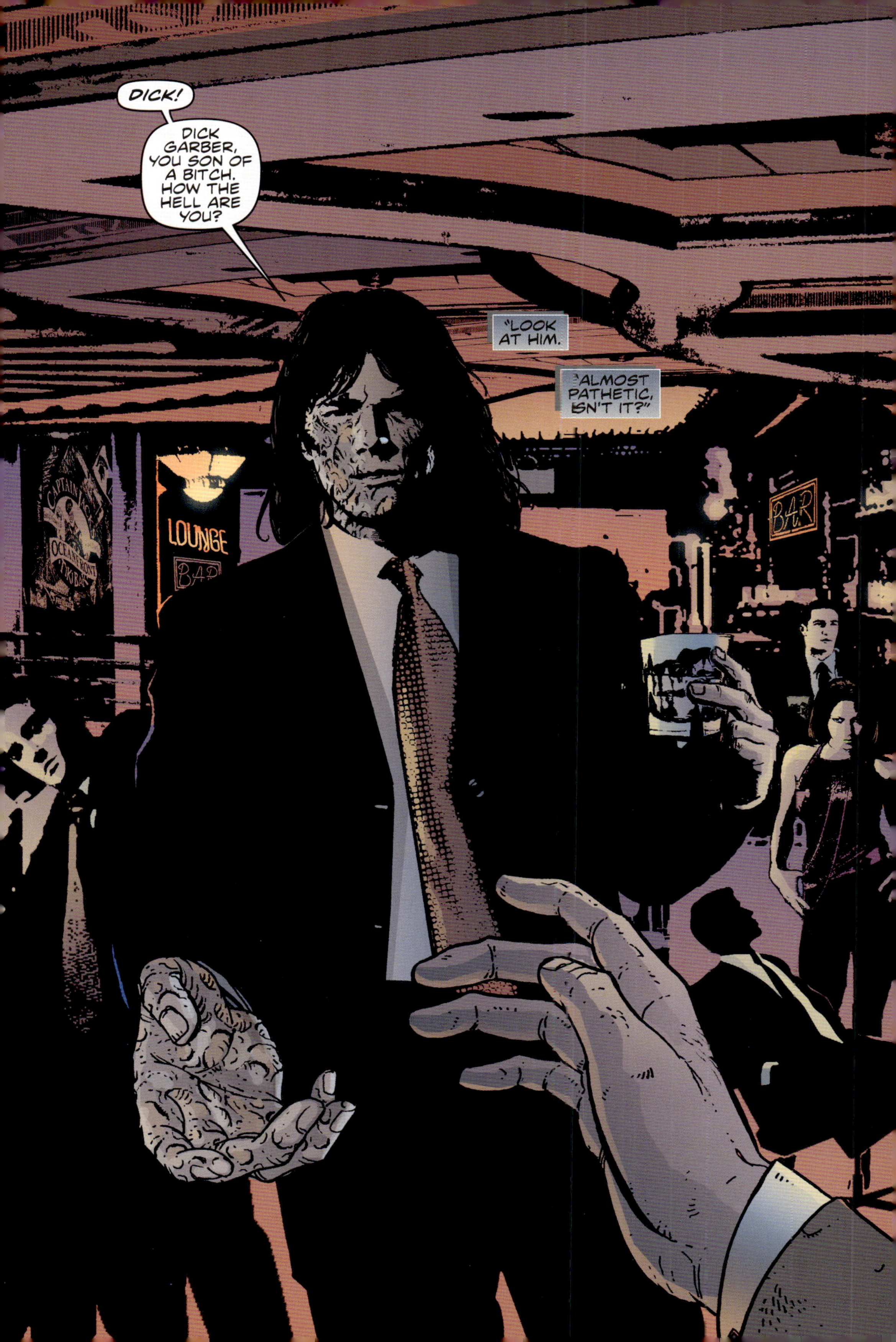
DICK!
DICK GARBER, YOU SON OF A BITCH. HOW THE HELL ARE YOU?
"LOOK AT HIM.
"ALMOST PATHETIC, ISN'T IT?"
LOUNGE
BAR
BAR

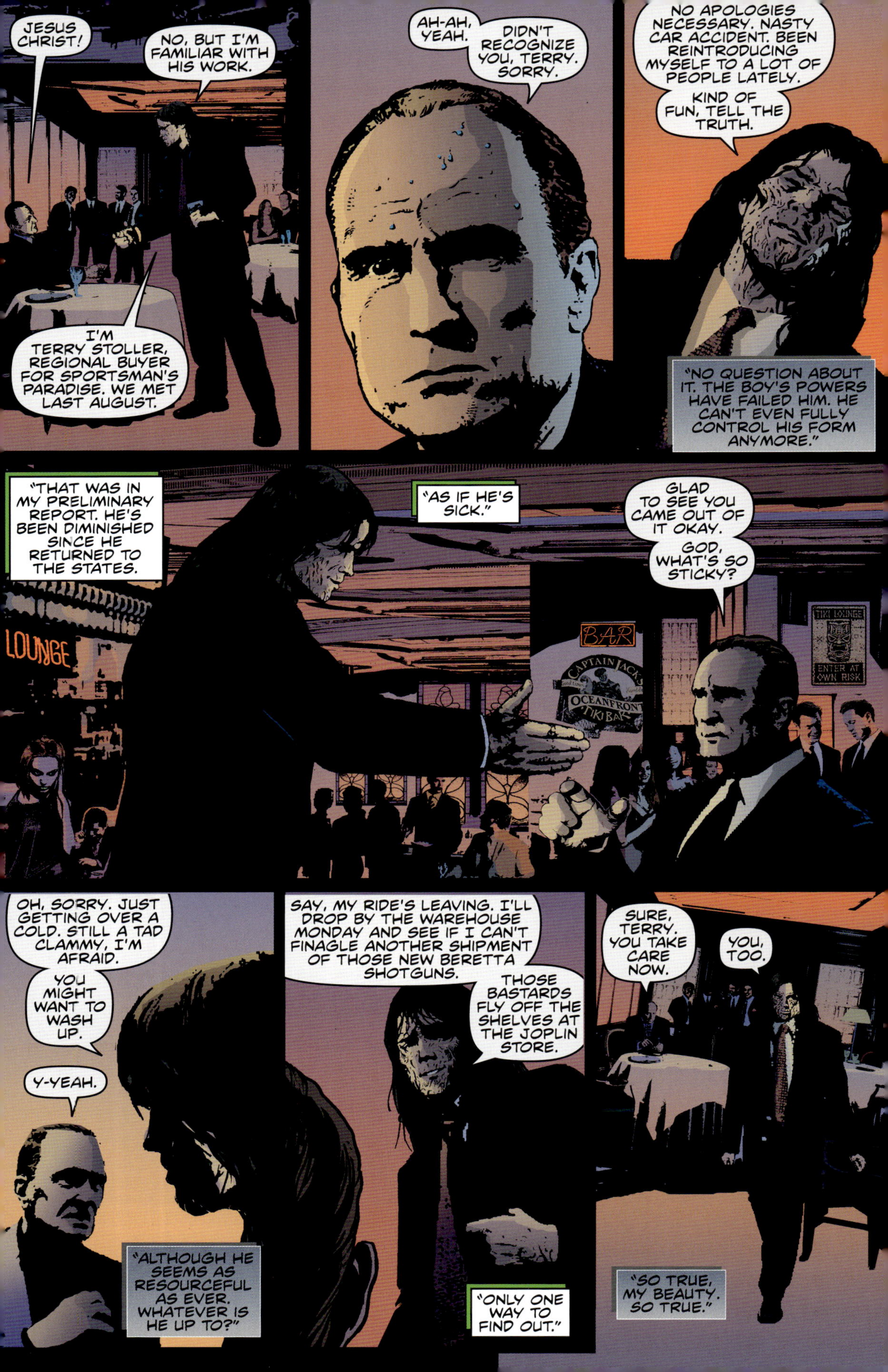
JESUS CHRIST!
NO, BUT I'M FAMILIAR WITH HIS WORK.
I'M TERRY STOLLER, REGIONAL BUYER FOR SPORTSMAN'S PARADISE. WE MET LAST AUGUST.
AH-AH, YEAH.
DIDN'T RECOGNIZE YOU, TERRY. SORRY.
NO APOLOGIES NECESSARY. NASTY CAR ACCIDENT. BEEN REINTRODUCING MYSELF TO A LOT OF PEOPLE LATELY.
KIND OF FUN, TELL THE TRUTH.
"NO QUESTION ABOUT IT. THE BOY'S POWERS HAVE FAILED HIM. HE CAN'T EVEN FULLY CONTROL HIS FORM ANYMORE."
"THAT WAS IN MY PRELIMINARY REPORT. HE'S BEEN DIMINISHED SINCE HE RETURNED TO THE STATES.
"AS IF HE'S SICK."
GLAD TO SEE YOU CAME OUT OF IT OKAY.
GOD, WHAT'S SO STICKY?
LOUNGE
BAR
CAPTAIN JACK'S
OCEANFRONT TIKI BAR
TIKI LOUNGE
ENTER AT OWN RISK
OH, SORRY. JUST GETTING OVER A COLD. STILL A TAD CLAMMY, I'M AFRAID.
YOU MIGHT WANT TO WASH UP.
Y-YEAH.
"ALTHOUGH HE SEEMS AS RESOURCEFUL AS EVER. WHATEVER IS HE UP TO?"
SAY, MY RIDE'S LEAVING. I'LL DROP BY THE WAREHOUSE MONDAY AND SEE IF I CAN'T FINAGLE ANOTHER SHIPMENT OF THOSE NEW BERETTA SHOTGUNS.
THOSE BASTARDS FLY OFF THE SHELVES AT THE JOPLIN STORE.
"ONLY ONE WAY TO FIND OUT."
SURE, TERRY. YOU TAKE CARE NOW.
YOU, TOO.
"SO TRUE, MY BEAUTY. SO TRUE."

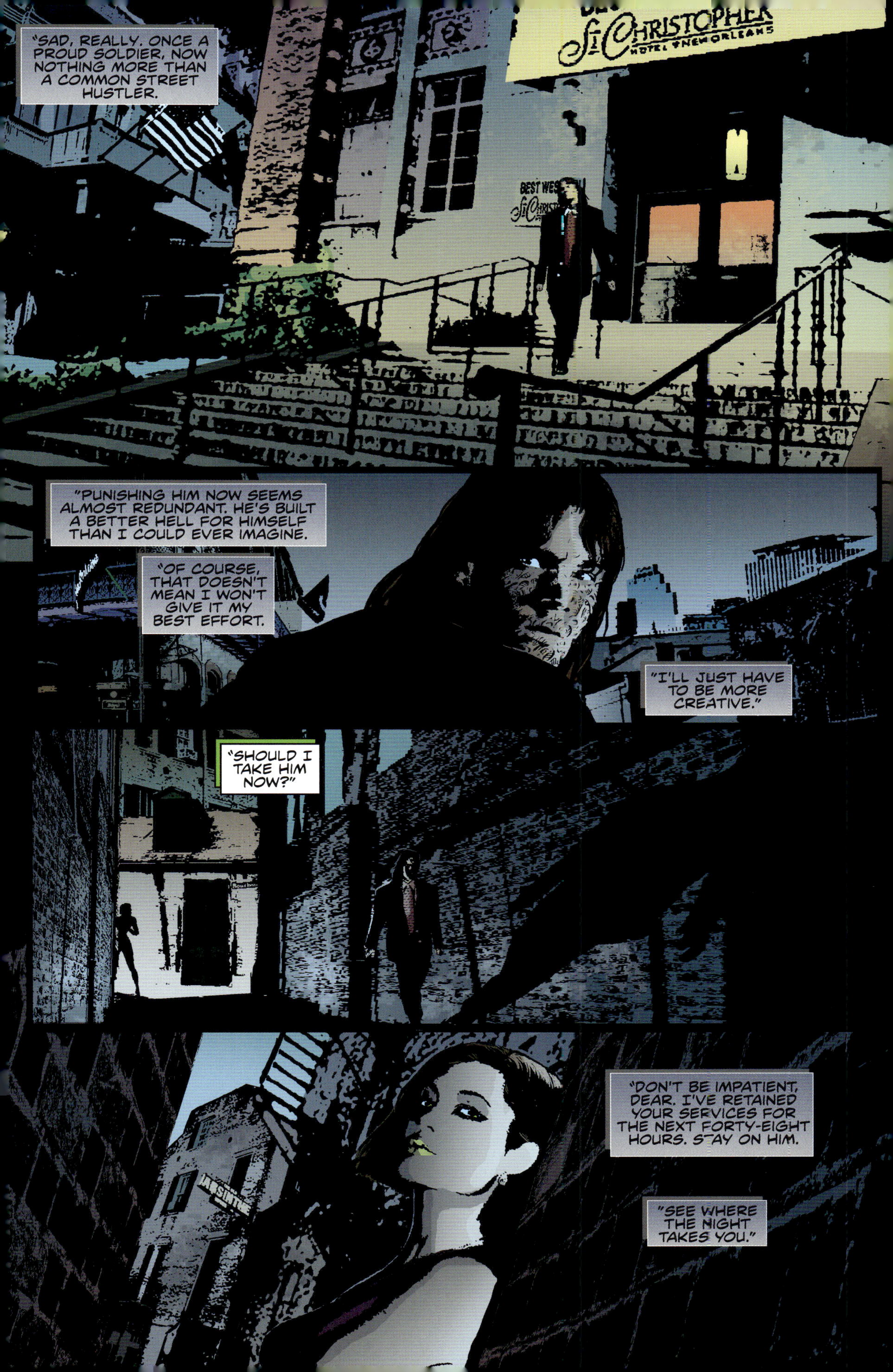
St. Christopher
HOTEL • NEW ORLEANS
"SAD, REALLY. ONCE A PROUD SOLDIER, NOW NOTHING MORE THAN A COMMON STREET HUSTLER.
"PUNISHING HIM NOW SEEMS ALMOST REDUNDANT. HE'S BUILT A BETTER HELL FOR HIMSELF THAN I COULD EVER IMAGINE.
"OF COURSE, THAT DOESN'T MEAN I WON'T GIVE IT MY BEST EFFORT.
"I'LL JUST HAVE TO BE MORE CREATIVE."
"SHOULD I TAKE HIM NOW?"
"DON'T BE IMPATIENT, DEAR. I'VE RETAINED YOUR SERVICES FOR THE NEXT FORTY-EIGHT HOURS. STAY ON HIM.
"SEE WHERE THE NIGHT TAKES YOU."

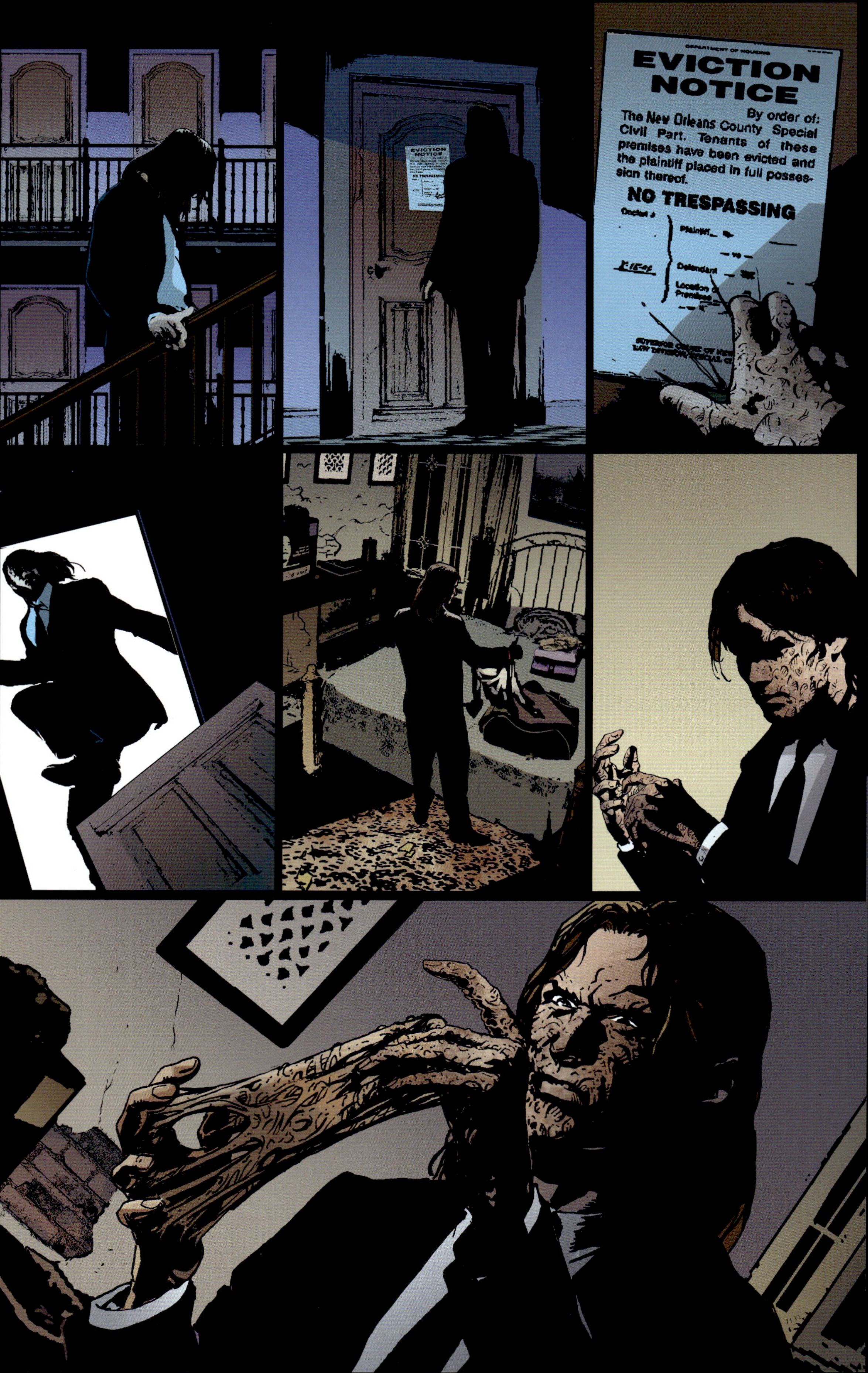
DEPARTMENT OF HOUSING
EVICTION NOTICE
By order of:
The New Orleans County Special Civil Part. Tenants of these premises have been evicted and the plaintiff placed in full possession thereof.
NO TRESPASSING
Plaintiff
Defendant

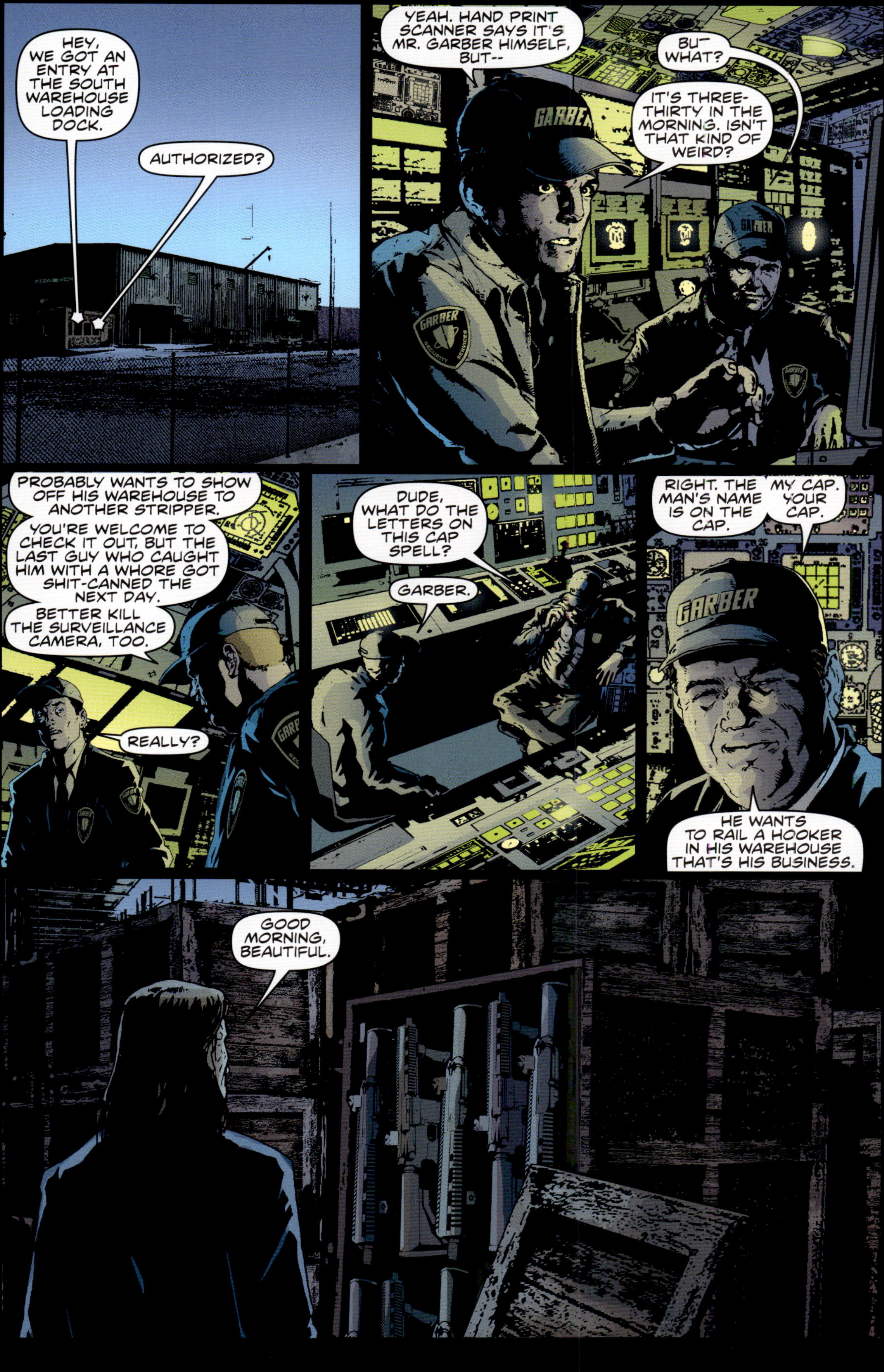
HEY, WE GOT AN ENTRY AT THE SOUTH WAREHOUSE LOADING DOCK.
AUTHORIZED?
YEAH. HAND PRINT SCANNER SAYS IT'S MR. GARBER HIMSELF, BUT--
BUT-- WHAT?
IT'S THREE-THIRTY IN THE MORNING. ISN'T THAT KIND OF WEIRD?
GARBER
PROBABLY WANTS TO SHOW OFF HIS WAREHOUSE TO ANOTHER STRIPPER.
YOU'RE WELCOME TO CHECK IT OUT, BUT THE LAST GUY WHO CAUGHT HIM WITH A WHORE GOT SHIT-CANNED THE NEXT DAY.
BETTER KILL THE SURVEILLANCE CAMERA, TOO.
REALLY?
DUDE, WHAT DO THE LETTERS ON THIS CAP SPELL?
GARBER.
RIGHT. THE MAN'S NAME IS ON THE CAP.
MY CAP. YOUR CAP.
GARBER
HE WANTS TO RAIL A HOOKER IN HIS WAREHOUSE THAT'S HIS BUSINESS.
GOOD MORNING, BEAUTIFUL.

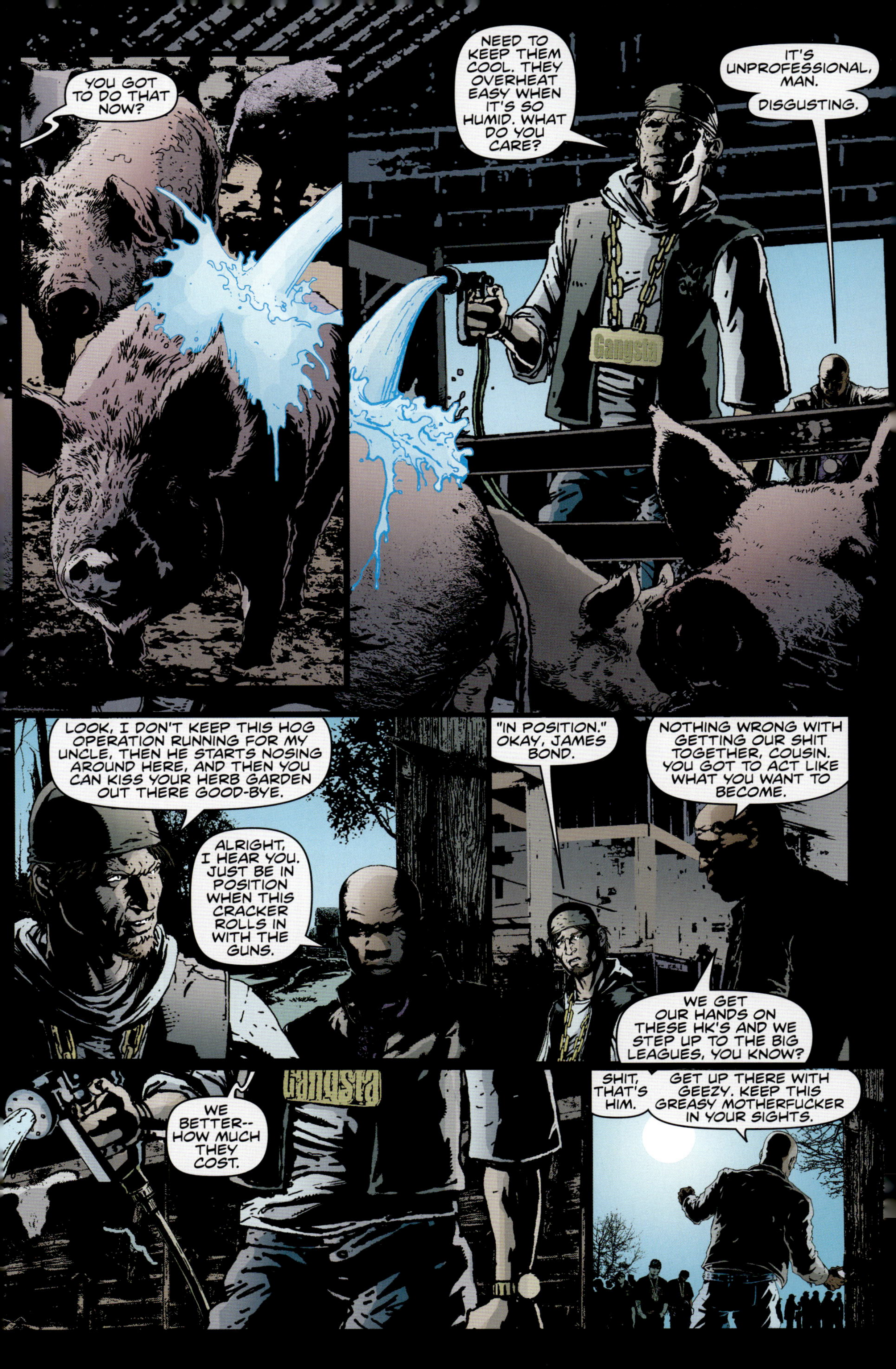
YOU GOT TO DO THAT NOW?
NEED TO KEEP THEM COOL. THEY OVERHEAT EASY WHEN IT'S SO HUMID. WHAT DO YOU CARE?
IT'S UNPROFESSIONAL, MAN.
DISGUSTING.
Gangsta
LOOK, I DON'T KEEP THIS HOG OPERATION RUNNING FOR MY UNCLE, THEN HE STARTS NOSING AROUND HERE, AND THEN YOU CAN KISS YOUR HERB GARDEN OUT THERE GOOD-BYE.
ALRIGHT, I HEAR YOU. JUST BE IN POSITION WHEN THIS CRACKER ROLLS IN WITH THE GUNS.
"IN POSITION." OKAY, JAMES BOND.
NOTHING WRONG WITH GETTING OUR SHIT TOGETHER, COUSIN. YOU GOT TO ACT LIKE WHAT YOU WANT TO BECOME.
WE GET OUR HANDS ON THESE HK'S AND WE STEP UP TO THE BIG LEAGUES, YOU KNOW?
Gangsta
WE BETTER-- HOW MUCH THEY COST.
SHIT, THAT'S HIM.
GET UP THERE WITH GEEZY. KEEP THIS GREASY MOTHERFUCKER IN YOUR SIGHTS.

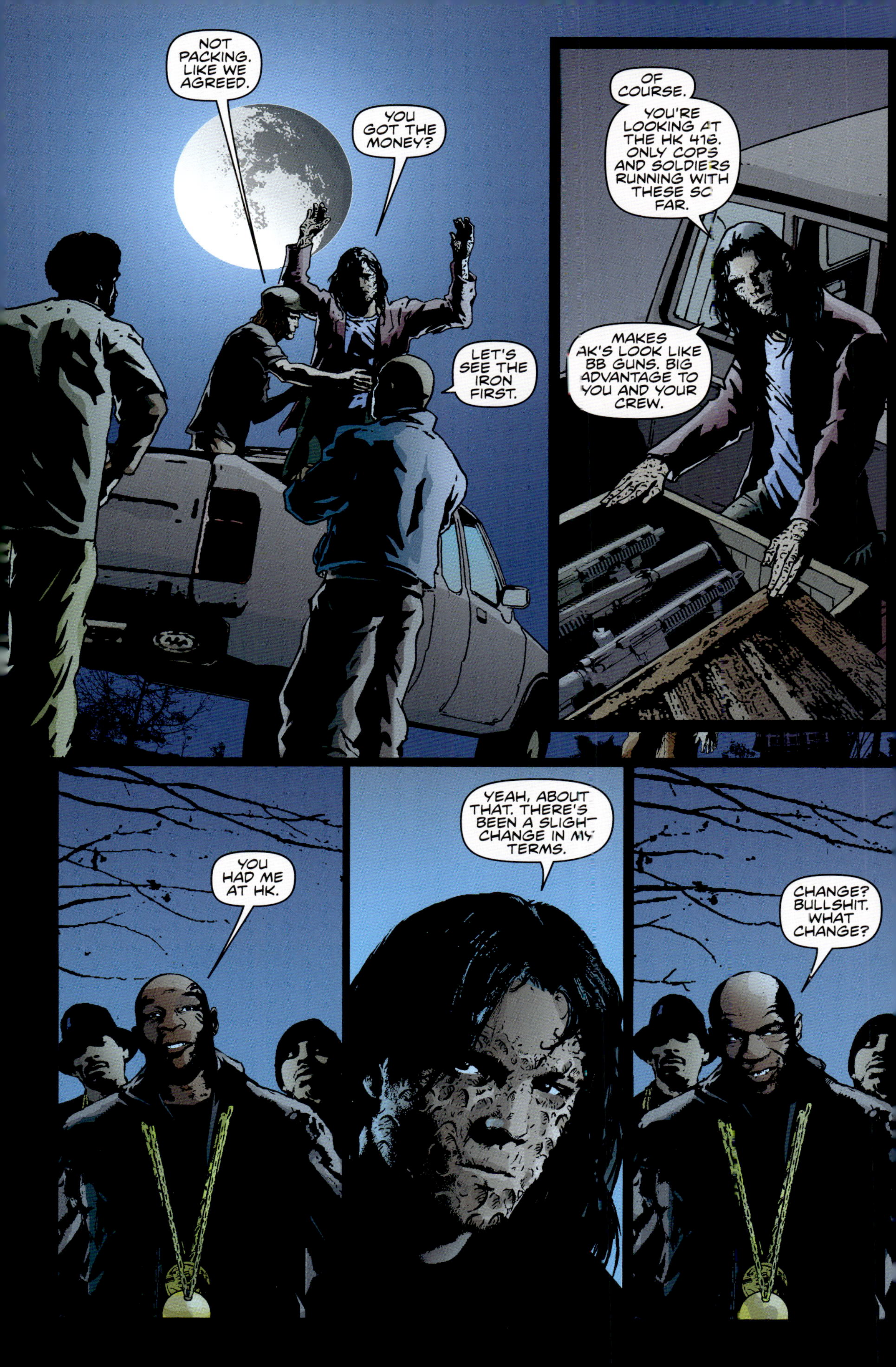
NOT PACKING. LIKE WE AGREED.
YOU GOT THE MONEY?
LET'S SEE THE IRON FIRST.
OF COURSE.
YOU'RE LOOKING AT THE HK 416. ONLY COPS AND SOLDIERS RUNNING WITH THESE SO FAR.
MAKES AK'S LOOK LIKE BB GUNS. BIG ADVANTAGE TO YOU AND YOUR CREW.
YOU HAD ME AT HK.
YEAH, ABOUT THAT. THERE'S BEEN A SLIGHT CHANGE IN MY TERMS.
CHANGE? BULLSHIT. WHAT CHANGE?

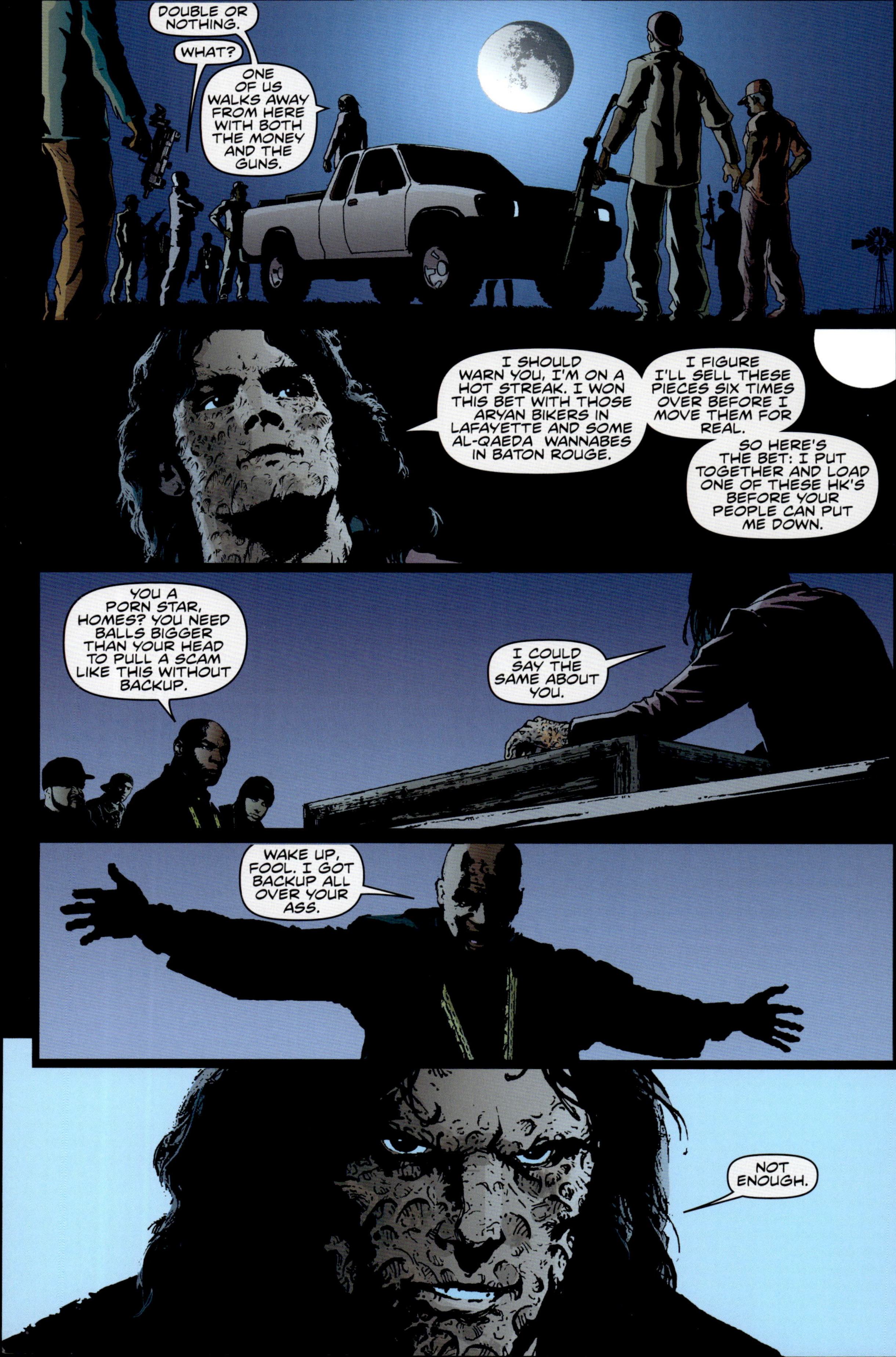
DOUBLE OR NOTHING.
WHAT?
ONE OF US WALKS AWAY FROM HERE WITH BOTH THE MONEY AND THE GUNS.
I SHOULD WARN YOU, I'M ON A HOT STREAK. I WON THIS BET WITH THOSE ARYAN BIKERS IN LAFAYETTE AND SOME AL-QAEDA WANNABES IN BATON ROUGE.
I FIGURE I'LL SELL THESE PIECES SIX TIMES OVER BEFORE I MOVE THEM FOR REAL.
SO HERE'S THE BET: I PUT TOGETHER AND LOAD ONE OF THESE HK'S BEFORE YOUR PEOPLE CAN PUT ME DOWN.
YOU A PORN STAR, HOMES? YOU NEED BALLS BIGGER THAN YOUR HEAD TO PULL A SCAM LIKE THIS WITHOUT BACKUP.
I COULD SAY THE SAME ABOUT YOU.
WAKE UP, FOOL. I GOT BACKUP ALL OVER YOUR ASS.
NOT ENOUGH.

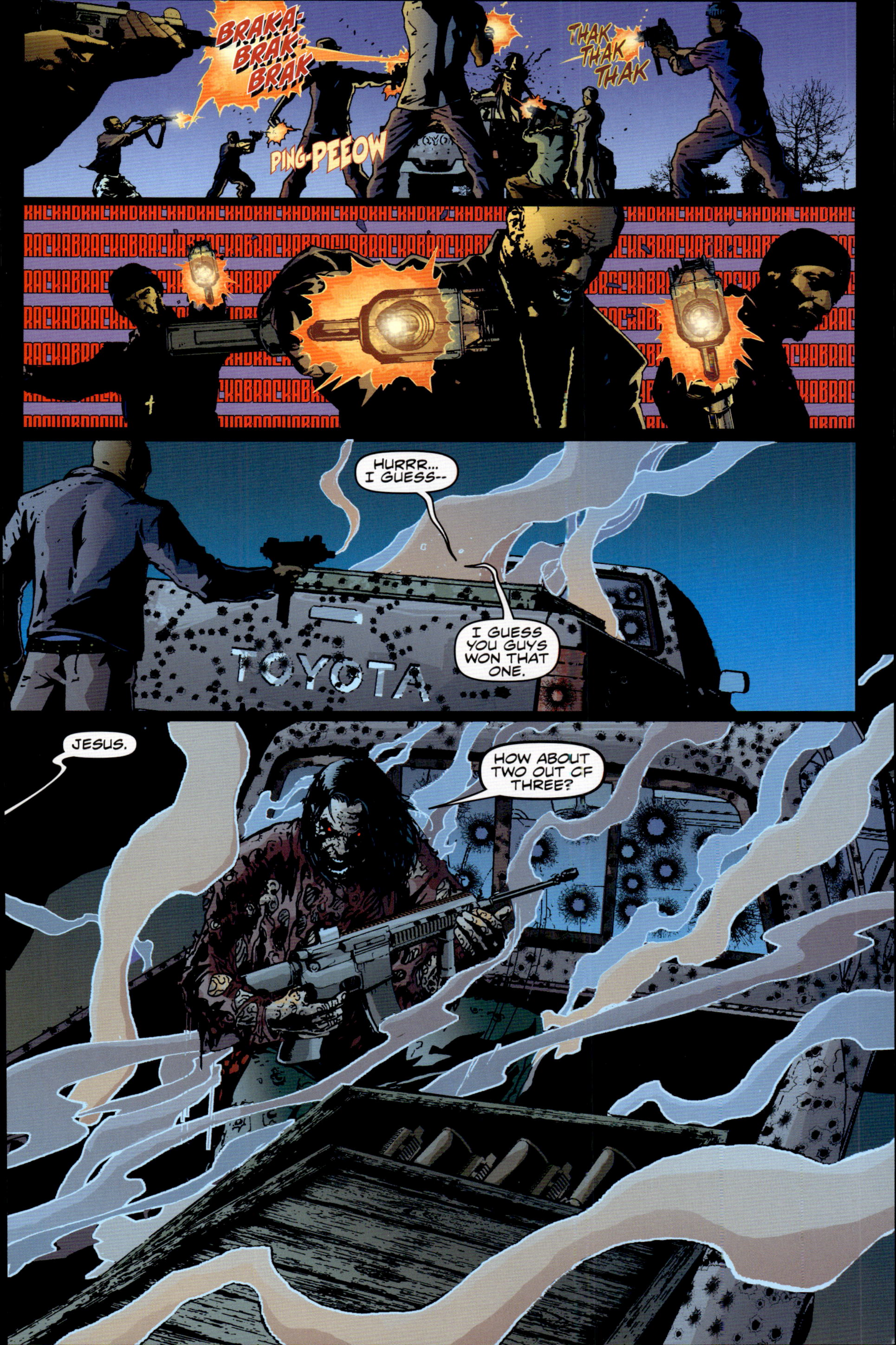
BRAKA-BRAK-BRAK
THAK THAK THAK
PING-PEEOW
HURRR... I GUESS--
I GUESS YOU GUYS WON THAT ONE.
JESUS.
HOW ABOUT TWO OUT OF THREE?

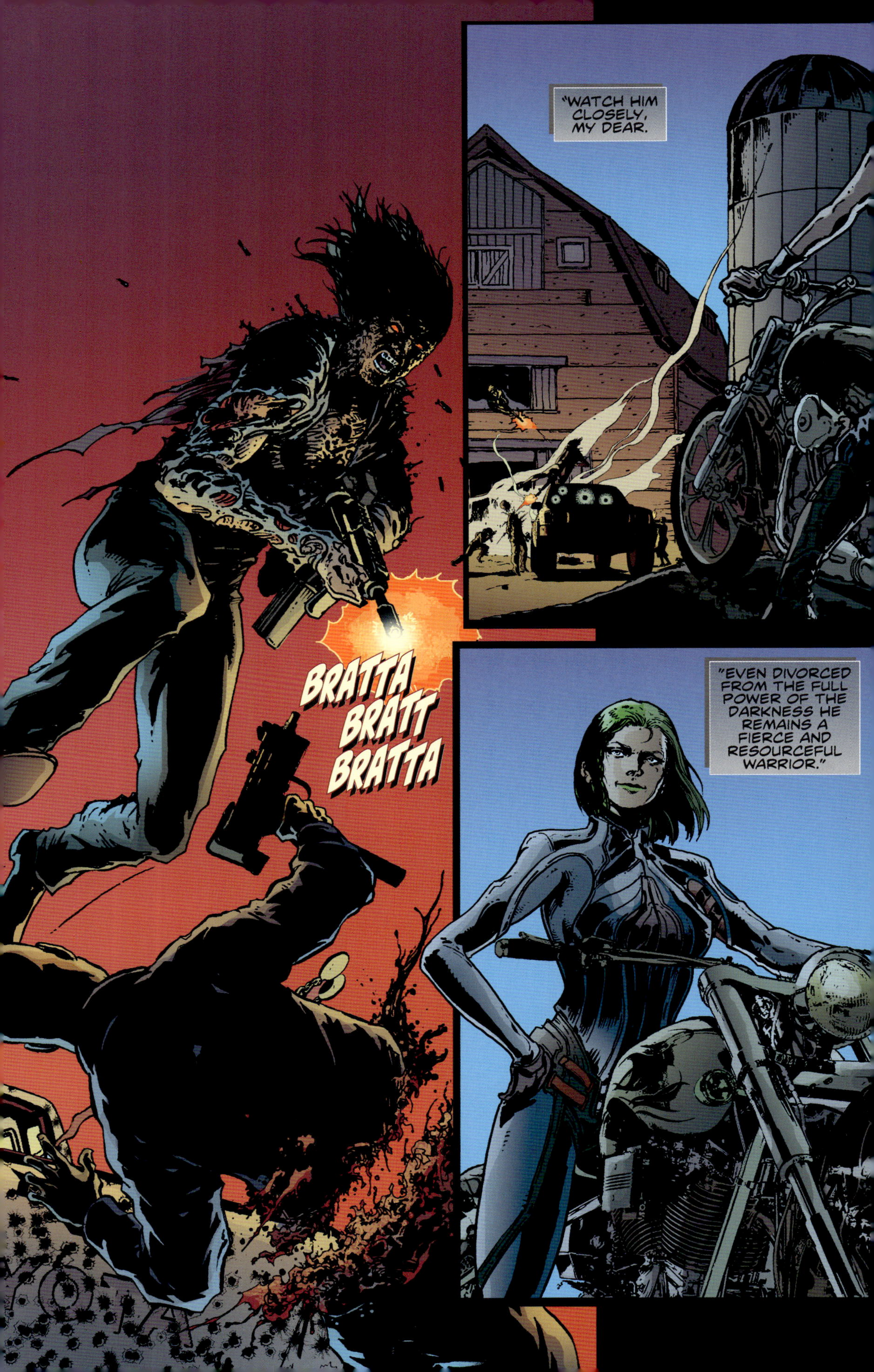
"WATCH HIM CLOSELY, MY DEAR.
BRATTA BRATT BRATTA
"EVEN DIVORCED FROM THE FULL POWER OF THE DARKNESS HE REMAINS A FIERCE AND RESOURCEFUL WARRIOR."

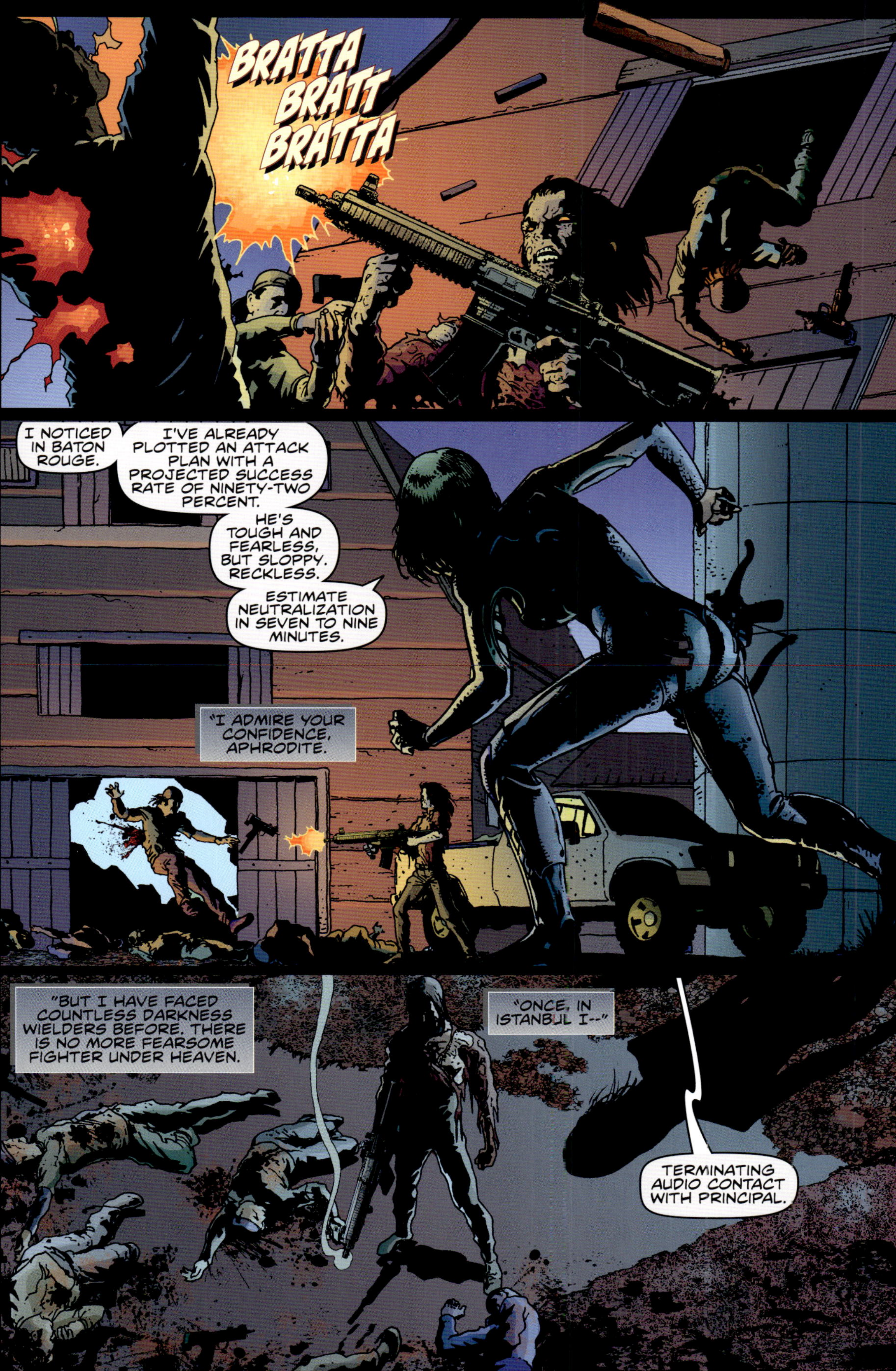
BRATTA BRATT BRATTA
I NOTICED IN BATON ROUGE.
I'VE ALREADY PLOTTED AN ATTACK PLAN WITH A PROJECTED SUCCESS RATE OF NINETY-TWO PERCENT.
HE'S TOUGH AND FEARLESS, BUT SLOPPY. RECKLESS.
ESTIMATE NEUTRALIZATION IN SEVEN TO NINE MINUTES.
"I ADMIRE YOUR CONFIDENCE, APHRODITE.
"BUT I HAVE FACED COUNTLESS DARKNESS WIELDERS BEFORE. THERE IS NO MORE FEARSOME FIGHTER UNDER HEAVEN.
"ONCE, IN ISTANBUL I--"
TERMINATING AUDIO CONTACT WITH PRINCIPAL.

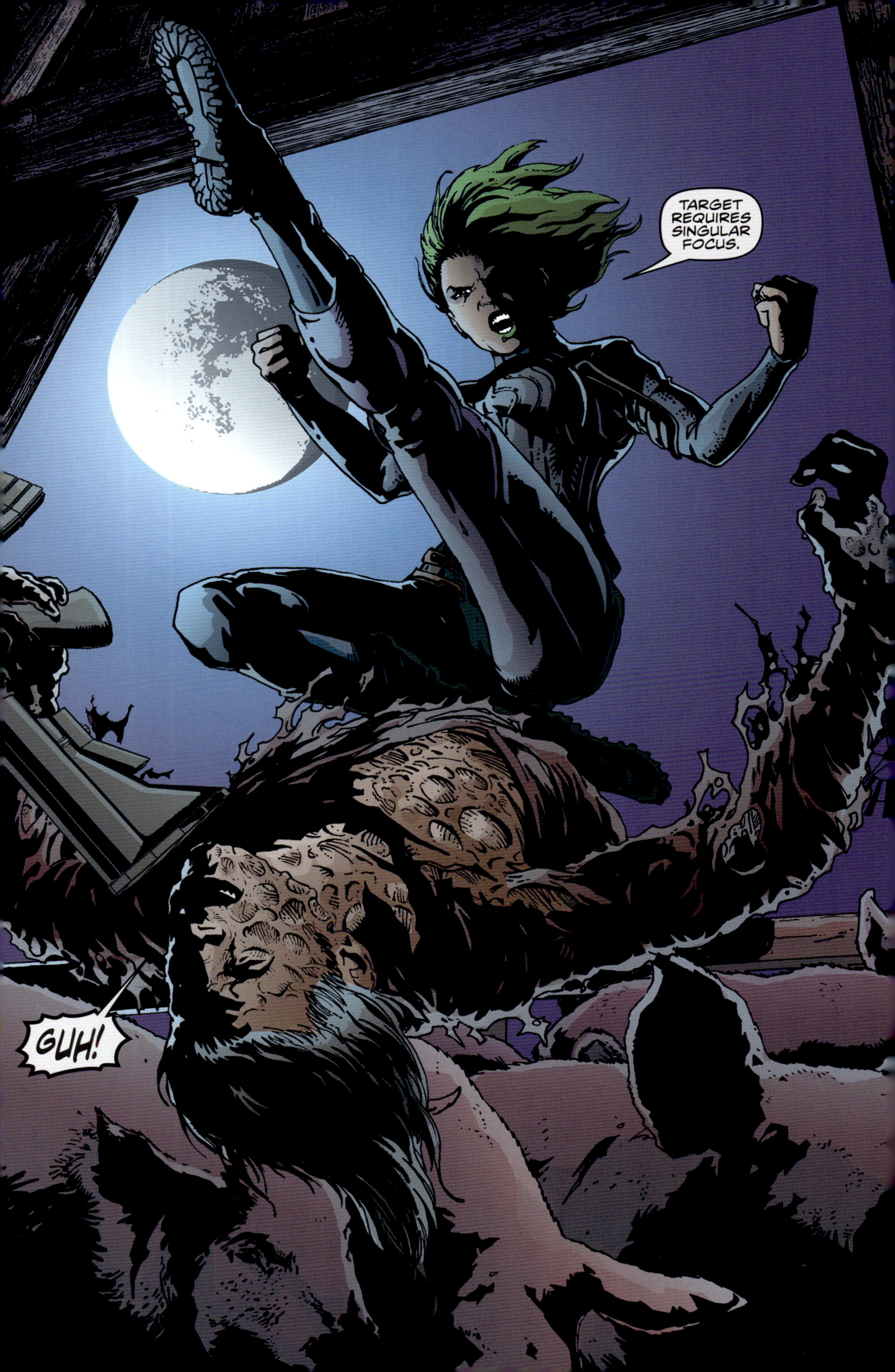
TARGET REQUIRES SINGULAR FOCUS.
GUH!

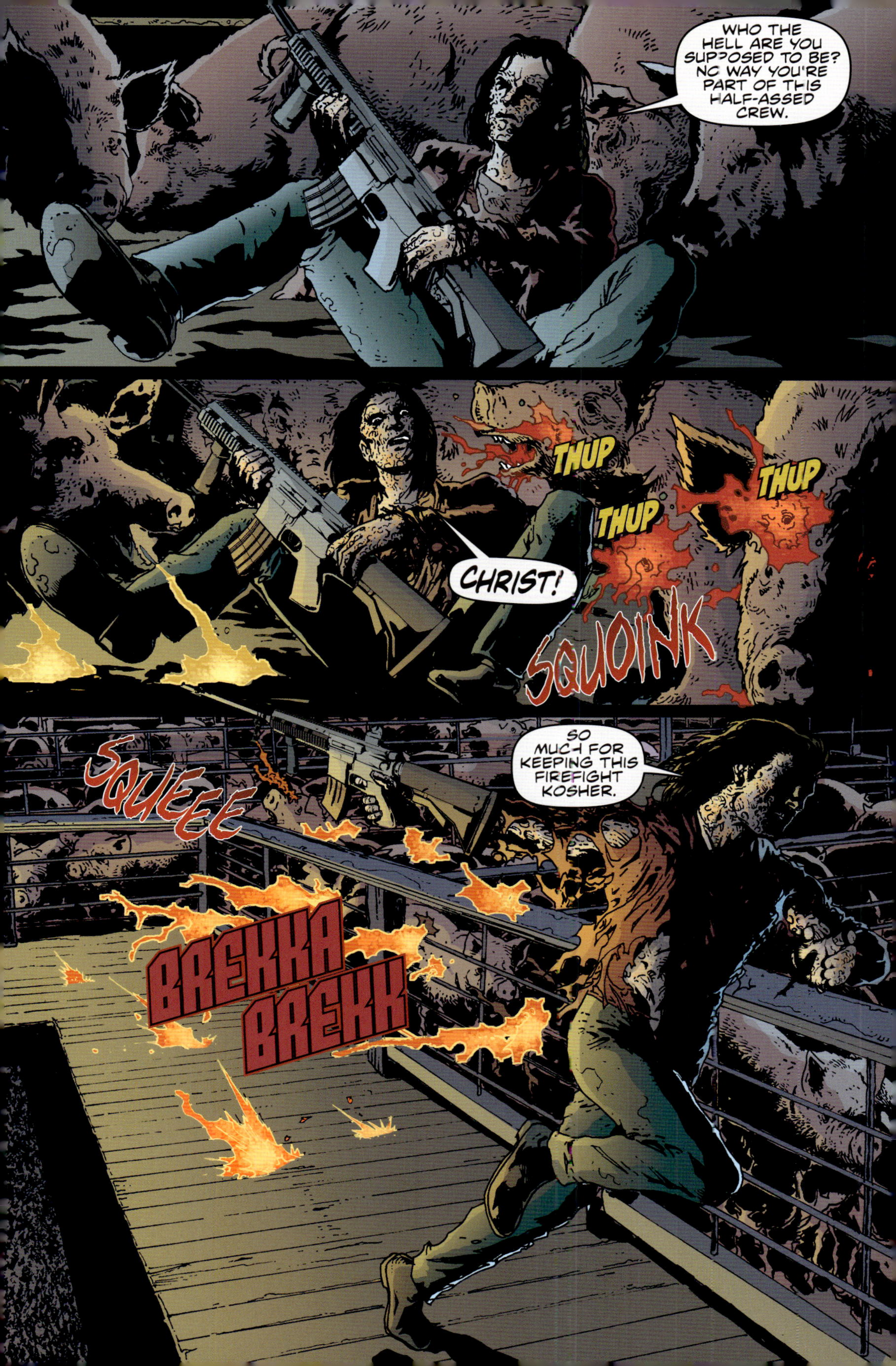
WHO THE HELL ARE YOU SUPPOSED TO BE? NO WAY YOU'RE PART OF THIS HALF-ASSED CREW.
THUP
THUP
THUP
CHRIST!
SQUOINK
SQUEEE
SO MUCH FOR KEEPING THIS FIREFIGHT KOSHER.
BREKKA BREKK

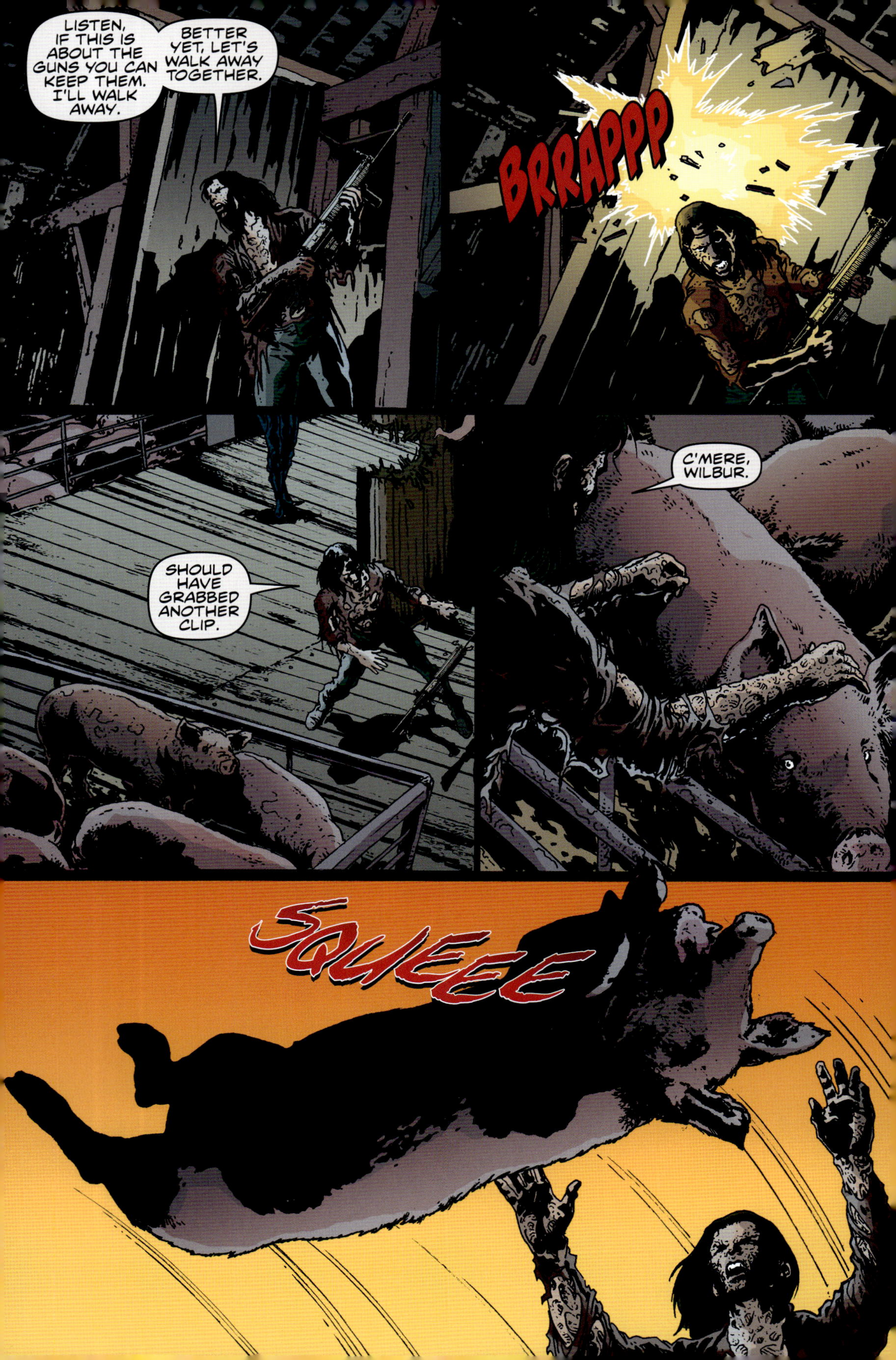
LISTEN, IF THIS IS ABOUT THE GUNS YOU CAN KEEP THEM. I'LL WALK AWAY.
BETTER YET, LET'S WALK AWAY TOGETHER.
BRRAPPP
SHOULD HAVE GRABBED ANOTHER CLIP.
C'MERE, WILBUR.
SQUEEE

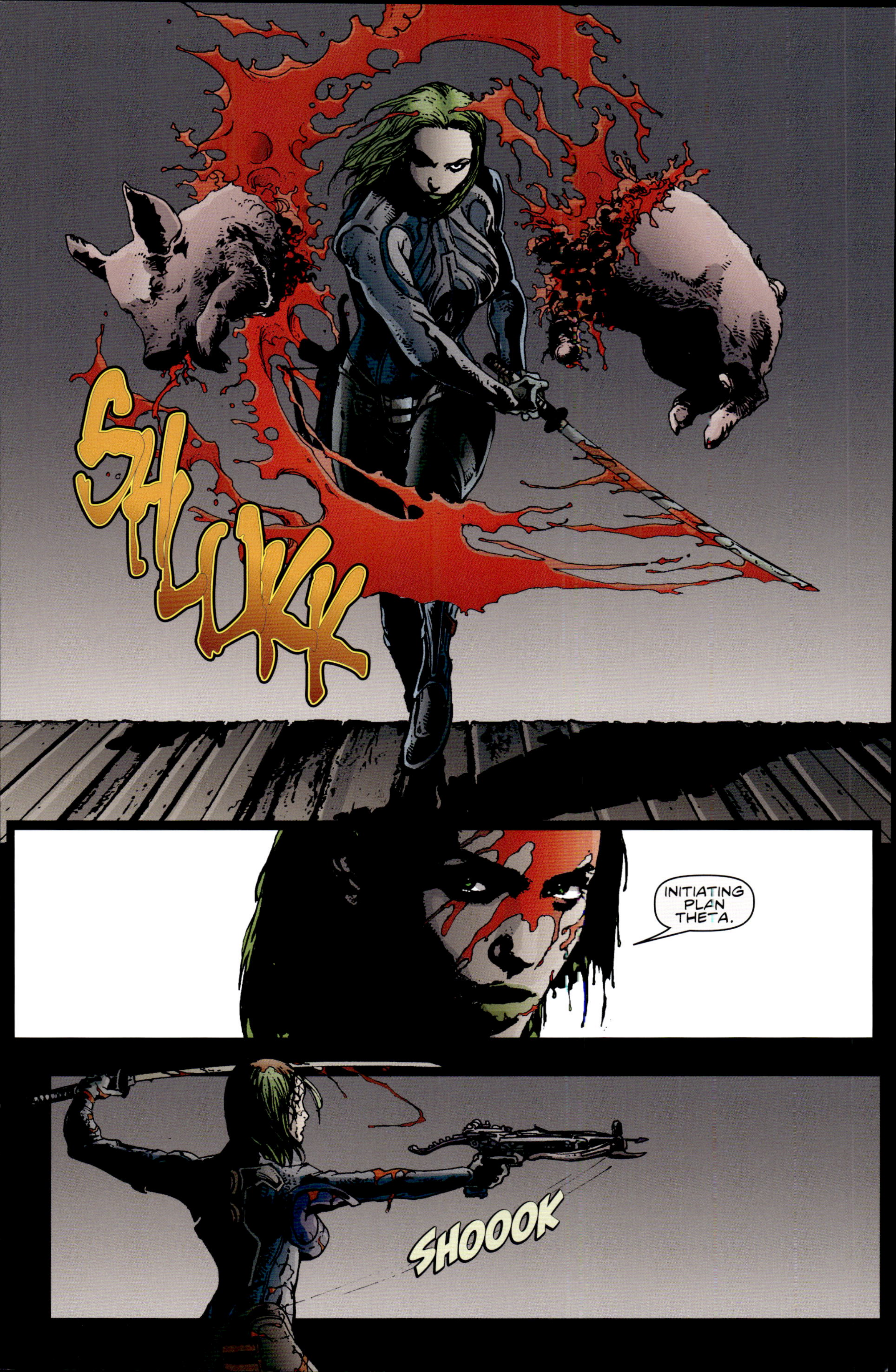
SHLUKK
INITIATING PLAN THETA.
SHOOOK

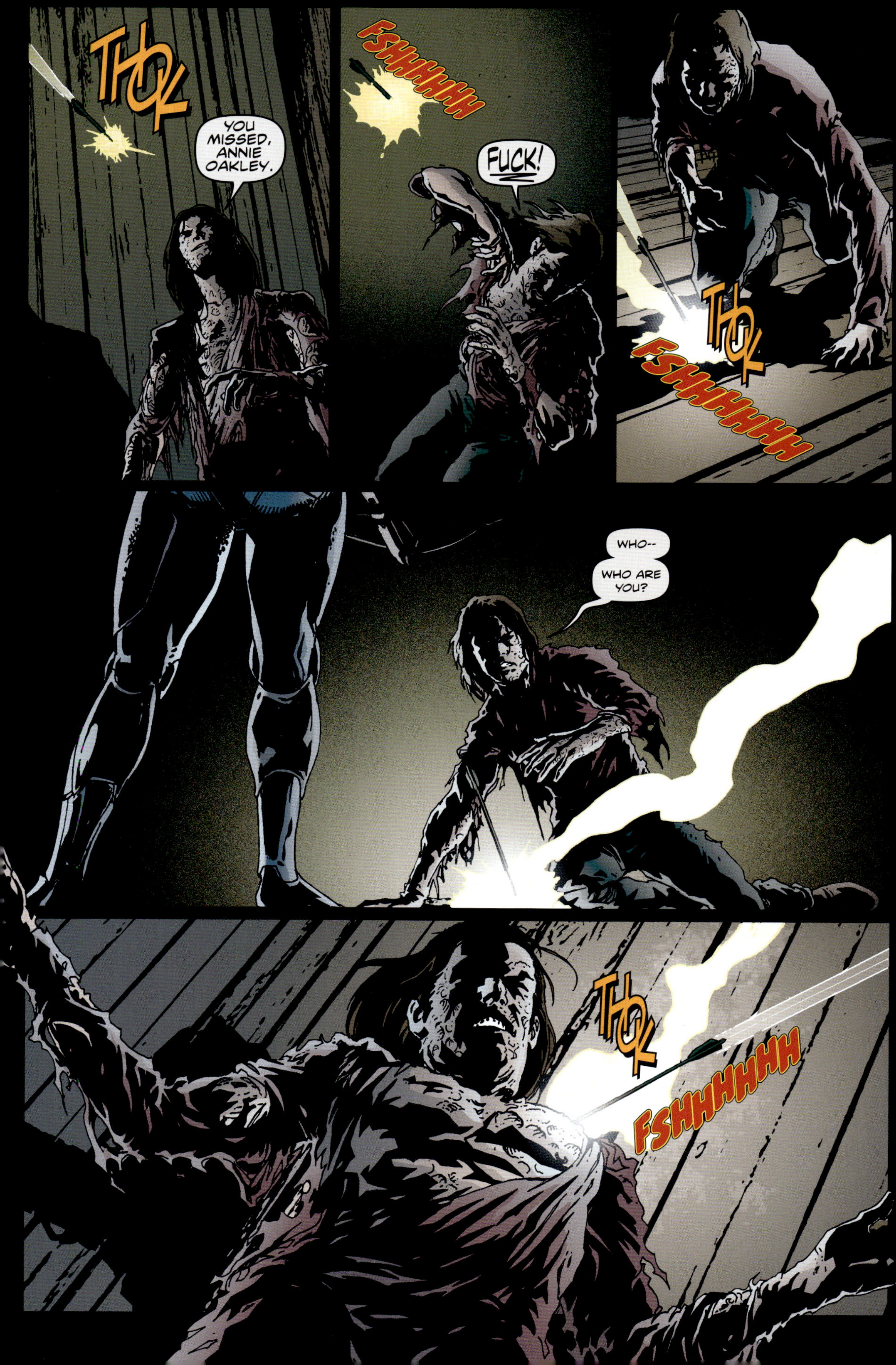
THOK
YOU MISSED, ANNIE OAKLEY.
FSHHHHHH
FUCK!
THOK
FSHHHHHHH
WHO--
WHO ARE YOU?
THOK
FSHHHHHH

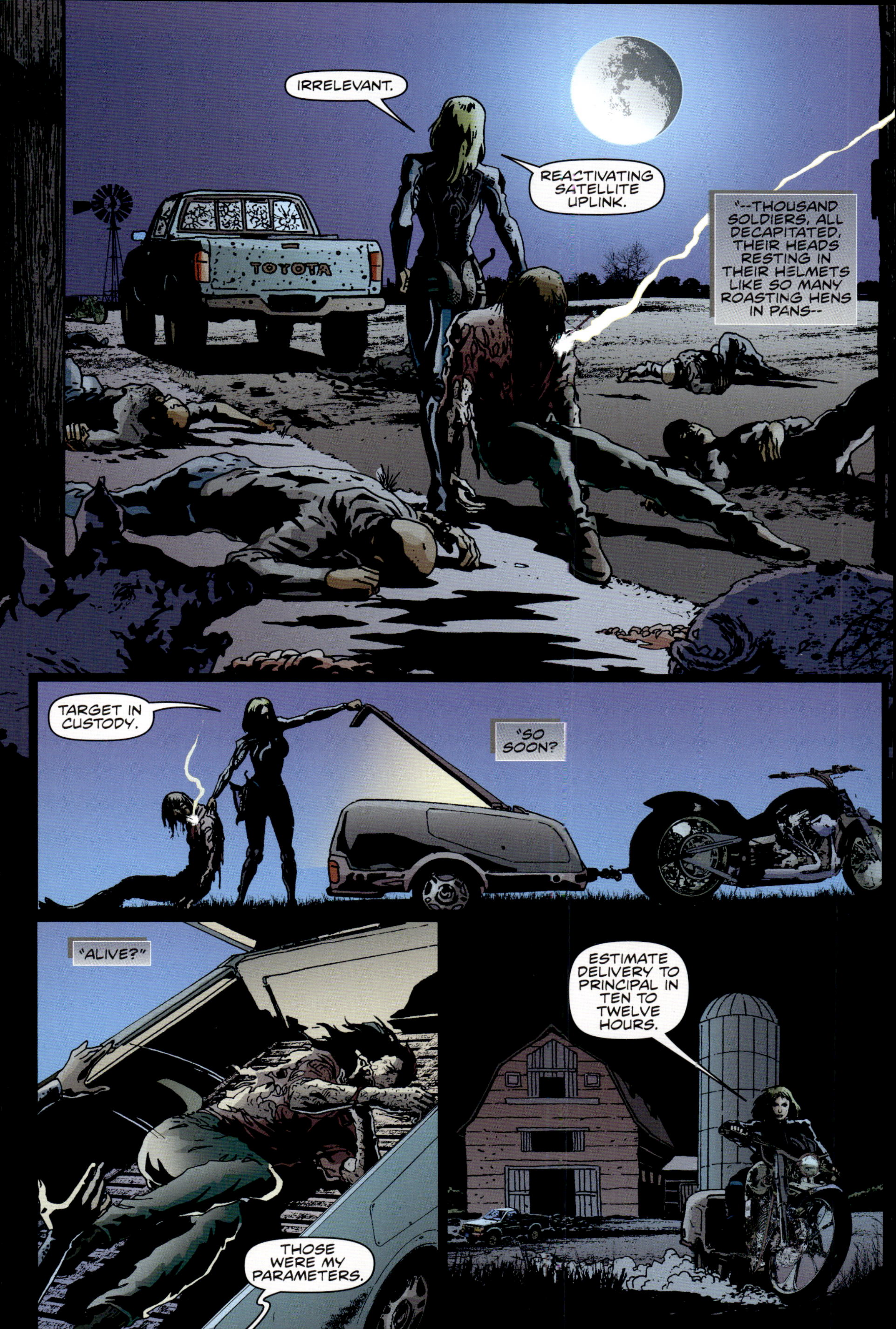
IRRELEVANT.
REACTIVATING SATELLITE UPLINK.
"--THOUSAND SOLDIERS, ALL DECAPITATED, THEIR HEADS RESTING IN THEIR HELMETS LIKE SO MANY ROASTING HENS IN PANS--
TOYOTA
TARGET IN CUSTODY.
"SO SOON?
"ALIVE?"
THOSE WERE MY PARAMETERS.
ESTIMATE DELIVERY TO PRINCIPAL IN TEN TO TWELVE HOURS.

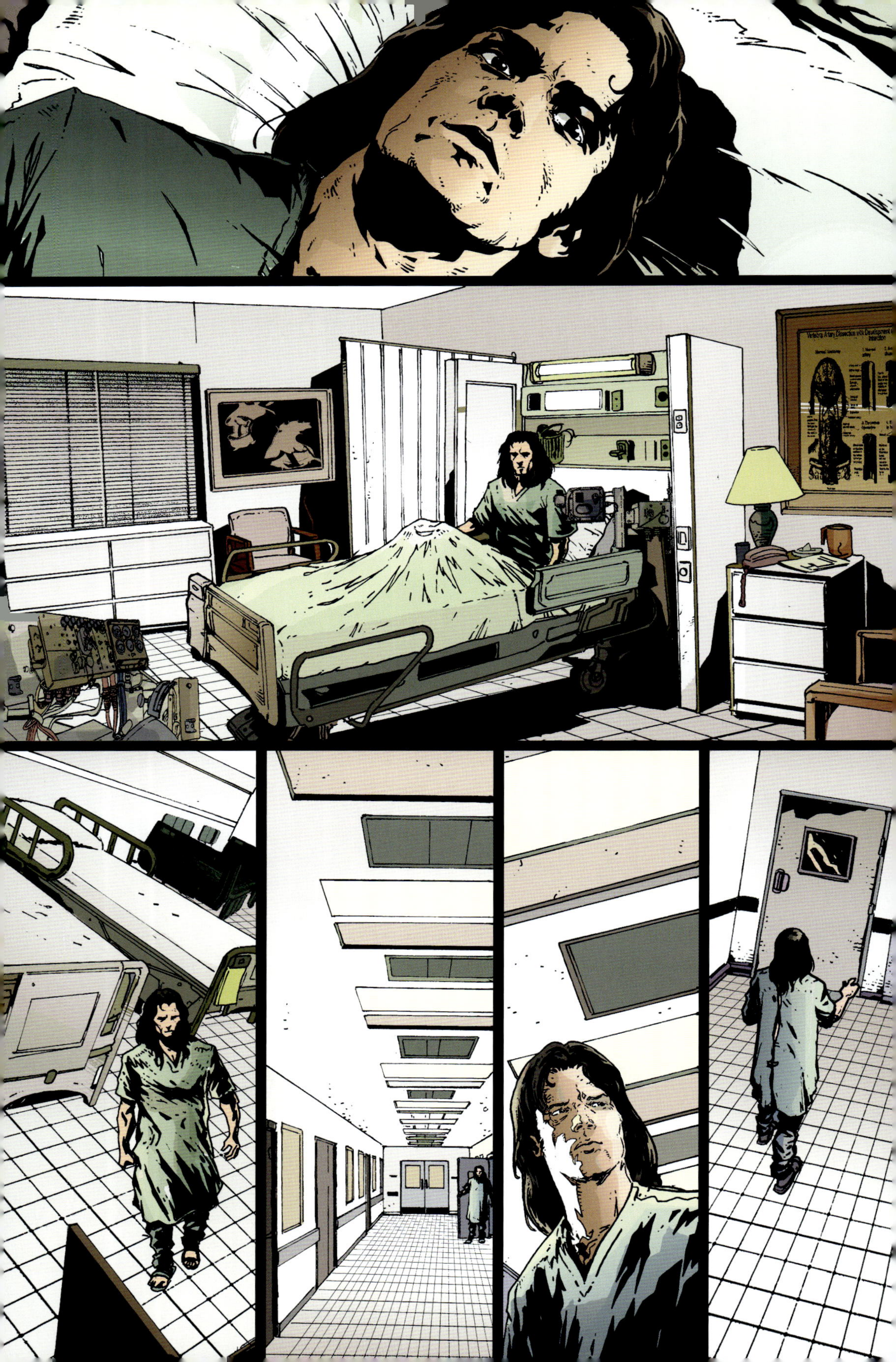

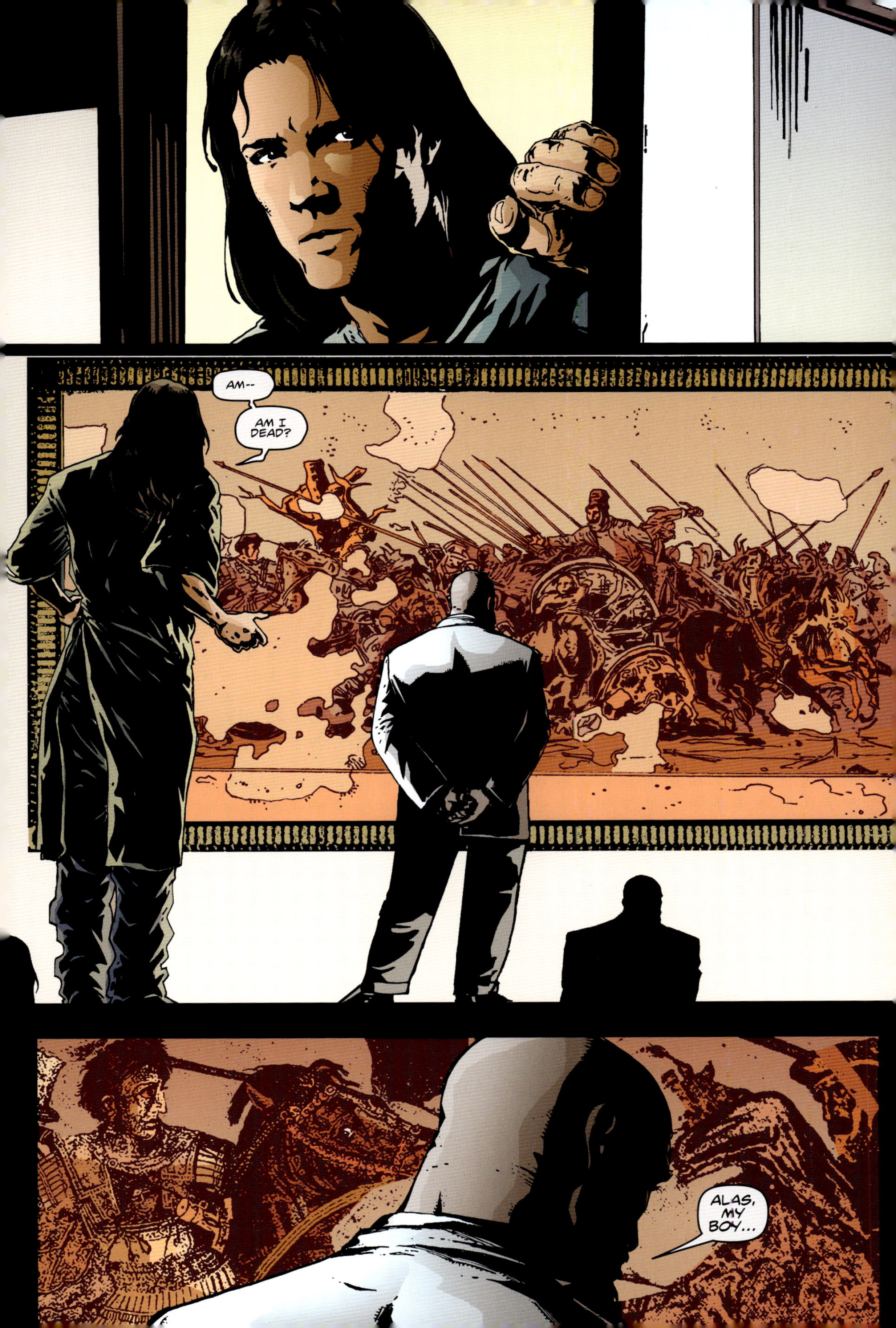
AM--
AM I DEAD?
ALAS, MY BOY...

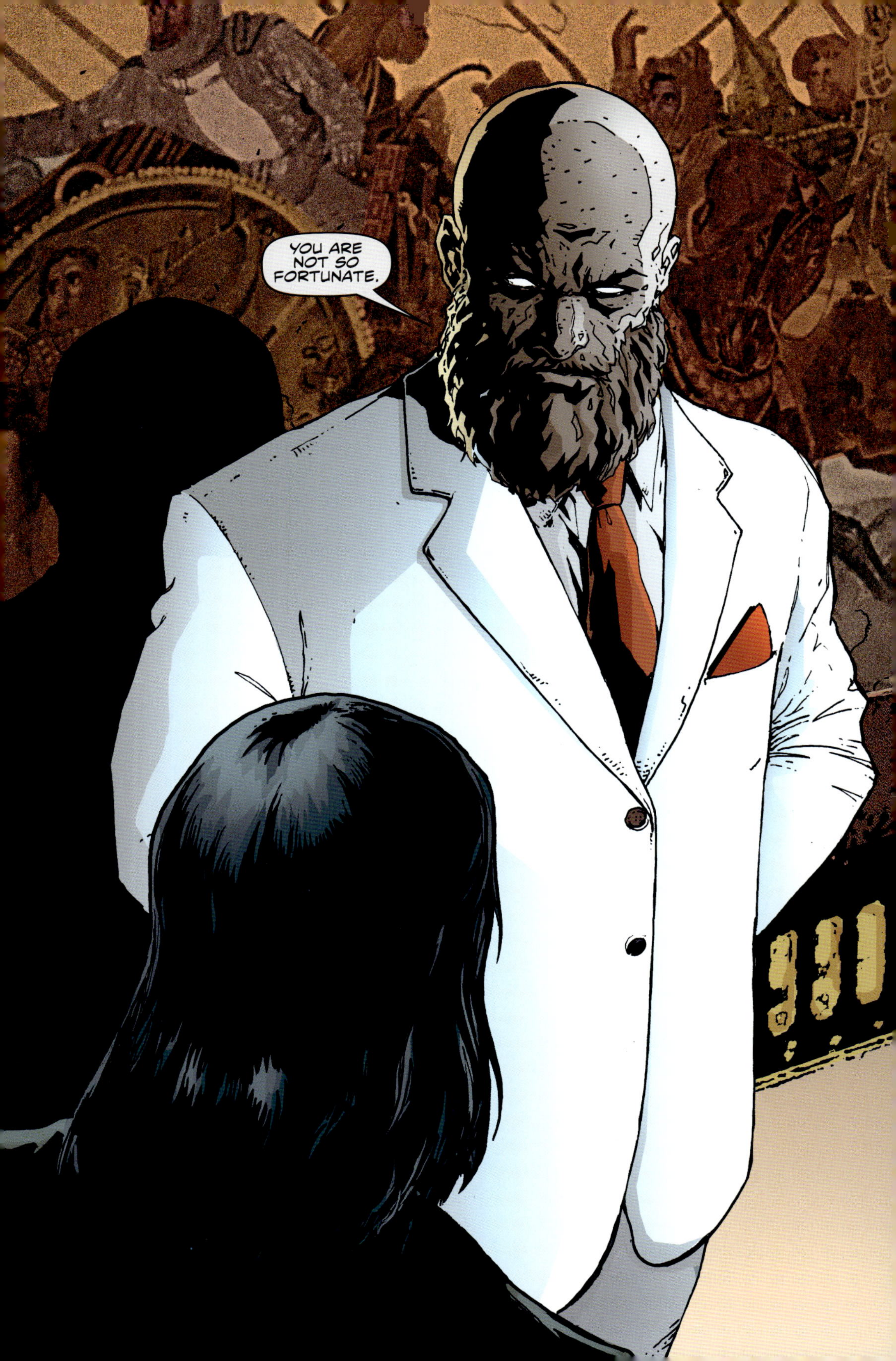
YOU ARE NOT SO FORTUNATE.

The Darkness Issue #73

cover art by: Jorge Lucas and Lee Loughridge

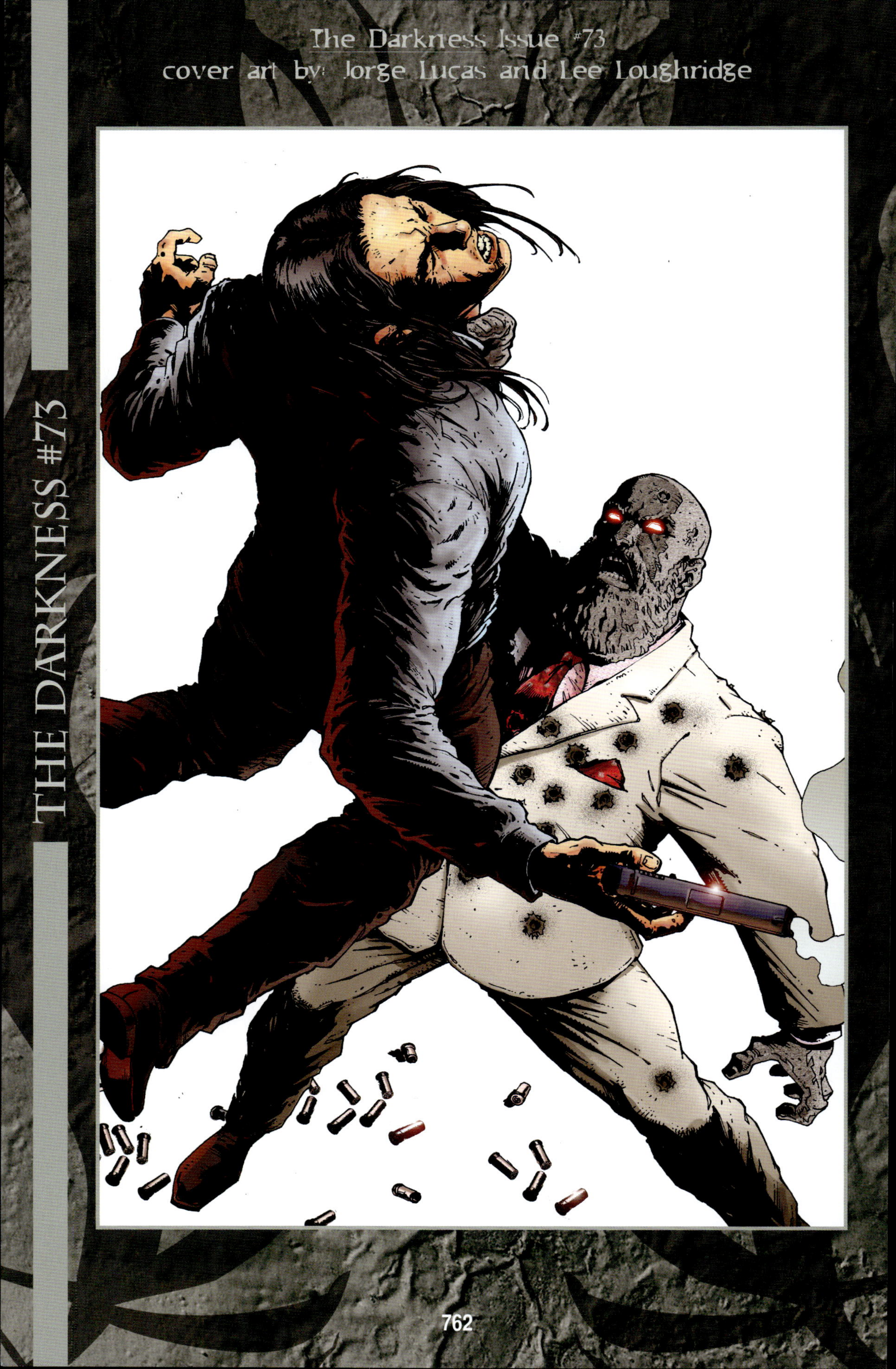

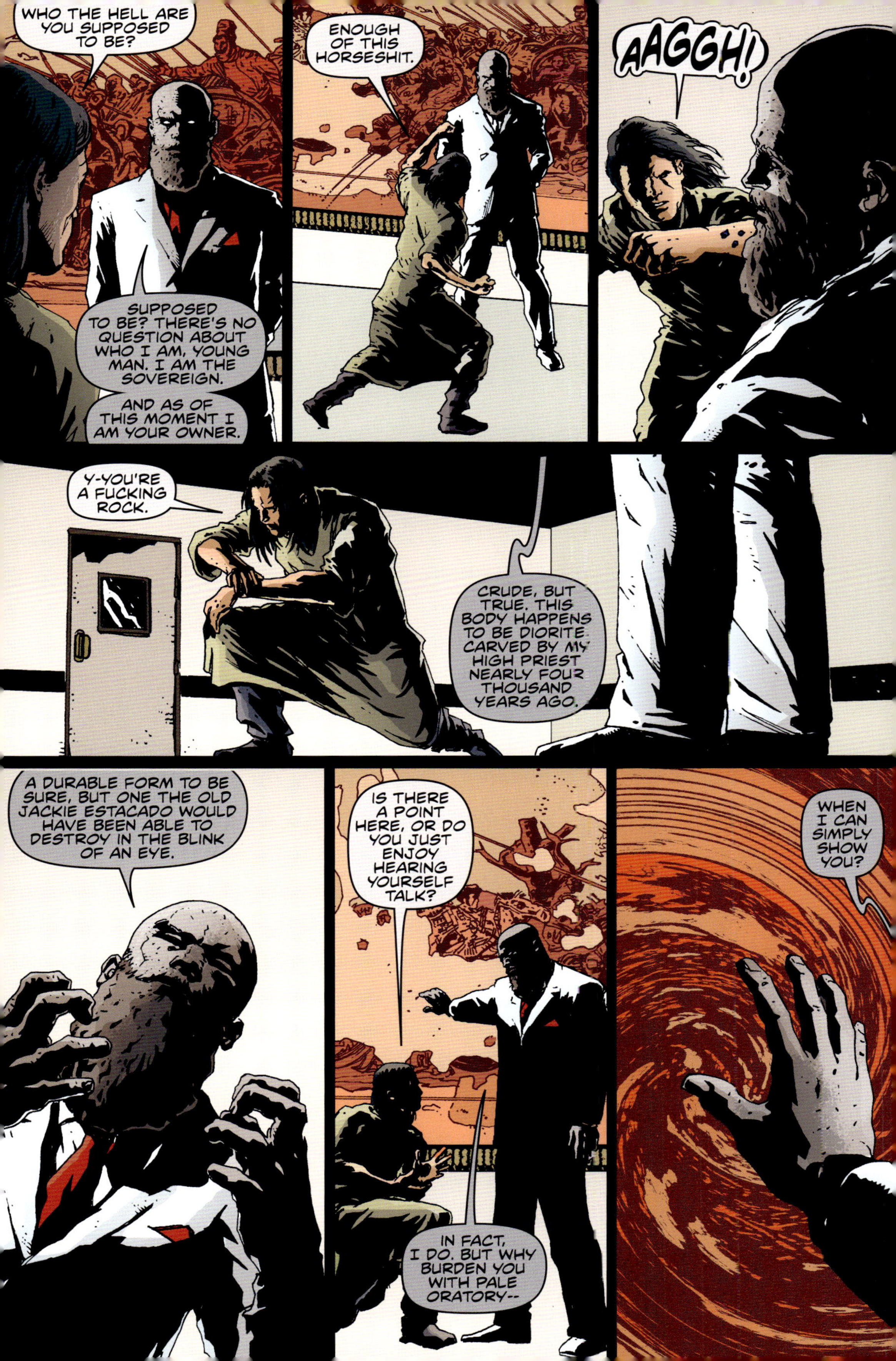
WHO THE HELL ARE YOU SUPPOSED TO BE?
SUPPOSED TO BE? THERE'S NO QUESTION ABOUT WHO I AM, YOUNG MAN. I AM THE SOVEREIGN.
AND AS OF THIS MOMENT I AM YOUR OWNER.
ENOUGH OF THIS HORSESHIT.
AAGGH!
Y-YOU'RE A FUCKING ROCK.
CRUDE, BUT TRUE. THIS BODY HAPPENS TO BE DIORITE CARVED BY MY HIGH PRIEST NEARLY FOUR THOUSAND YEARS AGO.
A DURABLE FORM TO BE SURE, BUT ONE THE OLD JACKIE ESTACADO WOULD HAVE BEEN ABLE TO DESTROY IN THE BLINK OF AN EYE.
IS THERE A POINT HERE, OR DO YOU JUST ENJOY HEARING YOURSELF TALK?
IN FACT, I DO. BUT WHY BURDEN YOU WITH PALE ORATORY--
WHEN I CAN SIMPLY SHOW YOU?

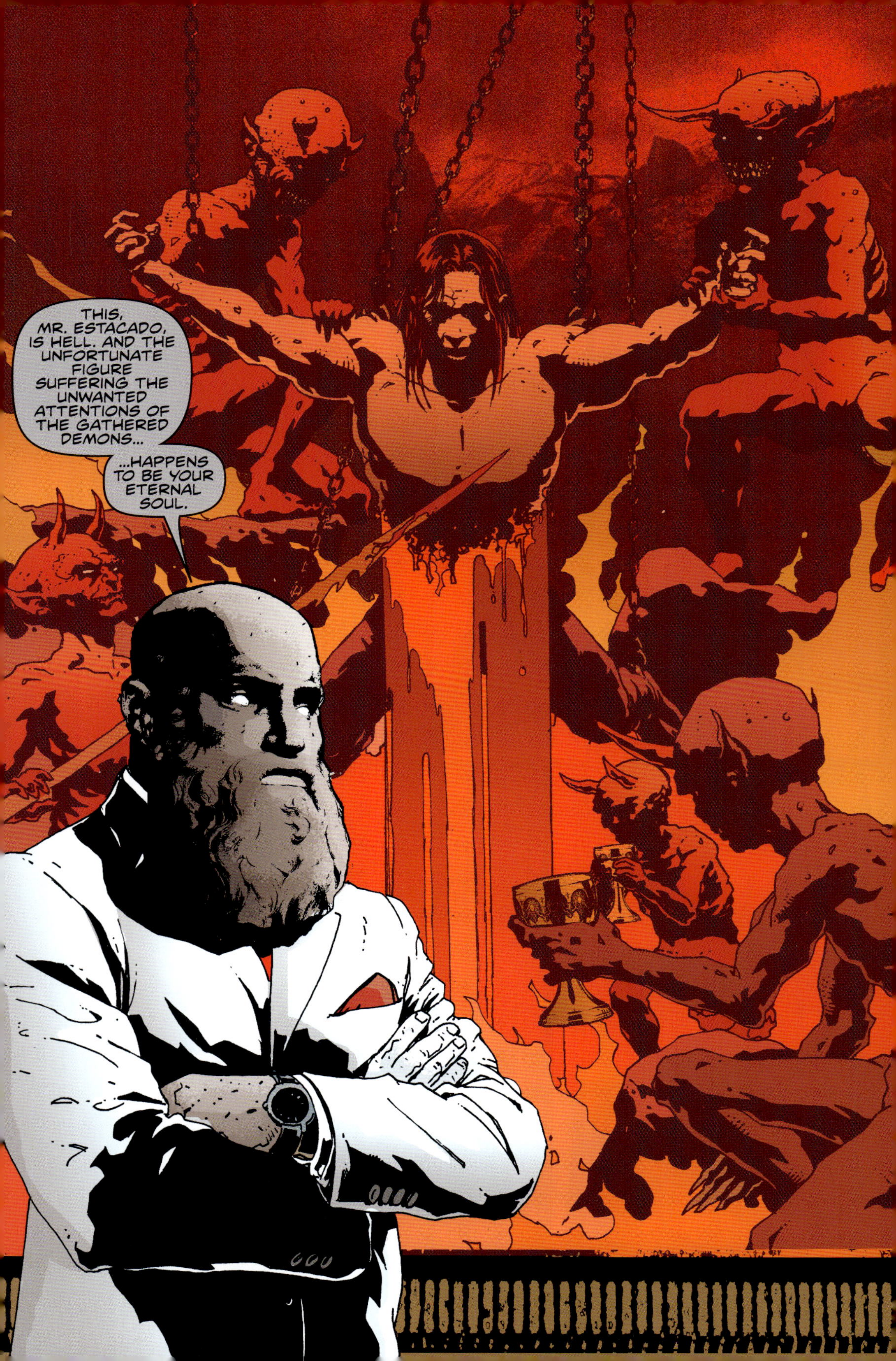
THIS, MR. ESTACADO, IS HELL. AND THE UNFORTUNATE FIGURE SUFFERING THE UNWANTED ATTENTIONS OF THE GATHERED DEMONS...
...HAPPENS TO BE YOUR ETERNAL SOUL.

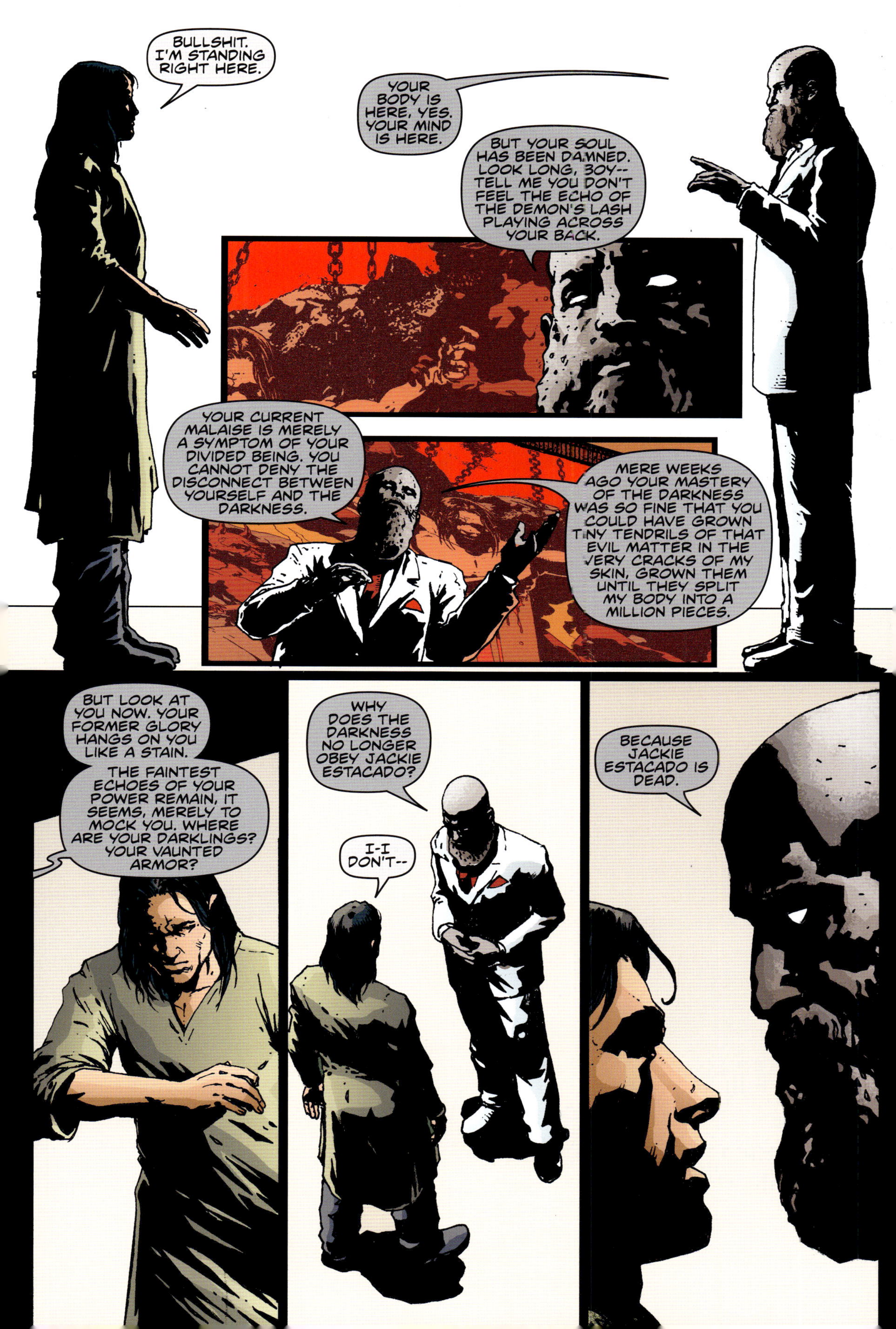
BULLSHIT. I'M STANDING RIGHT HERE.
YOUR BODY IS HERE, YES. YOUR MIND IS HERE.
BUT YOUR SOUL HAS BEEN DAMNED. LOOK LONG, BOY-- TELL ME YOU DON'T FEEL THE ECHO OF THE DEMON'S LASH PLAYING ACROSS YOUR BACK.
YOUR CURRENT MALAISE IS MERELY A SYMPTOM OF YOUR DIVIDED BEING. YOU CANNOT DENY THE DISCONNECT BETWEEN YOURSELF AND THE DARKNESS.
MERE WEEKS AGO YOUR MASTERY OF THE DARKNESS WAS SO FINE THAT YOU COULD HAVE GROWN TINY TENDRILS OF THAT EVIL MATTER IN THE VERY CRACKS OF MY SKIN, GROWN THEM UNTIL THEY SPLIT MY BODY INTO A MILLION PIECES.
BUT LOOK AT YOU NOW. YOUR FORMER GLORY HANGS ON YOU LIKE A STAIN.
THE FAINTEST ECHOES OF YOUR POWER REMAIN, IT SEEMS, MERELY TO MOCK YOU. WHERE ARE YOUR DARKLINGS? YOUR VAUNTED ARMOR?
WHY DOES THE DARKNESS NO LONGER OBEY JACKIE ESTACADO?
I-I DON'T--
BECAUSE JACKIE ESTACADO IS DEAD.

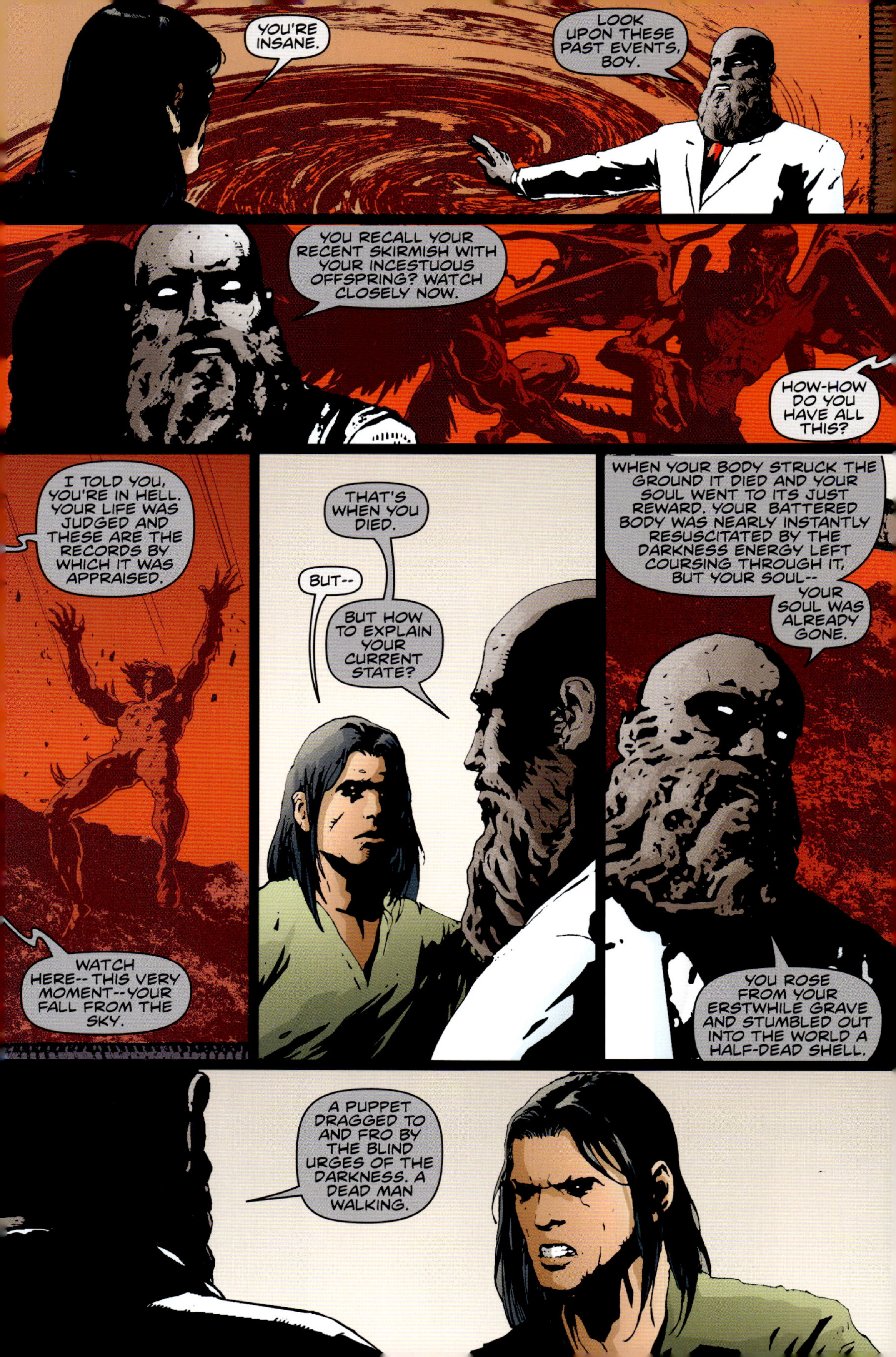
YOU'RE INSANE.
LOOK UPON THESE PAST EVENTS, BOY.
YOU RECALL YOUR RECENT SKIRMISH WITH YOUR INCESTUOUS OFFSPRING? WATCH CLOSELY NOW.
HOW-HOW DO YOU HAVE ALL THIS?
I TOLD YOU, YOU'RE IN HELL. YOUR LIFE WAS JUDGED AND THESE ARE THE RECORDS BY WHICH IT WAS APPRAISED.
WATCH HERE-- THIS VERY MOMENT--YOUR FALL FROM THE SKY.
THAT'S WHEN YOU DIED.
BUT--
BUT HOW TO EXPLAIN YOUR CURRENT STATE?
WHEN YOUR BODY STRUCK THE GROUND IT DIED AND YOUR SOUL WENT TO ITS JUST REWARD. YOUR BATTERED BODY WAS NEARLY INSTANTLY RESUSCITATED BY THE DARKNESS ENERGY LEFT COURSING THROUGH IT, BUT YOUR SOUL--
YOUR SOUL WAS ALREADY GONE.
YOU ROSE FROM YOUR ERSTWHILE GRAVE AND STUMBLED OUT INTO THE WORLD A HALF-DEAD SHELL.
A PUPPET DRAGGED TO AND FRO BY THE BLIND URGES OF THE DARKNESS. A DEAD MAN WALKING.

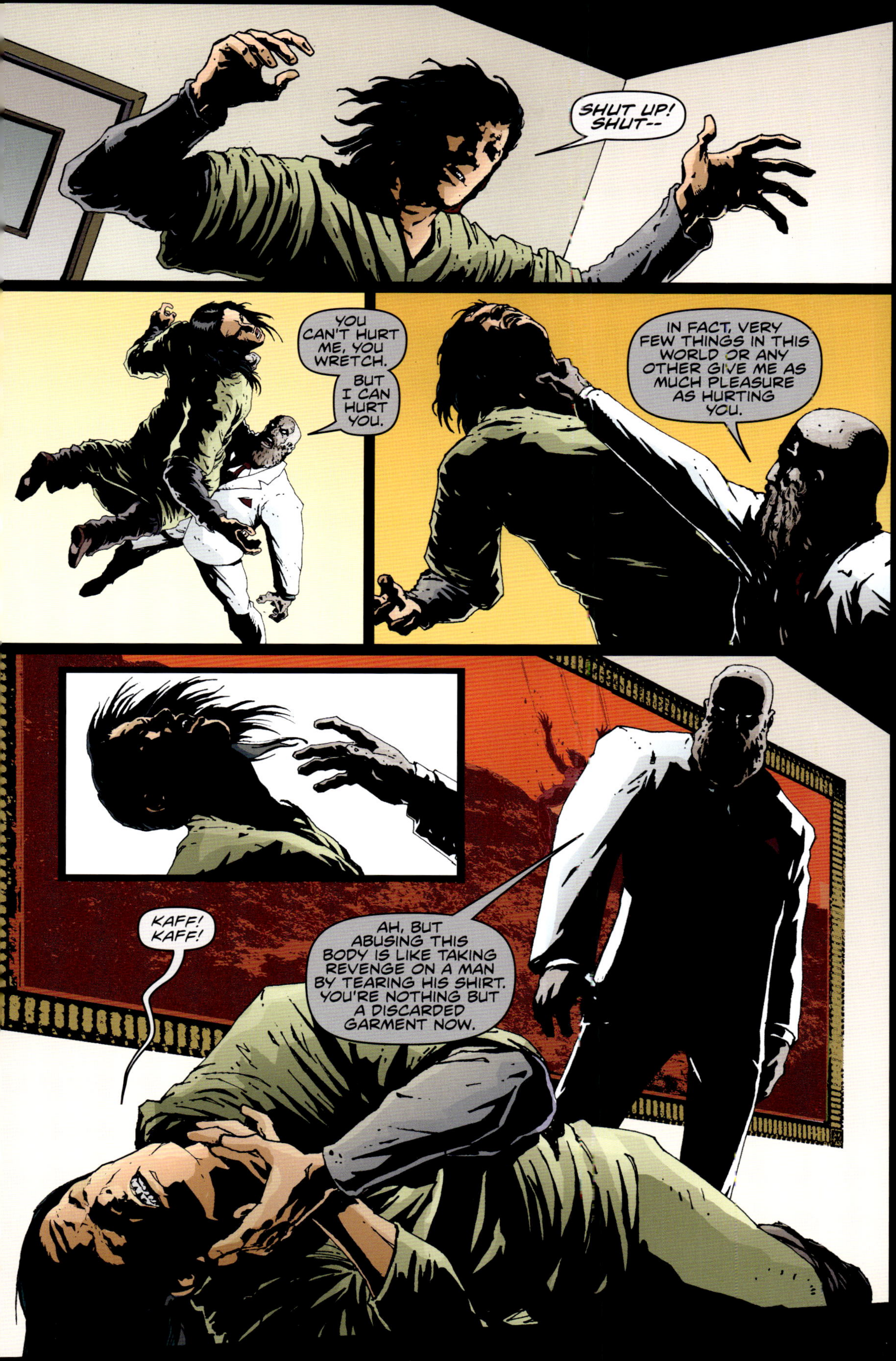
SHUT UP! SHUT--
YOU CAN'T HURT ME, YOU WRETCH.
BUT I CAN HURT YOU.
IN FACT, VERY FEW THINGS IN THIS WORLD OR ANY OTHER GIVE ME AS MUCH PLEASURE AS HURTING YOU.
KAFF! KAFF!
AH, BUT ABUSING THIS BODY IS LIKE TAKING REVENGE ON A MAN BY TEARING HIS SHIRT. YOU'RE NOTHING BUT A DISCARDED GARMENT NOW.

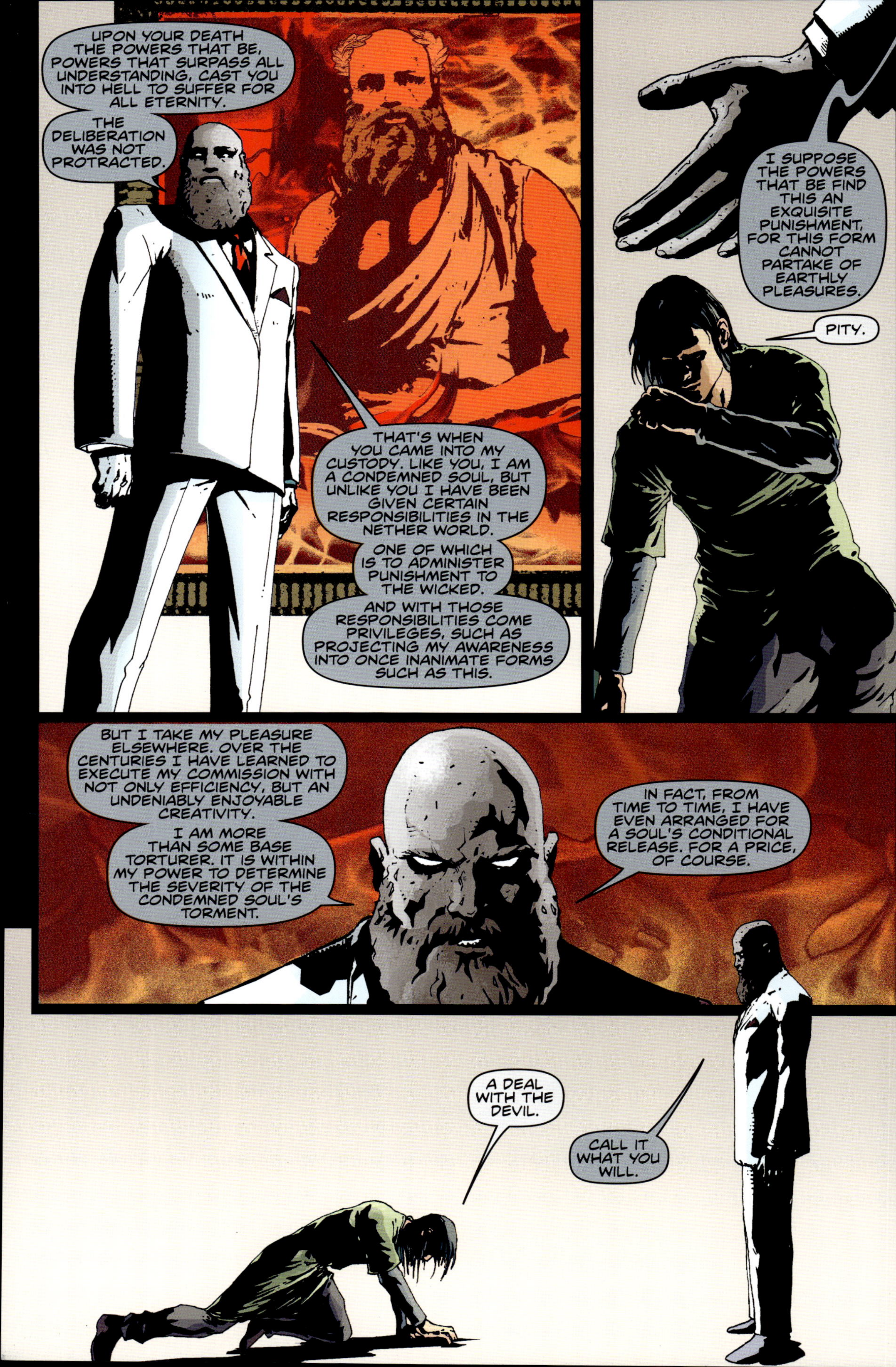
UPON YOUR DEATH THE POWERS THAT BE, POWERS THAT SURPASS ALL UNDERSTANDING, CAST YOU INTO HELL TO SUFFER FOR ALL ETERNITY.
THE DELIBERATION WAS NOT PROTRACTED.
THAT'S WHEN YOU CAME INTO MY CUSTODY. LIKE YOU, I AM A CONDEMNED SOUL, BUT UNLIKE YOU I HAVE BEEN GIVEN CERTAIN RESPONSIBILITIES IN THE NETHER WORLD.
ONE OF WHICH IS TO ADMINISTER PUNISHMENT TO THE WICKED.
AND WITH THOSE RESPONSIBILITIES COME PRIVILEGES, SUCH AS PROJECTING MY AWARENESS INTO ONCE INANIMATE FORMS SUCH AS THIS.
I SUPPOSE THE POWERS THAT BE FIND THIS AN EXQUISITE PUNISHMENT, FOR THIS FORM CANNOT PARTAKE OF EARTHLY PLEASURES.
PITY.
BUT I TAKE MY PLEASURE ELSEWHERE. OVER THE CENTURIES I HAVE LEARNED TO EXECUTE MY COMMISSION WITH NOT ONLY EFFICIENCY, BUT AN UNDENIABLY ENJOYABLE CREATIVITY.
I AM MORE THAN SOME BASE TORTURER. IT IS WITHIN MY POWER TO DETERMINE THE SEVERITY OF THE CONDEMNED SOUL'S TORMENT.
IN FACT, FROM TIME TO TIME, I HAVE EVEN ARRANGED FOR A SOUL'S CONDITIONAL RELEASE. FOR A PRICE, OF COURSE.
A DEAL WITH THE DEVIL.
CALL IT WHAT YOU WILL.

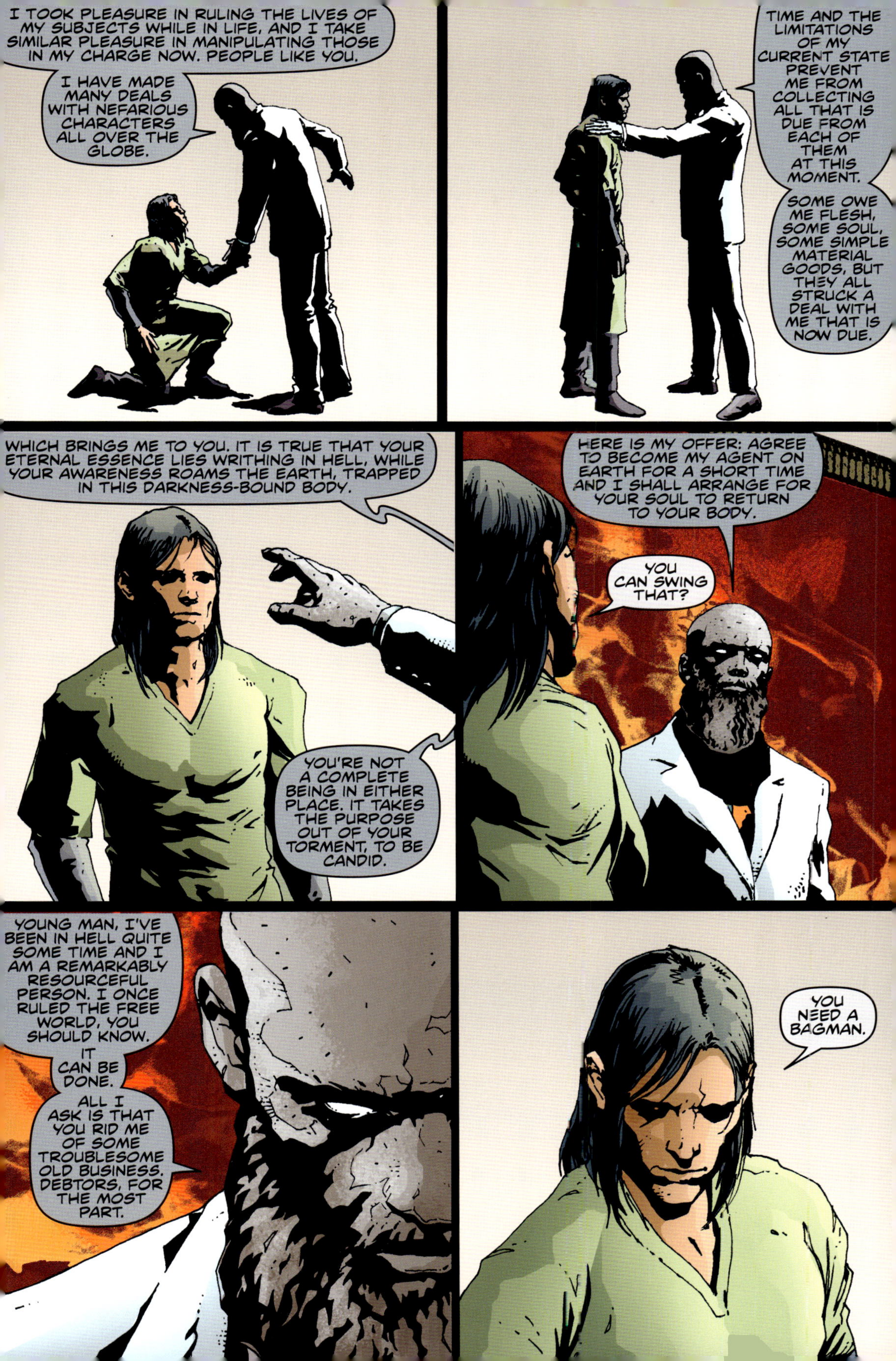
I TOOK PLEASURE IN RULING THE LIVES OF MY SUBJECTS WHILE IN LIFE, AND I TAKE SIMILAR PLEASURE IN MANIPULATING THOSE IN MY CHARGE NOW. PEOPLE LIKE YOU.
I HAVE MADE MANY DEALS WITH NEFARIOUS CHARACTERS ALL OVER THE GLOBE.
TIME AND THE LIMITATIONS OF MY CURRENT STATE PREVENT ME FROM COLLECTING ALL THAT IS DUE FROM EACH OF THEM AT THIS MOMENT.
SOME OWE ME FLESH, SOME SOUL, SOME SIMPLE MATERIAL GOODS, BUT THEY ALL STRUCK A DEAL WITH ME THAT IS NOW DUE.
WHICH BRINGS ME TO YOU. IT IS TRUE THAT YOUR ETERNAL ESSENCE LIES WRITHING IN HELL, WHILE YOUR AWARENESS ROAMS THE EARTH, TRAPPED IN THIS DARKNESS-BOUND BODY.
YOU'RE NOT A COMPLETE BEING IN EITHER PLACE. IT TAKES THE PURPOSE OUT OF YOUR TORMENT, TO BE CANDID.
HERE IS MY OFFER: AGREE TO BECOME MY AGENT ON EARTH FOR A SHORT TIME AND I SHALL ARRANGE FOR YOUR SOUL TO RETURN TO YOUR BODY.
YOU CAN SWING THAT?
YOUNG MAN, I'VE BEEN IN HELL QUITE SOME TIME AND I AM A REMARKABLY RESOURCEFUL PERSON. I ONCE RULED THE FREE WORLD, YOU SHOULD KNOW.
IT CAN BE DONE.
ALL I ASK IS THAT YOU RID ME OF SOME TROUBLESOME OLD BUSINESS. DEBTORS, FOR THE MOST PART.
YOU NEED A BAGMAN.

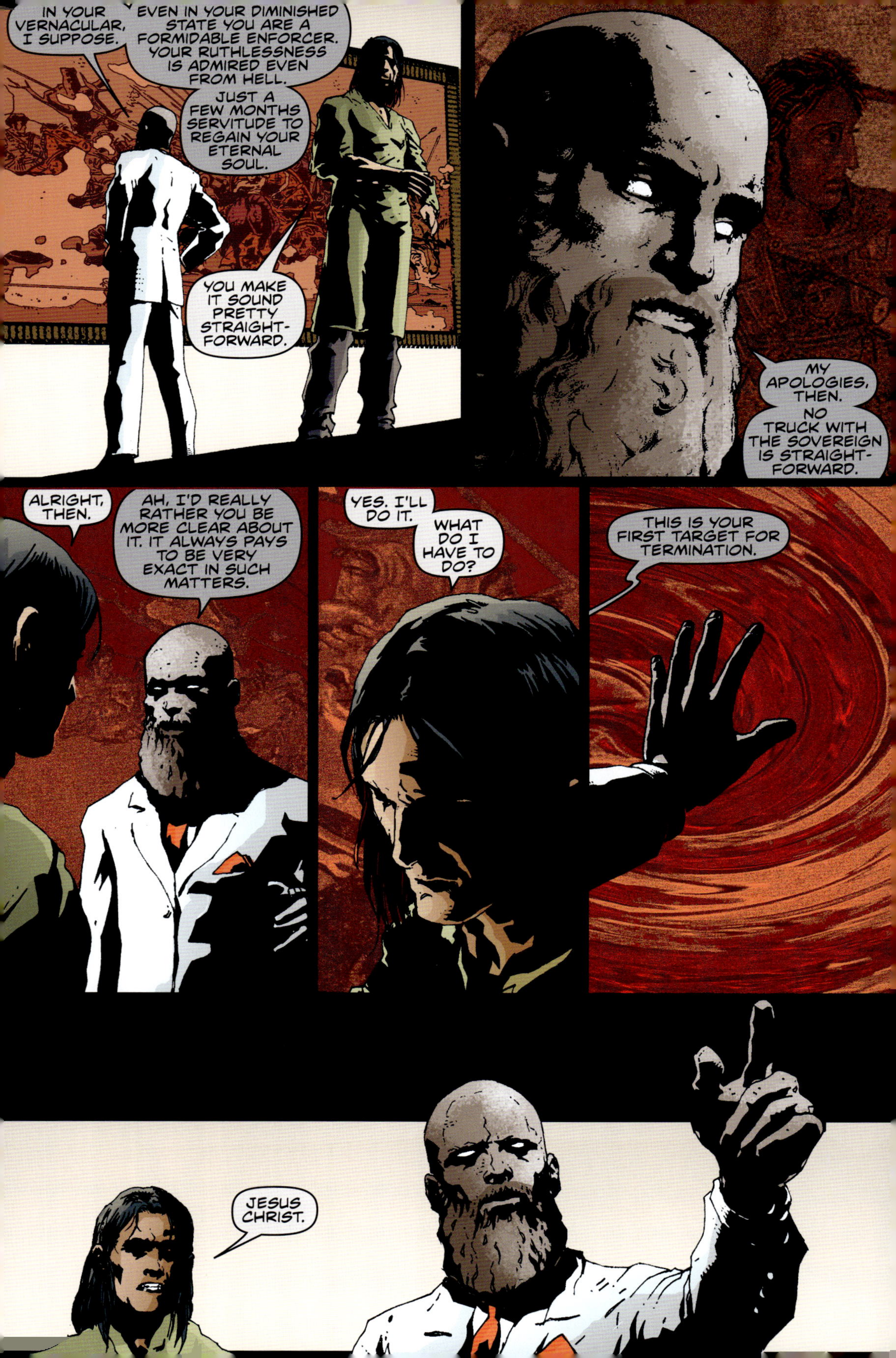
IN YOUR VERNACULAR, I SUPPOSE.
EVEN IN YOUR DIMINISHED STATE YOU ARE A FORMIDABLE ENFORCER. YOUR RUTHLESSNESS IS ADMIRED EVEN FROM HELL.
JUST A FEW MONTHS SERVITUDE TO REGAIN YOUR ETERNAL SOUL.
YOU MAKE IT SOUND PRETTY STRAIGHT-FORWARD.
MY APOLOGIES, THEN.
NO TRUCK WITH THE SOVEREIGN IS STRAIGHT-FORWARD.
ALRIGHT, THEN.
AH, I'D REALLY RATHER YOU BE MORE CLEAR ABOUT IT. IT ALWAYS PAYS TO BE VERY EXACT IN SUCH MATTERS.
YES. I'LL DO IT.
WHAT DO I HAVE TO DO?
THIS IS YOUR FIRST TARGET FOR TERMINATION.
JESUS CHRIST.

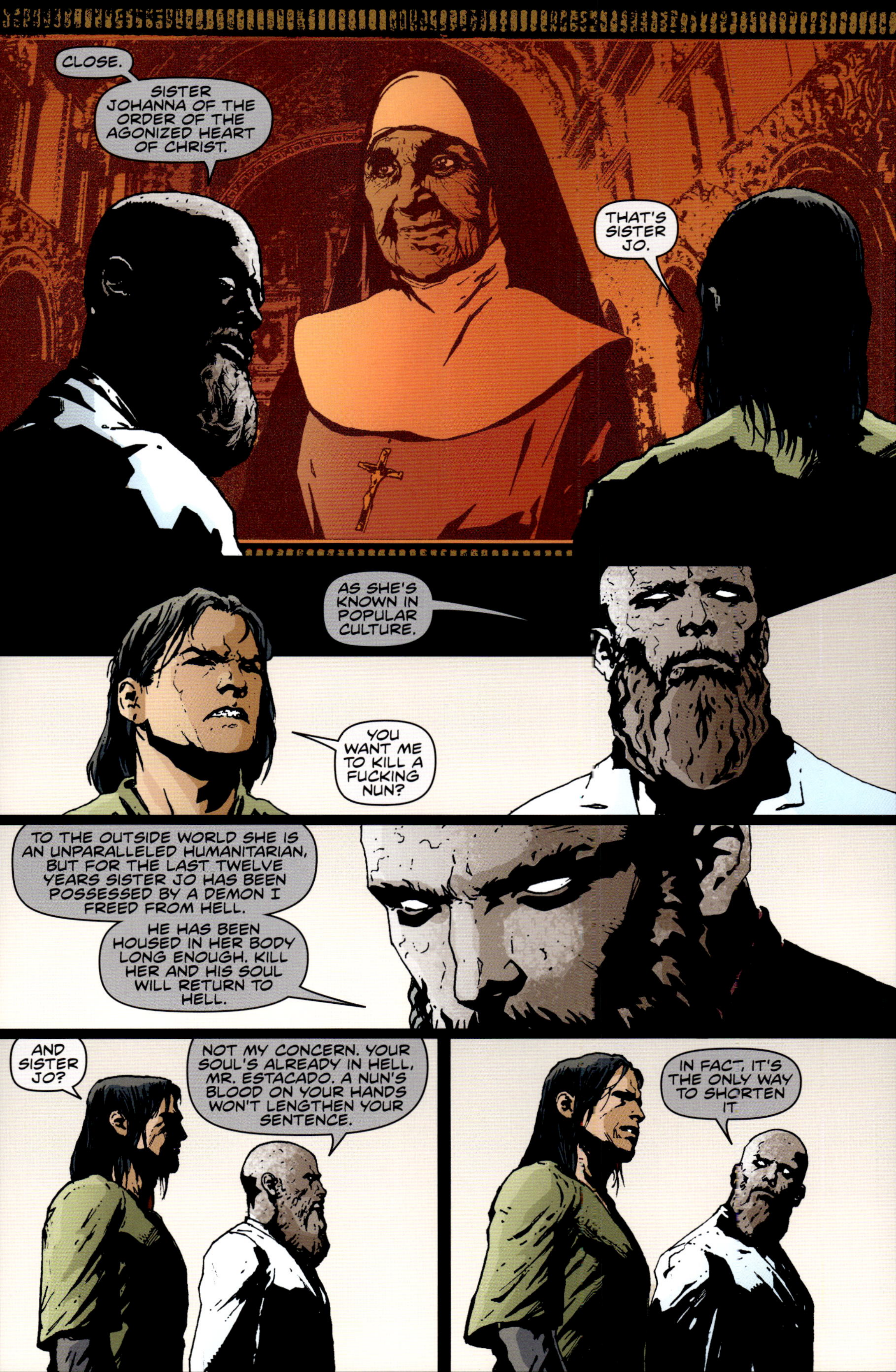
CLOSE.
SISTER JOHANNA OF THE ORDER OF THE AGONIZED HEART OF CHRIST.
THAT'S SISTER JO.
AS SHE'S KNOWN IN POPULAR CULTURE.
YOU WANT ME TO KILL A FUCKING NUN?
TO THE OUTSIDE WORLD SHE IS AN UNPARALLELED HUMANITARIAN, BUT FOR THE LAST TWELVE YEARS SISTER JO HAS BEEN POSSESSED BY A DEMON I FREED FROM HELL.
HE HAS BEEN HOUSED IN HER BODY LONG ENOUGH. KILL HER AND HIS SOUL WILL RETURN TO HELL.
AND SISTER JO?
NOT MY CONCERN. YOUR SOUL'S ALREADY IN HELL, MR. ESTACADO. A NUN'S BLOOD ON YOUR HANDS WON'T LENGTHEN YOUR SENTENCE.
IN FACT, IT'S THE ONLY WAY TO SHORTEN IT.

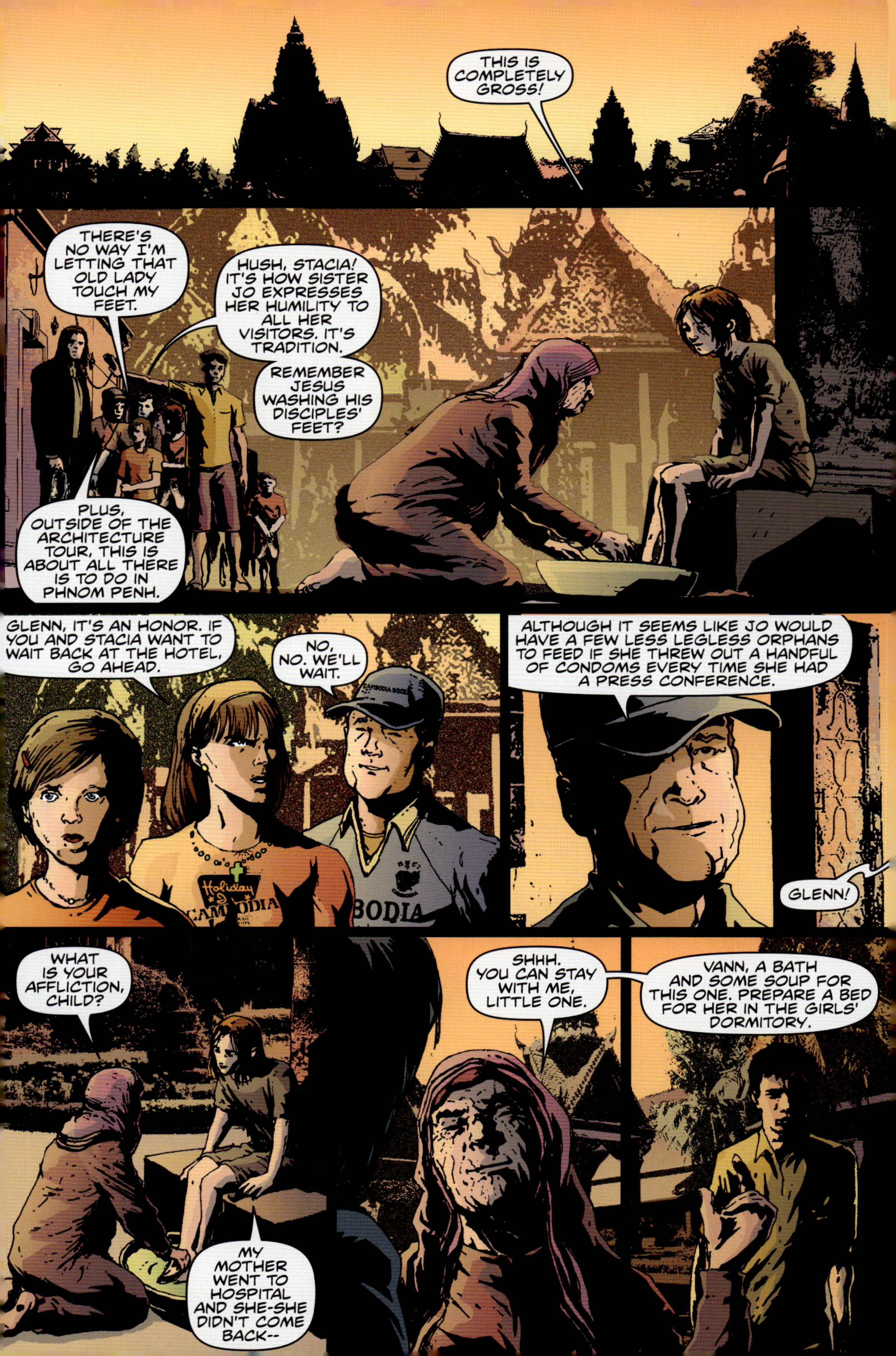
THIS IS COMPLETELY GROSS!
THERE'S NO WAY I'M LETTING THAT OLD LADY TOUCH MY FEET.
HUSH, STACIA! IT'S HOW SISTER JO EXPRESSES HER HUMILITY TO ALL HER VISITORS. IT'S TRADITION.
REMEMBER JESUS WASHING HIS DISCIPLES' FEET?
PLUS, OUTSIDE OF THE ARCHITECTURE TOUR, THIS IS ABOUT ALL THERE IS TO DO IN PHNOM PENH.
GLENN, IT'S AN HONOR. IF YOU AND STACIA WANT TO WAIT BACK AT THE HOTEL, GO AHEAD.
NO, NO. WE'LL WAIT.
ALTHOUGH IT SEEMS LIKE JO WOULD HAVE A FEW LESS LEGLESS ORPHANS TO FEED IF SHE THREW OUT A HANDFUL OF CONDOMS EVERY TIME SHE HAD A PRESS CONFERENCE.
GLENN!
WHAT IS YOUR AFFLICTION, CHILD?
MY MOTHER WENT TO HOSPITAL AND SHE-SHE DIDN'T COME BACK--
SHHH. YOU CAN STAY WITH ME, LITTLE ONE.
VANN, A BATH AND SOME SOUP FOR THIS ONE. PREPARE A BED FOR HER IN THE GIRLS' DORMITORY.

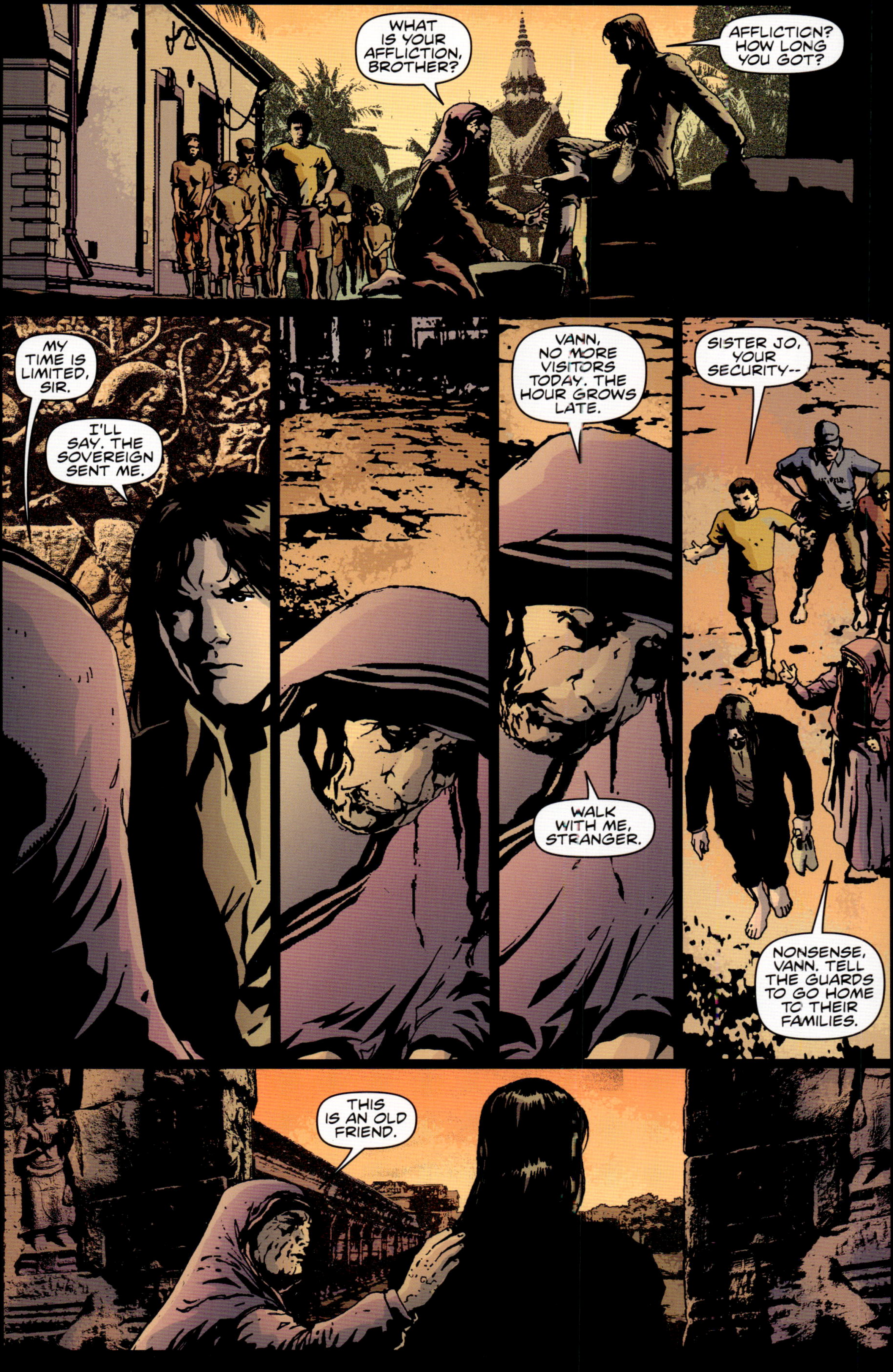
WHAT IS YOUR AFFLICTION, BROTHER?
AFFLICTION? HOW LONG YOU GOT?
MY TIME IS LIMITED, SIR.
I'LL SAY. THE SOVEREIGN SENT ME.
VANN, NO MORE VISITORS TODAY. THE HOUR GROWS LATE.
WALK WITH ME, STRANGER.
SISTER JO, YOUR SECURITY--
NONSENSE, VANN. TELL THE GUARDS TO GO HOME TO THEIR FAMILIES.
THIS IS AN OLD FRIEND.

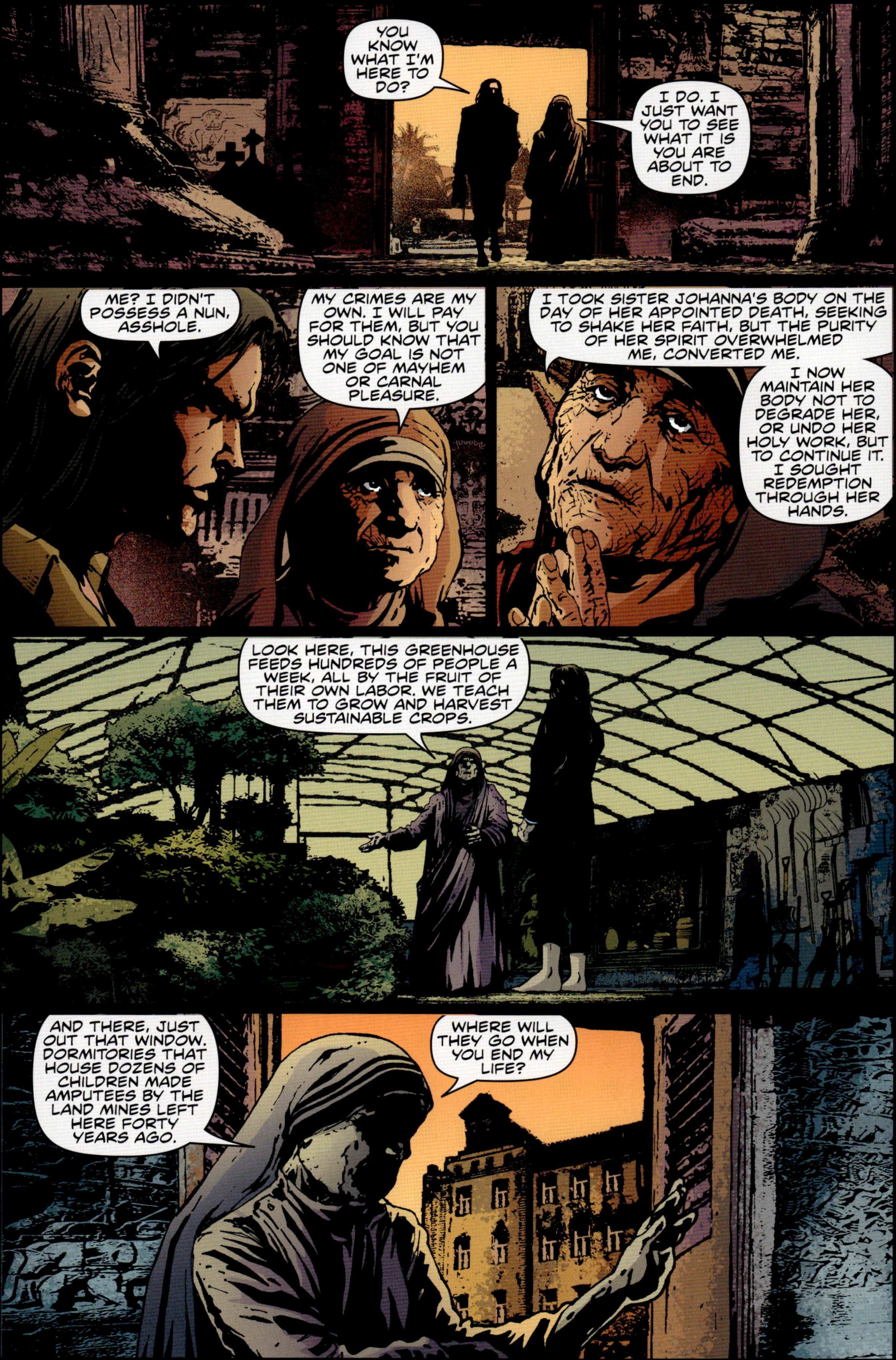
YOU KNOW WHAT I'M HERE TO DO?
I DO. I JUST WANT YOU TO SEE WHAT IT IS YOU ARE ABOUT TO END.
ME? I DIDN'T POSSESS A NUN, ASSHOLE.
MY CRIMES ARE MY OWN. I WILL PAY FOR THEM, BUT YOU SHOULD KNOW THAT MY GOAL IS NOT ONE OF MAYHEM OR CARNAL PLEASURE.
I TOOK SISTER JOHANNA'S BODY ON THE DAY OF HER APPOINTED DEATH, SEEKING TO SHAKE HER FAITH, BUT THE PURITY OF HER SPIRIT OVERWHELMED ME, CONVERTED ME.
I NOW MAINTAIN HER BODY NOT TO DEGRADE HER, OR UNDO HER HOLY WORK, BUT TO CONTINUE IT. I SOUGHT REDEMPTION THROUGH HER HANDS.
LOOK HERE, THIS GREENHOUSE FEEDS HUNDREDS OF PEOPLE A WEEK, ALL BY THE FRUIT OF THEIR OWN LABOR. WE TEACH THEM TO GROW AND HARVEST SUSTAINABLE CROPS.
AND THERE, JUST OUT THAT WINDOW. DORMITORIES THAT HOUSE DOZENS OF CHILDREN MADE AMPUTEES BY THE LAND MINES LEFT HERE FORTY YEARS AGO.
WHERE WILL THEY GO WHEN YOU END MY LIFE?

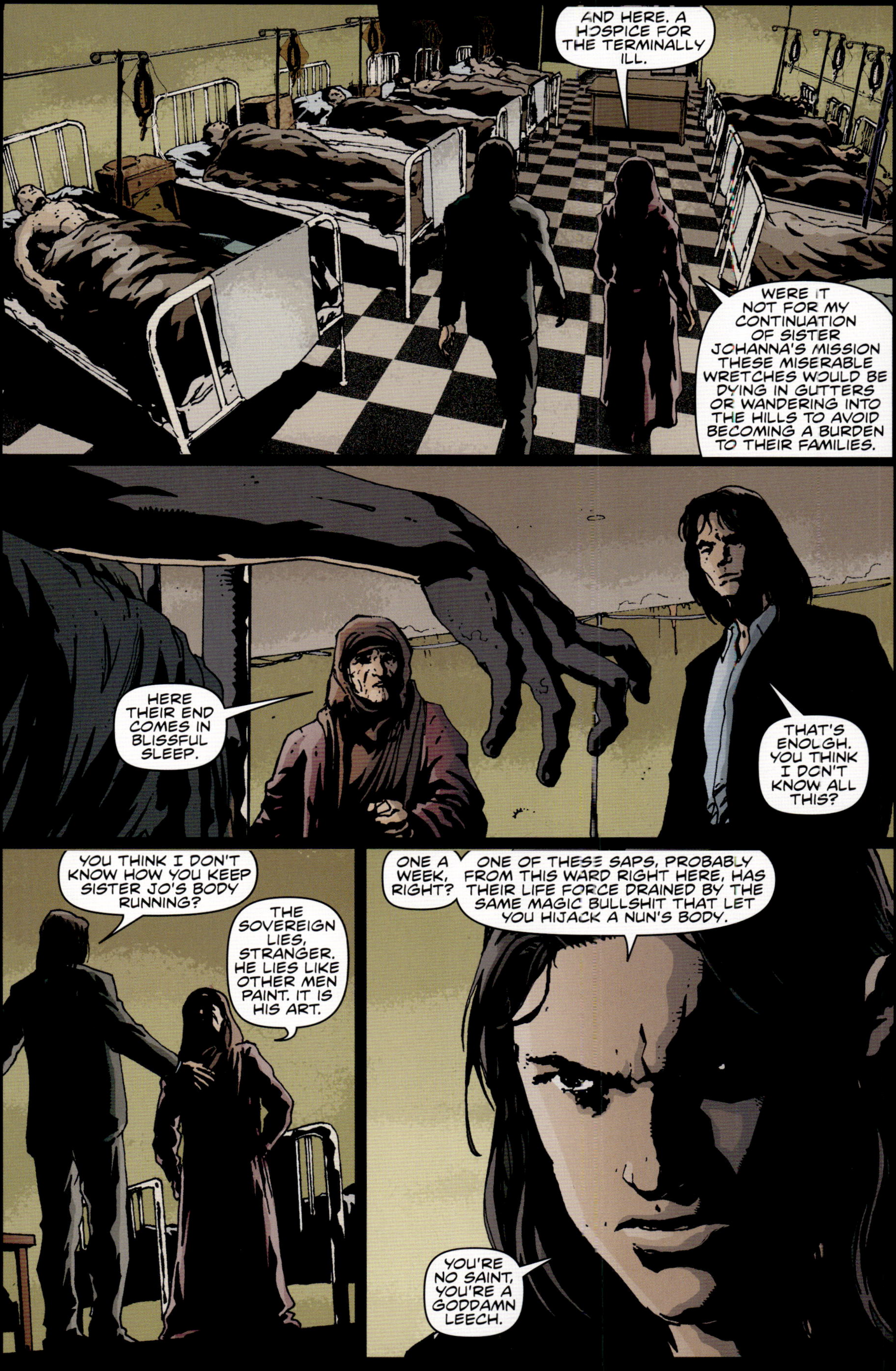
AND HERE. A HOSPICE FOR THE TERMINALLY ILL.
WERE IT NOT FOR MY CONTINUATION OF SISTER JOHANNA'S MISSION THESE MISERABLE WRETCHES WOULD BE DYING IN GUTTERS OR WANDERING INTO THE HILLS TO AVOID BECOMING A BURDEN TO THEIR FAMILIES.
HERE THEIR END COMES IN BLISSFUL SLEEP.
THAT'S ENOUGH. YOU THINK I DON'T KNOW ALL THIS?
YOU THINK I DON'T KNOW HOW YOU KEEP SISTER JO'S BODY RUNNING?
THE SOVEREIGN LIES, STRANGER. HE LIES LIKE OTHER MEN PAINT. IT IS HIS ART.
ONE A WEEK, RIGHT?
ONE OF THESE SAPS, PROBABLY FROM THIS WARD RIGHT HERE, HAS THEIR LIFE FORCE DRAINED BY THE SAME MAGIC BULLSHIT THAT LET YOU HIJACK A NUN'S BODY.
YOU'RE NO SAINT, YOU'RE A GODDAMN LEECH.

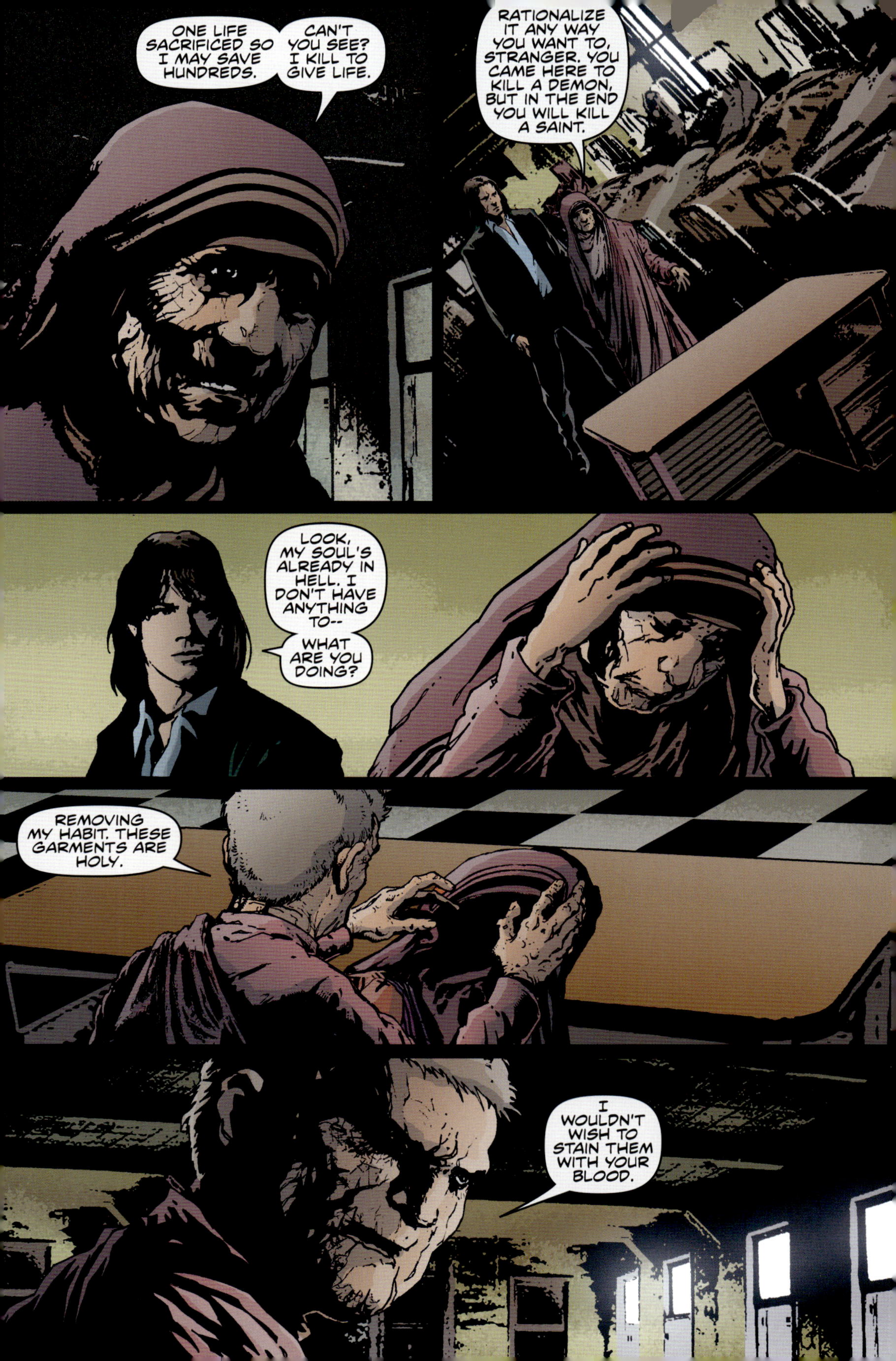
ONE LIFE SACRIFICED SO I MAY SAVE HUNDREDS.
CAN'T YOU SEE? I KILL TO GIVE LIFE.
RATIONALIZE IT ANY WAY YOU WANT TO, STRANGER. YOU CAME HERE TO KILL A DEMON, BUT IN THE END YOU WILL KILL A SAINT.
LOOK, MY SOUL'S ALREADY IN HELL. I DON'T HAVE ANYTHING TO--
WHAT ARE YOU DOING?
REMOVING MY HABIT. THESE GARMENTS ARE HOLY.
I WOULDN'T WISH TO STAIN THEM WITH YOUR BLOOD.

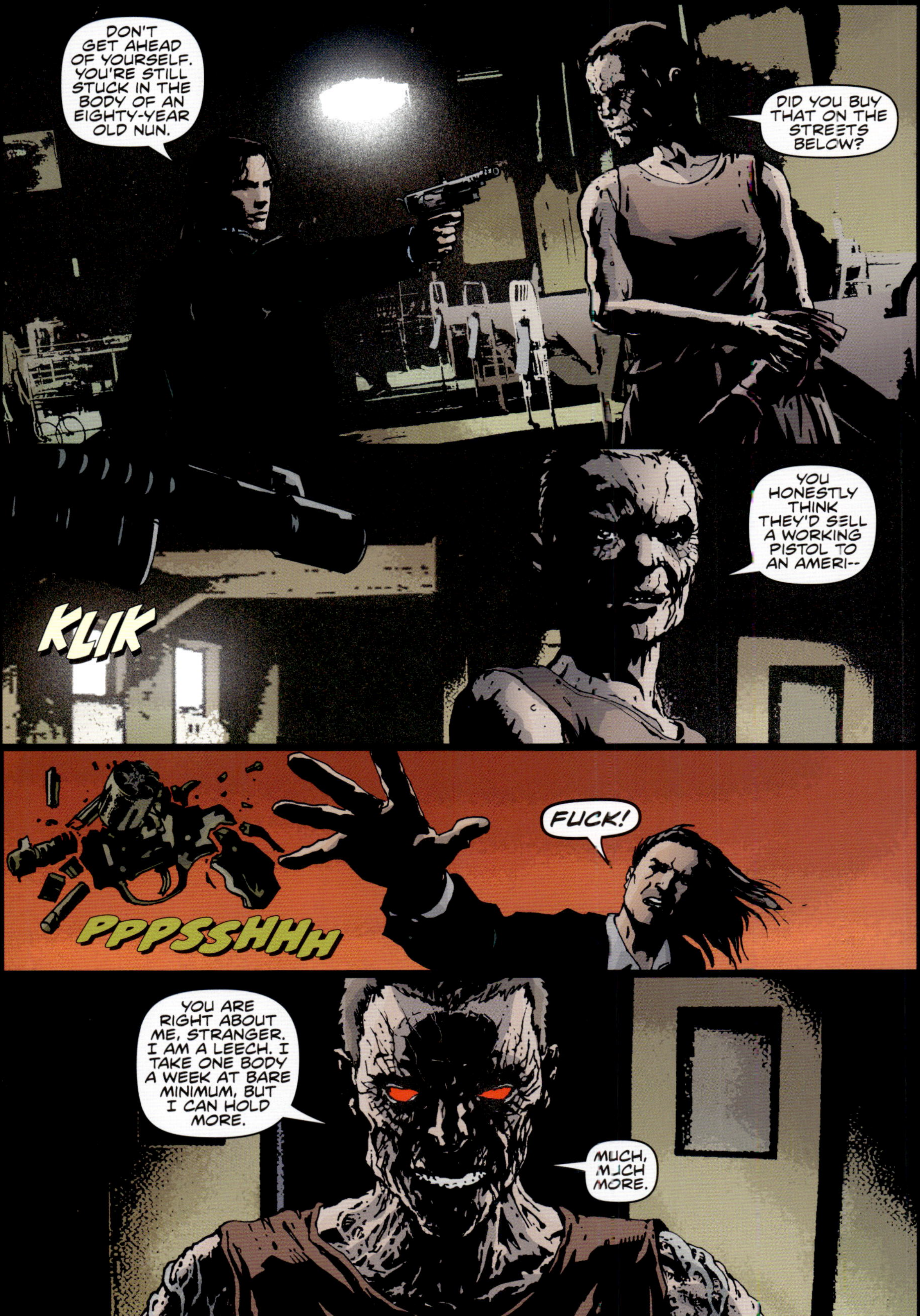
DON'T GET AHEAD OF YOURSELF. YOU'RE STILL STUCK IN THE BODY OF AN EIGHTY-YEAR OLD NUN.
DID YOU BUY THAT ON THE STREETS BELOW?
YOU HONESTLY THINK THEY'D SELL A WORKING PISTOL TO AN AMERI--
KLIK
FUCK!
PPPSSHHH
YOU ARE RIGHT ABOUT ME, STRANGER. I AM A LEECH. I TAKE ONE BODY A WEEK AT BARE MINIMUM, BUT I CAN HOLD MORE.
MUCH, MUCH MORE.

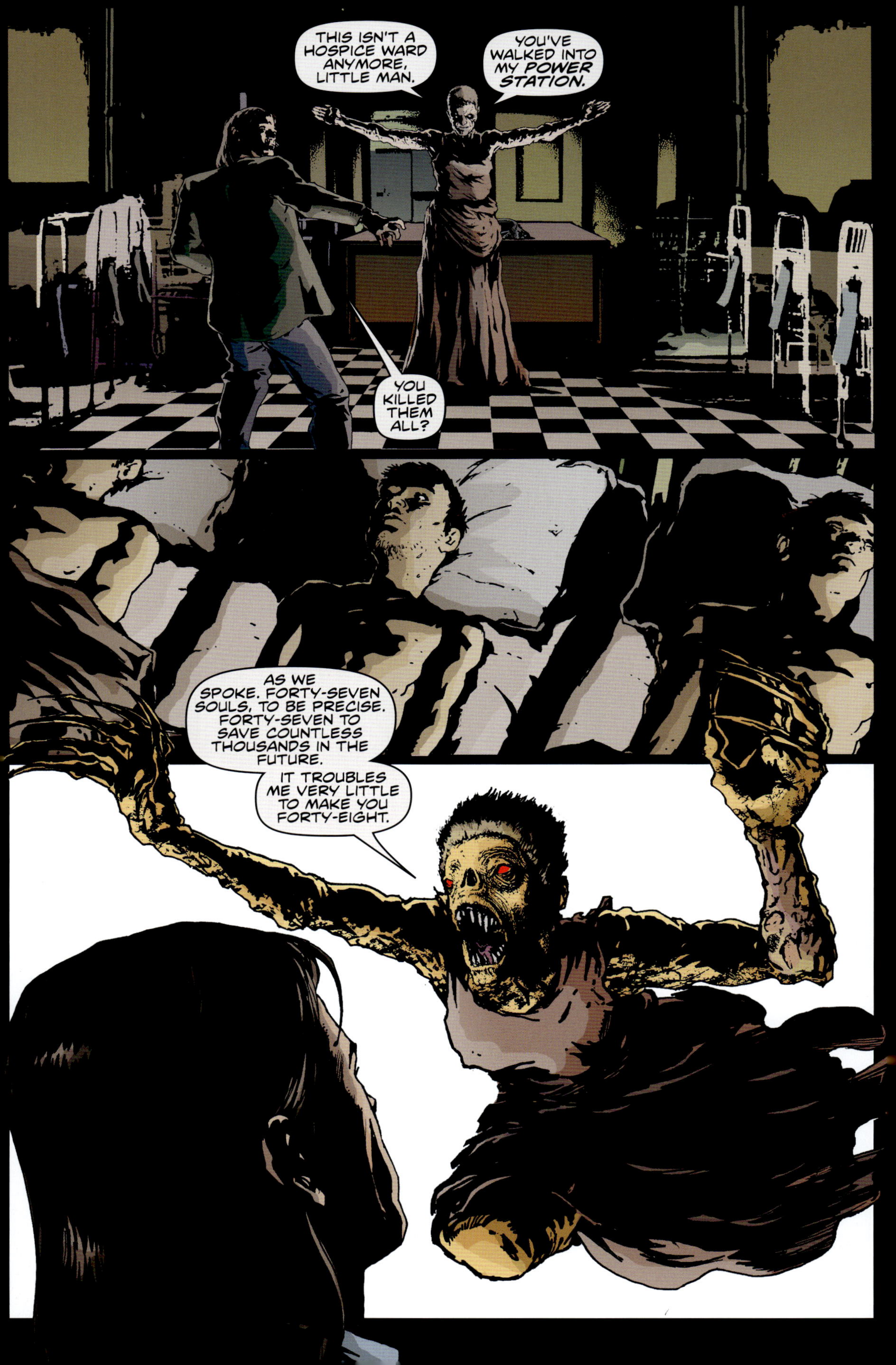
THIS ISN'T A HOSPICE WARD ANYMORE, LITTLE MAN.
YOU'VE WALKED INTO MY POWER STATION.
YOU KILLED THEM ALL?
AS WE SPOKE. FORTY-SEVEN SOULS, TO BE PRECISE. FORTY-SEVEN TO SAVE COUNTLESS THOUSANDS IN THE FUTURE.
IT TROUBLES ME VERY LITTLE TO MAKE YOU FORTY-EIGHT.

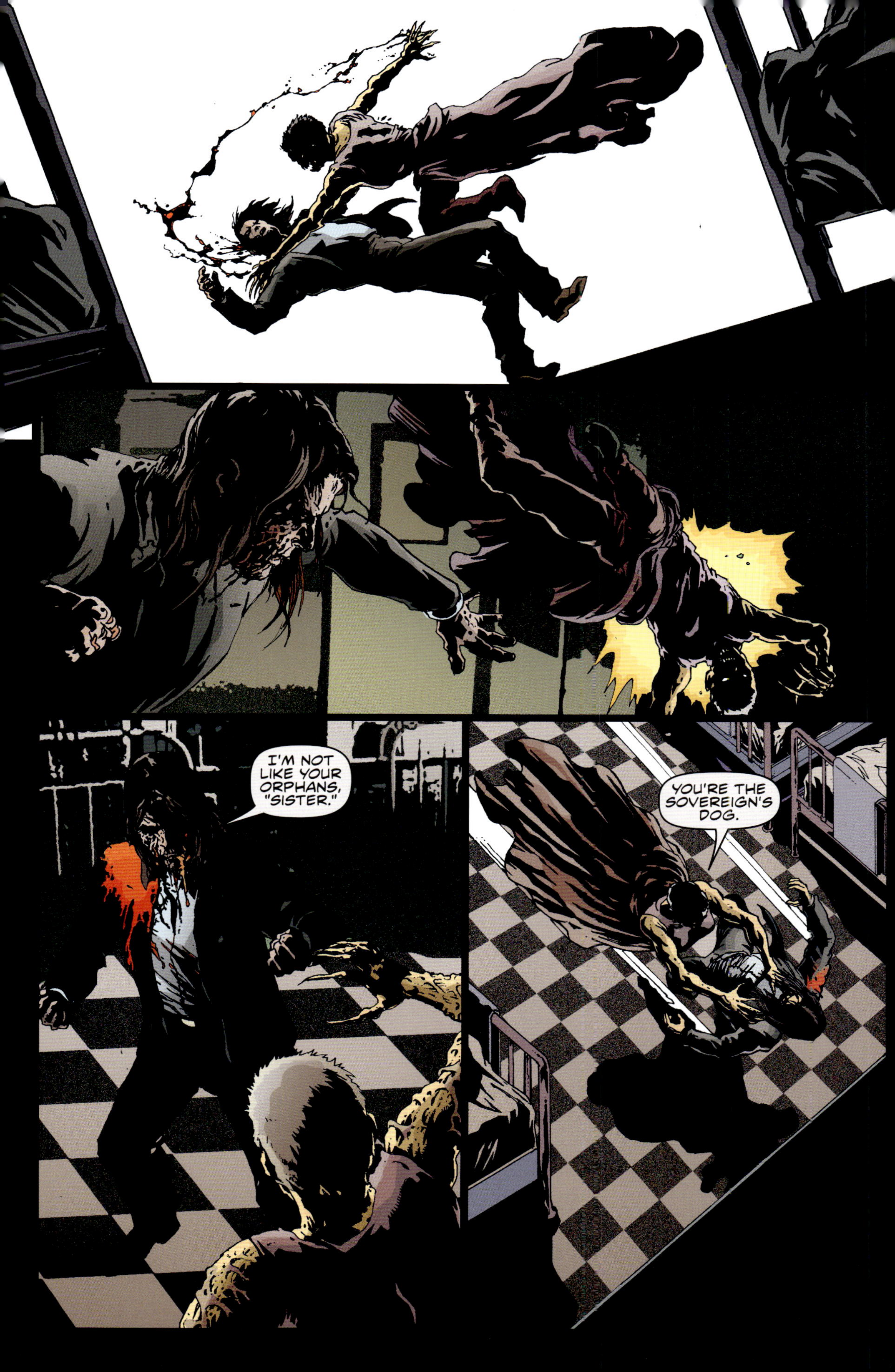
I'M NOT LIKE YOUR ORPHANS, "SISTER."
YOU'RE THE SOVEREIGN'S DOG.

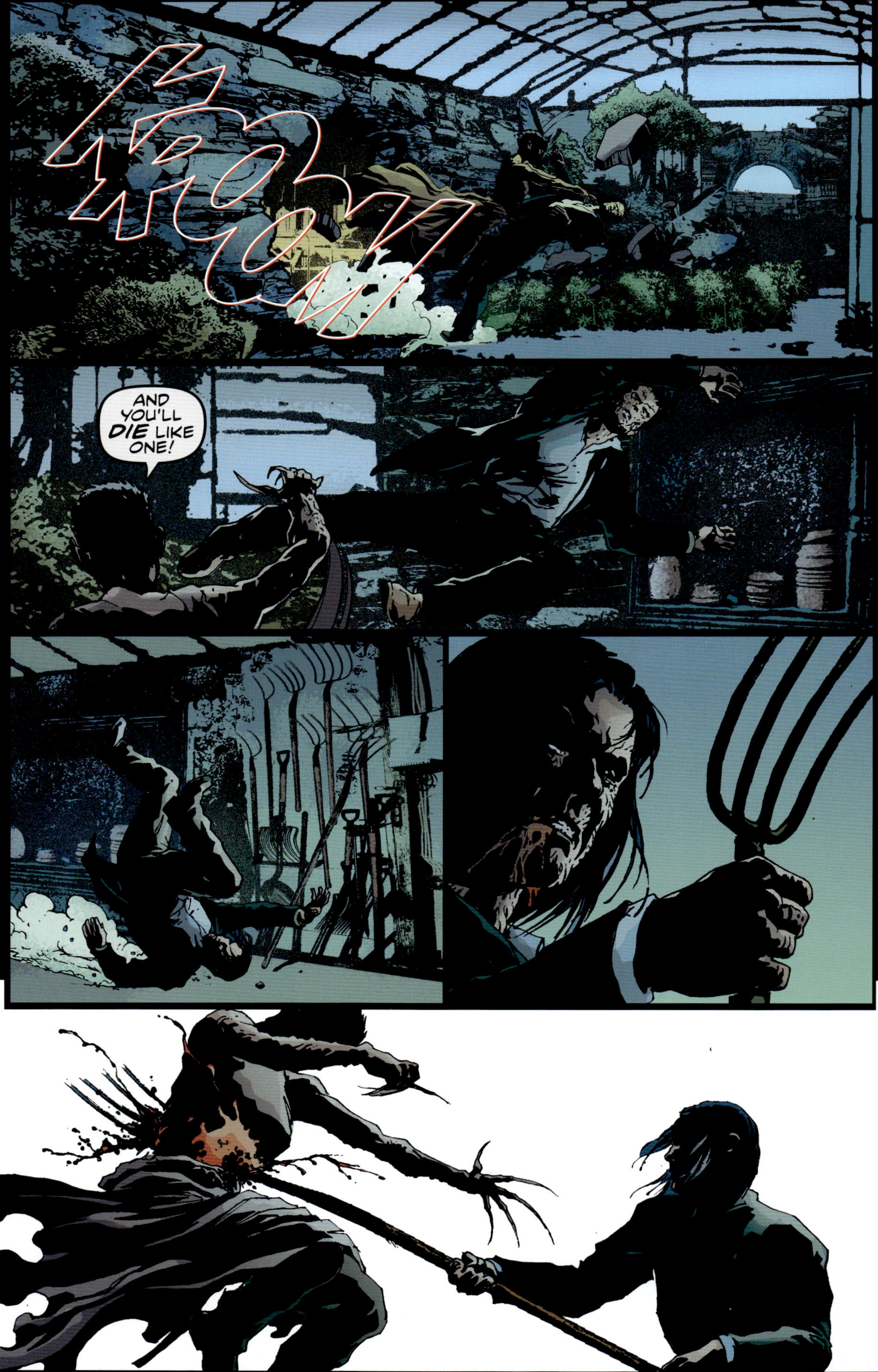
AND YOU'LL DIE LIKE ONE!

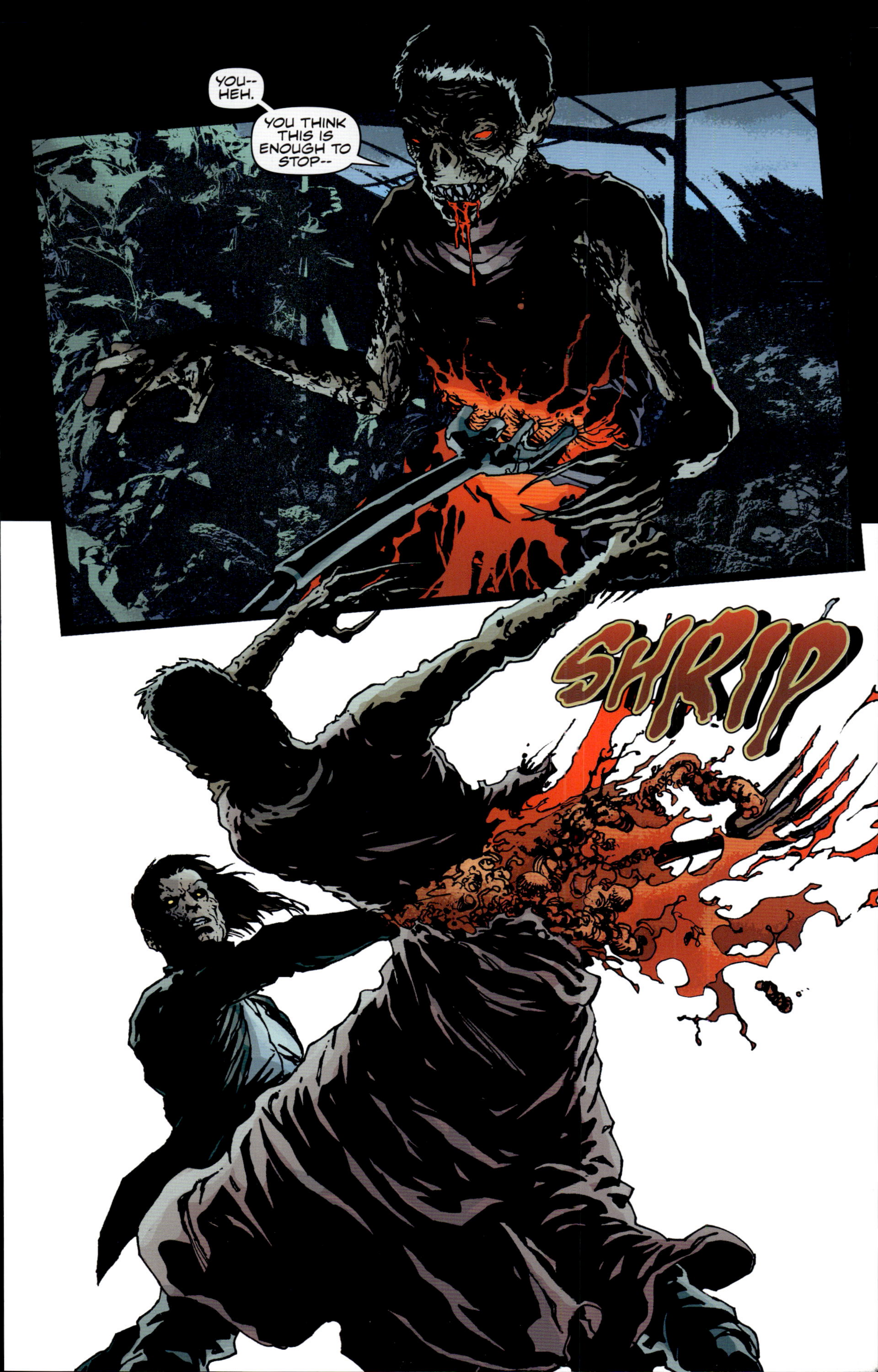
YOU-- HEH.
YOU THINK THIS IS ENOUGH TO STOP--
SHRIP

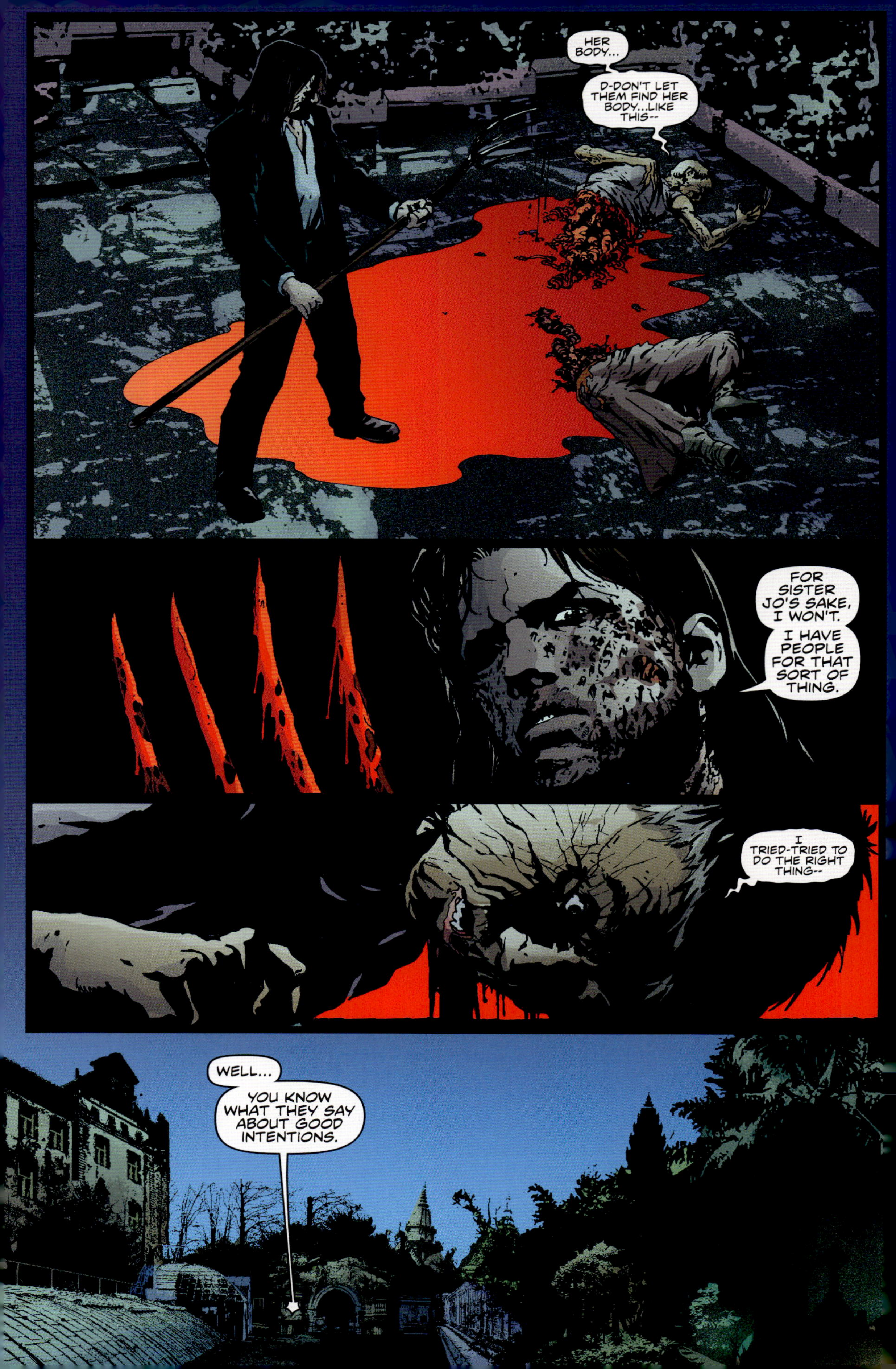
HER BODY...
D-DON'T LET THEM FIND HER BODY...LIKE THIS--
FOR SISTER JO'S SAKE, I WON'T.
I HAVE PEOPLE FOR THAT SORT OF THING.
I TRIED-TRIED TO DO THE RIGHT THING--
WELL...
YOU KNOW WHAT THEY SAY ABOUT GOOD INTENTIONS.

The Darkness Issue #74
cover art by: Frazier Irving

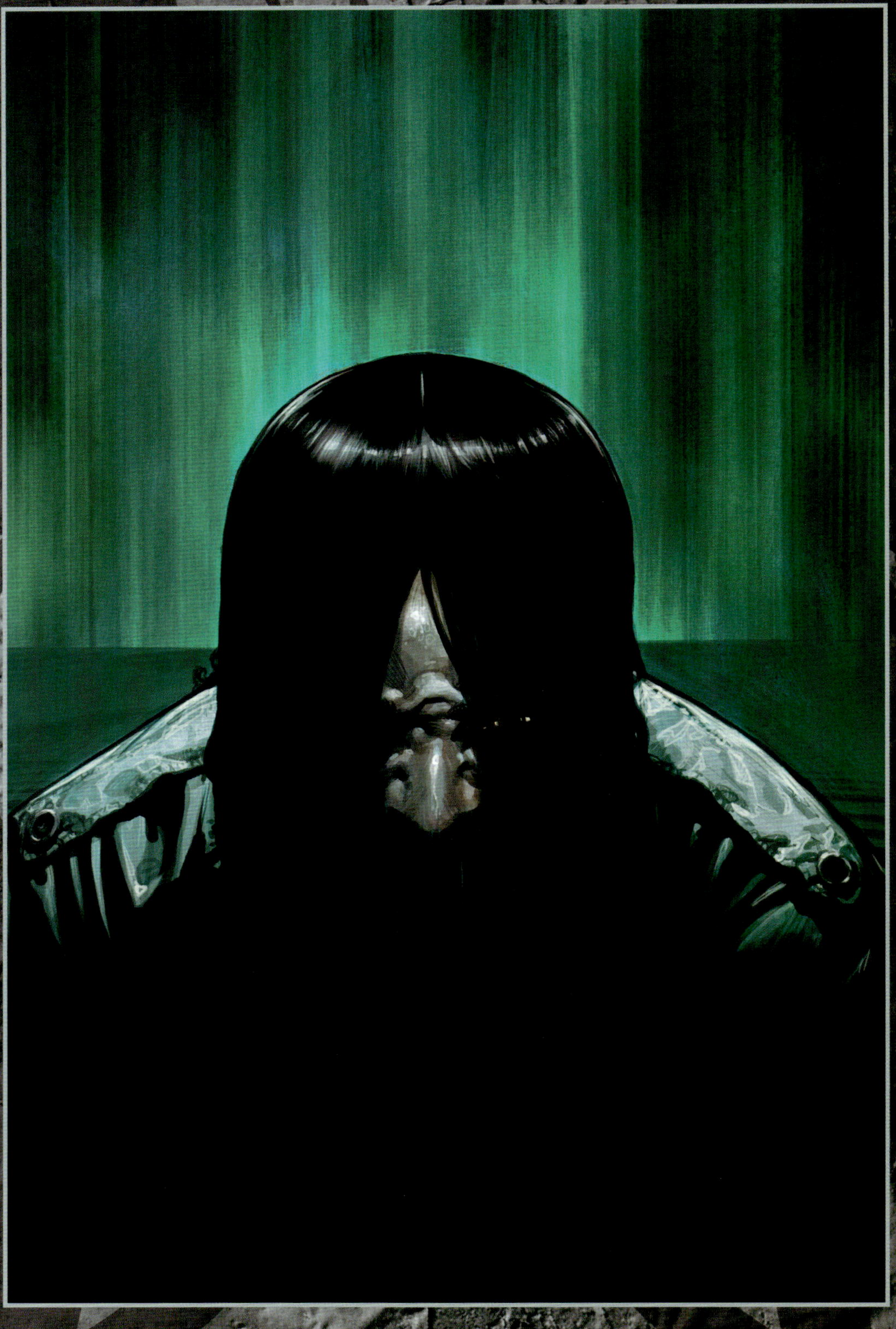

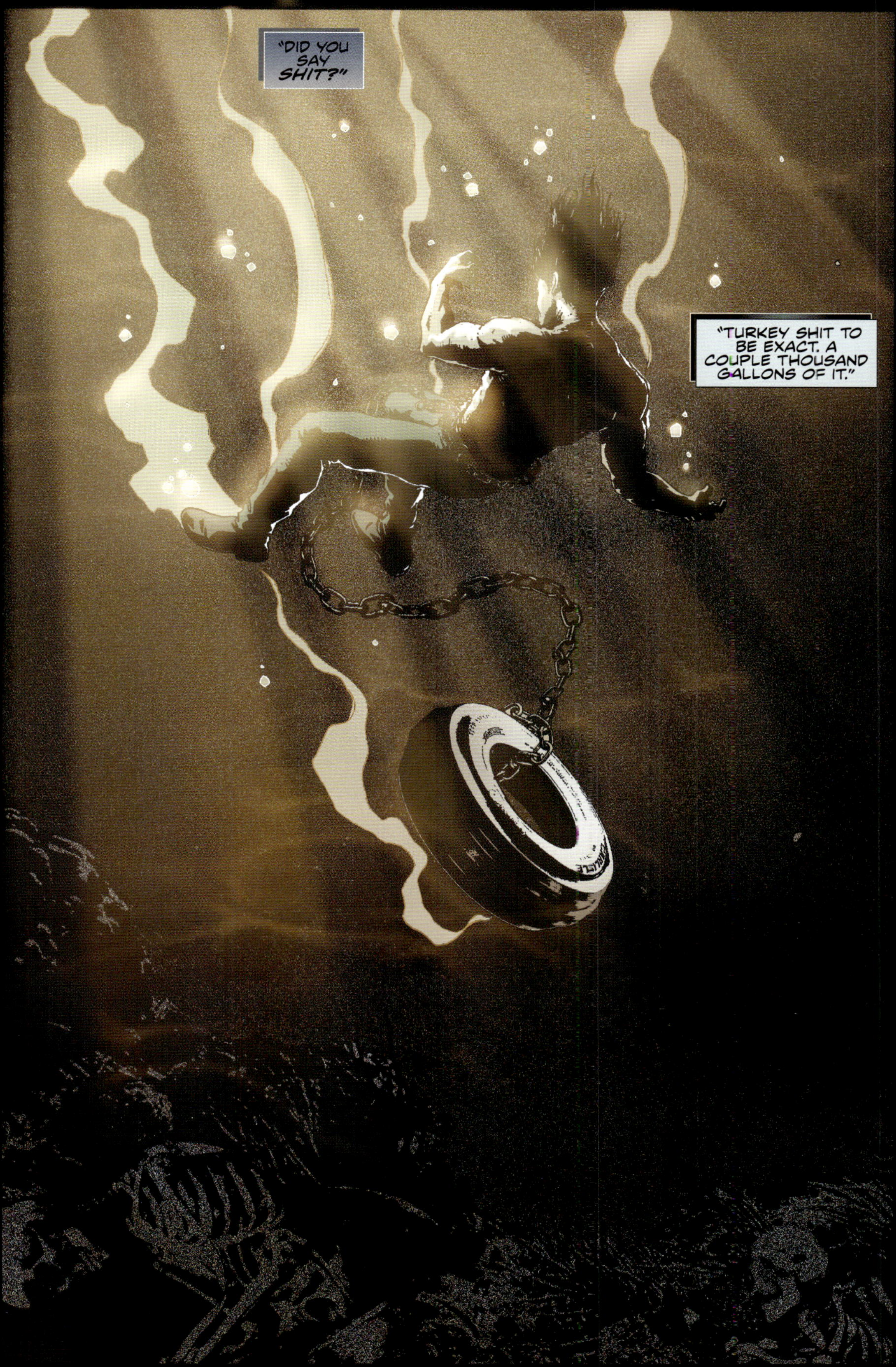
"DID YOU SAY SHIT?"
"TURKEY SHIT TO BE EXACT. A COUPLE THOUSAND GALLONS OF IT."

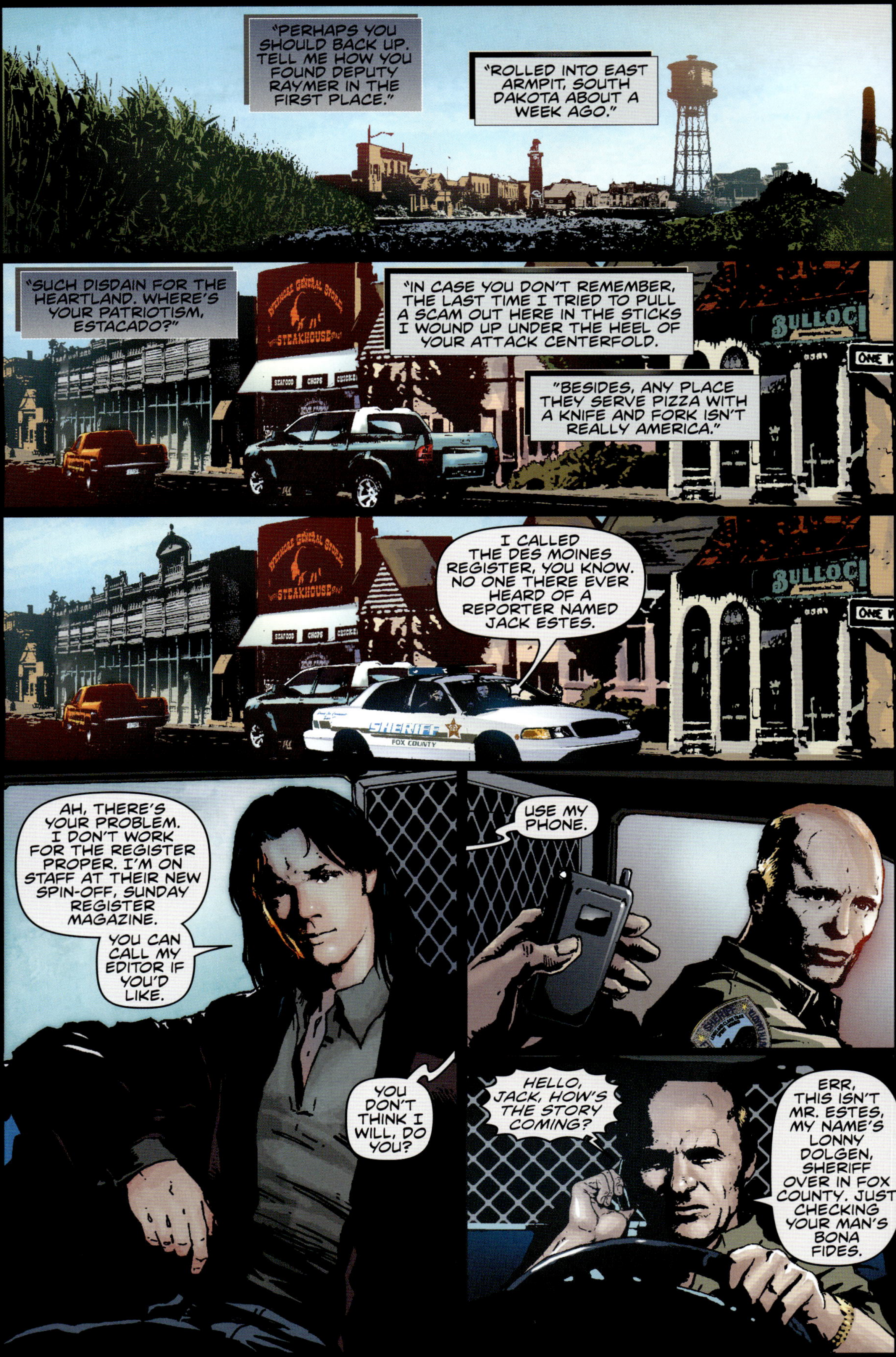
"PERHAPS YOU SHOULD BACK UP. TELL ME HOW YOU FOUND DEPUTY RAYMER IN THE FIRST PLACE."
"ROLLED INTO EAST ARMPIT, SOUTH DAKOTA ABOUT A WEEK AGO."
"SUCH DISDAIN FOR THE HEARTLAND. WHERE'S YOUR PATRIOTISM, ESTACADO?"
"IN CASE YOU DON'T REMEMBER, THE LAST TIME I TRIED TO PULL A SCAM OUT HERE IN THE STICKS I WOUND UP UNDER THE HEEL OF YOUR ATTACK CENTERFOLD.
"BESIDES, ANY PLACE THEY SERVE PIZZA WITH A KNIFE AND FORK ISN'T REALLY AMERICA."
STEAKHOUSE
SEAFOOD
CHOPS
BULLOC
ONE W
I CALLED THE DES MOINES REGISTER, YOU KNOW. NO ONE THERE EVER HEARD OF A REPORTER NAMED JACK ESTES.
SHERIFF
FOX COUNTY
AH, THERE'S YOUR PROBLEM. I DON'T WORK FOR THE REGISTER PROPER. I'M ON STAFF AT THEIR NEW SPIN-OFF, SUNDAY REGISTER MAGAZINE.
YOU CAN CALL MY EDITOR IF YOU'D LIKE.
USE MY PHONE.
YOU DON'T THINK I WILL, DO YOU?
HELLO, JACK, HOW'S THE STORY COMING?
ERR, THIS ISN'T MR. ESTES, MY NAME'S LONNY DOLGEN, SHERIFF OVER IN FOX COUNTY. JUST CHECKING YOUR MAN'S BONA FIDES.

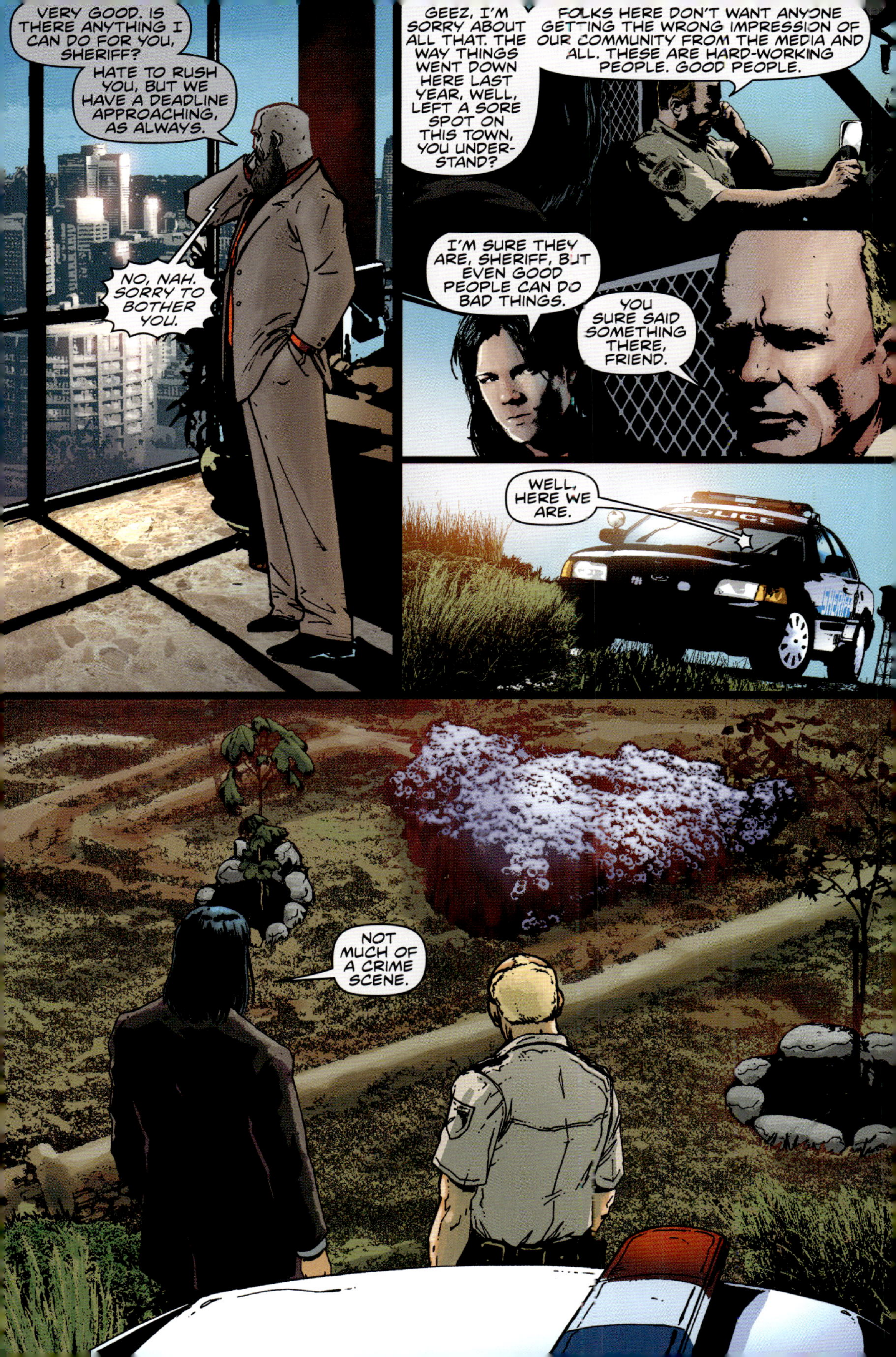

VERY GOOD. IS THERE ANYTHING I CAN DO FOR YOU, SHERIFF?
HATE TO RUSH YOU, BUT WE HAVE A DEADLINE APPROACHING, AS ALWAYS.
NO, NAH. SORRY TO BOTHER YOU.
GEEZ, I'M SORRY ABOUT ALL THAT. THE WAY THINGS WENT DOWN HERE LAST YEAR, WELL, LEFT A SORE SPOT ON THIS TOWN, YOU UNDERSTAND?
FOLKS HERE DON'T WANT ANYONE GETTING THE WRONG IMPRESSION OF OUR COMMUNITY FROM THE MEDIA AND ALL. THESE ARE HARD-WORKING PEOPLE. GOOD PEOPLE.
I'M SURE THEY ARE, SHERIFF, BUT EVEN GOOD PEOPLE CAN DO BAD THINGS.
YOU SURE SAID SOMETHING THERE, FRIEND.
WELL, HERE WE ARE.
POLICE
SHERIFF
NOT MUCH OF A CRIME SCENE.

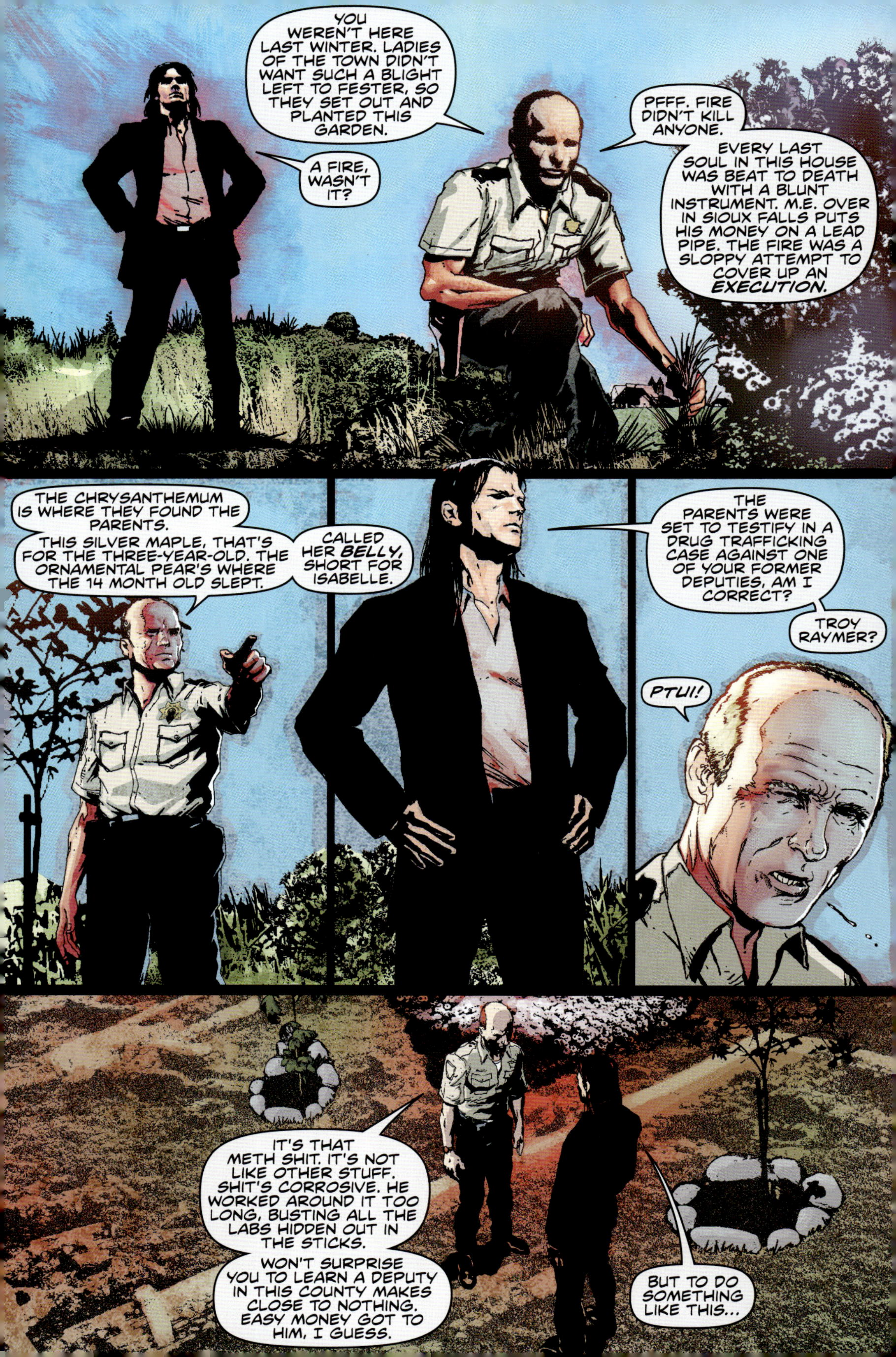
YOU WEREN'T HERE LAST WINTER. LADIES OF THE TOWN DIDN'T WANT SUCH A BLIGHT LEFT TO FESTER, SO THEY SET OUT AND PLANTED THIS GARDEN.
A FIRE, WASN'T IT?
PFFF. FIRE DIDN'T KILL ANYONE.
EVERY LAST SOUL IN THIS HOUSE WAS BEAT TO DEATH WITH A BLUNT INSTRUMENT. M.E. OVER IN SIOUX FALLS PUTS HIS MONEY ON A LEAD PIPE. THE FIRE WAS A SLOPPY ATTEMPT TO COVER UP AN EXECUTION.
THE CHRYSANTHEMUM IS WHERE THEY FOUND THE PARENTS.
THIS SILVER MAPLE, THAT'S FOR THE THREE-YEAR-OLD. THE ORNAMENTAL PEAR'S WHERE THE 14 MONTH OLD SLEPT.
CALLED HER BELLY, SHORT FOR ISABELLE.
THE PARENTS WERE SET TO TESTIFY IN A DRUG TRAFFICKING CASE AGAINST ONE OF YOUR FORMER DEPUTIES, AM I CORRECT?
TROY RAYMER?
PTUI!
IT'S THAT METH SHIT. IT'S NOT LIKE OTHER STUFF. SHIT'S CORROSIVE. HE WORKED AROUND IT TOO LONG, BUSTING ALL THE LABS HIDDEN OUT IN THE STICKS.
WON'T SURPRISE YOU TO LEARN A DEPUTY IN THIS COUNTY MAKES CLOSE TO NOTHING. EASY MONEY GOT TO HIM, I GUESS.
BUT TO DO SOMETHING LIKE THIS...

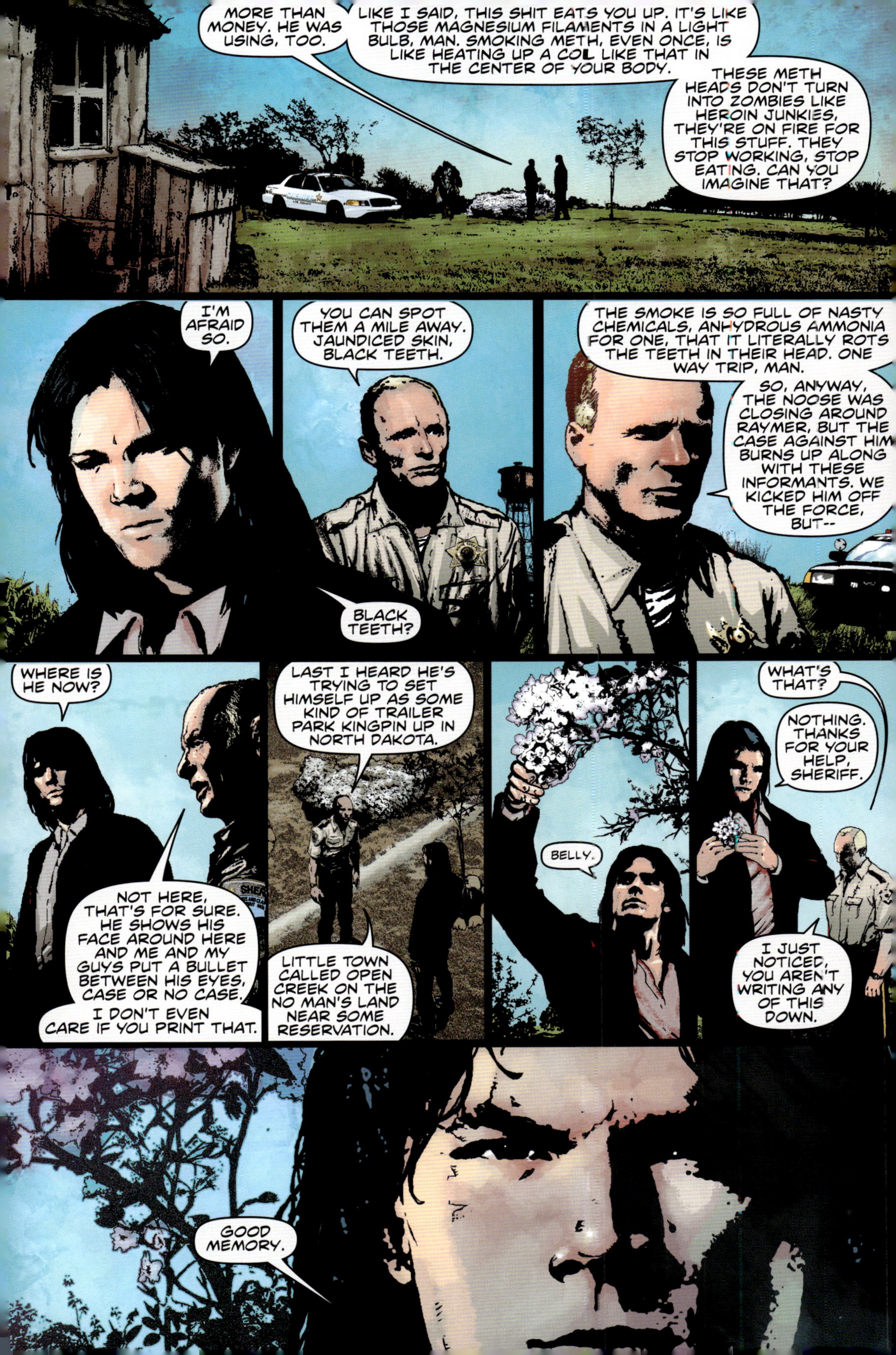
MORE THAN MONEY. HE WAS USING, TOO.
LIKE I SAID, THIS SHIT EATS YOU UP. IT'S LIKE THOSE MAGNESIUM FILAMENTS IN A LIGHT BULB, MAN. SMOKING METH, EVEN ONCE, IS LIKE HEATING UP A COIL LIKE THAT IN THE CENTER OF YOUR BODY.
THESE METH HEADS DON'T TURN INTO ZOMBIES LIKE HEROIN JUNKIES, THEY'RE ON FIRE FOR THIS STUFF. THEY STOP WORKING, STOP EATING. CAN YOU IMAGINE THAT?
I'M AFRAID SO.
YOU CAN SPOT THEM A MILE AWAY. JAUNDICED SKIN, BLACK TEETH.
BLACK TEETH?
THE SMOKE IS SO FULL OF NASTY CHEMICALS, ANHYDROUS AMMONIA FOR ONE, THAT IT LITERALLY ROTS THE TEETH IN THEIR HEAD. ONE WAY TRIP, MAN.
SO, ANYWAY, THE NOOSE WAS CLOSING AROUND RAYMER, BUT THE CASE AGAINST HIM BURNS UP ALONG WITH THESE INFORMANTS. WE KICKED HIM OFF THE FORCE, BUT--
WHERE IS HE NOW?
NOT HERE, THAT'S FOR SURE. HE SHOWS HIS FACE AROUND HERE AND ME AND MY GUYS PUT A BULLET BETWEEN HIS EYES, CASE OR NO CASE.
I DON'T EVEN CARE IF YOU PRINT THAT.
LAST I HEARD HE'S TRYING TO SET HIMSELF UP AS SOME KIND OF TRAILER PARK KINGPIN UP IN NORTH DAKOTA.
LITTLE TOWN CALLED OPEN CREEK ON THE NO MAN'S LAND NEAR SOME RESERVATION.
BELLY.
WHAT'S THAT?
NOTHING. THANKS FOR YOUR HELP, SHERIFF.
I JUST NOTICED, YOU AREN'T WRITING ANY OF THIS DOWN.
GOOD MEMORY.

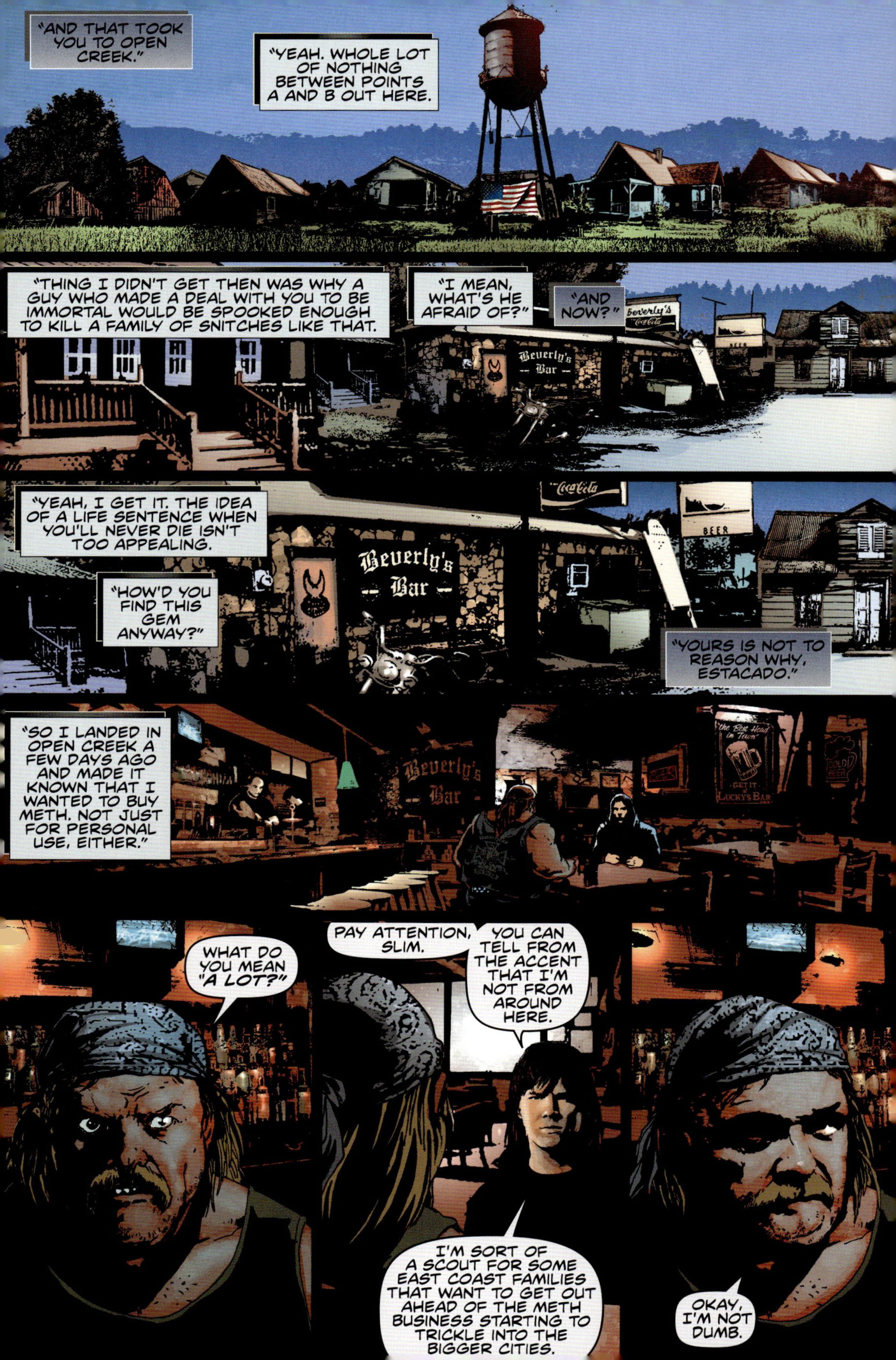
"AND THAT TOOK YOU TO OPEN CREEK."
"YEAH. WHOLE LOT OF NOTHING BETWEEN POINTS A AND B OUT HERE.
"THING I DIDN'T GET THEN WAS WHY A GUY WHO MADE A DEAL WITH YOU TO BE IMMORTAL WOULD BE SPOOKED ENOUGH TO KILL A FAMILY OF SNITCHES LIKE THAT.
"I MEAN, WHAT'S HE AFRAID OF?"
"AND NOW?"
Beverly's Bar
"YEAH, I GET IT. THE IDEA OF A LIFE SENTENCE WHEN YOU'LL NEVER DIE ISN'T TOO APPEALING.
"HOW'D YOU FIND THIS GEM ANYWAY?"
Beverly's Bar
BEER
"YOURS IS NOT TO REASON WHY, ESTACADO."
"SO I LANDED IN OPEN CREEK A FEW DAYS AGO AND MADE IT KNOWN THAT I WANTED TO BUY METH. NOT JUST FOR PERSONAL USE, EITHER."
Beverly's Bar
WHAT DO YOU MEAN "A LOT?"
PAY ATTENTION, SLIM.
YOU CAN TELL FROM THE ACCENT THAT I'M NOT FROM AROUND HERE.
I'M SORT OF A SCOUT FOR SOME EAST COAST FAMILIES THAT WANT TO GET OUT AHEAD OF THE METH BUSINESS STARTING TO TRICKLE INTO THE BIGGER CITIES.
OKAY, I'M NOT DUMB.

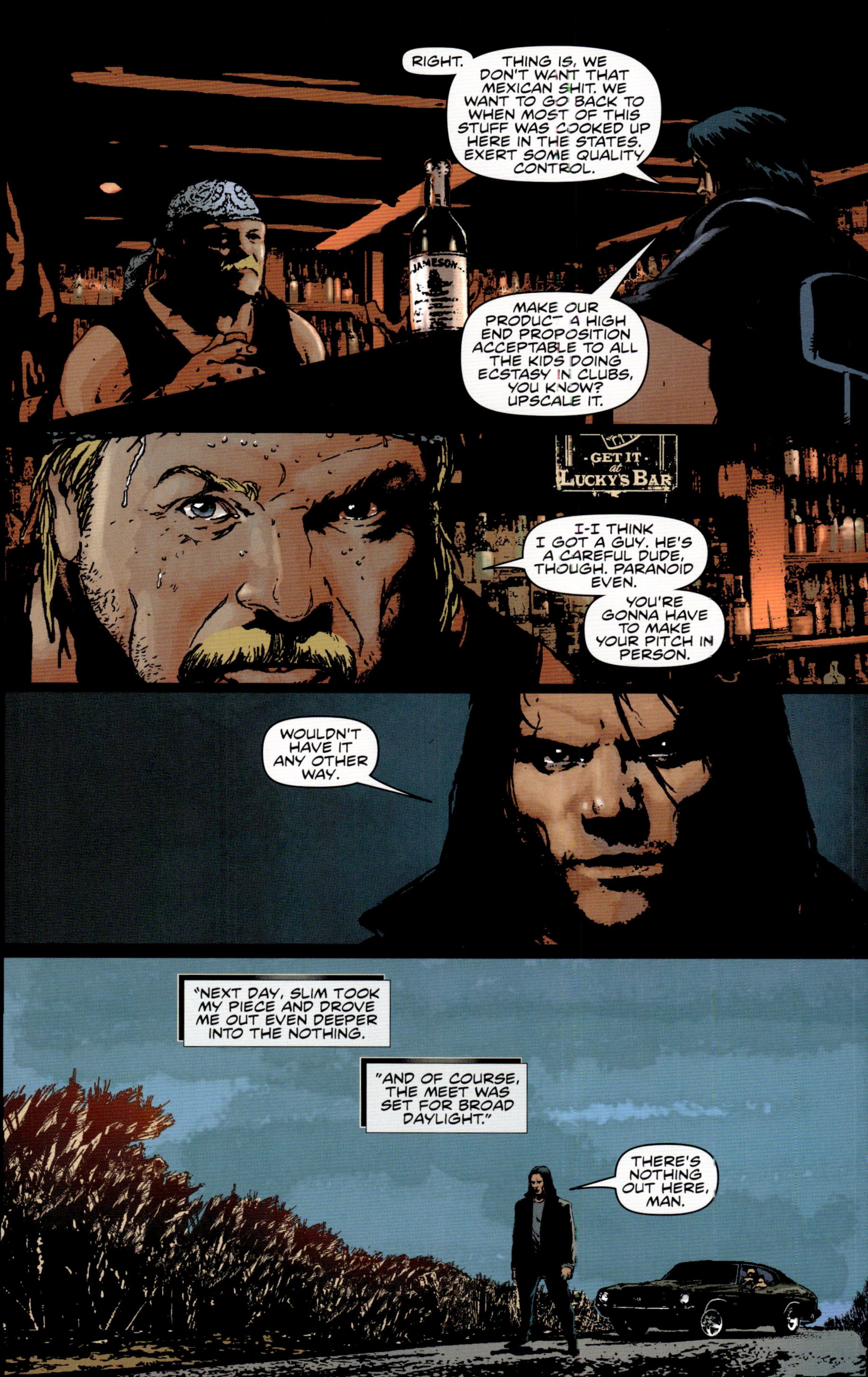
RIGHT.
THING IS, WE DON'T WANT THAT MEXICAN SHIT. WE WANT TO GO BACK TO WHEN MOST OF THIS STUFF WAS COOKED UP HERE IN THE STATES. EXERT SOME QUALITY CONTROL.
JAMESON
MAKE OUR PRODUCT A HIGH END PROPOSITION ACCEPTABLE TO ALL THE KIDS DOING ECSTASY IN CLUBS, YOU KNOW? UPSCALE IT.
GET IT at LUCKY'S BAR
I-I THINK I GOT A GUY. HE'S A CAREFUL DUDE, THOUGH. PARANOID EVEN.
YOU'RE GONNA HAVE TO MAKE YOUR PITCH IN PERSON.
WOULDN'T HAVE IT ANY OTHER WAY.
"NEXT DAY, SLIM TOOK MY PIECE AND DROVE ME OUT EVEN DEEPER INTO THE NOTHING.
"AND OF COURSE, THE MEET WAS SET FOR BROAD DAYLIGHT."
THERE'S NOTHING OUT HERE, MAN.

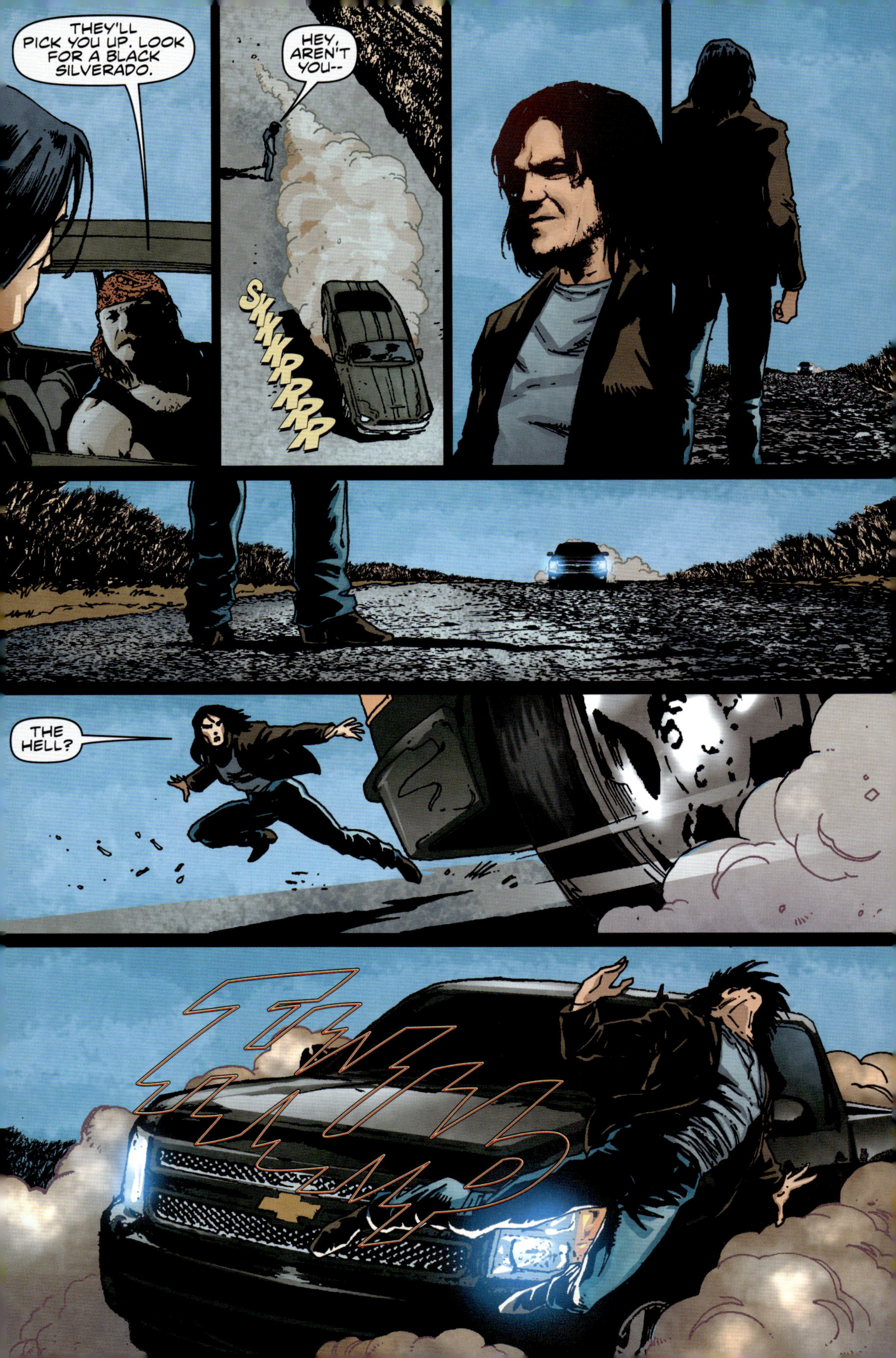
THEY'LL PICK YOU UP. LOOK FOR A BLACK SILVERADO.
HEY, AREN'T YOU--
SKKKRRRR
THE HELL?
THUMP

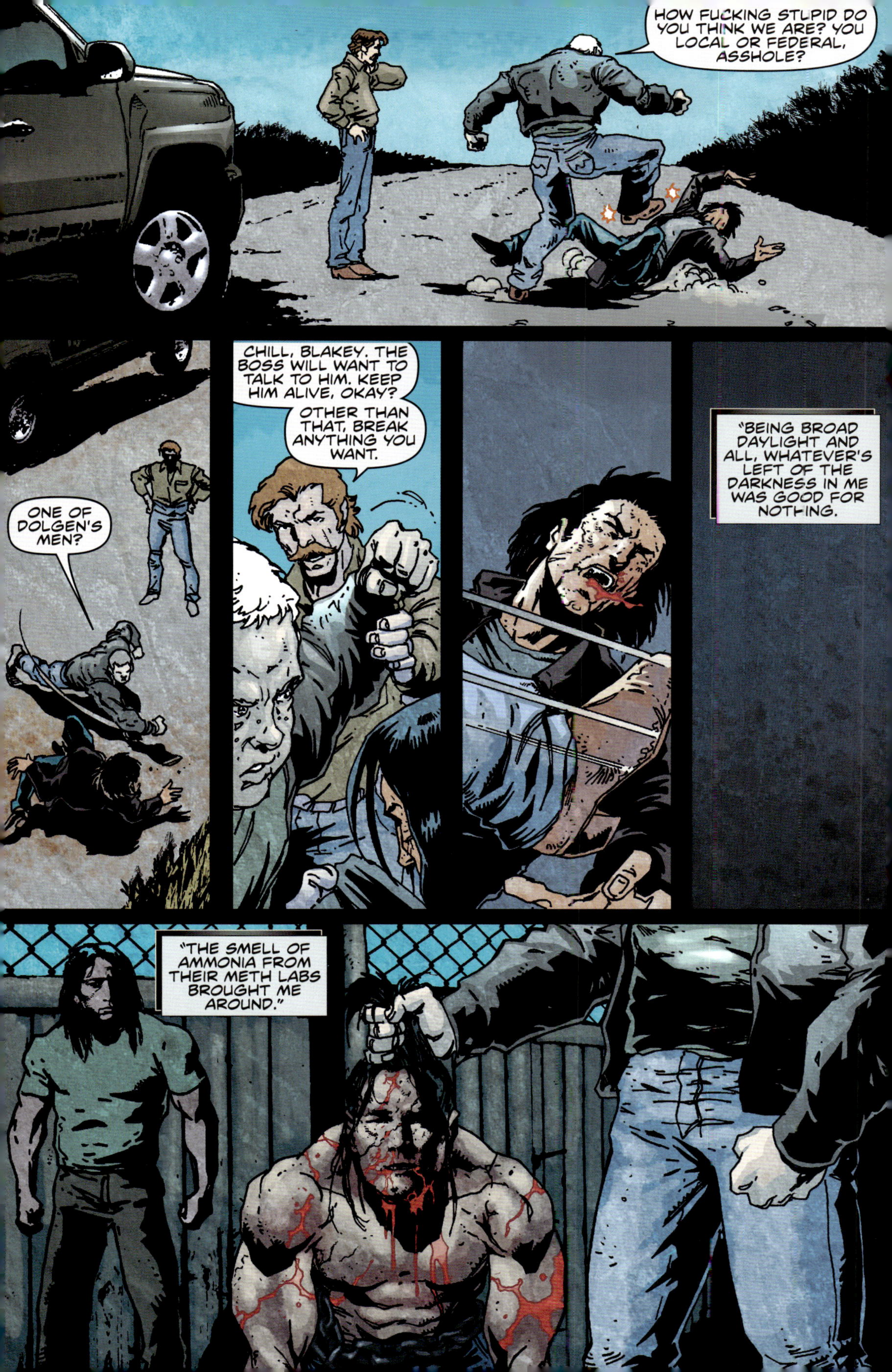
HOW FUCKING STUPID DO YOU THINK WE ARE? YOU LOCAL OR FEDERAL, ASSHOLE?
ONE OF DOLGEN'S MEN?
CHILL, BLAKEY. THE BOSS WILL WANT TO TALK TO HIM. KEEP HIM ALIVE, OKAY?
OTHER THAN THAT, BREAK ANYTHING YOU WANT.
"BEING BROAD DAYLIGHT AND ALL, WHATEVER'S LEFT OF THE DARKNESS IN ME WAS GOOD FOR NOTHING.
"THE SMELL OF AMMONIA FROM THEIR METH LABS BROUGHT ME AROUND."

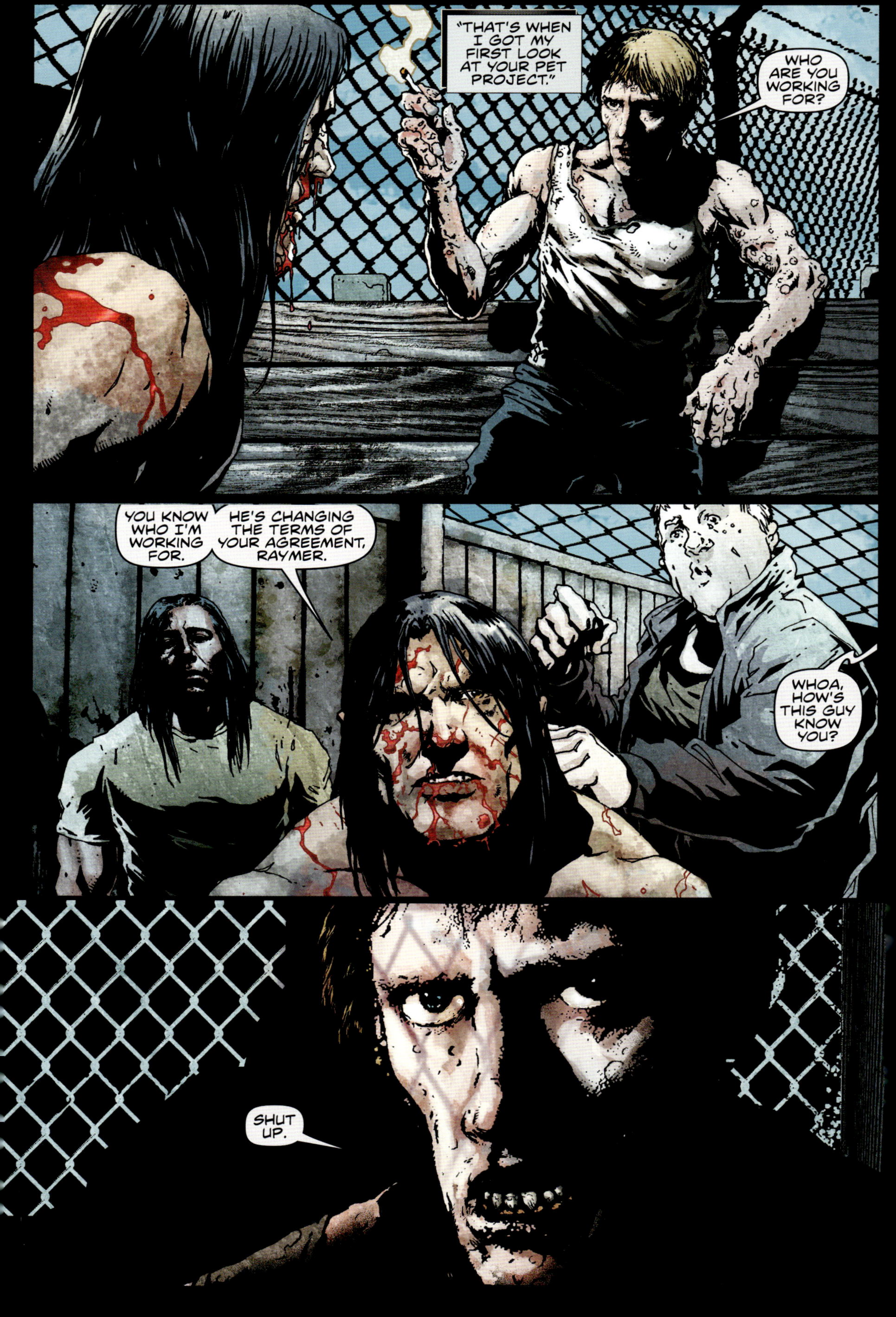
"THAT'S WHEN I GOT MY FIRST LOOK AT YOUR PET PROJECT."
WHO ARE YOU WORKING FOR?
YOU KNOW WHO I'M WORKING FOR.
HE'S CHANGING THE TERMS OF YOUR AGREEMENT, RAYMER.
WHOA, HOW'S THIS GUY KNOW YOU?
SHUT UP.

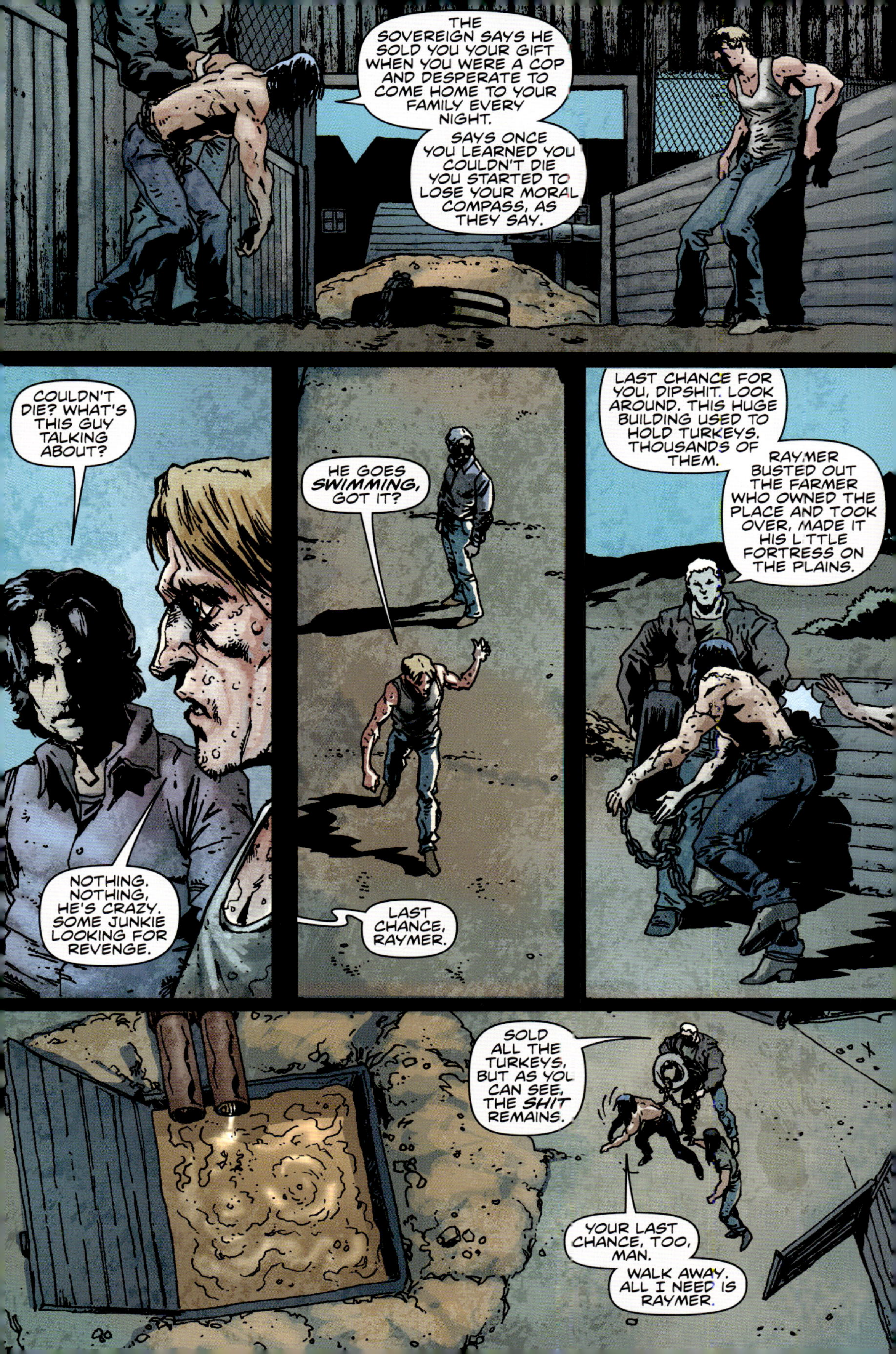
THE SOVEREIGN SAYS HE SOLD YOU YOUR GIFT WHEN YOU WERE A COP AND DESPERATE TO COME HOME TO YOUR FAMILY EVERY NIGHT.
SAYS ONCE YOU LEARNED YOU COULDN'T DIE YOU STARTED TO LOSE YOUR MORAL COMPASS, AS THEY SAY.
COULDN'T DIE? WHAT'S THIS GUY TALKING ABOUT?
NOTHING. NOTHING. HE'S CRAZY. SOME JUNKIE LOOKING FOR REVENGE.
HE GOES *SWIMMING*, GOT IT?
LAST CHANCE, RAYMER.
LAST CHANCE FOR YOU, DIPSHIT. LOOK AROUND. THIS HUGE BUILDING USED TO HOLD TURKEYS. THOUSANDS OF THEM.
RAYMER BUSTED OUT THE FARMER WHO OWNED THE PLACE AND TOOK OVER, MADE IT HIS LITTLE FORTRESS ON THE PLAINS.
SOLD ALL THE TURKEYS, BUT AS YOU CAN SEE, THE *SHIT* REMAINS.
YOUR LAST CHANCE, TOO, MAN.
WALK AWAY. ALL I NEED IS RAYMER.

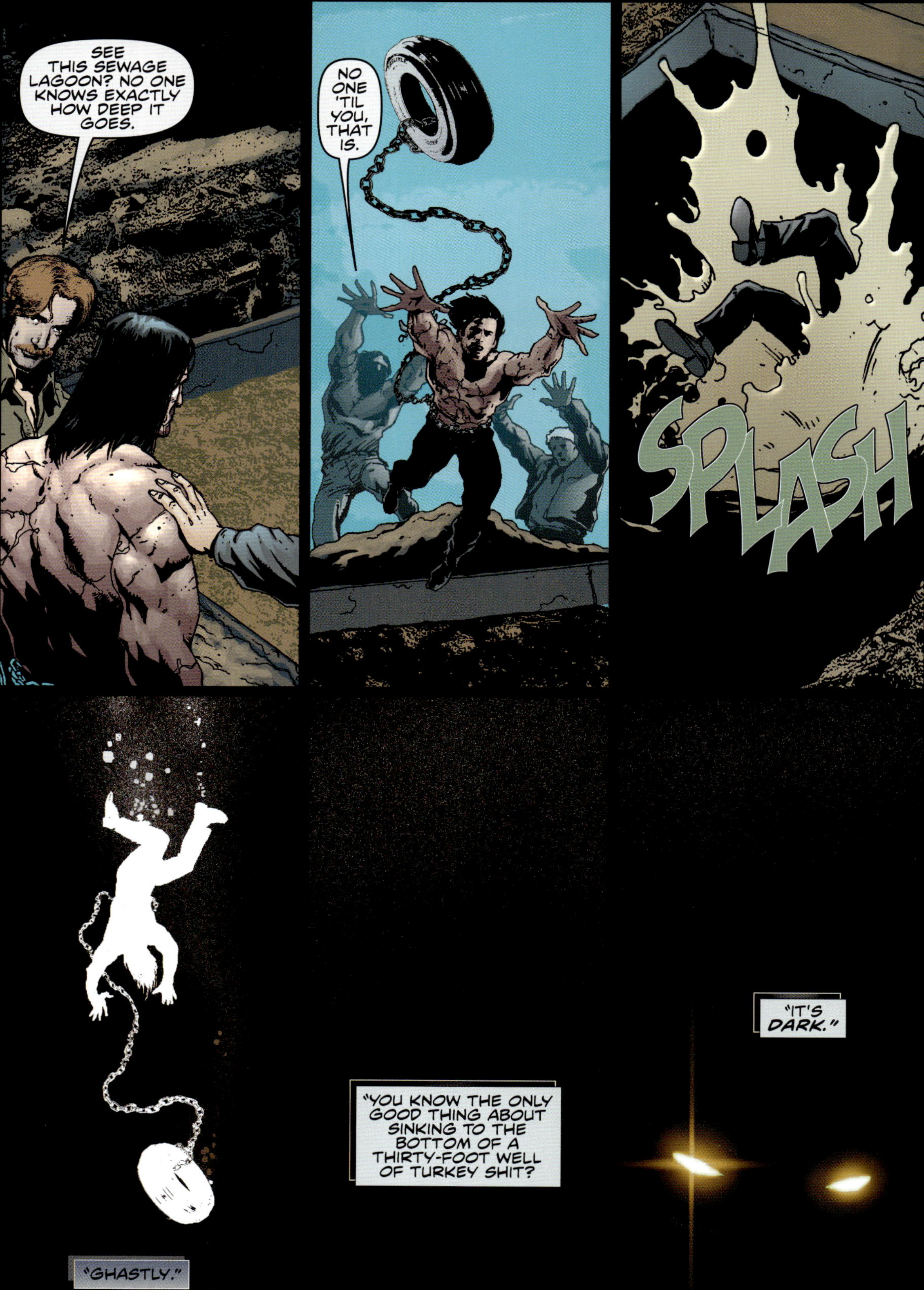

SEE THIS SEWAGE LAGOON? NO ONE KNOWS EXACTLY HOW DEEP IT GOES.
NO ONE 'TIL YOU, THAT IS.
SPLASH
"GHASTLY."
"YOU KNOW THE ONLY GOOD THING ABOUT SINKING TO THE BOTTOM OF A THIRTY-FOOT WELL OF TURKEY SHIT?
"IT'S DARK."

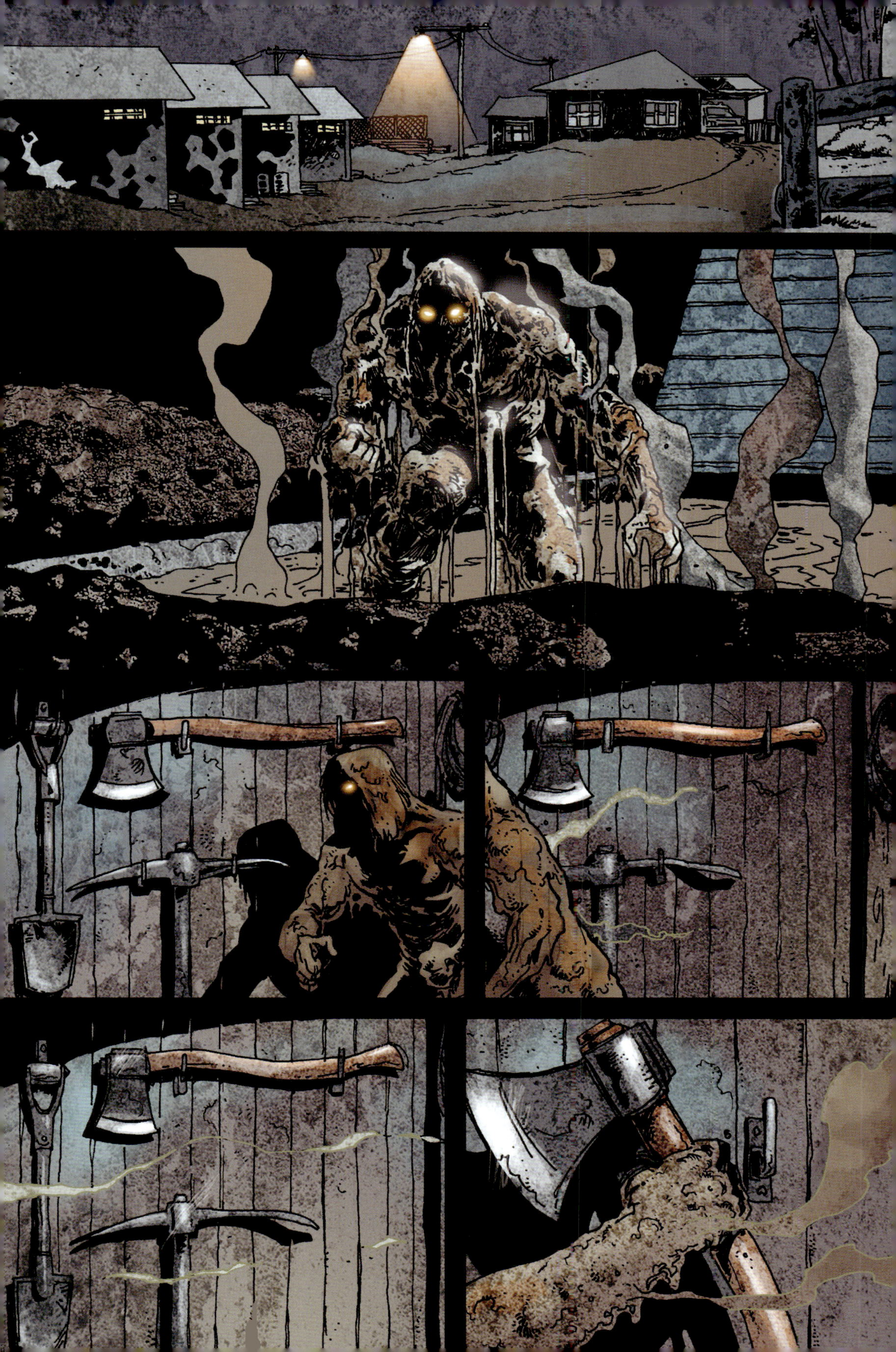

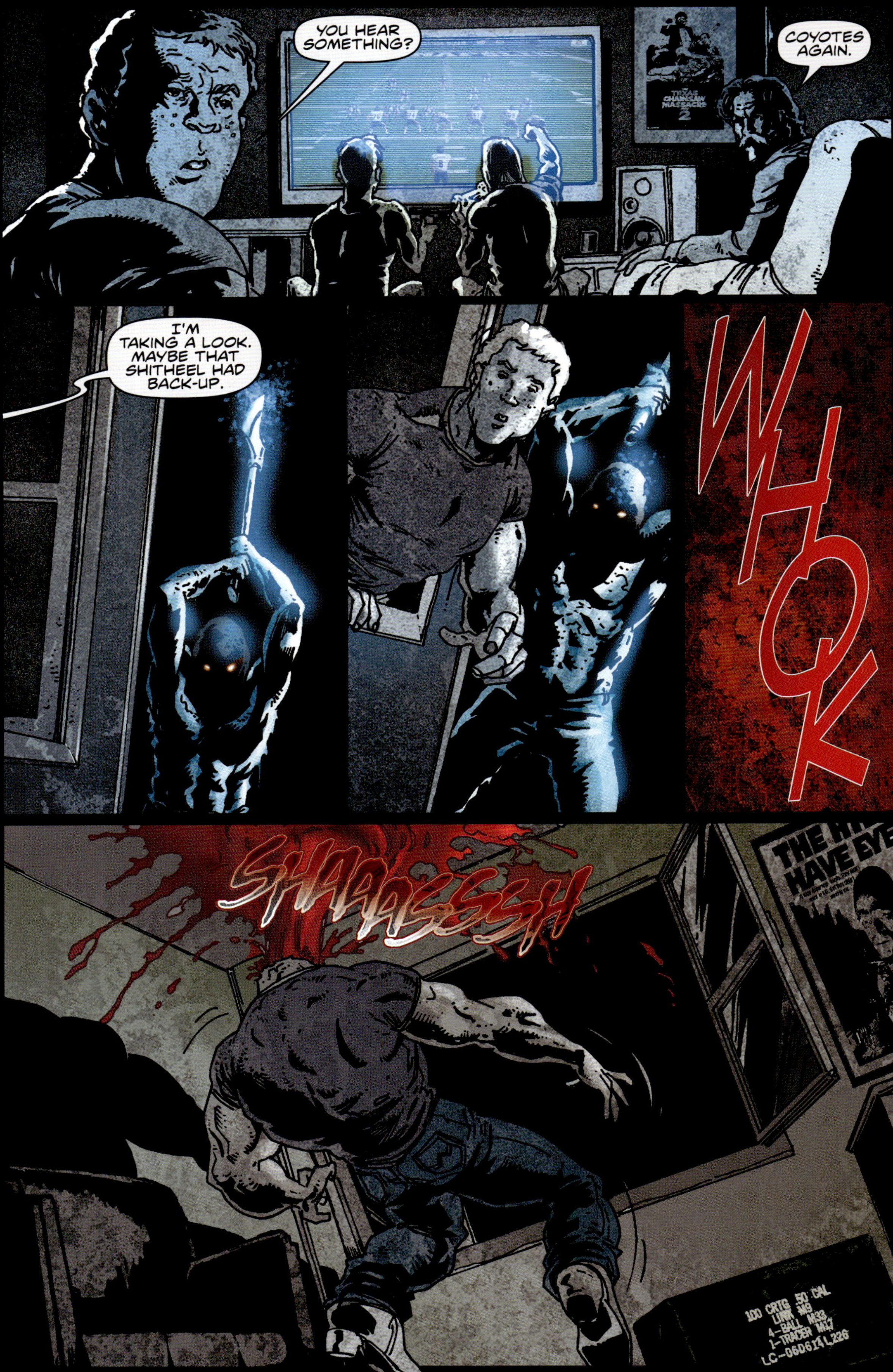
YOU HEAR SOMETHING?
COYOTES AGAIN.
THE TEXAS CHAINSAW MASSACRE 2
I'M TAKING A LOOK. MAYBE THAT SHITHEEL HAD BACK-UP.
WHOK
SHAAASSSH
THE HILLS HAVE EYES
100 CRTG .50 CAL
LINK M9
4-BALL M33
1-TRACER M17
LC-06G614L226

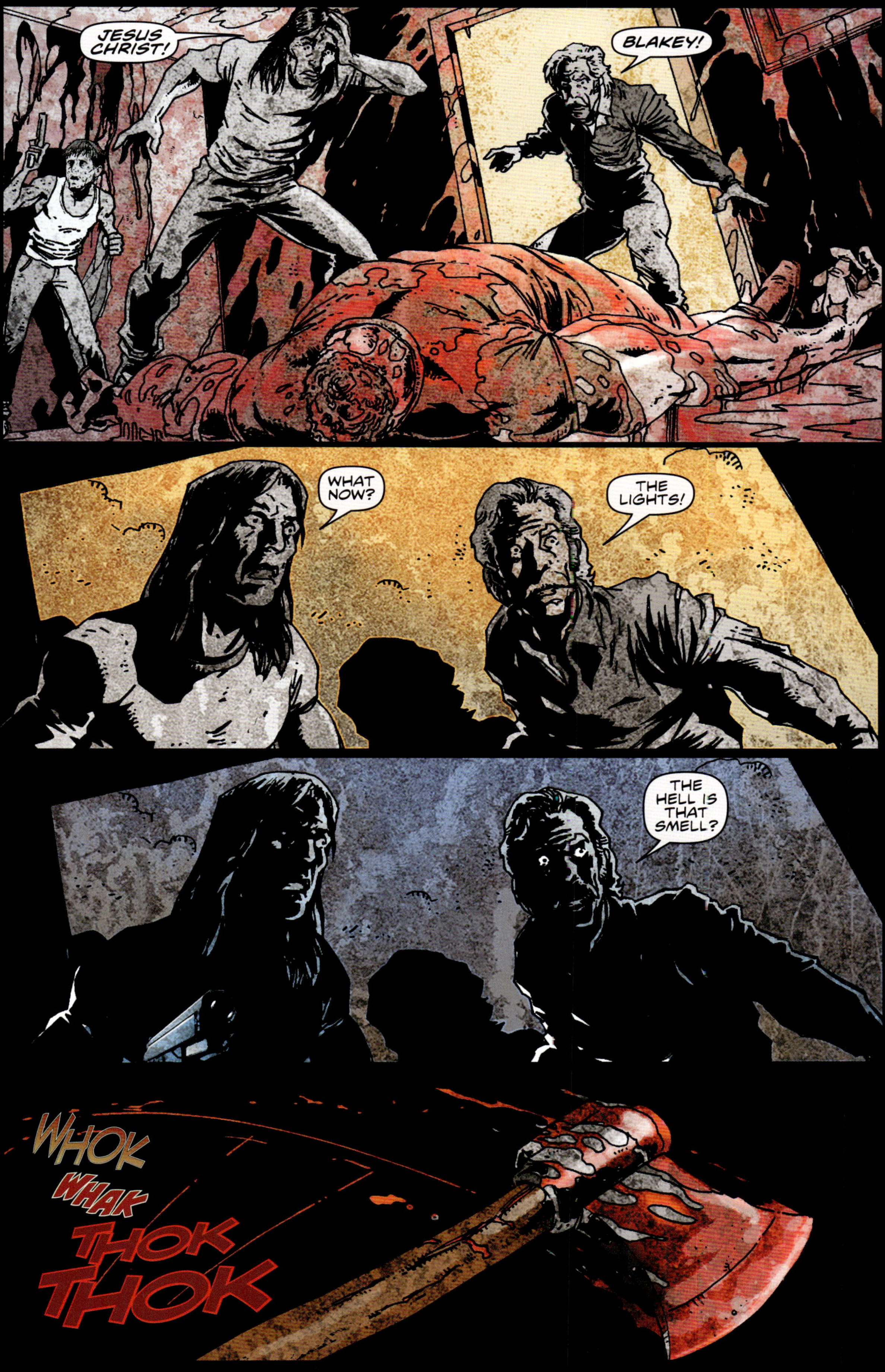
JESUS CHRIST!
BLAKEY!
WHAT NOW?
THE LIGHTS!
THE HELL IS THAT SMELL?
WHOK
WHAK
THOK
THOK

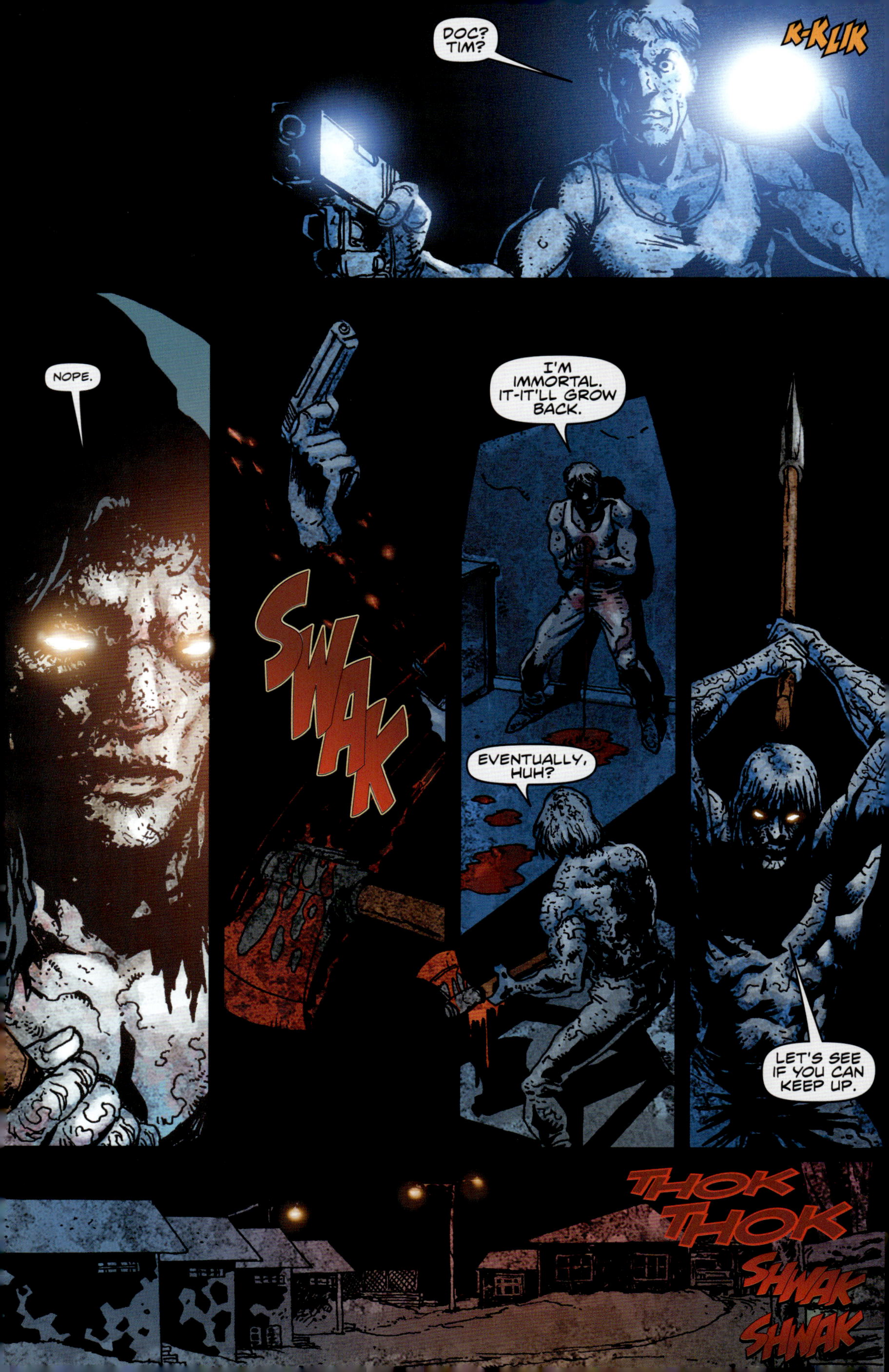
DOC? TIM?
K-KLIK
NOPE.
SWAK
I'M IMMORTAL. IT-IT'LL GROW BACK.
EVENTUALLY, HUH?
LET'S SEE IF YOU CAN KEEP UP.
THOK THOK
SHWAK SHWAK

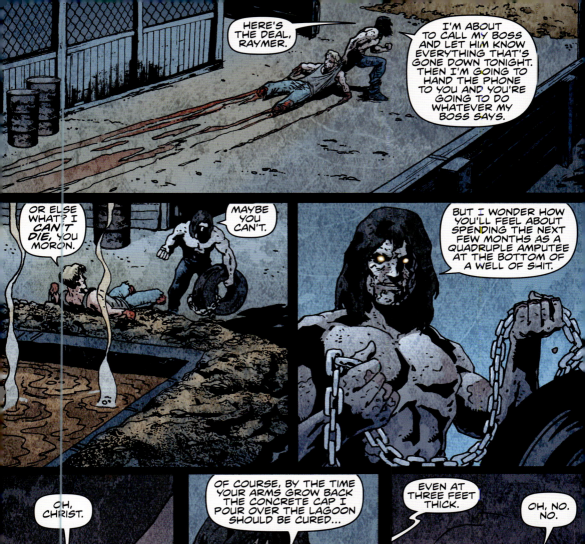

HERE'S THE DEAL, RAYMER.

I'M ABOUT TO CALL MY BOSS AND LET HIM KNOW EVERYTHING THAT'S GONE DOWN TONIGHT. THEN I'M GOING TO HAND THE PHONE TO YOU AND YOU'RE GOING TO DO WHATEVER MY BOSS SAYS.

OR ELSE WHAT? I CAN'T DIE, YOU MORON.

MAYBE YOU CAN'T.

BUT I WONDER HOW YOU'LL FEEL ABOUT SPENDING THE NEXT FEW MONTHS AS A QUADRUPLE AMPUTEE AT THE BOTTOM OF A WELL OF SHIT.

OH, CHRIST.

OF COURSE, BY THE TIME YOUR ARMS GROW BACK THE CONCRETE CAP I POUR OVER THE LAGOON SHOULD BE CURED...

EVEN AT THREE FEET THICK.

OH, NO. NO.

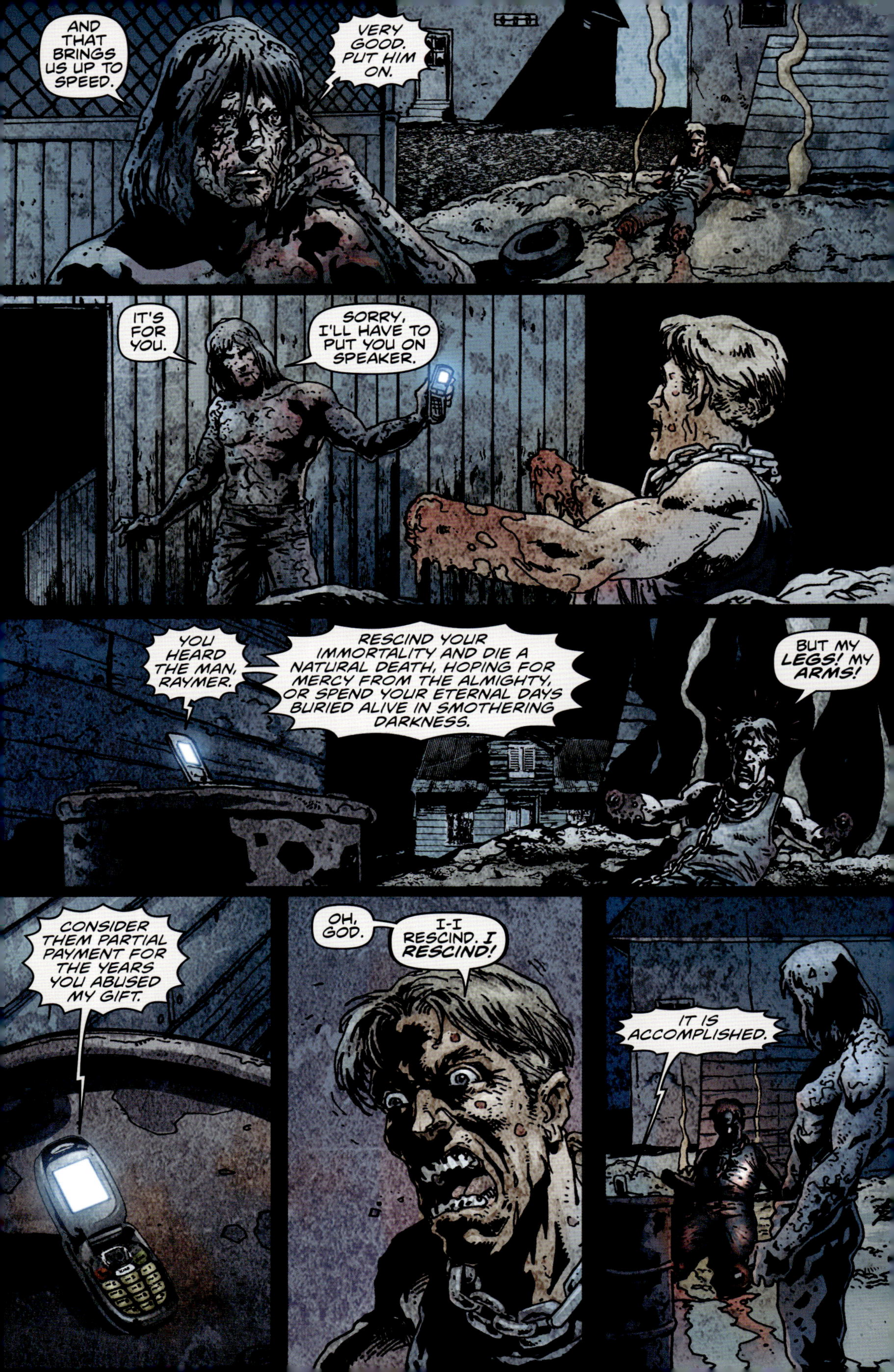

AND THAT BRINGS US UP TO SPEED.
VERY GOOD. PUT HIM ON.
IT'S FOR YOU.
SORRY, I'LL HAVE TO PUT YOU ON SPEAKER.
YOU HEARD THE MAN, RAYMER.
RESCIND YOUR IMMORTALITY AND DIE A NATURAL DEATH, HOPING FOR MERCY FROM THE ALMIGHTY, OR SPEND YOUR ETERNAL DAYS BURIED ALIVE IN SMOTHERING DARKNESS.
BUT MY LEGS! MY ARMS!
CONSIDER THEM PARTIAL PAYMENT FOR THE YEARS YOU ABUSED MY GIFT.
OH, GOD.
I-I RESCIND. I RESCIND!
IT IS ACCOMPLISHED.

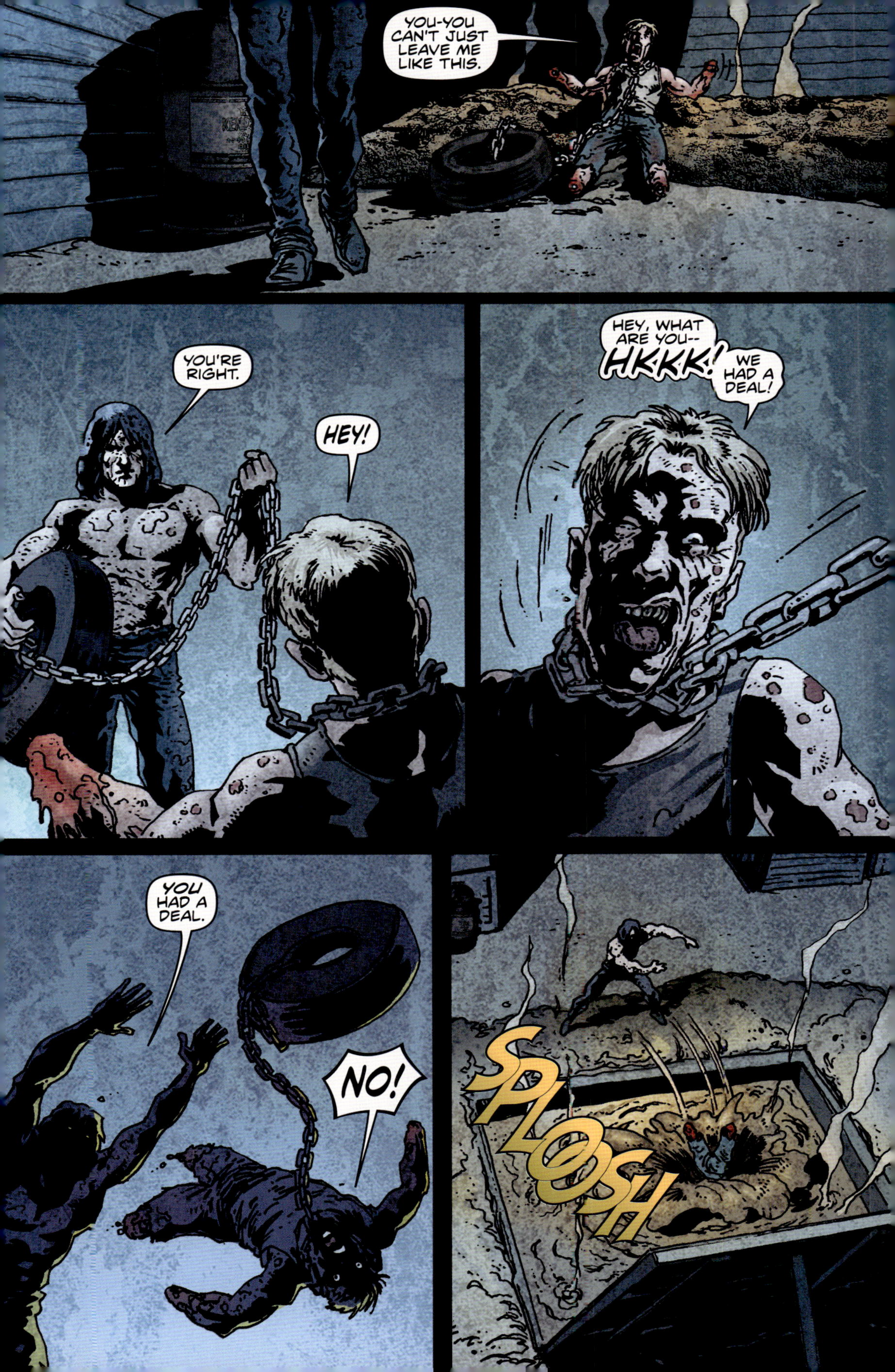
YOU-YOU CAN'T JUST LEAVE ME LIKE THIS.
YOU'RE RIGHT.
HEY!
HEY, WHAT ARE YOU--
HKKK!
WE HAD A DEAL!
YOU HAD A DEAL.
NO!
SPLOSH

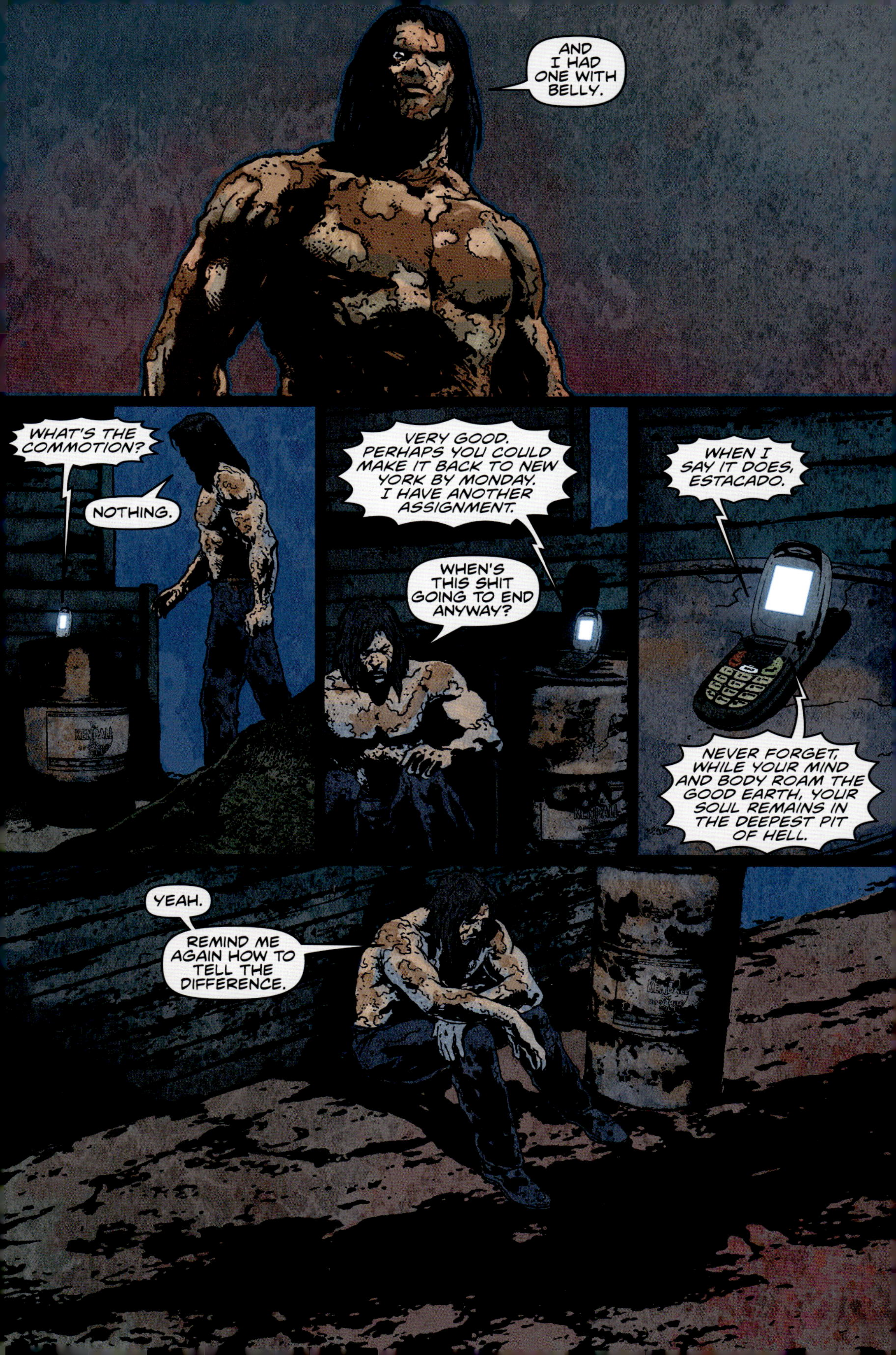
AND I HAD ONE WITH BELLY.
WHAT'S THE COMMOTION?
NOTHING.
VERY GOOD. PERHAPS YOU COULD MAKE IT BACK TO NEW YORK BY MONDAY. I HAVE ANOTHER ASSIGNMENT.
WHEN'S THIS SHIT GOING TO END ANYWAY?
WHEN I SAY IT DOES, ESTACADO.
NEVER FORGET, WHILE YOUR MIND AND BODY ROAM THE GOOD EARTH, YOUR SOUL REMAINS IN THE DEEPEST PIT OF HELL.
YEAH.
REMIND ME AGAIN HOW TO TELL THE DIFFERENCE.

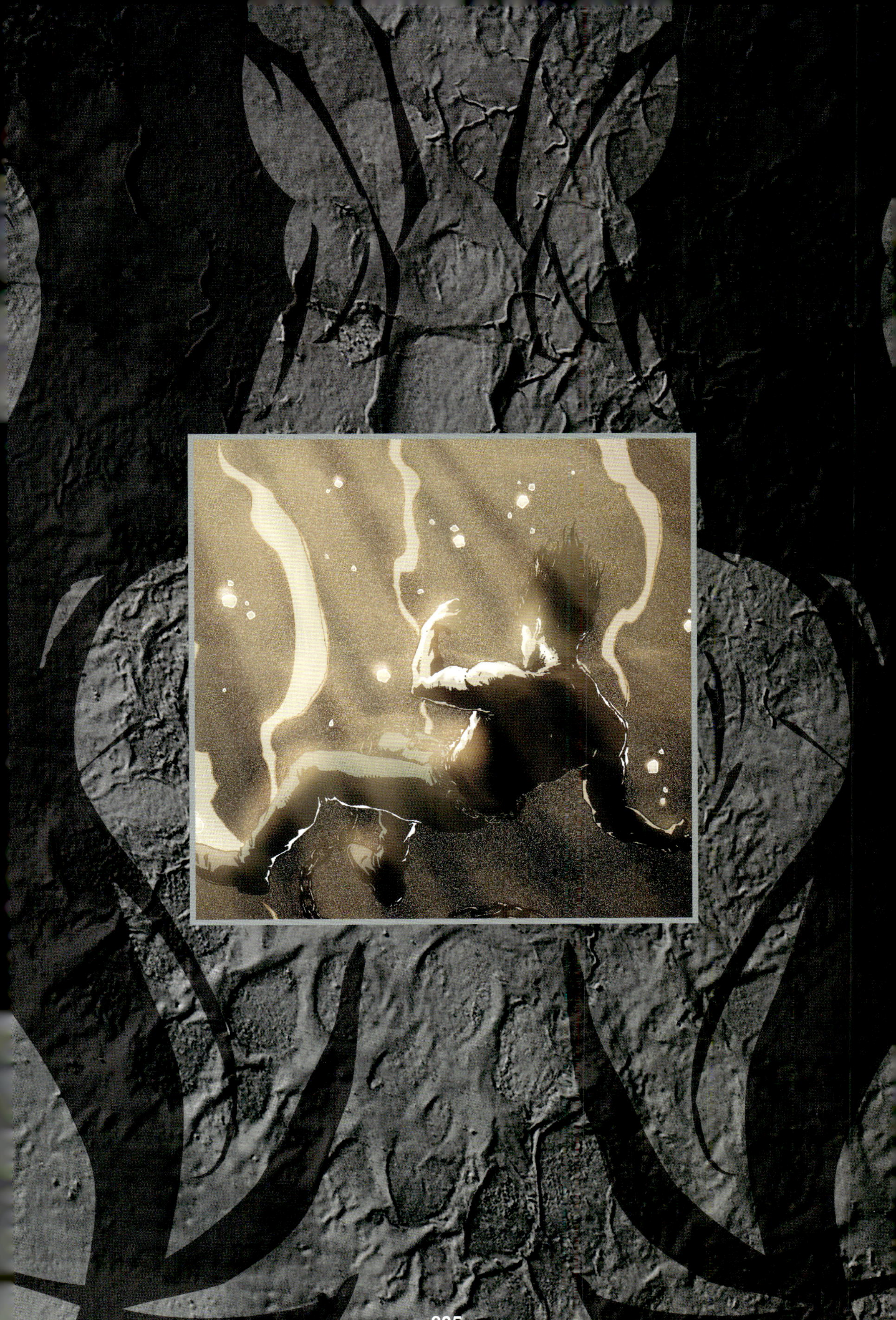

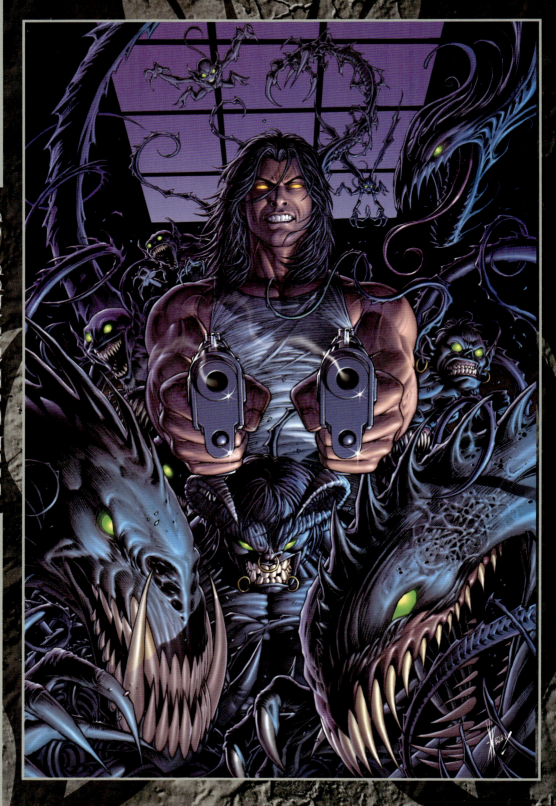

The Darkness Issue #75
cover art by: Dale Keown

THE DARKNESS #75

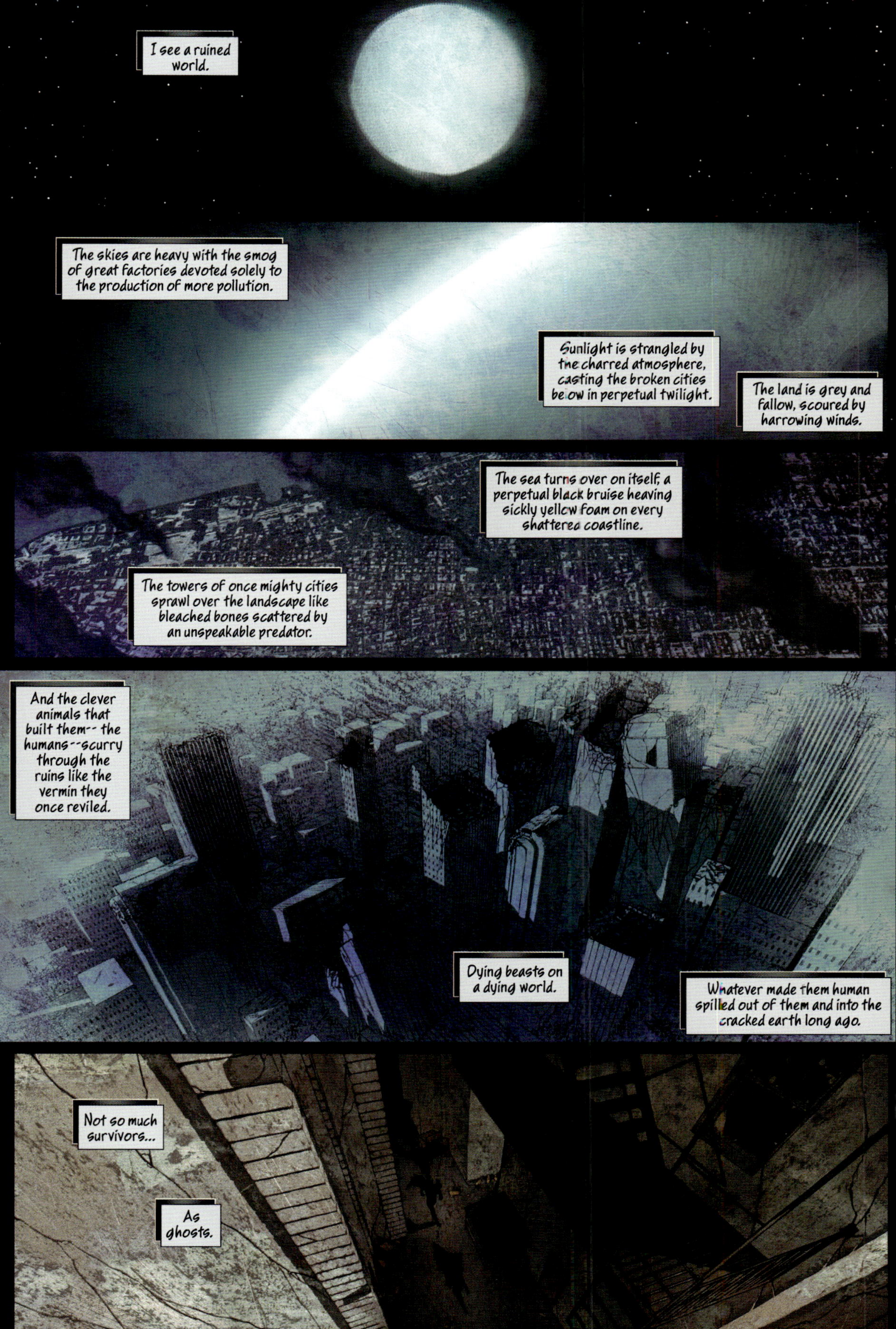
I see a ruined world.
The skies are heavy with the smog of great factories devoted solely to the production of more pollution.
Sunlight is strangled by the charred atmosphere, casting the broken cities below in perpetual twilight.
The land is grey and fallow, scoured by harrowing winds.
The sea turns over on itself, a perpetual black bruise heaving sickly yellow foam on every shattered coastline.
The towers of once mighty cities sprawl over the landscape like bleached bones scattered by an unspeakable predator.
And the clever animals that built them-- the humans--scurry through the ruins like the vermin they once reviled.
Dying beasts on a dying world.
Whatever made them human spilled out of them and into the cracked earth long ago.
Not so much survivors...
As ghosts.

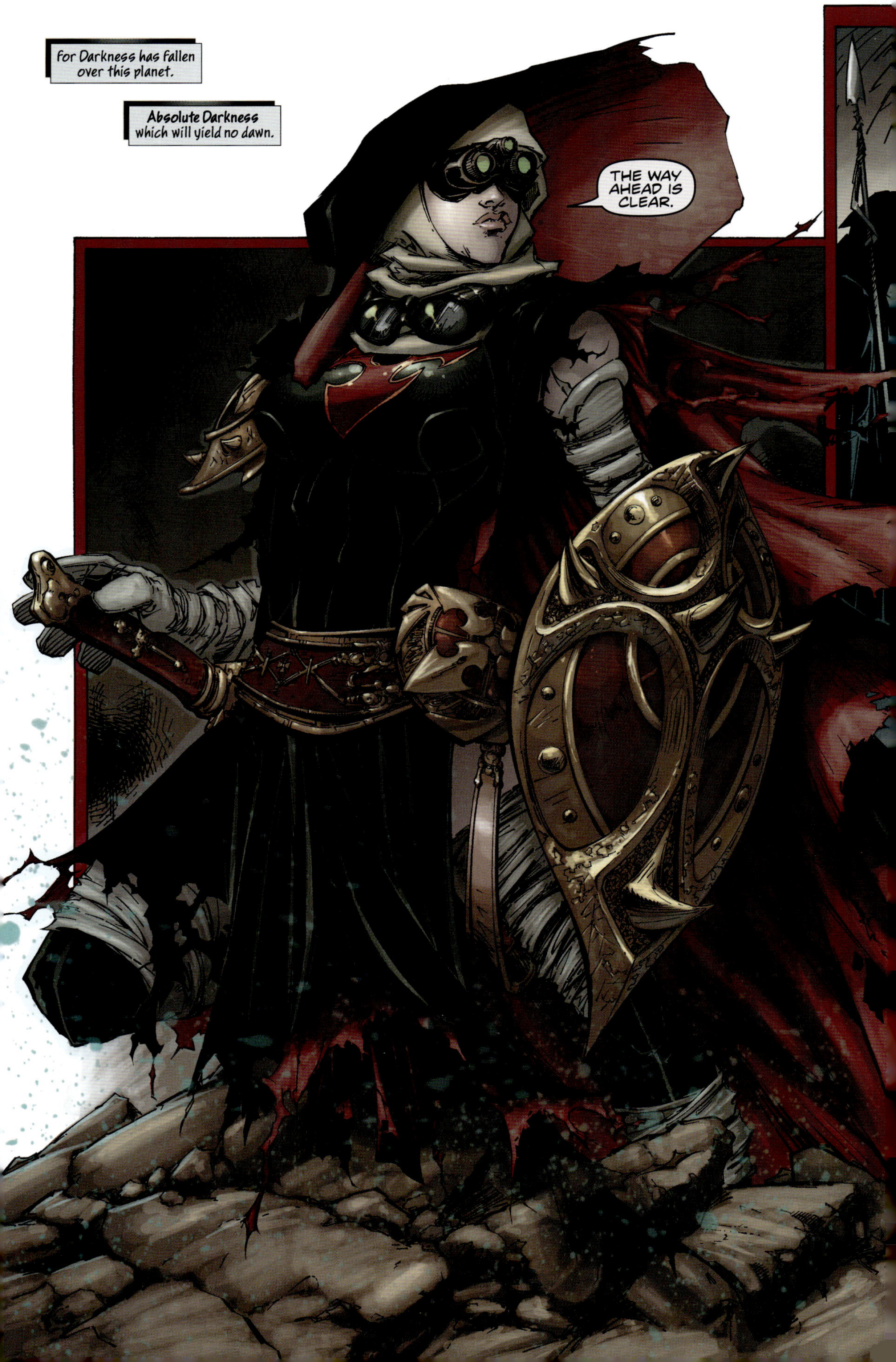
For Darkness has fallen over this planet.
Absolute Darkness which will yield no dawn.
THE WAY AHEAD IS CLEAR.

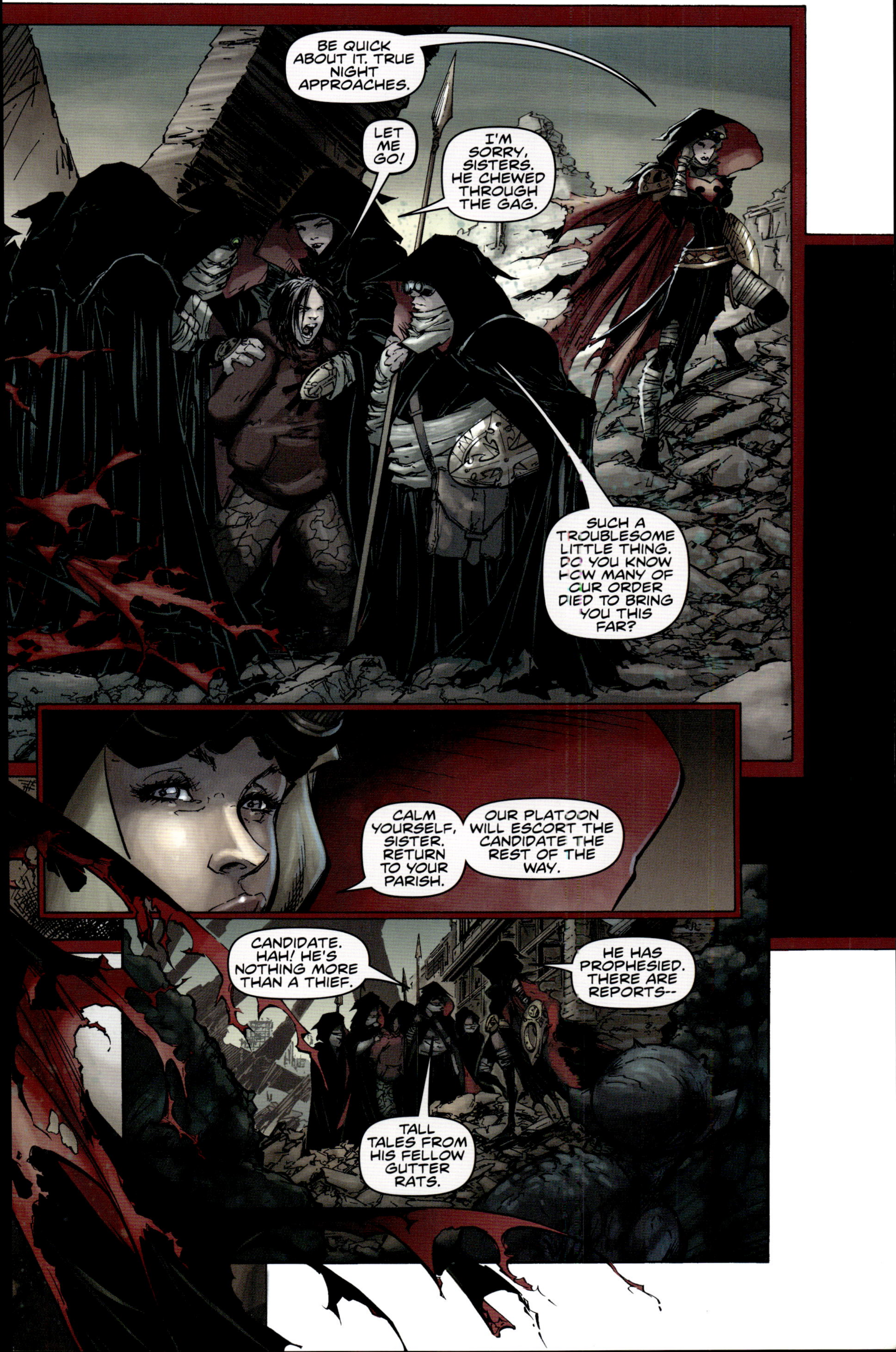
BE QUICK ABOUT IT. TRUE NIGHT APPROACHES.
LET ME GO!
I'M SORRY, SISTERS. HE CHEWED THROUGH THE GAG.
SUCH A TROUBLESOME LITTLE THING. DO YOU KNOW HOW MANY OF OUR ORDER DIED TO BRING YOU THIS FAR?
CALM YOURSELF, SISTER. RETURN TO YOUR PARISH.
OUR PLATOON WILL ESCORT THE CANDIDATE THE REST OF THE WAY.
CANDIDATE. HAH! HE'S NOTHING MORE THAN A THIEF.
HE HAS PROPHESIED. THERE ARE REPORTS--
TALL TALES FROM HIS FELLOW GUTTER RATS.

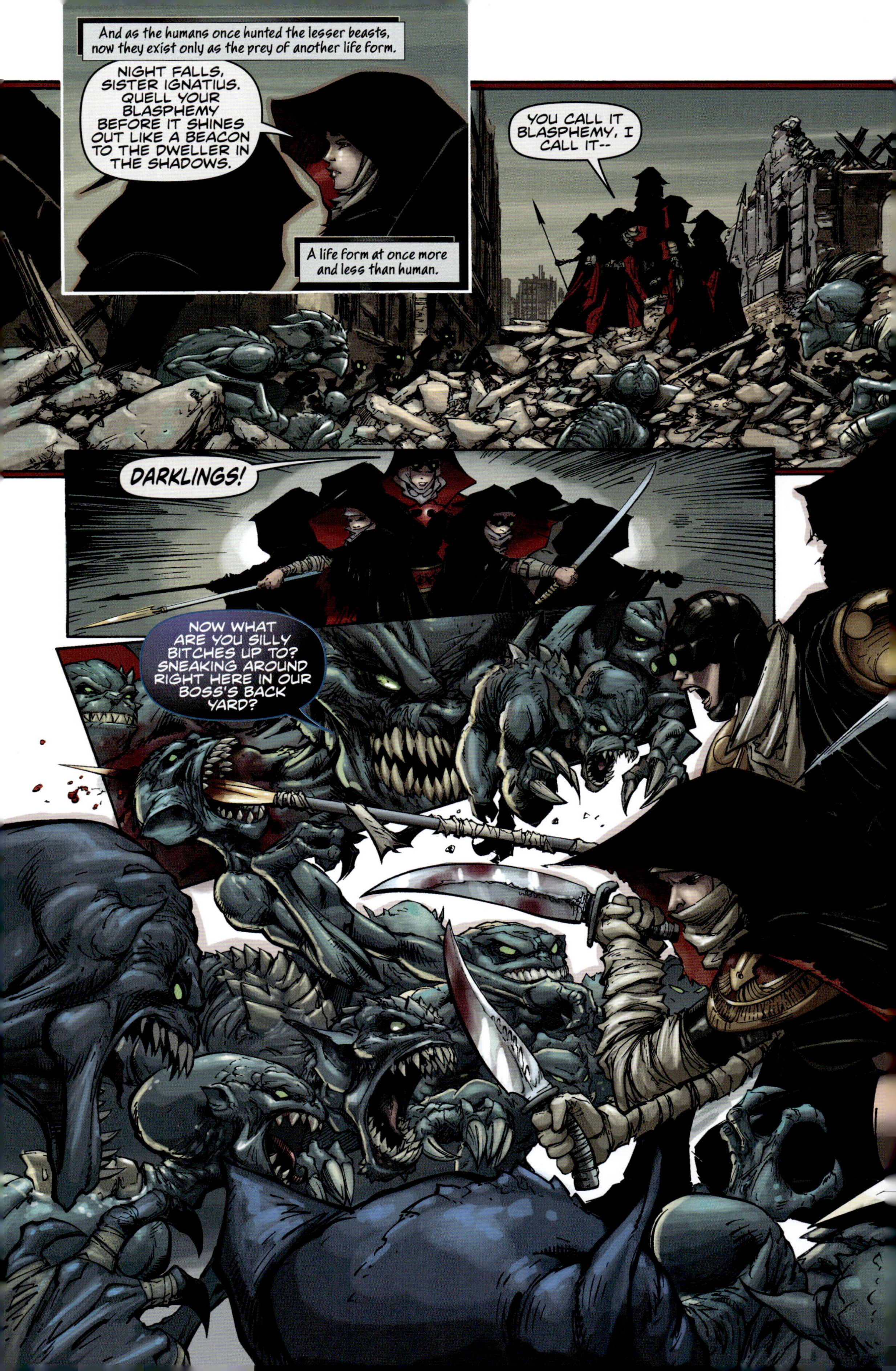
And as the humans once hunted the lesser beasts, now they exist only as the prey of another life form.
NIGHT FALLS, SISTER IGNATIUS. QUELL YOUR BLASPHEMY BEFORE IT SHINES OUT LIKE A BEACON TO THE DWELLER IN THE SHADOWS.
A life form at once more and less than human.
YOU CALL IT BLASPHEMY, I CALL IT--
DARKLINGS!
NOW WHAT ARE YOU SILLY BITCHES UP TO? SNEAKING AROUND RIGHT HERE IN OUR BOSS'S BACK YARD?

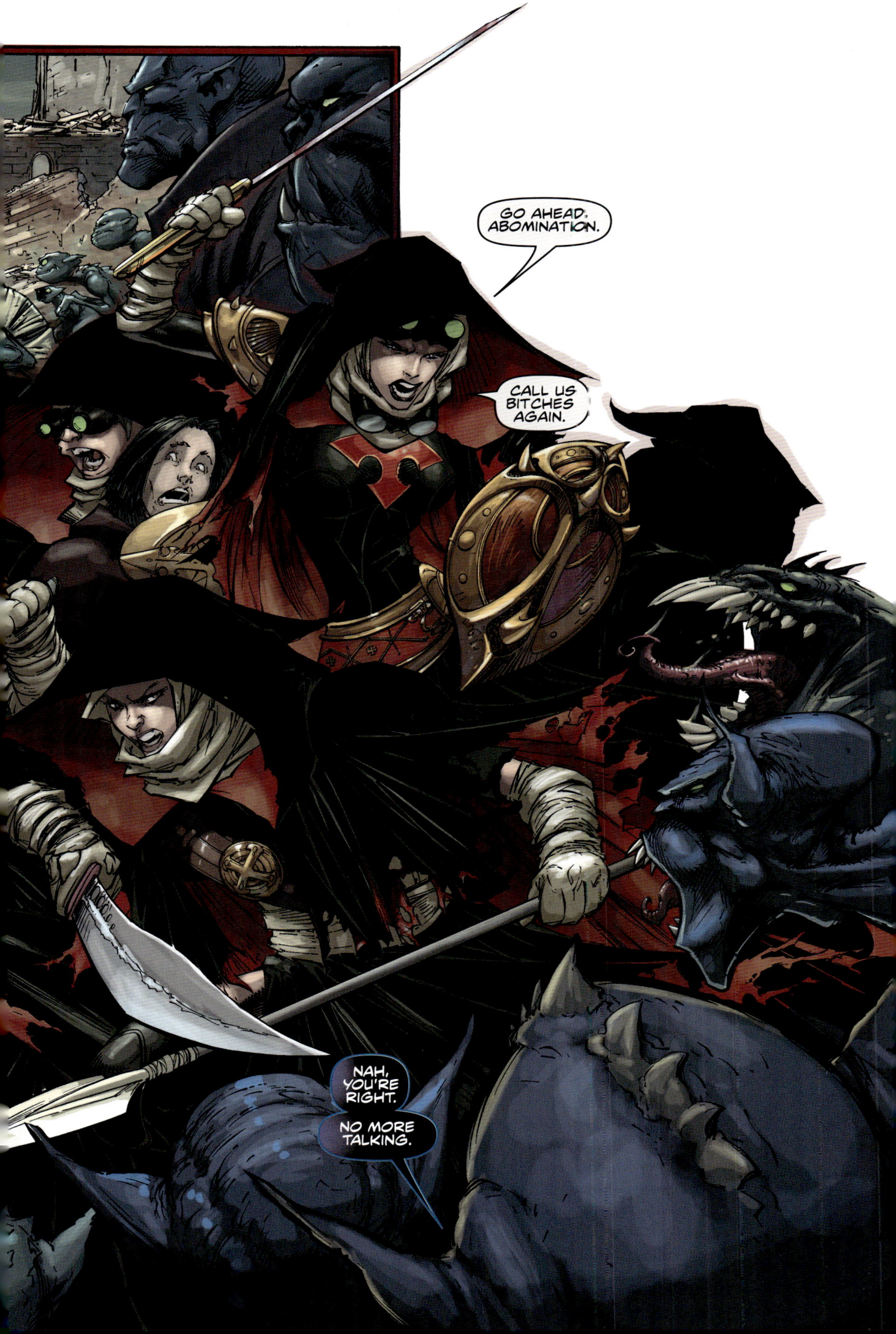
GO AHEAD, ABOMINATION.
CALL US BITCHES AGAIN.
NAH, YOU'RE RIGHT.
NO MORE TALKING.

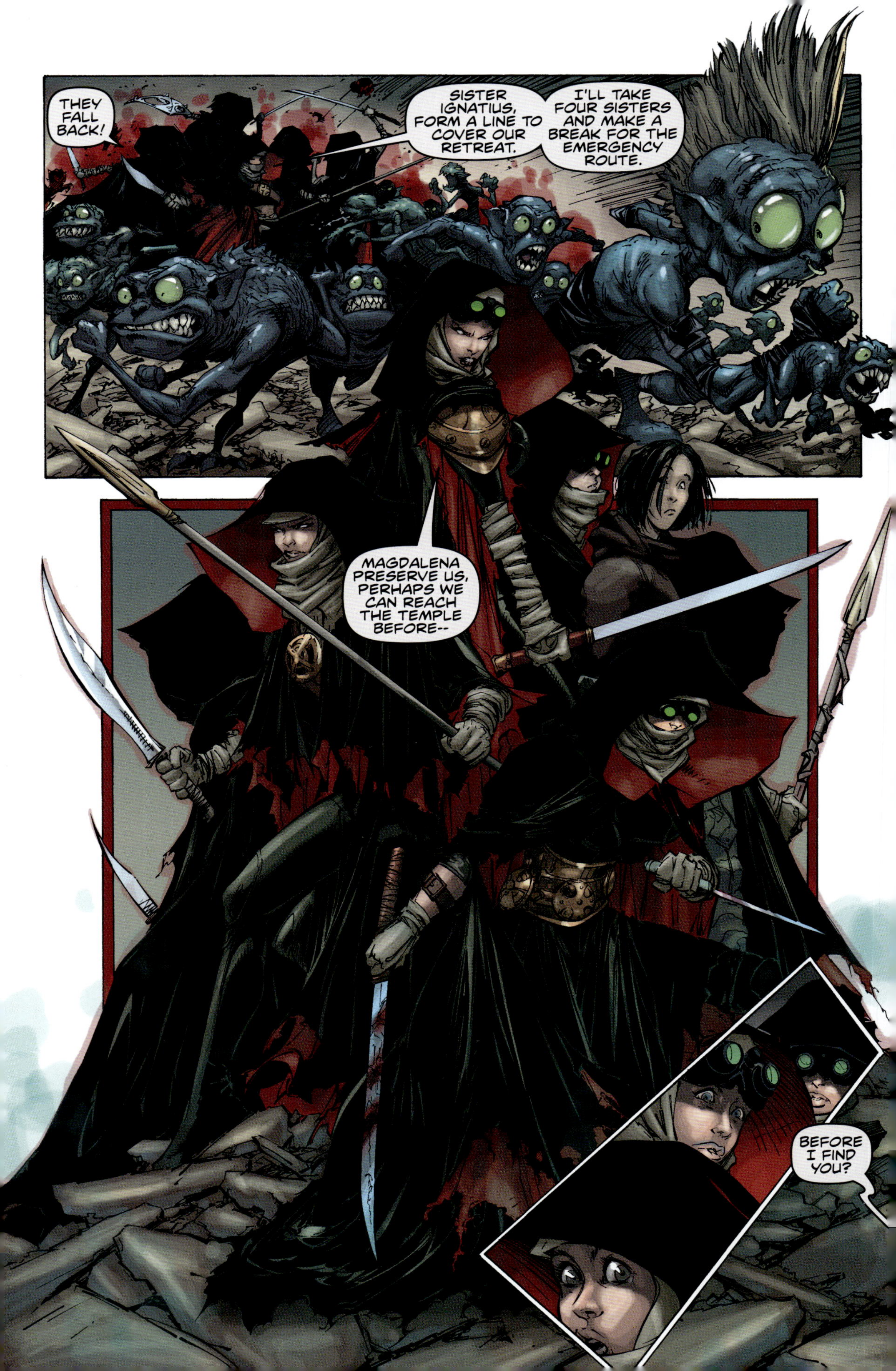
THEY FALL BACK!
SISTER IGNATIUS, FORM A LINE TO COVER OUR RETREAT.
I'LL TAKE FOUR SISTERS AND MAKE A BREAK FOR THE EMERGENCY ROUTE.
MAGDALENA PRESERVE US, PERHAPS WE CAN REACH THE TEMPLE BEFORE--
BEFORE I FIND YOU?

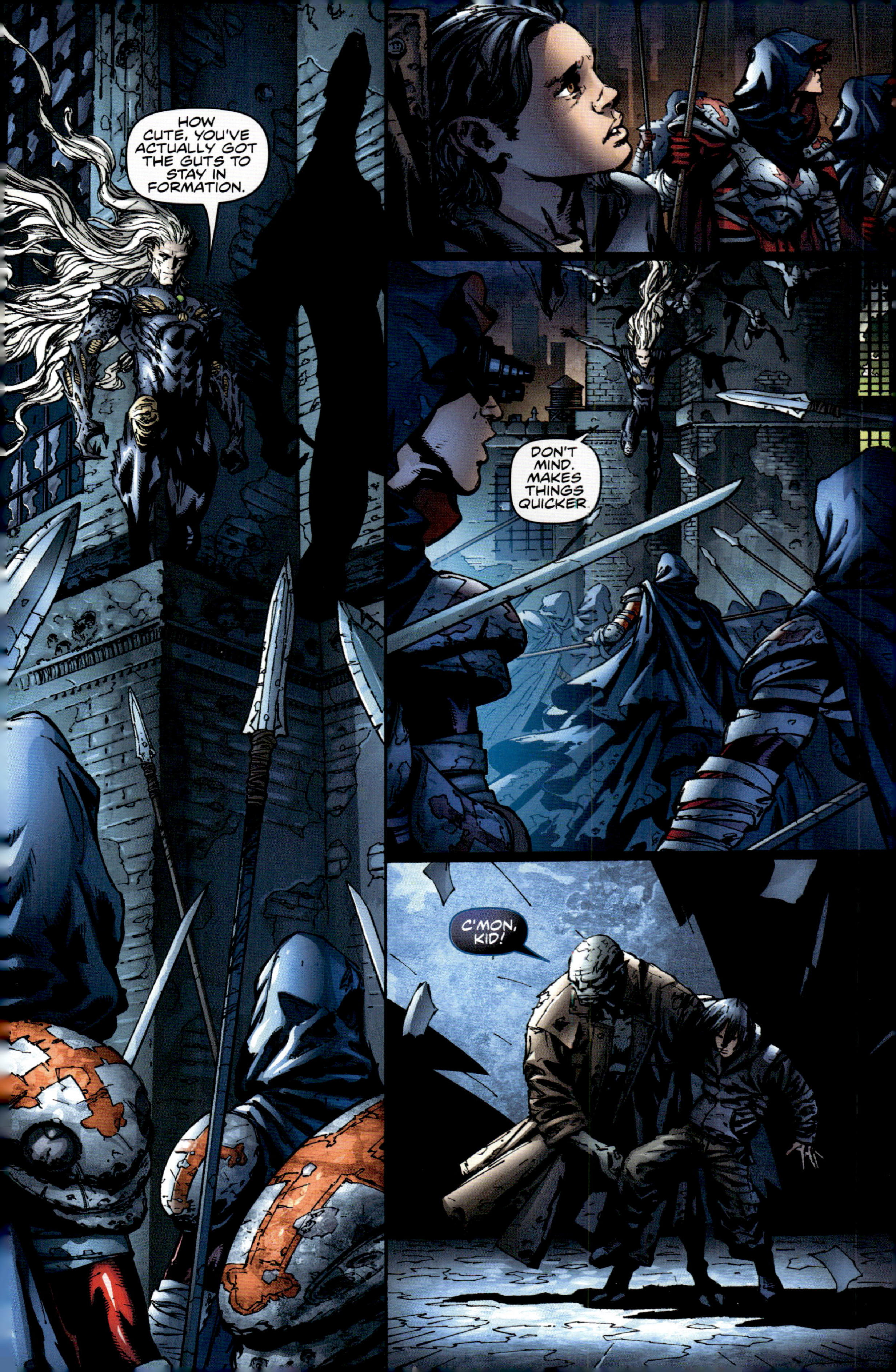

HOW CUTE, YOU'VE ACTUALLY GOT THE GUTS TO STAY IN FORMATION.
DON'T MIND. MAKES THINGS QUICKER.
C'MON, KID!

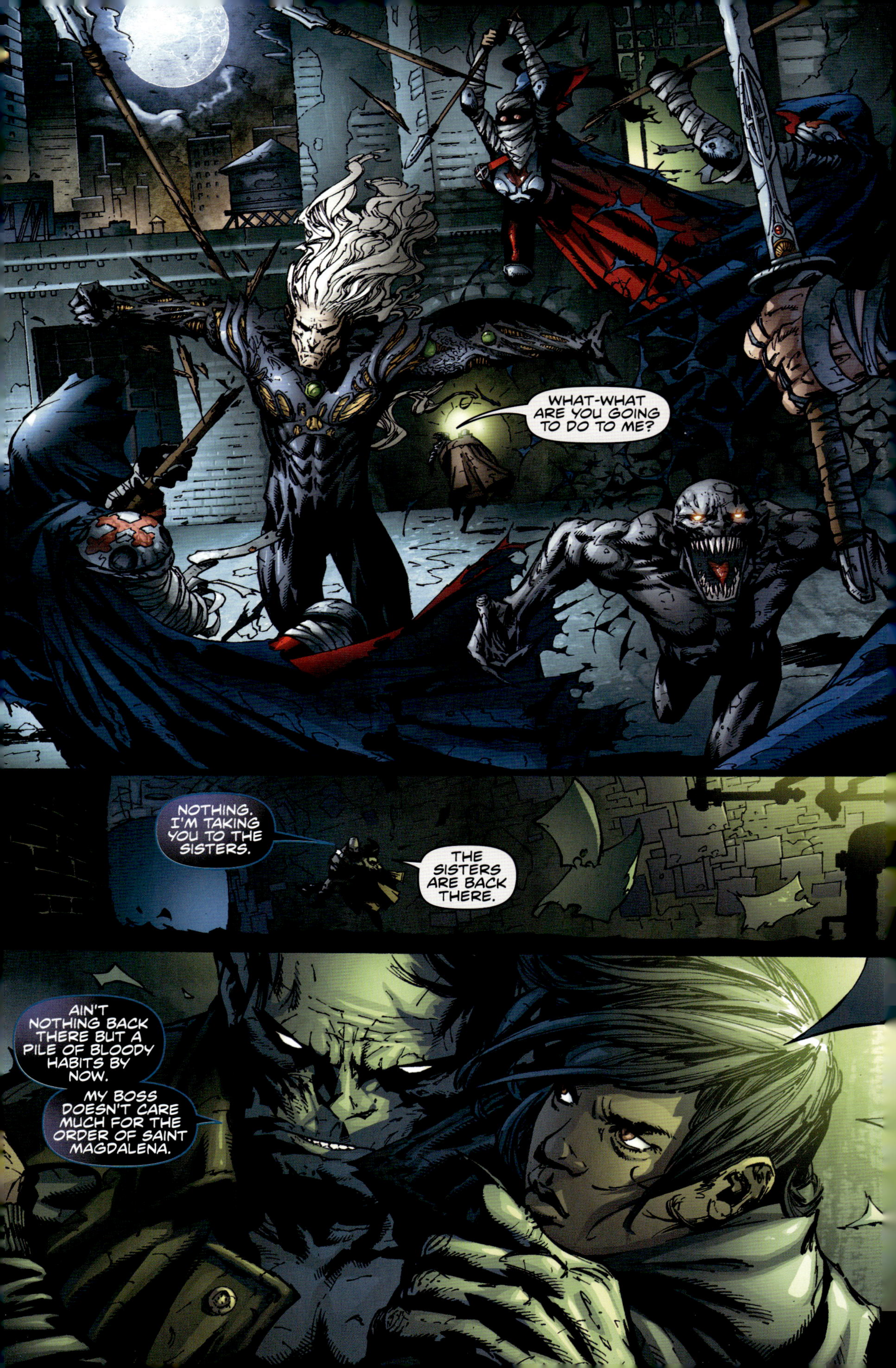
WHAT-WHAT ARE YOU GOING TO DO TO ME?
NOTHING. I'M TAKING YOU TO THE SISTERS.
THE SISTERS ARE BACK THERE.
AIN'T NOTHING BACK THERE BUT A PILE OF BLOODY HABITS BY NOW.
MY BOSS DOESN'T CARE MUCH FOR THE ORDER OF SAINT MAGDALENA.

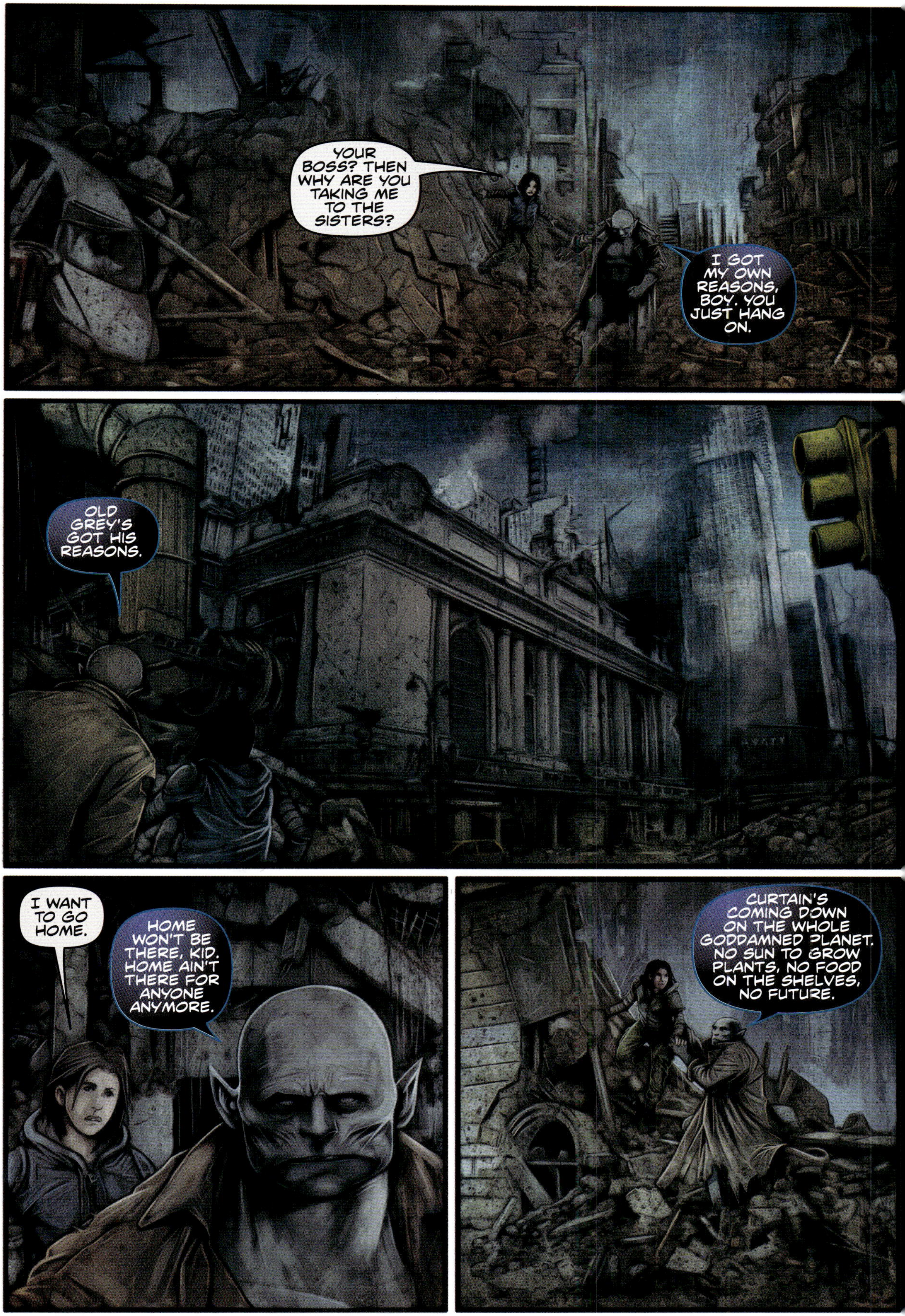
YOUR BOSS? THEN WHY ARE YOU TAKING ME TO THE SISTERS?
I GOT MY OWN REASONS, BOY. YOU JUST HANG ON.
OLD GREY'S GOT HIS REASONS.
I WANT TO GO HOME.
HOME WON'T BE THERE, KID. HOME AIN'T THERE FOR ANYONE ANYMORE.
CURTAIN'S COMING DOWN ON THE WHOLE GODDAMNED PLANET. NO SUN TO GROW PLANTS, NO FOOD ON THE SHELVES, NO FUTURE.

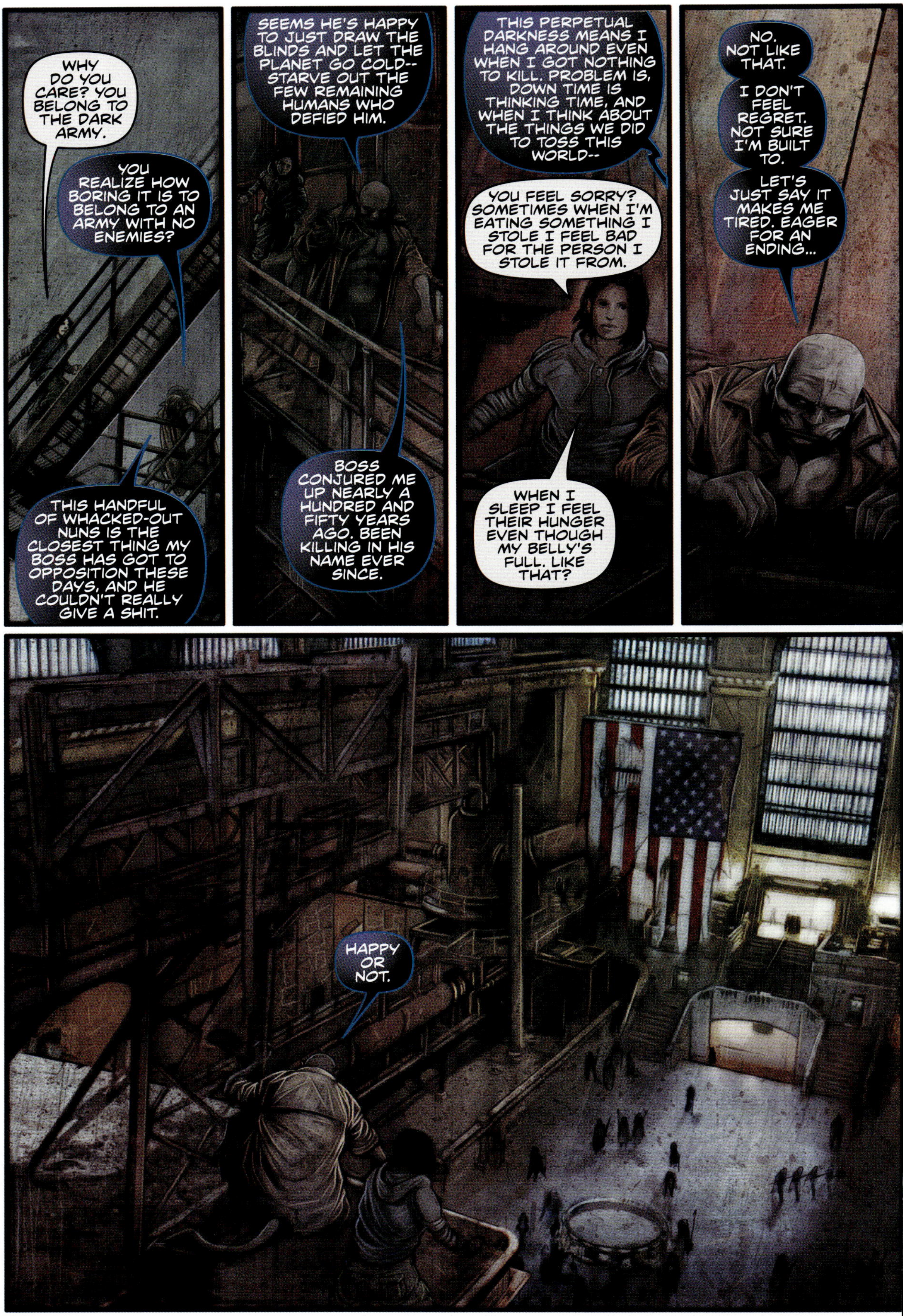

WHY DO YOU CARE? YOU BELONG TO THE DARK ARMY.
YOU REALIZE HOW BORING IT IS TO BELONG TO AN ARMY WITH NO ENEMIES?
THIS HANDFUL OF WHACKED-OUT NUNS IS THE CLOSEST THING MY BOSS HAS GOT TO OPPOSITION THESE DAYS, AND HE COULDN'T REALLY GIVE A SHIT.
SEEMS HE'S HAPPY TO JUST DRAW THE BLINDS AND LET THE PLANET GO COLD-- STARVE OUT THE FEW REMAINING HUMANS WHO DEFIED HIM.
BOSS CONJURED ME UP NEARLY A HUNDRED AND FIFTY YEARS AGO. BEEN KILLING IN HIS NAME EVER SINCE.
THIS PERPETUAL DARKNESS MEANS I HANG AROUND EVEN WHEN I GOT NOTHING TO KILL. PROBLEM IS, DOWN TIME IS THINKING TIME, AND WHEN I THINK ABOUT THE THINGS WE DID TO TOSS THIS WORLD--
YOU FEEL SORRY? SOMETIMES WHEN I'M EATING SOMETHING I STOLE I FEEL BAD FOR THE PERSON I STOLE IT FROM.
WHEN I SLEEP I FEEL THEIR HUNGER EVEN THOUGH MY BELLY'S FULL. LIKE THAT?
NO. NOT LIKE THAT.
I DON'T FEEL REGRET. NOT SURE I'M BUILT TO.
LET'S JUST SAY IT MAKES ME TIRED. EAGER FOR AN ENDING...
HAPPY OR NOT.

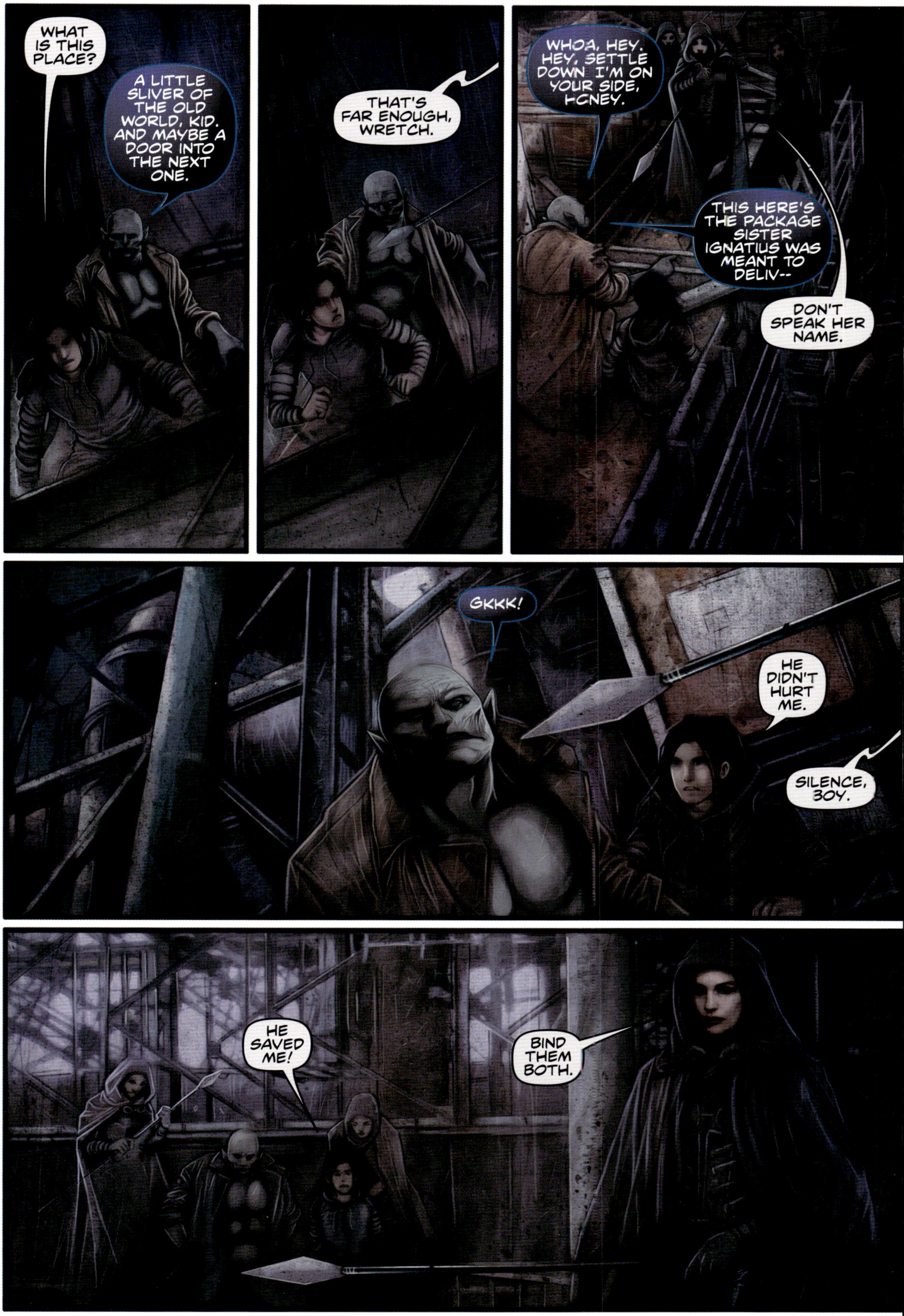
WHAT IS THIS PLACE?
A LITTLE SLIVER OF THE OLD WORLD, KID. AND MAYBE A DOOR INTO THE NEXT ONE.
THAT'S FAR ENOUGH, WRETCH.
WHOA, HEY. HEY, SETTLE DOWN. I'M ON YOUR SIDE, HONEY.
THIS HERE'S THE PACKAGE SISTER IGNATIUS WAS MEANT TO DELIV--
DON'T SPEAK HER NAME.
GKKK!
HE DIDN'T HURT ME.
SILENCE, BOY.
HE SAVED ME!
BIND THEM BOTH.

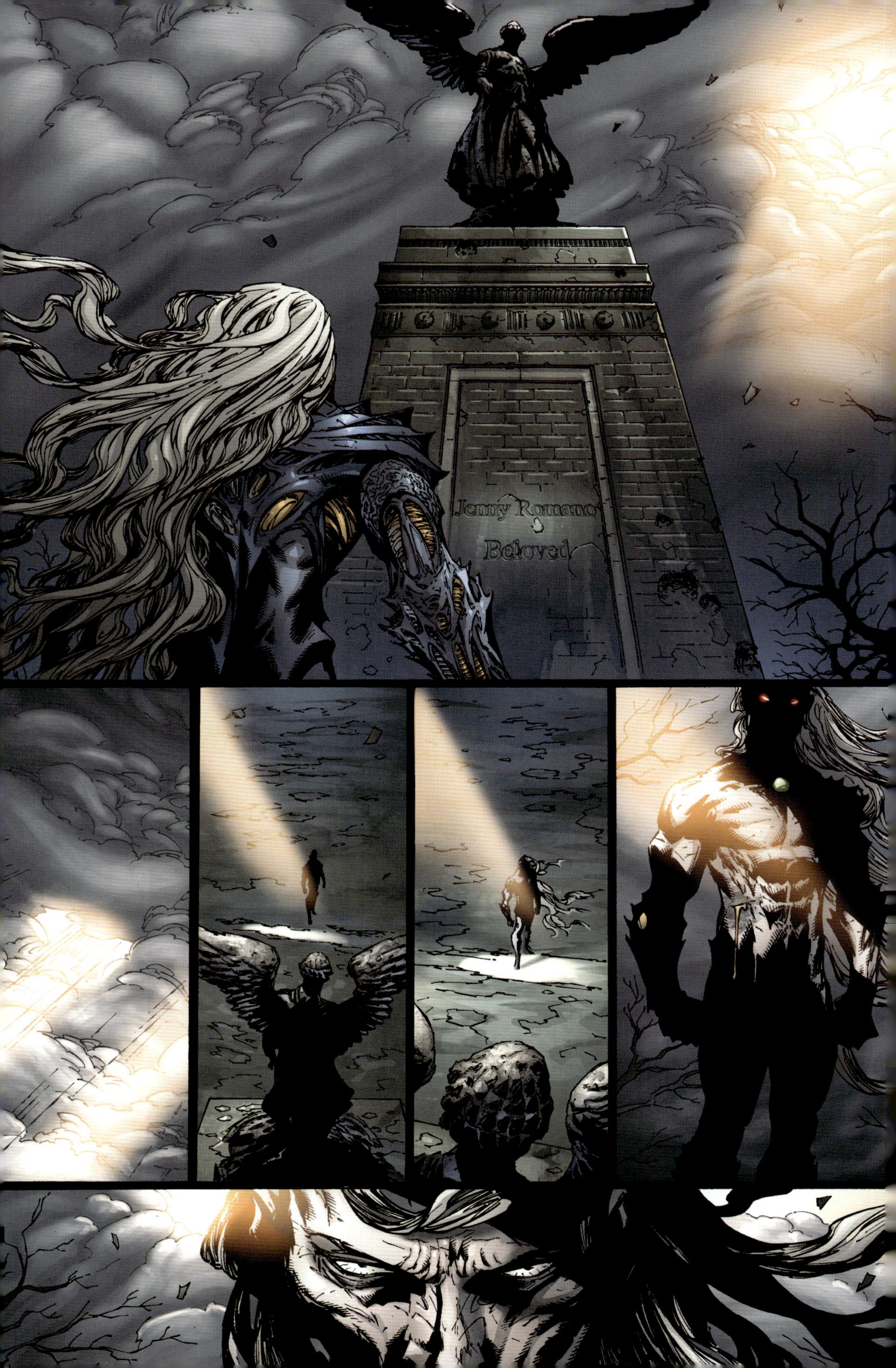
Jenny Romano
Beloved

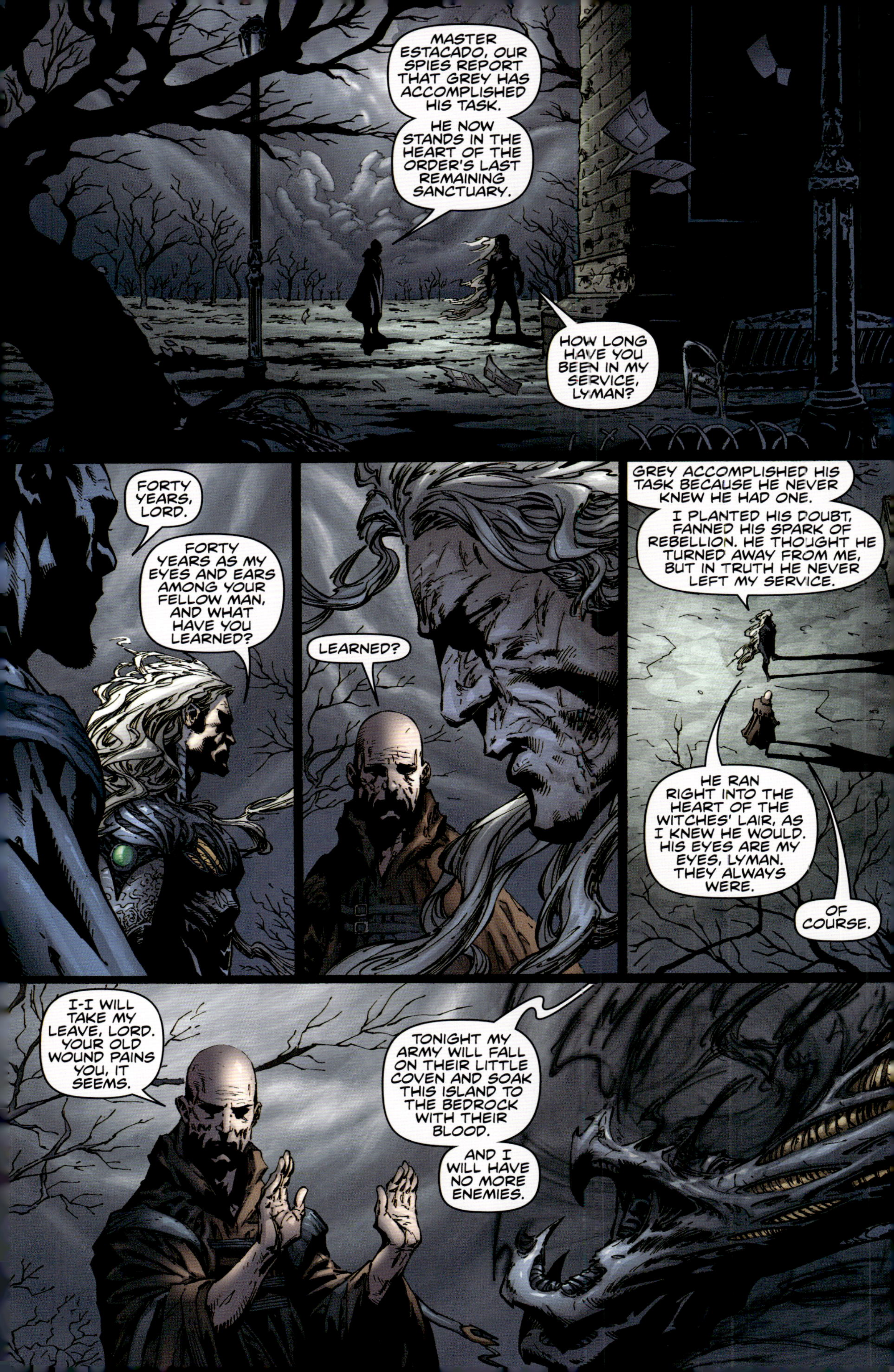

MASTER ESTACADO, OUR SPIES REPORT THAT GREY HAS ACCOMPLISHED HIS TASK.
HE NOW STANDS IN THE HEART OF THE ORDER'S LAST REMAINING SANCTUARY.
HOW LONG HAVE YOU BEEN IN MY SERVICE, LYMAN?
FORTY YEARS, LORD.
FORTY YEARS AS MY EYES AND EARS AMONG YOUR FELLOW MAN, AND WHAT HAVE YOU LEARNED?
LEARNED?
GREY ACCOMPLISHED HIS TASK BECAUSE HE NEVER KNEW HE HAD ONE.
I PLANTED HIS DOUBT, FANNED HIS SPARK OF REBELLION. HE THOUGHT HE TURNED AWAY FROM ME, BUT IN TRUTH HE NEVER LEFT MY SERVICE.
HE RAN RIGHT INTO THE HEART OF THE WITCHES' LAIR, AS I KNEW HE WOULD. HIS EYES ARE MY EYES, LYMAN. THEY ALWAYS WERE.
OF COURSE.
I-I WILL TAKE MY LEAVE, LORD. YOUR OLD WOUND PAINS YOU, IT SEEMS.
TONIGHT MY ARMY WILL FALL ON THEIR LITTLE COVEN AND SOAK THIS ISLAND TO THE BEDROCK WITH THEIR BLOOD.
AND I WILL HAVE NO MORE ENEMIES.

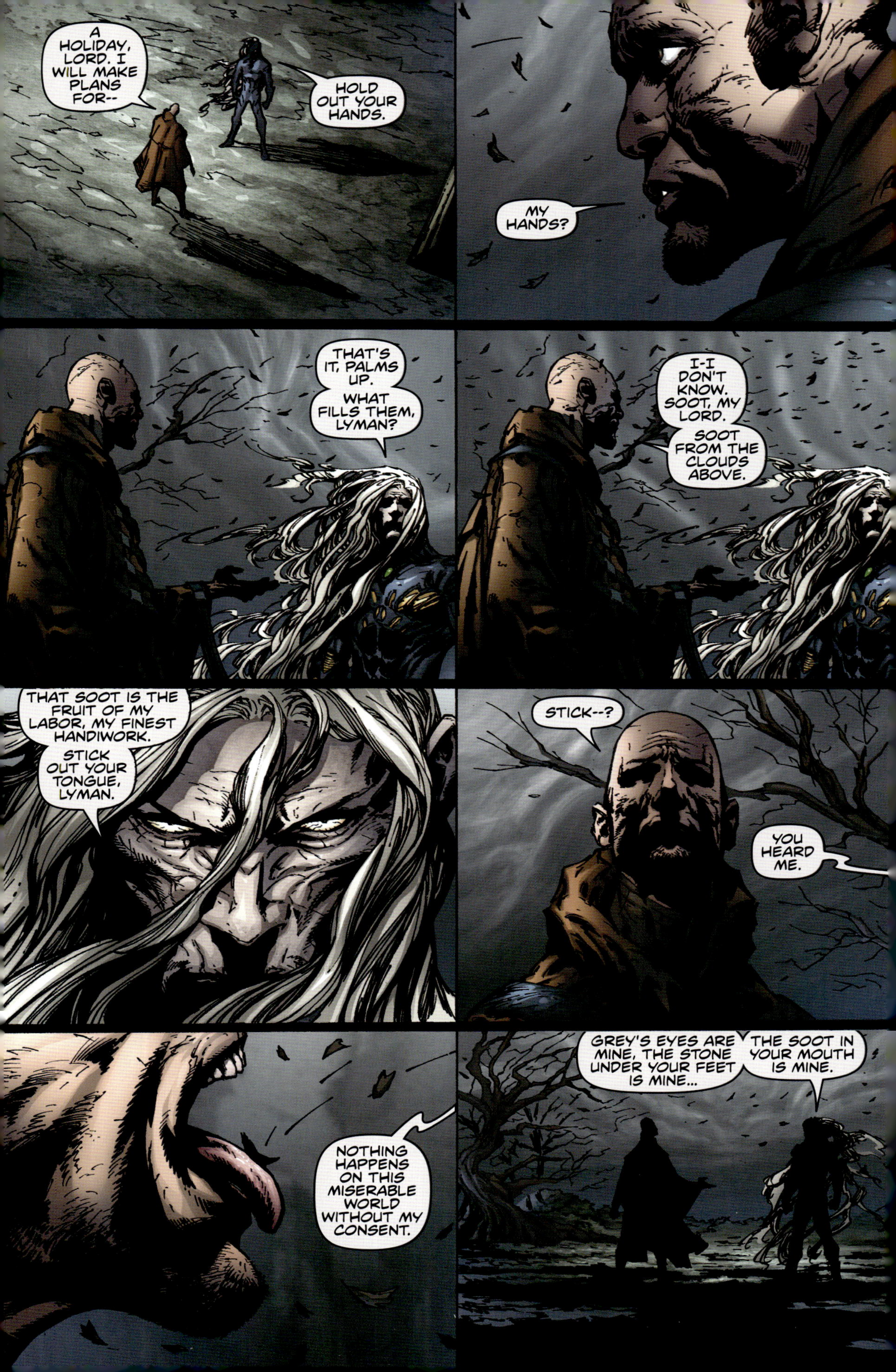
A HOLIDAY, LORD. I WILL MAKE PLANS FOR--
HOLD OUT YOUR HANDS.
MY HANDS?
THAT'S IT, PALMS UP.
WHAT FILLS THEM, LYMAN?
I-I DON'T KNOW. SOOT, MY LORD.
SOOT FROM THE CLOUDS ABOVE.
THAT SOOT IS THE FRUIT OF MY LABOR, MY FINEST HANDIWORK.
STICK OUT YOUR TONGUE, LYMAN.
STICK--?
YOU HEARD ME.
NOTHING HAPPENS ON THIS MISERABLE WORLD WITHOUT MY CONSENT.
GREY'S EYES ARE MINE, THE STONE UNDER YOUR FEET IS MINE...
THE SOOT IN YOUR MOUTH IS MINE.

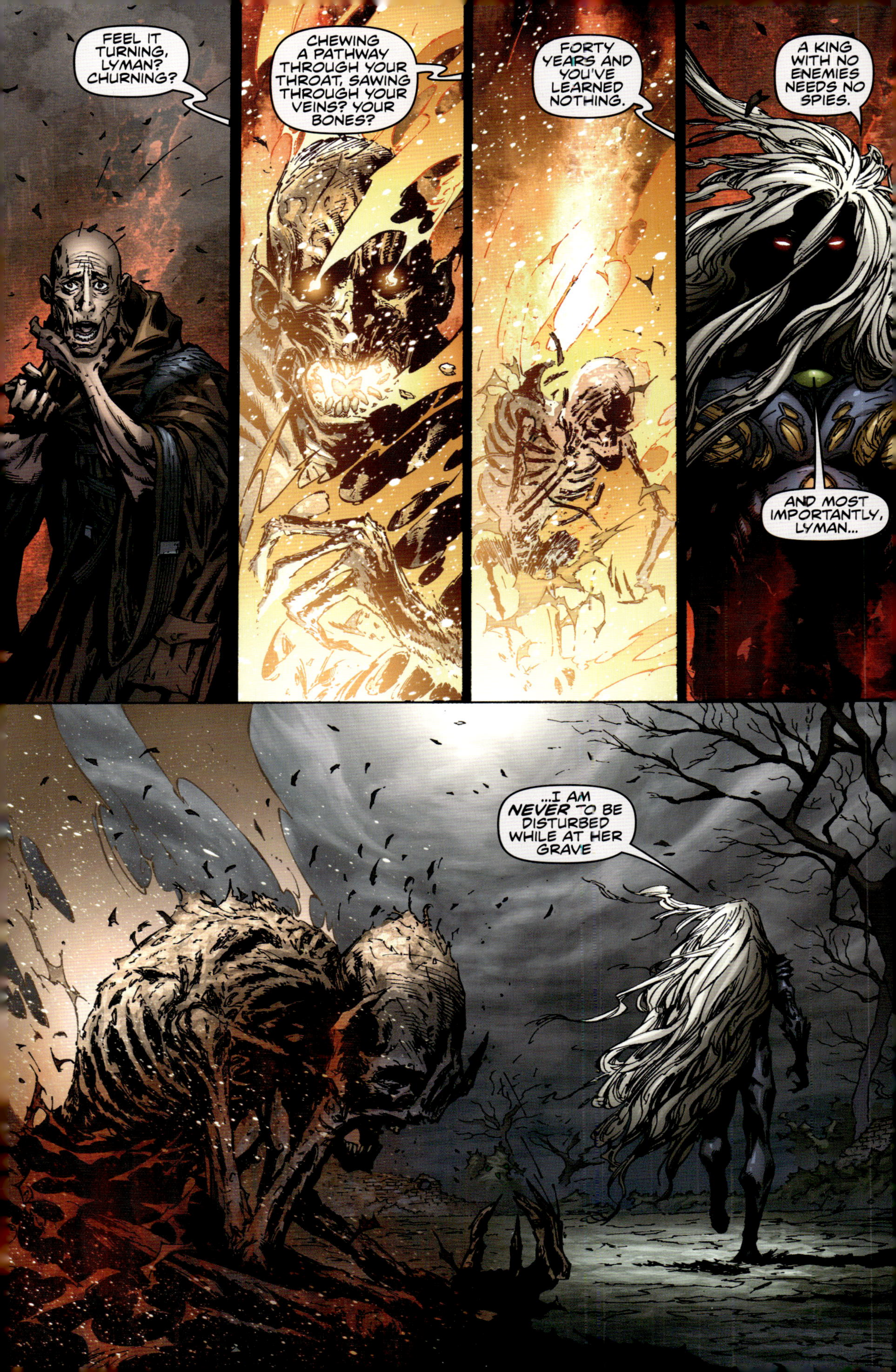
FEEL IT TURNING, LYMAN? CHURNING?
CHEWING A PATHWAY THROUGH YOUR THROAT, SAWING THROUGH YOUR VEINS? YOUR BONES?
FORTY YEARS AND YOU'VE LEARNED NOTHING.
A KING WITH NO ENEMIES NEEDS NO SPIES.
AND MOST IMPORTANTLY, LYMAN...
...I AM *NEVER* TO BE DISTURBED WHILE AT HER GRAVE.

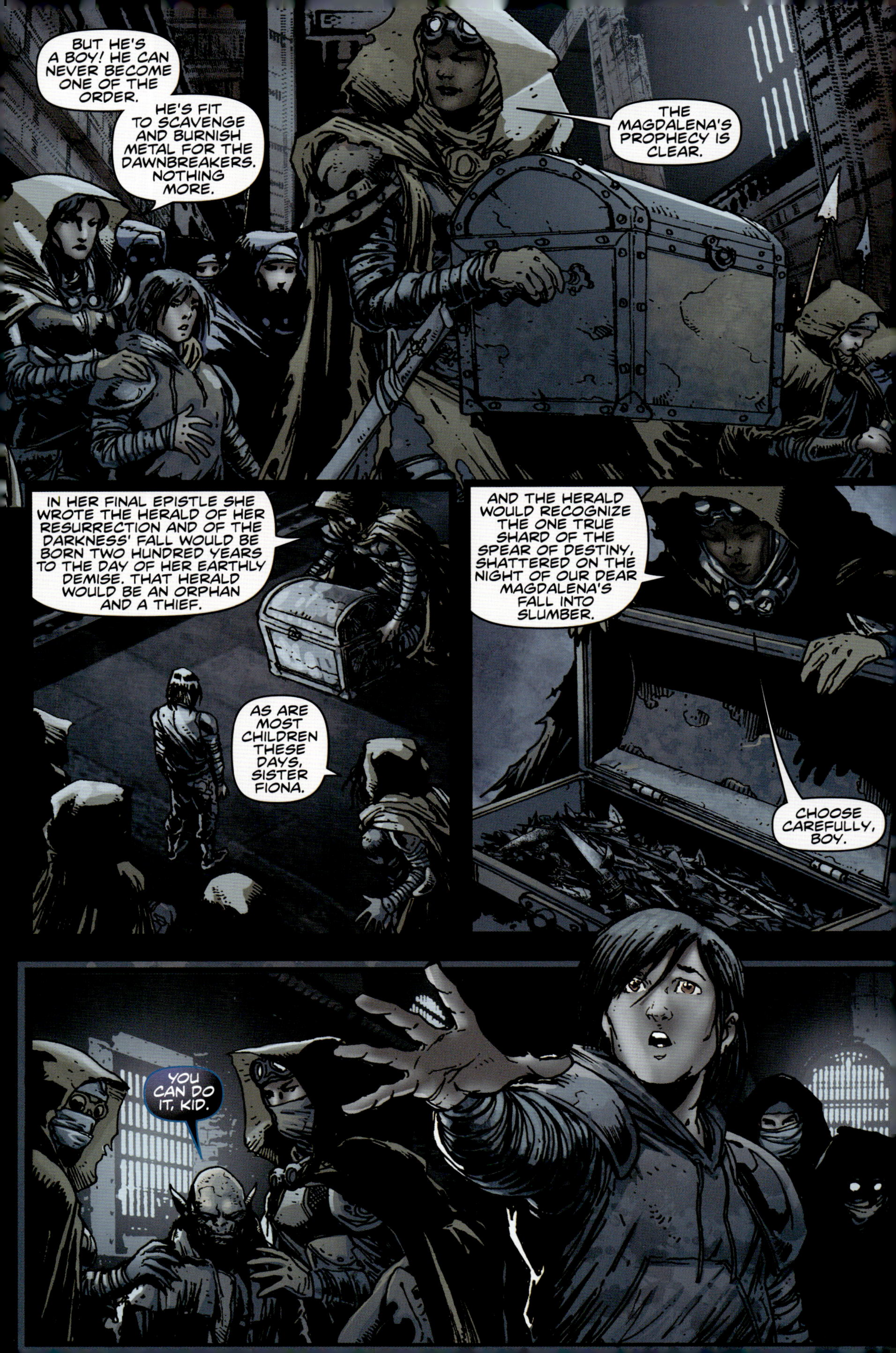
BUT HE'S A BOY! HE CAN NEVER BECOME ONE OF THE ORDER.
HE'S FIT TO SCAVENGE AND BURNISH METAL FOR THE DAWNBREAKERS. NOTHING MORE.
THE MAGDALENA'S PROPHECY IS CLEAR.
IN HER FINAL EPISTLE SHE WROTE THE HERALD OF HER RESURRECTION AND OF THE DARKNESS' FALL WOULD BE BORN TWO HUNDRED YEARS TO THE DAY OF HER EARTHLY DEMISE. THAT HERALD WOULD BE AN ORPHAN AND A THIEF.
AS ARE MOST CHILDREN THESE DAYS, SISTER FIONA.
AND THE HERALD WOULD RECOGNIZE THE ONE TRUE SHARD OF THE SPEAR OF DESTINY, SHATTERED ON THE NIGHT OF OUR DEAR MAGDALENA'S FALL INTO SLUMBER.
CHOOSE CAREFULLY, BOY.
YOU CAN DO IT, KID.

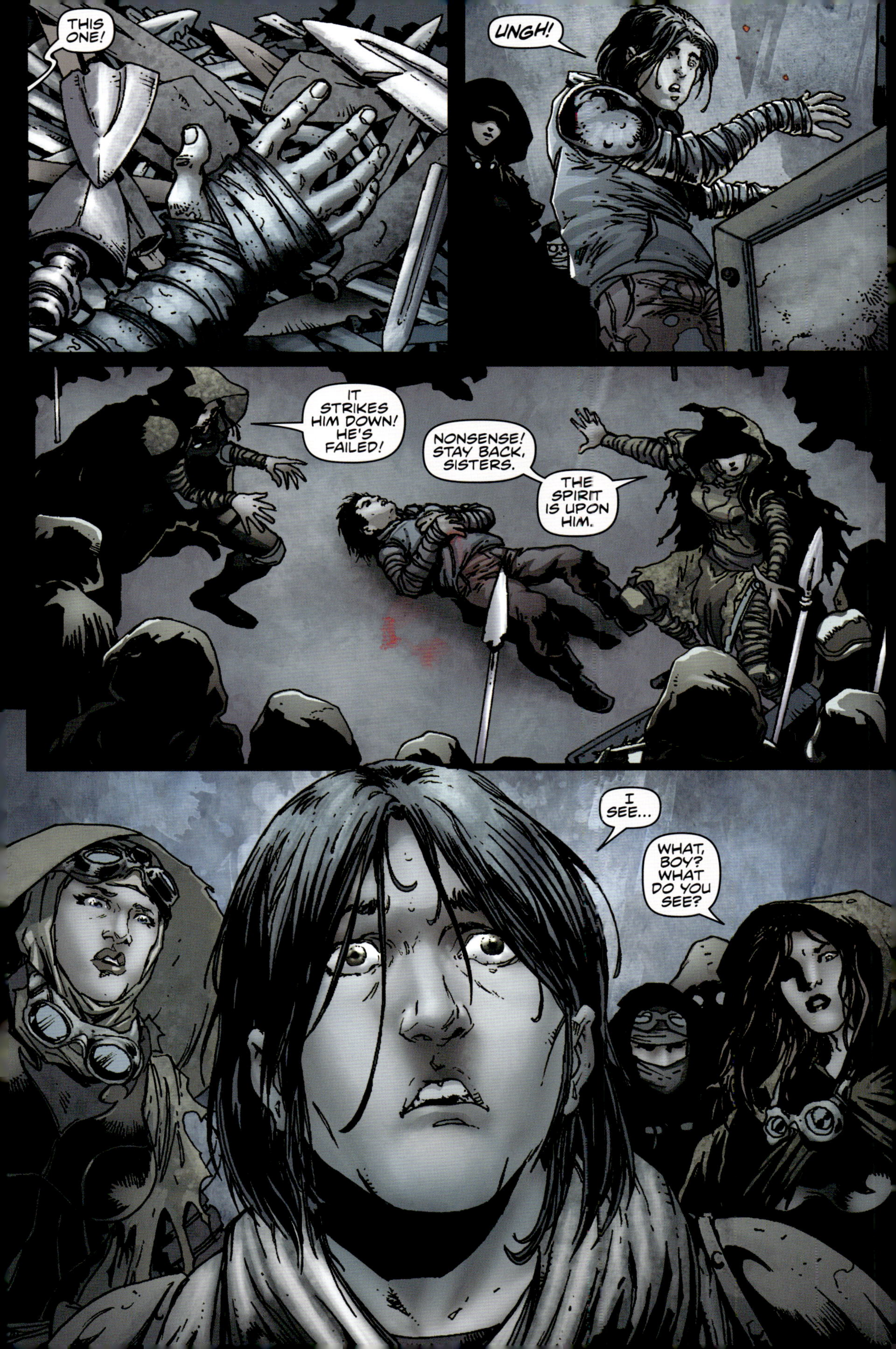

THIS ONE!
UNGH!
IT STRIKES HIM DOWN! HE'S FAILED!
NONSENSE! STAY BACK, SISTERS.
THE SPIRIT IS UPON HIM.
I SEE...
WHAT, BOY? WHAT DO YOU SEE?

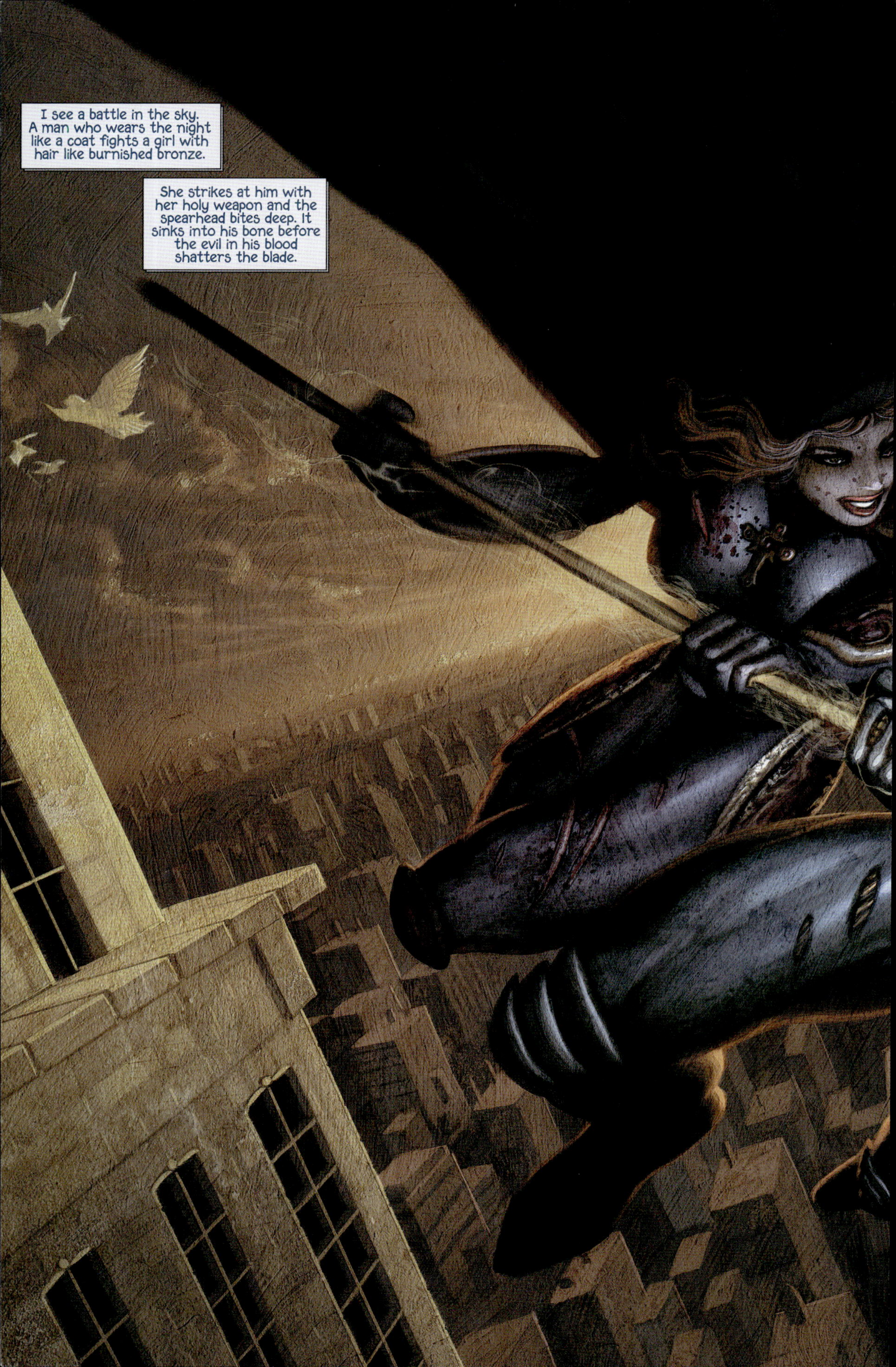
I see a battle in the sky. A man who wears the night like a coat fights a girl with hair like burnished bronze.
She strikes at him with her holy weapon and the spearhead bites deep. It sinks into his bone before the evil in his blood shatters the blade.

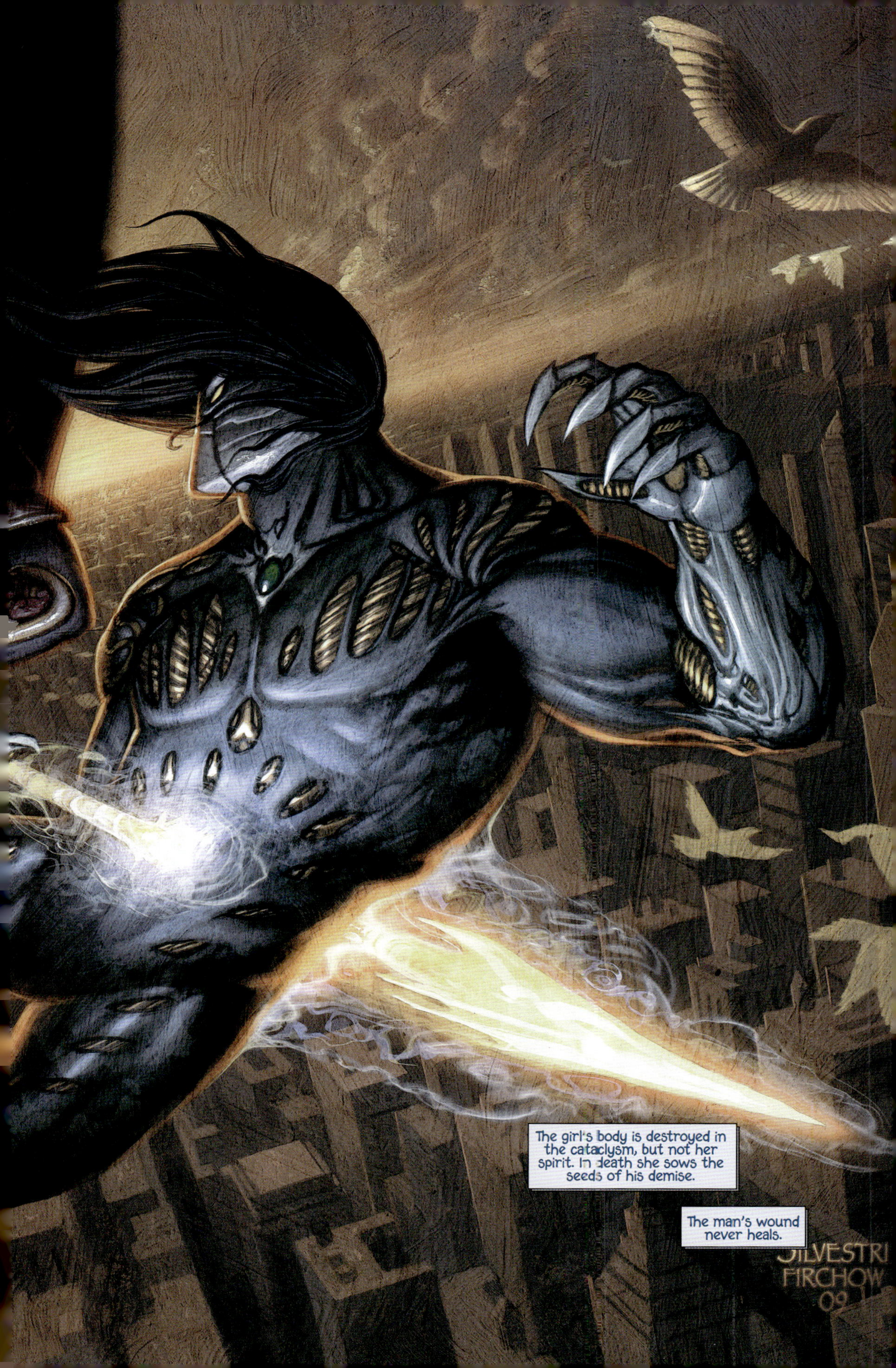
The girl's body is destroyed in the cataclysm, but not her spirit. In death she sows the seeds of his demise.
The man's wound never heals.
SILVESTRI
FIRCHOW
09

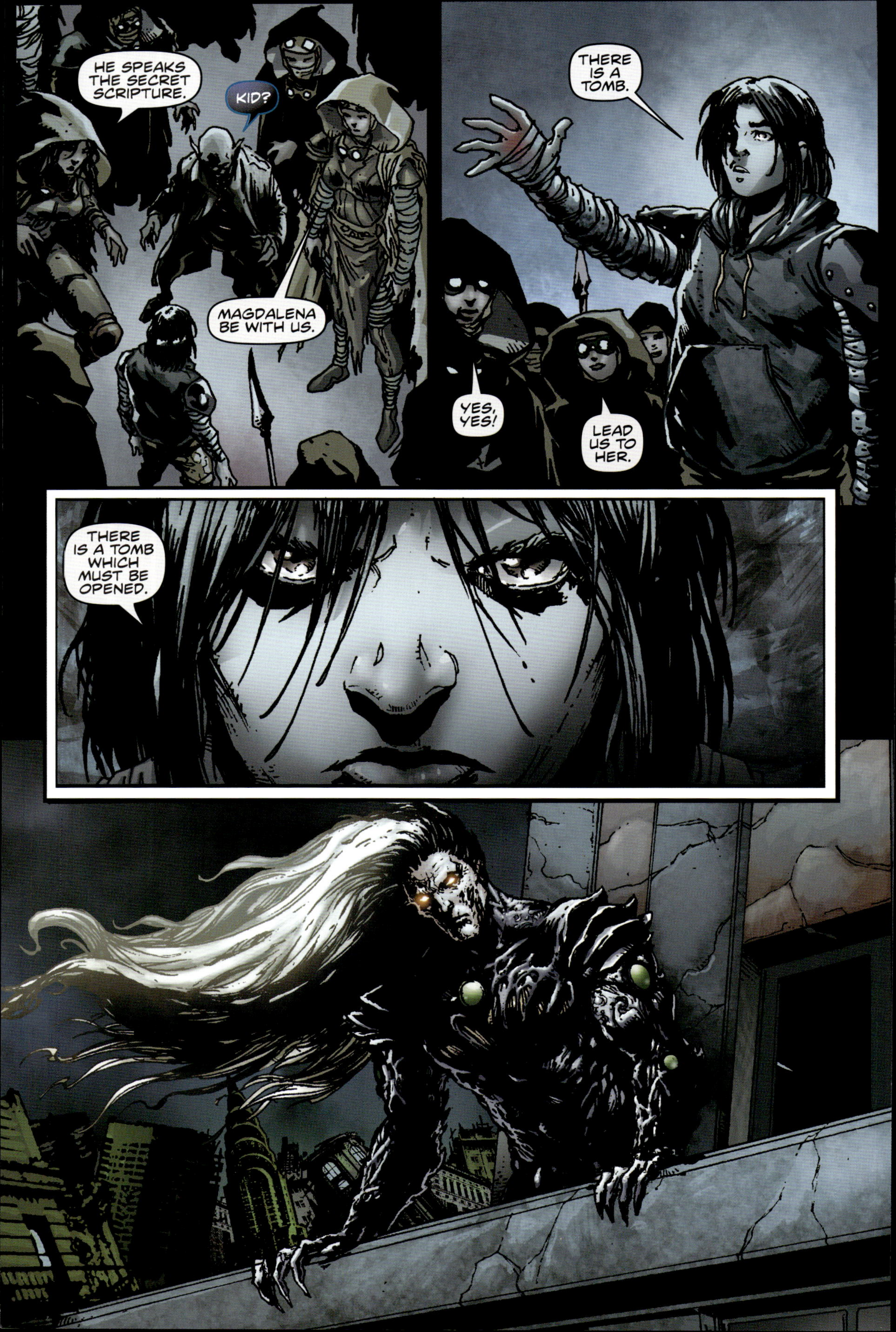
HE SPEAKS THE SECRET SCRIPTURE.
KID?
MAGDALENA BE WITH US.
THERE IS A TOMB.
YES, YES!
LEAD US TO HER.
THERE IS A TOMB WHICH MUST BE OPENED.

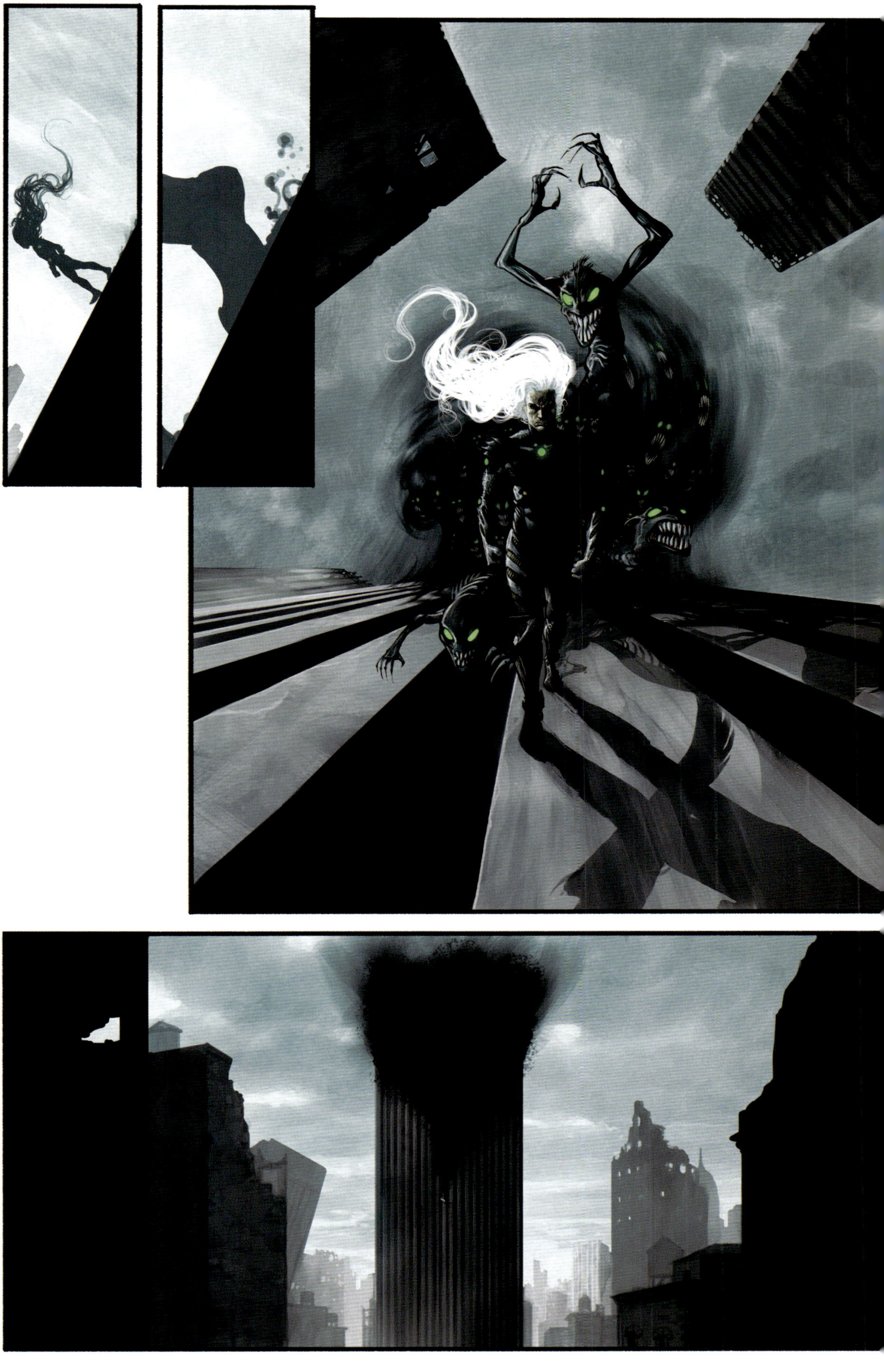

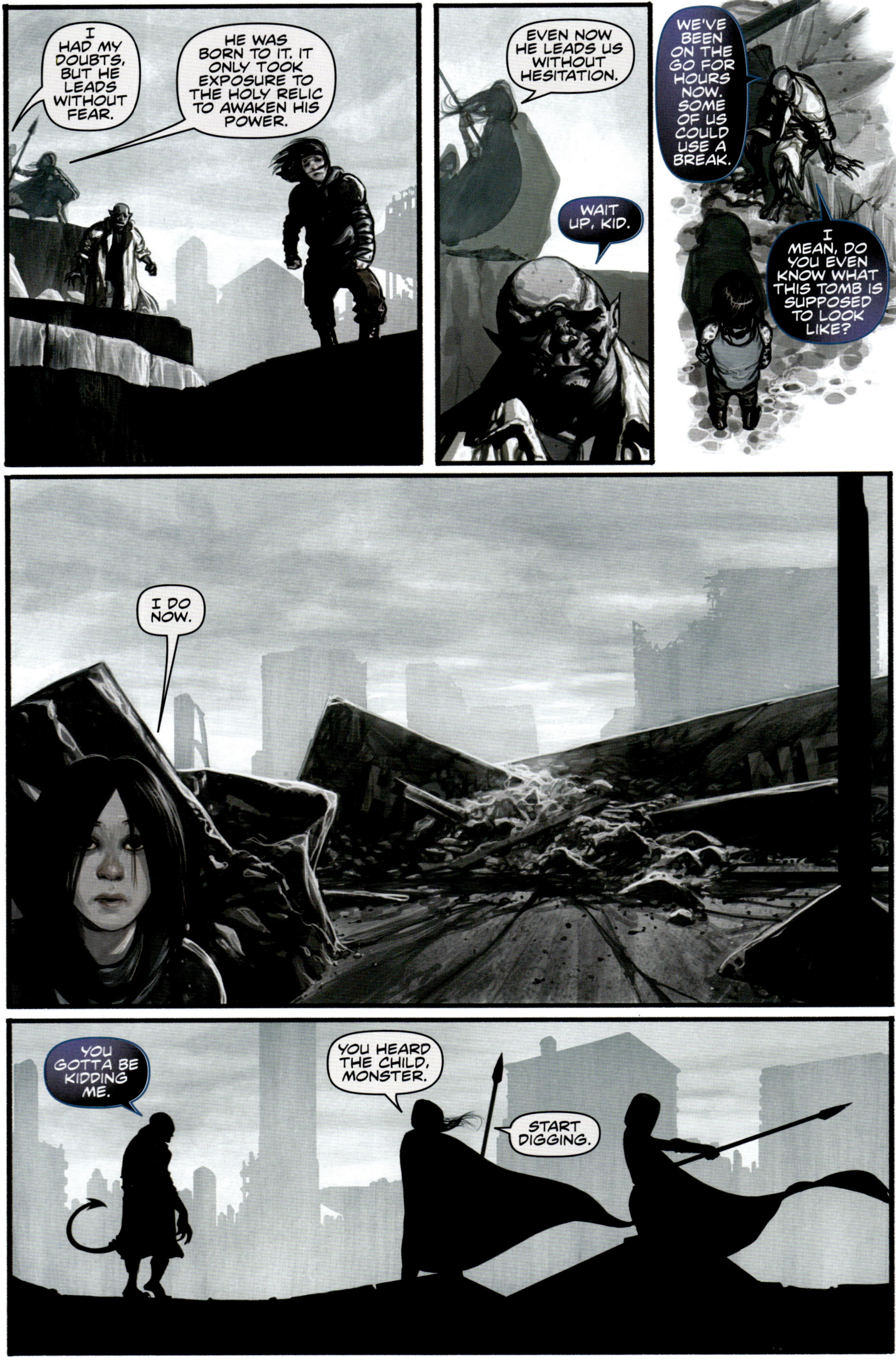
I HAD MY DOUBTS, BUT HE LEADS WITHOUT FEAR.
HE WAS BORN TO IT. IT ONLY TOOK EXPOSURE TO THE HOLY RELIC TO AWAKEN HIS POWER.
EVEN NOW HE LEADS US WITHOUT HESITATION.
WAIT UP, KID.
WE'VE BEEN ON THE GO FOR HOURS NOW. SOME OF US COULD USE A BREAK.
I MEAN, DO YOU EVEN KNOW WHAT THIS TOMB IS SUPPOSED TO LOOK LIKE?
I DO NOW.
YOU GOTTA BE KIDDING ME.
YOU HEARD THE CHILD, MONSTER.
START DIGGING.

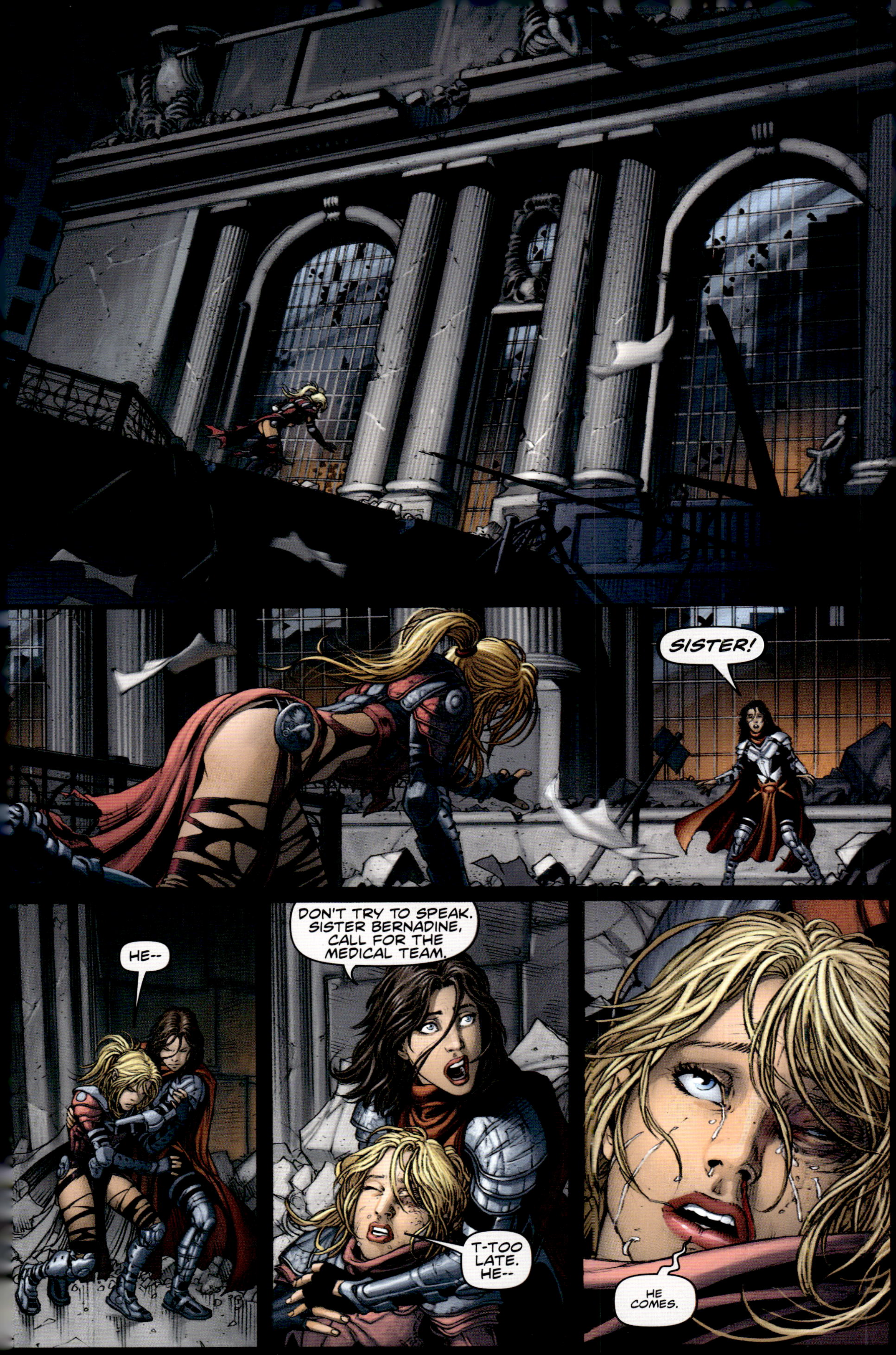
SISTER!
HE--
DON'T TRY TO SPEAK. SISTER BERNADINE, CALL FOR THE MEDICAL TEAM.
T-TOO LATE. HE--
HE COMES.

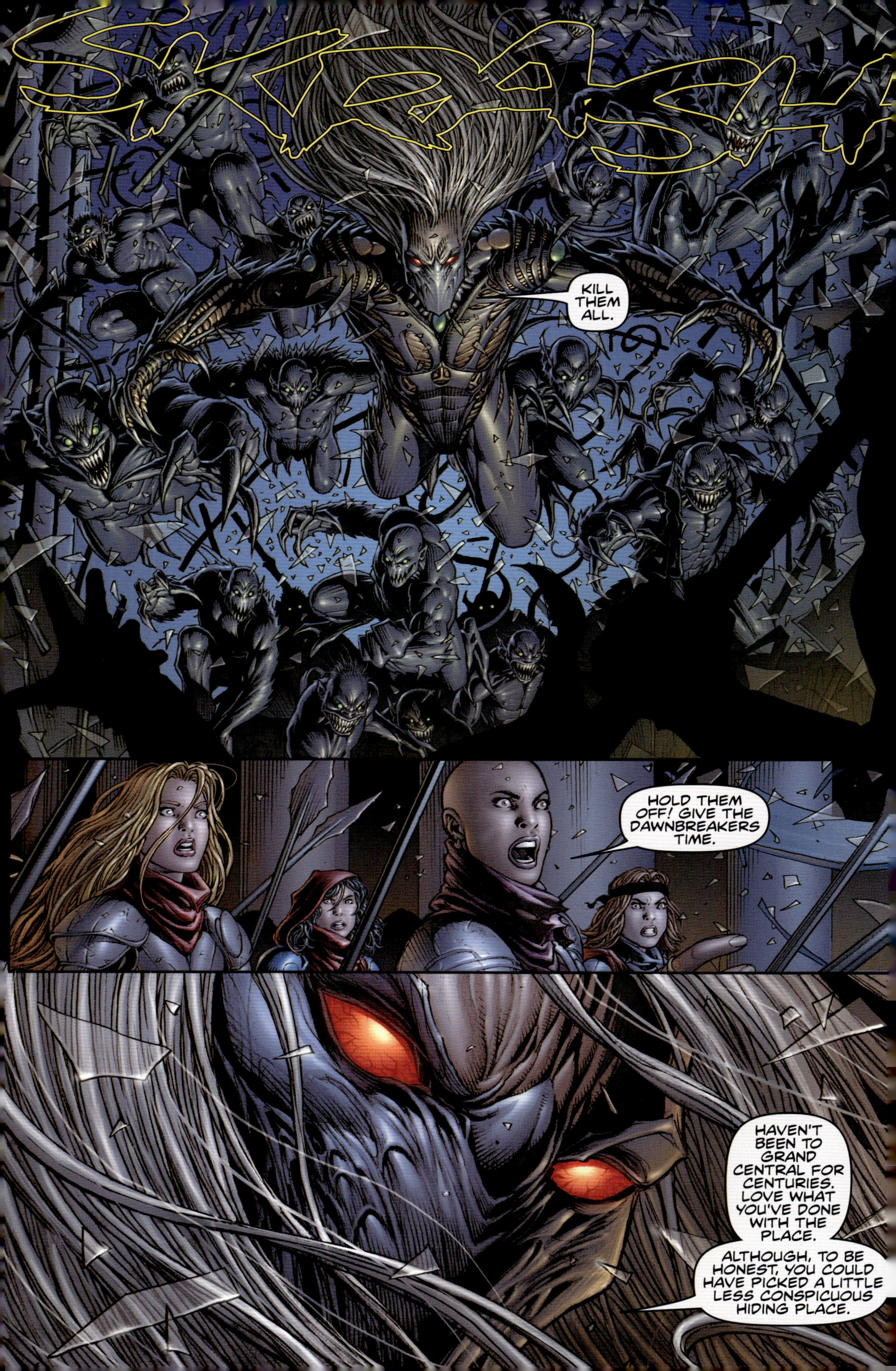
KILL THEM ALL.
HOLD THEM OFF! GIVE THE DAWNBREAKERS TIME.
HAVEN'T BEEN TO GRAND CENTRAL FOR CENTURIES. LOVE WHAT YOU'VE DONE WITH THE PLACE.
ALTHOUGH, TO BE HONEST, YOU COULD HAVE PICKED A LITTLE LESS CONSPICUOUS HIDING PLACE.

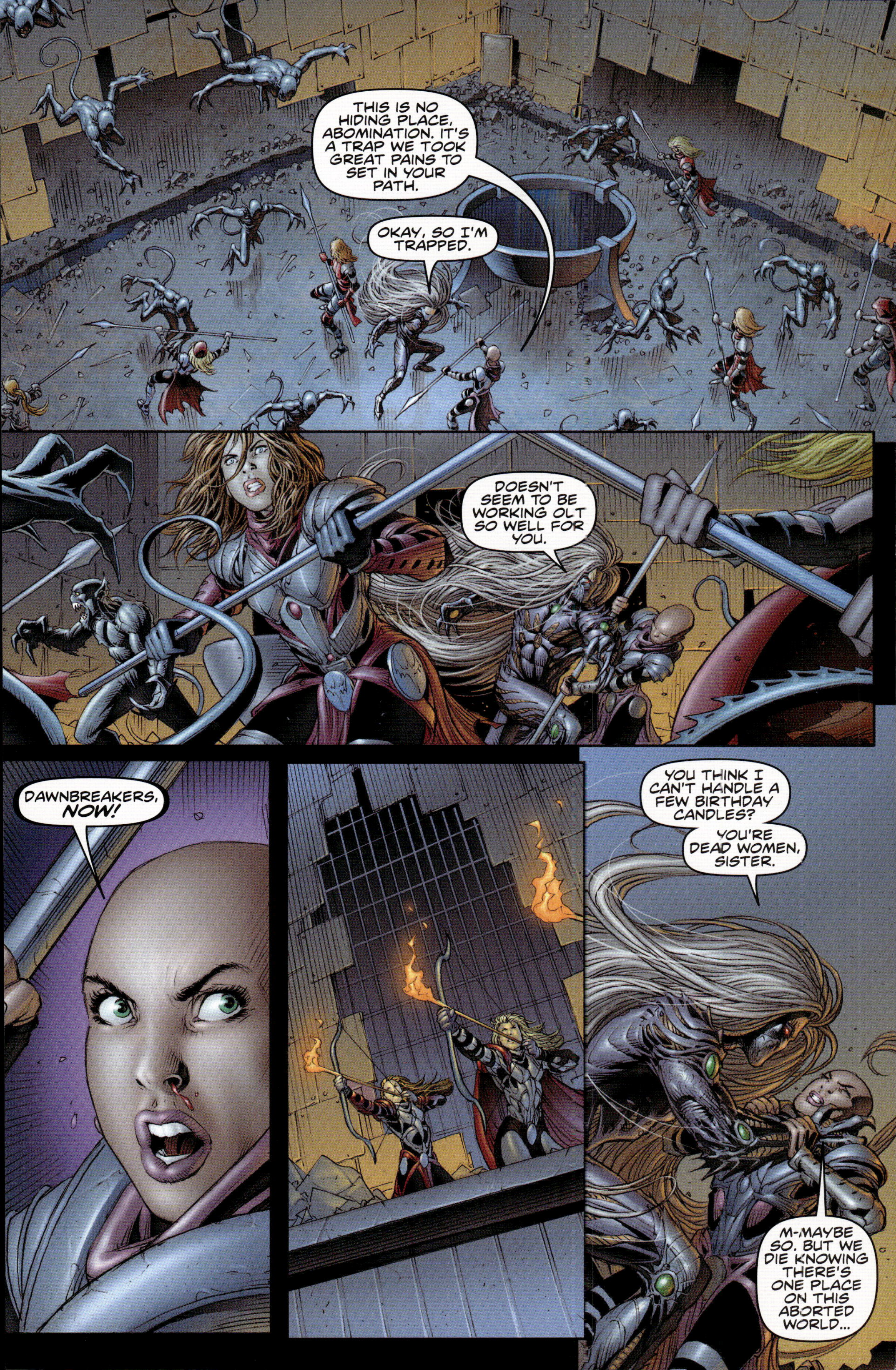
THIS IS NO HIDING PLACE, ABOMINATION. IT'S A TRAP WE TOOK GREAT PAINS TO SET IN YOUR PATH.
OKAY, SO I'M TRAPPED.
DOESN'T SEEM TO BE WORKING OUT SO WELL FOR YOU.
DAWNBREAKERS, *NOW!*
YOU THINK I CAN'T HANDLE A FEW BIRTHDAY CANDLES?
YOU'RE DEAD WOMEN, SISTER.
M-MAYBE SO. BUT WE DIE KNOWING THERE'S ONE PLACE ON THIS ABORTED WORLD...

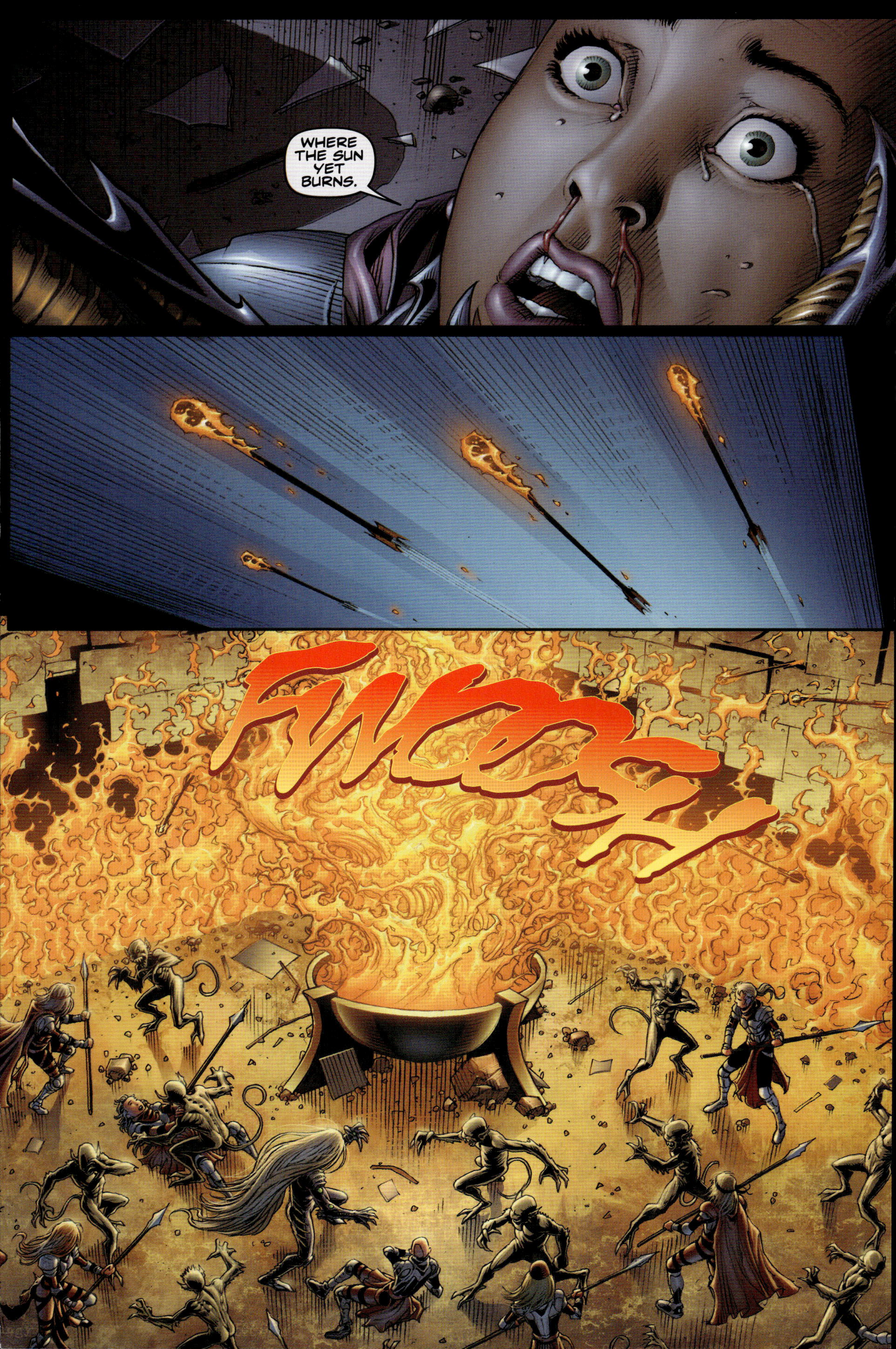
WHERE THE SUN YET BURNS.

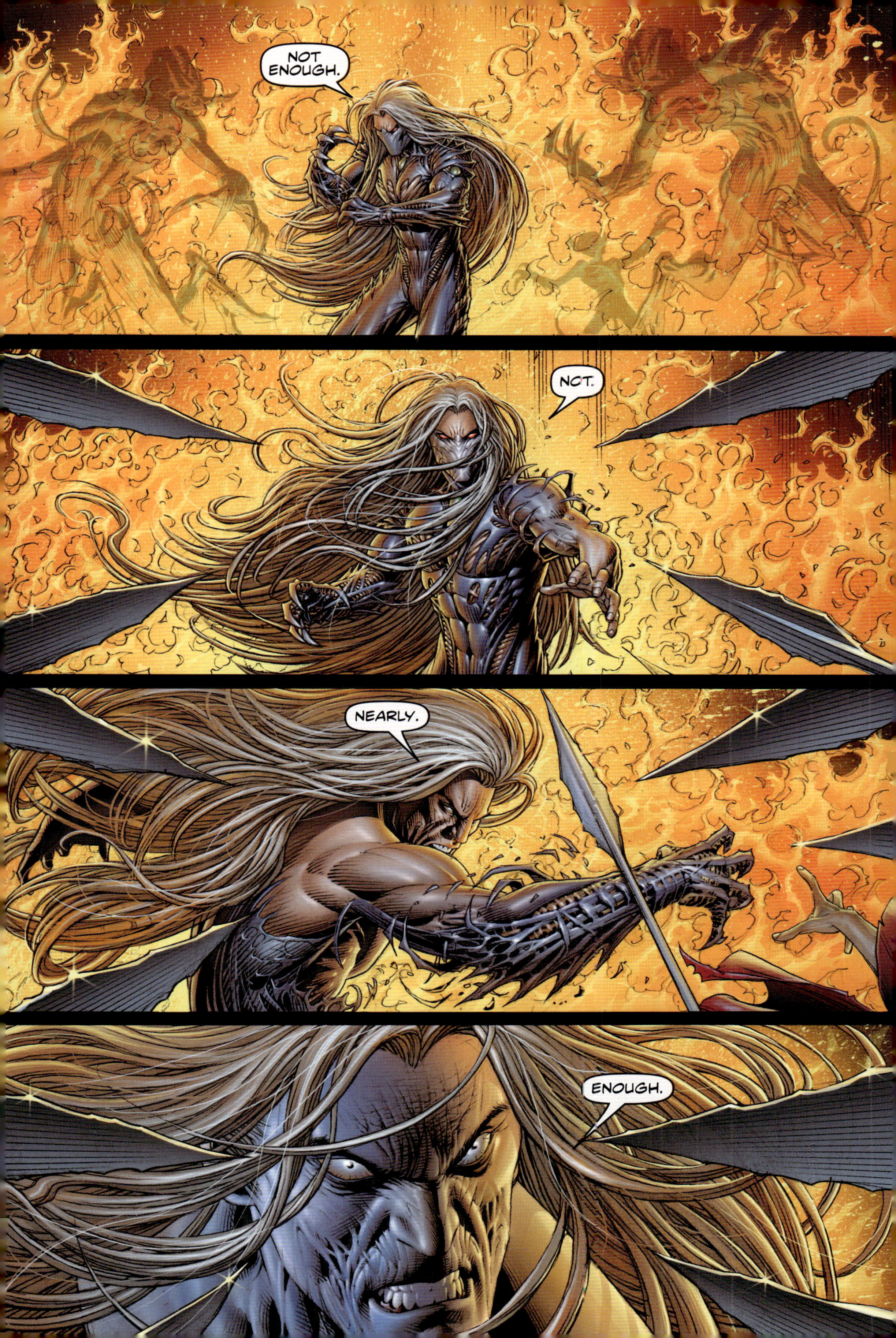
NOT ENOUGH.
NOT.
NEARLY.
ENOUGH.

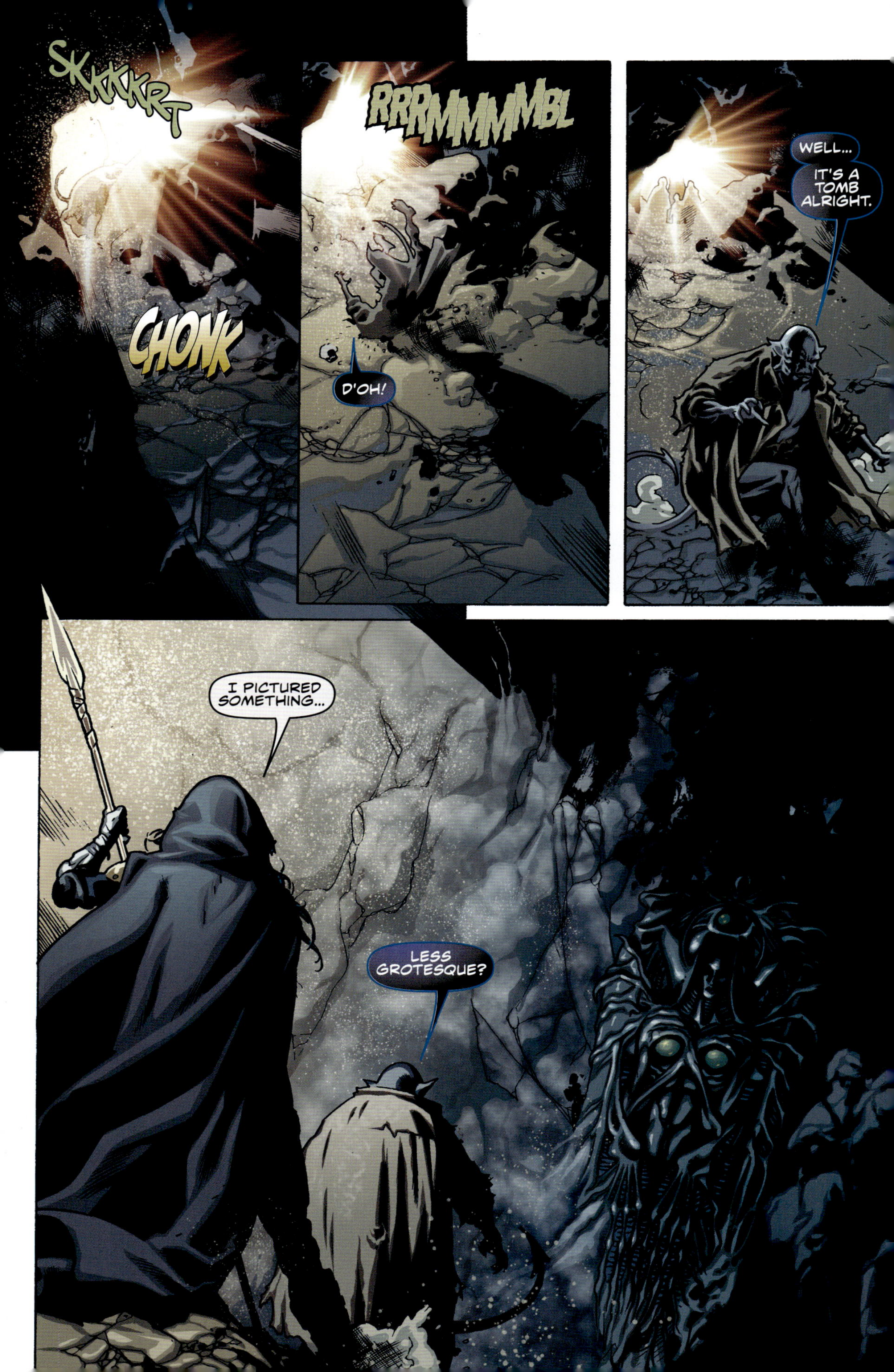
SKKKKRT
CHONK
RRRMMMMMBL
D'OH!
WELL...
IT'S A TOMB ALRIGHT.
I PICTURED SOMETHING...
LESS GROTESQUE?

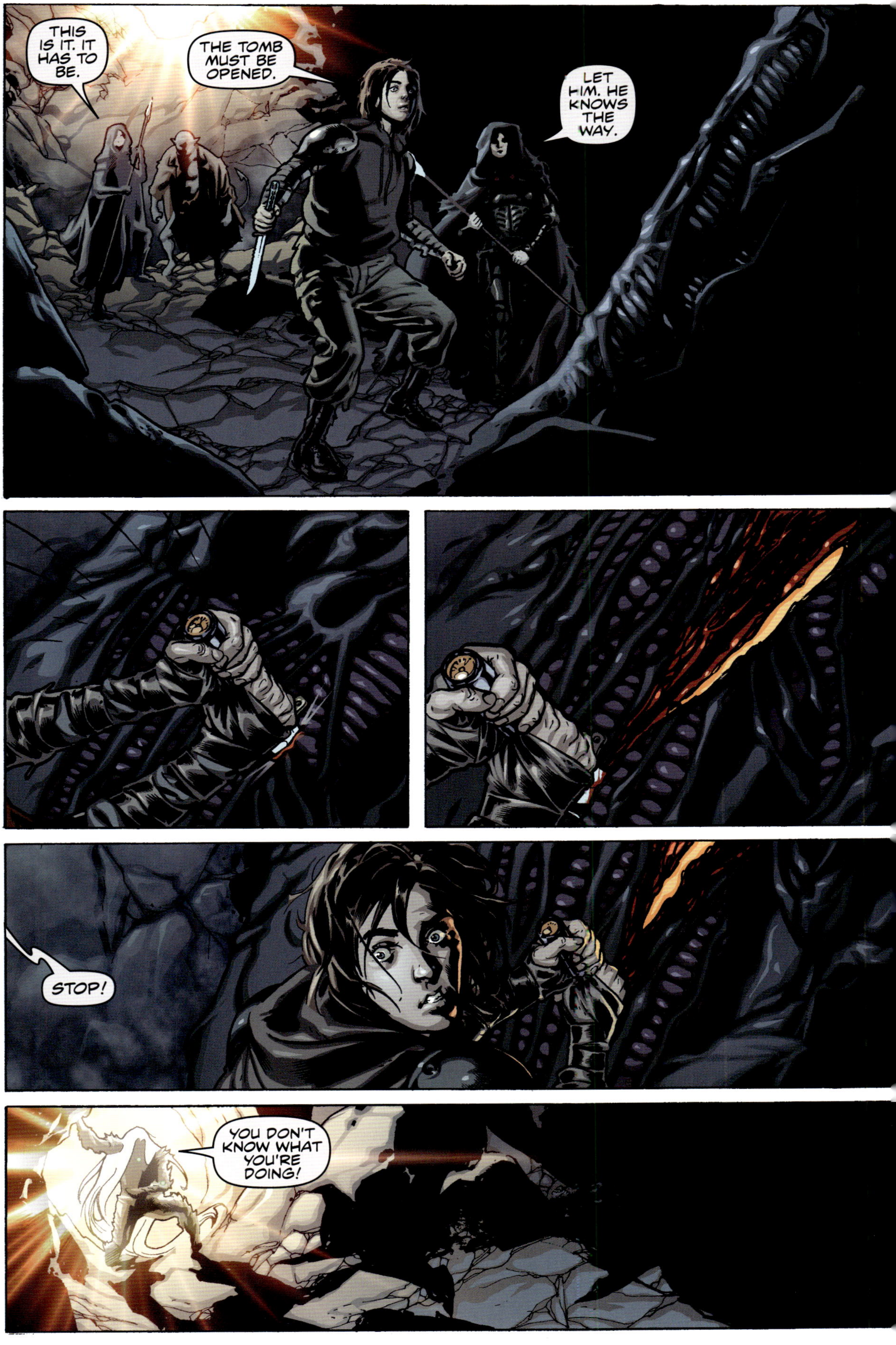

THIS IS IT. IT HAS TO BE.
THE TOMB MUST BE OPENED.
LET HIM. HE KNOWS THE WAY.
STOP!
YOU DON'T KNOW WHAT YOU'RE DOING!

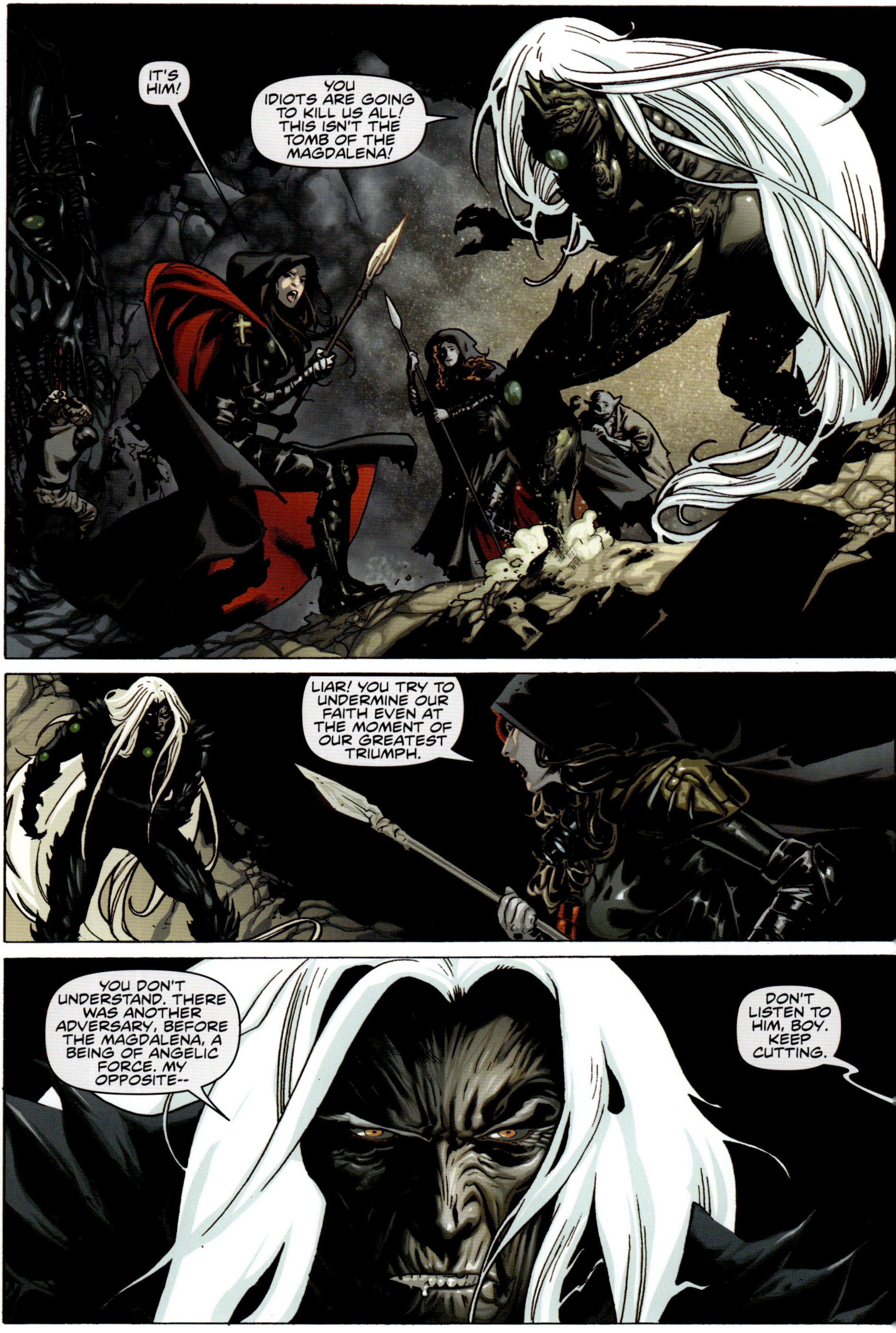
IT'S HIM!
YOU IDIOTS ARE GOING TO KILL US ALL! THIS ISN'T THE TOMB OF THE MAGDALENA!
LIAR! YOU TRY TO UNDERMINE OUR FAITH EVEN AT THE MOMENT OF OUR GREATEST TRIUMPH.
YOU DON'T UNDERSTAND. THERE WAS ANOTHER ADVERSARY, BEFORE THE MAGDALENA, A BEING OF ANGELIC FORCE. MY OPPOSITE--
DON'T LISTEN TO HIM, BOY. KEEP CUTTING.

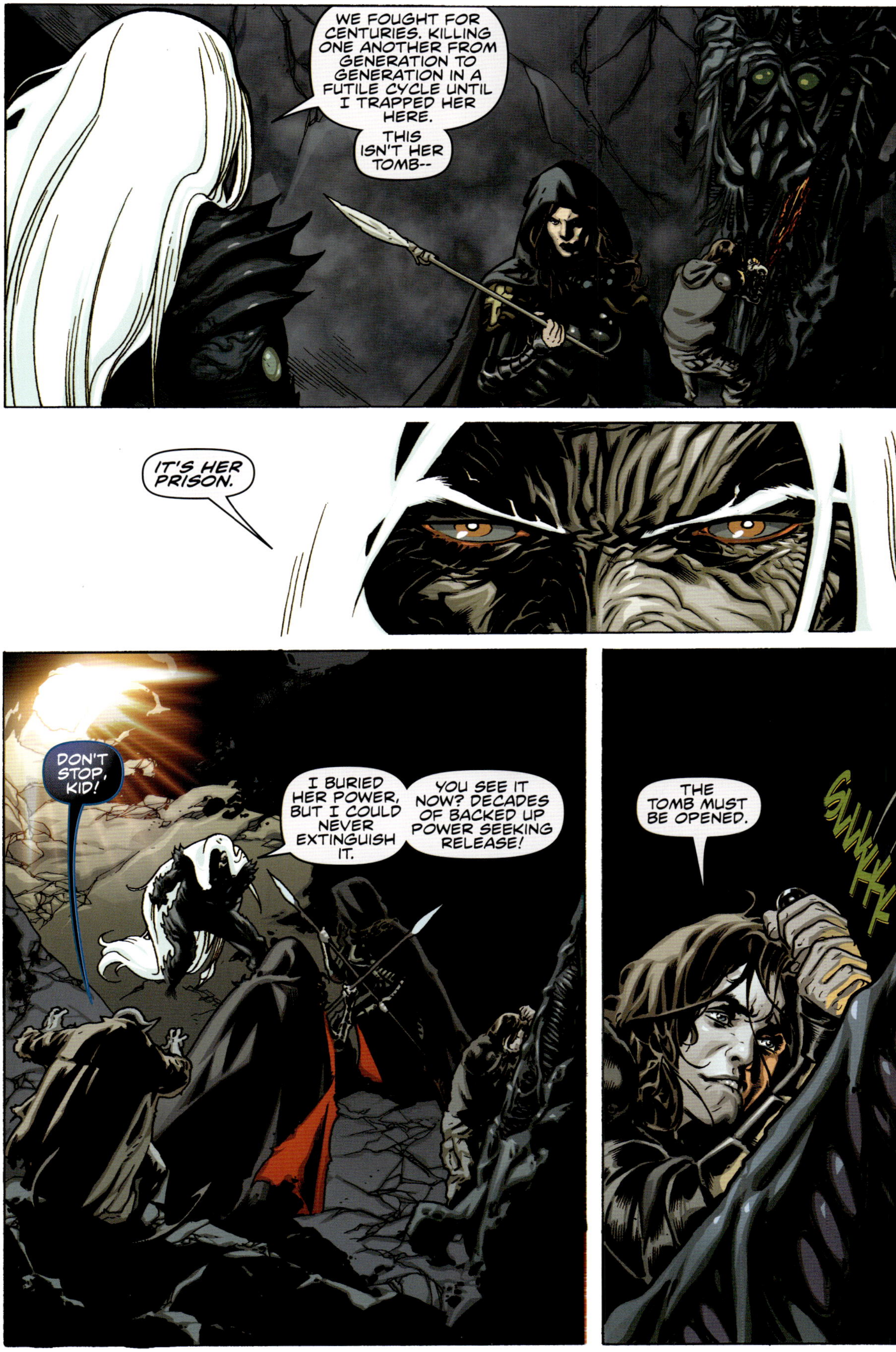
WE FOUGHT FOR CENTURIES. KILLING ONE ANOTHER FROM GENERATION TO GENERATION IN A FUTILE CYCLE UNTIL I TRAPPED HER HERE.
THIS ISN'T HER TOMB--
IT'S HER PRISON.
DON'T STOP, KID!
I BURIED HER POWER, BUT I COULD NEVER EXTINGUISH IT.
YOU SEE IT NOW? DECADES OF BACKED UP POWER SEEKING RELEASE!
THE TOMB MUST BE OPENED.
SHKKKK

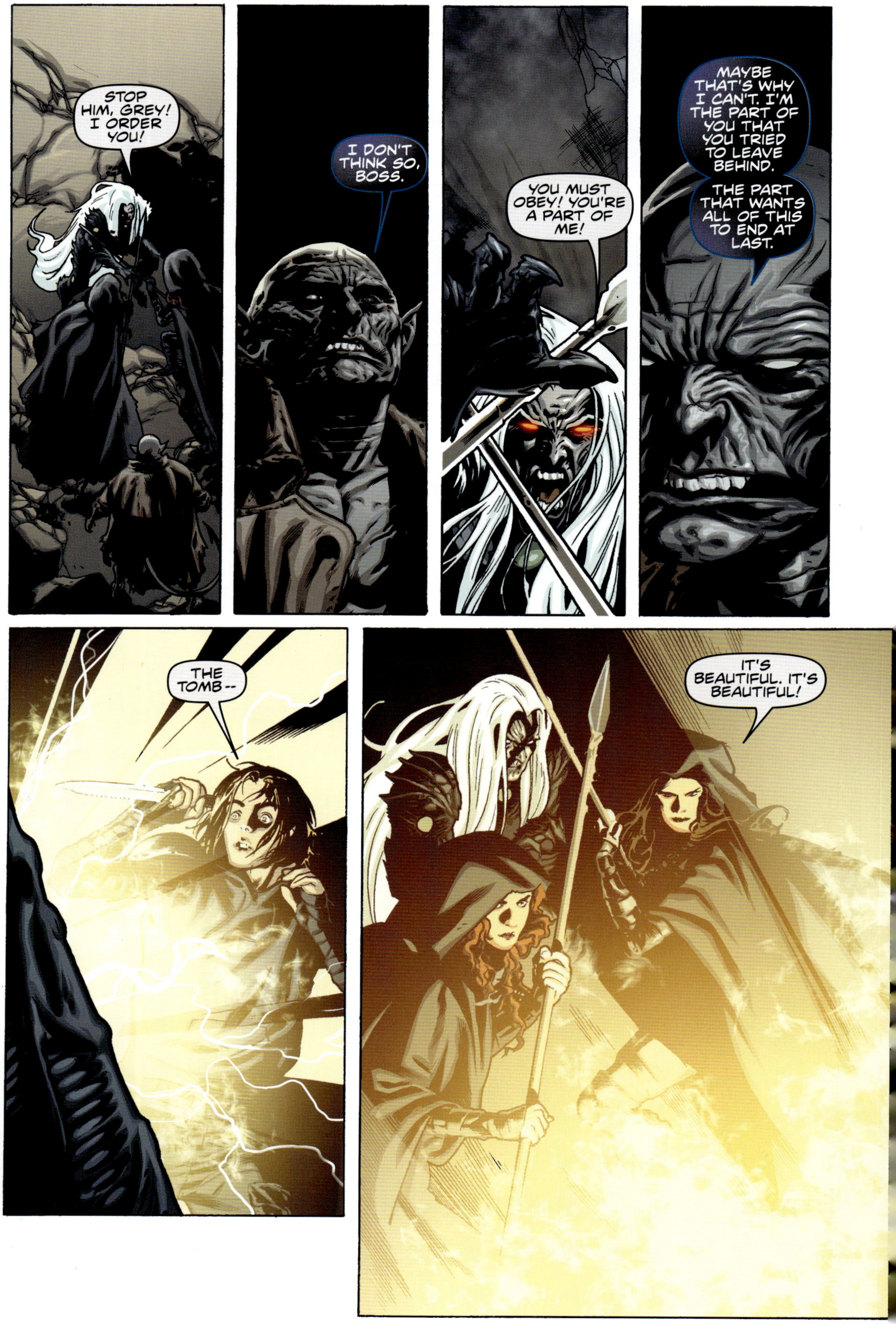
STOP HIM, GREY! I ORDER YOU!
I DON'T THINK SO, BOSS.
YOU MUST OBEY! YOU'RE A PART OF ME!
MAYBE THAT'S WHY I CAN'T. I'M THE PART OF YOU THAT YOU TRIED TO LEAVE BEHIND.
THE PART THAT WANTS ALL OF THIS TO END AT LAST.
THE TOMB --
IT'S BEAUTIFUL. IT'S BEAUTIFUL!

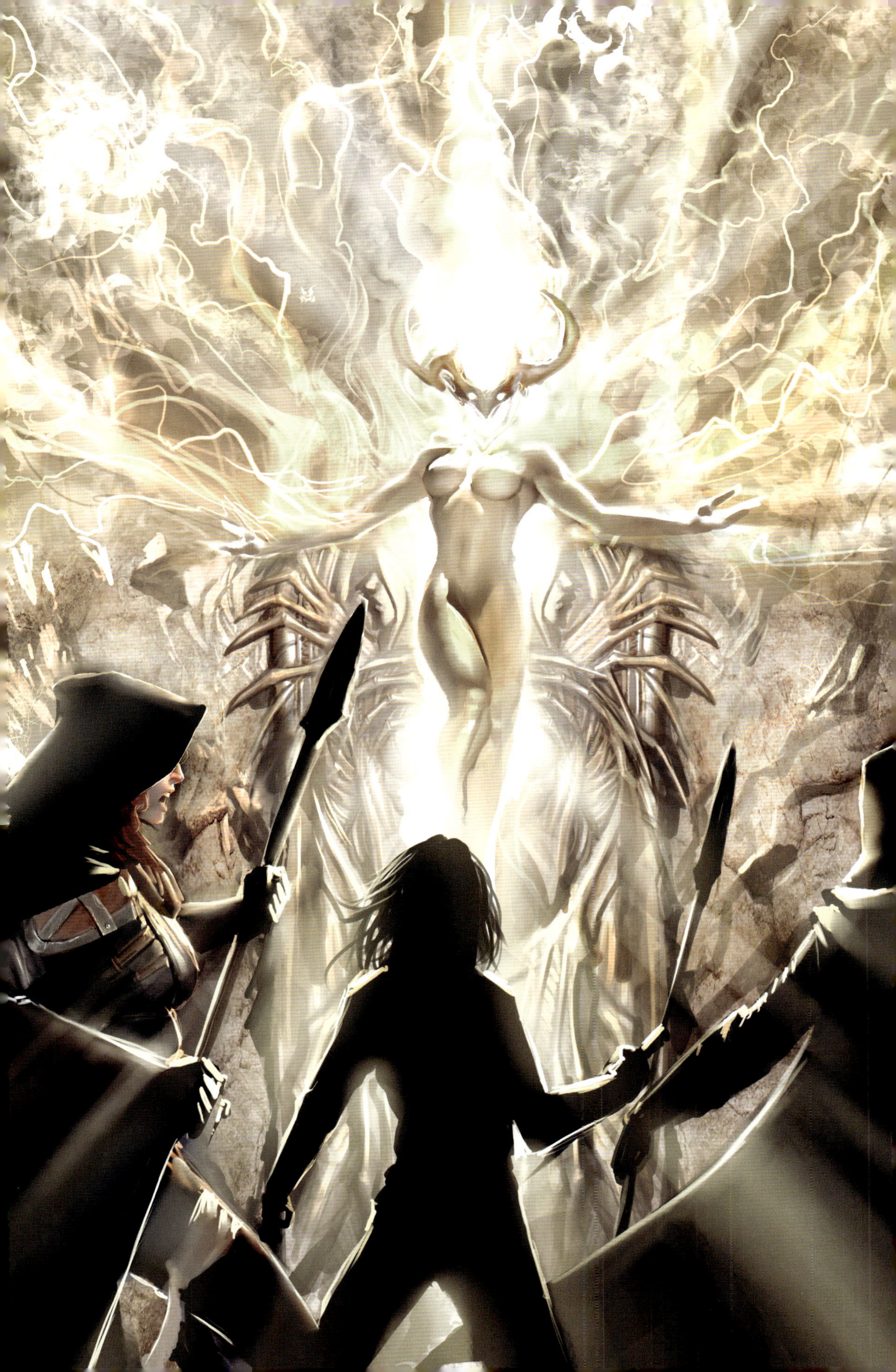

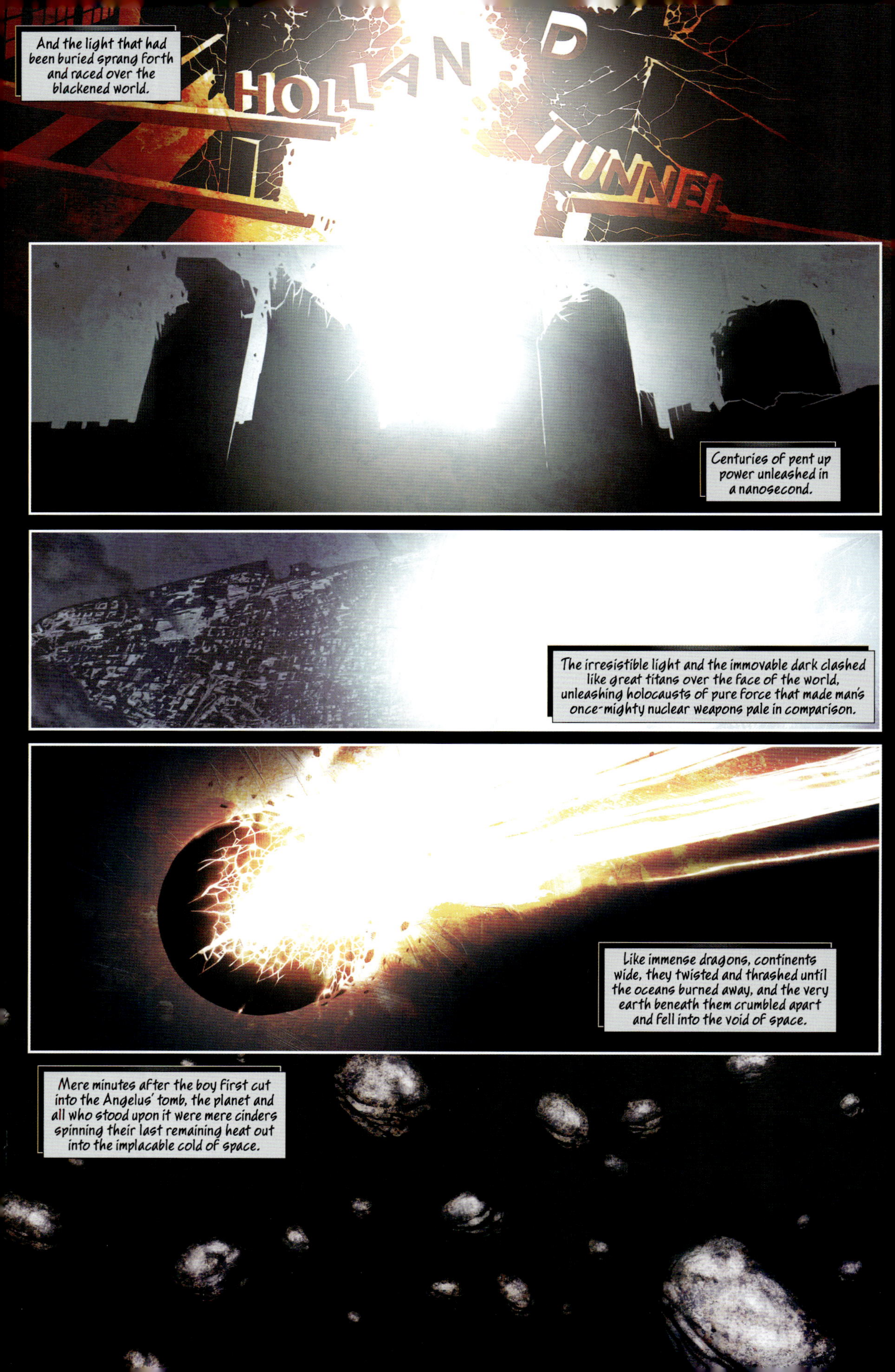

And the light that had been buried sprang forth and raced over the blackened world.
Centuries of pent up power unleashed in a nanosecond.
The irresistible light and the immovable dark clashed like great titans over the face of the world, unleashing holocausts of pure force that made man's once-mighty nuclear weapons pale in comparison.
Like immense dragons, continents wide, they twisted and thrashed until the oceans burned away, and the very earth beneath them crumbled apart and fell into the void of space.
Mere minutes after the boy first cut into the Angelus' tomb, the planet and all who stood upon it were mere cinders spinning their last remaining heat out into the implacable cold of space.

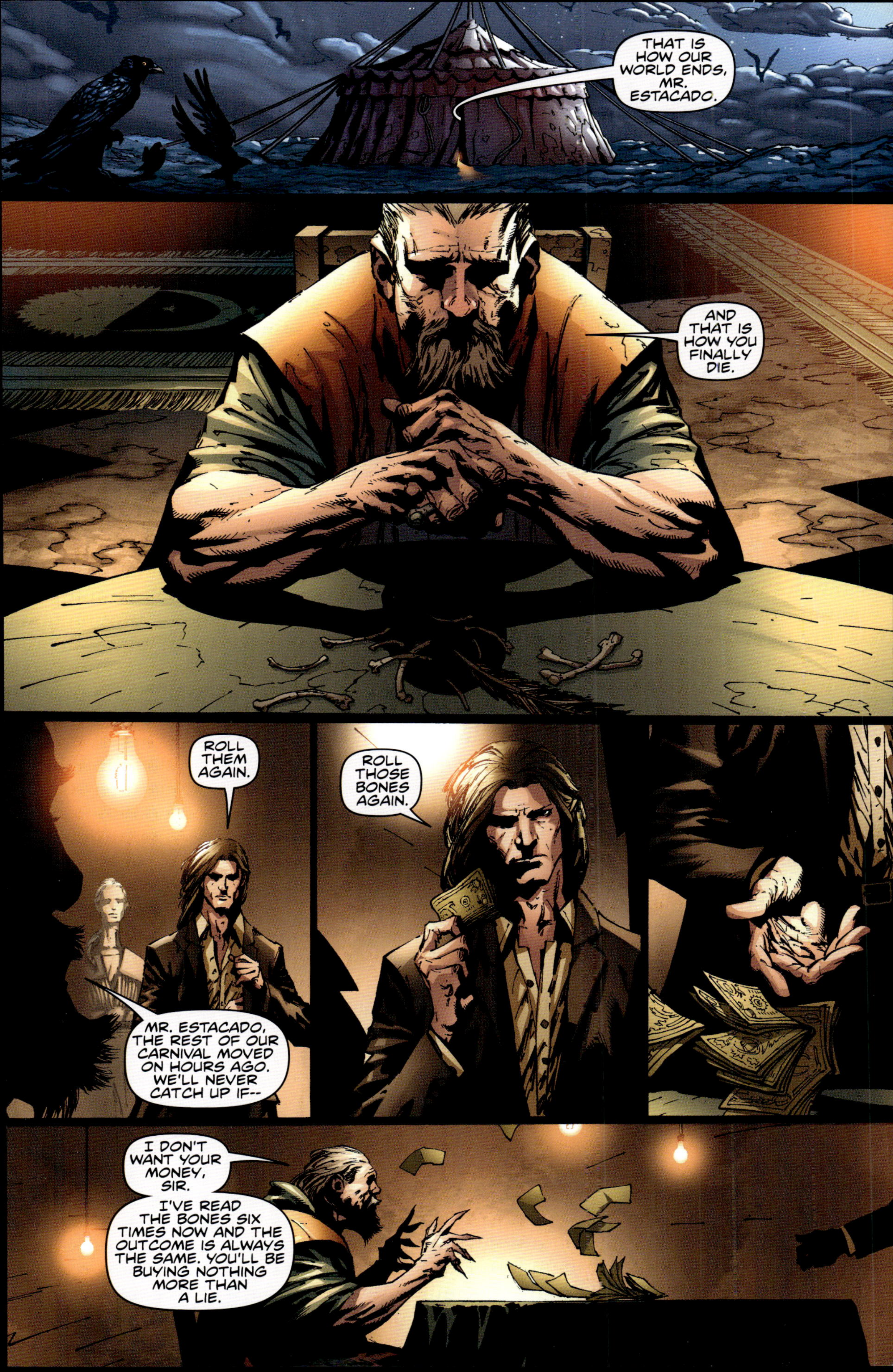

THAT IS HOW OUR WORLD ENDS, MR. ESTACADO.
AND THAT IS HOW YOU FINALLY DIE.
ROLL THEM AGAIN.
MR. ESTACADO, THE REST OF OUR CARNIVAL MOVED ON HOURS AGO. WE'LL NEVER CATCH UP IF--
ROLL THOSE BONES AGAIN.
I DON'T WANT YOUR MONEY, SIR.
I'VE READ THE BONES SIX TIMES NOW AND THE OUTCOME IS ALWAYS THE SAME. YOU'LL BE BUYING NOTHING MORE THAN A LIE.

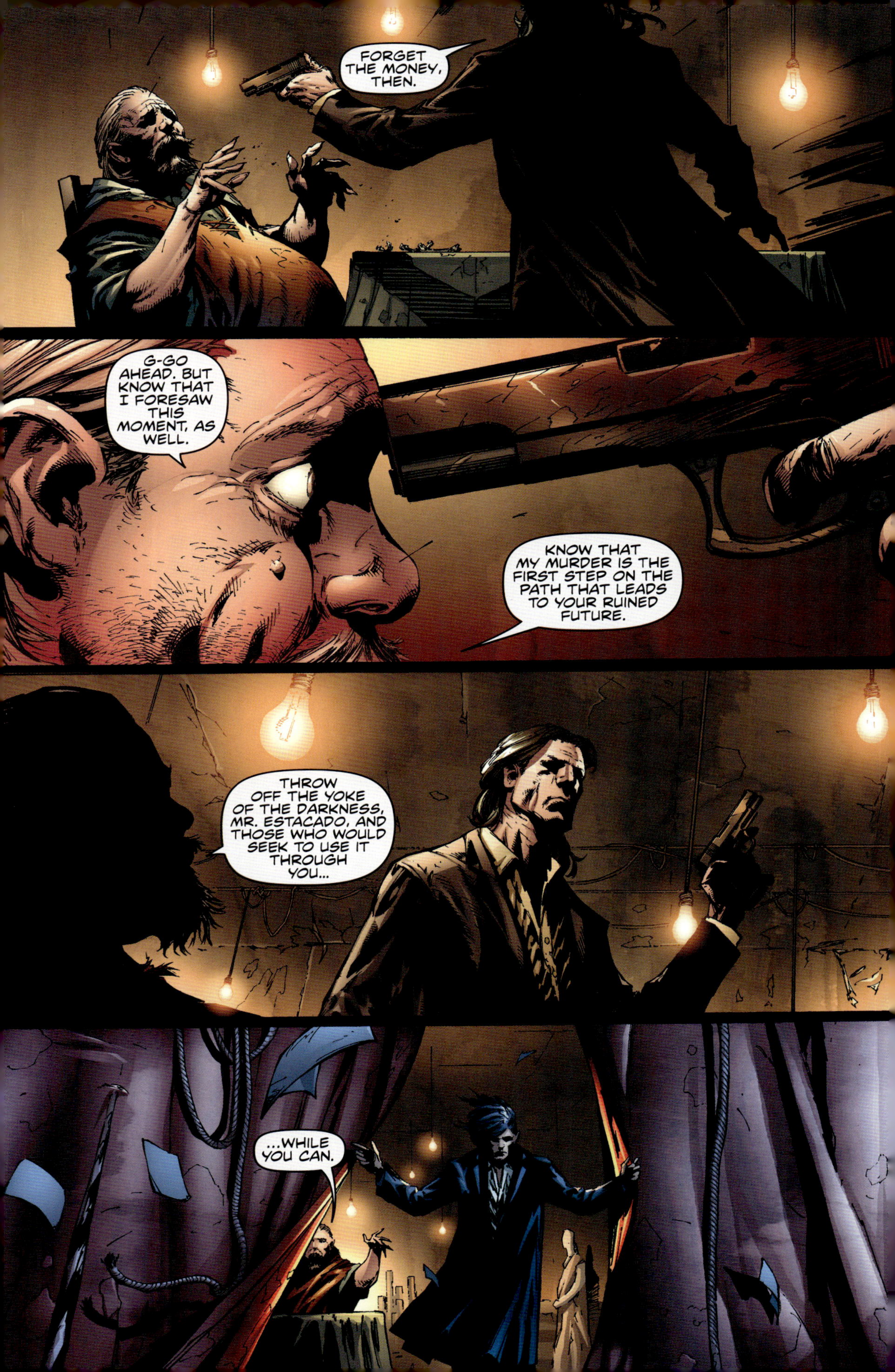
FORGET THE MONEY, THEN.
G-GO AHEAD. BUT KNOW THAT I FORESAW THIS MOMENT, AS WELL.
KNOW THAT MY MURDER IS THE FIRST STEP ON THE PATH THAT LEADS TO YOUR RUINED FUTURE.
THROW OFF THE YOKE OF THE DARKNESS, MR. ESTACADO, AND THOSE WHO WOULD SEEK TO USE IT THROUGH YOU...
...WHILE YOU CAN.

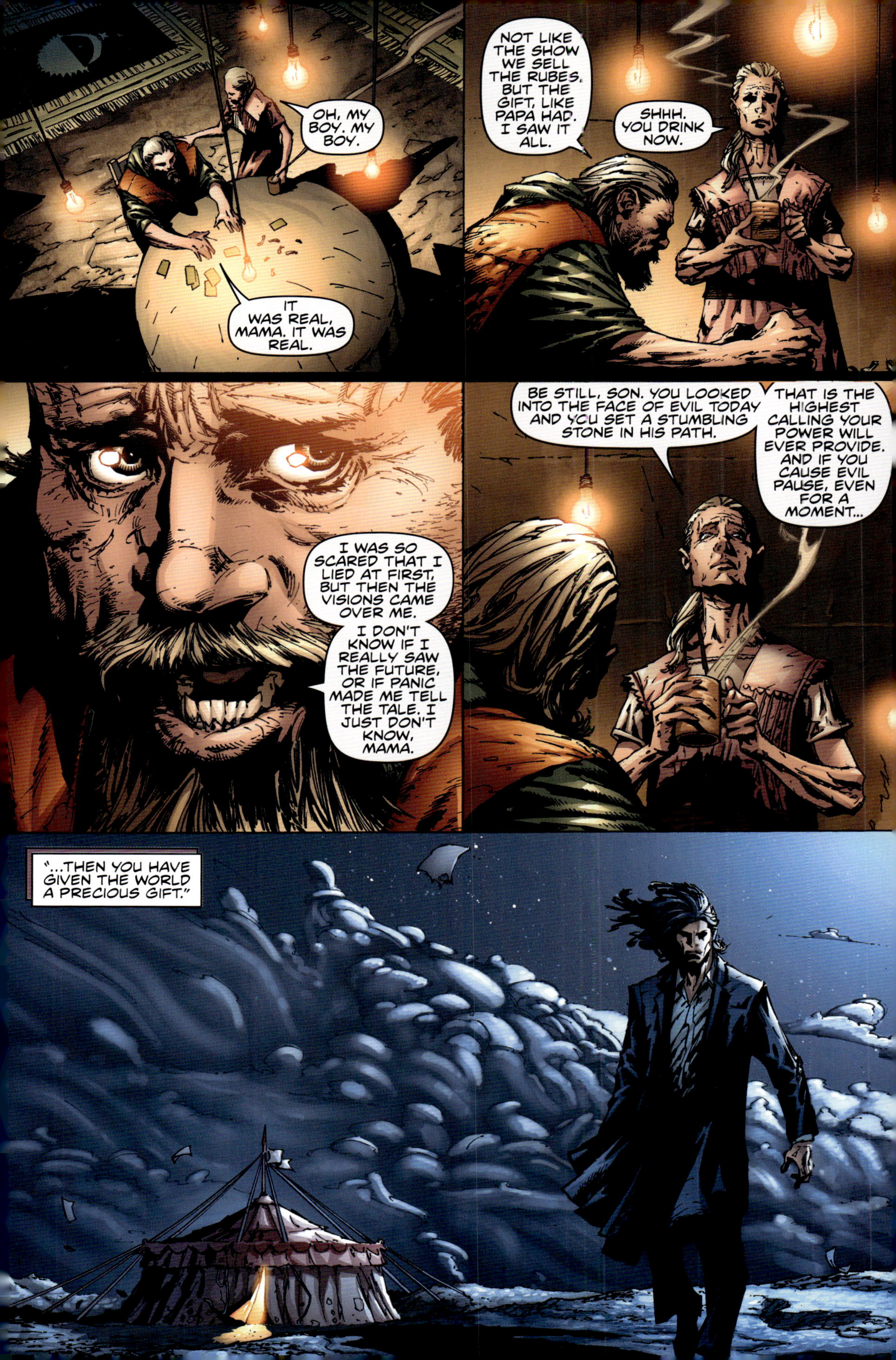
OH, MY BOY. MY BOY.
IT WAS REAL, MAMA. IT WAS REAL.
NOT LIKE THE SHOW WE SELL THE RUBES, BUT THE GIFT, LIKE PAPA HAD. I SAW IT ALL.
SHHH. YOU DRINK NOW.
I WAS SO SCARED THAT I LIED AT FIRST, BUT THEN THE VISIONS CAME OVER ME.
I DON'T KNOW IF I REALLY SAW THE FUTURE, OR IF PANIC MADE ME TELL THE TALE. I JUST DON'T KNOW, MAMA.
BE STILL, SON. YOU LOOKED INTO THE FACE OF EVIL TODAY AND YOU SET A STUMBLING STONE IN HIS PATH.
THAT IS THE HIGHEST CALLING YOUR POWER WILL EVER PROVIDE. AND IF YOU CAUSE EVIL PAUSE, EVEN FOR A MOMENT...
"...THEN YOU HAVE GIVEN THE WORLD A PRECIOUS GIFT."

The Darkness Issue #76
cover art by: Frazier Irving

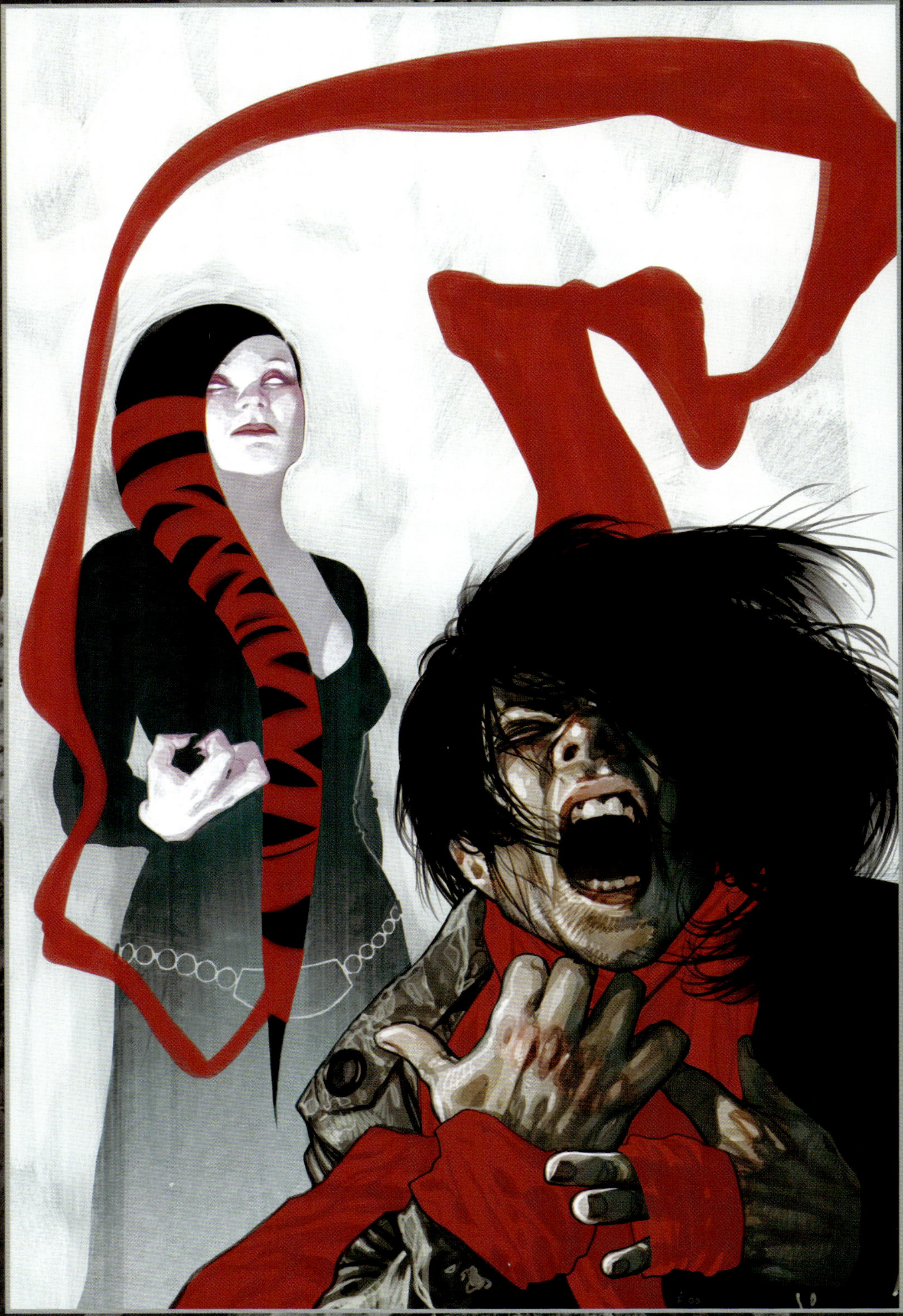

THE DARKNESS #76

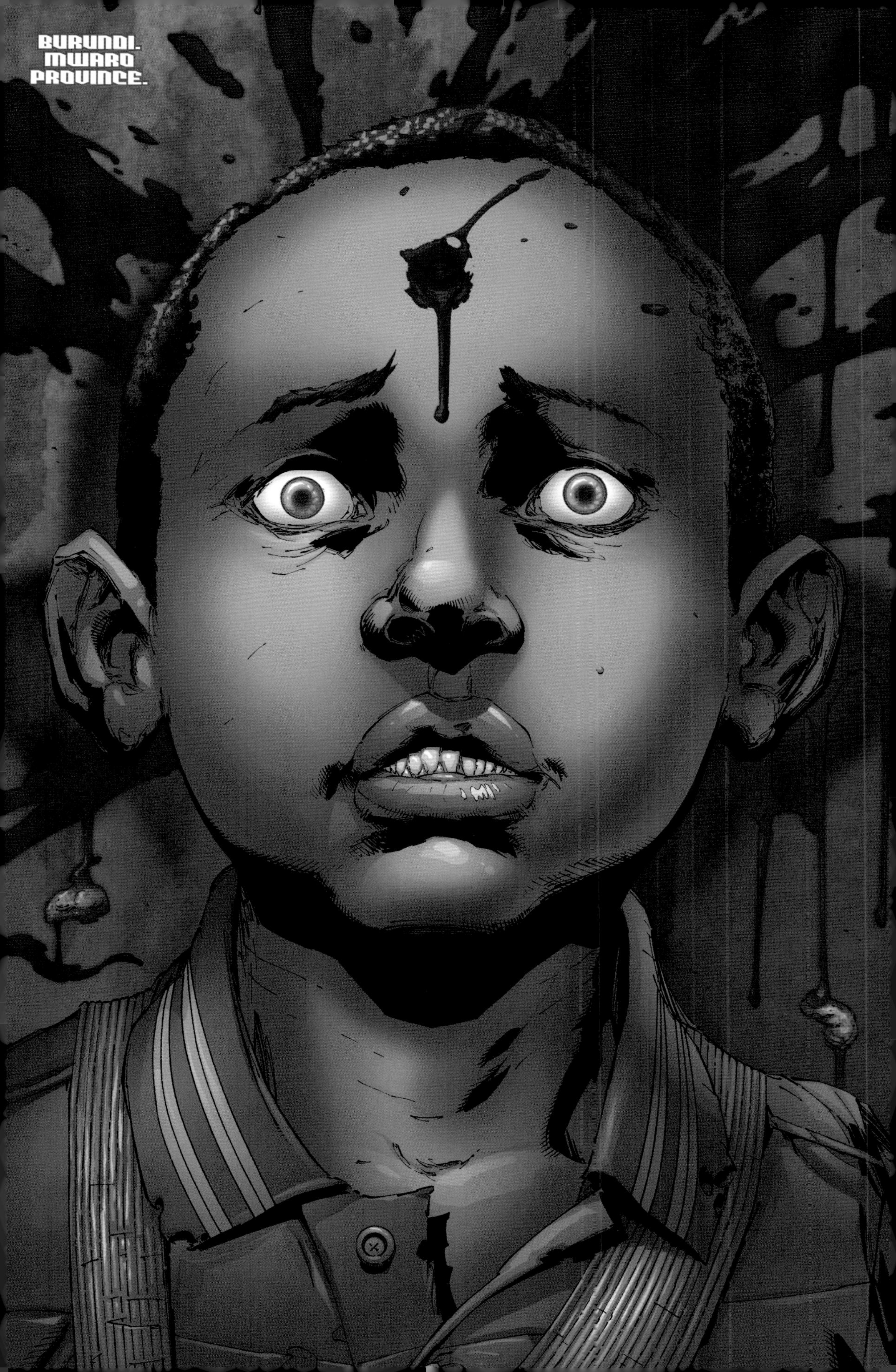
BURUNDI. MWARO PROVINCE.

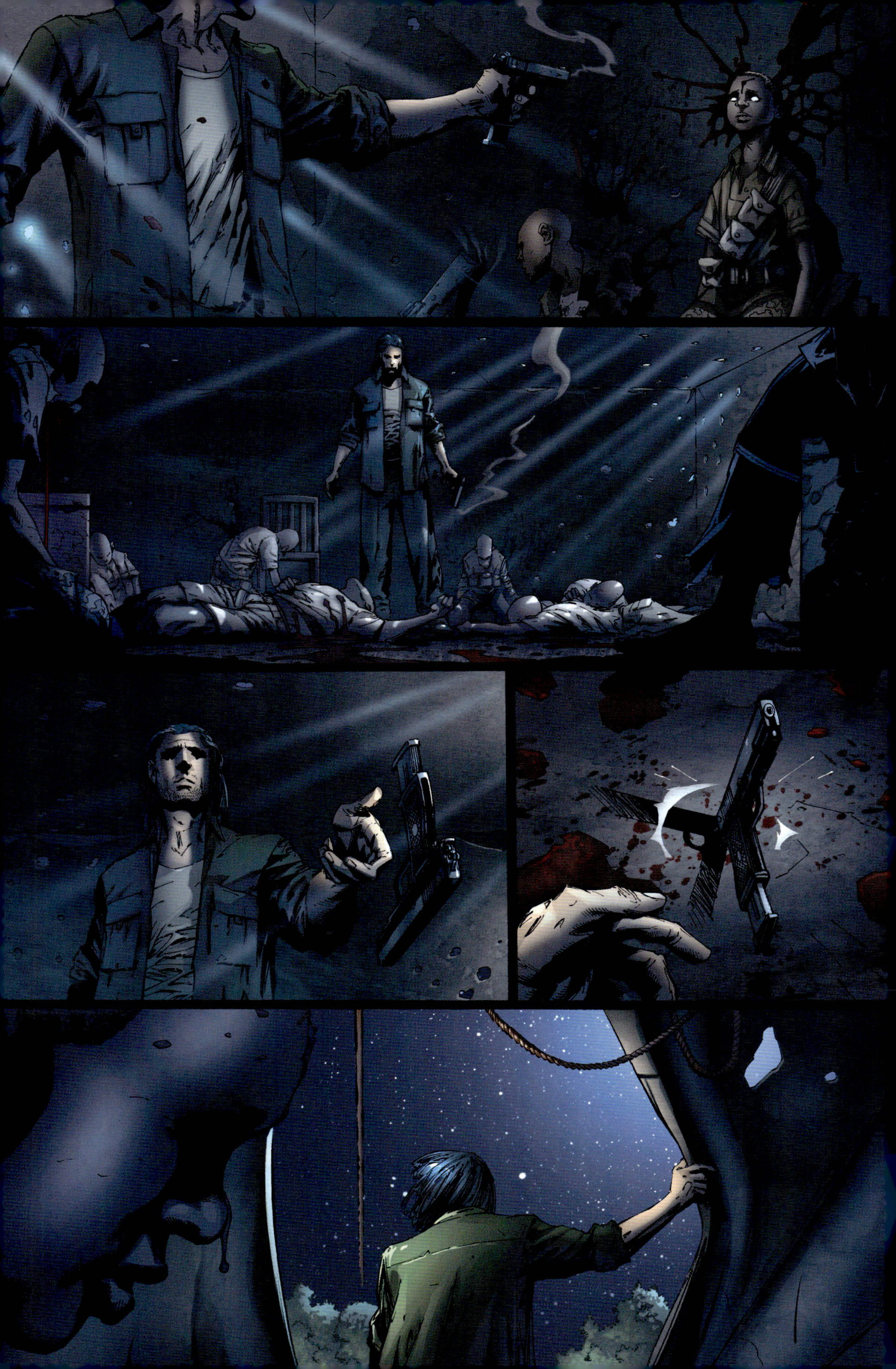

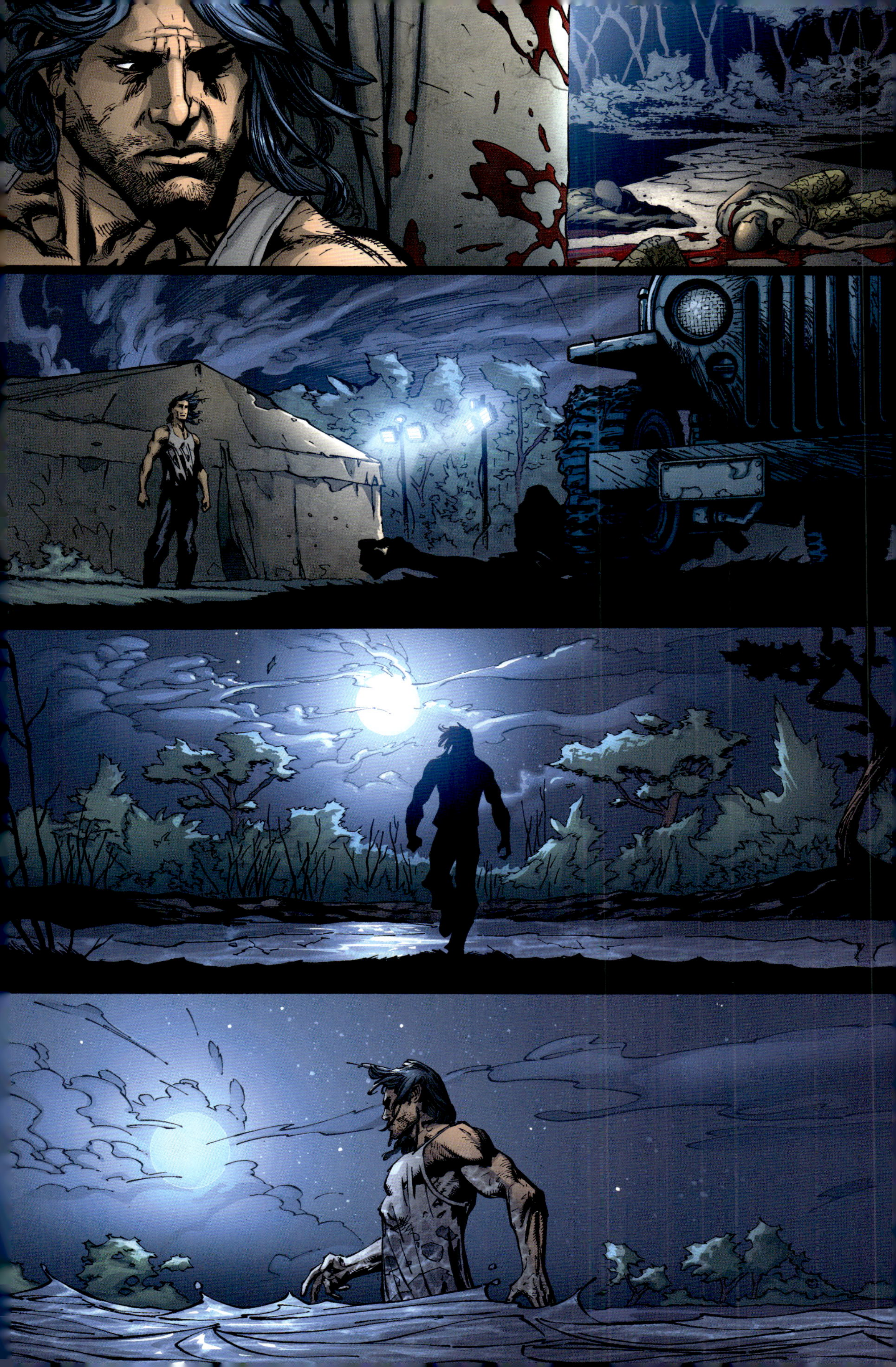

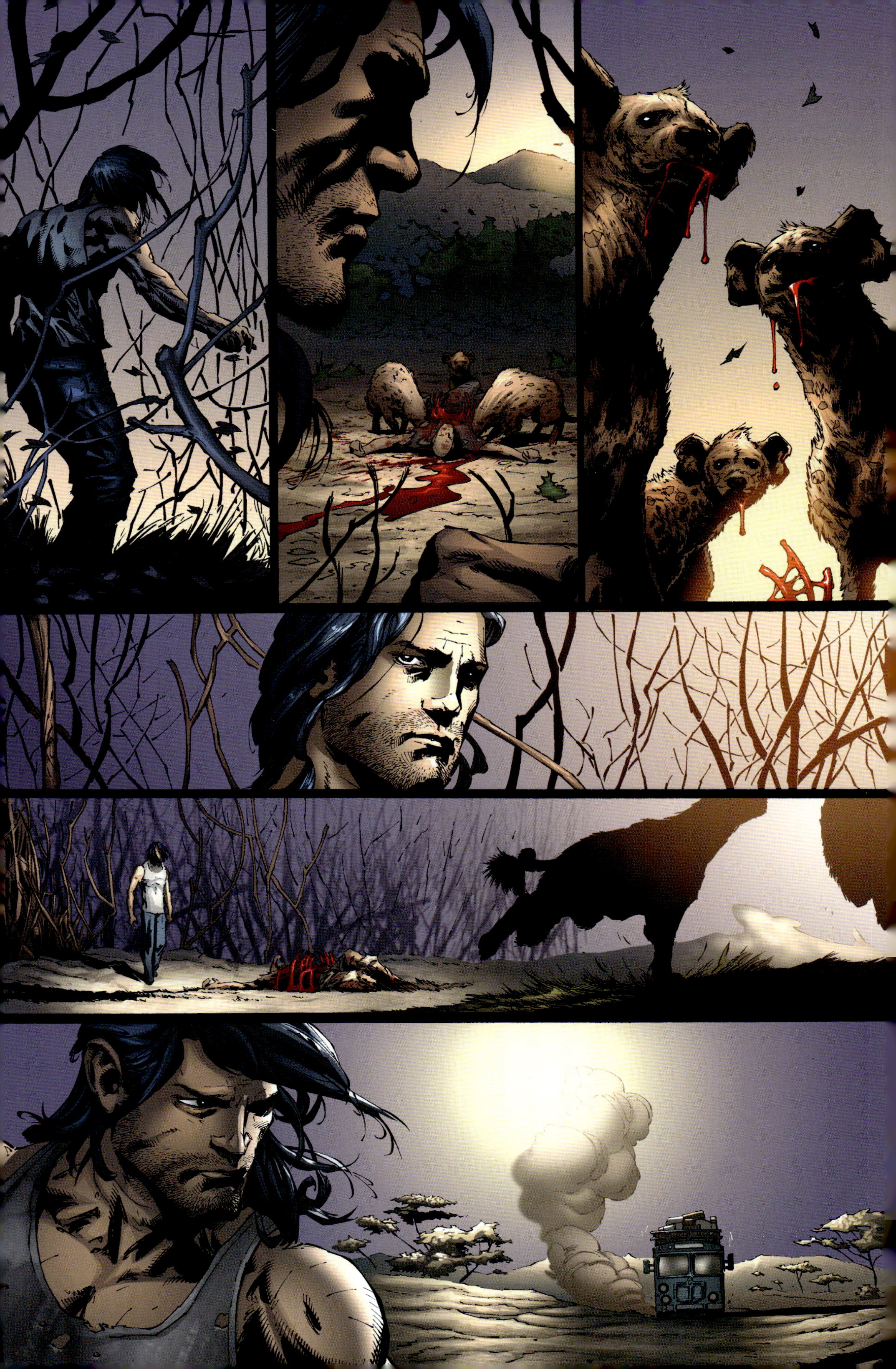

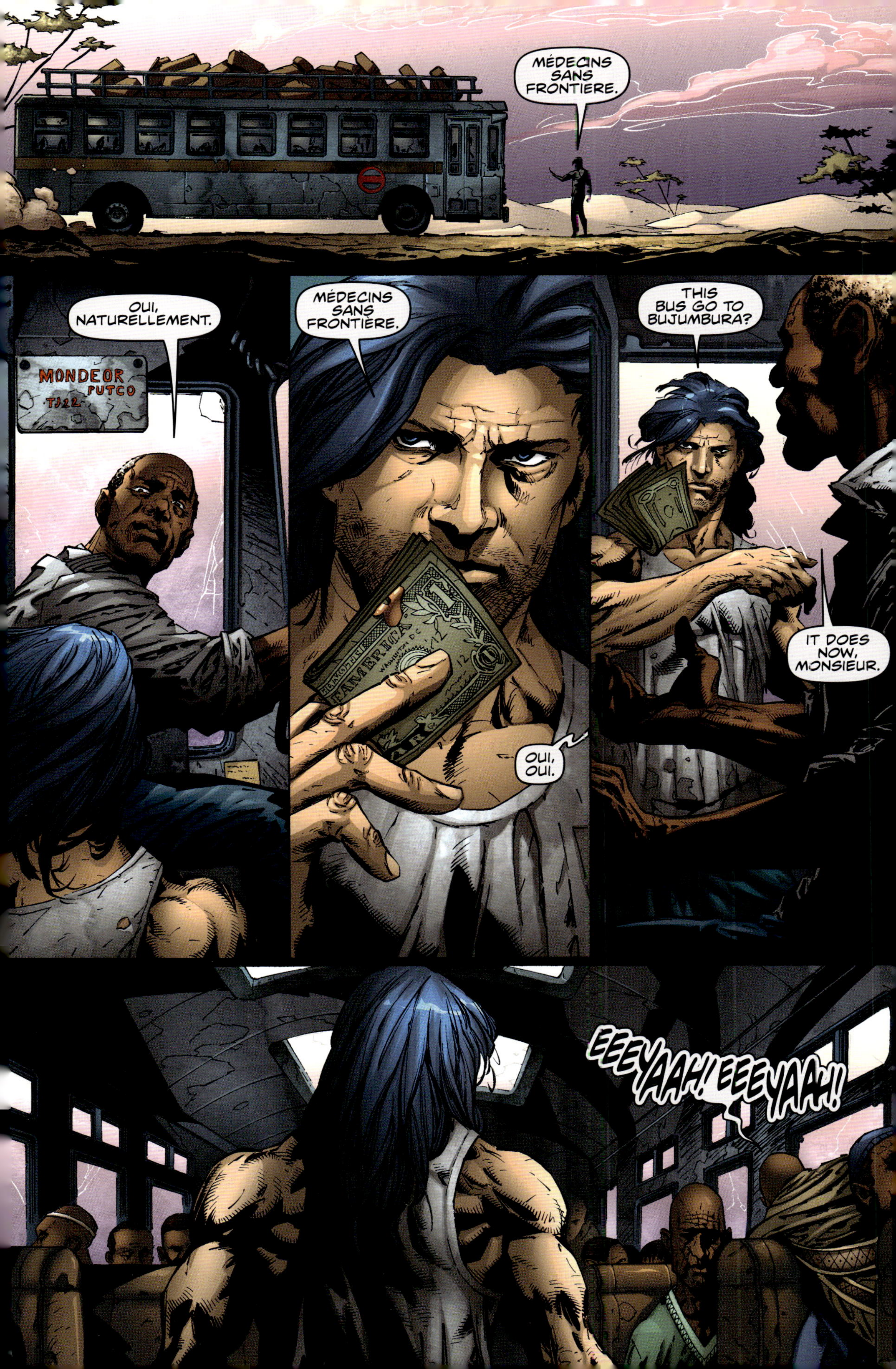
MÉDECINS SANS FRONTIERE.
MONDEOR PUTCO TJ22
OUI, NATURELLEMENT.
MÉDECINS SANS FRONTIÈRE.
OUI, OUI.
THIS BUS GO TO BUJUMBURA?
IT DOES NOW, MONSIEUR.
EEEYAAH! EEEYAAH!

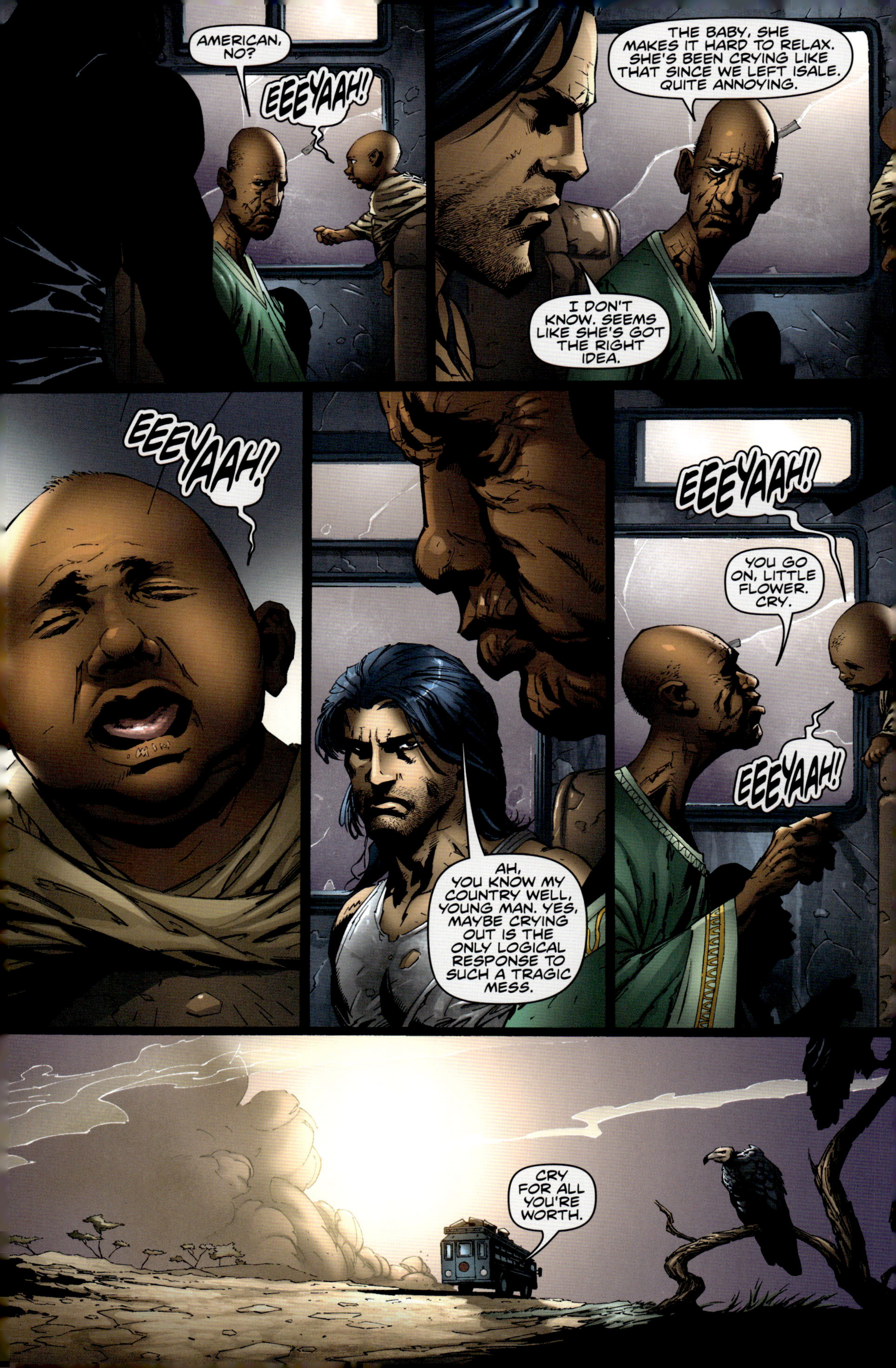
AMERICAN, NO?
EEEYAAH!!
THE BABY, SHE MAKES IT HARD TO RELAX. SHE'S BEEN CRYING LIKE THAT SINCE WE LEFT ISALE. QUITE ANNOYING.
I DON'T KNOW. SEEMS LIKE SHE'S GOT THE RIGHT IDEA.
EEEYAAH!
AH, YOU KNOW MY COUNTRY WELL, YOUNG MAN. YES, MAYBE CRYING OUT IS THE ONLY LOGICAL RESPONSE TO SUCH A TRAGIC MESS.
EEEYAAH!!
YOU GO ON, LITTLE FLOWER. CRY.
EEEYAAH!!
CRY FOR ALL YOU'RE WORTH.

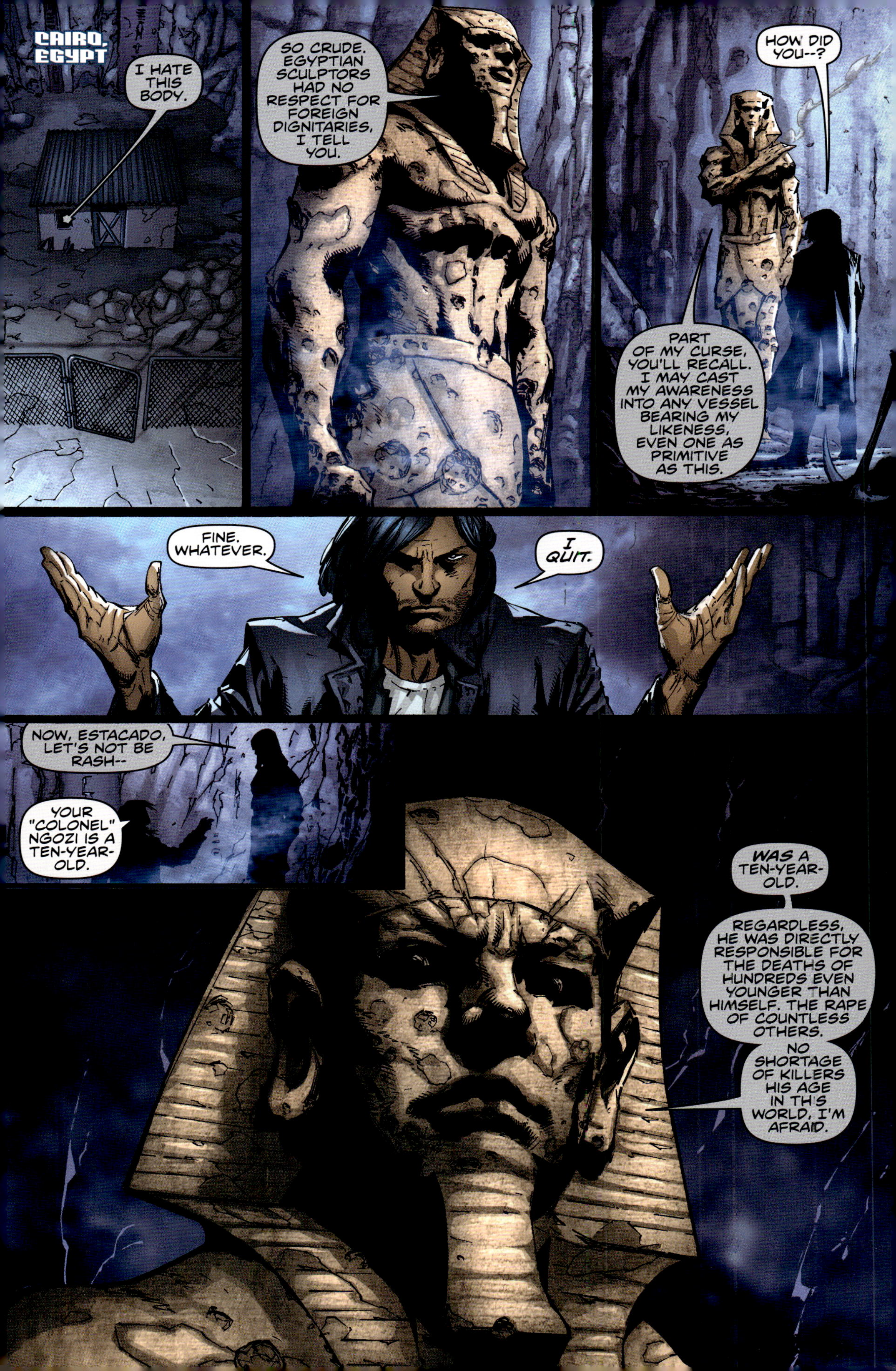
CAIRO, EGYPT
I HATE THIS BODY.
SO CRUDE. EGYPTIAN SCULPTORS HAD NO RESPECT FOR FOREIGN DIGNITARIES, I TELL YOU.
HOW DID YOU--?
PART OF MY CURSE, YOU'LL RECALL. I MAY CAST MY AWARENESS INTO ANY VESSEL BEARING MY LIKENESS, EVEN ONE AS PRIMITIVE AS THIS.
FINE. WHATEVER.
I QUIT.
NOW, ESTACADO, LET'S NOT BE RASH--
YOUR "COLONEL" NGOZI IS A TEN-YEAR-OLD.
WAS A TEN-YEAR-OLD.
REGARDLESS, HE WAS DIRECTLY RESPONSIBLE FOR THE DEATHS OF HUNDREDS EVEN YOUNGER THAN HIMSELF. THE RAPE OF COUNTLESS OTHERS.
NO SHORTAGE OF KILLERS HIS AGE IN THIS WORLD, I'M AFRAID.

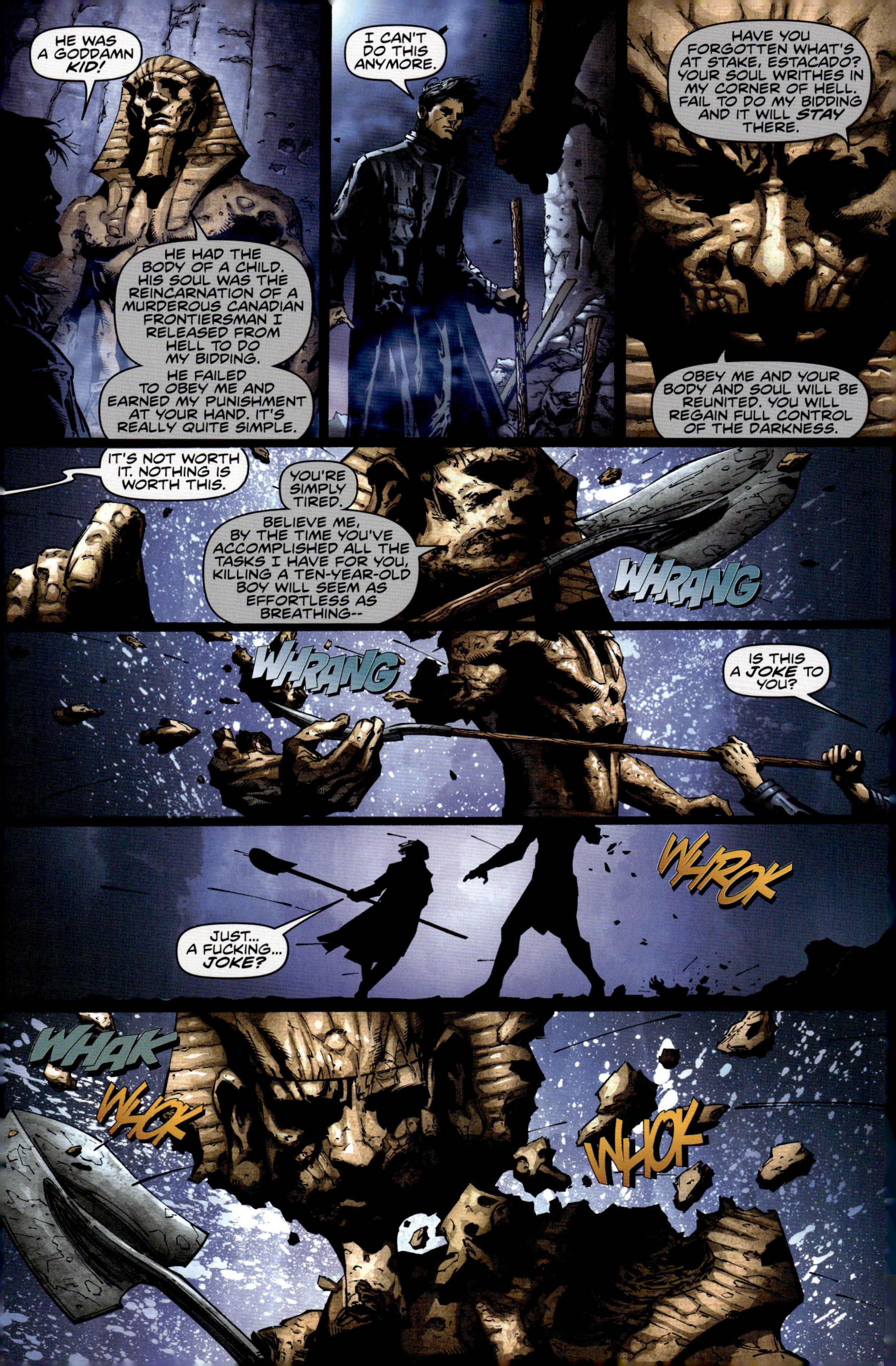
HE WAS A GODDAMN *KID!*
HE HAD THE BODY OF A CHILD. HIS SOUL WAS THE REINCARNATION OF A MURDEROUS CANADIAN FRONTIERSMAN I RELEASED FROM HELL TO DO MY BIDDING.
HE FAILED TO OBEY ME AND EARNED MY PUNISHMENT AT YOUR HAND. IT'S REALLY QUITE SIMPLE.
I CAN'T DO THIS ANYMORE.
HAVE YOU FORGOTTEN WHAT'S AT STAKE, ESTACADO? YOUR SOUL WRITHES IN MY CORNER OF HELL. FAIL TO DO MY BIDDING AND IT WILL *STAY* THERE.
OBEY ME AND YOUR BODY AND SOUL WILL BE REUNITED. YOU WILL REGAIN FULL CONTROL OF THE DARKNESS.
IT'S NOT WORTH IT. NOTHING IS WORTH THIS.
YOU'RE SIMPLY TIRED.
BELIEVE ME, BY THE TIME YOU'VE ACCOMPLISHED ALL THE TASKS I HAVE FOR YOU, KILLING A TEN-YEAR-OLD BOY WILL SEEM AS EFFORTLESS AS BREATHING--
WHRANG
WHRANG
IS THIS A *JOKE* TO YOU?
WHROK
JUST... A FUCKING... *JOKE?*
WHAK
WHOK
WHOK

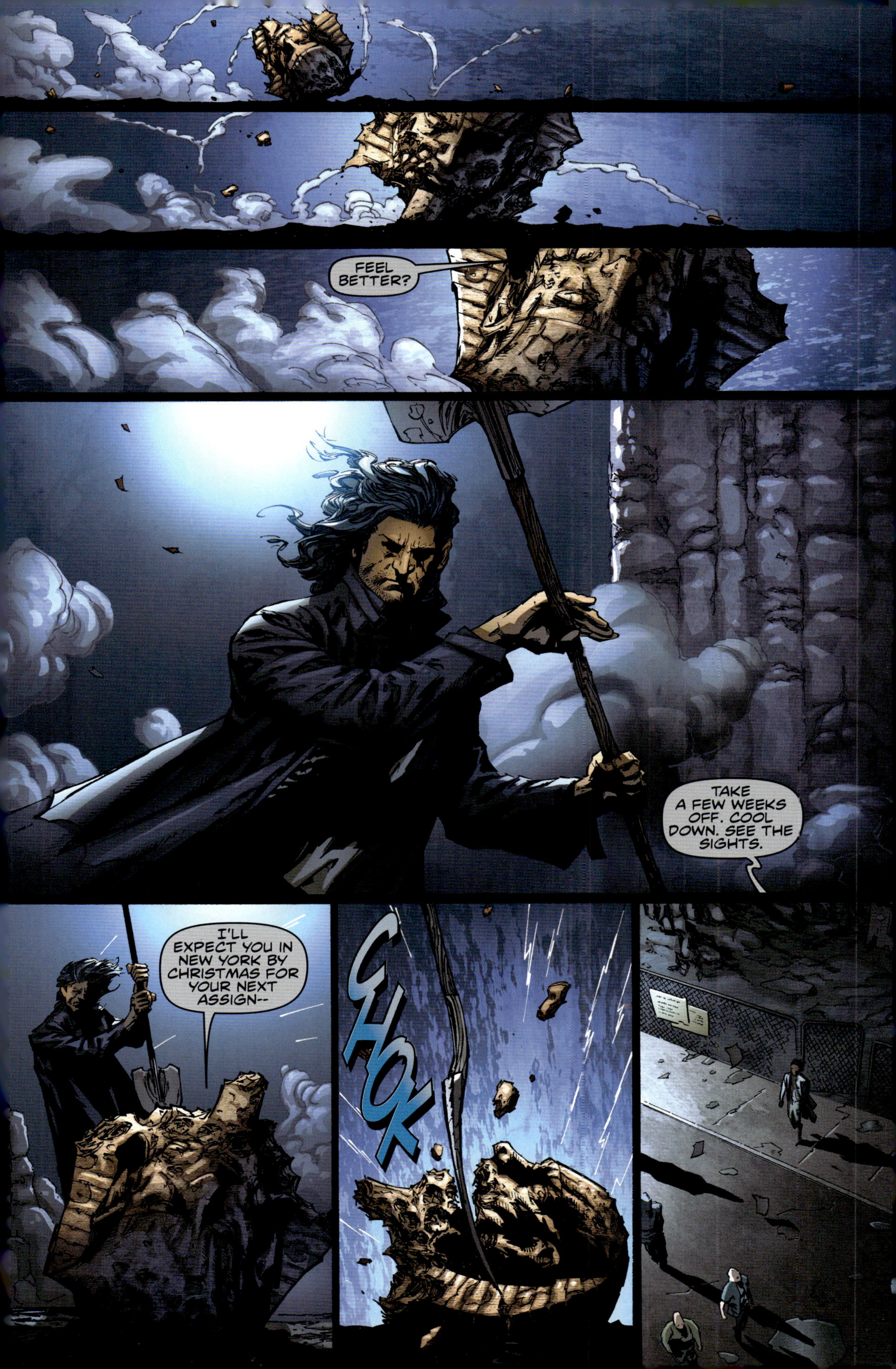
FEEL BETTER?
TAKE A FEW WEEKS OFF. COOL DOWN. SEE THE SIGHTS.
I'LL EXPECT YOU IN NEW YORK BY CHRISTMAS FOR YOUR NEXT ASSIGN--
CHOK

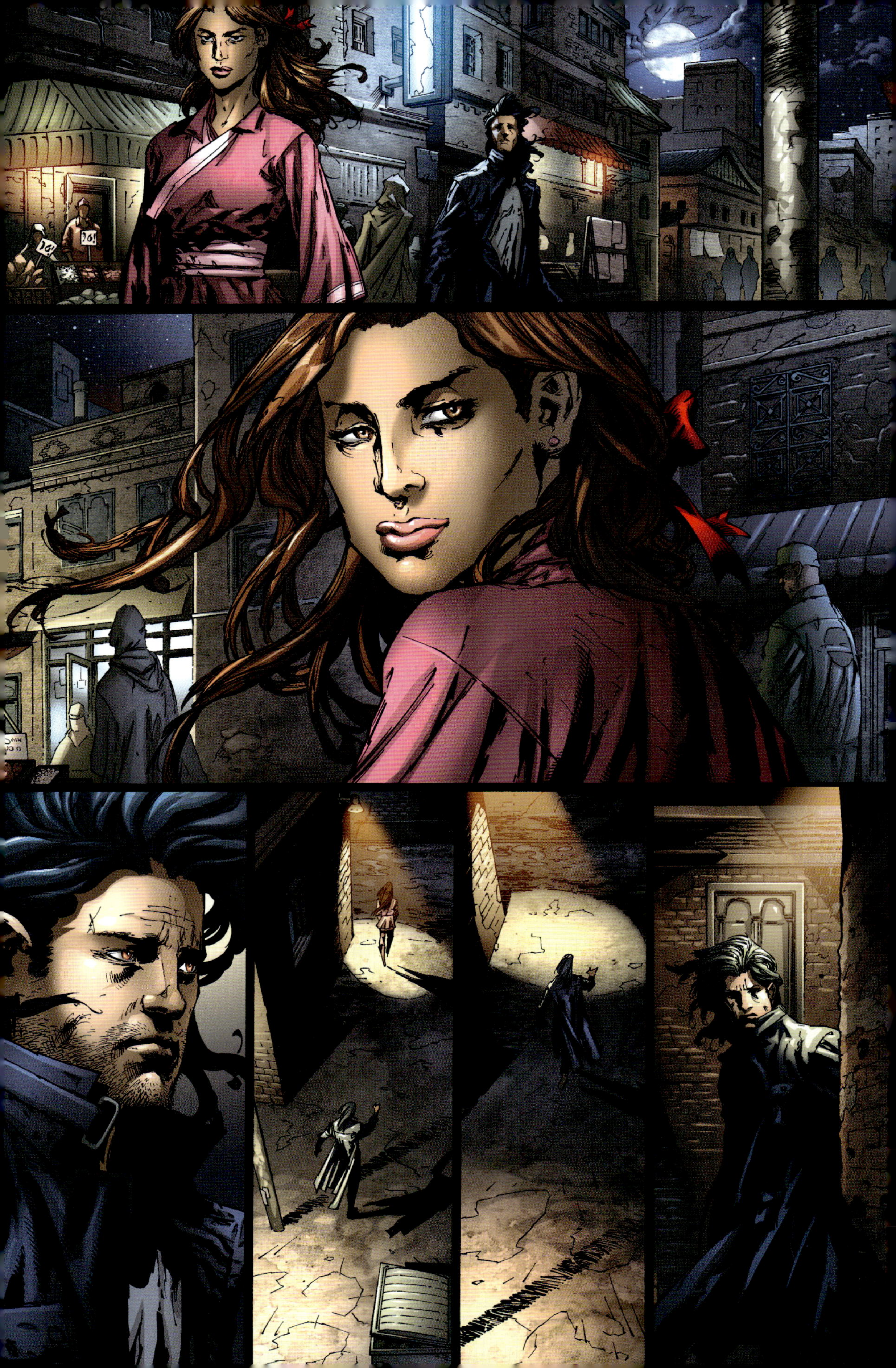

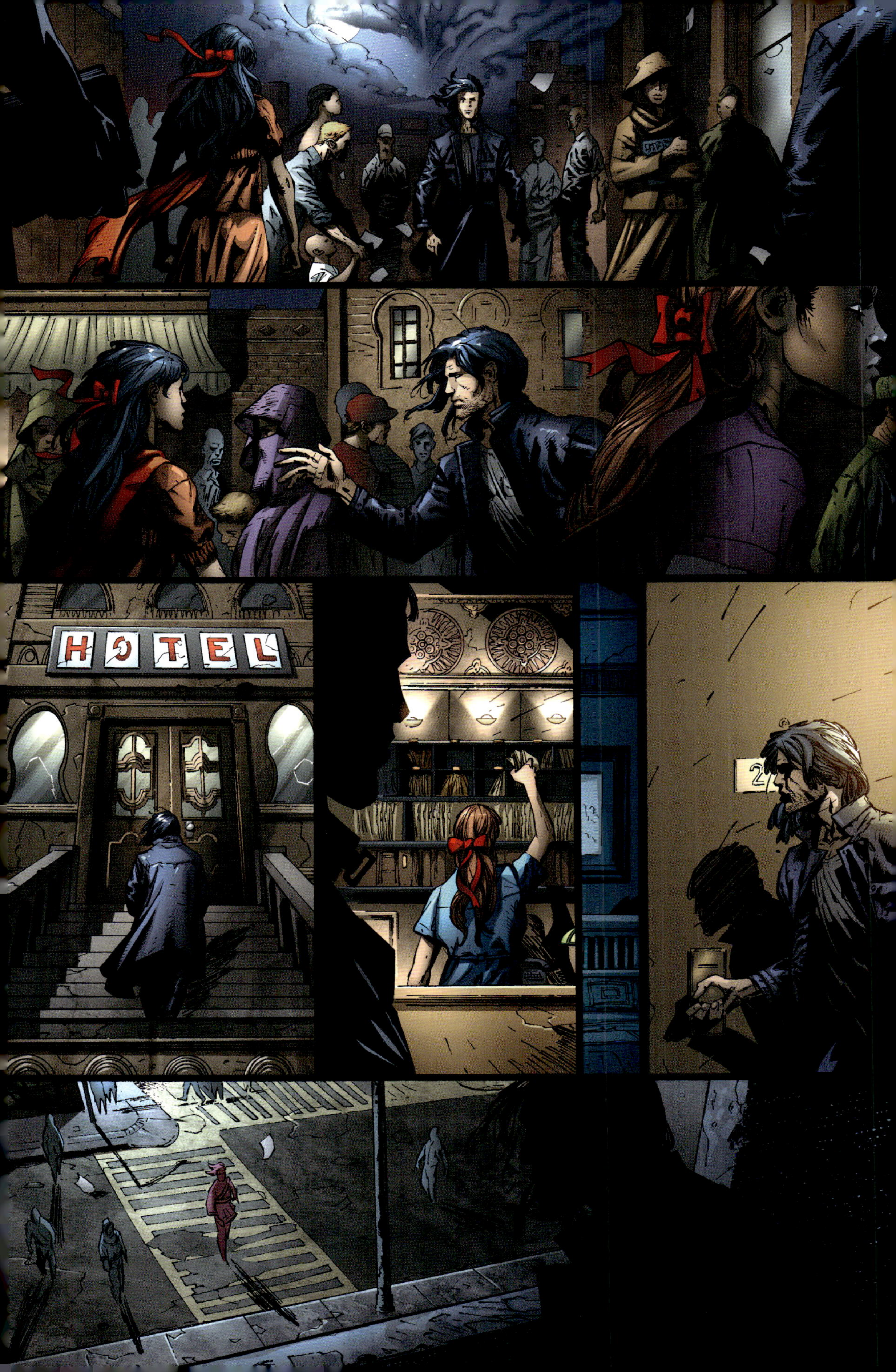
HOTEL

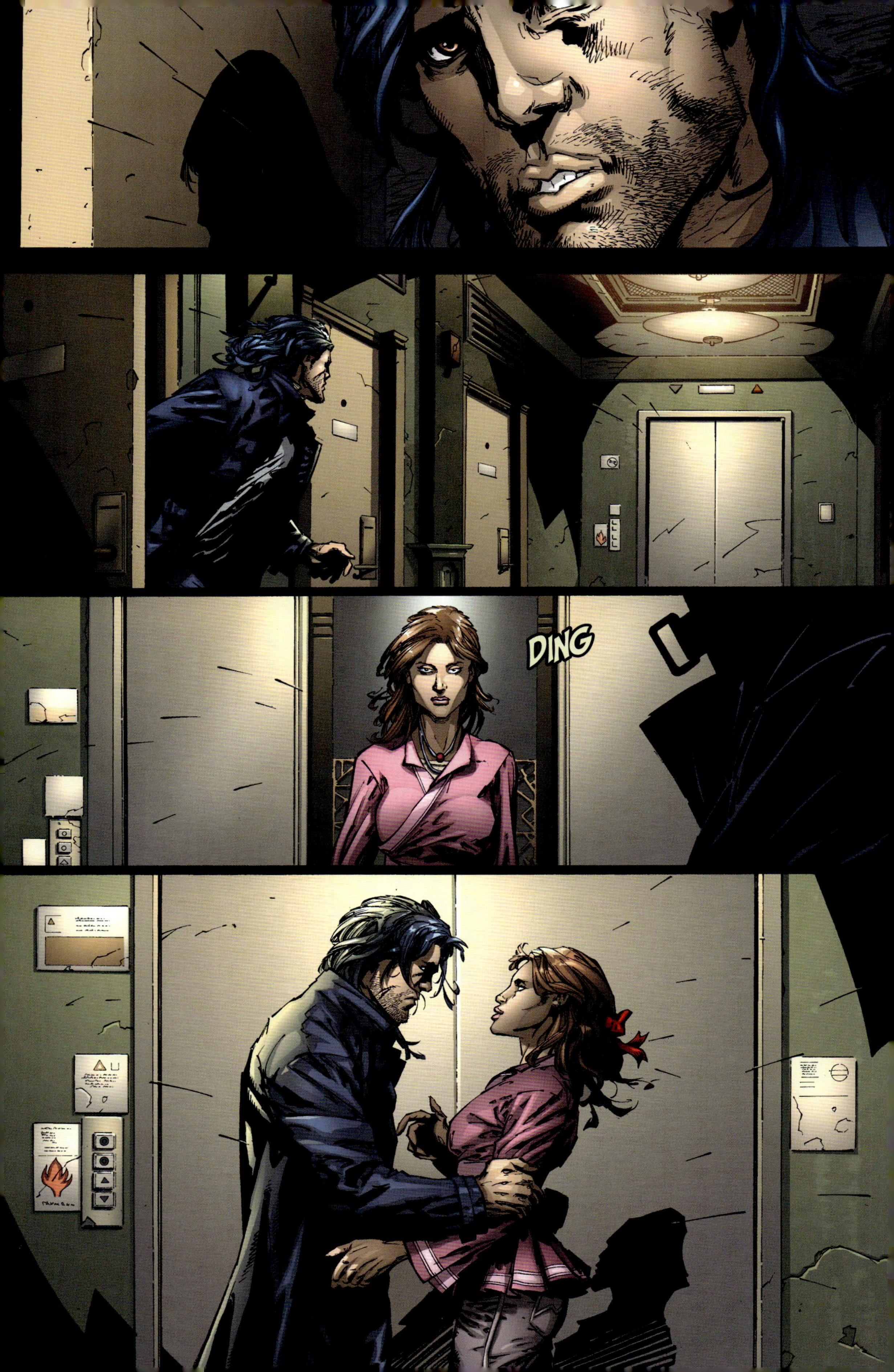
DING

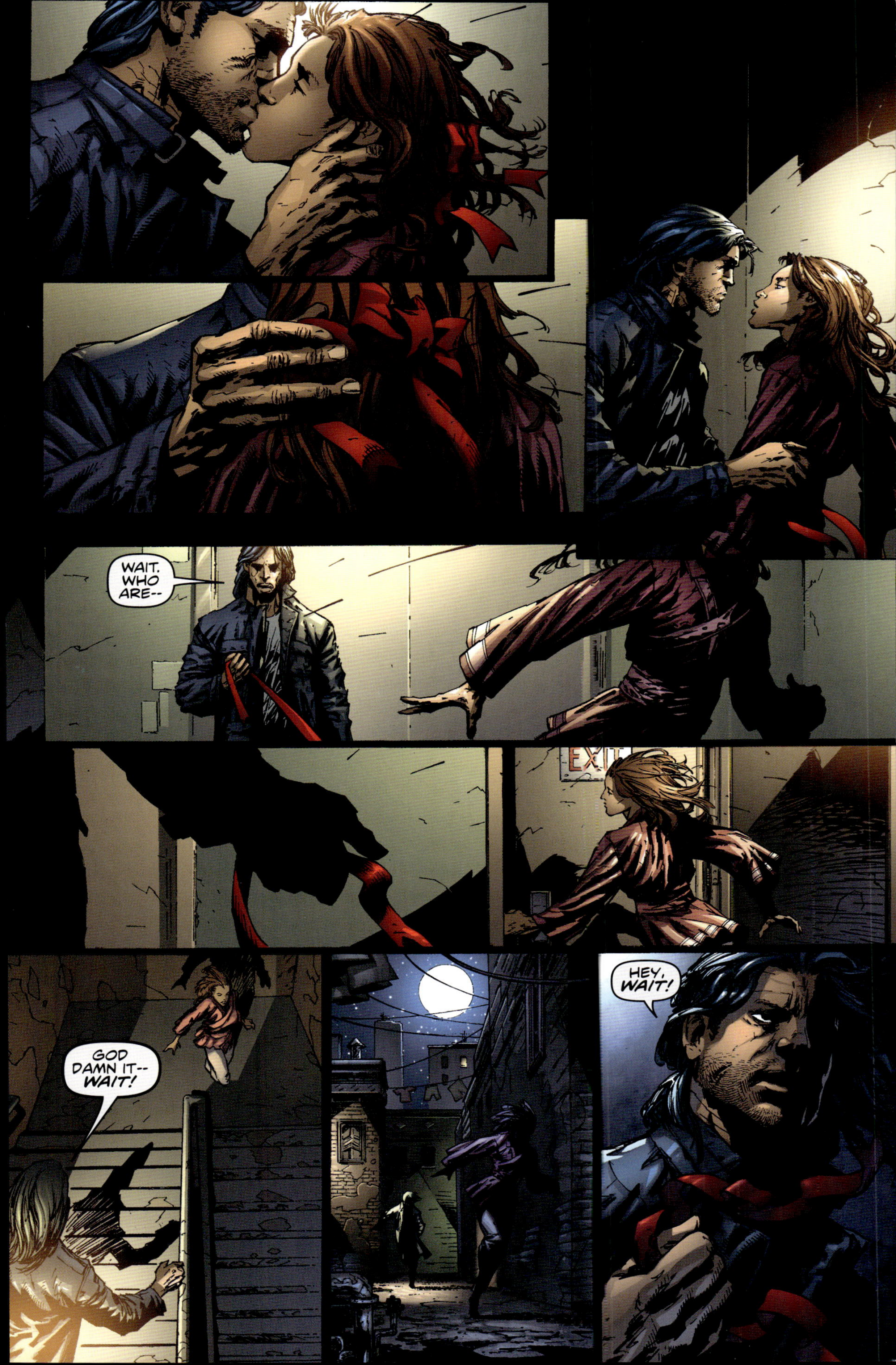
WAIT. WHO ARE--
GOD DAMN IT-- WAIT!
HEY, WAIT!

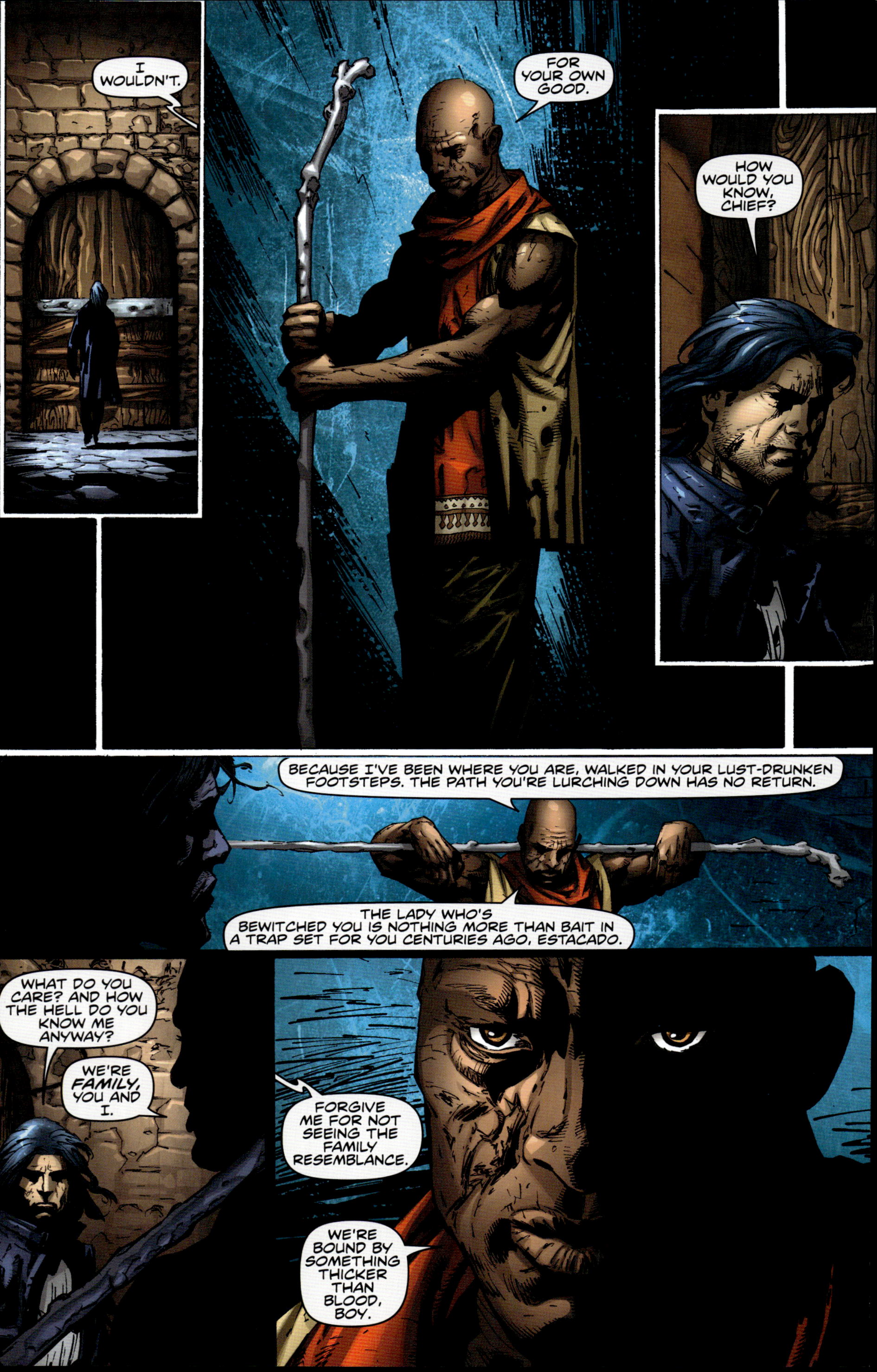
I WOULDN'T.
FOR YOUR OWN GOOD.
HOW WOULD YOU KNOW, CHIEF?
BECAUSE I'VE BEEN WHERE YOU ARE, WALKED IN YOUR LUST-DRUNKEN FOOTSTEPS. THE PATH YOU'RE LURCHING DOWN HAS NO RETURN.
THE LADY WHO'S BEWITCHED YOU IS NOTHING MORE THAN BAIT IN A TRAP SET FOR YOU CENTURIES AGO, ESTACADO.
WHAT DO YOU CARE? AND HOW THE HELL DO YOU KNOW ME ANYWAY?
WE'RE *FAMILY*, YOU AND I.
FORGIVE ME FOR NOT SEEING THE FAMILY RESEMBLANCE.
WE'RE BOUND BY SOMETHING THICKER THAN BLOOD, BOY.

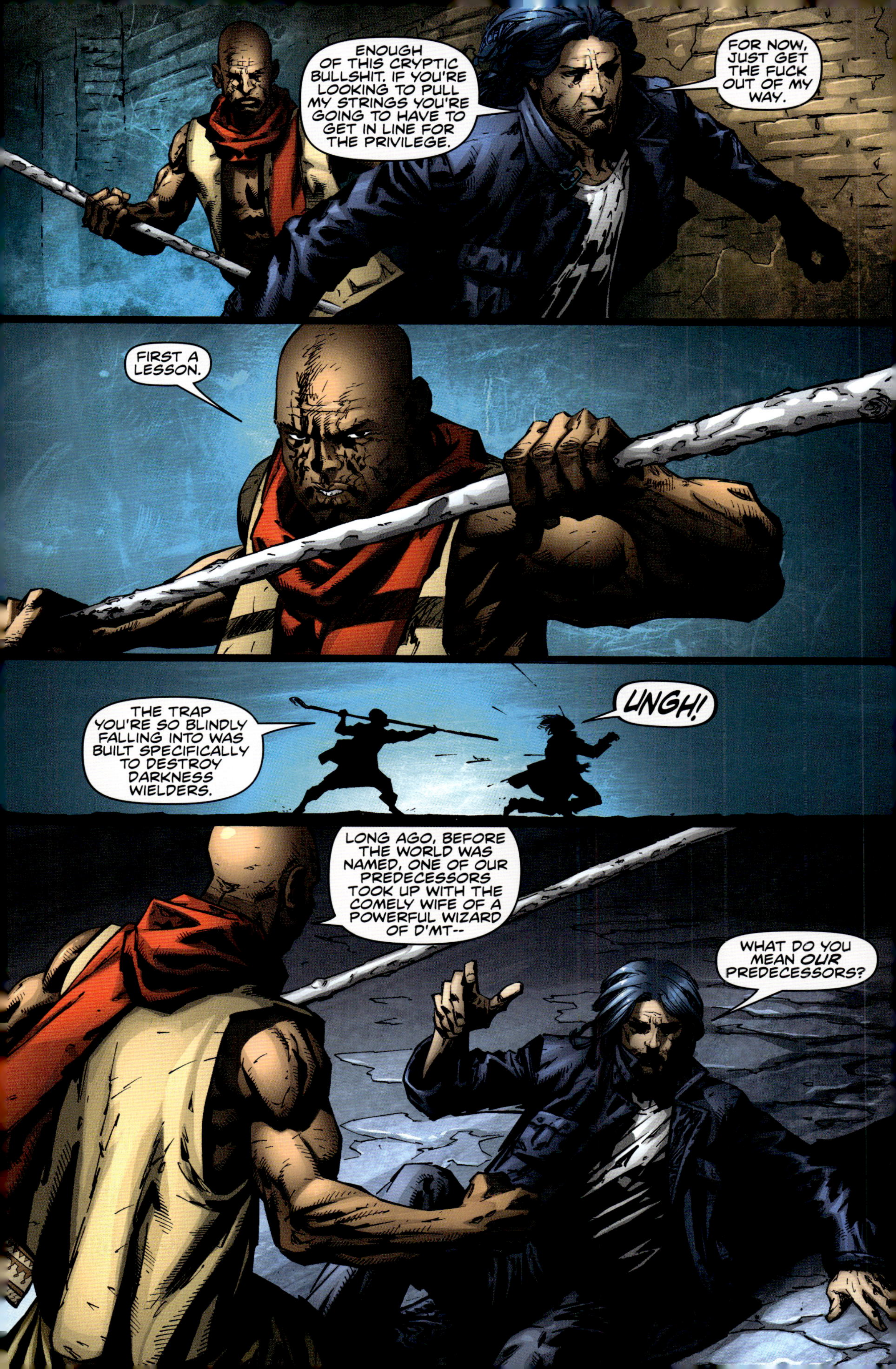
ENOUGH OF THIS CRYPTIC BULLSHIT. IF YOU'RE LOOKING TO PULL MY STRINGS YOU'RE GOING TO HAVE TO GET IN LINE FOR THE PRIVILEGE.
FOR NOW, JUST GET THE FUCK OUT OF MY WAY.
FIRST A LESSON.
THE TRAP YOU'RE SO BLINDLY FALLING INTO WAS BUILT SPECIFICALLY TO DESTROY DARKNESS WIELDERS.
UNGH!
LONG AGO, BEFORE THE WORLD WAS NAMED, ONE OF OUR PREDECESSORS TOOK UP WITH THE COMELY WIFE OF A POWERFUL WIZARD OF D'MT--
WHAT DO YOU MEAN *OUR* PREDECESSORS?

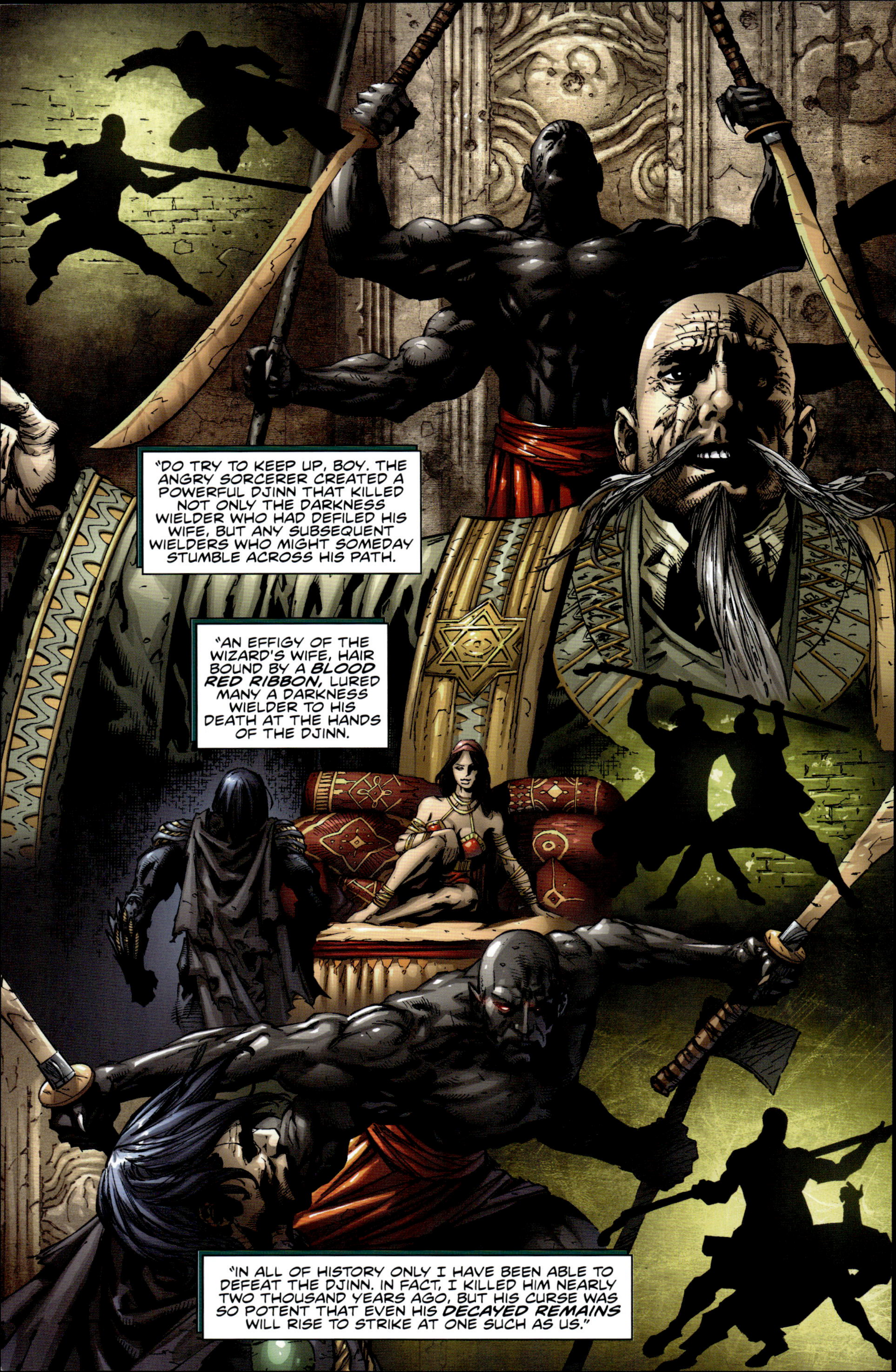
"DO TRY TO KEEP UP, BOY. THE ANGRY SORCERER CREATED A POWERFUL DJINN THAT KILLED NOT ONLY THE DARKNESS WIELDER WHO HAD DEFILED HIS WIFE, BUT ANY SUBSEQUENT WIELDERS WHO MIGHT SOMEDAY STUMBLE ACROSS HIS PATH.
"AN EFFIGY OF THE WIZARD'S WIFE, HAIR BOUND BY A BLOOD RED RIBBON, LURED MANY A DARKNESS WIELDER TO HIS DEATH AT THE HANDS OF THE DJINN.
"IN ALL OF HISTORY ONLY I HAVE BEEN ABLE TO DEFEAT THE DJINN. IN FACT, I KILLED HIM NEARLY TWO THOUSAND YEARS AGO, BUT HIS CURSE WAS SO POTENT THAT EVEN HIS DECAYED REMAINS WILL RISE TO STRIKE AT ONE SUCH AS US."

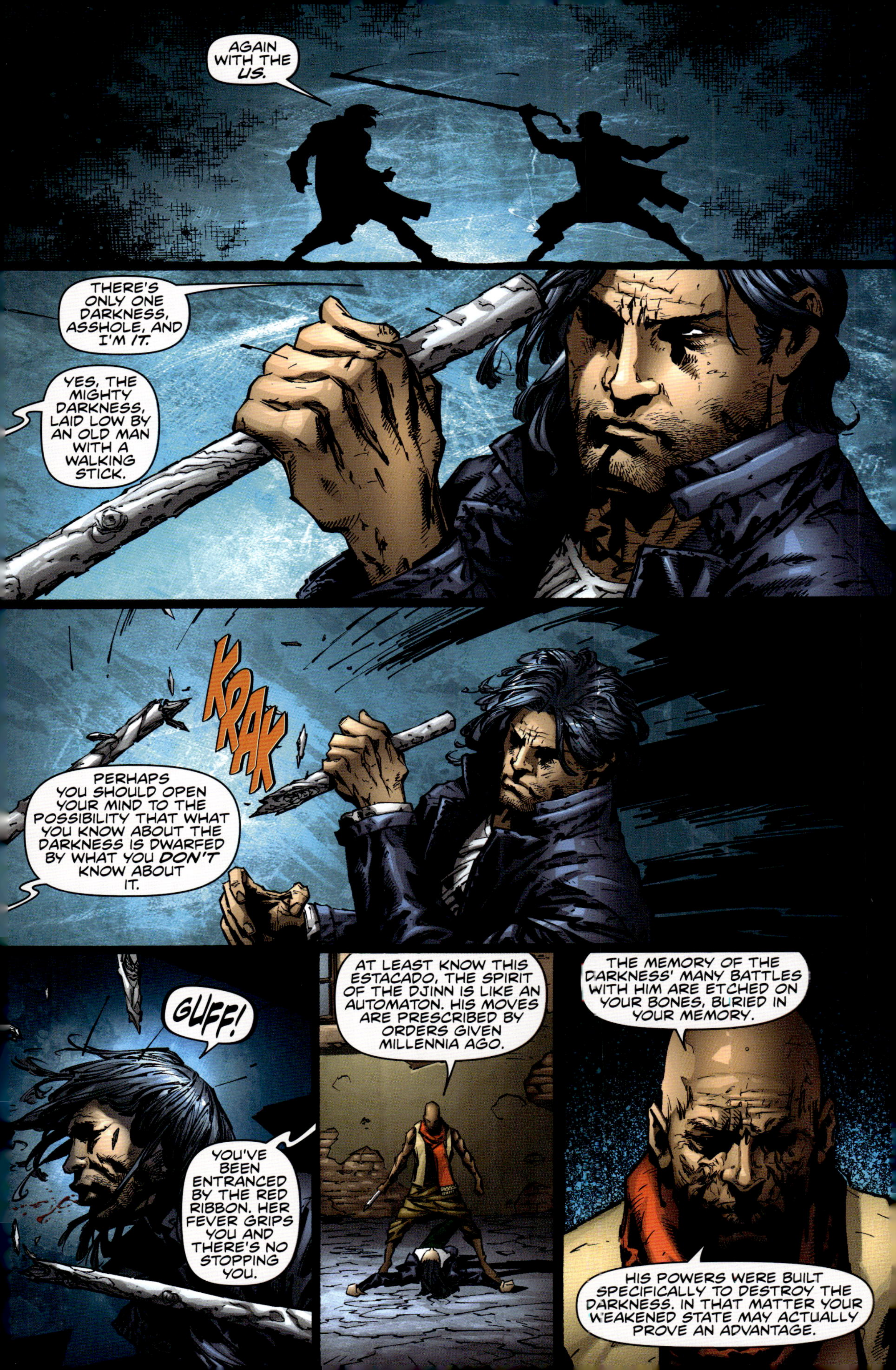
AGAIN WITH THE *US.*
THERE'S ONLY ONE DARKNESS, ASSHOLE, AND I'M *IT.*
YES, THE MIGHTY DARKNESS, LAID LOW BY AN OLD MAN WITH A WALKING STICK.
KRAK
PERHAPS YOU SHOULD OPEN YOUR MIND TO THE POSSIBILITY THAT WHAT YOU KNOW ABOUT THE DARKNESS IS DWARFED BY WHAT YOU *DON'T* KNOW ABOUT IT.
GUFF!
YOU'VE BEEN ENTRANCED BY THE RED RIBBON. HER FEVER GRIPS YOU AND THERE'S NO STOPPING YOU.
AT LEAST KNOW THIS ESTACADO, THE SPIRIT OF THE DJINN IS LIKE AN AUTOMATON. HIS MOVES ARE PRESCRIBED BY ORDERS GIVEN MILLENNIA AGO.
THE MEMORY OF THE DARKNESS' MANY BATTLES WITH HIM ARE ETCHED ON YOUR BONES, BURIED IN YOUR MEMORY.
HIS POWERS WERE BUILT SPECIFICALLY TO DESTROY THE DARKNESS. IN THAT MATTER YOUR WEAKENED STATE MAY ACTUALLY PROVE AN ADVANTAGE.

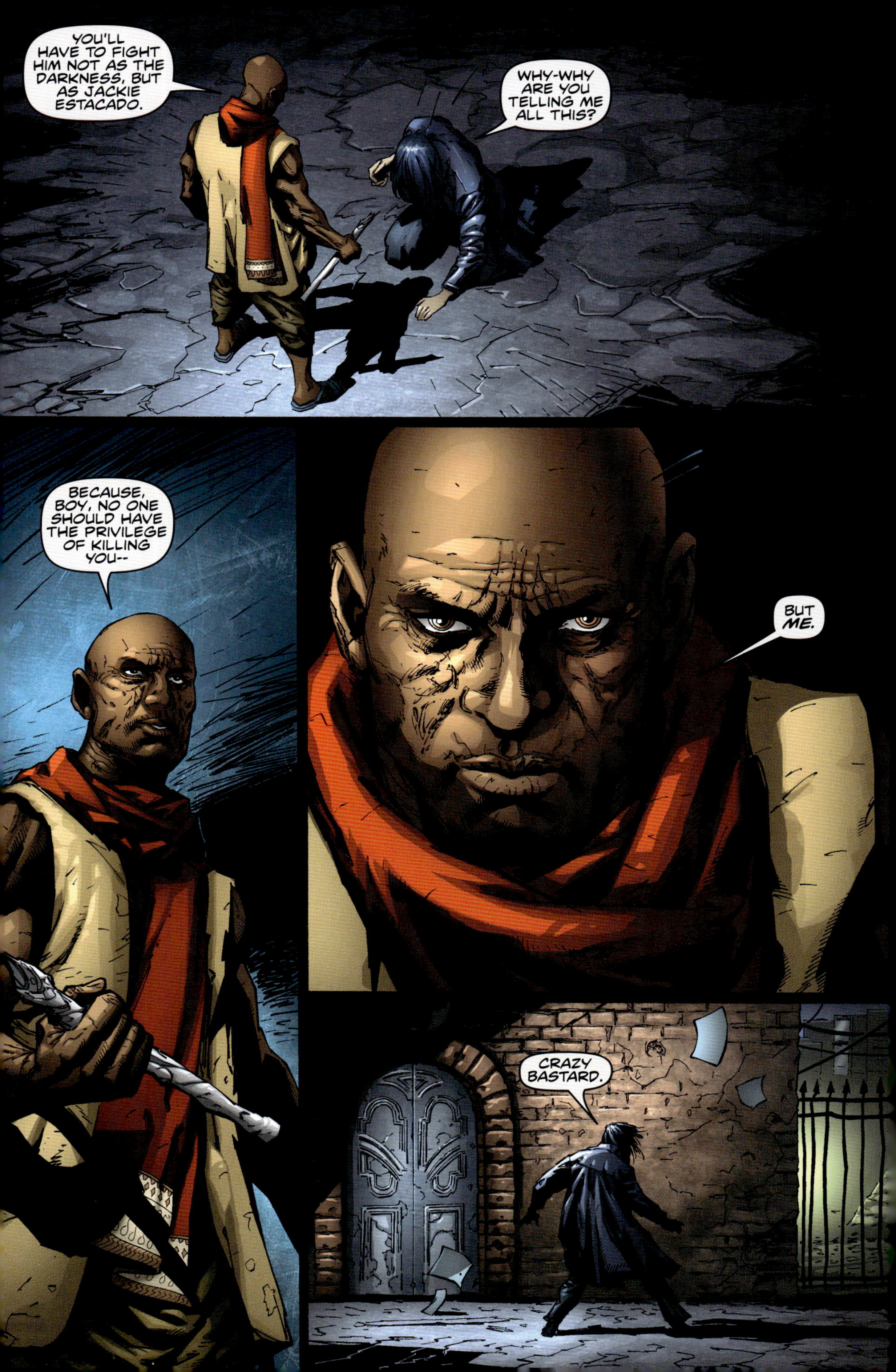
YOU'LL HAVE TO FIGHT HIM NOT AS THE DARKNESS, BUT AS JACKIE ESTACADO.
WHY-WHY ARE YOU TELLING ME ALL THIS?
BECAUSE, BOY, NO ONE SHOULD HAVE THE PRIVILEGE OF KILLING YOU--
BUT *ME.*
CRAZY BASTARD.

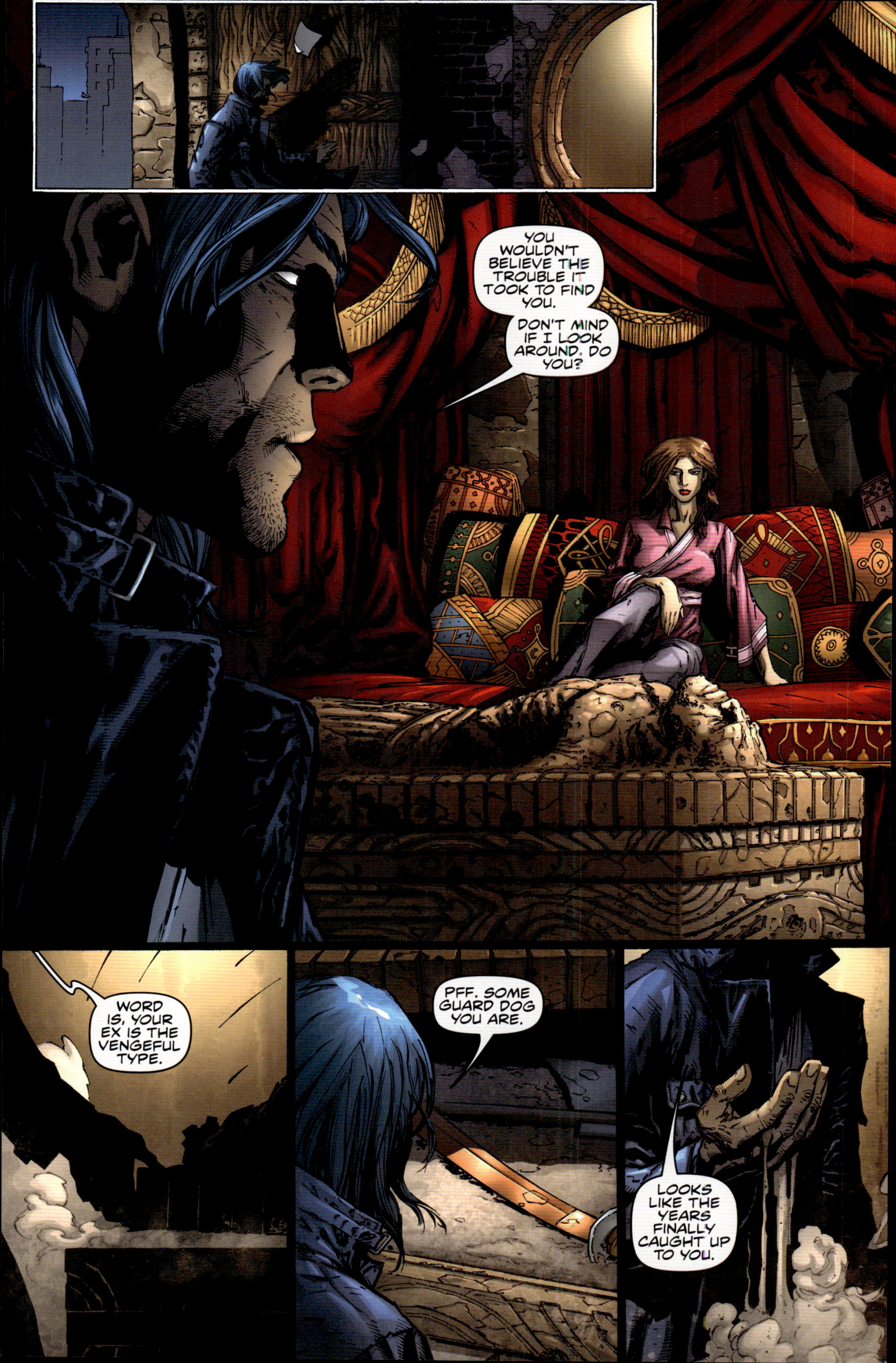
YOU WOULDN'T BELIEVE THE TROUBLE IT TOOK TO FIND YOU.
DON'T MIND IF I LOOK AROUND, DO YOU?
WORD IS, YOUR EX IS THE VENGEFUL TYPE.
PFF. SOME GUARD DOG YOU ARE.
LOOKS LIKE THE YEARS FINALLY CAUGHT UP TO YOU.

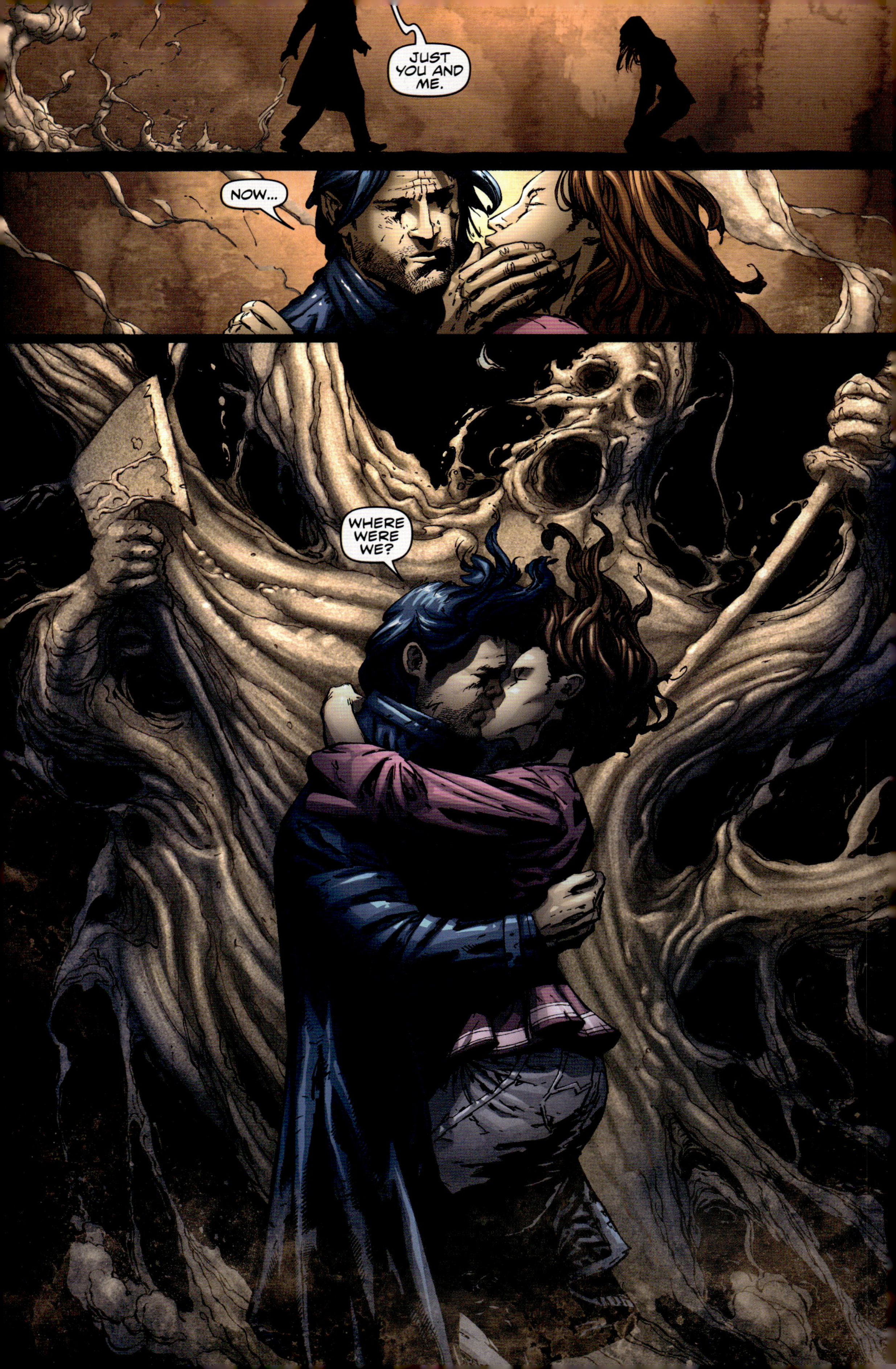
JUST YOU AND ME.
NOW...
WHERE WERE WE?

The Darkness Issue #77
cover art by: Frazier Irving

THE DARKNESS #77

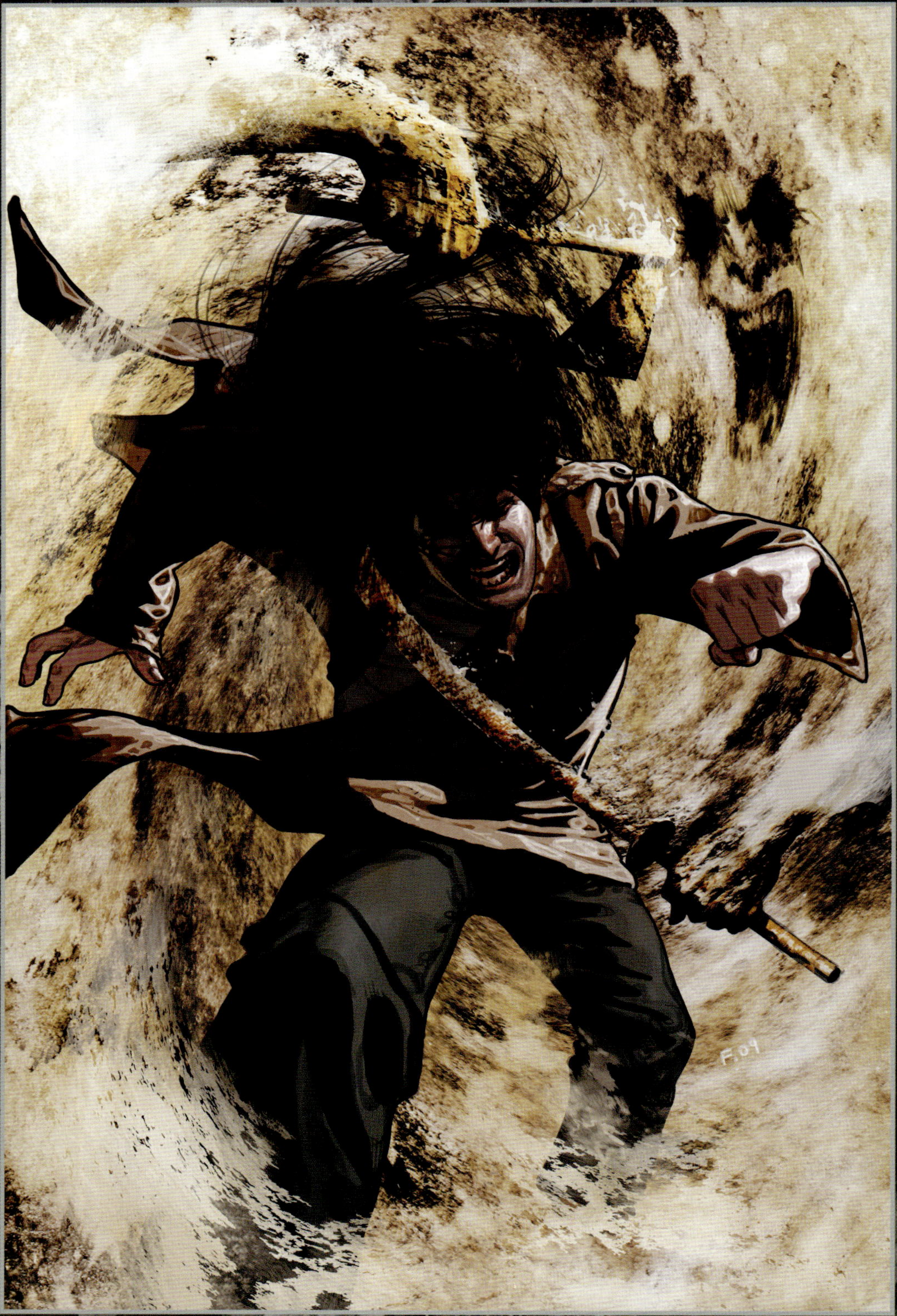
F.04

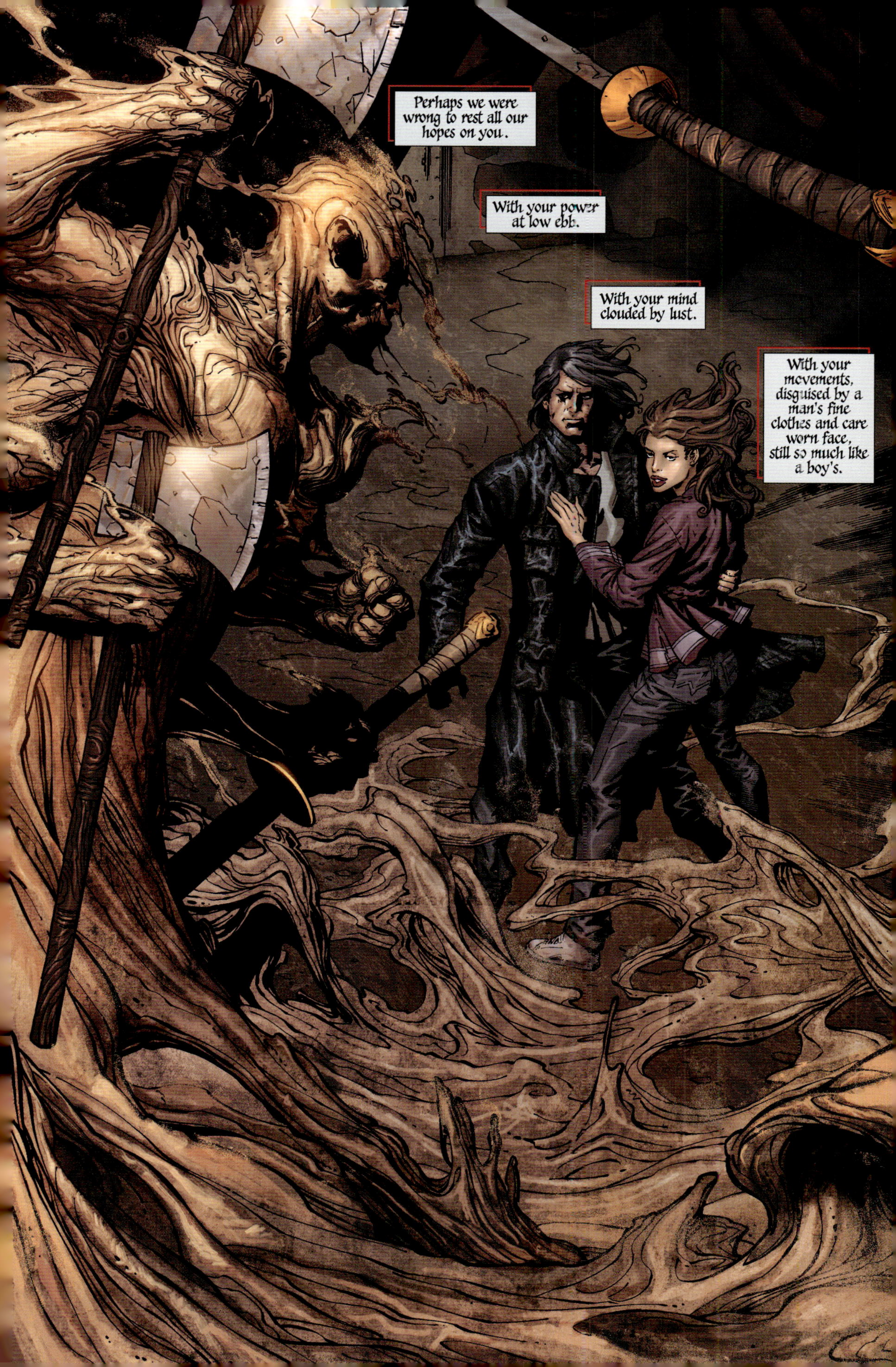
Perhaps we were wrong to rest all our hopes on you.
With your power at low ebb.
With your mind clouded by lust.
With your movements, disguised by a man's fine clothes and care worn face, still so much like a boy's.

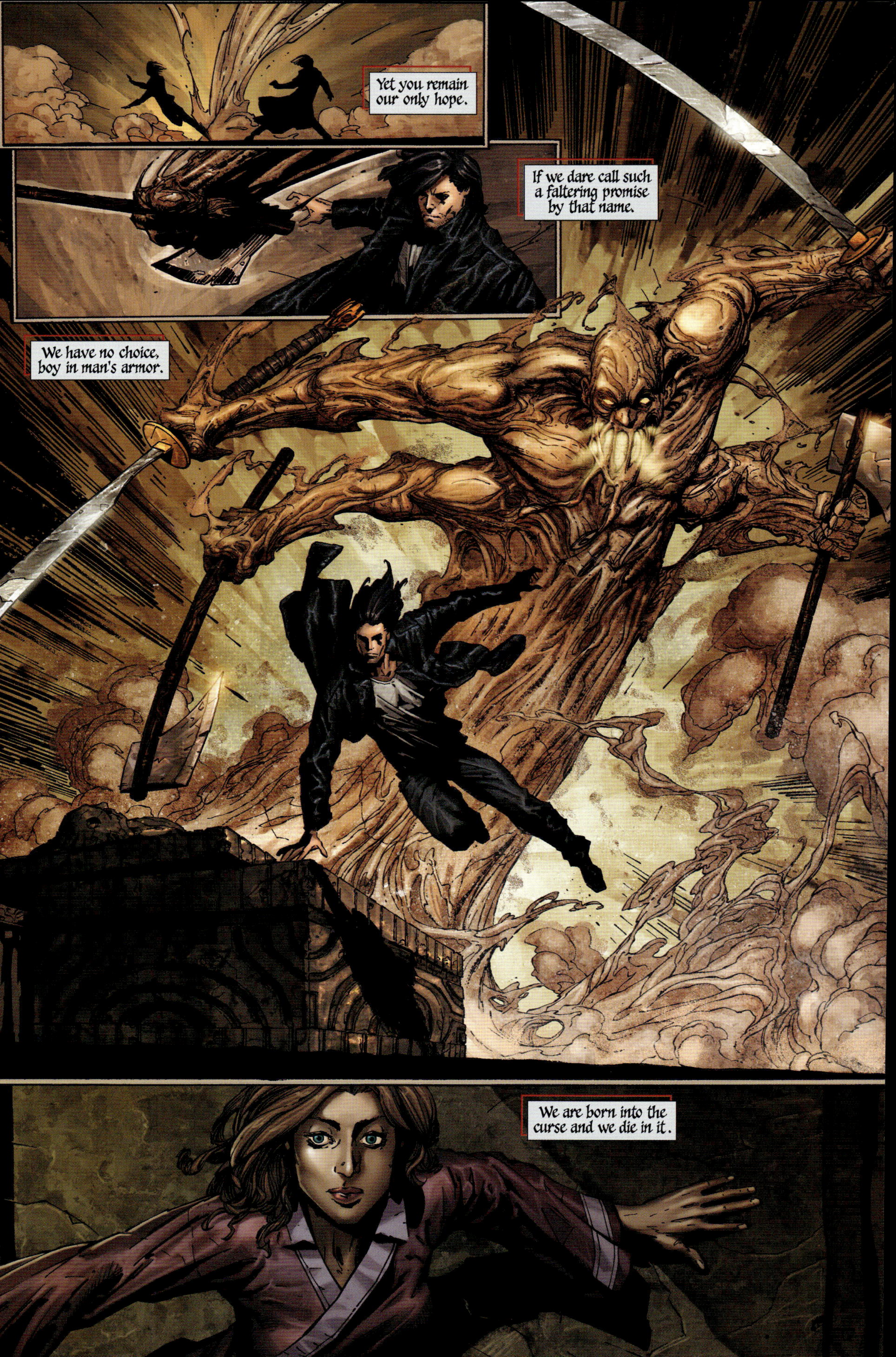
Yet you remain our only hope.
If we dare call such a faltering promise by that name.
We have no choice, boy in man's armor.
We are born into the curse and we die in it.

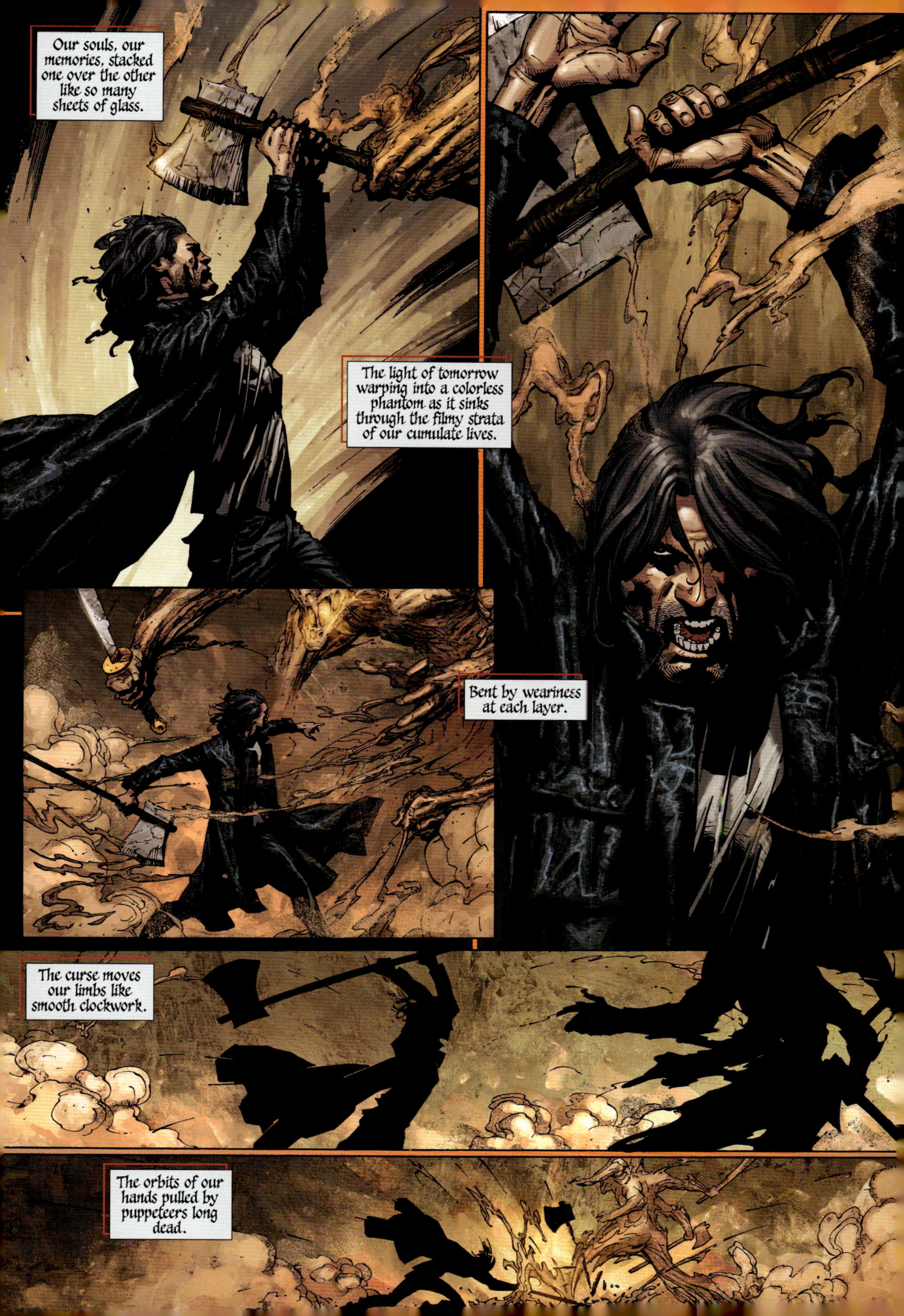
Our souls, our memories, stacked one over the other like so many sheets of glass.
The light of tomorrow warping into a colorless phantom as it sinks through the filmy strata of our cumulate lives.
Bent by weariness at each layer.
The curse moves our limbs like smooth clockwork.
The orbits of our hands pulled by puppeteers long dead.

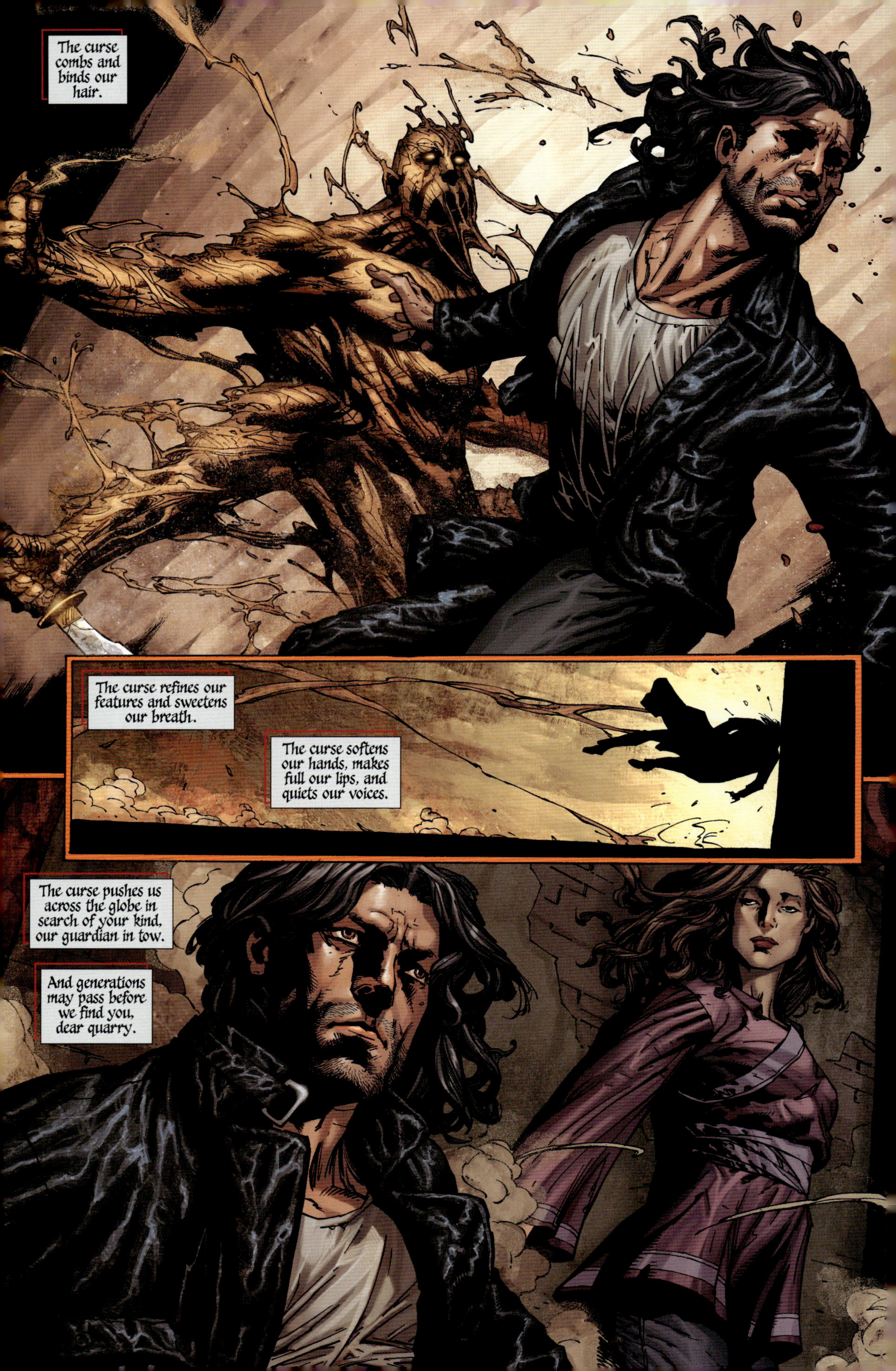
The curse combs and binds our hair.
The curse refines our features and sweetens our breath.
The curse softens our hands, makes full our lips, and quiets our voices.
The curse pushes us across the globe in search of your kind, our guardian in tow.
And generations may pass before we find you, dear quarry.

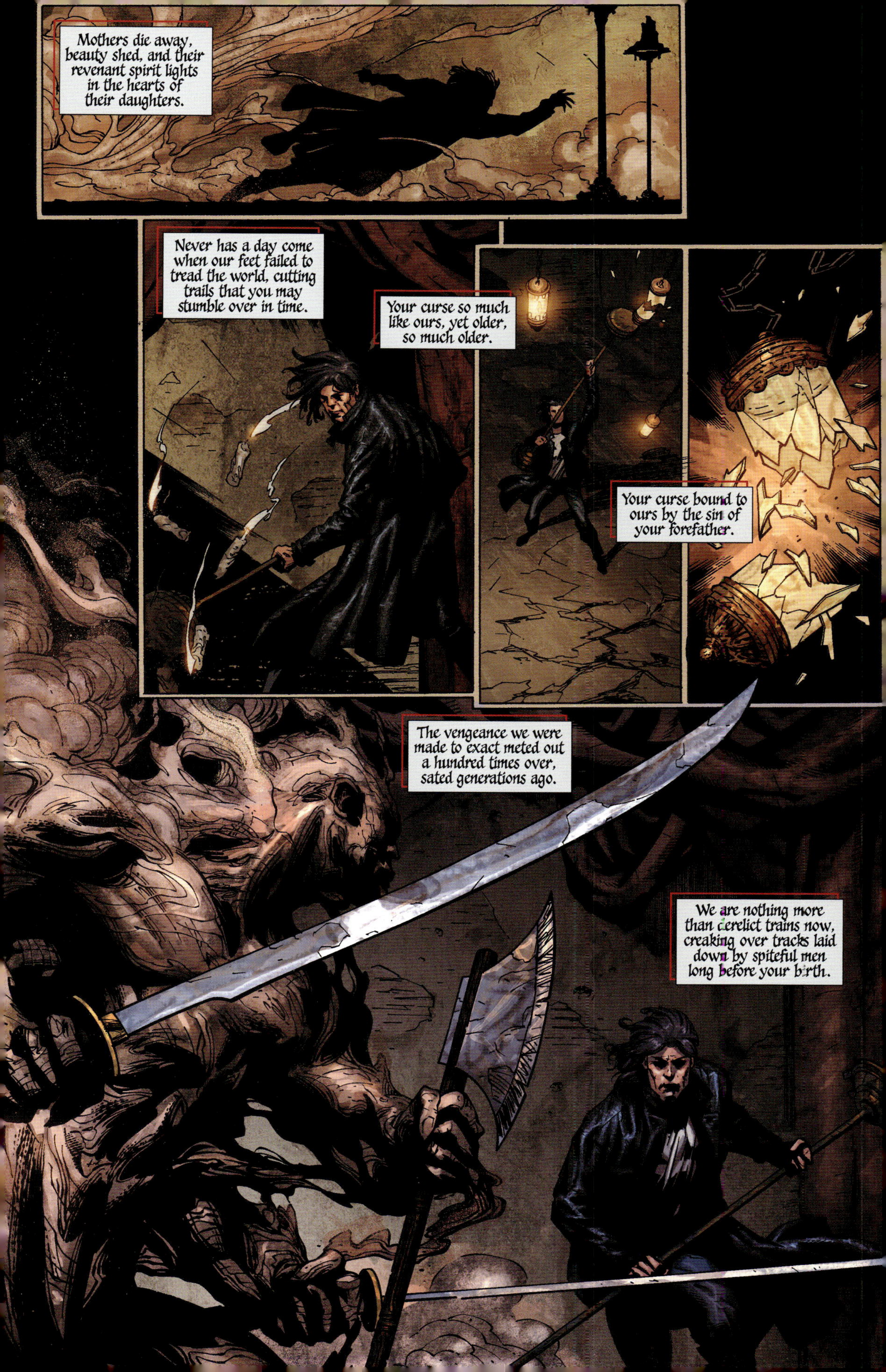
Mothers die away, beauty shed, and their revenant spirit lights in the hearts of their daughters.
Never has a day come when our feet failed to tread the world, cutting trails that you may stumble over in time.
Your curse so much like ours, yet older, so much older.
Your curse bound to ours by the sin of your forefather.
The vengeance we were made to exact meted out a hundred times over, sated generations ago.
We are nothing more than derelict trains now, creaking over tracks laid down by spiteful men long before your birth.

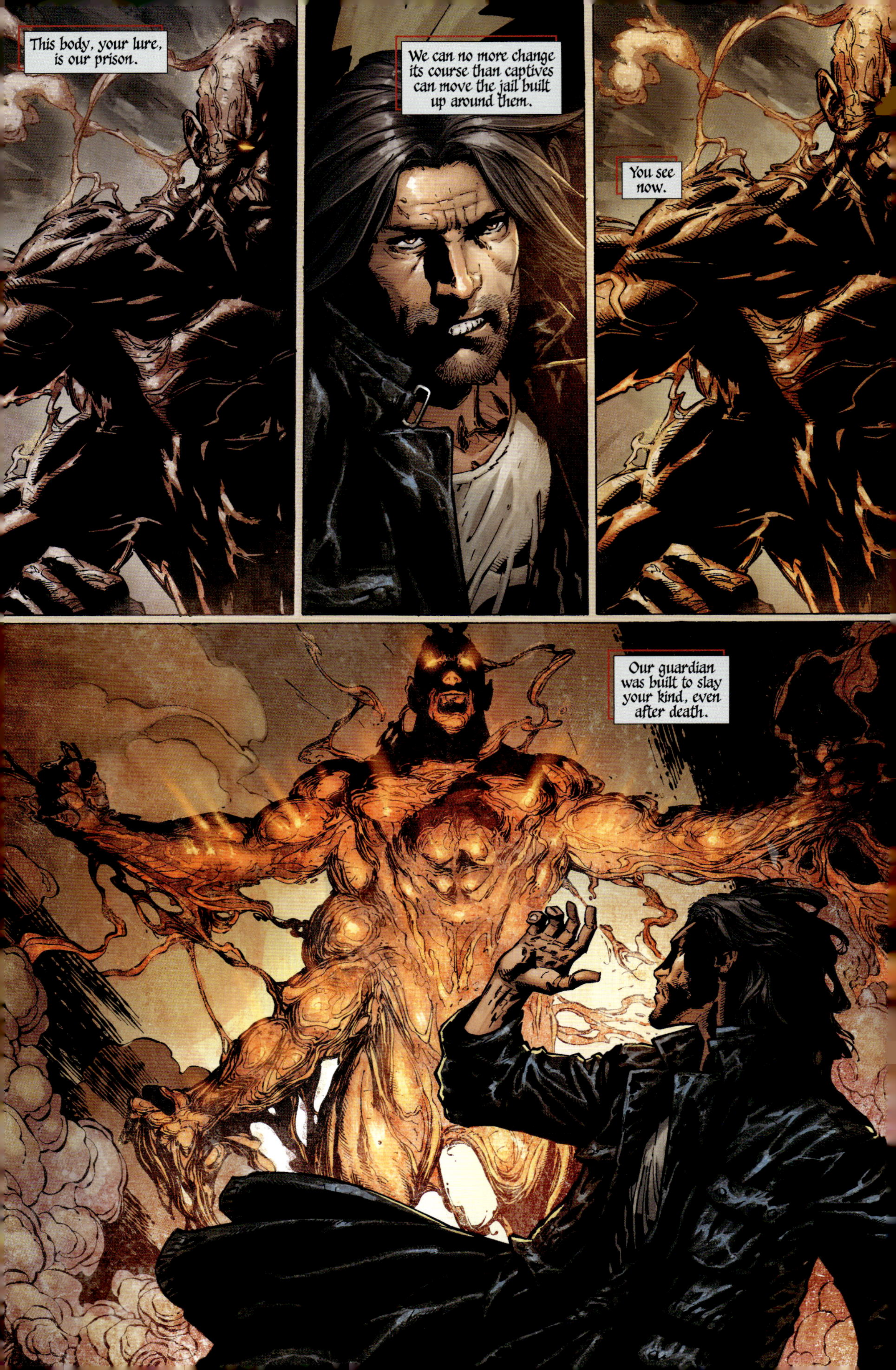
This body, your lure, is our prison.
We can no more change its course than captives can move the jail built up around them.
You see now.
Our guardian was built to slay your kind, even after death.

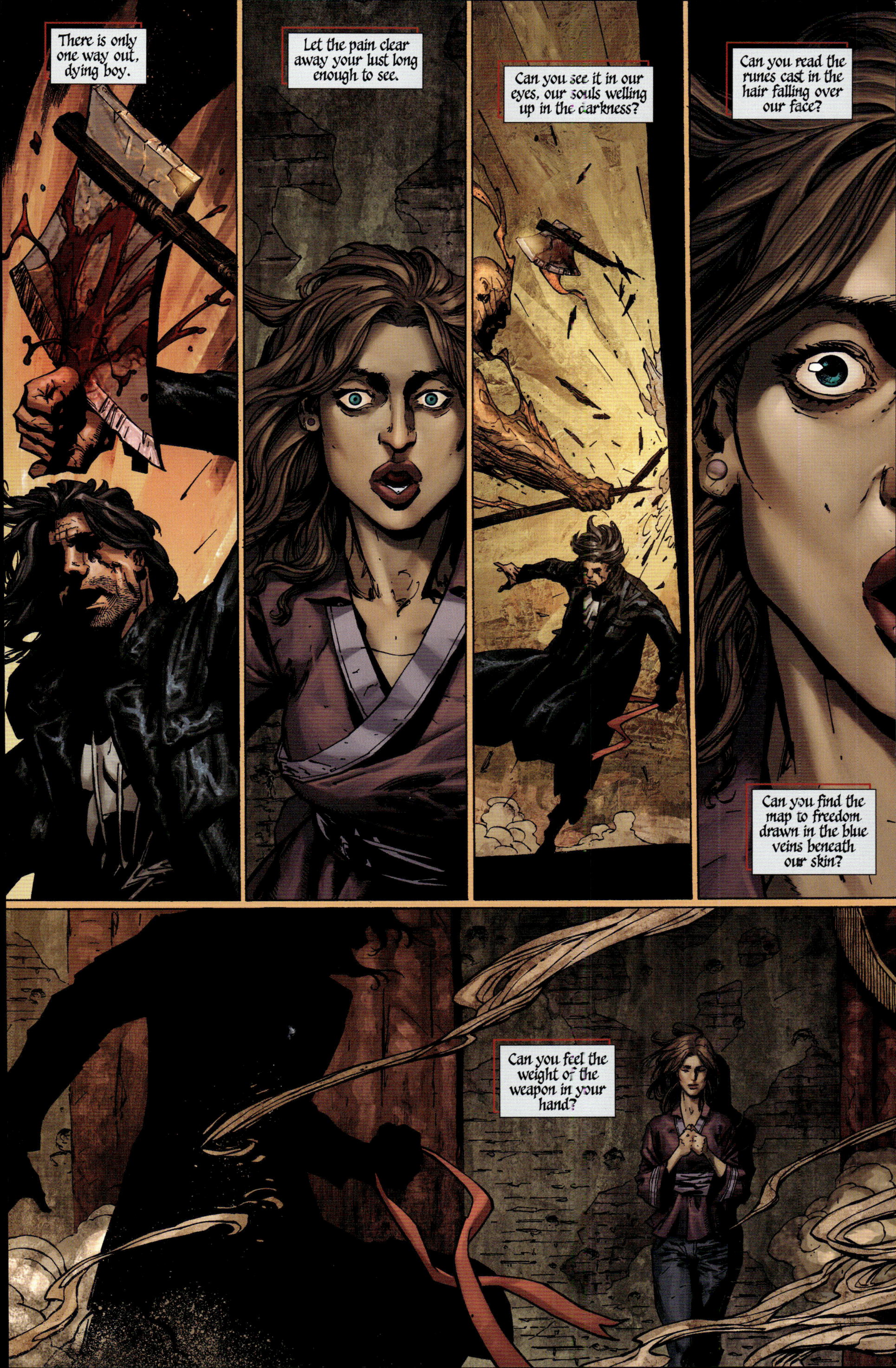
There is only one way out, dying boy.
Let the pain clear away your lust long enough to see.
Can you see it in our eyes, our souls welling up in the darkness?
Can you read the runes cast in the hair falling over our face?
Can you find the map to freedom drawn in the blue veins beneath our skin?
Can you feel the weight of the weapon in your hand?

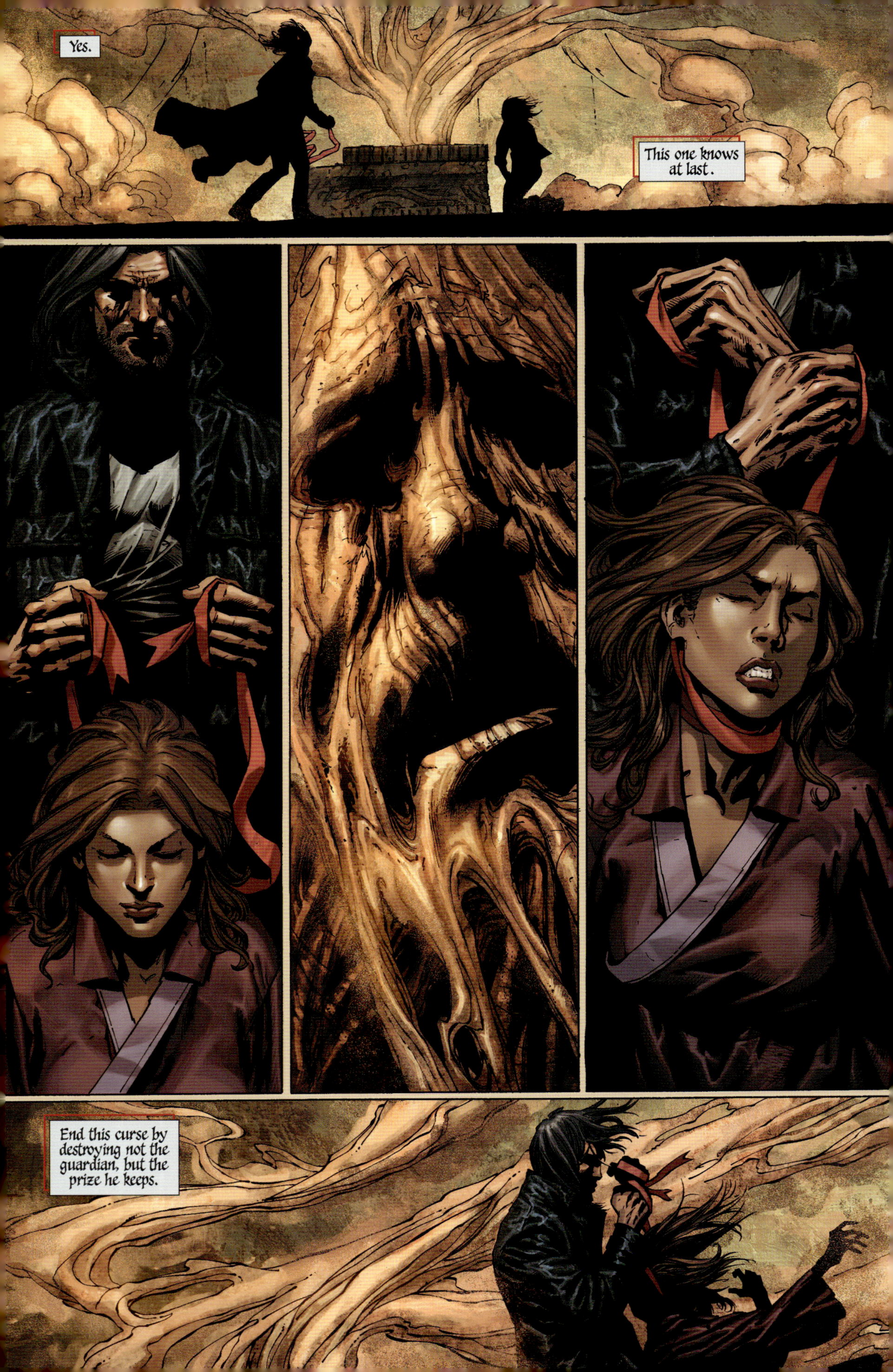
Yes.
This one knows at last.
End this curse by destroying not the guardian, but the prize he keeps.

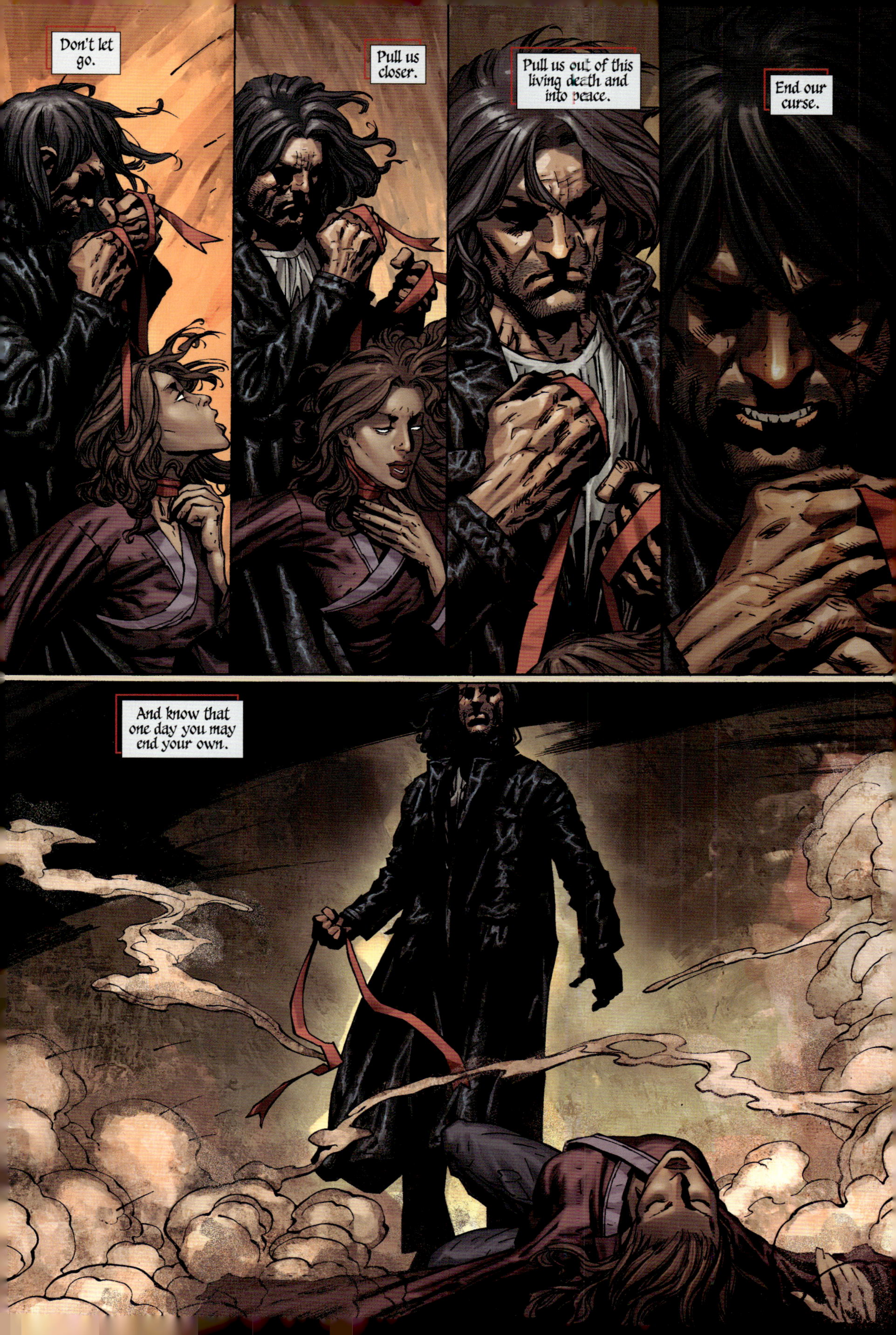
Don't let go.
Pull us closer.
Pull us out of this living death and into peace.
End our curse.
And know that one day you may end your own.

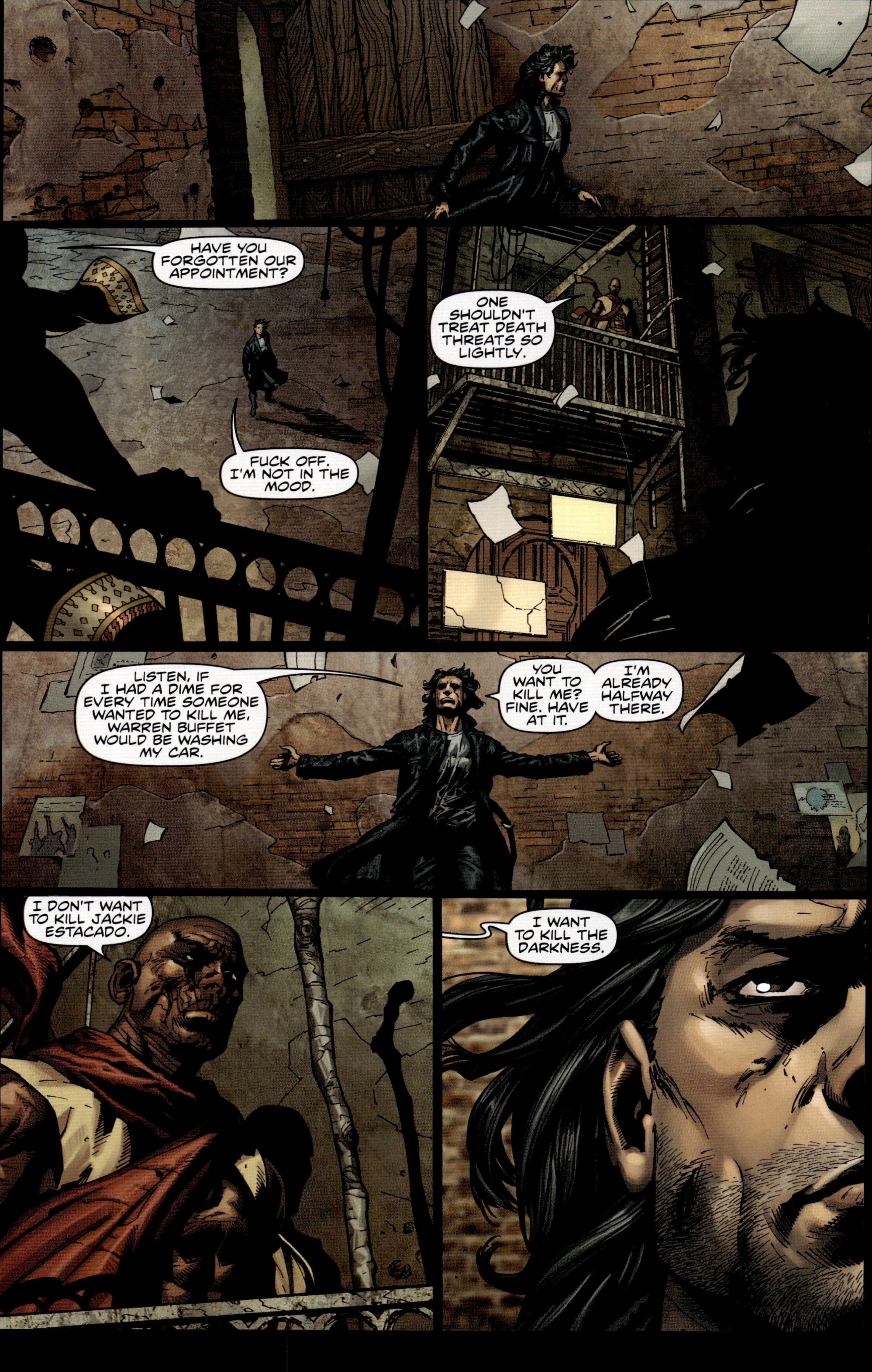
HAVE YOU FORGOTTEN OUR APPOINTMENT?
FUCK OFF. I'M NOT IN THE MOOD.
ONE SHOULDN'T TREAT DEATH THREATS SO LIGHTLY.
LISTEN, IF I HAD A DIME FOR EVERY TIME SOMEONE WANTED TO KILL ME, WARREN BUFFET WOULD BE WASHING MY CAR.
YOU WANT TO KILL ME? FINE. HAVE AT IT.
I'M ALREADY HALFWAY THERE.
I DON'T WANT TO KILL JACKIE ESTACADO.
I WANT TO KILL THE DARKNESS.

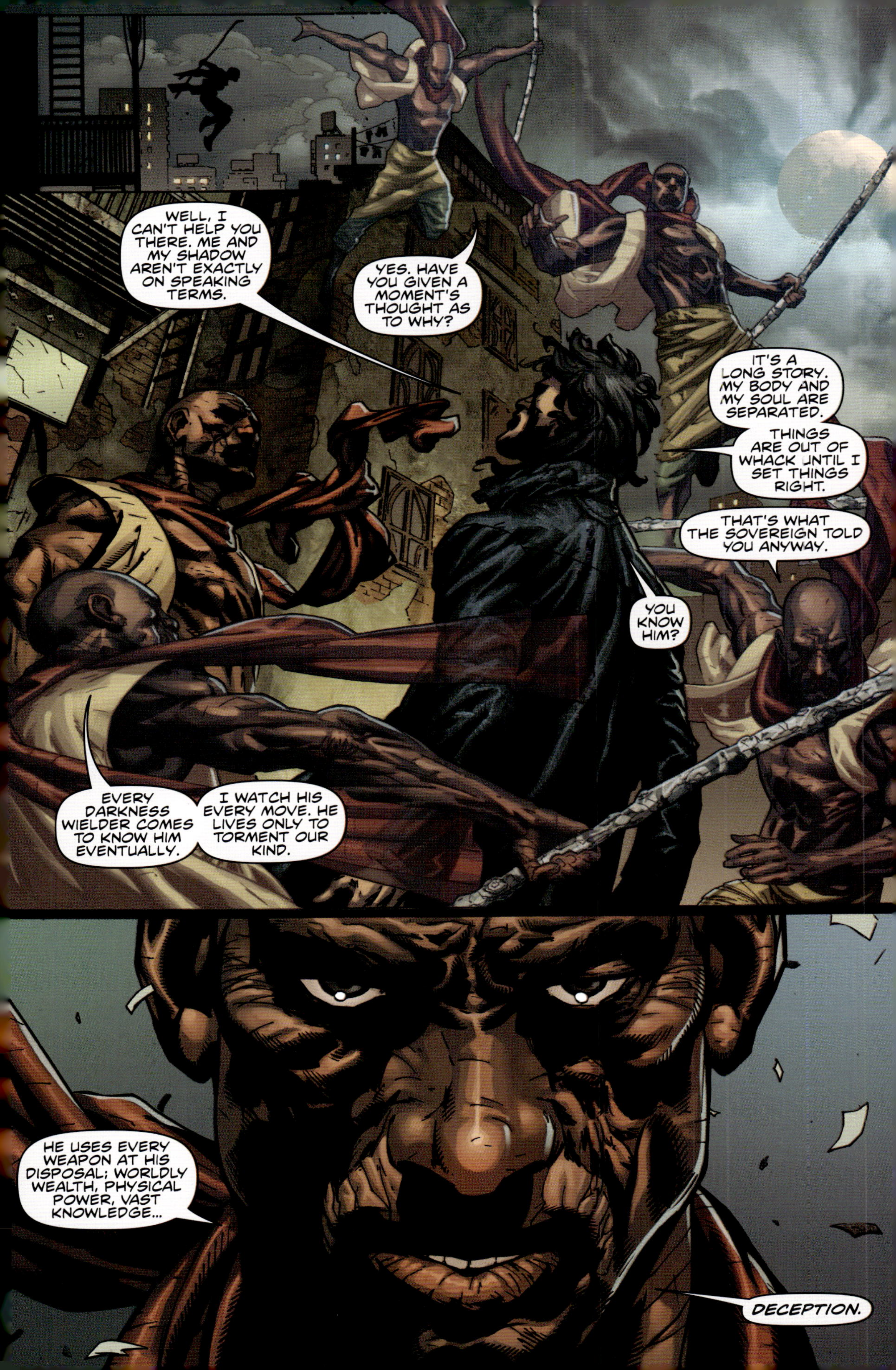
WELL, I CAN'T HELP YOU THERE. ME AND MY SHADOW AREN'T EXACTLY ON SPEAKING TERMS.
YES. HAVE YOU GIVEN A MOMENT'S THOUGHT AS TO WHY?
IT'S A LONG STORY. MY BODY AND MY SOUL ARE SEPARATED.
THINGS ARE OUT OF WHACK UNTIL I SET THINGS RIGHT.
THAT'S WHAT THE SOVEREIGN TOLD YOU ANYWAY.
YOU KNOW HIM?
EVERY DARKNESS WIELDER COMES TO KNOW HIM EVENTUALLY.
I WATCH HIS EVERY MOVE. HE LIVES ONLY TO TORMENT OUR KIND.
HE USES EVERY WEAPON AT HIS DISPOSAL; WORLDLY WEALTH, PHYSICAL POWER, VAST KNOWLEDGE...
DECEPTION.

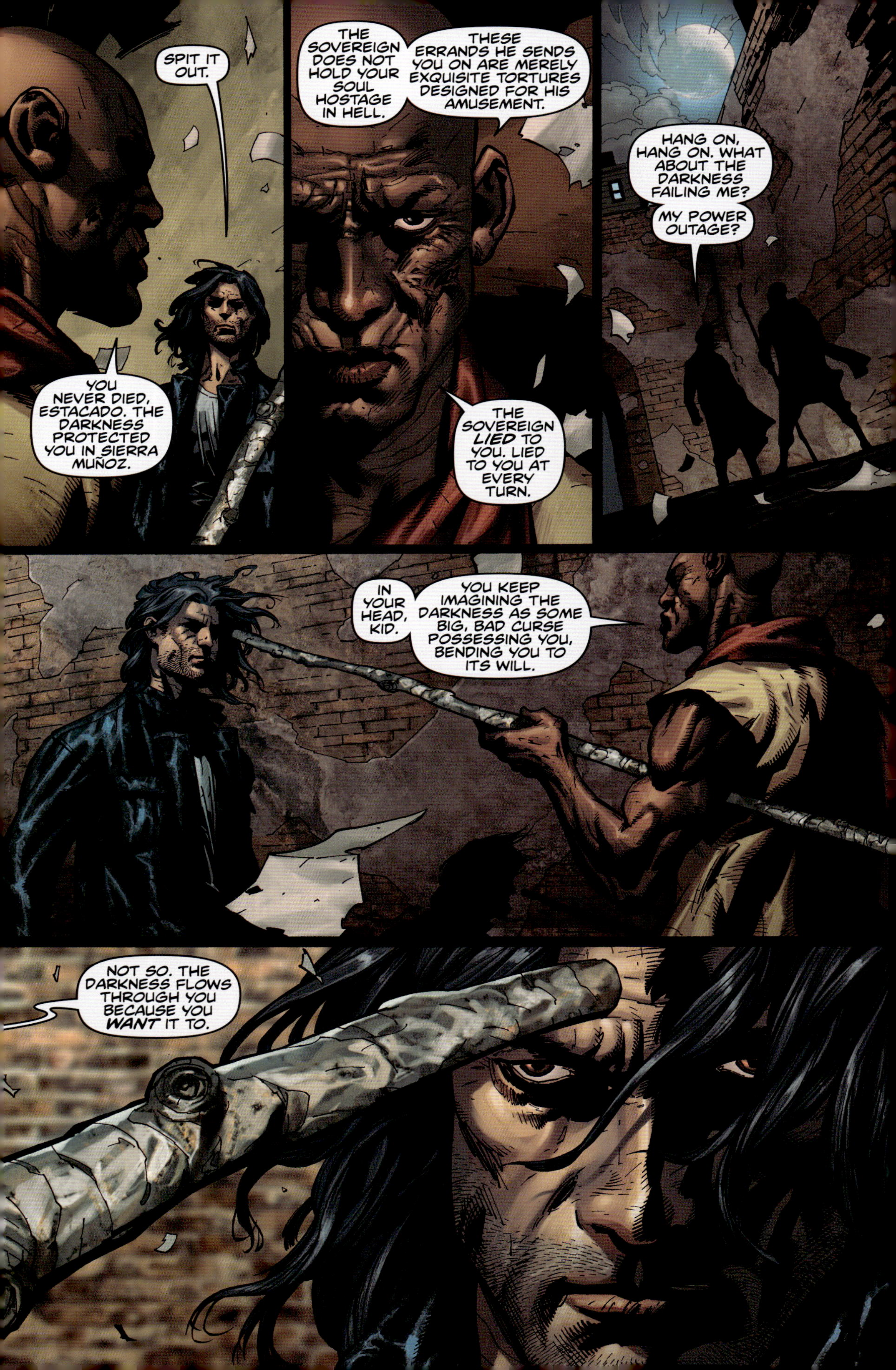
SPIT IT OUT.
YOU NEVER DIED, ESTACADO. THE DARKNESS PROTECTED YOU IN SIERRA MUÑOZ.
THE SOVEREIGN DOES NOT HOLD YOUR SOUL HOSTAGE IN HELL.
THESE ERRANDS HE SENDS YOU ON ARE MERELY EXQUISITE TORTURES DESIGNED FOR HIS AMUSEMENT.
THE SOVEREIGN *LIED* TO YOU. LIED TO YOU AT EVERY TURN.
HANG ON, HANG ON. WHAT ABOUT THE DARKNESS FAILING ME?
MY POWER OUTAGE?
IN YOUR HEAD, KID.
YOU KEEP IMAGINING THE DARKNESS AS SOME BIG, BAD CURSE POSSESSING YOU, BENDING YOU TO ITS WILL.
NOT SO. THE DARKNESS FLOWS THROUGH YOU BECAUSE YOU *WANT* IT TO.

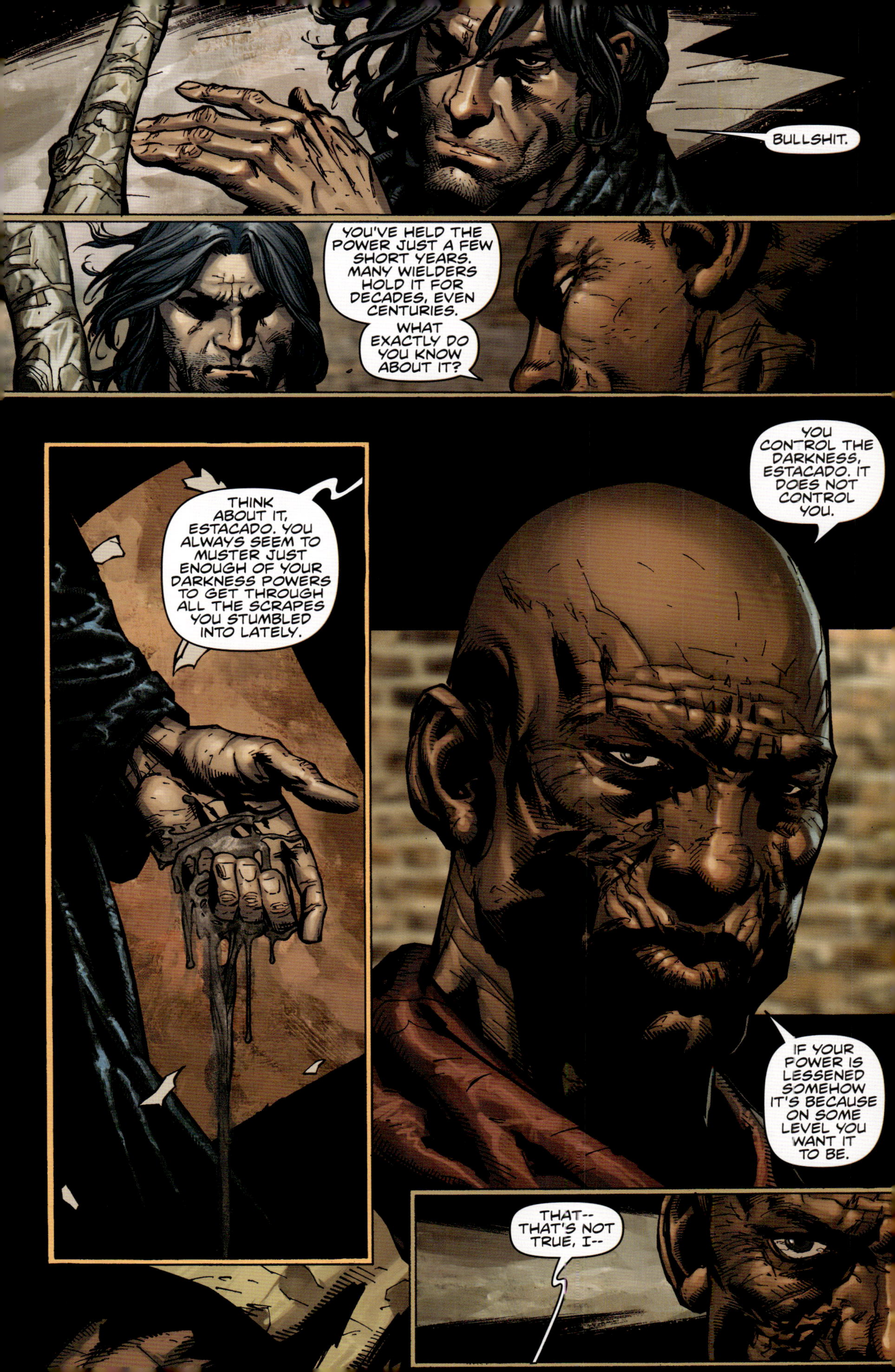

BULLSHIT.
YOU'VE HELD THE POWER JUST A FEW SHORT YEARS. MANY WIELDERS HOLD IT FOR DECADES, EVEN CENTURIES.
WHAT EXACTLY DO YOU KNOW ABOUT IT?
YOU CONTROL THE DARKNESS, ESTACADO. IT DOES NOT CONTROL YOU.
THINK ABOUT IT, ESTACADO. YOU ALWAYS SEEM TO MUSTER JUST ENOUGH OF YOUR DARKNESS POWERS TO GET THROUGH ALL THE SCRAPES YOU STUMBLED INTO LATELY.
IF YOUR POWER IS LESSENED SOMEHOW IT'S BECAUSE ON SOME LEVEL YOU WANT IT TO BE.
THAT-- THAT'S NOT TRUE, I--

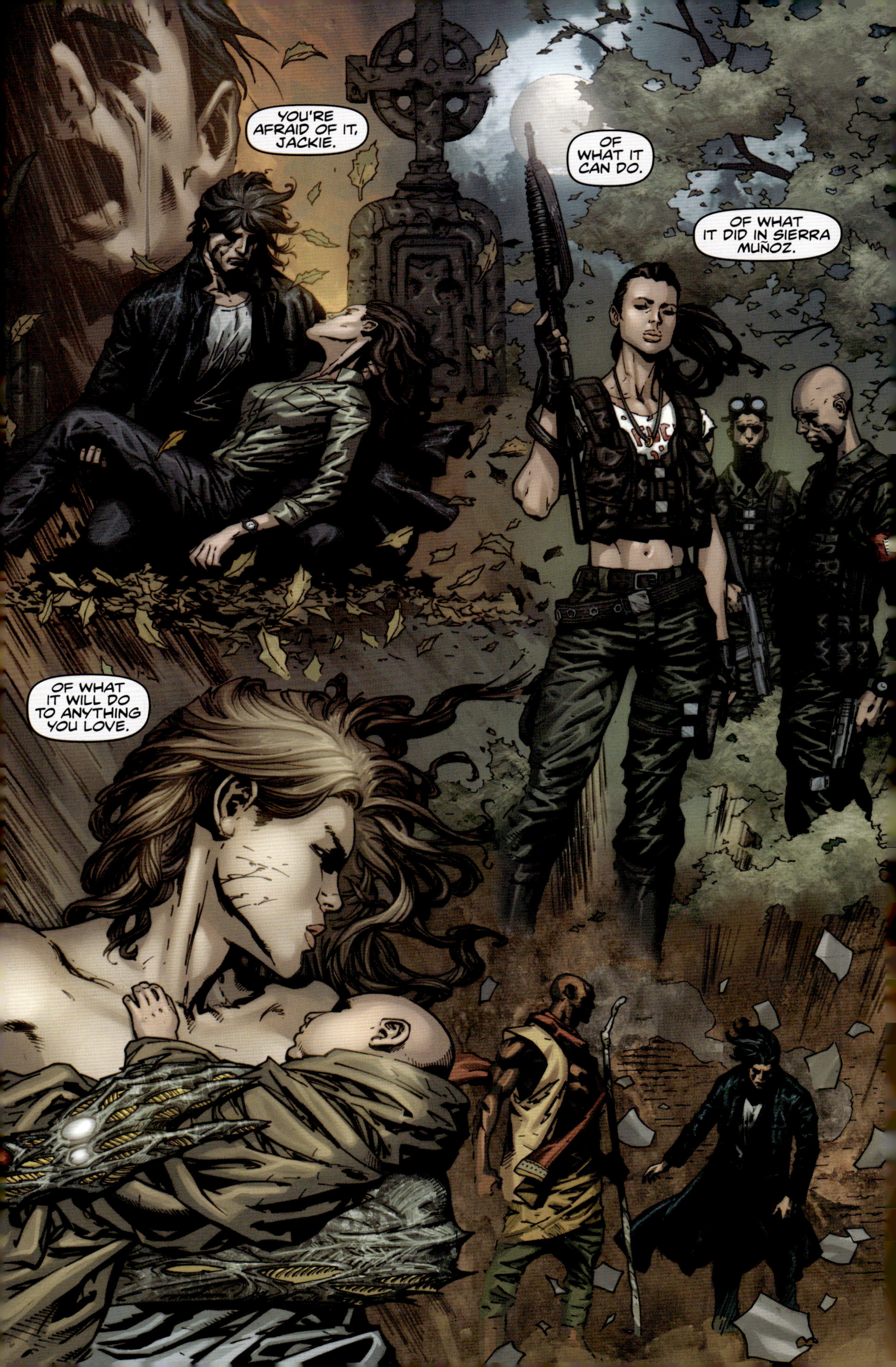
YOU'RE AFRAID OF IT, JACKIE.
OF WHAT IT CAN DO.
OF WHAT IT DID IN SIERRA MUÑOZ.
OF WHAT IT WILL DO TO ANYTHING YOU LOVE.

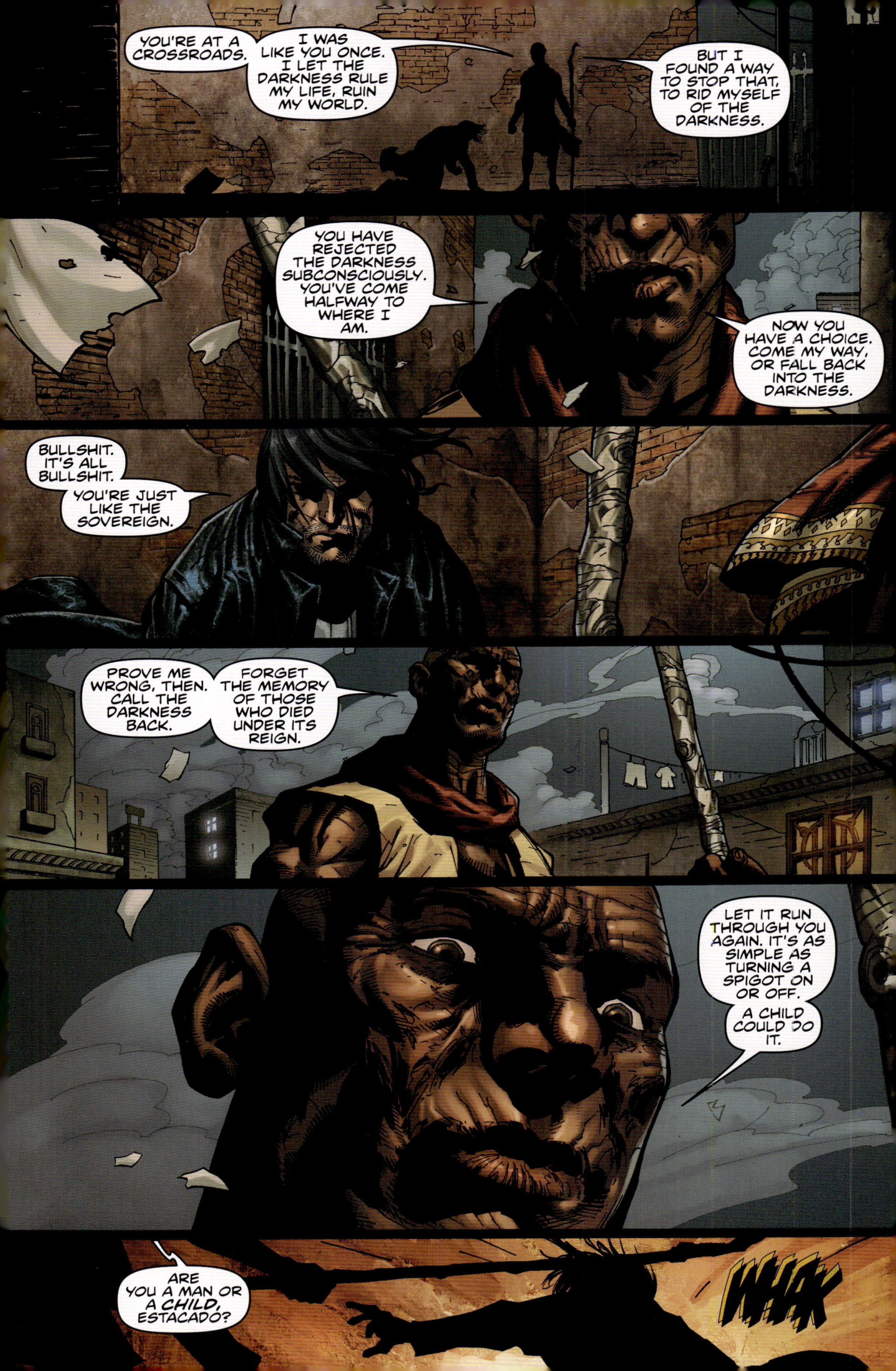
YOU'RE AT A CROSSROADS.
I WAS LIKE YOU ONCE. I LET THE DARKNESS RULE MY LIFE, RUIN MY WORLD.
BUT I FOUND A WAY TO STOP THAT, TO RID MYSELF OF THE DARKNESS.
YOU HAVE REJECTED THE DARKNESS SUBCONSCIOUSLY. YOU'VE COME HALFWAY TO WHERE I AM.
NOW YOU HAVE A CHOICE. COME MY WAY, OR FALL BACK INTO THE DARKNESS.
BULLSHIT. IT'S ALL BULLSHIT.
YOU'RE JUST LIKE THE SOVEREIGN.
PROVE ME WRONG, THEN. CALL THE DARKNESS BACK.
FORGET THE MEMORY OF THOSE WHO DIED UNDER ITS REIGN.
LET IT RUN THROUGH YOU AGAIN. IT'S AS SIMPLE AS TURNING A SPIGOT ON OR OFF.
A CHILD COULD DO IT.
ARE YOU A MAN OR A CHILD, ESTACADO?
WHAK

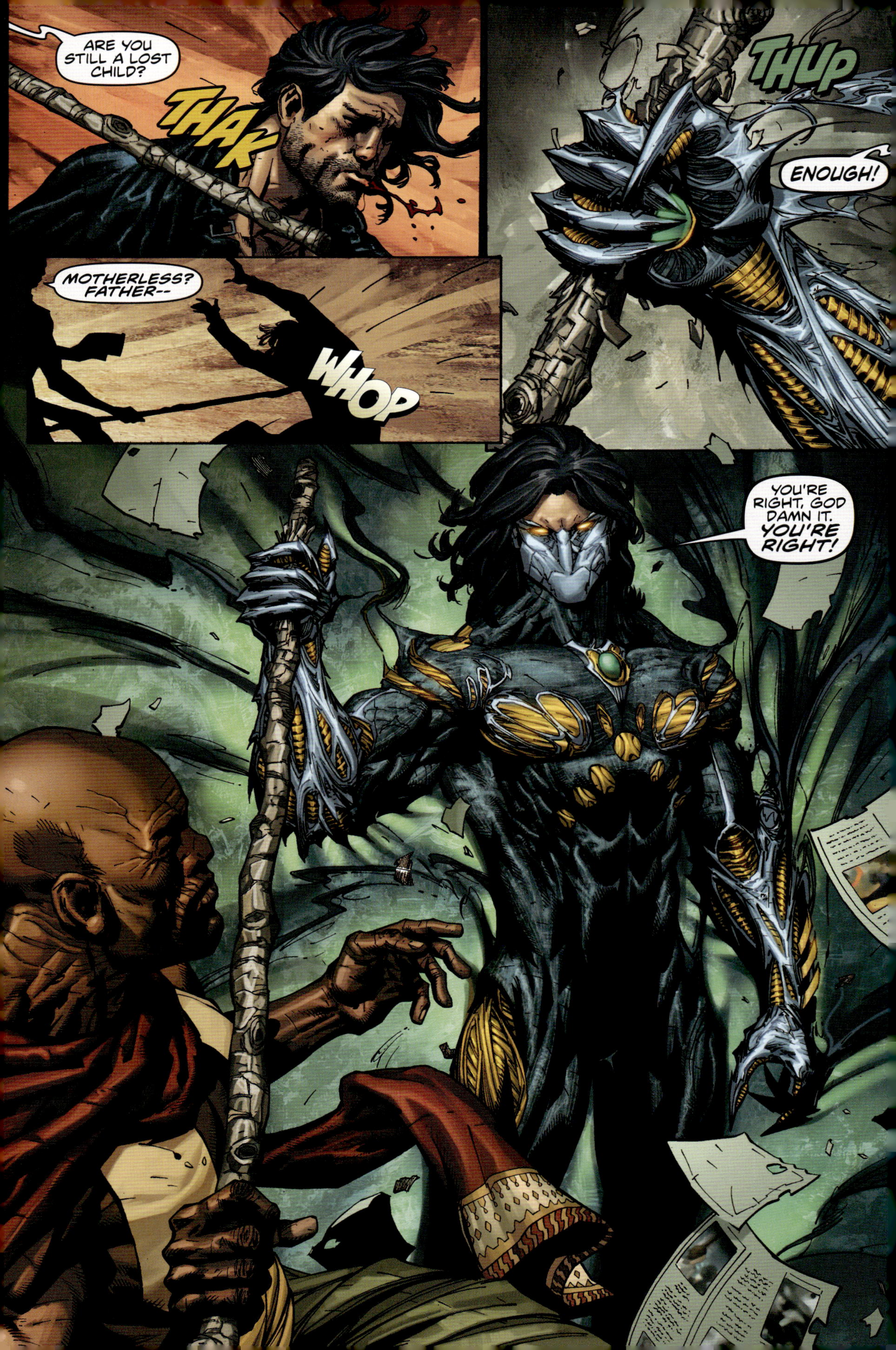
ARE YOU STILL A LOST CHILD?
THAK
THUP
ENOUGH!
MOTHERLESS? FATHER--
WHOP
YOU'RE RIGHT, GOD DAMN IT. YOU'RE RIGHT!

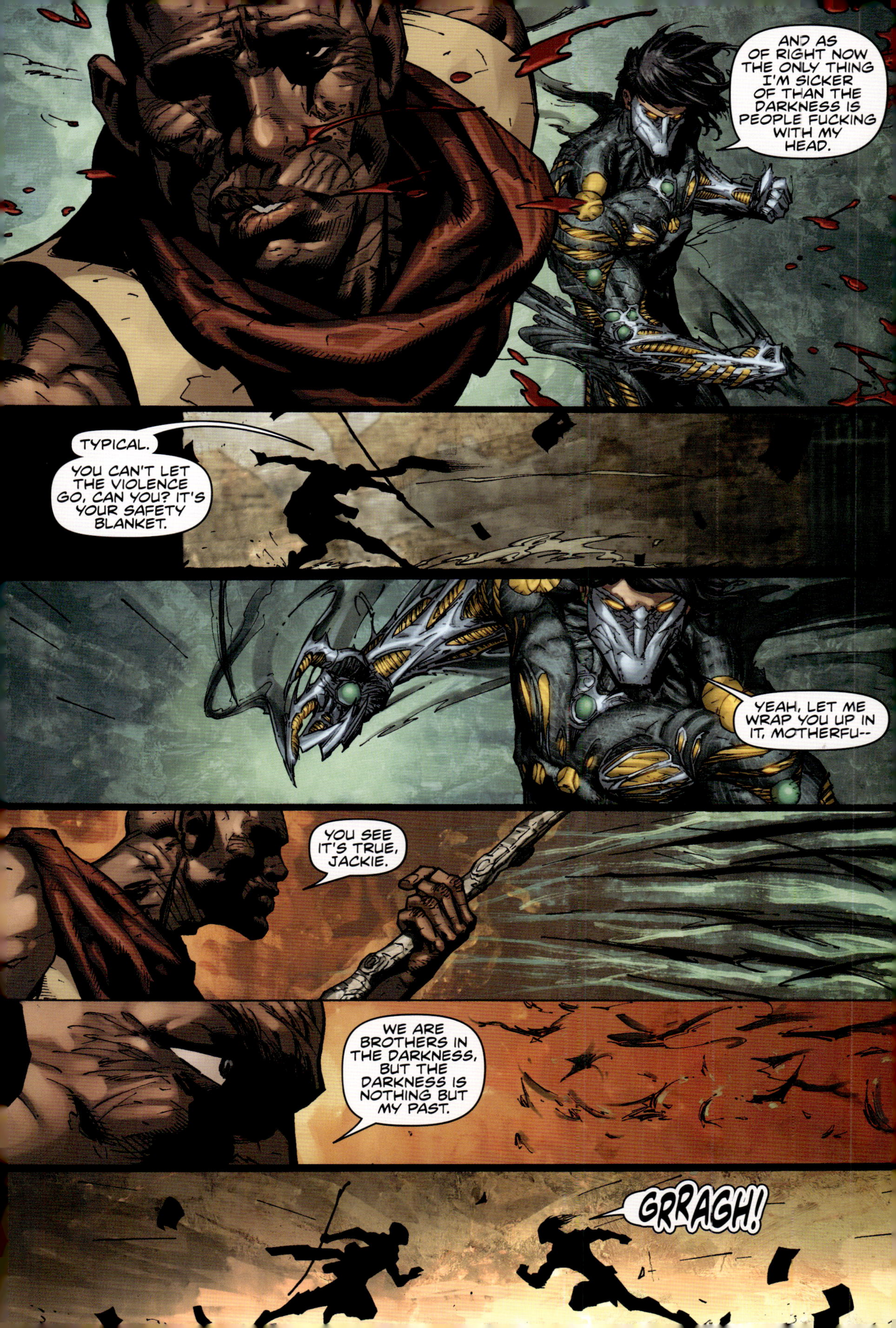
AND AS OF RIGHT NOW THE ONLY THING I'M SICKER OF THAN THE DARKNESS IS PEOPLE FUCKING WITH MY HEAD.
TYPICAL.
YOU CAN'T LET THE VIOLENCE GO, CAN YOU? IT'S YOUR SAFETY BLANKET.
YEAH, LET ME WRAP YOU UP IN IT, MOTHERFU--
YOU SEE IT'S TRUE, JACKIE.
WE ARE BROTHERS IN THE DARKNESS, BUT THE DARKNESS IS NOTHING BUT MY PAST.
GRRAGH!

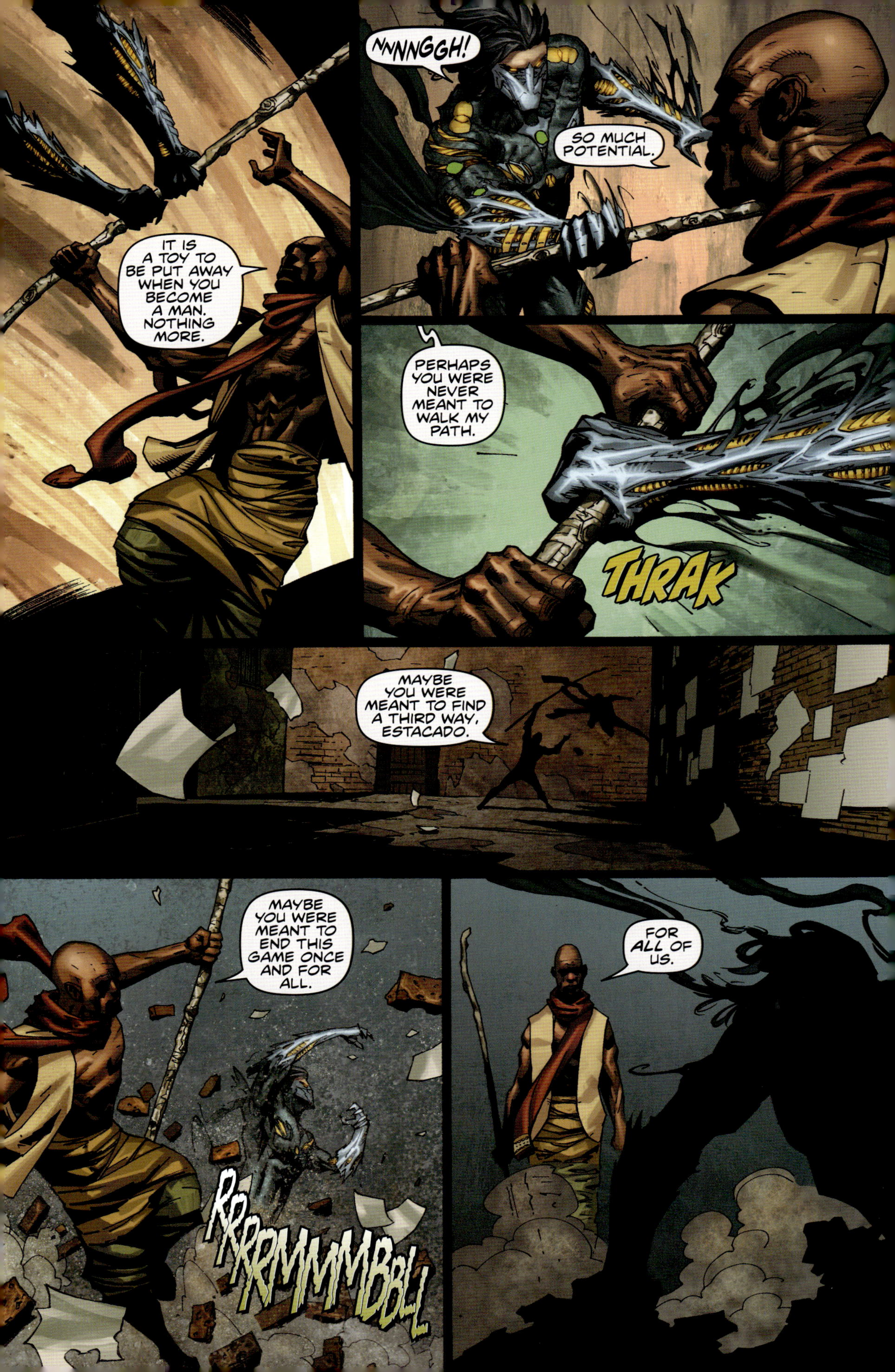
IT IS A TOY TO BE PUT AWAY WHEN YOU BECOME A MAN. NOTHING MORE.
NNNNGGH!
SO MUCH POTENTIAL.
PERHAPS YOU WERE NEVER MEANT TO WALK MY PATH.
THRAK
MAYBE YOU WERE MEANT TO FIND A THIRD WAY, ESTACADO.
MAYBE YOU WERE MEANT TO END THIS GAME ONCE AND FOR ALL.
RRRRMMMMBBLL
FOR ALL OF US.

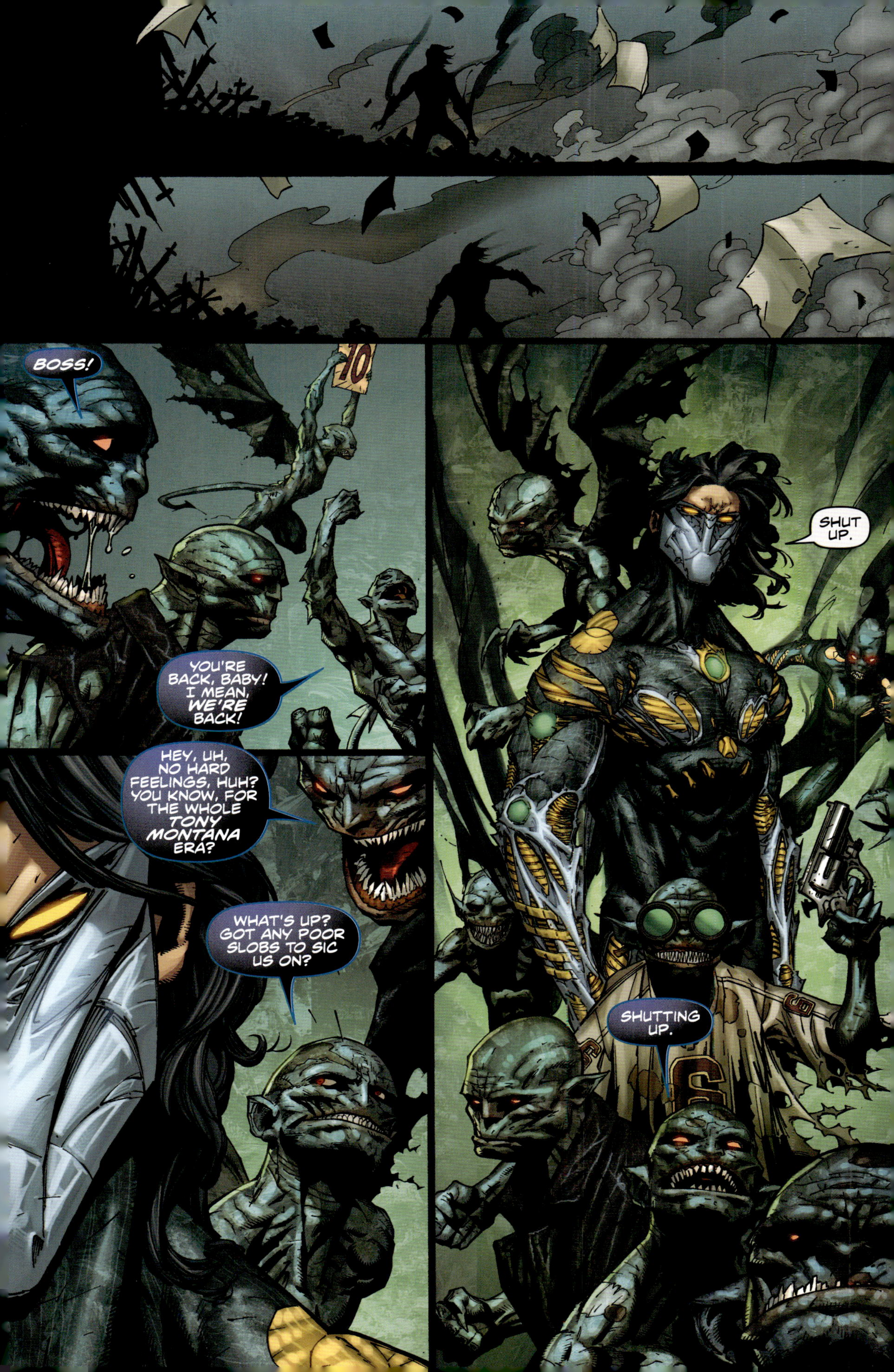
BOSS!
YOU'RE BACK, BABY! I MEAN, WE'RE BACK!
HEY, UH, NO HARD FEELINGS, HUH? YOU KNOW, FOR THE WHOLE TONY MONTANA ERA?
WHAT'S UP? GOT ANY POOR SLOBS TO SIC US ON?
SHUT UP.
SHUTTING UP.

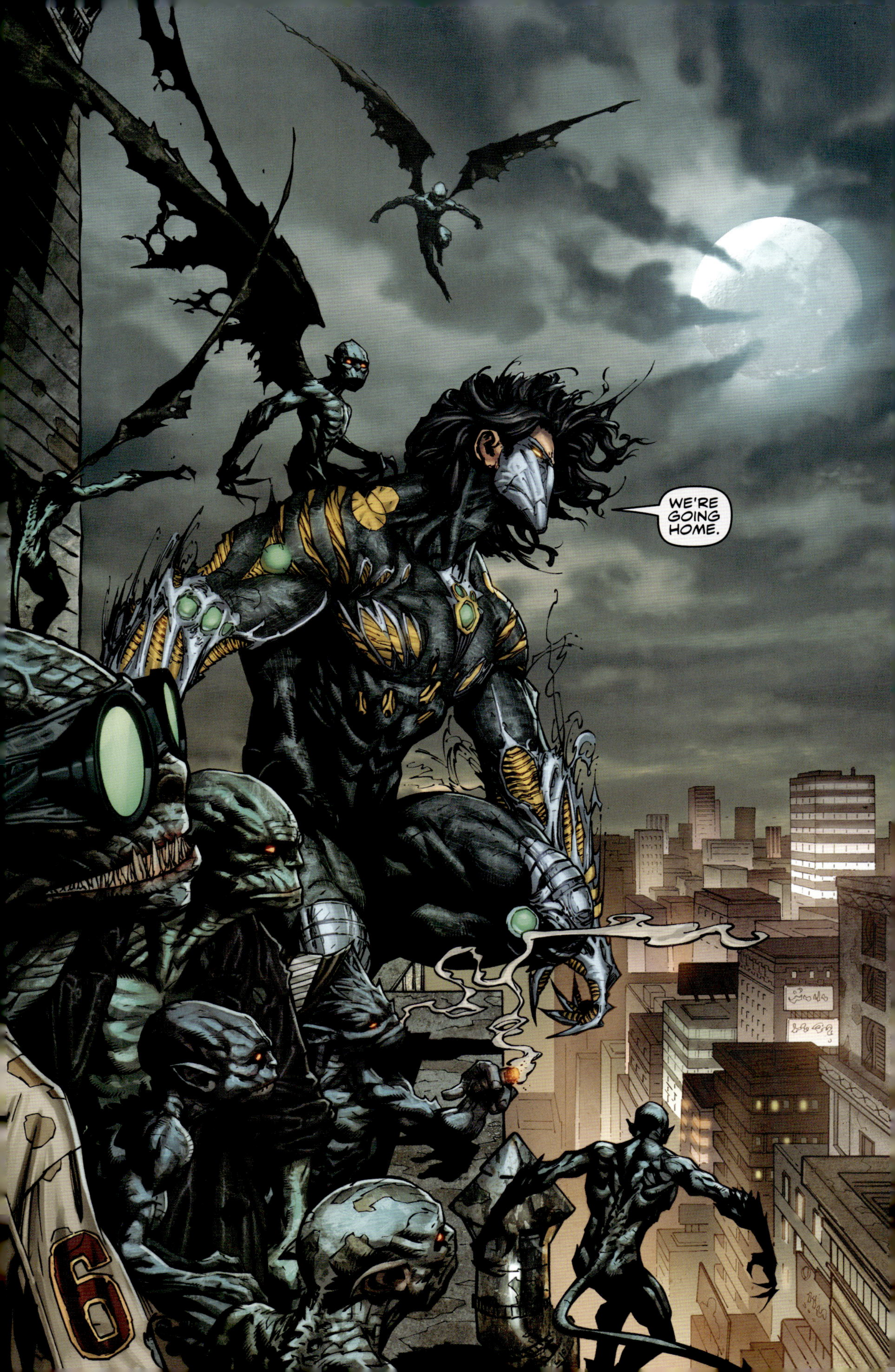
WE'RE GOING HOME.

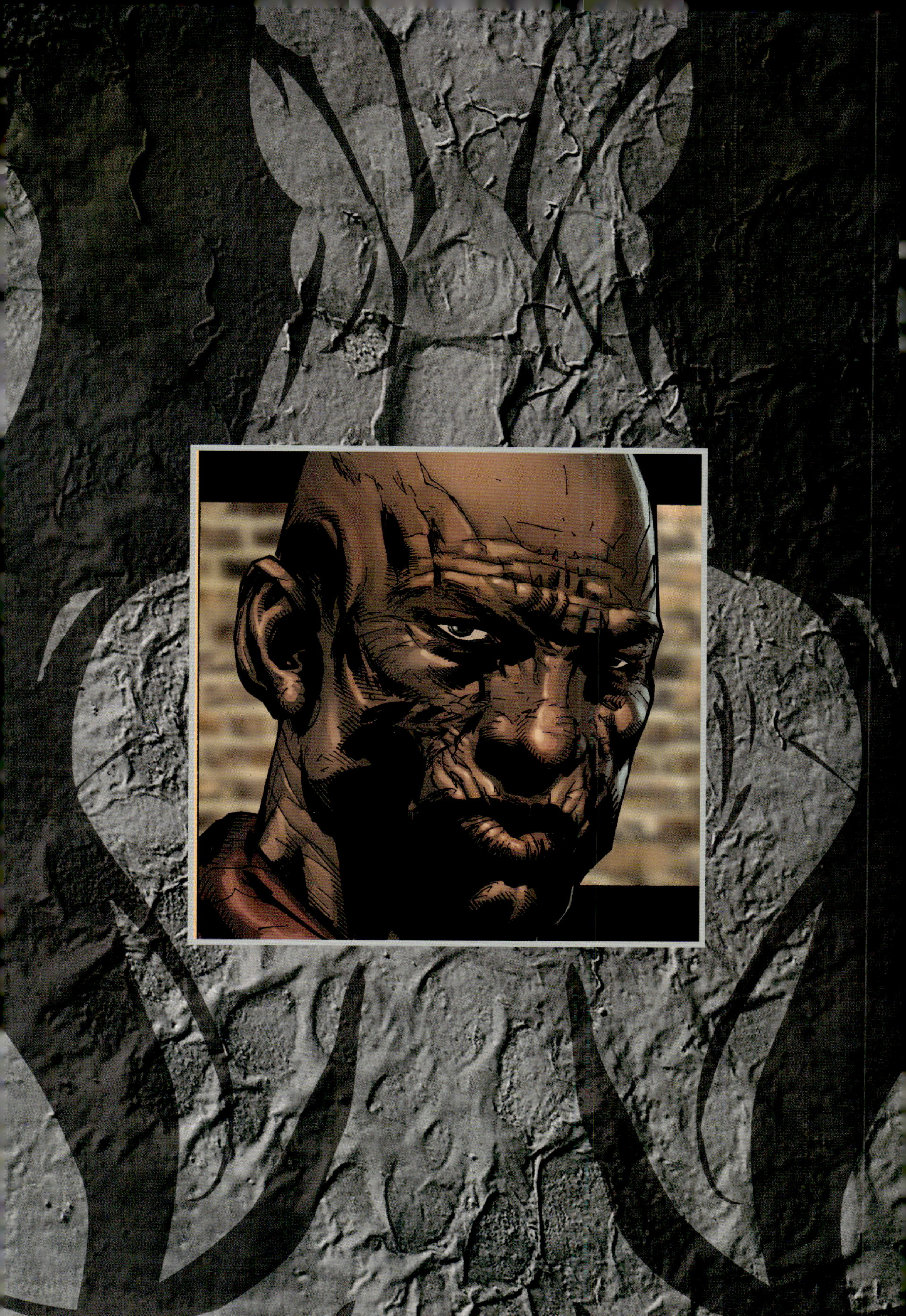

The Darkness Issue #78
cover art by: Michael Avon Oeming and Val Staples

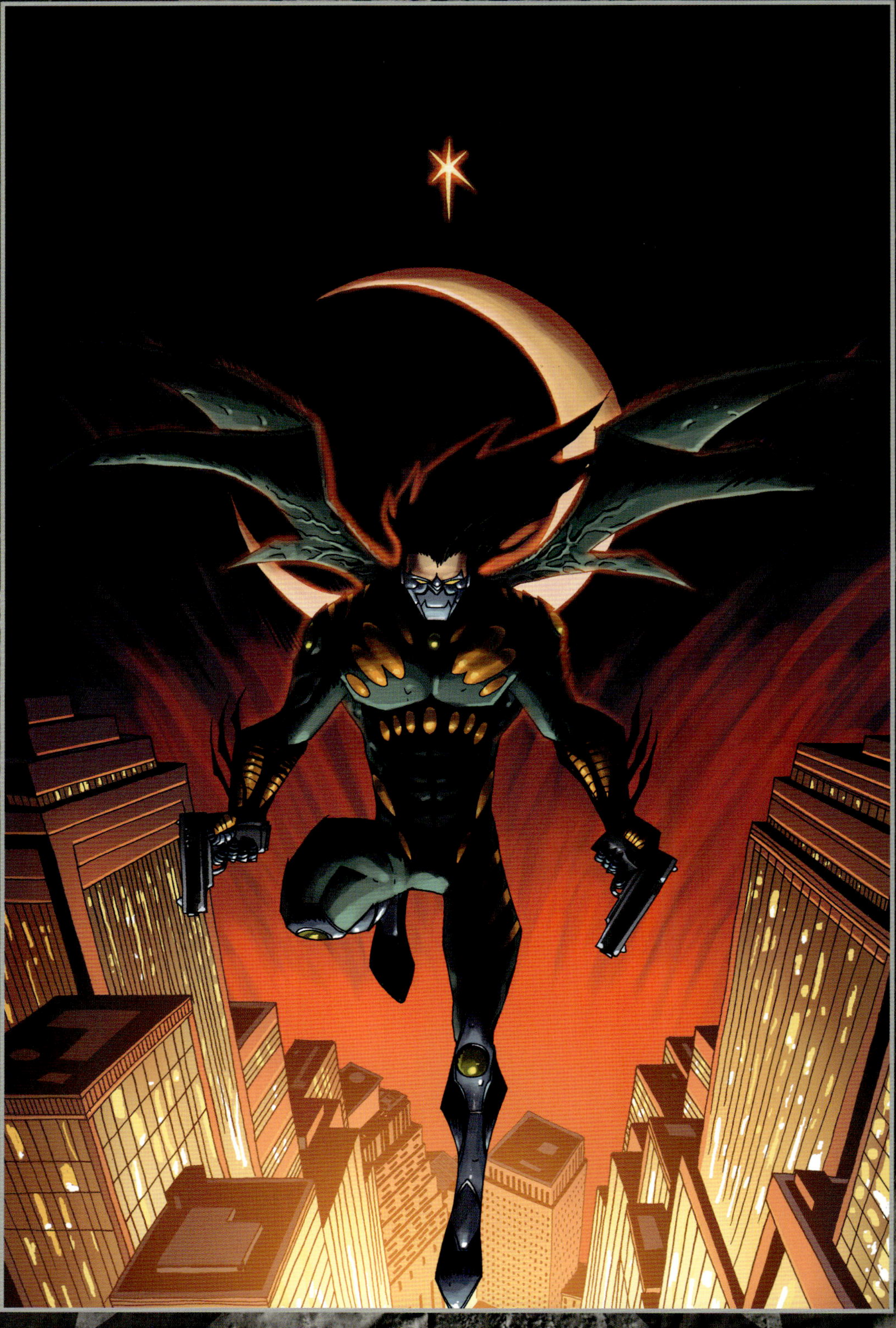

THE DARKNESS #78

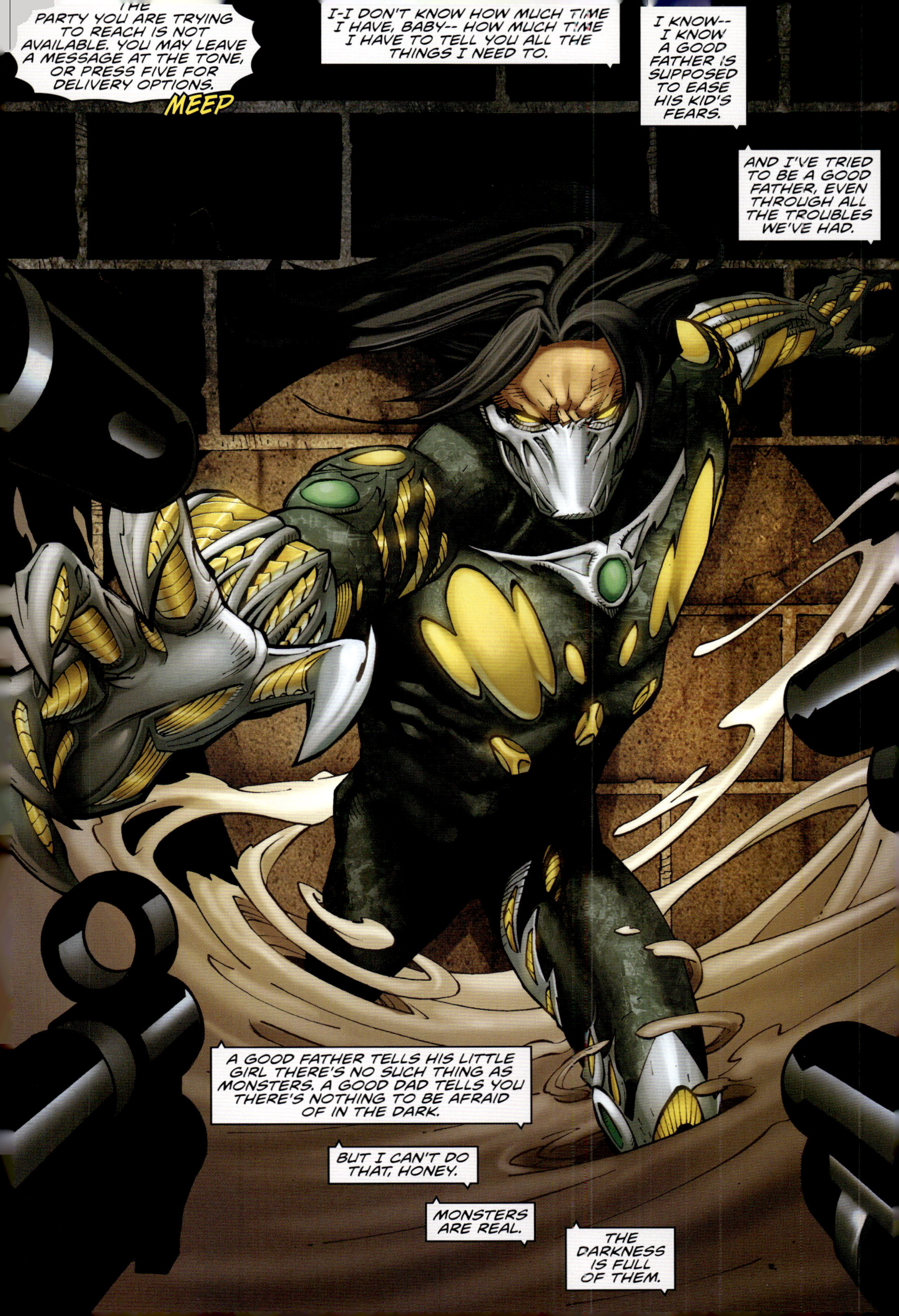
THE PARTY YOU ARE TRYING TO REACH IS NOT AVAILABLE. YOU MAY LEAVE A MESSAGE AT THE TONE, OR PRESS FIVE FOR DELIVERY OPTIONS.
MEEP
I-I DON'T KNOW HOW MUCH TIME I HAVE, BABY-- HOW MUCH TIME I HAVE TO TELL YOU ALL THE THINGS I NEED TO.
I KNOW-- I KNOW A GOOD FATHER IS SUPPOSED TO EASE HIS KID'S FEARS.
AND I'VE TRIED TO BE A GOOD FATHER, EVEN THROUGH ALL THE TROUBLES WE'VE HAD.
A GOOD FATHER TELLS HIS LITTLE GIRL THERE'S NO SUCH THING AS MONSTERS. A GOOD DAD TELLS YOU THERE'S NOTHING TO BE AFRAID OF IN THE DARK.
BUT I CAN'T DO THAT, HONEY.
MONSTERS ARE REAL.
THE DARKNESS IS FULL OF THEM.

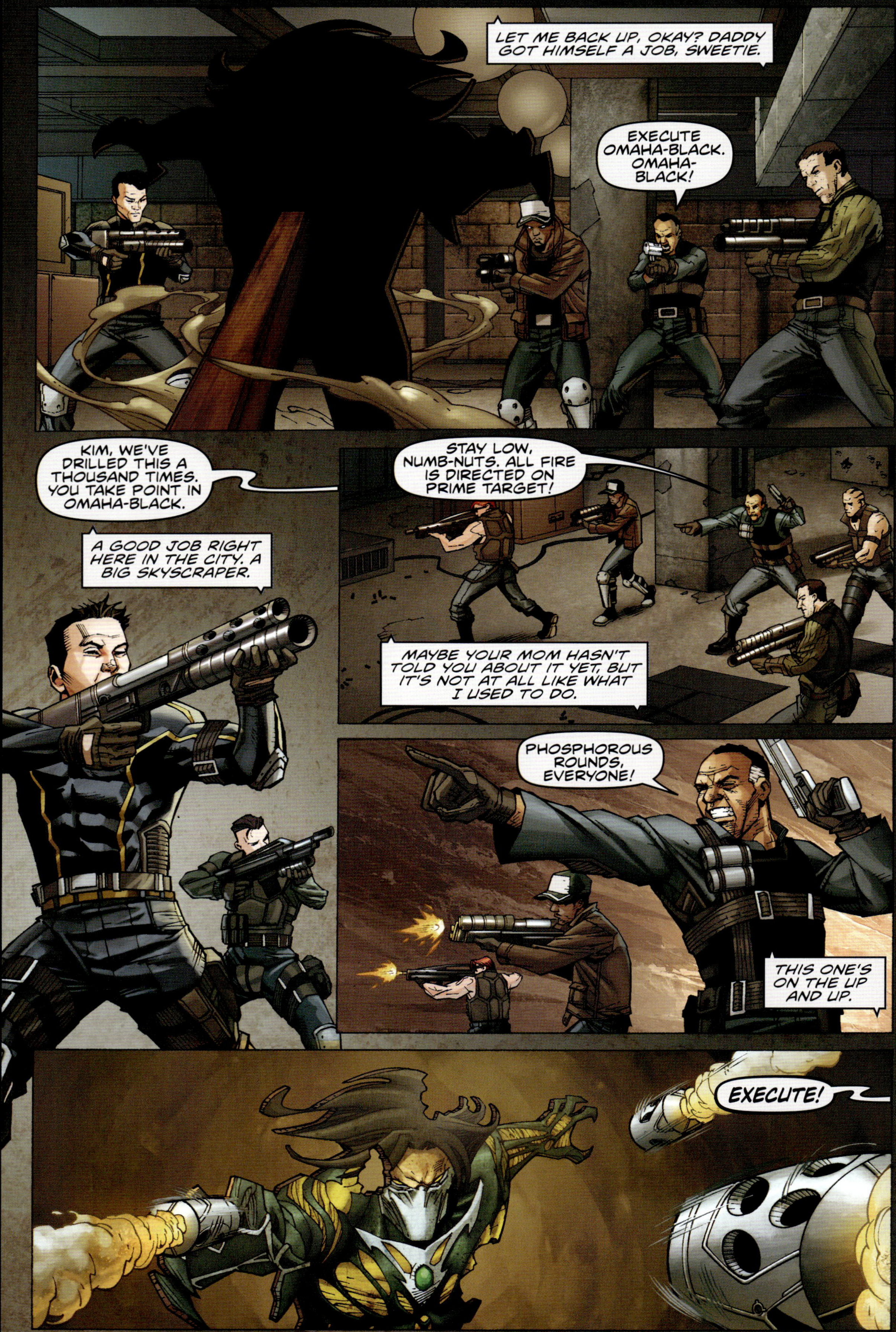
LET ME BACK UP, OKAY? DADDY GOT HIMSELF A JOB, SWEETIE.
EXECUTE OMAHA-BLACK. OMAHA-BLACK!
KIM, WE'VE DRILLED THIS A THOUSAND TIMES. YOU TAKE POINT IN OMAHA-BLACK.
A GOOD JOB RIGHT HERE IN THE CITY. A BIG SKYSCRAPER.
STAY LOW, NUMB-NUTS. ALL FIRE IS DIRECTED ON PRIME TARGET!
MAYBE YOUR MOM HASN'T TOLD YOU ABOUT IT YET, BUT IT'S NOT AT ALL LIKE WHAT I USED TO DO.
PHOSPHOROUS ROUNDS, EVERYONE!
THIS ONE'S ON THE UP AND UP.
EXECUTE!

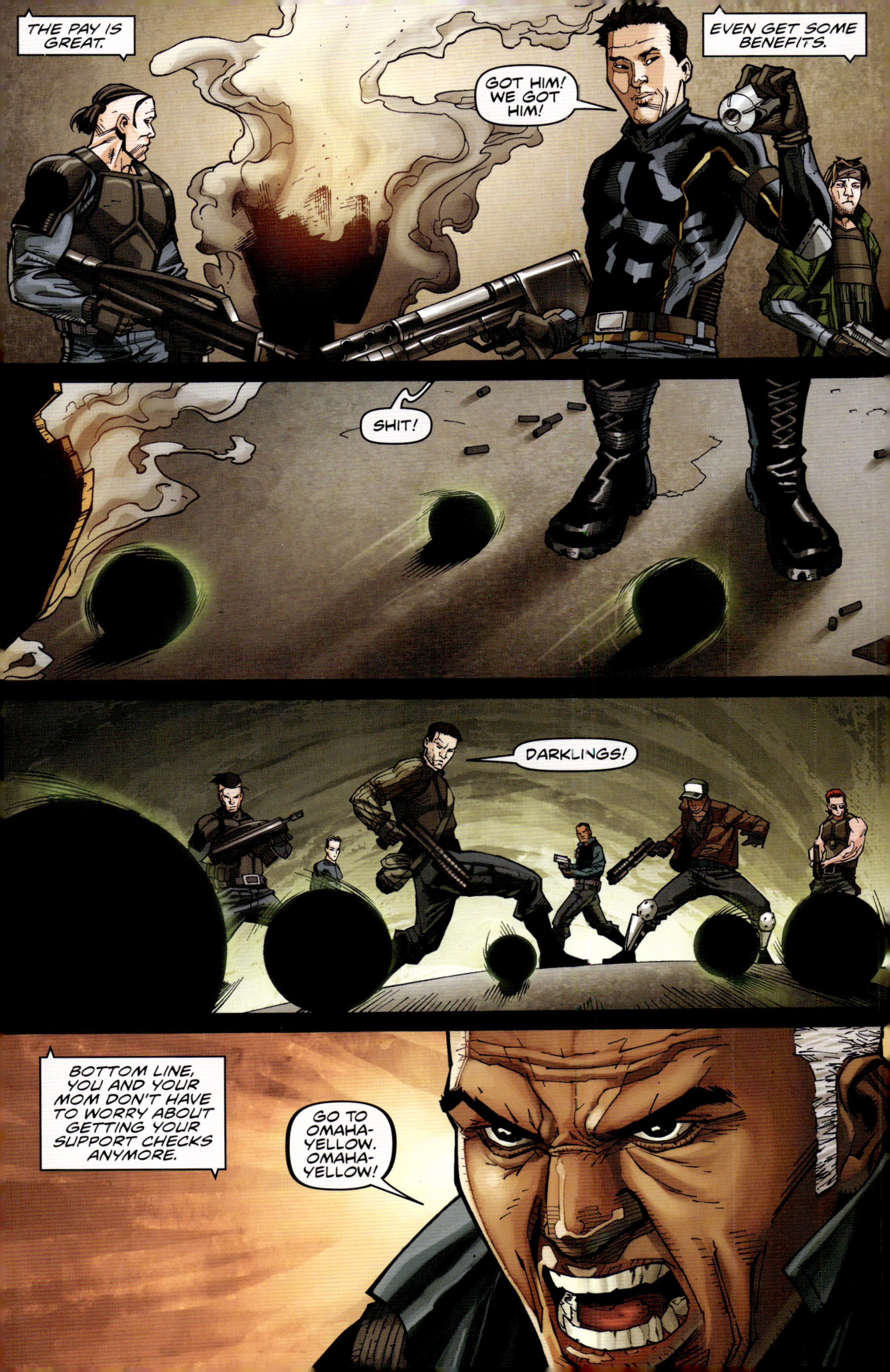
THE PAY IS GREAT.
GOT HIM! WE GOT HIM!
EVEN GET SOME BENEFITS.
SHIT!
DARKLINGS!
BOTTOM LINE, YOU AND YOUR MOM DON'T HAVE TO WORRY ABOUT GETTING YOUR SUPPORT CHECKS ANYMORE.
GO TO OMAHA-YELLOW. OMAHA-YELLOW!

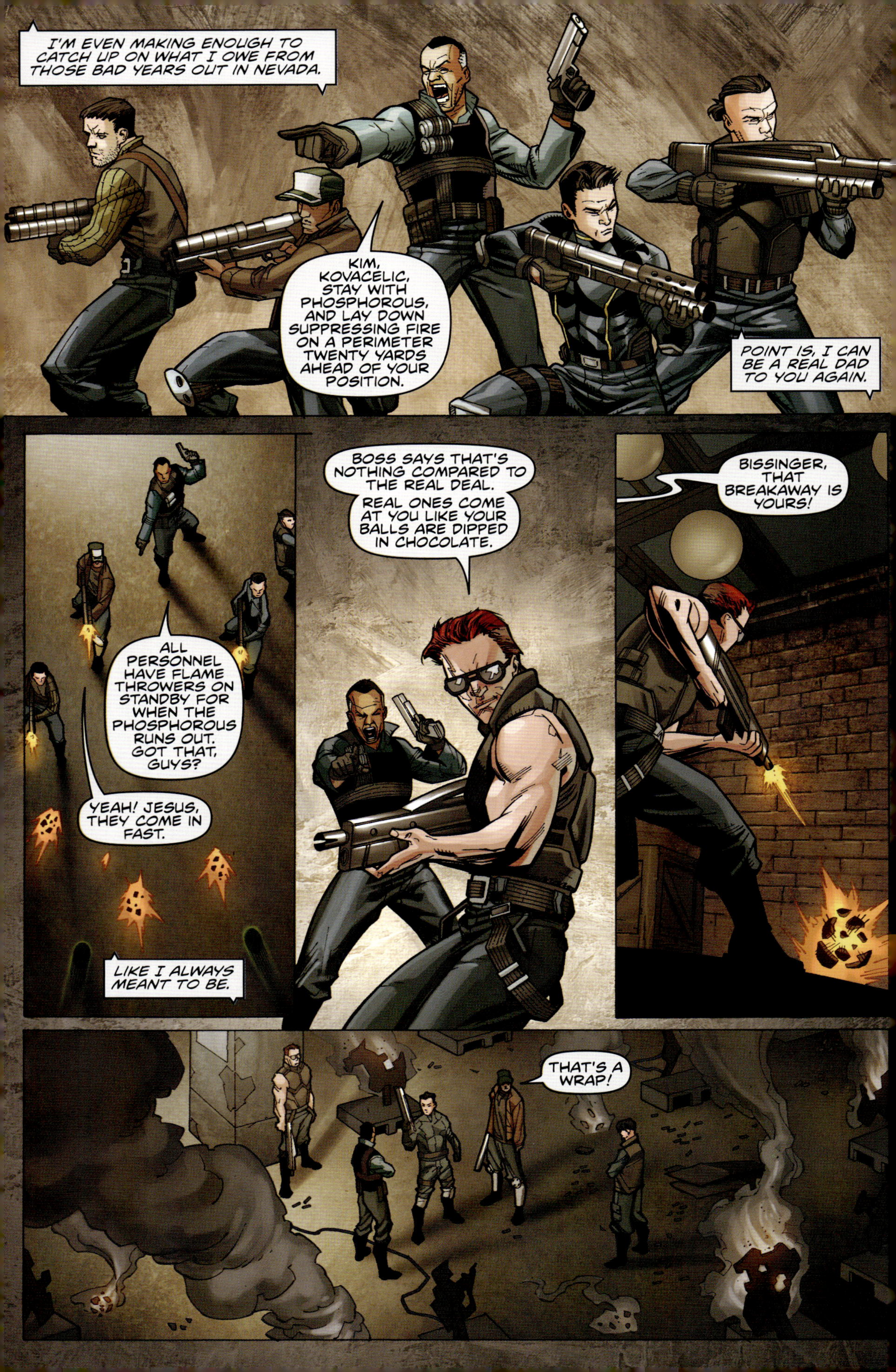
I'M EVEN MAKING ENOUGH TO CATCH UP ON WHAT I OWE FROM THOSE BAD YEARS OUT IN NEVADA.
KIM, KOVACELIC, STAY WITH PHOSPHOROUS, AND LAY DOWN SUPPRESSING FIRE ON A PERIMETER TWENTY YARDS AHEAD OF YOUR POSITION.
POINT IS, I CAN BE A REAL DAD TO YOU AGAIN.
ALL PERSONNEL HAVE FLAME THROWERS ON STANDBY FOR WHEN THE PHOSPHOROUS RUNS OUT. GOT THAT, GUYS?
YEAH! JESUS, THEY COME IN FAST.
LIKE I ALWAYS MEANT TO BE.
BOSS SAYS THAT'S NOTHING COMPARED TO THE REAL DEAL.
REAL ONES COME AT YOU LIKE YOUR BALLS ARE DIPPED IN CHOCOLATE.
BISSINGER, THAT BREAKAWAY IS YOURS!
THAT'S A WRAP!

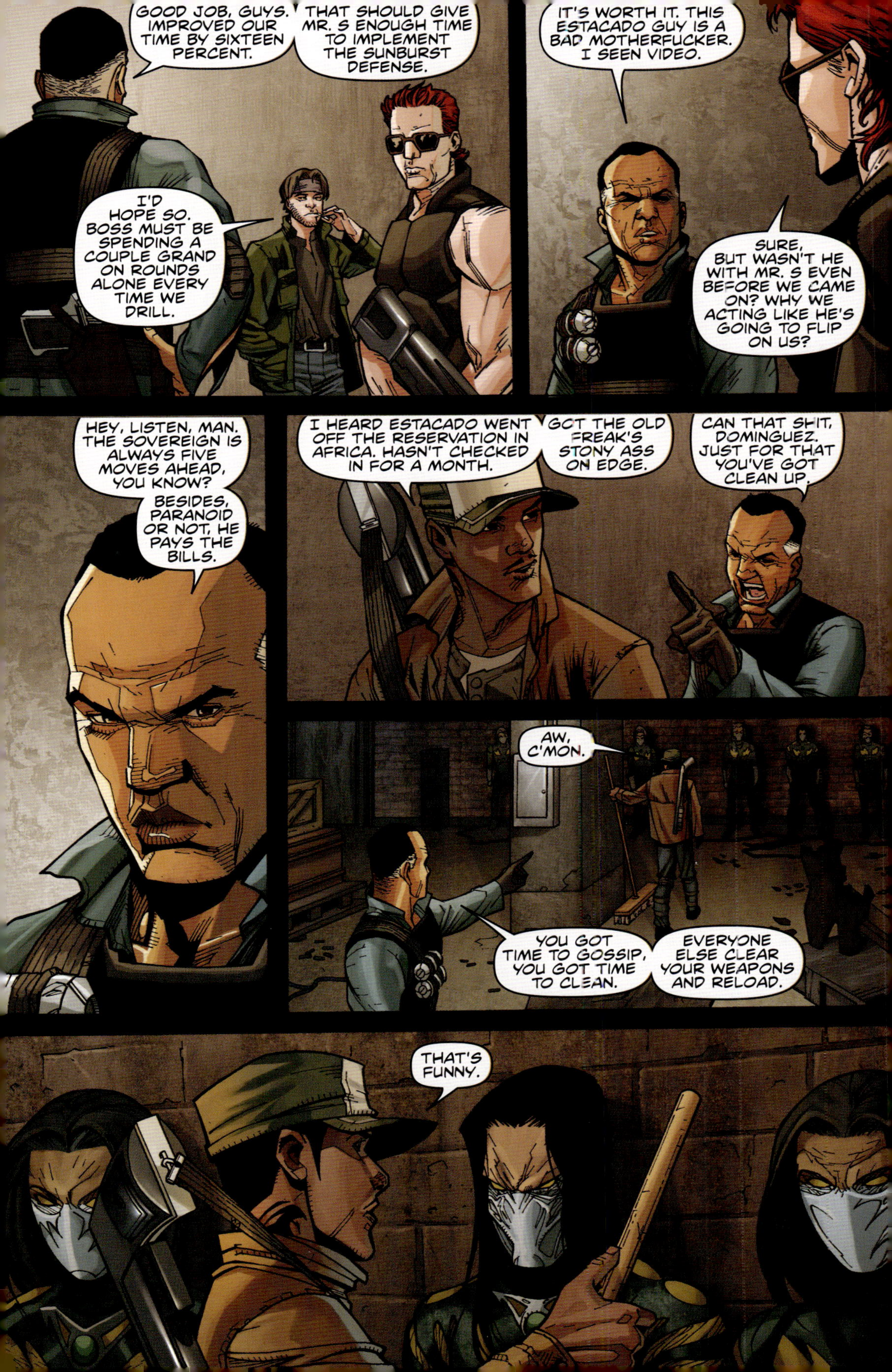
GOOD JOB, GUYS. IMPROVED OUR TIME BY SIXTEEN PERCENT.
THAT SHOULD GIVE MR. S ENOUGH TIME TO IMPLEMENT THE SUNBURST DEFENSE.
I'D HOPE SO. BOSS MUST BE SPENDING A COUPLE GRAND ON ROUNDS ALONE EVERY TIME WE DRILL.
IT'S WORTH IT. THIS ESTACADO GUY IS A BAD MOTHERFUCKER. I SEEN VIDEO.
SURE, BUT WASN'T HE WITH MR. S EVEN BEFORE WE CAME ON? WHY WE ACTING LIKE HE'S GOING TO FLIP ON US?
HEY, LISTEN, MAN. THE SOVEREIGN IS ALWAYS FIVE MOVES AHEAD, YOU KNOW?
BESIDES, PARANOID OR NOT, HE PAYS THE BILLS.
I HEARD ESTACADO WENT OFF THE RESERVATION IN AFRICA. HASN'T CHECKED IN FOR A MONTH.
GOT THE OLD FREAK'S STONY ASS ON EDGE.
CAN THAT SHIT, DOMINGUEZ. JUST FOR THAT YOU'VE GOT CLEAN UP.
AW, C'MON.
YOU GOT TIME TO GOSSIP, YOU GOT TIME TO CLEAN.
EVERYONE ELSE CLEAR YOUR WEAPONS AND RELOAD.
THAT'S FUNNY.

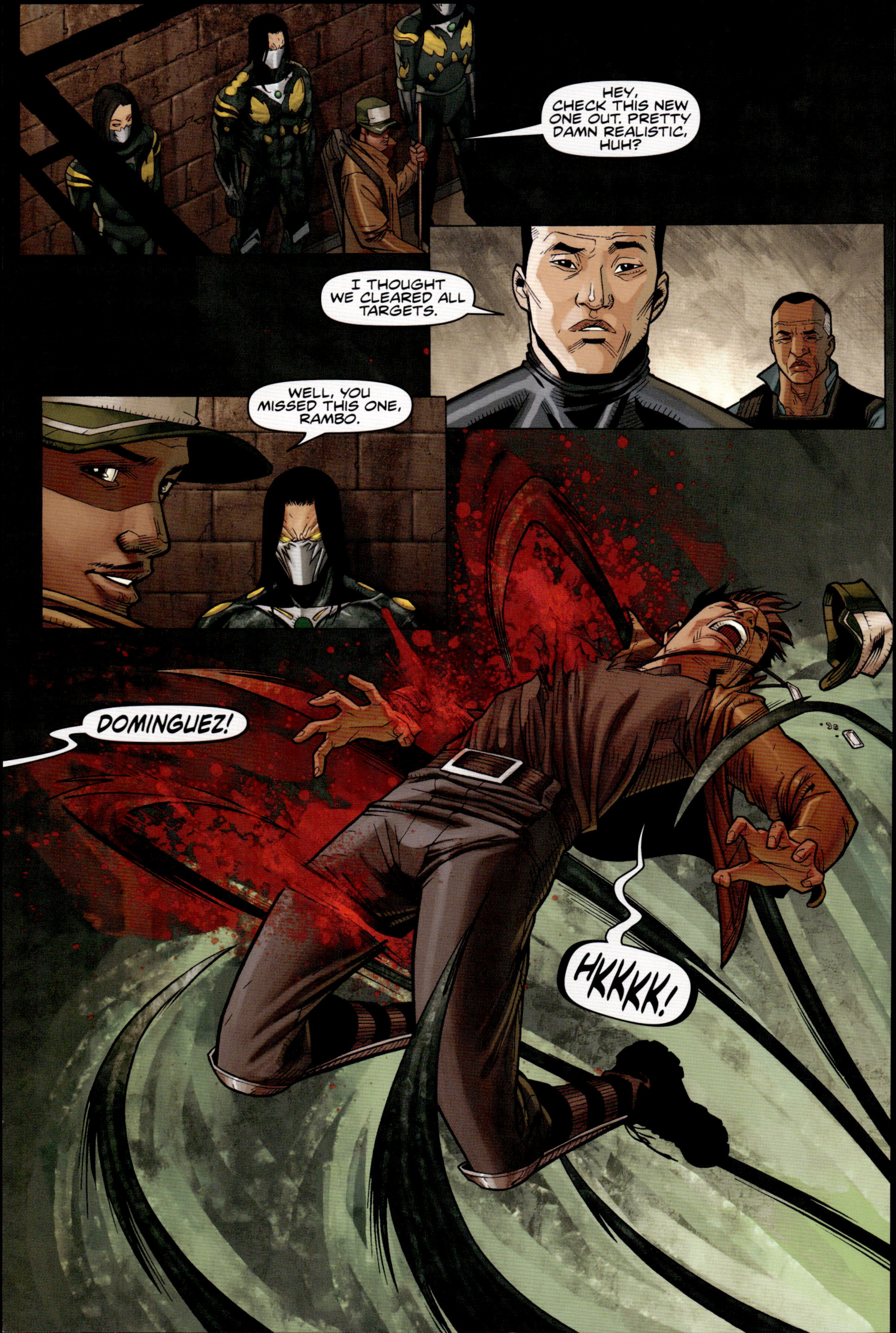
HEY, CHECK THIS NEW ONE OUT. PRETTY DAMN REALISTIC, HUH?
I THOUGHT WE CLEARED ALL TARGETS.
WELL, YOU MISSED THIS ONE, RAMBO.
DOMINGUEZ!
HKKKK!

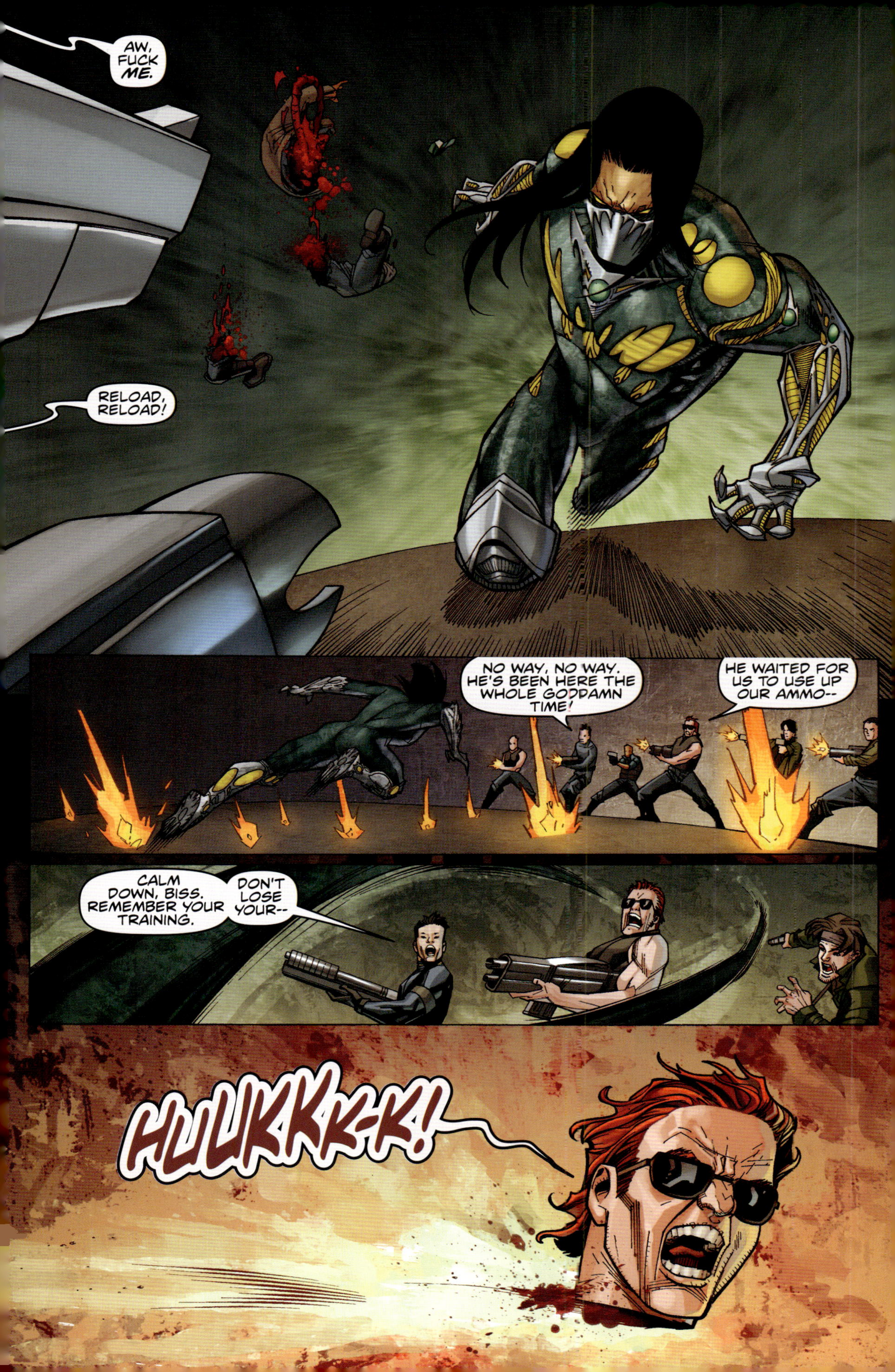
AW, FUCK ME.
RELOAD, RELOAD!
NO WAY, NO WAY. HE'S BEEN HERE THE WHOLE GODDAMN TIME!
HE WAITED FOR US TO USE UP OUR AMMO--
CALM DOWN, BISS. REMEMBER YOUR TRAINING.
DON'T LOSE YOUR--
HULKKK-K!

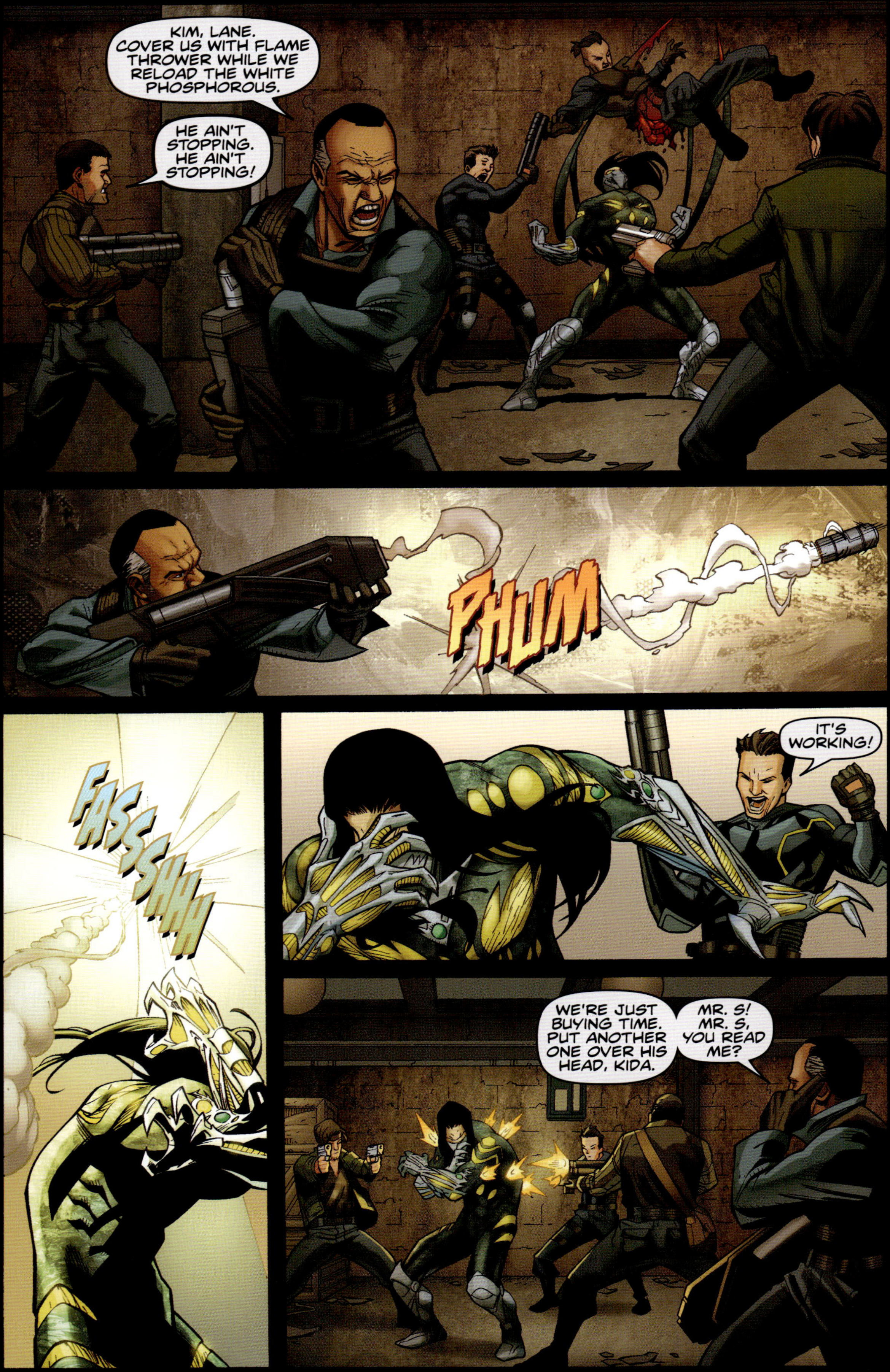
KIM, LANE. COVER US WITH FLAME THROWER WHILE WE RELOAD THE WHITE PHOSPHOROUS.
HE AIN'T STOPPING. HE AIN'T STOPPING!
PHUM
FASSSHHH
IT'S WORKING!
WE'RE JUST BUYING TIME. PUT ANOTHER ONE OVER HIS HEAD, KIDA.
MR. S! MR. S, YOU READ ME?

YES, MR. LOCKHART?

ESTACADO IS HERE. NOW.

SOMEHOW HE ENTERED THE COMPOUND AND IS ENGAGING US IN THE LIVE FIRE ROOM.

AH, I SEE.

WE NEED HELP. THIS GUY'S A FUCKING NIGHTMARE.

LIKE ALL DREAMS, MR. LOCKHART...

NIGHTMARES ARE CHASED AWAY BY THE DAWN.

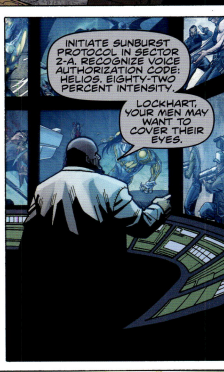

INITIATE SUNBURST PROTOCOL IN SECTOR 2-A. RECOGNIZE VOICE AUTHORIZATION CODE: HELIOS. EIGHTY-TWO PERCENT INTENSITY.

LOCKHART, YOUR MEN MAY WANT TO COVER THEIR EYES.

VVVMMMM

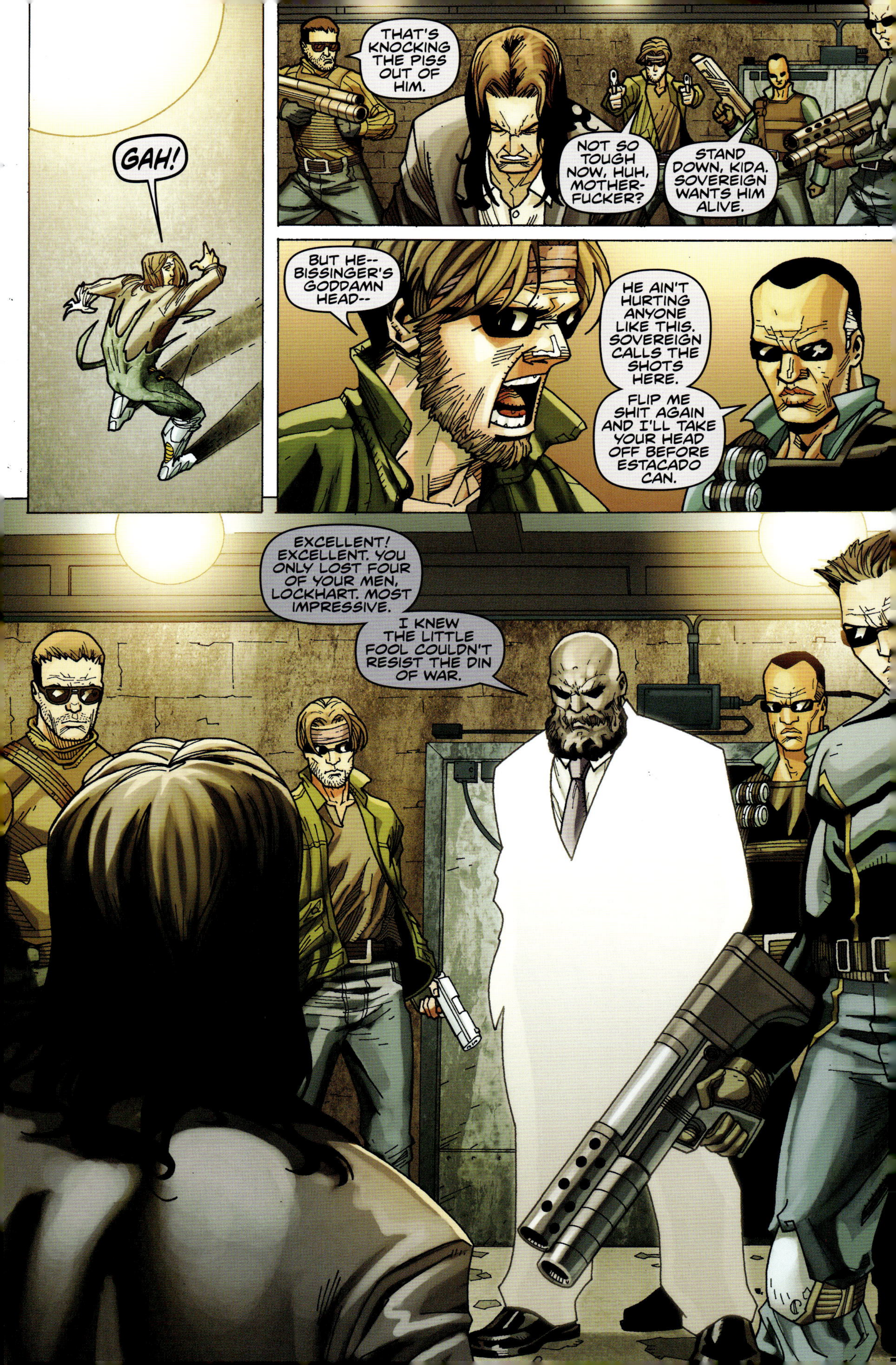
GAH!
THAT'S KNOCKING THE PISS OUT OF HIM.
NOT SO TOUGH NOW, HUH, MOTHER-FUCKER?
STAND DOWN, KIDA. SOVEREIGN WANTS HIM ALIVE.
BUT HE-- BISSINGER'S GODDAMN HEAD--
HE AIN'T HURTING ANYONE LIKE THIS. SOVEREIGN CALLS THE SHOTS HERE.
FLIP ME SHIT AGAIN AND I'LL TAKE YOUR HEAD OFF BEFORE ESTACADO CAN.
EXCELLENT! EXCELLENT. YOU ONLY LOST FOUR OF YOUR MEN, LOCKHART. MOST IMPRESSIVE.
I KNEW THE LITTLE FOOL COULDN'T RESIST THE DIN OF WAR.

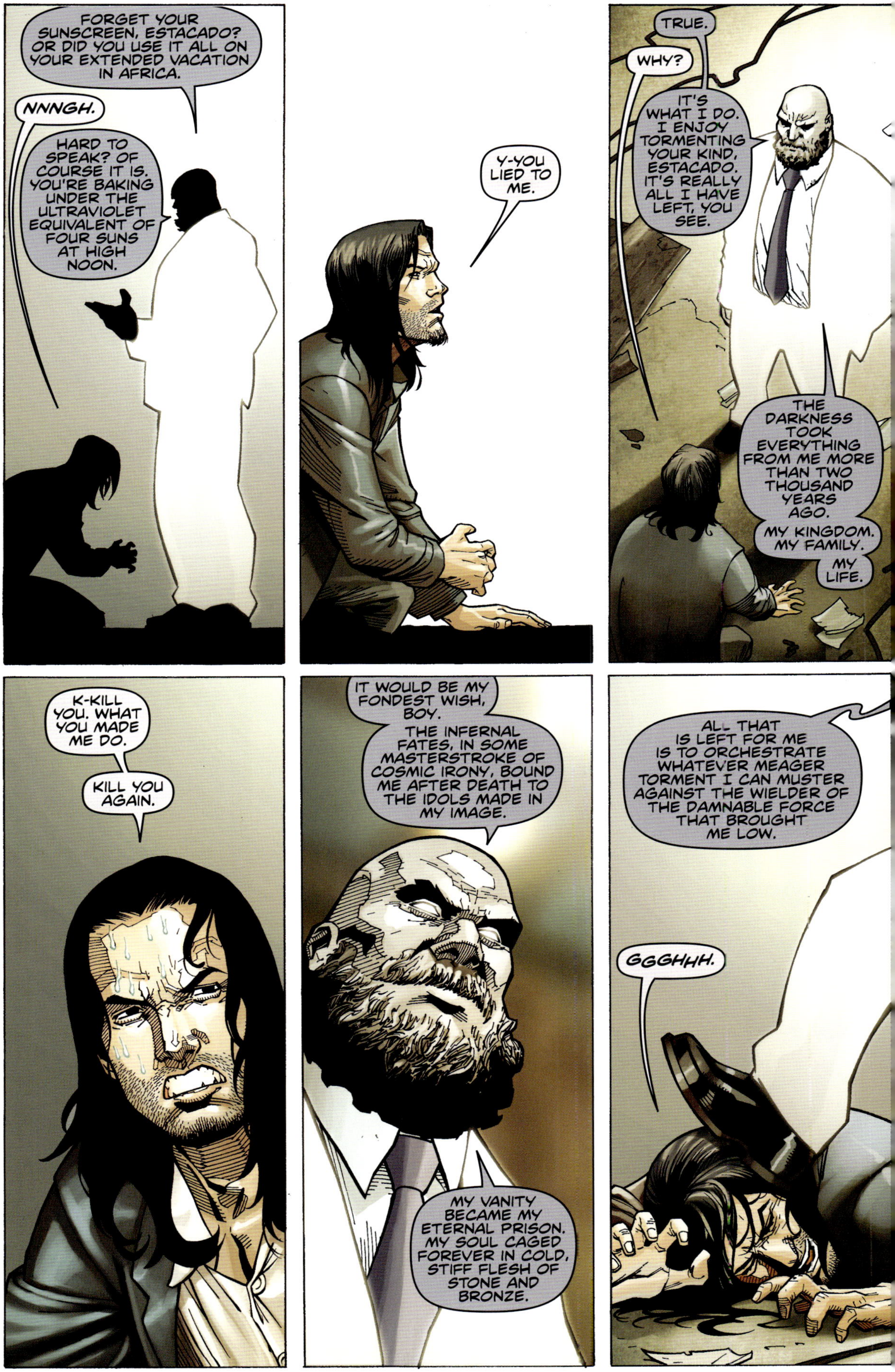
FORGET YOUR SUNSCREEN, ESTACADO? OR DID YOU USE IT ALL ON YOUR EXTENDED VACATION IN AFRICA.
NNNGH.
HARD TO SPEAK? OF COURSE IT IS. YOU'RE BAKING UNDER THE ULTRAVIOLET EQUIVALENT OF FOUR SUNS AT HIGH NOON.
Y-YOU LIED TO ME.
TRUE.
WHY?
IT'S WHAT I DO. I ENJOY TORMENTING YOUR KIND, ESTACADO. IT'S REALLY ALL I HAVE LEFT, YOU SEE.
THE DARKNESS TOOK EVERYTHING FROM ME MORE THAN TWO THOUSAND YEARS AGO.
MY KINGDOM. MY FAMILY.
MY LIFE.
K-KILL YOU. WHAT YOU MADE ME DO.
KILL YOU AGAIN.
IT WOULD BE MY FONDEST WISH, BOY.
THE INFERNAL FATES, IN SOME MASTERSTROKE OF COSMIC IRONY, BOUND ME AFTER DEATH TO THE IDOLS MADE IN MY IMAGE.
MY VANITY BECAME MY ETERNAL PRISON. MY SOUL CAGED FOREVER IN COLD, STIFF FLESH OF STONE AND BRONZE.
ALL THAT IS LEFT FOR ME IS TO ORCHESTRATE WHATEVER MEAGER TORMENT I CAN MUSTER AGAINST THE WIELDER OF THE DAMNABLE FORCE THAT BROUGHT ME LOW.
GGGHHH.

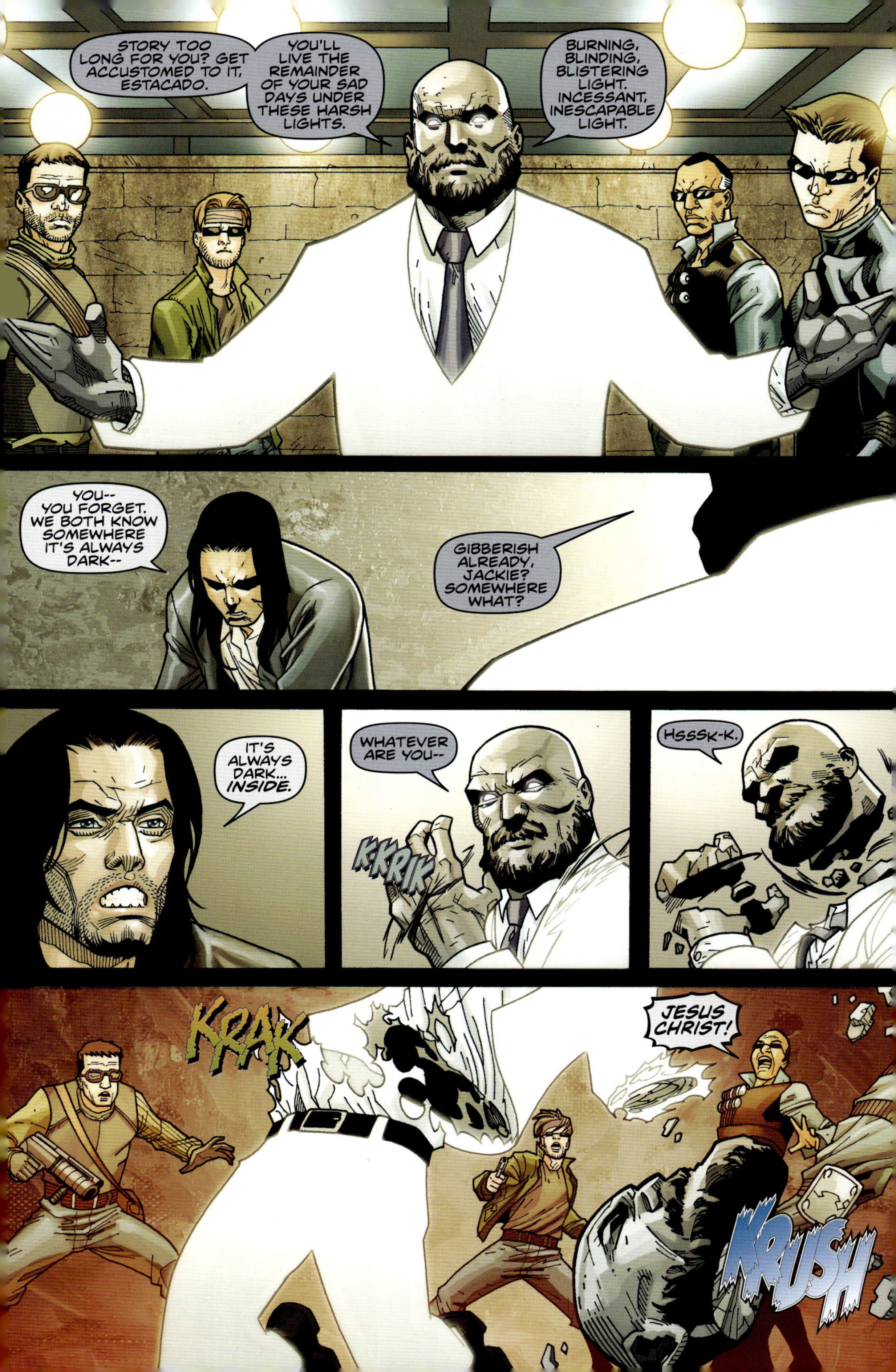
STORY TOO LONG FOR YOU? GET ACCUSTOMED TO IT, ESTACADO.
YOU'LL LIVE THE REMAINDER OF YOUR SAD DAYS UNDER THESE HARSH LIGHTS.
BURNING, BLINDING, BLISTERING LIGHT. INCESSANT, INESCAPABLE LIGHT.
YOU-- YOU FORGET. WE BOTH KNOW SOMEWHERE IT'S ALWAYS DARK--
GIBBERISH ALREADY, JACKIE? SOMEWHERE WHAT?
IT'S ALWAYS DARK... INSIDE.
WHATEVER ARE YOU--
K-KRIK
HSSSK-K.
KRAK
JESUS CHRIST!
KRUSH

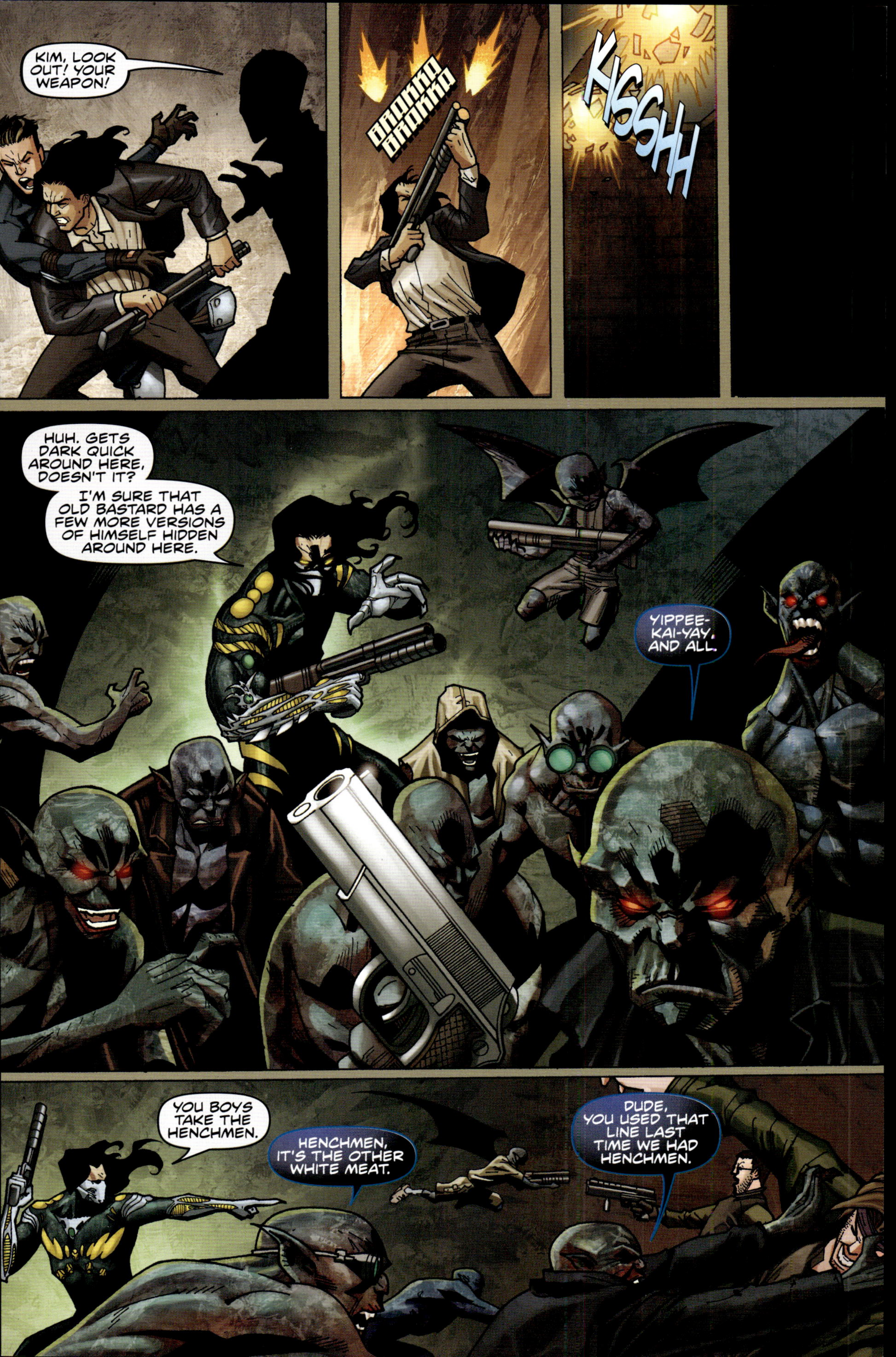
KIM, LOOK OUT! YOUR WEAPON!
BRAKKA BRAKKA
KISSHH
HUH. GETS DARK QUICK AROUND HERE, DOESN'T IT?
I'M SURE THAT OLD BASTARD HAS A FEW MORE VERSIONS OF HIMSELF HIDDEN AROUND HERE.
YIPPEE-KAI-YAY. AND ALL.
YOU BOYS TAKE THE HENCHMEN.
HENCHMEN, IT'S THE OTHER WHITE MEAT.
DUDE, YOU USED THAT LINE LAST TIME WE HAD HENCHMEN.

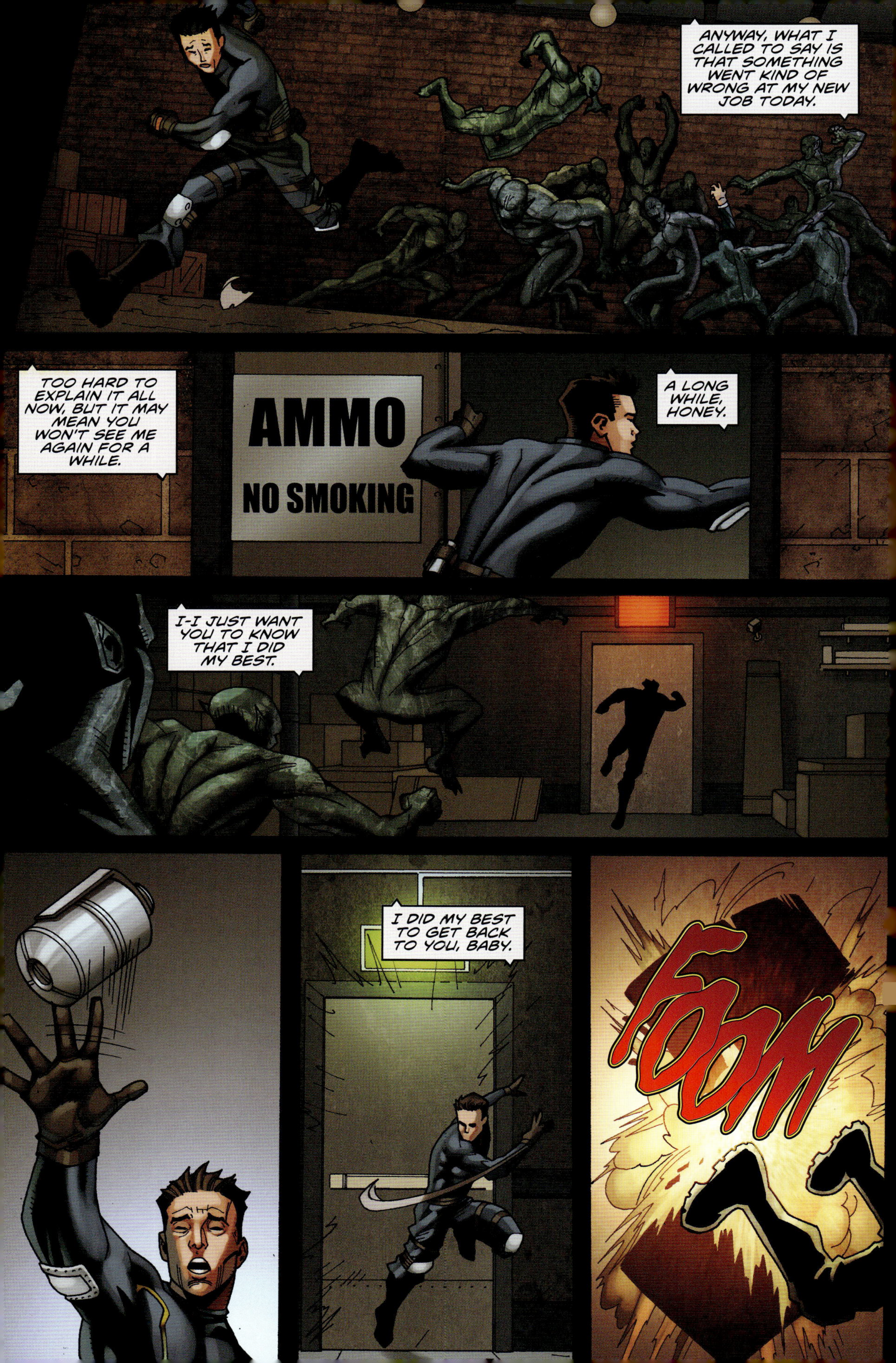

ANYWAY, WHAT I CALLED TO SAY IS THAT SOMETHING WENT KIND OF WRONG AT MY NEW JOB TODAY.
TOO HARD TO EXPLAIN IT ALL NOW, BUT IT MAY MEAN YOU WON'T SEE ME AGAIN FOR A WHILE.
AMMO
NO SMOKING
A LONG WHILE, HONEY.
I-I JUST WANT YOU TO KNOW THAT I DID MY BEST.
I DID MY BEST TO GET BACK TO YOU, BABY.
FOOM

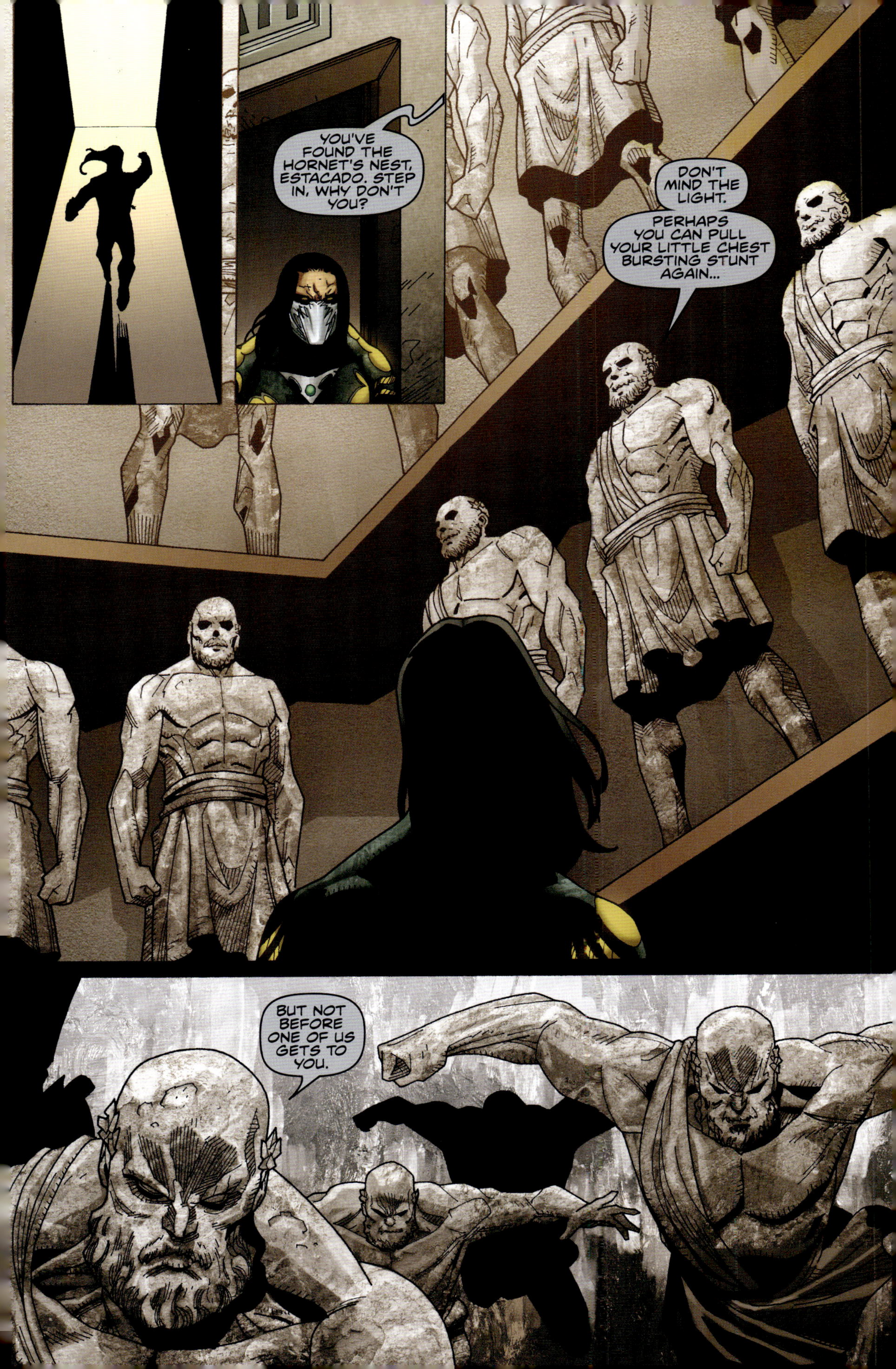
YOU'VE FOUND THE HORNET'S NEST, ESTACADO. STEP IN, WHY DON'T YOU?
DON'T MIND THE LIGHT.
PERHAPS YOU CAN PULL YOUR LITTLE CHEST BURSTING STUNT AGAIN...
BUT NOT BEFORE ONE OF US GETS TO YOU.

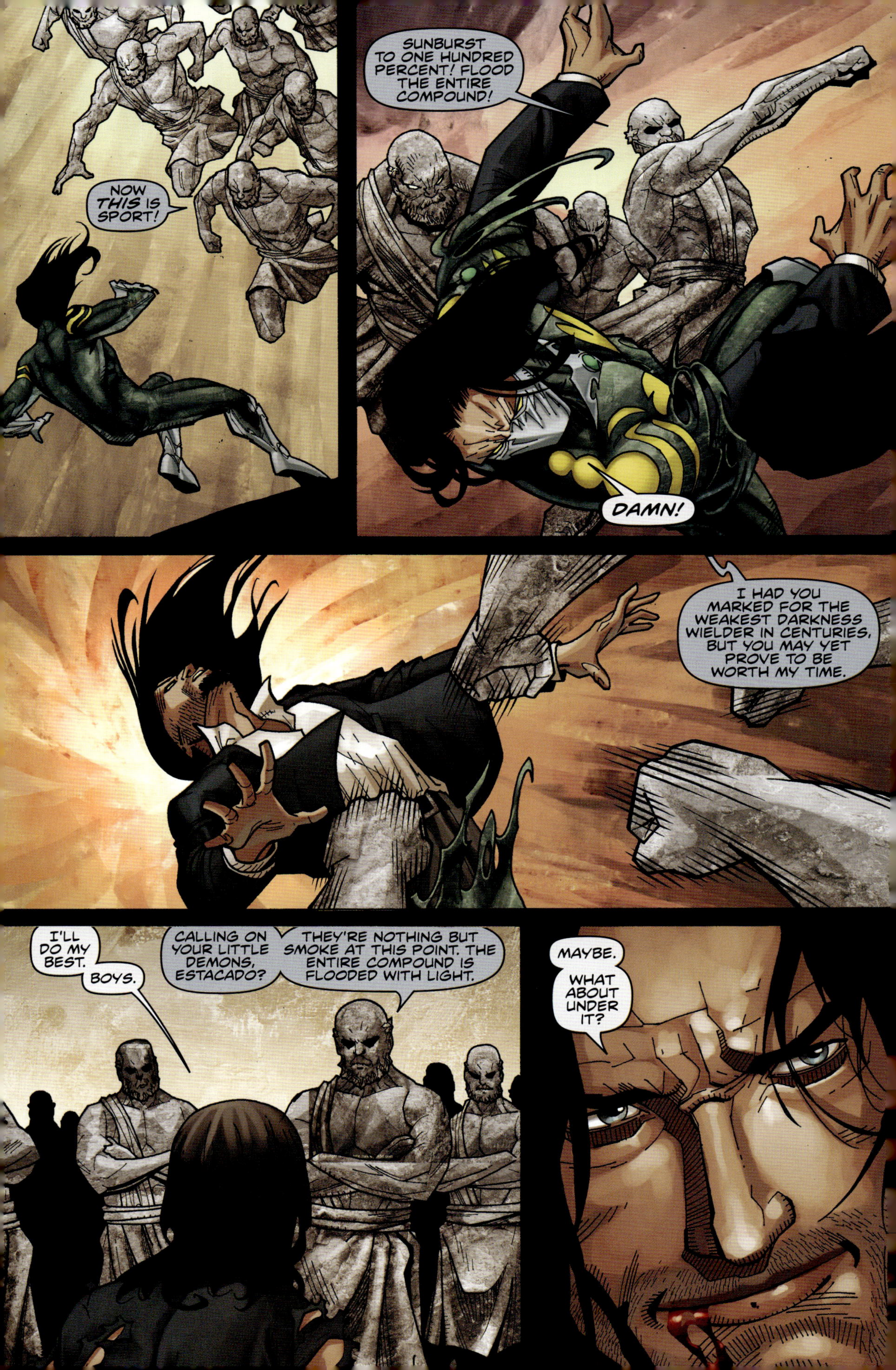
NOW THIS IS SPORT!
SUNBURST TO ONE HUNDRED PERCENT! FLOOD THE ENTIRE COMPOUND!
DAMN!
I HAD YOU MARKED FOR THE WEAKEST DARKNESS WIELDER IN CENTURIES, BUT YOU MAY YET PROVE TO BE WORTH MY TIME.
I'LL DO MY BEST.
BOYS.
CALLING ON YOUR LITTLE DEMONS, ESTACADO?
THEY'RE NOTHING BUT SMOKE AT THIS POINT. THE ENTIRE COMPOUND IS FLOODED WITH LIGHT.
MAYBE.
WHAT ABOUT UNDER IT?

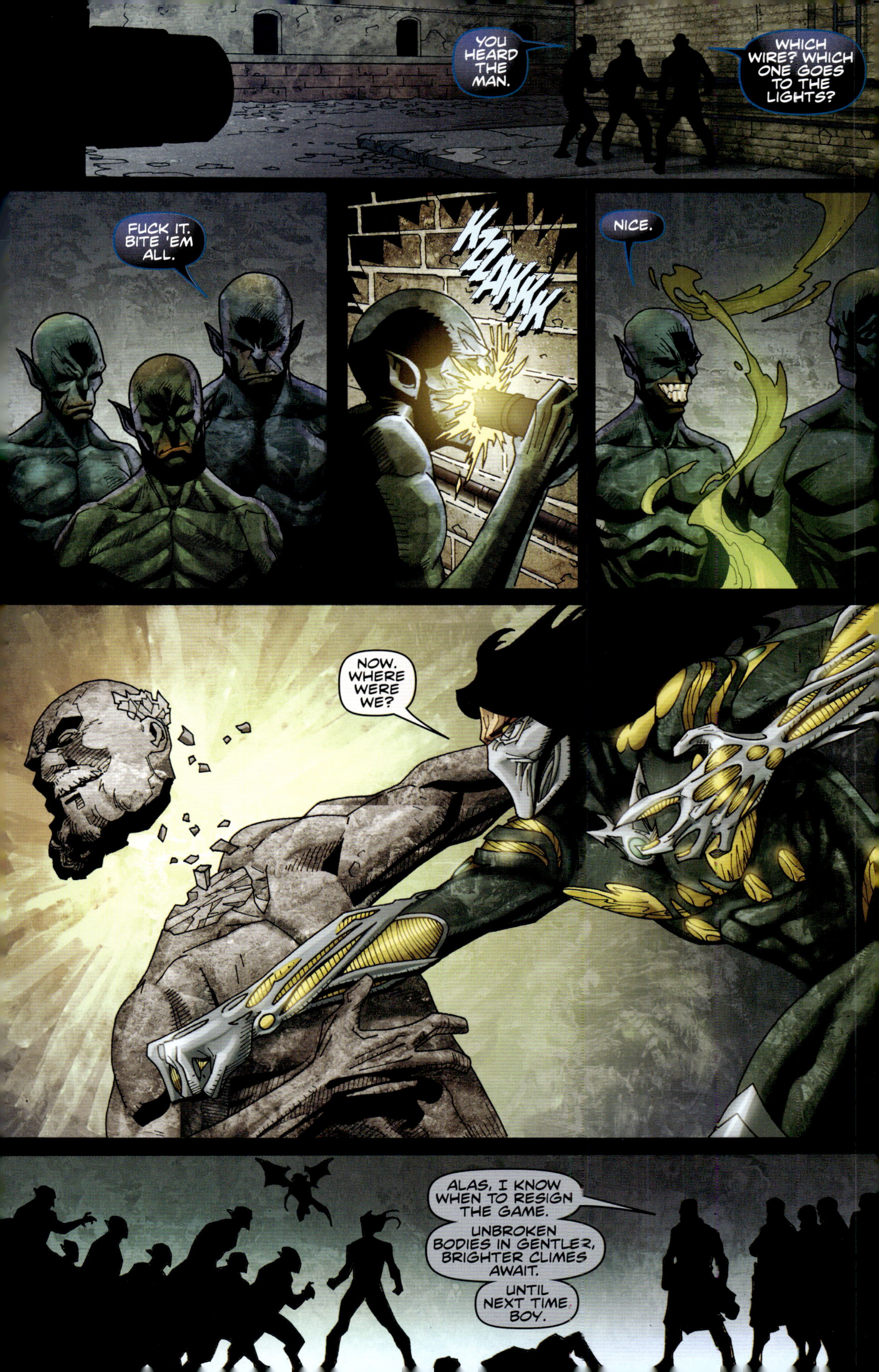

YOU HEARD THE MAN.
WHICH WIRE? WHICH ONE GOES TO THE LIGHTS?
FUCK IT. BITE 'EM ALL.
KZZAKKK
NICE.
NOW. WHERE WERE WE?
ALAS, I KNOW WHEN TO RESIGN THE GAME.
UNBROKEN BODIES IN GENTLER, BRIGHTER CLIMES AWAIT.
UNTIL NEXT TIME, BOY.

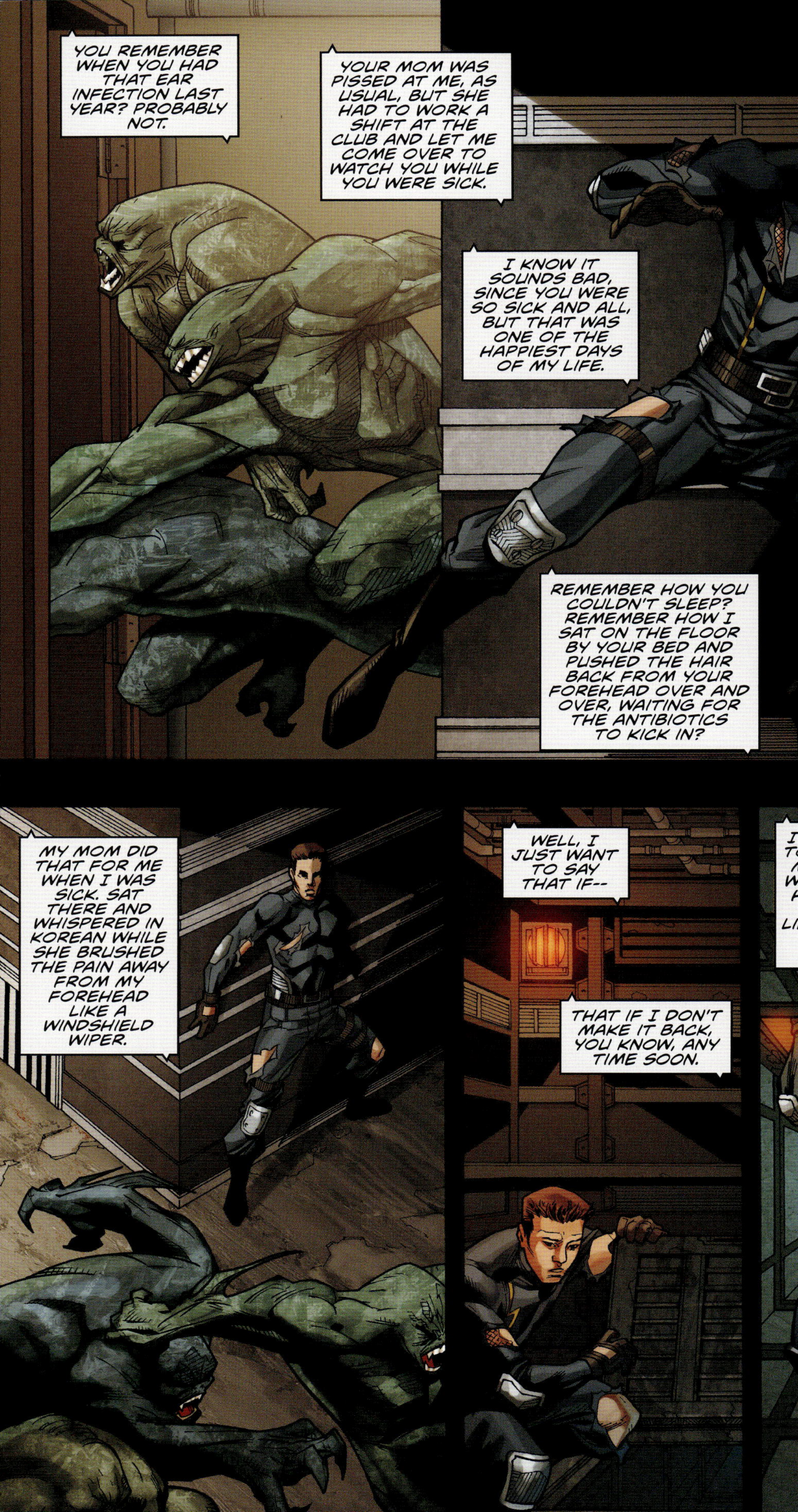
YOU REMEMBER WHEN YOU HAD THAT EAR INFECTION LAST YEAR? PROBABLY NOT.
YOUR MOM WAS PISSED AT ME, AS USUAL, BUT SHE HAD TO WORK A SHIFT AT THE CLUB AND LET ME COME OVER TO WATCH YOU WHILE YOU WERE SICK.
I KNOW IT SOUNDS BAD, SINCE YOU WERE SO SICK AND ALL, BUT THAT WAS ONE OF THE HAPPIEST DAYS OF MY LIFE.
REMEMBER HOW YOU COULDN'T SLEEP? REMEMBER HOW I SAT ON THE FLOOR BY YOUR BED AND PUSHED THE HAIR BACK FROM YOUR FOREHEAD OVER AND OVER, WAITING FOR THE ANTIBIOTICS TO KICK IN?
MY MOM DID THAT FOR ME WHEN I WAS SICK. SAT THERE AND WHISPERED IN KOREAN WHILE SHE BRUSHED THE PAIN AWAY FROM MY FOREHEAD LIKE A WINDSHIELD WIPER.
WELL, I JUST WANT TO SAY THAT IF--
THAT IF I DON'T MAKE IT BACK, YOU KNOW, ANY TIME SOON.

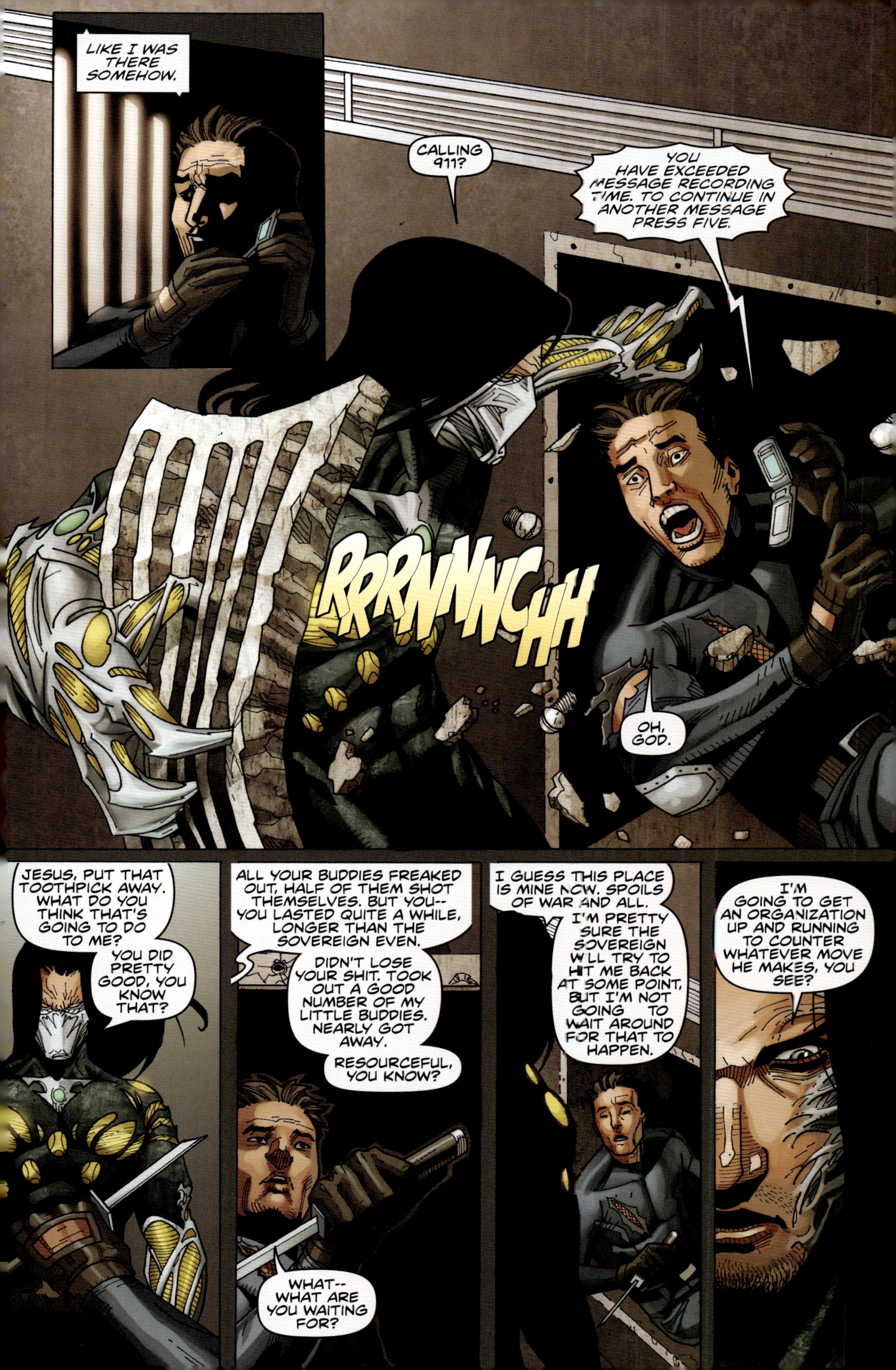
LIKE I WAS THERE SOMEHOW.
CALLING 911?
YOU HAVE EXCEEDED MESSAGE RECORDING TIME. TO CONTINUE IN ANOTHER MESSAGE PRESS FIVE.
RRRNNNCHH
OH, GOD.
JESUS, PUT THAT TOOTHPICK AWAY. WHAT DO YOU THINK THAT'S GOING TO DO TO ME?
YOU DID PRETTY GOOD, YOU KNOW THAT?
ALL YOUR BUDDIES FREAKED OUT, HALF OF THEM SHOT THEMSELVES. BUT YOU-- YOU LASTED QUITE A WHILE, LONGER THAN THE SOVEREIGN EVEN.
DIDN'T LOSE YOUR SHIT. TOOK OUT A GOOD NUMBER OF MY LITTLE BUDDIES. NEARLY GOT AWAY.
RESOURCEFUL, YOU KNOW?
WHAT-- WHAT ARE YOU WAITING FOR?
I GUESS THIS PLACE IS MINE NOW. SPOILS OF WAR AND ALL.
I'M PRETTY SURE THE SOVEREIGN WILL TRY TO HIT ME BACK AT SOME POINT, BUT I'M NOT GOING TO WAIT AROUND FOR THAT TO HAPPEN.
I'M GOING TO GET AN ORGANIZATION UP AND RUNNING TO COUNTER WHATEVER MOVE HE MAKES, YOU SEE?

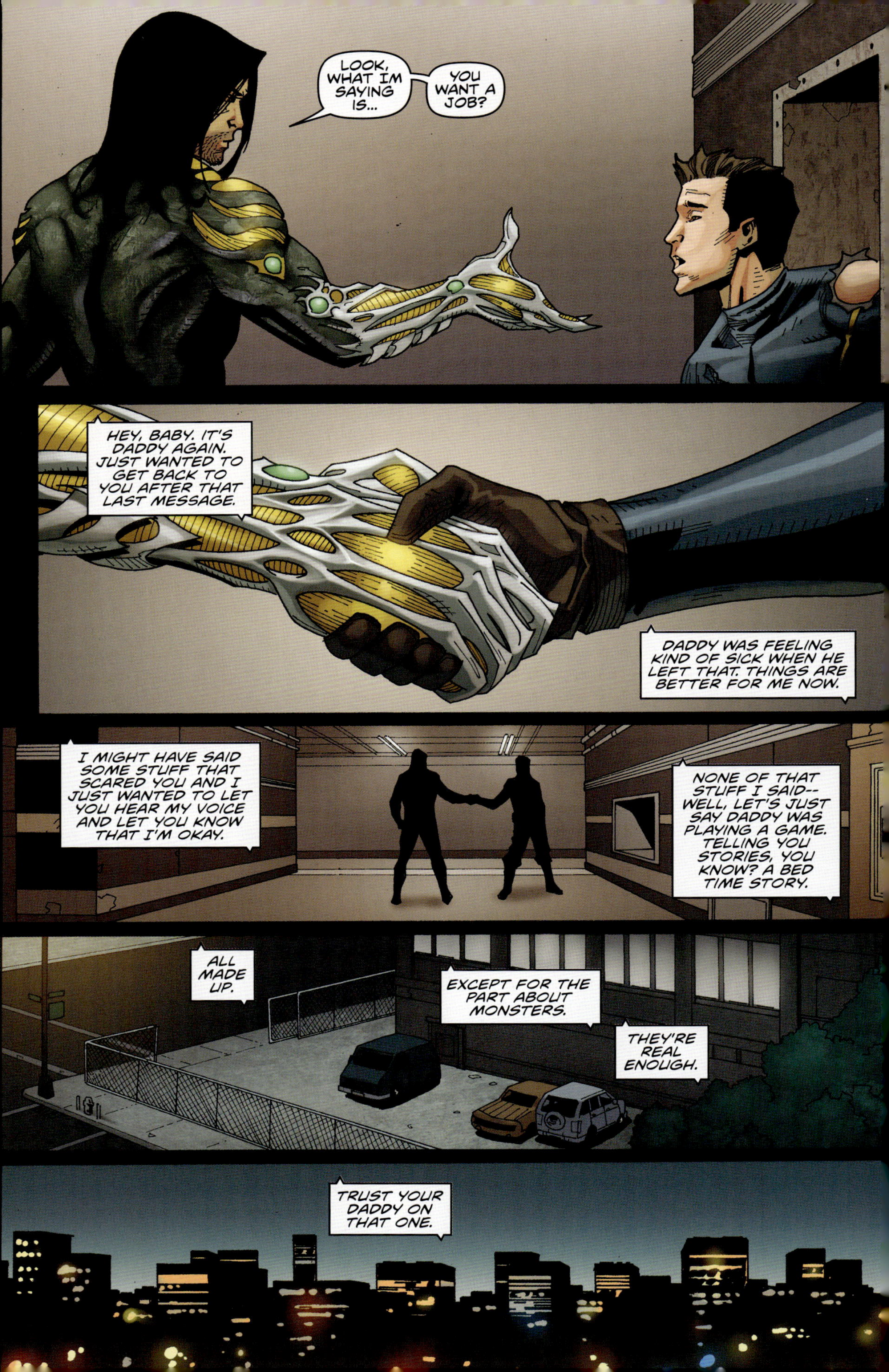
LOOK, WHAT I'M SAYING IS...
YOU WANT A JOB?
HEY, BABY. IT'S DADDY AGAIN. JUST WANTED TO GET BACK TO YOU AFTER THAT LAST MESSAGE.
DADDY WAS FEELING KIND OF SICK WHEN HE LEFT THAT. THINGS ARE BETTER FOR ME NOW.
I MIGHT HAVE SAID SOME STUFF THAT SCARED YOU AND I JUST WANTED TO LET YOU HEAR MY VOICE AND LET YOU KNOW THAT I'M OKAY.
NONE OF THAT STUFF I SAID-- WELL, LET'S JUST SAY DADDY WAS PLAYING A GAME. TELLING YOU STORIES, YOU KNOW? A BED TIME STORY.
ALL MADE UP.
EXCEPT FOR THE PART ABOUT MONSTERS.
THEY'RE REAL ENOUGH.
TRUST YOUR DADDY ON THAT ONE.

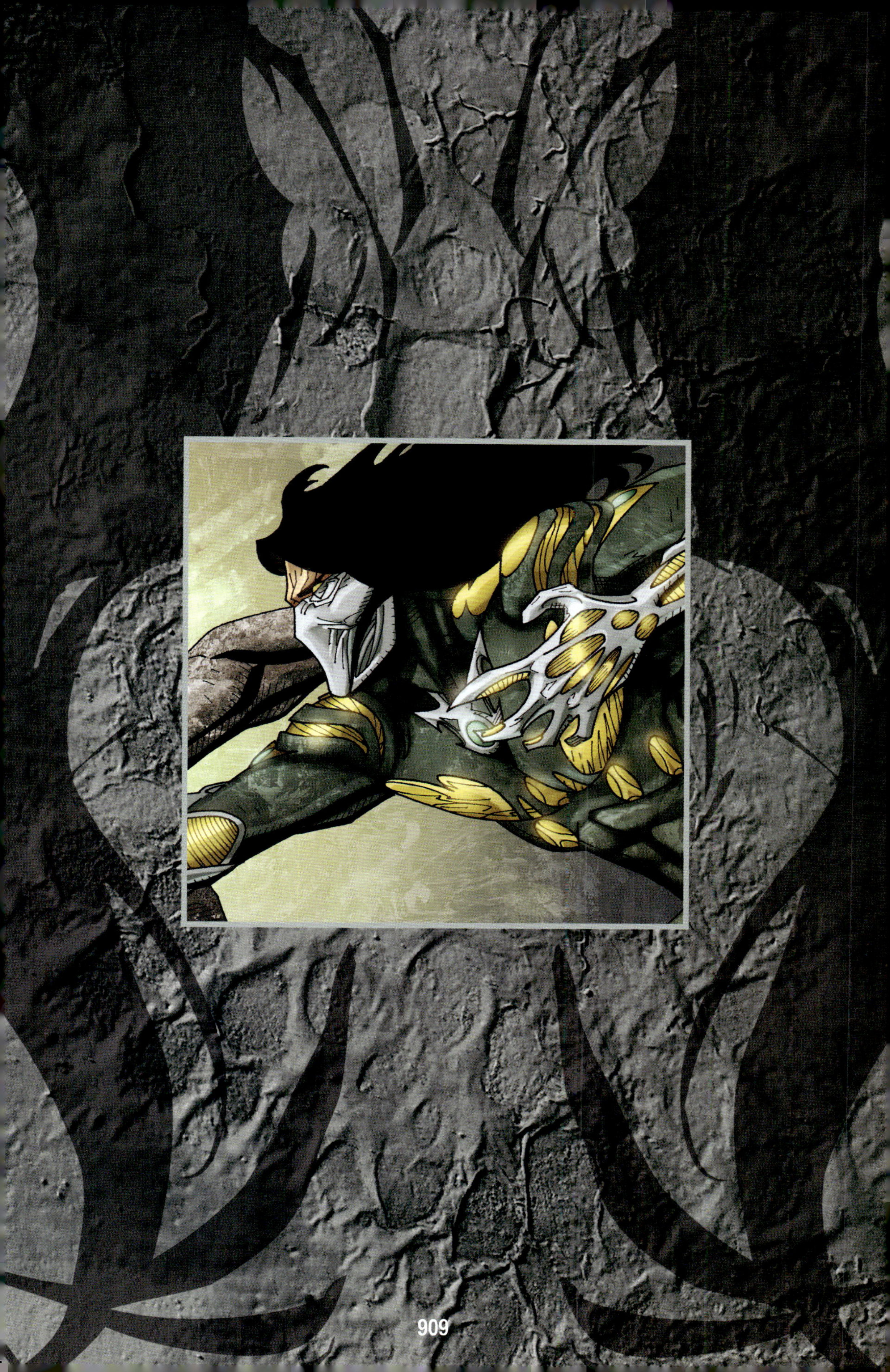

The Darkness Issue #79

cover art by: Jorge Lucas and Felix Serrano

THE DARKNESS #79

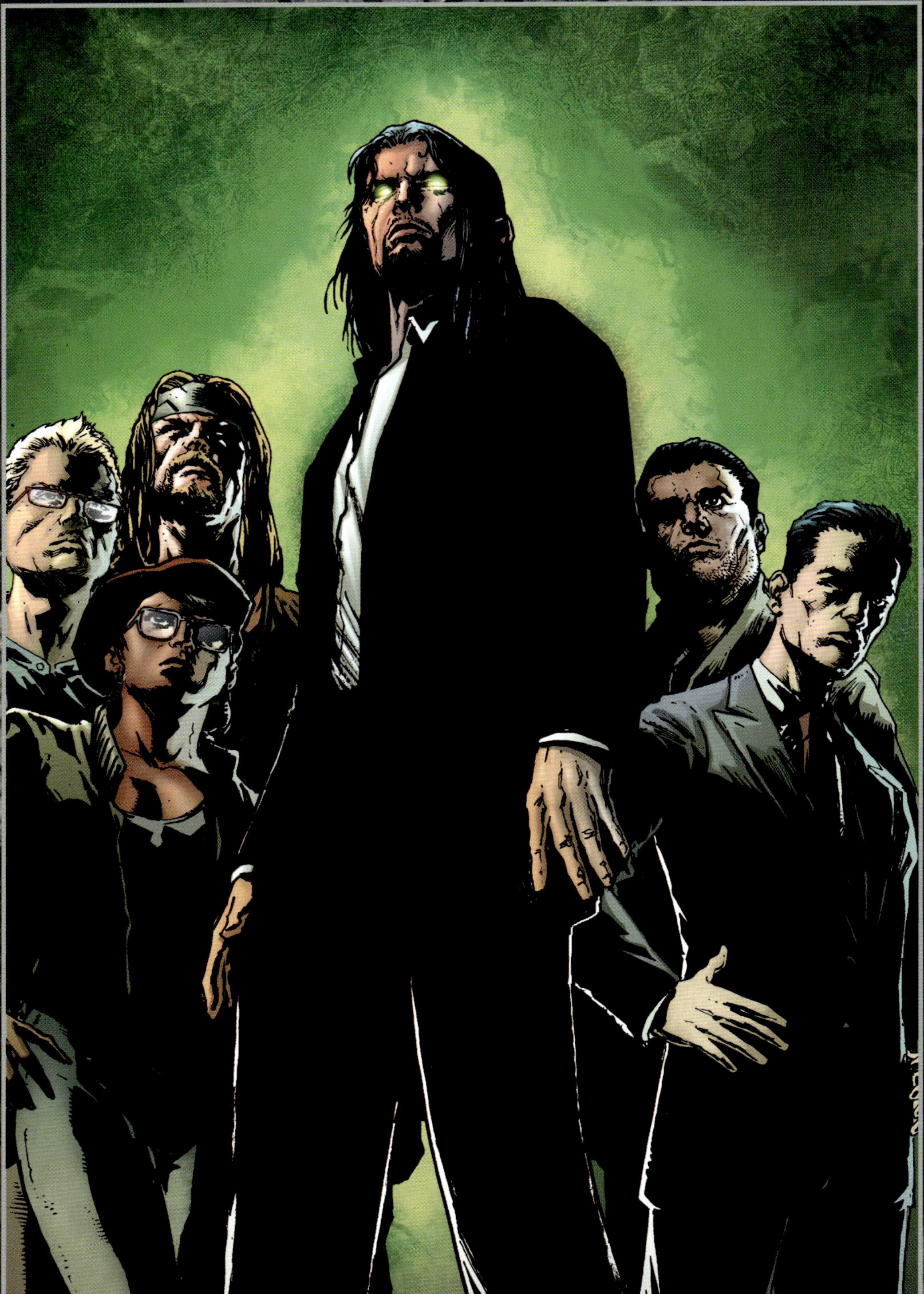

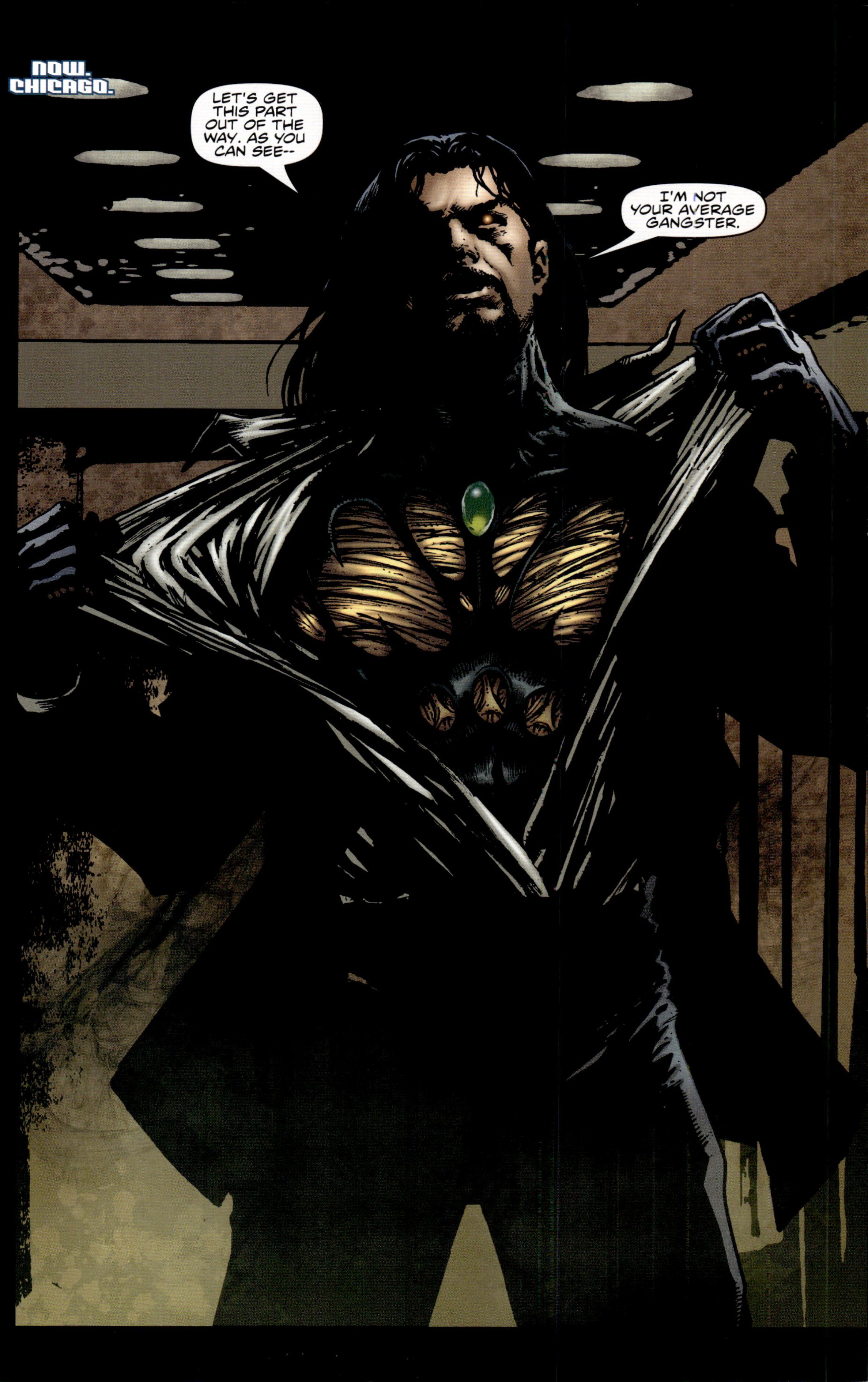
NOW.
CHICAGO.
LET'S GET THIS PART OUT OF THE WAY. AS YOU CAN SEE--
I'M NOT YOUR AVERAGE GANGSTER.

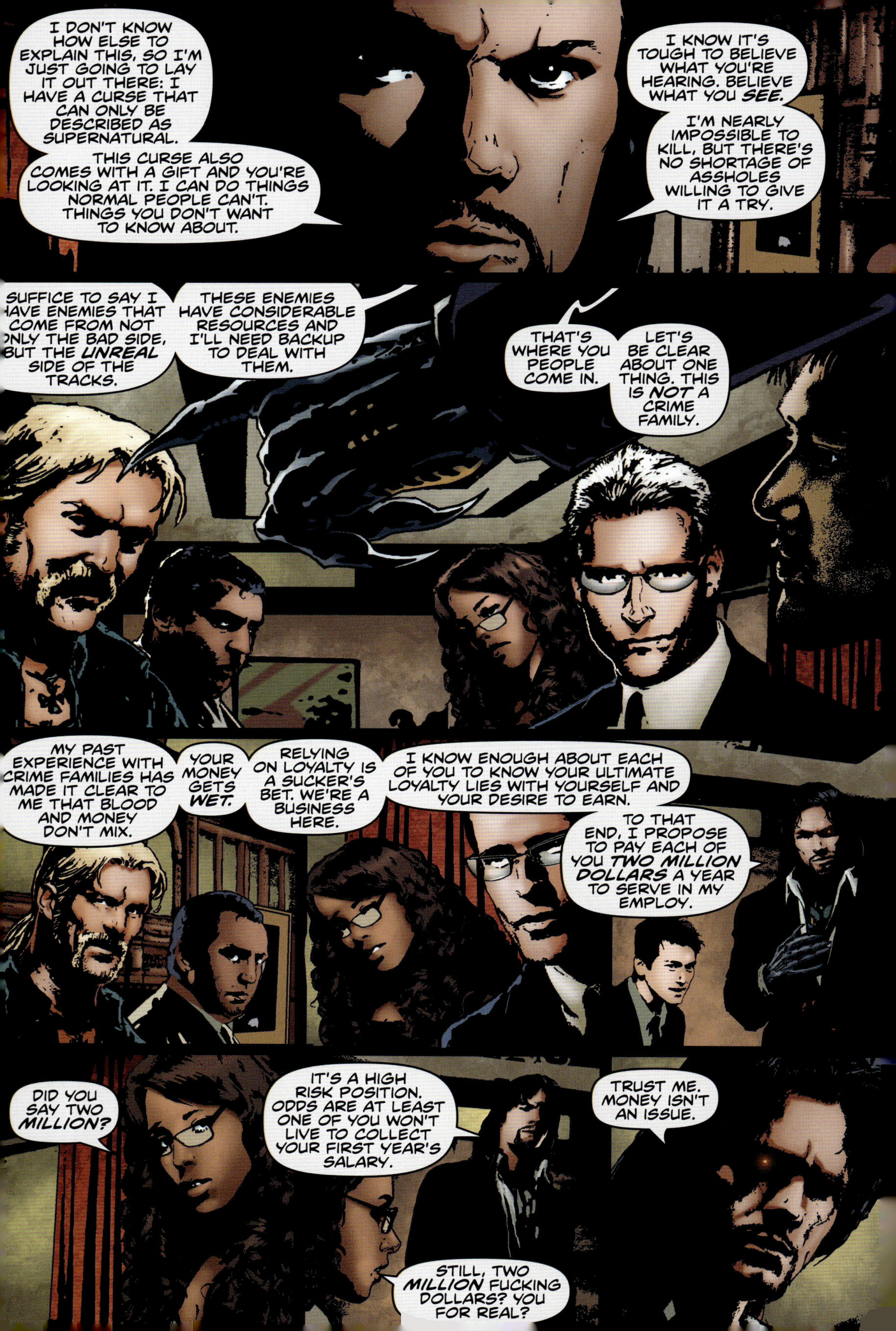
I DON'T KNOW HOW ELSE TO EXPLAIN THIS, SO I'M JUST GOING TO LAY IT OUT THERE: I HAVE A CURSE THAT CAN ONLY BE DESCRIBED AS SUPERNATURAL.
THIS CURSE ALSO COMES WITH A GIFT AND YOU'RE LOOKING AT IT. I CAN DO THINGS NORMAL PEOPLE CAN'T. THINGS YOU DON'T WANT TO KNOW ABOUT.
I KNOW IT'S TOUGH TO BELIEVE WHAT YOU'RE HEARING. BELIEVE WHAT YOU SEE.
I'M NEARLY IMPOSSIBLE TO KILL, BUT THERE'S NO SHORTAGE OF ASSHOLES WILLING TO GIVE IT A TRY.
SUFFICE TO SAY I HAVE ENEMIES THAT COME FROM NOT ONLY THE BAD SIDE, BUT THE UNREAL SIDE OF THE TRACKS.
THESE ENEMIES HAVE CONSIDERABLE RESOURCES AND I'LL NEED BACKUP TO DEAL WITH THEM.
THAT'S WHERE YOU PEOPLE COME IN.
LET'S BE CLEAR ABOUT ONE THING. THIS IS NOT A CRIME FAMILY.
MY PAST EXPERIENCE WITH CRIME FAMILIES HAS MADE IT CLEAR TO ME THAT BLOOD AND MONEY DON'T MIX.
YOUR MONEY GETS WET.
RELYING ON LOYALTY IS A SUCKER'S BET. WE'RE A BUSINESS HERE.
I KNOW ENOUGH ABOUT EACH OF YOU TO KNOW YOUR ULTIMATE LOYALTY LIES WITH YOURSELF AND YOUR DESIRE TO EARN.
TO THAT END, I PROPOSE TO PAY EACH OF YOU TWO MILLION DOLLARS A YEAR TO SERVE IN MY EMPLOY.
DID YOU SAY TWO MILLION?
IT'S A HIGH RISK POSITION. ODDS ARE AT LEAST ONE OF YOU WON'T LIVE TO COLLECT YOUR FIRST YEAR'S SALARY.
TRUST ME. MONEY ISN'T AN ISSUE.
STILL, TWO MILLION FUCKING DOLLARS? YOU FOR REAL?

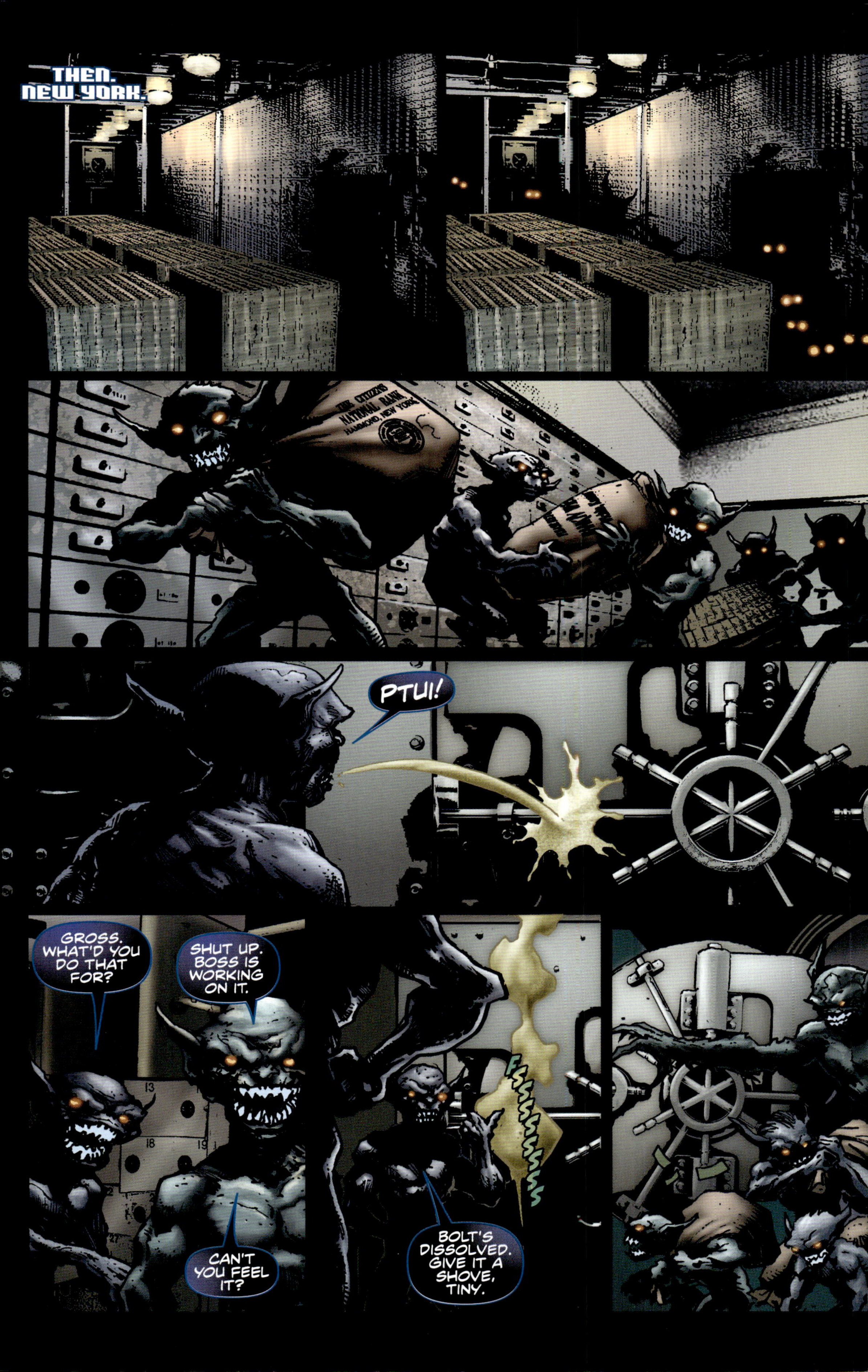
THEN. NEW YORK.
PTUI!
GROSS. WHAT'D YOU DO THAT FOR?
SHUT UP. BOSS IS WORKING ON IT.
CAN'T YOU FEEL IT?
BOLT'S DISSOLVED. GIVE IT A SHOVE, TINY.

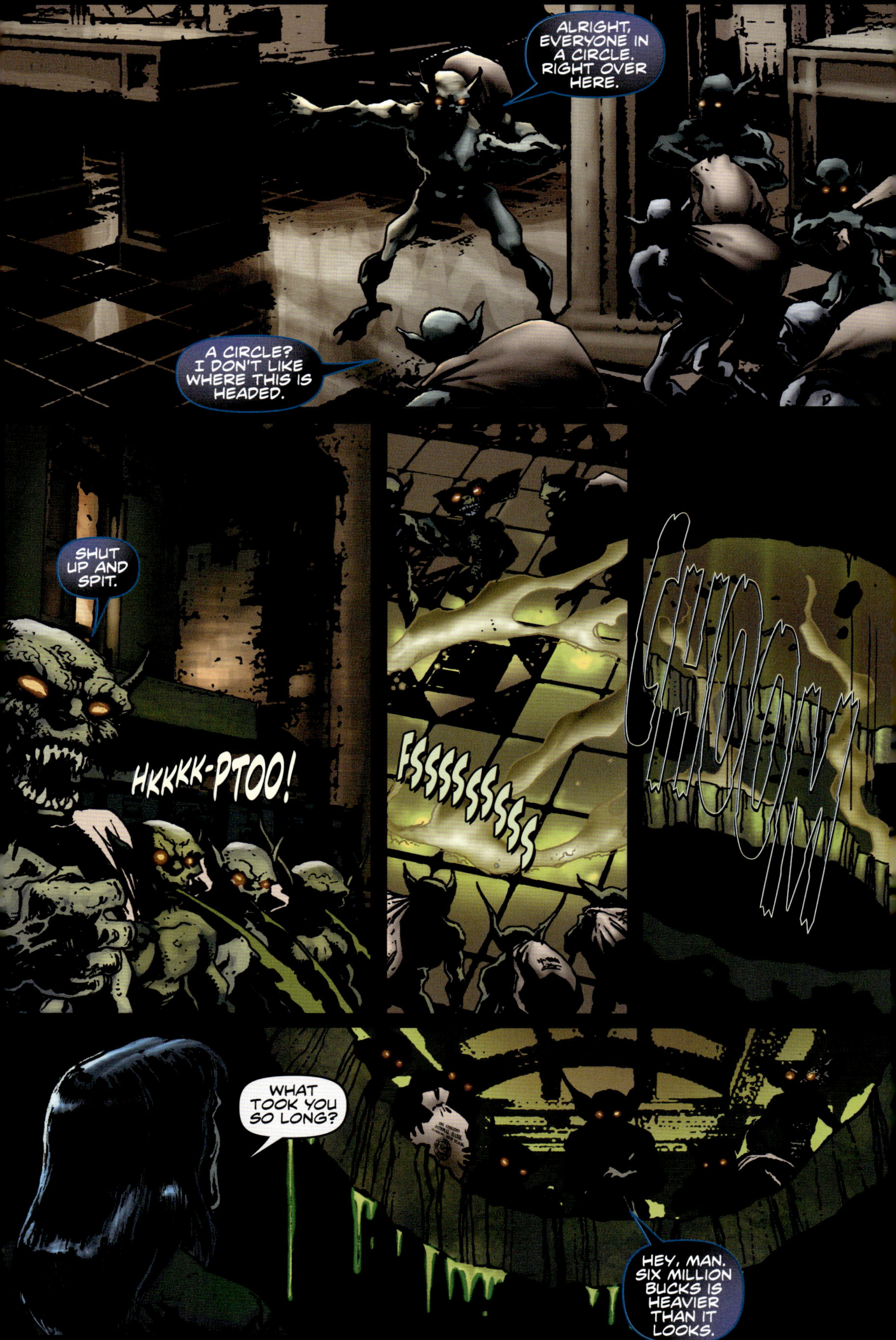
ALRIGHT, EVERYONE IN A CIRCLE. RIGHT OVER HERE.
A CIRCLE? I DON'T LIKE WHERE THIS IS HEADED.
SHUT UP AND SPIT.
HKKKK-PTOO!
FSSSSSSSSS
WHAT TOOK YOU SO LONG?
HEY, MAN. SIX MILLION BUCKS IS HEAVIER THAN IT LOOKS.

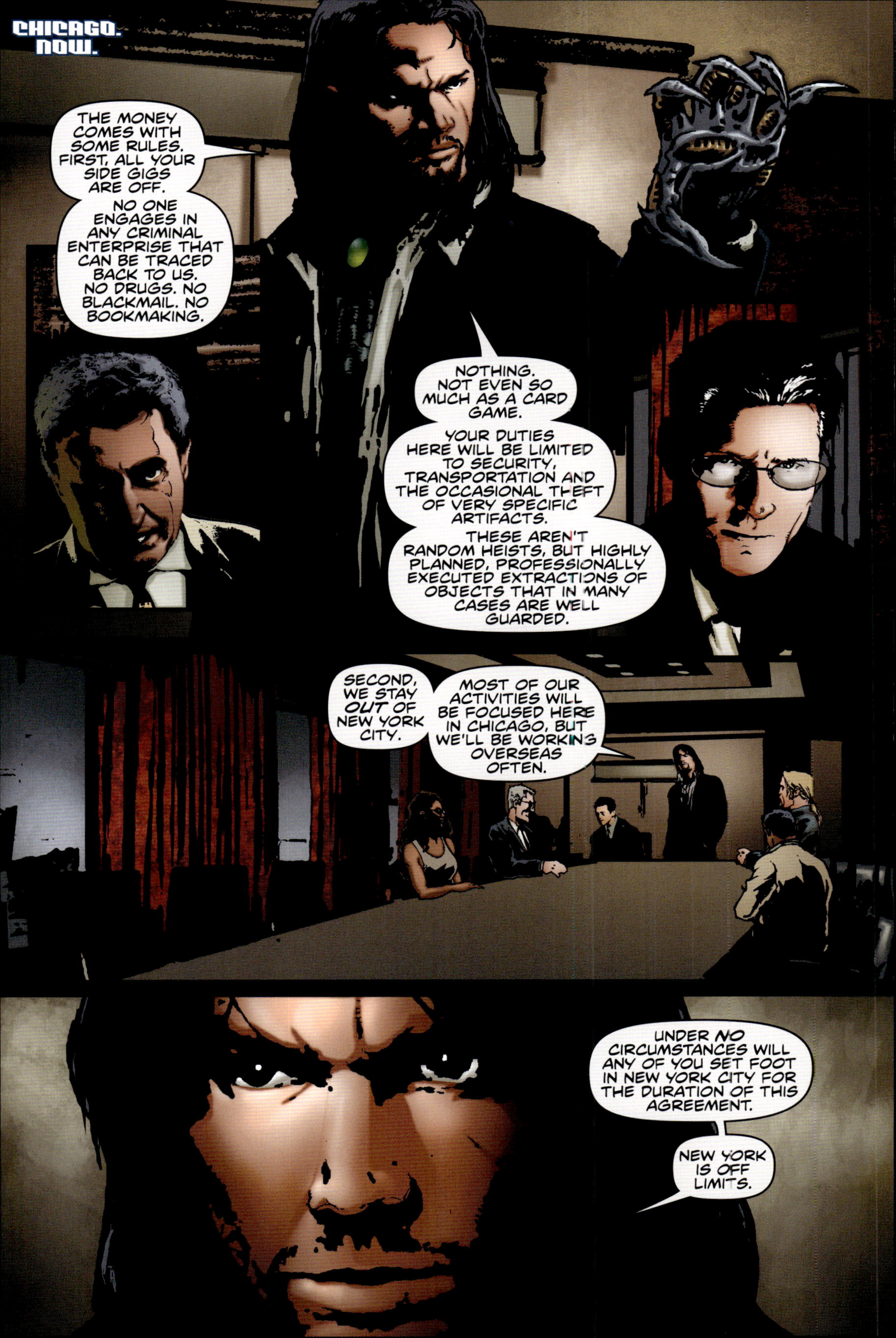
CHICAGO. NOW.
THE MONEY COMES WITH SOME RULES. FIRST, ALL YOUR SIDE GIGS ARE OFF.
NO ONE ENGAGES IN ANY CRIMINAL ENTERPRISE THAT CAN BE TRACED BACK TO US. NO DRUGS. NO BLACKMAIL. NO BOOKMAKING.
NOTHING. NOT EVEN SO MUCH AS A CARD GAME.
YOUR DUTIES HERE WILL BE LIMITED TO SECURITY, TRANSPORTATION AND THE OCCASIONAL THEFT OF VERY SPECIFIC ARTIFACTS.
THESE AREN'T RANDOM HEISTS, BUT HIGHLY PLANNED, PROFESSIONALLY EXECUTED EXTRACTIONS OF OBJECTS THAT IN MANY CASES ARE WELL GUARDED.
SECOND, WE STAY OUT OF NEW YORK CITY.
MOST OF OUR ACTIVITIES WILL BE FOCUSED HERE IN CHICAGO, BUT WE'LL BE WORKING OVERSEAS OFTEN.
UNDER NO CIRCUMSTANCES WILL ANY OF YOU SET FOOT IN NEW YORK CITY FOR THE DURATION OF THIS AGREEMENT.
NEW YORK IS OFF LIMITS.

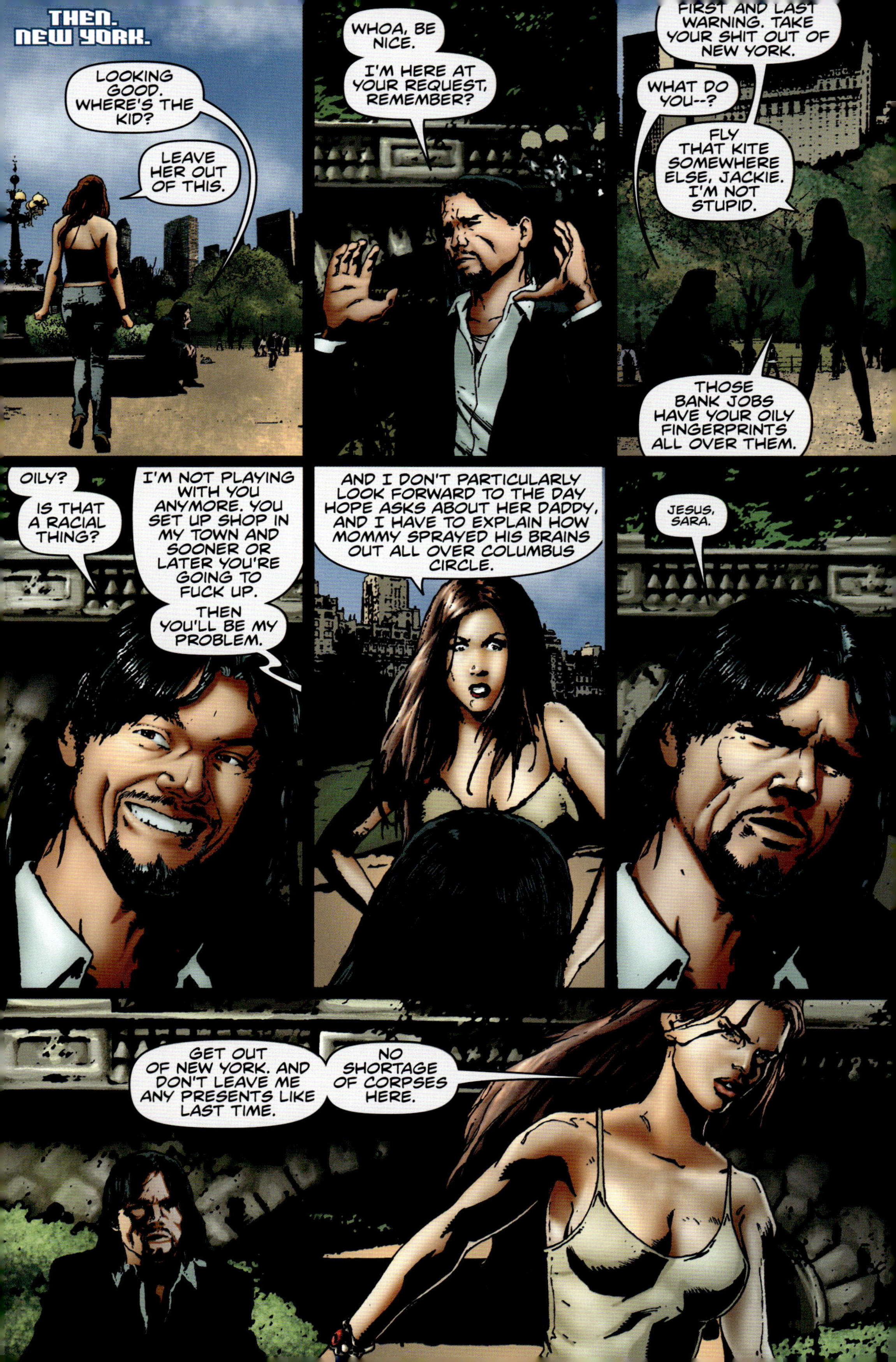
THEN. NEW YORK.
LOOKING GOOD. WHERE'S THE KID?
LEAVE HER OUT OF THIS.
WHOA, BE NICE.
I'M HERE AT YOUR REQUEST, REMEMBER?
FIRST AND LAST WARNING. TAKE YOUR SHIT OUT OF NEW YORK.
WHAT DO YOU--?
FLY THAT KITE SOMEWHERE ELSE, JACKIE. I'M NOT STUPID.
THOSE BANK JOBS HAVE YOUR OILY FINGERPRINTS ALL OVER THEM.
OILY?
IS THAT A RACIAL THING?
I'M NOT PLAYING WITH YOU ANYMORE. YOU SET UP SHOP IN MY TOWN AND SOONER OR LATER YOU'RE GOING TO FUCK UP.
THEN YOU'LL BE MY PROBLEM.
AND I DON'T PARTICULARLY LOOK FORWARD TO THE DAY HOPE ASKS ABOUT HER DADDY, AND I HAVE TO EXPLAIN HOW MOMMY SPRAYED HIS BRAINS OUT ALL OVER COLUMBUS CIRCLE.
JESUS, SARA.
GET OUT OF NEW YORK. AND DON'T LEAVE ME ANY PRESENTS LIKE LAST TIME.
NO SHORTAGE OF CORPSES HERE.

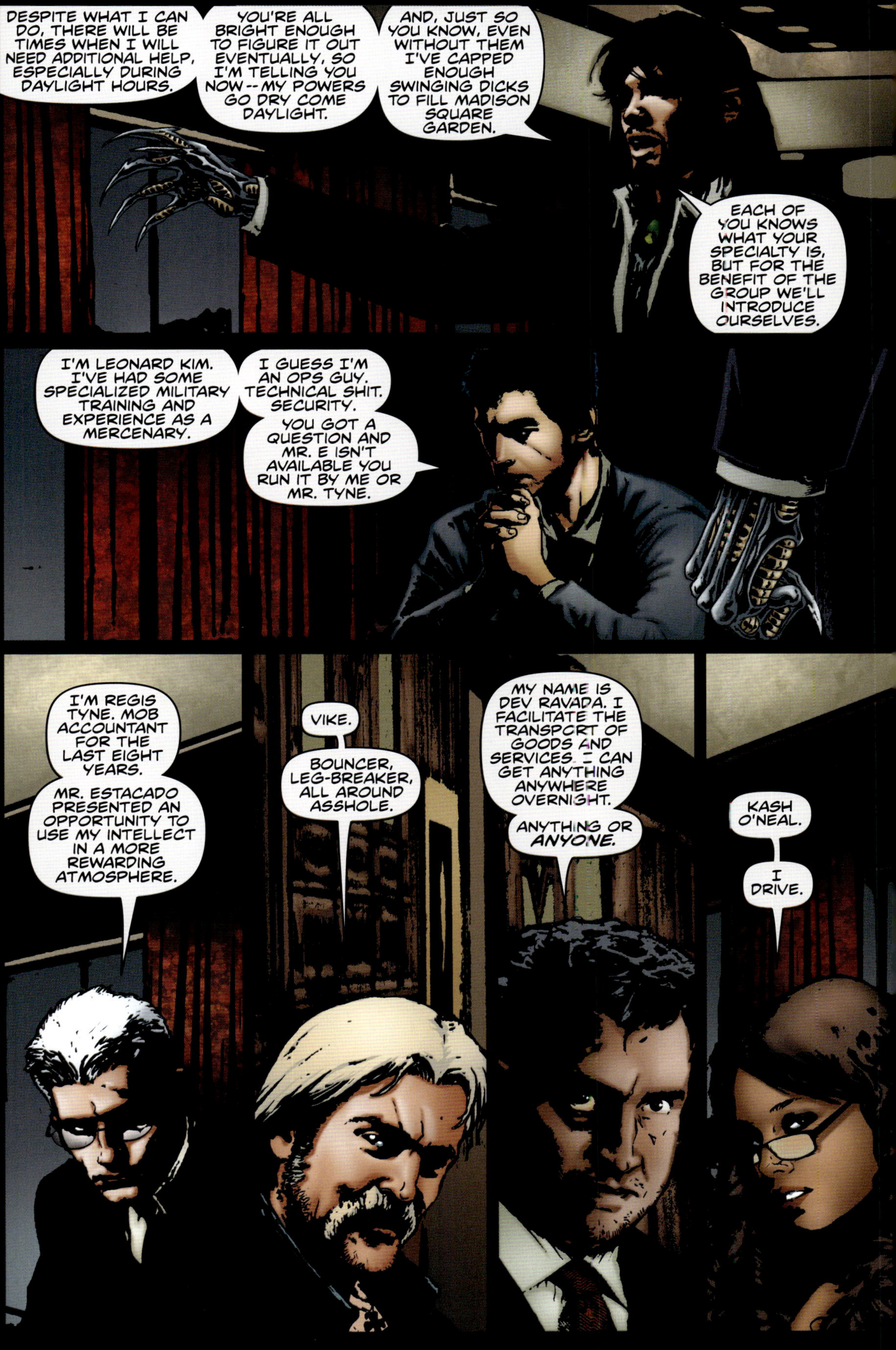
DESPITE WHAT I CAN DO, THERE WILL BE TIMES WHEN I WILL NEED ADDITIONAL HELP, ESPECIALLY DURING DAYLIGHT HOURS.
YOU'RE ALL BRIGHT ENOUGH TO FIGURE IT OUT EVENTUALLY, SO I'M TELLING YOU NOW--MY POWERS GO DRY COME DAYLIGHT.
AND, JUST SO YOU KNOW, EVEN WITHOUT THEM I'VE CAPPED ENOUGH SWINGING DICKS TO FILL MADISON SQUARE GARDEN.
EACH OF YOU KNOWS WHAT YOUR SPECIALTY IS, BUT FOR THE BENEFIT OF THE GROUP WE'LL INTRODUCE OURSELVES.
I'M LEONARD KIM. I'VE HAD SOME SPECIALIZED MILITARY TRAINING AND EXPERIENCE AS A MERCENARY.
I GUESS I'M AN OPS GUY. TECHNICAL SHIT. SECURITY.
YOU GOT A QUESTION AND MR. E ISN'T AVAILABLE YOU RUN IT BY ME OR MR. TYNE.
I'M REGIS TYNE. MOB ACCOUNTANT FOR THE LAST EIGHT YEARS.
MR. ESTACADO PRESENTED AN OPPORTUNITY TO USE MY INTELLECT IN A MORE REWARDING ATMOSPHERE.
VIKE.
BOUNCER, LEG-BREAKER, ALL AROUND ASSHOLE.
MY NAME IS DEV RAVADA. I FACILITATE THE TRANSPORT OF GOODS AND SERVICES. I CAN GET ANYTHING ANYWHERE OVERNIGHT.
ANYTHING OR *ANYONE.*
KASH O'NEAL.
I DRIVE.

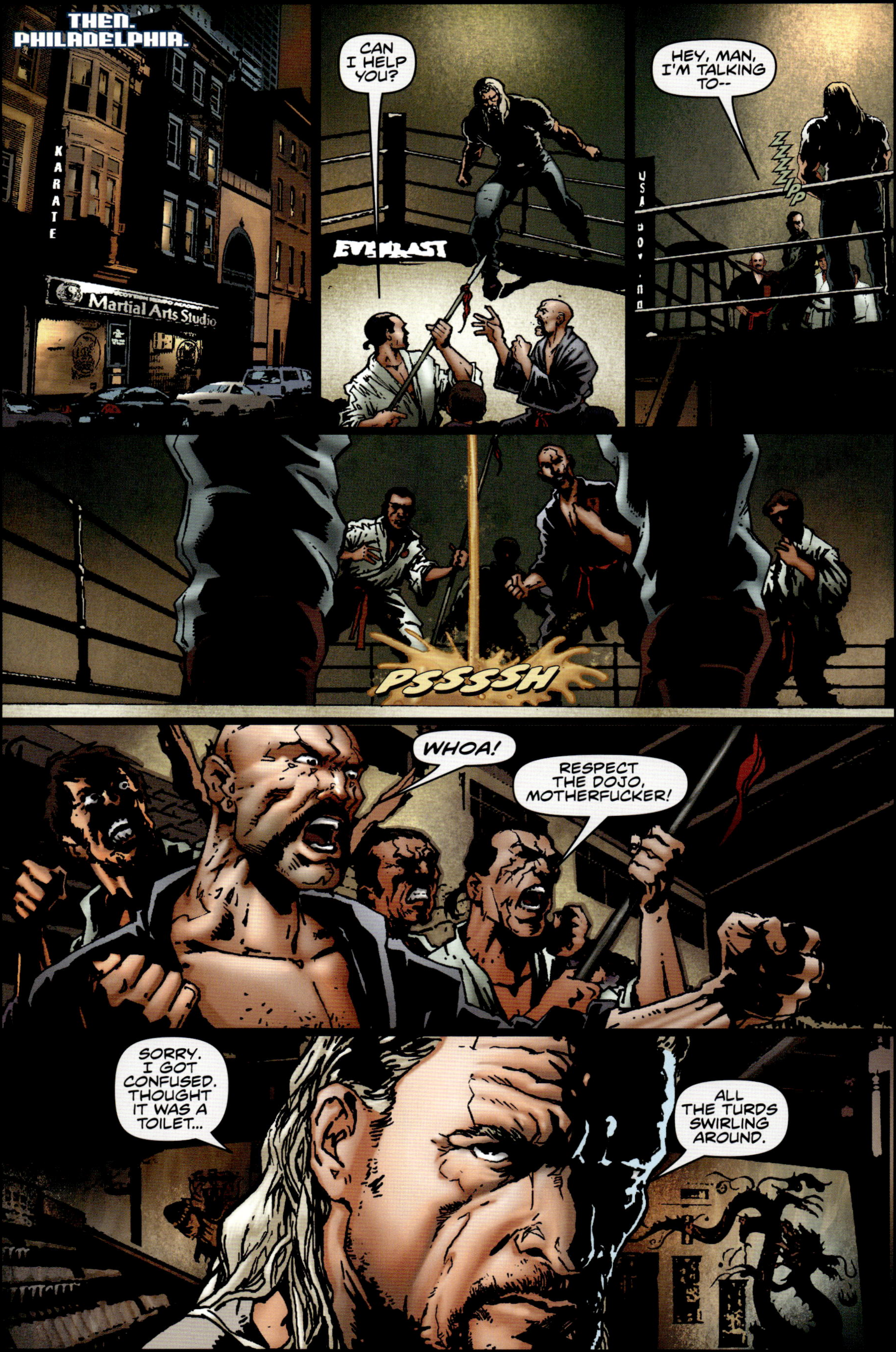
THEN. PHILADELPHIA.
KARATE
Martial Arts Studio
CAN I HELP YOU?
EVERLAST
HEY, MAN, I'M TALKING TO--
ZZZZIPP
PSSSSH
WHOA!
RESPECT THE DOJO, MOTHERFUCKER!
SORRY. I GOT CONFUSED. THOUGHT IT WAS A TOILET...
ALL THE TURDS SWIRLING AROUND.

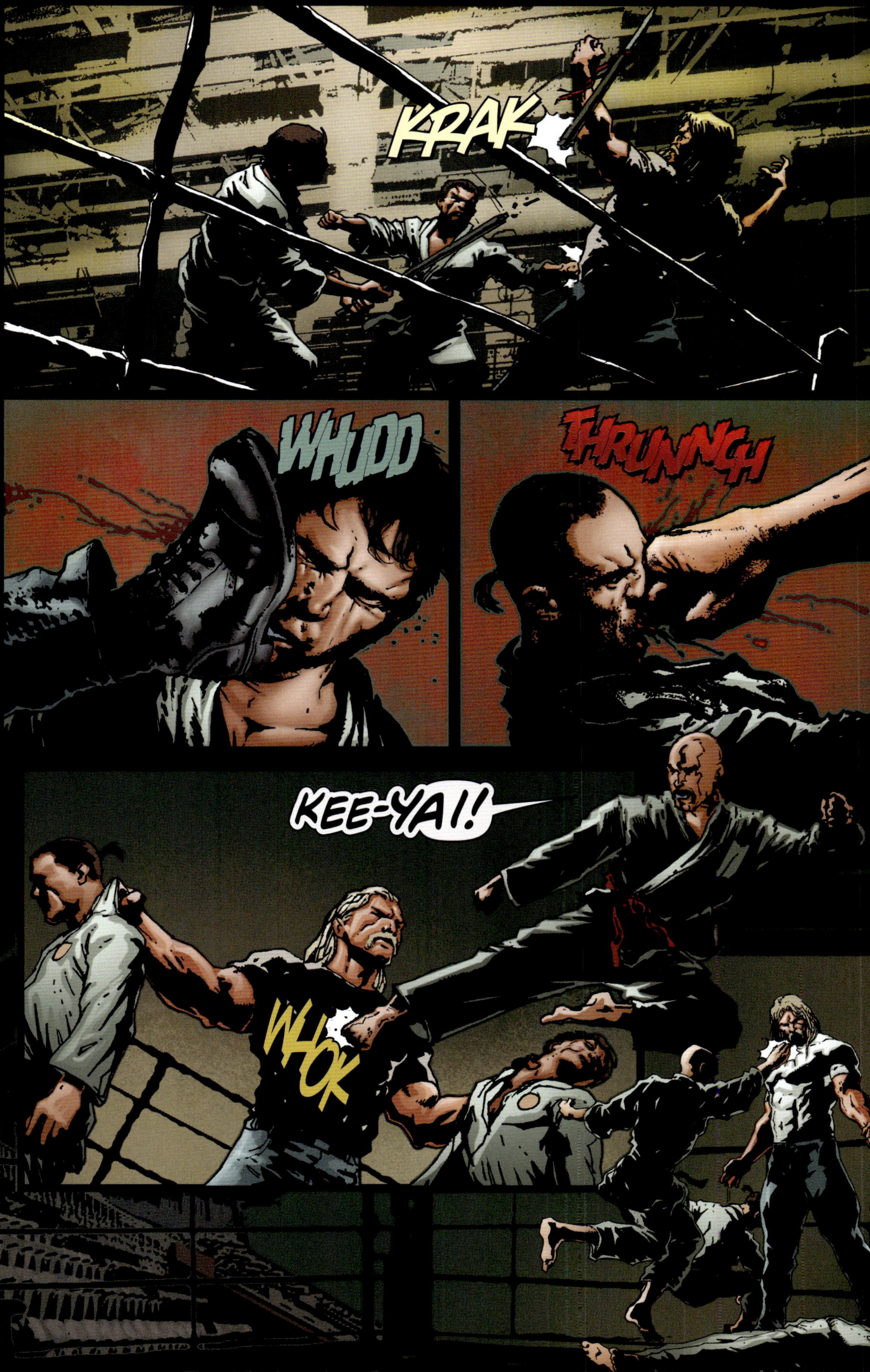
KRAK
WHUDD
THRUNNCH
KEE-YAI!
WHOK

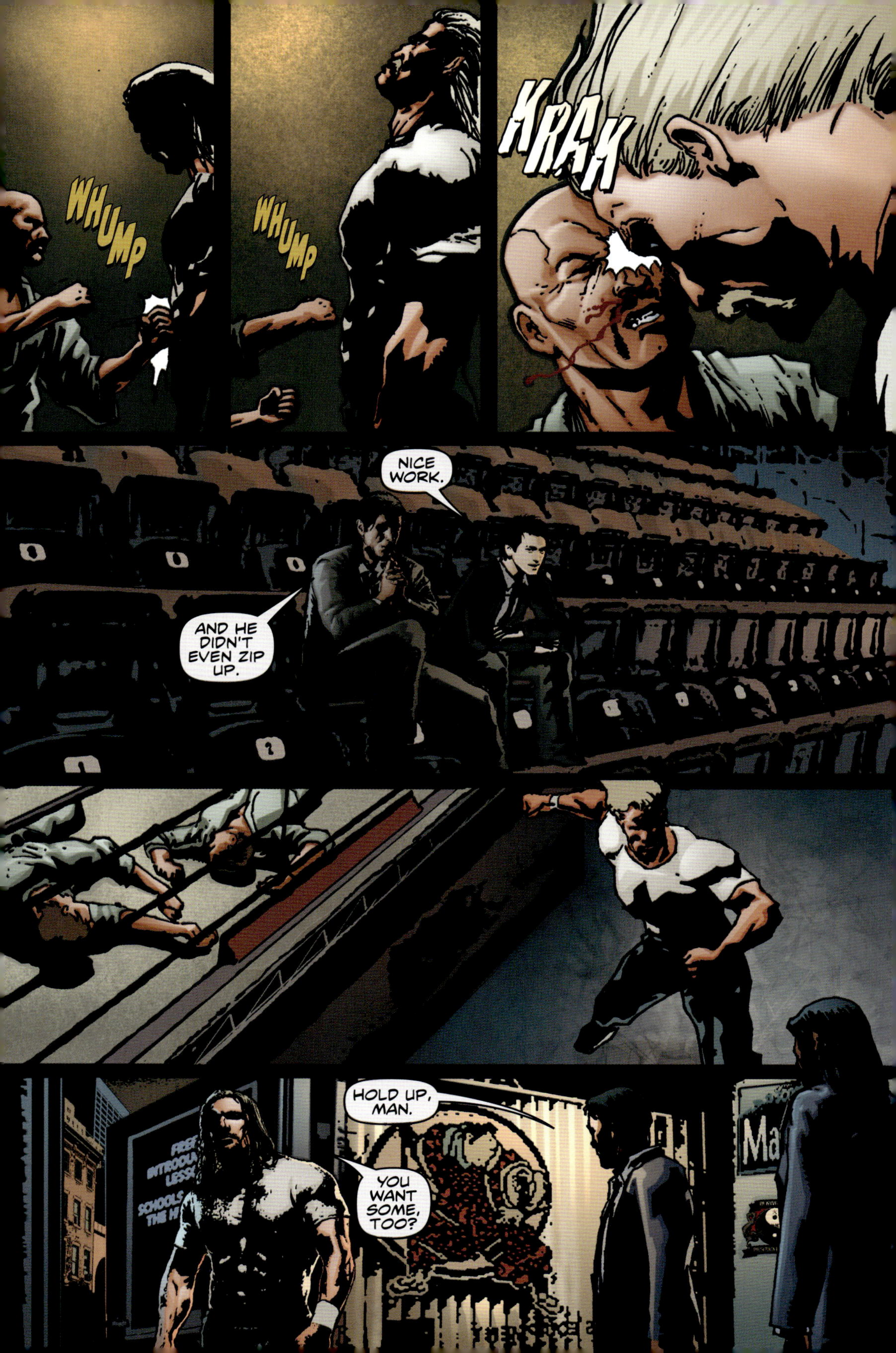
WHUMP
WHUMP
KRAK
NICE WORK.
AND HE DIDN'T EVEN ZIP UP.
HOLD UP, MAN.
YOU WANT SOME, TOO?

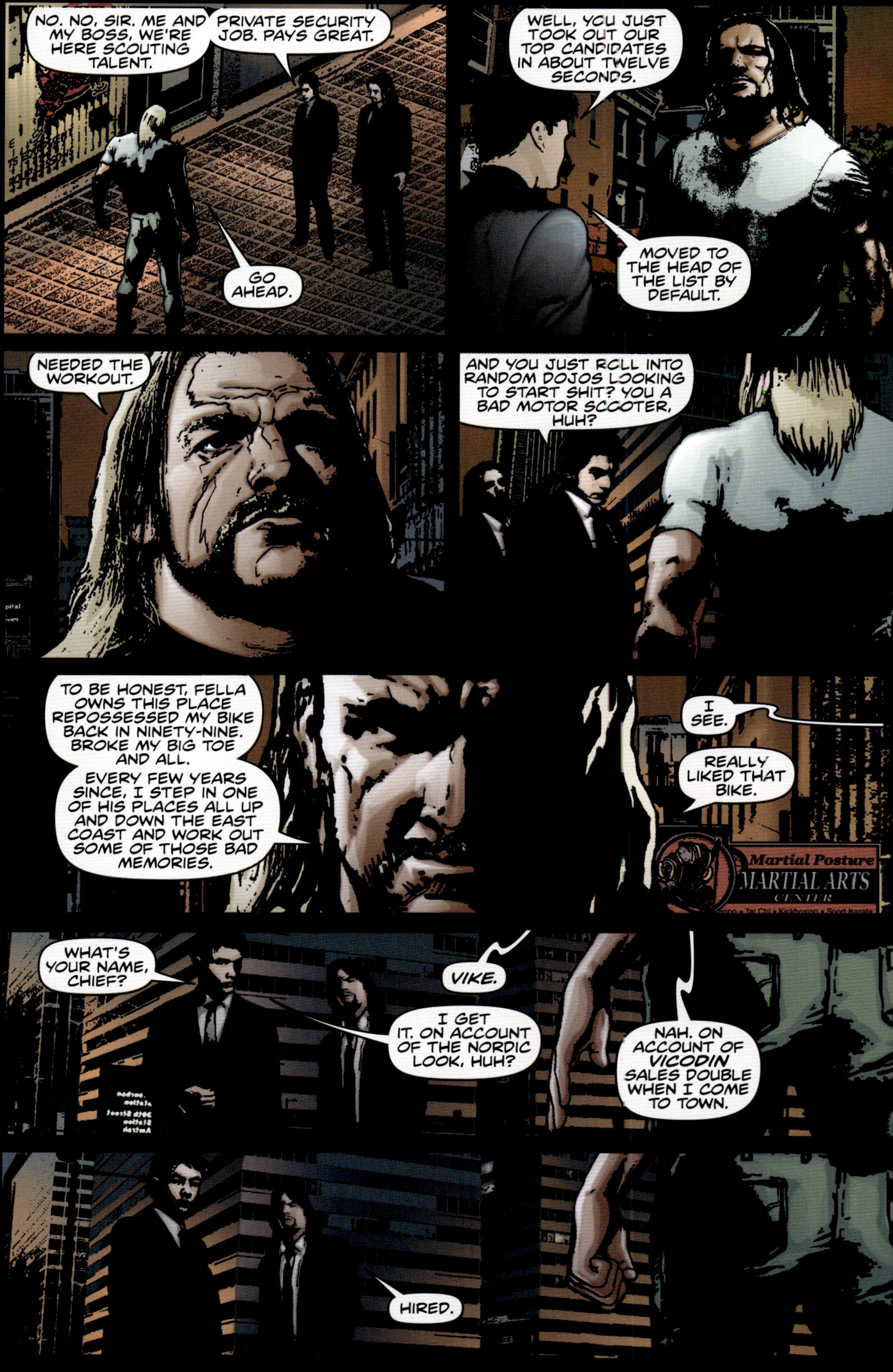
NO. NO, SIR. ME AND MY BOSS, WE'RE HERE SCOUTING TALENT.
PRIVATE SECURITY JOB. PAYS GREAT.
GO AHEAD.
WELL, YOU JUST TOOK OUT OUR TOP CANDIDATES IN ABOUT TWELVE SECONDS.
MOVED TO THE HEAD OF THE LIST BY DEFAULT.
NEEDED THE WORKOUT.
AND YOU JUST ROLL INTO RANDOM DOJOS LOOKING TO START SHIT? YOU A BAD MOTOR SCOOTER, HUH?
TO BE HONEST, FELLA OWNS THIS PLACE REPOSSESSED MY BIKE BACK IN NINETY-NINE. BROKE MY BIG TOE AND ALL.
EVERY FEW YEARS SINCE, I STEP IN ONE OF HIS PLACES ALL UP AND DOWN THE EAST COAST AND WORK OUT SOME OF THOSE BAD MEMORIES.
I SEE.
REALLY LIKED THAT BIKE.
Martial Posture
MARTIAL ARTS
CENTER
WHAT'S YOUR NAME, CHIEF?
VIKE.
I GET IT. ON ACCOUNT OF THE NORDIC LOOK, HUH?
NAH. ON ACCOUNT OF *VICODIN* SALES DOUBLE WHEN I COME TO TOWN.
HIRED.

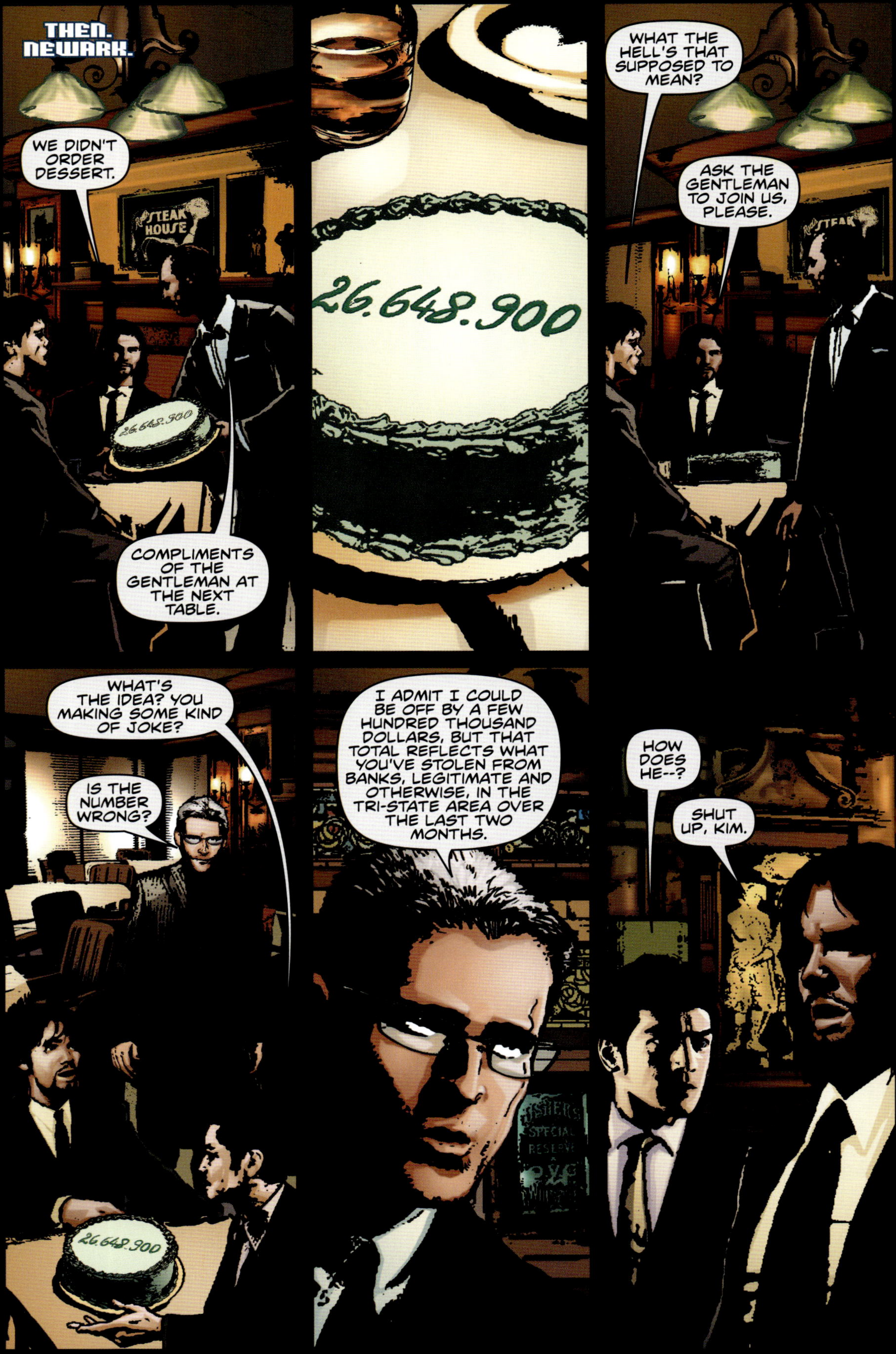
THEN. NEWARK.
WE DIDN'T ORDER DESSERT.
COMPLIMENTS OF THE GENTLEMAN AT THE NEXT TABLE.
26.648.900
WHAT THE HELL'S THAT SUPPOSED TO MEAN?
ASK THE GENTLEMAN TO JOIN US, PLEASE.
WHAT'S THE IDEA? YOU MAKING SOME KIND OF JOKE?
IS THE NUMBER WRONG?
I ADMIT I COULD BE OFF BY A FEW HUNDRED THOUSAND DOLLARS, BUT THAT TOTAL REFLECTS WHAT YOU'VE STOLEN FROM BANKS, LEGITIMATE AND OTHERWISE, IN THE TRI-STATE AREA OVER THE LAST TWO MONTHS.
HOW DOES HE--?
SHUT UP, KIM.

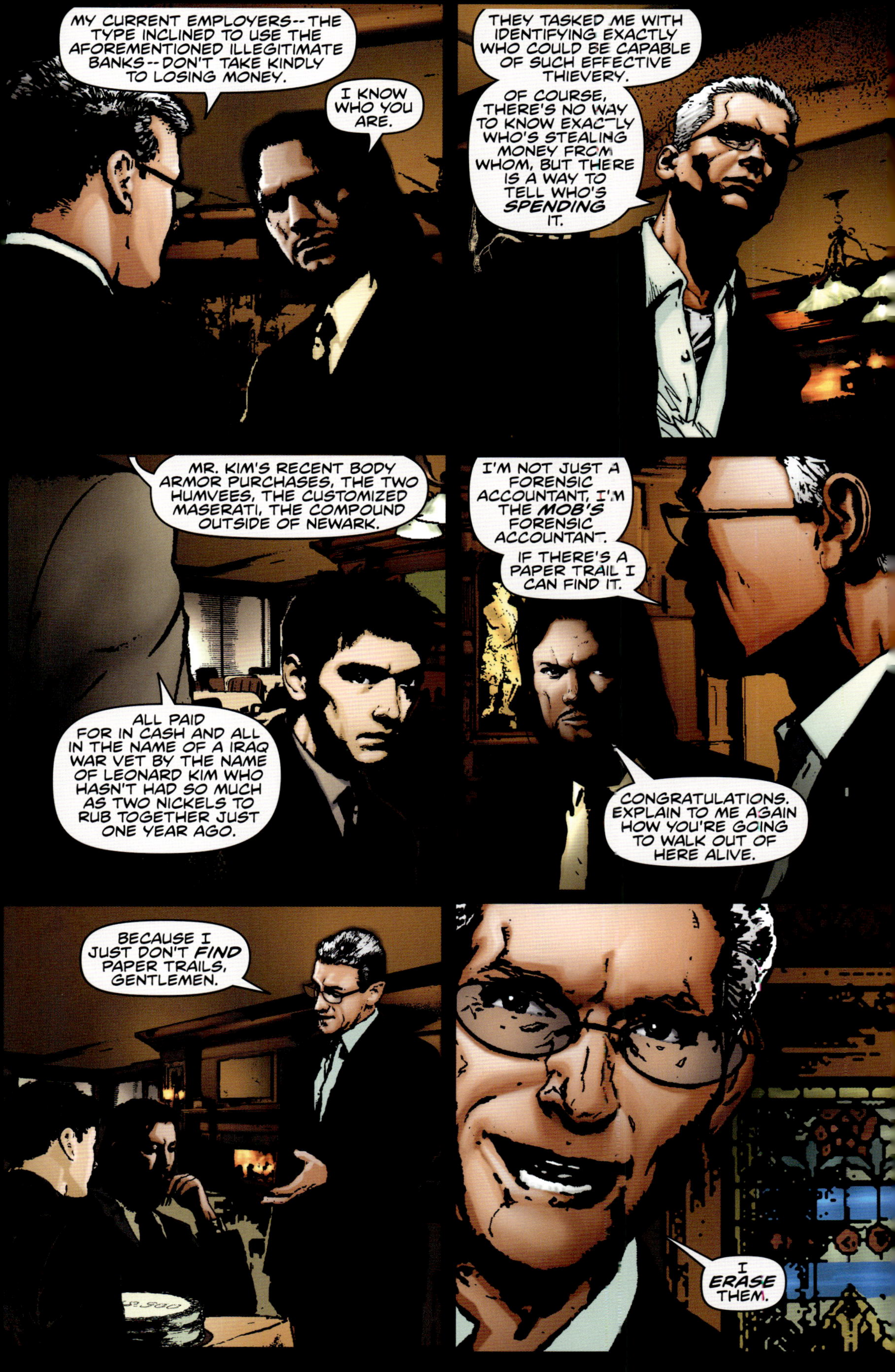
MY CURRENT EMPLOYERS--THE TYPE INCLINED TO USE THE AFOREMENTIONED ILLEGITIMATE BANKS--DON'T TAKE KINDLY TO LOSING MONEY.
I KNOW WHO YOU ARE.
THEY TASKED ME WITH IDENTIFYING EXACTLY WHO COULD BE CAPABLE OF SUCH EFFECTIVE THIEVERY.
OF COURSE, THERE'S NO WAY TO KNOW EXACTLY WHO'S STEALING MONEY FROM WHOM, BUT THERE IS A WAY TO TELL WHO'S *SPENDING* IT.
MR. KIM'S RECENT BODY ARMOR PURCHASES, THE TWO HUMVEES, THE CUSTOMIZED MASERATI, THE COMPOUND OUTSIDE OF NEWARK.
ALL PAID FOR IN CASH AND ALL IN THE NAME OF A IRAQ WAR VET BY THE NAME OF LEONARD KIM WHO HASN'T HAD SO MUCH AS TWO NICKELS TO RUB TOGETHER JUST ONE YEAR AGO.
I'M NOT JUST A FORENSIC ACCOUNTANT, I'M THE *MOB'S* FORENSIC ACCOUNTANT.
IF THERE'S A PAPER TRAIL I CAN FIND IT.
CONGRATULATIONS. EXPLAIN TO ME AGAIN HOW YOU'RE GOING TO WALK OUT OF HERE ALIVE.
BECAUSE I JUST DON'T *FIND* PAPER TRAILS, GENTLEMEN.
I *ERASE* THEM.

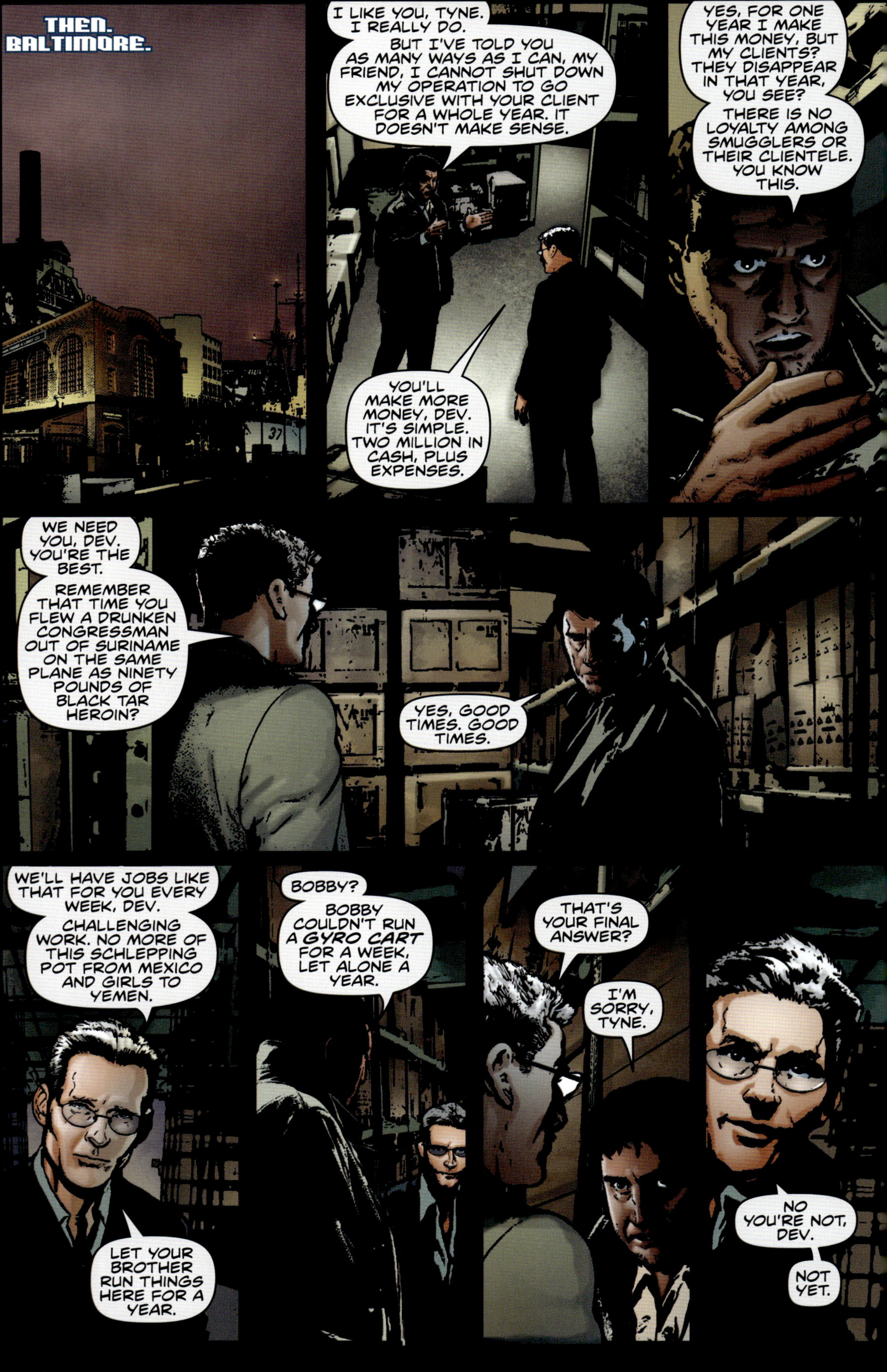
THEN. BALTIMORE.
I LIKE YOU, TYNE. I REALLY DO.
BUT I'VE TOLD YOU AS MANY WAYS AS I CAN, MY FRIEND, I CANNOT SHUT DOWN MY OPERATION TO GO EXCLUSIVE WITH YOUR CLIENT FOR A WHOLE YEAR. IT DOESN'T MAKE SENSE.
YOU'LL MAKE MORE MONEY, DEV. IT'S SIMPLE. TWO MILLION IN CASH, PLUS EXPENSES.
YES, FOR ONE YEAR I MAKE THIS MONEY, BUT MY CLIENTS? THEY DISAPPEAR IN THAT YEAR, YOU SEE?
THERE IS NO LOYALTY AMONG SMUGGLERS OR THEIR CLIENTELE. YOU KNOW THIS.
WE NEED YOU, DEV. YOU'RE THE BEST.
REMEMBER THAT TIME YOU FLEW A DRUNKEN CONGRESSMAN OUT OF SURINAME ON THE SAME PLANE AS NINETY POUNDS OF BLACK TAR HEROIN?
YES, GOOD TIMES. GOOD TIMES.
WE'LL HAVE JOBS LIKE THAT FOR YOU EVERY WEEK, DEV.
CHALLENGING WORK. NO MORE OF THIS SCHLEPPING POT FROM MEXICO AND GIRLS TO YEMEN.
LET YOUR BROTHER RUN THINGS HERE FOR A YEAR.
BOBBY?
BOBBY COULDN'T RUN A GYRO CART FOR A WEEK, LET ALONE A YEAR.
THAT'S YOUR FINAL ANSWER?
I'M SORRY, TYNE.
NO YOU'RE NOT, DEV.
NOT YET.

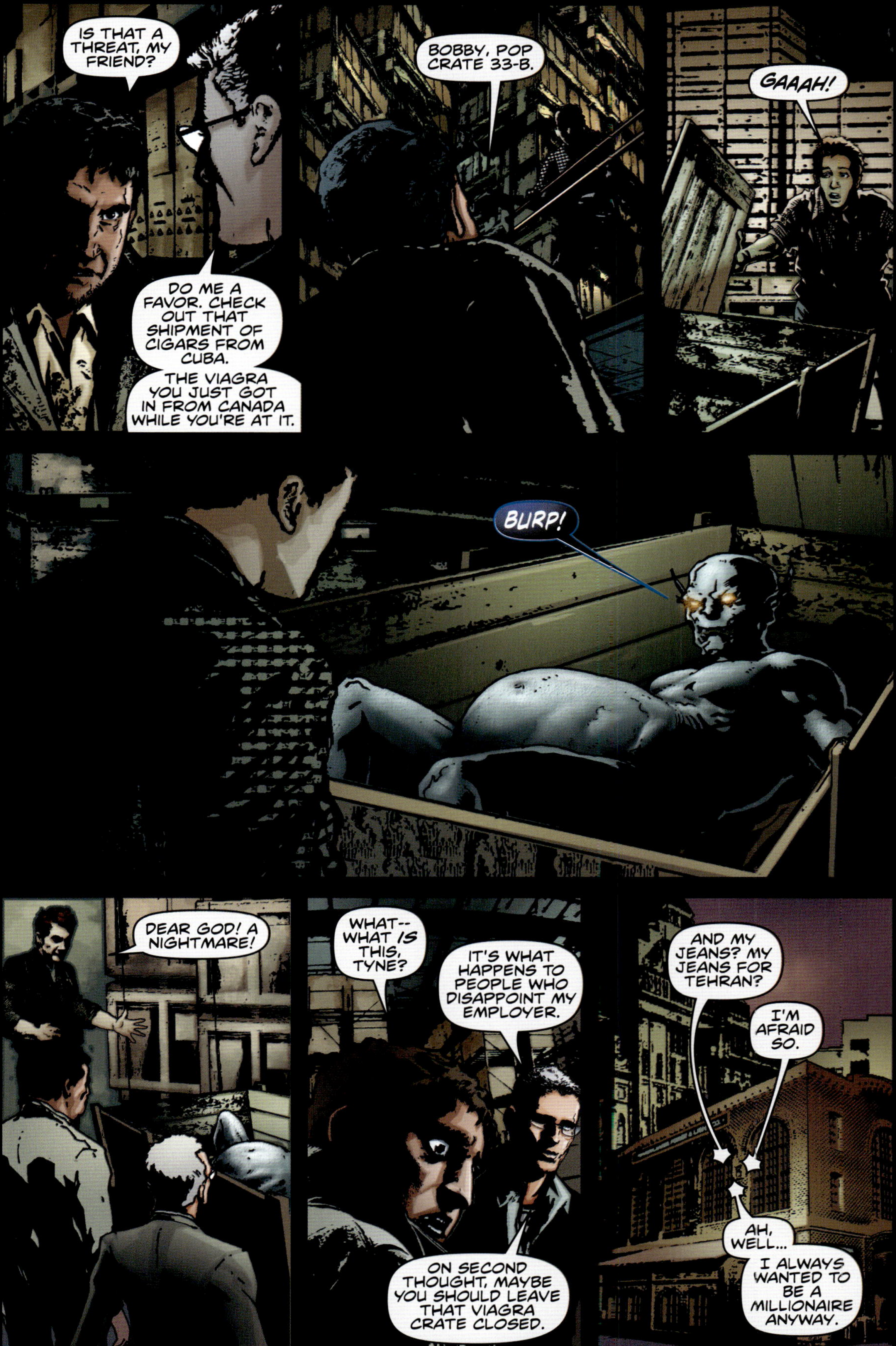
IS THAT A THREAT, MY FRIEND?
DO ME A FAVOR. CHECK OUT THAT SHIPMENT OF CIGARS FROM CUBA.
THE VIAGRA YOU JUST GOT IN FROM CANADA WHILE YOU'RE AT IT.
BOBBY, POP CRATE 33-B.
GAAAH!
BURP!
DEAR GOD! A NIGHTMARE!
WHAT-- WHAT IS THIS, TYNE?
IT'S WHAT HAPPENS TO PEOPLE WHO DISAPPOINT MY EMPLOYER.
ON SECOND THOUGHT, MAYBE YOU SHOULD LEAVE THAT VIAGRA CRATE CLOSED.
AND MY JEANS? MY JEANS FOR TEHRAN?
I'M AFRAID SO.
AH, WELL...
I ALWAYS WANTED TO BE A MILLIONAIRE ANYWAY.

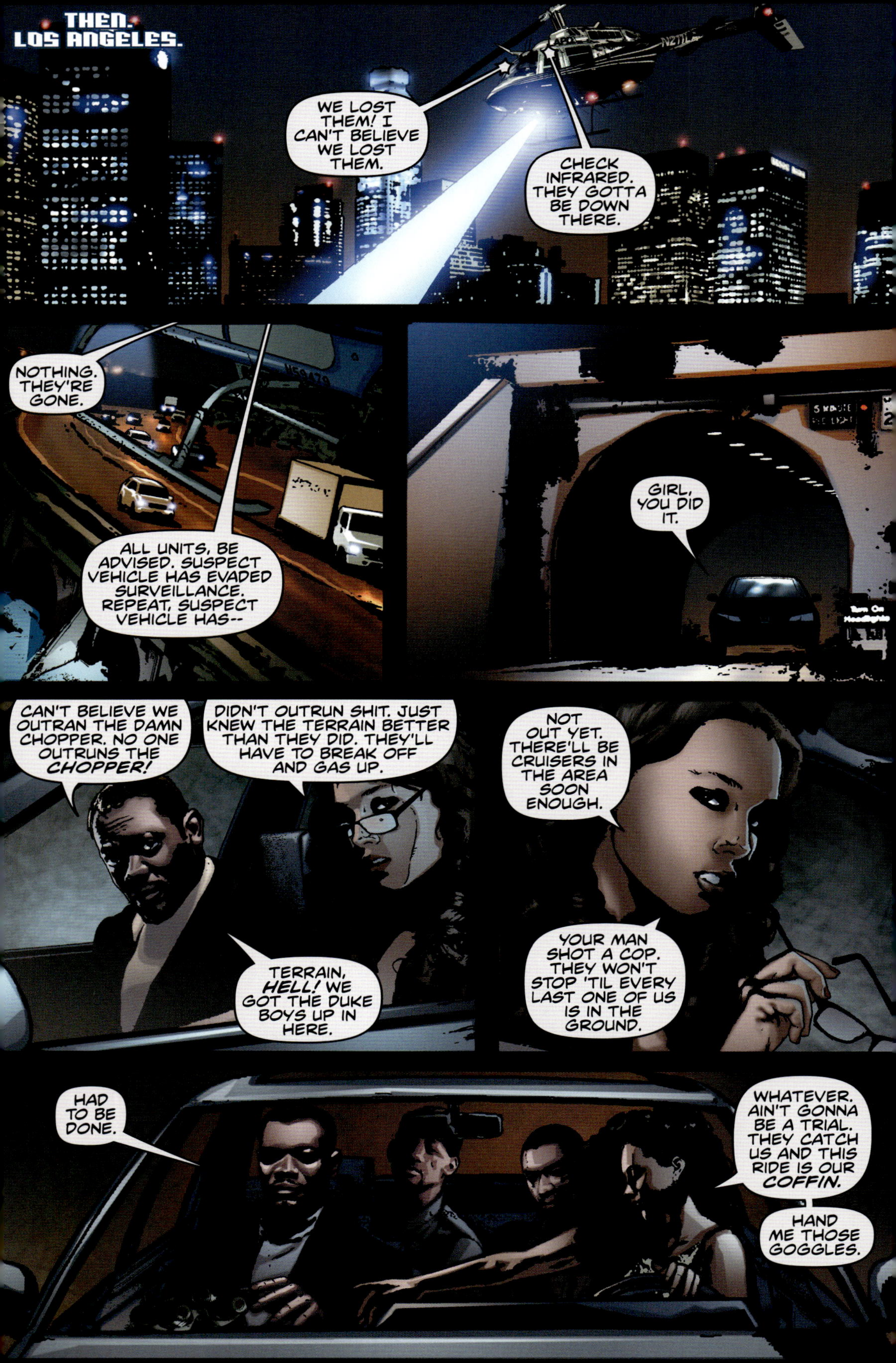
THEN.
LOS ANGELES.
WE LOST THEM! I CAN'T BELIEVE WE LOST THEM.
CHECK INFRARED. THEY GOTTA BE DOWN THERE.
NOTHING. THEY'RE GONE.
ALL UNITS, BE ADVISED. SUSPECT VEHICLE HAS EVADED SURVEILLANCE. REPEAT, SUSPECT VEHICLE HAS--
GIRL, YOU DID IT.
Turn On Headlights
CAN'T BELIEVE WE OUTRAN THE DAMN CHOPPER. NO ONE OUTRUNS THE CHOPPER!
DIDN'T OUTRUN SHIT. JUST KNEW THE TERRAIN BETTER THAN THEY DID. THEY'LL HAVE TO BREAK OFF AND GAS UP.
TERRAIN, HELL! WE GOT THE DUKE BOYS UP IN HERE.
NOT OUT YET. THERE'LL BE CRUISERS IN THE AREA SOON ENOUGH.
YOUR MAN SHOT A COP. THEY WON'T STOP 'TIL EVERY LAST ONE OF US IS IN THE GROUND.
HAD TO BE DONE.
WHATEVER. AIN'T GONNA BE A TRIAL. THEY CATCH US AND THIS RIDE IS OUR COFFIN.
HAND ME THOSE GOGGLES.

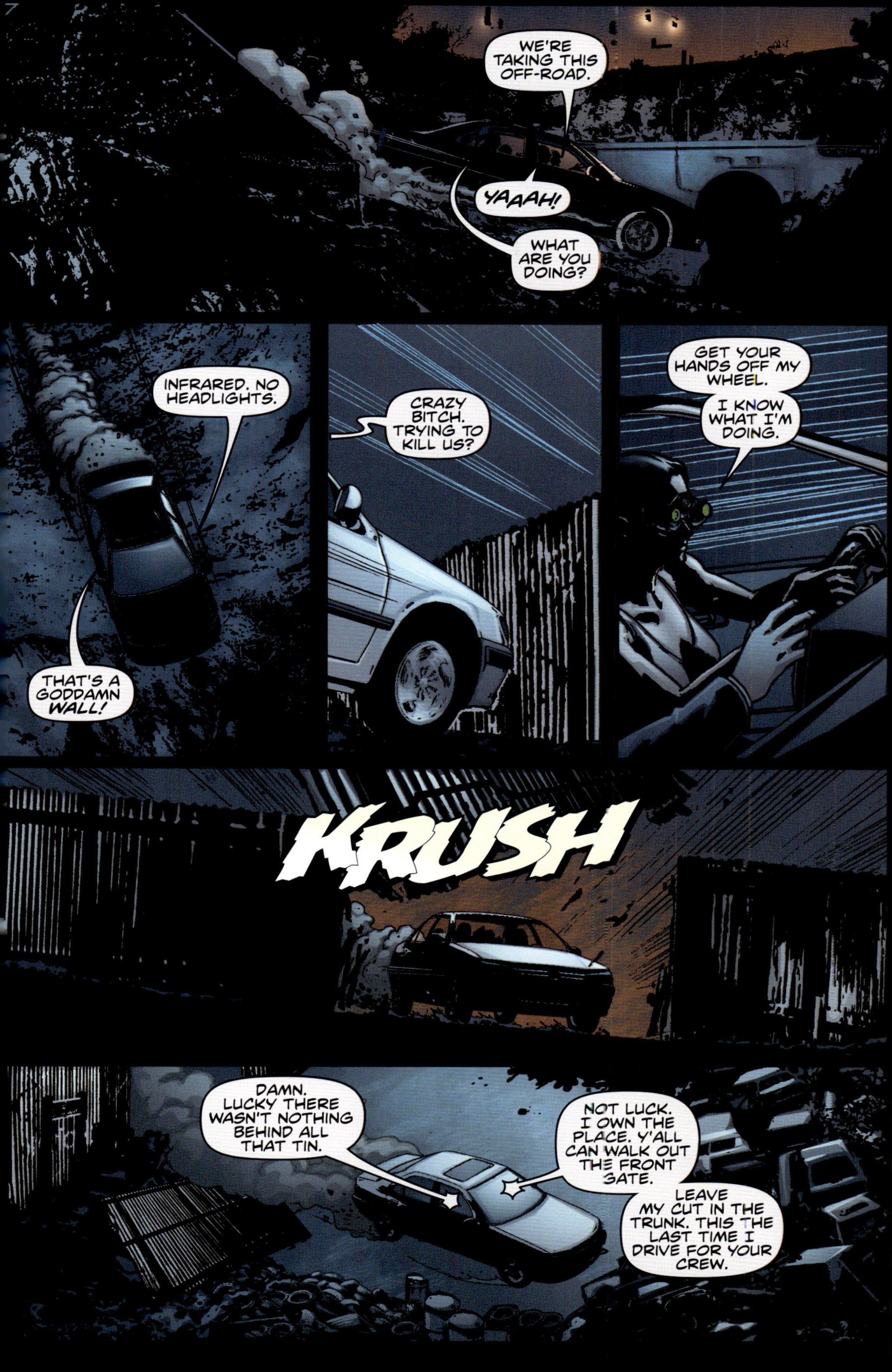
WE'RE TAKING THIS OFF-ROAD.
YAAAH!
WHAT ARE YOU DOING?
INFRARED. NO HEADLIGHTS.
THAT'S A GODDAMN WALL!
CRAZY BITCH. TRYING TO KILL US?
GET YOUR HANDS OFF MY WHEEL.
I KNOW WHAT I'M DOING.
KRUSH
DAMN. LUCKY THERE WASN'T NOTHING BEHIND ALL THAT TIN.
NOT LUCK. I OWN THE PLACE. Y'ALL CAN WALK OUT THE FRONT GATE.
LEAVE MY CUT IN THE TRUNK. THIS THE LAST TIME I DRIVE FOR YOUR CREW.

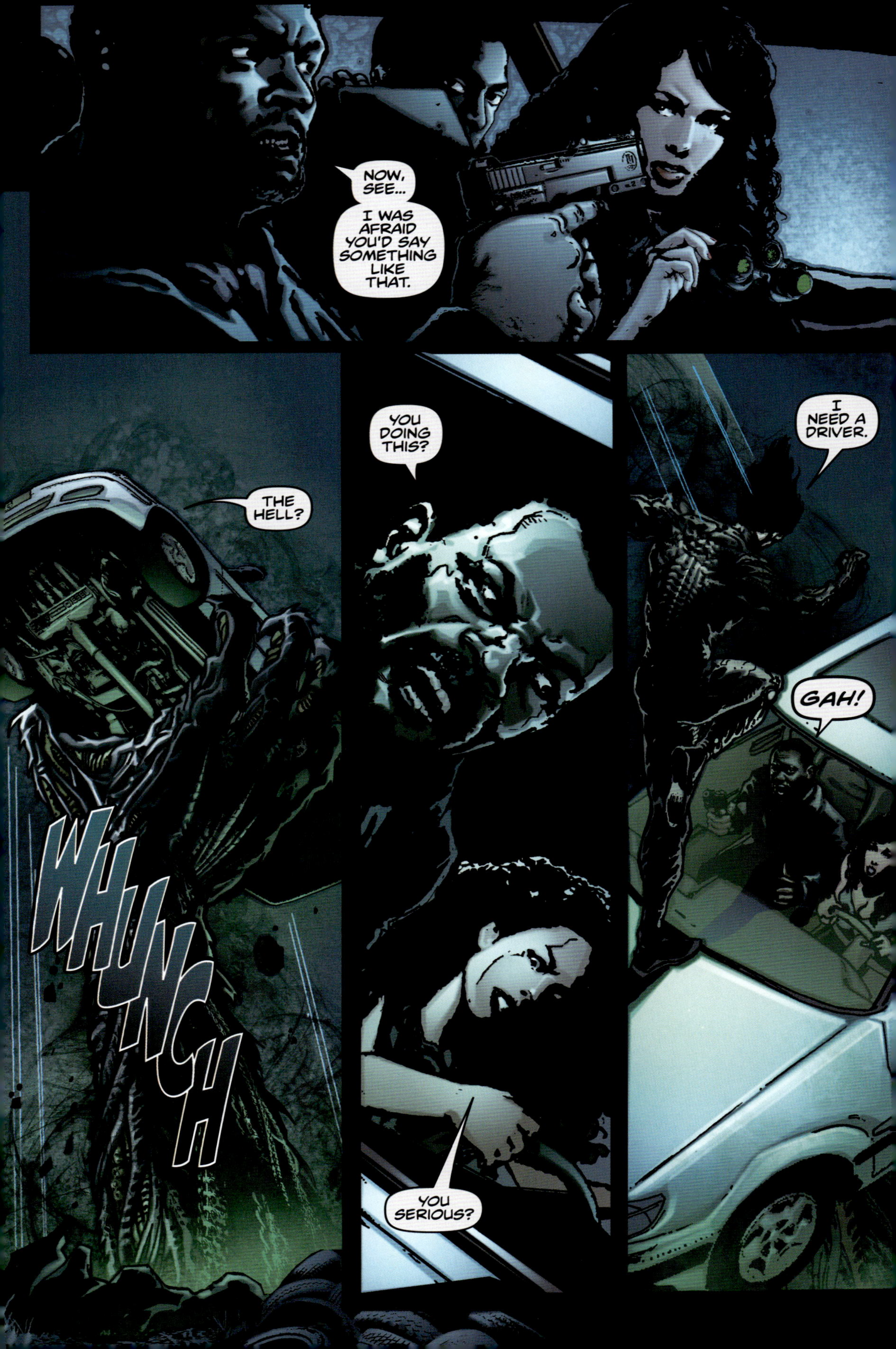
NOW, SEE...
I WAS AFRAID YOU'D SAY SOMETHING LIKE THAT.
THE HELL?
WHUNCH
YOU DOING THIS?
YOU SERIOUS?
I NEED A DRIVER.
GAH!

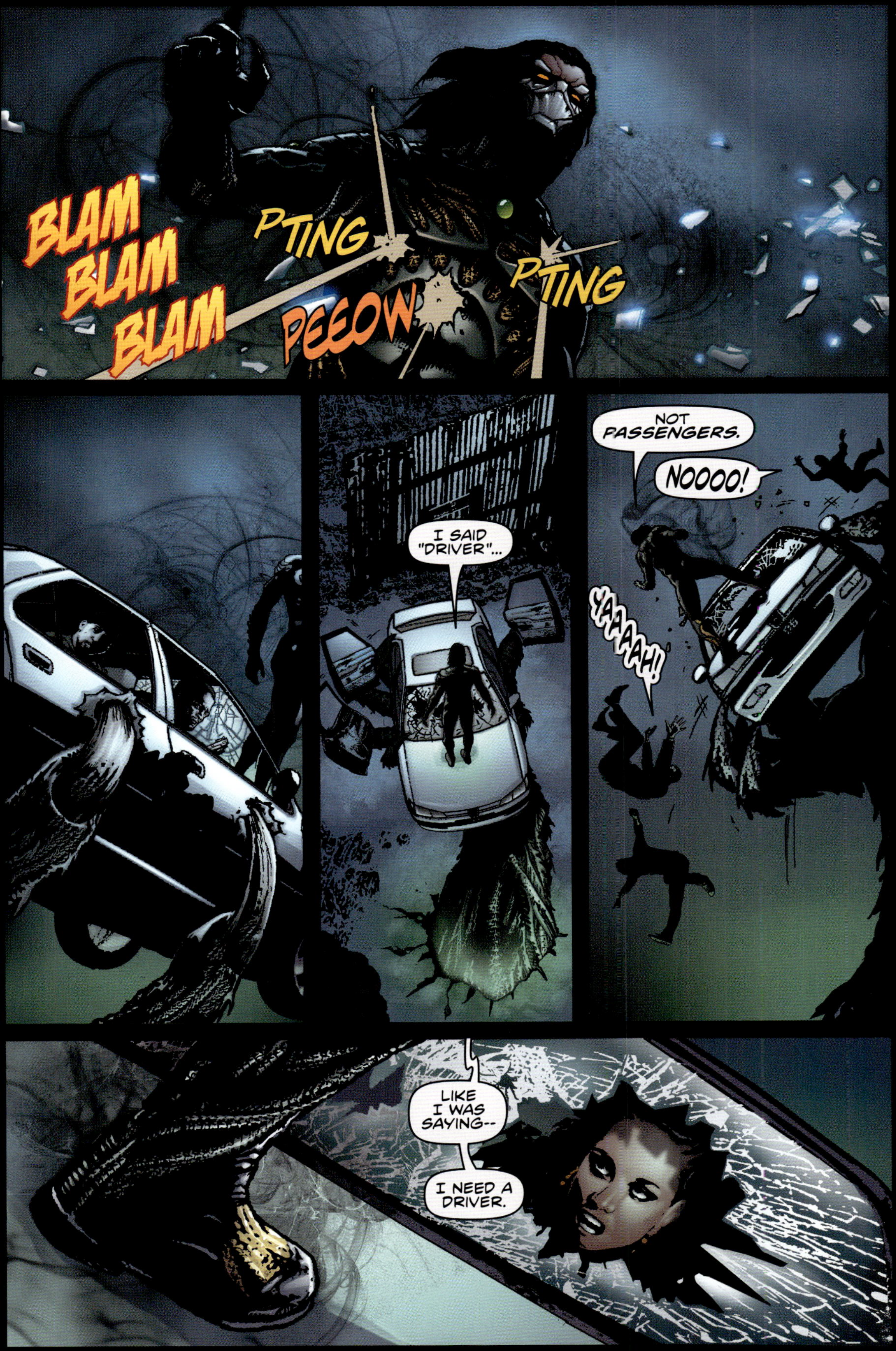
BLAM
BLAM
BLAM
PTING
PEEOW
PTING
I SAID "DRIVER"...
NOT PASSENGERS.
NOOOO!
YAAAAAH!!
LIKE I WAS SAYING--
I NEED A DRIVER.

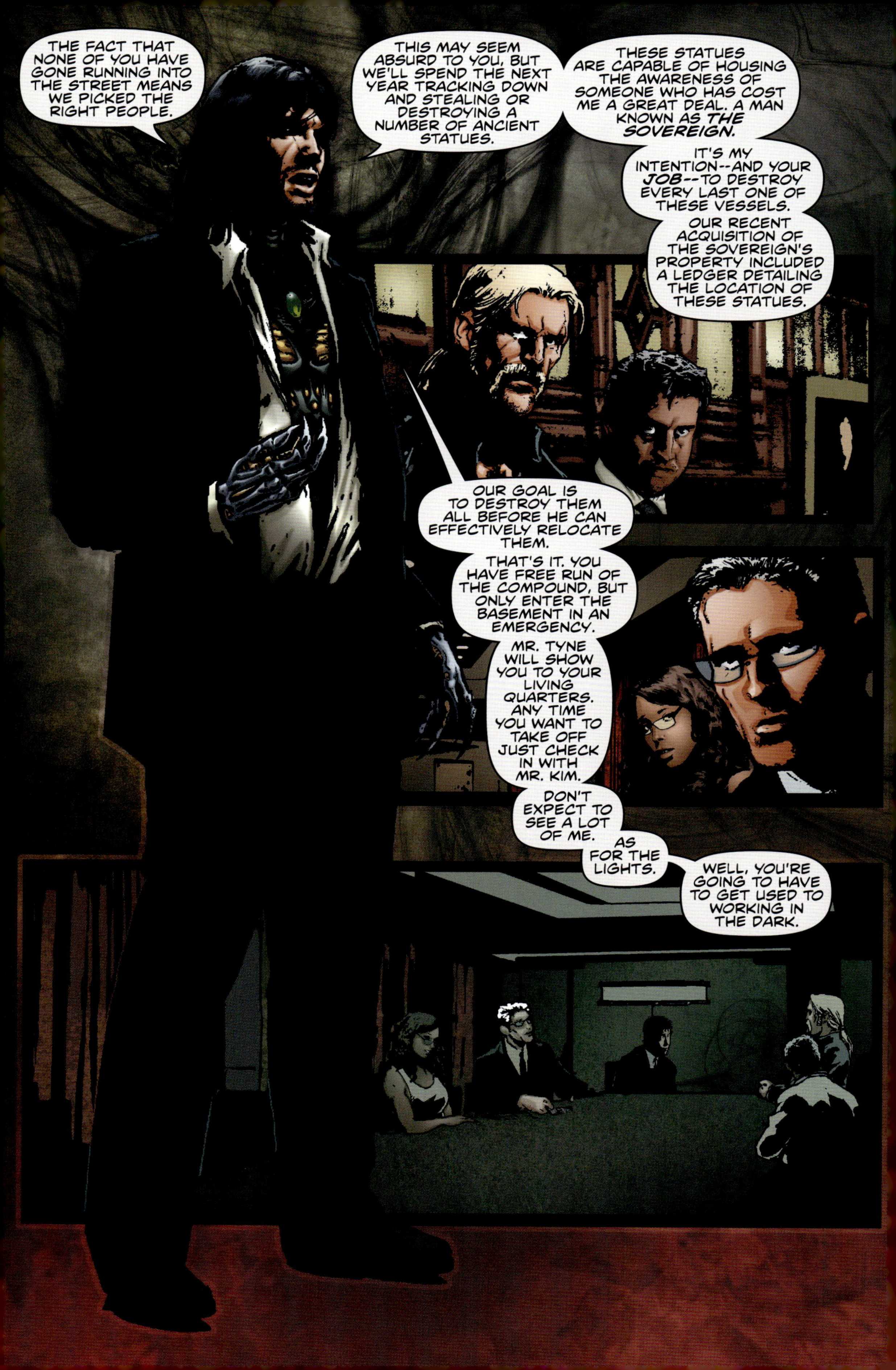
THE FACT THAT NONE OF YOU HAVE GONE RUNNING INTO THE STREET MEANS WE PICKED THE RIGHT PEOPLE.
THIS MAY SEEM ABSURD TO YOU, BUT WE'LL SPEND THE NEXT YEAR TRACKING DOWN AND STEALING OR DESTROYING A NUMBER OF ANCIENT STATUES.
THESE STATUES ARE CAPABLE OF HOUSING THE AWARENESS OF SOMEONE WHO HAS COST ME A GREAT DEAL. A MAN KNOWN AS *THE SOVEREIGN.*
IT'S MY INTENTION--AND YOUR *JOB*--TO DESTROY EVERY LAST ONE OF THESE VESSELS.
OUR RECENT ACQUISITION OF THE SOVEREIGN'S PROPERTY INCLUDED A LEDGER DETAILING THE LOCATION OF THESE STATUES.
OUR GOAL IS TO DESTROY THEM ALL BEFORE HE CAN EFFECTIVELY RELOCATE THEM.
THAT'S IT. YOU HAVE FREE RUN OF THE COMPOUND, BUT ONLY ENTER THE BASEMENT IN AN EMERGENCY.
MR. TYNE WILL SHOW YOU TO YOUR LIVING QUARTERS. ANY TIME YOU WANT TO TAKE OFF JUST CHECK IN WITH MR. KIM.
DON'T EXPECT TO SEE A LOT OF ME.
AS FOR THE LIGHTS.
WELL, YOU'RE GOING TO HAVE TO GET USED TO WORKING IN THE DARK.

The Darkness Issue #80
cover art by: Phil Hester and Admira Wijaya

THE DARKNESS #80

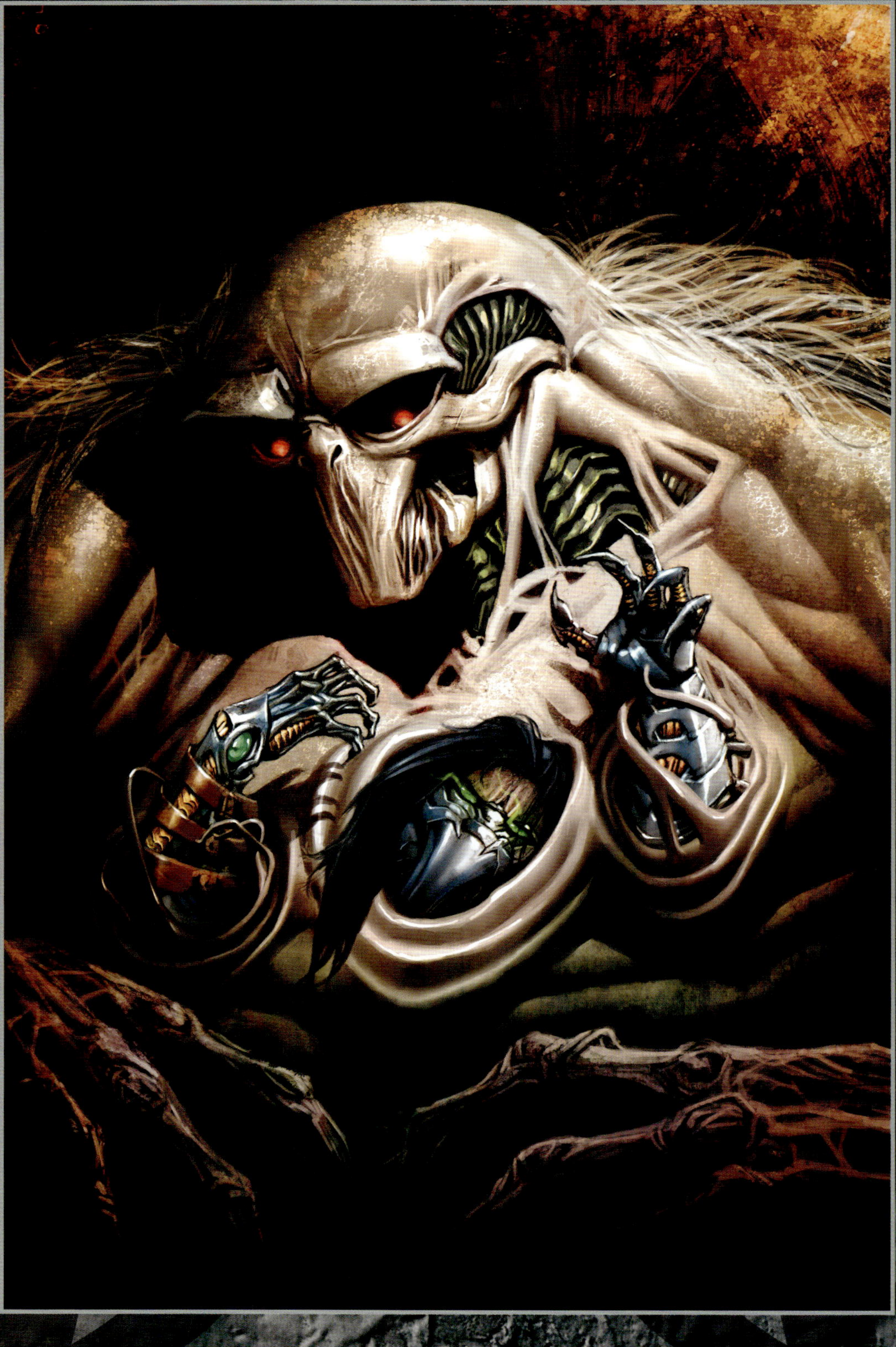

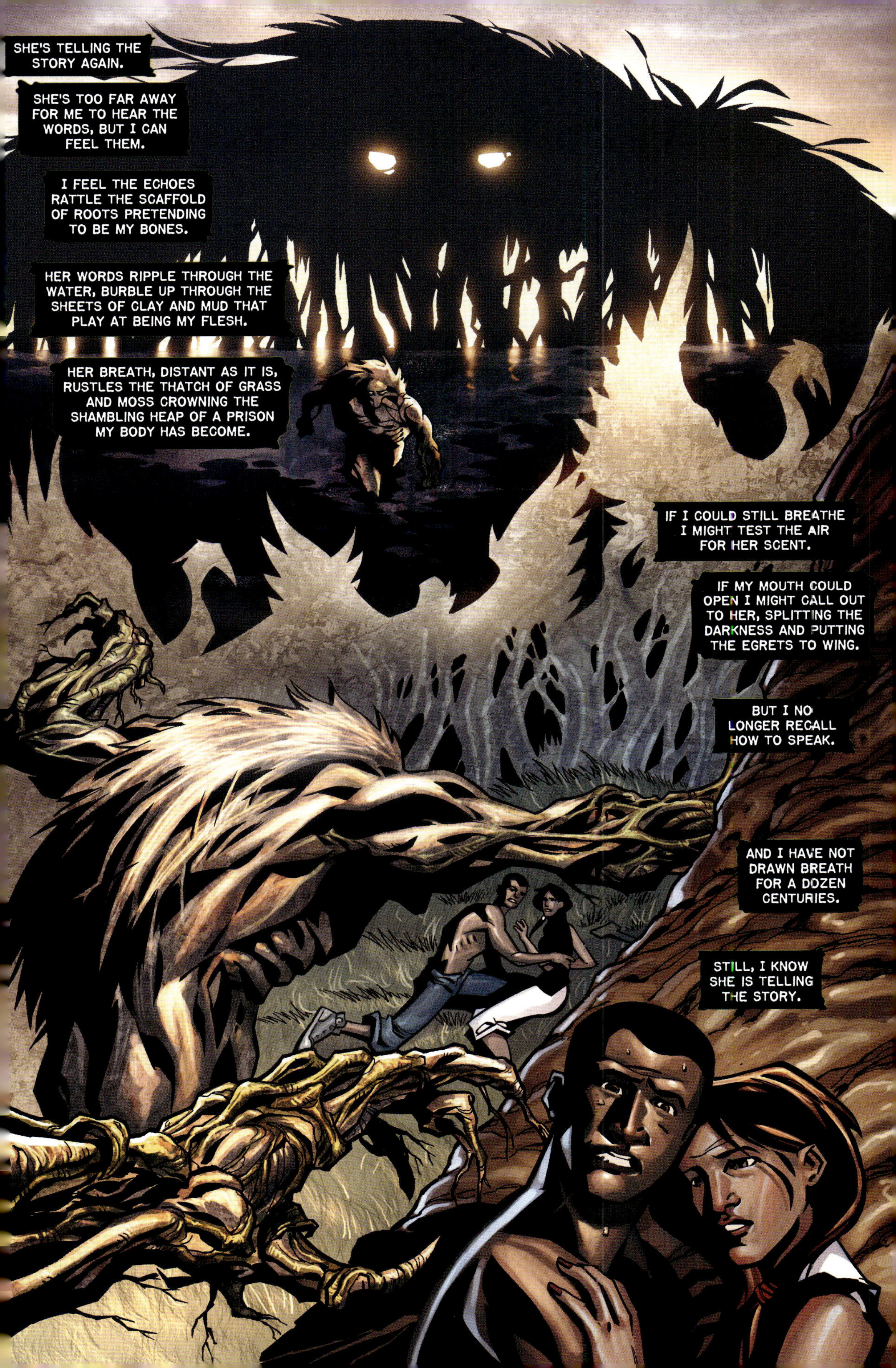
SHE'S TELLING THE STORY AGAIN.
SHE'S TOO FAR AWAY FOR ME TO HEAR THE WORDS, BUT I CAN FEEL THEM.
I FEEL THE ECHOES RATTLE THE SCAFFOLD OF ROOTS PRETENDING TO BE MY BONES.
HER WORDS RIPPLE THROUGH THE WATER, BURBLE UP THROUGH THE SHEETS OF CLAY AND MUD THAT PLAY AT BEING MY FLESH.
HER BREATH, DISTANT AS IT IS, RUSTLES THE THATCH OF GRASS AND MOSS CROWNING THE SHAMBLING HEAP OF A PRISON MY BODY HAS BECOME.
IF I COULD STILL BREATHE I MIGHT TEST THE AIR FOR HER SCENT.
IF MY MOUTH COULD OPEN I MIGHT CALL OUT TO HER, SPLITTING THE DARKNESS AND PUTTING THE EGRETS TO WING.
BUT I NO LONGER RECALL HOW TO SPEAK.
AND I HAVE NOT DRAWN BREATH FOR A DOZEN CENTURIES.
STILL, I KNOW SHE IS TELLING THE STORY.

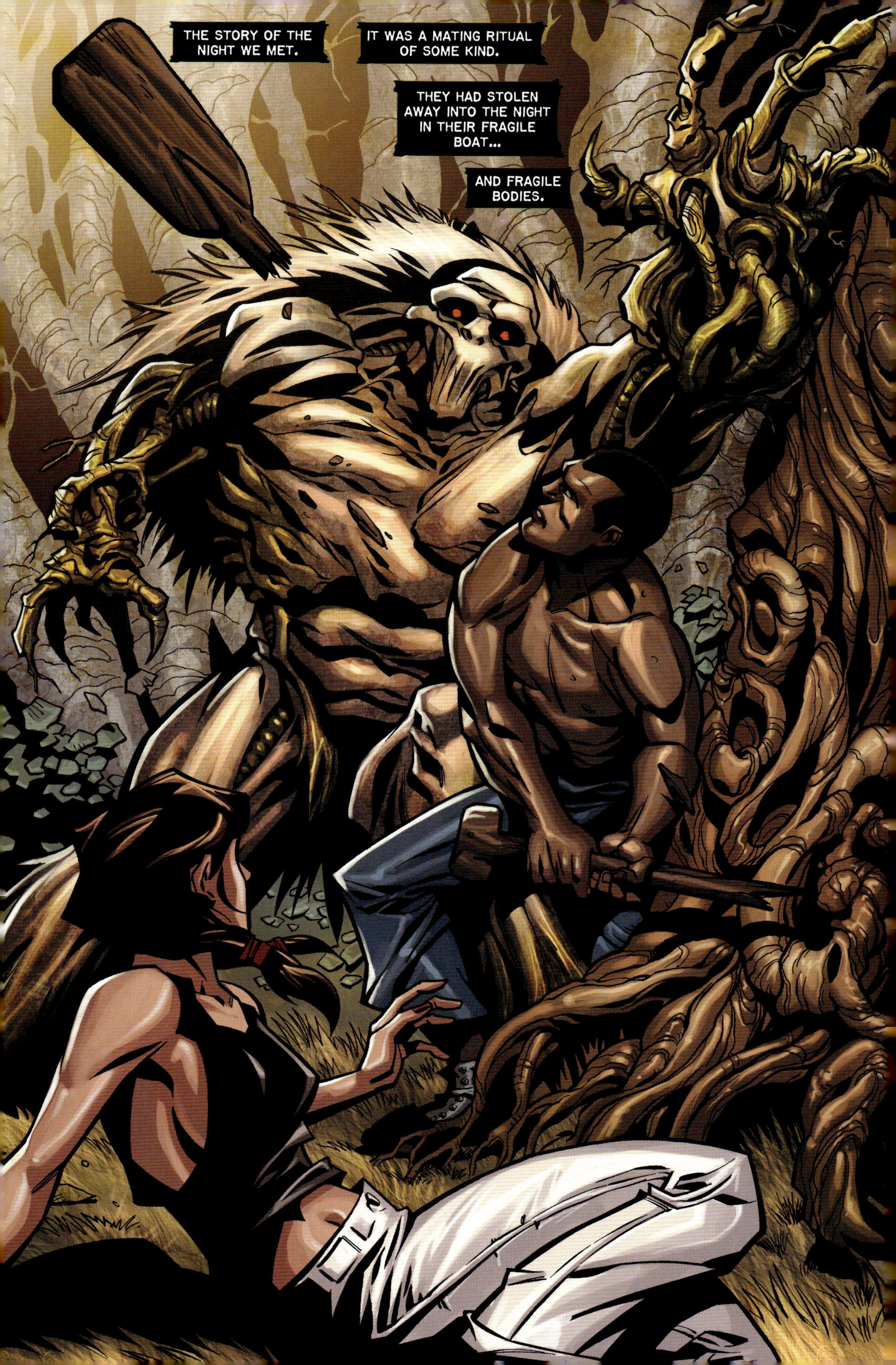
THE STORY OF THE NIGHT WE MET.
IT WAS A MATING RITUAL OF SOME KIND.
THEY HAD STOLEN AWAY INTO THE NIGHT IN THEIR FRAGILE BOAT...
AND FRAGILE BODIES.

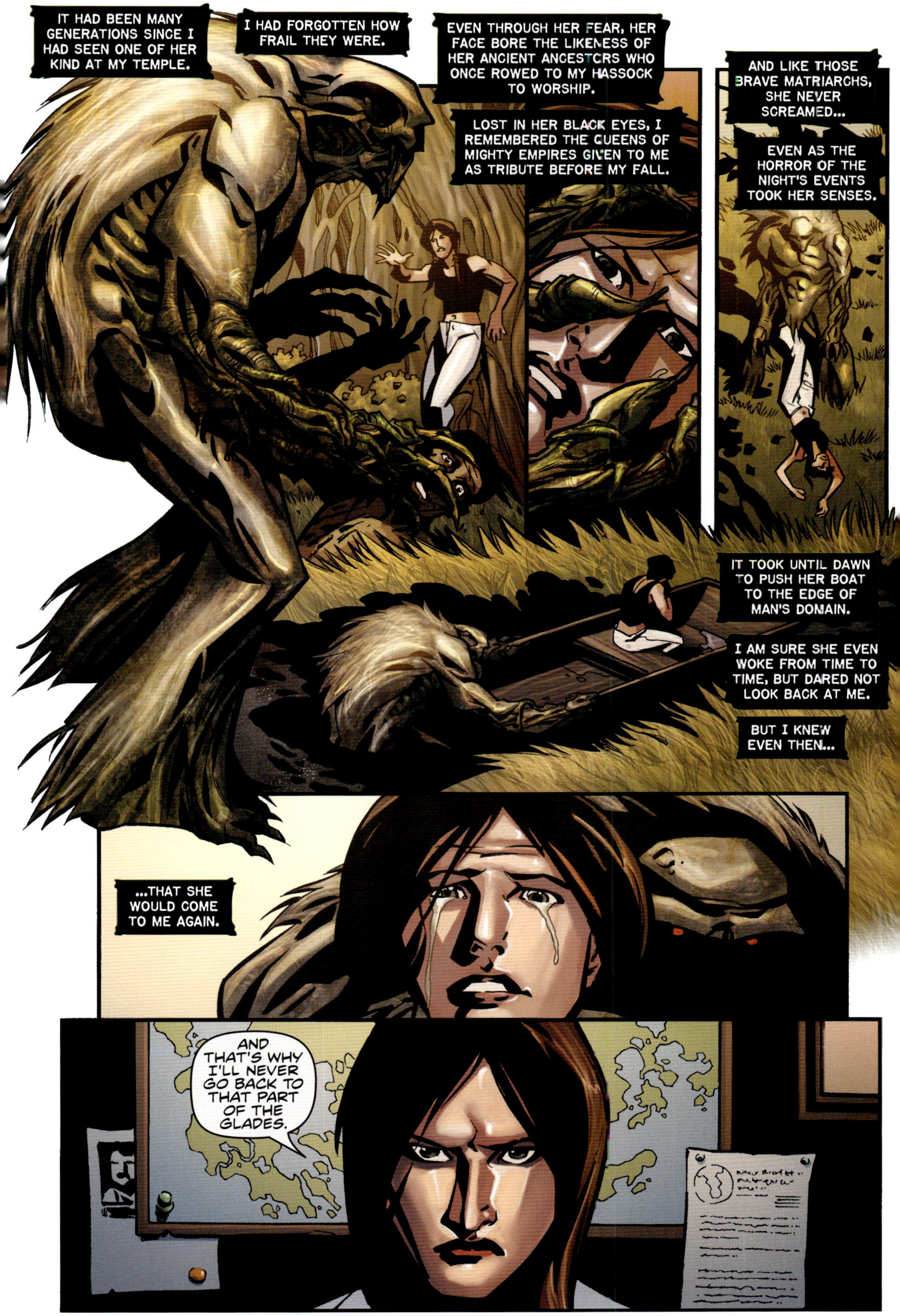
IT HAD BEEN MANY GENERATIONS SINCE I HAD SEEN ONE OF HER KIND AT MY TEMPLE.
I HAD FORGOTTEN HOW FRAIL THEY WERE.
EVEN THROUGH HER FEAR, HER FACE BORE THE LIKENESS OF HER ANCIENT ANCESTORS WHO ONCE ROWED TO MY HASSOCK TO WORSHIP.
LOST IN HER BLACK EYES, I REMEMBERED THE QUEENS OF MIGHTY EMPIRES GIVEN TO ME AS TRIBUTE BEFORE MY FALL.
AND LIKE THOSE BRAVE MATRIARCHS, SHE NEVER SCREAMED...
EVEN AS THE HORROR OF THE NIGHT'S EVENTS TOOK HER SENSES.
IT TOOK UNTIL DAWN TO PUSH HER BOAT TO THE EDGE OF MAN'S DOMAIN.
I AM SURE SHE EVEN WOKE FROM TIME TO TIME, BUT DARED NOT LOOK BACK AT ME.
BUT I KNEW EVEN THEN...
...THAT SHE WOULD COME TO ME AGAIN.
AND THAT'S WHY I'LL NEVER GO BACK TO THAT PART OF THE GLADES.

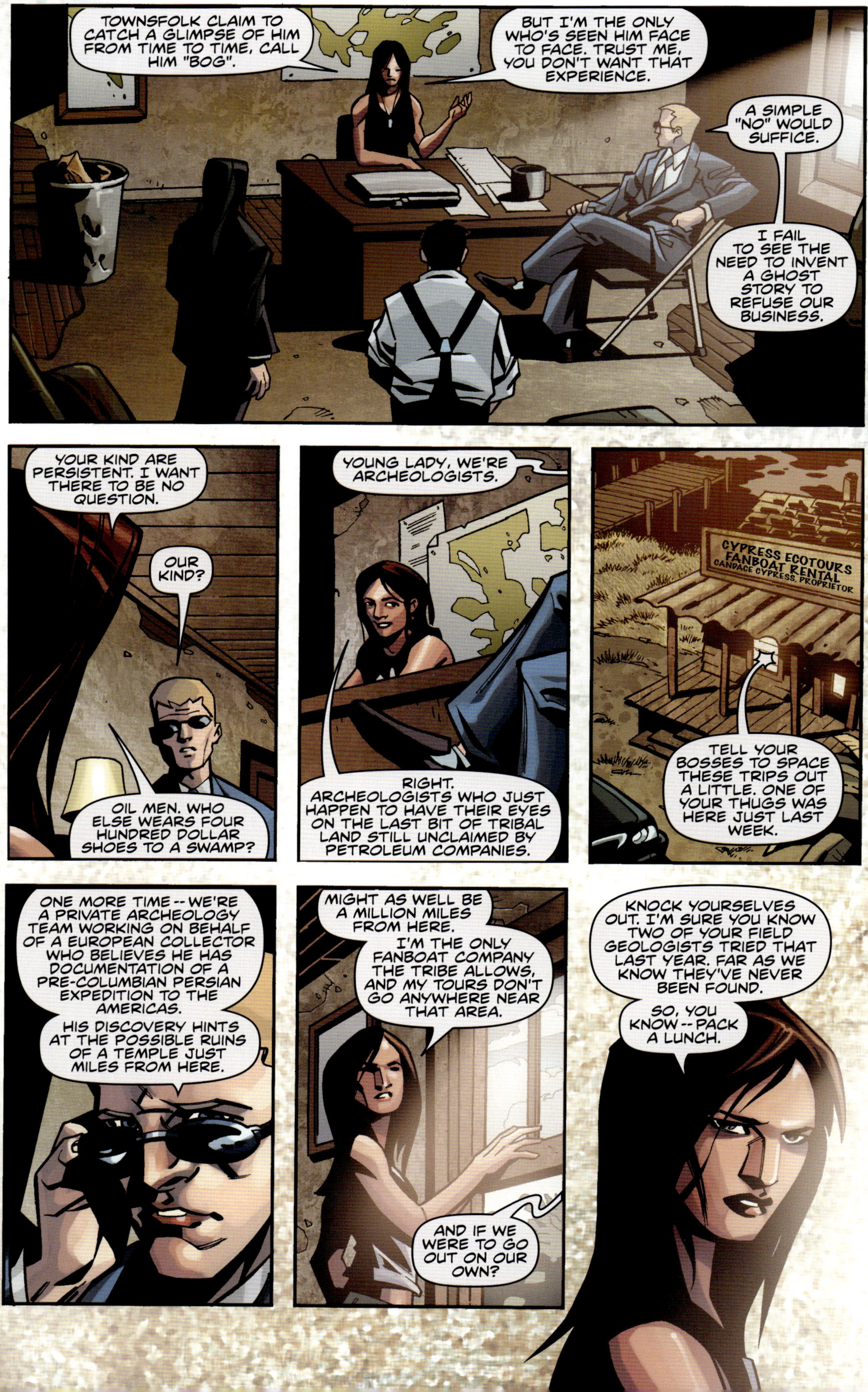

TOWNSFOLK CLAIM TO CATCH A GLIMPSE OF HIM FROM TIME TO TIME, CALL HIM "BOG".
BUT I'M THE ONLY WHO'S SEEN HIM FACE TO FACE. TRUST ME, YOU DON'T WANT THAT EXPERIENCE.
A SIMPLE "NO" WOULD SUFFICE.
I FAIL TO SEE THE NEED TO INVENT A GHOST STORY TO REFUSE OUR BUSINESS.
YOUR KIND ARE PERSISTENT. I WANT THERE TO BE NO QUESTION.
OUR KIND?
OIL MEN. WHO ELSE WEARS FOUR HUNDRED DOLLAR SHOES TO A SWAMP?
YOUNG LADY, WE'RE ARCHEOLOGISTS.
RIGHT. ARCHEOLOGISTS WHO JUST HAPPEN TO HAVE THEIR EYES ON THE LAST BIT OF TRIBAL LAND STILL UNCLAIMED BY PETROLEUM COMPANIES.
CYPRESS ECOTOURS
FANBOAT RENTAL
CANDACE CYPRESS, PROPRIETOR
TELL YOUR BOSSES TO SPACE THESE TRIPS OUT A LITTLE. ONE OF YOUR THUGS WAS HERE JUST LAST WEEK.
ONE MORE TIME -- WE'RE A PRIVATE ARCHEOLOGY TEAM WORKING ON BEHALF OF A EUROPEAN COLLECTOR WHO BELIEVES HE HAS DOCUMENTATION OF A PRE-COLUMBIAN PERSIAN EXPEDITION TO THE AMERICAS.
HIS DISCOVERY HINTS AT THE POSSIBLE RUINS OF A TEMPLE JUST MILES FROM HERE.
MIGHT AS WELL BE A MILLION MILES FROM HERE.
I'M THE ONLY FANBOAT COMPANY THE TRIBE ALLOWS, AND MY TOURS DON'T GO ANYWHERE NEAR THAT AREA.
AND IF WE WERE TO GO OUT ON OUR OWN?
KNOCK YOURSELVES OUT. I'M SURE YOU KNOW TWO OF YOUR FIELD GEOLOGISTS TRIED THAT LAST YEAR. FAR AS WE KNOW THEY'VE NEVER BEEN FOUND.
SO, YOU KNOW -- PACK A LUNCH.

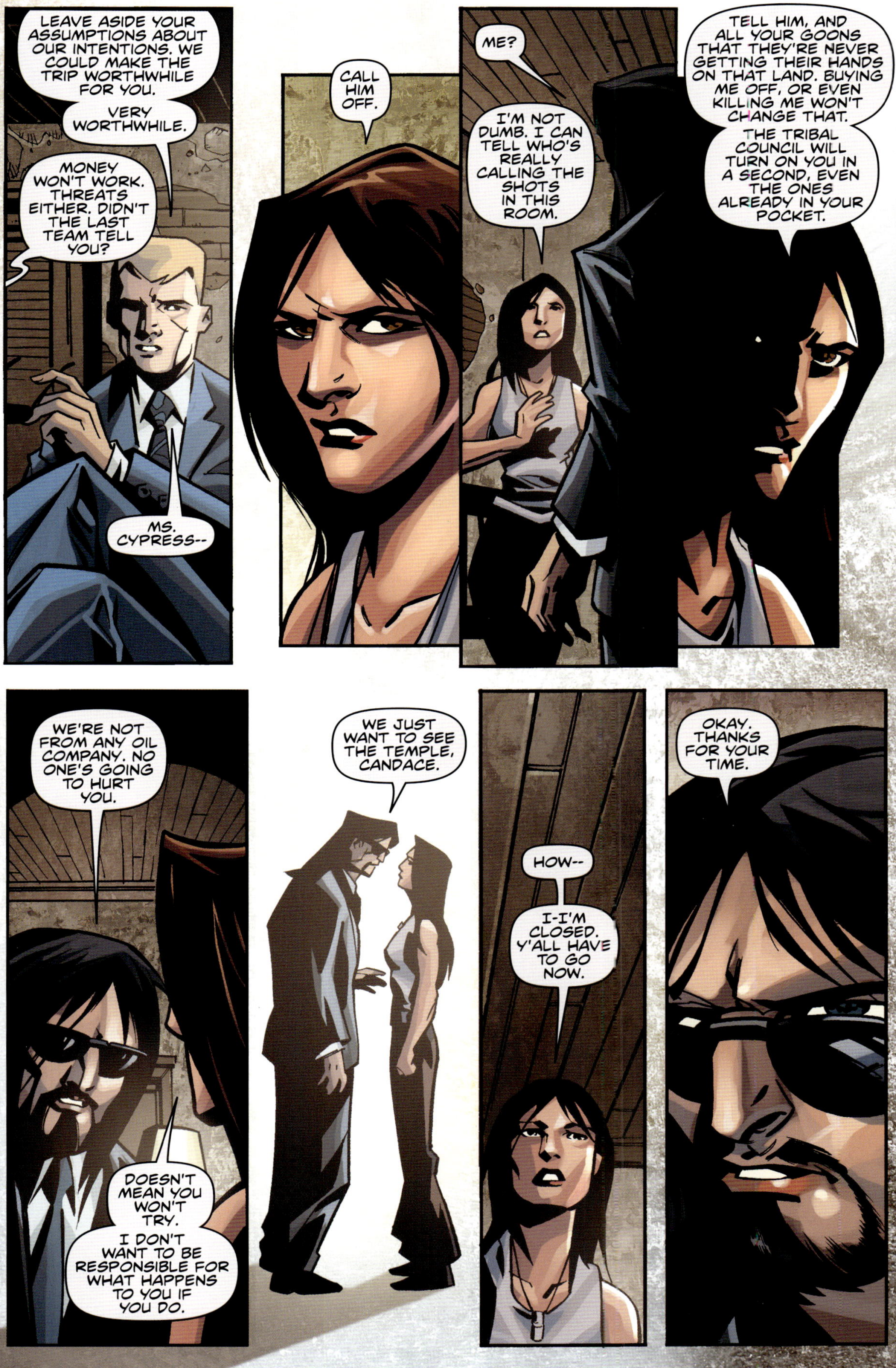
LEAVE ASIDE YOUR ASSUMPTIONS ABOUT OUR INTENTIONS. WE COULD MAKE THE TRIP WORTHWHILE FOR YOU.
VERY WORTHWHILE.
MONEY WON'T WORK. THREATS EITHER. DIDN'T THE LAST TEAM TELL YOU?
MS. CYPRESS--
CALL HIM OFF.
ME?
I'M NOT DUMB. I CAN TELL WHO'S REALLY CALLING THE SHOTS IN THIS ROOM.
TELL HIM, AND ALL YOUR GOONS THAT THEY'RE NEVER GETTING THEIR HANDS ON THAT LAND. BUYING ME OFF, OR EVEN KILLING ME WON'T CHANGE THAT.
THE TRIBAL COUNCIL WILL TURN ON YOU IN A SECOND, EVEN THE ONES ALREADY IN YOUR POCKET.
WE'RE NOT FROM ANY OIL COMPANY. NO ONE'S GOING TO HURT YOU.
DOESN'T MEAN YOU WON'T TRY.
I DON'T WANT TO BE RESPONSIBLE FOR WHAT HAPPENS TO YOU IF YOU DO.
WE JUST WANT TO SEE THE TEMPLE, CANDACE.
HOW--
I-I'M CLOSED. Y'ALL HAVE TO GO NOW.
OKAY. THANKS FOR YOUR TIME.

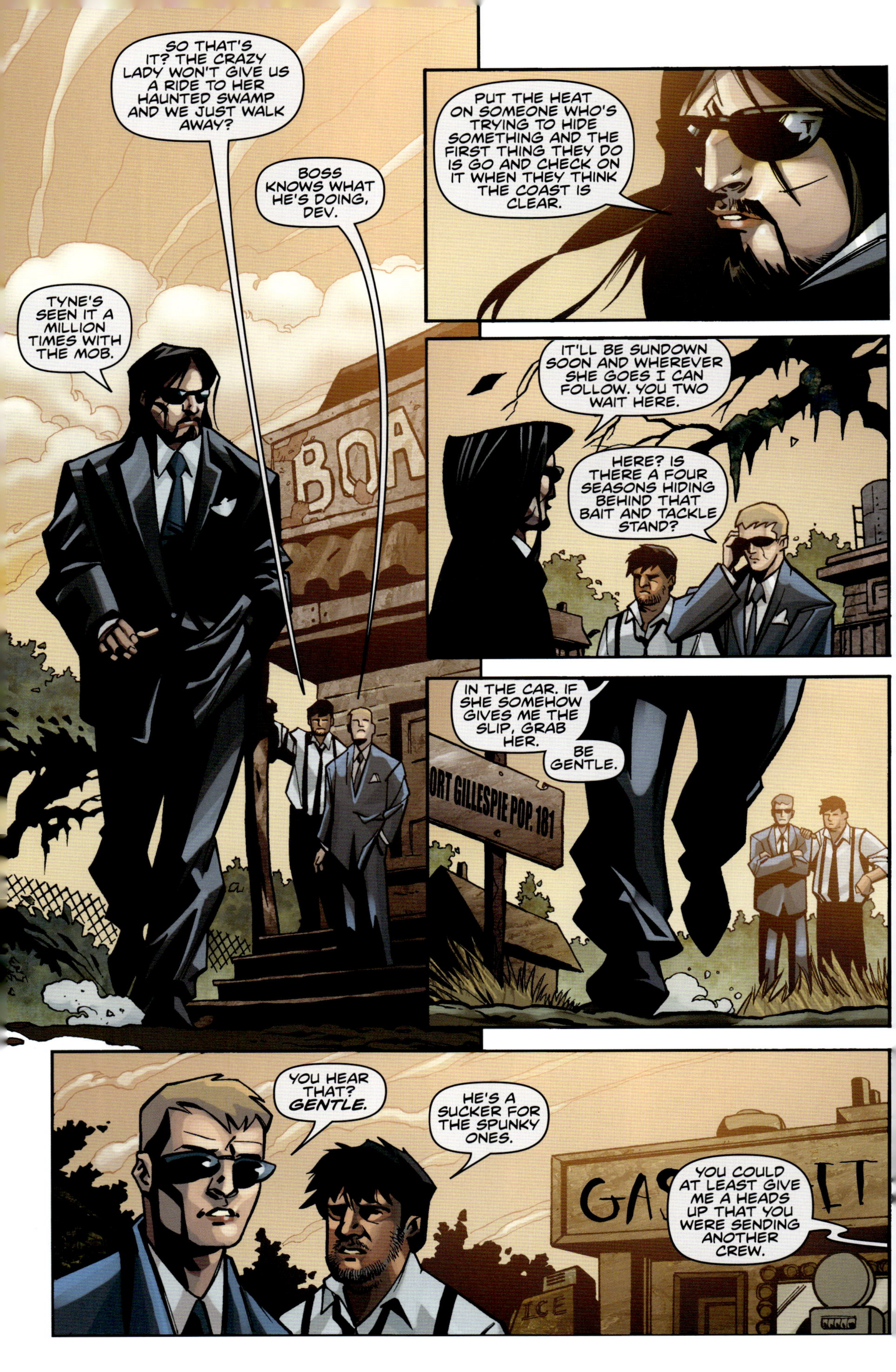
SO THAT'S IT? THE CRAZY LADY WON'T GIVE US A RIDE TO HER HAUNTED SWAMP AND WE JUST WALK AWAY?
BOSS KNOWS WHAT HE'S DOING, DEV.
TYNE'S SEEN IT A MILLION TIMES WITH THE MOB.
BOA
PUT THE HEAT ON SOMEONE WHO'S TRYING TO HIDE SOMETHING AND THE FIRST THING THEY DO IS GO AND CHECK ON IT WHEN THEY THINK THE COAST IS CLEAR.
IT'LL BE SUNDOWN SOON AND WHEREVER SHE GOES I CAN FOLLOW. YOU TWO WAIT HERE.
HERE? IS THERE A FOUR SEASONS HIDING BEHIND THAT BAIT AND TACKLE STAND?
IN THE CAR. IF SHE SOMEHOW GIVES ME THE SLIP, GRAB HER.
BE GENTLE.
ORT GILLESPIE POP. 181
YOU HEAR THAT? GENTLE.
HE'S A SUCKER FOR THE SPUNKY ONES.
YOU COULD AT LEAST GIVE ME A HEADS UP THAT YOU WERE SENDING ANOTHER CREW.
ICE

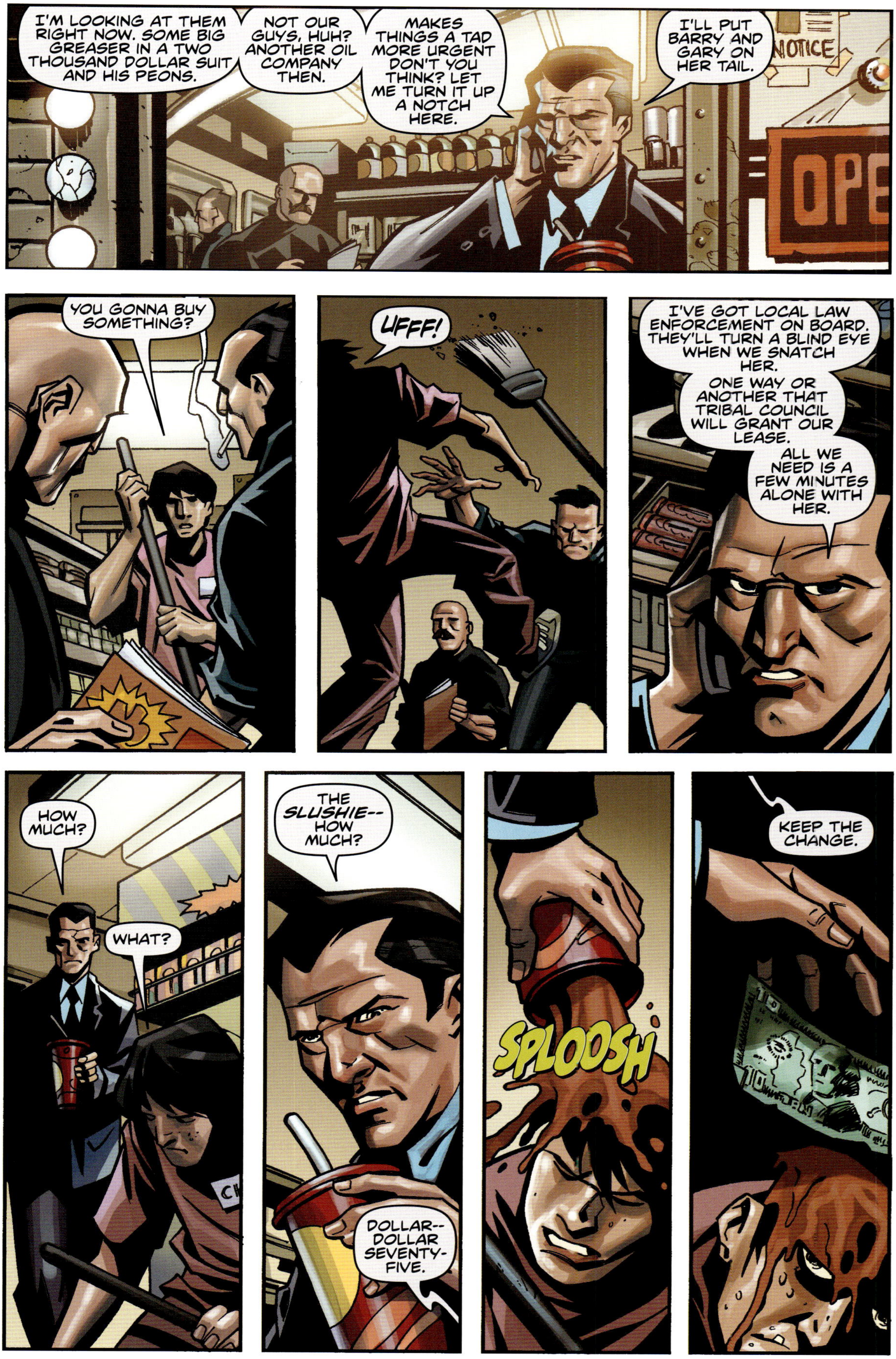
I'M LOOKING AT THEM RIGHT NOW. SOME BIG GREASER IN A TWO THOUSAND DOLLAR SUIT AND HIS PEONS.
NOT OUR GUYS, HUH? ANOTHER OIL COMPANY THEN.
MAKES THINGS A TAD MORE URGENT DON'T YOU THINK? LET ME TURN IT UP A NOTCH HERE.
I'LL PUT BARRY AND GARY ON HER TAIL.
NOTICE
OPE
YOU GONNA BUY SOMETHING?
UFFF!
I'VE GOT LOCAL LAW ENFORCEMENT ON BOARD. THEY'LL TURN A BLIND EYE WHEN WE SNATCH HER.
ONE WAY OR ANOTHER THAT TRIBAL COUNCIL WILL GRANT OUR LEASE.
ALL WE NEED IS A FEW MINUTES ALONE WITH HER.
HOW MUCH?
WHAT?
THE SLUSHIE--HOW MUCH?
DOLLAR--DOLLAR SEVENTY-FIVE.
SPLOOSH
KEEP THE CHANGE.

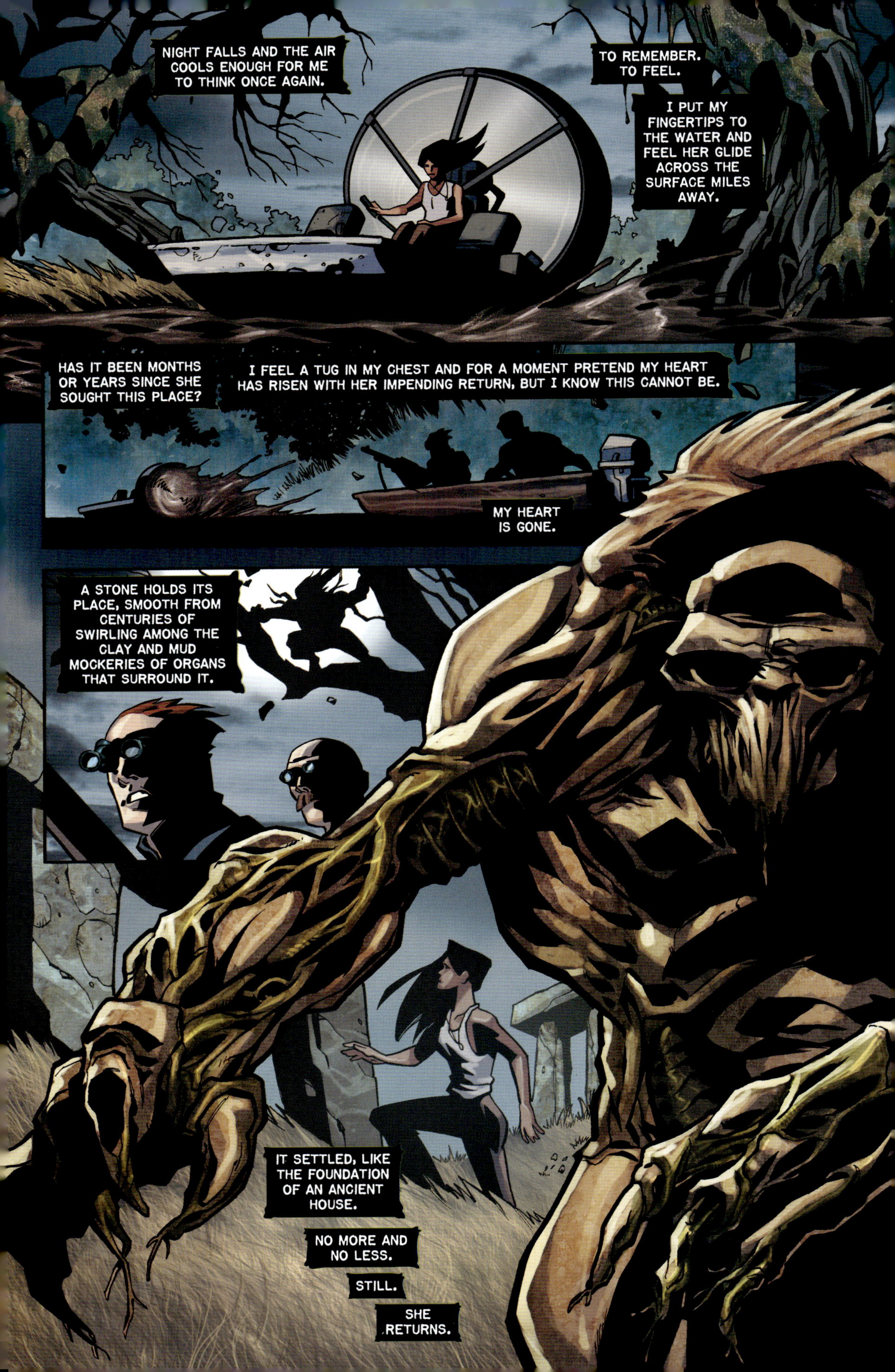
NIGHT FALLS AND THE AIR COOLS ENOUGH FOR ME TO THINK ONCE AGAIN.
TO REMEMBER. TO FEEL.
I PUT MY FINGERTIPS TO THE WATER AND FEEL HER GLIDE ACROSS THE SURFACE MILES AWAY.
HAS IT BEEN MONTHS OR YEARS SINCE SHE SOUGHT THIS PLACE?
I FEEL A TUG IN MY CHEST AND FOR A MOMENT PRETEND MY HEART HAS RISEN WITH HER IMPENDING RETURN, BUT I KNOW THIS CANNOT BE.
MY HEART IS GONE.
A STONE HOLDS ITS PLACE, SMOOTH FROM CENTURIES OF SWIRLING AMONG THE CLAY AND MUD MOCKERIES OF ORGANS THAT SURROUND IT.
IT SETTLED, LIKE THE FOUNDATION OF AN ANCIENT HOUSE.
NO MORE AND NO LESS.
STILL.
SHE RETURNS.

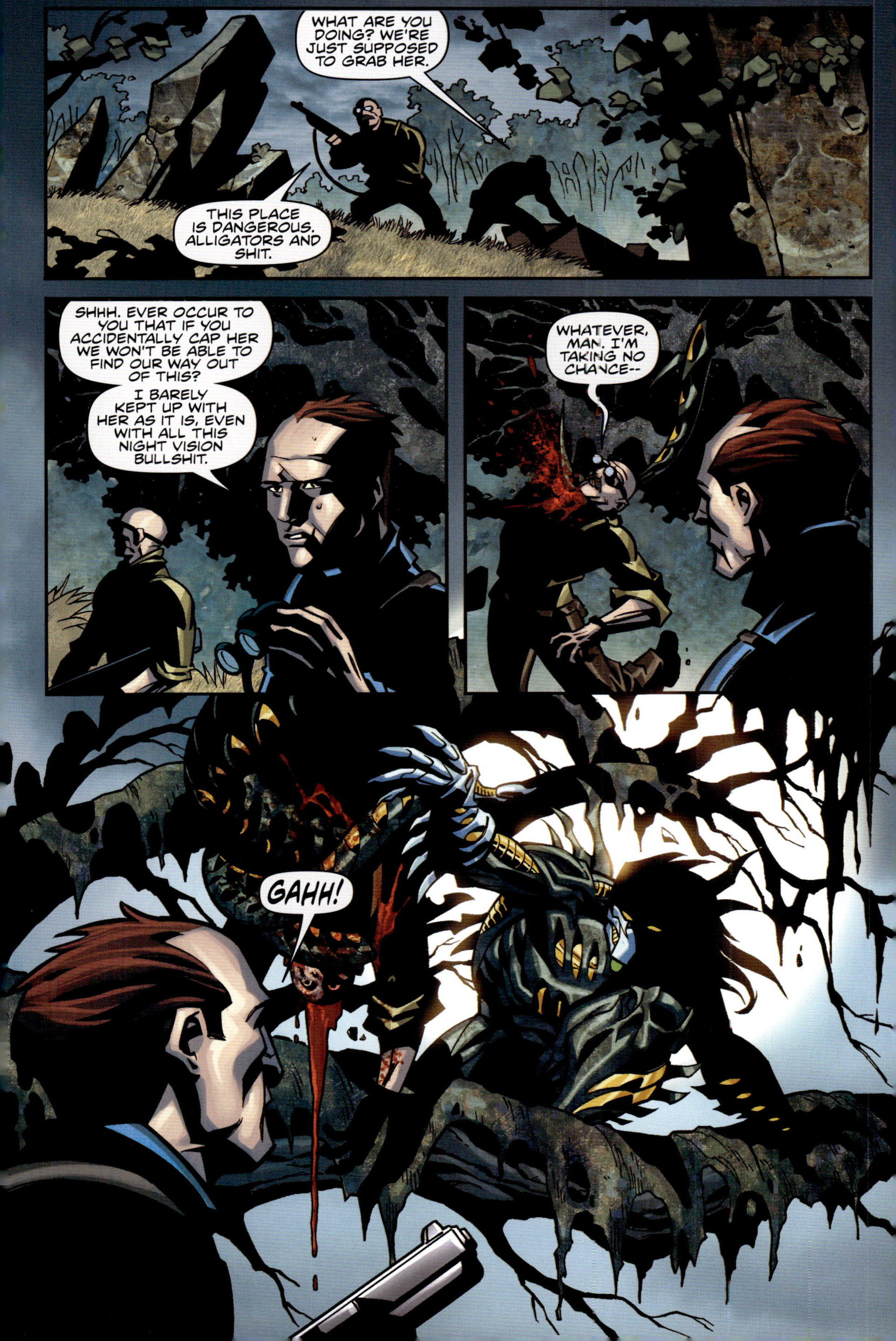
WHAT ARE YOU DOING? WE'RE JUST SUPPOSED TO GRAB HER.
THIS PLACE IS DANGEROUS. ALLIGATORS AND SHIT.
SHHH. EVER OCCUR TO YOU THAT IF YOU ACCIDENTALLY CAP HER WE WON'T BE ABLE TO FIND OUR WAY OUT OF THIS?
I BARELY KEPT UP WITH HER AS IT IS, EVEN WITH ALL THIS NIGHT VISION BULLSHIT.
WHATEVER, MAN. I'M TAKING NO CHANCE--
GAHH!

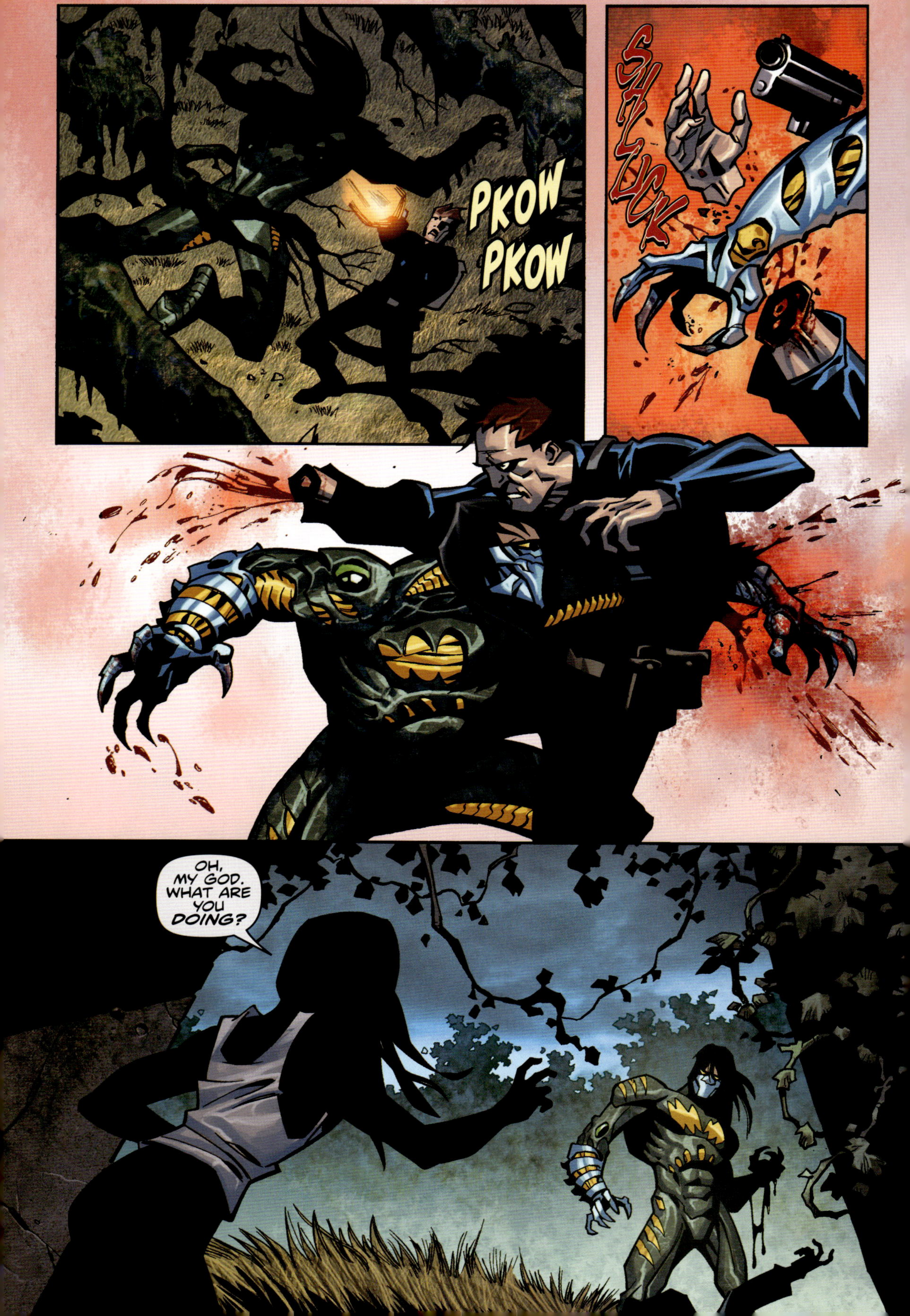
PKOW
PKOW
SHLUCK
OH, MY GOD. WHAT ARE YOU DOING?

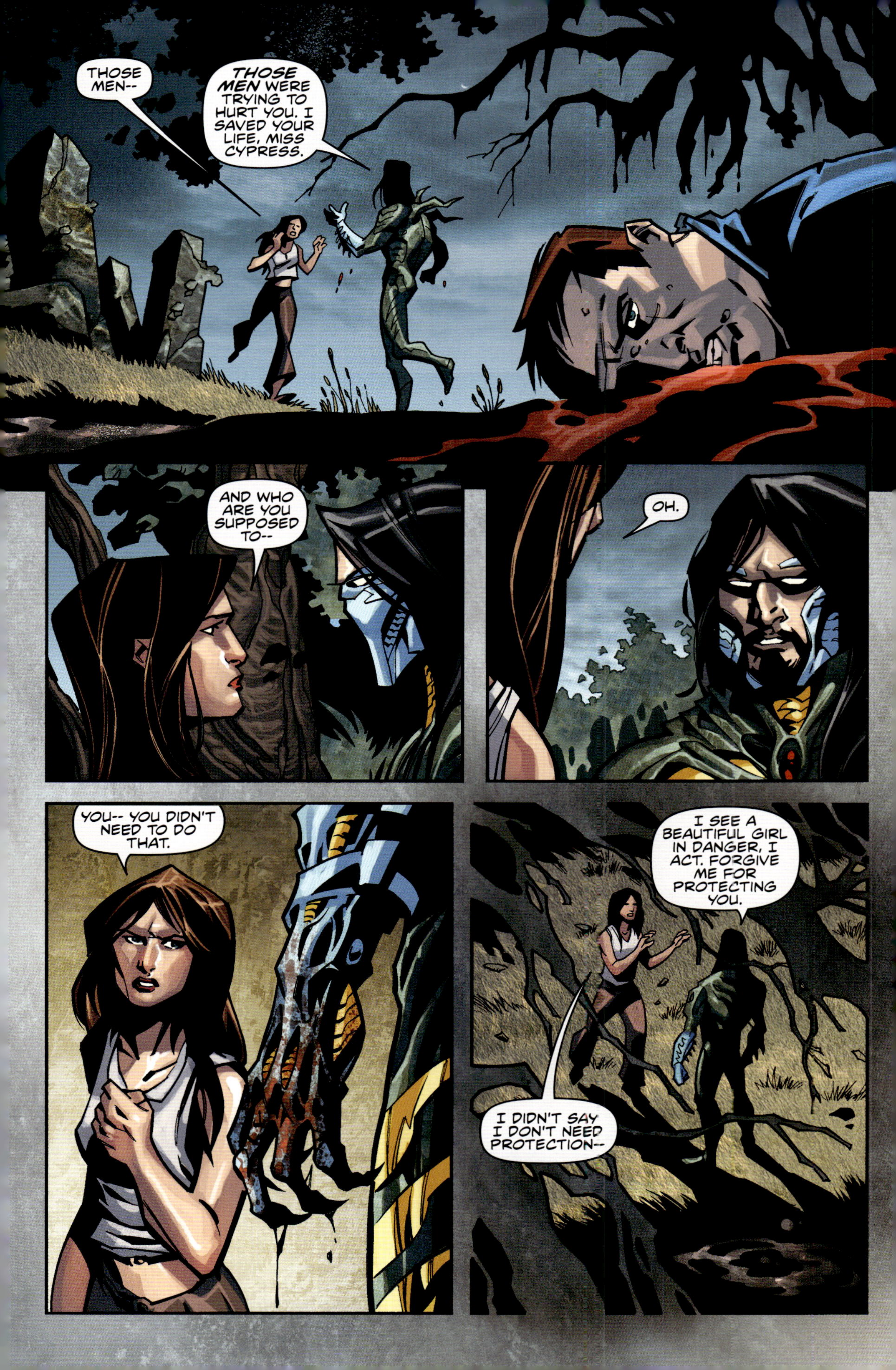
THOSE MEN--
THOSE MEN WERE TRYING TO HURT YOU. I SAVED YOUR LIFE, MISS CYPRESS.
AND WHO ARE YOU SUPPOSED TO--
OH.
YOU-- YOU DIDN'T NEED TO DO THAT.
I SEE A BEAUTIFUL GIRL IN DANGER, I ACT. FORGIVE ME FOR PROTECTING YOU.
I DIDN'T SAY I DON'T NEED PROTECTION--

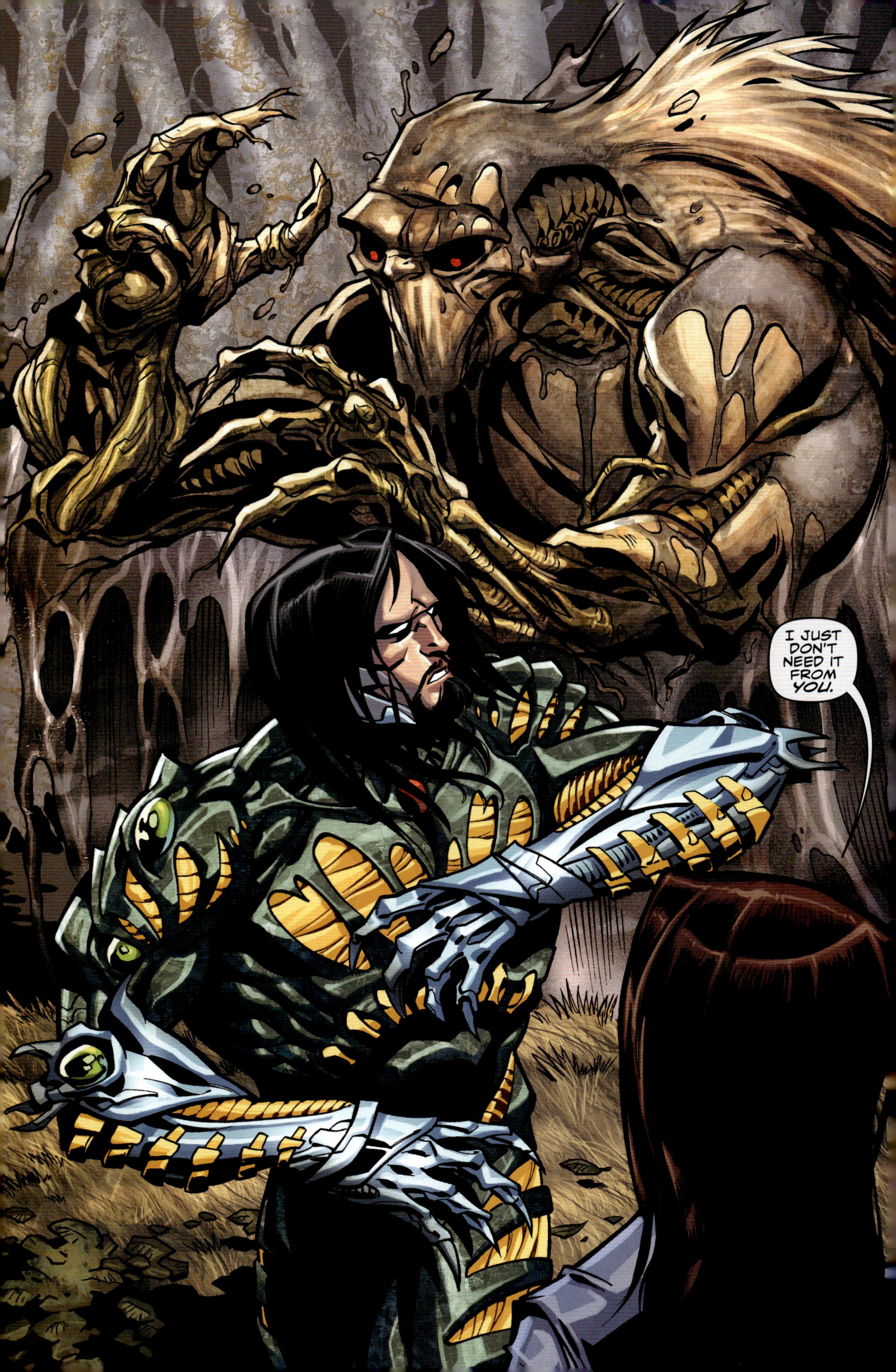
I JUST DON'T NEED IT FROM YOU.

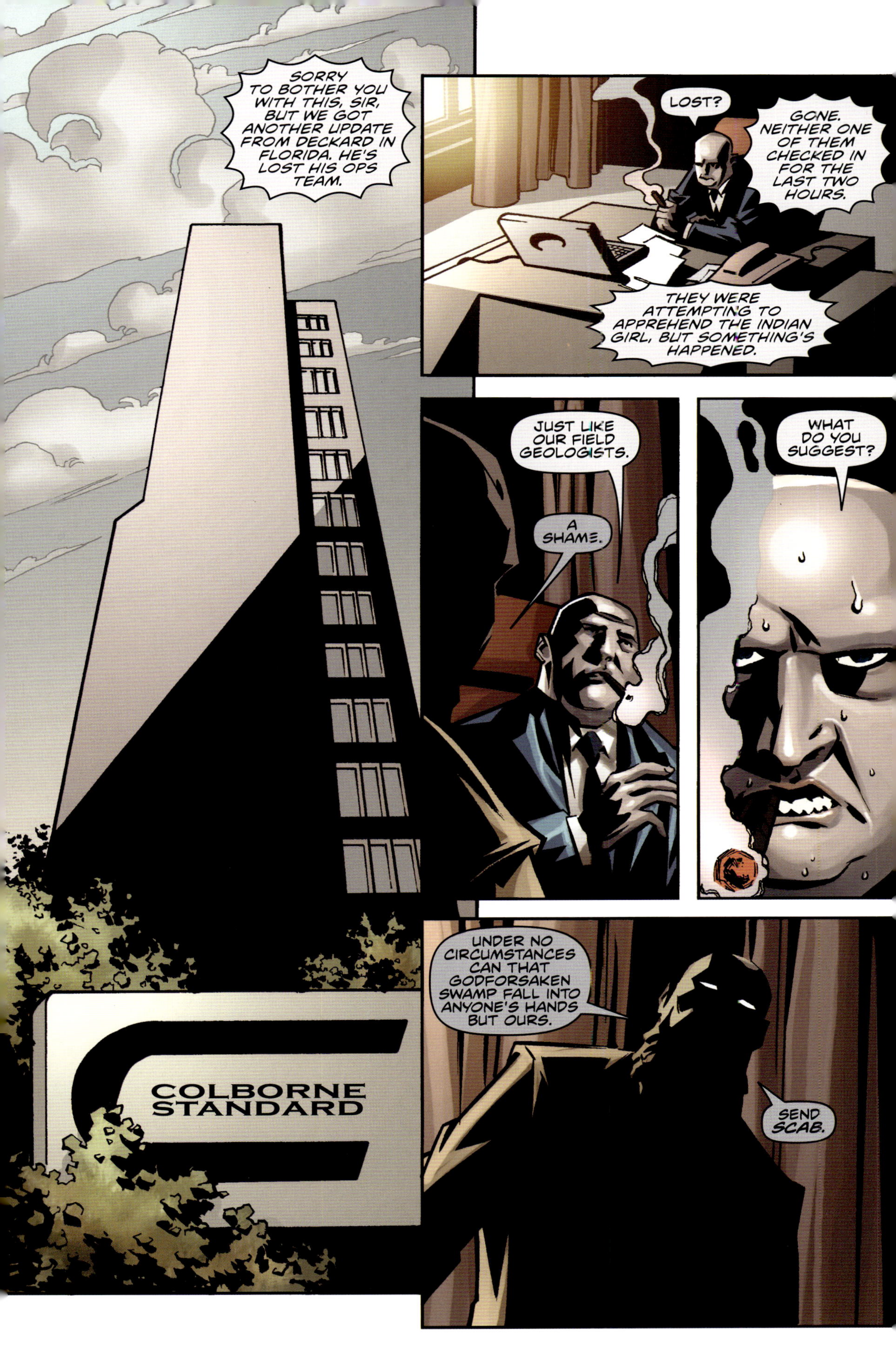
SORRY TO BOTHER YOU WITH THIS, SIR, BUT WE GOT ANOTHER UPDATE FROM DECKARD IN FLORIDA. HE'S LOST HIS OPS TEAM.
COLBORNE STANDARD
LOST?
GONE. NEITHER ONE OF THEM CHECKED IN FOR THE LAST TWO HOURS.
THEY WERE ATTEMPTING TO APPREHEND THE INDIAN GIRL, BUT SOMETHING'S HAPPENED.
JUST LIKE OUR FIELD GEOLOGISTS.
A SHAME.
WHAT DO YOU SUGGEST?
UNDER NO CIRCUMSTANCES CAN THAT GODFORSAKEN SWAMP FALL INTO ANYONE'S HANDS BUT OURS.
SEND SCAB.

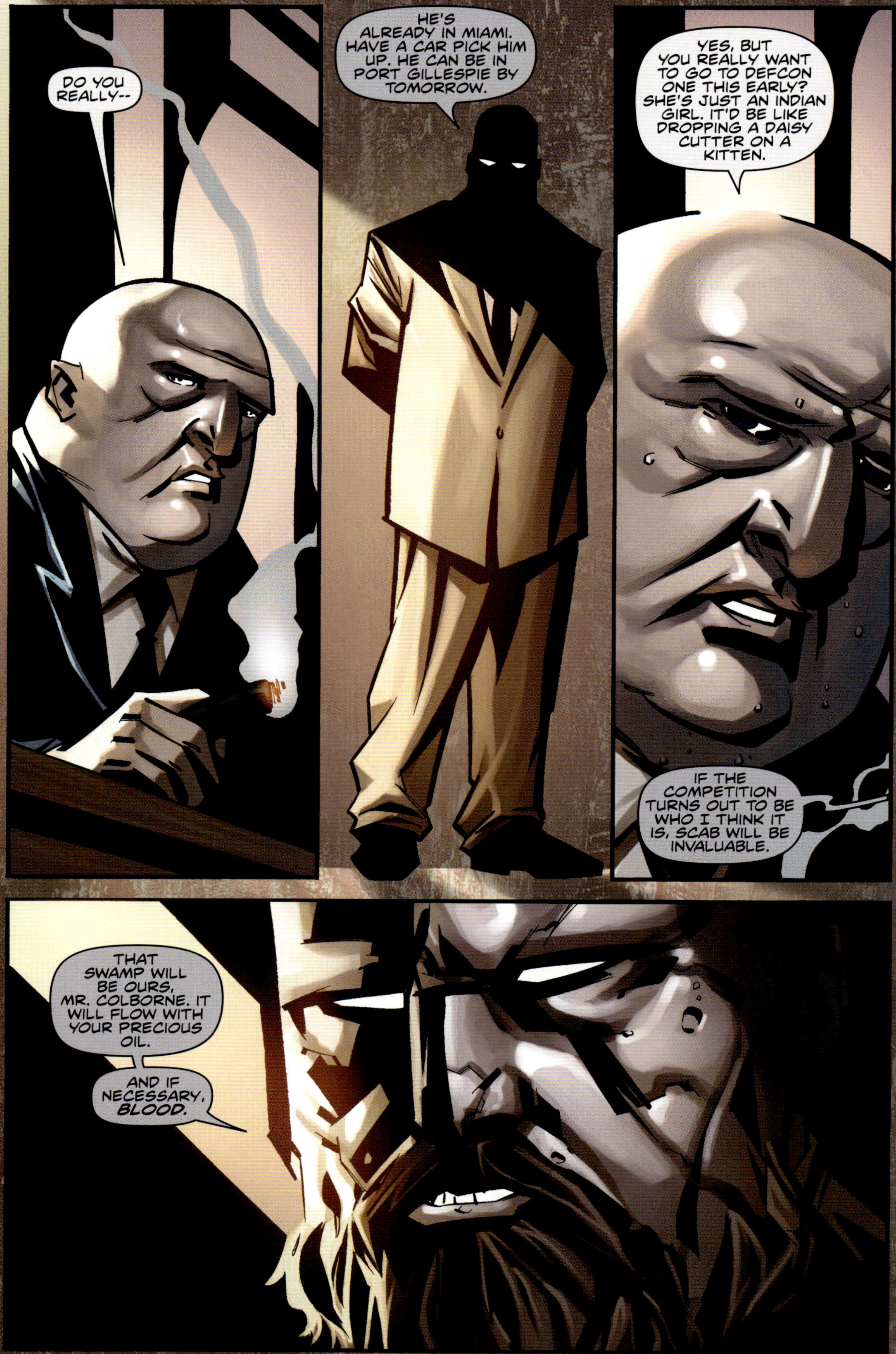
DO YOU REALLY--
HE'S ALREADY IN MIAMI. HAVE A CAR PICK HIM UP. HE CAN BE IN PORT GILLESPIE BY TOMORROW.
YES, BUT YOU REALLY WANT TO GO TO DEFCON ONE THIS EARLY? SHE'S JUST AN INDIAN GIRL. IT'D BE LIKE DROPPING A DAISY CUTTER ON A KITTEN.
IF THE COMPETITION TURNS OUT TO BE WHO I THINK IT IS, SCAB WILL BE INVALUABLE.
THAT SWAMP WILL BE OURS, MR. COLBORNE. IT WILL FLOW WITH YOUR PRECIOUS OIL.
AND IF NECESSARY, BLOOD.

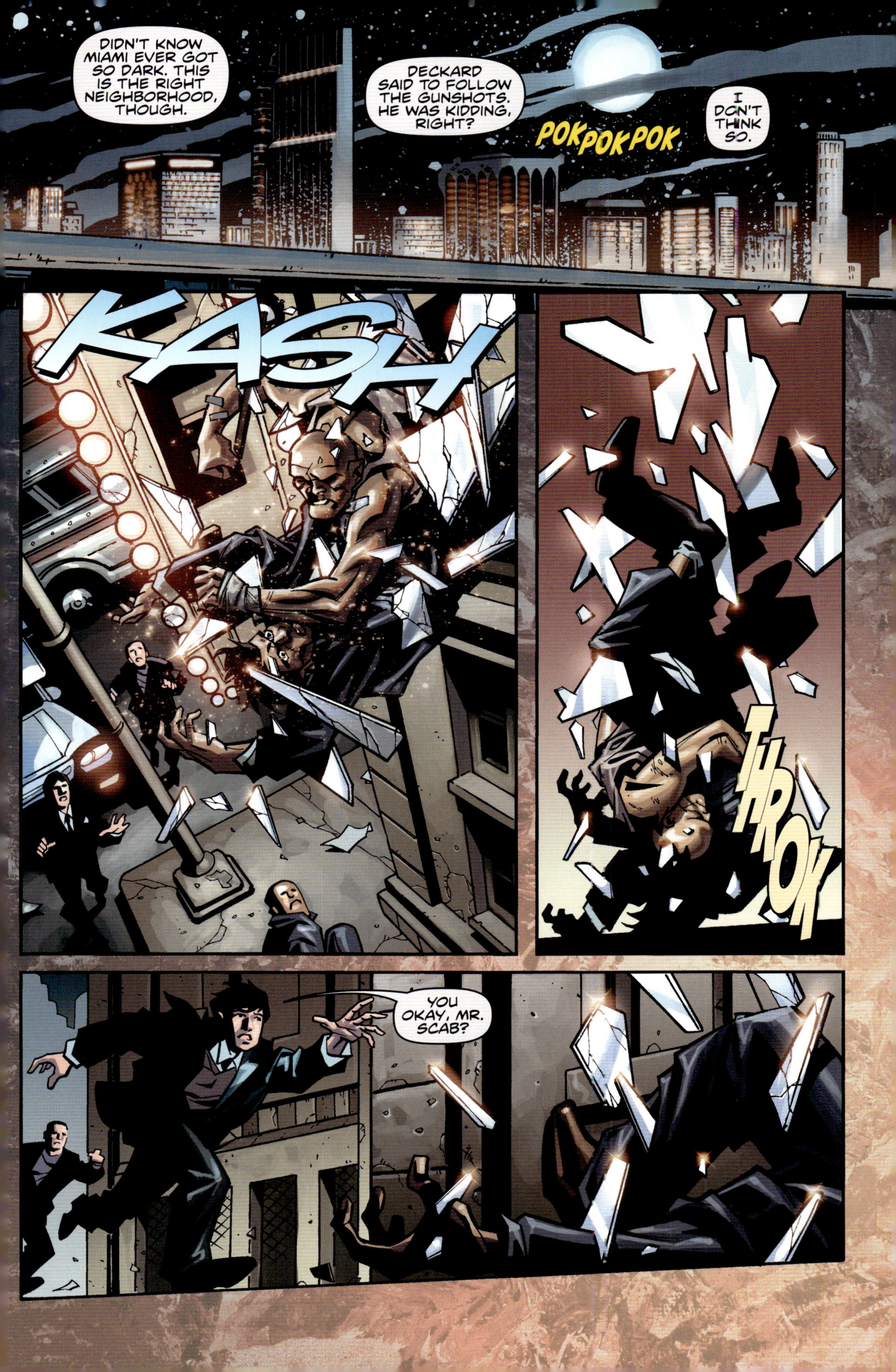
DIDN'T KNOW MIAMI EVER GOT SO DARK. THIS IS THE RIGHT NEIGHBORHOOD, THOUGH.
DECKARD SAID TO FOLLOW THE GUNSHOTS. HE WAS KIDDING, RIGHT?
POKPOKPOK
I DON'T THINK SO.
KASH
THROK
YOU OKAY, MR. SCAB?

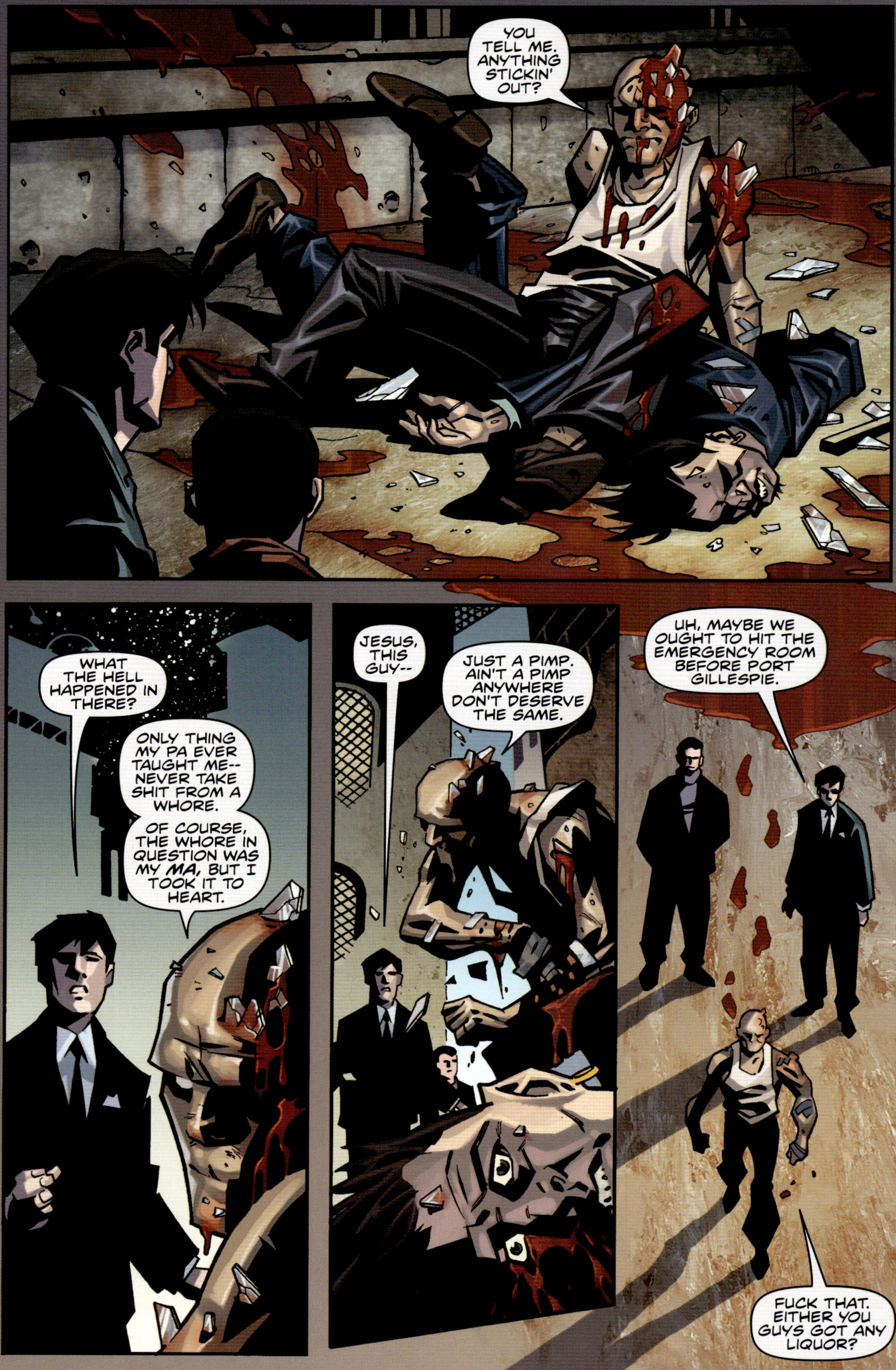
YOU TELL ME. ANYTHING STICKIN' OUT?
WHAT THE HELL HAPPENED IN THERE?
ONLY THING MY PA EVER TAUGHT ME--NEVER TAKE SHIT FROM A WHORE.
OF COURSE, THE WHORE IN QUESTION WAS MY *MA*, BUT I TOOK IT TO HEART.
JESUS, THIS GUY--
JUST A PIMP. AIN'T A PIMP ANYWHERE DON'T DESERVE THE SAME.
UH, MAYBE WE OUGHT TO HIT THE EMERGENCY ROOM BEFORE PORT GILLESPIE.
FUCK THAT. EITHER YOU GUYS GOT ANY LIQUOR?

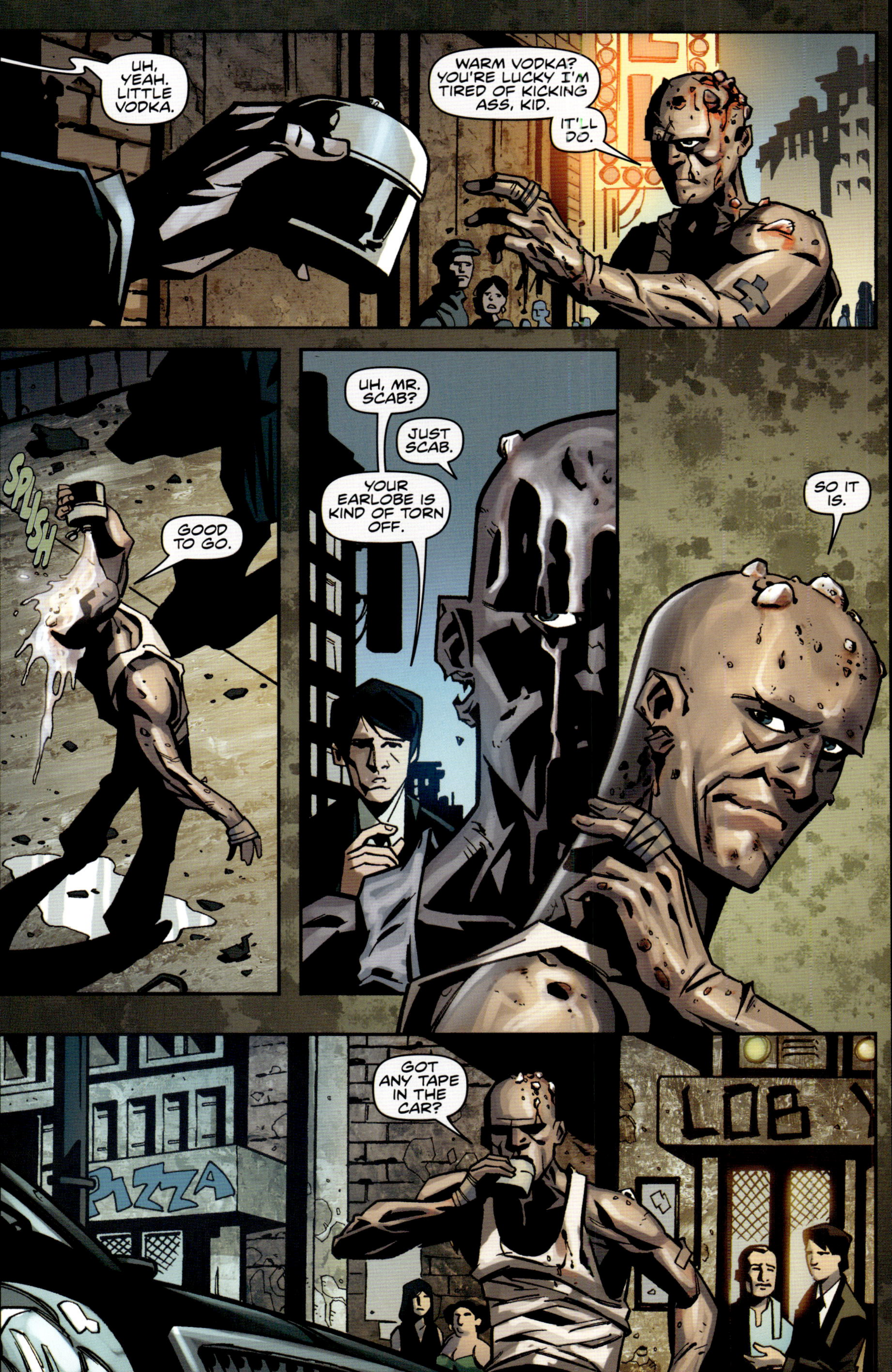
UH, YEAH. LITTLE VODKA.
WARM VODKA? YOU'RE LUCKY I'M TIRED OF KICKING ASS, KID.
IT'LL DO.
SPLISH
GOOD TO GO.
UH, MR. SCAB?
JUST SCAB.
YOUR EARLOBE IS KIND OF TORN OFF.
SO IT IS.
PIZZA
GOT ANY TAPE IN THE CAR?
LOB

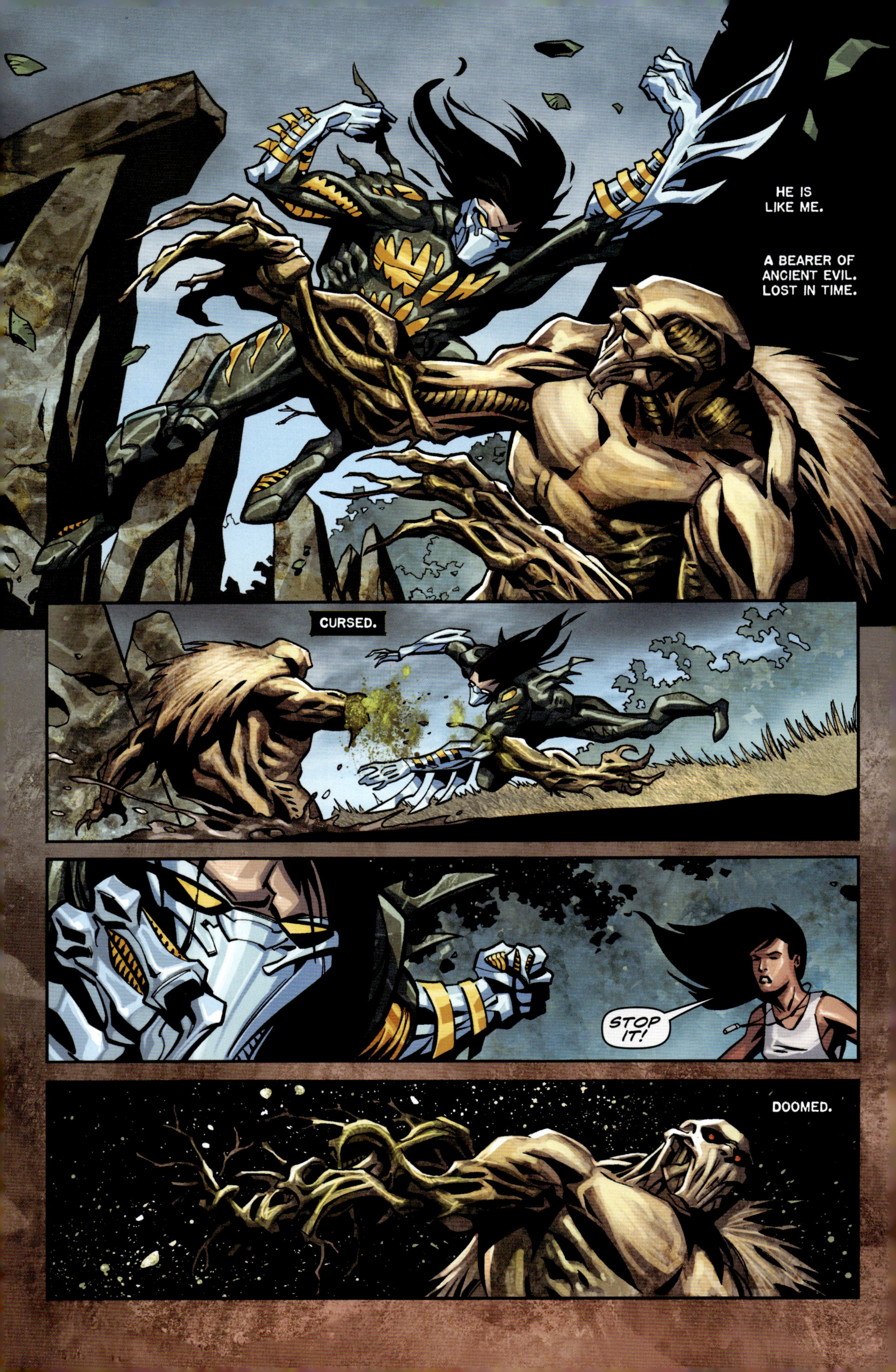
HE IS LIKE ME.
A BEARER OF ANCIENT EVIL. LOST IN TIME.
CURSED.
STOP IT!
DOOMED.

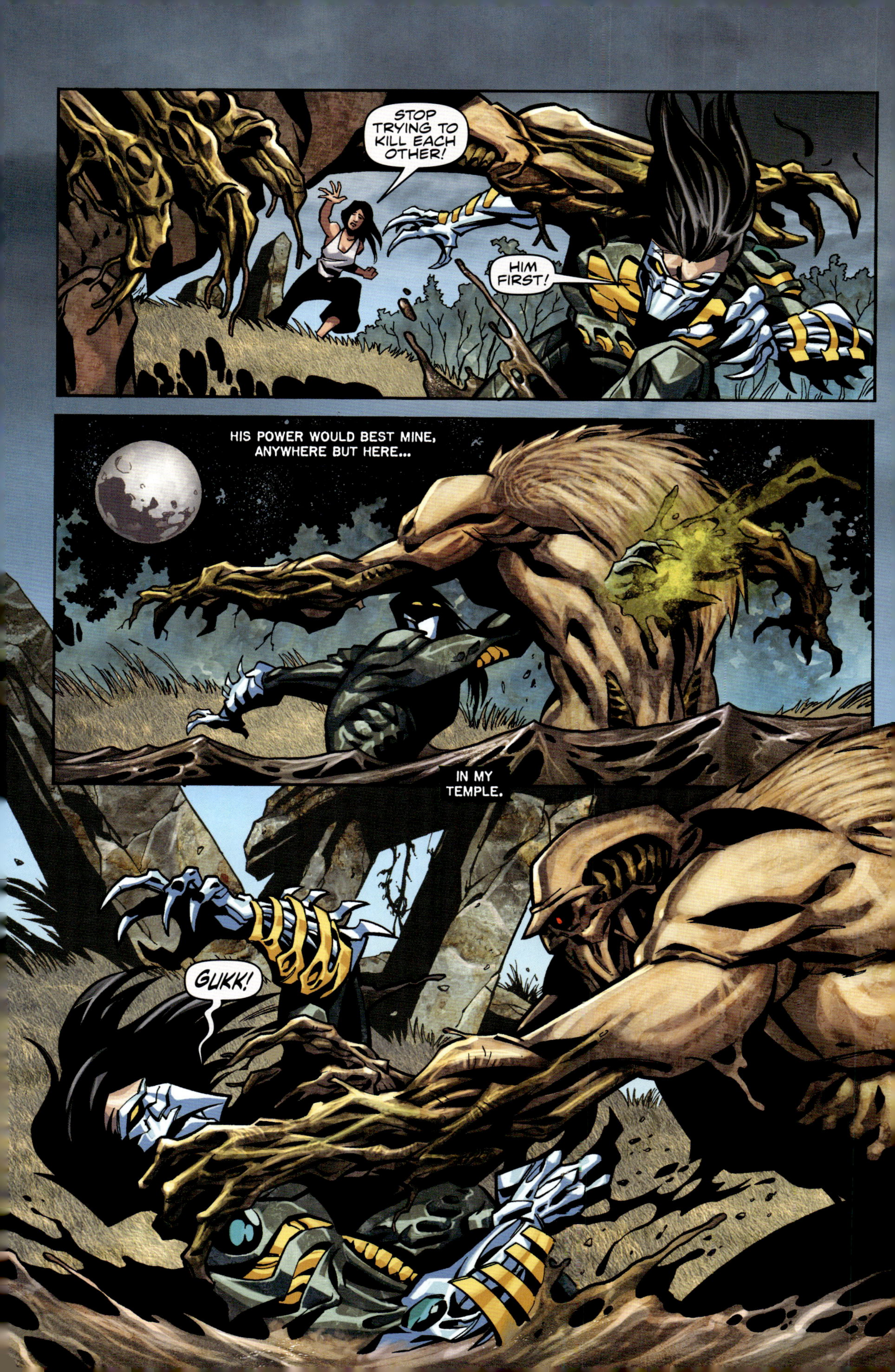
STOP TRYING TO KILL EACH OTHER!
HIM FIRST!
HIS POWER WOULD BEST MINE, ANYWHERE BUT HERE...
IN MY TEMPLE.
GUKK!

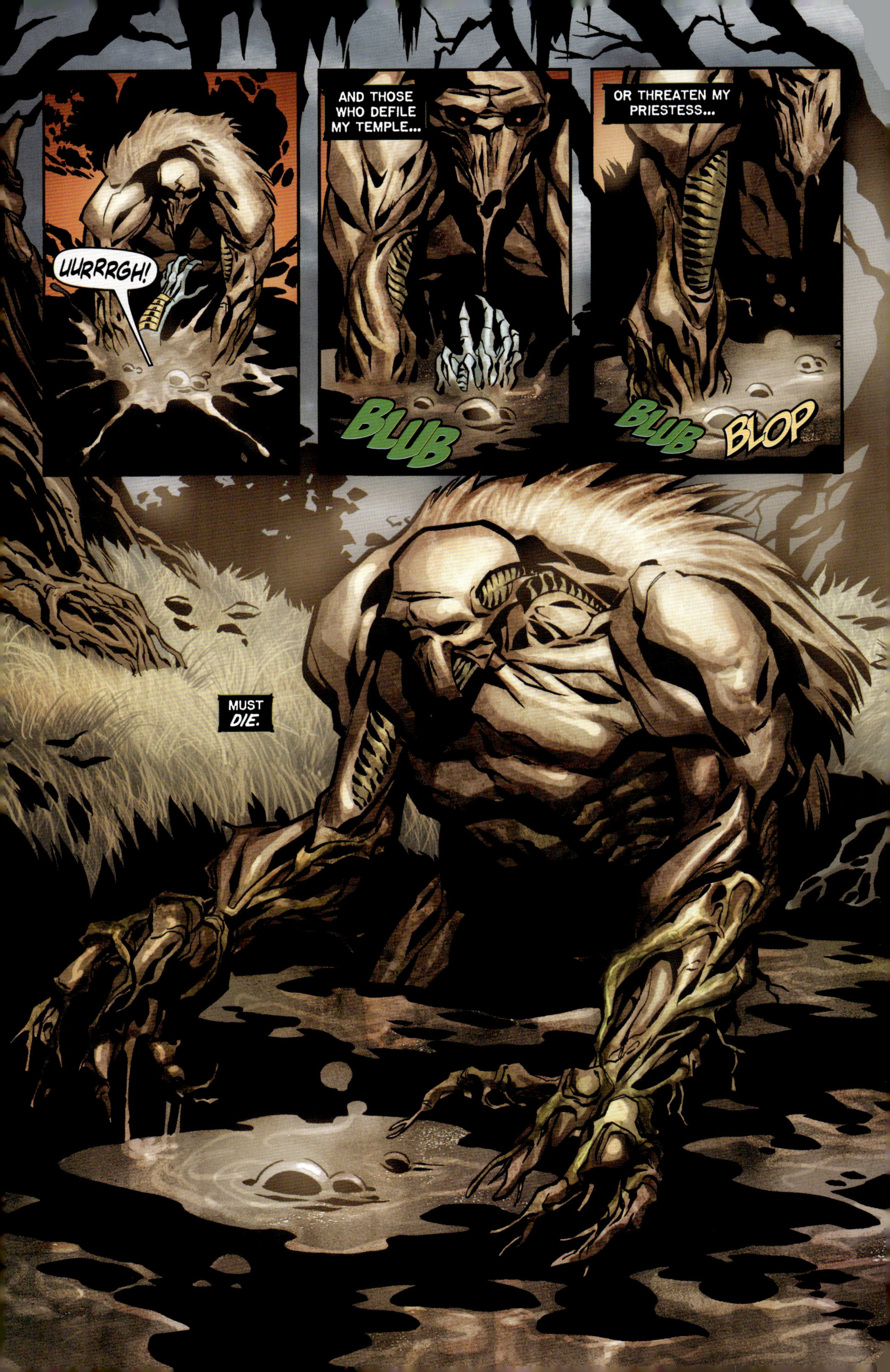
UURRRGH!
AND THOSE WHO DEFILE MY TEMPLE...
BLUB
OR THREATEN MY PRIESTESS...
BLUB
BLOP
MUST DIE.

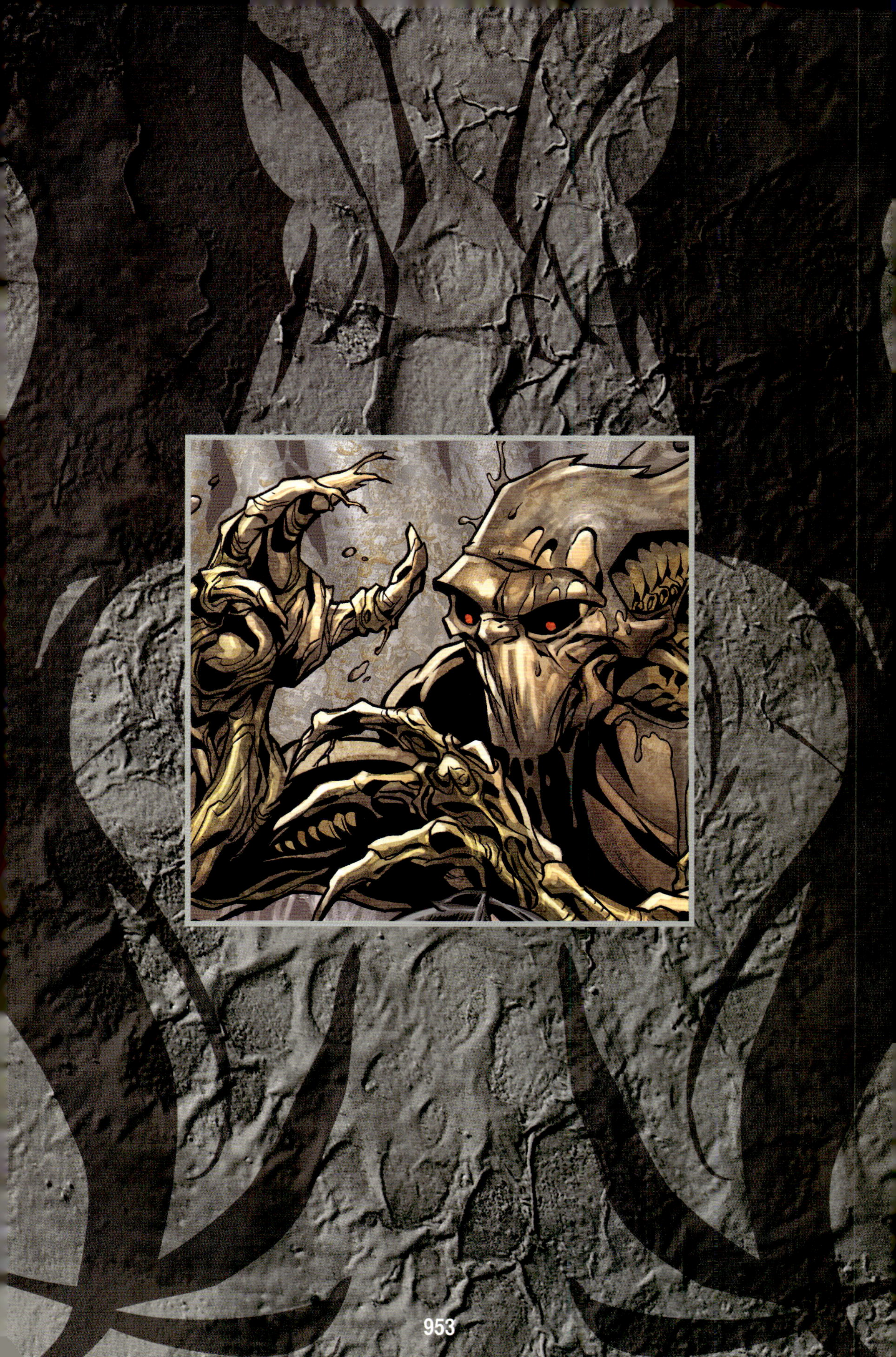

THE DARKNESS #81

The Darkness Issue #81
cover art by: Michael Broussard, Eric Basaldua
and Arif Prianto of IFS

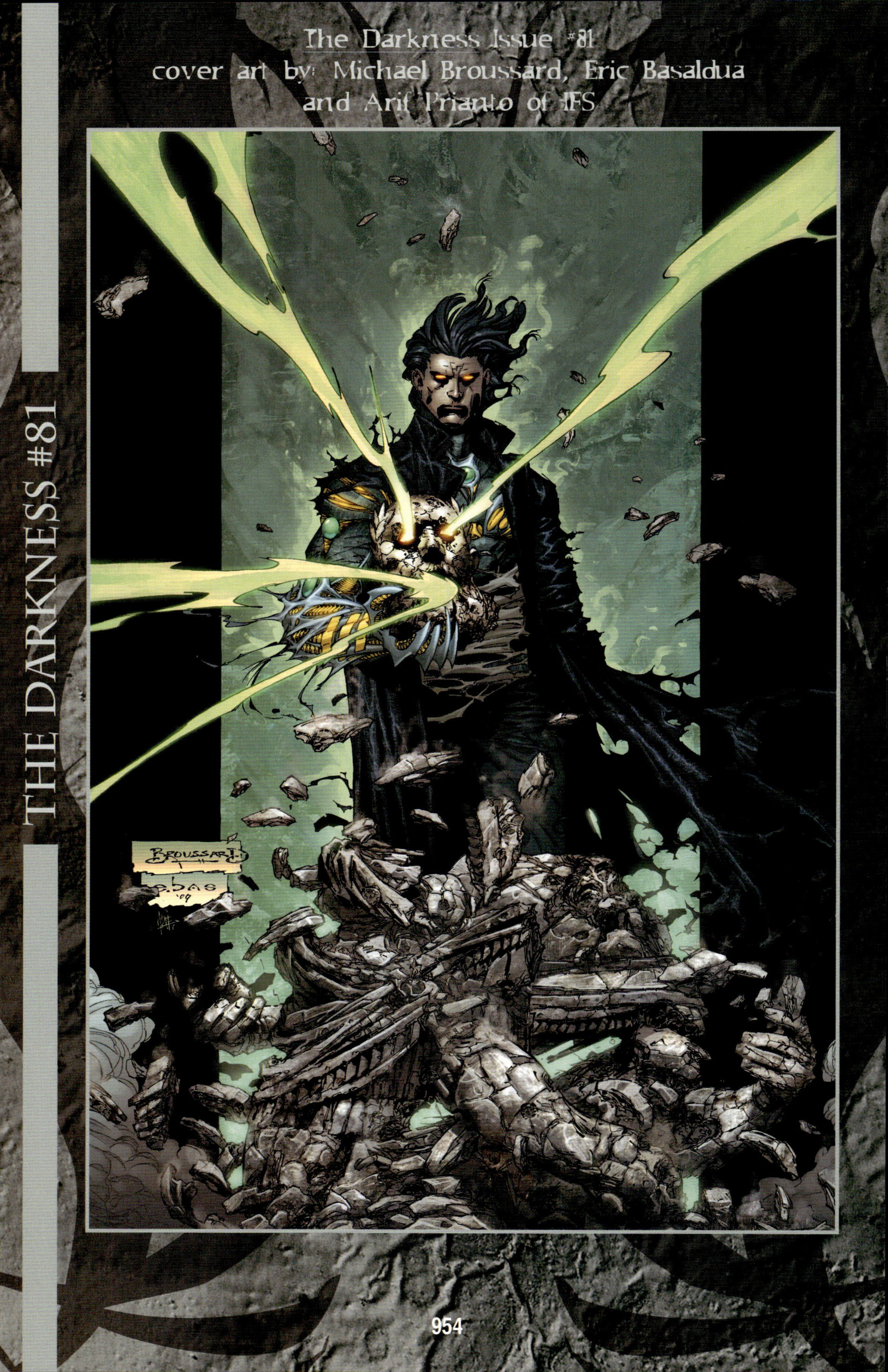
BROUSSARD

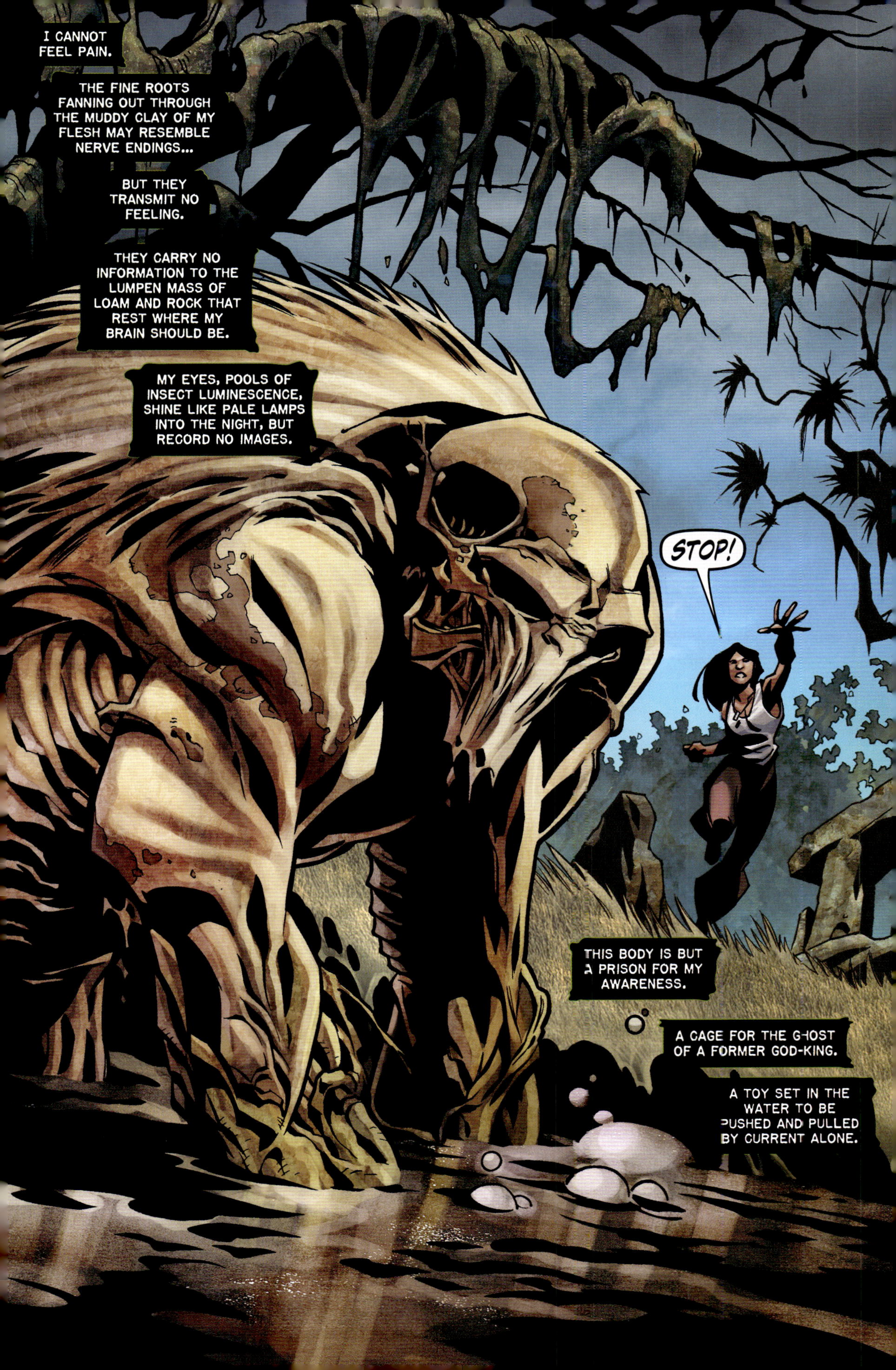
I CANNOT FEEL PAIN.
THE FINE ROOTS FANNING OUT THROUGH THE MUDDY CLAY OF MY FLESH MAY RESEMBLE NERVE ENDINGS...
BUT THEY TRANSMIT NO FEELING.
THEY CARRY NO INFORMATION TO THE LUMPEN MASS OF LOAM AND ROCK THAT REST WHERE MY BRAIN SHOULD BE.
MY EYES, POOLS OF INSECT LUMINESCENCE, SHINE LIKE PALE LAMPS INTO THE NIGHT, BUT RECORD NO IMAGES.
STOP!
THIS BODY IS BUT A PRISON FOR MY AWARENESS.
A CAGE FOR THE GHOST OF A FORMER GOD-KING.
A TOY SET IN THE WATER TO BE PUSHED AND PULLED BY CURRENT ALONE.

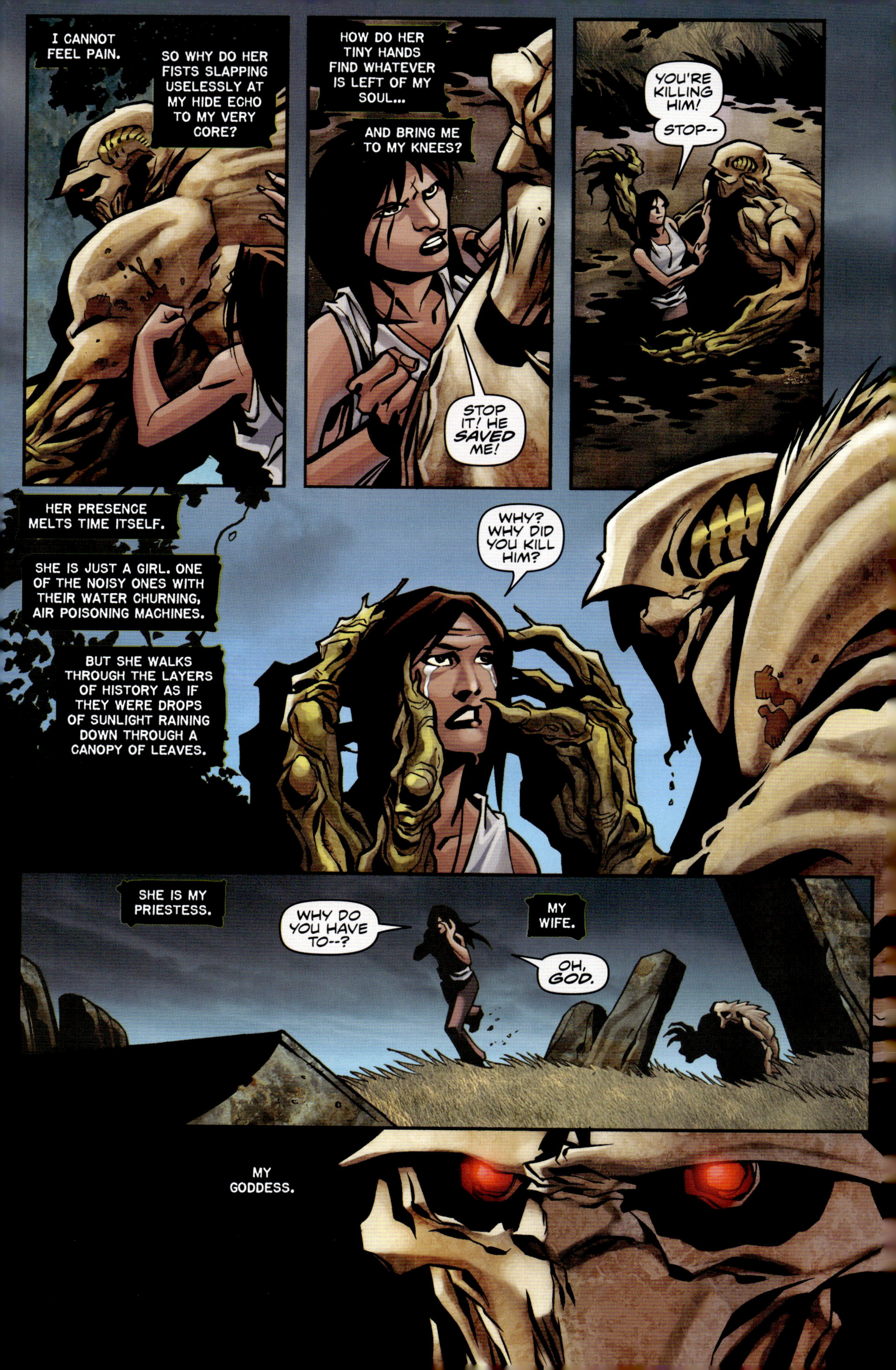
I CANNOT FEEL PAIN.
SO WHY DO HER FISTS SLAPPING USELESSLY AT MY HIDE ECHO TO MY VERY CORE?
HOW DO HER TINY HANDS FIND WHATEVER IS LEFT OF MY SOUL...
AND BRING ME TO MY KNEES?
STOP IT! HE SAVED ME!
YOU'RE KILLING HIM!
STOP--
HER PRESENCE MELTS TIME ITSELF.
WHY? WHY DID YOU KILL HIM?
SHE IS JUST A GIRL. ONE OF THE NOISY ONES WITH THEIR WATER CHURNING, AIR POISONING MACHINES.
BUT SHE WALKS THROUGH THE LAYERS OF HISTORY AS IF THEY WERE DROPS OF SUNLIGHT RAINING DOWN THROUGH A CANOPY OF LEAVES.
SHE IS MY PRIESTESS.
WHY DO YOU HAVE TO--?
MY WIFE.
OH, GOD.
MY GODDESS.

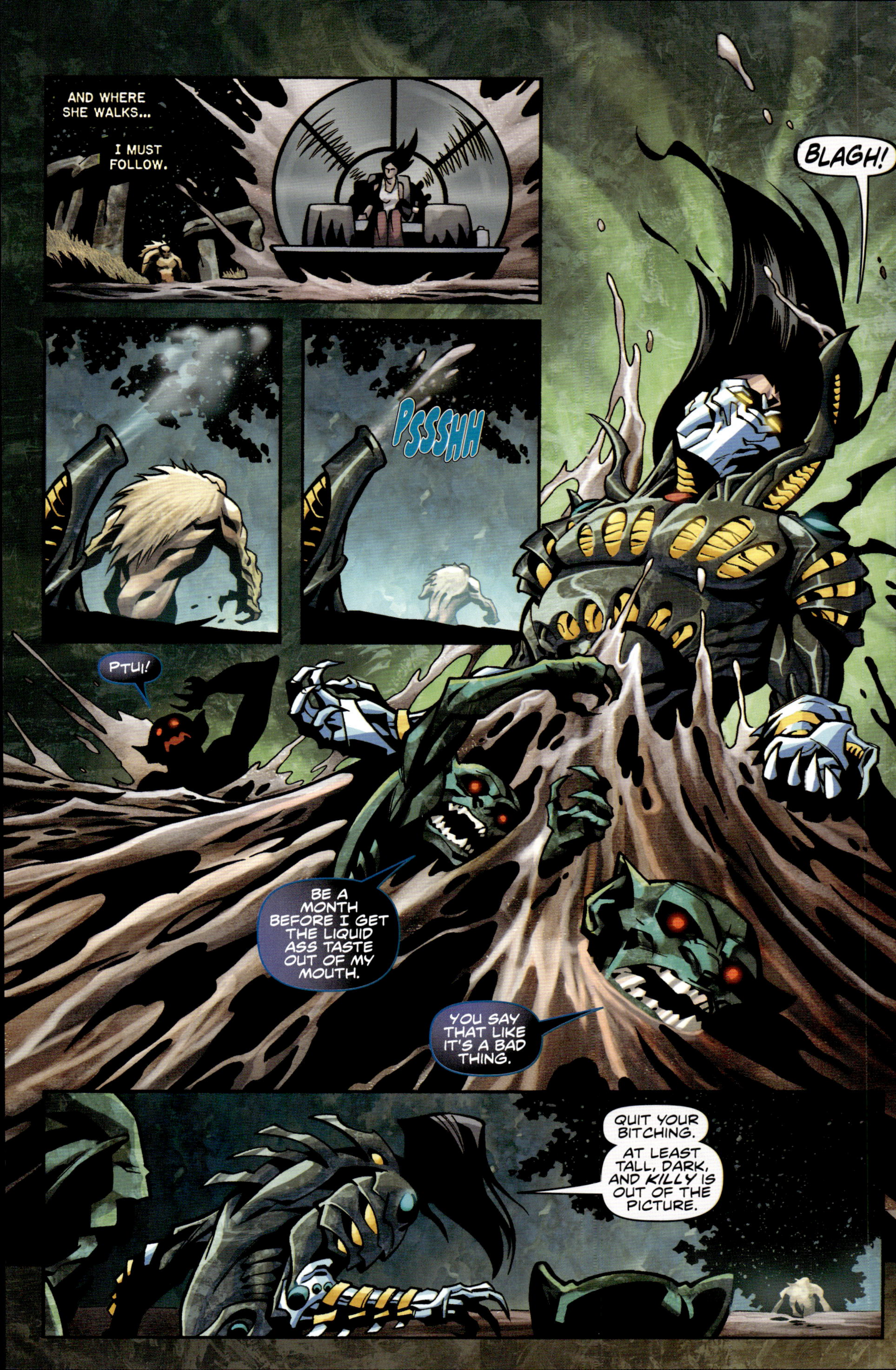
AND WHERE SHE WALKS...
I MUST FOLLOW.
BLAGH!
PSSSHH
PTUI!
BE A MONTH BEFORE I GET THE LIQUID ASS TASTE OUT OF MY MOUTH.
YOU SAY THAT LIKE IT'S A BAD THING.
QUIT YOUR BITCHING.
AT LEAST TALL, DARK, AND KILLY IS OUT OF THE PICTURE.

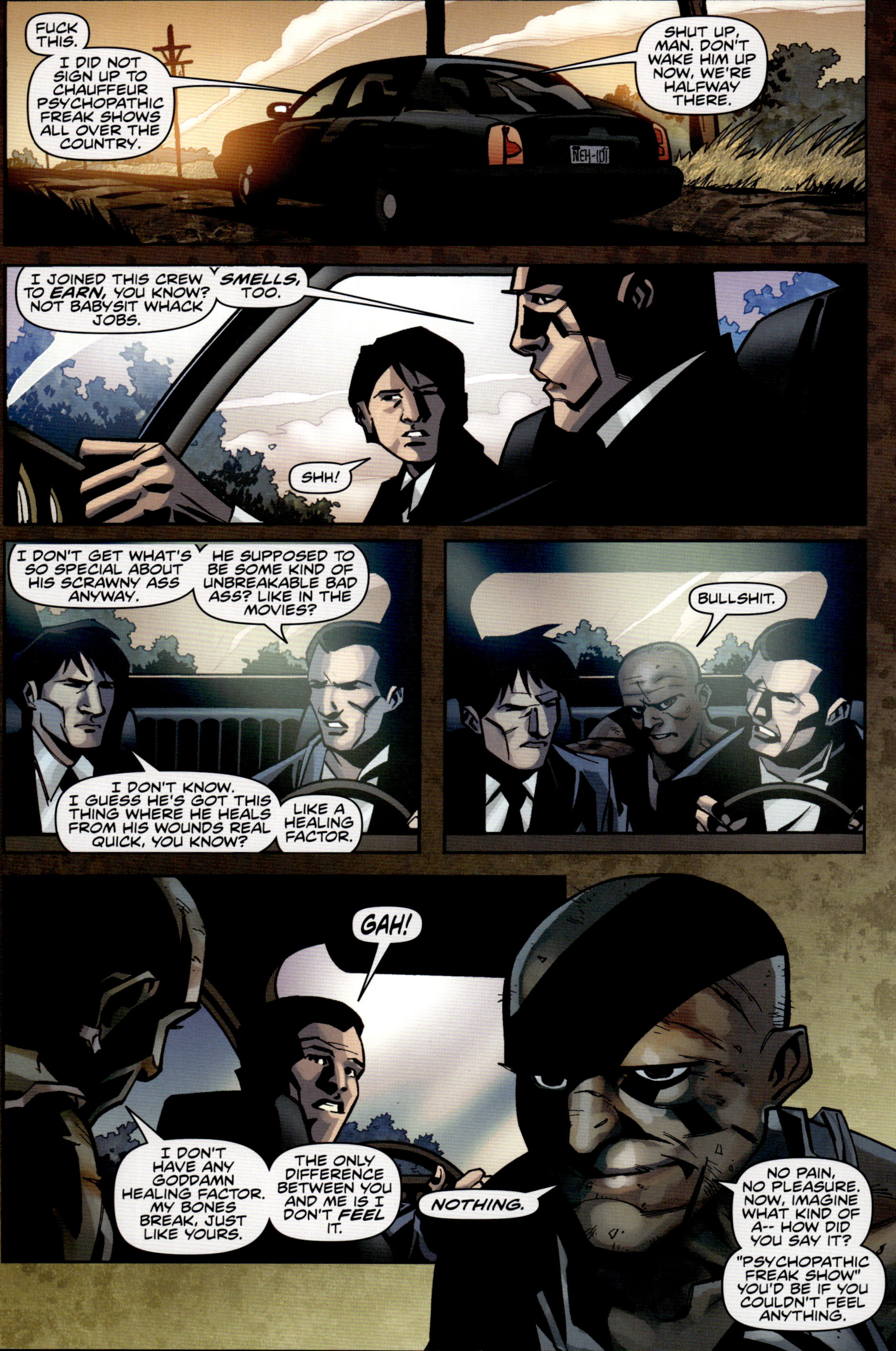
FUCK THIS.
I DID NOT SIGN UP TO CHAUFFEUR PSYCHOPATHIC FREAK SHOWS ALL OVER THE COUNTRY.
SHUT UP, MAN. DON'T WAKE HIM UP NOW, WE'RE HALFWAY THERE.
NEH-101
I JOINED THIS CREW TO EARN, YOU KNOW? NOT BABYSIT WHACK JOBS.
SMELLS, TOO.
SHH!
I DON'T GET WHAT'S SO SPECIAL ABOUT HIS SCRAWNY ASS ANYWAY.
HE SUPPOSED TO BE SOME KIND OF UNBREAKABLE BAD ASS? LIKE IN THE MOVIES?
I DON'T KNOW. I GUESS HE'S GOT THIS THING WHERE HE HEALS FROM HIS WOUNDS REAL QUICK, YOU KNOW?
LIKE A HEALING FACTOR.
BULLSHIT.
GAH!
I DON'T HAVE ANY GODDAMN HEALING FACTOR. MY BONES BREAK, JUST LIKE YOURS.
THE ONLY DIFFERENCE BETWEEN YOU AND ME IS I DON'T FEEL IT.
NOTHING.
NO PAIN, NO PLEASURE. NOW, IMAGINE WHAT KIND OF A-- HOW DID YOU SAY IT?
"PSYCHOPATHIC FREAK SHOW" YOU'D BE IF YOU COULDN'T FEEL ANYTHING.

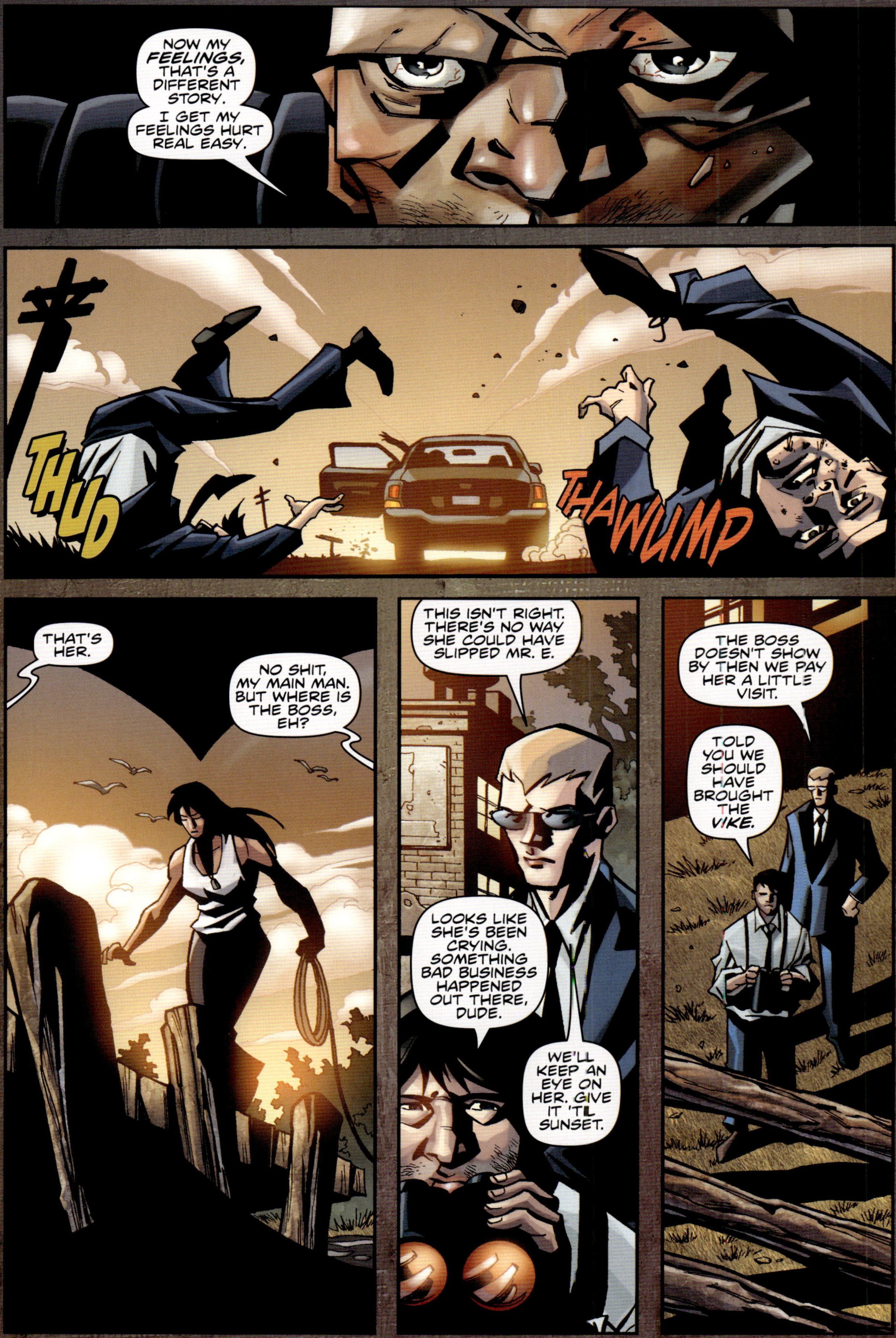
NOW MY FEELINGS, THAT'S A DIFFERENT STORY.
I GET MY FEELINGS HURT REAL EASY.
THUD
THAWUMP
THAT'S HER.
NO SHIT, MY MAIN MAN. BUT WHERE IS THE BOSS, EH?
THIS ISN'T RIGHT. THERE'S NO WAY SHE COULD HAVE SLIPPED MR. E.
LOOKS LIKE SHE'S BEEN CRYING. SOMETHING BAD BUSINESS HAPPENED OUT THERE, DUDE.
WE'LL KEEP AN EYE ON HER. GIVE IT 'TIL SUNSET.
THE BOSS DOESN'T SHOW BY THEN WE PAY HER A LITTLE VISIT.
TOLD YOU WE SHOULD HAVE BROUGHT THE VIKE.

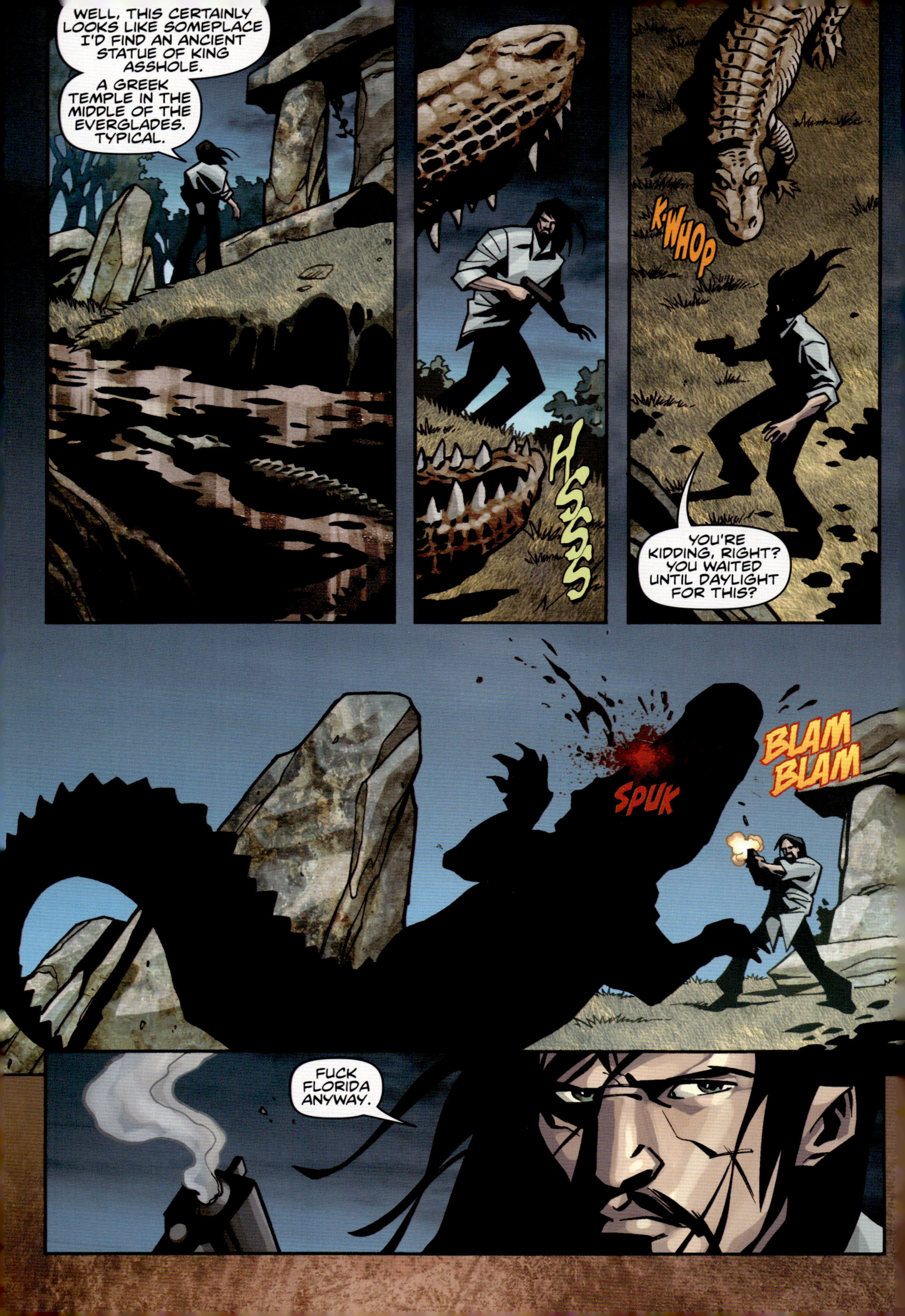
WELL, THIS CERTAINLY LOOKS LIKE SOMEPLACE I'D FIND AN ANCIENT STATUE OF KING ASSHOLE.
A GREEK TEMPLE IN THE MIDDLE OF THE EVERGLADES. TYPICAL.
HSSSS
K-WHOP
YOU'RE KIDDING, RIGHT? YOU WAITED UNTIL DAYLIGHT FOR THIS?
SPUK
BLAM BLAM
FUCK FLORIDA ANYWAY.

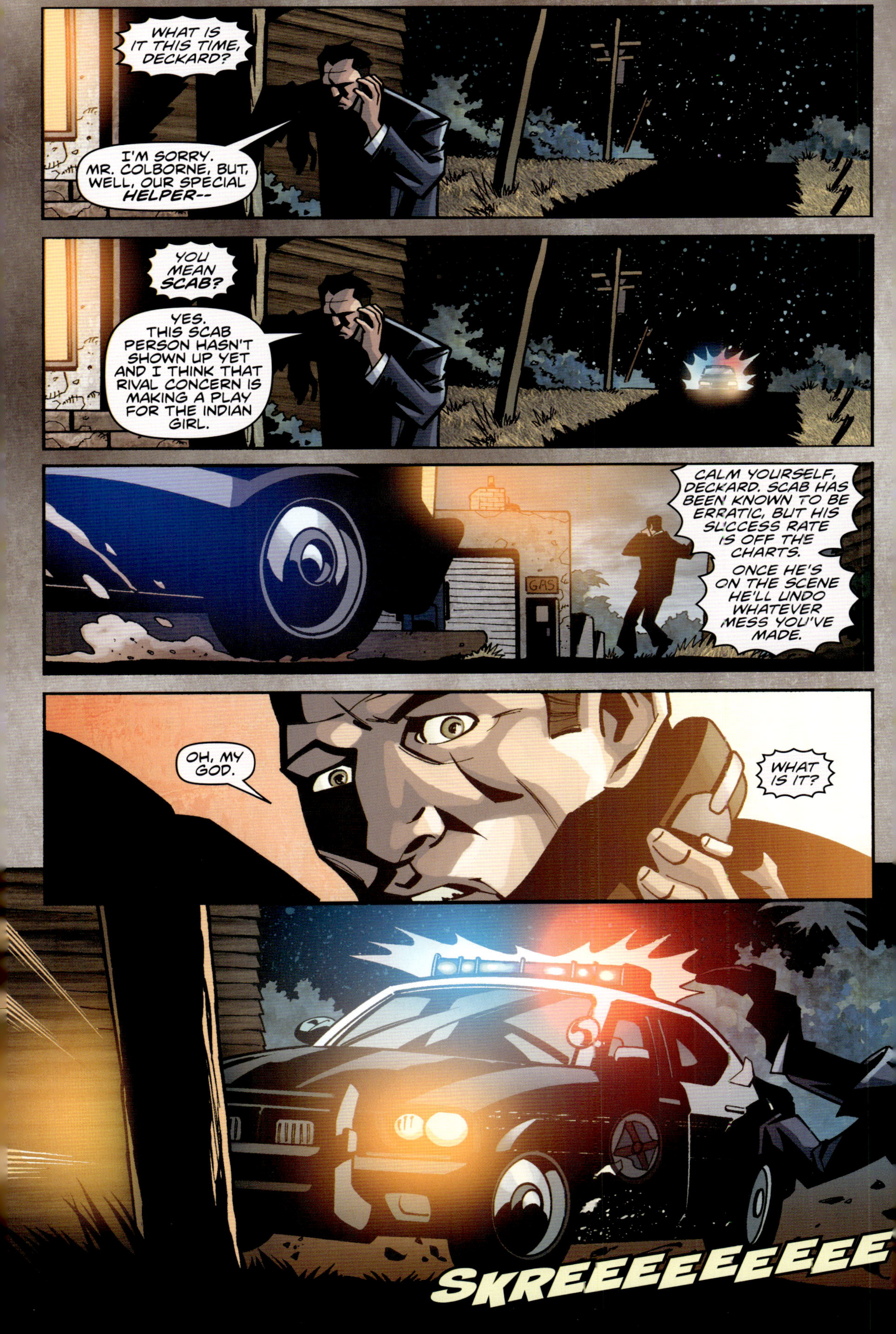
WHAT IS IT THIS TIME, DECKARD?
I'M SORRY. MR. COLBORNE, BUT, WELL, OUR SPECIAL HELPER--
YOU MEAN SCAB?
YES. THIS SCAB PERSON HASN'T SHOWN UP YET AND I THINK THAT RIVAL CONCERN IS MAKING A PLAY FOR THE INDIAN GIRL.
CALM YOURSELF, DECKARD. SCAB HAS BEEN KNOWN TO BE ERRATIC, BUT HIS SUCCESS RATE IS OFF THE CHARTS.
ONCE HE'S ON THE SCENE HE'LL UNDO WHATEVER MESS YOU'VE MADE.
GAS
OH, MY GOD.
WHAT IS IT?
SKREEEEEEEEEE

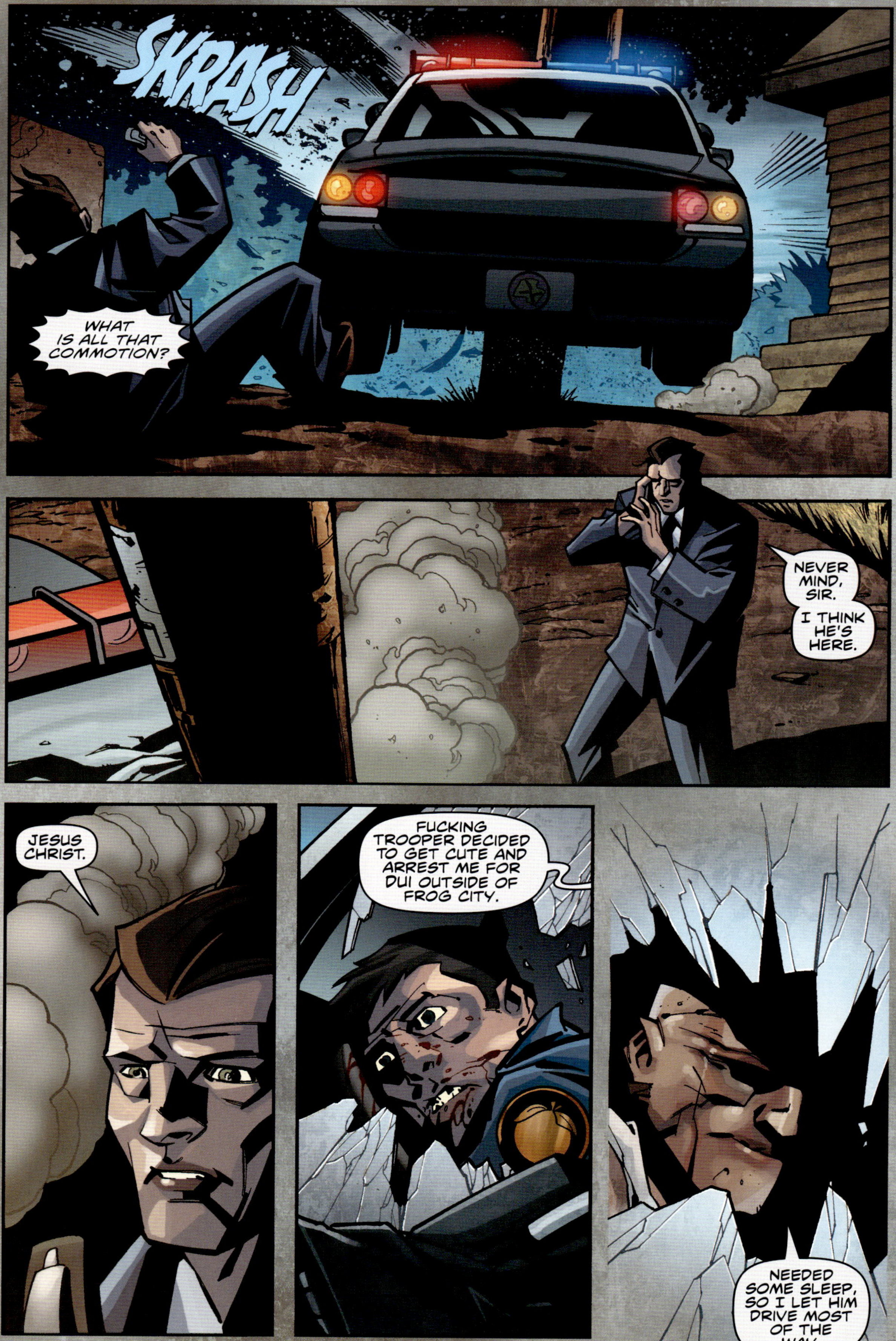
SKRASH
WHAT IS ALL THAT COMMOTION?
NEVER MIND, SIR.
I THINK HE'S HERE.
JESUS CHRIST.
FUCKING TROOPER DECIDED TO GET CUTE AND ARREST ME FOR DUI OUTSIDE OF FROG CITY.
NEEDED SOME SLEEP, SO I LET HIM DRIVE MOST OF THE WAY.

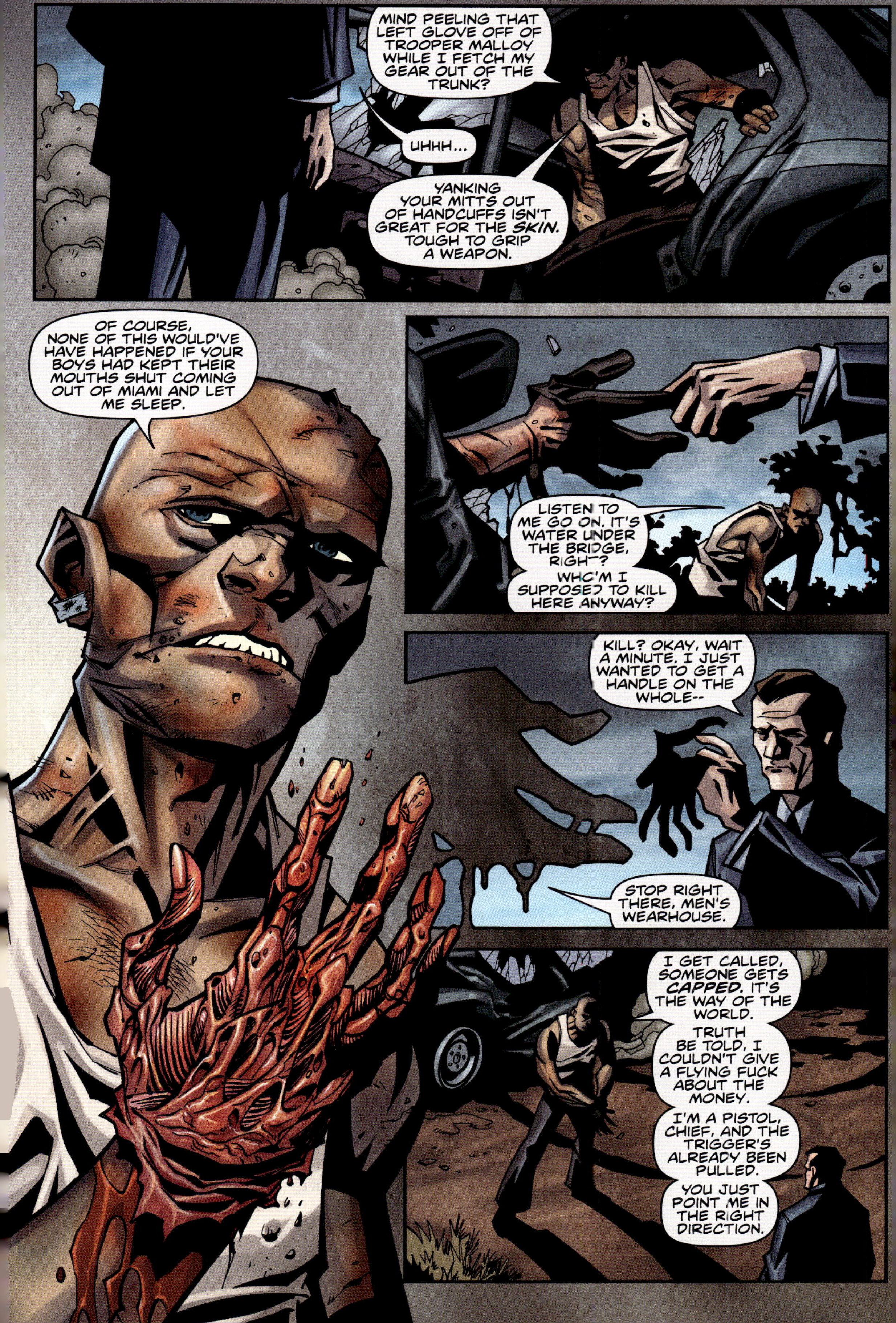
MIND PEELING THAT LEFT GLOVE OFF OF TROOPER MALLOY WHILE I FETCH MY GEAR OUT OF THE TRUNK?
UHHH...
YANKING YOUR MITTS OUT OF HANDCUFFS ISN'T GREAT FOR THE SKIN. TOUGH TO GRIP A WEAPON.
OF COURSE, NONE OF THIS WOULD'VE HAVE HAPPENED IF YOUR BOYS HAD KEPT THEIR MOUTHS SHUT COMING OUT OF MIAMI AND LET ME SLEEP.
LISTEN TO ME GO ON. IT'S WATER UNDER THE BRIDGE, RIGHT?
WHO'M I SUPPOSED TO KILL HERE ANYWAY?
KILL? OKAY, WAIT A MINUTE. I JUST WANTED TO GET A HANDLE ON THE WHOLE--
STOP RIGHT THERE, MEN'S WEARHOUSE.
I GET CALLED, SOMEONE GETS CAPPED. IT'S THE WAY OF THE WORLD.
TRUTH BE TOLD, I COULDN'T GIVE A FLYING FUCK ABOUT THE MONEY.
I'M A PISTOL, CHIEF, AND THE TRIGGER'S ALREADY BEEN PULLED.
YOU JUST POINT ME IN THE RIGHT DIRECTION.

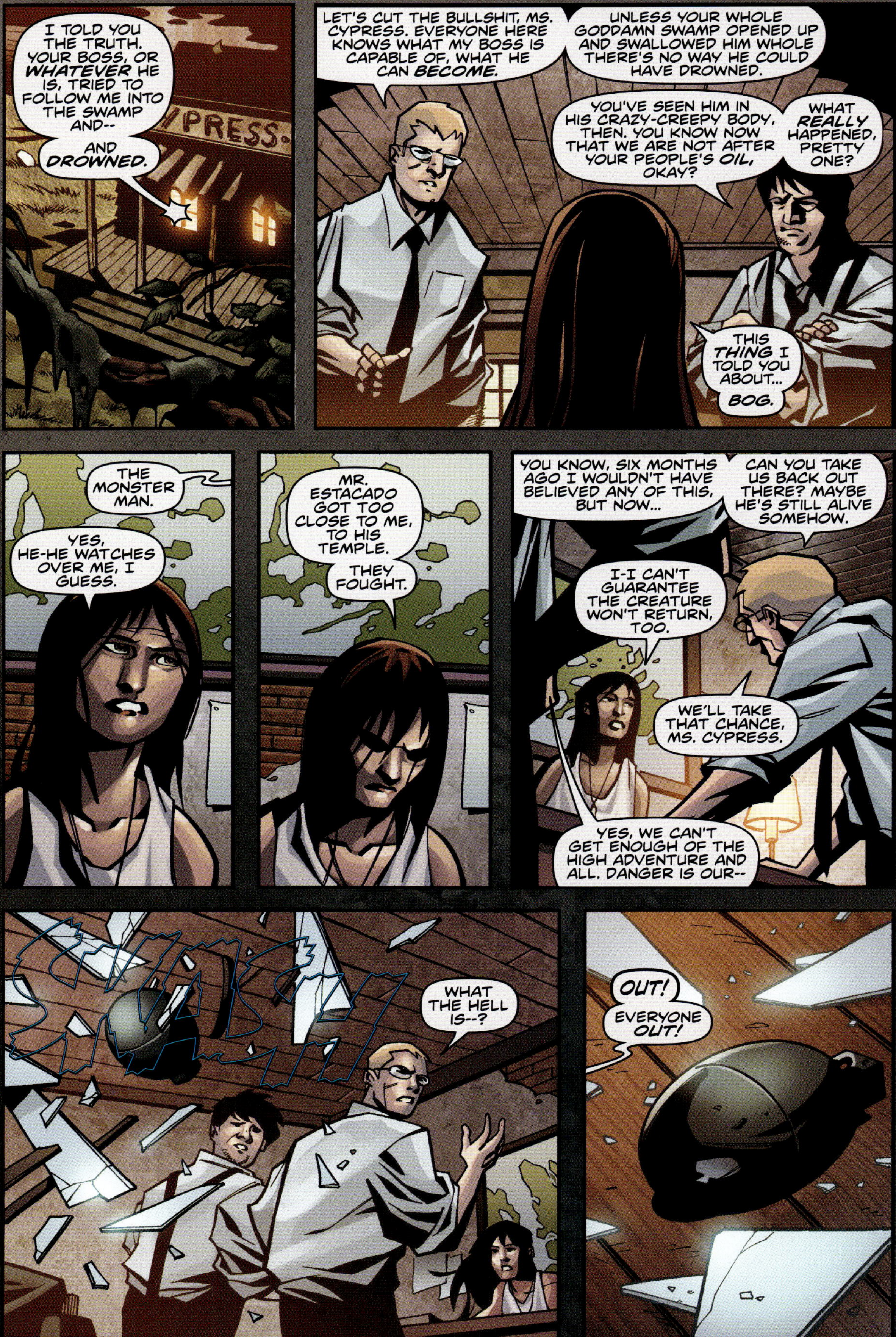
I TOLD YOU THE TRUTH. YOUR BOSS, OR WHATEVER HE IS, TRIED TO FOLLOW ME INTO THE SWAMP AND--
AND DROWNED.
PRESS
LET'S CUT THE BULLSHIT, MS. CYPRESS. EVERYONE HERE KNOWS WHAT MY BOSS IS CAPABLE OF, WHAT HE CAN BECOME.
UNLESS YOUR WHOLE GODDAMN SWAMP OPENED UP AND SWALLOWED HIM WHOLE THERE'S NO WAY HE COULD HAVE DROWNED.
YOU'VE SEEN HIM IN HIS CRAZY-CREEPY BODY, THEN. YOU KNOW NOW THAT WE ARE NOT AFTER YOUR PEOPLE'S OIL, OKAY?
WHAT REALLY HAPPENED, PRETTY ONE?
THIS THING I TOLD YOU ABOUT... BOG.
THE MONSTER MAN.
YES, HE-HE WATCHES OVER ME, I GUESS.
MR. ESTACADO GOT TOO CLOSE TO ME, TO HIS TEMPLE.
THEY FOUGHT.
YOU KNOW, SIX MONTHS AGO I WOULDN'T HAVE BELIEVED ANY OF THIS, BUT NOW...
CAN YOU TAKE US BACK OUT THERE? MAYBE HE'S STILL ALIVE SOMEHOW.
I-I CAN'T GUARANTEE THE CREATURE WON'T RETURN, TOO.
WE'LL TAKE THAT CHANCE, MS. CYPRESS.
YES, WE CAN'T GET ENOUGH OF THE HIGH ADVENTURE AND ALL. DANGER IS OUR--
WHAT THE HELL IS--?
OUT! EVERYONE OUT!

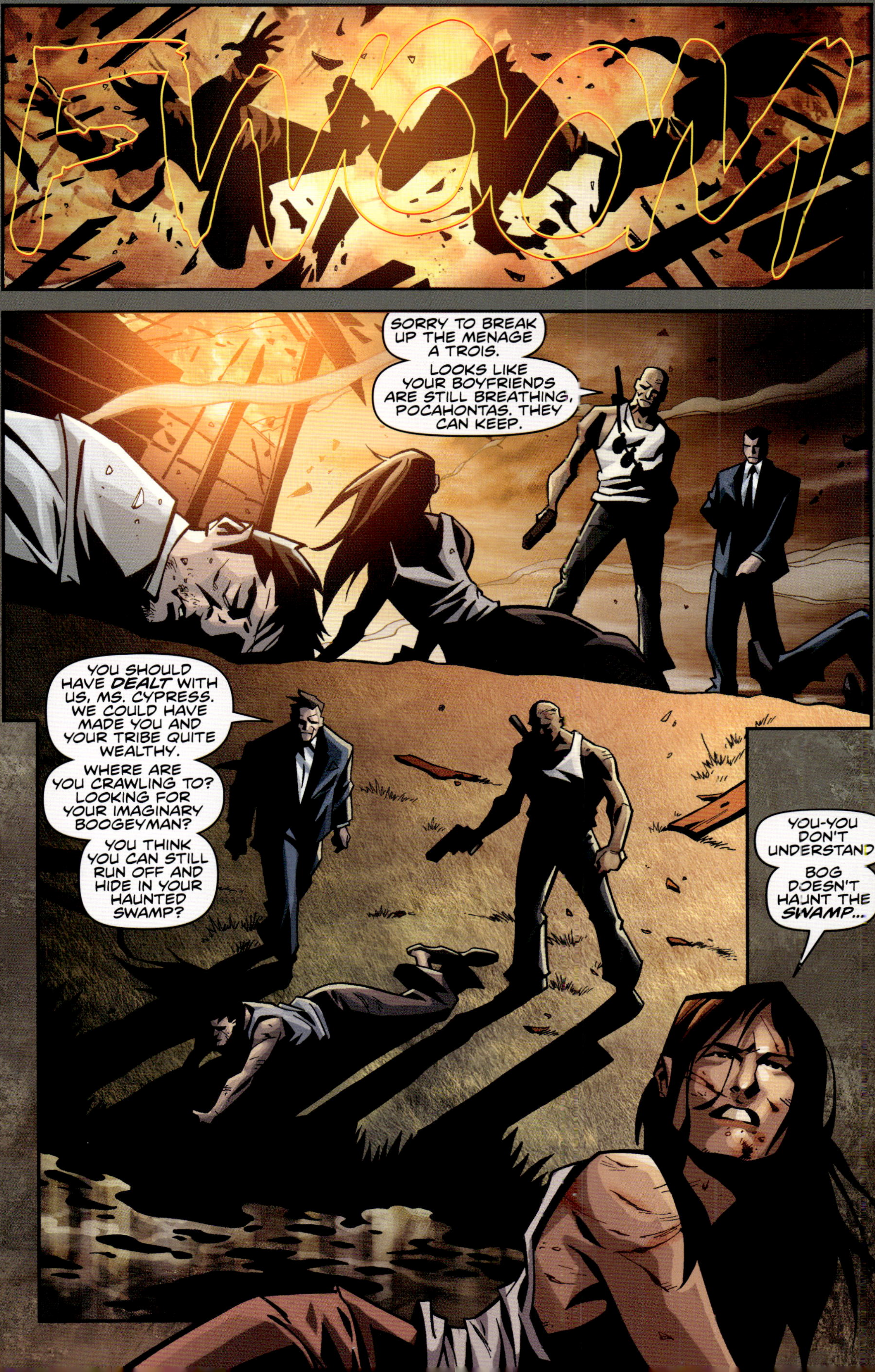
FWOOM
SORRY TO BREAK UP THE MENAGE A TROIS.
LOOKS LIKE YOUR BOYFRIENDS ARE STILL BREATHING, POCAHONTAS. THEY CAN KEEP.
YOU SHOULD HAVE DEALT WITH US, MS. CYPRESS. WE COULD HAVE MADE YOU AND YOUR TRIBE QUITE WEALTHY.
WHERE ARE YOU CRAWLING TO? LOOKING FOR YOUR IMAGINARY BOOGEYMAN?
YOU THINK YOU CAN STILL RUN OFF AND HIDE IN YOUR HAUNTED SWAMP?
YOU-YOU DON'T UNDERSTAND.
BOG DOESN'T HAUNT THE SWAMP...

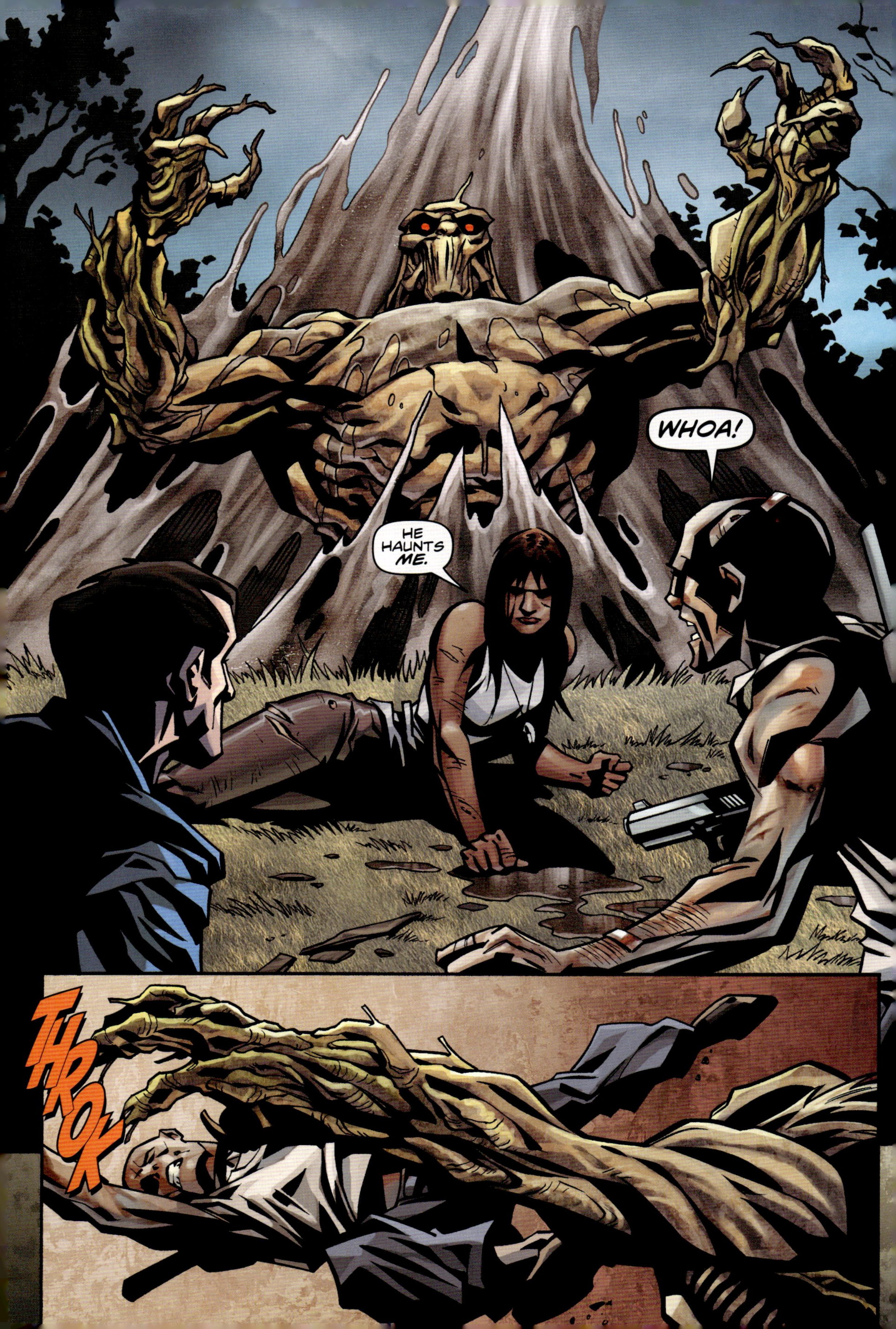
WHOA!
HE HAUNTS ME.
THROK

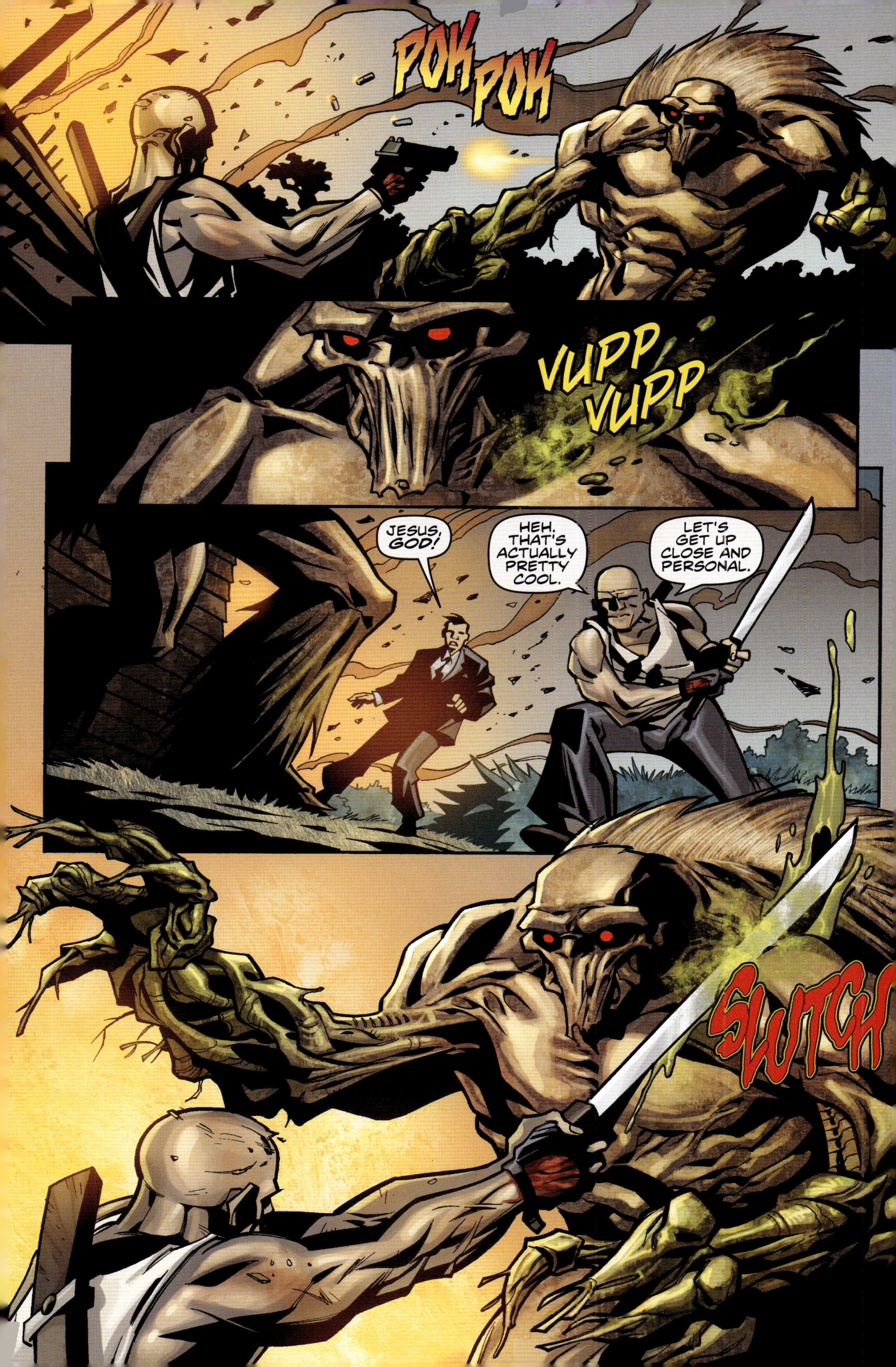
POK POK
VUPP VUPP
JESUS, GOD!
HEH. THAT'S ACTUALLY PRETTY COOL.
LET'S GET UP CLOSE AND PERSONAL.
SLUTCH

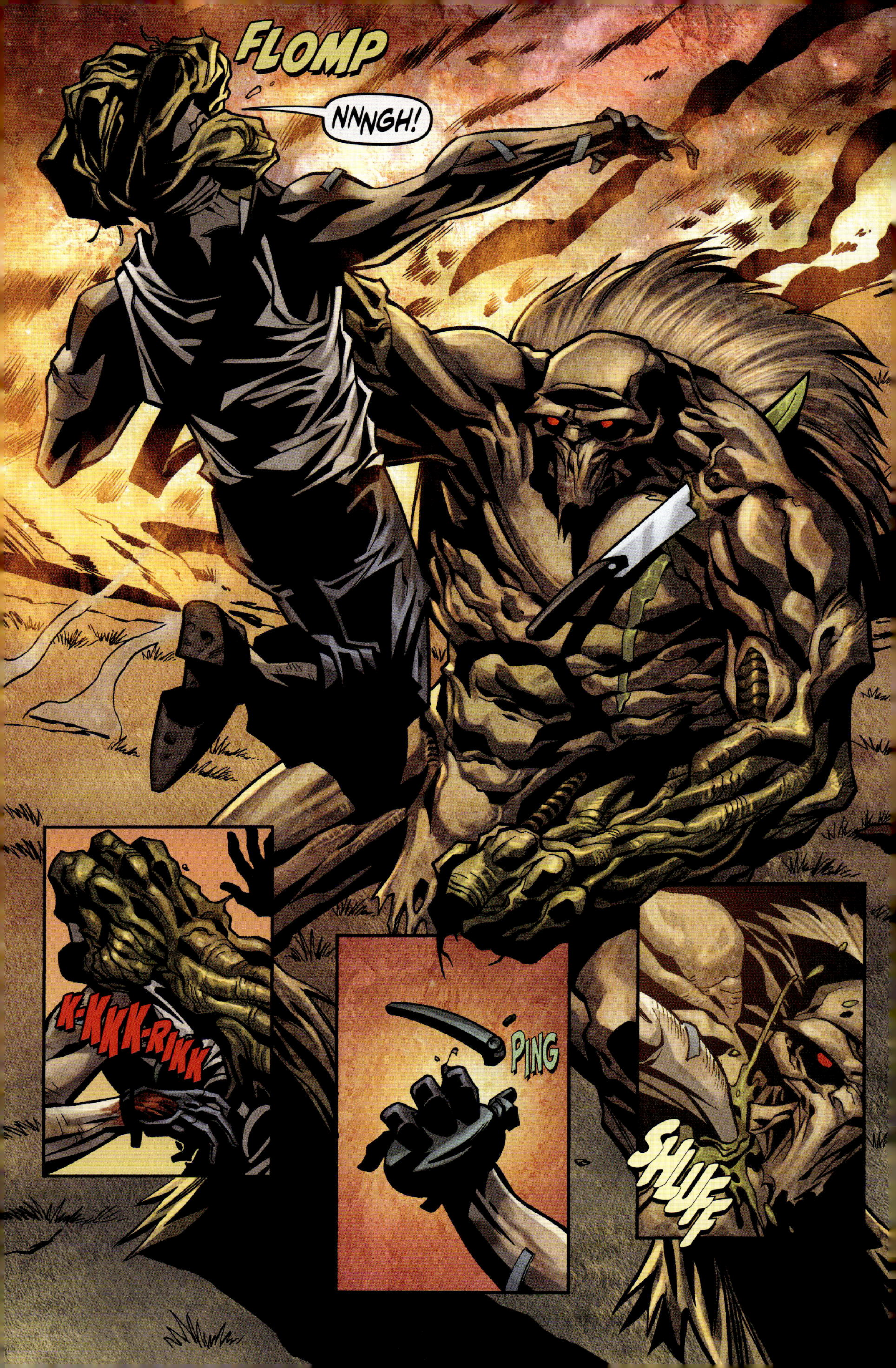
FLOMP
NNNGH!
K-KKK-RIKK
PING
SHLUFF

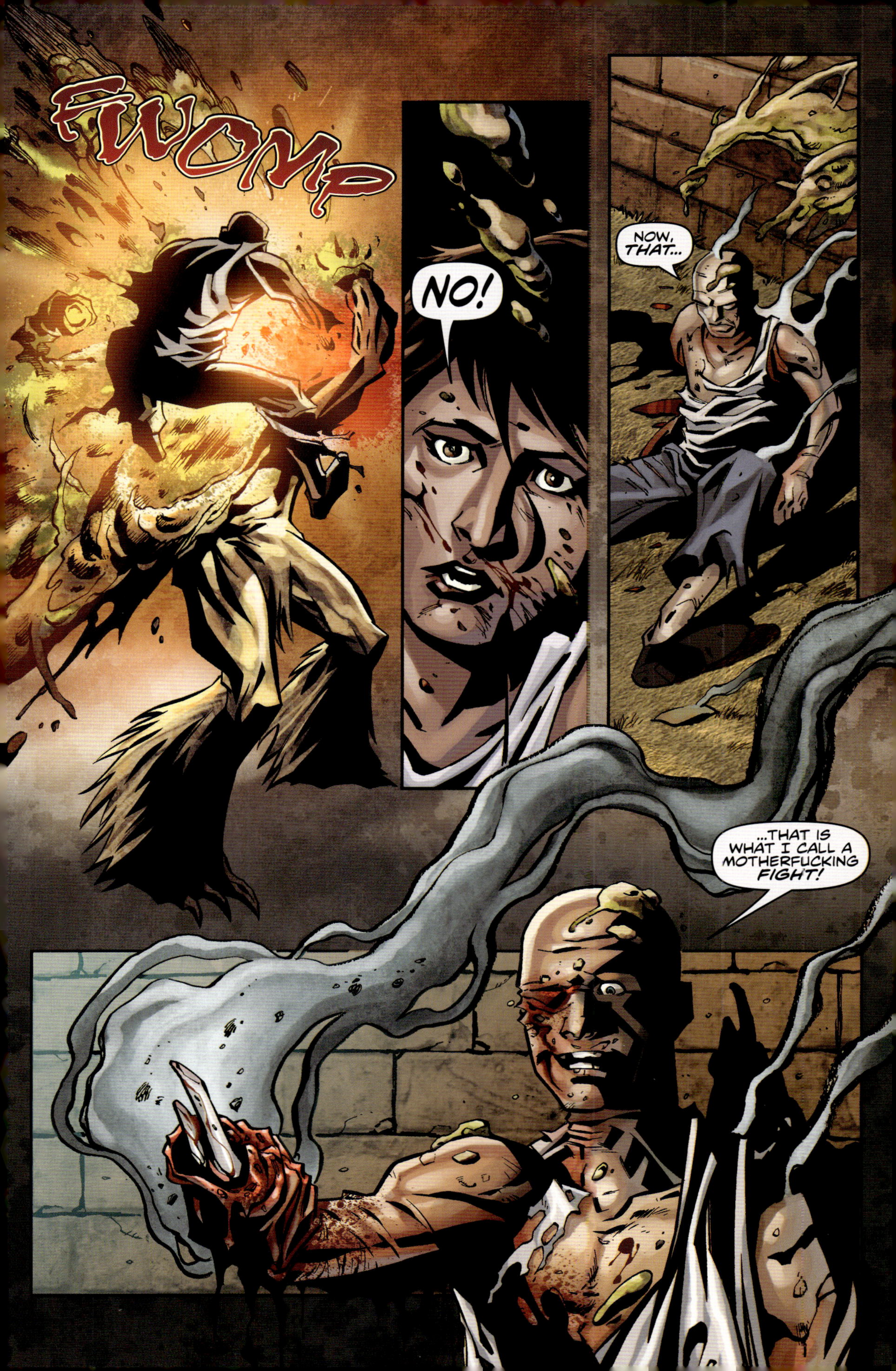
FWOMP
NO!
NOW, THAT...
...THAT IS WHAT I CALL A MOTHERFUCKING FIGHT!

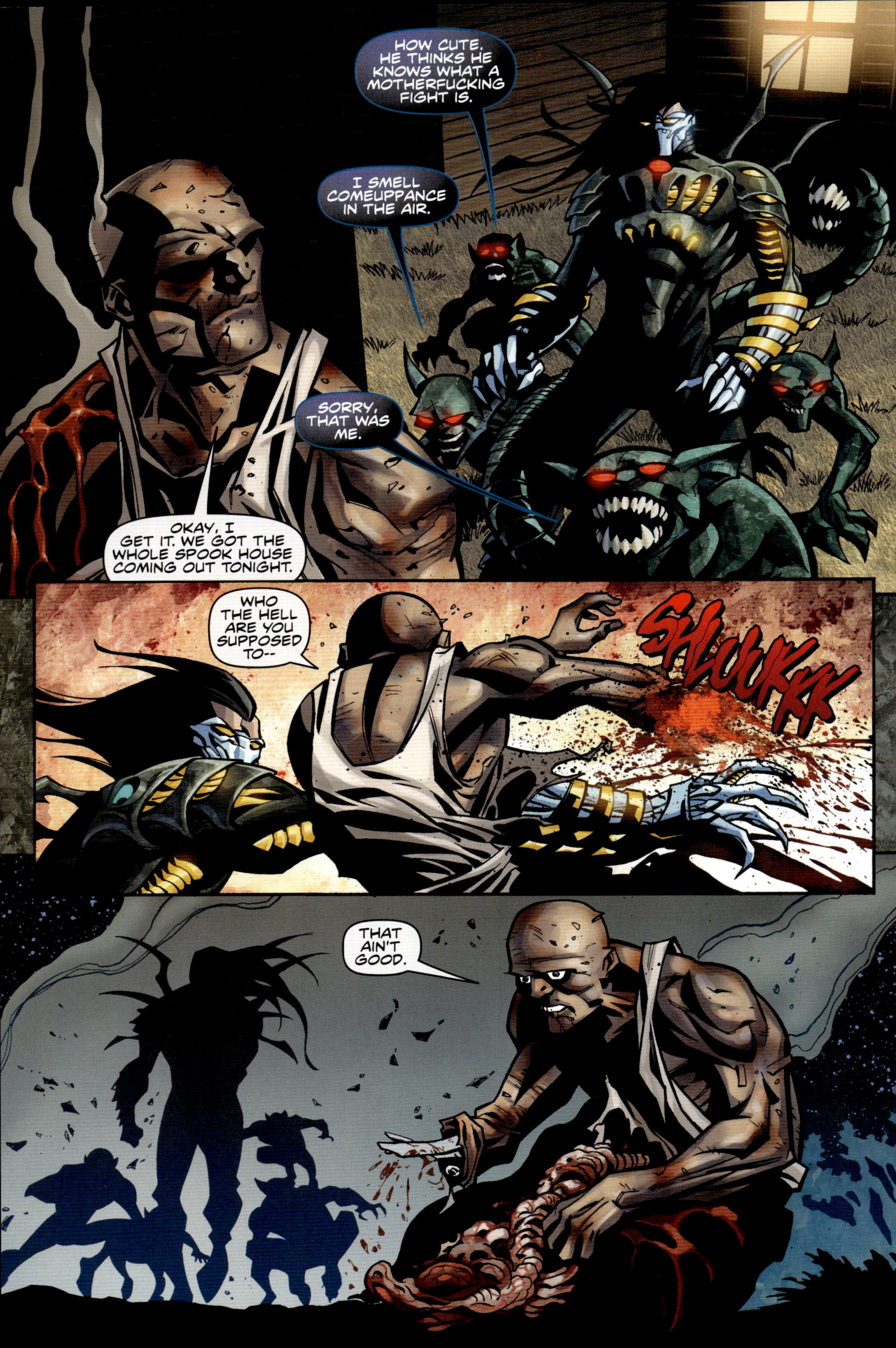
HOW CUTE. HE THINKS HE KNOWS WHAT A MOTHERFUCKING FIGHT IS.
I SMELL COMEUPPANCE IN THE AIR.
SORRY, THAT WAS ME.
OKAY, I GET IT. WE GOT THE WHOLE SPOOK HOUSE COMING OUT TONIGHT.
WHO THE HELL ARE YOU SUPPOSED TO--
SHLUUKKK
THAT AIN'T GOOD.

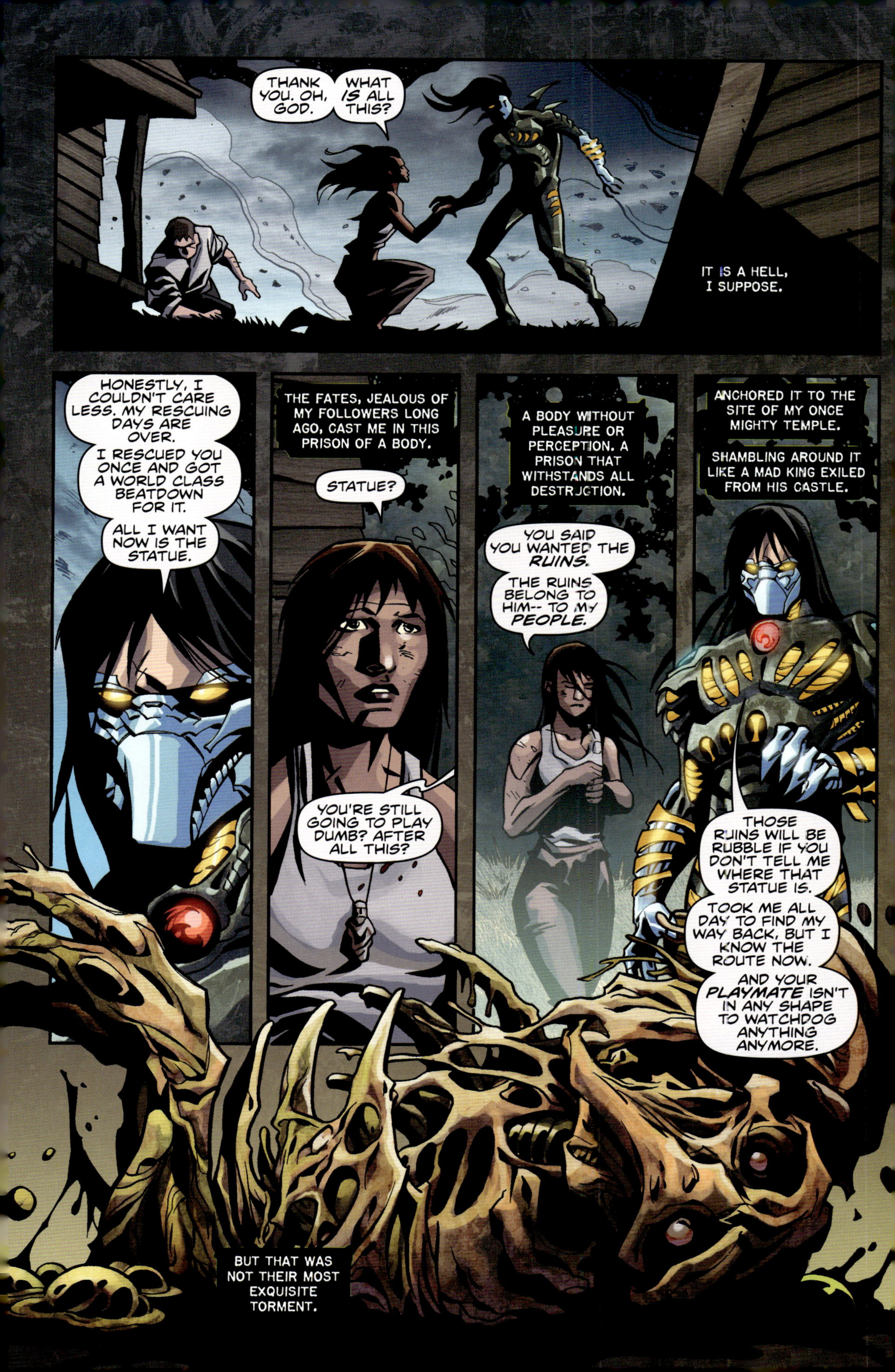
THANK YOU. OH, GOD.
WHAT IS ALL THIS?
IT IS A HELL, I SUPPOSE.
HONESTLY, I COULDN'T CARE LESS. MY RESCUING DAYS ARE OVER.
I RESCUED YOU ONCE AND GOT A WORLD CLASS BEATDOWN FOR IT.
ALL I WANT NOW IS THE STATUE.
THE FATES, JEALOUS OF MY FOLLOWERS LONG AGO, CAST ME IN THIS PRISON OF A BODY.
STATUE?
YOU'RE STILL GOING TO PLAY DUMB? AFTER ALL THIS?
A BODY WITHOUT PLEASURE OR PERCEPTION. A PRISON THAT WITHSTANDS ALL DESTRUCTION.
YOU SAID YOU WANTED THE RUINS.
THE RUINS BELONG TO HIM-- TO MY PEOPLE.
ANCHORED IT TO THE SITE OF MY ONCE MIGHTY TEMPLE.
SHAMBLING AROUND IT LIKE A MAD KING EXILED FROM HIS CASTLE.
THOSE RUINS WILL BE RUBBLE IF YOU DON'T TELL ME WHERE THAT STATUE IS.
TOOK ME ALL DAY TO FIND MY WAY BACK, BUT I KNOW THE ROUTE NOW.
AND YOUR PLAYMATE ISN'T IN ANY SHAPE TO WATCHDOG ANYTHING ANYMORE.
BUT THAT WAS NOT THEIR MOST EXQUISITE TORMENT.

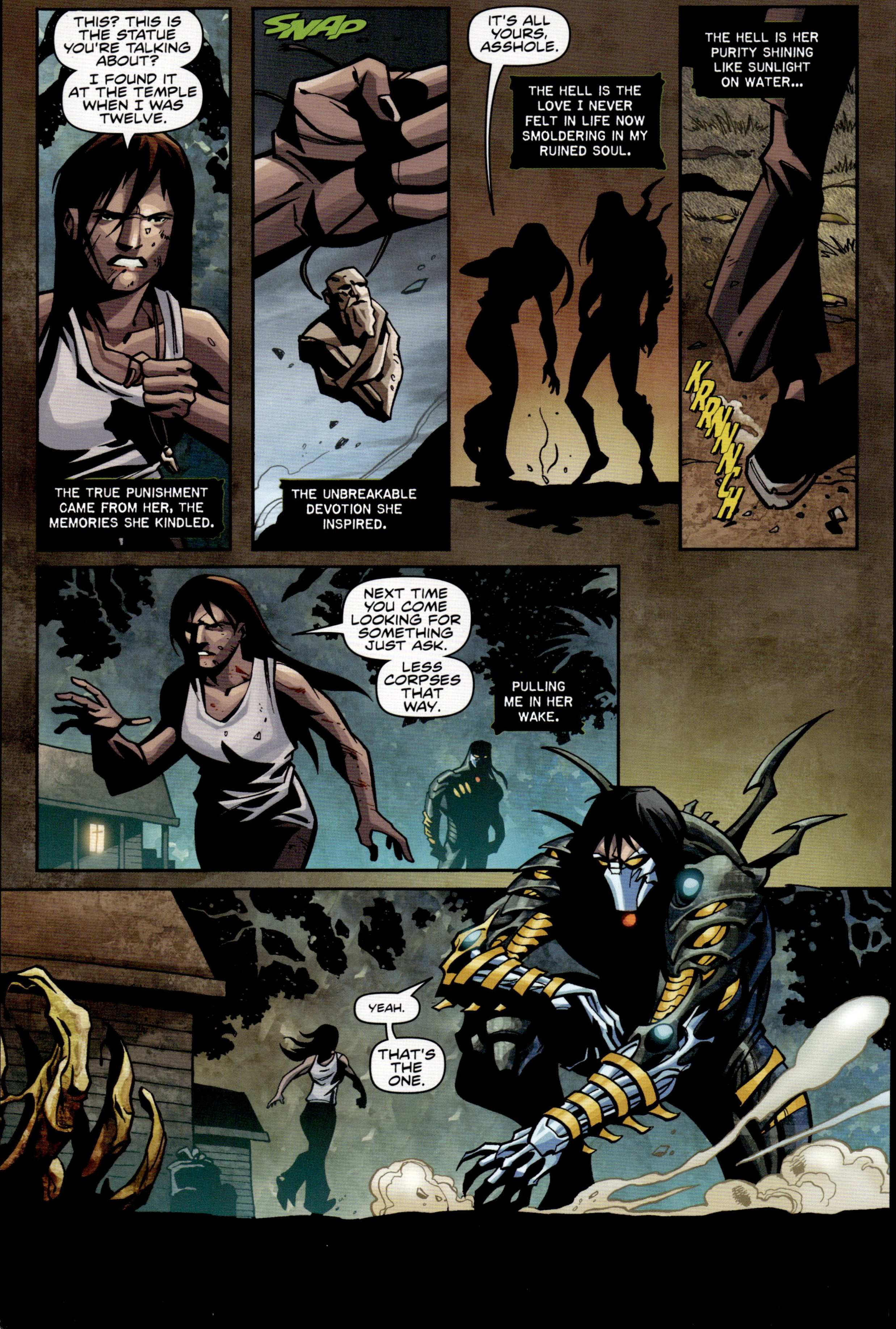
THIS? THIS IS THE STATUE YOU'RE TALKING ABOUT?
I FOUND IT AT THE TEMPLE WHEN I WAS TWELVE.
THE TRUE PUNISHMENT CAME FROM HER, THE MEMORIES SHE KINDLED.
SNAP
THE UNBREAKABLE DEVOTION SHE INSPIRED.
IT'S ALL YOURS, ASSHOLE.
THE HELL IS THE LOVE I NEVER FELT IN LIFE NOW SMOLDERING IN MY RUINED SOUL.
THE HELL IS HER PURITY SHINING LIKE SUNLIGHT ON WATER...
KRRNNNCH
NEXT TIME YOU COME LOOKING FOR SOMETHING JUST ASK.
LESS CORPSES THAT WAY.
PULLING ME IN HER WAKE.
YEAH.
THAT'S THE ONE.

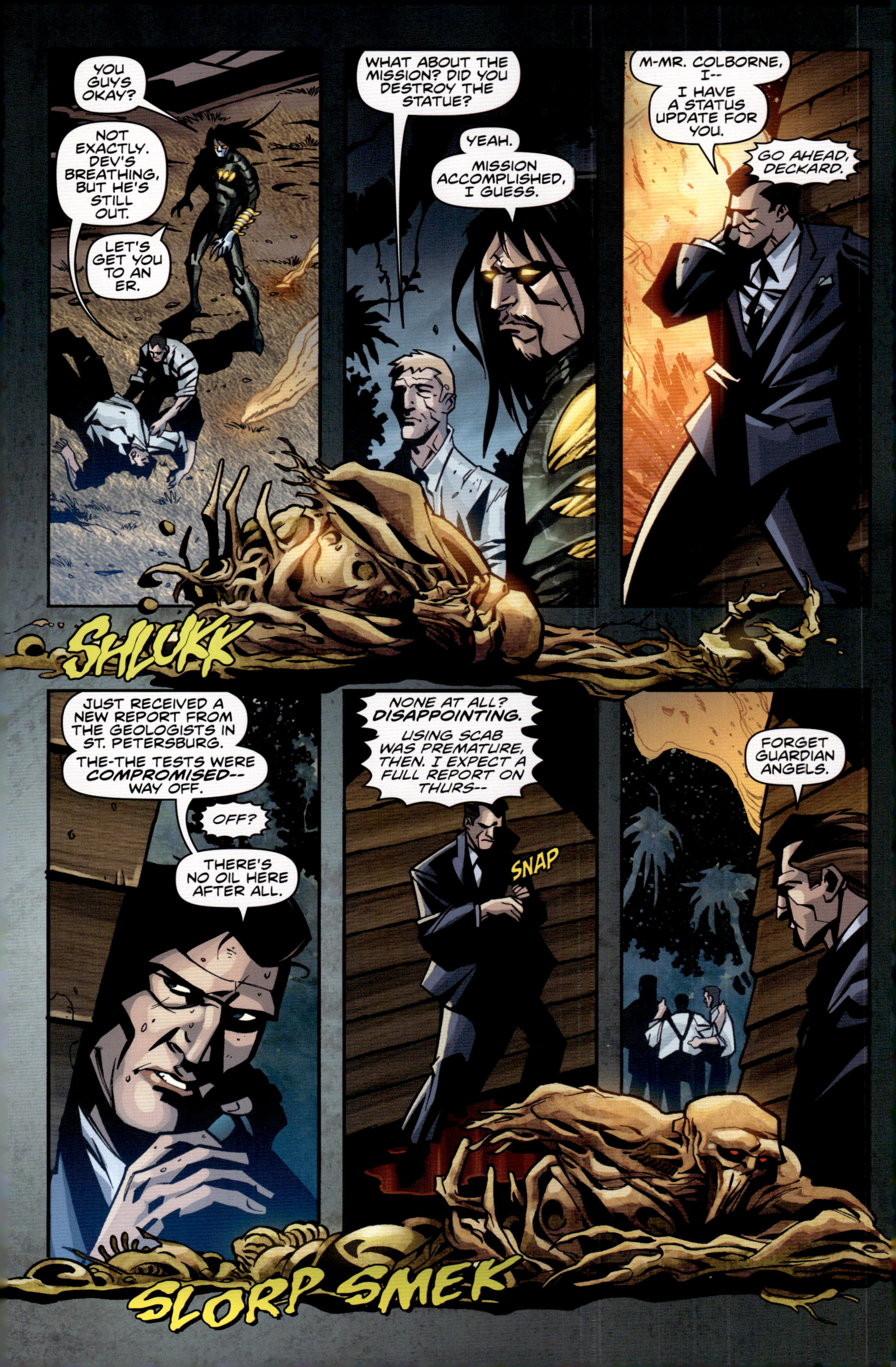

YOU GUYS OKAY?
NOT EXACTLY. DEV'S BREATHING, BUT HE'S STILL OUT.
LET'S GET YOU TO AN ER.
WHAT ABOUT THE MISSION? DID YOU DESTROY THE STATUE?
YEAH.
MISSION ACCOMPLISHED, I GUESS.
M-MR. COLBORNE, I--
I HAVE A STATUS UPDATE FOR YOU.
GO AHEAD, DECKARD.
SHLUKK
JUST RECEIVED A NEW REPORT FROM THE GEOLOGISTS IN ST. PETERSBURG.
THE-THE TESTS WERE COMPROMISED-- WAY OFF.
OFF?
THERE'S NO OIL HERE AFTER ALL.
NONE AT ALL? DISAPPOINTING.
USING SCAB WAS PREMATURE, THEN. I EXPECT A FULL REPORT ON THURS--
SNAP
FORGET GUARDIAN ANGELS.
SLORP SMEK

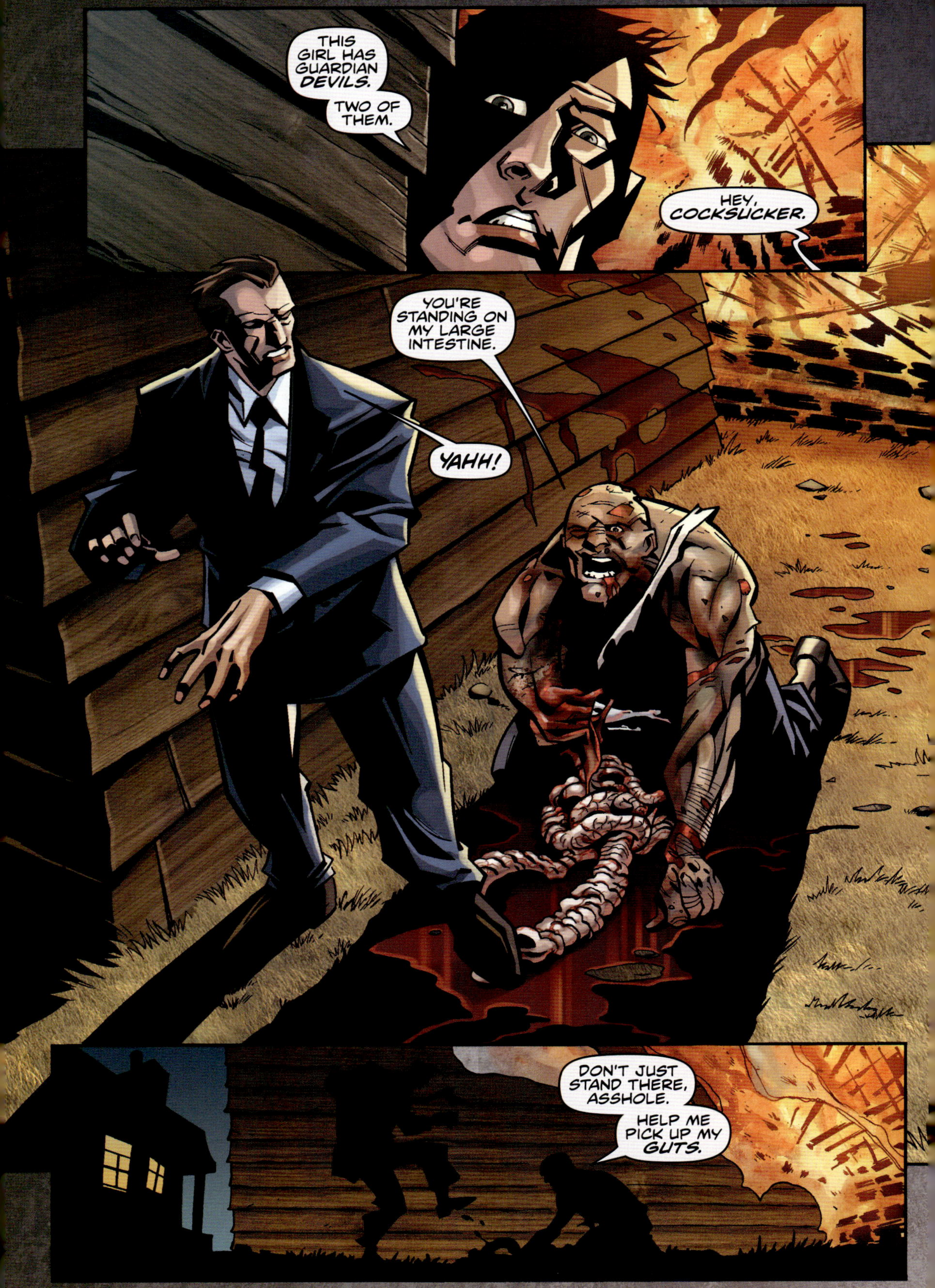
THIS GIRL HAS GUARDIAN DEVILS.
TWO OF THEM.
HEY, COCKSUCKER.
YOU'RE STANDING ON MY LARGE INTESTINE.
YAHH!
DON'T JUST STAND THERE, ASSHOLE.
HELP ME PICK UP MY GUTS.

The Darkness Issue #82
cover art by: Tom Feister

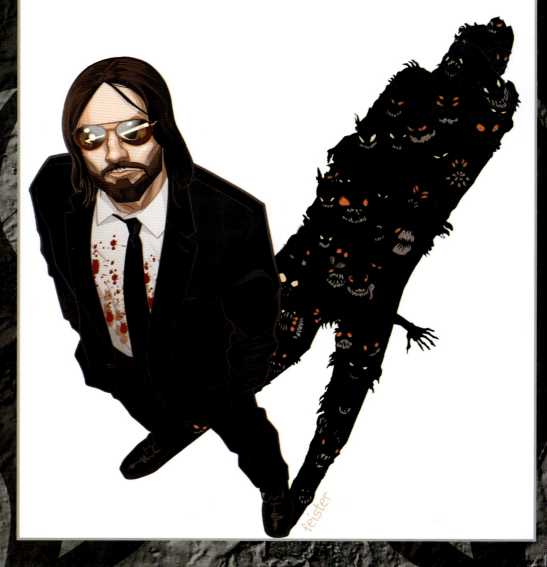

THE DARKNESS #82

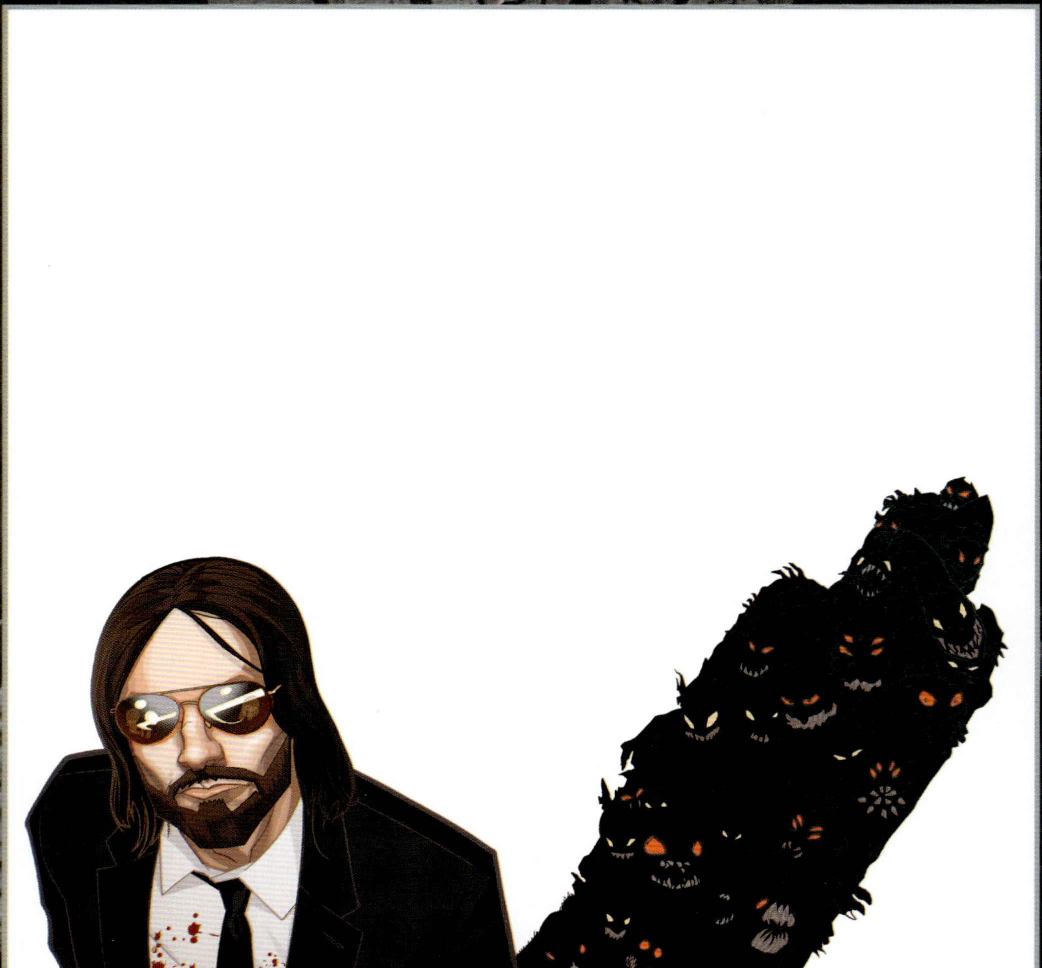
feister

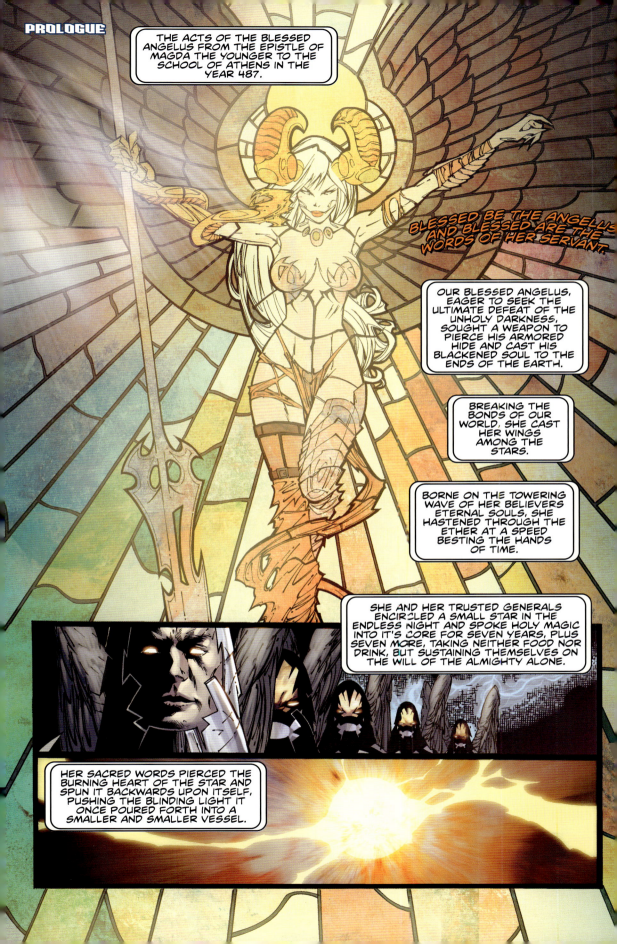

THE ACTS OF THE BLESSED ANGELUS FROM THE EPISTLE OF MAGDA THE YOUNGER TO THE SCHOOL OF ATHENS IN THE YEAR 487.

BLESSED BE THE ANGELUS AND BLESSED ARE THE WORDS OF HER SERVANT.

OUR BLESSED ANGELUS, EAGER TO SEEK THE ULTIMATE DEFEAT OF THE UNHOLY DARKNESS, SOUGHT A WEAPON TO PIERCE HIS ARMORED HIDE AND CAST HIS BLACKENED SOUL TO THE ENDS OF THE EARTH.

BREAKING THE BONDS OF OUR WORLD, SHE CAST HER WINGS AMONG THE STARS.

BORNE ON THE TOWERING WAVE OF HER BELIEVERS ETERNAL SOULS, SHE HASTENED THROUGH THE ETHER AT A SPEED BESTING THE HANDS OF TIME.

SHE AND HER TRUSTED GENERALS ENCIRCLED A SMALL STAR IN THE ENDLESS NIGHT AND SPOKE HOLY MAGIC INTO IT'S CORE FOR SEVEN YEARS, PLUS SEVEN MORE, TAKING NEITHER FOOD NOR DRINK, BUT SUSTAINING THEMSELVES ON THE WILL OF THE ALMIGHTY ALONE.

HER SACRED WORDS PIERCED THE BURNING HEART OF THE STAR AND SPUN IT BACKWARDS UPON ITSELF, PUSHING THE BLINDING LIGHT IT ONCE POURED FORTH INTO A SMALLER AND SMALLER VESSEL.

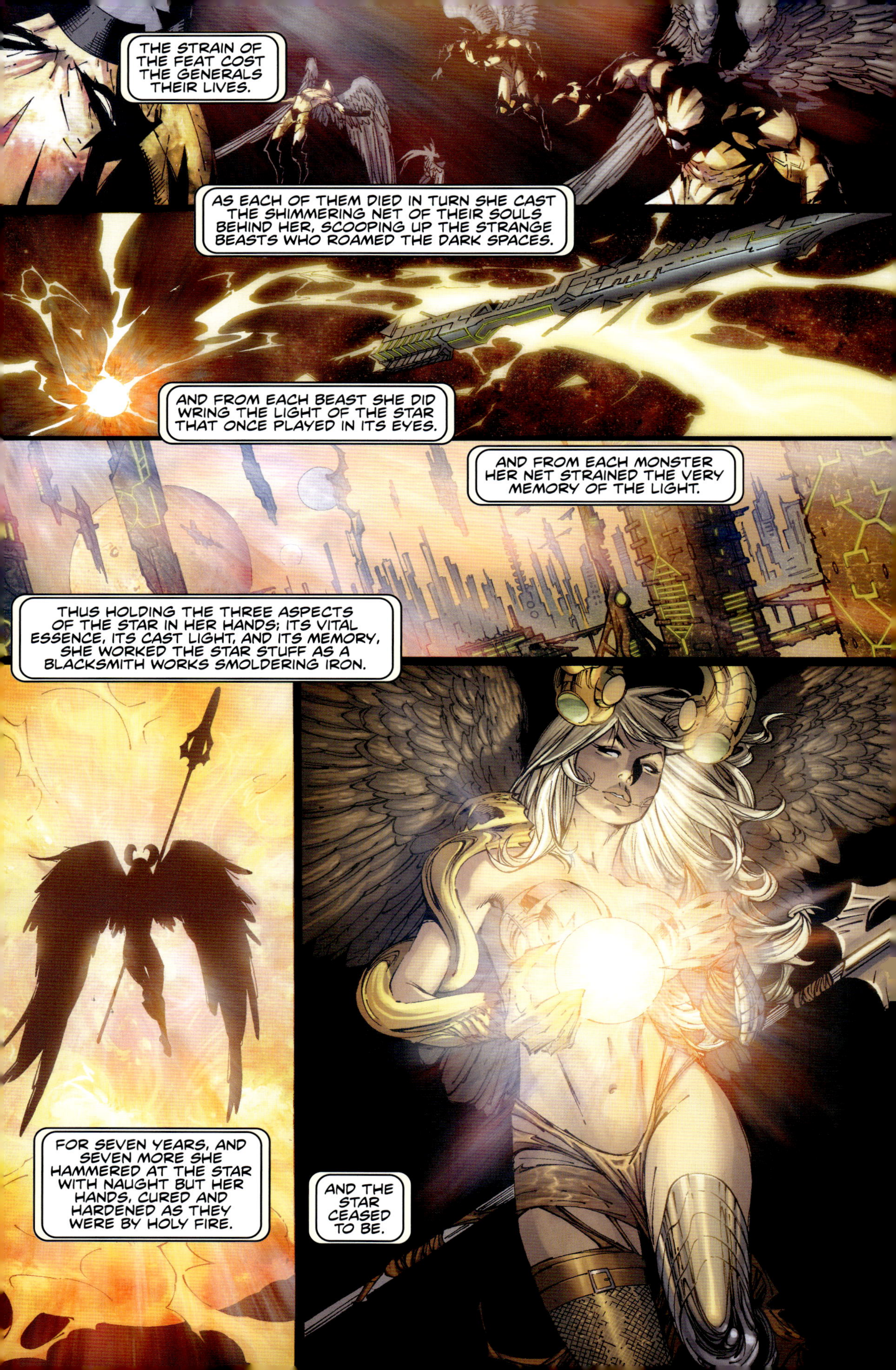
THE STRAIN OF THE FEAT COST THE GENERALS THEIR LIVES.
AS EACH OF THEM DIED IN TURN SHE CAST THE SHIMMERING NET OF THEIR SOULS BEHIND HER, SCOOPING UP THE STRANGE BEASTS WHO ROAMED THE DARK SPACES.
AND FROM EACH BEAST SHE DID WRING THE LIGHT OF THE STAR THAT ONCE PLAYED IN ITS EYES.
AND FROM EACH MONSTER HER NET STRAINED THE VERY MEMORY OF THE LIGHT.
THUS HOLDING THE THREE ASPECTS OF THE STAR IN HER HANDS; ITS VITAL ESSENCE, ITS CAST LIGHT, AND ITS MEMORY, SHE WORKED THE STAR STUFF AS A BLACKSMITH WORKS SMOLDERING IRON.
FOR SEVEN YEARS, AND SEVEN MORE SHE HAMMERED AT THE STAR WITH NAUGHT BUT HER HANDS, CURED AND HARDENED AS THEY WERE BY HOLY FIRE.
AND THE STAR CEASED TO BE.

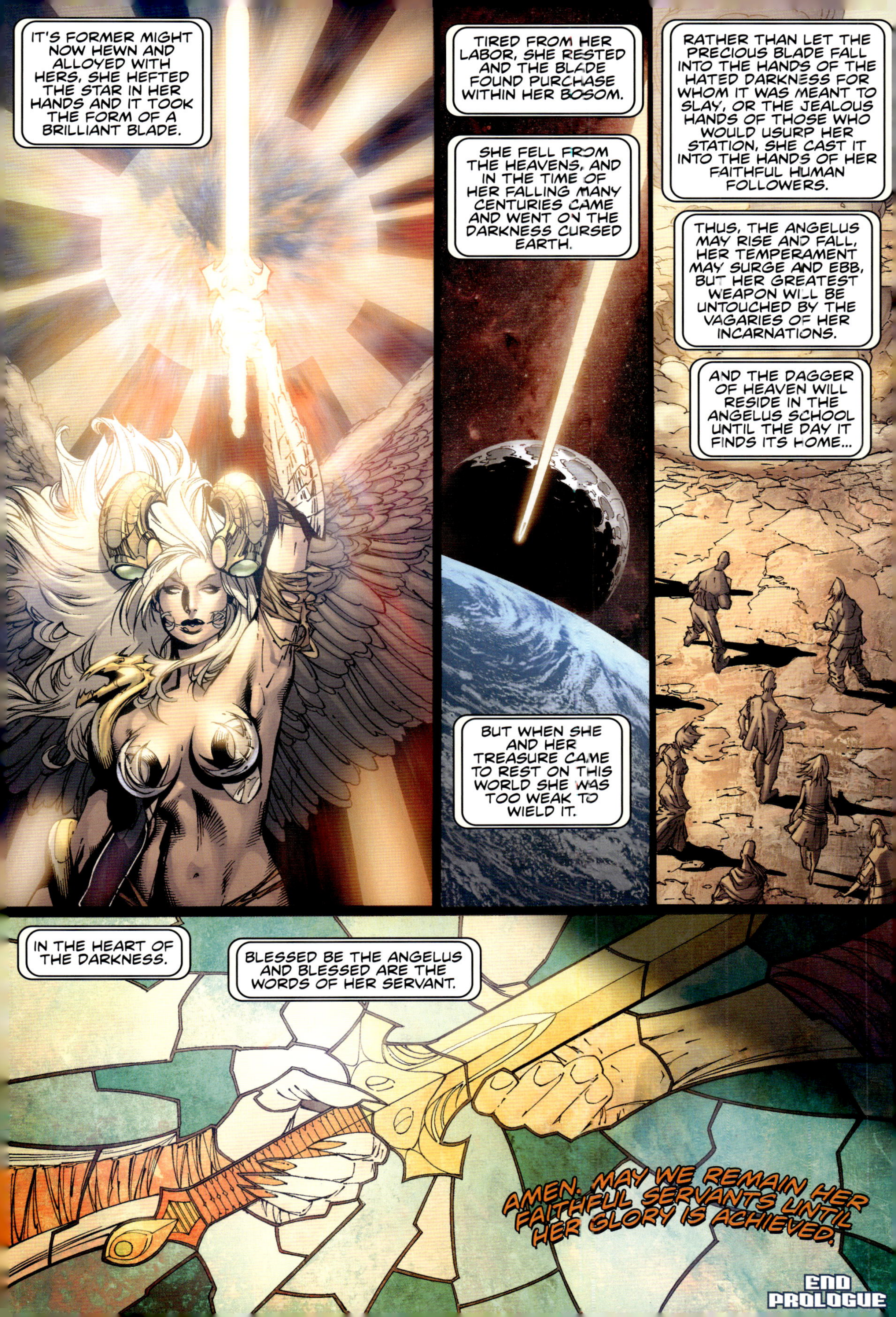
IT'S FORMER MIGHT NOW HEWN AND ALLOYED WITH HERS, SHE HEFTED THE STAR IN HER HANDS AND IT TOOK THE FORM OF A BRILLIANT BLADE.
TIRED FROM HER LABOR, SHE RESTED AND THE BLADE FOUND PURCHASE WITHIN HER BOSOM.
SHE FELL FROM THE HEAVENS, AND IN THE TIME OF HER FALLING MANY CENTURIES CAME AND WENT ON THE DARKNESS CURSED EARTH.
BUT WHEN SHE AND HER TREASURE CAME TO REST ON THIS WORLD SHE WAS TOO WEAK TO WIELD IT.
RATHER THAN LET THE PRECIOUS BLADE FALL INTO THE HANDS OF THE HATED DARKNESS FOR WHOM IT WAS MEANT TO SLAY, OR THE JEALOUS HANDS OF THOSE WHO WOULD USURP HER STATION, SHE CAST IT INTO THE HANDS OF HER FAITHFUL HUMAN FOLLOWERS.
THUS, THE ANGELUS MAY RISE AND FALL, HER TEMPERAMENT MAY SURGE AND EBB, BUT HER GREATEST WEAPON WILL BE UNTOUCHED BY THE VAGARIES OF HER INCARNATIONS.
AND THE DAGGER OF HEAVEN WILL RESIDE IN THE ANGELUS SCHOOL UNTIL THE DAY IT FINDS ITS HOME...
IN THE HEART OF THE DARKNESS.
BLESSED BE THE ANGELUS AND BLESSED ARE THE WORDS OF HER SERVANT.
AMEN. MAY WE REMAIN HER FAITHFUL SERVANTS UNTIL HER GLORY IS ACHIEVED.
END PROLOGUE

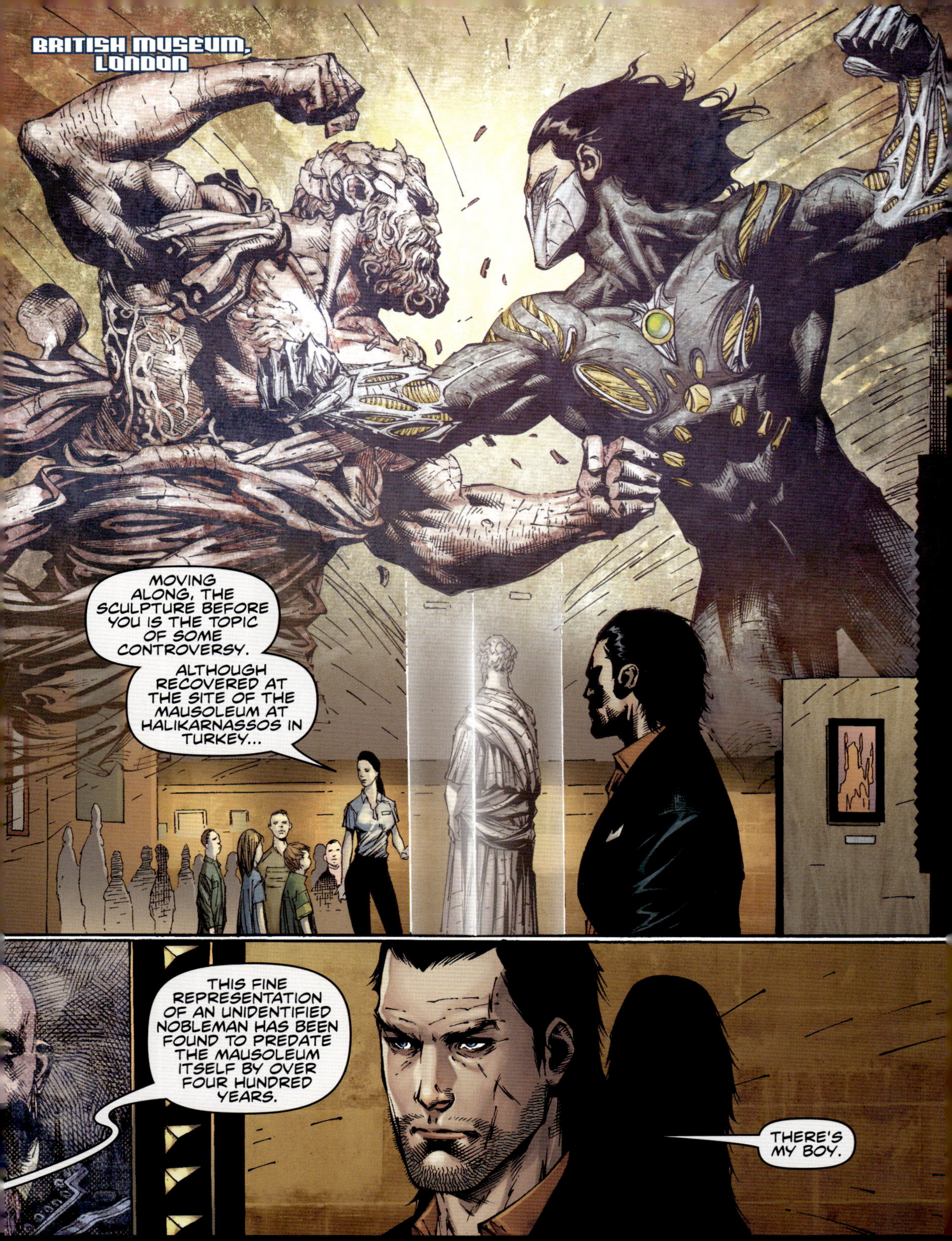
BRITISH MUSEUM, LONDON
MOVING ALONG, THE SCULPTURE BEFORE YOU IS THE TOPIC OF SOME CONTROVERSY.
ALTHOUGH RECOVERED AT THE SITE OF THE MAUSOLEUM AT HALIKARNASSOS IN TURKEY...
THIS FINE REPRESENTATION OF AN UNIDENTIFIED NOBLEMAN HAS BEEN FOUND TO PREDATE THE MAUSOLEUM ITSELF BY OVER FOUR HUNDRED YEARS.
THERE'S MY BOY.

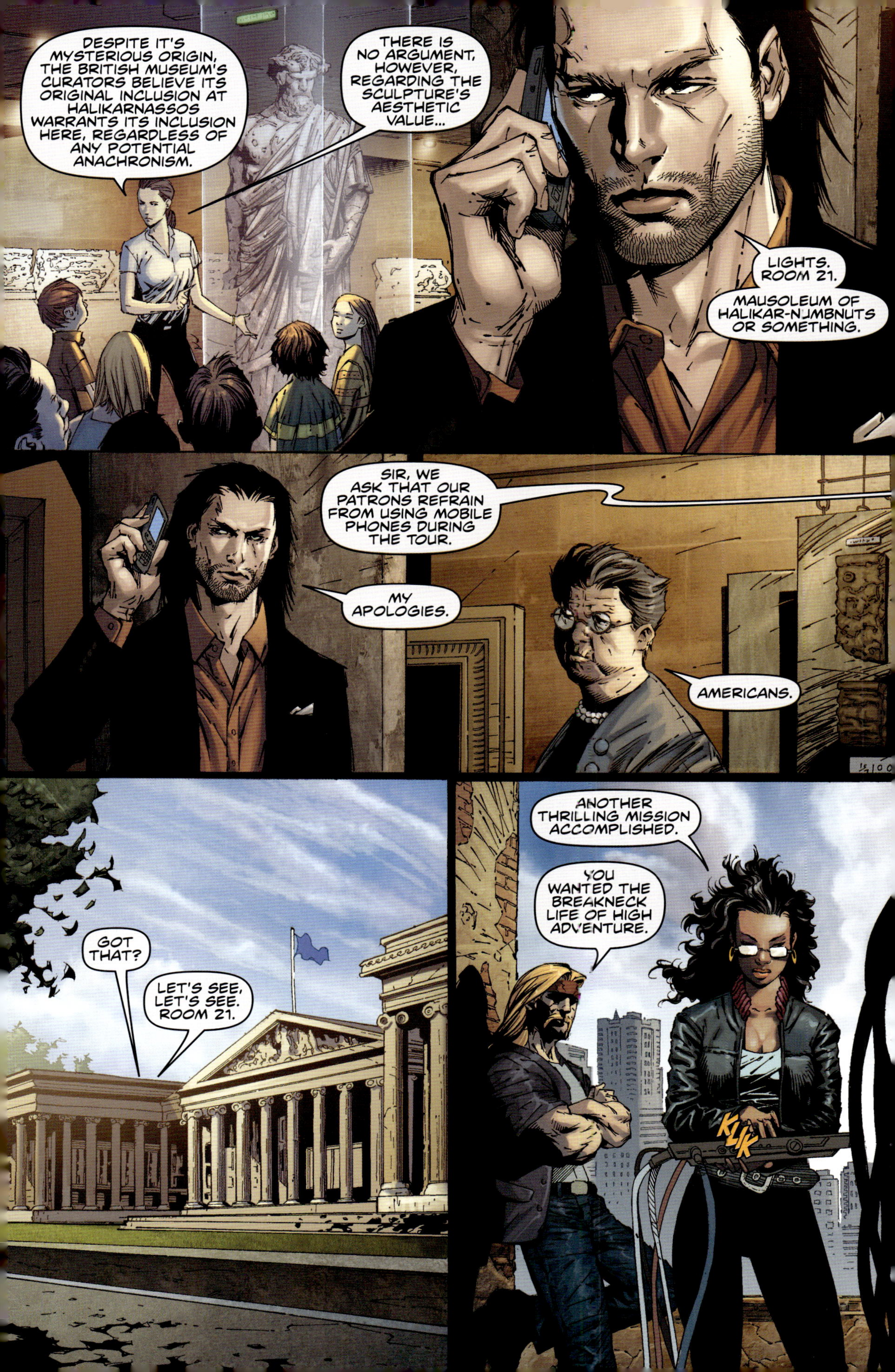
DESPITE IT'S MYSTERIOUS ORIGIN, THE BRITISH MUSEUM'S CURATORS BELIEVE ITS ORIGINAL INCLUSION AT HALIKARNASSOS WARRANTS ITS INCLUSION HERE, REGARDLESS OF ANY POTENTIAL ANACHRONISM.
THERE IS NO ARGUMENT, HOWEVER, REGARDING THE SCULPTURE'S AESTHETIC VALUE...
LIGHTS. ROOM 21.
MAUSOLEUM OF HALIKAR-NUMBNUTS OR SOMETHING.
SIR, WE ASK THAT OUR PATRONS REFRAIN FROM USING MOBILE PHONES DURING THE TOUR.
MY APOLOGIES.
AMERICANS.
GOT THAT?
LET'S SEE, LET'S SEE. ROOM 21.
ANOTHER THRILLING MISSION ACCOMPLISHED.
YOU WANTED THE BREAKNECK LIFE OF HIGH ADVENTURE.
KLIK

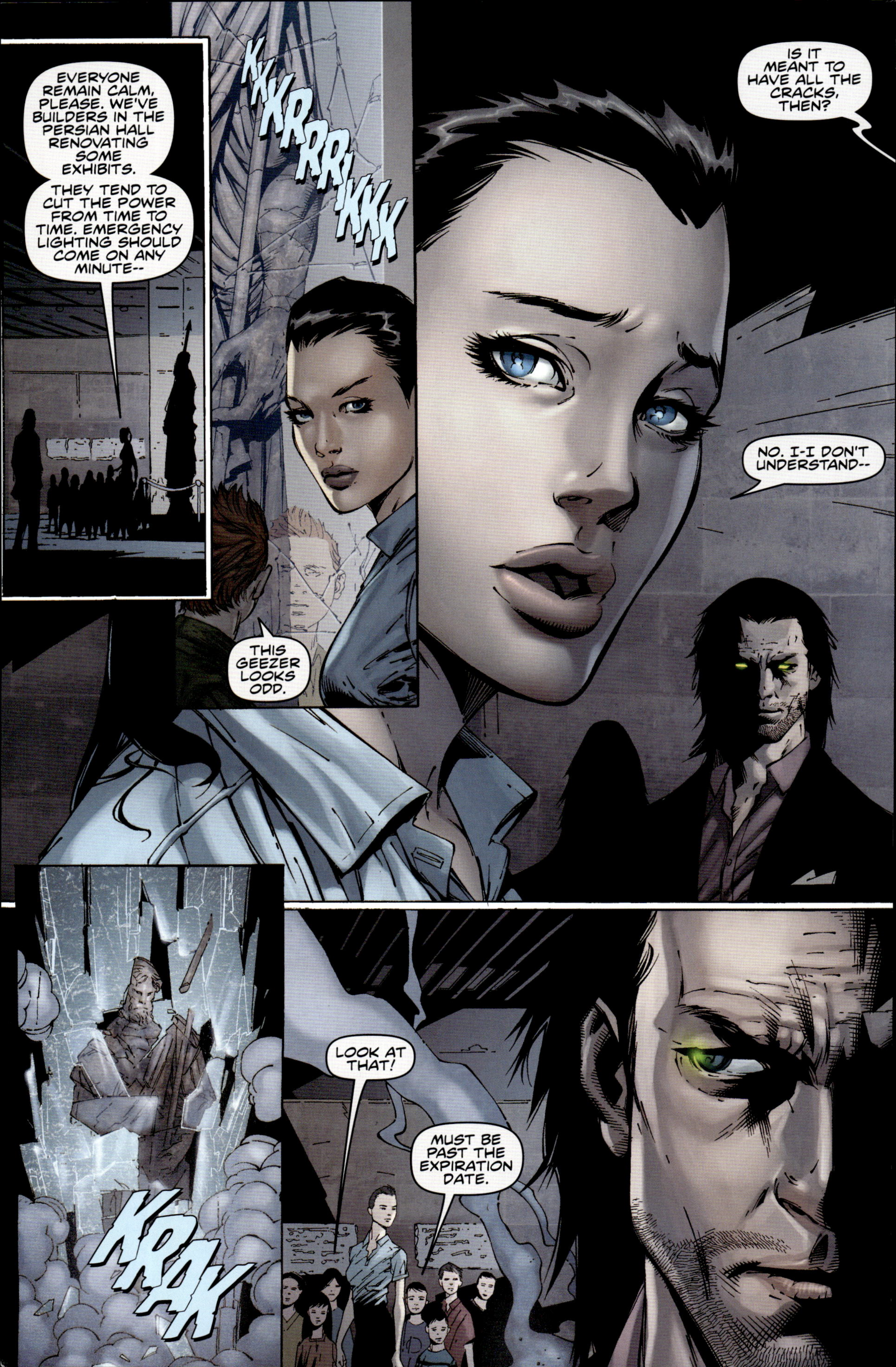
EVERYONE REMAIN CALM, PLEASE. WE'VE BUILDERS IN THE PERSIAN HALL RENOVATING SOME EXHIBITS.
THEY TEND TO CUT THE POWER FROM TIME TO TIME. EMERGENCY LIGHTING SHOULD COME ON ANY MINUTE--
KKKRRRIKKKK
THIS GEEZER LOOKS ODD.
IS IT MEANT TO HAVE ALL THE CRACKS, THEN?
NO. I-I DON'T UNDERSTAND--
KRAK
LOOK AT THAT!
MUST BE PAST THE EXPIRATION DATE.

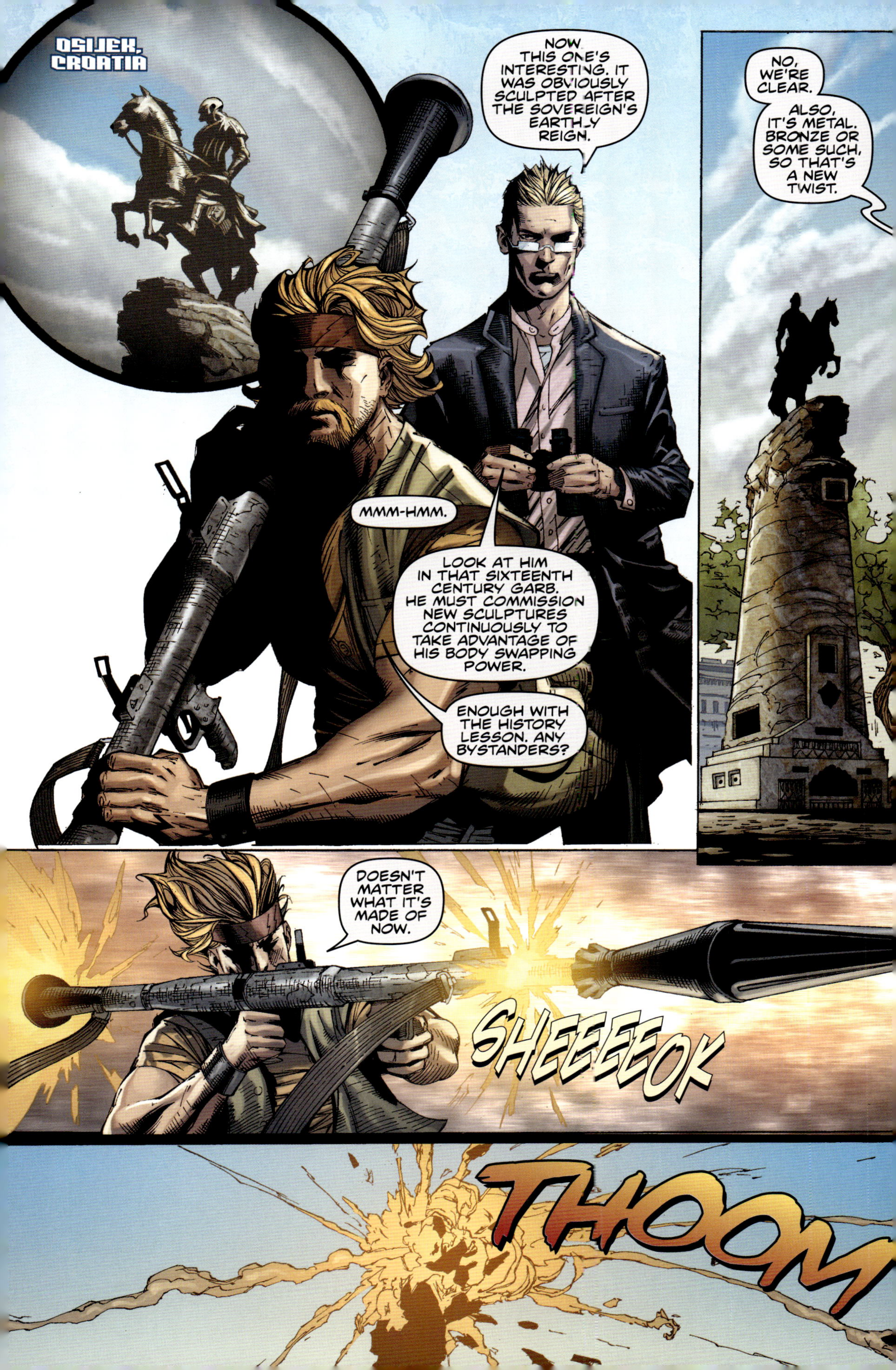
OSIJEK, CROATIA
NOW THIS ONE'S INTERESTING. IT WAS OBVIOUSLY SCULPTED AFTER THE SOVEREIGN'S EARTHLY REIGN.
NO, WE'RE CLEAR.
ALSO, IT'S METAL. BRONZE OR SOME SUCH, SO THAT'S A NEW TWIST.
MMM-HMM.
LOOK AT HIM IN THAT SIXTEENTH CENTURY GARB. HE MUST COMMISSION NEW SCULPTURES CONTINUOUSLY TO TAKE ADVANTAGE OF HIS BODY SWAPPING POWER.
ENOUGH WITH THE HISTORY LESSON. ANY BYSTANDERS?
DOESN'T MATTER WHAT IT'S MADE OF NOW.
SHEEEEOK
THOOM

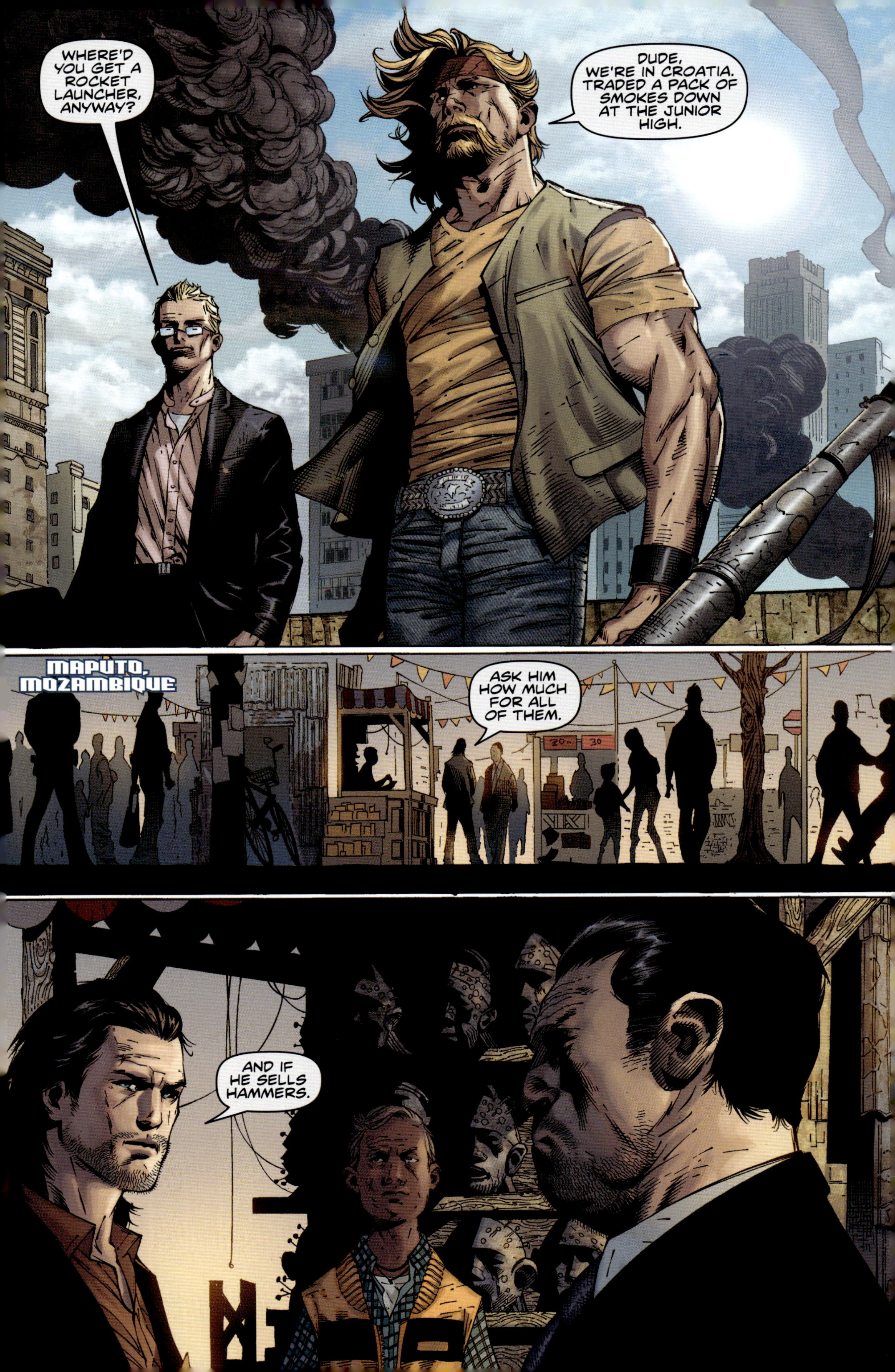
WHERE'D YOU GET A ROCKET LAUNCHER, ANYWAY?
DUDE, WE'RE IN CROATIA. TRADED A PACK OF SMOKES DOWN AT THE JUNIOR HIGH.
MAPUTO, MOZAMBIQUE
ASK HIM HOW MUCH FOR ALL OF THEM.
AND IF HE SELLS HAMMERS.

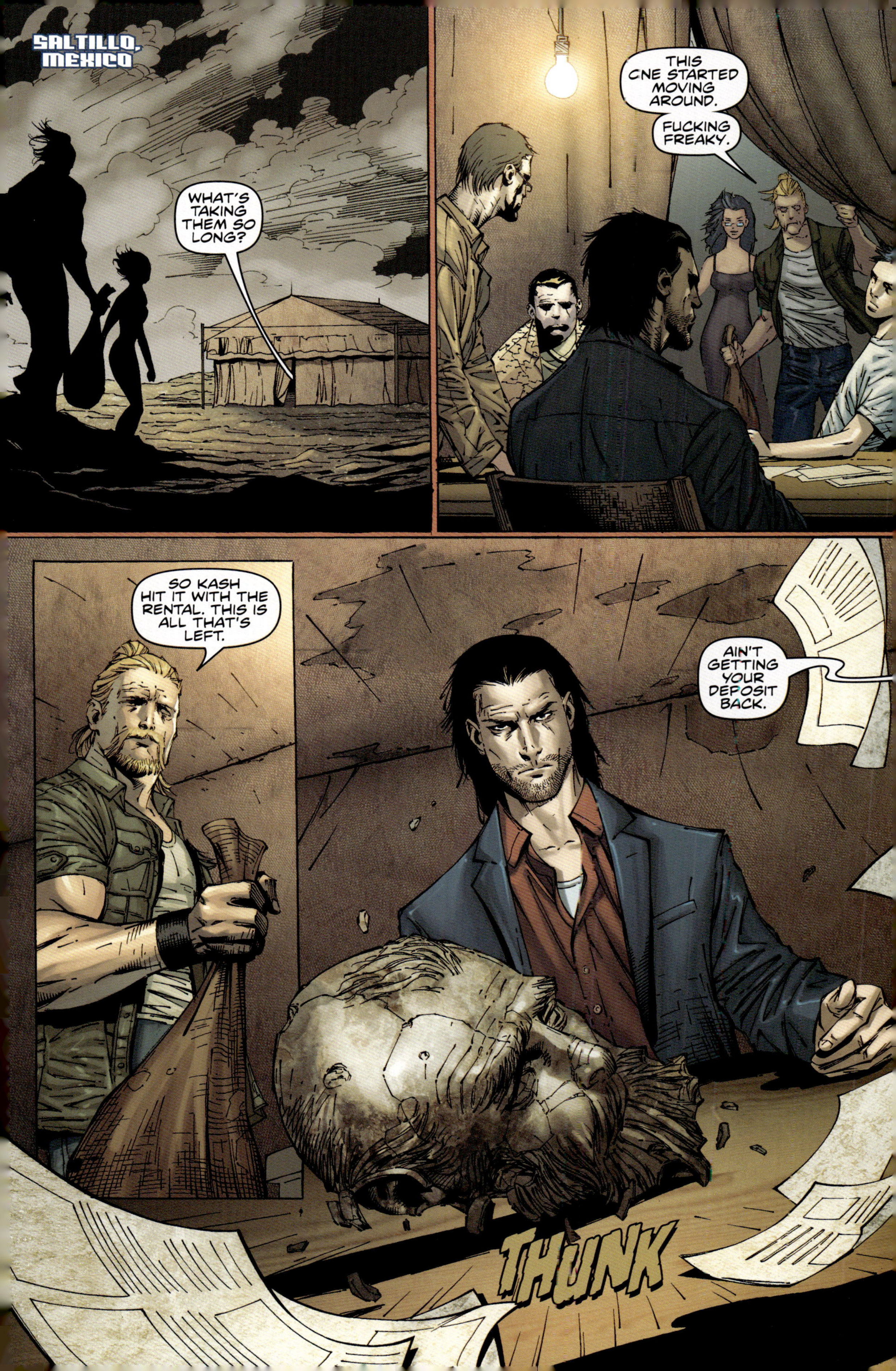

SALTILLO, MEXICO
WHAT'S TAKING THEM SO LONG?
THIS ONE STARTED MOVING AROUND.
FUCKING FREAKY.
SO KASH HIT IT WITH THE RENTAL. THIS IS ALL THAT'S LEFT.
AIN'T GETTING YOUR DEPOSIT BACK.
THUNK

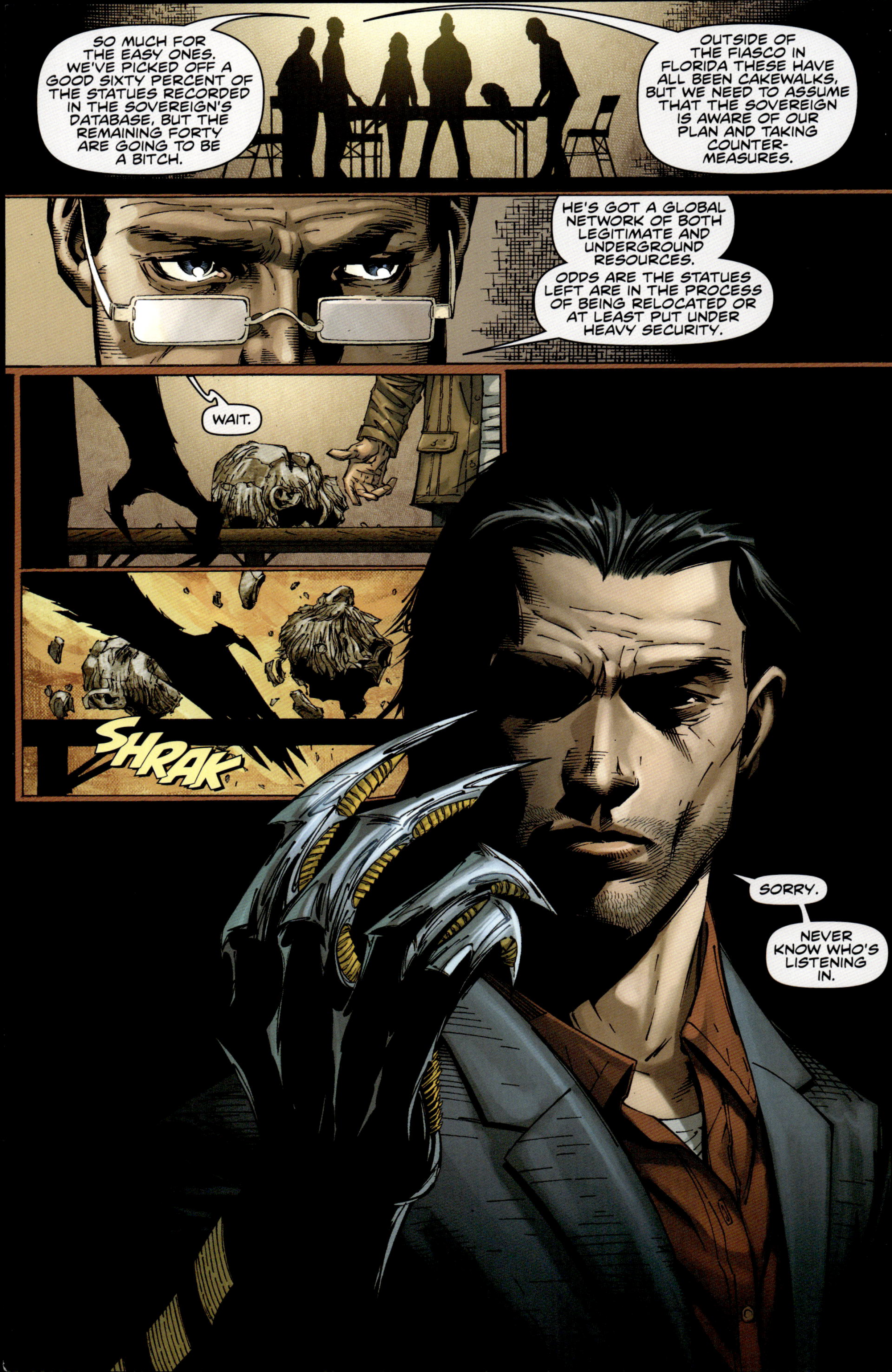
SO MUCH FOR THE EASY ONES. WE'VE PICKED OFF A GOOD SIXTY PERCENT OF THE STATUES RECORDED IN THE SOVEREIGN'S DATABASE, BUT THE REMAINING FORTY ARE GOING TO BE A BITCH.
OUTSIDE OF THE FIASCO IN FLORIDA THESE HAVE ALL BEEN CAKEWALKS, BUT WE NEED TO ASSUME THAT THE SOVEREIGN IS AWARE OF OUR PLAN AND TAKING COUNTER-MEASURES.
HE'S GOT A GLOBAL NETWORK OF BOTH LEGITIMATE AND UNDERGROUND RESOURCES.
ODDS ARE THE STATUES LEFT ARE IN THE PROCESS OF BEING RELOCATED OR AT LEAST PUT UNDER HEAVY SECURITY.
WAIT.
SHRAK
SORRY.
NEVER KNOW WHO'S LISTENING IN.

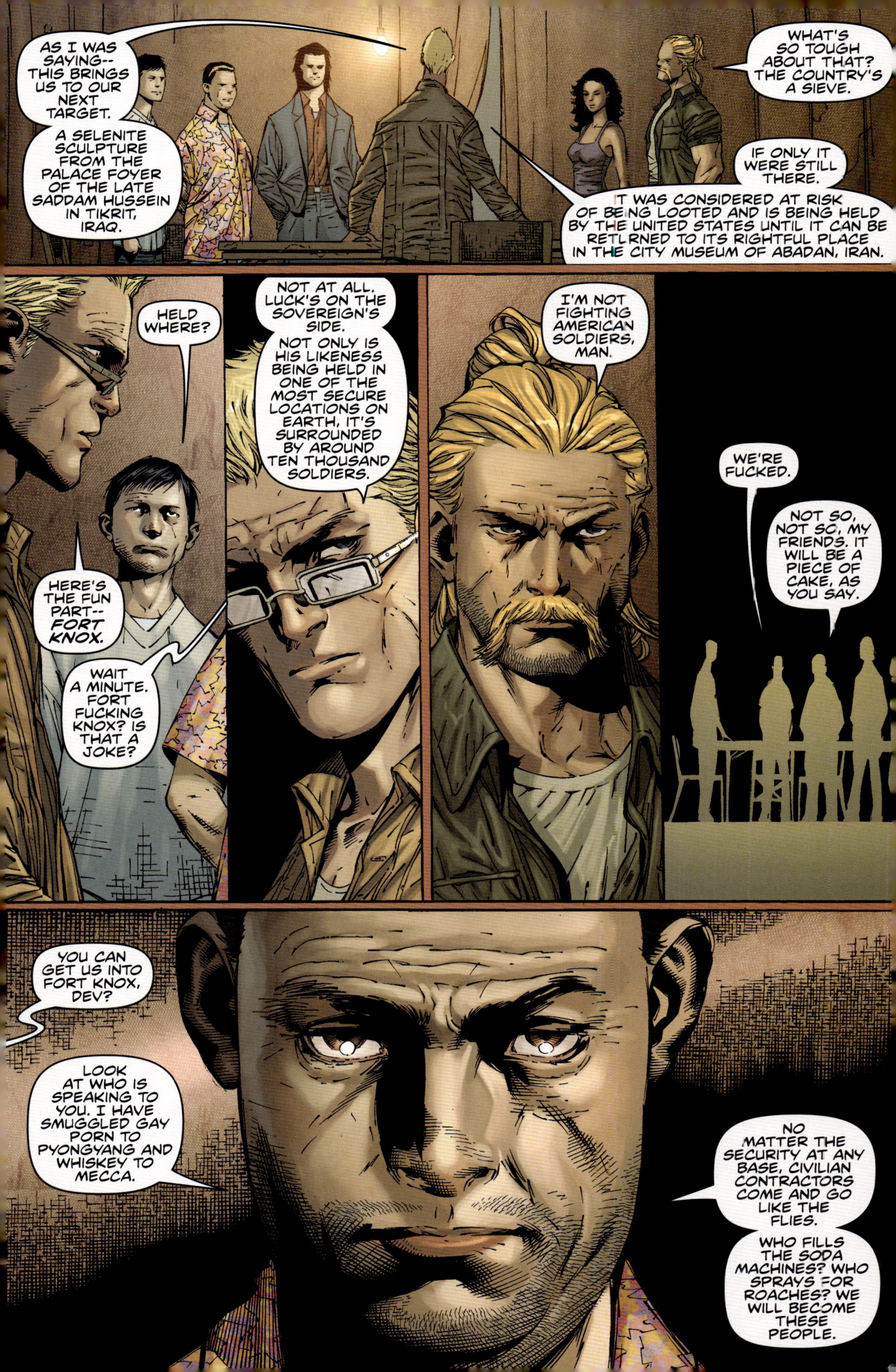
AS I WAS SAYING-- THIS BRINGS US TO OUR NEXT TARGET.
A SELENITE SCULPTURE FROM THE PALACE FOYER OF THE LATE SADDAM HUSSEIN IN TIKRIT, IRAQ.
WHAT'S SO TOUGH ABOUT THAT? THE COUNTRY'S A SIEVE.
IF ONLY IT WERE STILL THERE.
IT WAS CONSIDERED AT RISK OF BEING LOOTED AND IS BEING HELD BY THE UNITED STATES UNTIL IT CAN BE RETURNED TO ITS RIGHTFUL PLACE IN THE CITY MUSEUM OF ABADAN, IRAN.
HELD WHERE?
HERE'S THE FUN PART-- **FORT KNOX.**
WAIT A MINUTE. FORT FUCKING KNOX? IS THAT A JOKE?
NOT AT ALL. LUCK'S ON THE SOVEREIGN'S SIDE.
NOT ONLY IS HIS LIKENESS BEING HELD IN ONE OF THE MOST SECURE LOCATIONS ON EARTH, IT'S SURROUNDED BY AROUND TEN THOUSAND SOLDIERS.
I'M NOT FIGHTING AMERICAN SOLDIERS, MAN.
WE'RE FUCKED.
NOT SO, NOT SO, MY FRIENDS. IT WILL BE A PIECE OF CAKE, AS YOU SAY.
YOU CAN GET US INTO FORT KNOX, DEV?
LOOK AT WHO IS SPEAKING TO YOU. I HAVE SMUGGLED GAY PORN TO PYONGYANG AND WHISKEY TO MECCA.
NO MATTER THE SECURITY AT ANY BASE, CIVILIAN CONTRACTORS COME AND GO LIKE THE FLIES.
WHO FILLS THE SODA MACHINES? WHO SPRAYS FOR ROACHES? WE WILL BECOME THESE PEOPLE.

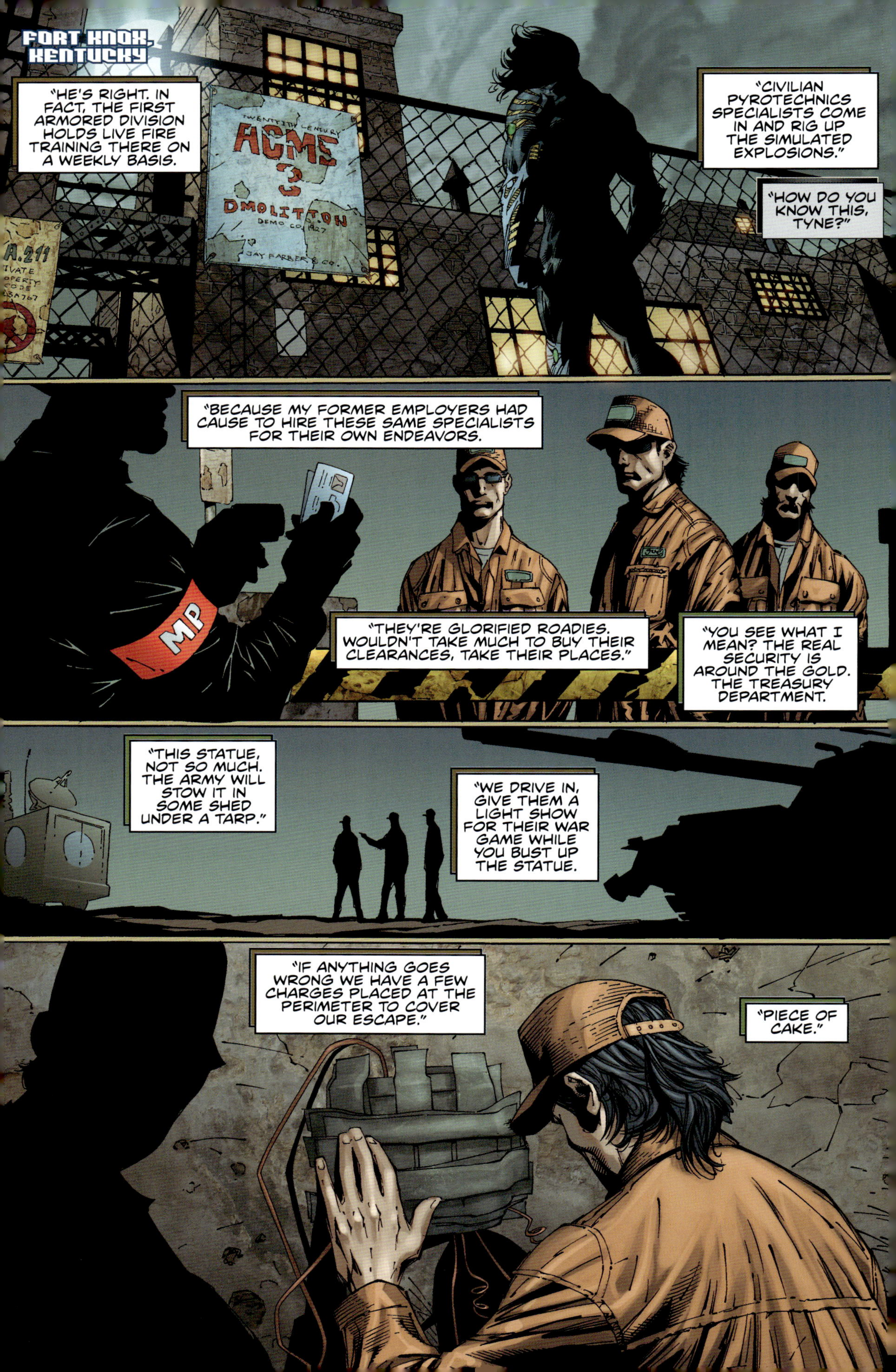
FORT KNOX, KENTUCKY
"HE'S RIGHT. IN FACT, THE FIRST ARMORED DIVISION HOLDS LIVE FIRE TRAINING THERE ON A WEEKLY BASIS.
TWENTIETH CENTURY ACME 3 DMOLITION DEMO CO. 1927 JAY BARBER & CO.
"CIVILIAN PYROTECHNICS SPECIALISTS COME IN AND RIG UP THE SIMULATED EXPLOSIONS."
"HOW DO YOU KNOW THIS, TYNE?"
"BECAUSE MY FORMER EMPLOYERS HAD CAUSE TO HIRE THESE SAME SPECIALISTS FOR THEIR OWN ENDEAVORS.
MP
"THEY'RE GLORIFIED ROADIES. WOULDN'T TAKE MUCH TO BUY THEIR CLEARANCES, TAKE THEIR PLACES."
"YOU SEE WHAT I MEAN? THE REAL SECURITY IS AROUND THE GOLD. THE TREASURY DEPARTMENT.
"THIS STATUE, NOT SO MUCH. THE ARMY WILL STOW IT IN SOME SHED UNDER A TARP."
"WE DRIVE IN, GIVE THEM A LIGHT SHOW FOR THEIR WAR GAME WHILE YOU BUST UP THE STATUE.
"IF ANYTHING GOES WRONG WE HAVE A FEW CHARGES PLACED AT THE PERIMETER TO COVER OUR ESCAPE."
"PIECE OF CAKE."

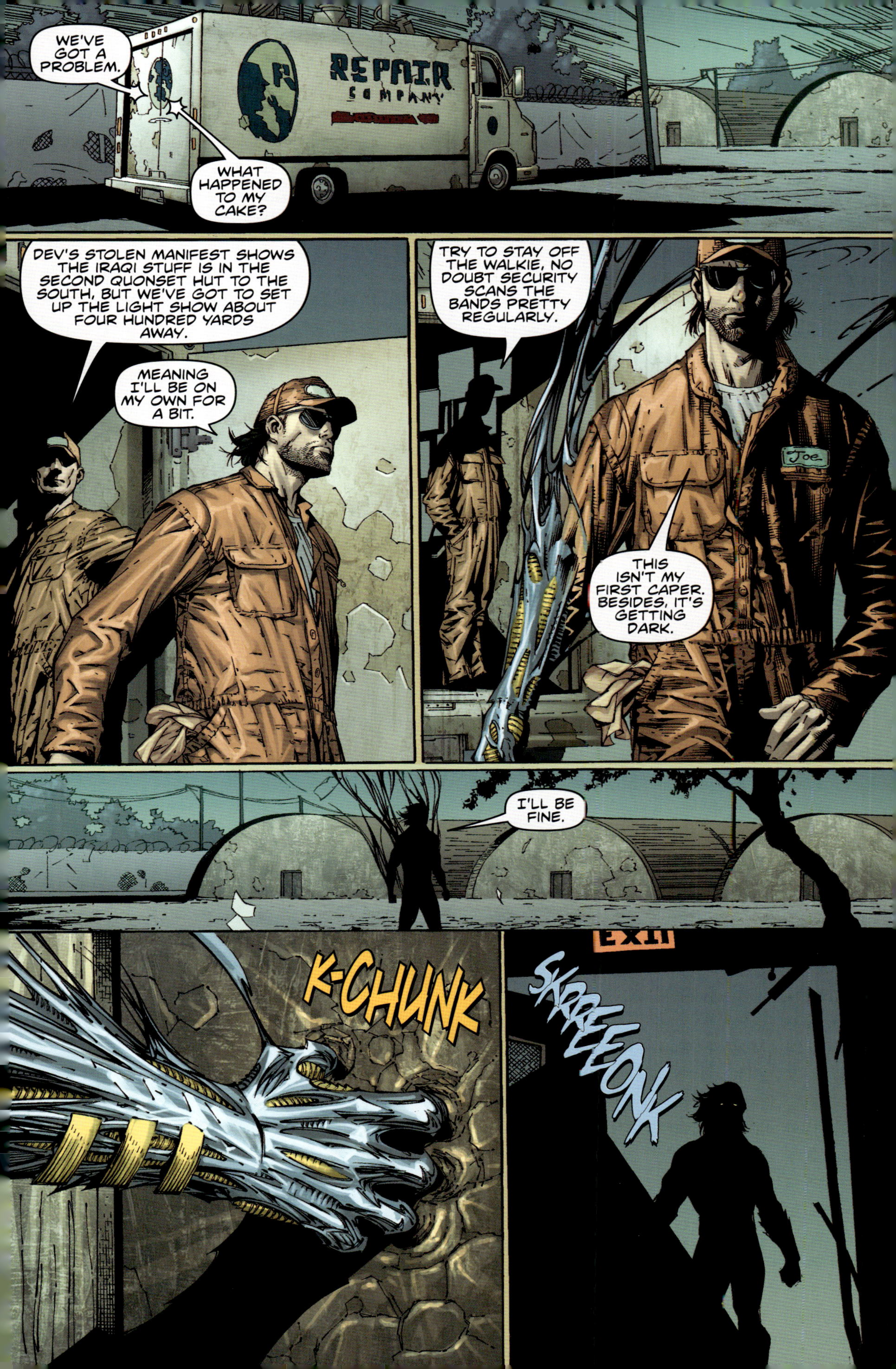
WE'VE GOT A PROBLEM.
REPAIR COMPANY
WHAT HAPPENED TO MY CAKE?
DEV'S STOLEN MANIFEST SHOWS THE IRAQI STUFF IS IN THE SECOND QUONSET HUT TO THE SOUTH, BUT WE'VE GOT TO SET UP THE LIGHT SHOW ABOUT FOUR HUNDRED YARDS AWAY.
MEANING I'LL BE ON MY OWN FOR A BIT.
TRY TO STAY OFF THE WALKIE, NO DOUBT SECURITY SCANS THE BANDS PRETTY REGULARLY.
Joe
THIS ISN'T MY FIRST CAPER. BESIDES, IT'S GETTING DARK.
I'LL BE FINE.
K-CHUNK
EXIT
SKREEEONK

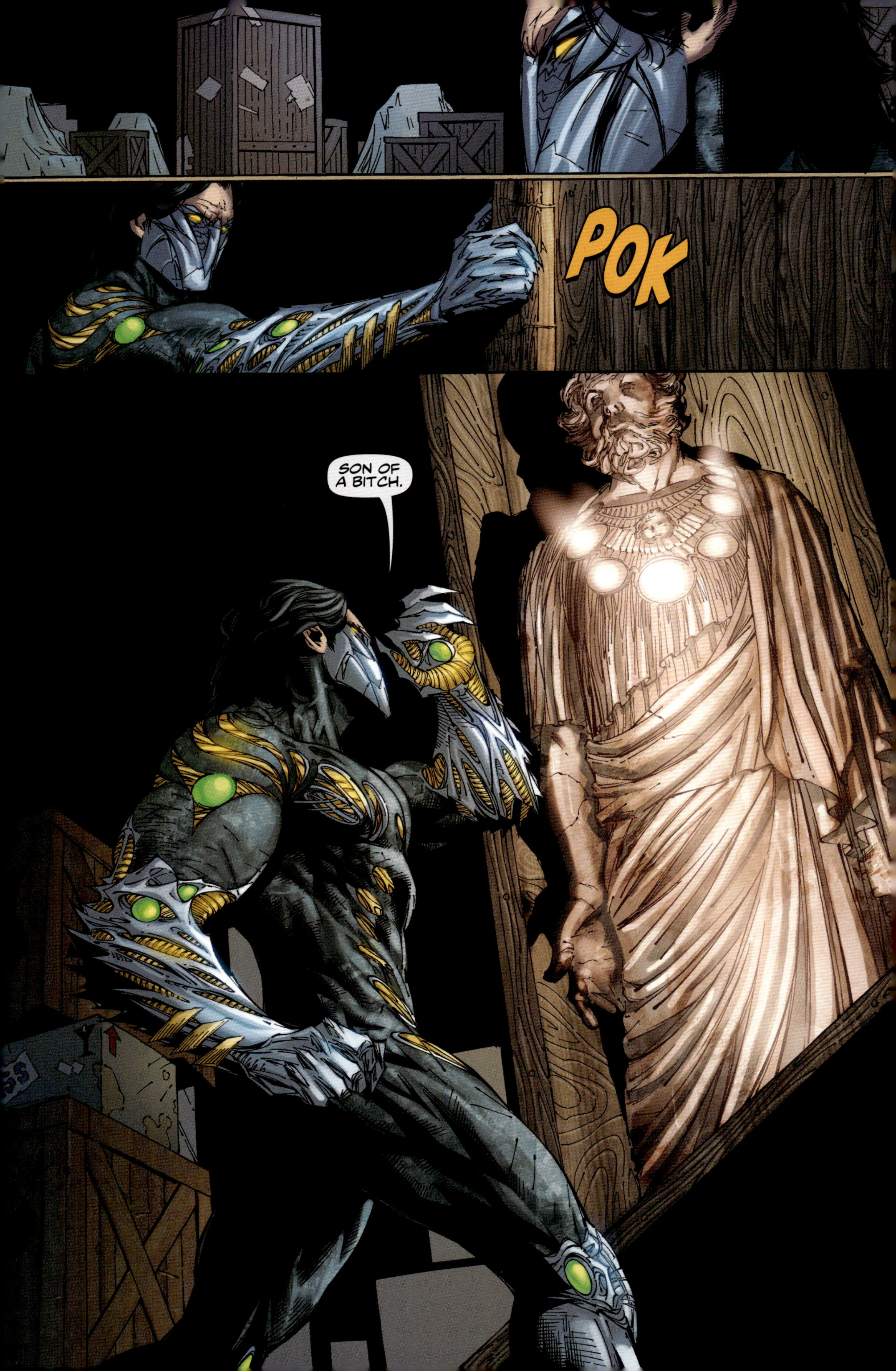
POK
SON OF A BITCH.

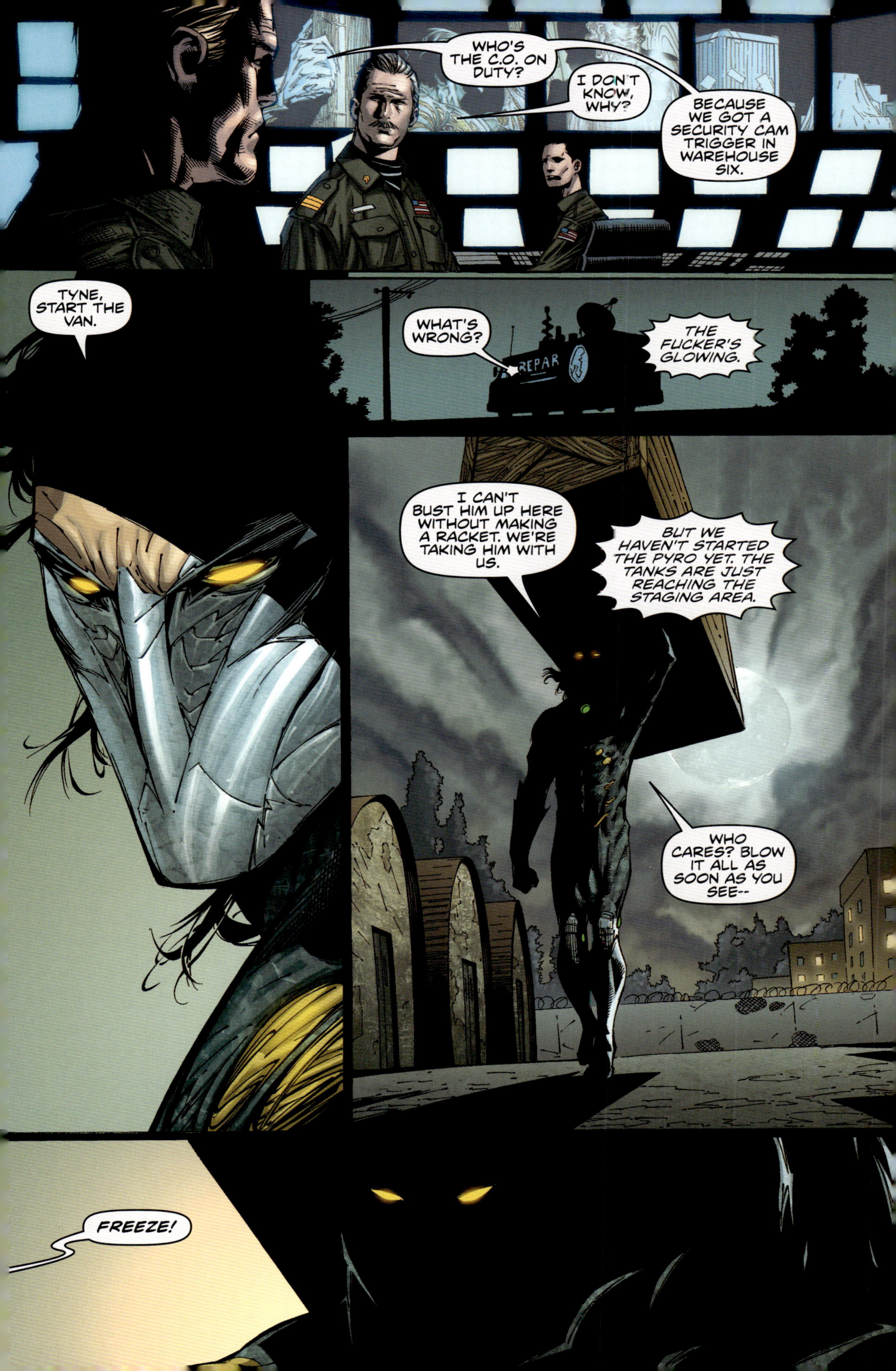
WHO'S THE C.O. ON DUTY?
I DON'T KNOW, WHY?
BECAUSE WE GOT A SECURITY CAM TRIGGER IN WAREHOUSE SIX.
TYNE, START THE VAN.
WHAT'S WRONG?
REPAR
THE FUCKER'S GLOWING.
I CAN'T BUST HIM UP HERE WITHOUT MAKING A RACKET. WE'RE TAKING HIM WITH US.
BUT WE HAVEN'T STARTED THE PYRO YET. THE TANKS ARE JUST REACHING THE STAGING AREA.
WHO CARES? BLOW IT ALL AS SOON AS YOU SEE--
FREEZE!

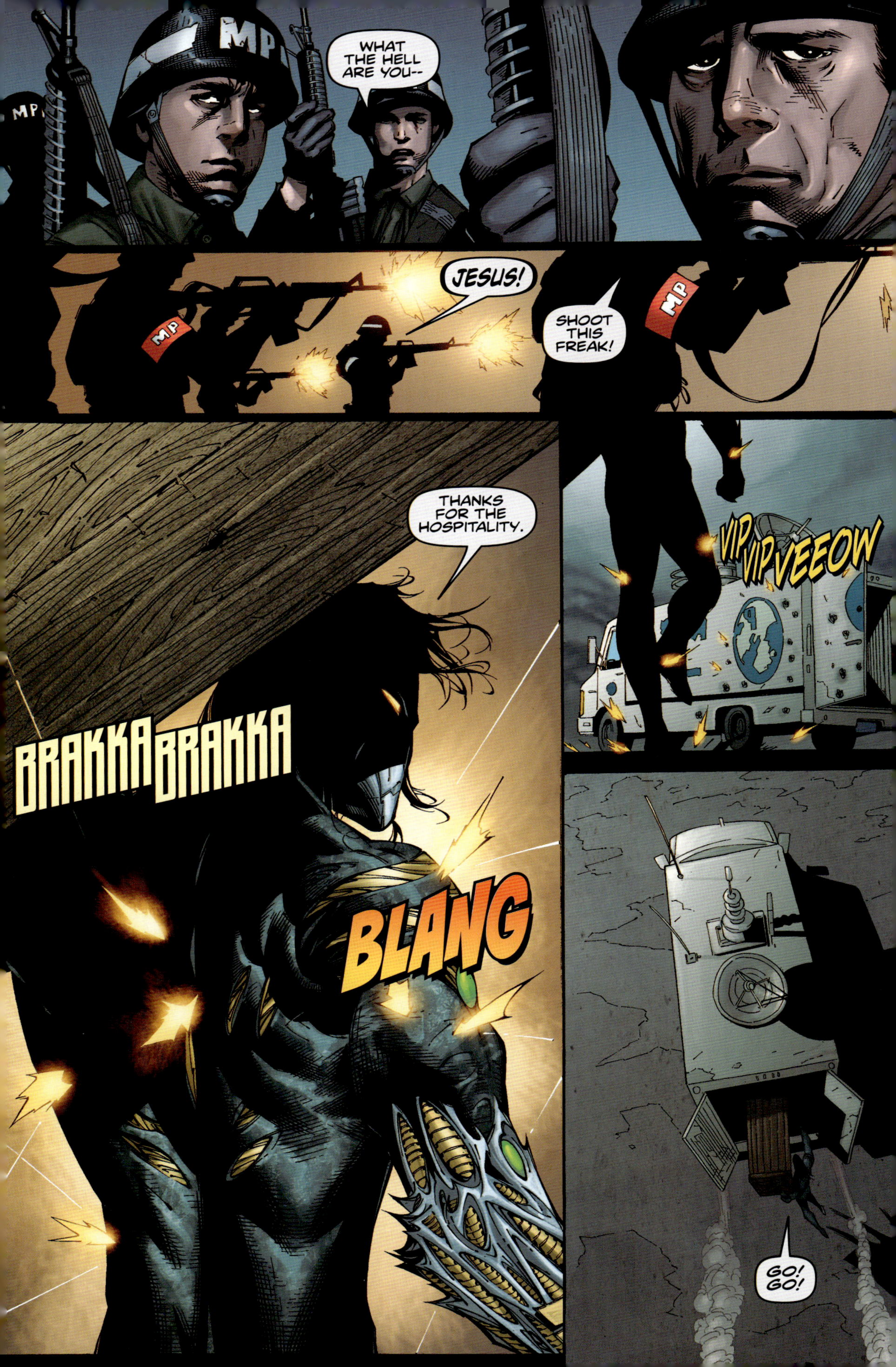
MP
MP
WHAT THE HELL ARE YOU--
JESUS!
SHOOT THIS FREAK!
MP
MP
THANKS FOR THE HOSPITALITY.
VIP VIP VEEOW
BRAKKA BRAKKA
BLANG
GO! GO!

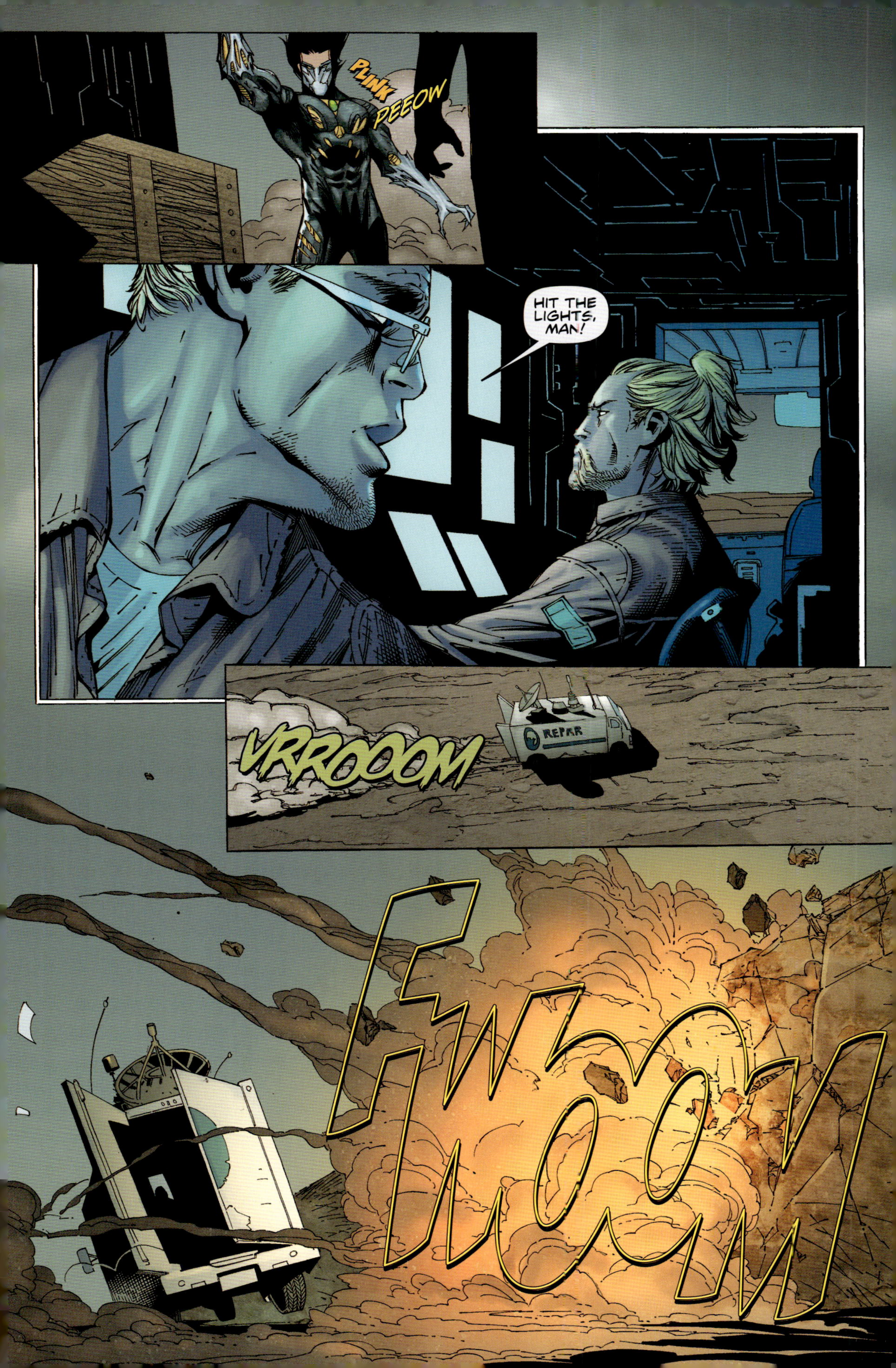
PLINK
PEEOW
HIT THE LIGHTS, MAN!
VRROOOM
REPAR
FWOOOM

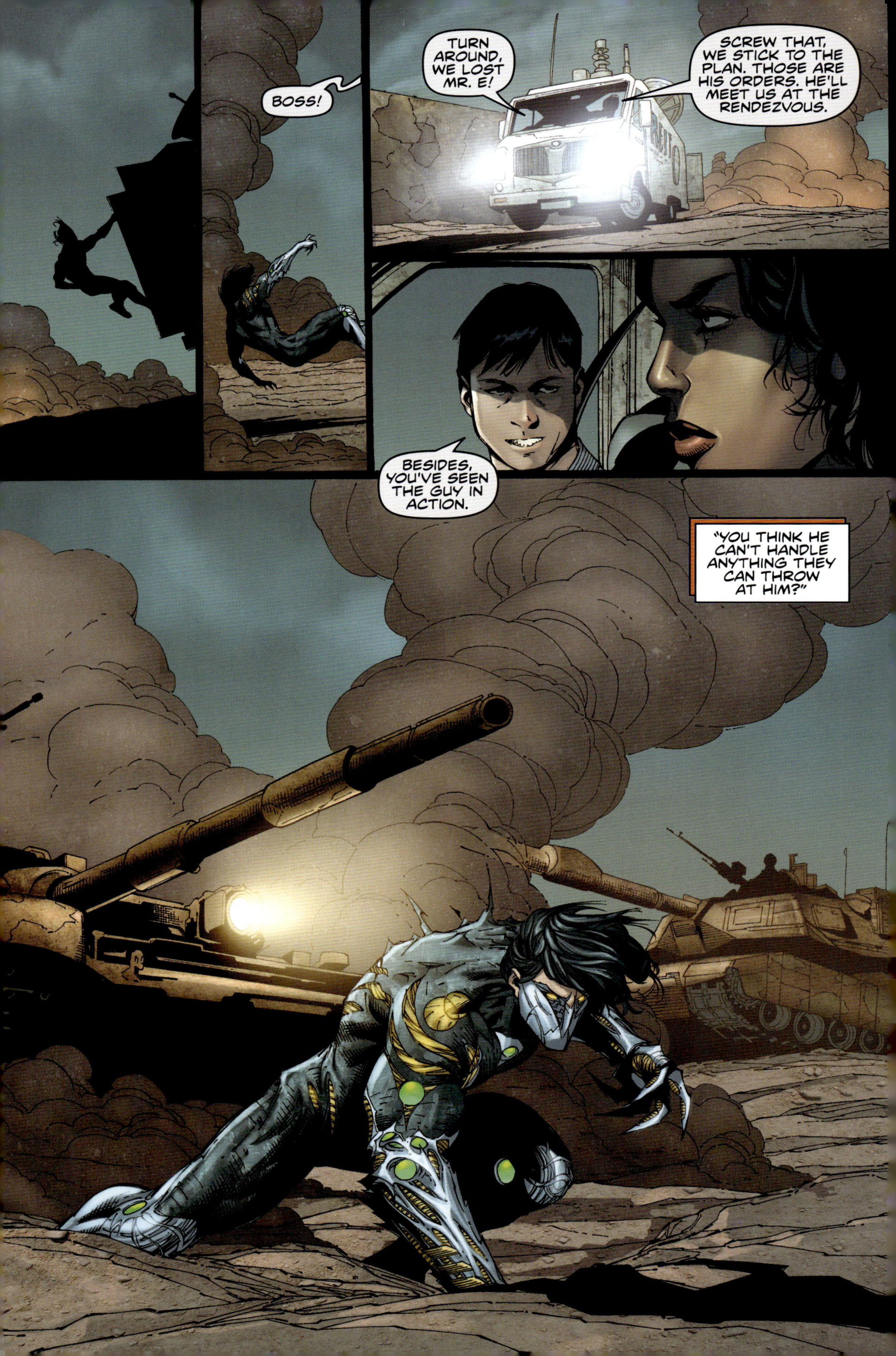
BOSS!
TURN AROUND, WE LOST MR. E!
SCREW THAT, WE STICK TO THE PLAN. THOSE ARE HIS ORDERS. HE'LL MEET US AT THE RENDEZVOUS.
BESIDES, YOU'VE SEEN THE GUY IN ACTION.
"YOU THINK HE CAN'T HANDLE ANYTHING THEY CAN THROW AT HIM?"

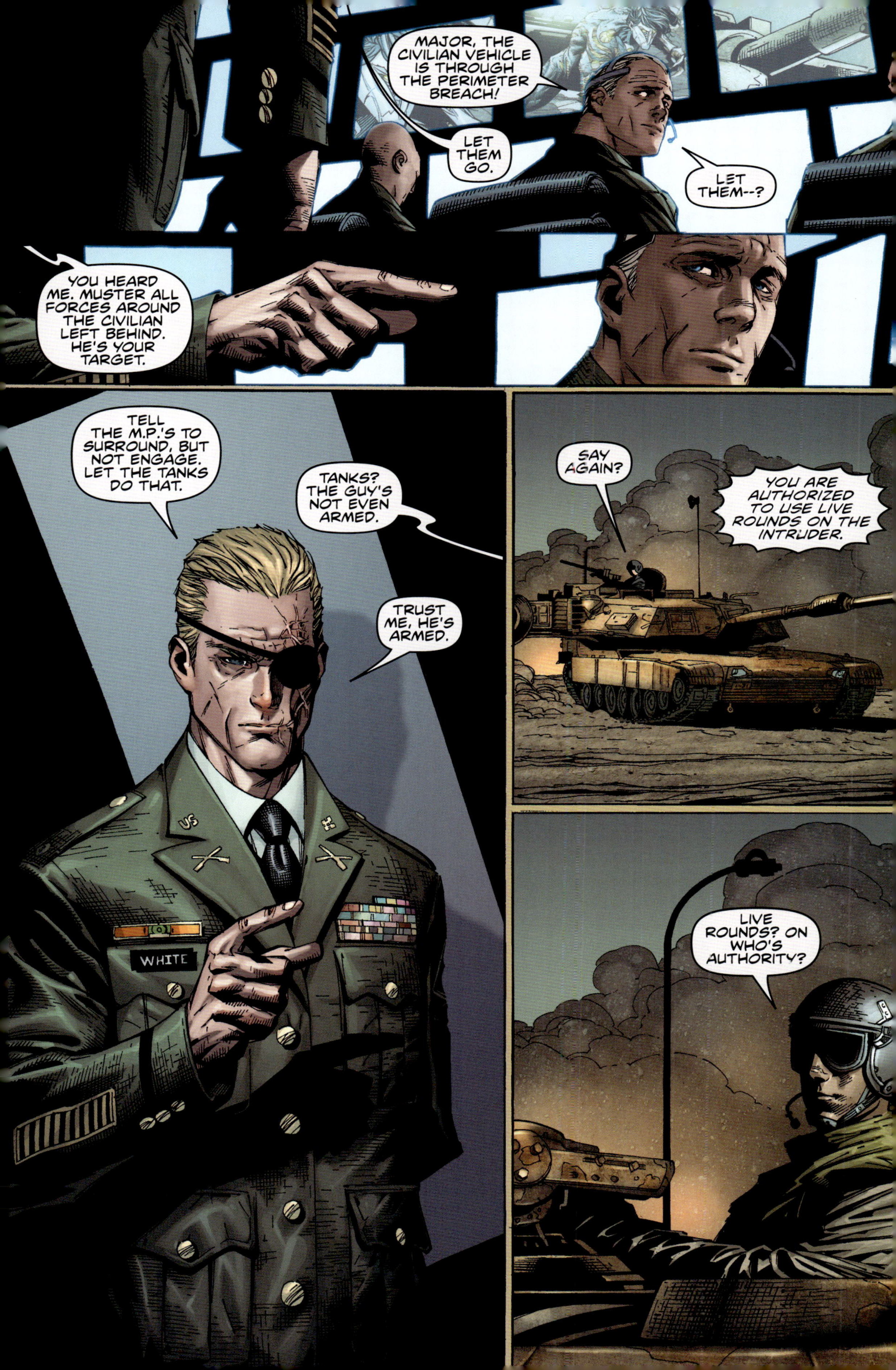
MAJOR, THE CIVILIAN VEHICLE IS THROUGH THE PERIMETER BREACH!
LET THEM GO.
LET THEM--?
YOU HEARD ME. MUSTER ALL FORCES AROUND THE CIVILIAN LEFT BEHIND. HE'S YOUR TARGET.
TELL THE M.P.'S TO SURROUND, BUT NOT ENGAGE. LET THE TANKS DO THAT.
TANKS? THE GUY'S NOT EVEN ARMED.
TRUST ME, HE'S ARMED.
WHITE
SAY AGAIN?
YOU ARE AUTHORIZED TO USE LIVE ROUNDS ON THE INTRUDER.
LIVE ROUNDS? ON WHO'S AUTHORITY?

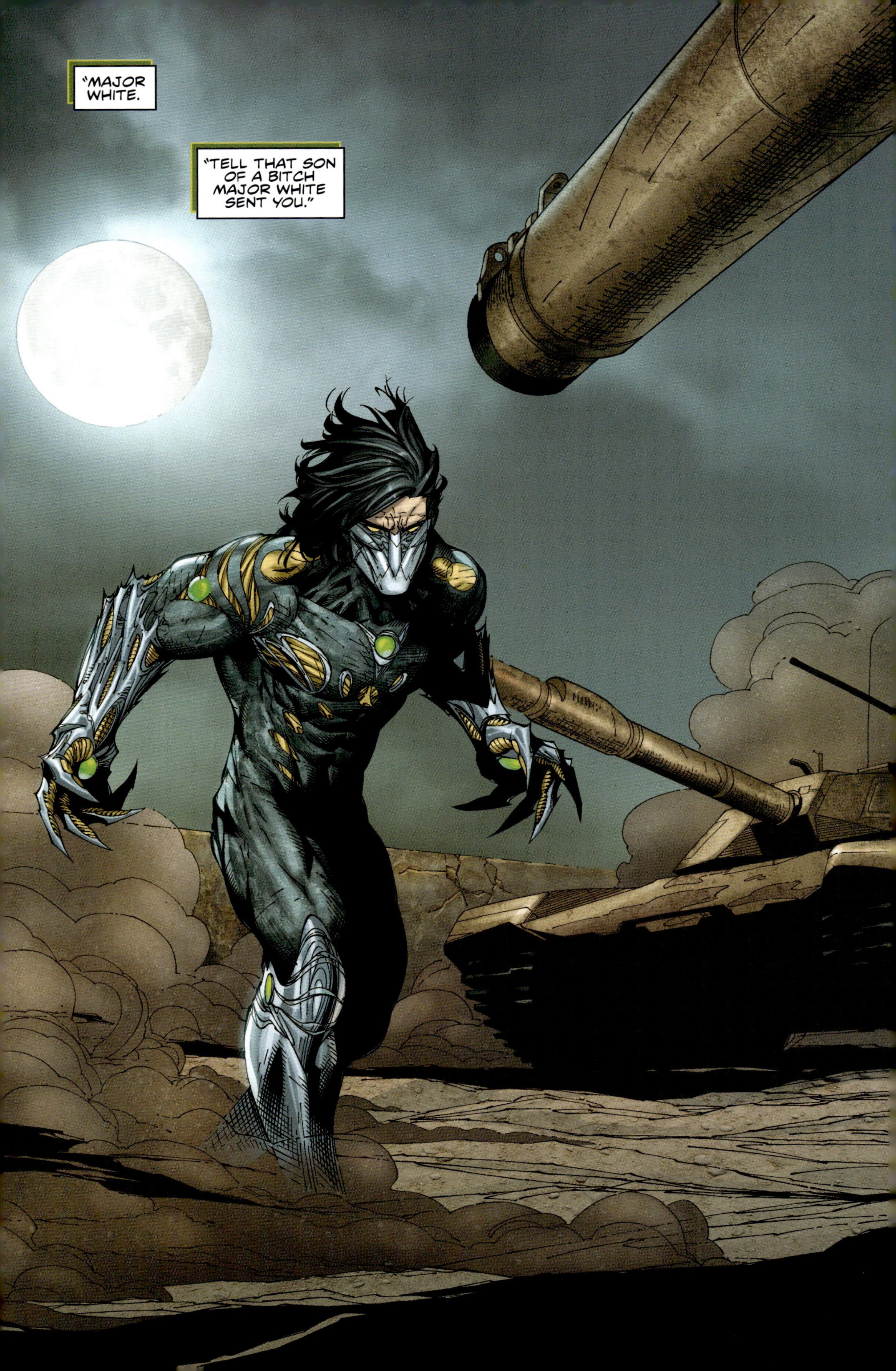
"MAJOR WHITE.
"TELL THAT SON OF A BITCH MAJOR WHITE SENT YOU."

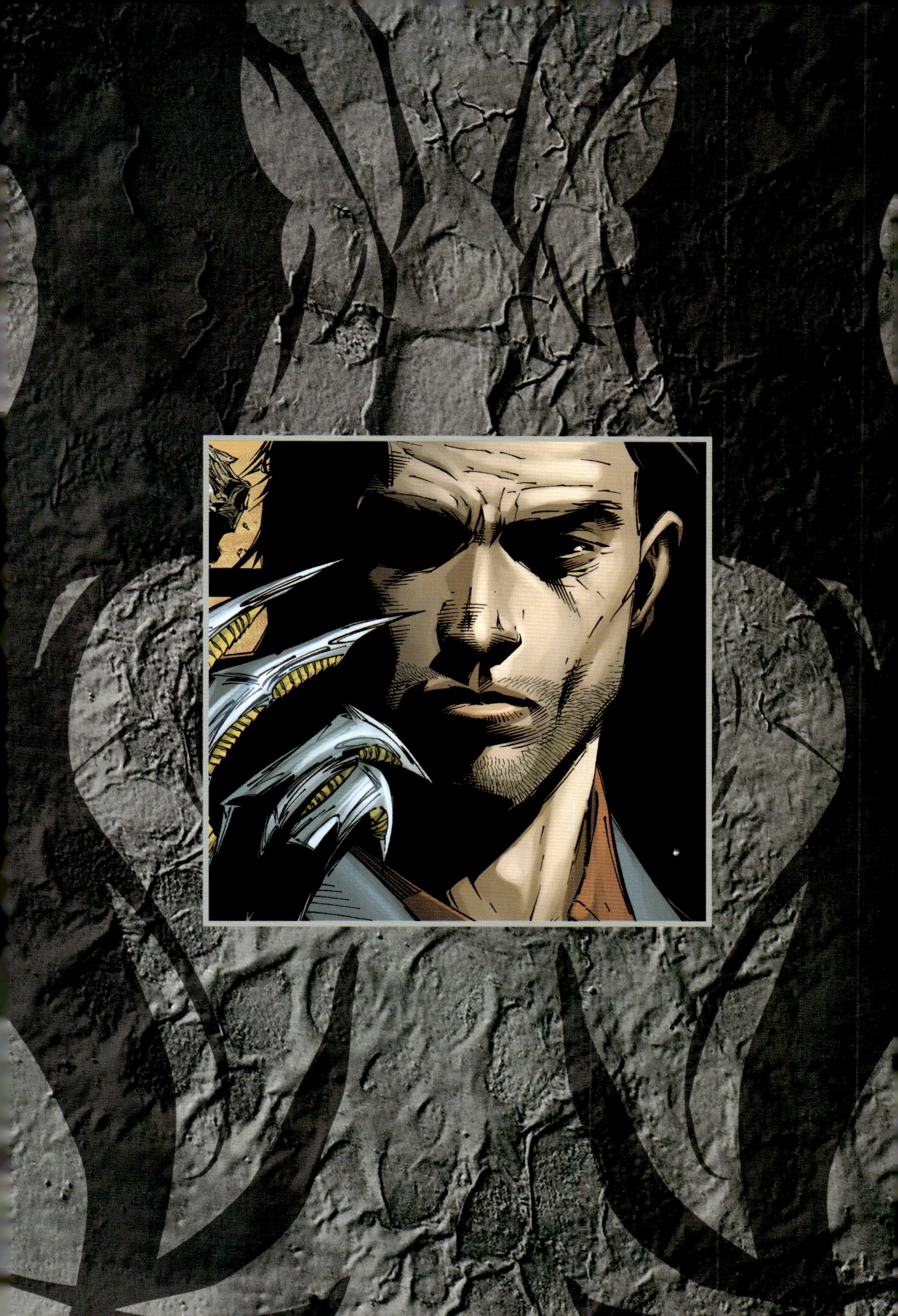

The Darkness Issue #83
cover art by: Dennis Calero

THE DARKNESS #83

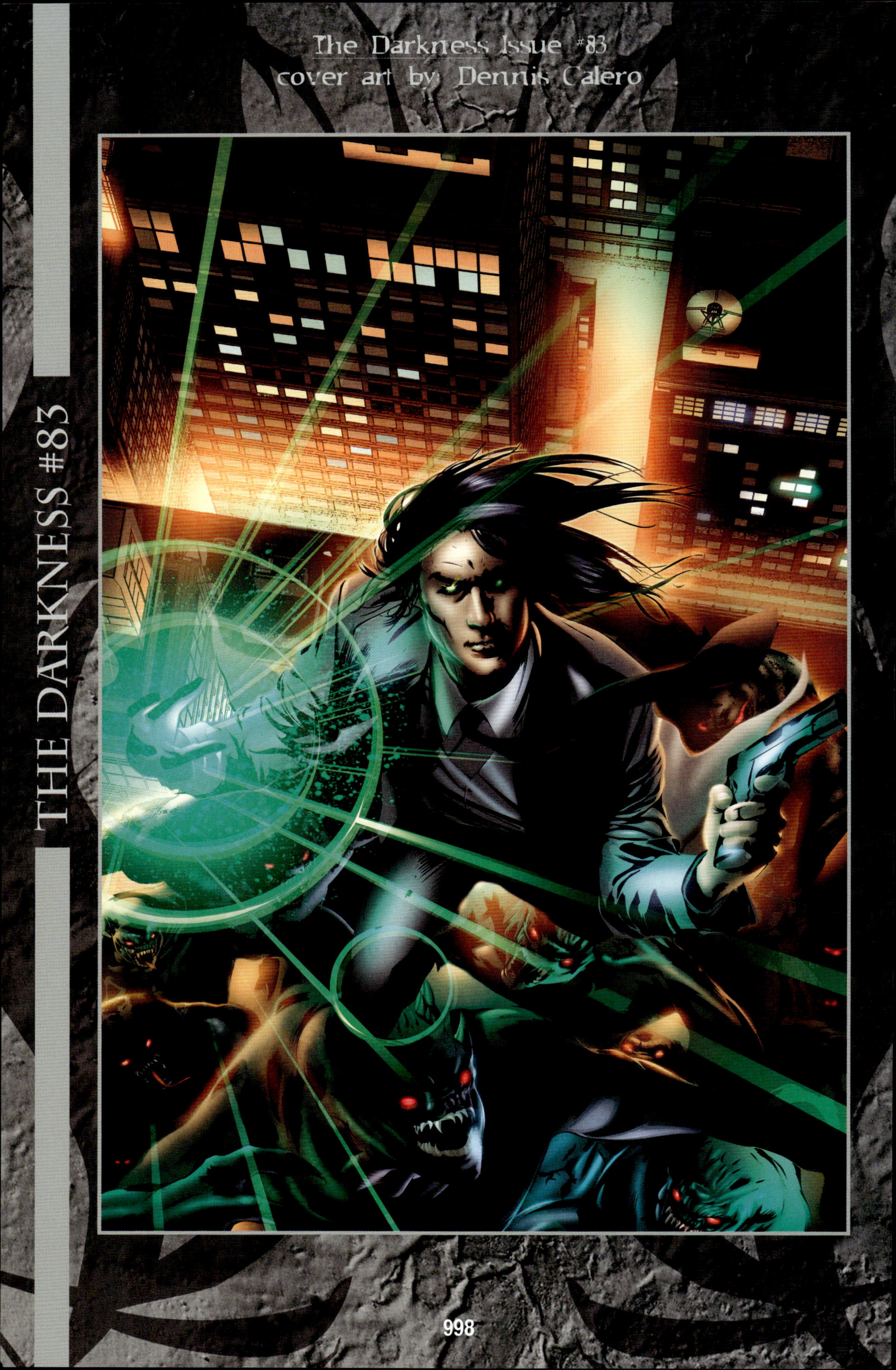

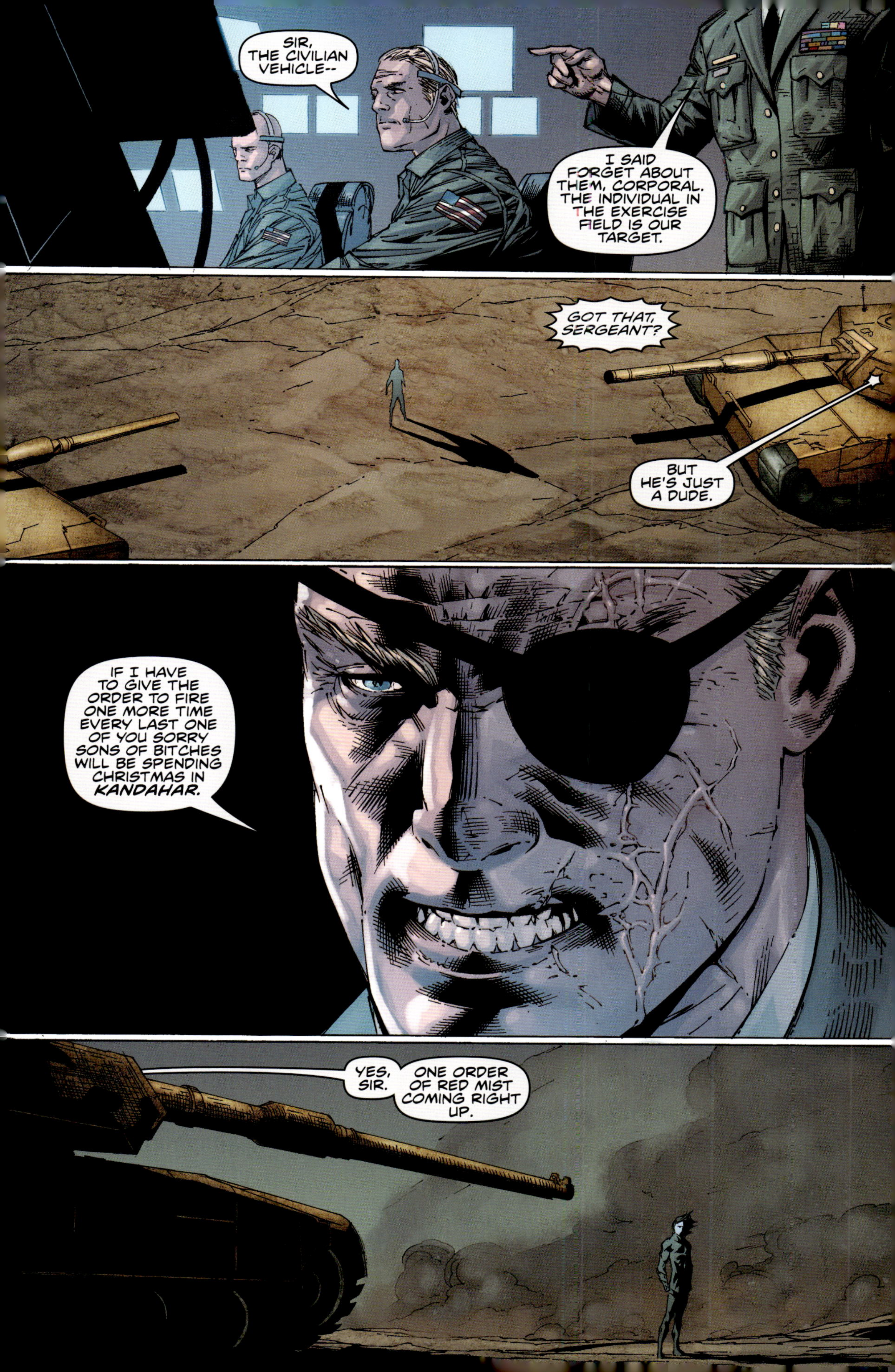
SIR, THE CIVILIAN VEHICLE--
I SAID FORGET ABOUT THEM, CORPORAL. THE INDIVIDUAL IN THE EXERCISE FIELD IS OUR TARGET.
GOT THAT, SERGEANT?
BUT HE'S JUST A DUDE.
IF I HAVE TO GIVE THE ORDER TO FIRE ONE MORE TIME EVERY LAST ONE OF YOU SORRY SONS OF BITCHES WILL BE SPENDING CHRISTMAS IN *KANDAHAR.*
YES, SIR.
ONE ORDER OF RED MIST COMING RIGHT UP.

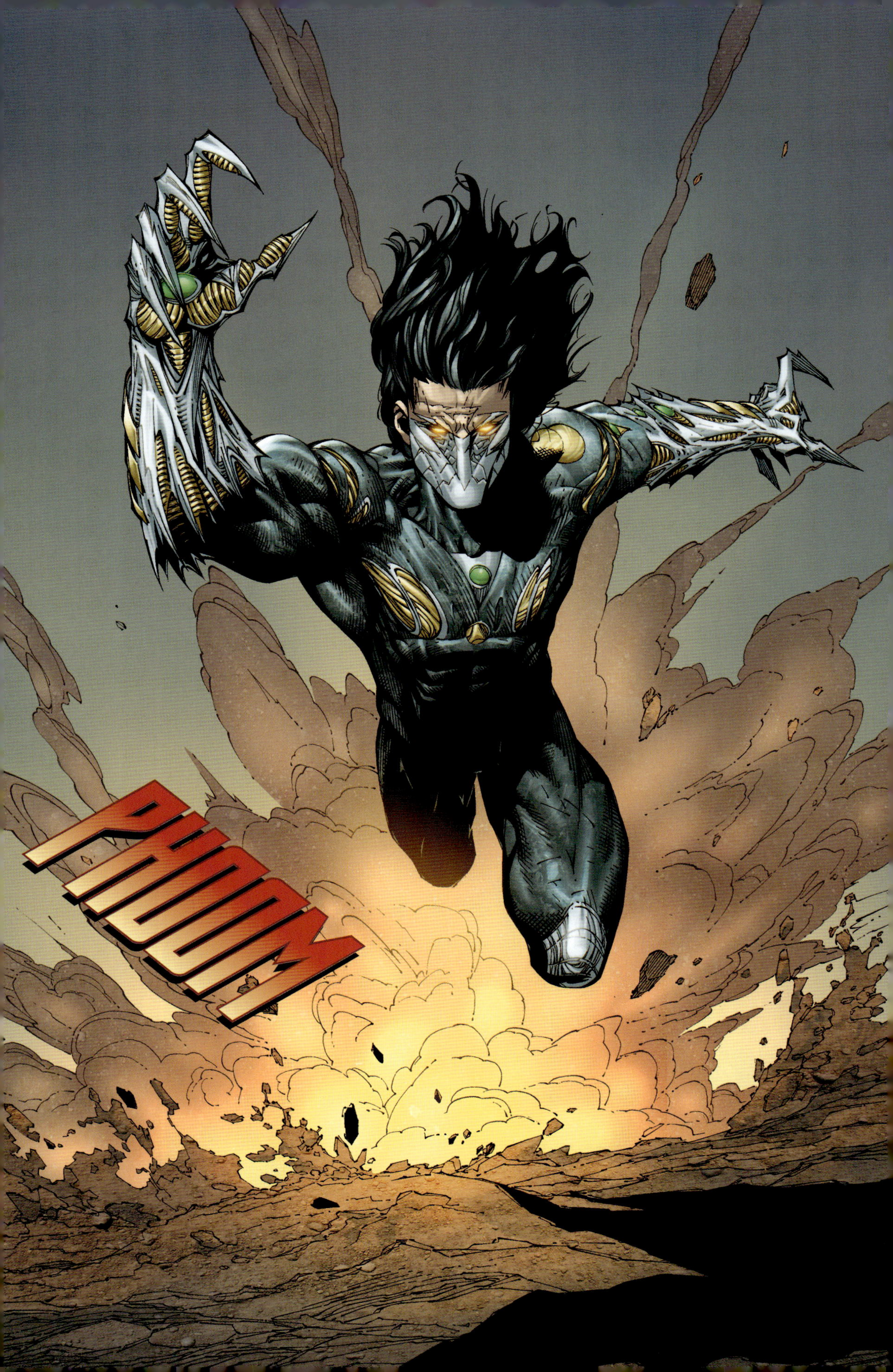
PHOOM

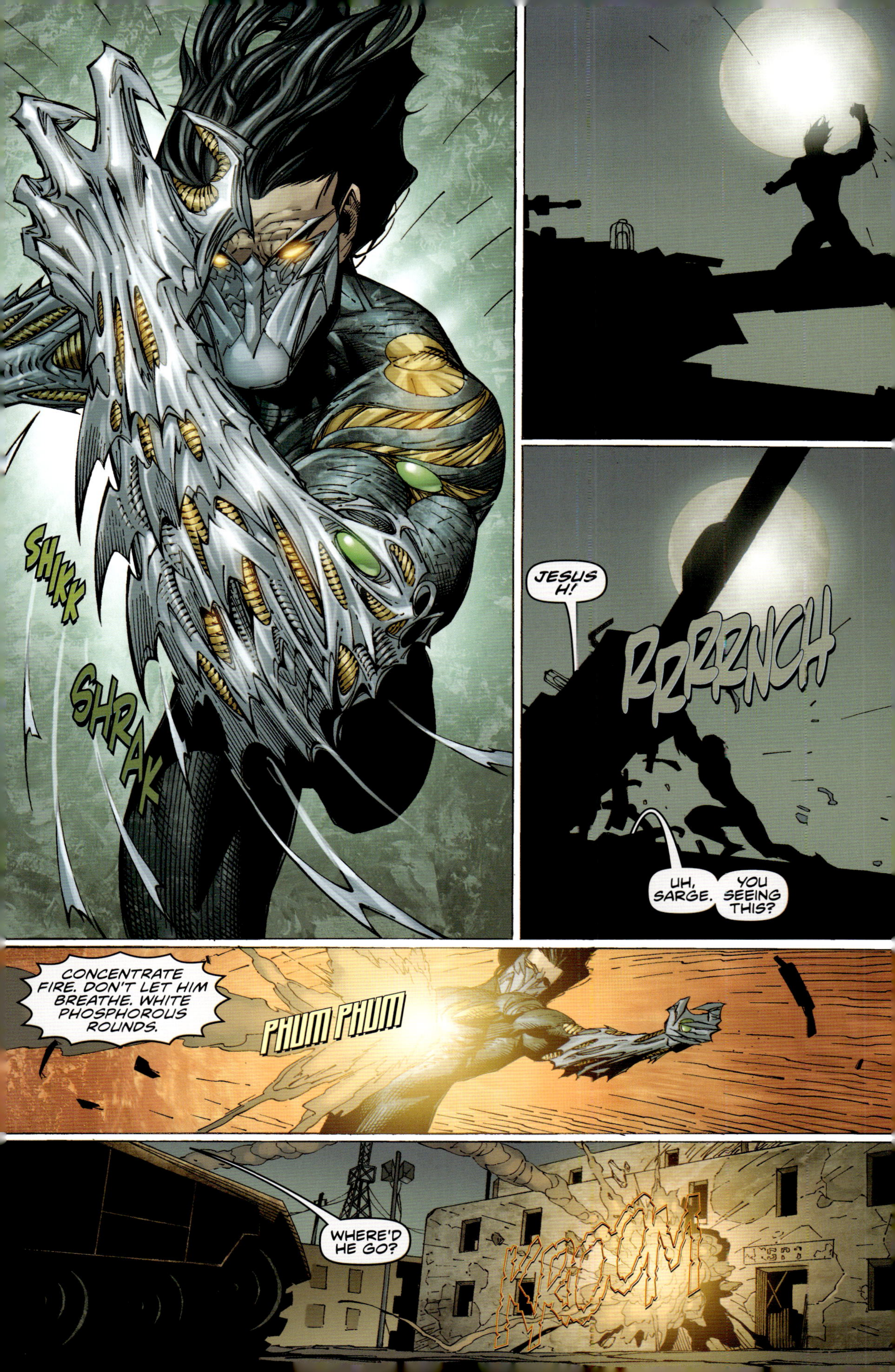
SHIKK
SHRAK
JESUS H!
RRRRNCH
UH, SARGE.
YOU SEEING THIS?
CONCENTRATE FIRE. DON'T LET HIM BREATHE. WHITE PHOSPHOROUS ROUNDS.
PHUM PHUM
WHERE'D HE GO?
KROOM

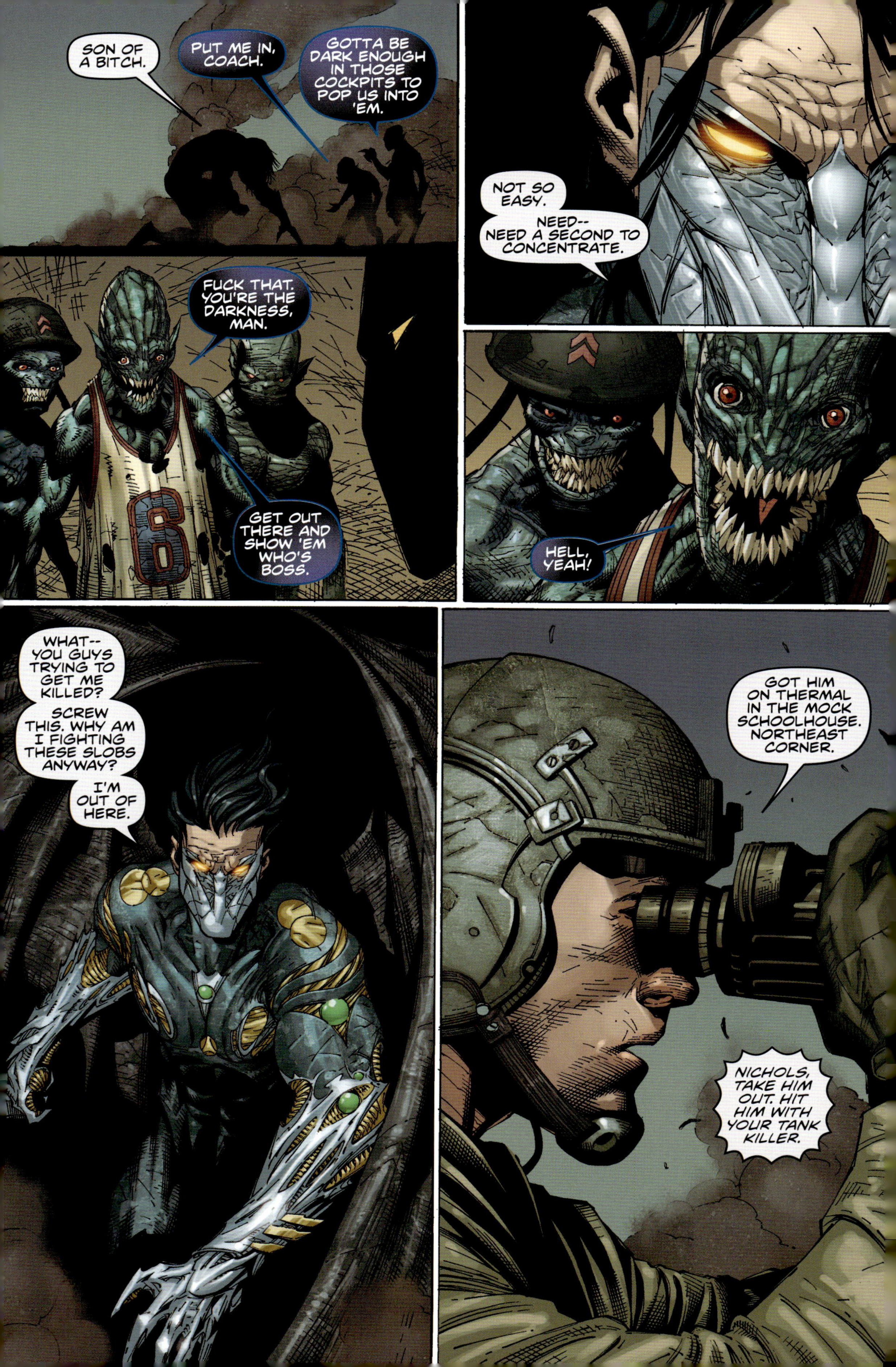
SON OF A BITCH.
PUT ME IN, COACH.
GOTTA BE DARK ENOUGH IN THOSE COCKPITS TO POP US INTO 'EM.
NOT SO EASY.
NEED-- NEED A SECOND TO CONCENTRATE.
FUCK THAT. YOU'RE THE DARKNESS, MAN.
GET OUT THERE AND SHOW 'EM WHO'S BOSS.
HELL, YEAH!
WHAT-- YOU GUYS TRYING TO GET ME KILLED?
SCREW THIS. WHY AM I FIGHTING THESE SLOBS ANYWAY?
I'M OUT OF HERE.
GOT HIM ON THERMAL IN THE MOCK SCHOOLHOUSE. NORTHEAST CORNER.
NICHOLS, TAKE HIM OUT. HIT HIM WITH YOUR TANK KILLER.

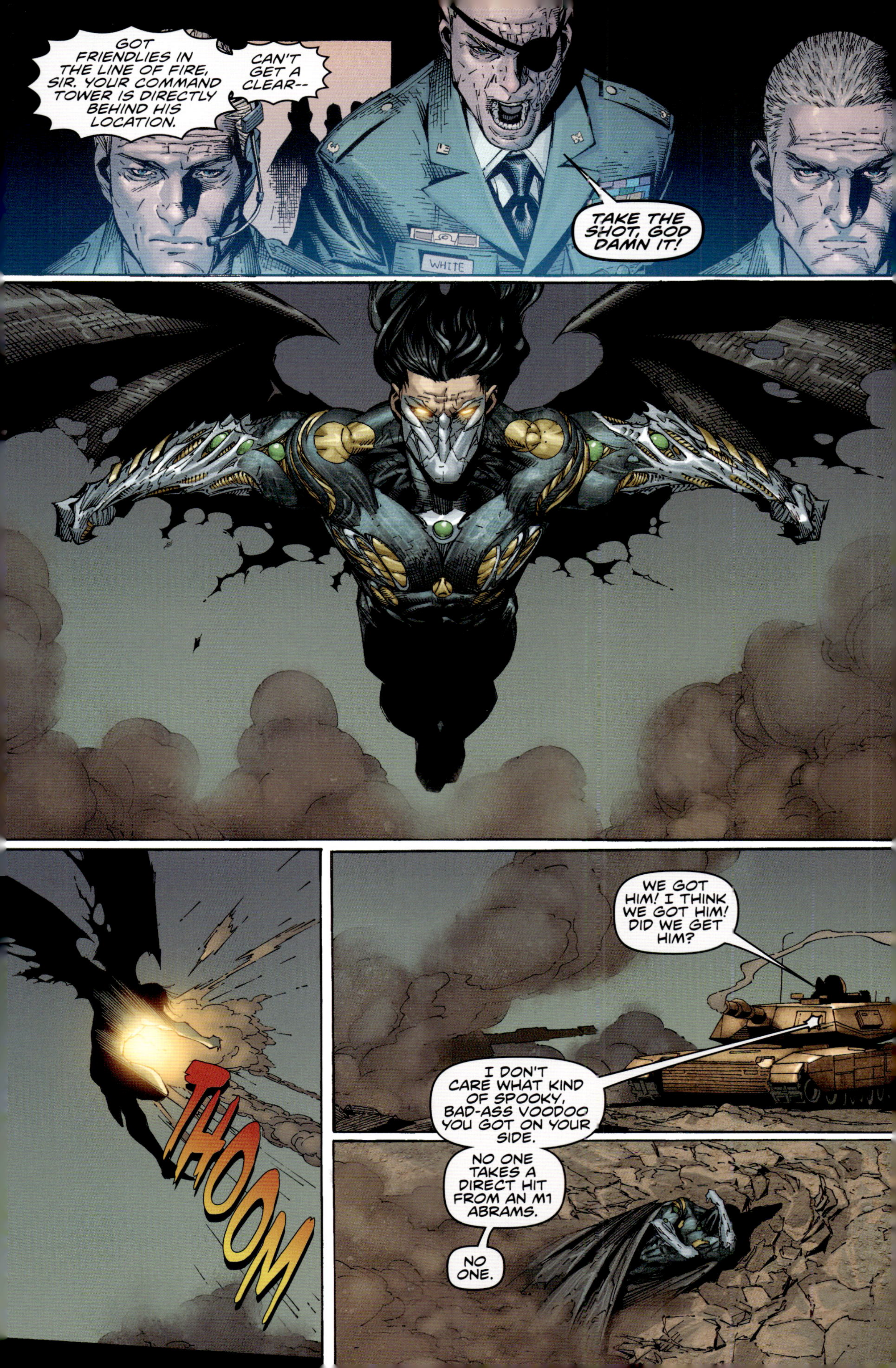
GOT FRIENDLIES IN THE LINE OF FIRE, SIR. YOUR COMMAND TOWER IS DIRECTLY BEHIND HIS LOCATION.
CAN'T GET A CLEAR--
TAKE THE SHOT, GOD DAMN IT!
WHITE
THOOM
WE GOT HIM! I THINK WE GOT HIM! DID WE GET HIM?
I DON'T CARE WHAT KIND OF SPOOKY, BAD-ASS VOODOO YOU GOT ON YOUR SIDE.
NO ONE TAKES A DIRECT HIT FROM AN M1 ABRAMS.
NO ONE.

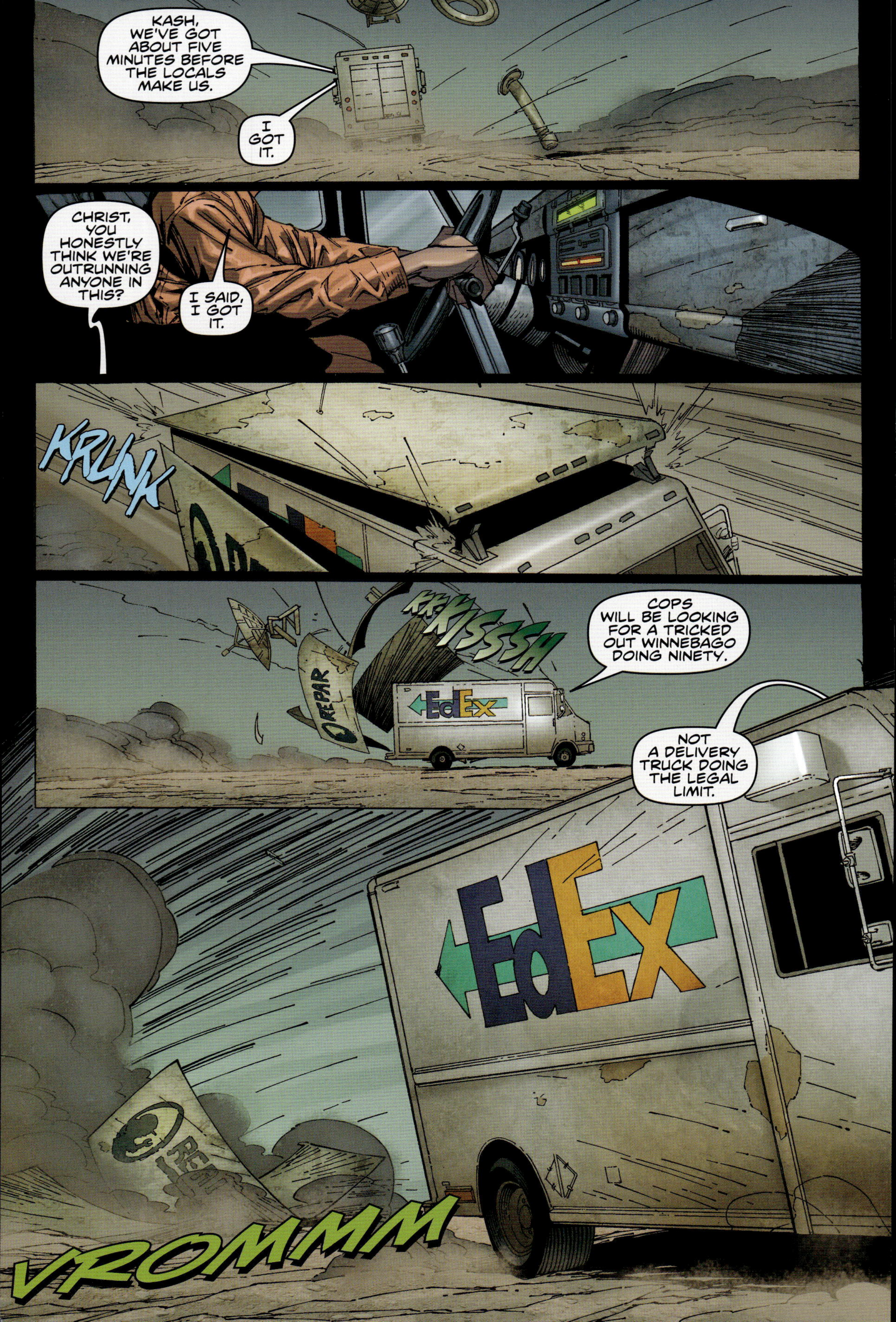
KASH, WE'VE GOT ABOUT FIVE MINUTES BEFORE THE LOCALS MAKE US.
I GOT IT.
CHRIST, YOU HONESTLY THINK WE'RE OUTRUNNING ANYONE IN THIS?
I SAID, I GOT IT.
KRUNK
KKKISSSH
REPAR
EdEx
COPS WILL BE LOOKING FOR A TRICKED OUT WINNEBAGO DOING NINETY.
NOT A DELIVERY TRUCK DOING THE LEGAL LIMIT.
EdEx
VROMMMM

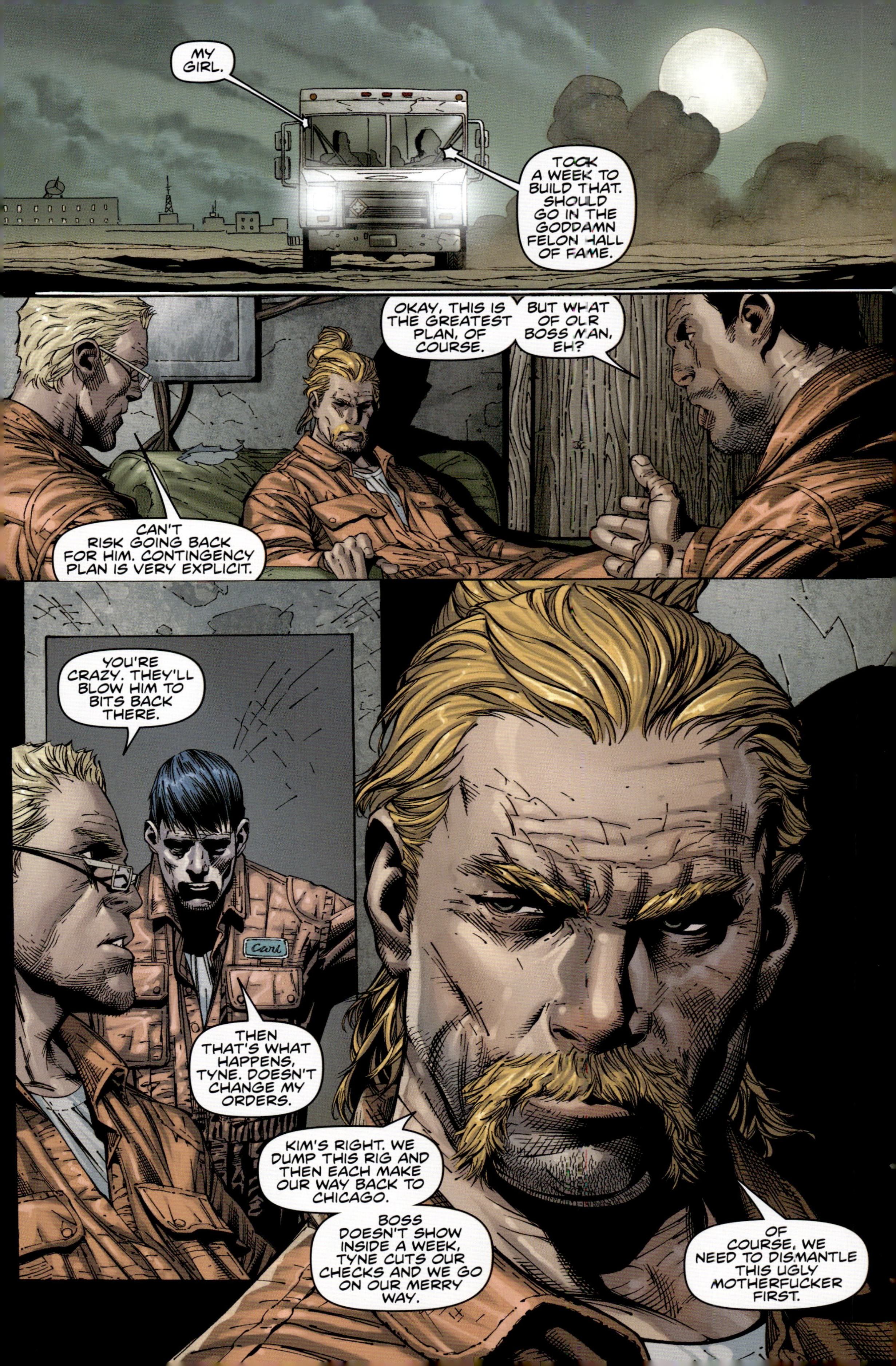
MY GIRL.
TOOK A WEEK TO BUILD THAT. SHOULD GO IN THE GODDAMN FELON HALL OF FAME.
OKAY, THIS IS THE GREATEST PLAN, OF COURSE.
BUT WHAT OF OUR BOSS MAN, EH?
CAN'T RISK GOING BACK FOR HIM. CONTINGENCY PLAN IS VERY EXPLICIT.
YOU'RE CRAZY. THEY'LL BLOW HIM TO BITS BACK THERE.
Carl
THEN THAT'S WHAT HAPPENS, TYNE. DOESN'T CHANGE MY ORDERS.
KIM'S RIGHT. WE DUMP THIS RIG AND THEN EACH MAKE OUR WAY BACK TO CHICAGO.
BOSS DOESN'T SHOW INSIDE A WEEK, TYNE CUTS OUR CHECKS AND WE GO ON OUR MERRY WAY.
OF COURSE, WE NEED TO DISMANTLE THIS UGLY MOTHERFUCKER FIRST.

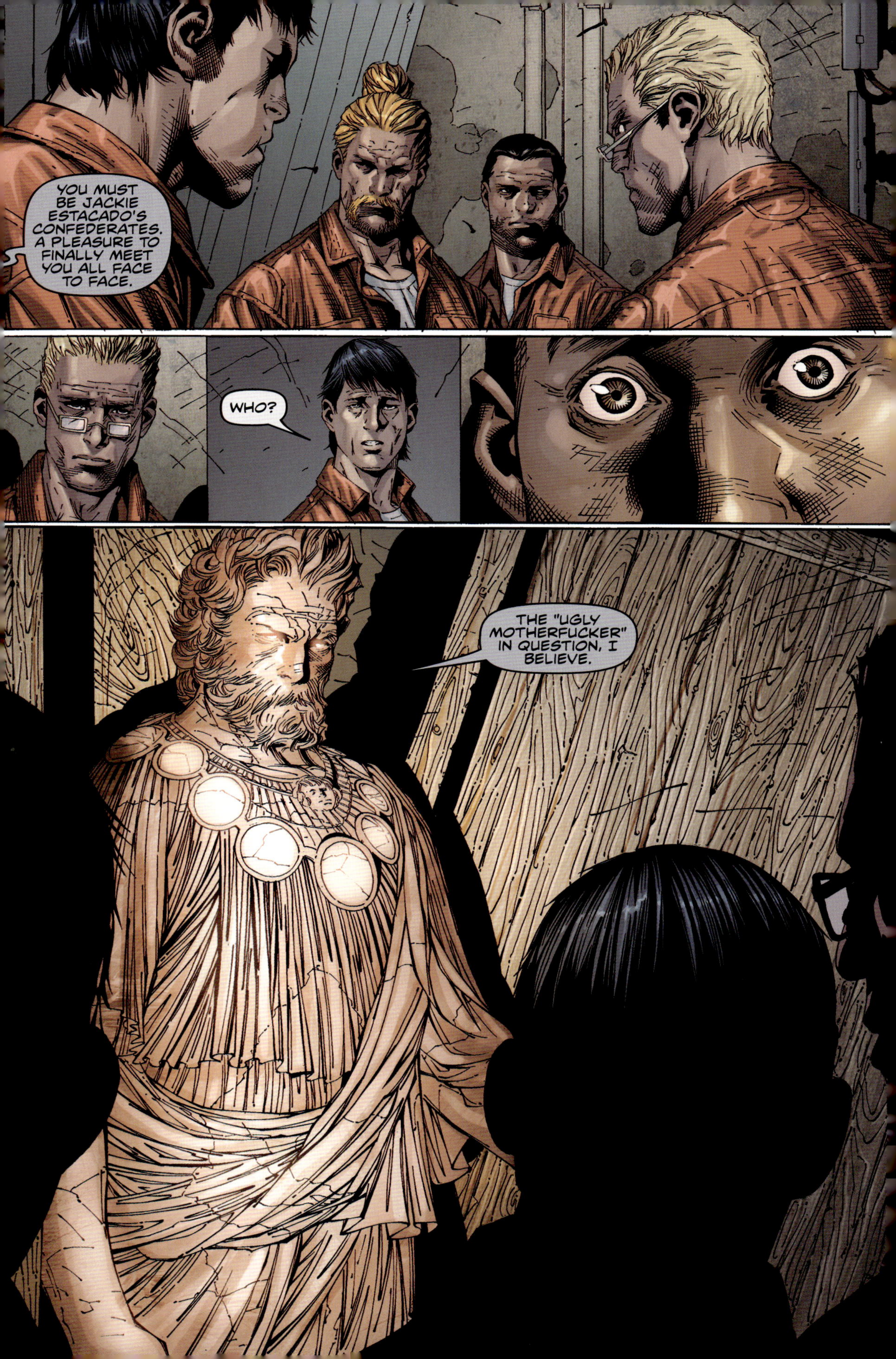
YOU MUST BE JACKIE ESTACADO'S CONFEDERATES. A PLEASURE TO FINALLY MEET YOU ALL FACE TO FACE.
WHO?
THE "UGLY MOTHERFUCKER" IN QUESTION, I BELIEVE.

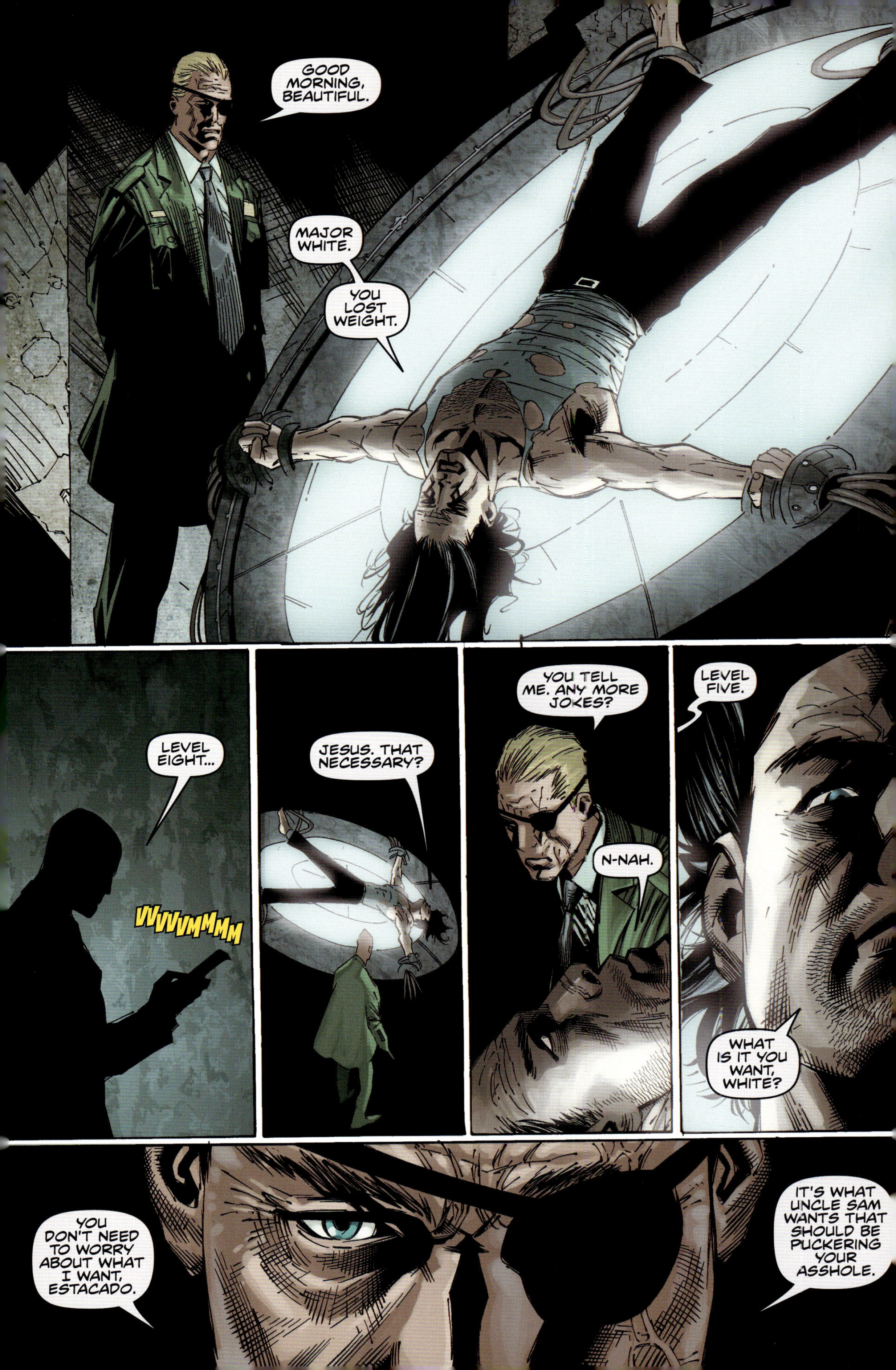
GOOD MORNING, BEAUTIFUL.
MAJOR WHITE.
YOU LOST WEIGHT.
LEVEL EIGHT...
VVVVVMMMM
JESUS. THAT NECESSARY?
YOU TELL ME. ANY MORE JOKES?
N-NAH.
LEVEL FIVE.
WHAT IS IT YOU WANT, WHITE?
YOU DON'T NEED TO WORRY ABOUT WHAT I WANT, ESTACADO.
IT'S WHAT UNCLE SAM WANTS THAT SHOULD BE PUCKERING YOUR ASSHOLE.

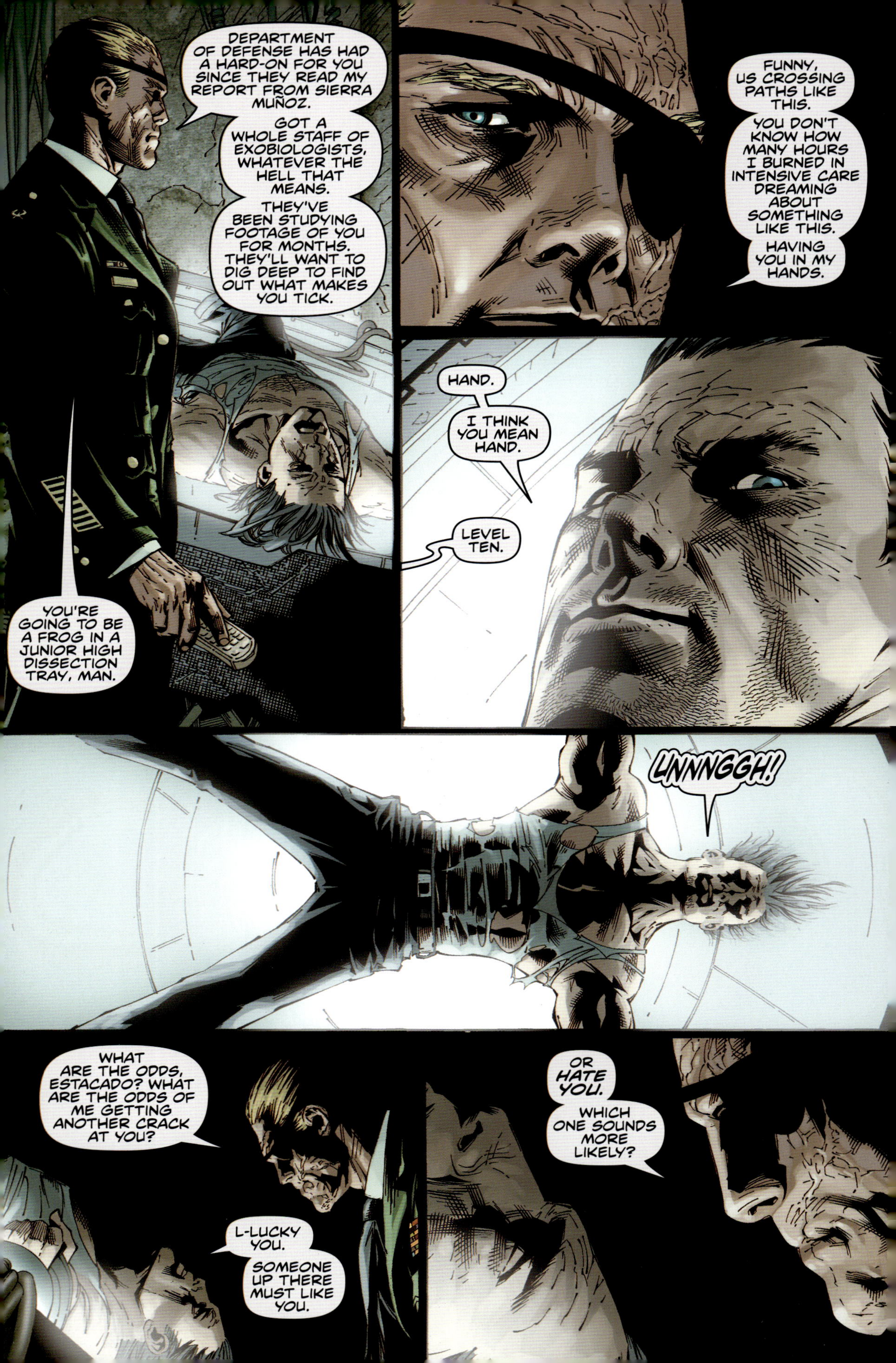
DEPARTMENT OF DEFENSE HAS HAD A HARD-ON FOR YOU SINCE THEY READ MY REPORT FROM SIERRA MUÑOZ.
GOT A WHOLE STAFF OF EXOBIOLOGISTS, WHATEVER THE HELL THAT MEANS.
THEY'VE BEEN STUDYING FOOTAGE OF YOU FOR MONTHS. THEY'LL WANT TO DIG DEEP TO FIND OUT WHAT MAKES YOU TICK.
YOU'RE GOING TO BE A FROG IN A JUNIOR HIGH DISSECTION TRAY, MAN.
FUNNY, US CROSSING PATHS LIKE THIS.
YOU DON'T KNOW HOW MANY HOURS I BURNED IN INTENSIVE CARE DREAMING ABOUT SOMETHING LIKE THIS.
HAVING YOU IN MY HANDS.
HAND.
I THINK YOU MEAN HAND.
LEVEL TEN.
UNNNGGH!
WHAT ARE THE ODDS, ESTACADO? WHAT ARE THE ODDS OF ME GETTING ANOTHER CRACK AT YOU?
L-LUCKY YOU.
SOMEONE UP THERE MUST LIKE YOU.
OR HATE YOU.
WHICH ONE SOUNDS MORE LIKELY?

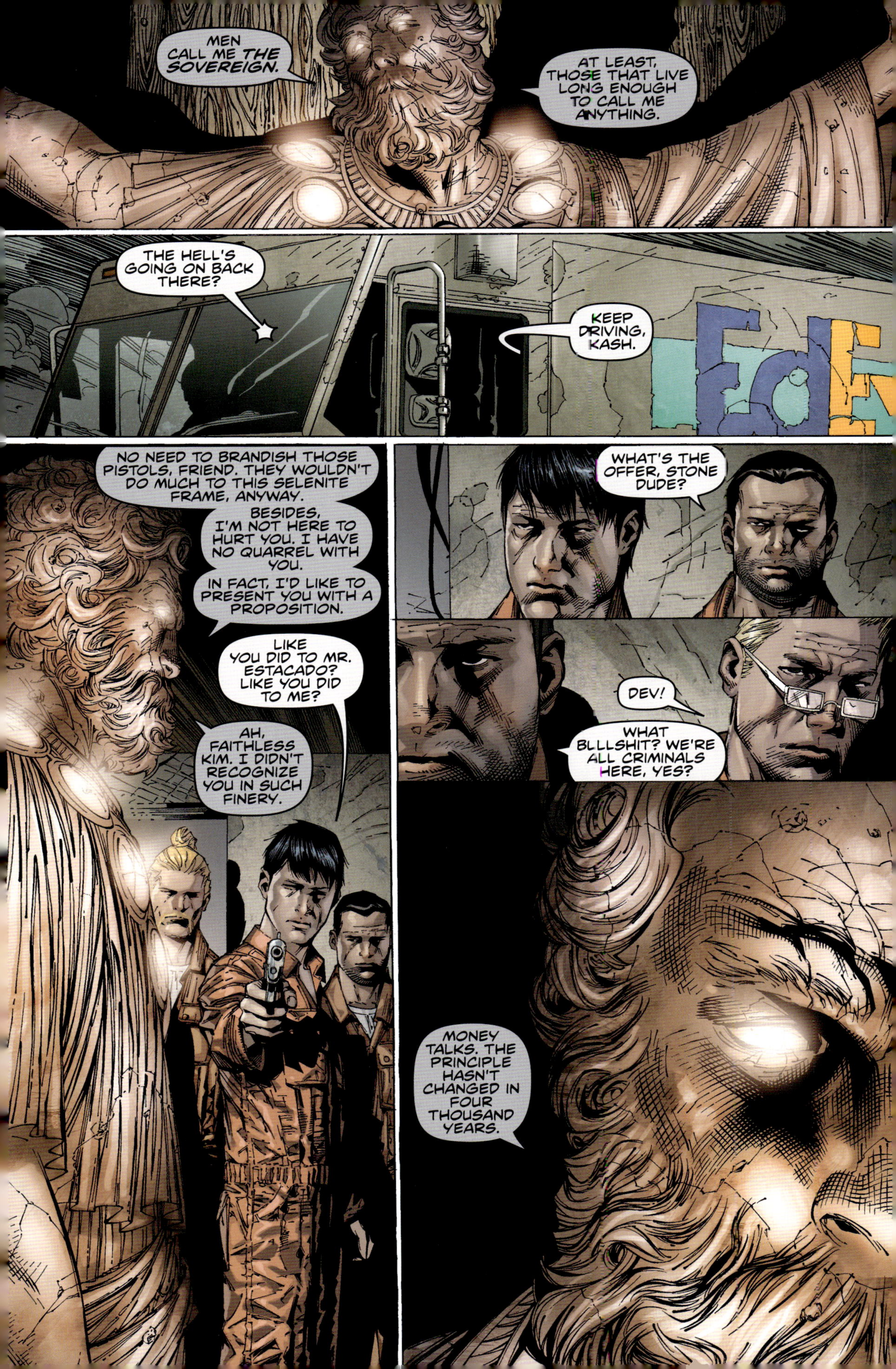
MEN CALL ME THE SOVEREIGN.
AT LEAST, THOSE THAT LIVE LONG ENOUGH TO CALL ME ANYTHING.
THE HELL'S GOING ON BACK THERE?
KEEP DRIVING, KASH.
NO NEED TO BRANDISH THOSE PISTOLS, FRIEND. THEY WOULDN'T DO MUCH TO THIS SELENITE FRAME, ANYWAY.
BESIDES, I'M NOT HERE TO HURT YOU. I HAVE NO QUARREL WITH YOU.
IN FACT, I'D LIKE TO PRESENT YOU WITH A PROPOSITION.
LIKE YOU DID TO MR. ESTACADO? LIKE YOU DID TO ME?
AH, FAITHLESS KIM. I DIDN'T RECOGNIZE YOU IN SUCH FINERY.
WHAT'S THE OFFER, STONE DUDE?
DEV!
WHAT BLLLSHIT? WE'RE ALL CRIMINALS HERE, YES?
MONEY TALKS. THE PRINCIPLE HASN'T CHANGED IN FOUR THOUSAND YEARS.

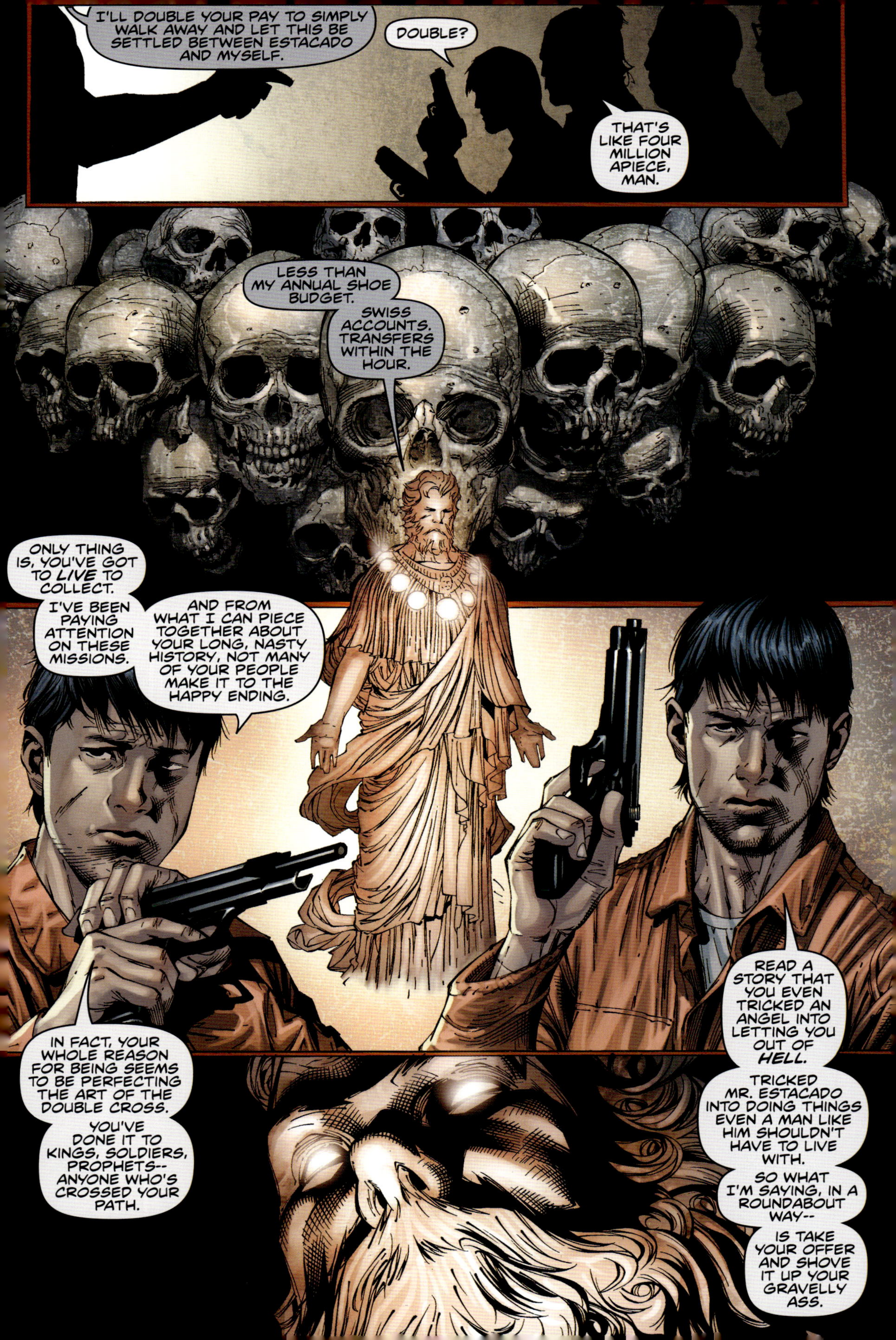

I'LL DOUBLE YOUR PAY TO SIMPLY WALK AWAY AND LET THIS BE SETTLED BETWEEN ESTACADO AND MYSELF.
DOUBLE?
THAT'S LIKE FOUR MILLION APIECE, MAN.
LESS THAN MY ANNUAL SHOE BUDGET.
SWISS ACCOUNTS. TRANSFERS WITHIN THE HOUR.
ONLY THING IS, YOU'VE GOT TO LIVE TO COLLECT.
I'VE BEEN PAYING ATTENTION ON THESE MISSIONS.
AND FROM WHAT I CAN PIECE TOGETHER ABOUT YOUR LONG, NASTY HISTORY, NOT MANY OF YOUR PEOPLE MAKE IT TO THE HAPPY ENDING.
IN FACT, YOUR WHOLE REASON FOR BEING SEEMS TO BE PERFECTING THE ART OF THE DOUBLE CROSS.
YOU'VE DONE IT TO KINGS, SOLDIERS, PROPHETS-- ANYONE WHO'S CROSSED YOUR PATH.
READ A STORY THAT YOU EVEN TRICKED AN ANGEL INTO LETTING YOU OUT OF HELL.
TRICKED MR. ESTACADO INTO DOING THINGS EVEN A MAN LIKE HIM SHOULDN'T HAVE TO LIVE WITH.
SO WHAT I'M SAYING, IN A ROUNDABOUT WAY--
IS TAKE YOUR OFFER AND SHOVE IT UP YOUR GRAVELLY ASS.

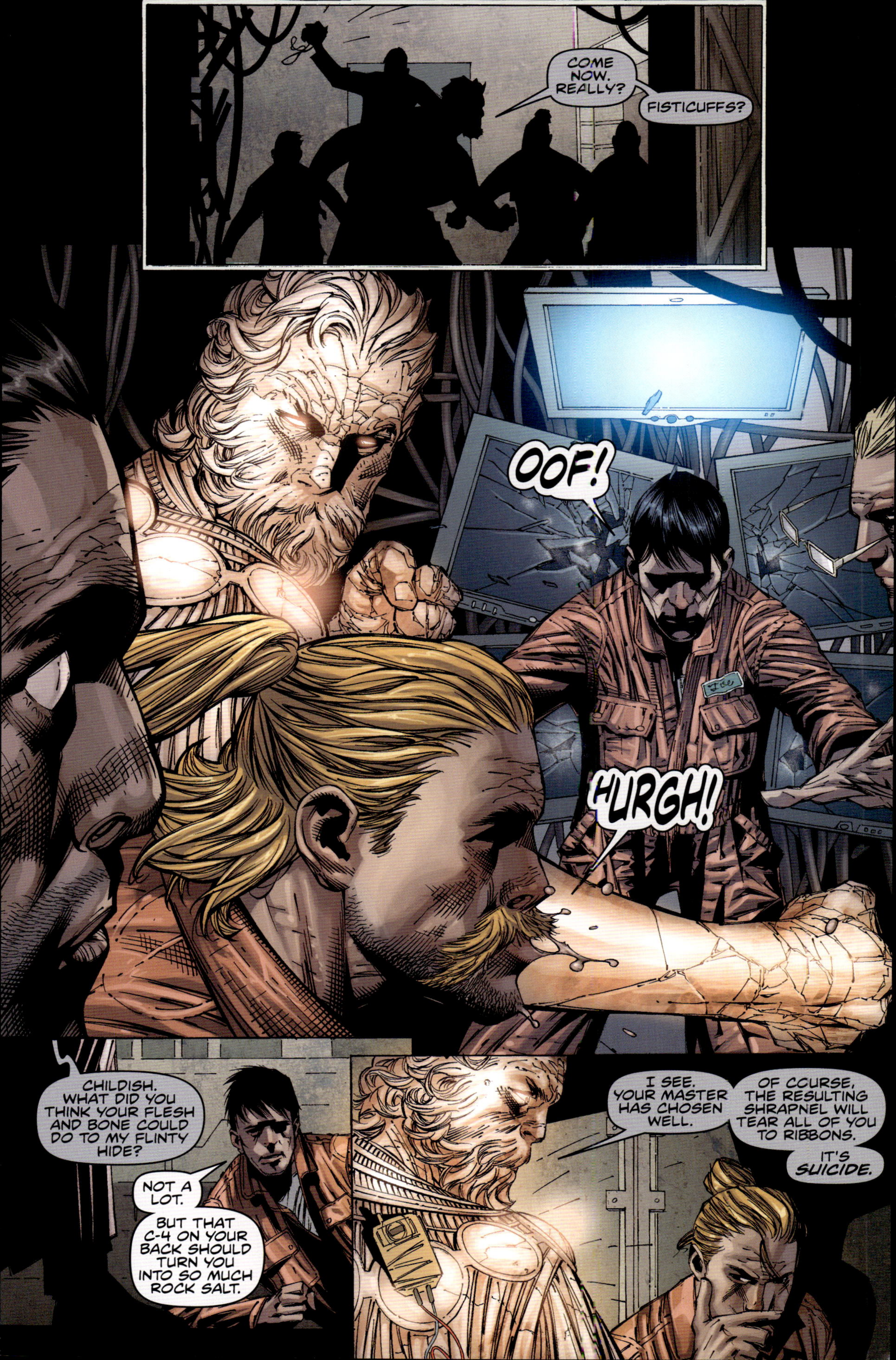
COME NOW. REALLY?
FISTICUFFS?
OOF!
HURGH!
CHILDISH. WHAT DID YOU THINK YOUR FLESH AND BONE COULD DO TO MY FLINTY HIDE?
NOT A LOT.
BUT THAT C-4 ON YOUR BACK SHOULD TURN YOU INTO SO MUCH ROCK SALT.
I SEE. YOUR MASTER HAS CHOSEN WELL.
OF COURSE, THE RESULTING SHRAPNEL WILL TEAR ALL OF YOU TO RIBBONS.
IT'S *SUICIDE.*

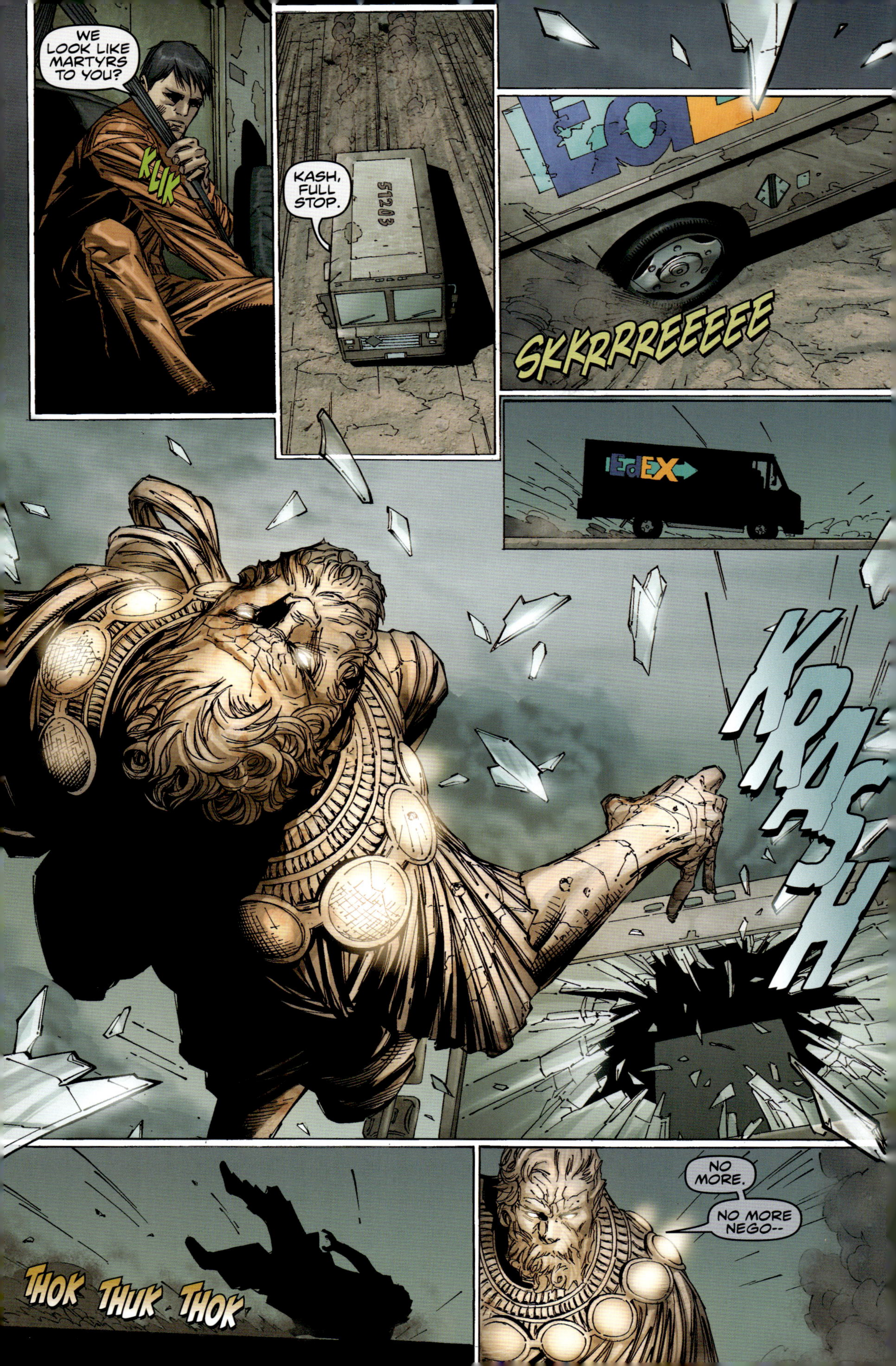

WE LOOK LIKE MARTYRS TO YOU?
KLIK
KASH, FULL STOP.
51203
SKKRRREEEEEE
FEDEX
KRASH
THOK THUK THOK
NO MORE.
NO MORE NEGO--

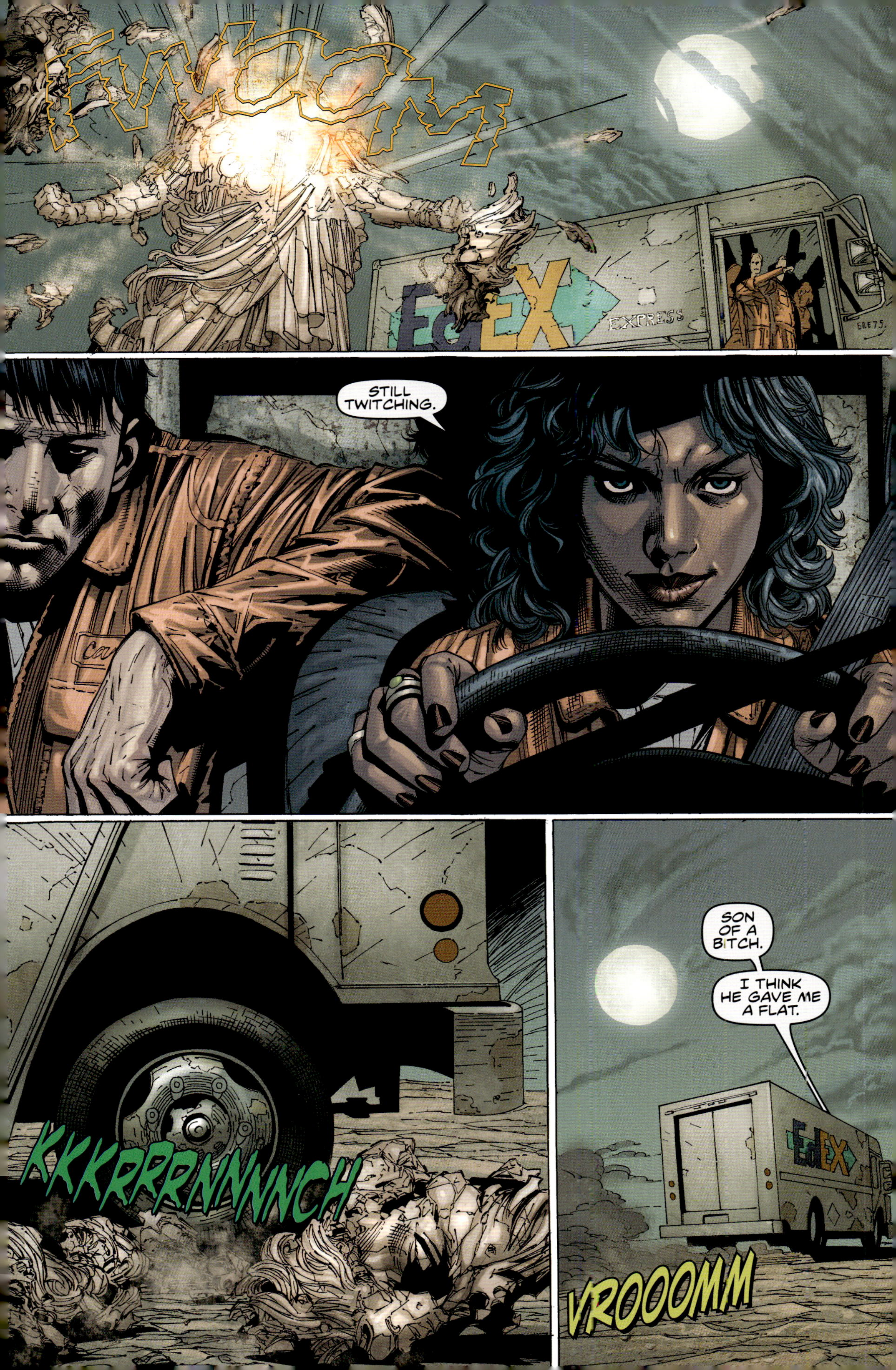
FWOOM
FEDEX EXPRESS
STILL TWITCHING.
KKKRRRNNNNCH
SON OF A BITCH.
I THINK HE GAVE ME A FLAT.
VROOOMM

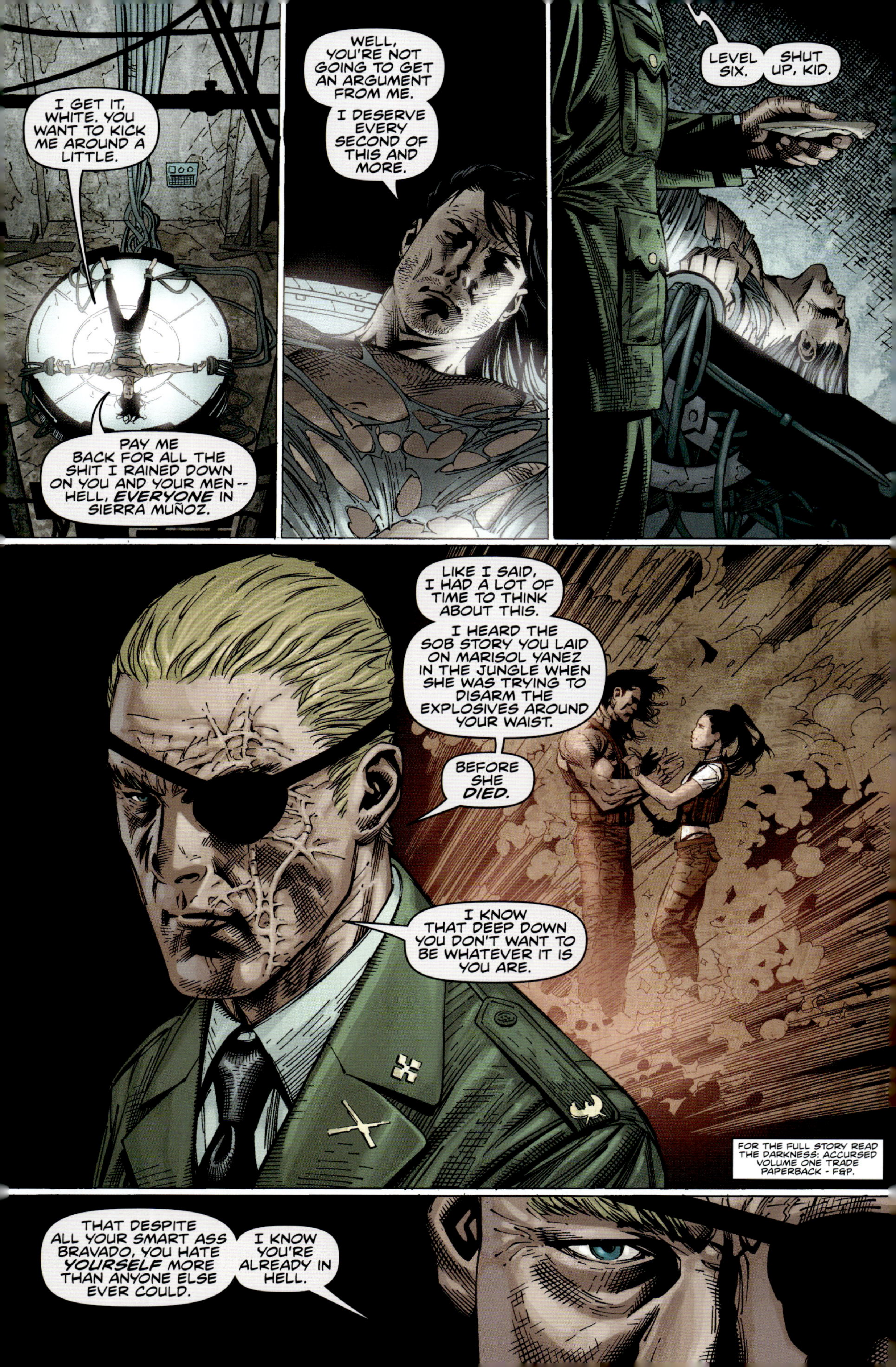
I GET IT, WHITE. YOU WANT TO KICK ME AROUND A LITTLE.
PAY ME BACK FOR ALL THE SHIT I RAINED DOWN ON YOU AND YOUR MEN -- HELL, EVERYONE IN SIERRA MUÑOZ.
WELL, YOU'RE NOT GOING TO GET AN ARGUMENT FROM ME.
I DESERVE EVERY SECOND OF THIS AND MORE.
LEVEL SIX.
SHUT UP, KID.
LIKE I SAID, I HAD A LOT OF TIME TO THINK ABOUT THIS.
I HEARD THE SOB STORY YOU LAID ON MARISOL YANEZ IN THE JUNGLE WHEN SHE WAS TRYING TO DISARM THE EXPLOSIVES AROUND YOUR WAIST.
BEFORE SHE DIED.
I KNOW THAT DEEP DOWN YOU DON'T WANT TO BE WHATEVER IT IS YOU ARE.
FOR THE FULL STORY READ THE DARKNESS: ACCURSED VOLUME ONE TRADE PAPERBACK - F&P.
THAT DESPITE ALL YOUR SMART ASS BRAVADO, YOU HATE YOURSELF MORE THAN ANYONE ELSE EVER COULD.
I KNOW YOU'RE ALREADY IN HELL.

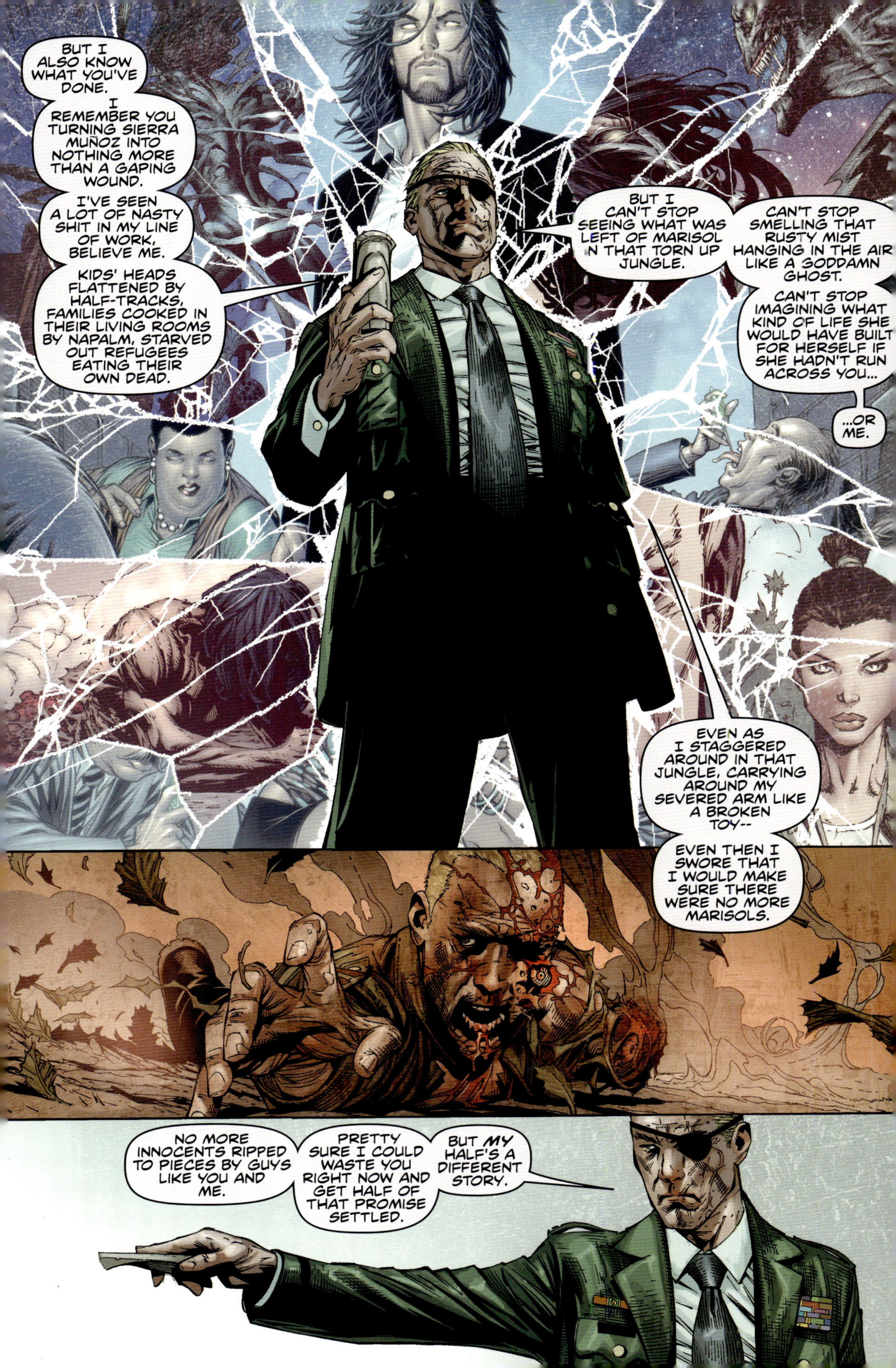
BUT I ALSO KNOW WHAT YOU'VE DONE.
I REMEMBER YOU TURNING SIERRA MUÑOZ INTO NOTHING MORE THAN A GAPING WOUND.
I'VE SEEN A LOT OF NASTY SHIT IN MY LINE OF WORK, BELIEVE ME.
KIDS' HEADS FLATTENED BY HALF-TRACKS, FAMILIES COOKED IN THEIR LIVING ROOMS BY NAPALM, STARVED OUT REFUGEES EATING THEIR OWN DEAD.
BUT I CAN'T STOP SEEING WHAT WAS LEFT OF MARISOL IN THAT TORN UP JUNGLE.
CAN'T STOP SMELLING THAT RUSTY MIST HANGING IN THE AIR LIKE A GODDAMN GHOST.
CAN'T STOP IMAGINING WHAT KIND OF LIFE SHE WOULD HAVE BUILT FOR HERSELF IF SHE HADN'T RUN ACROSS YOU...
...OR ME.
EVEN AS I STAGGERED AROUND IN THAT JUNGLE, CARRYING AROUND MY SEVERED ARM LIKE A BROKEN TOY--
EVEN THEN I SWORE THAT I WOULD MAKE SURE THERE WERE NO MORE MARISOLS.
NO MORE INNOCENTS RIPPED TO PIECES BY GUYS LIKE YOU AND ME.
PRETTY SURE I COULD WASTE YOU RIGHT NOW AND GET HALF OF THAT PROMISE SETTLED.
BUT *MY* HALF'S A DIFFERENT STORY.

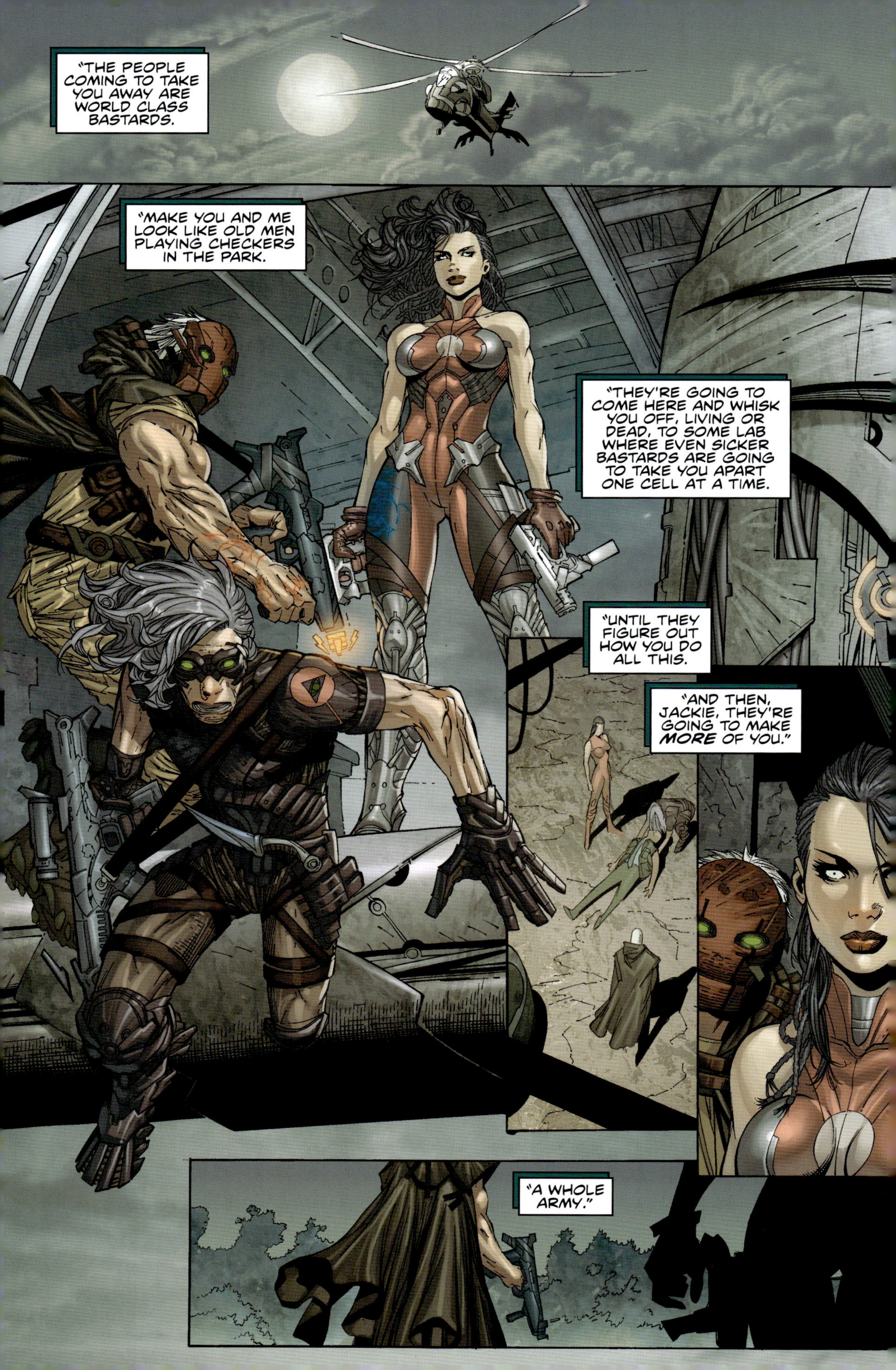
"THE PEOPLE COMING TO TAKE YOU AWAY ARE WORLD CLASS BASTARDS.
"MAKE YOU AND ME LOOK LIKE OLD MEN PLAYING CHECKERS IN THE PARK.
"THEY'RE GOING TO COME HERE AND WHISK YOU OFF, LIVING OR DEAD, TO SOME LAB WHERE EVEN SICKER BASTARDS ARE GOING TO TAKE YOU APART ONE CELL AT A TIME.
"UNTIL THEY FIGURE OUT HOW YOU DO ALL THIS.
"AND THEN, JACKIE, THEY'RE GOING TO MAKE *MORE* OF YOU."
"A WHOLE ARMY."

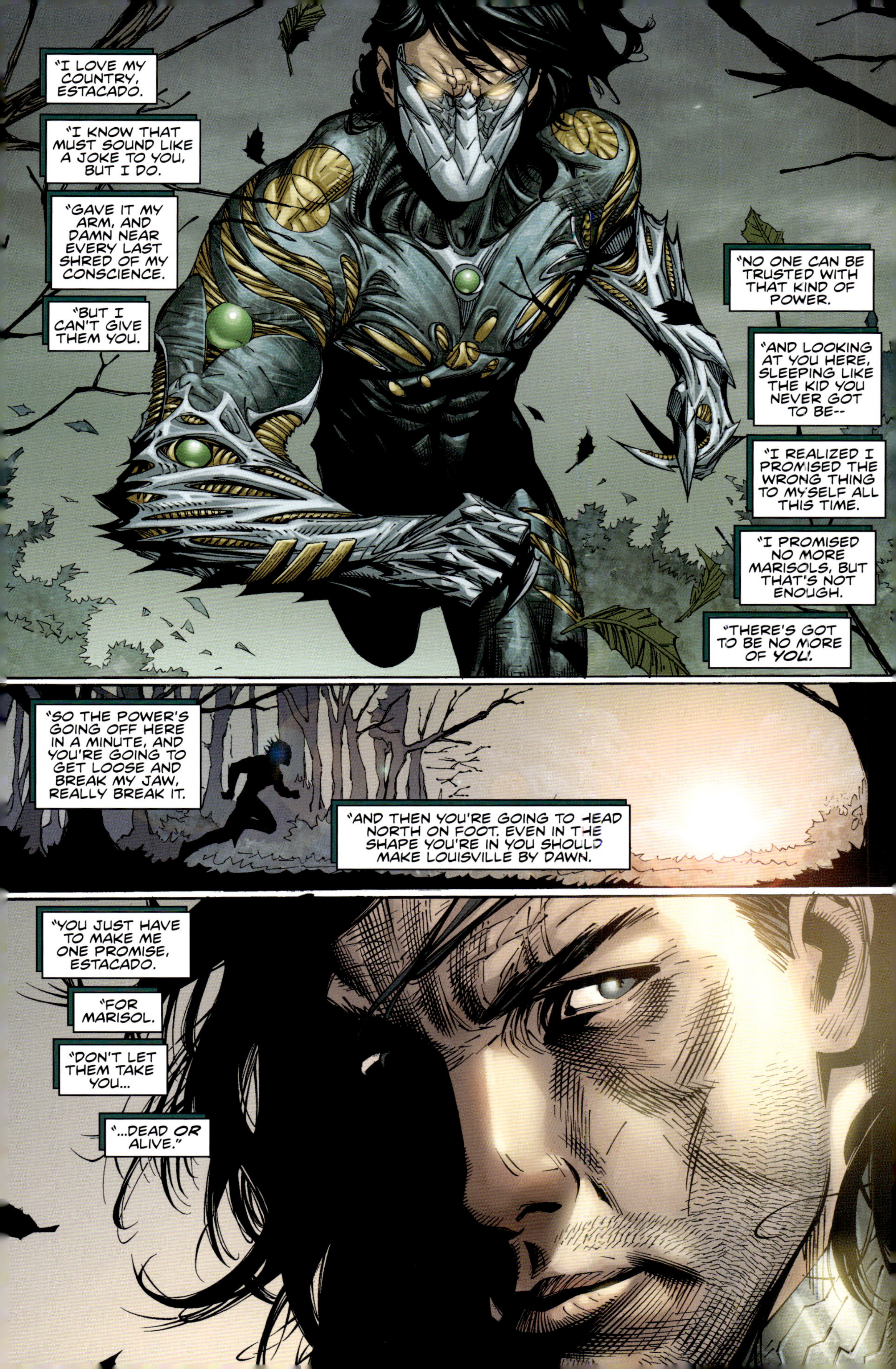
"I LOVE MY COUNTRY, ESTACADO.
"I KNOW THAT MUST SOUND LIKE A JOKE TO YOU, BUT I DO.
"GAVE IT MY ARM, AND DAMN NEAR EVERY LAST SHRED OF MY CONSCIENCE.
"BUT I CAN'T GIVE THEM YOU.
"NO ONE CAN BE TRUSTED WITH THAT KIND OF POWER.
"AND LOOKING AT YOU HERE, SLEEPING LIKE THE KID YOU NEVER GOT TO BE--
"I REALIZED I PROMISED THE WRONG THING TO MYSELF ALL THIS TIME.
"I PROMISED NO MORE MARISOLS, BUT THAT'S NOT ENOUGH.
"THERE'S GOT TO BE NO MORE OF *YOU*.
"SO THE POWER'S GOING OFF HERE IN A MINUTE, AND YOU'RE GOING TO GET LOOSE AND BREAK MY JAW, REALLY BREAK IT.
"AND THEN YOU'RE GOING TO HEAD NORTH ON FOOT. EVEN IN THE SHAPE YOU'RE IN YOU SHOULD MAKE LOUISVILLE BY DAWN.
"YOU JUST HAVE TO MAKE ME ONE PROMISE, ESTACADO.
"FOR MARISOL.
"DON'T LET THEM TAKE YOU...
"...DEAD *OR* ALIVE."

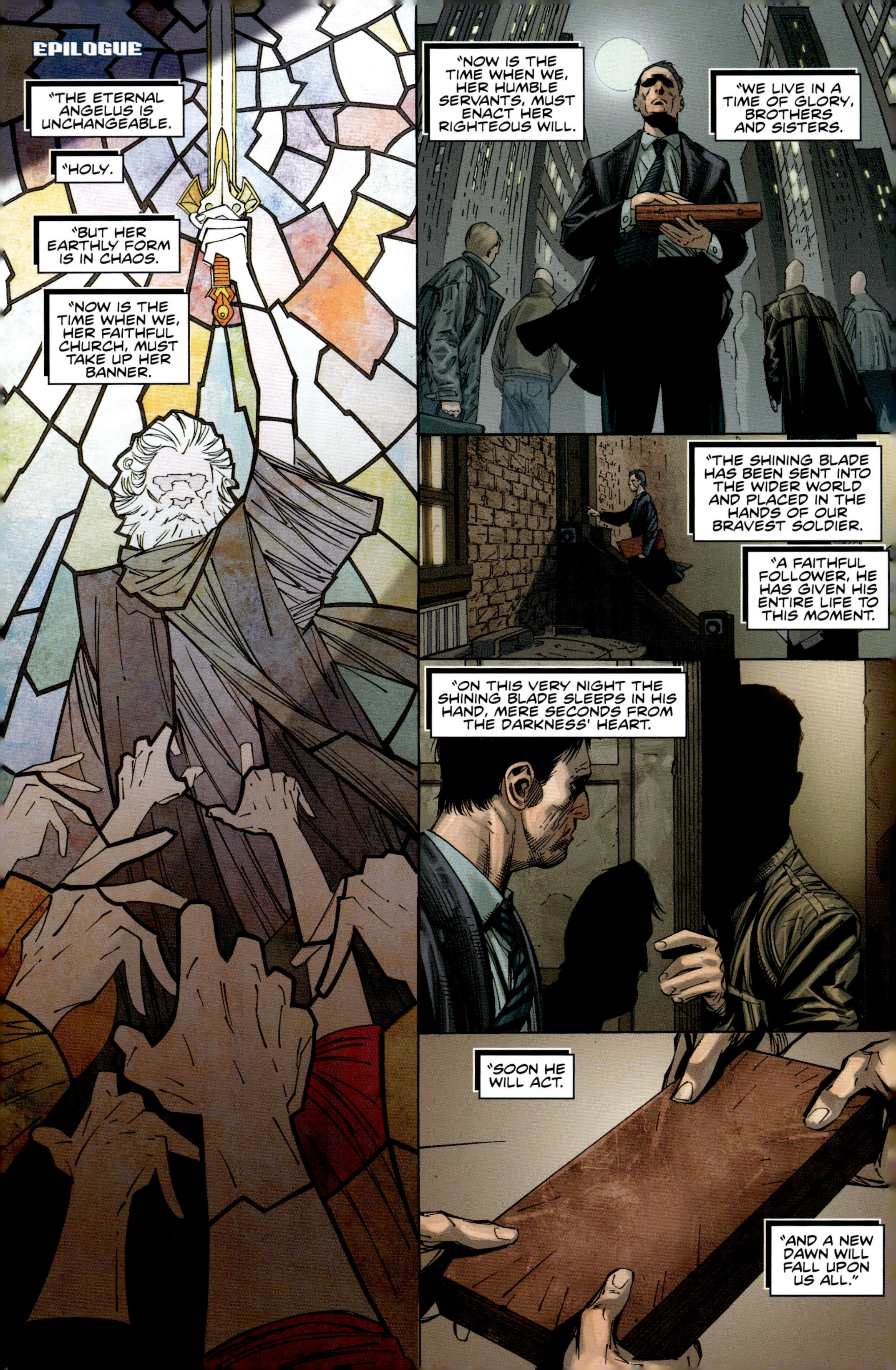
EPILOGUE
"THE ETERNAL ANGELUS IS UNCHANGEABLE.
"HOLY.
"BUT HER EARTHLY FORM IS IN CHAOS.
"NOW IS THE TIME WHEN WE, HER FAITHFUL CHURCH, MUST TAKE UP HER BANNER.
"NOW IS THE TIME WHEN WE, HER HUMBLE SERVANTS, MUST ENACT HER RIGHTEOUS WILL.
"WE LIVE IN A TIME OF GLORY, BROTHERS AND SISTERS.
"THE SHINING BLADE HAS BEEN SENT INTO THE WIDER WORLD AND PLACED IN THE HANDS OF OUR BRAVEST SOLDIER.
"A FAITHFUL FOLLOWER, HE HAS GIVEN HIS ENTIRE LIFE TO THIS MOMENT.
"ON THIS VERY NIGHT THE SHINING BLADE SLEEPS IN HIS HAND, MERE SECONDS FROM THE DARKNESS' HEART.
"SOON HE WILL ACT.
"AND A NEW DAWN WILL FALL UPON US ALL."

The Darkness Issue #84
cover art by: Bagus Hutomo of IFS

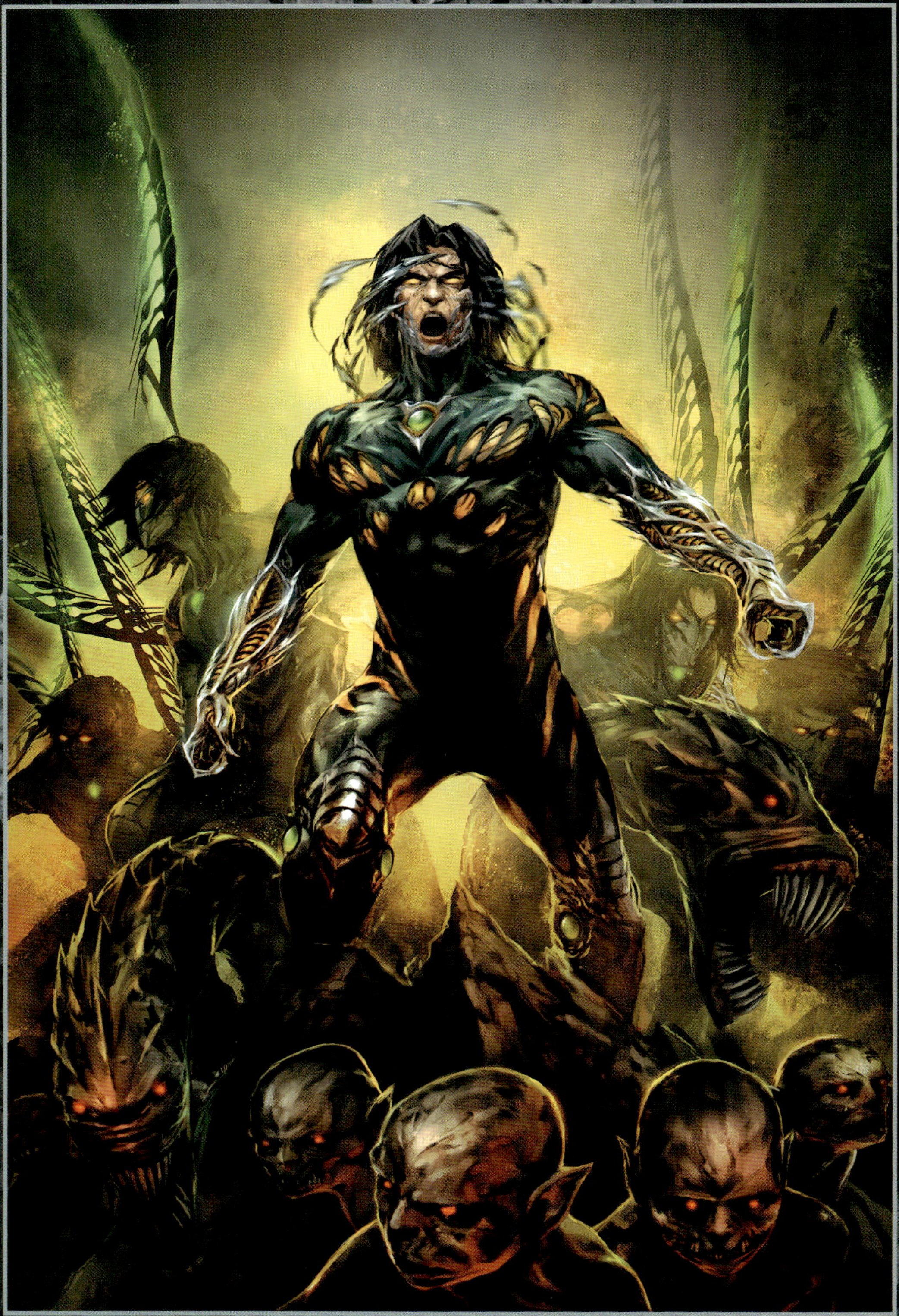

THE DARKNESS #84

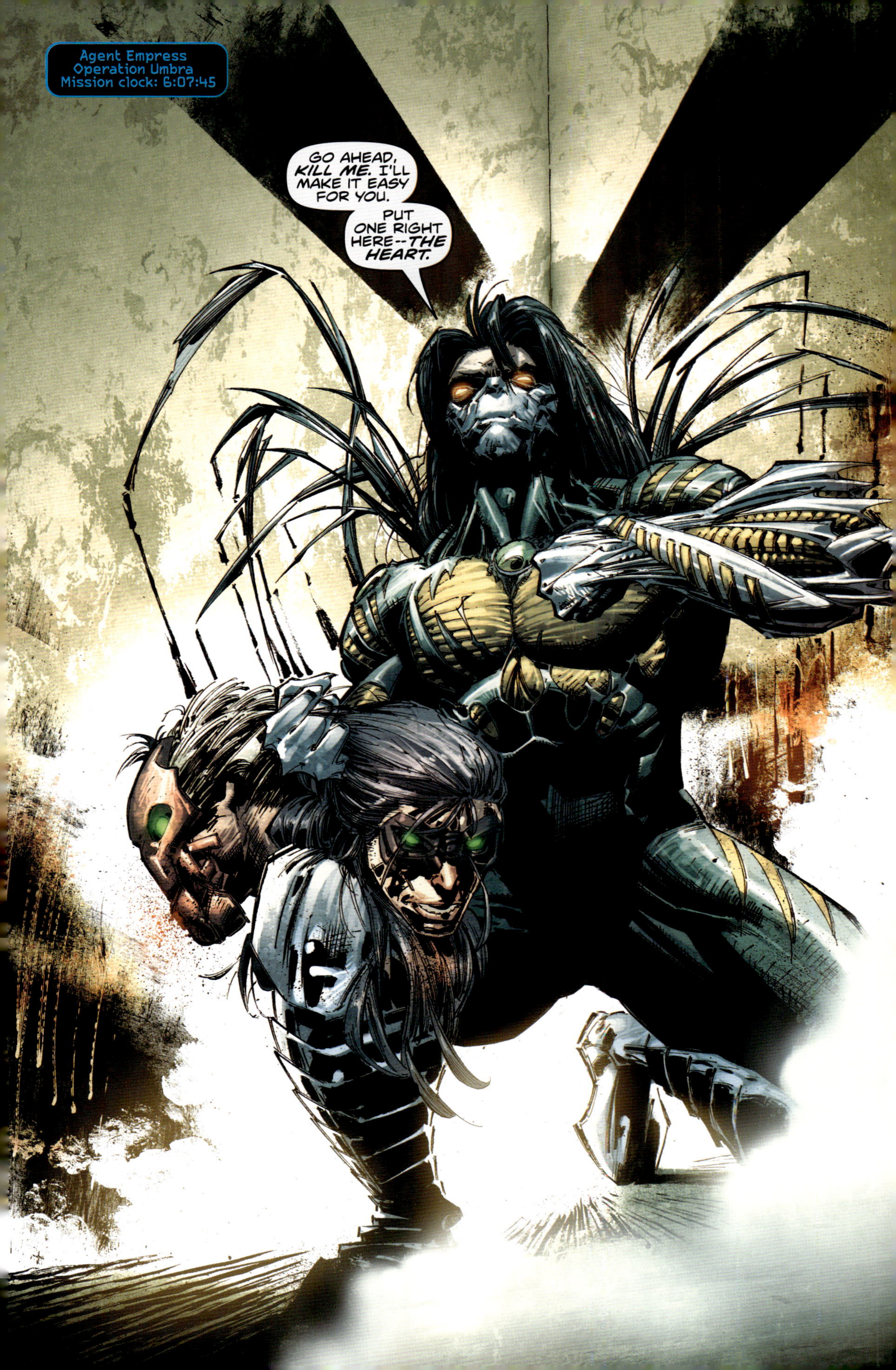
Agent Empress
Operation Umbra
Mission clock: 6:07:45
GO AHEAD, KILL ME. I'LL MAKE IT EASY FOR YOU.
PUT ONE RIGHT HERE--THE HEART.

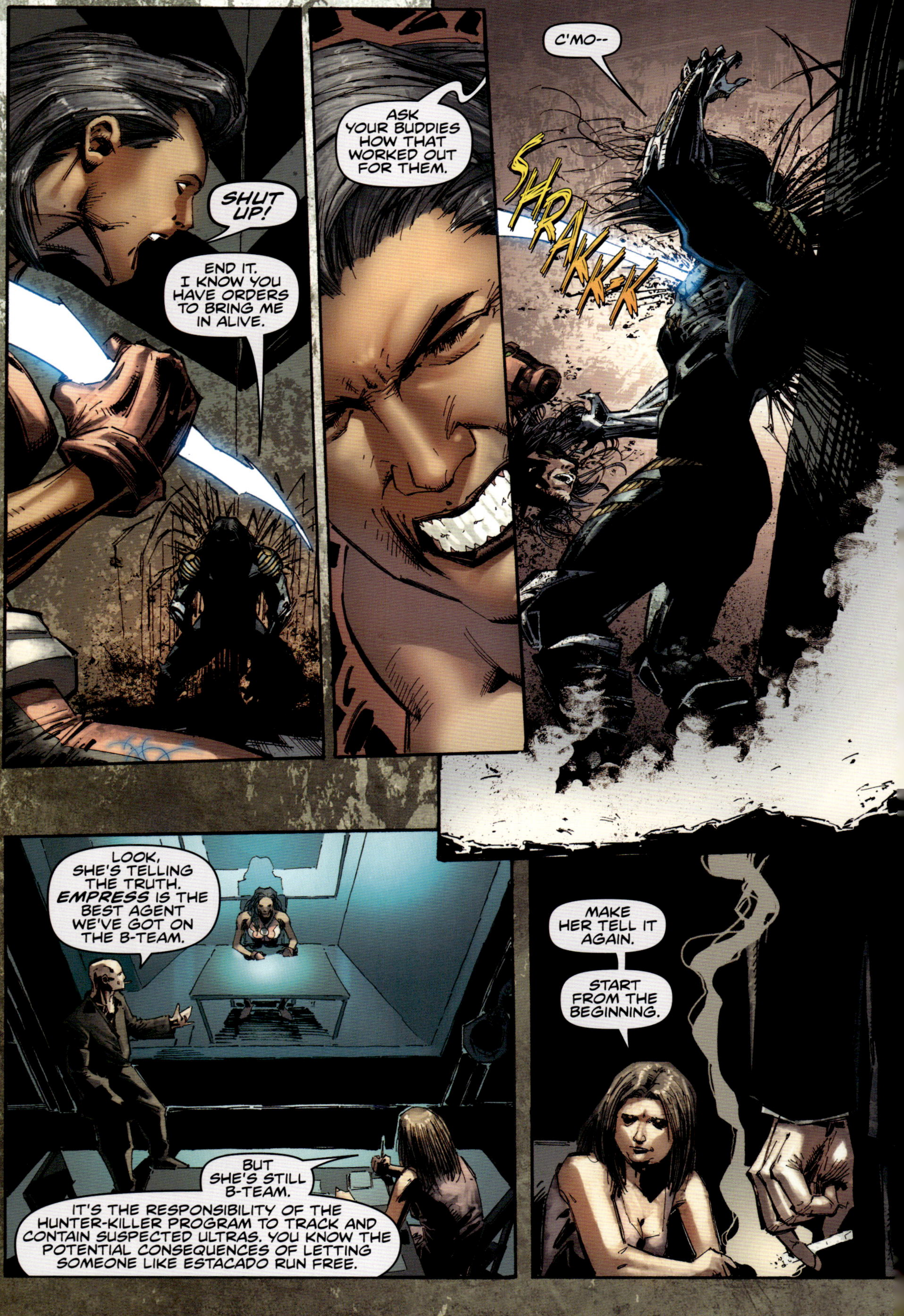
SHUT UP!
END IT. I KNOW YOU HAVE ORDERS TO BRING ME IN ALIVE.
ASK YOUR BUDDIES HOW THAT WORKED OUT FOR THEM.
C'MO--
SHRAKK-K
LOOK, SHE'S TELLING THE TRUTH. EMPRESS IS THE BEST AGENT WE'VE GOT ON THE B-TEAM.
BUT SHE'S STILL B-TEAM.
IT'S THE RESPONSIBILITY OF THE HUNTER-KILLER PROGRAM TO TRACK AND CONTAIN SUSPECTED ULTRAS. YOU KNOW THE POTENTIAL CONSEQUENCES OF LETTING SOMEONE LIKE ESTACADO RUN FREE.
MAKE HER TELL IT AGAIN.
START FROM THE BEGINNING.

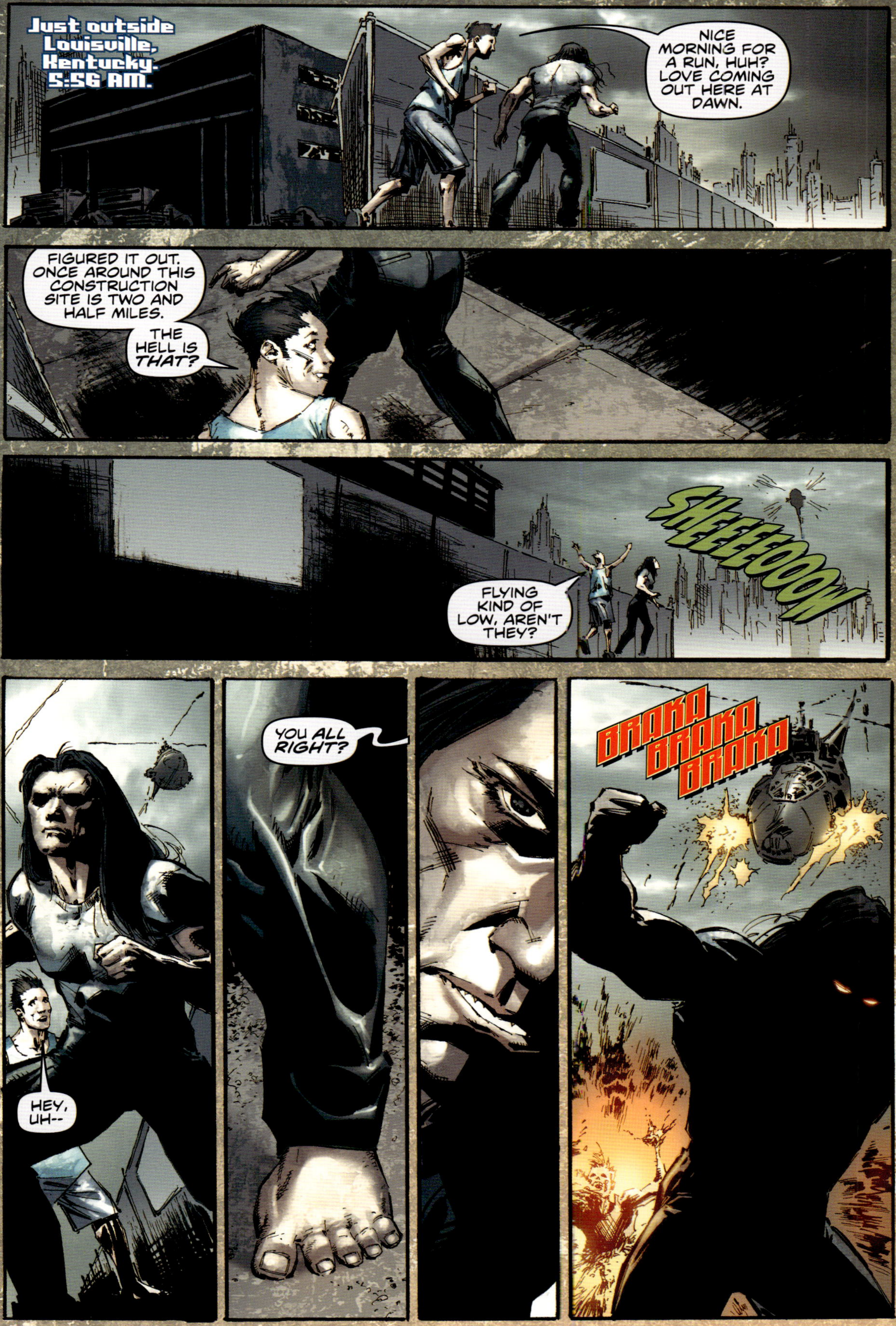
Just outside Louisville, Kentucky. 5:56 AM.
NICE MORNING FOR A RUN, HUH? LOVE COMING OUT HERE AT DAWN.
FIGURED IT OUT. ONCE AROUND THIS CONSTRUCTION SITE IS TWO AND HALF MILES.
THE HELL IS *THAT*?
SHEEEOOOW
FLYING KIND OF LOW, AREN'T THEY?
HEY, UH--
YOU *ALL RIGHT*?
BRAKA BRAKA BRAKA

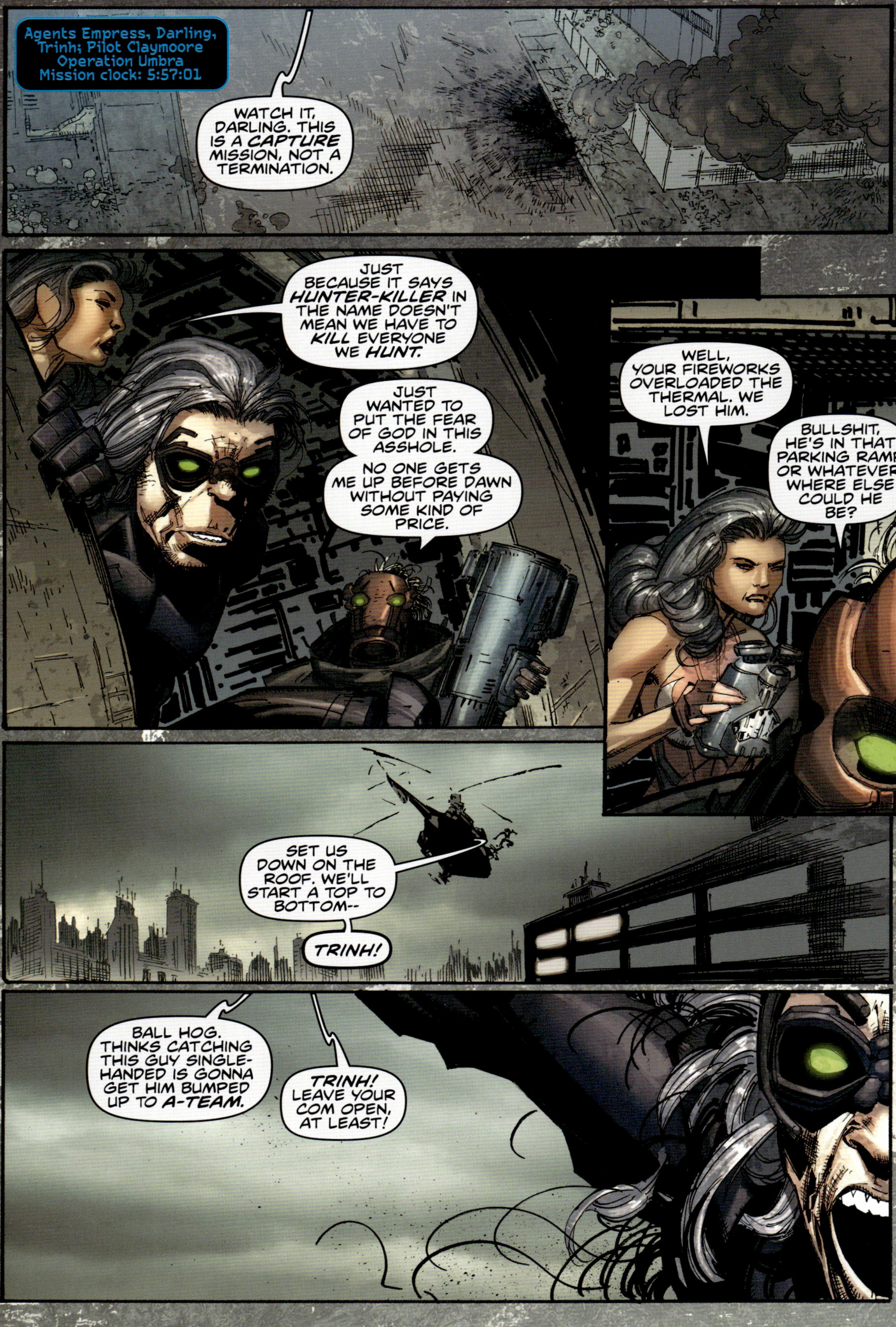
Agents Empress, Darling, Trinh; Pilot Claymoore
Operation Umbra
Mission clock: 5:57:01
WATCH IT, DARLING. THIS IS A CAPTURE MISSION, NOT A TERMINATION.
JUST BECAUSE IT SAYS HUNTER-KILLER IN THE NAME DOESN'T MEAN WE HAVE TO KILL EVERYONE WE HUNT.
JUST WANTED TO PUT THE FEAR OF GOD IN THIS ASSHOLE.
NO ONE GETS ME UP BEFORE DAWN WITHOUT PAYING SOME KIND OF PRICE.
WELL, YOUR FIREWORKS OVERLOADED THE THERMAL. WE LOST HIM.
BULLSHIT, HE'S IN THAT PARKING RAMP OR WHATEVER. WHERE ELSE COULD HE BE?
SET US DOWN ON THE ROOF. WE'LL START A TOP TO BOTTOM--
TRINH!
BALL HOG. THINKS CATCHING THIS GUY SINGLE-HANDED IS GONNA GET HIM BUMPED UP TO A-TEAM.
TRINH! LEAVE YOUR COM OPEN, AT LEAST!

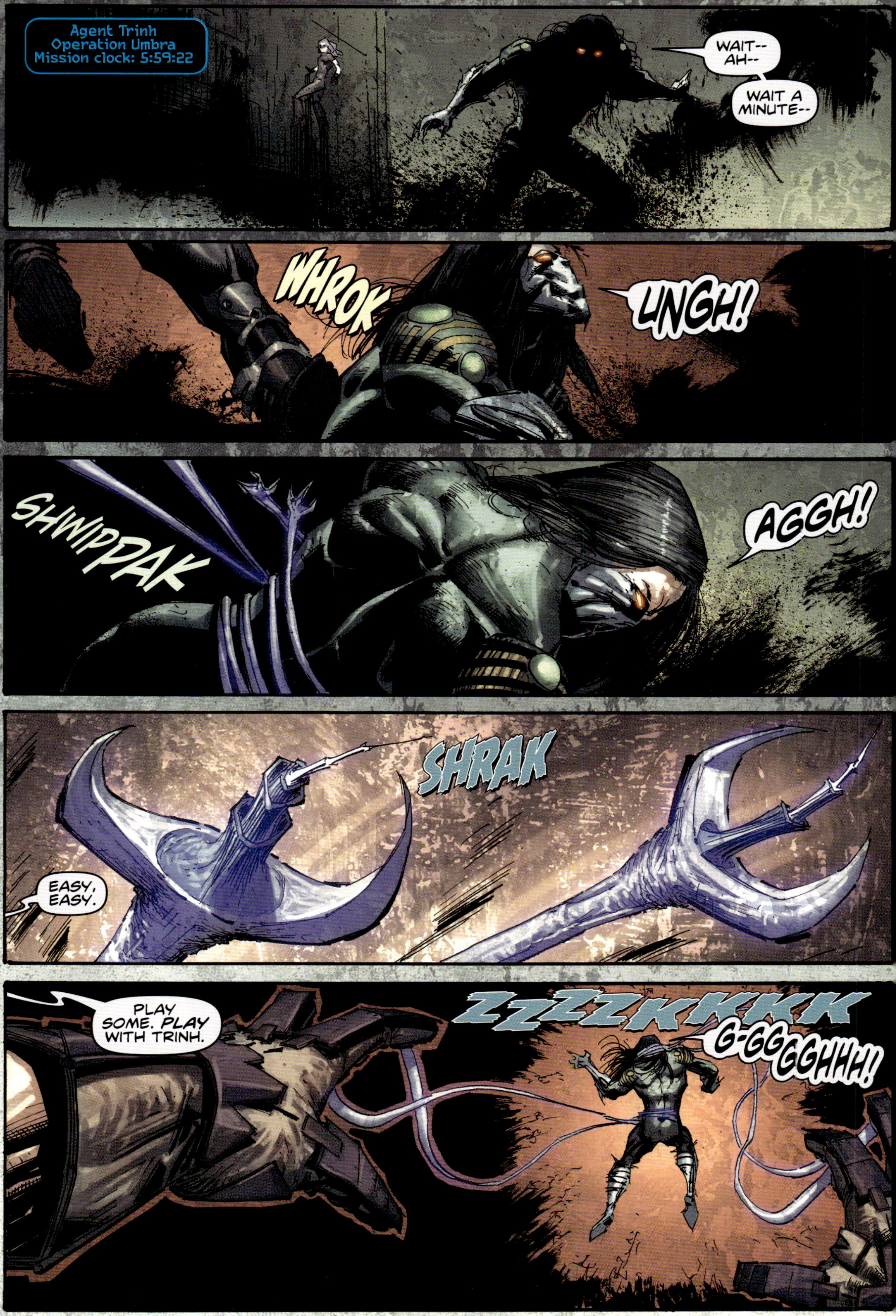
Agent Trinh
Operation Umbra
Mission clock: 5:59:22
WAIT--
AH--
WAIT A MINUTE--
WHROK
UNGH!
SHWIPPAK
AGGH!
SHRAK
EASY, EASY.
PLAY SOME. PLAY WITH TRINH.
ZZZZKKKKK
G-GGGGHHH!

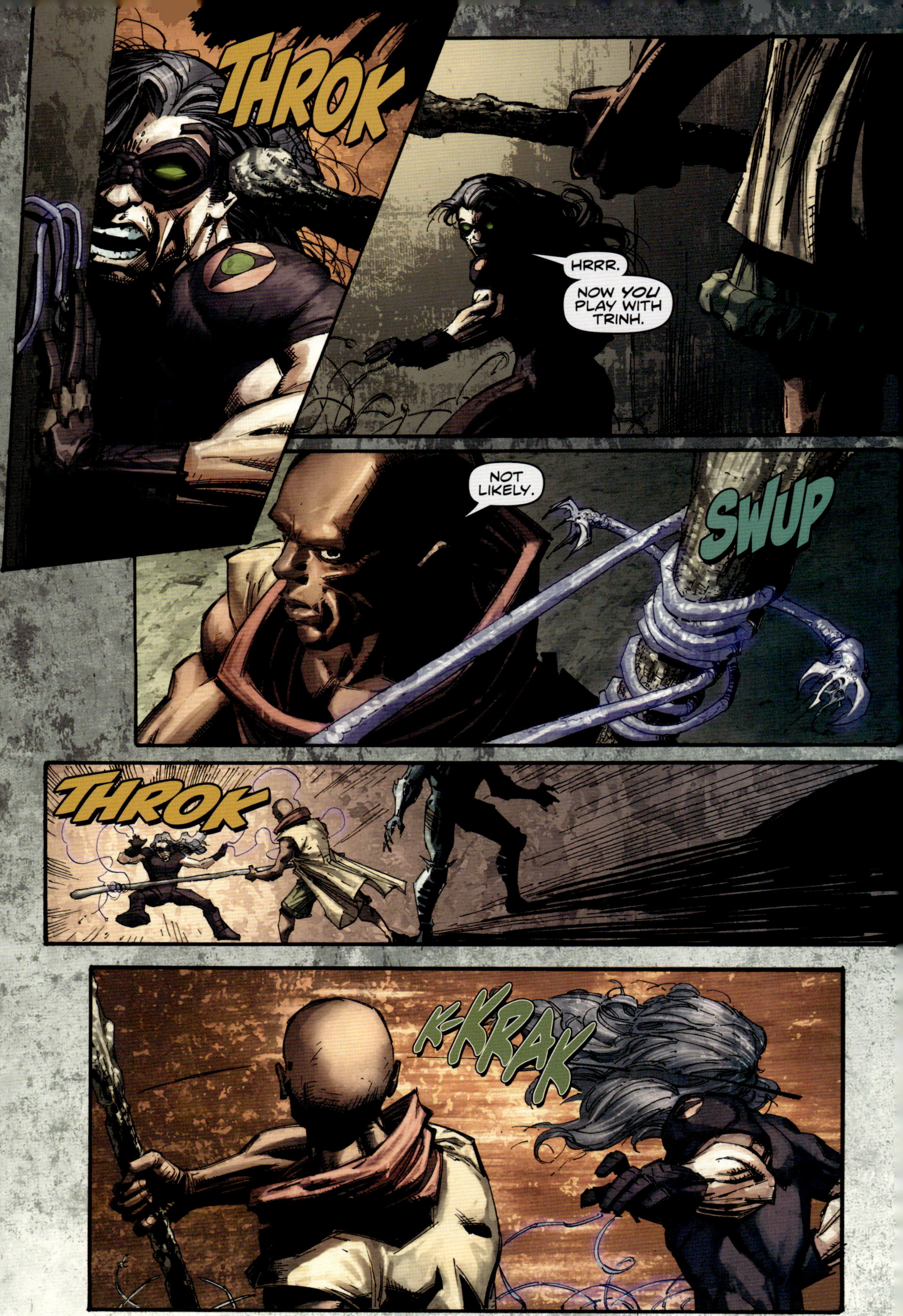
THROK
HRRR.
NOW YOU PLAY WITH TRINH.
NOT LIKELY.
SWUP
THROK
K-KRAK

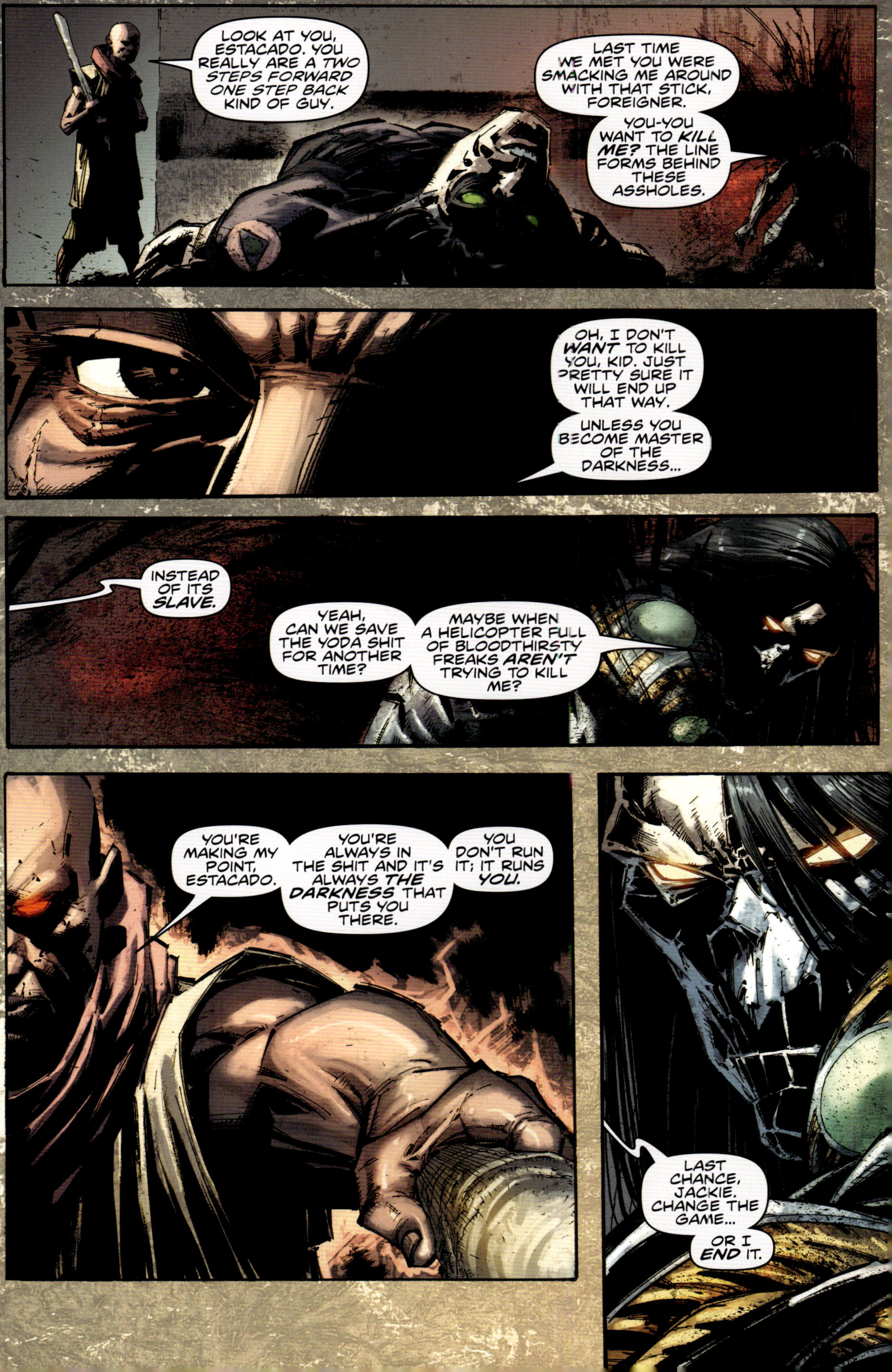
LOOK AT YOU, ESTACADO. YOU REALLY ARE A TWO STEPS FORWARD ONE STEP BACK KIND OF GUY.
LAST TIME WE MET YOU WERE SMACKING ME AROUND WITH THAT STICK, FOREIGNER.
YOU-YOU WANT TO KILL ME? THE LINE FORMS BEHIND THESE ASSHOLES.
OH, I DON'T WANT TO KILL YOU, KID. JUST PRETTY SURE IT WILL END UP THAT WAY.
UNLESS YOU BECOME MASTER OF THE DARKNESS...
INSTEAD OF ITS SLAVE.
YEAH, CAN WE SAVE THE YODA SHIT FOR ANOTHER TIME?
MAYBE WHEN A HELICOPTER FULL OF BLOODTHIRSTY FREAKS AREN'T TRYING TO KILL ME?
YOU'RE MAKING MY POINT, ESTACADO.
YOU'RE ALWAYS IN THE SHIT AND IT'S ALWAYS THE DARKNESS THAT PUTS YOU THERE.
YOU DON'T RUN IT; IT RUNS YOU.
LAST CHANCE, JACKIE. CHANGE THE GAME...
OR I END IT.

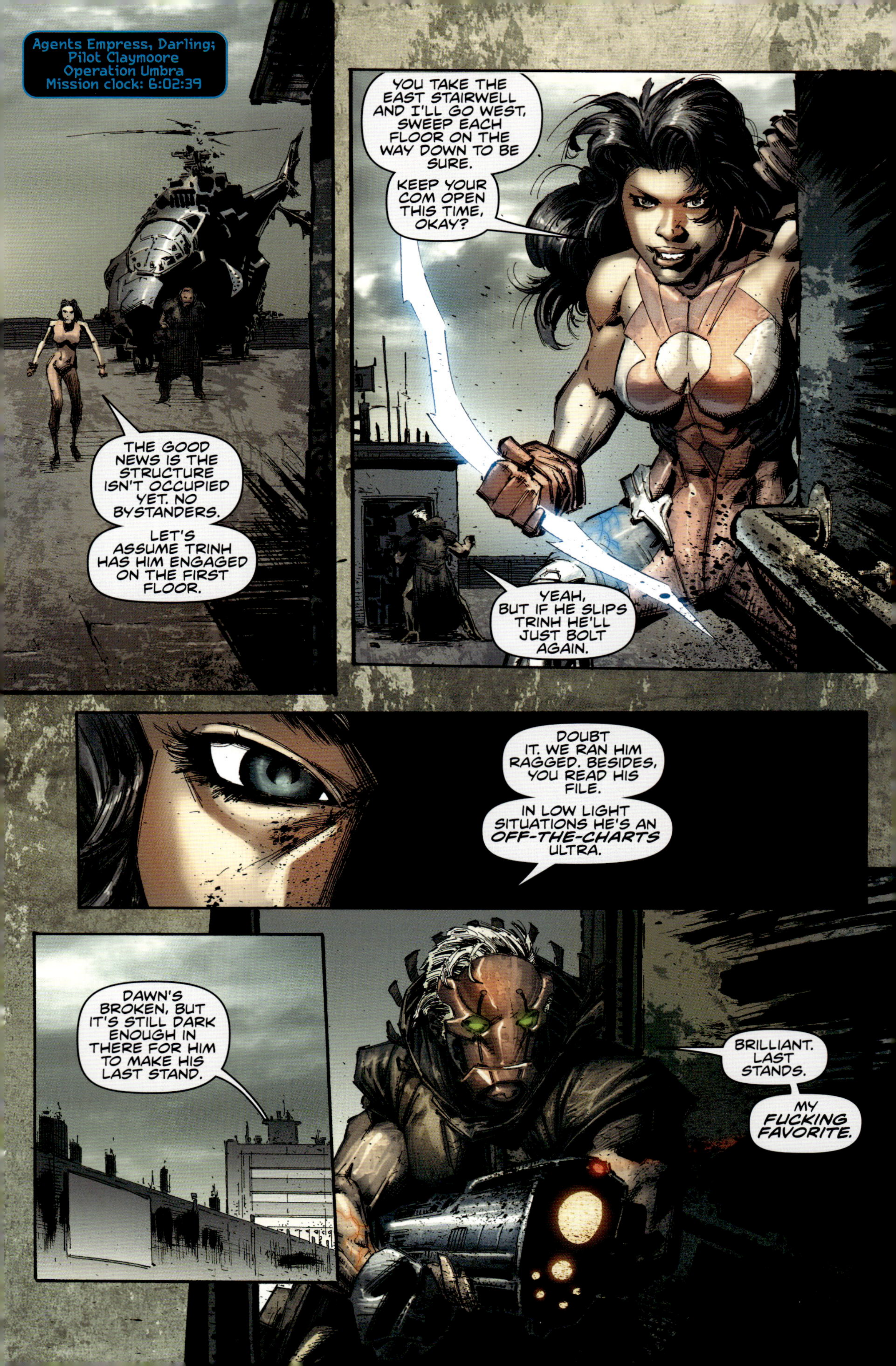
Agents Empress, Darling; Pilot Claymoore Operation Umbra Mission clock: 6:02:39
THE GOOD NEWS IS THE STRUCTURE ISN'T OCCUPIED YET. NO BYSTANDERS.
LET'S ASSUME TRINH HAS HIM ENGAGED ON THE FIRST FLOOR.
YOU TAKE THE EAST STAIRWELL AND I'LL GO WEST, SWEEP EACH FLOOR ON THE WAY DOWN TO BE SURE.
KEEP YOUR COM OPEN THIS TIME, OKAY?
YEAH, BUT IF HE SLIPS TRINH HE'LL JUST BOLT AGAIN.
DOUBT IT. WE RAN HIM RAGGED. BESIDES, YOU READ HIS FILE.
IN LOW LIGHT SITUATIONS HE'S AN *OFF-THE-CHARTS* ULTRA.
DAWN'S BROKEN, BUT IT'S STILL DARK ENOUGH IN THERE FOR HIM TO MAKE HIS LAST STAND.
BRILLIANT. LAST STANDS.
MY *FUCKING FAVORITE.*

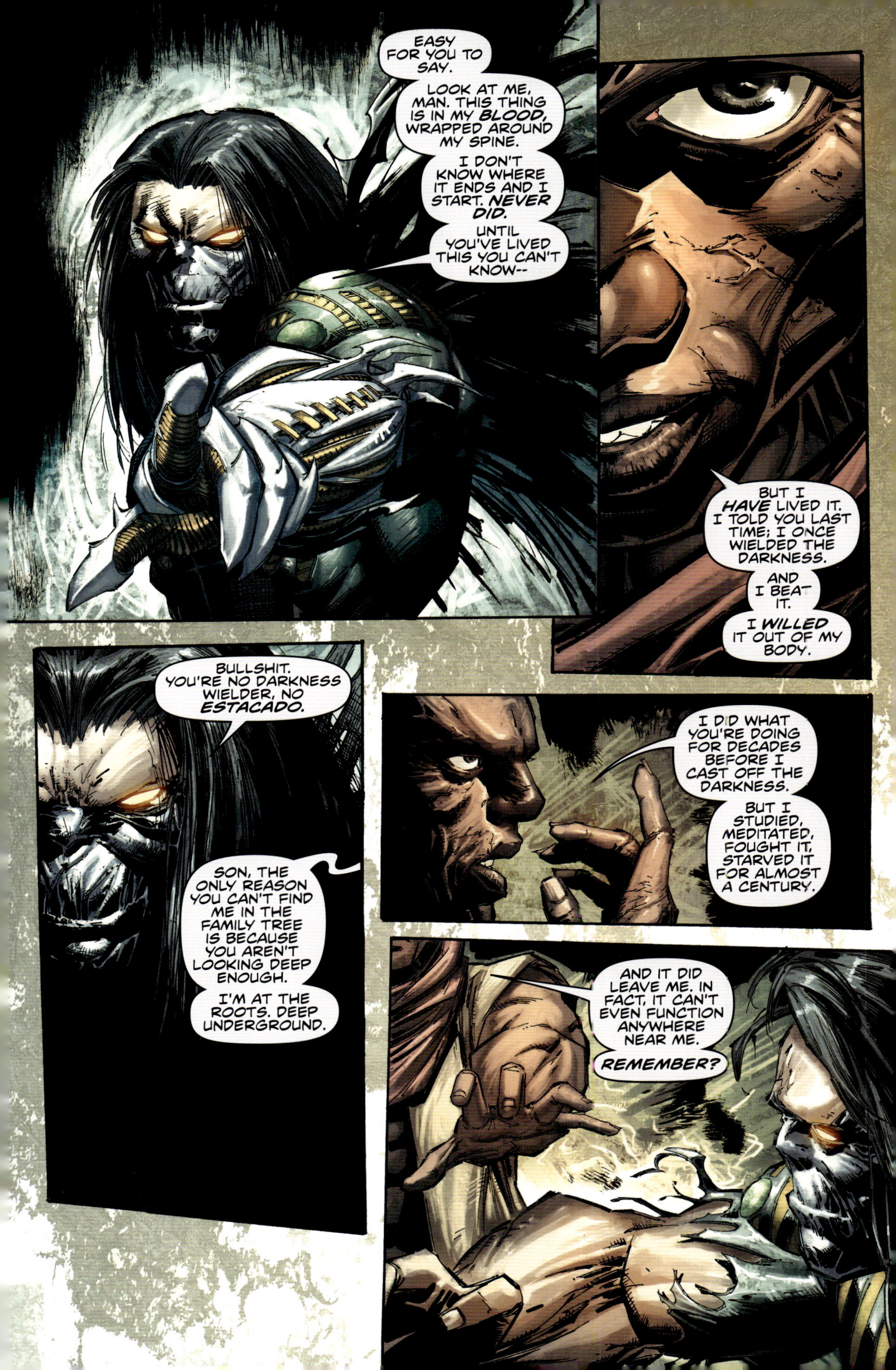
EASY FOR YOU TO SAY.
LOOK AT ME, MAN. THIS THING IS IN MY BLOOD, WRAPPED AROUND MY SPINE.
I DON'T KNOW WHERE IT ENDS AND I START. NEVER DID.
UNTIL YOU'VE LIVED THIS YOU CAN'T KNOW--
BUT I HAVE LIVED IT. I TOLD YOU LAST TIME; I ONCE WIELDED THE DARKNESS.
AND I BEAT IT.
I WILLED IT OUT OF MY BODY.
BULLSHIT. YOU'RE NO DARKNESS WIELDER, NO ESTACADO.
SON, THE ONLY REASON YOU CAN'T FIND ME IN THE FAMILY TREE IS BECAUSE YOU AREN'T LOOKING DEEP ENOUGH.
I'M AT THE ROOTS. DEEP UNDERGROUND.
I DID WHAT YOU'RE DOING FOR DECADES BEFORE I CAST OFF THE DARKNESS.
BUT I STUDIED, MEDITATED, FOUGHT IT, STARVED IT FOR ALMOST A CENTURY.
AND IT DID LEAVE ME. IN FACT, IT CAN'T EVEN FUNCTION ANYWHERE NEAR ME.
REMEMBER?

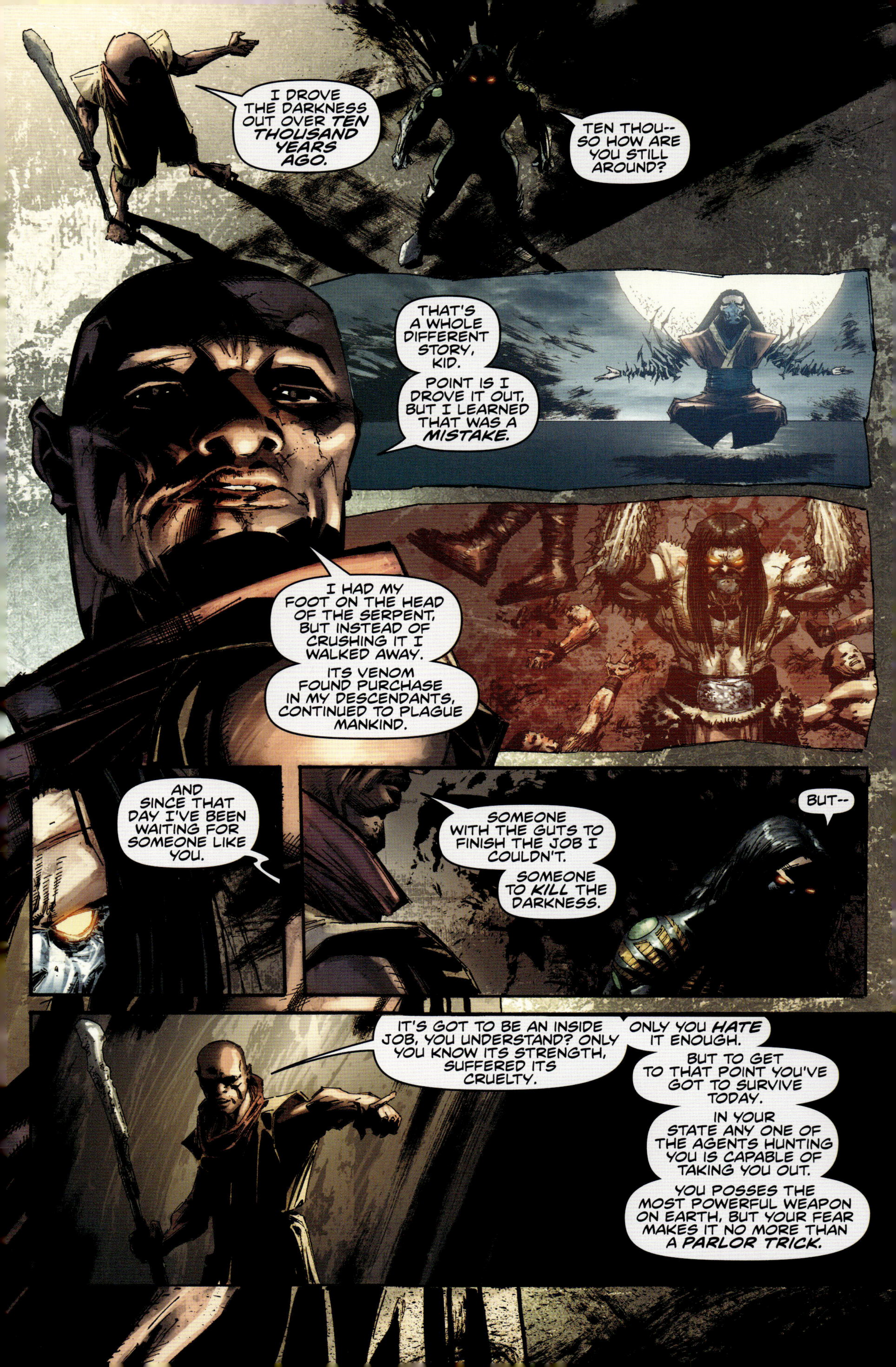
I DROVE THE DARKNESS OUT OVER *TEN THOUSAND YEARS AGO.*
TEN THOU-- SO HOW ARE YOU STILL AROUND?
THAT'S A WHOLE DIFFERENT STORY, KID.
POINT IS I DROVE IT OUT, BUT I LEARNED THAT WAS A *MISTAKE.*
I HAD MY FOOT ON THE HEAD OF THE SERPENT, BUT INSTEAD OF CRUSHING IT I WALKED AWAY.
ITS VENOM FOUND PURCHASE IN MY DESCENDANTS, CONTINUED TO PLAGUE MANKIND.
AND SINCE THAT DAY I'VE BEEN WAITING FOR SOMEONE LIKE YOU.
SOMEONE WITH THE GUTS TO FINISH THE JOB I COULDN'T.
SOMEONE TO *KILL* THE DARKNESS.
BUT--
IT'S GOT TO BE AN INSIDE JOB, YOU UNDERSTAND? ONLY YOU KNOW ITS STRENGTH, SUFFERED ITS CRUELTY.
ONLY YOU *HATE* IT ENOUGH.
BUT TO GET TO THAT POINT YOU'VE GOT TO SURVIVE TODAY.
IN YOUR STATE ANY ONE OF THE AGENTS HUNTING YOU IS CAPABLE OF TAKING YOU OUT.
YOU POSSES THE MOST POWERFUL WEAPON ON EARTH, BUT YOUR FEAR MAKES IT NO MORE THAN A *PARLOR TRICK.*

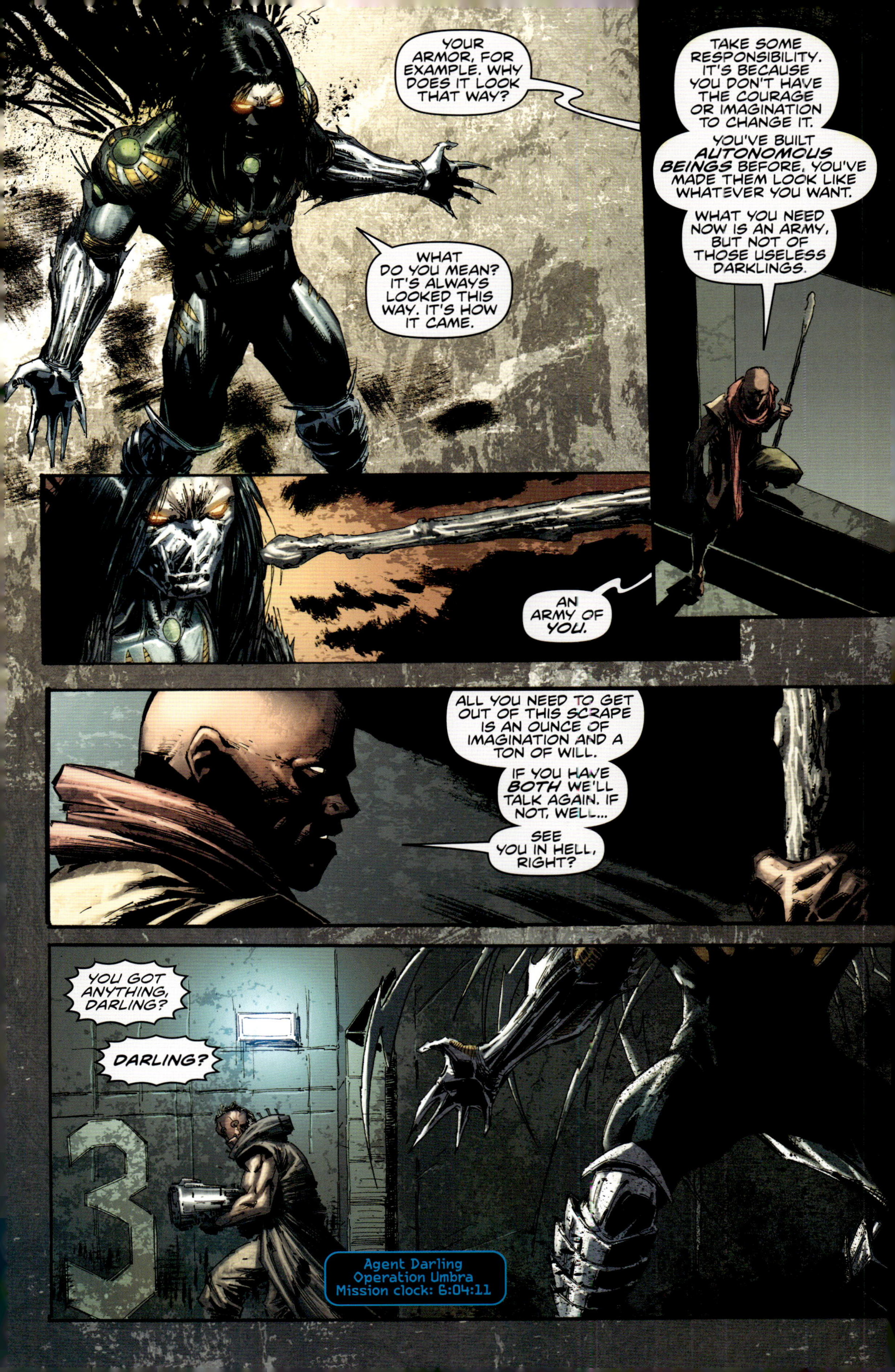
YOUR ARMOR, FOR EXAMPLE. WHY DOES IT LOOK THAT WAY?
WHAT DO YOU MEAN? IT'S ALWAYS LOOKED THIS WAY. IT'S HOW IT CAME.
TAKE SOME RESPONSIBILITY. IT'S BECAUSE YOU DON'T HAVE THE COURAGE OR IMAGINATION TO CHANGE IT.
YOU'VE BUILT AUTONOMOUS BEINGS BEFORE. YOU'VE MADE THEM LOOK LIKE WHATEVER YOU WANT.
WHAT YOU NEED NOW IS AN ARMY, BUT NOT OF THOSE USELESS DARKLINGS.
AN ARMY OF YOU.
ALL YOU NEED TO GET OUT OF THIS SCRAPE IS AN OUNCE OF IMAGINATION AND A TON OF WILL.
IF YOU HAVE BOTH WE'LL TALK AGAIN. IF NOT, WELL...
SEE YOU IN HELL, RIGHT?
YOU GOT ANYTHING, DARLING?
DARLING?
3
Agent Darling
Operation Umbra
Mission clock: 6:04:11

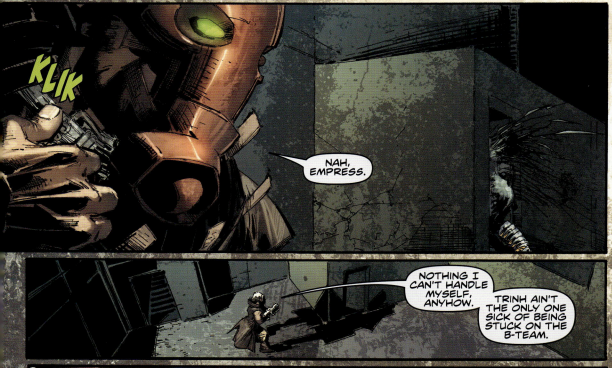

KLIK

NAH, EMPRESS.

NOTHING I CAN'T HANDLE MYSELF, ANYHOW. TRINH AIN'T THE ONLY ONE SICK OF BEING STUCK ON THE B-TEAM.

HA! I SEE YOU WORKING THERE. READ YOUR FILE. I KNOW YOU GET TOUGHER IN THE DARK.

TOO BAD YOU DON'T KNOW AS MUCH ABOUT ME. SEE, I CAN *HARDEN* UP THESE FISTS...

PUNCH THROUGH NEARLY ANYTHING.

THROK

THAT MEANS...

WHOK

I CAN SHED A LITTLE *LIGHT* ON YOUR HIDEOUT.

THRUNCH

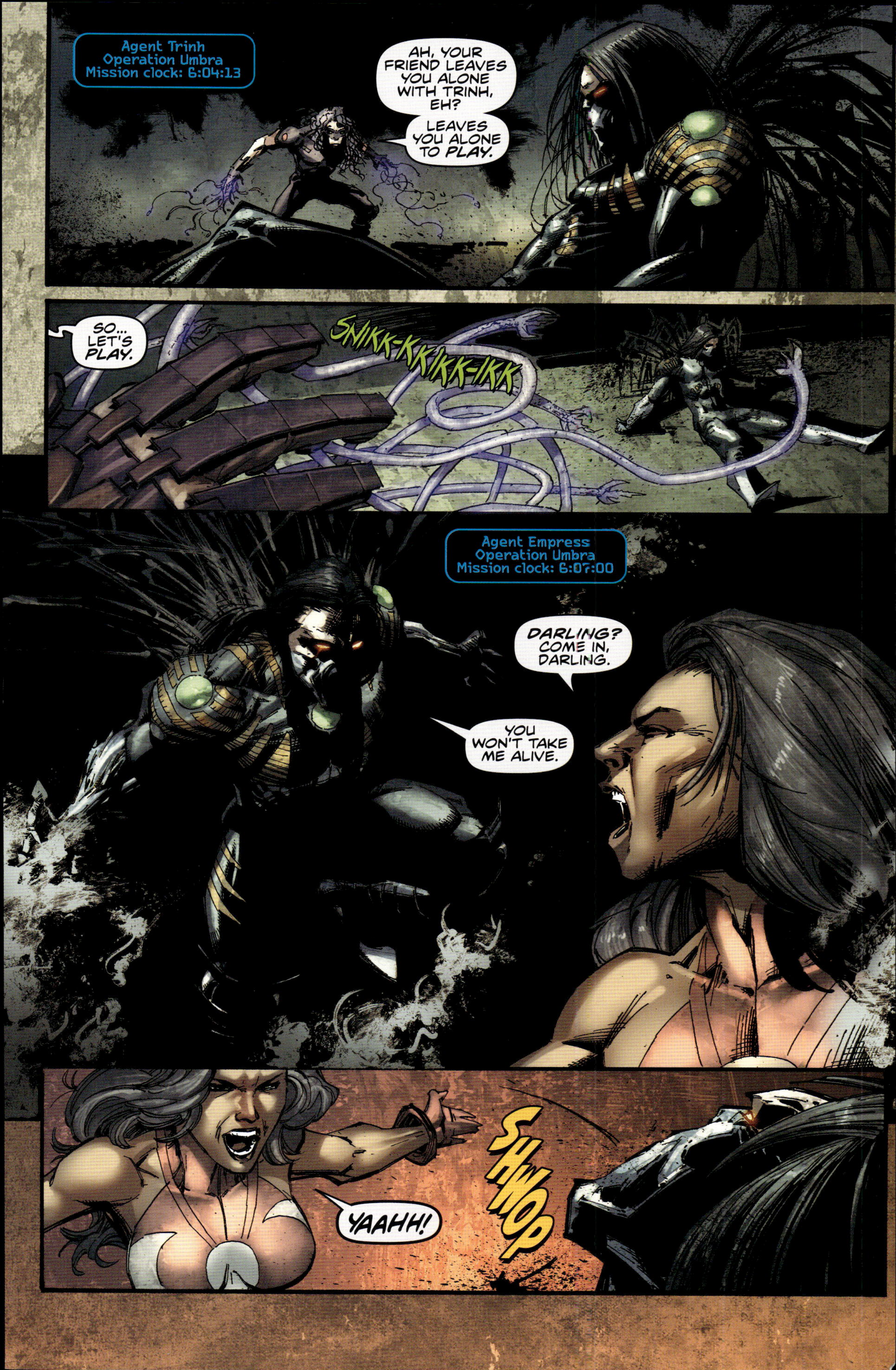
Agent Trinh
Operation Umbra
Mission clock: 6:04:13
AH, YOUR FRIEND LEAVES YOU ALONE WITH TRINH, EH?
LEAVES YOU ALONE TO PLAY.
SO... LET'S PLAY.
SNIKK-KKIKK-IKK
Agent Empress
Operation Umbra
Mission clock: 6:07:00
DARLING? COME IN, DARLING.
YOU WON'T TAKE ME ALIVE.
YAAHH!
SHWOP

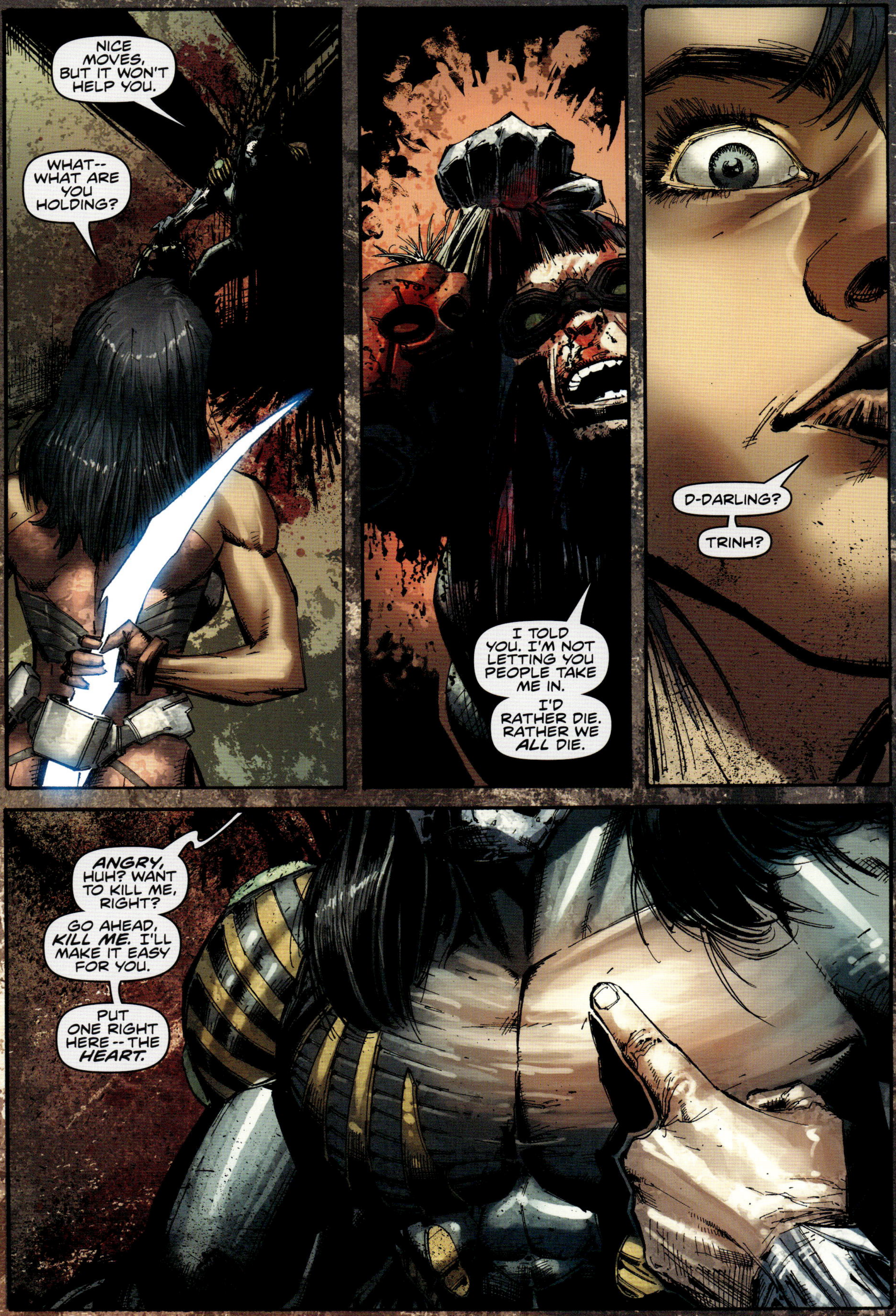
NICE MOVES, BUT IT WON'T HELP YOU.
WHAT-- WHAT ARE YOU HOLDING?
I TOLD YOU. I'M NOT LETTING YOU PEOPLE TAKE ME IN.
I'D RATHER DIE. RATHER WE *ALL* DIE.
D-DARLING?
TRINH?
ANGRY, HUH? WANT TO KILL ME, RIGHT?
GO AHEAD, ***KILL ME.*** I'LL MAKE IT EASY FOR YOU.
PUT ONE RIGHT HERE -- THE ***HEART.***

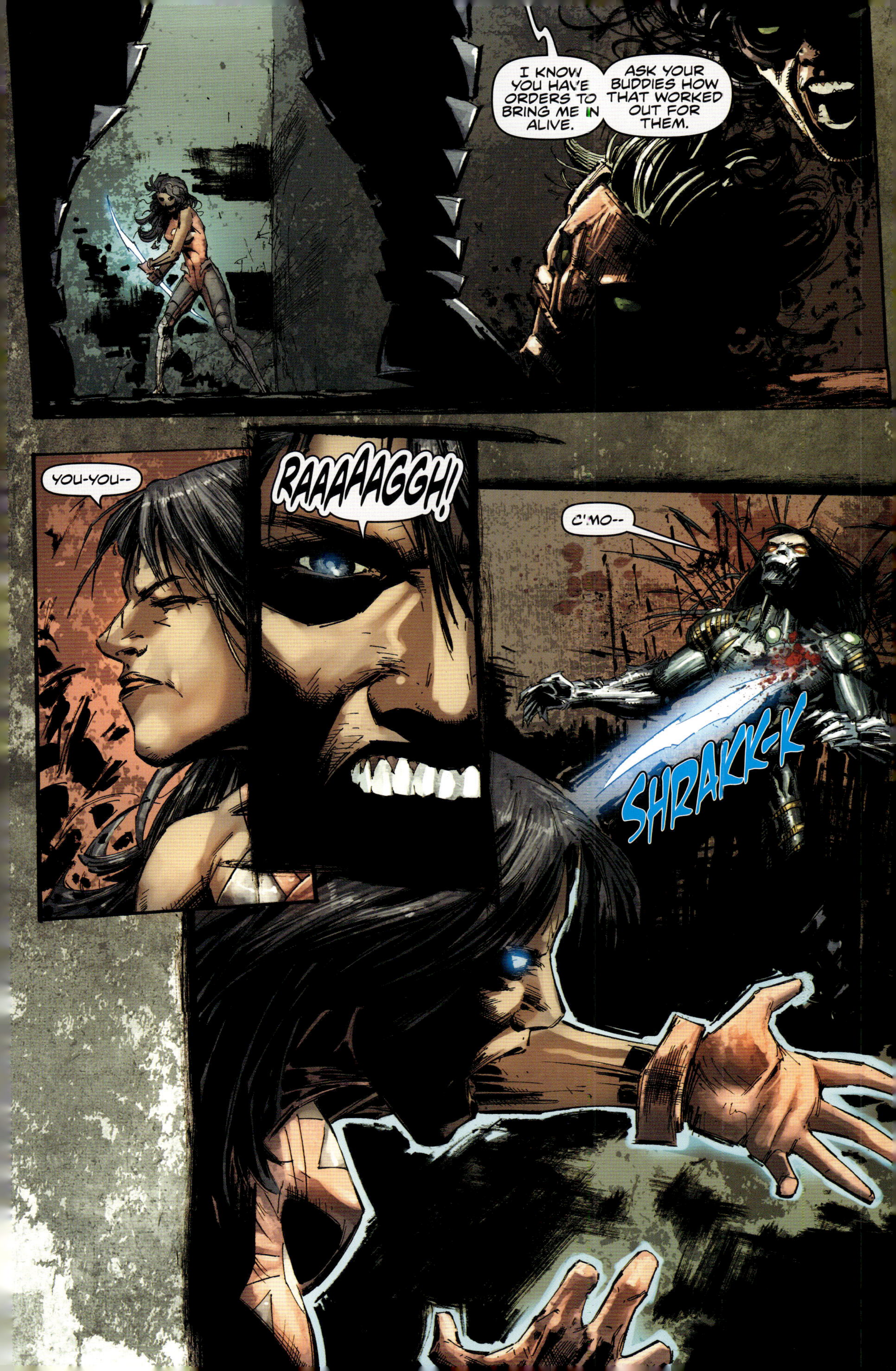

I KNOW YOU HAVE ORDERS TO BRING ME IN ALIVE.
ASK YOUR BUDDIES HOW THAT WORKED OUT FOR THEM.
YOU-YOU--
RAAAAAGGH!
C'MO--
SHRAKK-K

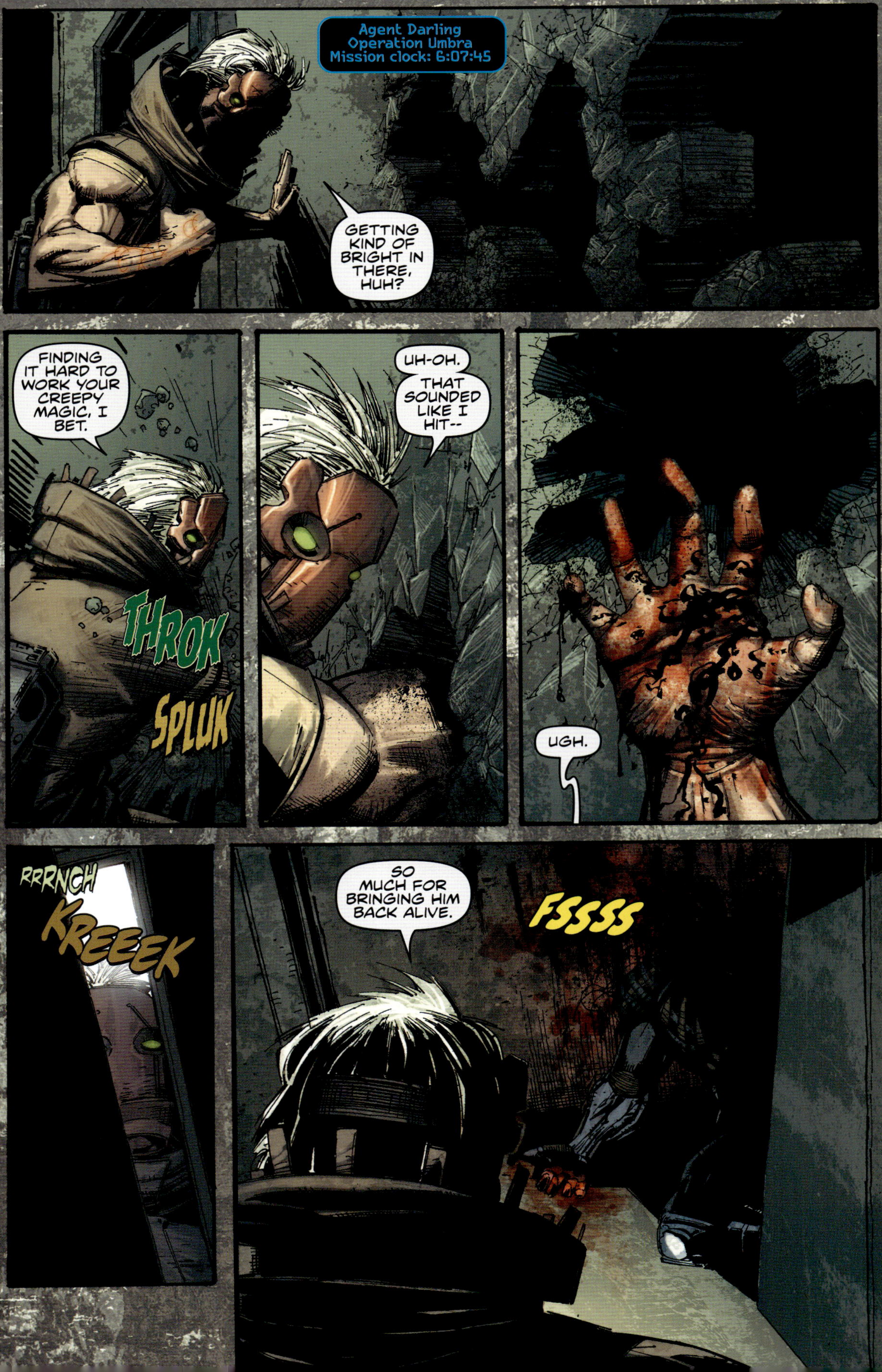
Agent Darling
Operation Umbra
Mission clock: 6:07:45
GETTING KIND OF BRIGHT IN THERE, HUH?
FINDING IT HARD TO WORK YOUR CREEPY MAGIC, I BET.
THROK
SPLUK
UH-OH.
THAT SOUNDED LIKE I HIT--
UGH.
RRRNCH
KREEEK
SO MUCH FOR BRINGING HIM BACK ALIVE.
FSSSS

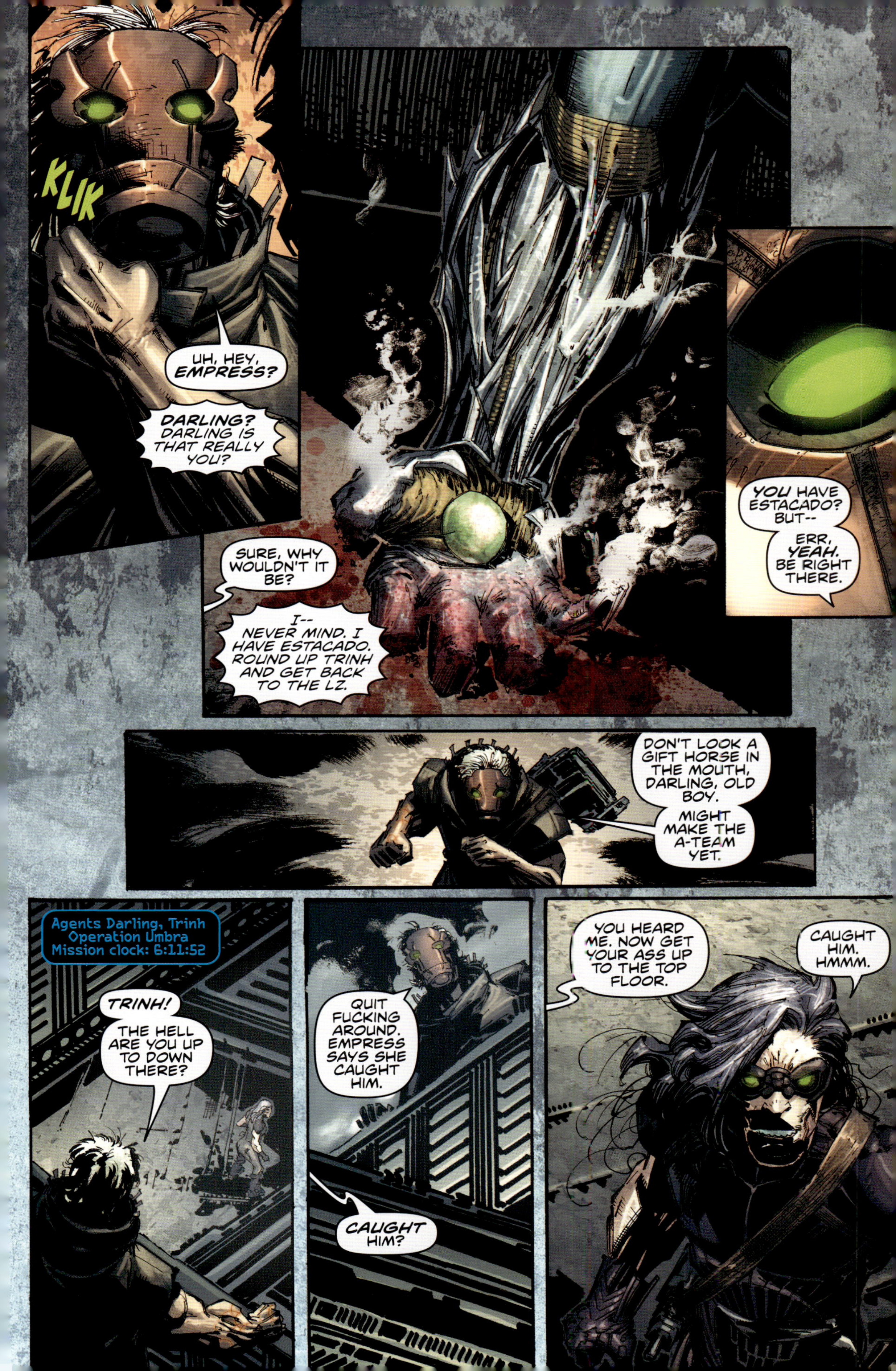
KLIK
UH, HEY, EMPRESS?
DARLING? DARLING IS THAT REALLY YOU?
SURE, WHY WOULDN'T IT BE?
I-- NEVER MIND. I HAVE ESTACADO. ROUND UP TRINH AND GET BACK TO THE LZ.
YOU HAVE ESTACADO? BUT--
ERR, YEAH. BE RIGHT THERE.
DON'T LOOK A GIFT HORSE IN THE MOUTH, DARLING, OLD BOY.
MIGHT MAKE THE A-TEAM YET.
Agents Darling, Trinh
Operation Umbra
Mission clock: 6:11:52
TRINH!
THE HELL ARE YOU UP TO DOWN THERE?
QUIT FUCKING AROUND. EMPRESS SAYS SHE CAUGHT HIM.
CAUGHT HIM?
YOU HEARD ME. NOW GET YOUR ASS UP TO THE TOP FLOOR.
CAUGHT HIM. HMMM.

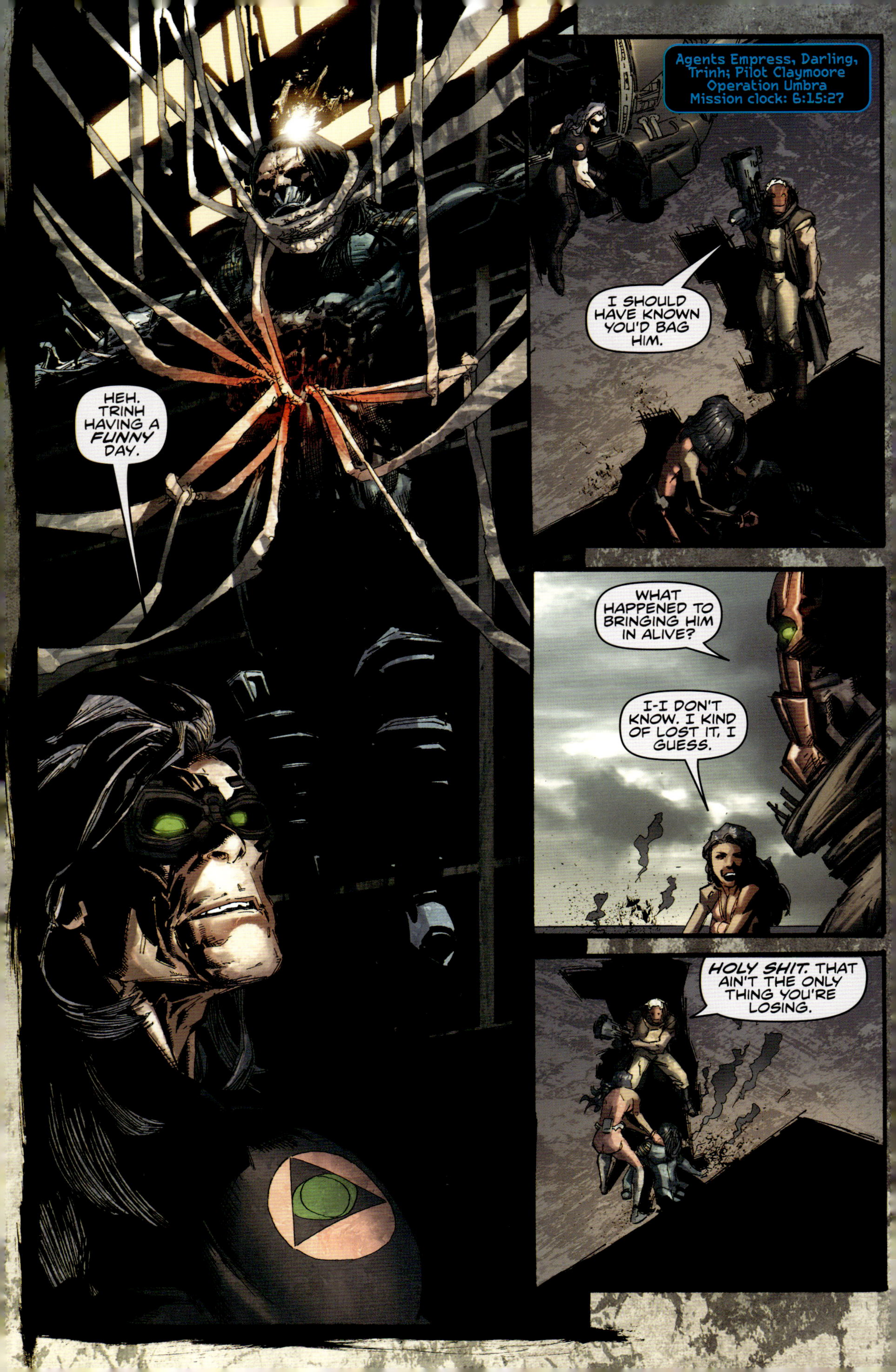

Agents Empress, Darling, Trinh; Pilot Claymoore Operation Umbra Mission clock: 6:15:27
I SHOULD HAVE KNOWN YOU'D BAG HIM.
HEH. TRINH HAVING A *FUNNY* DAY.
WHAT HAPPENED TO BRINGING HIM IN ALIVE?
I-I DON'T KNOW. I KIND OF LOST IT, I GUESS.
HOLY SHIT. THAT AIN'T THE ONLY THING YOU'RE LOSING.

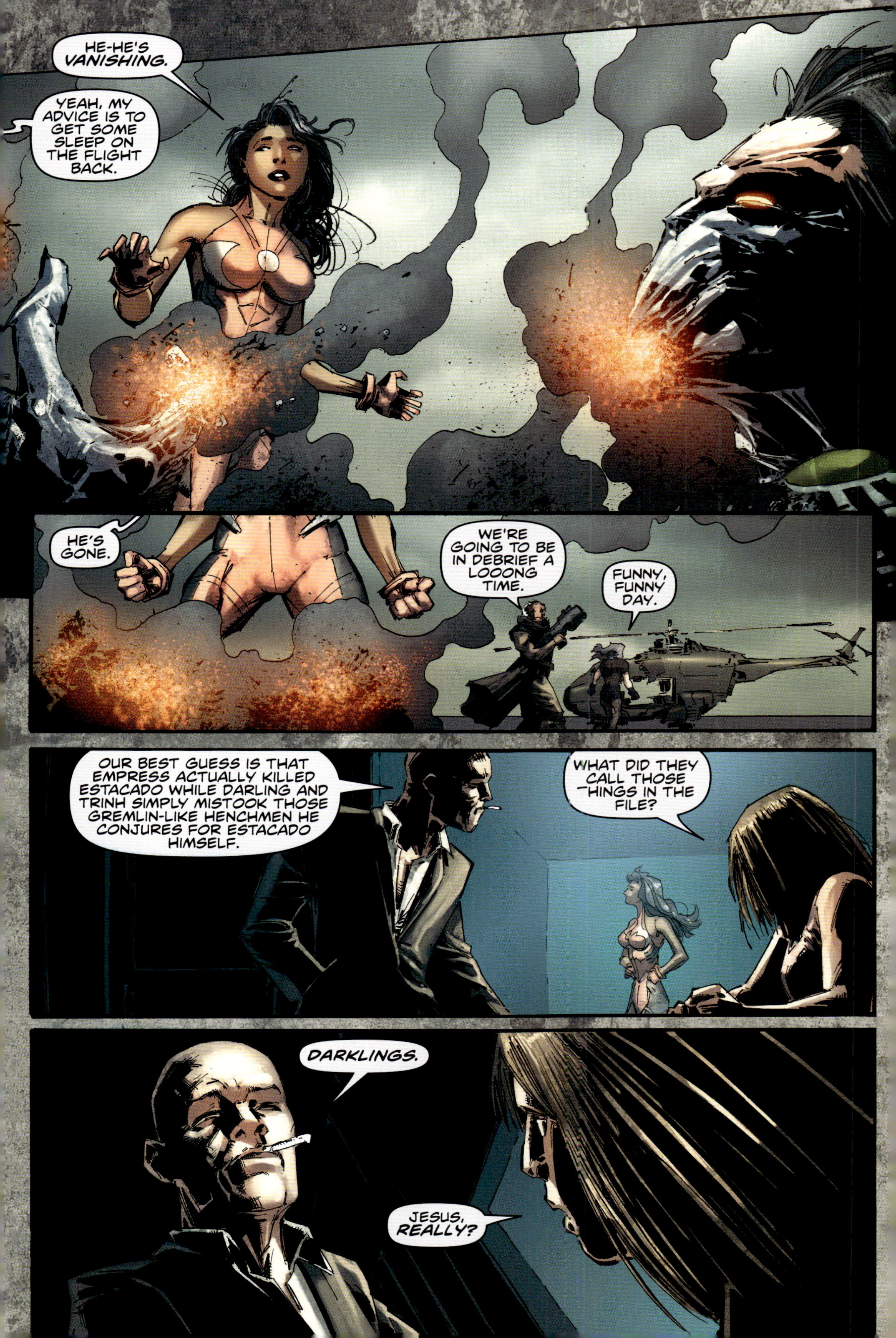
HE-HE'S *VANISHING.*
YEAH, MY ADVICE IS TO GET SOME SLEEP ON THE FLIGHT BACK.
HE'S GONE.
WE'RE GOING TO BE IN DEBRIEF A LOOONG TIME.
FUNNY, FUNNY DAY.
OUR BEST GUESS IS THAT EMPRESS ACTUALLY KILLED ESTACADO WHILE DARLING AND TRINH SIMPLY MISTOOK THOSE GREMLIN-LIKE HENCHMEN HE CONJURES FOR ESTACADO HIMSELF.
WHAT DID THEY CALL THOSE THINGS IN THE FILE?
DARKLINGS.
JESUS, *REALLY?*

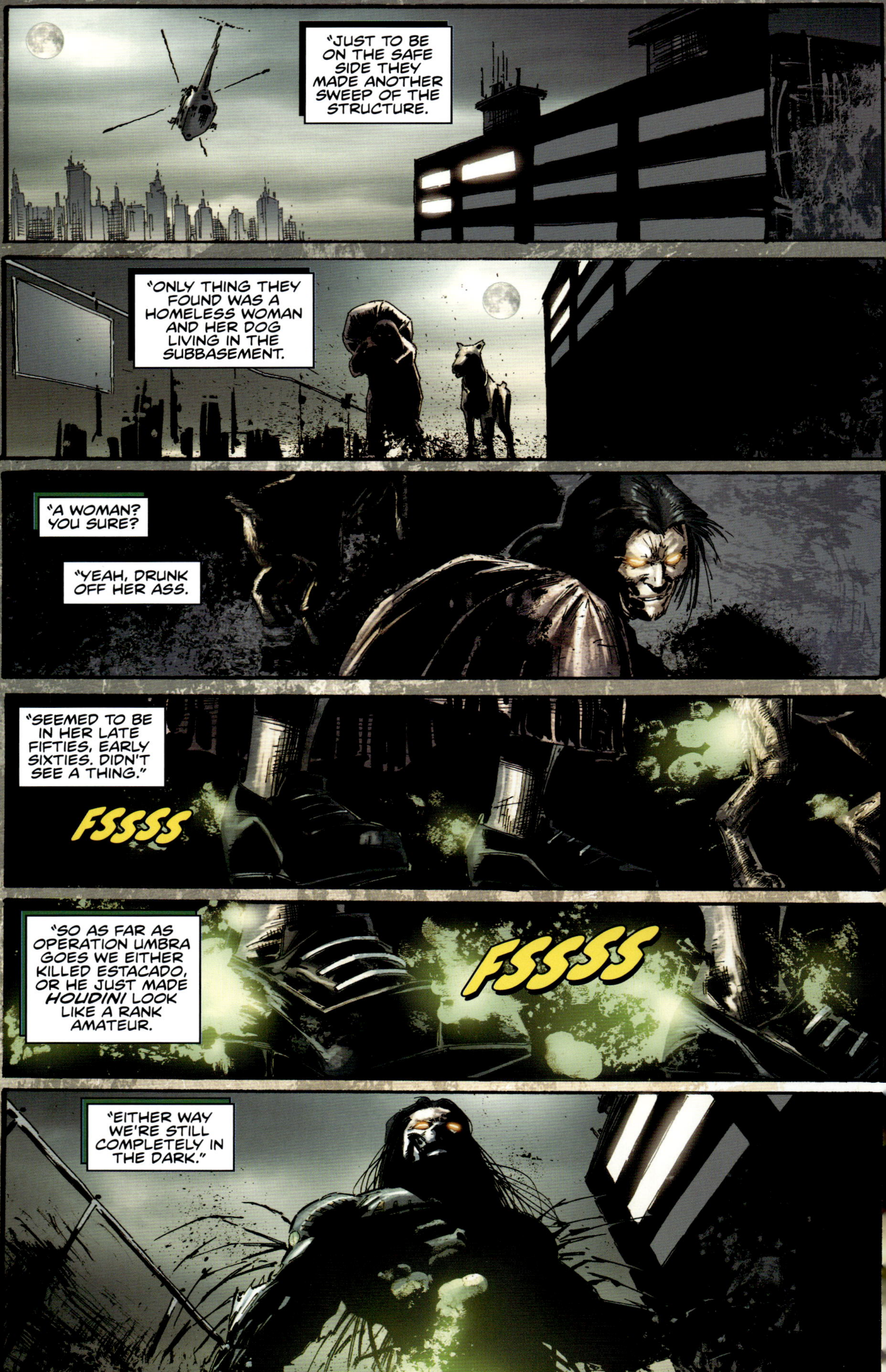
"JUST TO BE ON THE SAFE SIDE THEY MADE ANOTHER SWEEP OF THE STRUCTURE.
"ONLY THING THEY FOUND WAS A HOMELESS WOMAN AND HER DOG LIVING IN THE SUBBASEMENT.
"A WOMAN? YOU SURE?
"YEAH, DRUNK OFF HER ASS.
"SEEMED TO BE IN HER LATE FIFTIES, EARLY SIXTIES. DIDN'T SEE A THING."
FSSSS
"SO AS FAR AS OPERATION UMBRA GOES WE EITHER KILLED ESTACADO, OR HE JUST MADE HOUDINI LOOK LIKE A RANK AMATEUR.
FSSSS
"EITHER WAY WE'RE STILL COMPLETELY IN THE DARK."

The Darkness Issue #85

cover art by: Aaron Campbell and Felix Serrano

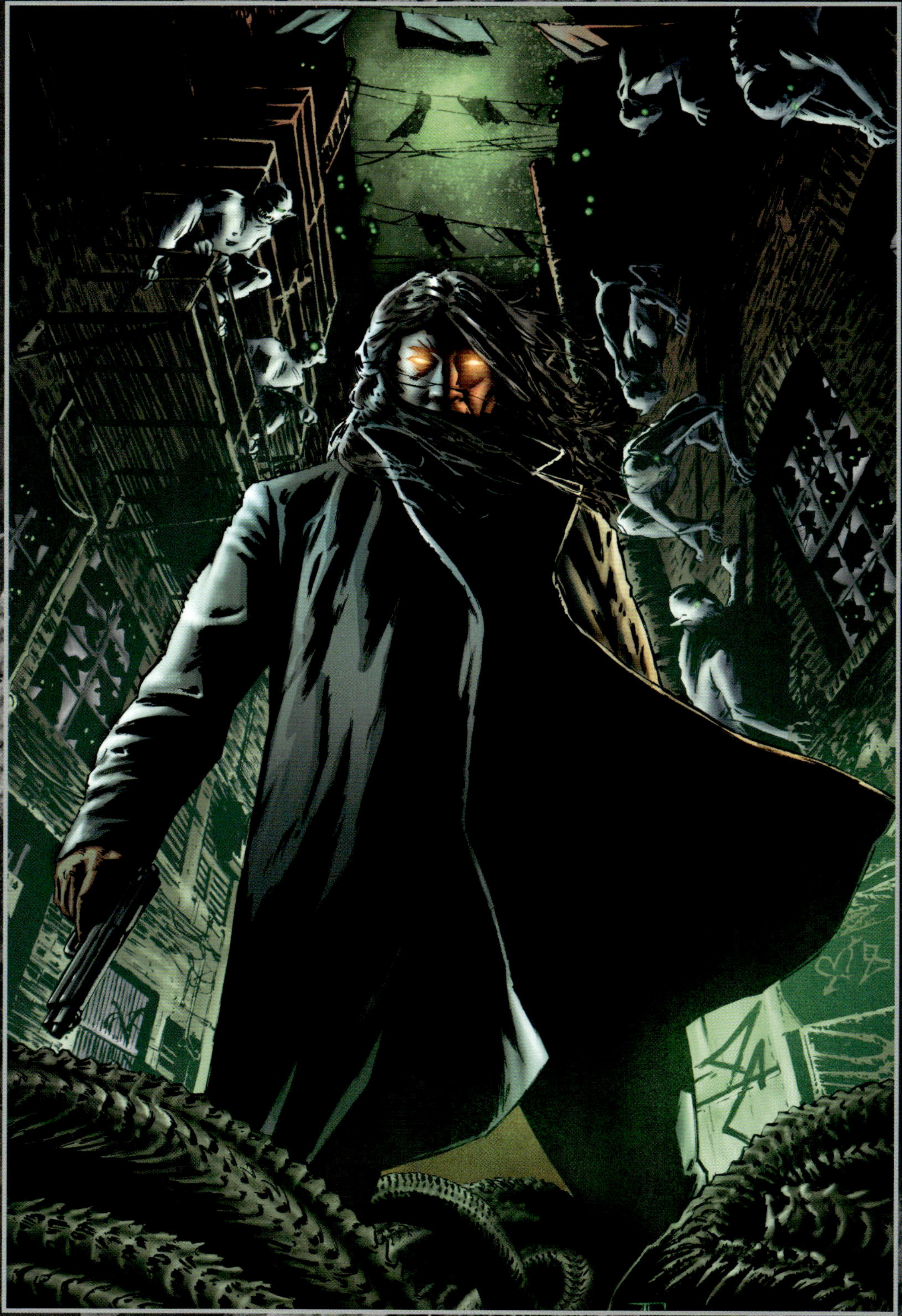

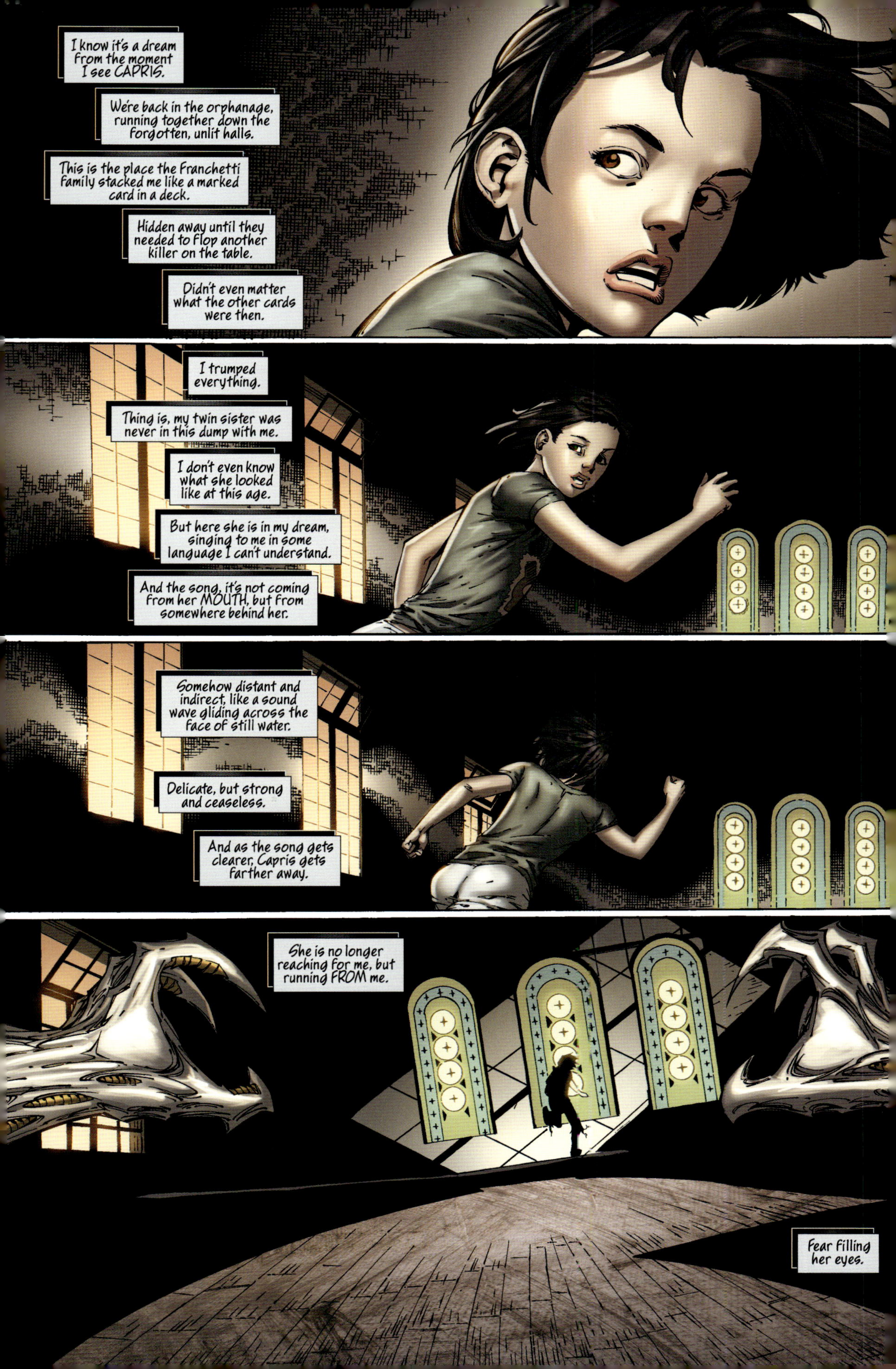
I know it's a dream from the moment I see CAPRIS.
We're back in the orphanage, running together down the forgotten, unlit halls.
This is the place the Franchetti family stacked me like a marked card in a deck.
Hidden away until they needed to flop another killer on the table.
Didn't even matter what the other cards were then.
I trumped everything.
Thing is, my twin sister was never in this dump with me.
I don't even know what she looked like at this age.
But here she is in my dream, singing to me in some language I can't understand.
And the song, it's not coming from her MOUTH, but from somewhere behind her.
Somehow distant and indirect, like a sound wave gliding across the face of still water.
Delicate, but strong and ceaseless.
And as the song gets clearer, Capris gets farther away.
She is no longer reaching for me, but running FROM me.
Fear filling her eyes.

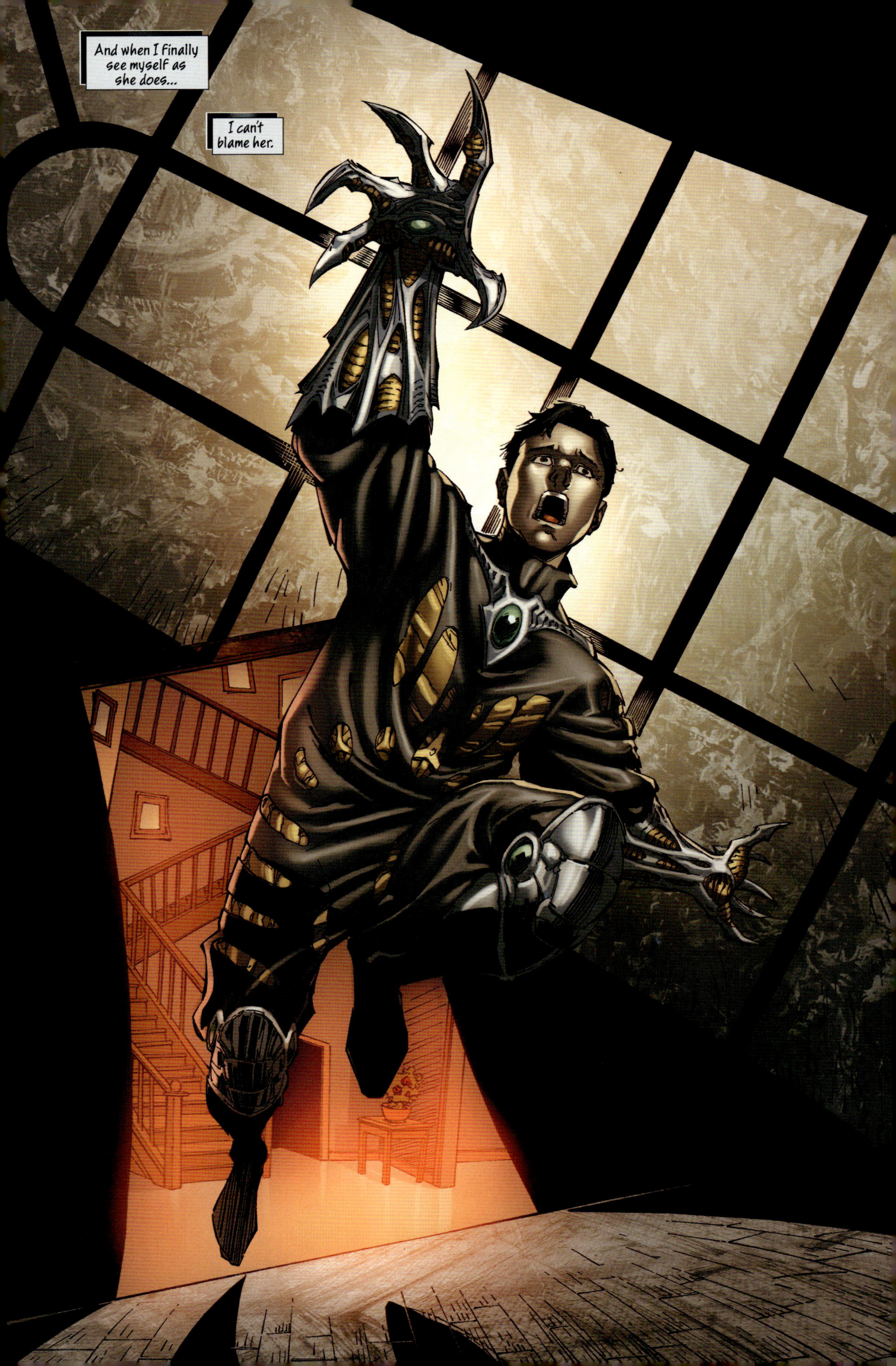
And when I finally see myself as she does...
I can't blame her.

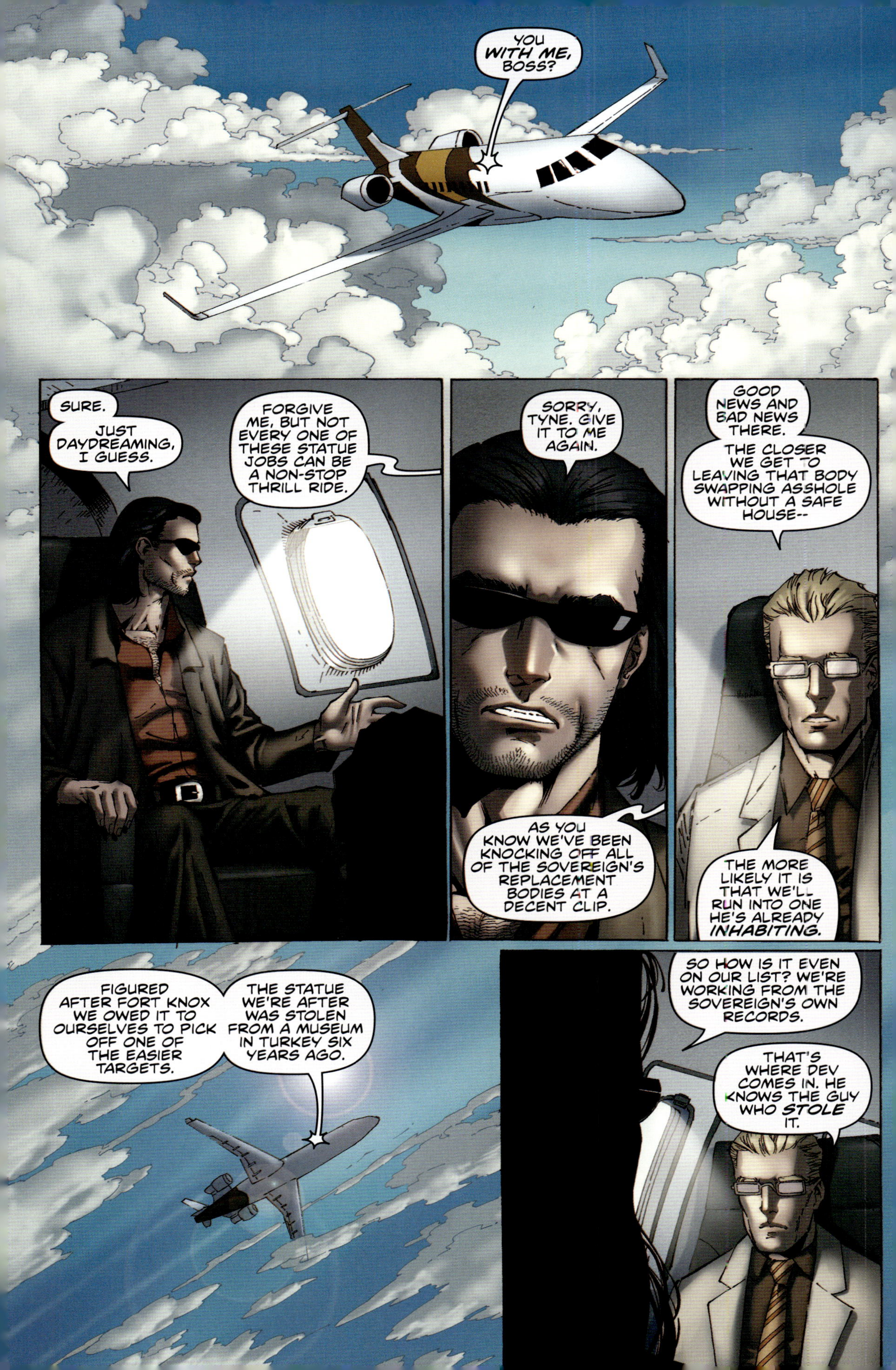
YOU WITH ME, BOSS?
SURE.
JUST DAYDREAMING, I GUESS.
FORGIVE ME, BUT NOT EVERY ONE OF THESE STATUE JOBS CAN BE A NON-STOP THRILL RIDE.
SORRY, TYNE. GIVE IT TO ME AGAIN.
AS YOU KNOW WE'VE BEEN KNOCKING OFF ALL OF THE SOVEREIGN'S REPLACEMENT BODIES AT A DECENT CLIP.
GOOD NEWS AND BAD NEWS THERE.
THE CLOSER WE GET TO LEAVING THAT BODY SWAPPING ASSHOLE WITHOUT A SAFE HOUSE--
THE MORE LIKELY IT IS THAT WE'LL RUN INTO ONE HE'S ALREADY INHABITING.
FIGURED AFTER FORT KNOX WE OWED IT TO OURSELVES TO PICK OFF ONE OF THE EASIER TARGETS.
THE STATUE WE'RE AFTER WAS STOLEN FROM A MUSEUM IN TURKEY SIX YEARS AGO.
SO HOW IS IT EVEN ON OUR LIST? WE'RE WORKING FROM THE SOVEREIGN'S OWN RECORDS.
THAT'S WHERE DEV COMES IN. HE KNOWS THE GUY WHO STOLE IT.

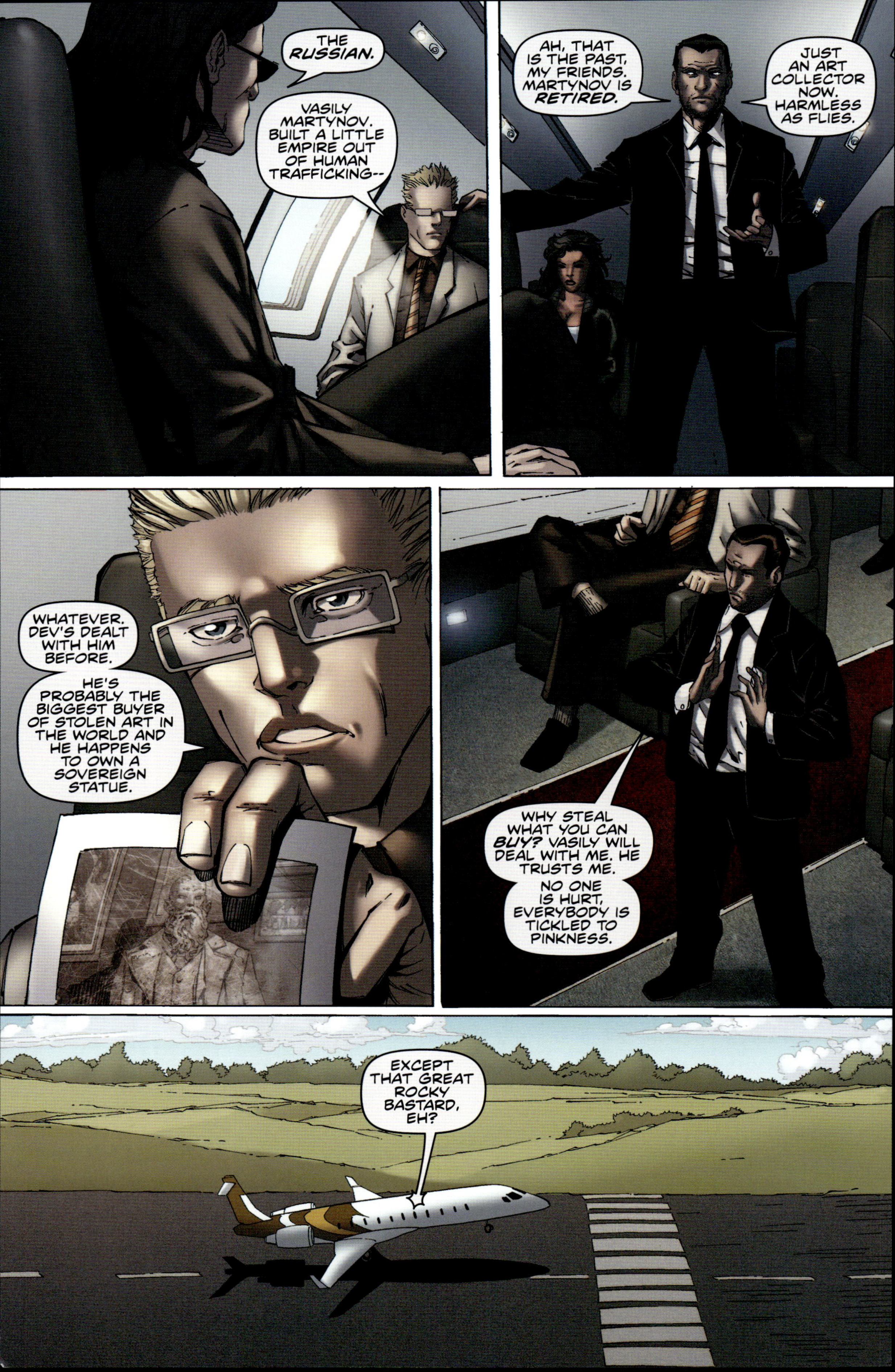
THE RUSSIAN.
VASILY MARTYNOV. BUILT A LITTLE EMPIRE OUT OF HUMAN TRAFFICKING--
AH, THAT IS THE PAST, MY FRIENDS. MARTYNOV IS RETIRED.
JUST AN ART COLLECTOR NOW. HARMLESS AS FLIES.
WHATEVER. DEV'S DEALT WITH HIM BEFORE.
HE'S PROBABLY THE BIGGEST BUYER OF STOLEN ART IN THE WORLD AND HE HAPPENS TO OWN A SOVEREIGN STATUE.
WHY STEAL WHAT YOU CAN BUY? VASILY WILL DEAL WITH ME. HE TRUSTS ME.
NO ONE IS HURT, EVERYBODY IS TICKLED TO PINKNESS.
EXCEPT THAT GREAT ROCKY BASTARD, EH?

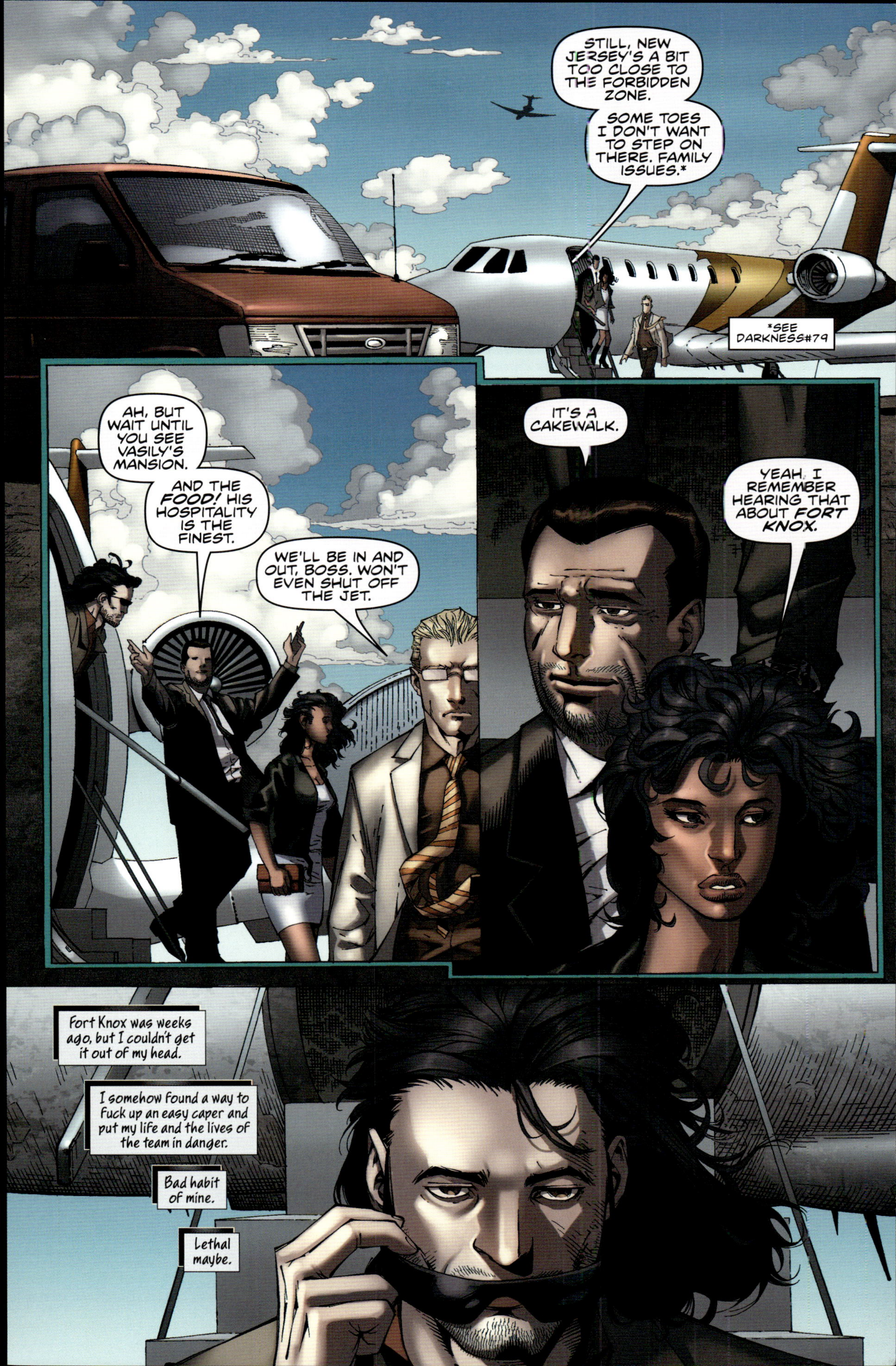
STILL, NEW JERSEY'S A BIT TOO CLOSE TO THE FORBIDDEN ZONE.
SOME TOES I DON'T WANT TO STEP ON THERE. FAMILY ISSUES.*
*SEE DARKNESS#79
AH, BUT WAIT UNTIL YOU SEE VASILY'S MANSION.
AND THE FOOD! HIS HOSPITALITY IS THE FINEST.
WE'LL BE IN AND OUT, BOSS. WON'T EVEN SHUT OFF THE JET.
IT'S A CAKEWALK.
YEAH, I REMEMBER HEARING THAT ABOUT FORT KNOX.
Fort Knox was weeks ago, but I couldn't get it out of my head.
I somehow found a way to fuck up an easy caper and put my life and the lives of the team in danger.
Bad habit of mine.
Lethal maybe.

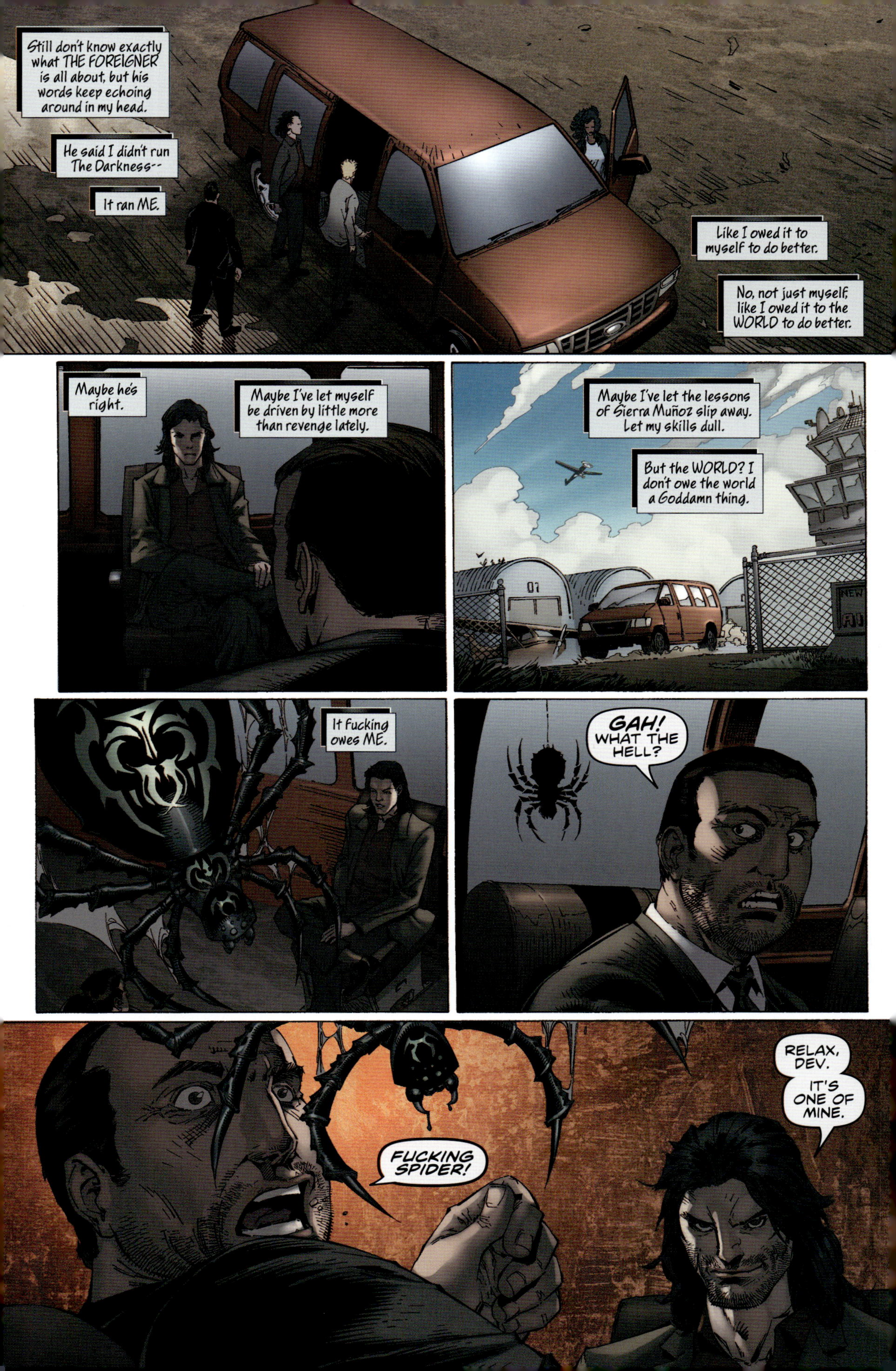
Still don't know exactly what THE FOREIGNER is all about, but his words keep echoing around in my head.
He said I didn't run The Darkness--
It ran ME.
Like I owed it to myself to do better.
No, not just myself. Like I owed it to the WORLD to do better.
Maybe he's right.
Maybe I've let myself be driven by little more than revenge lately.
Maybe I've let the lessons of Sierra Muñoz slip away. Let my skills dull.
But the WORLD? I don't owe the world a Goddamn thing.
It fucking owes ME.
GAH! WHAT THE HELL?
FUCKING SPIDER!
RELAX, DEV.
IT'S ONE OF MINE.

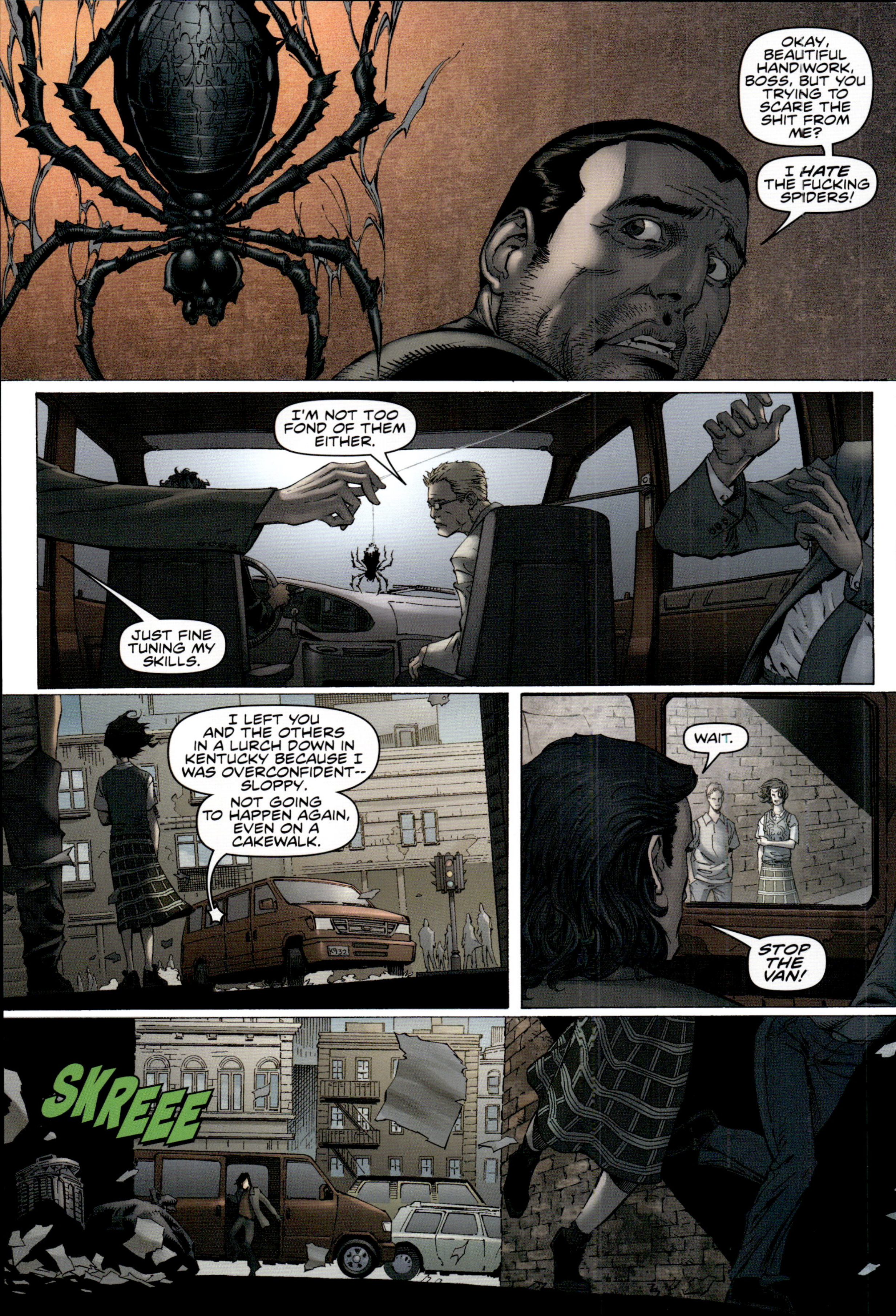
OKAY, BEAUTIFUL HANDIWORK, BOSS, BUT YOU TRYING TO SCARE THE SHIT FROM ME?
I HATE THE FUCKING SPIDERS!
I'M NOT TOO FOND OF THEM EITHER.
JUST FINE TUNING MY SKILLS.
I LEFT YOU AND THE OTHERS IN A LURCH DOWN IN KENTUCKY BECAUSE I WAS OVERCONFIDENT-- SLOPPY.
NOT GOING TO HAPPEN AGAIN, EVEN ON A CAKEWALK.
WAIT.
STOP THE VAN!
SKREEE

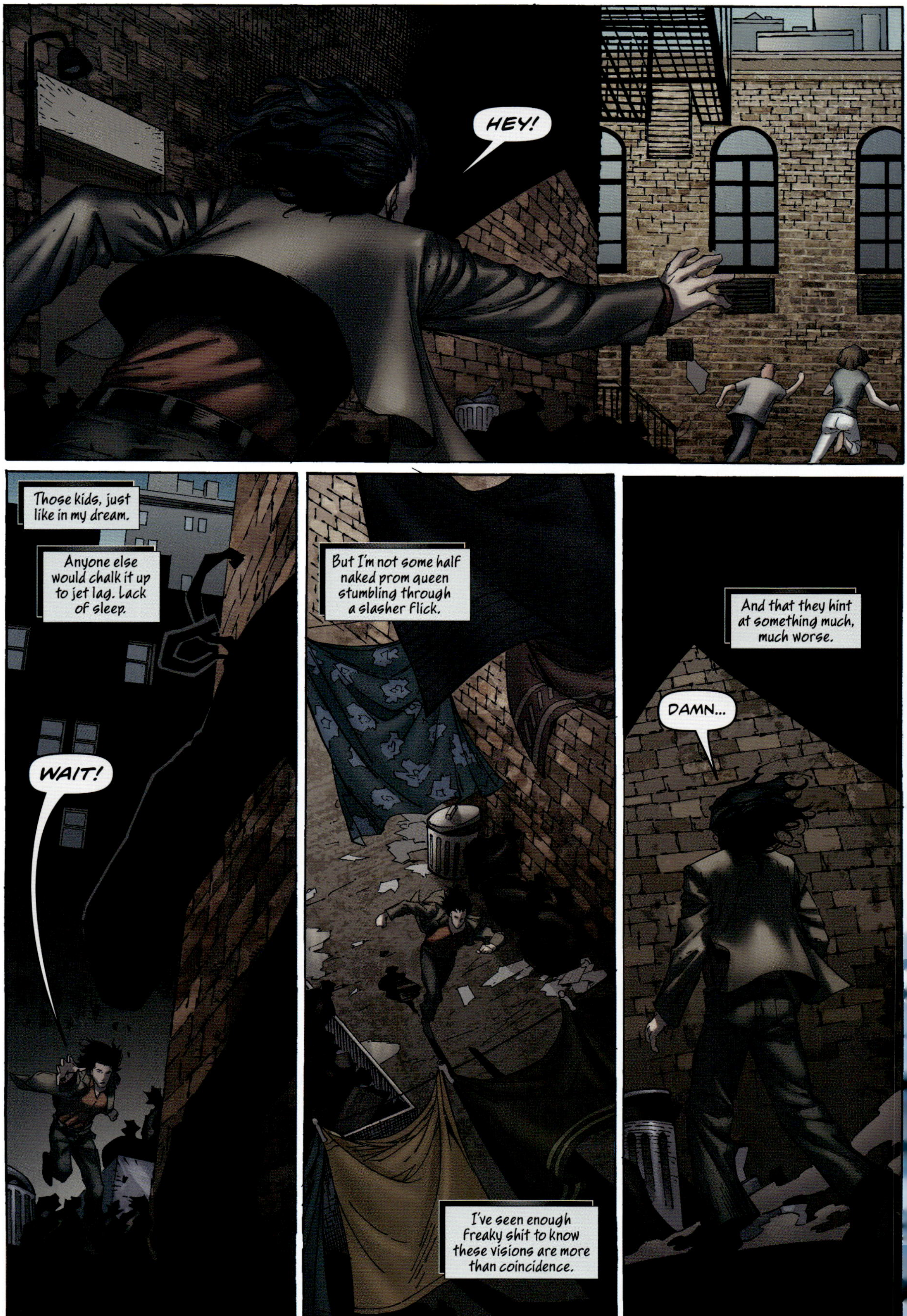
HEY!
Those kids, just like in my dream.
Anyone else would chalk it up to jet lag. Lack of sleep.
WAIT!
But I'm not some half naked prom queen stumbling through a slasher flick.
I've seen enough freaky shit to know these visions are more than coincidence.
And that they hint at something much, much worse.
DAMN...

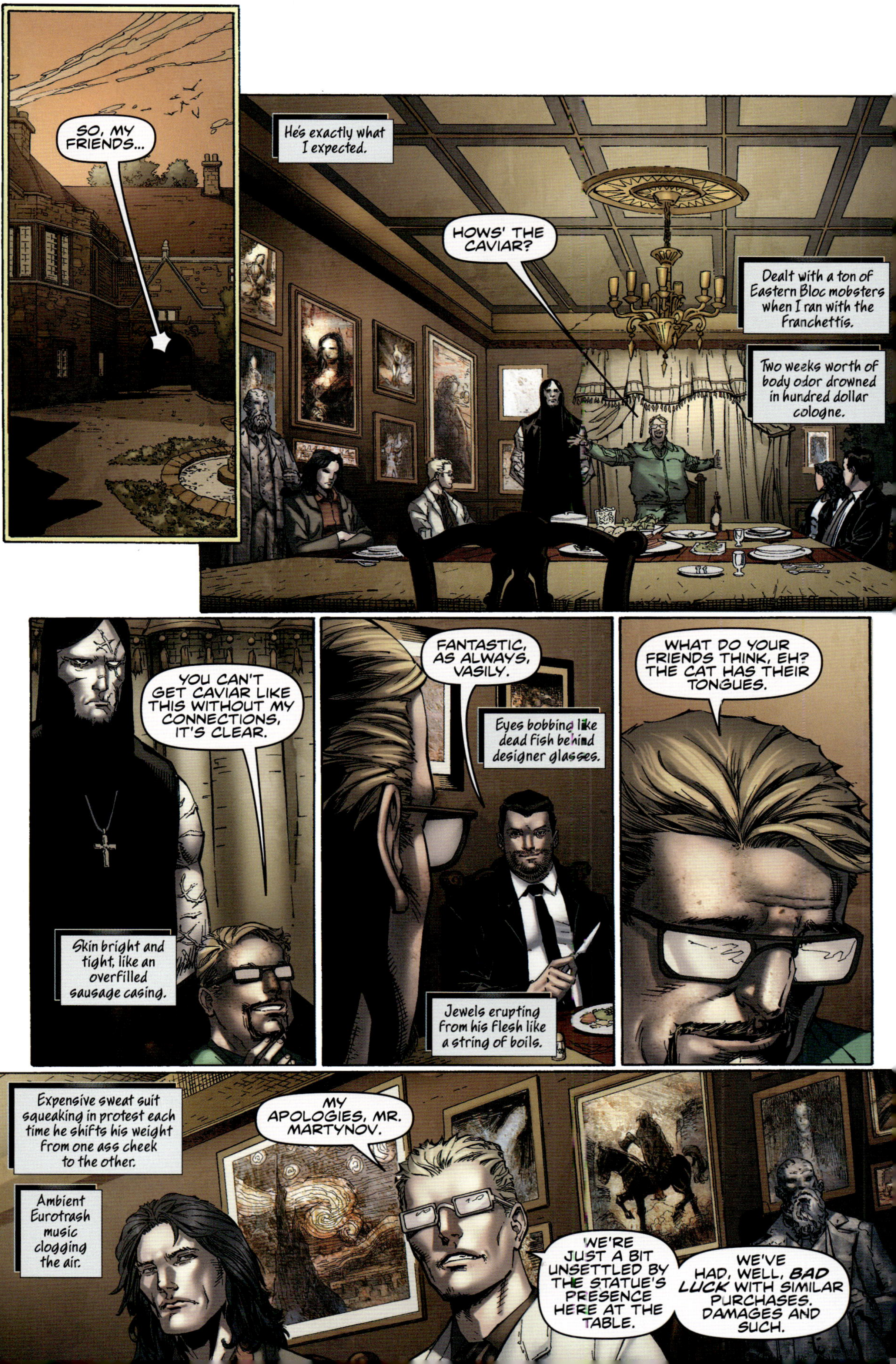

SO, MY FRIENDS...
He's exactly what I expected.
HOWS' THE CAVIAR?
Dealt with a ton of Eastern Bloc mobsters when I ran with the Franchettis.
Two weeks worth of body odor drowned in hundred dollar cologne.
YOU CAN'T GET CAVIAR LIKE THIS WITHOUT MY CONNECTIONS, IT'S CLEAR.
Skin bright and tight, like an overfilled sausage casing.
FANTASTIC, AS ALWAYS, VASILY.
Eyes bobbing like dead fish behind designer glasses.
Jewels erupting from his flesh like a string of boils.
WHAT DO YOUR FRIENDS THINK, EH? THE CAT HAS THEIR TONGUES.
Expensive sweat suit squeaking in protest each time he shifts his weight from one ass cheek to the other.
Ambient Eurotrash music clogging the air.
MY APOLOGIES, MR. MARTYNOV.
WE'RE JUST A BIT UNSETTLED BY THE STATUE'S PRESENCE HERE AT THE TABLE.
WE'VE HAD, WELL, BAD LUCK WITH SIMILAR PURCHASES. DAMAGES AND SUCH.

AH, IT WILL SECURED FOR YOUR VOYAGE, HAVE NO DOUBT.

ARVO WILL SEE TO IT BEFORE DESSERT.

But his attack dog...

Never seen anything like him.

WHY ISN'T ARVO EATING WITH US?

AH, HE IS A MYSTIC, YOU KNOW?

HOW TO SAY IT IN ENGLISH-- AN *ASCETIC*, YES?

NO DOUBT HIS MIND IS FLYING FREELY THROUGH SOME ENCHANTED PLANE, DINING ON AMBROSIA AND SOMA WITH HIS IMAGINARY GODS.

I DON'T KNOW. BIG FELLOW SEEMS PRETTY FIXATED ON WATCHING ME CHEW.

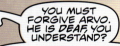

YOU MUST FORGIVE ARVO. HE IS *DEAF*, YOU UNDERSTAND?

MOST LIKELY HE IS TRYING TO READ YOUR LIPS. HE IS MY BODYGUARD, AFTER ALL.

HE'S QUITE GOOD AT IT. YOU SHOULD BE *FLATTERED*, MY FRIEND.

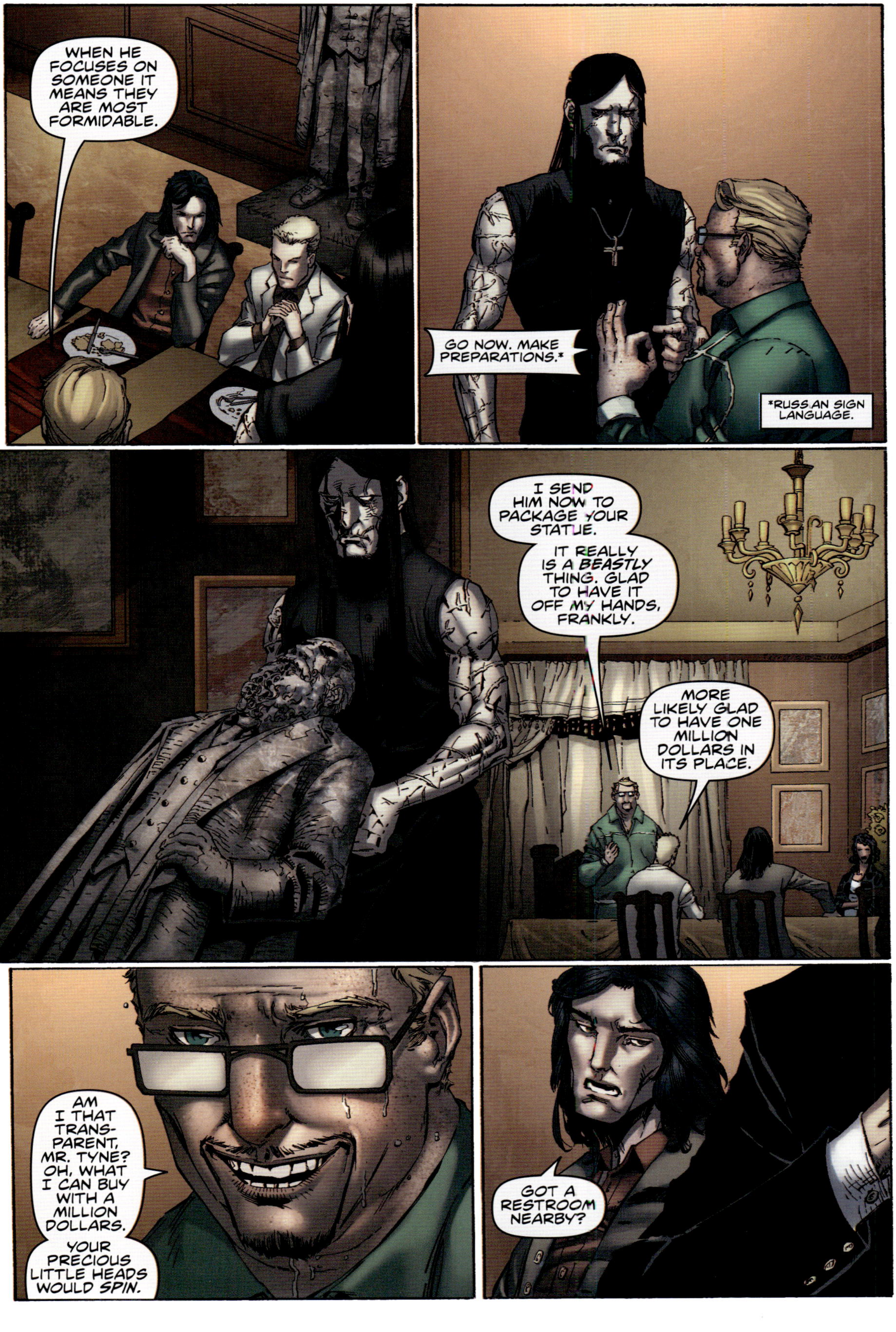
WHEN HE FOCUSES ON SOMEONE IT MEANS THEY ARE MOST FORMIDABLE.
GO NOW. MAKE PREPARATIONS.*
*RUSSIAN SIGN LANGUAGE.
I SEND HIM NOW TO PACKAGE YOUR STATUE.
IT REALLY IS A BEASTLY THING. GLAD TO HAVE IT OFF MY HANDS, FRANKLY.
MORE LIKELY GLAD TO HAVE ONE MILLION DOLLARS IN ITS PLACE.
AM I THAT TRANSPARENT, MR. TYNE? OH, WHAT I CAN BUY WITH A MILLION DOLLARS.
YOUR PRECIOUS LITTLE HEADS WOULD SPIN.
GOT A RESTROOM NEARBY?

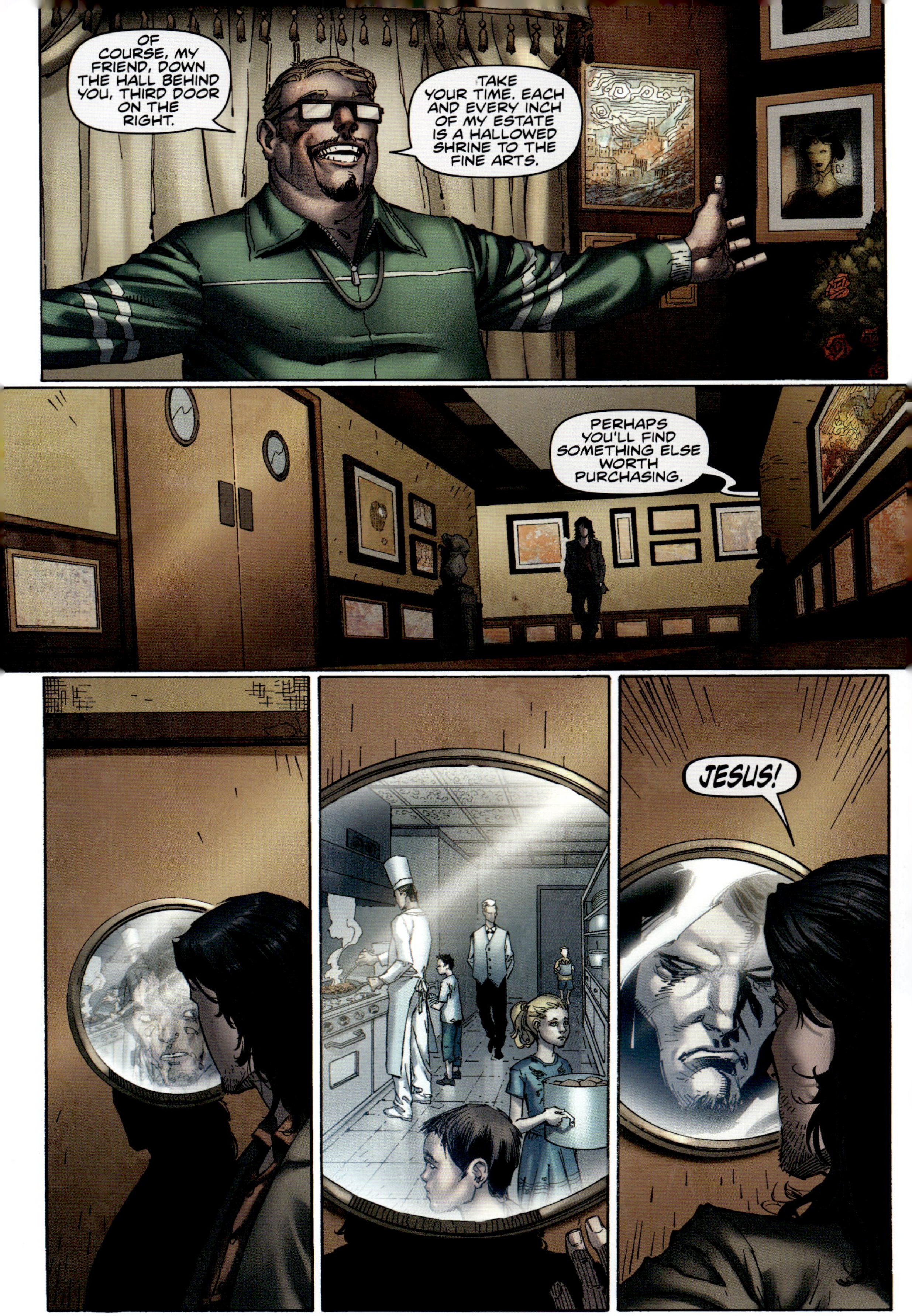
OF COURSE, MY FRIEND, DOWN THE HALL BEHIND YOU, THIRD DOOR ON THE RIGHT.
TAKE YOUR TIME. EACH AND EVERY INCH OF MY ESTATE IS A HALLOWED SHRINE TO THE FINE ARTS.
PERHAPS YOU'LL FIND SOMETHING ELSE WORTH PURCHASING.
JESUS!

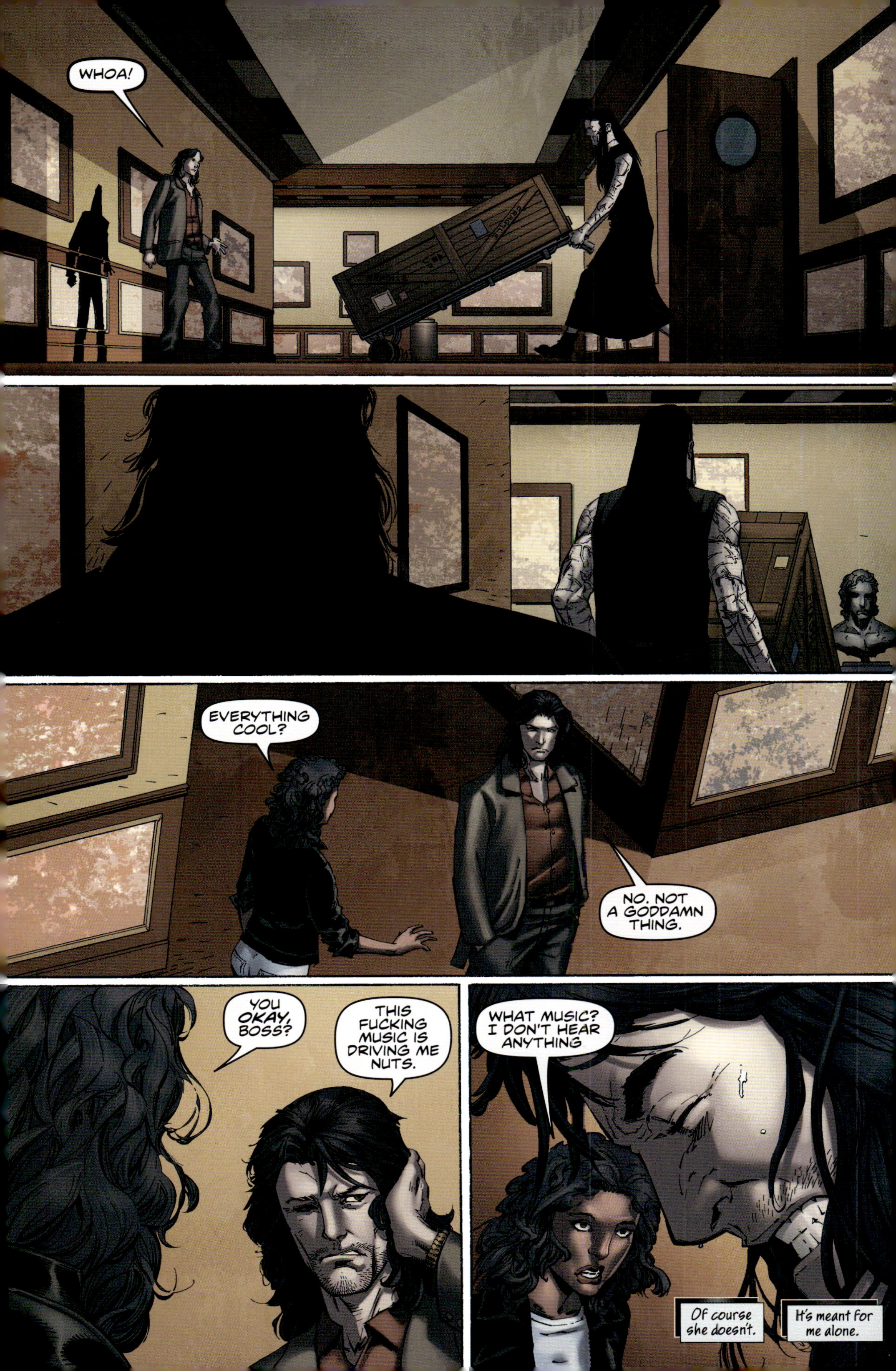
WHOA!
FRAGILE
EVERYTHING COOL?
NO. NOT A GODDAMN THING.
YOU OKAY, BOSS?
THIS FUCKING MUSIC IS DRIVING ME NUTS.
WHAT MUSIC? I DON'T HEAR ANYTHING
Of course she doesn't.
It's meant for me alone.

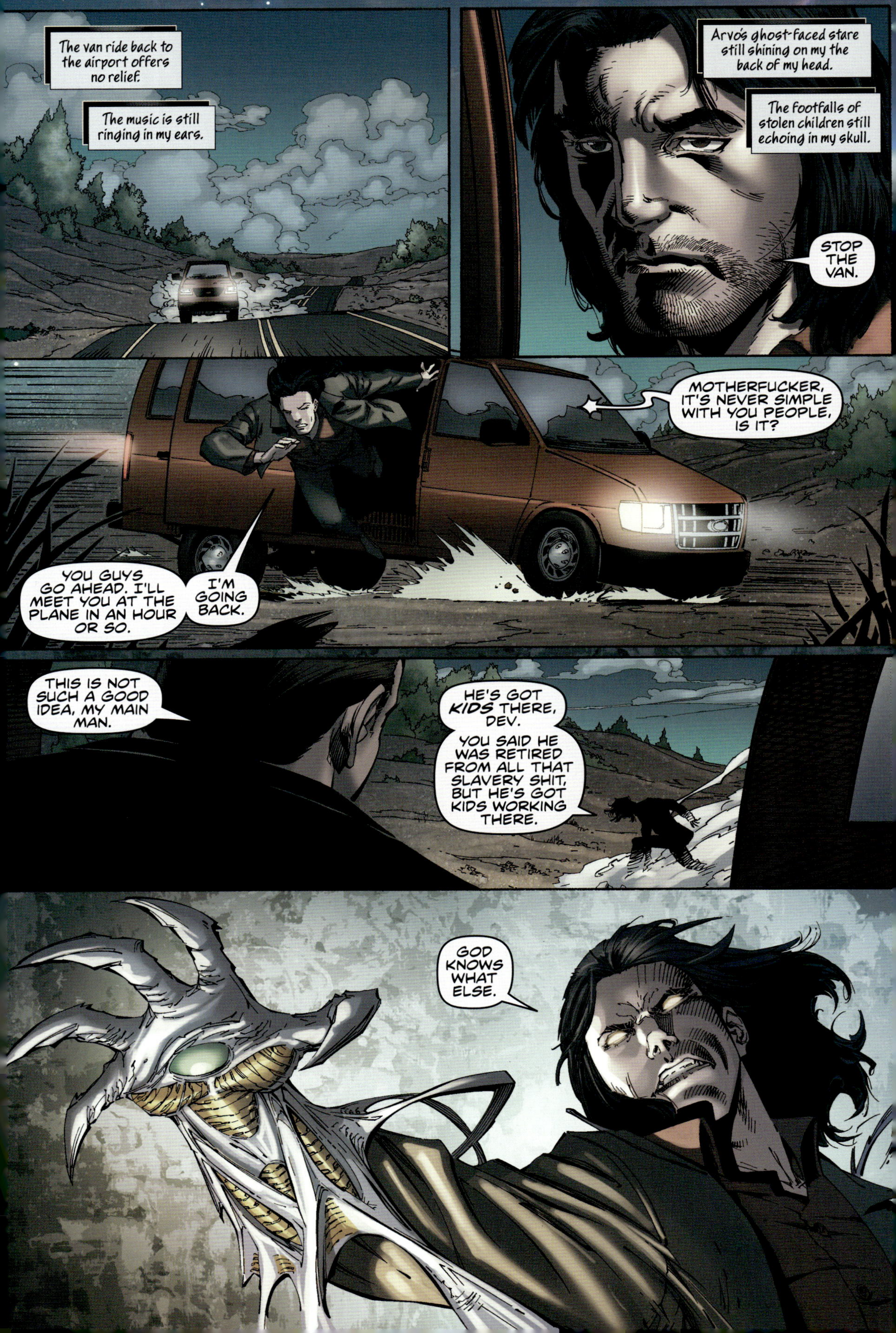
The van ride back to the airport offers no relief.
The music is still ringing in my ears.
Arvo's ghost-faced stare still shining on my the back of my head.
The footfalls of stolen children still echoing in my skull.
STOP THE VAN.
MOTHERFUCKER, IT'S NEVER SIMPLE WITH YOU PEOPLE, IS IT?
I'M GOING BACK.
YOU GUYS GO AHEAD. I'LL MEET YOU AT THE PLANE IN AN HOUR OR SO.
THIS IS NOT SUCH A GOOD IDEA, MY MAIN MAN.
HE'S GOT KIDS THERE, DEV.
YOU SAID HE WAS RETIRED FROM ALL THAT SLAVERY SHIT, BUT HE'S GOT KIDS WORKING THERE.
GOD KNOWS WHAT ELSE.

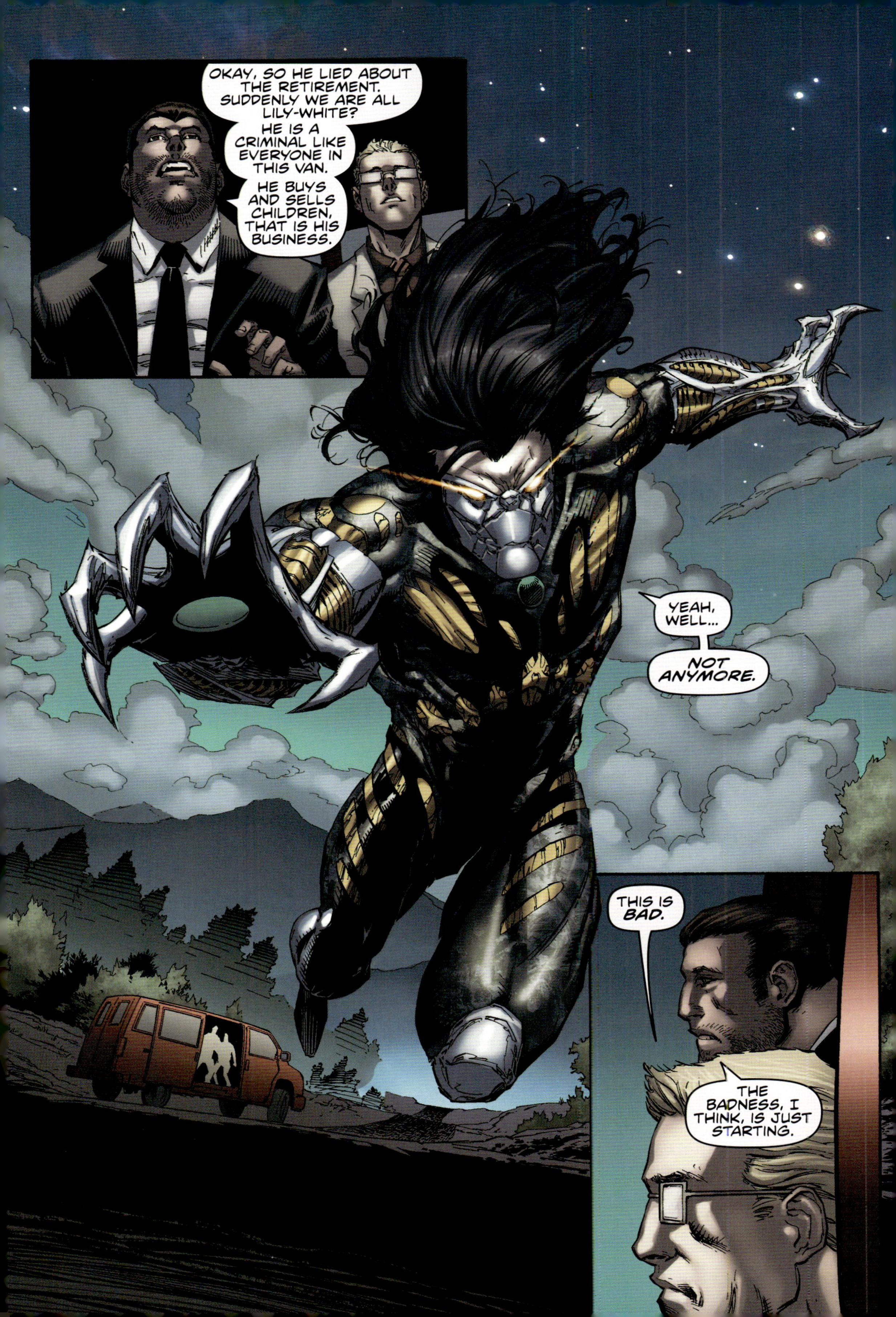
OKAY, SO HE LIED ABOUT THE RETIREMENT. SUDDENLY WE ARE ALL LILY-WHITE?
HE IS A CRIMINAL LIKE EVERYONE IN THIS VAN.
HE BUYS AND SELLS CHILDREN, THAT IS HIS BUSINESS.
YEAH, WELL...
NOT ANYMORE.
THIS IS BAD.
THE BADNESS, I THINK, IS JUST STARTING.

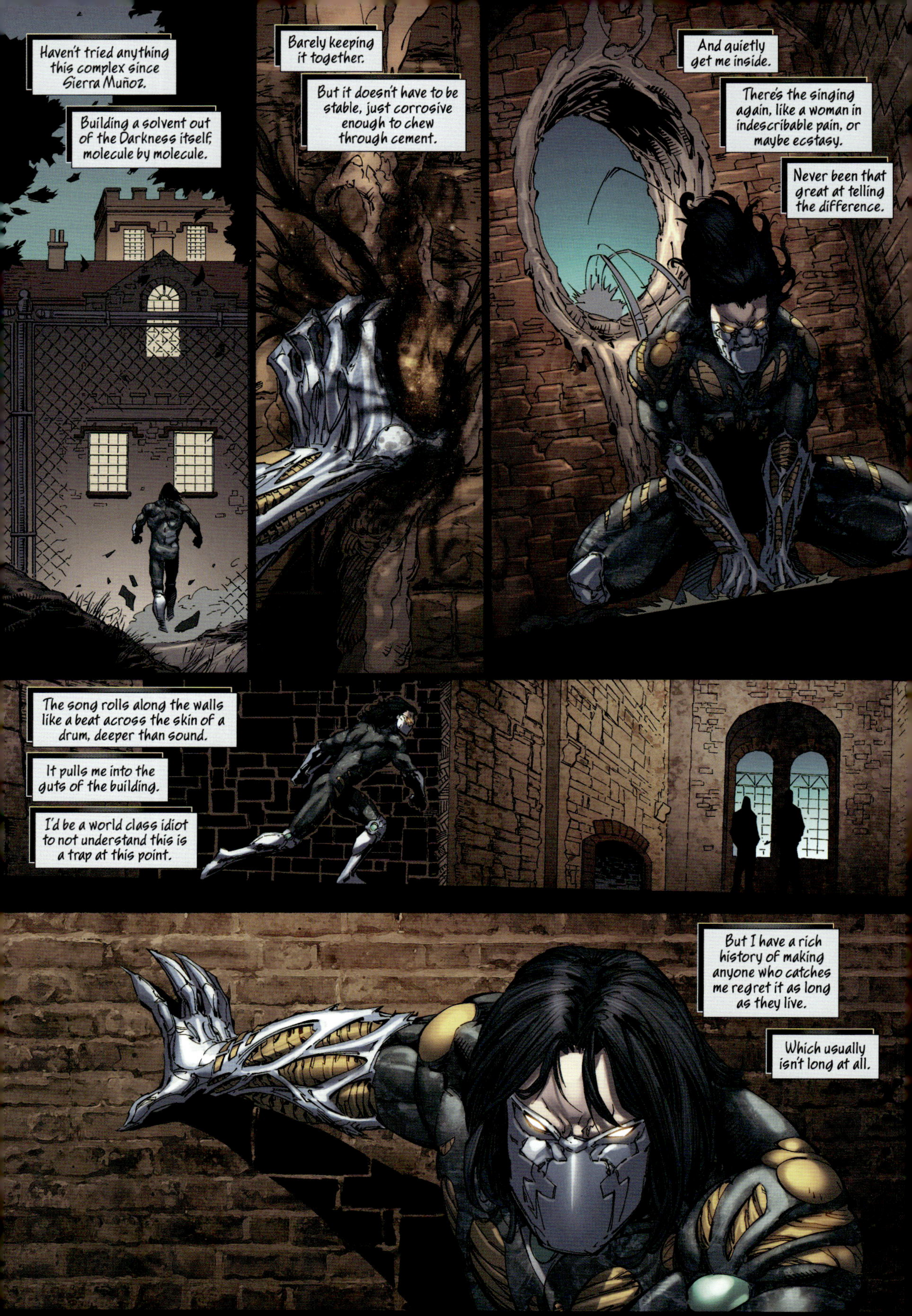
Haven't tried anything this complex since Sierra Muñoz.
Building a solvent out of the Darkness itself, molecule by molecule.
Barely keeping it together.
But it doesn't have to be stable, just corrosive enough to chew through cement.
And quietly get me inside.
There's the singing again, like a woman in indescribable pain, or maybe ecstasy.
Never been that great at telling the difference.
The song rolls along the walls like a beat across the skin of a drum, deeper than sound.
It pulls me into the guts of the building.
I'd be a world class idiot to not understand this is a trap at this point.
But I have a rich history of making anyone who catches me regret it as long as they live.
Which usually isn't long at all.

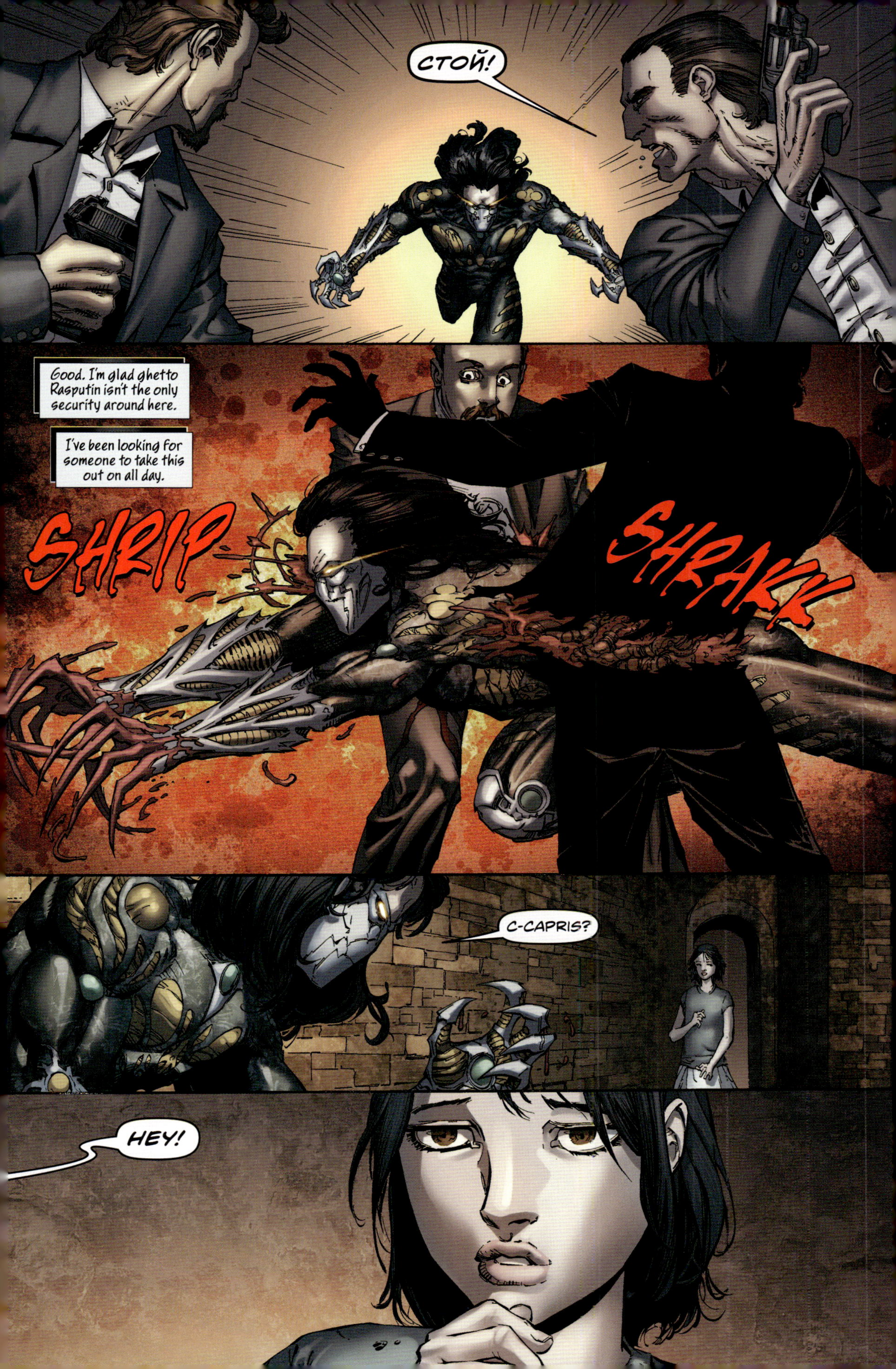

СТОЙ!
Good. I'm glad ghetto Rasputin isn't the only security around here.
I've been looking for someone to take this out on all day.
SHRIP
SHRAKK
C-CAPRIS?
HEY!

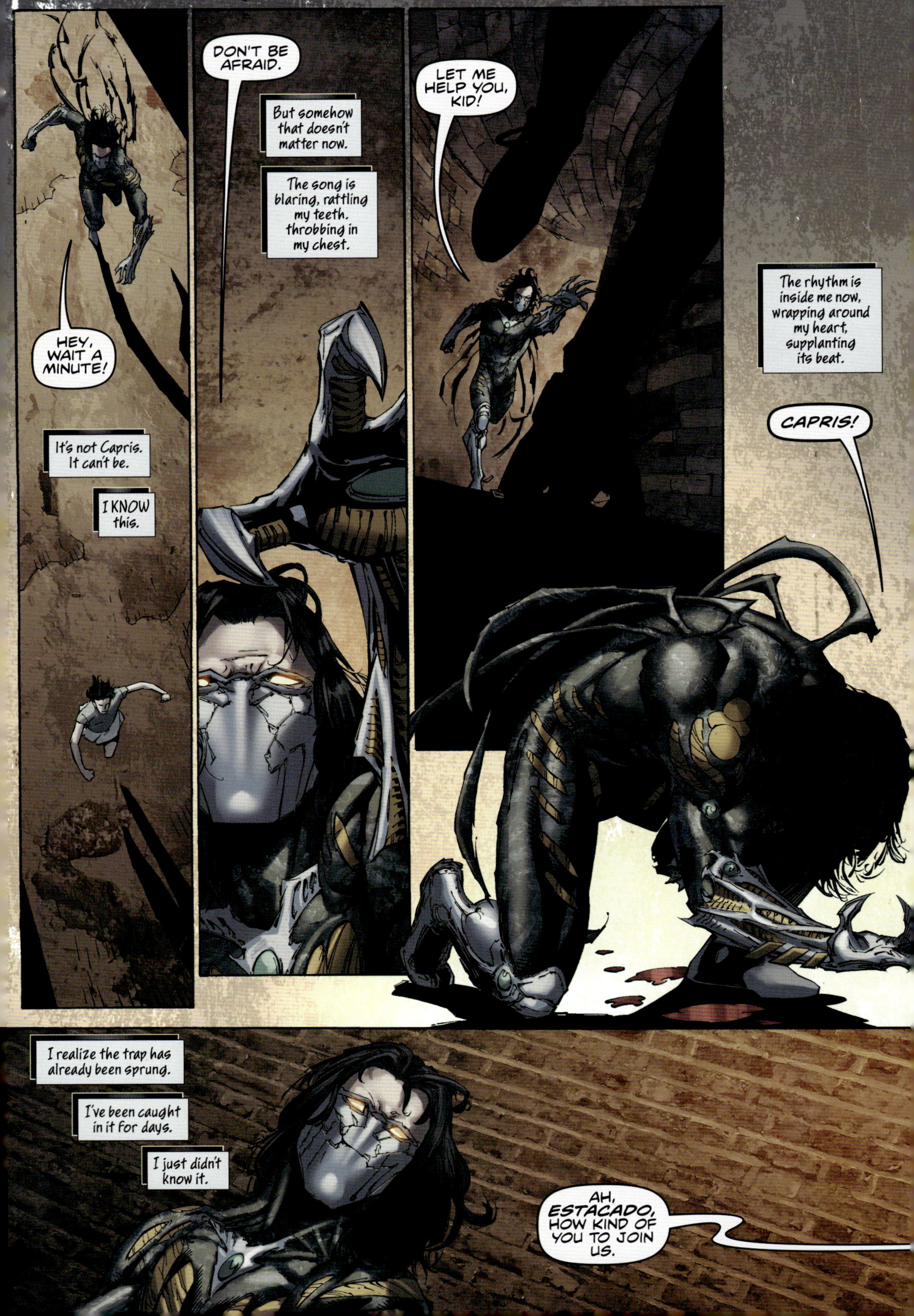
HEY, WAIT A MINUTE!
It's not Capris. It can't be.
I KNOW this.
DON'T BE AFRAID.
But somehow that doesn't matter now.
The song is blaring, rattling my teeth. throbbing in my chest.
LET ME HELP YOU, KID!
The rhythm is inside me now, wrapping around my heart, supplanting its beat.
CAPRIS!
I realize the trap has already been sprung.
I've been caught in it for days.
I just didn't know it.
AH, ESTACADO, HOW KIND OF YOU TO JOIN US.

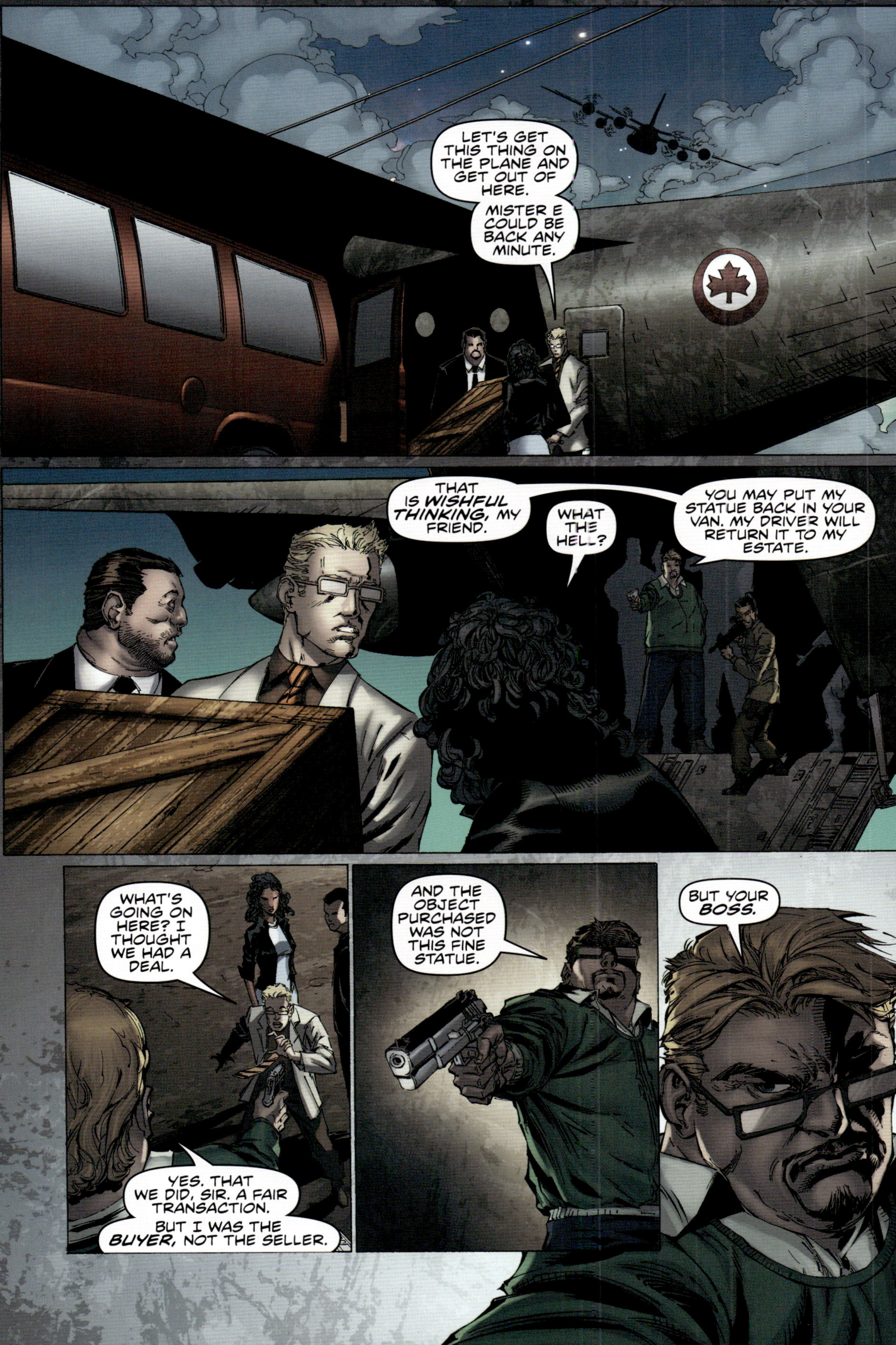
LET'S GET THIS THING ON THE PLANE AND GET OUT OF HERE.
MISTER E COULD BE BACK ANY MINUTE.
THAT IS WISHFUL THINKING, MY FRIEND.
WHAT THE HELL?
YOU MAY PUT MY STATUE BACK IN YOUR VAN. MY DRIVER WILL RETURN IT TO MY ESTATE.
WHAT'S GOING ON HERE? I THOUGHT WE HAD A DEAL.
YES. THAT WE DID, SIR. A FAIR TRANSACTION.
BUT I WAS THE BUYER, NOT THE SELLER.
AND THE OBJECT PURCHASED WAS NOT THIS FINE STATUE.
BUT YOUR BOSS.

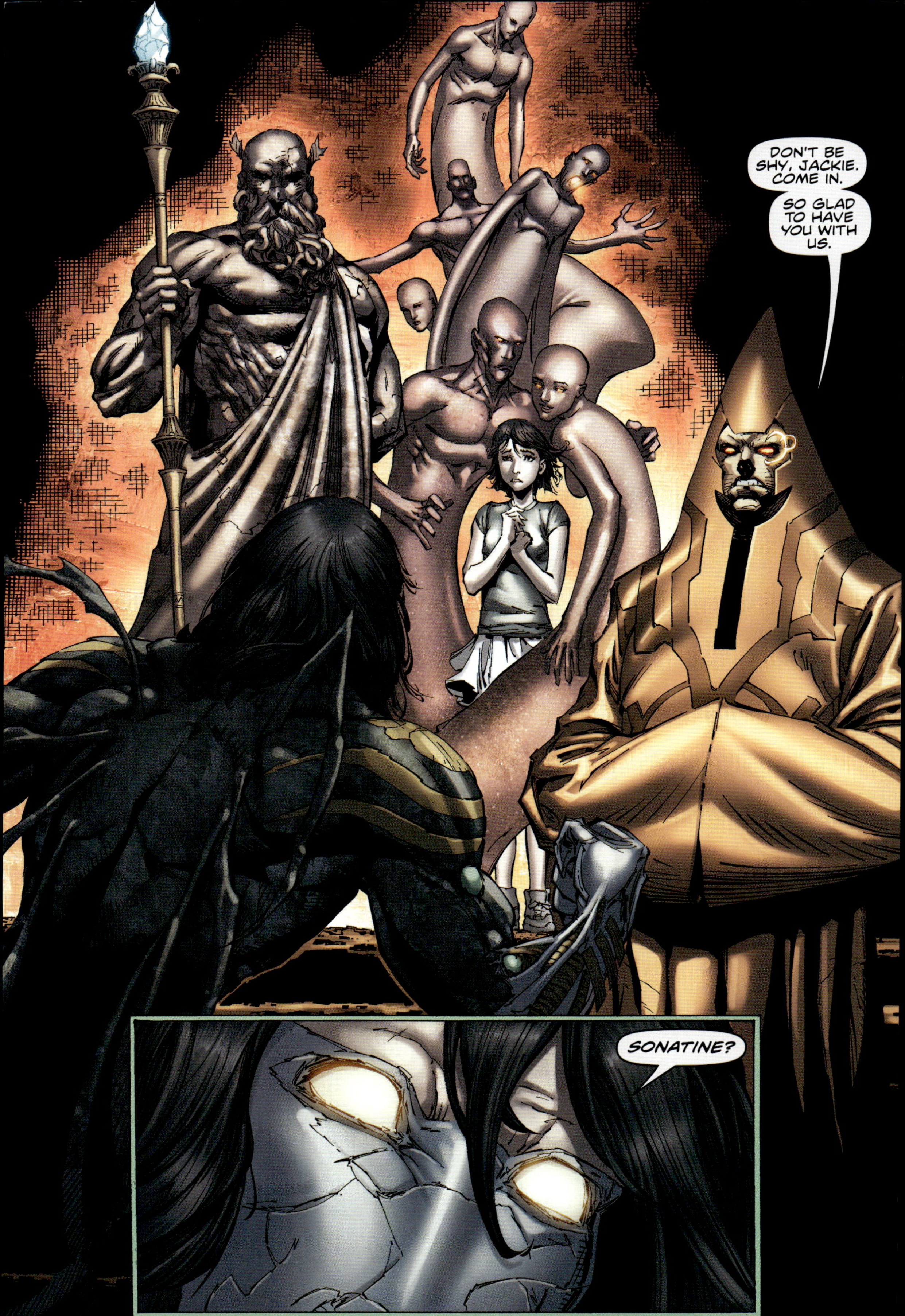
DON'T BE SHY, JACKIE. COME IN.
SO GLAD TO HAVE YOU WITH US.
SONATINE?

The Darkness Issue #86
cover art by: Rafael Albuquerque

THE DARKNESS #86

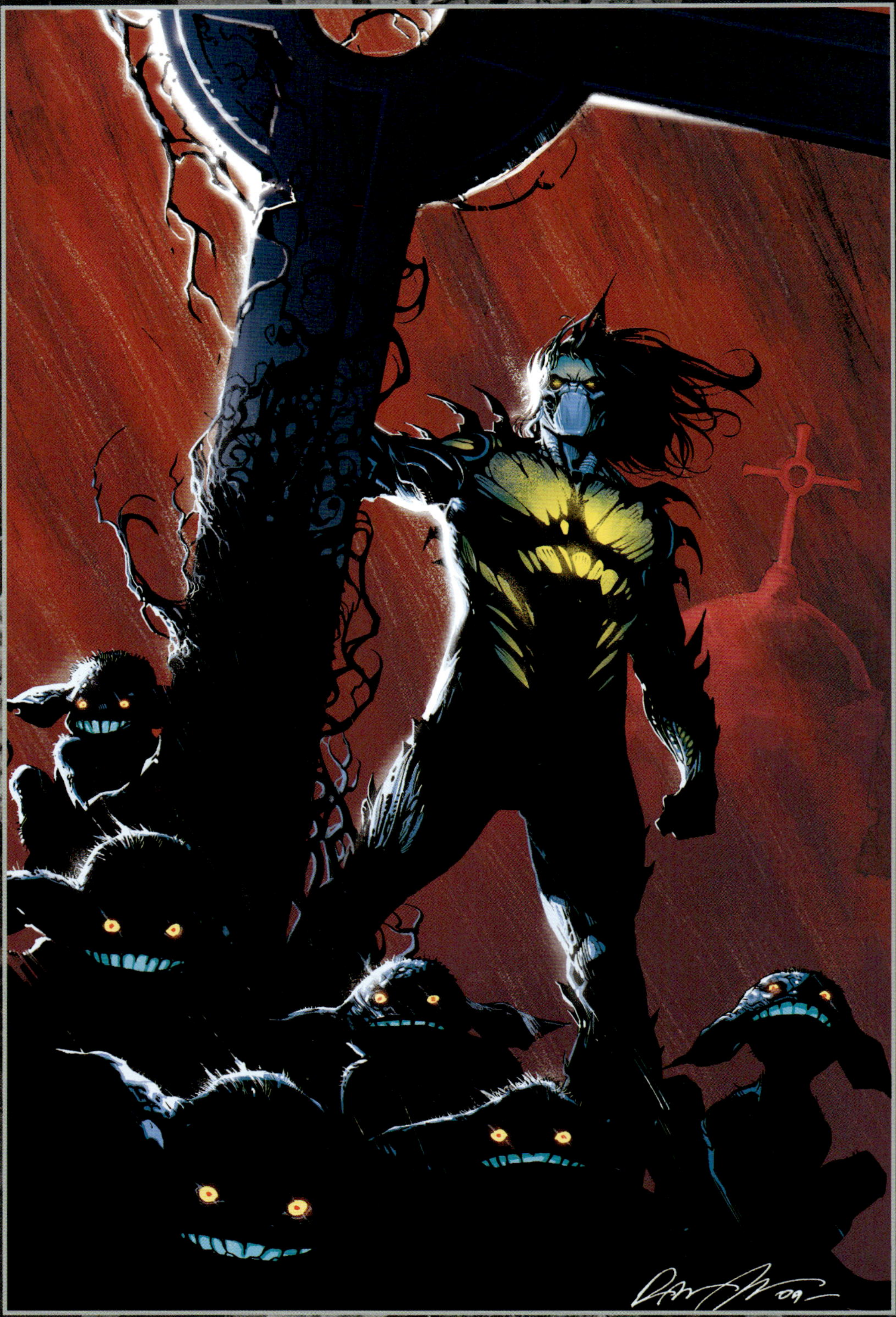

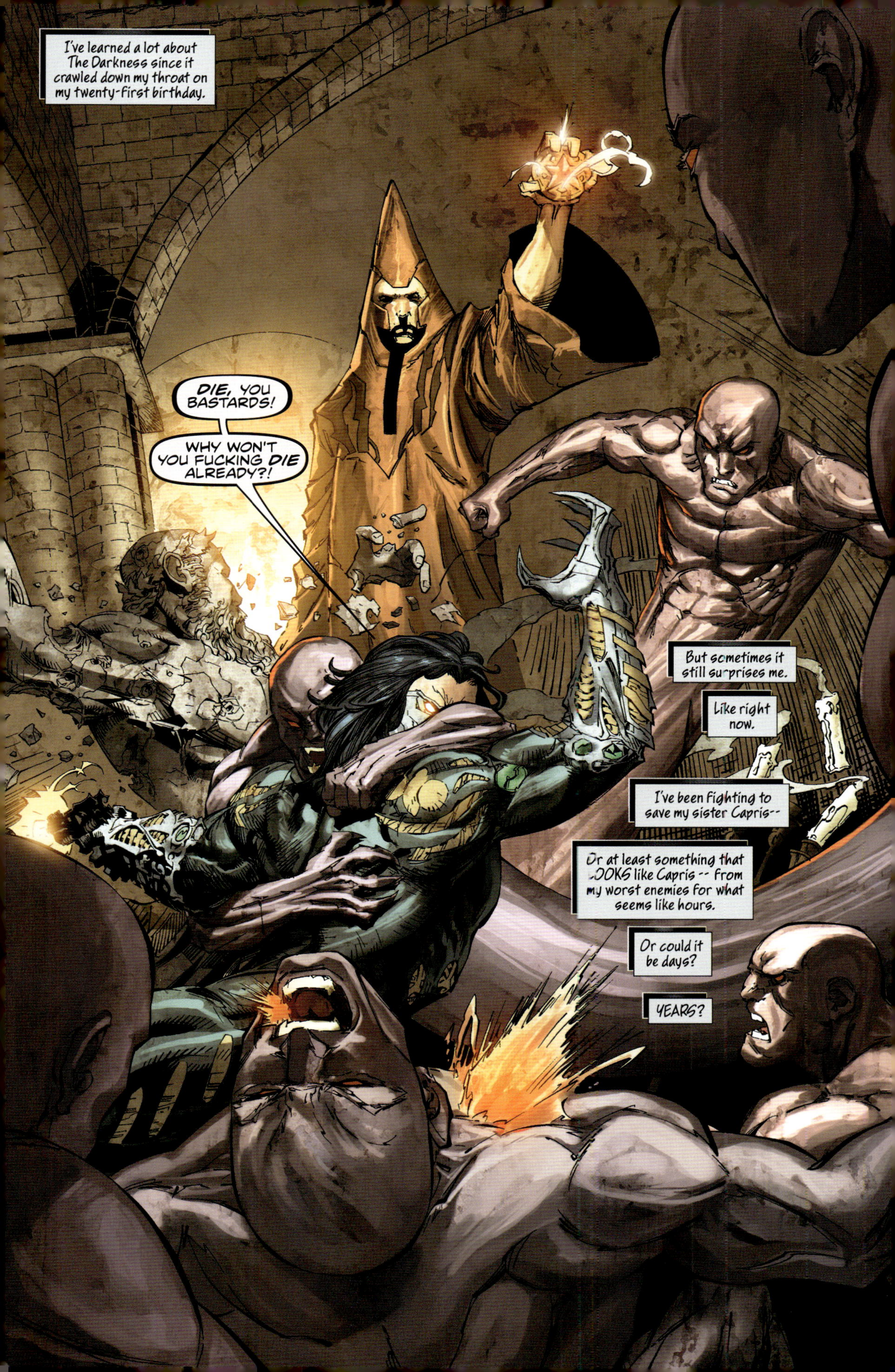
I've learned a lot about The Darkness since it crawled down my throat on my twenty-first birthday.
DIE, YOU BASTARDS!
WHY WON'T YOU FUCKING DIE ALREADY?!
But sometimes it still surprises me.
Like right now.
I've been fighting to save my sister Capris--
Or at least something that LOOKS like Capris -- from my worst enemies for what seems like hours.
Or could it be days?
YEARS?

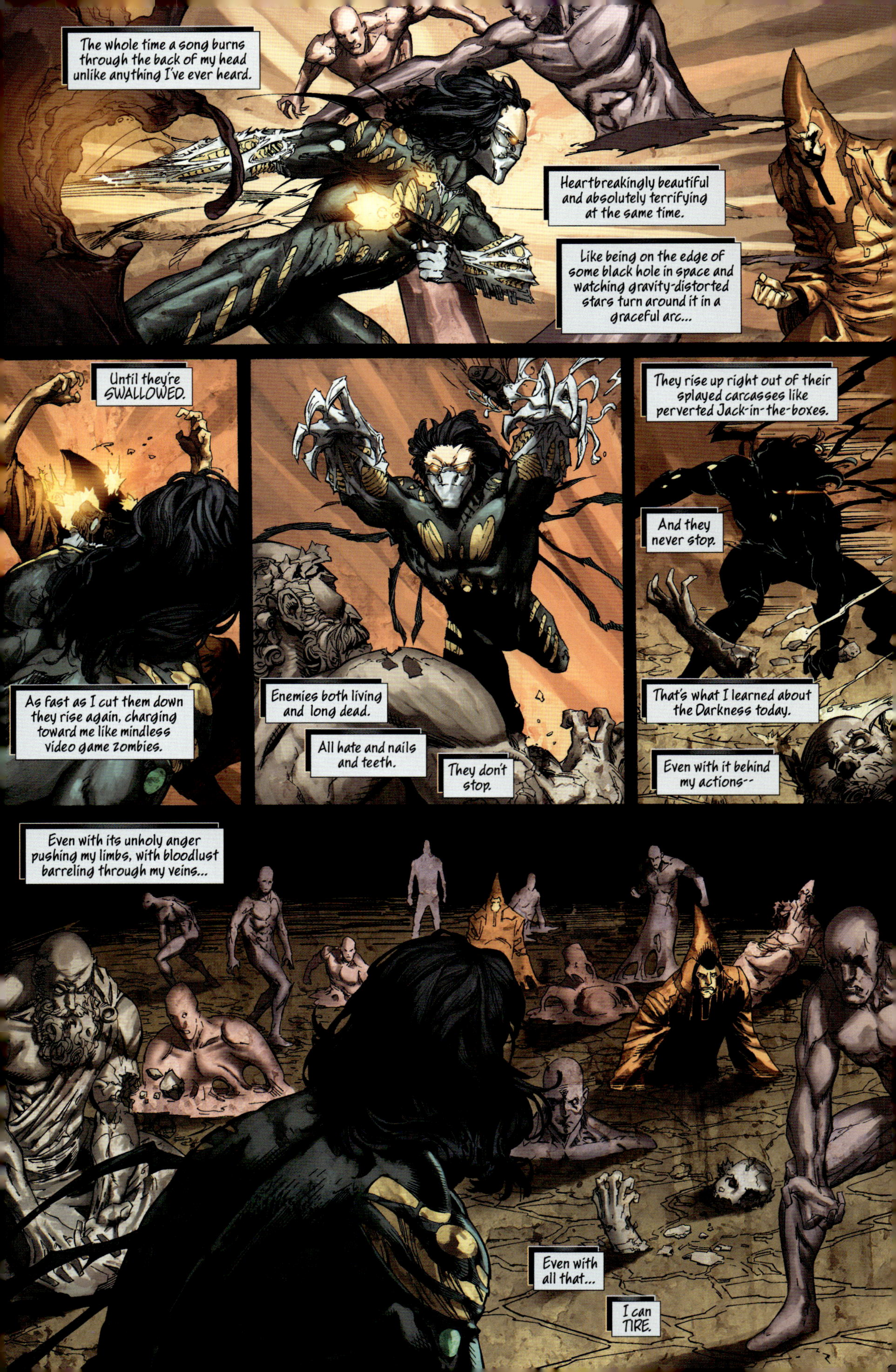

The whole time a song burns through the back of my head unlike anything I've ever heard.
Heartbreakingly beautiful and absolutely terrifying at the same time.
Like being on the edge of some black hole in space and watching gravity-distorted stars turn around it in a graceful arc...
Until they're SWALLOWED.
As fast as I cut them down they rise again, charging toward me like mindless video game zombies.
Enemies both living and long dead.
All hate and nails and teeth.
They don't stop.
They rise up right out of their splayed carcasses like perverted Jack-in-the-boxes.
And they never stop.
That's what I learned about the Darkness today.
Even with it behind my actions--
Even with its unholy anger pushing my limbs, with bloodlust barreling through my veins...
Even with all that...
I can TIRE.

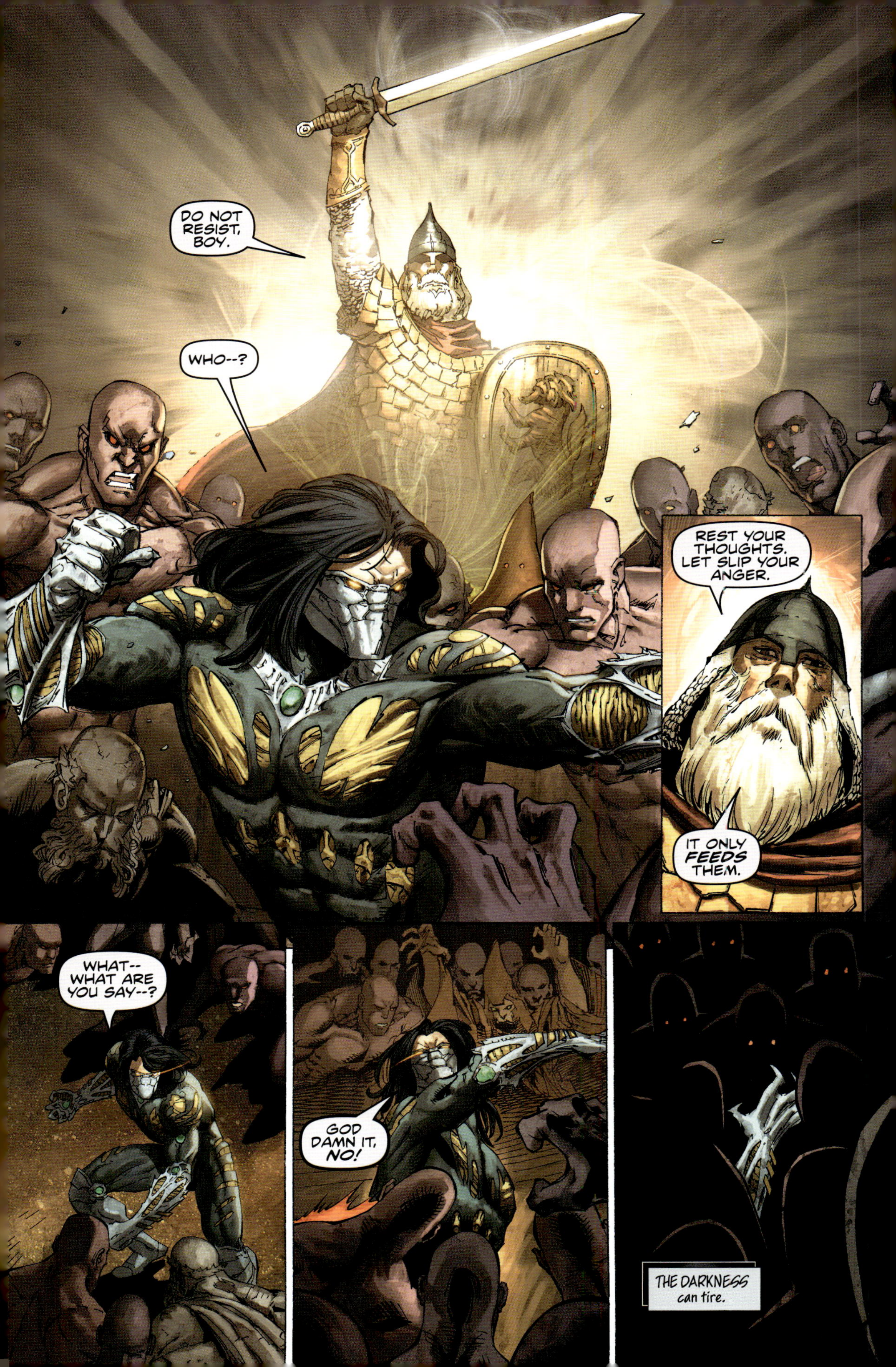
DO NOT RESIST, BOY.
WHO--?
REST YOUR THOUGHTS. LET SLIP YOUR ANGER.
IT ONLY FEEDS THEM.
WHAT-- WHAT ARE YOU SAY--?
GOD DAMN IT, NO!
THE DARKNESS can tire.

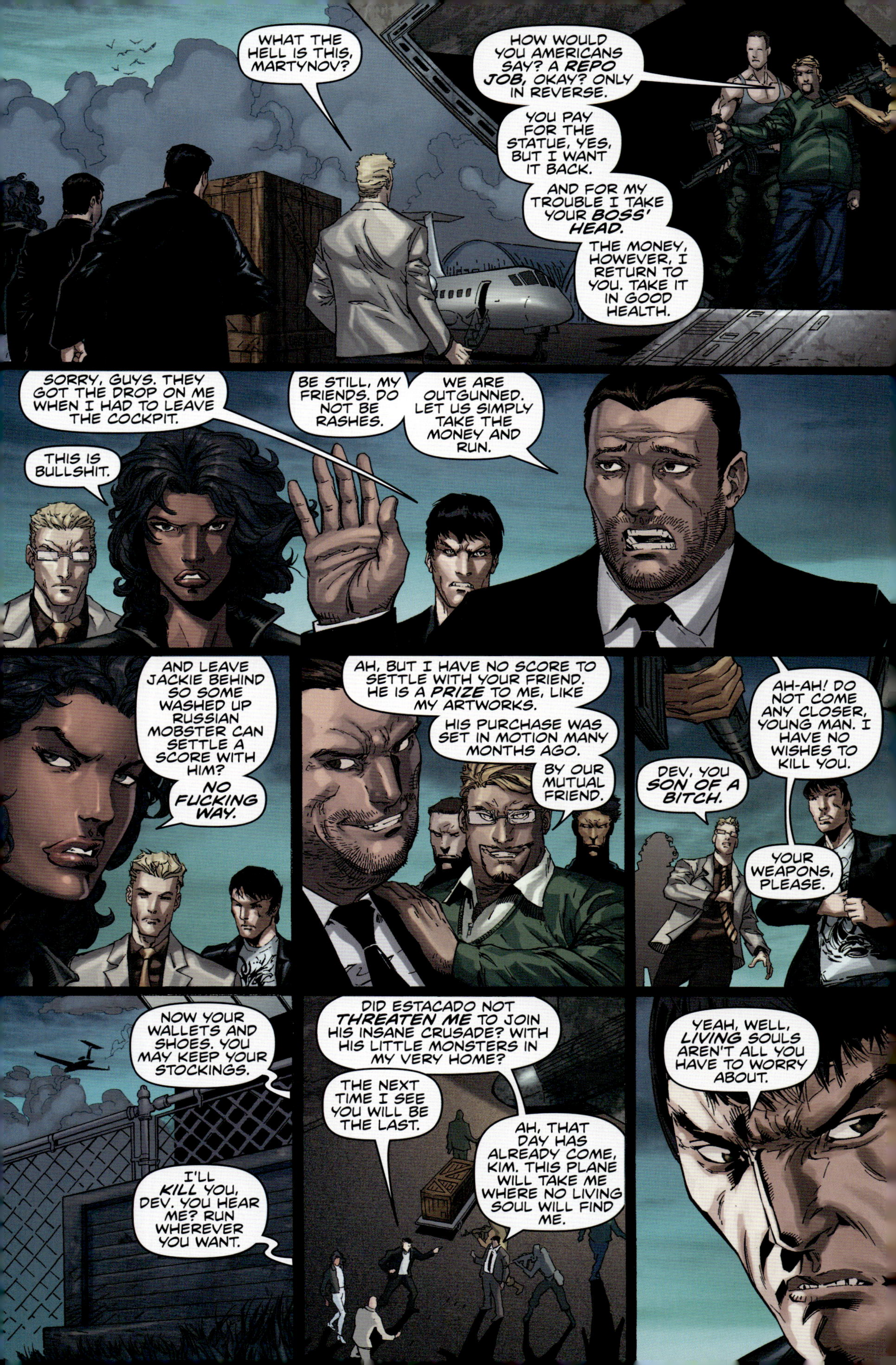
WHAT THE HELL IS THIS, MARTYNOV?
HOW WOULD YOU AMERICANS SAY? A REPO JOB, OKAY? ONLY IN REVERSE.
YOU PAY FOR THE STATUE, YES, BUT I WANT IT BACK.
AND FOR MY TROUBLE I TAKE YOUR BOSS' HEAD.
THE MONEY, HOWEVER, I RETURN TO YOU. TAKE IT IN GOOD HEALTH.
SORRY, GUYS. THEY GOT THE DROP ON ME WHEN I HAD TO LEAVE THE COCKPIT.
THIS IS BULLSHIT.
BE STILL, MY FRIENDS. DO NOT BE RASHES.
WE ARE OUTGUNNED. LET US SIMPLY TAKE THE MONEY AND RUN.
AND LEAVE JACKIE BEHIND SO SOME WASHED UP RUSSIAN MOBSTER CAN SETTLE A SCORE WITH HIM? NO FUCKING WAY.
AH, BUT I HAVE NO SCORE TO SETTLE WITH YOUR FRIEND. HE IS A PRIZE TO ME, LIKE MY ARTWORKS.
HIS PURCHASE WAS SET IN MOTION MANY MONTHS AGO.
BY OUR MUTUAL FRIEND.
AH-AH! DO NOT COME ANY CLOSER, YOUNG MAN. I HAVE NO WISHES TO KILL YOU.
DEV, YOU SON OF A BITCH.
YOUR WEAPONS, PLEASE.
NOW YOUR WALLETS AND SHOES. YOU MAY KEEP YOUR STOCKINGS.
I'LL KILL YOU, DEV. YOU HEAR ME? RUN WHEREVER YOU WANT.
DID ESTACADO NOT THREATEN ME TO JOIN HIS INSANE CRUSADE? WITH HIS LITTLE MONSTERS IN MY VERY HOME?
THE NEXT TIME I SEE YOU WILL BE THE LAST.
AH, THAT DAY HAS ALREADY COME, KIM. THIS PLANE WILL TAKE ME WHERE NO LIVING SOUL WILL FIND ME.
YEAH, WELL, LIVING SOULS AREN'T ALL YOU HAVE TO WORRY ABOUT.

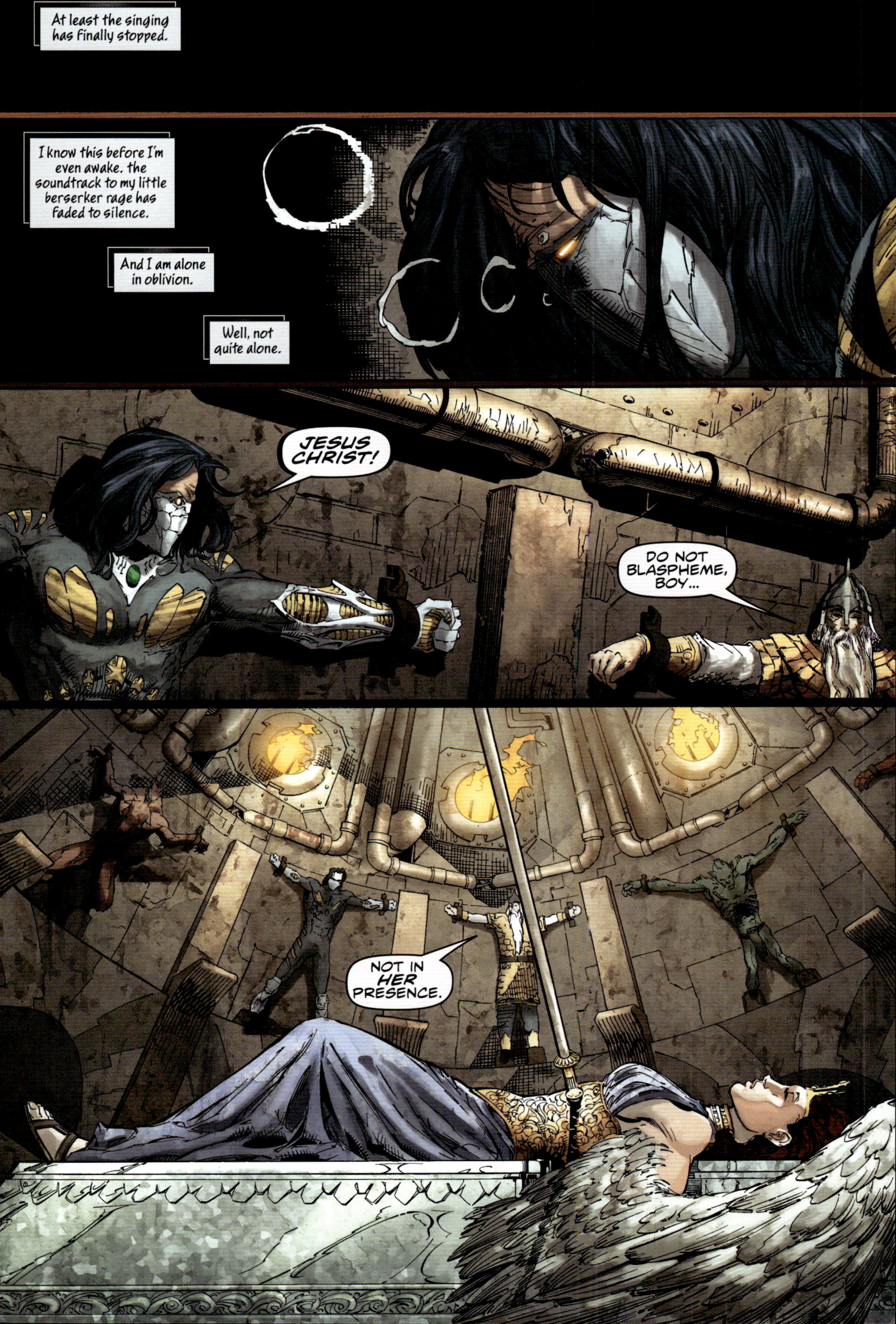

At least the singing has finally stopped.
I know this before I'm even awake. the soundtrack to my little berserker rage has faded to silence.
And I am alone in oblivion.
Well, not quite alone.
JESUS CHRIST!
DO NOT BLASPHEME, BOY...
NOT IN HER PRESENCE.

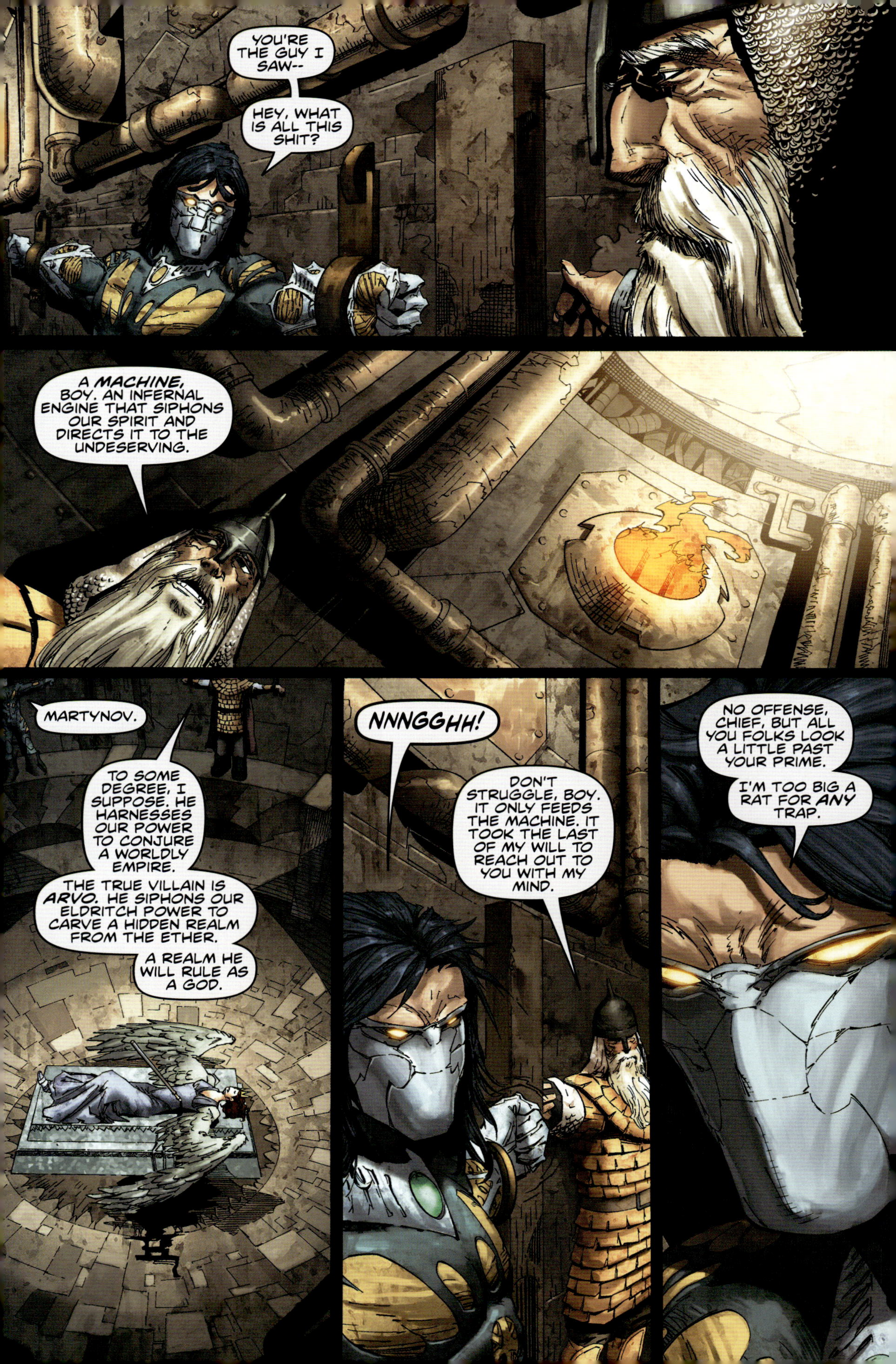
YOU'RE THE GUY I SAW--
HEY, WHAT IS ALL THIS SHIT?
A MACHINE, BOY. AN INFERNAL ENGINE THAT SIPHONS OUR SPIRIT AND DIRECTS IT TO THE UNDESERVING.
MARTYNOV.
TO SOME DEGREE, I SUPPOSE. HE HARNESSES OUR POWER TO CONJURE A WORLDLY EMPIRE.
THE TRUE VILLAIN IS ARVO. HE SIPHONS OUR ELDRITCH POWER TO CARVE A HIDDEN REALM FROM THE ETHER.
A REALM HE WILL RULE AS A GOD.
NNNGGHH!
DON'T STRUGGLE, BOY. IT ONLY FEEDS THE MACHINE. IT TOOK THE LAST OF MY WILL TO REACH OUT TO YOU WITH MY MIND.
NO OFFENSE, CHIEF, BUT ALL YOU FOLKS LOOK A LITTLE PAST YOUR PRIME.
I'M TOO BIG A RAT FOR ANY TRAP.

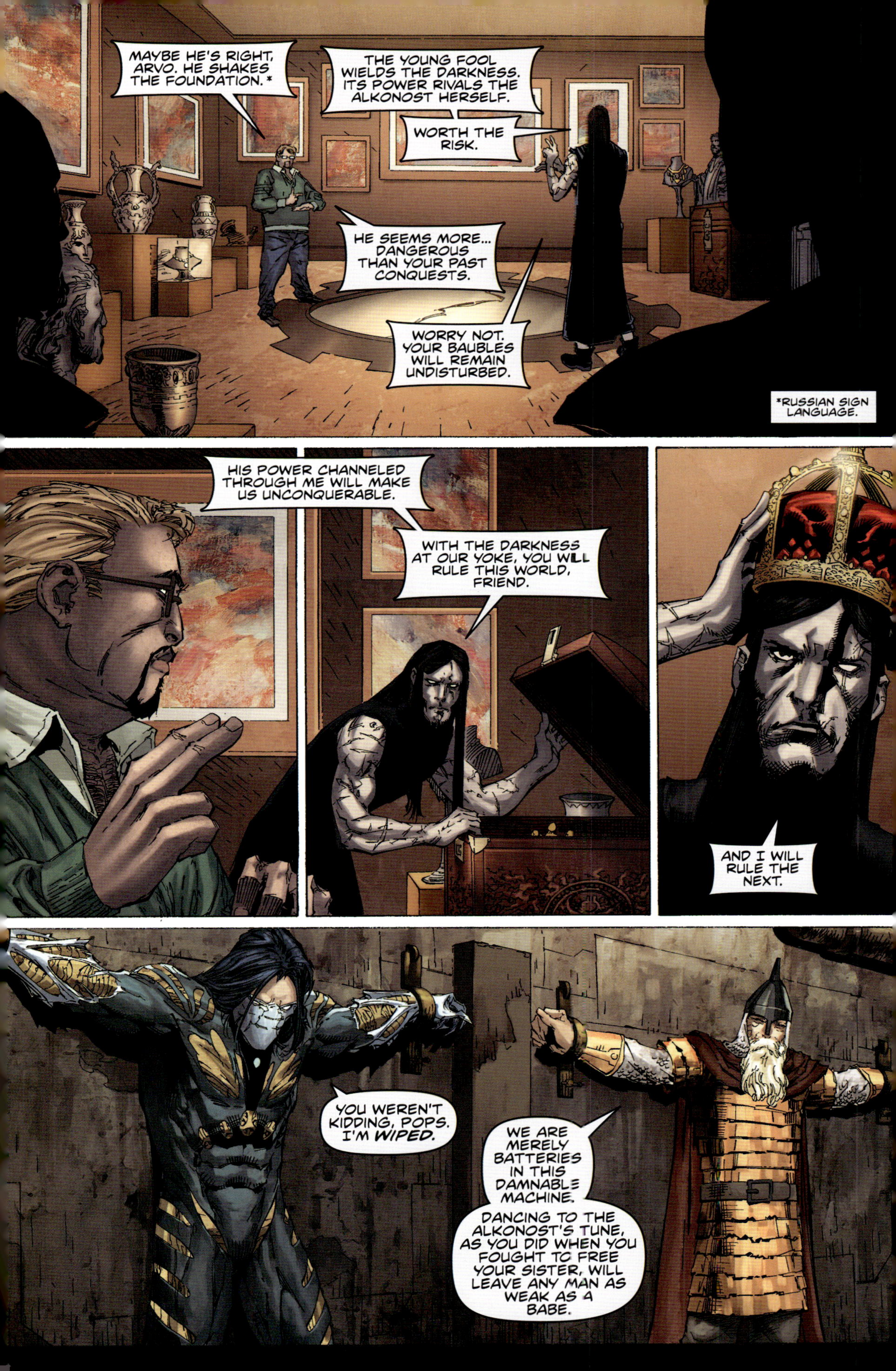
MAYBE HE'S RIGHT, ARVO. HE SHAKES THE FOUNDATION.*
THE YOUNG FOOL WIELDS THE DARKNESS. ITS POWER RIVALS THE ALKONOST HERSELF.
WORTH THE RISK.
HE SEEMS MORE... DANGEROUS THAN YOUR PAST CONQUESTS.
WORRY NOT. YOUR BAUBLES WILL REMAIN UNDISTURBED.
*RUSSIAN SIGN LANGUAGE.
HIS POWER CHANNELED THROUGH ME WILL MAKE US UNCONQUERABLE.
WITH THE DARKNESS AT OUR YOKE, YOU WILL RULE THIS WORLD, FRIEND.
AND I WILL RULE THE NEXT.
YOU WEREN'T KIDDING, POPS. I'M WIPED.
WE ARE MERELY BATTERIES IN THIS DAMNABLE MACHINE.
DANCING TO THE ALKONOST'S TUNE, AS YOU DID WHEN YOU FOUGHT TO FREE YOUR SISTER, WILL LEAVE ANY MAN AS WEAK AS A BABE.

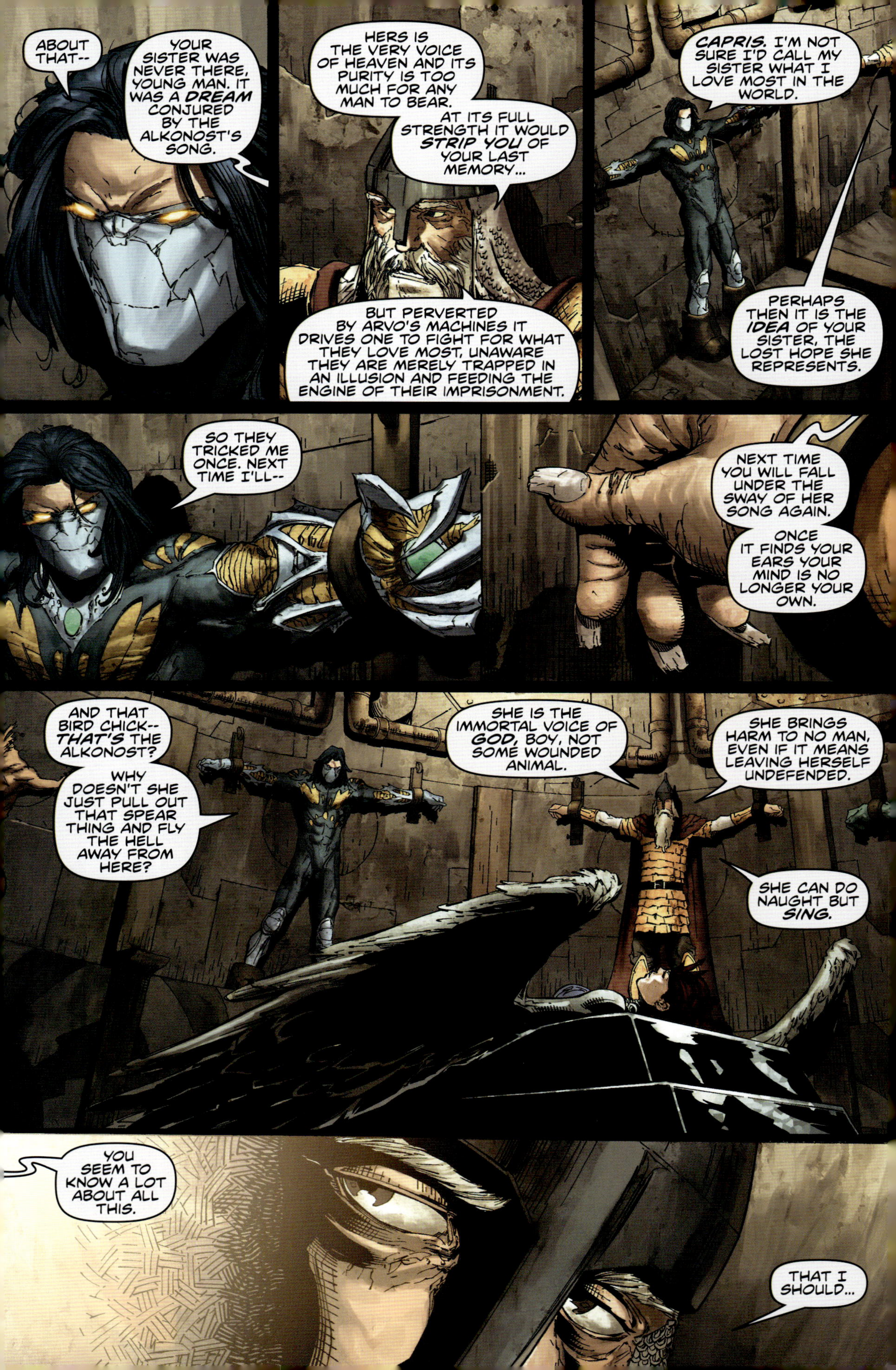
ABOUT THAT--
YOUR SISTER WAS NEVER THERE, YOUNG MAN. IT WAS A DREAM CONJURED BY THE ALKONOST'S SONG.
HERS IS THE VERY VOICE OF HEAVEN AND ITS PURITY IS TOO MUCH FOR ANY MAN TO BEAR.
AT ITS FULL STRENGTH IT WOULD STRIP YOU OF YOUR LAST MEMORY...
BUT PERVERTED BY ARVO'S MACHINES IT DRIVES ONE TO FIGHT FOR WHAT THEY LOVE MOST, UNAWARE THEY ARE MERELY TRAPPED IN AN ILLUSION AND FEEDING THE ENGINE OF THEIR IMPRISONMENT.
CAPRIS. I'M NOT SURE I'D CALL MY SISTER WHAT I LOVE MOST IN THE WORLD.
PERHAPS THEN IT IS THE IDEA OF YOUR SISTER, THE LOST HOPE SHE REPRESENTS.
SO THEY TRICKED ME ONCE. NEXT TIME I'LL--
NEXT TIME YOU WILL FALL UNDER THE SWAY OF HER SONG AGAIN.
ONCE IT FINDS YOUR EARS YOUR MIND IS NO LONGER YOUR OWN.
AND THAT BIRD CHICK-- THAT'S THE ALKONOST?
WHY DOESN'T SHE JUST PULL OUT THAT SPEAR THING AND FLY THE HELL AWAY FROM HERE?
SHE IS THE IMMORTAL VOICE OF GOD, BOY, NOT SOME WOUNDED ANIMAL.
SHE BRINGS HARM TO NO MAN, EVEN IF IT MEANS LEAVING HERSELF UNDEFENDED.
SHE CAN DO NAUGHT BUT SING.
YOU SEEM TO KNOW A LOT ABOUT ALL THIS.
THAT I SHOULD...

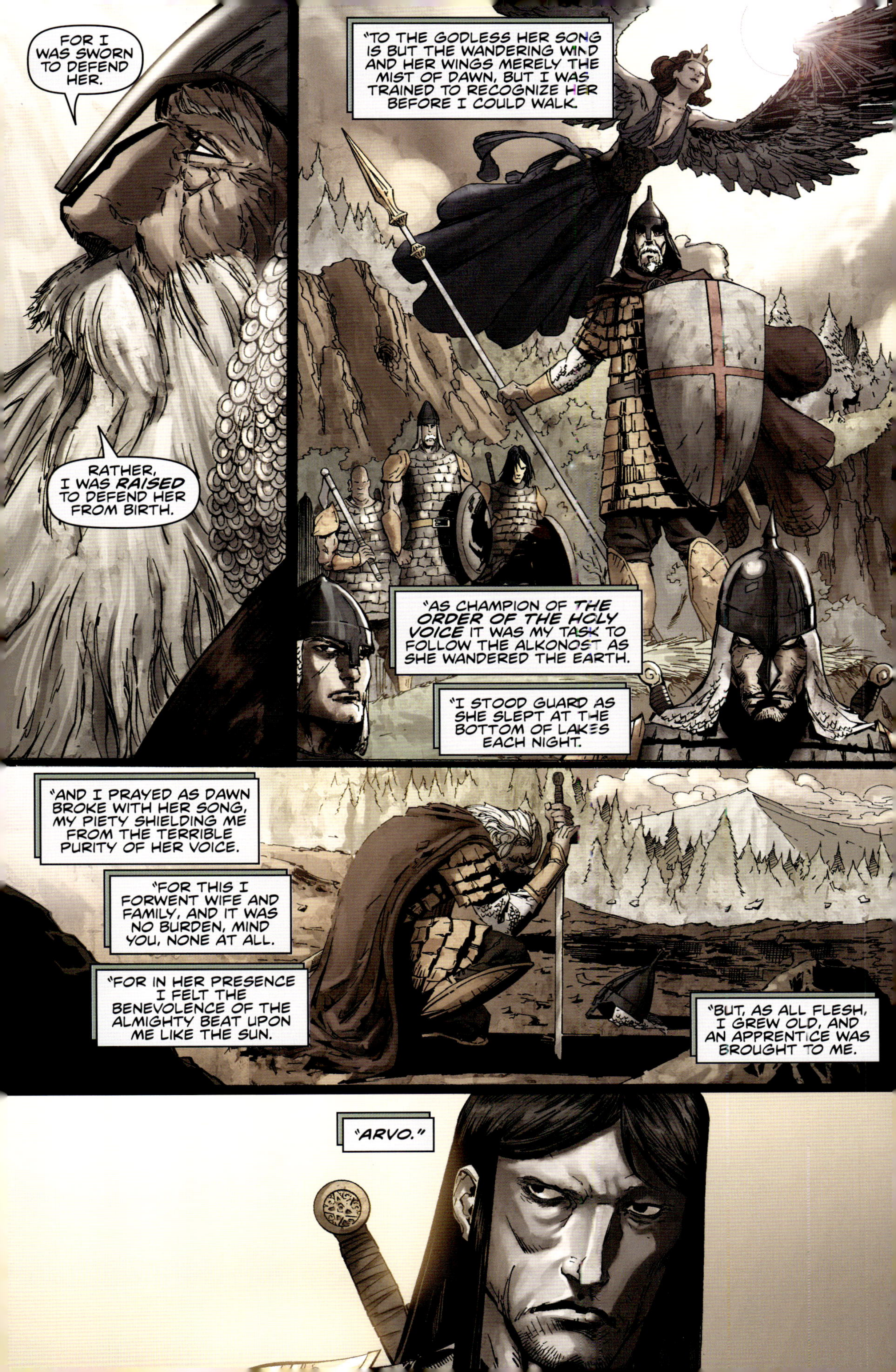
FOR I WAS SWORN TO DEFEND HER.
RATHER, I WAS *RAISED* TO DEFEND HER FROM BIRTH.
"TO THE GODLESS HER SONG IS BUT THE WANDERING WIND AND HER WINGS MERELY THE MIST OF DAWN, BUT I WAS TRAINED TO RECOGNIZE HER BEFORE I COULD WALK.
"AS CHAMPION OF *THE ORDER OF THE HOLY VOICE* IT WAS MY TASK TO FOLLOW THE ALKONOST AS SHE WANDERED THE EARTH.
"I STOOD GUARD AS SHE SLEPT AT THE BOTTOM OF LAKES EACH NIGHT.
"AND I PRAYED AS DAWN BROKE WITH HER SONG, MY PIETY SHIELDING ME FROM THE TERRIBLE PURITY OF HER VOICE.
"FOR THIS I FORWENT WIFE AND FAMILY, AND IT WAS NO BURDEN, MIND YOU, NONE AT ALL.
"FOR IN HER PRESENCE I FELT THE BENEVOLENCE OF THE ALMIGHTY BEAT UPON ME LIKE THE SUN.
"BUT, AS ALL FLESH, I GREW OLD, AND AN APPRENTICE WAS BROUGHT TO ME.
"ARVO."

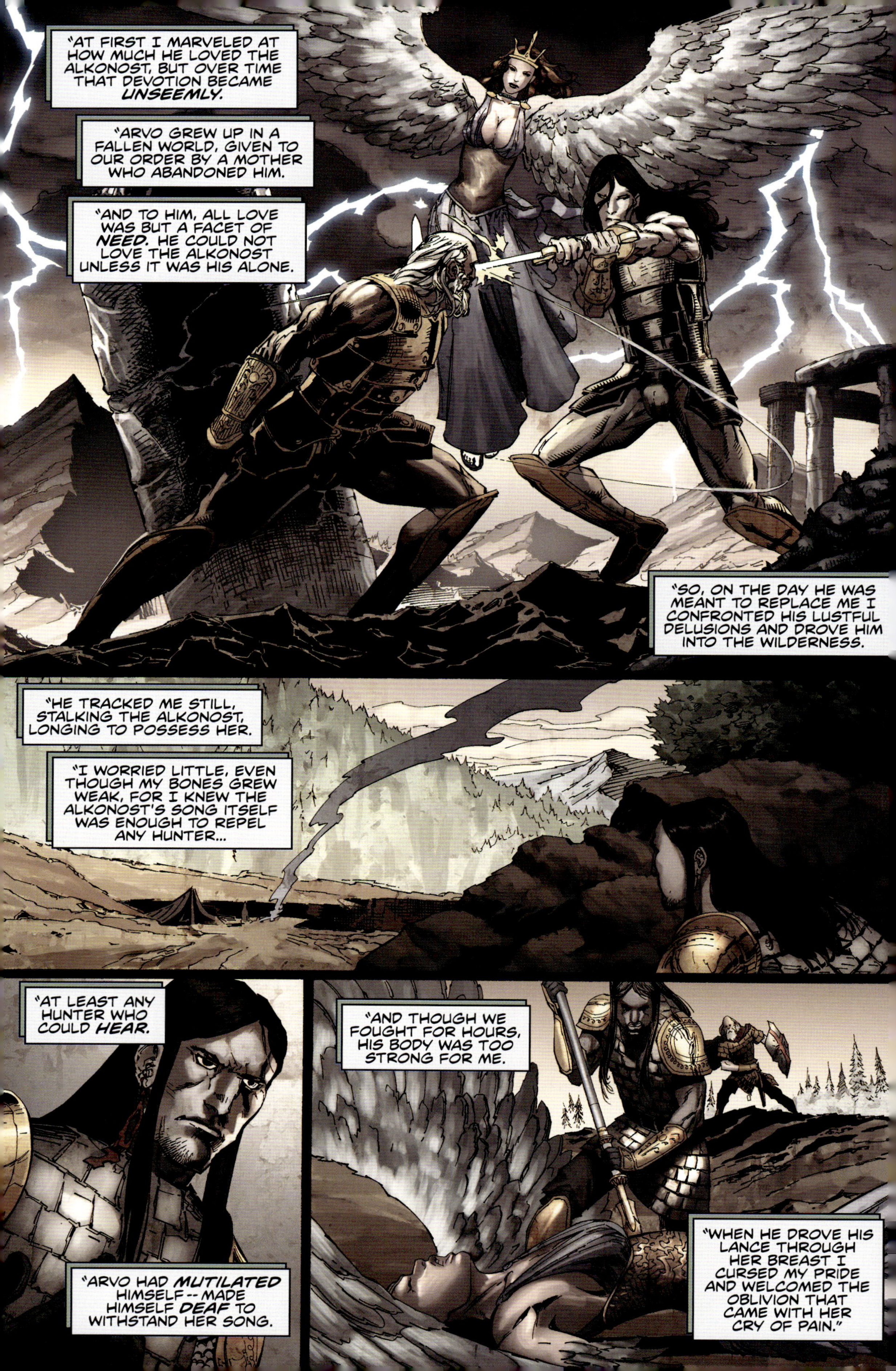
"AT FIRST I MARVELED AT HOW MUCH HE LOVED THE ALKONOST, BUT OVER TIME THAT DEVOTION BECAME *UNSEEMLY*.
"ARVO GREW UP IN A FALLEN WORLD, GIVEN TO OUR ORDER BY A MOTHER WHO ABANDONED HIM.
"AND TO HIM, ALL LOVE WAS BUT A FACET OF *NEED*. HE COULD NOT LOVE THE ALKONOST UNLESS IT WAS HIS ALONE.
"SO, ON THE DAY HE WAS MEANT TO REPLACE ME I CONFRONTED HIS LUSTFUL DELUSIONS AND DROVE HIM INTO THE WILDERNESS.
"HE TRACKED ME STILL, STALKING THE ALKONOST, LONGING TO POSSESS HER.
"I WORRIED LITTLE, EVEN THOUGH MY BONES GREW WEAK, FOR I KNEW THE ALKONOST'S SONG ITSELF WAS ENOUGH TO REPEL ANY HUNTER...
"AT LEAST ANY HUNTER WHO COULD *HEAR*.
"ARVO HAD *MUTILATED* HIMSELF -- MADE HIMSELF *DEAF* TO WITHSTAND HER SONG.
"AND THOUGH WE FOUGHT FOR HOURS, HIS BODY WAS TOO STRONG FOR ME.
"WHEN HE DROVE HIS LANCE THROUGH HER BREAST I CURSED MY PRIDE AND WELCOMED THE OBLIVION THAT CAME WITH HER CRY OF PAIN."

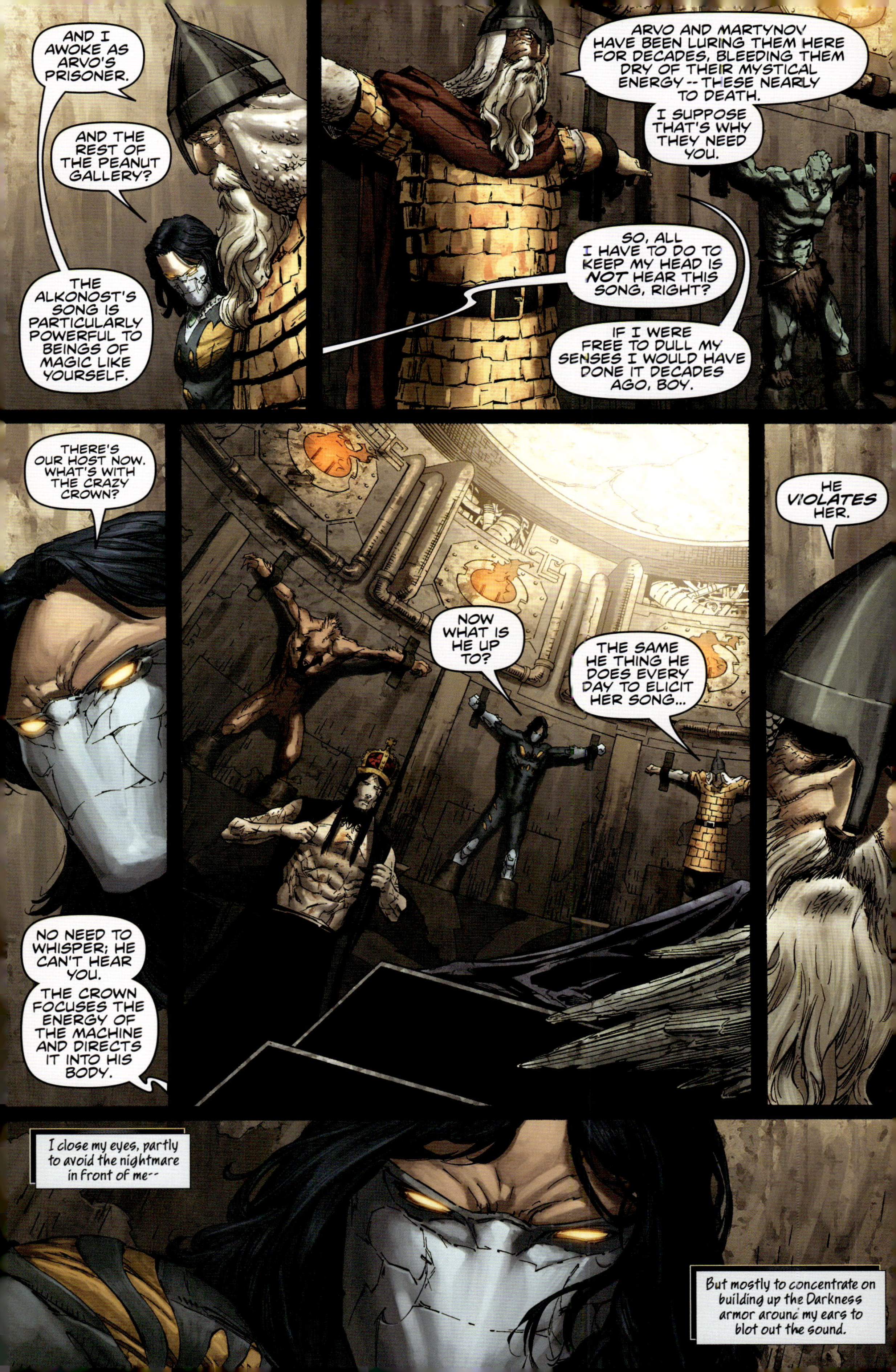
AND I AWOKE AS ARVO'S PRISONER.
AND THE REST OF THE PEANUT GALLERY?
THE ALKONOST'S SONG IS PARTICULARLY POWERFUL TO BEINGS OF MAGIC LIKE YOURSELF.
ARVO AND MARTYNOV HAVE BEEN LURING THEM HERE FOR DECADES, BLEEDING THEM DRY OF THEIR MYSTICAL ENERGY -- THESE NEARLY TO DEATH.
I SUPPOSE THAT'S WHY THEY NEED YOU.
SO, ALL I HAVE TO DO TO KEEP MY HEAD IS *NOT* HEAR THIS SONG, RIGHT?
IF I WERE FREE TO DULL MY SENSES I WOULD HAVE DONE IT DECADES AGO, BOY.
THERE'S OUR HOST NOW. WHAT'S WITH THE CRAZY CROWN?
NO NEED TO WHISPER; HE CAN'T HEAR YOU.
THE CROWN FOCUSES THE ENERGY OF THE MACHINE AND DIRECTS IT INTO HIS BODY.
NOW WHAT IS HE UP TO?
THE SAME HE THING HE DOES EVERY DAY TO ELICIT HER SONG...
HE *VIOLATES* HER.
I close my eyes, partly to avoid the nightmare in front of me--
But mostly to concentrate on building up the Darkness armor around my ears to blot out the sound.

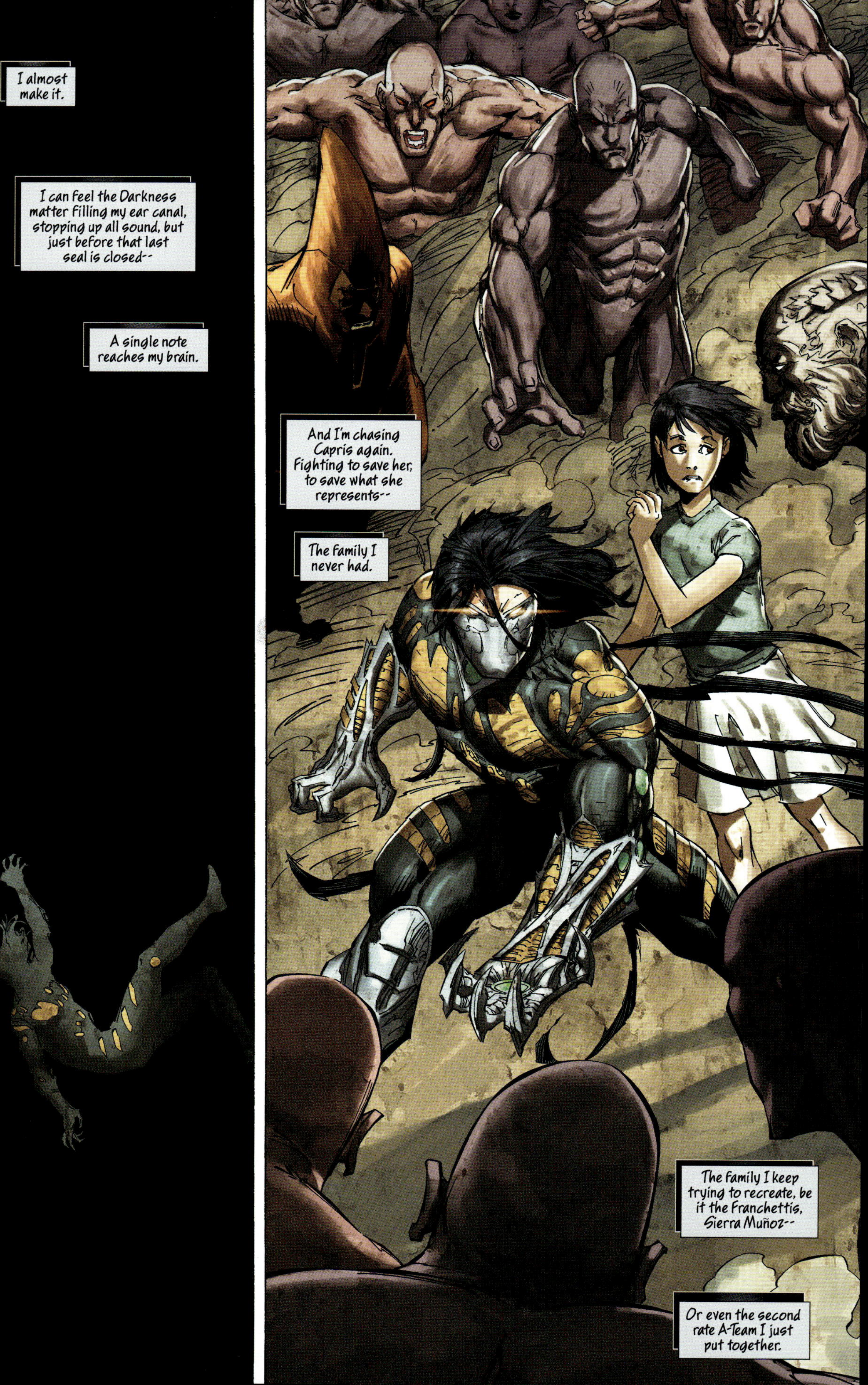

I almost make it.
I can feel the Darkness matter filling my ear canal, stopping up all sound, but just before that last seal is closed--
A single note reaches my brain.
And I'm chasing Capris again. Fighting to save her, to save what she represents--
The family I never had.
The family I keep trying to recreate, be it the Franchettis, Sierra Muñoz--
Or even the second rate A-Team I just put together.

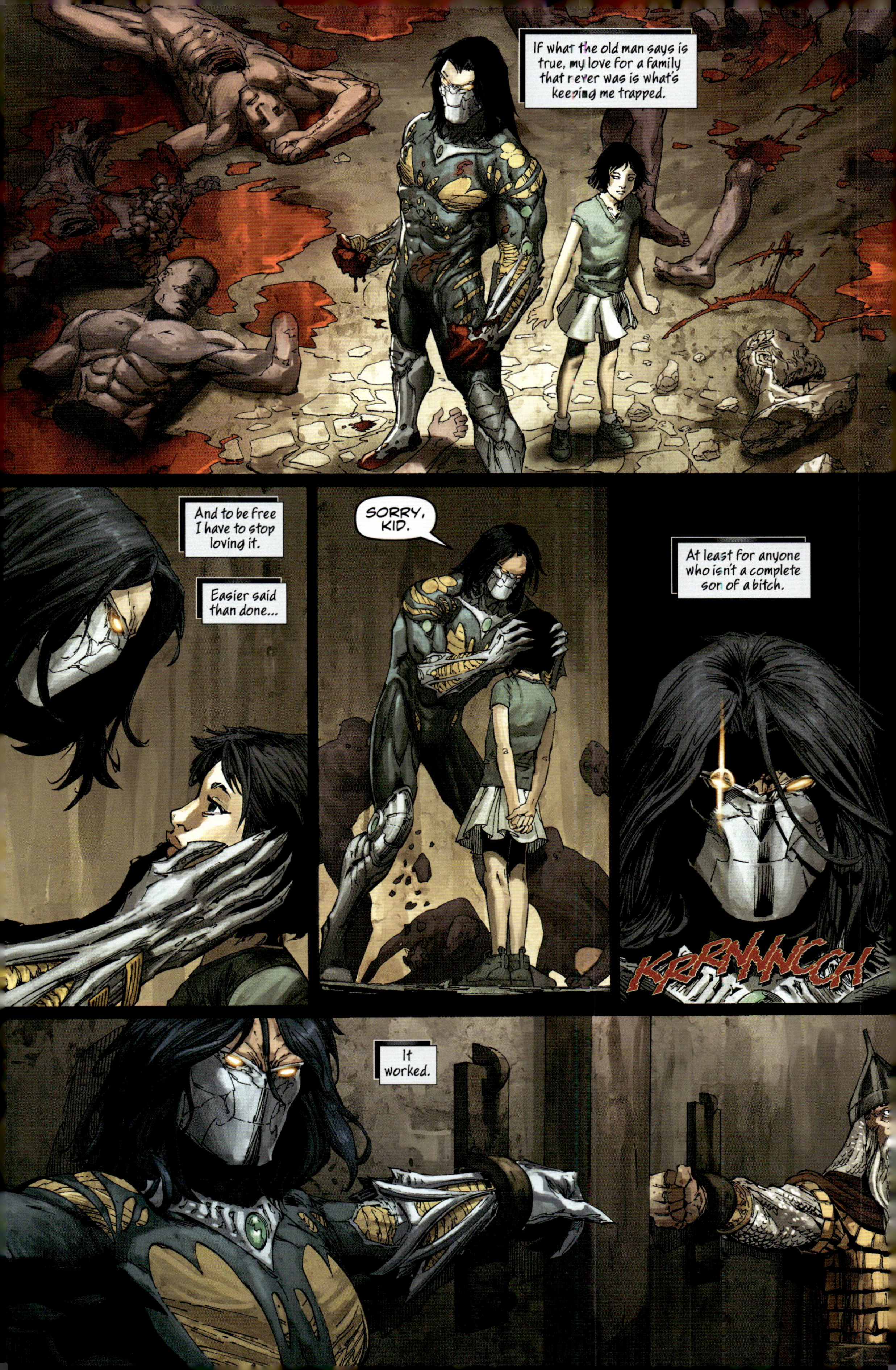

If what the old man says is true, my love for a family that never was is what's keeping me trapped.
And to be free I have to stop loving it.
Easier said than done...
SORRY, KID.
At least for anyone who isn't a complete son of a bitch.
KRRNNNCCH
It worked.

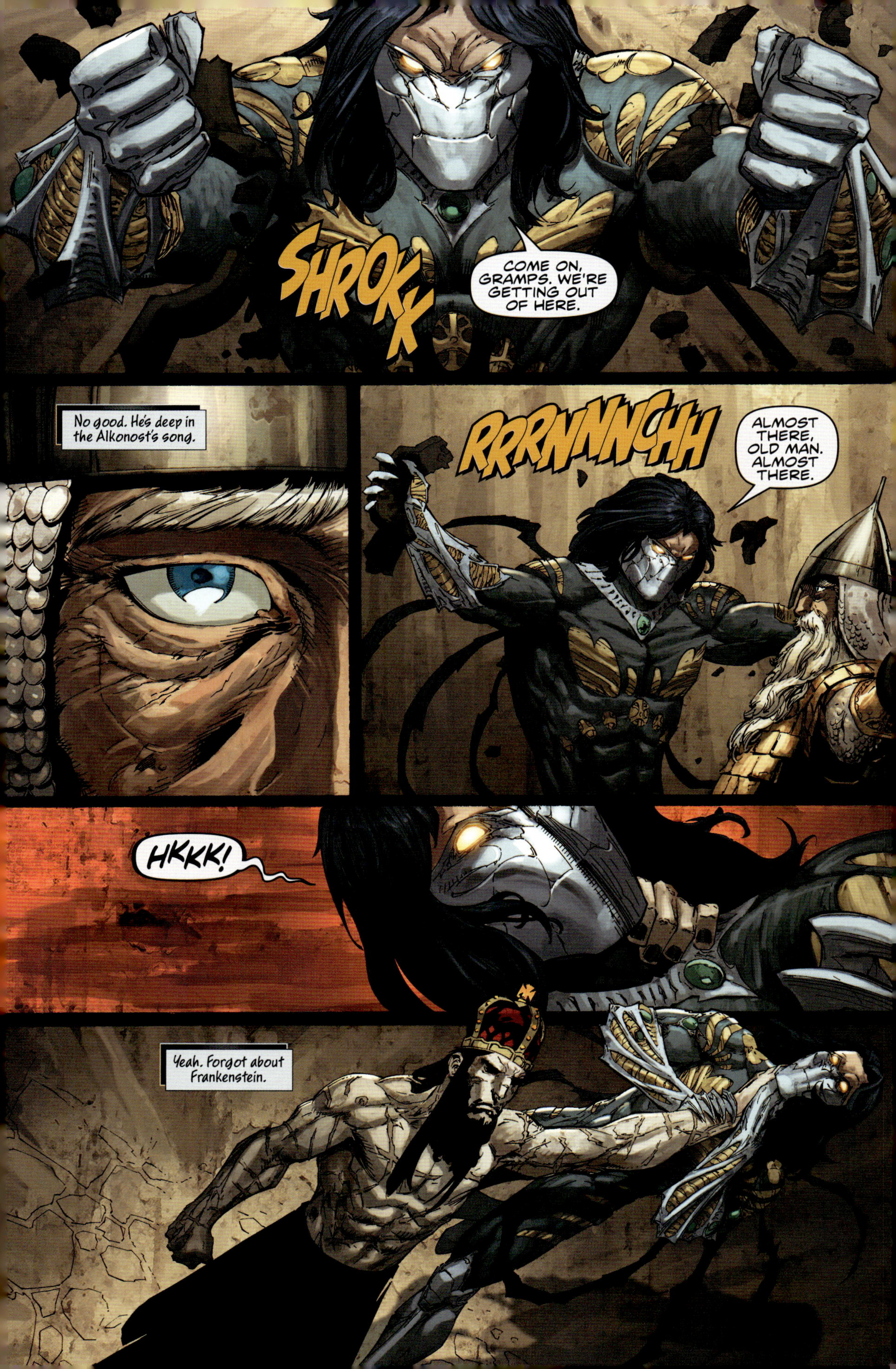
SHROKK
COME ON, GRAMPS. WE'RE GETTING OUT OF HERE.
No good. He's deep in the Alkonost's song.
RRRNNNCHH
ALMOST THERE, OLD MAN. ALMOST THERE.
HKKK!
Yeah. Forgot about Frankenstein.

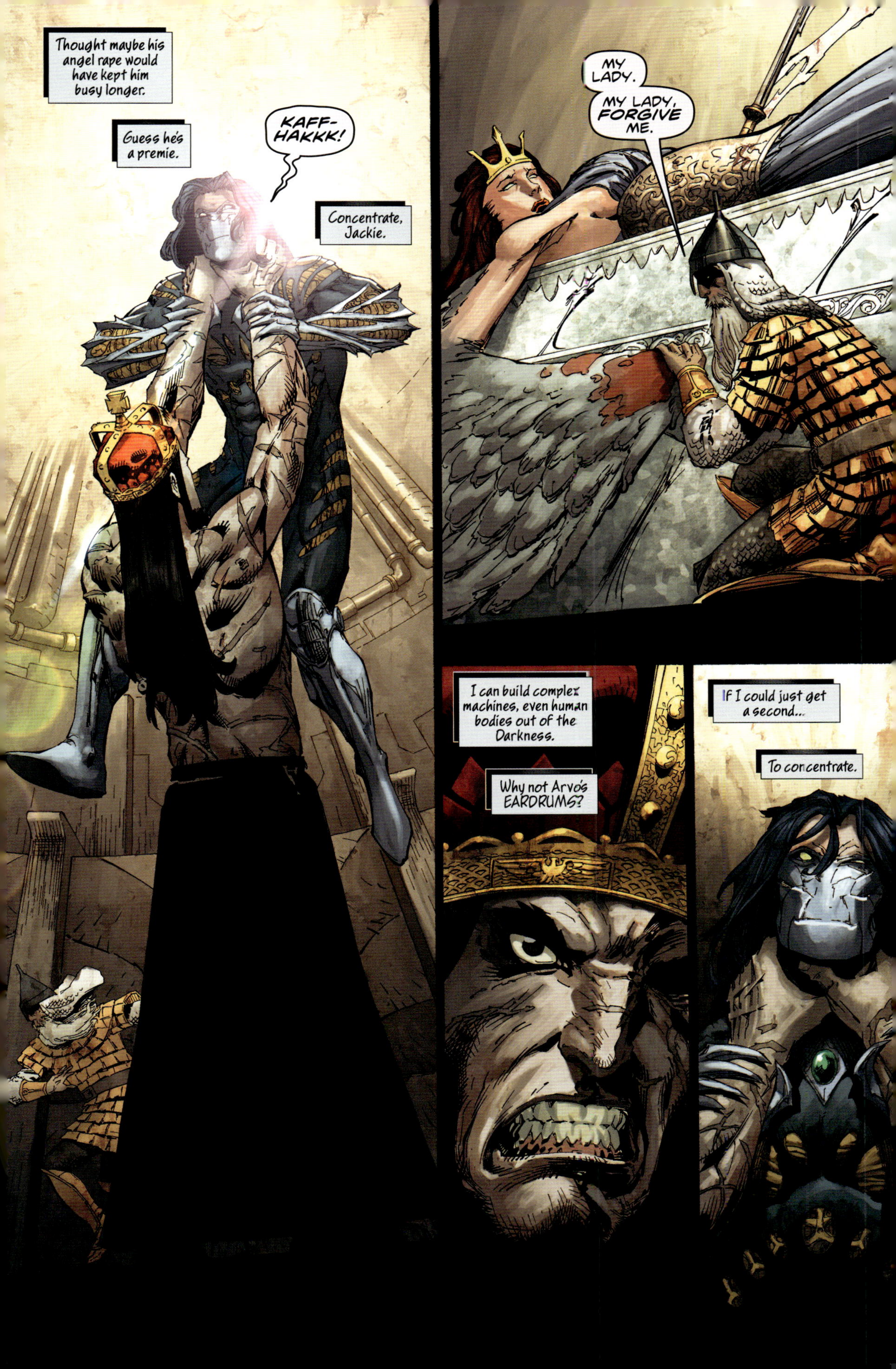
Thought maybe his angel rape would have kept him busy longer.
Guess he's a premie.
KAFF-HAKKK!
Concentrate, Jackie.
MY LADY.
MY LADY, FORGIVE ME.
I can build complex machines, even human bodies out of the Darkness.
Why not Arvo's EARDRUMS?
If I could just get a second...
To concentrate.

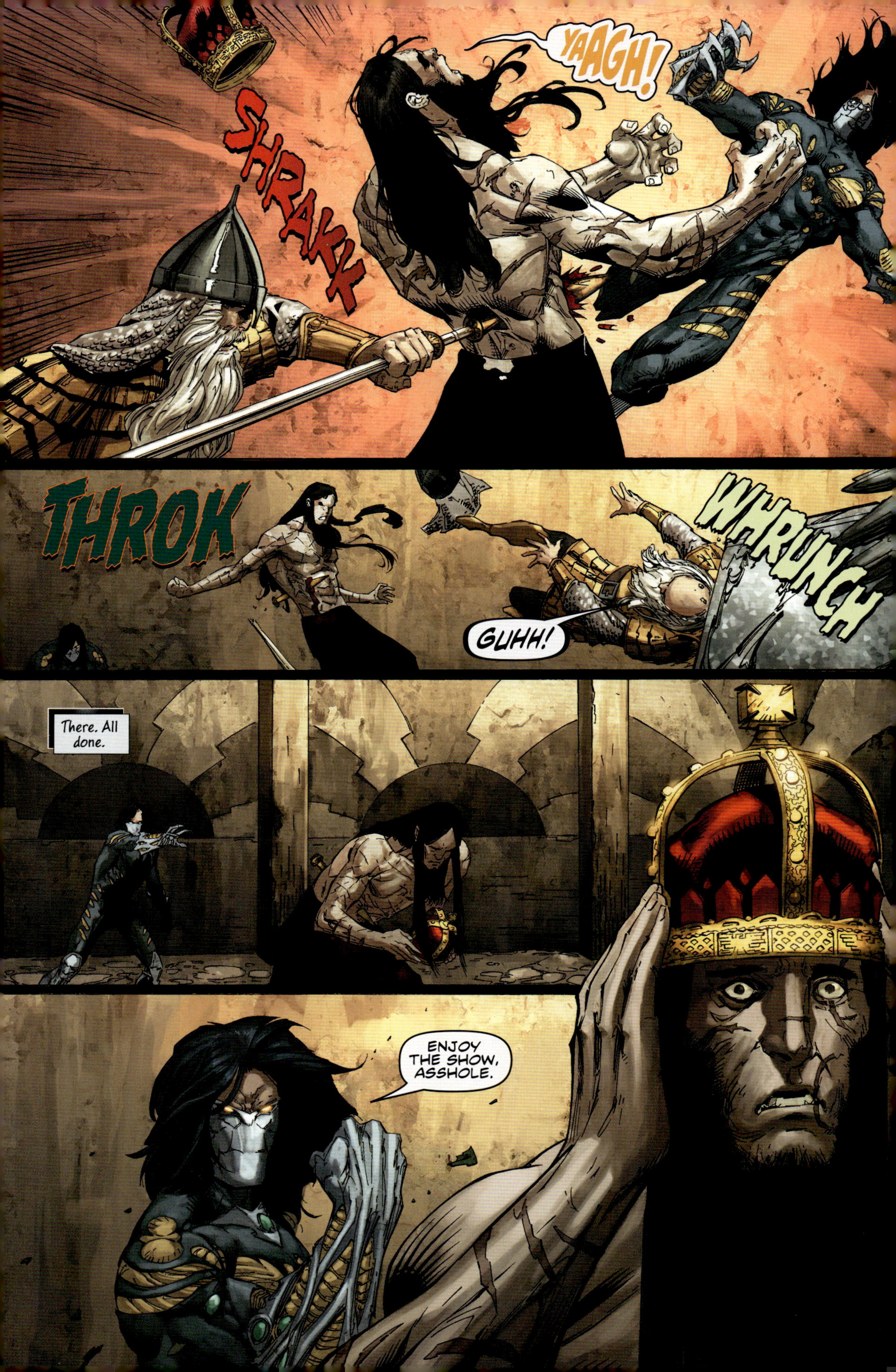
YAAGH!
SHRAKK
THROK
WHRUNCH
GUHH!
There. All done.
ENJOY THE SHOW, ASSHOLE.

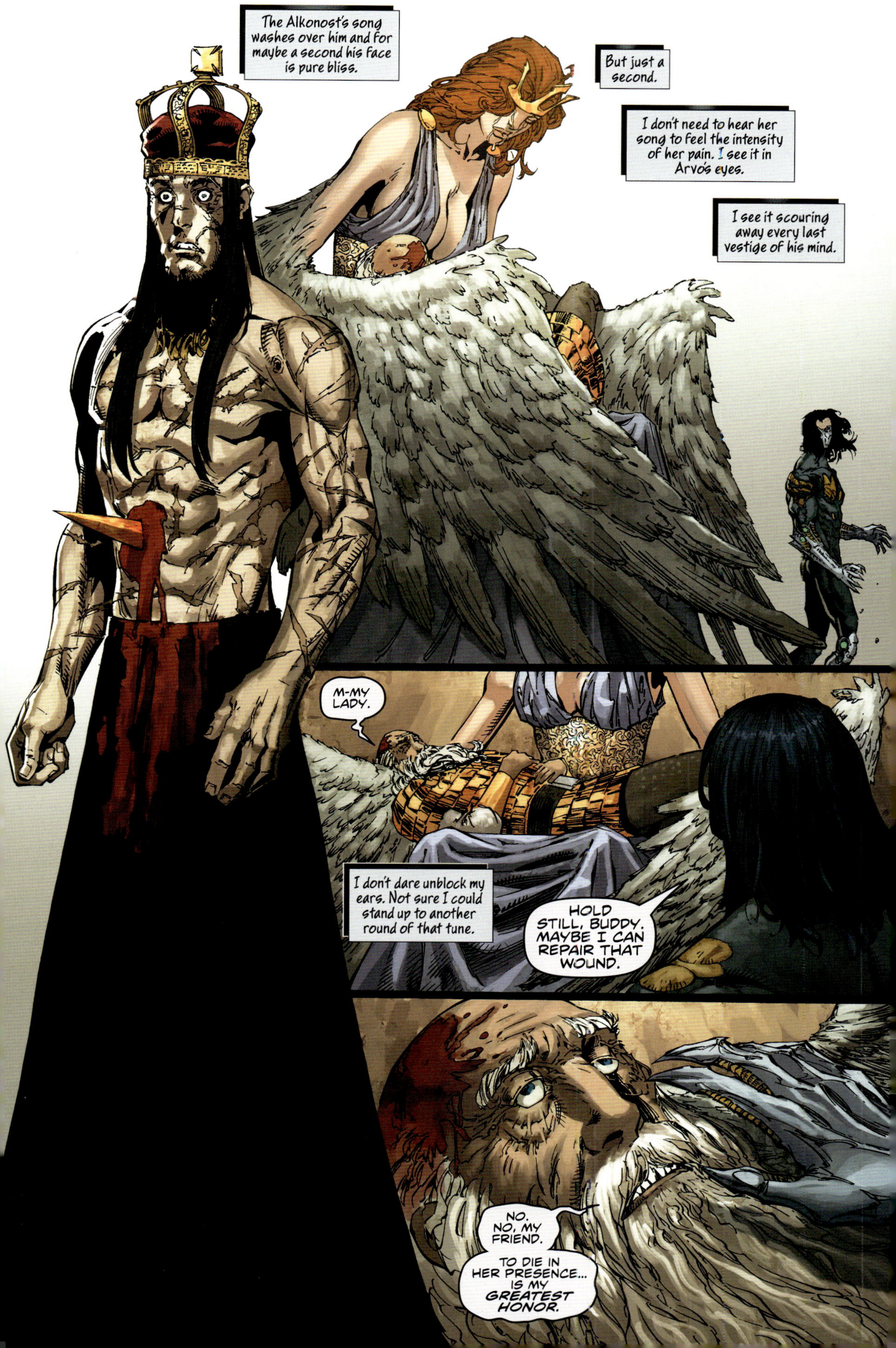
The Alkonost's song washes over him and for maybe a second his face is pure bliss.
But just a second.
I don't need to hear her song to feel the intensity of her pain. I see it in Arvo's eyes.
I see it scouring away every last vestige of his mind.
M-MY LADY.
I don't dare unblock my ears. Not sure I could stand up to another round of that tune.
HOLD STILL, BUDDY. MAYBE I CAN REPAIR THAT WOUND.
NO. NO, MY FRIEND.
TO DIE IN HER PRESENCE... IS MY GREATEST HONOR.

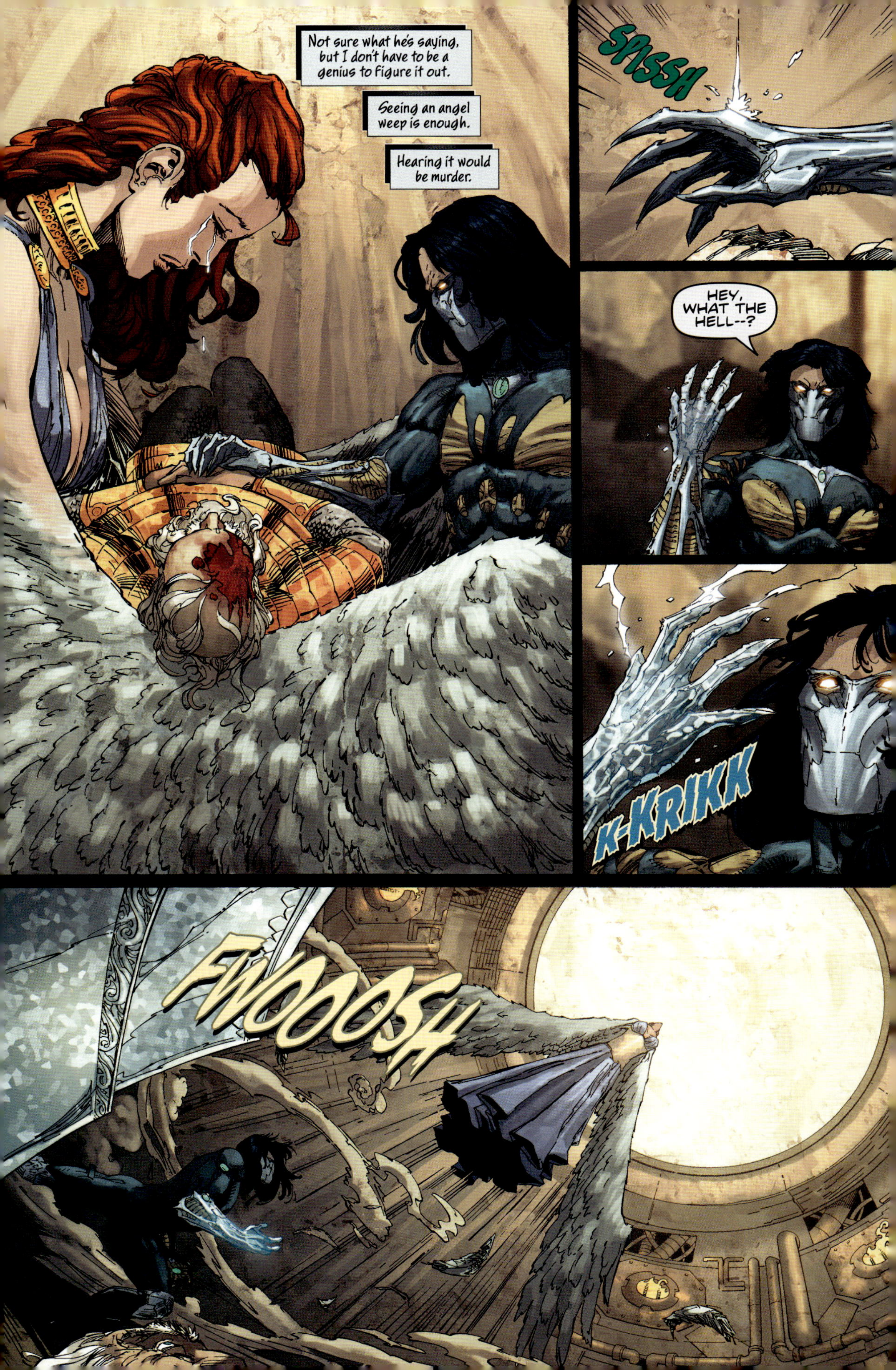
Not sure what he's saying, but I don't have to be a genius to figure it out.
Seeing an angel weep is enough.
Hearing it would be murder.
SPISSH
HEY, WHAT THE HELL--?
K-KRIKK
FWOOOSH

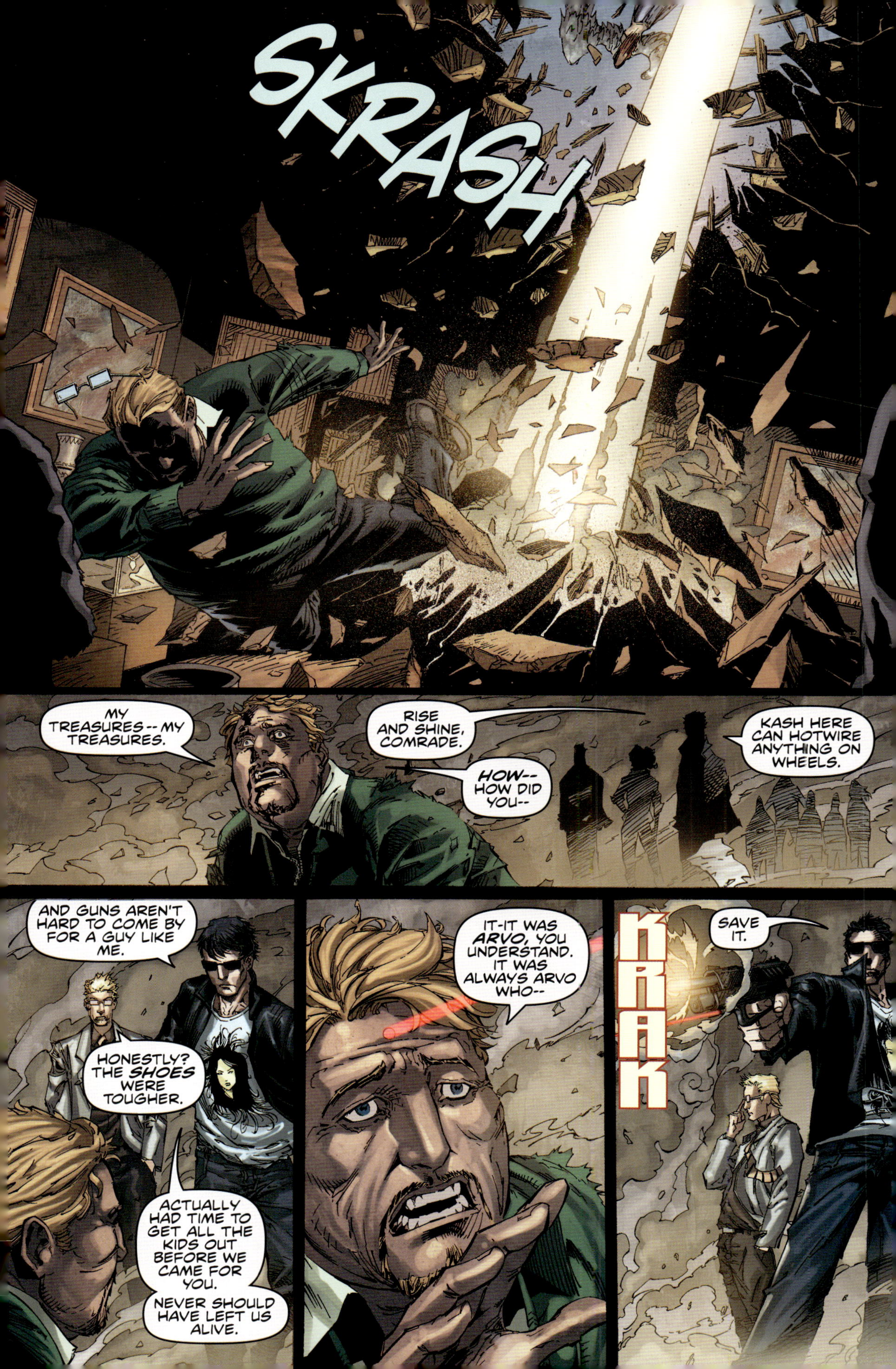
SKRASH
MY TREASURES -- MY TREASURES.
RISE AND SHINE, COMRADE.
HOW-- HOW DID YOU--
KASH HERE CAN HOTWIRE ANYTHING ON WHEELS.
AND GUNS AREN'T HARD TO COME BY FOR A GUY LIKE ME.
HONESTLY? THE SHOES WERE TOUGHER.
ACTUALLY HAD TIME TO GET ALL THE KIDS OUT BEFORE WE CAME FOR YOU.
NEVER SHOULD HAVE LEFT US ALIVE.
IT-IT WAS ARVO, YOU UNDERSTAND. IT WAS ALWAYS ARVO WHO--
KRAK
SAVE IT.

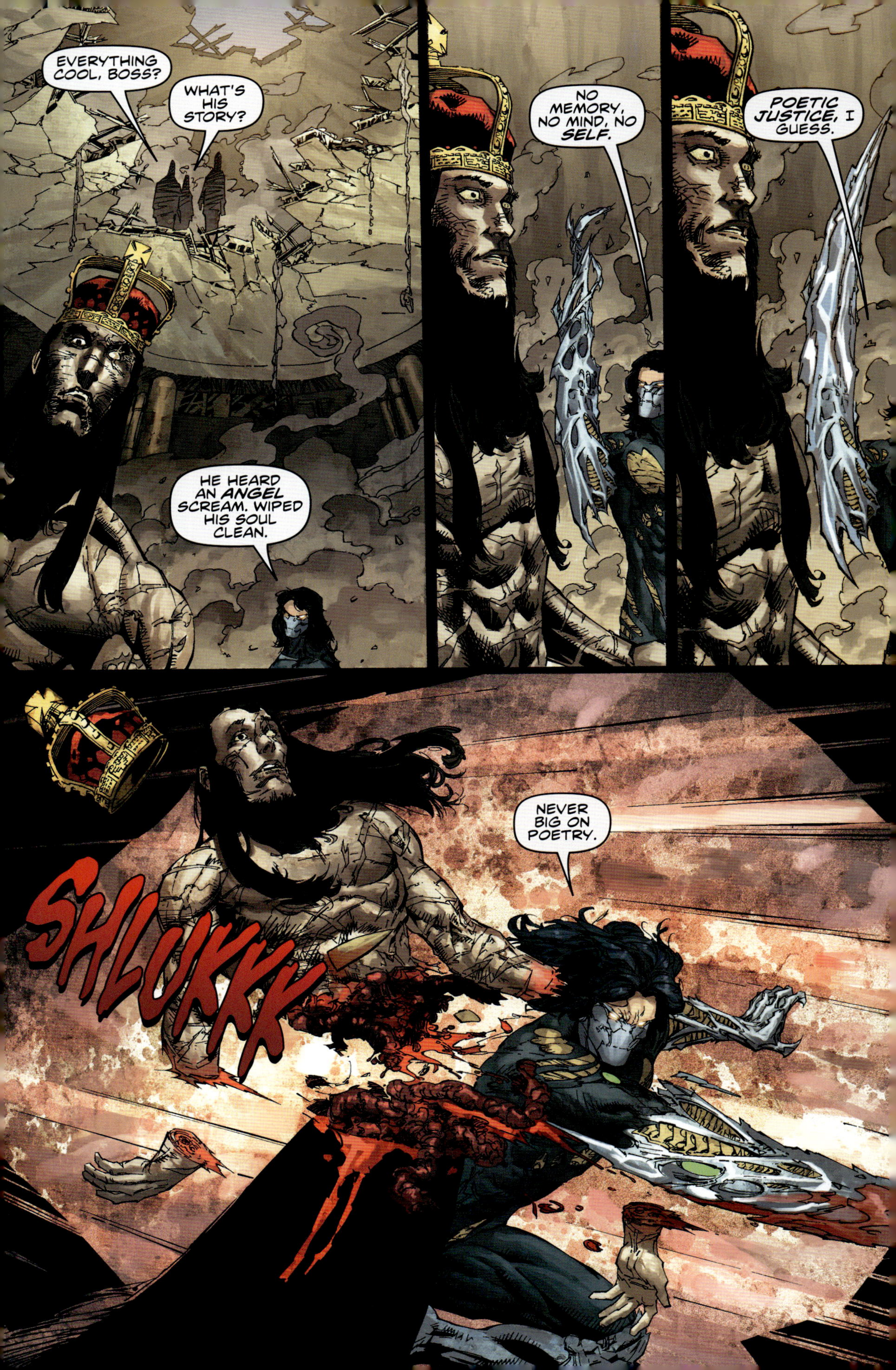
EVERYTHING COOL, BOSS?
WHAT'S HIS STORY?
HE HEARD AN ANGEL SCREAM. WIPED HIS SOUL CLEAN.
NO MEMORY, NO MIND, NO SELF.
POETIC JUSTICE, I GUESS.
NEVER BIG ON POETRY.
SHLUKK

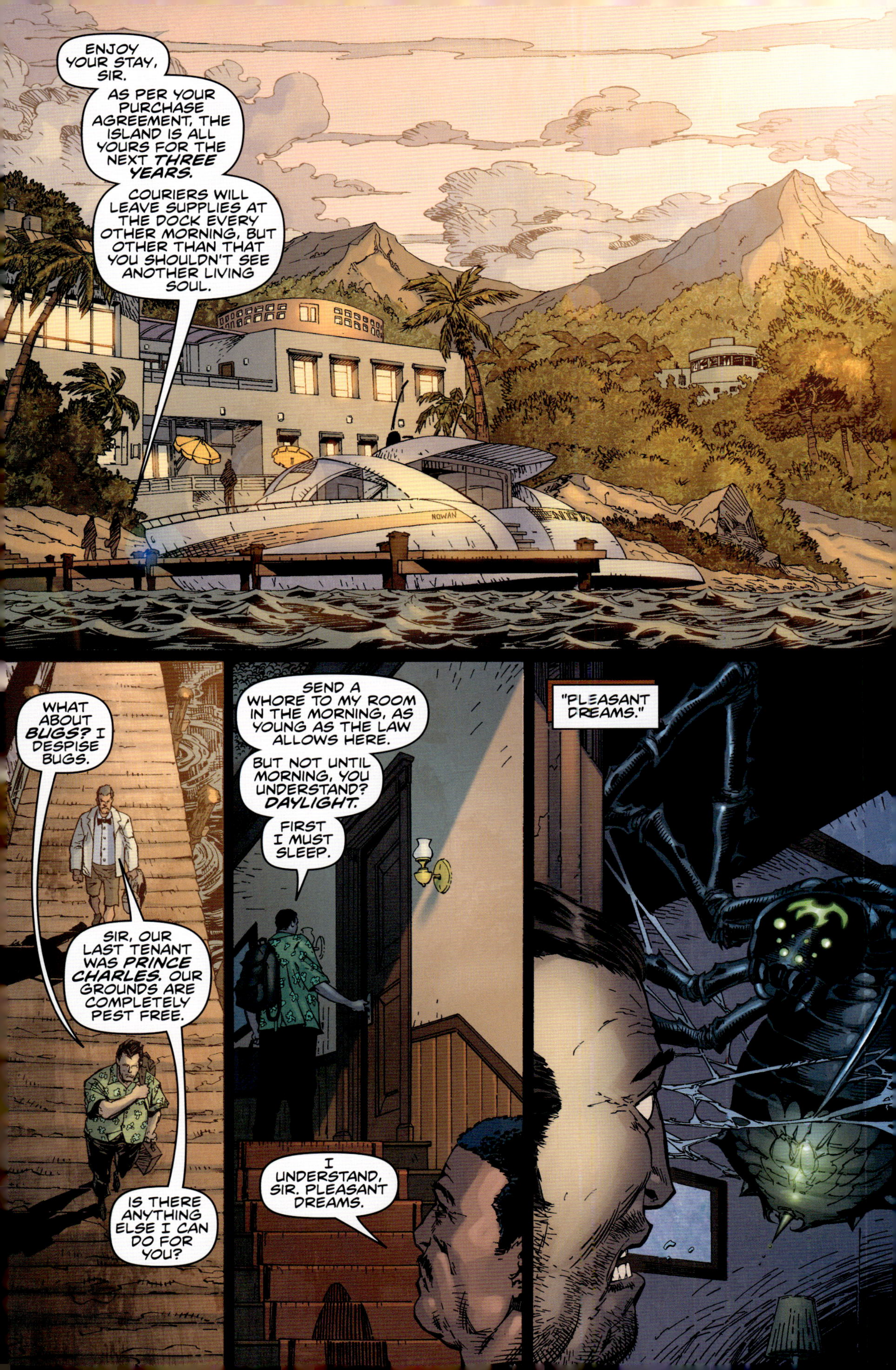
ENJOY YOUR STAY, SIR.
AS PER YOUR PURCHASE AGREEMENT, THE ISLAND IS ALL YOURS FOR THE NEXT *THREE YEARS.*
COURIERS WILL LEAVE SUPPLIES AT THE DOCK EVERY OTHER MORNING, BUT OTHER THAN THAT YOU SHOULDN'T SEE ANOTHER LIVING SOUL.
NOWAN
WHAT ABOUT *BUGS?* I DESPISE BUGS.
SIR, OUR LAST TENANT WAS *PRINCE CHARLES.* OUR GROUNDS ARE COMPLETELY PEST FREE.
IS THERE ANYTHING ELSE I CAN DO FOR YOU?
SEND A WHORE TO MY ROOM IN THE MORNING, AS YOUNG AS THE LAW ALLOWS HERE.
BUT NOT UNTIL MORNING, YOU UNDERSTAND? *DAYLIGHT.*
FIRST I MUST SLEEP.
I UNDERSTAND, SIR. PLEASANT DREAMS.
"PLEASANT DREAMS."

The Darkness Issue #87
cover art by: Dale Keown

THE DARKNESS #87

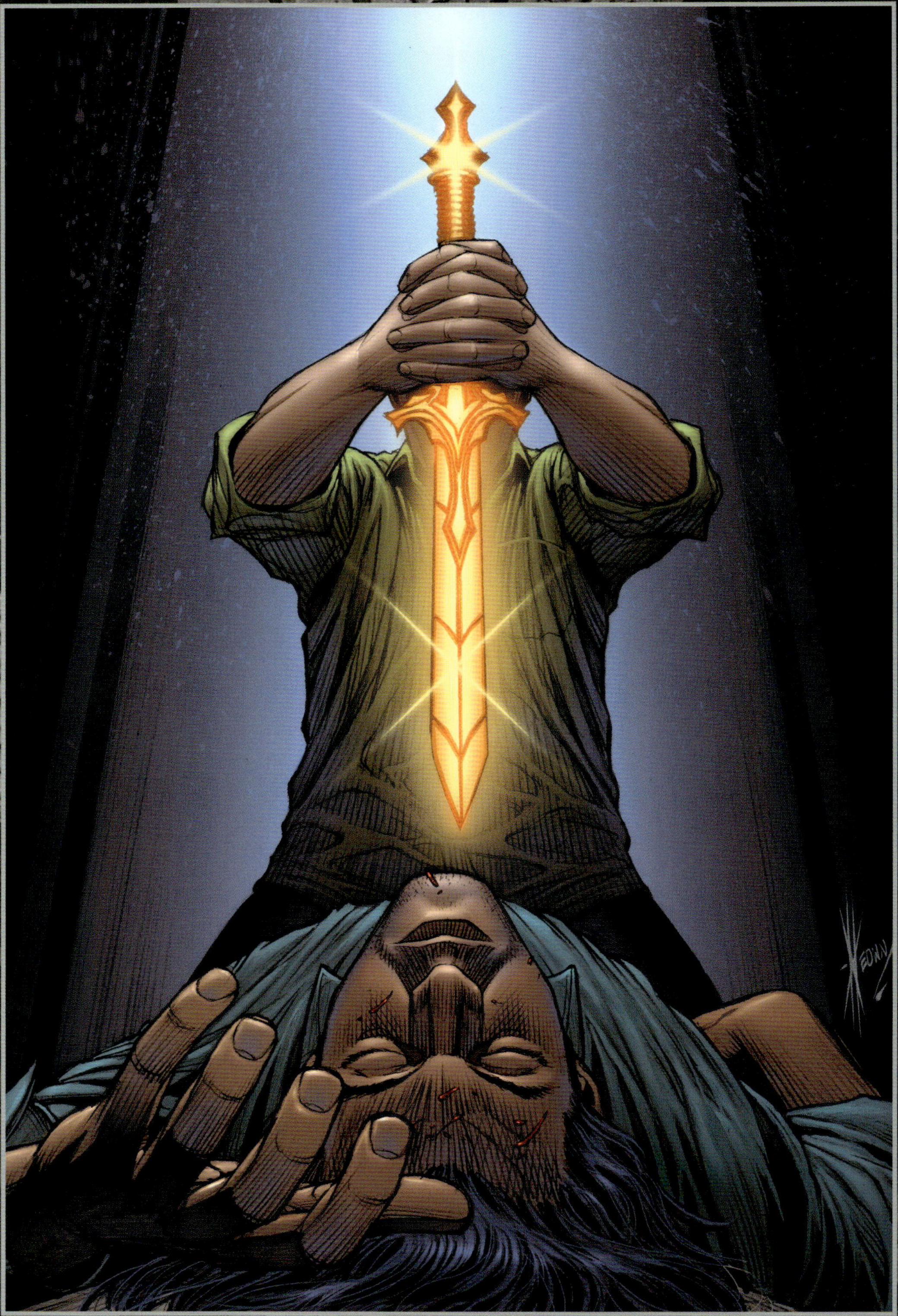

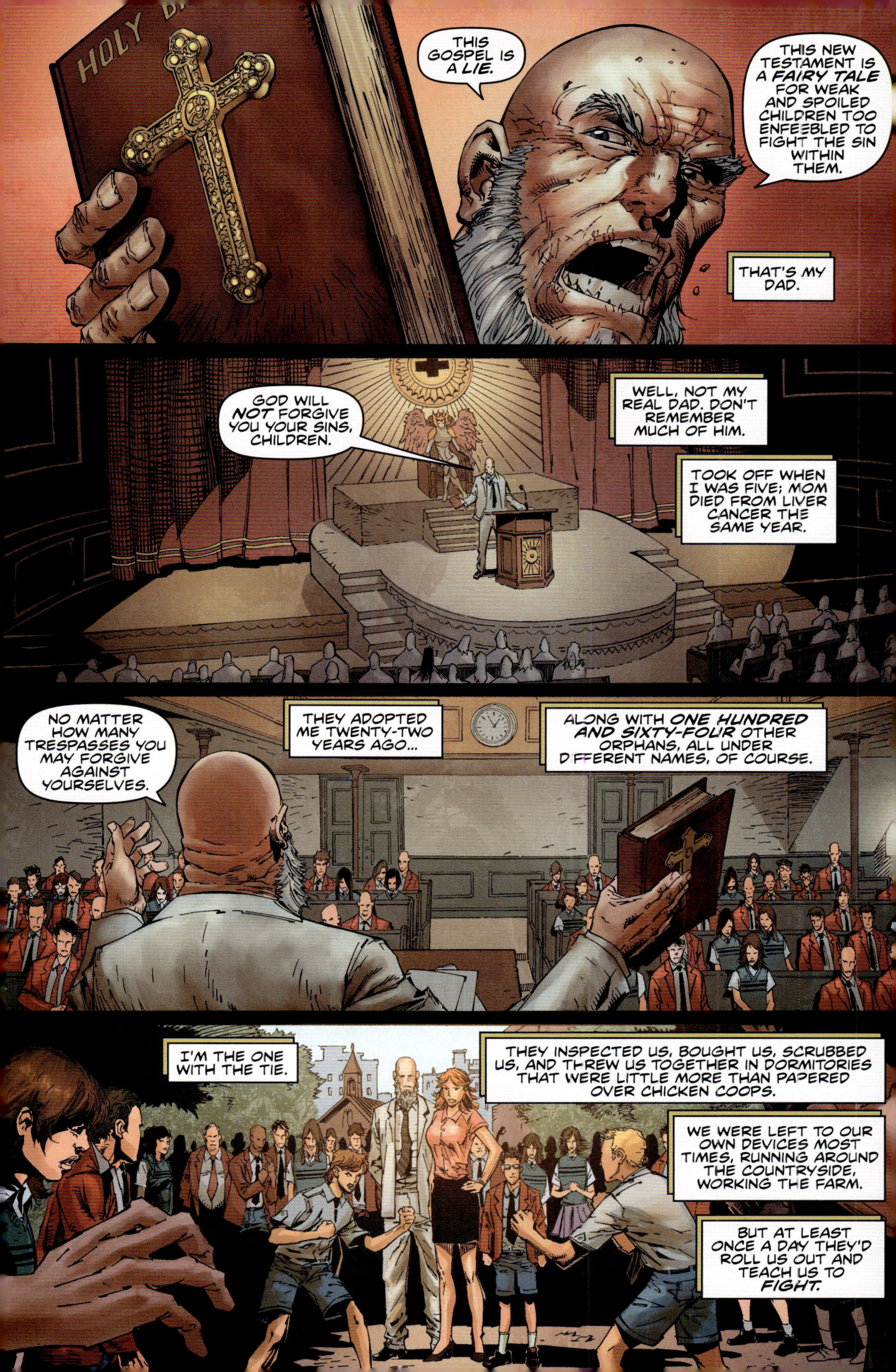
HOLY BI
THIS GOSPEL IS A LIE.
THIS NEW TESTAMENT IS A FAIRY TALE FOR WEAK AND SPOILED CHILDREN TOO ENFEEBLED TO FIGHT THE SIN WITHIN THEM.
THAT'S MY DAD.
GOD WILL NOT FORGIVE YOU YOUR SINS, CHILDREN.
WELL, NOT MY REAL DAD. DON'T REMEMBER MUCH OF HIM.
TOOK OFF WHEN I WAS FIVE; MOM DIED FROM LIVER CANCER THE SAME YEAR.
NO MATTER HOW MANY TRESPASSES YOU MAY FORGIVE AGAINST YOURSELVES.
THEY ADOPTED ME TWENTY-TWO YEARS AGO...
ALONG WITH ONE HUNDRED AND SIXTY-FOUR OTHER ORPHANS, ALL UNDER DIFFERENT NAMES, OF COURSE.
I'M THE ONE WITH THE TIE.
THEY INSPECTED US, BOUGHT US, SCRUBBED US, AND THREW US TOGETHER IN DORMITORIES THAT WERE LITTLE MORE THAN PAPERED OVER CHICKEN COOPS.
WE WERE LEFT TO OUR OWN DEVICES MOST TIMES, RUNNING AROUND THE COUNTRYSIDE, WORKING THE FARM.
BUT AT LEAST ONCE A DAY THEY'D ROLL US OUT AND TEACH US TO FIGHT.

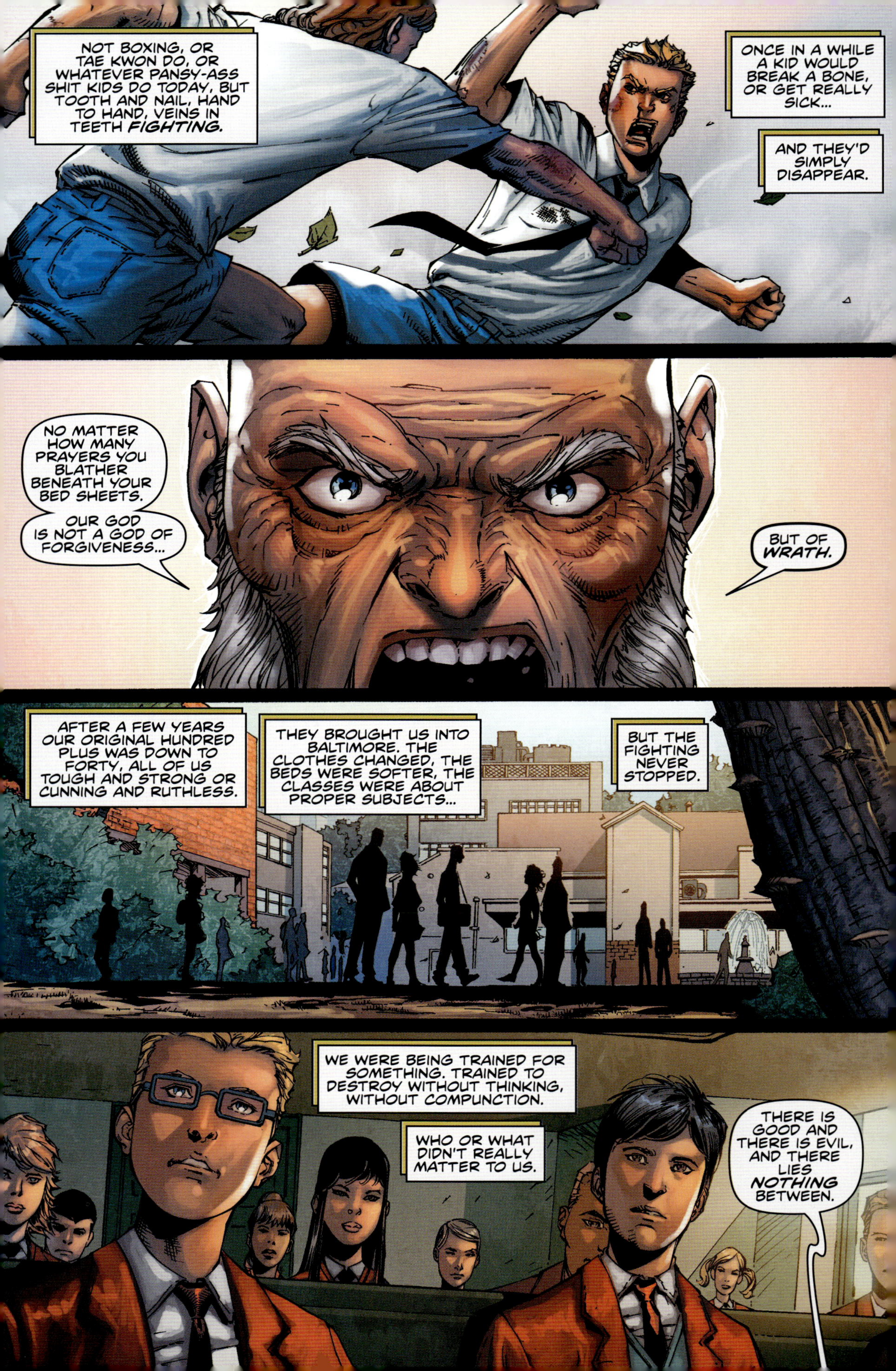
NOT BOXING, OR TAE KWON DO, OR WHATEVER PANSY-ASS SHIT KIDS DO TODAY, BUT TOOTH AND NAIL, HAND TO HAND, VEINS IN TEETH *FIGHTING.*
ONCE IN A WHILE A KID WOULD BREAK A BONE, OR GET REALLY SICK...
AND THEY'D SIMPLY DISAPPEAR.
NO MATTER HOW MANY PRAYERS YOU BLATHER BENEATH YOUR BED SHEETS.
OUR GOD IS NOT A GOD OF FORGIVENESS...
BUT OF *WRATH.*
AFTER A FEW YEARS OUR ORIGINAL HUNDRED PLUS WAS DOWN TO FORTY, ALL OF US TOUGH AND STRONG OR CUNNING AND RUTHLESS.
THEY BROUGHT US INTO BALTIMORE. THE CLOTHES CHANGED, THE BEDS WERE SOFTER, THE CLASSES WERE ABOUT PROPER SUBJECTS...
BUT THE FIGHTING NEVER STOPPED.
WE WERE BEING TRAINED FOR SOMETHING. TRAINED TO DESTROY WITHOUT THINKING, WITHOUT COMPUNCTION.
WHO OR WHAT DIDN'T REALLY MATTER TO US.
THERE IS GOOD AND THERE IS EVIL, AND THERE LIES *NOTHING* BETWEEN.

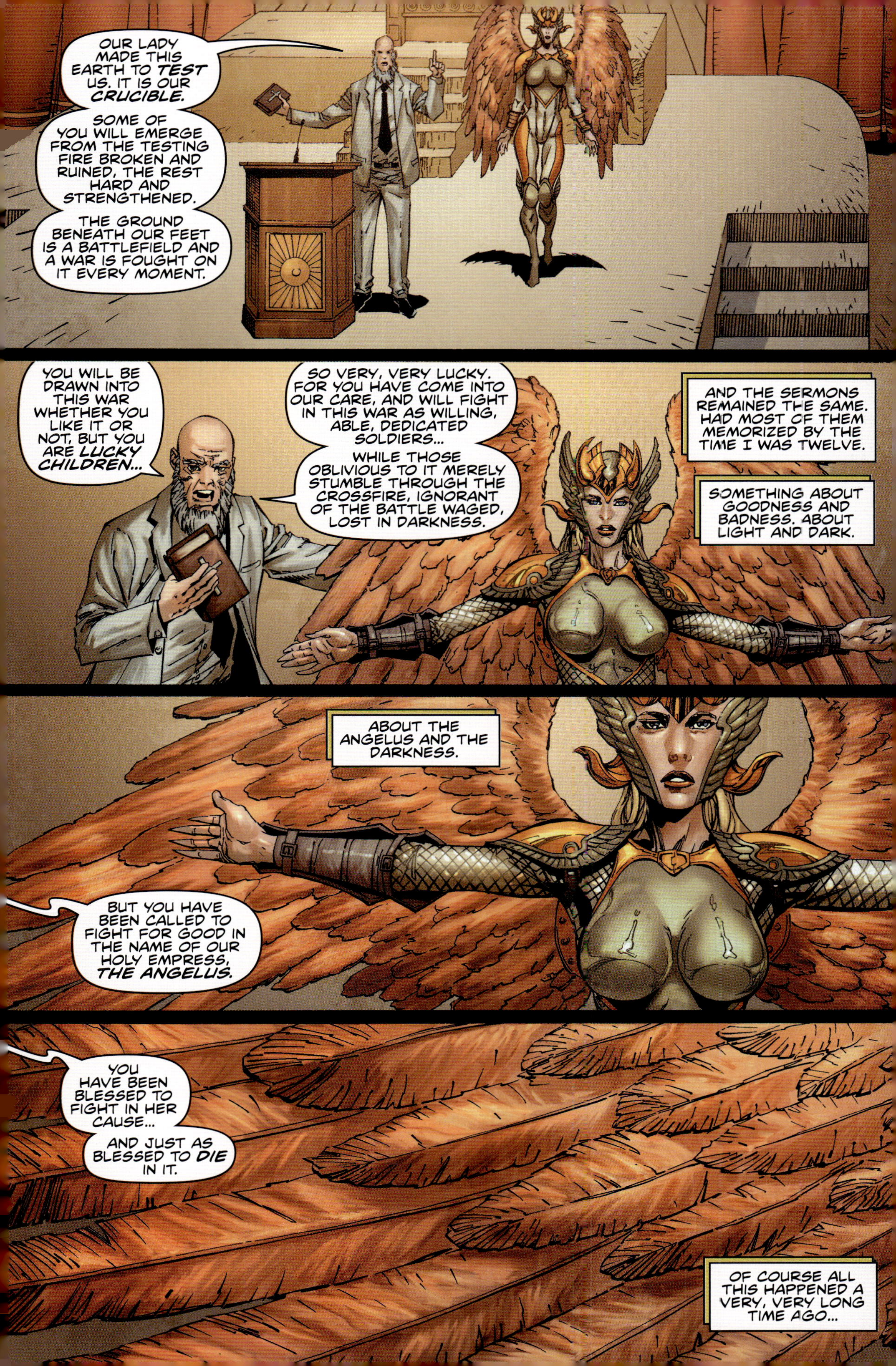
OUR LADY MADE THIS EARTH TO TEST US. IT IS OUR CRUCIBLE.
SOME OF YOU WILL EMERGE FROM THE TESTING FIRE BROKEN AND RUINED, THE REST HARD AND STRENGTHENED.
THE GROUND BENEATH OUR FEET IS A BATTLEFIELD AND A WAR IS FOUGHT ON IT EVERY MOMENT.
YOU WILL BE DRAWN INTO THIS WAR WHETHER YOU LIKE IT OR NOT, BUT YOU ARE LUCKY CHILDREN...
SO VERY, VERY LUCKY. FOR YOU HAVE COME INTO OUR CARE, AND WILL FIGHT IN THIS WAR AS WILLING, ABLE, DEDICATED SOLDIERS...
WHILE THOSE OBLIVIOUS TO IT MERELY STUMBLE THROUGH THE CROSSFIRE, IGNORANT OF THE BATTLE WAGED, LOST IN DARKNESS.
AND THE SERMONS REMAINED THE SAME. HAD MOST OF THEM MEMORIZED BY THE TIME I WAS TWELVE.
SOMETHING ABOUT GOODNESS AND BADNESS. ABOUT LIGHT AND DARK.
ABOUT THE ANGELUS AND THE DARKNESS.
BUT YOU HAVE BEEN CALLED TO FIGHT FOR GOOD IN THE NAME OF OUR HOLY EMPRESS, THE ANGELUS.
YOU HAVE BEEN BLESSED TO FIGHT IN HER CAUSE...
AND JUST AS BLESSED TO DIE IN IT.
OF COURSE ALL THIS HAPPENED A VERY, VERY LONG TIME AGO...

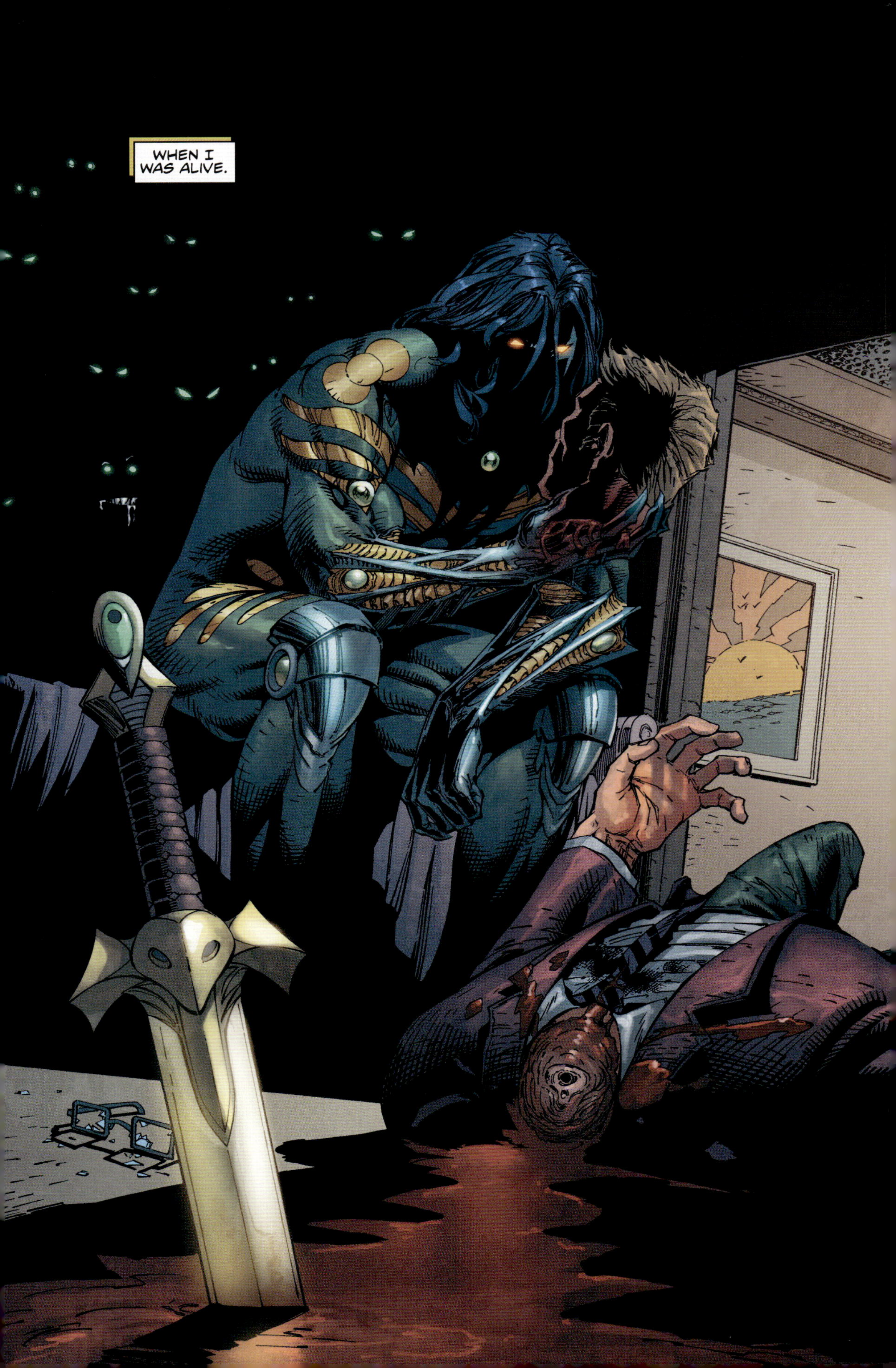
WHEN I
WAS ALIVE.

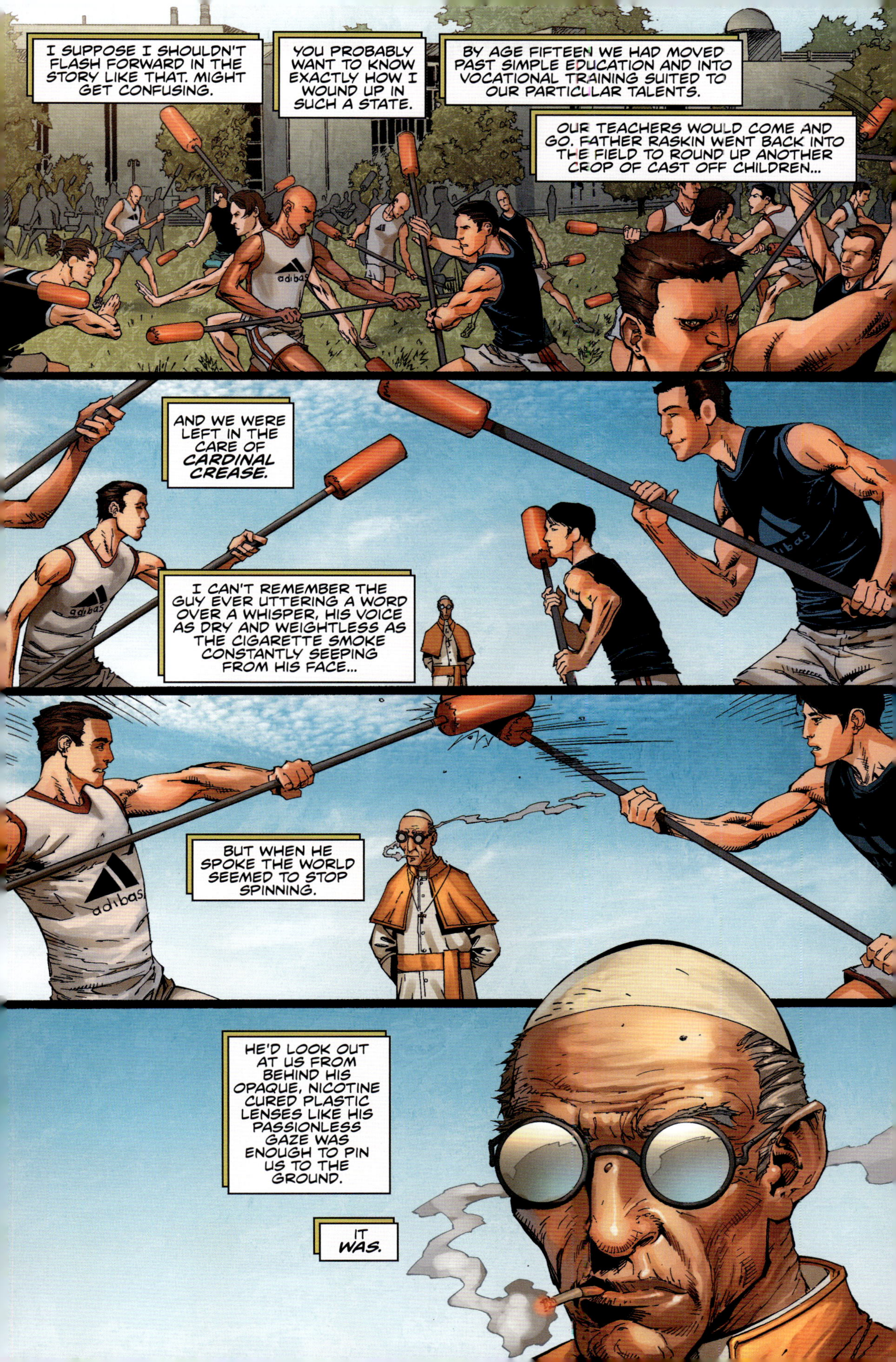

I SUPPOSE I SHOULDN'T FLASH FORWARD IN THE STORY LIKE THAT. MIGHT GET CONFUSING.
YOU PROBABLY WANT TO KNOW EXACTLY HOW I WOUND UP IN SUCH A STATE.
BY AGE FIFTEEN WE HAD MOVED PAST SIMPLE EDUCATION AND INTO VOCATIONAL TRAINING SUITED TO OUR PARTICULAR TALENTS.
OUR TEACHERS WOULD COME AND GO. FATHER RASKIN WENT BACK INTO THE FIELD TO ROUND UP ANOTHER CROP OF CAST OFF CHILDREN...
AND WE WERE LEFT IN THE CARE OF *CARDINAL CREASE.*
I CAN'T REMEMBER THE GUY EVER UTTERING A WORD OVER A WHISPER, HIS VOICE AS DRY AND WEIGHTLESS AS THE CIGARETTE SMOKE CONSTANTLY SEEPING FROM HIS FACE...
BUT WHEN HE SPOKE THE WORLD SEEMED TO STOP SPINNING.
HE'D LOOK OUT AT US FROM BEHIND HIS OPAQUE, NICOTINE CURED PLASTIC LENSES LIKE HIS PASSIONLESS GAZE WAS ENOUGH TO PIN US TO THE GROUND.
IT *WAS.*

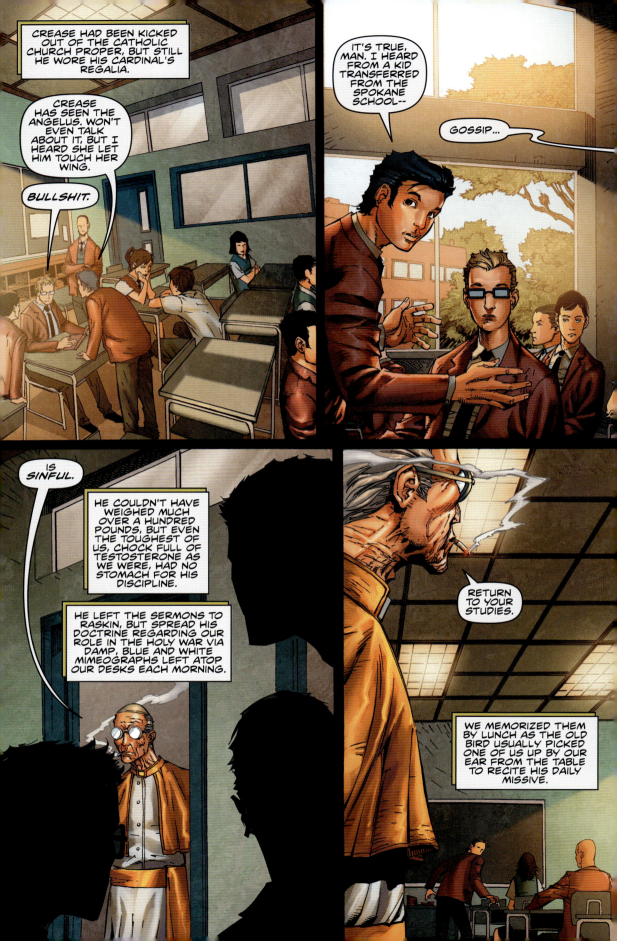

CREASE HAD BEEN KICKED OUT OF THE CATHOLIC CHURCH PROPER, BUT STILL HE WORE HIS CARDINAL'S REGALIA.

CREASE HAS SEEN THE ANGELUS. WON'T EVEN TALK ABOUT IT, BUT I HEARD SHE LET HIM TOUCH HER WING.

BULLSHIT.

IT'S TRUE, MAN. I HEARD FROM A KID TRANSFERRED FROM THE SPOKANE SCHOOL--

GOSSIP...

IS *SINFUL.*

HE COULDN'T HAVE WEIGHED MUCH OVER A HUNDRED POUNDS, BUT EVEN THE TOUGHEST OF US, CHOCK FULL OF TESTOSTERONE AS WE WERE, HAD NO STOMACH FOR HIS DISCIPLINE.

HE LEFT THE SERMONS TO RASKIN, BUT SPREAD HIS DOCTRINE REGARDING OUR ROLE IN THE HOLY WAR VIA DAMP, BLUE AND WHITE MIMEOGRAPHS LEFT ATOP OUR DESKS EACH MORNING.

RETURN TO YOUR STUDIES.

WE MEMORIZED THEM BY LUNCH AS THE OLD BIRD USUALLY PICKED ONE OF US UP BY OUR EAR FROM THE TABLE TO RECITE HIS DAILY MISSIVE.

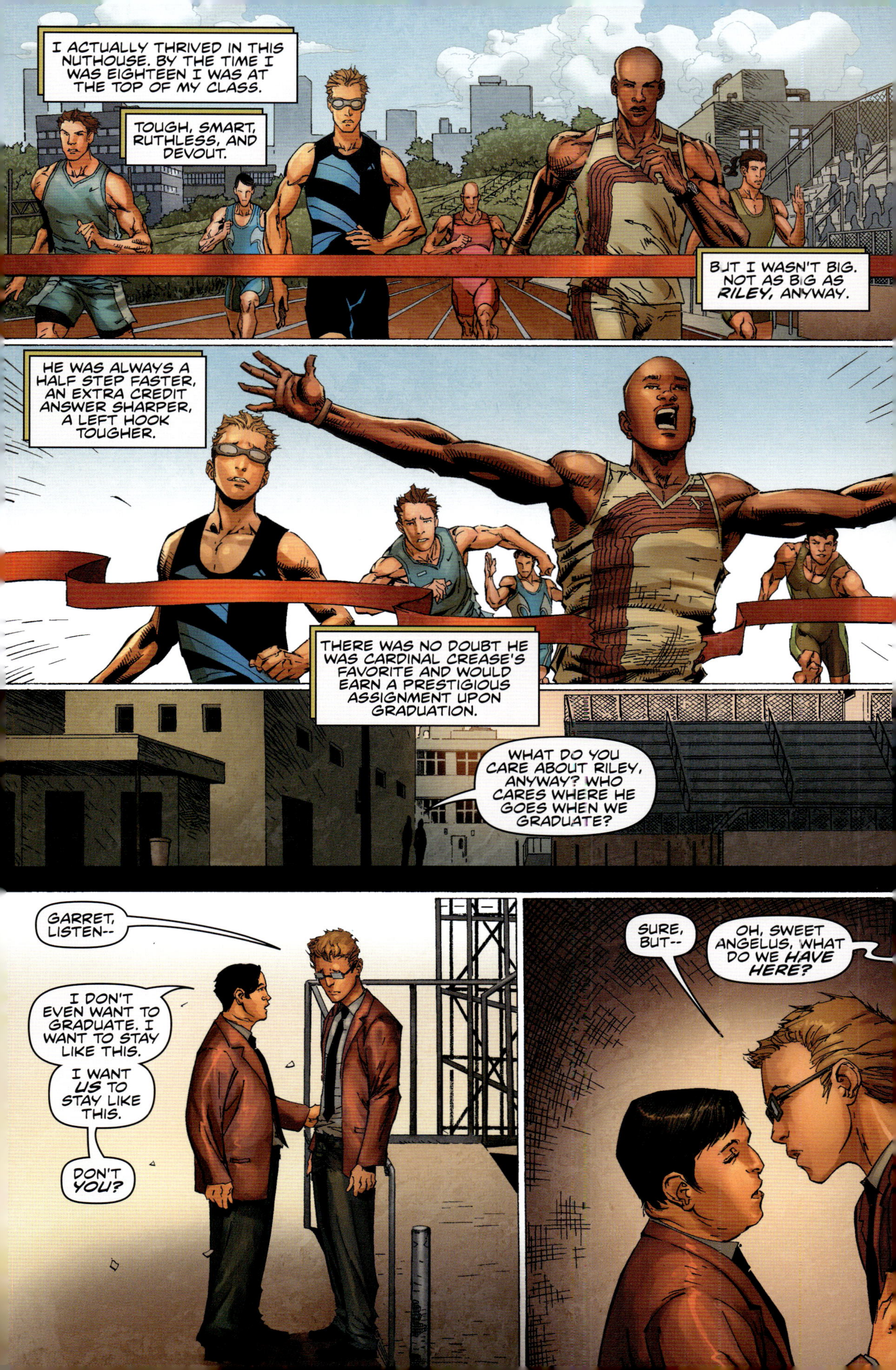
I ACTUALLY THRIVED IN THIS NUTHOUSE. BY THE TIME I WAS EIGHTEEN I WAS AT THE TOP OF MY CLASS.
TOUGH, SMART, RUTHLESS, AND DEVOUT.
BUT I WASN'T BIG. NOT AS BIG AS RILEY, ANYWAY.
HE WAS ALWAYS A HALF STEP FASTER, AN EXTRA CREDIT ANSWER SHARPER, A LEFT HOOK TOUGHER.
THERE WAS NO DOUBT HE WAS CARDINAL CREASE'S FAVORITE AND WOULD EARN A PRESTIGIOUS ASSIGNMENT UPON GRADUATION.
WHAT DO YOU CARE ABOUT RILEY, ANYWAY? WHO CARES WHERE HE GOES WHEN WE GRADUATE?
GARRET, LISTEN--
I DON'T EVEN WANT TO GRADUATE. I WANT TO STAY LIKE THIS.
I WANT US TO STAY LIKE THIS.
DON'T YOU?
SURE, BUT--
OH, SWEET ANGELUS, WHAT DO WE HAVE HERE?

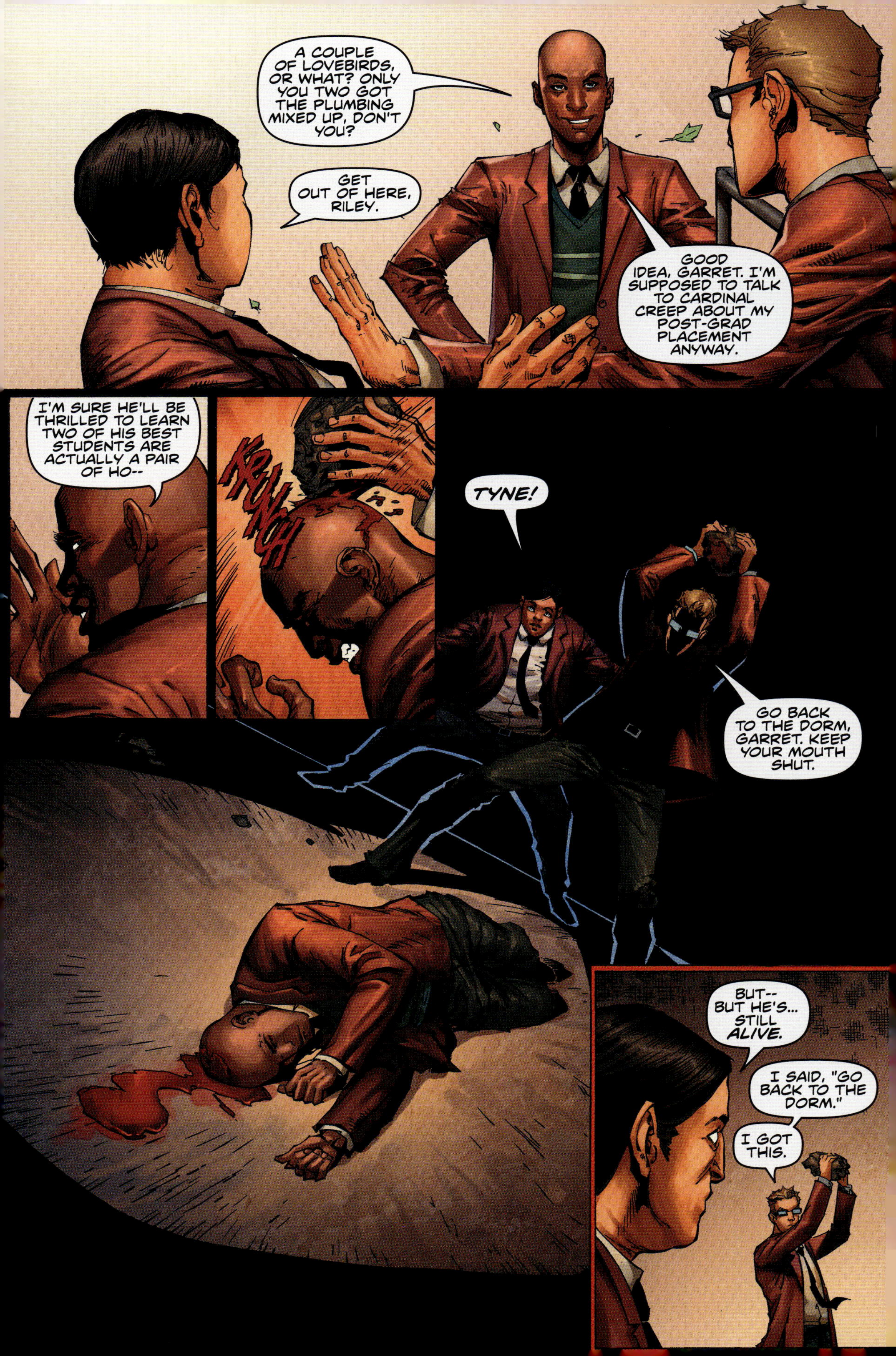
A COUPLE OF LOVEBIRDS, OR WHAT? ONLY YOU TWO GOT THE PLUMBING MIXED UP, DON'T YOU?
GET OUT OF HERE, RILEY.
GOOD IDEA, GARRET. I'M SUPPOSED TO TALK TO CARDINAL CREEP ABOUT MY POST-GRAD PLACEMENT ANYWAY.
I'M SURE HE'LL BE THRILLED TO LEARN TWO OF HIS BEST STUDENTS ARE ACTUALLY A PAIR OF HO--
KRUNCH
TYNE!
GO BACK TO THE DORM, GARRET. KEEP YOUR MOUTH SHUT.
BUT-- BUT HE'S... STILL ALIVE.
I SAID, "GO BACK TO THE DORM."
I GOT THIS.

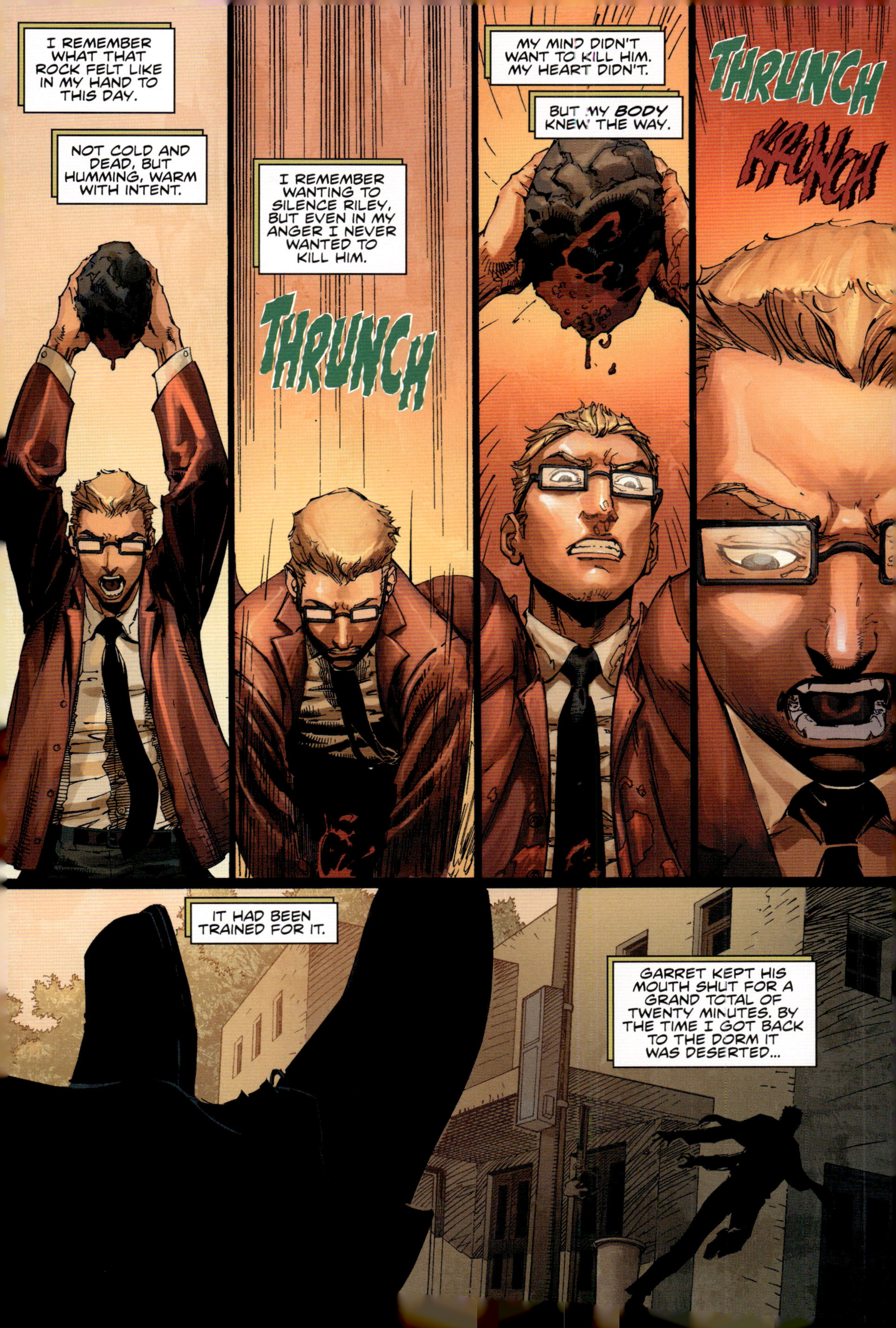
I REMEMBER WHAT THAT ROCK FELT LIKE IN MY HAND TO THIS DAY.
NOT COLD AND DEAD, BUT HUMMING, WARM WITH INTENT.
I REMEMBER WANTING TO SILENCE RILEY, BUT EVEN IN MY ANGER I NEVER WANTED TO KILL HIM.
THRUNCH
MY MIND DIDN'T WANT TO KILL HIM. MY HEART DIDN'T.
BUT MY *BODY* KNEW THE WAY.
THRUNCH
KRUNCH
IT HAD BEEN TRAINED FOR IT.
GARRET KEPT HIS MOUTH SHUT FOR A GRAND TOTAL OF TWENTY MINUTES. BY THE TIME I GOT BACK TO THE DORM IT WAS DESERTED...

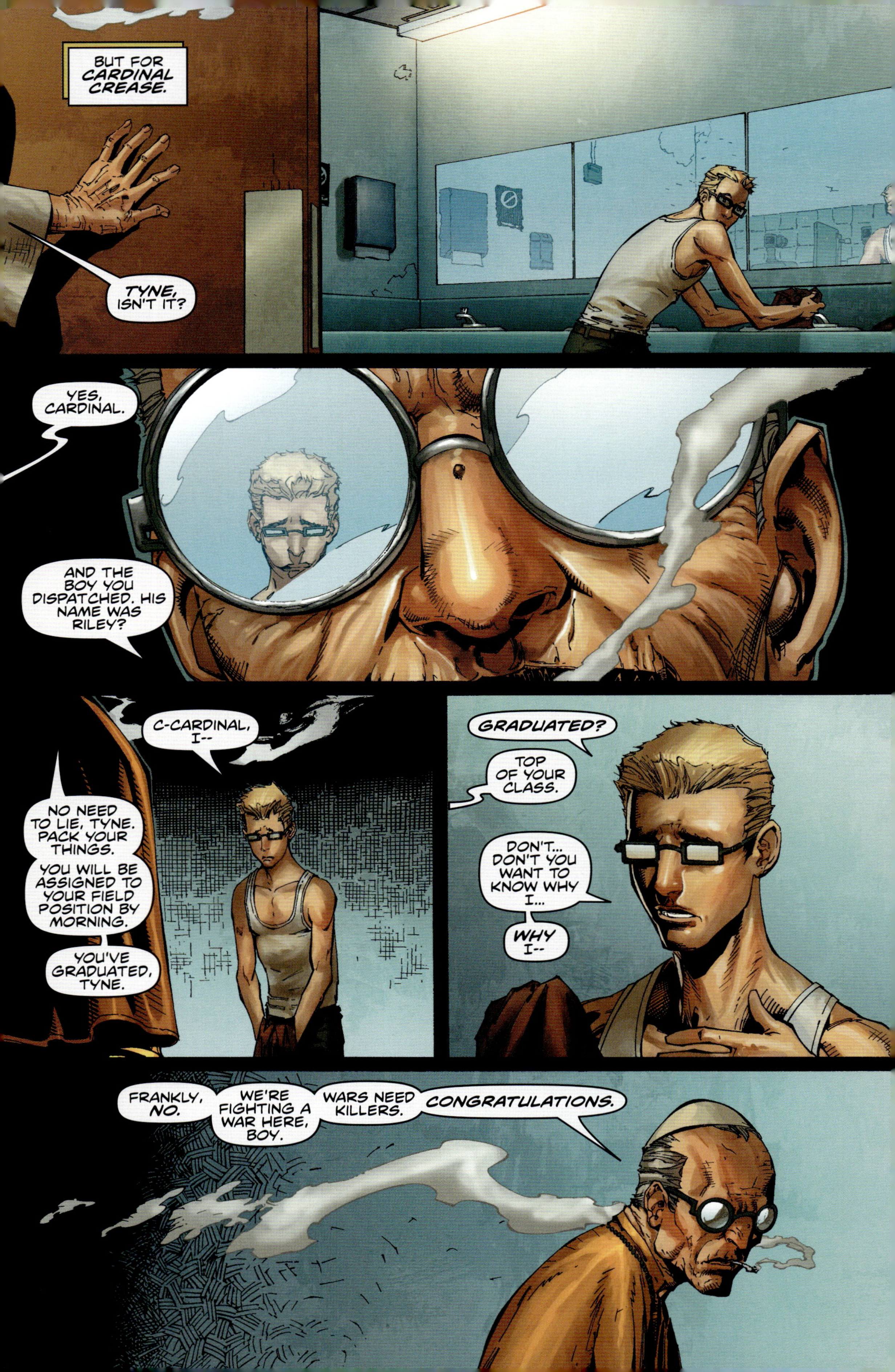
BUT FOR CARDINAL CREASE.
TYNE, ISN'T IT?
YES, CARDINAL.
AND THE BOY YOU DISPATCHED. HIS NAME WAS RILEY?
C-CARDINAL, I--
NO NEED TO LIE, TYNE. PACK YOUR THINGS.
YOU WILL BE ASSIGNED TO YOUR FIELD POSITION BY MORNING.
YOU'VE GRADUATED, TYNE.
GRADUATED?
TOP OF YOUR CLASS.
DON'T... DON'T YOU WANT TO KNOW WHY I...
WHY I--
FRANKLY, NO.
WE'RE FIGHTING A WAR HERE, BOY.
WARS NEED KILLERS.
CONGRATULATIONS.

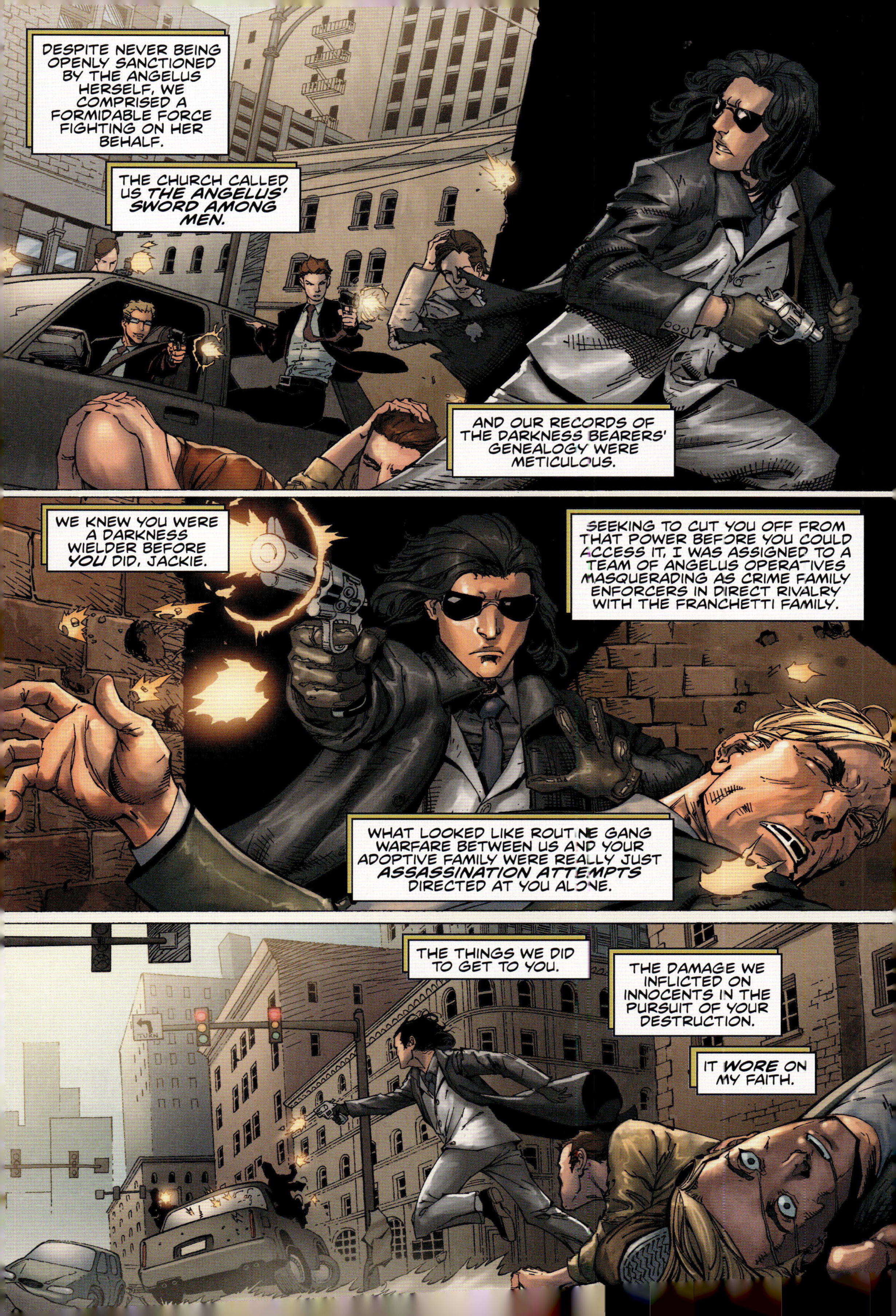
DESPITE NEVER BEING OPENLY SANCTIONED BY THE ANGELUS HERSELF, WE COMPRISED A FORMIDABLE FORCE FIGHTING ON HER BEHALF.
THE CHURCH CALLED US *THE ANGELUS' SWORD AMONG MEN.*
AND OUR RECORDS OF THE DARKNESS BEARERS' GENEALOGY WERE METICULOUS.
WE KNEW YOU WERE A DARKNESS WIELDER BEFORE *YOU* DID, JACKIE.
SEEKING TO CUT YOU OFF FROM THAT POWER BEFORE YOU COULD ACCESS IT, I WAS ASSIGNED TO A TEAM OF ANGELUS OPERATIVES MASQUERADING AS CRIME FAMILY ENFORCERS IN DIRECT RIVALRY WITH THE FRANCHETTI FAMILY.
WHAT LOOKED LIKE ROUTINE GANG WARFARE BETWEEN US AND YOUR ADOPTIVE FAMILY WERE REALLY JUST *ASSASSINATION ATTEMPTS* DIRECTED AT YOU ALONE.
THE THINGS WE DID TO GET TO YOU.
THE DAMAGE WE INFLICTED ON INNOCENTS IN THE PURSUIT OF YOUR DESTRUCTION.
IT *WORE* ON MY FAITH.

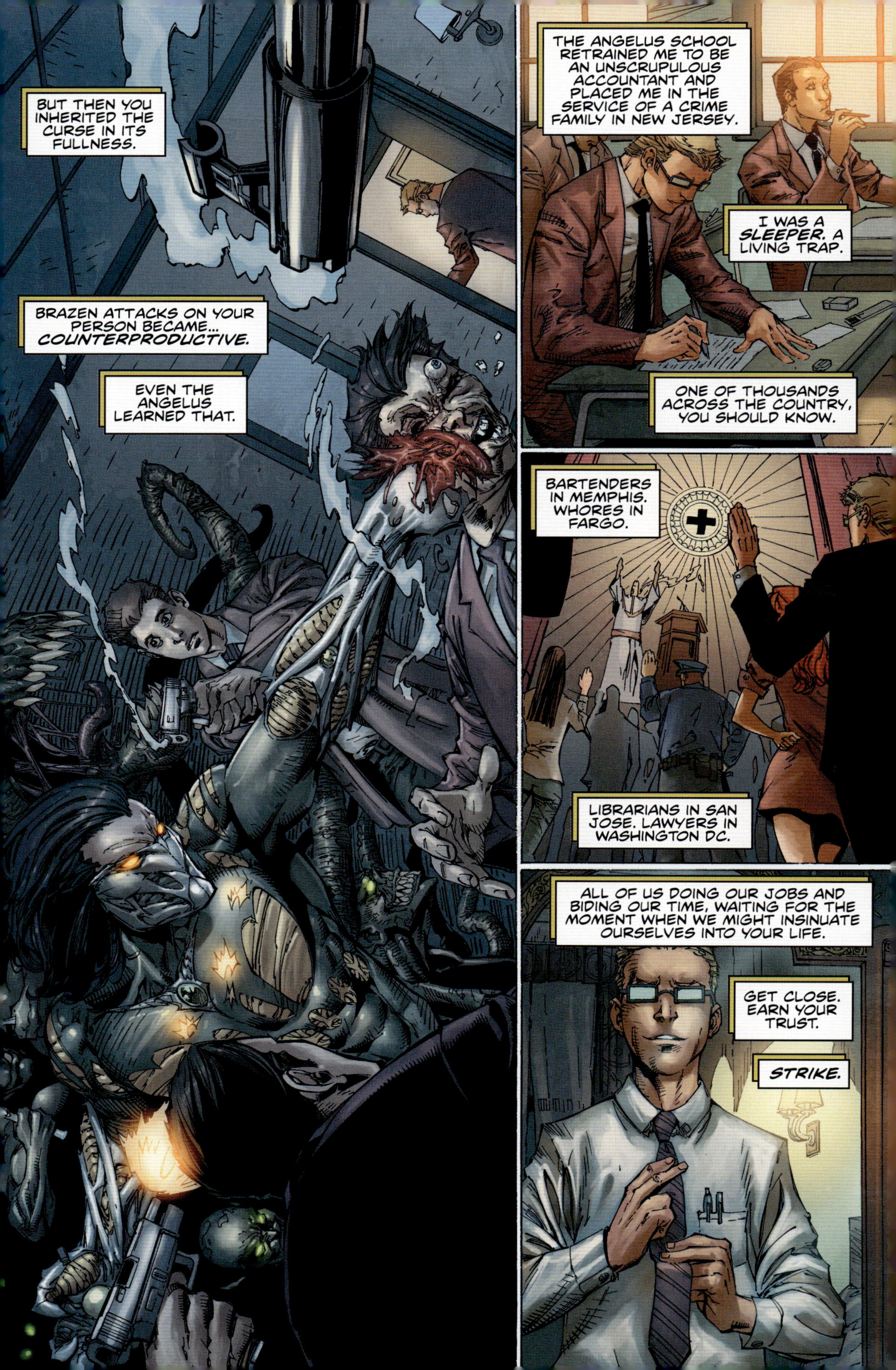

BUT THEN YOU INHERITED THE CURSE IN ITS FULLNESS.
BRAZEN ATTACKS ON YOUR PERSON BECAME... *COUNTERPRODUCTIVE.*
EVEN THE ANGELUS LEARNED THAT.
THE ANGELUS SCHOOL RETRAINED ME TO BE AN UNSCRUPULOUS ACCOUNTANT AND PLACED ME IN THE SERVICE OF A CRIME FAMILY IN NEW JERSEY.
I WAS A *SLEEPER.* A LIVING TRAP.
ONE OF THOUSANDS ACROSS THE COUNTRY, YOU SHOULD KNOW.
BARTENDERS IN MEMPHIS. WHORES IN FARGO.
LIBRARIANS IN SAN JOSE. LAWYERS IN WASHINGTON DC.
ALL OF US DOING OUR JOBS AND BIDING OUR TIME, WAITING FOR THE MOMENT WHEN WE MIGHT INSINUATE OURSELVES INTO YOUR LIFE.
GET CLOSE. EARN YOUR TRUST.
STRIKE.

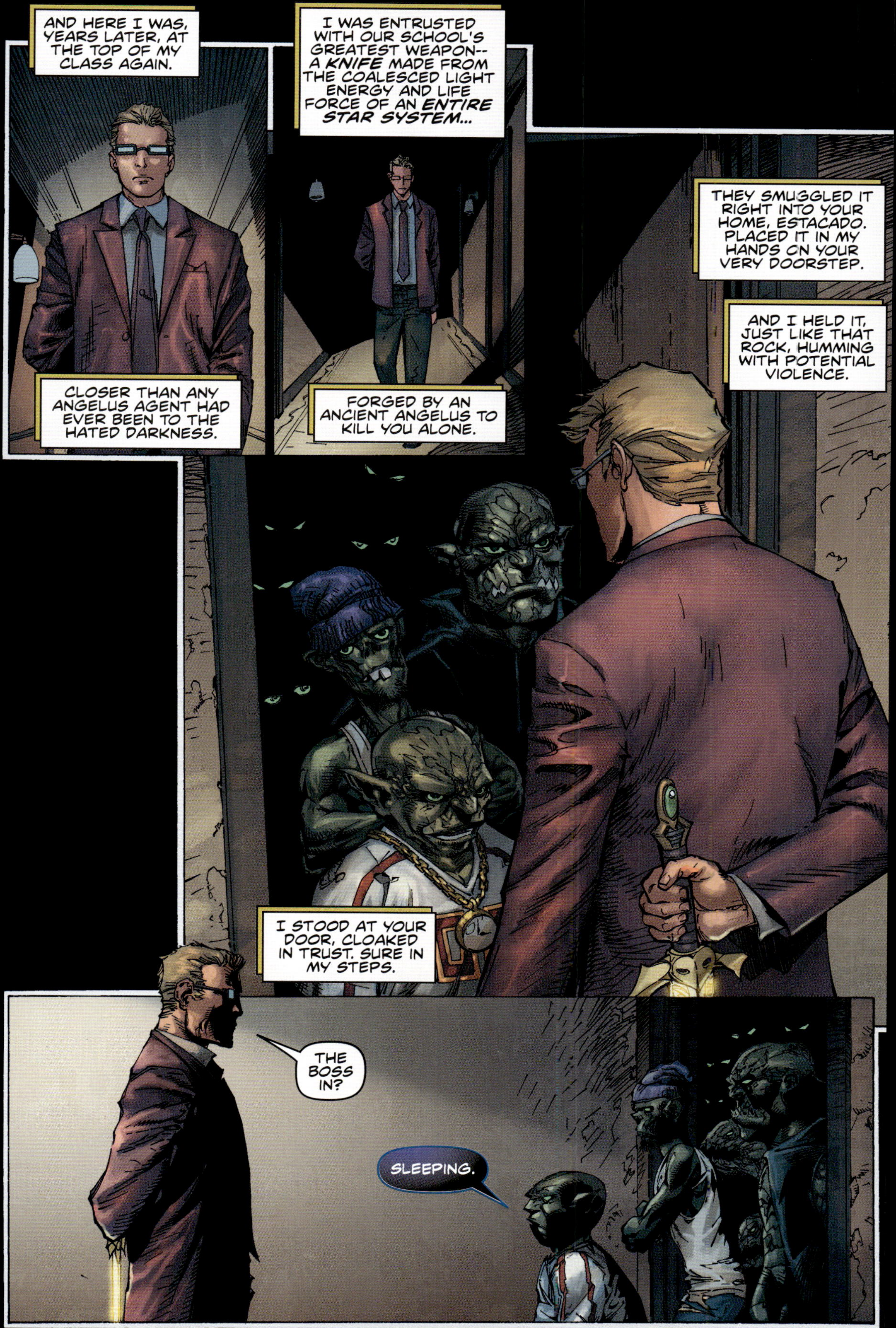
AND HERE I WAS, YEARS LATER, AT THE TOP OF MY CLASS AGAIN.
CLOSER THAN ANY ANGELUS AGENT HAD EVER BEEN TO THE HATED DARKNESS.
I WAS ENTRUSTED WITH OUR SCHOOL'S GREATEST WEAPON-- A KNIFE MADE FROM THE COALESCED LIGHT ENERGY AND LIFE FORCE OF AN ENTIRE STAR SYSTEM...
FORGED BY AN ANCIENT ANGELUS TO KILL YOU ALONE.
THEY SMUGGLED IT RIGHT INTO YOUR HOME, ESTACADO. PLACED IT IN MY HANDS ON YOUR VERY DOORSTEP.
AND I HELD IT, JUST LIKE THAT ROCK, HUMMING WITH POTENTIAL VIOLENCE.
I STOOD AT YOUR DOOR, CLOAKED IN TRUST. SURE IN MY STEPS.
THE BOSS IN?
SLEEPING.

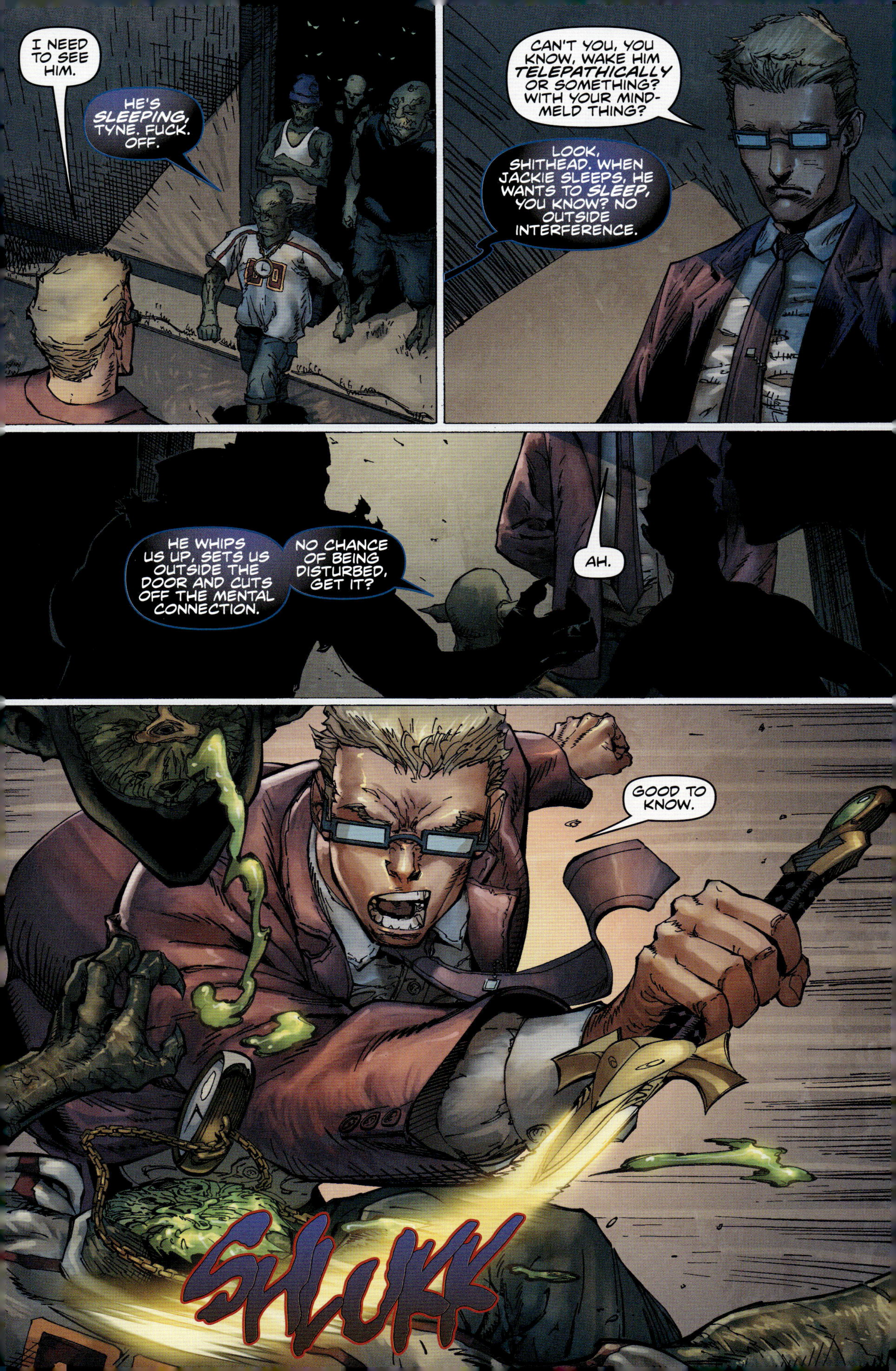
I NEED TO SEE HIM.
HE'S SLEEPING, TYNE. FUCK. OFF.
CAN'T YOU, YOU KNOW, WAKE HIM TELEPATHICALLY OR SOMETHING? WITH YOUR MIND-MELD THING?
LOOK, SHITHEAD. WHEN JACKIE SLEEPS, HE WANTS TO SLEEP, YOU KNOW? NO OUTSIDE INTERFERENCE.
HE WHIPS US UP, SETS US OUTSIDE THE DOOR AND CUTS OFF THE MENTAL CONNECTION.
NO CHANCE OF BEING DISTURBED, GET IT?
AH.
GOOD TO KNOW.
SHLUKK

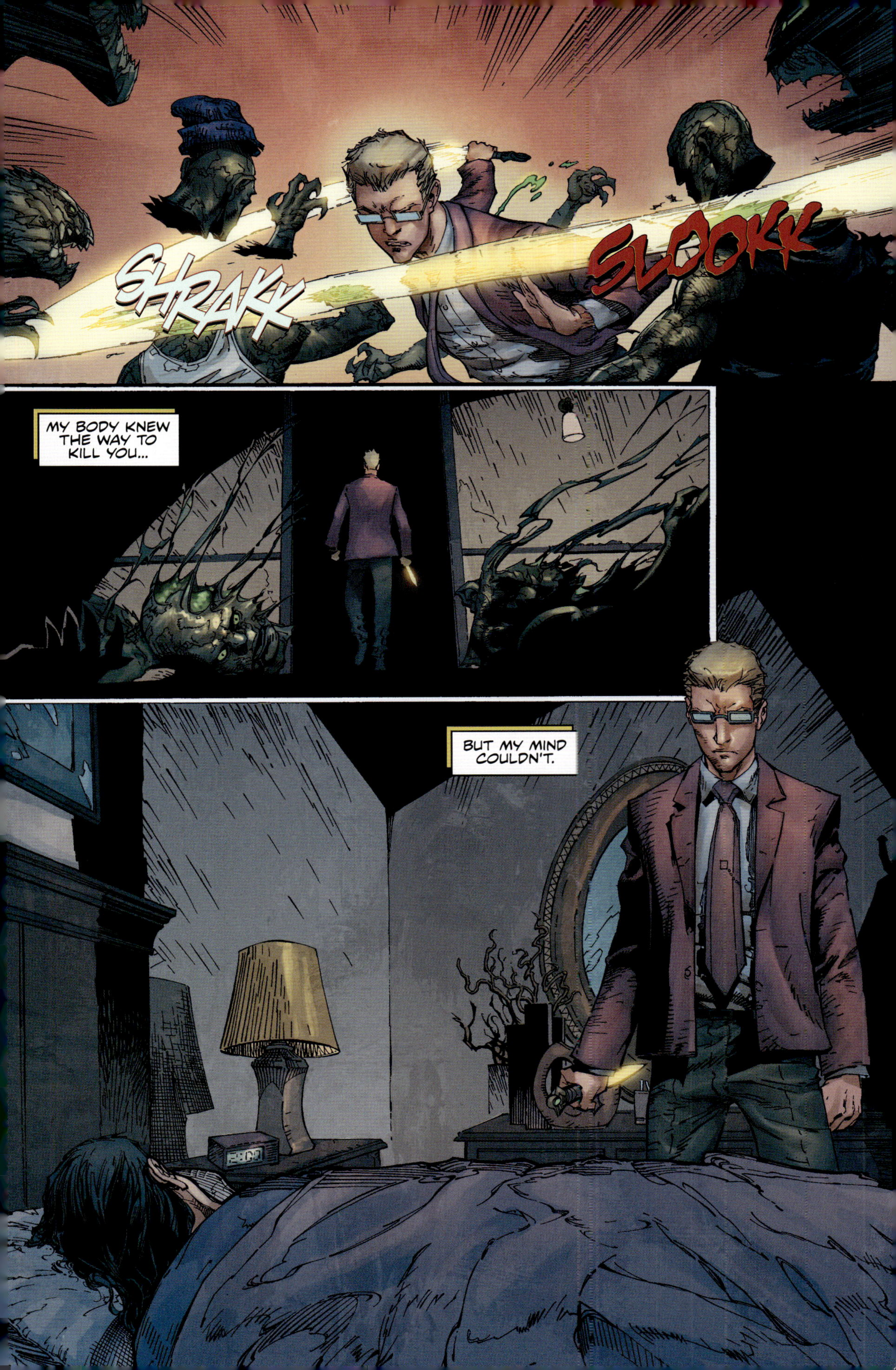
SHRAKK
SLOOKK
MY BODY KNEW THE WAY TO KILL YOU...
BUT MY MIND COULDN'T.

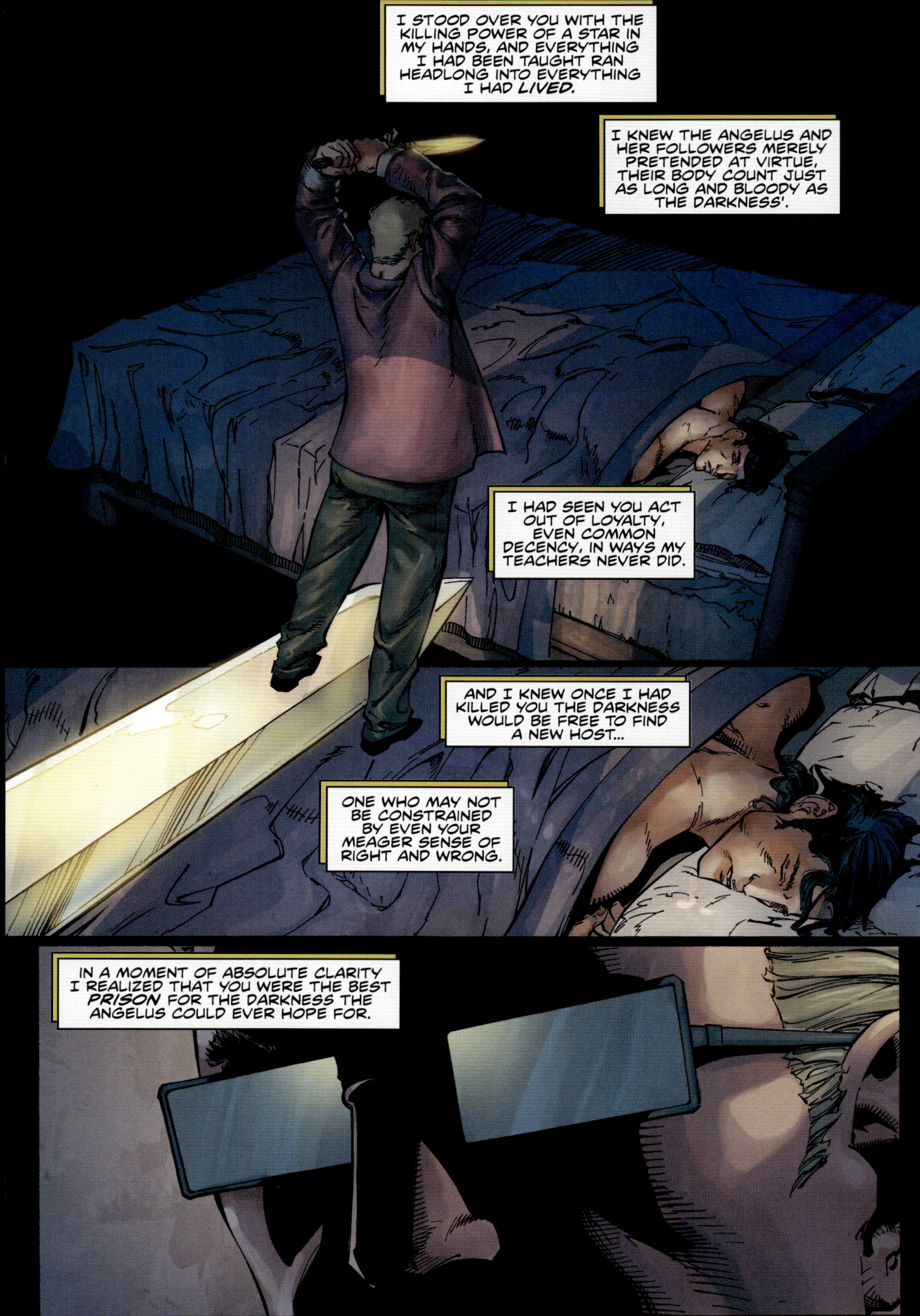
I STOOD OVER YOU WITH THE KILLING POWER OF A STAR IN MY HANDS, AND EVERYTHING I HAD BEEN TAUGHT RAN HEADLONG INTO EVERYTHING I HAD *LIVED*.
I KNEW THE ANGELUS AND HER FOLLOWERS MERELY PRETENDED AT VIRTUE, THEIR BODY COUNT JUST AS LONG AND BLOODY AS THE DARKNESS'.
I HAD SEEN YOU ACT OUT OF LOYALTY, EVEN COMMON DECENCY, IN WAYS MY TEACHERS NEVER DID.
AND I KNEW ONCE I HAD KILLED YOU THE DARKNESS WOULD BE FREE TO FIND A NEW HOST...
ONE WHO MAY NOT BE CONSTRAINED BY EVEN YOUR MEAGER SENSE OF RIGHT AND WRONG.
IN A MOMENT OF ABSOLUTE CLARITY I REALIZED THAT YOU WERE THE BEST *PRISON* FOR THE DARKNESS THE ANGELUS COULD EVER HOPE FOR.

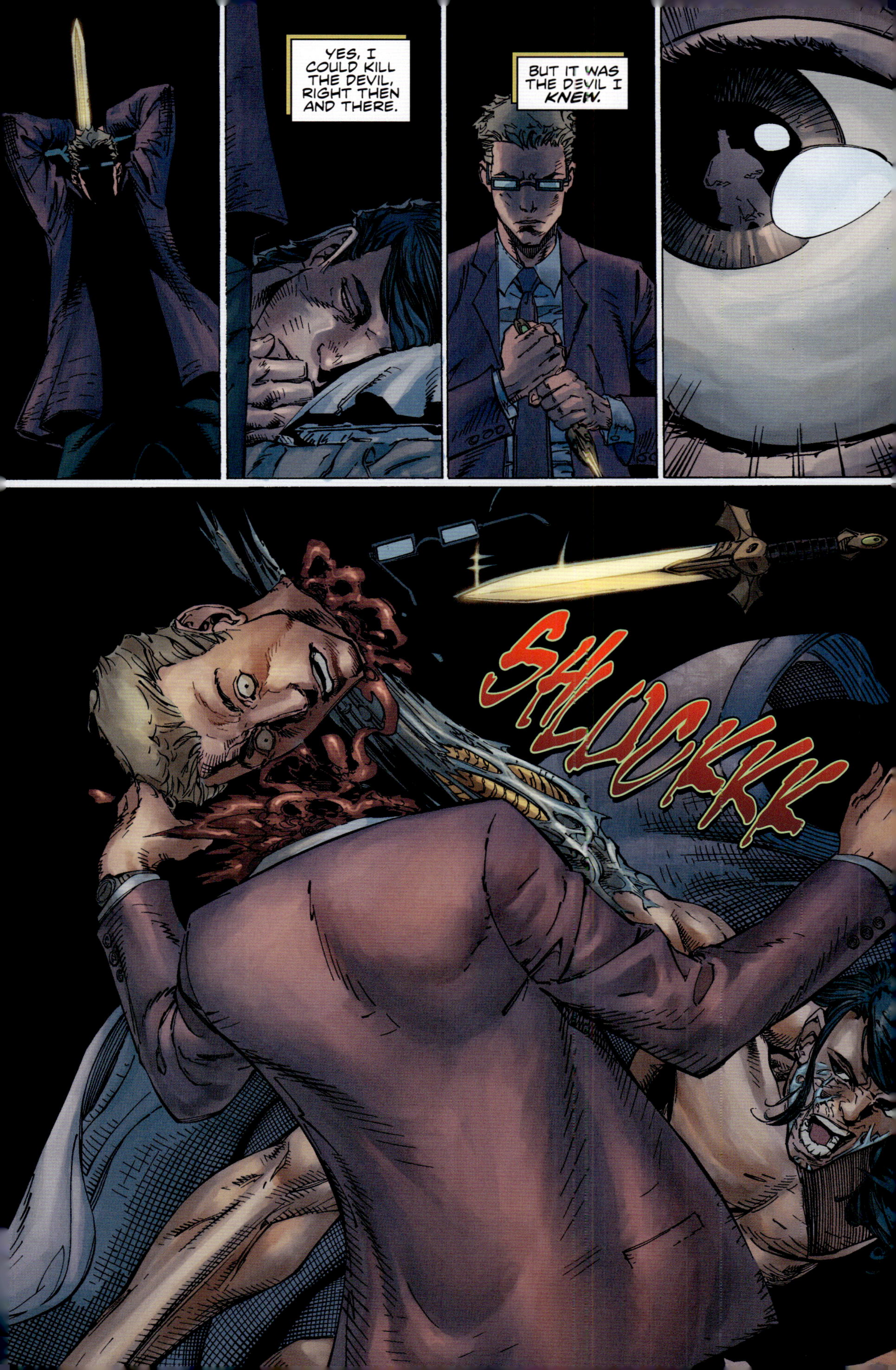
YES, I COULD KILL THE DEVIL, RIGHT THEN AND THERE.
BUT IT WAS THE DEVIL I *KNEW*.
SHLOCKKK

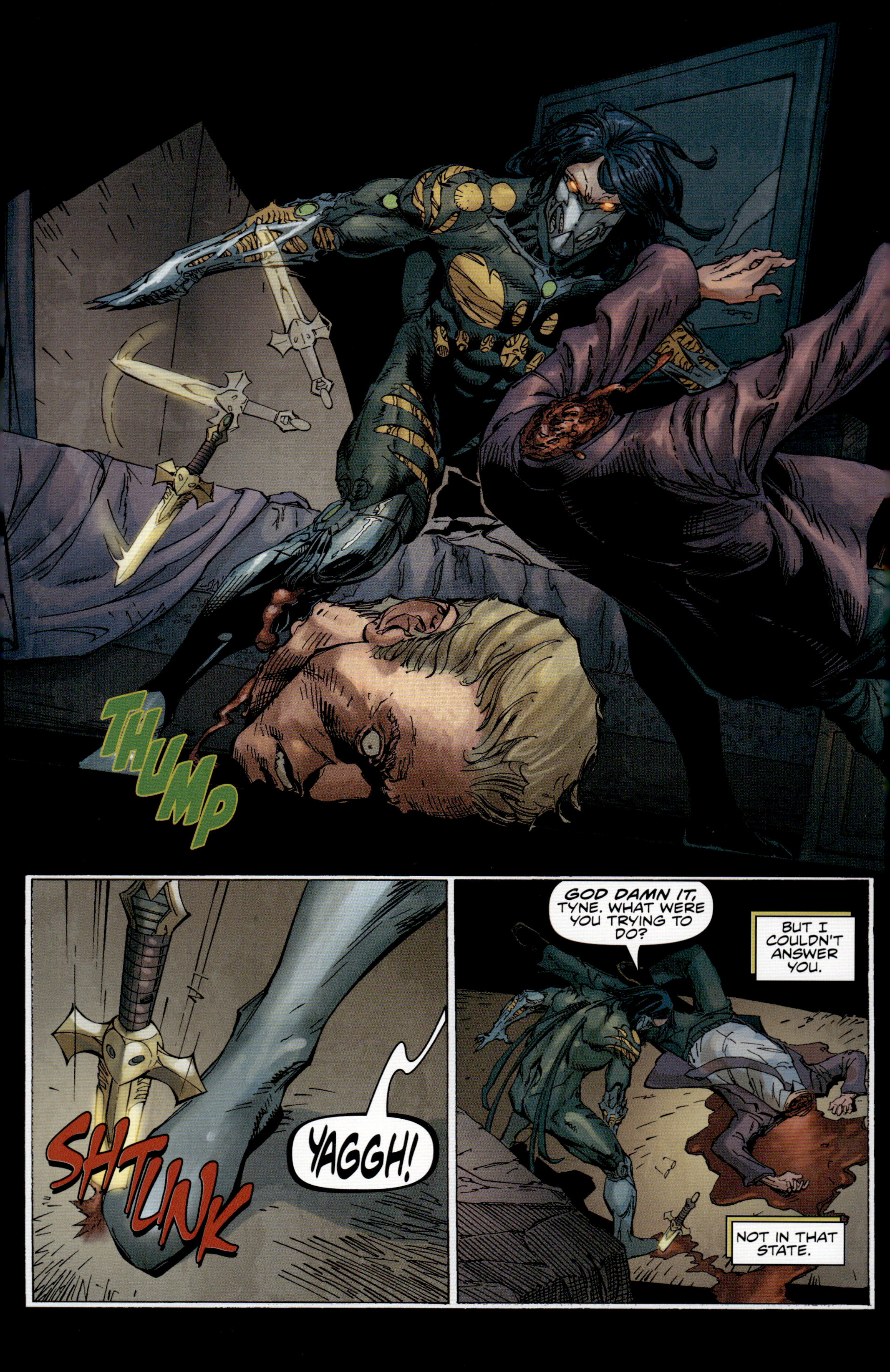
THUMP
SHTUNK
YAGGH!
GOD DAMN IT, TYNE. WHAT WERE YOU TRYING TO DO?
BUT I COULDN'T ANSWER YOU.
NOT IN THAT STATE.

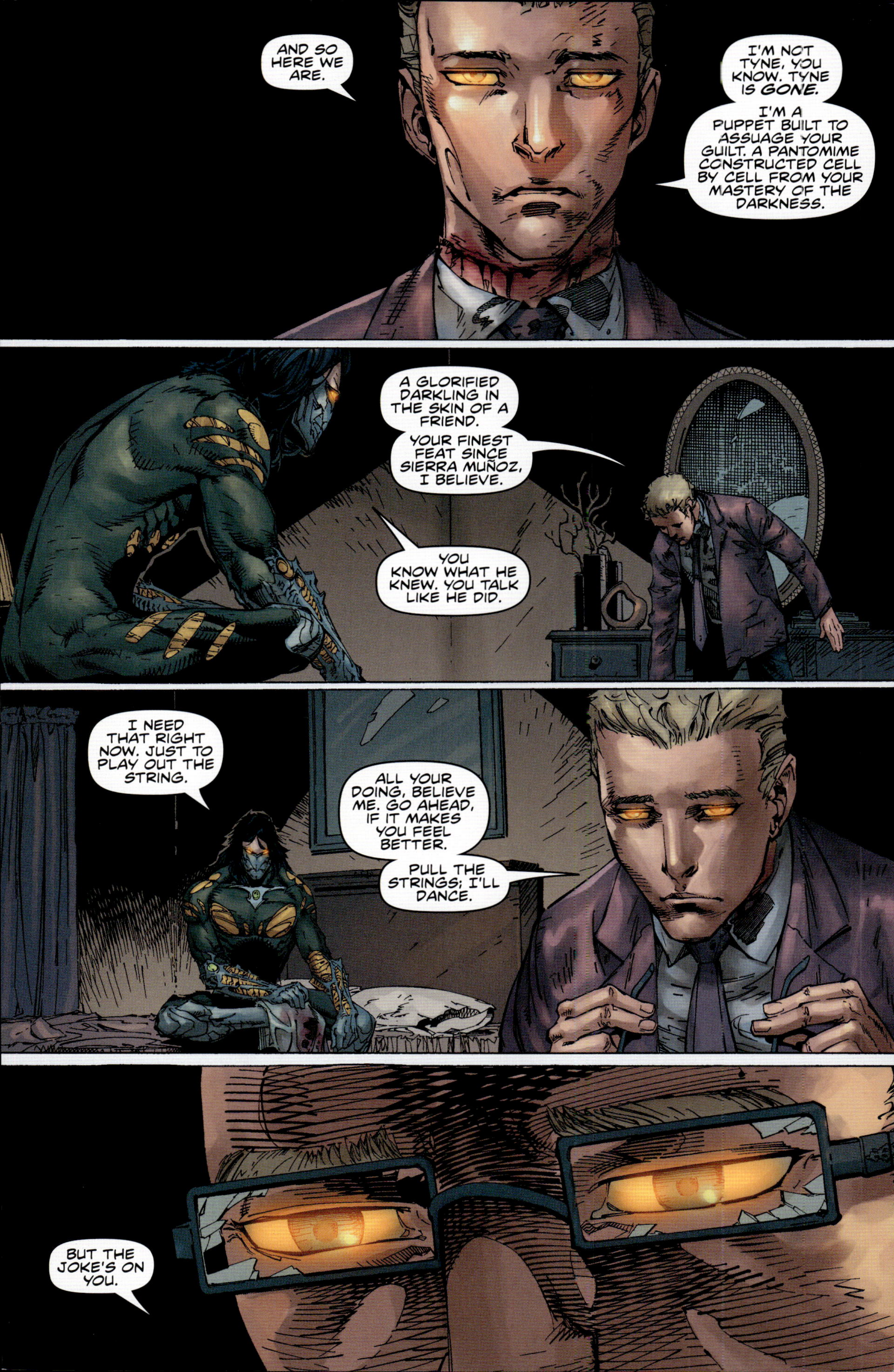
AND SO HERE WE ARE.
I'M NOT TYNE, YOU KNOW. TYNE IS GONE.
I'M A PUPPET BUILT TO ASSUAGE YOUR GUILT. A PANTOMIME CONSTRUCTED CELL BY CELL FROM YOUR MASTERY OF THE DARKNESS.
A GLORIFIED DARKLING IN THE SKIN OF A FRIEND.
YOUR FINEST FEAT SINCE SIERRA MUÑOZ, I BELIEVE.
YOU KNOW WHAT HE KNEW. YOU TALK LIKE HE DID.
I NEED THAT RIGHT NOW. JUST TO PLAY OUT THE STRING.
ALL YOUR DOING, BELIEVE ME. GO AHEAD, IF IT MAKES YOU FEEL BETTER.
PULL THE STRINGS; I'LL DANCE.
BUT THE JOKE'S ON YOU.

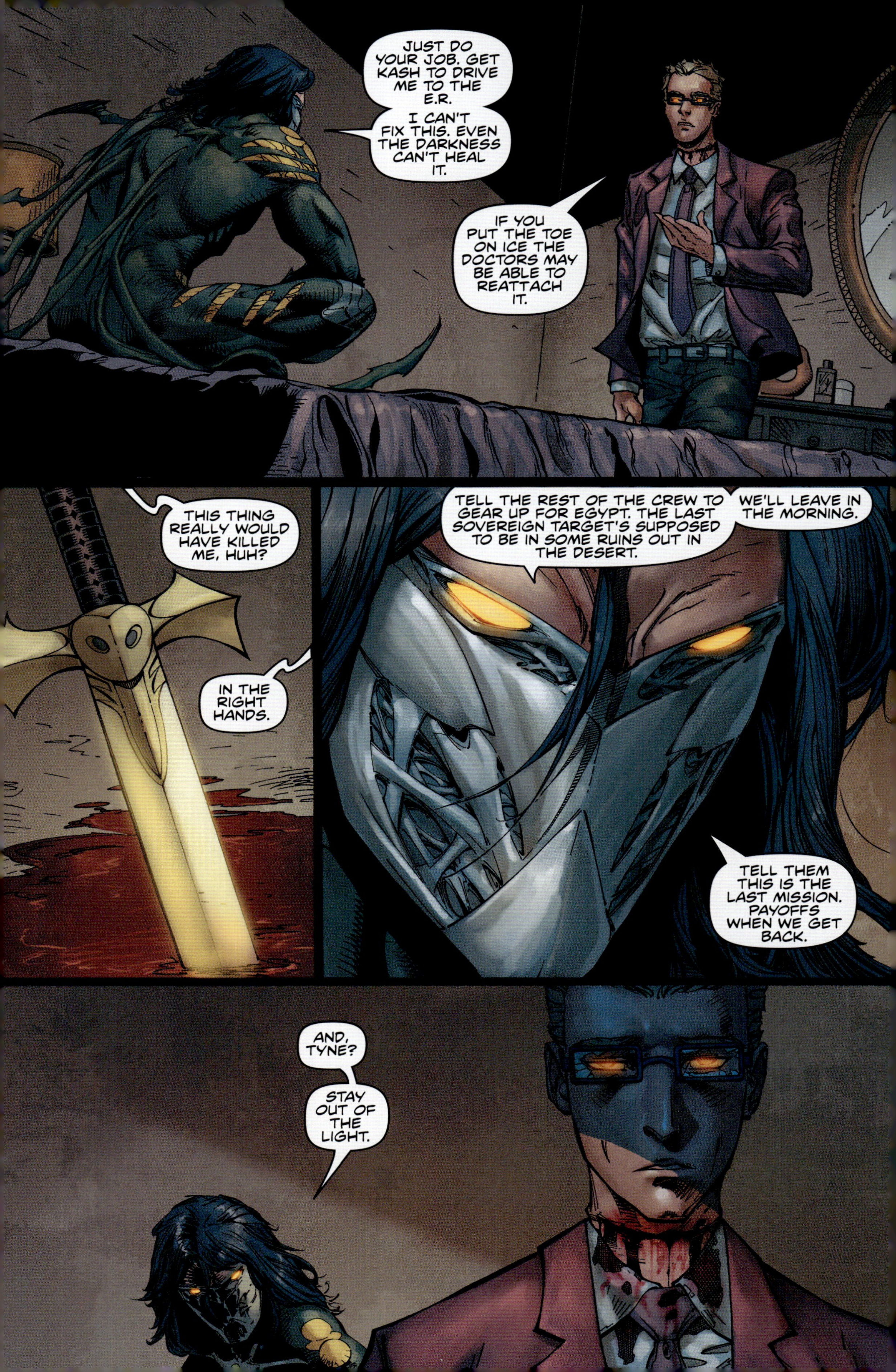
JUST DO YOUR JOB. GET KASH TO DRIVE ME TO THE E.R.
I CAN'T FIX THIS. EVEN THE DARKNESS CAN'T HEAL IT.
IF YOU PUT THE TOE ON ICE THE DOCTORS MAY BE ABLE TO REATTACH IT.
THIS THING REALLY WOULD HAVE KILLED ME, HUH?
IN THE RIGHT HANDS.
TELL THE REST OF THE CREW TO GEAR UP FOR EGYPT. THE LAST SOVEREIGN TARGET'S SUPPOSED TO BE IN SOME RUINS OUT IN THE DESERT.
WE'LL LEAVE IN THE MORNING.
TELL THEM THIS IS THE LAST MISSION. PAYOFFS WHEN WE GET BACK.
AND, TYNE?
STAY OUT OF THE LIGHT.

The Darkness Issue #88
cover art by: Matt Timson

THE DARKNESS #88

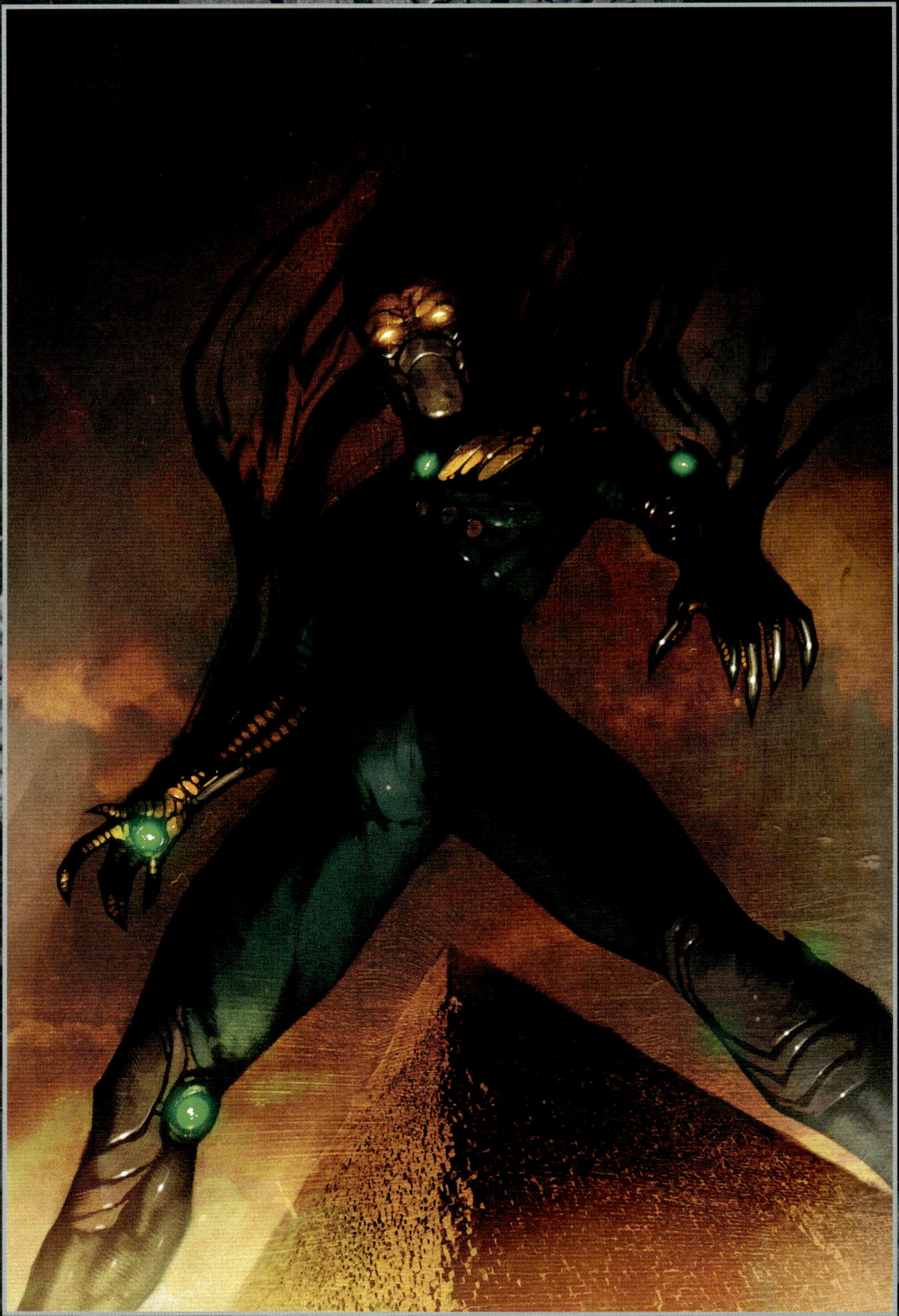

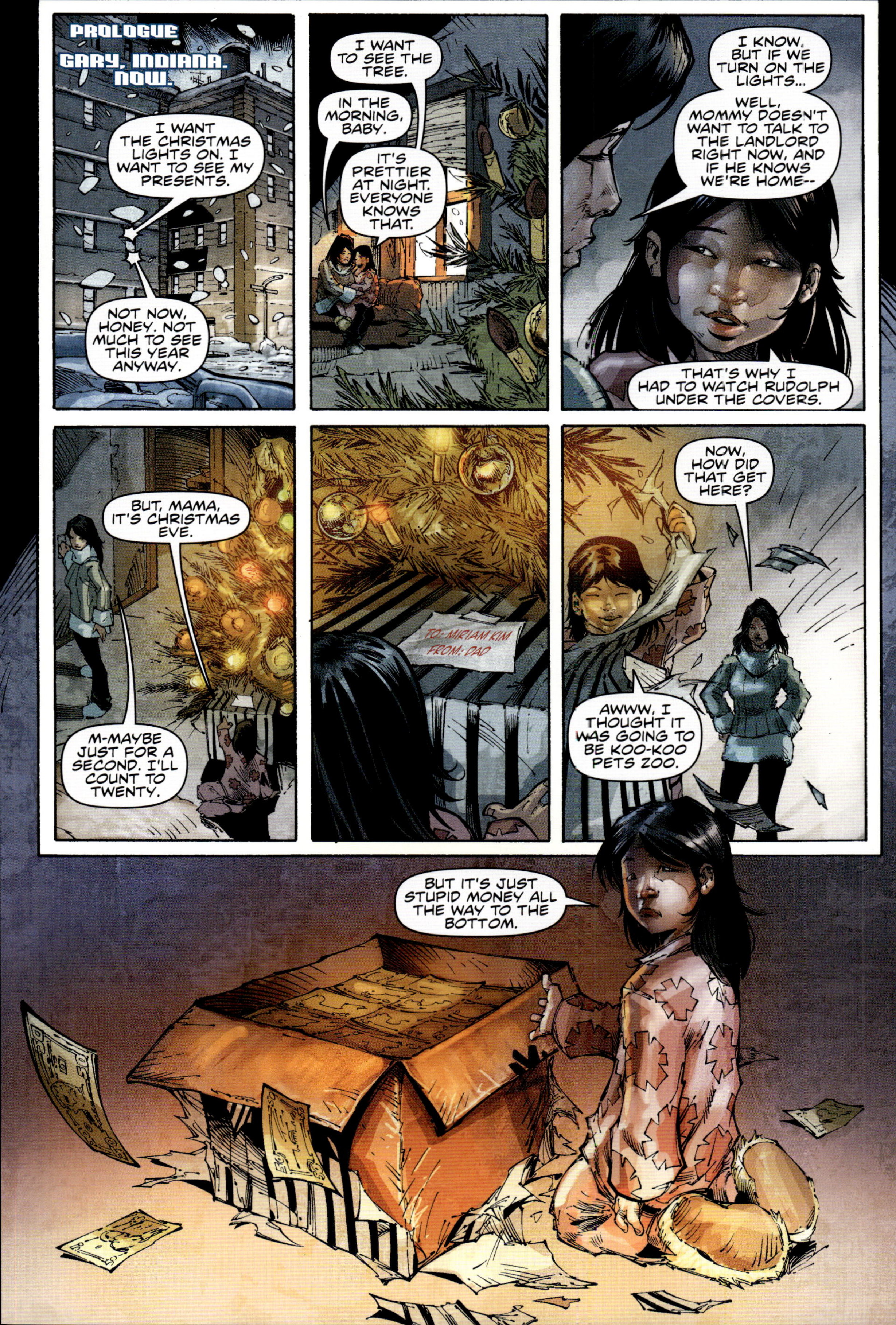
PROLOGUE
GARY, INDIANA. NOW.
I WANT THE CHRISTMAS LIGHTS ON. I WANT TO SEE MY PRESENTS.
NOT NOW, HONEY. NOT MUCH TO SEE THIS YEAR ANYWAY.
I WANT TO SEE THE TREE.
IN THE MORNING, BABY.
IT'S PRETTIER AT NIGHT. EVERYONE KNOWS THAT.
I KNOW. BUT IF WE TURN ON THE LIGHTS...
WELL, MOMMY DOESN'T WANT TO TALK TO THE LANDLORD RIGHT NOW, AND IF HE KNOWS WE'RE HOME--
THAT'S WHY I HAD TO WATCH RUDOLPH UNDER THE COVERS.
BUT, MAMA, IT'S CHRISTMAS EVE.
M-MAYBE JUST FOR A SECOND. I'LL COUNT TO TWENTY.
TO: MIRIAM KIM
FROM: DAD
NOW, HOW DID THAT GET HERE?
AWWW, I THOUGHT IT WAS GOING TO BE KOO-KOO PETS ZOO.
BUT IT'S JUST STUPID MONEY ALL THE WAY TO THE BOTTOM.

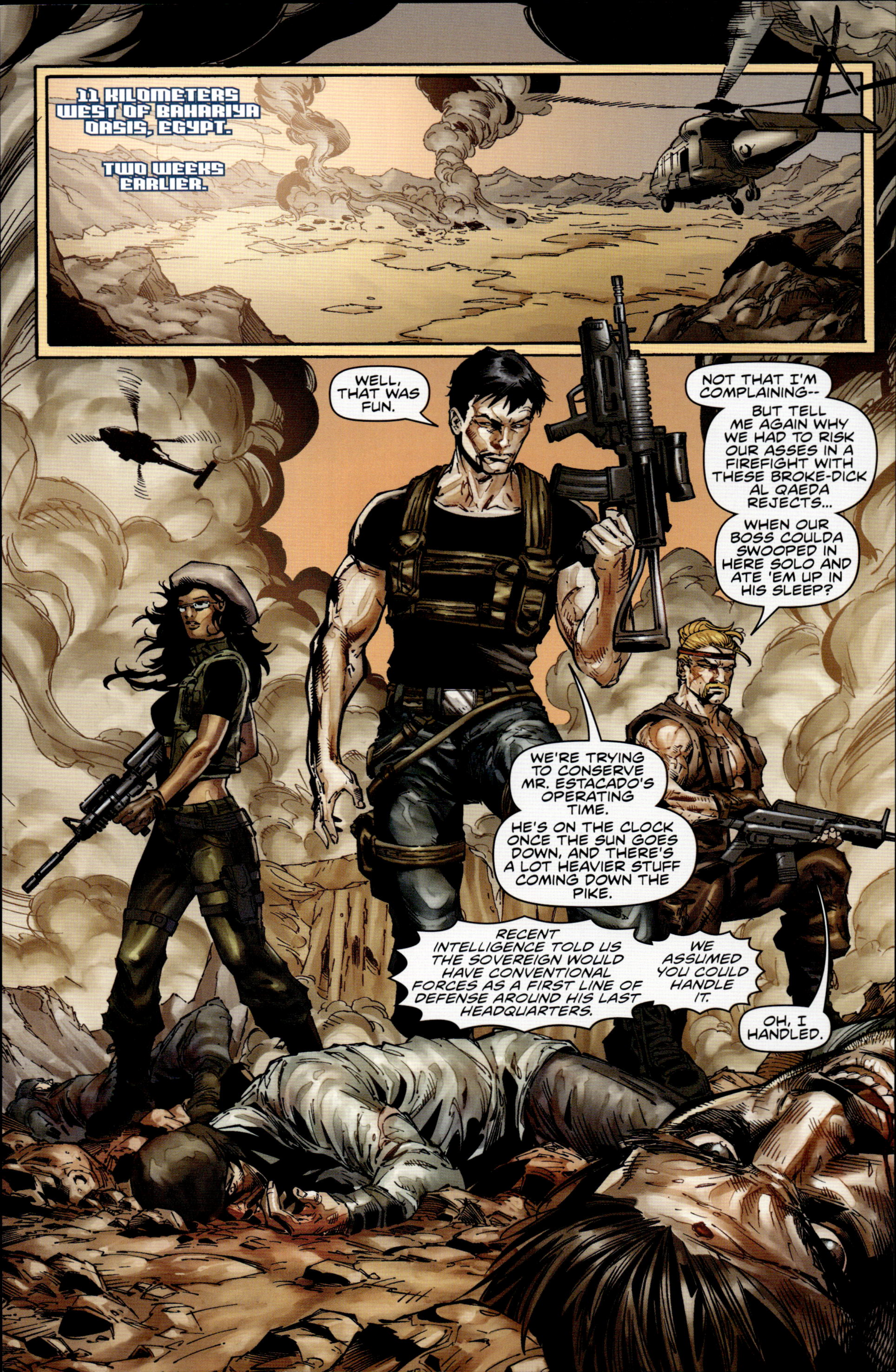
11 KILOMETERS WEST OF BAHARIYA OASIS, EGYPT.
TWO WEEKS EARLIER.
WELL, THAT WAS FUN.
NOT THAT I'M COMPLAINING--
BUT TELL ME AGAIN WHY WE HAD TO RISK OUR ASSES IN A FIREFIGHT WITH THESE BROKE-DICK AL QAEDA REJECTS...
WHEN OUR BOSS COULDA SWOOPED IN HERE SOLO AND ATE 'EM UP IN HIS SLEEP?
WE'RE TRYING TO CONSERVE MR. ESTACADO'S OPERATING TIME.
HE'S ON THE CLOCK ONCE THE SUN GOES DOWN, AND THERE'S A LOT HEAVIER STUFF COMING DOWN THE PIKE.
RECENT INTELLIGENCE TOLD US THE SOVEREIGN WOULD HAVE CONVENTIONAL FORCES AS A FIRST LINE OF DEFENSE AROUND HIS LAST HEADQUARTERS.
WE ASSUMED YOU COULD HANDLE IT.
OH, I HANDLED.

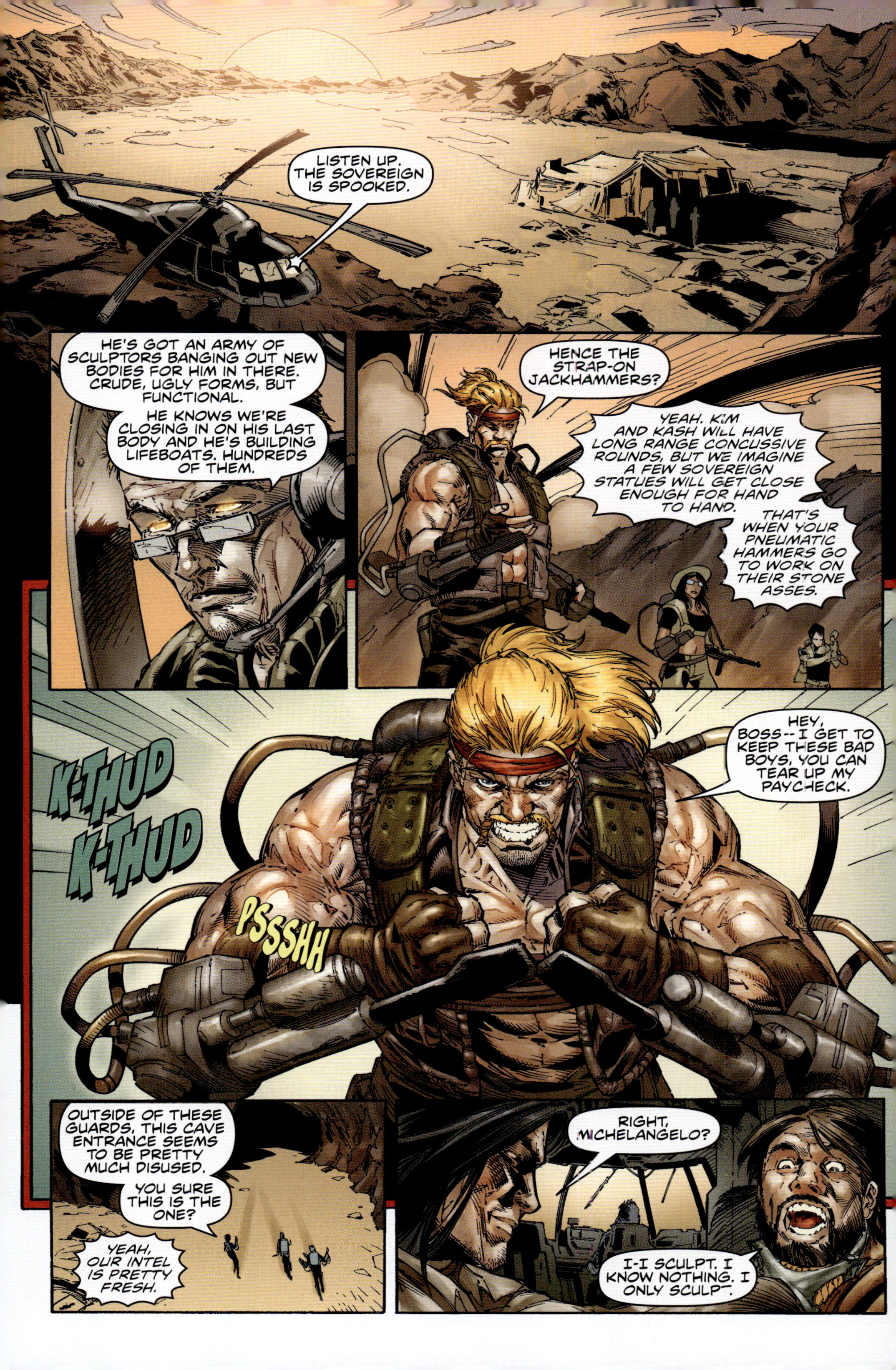
LISTEN UP. THE SOVEREIGN IS SPOOKED.
HE'S GOT AN ARMY OF SCULPTORS BANGING OUT NEW BODIES FOR HIM IN THERE. CRUDE, UGLY FORMS, BUT FUNCTIONAL.
HE KNOWS WE'RE CLOSING IN ON HIS LAST BODY AND HE'S BUILDING LIFEBOATS. HUNDREDS OF THEM.
HENCE THE STRAP-ON JACKHAMMERS?
YEAH. KIM AND KASH WILL HAVE LONG RANGE CONCUSSIVE ROUNDS, BUT WE IMAGINE A FEW SOVEREIGN STATUES WILL GET CLOSE ENOUGH FOR HAND TO HAND.
THAT'S WHEN YOUR PNEUMATIC HAMMERS GO TO WORK ON THEIR STONE ASSES.
K-THUD
K-THUD
PSSSHH
HEY, BOSS--I GET TO KEEP THESE BAD BOYS, YOU CAN TEAR UP MY PAYCHECK.
OUTSIDE OF THESE GUARDS, THIS CAVE ENTRANCE SEEMS TO BE PRETTY MUCH DISUSED.
YOU SURE THIS IS THE ONE?
YEAH, OUR INTEL IS PRETTY FRESH.
RIGHT, MICHELANGELO?
I-I SCULPT. I KNOW NOTHING. I ONLY SCULPT.

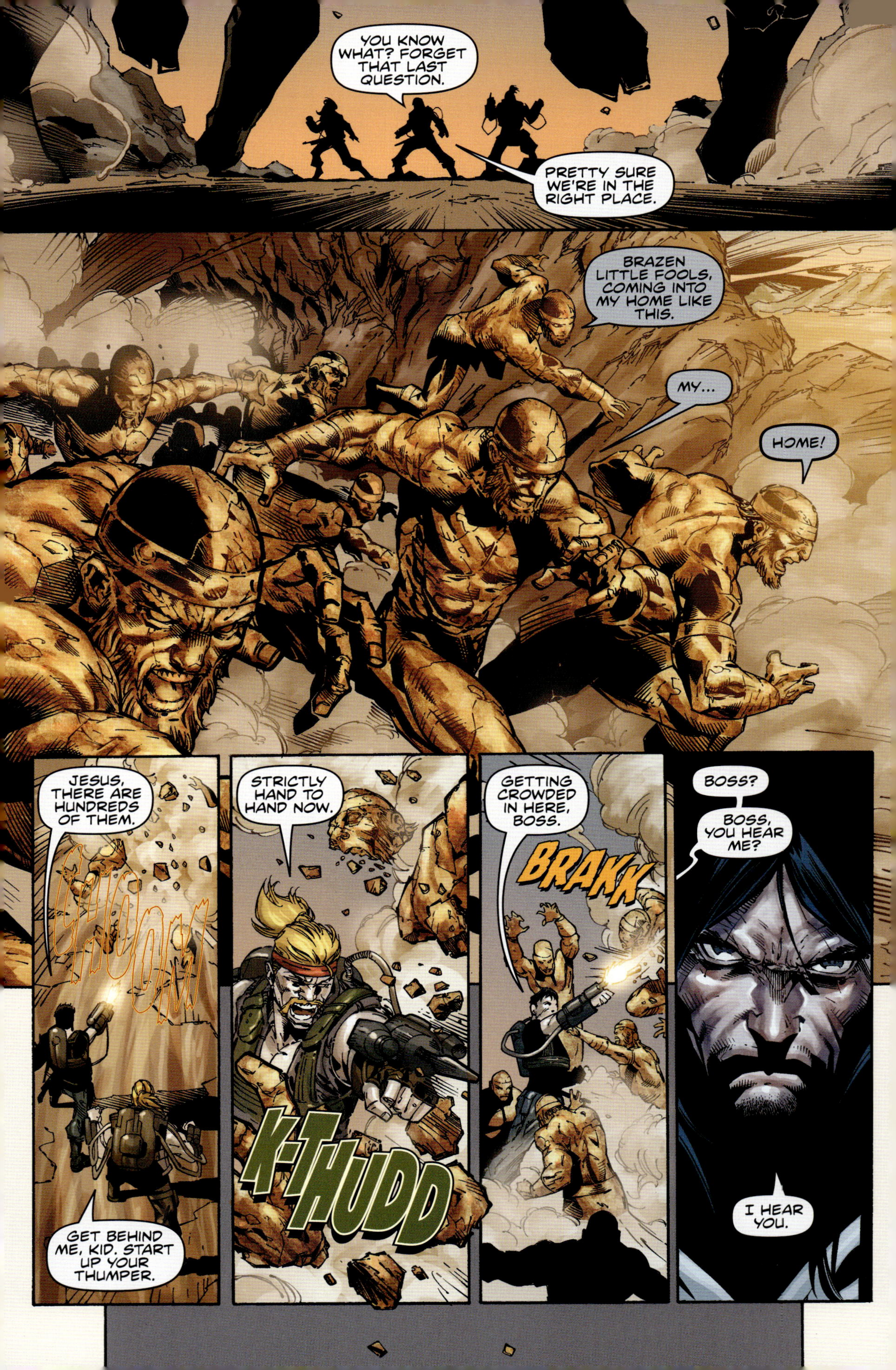
YOU KNOW WHAT? FORGET THAT LAST QUESTION.
PRETTY SURE WE'RE IN THE RIGHT PLACE.
BRAZEN LITTLE FOOLS, COMING INTO MY HOME LIKE THIS.
MY...
HOME!
JESUS, THERE ARE HUNDREDS OF THEM.
GET BEHIND ME, KID. START UP YOUR THUMPER.
STRICTLY HAND TO HAND NOW.
K-THUDD
GETTING CROWDED IN HERE, BOSS.
BRAKK
BOSS?
BOSS, YOU HEAR ME?
I HEAR YOU.

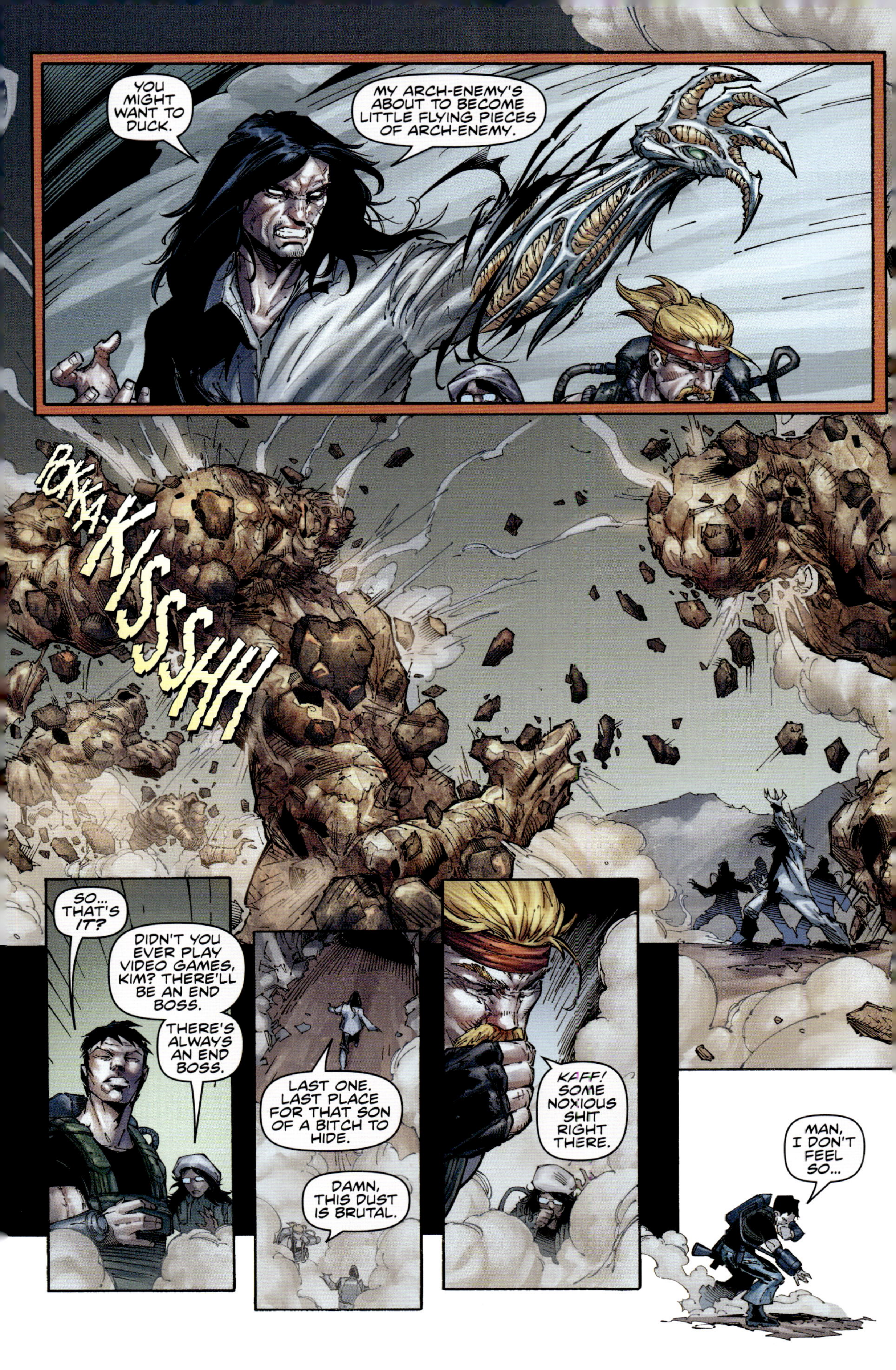
YOU MIGHT WANT TO DUCK.
MY ARCH-ENEMY'S ABOUT TO BECOME LITTLE FLYING PIECES OF ARCH-ENEMY.
POKKA-KISSSHH
SO... THAT'S IT?
DIDN'T YOU EVER PLAY VIDEO GAMES, KIM? THERE'LL BE AN END BOSS.
THERE'S ALWAYS AN END BOSS.
LAST ONE. LAST PLACE FOR THAT SON OF A BITCH TO HIDE.
DAMN, THIS DUST IS BRUTAL.
KAFF! SOME NOXIOUS SHIT RIGHT THERE.
MAN, I DON'T FEEL SO...

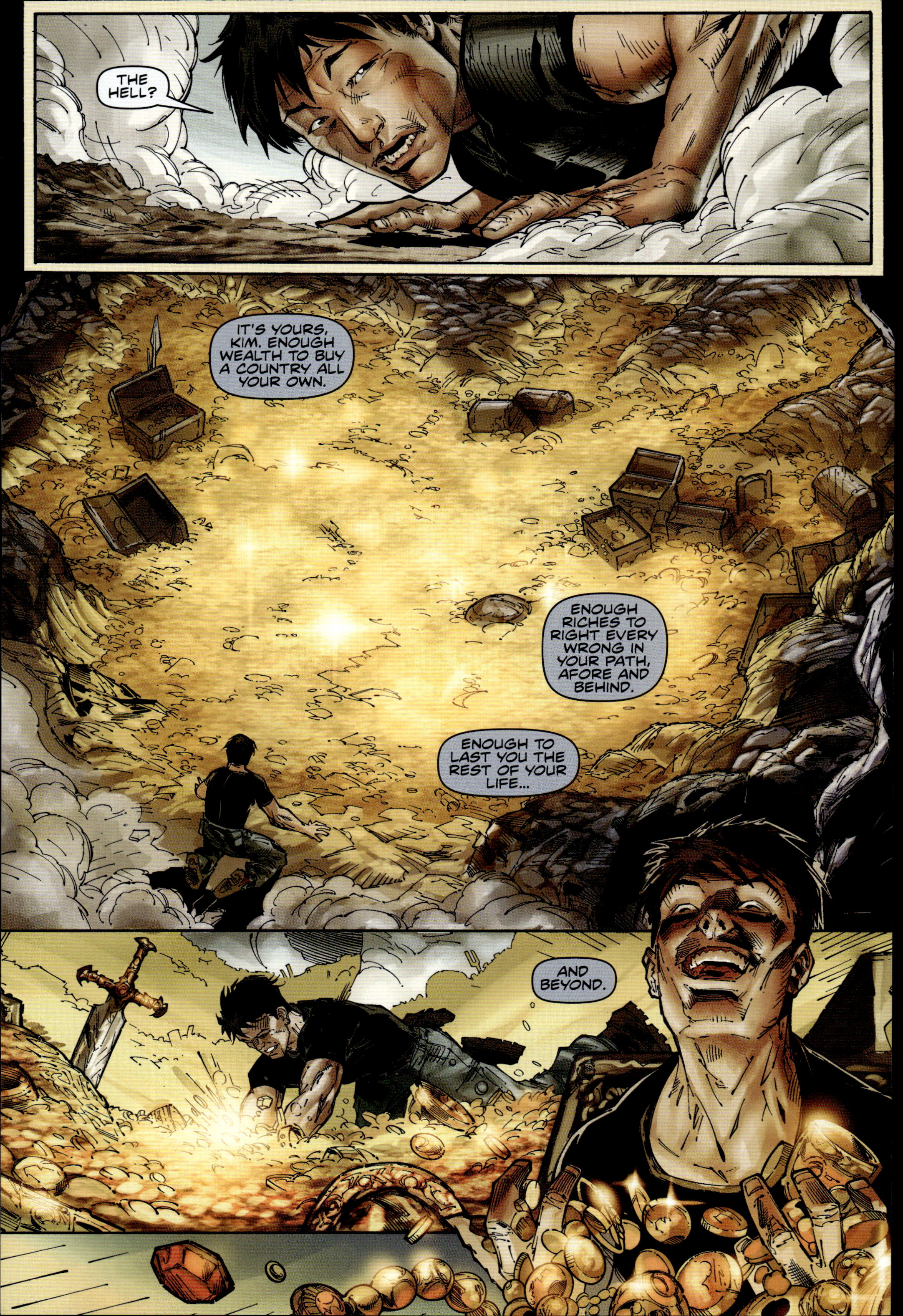
THE HELL?
IT'S YOURS, KIM. ENOUGH WEALTH TO BUY A COUNTRY ALL YOUR OWN.
ENOUGH RICHES TO RIGHT EVERY WRONG IN YOUR PATH, AFORE AND BEHIND.
ENOUGH TO LAST YOU THE REST OF YOUR LIFE...
AND BEYOND.

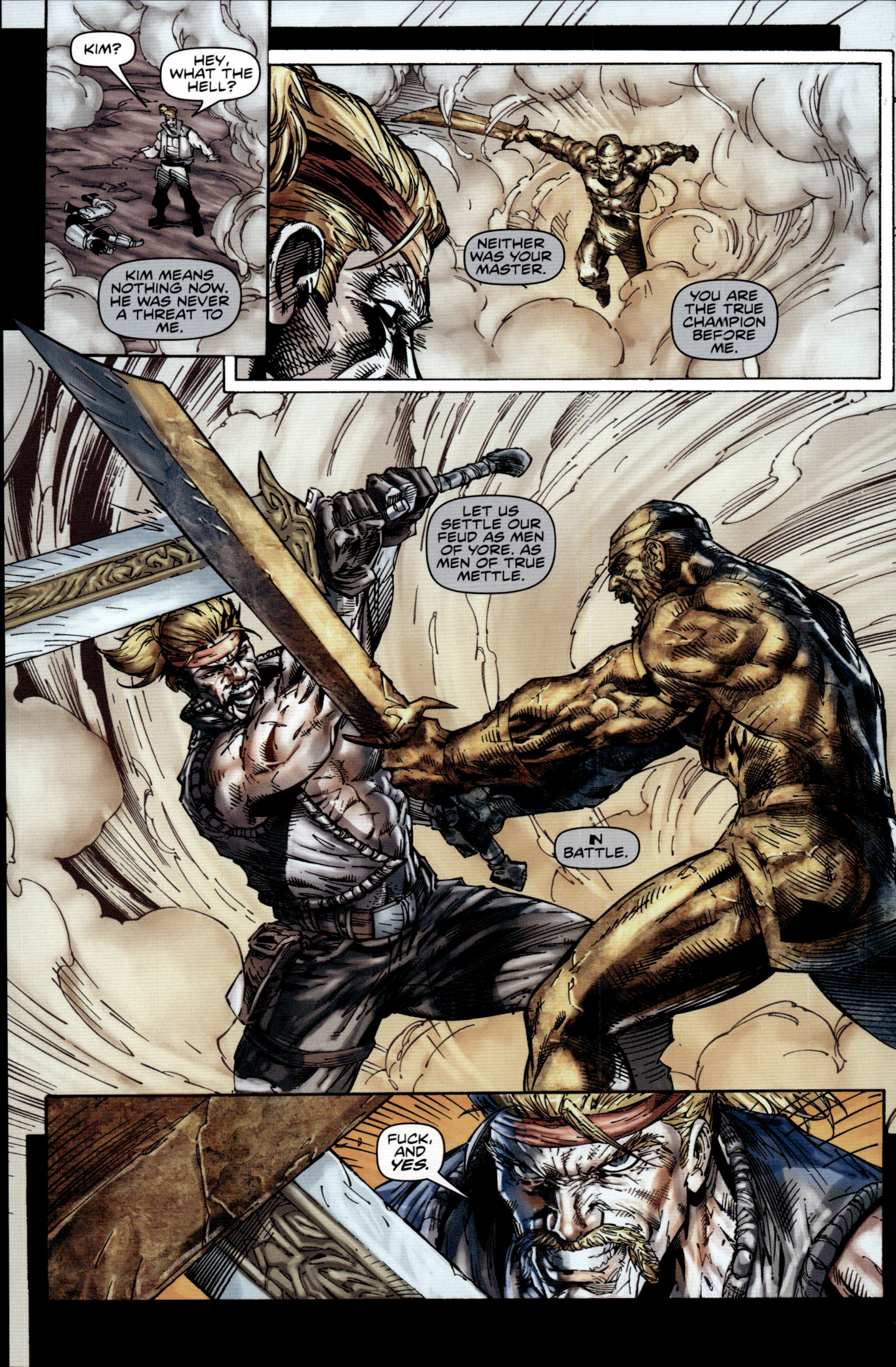
KIM?
HEY, WHAT THE HELL?
KIM MEANS NOTHING NOW. HE WAS NEVER A THREAT TO ME.
NEITHER WAS YOUR MASTER.
YOU ARE THE TRUE CHAMPION BEFORE ME.
LET US SETTLE OUR FEUD AS MEN OF YORE. AS MEN OF TRUE METTLE.
IN BATTLE.
FUCK, AND YES.

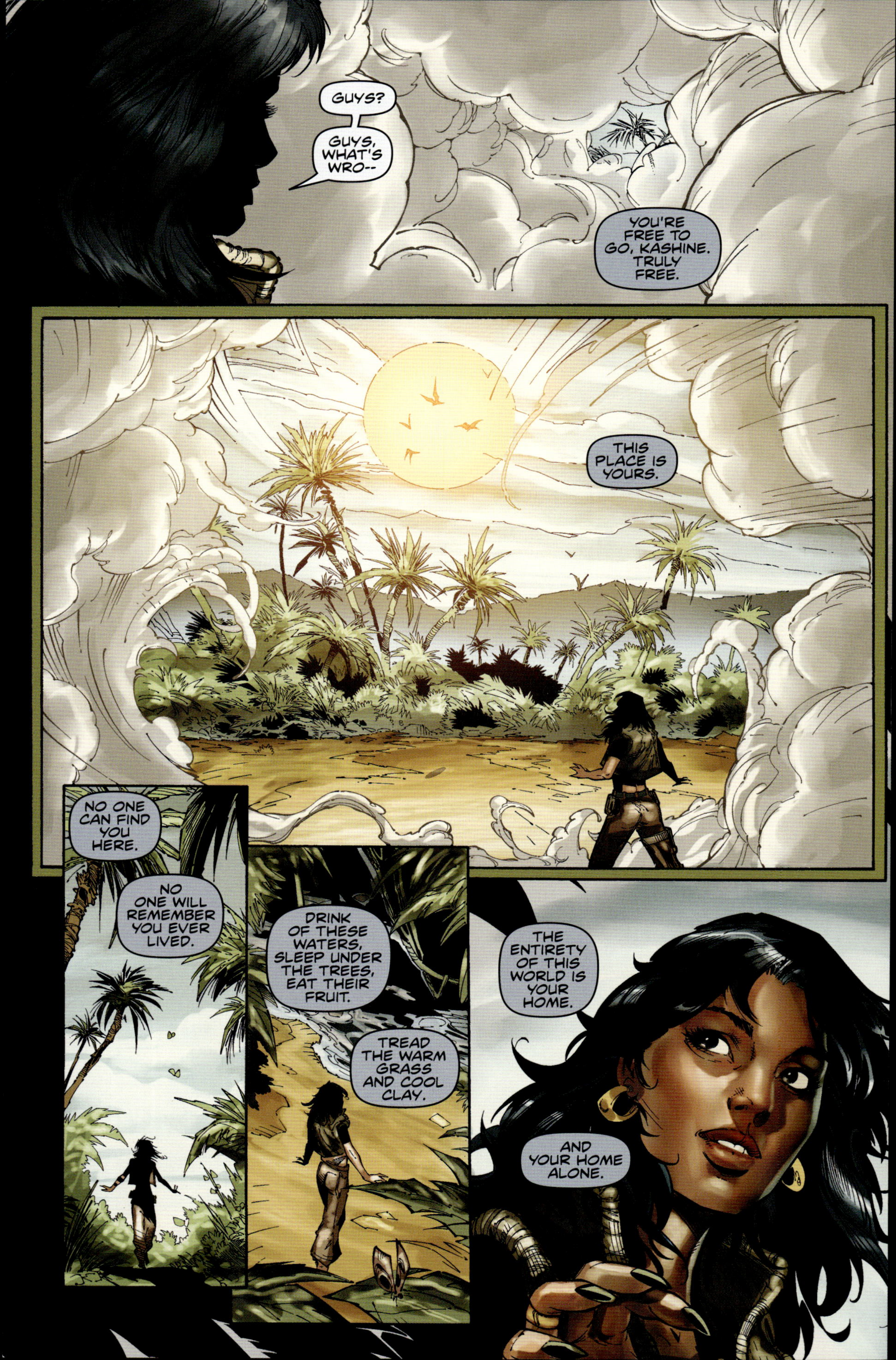
GUYS?
GUYS, WHAT'S WRO--
YOU'RE FREE TO GO, KASHINE. TRULY FREE.
THIS PLACE IS YOURS.
NO ONE CAN FIND YOU HERE.
NO ONE WILL REMEMBER YOU EVER LIVED.
DRINK OF THESE WATERS, SLEEP UNDER THE TREES, EAT THEIR FRUIT.
TREAD THE WARM GRASS AND COOL CLAY.
THE ENTIRETY OF THIS WORLD IS YOUR HOME.
AND YOUR HOME ALONE.

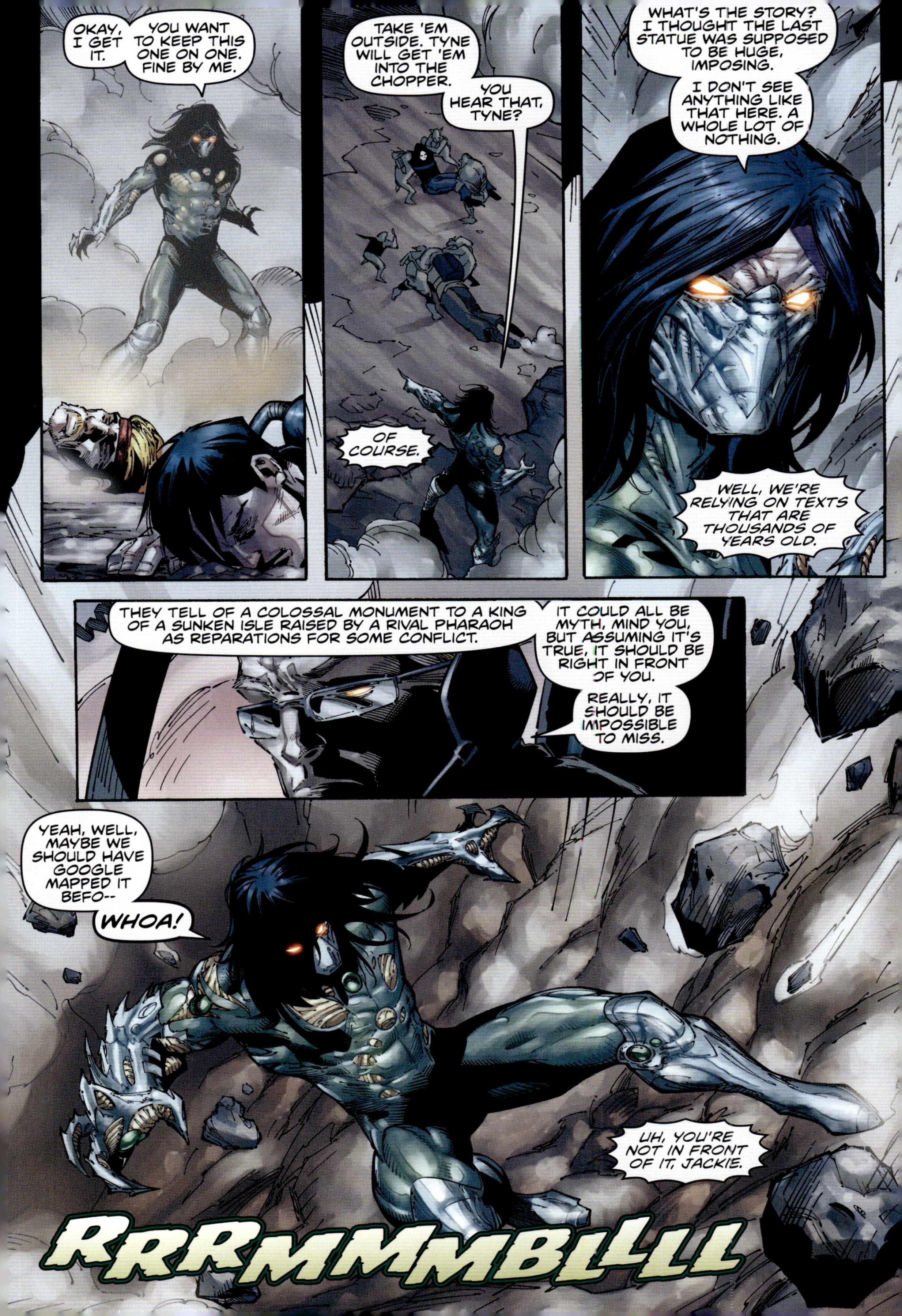
OKAY, I GET IT.
YOU WANT TO KEEP THIS ONE ON ONE. FINE BY ME.
TAKE 'EM OUTSIDE. TYNE WILL GET 'EM INTO THE CHOPPER.
YOU HEAR THAT, TYNE?
OF COURSE.
WHAT'S THE STORY? I THOUGHT THE LAST STATUE WAS SUPPOSED TO BE HUGE, IMPOSING.
I DON'T SEE ANYTHING LIKE THAT HERE. A WHOLE LOT OF NOTHING.
WELL, WE'RE RELYING ON TEXTS THAT ARE THOUSANDS OF YEARS OLD.
THEY TELL OF A COLOSSAL MONUMENT TO A KING OF A SUNKEN ISLE RAISED BY A RIVAL PHARAOH AS REPARATIONS FOR SOME CONFLICT.
IT COULD ALL BE MYTH, MIND YOU, BUT ASSUMING IT'S TRUE, IT SHOULD BE RIGHT IN FRONT OF YOU.
REALLY, IT SHOULD BE IMPOSSIBLE TO MISS.
YEAH, WELL, MAYBE WE SHOULD HAVE GOOGLE MAPPED IT BEFO--
WHOA!
UH, YOU'RE NOT IN FRONT OF IT, JACKIE.
RRRMMMBLLLL

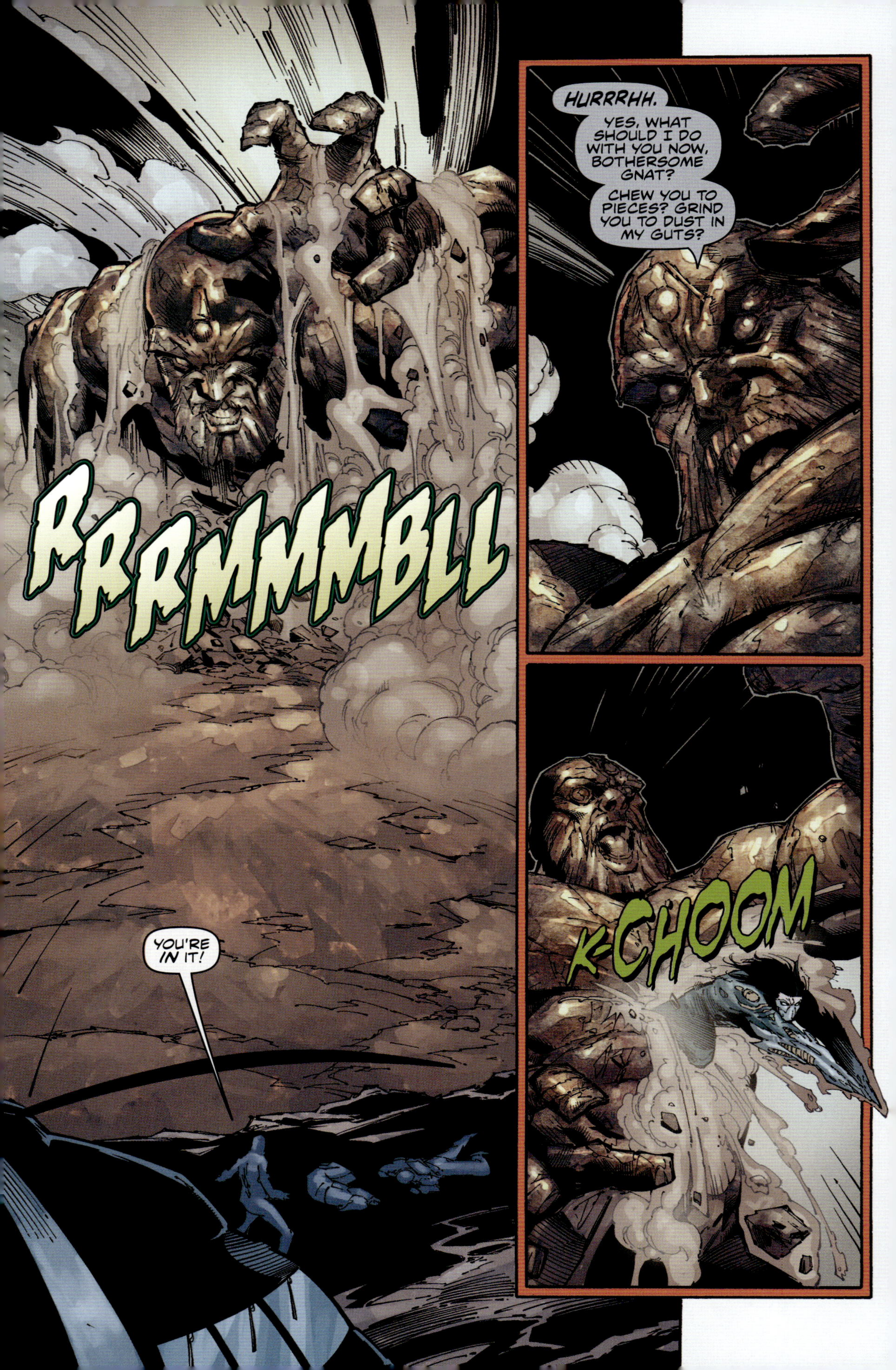
RRMMMBLL
YOU'RE IN IT!
HURRRHH.
YES, WHAT SHOULD I DO WITH YOU NOW, BOTHERSOME GNAT?
CHEW YOU TO PIECES? GRIND YOU TO DUST IN MY GUTS?
K-CHOOM

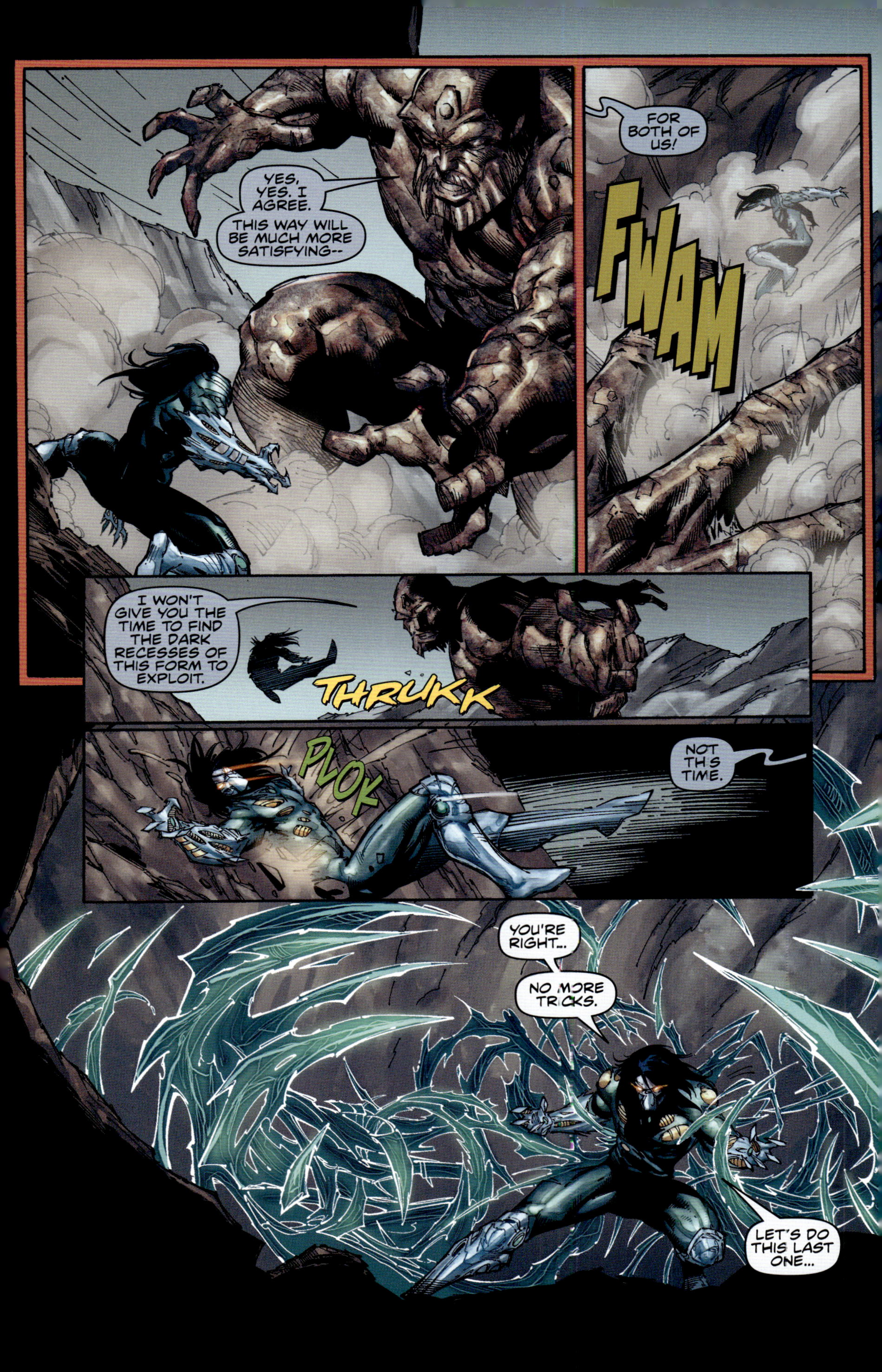
YES, YES. I AGREE.
THIS WAY WILL BE MUCH MORE SATISFYING--
FOR BOTH OF US!
FWAM
I WON'T GIVE YOU THE TIME TO FIND THE DARK RECESSES OF THIS FORM TO EXPLOIT.
THRUKK
PLOK
NOT THIS TIME.
YOU'RE RIGHT...
NO MORE TRICKS.
LET'S DO THIS LAST ONE...

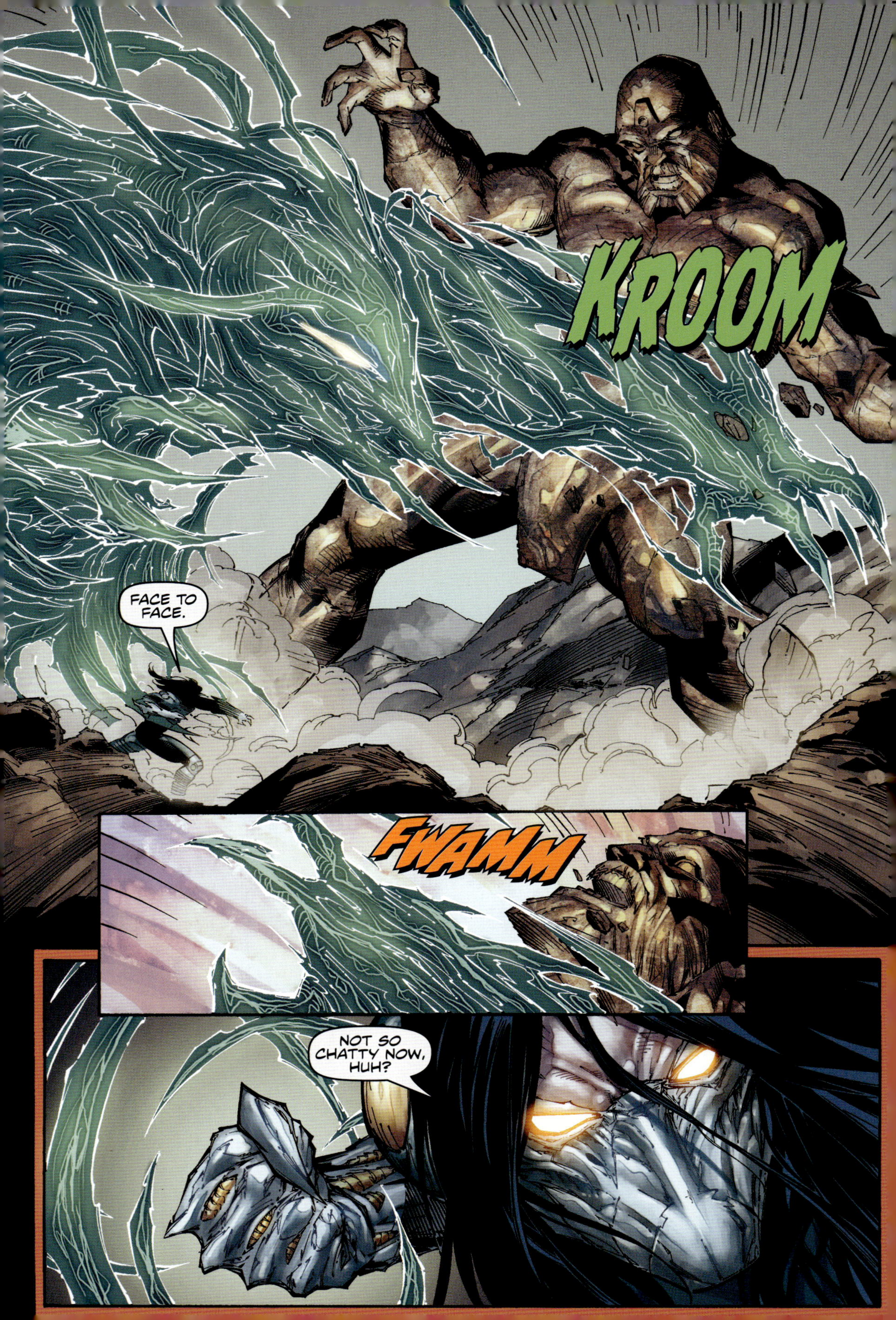
KROOM
FACE TO FACE.
FWAMM
NOT SO CHATTY NOW, HUH?

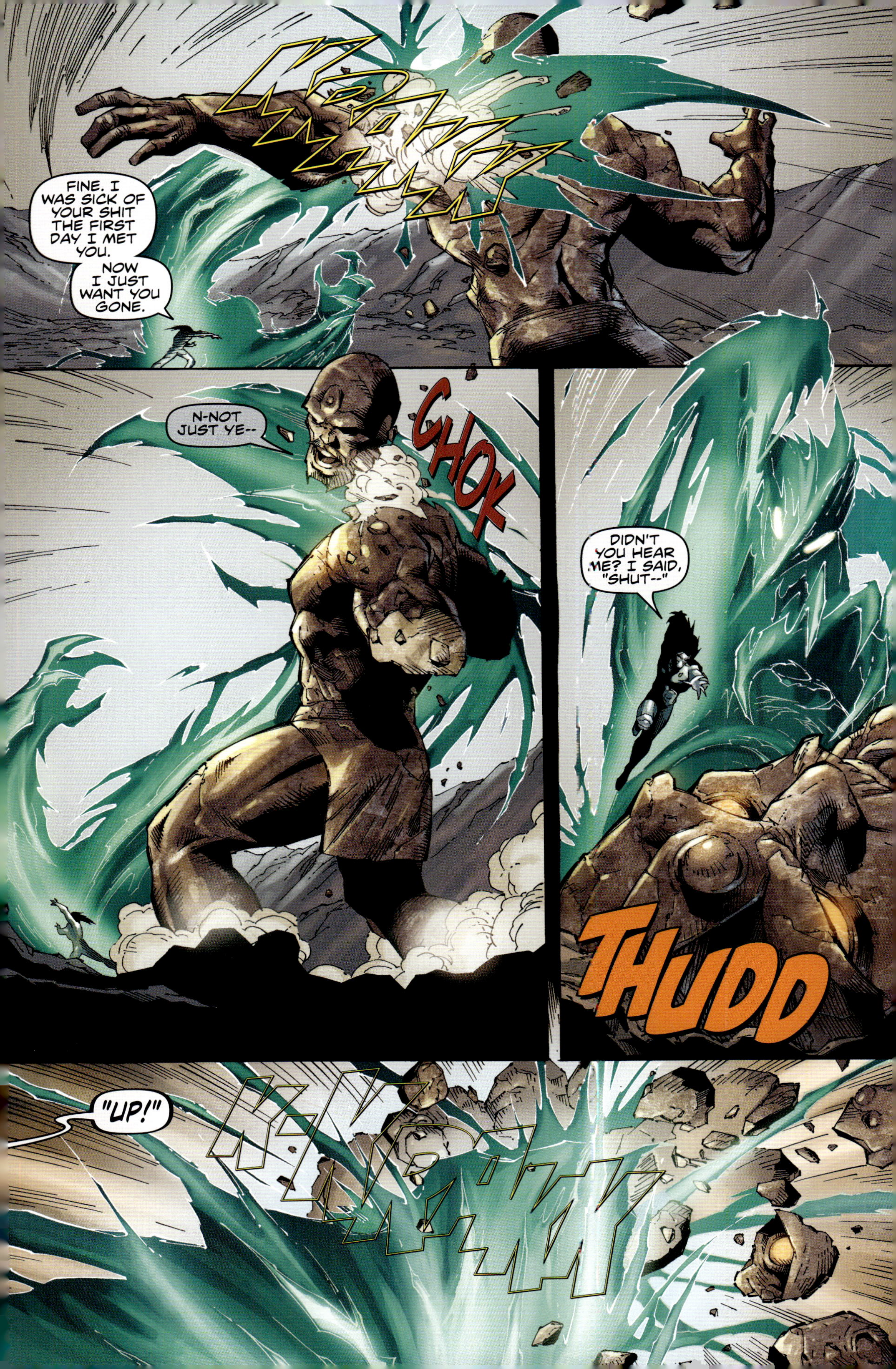
FINE. I WAS SICK OF YOUR SHIT THE FIRST DAY I MET YOU.
NOW I JUST WANT YOU GONE.
N-NOT JUST YE--
CHOK
DIDN'T YOU HEAR ME? I SAID, "SHUT--"
THUDD
"UP!"

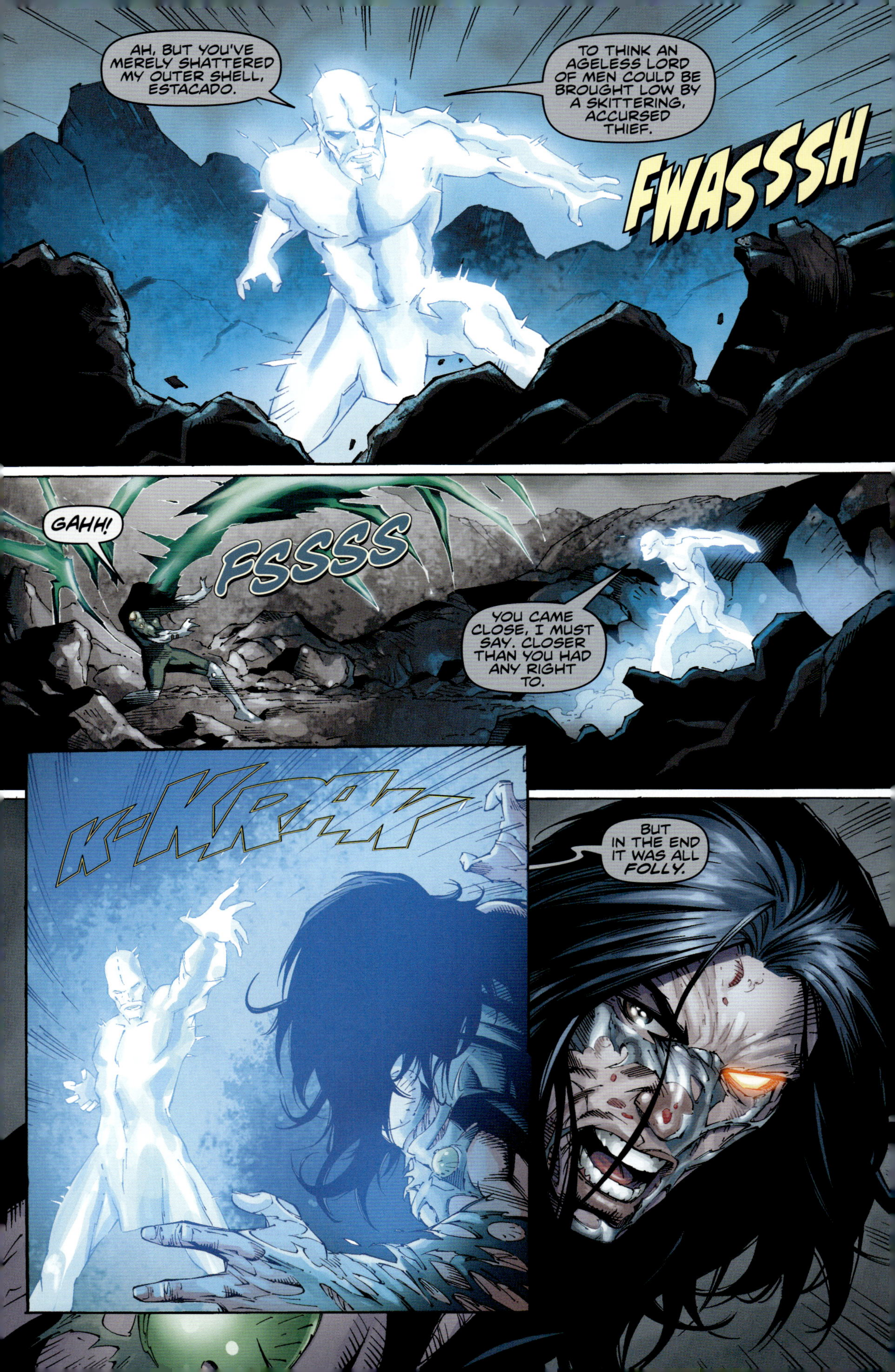
AH, BUT YOU'VE MERELY SHATTERED MY OUTER SHELL, ESTACADO.
TO THINK AN AGELESS LORD OF MEN COULD BE BROUGHT LOW BY A SKITTERING, ACCURSED THIEF.
FWASSSH
GAHH!
FSSSS
YOU CAME CLOSE, I MUST SAY. CLOSER THAN YOU HAD ANY RIGHT TO.
K-MRAK
BUT IN THE END IT WAS ALL FOLLY.

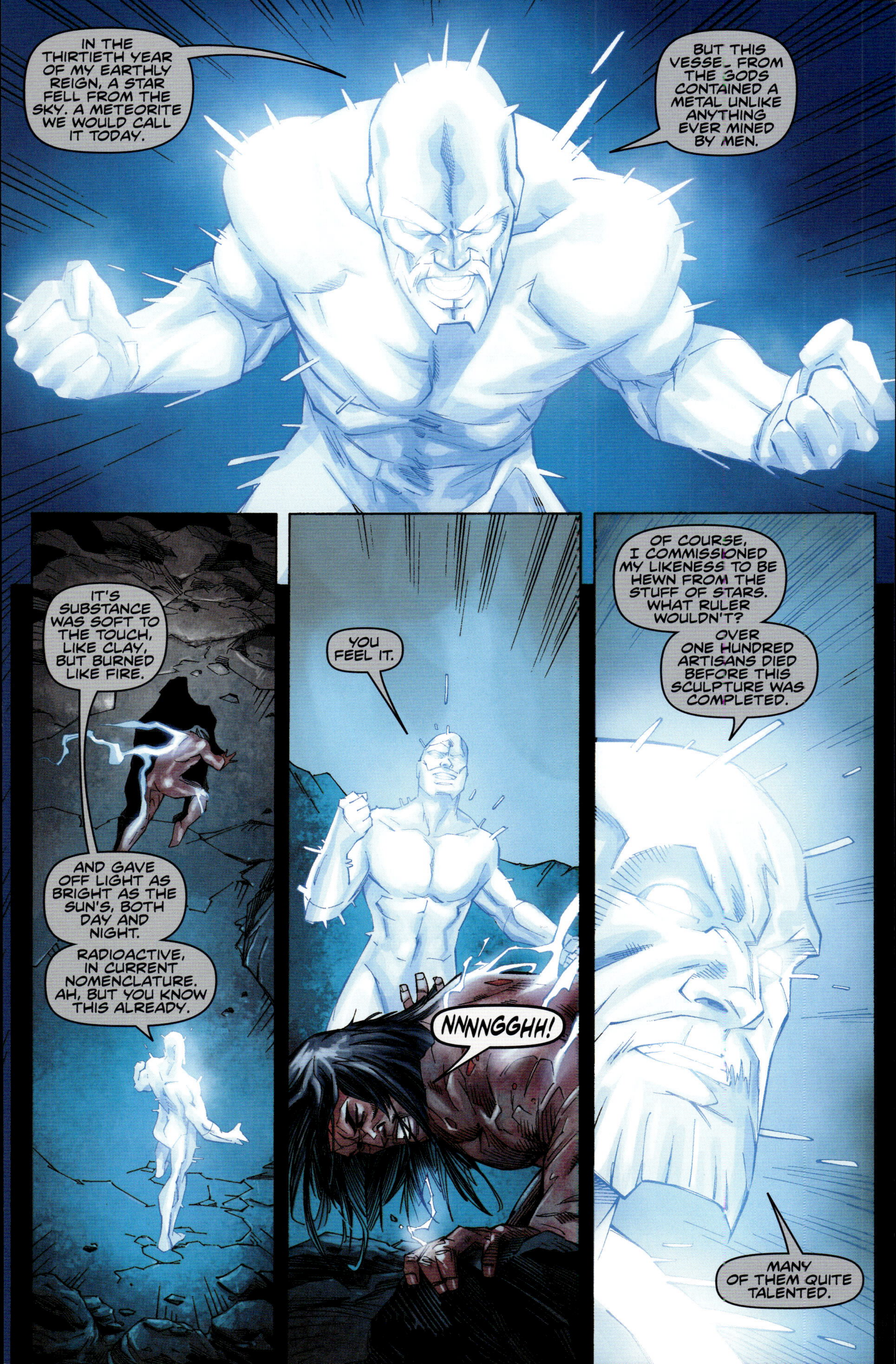
IN THE THIRTIETH YEAR OF MY EARTHLY REIGN, A STAR FELL FROM THE SKY. A METEORITE WE WOULD CALL IT TODAY.
BUT THIS VESSEL FROM THE GODS CONTAINED A METAL UNLIKE ANYTHING EVER MINED BY MEN.
IT'S SUBSTANCE WAS SOFT TO THE TOUCH, LIKE CLAY, BUT BURNED LIKE FIRE.
AND GAVE OFF LIGHT AS BRIGHT AS THE SUN'S, BOTH DAY AND NIGHT.
RADIOACTIVE, IN CURRENT NOMENCLATURE. AH, BUT YOU KNOW THIS ALREADY.
YOU FEEL IT.
NNNNGGHH!
OF COURSE, I COMMISSIONED MY LIKENESS TO BE HEWN FROM THE STUFF OF STARS. WHAT RULER WOULDN'T?
OVER ONE HUNDRED ARTISANS DIED BEFORE THIS SCULPTURE WAS COMPLETED.
MANY OF THEM QUITE TALENTED.

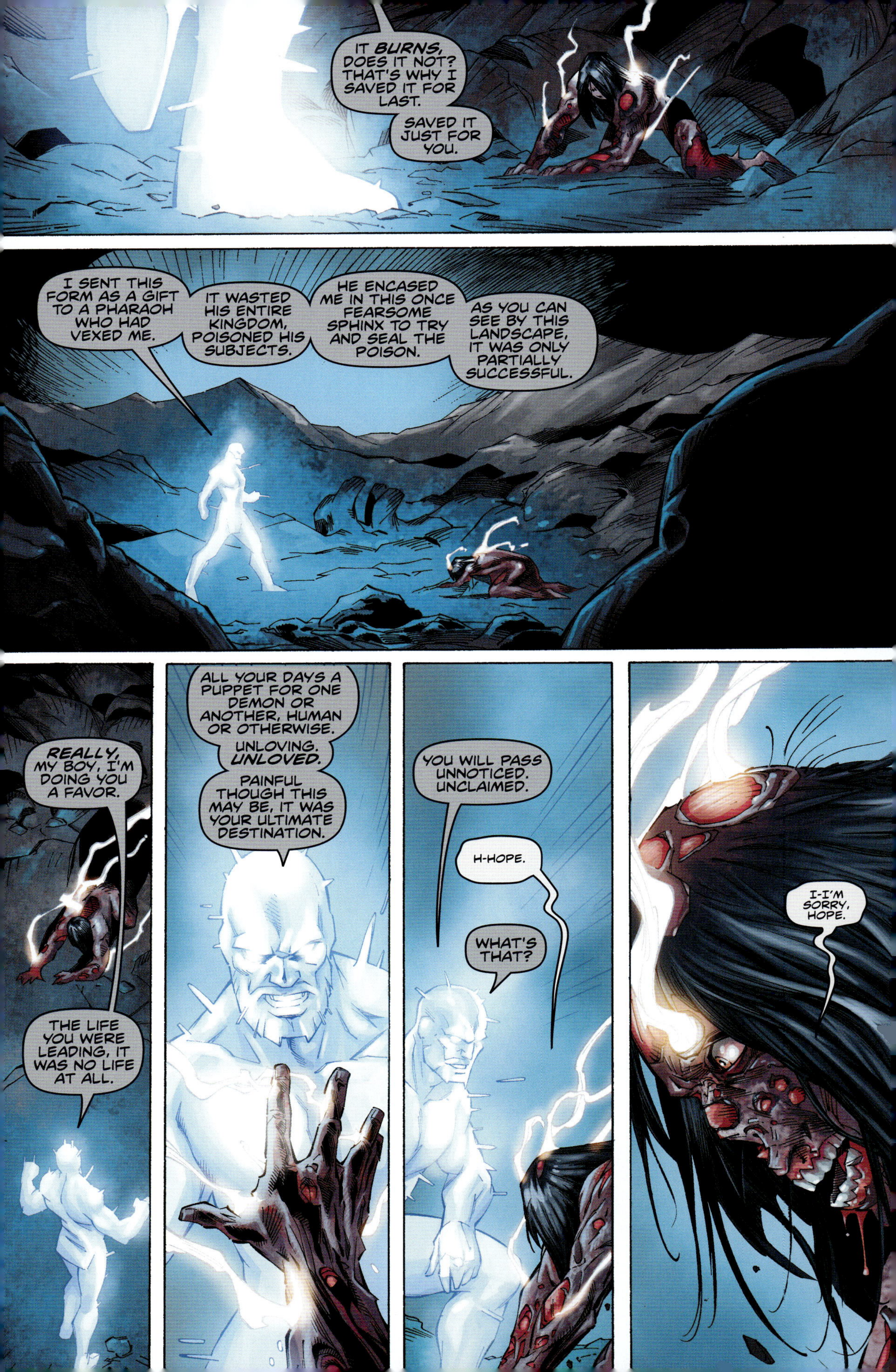
IT *BURNS,* DOES IT NOT? THAT'S WHY I SAVED IT FOR LAST.
SAVED IT JUST FOR YOU.
I SENT THIS FORM AS A GIFT TO A PHARAOH WHO HAD VEXED ME.
IT WASTED HIS ENTIRE KINGDOM, POISONED HIS SUBJECTS.
HE ENCASED ME IN THIS ONCE FEARSOME SPHINX TO TRY AND SEAL THE POISON.
AS YOU CAN SEE BY THIS LANDSCAPE, IT WAS ONLY PARTIALLY SUCCESSFUL.
REALLY, MY BOY, I'M DOING YOU A FAVOR.
THE LIFE YOU WERE LEADING, IT WAS NO LIFE AT ALL.
ALL YOUR DAYS A PUPPET FOR ONE DEMON OR ANOTHER, HUMAN OR OTHERWISE.
UNLOVING. *UNLOVED.*
PAINFUL THOUGH THIS MAY BE, IT WAS YOUR ULTIMATE DESTINATION.
YOU WILL PASS UNNOTICED. UNCLAIMED.
H-HOPE.
WHAT'S THAT?
I-I'M SORRY, HOPE.

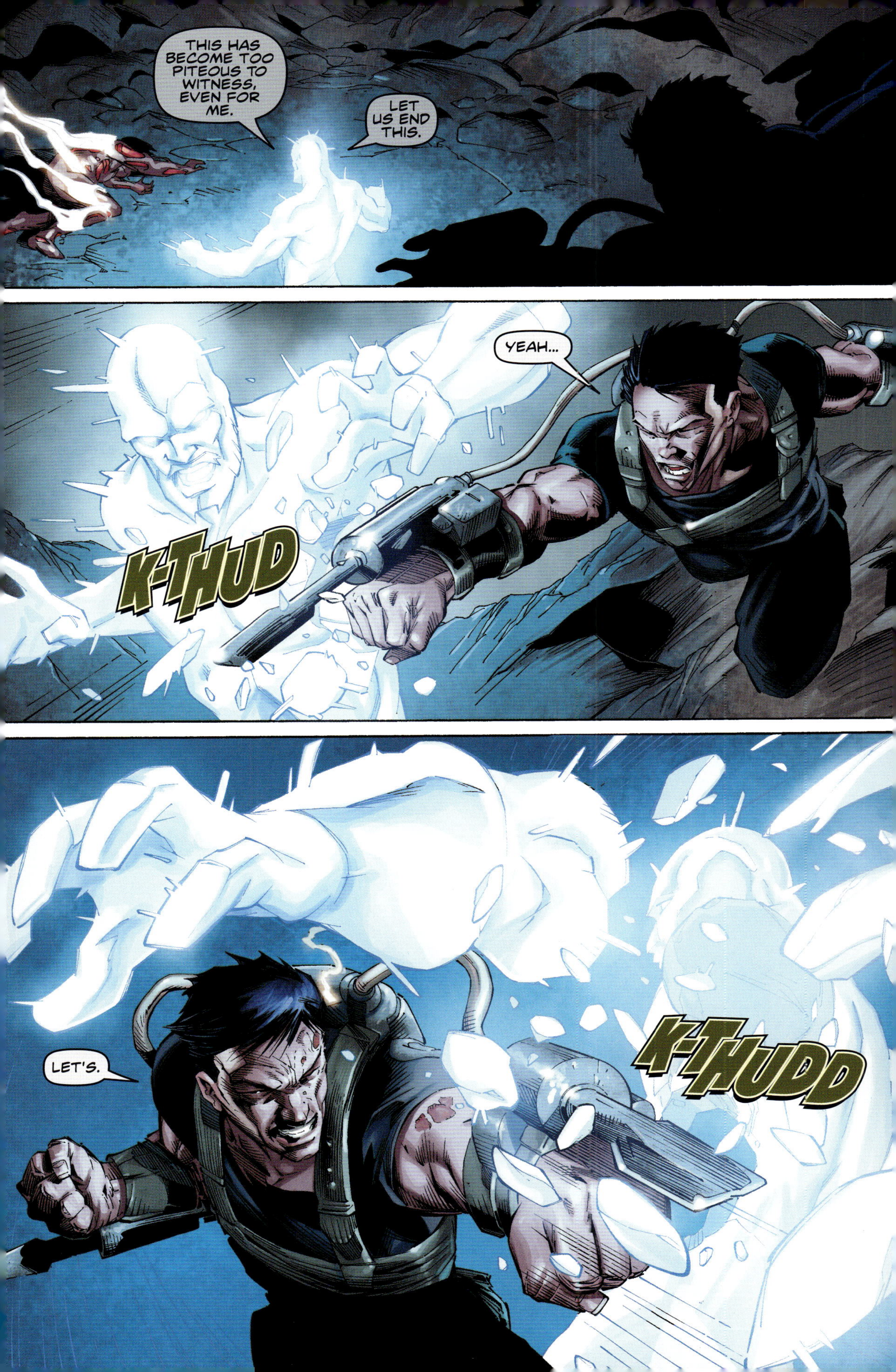
THIS HAS BECOME TOO PITEOUS TO WITNESS, EVEN FOR ME.
LET US END THIS.
YEAH...
K-THUD
LET'S.
K-THUDD

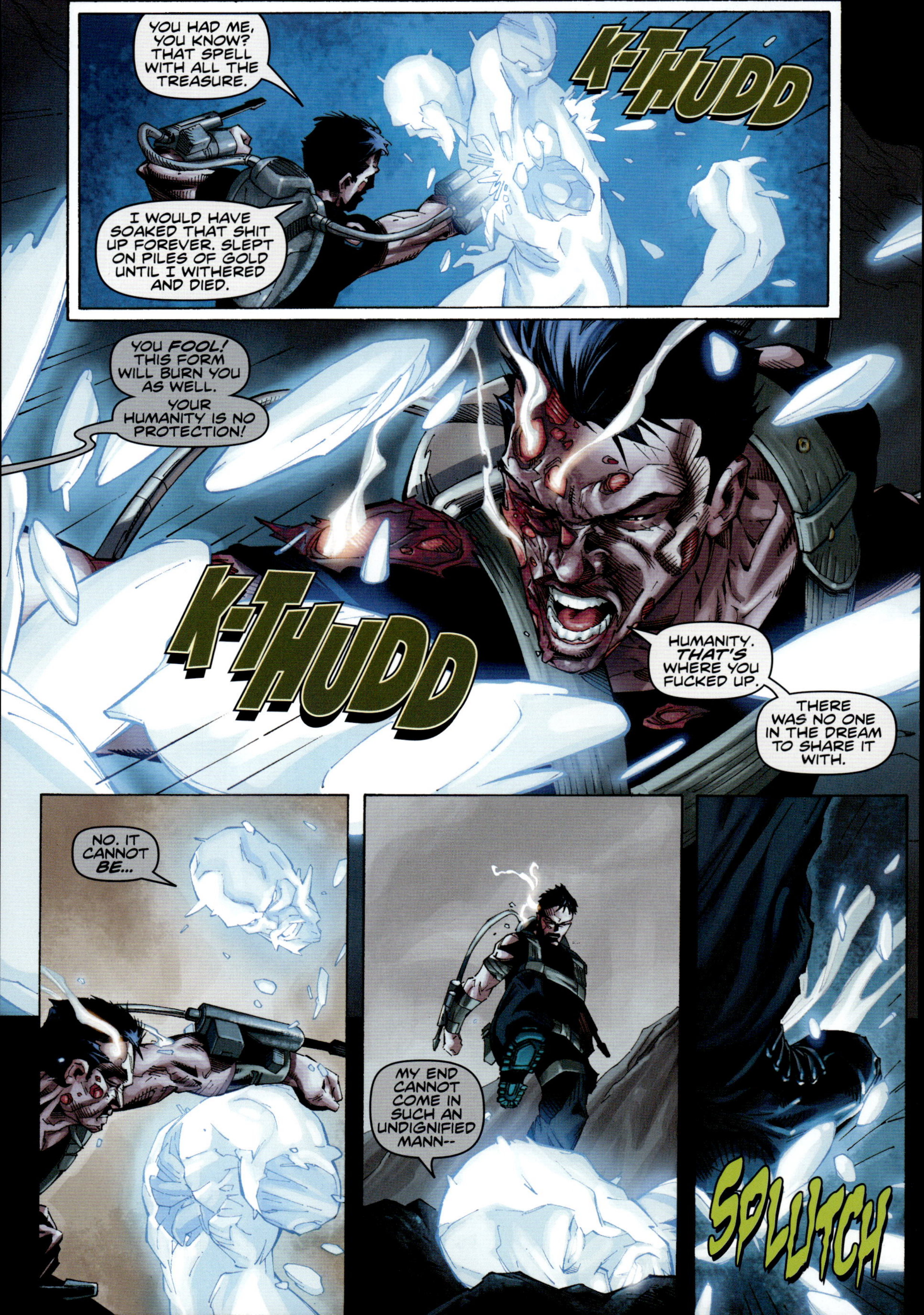
YOU HAD ME, YOU KNOW? THAT SPELL WITH ALL THE TREASURE.
K-THUDD
I WOULD HAVE SOAKED THAT SHIT UP FOREVER. SLEPT ON PILES OF GOLD UNTIL I WITHERED AND DIED.
YOU FOOL! THIS FORM WILL BURN YOU AS WELL.
YOUR HUMANITY IS NO PROTECTION!
K-THUDD
HUMANITY. THAT'S WHERE YOU FUCKED UP.
THERE WAS NO ONE IN THE DREAM TO SHARE IT WITH.
NO. IT CANNOT BE...
MY END CANNOT COME IN SUCH AN UNDIGNIFIED MANN--
SPLUTCH

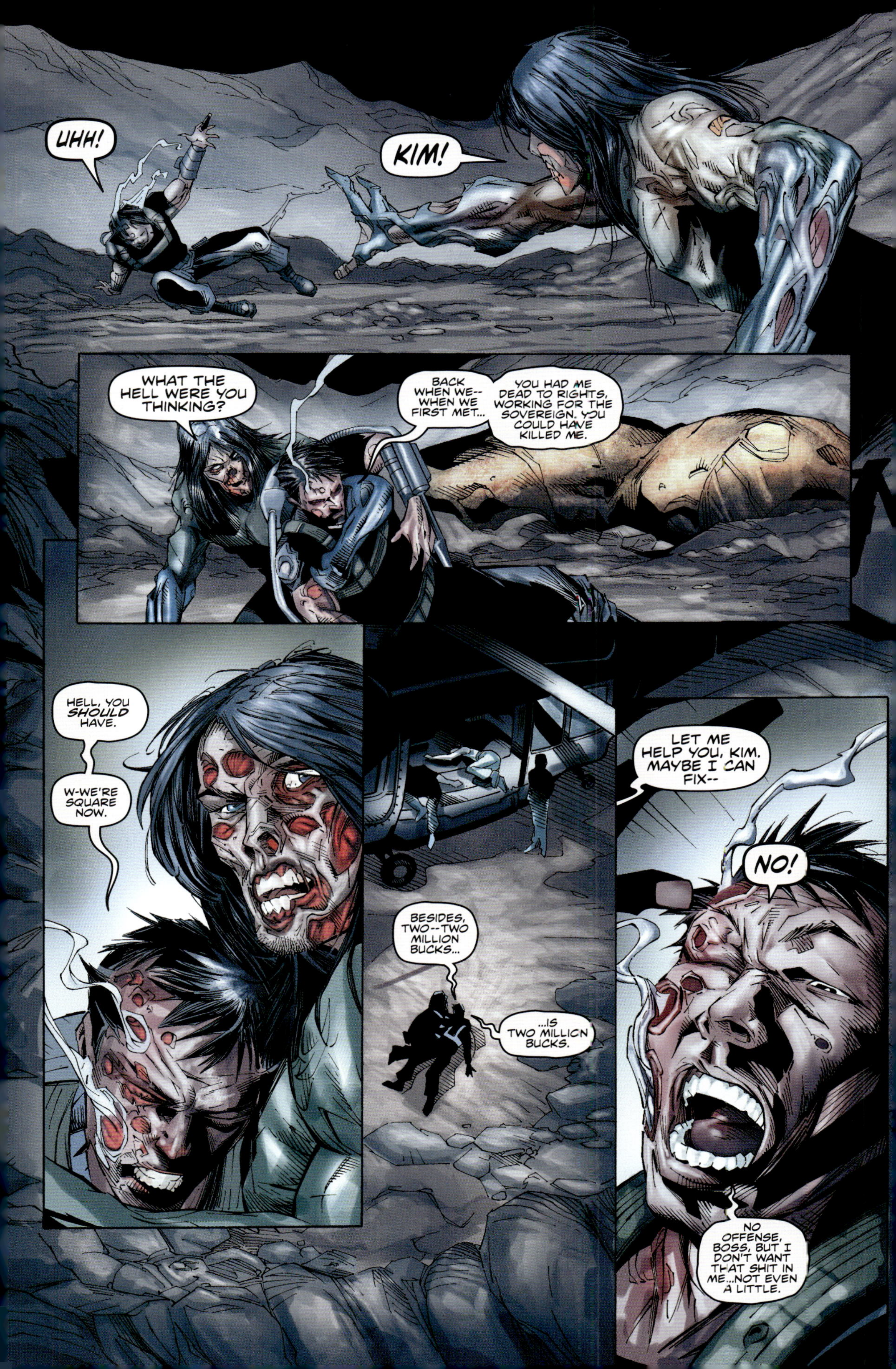

UHH!
KIM!
WHAT THE HELL WERE YOU THINKING?
BACK WHEN WE-- WHEN WE FIRST MET...
YOU HAD ME DEAD TO RIGHTS, WORKING FOR THE SOVEREIGN. YOU COULD HAVE KILLED ME.
HELL, YOU SHOULD HAVE.
W-WE'RE SQUARE NOW.
BESIDES, TWO--TWO MILLION BUCKS...
...IS TWO MILLION BUCKS.
LET ME HELP YOU, KIM. MAYBE I CAN FIX--
NO!
NO OFFENSE, BOSS, BUT I DON'T WANT THAT SHIT IN ME...NOT EVEN A LITTLE.

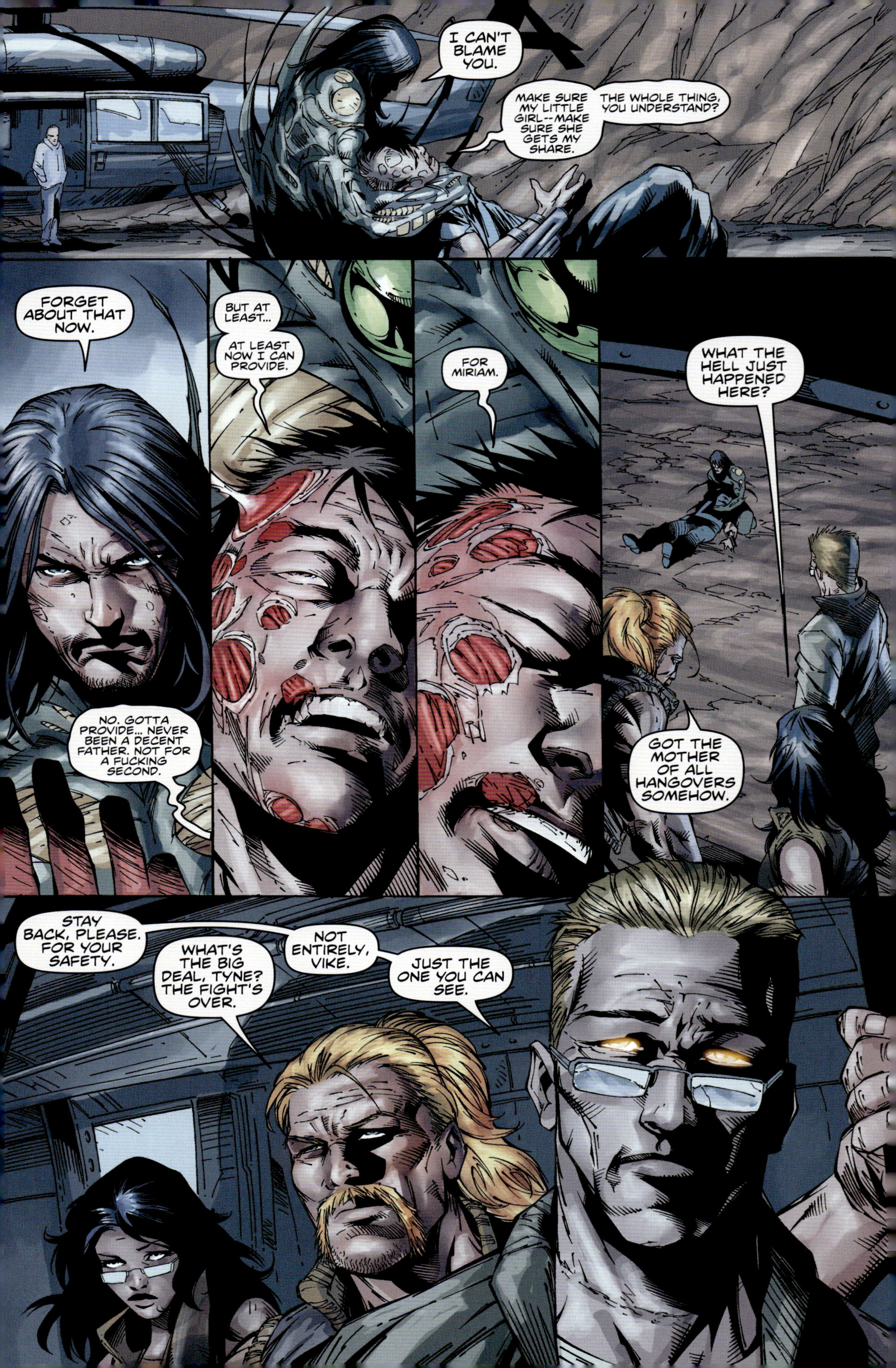
I CAN'T BLAME YOU.
MAKE SURE MY LITTLE GIRL--MAKE SURE SHE GETS MY SHARE.
THE WHOLE THING, YOU UNDERSTAND?
FORGET ABOUT THAT NOW.
NO. GOTTA PROVIDE... NEVER BEEN A DECENT FATHER. NOT FOR A FUCKING SECOND.
BUT AT LEAST...
AT LEAST NOW I CAN PROVIDE.
FOR MIRIAM.
WHAT THE HELL JUST HAPPENED HERE?
GOT THE MOTHER OF ALL HANGOVERS SOMEHOW.
STAY BACK, PLEASE. FOR YOUR SAFETY.
WHAT'S THE BIG DEAL, TYNE? THE FIGHT'S OVER.
NOT ENTIRELY, VIKE.
JUST THE ONE YOU CAN SEE.

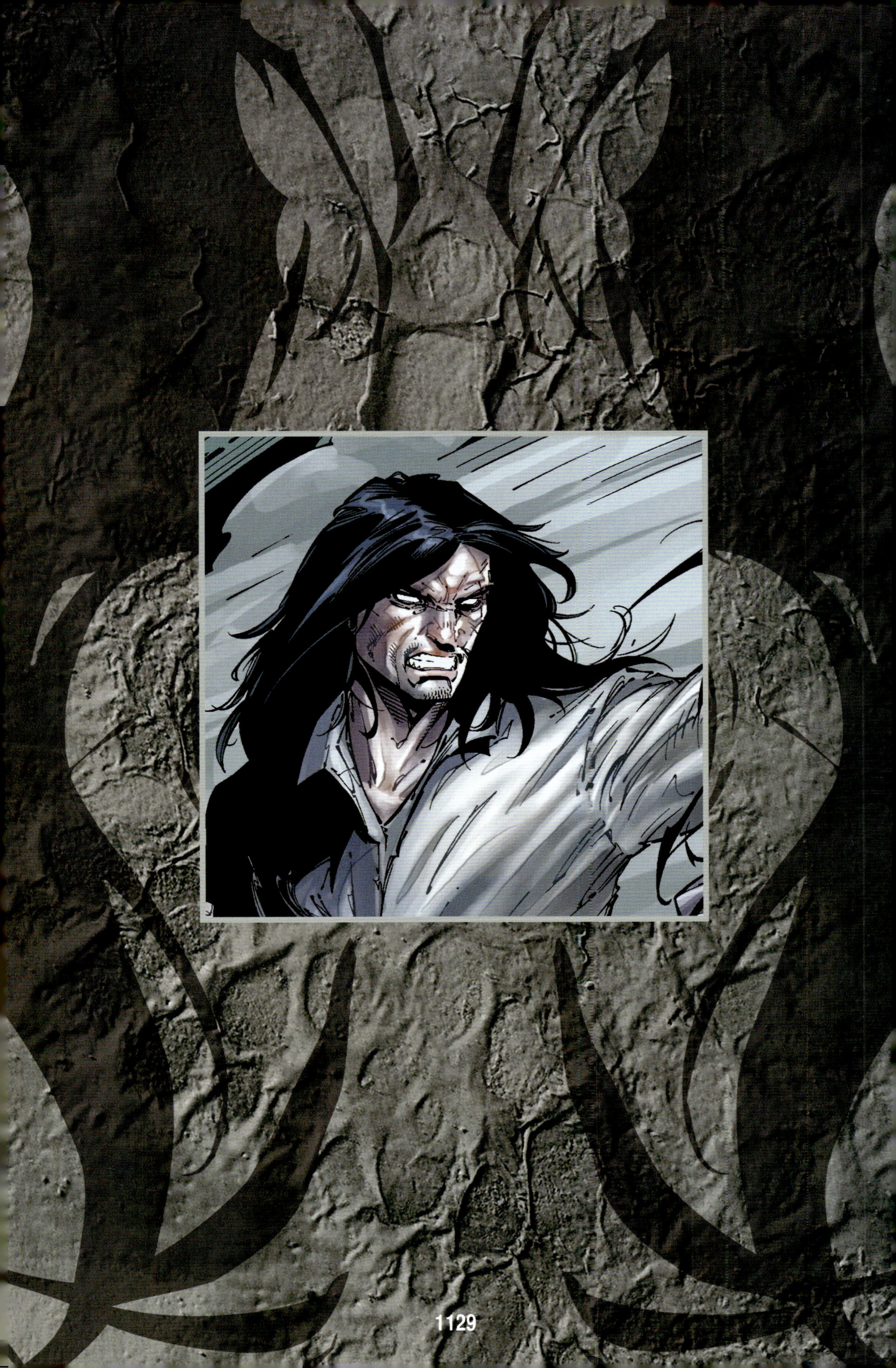

The Darkness Issue #89
cover art by: Matt Timson

THE DARKNESS #89

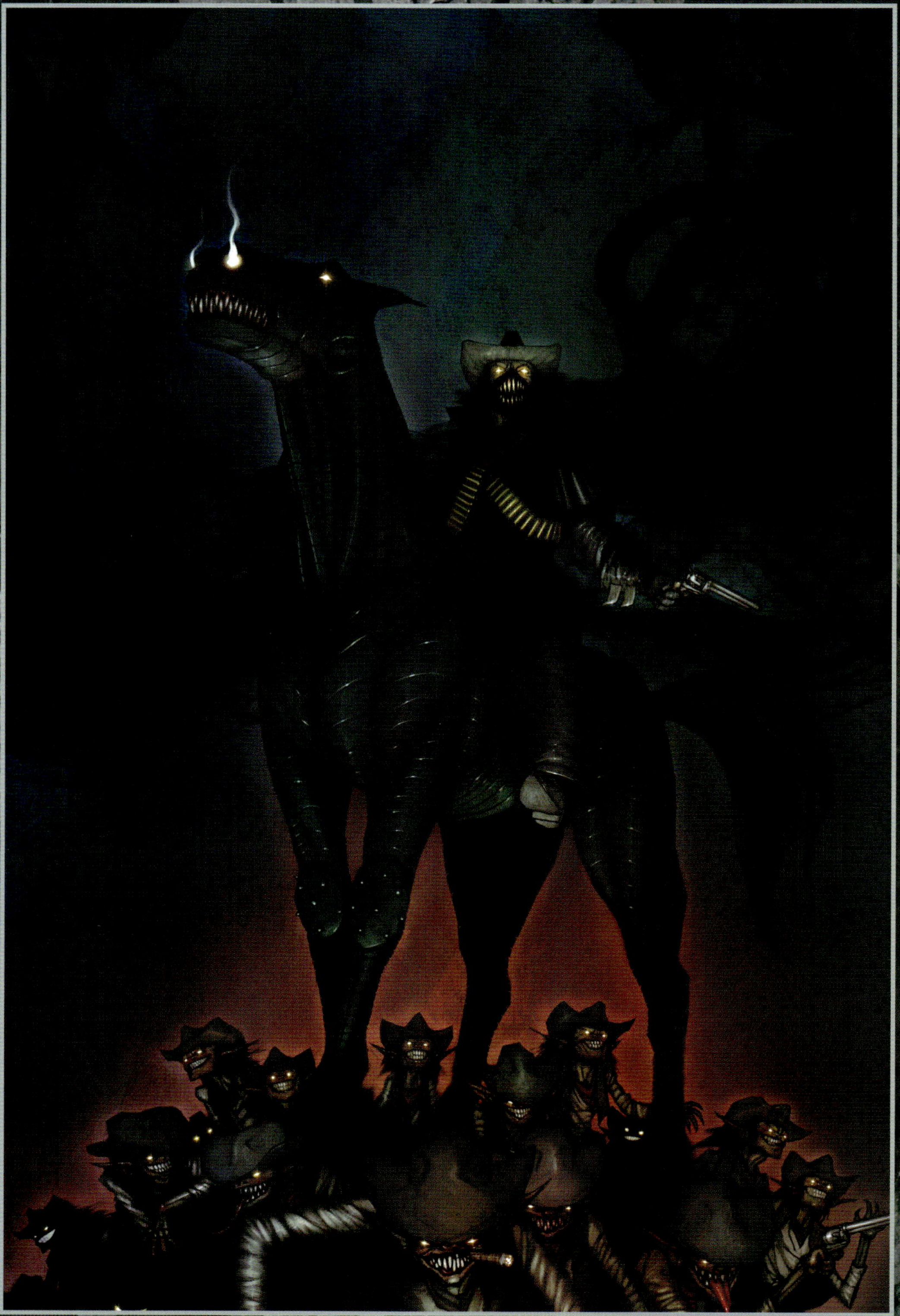

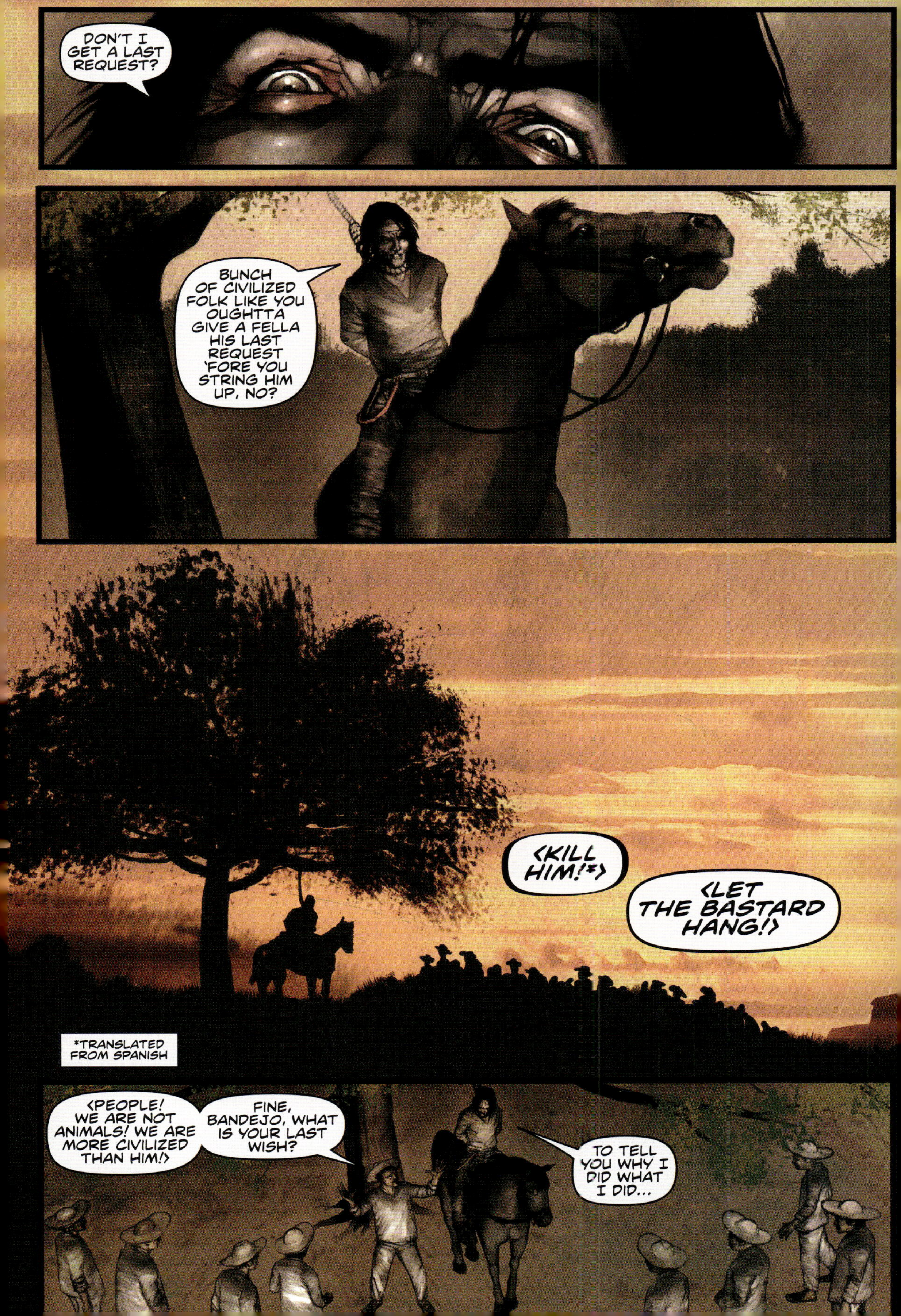
DON'T I GET A LAST REQUEST?
BUNCH OF CIVILIZED FOLK LIKE YOU OUGHTTA GIVE A FELLA HIS LAST REQUEST 'FORE YOU STRING HIM UP, NO?
<KILL HIM!*>
<LET THE BASTARD HANG!>
*TRANSLATED FROM SPANISH
<PEOPLE! WE ARE NOT ANIMALS! WE ARE MORE CIVILIZED THAN HIM!>
FINE, BANDEJO, WHAT IS YOUR LAST WISH?
TO TELL YOU WHY I DID WHAT I DID...

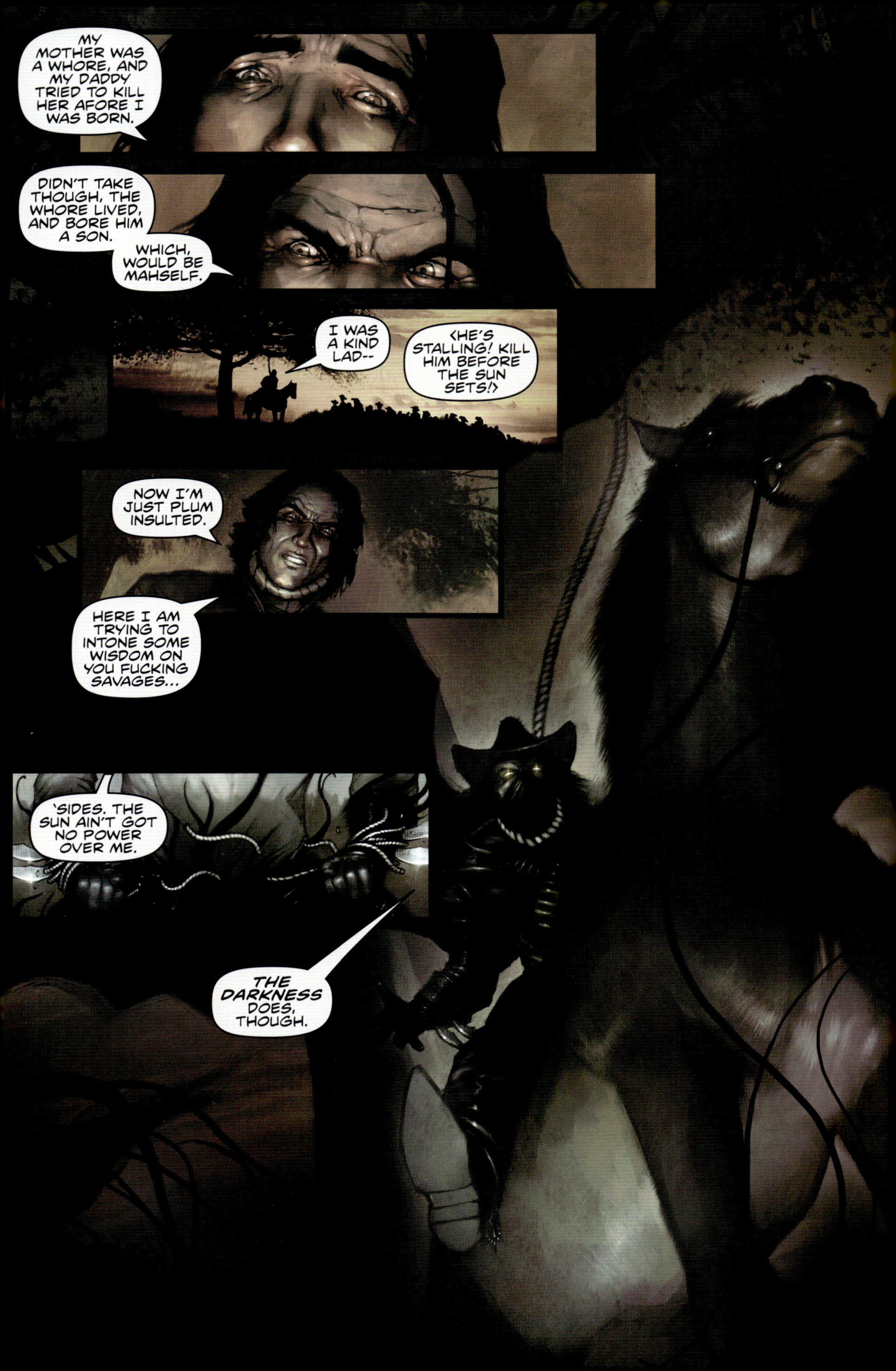
MY MOTHER WAS A WHORE, AND MY DADDY TRIED TO KILL HER AFORE I WAS BORN.
DIDN'T TAKE THOUGH, THE WHORE LIVED, AND BORE HIM A SON.
WHICH, WOULD BE MAHSELF.
I WAS A KIND LAD--
‹HE'S STALLING! KILL HIM BEFORE THE SUN SETS!›
NOW I'M JUST PLUM INSULTED.
HERE I AM TRYING TO INTONE SOME WISDOM ON YOU FUCKING SAVAGES...
'SIDES. THE SUN AIN'T GOT NO POWER OVER ME.
THE DARKNESS DOES, THOUGH.

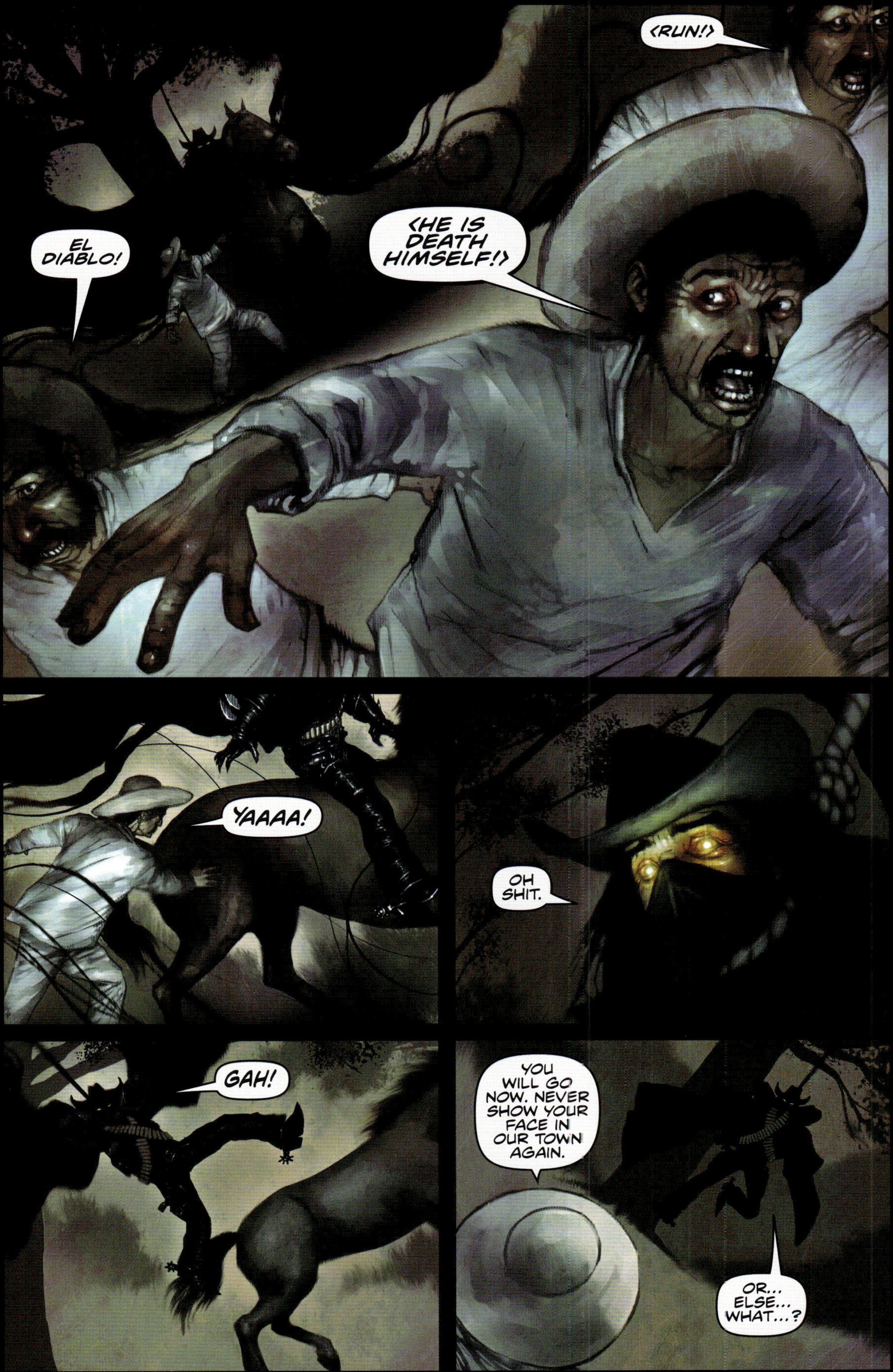

<RUN!>
EL DIABLO!
<HE IS DEATH HIMSELF!>
YAAAA!
OH SHIT.
GAH!
YOU WILL GO NOW. NEVER SHOW YOUR FACE IN OUR TOWN AGAIN.
OR... ELSE... WHAT...?

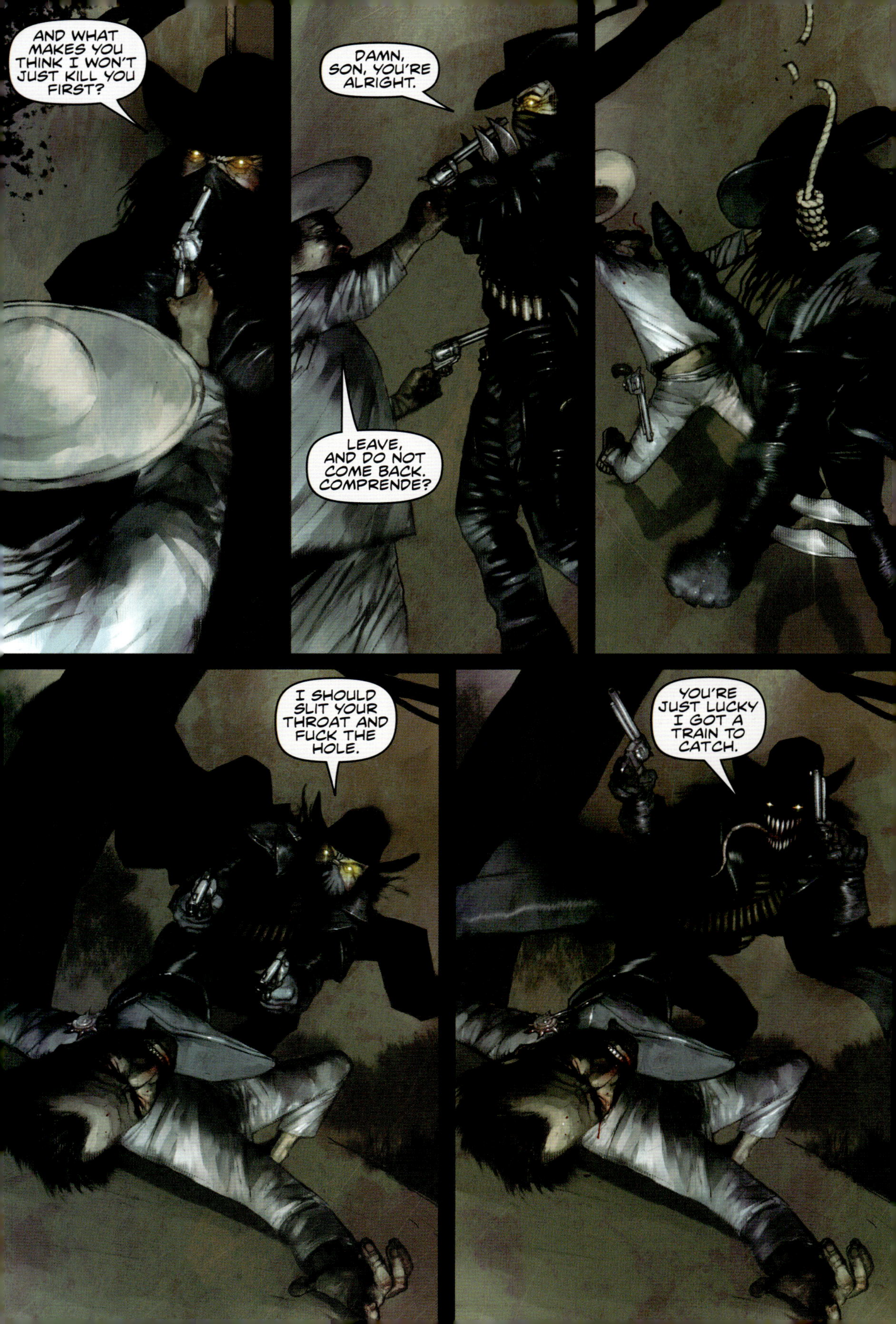
AND WHAT MAKES YOU THINK I WON'T JUST KILL YOU FIRST?
DAMN, SON, YOU'RE ALRIGHT.
LEAVE, AND DO NOT COME BACK. COMPRENDE?
I SHOULD SLIT YOUR THROAT AND FUCK THE HOLE.
YOU'RE JUST LUCKY I GOT A TRAIN TO CATCH.

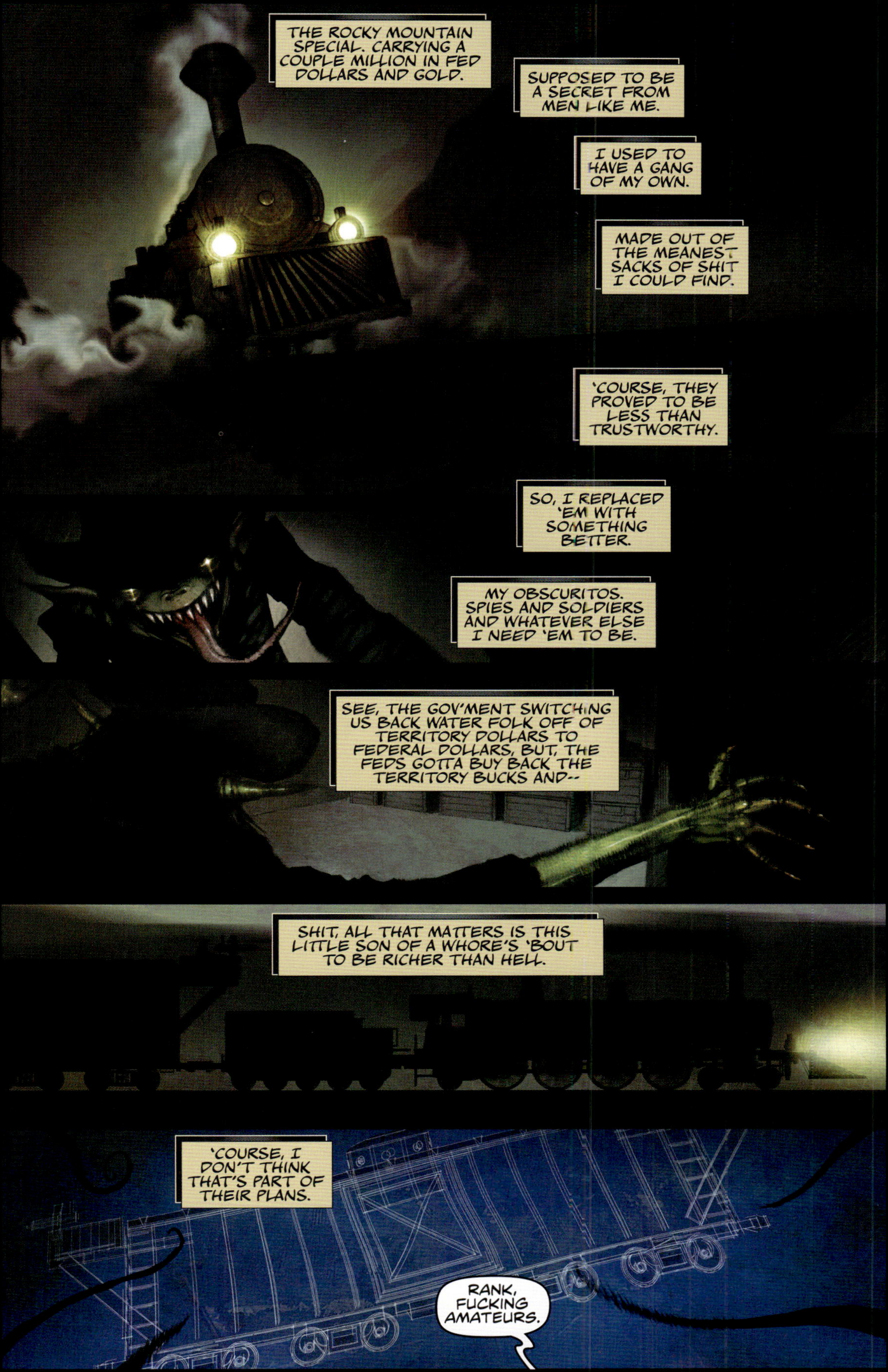
THE ROCKY MOUNTAIN SPECIAL. CARRYING A COUPLE MILLION IN FED DOLLARS AND GOLD.
SUPPOSED TO BE A SECRET FROM MEN LIKE ME.
I USED TO HAVE A GANG OF MY OWN.
MADE OUT OF THE MEANEST SACKS OF SHIT I COULD FIND.
'COURSE, THEY PROVED TO BE LESS THAN TRUSTWORTHY.
SO, I REPLACED 'EM WITH SOMETHING BETTER.
MY OBSCURITOS. SPIES AND SOLDIERS AND WHATEVER ELSE I NEED 'EM TO BE.
SEE, THE GOV'MENT SWITCHING US BACK WATER FOLK OFF OF TERRITORY DOLLARS TO FEDERAL DOLLARS, BUT, THE FEDS GOTTA BUY BACK THE TERRITORY BUCKS AND--
SHIT, ALL THAT MATTERS IS THIS LITTLE SON OF A WHORE'S 'BOUT TO BE RICHER THAN HELL.
'COURSE, I DON'T THINK THAT'S PART OF THEIR PLANS.
RANK, FUCKING AMATEURS.

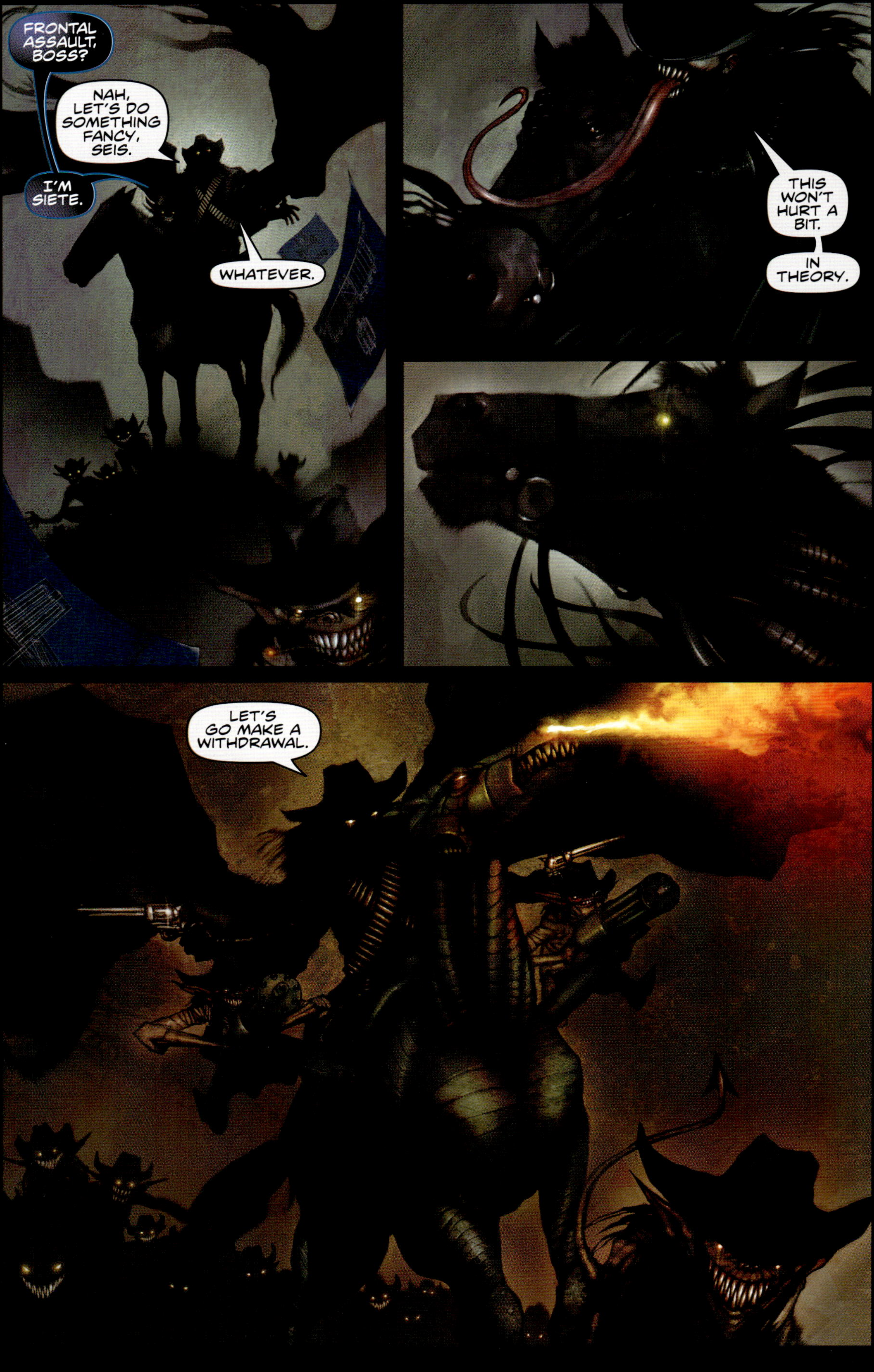
FRONTAL ASSAULT, BOSS?
NAH, LET'S DO SOMETHING FANCY, SEIS.
I'M SIETE.
WHATEVER.
THIS WON'T HURT A BIT.
IN THEORY.
LET'S GO MAKE A WITHDRAWAL.

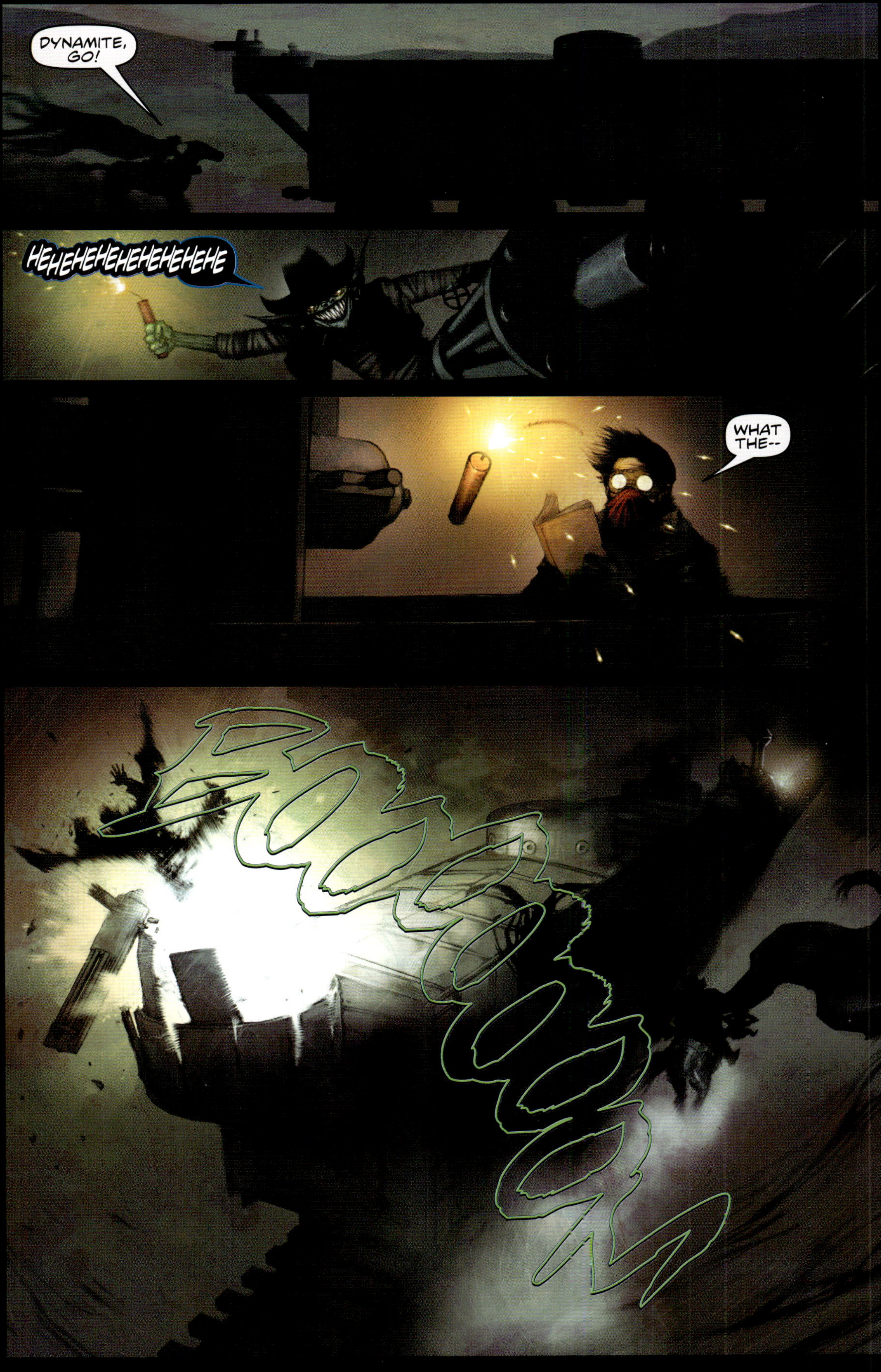
DYNAMITE, GO!
HEHEHEHEHEHEHEHEHE
WHAT THE--
BOOOOOOOOM

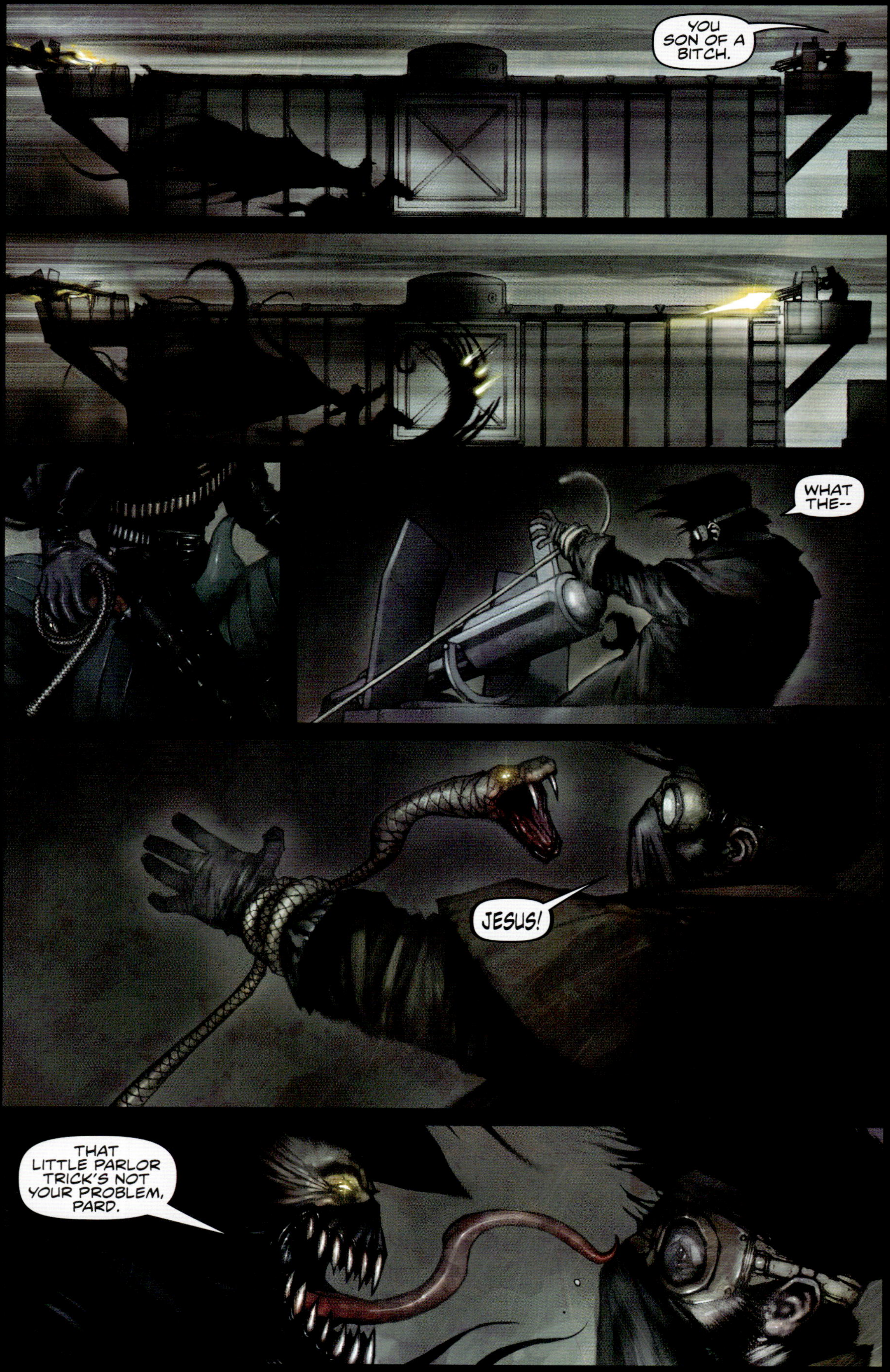
YOU SON OF A BITCH.
WHAT THE--
JESUS!
THAT LITTLE PARLOR TRICK'S NOT YOUR PROBLEM, PARD.

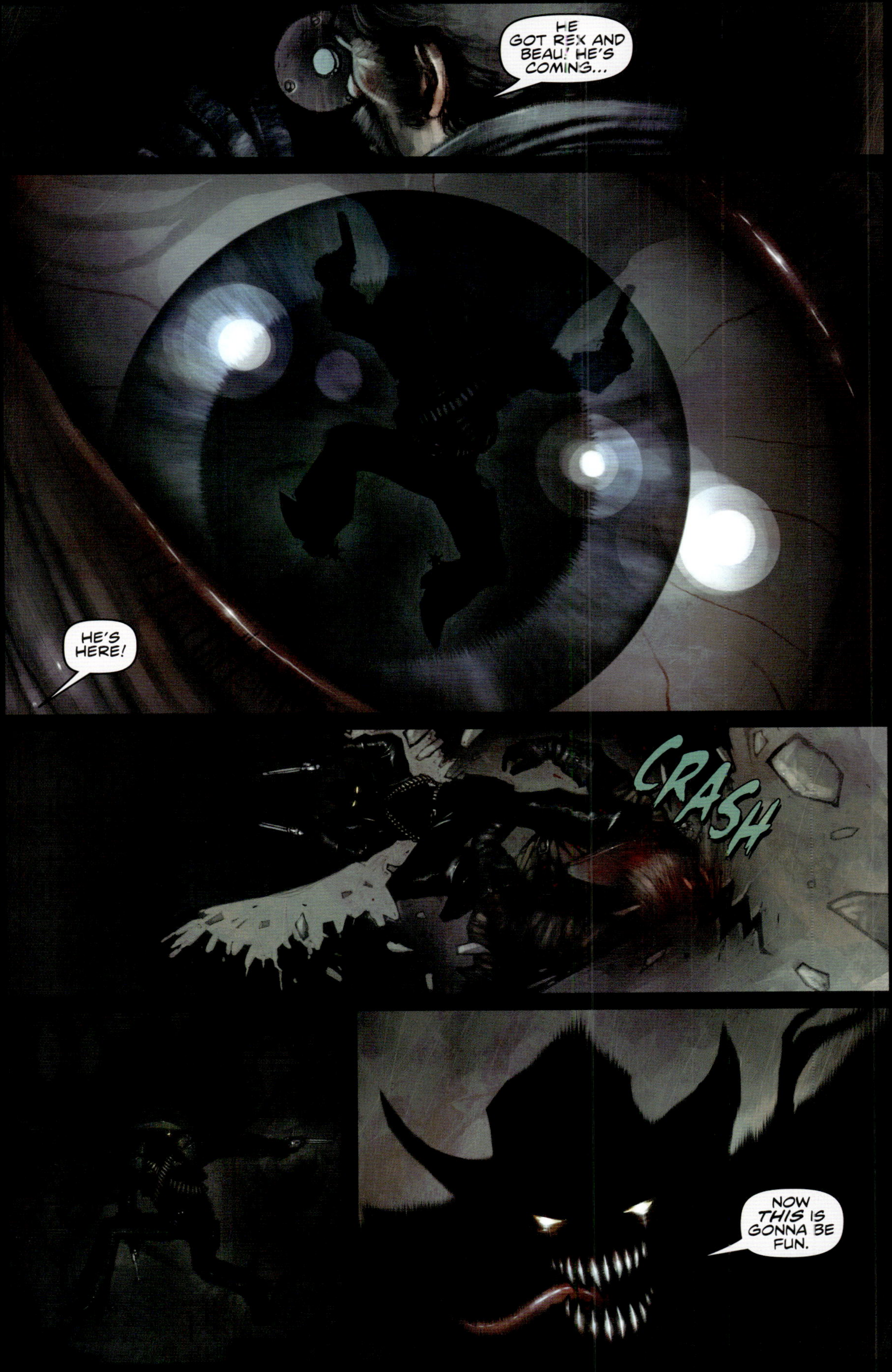

HE GOT REX AND BEAU! HE'S COMING...
HE'S HERE!
CRASH
NOW THIS IS GONNA BE FUN.

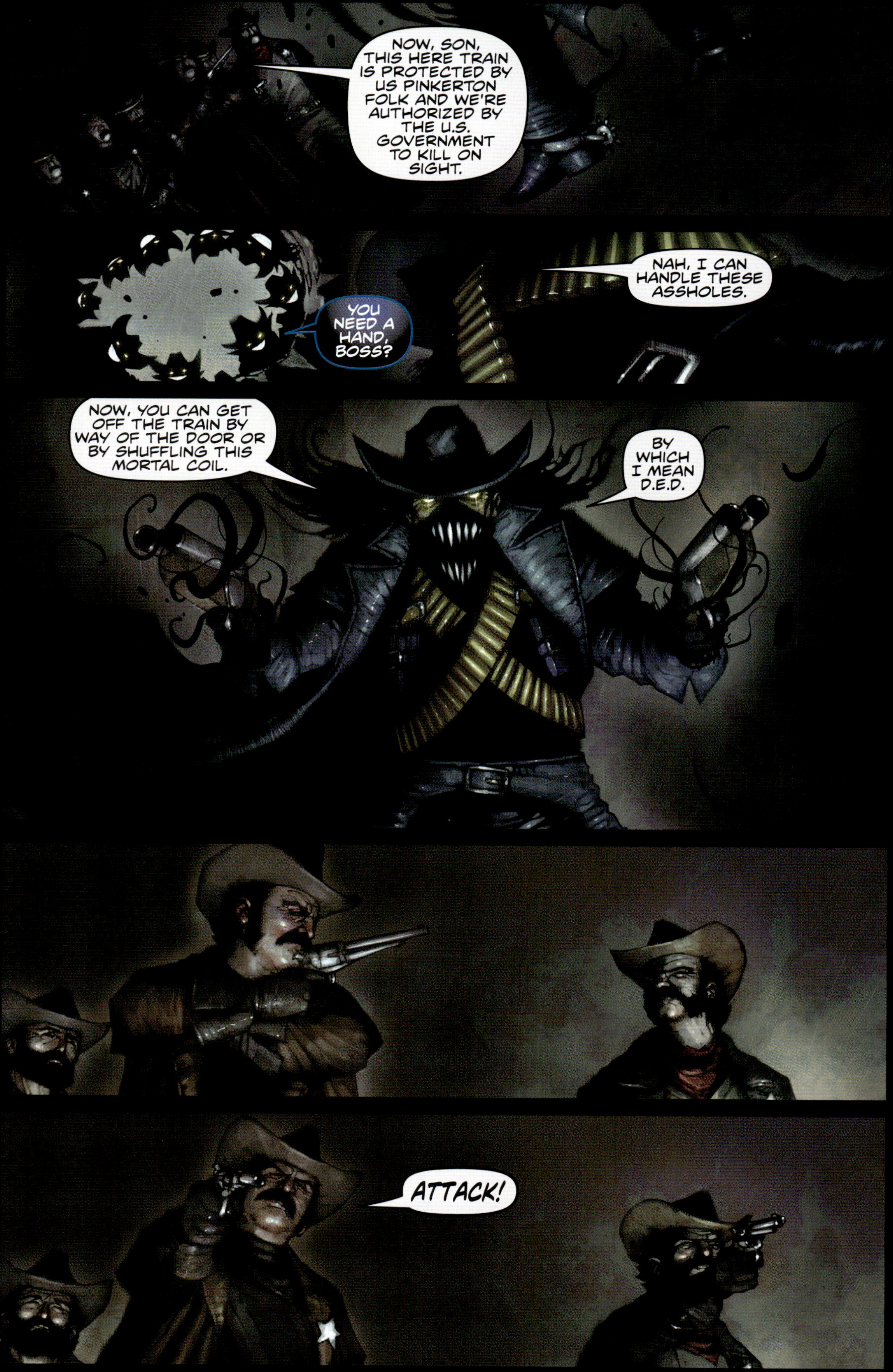
NOW, SON, THIS HERE TRAIN IS PROTECTED BY US PINKERTON FOLK AND WE'RE AUTHORIZED BY THE U.S. GOVERNMENT TO KILL ON SIGHT.
YOU NEED A HAND, BOSS?
NAH, I CAN HANDLE THESE ASSHOLES.
NOW, YOU CAN GET OFF THE TRAIN BY WAY OF THE DOOR OR BY SHUFFLING THIS MORTAL COIL.
BY WHICH I MEAN D.E.D.
ATTACK!

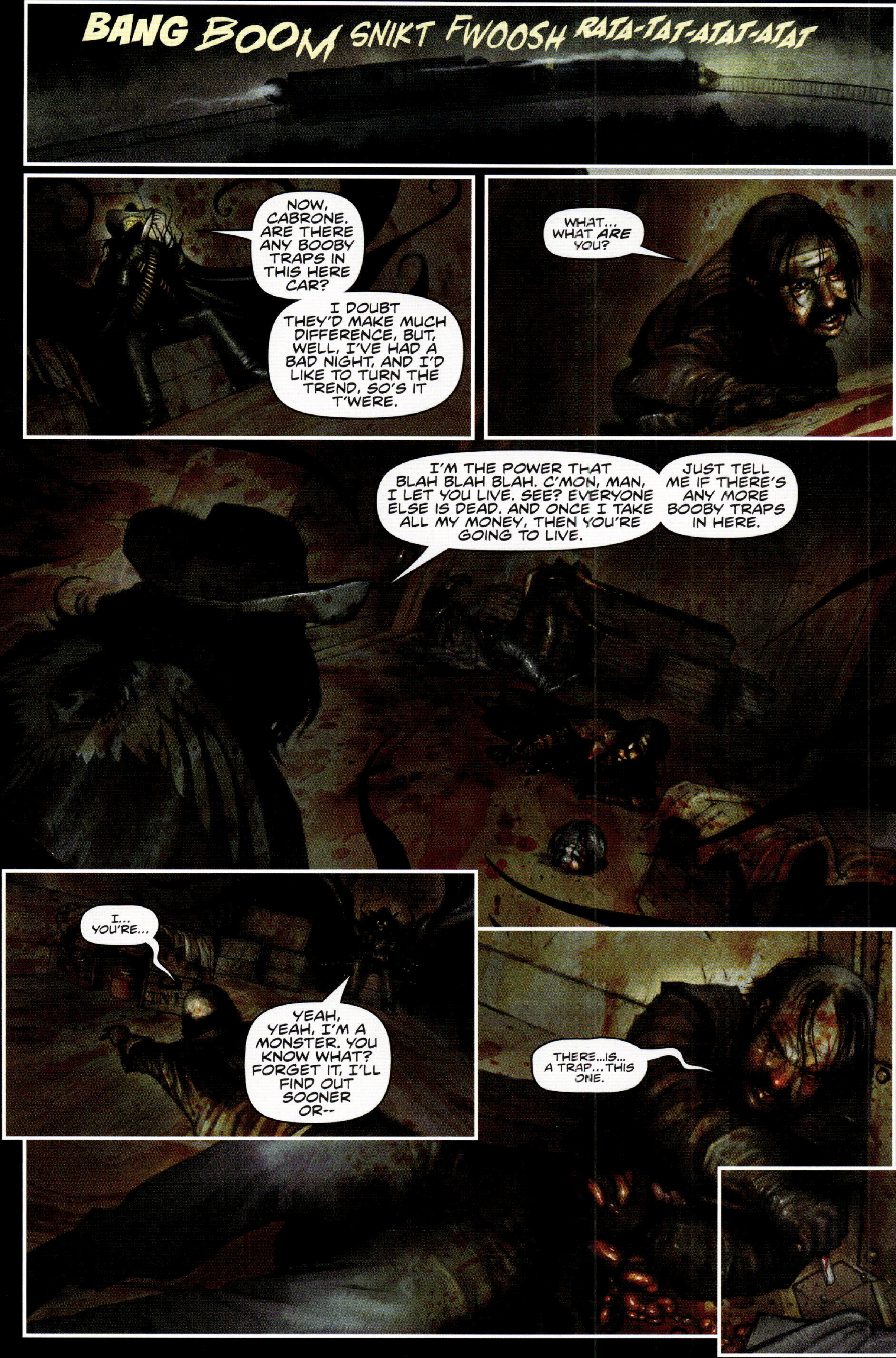
BANG BOOM SNIKT FWOOSH RATA-TAT-ATAT-ATAT
NOW, CABRONE. ARE THERE ANY BOOBY TRAPS IN THIS HERE CAR?
I DOUBT THEY'D MAKE MUCH DIFFERENCE, BUT, WELL, I'VE HAD A BAD NIGHT, AND I'D LIKE TO TURN THE TREND, SO'S IT T'WERE.
WHAT... WHAT ARE YOU?
I'M THE POWER THAT BLAH BLAH BLAH. C'MON, MAN, I LET YOU LIVE. SEE? EVERYONE ELSE IS DEAD. AND ONCE I TAKE ALL MY MONEY, THEN YOU'RE GOING TO LIVE.
JUST TELL ME IF THERE'S ANY MORE BOOBY TRAPS IN HERE.
I... YOU'RE...
YEAH, YEAH, I'M A MONSTER. YOU KNOW WHAT? FORGET IT, I'LL FIND OUT SOONER OR--
THERE...IS... A TRAP...THIS ONE.

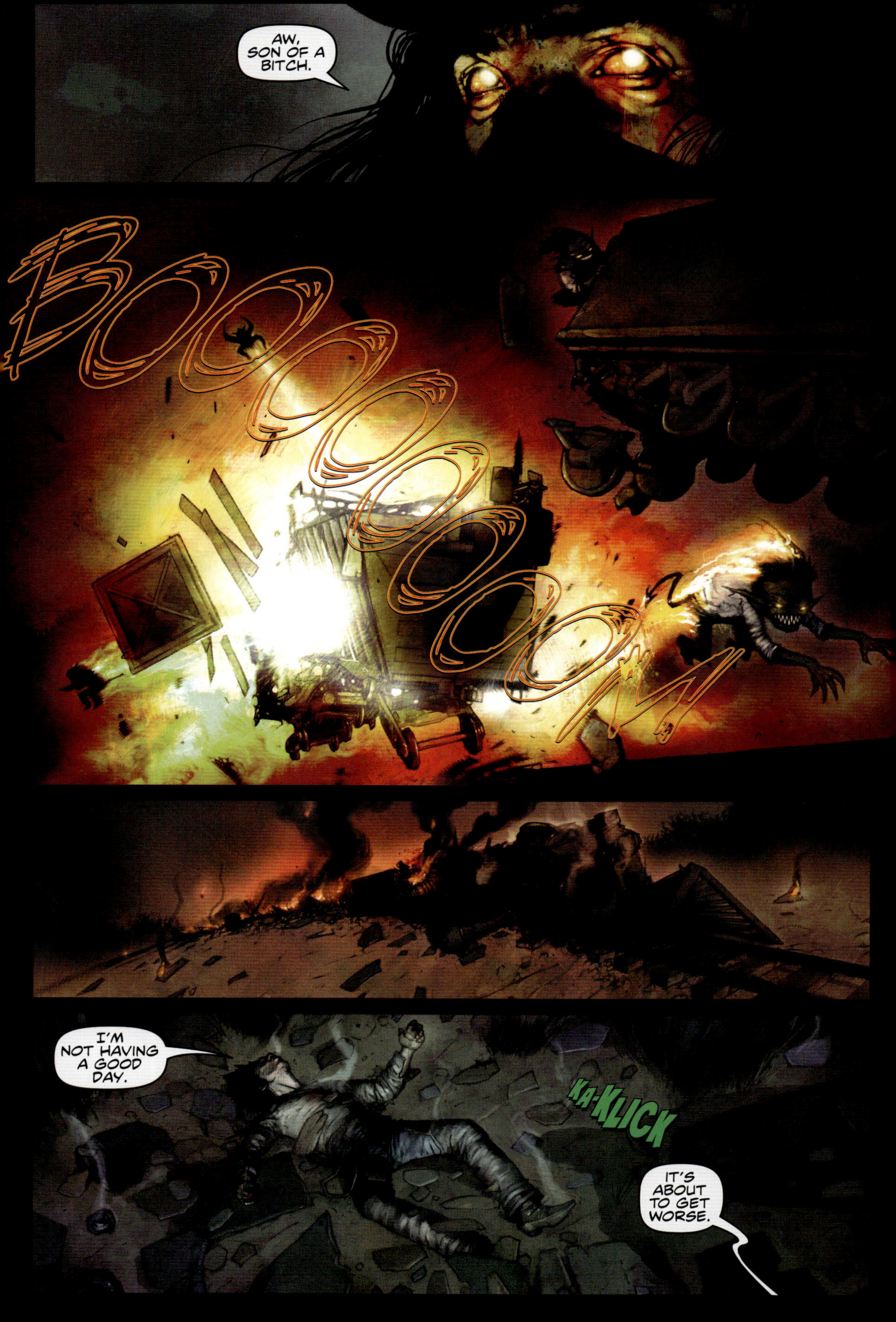
AW, SON OF A BITCH.
BOOOOOOOOOM!
I'M NOT HAVING A GOOD DAY.
KA-KLICK
IT'S ABOUT TO GET WORSE.

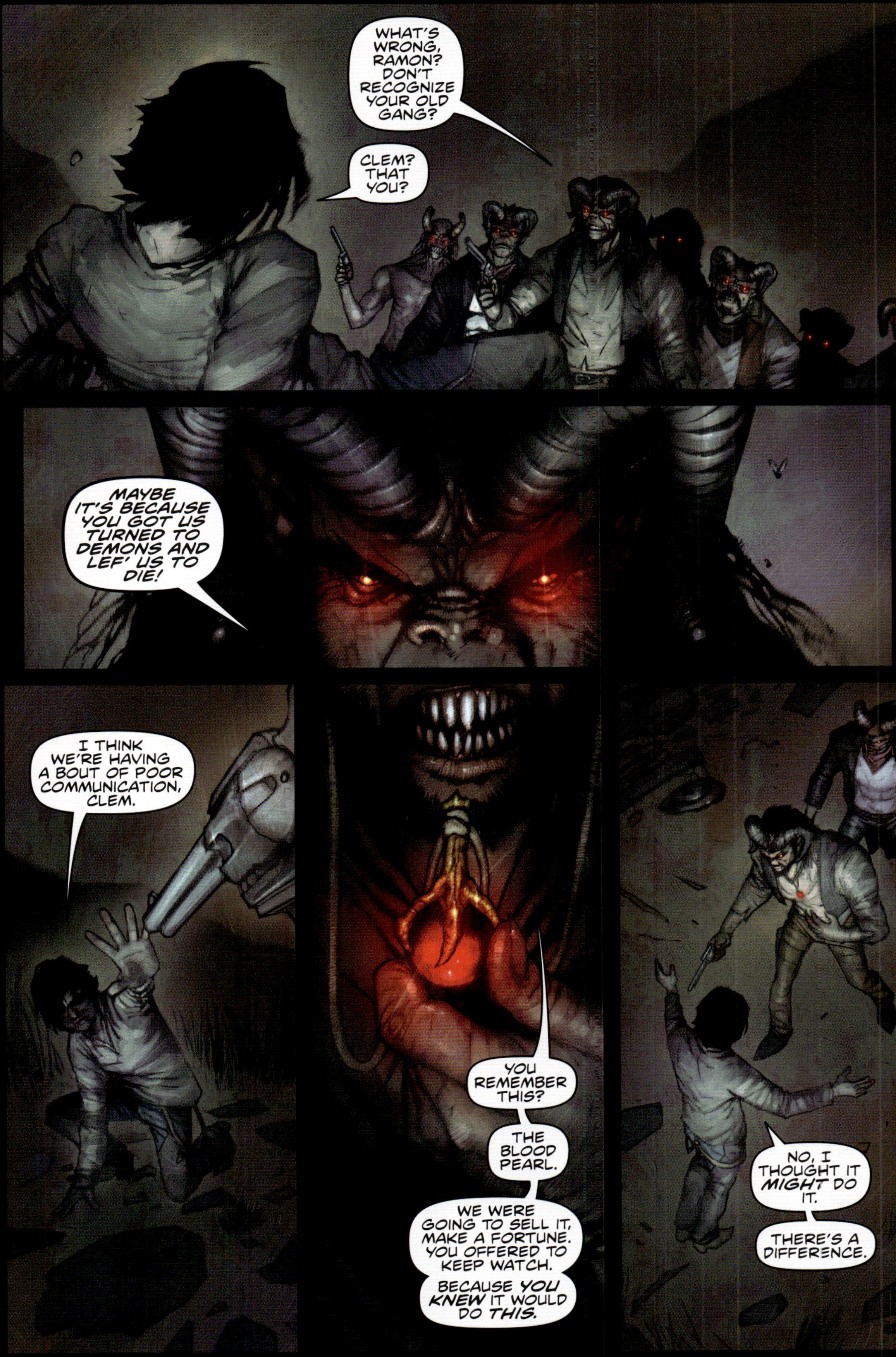
WHAT'S WRONG, RAMON? DON'T RECOGNIZE YOUR OLD GANG?
CLEM? THAT YOU?
MAYBE IT'S BECAUSE YOU GOT US TURNED TO DEMONS AND LEF' US TO DIE!
I THINK WE'RE HAVING A BOUT OF POOR COMMUNICATION, CLEM.
YOU REMEMBER THIS?
THE BLOOD PEARL.
WE WERE GOING TO SELL IT, MAKE A FORTUNE. YOU OFFERED TO KEEP WATCH.
BECAUSE *YOU KNEW* IT WOULD DO *THIS*.
NO, I THOUGHT IT *MIGHT* DO IT.
THERE'S A DIFFERENCE.

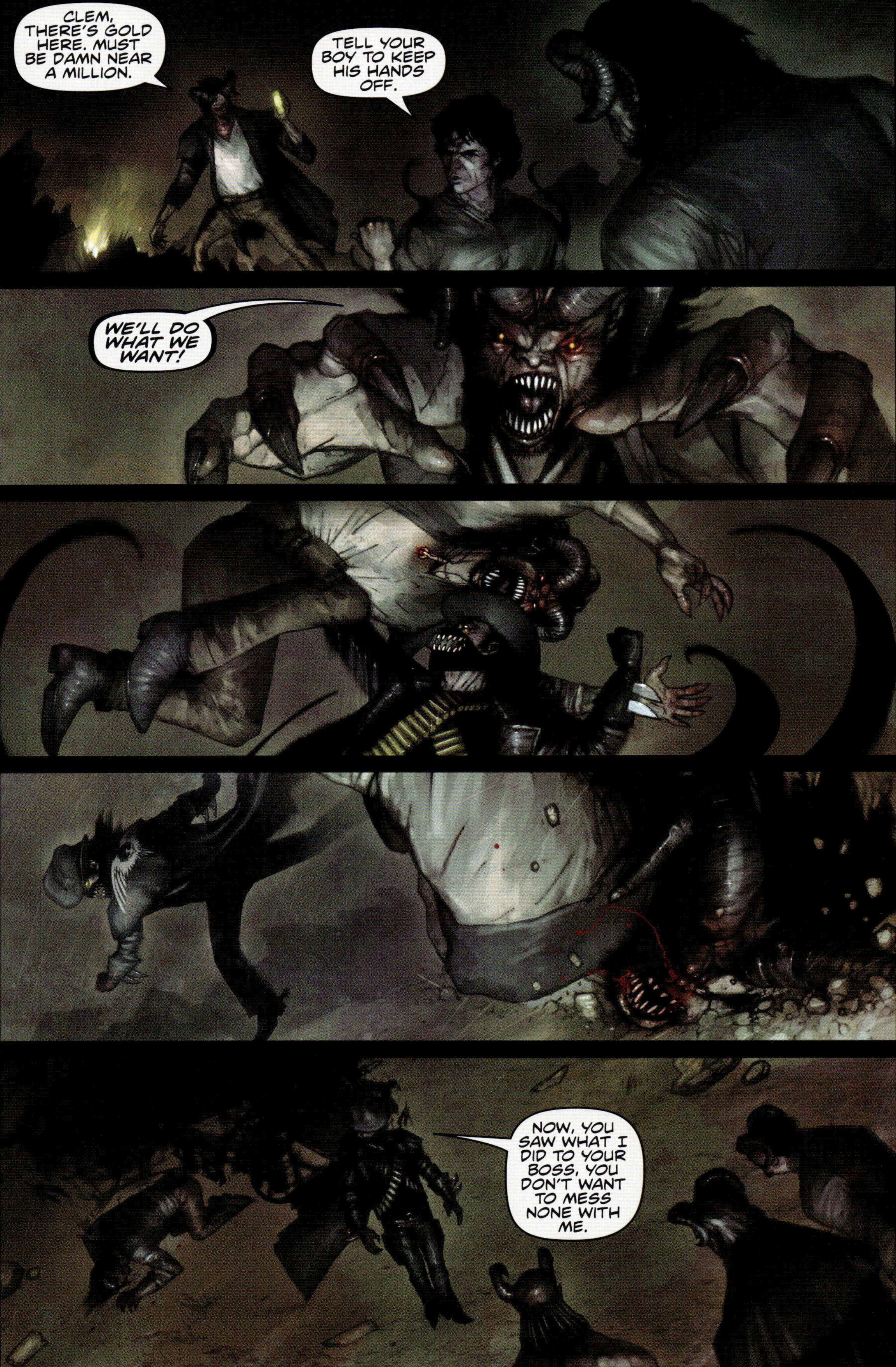
CLEM, THERE'S GOLD HERE. MUST BE DAMN NEAR A MILLION.
TELL YOUR BOY TO KEEP HIS HANDS OFF.
WE'LL DO WHAT WE WANT!
NOW, YOU SAW WHAT I DID TO YOUR BOSS, YOU DON'T WANT TO MESS NONE WITH ME.

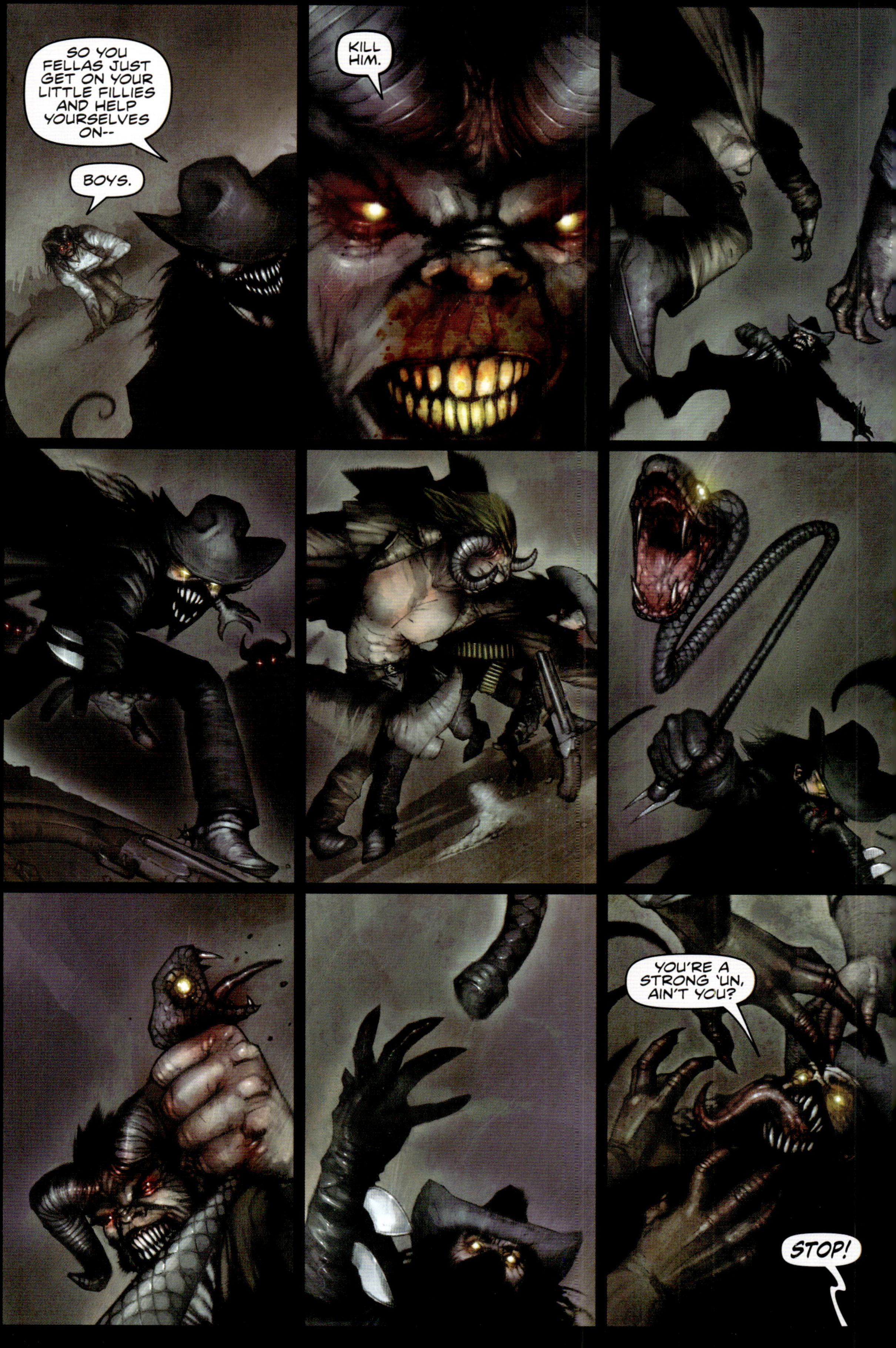
SO YOU FELLAS JUST GET ON YOUR LITTLE FILLIES AND HELP YOURSELVES ON--
BOYS.
KILL HIM.
YOU'RE A STRONG 'UN, AIN'T YOU?
STOP!

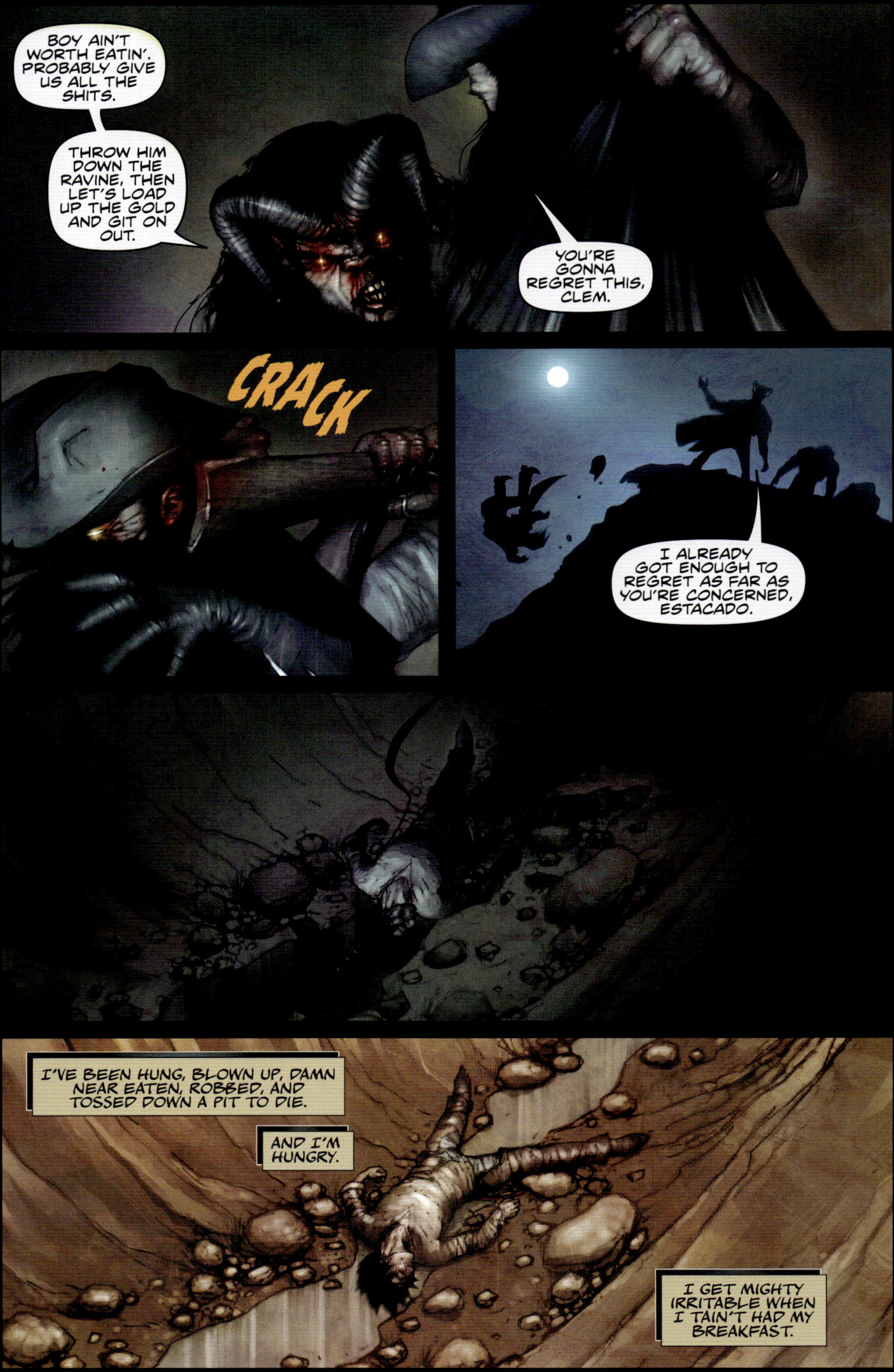
BOY AIN'T WORTH EATIN'. PROBABLY GIVE US ALL THE SHITS.
THROW HIM DOWN THE RAVINE, THEN LET'S LOAD UP THE GOLD AND GIT ON OUT.
YOU'RE GONNA REGRET THIS, CLEM.
CRACK
I ALREADY GOT ENOUGH TO REGRET AS FAR AS YOU'RE CONCERNED, ESTACADO.
I'VE BEEN HUNG, BLOWN UP, DAMN NEAR EATEN, ROBBED, AND TOSSED DOWN A PIT TO DIE.
AND I'M HUNGRY.
I GET MIGHTY IRRITABLE WHEN I TAIN'T HAD MY BREAKFAST.

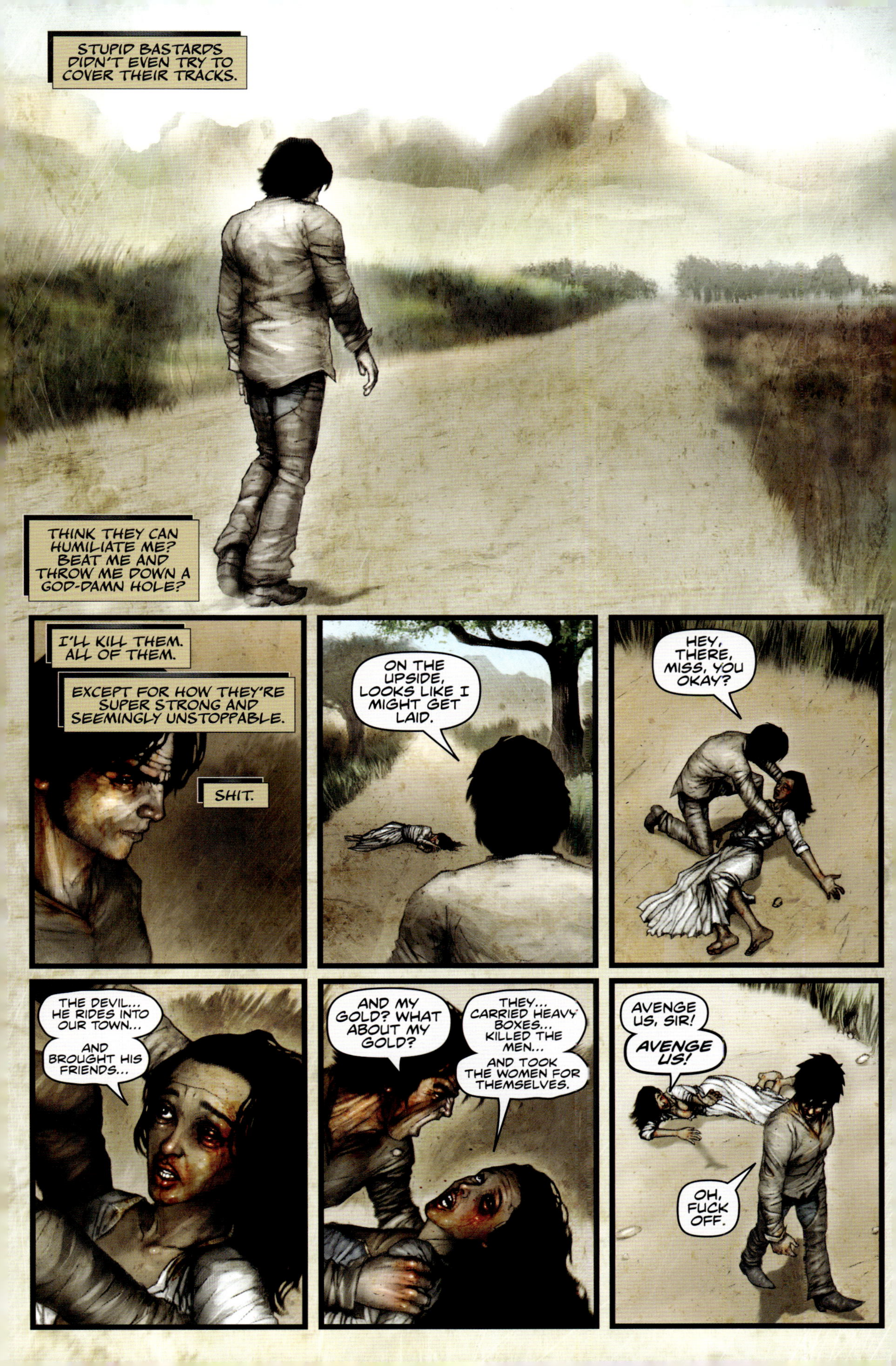
STUPID BASTARDS DIDN'T EVEN TRY TO COVER THEIR TRACKS.
THINK THEY CAN HUMILIATE ME? BEAT ME AND THROW ME DOWN A GOD-DAMN HOLE?
I'LL KILL THEM. ALL OF THEM.
EXCEPT FOR HOW THEY'RE SUPER STRONG AND SEEMINGLY UNSTOPPABLE.
SHIT.
ON THE UPSIDE, LOOKS LIKE I MIGHT GET LAID.
HEY, THERE, MISS, YOU OKAY?
THE DEVIL... HE RIDES INTO OUR TOWN...
AND BROUGHT HIS FRIENDS...
AND MY GOLD? WHAT ABOUT MY GOLD?
THEY... CARRIED HEAVY BOXES... KILLED THE MEN...
AND TOOK THE WOMEN FOR THEMSELVES.
AVENGE US, SIR!
AVENGE US!
OH, FUCK OFF.

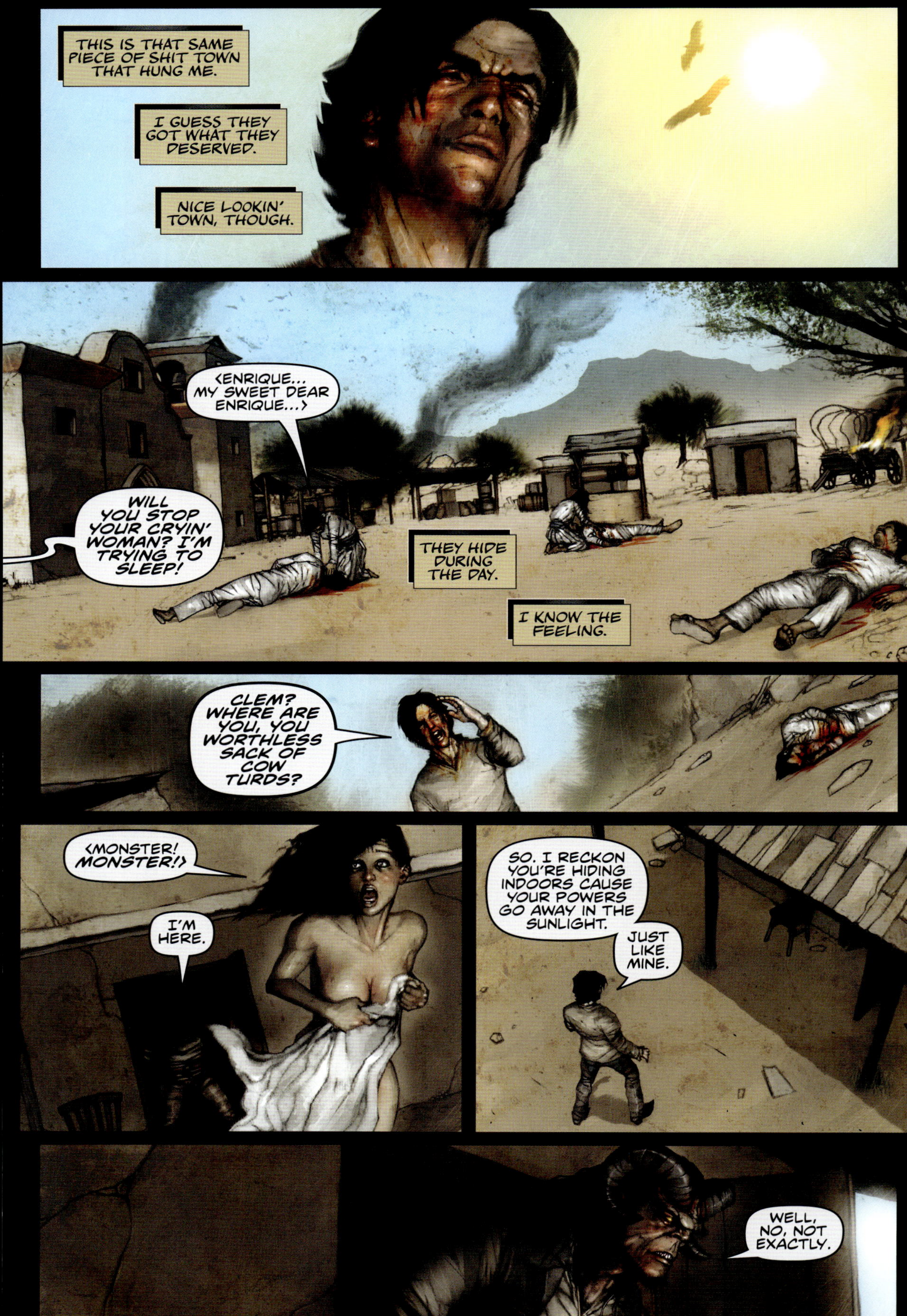
THIS IS THAT SAME PIECE OF SHIT TOWN THAT HUNG ME.
I GUESS THEY GOT WHAT THEY DESERVED.
NICE LOOKIN' TOWN, THOUGH.
<ENRIQUE... MY SWEET DEAR ENRIQUE...>
WILL YOU STOP YOUR CRYIN' WOMAN? I'M TRYING TO SLEEP!
THEY HIDE DURING THE DAY.
I KNOW THE FEELING.
CLEM? WHERE ARE YOU, YOU WORTHLESS SACK OF COW TURDS?
<MONSTER! MONSTER!>
I'M HERE.
SO. I RECKON YOU'RE HIDING INDOORS CAUSE YOUR POWERS GO AWAY IN THE SUNLIGHT.
JUST LIKE MINE.
WELL, NO, NOT EXACTLY.

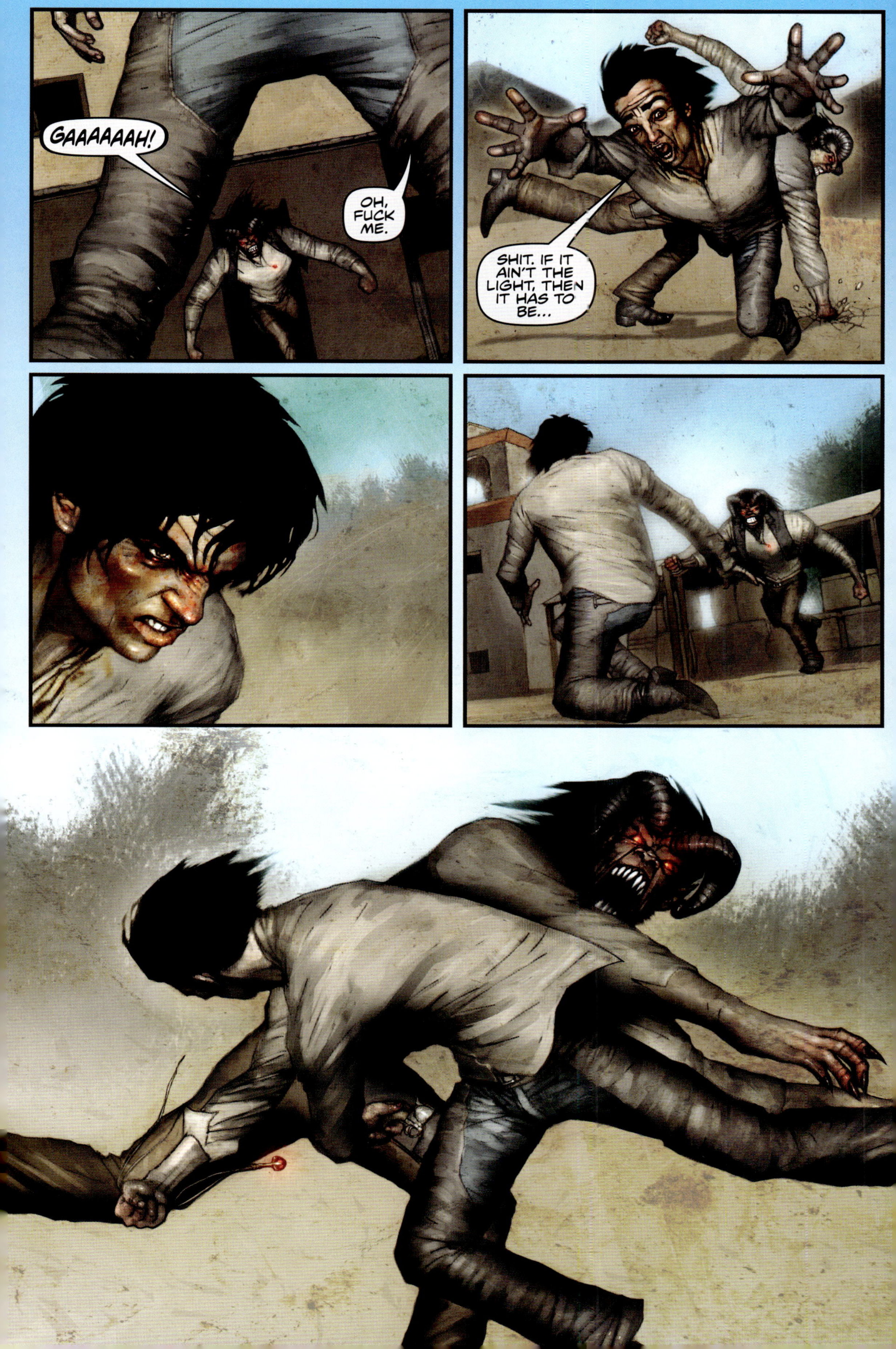
GAAAAAAH!
OH, FUCK ME.
SHIT. IF IT AIN'T THE LIGHT, THEN IT HAS TO BE...

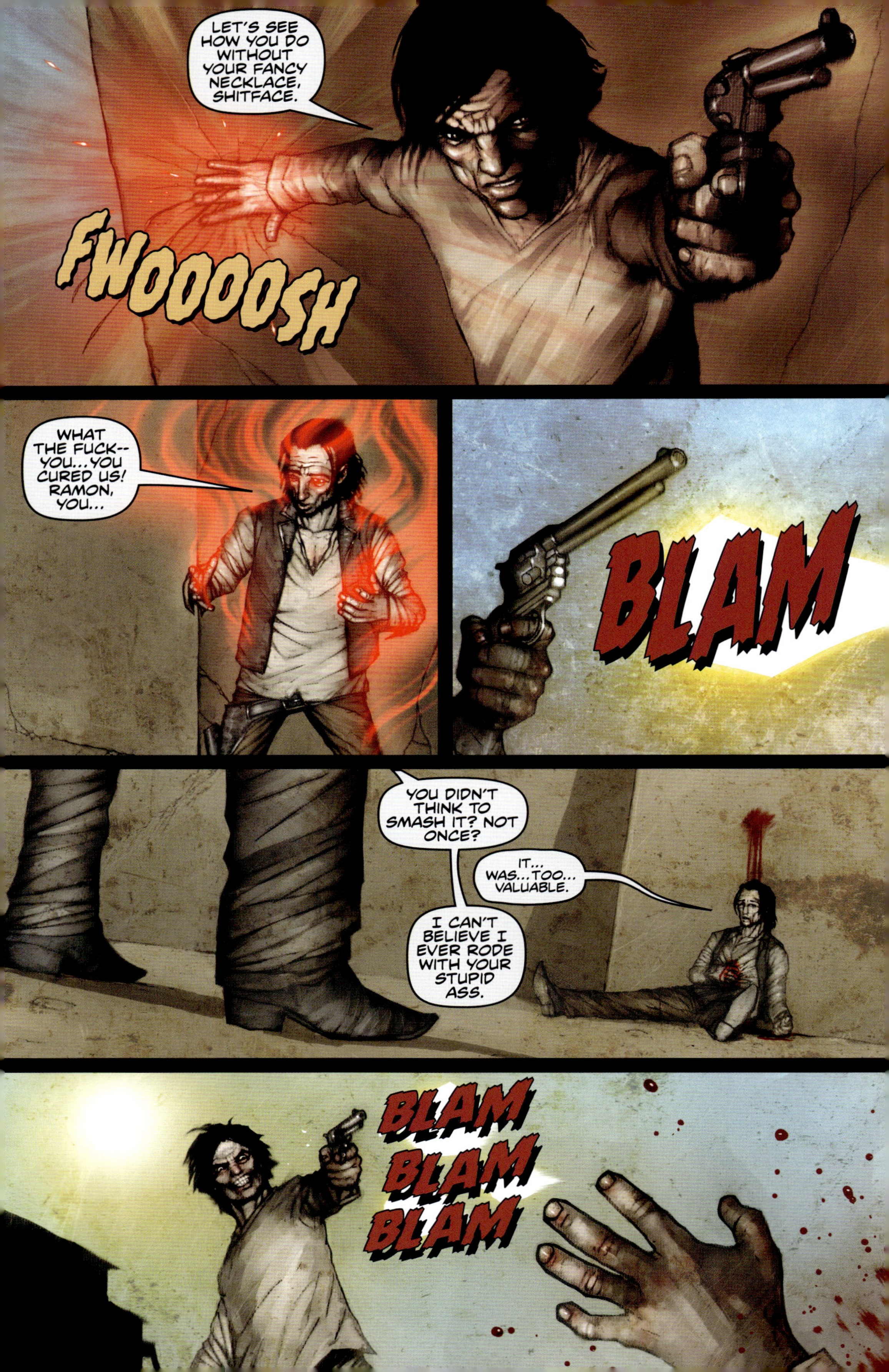
LET'S SEE HOW YOU DO WITHOUT YOUR FANCY NECKLACE, SHITFACE.
FWOOOOSH
WHAT THE FUCK-- YOU...YOU CURED US! RAMON, YOU...
BLAM
YOU DIDN'T THINK TO SMASH IT? NOT ONCE?
IT... WAS...TOO... VALUABLE.
I CAN'T BELIEVE I EVER RODE WITH YOUR STUPID ASS.
BLAM
BLAM
BLAM

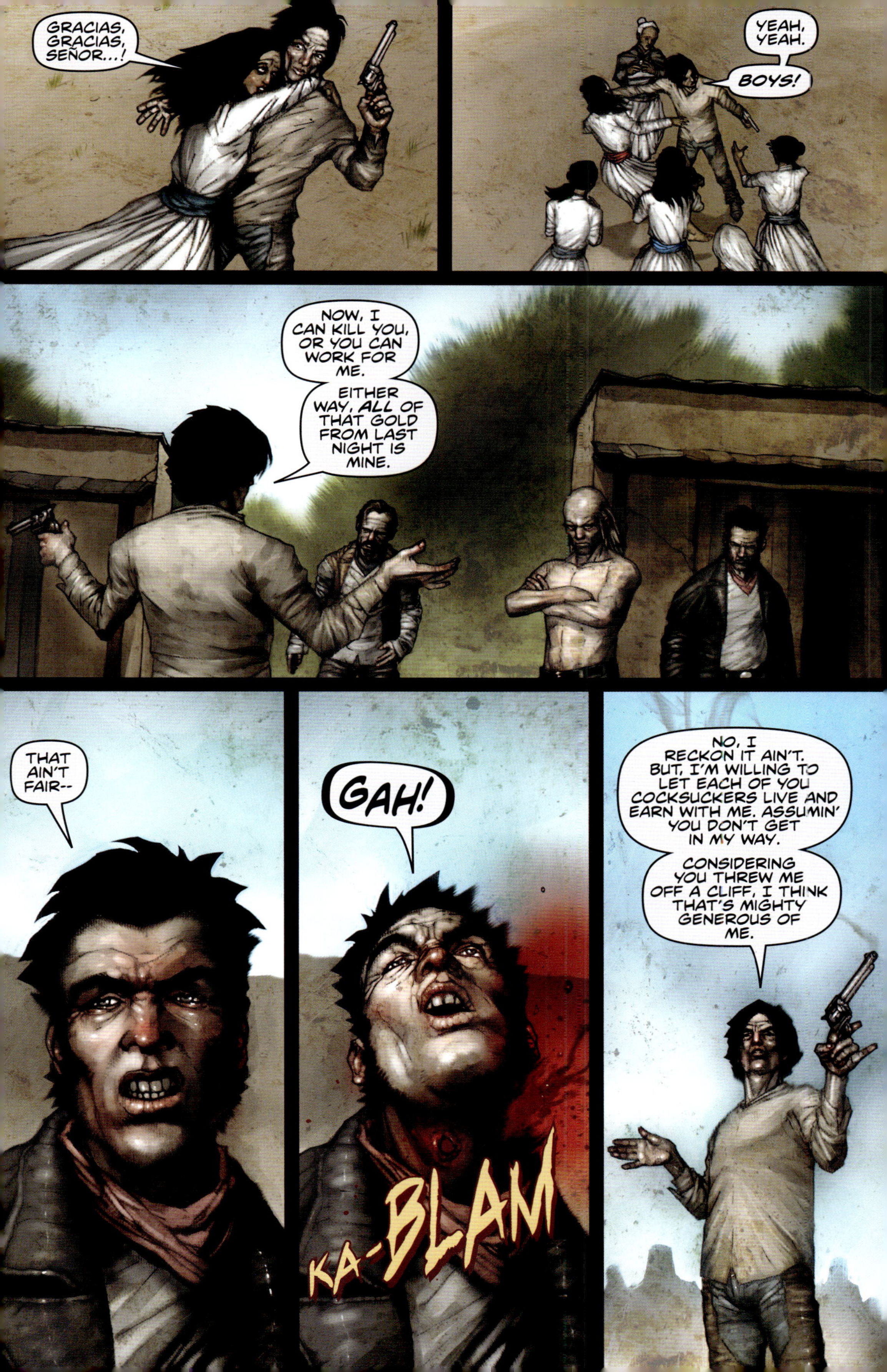
GRACIAS, GRACIAS, SEÑOR...!
YEAH, YEAH.
BOYS!
NOW, I CAN KILL YOU, OR YOU CAN WORK FOR ME.
EITHER WAY, ALL OF THAT GOLD FROM LAST NIGHT IS MINE.
THAT AIN'T FAIR--
GAH!
KA-BLAM
NO, I RECKON IT AIN'T. BUT, I'M WILLING TO LET EACH OF YOU COCKSUCKERS LIVE AND EARN WITH ME. ASSUMIN' YOU DON'T GET IN MY WAY.
CONSIDERING YOU THREW ME OFF A CLIFF, I THINK THAT'S MIGHTY GENEROUS OF ME.

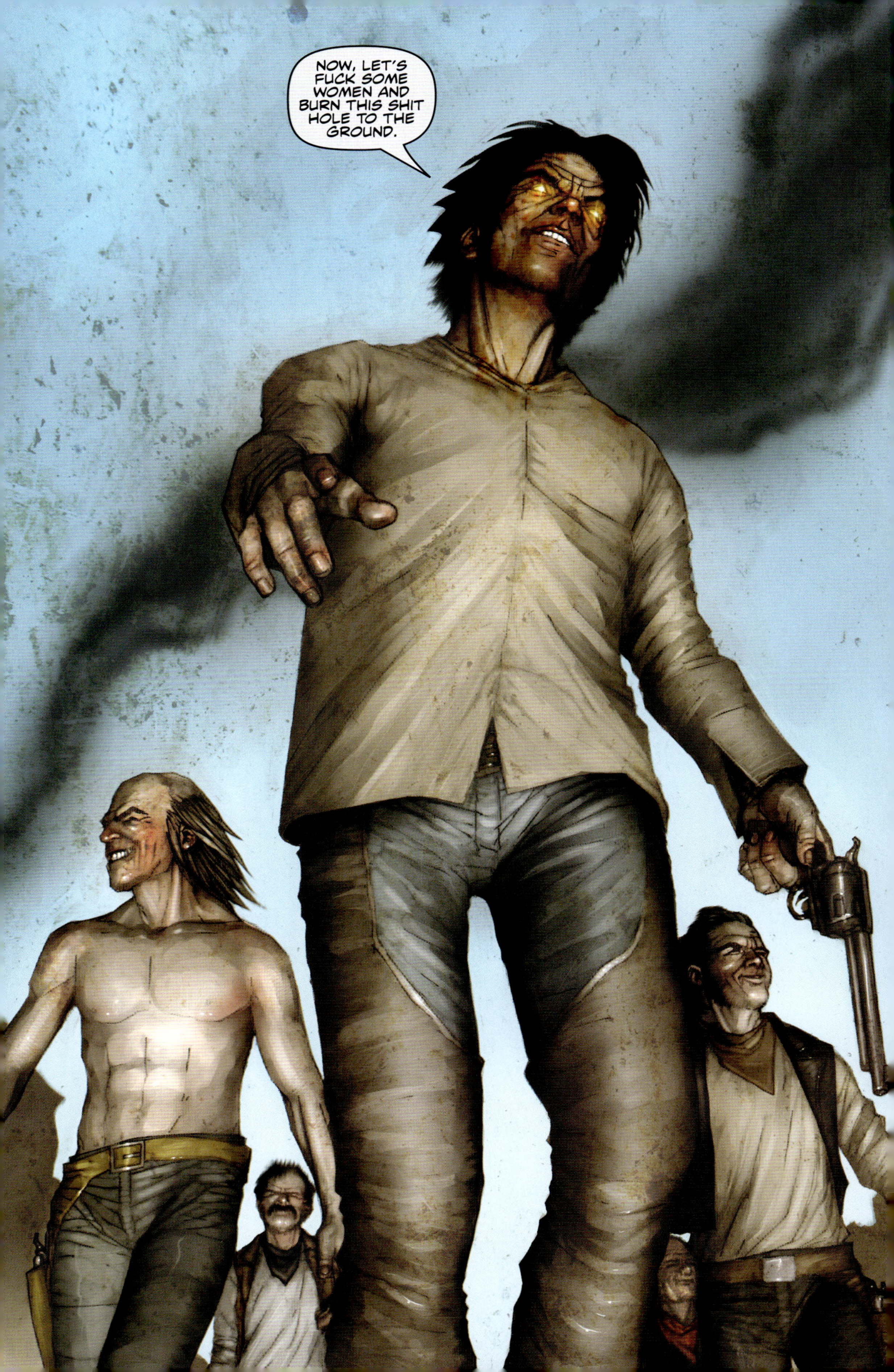
NOW, LET'S FUCK SOME WOMEN AND BURN THIS SHIT HOLE TO THE GROUND.

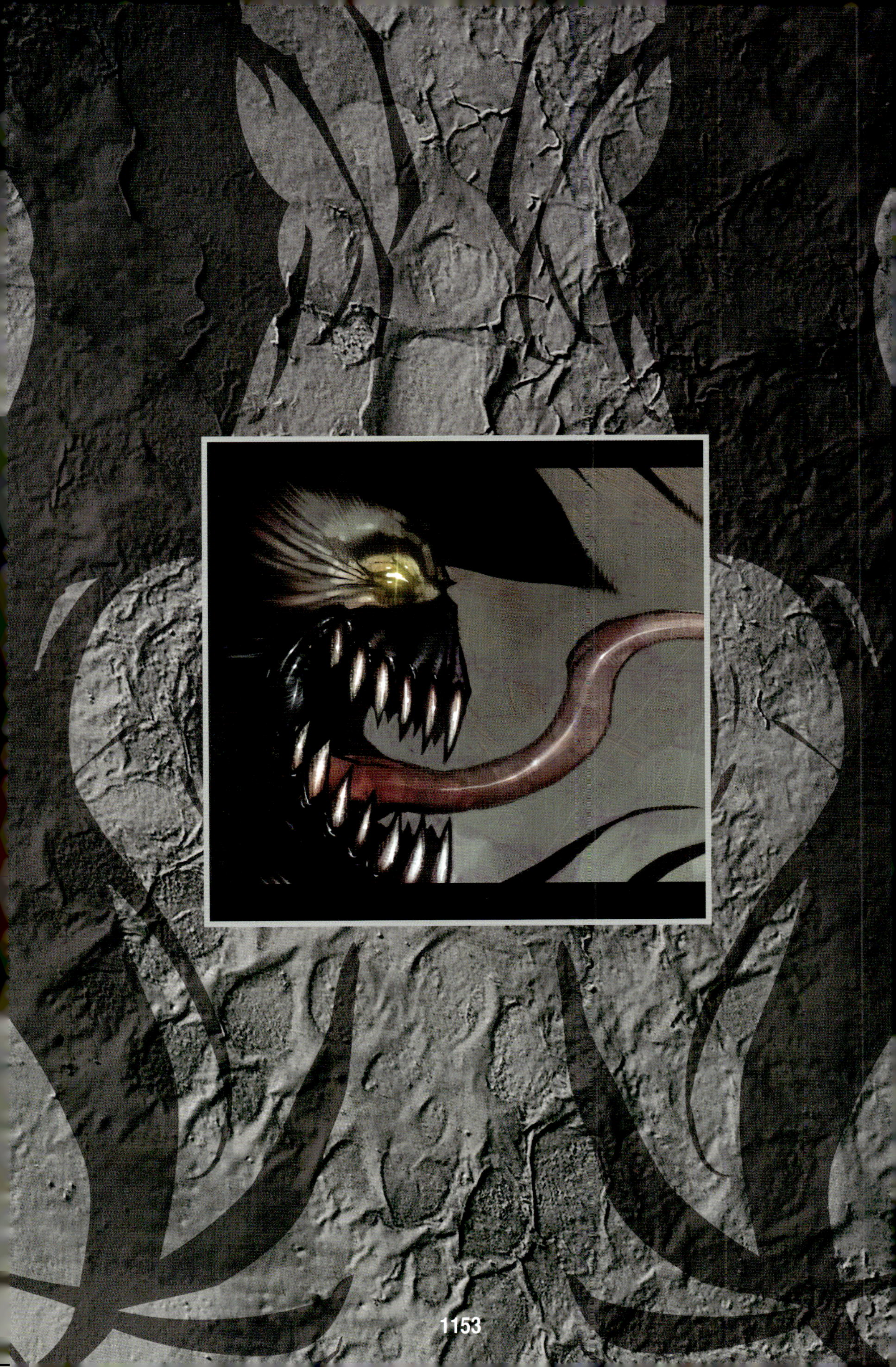

The Darkness: Lodbrok's Hand

cover art by: Michael Avon Oeming and Val Staples

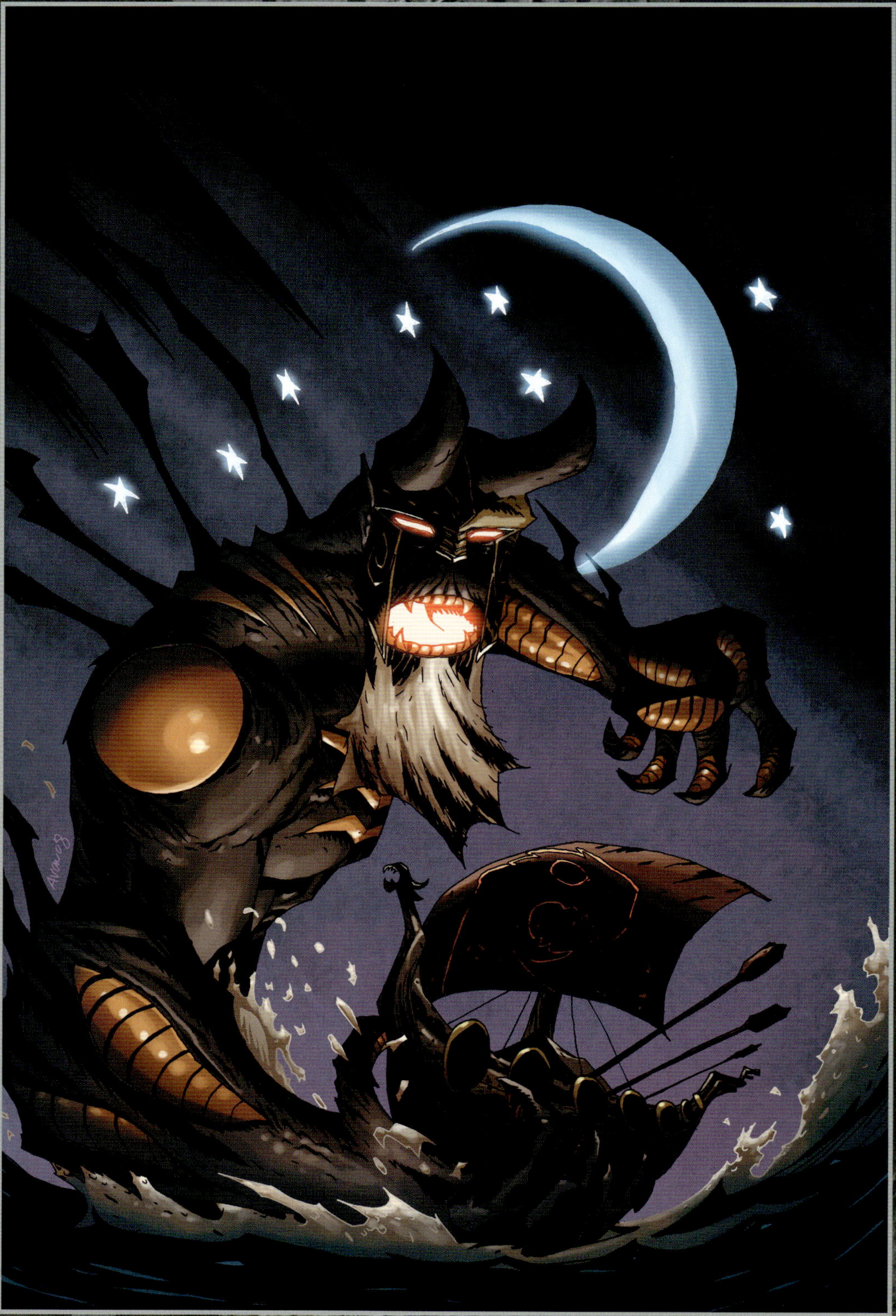

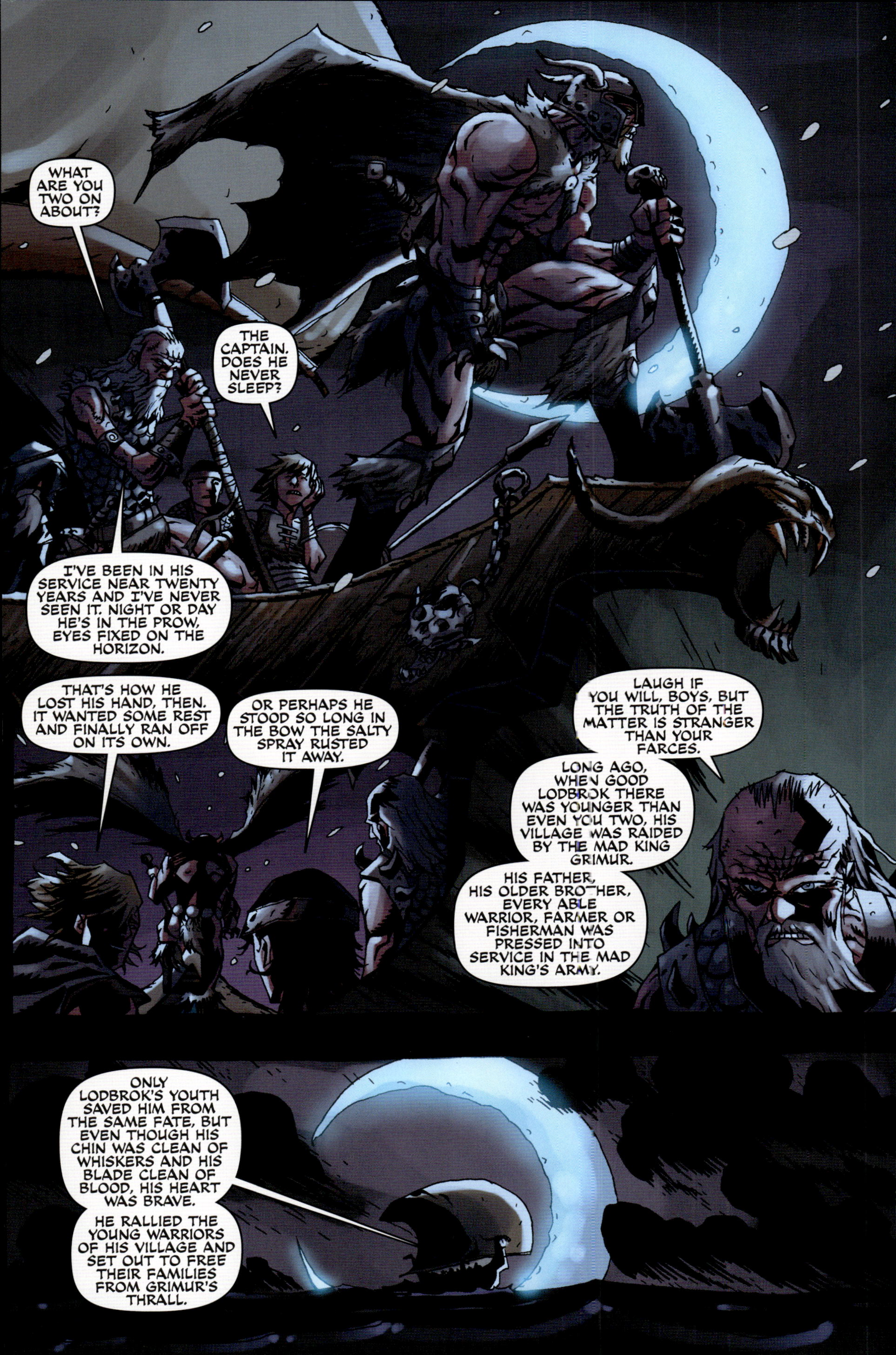
WHAT ARE YOU TWO ON ABOUT?
THE CAPTAIN. DOES HE NEVER SLEEP?
I'VE BEEN IN HIS SERVICE NEAR TWENTY YEARS AND I'VE NEVER SEEN IT. NIGHT OR DAY HE'S IN THE PROW, EYES FIXED ON THE HORIZON.
THAT'S HOW HE LOST HIS HAND, THEN. IT WANTED SOME REST AND FINALLY RAN OFF ON ITS OWN.
OR PERHAPS HE STOOD SO LONG IN THE BOW THE SALTY SPRAY RUSTED IT AWAY.
LAUGH IF YOU WILL, BOYS, BUT THE TRUTH OF THE MATTER IS STRANGER THAN YOUR FARCES.
LONG AGO, WHEN GOOD LODBROK THERE WAS YOUNGER THAN EVEN YOU TWO, HIS VILLAGE WAS RAIDED BY THE MAD KING GRIMUR.
HIS FATHER, HIS OLDER BROTHER, EVERY ABLE WARRIOR, FARMER OR FISHERMAN WAS PRESSED INTO SERVICE IN THE MAD KING'S ARMY.
ONLY LODBROK'S YOUTH SAVED HIM FROM THE SAME FATE, BUT EVEN THOUGH HIS CHIN WAS CLEAN OF WHISKERS AND HIS BLADE CLEAN OF BLOOD, HIS HEART WAS BRAVE.
HE RALLIED THE YOUNG WARRIORS OF HIS VILLAGE AND SET OUT TO FREE THEIR FAMILIES FROM GRIMUR'S THRALL.

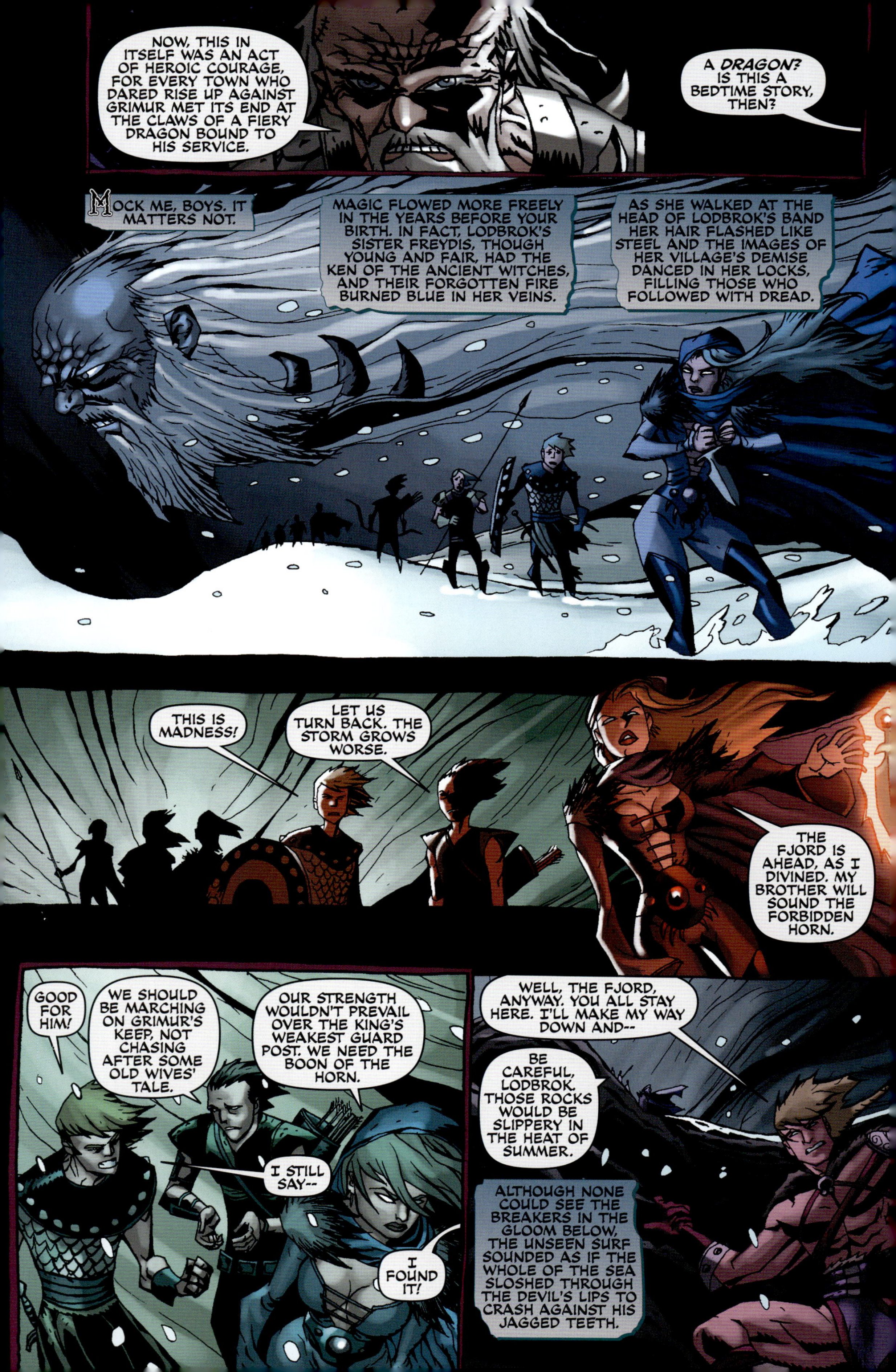
NOW, THIS IN ITSELF WAS AN ACT OF HEROIC COURAGE, FOR EVERY TOWN WHO DARED RISE UP AGAINST GRIMUR MET ITS END AT THE CLAWS OF A FIERY DRAGON BOUND TO HIS SERVICE.
A DRAGON? IS THIS A BEDTIME STORY, THEN?
MOCK ME, BOYS. IT MATTERS NOT.
MAGIC FLOWED MORE FREELY IN THE YEARS BEFORE YOUR BIRTH. IN FACT, LODBROK'S SISTER FREYDIS, THOUGH YOUNG AND FAIR, HAD THE KEN OF THE ANCIENT WITCHES, AND THEIR FORGOTTEN FIRE BURNED BLUE IN HER VEINS.
AS SHE WALKED AT THE HEAD OF LODBROK'S BAND HER HAIR FLASHED LIKE STEEL AND THE IMAGES OF HER VILLAGE'S DEMISE DANCED IN HER LOCKS, FILLING THOSE WHO FOLLOWED WITH DREAD.
THIS IS MADNESS!
LET US TURN BACK. THE STORM GROWS WORSE.
THE FJORD IS AHEAD, AS I DIVINED. MY BROTHER WILL SOUND THE FORBIDDEN HORN.
GOOD FOR HIM!
WE SHOULD BE MARCHING ON GRIMUR'S KEEP, NOT CHASING AFTER SOME OLD WIVES' TALE.
OUR STRENGTH WOULDN'T PREVAIL OVER THE KING'S WEAKEST GUARD POST. WE NEED THE BOON OF THE HORN.
I STILL SAY--
I FOUND IT!
WELL, THE FJORD, ANYWAY. YOU ALL STAY HERE. I'LL MAKE MY WAY DOWN AND--
BE CAREFUL, LODBROK. THOSE ROCKS WOULD BE SLIPPERY IN THE HEAT OF SUMMER.
ALTHOUGH NONE COULD SEE THE BREAKERS IN THE GLOOM BELOW, THE UNSEEN SURF SOUNDED AS IF THE WHOLE OF THE SEA SLOSHED THROUGH THE DEVIL'S LIPS TO CRASH AGAINST HIS JAGGED TEETH.

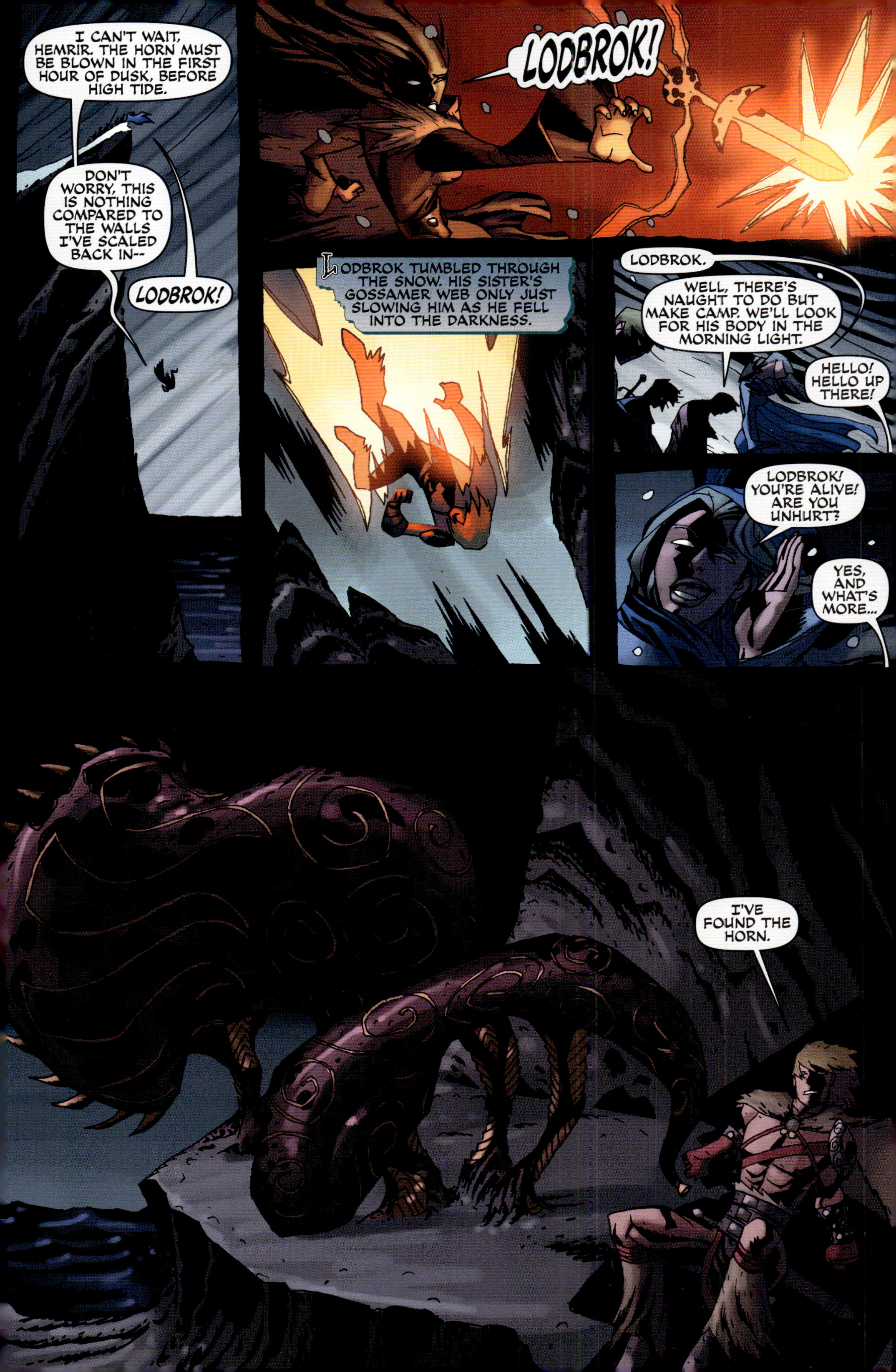
I CAN'T WAIT, HEMRIR. THE HORN MUST BE BLOWN IN THE FIRST HOUR OF DUSK, BEFORE HIGH TIDE.
DON'T WORRY, THIS IS NOTHING COMPARED TO THE WALLS I'VE SCALED BACK IN--
LODBROK!
LODBROK!
LODBROK TUMBLED THROUGH THE SNOW. HIS SISTER'S GOSSAMER WEB ONLY JUST SLOWING HIM AS HE FELL INTO THE DARKNESS.
LODBROK.
WELL, THERE'S NAUGHT TO DO BUT MAKE CAMP. WE'LL LOOK FOR HIS BODY IN THE MORNING LIGHT.
HELLO! HELLO UP THERE!
LODBROK! YOU'RE ALIVE! ARE YOU UNHURT?
YES, AND WHAT'S MORE...
I'VE FOUND THE HORN.

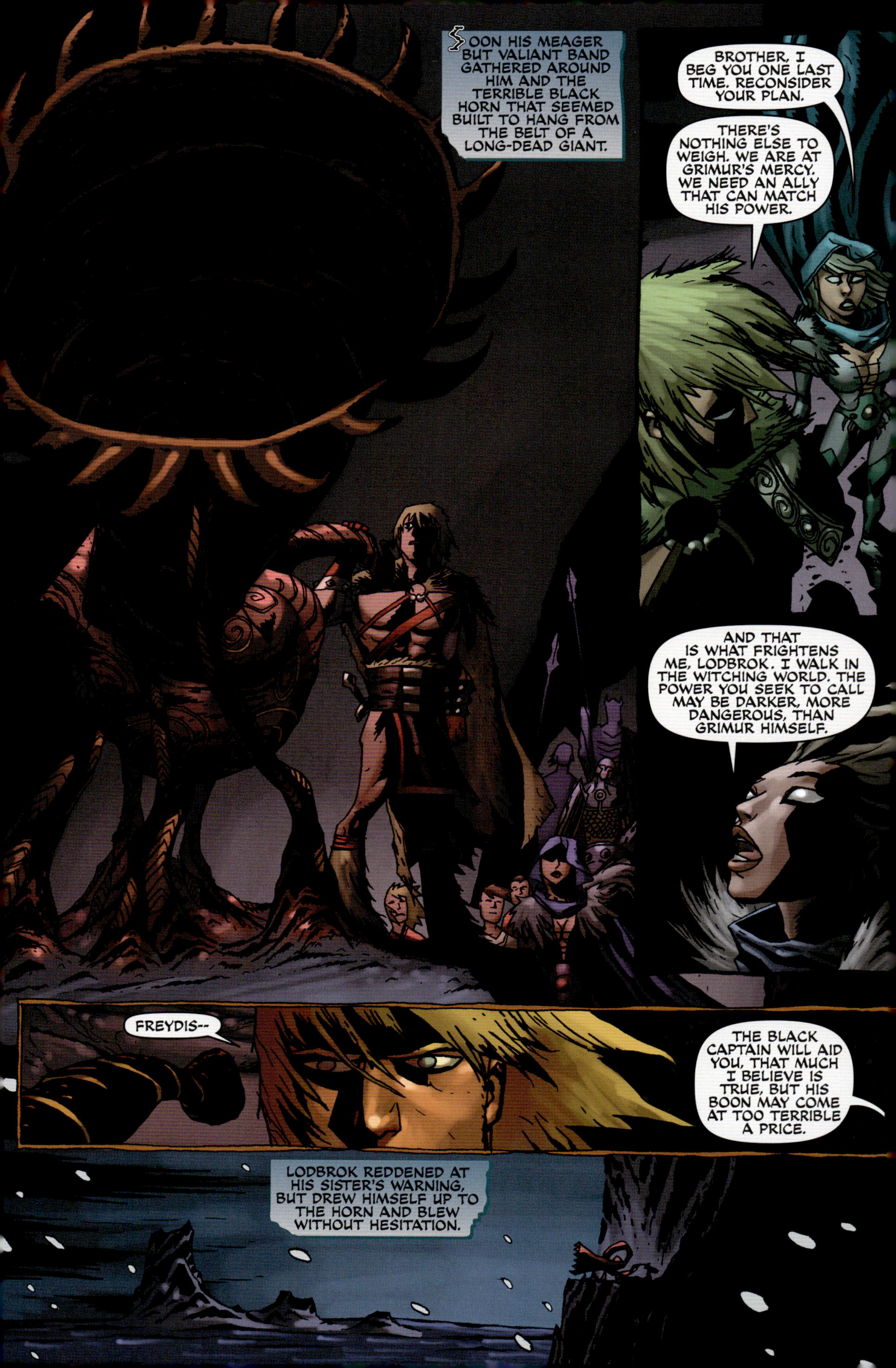
SOON HIS MEAGER BUT VALIANT BAND GATHERED AROUND HIM AND THE TERRIBLE BLACK HORN THAT SEEMED BUILT TO HANG FROM THE BELT OF A LONG-DEAD GIANT.
BROTHER, I BEG YOU ONE LAST TIME. RECONSIDER YOUR PLAN.
THERE'S NOTHING ELSE TO WEIGH. WE ARE AT GRIMUR'S MERCY. WE NEED AN ALLY THAT CAN MATCH HIS POWER.
AND THAT IS WHAT FRIGHTENS ME, LODBROK. I WALK IN THE WITCHING WORLD. THE POWER YOU SEEK TO CALL MAY BE DARKER, MORE DANGEROUS, THAN GRIMUR HIMSELF.
FREYDIS--
THE BLACK CAPTAIN WILL AID YOU, THAT MUCH I BELIEVE IS TRUE, BUT HIS BOON MAY COME AT TOO TERRIBLE A PRICE.
LODBROK REDDENED AT HIS SISTER'S WARNING, BUT DREW HIMSELF UP TO THE HORN AND BLEW WITHOUT HESITATION.

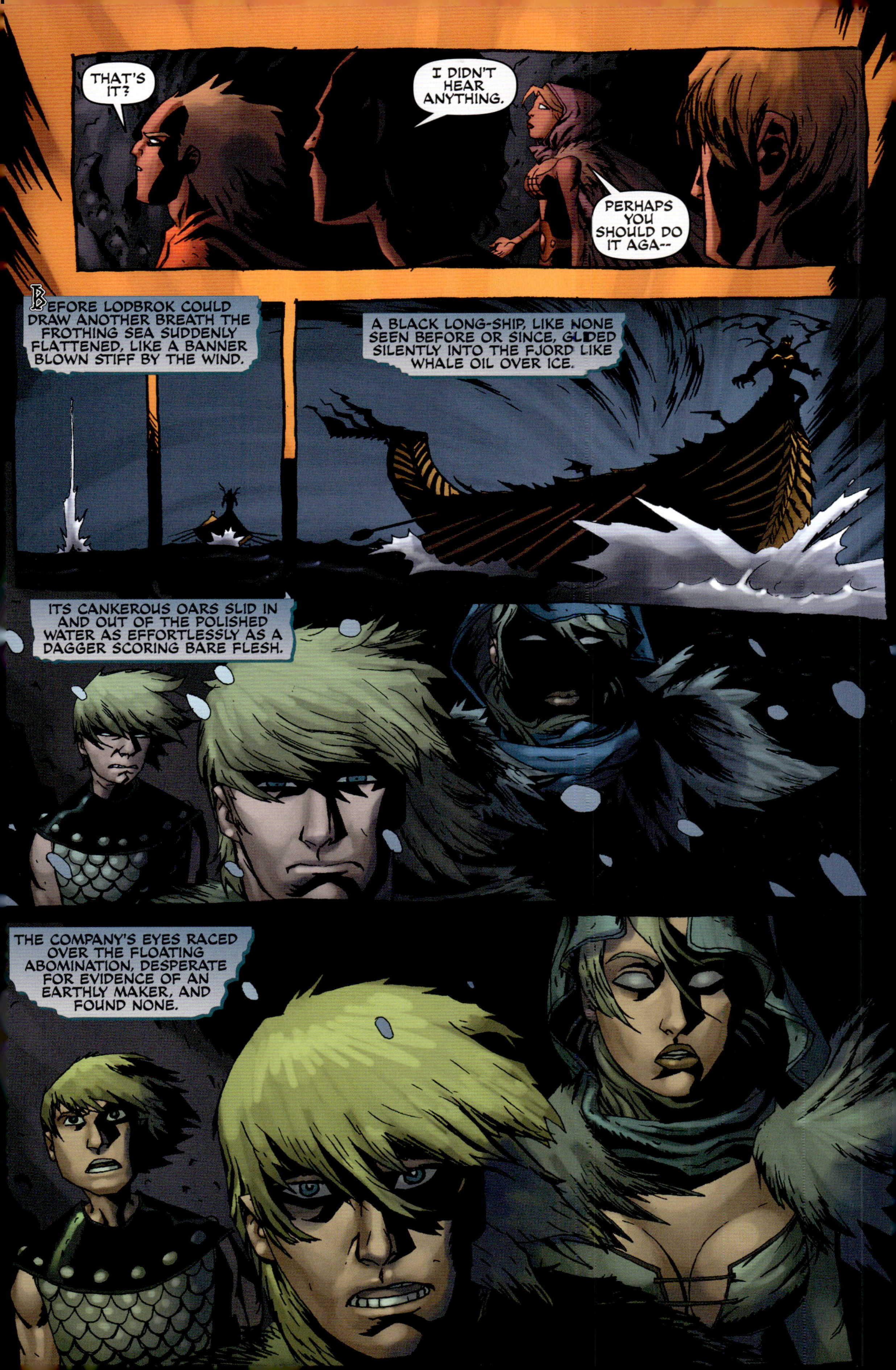
THAT'S IT?
I DIDN'T HEAR ANYTHING.
PERHAPS YOU SHOULD DO IT AGA--
BEFORE LODBROK COULD DRAW ANOTHER BREATH THE FROTHING SEA SUDDENLY FLATTENED, LIKE A BANNER BLOWN STIFF BY THE WIND.
A BLACK LONG-SHIP, LIKE NONE SEEN BEFORE OR SINCE, GLIDED SILENTLY INTO THE FJORD LIKE WHALE OIL OVER ICE.
ITS CANKEROUS OARS SLID IN AND OUT OF THE POLISHED WATER AS EFFORTLESSLY AS A DAGGER SCORING BARE FLESH.
THE COMPANY'S EYES RACED OVER THE FLOATING ABOMINATION, DESPERATE FOR EVIDENCE OF AN EARTHLY MAKER, AND FOUND NONE.

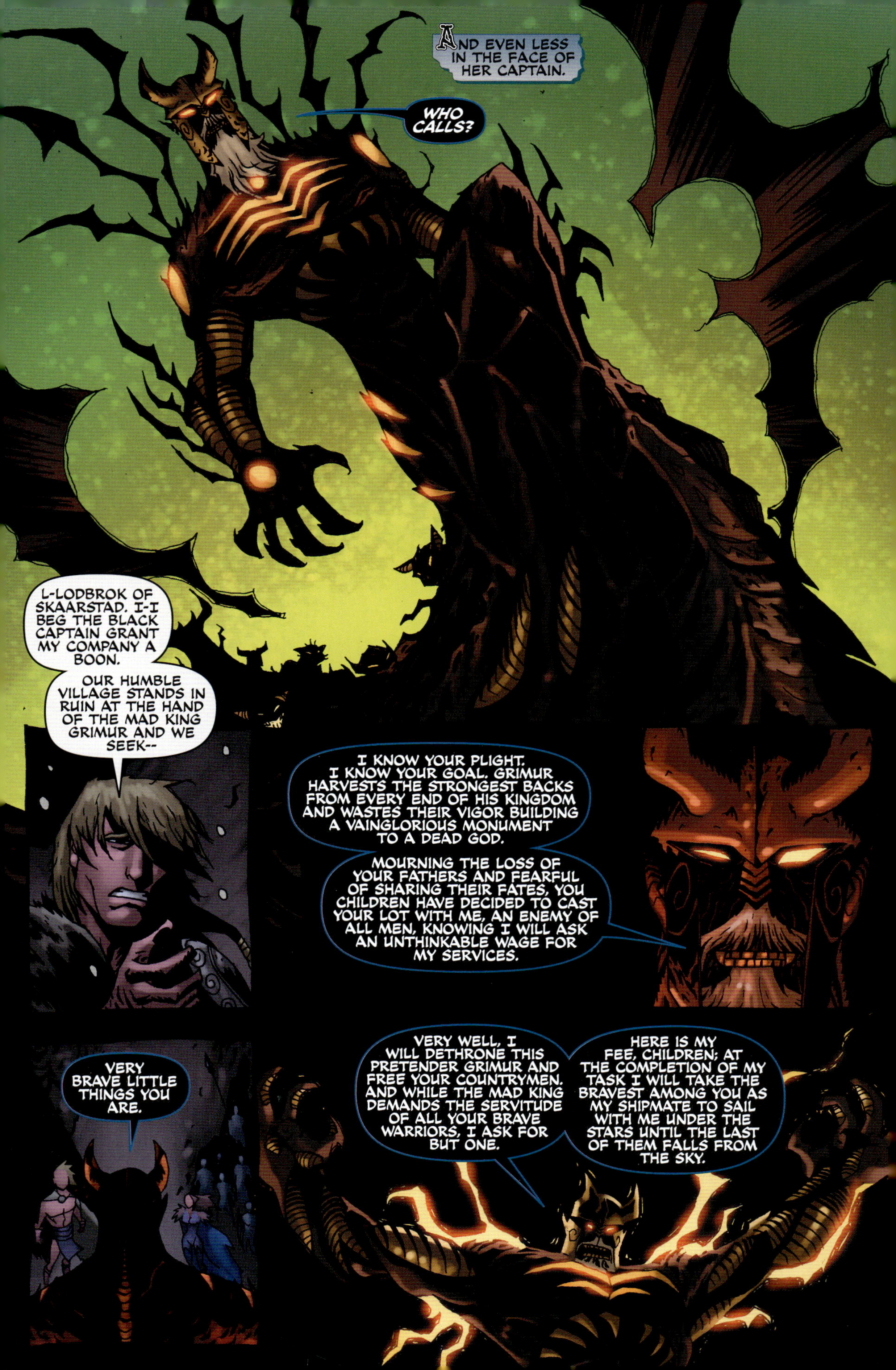
AND EVEN LESS IN THE FACE OF HER CAPTAIN.
WHO CALLS?
L-LODBROK OF SKAARSTAD. I-I BEG THE BLACK CAPTAIN GRANT MY COMPANY A BOON.
OUR HUMBLE VILLAGE STANDS IN RUIN AT THE HAND OF THE MAD KING GRIMUR AND WE SEEK--
I KNOW YOUR PLIGHT. I KNOW YOUR GOAL. GRIMUR HARVESTS THE STRONGEST BACKS FROM EVERY END OF HIS KINGDOM AND WASTES THEIR VIGOR BUILDING A VAINGLORIOUS MONUMENT TO A DEAD GOD.
MOURNING THE LOSS OF YOUR FATHERS AND FEARFUL OF SHARING THEIR FATES, YOU CHILDREN HAVE DECIDED TO CAST YOUR LOT WITH ME, AN ENEMY OF ALL MEN, KNOWING I WILL ASK AN UNTHINKABLE WAGE FOR MY SERVICES.
VERY BRAVE LITTLE THINGS YOU ARE.
VERY WELL, I WILL DETHRONE THIS PRETENDER GRIMUR AND FREE YOUR COUNTRYMEN. AND WHILE THE MAD KING DEMANDS THE SERVITUDE OF ALL YOUR BRAVE WARRIORS, I ASK FOR BUT ONE.
HERE IS MY FEE, CHILDREN; AT THE COMPLETION OF MY TASK I WILL TAKE THE BRAVEST AMONG YOU AS MY SHIPMATE TO SAIL WITH ME UNDER THE STARS UNTIL THE LAST OF THEM FALLS FROM THE SKY.

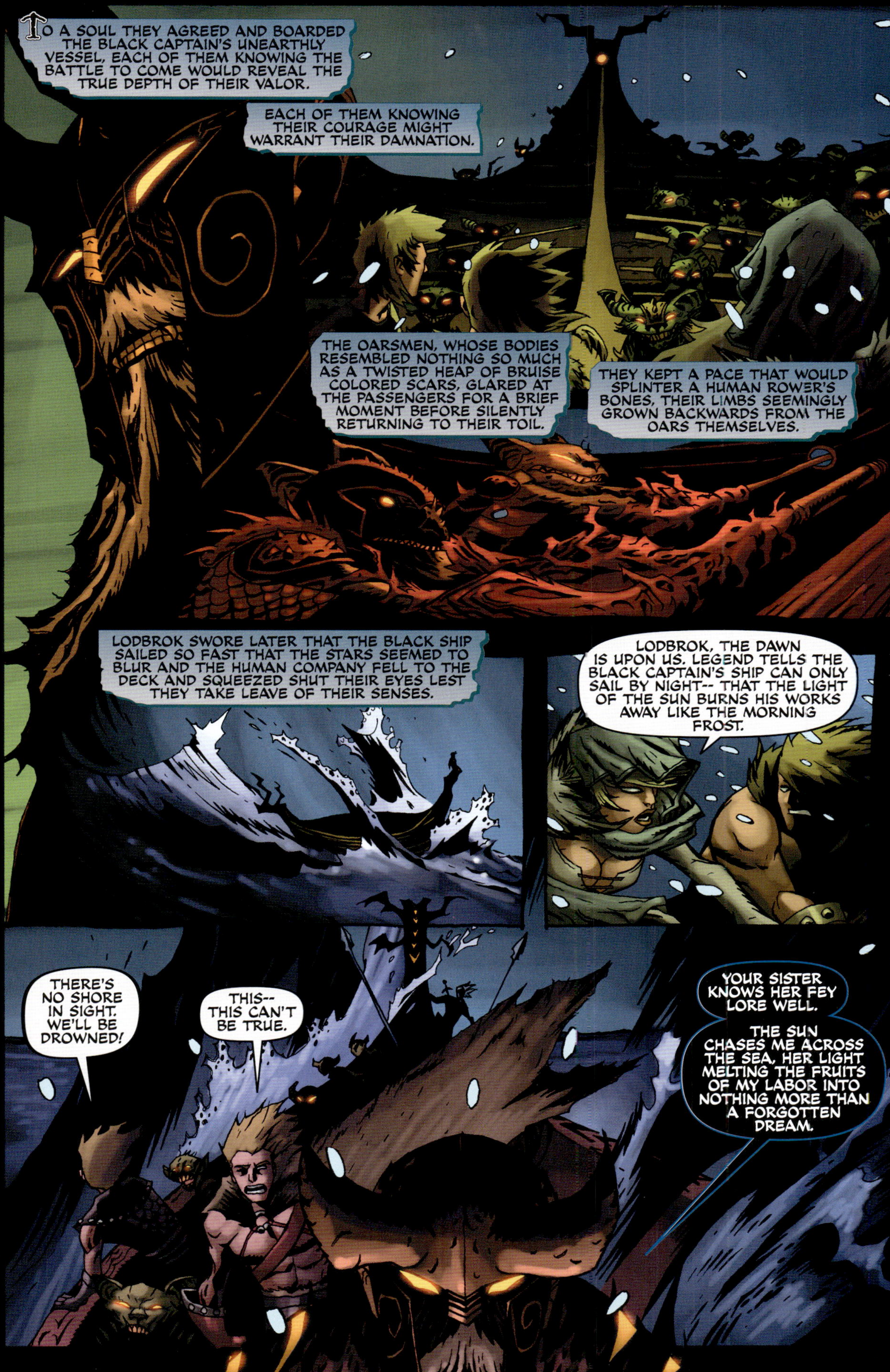
TO A SOUL THEY AGREED AND BOARDED THE BLACK CAPTAIN'S UNEARTHLY VESSEL, EACH OF THEM KNOWING THE BATTLE TO COME WOULD REVEAL THE TRUE DEPTH OF THEIR VALOR.
EACH OF THEM KNOWING THEIR COURAGE MIGHT WARRANT THEIR DAMNATION.
THE OARSMEN, WHOSE BODIES RESEMBLED NOTHING SO MUCH AS A TWISTED HEAP OF BRUISE COLORED SCARS, GLARED AT THE PASSENGERS FOR A BRIEF MOMENT BEFORE SILENTLY RETURNING TO THEIR TOIL.
THEY KEPT A PACE THAT WOULD SPLINTER A HUMAN ROWER'S BONES, THEIR LIMBS SEEMINGLY GROWN BACKWARDS FROM THE OARS THEMSELVES.
LODBROK SWORE LATER THAT THE BLACK SHIP SAILED SO FAST THAT THE STARS SEEMED TO BLUR AND THE HUMAN COMPANY FELL TO THE DECK AND SQUEEZED SHUT THEIR EYES LEST THEY TAKE LEAVE OF THEIR SENSES.
LODBROK, THE DAWN IS UPON US. LEGEND TELLS THE BLACK CAPTAIN'S SHIP CAN ONLY SAIL BY NIGHT-- THAT THE LIGHT OF THE SUN BURNS HIS WORKS AWAY LIKE THE MORNING FROST.
THERE'S NO SHORE IN SIGHT. WE'LL BE DROWNED!
THIS-- THIS CAN'T BE TRUE.
YOUR SISTER KNOWS HER FEY LORE WELL.
THE SUN CHASES ME ACROSS THE SEA, HER LIGHT MELTING THE FRUITS OF MY LABOR INTO NOTHING MORE THAN A FORGOTTEN DREAM.

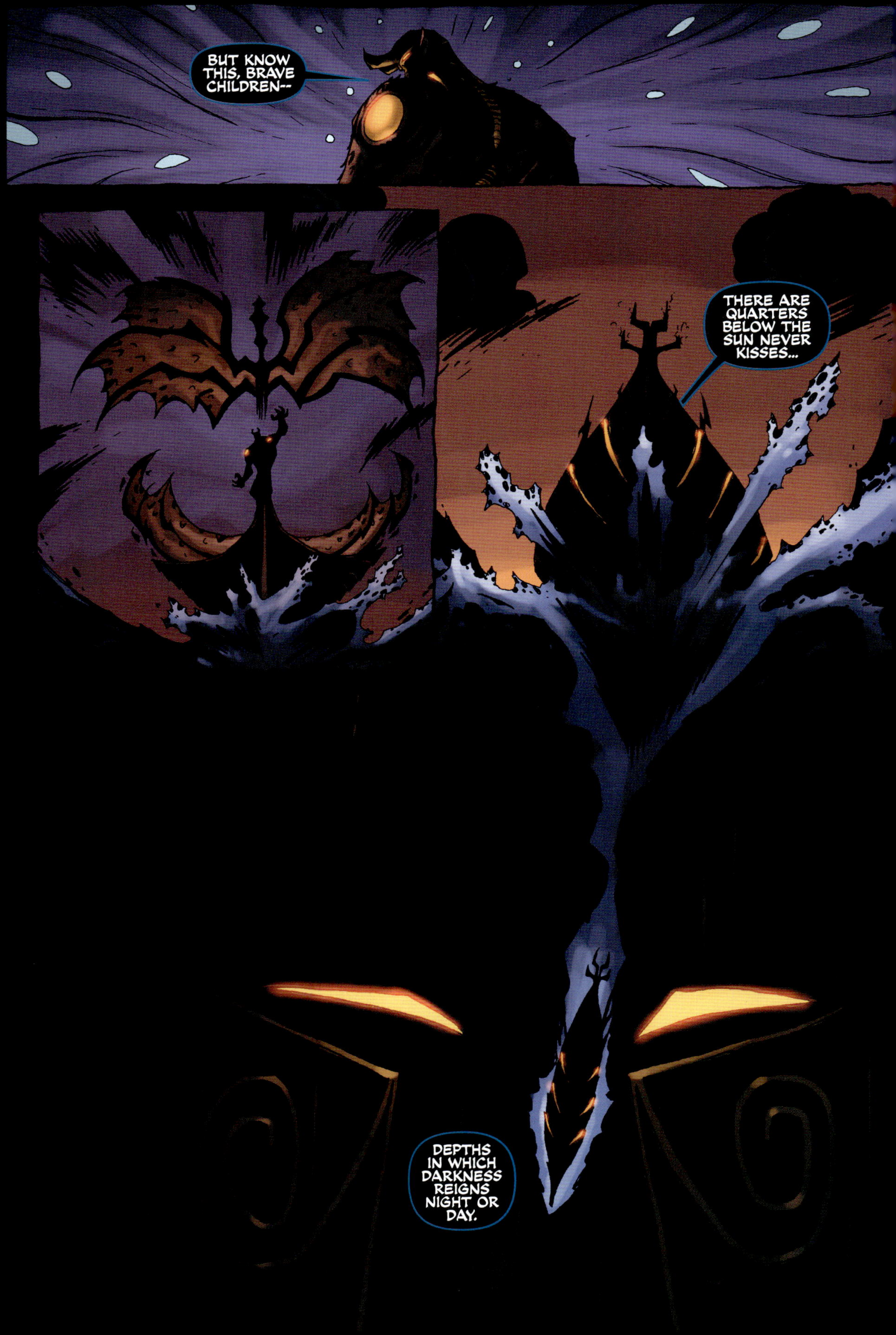
BUT KNOW THIS, BRAVE CHILDREN--
THERE ARE QUARTERS BELOW THE SUN NEVER KISSES...
DEPTHS IN WHICH DARKNESS REIGNS NIGHT OR DAY.

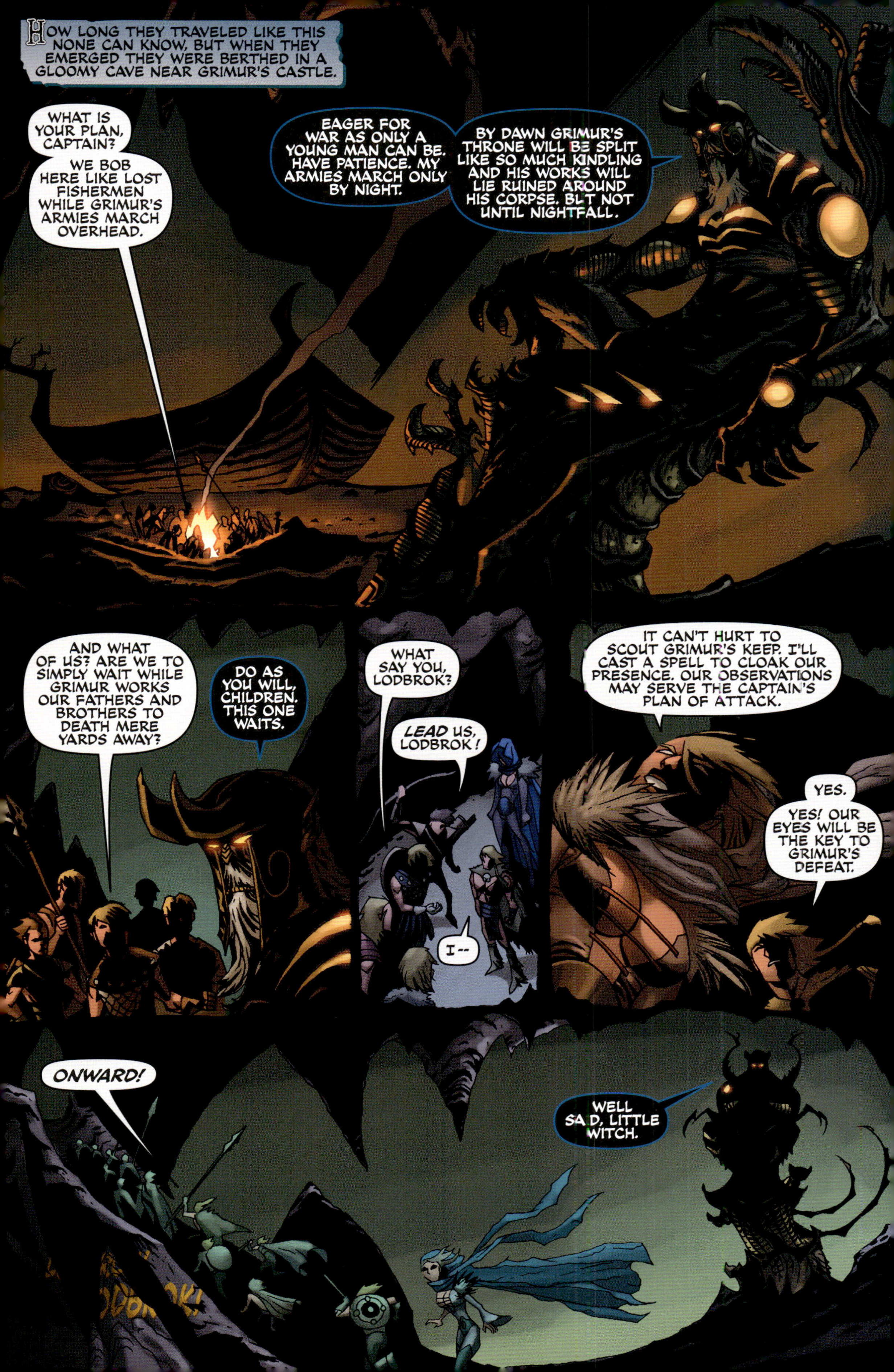
HOW LONG THEY TRAVELED LIKE THIS NONE CAN KNOW, BUT WHEN THEY EMERGED THEY WERE BERTHED IN A GLOOMY CAVE NEAR GRIMUR'S CASTLE.
WHAT IS YOUR PLAN, CAPTAIN?
WE BOB HERE LIKE LOST FISHERMEN WHILE GRIMUR'S ARMIES MARCH OVERHEAD.
EAGER FOR WAR AS ONLY A YOUNG MAN CAN BE. HAVE PATIENCE. MY ARMIES MARCH ONLY BY NIGHT.
BY DAWN GRIMUR'S THRONE WILL BE SPLIT LIKE SO MUCH KINDLING AND HIS WORKS WILL LIE RUINED AROUND HIS CORPSE. BUT NOT UNTIL NIGHTFALL.
AND WHAT OF US? ARE WE TO SIMPLY WAIT WHILE GRIMUR WORKS OUR FATHERS AND BROTHERS TO DEATH MERE YARDS AWAY?
DO AS YOU WILL, CHILDREN. THIS ONE WAITS.
WHAT SAY YOU, LODBROK?
LEAD US, LODBROK!
I--
IT CAN'T HURT TO SCOUT GRIMUR'S KEEP. I'LL CAST A SPELL TO CLOAK OUR PRESENCE. OUR OBSERVATIONS MAY SERVE THE CAPTAIN'S PLAN OF ATTACK.
YES.
YES! OUR EYES WILL BE THE KEY TO GRIMUR'S DEFEAT.
ONWARD!
WELL SAID, LITTLE WITCH.

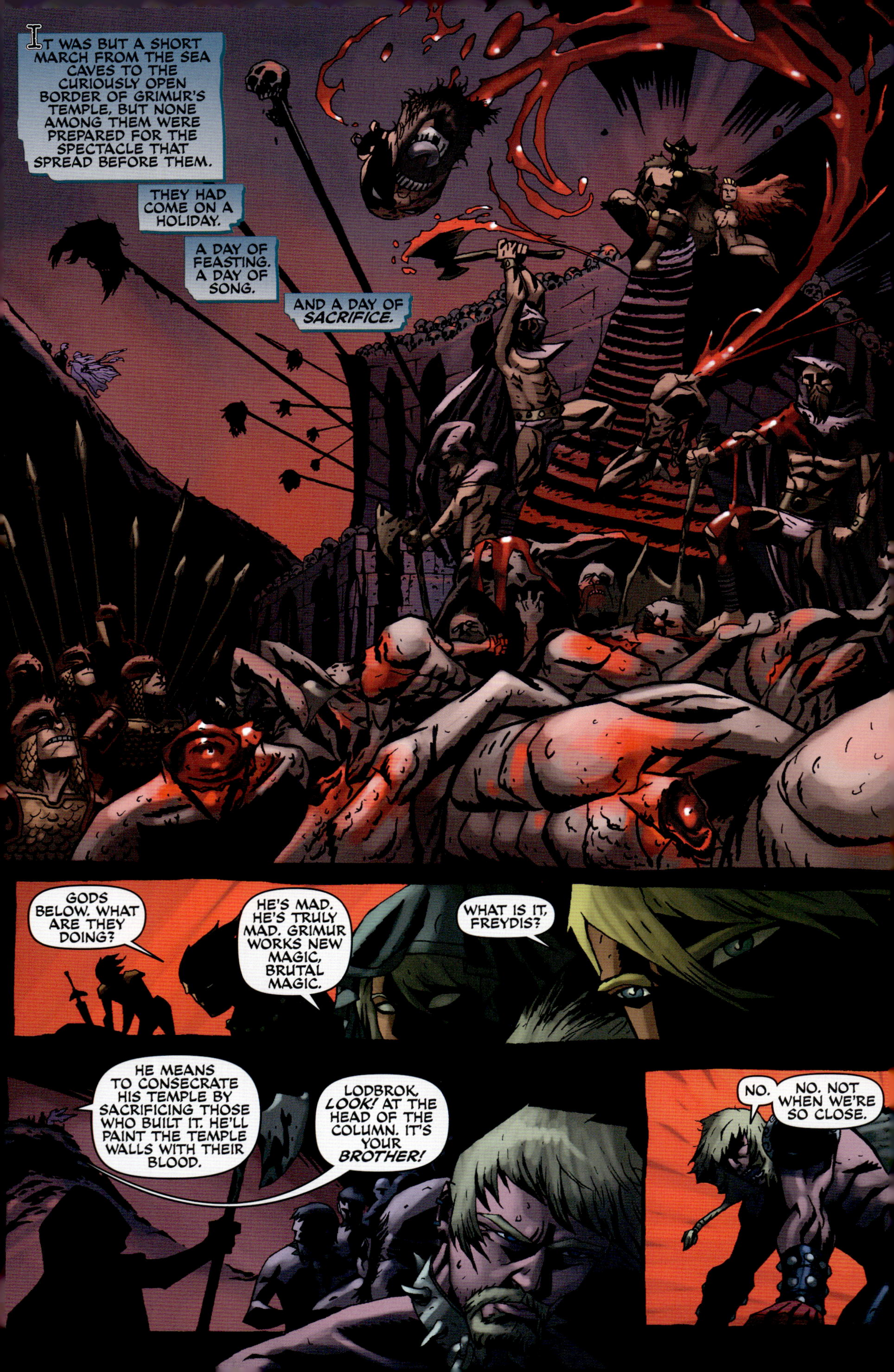
IT WAS BUT A SHORT MARCH FROM THE SEA CAVES TO THE CURIOUSLY OPEN BORDER OF GRIMUR'S TEMPLE, BUT NONE AMONG THEM WERE PREPARED FOR THE SPECTACLE THAT SPREAD BEFORE THEM.
THEY HAD COME ON A HOLIDAY.
A DAY OF FEASTING. A DAY OF SONG.
AND A DAY OF *SACRIFICE.*
GODS BELOW. WHAT ARE THEY DOING?
HE'S MAD. HE'S TRULY MAD. GRIMUR WORKS NEW MAGIC, BRUTAL MAGIC.
WHAT IS IT, FREYDIS?
HE MEANS TO CONSECRATE HIS TEMPLE BY SACRIFICING THOSE WHO BUILT IT. HE'LL PAINT THE TEMPLE WALLS WITH THEIR BLOOD.
LODBROK, *LOOK!* AT THE HEAD OF THE COLUMN. IT'S YOUR *BROTHER!*
NO.
NO. NOT WHEN WE'RE SO CLOSE.

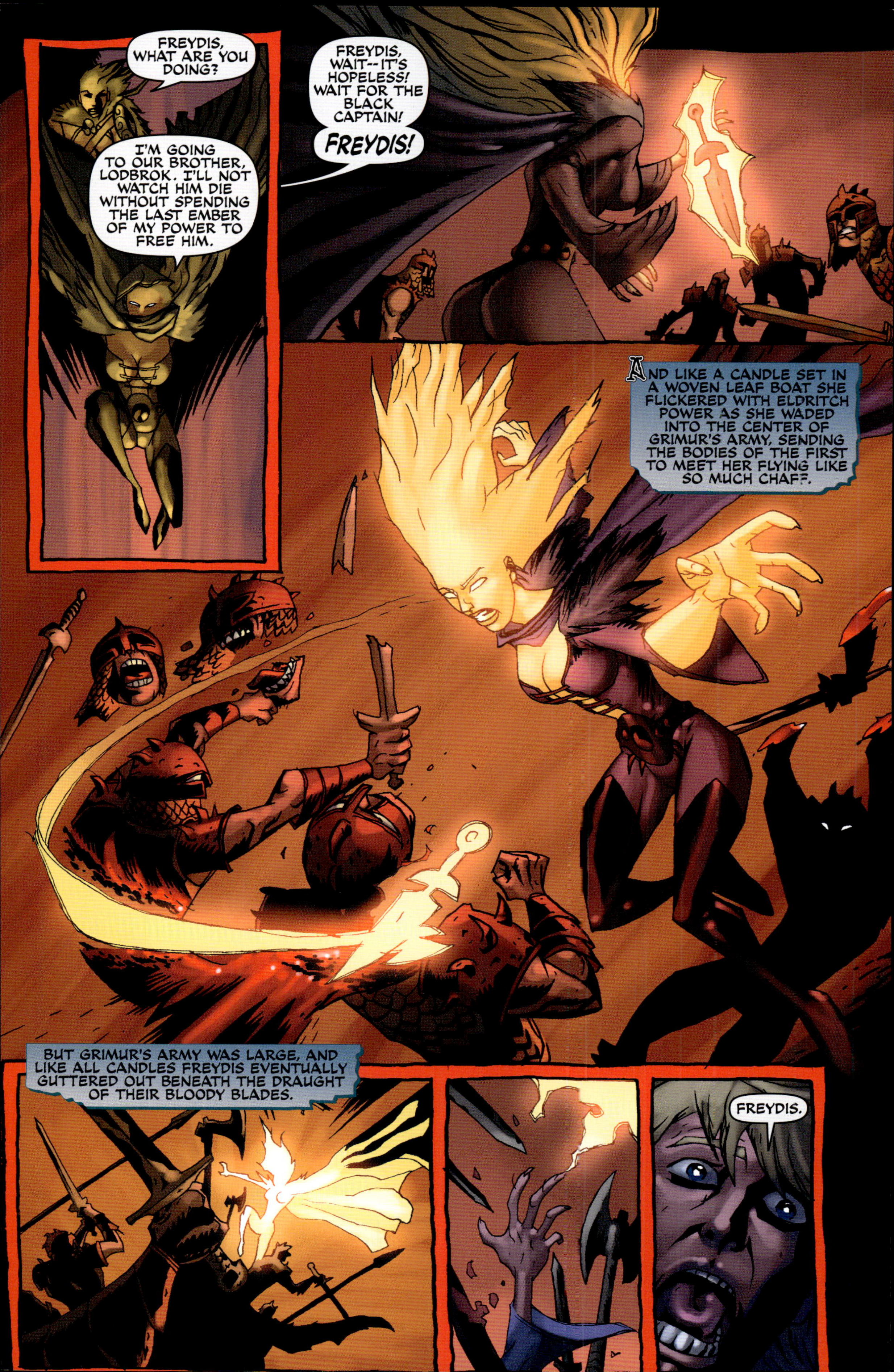
FREYDIS, WHAT ARE YOU DOING?
I'M GOING TO OUR BROTHER, LODBROK. I'LL NOT WATCH HIM DIE WITHOUT SPENDING THE LAST EMBER OF MY POWER TO FREE HIM.
FREYDIS, WAIT--IT'S HOPELESS! WAIT FOR THE BLACK CAPTAIN!
FREYDIS!
AND LIKE A CANDLE SET IN A WOVEN LEAF BOAT SHE FLICKERED WITH ELDRITCH POWER AS SHE WADED INTO THE CENTER OF GRIMUR'S ARMY, SENDING THE BODIES OF THE FIRST TO MEET HER FLYING LIKE SO MUCH CHAFF.
BUT GRIMUR'S ARMY WAS LARGE, AND LIKE ALL CANDLES FREYDIS EVENTUALLY GUTTERED OUT BENEATH THE DRAUGHT OF THEIR BLOODY BLADES.
FREYDIS.

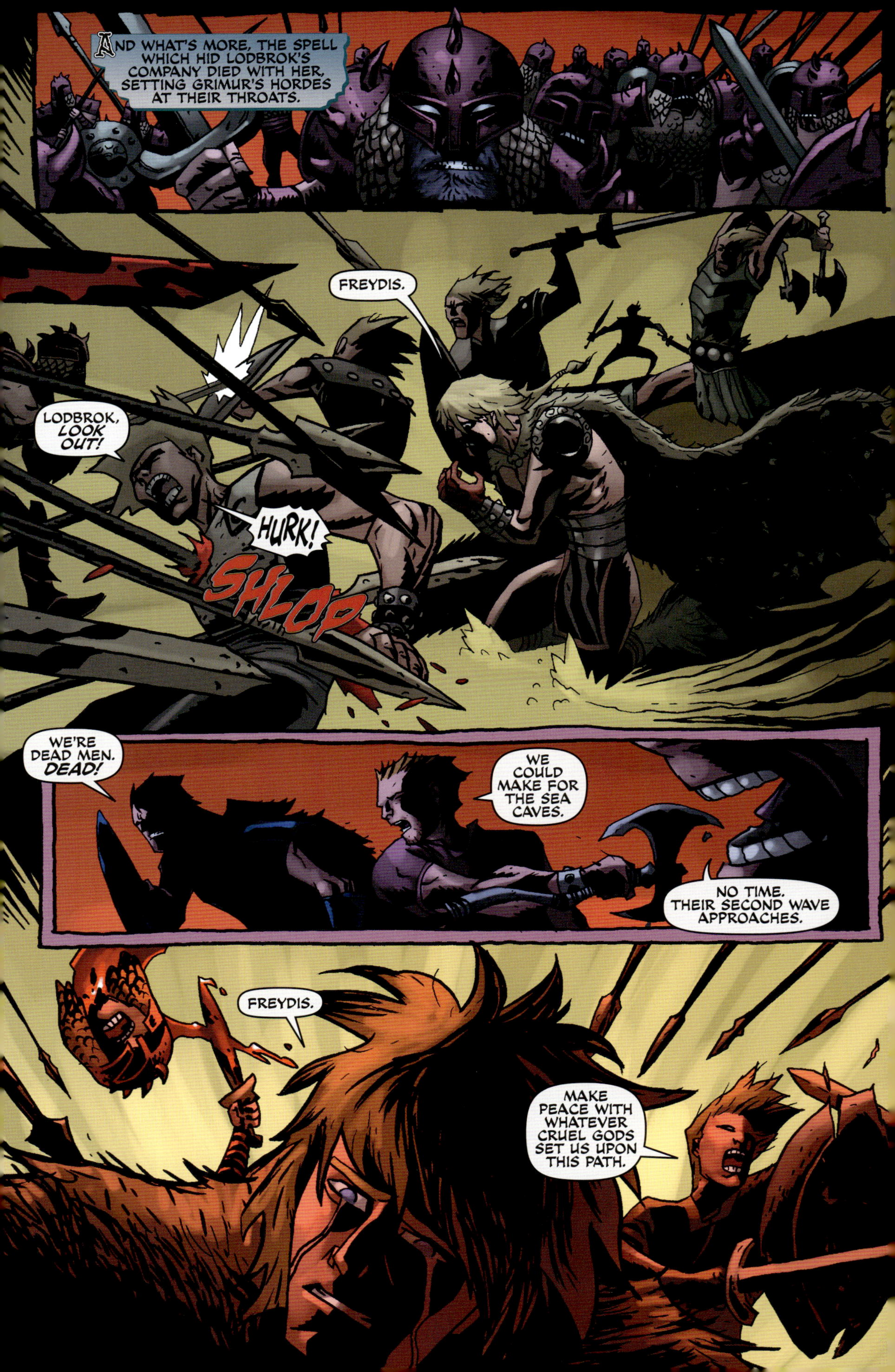
AND WHAT'S MORE, THE SPELL WHICH HID LODBROK'S COMPANY DIED WITH HER, SETTING GRIMUR'S HORDES AT THEIR THROATS.
FREYDIS.
LODBROK, LOOK OUT!
HURK!
SHLOP
WE'RE DEAD MEN. DEAD!
WE COULD MAKE FOR THE SEA CAVES.
NO TIME. THEIR SECOND WAVE APPROACHES.
FREYDIS.
MAKE PEACE WITH WHATEVER CRUEL GODS SET US UPON THIS PATH.

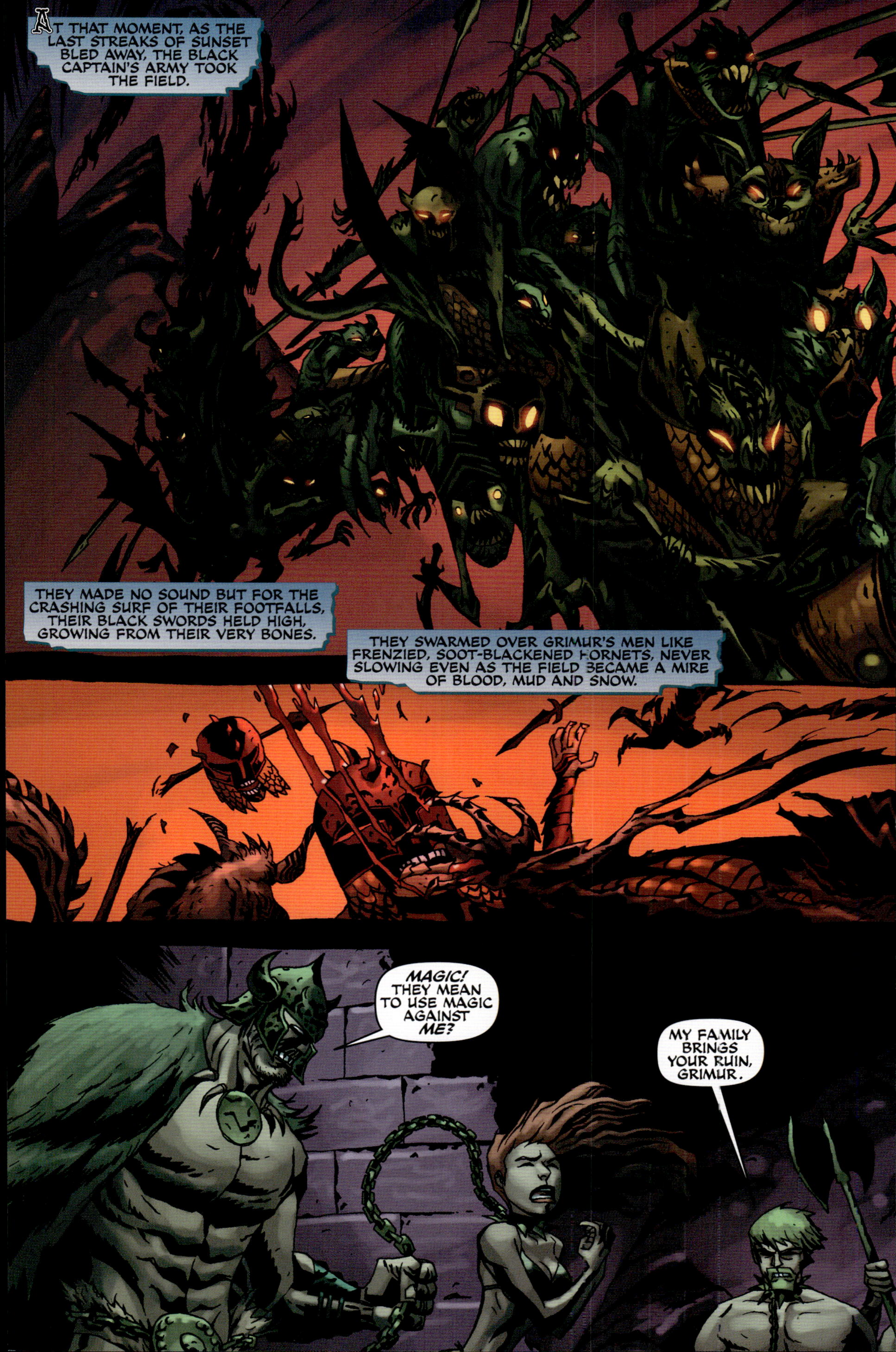
AT THAT MOMENT, AS THE LAST STREAKS OF SUNSET BLED AWAY, THE BLACK CAPTAIN'S ARMY TOOK THE FIELD.
THEY MADE NO SOUND BUT FOR THE CRASHING SURF OF THEIR FOOTFALLS, THEIR BLACK SWORDS HELD HIGH, GROWING FROM THEIR VERY BONES.
THEY SWARMED OVER GRIMUR'S MEN LIKE FRENZIED, SOOT-BLACKENED HORNETS, NEVER SLOWING EVEN AS THE FIELD BECAME A MIRE OF BLOOD, MUD AND SNOW.
MAGIC! THEY MEAN TO USE MAGIC AGAINST ME?
MY FAMILY BRINGS YOUR RUIN, GRIMUR.

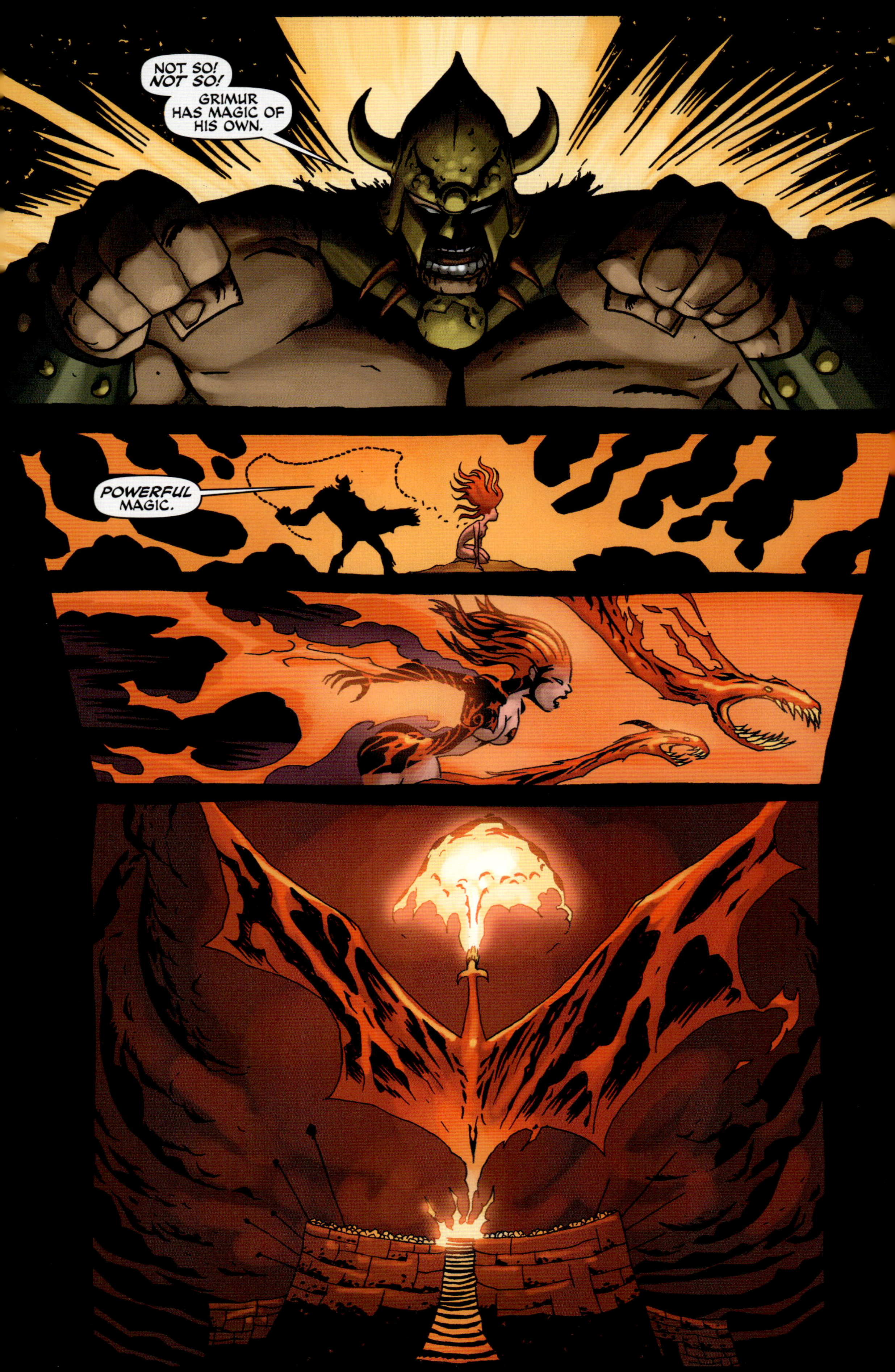

NOT SO! NOT SO! GRIMUR HAS MAGIC OF HIS OWN.
POWERFUL MAGIC.

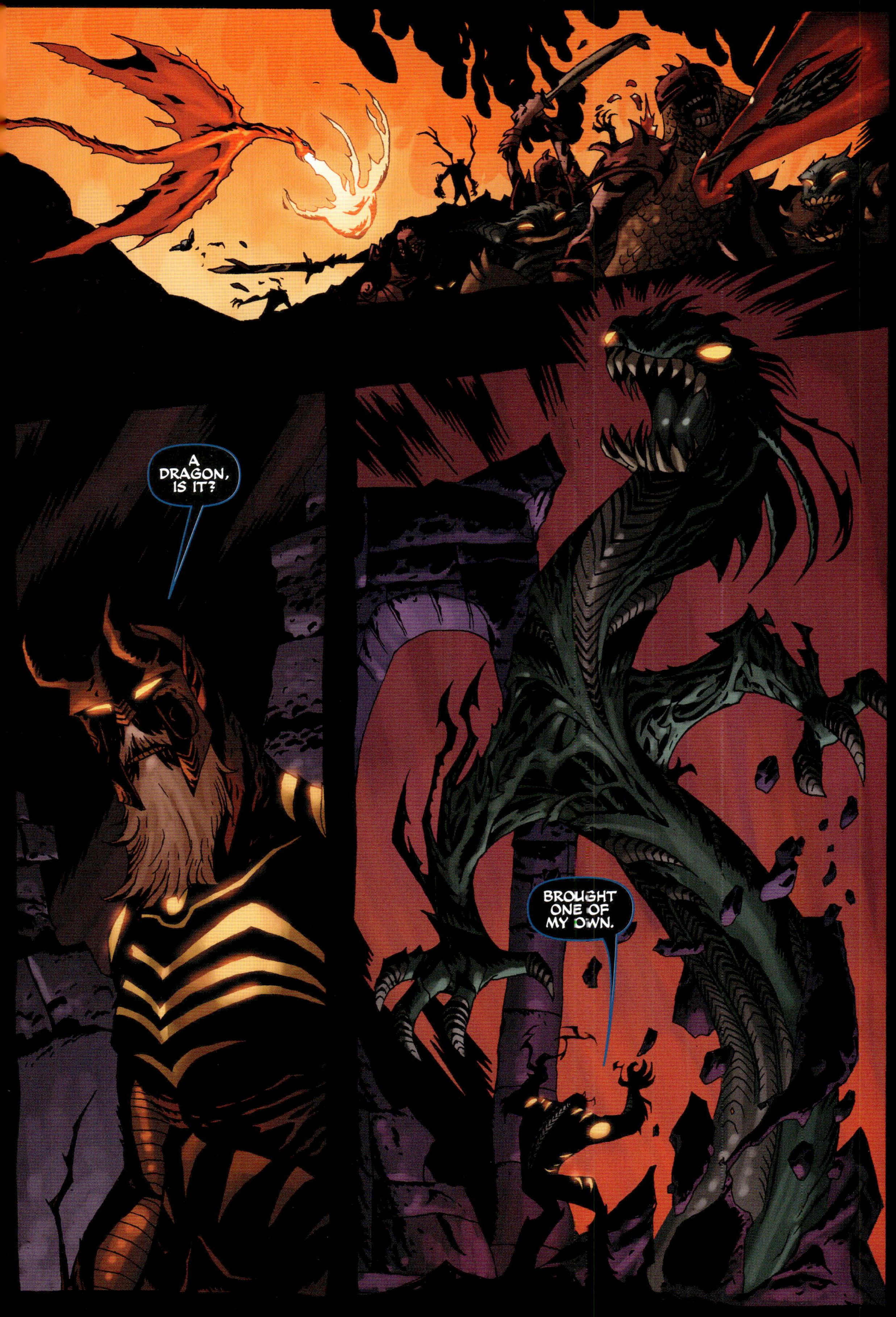
A DRAGON, IS IT?
BROUGHT ONE OF MY OWN.

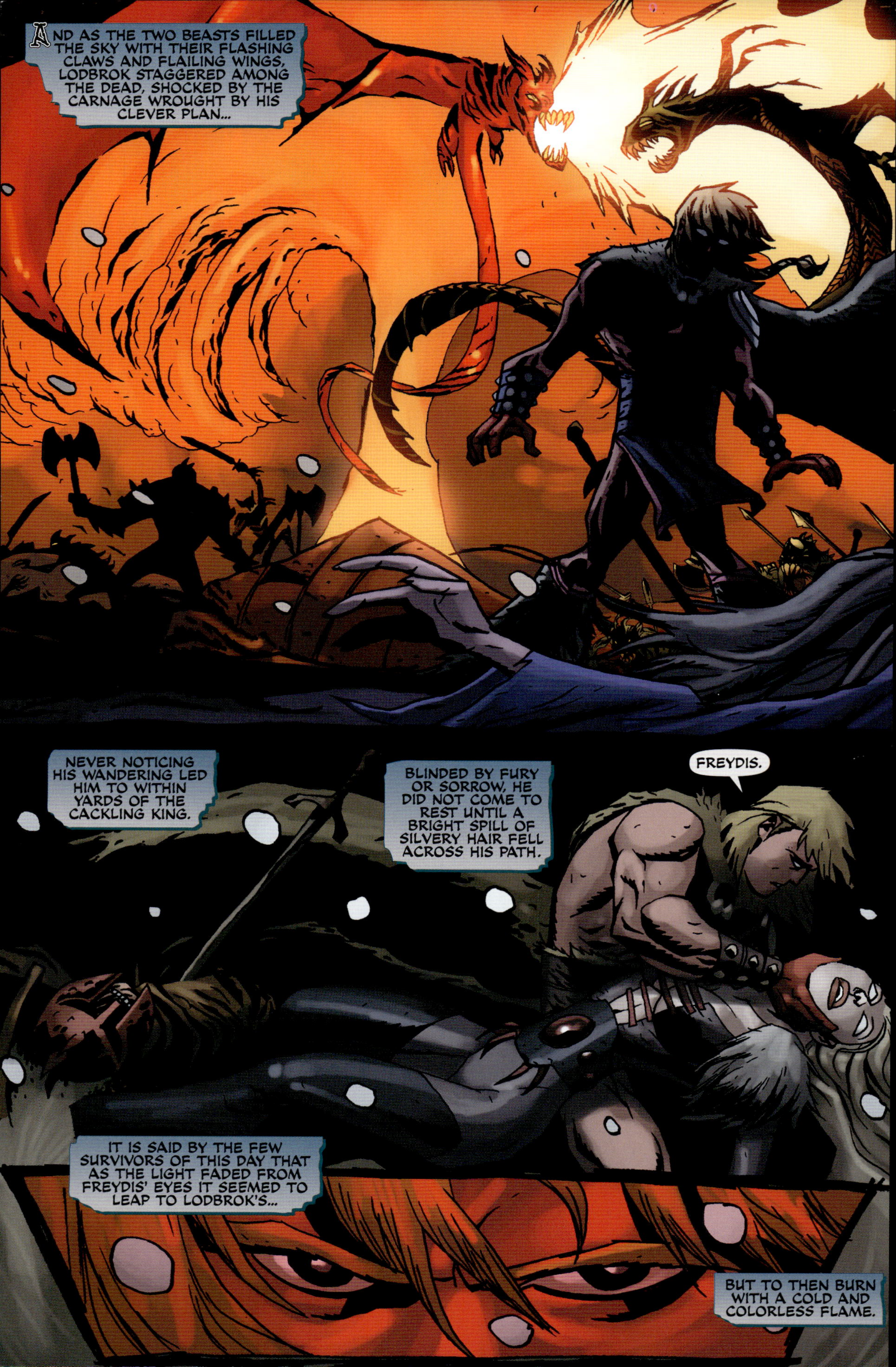
AND AS THE TWO BEASTS FILLED THE SKY WITH THEIR FLASHING CLAWS AND FLAILING WINGS, LODBROK STAGGERED AMONG THE DEAD, SHOCKED BY THE CARNAGE WROUGHT BY HIS CLEVER PLAN...
NEVER NOTICING HIS WANDERING LED HIM TO WITHIN YARDS OF THE CACKLING KING.
BLINDED BY FURY OR SORROW, HE DID NOT COME TO REST UNTIL A BRIGHT SPILL OF SILVERY HAIR FELL ACROSS HIS PATH.
FREYDIS.
IT IS SAID BY THE FEW SURVIVORS OF THIS DAY THAT AS THE LIGHT FADED FROM FREYDIS' EYES IT SEEMED TO LEAP TO LODBROK'S...
BUT TO THEN BURN WITH A COLD AND COLORLESS FLAME.

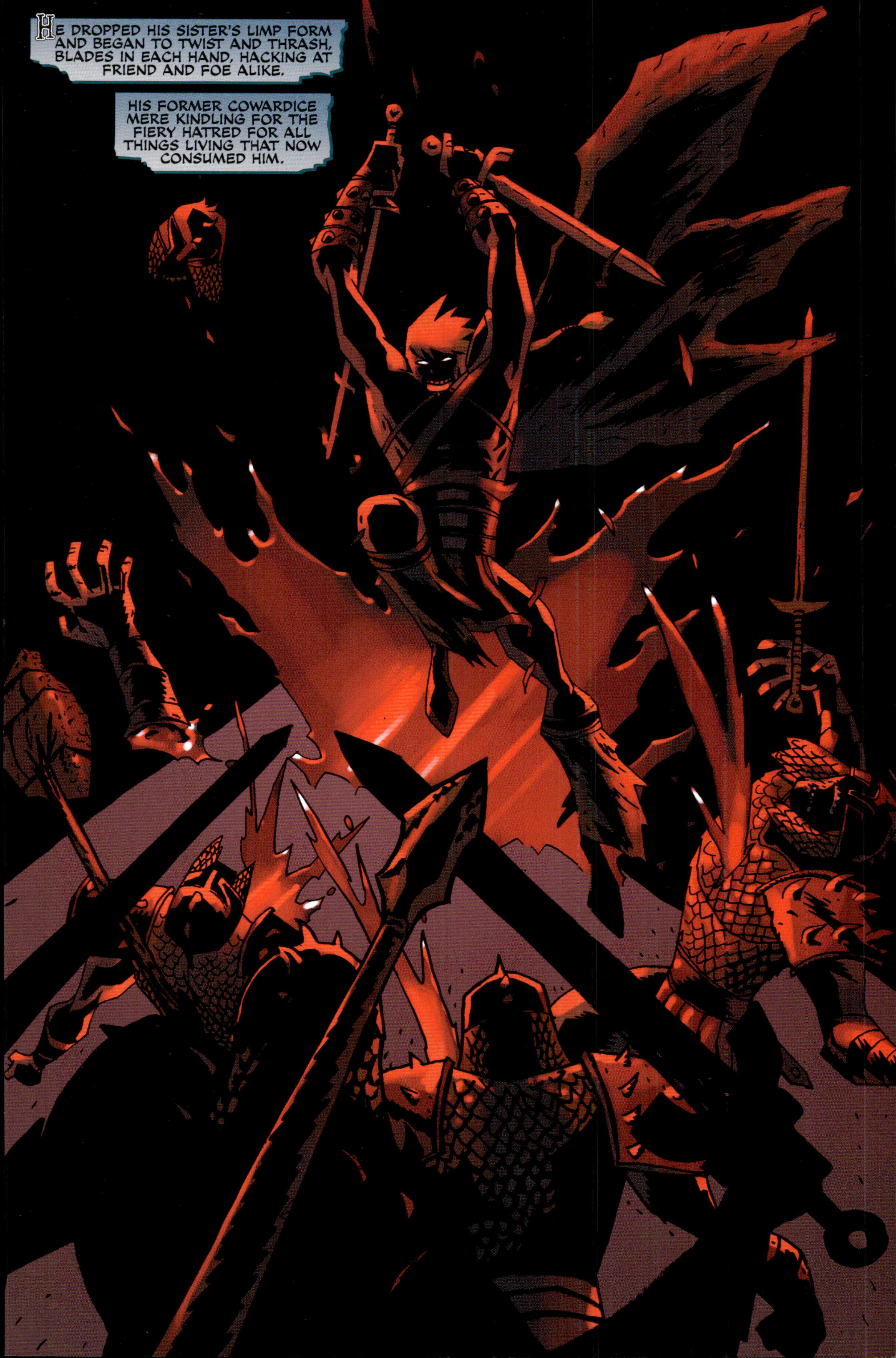
HE DROPPED HIS SISTER'S LIMP FORM AND BEGAN TO TWIST AND THRASH, BLADES IN EACH HAND, HACKING AT FRIEND AND FOE ALIKE.
HIS FORMER COWARDICE MERE KINDLING FOR THE FIERY HATRED FOR ALL THINGS LIVING THAT NOW CONSUMED HIM.

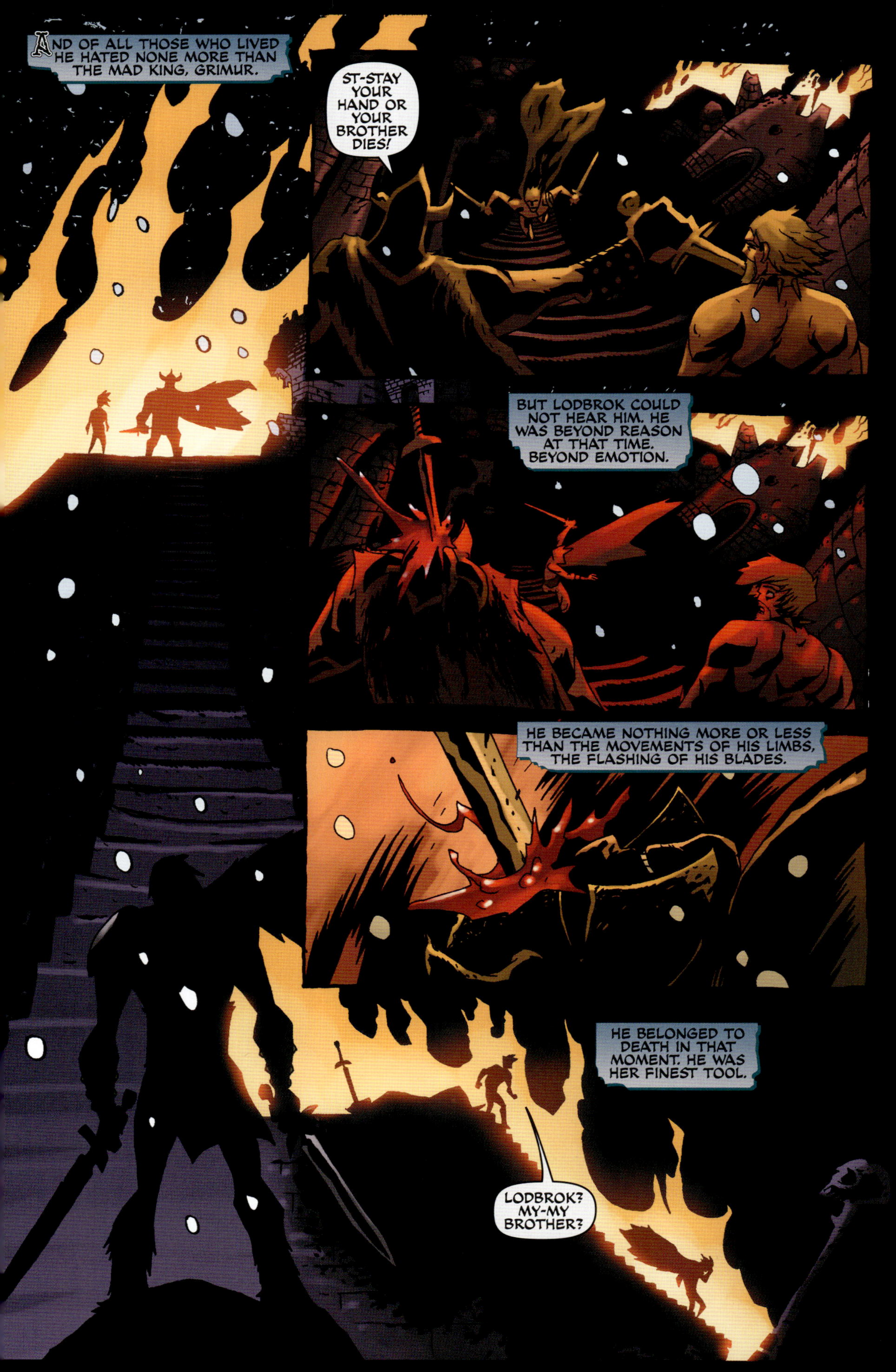
AND OF ALL THOSE WHO LIVED HE HATED NONE MORE THAN THE MAD KING, GRIMUR.
ST-STAY YOUR HAND OR YOUR BROTHER DIES!
BUT LODBROK COULD NOT HEAR HIM. HE WAS BEYOND REASON AT THAT TIME. BEYOND EMOTION.
HE BECAME NOTHING MORE OR LESS THAN THE MOVEMENTS OF HIS LIMBS, THE FLASHING OF HIS BLADES.
HE BELONGED TO DEATH IN THAT MOMENT. HE WAS HER FINEST TOOL.
LODBROK? MY-MY BROTHER?

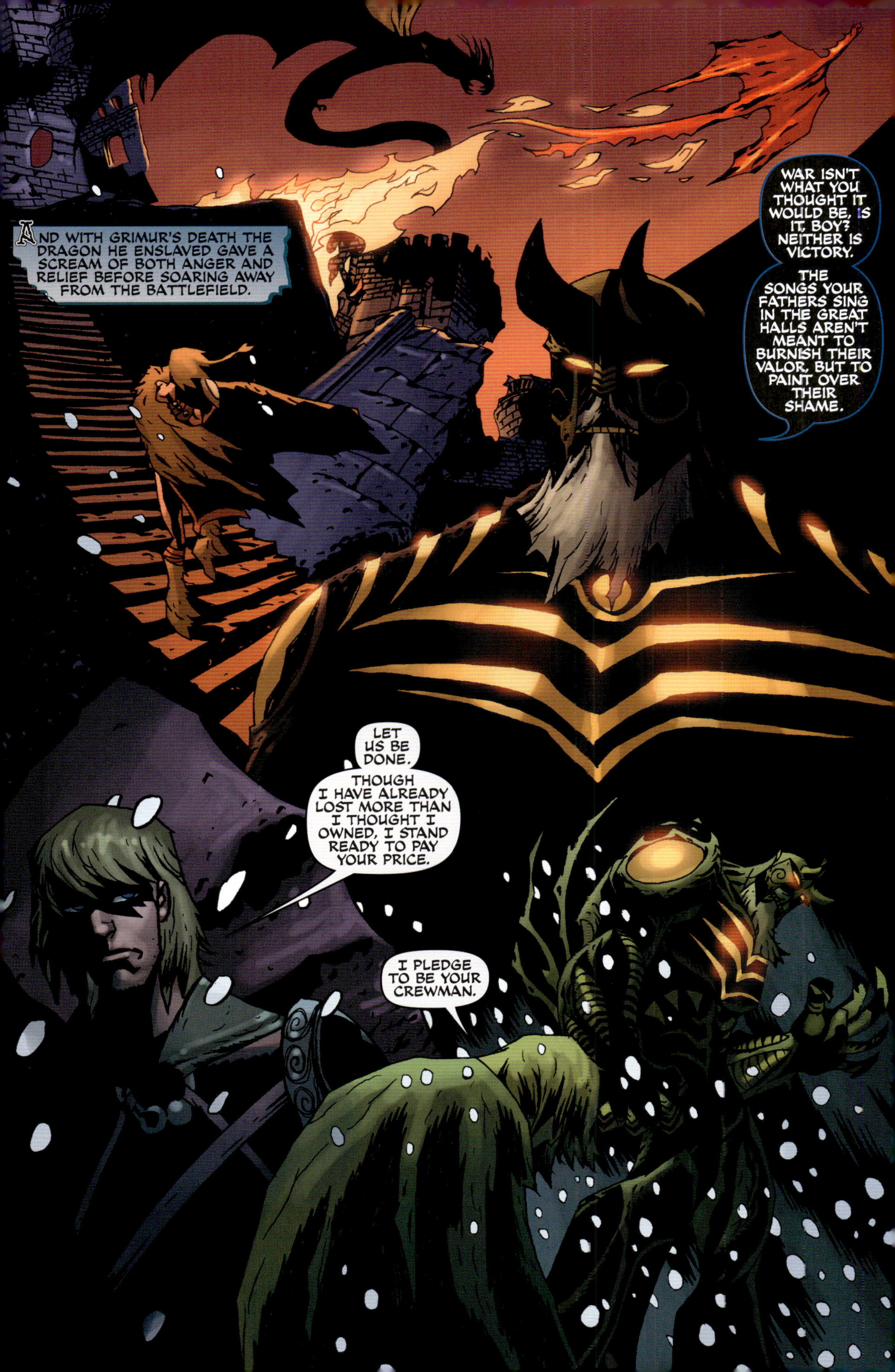
AND WITH GRIMUR'S DEATH THE DRAGON HE ENSLAVED GAVE A SCREAM OF BOTH ANGER AND RELIEF BEFORE SOARING AWAY FROM THE BATTLEFIELD.
WAR ISN'T WHAT YOU THOUGHT IT WOULD BE, IS IT, BOY? NEITHER IS VICTORY.
THE SONGS YOUR FATHERS SING IN THE GREAT HALLS AREN'T MEANT TO BURNISH THEIR VALOR, BUT TO PAINT OVER THEIR SHAME.
LET US BE DONE.
THOUGH I HAVE ALREADY LOST MORE THAN I THOUGHT I OWNED, I STAND READY TO PAY YOUR PRICE.
I PLEDGE TO BE YOUR CREWMAN.

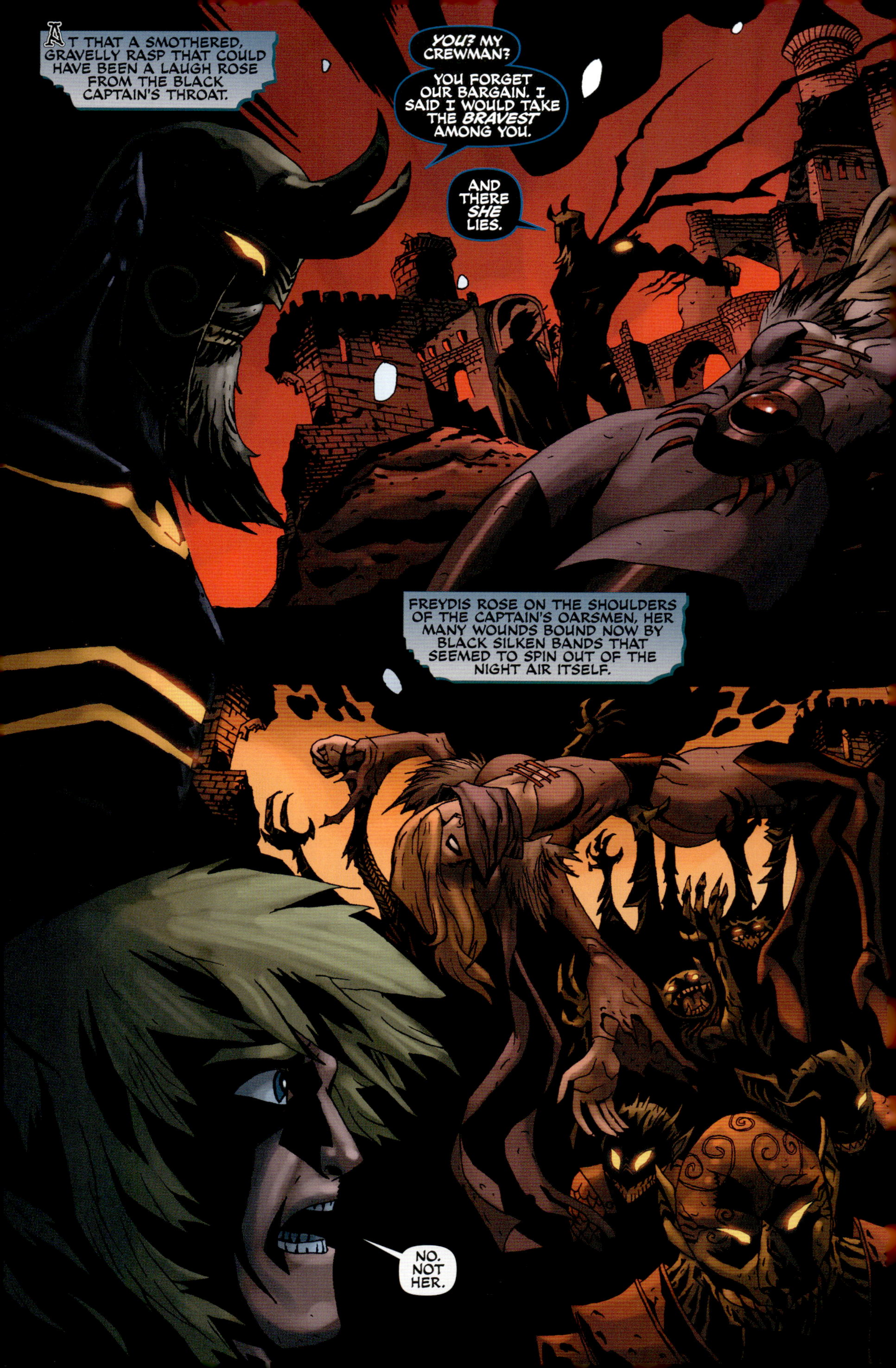
AT THAT A SMOTHERED, GRAVELLY RASP THAT COULD HAVE BEEN A LAUGH ROSE FROM THE BLACK CAPTAIN'S THROAT.
YOU? MY CREWMAN?
YOU FORGET OUR BARGAIN. I SAID I WOULD TAKE THE BRAVEST AMONG YOU.
AND THERE SHE LIES.
FREYDIS ROSE ON THE SHOULDERS OF THE CAPTAIN'S OARSMEN, HER MANY WOUNDS BOUND NOW BY BLACK SILKEN BANDS THAT SEEMED TO SPIN OUT OF THE NIGHT AIR ITSELF.
NO. NOT HER.

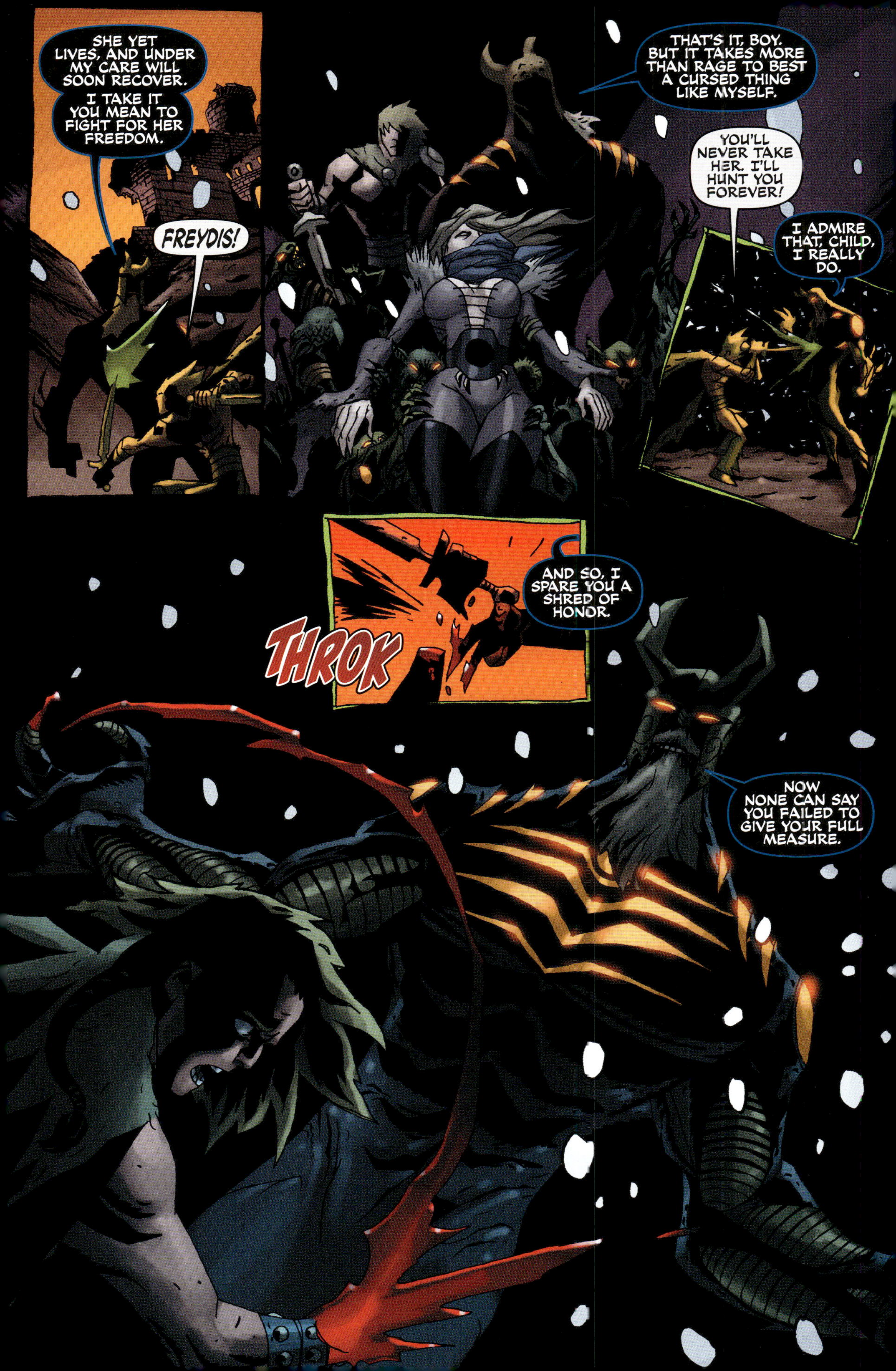
SHE YET LIVES, AND UNDER MY CARE WILL SOON RECOVER.
I TAKE IT YOU MEAN TO FIGHT FOR HER FREEDOM.
FREYDIS!
THAT'S IT, BOY. BUT IT TAKES MORE THAN RAGE TO BEST A CURSED THING LIKE MYSELF.
YOU'LL NEVER TAKE HER. I'LL HUNT YOU FOREVER!
I ADMIRE THAT, CHILD, I REALLY DO.
AND SO, I SPARE YOU A SHRED OF HONOR.
THROK
NOW NONE CAN SAY YOU FAILED TO GIVE YOUR FULL MEASURE.

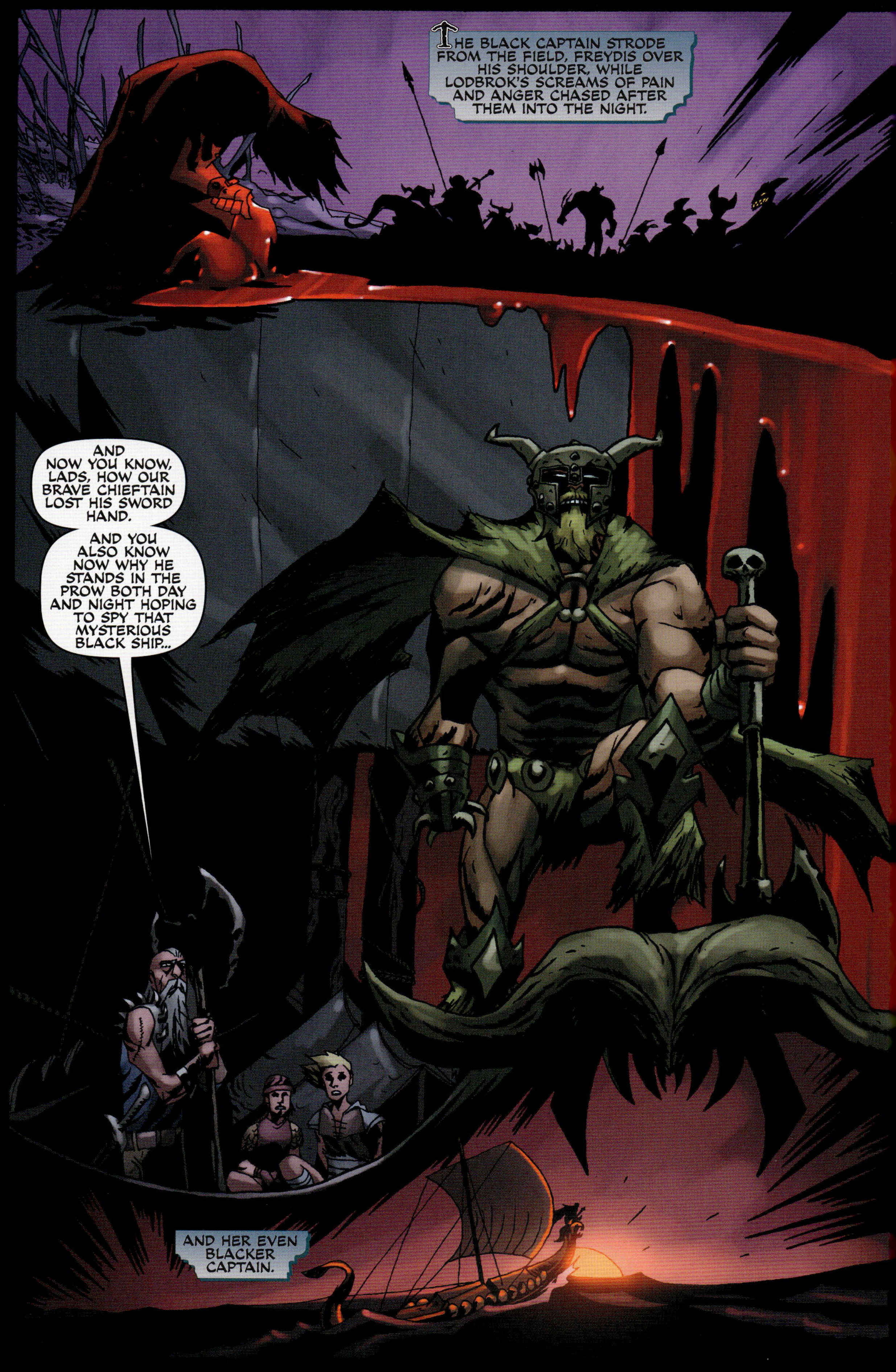
THE BLACK CAPTAIN STRODE FROM THE FIELD, FREYDIS OVER HIS SHOULDER, WHILE LODBROK'S SCREAMS OF PAIN AND ANGER CHASED AFTER THEM INTO THE NIGHT.
AND NOW YOU KNOW, LADS, HOW OUR BRAVE CHIEFTAIN LOST HIS SWORD HAND.
AND YOU ALSO KNOW NOW WHY HE STANDS IN THE PROW BOTH DAY AND NIGHT HOPING TO SPY THAT MYSTERIOUS BLACK SHIP...
AND HER EVEN BLACKER CAPTAIN.

The Darkness: Shadow anf Flame
cover art by: Jorge Lucas and Felix Serrano

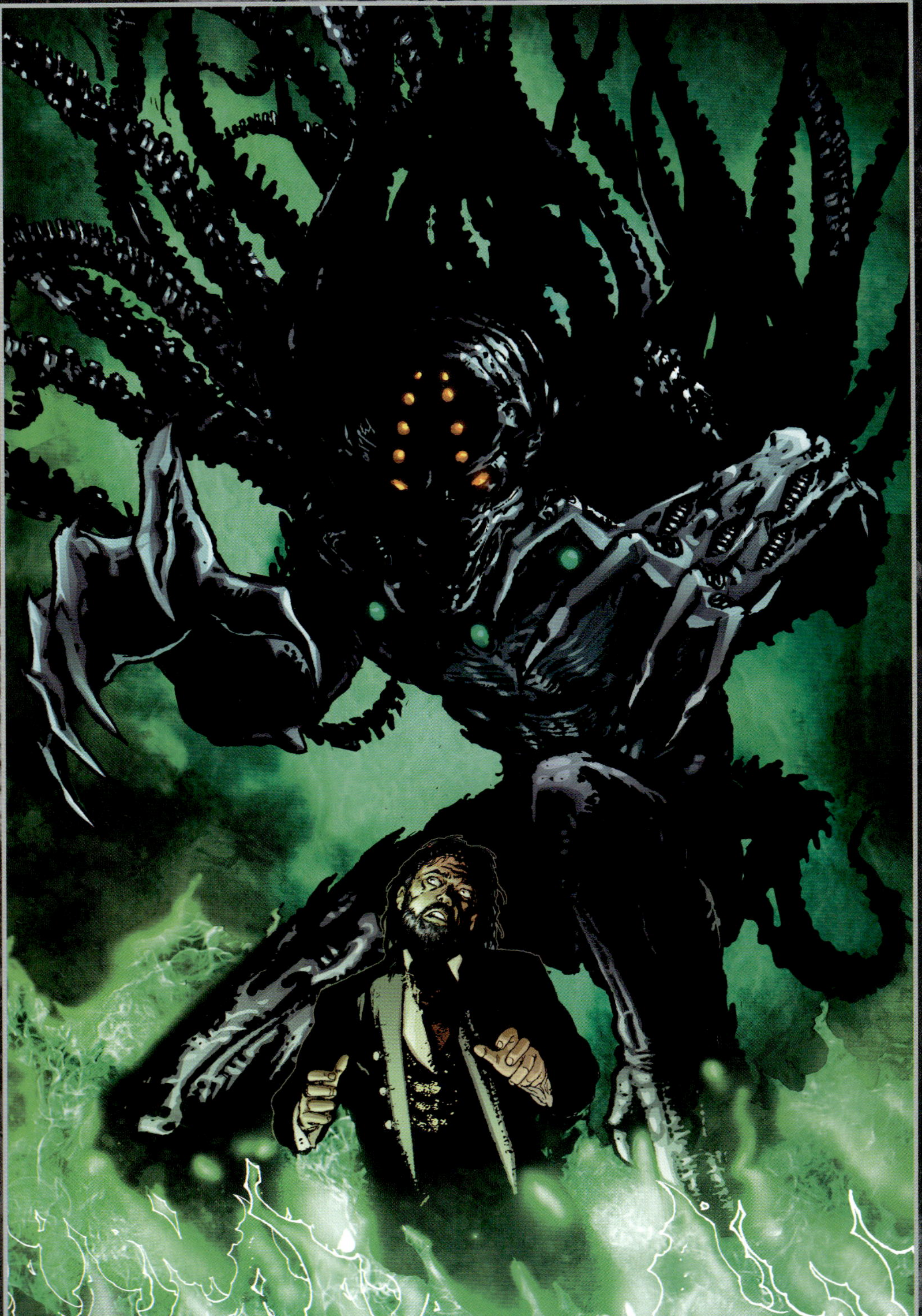

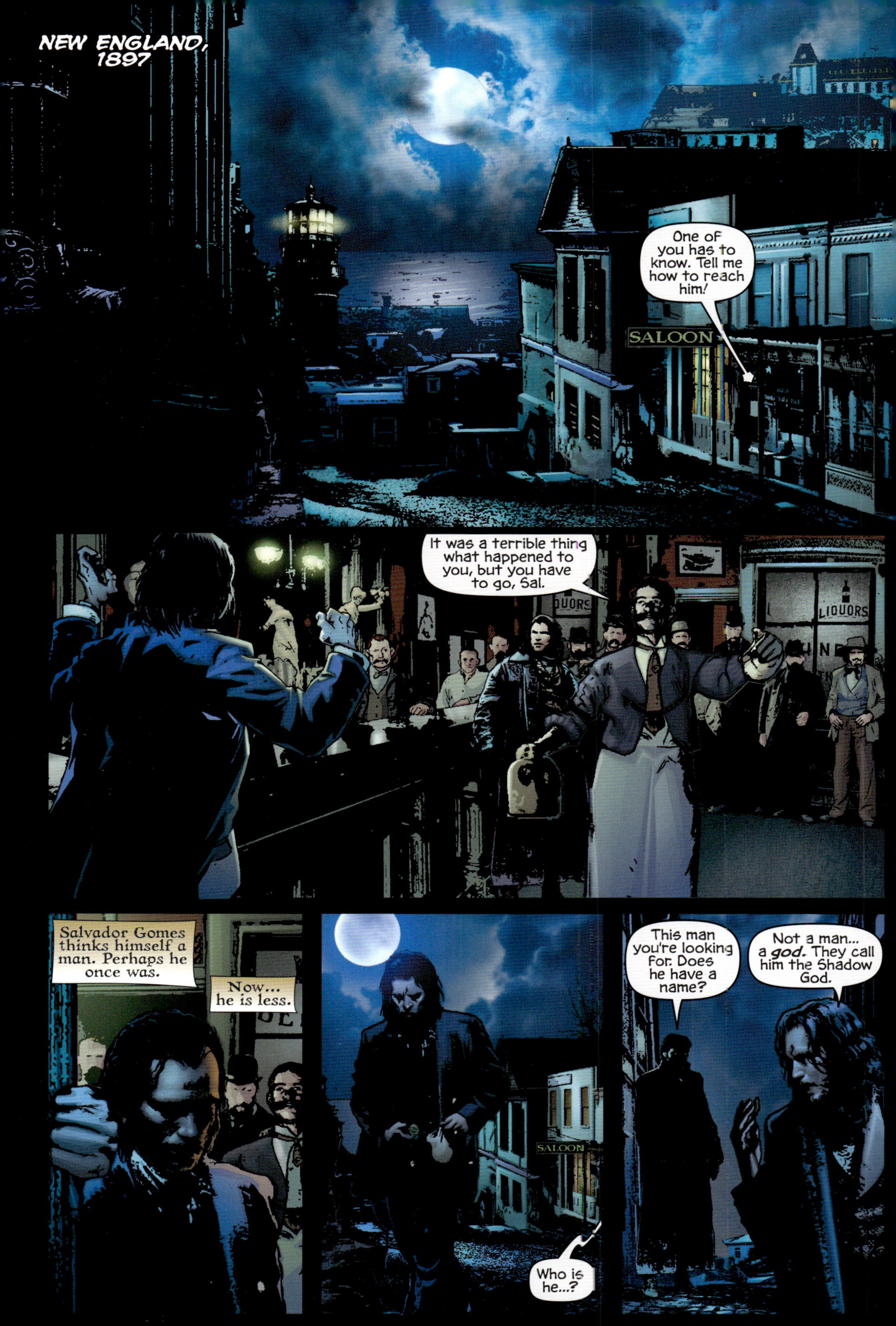

NEW ENGLAND, 1897
One of you has to know. Tell me how to reach him!
SALOON
It was a terrible thing what happened to you, but you have to go, Sal.
LIQUORS
Salvador Gomes thinks himself a man. Perhaps he once was.
Now... he is less.
SALOON
Who is he...?
This man you're looking for. Does he have a name?
Not a man... a ***god.*** They call him the Shadow God.

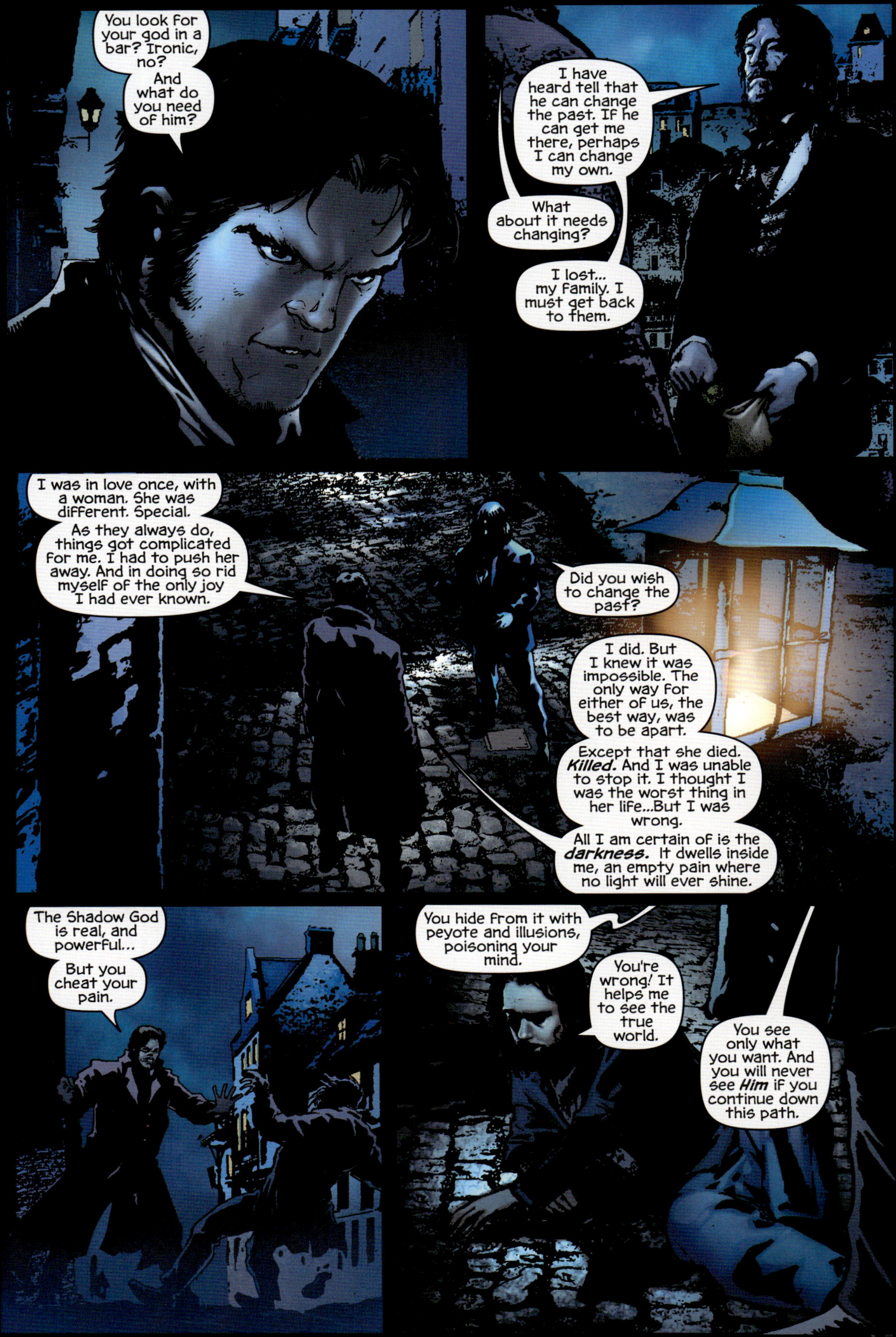

You look for your god in a bar? Ironic, no?
And what do you need of him?
I have heard tell that he can change the past. If he can get me there, perhaps I can change my own.
What about it needs changing?
I lost... my family. I must get back to them.
I was in love once, with a woman. She was different. Special.
As they always do, things got complicated for me. I had to push her away. And in doing so rid myself of the only joy I had ever known.
Did you wish to change the past?
I did. But I knew it was impossible. The only way for either of us, the best way, was to be apart.
Except that she died. *Killed.* And I was unable to stop it. I thought I was the worst thing in her life...But I was wrong.
All I am certain of is the *darkness.* It dwells inside me, an empty pain where no light will ever shine.
The Shadow God is real, and powerful...
But you cheat your pain.
You hide from it with peyote and illusions, poisoning your mind.
You're wrong! It helps me to see the true world.
You see only what you want. And you will never see *Him* if you continue down this path.

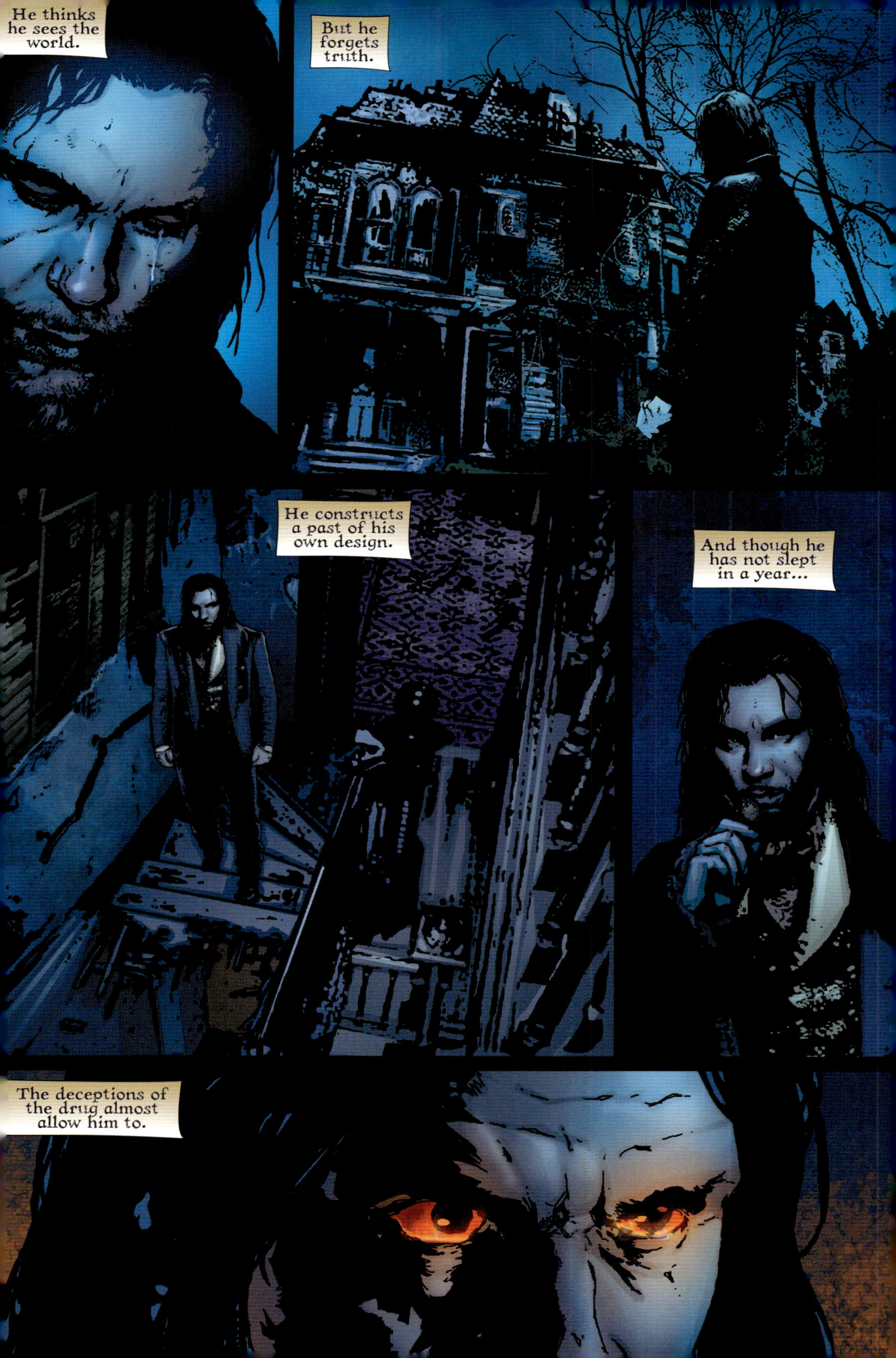
He thinks he sees the world.
But he forgets truth.
He constructs a past of his own design.
And though he has not slept in a year...
The deceptions of the drug almost allow him to.

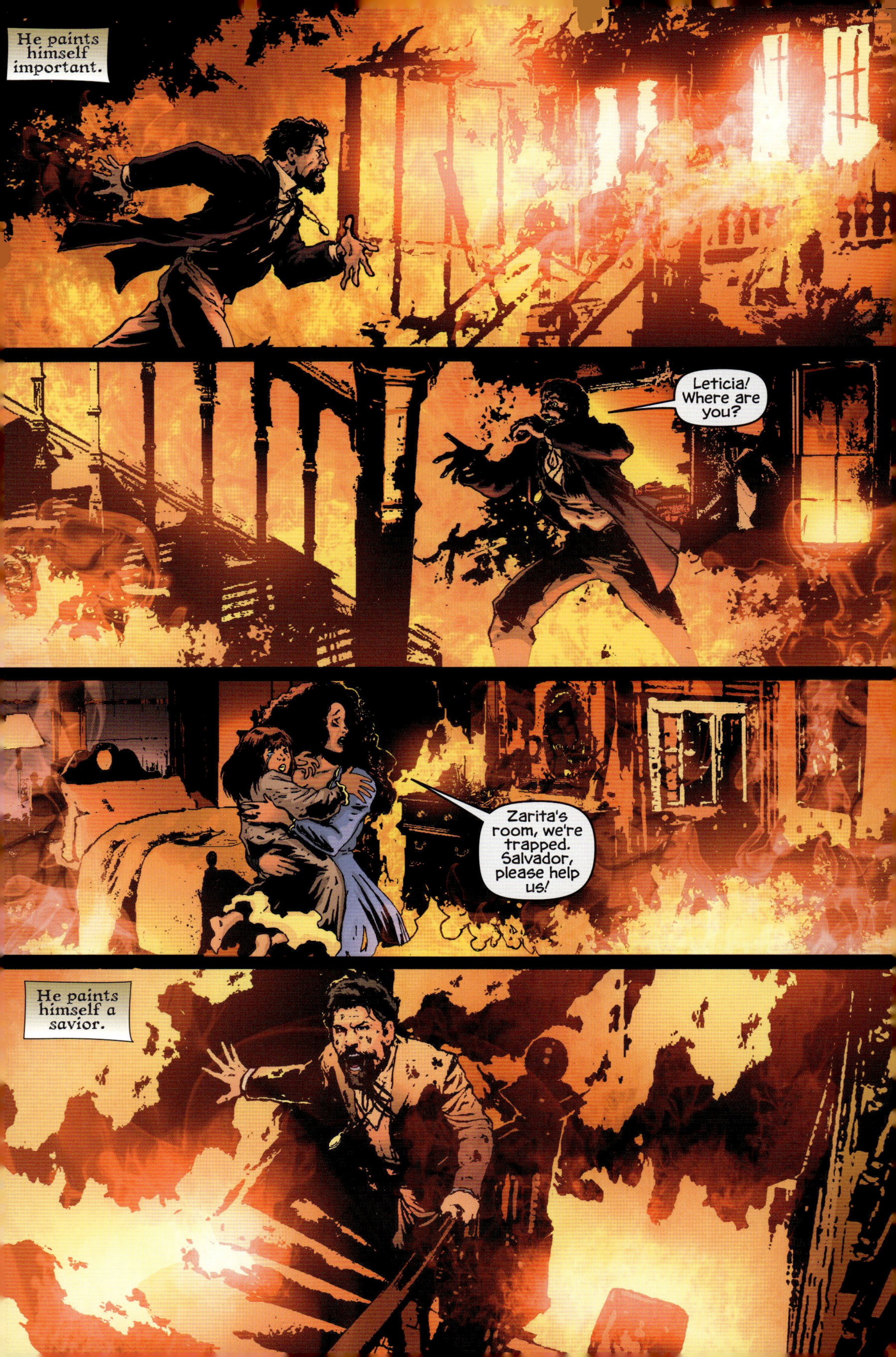
He paints himself important.
Leticia! Where are you?
Zarita's room, we're trapped. Salvador, please help us!
He paints himself a savior.

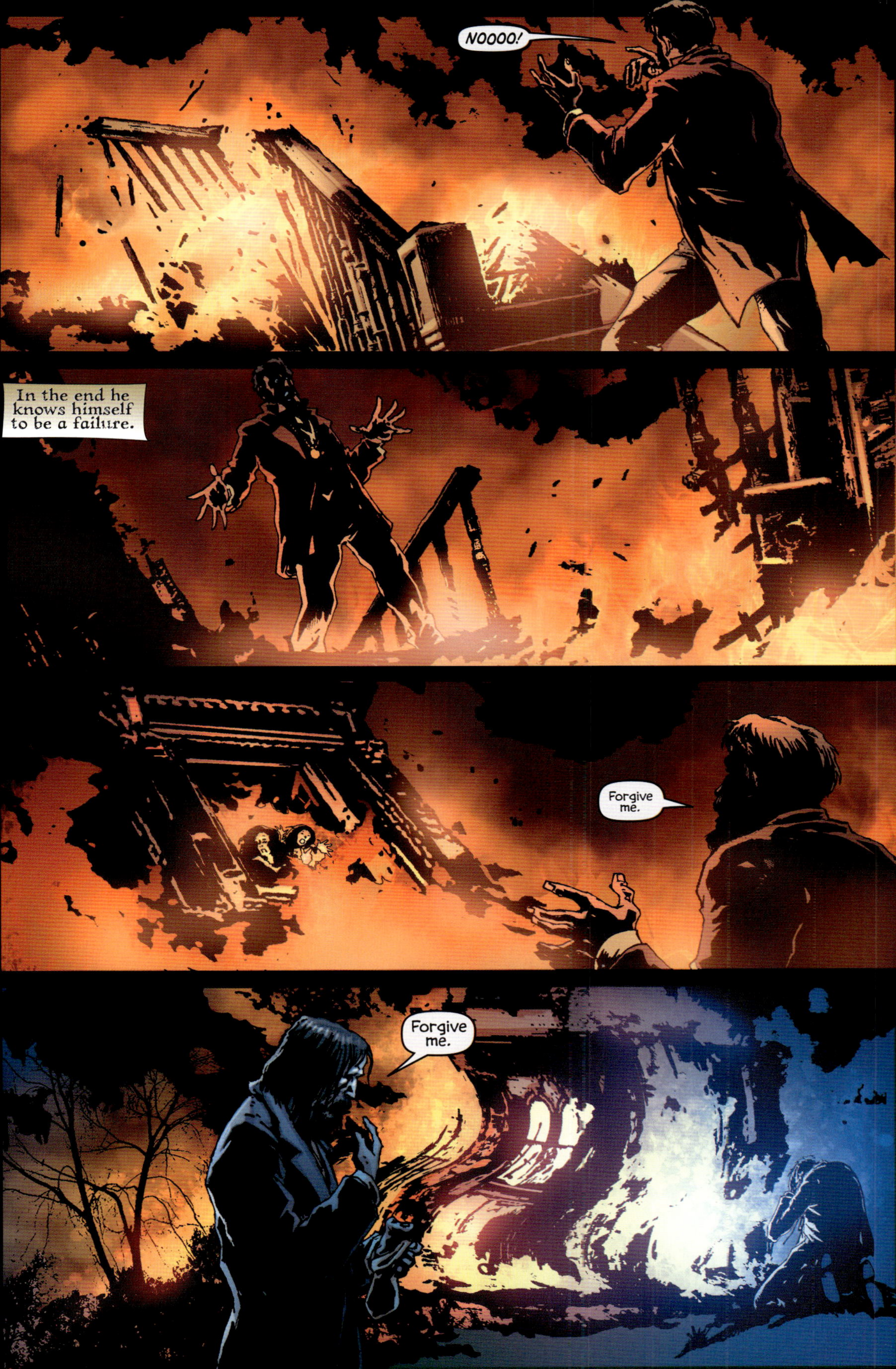
NOOOO!
In the end he knows himself to be a failure.
Forgive me.
Forgive me.

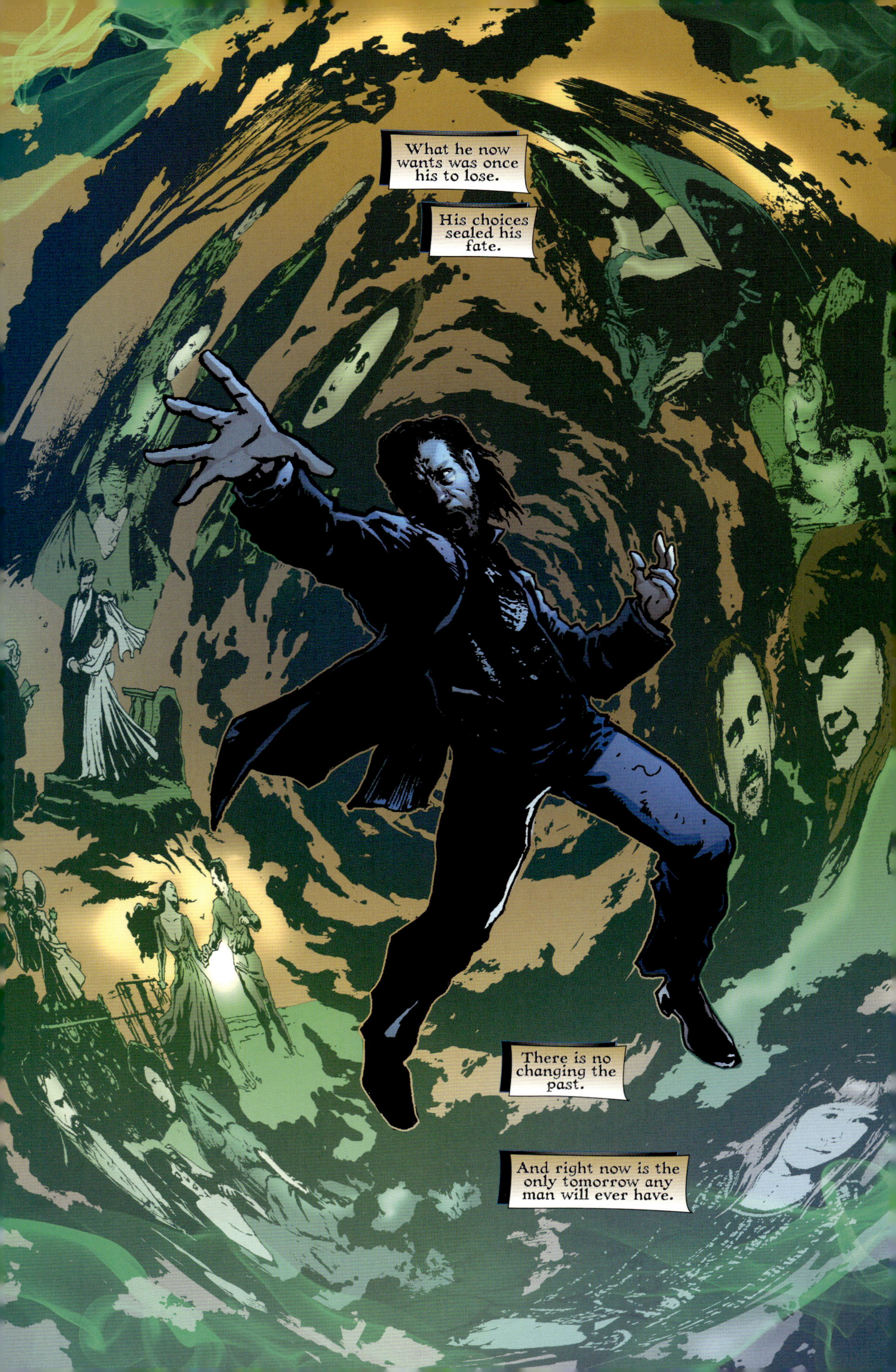
What he now wants was once his to lose.
His choices sealed his fate.
There is no changing the past.
And right now is the only tomorrow any man will ever have.

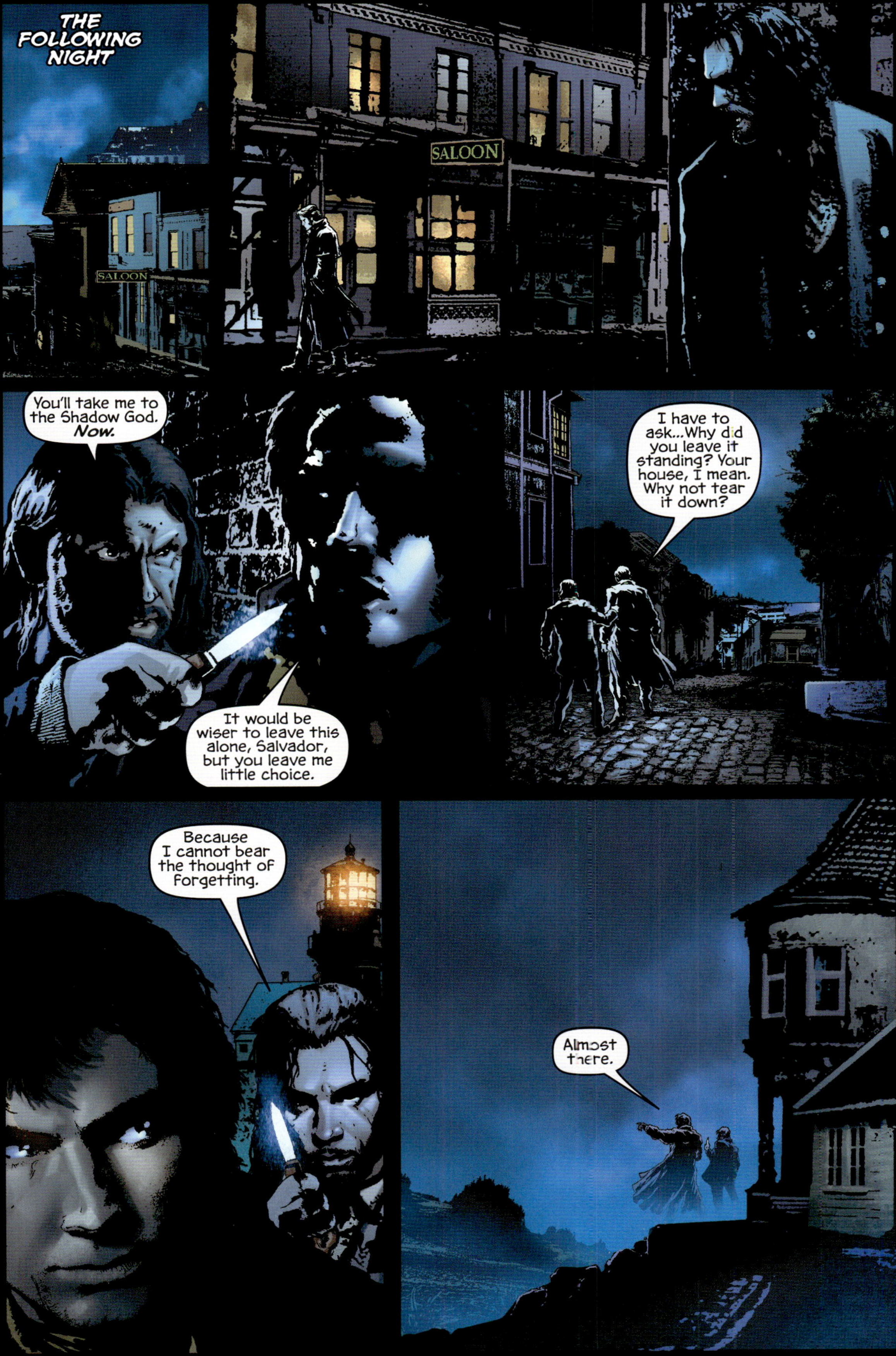
THE FOLLOWING NIGHT
SALOON
SALOON
You'll take me to the Shadow God. *Now.*
It would be wiser to leave this alone, Salvador, but you leave me little choice.
I have to ask...Why did you leave it standing? Your house, I mean. Why not tear it down?
Because I cannot bear the thought of forgetting.
Almost there.

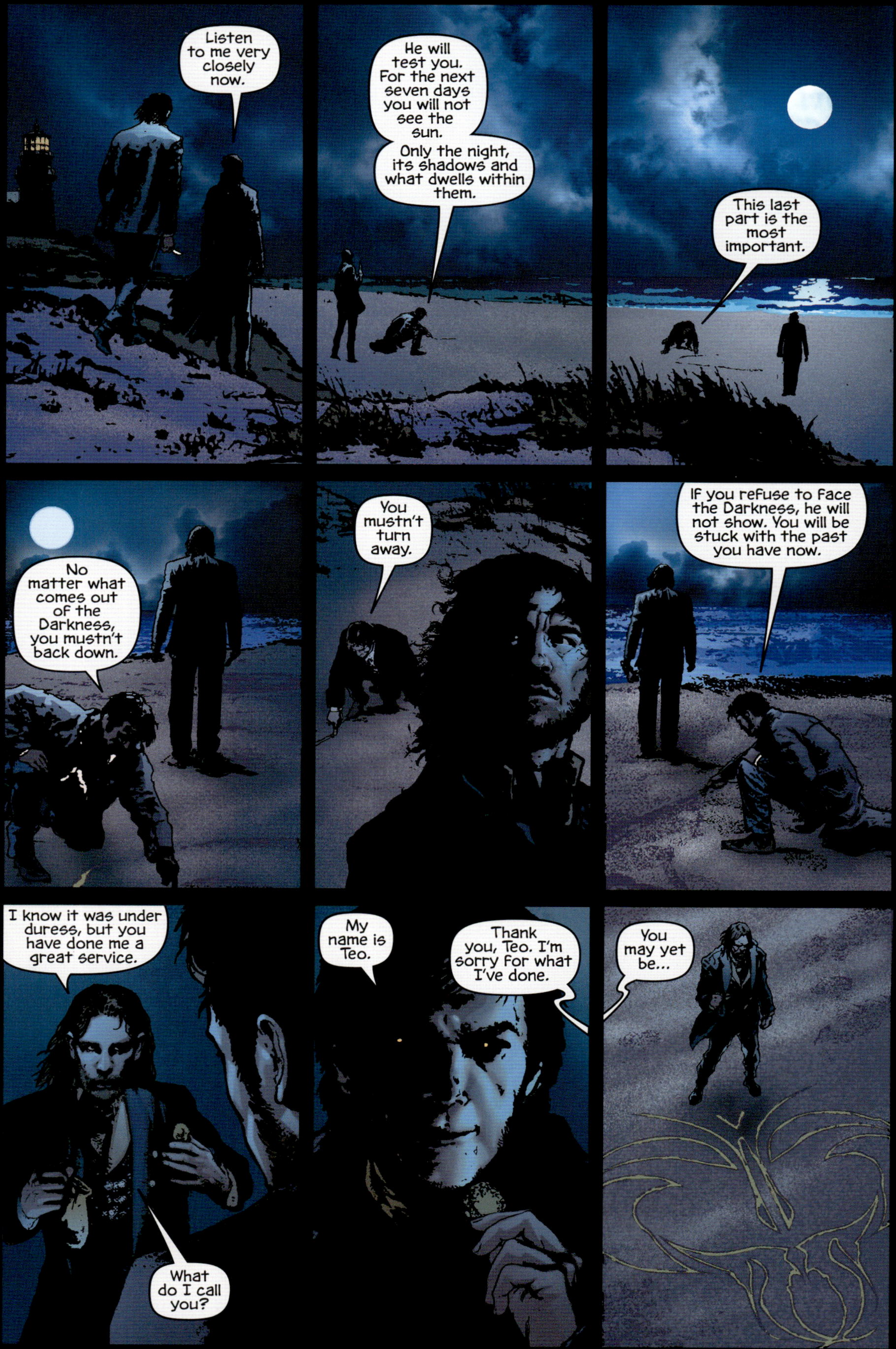
Listen to me very closely now.
He will test you. For the next seven days you will not see the sun.
Only the night, its shadows and what dwells within them.
This last part is the most important.
No matter what comes out of the Darkness, you mustn't back down.
You mustn't turn away.
If you refuse to face the Darkness, he will not show. You will be stuck with the past you have now.
I know it was under duress, but you have done me a great service.
What do I call you?
My name is Teo.
Thank you, Teo. I'm sorry for what I've done.
You may yet be...

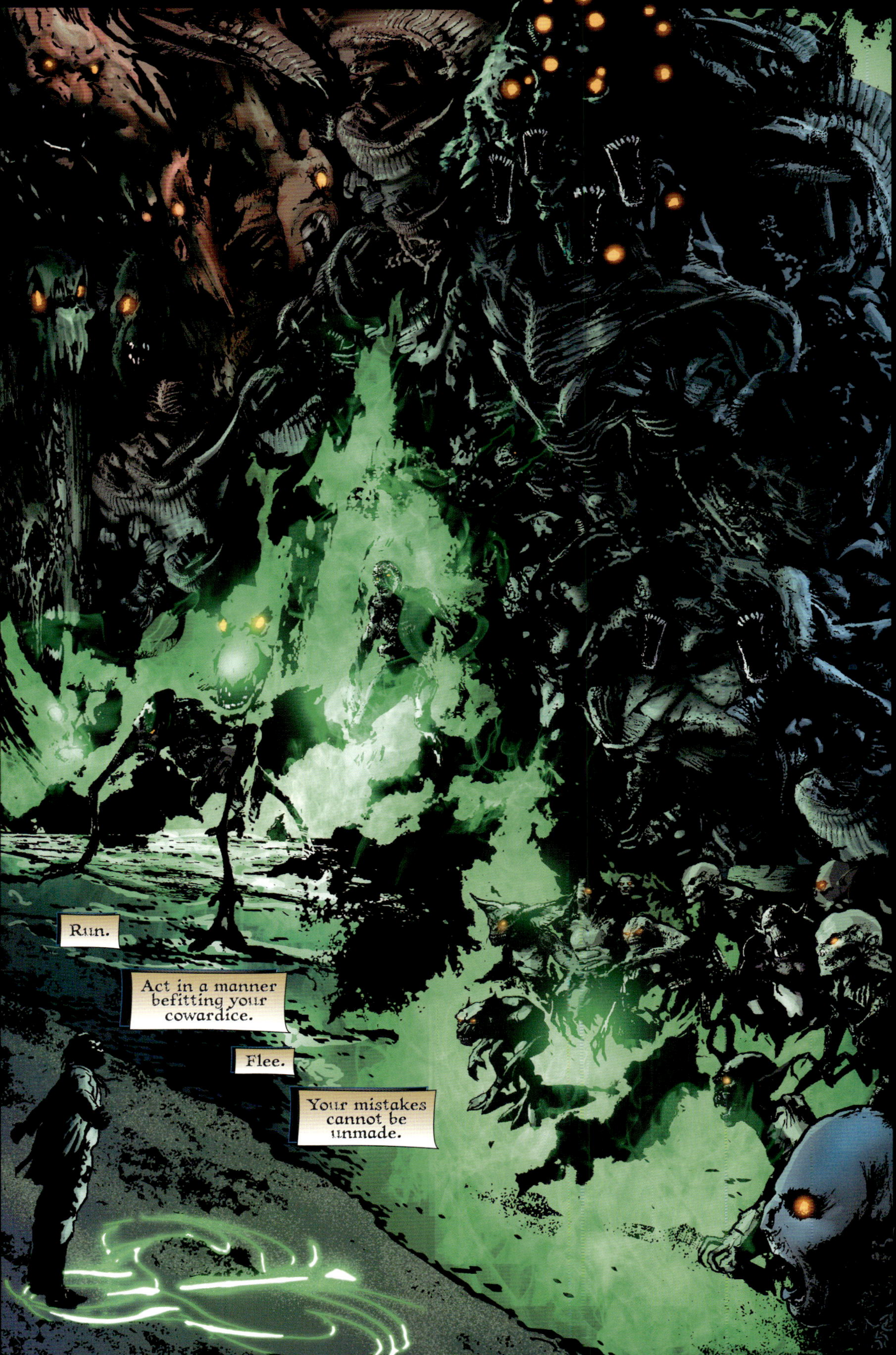
Run.
Act in a manner befitting your cowardice.
Flee.
Your mistakes cannot be unmade.

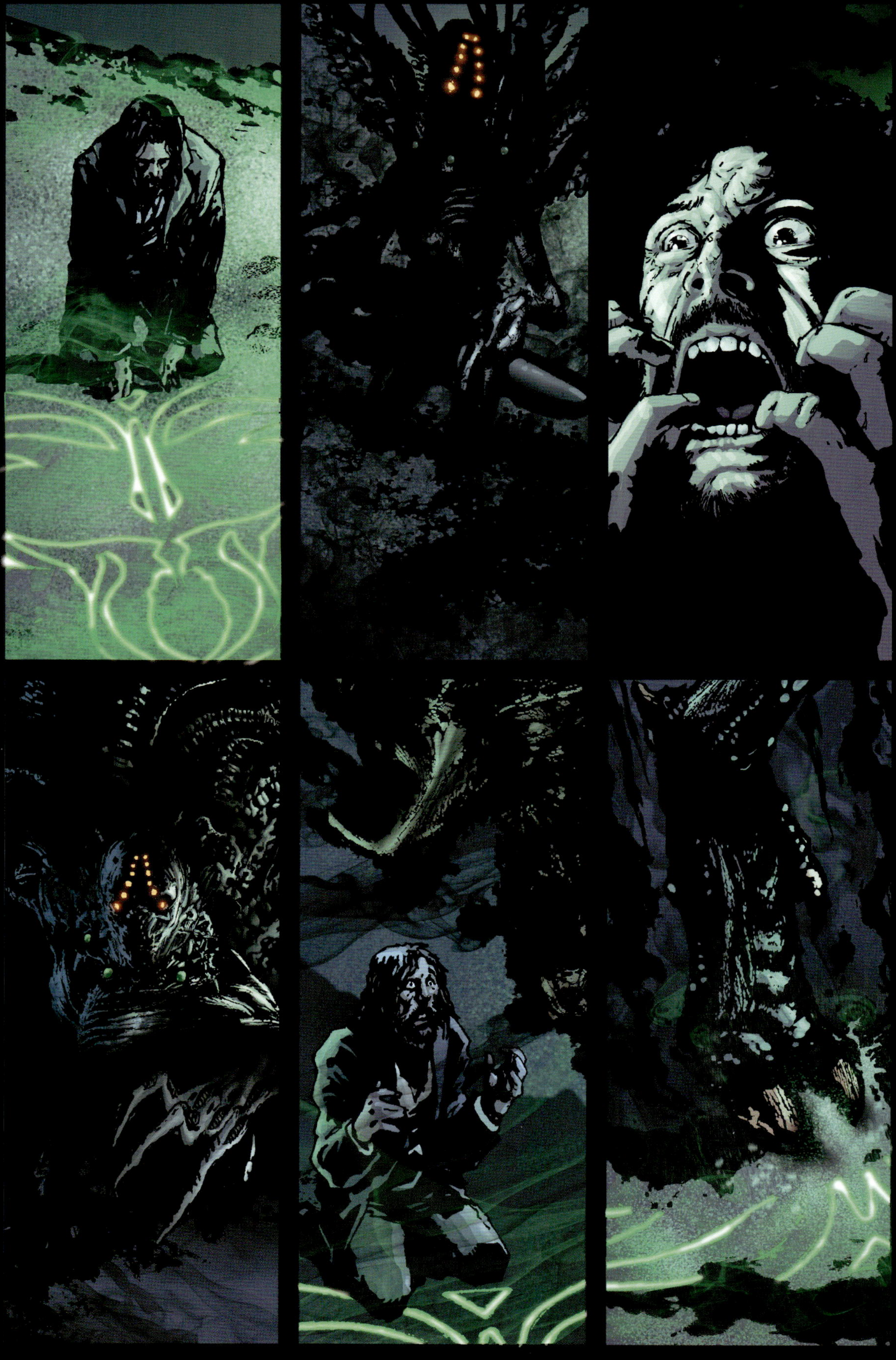

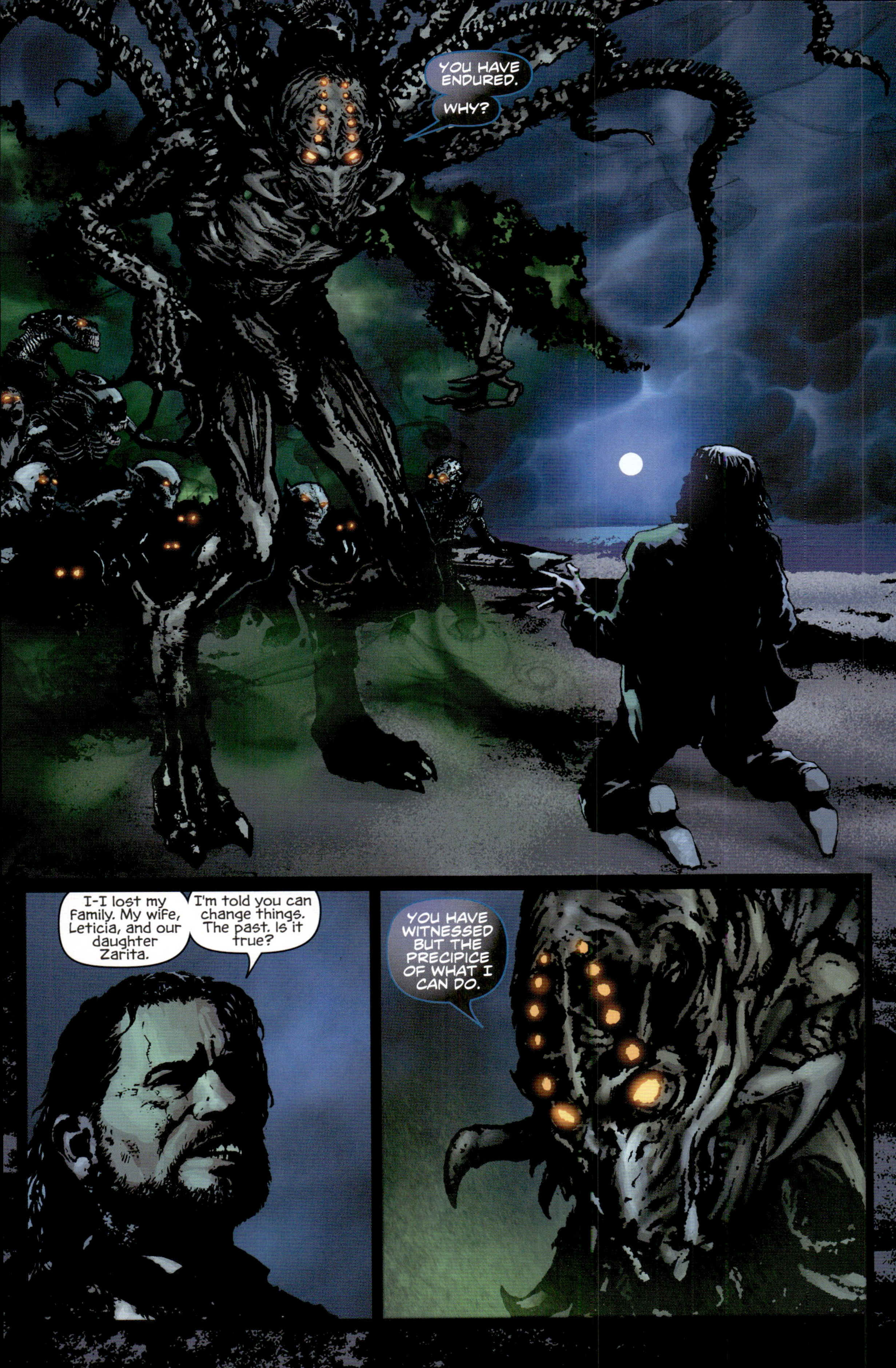
YOU HAVE ENDURED.
WHY?
I-I lost my family. My wife, Leticia, and our daughter Zarita.
I'm told you can change things. The past. Is it true?
YOU HAVE WITNESSED BUT THE PRECIPICE OF WHAT I CAN DO.

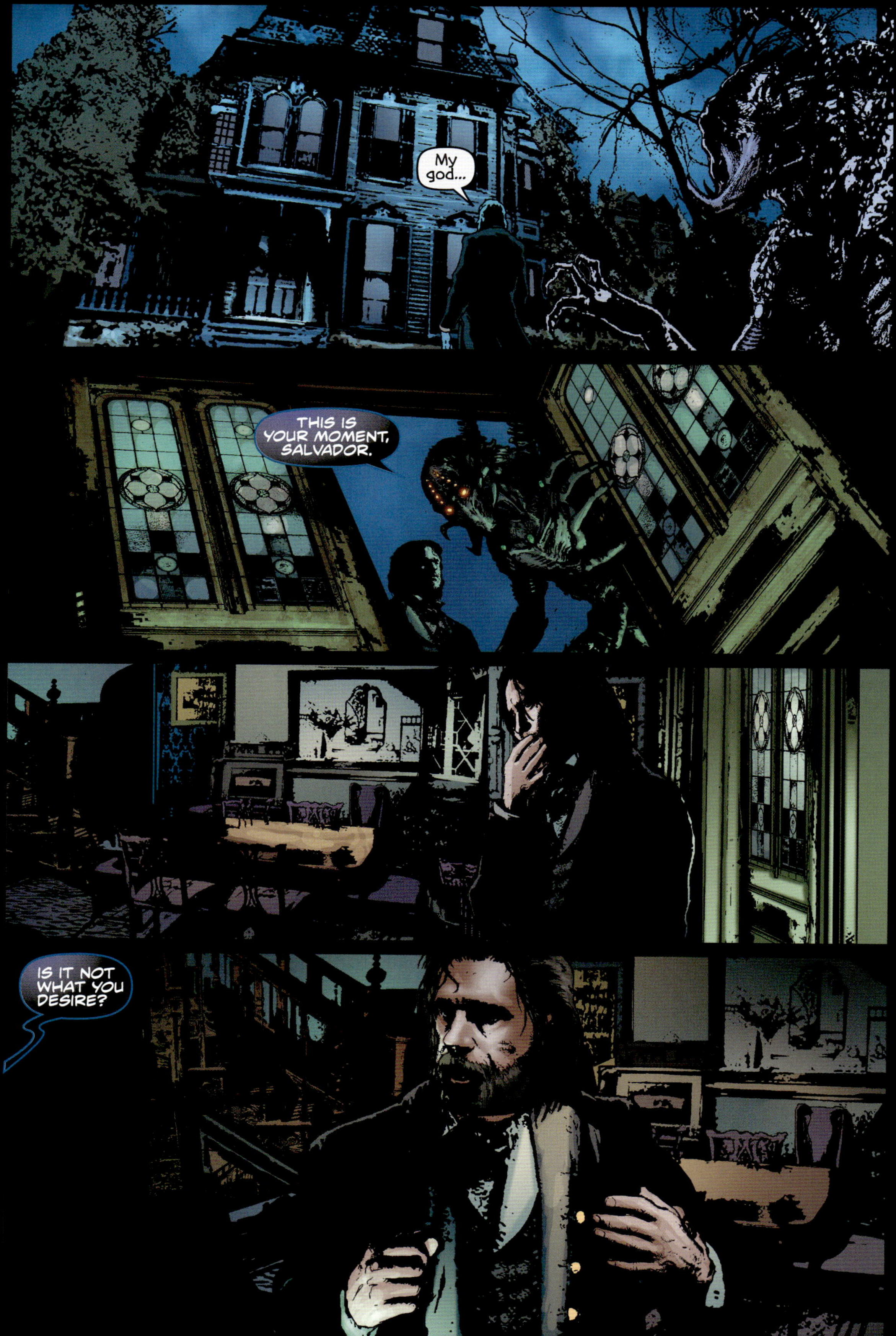
My god...
THIS IS YOUR MOMENT, SALVADOR.
IS IT NOT WHAT YOU DESIRE?

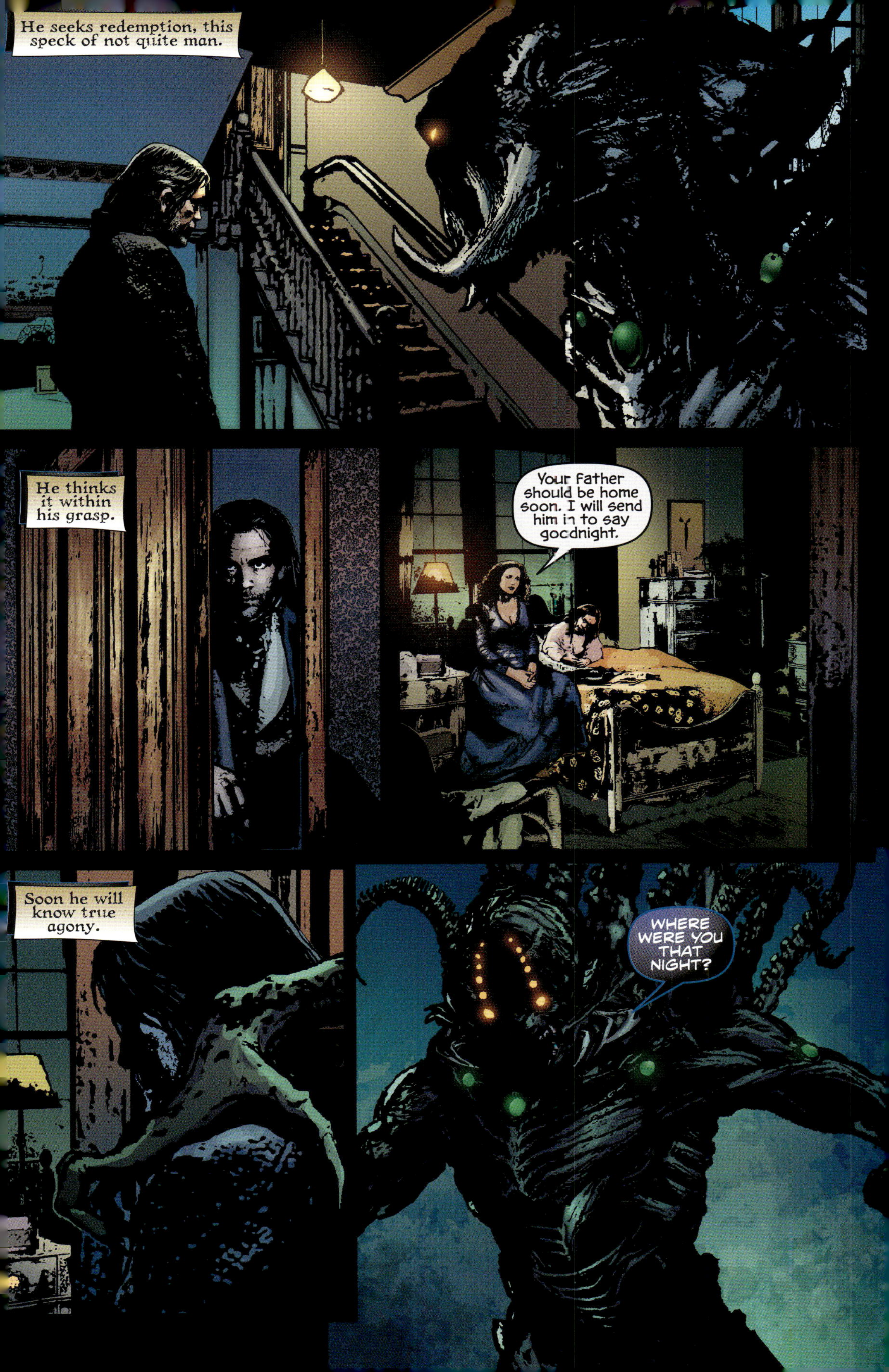
He seeks redemption, this speck of not quite man.
He thinks it within his grasp.
Your father should be home soon. I will send him in to say goodnight.
Soon he will know true agony.
WHERE WERE YOU THAT NIGHT?

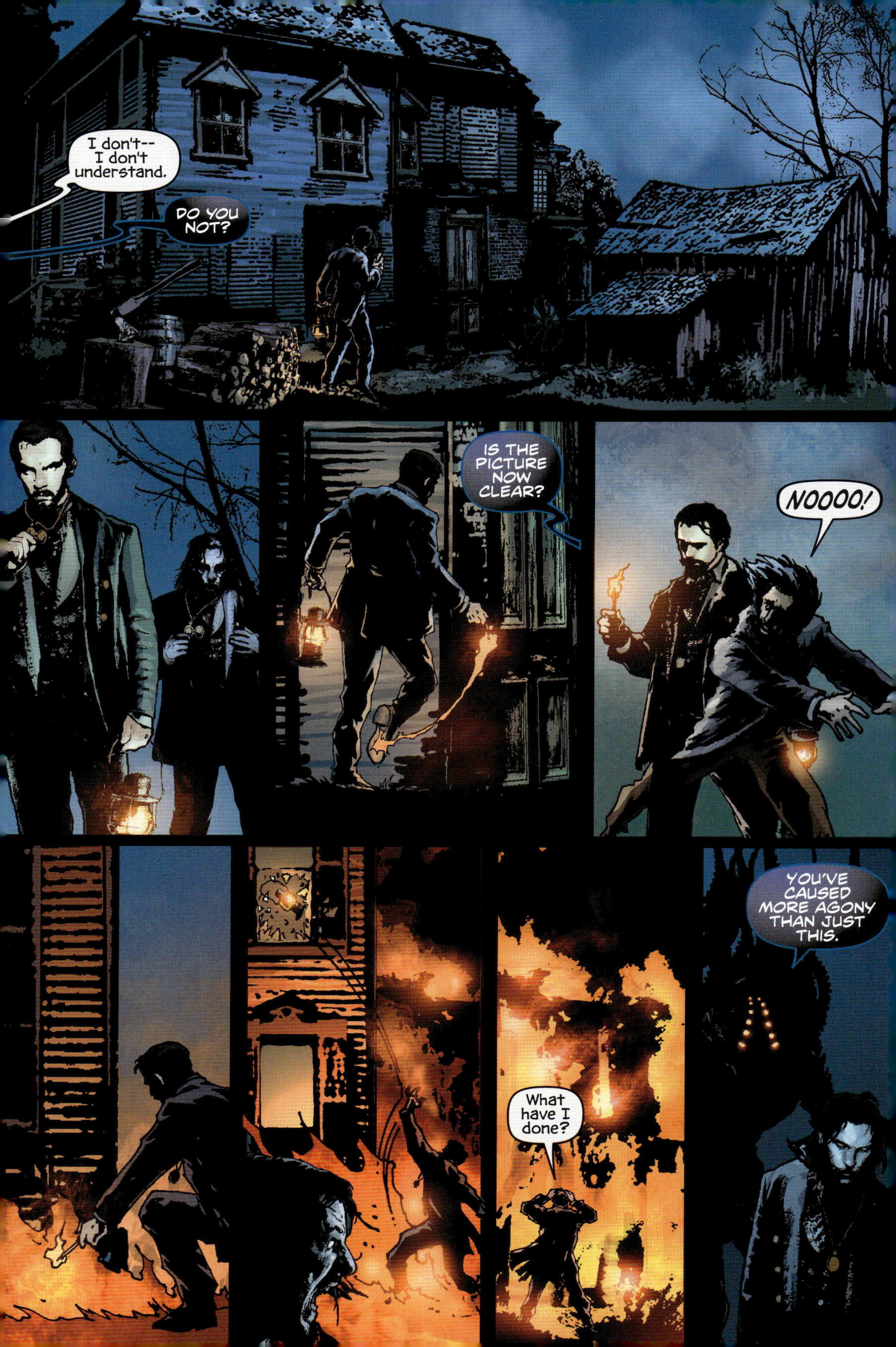
I don't-- I don't understand.
DO YOU NOT?
IS THE PICTURE NOW CLEAR?
NOOOO!
YOU'VE CAUSED MORE AGONY THAN JUST THIS.
What have I done?

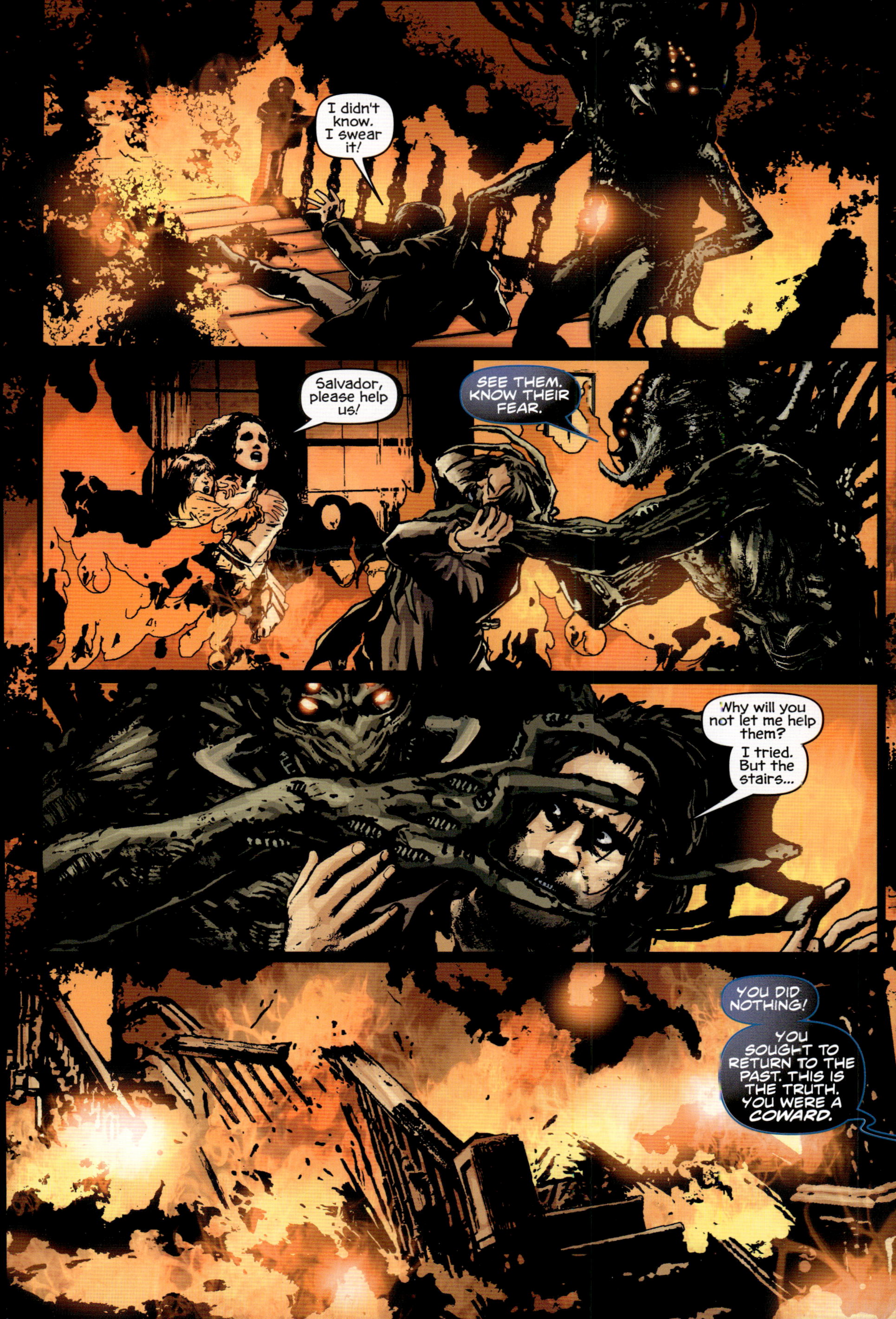
I didn't know. I swear it!
Salvador, please help us!
SEE THEM. KNOW THEIR FEAR.
Why will you not let me help them?
I tried. But the stairs...
YOU DID NOTHING!
YOU SOUGHT TO RETURN TO THE PAST. THIS IS THE TRUTH. YOU WERE A COWARD.

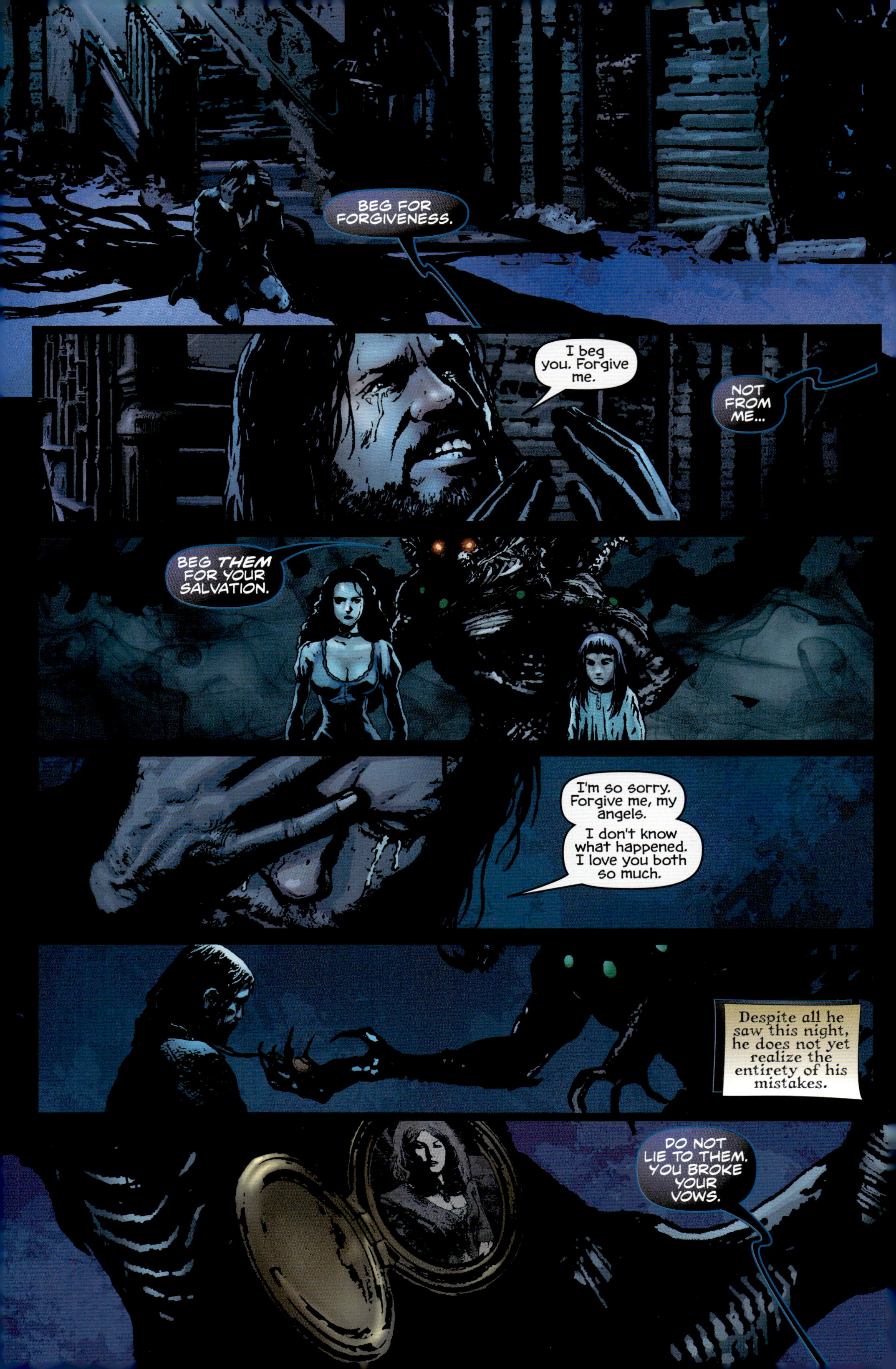
BEG FOR FORGIVENESS.
I beg you. Forgive me.
NOT FROM ME...
BEG *THEM* FOR YOUR SALVATION.
I'm so sorry. Forgive me, my angels.
I don't know what happened. I love you both so much.
Despite all he saw this night, he does not yet realize the entirety of his mistakes.
DO NOT LIE TO THEM. YOU BROKE YOUR VOWS.

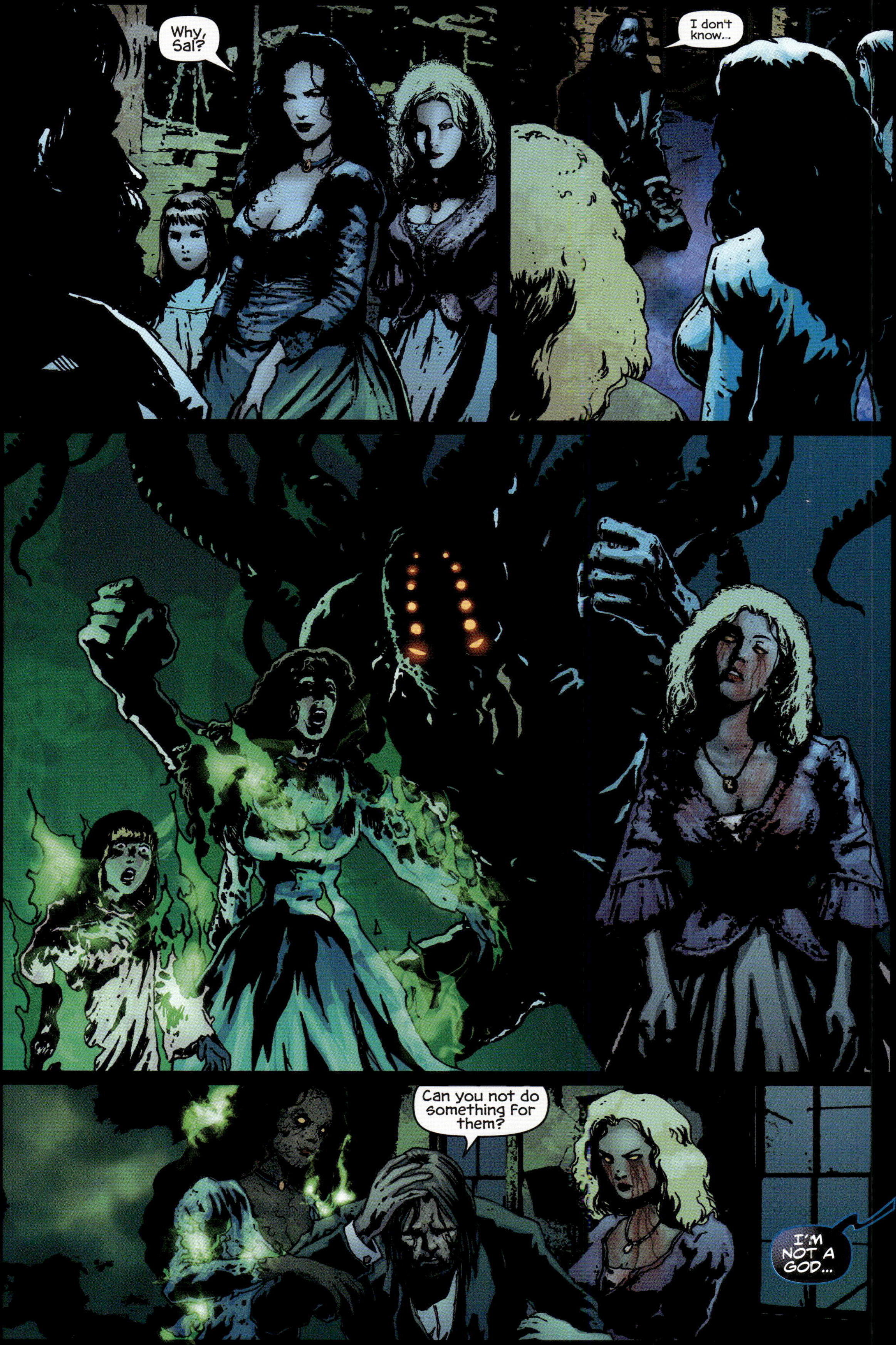
Why, Sal?
I don't know...
Can you not do something for them?
I'M NOT A GOD...

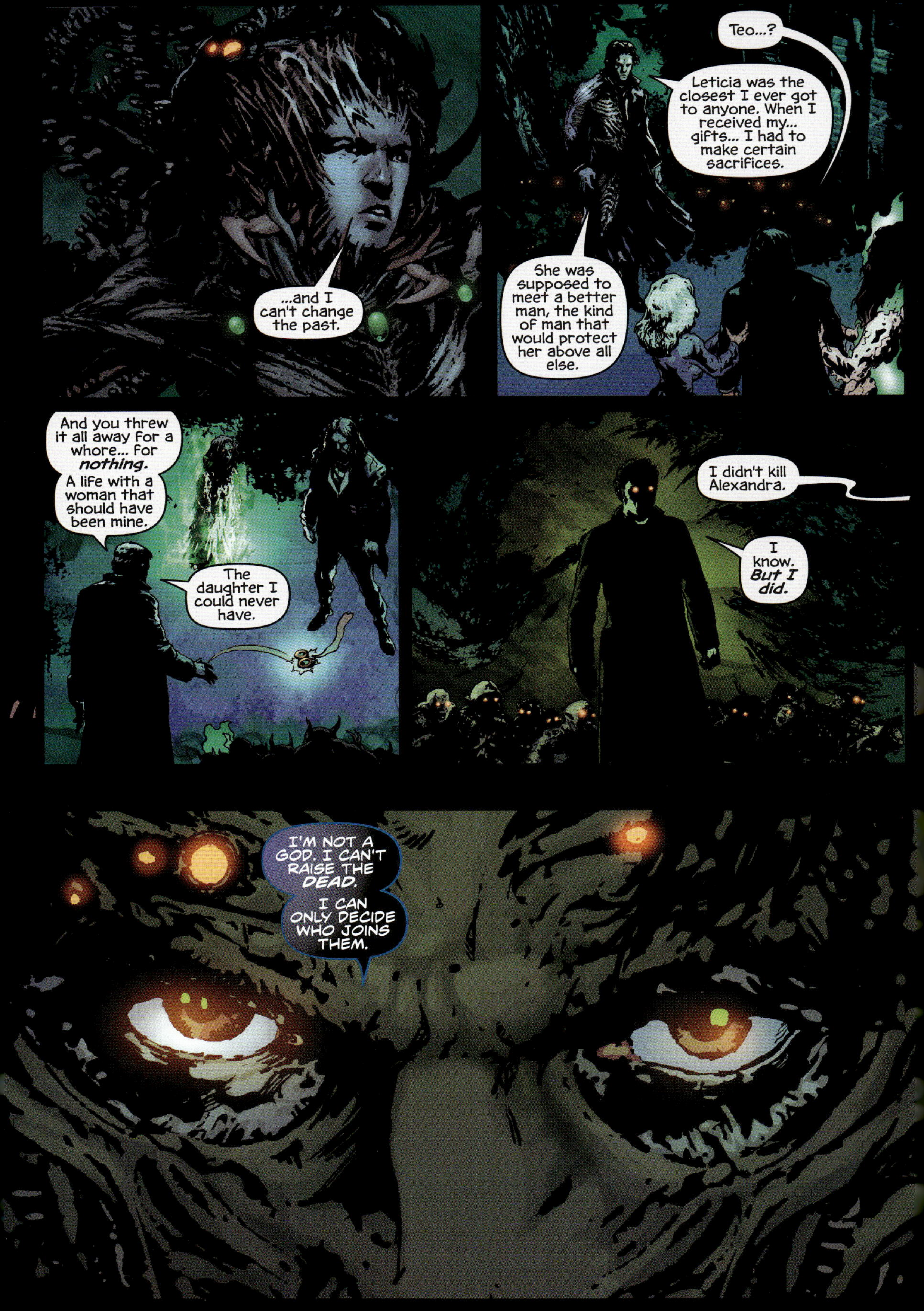
...and I can't change the past.
Teo...?
Leticia was the closest I ever got to anyone. When I received my... gifts... I had to make certain sacrifices.
She was supposed to meet a better man, the kind of man that would protect her above all else.
And you threw it all away for a whore... for *nothing.* A life with a woman that should have been mine.
The daughter I could never have.
I didn't kill Alexandra.
I know. *But I did.*
I'M NOT A GOD. I CAN'T RAISE THE *DEAD.*
I CAN ONLY DECIDE WHO JOINS THEM.

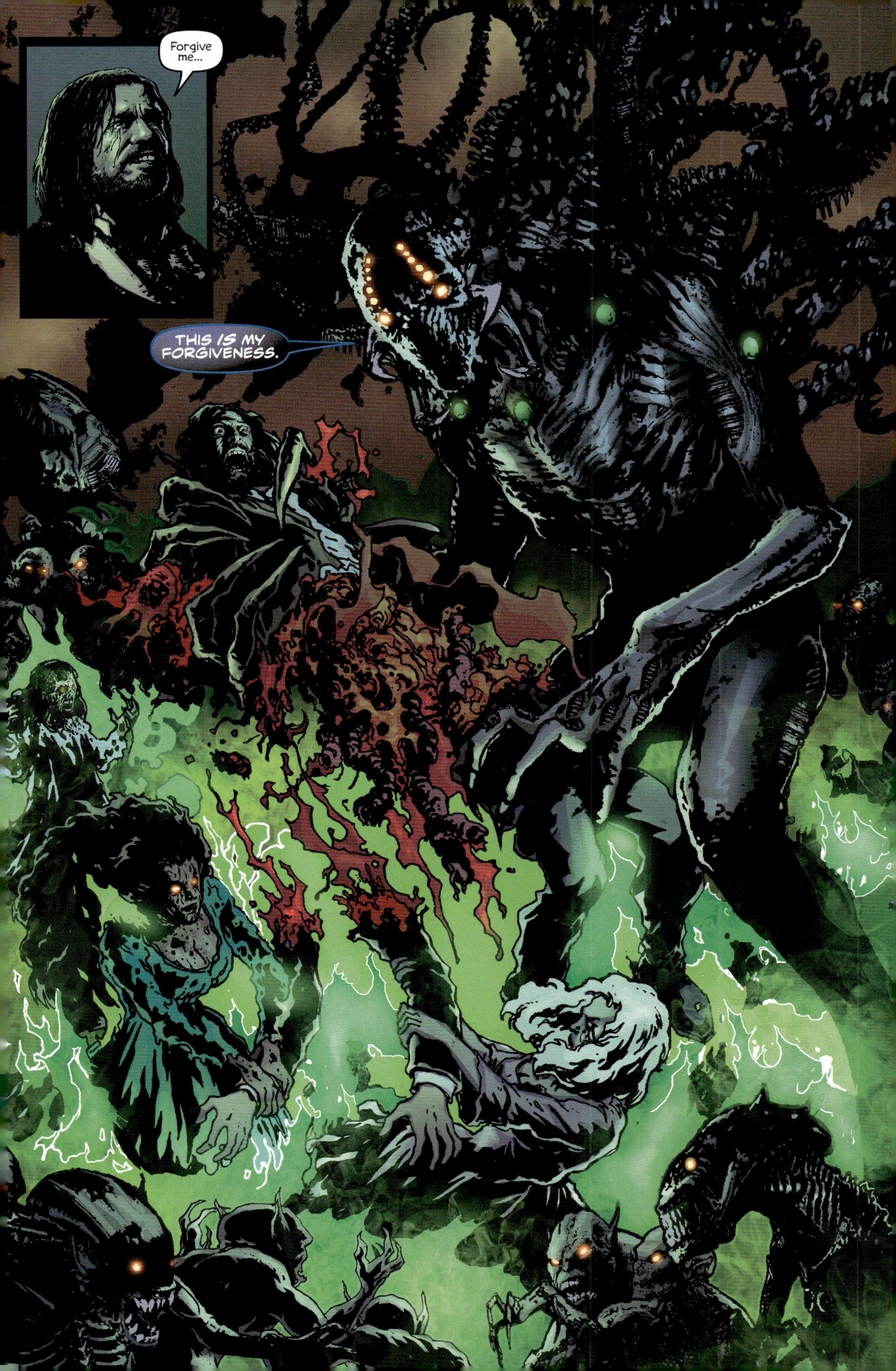
Forgive me...
THIS IS MY FORGIVENESS.

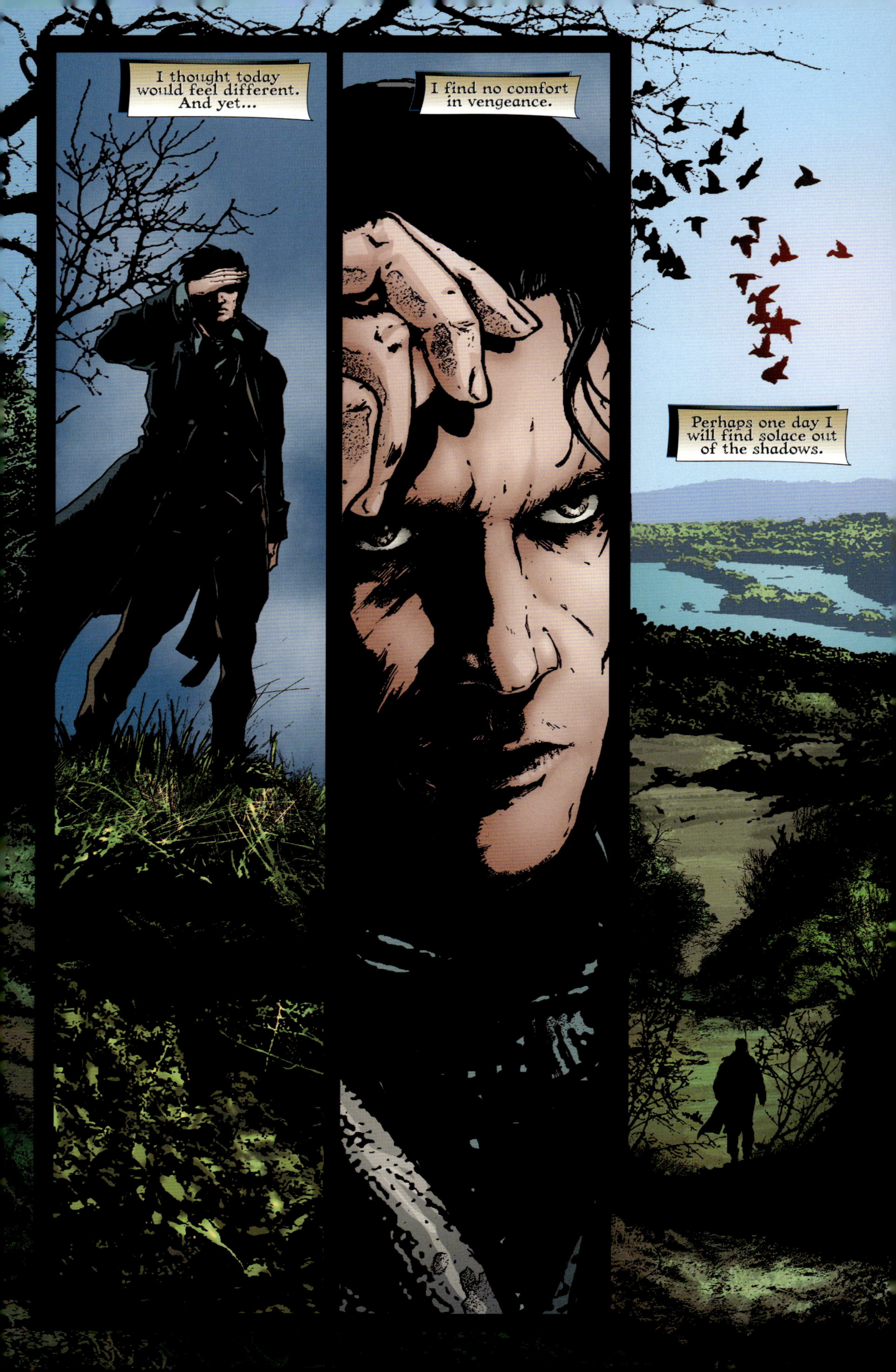
I thought today would feel different. And yet...
I find no comfort in vengeance.
Perhaps one day I will find solace out of the shadows.

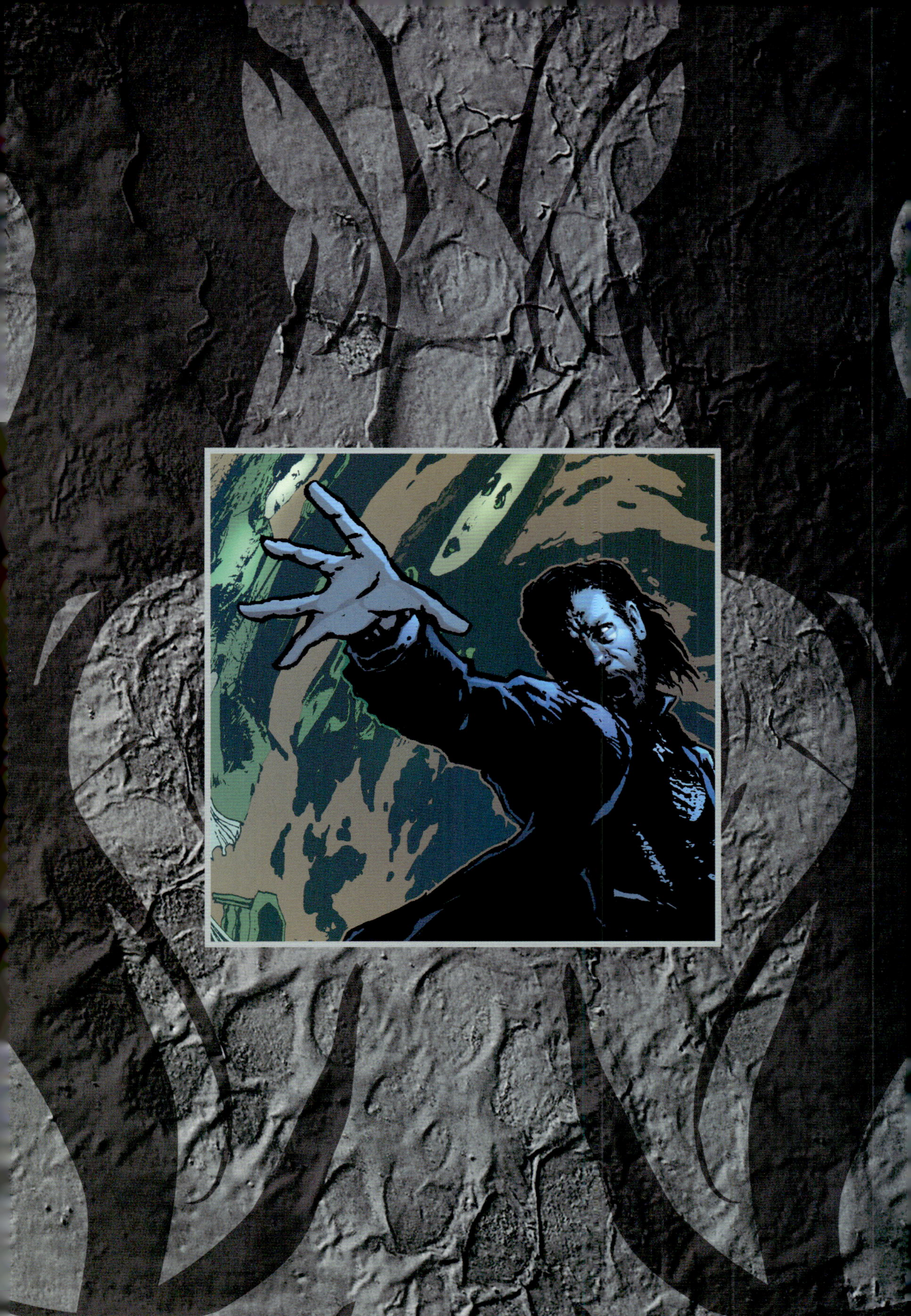

The Darkness: Butcher
cover art by: Michael Broussard, Larry Molinar
and Mark Prudeaux

THE DARKNESS: BUTCHER

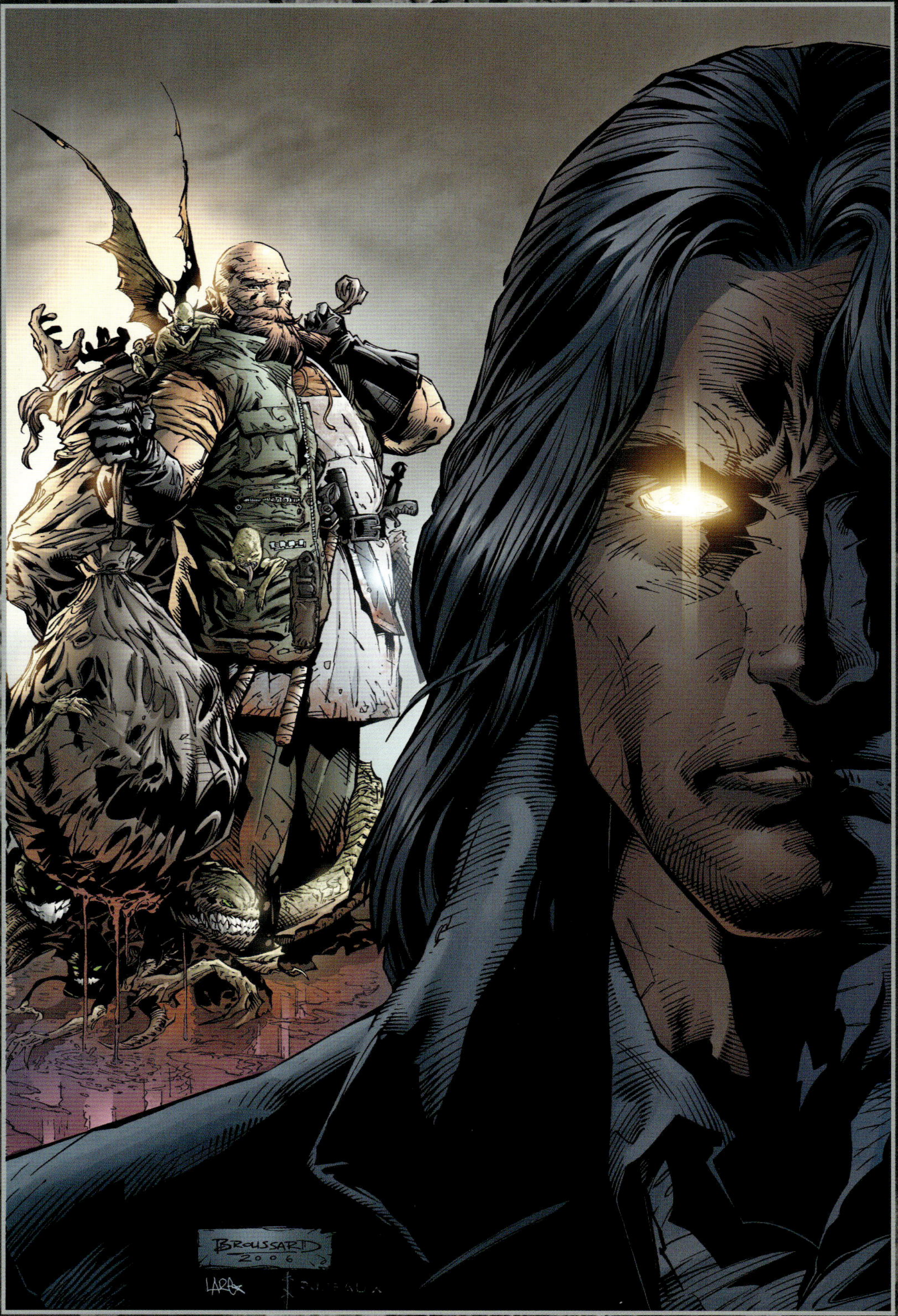
BROUSSARD
2006

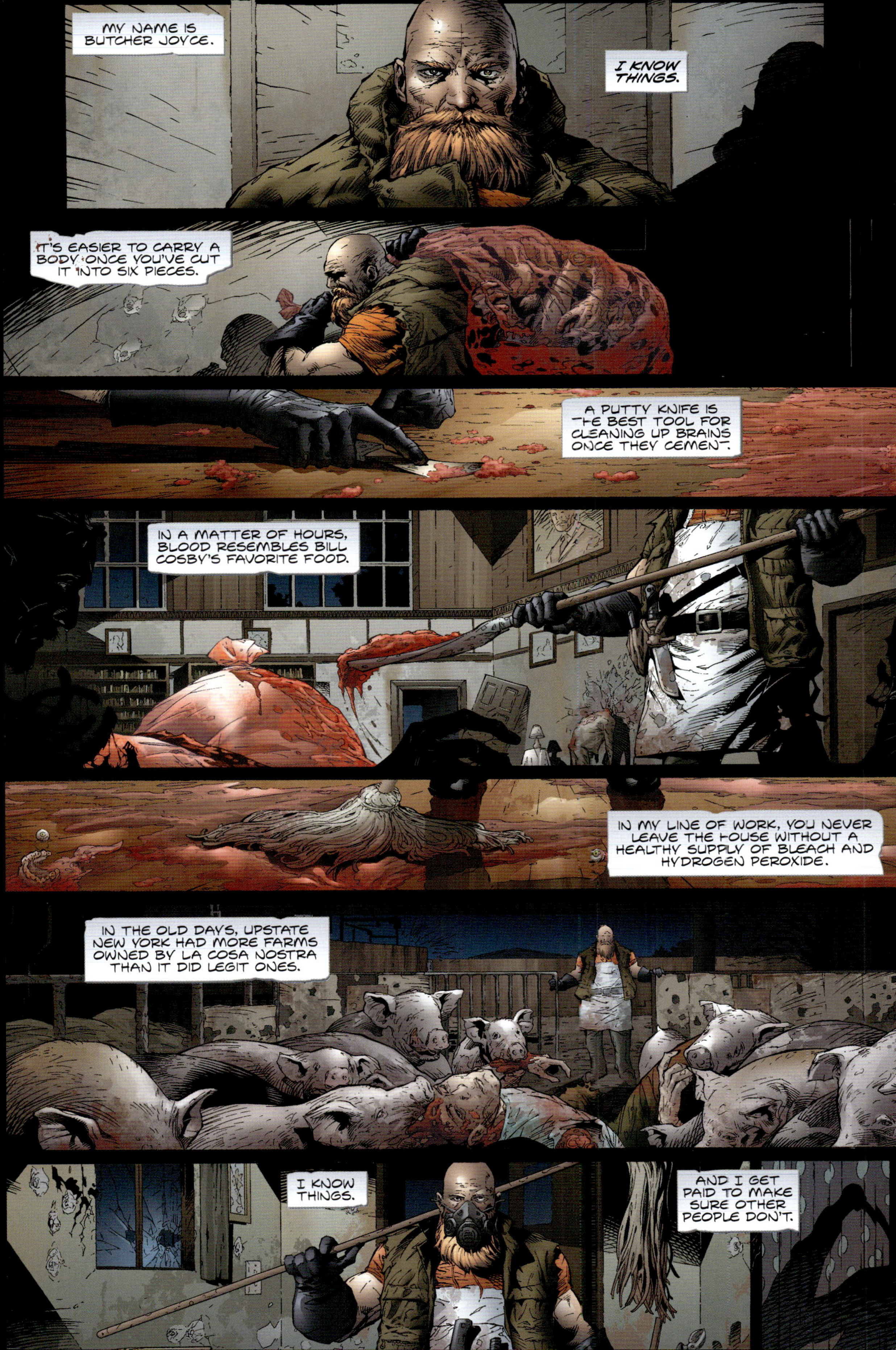
MY NAME IS BUTCHER JOYCE.
I KNOW THINGS.
IT'S EASIER TO CARRY A BODY ONCE YOU'VE CUT IT INTO SIX PIECES.
A PUTTY KNIFE IS THE BEST TOOL FOR CLEANING UP BRAINS ONCE THEY CEMENT.
IN A MATTER OF HOURS, BLOOD RESEMBLES BILL COSBY'S FAVORITE FOOD.
IN MY LINE OF WORK, YOU NEVER LEAVE THE HOUSE WITHOUT A HEALTHY SUPPLY OF BLEACH AND HYDROGEN PEROXIDE.
IN THE OLD DAYS, UPSTATE NEW YORK HAD MORE FARMS OWNED BY LA COSA NOSTRA THAN IT DID LEGIT ONES.
I KNOW THINGS.
AND I GET PAID TO MAKE SURE OTHER PEOPLE DON'T.

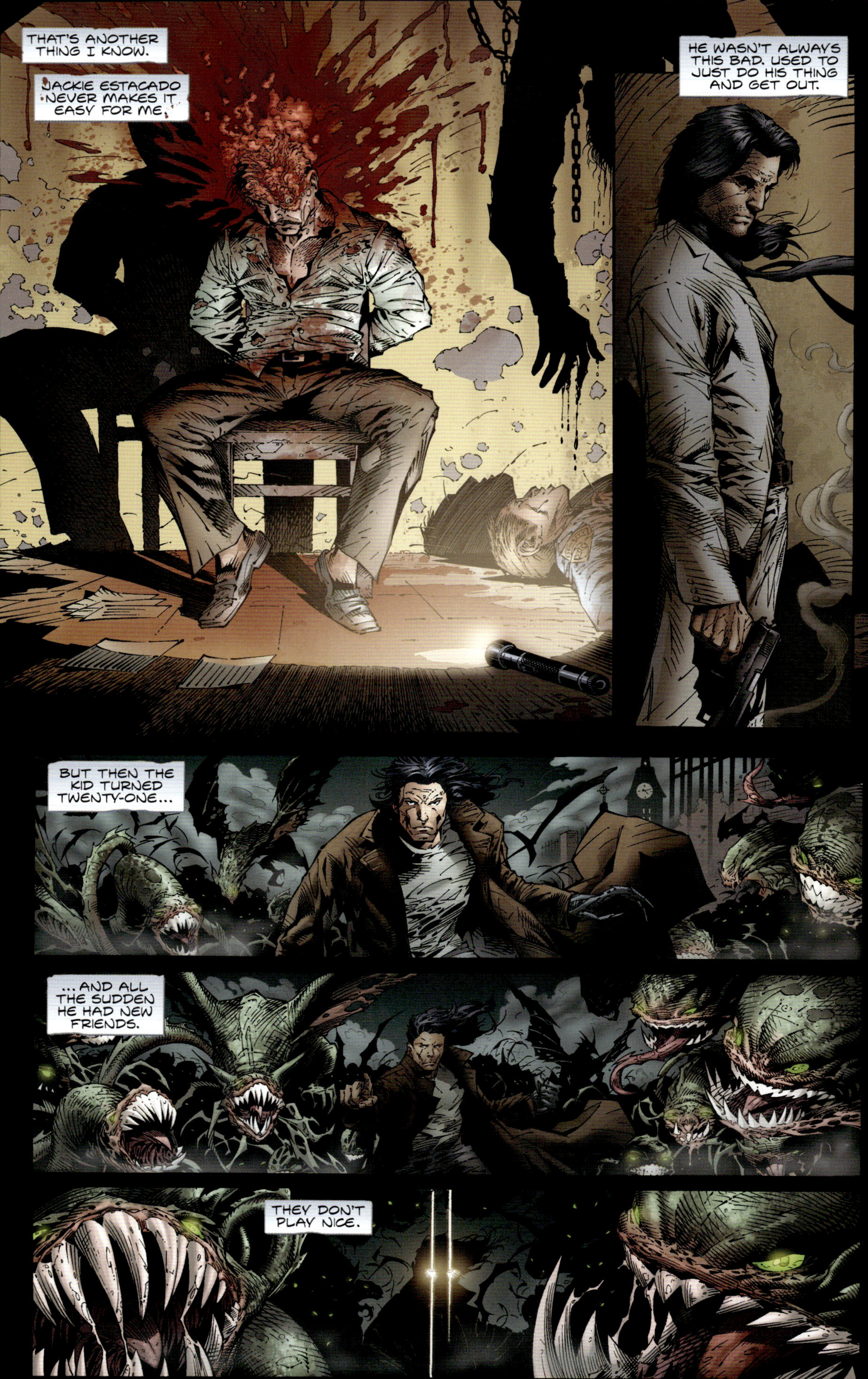
THAT'S ANOTHER THING I KNOW.
JACKIE ESTACADO NEVER MAKES IT EASY FOR ME.
HE WASN'T ALWAYS THIS BAD. USED TO JUST DO HIS THING AND GET OUT.
BUT THEN THE KID TURNED TWENTY-ONE...
...AND ALL THE SUDDEN HE HAD NEW FRIENDS.
THEY DON'T PLAY NICE.

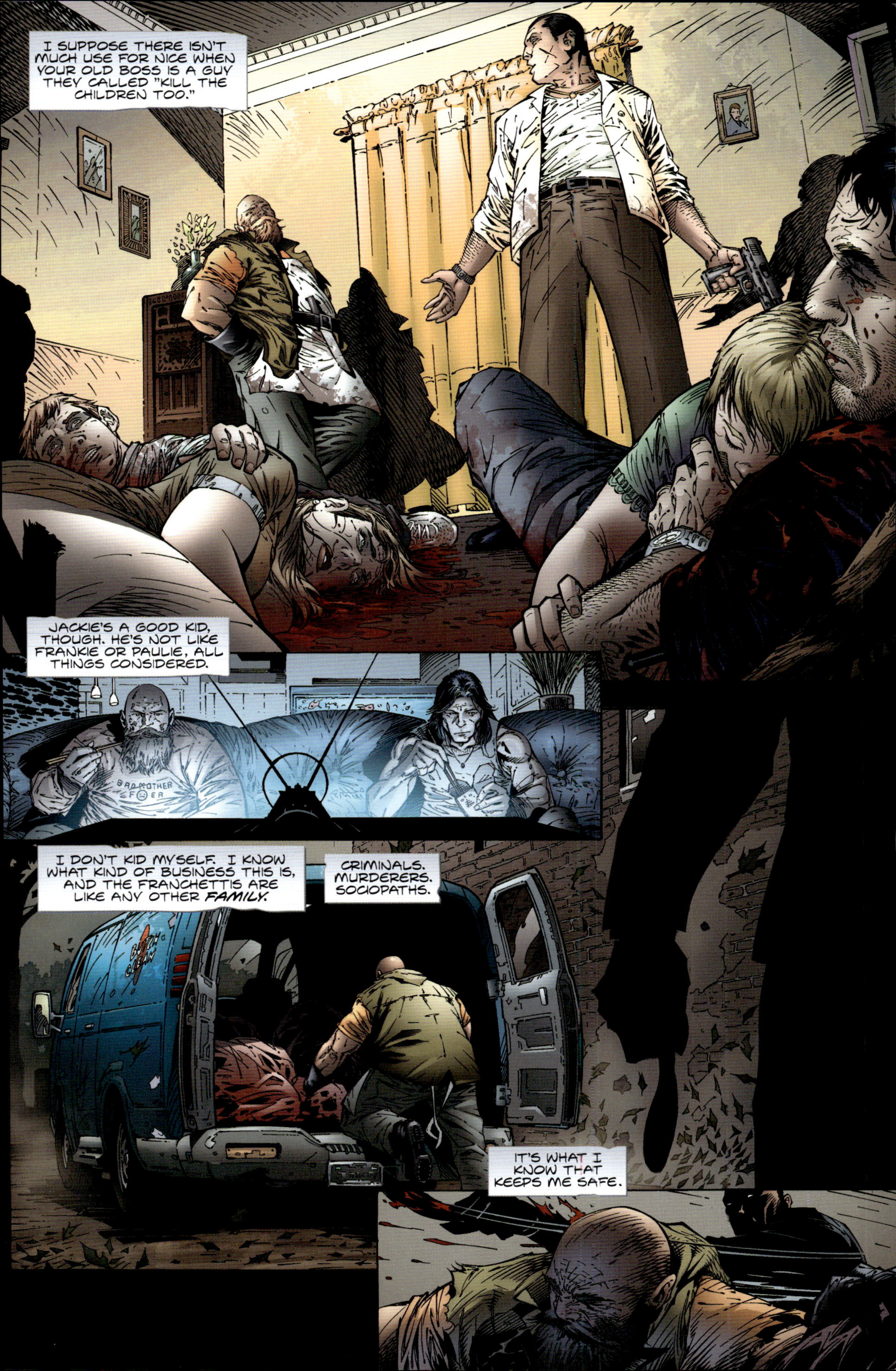
I SUPPOSE THERE ISN'T MUCH USE FOR NICE WHEN YOUR OLD BOSS IS A GUY THEY CALLED "KILL THE CHILDREN TOO."
JACKIE'S A GOOD KID, THOUGH. HE'S NOT LIKE FRANKIE OR PAULIE, ALL THINGS CONSIDERED.
BAD MOTHER F☹ER
I DON'T KID MYSELF. I KNOW WHAT KIND OF BUSINESS THIS IS, AND THE FRANCHETTIS ARE LIKE ANY OTHER *FAMILY.*
CRIMINALS. MURDERERS. SOCIOPATHS.
IT'S WHAT I KNOW THAT KEEPS ME SAFE.

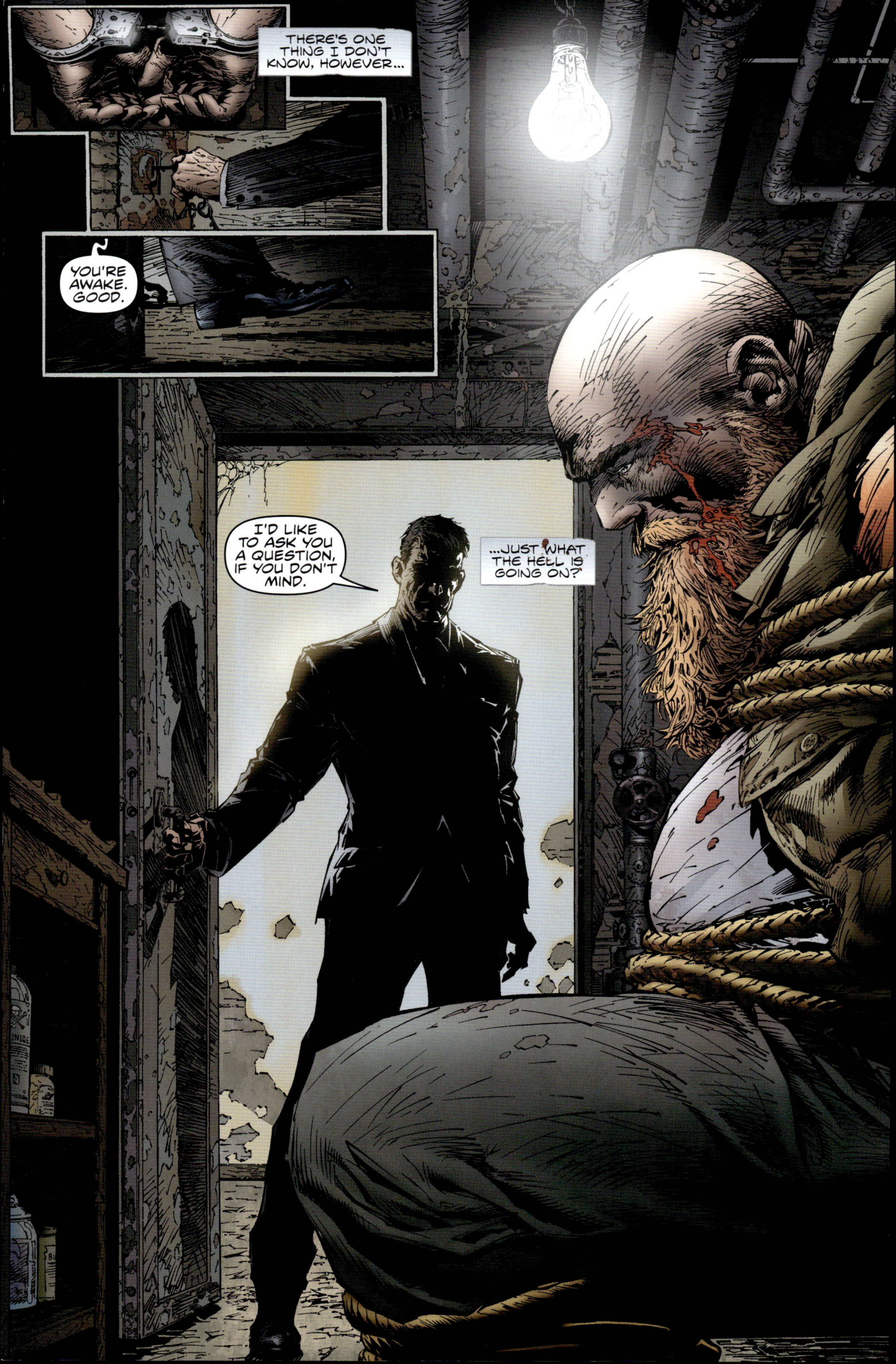
THERE'S ONE THING I DON'T KNOW, HOWEVER...
YOU'RE AWAKE. GOOD.
I'D LIKE TO ASK YOU A QUESTION, IF YOU DON'T MIND.
...JUST WHAT THE HELL IS GOING ON?

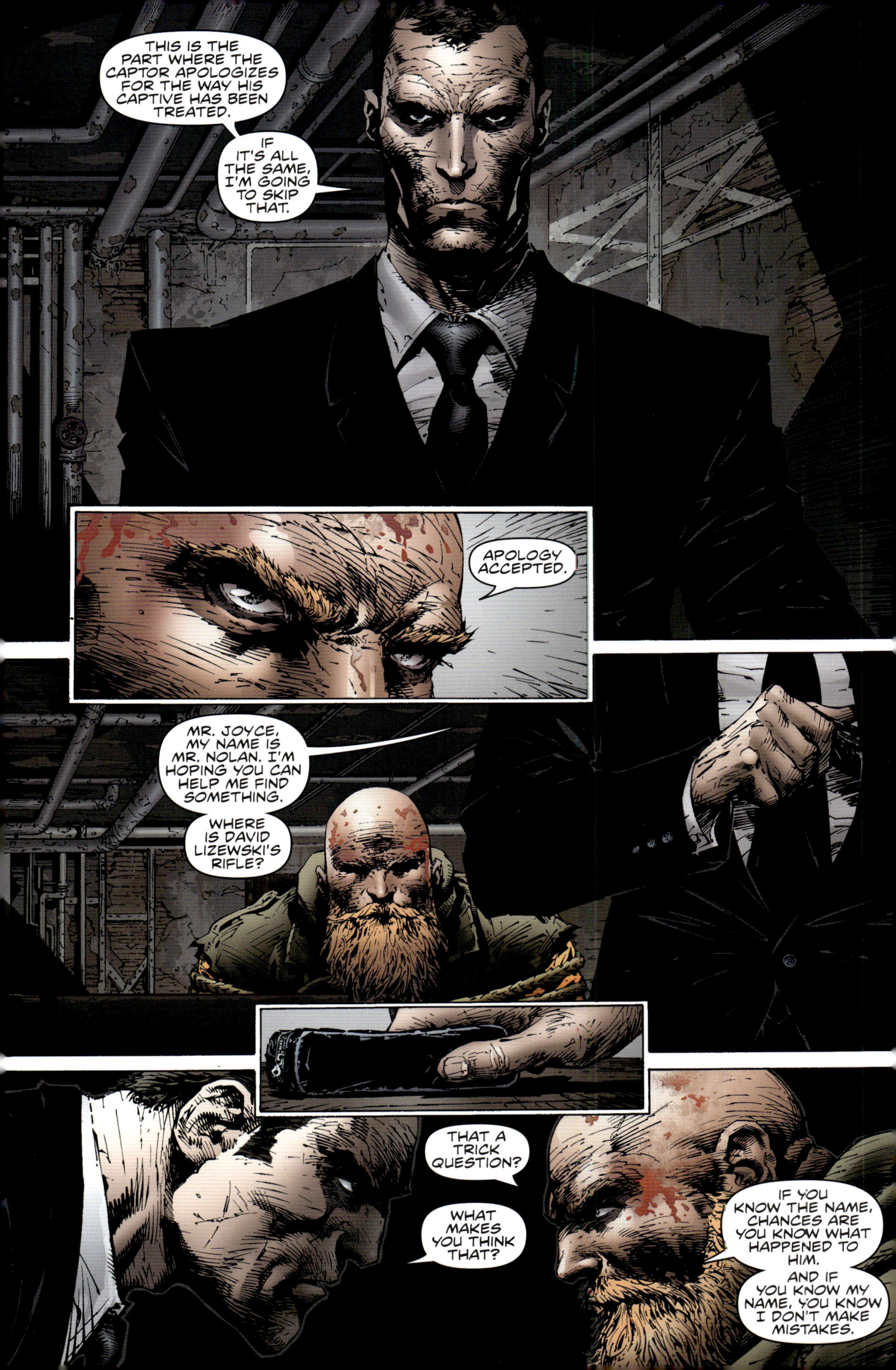

THIS IS THE PART WHERE THE CAPTOR APOLOGIZES FOR THE WAY HIS CAPTIVE HAS BEEN TREATED.
IF IT'S ALL THE SAME, I'M GOING TO SKIP THAT.
APOLOGY ACCEPTED.
MR. JOYCE, MY NAME IS MR. NOLAN. I'M HOPING YOU CAN HELP ME FIND SOMETHING.
WHERE IS DAVID LIZEWSKI'S RIFLE?
THAT A TRICK QUESTION?
WHAT MAKES YOU THINK THAT?
IF YOU KNOW THE NAME, CHANCES ARE YOU KNOW WHAT HAPPENED TO HIM.
AND IF YOU KNOW MY NAME, YOU KNOW I DON'T MAKE MISTAKES.

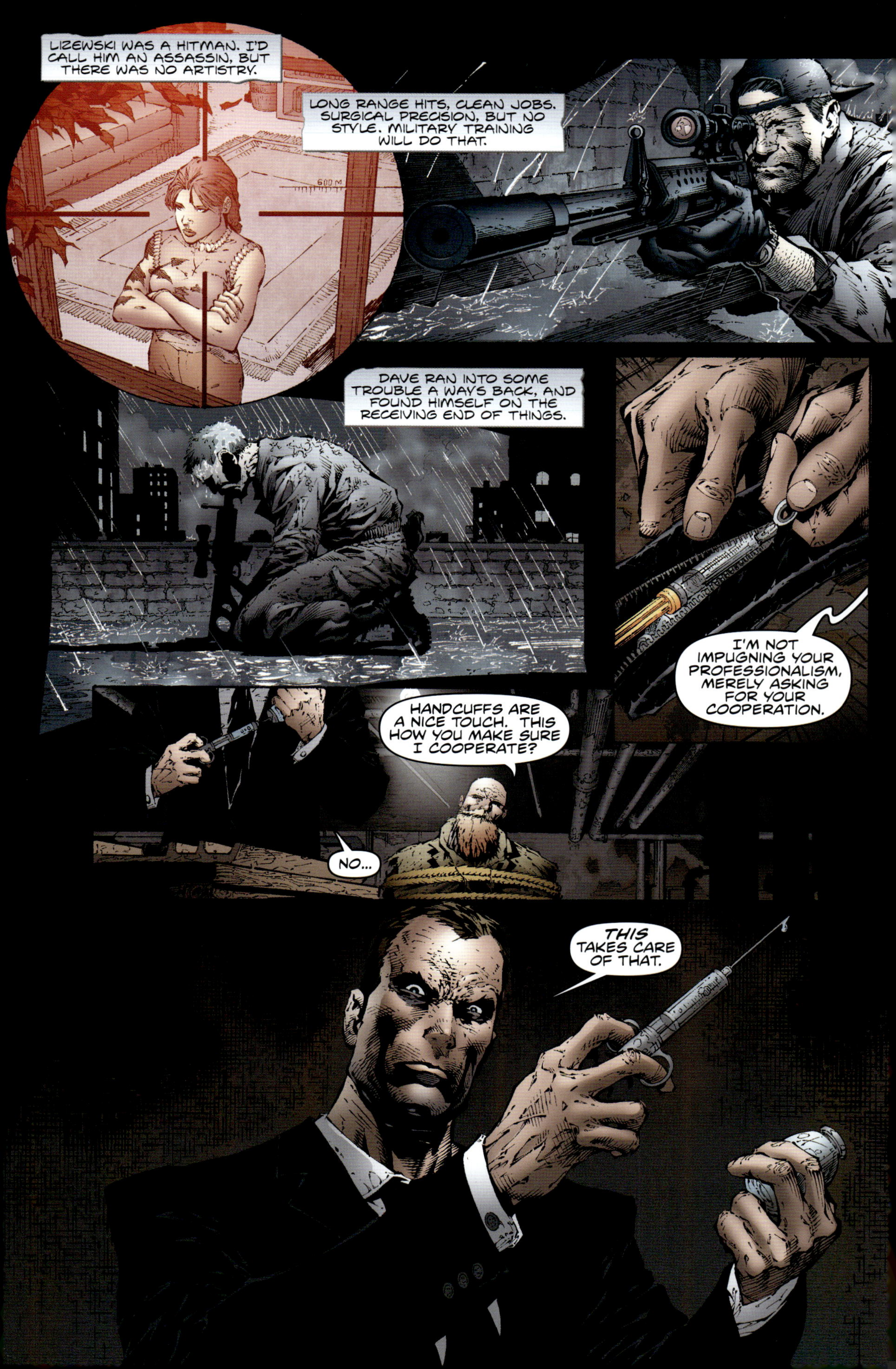
LIZEWSKI WAS A HITMAN. I'D CALL HIM AN ASSASSIN, BUT THERE WAS NO ARTISTRY.
600 M
LONG RANGE HITS, CLEAN JOBS. SURGICAL PRECISION, BUT NO STYLE. MILITARY TRAINING WILL DO THAT.
DAVE RAN INTO SOME TROUBLE A WAYS BACK, AND FOUND HIMSELF ON THE RECEIVING END OF THINGS.
I'M NOT IMPUGNING YOUR PROFESSIONALISM, MERELY ASKING FOR YOUR COOPERATION.
HANDCUFFS ARE A NICE TOUCH. THIS HOW YOU MAKE SURE I COOPERATE?
NO...
THIS TAKES CARE OF THAT.

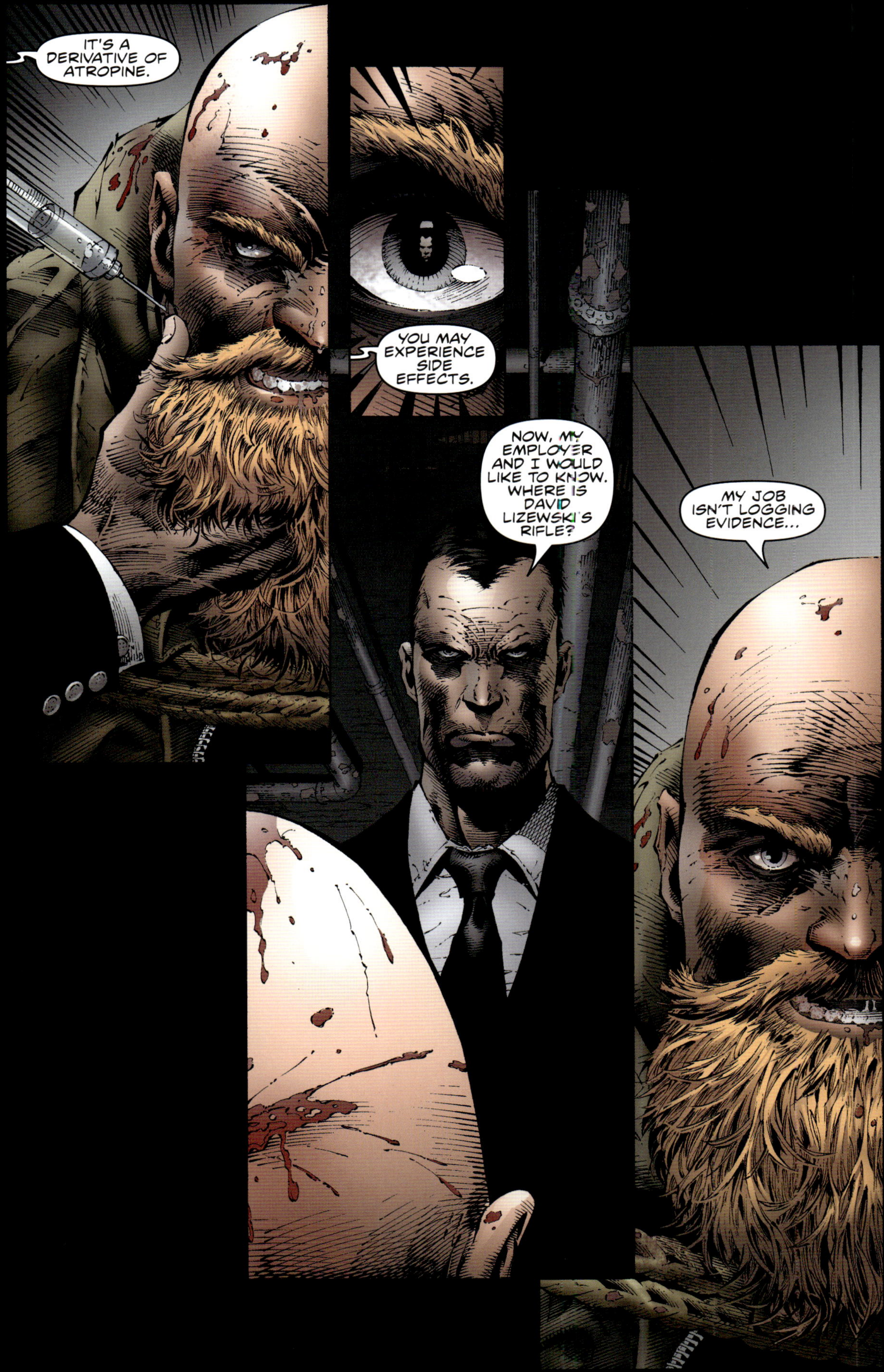
IT'S A DERIVATIVE OF ATROPINE.
YOU MAY EXPERIENCE SIDE EFFECTS.
NOW, MY EMPLOYER AND I WOULD LIKE TO KNOW. WHERE IS DAVID LIZEWSKI'S RIFLE?
MY JOB ISN'T LOGGING EVIDENCE...

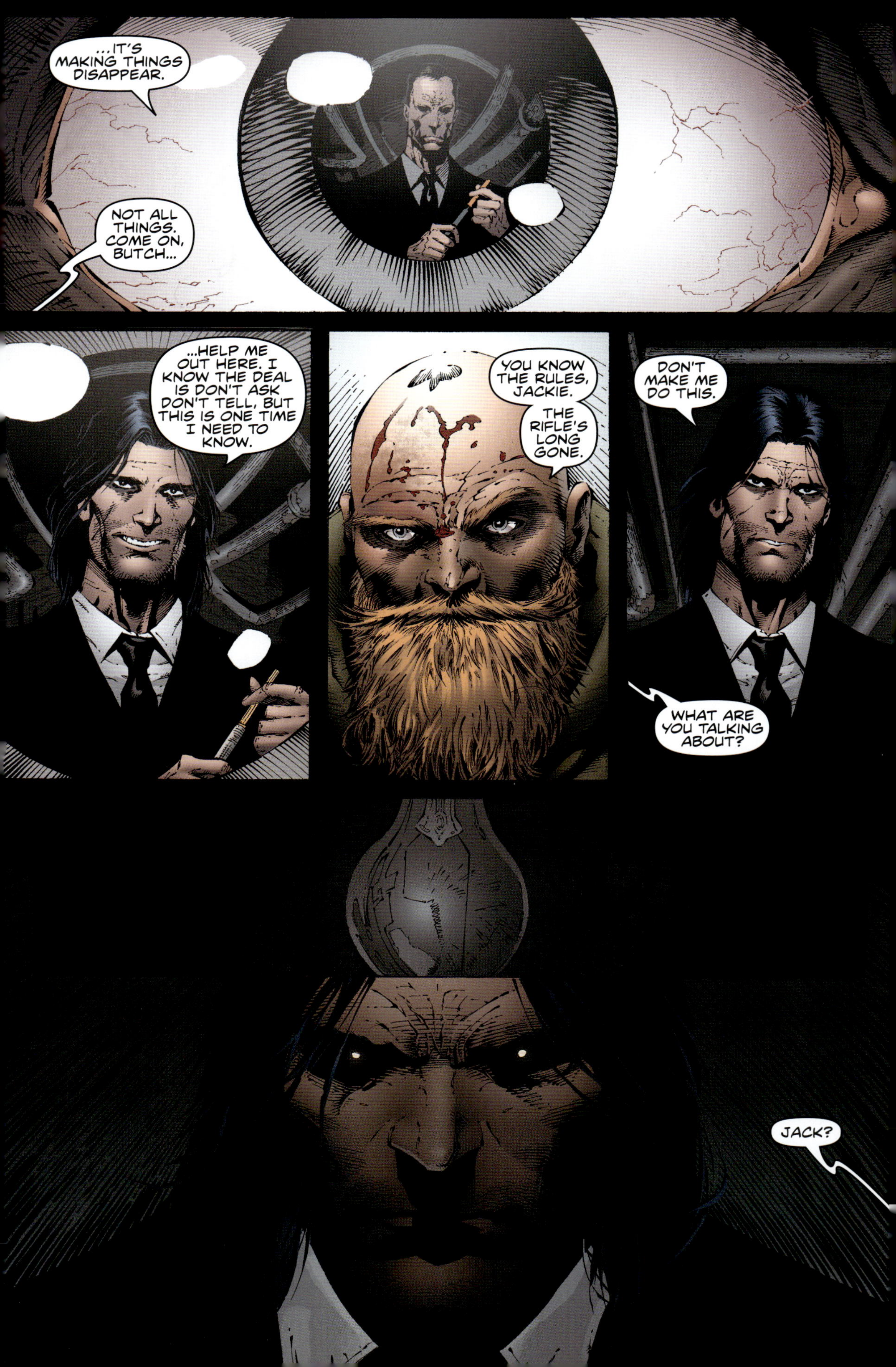
...IT'S MAKING THINGS DISAPPEAR.
NOT ALL THINGS. COME ON, BUTCH...
...HELP ME OUT HERE. I KNOW THE DEAL IS DON'T ASK DON'T TELL, BUT THIS IS ONE TIME I NEED TO KNOW.
YOU KNOW THE RULES, JACKIE.
THE RIFLE'S LONG GONE.
DON'T MAKE ME DO THIS.
WHAT ARE YOU TALKING ABOUT?
JACK?

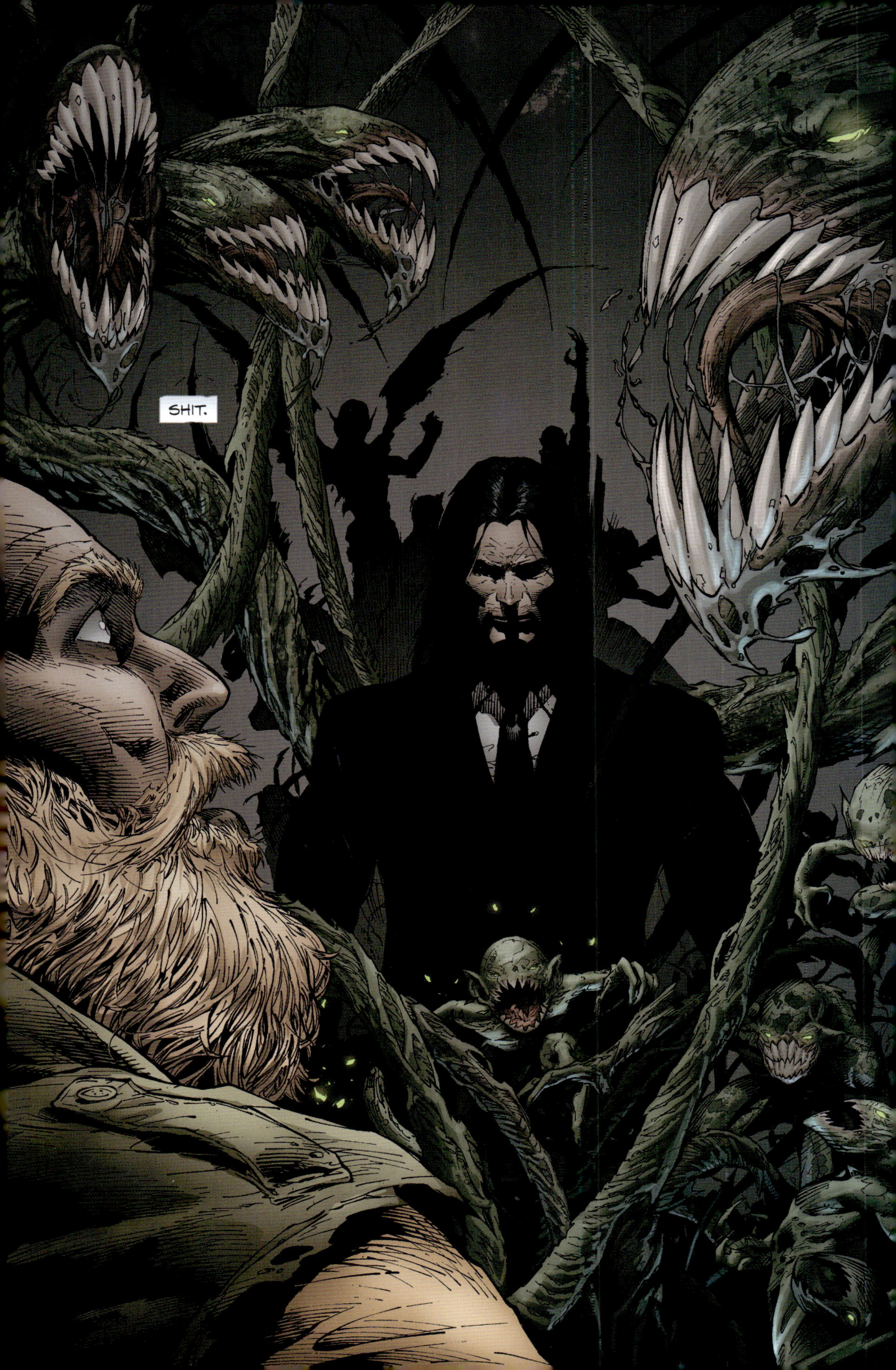
SHIT.

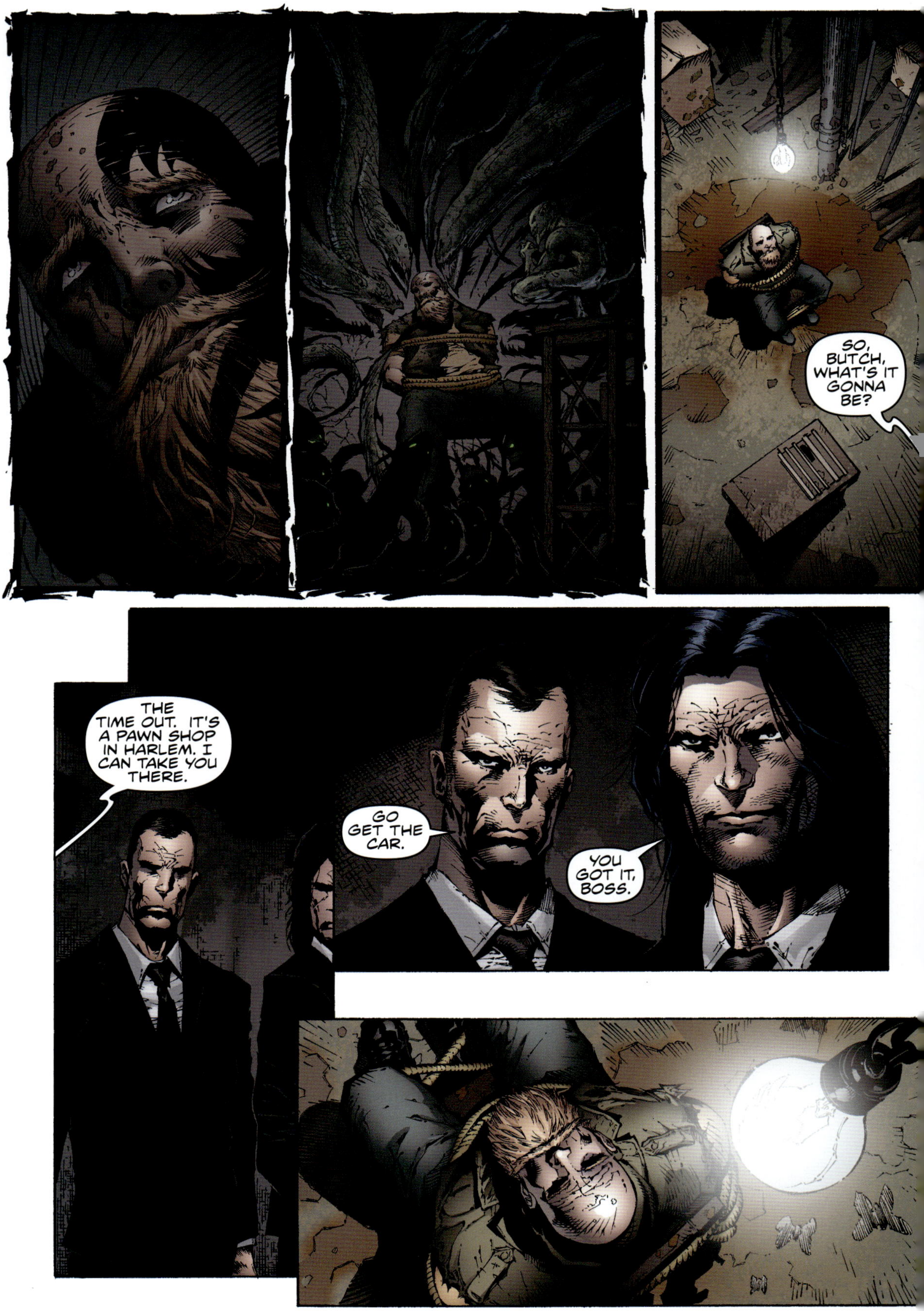
SO, BUTCH, WHAT'S IT GONNA BE?
THE TIME OUT. IT'S A PAWN SHOP IN HARLEM. I CAN TAKE YOU THERE.
GO GET THE CAR.
YOU GOT IT, BOSS.

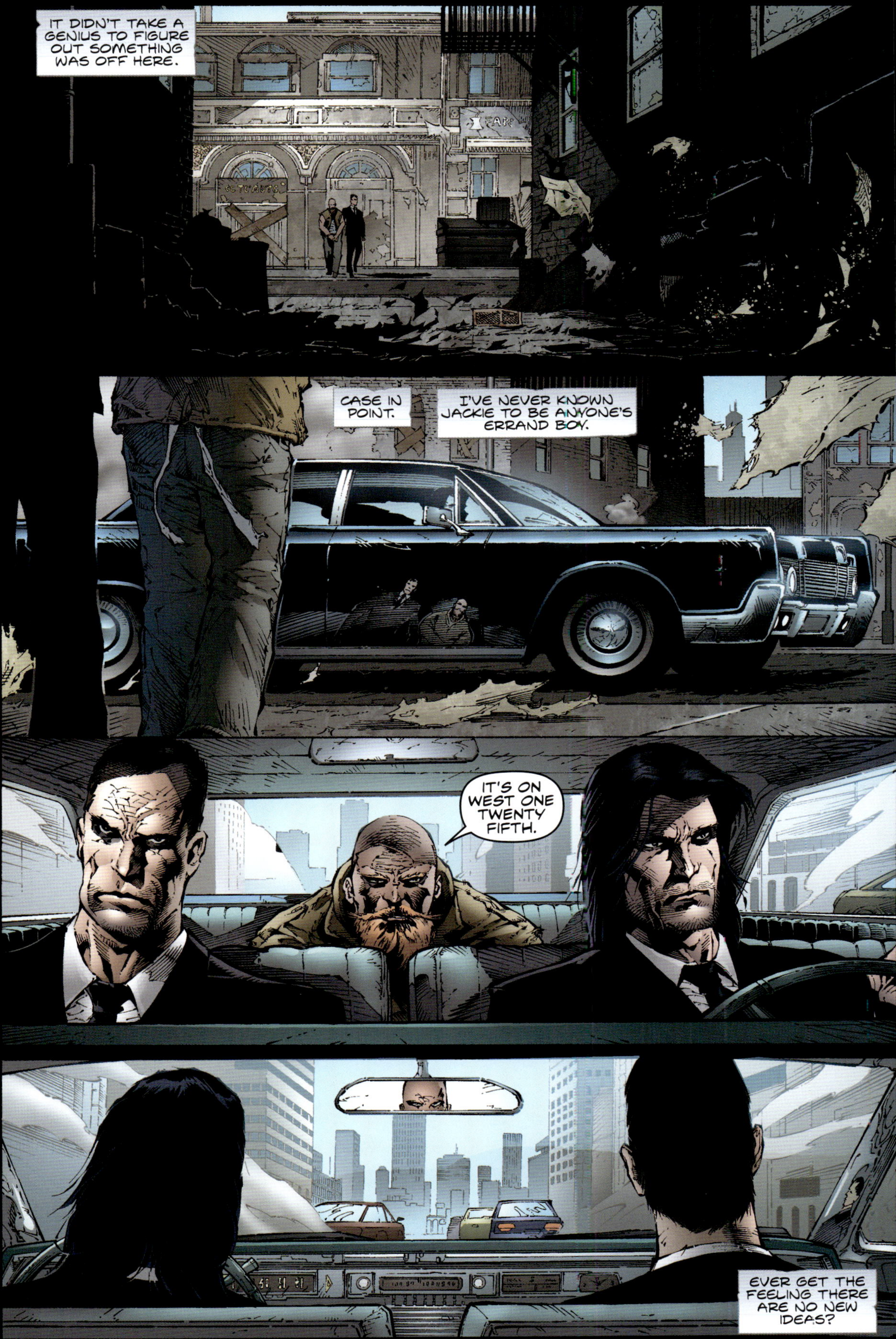
IT DIDN'T TAKE A GENIUS TO FIGURE OUT SOMETHING WAS OFF HERE.
CASE IN POINT.
I'VE NEVER KNOWN JACKIE TO BE ANYONE'S ERRAND BOY.
IT'S ON WEST ONE TWENTY FIFTH.
EVER GET THE FEELING THERE ARE NO NEW IDEAS?

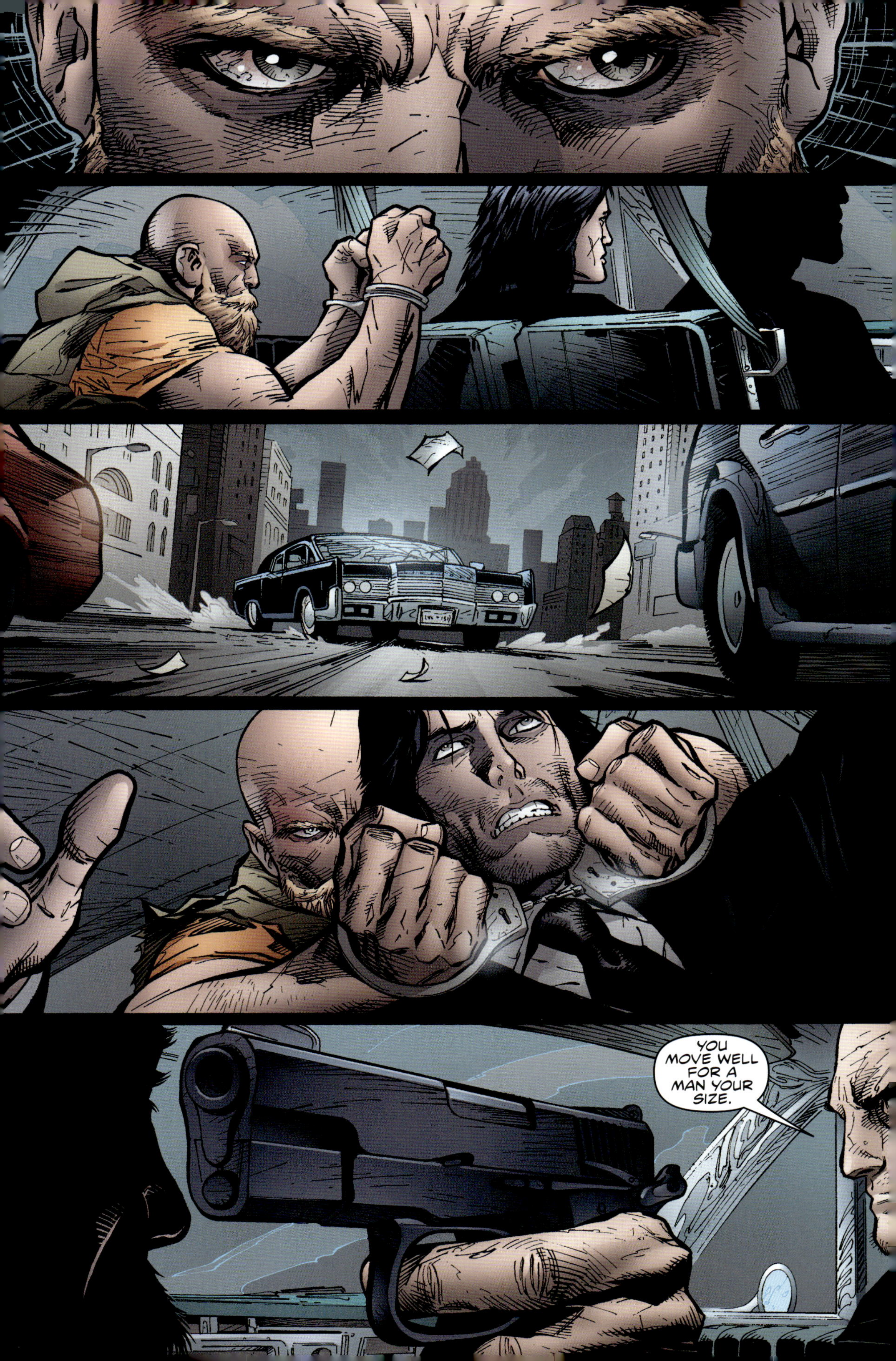
YOU MOVE WELL FOR A MAN YOUR SIZE.

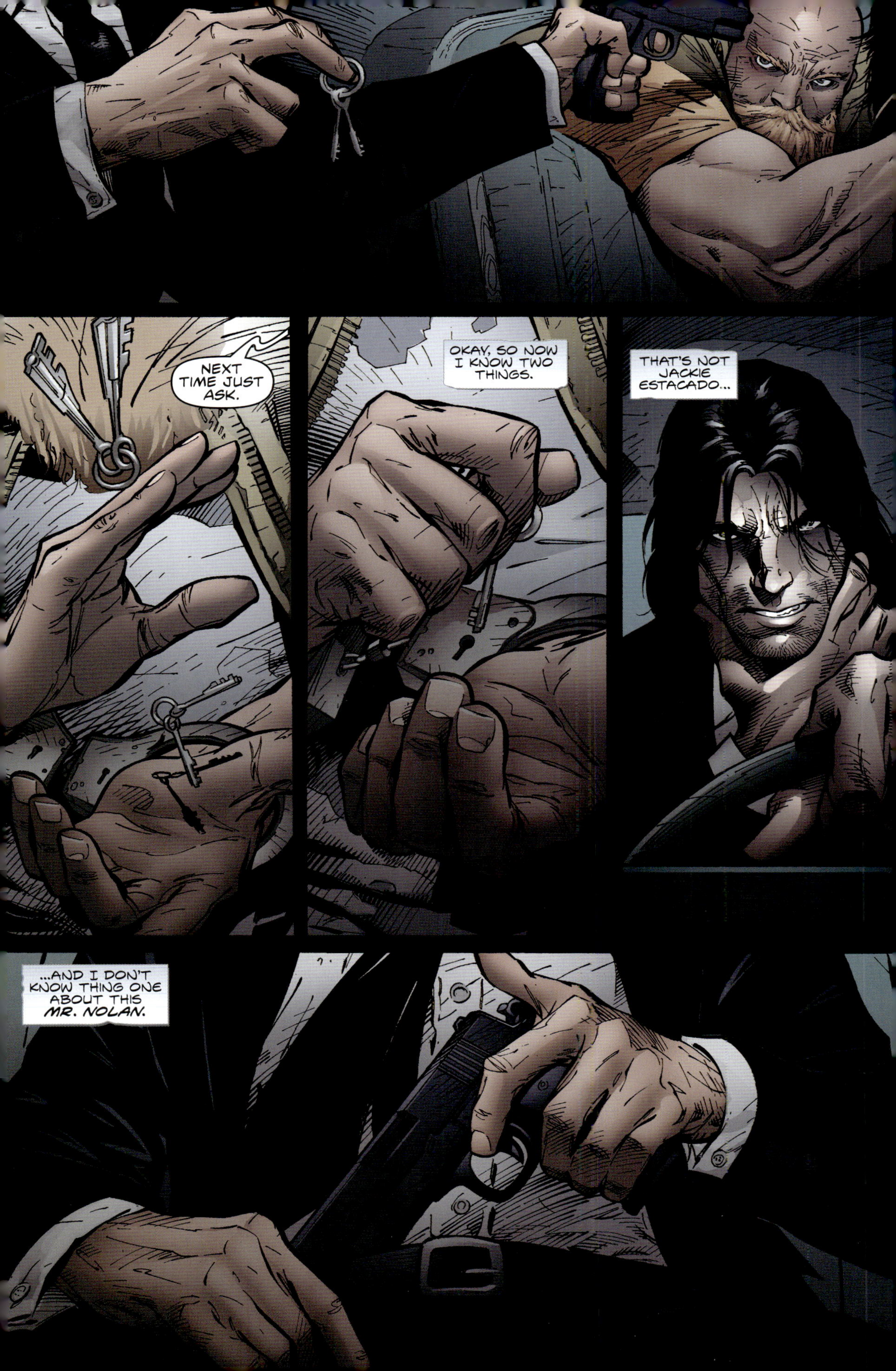
NEXT TIME JUST ASK.
OKAY, SO NOW I KNOW TWO THINGS.
THAT'S NOT JACKIE ESTACADO...
...AND I DON'T KNOW THING ONE ABOUT THIS MR. NOLAN.

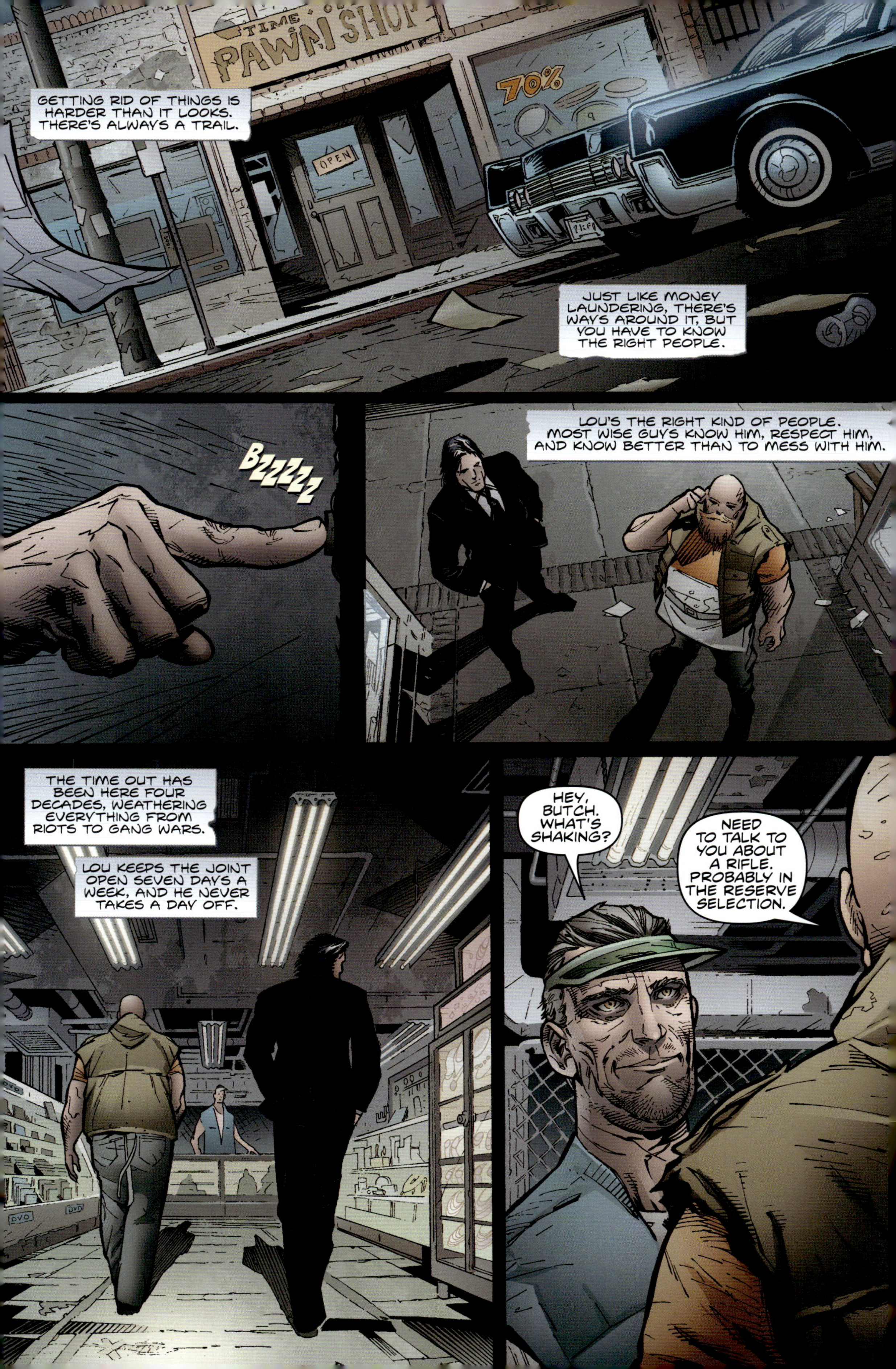
TIME OUT PAWN SHOP
GETTING RID OF THINGS IS HARDER THAN IT LOOKS. THERE'S ALWAYS A TRAIL.
OPEN
70%
JUST LIKE MONEY LAUNDERING, THERE'S WAYS AROUND IT, BUT YOU HAVE TO KNOW THE RIGHT PEOPLE.
BZZZZZ
LOU'S THE RIGHT KIND OF PEOPLE. MOST WISE GUYS KNOW HIM, RESPECT HIM, AND KNOW BETTER THAN TO MESS WITH HIM.
THE TIME OUT HAS BEEN HERE FOUR DECADES, WEATHERING EVERYTHING FROM RIOTS TO GANG WARS.
LOU KEEPS THE JOINT OPEN SEVEN DAYS A WEEK, AND HE NEVER TAKES A DAY OFF.
HEY, BUTCH. WHAT'S SHAKING?
NEED TO TALK TO YOU ABOUT A RIFLE. PROBABLY IN THE RESERVE SELECTION.

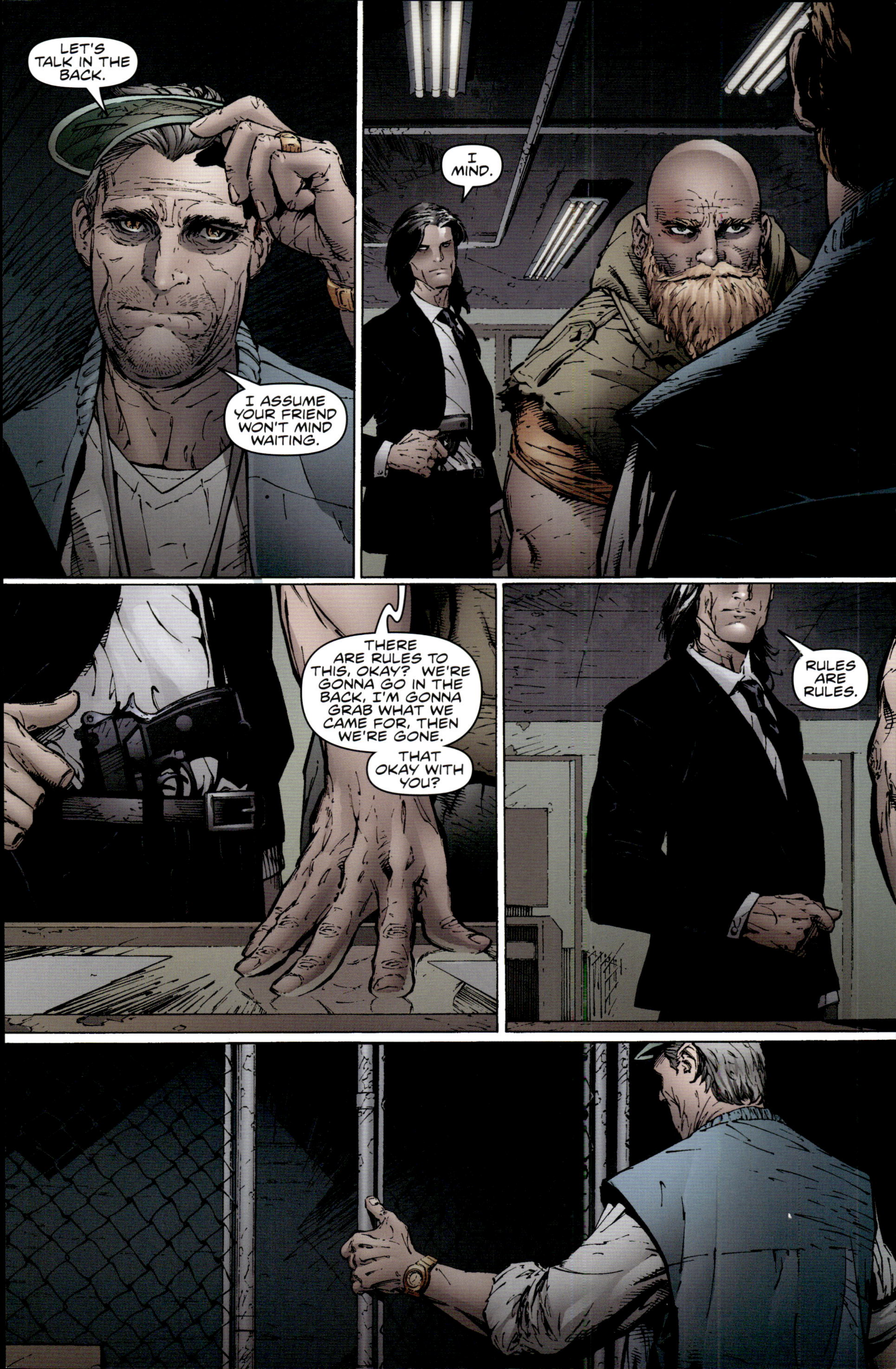
LET'S TALK IN THE BACK.
I ASSUME YOUR FRIEND WON'T MIND WAITING.
I MIND.
THERE ARE RULES TO THIS, OKAY? WE'RE GONNA GO IN THE BACK, I'M GONNA GRAB WHAT WE CAME FOR, THEN WE'RE GONE.
THAT OKAY WITH YOU?
RULES ARE RULES.

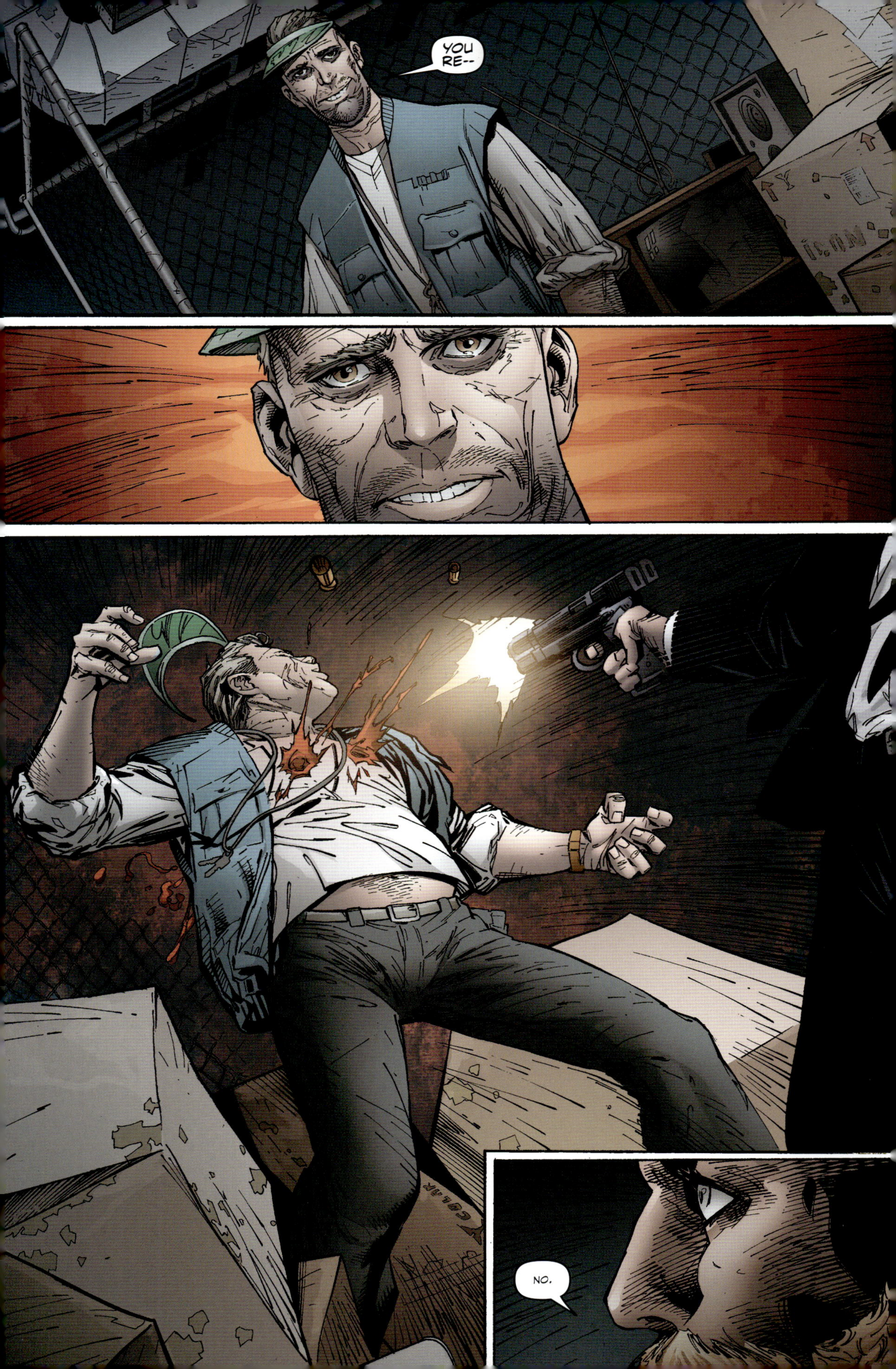
YOU RE--
NO.

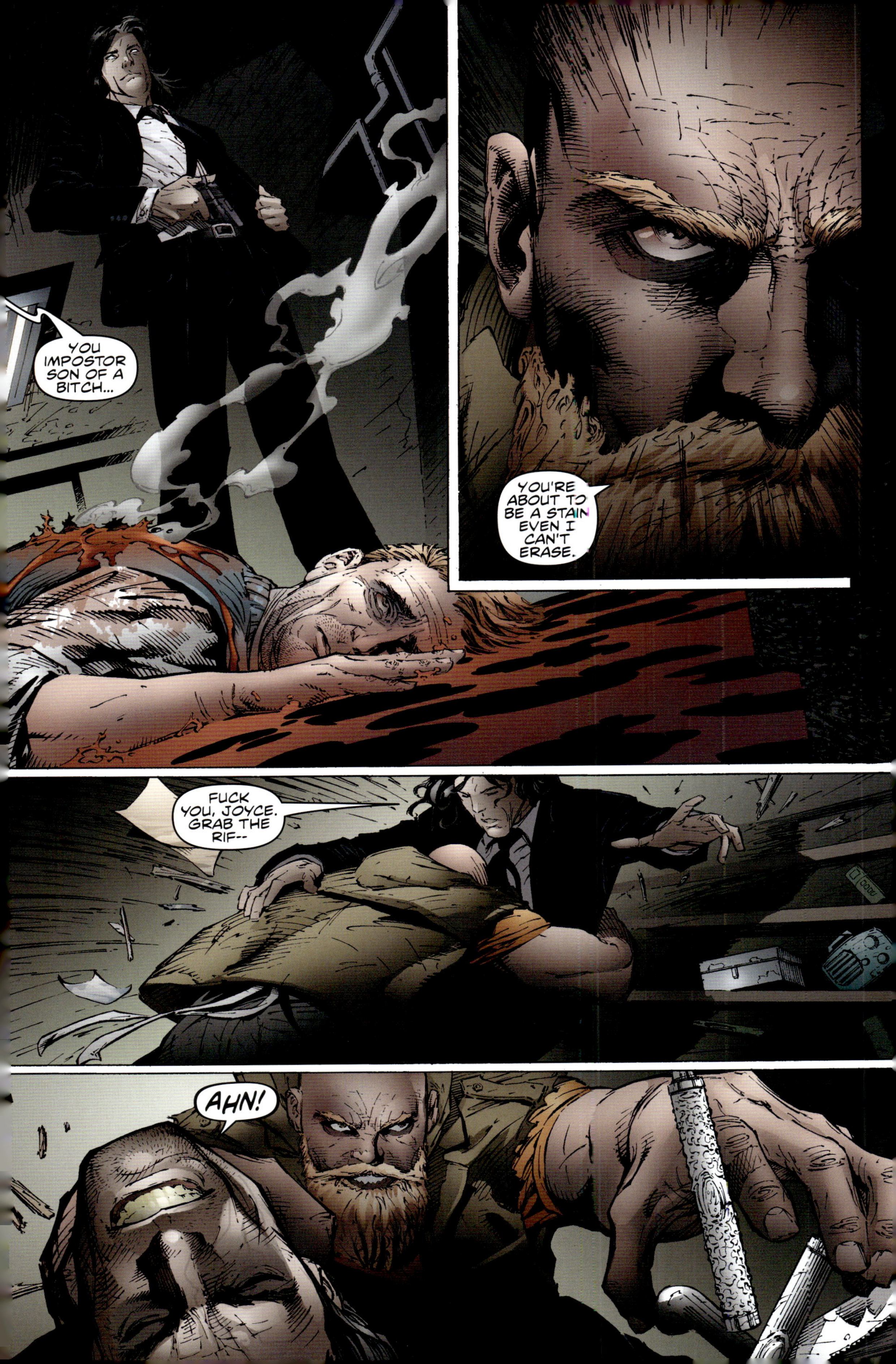
YOU IMPOSTOR SON OF A BITCH...
YOU'RE ABOUT TO BE A STAIN EVEN I CAN'T ERASE.
FUCK YOU, JOYCE. GRAB THE RIF--
AHN!

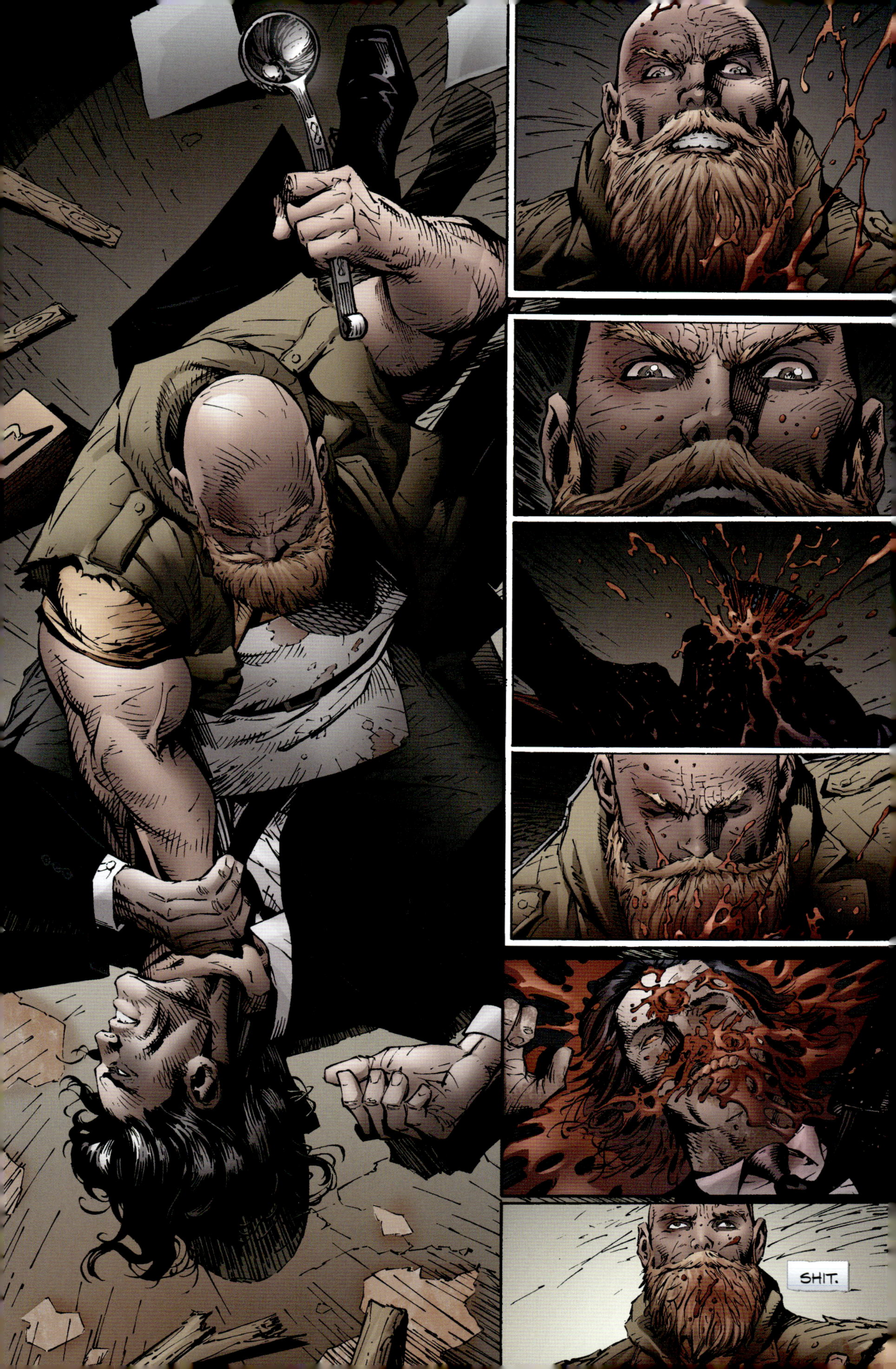
SHIT.

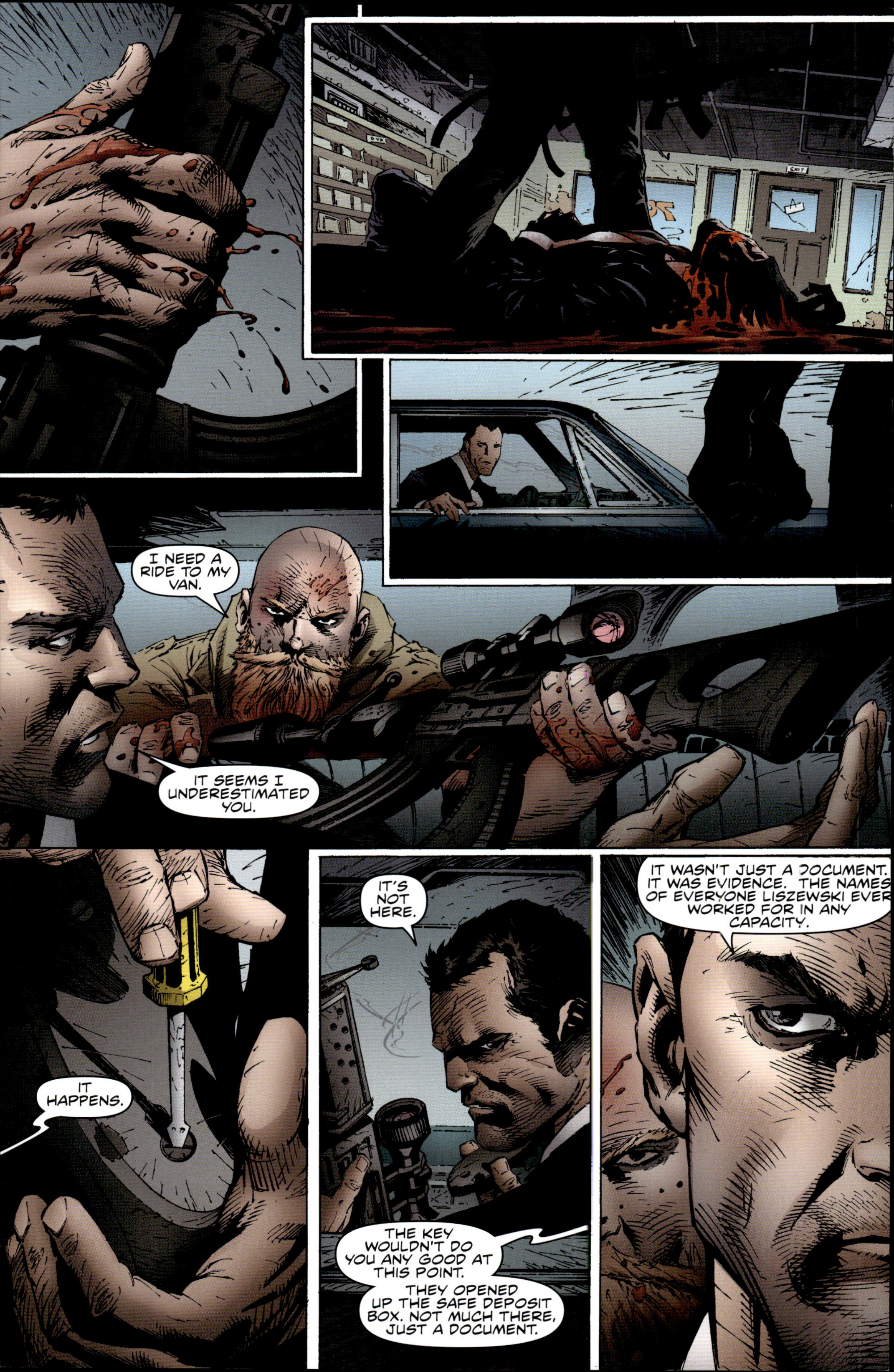
I NEED A RIDE TO MY VAN.
IT SEEMS I UNDERESTIMATED YOU.
IT HAPPENS.
IT'S NOT HERE.
THE KEY WOULDN'T DO YOU ANY GOOD AT THIS POINT.
THEY OPENED UP THE SAFE DEPOSIT BOX. NOT MUCH THERE, JUST A DOCUMENT.
IT WASN'T JUST A DOCUMENT. IT WAS EVIDENCE. THE NAMES OF EVERYONE LISZEWSKI EVER WORKED FOR IN ANY CAPACITY.

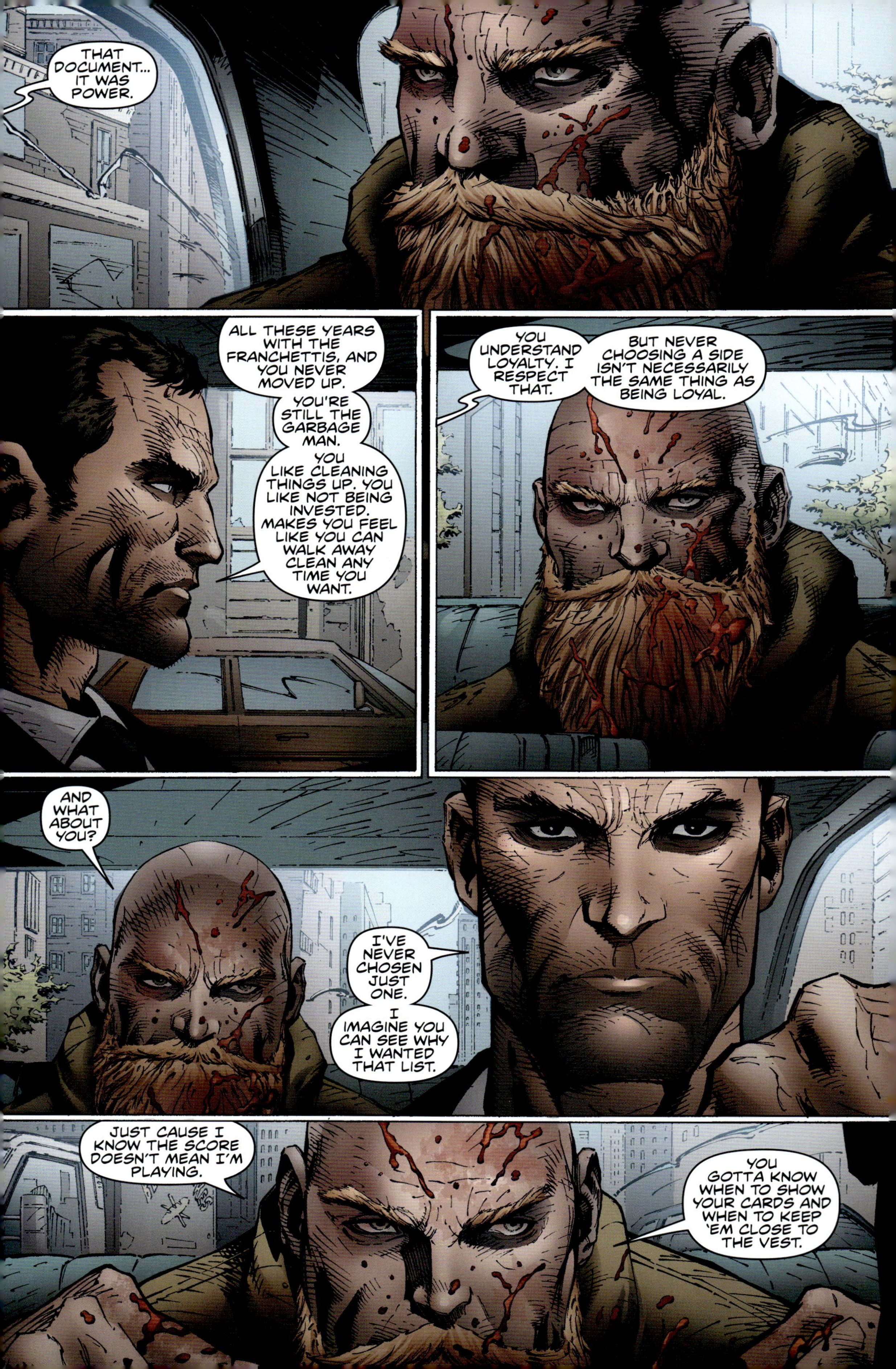
THAT DOCUMENT... IT WAS POWER.
ALL THESE YEARS WITH THE FRANCHETTIS, AND YOU NEVER MOVED UP.
YOU'RE STILL THE GARBAGE MAN.
YOU LIKE CLEANING THINGS UP. YOU LIKE NOT BEING INVESTED. MAKES YOU FEEL LIKE YOU CAN WALK AWAY CLEAN ANY TIME YOU WANT.
YOU UNDERSTAND LOYALTY. I RESPECT THAT.
BUT NEVER CHOOSING A SIDE ISN'T NECESSARILY THE SAME THING AS BEING LOYAL.
AND WHAT ABOUT YOU?
I'VE NEVER CHOSEN JUST ONE.
I IMAGINE YOU CAN SEE WHY I WANTED THAT LIST.
JUST CAUSE I KNOW THE SCORE DOESN'T MEAN I'M PLAYING.
YOU GOTTA KNOW WHEN TO SHOW YOUR CARDS AND WHEN TO KEEP 'EM CLOSE TO THE VEST.

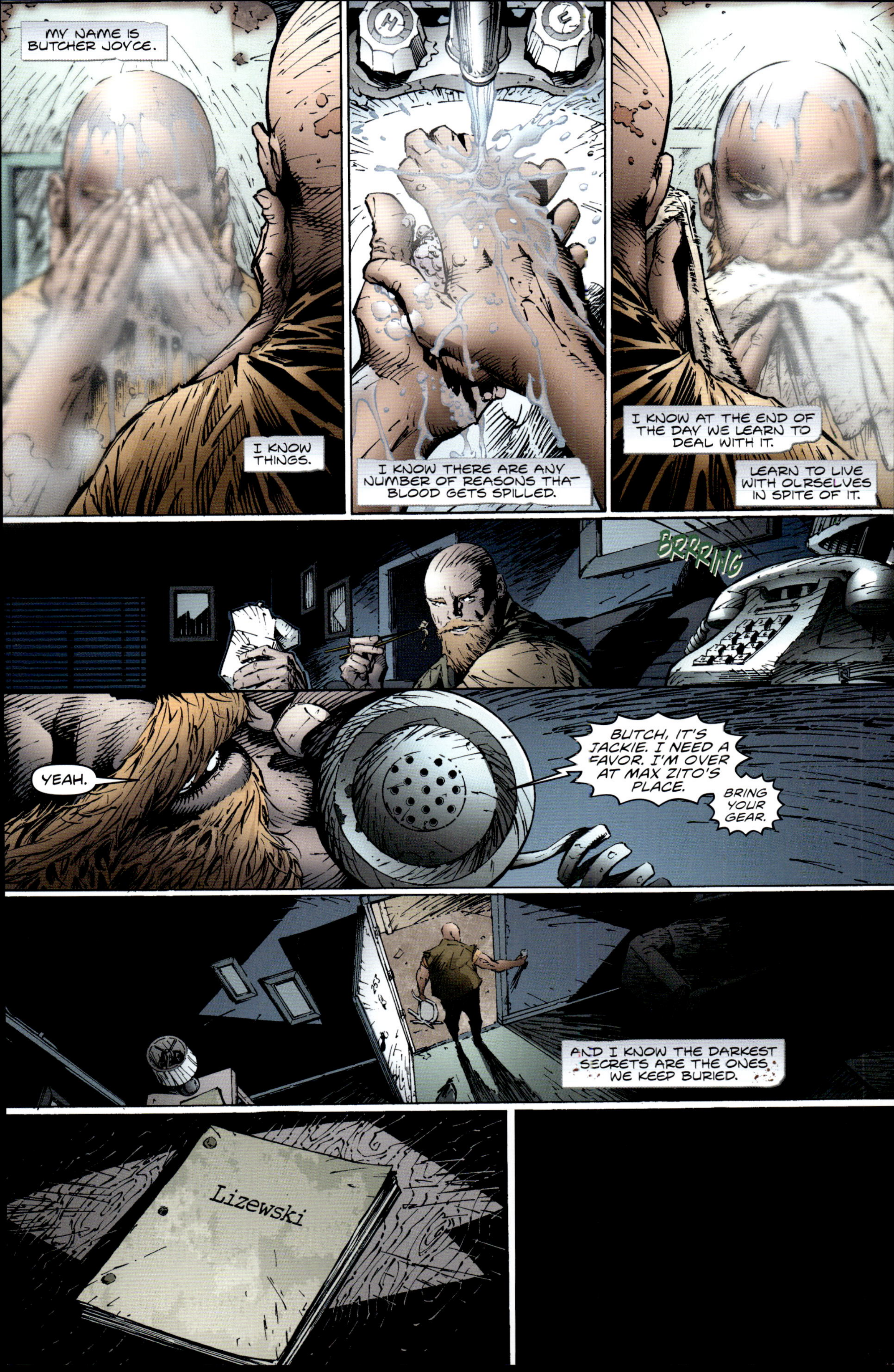
MY NAME IS BUTCHER JOYCE.
I KNOW THINGS.
I KNOW THERE ARE ANY NUMBER OF REASONS THAT BLOOD GETS SPILLED.
I KNOW AT THE END OF THE DAY WE LEARN TO DEAL WITH IT.
LEARN TO LIVE WITH OURSELVES IN SPITE OF IT.
BRRRING
YEAH.
BUTCH, IT'S JACKIE. I NEED A FAVOR. I'M OVER AT MAX ZITO'S PLACE.
BRING YOUR GEAR.
AND I KNOW THE DARKEST SECRETS ARE THE ONES WE KEEP BURIED.
Lizewski

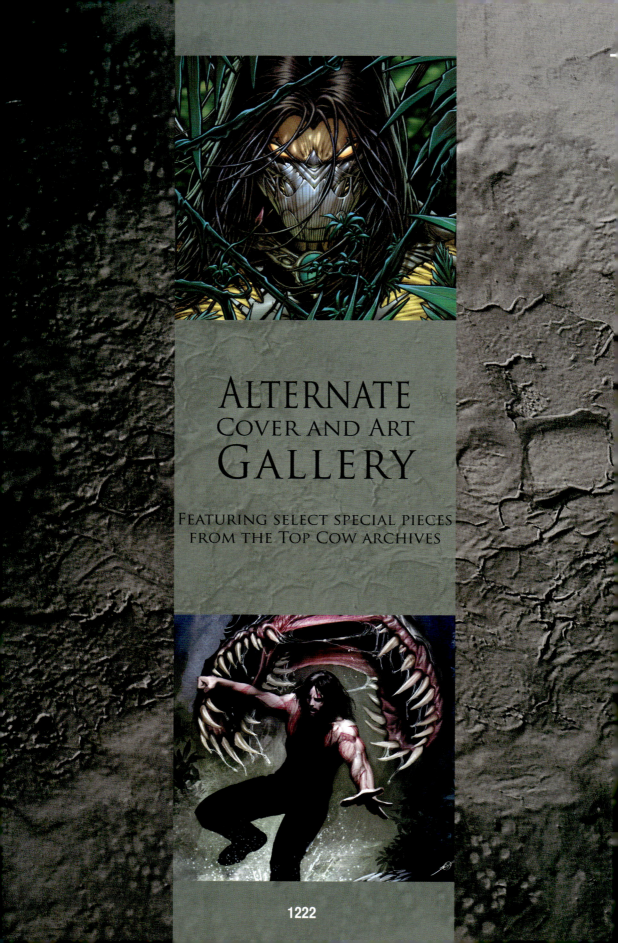

ALTERNATE
COVER AND ART
GALLERY

FEATURING SELECT SPECIAL PIECES
FROM THE TOP COW ARCHIVES

Issue #1 Holofoil COVER VARIANT

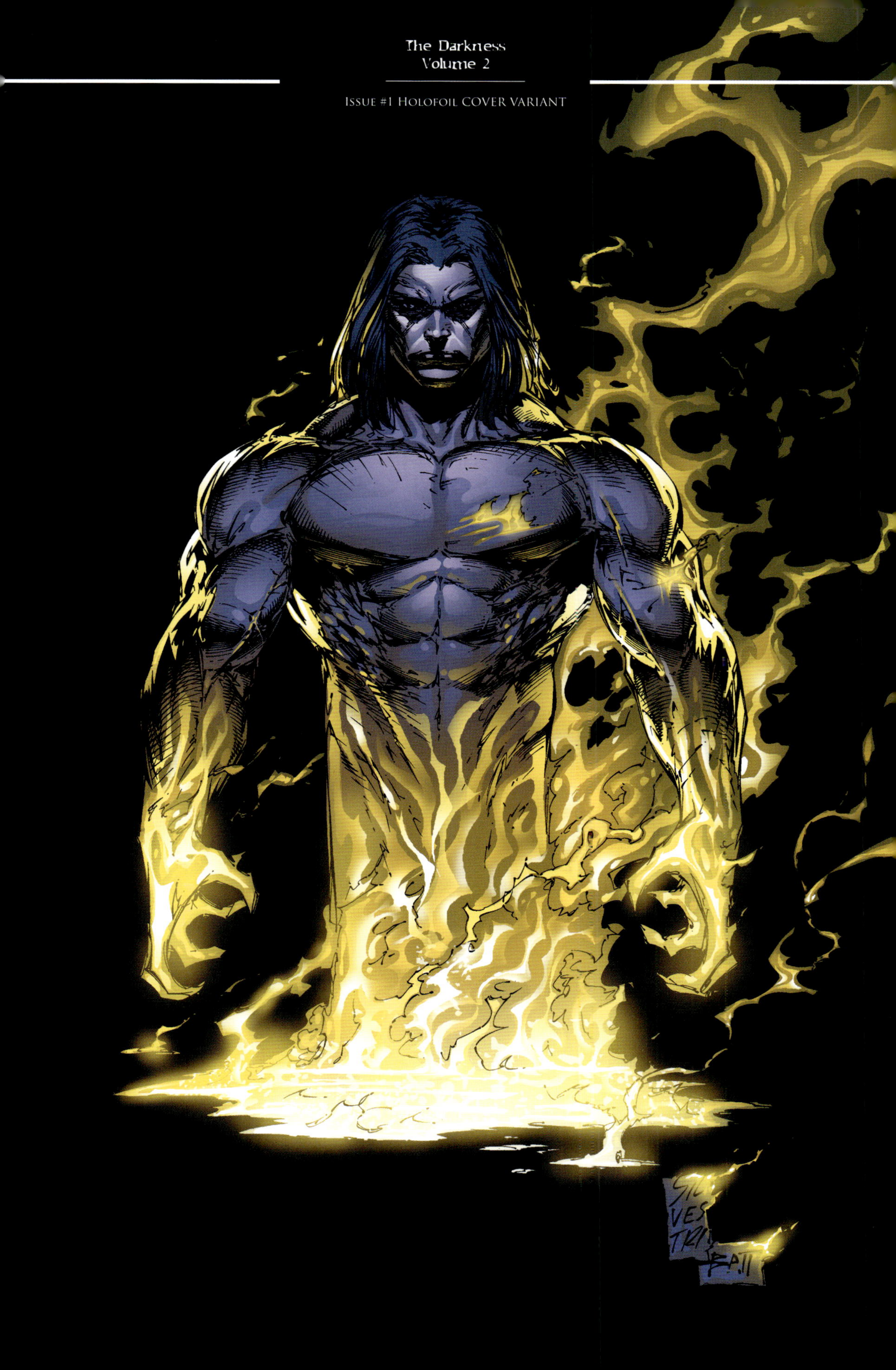

Issue #1 E3 Exclusive pencils

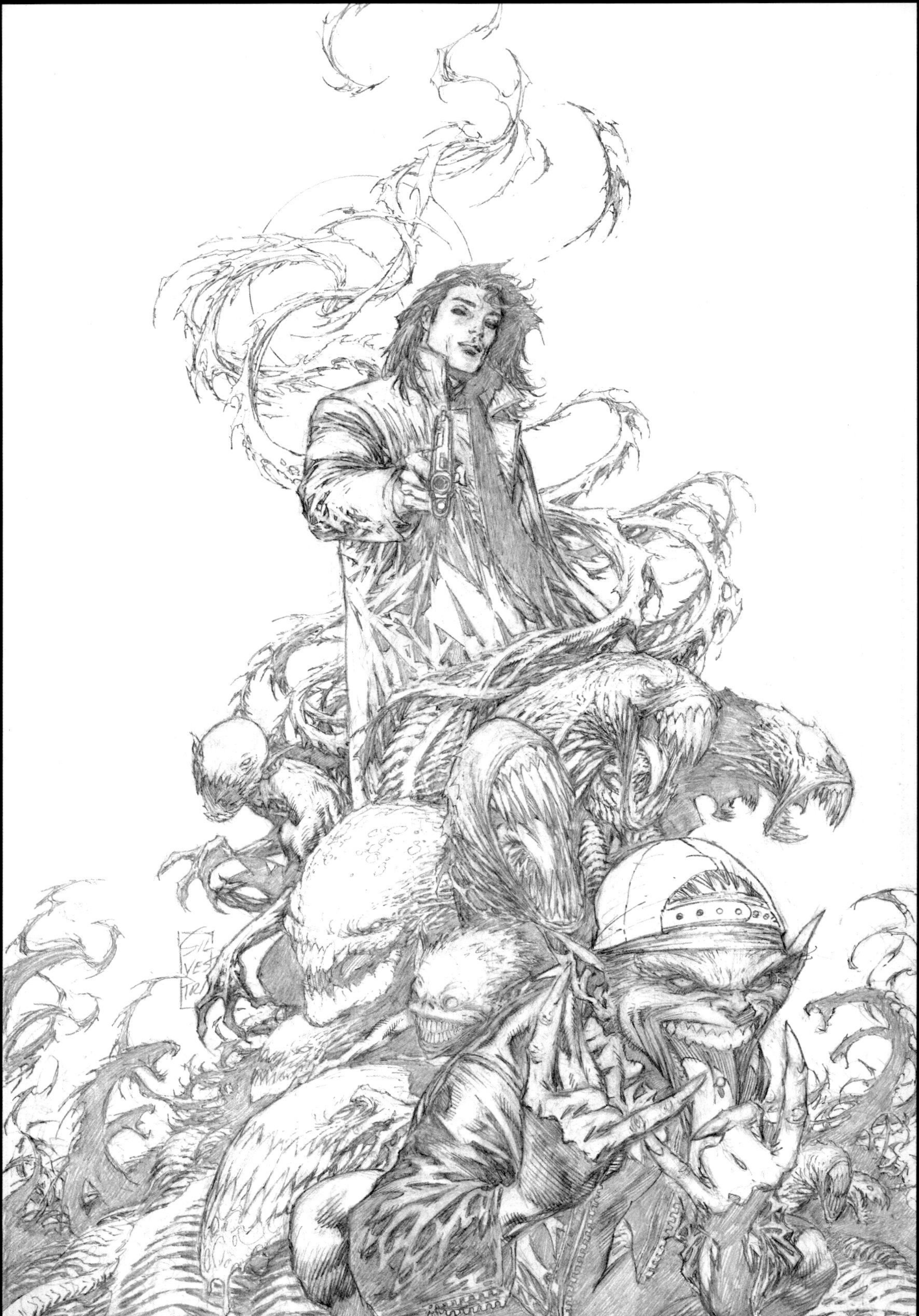
SILVESTRI

The Darkness
Volume 2

Issue #1 E3 Exclusive

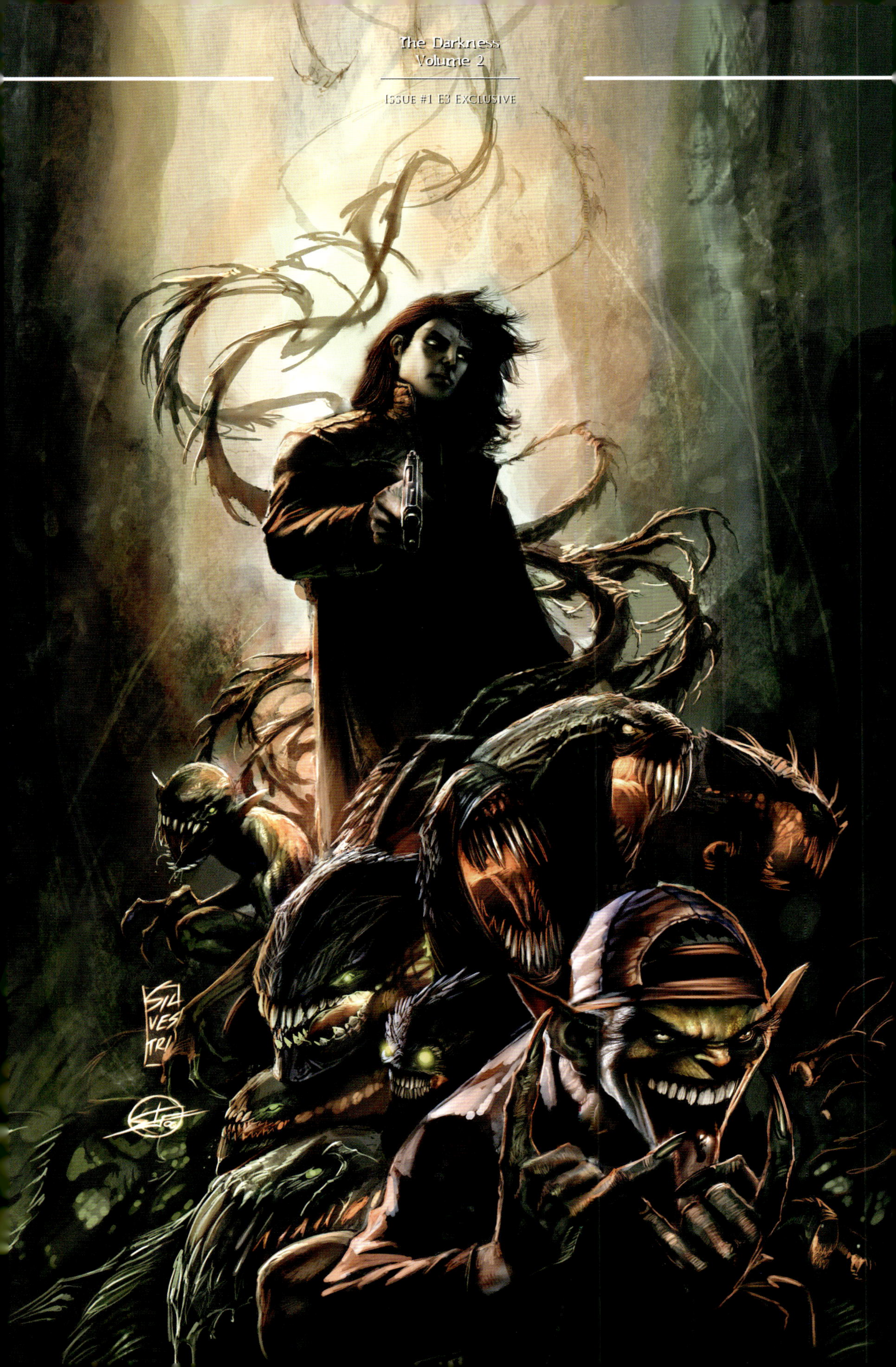

Issue #1 Sketch Variant

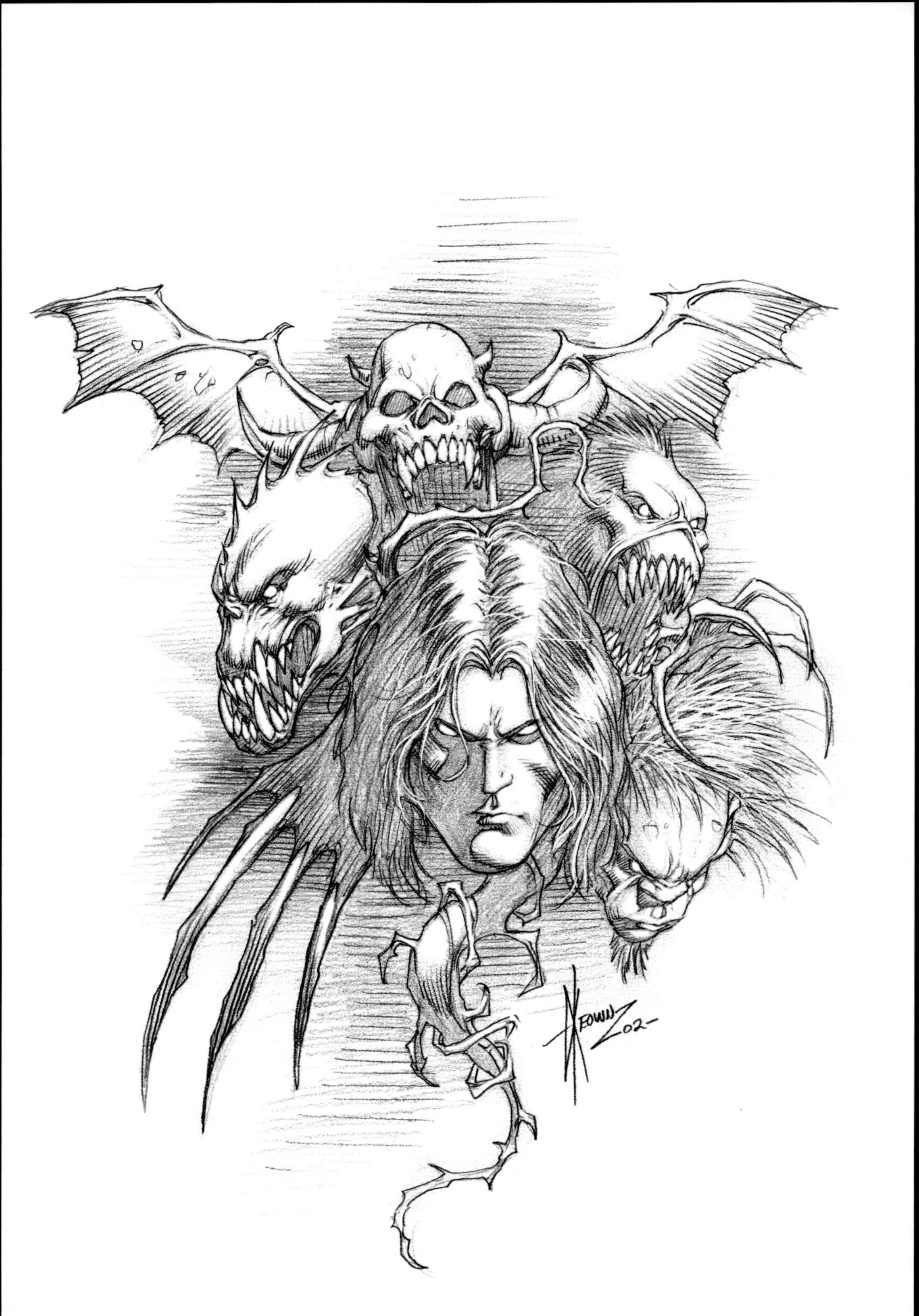

ISSUE #1 POSTER VARIANT

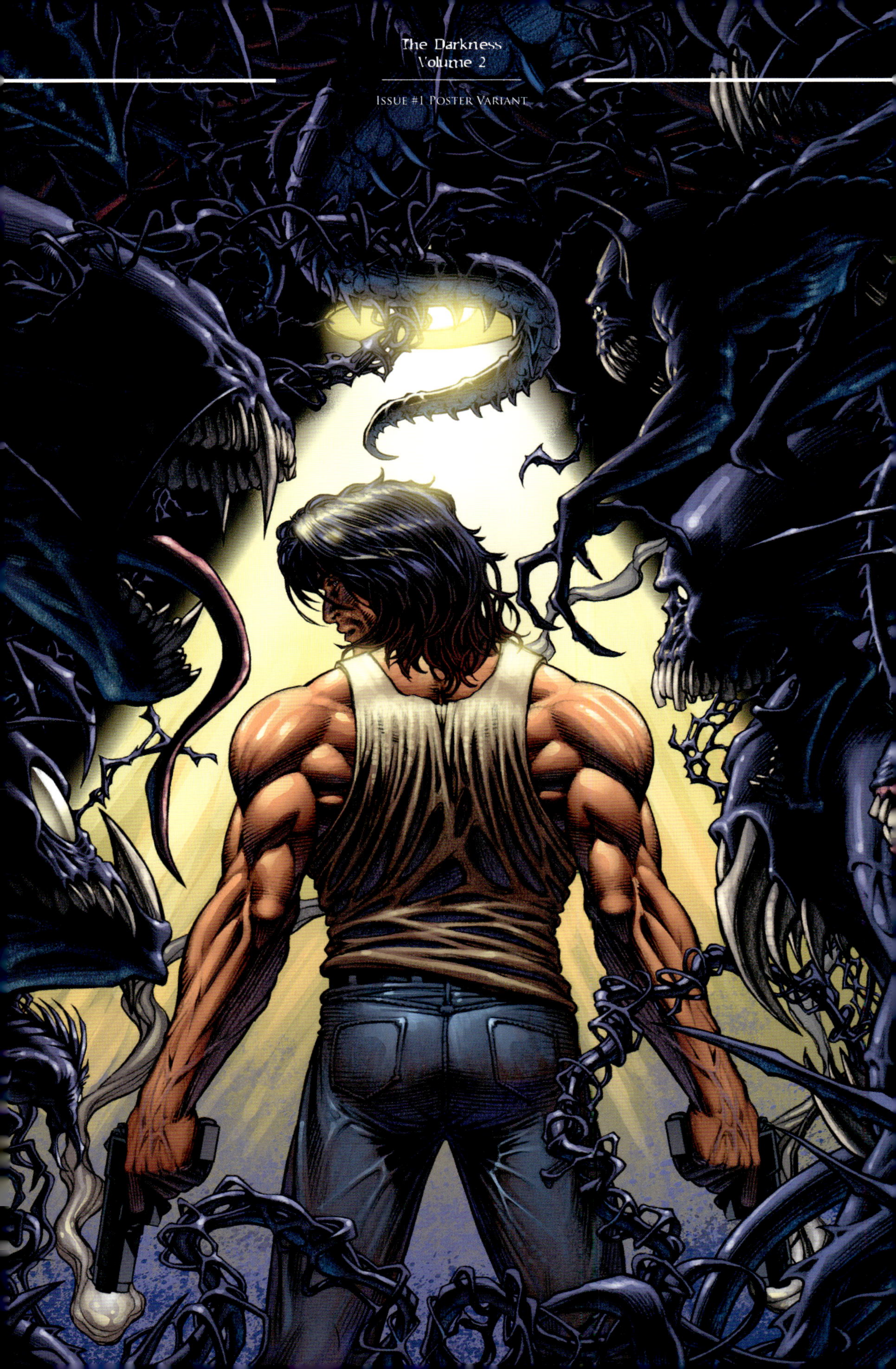

Issue #2 MegaCon Exclusive

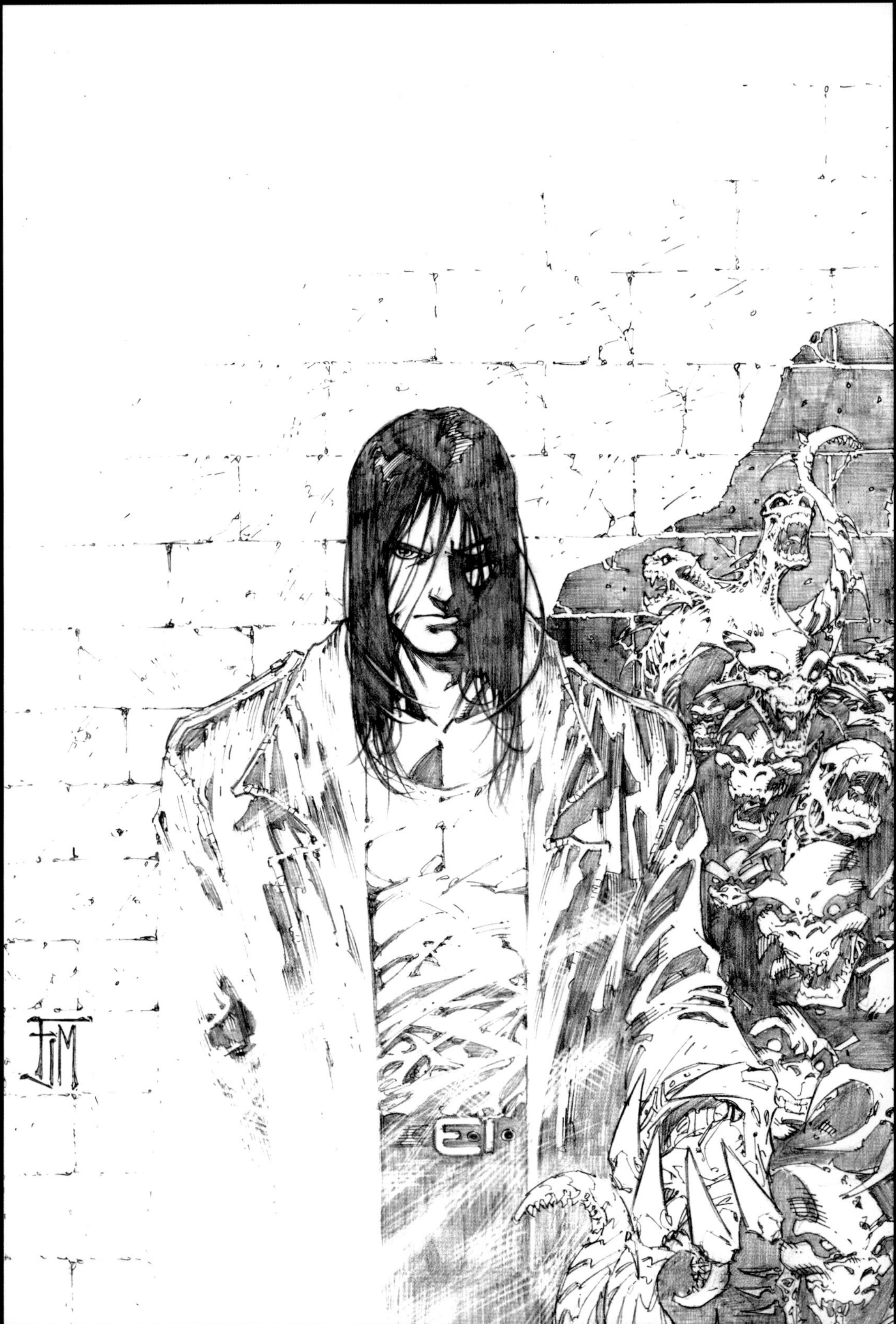

The Darkness
Volume 2

Issue #7 eBas Variant

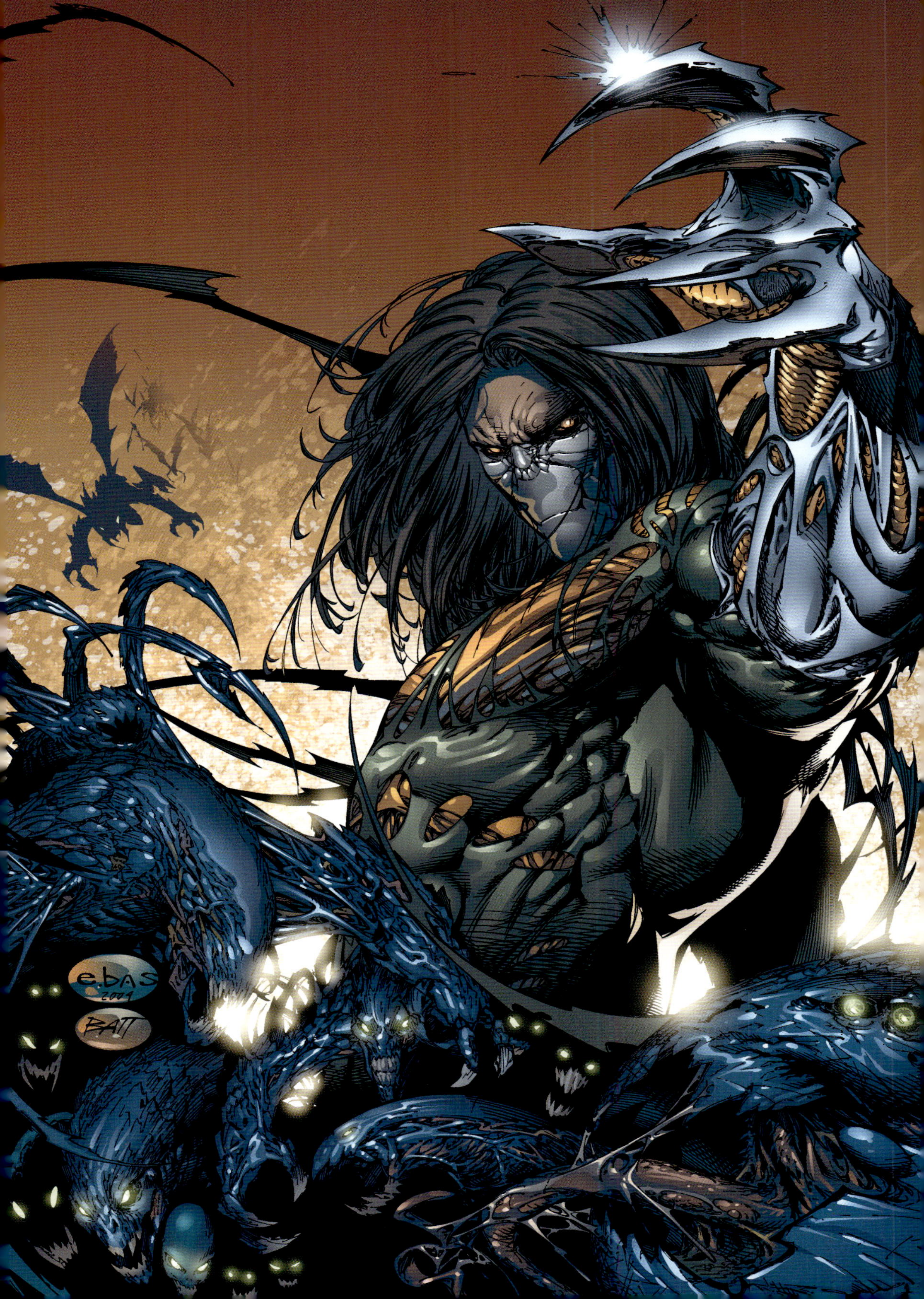
e.bas
2004
BATT

The Darkness
Volume 2

Issue #5 Chibi Variant

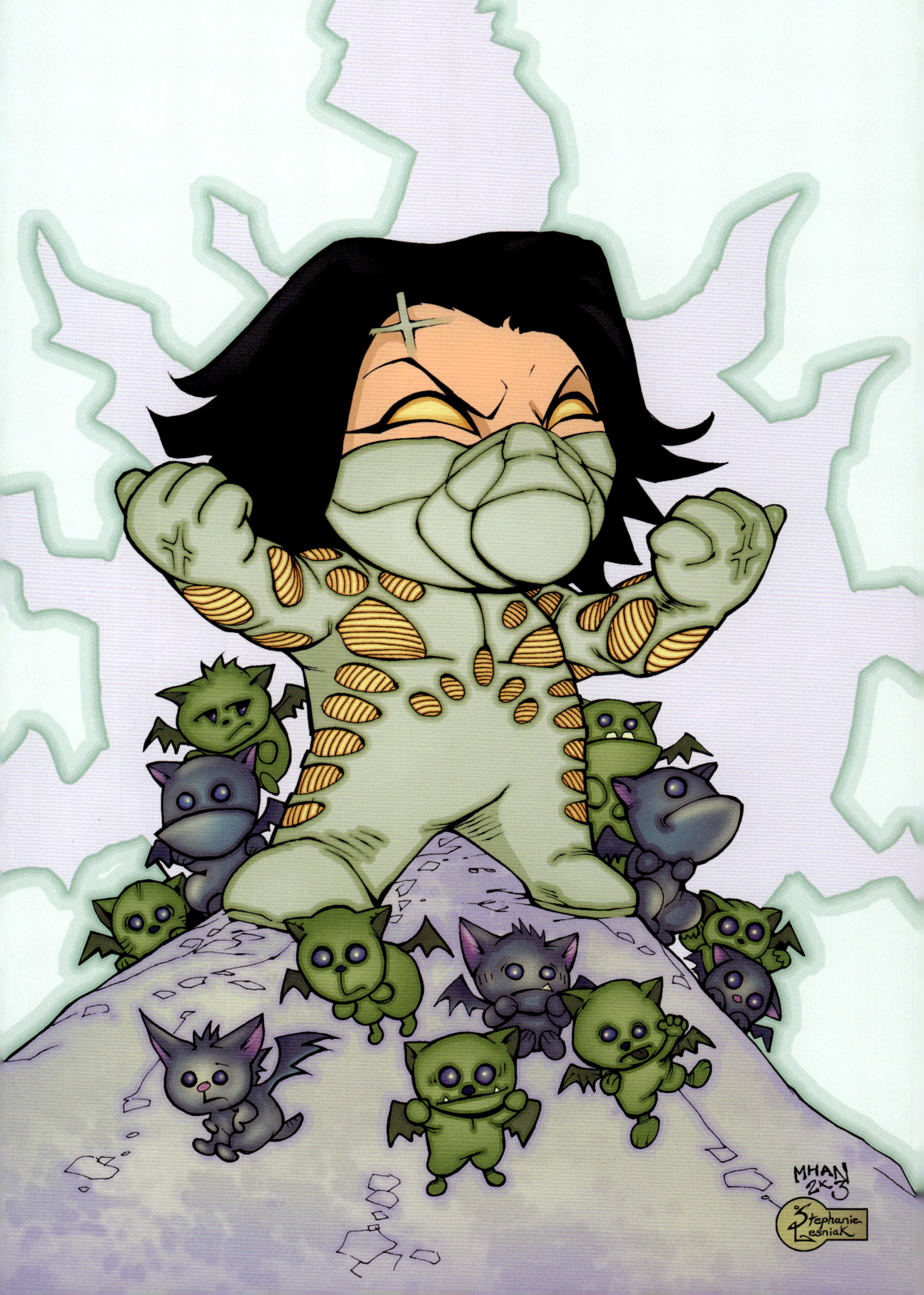
MHAN
2K.3
Stephanie
Lesniak

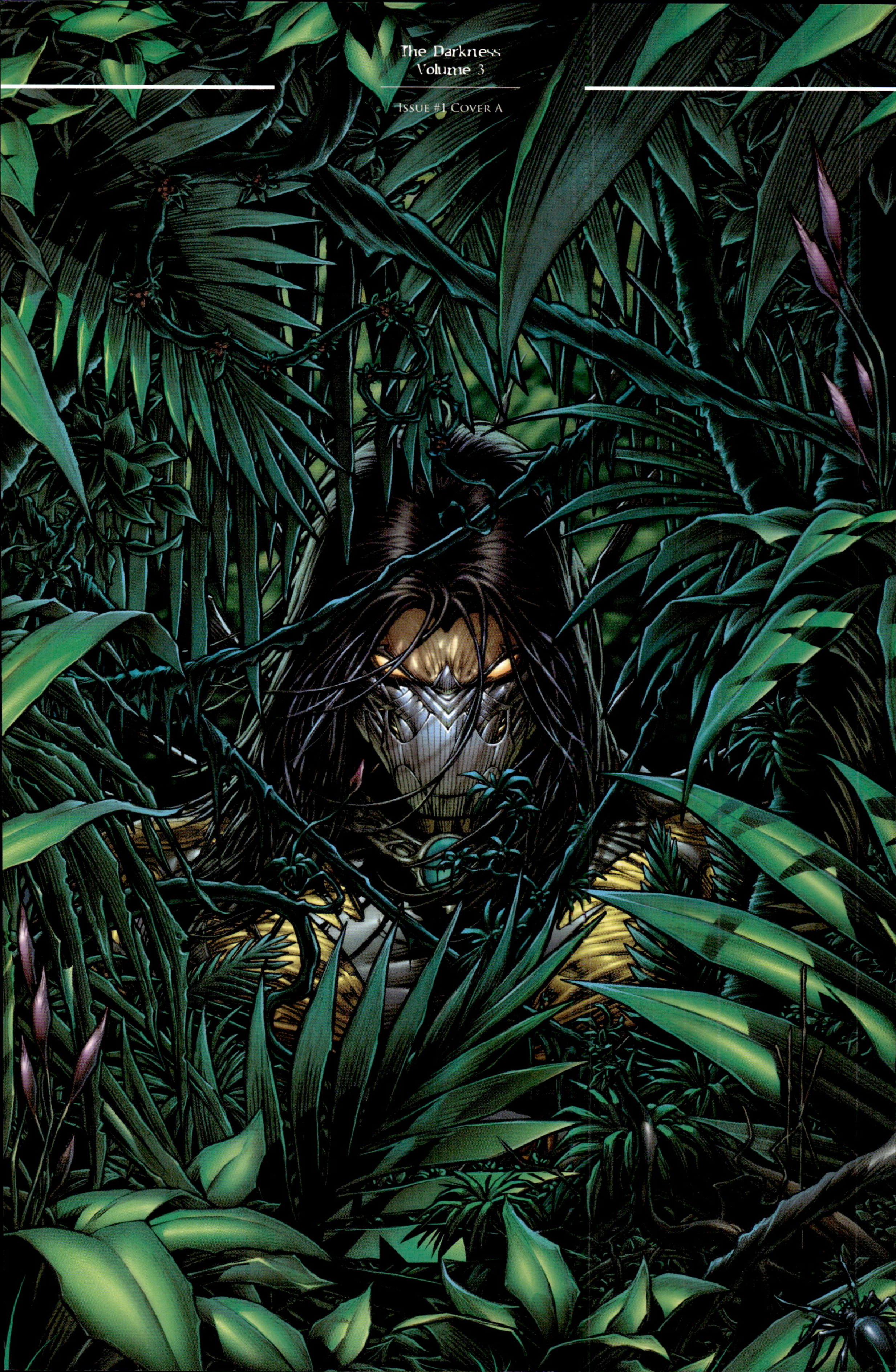
The Darkness
Volume 3
Issue #1 Cover A

The Darkness
Volume 3

Issue #1 Cover C

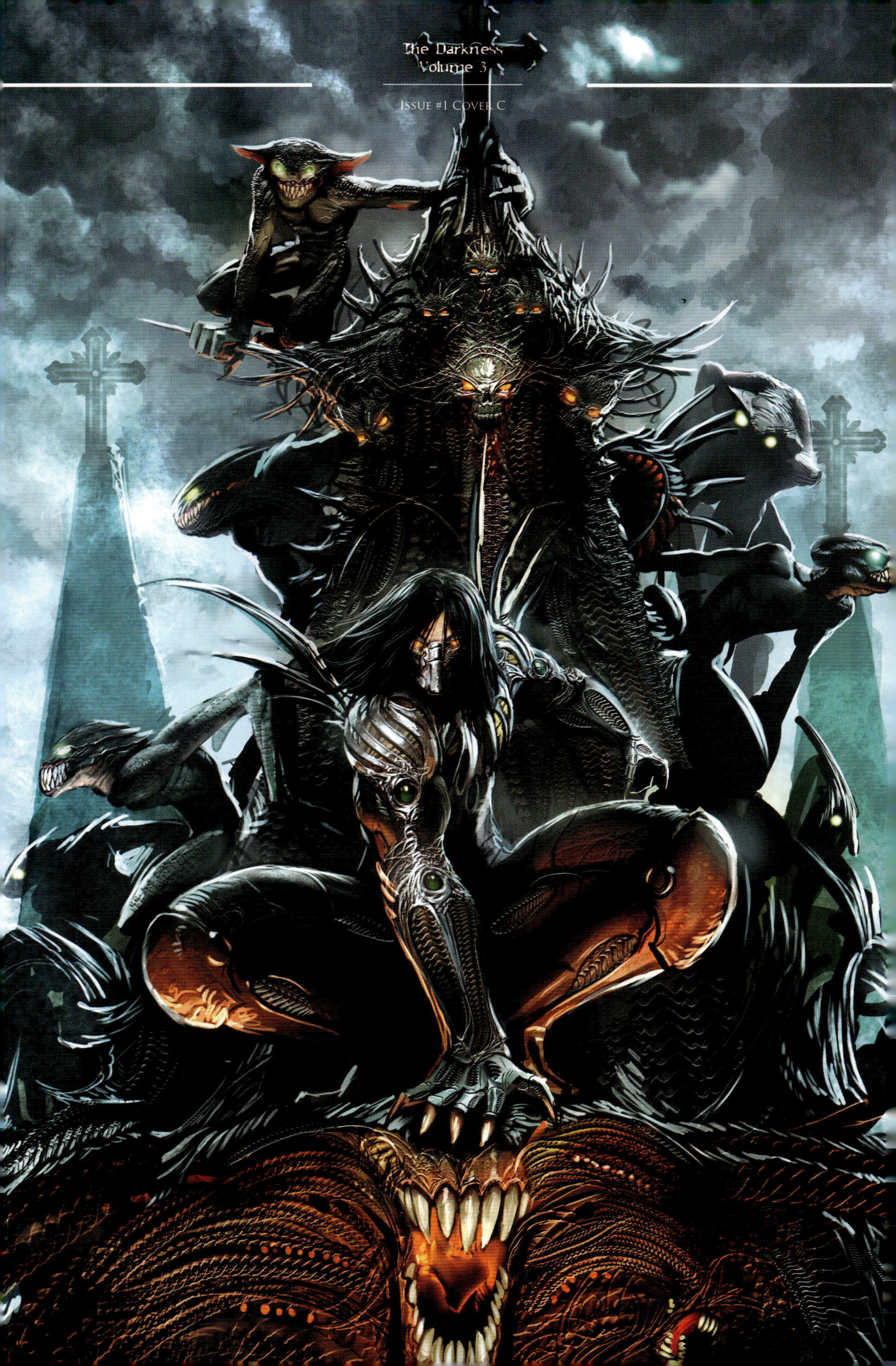

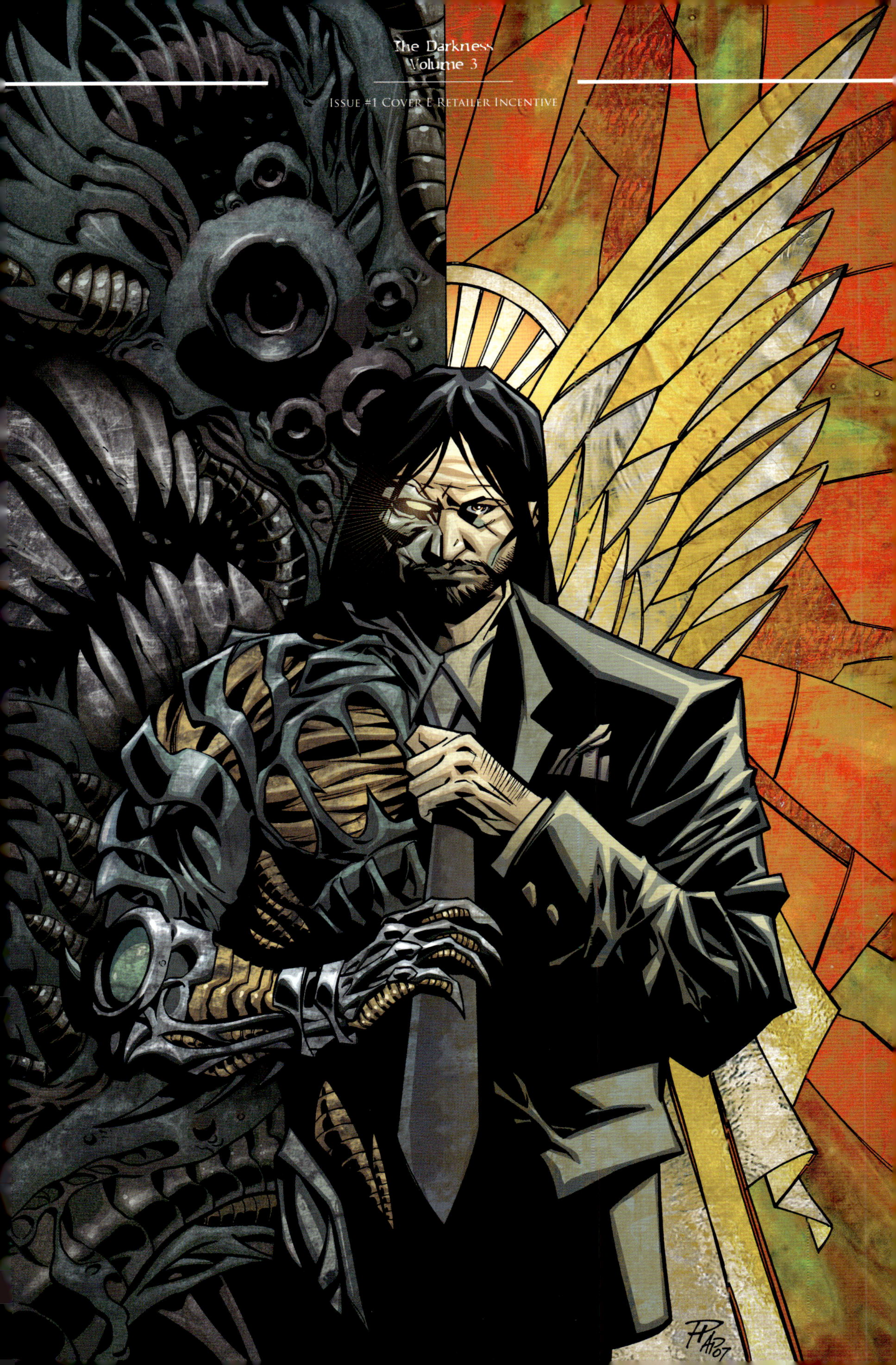

The Darkness
Volume 3

Issue #1 Cover E Retailer Incentive

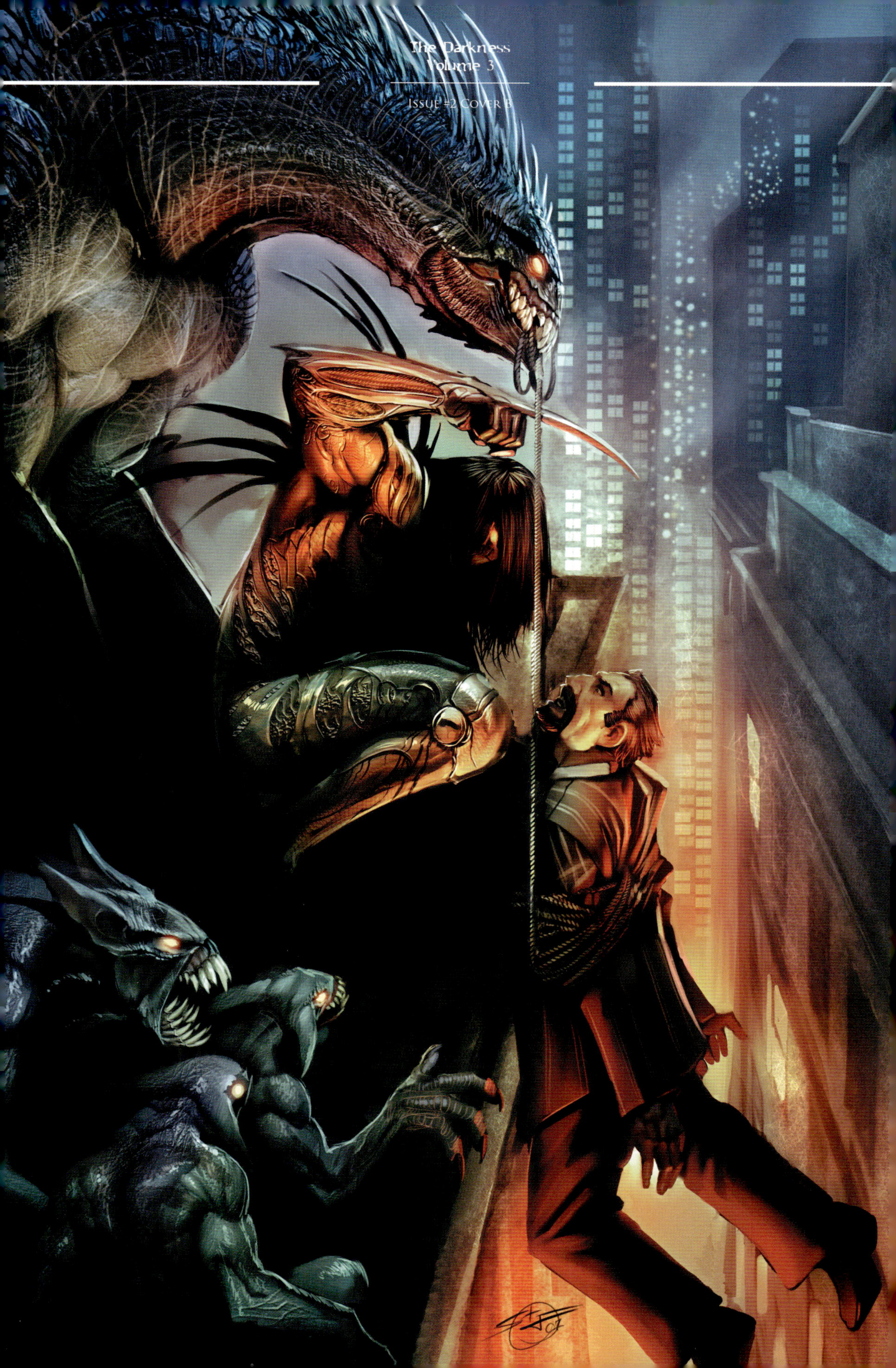

The Darkness
Volume 3

Issue #2 Cover B

The Darkness
Volume 3

Issue #2 Cover C WonderCon Exclusive

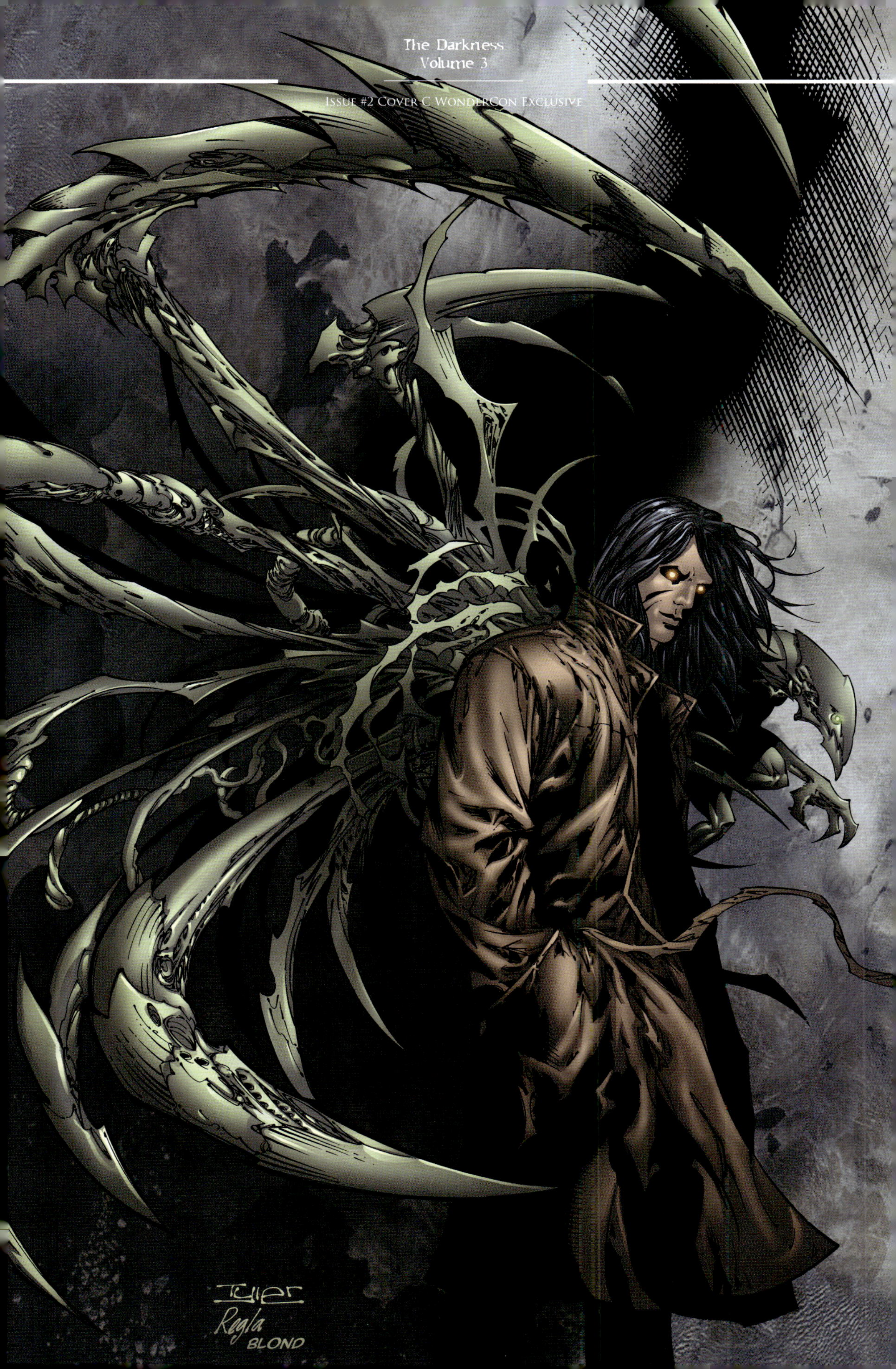
Tyler
Regla
BLOND

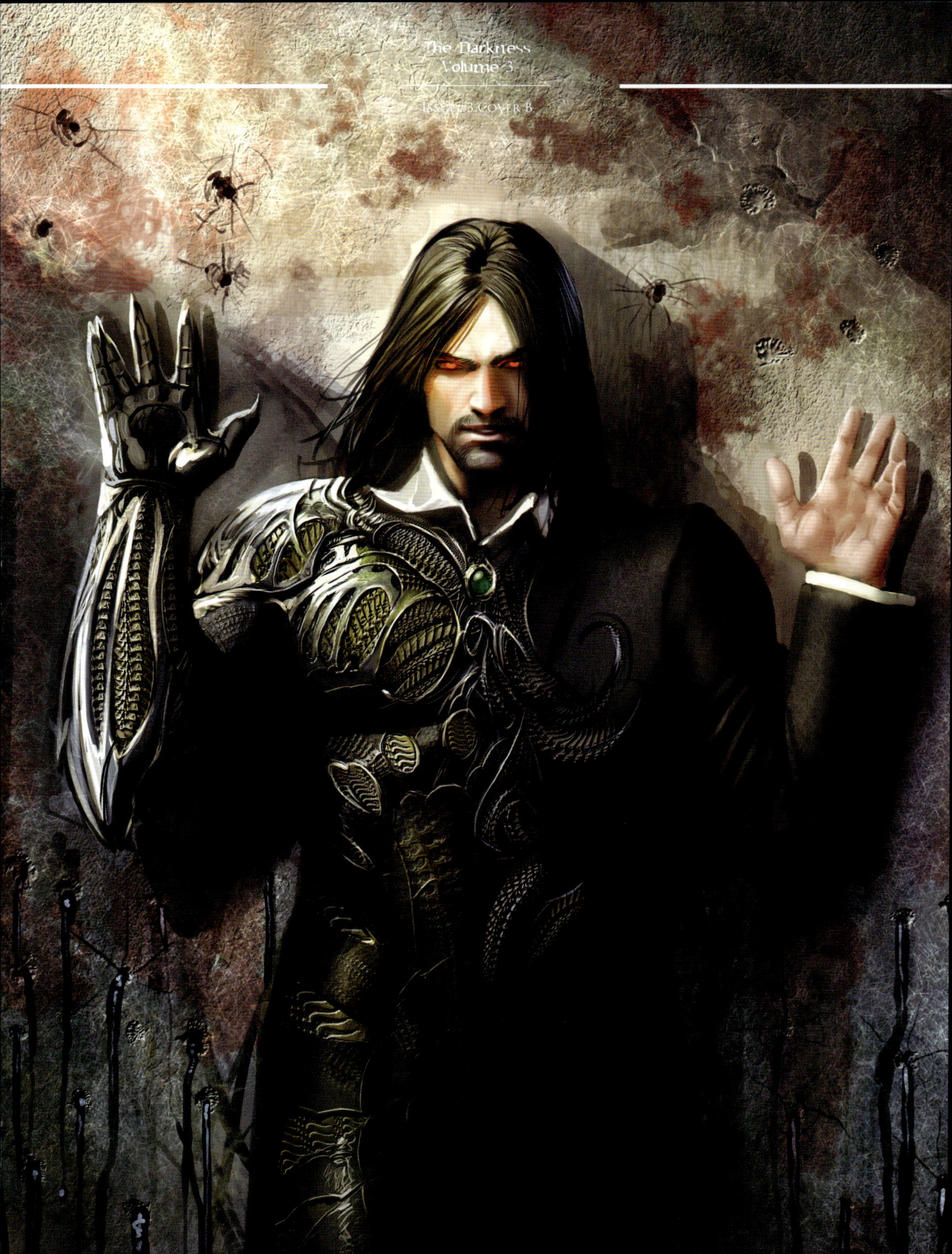

The Darkness
Volume 3

Issue #3 Cover B

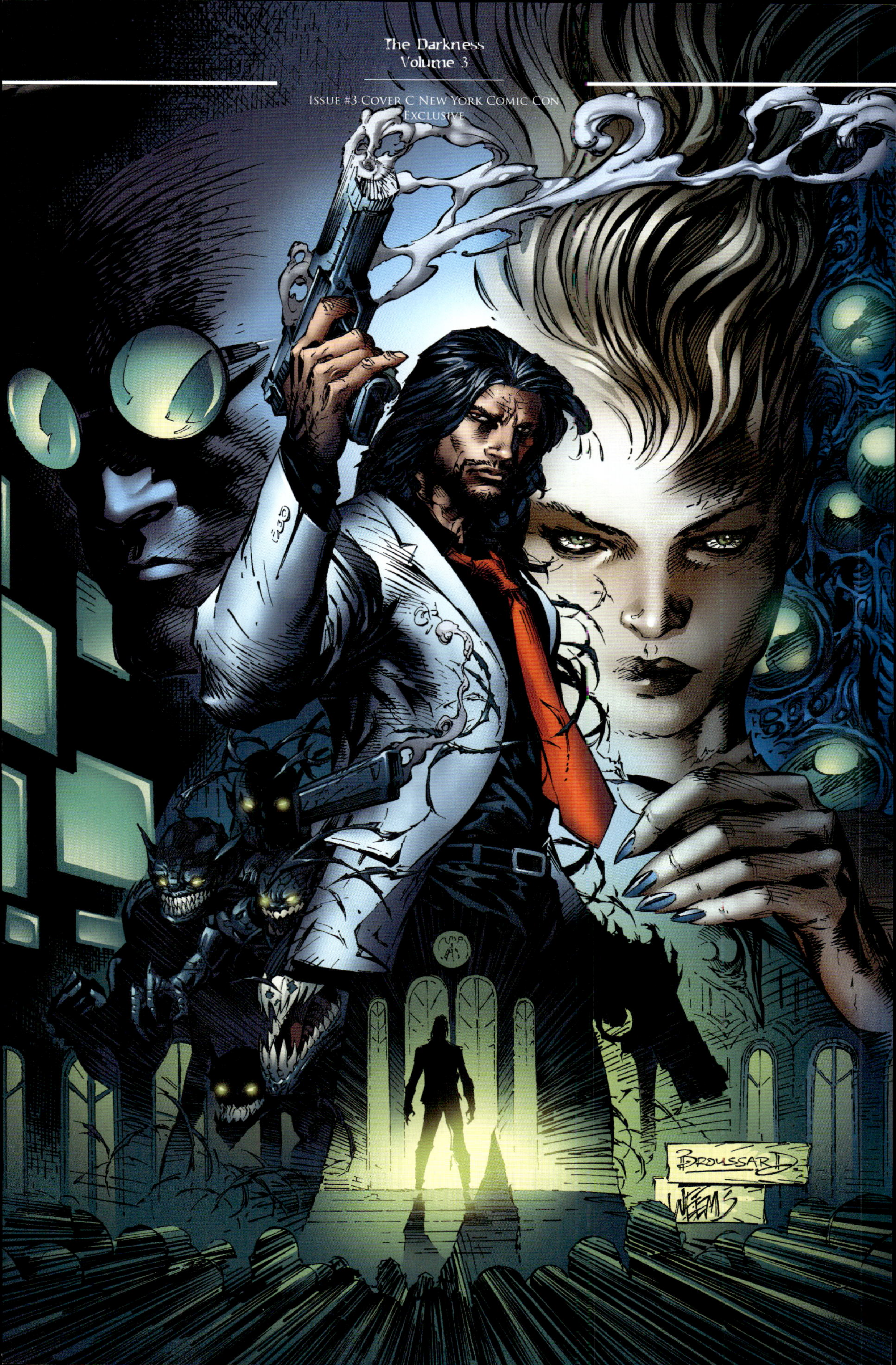
BROUSSARD
WEEMS

The Darkness
Volume 3

Issue #3 Cover C New York Comic Con Exclusive

Issue #4 Cover B

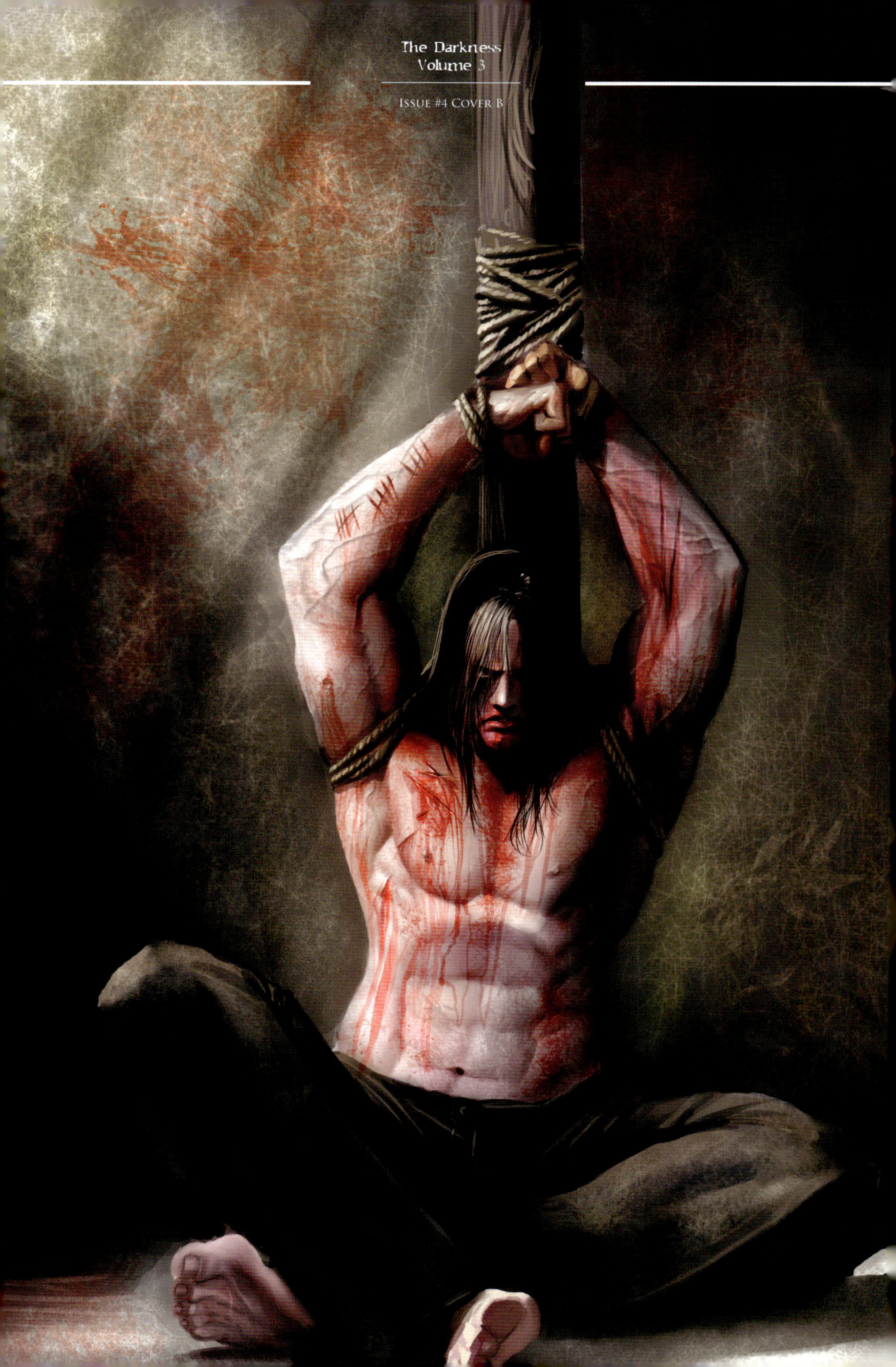

The Darkness
Volume 3

Issue #4 Cover C Wizard World
Chicago Exclusive

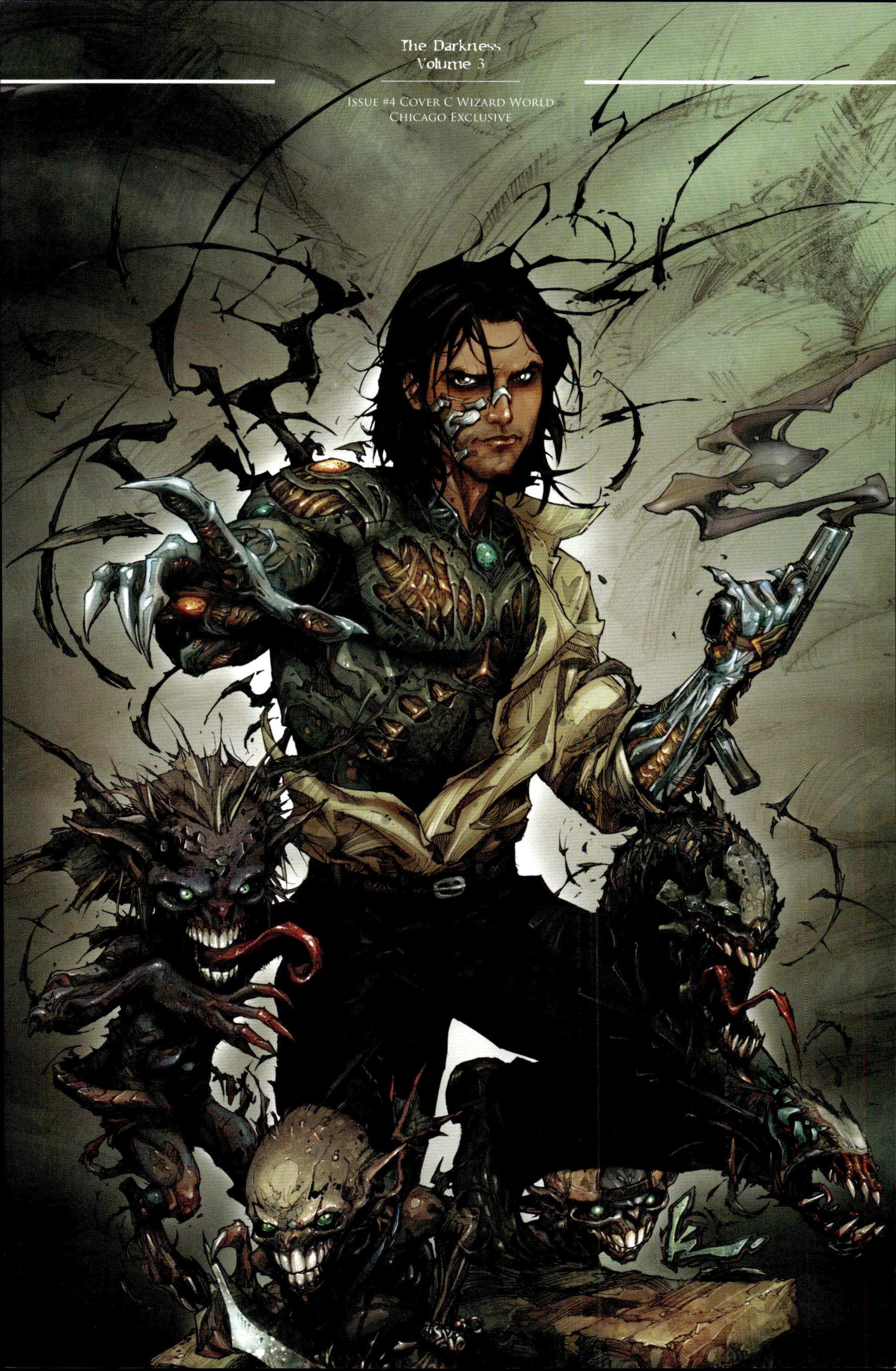

Issue #5 Cover B

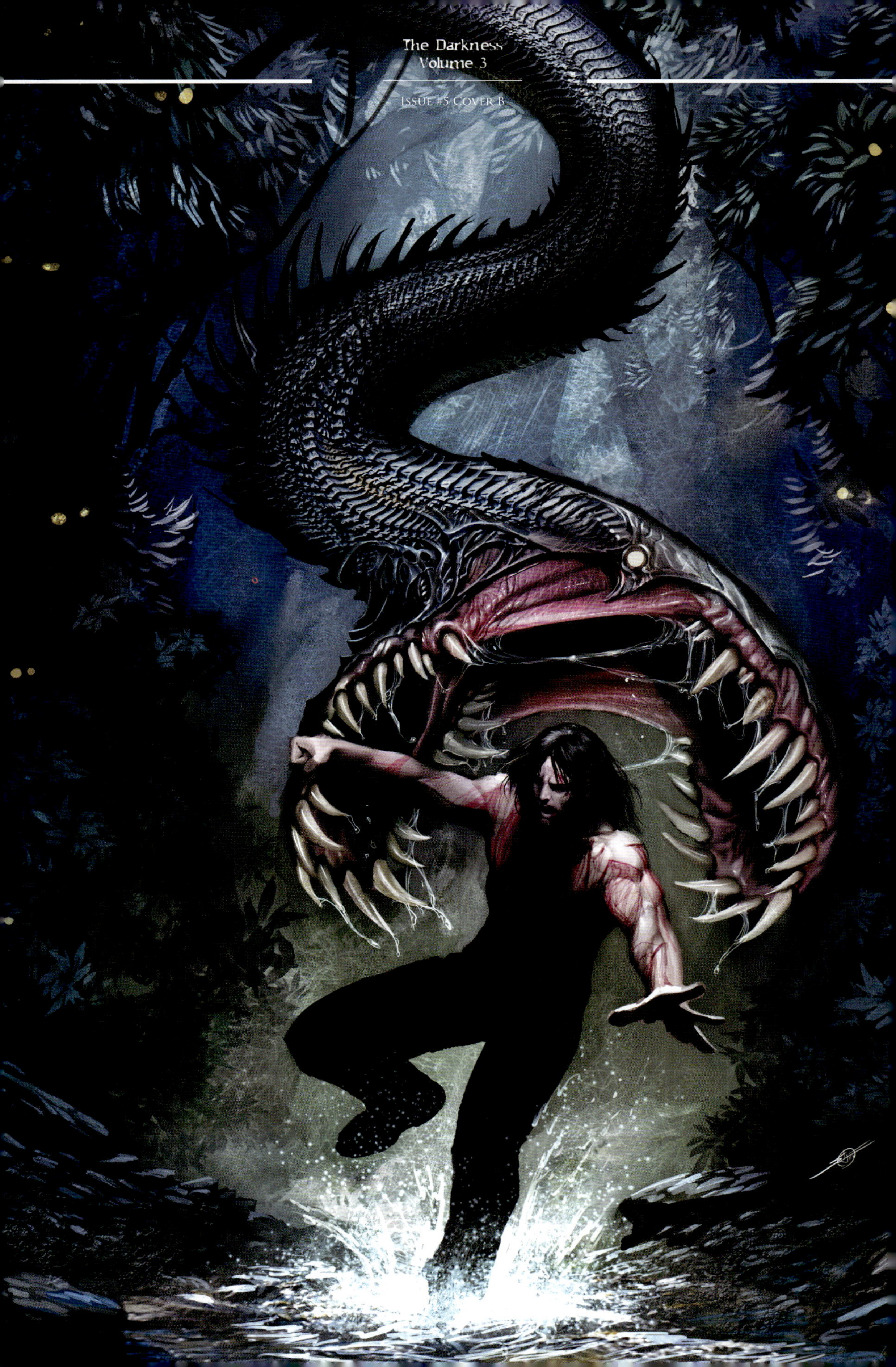

The Darkness
Volume 3

Issue #6 Cover B

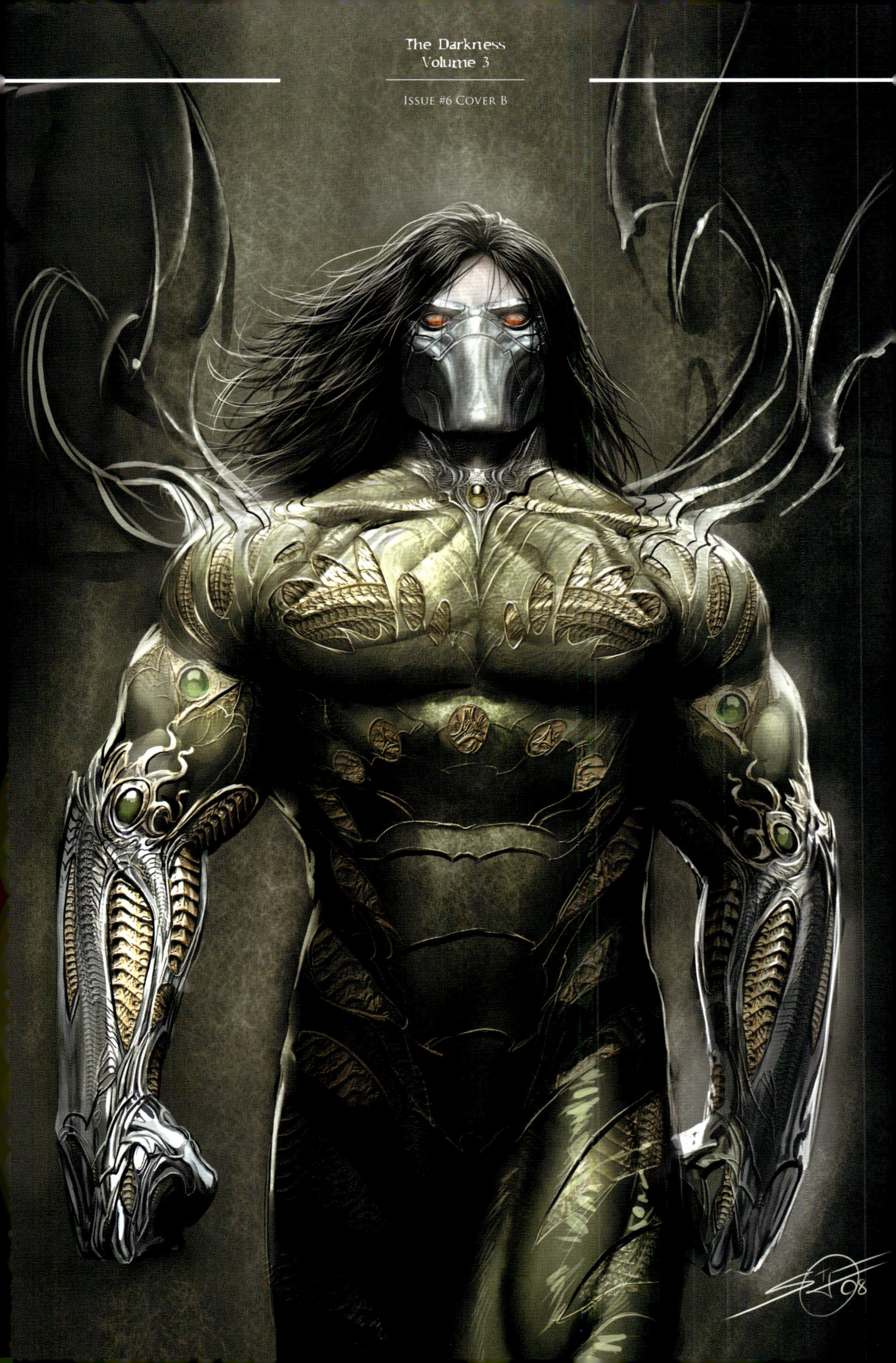

Issue #7 Cover B

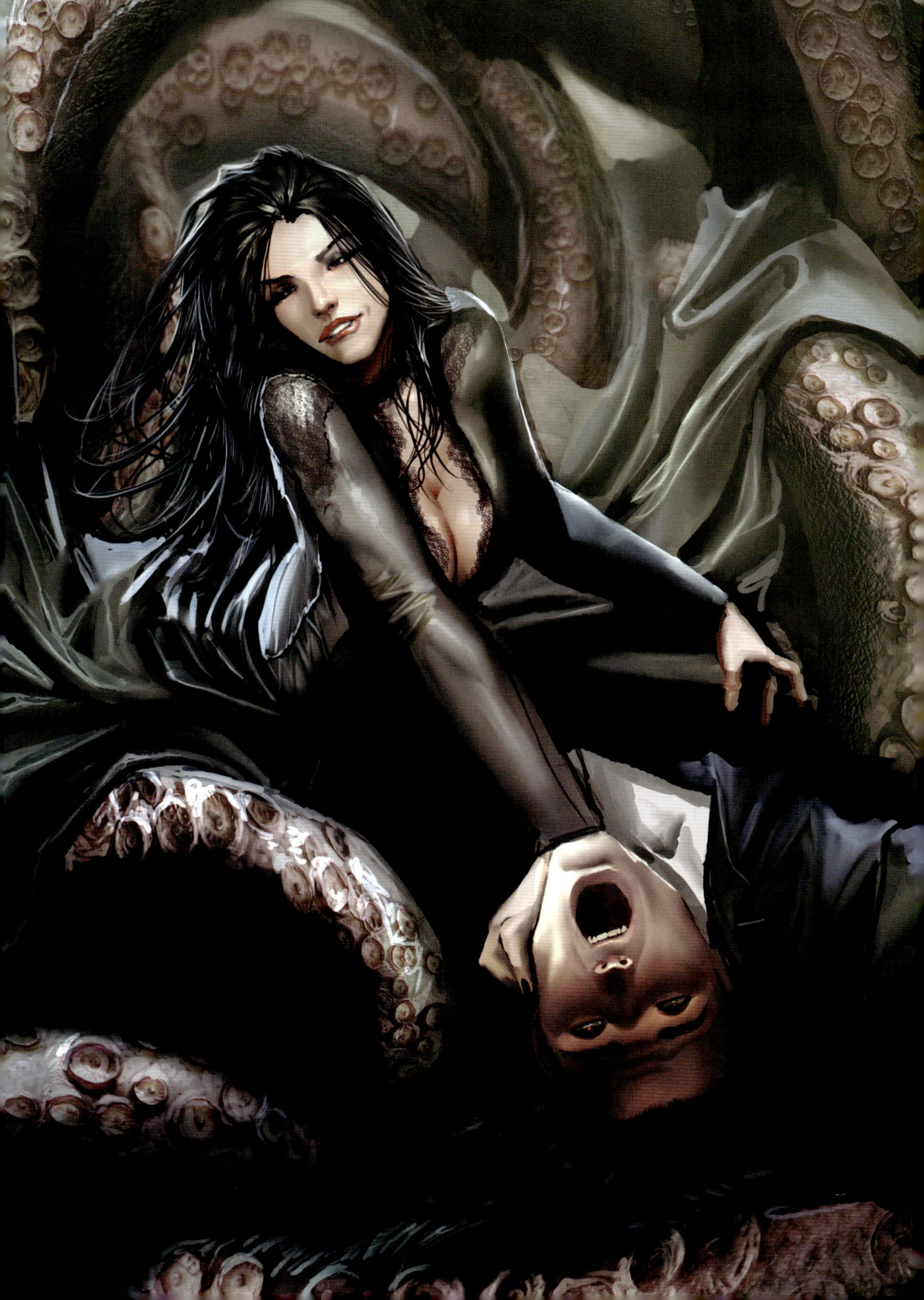

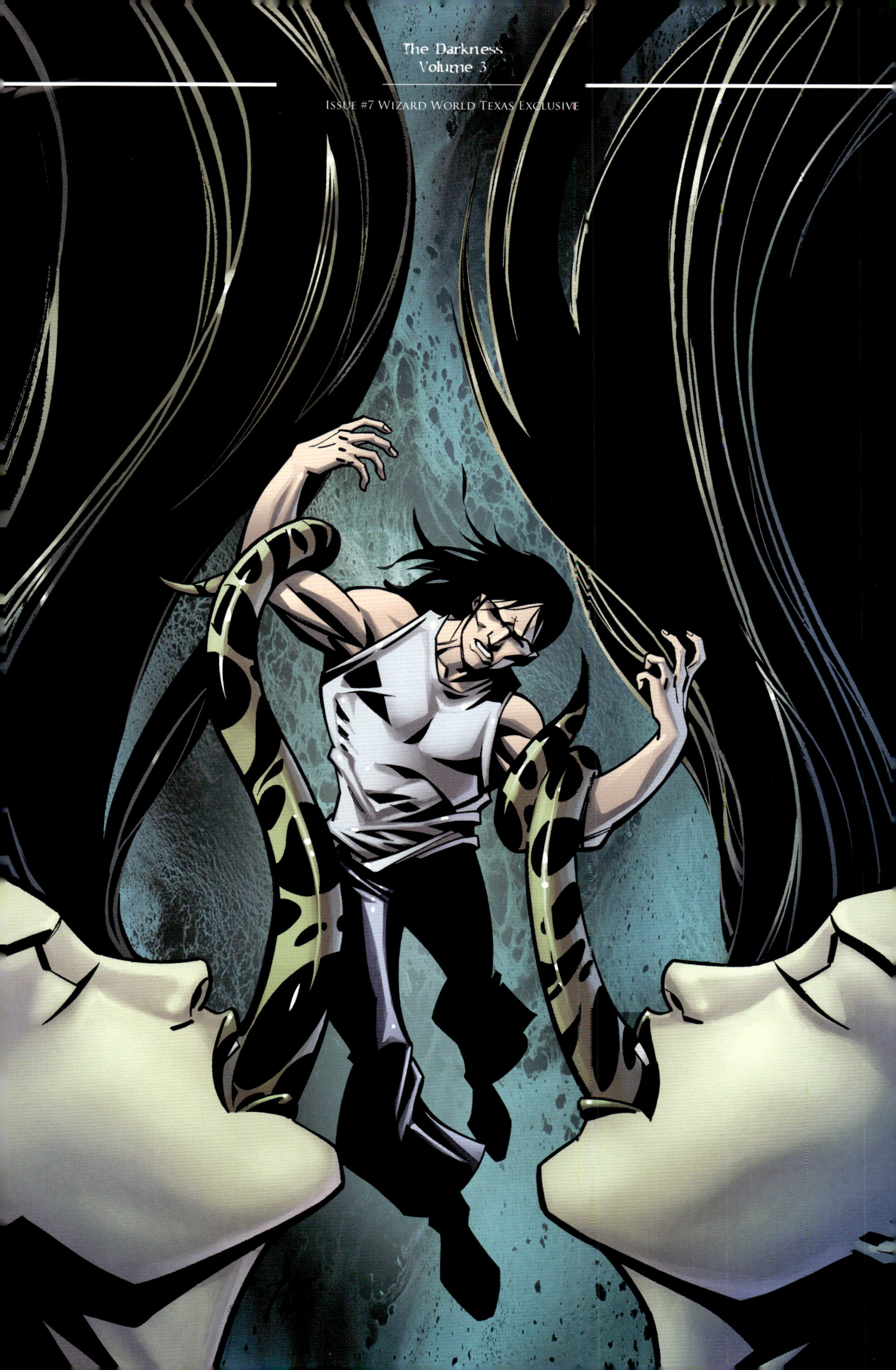
The Darkness
Volume 3
Issue #7 Wizard World Texas Exclusive

The Darkness
Volume 3

ISSUE #8 COVER B

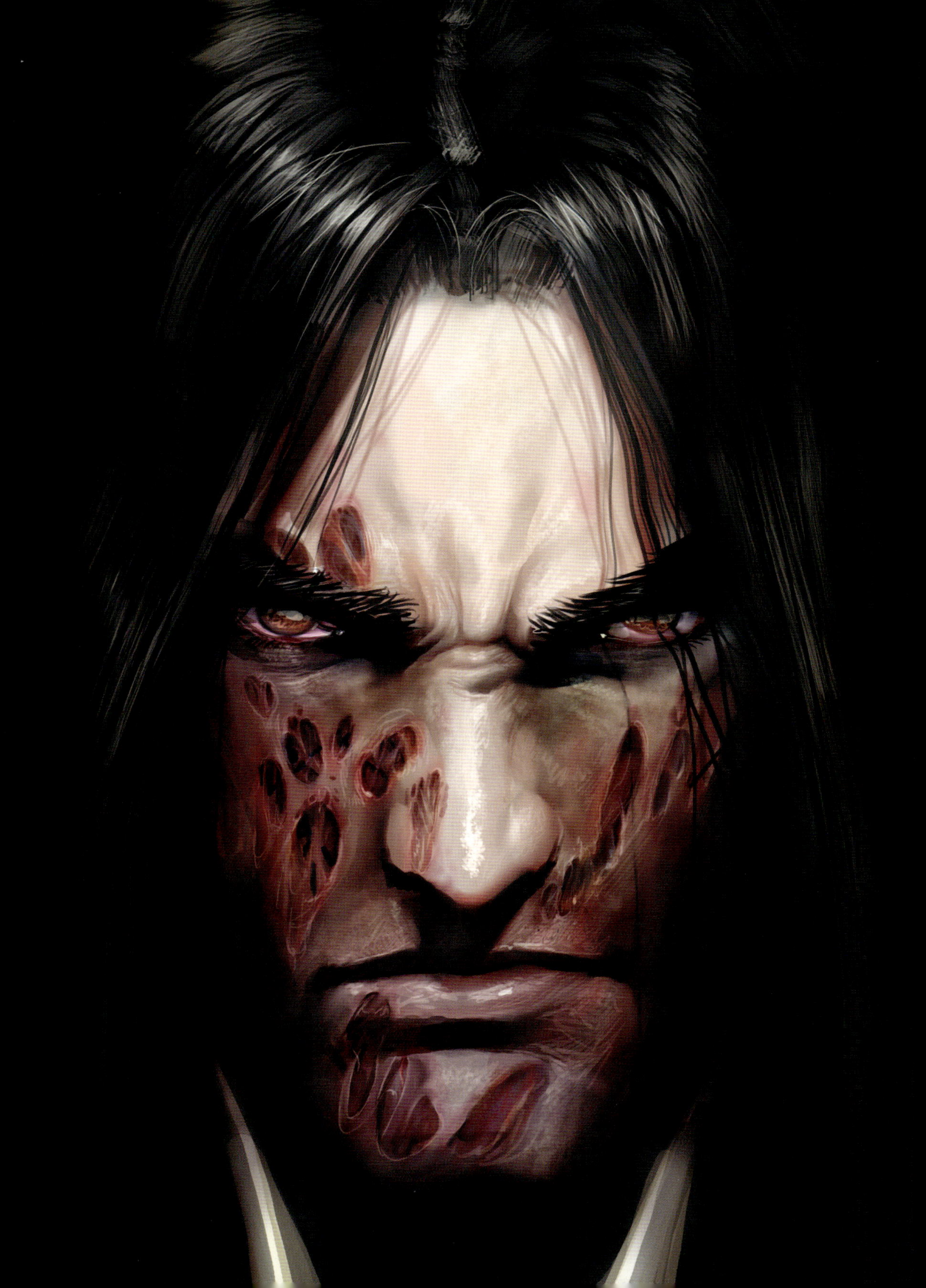

Issue #9 Cover B

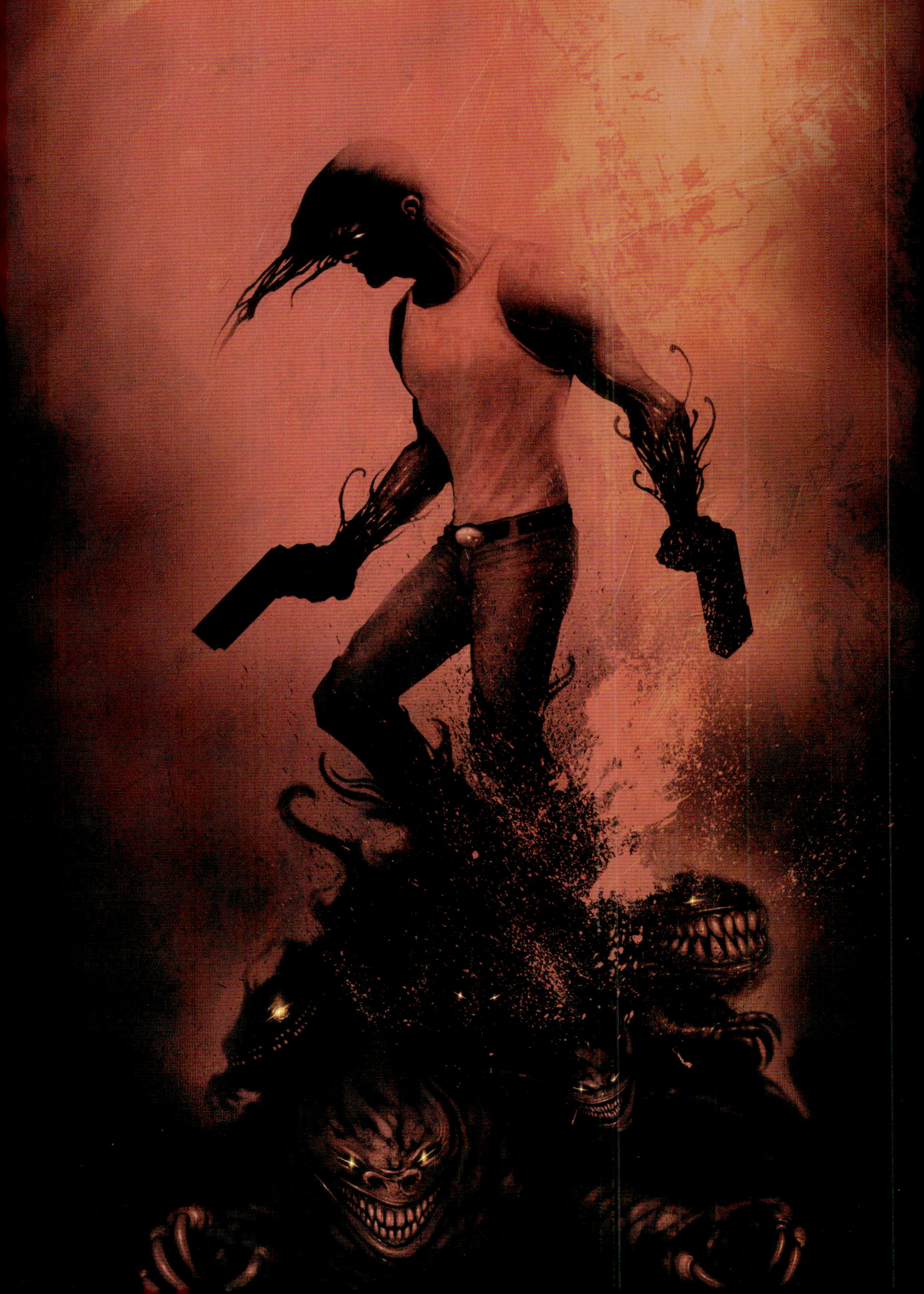

Issue #75 Cover A

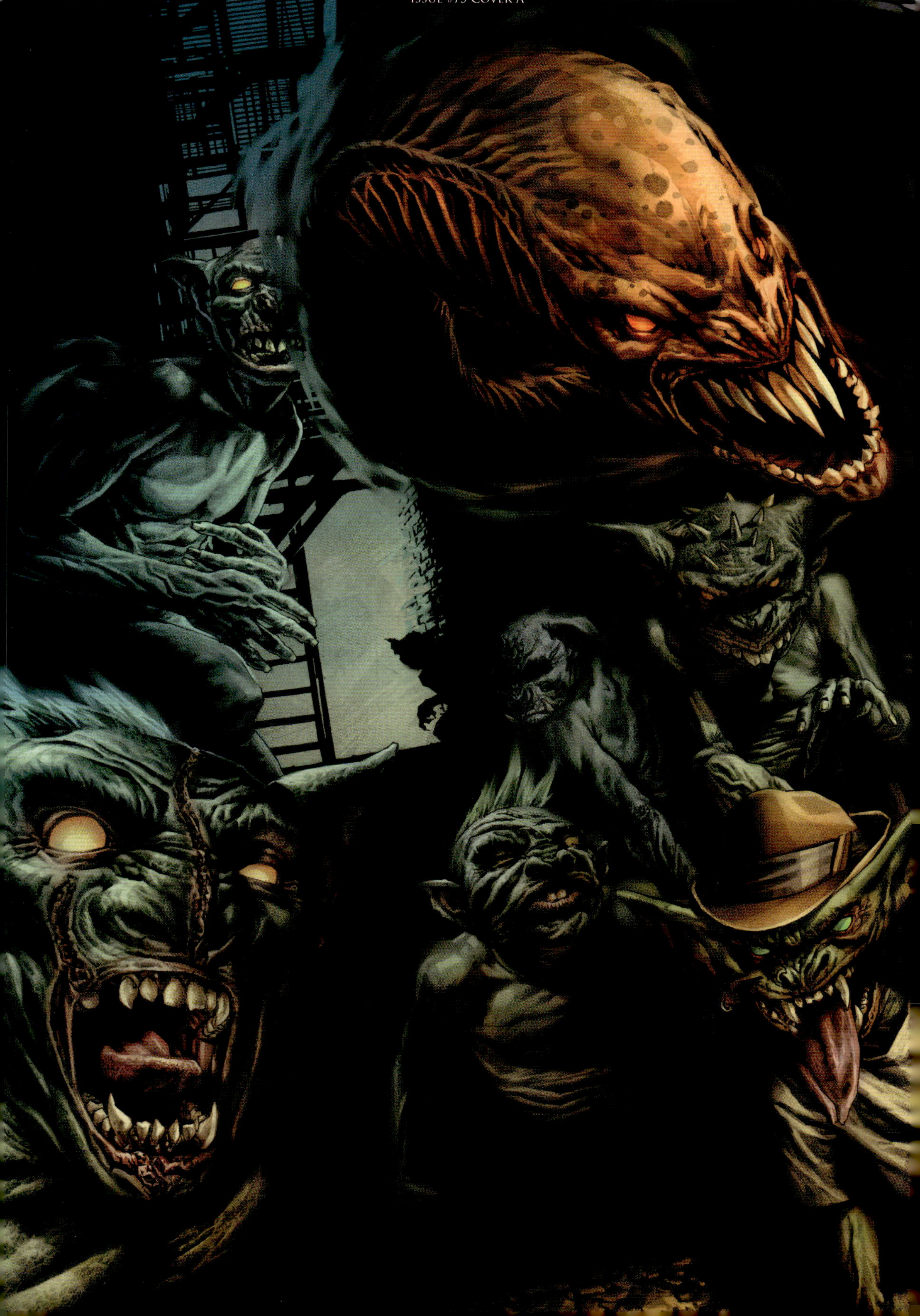

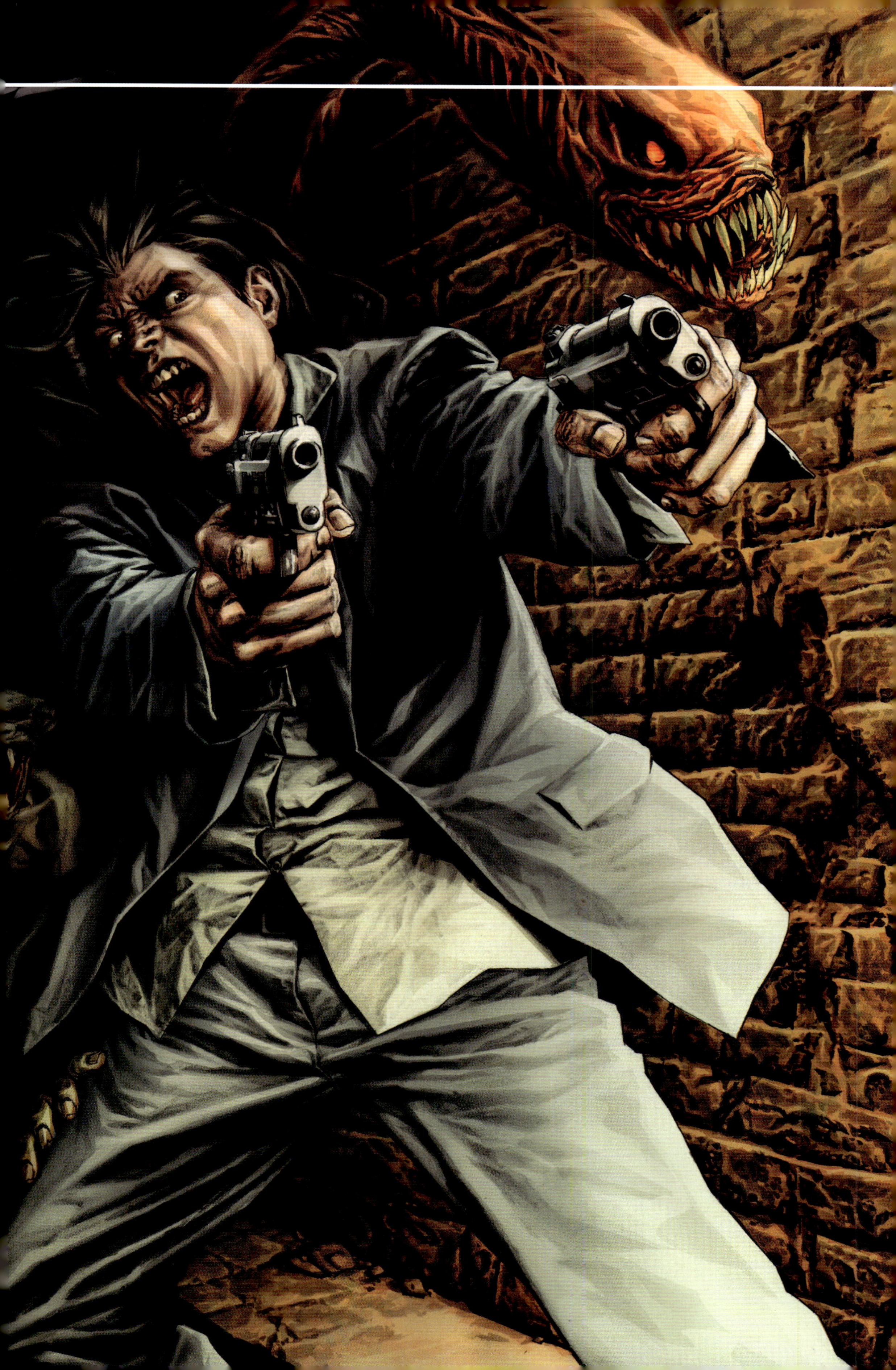

Issue #75 Cover C

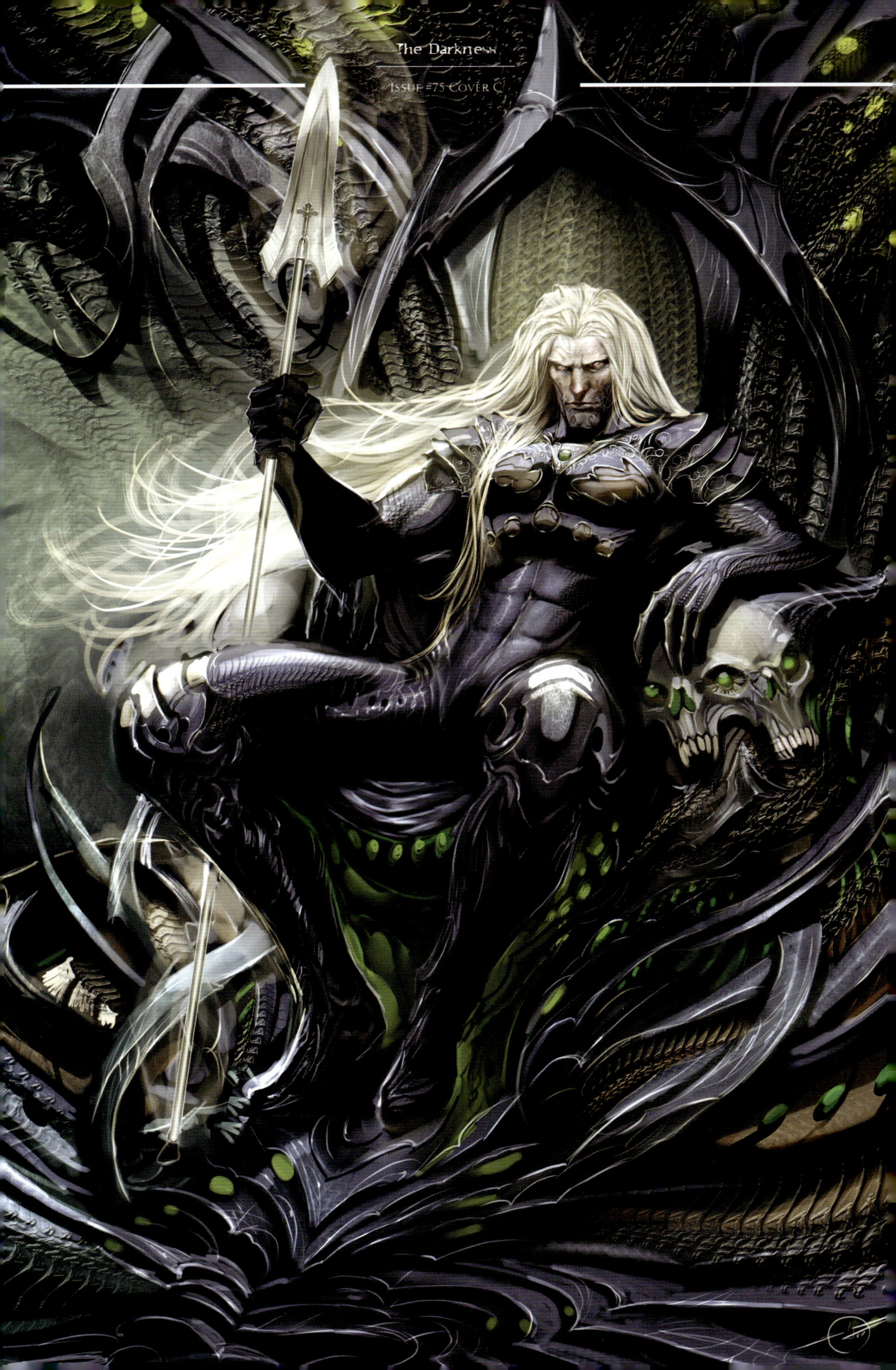

Issue #75 Cover D

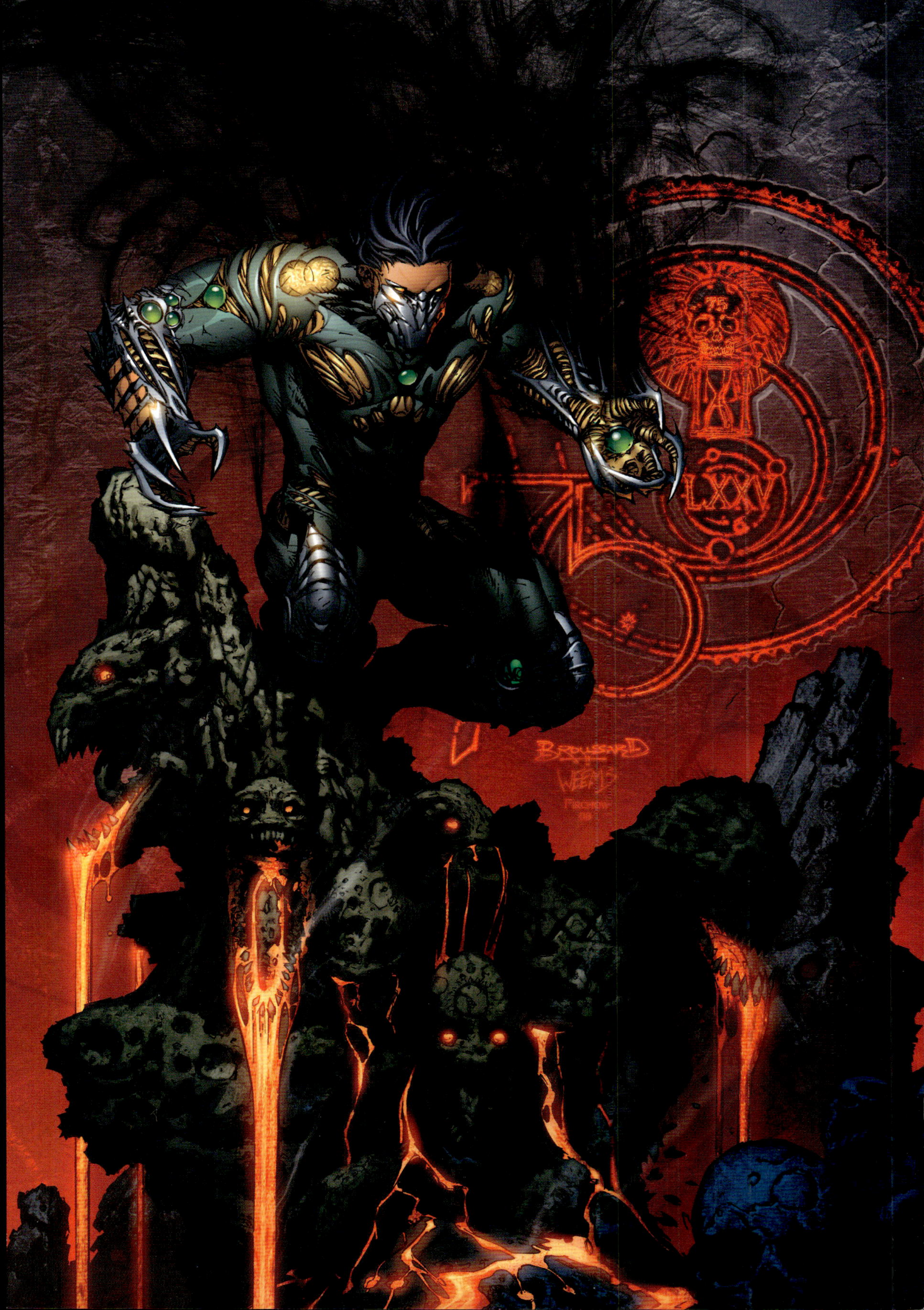
LXXV

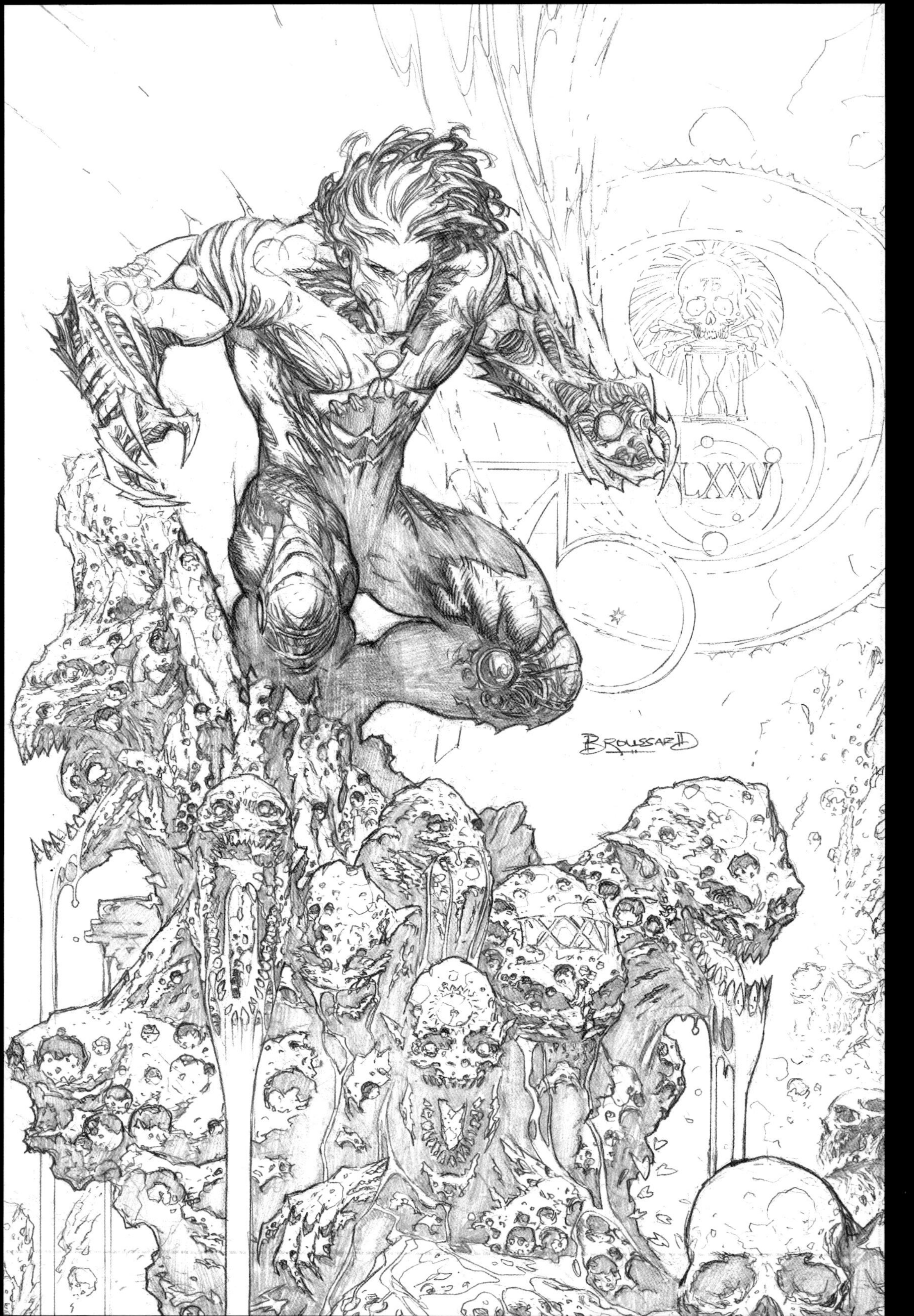
75
LXXV
BROUSSARD

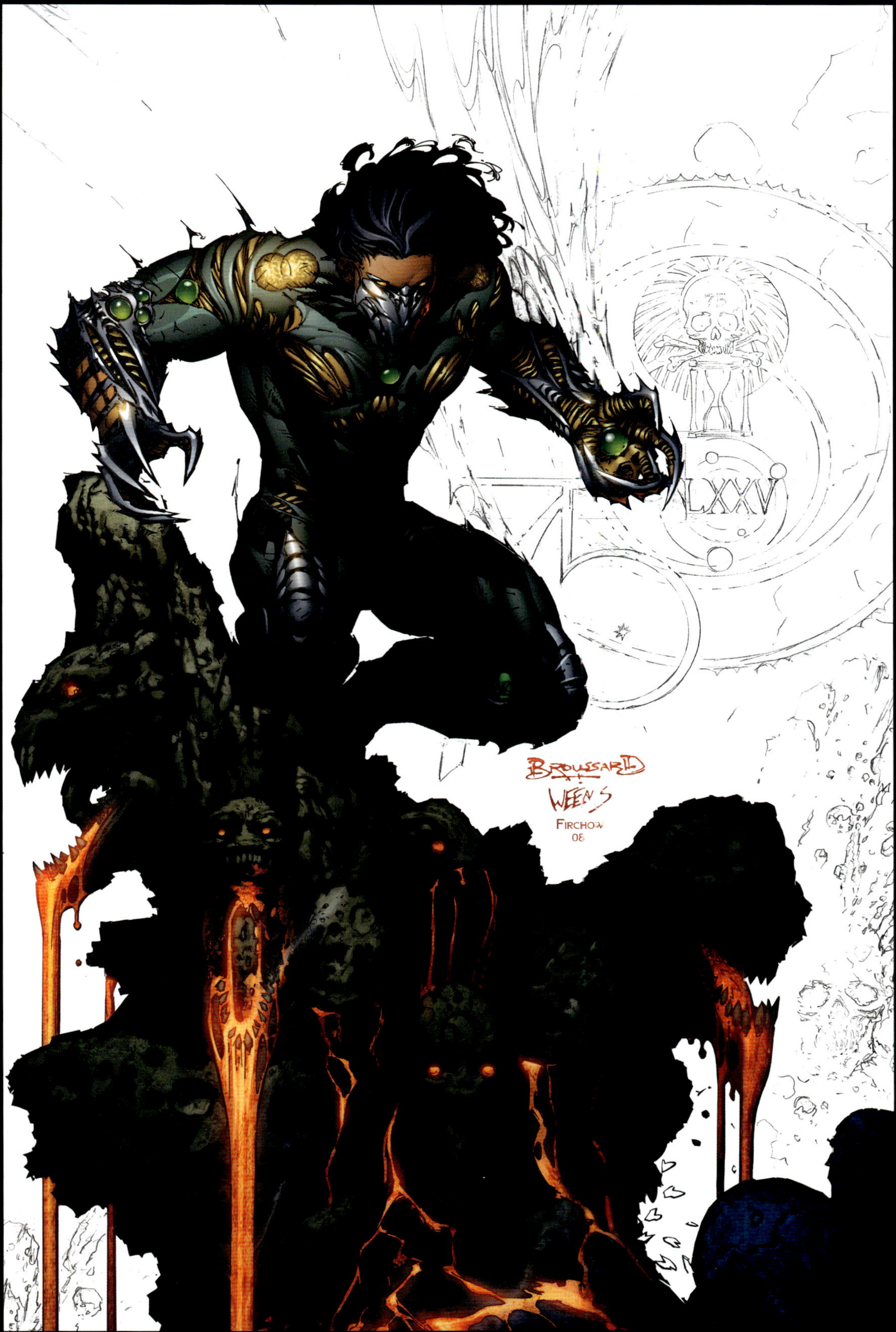
LXXV
BROUSSARD
WEEMS
FIRCHOW
08

Issue #75 Cover G
New York Comic Con Exclusive

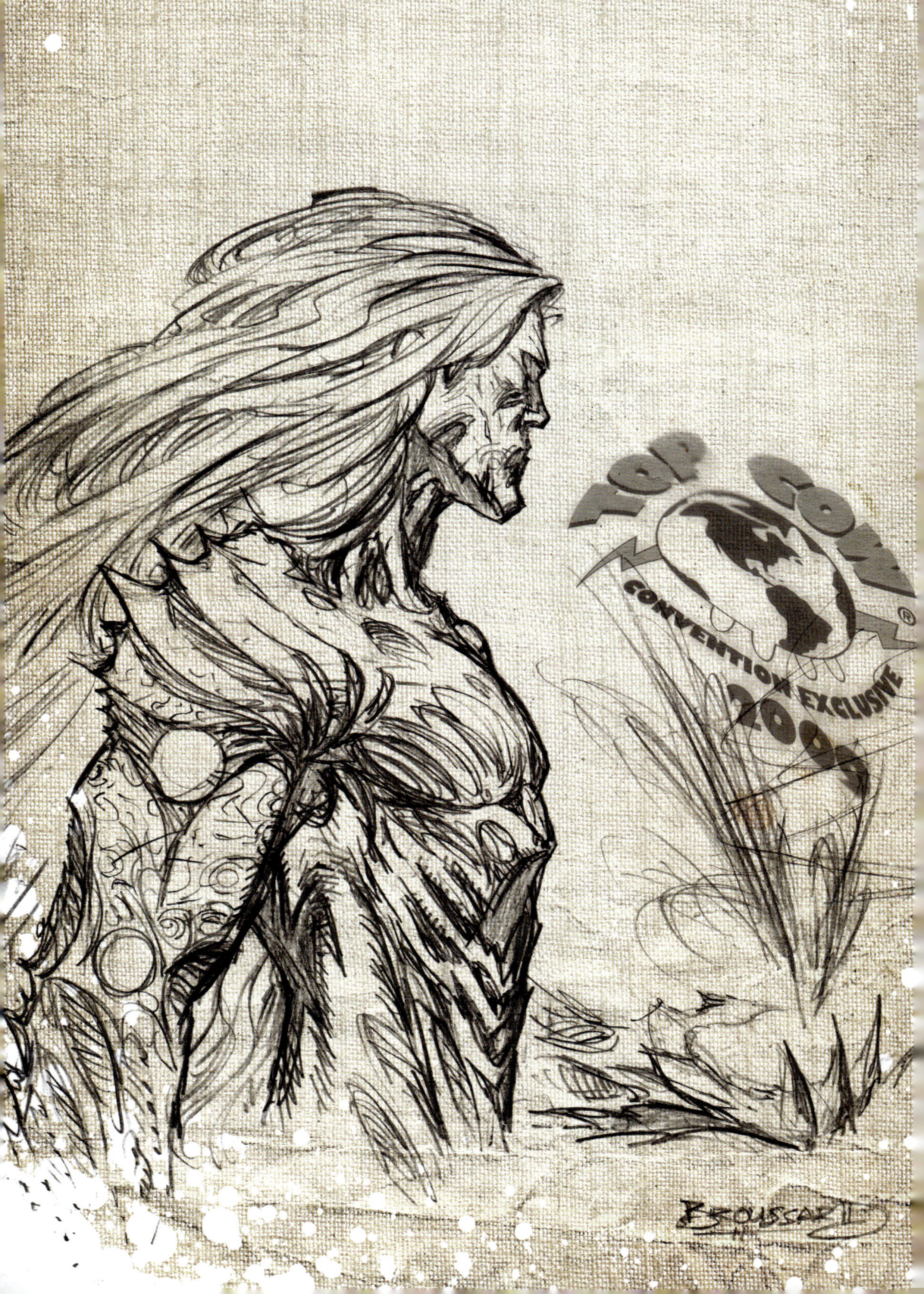
TOP COW
CONVENTION EXCLUSIVE
BROUSSARD

Issue #76 Cover B

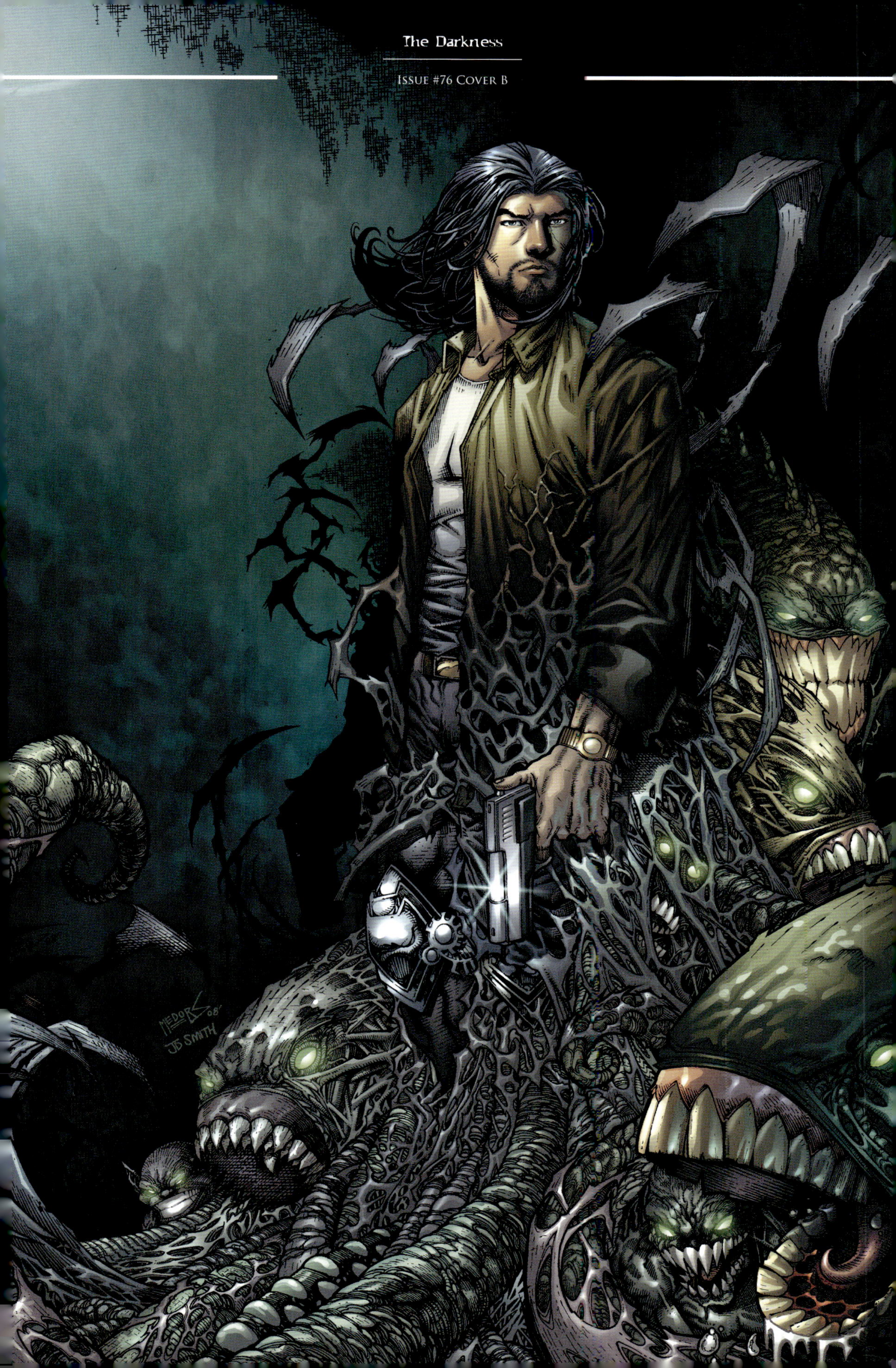
MEDORS '08
JB SMITH

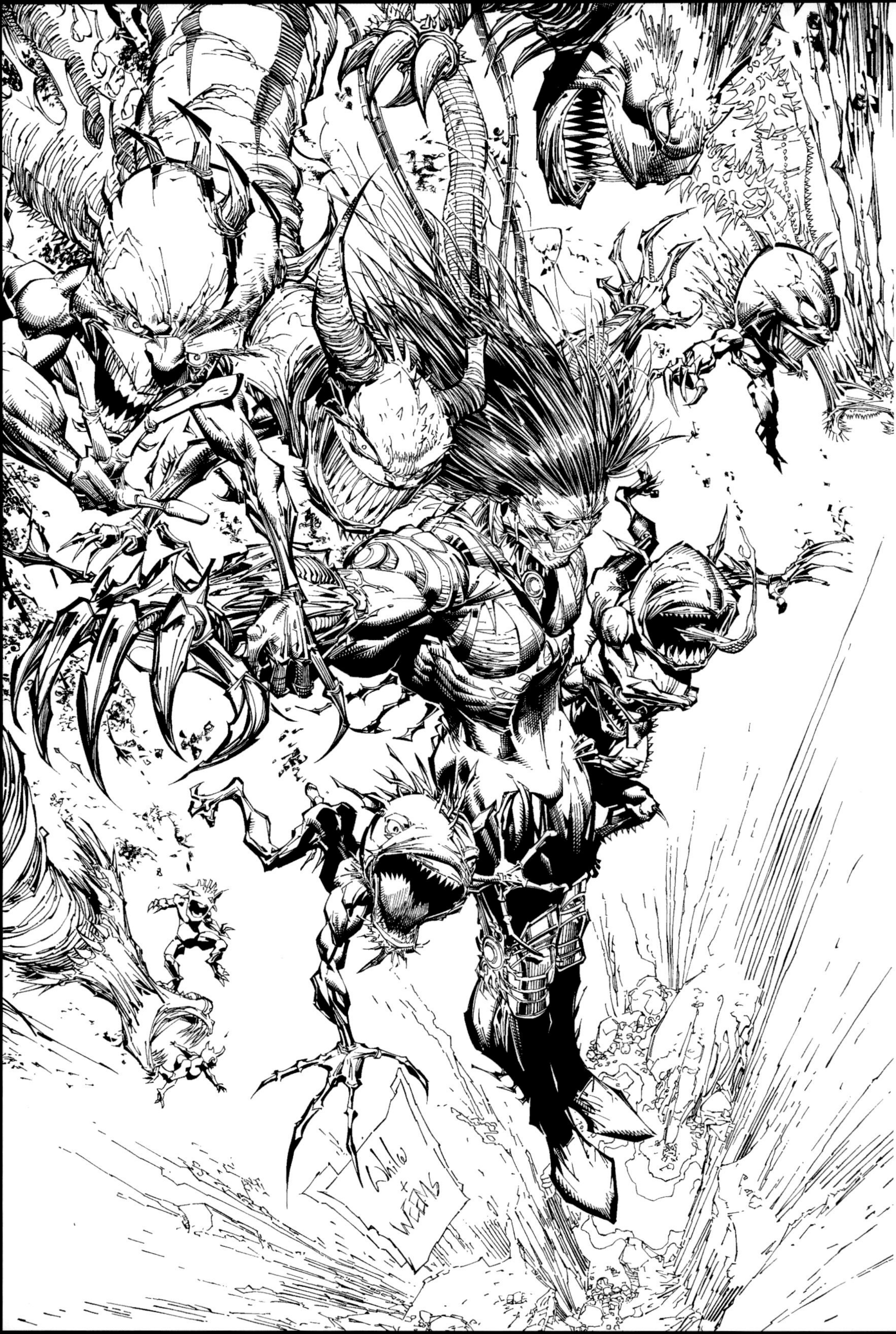
White
+
Weems

Issue #79 Cover B

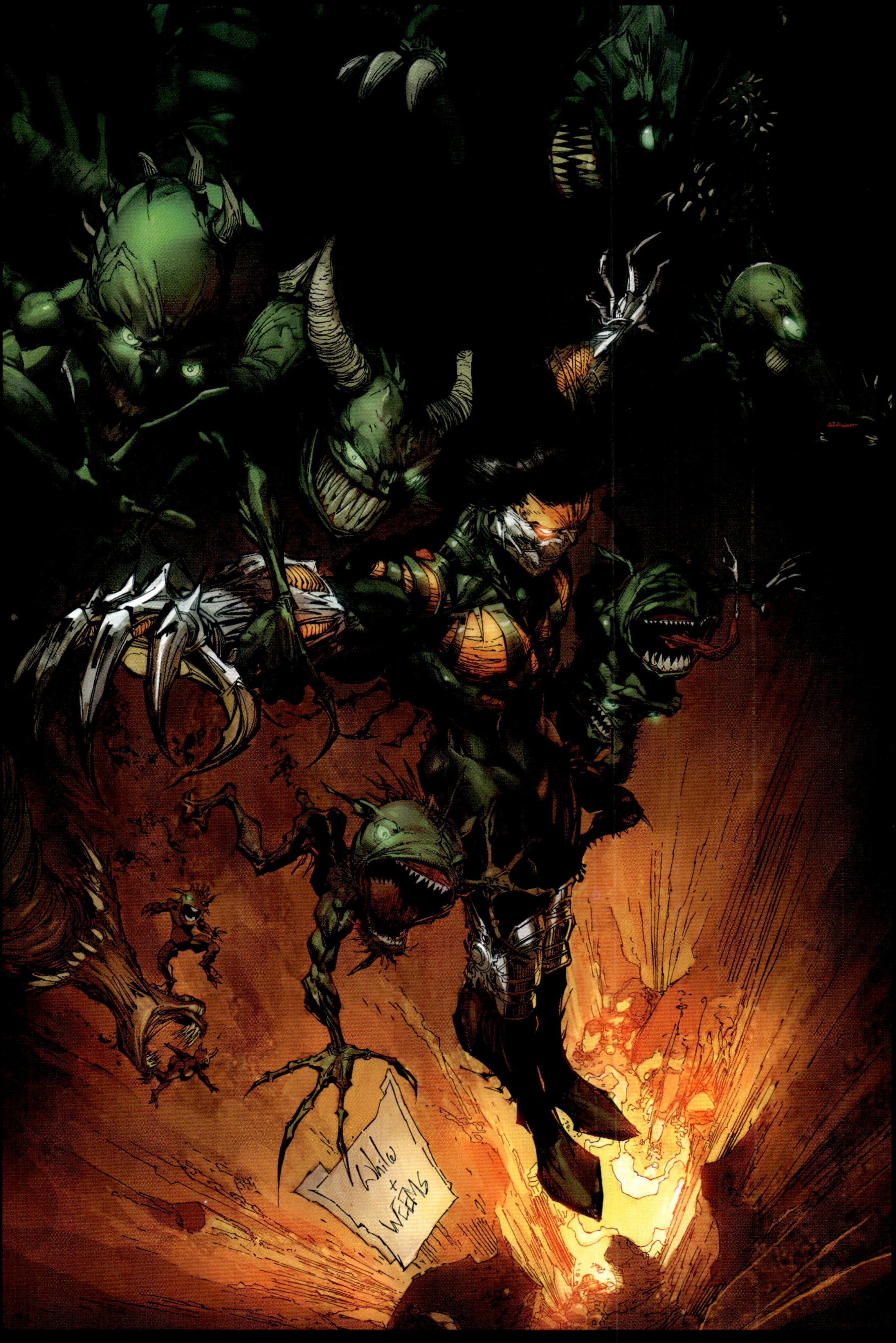

Issue #80 Cover C All Beef Edition

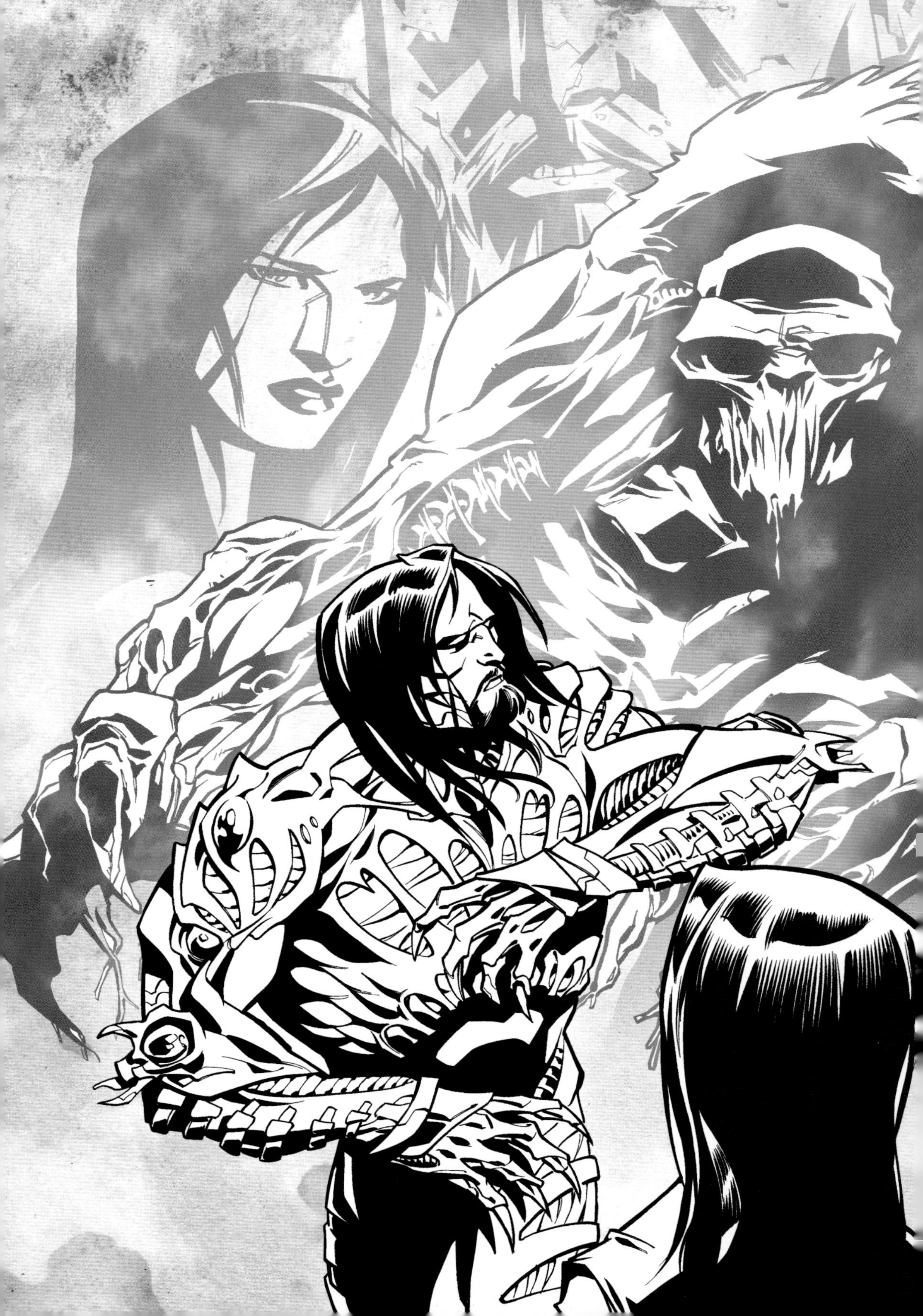

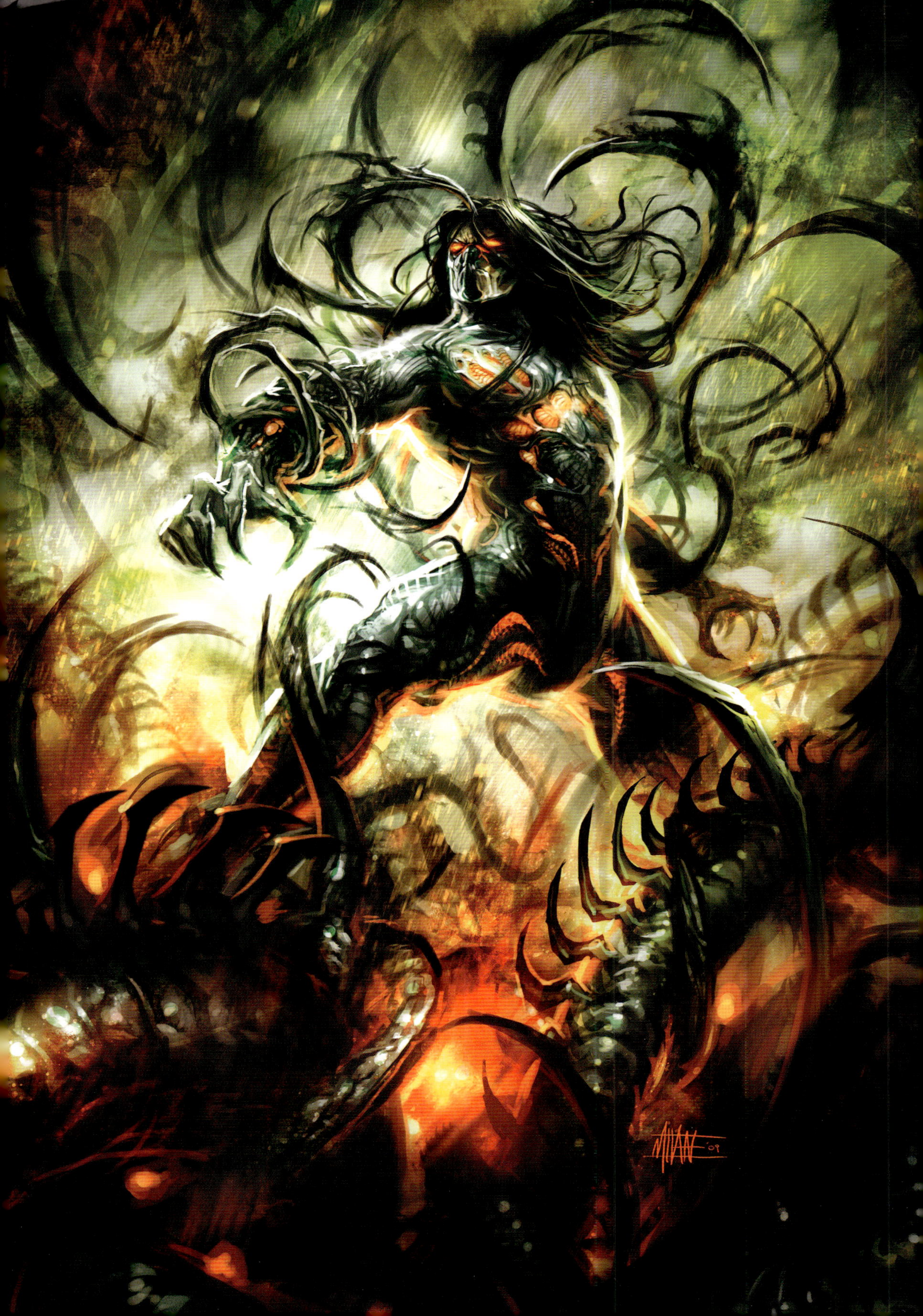

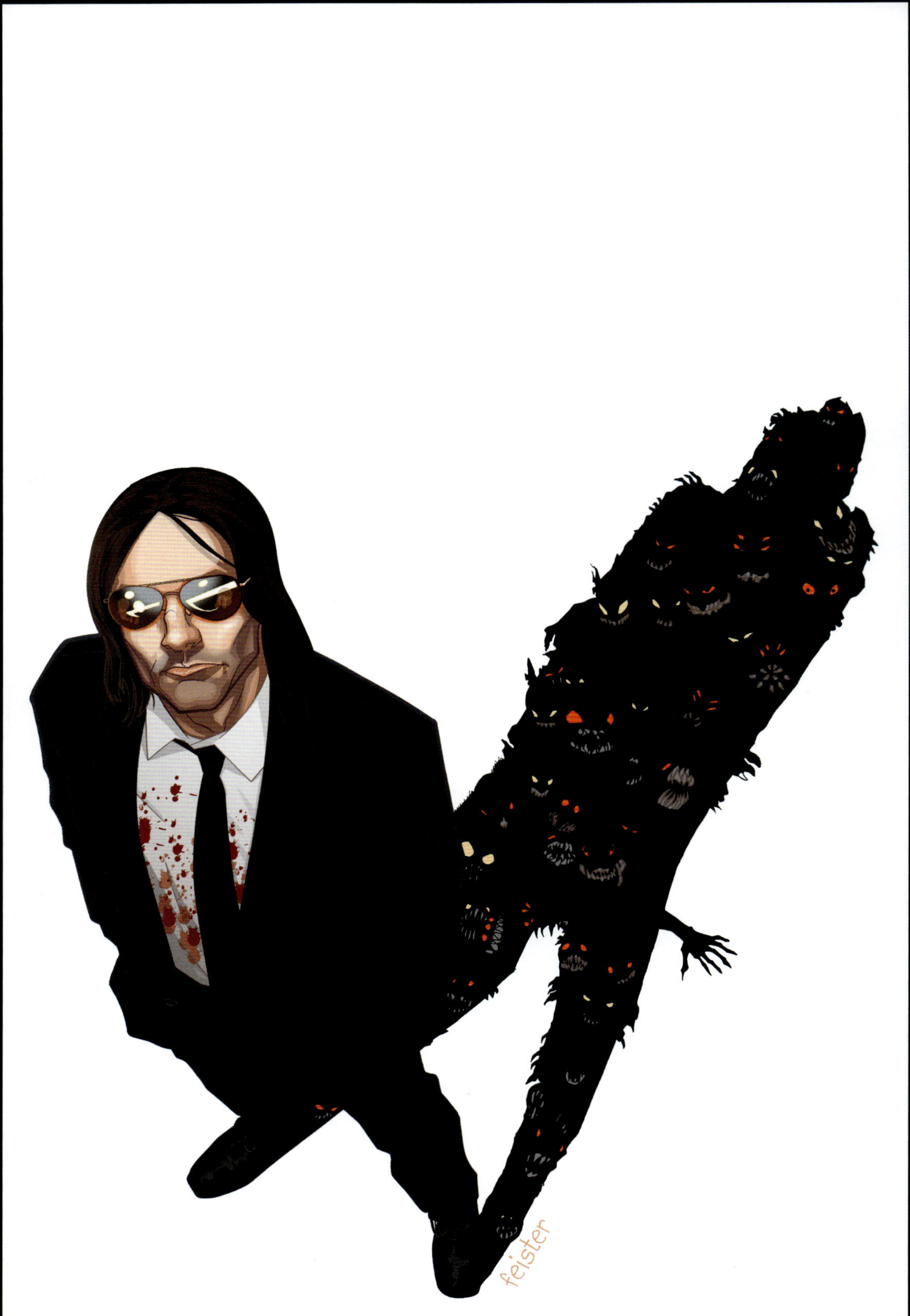
feister

The Darkness

Issue #83 Cover B
Emerald City Comic Con Exclusive

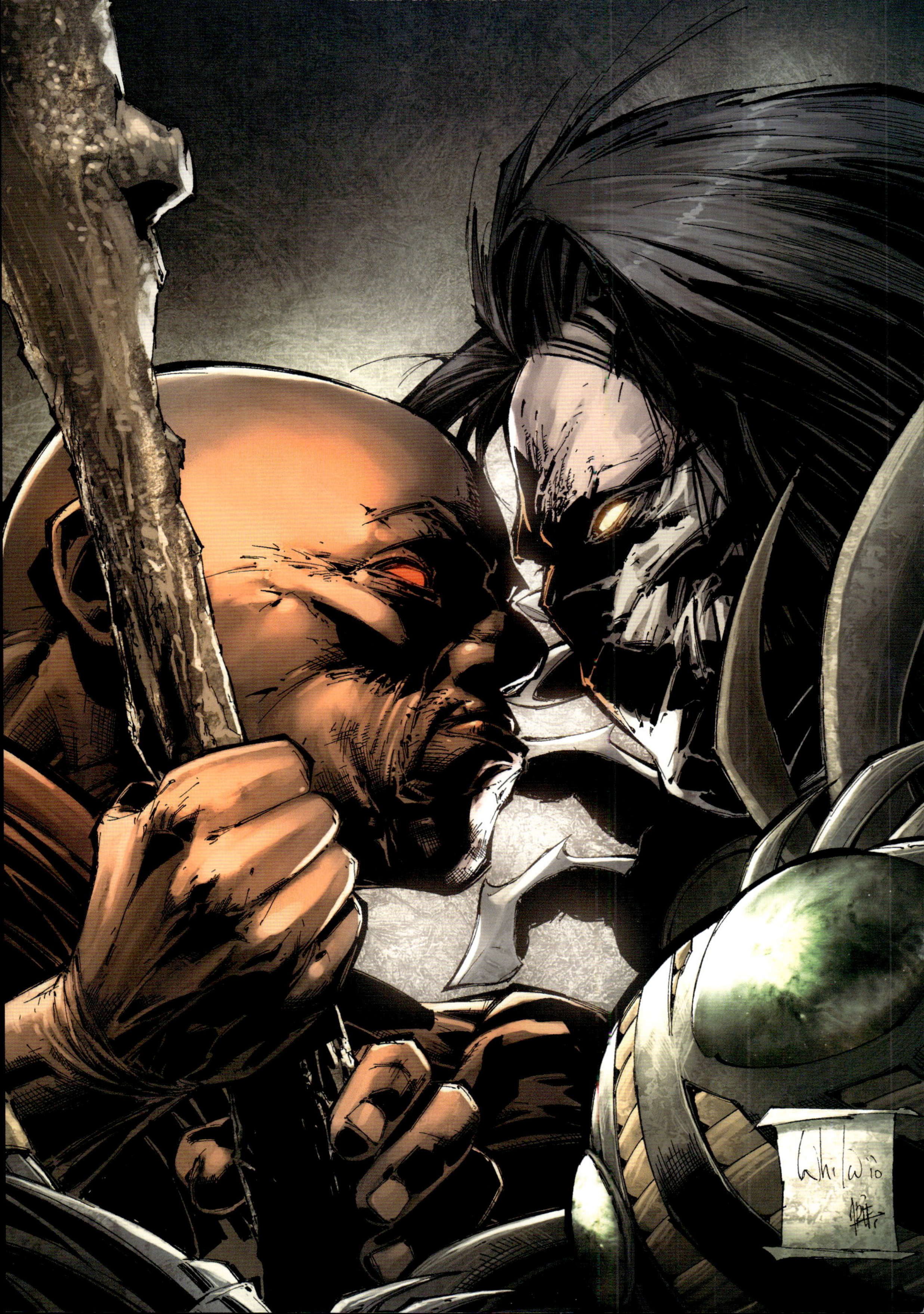

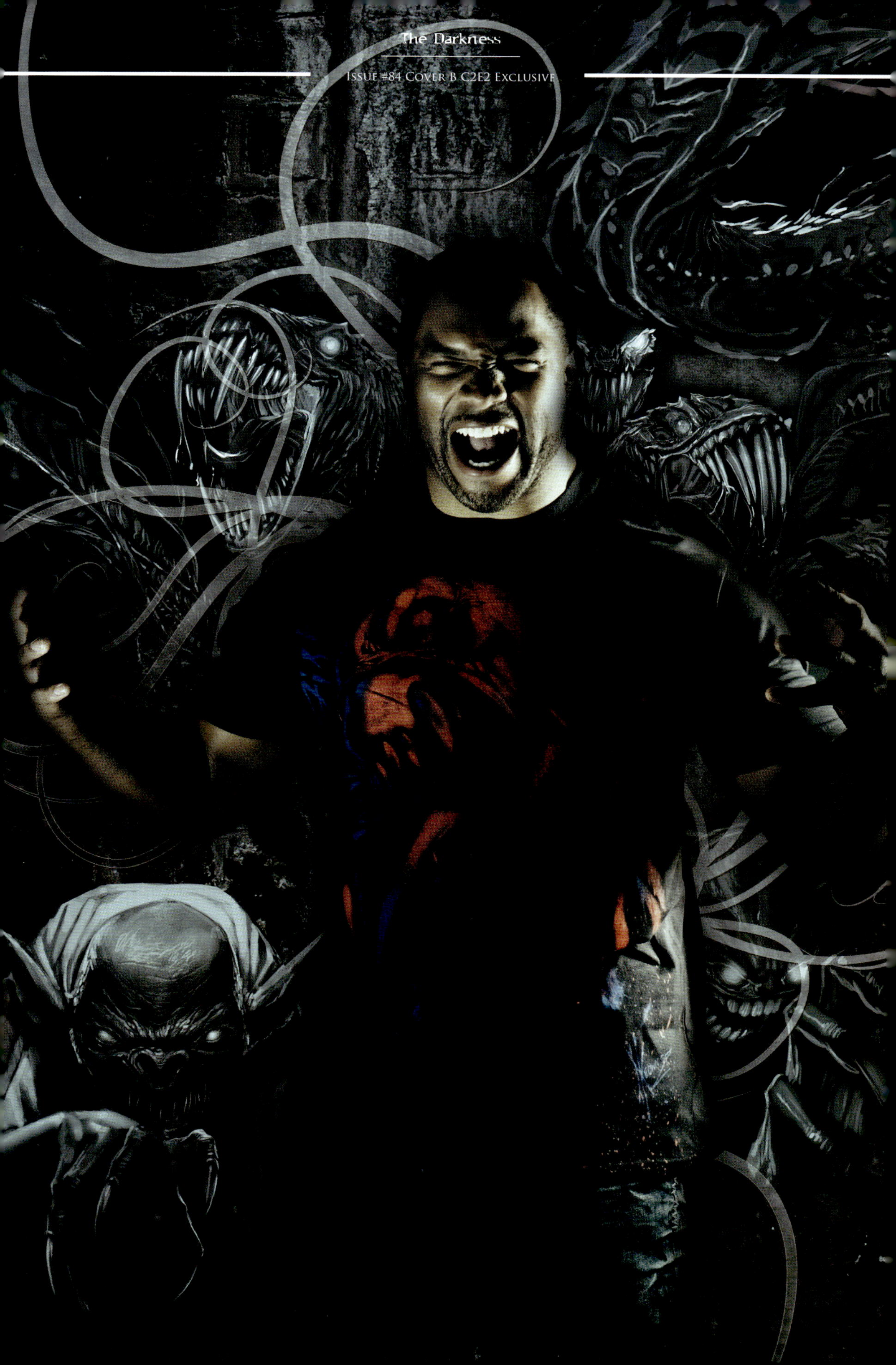

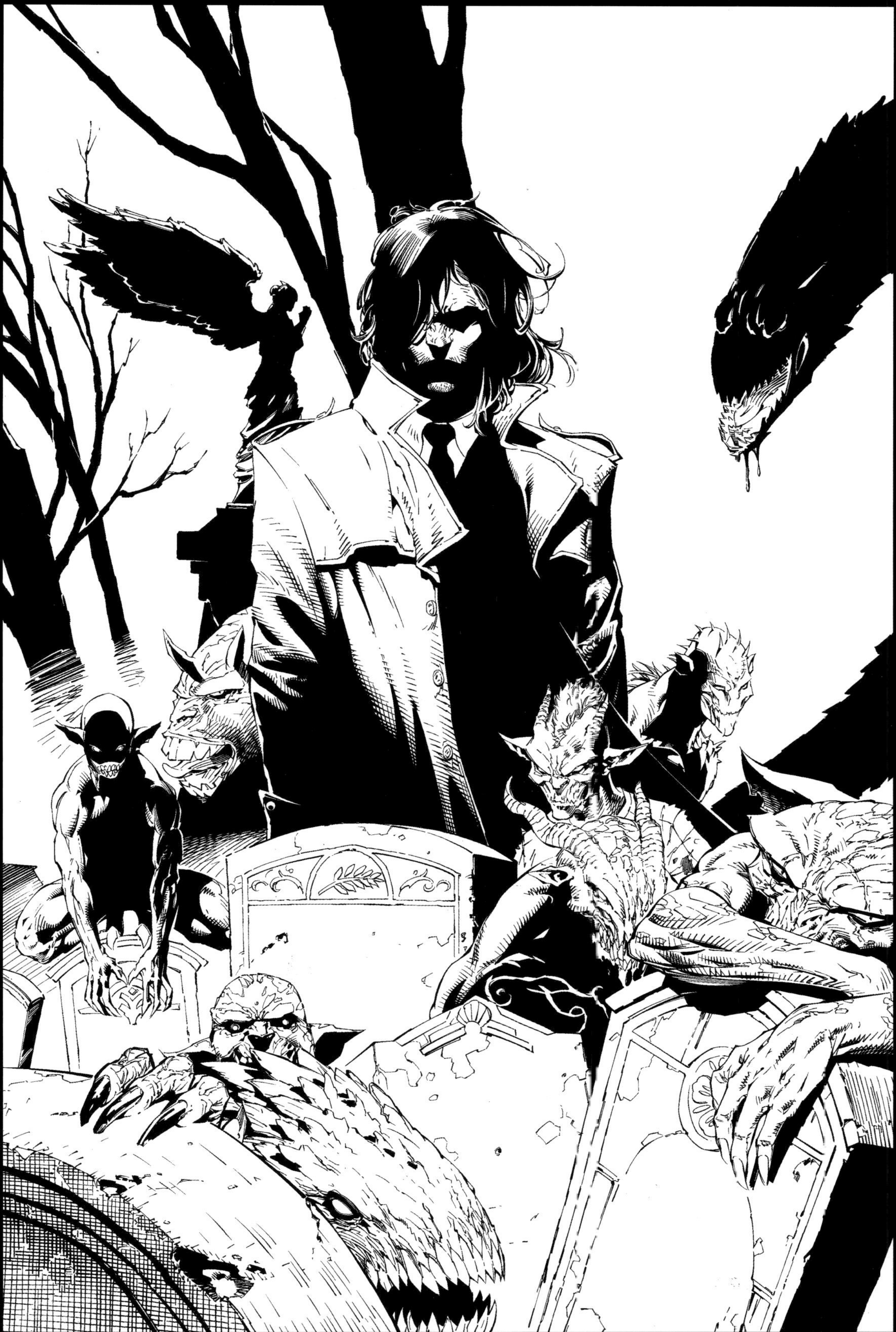

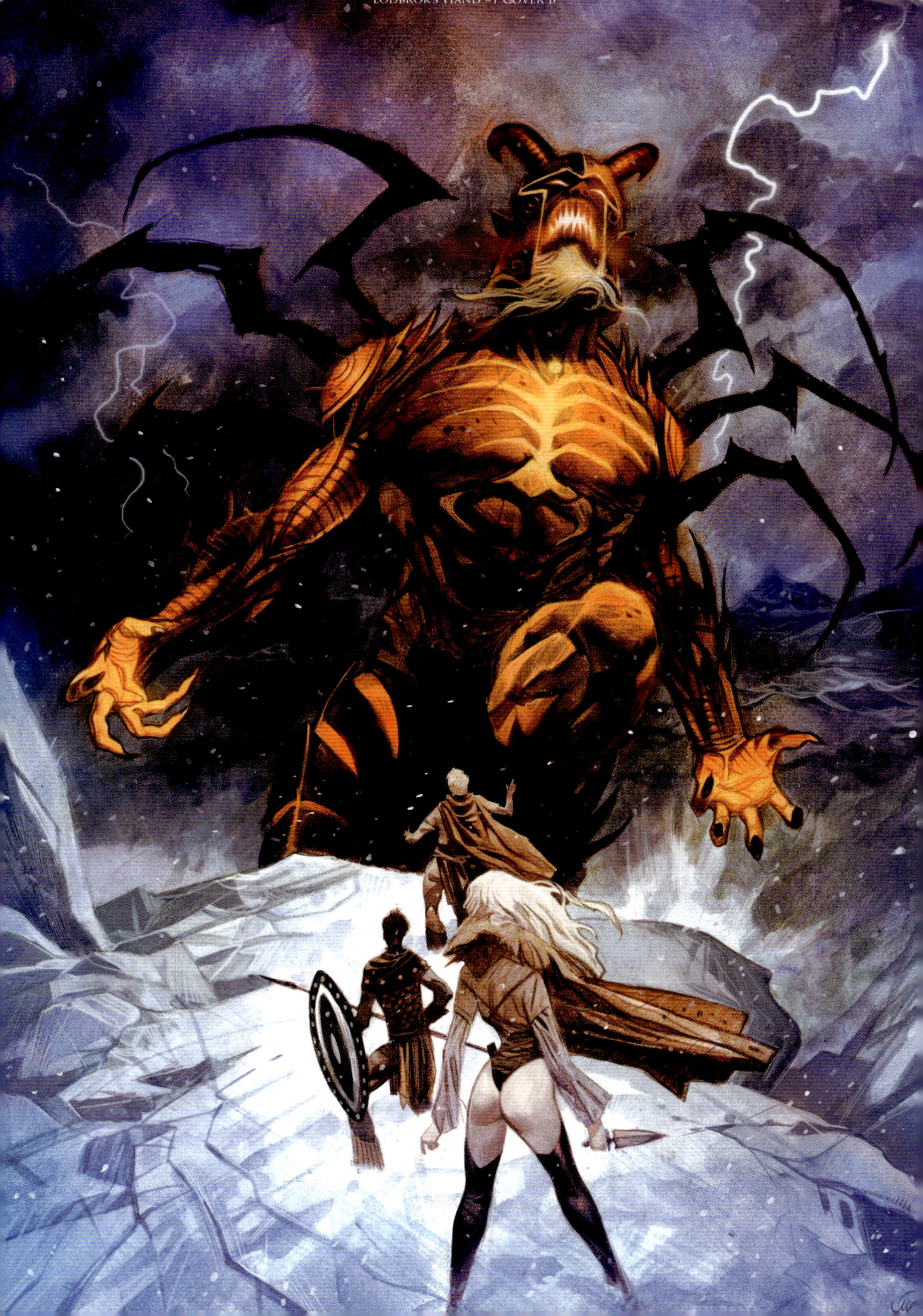

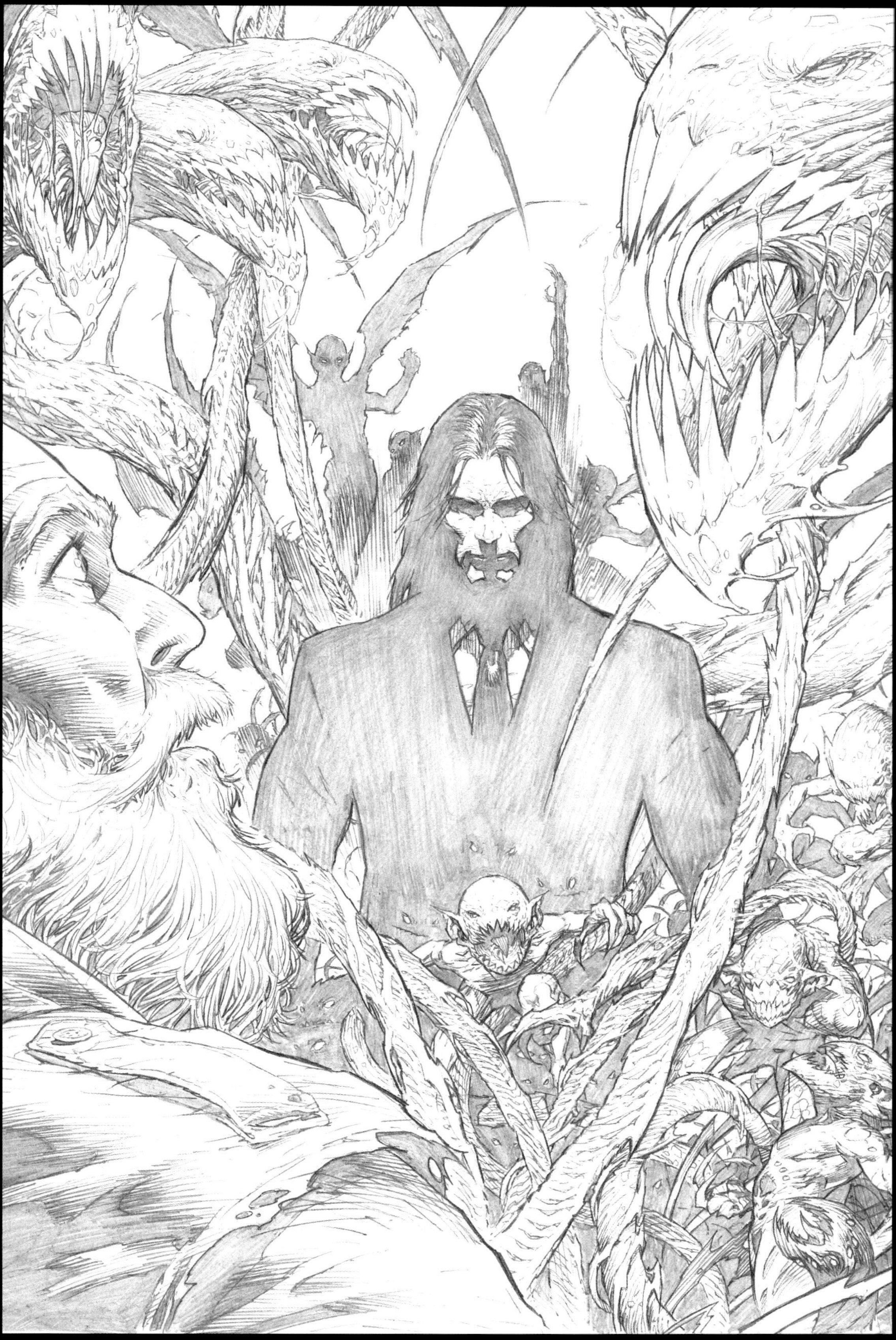

THE DARKNESS #41-64 ORIGINALLY PUBLISHED
IN SINGLE ISSUE FORMAT AS
THE DARKNESS VOL. 2 #1-24.

THE DARKNESS #65-74 ORIGINALLY PUBLISHED
IN SINGLE ISSUE FORMAT AS
THE DARKNESS VOL. 3 #1-10

THE DARKNESS
ISSUE #41-#44 CREDITS

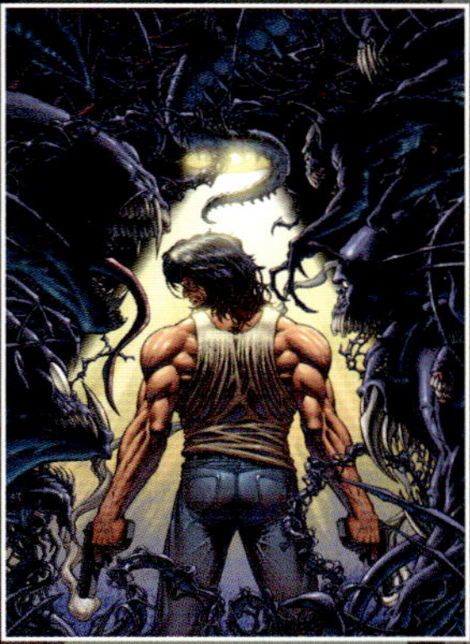

THE DARKNESS ISSUE #41

Paul Jenkins_ story
Dale Keown_ pencils
Matt Milla_ colors
Robin Spehar with
Dreamer Design's Dennis Heisler_ letters

Originally published December 2002

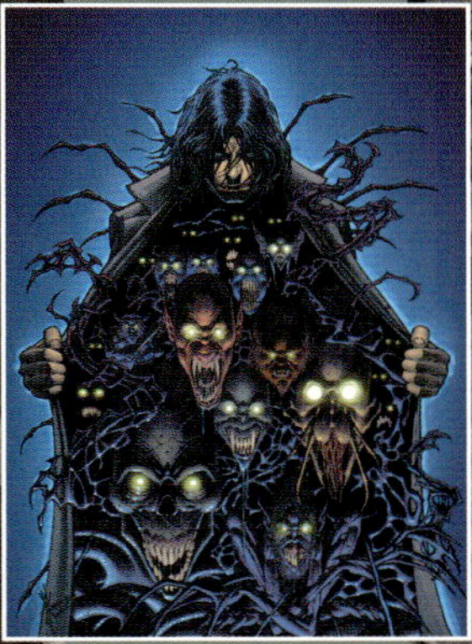

THE DARKNESS ISSUE #42

Paul Jenkins_ story
Dale Keown_ pencils
Matt Milla_ colors
Robin Spehar with
Dreamer Design's Dennis Heisler_ letters

Originally published February 2003

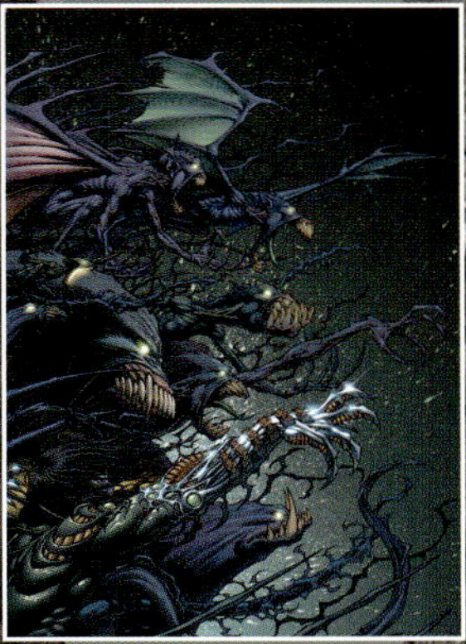

THE DARKNESS ISSUE #43

Paul Jenkins_ story
Dale Keown_ pencils
Matt Milla_ colors
Robin Spehar with
Dreamer Design's Dennis Heisler_ letters

Originally published May 2003

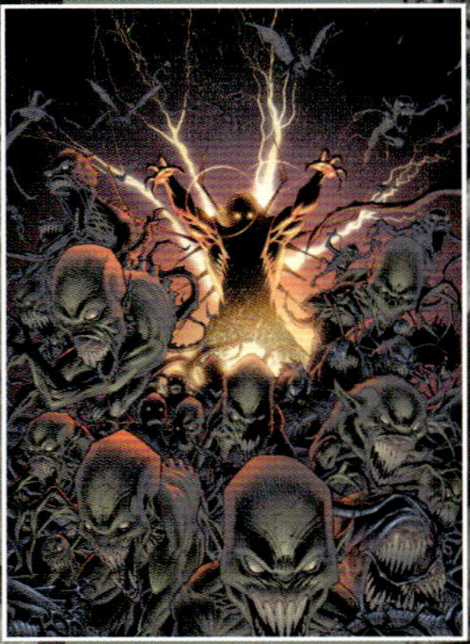

THE DARKNESS ISSUE #44

Paul Jenkins_ story
Dale Keown_ pencils
Keu Cha_ pencil assists
Matt Milla_ colors
Robin Spehar with
Dreamer Design's Dennis Heisler_ letters

Originally published July 2003

THE DARKNESS
ISSUE #45-#48 CREDITS

THE DARKNESS ISSUE #45

Paul Jenkins_ story
Dale Keown_ pencils
Keu Cha_ pencil assists
Matt Milla_ colors
Robin Spehar with
Dreamer Design's Dennis Heisler_ letters

Originally published September 2003

THE DARKNESS ISSUE #46

Paul Jenkins_ story
Dale Keown_ pencils
Matt Milla_ colors
Robin Spehar with
Dreamer Design's Dennis Heisler_ letters

Originally published December 2003

THE DARKNESS ISSUE #47

Paul Jenkins_ story
Eric 'eBas' Basaldua_ pencils
Mike Choi_ pencil assists
Matt 'Batt' Banning, Rick Basaldua, Scott Hanna_ inks
Matt Milla_ colors
Robin Spehar with
Dreamer Design's Dennis Heisler_ letters

Originally published March 2004

THE DARKNESS ISSUE #48

Paul Jenkins_ story
Romano Molenaar_ pencils
**Matt 'Batt' Banning, Tom Bar-Or, Rick Basaldua,
Kevin Conrad, David Rivera, Joe Weems**_ inks
Matt Milla_ colors
Robin Spehar with
Dreamer Design's Dennis Heisler_ letters

Originally published April 2004

THE DARKNESS ISSUE #49

Paul Jenkins_ story
Steve Cummings_ pencils
Rick Basaldua, Jonathan Sibal_ inks
Matt Milla_ colors
Robin Spehar with
Dreamer Design's Dennis Heisler_ letters

Originally published May 2004

THE DARKNESS ISSUE #50

Ron Marz_ story
Martin Montiel_ pencils\
Matt 'Batt' Banning, Jay Leisten,
Sal Regla, Jonathan Sibal_ inks
Matt Milla_ colors
Robin Spehar with
Dreamer Design's Dennis Heisler_ letters

Originally published June 2004

THE DARKNESS ISSUE #51

Ron Marz_ story
Martin Montiel_ pencils
Matt 'Batt' Banning, Tom Bar-Or, Rick Basaldua,
Jay Leisten, Jonathan Sibal_ inks
Matt Milla_ colors
Robin Spehar with
Dreamer Design's Dennis Heisler_ letters

Originally published June 2004

THE DARKNESS ISSUE #52

Ron Marz_ story
Martin Montiel_ pencils
Matt 'Batt' Banning, Tom Bar-Or_ inks
Matt Milla_ colors
Robin Spehar with
Dreamer Design's Dennis Heisler_ letters

Originally published August 2004

THE DARKNESS
ISSUE #53-#56 CREDITS

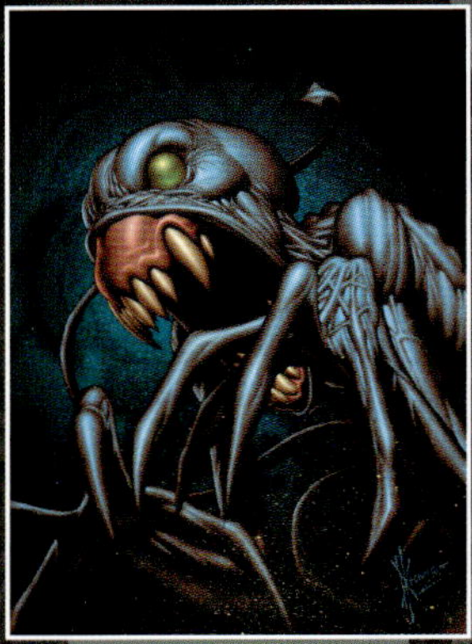

THE DARKNESS ISSUE #53

Ron Marz_ story
Martin Montiel_ pencils
Matt 'Batt' Banning, Tom Bar-Or_ inks
Matt Milla_ colors
Robin Spehar with
Dreamer Design's Dennis Heisler_ letters

Originally published September 2004

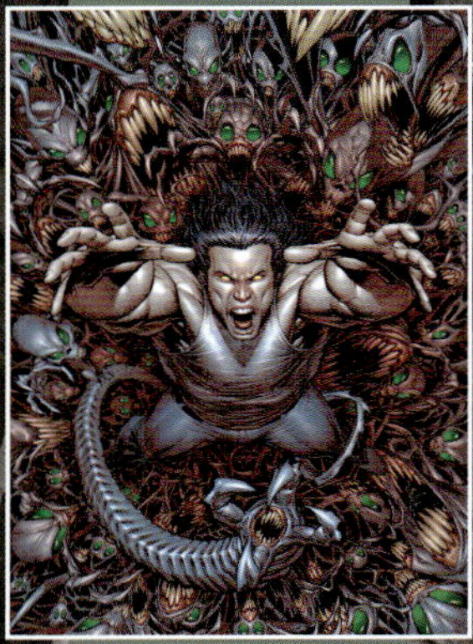

THE DARKNESS ISSUE #54

Frank Tieri_ story
J. J. Kirby_ pencils
Jay Leisten, Jonathan Sibal_ inks
Matt Milla_ colors
Robin Spehar with
Dreamer Design's Dennis Heisler_ letters

Originally published September 2004

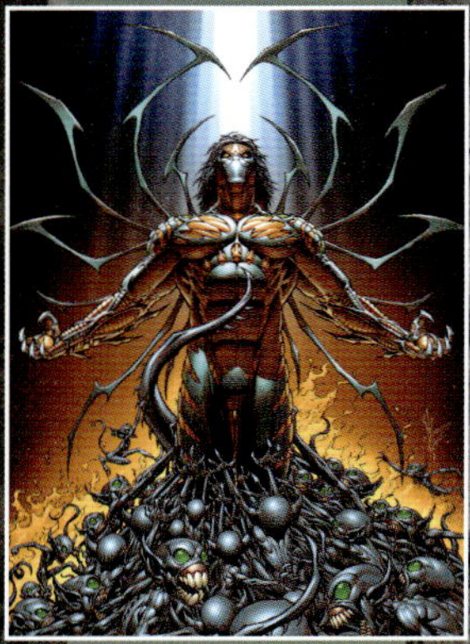

THE DARKNESS ISSUE #55

Frank Tieri_ story
Martin Montiel_ pencils
Tom Bar-Or_ inks
Matt Milla_ colors
Robin Spehar with
Dreamer Design's Dennis Heisler_ letters

Originally published October 2004

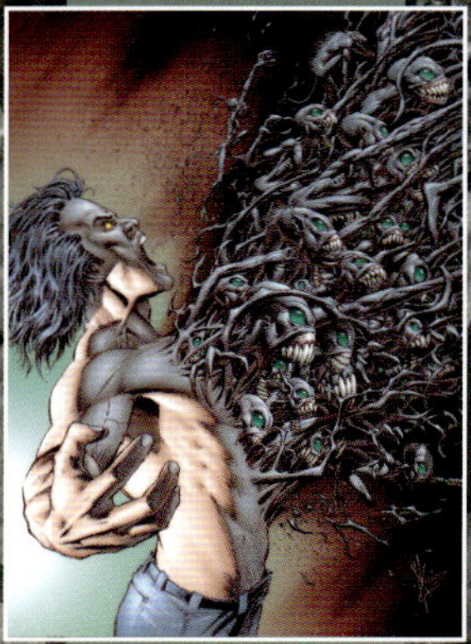

THE DARKNESS ISSUE #56

Frank Tieri_ story
Matin Montiel_ pencils
Matt 'Batt' Banning, Tom Bar-Or_ inks
Matt Milla_ colors
Robin Spehar with
Dreamer Design's Dennis Heisler_ letters

Originally published November 2004

THE DARKNESS
ISSUE #57-#60 CREDITS

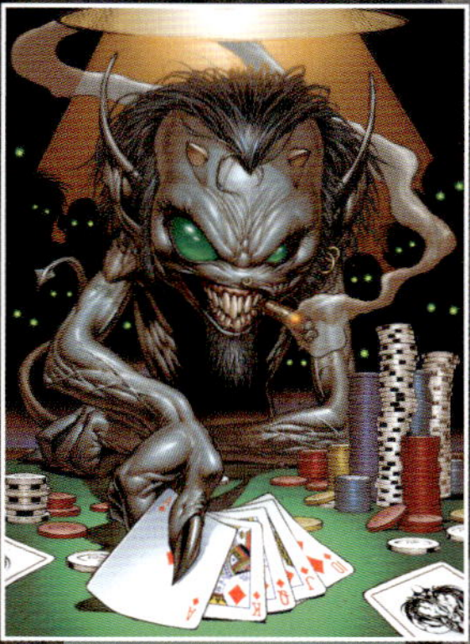

THE DARKNESS ISSUE #57

David Lapham_ story
Brian Denham_ line art
Matt Milla_ colors
Robin Spehar with
Dreamer Design's Dennis Heisler_ letters

Originally published December 2004

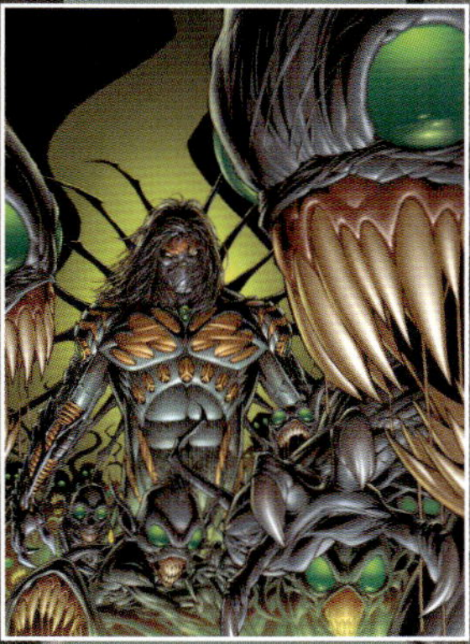

THE DARKNESS ISSUE #58

David Lapham_ story
Brian Denham_ line art
Matt Milla_ colors
Robin Spehar with
Dreamer Design's Dennis Heisler_ letters

Originally published February 2005

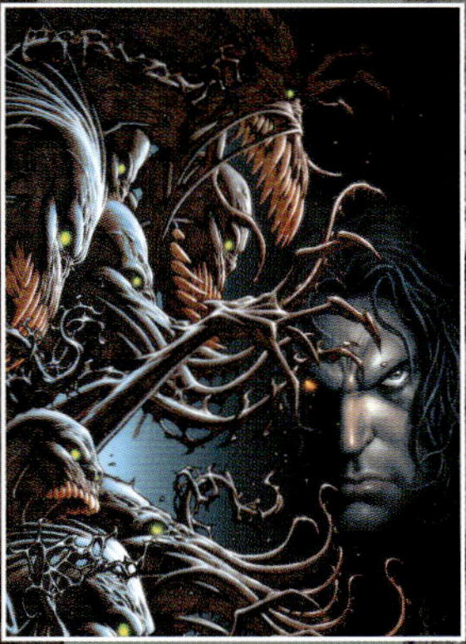

THE DARKNESS ISSUE #59

David Lapham_ story
Brian Denham_ line art
Sonia Oback_ colors
Robin Spehar with
Dreamer Design's Dennis Heisler_ letters

Originally published March 2005

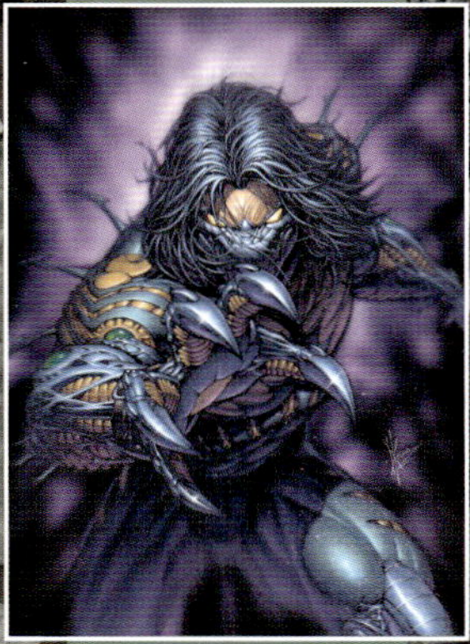

THE DARKNESS ISSUE #60

David Lapham_ story
John Lucas, William Walden_ pencils
Tom Bar-Or, Rick Basaldua, John Lucas, Ronald Paris, Mark Prudeaux_ inks
Sonia Oback_ colors
Robin Spehar with
Troy Peteri_ letters

Originally published June 2005

THE DARKNESS
ISSUE #61-#64 CREDITS

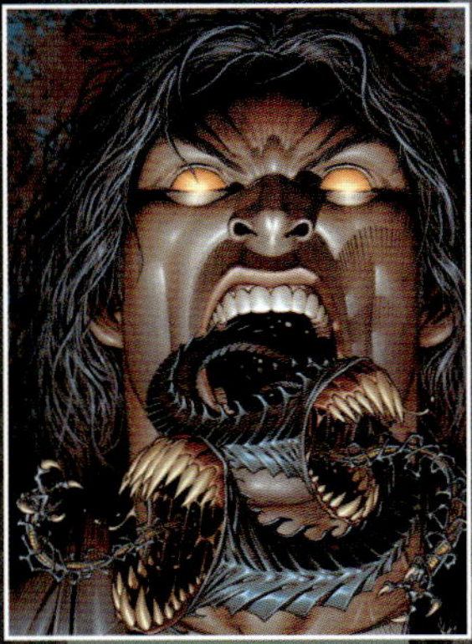

THE DARKNESS ISSUE #61

Brian Buccellato_ story
Francis Manapul_ pencils
Kevin Conrad, Robert Hunter, Jay Leisten_ inks
Brian Buccellato_ colors
Troy Peteri_ letters

Originally published August 2005

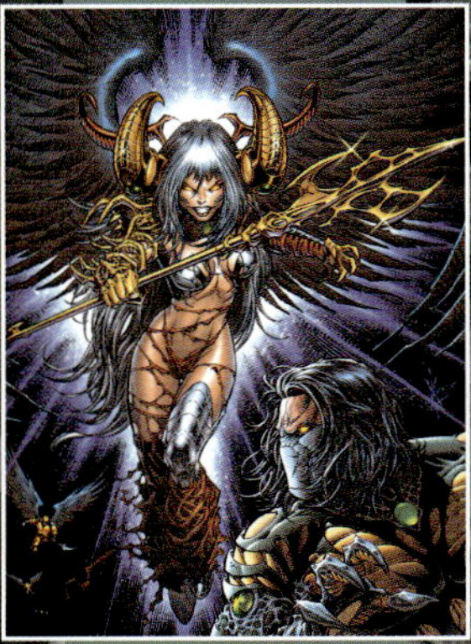

THE DARKNESS ISSUE #62

David Wohl_ story
Martin Montiel_ pencils
Jay Leisten_ inks
Sonia Oback_ colors
Troy Peteri_ letters

Originally published September 2005

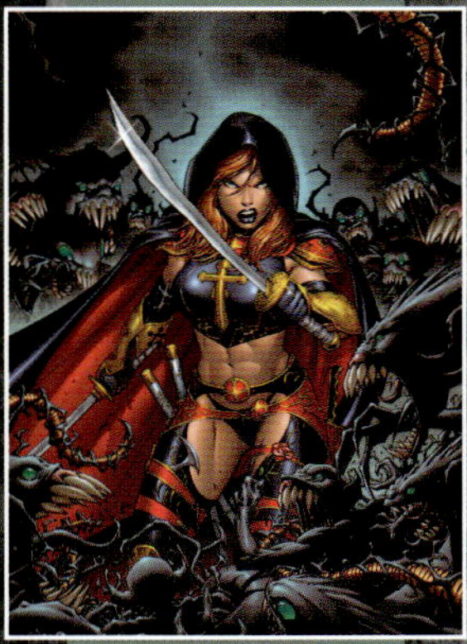

THE DARKNESS ISSUE #63

David Wohl_ story
Martin Montiel_ pencils
Jay Leisten_ inks
Sonia Oback_ colors
Troy Peteri_ letters

Originally published October 2005

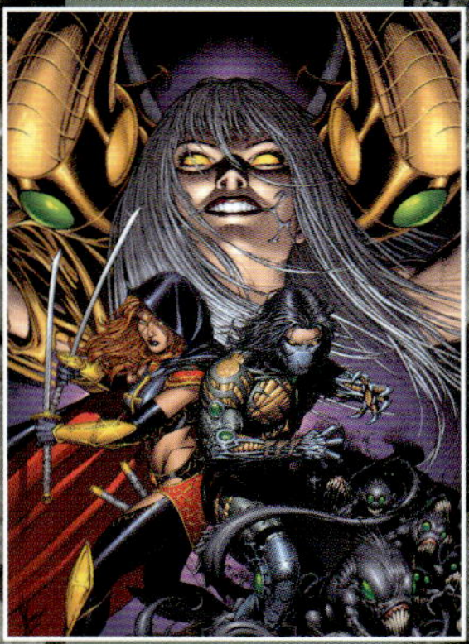

THE DARKNESS ISSUE #64

David Wohl_ story
Martin Montiel_ pencils
Jay Leisten, Roland Paris_ inks
Sonia Oback_ colors
Troy Peteri_ letters

Originally published November 2005

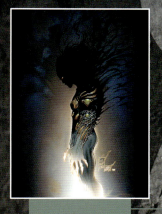

THE DARKNESS
ISSUE #65-#68 CREDITS

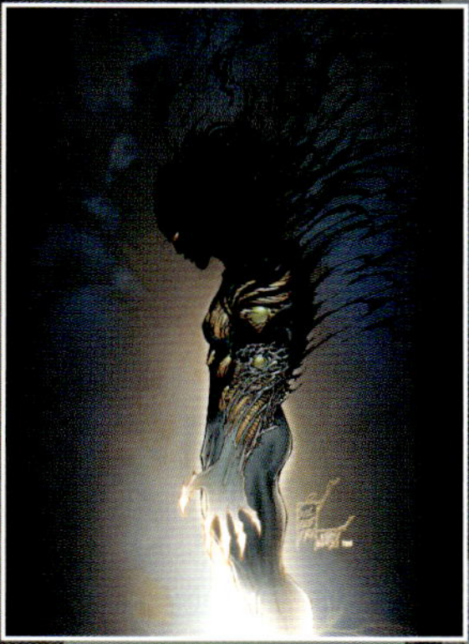

THE DARKNESS ISSUE #65

Phil Hester_ story
Michael Broussard_ pencils
Ryan Winn_ inks
Matt Milla_ colors
Troy Peteri_ letters

Originally published December 2007

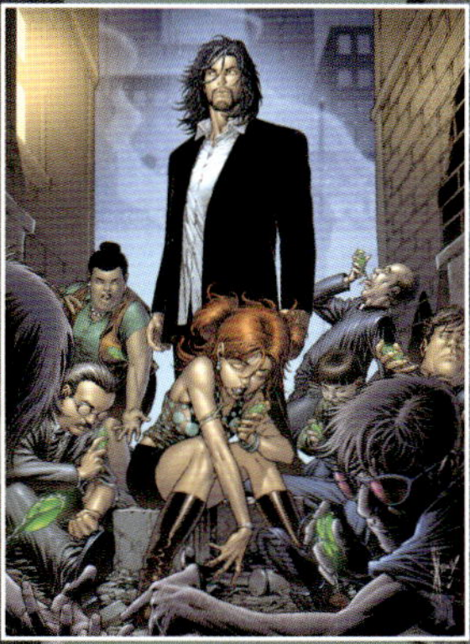

THE DARKNESS ISSUE #66

Phil Hester_ story
Michael Broussard_ pencils
Ryan Winn_ inks
Matt Milla_ colors
Troy Peteri_ letters

Originally published February 2008

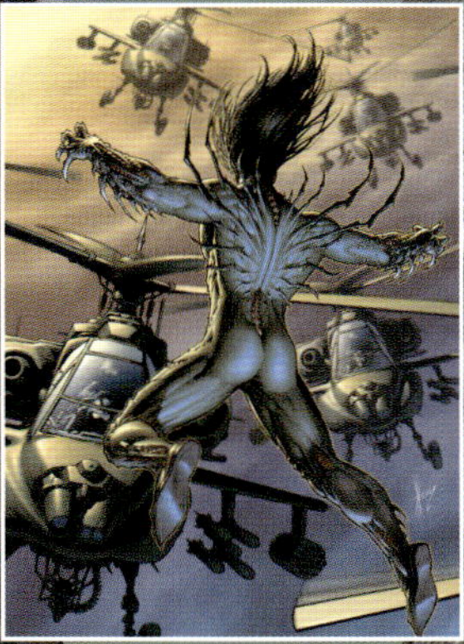

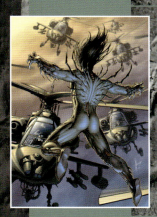

THE DARKNESS ISSUE #67

Phil Hester_ story
Michael Broussard with **Dale Keown**_ pencils
Ryan Winn with **Joe Weems**_ inks
Matt Milla_ colors
Troy Peteri_ letters

Originally published April 2008

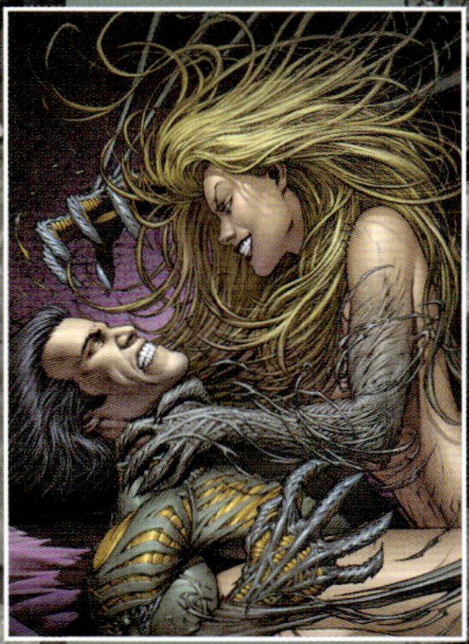

THE DARKNESS ISSUE #68

Phil Hester_ story
Michael Broussard_ pencils
Ryan Winn_ inks
Matt Milla_ colors
Troy Peteri_ letters

Originally published June 2008

THE DARKNESS
ISSUE #69-#72 CREDITS

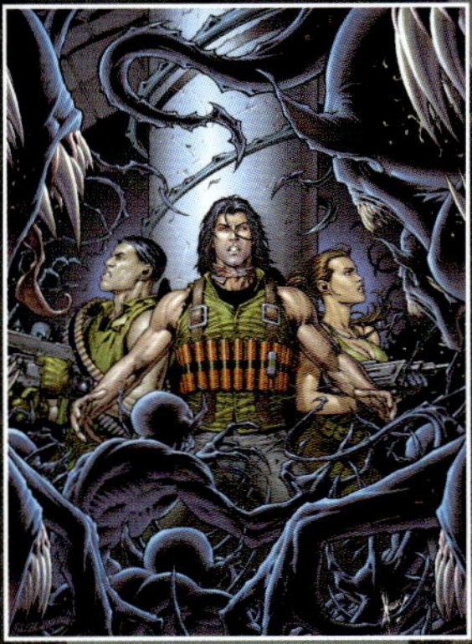

THE DARKNESS ISSUE #69

Phil Hester_ story
Michael Broussard_ pencils
Ryan Winn_ inks
Sheldon Mitchell_ colors
Troy Peteri_ letters

Originally published September 2008

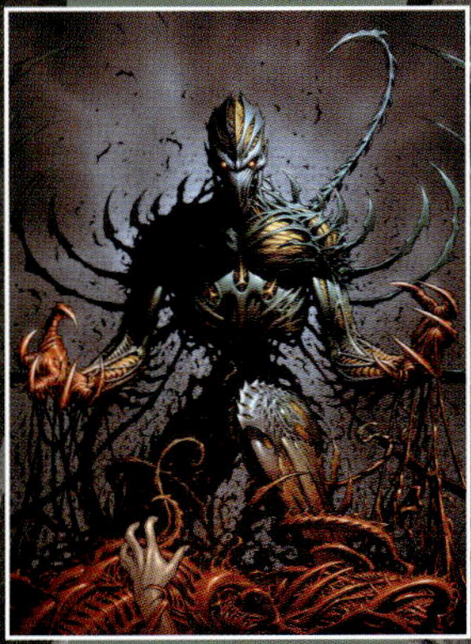

THE DARKNESS ISSUE #70

Phil Hester_ story
Michael Broussard_ pencils
Ryan Winn_ inks
Sheldon Mitchell_ colors
Troy Peteri_ letters

Originally published October 2008

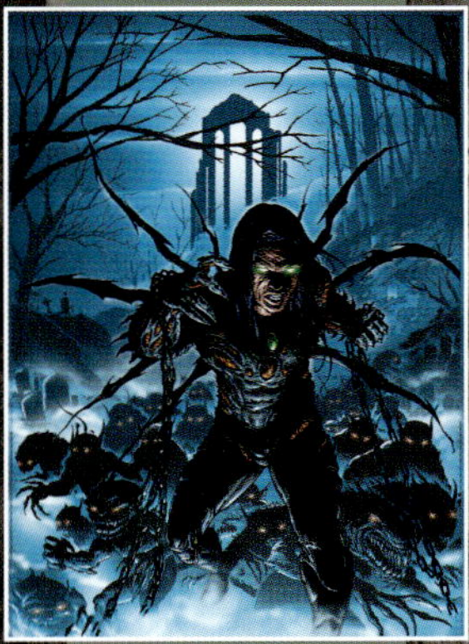

THE DARKNESS ISSUE #71

Phil Hester_ story
Jorge Lucas_ line art
Lee Loughridge_ colors
Troy Peteri_ letters

Originally published November 2008

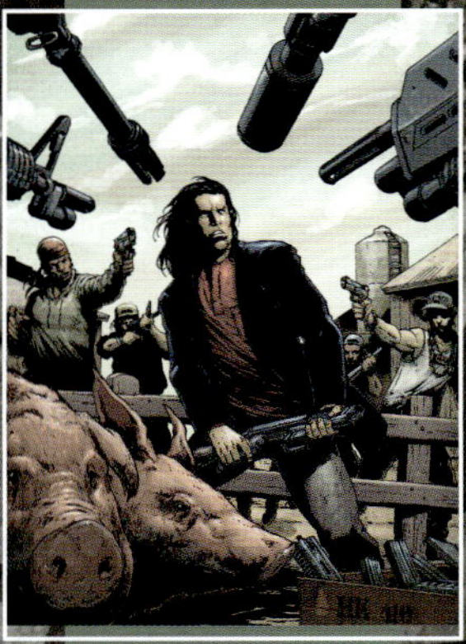

THE DARKNESS ISSUE #72

Phil Hester_ story
Jorge Lucas_ line art
Lee Loughridge_ colors
Troy Peteri_ letters

Originally published December 2008

THE DARKNESS

ISSUE #73-#76 CREDITS

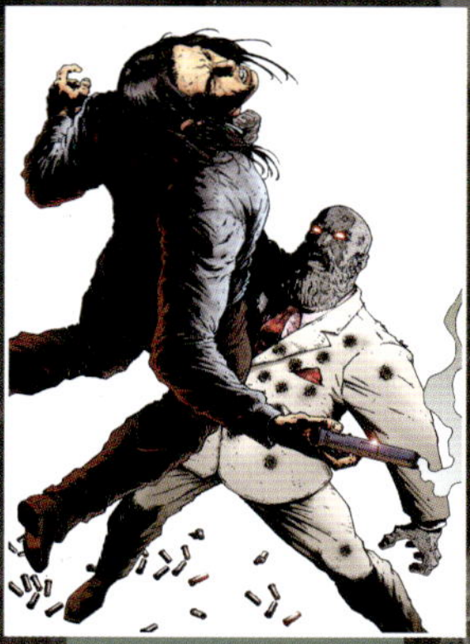

THE DARKNESS ISSUE #73

Phil Hester_ story
Jorge Lucas_ line art
Lee Loughridge_ colors
Troy Peteri_ letters

Originally published January 2009

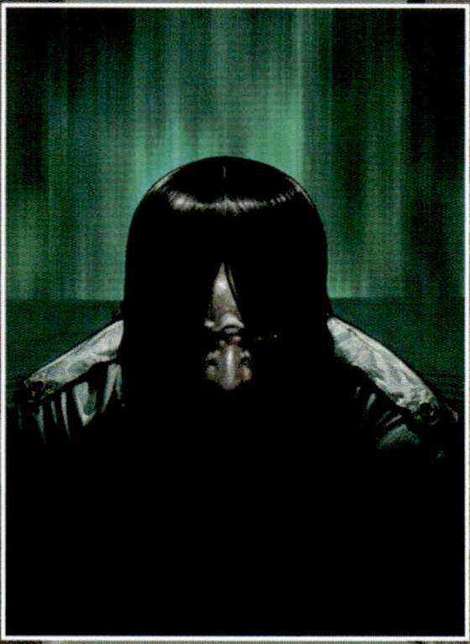

THE DARKNESS ISSUE #74

Phil Hester_ story
Jorge Lucas_ line art
Felix Serrano_ colors
Troy Peteri_ letters

Originally published February 2009

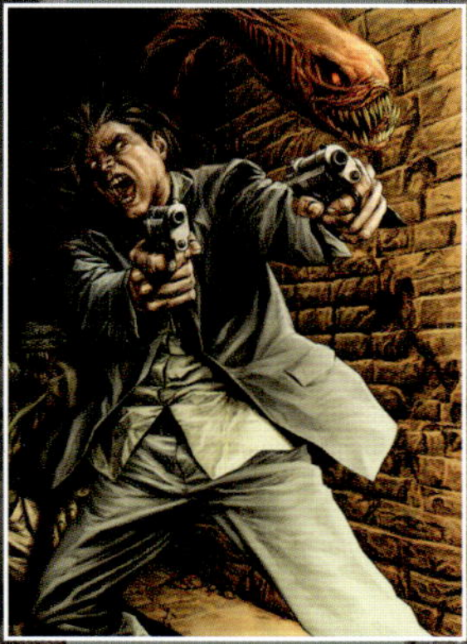

THE DARKNESS ISSUE #75

Phil Hester_ story
Matt Timson_ art & pencils (pages 1 & 34)
Joe Benitez_ art & pencils (pages 2-6)
Michael Broussard_ art & pencils (pages 7-8, 12-15, & 35-37)
Lee Carter_ art & pencils (pages 9-11)
Jorge Lucas_ art & pencils (pages 16-17 & 20)
Marc Silvestri & Steve Firchow_ art & pencils (pages 13-19)
Frazier Irving_ art & pencils (pages 21-22)
Dale Keown_ art & pencils (pages 23-27)
Ryan Sook_ art & pencils (pages 28-32)
Stjepan Sejic_ art & pencils (page 33)
Joe Weems_ inks (pages 2-6)
Ryan Winn_ inks (pages 7-8, 12-15 & 35-37)
Edgar Delgado_ colors (pages 2-6)
Benny Fuentes_ colors (pages 7-8, 12-15 & 35-37)
Felix Serrano_ colors (pages 16-17 & 20)
Steve Firchow_ colors (pages 23)
Dale Keown_ colors (pages 24-27)
Dave McCaig_ colors (pages 28-32)
Troy Peteri_ letters

Originally published February 2009

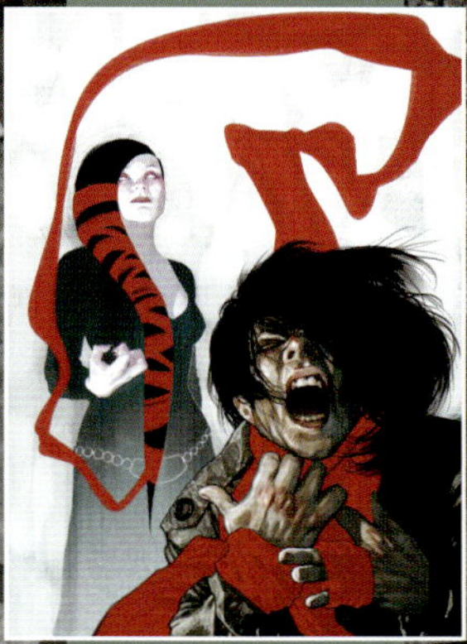

THE DARKNESS ISSUE #76

Phil Hester_ story
Michael Broussard_ pencils
Ryan Winn_ inks
Benny Fuentes_ colors
Troy Peteri_ letters

Originally published March 2009

THE DARKNESS ISSUE #77

Phil Hester_ story
Michael Broussard_ pencils
Ryan Winn_ inks
Arif Prianto of IFS_ colors
Troy Peteri_ letters

Originally published May 2009

THE DARKNESS ISSUE #78

Phil Hester_ story
Nelson Blake II_ pencils
Ryan Winn_ inks
Arif Prianto of IFS_ colors
Troy Peteri_ letters

Originally published July 2009

THE DARKNESS ISSUE #79

Phil Hester_ story
Jorge Lucas_ line art
Felix Serrano_ colors
Troy Peteri_ letters

Originally published August 2009

THE DARKNESS ISSUE #80

Phil Hester_ story
Phil Hester_ pencils
Ande Parks_ inks
Sakti Yuwono, Arif Prianto & Admira Wijaya of IFS_ colors
Troy Peteri_ letters

Originally published September 2009

THE DARKNESS ISSUE #81

Phil Hester_ story
Phil Hester_ pencils
Ande Parks_ inks
Sakti Yuwono, Arif Prianto & Admira Wijaya of IFS_ colors
Troy Peteri_ letters

Originally published November 2009

THE DARKNESS ISSUE #32

Phil Hester_ story
Michael Broussard_ pencils
Rick Basaldua_ inks
Arif Prianto of IFS_ colors
Troy Peteri_ letters

Originally published January 2010

THE DARKNESS ISSUE #33

Phil Hester_ story
Michael Broussard_ pencils
Rick Basaldua_ inks
Arif Prianto of IFS_ colors
Troy Peteri_ letters

Originally published March 2010

THE DARKNESS ISSUE #34

Phil Hester_ story
Whilce Portacio_ line art
Arif Prianto of IFS_ colors
Troy Peteri_ letters

Originally published April 2010

THE DARKNESS
ISSUE #85-#88 CREDITS

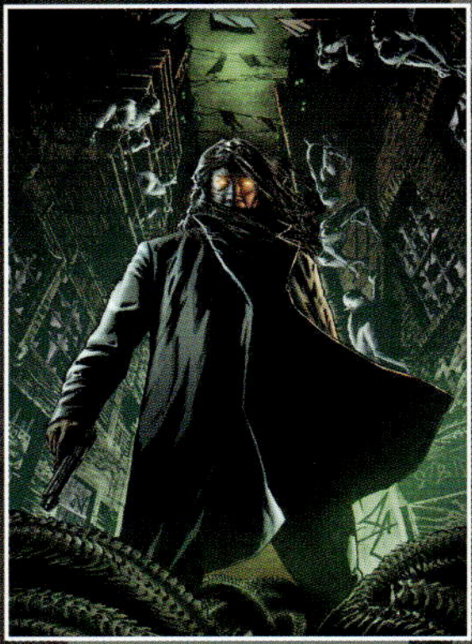

THE DARKNESS ISSUE #85

Phil Hester_ story
Sheldon Mitchell_ pencils
Rick Basaldua, Joe Weems, Ryan Winn_ inks
Arif Prianto of IFS_ colors
Troy Peteri_ letters

Originally published July 2010

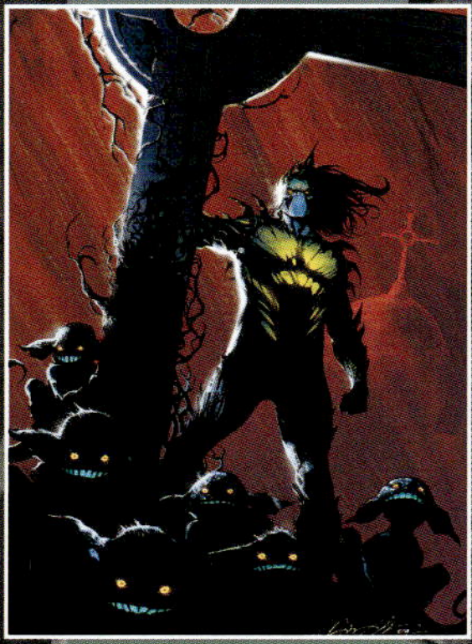

THE DARKNESS ISSUE #86

Phil Hester_ story
Sheldon Mitchell_ pencils
Joe Weems, Ryan Winn, Rick Basaldua_ inks
Arif Prianto of IFS_ colors
Troy Peteri_ letters

Originally published September 2010

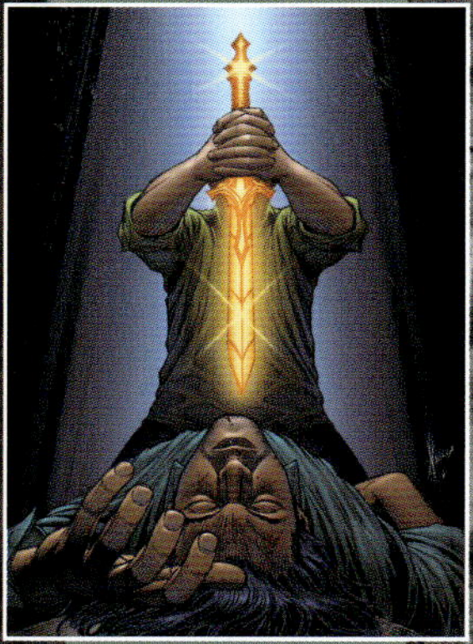

THE DARKNESS ISSUE #87

Phil Hester_ story
Sheldon Mitchell_ pencils
Joe Weems_ inks
Arif Prianto of IFS_ colors
Troy Peteri_ letters

Originally published December 2010

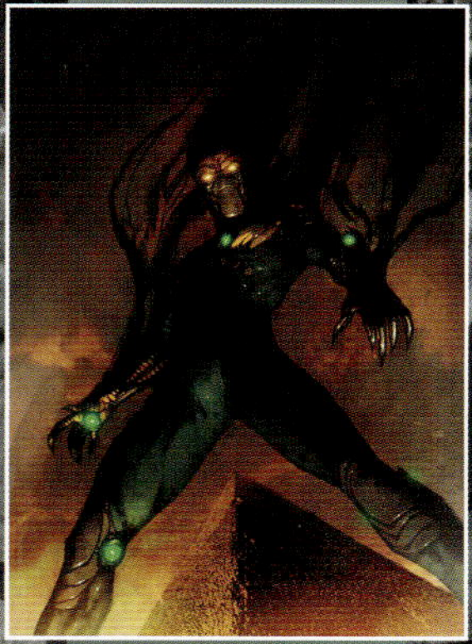

THE DARKNESS ISSUE #88

Phil Hester_ story
Romano Molenaar_ pencils
Rick Basaldua, Jason Gorder, Sal Regla_ inks
Arif Prianto of IFS, Michael Atiyeh_ colors
Troy Peteri_ letters

Originally published December 2010

THE DARKNESS

ISSUE #89, THE DARKNESS: LODEROK'S HAND, THE DARKNESS: SHADOWS AND FLAME, THE DARKNESS: BUTCHER CREDITS

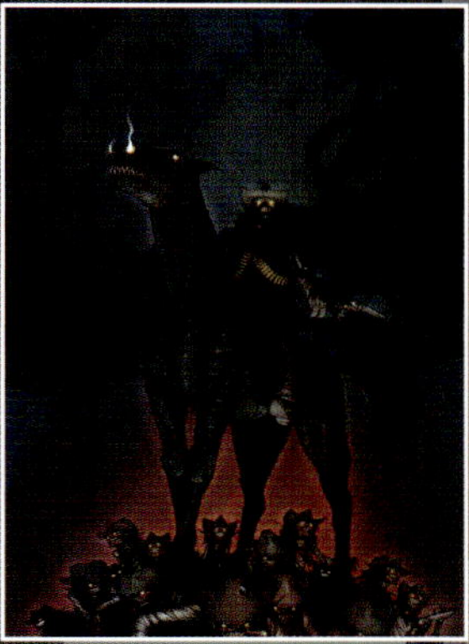

THE DARKNESS ISSUE #89

Joshua Hale Fialkov_ story
Matt Timson_ art
Troy Peteri_ letters

Originally published January 2011

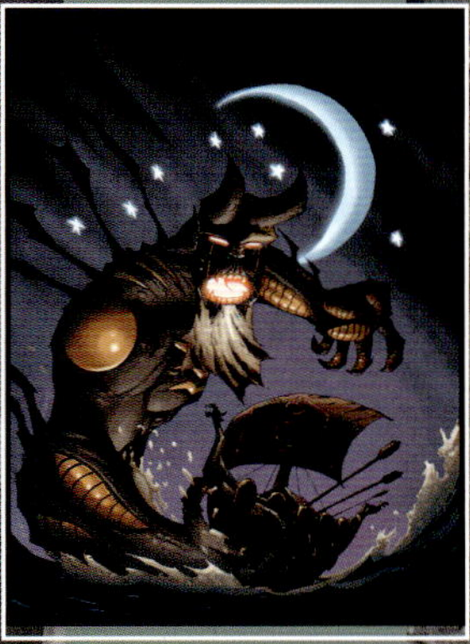

THE DARKNESS LODBROK'S HAND

Phil Hester_ story
Michael Avon Oeming_ line art
Val Staples_ colors
Troy Peteri_ letters

Originally published December 2008

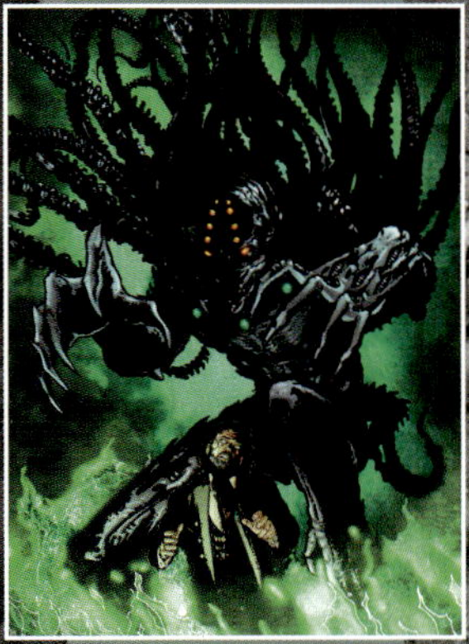

THE DARKNESS SHADOWS AND FLAME

Rob Levin_ story
Jorge Lucas_ line art
Felix Serrano_ colors
Troy Peteri_ letters

Originally published January 2010

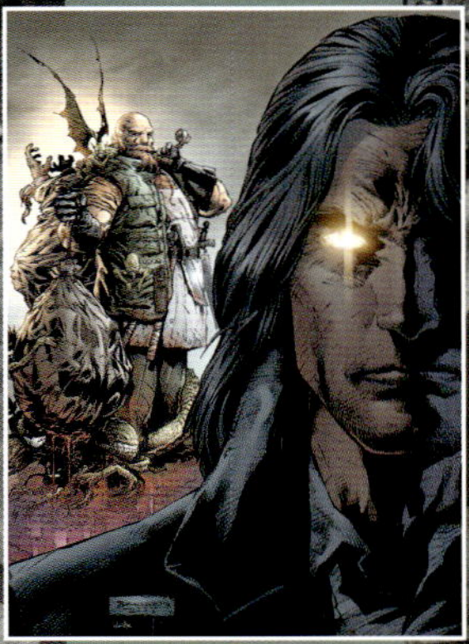

THE DARKNESS BUTCHER

Rob Levin_ story
Michael Broussard_ pencils
Jay Leisten_ inks
Larry Molinar_ colors
Troy Peteri_ letters

Originally published April 2008

Explore more about The Artifacts within the Top Cow Universe!

Ron Marz • Michael Broussard
ARTIFACTS
volume 1
FEATURING AN INTRODUCTION BY
MARC SILVESTRI

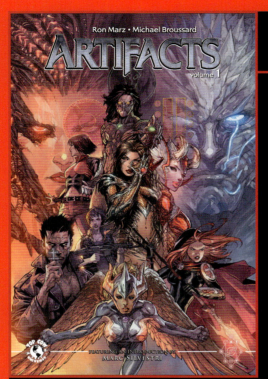

Artifacts
Volume 1

written by:
Ron Marz
pencils by:
Michael Broussard & Stjepan Sejic

When a mysterious antagonist kidnaps Hope, the daughter of Sara Pezzini and Jackie Estacado, Armageddon is set in motion. Featuring virtually every character in the Top Cow Universe, Artifacts is an epic story for longtime fans and new readers alike.

Collects issues #0-4

(ISBN 978-1-60706-201-1)

RON MARZ • STJEPAN SEJIC
ANGELUS

RON MARZ • STJEPAN SEJIC
BROKEN TRINITY

Angelus
Volume 1
written by:
Ron Marz
art by:
Stjepan Sejic

Collects issues #1-6

ISBN#
978-1-60706-198-4

First Born
Volume 1
written by:
Ron Marz
art by:
Stjepan Sejic

Collects First Born issues #0-3 & Witchblade issues #110-112

ISBN#
978-1-58240-864-5

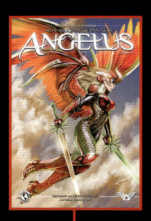

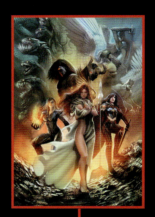

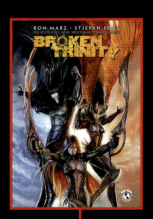

Broken Trinity
Volume 1
written by:
Ron Marz with Phil Hester & Bryan Edward Hill
art by:
Stjepan Sejic & more

Collects issues #1-3, Broken Trinity: The Darkness #1, Broken Trinity: Witchblade #1, Broken Trinity: The Angelus #1 & Broken Trinity: Aftermath #1

ISBN#
978-1-60706-198-4

Ready for more? Jump into the Top Cow Universe with *Witchblade*!

RON MARZ • MIKE CHOI
WITCHBLADE
VOLUME 1
FEATURING AN INTRODUCTION BY
RON MARZ

Witchblade
volume 1 - volume 8

written by:
Ron Marz
art by:
Mike Choi, Stephen Sadowski, Keu Cha, Chris Bachalo, Stjepan Sejic and more!

Get in on the ground floor of Top Cow's flagship title with these affordable trade paperback collections from Ron Marz's series-redefining run on Witchblade! Each volume collects a key story arc in the continuing adventures of Sara Pezzini and the Witchblade, culminating in the epic 'War of the Witchblades' storyline!

Book Market Edtion, volume 1
collects issues #80-#85
(ISBN: 978-1-58240-906-1) $9.99

WITCHBLADE
VOLUME 2

volume 2
collects issues #86-#92
(ISBN: 978-1-58240-886-6)
U.S.D. $14.99

WITCHBLADE
VOLUME 3

volume 3
collects issues #93-#100
(ISBN: 978-1-58240-887-3)
U.S.D. $14.99

WITCHBLADE
VOLUME 4

volume 4
collects issues #101-109
(ISBN: 978-1-58240-898-9)
U.S.D. $17.99

WITCHBLADE
VOLUME 5

volume 5
collects issues #110-115,
First Born issues #1-3
(ISBN: 978-1-58240-899-6)
U.S.D. $17.99

WITCHBLADE

volume 6
collects issues #116-#120
(ISBN: 978-1-60706-041-3)
U.S.D. $14.99

RON MARZ • STJEPAN SEJIC
WITCHBLADE
VOLUME 7

volume 7
collects issues #121-#124 &
Witchblade Annual #1
(ISBN: 978-1-60706-058-1)
U.S.D. $14.99

WITCHBLADE

volume 8
collects issues #125-#130
(ISBN: 978-1-60706-102-1)
U.S.D. $14.99

The Top Cow essentials checklist:

Artifacts Volume 1
(ISBN: 978-1-60706-201-1)

Art of Top Cow Softcover
(ISBN: 978-1-60706-099-4)

Broken Trinity Volume 1
(ISBN: 978-1-60706-051-2)

The Darkness: Accursed Volume 1
(ISBN: 978-1-58240-958-0)

The Darkness: Origins Volume 1
(ISBN: 978-1-60706-097-0)

First Born
(ISBN: 978-1-58240-854-5)

Freshmen Volume 1
(ISBN: 978-1-58240-593-3)

Magdalena Volume 1
(ISBN: 978-1-60706-206-6)

Rising Stars Volume 1
(ISBN: 978-1-58240-172-0)

Wanted
(ISBN: 978-1-58240-497-4)

Witchblade: Origins Volume 1
(ISBN: 978-1-58240-901-6)

Witchblade: Redemption Volume 1
(ISBN: 978-1-60706-193-9)

For more info , ISBN and ordering information on our latest collections go to:

www.topcow.com

Ask your retailer about our catalogue of our collected editions, digests and hard covers or check the listings at:

Barnes and Noble,
Amazon.com
and other fine retailers.

To find your nearest comic shop go to:

www.comicshoplocator.com